PEARLS

PEARLS

CELIA BRAYFIELD

ISBN-13: 9781492781196

For Chloe

CONTENTS

Prologue   ix
Chapter One   1
Chapter Two   13
Chapter Three   24
Chapter Four   38
Chapter Five   52
Chapter Six   71
Chapter Seven   88
Chapter Eight   111
Chapter Nine   129
Chapter Ten   146
Chapter Eleven   172
Chapter Twelve   191
Chapter Thirteen   214
Chapter Fourteen   229
Chapter Fifteen   248
Chapter Sixteen   262
Chapter Seventeen   280
Chapter Eighteen   294
Chapter Nineteen   314
Chapter Twenty   335
Chapter Twenty-One   357
Chapter Twenty-Two   379
Chapter Twenty-Three   404
Chapter Twenty-Four   428
Chapter Twenty-Five   442
Chapter Twenty-Six   459
Chapter Twenty-Seven   471
Chapter Twenty-Eight   492
Chapter Twenty-Nine   507

PROLOGUE

CATHERINE BOURTON was so beautiful that men seldom realized she had any other qualities until it was too late. Her oval face, with its creamy olive complexion, was one of *the* faces of the eighties – so *Time* magazine had said. But her bronze-brown eyes seemed to know much more than they saw; they hinted at the ancestry of the Bourton family, rich Italians grafted to the British aristocracy by Queen Elizabeth I to dissuade them from bankrolling the Spanish Armada.

Such beauty made men vulnerable. Even a man like Mr Phillips, the Crown Jeweller of Great Britain, whose daily round was largely devoted to considering the effect of the world's most famous jewels on the world's most beautiful women, temporarily forgot the purpose of their meeting in his cramped oval office over-looking Regent Street.

In the concrete canyons around Wall Street, the presence of Catherine Bourton could render innumerate any of the men who had dollar signs where their wives presumed their hearts to be; in a boardroom in the City of London, captains of industry would meander through their agenda muttering compliments and vying for her attention if Catherine Bourton was among them; the two men in Mr Phillips' gilded candy-box at Garrard's were lost the instant she joined them.

The power of her beauty came from the combination of the symmetrical purity of her High Renaissance face with the sensual promise of her mouth. Catherine Bourton's mouth looked soft and crumpled, as if it had just been kissed and would respond favourably to being kissed again. The top lip was a little wider and fuller than the bottom lip, giving her an ineradicable smile. *Time* magazine had called her the Mona Lisa of Wall Street. Catherine had not been surprised. She had been called the Mona Lisa of somewhere or other ever since she could remember.

Nowadays, her reputation came before her. Mr Phillips had first met her when she was a debutante; pretty, he remembered, but not more distinctive among the crop than one of the spring daffodils in Hyde Park. Like many men after him, Mr Phillips had misjudged her. She had seldom been out of the headlines since their first meeting, on so many different counts – her marriage, her divorce, her adventures in the City, her glittering connections, and the suspicion that she was the architect of some of the most conspicuous personal fortunes in the world.

Since generosity and fair-mindedness were among Catherine's other qualities, she seldom brought her sexual attraction into play unless all other tactics had failed. She had found that this was also more efficient. She was dressed to underplay her allure, in a plain, black linen suit from Chanel, with her straight brown hair cut in a simple bob.

She wore square-cut diamond earrings, very fine blue-white stones of the first water, because she knew that a jeweller, even Mr Phillips at Garrard's, judged people largely on their jewellery. Just as the plain cut of the diamonds only emphasized their quality, so the simplicity of her dress only made her seem more attractive. She considered this Catch 22 typical of the double binds which affect a woman in a man's world; it left her only two possibilities – to win like a man, or to win like a woman.

She liked to win; situations in which winning was neither necessary nor possible disturbed her, and she had come to Garrard's to deal with what she suspected was a major problem of this kind.

'So, Mr Phillips, what can you tell me about our pearls?' she began, taking the hard upright chair by his desk. 'I've broken my schedule and flown back to London specially to get your opinion. When I spoke to my sister in New Orleans this morning she was dying to know what you've found out. It's not every day we both wake up in the morning and find someone's hidden a pair of pearls under our pillows. Did the tooth fairy get her deliveries mixed up? Or do you think there's a logical explanation?'

She talked about her sister with the same kind of adoration that Mr Phillips associated with young brides talking about their husbands; there could be no doubt that this was the most thrilling, the most precious, the most extraordinary person in her world. Mr Phillips was aware that some of his younger staff, who followed pop music, shared Catherine Bourton's high opinion of her sister Monty; however, Mr Phillips himself knew nothing about popular music or its stars.

He was a fine looking man with the military haircut and shiny shoes of all British courtiers, and he opened his dog-eared file with a nervous snuffle. The August heat made his office stuffy and the plastic desk fan which stirred the sticky air also propelled dust into the atmosphere.

'I've asked Mr Jerryman, our chief pearl trader, to join us.' He indicated the wiry, white-haired man at his side, who took a small, polythene envelope from the inside pocket of his black jacket.

'He has examined them and, broadly speaking, the news is that you have a pair of very fine, pink pearls, teardrop shape, probably of oriental origin . . .'

'And worth?' Catherine knew that when an Englishman said 'broadly speaking' and called in a second opinion, she was to be treated to a round of ancient British bullshit.

'The price, you mean?' Mr Phillips seemed faintly offended that money should be mentioned in the presence of such glorious jewels.

Mr Jerryman tipped the pearls out of their protective plastic envelope into his hand. Against his papery skin the lustrous gems glowed like living things. 'Pearls are very hard to price, very hard.' Mr Jerryman shook his head and smoothed his slicked-down white hair. 'The great pearls, like La Peregrina, which Richard Burton gave to Elizabeth Taylor, are almost personalities in their own right. They are more or less priceless.'

'Well, how do these two compare to La Peregrina?' Catherine disliked imprecision, especially about money.

'We think they compare very well.' Mr Phillips twinkled at her and took off his glasses for emphasis. 'Don't we, Mr Jerryman?'

Cradling the pearls in his palm Mr Jerryman gently pulled a cream silk handkerchief from his pocket and spread it on the small table by the grimy window. 'We always look at pearls against a pale background such as this,' he picked the two jewels out of his hand and placed them on the cloth with reverence, 'because a pearl is a responsive surface, and it tends to take on the colour and texture of whatever it is displayed against. That's why, of course, pearls look so good against a – er – a lady's . . .' he paused, embarrassed.

'Skin?' Catherine suggested, amused.

'Quite so. Now the first question to consider is whether these are completely natural pearls, or whether they are cultured. And there is no doubt that these are natural pearls because of their size.' Catherine gave him her most patient smile. 'They are each around 200 carats, which means they must be among the largest pearls ever fished – and you simply do not get cultured pearls that large. Only the biggest species of oyster, called *Pinctada maxima,* can make a pearl of this size, and that species does not take kindly to interference, so they are never used for culturing.'

'And, apart from the size, of course, there are the X-rays.' Mr Phillips undipped two small plates, no bigger than dental X-rays, from the file and held them up against the occluded light of the begrimed window. Catherine saw that each pearl showed a succession of faintly marked rings, like the annual rings of a treetrunk. 'A cultured pearl is achieved by seeding the oyster with a tiny piece of grit.' Phillips waved his pen over the X-rays with authority. 'In consequence, that impurity always shows up on the plates – but in this case there's nothing, so we can be sure they're natural pearls.'

'And the third check is on the specific gravity,' the older man resumed. 'Natural pearls are always just a tiny bit heavier for their size, because they are solid nacre.'

'Nacre, what's that?' Catherine enquired pleasantly. Encouraging a display of technical knowledge always gave the boys confidence. Meetings, like everything else about business, were a game to her, and the first rule was to leave the guys their balls.

'Nacre is the stuff the mother oyster makes the pearls with – it's built up in layers around the centre. See here on the X-ray, these little rings?' Mr Phillips gestured again with his fountain pen.

'Chemically it is mostly just calcium carbonate – the same as blackboard chalk or the granite kerbstones down there on Piccadilly Circus,' Mr Jerryman warmed to his favourite subject. 'The magic ingredient of nacre is something called conchiolin, a protein secreted by the oyster's tissues to bind it all together.'

'Does it *tell* you anything?' prompted Catherine blandly. 'My sister and I are just longing to know about these pearls. They're the most mysterious thing that's ever happened to us.'

'Why, yes, it tells us quite a lot. We can get some idea of the pearl's age from the nacre, because it builds up at about a thousand layers a year; but any pearl this size will have come from a bed undisturbed for decades.' Mr Jerryman turned the jewels over on the silk with a gesture of affection. 'The colour gives us some clues, too – it's partly due to pigment in the nacre, and partly determined by the way the light is refracted between the outer layers. These are a very rare colour – almost apricot, don't you think?'

Mr Phillips unfolded his gold-rimmed half-glasses and put them on again to peer closely at the pearls. 'Yes, apricot's about right – creamy-golden with a touch of pink in there.'

'But, what does that mean?' Catherine gave Mr Phillips' elaborate ormolu clock a marked glance – for how much of this minuet did she have time?

'These must have been made by the gold-lipped sub-species of *Pinctada maxima*, which narrows down the country of origin for you,' the white-haired jeweller explained. 'And you only find the gold-lipped pearl oyster off Burma, Thailand and the Indonesian islands. Now, I have some contacts out there, and I've sent a few telexes, but no one's got any information. Which I regard as highly significant.' Mr Phillips removed his spectacles to underline the seriousness of his pronouncement, 'because when a pearl this size is found – which is very rare, maybe once in twenty years – they know about it in every bar in Tokyo by the end of the week. Fishing up a perfect pair like this ought to have been headline news around the world. I'd be most surprised if these two had been traded on the open market.'

'Are you saying they're stolen?' The idea did not appear to disturb Catherine Bourton as much as the two men had feared.

'Not necessarily, but they must have been acquired by some private means – unless the tooth fairy has taken up pearl fishing in her spare time.' They laughed, pleased that the awkward moment had passed.

'And you're sure they're quite new – not antique? My sister and I thought perhaps they might turn up in your records somewhere.'

'We checked our ledgers, of course,' Mr Phillips was anxious not to appear negligently complacent in his expertise, 'and I've checked with Sotheby's and Christie's for you as well, but I didn't expect they would find them. We were sure they hadn't been out of the sea very long. It's what we call the lustre, you see, that gleam they have that's strong and gentle at the same time; it fades if the pearls aren't worn next to the skin once they're out of the oyster. I got these others out of our safe to show you what we mean.' He reached into his desk and pulled out a pair of pearl drop earrings set with diamonds.

Catherine noticed immediately that the large pale pearls were identical to those worn by a prominent European princess whose signed photograph was half-hidden by the pile of papers on the desk. She also noticed that the pearls were dull, not shiny like the ones she had brought them. She could see her face in those shiny surfaces.

The Garrard's ledgers, she knew, recorded almost every major jewel in the world. They were large vellum-paged account books, bound in leather the colour of autumn leaves, which recorded the history of the world's ruling classes as accurately as any history book. The early volumes, from the first entry in 1730, related to the crown jewels of Great Britain, a hoard increased at each dynastic marriage. Then the wealth of the British Empire appeared, in the form of maharajahs' rubies and the Koh-i-Noor diamond, set in 1853.

From the turn of the century, the once-crowned heads of Europe came to Garrard's to sell what jewels they had been able to salvage from their revolutionary deposers. The ledgers even recorded the shameful affair of the Imperial Russian jewel-case, sent for sale, on behalf of the Tsar's family, by Britain's Queen Mary only after she had picked the choicest items for herself. Of late, many of the ledger entries recorded the creation of state regalia for the new countries of the third world; but there was still some business accruing from royal patronage – like the diamond and drop-pearl tiara given by the Queen to the Princess of Wales on her wedding.

'See the difference? These were collected by Elizabeth of Bohemia in the seventeenth century. Mind you, don't say I said that because *she* tells everyone they were the Empress Josephine's.' He glanced at the princess's photograph. 'But she won't wear them, and they'll never get that shine back now.' He shook his head, implying that the foolishness of princesses was an occupational hazard.

'Do you think ours have ever been worn?'

'No, frankly, I doubt it. I'll tell you why. They're the same weight as La Peregrina, which used to belong to the Duchess of Abercorn, and I remember her telling me that she had to have it bored because it was too heavy to stay in a claw setting and she once lost it down the side of a sofa-cushion in Buckingham Palace. She was always losing it, in fact. These two haven't been bored, so I doubt they've ever been worn. We'd be happy to set them for you, of course. Splendid pair of earrings – had some nice little diamonds in last week, set them off a treat . . .'

Catherine smiled with polite regret, and opened her briefcase to take out two white leather jewel-boxes. She reached forward, picked up the pearls, and fitted each one into the little nest of black velvet inside its box, and put them back in the briefcase. 'But, I'm sure that boring them will reduce their value?'

The two men nodded as she rose to her feet and moved towards the door.

'And my sister and I would like to find out who gave them to us before we do anything else. Now, if I've remembered correctly, we know that these pearls must be newly discovered, from somewhere in Burma, Thailand or Indonesia, and perhaps stolen or at least sold privately, and they've never been worn.'

'I'd guess from a small fishery,' added the older man, tucking his handkerchief back into his breast pocket. 'They'd never have been able to keep the discovery secret in a big operation.'

Catherine thanked the two men with such grace that they were at once convinced they had solved the entire mystery of the pearls. Mr Phillips escorted her through the blue-walled enclave which the Garrard's staff call the royal enclosure and watched as she walked briskly but unevenly out into Regent Street. She had a very slight limp.

Her office was in Pall Mall, on the sixth floor, high above the gentlemen's clubs and the traffic.

'Any joy, Mum?' her son Jamie called as she closed the plain glass door with CBC Investment Consultants painted on it in small silver letters. Jamie looked up from the word processor with his father's light-blue eyes, all the more startling against his curly black hair.

'A little joy. Curiouser and curiouser, really. How's the bulletin?' Her son spent his Oxford vacations helping out around her office, and this year she had entrusted him with the job of preparing the monthly digest of market trends which was mailed to all their clients.

'Er, not too bad. Put it this way – I thought an essay crisis was a good excuse for a nervous breakdown until I got into currency forecasts.'

She walked round behind him, noticing how broad his shoulders were now as she peered over them at the screen. 'We're calling the Yen bullish, are we?'

'I think so, it looks quite strong after oil prices came down last week.' He looked up at her, compressing his thick, black brows with anxiety.

'And you're sure that's valid?'

'Pretty sure – I'm not basing it all on Chicago if that's what you mean. Don't you agree?'

'Yes, darling, of course I agree. I'm just testing. Can you tone this bit down? Your grandfather will kill us if we talk about the British having a blinkered obsession with short-term credit. You *are* right, just put it more diplomatically.' She patted his sunburned arm affectionately and wandered across to the other side of the office, idly picking up pieces of paper and reading them without taking in their contents.

'What time's your flight?' Jamie spoke without taking his eyes off the screen as he made the corrections.

'Couple of hours – I'll have to leave soon. Make sure the receptionist gets fresh flowers tomorrow, won't you, darling? Those lilies look rather tired.' She gazed out of the window at the handsome facgde of the Athenaeum Club across the road.

Her son abruptly switched off the word processor. 'You're worried, aren't you? Come on, what's on your mind?' He came over and put his arms around her. 'Is it the pearls?'

'Yes, I suppose so. It's just so strange, Jamie. Nothing like this has ever happened before. There's no reason, no meaning – I can't understand it. They said they were *priceless* at Garrard's. Who would give Monty and me two priceless pearls?'

'Probably some secret admirer.'

'Don't be silly, no one could possibly fancy both of us. No one would dare.' She laughed, trying to break her mood of anxiety.

'Didn't they give you anything else to go on at Garrard's?'

She shook her head and shrugged her shoulders. 'Nothing much. They just tried to persuade me to have them bored and made into a pair of earrings.'

'Well, why don't you do that?' He squeezed her protectively and she smiled with unease. Catherine still had difficulty in bridging the gap in her mind between this brawny young god and the little boy with busy knees in a pedal-car who used to cry when he ran into a tree.

'Go on,' he urged, 'you and Monty could wear them for six months each, every year.'

Catherine gave another nervous laugh. 'Listen, I've called my sister all sorts of things in my life, but the twinset-and-pearls-type is something she'll *never* be.'

In a cave of light in the middle of the vast auditorium a woman in a pink jacket was punching the air in time to the beat. Twenty thousand voices were roaring for her. Her hips ground to and fro as she stamped the rhythm.

'*Was it good for you too?*' Monty yelled, and the crowd rose up like a wave and howled. She flung back her head and felt the sweat trickling down her neck, her back, between her breasts. She snapped her head upright. 'Shall we do it again?' Another full-throated roar answered her, and she turned and pulled the band together with a wave of her arm. The crowd were clapping the time, whistling, screaming, stamping the floor, swaying like a cornfield in a storm as the lights played over them.

Sometimes Monty thought she could die like this, on stage, with her people, all burned up with the noise and the music and the lights. Other times, she felt as if she *was* going to die, right there, as if her heart were going to stop or her brain burst with excitement and exhaustion. Her voice was raw now, at the end of her third night at the Superdome, but she liked the way it sounded. Raw was good for 'Man Beats Woman', her first big hit in the States, the song she always sang for her second encore. Deliberately, she slipped control of her voice and heard the sound tear out of her.

Winston, her drummer, was playing like a madman, his shirt flapping wet with perspiration. She danced across the stage and wound her arms around Stas at the keyboards as he launched into an orgasmic build-up of scales. The crowd was a sea of reaching hands as she moved forward to the edge of the stage, slipping off her jacket. P. J. and Barbara shared a mike to her left, their legs working like pistons in their long, white skirts. Monty whirled her jacket around her head, her whole body whipped into curves by the motion; then she flung it out into the crowd and the arms folded over it like a sea anemone's tentacles.

One last chorus. In a white T-shirt and black trousers, her cropped, black hair slick with sweat, she stomped backwards and the guitarists moved in from each side to join her for the triumphant final chord. All right! All right. Breath tore into her chest and blood thundered in her ears as she bowed to the tempest of applause.

Better bring them down gently now. A word to Tony, the lead guitar, and then Monty sat down at the edge of the stage and they killed most of the lights. Someone brought Monty her own guitar and she checked the tuning, gaining time to get her breathing more relaxed. Already the crowd was settling, knowing what was to come.

'This song is very important to me,' she told them, aware that most of them knew the story and anticipating the murmur of response. 'It's a song about who we are and what we're doing here. It's called "Broken Wings", but I always think of it as Joe's song.' She looked away to the right, and there was Joe at the edge of the stage, tipping her an easy, little salute with a kiss in it. Then she forgot him, and concentrated on the song; why did I ever write something with such damned difficult intervals, she wondered.

Ten minutes later Monty erupted into her dressing room, filling the small space with the surplus energy of her stage personality.

'Cathy!' she hurled herself into her sister's arms and at once Catherine's white Armani shirt was mottled with sweat and creased by Monty's passionate embrace. 'Darling, darling Cathy! You made it! You look wonderful! Doesn't she, Joe? What's the news – about the pearls?' The veins in Monty's neck stood out, she was gleaming with sweat and her arms were shaking with exhaustion as she hugged her sister closely. Cathy could feel the force of her sister's heartbeats; not for the first time, she envied Monty her ability to surrender herself completely, body and spirit. Her eyes looked more cat-like than ever, their pupils dilated with the high of performing.

'You're coming home with us, aren't you?' Monty continued, talking too loud and too fast. 'Say you'll stay, Cathy. I'll scream if you've got to go back to New York to do business. I miss you so much. Did you have a good flight? Tell me – what did they say? About the pearls, what's happening, what are they?'

'Not very much, nothing to go on. I'll tell you tomorrow. You were great, Monty. What a crowd. Are they always like that?' Catherine knew it would be hours before her sister came down and was calm enough to put two sentences together. She was like another person after a concert, jittery and explosive, on an emotional razor-edge, ready to plunge from the great high to the great low if she was not handled carefully.

Joe always knew how to calm her. Cathy was never completely at ease in her sister's world; nor was she completely at ease with Joe. Despite her best intentions, she was jealous. The sisters were so close Cathy often felt as if they were twins, psychically connected even when they were apart. Cathy had never found such intimacy with another adult, but Monty had Joe, and now they had a baby, too.

They were carried away in a river of people, swept through the concrete bowels of the Superdome and out into a limousine, then away to an airport and into a jet. Monty at last fell asleep on Joe's shoulder, her lashes curling on her flushed cheeks.

It was still dark when they emerged in the furnace of the Phoenix night, to be driven through the stark landscape to the home which Monty and Joe had built in the mountains. By the time they arrived, Catherine felt as if she were on another planet, not just because the house was walled with black lava rock: their world was one of extremes – but then so was the world of money, where Catherine lived. The difference was that Catherine succeeded because she remained apart from the craziness, while Monty had won by surrendering herself to it.

Joe, Monty's lover and manager, was one of those men whose sexual aura hung brooding like summer lightning in the atmosphere. Maybe it was because that narrow face, with its black eyes and full, curving lips, had also launched thousands of album covers in its day. Catherine was well acquainted with the power of a public image; that was not the whole story with Joe. He was the most disturbing man she had ever met.

She watched him the following afternoon, patiently feeding some mashed banana to Paloma, his baby daughter, and wondered how it could be that his clothes gave the impression that they covered his flesh unwillingly.

'She's a lovely baby, Monty.'

'C'mon, you hate babies.' Monty smiled fondly up at the messy tableau from the black leather sofa.

'Yes, but as babies go she's adorable.'

Monty sat forward, dismissing the ritual exchange of compliments. 'The pearls, Cathy, we've got to know *why*. Nobody would give us both a present like that for no reason. They've got to have some meaning.'

'I know that, Monty – but *what*? What have we two got in common, for heaven's sake? We've lived totally separate lives for twenty years, almost.'

'I think that's the key to it.' Joe put down the dish and walked down the wide, wooden steps to the level where the sisters were talking. 'The *only* thing you two have in common is your blood. Sure, everyone knows how close you are, but there's no other link between you at all except that you're children of the same parents. Apart from that, the only thing that's the same in both your lives is that they just don't make any sense.'

'What do you mean?' Cathy felt as if she were being criticized, then realized that she wasn't. It was hard to tell with Joe.

'What I mean is, from what Monty's told me, you've both had turning points in your lives where something pulled you back from the edge – and it wasn't anything ordinary.'

'You mean, like me and the smack?' asked Monty. Cathy flinched inwardly; she was always disturbed by the matter-of-fact way her sister could talk about having been a heroin addict.

'Yes, you and the smack, and what about you, Cathy?' Joe's even, velvety voice was devoid of accusation, but Cathy knew she must also make her confession.

'We've never really understood . . .' she paused, not liking to remember past pain. 'Well, I've got away with far more than I've had any right to, businesswise, I suppose.'

Joe, pitiless, said nothing, hoping to pull a more specific declaration out of her, but the baby, furious that the supply of dinner had dried up, squawked and splatted its small hand into the dish, then hurled it off the tray. The awkward moment passed, and Joe went to wipe up the floor.

Beyond the room's glass wall, the searing colours of the Arizona sunset, bands of orange and neon pink, were intensifying out of the pure blue sky of daytime. Monty sighed and got up to get her sister a drink.

'Do you remember Daddy telling us that the sun went down with a green flash in the tropics?' She handed Cathy a Scotch and water, half-and-half, with one ice cube, and poured Coke for Joe and herself. 'I've seen every colour of the rainbow out there, but never green. I'm sure the green flash was just one of those old colonial myths they were all so keen on.'

Cathy sipped her drink thoughtfully. 'Daddy never told us anything very much about Malaya, did he? When I think about it, all he ever mentioned were romantic little things like that.'

'Wasn't he some kind of war hero?' Joe strolled down into the conversation with a cleaned-up Paloma tucked contentedly into the crook of his arm.

'Yes, but he never talked about that either. And Mummy never told us anything because she hated the place. All I can remember is our *amah* and her black trousers.' Cathy paused, scanning her childhood memories rapidly. She looked at Joe and Monty, now sitting side by side on the leather cushions watching fondly as Paloma crawled around the floor. Sometimes Joe seemed like a cross between Freud and Buddha; he knew the answers to everything. How could her sister live with anyone so disturbingly enlightened? Maybe I just don't like men who're smarter than I am, Cathy thought. Then Monty jumped up, fired by the new idea.

'You're right, Joe! Of course. We've no idea what Daddy's life was like out in the East, and he didn't tell us anything, not even what he did during the Japanese occupation to get his D S O. He never even told Cathy anything, and he was so close to her. He never saw any of his old army friends, and there weren't any books in the house about the Malayan campaign. Now I think about it, it's obvious! *And* the one thing the Garrard's people could tell us was that the pearls must have come from the East somewhere – Thailand or Burma, didn't they say? That's just north of Malaya. There *must* be a link.'

Monty's enthusiasm always charmed Cathy, whose temperament was naturally cool.

'Not necessarily,' she said. 'But there *might* be some connection.'

'Private detectives!'

'Monty, for heaven's sake, this isn't a soap opera.'

'I know, but there must *be* private detectives.'

Cathy smoothed her blue silk skirt as she considered the next step. 'It's so melodramatic, I'm sure they're all bone-thick ex-cops anyway, all thinking they're Humphrey Bogart, and trying to charge $100 a day plus expenses.' She recognized that she was being unreasonable, and shook her head. 'Do you know what really bothers me, Monty? I've never felt that Daddy killed himself just because he got into debt. He'd have just laughed it off and charmed someone into lending him more money. There was something worse, I'm sure of it.'

'And you're scared of finding out what it is?' Monty took her sister's slender, straight-fingered hands in her own.

'I am scared, yes. You're the only person I'd admit it to, but I'm really frightened. I've got this awful feeling about the whole business. My intuition is just screaming NO.'

The three of them were silent. Cathy was always so calm, so decisive, so economically poised as she shifted millions of dollars around the world for her clients; Monty knew that her sister could feel as terrified as any other woman inside but very seldom showed it: so this admission of fear was a shock.

The baby tumbled off the bottom step of the short flight which separated the two areas of the vast living space; she whimpered because she had bumped her head. Joe jumped up and scooped the infant into his arms.

'What do you feel about it all, Monty?' he asked as he sat down again. She looked into his eyes and Cathy felt the intensity of their intimacy like a spark passing between them.

'I have a strange feeling, too, but it's not scary. It's more like I'm being called in, or called home, or something. I feel as if something is coming full circle. Like you, I suppose, I think maybe we'll be able to understand some things that we couldn't before. But I'm not scared – just for once.'

Throughout their lives it had been Cathy's job to look after her younger sister, and the responsibility had become a habit. Cathy resolutely shook off her forebodings.

'Somewhere in the world there must be a private detective who hasn't walked out of a bad film. You're right, Monty, we might as well start by investigating the eastern connection. And why Daddy died. There might be something – anyway, that's all we've got to go on.' She stood up with a swish of silk, her dark brown hair swinging into place as she moved. 'I've got a couple of clients who're big in Hong Kong, I'll ask their advice. I'll brief someone, and get a report when I'm in Singapore next month for the tin crisis conference, and then we can all meet up at the opening of the Shahzdehs' new development.'

Joe and Monty smiled at each other; Cathy had a kind of puritanical guilt about taking holidays, and they had been hoping she would overcome it to take up an invitation issued by one of her oldest clients, an Iranian couple whose multifarious interests included a chain of luxury resort islands.

'Isn't it so typical of my work-obsessed sister to think of a jet-set playground as just another development?' Monty chinked the ice in her drink happily.

'OK, it's a deal,' said Joe. 'I'm glad you're coming to the Shahzdehs' new island, it sounds like quite a place.'

Monty's butterfly mind had already settled on a new idea. 'Cathy, can I ask you something, sister-to-sister?'

'If you can't, I don't know who can.'

Monty pointed to the baby's neatly diapered rear, as Paloma crawled towards the steps once more. 'Did it ever bother you to have that mark on your thigh?' In the centre of the child's plump upper leg was a light-brown, leaf-shaped birthmark. Cathy involuntarily slid her hand under her own right thigh, where she too had an area of darker pigmentation.

'Only when we were all wearing mini-skirts and bare legs, in the sixties. That was the only time it showed. I forget about it mostly.'

Monty frowned, knowing her sister's capacity for camouflaging the smallest area of vulnerability. Joe was staring at the ceiling; Monty knew he thought she was obsessed with the baby's birthmark. She had been fretting over it, and wanting to see a specialist, ever since the birth. Monty's own version of the mark was a much narrower shape, darker, but higher up, on her right buttock, so that it was never visible unless she wore a brief bikini or leotard.

'You're sure – you didn't feel it was a disfigurement?' her voice faltered on the word.

'No, honestly, Monty, I was hardly aware of it. It's something I never give a thought to.'

Later, however, Cathy lay awake in the night thinking about the pale brown stain on her skin. She had dreamed vividly of watching herself from behind, diving into a swimming pool, with the birthmark showing darker because she was sun-tanned. Accompanying the dream were feelings of violent emotional disturbance – anger, anxiety and acute insecurity. Monty said that everyone dreamed a lot in Arizona; she had a theory that the elemental landscape, all air, fire and earth, put people in closer touch with their hidden emotions.

Perhaps she was right, Cathy thought, sitting up in bed and pulling the white quilt up to shoulder level. She switched on the concealed lighting in the white wall behind the bed and reached for the folder at her bedside. It contained the draft of the prospectus for her new venture, a private bank. In the years during which Cathy had dealt successfully with some of the wealthiest but most wayward people in the world, she had become convinced that the bank would be a logical develop-ment of the service she already provided for her clients. Now other firms were get-ting to the same place, and it was time to act before her market began to be eroded. Cathy knew she would never be in quite such a strong position again.

She was a wealthy woman, certainly, the richest self-made woman in Britain. But money did not buy friends, it just got you smarter enemies. Human nature didn't change – especially male human nature.

Even the prospectus could not engage her tormented mind and Cathy's thoughts strayed. A name floated out of her unfocused memories of her father – William Treadwell. He was the man to whom her father had been closest out in the East; maybe she could trace him.

Because Treadwell had changed his name and adopted the native religion, Daddy had talked about him as if he had contracted some chronic illness. They must have been close, or her father would never have felt so strongly about Treadwell's change of faith. She tried to remember more. Treadwell had taught her father to play chess. Cathy smiled with affection for her dead father. She also remembered her husband accusing her: 'You don't love me,' he had raged, 'you can't love me, or any other man. There's only one man you'll ever love, Cathy, and he's dead. That's your little tragedy, darling.' The harsh words, spoken in anger so long ago, no longer wounded her. What her husband had said was untrue; she could love. She loved her son more than his father would ever be able to comprehend, but there would never be anyone in her life quite as dazzling as Daddy, of course. She had accepted that.

CHAPTER ONE

'I SEEM to be in trouble.' The forelock of James Bourton's greying dark hair fell into his line of vision as he leaned over the chessboard. He picked up his one remaining bishop, moved it halfway across the board, saw danger and retreated.

A few pink petals from the rose which climbed the grey-stone façade of their house fell on to their table on the terrace, and James picked them off, playing for time. Cathy wondered if her father was putting on a show of floundering in defeat for her benefit. She hoped not. She was sixteen, and no longer wanted concessions of that kind. She watched him with patience, folding her arms across the bib of her navy school tunic to keep warm. The heat of the September day was fading.

When she had been a little girl, it had been different. She could not bear to lose at any game, and had cried and screamed, 'It's not fair!' if she was check-mated. Her father had indulged her, surrendering with a show of despair at the end but putting up just enough of a fight for her to feel her triumph was genuine.

'Dash it, you've done it again,' he would murmur in a pained voice. 'Run off the board by my own daughter!' he would protest, pretending an agony of disgrace.

'But Daddy,' Cathy would say with childish forthrightness which persisted long after she should have learned tact, 'I only won because you were absolutely *stupid*.'

'In victory, magnanimity,' he advised her, making room for her on his lap so she could give him a kiss. He smelt of the cologne from his Curzon Street barber, of cigars, and, after lunch, of brandy. His cheeks were cool and smooth, never scratchy with stubble like Uncle Hugo's.

Cathy began to beat her father for real shortly after she went to boarding school, but he would still lounge back in his chair, blow smoke-rings from his afternoon cigar, and give her advice from a position of superiority.

'Always think two moves ahead,' he counselled in lordly tones. 'Put yourself in your enemy's shoes. Think about what I'm up to as well as what you're going to do about it,' he told her, narrowing his bright brown eyes. Then his attention would wander and she would be able to take his queen in two moves.

'That's the spirit, princess. Do as your father says, not as he does.' And he would beam with pleasure, tickled pink that his daughter had such ability. His

1

concentration span was short, and, unlike Cathy, he saw no point in winning a game, only in passing his time enjoyably.

The last chess game of the school holidays had become a ritual, as much a part of the process of saying goodbye to home as taking her pony down to the livery stable and kissing his silky nose. Their mother would leave for her afternoon at the bridge club, and Monty would vanish upstairs to her piano. This was the last precious time which Cathy would spend alone with her father for some months.

'All right, you've got me. I surrender. Hang out the white flag.' James tossed the hair out of his eyes and they smiled at each other with satisfaction. 'I never mind losing to the most beautiful girl in the world. Come and give your poor father a kiss.'

From the uppermost window, under the graceful gothic curve of the gable, cascades of notes sounded from the piano. Monty was attacking an elaborate Chopin fantasy much too fast, slurring across the passages she could not remember and guessing the chords until at last the piece collapsed in hopeless dissonance. Monty said, 'Hell,' loudly enough to be heard outside, slammed down the piano lid, then slammed it up again and started picking out a different tune. James hummed it.

'Isn't that something by those dreadful insects – what are they called?' Cathy knew he was teasing her.

'The Beatles, Daddy. Yes, she can play all their songs.'

'They're still the latest thing, are they?'

'They've been number one for weeks.'

'Ridiculous name. I suppose you teenagers like that sort of noise.' He tossed the last two inches of Havana into the herbaceous border.

'We're not teenagers, Daddy.'

'Of course you are, you're sixteen and fifteen, that makes you teenagers.'

Cathy wriggled on the Georgian garden bench. She had a knack of seeing life very clearly which adults often found embarrassing. 'You know what I mean, we aren't *really* teenagers.' What she meant was that teenagers were virtually a new social class. The granddaughters of a Duke, educated at the boarding school which was shortly to be attended by the Queen's own daughter, had their position in society predetermined.

Whatever their social background or education, teenagers shared the same interests and rejected everything their parents held dear. Teenagers, by definition, had rows with their parents and wore outrageous outfits. They had jobs which paid them as much as £20 per week – leaving plenty of money to spend on clothes and records – but their attitude to work was irresponsible. They skipped from one job to another, contributing as little as possible and always looking for excitement rather than secure employment with a pension afterwards.

Girl teenagers wore corpse-pale make-up, near-white lipstick and thick black eyeliner; the boys wore hair so long it almost brushed their shirt collars, and cuban-heeled boots with chisel toes. At weekends, teenagers hung around coffee bars in gangs. Above all, teenagers liked pop music. They bought singles by the million for 6s 3d each, and played them on automatic record players. Teenagers despised BBC light music programmes hosted by middle-aged men with patronizing, upper-class voices. Instead, they tuned their transistor radios to Radio Luxembourg, a station which transmitted pop music all night from the tiny principality on the Continent, beyond the censorship of British broadcasting laws.

James half-approved of what he called the teenage thing. He bought Monty a transistor radio for her fourteenth birthday, and silenced his wife with a glare when she objected to the noise. Without ever analysing his knowledge, James recognized that teenagers were essentially non-conformist, and his two daughters, high-spirited as they might be, were nice, upper-class girls, conformist to the tips of their unvarnished fingernails.

'Why shouldn't they enjoy themselves?' he argued with his wife. 'There's no harm in listening to music. They'll grow up soon enough.'

Bettina pinched her lips, making the coral lipstick run further into the deep wrinkles around her once pretty mouth. 'Nice young men nowadays . . .' she began, but James cut off her sentence.

'Nice young men nowadays aren't going to want to marry a pair of stick-in-the-muds,' he told her, suddenly vicious.

Bettina wanted her daughters married as well and as quickly as possible, so that she could consider her duty as a mother discharged. The sisters had sensed their mother's hostility in their earliest childhood, and drawn closely together to protect themselves against her. In those days their father had been a virtual stranger, whose weekend visits were like interludes of dazzling sunlight in a life overcast with their mother's dislike.

As they matured from perplexing bundles of childish passion to pleasing pre-adolescents, James discovered that his daughters were delightful companions. Just as his own lust for living was waning, their enthusiasm refreshed it. Even their faults entranced him; if Cathy was outspoken to the point of rudeness and Monty increasingly rebellious, they were only expressing his own frustrated feelings. He began to realize that the two girls were the best achievement of his life. They were also the only women whom he could love with all his heart; he was never anxious to be left alone with his wife, whom he did not love at all.

To everyone but his wife, Bettina, James Bourton was the most charming man imaginable. In middle age he was wiry and energetic, with spontaneous good manners and flattering attention for everyone from the new traffic wardens who put tickets on his Bentley all over the City to the Chairmen of his boards.

One enthusiasm after another caught James's fancy, and in consequence he passed on to his elder daughter a broad-based education in gentlemanly pursuits;

at sixteen she could hold a competent discussion with anyone about the right trout fly to use, the best claret to drink or the most likely horse to back. She was slow to acquire the ladylike cunning to hide this knowledge, but most of her father's friends found her girlish frankness charming and would only laugh when she earnestly explained exactly where they had gone wrong.

Cathy also learned something else from mixing in her father's world. She learned that he was a failure. He was well-liked, and valued for his name and connections, which were worth a great deal in the City of London in 1963. But his colleagues thought James a lightweight, lacking in judgement and insufficiently aggressive in business. Every now and then she would catch a patronizing note as someone spoke to him, and she would burn inwardly with anger. Didn't they realize that her father was the most marvellous man in the world?

'Well – all good things must come to an end.' James stood up and took her arm as they strolled indoors. 'Go and see if your sister's ready. I've got to speak to your headmistress about her and we'd better not be late if I'm going to tackle the dragon in her lair.'

Nominally, James was a director of a large merchant bank, two new Unit Trust companies and an old-established insurance brokerage house. Lord James Bourton was a name which looked well on the letterheads, and James himself looked well at board meetings, excavating neat holes in the ends of his cigars with a gold penknife to mask his boredom. He looked best of all in the bank's box at Ascot, or watching polo on Smith's Lawn at Windsor, or running a fluent, amusing conversation around the long, mahogany dining table of his club. Any habitat of the British aristocracy was natural to him, and the traditional plumage also became him more than it became most men; Cathy thought he looked finest in full evening dress, with diamond studs twinkling below his crisp white tie and discreet medal ribbons reminding everyone that this dandy had also served his country.

As soon as the girls were old enough, James took them with him to lighten some of the ceaseless round of entertaining which was his primary business function. Bettina never spent more time with her husband than necessary; Monty was easily bored, and then became sulky, announcing that she didn't want to dress up and go out with her father any more; but Cathy was always delighted with any excuse to enjoy his company.

The road that led to Benenden School was like the road to Manderley, a mysterious, private highway overhung with beech trees and rhododendron bushes. Monty always had a sense of foreboding as they drove down the dark-green tunnel, leaving the fertile Kent countryside behind in the mellow autumn sunshine. The wall of vegetation enclosed the school completely, cutting it off from life in the real world outside.

She shrank down into the corner of the Bentley as it emerged into the avenue of lime trees that connected the group of red-brick school buildings; the main building was a castellated edifice with Jacobean pretensions. Monty thought it a hypocritical sham, and held the same opinion of most of the activities promoted within its walls. Most of all, she dreaded the swamp of boredom which waited behind the diamond-paned windows. The endless afternoons spent acquiring useless facts or redundant skills would, she knew, plunge her into a lethargy which was as painful and exhausting as an illness.

Cathy got out first. Her house, Etchyngham, was a building at the far end of the lime avenue. Etchyngham's colour was pink, and Cathy looked almost pretty with a pink belt and tie on her navy uniform. Monty's house, Guldeford, had orange accessories. She hated orange. It made her look sallow. Monty knew the teachers kept her in Guldeford House because it was part of the main school building and she would be under their noses. The school's biggest troublemaker, Serena Lamotte, who called herself Swallow, was in Guldeford House for the same reason. Monty and Swallow were becoming good friends.

Once the girls had kissed him goodbye and vanished inside their respective houses, James strolled towards the headmistress's study, trying to put himself in the right frame of mind to win Monty the approval of those in authority over her. The reason he found this difficult was that he felt his younger daughter's spirit was her most valuable quality. He envied her courage to rebel; he could not help reflecting that his own life would have been very different, and probably far more satisfying, if his character had contained a similar measure of fire. He saw no reason at all why she should obey the school rules. If his bond with his elder daughter was founded on complementary personalities and interests, James's attraction to Monty was the yearning of a reluctantly domesticated personality for one which was fighting to remain untamed. Cathy shared this feeling. They both knew that Monty was in some way special, and protected her accordingly.

In the headmistress's study James began to play the part of the concerned parent.

'Quite frankly, Lord James, I am not at all sure that we will be able to do much more for Miranda,' Miss Sharpe began with an expression of discomfort.

Miranda was Monty's real Christian name. Monty, the nickname of Britain's great World War II general, had been the name her father had called her after a holiday at Deauville, where he had listened to his seven-year-old daughter ordering her older sister and her cousins to scramble up and down sand dunes in a game they called Desert Rats. The name seemed more appropriate as Miranda grew older, more independent, more awkward, and more uncontrollable.

'It isn't just a question of position badges and detentions, or even of the smoking. It's her general attitude. We stress personal integrity here and we have to consider the other girls. Does she smoke at home, do you know?'

'Certainly not.' James knew perfectly well that Monty's recent passion for long walks was entirely inspired by the fact that she could smoke undetected out of doors. 'We've had some long talks during the holidays, and Monty has promised to turn over a completely new leaf.' He beamed with confidence, baring fine white teeth, one of which was chipped. 'I'm sure you'll find the smoking was just a youthful experiment.' The smile widened and the lines which crisscrossed his otherwise boyish face deepened. Miss Sharpe smiled back. 'Monty really lives for her music, and my wife and I are tremendously appreciative of everything you've done for her here. I'm quite sure you will have every reason to be proud of her. She's quite determined to make a new start.' Like all successful seducers, James's blandishing sincerity was due to the fact that he believed every word he said at the time he said it, and Miss Sharpe's shrewd schoolmistress's sense about difficult girls was overwhelmed.

'I've been meaning to congratulate you on your Oxford and Cambridge results,' he went on. 'You must be very pleased. I think Cathy's rather looking forward to the Sixth Form.'

'Will she be considering university?' The annual tragedy of Miss Sharpe's life was that the parents of so many of her competent girls took them away from the school at fifteen or sixteen and sent them to finishing schools or tossed them into the debutante season, considering any proof of intellect as at best irrelevant and at worst something more damaging to the girl's marriage prospects than congenital insanity. Many of the school staff would have been married if their fiancés had not died in the war. Their careers were a forced choice, and they felt in no position to argue with the girls' parents.

'We'll leave university up to her – I think that's wisest, don't you? I see you've started work on the new house – how *is* the appeal going?' James was subtly reminding Miss Sharpe that his contribution to the fundraising had been handsome and early, allowing her to approach other parents with a high benchmark to indicate the size of donation required. Such generosity was to be expected of a man of his means and social position, but with Monty under threat of expulsion, this seemed to her father an expedient moment to bring up the subject of the school's gratitude.

Having conducted this delicate conversation with his usual panache, James stepped out and into the Bentley, and ordered his driver to take him on to London, leaving Miss Sharpe with the afterglow of his smile and a sense of obligation towards both his daughters.

'God, another term in this bloody hellhole!' Monty flopped down on her bed with a screech of springs, and scowled across the stack of luggage at two of the girls who shared her dormitory. One of Benenden's idiosyncrasies was that girls were quartered in small dormitories of three or four, and their ages were mixed.

The fifteen-year-old Monty found herself billeted with Frances Graham, the timid twelve-year-old daughter of a British Ambassador, and Camilla Carstairs, a devastatingly pretty blonde who was school captain of lacrosse, the apple of the English mistress's eye, and the daughter of a judge.

'Do you have to swear?' Camilla demanded in her strangled drawl. Monty ignored her.

'Whose is all this stuff?' Monty pointed at six pieces of matching, white leather luggage stacked higgledy-piggledy by the unoccupied bed.

'The new girl's, I suppose.' Camilla took her brown canvas lacrosse boots, temporarily clean of the mud that would cake their studded soles for the rest of the term, out of her much- mended case and put them into the bottom of her cupboard. Most of the girls at Benenden had luggage which was good quality but old, handed down by their parents. The heap of white cases, however, was obviously brand new and each gleaming side was embossed with the gilded initials R. E. E.

Monty sauntered across the room and ran her finger over the monogram on the smallest case.

'Her parents must be loaded.'

'Of course they're loaded, they're Jewish. Don't you remember Miss Sharpe giving us a pi-jaw about her at the end of last term?' Swallow Lamotte, skinny and tousle-haired with thick lips like a goldfish, came in and sat on Monty's bed.

'They own half of P & G, don't they?' Pearce & Goldsmith, or P & G for short, was a rapidly growing chain-store selling cheap, serviceable clothes of remarkable quality, considering their price.

'She won't be short of anything, anyway. Did you bring any chocolate?' She rummaged in Monty's tuckbox.

The porter struggled through the doorway with the last and largest of the white cases. Monty lethargically snapped open her own case, a scuffed, pigskin legacy from James, and began stuffing away her clothes.

'Why are they making such a fuss about her, anyway? She can't be any different from the rest of us.' She tossed her newly acquired black stockings on to a high shelf, followed by the ferocious girdle which held them up. It was a surgical greyish-white, with a flat satin panel in front and wide flanges of rubbery elastic around the sides. Monty was grateful for the way it flattened the obstinate curve of her stomach, but loathed the way it imprinted hideous red weals on her body. To add what the manufacturers hoped was a feminine touch, the suspenders were veiled with scraps of satin ribbon which frayed unattractively.

'I see your mother bought you a bra at last.' Swallow opened a packet of biscuits.

'She made enough fuss about it.' Monty showed them the heavy contraption which, she hoped, flattened her breasts back to nothing.

'She's the first Jewish girl they've had since the war, and they're afraid she'll be bullied – that's why they're making all this fuss.' Camilla closed her suitcase and pushed it under her bed, then dragged her trunk towards her and began opening its brass locks. Inside were books, supplies of jam and chocolate, and the filthy, one-eared teddy bear she placed proudly in the centre of her pillow. 'She's seeing the housemistress now and I've got to go and fetch her at half past and show her round.' Vigorously, Camilla brushed specks of fluff off the long navy cape the girls wore outdoors in winter, and hung it on the rail of her washing cubicle.

'Look here, Monty, this won't do at all,' she said with irritation. 'I'm dormitory monitor, I'm responsible for keeping the place decent and I'm not having you turn it into a pigsty on the first day of term. You can jolly well take all those down again and fold them up neatly.' She pointed at the crumpled mess of shirts, vests, and underwear in Monty's cupboard.

With bad grace, Monty pulled down the mass of tangled clothes and began folding each garment as slowly as she could.

'Camilla, why do they think she'll be bullied because she's Jewish?'

'Some people are a bit funny about Jews, that's all.'

'But why? Hitler hated the Jews, and we fought Hitler so why do we hate the Jews, too?'

'We don't. They've just come over here from Europe and made a lot of money and some people don't like it, that's all.'

'But if they were going to be put in concentration camps to die it was sensible to come over here, surely?' Monty knew perfectly well what Camilla was going to say next; she was hoping that by spinning out the conversation she could postpone the job of tidying her cupboard. The plan worked. Camilla suddenly checked her watch and jumped up.

'Cripes – I'll be late!' She sprinted off down the corridor on solidly muscled legs.

Swallow pulled back Camilla's bedcovers and sprinkled some biscuit crumbs between the sheets.

'Sweet dreams, Sergeant Major,' she said, punching the teddy bear in its stomach.

Monty shoved her clothes back and wondered what the new girl would be like. She didn't know any Jewish people, or anything about them, except what she remembered from her lessons; they had read *The Merchant of Venice* in English, and in history lessons had learned that Disraeli bought the Suez canal for Britain with the Rothschilds' money. All Monty really knew about Jewish people was that they were different, and she knew, too, that she was different; she was beginning to look on herself as a lonely, misunderstood figure, forever alienated from quiet sleek-haired girls like Camilla or Cathy, whose souls were as well-ordered as their cupboards, with no tangled masses of doubt shoved away out of sight.

It was easy for the other girls to keep to the school rules, to be quiet, tidy, hard-working and obedient, but Monty found all that impossible. The rules were stupid, she thought and the teachers were, too; and what was the point of tidiness as long as you could find your clothes when you needed them?

Half an hour later Camilla returned, bringing with her the new girl. 'This is Rosanna Emanuel,' she said formally, as Monty and Swallow looked up.

'How do you do.' Rosanna advanced and shook hands with each of them in turn, stepping around her white mountain of luggage as she went. Her face was fine and delicate, with a fierce beauty which made Camilla's Anglo-Saxon prettiness look suddenly insipid. Her hair was curly and the weight of it was drawn into a ponytail of glossy ringlets, while curly tendrils framed her face.

Her clothes, however, were unlike anything that Monty, Camilla or Swallow had ever imagined. They watched in fascination as Rosanna methodically opened her cases and took possession of the modest allocation of space Benenden offered each student.

From the biggest case came an immaculate array of school uniform, the tunics altered by her mother's dressmaker to fit and flatter. In fact, when Monty looked closely, she saw that the plain, navy pinafore had been copied in fine wool gaberdine, instead of the standard-issue serge from Debenham & Freebody. Rosanna had a crisp, white poplin blouse for every day of the week, and these too had been made for her. The next case held her cape, and 'flaps' – an immense circular skirt in the house colour which was worn for the weekly dancing class. Never had Guldeford orange seemed so bright.

'Do we really have to wear these?' she asked Monty, holding up the hideous jelly-bag hat that went with the outdoor cape. Monty nodded.

Next came the velvet dress the girls wore for church on Sundays. This had a half train at the back, and a silk collar. The dresses came in harsh blue, red or green, and most girls had only one. Rosanna had three, one in each colour, and the hues were considerably more subtle. All in all, Rosanna's uniform was perfectly in accordance with the school list, but not quite right. It was better. According to the arcane conventions of the British upper class, better was wrong.

'Did you get all that at Debenham & Freebody's?' Swallow asked out of curiosity.

'Oh no – we hated their things. Mummy bought one of everything and then gave them to her dressmaker to copy. Where do we put empty cases?'

'Under the bed. You can put some of yours under mine, if you like.' Monty swung aside her legs and drew up her bedcover.

'That's *terribly* kind of you.'

It was all wrong – not wrong as it would have been if Rosanna could not have been expected to know any better, as if her father were a workman or a foreigner or something. It was wrong because one shouldn't say 'dressmaker' but talk about

9

'this little woman who makes my mother's frocks'; neither should one display emotion, even a mild emotion such as gratitude. 'Terribly kind' was incorrect. The right way was to mutter 'thanks' and get on with unpacking. It was wrong to be effusive, wrong to exaggerate, wrong to mind so much how you looked that you took care and spent a lot of money and were not ashamed to say so.

Monty, Swallow and Camilla had been brought up in the curious way the English aristocracy raised their children. All but their most basic needs would be ignored until they were old enough to be mated. They had eaten in the kitchen or the nursery with their nannies, seldom in the dining room with their parents; they had been dressed in ugly, practical clothes, some of which were expensive, but none of which were stylish or pretty. Vanity was discouraged as an unnecessary vice, and in some nurseries looking in the mirror was not allowed. There was no question of girls wearing what they wanted; they had to have roomy heavy shoes, stout tweed skirts and shapeless heavy coats.

For entertainment they were simply turfed out of doors, and for company they had been left to their parents' servants. The girls were encouraged to lavish their emotions on dogs and ponies, thus ensuring that boys and sex were excluded from their interests. At the age of seventeen these ugly gauche grubs would be brought indoors, washed, taught the rudiments of social skills, kitted out in adult finery, told that they were butterflies and released to mate in the desperately short debutante season, after which their parents would give them no more money or attention.

'When are you going to wear *that*?' asked Camilla with a sneer. Rosanna hung up a full-skirted, strapless cocktail dress of black grosgrain.

'The opera. My father's coming to take me to the opera on my first weekend out. Mummy's sure I'm going to be terribly homesick.'

'Gosh, you lucky thing.' Now Monty was frankly envious. 'I've never been to an opera. Is it nice?'

'Some of it is. I like Mozart best, but the singers are all so fat and ugly that I usually end up watching with my eyes shut.' Monty laughed, the others did not.

'Is that your fiddle?' Monty indicated the black violin case, the only item among Rosanna's luggage which was not spanking new.

'Well, sort of. I'm not terribly good. I don't practise enough.' Rosanna stowed another empty case under Monty's bed and turned to the next full one, which contained only her underwear, packed in crisp sheets of blue-white tissue paper. First came knitted wool vests and long, matching camiknickers, trimmed with pink lace.

Swallow snorted. 'You'll certainly need *them*.'

'Is it *very* cold here?' Rosanna's eyes widened, fearful of discomfort.

'Bloody arctic,' Monty confirmed.

'And is there a lot of lacrosse? We didn't play games much at my last school.'

'You haven't missed a thing, I promise. We've got lacrosse every day this term. It's called lax, actually, not lacrosse.'

Rosanna smiled, grateful for this tiny measure of initiation into the school customs. 'Does everybody have to play?'

'Everybody. Camilla's the school captain. They let you off if you're injured, though.'

'What about if you're having a bad period – I have awful periods, absolute agony and they go on for days.'

'No good, they still flog you out into the mud.'

Rosanna shuddered, and put away three matching sets of white lace, French brassières, panties and garter belts. The brassières were daringly wired to make her already full breasts look even more luscious, and had pink satin rosebuds with green satin leaves sewn between the cups.

Next out of the case was a long, white lace corselette, with bones from breast to hip level, and dangling suspenders.

'Gosh, that's *beautiful*. I've never seen anything like that except on Brigitte Bardot posters.' Monty fingered the outrageously adult garment gingerly. 'Are you really going to wear it?'

'Of course I am, I need it. I've got a horribly fat stomach and no waist at all.' Rosanna pulled in her uniform to show them.

By the time the supper bell rang at 7.30 Rosanna had also unpacked thick, black stockings of pure silk, not of itchy cotton like Monty's, and an ivory-handled manicure set in a white leather case. In her washing cubicle was her pure bristle toothbrush and a tiny tube of red toothpaste which was supposed to make her teeth sparkle. Across the greyish-yellow candlewick bedspread lay a thick, red merino dressing gown and a Swiss cotton nightdress.

Camilla treated each item as a personal insult. Swallow sulked with jealousy. Monty felt as if someone had raised the corner of the dust sheet which had been draped over her future.

They trooped down to the oak-panelled dining hall, each girl carrying her own napkin in a napkin ring. In keeping with the rest of their possessions, the Benenden girls' napkins were frayed damask squares belonging to long worn-out sets of their parents' table linen, and they were rolled lopsidedly into rings of painted wood or scratched horn.

Miss Sharpe was clearing her throat to say grace as Monty and Rosanna slipped into the last two places at their table. '*Per Jesum Christum Dominum nostrum,*' she finished, as, one by one, the pupils standing with bowed heads stole furtive glances at the new girl.

Rosanna's napkin was of new Irish linen, with an elaborately embroidered R in one corner. Her napkin ring, on which her initials were engraved, was thick and heavy, and it gleamed with the unmistakable soft intensity of solid silver.

There was a hostile silence at Rosanna's table as the other girls appraised her prettiness, her elegance and her obvious wealth.

'I say,' brayed a voice from the table's end, 'I thought all Jews had *horns*.'

Rosanna looked up and smiled.

CHAPTER TWO

E VERY MARRIAGE has a secret contract between wife and man which has nothing to do with any of the purposes of matrimony set out in the prayer book. The unwritten contract between James Bourton's parents required his father to provide the means for his mother to satisfy her ambitions. She wanted to be a successful woman, a great society beauty around whose feet the most powerful men would grovel in adoration.

Since love affairs were the prerogative of married people, Lady Davina chose her husband without delay. The young Duke of Witherham could give her everything else she needed – entrée to court circles, political contacts, several impressive houses and the wealth to create a lavish backdrop for her personal pageant. She swiftly overpowered him with a barrage of flattery and flirtation, which he accepted as no more than his due.

After their marriage, however, Davina discovered that her husband would not fulfil his part of the matrimonial bargain because he did not understand it; he had no appreciation of the importance of flowers, jewels, love-letters and clandestine trysts which would be common knowledge from Piccadilly to Kensington the next day. He rightly assumed that his wife had no intention of rejecting him, his wealth and his title, and was therefore deeply puzzled when she solicited the advances of other men. He did not realize that his wife was an ambitious but cowardly woman who was unable to seek fulfilment outside the traditional arena of feminine manipulation.

The women in her circle understood perfectly the kind of supremacy Davina was trying to establish, and counterattacked in the same style, with more outrageous clothes, more notorious exploits and more scandalous liaisons.

The Duke turned mulish, and rejected the London social scene for the enjoyment of his country estates. Davina detested the country. She became cold and waspish, and distracted herself by refitting his country seat, Bourton House, at terrifying expense. When his wife pushed him towards public life, the Duke resisted with oxlike cussedness. With the perverse cunning of a man who chooses to escape his wife's dominion by assuming dullness, he scotched her ambitions by sticking at the social level of a country squire. When she began to launch herself at their male weekend guests in a flurry of seductive sweet talk, he took it as permission to begin an affair with the wife of the local hunt-master.

To these injuries, further insult was added on a blustery, autumn afternoon in 1918. Davina had been convinced that her second child would be a girl. Her Grace at once directed that her second son be dressed in petticoats, and referred to him thereafter as Jane. From the cradle, James Bourton's sexuality was warped.

'I shan't waste any more time having children,' Davina told her husband. 'We shall just have to make do with what we've got. I've far more important things to think of than babies.' She never considered divorce; divorced women were not received at Court. Divorce was for Americans. Davina was determined to shine in society in spite of her husband.

Lord James Bourton joined his brother Hugo, the three-year-old Marquess of St Elians, in the nursery, where the younger boy became highly popular. As a baby he was plump and smiling; as a toddler he was an irresistible little animal, winning all kinds of concessions from the nurserymaids with his sweet ways. As a small boy, with a gold watchchain gleaming across the little waistcoat he could wear when his mother was absent, he was the personification of masculinity in miniature, and the stolid Hugo watched with envy as James was bounced and tickled and drawn into romps which grew increasingly less innocent. Virginity was something he never knew about until many years after his own had been debauched by a succession of bored, simpleminded servant girls.

The nannies – and there were so many of them that the two boys could never remember any by name – were tyrannized by the Duchess, who would descend from London with an avalanche of petty impositions. 'Hugo must always wear green, it suits his complexion,' she would command, 'and the children must learn Italian. I shall take them to Venice in the spring.' Then she might light on some extravagance. 'Why on earth is the nursery fire so high? Are you trying to burn the house down, Nanny? No more than *one* bucket of coals a day, if you please.'

Stinginess was followed by generosity. 'Nanny, your hands are simply blue with cold. Ask my maid for my old muff as soon as we get back.' In another two days, she would forget and accuse the bewildered servant of having stolen the muff, often in vulgar terms that advertised the blatant greed of her own nature.

Davina, Duchess of Witherham, could never have enough of anything that gave a woman status. She pestered her lovers for flowers and her husband for jewels, wrecked the estate's accounts by requisitioning sums for a swimming pool or a rose arbour, stuffed whole rooms with clothes which she seldom felt flattered her enough. She bought hunters which she could not ride and took lavish holidays in Europe on which she inevitably fell ill, saw nothing and was a whining burden to her companions.

Most of all, she could not have enough of men. Without her husband, the highest echelons of society were closed to her. Instead she joined the vivid coterie of adventuresses around the Prince of Wales. Denied fame, she chose notoriety. Other bright young things might dance on the tables at the Embassy Club, but Davina was to be found underneath, riding her latest conquest with shrieks not sufficiently stifled to preserve their privacy. One bold man who refused her at the last fence almost died of shame when she bit off his fly buttons. It was rumoured that at her bedside she kept a silver sugar shaker filled with cocaine, which she sprinkled on her lovers' erections to make them last longer.

When Davina heard this story she played it up to the hilt, carrying a tiny sugar shaker in her purse. What was important to her was not to make love, but to be seen to be made love to – was not that the greatest tribute a woman could collect? As a great beauty, Davina was entirely her own invention. She demanded that Cecil Beaton photograph her; the session was lengthy and unsuccessful. 'You can't catch the beauty of a woman's soul if she hasn't got one,' he said afterwards.

Without her repertoire of erotic blandishments she was nothing but a woman with thin brown hair and muddy green eyes, the size of whose hips was accentuated by the sway-backed stance she imagined was regal posture. She had fine breasts in the twenties, when it was fashionable to be flat-chested, and by the early thirties, when a soft swelling below the crêpe-de-chine was again desirable, her bosom had deflated. Nature, at least, would not be ordered to her own ends.

She looked upon her sons as merely two more males whose sexuality could be turned to her advantage. She conducted coquettish enquiries into the progress of their adolescence. Hugo, a naturally prudish creature, found her embarrassing before he was old enough to know why.

James, as an infant, offered her the purest love she would ever inspire. His earliest memory was of standing in adoration beside his mother's dressing table, handing her maid the hairpins as she dressed Her Grace's hair around a glittering tiara. He was about four years old, and if her lovers had noticed a slight wattling of the skin of her eyelids, she was still as beautiful as a goddess to her younger son.

Hypnotized with wonder, James reached up to touch the tiara. His mother, infuriated, seized a pin from the maid and stabbed it into her son's pudgy hand, then ordered the nursemaid to remove him and pulled her silken skirts away from the bleeding child. Accustomed to such female treachery, James never felt safe with any woman.

When he was about to go to Eton, Davina ordered his hair to be cut and had him dressed as a boy at last. For the first time she noticed that her younger son had a great deal of charm, and worshipped her as lavishly as her overbred Pomeranian puppy.

Eton, like most other great British boys' schools in the thirties, was an all-male community with a hierarchy of sexual domination like that of a troop of baboons. The older boys buggered the younger boys to reinforce their authority. The juniors were required to act as servants to the older boys to make their submission formal. James, good-looking, good-natured and piquantly manly even at the age of thirteen, caused quite a stir. He had no fear of his own sex, and promptly escaped into an affair with Cosmo Flett, a cultivated senior boy who was unpopular because of his brains and ugliness. Cosmo protected him, read him poetry, and got a broken nose in the cause of defending their love, after which they were left alone.

In the vacations, however, there was no escape from the hall of mirrors which forever disorients young men of precocious sexual allure and stunted emotional growth. His mother was always waiting for him, with presents, new clothes, and teasing compliments.

'My gorgeous boy,' she murmured, messing his dark hair. 'I'm too, too jealous of you with all your little friends. Won't you keep your poor mother company just a tiny bit?'

He was paraded through her London life of nightclubs and cocktail parties almost as a proof of her desirability, as if to show her disenchanted lovers that she deserved only young flesh of the standard she herself had created.

This period of favour ended sharply when James fell deeply into calf-love with one of his mother's friends, a pale, plump woman of forty who hung on his arm, squeezing herself against his awkward elbow and making knowing, I-can't-help-myself eyes at all their acquaintances. Furious at this double betrayal, Davina raged at the woman, who crumpled before a social *force majeure* and went back to her husband.

James, who had believed himself truly in the grip of romantic passion, stayed in bed at Bourton House for a month then made a clumsy attempt to shoot himself, blistering the newly painted library ceiling with lead pellets. His mother was briefly concerned, which restored his cheerfulness.

He was young, healthy, sensual and driven by an obscure anxiety about women. However, the more time he spent in female company the more he grew aware of the power of his charm, and he began to use it. His seductions were initiated by a desperate feeling that a woman was 'safe' only if she were squirming helplessly beneath him, gasping that she loved him and begging to do whatever he wanted. Out of bed he was often petulant and jealous, quick to suspect unfaithfulness and eager to make love again to obliterate the suspicion.

He became engaged, then broke it off cruelly, and the Duke ordered his younger son back to Bourton House, where the housemaids squabbled for the honour of taking up his morning tea. James was becoming more and more attractive to women as hard muscles filled out his small, slim frame and his dark spaniel's eyes learned to plead from below his tousled forelock.

Soon there was a pregnant housemaid to marry off hastily and a jealous footman, and Davina, still seething with rejection, began to demand that James be banished. Hugo, his older brother, whose temperament was placid and pompous, supported her and James sealed his own fate by paying marked attention to his father's mistress.

His mother manoeuvred him towards the army, but James stubbornly resisted. She launched half a dozen different schemes to find him posts in America, India or Australia. He conspired with Cosmo, now a Cambridge undergraduate with remarkable contacts, to have himself rejected by the Foreign Office.

Malaya was James's own idea; he had no idea where it was, but it was somewhere of which his mother had not thought.

'I had an interview yesterday,' he announced to his astonished family one Saturday at breakfast. 'And I've been offered a job.'

'Marvellous, darling,' his mother spoke in the threatening tone of voice with which she greeted all bids for independence among her menfolk.

'Exactly what kind of fool has decided to employ you?' asked his father, piling his plate with slabs of ham.

'The fool who is recruiting staff for the Hong Kong and Shanghai Bank.' James buttered a piece of toast with precision.

'Does he know you can't add up for toffee?' Hugo's habitual jealousy of his brother had deepened.

'He doesn't seem worried about that. All they did was give me a hearing test to see if I'd be able to understand Chinese. They said I came out of it rather well.'

His father grunted as he sat down. 'We'd better be grateful there's something you can do, I suppose.'

Davina commanded the table's attention with a raised voice. 'You can't *possibly* go to a country like that, James. There's a civil war and pirates and heaven knows what. The disease! And the East is an absolute *sink* of iniquity.'

'Certainly hope so,' James murmured, reaching for the marmalade. 'You're quite wrong, Mother,' he continued, applying a generous coating of the darkbrown conserve to his toast. 'There hasn't been any civil war since Malaya became a British protectorate, in 18 . . . er, well, a long time ago.'

'Tosh,' pronounced his brother, asserting his challenged superiority. 'Own up – you haven't a clue where you're going.'

'Don't you bet on it. Malaya is a pearshaped peninsula slightly smaller than the American state of Florida, which lies to the south of Siam.' James rattled through the information on the cyclostyled sheet provided by the Hong Kong and Shanghai Bank. 'The country produces half the total world production of tin and four-fifths of the total world production of rubber. On the ancient trading routes linking East and West, it is the meeting place of many races where men of all complexions live as friends. Eighty per cent of the country is covered with jungle and . . .' At last he paused; the only remaining fact about his destination which he could remember was that there were over two hundred species of dragonfly there.

'You're *completely* mad,' interjected his mother. 'You haven't the faintest notion of what you're doing. I shall telephone this bank tomorrow and tell them you've changed your mind.'

'Leave the boy alone,' his father broke in with unusual ferocity. 'Let him go to hell his own way. There's damn all he can do around here. At least he's shown initiative.'

Despite his bravado in front of his family, James was nervous of travelling half-way round the world to a new life in a country that was little more than a name to him. When he returned to London he went to the Botanical Gardens at Kew, and walked in wonder from the cool house to the temperate house to the sub-tropical house until finally he stood below the soaring palms of the largest, hottest, most humid greenhouse of all and looked at a small tree with feathery green leaves before which stood a plaque inscribed *Federated Malay States*. Beside this tree was a banana plant.

The greenhouse was filled with the murmuring sounds of water which dripped incessantly from a million leaves and trickled away under the wrought-iron covers of the drainage channels. James felt his shirt stick to his back and a collar of perspiration form around his neck. This sample of the environment which lay ahead of him acted as a solemn reassurance that he was making a wise decision.

Two weeks later, with a steel-lined trunk containing eighteen stiff shirts, thirty-six stiff collars, a solar topee and a padded jacket designed to protect his spine from the burning tropical sun, James embarked on the P & O liner at Southampton with a sense of release that was the nearest thing to total ecstasy he had ever experienced.

Georgetown, the colonial capital of Penang Island, delighted him as much as if it had been a toy town arranged entirely for his amusement. The grey-stone fort, with its guns pointing seaward, made him imagine distant junks loaded with Arab pirates heaving over the shimmering horizon.

In the solid buildings of the commercial district he felt the pulse of international trade, and saw himself as an intrepid agent of enterprise. He took a rickshaw down Pitt Street and was thrilled at the sight of the Chinese temple belching clouds of incense, and the Indian temple painted in pastel colours like a vast icecream cassata, and the food-hawkers selling green coconuts or tiny kebabs grilled on charcoal braziers. The exotic-looking crowds enthralled him; the savagery in the town's air exhilarated him. The sobriety required by his new profession was a welcome yoke. James felt that at last he was living real life.

At the bank, he supervised a room full of Chinese clerks twice his age. At first he was well thought of, not least because he had an ear for the subtle tones of Oriental languages, and could soon talk enough Cantonese to converse with the clerks.

Within six months, however, nemesis caught up with him.

'Bourton, you have done well, and I don't want you to think we aren't pleased with you,' began his supervisor, perspiring in the afternoon heat of the ovenlike office on Queen Street. 'But we can't have our chaps getting married the minute they come out.'

'I'm not getting married, sir.'

'Well, then what the devil are you playing at?' James was genuinely perplexed. He knew, of course, that it was a condition of his employment that he should remain unmarried for his first four years in the East.

The custom, he had soon discovered, was for the young British bank employees to work a lot, exhaust themselves in sport, and make forays among the Chinese prostitutes who waited patiently in rickshaws by the port. At the end of their first tour the young men took a six-month vacation in England, during which the more personable ones would succeed in getting engaged. The poorer, shyer and less good-looking ones would have to wait another four years, for their second long leave. James, eager to do well in his new life, had behaved with perfect propriety and was conducting a chaste romance with a girl called Lucy Kennedy, whose father was a senior civil servant.

'I'm sorry, sir, I don't know what all this is about.'

'You've been seeing a great deal of Lucy Kennedy, you don't deny that, I suppose.'

'No sir, of course not. She's a very sweet girl.'

'Sweet she may be, but she's putting it about that you're engaged. Where d'you suppose she came by that idea?'

'Honestly, sir, I swear I've never mentioned anything of the sort to her.'

His supervisor, a pale Scot with the exhausted look which white men of long residence in the tropics often acquire, questioned James's sincerity with washed-out blue eyes before giving a grudging grunt of satisfaction.

'I believe you're telling the truth, but you'd better find Miss Kennedy and get to the bottom of this smartly before I have her father to reckon with. The bank is one of the biggest British establishments in the East, people look to us as an example, and we can't have a pipsqueak like you muddying the water.'

'Look here, Lucy,' James said awkwardly, stumbling over a fallen palm-frond as they walked in the garden of her father's white-pillared mansion, 'have you said anything about us?'

'Oh don't be angry, James, I only told Mummy. I was so excited I had to tell someone,' She skipped with happiness at his side.

'But, Lucy, there's nothing to tell.'

Doubt suddenly fogged her adoring eyes. Her plump lower lip quivered and she pulled nervously at her neatly marcelled silver-blond bob. 'What do you mean, there's nothing to tell?'

James stopped walking and took her hands. 'I can't get engaged, Lucy, you know that.'

'But you asked me, James.' Huge tears suddenly appeared in the corners of her grey eyes.

'Lucy, I swear, I never asked you. There's nothing further from my mind, I promise you.'

'But don't you love me, James?' Tears were now pouring freely down her plump cheeks. In another anguished ten minutes the mystery was solved. The previous Saturday James had taken her to the weekly dance at the E & O Hotel, and at the end of the evening they had walked out on the stone-walled terrace above the sea, listening to the soothing splash of the waves and the crickets chirping in the coconut palms.

'I do love the East, Lucy, don't you?' he had said taking a deep, happy breath of the fragrant air. 'I shouldn't mind if I stayed here the rest of my life.' And Lucy had squeaked delightedly and planted a wet kiss on his uncomprehending cheek. To a girl of seventeen with few brains and nothing but marriage on her mind, his idle words had been a proposal.

Lucy howled and screamed and cried her eyes out; her father angrily attacked James's supervisor, who defended James as firmly as he could without implying that the girl was an idiot. James, thoroughly frightened, swore to himself that he would not go near a white girl again for the rest of his four years. He drank a great deal of whisky, played rugger and cricket and a great many games of billiards at the Penang Club and sobered up by long tramps in the cool, jungle-covered mountain-side reached by a ratchet-railway from the town.

His luck did not hold. He lodged in a small villa with three other boys from the 'Honkers and Shankers'. Next door lived a lanky Eurasian woman, half Russian and half Thai, married to the Dutch purser on one of the steamships which shuttled up and down the Straits of Malacca between Penang in the north and Singapore Island in the south. She was bored, lonely and often drunk while her husband was away, though when he returned to their yellow-painted Chinese house they had screaming arguments which sent the chickens in the garden squawking for cover.

One evening the four young Englishmen were sitting at their dinner table, gently stupefied with heat, food and drink. The Eurasian woman appeared at their door in a crumpled, pink silk peignoir with a half-drunk bottle of brandy in hand.

She sat on the table, began slurring and hiccupping through her life history, then collapsed face down in a plate of melted icecream.

The four eighteen-year-olds, thoroughly drilled in their duty to see a lady home, rose shakily and carried her round to her door, at which instant her husband returned. The woman's eyes flickered open and she accused the boys of raping her, speaking in Dutch which they did not understand. The Dutchman stomped into his house, came out with a pistol and fired wildly, wounding one of James's companions.

The police were called and the next morning James was once again protesting his innocence to his supervisor, who shook his head.

'I'm sorry, Bourton, there's nothing I can do. A scandal like this is something the bank will not tolerate. You know damn well it's your duty to observe decent social standards and maintain the reputation of the white man in the community. You'll have to go, I'm afraid. You'll get three months' pay and you'll have to ship home in four weeks or pay your own passage.'

'If I decide to stay, sir . . .'

The older man interrupted him with rough sympathy. 'If you decide to stay, you'll have a devil of a job finding anyone to take you on, at least in Penang. You might get a Civil Service job if you got your father to pull strings for you in London, but you've blotted your copybook pretty thoroughly and you can't expect promotion until you've lived all this down.'

James's pleasant features looked miserable and his shoulders hunched unhappily inside his white shirt.

'Don't want to go home, is that it?'

'Not much, sir.'

'Got a taste for the East, have you? Well, if you think you could stand more, you could get yourself taken on at a rubber estate. Nobody gives a damn what you get up to out in the jungle.'

A week later a note was delivered to James suggesting that he meet a Mr C. Douglas Lovell at 6 pm at the Criterion Tiffin and Billiard Rooms on Beach Street. He found a tall man with thick white hair and moustache taking bets with two Chinese businessmen on the last frame of their game.

'Boy, stengah for my young friend here. Be with you in a moment, laddie, just a bit of business to attend to.' He prowled smoothly to the end of the table, lined up the shot through half-closed eyes, and briskly sent the balls clicking towards their pockets. The 'boy', a sixty-year-old Chinese with skin the colour of a finnan haddock, brought James his stengah, a small whisky well diluted with water. Douglas Lovell collected a handful of dollars from each businessman, the three men bowed to each other, and he joined James at the bar.

'Chap at Honkers & Shankers tells me you've had a spot of bother.'

'You could say that, sir.'

'Makes two of us. One of my chaps popped his clogs last week. Cerebral malaria, pretty vile way to go.' He gulped down half his stengah. 'Not afraid of hard work, are you?'

'No, sir.' James's leaden mood began to lift.

'Well, you'd better be telling the truth. I don't employ any idle blue-bloods on my estate. You'll be up at five every day of the week, including Sunday. Highest-paid form of unskilled labour, my rubber assistants. You'll get a hundred and fifty dollars a month plus another ten if you can pass the Tamil exam. Got an ear for languages, I'm told.'

'They do seem to come easily to me, sir. Where exactly is your estate?'

'Take a day – best way, steamer to Port Swettenham, train through K L and then it's about an hour. They've promised us a road next year but I'll believe it when I see it. We've got our own club, our own billiard table and you get two free days a month if you want to go down to K L and beat it up. What do you say?'

James was torn between the feeling that he wanted to be at the heart of the country and to know the mysteries of misty jungle-covered hills of the mainland, and the recognition that a rubber planter was looked upon as something of a social misfit. Although at home he had had no contact with the kind of people who were in trade, and was therefore blithely unaware of the professions which could be considered suitable for a gentleman, and those which represented a definite loss of social status, he had heard men at the Club talk about rubber planters disparagingly. 'The kind of man that marries a barmaid' was the judgement on the white men, mostly British, who marshalled thousands of Asiatics to tap millions of trees to stack the dockside at Penang with bales of latex sheets awaiting shipment to America and Europe.

Douglas Lovell, however, did not look like the kind of man who married a barmaid; his commanding bearing and clipped speech said 'army' as clearly as a uniform. James liked his directness and felt the lure of the unknown East. Only a vague premonition of his parents' disapproval held him back.

'Look, young man,' Douglas Lovell spoke in an unexpectedly quiet voice, 'you won't get a better offer. I'd heard the story of that Dutchman's wife from three separate people before I left K L. I don't doubt it sounded ten times worse than it was, but the point is you're finished out here in the kind of job you came out to do.'

'I know that, sir, but it's not fair. It was all a put-up job . . .'

The older man cut him short with an irritated wave of his glass. 'Life's not fair, my boy, and the trick of it is to be in the position to be able to say what's fair and what's not for the other poor buggers, instead of having to take another man's justice. I make the rules of my estate, and I don't give a damn what you get up to as long as we meet our latex quota and the coolies don't shit on the road. Now, d'you want a job or don't you?'

James made up his mind in a rush, swallowing a sense of offence at the implication that he would welcome a relaxed moral climate. 'Yes, sir, I do want it.'

'Good. I'm told your family have a bob or two but somehow I didn't think you were the type to be a remittance man.' James was flattered, puzzled and startled as the older man put out his hand to shake on the deal.

'May I ask what a remittance man is?'

'Young fool shipped out East by the family to save them further embarrassment, spends his allowance on opium and taxi-dancers and dies young. Buried one once, found him dead in a shack on the edge of the jungle. Took three months to get the body identified. You're not that type. Ask too many questions.'

James was indeed quivering with curiosity about every corner of the new world for which he departed the next day. With his new job he acquired a tin-roofed bungalow built on stilts, on the edge of virgin jungle. At noon the silence was so profound he felt he could hear the vast primaeval forest grow. All day moisture dripped from green leaves and shifting mists mantled the ancient treetops. There was a clean, earthy smell. When he was on his own under the green canopy, James felt as pure as Adam in the Garden of Eden.

CHAPTER THREE

'WAIT FOR me!' called Rosanna, running up the avenue of lime trees. Cathy and Monty, swathed in their capes and scarves against the raw February cold, were tramping arm in arm ahead of her. Together, they stopped and turned, two figures dwarfed by the massive trees. Cathy, at 5ft 7in, taller than her sister by a generous hand's-breadth, rubbed Monty's bare hands to warm them while they waited. Monty often forgot her gloves, no matter how cruel the weather.

'Hurry up, we're freezing,' she yelled in the teeth of the blustering wind. Rosanna, brown curls tangled, caught up with both sisters and pulled a sheaf of magazines from under her cloak.

'I've got *Swoon, Honey, True Romance* and *Teengirl.*'

'Fab. Let's get inside before we freeze to death.'

In the years to come the first thing all three of them would remember about Benenden was the cold. Icy winds which originated from Central Europe blew over the flat Kent fields and scoured the school grounds unmercifully, chilling the red-brick buildings.

In the winter mornings the tip of Rosanna's nose would hurt with the cold, Cathy's toes would be blue and Monty would lie like a corpse under her bedclothes trying to conserve the pitiful glow of her body warmth in the clammy chill of the sheets.

Rosanna returned from the Christmas holidays with fur slippers and a thick, pink cashmere blanket which she added to the permitted quota of coverings on her bed with considerable guilt. Unlike Cathy and Monty, she had not been toughened by merciless English nannies and lectured about the virtue of sensual deprivation. Desperate as she was to fit in with the other girls, Rosanna drew the line at freezing half to death. In every other way she tried as hard as she could to be exactly like the others. At breakfast she ate every scrap of bacon, conscious that she was being watched. At prayers in the chapel she could clearly be heard singing 'There is room in my heart for Jesus'. At Christmas, when there was a candlelit carol service, followed by an icecream and treacle treat, Rosanna sang a solo.

This show of conforming to an alien religion was something Rosanna put on almost by instinct. Her family came from the waves of Jewish immigrants who had fled persecution in Europe over the last half century; her mother still spoke with a distinct Austrian accent. Their aim was to follow the Rothschilds, Prime Minister Disraeli and all the ancient Jewish dynasties in Britain by seeming to be merely English people of Jewish extraction. A Jewish person should not be any more conspicuous in the community than the few acres of wheat which a great banking family reserved for the Chief Rabbi's Passover cakes were obvious among the rest of their country estate.

The only concession which the school made to Rosanna's religion was to allow her to stay behind on Sunday when the other girls had to walk two miles to the village church. Even then, she was so eager to be like the others that she walked through the dank countryside with them, and went to the half- timbered newsagent's shop to buy sweets and romance magazines while they attended the service.

They wore thick navy-blue bloomers, called 'wovs', which did not quite cover their legs to the tops of their stockings, so throughout the long tramp there was always a band of icy naked, goosepimpled flesh around their thighs.

At first Monty and Cathy were enthralled by Rosanna's wardrobe but slightly in awe of her. Rosanna, in turn, did not dare to dream of entering the charmed territory of the sisters' relationship. They were closer to each other than the most devoted friends, bound together by a deep emotion which was like a force-field that repelled intruders. They had no particular favourites among their classmates, but spent all their free time in each other's company, talking for hours with such close rapport that their conversations seemed to be in a private dialect. Sometimes they behaved as if they were a single person; if Monty was penalized for infringing school rules, Cathy would seem pained by the injustice; if Cathy collected a prize for her work, Monty would glow with pride.

A few days after Rosanna arrived, the two sisters united in sympathy for her against the subtle rejection of many of the other girls. They seemed to recognize an affinity with her, and Monty, as always, acted for both of them and made the first move.

'Come and join the madrigal society,' she had invited Rosanna abruptly. 'I'm sick of being the only contralto who can sing in tune, and they won't let me be a soprano because there are too many of them already,' she explained, half apologizing, wanting to say they would like to be friends but shy of making the commitment clear. As the outcast and the rebel, Rosanna and Monty were predestined friends. Their love of music settled the matter.

Rosanna was conscientious and quiet and the teachers approved of her; Cathy liked her because she was bright, and in the same classes as she was. Cathy had been feeling more and more isolated by the fact that the work other girls found hard she could do easily, and she was glad of companionship in the top grades. No one in the school could beat Cathy at mental arithmetic, but Rosanna came close.

The rest of the school did not openly reject their first Jewish companion, but they did not accept her either. No one walked with her to the village, offered to partner her in lacrosse or gave her a slice of their birthday cake. They treated her as good English girls treated any other embarrassment – as if she did not exist.

Halfway through the autumn term Swallow Lamotte was suddenly expelled. Monty came in from lacrosse one afternoon and found Swallow, red-faced and truculent, slamming clothes into her trunk. 'Just remember, love, they can't actually *kill* you,' she called defiantly to Monty as she ran downstairs to her father's car.

'But what did she *do?*' Rosanna asked Camilla in the darkness after lights out. Even the girl who had talked to newspaper reporters about Princess Anne had not been expelled. Camilla knew but found she couldn't quite say the words. '*Elle n'est plus vierge,*' she whispered finally, and refused to say any more.

There was instantly a storm of speculation which roared through the upper school for days.

'But what did she actually *do?*'

'Who did she do it with, that's the point.'

'Do you suppose it was – no, it couldn't have been.' The Benenden community included only four men, an elderly physics teacher who scarcely counted as a member of the male sex, a young chaplain who played the guitar, with whom three-quarters of the girls were in love and the two plain-clothes detectives who shadowed the young Princess. It was inconceivable that any of these males would have had a sexual relationship with a pupil.

As to what Swallow might actually have done to cease being a virgin, they had no clear idea. Sex was a mystery to them, intriguing because it was forbidden, part of the unknown territory of maturity from which they were deliberately barred. Their biology lessons were evasive. Their school books were censored; even the word 'breast' was expurgated from their editions of Shakespeare. Sex was taboo; romance was considered harmless.

By 4 pm, the magazines had been read, swapped and exhausted, and the three girls drooped around the dormitory, suffering the excruciating boredom of the green room of womanhood.

'Do you think people *really* do things like this?' Monty thoughtfully reached for her contraband copy of *Lady Chatterley's Lover* with a frown. They had all read it, especially the page with the word 'fuck' on it eight times. They did not understand it.

'I'd never do anything like that,' said Cathy firmly.

'I can't see Simon doing *anything* like that,' giggled Rosanna.

Because she had an elder brother, Rosanna was regarded as an expert on everything to do with love, a subject about which all the girls lived in a ferment of impatient curiosity. They discussed endlessly the right ways to behave when you were overwhelmed by rightful passion.

'Would you let a boy kiss you?' asked Rosanna.

'Yes, if we were in love.' Monty rummaged around in one of her drawers for a bag of marshmallows and offered them to the others.

'I bet you would anyway if he looked like Brian Jones,' needled Rosanna.

'If he looked like Brian Jones, I'd be in love with him anyway. I'd let him do *any-thing* if he looked like Brian Jones.' Monty cast languorous eyes up at the picture of the prettiest member of the Rolling Stones which she had taped inside her ward-robe. She knew it was her role to shock the others. Pin-ups were forbidden, as were make-up, scent and letters from boys.

'That's awful. Only an absolute slut would behave like that.' Cathy spoke with concern and Monty, who had intended to worry her sister, gave a chuckle of satisfaction.

'My mother says you must never let a boy touch you or you'll be spoiled and no one will want to marry you.' Rosanna listlessly opened another fashion magazine. 'She's terrified I'll be a tarnished bride.'

'I don't think you should kiss a boy unless you're engaged,' agreed Cathy.

'But if you never find anything out before you get engaged, how do you know you really love each other?' Monty flicked through pages of tall, blonde girls with smudgy, black eyeliner, posing knock-kneed in mini-skirts.

'You just *know*, that's all. I'm sure I'll know. I'll feel all swoony and weak, like fainting when he holds my hand.' There was a silence as the three girls tried to imagine feeling wildly, passionately in love. They couldn't.

'Let's try that,' Rosanna suggested, pointing to a page in Monty's magazine which demanded in big black type, 'Should *you* wear a mini-skirt?'

'What do you have to do?'

'It tells you – I'll get my tape-measure.' Cathy ran off to her own dormitory and came back with the measuring tape she used for dressmaking. She measured Monty's legs at the thigh, knee, calf and ankle, then did the same for Rosanna; Monty measured Cathy's legs and finally they lined up in front of the mirror in the corridor and looked intently at their reflections.

'It says here,' Cathy read from the article, 'that perfect legs should meet only at the knee and ankle.' They gazed solemnly forward; Rosanna's plump legs met most of the way down; Monty's legs were also plump, but bowed so there was a tiny gap at the level of her knees. Cathy's legs were perfect – slim, straight and gracefully proportioned.

'But I've got this,' she moaned, twisting around to point to the faint gold impression of the birthmark just above the back of her right knee.

'Do you suppose,' Monty pulled at the skirt of her unflattering navy tunic, 'that anyone would notice if we put up the hems a bit? Our legs would look longer. We could do it just a little at a time, I bet Grice wouldn't spot it.'

Miss Grice was their housemistress, an unsmiling, ruddy-cheeked woman who taught lacrosse. Monty called her 'the Voice of Doom', because her voice, bellowing, 'Swing, girls, *swing,*' across the muddy pitch, could be heard every afternoon throughout the school grounds.

Cathy, who sewed the most neatly, took up all three tunics one inch, and the three friends self-consciously went in to supper. No one noticed.

That night they crept out of their dormitories, leaving pillows under their blankets in case anyone peeped in to check that all was well, and scuttled down the corridor to the laundry room, where they locked the door, jammed towels at the top and bottom to block out the merest crack of illumination, then put on the light. Working in a froth of excitement, Cathy pinned, Monty pressed, Rosanna tacked, Cathy stitched and then Monty pressed the tunics for the last time.

'Two inches isn't much, is it?' Rosanna held her finished uniform against her waist and tried to judge the skirt length.

'Look, we've got to be absolutely dead-pan at breakfast,' warned Monty. 'No giggling. Poker faces. We mustn't look as if anything's going on.'

Simmering with delicious excitement, they appeared at breakfast next morning, feeling as if their newly revealed kneecaps were glowing neon-bright. None of the teachers noticed, but one or two of the other girls shot startled, envious looks at the immaculately raised hems. Monty grew blasé and crossed her legs with panache as she sat in a deep chintz-covered armchair at morning break. At lunchtime, one or two of the girls tackled them, but they pretended innocence.

'Another inch, Cathy, go on; we're bound to get away with it,' Monty's eyes were bigger and rounder than ever with the thrill of challenging authority.

'No,' said Cathy firmly, 'it's all round the school already: some little sneak's bound to tell on us.'

'Rubbish. No one can prove anything. We've just grown a bit taller, that's all. There's nothing wrong with altering your uniform, anyway. No one's said anything about Rosanna's being more fitted.' Cathy dug her heels in and Rosanna, anxious not to be conspicuous, agreed.

'We've proved our point, we've got away with it. Let's stop now,' she urged Monty, pulling her red dressing gown around her.

'I think you're both absolute *weeds,*' sulked Monty. After lights-out, she went alone to the laundry room by torchlight and turned up the hem of her tunic another inch.

As the four hundred girls stood quietly waiting for Miss Sharpe to say grace, Grice, the housemistress walked suspiciously round the table, eyeing every girl's hemline. As Cathy had predicted, the secret had been guessed and communicated. Monty felt the hairs on the back of her neck prickle as Miss Grice approached, then heard her voice, for once low but still hectoring, say, 'See me after breakfast, Miranda, if you please.'

'I suppose you think that tampering with the school uniform's very clever?' she snapped, walking to and fro across the worn carpet in her study. 'Well, let me tell you that it isn't. What have you got to say for yourself?'

'It's the fashion, Miss Grice.' Monty's line in disciplinary encounters was what was called dumb insolence – the pretended innocent put-down of the enemy.

'You'll have plenty of time for fashion when you've left school, and we're not bothered with you any longer. While you're here, you'll obey the rules.' Monty's eyes glazed and she gazed vaguely at Miss Grice, seeing her as a gesticulating doll about four inches high. 'You'll stay in detention this afternoon and put that hem down, and bring it to me when you've finished. And you'll learn a hundred lines by tomorrow – I've marked the page.' The worst punishment that was ever given to a girl at Benenden was to learn poetry by heart.

In the beginning, Monty had simply been given a fat, blue book and told to learn a poem from it. She soon became proficient in all the poems of less than ten lines in this weighty volume. Miss Grice's next manoeuvre had been to set a fixed number of lines to be memorized. Monty had countered by picking the most explicit love poems she could find and reciting them slowly, stone-faced, while looking Miss Grice straight in the eye as she intoned, '*Enter these arms, for since thou thought it best, not to dream all my dream, let's act the rest.*' She had an excellent memory.

Miss Grice's latest strategy was to specify precisely the lines she wanted Monty to learn, in a romantic Scottish ballad with a galloping metre. Thus the girls were even more firmly instructed that romance was right and sex was wrong.

'Rotten, old boot,' Cathy consoled her sister. 'I'll do the hem for you.'

'You can't, she wants to stand over me.' Monty sulkily opened the poetry book. 'Oh God, what slop. Young Lochinvar.'

'Didn't you learn that last term?'

'Yes, the old bat must've forgotten.' Monty was rapidly scanning the lines.

'Never mind, Monty.' Rosanna huddled thankfully inside her scarlet robe. 'She's just jealous. I mean, who'd want to look at *her* legs?' They all shrieked with laughter.

'Ugh. Don't, what a disgusting thought. Not before supper, please Rosanna.'

'*Oh young Lochinvar is come out of the West. Through all the wide border his steed was the best,*' muttered Monty rapidly.

'Grice's knees go blue in the cold, you know, and her varicose veins stick out. I've watched them.' Rosanna pulled out a magnifying mirror and tweezers and began to tweak at her thick glossy eyebrows.

'Those revolting divided skirts of hers are shorter than a mini-skirt anyway; what's this for?' Cathy picked up a strange implement from the bagful of cosmetic instruments designed to enhance Rosanna's looks without breaking the no make-up rule.

'*Oh come ye in peace here or come ye in war, Or to dance at our bridal, young Lord Lochinvar?*' Monty raced through the poem in a rapid chant.

'Eyelash-curlers – look, you do it like this.' Rosanna picked the curlers up and demonstrated. 'Then you put some of this cream on at night and you get really thick eyelashes.'

'You've got really thick eyelashes, anyway.' Cathy looked at her own face in the magnifying mirror. Her skin was the colour and texture of creamy new milk. The natural shade of her lips was cinnamon pink, and above her short, straight nose her eyes gazed out, rayed in shades of brown from dark clove to bright topaz. Cathy liked her looks. For the sake of politeness she echoed the others' moans about their imperfections, but deep down she was prepared to believe she was beautiful. Of course, eyelashes could never be too long or too thick, and hers might look even better if they curled more. Hopefully, she dabbed on some of the black cream.

'*She looked down to blush, And looked up to sigh. With a smile on her lips and a tear in her eye. He took her soft hand 'ere her mother could bar . . .*' Monty gabbled on as fast as she could, then threw the poetry book across the room with a yell of triumph. 'Know it, know it. Can I have some of that?'

'You don't need it either.' Cathy handed the tiny pot to her sister.

'I bet you wouldn't do what she did.' Monty smeared the cream generously over her lids and studied the effect in the mirror. Her lashes stuck together in spikes, making her eyes look like big black stars. Impatiently, she pushed away the tangle of black curls which hung almost to the wide bridge of her nose. *Why* didn't her hair fall in a sleek curtain down to her eyebrows, like that of the models in the magazines? Like Cathy's did?

'Do what?'

'Run off with your secret lover on your wedding day.'

'I'd be marrying my secret lover, anyway.' Cathy made remarks like this with a solemnity which never sounded complacent, only serenely confident.

If sex and love were enthralling, marriage was their greatest fascination, and they all felt they knew everything about it. Except of course, the only important thing – *whom* they were going to marry. There were innumerable ways of consulting fate on this. Although they scoffed loudly at superstition, and dared each other to walk under ladders or leave spilled salt untouched, the girls would count cherry stones, study astrology or carefully peel the skin off an apple in an unbroken ribbon. Then you had to swing it three times round your head and let it fall behind you. The shape of the fallen peel foretold the initial of your future husband's name.

The peel always fell in a wobbly curve, so that many of the girls seemed to be destined to marry a Charles or a William. In view of the narrow range of boys' names considered acceptable in their social echelon it was probably quite an accurate prediction.

Their romance-sodden languor increased as the weather grew warmer. When Midsummer's Eve came in the ripe heat of June, they decided to try the ultimate prediction.

'What you have to do,' Cathy explained, 'is sit in front of a mirror, with another mirror behind you, in your nightdress on Midsummer Night, with your hair unbound, and a candle on either side of you. Then you look in the mirrors and at midnight you see your husband's face behind you.'

'How spooky, I wouldn't dare,' said Rosanna, shivering in imagined horror.

'Well, I don't care about getting married anyway. You do it, Cathy.' Monty, suddenly annoyed by the complacent way her sister talked about the whole business of marriage, wanted to challenge her. 'Come on, where shall we do it?'

'Well, we can't do it in the corridor because someone's bound to hear us – where else is there a big mirror?' Rosanna was always practical.

'The boot room, but . . .'

There was unspoken agreement that the boot room was much too prosaic. 'You'd need a big mirror or you wouldn't be able to see him properly.'

'What about the headmistress's cloakroom?'

'Monty!' Rosanna squealed in horror.

'There's a big mirror on chains in there. We could take it down easily between us.' Monty looked challengingly from Cathy to Rosanna.

'I know – we could take it to that room under the stage. There's another mirror there – the one we use to check our costumes. No one would find us.' This was indisputable. The room under the stage in the great hall was accessible only from a trap-door in the corridor outside.

Under Monty's generalship, the scheme took on wilder and wilder proportions. The following day they took a pair of 3ft candles in brass candlesticks from the chapel. They synchronized their watches like commandos and met at eleven o'clock on Midsummer's Eve at the bottom of the stairs, with their cloaks over their nightdresses, or, in Rosanna's case, over her baby-doll pyjamas.

'Walk on the grass, then no one will hear us,' commanded Monty in a whisper. They ran furtively down the avenue of trees; the limes were beginning to flower and the air was sticky and tartly-scented with their pollen.

By the dim beams of their pocket torches they tiptoed through the corridors to the cloakroom by the headmistress's study.

'Careful, the chains will rattle,' panted Monty as she and Rosanna struggled to hold the heavy looking-glass. With Cathy holding the chains, they carried the mirror crabwise down the corridor. Cathy heaved at the brass ring in the floor which opened the trap-door, and they slowly negotiated the steps into the ominous darkness below.

'That torch is useless. Light the candles, Rosanna.' There was a scrape of a match, a flare of light, then darkness.

'Blast, dropped it. Hang on. I'll try again.' This time the wick caught light, and when Rosanna held the candle up they could make out the huge wicker baskets which held the costumes for the school plays.

'Cathy, shut the trap-door and then no one will be able to hear us.' Monty began pulling the creaking skips together. Soon the scene was set according to Cathy's instructions, and the flickering reflections of the candlelight shone around the dark cellar.

Monty found a dusty, Elizabethan-style stool and planted it between the mirrors. 'There you are, Cathy – take off your cloak.' Cathy, shivering slightly in her sprigged cotton nightdress, sat down and Rosanna brushed her loose straight hair for her.

'Move back you two, I can see you in the mirror.' They drew back.

'What time is it? I can't see.' Rosanna peered at her tiny enamel-faced wrist-watch by the light of the nearest candle.

'Ten to twelve.'

A solemn silence fell as they settled down to wait for midnight with mounting apprehension. Cathy, her lips quivering with nerves, gazed into the mirror, trying to concentrate on the black space behind her head instead of on her pale oval face reflected to infinity.

She looked like a bride already, Monty thought wistfully, wishing her own hair was smooth and straight, her own nose fine and small, and her skin creamy and absolutely without pimples, as Cathy's was. For all she envied it, Cathy's effortless beauty was something of which she felt vicariously proud.

Rosanna worried that she would be unable to find a husband to match her parents' detailed demands; Monty, secretly convinced that no one would ever want to marry a fat, frizzy-haired, bow-legged creature like herself, and utterly determined not to end up like her own mother, had great misgivings about the whole idea of getting married. But Cathy had always been quietly confident of her future, and unconsciously the trio had elected her as the bride-to-be.

There were noises in the still night. The wicker baskets gave tiny creaks. Above them, the polished oak floorboards settled with occasional groans. A hunting owl shrieked in the park outside.

'What's the time now?' Cathy whispered, her voice hoarse with tension.

Rosanna held her watch towards the light again. 'One minute to go.'

Cathy gazed intently into the mirror before her. Clearly they heard the distant whirring of weights as the school clock prepared to strike. As if pulled by an invisible thread, the three girls leaned forward and stared into the mirror's depth. The candles guttered, the clock struck and a pale shape appeared momentarily in the reflected dark.

Suddenly, Cathy screamed, half-jumped to her feet and shrieked again with fright. Rosanna screamed too, and fell back against a basket. Monty turned round, wide-eyed with terror, and gazed straight at a furious Miss Grice, who demanded:

'What in the world are you girls doing?'

'I've never been so pleased to hear the Voice of Doom, I can tell you,' Monty tried in vain to lighten their mood as they waited outside the headmistress's room the next morning. Girls gazed curiously at them as they passed, knowing that they must have done something dreadful to be waiting there.

The oak door opened violently and Miss Sharpe's voice called them in.

'Never in all the time I have taught at this school have I heard of anything so stupid.' Her tone was icy with contempt and her blue eyes glared at them one after the other. 'Quite apart from the fact that you have desecrated the chapel, stolen school property and broken school rules, you could have burned the whole school down.'

Cathy and Rosanna looked uncomfortably at their shoes. Monty, glazed-eyed as usual, comforted herself with a daydream of the school consumed by flames, and Miss Sharpe's charred body tumbling from the castellated parapet.

'I don't know what you were all doing and frankly I don't want to know. Take that smirk off your face, Catherine.' Cathy's long, upturned top lip always made her seem to be smiling when she wasn't, and she no longer tried to explain. 'I'm surprised at you, *especially* you, Catherine. This sort of behaviour is quite out of character. And you, Rosanna, you've made a very good start here and I hope you're not going to spoil it.' Oh dear, thought Cathy, she's going to come down hard on Monty. 'But I've seen quite a lot of you recently, Miranda, haven't I?'

Why does she always use those mealy-mouthed expressions, wondered Monty with contempt. Miss Sharpe continued, 'I had thought all this teenage rebellion, or whatever you choose to call it, was over, but I can see now that you haven't changed and I'm beginning to wonder if you ever will change, Miranda.'

Same old story, Monty thought. Can't she come up with anything new?

'You will all be confined to the school for the rest of the term,' Miss Sharpe announced at last. 'I shall be writing to your parents, of course, and if there is any repetition of these escapades, I shall suspend you immediately. As for you Miranda, I really don't think there is anything more we can do for you here. You will be allowed to sit your exams, but we shall not expect you back next term.'

As if sitting bloody exams was a treat, sneered Monty to herself. As if I wanted to come back here.

Cathy, usually the first to raise the spirits of the other two in times of gloom, said nothing as they walked back to their lessons. Monty, full of brittle bravado, demanded, 'So did you see anything in the mirror, after all?'

Cathy shook her head. 'Only Grice. It's only a superstition, anyway, isn't it?'

'You really didn't see a thing?' Monty pressed her sister, sensing that she was keeping something back.

'No, of course I didn't. Didn't you hear what I said?' Cathy spoke with irritation, and Monty let the matter drop. They walked on in silence until they parted to make their way to the classrooms. Cathy probed her memory, trying to bring back the picture she had seen before the panic of discovery made everything unclear. She had an indelible impression of a small man with greying hair and an aura of vitality. The only man she knew who matched the picture was her father.

Arches of bright sunlight, the light, rich sun of Paris in summer, lay across the narrow pavement, shaped by the graceful arcades of the Rue de Rivoli. The boutiques selling leather, luggage and elegant but useless gifts pulled their blinds halfway down to protect their stock from the sunlight, but James Bourton's eye was not distracted by the gilded nicknacks on display.

He walked slowly around the Place Vendôme to the Ritz, and ordered himself a whisky-soda at the bar. The barman knew him well. Milord James was almost the last of the real English clientele, elegant, cultivated, free-spending, and a pleasure to serve. Naturally, he always put up at the Ritz. They had had the honour of serving him for almost twenty years.

He seemed a little abstracted today, the barman noticed as he returned to his position midway down the gleaming counter, perhaps even a little pale. Many men needed a drink to help them accept bad news, but the barman was not the sort who cared to listen to his customers' troubles; their difficulties were always to do with money or with women, neither of which was susceptible to reason or really important. James drank his whisky rapidly and ordered another, then a third. Had the barman looked closely, he would have seen that not only was his customer pale beneath his permanent light tan, but that the beautifully manicured hand clamped around the glass was shaking violently enough to make the ice ring against its sides.

After the third whisky James slipped off the bar stool, telling the barman to send the bill to the hotel cashier immediately as he was checking out straight away. Half an hour later, while a maroon-uniformed porter wheeled his bags out into the Place Vendôme, James settled the bill rapidly and took a taxi to Orly airport.

Within three hours he was at his desk in his office in London Wall, thanking his secretary for his afternoon tea.

'You've had an awful lot of telephone calls, Lord James.' She gazed over the massive mahogany desk adoringly. All the other secretaries in the firm envied her position; James Bourton was charming, kind, good-looking and, at almost fifty, so thrillingly sexy. The other directors were pompous, had spreading bellies and dandruff on their collars; none of the office girls could quite understand why they all subtly disparaged James.

'Mr Hodge from the Allied Bank called three times; he says it's urgent. Your solicitors have called twice, and they want you to ring back. And a man came in to see you – he wouldn't say what it was about, only that you weren't expecting him and he'd pop in again.'

'I think I know what it's about; is this the rest of the mail?' The letter from Benenden was on top of a pile that filled his correspondence tray. She nodded her neatly groomed blonde head.

'Now, I want you first of all to go over to accounts and get me some cash.' He scribbled an authority on a slip of paper and handed it to her. 'I've some clients to take out this evening and the banks are shut. After that, I'll give you a packet that has to go by registered post straight away.

'Then I'd like you to slip over to Piccadilly and pick up this order at Paxton and Whitfield.' One of James Bourton's many indulgences was the finest cheese from the Jermyn Street shop. The secretary looked at the paper he handed her but did not ask herself why a man recently returned from France should order Camembert in England. 'Don't bother coming back to the office. I'll be gone by the time you get here and it'll be better off in your refrigerator overnight. Give it to me tomorrow.' She nodded eagerly, and tripped off down the corridor, returning in ten minutes with two thousand pounds in twenty-pound notes. There was nothing unusual about Lord James asking for so much folding money. He would often drop considerably more than that sum in an evening when he was entertaining clients with a taste for gambling.

With his secretary out of the room, James fumbled in his desk drawers and found a half-empty cigar box. He transferred the remaining cigars to the humidor on a side-table, packed the money tightly into the box, and wrote a card saying simply, 'This is for you'. He taped the box shut, pushed it clumsily into an envelope and addressed it to Mrs Mae Brown at an address in Bayswater.

Once his secretary had left to post the packet and buy the cheese, James locked his office door and went back to his desk. He raked briefly through his mail with hands that still trembled and had difficulty opening the envelopes. For some months now he had asked the girl to leave his mail unopened. He opened the letter from the school with agitation, then smiled and discarded it.

The telephone rang at 5.15 pm, but he did not answer it. By 6 pm, the office was silent and empty, and the street below full of purposeful bustle as people crowded towards the railway stations on their way home. James sat still in his chair, his eyes fixed on the framed citation for his wartime decoration. It was the only thing hanging on the blue, silk-papered wall that was not beautiful, but for once he did not want to enjoy his paintings.

When his secretary went to open the office next morning she found the door locked. No doubt Lord James had not yet arrived. She called his flat in Albany, but the cleaner answered and said she didn't think Lord James had come home from France. Alarmed, the secretary called the building's caretaker, who came up with a spare key and opened Lord James's office.

Forty-eight hours after punishing the three girls, Miss Sharpe again sent for Cathy. As soon as she entered the headmistress's office, Cathy knew that something was seriously wrong; her first instinct was to think that Monty had run away.

'Do you know where your sister is?' There was definitely something amiss. Miss Sharpe's normally piercing glance was jumping nervously around the room and her voice sounded half-strangled.

'No, Miss Sharpe, I haven't seen her all afternoon.'

'You must find her at once. I've had a telephone call from your mother. She wants you to come home immediately.'

'Is something wrong?' Cathy was by now absolutely sure that something had happened. Miss Sharpe suddenly looked directly at her and her voice cracked as she spoke.

'There is, Catherine, but I'm afraid you must wait for your mother to tell you what it is. She will be here to fetch you in forty minutes. All I can say is that I am most dreadfully sorry for you both. Now hurry and find your sister.'

Cathy ran down out of the square, mock-Tudor, stone doorway and around the creeper-covered window bay at the front of the main building. Spurts of gravel shot across the lawn behind her as she raced round the corner, then dodged through a crowd of younger girls packed into the narrow passageway between two wings of the rambling red-brick building.

At the back of the complex was the music wing, where Monty was sure to be found. Whenever her sister was worried about something – and for all her outward defiance, Cathy knew Monty was worried about what their parents would say when they got Miss Sharpe's letter – she usually buried herself in the music wing, to play the piano for hours. She found both Monty and Rosanna on the top floor of the stuffy building, contentedly practising a piece of Mozart. Cathy paused for a second and watched them through the glass panel in the door. Her sister's face, for once devoid of cynicism, defensiveness and rebellion, looked calm and at peace as she followed the line of notes on the sheet music. Rosanna swayed slightly with each stroke of her bow.

Cathy tapped at the door and they stopped playing and looked up. She went in. 'Monty, I don't know what's up but Mummy's coming to get us and we've got to pack.'

Within an hour their mother was standing awkwardly beside the Bentley as the porter loaded the girls' suitcases. Bettina Bourton was a dumpy woman with hair dyed a harsh honey-brown to hide the grey. Her mouth was set in a thick, carmine line. Her vague blue eyes, which always had a look of suppressed anxiety, now registered barely controlled panic.

'Come and sit down a minute,' she said, brusque in her agitation. They sat one on each side of her on a stone bench, watching their mother twist the sapphire and ruby eternity rings which cut into her plump fingers.

Suddenly, Bettina caught her breath and began to speak, slurring her words in distress. 'Your father's dead. His office telephoned this morning. They say we've got to go home and wait because the police want to see us. Don't ask me what it's all about because . . .' She gulped air again then spluttered into tears.

Numb with shock as she was, Cathy gave her mother a calming embrace and patted her arm, muttering, 'There, there.'

Monty sat in silence. She was sure that the school's letter had somehow killed her father, that her bad behaviour was responsible for his death.

Then Cathy and Monty looked at each other over their mother's bowed head, silently sharing the sense of desolation that slowly welled up to swamp their initial reactions. We're alone now. Don't leave me, their wide, dark eyes implored each other. I won't leave you, each responded; I love you, we'll always be together.

Inside his office, James Bourton's body lay slumped across his desk, a red mess where his head should have been. The blue silk-paper of the wall to the left, the leather-bound books in the bookcase, the correspondence in the tray and the blotter were caked with dried splashes of blood and fragments of brain. Clamped in his right hand with the reflex grasp of death was his army pistol. James Bourton had shot himself.

Chapter Four

SOUR WHISKY surged in James Bourton's stomach, then died down. At twenty-two, a hangover felt good. Standing in the cool pre-dawn darkness in a white shirt and crisp khaki shorts, he supervised the muster of two hundred coolies with the impression that he was enjoying the masculine pleasures of drink and domination simultaneously.

His woman was waiting in the slow-moving line of Tamils which stretched away into the darkness of the muster ground beyond the pool of light from the hissing pressure lamp. Selambaram, the conductor, or overseer, called the name of each man or woman in turn and those who were fit to work stepped forward. Each tapper carried two buckets for latex; the weeders each held the heavy hoe used to keep the long, dim corridors between the rubber trees free of the infiltrating plants which tried eternally to reclaim the land for the jungle.

'Is that right?' James demanded, as Damika, his mistress, impassively answered in her turn and moved away with the kerosene cans she used as buckets; her sari, stiff with dried latex, rustled at each step. James's finger pointed to the line opposite her name in Selambaram's book. The neatly ruled double page had a column for each day of the month, and further columns to note the total wage due at the month's end, how much of the wage was to be taken in the form of dry rice, and the proportion the coolie had requested as an advance on the twentieth day of the month. Damika had taken half her wages in advance.

'It is correct, *tuan.*' Selambaram continued to call the roll of the labourers in James's control, his popeyed, almost black face expressionless.

'Why has she taken so much?'

'You must ask the woman, *tuan.* I do not know.' James was suddenly agitated by obscure suspicion, which grew stronger as the woman faded into the darkness.

At 5.30 am, when the long process of muster was completed, James mounted his motorbike and sped away down the red earth road, riding past the line of coolie shacks and out to a crossroads where he slowed to negotiate the muddy gullies carved by the heavy tropical rain. From the intersection, the downhill fork led to the railway track, the others to outlying areas of the plantation. James turned uphill. The sad liquid whoops of gibbons sounded from the jungle to his right.

Soon the sun would rise behind the mountains; a smear of colourless light waxed among the dark-grey clouds, and the voices of the monkeys were gradually joined by the noise of the millions of insects which announced the dawn.

On his left the rubber trees stood in orderly rows, their slim grey-brown trunks all forked at the same level, their leaves mingling at a height of forty-five feet to cast unbroken shadow over the plantation. Each tree was marked with an identical swathe of scarred bark, like a sarong wrapped around the bole of the trunk.

On the terraced hillside James saw some of his coolies working. Damika, he knew, would be further down, and he bumped and skidded onwards until the headlamp picked out the turquoise shades of her sari as she bent intently over her knife and cut into the bark of a tree. Tapping rubber was skilled work – too deep a cut would damage the tree, too shallow an incision would not produce enough of the creamy sap to fill the cup which was delicately fixed on two wires around the trunk. Only an inch-wide strip of bark could be cut each month. Anxious as he was, James waited until the woman had made her cut, finishing with a twist of the knife to make a curl of bark down which the white sap would run into the conical metal cup below.

She straightened her body and pushed the swathe of sari fabric more securely on to her left shoulder, her metal bangles sounding faintly in the quiet half-light.

'Why have you asked the conductor for money?' James demanded. His suspicion was formless; there was no logic in it. The woman was poor and powerless, virtually a slave, yet she could provoke in James the fear of all her sex which was buried in his subconscious.

'I have earned the money, *tuan*, and I need it.' Was her glance startled or guilty? It was too dark for him to tell.

'But I give you money, I have given you a lot of money. What has become of it?'

'The money you give me I give to my husband, *tuan*.' Her round, black eyes were, as far as he could judge, amiably blank, as always.

'You and your husband earn good wages here. You have not been sick. What has your husband done with my money?'

'*Tuan*, he gives it to Chung Li, the labour contractor. We owe him money.' James, now in his second tour of duty as an assistant on the Bukit Helang estate, knew Chung Li, the biggest contractor in the district, who shipped in the Tamil workers from South India or Ceylon.

'Why do you owe money to Chung Li?'

'It is according to our contract, *tuan*. We must pay him back the money he has spent to bring us here, on our steamer passage and our food on the journey.'

'How much do you have to pay him?' James's eyes wandered to the well-formed, brown arms and the band of naked flesh between the tightly wound waist of her sari and the short blouse that covered her shoulders and breasts.

'We must pay him half of our wages for three years. After that nothing, unless we wish to return home.'

'Chung Li is the son of a dog. He is paid well by *tuan besar* for finding workers for the estate. I did not know he took payment from the workers, too.'

'Chung Li is a good man, *tuan*. Before his men came to our village we had no food. My husband and I had no children, because all my babies died. They were too small and we did not have enough to eat.' An anxious note crept into her voice at the memory. 'Now I have two fine sons, we eat rice every day, and there is enough even for my husband's mother. The *tuan* is also good to us and we are grateful for his kindness.' Unconsciously her fingers swung the gold metal earring in her right ear, which James had bought her to match the one in her left ear.

James yawned, his anxiety forgotten, and tasted the bile from his uneasy stomach. His obscure fear that the woman was somehow betraying him had faded with the dawn shadows, and he was no longer interested in what she was saying. The faint aroma of the coconut oil she used to dress her long black hair, and the musky odour of her flesh, drifted to his nostrils. He felt the skin around his balls shiver.

The woman sensed his loss of interest and her own anxiety subsided. Then they heard a distant whirr; there was a call from the track uphill, and a foreman on a bicycle appeared, pedalling fast. As he approached James, he braked and jumped off the bicycle as a sign of respect for a European.

'*Tuan besar* asks for you, *tuan*. There is trouble where they are cutting the trees.' *Tuan* was a short form of the Malay word *tuanku*, meaning a prince, and was the usual form of address from an Asian to a white man. *Besar* meant big, and *tuan besar* meant Douglas Lovell, the estate manager and lord of more than all he could survey in this isolated region.

James mounted his mud-spattered Triumph and roared away. His closest friend among the eight assistants on the estate was Gerald Rawlins, currently on his first leave in England. In his absence James had kept an eye on his coolies, and put in hand the work of clearing a new patch of jungle for planting. This ground was now a mass of felled vegetation. A gang of Tamils was hacking the branches off a fallen tree, another group urged on a pair of lugubrious water buffalo yoked to a bare trunk by rusty chains.

In the middle of the clearing stood the *tuan besar*, Douglas Lovell, in grimy, fawn riding-breeches and a sweat-stained shirt. Around him in sullen silence waited the band of Malay contrac-tors who had been hired for the work of tree-felling. Behind them a single tree, its trunk massively gnarled and covered in flaking, bone-grey bark, stretched two hundred feet into the cloudy sky.

'Took your time,' grunted Douglas Lovell. 'Tell me what these fellas are getting excited about, will you? They're jibbing at the last tree.'

James approached the group of Malays, trying to look unconcerned, and asked for the foreman. A man of about thirty-five, with a coarse, broad face and several teeth missing, greeted him, and James walked with him a little way from the group. Racking his brains for the right way to handle the situation, James began, 'You and your men have done a fine job. You have cleared this area more quickly than I expected.'

'Good men work well for a good master, *tuan*' the foreman answered.

Encouraged, James went on, 'Maybe if I ask *tuan besar* myself he will give you a bonus.'

'*Tuan besar* will not agree. We will be contented with the price on which we shook hands, and as we have worked fast the benefit will be ours, and we will return to our village.'

So this was not a strategy to get more money; James gave the foreman his most beguiling smile and made an oblique request for further information. 'The questions of the *tuans* are as foolish as the questions of a child, I know. I myself am scarcely more than a child,' he remarked in a matter-of-fact tone.

The foreman beamed patronizingly at James and laughed. James tried to look grave rather than triumphant as the man explained: 'This tree is the home of a ghost. My men will not harm it, for fear of disturbing the ghost which will come in the night and drink their blood.'

James nodded and said, 'The forest is full of spirits and it is foolish to annoy them.' The foreman also nodded, looking relieved, and there was a perceptible release of tension as James jumped nimbly over a fallen trunk and reported back to Douglas Lovell.

'Damn superstitions,' the manager muttered, settling his finger-marked topee further back on his head. 'I'd never have employed Malay labour myself, too damn idle.' He looked up the vast length of the treetrunk, narrowing his eyes against the glare of the sky. 'Any suggestions, Bourton? We've got to get this bugger down somehow.'

'Well, sir, the Chinese don't care about the forest ghosts. These men have finished the job otherwise, and in good time. Why don't we pay them off and see if we can hire some Chinese instead.'

'Damned expensive.'

'If we let the Tamils do it they'll botch it. And I'll get a good price, sir.'

The older man smiled at the slim youngster. 'You sound like a bloody Chinese shopkeeper yourself. Very well.'

A few years in the enclosed multi-stranded community of the Bukit Helang estate had transformed James from a weak and wary boy into a man. All the sullen resistance which had stunted his abilities at school in England was charmed away by the challenges of a new environment; he had grown steadily confident as he discovered that his name, his lineage and his wealth were of no consequence to his fellow planters, but his quick mind, sensitive ear and his practical courage were rewarded by Douglas Lovell's blunt praise and the quick obedience of the men whom he commanded.

Above all, this was a man's world, free of the complications of women. Of the fifteen men in Douglas Lovell's employ, only one, Anderson the doctor, was married, and his wife had the flat-chested, striding manner of an Englishwoman who has elected to un-sex herself for the sake of convenience.

Douglas Lovell ruled his kingdom like a natural imperialist restrained by common sense. He threatened to flog bad coolies, but never did so. An army bugle woke the estate every day for muster.

The memory of the rubber slump of the early thirties remained fresh, and Bukit Helang still ran at scarcely half its capacity, filling a fixed production quota dictated by the rubber company in London. There was a large bulletin board in the white-pillared shade of the estate office, where every day a clerk posted the size of the day's crop, the price of rubber, the number of coolies working and the profit made.

James had never before won approval for his abilities rather than his charm, or felt himself to be engaged in useful, productive work. The experience improved his spirit immensely. Above all, he was admired as a linguist. The basis of this gift was his acute and subtle ear; at Eton he had learned only one foreign language – French – which was taught from books and blackboard by an Englishman with a vile accent that confirmed the boys in the notion that the wogs began at Calais. Now, however, he had no difficulty in learning to speak the oriental languages by listening to the speech of the natives.

'You've got the gift of tongues all right,' another junior assistant had observed in admiration, as he came upon James one day quizzing Ahmed his houseboy in fluent Malay. James himself had been astonished at the ease with which the new languages around him flowed into his mind. At times he was aware of thinking in a mixture of Malay, Cantonese and Tamil, as he gave his men instructions, or of having forgotten the English word for some familiar object, as he dined and drank with the other assistants. His absorption of Oriental speech was instinctive and completely phonetic, however, and when he came to sit the Incorporated Society of Planters' Tamil examination for the first time, he failed.

Douglas Lovell was concerned. 'Chap like you saves a manager a hell of a lot of bother,' he observed from the back of the stocky dun pony on which he made his morning round of the estate.

James walked respectfully by the ambling pony's side. 'I'm sure I'll pass next time. I've just got to flog through the grammar, sir.'

Douglas Lovell paused to watch a group of Tamils weeding the avenues between the rows of young trees. 'Tell 'm to leave the young grass,' he ordered

James. 'Rain'll wash all the soil away if they clear down to bare earth.' When James returned to his side he continued, 'As far as I'm concerned, it's your Malay that's most useful. Never could get the measure of the Malays. Language is easy enough, I'm told, but half the time they're talking in riddles.'

'It's their idea of politeness, sir. They think it's discourteous to ask direct questions. And they have these funny little poems that they all seem to know, and sometimes instead of saying something outright they'll just make some reference to a poem and everything's understood.'

'Hrmph. Not by me, it isn't. Anyway, as far as the Board are concerned, I can't promote you if you don't get the Tamil exam, so you'd better crack on with it.' They walked slowly onwards and the pony swished its pepper-and-salt tail in irritation at the flies. Next to the young rubber was an expanse of older, almost exhausted trees where a solitary Tamil woman crouched as she emptied the half-full cups of latex into her bucket.

'When I first came out here,' Douglas Lovell spoke slowly with light but unmistakable emphasis, 'my manager told me the best way to polish up my Tamil was to get myself a sleeping dictionary.'

'A what, sir?'

'Sleeping dictionary. Native woman. Best place to learn any language is in bed, y'know.' James looked at his boots to hide what he was sure was a blush, and Douglas Lovell looked resolutely between the pony's dark-tipped ears. 'Of course, some fellas don't find 'em very attractive.' There was a pause.

'I think some of them are quite beautiful, actually.'

'You're quite right. Well, if you see one that takes your fancy, here's how it's done.' Briskly he prodded the pony forward, pulled up by the Tamil woman and felt in his breeches pocket for a 20 cent coin, which he tossed into the half-full latex cup in her hand. When she looked up, he nodded towards James and indicated with a jerk of his cane that the initiative came from the younger man, who stood by in frozen fascination.

'If she takes the money, the foreman'll have her cleaned up at the end of the day and sent round to your bungalow. Make sure you pick a married woman, or there's a devil of a fuss.' He turned the pony. 'Best of luck.' He cantered fast up the track without looking back.

The woman looked at James with expressionless round eyes, then picked the coin out of the cup of sticky white sap with a hesitant smile.

Despite his total trust in his new boss, and despite knowing that Douglas Lovell was almost an absolute monarch James barely believed that the woman would come, and half hoped she would not. But, as soon as Ahmed had cleared away his dinner dishes and lit his Java cheroot, Damika walked gracefully out of the darkness up to the verandah steps. He was reassured to see that she had dressed up, with a waxy, white frangipani flower in her black hair and ankle bracelets which chinked softly at each barefoot step. For a few moments there was no sound except the shrilling of the night insects and no movement but the flicker of a bat across the light from the kerosene lamp. Then Ahmed in the kitchen quarters clashed some pans, as if to confirm his tactful preoccupation outside, and James threw the cheroot away, stood up and led Damika into his bedroom.

She helped him unwind the length of her sari, showing neither nervousness nor attraction, and he felt her flesh, cool and firm where he had anticipated a hot softness like rotting fruit. She was not embarrassed either by her nakedness or his, but sighed quietly as he fished in the knot of hair at the nape of her neck for the restraining pins.

Suddenly James was filled with a huge surge of desire. It came with the realization that this woman was a creature completely in his power. His first instinct was to extricate his throbbing penis from his clothes and plunge into the acquiescent flesh before him, but he paused, wanting to glory in complete ownership, the simple pragmatism of the transaction, the fact that he did not need to charm or flatter, scheme or beg, to get possession of this body, and that when the act was over there was no harm she could do him.

He made her sit on his canvas stool and spread her hair around her shoulders, feeling its oiled heaviness. He stroked her arms and breasts, moving the lamp closer to see the mahogany tints of her skin. He pulled at her nipples to see if they would harden, licked, then bit them to try their taste. He pushed her thighs apart, using the commanding firmness of a farrier making a horse pick up its feet, and observed the sparseness of her pubic hair, and the unexpected pinkness of the inner flesh which he probed with his fingers. Where her skin wrinkled, it was velvet black and the folds were smooth and even. He felt his blood roaring in his veins like a river of fire which incinerated everything it touched. Unsteadily, he stood up and motioned her to lie down on his bed, then scrambled between her legs and thrust into her with a sensation of instant release like blinding light.

A few moments later he sat up, dazed, and watched her methodically replace her long earrings, check the tiny, metal flower which pierced her short straight nose, and coil her hair. Mutely he searched for the hairpins he had dropped on the polished hardwood floorboards and handed them to her, then watched as she folded her sari fabric into fanlike pleats and wound the garment around herself. She turned and moved towards the door.

'Are you going?' he asked, clearing his hoarse throat as he spoke.

She looked confused. 'I am going, but I can stay if you wish.'

'Yes, stay. Sleep here with me.'

Without emotion, she returned and unwound the sari. Young, physically healthy and emotionally maimed, James felt the burning river of lust carry him swiftly onwards. He also felt a guilty gratitude towards Damika which he now showed in a fever of caresses which seemed to surprise her. He entered her twice more, then fell asleep. She slept on the mat at his bedside until 4.30 am, when Ahmed, quiet as a cat, shook her awake and she returned to her husband's shack to cook their morning rice.

As soon he had finished taking muster that morning, James tracked her down and dropped another 20 cent coin into her latex cup.

That had been two years ago. He had discovered, to his amusement, that she was illiterate and no help to his mastery of Tamil. Occasionally he bought her a tortoiseshell hairpin or a bangle, with which she was gratifyingly happy. During the day he gave her no thought whatsoever, beyond making the decision whether or not to summon her.

'Bloody glad you're back, Gerald. It's been a blasted nuisance keeping an eye on your patch for six months,' shouted James over the pandemonium of the railway station at the capital, Kuala Lumpur. A swell of people and luggage surged below the pointed arches of white stone. The two men pumped hands and slapped shoulders happily, then turned to follow the porters who were carrying Gerald's battered trunk and two new suitcases through the throng. The length of the train was divided by race, with the Tamils milling around the third class, Chinese families greeting each other at the second class, and Europeans summoning porters to first class; a Malay rajah, his retinue and his polo ponies occupied two special carriages. At the front of the engine a group of Tamil sweepers with baskets and buckets were swabbing the remains of a wandering goat off the buffers amid gently rising steam.

'Not there,' bellowed Gerald at the porters' backs as they swerved towards the exit. 'James, get them over to the left-luggage office. No sense putting up anywhere if we're to be back at Bukit Helang in the morning.'

James passed Gerald the luggage receipts and the two men strolled out into the early evening bustle of Kuala Lumpur, always called simply K. L. by the British. They climbed into a rickshaw pulled by a sweating Chinese and Gerald looked fondly around him, as he brushed railway smuts from his crumpled white trousers.

'Damn sight prettier than Victoria Station,' he said, indicating the cream and white minarets of the railway terminus. 'My God, it was cold back home, I'd forgotten how cold. Are we going to the Dog?'

'Where else – the fatted calf for the prodigal son.'

'Not prodigal for long now, old boy.' Gerald screwed his freckled face into a hearty wink. 'There's a little girl back home with my ring on her finger, choosing her trousseau and packing her trunks . . .' James let out a yell that momentarily startled the sweating rickshaw puller, who half-halted and flung them forward.

'You clever sod, Rawlins, you've cracked it.'

'Did just what the *tuan besar* advised, old boy. Put up at my aunt's in Guildford, had tea every day in a little tearoom opposite the hospital and bingo! Got myself a nice little nurse in ten days flat.' He sat back on the oilcloth-covered seat, grinning, and James thumped his knee in congratulation, knowing how eager Gerald had been to find a wife.

At the club, James ordered champagne and they settled into rattan chairs on the verandah. On the playing field a cricket match between two teams of police cadets was drawing to a close.

The Dog, formally the Spotted Dog, or even more formally the Selangor Club, was an ever-growing complex of bungalows fronted with black and white, mock-Tudor timbering. Its verandahs faced the spacious, green cricket field, and beyond the far boundary the mellow sunlight burnished the pink and white façade and the copper domes of the palace of the state ruler.

'Spotted' suggested the Club's character; albeit a smart establishment, it admitted both *tuan besars* and juniors, and was technically open to Asiatic members as well, although they were few in number. Most of the European clubs in Malaya were either strictly for whites, or specified either big or little *tuans* only, to avoid the embarrassment of social exchange among non-equals. Britain had transplanted its class system to the Empire, along with its notions of business, government and social service.

'So, when's the wedding?'

'Betty – she's called Betty – is booked on the boat in six weeks' time, so she'll be out by October. Mother's as pleased as a cat with two tails, running round Penang arranging the wedding and firing off letters all over the show.' Gerald's family, for three generations employed in the East, was scattered across half the globe. 'I've bought her a present,' he went on, fishing in the pocket of his creased, cream jacket. 'Picked it out at Simon Artz in Port Said. You know about this stuff, d'you like it?' He produced a small, blue velveteen case and prised it open awkwardly with his blunt, freckled fingers. Inside was a cocktail watch of silver metal, its ornate bracelet encrusted with sparkling stones.

'I say, *isn't* that splendid.' James picked up the watch and unobtrusively searched for a hallmark. 'Your Betty should be absolutely delighted. It's charming, first-class.' The watch was not hallmarked, the stones were marcasites at best and Gerald was yet another of the suckers to have found a glittering bargain at Simon Artz's renowned general store on the Suez Canal, but James was too much of a gentleman to say so.

The cricket match ended in a ragged round of muted applause and the white-coated umpires presided as the stumps were drawn out of the coarse turf. The light of the tropical day faded quickly and they moved into the bar. James saw a familiar, gangling figure in the doorway.

'Treadwell! Just the man we need. Come and toast Gerald's future happiness, he's got himself hitched first shot. Boy, another bottle here, if you'd be so kind.'

'You'll never get it right, Bourton,' the lanky Australian folded up like a collapsing deck-chair as he sat, 'your la-di-dah manners don't cut any ice with the natives, y'know.'

Like many bachelor friendships, the oddly matched threesome passed much time in ritual insult, lest anyone should suspect there was affection between them.

'When I want a lecture on etiquette from a bloody convict I'll ask for it. To the bridegroom!' They clinked their Selangor pewter tankards and gulped champagne.

'Now listen, Bill,' James leaned forward, realizing he'd better get important matters out of the way before they were too drunk to remember anything, 'I need your help. Can you spare me a couple of your Chinese lumberjacks for a day? Our fellows got spooked by one of those blasted spirit-house trees and I need a pair of decent, sensible men from outside to fell it.'

'Sure, I'll find you a pair who'd chop up their own grandmothers for ten dollars.'

'Good man, I knew you'd be able to help.'

'Not much good sweating out my life in the lumber trade if I can't help out my pals, is there?' For all his studied lack of pretension, Bill Treadwell was a botanist, an expert in the diseases of hardwood trees, employed in a research project for London University. James, with no desire to get married, had seen no need to return to England for the vacation at the end of his first tour of duty, and instead had spent some time in the forest with Bill.

The two men's friendship had been founded on month-long treks into the jungle; they had lived off rice, fern-tips and what James could shoot; they had attempted to catalogue the hundreds of birds and insects which had fluttered or crawled across their tracks; they had followed tantalizing pathways made by the jungle animals which had abruptly vanished in the walls of vegetation; they had leaped back in terror from the sweeping horns of a *selandang*, the Asian wild ox, enraged when they disturbed it at a hidden wallow; they had strained eyes and ears in vain for an elephant or a tiger and surmised that the distant patter of falling leaves was the step of the tiny mouse-deer. Humbled in the hushed cathedral of nature, they had shared the natives' superstitions and lain unsleeping in the night, telling each other what they knew of the folklore and mythology of the Malayan people. The Australian's erudition and his taste for serious talk had fed James's hungry mind and stimulated the fine intellect which his own native culture had stunted.

A boy slipped past with a salver of curry puffs, reminding them that they could drink more if they lined their stomachs. James ordered some.

'So there'll be no tempting you on one of our jungle hikes now, I suppose?' Bill stuffed the corner of a spicy patty in his mouth and bit it off, waving the remaining fragment at Gerald.

'No, I'm going to settle down and be an old married man,' he replied.

'Shame!' James shouted.

'And there'll be no popping down to old Mary's tonight, I take it?' Bill swallowed down the rest of his curry puff, crinkling his shrewd, blue eyes.

'Well,' Gerald knitted his pale eyebrows, 'I don't think I'll get carried away with this marriage thing just yet – no sense in too much of a good thing is there?'

'I'm relieved to hear it. You had me worried there for a while.' Their custom was to meet in Kuala Lumpur once a month and, emboldened by drink and each other's company, to end the evening at a dilapidated whorehouse in the Chinese quarter, whose official name was the Bright World of Much Happiness, but which was widely known as Mary's.

The curry puffs made them thirsty, and James ordered more champagne, which made them thirstier still, so they ordered stengahs. There was a rowdy commotion as two groups of men started a pitched battle around the doorway of the reading room, spitting whisky at each other from between their teeth. Behind James, a trio of French planters drew closer together in disapproval and carried on discussing whether sex was more important to men or to women.

'How's . . .' Gerald belched gently, 'how's old Douglas Lovell been struggling on without me?'

'Pretty fair. Got himself a new pony from India and a new mistress from Siam, so he's feeling rather good, I should say.'

'He'll be the last of the uncrowned kings of Malaya. I'm glad I've had the chance of serving under him, y'know. Dying breed, marvellous man.' Gerald's pale, slightly bulbous eyes misted with drink and sentiment.

'You're a dying breed yourself, Rawlins.' Bill Treadwell pulled his nose out of his glass and put the drink down with excess precision.

'Don't start . . . you colonials have always got a bee in your bonnet about something.' James pulled in his chair as the whisky–spitting war escalated into the room.

'S'true. Ten years' time the *tuans* 'll be dying out like dinosaurs.'

Gerald's amiable round face flushed with drunken irritation. 'Listen, if we British weren't here this country would be nothing. There'd be no tin-mining . . .'

'Chinese found the tin, Chinese can mine it.'

'. . . there'd be no rubber . . .'

'Don't need white skin to plant trees, do you?'

'. . . and there'd be civil war from one end of the peninsula to the other. Dammit, man, we're only here because the Rajahs asked for British soldiers to stop their people massacring each other.' Gerald's freckled fist hit the rattan table for emphasis.

Bill Treadwell sat back like a bemused schoolmaster with a particularly obdurate class of dullards. 'The sun will never set on the British Empire, hey? Or the British umpire either?' The cricketers, now bathed and changed, were coming into the bar and acknowledging greetings around the room. Treadwell leaned towards

Gerald to give his argument emphasis. 'It'll happen all right, but you don't understand why. You don't even understand what you don't understand. You think that the Malays are like children because they smile a lot and believe that trees have spirits. You can't see what it is that makes them a nation.'

'Well, they're not a bloody nation, they're a bunch of bloody savages from every uncivilish – uincivilized race East of Suez.' Gerald spluttered more and more, as his anger flared. 'The Chinese chop each other up in tong wars, the Tamils worship cows and the damn Malays sit in their *kampongs* doing bugger all. Country would've gone to hell but for the British.'

There was a crash, and more boisterous shouting, as the whisky fighters barricaded the reading-room door with an upended leather sofa.

'For heaven's sake, don't you see it doesn't matter? The Malays got their religion from Arab pirates, their art from Indonesia, and their language from Persia; there are people in the jungle who don't know how to make fire and whose babies are born pink-skinned. They've been colonized by the Siamese, the Portuguese, the Chinese, the Dutch and your mob, and none of it makes any bloody difference. The way the Malays think, all that's totally insignificant. This is their land and they'll be here when you and King George and the British Empire are just another folk memory.'

Gerald squirmed angrily in his chair, not noticing that James, who had the ability to hear two conversations at once, had tuned out of the often repeated argument, and was listening to the French planters continue their debate on love.

'You're forgetting one thing,' Gerald said finally, stifling another belch. 'You're forgetting that we love this bloody country.'

The Australian leaned forward, not too drunk to hear the catch of emotion in his friend's voice. 'I know, chum. I know you bloody love it. You shut your eyes on misty mornings and look at the brown cows and the green *padi*fields and you think you're living in England, you think you're at home.'

There was a massive roar of drunken triumph as one army succeeded in shoving aside the upended sofa and storming over it into the reading room.

'But you aren't at home, mate. You're in some other blighter's home. And you love it for what you can get out of it, oh, yes, you do.' He raised a bony hand to quell Gerald's indignant protest. 'You love Malaya because you can live like a king out here and back home you'd be cooped up in a stinking office pushing paper.'

'That's rot, Treadwell . . .'

'But the Malay loves Malaya because the land is part of his soul. Doesn't matter to him who lines their pockets, mining tin or planting rubber, it's his country.'

Gerald slumped back, shaking his tousled ginger hair. 'I don't understand. I don't understand you and I don't understand the bloody Malays either.'

With an exasperated gesture, Bill shoved his hornrimmed spectacles back to the bridge of his sun reddened nose. 'You'll never understand the bloody Malays until you live their life, take their religion and become one of them. That's what it's all about. For Christ's sake, why do I have to explain this to a pair of bloody Brits. Look at yourselves, man.'

The French planters concluded that love was more important to a woman than to a man because a woman had a greater capacity for sensual enjoyment. An armistice was called in the reading room and the whisky-sodden army came tottering out in twos and threes, laughing uproariously. James suddenly switched his attention to what the Australian was saying.

'What about us, you old sheepshagger? You two must be as pissed as rats.'

'Well, look at you both. You're as swarthy as a bloody Eyetie. Where're your folks from originally?'

'Italy, France – my mother's side are Huguenot, my father's came from Florence.'

'And look at him . . .' Treadwell's bony finger pointed at Gerald, 'red hair, fair skin –'

'*The Celt in all his variants from Builth to Ballyhoo, His mental processes are plain – one knows what he will do*,' quoted James. 'I know what you're getting at. Here we are calling ourselves Anglo-Saxon and Church of England when we're no more Anglo-Saxon than a Chinese rickshaw boy, and we've cobbled our religion together same as the Malays have stuck a bit of Hinduism and a few of their old spirit cults into Islam. But we're English because we think English and . . .'

'And drink Scotch,' Gerald finished defiantly, signalling to the distant boy. 'How about one for the road?'

'Well, thank Christ for the upper classes,' muttered the Australian, giving James a wink as he emptied his glass.

Later they stumbled under the string of fairy lights above the wrought-iron gate of Mary's. Mary, a dumpy Eurasian with skin like yellow leather, shouted to the girls to bring out bottles of warm beer and crank up the gramophone, and as they moved lethargically to obey she sat down opposite the men at the tin table.

'I got a very nice girl, new girl . . .' She looked from one man to the other as if trying to hypnotize them into believing her.

'What is she?' James's tone was businesslike.

'She's Malay, but nice, very pretty, you like.' The three men shook their heads. 'Very pretty girl, you see, I call her . . .' Mary signalled across the room and they waited uncomfortably. In a few moments a woman in a tight orange jacket and flowered sarong appeared and stood hesitantly in the side doorway. James judged her to be at least thirty-five, since she had lost the lamblike plumpness of young Malay girls but was not much wrinkled.

'Does she know how to kiss?' asked Gerald, who had discovered during his courtship in Guildford that kissing was quite pleasant. In general, the Malay whores did not kiss and tended to be uglier and older than the Chinese.

'She do anything,' Mary promised confidently. Gerald shook his head.

'What about Sally?'

'Sally – ah, you mean Sui Li. She busy.'

'Busy long?'

Mary paused for thought. 'Not busy much longer, I think. You want her after?'

'Yes, she's worth waiting for." Gerald swigged with bravado.

'And your friend?' Mary looked at James, who was still considering the Malay girl. Her skin was a light-walnut shade and she had a high-cheekboned face which argued some Mediterranean blood.

'Where's she from, Mary?'

'I don't ask. She come yesterday, tell me husband die.' There was little point in asking further, since he knew he would probably not be told the truth. James liked the girl's diffidence, disliked her maturity, and didn't much care for the Chinese whores who were as skinny as cats.

'She'll do,' he said, giving Mary some notes and disappearing with the woman up the house's sloping stairs.

'Since you're so clever' Gerald turned to Bill, 'you tell me this. Why're all the Malay girls so bloody ugly?'

'Easy. Malay women only go on the game if they're widowed or divorced, no male relative to support them, and got no hope of getting another husband. Your Malay, being a Moslem, doesn't care for divorced women because he thinks they know too much. Specially in the little villages – they've got a saying that a wife who's lost her husband is as frisky as a horse that's thrown its rider. The peasants get together and throw the girl out of the village before she gives the married women ideas. But with the Chinese it's all down to money – Chinese girl thinks she can make more money spreading her legs than selling mangoes, she's away. Half of them are sold by their mothers, if they're pretty.'

'So, what's your fancy? You've been bloody quiet sitting there.'

'I'll sit this one out, I think.' Treadwell's tone was grim, and Gerald was about to ask the reason when Sui Li appeared in a skintight pink cheongsam. She greeted him with delighted shrieks, to emphasize her popularity and consequent prosperity to the other girls, and dragged him happily up the stairs to her room. Underneath her cheongsam she was naked, but in the few moments it took her to peel it off, Gerald slumped down on the bed and fell asleep.

Downstairs Bill Treadwell waited, reflectively sipping his beer. For all he had drunk, he felt sober. He took off his hornrimmed spectacles and put them in the breast pocket of his jacket. Mary's, with its peeling Tiger beer posters and languid whores, faded to an indistinct blur.

CHAPTER FIVE

FOR MONTY, the worst thing about her father's death was that it left her alone with her mother. There was her sister, of course, but Cathy was different. She was not a combatant in the unending war with Bettina which was the real focus of the Bourton family's energy. To a casual friend, it would seem that both the Bourton daughters were caught up in competition for the love of their bewitching father. The truth was much darker than that. James and his girls were united in resistance to Bettina's hatred.

The family had no casual friends, because Bettina froze them off with calculated social inadequacy. She had made an offensive weapon of her shyness. Their house was a tall, grey-stone building of exceptional elegance and charm, built to nestle in a spinney at the foot of the Downs to the north of Brighton, on the outskirts of a village of red-brick cottages. The graceful aspect of the house suggested that life within was all civilized happiness. Very few people ever entered it. Those who did noticed that Bettina outwardly observed all the conventions of motherhood, while at the same time persecuting her family with cold passivity.

The girls responded by drawing together for emotional support. Before they dared to express in words the conviction that their mother did not like them, they shared the knowledge subconsciously; it was an awful secret which they kept together.

James all but deserted his home while the girls were small, spending most of his time in London. Cathy grew up with the futile notion that if she were as good as she possibly could be, maybe one day their mother would love them and their father would come back. She became a high-spirited girl with great gifts of pleasing, and in due course James began to take pleasure in her company.

Monty scorned to please. She attacked. She wanted more than mere survival. She wanted revenge. By instinct she saw that Bettina's façade of parenthood masked relentless ill-will.

'Witch,' she screamed at her mother in her frequent childhood tantrums. 'Witch! Witch! Wicked, wicked witch! I hate you! I'm going to burn you all up.'

Bettina never replied. She continued on her daily routine, as if she were a planet moving obliviously in its orbit. Her mornings were spent in her room; in the afternoon she would set off for the bridge club and she would not return until late at night. She and James had separate bedrooms. They seldom shared a meal. Rarely, James would suggest an outing for the whole family, in which Bettina would at once refuse to take part. She never accompanied him anywhere. The family came together only at Christmas.

The wifely duty of decorating the house was also something she avoided, with the result that James and his mother, Davina, had created the interior together. James's taste was for rich, highly-coloured furnishings and exotic pieces of furniture. Davina introduced fleets of silver photograph frames, collections of Sevres porcelain, wistful watercolour portraits of their distant relatives and odd items which she felt she could purloin from Bourton without their Uncle Hugo noticing. One of these stolen treasures was an oil painting of a bright-eyed, white lap-dog which, Davina told them, with great pride, had belonged to Madame de Pompadour. It was the only one of her additions which could hold its own against James's emerald brocade curtains and inlaid Chinese cabinets.

The girls grew up in a riot of ill-matched luxury. Their mother's conversation was a stream of platitudes directed at nullifying all communication. If Monty complained her tennis clothes were sweaty, Bettina would say, 'Nonsense. Horses sweat. Gentlemen perspire and ladies gently glow.' If Monty said she was hungry, Bettina would at once tell her, 'You can't be hungry. You've no idea what hunger is.' If any member of the family attempted to involve her in a decision, Bettina would refuse, saying, 'It's no use, I never discuss anything with my relatives. It only leads to arguments.'

Bettina also refused to acknowledge either daughter's approach to womanhood. Cathy and Monty knew, from the experience of their friends at school, that they would probably begin to menstruate some time, and one morning, Monty woke up in pain to find her bedclothes soaked with scarlet blood. Cathy called their mother, who looked at the mess with distaste, said nothing and walked away. Half an hour later the housekeeper appeared to strip the bed, and gave Monty one of her own sanitary towels. Monty was made to feel she had done something offensive.

'Anyone would think I'd started just to upset her,' snarled Monty. 'She ought to be pleased. I'll be grown-up soon and then she won't have to bother with me any more.'

Cathy and Monty were sent to boarding school when they were six and five years old respectively. They passed most of their summer vacations with their uncle's family at Bourton. The piano lessons were started in the remaining holidays as a solution to the problem of getting the children out of their mother's way. Cathy was easily pleased with her pony. But Monty was frightened of horses and said that riding hurt her rapidly developing breasts, a ploy she knew would work because

Bettina would evade discussion on so embarrassing a subject. Instead, she was put on the country bus to the next village, where an elderly woman gave piano lessons in the church hall.

'I can do tunes now,' Monty announced to her sister shortly after her tenth birthday. 'It's as easy as anything. My teacher says I've got perfect pitch because I can sing whatever she plays. She says I've got a very good ear.'

Cathy looked at each side of her sister's head, pushing back her dark curls to look at her ears. 'Which one is it?' she asked with curiosity.

'Not my *real ear*, silly, ear for music. Don't you know anything?' Proud as she was of her smart older sister, Monty enjoyed mastery of something at which Cathy did not shine.

No one except Cathy had any notion of the pleasure Monty found in music until the teacher by chance met James at a village fete. 'You must be so proud of Miranda's playing,' the grey-haired spinster told him, taking the money for his guess at the weight of her almond-paved Dundee cake. 'She's such a *pleasure* to teach. She's developing real musical sensitivity, you know – unusual for a child of her age. She needs to practise more, of course . . . I expect you'll be getting a new piano, soon?'

'A new piano?' James was puzzled. He spent so little time at home that he could not be sure, but his recollection was that there was no piano in his house. The music teacher knew this perfectly well, and had fifty years' experience of manipulating wealthy, philistine parents for the benefit of their talented offspring. Soon a handsome, French satinwood piano with ormolu candelabra appeared in the house.

Monty's joy in the instrument made Bettina feel thwarted and angry; but she could not defy James. She had been outmanoeuvred for the first time, and every hour Monty spent at the yellowed keyboard pressed home the advantage.

Now there was no James to save Monty from the cold antagonism of her mother. As she took her place in the limousine that drove the bereaved family of Lord James Bourton home from the suburban crematorium where his widow had directed that his remains be summarily reduced to ashes, Monty felt desolate. She was unprotected. She flinched as a group of photographers who had been waiting at the gates to their home crowded round the car and Cathy pulled down the limousine's blinds with angry force.

Throughout the terrible summer, Monty and Catherine scarcely left each other's company. Day after day they watched a succession of small black cars drive tentatively up to the house. Out of the cars climbed dark-suited men, who raised the gleaming door-knocker with bowed heads, knowing they were bringing bad news. They gave their names to the housekeeper in embarrassed voices, and she showed them into the drawing room where they had long meetings with Bettina.

Bettina would tell the girls nothing, nor discuss anything with them. Her face set in a blank mask, she came and went without saying where she was going or why.

'This is nothing to do with you,' she told Cathy with savagery. 'There's nothing to do and nothing to tell. Stop pestering me.'

In the first few weeks the girls cried a great deal, especially at night when they woke up at intervals and the darkness was full of shapeless horrors. Monty moved her bed into Cathy's room, because anything was better than waking up and crying alone.

'If only we *knew*,' muttered Cathy, tears seeping from the corners of her eyes and trickling down her temples to wet her hair. 'Why would Daddy do such an awful thing? Surely he must have known that whatever he had done we would always love him? He must have been so unhappy.'

'We'll know when they finally have the inquest.' Monty knew she was offering small comfort. 'Don't cry, *please*, Cathy, I can't bear it if you cry too.'

'But *when* are they going to have the inquest? It's been weeks now, they don't seem to know anything.'

'I don't believe he killed himself.' Monty was still haunted by the idea that she had somehow killed her father and determined to argue herself out of it. 'He didn't have any reason, he didn't have any problems. And he didn't leave a note. They must think someone killed him, or why were the police here?'

'Were the police here?' Cathy sat up and fumbled for a tissue in the darkness.

'Yes, I asked Mrs Armstrong and she wouldn't answer. Mummy's told her not to talk to us about anything. But chatted up the driver and he told me. You could tell, anyway – they all wear blue nylon shirts.'

Cathy switched on the light, and at the sight of each other's tear-streaked faces the girls cried again, hugging one another for comfort.

'It's no good, crying's no good,' Cathy said at last. 'We've got to wait it out, that's all. Someone's bound to tell us before the inquest. They won't want us to read it in the newspapers.'

The days dragged on, hot and overcast. Their mother made telephone calls behind closed doors. She seemed to age before their eyes, shrinking inside her flower-printed cotton dresses. Her hair collapsed in lifeless strands, despite its dye and permanent wave, and the skin of her neck began to fall into slack folds around the sinews. She sat at dinner with them making hesitant rushes at small-talk, sipping continually from a very small glass of water, which she would leave the room to refill herself.

The sisters saw nothing odd in this behaviour, because the very small water-glass had been one of Bettina's idiosyncrasies for as long as they could remember. But in the long limbo of anguish, they sought any distraction, and one evening, when Bettina was called away from the dinner table to another hushed telephone call, Monty picked up the glass, sniffed it, then sipped it.

'Taste it,' she passed the glass steadily to Cathy, 'it's vodka or something. She must have a bottle hidden somewhere.'

At home the girls were allowed aperitifs before dinner, or a glass of wine, but neither of them really liked the taste of alcohol. Sometimes, if James had opened a particularly fine vintage, he would insist that they sip it, saying, 'Never hurts to know a good wine.' Neither of them had ever done more than taste spirits, and they had only the vaguest idea of how drink was measured, how much was too much.

'She can't . . .'

'. . . can't be an alcoholic? I bet she's hiding the bottles in her room.'

'She can't be. I've never seen her drunk, at all.' Cathy thought alcoholics were people who collapsed in the gutter, not women who drank steadily in secret just to be able to put on a show of being normal.

'Oh can't she? You know she never kisses us, don't you? She must be afraid we'll smell it on her breath.'

'Don't be so dramatic, Monty.' Cathy's conviction was wavering. Now that there was an explanation for their mother's odd behaviour, Cathy's acute mind quickly arranged the evidence to support it, remembering the amount of time Bettina spent isolated in her own room, the occasions when she had not seemed to understand what they were saying or made responses which had not made sense.

'I'll find out, if you don't believe me.' Monty swiftly threw down her napkin and ran out of the room. Their mother's muted voice sounded occasionally behind the closed door of the drawing room. Monty ran upstairs and slipped into Bettina's bedroom. A few moments later she reappeared brandishing a half-empty gin bottle in her hand.

'There. It was inside her dressing-table drawer. And there's an empty one in a Harrods bag in there, too.' She planted the bottle in the middle of the gleaming, mahogany table. Cathy looked at it as if it were a snake.

'So what we know now,' she drew in a slow, shuddering breath, 'is that you are sixteen and I am seventeen, our father is dead, and our mother drinks.'

'Maybe she'll drink herself to death.' Monty immediately regretted speaking so harshly, as she saw her sister's eyes brim with tears once more. 'Oh come on, Cathy. She's not going to take care of us; no one ever took care of us. We were all right as long as we had Daddy, but we're both on our own now – it's up to us. We've still got each other, that's the main thing.'

A few moments later Bettina came back to find her daughters sitting in silence. She ignored them, and the accusing bottle in the table centre. 'If you've finished dinner you'd better go up and pack,' she announced grimly. 'We're going to Bourton tomorrow.'

'Have they found out anything, Mummy?'

'They've found out why he did it, if that's what you mean. It is none of my business. Your Uncle Hugo is going to speak to you.'

In the past, they had always gone to Bourton at Christmas and in the summer vacation. Cathy never thought of it without remembering the first time they arrived there, when she was very small, and the family had just come home from Malaya. In the evening darkness, the car headlights had caught the eyes of a group of deer on the estate road in front of them and her father had wound down the window and lifted her up, so she could hear the soft rumble of their hooves as they leaped across the road. It was like driving into the England of her story books, a place full of princes and castles and enchantment.

Now, however, it was high summer, and the grass of the park was baked to gold and the estate road was clogged with buses full of tourists. The yellow-stone house rose out of the throng of trippers like a square cake rising inside its frill. A rank of lichen-spotted statues guarded the terrace and two fountains spouted continuously during opening hours.

The family lived in the North Wing, which was at the back and comprised about one third of the house. The middle third was closed: eighteenth-century, hand-painted Chinese wallpaper was boarded over, plastic sheeting covered holes in the roof and dead leaves had collected in the central courtyard. The South Wing at the front was crammed with paintings which had been too important to sell without scandal, and furniture too ugly to sell at a reasonable price; this was open to the public.

The National Trust owned the house; Uncle Hugo, the Duke of Witherham, owned the estate, or what was left of it. With ruthless management it yielded enough to keep him, his wife Pamela, their two children and the seventy-four-year-old Dowager Duchess, in what they defined as comfort. This meant that the stairs were uncarpeted and the bedrooms unheated, but there were hunters for Pamela, shooting for Hugo, and Davina retained all her jewellery but could not afford to insure it.

Cathy and Monty sat side by side in hard chairs in their uncle's office.

'This is a frightful business about your father,' Uncle Hugo began. 'Your mother just can't cope, so she's asked me to talk to you. I'm afraid you're going to have to prepare yourselves for quite a few changes.' He got up from his lopsided swivel chair, and walked round to the front of his desk, on which he perched his heavy, tweed-trousered backside with a clumsy pretence of informality. 'None of us had the least idea; heaven knows how he managed it all, without us finding out.'

Cathy whose sensitivity to adult preoccupations made her wise beyond her years, could tell that Uncle Hugo blamed himself for not having known whatever it was, but was trying to cover this up.

'The thing is, my dears, your father wasn't quite as clever as he thought he was, when it came to business. He really was rather at sea in the City, you know, and – um –' there was no kind way to say it, and kindness, in any case, was something Hugo had never valued '– he lost rather a lot of money. A great deal of money. Of course he liked to live well.'

'But he inherited all that money from our grandfather.' Cathy's earnest bewilderment made her uncle even more uncomfortable.

'Not exactly, my dear, you don't quite understand. You and your sister inherited the money, it was in trust for you both. Really your father had no right to it.'

'Uncle Hugo, do you mean something has happened to our grandfather's money?'

'Yes, my dear, I'm afraid, I do. There are firms which will lend money and which specialize in finding the weak spots in other people's legal arrangements. It seems that your father had consulted one of these outfits, and taken, over the years, a series of loans against your trust. He'd covered his tracks thoroughly, so it has taken the police some time to get all the facts. He was being pressed quite savagely by these people and there's . . .' he paused, wondering if the full extent of their father's agony was something the girls ought to know.

How vividly they looked like their father, Hugo thought, as he watched the two bewildered girls shrink together and link arms. Cathy had that meandering top lip which had always made James seem to be smiling, and her hair, though definitely brown rather than James's jet black, had the same heavy texture; and yet, she had a directness, a collected manner, which was nothing like her father's flighty charm. The younger girl seemed at first glance not to take after her father at all, although she had his unruly curls. She also had his devilment. Hugo could see in her eyes the defiance that he remembered blazing from the eyes of the small brother who had shared his nursery many years ago.

'But Uncle Hugo, aren't trusts supposed to stop people using up all their money?' Cathy had a frustrating sense that embarrassment was making her uncle hold back the most important information.

'Yes my dear, they are. I promise you, we've thrashed out the whole affair with the lawyers at Pasterns and there's no way round it. When your grandfather set up the trust he was thinking mostly of persuading your father to settle down to a decent family life. He was rather the black sheep in those days.' Pasterns were the unimpeachable firm of solicitors who handled all the Bourton family's business, as well as that of half the remaining landed gentry in England. 'Your father was a very persuasive man, don't forget. He never had any trouble getting people to lend him money. He led us all to understand he'd made his fortune in the East.'

Hugo blamed himself. There was something inevitable about this tragedy: it had been foreshadowed for half a century by James's recklessness and peculiar lack of moral sensitivity. In a sense the rest of the Bourton family had lived as if walking on eggshells, waiting for James sooner or later to pay the penalty for his careless hedonism.

Hugo ploughed on with his task. 'I must tell you this, my dears, because you've got to hear it from one of the family. At the time he died your father had pretty much come to the end of the line. The police know that he had been to see one of these Arab financiers in Paris, and we can only presume he was trying to borrow more money. He was starting to default on some of the repayments on these loans.'

Four innocent, questioning, dark-brown eyes were fixed on him; a more sensitive man would have wept, but Hugo had no emotion to show; as the head of the family he felt only a dogged compulsion to fulfil his responsibility.

Cathy met his gaze calmly. 'Yes, Uncle Hugo, what else?'

'There is some question of blackmail, I believe, but it seems unlikely that the police will get to the bottom of it because the outfit is based abroad and they're getting no cooperation from the police at the other end. We may never know exactly what kind of mess your father was in.'

He means we're broke, thought Cathy. That's why he's rambling around and looking so uncomfortable. The idea did not disturb her. Money, to the sisters, was something you spent on magazines and records and cinema tickets, not something which determined your social position, your marriage prospects, your health or your happiness. Money was the only topic which was more strictly taboo than sex in the girls' artificially prolonged childhood.

'How much have we got left?' asked Monty in a rush.

'Nothing. Nothing at all. I'm very sorry, my dears, but it's all gone.'

Cathy's mind was, as always, racing pragmatically ahead.

'We can sell the house . . .' she began in a constructive tone.

'Your father bought the house with a mortgage from the trust, to provide you all with a home. It has appreciated, of course, but his personal liabilities will more than swallow that up. I shall have to reach into my own pocket to stop his estate being declared bankrupt.'

'So what's going to happen to us?' Monty's full mouth set in an angry bow. 'I suppose you and Mummy have got it all planned?'

'Not quite. We decided to get this business over with before the inquest, then make our plans.' Hugo looked awkwardly at Cathy, who was fumbling in the flounced sleeve of her dress for a handkerchief.

'Poor, poor Daddy,' she whispered, catching the first tears as they fell. Monty hugged her awkwardly and glared at Uncle Hugo.

'Papa says your father is worse than a criminal. He says he sold your birthright for a mess of pottage,' announced their fourteen-year-old cousin Edward in a nasty tone of triumph. 'He says you're absolute paupers and we'll have to be kind to you, but I shan't let you ride my new pony because you'll ruin its mouth.

'Shut up, squirt!' Monty kicked him with her new, Louis-heeled shoe. 'We shan't have to go to school any more, so think of that when your stupid pony's bucked you off!'

Cathy and Monty had nothing but a blood tie in common with their cousins. Caroline and Edward were beefy children who lacked all the intelligence, sensitivity and charm of the Bourton girls but were happily too far sunk in bovine complacency to realize it.

The four of them were sitting in the stuffy hayloft above the stables, a favourite hiding place at Bourton. Monty watched with distaste as Caroline, Edward's older sister, scrubbed a bridle with saddle soap, shoving strands of her coarse, brown hair out of her face. She was sallow-skinned and pearshaped like her father, and her old putty-coloured jodhpurs did not improve her silhouette.

'Are you really not going back to school? Oh damn!' Brusquely Caroline bit off a broken fingernail, then wiped her soapy mouth on her sleeve.

'We've got to go to secretarial college. Then we'll be able to get jobs if we don't get married.' Cathy lay listlessly across the highest bales of sweet-smelling hay, watching a swift dart to its nest through a hole left by a missing slate.

'Your mother does go on about you getting married.' Caroline was trying to be sympathetic.

'She wants to get rid of us. She always has. She's obsessed with it. She must be crazy – who'd get married just to play bridge all day?' Monty was dying for a cigarette, but could not be bothered to get up and go outside.

'Beggars can't be choosers,' sneered Edward. 'Who'd marry you two, anyway, now you haven't got any money? You're a dead loss.' He dodged Monty's foot by rolling over on the floor, wisps of hay sticking to his checked shirt.

'I suppose you think you'll be the answer to a maiden's prayer yourself.' His sister dunked the snaffle in a bucket of water, then hung the damp bridle up on a nail to dry.

'My mother says your mother won't be bringing you out either.'

'I don't think she was very keen on the idea, anyway. You know she's terrified of society, as she calls it.' Cathy rolled over on her stomach and watched her cousin go to work lathering her jumping saddle. 'It would have been fun, though.'

'Yes, it would.' Caroline stood up and hoisted a fallen bra-strap back into place under her blouse. 'It'll be a frightful bore going to all those cocktail parties on my own.'

All Caroline's sentimental potential was absorbed by her animals; admitting that she would have liked to share her debutante season with her cousins was, by her standards, an emotional outpouring. Cathy smiled, grateful for what she recognized as sympathy.

'Can I light a fag in here?' Monty already had a Consulate between her lips, and snatched the packet out of Edward's reach. 'You're too young. Buy your own.'

To one member of the Bourton family, however, a debutante season for Cathy and Monty was strategically essential. The Dowager Duchess, who had long ago rejected the notion of being a dowager and insisted on her own title of Lady Davina, had been looking forward for years to piloting the girls through their maiden voyage in society. The prospect of instructing the uncouth Caroline in the art of ensnaring the best possible husband was considerably less promising than that of launching her more attractive cousins. She had watched them begin to bloom and longed to teach Monty the best way to play on her catlike sensuality, and to show Cathy how to withdraw when her wistful beauty caused havoc.

Now that every trace of her own physical charm had withered, Davina was enduring an enforced loss of feminine status. She had fought frantically against advancing age, with diets, cosmetics, couturiers and plastic surgery. It was a useless struggle. Now that she was no longer sexually desirable, she was not noticed.

She tasted bitter humiliation every time she entered a crowded room and no men registered her arrival. She felt as if she had gradually ceased to exist. Having spent all her life practising the art of seduction, she was unable to relate to men in any other way, and she despised the company of women. Her pretty granddaughters were her last hope.

'Of course, they must *all* come out!' Lady Davina's bracelets clashed as she reached for her glass at dinner. Hugo glowered up the length of the table at his mother. She was, in effect, proposing that he pay for all three girls, and he knew that with Lady Davina in charge of the operation he would have to find tens of thousands of pounds for dresses and parties in addition to the money he was now obliged to divert to paying James's debts and securing rudimentary job-training for James's daughters.

'Mother, I've told you before it's out of the question.'

'I was not consulted. Caroline can't possibly come out on her own. She's incapable of catching anything with less than four legs. She'll simply be asked to a succession of dreary hunt balls. Hopeless!'

Caroline's mother, a tall, brown-haired woman with the same yellow skin as her daughter, pressed the bell on the floor with her foot and the butler appeared to clear away the goldrimmed Minton plates. Dinner at Bourton was almost always tinned soup followed by game; Hugo justified the staggering sum he spent on shooting by bringing hundreds of birds back to be hung in the game larder until semi-putrid, when they would be drawn, plucked and stored in the walk-in freezer. This evening they were eating curried grouse. Monty quite liked it. If you mixed in enough chutney, you couldn't taste the grouse at all.

'I simply cannot afford to bring out three girls. You must be reasonable, Mother.' In the shadowy radiance from the candelabra, which had been converted to electricity but for economy's sake was run on half the right number of light bulbs, Hugo looked exactly like a wicked uncle, with his heavy features, beaky nose and blue jowls.

'I am being reasonable, Hugo. It will be a complete waste of money to bring out Caroline by herself. And three girls will cost you hardly any more than one.' Lady Davina's Pomeranian dog jumped off her lap, dislodged by her arthritic gesticulations.

'The money simply isn't there, Mother.'

'Nonsense. One can always find money from somewhere. I shall sell some jewellery.' This was Davina's ultimate weapon. Almost all her jewellery was what an auctioneer would describe as important; the sale would make headlines. Lady Davina herself, although long past the age of scandalous behaviour in nightclubs, was still a name known to society columnists. She chafed in the obscurity of a dowager, and would seize any opportunity to be talked about once more. Hugo sawed into a grouse leg with resignation. His mother was right as usual. Family prestige was the issue.

'On the other hand, it won't look very good if the girls don't come out after all this business.' He forked a sinewy morsel into his mouth and chewed it vigorously. 'They're on at me to fell some more of the West Wood this year.'

'Then that's settled.' Davina swivelled her mud-coloured eyes, beaded with black mascara, towards Cathy and Monty and gave them an enormous, theatrical wink. 'The three of you can have a season next year.'

'Two.' Monty looked firmly at her grandmother. 'You're not trailing me round that cattle market.'

'Miranda!' Bettina, sitting in unsteady silence opposite her daughters, spluttered to life. 'How dare you be so ungrateful! You wicked children – you'll do exactly as you're told. It's the least you can do, after all this mess. Apologize to your grandmother this minute.' Monty's defiant stare raked round the table like a machine gun.

'Be quiet, Mummy. I'm saving Uncle a lot of money, so you can't complain. I'd rather die than be tarted up in a white frock and led off to be mated like a prize heifer.'

Lady Davina scooped up her lap-dog and gave a tight, blood red smile. 'As you wish, Miranda. I shall have quite enough to do with your sister and Caroline.'

Davina's energy was suddenly phenomenal; she itched to relive the sexual and social triumphs of her own nubile years. Monty's defection made little difference, since she knew that attractive sisters close in age were often invited together, even if only the elder was officially coming out – and what young girl would be able to resist going to glittering balls and riotous parties all summer long? The endless, ill-defined medical conditions which had for years restricted Davina's existence, mysteriously abated. Lounging on the blue velvet daybed by the drawing-room fire, with the Pomeranian at her feet and a copy of *The Tatler* on her lap, she telephoned ceaselessly around the country, activating the network of acquaintances she had first made during her own season before the First World War.

'Nancy! Too divine. Yes we shall certainly see you at Fugborough for Fiona. In May, you said?' She covered many pages of thick, blue writing paper with notes in arthritic script.

'So sick-making, they can't be presented. Never mind, Thelma darling, we shall make do – now who is this little man with a list?'

She was particularly gushing with the friends she knew to have eligible sons and grandsons. 'Nothing makes you more popular than knowing heaps of young men – now where's Marina's number, I'm sure they've got three, but perhaps Charlie is still at Eton . . .'

Cathy and Caroline were summoned to her bedroom, chilly, stuffy and smelling of stale Schiaparelli scent, and made to try on jewellery.

'Remember, Caroline, never emeralds for you – they make your complexion look like dishwater.' Immune to such abuse, Caroline pulled off the necklace and stepped forward to replace it in its box, treading on the dog which yelped and scuttled under the pink chintz skirts of the dressing table. 'Pearls for daytime, of course, and always diamonds for evening, but remember that at your age, *you* must shine, not your jewellery.' Catherine tentatively picked up a collar of baguette diamonds, showy in the severely Art Deco style.

'Certainly not, most unsuitable.' Lady Davina took it from her and picked out a modest Victorian pendant instead. She obviously intended to keep the best pieces for herself.

'Thank you, Grandmother, it's really pretty.' Cathy held the almost invisible gold chain against her throat and admired the small rubies and even smaller diamond sparkling on her smooth skin.

'I think you had better call me Didi, darlings, everyone always does.' Lady Davina made this suggestion in carefully casual tones, inwardly appalled at the prospect of being called 'Grandmother' in public.

In a week, she had acquired all the vital information she needed to lay the ground to plan the season. Although trained from puberty to present a façade of adorable idiocy, and now able to add the dimension of approaching senility to the performance, Lady Davina had a magnificent memory. Soon she had stored in it the names of the two-hundred-odd girls who were to come out the next year, as well as the likely dates for their dances. This data she added to the encyclopaedic store of information she had amassed about the wealth, property, estates and connections of each family. From a society columnist in London she then acquired 'the List' – a roll of young men's names which came with the unwritten guarantee that every one was a sound prospective husband, with a decent family and reasonable wealth behind him and no known social vices.

'*Three* earls,' she announced, setting down her translucent, porcelain teacup with a tremulous hand. 'You should be able to manage one easily, Catherine. I shall be most disappointed if you let me down.' Cathy nodded uncertainly. She felt crushed by the responsibility she now had to restore the family's name and fortune by marrying gloriously. Her thrilling, romantic dreams were all too quickly turning into frightening reality. 'Who are they, Didido we know any of them?'

'Sholto Mayleigh Shillingworth – over thirty, I should say. The longer a man stays unmarried, darling, the harder he is to catch. Andrew Downcliffe's people own half of Ayrshire, but you won't want to live in Scotland if you can avoid it. Then there's Charlie Coseley, in banking, I believe.'

'He's a dreamboat,' said Caroline suddenly, giving her first evidence of interest in flesh that was not equine. 'His cousin was at school with us and I saw him once when he came to take her out.'

Monty spent three or four days sulking and smoking, wandering aimlessly around the estate feeling irritated by the noisy busloads of tourists. She was not only bored but wrapped still in a blanket of guilty sadness which muffled the effect of the outside world upon her. She was sullen with the adults of the family, contemptuous of Caroline and vilely rude to Edward. No one took much notice of her, except Cathy.

'Please, Monty, won't you change your mind? It won't be any fun coming out without you,' Cathy pleaded, finding her skimming pebbles into the lake one afternoon.

'But it won't be any fun for me, don't you see? I'm not pretty like you, you'll get all the boys and I'll just be stuck with Caroline and the rest of the no-hopers.' Monty let fly a stone at exactly the right angle and it bounced across the water much further than she had intended, frightening a moorhen.

'You won't – don't be silly. You'll probably do much better than me. Rosanna said her brother thought you were fabulous looking when he came to take her out from school.'

Monty sniffed, unconvinced. They both knew that Cathy, with her slim, coltish legs, her swinging straight hair, beautiful complexion and boyish figure, was so pretty she could have stepped straight from the pages of *Vogue*. What Cathy recognized, but Monty refused to believe, was that Monty was just as attractive, but in a lush, sensual way that was not, at the time, particularly fashionable.

'You're only saying that to be nice,' Monty stooped to pick up some more pebbles.

'No I'm not. Oh please, Monty. I'll hate it without you.'

'But why are you doing it? You wanted to go to university.'

'I know, but it's different now, isn't it? Can't you see if one of us doesn't get married to someone rich soon we'll be stuck living on Uncle Hugo's charity. And everyone will point at us as the daughters of the Suicide Peer.' This was the name the newspapers had found for their father. Rumours about his death were still appearing in print.

'Anyway, what good would university do me? I'd only get a lot more useless exams while everyone else was getting the best men. *Please*, Monty.'

Monty shook her head. 'I'd only do something awful and get you a bad name. All those chinless wonders would drive me nuts. It's your choice, Cathy, but not mine.'

A few days later, Monty wandered out of the estate to the side of the main road, and casually stuck up a thumb as she had seen hitchhiking servicemen do. Instantly a car stopped for her.

'Where to?' The driver was a plump, golden-haired man of about forty, in tweeds. Monty, thrilled with the sudden success of her half-planned scheme, looked wildly at the signpost across the road. It said Frome 7 1/2, Bath 80, Exeter 110.

'Exeter,' she said with what she did not realize was a ripe, inviting smile.

'Hop in.' He took a pile of papers from the passenger seat and flung them in the back, on top of a heap of small brown, cardboard boxes.

He was a salesman for a firm manufacturing agricultural pharmaceuticals, jolly, stupid but worldly enough to recognize Monty straight away for a posh piece kicking over the traces.

'Live round here? Had a row with your family?' He offered her a strong cigarette, stabbed in the dashboard lighter then flipped it out and held it for her, while steering with one negligent finger. Monty inhaled deeply, feeling fabulously adult.

When they reached the town two hours later he bought her a hamburger in a coffee bar.

'Seen that, have you?' he asked casually as they went past the cinema where a Beatles film was playing.

'Not yet,' she answered.

They sat in the back row and watched John Lennon playing a harmonica in a train. After a while the man's left hand, moving as if of its own volition, appeared on her shoulder. Full of delicious anticipation, Monty turned her face towards him; his thumb gently tipped up her chin and suddenly they were kissing.

My first real kiss, she realized with mounting excitement, eagerly parting her lips. Obviously that was the right thing to do, because his hot tongue snaked into her mouth immediately. Out of the corner of her eye she could see Ringo Starr on the screen, with arms outstretched, whirling around like a helicopter rotor, but she was much more aware of the delicious, tingling excitement in her limbs. She tried putting her tongue in his mouth, and was rewarded by a crushing embrace.

In the afternoon, the small country cinema was almost empty. The man's firm, fat fingers undid her blouse and began stroking her breast over her bra, then dipped experimentally inside the cup. Is he going to take my bra off, Monty wondered, undecided if she wanted him to try, but longing to feel him touch her naked flesh.

What she didn't know was that in fifteen years on the road the man had picked up and made love to enough girls to know an over-eager virgin when he kissed one and, being fundamentally decent and the father of girls who would soon be Monty's age, he had no intention at all of taking this puss for the hot number she was obviously pretending to be. They necked pleasantly through the rest of the movie, by which time Monty's knickers were damp with excitement. Then he drove her to the edge of the town, and she hitched a ride back to Bourton, arriving in perfect time to change for dinner, at which she was unexpectedly pleasant to everyone.

Monty now had an excited sparkle about her which subtly signalled her craving for sexual adventure to every boy interested enough to read the signs. A youth who served behind the bar at the Bourton Arms, the pub outside the estate gates where she was in the habit of buying her cigarettes, asked her if she wanted to go for a ride on his motorbike and a couple of days later kissed her as they leaned on a gate from which there was supposed to be a view over five counties. He was rather clumsy and smelt of pickled onions.

The French tourist who asked if he might take her picture by the rotunda was much more accomplished and could unfasten her bra with one adroit hand. He was very persistent about trying to pry inside her knickers, which Monty eventually allowed him to do.

By the time the girls had to go up to London, Monty had also tried her new found allure on a Cockney coach-driver, a suave young expert in nineteenth-century militaria who came to value the Witherham collection and one of Uncle Hugo's shooting chums who visited for a weekend without his wife. She felt slightly ashamed, madly attractive and tremendously powerful with her newly-discovered seductive ability. She was more than half regretful that she was not coming out. She longed passionately to find someone she liked enough to whom to lose her virginity. Preferably someone who looked like Brian Jones.

'This is my brother Simon.' Rosanna Emanuel's demeanour was excessively formal, in order that her brother should not realize how much and how intimately he had been discussed in Benenden dormitories.

'Hello,' said Simon ceremonially shaking hands and hoping that Cathy and Monty should not realize how much and how intimately he and his friends had in their turn speculated about his sister's friends.

'There is not the slightest use in dining with a Jewish family,' Lady Davina had warned. For once, Cathy had argued with her.

'We were tremendous friends at school and it would look awful if we didn't see her now we're in London for a year. Besides, Rosanna's a very good influence on Monty.'

'Never confuse friendship with social climbing,' was their grandmother's reply, but she let them go, knowing that forbidding the association would only make it more alluring.

And so Cathy and Monty had walked across Hyde Park, from the Bourton family's small house in Trevor Square to the Emanuels' large apartment by Marble Arch. It was double-glazed and lavishly heated, with sumptuous deep-pile carpets. There were small silver dishes of chocolates everywhere.

Mrs Emanuel was a tiny, vivacious woman with a strong foreign accent of which both her children were violently ashamed. She had arrived in London in the late thirties from Vienna, one of the hundreds of educated girls from Germany and Austria who had taken jobs as domestic servants to circumvent the British immigration law and escape Nazi persecution. Having married into the Emanuel family, prominent among the rising tycoon class of British Jews, she found fuel for her bottomless feelings of insecurity as well as scope for her limitless social ambition.

It was soon clear that Simon was a major irritation in his mother's life. 'Why don't you cut your hair?' she asked him bluntly as soon as they sat down to lunch. 'You promised me, Simon. No nice girl wants to go out with a boy with long hair. Tell me, Catherine, what do you think?'

Cathy was startled by the directness of this attack and the unembarrassed way that she, a stranger in the house, had been invited to contribute to a personal argument. In her own family no intimate matter was ever mentioned to guests; indeed, most intimate matters were never discussed at all. Cathy struggled with the majolica asparagus-tongs to give herself time to think.

'Quite a lot of boys do wear rather long hair nowadays,' she began diplomatically.

'But not as long as Simon's surely. Look it's falling right over his collar now.'

Simon squirmed in his chair. His glossy black hair covered his ears and the back of his collar, in a laboriously groomed bob. His head was neat and his features regular, almost classical in proportion: he looked like a pre-Raphaelite knight. Nothing like Brian Jones, Monty acknowledged, but pretty groovy all the same.

'I think people don't really mind long hair as long as it's clean and well-cut. What a beautiful chandelier, Mrs Emanuel, is it Venetian?' Cathy's attempt to change the subject was defeated at once.

'Long hair, it looks dirty – ugh. You must go to the barber with your father tomorrow, Simon. Joseph, you must take Simon with you. See that he goes. When you are working in your father's office, Simon, you must look decent.'

'But I'm not working in the office, and I'm not going to work in his office, ever.' Simon glared at his mother from under the coal-black sweep of his eyebrows. Angrily she clutched at the swag of gold chains at her throat.

'And what else are you going to do with your life? You are not such a clever boy, you know. You are thrown out of school, you don't take your exams, we send you to college for special teaching and you don't do any work. So who will give you a job if your father does not?'

Simon shrugged his broad shoulders. 'There are plenty of jobs.'

'But a *good* job, Simon. Ach, if only you were like your sister, she is such a good girl. Why do you want to go to strangers when your father needs you to help him?'

'He doesn't need me and I don't want to sit in an office all day for the rest of my life.'

Mrs Emanuel's tiny hand grasped her necklace tight in fury. 'And what do you want, may I ask? Don't tell me, I know. You want to be one of those filthy pop singers. Ridiculous. Disgusting! Joseph, you must stop him . . .'

Simon's father, a pale, quiet man, had munched stolidly through the sumptuous meal as his wife and son continued their squabble. The three girls, all acutely embarrassed, lowered their eyes and said nothing.

Coffee, served in tiny cloisonné cups with *petits fours*, was taken in the sitting room. As soon as it was poured, Rosanna said, 'Would you like to see my clothes?' and the girls escaped.

Rosanna's bedroom was a tent of white cotton lace; she had a huge dressing room, where racks and racks of beautiful garments hung, protected by plastic bags.

'Will you be getting lots of new clothes now you're coming out?' she asked Cathy.

'Didi says I need at least six ball-gowns, plus cocktail dresses, of course. She's taking us to Hartnell next week.' Cathy pulled a face, wistfully spreading the skirt of a pink flowered gown.

'She can't possibly take you to that ghastly placewhy *the Queen* dresses there.' There was no greater condemnation. 'Why don't you come with me to Jane & Jane – they've got beautiful things.'

'Mmmn.' Cathy longed to go round the mushroom crop of new fashion designers whose provocatively pretty clothes filled the fashion magazines. She could already, in her mind's eye, imagine the ghastly dress which would be bought for her at Hartnell, no doubt with pale-blue chiffon swagged over the bust and sequins everywhere. But there was a problem.

'Oh do come, Cathy; you *can't* come out in Hartnell.'

'I've got to. Didi gets a discount.'

'Pouf.' Rosanna had never in her young life owned anything bought for the full retail price. 'I'll get you a discount, if that's all you're worried about. And Daddy says the mark-up on Hartnell is ridiculous, anyway.'

'Are you sure? I've only got the teeniest dress allowance, we can't afford anything really. Caroline's got five thousand for her clothes, and she'll look awful in everything. I do hate being a poor relation.' She tried on a bonnet smothered in cotton lace flowers. The price tag was still attached – it read 25 guineas.

'We'll get you a nice rich husband and then you'll be all right,' Rosanna reassured her, echoing the advice which her mother had hammered into her, which her grandmother had given her mother, and which had held true for generations of women before them. 'And clothes cost nothing nowadays – look,' she pulled out a black-and-white, flower-printed smock, 'from that Laura Ashley shop by South Kensington station – guess how much? *Two pounds.*'

Monty felt oppressed by the glorious abundance of Rosanna's wardrobe and determined to stamp out the painful wish that she too could come out. She wandered down the apartment's corridor. Faint sounds of music came from a half-open door – a few single notes, an experimental wail or two, some rhythmic strumming. Curiously, Monty pushed the door open.

'Oh, hello.' Simon scrambled awkwardly upright and put his guitar down. 'Listen, I'm sorry about my mother.'

'She's just as bad as mine, actually.'

'*Nobody* is like my mother.' Of this Simon was perfectly certain.

'Mine's awful, just the same. She drinks, you know.' Monty had never told anyone that, or even said the words out loud.

'That's terrible. Though I think I'd like my mother better if she did drink, then at least she'd have an excuse for being diabolical.'

There was an awkward silence.

'What did she mean about you getting thrown out of school?'

'I got expelled.'

'They were going to expel me from Benenden, too. What did you do?'

'Oh, smoking and things. And I tried to buy some pot.'

Monty was impressed. Buying pot was a glamorous misdemeanour. Nothing was more effective in shocking the older generation than drugs. She looked at Simon with silent respect. He changed the subject before she asked more questions which might have forced him to admit that he had paid £20 for a bouillon cube in a piece of crumpled foil.

'Do you want to hear my new Rolling Stones LP?' he asked.

'Which one is it?' There had been an abrupt withdrawal of money for records since her father's death; even if the Radio Luxembourg DJs had called the album repetitive and boring, Monty was dying to hear it.

'The Beatles want to hold your hand, the Stones want to burn your town,' quoted Simon, reverently placing the disc on his teak-veneered stereo.

'You're really lucky to have your own stereo.' Monty made herself comfortable on the end of the bed and looked around. Simon's room was large and immaculately neat, with an intriguing rank of guitars and attachments against one wall and the biggest collection of records Monty had ever seen, methodically stored beside them.

'They had to buy me a stereo – they were sick of me playing Fats Domino in their sitting room. They had to sound-proof my room, too.' Simon sat at the other end of the bed and played along with Mick Jagger's voice.

Groovy chick, he thought, surreptitiously eyeing Monty's clinging ribbed sweater, mini-skirt and white boots. Dare I ask her out? What if she turns me down?

CHAPTER SIX

WHEN SHE embarked on the P & O liner *Carthage*, Betty Clare was eighteen years old and full of dreams. From Gerald's descriptions of Penang she imagined an enchanted island like a child's drawing, a heap of green hills piled up in the middle of an azure sea, crystal waves lapping at its sparkling beaches. 'The Pearl of the Orient,' she had murmured to herself each night, looking at the small, blurred photograph of Gerald posed cheerily on a seaside terrace by a palm tree.

Gerald was the chief element of this paradise, of course; so strong, so manly, waiting for her with loving arms and a faithful heart. True, his face was not distinct in the photograph and she could not now remember it clearly. It was six months since their courtship, almost a year since he had come running after her down Guildford High Street, to return the gloves she had left behind in the tearoom. She remembered how the weak English sun shone on the gold hairs on the back of his hand, and the ruddiness of him in general. He had seemed so vibrant and healthy against the pallor of her existence in a small town whose life was overshadowed in every respect by London, an hour away on the railway.

Betty's family were not wealthy and her cabin on the liner was not large. In fact, the bright blue tin trunks which contained her wedding clothes, her trousseau and her wedding presents almost filled it up, leaving just a narrow corridor beside her bed. Anxiety that these precious belongings would be somehow lost or damaged made her suffer this crowding rather than send the trunks to the hold. She marked them all 'Wanted on Voyage', and opened one on the first night at sea so that the sight of her pink linen-look going-away dress could comfort her in this strange metal cell which hummed and smelt of oil.

The trunks had another advantage; they put a barrier between Betty and the girl with whom she had to share the cabin. There was no doubt that Heather was 'fast'. She wore slacks all day, smoked cigarettes at table and painted her nails.

'Getting married, love?' she enquired at the sight of the bridal supplies, and added coarsely 'Love, money or a bun in the oven?'

'Pardon?' Betty had no idea what she meant, but the tone was unpleasant.

'Skip it.' Not bad-hearted, Heather sensed she had given offence. 'Oh *ho!* she crowed as they became acquainted. 'Padre's daughter, eh? Well, you know what they say . . .' She slapped Betty's knee as if being the daughter of an army chaplain was something Betty had done on purpose to amuse future acquaintances. 'It's a great institution, marriage, so they tell me. I'm just not ready for the institution yet.'

'Why are you travelling East?' Betty changed the subject.

'I'm getting out while the going's good, love. Going to stay with my aunt and uncle in Hong Kong. You won't catch me waiting around London for the Germans. I expect that's why your folks are keen to pack you off, too.'

'My father says another war is out of the question now the Germans have promised us they won't invade any more countries.'

'Well, love, I'm not going to stick around to find out if they promised with their fingers crossed.' Heather dabbed another layer of orange powder over her nose and snapped her compact shut. At the end of the corridor outside, a bugle was blown to signify the second sitting in the dining room. 'Are you coming to dinner, or what?'

Betty was still wearing her twinset and skirt. Heather had changed into a bias-cut gown with a bolero in a red rayon fabric embossed with flowers. Her scent almost drowned the faint atmosphere of engine oil which pervaded all the second-class cabins.

'I thought one didn't dress for dinner on the first night at sea?'

'*One* may wear what *one* likes, and I can't see any point in looking like a frump myself.'

They walked up the narrow tube of a corridor, feeling the odd shifts of the floor as the great ship rode the ocean.

'Your fiancé must be mad to let you come out East alone,' Heather offered by way of conversation at dinner. It was well known that aboard ship the combined effect of warm, starry nights, the boredom and the fact that there were so many men – particularly young men, setting off to make their fortunes in the colonies, full of high spirits and hearty appetites – made it dangerous for an engaged girl to travel alone to a wedding in the East.

'Isn't he worried you'll come down the gangplank on another man's arm?'

Betty creased her rose-petal lips in a complacent smile. 'My father has asked a missionary friend of his to take care of me, so I'll be quite safe. Mr Forsyth, he's called. They were at the theological college together. He's sent me a card already.' She showed the pasteboard oblong to Heather, who sniffed and dismissed Betty as a dead loss. She was looking at the pan of flaming *crêpes suzette* as if it were going to burn her, Heather thought.

There were two reasons why an Englishwoman should be happy to go East – the men and the luxury. Both were in much more lavish supply than in depression-starved Britain, where a generation of men had been wiped out by World War I.

The P & O voyage was just a foretaste of the good life ahead, with dancing every evening and attentive servants fulfilling every wish of even the second-class passengers.

'*Servants!* You will have servants!' Betty's mother and her aunts had exclaimed when she told them her young man wanted to marry her and take her out East. Not having servants was a greater shame to them than having to keep rabbits. Even the most junior professional man should have been able to afford a cook or a maid, but their household could not. 'You can't get good servants nowadays,' was the refrain with which they comforted themselves. Servants were the God-given right of the middle class, a right of which they had been cheated despicably by fate.

'You must learn how to manage them,' her female relations had warned her, 'native servants – give them an inch and they'll take a mile. You must be firm, Betty. Strict but fair. Make them do everything to your satisfaction every time.' And her mother had given her a little manual called *The Housewife's Friend,* one of her own wedding gifts for which she had had no use, a slim book written for those unfortunate girls who married in the twenties with the expectation of keeping only one maid.

The three women hated Betty's father for being so inconsiderate as to have been gassed in Flanders and for being a virtual invalid now. With every chip of green soap they cut to wash clothes and every dab of blacklead with which they anointed the kitchen range, every fire they laid and every mattress they turned, their resentment intensified so that Betty had been raised in a climate of vinegary aversion to all that was male. She did not yet consciously endorse this dislike. She was barely aware of it; but anything that was aggressive, strong, loud or vigorous disturbed her.

The next day they entered the Bay of Biscay, and the liner's vast structure began to stagger and groan like a beast in its death throes. Betty was piteously sick. Heather comforted her, wiping her face and fetching glasses of soda water to settle her heaving stomach. When she was once again fit to stand, Betty disliked her robust cabin-mate even more. She was quite obviously one of the wicked who flourished like a green bay tree.

Mrs Clare had warned her daughter. 'You may meet some very strange people on the ship. Travelling throws you together with all sorts and you can't always choose your company. Just take no notice of them, dear.' Mrs Clare firmly believed that evil ignored would melt away of its own accord, and so it was with Heather, who took up with the junior purser soon after Bilbao and thereafter appeared in the cabin only to change her clothes.

Once the ship was out of the angry, grey waters of Biscay, and she was restored to health and confidence, Betty found her protector, a short man with white hair and grey eyes. The Reverend John Forsyth was on his way to Shanghai to resume his work at the Christian mission.

'I shall be glad to get back to a city I know,' he told her. 'I hadn't seen London for seventeen years, and I couldn't get used to it at all. So much building going on. So many motor cars everywhere. My mother's house used to be in the middle of green fields, and now there's nothing but strips of mean little houses as far as the eye can see. Do you play bridge, Miss Clare?'

Betty gave the pack on the table in front of the Anglican priest a doubtful look. 'I've never played cards at all. My father is very against gambling.'

'Bridge isn't gambling, my dear young lady. It's first-class intellectual exercise. Mental callisthenics. Let me explain . . .' With a supple sweep of his small hands, Mr Forsyth scooped up his game of patience and began to deal out the cards anew.

He was a superb companion for anyone, particularly for this shrinking, immature girl on a voyage of alarming sensations. There was a tradition among the colonists that the old hands initiated the young in the mysteries of the East and the Reverend John Forsyth had an inexhaustible repertoire of stories and the sensitivity to select anecdotes which would instruct her in alien ways without filling her with shapeless dread. He was witty but without malice, and worldly without disdain for her ignorance, which was profound.

Her father and stepmother had taken the greatest care to shield the only child of their house from every influence of the world, the flesh and the devil, and instead of knowledge had filled her head with precepts by which they hoped she would live a virtuous life. As a result, her ignorance was of the most dangerous kind, perpetuated by a lack of imagination, buttressed by fear of the unknown. Miss Clare, her chaperon realized, had perfected the mental trick of not perceiving anything that might disturb her; thus, for instance, she had no curiosity about the reason why the flashy Heather had abandoned their shared cabin, or where or with whom she might be sleeping.

She had a charming maidenly serenity which quite captivated their bridge partners, Miss Rogers and Miss Westlake. Betty had no curiosity about them either, and did not remark the unusual enthusiasm with which they insisted she visit them in Singapore, or ask herself why two relatively well-off English ladies should choose to live together abroad, or why two women in their thirties who took care to wave their hair and make up their faces should nevertheless prefer to pass the voyage playing bridge with an elderly missionary and a prim girl rather than amuse themselves in the society of the plentiful young men. Like Queen Victoria, Betty had never heard of lesbians and would not have believed the truth if anyone had explained it to her.

The *Carthage* put into Port Said for coal and as the ship halted in the harbour, the cheerful warmth of the Mediterranean gave way to a fierce, stifling heat. The ship's officers exchanged their evening dress for short white jackets which reached only to the waist, and in the first class the ladies sent their furs to the ship's cold store for the rest of the voyage.

In Betty's cabin, a steward came to close all the portholes. 'They say it's to keep the coal dust out, Miss, but tell you the truth, it's to keep out them gippo thieves,' he told her. 'You'll be all right to open up once we're at sea again.' Her cabin was like an oven, and Betty felt nauseous and giddy. There seemed to be no cool place on the whole ship. The decks beneath her feet were like hot coals.

Mr Forsyth found her sitting on a steamer chair under a sun canopy.

'I was hoping to take you ashore to see the sights. There's rather an interesting mosque here and ladies usually enjoy the shopping.' She shook her head.

'I couldn't, Mr Forsyth, you go on without me.'

'Not up to it? It's just the heat, you know. You're not accustomed to it. Take a bath and lie down for an hour or so. I'll tell you my adventures at dinner.' Deliberately, he withheld his sympathy. This child would withdraw permanently into all manner of fearful illnesses unless her retreat was cut off by someone kind enough to be cruel. At dinner she was wan and ate almost nothing, but he walked her to the card room all the same, using the authority of his quasi-parental position to insist.

Thus impelled, Betty bore up through the smothering heat of the Suez Canal, and once the *Carthage* passed the sunbaked rock of Aden and began to cross the Indian Ocean, the air became more refreshing. The four bridge players fell more and more into the routine of the hot, listless days and cool velvet nights. The endless time was marked by daily rituals – the cocktail hour before each meal, the afternoon siesta, the daily sweepstake on the number of miles the ship had sailed.

The passengers felt a growing sense of freedom, isolated in their own little world of ease and comparative luxury. The tentative attractions of the Mediterranean waters became fierce flirtations, while love affairs begun earlier hit stormy waters. Heather reappeared in the cabin and started slamming drawers open and shut as she redistributed her belongings.

'You can keep your shipboard romances,' she told Betty. 'Men are all the same – selfish brutes. I told him, it'll be me that's left holding the baby. Fine start to a new life that'll be. Stuck on the wrong side of the bloody earth; with a squalling brat.'

Her resolve lasted only two days, and then Betty had the cabin to herself once more and Heather and the junior purser were again a regular feature of the second-class dining room – where his duties included playing Ivor Novello selections on the piano after dinner and she draped herself adoringly over the back of a chair to watch him.

Betty told her bridge friends the story. 'I think she's awfully silly; how could she have a baby if she wasn't married?' she asked with contempt, and Mr Forsyth, Miss Rogers and Miss Westlake glanced at each other from behind their cards. The four had become thoroughly fond of each other, as disparate strangers will when forced together by circumstances.

As soon as Betty said goodnight, Miss Rogers opened the subject. 'Do you suppose that our young friend knows what to expect from the physical side of marriage?' she asked, putting a pin back into her stylishly rolled hair. Mr Forsyth shook his head.

'I think she's as innocent as a newborn lamb.' Miss Westlake nodded, checking her diamanté dressclip to cover her embarrassment.

'Green as grass, if you ask me.'

There was a pause as they contemplated the implications this discovery had for their little square of friendship.

'There's a certain sort of girl, in my experience, who isn't cut out for a honeymoon. I was dreadfully naive myself and of course, my mother told me nothing, nothing at all . . . Frankly, it was a beastly experience.' Miss Rogers' crimson mouth puckered in amusement at her own choice of words, and Miss Westlake's willowy figure swayed towards her in sympathy.

'Do you suppose we should talk to her?' he asked with a plain sincerity which acknowledged his own sex's ineptitude in emotional matters.

Simultaneously, the two women nodded. 'She looks up to *you* as a father figure,' said Miss Westlake, 'and I'm afraid if one of us tackled it she might – well, we could – well, you know, our experiences of marriage haven't been very good, I'm sorry to say. And she is such a cowering little thing.'

The elderly man of God accepted the truth of what she said with regret. Like most men, he would rather face a shipload of Yangtze pirates armed to the teeth than a woman with urgent emotional needs.

'I'll have a little talk with her tomorrow,' he agreed, with resignation.

'Tell me, my dear,' he began next day, finding Betty under the sun-canopy for her usual siesta, 'were you close to your mother? Could you talk to her about life when something worried you?'

'Oh, yes. My mother's a wonderful woman, my father says she's the light of his life.'

He smiled, noticing that the only response her creamy complexion had made in two weeks of roasting sun was to produce a tiny dusting of freckles, like toast crumbs, over the bridge of her upturned nose. He thought her a pastel, passive, pretty little thing, made for muted emotions and narrow horizons, hardly strong enough for life at all.

'So your parents have a very happy marriage?'

'Oh, yes.'

'I expect your mother told you all the secrets of her success before you set off?'

Betty was earnestly trying to follow the vicar's train of thought. She had been brought up to expect sermonizing from older people, and it had, in truth, seemed strange to her that this very wise adult had treated her like an equal when he was so obviously superior to her in every way.

Now he was beginning to sound like an adult should. Eagerly she followed his lead. 'Oh yes. She told me always to wear plenty of scent – look.' Quick as a bird, she dipped into her handbag and brought out a bottle of Yardley's Lavender. 'And to make sure my husband never saw me doing anything undignified, like cleaning my teeth. She said that being slovenly about that sort of thing killed all the magic in a marriage.'

'I expect that's very true. The happiest marriages have always been between people who knew the difference between intimacy and familiarity, I think. One breeds respect and the other breeds contempt. People say that if there's trouble in a marriage, it's usually in the bedroom, but in my experience the rot starts in the bathroom first.' Mr Forsyth was rather pleased with this quip, but Betty's periwinkle eyes became shadowed with anxiety. He at once abandoned vanity, kicked himself for this besetting sin, and returned to the awkward task in hand.

'Did your mother also mention the bedroom side of things at all?'

'Oh yes, she was quite frank about it. She said that my husband would make demands on me, but it would be ail right, I would just have to not mind, just not let it upset me.'

'How very sensible. And did she explain to you what these demands . . . the sort of thing she was talking about?'

'Well no. I never thought to ask her.'

'I'd like to explain, Miss Clare. I have found that some men place great importance on this aspect of marriage, and when their wives can share in it with joyful acceptance there is a great deal of happiness to follow.' He spoke with a tinge of wistfulness. His own marriage had been ecstatic but short. His wife had died of malaria three months after arriving in the East.

He proceeded with the utmost finesse, first drawing to Betty's attention the difference between the boy babies and the girl babies in the hospital where she worked. Betty's nursing career had been abandoned instantly Gerald had proposed to her, and so amounted only to three months of theoretical lessons on hygiene. She had, however, observed that boy babies and girl babies were differently made, but attached no importance to the anatomical aberration. In fact, she had assumed that the boy baby's penis was some superfluous fold of skin which would disappear before adulthood.

Next the patient priest asked her if she had ever seen animals mating, which she said she had. Her home had tottered on a knife-edge of destitution all her life, with her father's army pension supporting himself, his wife, his two spinster sisters and his daughter. To be sure of eating meat, they had kept rabbits in their back garden, and the breeding, rearing and slaughter of these animals was her father's most meaningful occupation. Mating the rabbits meant that her father put on big, leather gloves, pulled the buck rabbit out of his hutch and tossed him, kicking frantically, into a hutch with a female. They would settle down to munch bran together for a week, and then the buck would be put back in his own hutch. Sometimes he would bite the female, and sometimes he bit Betty's father.

Betty had many times seen rabbits copulate, a process which they accomplished in twenty seconds without any excitement or change of expression. Thick fur hid all the organs employed. Mr Forsyth very carefully explained that mating was mechanically the same process in humans, but that the species to whom God gave dominion over the animals usually went about things with some physical expression of affection. Betty seemed to be following him easily so he mentioned that she might perhaps have enjoyed kissing her fiancé, at which she blushed attractively.

'You will probably find it all rather strange at first,' he finished, smiling with relief at a difficult assignment accomplished to the limit of his skill. 'Because explanations are all very well but one person can't really convey very much to another. Experience is everything, I've found. Ah – look there – the flying fish have come back.' And out on the bright surface of the sea three quivery flashes of light skittered away from the ship's wash. In an instant the silver streaks sank back into the sea, and everything the kind Reverend Forsyth had said to Betty vanished similarly in the morass of her ignorance. The facts of life, without any context of sexual knowledge, held no significance for her. She imagined that once married, she and Gerald would, like rabbits, browse contentedly side by side.

At last they approached the island of Penang. The sky was a hazy turquoise and the sea its greyish reflection. The water, Betty noticed, was not clear but opaque and souplike. For twenty-four hours the liner had sailed between green islands just like those of her childish vision, and now, at last, it was slowly reaching its destination.

Green hills were visible in the cloudy distance. Ahead of the liner was the quay of Georgetown, with its row of stone buildings, one of which was pillared and had a thick square tower topped by a dome. Betty liked them; the buildings were solid, and not much decorated, the utilitarian architecture of trade. They looked like the banks at home, only they were brilliantly white not grimed and soot-streaked. Beyond them was the massive greystone wall of Fort Cornwallis, its cannons commanding the flat stretch of water between Penang Island and the misty, palm-edged mainland of Malaya.

As the ship drew closer to the shore and swung ponderously round into alignment with the pier, she saw a lower layer of buildings, mostly of weathered wood – warehouses and port offices thronged with people. Mr Forsyth pointed out to her the settlement of Chinese shacks built on stilts over the water itself. 'Very ingenious people,' he explained. 'The land is all owned by landlords who want to charge them rent to build on it – so they build their houses over the water where it's free.'

As she docked, the ship was besieged by bumboats full of hawkers selling snacks and curios. Garbage scows moored at one end of the liner and black birds swooped down on the rubbish like huge flies.

At the mahogany rail Mr Forsyth scented the tepid breeze with delight. 'Smell it,' he told her, 'that's the smell of the East. Blossoms and spice woods from the jungle, rubber and coconut fibre from the wharf, charcoal smoke, the mist on the mountains – whenever I smell that, I know I'm home.'

Betty smelted the breeze uncertainly. It did have an odour, something damp and almost intimate. It did not seem pleasant to her. In the crowd of people pressed at the pierside she could not see Gerald and uneasy impatience filled her. Why did everything take so long on this ship? Why did they have to wait for a hundred coolies to scramble on and off before the passengers could disembark?

Below her, three small Chinese boys in a dilapidated sampan were shrieking and performing acrobatic tricks, calling for the curious passengers to throw them money. More urchins were jumping into the water from the end of a vacant pier. As Betty watched, there was a crescendo of screaming and violent activity in the boats at the waterside; men began to beat the water with bamboo poles and a dripping child was pulled out and carried away by howling women.

'What are they doing, what's the matter?' she asked the missionary with alarm.

'Sea snake, I expect – they used to have a lot of them in Penang – yes, look, there it is, they've caught it.' Betty stepped back and gasped with disgust as the men in the boat awkwardly flung a huge black serpent on to the pier with their poles. It writhed and lashed itself over and over until other men with cleavers hacked at it and eventually chopped it into pieces; then the crowd closed around the dreadful sight and hid it.

'Bit of a shock, isn't it?' Mr Forsyth calmed her in his non-committal style. 'You're lucky to have seen it, you know, there are hardly any of them left now.'

At last the waiting in the sticky heat was over, the gangplanks were lowered, and Betty said a tremulous temporary goodbye to her friends and walked forward. Halfway down she saw Gerald, eager, smiling, spruce in his white suit, and holding out his arms just as she had seen him in her dreams.

The etiquette for a beach wedding was entirely designed to delight the bride-to-be who shipped out from England before she embarked on the hazards of life as a memsahib in the Crown Colony. Gerald and his mother drove Betty straight to the cool palm-shaded haven of the E & O Hotel, where smiling porters in uniform took up her trunks, deft maids unpacked them and her wedding clothes were removed, pressed and returned looking as fresh as they had in Debenham & Freebody's in London such a very long time ago.

Gerald's mother, the image of her son and as tall as he, but with more presence, had organized the entire affair. Betty felt, the next day, as if she were going to be married in a bower of orchids. Her bouquet was the largest mass of blooms she had ever seen, smelling quite violently of jasmine, and with fragile English flowers next to succulent, tropical blossoms.

In St George's Church, two days later, the Reverend John Forsyth marched her up the aisle. Elizabeth Louise Clare took Gerald Arthur Rawlins to be her lawful wedded husband according to God's holy ordinance, and posed with him afterwards on the white-pillared rotunda in the shade of the huge churchyard trees, surrounded by strangers, and half-hallucinating with the heat. Her dress was of thick ivory satin, fitted tightly at the sleeves and waist and, on the advice of Gerald's mother, she wore a long cotton slip underneath it to prevent perspiration stains.

'After all,' the older woman advised, 'you don't want to bring your dress halfway round the world and be photographed in it for ever more with sweat marks round your waist. You'll learn not to buy tight-fitting dresses out East.'

They were photographed again in rattan chairs by a frangipani bush on the hotel terrace, Gerald with his bow tie askew and Betty smiling trustfully at the Chinese photographer. They were both overshadowed by the commanding bulk of Gerald's mother behind them, while Mr Forsyth sat awkwardly beside the bride.

Indoors it was cooler, with fans whirring endlessly to stir the clammy air. Her wedding breakfast was a procession of dishes traditional to the colony – fierce mulligatawny soup, hot curry, roast beef and finally icecream with a strange white jelly next to it. Gerald spooned everything down with enthusiasm. He had not had much of a stag night, by comparison with an evening with James and Bill in K. L., but a few boys from the Cricket Club had got up a party, and he had the kind of minor hangover which made him hungry. He noticed his bride looking at her plate in hesitation.

'It's traditional – mangosteen and icecream – delicious, try it.' He scooped up half the pale fruit and tried to feed it to her. It looked like a foetus, something unborn, like the most horrible thing Betty could remember having seen.

'No, please, Gerald, I'm really not hungry . . .' she whispered, pleading.

'Nonsense, open wide.' Fearful of offending him, she parted her lips and gulped the spoonful down. Her head swam and she half-stood up, thinking she was going to be sick. Instead she fell limply forward in a faint.

Gerald's mother had her taken upstairs to her room and brought her round with a little bottle of sal volatile. In her overbearing way she was concerned about Betty.

'There are only two types of women in the tropics. Those who cope, and those who don't. If you make up your mind you're going to cope, you will. Take it easy the first couple of days, *always* have a lie-off in the afternoons and whatever you do, don't drink unless you are accustomed to it. You'll get used to the heat, I promise you. Everybody does. But no more fitted frocks, I think.' And she went through

Betty's trunks and found an afternoon dress of cheap blue-and-white silk for her to wear in place of the pink linen suit, which had seemed so cool in London, but now felt as hot as a blanket.

They were pelted with confetti and driven away in the handsome, black Jaguar which belonged to Gerald's father.

Penang seemed to Betty to be divided into districts of three distinct types. There was the crowded, red-roofed hugger-mugger of Chinatown, the stone-built, white-washed solidity of the British mercantile quarter and now the area through which they drove, where broad avenues were shaded by massive trees and lined with immense mansions. These were far more impressive than anything she had ever seen in her life. Even Buckingham Palace, to which her father had once taken her, seemed shabby in comparison.

'Who lives there?' she asked Gerald, as they passed a huge turquoise palace.

'Oh, that's the great Mr Choy,' he told her. 'Made his money in lumber and tin. And rubber, of course. He owns the neighbouring estate to ours. All these houses belong to the Chinese millionaires, except that one. That's the Governor's.' He pointed out a long building with one square turret.

'They're very grand, Gerald,' she said doubtfully, meaning that these huge, coloured, decorated palaces awed her. Although their style aped the pale colonial buildings of the British, rather than the Chinatown houses which had upswept eaves and carved gilded dragons on their roofs, it was still threateningly alien to her eyes. There was too much stucco, there were too many balconies – the ostentation was blatant, almost savage.

They arrived at their honeymoon hotel in time for the afternoon lie-off, and Gerald went for a swim in the milky sea. He felt rather lonely cavorting in the waves like a solitary, sporting porpoise, but Betty had almost flinched when he said, 'Fancy a dip?'

'But the water's *deep*, Gerald,' she protested. 'Please, please, you must be careful.' It made him feel manly to pat her little hand in reassurance before striding down the sand.

He enjoyed showing her the wonders of the country where he had been born, expecting her to feel the thrills he remembered experiencing when he had finally returned to Penang after ten years in England, attending school and being farmed out to relatives every holiday. He made her sit on the terrace overlooking the beach and watch the flaming sunset.

'Better than Guy Fawkes Night, eh?' he remarked as the violent orange panorama faded to an apricot blush behind the black clouds.

'Wonderful,' she agreed.

'And see the moon's the wrong way up?' He waved his glass at the vaporous crescent rising above the dark hills.

'Lovely.' She nodded. Some large insects were flying into the lamplight. The strangeness of everything overwhelmed her and she momentarily yearned with all the power of her feeble heart for a clean British sea-breeze and a good grey sky of home.

Cheerfully, Gerald prattled at her during dinner, drinking whisky-and-water throughout, and then they danced to the gramophone on the terrace. He pressed his cheek to hers and a film of sweat at once formed between them, plastering her hair flat, but Gerald didn't seem to mind. Betty closed her eyes and tried to recapture the wonderful, melting, giddy feeling she had felt when he had kissed her at home, but it would not come back. Instead, a pool of apprehension welled up in her stomach.

'Shall we turn in?' he murmured after an eternity of swaying back and forth. In the bedroom he left her to change into her night-clothes alone, as much to mask his own nervousness as out of consideration for hers. 'For heaven's sake, go easy on the girl,' his mother had commanded, and Gerald, who had never had sex with a woman who was not a prostitute in his life, was now in a storm of confusion at the prospect of deflowering his wife. He loved Betty so much, he thought; her sweetness and shyness wrenched his decent soul. He wanted sex, sex was what men did with their wives – except that it was a filthy, shameful thing he had only done with those creatures at Mary's. Oh God, why had he ever had anything to do with all that? He was ashamed and he felt drunk, far drunker than he should have been on a few glasses of whisky.

In bed, he held Betty in his arms and kissed her, feeling his desire wavering, like the moonlight until finally it subsided. Then he fell asleep, and later so did Betty, content that her duty as a wife had been accomplished.

She opened her eyes in complete darkness, aware that her nightdress was being dragged up above her knees and a weight was crushing her chest so that she could hardly breathe. In terror, she flailed her arms and legs, but the weight was not dislodged and she heard Gerald urgently whispering, 'Betty, oh Betty, I love you.' There was a wave of stale whisky vapour from his mouth, and Betty lay inert as he pressed his lips on hers with force.

Her husband's body rolled back and forth on hers, and then to her horror his leg shoved between her knees, and he pushed apart her thighs and pulled at the nightdress, baring beneath the sheet that nasty part of her body for which she had no name. Why did he want to expose the place where disgusting bodily functions were performed? Revulsion paralysed her. She felt as if she were going to choke.

Then he half-rolled off her; she drew a gasping breath, then there was something else, some hot, hard, rubbery thing stabbing and hurting at that awful place. Sharp flashes of pain shot up towards her belly. The thing was tearing against her dry flesh. Sweat poured from Gerald's face and dripped on to her, adding its acrid smell to the stink of liquor. In the darkness, her husband was grunting like a beast possessed by demons. Then the crushing weight of his body was on her again, there was terrible burning pain, then Gerald cried out, stopped rolling and lay still.

Betty lay shaking under his body, crazed with panic. Was he dead, or ill, or mad? Why had he done that revolting thing to her? What had he attacked her with? Gerald rolled off his wife and drifted obliviously towards sleep. At the back of his fuddled mind he realized that something had not been the same as doing it with the girls at Mary's, but perhaps, he reasoned, white women were different.

From Gerald's descriptions Betty had imagined the rubber estate like the plantations in *Gone With The Wind,* a vast acreage of orderly vegetation dominated by a gracious white house. She saw herself, like Melanie Wilkes, with a pony and trap and a loyal native servant, performing charitable deeds among the plantation workers.

At first her expectations were fulfilled. After the Malay kampong with its dark wood cottages like gingerbread houses, the red dirt road to Bukit Helang curved between attractive fields of saplings and broadened at the hilltop into a spacious compound. Some amiable brown cows grazed in front of the plantation house; the buildings were spacious, pillared and shuttered, and shaded by a row of royal palms. But the ox-cart which carried them and their belongings continued past the main settlement and on to a single-storey, tin-roofed bungalow a quarter of a mile beyond, on the edge of the towering jungle.

Two young Asiatics in starched white jackets stood beside the front steps to welcome them. 'Ah Kit, my – our – boy,' Gerald presented him, 'and Hassan is the gardener.' They bowed and Betty nodded at her servants.

Jungle she had conceived as a kind of endless flowering shrubbery. Instead, it was an impassive, grey-green wall all around them, tall and dark and full of unseen life which gibbered incessantly, by day and night. It sounded to her as if a million banshees were cackling with glee at her unhappiness. There was no animal ever to be seen, and few birds. No flowers ever bloomed, except some unearthly dead-grey orchids flopping from a high fork of a tree.

When the lamps were lit at night, great bugs would blunder into the bungalow unless the long rattan blinds were pulled securely down around the balcony rail. Even so, Betty at first saw a spider under every cushion and a scorpion in every corner. She suffered tortures of continence in the night because the bathroom floor was slatted and she could not look at it without fearing that a snake would slither through the gaps.

There was only one other white woman on the estate, Jean Anderson, the spare, middle-aged wife of the plantation doctor. They were a kindly couple who took Betty under their wing at once. Dr Anderson was short and plump, with round cheeks that flamed rosily through his deep tan, and thinning, fair hair. They had a gramophone and a selection of lovingly preserved recordings of popular ballads and light opera, and in the evenings they preferred to sit quietly enjoying each other's company and the music, rather than join the boisterous company of the other planters. Betty sometimes heard snatches of Gilbert and Sullivan wafted through the trees on freak currents of air.

The Andersons' bungalow was the nearest and every morning, when her husband had left after his breakfast, Betty would hear the rattle of Jean's bicycle and her brisk greeting to Ah Kit.

'There's a sort of tradition that we speak Malay to the servants,' she told Betty after watching her struggle in vain to tell Ah Kit how to use the refrigerator. This luxury had been Gerald's parents' wedding gift to them, but the houseboy cooked complete meals for a week and stored them in the whirring white box, distressing Betty's notions of hygiene. 'I'll write down some of the basic phrases and, if you get into a pickle, it'll help you out. Don't be disturbed, they all think the fridge keeps food indefinitely.'

'He looks so – well, so sneering and superior,' Betty confessed.

'The Chinese are always sure that they are very, very superior people, which makes them first-class servants. You can be great friends with them, and there's never any need to nag them because their standards are terrifically high.'

'But whenever I go to tell him something he acts as if I'm insulting him.'

'What do you do – go out to his quarters?'

'Well, of course.' Betty answered with blank surprise.

'Never do that, dear. We don't. You just don't go out to the servants' quarters. That's their home and you don't invade. Call him, always, and he'll come out smiling.'

And Betty did as the older woman counselled, and saw Ah Kit run out of his hut, buttoning his immaculate, starched jacket as he did so. He cooked in the open between the two dwellings, on a charcoal fire in a kerosene tin, first chopping his ingredients with a cleaver on a tall wooden block. Betty was quite glad that Ah Kit's domain was out of bounds; once she was sure she had seen him put a frog on the chopping board.

She looked out one morning and saw quantities of their rice and flour spread out on table cloths on the lawn of coarse jungle grass. She ordered Ah Kit to put the stores back in their tins at once but he fired off a torrent of Malay then tried to explain to her again, speaking slowly, before giving up and walking away.

'He's quite right,' Jean told her when she came over. 'When it's a nice, hot, sunny day and set fair they ought to take the chance to put the dry goods out in the sun. You can't stop the weevils and maggots breeding in this climate, but if you spread the stores in the sun then the creatures crawl away, and you can sieve it all and put it back in the containers. Housekeeping out here is an eternal battle with the insects, you'll find. I used to think Malaya was built on an antheap when I first came out.'

Her friendly neighbour could help with household hints, but not with the physical discomfort. Betty soon became accustomed to feeling a band of sweat-soaked fabric behind the belt of her dress, and to changing her clothes completely three times a day. If she wore cool, sleeveless frocks, her pale arms were smothered with an itchy heat rash, and if she covered them up, she sweltered. Her toes blistered and her eyelids puffed, the delicate membranes irritated by the brightness and the dust.

Worst of all, much the worst, were the nights. By the time they arrived at Bukit Helang, Gerald had realized that he could not penetrate his wife – at least, not without inflicting an inhuman degree of suffering on her – and Betty had recognized that the revolting thing Gerald did to her in bed at night was what a husband had a right to ask of his wife. She willed herself not to mind, but it was not enough. Gerald fussed with her and tormented her and only stopped if she cried or told him she couldn't bear the pain any more. Her deeply instilled ideals of duty made it impossible to hate her husband, and instead she gave way to apathy.

The disaster of their intimate life quickly became a secret that the two conspired to keep, and in company they held hands and kissed like model honeymooners. James with his perception, Douglas Lovell with his experience, Dr Anderson with his medical training and Jean with her sympathy, all missed the couple's reluctance to be left alone together. Gerald took to acting the expansive host, and invited James or one of the other young assistants over for meals. He drank more and more, and his humour became sarcastic, while Betty grew thin and listless, sleeping in until after ten in the mornings and prolonging the afternoon lie-off, until she did little more than get up and dress for their meals.

Three months after their wedding the news came that Britain was at war with Germany, grinding Betty deeper into her despair. Although she hated the notion of displeasing Gerald, she had lately started rehearsing in her mind a speech to him in which she admitted that she was a failure as a wife and asked to be sent home. Now there was no chance of that. She was condemned to this terrible place.

In the end, it was Betty's feeble temperament itself which saved their marriage. Each evening, the young assistants would play tennis on the two courts which Douglas Lovell had levelled and turfed beside the plantation office. Betty was incompetent at all physical sports, but she came with Gerald for the distraction and usually sat and drank lemonade beside the court in the shade of the casuarina trees. Even here the jungle was barely held back. Banks of ferns crawled towards the clipped lawn like clawing hands outstretched to repossess their territory. Lassoes of blue convolvulus lay over the garden shrubs.

Betty watched Gerald and James play, James darting like a bird across the back of the court while Gerald panted to and fro near the net, joking with his opponent. She felt a tickling at the nape of her neck, so light it could have been a falling hair, and put up her hand to remove it.

With repellent speed a bloated creature clambered down her arm and fell into her lap. Its body was a pallid green bladder covered with spines, its shape so bizarre it seemed to have no head or legs, and to move itself in convulsions. Betty was stiff with fear. Her lips stuck to her teeth and she was unable to cry out. At that moment, the boy came up with her lemonade and she dumbly implored him with her eyes. Laughing, he fished up the vile creature with his napkin and showed it to her on his tray.

'Leaf insect, madam,' he told her with pride. The thing was as big as a dinner plate.

Betty leaped to her feet, screaming and scraping at the skirt of her dress as if the animal were still stuck to it. She lost her breath, gasped for air, gasped again, screamed for Gerald, tried to stop, gulped air once more and fell into a chaotic pattern of screaming and gasping which she could not control. Within half a minute she collapsed unconscious.

Anderson the doctor was fetched and Betty was carried home and put to bed. Ah Kit's wife was instructed to sponge her body with tepid water to cool her, and the doctor gave her an injection.

'If I'm right, this was just a hysterical thing,' he told Gerald. 'She was hyperventilating, which caused her to pass out, but there's nothing serious amiss. Keep her calm and she'll be as right as rain tomorrow. I've given her a mild sedative, that's all.'

After the doctor had gone, and he had eaten and drunk dinner alone, Gerald sat on the end of the bed and looked at his wife. Her face was still flowerlike in its innocence, in spite of the weight she had lost in the last weeks. She was loosely wrapped in a sheet, on the doctor's instructions. Gerald had never seen his wife naked, and among the bewildering turmoil of his thoughts about her and their failed love life was that germ of suspicion that white women somehow were made differently from Orientals.

Slowly he pulled back the sheet. Betty stirred but did not wake. Even in the gold lamplight she seemed as pale as milk and her nipples were the fresh pink of rose petals. With curiosity, Gerald stretched out his hand and felt between her legs. Betty murmured and turned her head, but her eyelids did not flicker. Carefully he felt between each moistening fold, at last deciding that there was no difference. Now he was aroused but perplexed – was it right to have sex with a woman who was unconscious, even if she was your wife?

In fact, Betty was not completely unconscious. She was aware of Gerald touching her as if it were happening far away. She felt no disgust or fear, and no pain when he eventually unbuttoned himself, got on top of her and penetrated her with a brief yelp of triumph. It all seemed like a dream and of no consequence, but she was aware that he seemed pleased with her.

Neither Gerald nor Betty ever referred to this incident, but the next night Gerald again succeeded in having full intercourse with his wife, and the spasm of fright which had closed her vaginal muscles tight against him never returned. He found, in the next few months, that the process was a good deal easier if he felt around between her legs first. Betty never came to enjoy any of this, but she could appear accepting enough to make Gerald feel happy about doing it.

Six months later, the older Mrs Rawlins travelled to Bukit Helang to stay with her son and was reassured by the harmony of his household. Betty spoke creditable kitchen Malay to Ah Kit and Gerald was in high good humour most of the time. On the balcony a pied jumbul bird piped in the morning sun and the gardener tended a new row of bright orchids in pots. Little Betty found herself co-opted into the honourable association of the Mems who coped.

CHAPTER SEVEN

G IGGLING WAS not on the curriculum at St John's Secretarial College in Kensington, but it was the only activity to which the students devoted much time. None of the girls really worked. Many flounced late through the door, signed the register and ran straight out again to head for Chelsea and the new boutiques full of skimpy mini-dresses designed exclusively for the near-pubescent figure.

The teachers, embittered petit-bourgeois spinsters with the impossible job of training butterfly-witted debutantes, hounded the more docile through lessons in book-keeping and office practice with grim disapproval. On the days after the big debutante dances the only girls in the college would be the foreigners and one or two from the suburban middle classes.

It was becoming fashionable by 1964 for a debutante to have a job. 'Hopes to work with children' or 'already signed by London's top model agency' was the sort of thing to appear after your name, age and parentage in the caption to your picture in the society magazines, *The Tatler* or *Queen*.

The students at St John's adopted these poses without having the slightest anticipation that they might ever want or need a job. They were content with their destiny as future wives and mothers who would be maintained as their husband's most expensive status symbols. They expected to spend money – on clothes, jewels, homes and amusements – but never, ever to make money.

This affectation of work was to the aristocracy another amusing pastime, part of the trendy acquisitive spirit of the age. It never occurred to most of them that they might actually *need* to work one day, at least in the sense of getting up before 11 am on a regular basis.

As they waited every day for the 73 bus to take them down Knightsbridge to St John's, Cathy, Caroline and Monty saw the signs of the times: when a Rolls Royce drove past them it might as well contain a chauffeur and a silver-haired, sober-suited businessman as a pop-group manager in his twenties, with a flowered shirt, driving himself. Grimy workmen's tea bars closed, and re-opened as Continental-style pavement cafés serving frothy cappuccino.

Londoners were longing to sit in the sun. In the entire twentieth century, until that enchanted era, no ordinary person in Britain had lived very far from the threat of poverty or death. War, slump, more war, more slump – now the country was famished for pleasure, frivolity and abundance.

There was wealth for the making, goods to be bought, plenty of everything for everyone. Foreign countries meant holidays, not battle fronts. The streets were clogged with cars, the shops stuffed with clothes. There was no need to save, no need to deny yourself any longer.

Material goods were not the only pleasures which were at last off-ration; sex was to be available too, without guilt, shame or danger. Thanks to the Pill, love would soon be free for all.

The debutante season danced to the relentless rhythm of swinging London. Instead of a dance band, girls were starting to demand pop groups to play at their balls.

Lady Davina was put out to find that, instead of shepherding two demure girls in pastel chiffon through a succession of decorous balls, she must instead release Cathy and Caroline into motley assemblies of men with jewelled cufflinks and girls in cotton frocks – full length, high-waisted cotton frocks, pretty in a Bo-Peep way, to be sure, but nothing which accorded with her notion of glamour.

Each morning she made them visit her bedroom, a stuffier, more heavily scented reproduction of her chintz-swagged quaters at Bourton House. While the Pomeranian wheezed in the folds of her pink satin quilt she lectured them in the art of catching a prize man.

'Never let a man know you're on a diet,' she ordered, sipping tepid Lapsang Souchong from a chipped Minton cup. 'Men like to see a girl eat heartily, they think it shows *animal appetites*. Of course you don't eat a thing when you're at home, not a scrap! But *he* must never know that.'

There was a muffled gurgle, like distant plumbing, from below the quilt. The dowager's persecuted bowels, accustomed for decades to a diet rich only in liquids and laxatives, evidently had their own views on her philosophy.

'Never talk to a man about business, money, politics or religion. If *he* wants to talk about those things, of course you listen. Listen properly. Make notes afterwards of what he's said,' her pointed, red tongue flickered over her dry lips. 'But *never* put forward your own opinions. Leave men's things to men – heaven knows why they find them so fascinating. If you must talk, talk about charming topics of no consequence.'

'Ask who he hunts with, you mean?' said Caroline.

Lady Davina snorted. 'Of course not!'

'What sort of things, then?' Monty picked at a crushed satin rosette on the quilt, trying not to sound as sarcastic as she felt. Lady Davina rallied her quavering voice.

'Gossip!' she exclaimed, 'Talk about people you know, tell little stories, amuse him! Think of yourself as Scheherazade, soothing your weary Sultan with tales c

1001 Nights! And flatter him, always flatter him. A woman should be able to make a man *worship* her.'

Cathy, who absorbed these lessons with considerable misgiving since she always had difficulty inhibiting herself from saying what she thought, silently racked her brains for spellbinding anecdotes of typing classes at St John's.

'I hate flattery – it's insincere,' she protested, as she admired her new Sassoon haircut in one of Lady Davina's cherub-infested mirrors.

'Nonsense! In courtship one must always be accommodating – you do *not* need to be sincere.'

Yet more embarrassing than these morning lectures were the evening excursions on which Lady Davina occasionally took them. They would go to the Mirabelle or the Caprice, gilt-encrusted old-fashioned restaurants to which diners still wore evening dress, whose head waiters took pleasure in barring a man with long hair or without a tie. In stiff cocktail dresses, with velvet bands in their hair, Cathy, Caroline and Monty sat beside their overexcited chaperone as she instructed them in the ladylike arts of seeming to eat, seeming to drink and seeming to be merry when in fact you ate no food, drank only water and had a raging migraine.

Worst of all were the occasions when one of Lady Davina's few surviving admirers creakily lowered his shrivelled body into a chair beside her. Her animation became more vivid, her voice louder as she whooped and shrieked flirtatiously, heaping ridiculous flattery on the withered specimens of manhood temporarily within her grasp. 'Johnnie!' she would simper *fortissimo,* 'you wicked, divine man! How I long for those wonderful weekends we used to have! You were such a *naughty* boy, you know!' and Johnnie, or Gervase, or Ralphie, would twinkle a bleary eye and mumble some chivalrous rejoinder.

'They must be dumb to fall for it – she's as subtle as a brick,' Monty disapproved.

'They do fall for it, though.' Cathy thoughtfully stroked her hair. 'I know it's nauseating, but it works.'

They went to one or two London balls in preparation for the Season to come in the New Year, but the real social business of the autumn months were the tea parties, at which the rising debs practised social skills and sought pledges of support for their planned cocktail parties and dances.

Caroline's strategy was unsubtle bribery. 'Do come to Bourton,' she virtually ordered her new acquaintances. 'The hunting's first-class, everyone says so, and Daddy's promised he'll turn the heating on for the swimming pool.'

'I'd wish you'd find out who they are first,' Cathy complained in the taxi back to Trevor Square. 'We don't want a room full of dowdy lumps who haven't got any brothers.'

'The girls are only a way to get at the men,' Lady Davina had advised them, and Cathy, with single-minded tact, sifted every room for relatives of the three young earls.

Anthea Downcliffe, plump, mousey-haired and totally at sea in London after the enclosed Ayrshire set, was easy to befriend and pathetically grateful for the patronage. Lady Davina, on hearing that Sholto Mayleigh Shillingworth went two or three times a year to a shady health farm for colonic irrigation, removed him from the guest-list and refused to explain why. 'A dead loss, my darlings. Trust me,' she trilled.

The nearest relative of the Coseley clan was the cousin of Charlie the dream-boat, a showy long-legged blonde who seemed dauntingly impeccable in her Courrèges shifts. Cathy was surprised, when, after three or four weeks of tea parties, this girl had come across a Pimlico drawing room, introduced herself as Venetia Mountford, and said vaguely, 'I hope you're coming to my dance, and your sister. I hear she's terrific fun.'

'I'm coming out with my cousin. Weren't you at school together?' Cathy generously indicated Caroline towering over a stockbroker's daughter with teeth like a beaver, who, Cathy recalled with relief, did have a brother.

'Oh, Caroline.' Venetia peered across the room and added with ill grace, 'Her, too, of course. I'll ask Mummy to invite all three of you.' This she did, but her dance was almost at the end of the summer and Cathy knew she had to meet Charlie earlier than that to be in with a chance.

The real significance of Venetia's approach, as Lady Davina at once knew, was that Cathy and Monty were acquiring a little mystique in the new Season's coterie. The mothers liked Cathy's beautiful manners which secured a gratifying array of engraved invitations tucked into the gilt looking-glass at Trevor Square by Lady Davina. The society photographers liked her face, which was of the small-featured kind that photographed exquisitely. She was taller than average, slim, long-legged and well-groomed. Tim Studd, the top society photographer, singled her out at once and spent an afternoon taking pictures which he sent out to glossy magazines.

The debutantes' brothers, however, were attracted by Monty's air of rebellious sensuality, and Lady Davina watched complacently as a knot of red-faced suitors gathered. At the few dances they had attended, Monty was invariably swept on to the floor at once, where she danced the Frug or the Twist with increasing abandon. By 10.30 she would be necking, tousle-haired and conspicuous, with her last partner. Strictly chaperoned as they were, there was no opportunity for more than kissing, but Monty was the picture of erotic invitation and it took only a few weeks for the word to get round that the younger Bourton girl was 'likely'. 'I hear she's terrific fun' in fact meant 'my brother wants to lay her'.

Monty was one of the handful of mildly notorious girls coming out in 1964 who was straightforwardly seeking sexual experience. She knew, with the instinct of a child, that anything so fervently forbidden by adults must be of crucial importance and she yearned with the emotions of a woman to begin what she thought was the real business of a woman's life – the business of love. Most of the debs were less impetuous in moving into the sexual arena – some were scared, some were ignorant, a few were frigid, and most had been taught to preserve their virginity at all costs, because it was the most valuable inducement they could offer a prospective husband.

'Remember, my dear, beauty is only *sin* deep!' Roguishly Lady Davina advised them as they set out for their first dates. 'No one wants something that's simply given away.'

Even Caroline could see, however, that whatever Monty looked as if she might be prepared to give away was a very popular commodity.

However abandoned she appeared, Monty was in no hurry to explore the mystery of love with any of her overexcited, sweaty-handed dancing partners. Much as she sneered at Cathy's romantic chastity and made jokes about the dream lover who looked like Brian Jones, she too was waiting for the one man she could name as *the* great love. She made more and more daring experiments with her body, while still looking for a man to whom she could commit all of herself, heart, mind and excitable flesh. She felt somehow incomplete, and reasoned that sexual initiation would supply what she lacked.

In the meantime, all her doubts and worries focused in complete terror of pregnancy. Such was the level of sexual sophistication among her peer group that many of them shared her nightmares when they had engaged in nothing more serious than a kiss. Pregnancy seemed like awful retribution for sex, a punishment for doing what parents forbade. It meant the end of everything – fun, good looks, pretty clothes, parties, romance, possibilities and, of course, marriage. Life after pregnancy was never envisaged in detail, only as a black expanse of failure.

In the beginning, Monty never intended her dream lover to be Simon Emanuel, who was not blond, or vaguely menacing, or provocatively thin like Brian Jones, but dark, robust and as sweet as a puppy when he tried to amuse her. The expensive coaching college where he was being crammed for his exams was not far from St John's, so they met a few times in the Kensington coffee bars, then walked across the park, kicking up the dead leaves, to the Emanuels' apartment, where they played records for hours.

Over Christmas, everything changed. Cathy and Monty travelled to their home, which would be sold at auction in a few more weeks. There were already grimy squares on the walls where some of the paintings had been removed, and some of the furniture had been labelled. They were hardly inside the door when Cathy mentioned Rosanna's name in conversation and their mother exploded with anger.

'The Emanuels are the scum of the ghettos of Europe!' Her watery blue eyes were livid with a fury of which the sisters had never dreamed her capable. She was in a mood of simmering resentment against her dead husband and, by extension, the two girls as well. Three months alone in the house, undertaking the enforced dismantling of her home and the comfortable life she had enjoyed there, had bred first fear then anger in her mind. She had drunk even more than usual, and even now the spirituous tang was distinct on her breath. 'I can't think what Davina is doing allowing you to associate with those people,' she continued. 'At school you meet all sorts, you can't avoid it, you have to mix with them. But if this is her idea of bringing you out it certainly isn't mine.'

'But, Mummy, it would be awfully rude . . .' Catherine began, astonished at the ease with which an adult would betray her own principles for the sake of prejudices.

'I'm sure they'd *quite* understand. You don't need to say anything. Just don't go there again.' Bettina pinched her lips viciously together, deepening the wrinkles which bitterness had deepened around her mouth.

'Rosanna's my friend and if I want to see her I will,' Monty snapped, throwing her coat on to the oak table in the hall and running angrily upstairs. In front of her was a pale space against the pink wallpaper where her piano had been. There was an instant's silence and then Monty shouted even more loudly, 'And what have you done with *my* piano?'

Bettina stuck her nose in the air and walked into the drawing room without answering. Monty flung down the stairs in pursuit of her mother. 'I said, *what have you done with my piano?*'

'Don't speak to me in that tone of voice, Miranda.'

'What have you done with my piano?'

Bettina rearranged the dried flowers in a silver rose bowl, still silent. It was difficult to believe that she wasn't enjoying wounding her daughter, and Monty was inflamed with rage. Suddenly, she shoved her mother with violence and Bettina fell into the depths of the sofa.

'Answer me, you bitch!'

'Monty!' Cathy was shocked.

'I want to know what you've done with it!' Monty kicked her mother's feet in fury.

'It is not *your* piano, Miranda.' The older woman's jaw juddered with anger as she spoke. 'None of this is ours any more, don't you understand?' Her tone was pleading now; she was playing for Monty's sympathy, but Monty was pitiless where her mother was concerned.

'Oh I understand all right. You and Daddy have spent all our money so we've got nothing. That's perfectly clear, thank you. Where is it?' Monty's face was becoming chalk white, her eyes wide. She already knew the answers; inside her anguished mind, she was searching for a course of action, but could find nothing. Rage and frustration seethed like corrosive acids in her head.

'Your piano has been sold, Miranda. And we didn't get very much for it, either. Everything in this house has been sold.'

'But not everything has been taken away, has it?' Monty's tone was ugly. 'Only my piano. *This* hasn't gone for instance.' She kicked the occasional table over, sending the rose bowl and dried flowers flying. 'And this hasn't gone yet, has it?' She seized the chintz frill around the sofa and ripped it. 'And we've still got bookcases, haven't we?' She grabbed the poker and smashed the glass front of a bookcase. 'Who are you trying to kid, Mummy? You got rid of the piano because you'd like to get rid of me, didn't you? Well, you've succeeded. I'm going. And I'll never speak to you again.' She ran out of the drawing room, slamming the door loudly enough to rattle the windows, and bolted out of the house, leaving the front door open to the chill of the December air.

Bettina gave a satisfied sigh, and patted her hair into shape as she got off the sofa. Catherine looked at her mother with astonishment realizing that Monty's ridiculously dramatic words were perfectly accurate, and that the sale of the piano had indeed been a calculated stab at her sister's only area of vulnerability. Cathy suddenly had an insight into the side of her sister she found difficult to understand; she realized that Monty's pose of rebellion was not just self-dramatization. Her sister had simply decided to fight hate with hate.

Monty's fleeing footsteps could be heard with diminishing volume as she ran coatless down the gravel drive.

'Shouldn't we do something?' Cathy asked, feeling uncomfort-able.

'I think quite enough has been done for Miranda already,' their mother replied. 'You girls think you know everything, I'm sure, but you can't begin to understand . . .' she paused as if she had lost the thread of what she wanted to say, then started on a different tack. 'I haven't started on your rooms, so you'd better begin packing up directly.'

Miserably, Cathy went upstairs and began to take down from the picture rail the row of rosettes she had won with her ponies. Without her father, there seemed to be a horrible vacuum in the house. She felt desperately alone; but it was no good feeling sad. There was work to be done, the whole of her childhood to be packed up and stored away. Then she must get on with her grown-up life, which meant making the marvellous marriage that everyone expected of her.

She scraped her sleeve across her cheeks to wipe away the tears which refused to be held back, and reached for the framed photograph hanging below the rosettes; it showed her winning the first prize, in the novice class of the Pony Club gymkhana, which her father had presented. James stood smiling at the pony's head, and Cathy was holding up the little silver cup in a gesture of innocent triumph. The pony stood square and still, its ears forward and eyes alert. It was a picture of perfection. Should I keep it or throw it away, Cathy wondered. She put it with the rosettes on the pile of things she intended to throw away. She had more important prizes to think of now.

Monty strolled down the lane, not caring that her shoes were letting in water. She felt peculiarly exhilarated, almost lightheaded. Without the burden of obligation to a parent she loathed she felt as weightless as the seagulls planing over the bare ploughed fields. She had no money, no coat and no idea what she was going to do, and it was thrilling. She stopped a delivery van which was going to Brighton, and at Brighton ran on to the station platform in time to jump on the London train. She hid from the ticket collector in the lavatory, told the man at the barrier she'd lost her coat and the ticket with it, and then walked to Trevor Square. The house was dark and shuttered; Lady Davina and the staff had gone to Bourton House. Still elated, but by now very cold, Monty walked on, across the park to the Emanuels' apartment.

'But she will worry, your poor mother.' Mrs Emanuel looked like an anxious pullet uncertain where the fox was lurking. To get involved in the Bourton family squabbles, and on the wrong side, was no part of her social game plan. 'You must telephone her at once.'

'I'd much rather not, I'd only be rude to her.' Monty felt her fingertips ache as they thawed in the heavy warmth of the apartment.

'But what will you do? Where will you go? You can stay here, of course . . .'

'I love the way my mother says you can stay here when what she means is you can't.' Simon slouched by the window, pretending to look at the gaslights reflected in the distant Serpentine.

'Simon! Don't put words in my mouth. That's not what I said, of course Monty can stay. You're very welcome, dear, of course.' Mrs Emanuel was angry with herself for being outmanoeuvred, but disguised this by fussing, 'You poor girl, you must be frozen to death.' She pressed the brass bell-push and an immaculately uniformed maid appeared.

'Please draw Miss Bourton a bath. And, Rosanna, go with her, see if you can find her something to wear.' Given the extent of Rosanna's wardrobe this was hardly a heavy imposition.

Mr Emanuel, as usual, said nothing, while his wife fretted. 'It will all blow over in the morning, my dear,' was all he contributed to soothe her distress.

The next day Monty phoned Cathy when she was sure that Bettina would be out playing bridge. Cathy was still shocked by the realization that her mother had deliberately provoked Monty's rebellion, and felt she had to take control. She proposed calling Lady Davina and Mrs Emanuel, and negotiating a compromise.

'Look, you can't impose on Rosanna's family. What do you want to do?' she asked her sister.

'I don't know, Cathy.' Monty's voice was unusually quiet. 'I'm not ever going back to the house, or ever living with that woman again.'

'Mmm, but you'll stay at St John's?'

'I suppose so.'

'Well, we'll have to go back to Trevor Square next term, anyway, because Mummy's flat won't be ready.' Bettina had bought a tiny apartment in Brighton, where she would be able to keep up attendance at the bridge club.

'But what about Christmas?' Cathy was anxious for herself as well as her sister. 'You *can't* not be with your family at Christmas.'

'*What* family? – you're the only family I've got, Cathy. You're the only one who really cares. Isn't that what a family is – people who care about each other?'

Cathy telephoned Lady Davina, who in turn rang Mrs Emanuel and patronized her so lavishly that she was reassured about her role in the drama and agreed to have Monty until the Trevor Square house was open again in mid-January.

The Emanuels were acutely uncomfortable with their guest, but hid the fact by spoiling her. Behind closed doors, Rosanna wrangled with her parents over the best way to integrate the stranger into their household at Chanukah, the Jewish festival of lights which the Emanuels, like many liberal families in British Jewry, used as a pretext for following the secular forms of Christmas.

The apartment's vast sitting room looked like a Hollywood set for Queen Victoria's Christmas, with a massive fir tree smothered in swags of ribbon and gifts wrapped exquisitely by Rosanna. Monty adored the lavishness of it all, and the genuine religious feeling she detected in the domestic ceremonies of lighting candles and singing songs. The Emanuels seemed to her to be much more like a real family than her own, even if Mrs Emanuel did make monstrous attempts to direct her children's lives. Fifty people, all related to the family, sat down to Christmas dinner. Monty looked on enviously as the succession of uncles, aunts, cousins crowded through the door for the week of banqueting which followed.

'You've got an awful lot of family,' she said to Simon one morning as they were awaiting the day's influx of relatives.

'Too much.' He stood sourly by the window. 'I'm sick of them all asking me when I'm going to join the business. My mother puts them up to it – it's just another of her ways of pressuring me.'

Mrs Emanuel anxiously spoiled Monty, fearful that she was in some way a spy in their midst who would catch the family out in its great pretence of fitting into British society. Monty was taken to the opera, to recitals, to concerts, to half a dozen parties whose extravagant elegance dazzled her.

'Rosanna – have you done your practice? Rosannago do your practice now, later you will be too tired.' Every day Mrs Emanuel unnecessarily nagged her daughter towards perfection. One evening a famous soprano came to the house to hear Rosanna sing and both parents anxiously questioned her about Rosanna's training. Should she study in Paris? in New York? Vienna? How good was she, really, no really, how good?

Monty was entranced. Accustomed to Bettina sneering, 'Must you play that ghastly piano?' or 'Stop banging that damn piano, for heaven's sake,' it seemed like a dream of good fortune to be born into a family where music was a valued talent not a dangerous vice.

'Now, Monty, you must play with Rosanna,' Mrs Emanuel commanded one day.

'Yes, play for us, we want to hear you – Rosanna is always better with her friends,' Mr Emanuel added, and so Monty sat down at the velvet-black grand piano and accompanied Rosanna in one of their school pieces.

'But you play beautifully, doesn't she. Mother?' Mr Emanuel became talkative with surprise and indignation. 'Why don't your parents make you study?'

The fact was that neither her mother nor, when he was alive, her father, had the faintest notion of the value of art, talent or study. Monty sensed that her present audience would not understand that. Instead she said, 'We aren't a very musical family, I suppose.' Mr Emanuel shook his head in wonder.

'She sings beautifully too, don't you, Monty?' Rosanna was full of encouraging enthusiasm.

Before Monty had time to feel embarrassed, Rosanna played the introduction to one of the madrigals they had sung at school and took the soprano part so that Monty had to sing in the lower registers which showed off the mature tone of her voice. It was an idiotic song full of 'hey-nonny-noes' and Monty hated it, but Rosanna's parents applauded them with admiration.

'Wonderful! Wonderful voice you have! Doesn't she, Joseph?'

'Lovely, my dear, quite lovely. And you haven't studied at all?' He plainly found this an extraordinary example of parental neglect. The next day, after a secret conference with Rosanna, Mr Emanuel suggested that Monty join his daughter at her singing lessons during the holiday, and for a fortnight they shared a daily lesson with the Covent Garden soprano who came to the apartment to teach them.

The Emanuels treated her as a charity case, a poor child deprived of music. Except Simon. Simon treated Monty as young men often treat women with whom they are acutely in love; he barely spoke to her, fidgeted when she was around and stared at her when he thought she wasn't looking.

'Do you want me to show you how to play the guitar?' Simon appeared in the sitting room one afternoon. The weak winter sun streamed in from the leafless park outside. Rosanna and her mother had gone to Fortnum and Mason to exchange unwanted presents and Monty was amusing herself at the piano.

'Fabulous!' She got up and went to sit beside Simon on the sofa, taking up the Spanish guitar he handed to her. By now, Monty knew enough about men to know that this was one of those invitations not to be taken at face value.

'Press harder,' Simon ordered, positioning the fingers of her left hand, 'use the tips of your fingers.' He put his arm around her to show her how to press the strings against the frets in the neck.

'But my fingers aren't strong enough,' Monty complained. She smelt the faint, rich aroma of his body and the vague scent of aftershave, felt the warmth of his flesh through his cashmere sweater. Monty's interest in the guitar began to evaporate.

'Your fingers will get stronger in time, and the tips will harden. Here, feel how mine are.' Obediently she touched his fingers with hers, then looked up towards him as their hands interlaced. Simon put the guitar down on the floor and pulled her towards him, breathless with elation. Monty opened her lips under his and lay back on the sofa, her senses swimming. The warm silence of the apartment seemed to roar in her ears as she surrendered to the responses of her body. Whatever it was that had held her back with the boys at the dances, it had gone now. Kissing Simon felt right.

'I feel as if I've known you all my life,' she murmured as they finally drew apart.

'Me too. You've got fantastic eyes.'

'They turn up though.'

'That's what I like about them.' Monty smiled. All the boys said she had fantastic eyes. Whatever dumb magic they had, she was glad it worked on Simon too.

They kissed again and she felt his hand hover over her breast, not daring to caress, so she arched her back and pressed her body against him. Simon, used to the elaborate teases of the 'nice' girls he had kissed before, felt ready to explode with lust and gratitude.

For an hour they revelled in their new conspiracy, then tidied the sofa and went to make coffee in the immense kitchen, where Rosanna and Mrs Emanuel found them on their return. Monty and Simon put on what they thought was an Oscar-winning performance of innocence, in which their complicity was blatantly apparent.

Monty could not sleep that night. She went into the marble- tiled guest bathroom and looked at herself in the mirror. She felt different, but she couldn't see it. Somewhere on her face it must show – how could she look the same when inside she was in love for the first time?

At the first opportunity, Mrs Emanuel said to her son, 'Monty is a very nice girl, Simon, but you won't get too fond of her – Simon – promise me? You understand me, Simon?'

'Of course, Mother, I promise, don't worry,' he answered lightly. It was not a false vow. No degree of fondness would be too great for Monty, Simon thought.

'I'm in love,' Monty told her sister three months later. They were back at college, and back at the Bourton house in Trevor Square under Lady Davina's critical eye. Simon had taken Monty out as often as he dared, while Cathy had stayed in, with a borrowed sewing machine, painstakingly copying some of Rosanna's prettiest dresses; she had discovered that even at wholesale prices the frocks she liked best were too expensive.

With great care, Monty zipped up her sister's white dress for Queen Charlotte's Ball.

'With Rosanna's brother?' Cathy pulled up the long white gloves, which reached over her elbows.

'Yes, with Simon. Oh, Cathy, don't you think he's dishy?'

'I suppose he is good-looking but Mummy'll never let you marry him.' She pulled critically at the thick garland of artificial gardenias around the dress's scooped neckline.

'I don't want to marry him, I'm in love, that's all. You look fab. The chinless wonders won't be able to resist you.' Monty accepted Cathy's ambition although she did not share it. Her sister's marriage had become the preoccupying business of them both.

Cathy studied her reflection in the murky depths of the glass in her room at Trevor Square. Under the white silk gown her figure was as slender as a model's. In fact, Cathy had already been invited by a society magazine to model some clothes for a special feature on model debutantes. Her glossy dark hair, cut in a geometric bob by Vidal Sassoon, swung against her faintly hollow cheeks, contrasting with her pale pink lipstick. Her eyes seemed smoky and enormous.

'I think I'll do.' She smiled with satisfaction and gave Monty a hug. 'You won't do anything stupid, Monty darling, will you?'

'If you mean don't get pregnant, don't worry. We're being very careful. Aren't you dying to be in love, Cathy?'

Cathy sighed. She could see her sister glowing with excitement, and longed to feel the same way, but she knew that her own emotional make-up was different. In the bottom of her heart, Cathy wondered if she were capable of such violent feelings.

'He'll come soon, I just know he will,' Monty promised her.

'Who will?'

'Mr Right.'

'*The Earl* of Right, you mean.' They caught each other's eyes in the mirror and giggled.

Queen Charlotte's Ball at the beginning of April marked the official start of the debutante season. Cathy joined forty other selected maidens in white gowns to pull a vast cardboard wedding cake across the ballroom floor with white ribbons. William Hickey of the *Daily Express*, the most influential gossip column, tipped her for the 'Deb of the Year' title and, to Monty's fury, printed a picture of both of them with a caption reading 'Cathy and Miranda, daughters of the suicide peer, Lord James Bourton.'

Caroline, ignored by the photographers, and not selected for the cake ceremony, stamped grimly off to college next morning while the Bourton sisters were awarded breakfast in bed by Lady Davina.

'And Charles Coseley has accepted!' she triumphed, waving a sheet of blue embossed writing paper which bore two lines of the electro-cardiograph handwriting boys acquired at Eton. 'Now don't let us down, Cathy. We're relying on you.'

As the previous autumn's tea parties had progressed, Lady Davina had decided on a late July dance for Cathy and Caroline. The funds from the felling of the West Wood would provide for a thousand guests and, as she had watched Cathy quietly charm and manipulate the girls who were prime targets, Lady Davina had realized that there would be no trouble in pledging a handsome number of return invitations.

There would be no trouble, either, in making the Bourton dance one of the grandest of the season. After sympathizing with Caroline's mother over the strain and bother of organizing it all, and hearing Lady Davina make all manner of old-fashioned suggestions, Cathy calmly took control of the operation. She hired a young cousin of the Queen to organize the affair and between them the dance was planned in elaborate details; a discotheque, a pop group, an immense dance floor laid over the priceless parquet of the ballroom, garlands of flowers around every table, a small fun fair set up in the home paddock and a second dance floor of Perspex built over the top of the ornamental lake.

'Darling, aren't you the teeniest bit nervous? I was simply shattered with nerves before my dance.' A germ of doubt nagged Lady Davina as she watched her protegee approach her great day so calmly. Was this completely normal? Suppose all the serenity suddenly collapsed and she cracked up at the last moment?

'I suppose I should be wound up, but I don't feel it, honestly. We've planned everything for months, there's nothing we've forgotten, I've done everything you said, now . . .' Cathy didn't finish. She couldn't think of an elegant way to say that the only thing she cared about was getting Charles Coseley to ask her to dance.

She had made a close friend of his cousin Venetia, scanned the society magazines for snippets of gossip and subtly but relentlessly turned every conversation to the end of finding out everything she could about her target.

Charles Coseley, the Earl of Laxford, was twenty-nine, and personally worth £15 million; when he succeeded to his father's title of Marquess of Shrewton, he would also inherit houses in London, Wiltshire and Yorkshire, with a total fortune of over Â£200 million. There was a villa in the South of France, and a yacht; Charlie Coseley liked gambling, dancing, polo, shooting, crashing his E-Type Jaguar and, most of all, girls. He'd been out with all the most glamorous girls of the previous Season and none of them had lasted more than six weeks.

'Charlie's awful, really, you must warn your sister,' Venetia told Cathy one afternoon when they had returned to Trevor Square after an exhausting afternoon scouring the Chelsea boutiques. 'He just goes for one bird after another, drives them crazy with flowers and phone calls, then as soon as he's got them – bang, finished, all over.'

'How odd.' Cathy widened her eyes inquiringly at Venetia; she knew all she had to do was look receptive and she'd be told everything she needed to know.

'He pesters them to sleep with him and then as soon as they do, he's off. My uncle and aunt are getting rather worried, actually. He is the heir, after all.'

'Mmmn.' Cathy passed Venetia a dark blue china mug with 'opium' written on it in large gold letters. It contained tea. They had bought the mug in Carnaby Street. 'And he goes a bit far, really,' Venetia continued contentedly. 'He's so good-looking he can get any girl he wants and they're all heartbroken. Some stupid little dolly tried to commit suicide when he dumped her last year.'

'Good heavens. Does he sleep with *all* his girlfriends?'

'Absolutely.'

'Sugar?'

Following Lady Davina's advice, Cathy read the polo reports in *The Field* every week and demanded that all her dates should take her to the Garrison and the Saddle Room, the nightclubs Venetia said Charlie frequented. She saw him once or twice, always with a different, stunning girl, but he obviously never noticed her. She realized that she was not his type of girl at all. He went for the girls in the shortest mini-skirts and the most transparent dresses, with the longest blonde hair and the most heavily made-up eyes. Cathy felt awkward in very revealing clothes and knew that an understated, natural style of dress suited her best.

'How the hell am I going to get him when he doesn't even know I exist?' Cathy asked herself in desperation as she watched Charlie's elegant limbs vibrating through the Shake on the Saddle Room's dance floor. Opposite him was yet another rangy blonde, wearing a gold crochet dress over a hideous, flesh-coloured bodystocking.

'What are you looking so moody about?' Cathy's date drawled rudely. 'I hate moody birds, come on and dance.' They edged into the crowd and Cathy flung herself into sensual gyrations, hoping to catch Charlie's eye at last but succeeding only in winding a young Guards officer on her left.

'How much money do you think she paid for that old rope?' she bitched as Charlie and the blonde left the floor. The glittering crochet dress attracted everyone's attention.

'Well, it won't be enough to tie old Charlie down, whatever it cost,' her date answered with envy.

In the taxi home afterwards Cathy sat inertly while her date half-smothered her with kisses. She felt nothing except rather sticky around the face; she was deep in thought, pondering the impossible problem of Charlie Coseley, the man she loved, whose fortune would save her family.

Simon took Monty to the Ad Lib Club, a dark penthouse high in a modern skyscraper where the pop groups played, and those who were not playing came to drink Scotch and Coke and mingle. It was the exclusive haunt of the new meritocracy; everyone was hustling or being hustled. Like a shoal of piranhas the success-hungry crowd fastened on the stars – George Harrison in a pair of jeans, Mick Jagger in a flowered shirt, David Bailey with Jean Shrimpton.

Simon Emanuel, his arm around Monty, was there to fix a niche for himself in the music business. Since the name 'Emanuel' meant money, there were plenty of two-bit shysters to take him on, but Simon was after the musicians and that was harder.

'They think I'm just a rich Jewish kid trying to buy into the scene,' he told Monty. 'I know they'd change their tune if they heard me play, but I can't just get on stage and jam with the Stones.'

'Why not?' said Monty. 'Everyone else does.' It was one of the Ad Lib's unique attractions.

'Yes, but they're different.' Simon meant that the Stones, the Animals, the Kinks, and all the rest were lean, mean, working-class kids, who were more hostile to outsiders even than the traditional élite. From the perspective of the music business, he was on the wrong side of the class barrier.

Monty and Simon would leave the Ad Lib at three or four in the morning, and stay together in the dangerous darkness of Trevor Square kissing and petting until the dawn. At first, they were frightened of discovery, but then Monty realized that Lady Davina took a sleeping pill every night.

'She wouldn't wake up if the house was burning down,' laughed Monty, sinking into Simon's arms with abandon.

'But what about Cathy and Caroline?' Simon unbuttoned her satin blouse.

'They sleep like logs and anyway they wouldn't tell on us. I do love you, Simon.' The satin blouse slithered to the floor, to be joined by Monty's black boots, white tights and the eighteen-inch wide strip of plum velvet that was her skirt. They undressed each other little by little, then embraced on the threadbare Turkey rug in front of the warm ashes of the fire. To be together, to touch and hold and caress each other – it was all ecstasy, but they dared not make love properly in case Monty got pregnant; they dared not even tell each other how much they yearned to go all the way.

'Why do you love me?' Monty asked, snuggling close.

'I don't know, you're not like other girls, that's all.' He stroked the soft curve of her hip, gingerly slid his hand between her thighs.

'You're not like other boys, either, that's why I love you.' Monty reached into the darkness and held the shaft of eager flesh as it swelled in her hand, wondering how it would feel to have it inside her body. It seemed silly to be so close and to love each other so much and to deny themselves the ultimate intimacy. It did not occur to either of them that the most powerful force binding them together was the disapproval of their families. Monty would have been outraged at the suggestion that she cared enough about Bettina's opinion to flout it.

By the time the crocuses in Hyde Park were fading, the 1965 Season was under way, and the mirror at Trevor Square was half-obliterated with invitations. All over England and Scotland, houses filled at the weekends with extraordinary mixtures of people whose only common link was some connection with the aristocracy. Unregenerate landed gentry, their faces reddened by the winter's hunting, rubbed shoulders with long-haired jeunesse dorée in velvet jackets. Elderly men who had danced with girls who had danced with Edward VIII frowned at youths in hipster trousers and lace shirts. Women with legs as thick and knotted as ancient oaks smiled wistfully at girls whose sapling thighs were displayed in patent leather boots. Dior swirled disdainfully past Biba; diamonds blazed at plastic flowers, and whiffs of marijuana percolated into the musty folds of tapestries.

There was a ball every Saturday and besides the dance itself, there would also be the house party, a raucous random selection of revellers billeted on the home of a guest who lived near the host, who were given dinner before the dance and a bed for the night after it, with the requisite amount of chauffeuring and chaperonage. In the Season the entire British upper class conspired to get its young mated without undue incident.

The race was on among the young girls to see how far they could go with drink, drug-taking or sexual experiment, without spoiling their chances with the wealthiest men in the pool. In six months or so their social careers would be determined and many would have acquired newspaper cutting files which would pursue them for the rest of their lives.

Cathy and Caroline went first to a couple of dull dances for Caroline's hunting chums at the other side of the country, where they sipped fruit-punch that was virtually alcohol-free, panted through the Benenden repertoire of Scottish reels and were in bed by 2 am and up the next day in time for a scavenger hunt. These were childish, boisterous and inelegant affairs, no preparation for what was to come.

Then they went to the first big private ball of the season, for the daughter of a wealthy Member of Parliament in Cornwall. Monty was asked as well.

'Six hours on this bloody train!' Caroline shoved her suitcase into the luggage rack and plumped down to read a riding magazine.

'It'll be worth it. Lucy knows an awful lot of people, and we're terribly lucky to be invited. Half the college is sick with jealousy.'

'Hmph. You mean Lucy knows Charlie Coseley so we've got to struggle up the length of the country so you can chase after him.'

'Oh come on, Caroline, we'll be staying in a castle. It'll be really romantic.' Monty gazed out of the window at the grey London suburbs.

'I suppose you've got Simon invited.' Caroline flicked over a page of light hunters.

'I didn't need to get him invited.' Monty complacently turned towards her cousin. 'Lucy Limpton's dying to get her paws on him because he's an Emanuel.'

Cathy gazed wistfully out of the window. In her heart of hearts she was beginning to admit that she might be stupid to pin all her hopes on landing the catch of the season; but when she compared Charlie's flashing smile and crisp, gold curls to her slobbery, importunate dates so far, she shuddered. She was beginning to feel nauseated by the mere smell of them.

Catching Charlie was also a question of pride; Cathy smarted at the patronizing expressions of sympathy she got from well-meaning acquaintances: 'Such a shame about your poor father – nothing in the stories, I suppose?' was the line, vulgar curiosity masquerading as good manners. She smothered flaring anger every time she passed a knot of strangers and they exchanged comments in low voices, and she heard, or thought she heard, the words 'suicide peer' yet again. She wanted to show them all that she was a force to be reckoned with, not just a minor figure in a shameful scandal.

It was a small grey castle, taller than it was wide, built at the tip of a steep inlet of sea. On the steps, Cathy straightened her immaculate camel mini-skirt, glad now that she had shortened it as much as she dared, and aware how fine her legs looked in their cream tights and white boots, and how her superbly cut hair would fall silkily back into shape no matter how the relentless wind from the Atlantic whipped it about her head. Was *he* watching, perhaps, from the narrow windows?

'For heaven's sake stop mooning,' snapped Caroline, 'I'm turning blue.'

'The wind is a little fresh today.' Their host Sir John Limpton had appeared, to lead them indoors. 'We're so lucky here in the West: the gulf stream keeps the sea warm so it never gets really cold.' He was a tall man with hollow cheeks and thinning dark hair. The girls looked at each other and smothered laughter as he led them down dank corridors whose stone walls seemed to be sweating chill. What was the man's notion of real cold?

Sir John lingered just an instant waiting for the footman to bring up the last suitcase, really wanting to look at Cathy's legs. In Chelsea, there were many girls, and they all wore a skirt no more than halfway down their thighs. But what Chelsea girls considered mere fashion, older men interpreted as invitation. Sir John's life was lived in Westminster and the country where there were few girls, and none who showed so much as their knees. He was virtually hypnotized by the pale, slender limbs before him; Cathy was both gratified and disturbed when she noticed him direct a furtive glance at her thighs as he pretended to supervise the footman with their cases.

The dance was dazzling, and even Caroline admitted that the journey had been worth it. There was champagne, a piper at dinner, salmon and venison from the estate; and then half the Opposition front bench seemed to be in the ballroom demonstrating their skill at the Watusi.

Young couples who were already paired off, but by tradition lodged in separate house parties, made their way down the icy corridors looking for a convenient place to make love before getting dressed again and scampering down to the ballroom in time for the toast to the debutante and her future.

Charlie Coseley arrived with the first house party; he had had a row with the red-haired actress who came with him, danced with four or five different girls then swept Lady Limpton on to the floor for an abandoned smooch. This was not unusual: it was considered good form for the men to flirt with their hostess.

Simon arrived late, ran from hall to crowded hall like a seeking gundog until he found Monty, and then pulled her outside. On the gravel, stood a sleek, dark car. 'Get in!' He pulled open the passenger door with care. Monty looked at him, not understanding.

'But whose is it, Simon? Have you borrowed it?'

'Nope. I've bought it.'

'But it's an Aston Martin!'

'So what?' He ran round to the other side and climbed in beside her. 'My grandmother left me some money. It's been in trust for me for years, until I was twenty-one. So now I'm twenty-one!' He dragged her uncomfortably towards him across the gearstick, kissed her with a new mastery, then broke off and started the engine with a roar. The powerful headlamps caught the stone parapet, the drawbridge and the close-pressed firs beyond. Wild with his new freedom, Simon drove them away.

'Where are we going?' Happily Monty settled in the low-slung seat.

'Anywhere! Let's just *go!*' Simon jammed a tape into the player and loud music filled the car. Monty giggled.

'It's just like a little house.'

'You can put the seats down to make a bed, too.' He reached over and squeezed her thigh.

They sped along narrow stone-walled roads and, after Simon had nearly slaughtered a sheep, Monty persuaded him to drive less fast. They found a spectacular beach of fine silver sand, pulled off their clothes and leapt into the boisterous sea, exhilarated by the April cold and by the gloriousness of feeling like the only two figures in the landscape.

Later, cocooned in the car with Monty's Biba ballgown as a blanket, Simon said, 'There's something I want to ask you.' He's going to ask if we can make love properly, Monty thought thankfully. But instead, he asked, 'If I buy an apartment, will you come and live with me?'

'Can you really buy an apartment?' Monty said, testing this wonderful dream.

'Yep. I've got enough money for a deposit, and I went to see an accountant who says I can easily get a mortgage once I go to work for my father.'

'But I thought you didn't want to go into the business?'

'I don't, but nothing's happening for me with music right now.'

'But you'll get a break soon, Simon, I know you will. It's only a matter of time.' Monty felt as if he were proposing to renege on their shared faith. They both agreed that rejecting the world of their parents was the beginning of wisdom.

'Are you saying no, Monty?' His voice shrank to a fearful half-whisper. He desperately wanted her to live with him, but knew that her family, as well as his, would be enraged.

'Oh, darling Simon, no – I mean, yes – I mean of course I'll come and live with you. I love you, don't I?' Their lips met for a long, uncomfortable and passionate kiss. Monty felt her skin chilled and gritty from the sand of the beach, and she was suddenly worried by a new thought.

'Simon, I'm going to have to go on the Pill, aren't I?'

'We can be careful, darling, just like now.'

'Uh huh – maybe *you* can be careful, but I can't. Not if I'm living with you, Simon. Can't you see how awful it would be? We'd just be dying to do it properly all the time. I'll *have* to get the Pill somehow.' But where was she going to get the Pill without being married?

At 4 am the castle was still ablaze with lights. The discotheque was quiet, and in the dining hall liveried servants were setting out a line of silver chafing dishes for the breakfast. Cathy and Caroline trudged up the stairs to their room, footsore and dejected. Ahead of them on the first-floor landing a group of smart London guests were shrieking with merriment at one boy who had taken some LSD. Acid was the new diversion for the more daring men, who gaily ravaged their nervous tissues with weekend after weekend of trips, to the entertainment of the more timid onlookers.

'I think I must be the only girl in the room Charlie didn't dance with,' Cathy paused to take off her shoes. 'He had a stinking row with that actress, got frightfully drunk and grabbed every bird he could reach – but not me.' She looked exhausted but still luminously beautiful. Her hair was pinned up in a pile of glossy curls, and sprinkled with tiny white silk flowers. Her dress was of the palest pink slub silk, with a high waist, long, fitted sleeves and rows of minute buttons at the wrists and down the back. It was a dress she had made herself and it had taken hours of labour to cover every tiny button and stitch the exquisite silk flowers on to hairpins.

'Never mind,' Caroline consoled her, 'he was obviously too sloshed to notice that you were the most beautiful girl in the room.'

'I've got a filthy headache, too. I don't think much of Lucy's father's taste in champagne.' At the top of the ugly oak staircase they turned along the corridor to their allotted bedroom, and opened the door on a self-conscious attempt at an orgy. The air was foetid with marijuana and ten or twelve people were lying on the floor watching the actress who had come with Charlie Coseley. She was naked except for a smudged layer of body paint, and she was ineffectually trying to touch up the design on her buttocks in the mirror.

'You shouldn't have sat down, April,' sniggered a man in a polo-necked evening shirt, passing the joint, 'spoiled my work of art.'

Caroline stomped undaunted into the laughing circle.

'Look, this is our room. Go and find somewhere else to play.'

They laughed helplessly, some coughing in the fumes.

'Oh cool it, Caro, siddown and have a smoke.'

'No thank you.'

'No *thank you*!' he mimicked her prim tone, to gales of giggling. The handle of the bathroom door rattled noisily then there was pounding from the other side and cries of 'Open up!' Nobody took much notice.

At last the boy in the polo-necked shirt struggled to his feet and tried the door. "Slocked. Where's key?' There were louder shouts and more knocking.

'Help! Let us out – Jeremy's having a bad trip.'

Another man blundered across to join the struggle and together they smashed the door lock with the leg of a massive carved chair.

Three people squeezed simultaneously through the splintered doorway. 'Oh God, you're all *orange*!' the first man shouted happily, then pitched over the nearest pair of legs and sprawled on the carpet, his limbs rowing back and forth like those of an upturned beetle.

Behind him stood Monty's school friend, Swallow Lamotte, her strawy blond hair now waist length. Apart from a man's black bow tie dangling loose down to her nipples, she was wearing nothing. The man with her wore only his socks and a mass of shaving foam around his lower belly.

'Oh hello, you two. I was just trying to trim Jeremy's pubes for him. Terrible vibes in here. What's up?' Swallow's taste for debauchery couldn't overcome her basic common sense, nor her sensitivity to social atmosphere.

'We want to go to bed, that's all.' They all sniggered and Cathy bit her tongue with embarrassment at her unthinking choice of words. 'This *was* our room,

Swallow.' Her head throbbed unbearably and she rested her cheek against the chill stone doorway for some relief.

'Plenty of room!' slurred the ginger-haired actress generously. 'Join th' party.' She waved towards the bed. For the first time they noticed that it was occupied by a couple. The girl was virtually unconscious, and the man, grimly drunk, was grinding his limp penis against her trying to get an erection. He looked round at Caroline, suddenly cheerful at the promise of more lively company, then rolled off and picked up a half-empty bottle of brandy beside the bed.

'Lots of room – have a drink, you two. Whass yer name?'

'Your best bet is to kip down in the housekeeper's room,' Swallow briskly advised. 'Ground floor, north wing, down the passage at the back of the dining hall. Just take your night clothes, I'll make sure the rest of your stuff is OK.' She stepped over the sprawled bodies and showed Caroline and Cathy out of the rooms like a gracious hostess. 'You can ask the housekeeper for an aspirin, she's bound to have one. See you in the morning.'

They walked slowly back to the staircase, too shocked and too tired to say very much. The room which they presumed to be the housekeeper's, on the ground floor off a corridor which led to the kitchen, was at least warm, heated by a substantial coal fire. There was one ordinary bed and a sofa, on which Caroline flopped to give the miserable Cathy the better berth.

Cathy first searched the spartan bathroom for aspirins. She found these, took the tablets and then roused the drowsy Caroline to unbutton her dress. Miserable as she was, Cathy looked in the closet for a hanger, but then found that the rail in the closet was too low for the long gown to hang without crumpling. She decided to hang the dress in the bathroom, from the head of the ancient shower fitment which drooped like a sunflower over the tub.

Caroline was already asleep, snoring gently, and Cathy was just on the point of drifting into slumber when the door of the room crashed open, and a wedge of harsh light penetrated the darkness. A tall figure lurched through the doorway, holding the door handle for support.

'Fucking buggering hell!' it swore as its unsteady legs collided with Caroline's outstretched calves and half-dislodged her from the sofa. Three more staggering steps took the figure to the bathroom door.

'Whatever is going on? What do you think you're doing?' Caroline demanded in ringing tones as the bathroom door smashed into the wall and the figure half-fell through it. There was the sound of a man about to throw up, followed by the unmistakable sound of badly aimed vomit splattering porcelain. The smell of semi-digested food soused in liquor pervaded the room.

Cathy sleepily sat up. 'What's the matter?' she asked, her eyes flickering open, feeling instantly angry. 'What the hell do you mean by barging into our room like this? You're smashed out of your skull! How dare you charge into our bathroom? If you've ruined my dress . . .' She scrambled out of bed, impatiently disentangling the ruffled skirt of her white Victorian nightgown.

'Now look here . . .' Caroline picked herself up from the floor and put on the light. She stood like an angry Valkyrie by the open door, her beefy shoulders straining at the armholes of her blue Laura Ashley nightdress.

The intruder was leaning against the bathroom door, extremely drunk, wiping his chin with the skirt of Cathy's exquisite pink gown. The rest of the dress was soaked with the foul-smelling contents of his stomach. Charlie Coseley had evidently drunk a lot of red wine that evening.

'You've *ruined* my dress! You pig! You revolting pig!' She felt as if she were incandescent with fury. Cathy scarcely realized it, but weeks of yearning for this man to notice her had brought her to a state where she detested him so passionately that she was ready to pull out his gorgeous blond curls with her own hands.

'Mishtake . . .' slurred Charlie, letting go of the bathroom door and taking a few steps into the room. Ahead of him loomed Caroline, her arms outstretched as if to head off a bolting pony. 'Shorry . . .' Charlie turned towards Cathy, making a helpless gesture with his hands.

'You're not getting away with this! How dare you behave so disgustingly? You're not fit to belong to the human race!' Cathy raged, almost enjoying herself.

'Anyone ever tell you . . .' Charlie advanced one step towards her, pointing a wavering finger, 'anyone ever tell you . . . you're beautiful when you're . . . hup! beautiful when you're angry? Whassyourname, anyway? Don'I know you?' He looked mildly confused. He raised the pointing finger again, then fell forward across the sofa.

'Zonked out,' Caroline pronounced, inspecting the body with satisfaction.

'So much for the Earl of Right,' Cathy sneered, giving the prone form a disdainful prod with her foot. 'What an animal.'

'Oh cripes, look.' Caroline picked up a messy but once expensive pigskin shaving-bag. 'Maybe this really was his room in the first place.' She opened the closet, and pulled out a tweed sports jacket and a pair of cavalry twill trousers. 'Yes, look, here are his clothes.'

'Well, that's not our fault. If he'd been nicer to that April bird we wouldn't have been turned out of our own room in the first place.' Cathy pressed the bell for the servants with a bravura gesture. Looking like a Parisian soubrette with tousled hair and lace trimmed gown, she stared miserably at the sprawled body of the man on whom she had set her heart. 'I'm bloody well going to send him a bill.' She picked up the stinking ruin of her dress between finger and thumb, then sadly let it drop. Caroline belted her ugly plaid dressing gown with a decisive gesture and strode towards the door.

'Caro, where are you going?'

'I'm going to make a scene, that's where I'm going.'

A few minutes later an elderly maid appeared, expressed anguish over Cathy's soiled dress and took it away. Two more servants, and the housekeeper herself, followed to clean the bathroom. Two footmen carried Charlie out of the room. Then Caroline reappeared, with their host, Sir John Limpton, who immediately sat down on Cathy's bed, took her hand, and offered an emotional apology. 'Your cousin has explained everything and I regret most profoundly that this should have happened under my roof. The young fool should have known better. You can be sure that I shall have a few words with him in the morning. More than a few words. Considerably more. I knew your father, of course, don't know if he ever mentioned me. Terrible business . . .' He shook his head and rambled on for five minutes more, then pulled himself together and departed.

'*Caro!* Whatever did you tell him to get him crawling like that?' Cathy now wished desperately that the whole affair were just a bad dream. She felt ravaged with embarrassment, and furious with herself as well as with Charlie. In a few intemperate instants, she had blown her chance of landing Britain's most eligible Earl.

'I just said you were really upset, and – ah – well, it all got a bit out of hand, I was pitching it strong for the housekeeper when old Sir John loomed up and wanted the whole story. He was absolutely livid. I think he's got a soft spot for you, Cathy.'

Smarting with failure, Cathy decided to scuttle back to London as early as she could the next day, fearful that Charlie would come round before she left. When he did regain consciousness, which was towards the end of Sunday afternoon, he received a thunderous lecture from his host, who was also a friend of his own father. As a result, Cathy received a large bouquet on Monday, accompanied by a colossal, pink velvet stuffed pig, wearing a white tutu and a label which read, 'This little pig says he's sorry.' Shortly after they were delivered, the telephone rang.

'I wouldn't blame you if you said you never wanted to see hide or hair of me ever again,' said Charlie humbly, 'but if you think you could bear it, perhaps you would have dinner with me and tell me how I can make it up to you for ruining your dress?'

CHAPTER EIGHT

SINGAPORE IN 1948 was like a smashed wasps' nest. Huge ruined buildings, once creamy colonial white and now scarred with the shrapnel of World War II air raids, awaited demolition. Thousands of people, mostly of Chinese origin, scurried around building sites, gathering up rubble with their bare hands, carrying it away in wicker baskets, driving bulldozers and bullock-carts to and fro as they toiled to create a new city.

The water of the harbour was calm as it had been through the preceding centuries, when the ships of five continents had crossed its scummy surface. The corpses of twenty thousand citizens of the city, machine-gunned by the Japanese, now lay below the flotsam on the docile waves, but those who lived on remembered the dead with their ancestors but turned their energies to work. While Europe built war memorials, Singapore had decided to construct its glittering future. The docks were to be rebuilt, the airport resited, the notorious internment camps destroyed but not commemorated. The city at the axis of the East's great trading routes was preparing to welcome oil-tankers instead of tea clippers, jet aircraft in place of rusty tramp steamers. Singapore wanted to forget the past and embrace the future.

For the present, there were the British Tommies, thousands of loud, slow-moving men in khaki shorts, their pale, northern skins fried red in the tropic sun. They had come to drive out the Japanese, stayed to supervise the repatriation of the prison camp survivors, and now arrived in renewed numbers to fight the Communist guerrillas who threatened mainland Malaya across the calm, pale grey waters of the Straits.

The soldiers were mostly conscripts aged under twenty, eager to sample the marvels of the East, equipped with malaria pills and homilies about the danger of diseased foreign whores. Penicillin had been available for a mere three years, and its power to destroy the bacteria causing gonorrhoea and syphilis seemed a claim rather than a reality. The Tommies' word for a woman was 'bint', from the Arabic name prefix '*binti*' meaning 'daughter of'.

Throughout the air raids, blackouts, blockades and invasions of the war years, Singapore had maintained its purposeful dedication to business. War was a tonic to trade. Now the Indian jewellers on Arab Street displayed in their plate-glass cases an unprecedented range of wares: the portable wealth of Eurasian concu-bines hastily cashed in when the girls' protectors fled the Japanese advance, the slim, gold wedding rings sold for medicines by the starving nuns in the internment camps, Dutch cigar cases, Australian watches, Russian icons, Chinese jade. The passport to the city was something to sell.

Into the small, curving river which slipped through Chinatown sailed a high-powered Malay fishing-boat bringing a few passengers from the mainland. The pet-rol engine idled and spluttered as the boat nosed to a landing between the ranks of sampans at the quayside, and the fisherman's boy helped the passengers mount the rough steps made from railway sleepers. The last to alight was a woman of per-haps twenty, who climbed with difficulty because of her tight brown sarong. The boy ran down again to collect the palm-leaf bag which bulged with her possessions.

Bemused by the throng of rickshaws and bicycles along the quay, the girl looked wonderingly at the façade of shuttered shop-houses in front of her, the three- or four-storey buildings incorporating warehouses and teashops behind a shabby arcade of columns. The walls were covered with peeling layers of cigarette posters and advertisements for American films.

'Can I help you – perhaps you have lost your way?' A plump Eurasian woman in a navy print dress spoke to her in English.

'Thank you.' The girl turned in relief. 'I am looking for a cheap lodging-house, if you know of one.'

'Singapore is full of cheap rest-houses. Do you want to stay in any particular part of town? Perhaps you have friends in the city?'

'No, no friends. I have to find work, so I want to be near the centre, that's all.' She was neatly formed, with a high-cheekboned, heart-shaped face.

'I rent a few rooms in my house – only young ladies, of course. One of them has just left me to go back to her village and get married. Perhaps you would like to see her room?'

The girl hesitated. Apart from the fact that she spoke English well, everything about her indicated a village girl of little sophistication. She had few clothes in her bag, wore no jewellery or accessories of Western manufacture, and her silhouette showed no evidence of a bra. Her figure-hugging black *bhaju* and printed sarong were in traditional Malay style; the long line of buttons down the *bhaju* front were, the woman noticed with a covert glance, hand-made of braided thread. But village girl or not, she was suspicious of this sudden good luck. Good. She had common sense as well.

'If you wish, I will give you my address and you can call later to see the room. But I am on my way home now and we could take a rickshaw together?' No pres-sure, not at this stage, not with a Malay. Had she been Chinese the woman would have hectored a little, but the timid Malay girls needed more careful manipulation.

'That's very kind of you.'

'So will you come now with me?'

'Why not.' She picked her bag up decisively, and the Eurasian woman hailed a rickshaw.

'My name is Anna Maria,' she said, holding out a hand, 'Spanish name. My mother is from Madrid.' A European connection was always reassuring, she found; in fact, her mother was a Filipino housemaid. As the rickshaw boy ran through the thronged streets Anna Maria appraised her catch out of the corner of her eye. Slim, graceful but with that bit of extra flesh the British liked; a real little bosom, infact.

'Excuse me asking, but are you Malay?'

'Yes, I come from Pahang, south Pahang.' She had named one of the less developed areas on the east side of the peninsula.

'May I ask your name?' It was an intrusive question, but the girl rallied to answer, evidently understanding that city people were more outspoken than country folk.

'I am Ayeshah binti Mohammed,' she answered, as if she had rehearsed the sentence. Anna Maria had heard so many false names she scarcely bothered to register suspicion.

'And are your mother and father still living?'

'My mother only.'

'You are very pretty, very nice.'

The girl barely reacted. Most young Malay girls giggled at compliments but there was a hard core here, a passive negation in her manner. Yet she *was* pretty, and Anna Maria was sure she had European blood in her family somewhere; her skin was dark olive, her nose slightly upturned but sharp at the bridge not broad, her eyes round and her hair finer than that of most full-blooded Asiatics.

'A pretty girl like you should have a husband.' Another bleak silence. That was it then. Husband had run away, maybe chopped up by the terrorists, who could say?

'What work are you hoping to find?' The rickshaw boy was pacing steadily past the conglomeration of white buildings that formed Raffles Hotel. A Union Jack hung limply from a pole over the entrance.

'Maybe I can be *amah* in an English house. I speak good English, I work hard.'

Anna Maria drew in a hissing breath and shook her head.

'Very hard work to find. Do you have references? Someone who can introduce you?'

The younger woman's proud poise wavered as she shook her head. References were something that had never occurred to her.

Anna Maria's house was a weatherbeaten, turquoise building in the old colonial-Georgian style, with semi-circular fan lights above the upper windows. Ferns gushed from the clogged guttering. Ayeshah's room was a small one at the back, with a high window, one foot square, bare floor boards and an iron bed. The

Chinese disliked building houses with big windows at the back, in case they gave access to bad spirits. Ayeshah walked around it with an animal-like curiosity, agreed the rent and closed the door behind Anna Maria with a calm finality which inhibited any further overtures.

Next morning, trim and serious in a fresh sarong, Ayeshah asked Anna Maria how to get to the quarters where the rich Europeans lived, and walked off briskly. All day she tramped from one villa to another, knocking on doors with diminishing confidence. In most houses she never saw the owners, only the Chinese houseboys who brusquely sent her away, angry that some stupid village girl should not understand the system of nepotism and introduction which regulated candidates for household jobs.

She had known, of course, that in leaving the village and coming to a town she was leaving a rural Malay life, and moving in to a harsh Chinese world, but she had not expected to feel so much of an alien. At night Ayeshah returned, overwhelmed by her failure and by the horrible size of the city, which had been quite outside her ability to imagine. The grey paved streets seemed to extend for ever in all directions, crowded with busy people who had no pity for her strangeness.

She bought rice for a few cents from a hawker. It tasted smoky and rancid, as if it had been cooked with dirty oil, and it was expensive, but she was too hungry to care.

'Maybe you will be luckier in the Chinese houses,' Anna Maria suggested. While Ayeshah was out, Anna Maria had gone into her room, using her duplicate key, and examined her small bag of belongings. She found the money in the pillow lining. There was more than she had expected, enough for a month if the girl were careful, which she seemed to be.

With new heart, waving gaily to Anna Maria as the landlady leaned out of her first-floor window to hang her canary's cage in the sun, Ayeshah set off the next morning for Emerald Hill. Again she went from door to door, this time of smartly painted terraced villas with small gardens; she quickly realized that each house had only one or two servants. The houseboys were older and angrier than the others, the doors slammed behind her instead of closing civilly.

At the end of the day she was so tired that she spent precious dollars on a rickshaw back to Anna Maria's street. She had found out that seven other girls also lived there, but when she left in the morning they were all asleep, and none of them were in when she returned in the evening. By the time the other lodgers clattered up the bare wood stairs, Ayeshah was sleeping the sound sleep of a young, healthy and exhausted girl. When she paid the rickshaw boy she asked him where the richest people in Singapore lived, and how she should get there.

Next day Ayeshah took a bus ride out to the prosperous suburb the rickshaw driver had named, and continued her pilgrimage in search of work, walking through huge gardens with swimming pools, to knock at the servants' entrances of vast, pastel mansions owned by Chinese millionaires. By now, although she did not know it, she had a pleading look in her eye and a plaintive tone in her voice that invited yet more rejection. The butlers were grave, polite but regretful. Returning at the end of the hours of daylight she lost her way, and wandered the empty streets for hours, panic fluttering in her chest, until at last the slope of an avenue was familiar and she found the bus-stop.

From the bus-stop in Victoria Street there was only a short distance to walk to Anna Maria's house, but now it was quite dark and the bars were filling with seamen and soldiers. She passed the junction of Bugis Street, scenting noodles from the food hawkers' barrows, and paused; should she spend more money on food?

A large rat stuck its nose out of the deep guttering by her feet, took fright and retreated. As Ayeshah was counting her money there was shouting in a bar to her left, then fighting men fell out into the street. Chinese and Malays were punching and butting each other, some waving broken bottles. Tension between the two races ran high in the city, needing only an incident to transform hatred into violence. The fighting men crashed to the ground at Ayeshah's feet. Totally unaccustomed to both drunkenness and violence, she stumbled away in horror as the bigger man knelt on the other's chest and repeatedly smashed his head on the granite paving-stones. Ayeshah ran home as fast as her swathed sarong would allow and bolted up the stairs.

Anna Maria sat at her dilapidated roll-top desk on the first-floor landing, with a lean, brown-skinned Chinese man in a black suit. As Ayeshah breathlessly scrambled to the top of the stairs, they turned and rose as if they had been waiting for her.

'Poor girl, have you had an accident?' Anna Maria rushed to her side and made her sit down. Ayeshah recovered her breath; she saw that blood from the street fight had splashed her feet and legs. An instant later she realized that she had dropped all her money in terror.

'No, please. I am quite all right. I just saw some men fighting in the street and it frightened me.'

'Sit, please. Have some tea.' Anna Maria poured the translucent brew into a tiny rose-printed cup. 'You are sure you are not hurt?'

Ayeshah sipped and shook her head. The tea was tepid and bitter, witnessing a long wait. She sensed that there was business to be done with the Chinese, and looked at him expectantly.

'May I introduce my good friend Hong Seung? He has come here asking my help and I suggested that he should wait and meet you.' Hong Seung was courteous. He offered her an English cigarette which she refused with a giggle that seemed to reassure them all.

'My honoured friend Anna Maria,' they half-bowed to each other, 'says you are looking for work. I heard this and thought it was good luck, for I need a girl to work for me. I own a laundry, not far from here. My business is good and I need one more girl to wash. Too many boys in my family and no girls. Girls wash better. I think I ask Anna Maria, she know plenty girls.' Relief cleared Ayeshah's panic-filled head instantly.

'What will you pay me?' she asked stiffly.

'I am still a poor man, I cannot pay much – five dollars is all I can manage.'

It was, she knew, more than an *amah's* wages, but then she had to pay Anna Maria and buy her own food. Still, it was enough. She nodded. Anna Maria and Hong Seung smiled at each other.

'You come tomorrow,' said Hong Seung, showing a mouth full of gold teeth. Stupid girl, he thought, I would have paid her six if she had asked for it.

Hong Seung's laundry was a traditional Chinese shop-house under a stucco arcade, with a slab of granite as a bridge over the deep monsoon drain and a red tin shrine tacked to a pillar with dying flowers and burning joss sticks on it. In the front of the shop four men in singlets and shorts ironed on tables, with modern irons wired to the electric lighting circuit in the ceiling.

At the back of the building was a courtyard where the laundry was washed and dried. At intervals bicycle carts drew up at the wrought-iron gate in the back alley, and huge bundles of sheets, table cloths and soiled uniforms were dragged inside the yard.

It was not easy work. First the bundles had to be sorted and counted. The washing was then boiled in huge old-fashioned coppers, with fragments of soap chopped with a cleaver from big brown blocks. When it was judged to be clean, Ayeshah had to reach into the boiling water with her bare hands and pull the linen out, then rinse it in clear water at the shallow sinks against the wall.

There was one tap at the side of the yard. The heavy, wet sheets were fed through a mangle, and stretched on bamboo poles to dry. There were two children to help her, a six-year-old to fan the fires under the coppers and keep them fed with charcoal, and a girl of eight.

At the end of the first day, Ayeshah's hands were scalded red and her back ached painfully. She was tottering with exhaustion by the time she spread the last sheet on its pole. The courteous Hong Seung was not about, but his mother, a vastly fat woman with grey hair in a bun, glowered at her.

Next morning she was greeted by a screaming tirade from the old woman, most of which she could not understand. What, finally, she made out was that she had muddled up two bundles of laundry. There was no system of laundry marks, and she was expected to be able to tell each customer's sheets by eye alone.

The older child went silently about her work, but the younger one watched her with something more than curiosity. Tired, demoralized, disoriented, with an inner core of numbness from a much greater wound, Ayeshah unresistingly let events take their course.

Somewhere in her thoughts she knew with complete certainty that she was being tricked, that she had been marked as a victim from the moment she met Anna Maria at the quayside. Somewhere else in her mind she was willing to assign her destiny to others. Her will had been drained by a vast grief; while her physical being could be a puppet, her soul was hiding, repairing its wound. It was immaterial who pulled the strings.

At the end of the day a bundle of gravy-stained table cloths arrived, and Ayeshah left them soaking overnight. In the morning, she found that a blue *amah's* blouse had been in the bundle, and had stained the entire copperful of white linen, which now included two fine gentlemen's shirts.

'Quickly,' she ordered the elder child, 'fill the copper with fresh water and boil these again – maybe we can get the stains out.' The child shrugged and did what she asked without any sense of urgency.

Ayeshah battered frantically at the shirts on the washing stones, and got them back to an even, slightly tainted whiteness. By the evening the backs of her hands were covered with small blisters from repeated immersion in the scalding water. Larger blisters were swelling painfully under some of her cuticles. When she woke the next morning her hands were crusted where the blisters had wept. When she tried to move her fingers, the pain was like fire.

'Where is Hong Seung?' she asked the fat woman at the week's end. To her surprise her employer materialized at once from the front of the shop.

'Forgive my weakness and foolishness,' she began, half muttering words she sensed were useless, 'but I cannot do this work. It is too hard for me – now I can't put my hands in the water at all, you see.' She held her hands out, and Hong Seung made a show of turning on the single naked light bulb to examine them.

'Bad.' He nodded. 'Hands no good, too soft.'

'So I cannot work here any more,' Ayeshah's voice sounded a little more confident, now the Chinese had accepted her incapacity.

'No more work,' he agreed.

'We agreed my wages would be five dollars,' Ayeshah followed up nervously again.

'You want money?' Hong Seung reached into the pocket of his shirt and pulled out a folded scrap of paper. Resting it on a three-legged table, he took a pencil stub from behind his ear and covered the paper with Chinese characters.

'Solook,' he motioned to Ayeshah to read over his shoulder.

'Two loads washing you mix up – deliver late, customer angry, not pay. Ten dollar. Table cloths stain, no good any more. Eighteen dollar. Two shirts no good, very expensive shirt, customer very angry. Forty dollar. Use much soap, we say one dollar. Sixty-nine dollar. You earn five dollar, OK. You pay me sixty-four dollar now, please.'

One by one the other laundry workers gathered round. Ayeshah looked in horror from one angry face to another. They yammered at each other in Chinese, went over Hong Seung's figures among themselves, nodded and smacked the paper emphatically to express their agreement. Ayeshah caught words she knew, 'lazy', 'stupid girl', 'much money'. She began to cry. Finally Hong Seung marched her back to Anna Maria's house.

'Bad girl, she bad girl,' he shouted, shoving her up the stairs, 'she get money now, pay me.'

Choking back her tears, Ayeshah ran upstairs to her room and felt inside the pillow case. There was nothing there. Frantically she pulled out the pillow, turned the threadbare covering inside out and shook it. She looked under the bed, pulled the sheet off the grimy mattress, turned out her bag, scattered her clothes. Her money was gone.

Anna Maria was standing with Hong Seung in front of the littered desk when Ayeshah came down stairs. She was angry, but restrained by her harboured sense of predestination.

'Anna Maria,' she said, trying not to sniff. 'Someone has stolen my money.'

'Nonsense. You're lying. You had no money,' Anna Maria shouted in anger, no longer poised or sophisticated. 'You came here with a handful of dollars and now you can't pay me for the room. I've heard that story before, miss.'

'But I had a lot of money – in my pillow.'

'You had nothing. I know, I changed your linen. Stupid girl, you think you can swindle me? Or my friend Hong Seung? Prison is the place for girls like you.'

Roused by the shouting, two of the other lodgers appeared, sleep-smudged faces leaning over the top floor banister rail.

'Susie! Get dressed and go and find a constable.'

'No, no please,' Ayeshah was so scared she could hardly put the words together. 'I'll pay you, both of you. My hands will be good soon, I'll work hard . . .'

Hong Seung spat. 'Hands no good, too soft.'

A lanky Chinese girl came down the stairs yawning and scrab-bling inside a white plastic handbag.

'You want I go to police house?' she asked Anna Maria.

'Yes – go now, tell them to come and arrest this little thief. Hurry up!'

Ayeshah screamed and flung herself at Anna Maria, who furiously shoved her away so she fell in a sobbing heap on the stairs. Three more girls watched from the top floor, muttering excitedly. Hong Seung, Anna Maria and the scrawny Chinese girl talked briskly, deciding something among themselves. Then Susie helped Ayeshah up.

'OK. All fixed,'Anna Maria announced. 'You work with Susie at the dance hall. If you're good and work hard, get lots of tips, you can pay us what you owe. You're very lucky, Susie is sorry for you, she has asked us to be kind. Myself, I would have you arrested, but she says no. Do what she says and maybe you won't have to go to prison.'

There was more discussion between Hong Seung and the Chinese girl, and eventually they seemed to reach an agreement and the laundry-owner left. Susie pulled Ayeshah upstairs with her and made her sit on her bed while she finished her preparations for the night's work. She scooped up swags of her coarse black hair and pinned them into a chignon like those worn by the European women, then began spitting into a little case of mascara, and stirring up a paste with a brush. Ayeshah was fascinated, in spite of the horrors of the argument with Hong Seung and Anna Maria. She had never seen a woman use makeup before.

Two other girls sat with her, smoking English cigarettes. They pinched her arms and the upper swell of her breast, laughed, and nodded encouragingly.

'Pretty titties,' said one, 'Tommies will like.' Susie smiled at her in the pink-tinted mirror. 'We get brassiere tomorrow. Tommies like brassiere, make titties bigger.' She rolled up her pink sweater and showed Ayeshah a white cotton bra of near-surgical strength hanging loose over her own concave chest and forming a bridge of greyish elastic between her sharp shoulder-blades.

They took a taxi to the dance hall, an extravagance which hinted to Ayeshah that she was moving into a more lavish world. The Miss Chatterbox Rendez-Vous was a big smoke-tainted room with flapping Shanghai doors at the entrance like the doorway of a cowboy saloon. There was a space cleared for dancing in the middle of the room, a modern jukebox, and a row of tin tables, some covered with oilcloth. Each girl planted her handbag by a seat at the table before joining the gossiping group around the jukebox. They played wailing Chinese ballads until the first British soldiers began to slope in, then switched to Western big band music.

Susie rapidly instructed her in the art of making 'plenty dollar' as a taxi-dance girl.

'Choose young boy only,' she advised, 'he come quick, no trouble. Be sweet with him, when he say "Missy, you pretty," you ask him if he like long time, all night. Ask ten dollar for make love, five more dollar all night. You must get money first – very important.'

She opened the white plastic handbag and groped among the mess of cosmetics inside. 'Here. Put rubber johnny, then you never get sick.' She put a packet of three contraceptives in Ayeshah's barely comprehending hand, looking at her curiously. Pretty girl, but very quiet. No wonder the Chinese were the best taxi-dance girls; they knew it was important to smile a lot and be brisk and businesslike.

Ayeshah watched blandly as Susie began work. A meaty middle-aged sergeant approached her with a book of paper tickets in his hand. She tore one out, tucked it into her handbag and danced with him, gazing blankly into space and holding him at arms' length. When the song finished, she returned quickly to her seat and took a ticket from a skinny private with the prematurely aged look of lifelong borderline malnutrition. She snaked her body close to him, grinding her pelvis into his. She gazed glaze-eyed over the boy's shoulder, but her right hand, Ayeshah noticed, was between their bodies, hard at work. At the end of the music they had a short discussion and Susie triumphantly came back to collect her handbag.

'Be lucky!' she called to Ayeshah, giving her a wink over her shoulder as she tripped out of the door on the boy's arm. Ayeshah smiled a tight, nervous grimace and looked up to see another soldier, slight with curled fair hair, with a dance ticket in his outstretched hand. She took it and, having no handbag, rolled it into the waist of her sarong.

Western dancing was not so different from the Malay *joget*, she found, but harder to do with your bodies pressed together. The fair soldier smelt nauseatingly of beer; he was sweating and breathing heavily; his penis was hardening fast – she could feel it against her body. Timidly, Ayeshah slid her hand to the man's crotch as she had seen Susie do, wincing with pain as she scraped her blistered skin. Fortunately, he seemed not to notice her clumsy hesitancy.

'How much is it?' he asked, giving her a smile and pulling away a little to look at her with those funny blue eyes. She said ten dollars, and he nodded and turned for the door, wrapping her arm over his proprietorially. The men she assumed were his friends shouted things as they walked into the street.

In the taxi he at once unzipped his trousers and pulled her hand to his crotch, not seeming to notice the weeping blisters. He flipped half the buttons of her blouse open, muttering 'Gor!' as he felt her naked breasts. Was this the time to make him pay for all night, she wondered, fumbling desperately in the mess of unfamiliar garments for the slim, rubbery penis, which was already oozing drops of fluid. Susie was right about choosing the young ones.

In her room, breathing louder still, he helped her undo the remaining buttons, impatiently tugged the sarong off, then tore frantically at his own clothes, in his impatience getting his trousers tangled with his heavy boots. Ayeshah remembered Susie's advice, and reached for the packet of contraceptives which had fallen to the floor from the sarong folds. He snatched the packet from her and pulled the sleeve of powdered rubber over his penis with shaking fingers.

'You pay now, please,' she half whispered, and he stuffed notes in her hand. Then he was on top of her, stabbing wildly around her soft entrance, muttering incoherently with the anxiety that he was going to climax before getting inside the body he had hired. Ayeshah felt no pleasure, no pain, nothing beyond the discomfort of the prodding penis. He was much clumsier than her husband and automatically she helped him.

'Easy does it,' she said, the English phrase rising like a forgotten memory. With delicate fingers she guided him, and after a few violent plunges it was over. She slid from beneath him and got off the bed at once, not quite believing that she had done what she had done. The man too sat up, found cigarettes and matches, lit up, doubled the pillow over and lay back, an arm behind his head. He looked at her.

Once, in the village, a Japanese truck had killed one of her father's buffalo. By the time she and her brother had found the stiff-legged carcase, a monitor lizard had already gorged on it and was standing aggressively over the remainder. They had laughed to see the great jungle scavenger, already stuffed with food, greedily raking the meat with its swivelling reptile eyes, too full to eat more but too obsessed with the prospect of plenty to know that it had eaten enough. The lizard had been as big as a man. This man was looking at her now with the same greedy fascination.

'Well, kitten,' he said, blowing out a stream of blue smoke. 'How about all night, then?'

'Ten dollars.' Ayeshah hardly knew she'd said it. He licked his lips, his eyes roaming hungrily over her flesh.

'The other girls ask five.' The pained tone in his voice pleased her. So it hurt to give money – well it felt good to hurt a man, especially a white man.

'I ask ten.' She smiled, exhilarated. Ayeshah had animation now, the puppet no longer needed her strings to be pulled.

'I'll want my money's worth.'

'Of course.' She walked back to the bed and sat on the hard edge, picked the cigarette from between his fingers, put his hand on her breast and crushed her flesh into his fingers. 'Give me all the money now.' He gave it to her, feeling a big man, enhanced in his reputation as a jammy sod, having found a more expensive, better-looking tart than those Chinese bints with toastrack ribs.

Susie took Ayeshah to the Chinese doctor who gave her a bottle of blackish liquid to heal her hands. The wound in her soul seemed to mend as fast, as she acquired the skill of getting money out of men, Western men. Every dollar Ayeshah tucked into her new red plastic handbag seemed to give her more drive. Her aptitude was astonishing, Hong Seung told Anna Maria. His brother (who owned the Miss Chatterbox Rendez-Vous) reported that she was the most popular girl there, making so much money she barely bothered to collect the 20 cents per ticket that she earned for the dancing only. His brother didn't like it, when she turned up every few weeks with a stack of tickets to demand her dollars.

The other girls didn't like her either. When they tried to charge her prices, the soldiers just laughed. They were in awe of her ability to do business. Ayeshah was so unlike the lazy Malay girls; they were never good whores, they always had a bad conscience about the work and a sort of wistful apathy that the Tommies did not like.

'She is more like a Chinese, she thinks only of good business.' Anna Maria approved. 'But she sees with Western eyes. I have noticed this. I too, see that-way. Now she buys clothes and she chooses what pleases the British. But to the Chinese I think she looks ugly.' Hong Seung nodded, holding out his cup for more tea. Ayeshah's working dress was a skintight, scarlet silk cheongsam embroidered with chrysanthemums, an old-fashioned party dress to his eyes. The Chinese girls mostly wore Western dress, but sweaters and skirts looked wrong on them, accentuating their bow legs or concave chests. The cheongsam made Ayeshah look even less oriental, setting off the poise of her head and her rounded breasts, but it matched exactly the British boys' vision of an exotic oriental woman. In addition she had developed a proud, mysterious smile which seemed to promise numerous delights. The boys were too young and too drunk to find those delights, but this did not seem important.

Money gave Ayeshah an almost physical thrill. In the village, money had been almost irrelevant. The *padi* fields, the chickens, her little garden had provided a rich abundance of food; your husband made anything you needed, or you traded something you had for it. Before leaving the village, she had scarcely ever handled more than two dollars. But in the city, she realized by instinct, money was everything, and so easy to get.

Once or twice, when an unusually drunk soldier had passed out in her room, she had got dressed again and gone out to work Bugis Street, perching at the food-hawkers' tables to pick up merchant seamen and taking customers into a side alley for sex in a doorway. They liked you to do it with your mouth, and were older and slower than the soldiers, but she could double her money for the night with two or three of them.

The Chinese doctor gave her a medicine she served to her clients as snake wine, the famous Eastern aphrodisiac. It was expensive, and all it did was to make them sleep, but they dreamed orgiastically and never complained. The doctor treated her with extreme courtesy because she was a good customer, but in private he despised her as an unenlightened amateur courtesan who had no interest in the erotic arts. This was because she showed no interest in the medicine which he himself had formulated which could prolong the rigidity of the Jade Stalk all night.

Acquiring financial sophistication from a starting point of almost total ignorance, Ayeshah developed a natural fascination with all the ways of money. For the first month, afraid that her new-made riches would go the same way as the money she had hidden in her pillow, she carried it in the lining of her handbag. She grew increasingly fearful of theft and wondered where she could hide the money. Where did Susie keep hers? Susie could not advise her – most of her earnings were sent to Shanghai, to the parents who had sold her to a pimp five years earlier.

Ayeshah dared not ask the treacherous Anna Maria, but she knew she must secrete her rent money somewhere. One week Ayeshah paid Anna Maria a month's rent in advance, then woke early and watched her landlady all day through the crack of her door until she saw her lock her own rooms and prepare to go out. Ayeshah followed Anna Maria, in her distinctive black-and-white frock, through the crowded streets to Orchard Road, where she went into a modern building with heavy, wooden doors. A few moments later she came out and returned to her house.

The building, Ayeshah discovered, was a bank. Inside, a clerk, a clean and prosperous-looking Chinese boy, explained that banks would store her money for her and even pay her to do it. It seemed too good to be true. At Miss Chatterbox's, Ayeshah asked the other girls, who were scornful and said banks were for Europeans and could not be trusted.

'Stupid women, what do you know?' sneered Ali, the Malay waiter. 'Banks are safe even in war, I know. In my village the district officer went to the planters' club when the Japanese came and took all the whisky and put it in the bank. When the Japanese left it was all there, and he sold the batch for a much higher price.'

'But all the banks are Chinese?' Ayeshah was unable to believe in the trustworthiness of such a mercantile race.

'Not all, we have Malay banks too, Bank Bumiputra is very big, as big as the Chinese banks.'

And so Ayeshah, with relief, emptied the notes from her handbag lining on to the counter of the Bumiputra Bank and opened an account. Because she did not read very well, Ali, the waiter, helped her with the forms. Figures, however, gave her no trouble, and she read and re-read her first bank statement like a holy man reading the Koran.

Two years later Ali arrived at Miss Chatterbox Rendez-Vous at 4 pm to open up, and found the owner, Hong Seung's brother, in bloody joints all over the room. He had been ritually murdered by members of a rival tong, another victim of the endless trade vendettas between the Chinese secret societies. Ali had barely mopped up the blood by the time the first Tommies sauntered through the Shanghai doors. There were more of them than ever now, and on the mainland the Communists were waging a full-scale war.

Ayeshah anticipated that Hong Seung would take over his brother's business, but she returned to Anna Maria's to find her landlady's room stoutly locked and a fat Sikh sprawled on the chair before her desk.

'May I introduce myself?' he spoke elaborately formal English. 'Anna Maria is taking a holiday in Hong Kong and you will pay your rent to me while she is away.'

Ayeshah nodded noncommittally. 'Is there news of her friend Hong Seung?' she asked. 'On holiday' undoubtedly meant that whatever business had got the brother into trouble had also given Anna Maria a fright, and would certainly implicate Hong Seung too.

'He also visits with his family.' The Sikh smiled broadly beneath his crisp, white turban, implying that the evil ways of the Chinese always brought them their just deserts in the end.

From habit, Ayeshah and Susie went to Miss Chatterbox's as usual the next day, and found bamboo scaffolding outside and a band of coolies hacking at the walls. On the opposite pavement, a tall, slender man in a spotless white suit was examining a large plan with a European man. When he saw the girls he quickly crushed the sheet of paper into the white man's arms and called to them.

'*Mesdemoiselles!* Over here, please!' He shook their hands in turn. 'I am Philippe Thoc and this is now my club. How do you do.' His English had a strong accent they did not recognize, but from his name they guessed him to be at least half Vietnamese.

He bought them tea in a shop across the road. 'Unhappily it will be two or three weeks, I think, before we can re-open again, but I hope you will consider it worth your while to wait.' He offered fat French cigarettes, in a gold case, which they took out of politeness and smoked cautiously. 'When we open the club it will be quite different. My plan is to have a club for officersno more smelly soldiers, getting drunk and making trouble.' His eyes sparkled enthusiastically under long, ivory lids, and Ayeshah and Susie felt themselves drawn into his vision without really understanding it. 'No more taxi-dance – it's not chic. My plan is for a real nightclub with hostesses, a nice little band, a nice bar. We will serve only champagne. All I need is pretty girls like you, with good English, a little charm. And clean.' He lolled back on his chair and watched the girls smile guardedly back at him.

The Eurasian one – and now that Ayeshah's nocturnal way of life had removed her from day-long sunlight it was not possible to say with certainty that she was a Malay – was ideal, he thought. Pretty cat-face, intelligent, you could see it in the eyes, but not tough. Nothing special about the Chinese, but girls had their little attachments and it was wise to respect them.

For two weeks Philippe paid six of the girls half wages to be sure of having a skeleton staff. He hired two more waiters, and a Filipino jazz combo. The outside of the club was painted vivid pink, with the window and door frames in shiny black, and a black canopy over the door and the pavement. A pink neon sign proclaimed simply 'Club'. Philippe lectured the girls for hours on their duties as hostesses, and posted a long list of rules for them in the newly constructed office above the bar. No talking except in English, no powdering their noses at the tables, no girl to wear laddered stockings or clothes which needed mending. Evening dress to be worn all the time. Girls must smile. Girls must be polite.

'He's mad,' said Susie flatly. 'Where he think we will get money to buy dresses that he wants?' Ayeshah shrugged, pausing as she tried a new eyebrow pencil.

'He's been paying us to do nothing for a fortnight, don't forget. I don't think he's so crazy; he told me he ran a club like this in Saigon and made a lot of money.' Philippe talked a lot about his club in Saigon, and about Paris, the place where he had been born. Ayeshah had no idea where Paris was, but he made it sound as if the streets were paved with gold. She was impatient to find out what reality lay behind the talk of elegance, wealth and high society.

Crossly, Susie stubbed out her cigarette. Philippe wore a heavy gold watch and gold cufflinks. His clothes were of a quality neither of them had ever seen. It seemed likely that he had recently made a lot of money. 'If he do so well in Saigon, why he leave?'

'Who can say? I suppose there was some trouble. It isn't our business.' Ayeshah kept her eyes on her reflection in Susie's pink mirror. 'Take my old, red dress if you like. I'll buy a new one.'

What she did not tell Susie was that Philippe had twice taken her for a cocktail at Raffles Hotel. He had shown her the immense ballroom with a polished floor gleaming like a lake, and the swimming pool and the terrace shaded by the fan-shaped traveller's palms. Talking non-stop in his curious accent, he opened her mind to the world beyond the island of Singapore, and hinted that, if she threw her lot in with him, she would have a passport to wealth and enterprise beyond her dreams.

Philippe had three reasons for doing this. One was that he sensed that the other girls admired her, and that they would do what she said. The second was that he saw exactly how her sensual appeal could be marketed. The third was that she appealed to him sexually. There was something else, of which even this experienced pedlar of flesh was unaware. The wider the vistas he painted for her and the better Ayeshah understood what he could do for her, the more uneasy she became about their relationship. She did not want a man to have power over her, any kind of power, physical or financial.

'See that boy?' he asked her, pointing with his cigarette at the Raffles *maître d'hôtel*, who was showing a party of Europeans to seats on the terrace. 'How would you like to do what he does?'

Ayeshah was puzzled. 'Just that?'

'Maybe a few other things. Look after the other girls. Help me in the office, perhaps. It's an easy job – all you have to do is remember the customers, smile at them, keep them happy.'

She pursed her lips doubtfully, a mannerism which she had observed that Western men found very attractive. Philippe responded with the leap of interest she recognized. Then he asked her to dance. He moved with a pleasing, confident grace but his hands held her with a faint tremor, like rushes shivering in the breeze. Ayeshah dipped her eyelids, then again caught his glance, and smiled.

Later he took her back to Anna Maria's and disappeared into the noisy Singapore night. Ayeshah pondered. It gave her no trouble at all to open her legs for the Tommies and take dollars in exchange; but this was an involvement, bound up with the possibility of much bigger money, an entree into a more prosperous world, perhaps a new life far away from this tawdry city. She sensed something in Philippe which was beyond the thrall of physical attachment, beyond the reason of business. Some part of him was beyond control, and that was what she didn't like. She did like his neat head, covered in close curls that brilliantine could not flatten, his mobile face and flat, ivory-skinned body.

When the club opened, Ayeshah, in a new, black brocade cheongsam with frangipani flowers pinned in her chignon, welcomed the customers and seated them as Philippe prompted. The soft, mysterious allure she projected intensified as her confidence grew. Philippe congratulated himself on his judgement and ached to hold the rounded body which the tight dress simultaneously displayed and concealed. She evaded him with a show of flower like modesty which whipped his senses.

She was eager to learn how to cash up the till at the end of the evening, and so was able to evaluate the club's success. The first week, in which Philippe bought his friends drinks all night, was bad. The second week was worse, because few people came to the club. Then one or two friends of friends returned, and a regular clientele was established. Ayeshah was impressed. They were men with gold watches and gold cigarette cases, some in uniforms decorated with gold braid. They spent lavishly. They wore silk socks. They invited the girls to private parties in luxurious mansions, and sent their chauffeurs to collect them.

Ayeshah decided that Philippe's hints of glamour and prosperity had a basis in fact, and calculated that he was an opportunity she could not allow to pass. She relaxed the barrier of reserve she had put up against him. At the end of the club's sixth week, they worked out the accounts together, in the dead of night. When the final figure, a profit well above his projections, was written down Philippe threw aside his pencil and embraced her with joy. Instantly they were kissing, something she had not done for years, because she never kissed the Tommies. The feeling was sweet but the memories were painful; Ayeshah stamped them down and let physical sensations swell up to numb her mind. He picked her up and carried her slowly upstairs to his apartment.

Philippe was a delicate, elaborate lover, an erotic gourmet who delighted in finding new sensations for her to try. In his bedroom on the top floor, he nuzzled and nibbled her body with his pearly teeth, laughing with delight. Ayeshah found it relaxing to do nothing and have no concern over the progress of their lovemak-ing, no need to finish and get on to more business. It was also curious to have thrilling sensations aroused in her body while her mind was detached. Her deadened senses came to life with feelings that were close to physical pain, as if scarred limbs were bending across their wounds.

It was almost midday before they came downstairs, to Ali's knowing smiles and Susie's black sulk. Next day Philippe gave Susie the sack and hired in her place an angular Goanese girl with inch-long fingernails.

Philippe had no idea that the captivatingly primitive beauty whom he intended to transform into his ideal companion was already anticipating the day when he would have outlived his usefulness. He was not much concerned that her sexual response to him was muted, since in his experience a young whore who had detached herself from her body in this way could easily be reawakened by a patient, skilful lover.

He was momentarily concerned when he entered the club one evening and found her in a state of great agitation, squabbling with Ali, the barman, and rushing around the small, dark room like a furious cat, too disturbed to register his arrival.

'A man came to see her today, that's what's upset her,' Ali told him. 'Tall, thin European with glasses – I've seen him before. Always the same reaction, Ayeshah's like a witch for hours afterwards.'

'Who is he?'

Ali shrugged. Philippe assumed that her visitor was an old protector. He judged that the situation required instant action, and, catching her by the elbow, hustled her upstairs.

'I don't care for you entertaining your lovers while I'm out,' he told her, shoving her into their room and twisting her arm painfully.

'I have no lover, you're crazy,' she told him, struggling with all her strength.

He slapped her face hard, but carefully, so she would not be marked. 'It's of no interest to me who he is, but if he comes here again he can take you with him. I shall throw you out on the street, just like that. You belong to me and I won't have you making a fool of me. Understand?'

She stopped twisting in his grasp and, although she was shaking with anger he saw to his surprise a flash of intense calculation in her eyes.

'The man who came today was not my lover. I had a lover once, but not this man. He only brings me news of my village, my family, that's all.' There was a hint of desperation in her voice as she continued. 'If you think I'm lying, I will make sure when he comes again that you are here. But I need to see him – don't you understand, Philippe? How else will I know how my – my family is?'

Philippe was startled. He had expected screams, rage, an attack with her fingernails, in short a classic jealous fight, a struggle over the demarcation lines of their relationship in which he would assert his strength and Ayeshah would capitulate after a routine display of temperament.

'You little whore!' He hit her again, less carefully. 'Don't lie to me – do you think I'm stupid, eh?' He raged on, fighting his own sense of bewilderment as much as Ayeshah, who did not resist him and barely responded. Eventually he tired of the one-sided drama and half threw her down the narrow staircase, commanding her to continue her work.

Philippe rapidly forgot the incident. He forgot many things of significance. Soon Ayeshah identified the section of his soul which was out of her grasp; every night Philippe smoked opium at an expensive parlour uptown. He traded the drug, and others, to wealthy Europeans. The discovery pleased her – now she knew she could destroy Philippe when the time was right.

CHAPTER NINE

'THAT YOUNG lady will be a countess before the end of the season.'

In the cacophonous bustle of her dance, Cathy's sharp ears picked out the conversation between her mother and a distant Bourton relation. There was no doubt they were talking about her. Everyone was talking about her and Charlie Coseley. The previous week, William Hickey had named her 'Deb of the Year', printing the picture taken by Tim Studd and a caption mentioning that she was 'escorted everywhere by Charles Coseley, 29, Britain's most eligible Earl and the heir to the Marquess of Shrewton. Friends expect a wedding announcement soon.'

Bettina looked more relaxed than Cathy had seen her for months. She was not drunk; she was conspicuously sipping only orange juice, but that in itself meant nothing. Cathy could tell that her mother was sober because the self-pitying mood and vicious tone into which she fell when intoxicated were absent, and instead her behaviour was grimly reserved.

'I'm quite sure Cathy will play her cards right – no doubt about that. She's always known exactly how to get her way,' she heard Bettina answer with complacent spite.

'She has certainly made the Coseley boy come to heel,' the other woman continued. 'No more Chelsea tarts and nightclubs, so they tell me. His parents must be delighted, after all this time. The only son, of course.'

Cathy moved out of earshot, hurrying to the kitchen to check that the caterers were coping with the antiquated equipment. They had imported a battery of portable ovens powered by bottled gas to be sure of getting five hundred portions of quail stuffed with grapes to the tables at an acceptable temperature. The old kitchen, fitted out by Lady Davina in the twenties with the latest thing in solid oak cabinets, was as hot and crowded as hell and, she realized, no place for a girl who wanted to keep her blue Laura Ashley gown in milkmaid-fresh condition.

'Darling, where have you been? They're playing "Pretty Flamingo" and I've been looking for you everywhere. Stop being the perfect hostess and take care of me.' Charlie swirled her into his arms and started nuzzling her neck in the way he knew made ordinary girls go limp in his grasp and start begging for sex. He caressed Cathy without any expectation that she would do this. In three months of intensive courtship she had often gone limp in his arms, but stead-fastly refused to have sex. The defence of Cathy's virginity had been conducted according to rules of battle which, had either of them realized it, were as time-honoured as any principles of military strategy. They followed the pattern of relationships of young men and women which had changed very little in 2000 years of history.

Charlie at first had no greater interest in Cathy than in any other pretty, attain-able girl. He expected to seduce her within a few weeks and forget her just as quickly. He had taken her to dinner and on to Annabel's twice, frightened her a little by driving his E-Type Jaguar at 100 mph along Chelsea Embankment, kissed her very thoroughly at his pad, cursed the invention of pantyhose and said, 'Let's go to bed.'

'No,' said Cathy.

Charlie did a lot more kissing, throwing in a few of the tricks he knew were good for raising the temperature, like squeezing her breasts and tracing whorls in her ear with his tongue. Cathy was far too strung out with anxiety to respond.

'No, please, Charlie,' she said, 'I don't like it.' This was not the correct reaction. Most girls said no but implied that Charlie should not abandon hope – they said, 'I don't know you well enough.' That was the approved code.

Cathy wriggled away as soon as Charlie started snaking his hand under her skirt. At this point, the limited intellectual faculty possessed by Britain's most eli-gible earl acknowledged the possibility that he was dealing with a girl of little sexual experience.

'You're not a virgin, are you?' he demanded.

'Yes, of course,' Cathy replied. He pulled away and took his hands off her.

'But why? Don't you want to lose it?'

'No – not until my honeymoon. I want to wear white on my wedding day and deserve it.'

'My God, how can you be so straight? For Christ's sake, it's 1965. Look, don't worry, I'll be very gentle, I promise. You'll love every minute of it.' He pulled her close to him again and pulled up her skirt with determination. 'Let me make love to you, Cathy. You're driving me crazy.'

'No, Charlie, stop doing that.'

'Why? Don't you like it?' He trickled his fingers up the inside of her thigh with all the erotic skill he could summon.

'Of course I like it, but what's the point if it's not leading anywhere?'

'Only because you won't let it. Oh come on, Cathy. Let me turn you on. I'm a fabulous lover, everybody says so.'

'Go and screw everybody then, if they like it so much.'

'Well, you're certainly a waste of time, aren't you?' he snarled crossly.

Oh heavens, she wailed inwardly, there I go again. Why, why, why can't I keep my big mouth shut? Charlie angrily marched her out to his car, and drove her home in hostile silence.

But the next day, he called her again, and the next evening he attacked her again, this time calling her boring, straight and probably frigid. Cathy was unmoved. She knew Charlie could date dozens of exciting, switched-on and undoubtedly unfrigid girls if he wanted to, but it seemed wise not to tell him this.

Then Charlie switched to the soft approach, and told her he loved her, that she was beautiful, that he'd never met anyone like her and couldn't get her out of his mind. The last two statements were perfectly true. He was aroused and challenged by her virginity and his days at the bank were increasingly passed in daydreams about her ecstatic surrender to him. Behind these fantasies was his belief that since she was a virgin she would be absolutely overpowered with grateful lust once he had initiated her in the delights of sex.

'You'll always remember me,' he told her with mysterious delight. 'Girls always remember the first.' He made a private joke of the idea of her passionate capitulation, but Cathy realized he was half-serious and would not play. He sent her flowers and took her to a chic little jeweller in Beauchamp Place where he bought her a heartshaped gold pendant studded with diamonds.

On his vast, brown velvet sofa he persuaded her to undress little by little, kissed every inch of her and raved over the perfection of her body. Cathy's anxiety faded and her body began to respond to his caresses.

'You'll be wonderful in bed,' he told her. 'You're made for it, darling. It'll be like fucking hot velvet. Oh God, Cathy, *please*.'

'No, Charlie. For heaven's sake, why can't you understand that I mean what I say?' She was sharp because it was an effort now to master her senses. Instantly Charlie was angry again, and dumped her back at Trevor Square.

'Fear nothing, he'll call,' Lady Davina reassured her, knowing exactly what point in the game her protégée had reached.

'I hope so. I do love him,' Cathy sighed.

'What you feel is irrelevant. We must make *him* love you.' And Lady Davina made her return the diamond heart, then bought her a new dress, and took her racing to Royal Ascot, which Cathy found boring and exhausting. Charlie called the house every day, then in desperation called her at Bourton at the weekend. By the time Cathy was found, he was almost angrier than before.

'Where the hell have you been?' he snapped, as if their estrangement had been her caprice alone.

Infuriated as he was, Charlie never used force to get his way because he regarded rape as an admission of failure. He was coming to appreciate that Cathy had a strength of character which he had overlooked. She also had a sharp tongue and a disturbing propensity for telling the truth. Charlie's sex life was operated for public effect, and he was afraid she might make him look foolish if he broke too many rules. Cathy had a core of still seriousness which a more sensitive man would have appreciated at once. Charlie had come upon it slowly, unsuspectingly, and it drew out of him the unaccustomed emotion of respect.

He turned his frustration into humour. 'This man will self-destruct in five seconds if you don't sleep with him,' he intoned like a robot, shuffling along the hall at Bourton.

'Give me your body or I'll join the French Legion,' he demanded, flinging himself on to his knees at her feet in the drawing room.

'If you don't promise to sleep with me now I'll take off all my clothes and dance on the table,' he scribbled on a menu card during a particularly dreary house-party. Cathy laughed, loving him all the more, and relaxed with him so much that eventually one night, in his arms, she felt her body mysteriously align itself, tissue by tissue, into a perfect ring of ecstasy, and then convulse in an orgasm. Charlie was almost as impressed as she was. He had never been positively aware of a woman climaxing with him before, having always ploughed on more or less regardless of his partners' responses.

'Oh God, this is such a waste, darling,' he murmured as he lay next to her.

Inside her own head Cathy heard the voice of Lady Davina counselling, '*Never* speak too soon. Make it clear you will only give yourself to your husband, then say nothing further. Just leave him to work it out.' She sighed, depressed by the sadness following the release of her sexual tension.

And so now she sank reluctantly on to his lap in an alcove in Bourton House and pulled away his fingers as they fumbled with the buttons down the front of her dress. 'Don't undress me here, Charlie. Everyone can see us. Stop it.'

'Stopit, stopit, stopit!' he squawked. 'Who taught this bird to talk? Can't it say anything else?'

'You know I can't. Oh please, Charlie, don't start this argument again, not at my dance. I can't bear it.'

'*You* can't bear it,' he sneered, petulant and rejecting once more. 'At least you're getting your oats. Ungrateful cow.'

'That's not fair, Charlie.'

'Well, *you're* not fair, either.'

'Yes I am. It's my body, and my life, and what I choose to do with them is my affair and nobody else's, and just because you don't like it, you haven't got the right to complain.'

He stood up and glared at her. 'Who's complaining?' Insultingly he thrust his crotch at her face, 'I'm not complaining. Some day you'll find out what you've missed.' He spun round and walked away, leaving her feeling helpless and angry.

The discotheque was throbbing at full volume in the ballroom, where Charlie hauled a bedraggled girl in a semi-transparent smock on to the dance floor. She'd been had by half the men in London already, he knew. Within three dances she had agreed to leave with him. In the carpark he suddenly shoved her down against the body of his Jaguar, and screwed her with violence.

He drove back to London, making her roll joints, and then suck on his penis as he took the car around the clock. In his apartment, he demanded that she perform every degrading act he could think of, and a few she eagerly suggested in addition.

In the middle of Sunday morning, he ordered her to leave without warning, and spent the rest of the day drinking vodka by himself. Next morning, he went to the bank with a vicious headache and a sense of self-disgust.

He held out until Tuesday evening, when he telephoned Cathy and said. 'I'm sorry, darling, I behaved like a spoilt child.' Cathy said nothing, holding her breath. 'Look, Cathy, I want you to meet my parents. Father usually has some people up to shoot at the beginning of August. Will you come and stay?'

'I'd love to.' Cathy didn't dare say any more in case he heard the triumph in her voice. From that moment they both knew exactly where their relationship was heading.

The Marquess of Shrewton, Charlie's father, was a slender, colourless man whose chilly manner disguised much generosity of spirit. He liked Cathy immediately, which did not surprise her since most older men liked her, and he lost no time in talking to her about her relationship with Charlie, which did surprise her since she had expected this approach from his mother. Engagements, after all, ought to be girl talk. Lord Shrewton evidently saw this as a business matter. He looked at Cathy with intense curiosity.

'I knew your father, of course,' his voice was clipped and precise. 'Terrible tragedy. What was behind it, did anyone ever find out?'

'Money. He didn't have much and he spent much more than he had.'

'Didn't the police have some suspicion about blackmail?'

'We were told they did, but they couldn't prove anything.'

The Marquess was looking directly into her eyes. Suddenly Cathy felt as if she were being interrogated.

'Wasn't there some connection with Paris?' he asked.

'There was supposed to be, because he'd been in Paris on the day he . . .' she paused, the grief making it hard to talk even though Daddy had died over a year ago '. . . the day he died,' she finished, summoning all her self-control. Lord Shrewton said nothing but waited for her to continue. 'The police said they couldn't get any cooperation from the French, so they couldn't take things any further. We didn't think there was anything in it, anyway.'

'Why not?'

'Who would want to blackmail Daddy?' she asked, feeling pitifully young and naive.

'You couldn't think of anyone who might want to do that, is that what you're saying?'

'Yes,' Cathy almost whispered. She sensed an odd, almost obsessive, quality in his questioning, but so many people were curious about her father's suicide, though too embarrassed to question her, that it was almost a relief to be openly cross-examined. And, she acknowledged, he had a right to know all the material facts about her background.

Suddenly Lord Shrewton stepped back and smiled with reassurance. 'I should think you're probably right. Your father was very well liked in the City, and the police aren't always as clever as they think they are, in my experience. What about your father's estate – it hasn't been declared bankrupt, I take it?'

'No, we missed that by the skin of our teeth. Daddy's insurance policies were enough to cover what was owing, though they made an awful fuss about paying up. I think the accountants had to juggle the tax around. We had to sell a lot of things, of course. The house and everything.'

'That's too bad. But your mother's coping well, I hear.'

'She's moved into a little flat in Brighton.' Cathy hesitated. This was not the time to confess that if she married into the family she would be extending the blood tie to a chronic alcoholic, but not to mention it seemed like a lie. She compromised. 'I think she gets very down sometimes.'

'To be expected. Terrible shock. You realize you're nothing like the usual run of my son's girlfriends, don't you?'

'Well, so they tell me.'

'They tell you absolutely right.' A pale smile shone behind Lord Shrewton's hornrimmed glasses. 'Dreadful creatures, most of them. My wife didn't share my opinion, but I couldn't see any of them settling down to married life very well. Do you like children?'

'In moderation.' Cathy had no experience of children at all, but saw herself as a wife with two immaculate offspring in velvet-collared coats, shopping serenely in Knightsbridge and feeding the ducks on the pond in Kensington Gardens.

'In moderation.' The Marquess echoed her answer with irony. 'If you want my advice you'll get your family over with as fast as possible then get on and enjoy yourself.' He made a vague gesture around the landscape outside the windows.

Cathy understood him perfectly. What he was saying was that she could do what she liked as long as she gave him an heir to the title and estates. This implied that there might be something distasteful, or to be avoided, in marriage to Charlie, but Cathy was sure she had already seen him at his worst and was confident that he would change once they were married. Marriage to Charlie, as she imagined it, would be an endless tunnel of soft, pink bliss. If only he would ask her.

The next morning, Lord Shrewton telephoned his solicitor in London and then went to find his wife in the winter garden where she was supervising the potting up of the next year's bulbs. Charlie's mother was a plump honey-blonde with a smile as rich as butter, which always seemed a little thinly spread when it was directed at her husband.

He sat her down on the window seat and told her his plans. 'It's all settled,' he began, characteristically abrupt. 'I want to move quickly or the Bourton girl will think better of it. She's sound and sensible, good family, apart from that business with her father; there's no money, of course, but she's the best we'll get, in my opinion. Charlie seems struck, don't you think?'

His wife agreed with reluctance. 'He's gaga over all of them in the beginning.' She disliked Cathy for exactly the same reasons that her husband favoured her; the Marchioness preferred her son to associate with trashy girls so that she could remain the queen of his heart. Cathy, because Charlie was powerfully attracted to her, represented competition for his affections.

'Well if he's gaga enough to marry her, we can redraw the trust, buy them their own London home and increase his personal allowance quite substantially. The lawyers agree with me that the main concern expressed in the trust document is safeguarding the estate as a whole, and when there's an heir, the whole picture changes again.'

His pale grey eyes were gleaming with relish for the unsubtle strategy he had proposed; Lord Shrewton was disturbed by what he could not control, and the notion that all the care he and his forebears had devoted to the establishment of the Coseley fortune might be dissipated in a single generation by the ungovernable stupidity of his only son had unsettled him profoundly for almost ten years. As in many British families, the Coseleys' wealth was tied up in a tangle of legal arrangements, and an addition to the family could provide a useful way of extending this web and restraining the more spendthrift inheritors of the fortune.

He had also observed that his foolish wife took a perverse pride in Charlie's promiscuity. Although Lord Shrewton had consulted her out of innate courtesy, he allowed her no opportunity to object. That afternoon during the shoot, he paired off with Charlie and made plain the fact that the guardians of his inheritance were prepared to offer him a substantial bribe to marry Cathy.

'Oh well, I suppose everyone's got to make the same mistake once,' Charlie acceded after a thoughtful ten-minute silence, in which he balanced the allowance on offer against the money he was accustomed to drop at chemin-de-fer. 'And once I'm hitched you'll all have to stop bleating at last.'

The next day, the August sun blazed in a cloudless sky and the bracken gave off a rich fragrance in the heat. Long alleys had been cleared in the gorse for the convenience of the guns, and Charlie set off for the most distant of them with Cathy bouncing beside him in an old shooting-brake.

Part of Charlie's charm was his confident mastery of momentous occasions; where other, more sincere men were made clumsy and speechless by emotion, he was left in control by his lack of feeling.

'Isn't this bliss?' he murmured at midday, pulling her close to him as they lay on the grass. Invisible in the blue heaven above them a skylark was singing. 'I'd like to lie here forever with you.' He kissed her lips, then her eyelids, then the hollow of her throat. They had almost finished a bottle of very fine champagne, packed in the lunch hamper in an antique silver cooling-jacket so that it remained icy enough to mist the sides of the silver beakers. 'I love you, Cathy.' He'd said it a hundred times before to other girls but she never suspected the fluent ease with which the words rolled from his tongue.

Cathy nestled in his arms, expecting now to feel his deft fingers slip her blouse buttons undone, anticipating the delicious crawl of a caress on her sun-warmed skin. She could hear bees droning faintly, and, to her left, the gun-dog panting in the heat. I can't stand much more of this, she thought, feeling the ache of desire begin again. Why didn't Didi tell me it was going to be such hell? I want him so much I feel as if I am about to burst into flames. Instead of the expected moves, she felt Charlie take her left hand and kiss the palm of it, then sit up, and press the fingers against his cheek. With surprise, she looked up into his chalky blue eyes. 'Darling, I want us to be together always, forever. I want to spend the rest of my life with you, Cathy. Will you marry me? Say you will, please, darling Cathy.'

'What?' She had visualized him saying the words so often, but now when she really heard them she could hardly believe it.

'Not "what", you idiot. "Yes!" Say "Yes, Charlie".'

'Oh yes, Charlie!'

'Yes what?'

'Yes, I'll marry you.'

'And then what?'

'We'll be married?'

'Yes, and then what?'

'We'll have children?'

'No, much more important . . .'

He pushed her back on the scented grass. 'I'll give you something?'

'A ring?'

'More important. Can't you guess? I'll show you. Shut your eyes.'

The sun shone red through her closed eyelids. She heard him moving rapidly nearby, then there was something hot and smooth touching her lips.

'Have some to try now,' he suggested, devilment in his voice. She snapped her eyes open. He had pulled off all his clothes and was holding the neat, narrow head of his erect penis to her mouth.

'Trust you!' Cathy hit him as hard as she could and jumped to her feet. 'Trust you to think of some schoolboy gag to spoil everything.'

He capered around her chanting, like a Cockney barrow boy: 'Try before you buy! Nice 'n' ripe 'n' juicy! Fresh pricks – they're luvverly! Get your fresh prick 'ere!'

The dog, alarmed, scrambled up and bolted straight behind his feet, and the naked Charlie tripped and fell into the wall of harsh bracken with a yell.

Cathy was laughing as she pulled him upright when a group of beaters appeared at a crossroads in the covert and stood stock still with embarrassment. Charlie addressed them with exuberance.

'Don't think the worst of this lovely girl, gentlemen. Allow me to introduce her to you. You should be the first to know. My wife-to-be, the pure, the delightful Miss Catherine Bourton!' To Cathy's amazement the men who were wearing caps tugged at the peaks and the group made a general bow in her direction. 'Soon, of course, to be the new Countess of Laxford!'

The months that followed sped past like the landscape outside an express train. A marriage between two great families like the Coseleys and the Bourtons is generally a matter for lengthy and detailed negotiation on a scale which would not be inadequate for the United Nations General Assembly. Mr Napier, the most junior of the solicitors at Pasterns who dealt with the Bourton trust, spent several afternoons with the Coseley lawyers finding the most advantageous way to join the two of them in law.

'Why is it so difficult? I thought I had no worldly goods to endow anyone with,' Cathy asked.

'It's largely a notional issue, of course. The Coseleys are after some fancy footwork to help them, though it would involve the technical bankruptcy of your father's estate, which I assumed you wouldn't want. But there may be other ways we can accommodate them.'

Cathy felt at times as if she were being made to do a quickstep in a social minefield. The next delicate matter to be resolved was that there was simply no money available for the wedding and reception from the traditional source of matrimonial finance, the bride's father.

'Why be such a perfectionist, darling?' reasoned Davina, who had lived a life of triumphant extravagance. 'You don't need a ghastly gaggle of children following you up the aisle. Two bridesmaids will be quite enough. And you can economize on the flowers and . . .'

'I don't feel I want to make compromises about my wedding.' Cathy eyed the budget with anxiety. 'My wedding day is something I'll remember for the rest of my life.'

'But it is only *one* day, darling, and I'm sure you'll be far too busy to remember anything about it. All I can remember about my wedding was the awful smell of the flowers – hyacinths, I think they were. Too sick-making. I nearly fainted.'

Now that the season was over, Cathy, Caroline and Monty were still living with their grandmother at Trevor Square. But while Caroline and Monty were reluctantly dragging themselves through the last weeks of secretarial college, Cathy had been sent to a cooking school in Chelsea to learn the art of finding her way to a man's heart through his stomach.

'It's quite obvious Didi thinks her job's finished now that I'm engaged,' she confided to Monty when they met for a lunchtime cappuccino in a coffee bar. 'Do you know, they even tried to make me get married in the chapel at Bourton? You couldn't get more than fifty people in there if you herded them in at gunpoint.' Monty sprinkled brown sugar over the foam in her cup, then started skimming it off with her spoon.

'How can you stand it, Cathy? They're treating you like a prize heifer. I bet the Coseley mob will be the same, once you've given them their heir. Off to the abattoir with the useless carcass once the bull-calf is weaned.'

'Monty! Don't say such awful things. I know you don't mean them.'

'You know I mean every word, that's the trouble.'

Cathy was half-admiring, half-disapproving of her sister's talent for outrage. 'You're not really going to move in with Simon, are you?' she asked. 'There'll be hell to pay. Mummy will go mad.'

'Well, he's found the perfect apartment now, and it'll be decorated the way he wants soon. But Mummy is the least of my worries. I've simply got to get the Pill somehow. There's no way I can live with Simon and sleep with him every night and not go all the way.'

'Well why don't you get married?'

Monty frowned. The truth was that she could not believe a man would ever want to marry her, because she was wicked and rebellious and not as pretty as Cathy. But she told Cathy what she told herself. 'You don't understand. I don't believe in marriage. I want to live with a man because I love him and want to be with him, and I want him to live with me for the same reason, and that reason only, not a legal obligation. And I don't want to end up bitter and frustrated like our mother, or an old harpy like Simon's mother. Isn't that enough reason?'

'But it isn't being married that makes them so awful . . .' Cathy paused. She could think of no apparent reason why none of the married women they knew presented the picture of perfect contentment which she imagined a wife became for life on her wedding day. She changed the subject. 'Do you know what I'm really going to hate about marrying Charlie? I'll hate missing you, I know I will.'

'But you won't miss me – I'll be around.'

'I know, but it won't be the same. You don't like Charlie, do you?'

'I don't have to like him, you're the one that's marrying him. But I won't stay away just because of Charlie. You'll see, we'll have lots of time to be together, probably more than now because you won't be studying. And you'll be able to tell me all about married life.' Monty squeezed her sister's narrow, long-fingered hand in sympathy, noticing that she had been biting her nails. This little lapse from perfection was touching.

'Will you do something for me, Monty – a favour? A big favour?'

'What?'

'Don't move in with Simon until after the wedding. Please, Monty. There'll be such rows and it's bad enough now, with everyone squabbling about the guest-list.'

Monty agreed. 'OK. For you. I wouldn't do it for anyone else, mind. Even Simon can't move in yet. The flat's going to be full of builders for a couple of months, anyway.' In a matter-of-fact tone, Monty went on. 'Have you done it with Charlie yet?'

'Done what? Should you really eat all that sugar, if you're supposed to be on a diet?' Cathy was acting dumb out of hostility. Monty dunked another spoonful of demerara sugar in her cup.

'I mean, big sister, are you still in a state of maiden grace?'

'It's none of your business.'

'Go on – tell. I bet you're not. I bet you've let him have his evil way with you.'

'I bet *you're* not.'

'Yes I am. I'd give anything not to be, though.' Monty sighed.

Merely thinking about making love launched a visible ripple of langour over her features. Cathy did not care for her sister's capacity for sensuality, mainly because Charlie had called her frigid so many times that she was beginning to fear that she might be sexually inadequate in some way.

'Well, why don't you go on the Pill?'

'You can't buy it in Woolworth's, you know. You have to get it from a doctor, and the doctor won't give it to you if you aren't married.'

'There must be some doctors who won't ask questions.'

'But where do I find one?'

Cathy shrugged. 'Isn't there something else you can do not to get pregnant? French letters or something?'

Monty gave a pout of distaste. 'I want it to be beautiful, the first time Simon and I really make love. I want it to be a way of expressing everything we feel about each other; like a sacrament – the outward and physical sign. Sordid bits of rubber would spoil it.'

'Still, at least you wouldn't have to worry about getting pregnant.'

'Oh yes we would. Simon says half the contraceptive factories have been infil-trated by Catholics who don't approve of birth control so they deliberately put holes in them.'

They were talking in quieter and quieter voices. The practical aspects of sexual intercourse were not a subject fit to be discussed in a public place by young women.

'You don't really believe that, Monty?'

'No of course not – but what I hate are all those awful sniggering schoolboy jokes about French letters. They aren't anything to do with how Simon and I feel about each other. Surely, you *love* Charlie, don't you feel the same?' Monty spoke as if she found it very difficult to believe that anyone could love Charlie Coseley. Her disapproval was so obvious that her sister was offended.

'When Charlie and I go to bed, I'll be offering myself to my husband on our wedding night,' Cathy snapped. 'It's not the same thing at all.'

Monty snatched up the gauntlet. 'No it isn't, is it? You're just trading sex for his name, his title and his money, and he's just out to fuck everything that moves and the only reason he's marrying you is that it's the only way he'll get into your knickers. That's not my idea of love.'

'It's none of your damn business, Monty.' Cathy coldly paid for their coffees and stood up, tucking a threepenny piece under her saucer for the waitress. 'You're just jealous because I'm getting married and you're not.'

They walked along the crowded King's Road to Sloane Square, both aflame with hostility.

'You're the one that ought to be jealous! You must be the only bird in London who doesn't know what Charlie's up to,' Monty snarled. 'Try going round to April Henessy's house, and see whose E-Type is parked outside!'

As they reached the square, Cathy dealt her sister a ringing slap in the face, then without a word turned and vanished through Peter Jones, the store where the furnishings for her future home were to be made. She was violently angry because Monty had voiced a doubt which had been nagging at her for weeks. Once he had put the massive, sapphire engagement ring on her finger, Charlie's playful resigna-tion had switched to a mood of angry impatience.

'What the hell are you keeping it for now?' he had yelled at her with fury when she again refused him. 'You've got the ring on your finger, that's what you wanted, isn't it? What do you think you've got between your legs, anyway – the Crown Jewels?' Once more he had left her on a note of savage petulance, but this time the telephone had not rung again the next day, or even the next week. She saw a picture in the *Daily Express* of Charlie with his polo team in Paris, and told herself this was the explanation.

He had reappeared after a fortnight in a much more pleasant mood, but there had been none of the irresistible apologies to which she had become accustomed, just an offhand resumption of the outward show of their relationship, with dates in London and weekends at one or other of the Coseley houses. He no longer pressured her for sex, or tried to cut her out of the herd of their friends to be alone with her at every opportunity. In fact, he treated her as if she were barely present in his life. Maybe Monty was right, maybe there was another woman.

With sudden weariness she made her way to the soft furnishings department and tried not to think of Charlie at all as she ordered curtains for the impressive house he had bought in Royal Avenue. Worst of all, Monty was the only person in whom Cathy dared to confide, and Monty, although she had tried to hide it until now, hated Cathy's husband-to-be with a contemptuous passion. The warm, unquestioning love of her sister seemed to be threatened by the commitment she wanted to make to her future husband. She was dismayed; life without Monty being always there for confidences and support suddenly looked bleak.

Cathy sighed as she signed the order form, no longer excited by the twenty-five-foot sweep of turquoise silk she had decided upon for the drawing room curtains, or the question of when and how they should be lined, interlined, weighted, headed, hung and allowed to drop before they were hemmed.

One winter weekend, Lord Shrewton led her into the library for a private talk.

'I don't know if you've heard from our people yet, but they seem to have reached an agreement on the marriage settlement and I wanted to have a word with you about it. I don't suppose,' he gave her his wintery twinkle of a grin, 'my son has mentioned any of the details, if he even understands them. Briefly, I would have liked to be able to frame the arrangements more precisely so that you would be taken care of if – in the unhappy event of – should it happen that . . .'

'If we ever got divorced, you mean?' Cathy broke in to help him.

'Precisely. It seems a little cold-blooded to talk about divorce before the wedding and of course we sincerely hope the arrangements are never put to the test. But I wanted to explain to you that the whole thrust of the trust deeds with which Charlie's money is tied up is towards the long-term interest of the family, rather than individuals. I gather the lawyers have decided to continue in the same vein, and detail a separate provision for your heir, assuming you have one.'

Cathy grasped his concern immediately. 'I think it was just the same for me in my family. All the money was really ours, not our father's.'

'Precisely. Rather than make a separate provision for you as Charlie's wife, the lawyers have agreed that everything will go to your heirs. But one assumes the children will stay with the mother so it will come to the same thing if – er – well –'

'Yes, I understand.'

'Excellent. You're very quick on the uptake. Maybe you'd like to come and work for me in the bank one day. Some of our chaps seem to have difficulty getting the gist of a bus ticket.' He poked the fire briskly and rubbed his hands. 'All the preparations going well? Worse than starting a war, planning a wedding, so they tell me.'

The more Cathy saw of her future father-in-law, the easier she felt with his practical style. She didn't find him frightening any more; in fact, it amused her to see him snap comments and bark orders, now that she understood he deliberately used his intimidating persona to get what he wanted with the minimum fuss. Cathy felt brave enough to confide at least one of her worries to him.

'Do you think we ought to have the wedding at Bourton? All my family are absolutely set on it, but I know Charlie wants a big London wedding. What do you think?'

'I think it's your wedding and you should have whatever you want. And I suppose you want what Charlie wants, am I right?' She nodded eagerly.

'Well, I don't see why the Bourton family should foot the bill for my son's extravagant tastes. I don't suppose Hugo Bourton does either, if I know your uncle. We'll see what we can do.' She darted forward and gave his smooth, dry cheek a quick kiss of gratitude, causing the astute Marquess to blush.

The next week Cathy got a letter from Mr Napier at Pasterns enclosing a bundle of legal papers which she dutifully attempted to read, and with a final paragraph informing her that ten thousand pounds was being transferred to her bank account as a personal gift from the Marquess of Shrewton. He also offered an apartment in one of the estate's London terraces in Belgravia to Bettina.

That evening there was also a strangled telephone call from Charlie's mother, suggesting that the wedding reception be held at the Coseleys' London home. 'After all,' she explained, 'it *is* one of the few ballrooms in London still in private hands, and it seems such a shame that we hardly ever use it.'

In the dreary winter, Cathy learned how to make waterlilies out of tomatoes and baskets out of lemons in the cookery school, and spent hours with Lord Shrewton's secretary checking the list of wedding guests. She addressed five hundred and twenty-three engraved invitations with her own aching hand, went to Garrard's with Lady Davina to choose a tiara that would sit attractively under her veil, without making her feel as if her head were being sliced open like a breakfast egg.

From Jean Muir, she ordered a high-waisted wedding dress of heavy white silk which made her appear slimmer and more graceful than ever, and six small lace-bordered gowns in forget- me-not blue for the bridesmaids. She talked bouquets, posies, buttonholes and table centres with the florists, *suprêmes de volaille* with the Coseleys' cook, and crowd-control with their butler.

All this Cathy did quite alone. She apologized to Monty and the sisters fell into each other's arms with tears in their eyes, promising never to fight again, but Cathy did not dare test her sister's goodwill by asking for her help with the wedding. Bettina abruptly refused the offer of a London apartment, preferring to remain with her bridge club circle. Caroline was grimly jealous. Lady Davina absorbed with her next charity ball, the Marchioness, passive and hostile.

Monty kept her word and told Simon that she would not move in with him until after the wedding, but there remained a definite estrangement between the sisters which wounded Cathy more than she would admit. She had decided to have six little bridesmaids and two pages, chosen from the plentiful supply of infants in distant branches of their families, but wished now that she had made Monty her bridesmaid as well, to keep her close through the ordeal. Charlie became more and more detached, and arrived an hour late for their interview with the vicar of the Holy Trinity, Brompton.

Cathy awoke on the morning of her wedding day with a bleak sense of abandonment which she promptly crushed.

'This *is* the happiest day of my life,' she willed herself to believe, and fixed a serene smile under her veil as she took Uncle Hugo's arm and set off between the endless corridor of men in morning suits and women in petal hats. A twinge of panic made her heart jump when she saw no one at the end of the aisle, but then Charlie, looking more handsome than ever, moved into her field of vision, and turned to smile at her. 'That's bad luck, he shouldn't do that!' she thought, half expecting the quiet phalanxes of guests to collapse in disarray at this impudent breach of convention; but, glancing from the corners of her eyes through the mist of her veil, she read only bland approval around her.

They halted, Uncle Hugo released her from his arm, and Charlie on the other side at once squeezed her hand and gave her a quick, unrehearsed kiss. For once she was grateful for his uncontrollable physicality.

The day went on more and more like a play in which she was both performing and watching, a series of tableaux which she was able to view and experience at the same time. At the church steps the warm June breeze caught her silk tulle veil and she felt it tug at its moorings in the piled coils of her hair. Charlie pulled her into his arms in the car, confetti spilling from the creases in his grey Blades suit, and teased her by tugging open the zip down the back of her dress.

In the ballroom, where the pillars were swagged with garlands of white carnations, Cathy stood in the receiving line until her Louis-heeled satin pumps pinched her toes like red hot irons. When the last guest had been greeted and launched into the room, she brightened her smile and dutifully worked her way around the circuit of congratulating strangers until, with relief, she saw Monty with Simon and Rosanna in a group apart. Monty looked both decorous and sexy in an Ossie Clark crêpe dress printed with tendrilling vines.

'You haven't got a drink.' Simon at once halted a waitress and gave Cathy a glass of champagne. 'Stop being perfect and talk to us. Do you realize you've got half the Shadow Cabinet here?'

'Of course she does, she wrote the invitations.' Monty nudged him affectionately in the ribs as she raised her own glass. 'Here's to wedded bliss, Cathy – may it
be everything you ever hoped.' She spoke warmly, wanting to heal the breach that
had opened between them.

Cathy surveyed the crowded room, noticing several groups of men whose faces
were vaguely familiar from television newsreels and who were set apart by the indefinable aura of power around them. Simon was right. A large proportion of the
Conservative politicians swept out of office by Harold Wilson's government had
gathered to drink to their health.

'You're right, Simon: how awful of me, I must have written the names not realizing who they were.'

'Well, I don't suppose Charlie introduced you to the Shadow Chancellor during an evening at Annabel's.' Simon gulped down a canapé and licked his fingers.

'They're not Charlie's friends – they're his father's, surely,' Rosanna suggested
and Cathy nodded.

'I thought I was just marrying a man. I forgot I was marrying a merchant bank
as well.'

'Oh boy, try being Jewish,' Rosanna laughed, 'then you'll really know that family means business. Sometimes my father and his friends make me feel as if they're
planning a merger rather than a wedding for me and Simon.' Rosanna, to the
ecstatic delight of her mother, had just announced her engagement to a stocky
young man whose mother's cousin had married a Rothschild.

'Yes, but family isn't so important with us. This is more like the sort of thing my
father used to talk about. When I said I didn't want to be a deb, I remember him
telling me, "Don't write the Season off as mere frivolity. When people reach into
their pockets to make a splash there's always more to it than fun and games. They
want the world to know something about them."'

'Or prove that the upper classes still have the upper hand. Is your eyelash O
K?' Monty carefully pressed a straying corner of her sister's false eyelash back into
place.

At last it was almost over. The three-tiered cake was cut, the speeches made,
the bride and groom toasted and the overtired tiny bridesmaids led away to grizzle
out of earshot. Cathy left the ballroom, kicked off her shoes, and ran up to the
bedroom where her going-away dress was ready.

Monty followed her and flung her arms around her. 'I'm sorry I've been such a
pig, Cathy. I've been awful, I know I have. I just couldn't bear to think I was losing
you, that's all.'

Cathy felt light-headed with relief as the anxiety of the past months melted away.
'I felt just the same,' she told her sister. 'I couldn't bear thinking that you hated me
because you hated Charlie. Oh, darling Monty, let's not be so stupid ever again.'

To Monty's surprise, she saw tears glistening in her sister's almond-shaped eyes. 'Hey, hey,' she soothed her, reaching for the tissues. 'Don't cry, your eyelashes will fall off.'

A few moments later, the hairdresser arrived to unpin Cathy's false curls and brush out her hair. He was followed by Caroline, who began packing away the wedding regalia with workmanlike bustle; then Lady Davina appeared, and finally Charlie who babbled incoherent compliments and fumbled at the buttons on her beige Courrèges shift. At the top of the stairs which led down to the ballroom Cathy looked round for Monty and mischievously hurled her bouquet in her sister's direction; the guests surrounding her stood back and she was obliged to catch the flowers.

On the Comet to Nice, Cathy and Charlie slept like exhausted children, but when they arrived at the Coseleys' villa in Antibes, the warm, flower-scented air of the Côte d'Azur revived them. Charlie carried his bride over the threshold, dumped her in the middle of the vast, Art Deco bed, dragged off her knickers and set about consummating their marriage with no further wasted effort. He took about ninety seconds Cathy felt no pain and was almost delirious with the happiness of being desired.

For the next ten days, Charlie made love to her constantly, in bed, on the floor, on the massive, veneered dining table, on the beach, in the water, on the yachts of the various friends who were moored in the enchanting harbour. At dinner he would pull her hand under the table to his crotch, in the car his hand would stray past the gearshift to her thigh and in the powerboat he made her take the wheel and joyfully ripped away her pink gingham bikini, while she struggled to control the juddering shell on its crashing course through the waves.

She adored him more than ever. They had one fight, when they had drunk too much, over whether the moon was waxing or waning. Charlie punched her viciously in the side of the head then collapsed in grovelling apologies and made love to her with even more passion than before.

Two weeks after they came home to the impressive house in Royal Avenue, Cathy picked up a lipstick from the floor of his E-Type. It was a pearlized apricot shade which she did not wear. Charlie said it belonged to his secretary, and Cathy never considered disbelieving him.

Six weeks after their return, Cathy realized that the box of tampons she had bought before her wedding was still unopened. Two weeks later, she went to see her doctor, who asked her to come back in three days. 'Congratulations, Lady Laxford,' he said beaming as she walked into his consulting room. 'You're about to start a family.'

Chapter Ten

'**O**UR FIRST priority is to maintain the economy, and as far as we're concerned at Bukit Helang that means keeping up our rubber output, meeting our quotas and exceeding them if we can.' Douglas Lovell's shoulders, normally braced, were bowed and he spoke seriously. 'In the event of an enemy invasion, Malaya will be defended by the British Army; so will the rest of the Empire, most of Europe and half bloody Africa by the looks of things. The Army runs on rubber tyres, and our war service will be done better here than anywhere else. So any young fool thinking of running off home to enlist can think again – they're sending back any man who tries it.' The elderly manager glared fiercely at the men who had assembled in his office at the hour normally devoted to tennis.

Japanese troops were fighting in Burma, a few hundred miles to the north, and all over Malaya the Europeans were anticipating a call to arms.

'Strategically, because of our remote position we're not as important as the estates near the coast or the border,' he continued. 'We'll form our own detachment of the Federated Malay States Volunteer Force and organize our people for military training. Bourton, I'm seconding you to the District Officer to help organize an intelligence effort – he needs a linguist. Rawlins, Wilson and McArthur, you're to work with the Civil Defence Committee. I want plans for defence works on the estate on my desk as soon as you can. Anderson – pick out a dozen bright boys and give 'em First Aid training. I want parades every Sunday morning, drill in the evening – fight out a timetable among yourselves.'

The tennis nets had already been struck and stored, and within a fortnight the white lines of the courts were all but invisible, and the turf itself worn to its roots by marching feet. Beside the board on which he marked the rubber prices, Douglas Lovell set up a bulletin board where he posted news of the progress of the war.

'Two battleships of the Royal Navy, HMS *Repulse* and HMS *Prince of Wales*, are sailing to join the Far Eastern fleet where they will strengthen the defences of Singapore Island,' proclaimed a notice which was embellished with a thick red border and star. Gerald Rawlins read it out with satisfaction. 'That'll show the Japs we mean business. They'll think twice about sticking their nose in Malaya now.'

'Does it say anything about aircraft?' asked Bill Treadwell, peering as he scanned the typed lines. 'Not much use sending battleships without some air cover.'

As a European closely involved in Malay affairs rather than an employee of a foreign trading interest, Treadwell had been called to Singapore and given some rudimentary propaganda training then returned to Perak to whip up support in the largely uninterested Malay community. His weekends were spent touring the state making speeches and distributing leaflets and posters.

Gerald stood self-importantly in front of the bulletin and spoke to his friend as if to a particularly obtuse corporal.

'Don't be daft, man, Jap pilots are all short-sighted. They couldn't bomb a battleship at sea any more than you can read that notice without your glasses. That's if their planes can stay airborne long enough to get out to sea in the first place.' He picked up a swagger stick and military cap and tucked them under his arm.

The Australian shook his head with a smile. 'What I like about you, Rawlins, is your cock-eyed optimism, your pea-green innocence and your astounding ability to swallow any crap that's handed down to you as long as its got Made in England stamped all over it.'

'Careless talk costs lives, old man.' Gerald did not smile and he glanced uneasily around the office.

'Careless talk costs lives all right, especially if it's written up on the wall and signed C-in-C British Forces, Singapore,' Bill rejoined, deliberately not lowering his voice. 'If I were you I'd give some thought to sending your wife away while you still can.'

They walked out into the bright heat of morning and turned towards the parade ground. Douglas Lovell insisted that the Sunday parade take place at 11 am in the full heat of the day, to accustom the volunteer soldiers to the worst that the climate could inflict on them.

'Don't think I haven't thought of that already.' Gerald flapped his hat at a dog that had strayed from the coolie lines. 'Now Betty's in the family way, I'd give anything to have her safe and out of here. But she won't leave. Took on so much when I suggested it, I let the subject drop.'

'Women!' Bill spoke in tones of light-hearted despair which alluded to the well-known propensity of the weaker sex for persecuting the stronger with their weakness.

'Said she'd go to pieces if she had to leave me,' Gerald admitted with pride. 'She's got a point. She can hardly go back home, and if we got her on a boat to Colombo or Durban or somewhere she'd be billeted on some of my family who'd be total strangers to her. Betty just isn't the sort who can take all that in her stride. She's delicate.'

On the trampled turf forty men in makeshift uniforms lined up, trailing spades, sticks and dummy weapons carved from plywood packing cases.

'All Chinese?' Bill enquired, at last taking the trouble to put on his glasses.

'Mostly. One or two of the conductors, a few Malays. Most of them don't seem to care.' As a captain of this ragged fighting force, Gerald strutted along with greater self-importance as he approached his command.

'Can't blame them – it's not their war, after all. One master's the same as another to a coolie.'

'Don't get me wrong, Bill, it's not the Tamils I blame, I'm right with you on that one. But you'd think the Malays would stand up and fight – it's their damn country, after all. They've had nothing but good from the British, now they won't lift a finger.' He halted at the edge of the levelled ground. 'You're not joining us, I take it? Don't fancy a spot of exercise to whet the appetite for lunch?'

'No fear. In intelligence, our function is merely to observe, not engage the enemy.' And Bill threw him a salute that was only just short of insolent and lounged over to a bench in the shade of the casuarina trees, watching Gerald march stiffly forward as a sergeant called the men to attention.

An hour later, dripping with perspiration, they returned to Gerald's bungalow for him to change, then set off with Betty up the rutted track to James's house. Gerald's proudest possession was his new car, a dusty Model T Ford bought from another junior assistant at the start of the war. It struggled pluckily up the red earth lane, bucking over deep channels cut by the rivulets of water which coursed down the hillside after every rain storm.

'James, you idle bastard – on your feet!' he shouted in greeting as he mounted the verandah steps. But instead of James, Ahmed, the houseboy came running from his quarters.

'*Tuan* Bourton present his apologies, *tuan*. Gone this morning to Kampong Malim on defence business. Back noon, he say. *Tuan* Anderson has just arrived.' The plump doctor and his wife were already settled in the shady interior with drinks in their hands.

'Well, here's a fine to do! Asks his friends over for tiffin then clears off.' Gerald flopped into one of the rattan chairs and motioned the others to do the same. 'Now I ask you, is that the act of a gentleman?'

'The boy's flapping because James left no orders about lunch, either.' Jean Anderson crossed her thin legs primly. 'He simply tore off and forgot about us, I suppose.' Sunday lunch scarcely required specific instructions from James; the estate community ate in each other's homes in rotation, but the menu was always the traditional curry tiffin – chicken in spiced sauce, rice, and bowls of coconut, banana, chutney and sliced salad vegetables, followed by fruit and a sago pudding known as *gula malacca*.

Ahmed reappeared with a tray of gin pahits, lukewarm cocktails of gin, water and pink Angostura bitters which were customary before most of the planters' meals.

'I'll never let him call me an uncouth colonial again,' Bill lifted his glass in salute. 'Your health, Captain, Doctor. Here's to our future generation.'

Betty blushed as he glanced at her. It was only a month since Dr Anderson had confirmed her pregnancy, and she was not yet accustomed to the role of mother-to-be in her small community. She felt sick most of the day, as much from nerves as anything else. Anderson was the only man with whom she felt at ease; bluff and hearty in company, he was comfortingly tactful when they were alone together. She found that the touch of his small hands, delicate, confident and cool in spite of the climate, was enough to calm her. He anticipated all the alarms and discomforts of her condition, so that her pregnancy seemed like a delightful secret she could share with him alone.

Anderson was concerned about her. Although she was healthy and followed his instructions with childlike trust her emotional inadequacy worried him far more than her physical condition. He had directed her to join his First Aid classes and was pleased to see that having work to do calmed her anxiety.

The men's conversation rambled on, by tacit agreement avoiding all issues of importance in front of the women. Betty had the effect of dominating the company around her merely by her timidity; the prospect of alarming this frail creature was so self-evidently dreadful that menfolk automatically talked in nursery terms.

Bill told a rambling story of his one encounter with a tiger, when he had all but fallen over the dozing beast in the deep jungle. 'Dunno who was more surprised, me or the tiger!' he finished cheerily. He always finished the story that way, and Gerald, who had heard it many times before, was roused from inertia by irritation.

'Damn James, how long is he going to be? The *kampong's* only half an hour on that bike of his.'

Boredom settled over them like the clouds of white water vapour that mantled the jungle after rain. To Betty, the life of a memsahib, with its boredom and total inactivity, was almost a comfort; the heat, idleness, unvarying landscape and unchanging company held her secure in a blanket of predictability.

They fell silent, and in time became aware of the quiet crooning of a chicken that picked its way around the scarlet canna lilies at the bottom of the steps. When the boy brought another round of pahits, the doctor ordered him to fetch some bread, and in a few moments Ahmed returned with some small, half-leavened Malay loaves that were like flattened dinner rolls.

'Ever seen a chicken get drunk?' Anderson asked them, winking one eye. His sun-reddened face was creased with deep lines already, and when he winked half of it seemed to vanish in a knot of wrinkles.

On the rattan sideboard stood an array of bottles. The doctor selected a full bottle of navy rum and splashed it liberally over the bread, then threw one of the sodden loaves down to the chicken. It ran eagerly forward, gave a wary peck, then began gobbling the treat as fast as it could. Two more chickens scuttled out from under the house and Anderson tossed them another rum-soaked loaf.

'Take it easy, fellas,' he advised. 'Don't choke on your last supper.'

'They love it, don't they?' Gerald was excited as a child at the spectacle. 'Look at them put it away. Go on, give 'em another one.'

'Really – you men act just like infants at times,' Jean protested, glancing uneasily at Betty in case this cruel entertainment upset her; such was Betty's confidence in a professional man that she was looking with fascination from the birds to the doctor, showing no sign of repulsion.

The first chicken was by now visibly affected by the rum and aimed inaccurate pecks at the latecomers as they struggled for more bread. By the time the loaves were finished, all three birds were flustered and noisy.

'My grandfather used to do this back home,' the doctor observed, delighted. 'The real joke is when they start thinking they can fly.' He walked down the steps and the birds scattered frantically as he began driving them forwards with outstretched arms. 'Shoo, shoo, chick, chick chick.'

'Chick- chick- chick- chick- chick- chick- chick- chick- chicken!' sang Gerald. Betty began to giggle as the birds scrambled unsteadily forwards, flapping and squawking as they went. Anderson lunged for the nearest one, which evaded him with a frantic cry, then fell over its own feet in a drunken panic. Gerald and Betty laughed aloud as he grabbed the intoxicated birds and perched them on the bamboo fence bordering James's garden. They flapped crazily and plummeted to the ground in untidy heaps, then staggered on to their feet and lurched forward, one dragging a paralysed wing on the ground.

One bird flapped up to the fence of its own accord and evacuated messily over the doctor's boots, an act which looked so much like defiance that Gerald and Betty fell back in their chairs, wiping their eyes with mirth. Below them Ahmed appeared, doubled up with laughter and holding his sides.

'Pass me my rifle, Rawlins,' Anderson commanded, 'time to get on with the lunch.' From the steps he took aim and succeeded in hitting two of the birds. The third flapped in a frenzy of fear towards a length of fallen palm trunk, jammed itself head first into a narrow gap between the billet and the fence, struggled and was still.

Anderson walked over and prodded the inert bundle of feathers with his rifle.

'Died of fright.' He pulled out the body and held it by his neck, then picked up the remaining corpses and handed the three birds to the boy. 'There you are. Start cooking and *tuan* Bourton'll be back before they're ready. That's the trouble with chickens,' he tramped up the verandah steps once more, 'no guts. Lie down and die at the minute anything scares 'em.'

'Chicken-hearted.' Gerald put down his empty glass. 'Boy! More pahits!'

Half an hour later the distant purr of James's motorbike sounded through the perpetual churring of the jungle insects and he bounced into the shade of the bungalow, apologizing and calling for Ahmed and galvanizing them all anew with his energy. Betty brightened immediately as he fussed over her, enquiring at length about her health.

'What kept you?' Gerald demanded.

'Bad business.' James took a gulp of his drink. 'Man down in the village came to the police house with his son – real bad hat, off smuggling buffalo over the Siamese border most of the year. Anyway, the boy had been over the border on some shady business or other, and came back swearing that he'd seen the Japs clearing airstrips in the jungle up in the north east. The old man insisted he tell his tale to the authorities and they got me down to show the flag and put the fear of God in him.'

'Do any good?' Bill took out his glasses and began to polish them slowly with his handkerchief.

'Hard to tell. I'm inclined to believe the boy was telling the truth, but it doesn't make any sense, does it? If the Japs come, that'll be the last route they'll choose. It's virgin jungle all the way, right down to the beaches. Totally impassable.'

'Monsoon's starting anyway,' Anderson, who had lived on the east coast a few years earlier, spoke with authority. 'Landing from the sea would be out of the question – forty-foot breakers pounding the beaches from now until Christmas.'

'Fellow was a fifth-columnist. You should have had him shot.' Gerald stood up with indignation.

'Good old Gerald.' Bill pushed his spectacles back into pos ition. '*Pax Britannica* at any price. Just what we need to turn the Malays against us at the wrong moment.'

'What's your reading of the situation, Bill? Are the Malay leaders going to back us? And what's the word from aboveany orders for us in case of in . . .' he checked himself from saying the word 'invasion' '. . . if the worst came to the worst?'

'I've just sent Singapore a report saying the best help we'll get is probably from the Communists. They're violently anti-British now, of course, but my guess is they'll swing round if the Japs' do invade.'

Gerald snorted with contempt. 'Handful of barmy Chinese troublemakers.'

'More than a handful, and they can make trouble for the Japanese just as well as for us if it suits them. The Malays will just sit in their *kampongs* and grow rice, and keep themselves to themselves like they do now.'

Ahmed at last announced lunch and they sat down to a table set with a few small articles of silver from Bourton House and gaudy tropical flowers arranged in jampots.

'Surely, you don't *really* think the Japanese will come?' Betty asked, putting down her fork. She had no appetite.

'They wouldn't dare,' Gerald reassured her at once, reaching out to pat her hand.

'Malaya's impossible to invade,' Dr Anderson spoke with his usual confidence. 'Mountains, jungle, swamps – the country's a natural fortress. Nothing to worry about, my dear.'

'What do you think, James?' Bill was really asking whether they could decently say what was on their minds in front of Betty.

James smiled at her, his wide, frank, irresistible smile. 'I'm absolutely certain the Japs will try it,' he said gently. 'Won't you let us send you away, Betty? This will be no place for a woman when the fighting starts.'

Her brow puckering in anxiety, she turned to the fourth man. 'Do you think so, Bill?'

'Yup. I've always said it was only a matter of time once Tojo the warlord took over. Malaya's too valuable – they want the rubber, the tin, the rice, everything; to starve us as well as to supply themselves.'

'But they say on the radio that the defences of Malaya are impregnable.' Betty looked from one man to another for reassurance.

'They're only trying to keep morale up,' James explained. 'It's true, no one will ever conquer the jungle. But they will have a damn good try. You see, if the Japs control Malaya, they will control almost all the rubber in the world, which means they can virtually stop any army in its tracks and knock the bottom out of our automobile industry as well. And what's bad for General Motors is bad for America, don't you see?'

Gerald regarded his friends with contempt. 'What's the matter with you two – going off your heads? The Japs aren't at war with America, they'll never be at war with America. You're crazy.'

They ate on in silence, then dispersed for the afternoon lie-off while James remained at the table to write a report of the morning's interrogation. Soon the even rise and fall of Gerald's snores filled the house.

'What are you doing?' Betty, wan and in stockinged feet, reappeared in the doorway.

'Just a report on this morning's activities.' He blotted the page neatly and reached for an envelope. 'I'll send it down to Singapore tonight.'

'Then you don't think that boy was a fifth columnist?'

'No I don't. He's not the type. It seems to me if you're going to hire an agent to spread alarm and despondency in the population, the last sort you'd go for would be a virtual bandit.' She nodded, marvelling at his astuteness; men knew such a lot of things, especially James who was never ill at ease in any situation.

'You're right, I suppose.' Betty sat on the edge of the nearest chair and watched as he sealed the letter.

'Can't you sleep?' he asked. She shook her head and smiled apologetically. 'I'll get Ahmed to make you some barley water, that'll perk you up.'

'No, please, I don't want to be any trouble.'

'It's no trouble. Come and make yourself comfortable on the verandah. You're not just putting a brave face on things, telling us you feel fine?'

'I haven't got a brave face to put on, James.' She ran her fingers through her hair with a weary gesture. She pinned up her curls carefully every night, but the heat and humidity of the climate invariably relaxed them, so that by the evening her hair was a mess of lank, brown locks which embarrassed her with its disorder.

She need not have worried on James's account; having found extraordinary sexual satisfaction with native women, he no longer had any desire for females of his own race, of whom he had a disabling fear. He treated Betty with all the chivalrous attention he had been trained to show to a woman, enhanced by a neurotically exaggerated respect. This alone, in comparison with Gerald's hearty insensitivity, was more than enough to make Betty half in love with him.

James sent the boy away with his letter and returned to sit by her in the cool of the main room.

'I know it's none of my business,' he began, looking intently at the polished floorboards to hide his awkwardness, 'but what *are* you going to do, Betty? When the baby comes, I mean. I don't know much about these things, but it's madness to think of staying here too much longer. Won't you even go to Singapore?'

'A wife's place is with her husband, and I shall stay with Gerald.' She spoke as if he had offended her.

'But we'll all be called up, all of us volunteers, if there is an invasion.'

'I wouldn't know what to do without Gerald.' With maddening stubbornness, Betty avoided James's eyes and gazed out of the doorway at the heat-shimmering garden and the jungle beyond.

'My dear Betty, you may have to find out in an awful hurry. You need people to take care of you, a doctor . . .'

'I'm sure Dr Anderson will look after me beautifully.'

'But what if he's called up? He may well be, you know.'

'I shall manage. I can't leave my husband. And besides, what if the Japanese attack Singapore?'

'Singapore will never fall, Betty. I'm sure you'd be much safer there.'

'I think you're being very disloyal, talking like that. There won't be any invasion. There can't be.' And she turned to look at him with calm, crazy defiance. It gave her a perverse sensation of power to have so many people expending their energy on changing her mind – above all James, with his good looks, natural superiority and crested silver cutlery.

In the months that followed Betty rebuffed many more concerned advisers with the same stubborn irrationality. 'My mind is made up, I shall stay with my husband,' she repeated as more and more reports came of Japanese preparations north of the Siamese border. 'Dr Anderson agrees with me that I mustn't travel,' she announced.

She parroted the official line on every new development. 'They're on naval exercises – nothing to worry about,' she announced with finality when Japanese warships were sighted off the monsoon-lashed east coast, 'they won't come near Malaya.' Gerald was driven to desperation by his conflicting impulses to protect his wife and to uphold morale. She was daring him to admit that the official bravado was false.

Betty's vulnerability cowed them all. Even Douglas Lovell had an almost superstitious fear of her, calling her a 'stupid little mare' under his breath but never daring to voice his opinions outright. The doctor's wife, as the only other European woman on the estate, acquired a tacit but compelling moral responsibility for Betty, and so the question of either woman leaving was in the end never raised again.

Her pregnancy developed, increasing her discomfort as the baby grew. Worse than the weight of it, the aches and strains and violent flushes of heat, was the shamelessness of her condition, the fact that she could not conceal the ugly swelling that proclaimed her state to all at a glance. She tried to think of the baby, the sweet, little mite in its white lace gown, but could not relate that picture to the ugly bulk of her body.

On December 7th, 1941, the radio announcer at last dropped his tone of fatuous cheerfulness, and announced that Japanese troops had crossed the border in the north east, near Kota Baharu, and were engaged in fierce fighting with the British.

Next day came the news that the American fleet had been bombed the previous day in Pearl Harbor. A few days later, it was announced that the Malayan peninsula's naval defence, the two battleships *Prince of Wales* and *Repulse,* had been sunk by Japanese warships.

A profound depression settled on the European community, which deepened as it became clear that the Japanese were advancing steadily down the east side of the peninsula. The radio talked of 'firm stands' and 'strategic retreats' until it became obvious that the defending forces were in chaos and the Japanese army, on foot and on bicycles, using the beaches and the coconut groves, were sweeping down the east coast.

Then the west coast, too, began to fall. Penang was severely bombed, and the island's Military Commander at once ordered all the European women and children to be evacuated to safety in Singapore, making no provision whatever for the Asiatic population.

James walked out of his bungalow for a Sunday parade and did not return; he was ordered to Singapore to join Bill Treadwell in new intelligence work. A week later, Douglas Lovell read out orders for all the planters to abandon the estate and join an armoured car unit bound for the east coast.

'Time for us to see the little men off,' he concluded with relish. Only Gerald was allowed leave to return to his home and say goodbye to his wife, the extent of this compassion being justified by the need for one assistant to supervise the burning of the remaining stock of rubber.

'You and Jean had best make for Singapore,' he told Betty. 'You'll be quite safe there until the fighting is over.'

Dumb with apprehension, but never doubting that this was merely a temporary parting, Betty kissed him goodbye. Jean Anderson stayed with her that night and helped her pack small suitcases with clothes for herself and the baby. The next day they were driven to the railway line and boarded the train, heading first for Kuala Lumpur, where they would transfer to the Singapore express.

Ahmed wrapped the Bourton silver in canvas, buried it under James's bungalow and followed the terse order of the British governors to the native population – *pergi ulu*, go into the jungle. Ah Kit, Gerald's boy, took the wheels off the Model T and put wood blocks under the axles. He left with Ahmed, the picture of dejection.

'Cheer up, man,' Ahmed told him as they turned their backs on the plantation. 'There'll always be an England.'

On either side of the train as it crawled southwards, the sleeping green jungle was unchanged, but sometimes they heard gunfire or aircraft in the distance and at every halt more Europeans climbed aboard, bringing with them news of Japanese bombers attacking to the north and district hospitals filling with wounded only to empty again when another evacuation was ordered.

Betty, in the seventh month of her pregnancy, sat silently by a window and listened as Jean exchanged news with the other passengers. The weight of the baby under her blue-and-white striped smock pinned her down and inhibited her breathing. Occasionally, the baby moved, thrashing like a big fish in a net and making her gasp.

At Kuala Lumpur, the express was steaming quietly but the platform was a mêlée of people cramming themselves and their possessions aboard. There was a lengthy delay. The train driver too had obeyed the authorities' command and fled to the jungle.

At last two British soldiers climbed on to the footplate, stripped to the waist, and began to stoke the engine.

Slowly the crammed carriages travelled south, the ominous tranquillity of the jungle all around. Night fell, but Betty, more and more uncomfortable with the heat and pressure of the baby, was unable to sleep.

At one station a party of footsore Australian nurses boarded. They were drenched from a savage squall of rain and brought with them a crazy selection of supplies; they had carried hundreds of packets of cigarettes, and a complete Christmas dinner, cooked and not yet eaten, down a branch line from the bombed-out station of a coastal town. In the dawn light they heated the meal on the train's boiler, carved it with a penknife and shared it around the carriage. Jean Anderson produced a bottle of whisky to wash their breakfast down.

'We couldn't let the Japs get their hands on our mince pies,' one girl explained. 'It's Christmas, after all.'

The jungle gave way to the houses of the coastal town of Johor Baharu, which was choked with refugees. Singapore lay a few miles away at the end of the causeway and as the train inched onwards, a mood of nightmare gaiety infected the passengers. The nurses stood at the carriage door throwing packets of cigarettes to the huge, disorderly queue of people which shuffled across the causeway to safety in Singapore.

There were Malay families riding on ox-carts piled with their possessions, Chinese on bicycles with cages of pullets strapped to the handlebars, and a never-ending line of Morris and Ford cars loaded to the gunwales with white faces which smiled in relief as they approached sanctuary.

Betty slumped against the window, craving air and the coolness of the glass against her burning skin. The baby was still now but her back ached and she shifted heavily to try to find a more comfortable position.

'All right?' Jean leaned across to pat her hand. 'It won't be long now.'

'It's going so slowly.' Betty spoke peevishly, as if the train were dallying on purpose to annoy her.

'There's thousands of people, and they're all walking on the tracks. We'll be there soon.'

Betty stared at her dully, with a detachment that made her resemble a small, stupid cow. Her face was quite expressionless, but she had a stricken look which alarmed Jean.

Slowly, Betty looked round to the end of the carriage where the toilet was, then struggled to her feet without saying anything and made as if to push through the passengers in that direction. There was a patch of moisture on the seat where she had been sitting.

'Are you sure you're all right dear?' Anxious now, Jean pulled at her hand. There was no room for the two of them to stand in the crammed carriage.

'I felt something,' Betty said, too embarrassed to say any more.

'What sort of something – a pain?' Jean gently pulled her back to her seat.

'No, not a pain. My back aches a bit. It was something else.'

One of the nurses, a broadfaced, competent girl, leaned across towards her. 'What kind of something else? Was it like a trickle?'

Betty looked uncomfortably at the two women, not wanting to answer them in case they should confirm her worst fears.

'I'm all right, really,' she told them. 'My back aches, that's all. The baby's not due for weeks yet.'

The nurse stood up and stepped towards her. 'Come on – you don't want to take any chances do you? What did it feel like – was it like liquid?'

'Her seat was wet,' Jean put in, her voice low. Betty shot her a glance of total hatred.

'Have you been having any pains at all, any pains before?' persisted the nurse.

'No, no. Nothing. I'm fine, honestly. There's no need to worry about . . . uhup!' She caught her breath as a strong cramp emphatically seized her guts. The nurse quickly put out a hand and felt her belly, then glanced down at the watch pinned to the bib of her crumpled apron. She waited in silence until the onset of the next contraction.

'Seven minutes! Holy smoke – why didn't you say anything before?'

At the end of the causeway Betty, now weeping and scarlet in the face with the heat of her contractions, was helped off the train and into a loaded car. With Jean and the nurse gamely hanging on to the running board, they drove through cratered streets to a hospital which was already crowded with casualties of every race, who had been injured in the air-raids.

'There's nowhere to put her,' a Chinese sister said with calm authority, as they half-dragged Betty into the building. 'The best we can do is a trolley at the end of the corridor. The theatre was hit this morning, but our equipment is OK, mostly. Lucky for you this was a maternity hospital before.'

Betty screamed as another wave of pain engulfed her.

'Try to keep her quiet,' were the sister's final instructions. 'And when the next raid comes take cover where you can.'

Night fell quickly, and Betty began to vomit continuously, bringing up yellow bile and mucus once her stomach was empty. Tears flowed down her cracked cheeks and she began to call out incoherently, no longer able to control herself enough to speak. Her eyes rolled and the lids flickered irregularly.

'She's burning hot all over.' Jean quickly tucked a kidney bowl under Betty's chin and supported her as she spat feebly into it. 'Do you think she can hold still long enough for us to take her temperature?'

'She's so far gone, she might bite the thermometer.' The nurse shook her head.

'We can try in the armpit, maybe.'

The thermometer confirmed their fears.

'She's running an almighty fever – this baby had better not take much longer.'

The nurse propped the delirious woman's knees apart and examined her internally. 'It's a normal presentation, that's one good thing. But she's so weak and she's getting really dehydrated.'

They fetched water, stripped Betty's inflamed body and sponged it to cool her. They made her drink, but she brought back the liquid at once.

The lights failed, then glimmered feebly, then failed again. An air-raid warning was called, and in a short time, the ground shook and the roar of bombs drowned their voices; at the end of the corridor a window blew out, showering them with broken glass, and all the time Betty groaned and cried out.

'I wish to God I could remember my midwifery training,' the Australian said, ducking perfunctorily behind the trolley as another explosion shook the building. 'There's got to be some way to help her.'

They tried to raise the tortured body to let gravity help its weakening muscles, but Betty screamed like an animal and bit Jean's arms in a frenzy of pain. Then at last there was an alteration in the tenor of her cries, and the nurse pulled apart her knees once more in time for the small body, sticky and blackened with viscous secretion, to slide head first into her hands. She worked deftly to clean out its gaping mouth and bubbles of dark mucus appeared.

'There's breath in the lungs,' she said, 'so far so good.'

'Oh heaven – look.' Jean wiped part of the infant's back clean with the corner of the sheet; along half the length of the scrawny body was a visible deformity, an area of puckered flesh along the line of the backbone. 'What is it?'

The nurse shook her head. 'I've never seen that, but they told us about some kind of spinal malformation. The neural tube hasn't formed properly.' Very tenderly she laid the baby down and folded its tiny legs towards its body. She held it upright and rested its feet on the trolley. It hung limp between her hands, snuffling feebly like a kitten. 'It's way too early, but it ought to be able to move a little – I think it could be paralysed.'

In the wreck of the operating theatre, she hunted for oxygen, but the cylinder was empty. As the noise of the bombing receded, the cries of the injured grew louder, and a new influx of patients crowded into the teeming building. They cleared the baby's throat of mucus and tried to breathe life into the weak lungs, but in a few more moments the infant's slender hold on life slipped and it died.

Betty lay inert on the trolley, flushed with fever, her lips stretched wide over her even teeth. After she had passed the afterbirth, she began to haemorrhage and the nurse, at the limit of her own endurance, summoned the last of her control to give her an injection.

'Don't you die on me now, you little cow,' she snarled under her breath as she swabbed the puncture. 'You die on me now and you'll be sorry, you see.'

James saw the Japanese army for the first time as he lay beside the trunk of a fallen tree on the bank of a wide, brown river. Out of sight of the bridge a hundred yards upstream, he stretched full length in the mud, blinking to keep his eyes focused.

In his line of vision hung a slender black snake, immobile and precisely straight like a plumb line, hanging from a branch over the broad channel. James was distracted by the reptile for an instant, then the distant glint of the sun on weapons pulled his attention back to his objective. A disorderly column of soldiers in khaki was advancing rapidly across the wide span of planks.

He gave the signal, then crawled back into the covering jungle and ran along the barely visible track, hearing as he went the roar of the explosion as the bridge was blown. Behind him came the fast, light footsteps of Ibrahim, the man he had charged with detonating the long cordtex fuse. Without speaking, the two men ran on through the forest, ducking and twisting around low branches, their feet slipping on the litter of damp leathery leaves and slimy sticks. Finally the light undergrowth of the virgin jungle gave way to a wall of plants whose leaves were bordered with savage thorns. The razor-sharp fronds and tangled roots disguised pools of mud which sucked at their feet as they followed a hidden pathway.

Their camp was skilfully concealed in this impassable thicket of secondary jungle. At the base of a rocky outcrop Bill, waiting with the Chinese wireless operator, greeted them with repressed anxiety.

'What luck this time?' he asked brusquely.

'Sounded good, but I couldn't see much,' responded James. He bent down to pull a leech off his leg and the glistening ribbon of black rubbery tissue curled angrily around his hand, searching for blood with its primitive sensory organs.

'The bridge is all gone,' Ibrahim confirmed. 'I think everything went up. Many Japanese die.' He pulled a bottle of iodine from the metal box of medical supplies and handed it to James.

'Did they come after you?'

'I heard shots behind us, but they faded away. You can't hear anything in this jungle, Bill, you know that. Sounds just get smothered.' James applied the disinfectant to the bleeding spot from which he had detached the leech.

His friend, now his commanding officer, Major Bill Treadwell of the Special Operations Division, pressed on, 'And what about the grenades?'

'Very good,' Ibrahim told them. 'I saw them go like we think, explosions all up the road. The Japanese were in confusion, running around everywhere like chickens.' They laughed together; being trained in the British army ideal of smartness and discipline, the makeshift uniforms and ragged drill of the Japanese amused them.

In a couple of hours two more Chinese members of their party arrived from stations on the far side of the bridge. Their reports were encouraging. The long column of invading troops had halted and bivouacked untidily by the roadside while despatch riders on bicycles rode aimlessly up and down. Five or six of the enemy had been killed at the bridge and the necklace of grenades strung out along the roads had killed a dozen more and wounded others.

'Did we get any vehicles?' Bill asked. 'Or were this lot on bicycles too?'

'All bicycle,' was the answer, 'bicycle or walk. No car, no tank.'

'Can you beat the Nips? They're trying to take over the country with plimsolls and cycle clips.' Bill laughed in grudging appreciation, but his expression was grim.

The previous day they had seen an Indian division retreat down 'their' road, ranks of Punjabi soldiers in turbans pouring southwards to Singapore. They had made cautious contact, identifying themselves only as members of the Volunteer Force.

'I'm glad to hear Singapore's sending somebody north,' the British officer spoke with doubt and irritation. 'Our orders have been just withdraw, withdraw, withdraw, nothing else for days. My chaps are pretty brassed off, I can tell you.'

'Not as brassed off as they'd be if they'd had a few days in the jungle,' James remarked to Bill afterwards. The Indian regiments had been welcomed when they had arrived as evidence that at last the War Office had accepted the fact that Malaya was vulnerable. Even before the fighting began, however, it became obvious that these soldiers, the finest in the world on their own native mountains, had received no training in the very different techniques of jungle warfare.

Darkness fell, and the noise of the daytime insects was replaced by the strident night sounds of the jungle. They brewed tea, and Bill ordered a tin of pineapple to be opened in celebration.

'Third time lucky, eh?' he said, stirring sugar into his tin mug. 'Three bridges in ten days – I think that's pretty good going. Buck up, James.'

'Damn!'

'Now what is it, mate?'

'I'm sorry, Bill, I've cut myself on the tin opener. Here you'd better take over. That bloody wax.' Their canned stores were coated in wax as a protection against rust. The jungle air, heavy with moisture all the time, was enough to destroy clean metal in a matter of weeks: even stainless steel razor-blades, left unwaxed, would become spotted with rust overnight. Flesh itself decayed almost as fast. Every scratch or insect bite had to be carefully treated with disinfectant, and James winced as he dripped iodine on the cut in his palm.

'Haven't smelt that since they patched us up after games at Eton,' he said, taking his share of the pineapple and sucking the juice from it. In fact, the life of a jungle guerrilla to date seemed very much like his time at school. There was schoolboy pleasure in the secrecy procedures of an undercover operation, the code names, the ciphers, the passwords and the manuals stamped 'Top Secret'.

Every young Briton of the ruling class was trained from child-hood to defend the Empire, and the rudimentary military training on the plantation tennis courts was just a continuation of the cadet exercises which James had done on the school playing fields. In Singapore, at the 101 Special Training School on an isolated peninsula, he had sat through lessons in demolition, sabotage, weapons, unarmed combat and jungle survival in the same fog of unfocused boredom in which he had passed his days at Eton avoiding Latin syntax.

Most like school, however, was the rigid military hierarchy and the absurd, degrading wrangling in which Special Operations Division had been caught up. They had been forced to scheme like desperate spinsters in order to per-suade their superiors to order undercover units into the jungle. But while the Japanese army swept down the Malayan mainland like a whirlwind, the military commanders had bickered over niceties of administration, making the final decision only at the eleventh hour. A mixed force of Europeans and a last-min-ute conscription from the Communist Party of Malaya had been hastily trained and sent into the field, but the sense that this effort was too little and too late haunted them all.

Their stores would last them for three months, but Bill insisted that they con-serve as much as possible and start to live off the jungle, so the supplies had been wrapped in gunny bags and hoisted high in the forest canopy for safety. The canned pineapple was a luxury. They ate fern-tips and bamboo-shoots, and cheated with rice bought from Chinese smallholders who supported the Communists.

The wireless was their only link with what was going on in Singapore; it was an awkward mass of equipment which weighed 48lb and was best carried on a bicycle because it was almost too heavy for one man. Worst of all, it ran on batter-ies, and when the batteries failed they would need to be recharged or replaced. Bill ordered minimal use of the equipment – a contact every three days.

The Japanese were offering a bounty for every captured white, and as Europeans James and Bill were instantly conspicuous and vulnerable to betrayal. They adopted Malay dress; Bill dyed his yellow hair black and stained his skin. His height and light eyes made his disguise useless except at a distance, but James had been able to transform himself more successfully.

Alone among the undercover parties, they had been given a container of tab-lets which their instructing officer had discouragingly informed them were 'some dope London wants us to try out – supposed to darken your skin. Never had a field trial so heaven knows how it works. Might come in handy for disguise, if it does any good.' The canister was labelled Trisoralen.

James experimented with the drug at once, and found that it darkened his olive skin to an agreeable café-au-lait, although he felt nauseated and giddy at times. After a month, however, these effects were wearing off.

'Joking apart, Bill, I reckon the dope's pretty good.' He pulled up his shirt-sleeve and showed a smooth, brown arm. 'I reckon I can tolerate it, and I'm having to take less and less of it to keep the colour up.'

'Your own mother wouldn't know you; how many are you taking?'

'Four a day now. I was on twelve at the beginning.'

'How much have we got left?'

'Eleven tins, 100 tablets a tin, plus a handful I've got here.' Fearful that the tablets might degenerate in the humid heat, James had meticulously wrapped each day's dose in tinfoil and stored them in an airtight tin, which had once held Craven A tobacco.

With his curling dark hair, ready smile and the curve of his slightly bowed legs outlined by his clinging sarong, James appeared a very passable Malay. His British stride had been modified to the swaying, graceful walk imposed by his native dress. It seemed to the others as if he even smelt like a Malay, because the village dogs seldom barked at him as they did at Bill.

With Ibrahim and the Chinese, he could move freely in the towns unremarked among the crowds of refugees. Communist supporters gave them information, and there was much that they could see with their own eyes. Thousands of enemy troops poured southwards, with heavier guns and vehicles landed from the sea on the wide, white beaches.

At the end of January came the news that the British had abandoned their last fingerhold on the mainland, retreated to the island of Singapore, and blown up the causeway. The city was under heavy mortar fire as well as air attack, and the European women and children were being evacuated with all speed.

On February 15th they got the news that the defending forces had capitulated. The impregnable fortress had fallen. It was the worst day of James's carefree young life.

'We just cleared out, buggered off. We did nothing, nothing worthwhile.' He blew furiously at the sulky fire, making the damp wood burst into flame.

'It's London – London sold us down the river. That bastard Churchill had the East written off from the start.' The firelight glinted feebly on Bill's spectacles.

'You know what Malay people call this time?' Ibrahim asked them. 'They speak of *tarek orang puteh lari* now.'

'The time when the *tuans* ran.' James nodded. 'They're right.'

'Well, we ain't running. We're all that's left, we're on our own, and it's up to us.'

'I suppose before this I was proud to be British, although I couldn't go along with all that land-of-hope-and-glory stuff of Gerald's.' James's voice shook with shame and anger. 'But not now, not after this.'

'Yeah, well, if you're feeling sick, think how Gerald must be taking it. Poor bastard. I wonder where he is.'

A river of men, defeated troops marching doggedly in unison, flowed eastwards across Singapore island, periodically clearing the highway to let through the ambulances which carried their wounded. Once they had accepted the Allied surrender, the Japanese issued a general order that all men of the conquered army were to march out to the Changi district, where there was a civilian prison and a military barracks.

The march continued for three days, over bomb-cratered roads obstructed with rubble, twisted tram cables and fallen telegraph posts. The men marched past ruined houses and burned-out vehicles, with the ghastly stench of decaying corpses in their nostrils. Every white man on the island joined the march, from the age of twelve upwards, soldiers and civilians marching separately.

Gerald marched with a blank mind, all his energy concentrated on forcing his shaking legs to walk. Beside him Douglas Lovell strode in silence, his eyes staring ahead. From behind them came the sound of bagpipes and the regular tramp of the Gordon Highlanders.

Once they were out of the city the march became easier. The roads were less damaged, and from the villages and coconut plantations people came out with food and water which they thrust into the men's hands despite the angry orders of the Japanese. Every house along the route flew a red-and-white Japanese flag.

Gerald took a tin of lukewarm water from a Chinese boy and paused to drink.

'Don't stop,' Douglas Lovell snapped at once. 'Stop now and you'll never get started again. Keep moving, man.' Obediently Gerald shuffled onwards. Neither man had slept for more than a few hours in the past ten days. Exhaustion blurred their vision and dulled their senses, so they walked as if in a mist, with the insistent wail of the bagpipes pushing them forward.

At last they heard an order to halt, and waited in lines in the blazing sun until a subaltern with a clipboard worked his way round to them, asked for name, rank, number and regiment, and assigned them billets in the barracks.

'It's not Raffles, but it's all we can do for now. We've got more than fifty thousand men here and only space for a fifth of that number. You'll get enough room to lie down in, and that'll be it,' he told them. 'Report to your CO as soon as you can.'

'CO be damned,' Gerald muttered. 'He can look for me if he wants me.' They had no idea of the identity of their present Commanding Officer; the unit's original commander had been killed during the shelling of one of the many positions they had attempted to hold in their chaotic retreat.

Inside the barracks, a single-storey, concrete building with a tin roof, Gerald lay down on the dirty stone floor and fell into a heavy sleep, oblivious of the milling men around him piling up their equipment and claiming their own territory.

Douglas Lovell woke him the next day. 'They're issuing rations. On your feet, Rawlins.' Gerald sat up, rubbing his puffy eyes and scratching his unshaven face. They joined a long, sweating queue of men with mess tins and ate their portions of watery rice, boiled without salt, with distaste. It was sufficient nourishment to make Gerald feel refreshed, and the thoughts which he had been able to ignore came to the front of his mind.

'I'm going to take a stroll, see what I can see,' he told Douglas Lovell. 'I've got to find out about Betty. If every man in Singapore is in this damned place there must be someone who saw her. And if Anderson made it, he'll be with the wounded, don't you think?'

With stolid persistence, Gerald began to ask every man in the barracks if he had encountered a brown-haired, blue-eyed, pregnant Englishwoman named Betty in the panic-stricken disorder of Singapore. Douglas Lovell went with him.

They joined a teeming mass of servicemen who were coming to terms with defeat. For most of them this meant thinking the unthinkable. For weeks they had been fired with confidence by propaganda and morale-boosting speeches in which the possibility of a Japanese victory had never been mentioned. Now it was a reality and the fall of Singapore also implied a loss of faith in their leaders. Immense crowds of captives walked around continuously in search of reassurance against the fearful uncertainty which they shared.

Each man felt as anonymous as a single ant in an anthill, despite their diversity. There were freckled Scots, scrawny Cockneys, fat planters, pallid civil servants, young police cadets and elderly clergymen. Rank, regiment and social standing were suddenly irrelevant. They were all prisoners.

Several of the barracks buildings were in use as hospitals, packed with wounded and dying men. The first medical centre which Gerald visited was full of Australian troops, but in the second their spirits lifted instantly when they recognized Anderson's small, rounded figure crouched beside a patient at the end of the stuffy room. There was scarcely room to walk between the wounded men who lay on the stretchers and makeshift rope beds, flapping weakly at the flies.

The two men waited until Anderson could be absent for a few minutes. He joined them outside the building and shook hands vigorously, saying, 'My goodness, my goodness,' over and over again.

'Did you get any news of Jean?' Gerald asked at once.

'I saw her for a few hours when we reached Singapore; she got news that our unit had arrived and hunted us down.' Anderson still held Gerald's hand and arm, debating with himself whether to pass on the news that Betty had lost their baby. 'She'd been with Betty and I'm hopeful they both got away to sea,' he added, deciding against passing on the bad news. The doctor had been sent directly to a field hospital from the rubber estate, and during the British troops' flight and the shelling of the city he had seen so many good men die that the loss of an ailing infant to a healthy young couple seemed less of a tragedy than a blessing in the present situation.

Gerald looked at his cracked, mud-caked boots in silence for a few moments, sensing what he had not been told. 'As long as Betty's all right . . .' he muttered.

The following day, Gerald found another group of Volunteers, mostly planters like himself, all of whom were anxious about their families and friends. They sat talking for hours in the meagre shade of a squat palm tree, desperate for some hint of the welfare of their wives and children. There was nothing else to do, and nothing else to think about except their own unimaginable fate.

'It's damn useless standing here jawing,' Douglas Lovell said at last. 'The thing to do is post a list of all the relatives. There'll be Red Cross workers of some kind once this place is organized. And there are two thousand women in the civilian camp hereabouts, so I've heard. If we can get in contact with them and get their names, that'll be a start.'

'How do you propose doing that?' Gerald sneered, suddenly made vicious by his sense of powerlessness. 'Ask the Japs if we can invite the ladies over for tea?'

'Damn your insolence! Don't you know the way to speak to a superior officer?' the older man snarled, and Gerald flinched and looked apologetic, responding instinctively to the military tone of the reproach. Douglas Lovell once more assumed the responsibility of command. He outranked all the survivors of the Volunteer Force, and knew by instinct that if these demoralized men, in their overcrowded, deprived conditions, were not immediately held together with discipline, they would degenerate to the level of animals.

'I want all the writing materials we've got,' he ordered them, 'and all the food. You –' he pointed at a skinny young man whose shoulders were straightening visibly at the sound of commands, 'will be our quartermaster in charge of rations. And tomorrow morning, instead of sitting around gossiping like a bunch of washerwomen, there'll be half an hour of physical jerks. We must keep ourselves fit at all costs; there'll be an Allied landing and we must be ready to do our bit. And you, Rawlins, you'll beg, borrow or steal a razor and shave off that fuzz. If you wanted to grow a beard, you should have joined the navy.'

Soon the other commanders also brought their men into line and the vanquished army began to adapt to the prison camp. At first there were few Japanese to guard them, and while the enemy officers harangued them with barely comprehensible speeches about the shame of defeat and the greater shame of not committing suicide rather than be captured, the Japanese soldiers proved to be peasant types who were seldom wantonly cruel.

Within a few weeks, the Japanese ordered their captives to form work-gangs for forced labour in the Singapore docks. Smuggling began in earnest; every man who marched out of the compound returned with food, cigarettes or information pressed upon them by loyal citizens of the city.

With ingenuity which surprised Douglas Lovell, Gerald got himself included in one of the earliest labour-gangs and bribed a Chinese youth to ask at the hospital where Anderson told him Betty had been taken for news of their wives.

'They're OK,' he told Anderson on his return one night. 'They got on a navy ship with the hospital nurses – the HMS *Marco Polo*. They were trying to get to Colombo. Betty and Jean are OK.' His ruddy face, for weeks drawn with anxiety, was now creased in a permanent smile and Anderson slapped him on the shoulder, thinking that there would be little benefit to Gerald in speculative talk about mine-fields and enemy warships. What the man could not imagine could not hurt him.

'That's splendid news,' the doctor said in a quiet voice. 'Absolutely splendid. They're safe – thank heaven for that.'

Betty had only been in the water for twenty minutes, and already it no longer felt warm but icy cold. Her arms and legs were numb, her body was so chilled that it felt insubstantial but in the core of her abdomen an excruciating agony raged like an inner inferno. The waves lapped below her chin, sometimes splashing into her scarlet face. Her lips, deeply cracked after days of fever, were sore and swollen from the salt water. Mercifully, she was scarcely aware of the scene of desolation around her.

The indigo sea was full of floating debris from the stricken *Marco Polo*, like most of the ships at the tail end of the escape fleet from Singapore she was a rough-and-ready coastal freighter hastily commandeered by the navy to evacuate civilians from the besieged city.

Jean Anderson and Betty had been evacuated from the hospital with the handful of European nurses who had remained there. After the birth of her child, Betty had been seriously ill with an internal infection, but when the announcement was made at the head of the crowded corridor that patients capable of walking would be evacuated, Jean hauled her bodily off the bed and forced her to stand.

They had been bundled first aboard a heavily loaded launch which had ploughed from ship to ship in the crowded harbour until the commander of the *Marco Polo* agreed to take its human cargo. They set sail with two other ships, all crammed with women and children, but the desperate flotilla had separated outside the harbour, hoping to ensure by scattering that at least some of the craft would evade the Japanese warships and reach safety. The unlucky *Marco Polo* had very soon encountered a small patrol of Japanese warships, and the first shell had holed her, tearing the rusty fabric of the ship as if it were paper.

Now her surviving passengers, Jean and Betty among them, were buoyed up in the water by their cumbersome green, canvas life jackets and bobbed on the waves like so much flotsam among the splintered planks of the old freighter. The Japanese cruiser which had fired on their ship was invisible over the horizon, but three aeroplanes, like evil insects, droned louder and louder above them in the sky as they bore down on the helpless survivors.

The ship was listing and her bows were already below the surface. As Jean watched, the rusty stern slowly rose up in the water and the ship poised vertically for an instant before slipping swiftly down below the waves in terrifying obedience to the law of gravity.

'There she goes. That's the end of the *Marco Polo*,' gasped Jean at Betty's side, struggling to point across the surface as the swell bore them up and they saw the last few feet of the vessel's upended stern as it vanished into the swirling water. An instant later nothing remained where the ship had been except a pall of black smoke in the air and a spreading oil slick on the surface of the water. The stink of fuel and of burning debris filled their lungs at every breath, and Betty began to cough.

'Stop it, Betty, you must stop it,' the older woman pleaded, keeping a firm hold of the tapes securing Betty's canvas and cork life-jacket.

'I can't stop it.' Betty miserably wiped a stream of mucus from her nose into the oily water and coughed again and again.

'You must stop it, you silly girl. You've *got* to save your strength, and if you keep gasping and spluttering like that you'll get sea water in your lungs,' Jean snapped at her friend without sympathy. In the past few weeks Betty had eroded almost all the gallant woman's patience with her selfish refusal to fend for herself. Too late, Jean had realized that Betty's strategy for survival was simply to demand that stronger people take care of her.

With a roar the aircraft swooped down from the sky and spewed bullets over the water fifty yards away from them. Choppy waves spread out from the impact, washing into Betty's face, and half filling her mouth with a vile emulsion of fuel and brine as if to prove Jean right. The lake of oil which marked the *Marco Polo's* grave ignited; above the slap of water and the snarl of the aircraft they heard faint screams from the survivors who were burning in the water.

'Thank God they got us off first,' Jean murmured to herself, hoping Betty was too far gone in her fever to register the horror around her. Her head was lolling heavily forward now and Jean saw that she was becoming unconscious.

'Here you are, ma'am, catch hold of this.' A seaman, swimming strongly, approached pushing a stout wooden door from the ship. 'Can we get her on it, d'you think, if we push her up together?' With desperate determination they manoeuvred Betty's awkward body on to the half-submerged surface, skinning their hands and exhausting their strength in the process. The seaman's face and neck were burned raw on one side.

The enemy aircraft did not return, and a weird peace settled over the water as the floating survivors fell silent and were separated from each other by the strong currents. The overcast sky darkened, and squalls of rain harrowed the ocean surface. Jean copied the seaman and opened her mouth to catch the sweet water.

'Can you tell which way we're drifting?' she asked him.

He shook his head. 'Makes no odds. Whether we're carried back to Singapore or the islands, or swept over to Sumatra, the Japs'll be waiting.'

'How long can we survive in the water?' Jean's tone was as calm and conversational as if she were asking the time. She no longer felt cold, only tired, but her arms and hands ached from the effort of clinging to the side of the floating door.

'A day, two days . . . we'll be in luck if it rains again.'

Darkness settled swiftly over the waves; the moon and stars were hidden behind thick clouds and more rain fell. Manipulating her wet possessions with great difficulty in the faint radiance that persisted, Jean pulled her powder compact from the bag she had tied around her waist and caught a trickle of rainwater in the lid. It cost her a supreme effort of strength to tip the precious fluid between Betty's lips.

Soon after falling back into the black water Jean felt the cold, hard snouts of fish butting against her legs. The seaman could feel them too: she heard him swear under his breath.

'Beg pardon, ma'am. I don't fancy being a fish's breakfast just yet. Keep kicking your legs and the shoal will swim on.' Jean did as he suggested and the underwater battering stopped.

Shortly after dawn the seaman pointed to a barely visible black line at the horizon.

'That's land, at any rate,' he told Jean, suppressed hope in his voice. 'We're getting closer to it, and all. Let's pray to God the current will carry us in.'

The line thickened quickly and the outlines of palms and other trees became visible, and soon the green of the forest stood out distinctly against the blue of the sea. For a tantalizing hour the current carried them along parallel to the coastline; eagerly they wasted their remaining strength trying to swim to the shore, but the water was too powerful. At last they were borne close to a sandspit and, dragging the unconscious Betty on her makeshift raft, Jean and the seaman waded into shallow water and stumbled on to dry land.

They sat thankfully on the silted strip of gravel, feeling the warmth of the mid-morning sun bring life back to their limbs and wordlessly watching white streaks of salt crystallize on their legs and arms. The seaman pulled off the burned remnant of his shirt, squeezed water from it and spread it over Betty's face to protect her from the sun.

Bright as the sunlight was, it was kinder to their eyes on the brownish beach than it had been in the glittering water. Jean picked at the tight knots of her life-jacket with weak but persistent fingers, and at last was able to remove the heavy device which had saved her life. Feeling her strength return, and sensing a sweet, muddy smell in the air, she scrambled upright and looked around them.

'Heavens, we're at the mouth of a river!' she exclaimed. 'And I can see some houses and boats, quite a lot of boats. And people!'

'Can they see us?' The seaman rose to his feet and strained his eyes in the direction in which Jean was looking. In the middle of the small estuary an elderly Malay fisherman was sculling a small boat out to sea; they watched his slow progress in silence until the seaman at last judged that he could see them, and began to shout. With maddening slowness the bowed figure straightened above its oar, and finally made a tentative gesture of recognition.

The villagers gave them rice, eggs and dried fish to eat but treated them with embarrassed diffidence; the ocean current had carried them to the coast of Sumatra, where the Japanese were already in occupation and had demanded that all Europeans should give themselves up. Jean was still pushing rice into Betty's mouth when four Japanese soldiers on bicycles arrived, summoned by the village policeman.

A young man offered to transport Betty in a rough handcart which ran on a pair of bicycle wheels, and in the smothering heat of the afternoon the soldiers and their captives marched slowly along a road by the riverside. Jean became aware that she had a painful expanse of raw flesh, like a high collar, at the top of her neck, where the coarse canvas of the life-jacket had rubbed away her skin.

They spent the night with seventy other wretched Europeans in a derelict wooden cinema, and Jean noticed that Betty was no longer burning with fever. A night in the cold salt water had reduced her temperature. She was conscious and lucid in the morning, but remembered nothing of their escape from Singapore, or of the weeks she had spent in the hospital after the birth of her child; Jean told her very little, believing that forgetting was nature's way of protecting a feeble mind from knowledge it could not bear.

In the morning the Japanese arrived in force, and marched them all onwards without pity. The strongest men among the captives took turns to carry Betty between them. They reached the small town of Muntok and were ordered to line up in front of the prison building, in peacetime a warehouse where spices had been stored.

The men were marched away, and the women ordered into the grim, harsh-smelling interior of the building.

'It's like a fish shop – I shall feel like a cod fillet lying down there!' exclaimed a fleshy, grey-haired Englishwoman, pointing at the sloping slabs of concrete on either side of the long, bare room.

Rain began to fall, pattering ceaselessly on the tin roof and dripping down the walls. The captives were of every age and nationality; many were mothers with babies which screamed with hunger throughout the night. In the atmosphere of hellish despair the women's clothing still performed the heraldic function of femininity, and signalled the crucial facts about the people who owned the garments. In the gloom, Jean noticed the tattered grey uniforms of Australian army nurses, the black habit of a nun, and one or two bedraggled silk dresses which had no doubt fluttered elegantly in the mild breeze of Singapore's Tanglin Club a few days earlier while the owners watched the bombing across the bay.

After a week of fetching food and water for her, supporting her as she staggered to the open latrine outside, and silently willing her to recover, Jean was relieved when Betty's strength returned.

'Was there any news of Gerald?' she demanded one day, and Jean told her that she had tracked her own husband down at his hospital unit, and he had told her that Gerald and the rest of their volunteer company had reached Singapore safely.

'I suppose he'll be a prisoner-of-war now,' Betty sighed, not unhappily. No one had repeated to her the stories of Japanese atrocities which were circulating the camp. 'We'll just have to wait until the war is over. It won't be long, Jean, will it?' Her eyes, as blue and blameless as ever, looked for reassurance and Jean reached out a freckled hand to pat her arm. Betty might have her strength back, but she was still living in the mood of unrealistic detachment that had characterized the months of her pregnancy.

The camp had no supplies of any kind. The women slept in their clothes, and improvised cooking, eating and toilet utensils from what they had brought with them. The only food was a meagre ration of adulterated rice dispensed daily by the guards, and some of the more improvident captives began trading with daring Chinese who came to the perimeter fence in darkness with food, clothing and drugs for sale.

One day some Japanese soldiers inexplicably threw a whole basketful of bread scraps over the fence of the prison compound, and Jean was pleased to see Betty join the rush to gather the food, but shocked when she realized that Betty was swallowing crusts whole as she pretended to help the other women.

The next day Jean was startled to see Betty wearing a fresh, almost white, blouse.

'I didn't know you had that with you – what luck,' she commented with suspicion. They had boarded the *Marco Polo* with almost all the possessions they had brought from the rubber estate, but, like most of the survivors of the bombed freighter, Betty had seized the nearest, smallest bag before taking to the water.

Jean had been exasperated to open it and find nothing inside but a wad of sodden baby-clothes.

'Yes,' Betty agreed brightly, 'wasn't it lucky? I found it in my case.' Jean was almost sure she was lying, and had snatched the blouse from the washing-lines that now festooned the outside of the building.

'Your friend will make herself most unpopular if she doesn't mend her ways,' commented the thickset Englishwoman who had compared their accommodation to a fish shop. 'I'd have a word with her if I were you – in a place like this feelings tend to run very high, you know.'

'She doesn't mean any harm,' Jean apologized, knowing that the woman's advice was sound but still feeling loyal to Betty. 'She's been terribly ill, she lost the baby she was carrying and she just hasn't got any strength, you see. My husband – he's a doctor, her doctor – used to say she hadn't the strength of a newborn lamb. He meant mentally, of course, not in the physical sense. She isn't strong enough to be unselfish. She can't do anything for herself in life, just survive, that's all.'

The older woman glanced down the length of the prison building, taking account of the sick and injured, the fretful children, the drawn faces and tattered clothes, the shins already blistered with tropical ulcers and the bones beginning to poke through dwindling flesh. 'That's all any of us can do – survive,' she said, her pale lips set in a grim half-smile. 'I wouldn't be surprised if your friend turned out to be a great deal stronger than you imagine.'

Chapter Eleven

EVERY DAY on her way to college Monty passed a brass plate beside a black front door halfway down an elegant Kensington terrace. The inscription on it read, 'Dr Mary Wilson, MD, FRCS, FRCOG.'

'What do you suppose FRCOG means?' she asked Rosanna as they idled past one day, on their way to the coffee bar. 'FRCS is Fellow of the Royal College of Surgeons, I know that much.'

'FRCOG is Fellow of the Royal College of Obstetricians and Gynaecologists,' Rosanna told her. 'I know because I've got to see Mummy's gynaecologist before I get married and he's got those letters too.' Rosanna did not explain, but Monty could guess, that the purpose of this visit was to be prescribed the birth control pill. Already the Pill was so much identified with sexual licence that admitting to taking it was rather like wearing a placard saying 'nymphomaniac'.

Next day Monty went to Woolworth's and bought a cheap ring with one red stone and two white ones. She found Dr Wilson's telephone number in the directory and made an appointment, saying, 'It's because I'm getting married soon,' to the receptionist.

A week later she rang the bell and was admitted through the black door and sat down in the doctor's waiting room. In the middle of the room was a large, battered rocking-horse. There was a huge pile of dog-eared comics on the table, and a set of sentimental bunny rabbit pictures around the walls. Monty felt ill at ease in this nursery atmosphere.

The doctor was a tall, white-haired woman with a beautiful complexion and gold half-glasses. 'I came to see you because I'm getting married soon and my fiancé and I don't want to start a family just yet,' Monty told her, trying not to sound as if she had rehearsed the speech for a week. 'We think we're too young and haven't got a proper home yet, as my fiancé may be posted abroad soon.'

The doctor gave a warm smile. 'Well, that's not a great problem nowadays. I expect you've heard of the birth control pill? Let me just examine you. Slip off all your clothes below the waist and pop up on the couch.'

Monty felt first the doctor's gentle fingers, then a metal instrument inside her. No one's been in there except Simon before now, she thought. The doctor removed the instrument and decorously folded Monty's knees together.

'Well, you shouldn't have any trouble at all when you do want to have babies,' she said with approval. 'All present and correct inside, good childbearing pelvis, plenty of room.'

Monty smiled back at her, trying to look sincerely complimented, hoping the doctor was not going to need a reminder about the purpose of the visit.

'Now, I'll write you a prescription,' Monty heard her say with relief, 'for three months' supply, but I want you to come back after the first month and let me see how you're getting on. Are your periods regular?'

'Fairly regular.' She thought of the endless days of anxiety every time her period was late, the morbid scouring through her diary to verify the date she was due.

'You must start taking the pills five days after the beginning of your next period – assuming the wedding isn't far off?' Monty nodded.

Filled with delight and relief, she walked around the corner to the chemist, paid them £10, and came out with three pink cartons marked Ovulen in a discreet, plain white paper bag. In the privacy of her bedroom at Trevor Square, she looked at the little foil pack, with twenty-one tiny tablets in their plastic bubbles – so neat, so painless, so efficient.

Soon afterwards it was Simon's twenty-second birthday. Monty surreptitiously took his front-door key off his keyring for a few hours and had it copied. His parents, reassured now that he had started work in P & G's offices, agreed he could celebrate with Monty.

'I'll come round to the flat at seven,' she told him. 'I've got a special surprise for you!'

But at four in the afternoon, she called a taxi, loaded her suitcases into it, and drove round to the apartment, where she installed all her belongings in the wardrobes. On the bed she put black satin sheets, a gift from Cathy who had said, 'I don't see why you shouldn't have non-wedding presents as well as wedding presents.'

A great deal of the bedroom space was taken up with tape- recorders and stereo equipment. Monty slipped a special tape on the machine by the bedside, and adjusted it to play the instant the switch was pressed. She arranged a giant ribbon and bow of red crêpe paper across the bed, with a huge label reading 'Happy Birthday, Simon'. Then she took a shower, washed her hair, did her make-up and slithered naked between the sheets to wait for Simon.

When she heard the key in the lock, she leaned over and turned on the tape-recorder and her own voice sounded out, singing 'Happy Birthday' and accompanied by a laboriously compiled 4-track recording of herself on piano and guitar.

Simon burst into the bedroom with delight, jumped on to the bed, and hugged her. There wasn't a great deal of point in saying anything while the music played, but when it finished Monty got in first.

'Do you like your present?'

'Love it.' He started kissing her in the slightly cautious way into which they had fallen, knowing that there was no purpose in invoking too much desire.

'You haven't had the best yet.'

'What's that then?'

'Can't you guess?' He looked round the room thoughtfully, then saw one of the closet doors ajar. When he opened it an untidy jumble of Monty's clothes fell out.

'You've done it! You've moved in! Yippee!'

'That's not all – are you sure you can't guess?' How could he be so dumb? 'It's something you can't see.'

'You mean that I have got to look for it, you've hidden it?'

'No.'

'I give up then, what is it?'

'Well, come here.' Monty stretched out a hand and pulled him back to the bed. 'I'm your present you see and now you can have all of me. I'm taking the Pill.' He paused in surprise, then hugged her with tenderness. 'Are you all right – I mean, is it all right – I mean, do you feel OK?'

'Yes, of course I feel OK. I feel wonderful, great, absolutely fab. It's really easy.'

He held her very close and the room seemed to pulse with their heartbeats. At last Monty could bear it no longer.

'Don't you want your birthday present then?'

'Darling darling Monty, of course. Always. I'll want you forever.'

The next day, after agreeing that they wanted to wake up next to each other for the rest of their lives, they set about creating the formal reality of their relationship. Simon introduced her to his cleaning lady, and took the tiny card saying S. Emanuel out of the rack by the doorbells, turned it over, wrote Miss M. Bourton and Mr S. Emanuel on the blank side, and inserted it with a flourish. Then he went to the office and spent the whole morning having Monty's name added to his charge accounts. He had no intention of making any announcement to his parents about his new status; the first rule of Simon's relationship with his mother and father was never to tell them anything important.

Monty went to college and used her typewriter to write a letter to Bettina. 'Dear Mummy,' she wrote. 'Simon and I have decided to live together because we love each other. My new address is Flat 4, 112 Rowan Court, London W8, telephone Western 2768. I'll come down in a week or two to get the rest of my things.' Then she hesitated. 'Much love' didn't seem quite right. It certainly wasn't accurate, since she felt nothing but contempt and dislike for her mother. The vision of that pasty face under its frill of ill-crimped, brown curls made her shudder. Instead, she left the space at the end of the letter blank, and merely signed her name.

Two days later she was aware of someone watching her as she opened the door to the house, and no sooner had she shut the apartment door than the doorbell rang. It was Lady Davina.

'Your mother has sent me to talk sense into you, but I don't suppose it will do any good,' she began, pulling off her brown suede gloves. 'You've always been determined to go to hell your own way and as far as I'm concerned there's no reason anyone should try to stop you. I shan't sit down, I'm not staying . . .' She peered around the apartment with curiosity, which was obviously the main motive for her visit, and Monty wished that the cleaner had not been in to arrange the cushions neatly and remove the ashtrays. 'But you must consider your mother, Miranda.'

'Why?' Monty lit up a cigarette and blew smoke in Lady Davina's direction. 'She never considered me.'

It was a hard assertion to contradict and the older woman did not try.

'And your position, and the rest of the family. We've done everything we can to get you settled and you're simply throwing yourself away on this Jewish boy. I've no doubt they're perfectly nice people, but this idea of – of . . .'

'Living in sin?' Monty smiled grimly, feeling elated by the nicotine. 'That's the difference between me and my mother – I call it love, she calls it sin.'

'Don't be so ridiculous. You've no idea what love is. Decent people will cross the street rather than speak to you. And you won't get a job anywhere. You haven't a penny to bless yourself with, don't forget. You'll simply be a kept woman.'

'Well, I'd rather be kept by a man who loved me than by a man who's only fulfilling his legal obligation. Now would you like to look around our bedroom before you leave?'

'There's no need to take that attitude, Miranda. I'm only doing my best to prevent you from making a dreadful mistake which you will regret for the rest of your life.'

As she left, her grandmother fastidiously pulled her coat around her, as if to avoid so much as brushing the door jamb of this immoral dwelling with her skirts. Monty shut the door with a feeling of triumph, conscious that she had won her first battle with the old order.

As the weeks passed, she felt less and less inclined to fetch her few remaining possessions from her mother's home, particularly since Simon took delight in buying her whatever she wanted. Their Saturdays were orgies of consumption, spent floating up and down the King's Road, meeting friends, choosing clothes and hoping to spot Michael Caine or Julie Christie among the glamorous throng which spilled off the pavements almost under the wheels of the Rolls Royces and Jaguars in the road.

Only two of her grandmother's words had any impression on Monty, and they were the phrase 'kept woman'. Monty's secretarial college fees were paid to the end of term and she kept up the farce of her attendance, often asking another girl to sign her name in the register and doing nothing all day but sleeping late, meeting Simon for lunch, then whiling away the afternoon windowshopping. But a kept woman, with its connotations of concubinage, was the last thing she intended to be.

'Why not? He's loaded isn't he?' Swallow, her old school friend, lay back on the floor cushion and expertly sealed a fresh joint with her tongue.

'You don't understand. I don't want money to be part of why we're together.'

'You're too pure to live, my girl, that's your trouble.' Swallow lit up and inhaled deeply.

'It's like – to live outside the law you must be honest. I just don't want to have to depend on Simon. What to do, though? I'd hate an office job. I'm too fat to be a model.' Monty looked with distaste at her rounded breasts, which had developed alarmingly since she had moved into Simon's apartment. Her legs had also thickened and her waist was threatening to disappear completely. The scales in the doctor's surgery showed that she had gained 101lbs in the six weeks since she started taking the Pill. She waved the joint away.

'I'll only get the munchies.'

'Come and help me for a bit,' Swallow suggested. 'We can split the proceeds.'

'Why – what are you doing?'

'Finding houses for chemin-de-fer parties mostly, but that won't last long, now they've made gambling legal. People keep asking me to organize things for them, Monty. They think I'm the only person in Chelsea cool enough to know where to find things and together enough to deliver them. I was thinking of making a business of it. Call it Something In The City maybe. Strictly for freaks, you know – no straights allowed through the door.'

Monty felt this sounded too good to be true, but two days later Swallow telephoned. 'I've got an office and they're putting the phone in tomorrow. Are you going to come in with me, Monty? I've got to do six hampers for Glyndebourne and find a miniature Rolls Royce for some pop manager who wants it so John Lennon won't have the only one in London. *Please* come in on it, Monty. It'll be a gas.'

And it was. It was the sort of job Monty never really believed could exist, starting any time between 10.30 and 11 o'clock in the morning and dealing exclusively with groovy people who knew each other only by their Christian names and worked to the ceaseless beat of the new pirate radio stations. It was also the sort of job she needed to cope with the lifestyle she and Simon fell into as easily as flies drowning in jam. Every evening they would make love, then dress and go out to one of the new raffish rock nightclubs where the music was overpowering. There they would fall in with a crowd of their friends, perhaps go to someone's place to take drugs or listen to music, and then come back to their own apartment in the dawn hours to shower, make love again, and go to work.

At weekends, and in all their unstructured time, they sat around the apartment playing records, making music or experimenting with song-writing. Simon composed long, rambling songs with clever guitar breaks and very few words. Monty found she could write nothing but pretty ballads about love.

When they were exhausted, they either slept or bought some speed. They smoked marijuana continually in private. If Simon was bored he would take some LSD, but Monty tried it once, was overwhelmed with mad terror and never dared to do it again. Their ideal was a way of life which challenged established authority and the drugs were an essential part of that. Since Simon was known as a rich boy there was no shortage of people pressing him to buy every kind of mood-altering or mind expanding chemical. Their favourite dealer was a Cypriot boy they called Tony the Greek, who got into the habit of dropping into the apartment on Sunday afternoons with a briefcase of samples and a dog-eared pharmacological encyclopaedia in which to check out his wares.

Drugs did not interest them nearly as much as sex, although both were new universes to be discovered for the first time. 'Before I met you, my life was like black and white TV – now it's all colour,' Monty said one morning as she lay in his arms. 'Do you suppose it was ever like this for the people before? I can't imagine my mother ever feeling like this.'

'Nor mine,' murmured Simon, tracing the outline of a nipple with his finger and watching the magic spot of flesh pucker in response. 'Rosanna and I used to wonder how we ever got to be born.'

'So did we.'

They set about exploring the secret realm of sexuality, seeking to elaborate the physical expression of their love and feeling a sense of duty towards the unknown dimensions of human experience which had at last become available. First they learned what they could from each other.

'What does it feel like when you come?' Monty asked Simon. He paused for thought, screwing up his eyes.

'Like my spine's melting in the middle of an earthquake.' It sounded impressive. 'What does it feel like for you?'

'Different. It's like waves.' It sounded very dull by comparison. 'It feels like a giant sea-anemone exploding inwards.' She could see he thought she was exaggerating. 'Well, it feels like that sometimes, anyway. It felt like that last night.'

'What did it feel like this morning?'

'Bit of a non-event, really.'

'You made enough noise about it.'

'Well, I thought you'd be disappointed if I didn't.'

'I'm disappointed it was a non-event.' He pulled her towards him and began kissing her nipples. 'Let's see if we can catch a sea-anemone.'

'No, Simon, *please*, not yet. I'm so sore, I can hardly sit down as it is. Darling, don't be disappointed, it just is a non-event sometimes, that's all.'

Guilt about this enjoyment of forbidden fruit stalked them patiently. Every Friday night Simon went home for the traditional Sabbath supper, and sat at the place at the dining table which had been his since babyhood. He listened to his mother calling Monty a whore, and defended his love for her silently by throwing a switch in his mind and picturing Monty, laced in the black leather corset of a dominatrix, her eyes hot and blank with lust.

As midnight approached Simon would escape his mother's mounting hysteria and drive fast and thankfully to the apartment, to find Monty sleeping sweetly in one of his dirty shirts, which she had taken to bed with her for the comforting smell of him. In a maelstrom of confusion he disapproved of himself for thinking filthy things about the girl he loved, reproached himself for making his mother unhappy and usually ended up rolling a substantial joint to calm himself.

Monty's guilt was a far more stealthy animal, which operated by turning her own emotions against her. She began to worry about what Simon was doing every moment that he wasn't with her, and took to telephoning his office several times a day, 'just to talk,' as she said. The voice of his secretary preyed on her mind and she couldn't get rid of the idea that she was having an affair with him. 'It's ridiculous,' she told herself with anger, but the fear would not go away, until she found herself making sneering remarks to Simon about his 'office wife'.

'No wonder you're in such a hurry to get to the office,' she snapped one morning as he dressed. 'Not worth wasting time in bed with me when there's a hot little number waiting for you up there, I suppose.'

Simon ignored her and started tying his flower-printed tie in the bathroom. 'What am I saying?' Monty asked herself in panic. Nevertheless, she got out of bed and followed him. 'Why don't you just tell me?' she said with a threat in her tone. 'I don't mind you fucking someone else, I do mind you lying to me. We're supposed to trust each other, remember?'

'Monty, for the last time, I'm not fucking anybody else. Yours are the only knickers I'm interested in getting into. For Christ's sake, what's the matter with you?'

Tears began pouring down her cheeks. 'I don't know,' she whispered. 'I'm sorry, Simon, truly I am. I just can't help it.'

At work, it was as bad. Monty burst into tears every time she dialled a wrong number on the telephone, or if she broke a fingernail or put down her keys and could not remember where they were. One morning, she arrived for work at 12.30, unacceptably late even by the relaxed standards set by Swallow. As usual nowadays, she was crying. Swallow closed the office for lunch and took her to the café next door.

'Look, you've got to get yourself sorted out, Monty. What's the matter?'

Monty's face crumpled again and she howled with sobs. Eventually she gained enough control over herself to gasp, 'I don't know what's the matter, Swallow. If I did, don't you think I'd stop? I hate being like this. I cry so much it's not worth putting on mascara in the morning. I'm saying such crazy things I don't know how Simon puts up with me. This morning I just couldn't get out bed, I couldn't. What is it, Swallow – am I going mad or something?'

The next day, Swallow thumped a copy of *Queen* magazine down on her desk. 'Page 63 – read it,' she ordered. 'It's the answer to all your problems. Go on, read all of it. I'll do the phones for a while. Go outside and read it.'

Monty took the magazine round to the café and read through the article. 'Side-effects of the birth control pill can include skin rashes, varicose veins, weight gain, tenderness of the breasts, nausea and depression,' she read. 'Depression is a little-known psychological condition which can take many forms including melancholia, lethargy, loss of energy, and the feeling that life is no longer worth living.'

She turned the page, her eyes devouring the elegant black type. 'Doctors who prescribe the birth control pill are often reluctant to advise their patients of these side effects in case they experience them through the process of suggestion.' She finished her coffee and ran back to the office.

'Swallow! Do you really think . . .'

'Yes of course I do. Look, it's everything, isn't itcrying and flopping around everywhere? If I were you I should go back to that lovable doctor of yours right away.'

The doctor nodded wisely, and said, 'Quite a few of my patients have reported this type of thing – I'll give you a cap instead. It's not quite as effective, but you and your husband will be starting your family soon, I expect.' And she gave Monty a diaphragm that was perhaps a little smaller than the ideal size for her inner dimensions; the next size up would have been perfect, but the doctor did not have a diaphragm of that size in her small stock of contraceptives. 'Be very careful to check that it is in position correctly,' she warned as Monty left.

In two weeks Monty's ankles were delicately delineated once more, her waist was as small as it had ever been, the beginnings of her double chin had vanished and she was 10lbs lighter. The vale of tears through which she had passed seemed like a bad dream, and she kissed Simon goodbye each morning without a pang of the crazy jealousy that had overpowered her before. She did not, however, tell Simon why she had suddenly returned to her old, slender, smiling self.

Their love life, temporarily inhibited by Monty's depression, soon began to reach new heights. Secure in their love once more, they began eagerly to explore the limits of their feelings.

Like the enthusiastic students they were, they tried to read up their subject. They discovered a small magazine written by doctors with an extensive correspondence section full of letters by men whose wives liked wearing rubber or having sex with Alsatian dogs.

Through an advertisement in an underground newspaper, Monty ordered a book called *The Eastern Encyclopaedia of Erotica* which was thin, limp and rather smudgily printed.

'The Lingam sweetens the Yoni with its tears,' she read, puzzled.

'It's got one hundred and twenty-three positions.' Simon eagerly took the book away from her. They tried a few positions, and gave up during 'The Way of the Enlightened', which required them to sit naked, cross-legged and face to face with their palms pressed together, and meditate until they achieved simultaneous orgasm.

'Maybe it works in a hot climate,' said Monty, scrambling into her clothes with a shiver.

'Maybe we weren't meditating properly,' Simon suggested.

Next they sent away to Sweden for a pornographic magazine catalogue, and ordered three volumes called *Forbidden Lust, Swedish Weekend* and *Rule of the Lash,* which were easier to understand than the *Eastern Encyclopaedia* but still rather small and grubby.

They scoured the city for erotic films, sitting through endless dreary masterpieces of Czech cinema because the Sunday newspapers had described them as explicit. Then they discovered a sex shop, with black windows and a small sign saying 'Marital Aids' on the door. They decided to buy a vibrator, having read extensive testimonials to their erotic capabilities in the medical magazine.

'You ought to buy it, you'll be getting more out of it, and anyway I paid for the books,' Simon announced, half-pushing her towards the doorway. Almost speechless with embarrassment, Monty walked in and hurriedly picked the first instrument she saw in the display. It was black, with gold bands, and the name on the box was Non-Doctor.

Simon was very quiet for a week, until Monty said, 'It's different, I suppose, but I think I prefer you, darling. All those women who have multiple orgasms with them must be making it up. I can't manage more than two.' A week later the battery ran down, and they never bothered to buy a new one.

In time, Monty noticed that the weight which she had lost was beginning to creep back. Then she noticed something much more worrying. She had grown out of the habit of watching the calendar, but now there was no doubt that her period was late. At last she could not evade the terrible truth that, vague as she was about dates, she had not had a period for a full six weeks.

'The doctor will give you something,' Swallow told her with confidence. 'They have a pill that can make your period start if it's late.'

'I can't go back to that doctor. She thinks I want to get pregnant. Her bloody surgery looks like a nursery as it is.' Monty could just imagine the conversation.

'Well, go to my doctor, then. Old Dr Robert will come up with something, I'm sure.'

Monty shook her head. 'I want to think about it. I rather like the idea of having Simon's baby. I can see it inside me, all curled up like a miniature Simon already.'

Swallow snorted with contempt. 'You'd better think fast, girl. They won't be able to give you an abortion if you leave it too long, you know.'

The more Monty thought about the baby, the more wonderful it seemed, especially since Cathy was now pregnant, too. She thought how wonderful it would be to share the experience with her sister. By the end of the day she was imagining herself as a triumphantly pregnant bride – or perhaps they could get married after the birth, when their child was old enough to stand beside them in white rompers.

That evening the telephone rang.

'Monty, it's me, Rosanna. Tell Simon the minute he gets in to come home at once.'

'What's the matter? You sound terrible.'

'Father's collapsed. The doctors are with him now.'

'Is he . . .' Dead seemed a tactless word.

'He's alive but he looks awful.' Rosanna gulped at the end of the line and finished hurriedly, 'Just get him to phone, Monty. Our mother is going mad.'

Simon came in shortly afterwards, and Monty sent him out again as she had promised, sensing that the Emanuel family was drawing together at a time of crisis. At midnight he telephoned from the hospital to say he would not be back that night, and he returned next morning, drawn and looking older.

'He's had a heart attack,' he told her, slumping on to the sofa with relief. 'They're going to keep him in hospital at least a month. Apparently it's quite a good sign that he's in his sixties, because there's more hope the later they start. The doctor said he might be dead already if he was forty-five.'

The carefree pattern of their life abruptly changed, with Simon now rushing to the hospital every evening to sit at the bedside of the weak, yellow-skinned hulk which looked so unlike his father. Monty barely saw him, and felt wound taut with anxiety as the days stole by and her period still did not come.

One evening Rosanna called in on her way home. 'I can't face Mother just yet,' she said, dropping her music case on the kitchen worktop. 'Let's have a quick coffee to give me strength. She's been howling like a banshee for days. She's absolutely hysterical. You can't imagine what it's like.'

Mechanically, Monty filled the Italian percolator and set it over the heat. Rosanna talked on as the coffee was made then said, 'You're very quiet, Monty. Is everything all right?'

'Mmm, yes, everything's fine.' As she opened the refrigerator to get the milk, she felt a wave of nausea. She pushed the bottle on to the breakfast bar with haste and ran to the bathroom, fearing that she was going to be sick; nothing happened.

Rosanna looked closely at her friend. 'Are you sure you're all right? You look a bit puffy about the face.'

The weight of her secret was becoming unbearable, so Monty decided to share the burden with her friend. 'I think I'm pregnant, Rosanna, my period's weeks late.'

'My God, I'm so sorry,' Rosanna pressed her hands with ready sympathy. 'How terrible for you. What are you going to do?'

Monty shook her head. 'I don't know. Simon's so upset about his father, I daren't even tell him at the moment. We'll have to get married, I suppose.'

'But I thought you didn't want to get married!' Rosanna looked positively shocked.

'I didn't, but I think it's different if you've got children, don't you?'

Before her disbelieving eyes, her friend was transformed into a dynamic, decisive, young woman in whom it was possible to see her mother's ruthless adherence to the dynastic principle. Rosanna began quietly, 'Simon can't marry you, Monty.' She put up a hand to quell the indignant question on Monty's lips. 'You don't understand, and it's our fault, not yours. Simon can't marry you because he's Jewish, and a Jewish man has to marry a Jewish woman.'

'But not nowadays, surely?'

'Believe me, nowadays more than ever. One of our cousins married out and you know what the family did? They sat Shivah for him. That's what you have to do when people die, Monty. The idea was that he was dead to his family. They sat in mourning for him for a week.'

'But that's . . .'

'That's the way it is, Monty. Didn't you realize? I suppose not. We've tried so hard to fit in, and tried to pretend there isn't any difference between us, and really there is, and this is part of it.' She pushed away her cold coffee. 'Do you know what I think you should do? Get rid of it, as fast as you can. And don't tell Simon. It'd kill my father if he ever found out, my mother would go mad – madder than she is going already, that is.' She pulled a face to acknowledge that Mrs Emanuel's mental stability was almost beyond prediction.

'But worst of all, *think* what it would do to Simon. Right now, anyway – he'd be in agony. You can't do it to him, you just can't.'

Monty nodded in agreement. She loved Simon too much to inflict any more emotional torment on him. Rosanna hugged her and they both sighed.

'Poor, poor Monty. How could you have been so *stupid?*'

That was the question everybody asked her.

'How could you have been so stupid?' asked Swallow's doctor. 'In a few months this Abortion Act should be law and there would be no problem. But now, my dear, I'm afraid you're going to have to jump through quite a few hoops. You must see one of my colleagues. He won't be very difficult, but then you'll be interviewed by a panel and they can be a bit sticky.'

'What do I have to say?' Monty felt acutely anxious – suppose they refused to let her have an abortion? Now that the happy vision of having Simon's baby had faded, she once more saw pregnancy as a disaster.

'Just look miserable and answer their questions. Cry a bit, if you can. We've got to prove that having the baby will be injurious to your physical or mental health, and since you're obviously in the pink, we'll have to go for the mental angle. Just keep saying you don't know what'll you'll do, you won't be able to cope, that sort of thing.' Monty nodded and he gave her a sympathetic pat on the shoulder.

'Don't worry, they won't turn you down. Now, I'm afraid, I'll have to ask you for twenty guineas.'

The second doctor barely raised his eyes from his prescription pad to listen to her as he wrote out his recommendation, and at the end of the week, Monty found herself standing in a huge, mahogany-panelled room in a large London hospital looking at three flint-faced men and one woman. The woman was the most vicious.

'You girls think you can get away with anything nowadays,' she said in lofty tones. 'If you want to know what I think, you're a selfish, irresponsible little hussy.'

Monty had no difficulty in crying at this point but in the end the woman's spite defeated itself because her three male colleagues overruled her. Nevertheless, she had the final say.

'We have decided, *Miss* Bourton, to recommend that your pregnancy be terminated,' she announced, 'and frankly I cannot imagine how a girl stupid enough to become pregnant in this way could ever prove an adequate mother. And for the future, remember that the best contraceptive is the word "no". Fortunately, there's a very good chance you won't be able to conceive again.' The doctor believed this final statement implicitly. It was an opinion she based on statistics relating to illegal abortions, which were frequently followed by infection. She felt it was important to punish these girls by scaring them, so that they would be more careful in future.

Soon afterwards, Monty told Simon she was going to see her mother for a couple of days, was admitted into the dingy, Victorian hospital, and had his child scraped out of her body. She had spent a total of 160 guineas getting rid of the baby she wanted to have. The pain was no worse than the worst period cramps, and she put a brave face on the affair, treating it as just another adventure on the long journey to the promised land of free, true, modern love.

Once the initial relief of not being pregnant any more had faded, she felt tired. She wanted very much to tell Cathy everything, and could hardly believe the cruelty of fate in making it impossible for her to tell either Simon or her sister, the two people who loved her most, about what she had done. Cathy was now attractively advanced in her own pregnancy, with a taut oval bulge under her maternity smocks. Her hair shone more glossily than ever, though she tied it back at the nape of her neck with a bow of navy-blue ribbon. Her complexion glowed with health and her normal air of serenity was enhanced. Monty was tortured with envy of her sister, and saw her less often because it was very painful to look at Cathy's layette and the wicker crib decorated with ruffles of white broderie anglaise and know that her own baby no longer existed.

The tiredness persisted; Tony the Greek always had an array of amphetamines to sell, and she started taking some speed to keep awake in the evenings. In the beginning, one little apricot tablet would keep her alert. A few weeks later, she was taking three or four of the stronger, blue tablets every night, Simon, still preoccupied with his father's illness, hardly noticed that she was either lethargic or jittery. Swallow, however, saw that something was wrong.

'Did you type this?' she asked Monty, passing an invoice over the office. Monty looked at the address and saw that it was a meaningless jumble of letters.

'Sorry, Swallow, I must have done. I'll do it again right away.' She rolled a sheet of paper into the battered typewriter and started to hit the keys, but her fingers would not coordinate properly. Swallow watched her.

'What were you and Simon doing last night?'

'Simon went to see his parents. I didn't do much – why?'

'Seen Tony the Greek lately?'

'Oh c'mon, Swallow, don't get heavy with me.'

Swallow snorted and pushed her tousled blonde hair back with an impatient gesture. 'I don't know what dope you're doing, but it's screwing up your mind, whatever it is. I'd give it a rest, if I were you.'

Monty knew this was good advice, and was herself concerned that her mind seemed to be falling to pieces, and her heart, instead of beating steadily, seemed to be trying to flip, flop and fly inside her chest. She decided to stop using speed, and threw all the multi-coloured amphetamine tablets in the apartment down the lavatory.

Immediately, she crashed into the worst depression of her life. This time she was too anguished to cry. Instead she sat for hours when she was on her own, feeling abandoned and so lonely and unlovable that she wanted to die. But she was also convinced that she was too weak and ineffectual to kill herself, and so remained marooned in complete misery.

This time Simon came to her rescue, and insisted that she tell the doctor that she was ill.

'But I'm not ill,' she protested, 'I just feel a bit down, that's all.'

'Darling, you *are* ill and I'm sure the doctor can give you something,' he insisted, holding her tenderly. 'Do you want me to come with you?'

'No, no,' she protested, frightened that he would find out about the abortion. 'I'll go and see Dr Robert tomorrow darling, I promise.' Simon's so adorable and kind, she thought, I don't deserve him.

Swallow's Dr Robert preferred consultations in the bar of the local pub, and dispensed his medicines from a large wooden chest in the back of his car. 'The depression's just a reaction to coming off the speed,' he said briskly, counting out some red-and-white capsules into a container. 'These will take care of that. Then if you're still feeling a bit shaky, take these – Mother's Little Helper, known as Librium in the trade.' He tipped a handful of green and brown capsules into another bottle. 'But *don't* do any fun drugs while you're taking these, or you'll get some pretty weird reactions. Now what contraception are you using?'

Monty showed him the pills she had taken when she moved into Simon's apartment, which she had just begun to use again.

'Ovulen!' he said with disgust. 'No wonder you went off your rocker. There's enough in them to suppress ovulation in a sperm whale. See how you get on with these – they've just brought them out.' Over the beer-stained table he tossed three green packets with another name on them.

The red-and-white capsules immediately made her feel better, but when they were finished Monty felt as if her nerves were as taut as guitar strings. She was snappy with Simon and rude to Swallow's clients, and so she decided to take the Librium capsules to calm herself. Immediately she felt normal – at least, she thought she felt normal; it was so long since she had started taking substances which made her feel different that she could not exactly remember how it felt to be normal.

Simon's father was discharged from hospital and made a good recovery from his heart attack. Simon paid Monty more attention, and took the doctor's warnings about mixing drugs so seriously that he stopped smoking marijuana himself.

'If you smell it in the apartment you'll just want some. I'm not going to lead you into temptation,' he said, stroking her hair. 'From now on I'm smoking straights until you're really OK.'

'But won't you miss it?' She wound her arms around his waist, noticing that all the meals he had eaten at his parents' home recently had made him plumper. 'Why don't I try to make some hash fudge? Then you can just have a little nibble now and then.'

He agreed, and on Saturday, while Simon was out, Monty ground some grass to powder in the coffee mill and shook it into a pan of hot chocolate fudge mixture.

She tipped the fragrant sludge into a tray to cool, scraped out the saucepan and licked the spoon. The taste was both bitter and sickly, and she pulled a face. She added some cream, and tasted it again; it was blander but still not very appetizing. A slug of brandy finally made the flavour acceptable. Then, with a couple of hours to kill, Monty left the fudge to set and took a taxi to Knightsbridge to cruise around the shops.

Half an hour later she was standing in the cool marble cavern of the butcher's department in Harrods, choosing some steak for their supper, when the smell of meat became so strong that she felt sick. Quickly she walked away into the next hall. This was the fish department: the stink of fish was so vile that Monty began to retch.

She hurried towards the exit from the store, but felt as if the crowds of people were going to crush her. She retreated on legs that felt as if they were made of sponge, and blundered into the cheese department, where the noise of thousands of shopper's feet clattering on the tiles was deafening. The uniformed floorwalker gave her a hostile look and Monty knew at once that he was going to arrest her for shoplifting and have her ignominiously thrown into the street. He strode towards her with a threatening expression and Monty struggled away from him through the crowds. She half-ran into the flower hall, and hid herself, trembling, behind a line of potted palms, until he had passed.

Despite her deranged senses, part of her mind was working logically. She remembered tasting the hash fudge, licking the spoon clean two or three times. There must have been more grass in that mixture than I thought, she told herself. Now it's reacting with the Librium. This is what Dr Robert warned me would happen.

From the corner of her eye, she saw a pool of gleaming red liquid spreading across the floor from the archway to the meat department. It was blood. She could smell it now. Resolutely, Monty turned to face the archway and willed herself to see that there was nothing there. It's a hallucination, she told herself. As soon as she turned back, she knew that the ghastly tide of blood was rising again and felt full of dread. Desperate to make her mind behave, she shook her head violently.

'Monty! Whatever's the matter?'

Feeling a colossal wave of relief, Monty flung herself into Cathy's arms. She was safe at last. Peering into Cathy's eyes through a chemical fog, she pleaded:

'Take me away, Cathy, I don't feel very well. I need to lie down somewhere. Please take me out of here.'

Cathy took her firmly by the arm and they walked together out of the store and took a cab to Royal Avenue, where Monty lay down in a dim bedroom with the curtains closed until, four hours later, the effect of the drug cocktail subsided. What remained was an overpowering desire to talk.

'What is it – what made you ill, Monty?' Cathy sat heavily on the end of the bed and stroked her sister's feet in their striped Biba pantyhose.

'It was an accident,' Monty explained. 'I ate some dope I was using to make fudge for Simon, and it reacted with some tranquillizers the doctor gave me. Thank heaven you saw me.' She giggled, still feeling strange. 'I was seeing all kinds of crazy things.'

Cathy eyed her sister with concern. 'What did you need tranquillizers for?'

Monty said nothing, but the truth was burning in her head like a fire behind a door. 'Come on,' Cathy persisted. 'You can tell me, whatever it is. It's OK.'

Monty took a deep breath and started to speak, avoiding her sister's eyes. 'I got pregnant, Cathy, and I got rid of it; I had to, Simon's father was ill and he was under so much strain I couldn't bear to add to his problems and Rosanna said that if we got married he'd be dead to his family.'

'But why ever didn't you tell me?' Cathy's voice was full of wholehearted sympathy.

'I *couldn't*, Cathy – how could I? You'd have disapproved, I know you would.'

'No I wouldn't, you know I wouldn't. Oh, poor Monty, how awful for you. And I was chattering on about my baby – you must have felt terrible.'

Monty felt tears forming in her eyes. 'I thought it would be all over, and I wouldn't feel anything, like having a tooth out, that's all. I didn't realize I'd feel so bad.'

Because she herself was carrying a child, Cathy knew exactly how powerful were the emotions which her sister had tried to deny.

Monty looked closely at her sister, noticing that the bloom of pregnancy had faded a little and there were violet shadows under her eyes. Monty blinked to make sure of what she was seeing: under the serene sweep of her black eyebrows, Cathy's deep eye-sockets were tinted an unattractive yellowish green, and there were dark red contusions around her slightly swollen eyes. Saying nothing, Monty touched her sister's bruised face.

'Did Charlie do that?'

Cathy nodded. 'We had a row. It was my fault, I provoked him.'

Monty's broad upper lip curled momentarily with contempt but she checked herself from criticizing her sister's husband and simply reached forward to hug Cathy.

'Life isn't too great for either of us, is it?'

'Things aren't how I expected them to be,' Cathy admitted.

'The worst thing was not being able to tell you,' Monty said. 'I felt as if having to keep the secret was pushing you away, somehow.'

'Well, don't do it again,' Cathy said, with mock primness. 'No more secrets in this family.'

They spent a few more hours with each other, feeling immeasurably secure just because they were together. When Monty left she kissed her sister warmly, and said, 'You've always got a home with us, you know, if anything . . . happened.' She walked backwards down the street, seeing Cathy, a rotund but still graceful figure in cornflower blue, waving from the doorway.

For a month the only drugs Monty took were her contraceptive pills. Then she started to smoke hash again. She felt happier than she had done for some time, but not as happy as when she had first moved in with Simon. He was just as loving, kind and fascinating, but the joy was gone. Monty waited, confident that the magic would return, but the weeks went by and gradually Simon seemed to drift away from her. The secret of her abortion was dividing them, just as it had temporarily separated her from Cathy.

Instead of seeing Simon as the most perfect person in the universe, Monty began to criticize him. 'If you really want to be a musician you should do it,' she said to him one day. 'Just go in and chuck your job. Quit. Go for broke. Then you'll *have* to be a success.' She felt obscurely unhappy when he did exactly what she said, and a few days later attached himself to a group of boys whose second-rate band occasionally opened evenings at the Speakeasy, one of the clubs they frequented.

'They're pathetic,' she said, 'they're only hanging round you because they know you've got money and connections.'

'Well, that's as good a reason as any,' Simon replied. 'At least, they're smart enough to know what I can be useful for, instead of writing me off as some rich kid amusing himself with a guitar.'

There were four of them: Rick the singer, who also played lead guitar, Cy and Pete on rhythm and bass, and a drummer whom Monty disliked most of all.

'He smells,' she complained, 'and he's out of time.'

'All he needs is more rehearsals,' Simon told her.

'All he needs is a lobotomy,' Monty rejoined. Before long they all agreed with her.

'I'll put the word out,' Rick said with finality. 'There's a couple of blokes I know might be interested.' He was a slim, square-shouldered kid with thick brown hair that bounced in tight ringlets to his shoulders. Monty rather liked him. Although he was no older than she was, he had a sinewy maturity which made Simon appear callow and over-privileged in comparison. ''Ullo, darlin', 'ow're yer doin'' was Rick's standard greeting, an amiable exaggeration of his rough accent.

Before long they were approached by a man called Nasher who played with a jazz-oriented group from Newcastle which had been struggling round the circuit of small clubs and pubs that now lay ahead of them. Nasher was in his late twenties, with a square jaw and a face whose expression seldom changed.

'If I joined you, we'd be the best fuckin' rock'n'roll band in the world,' he announced in his sing-song Tyneside accent.

'I like a modest bloke, myself,' Rick approved.

'There'll be A & R men coming out of the woodwork to sign us,' Nasher told him.

'And besides,' Pete, always the practical one, scraped a thumbnail down his two-days' growth of stubble, 'your lead singer's wrecking himself on speed. He'll be a basket case in six months. You want a clean-living mob like us.'

'We aim to make a lot of bread and stay alive long enough to count it.' Cy gave the group his most satanic leer. With his lank black hair and hollow cheeks he already looked like a zombie, although his peculiar green eyes gleamed with vitality.

Nasher joined them. Simon bought him a new drum kit for £70; and spent almost £1,000 on clothes and stage equipment, including two amplifiers that were bigger than anything a band of their modest stature had ever used before.

'What are we going to call ourselves, then?' Nasher demanded one evening. Now, instead of going to a smart nightclub every night, Monty and Simon spent their evenings in pubs with the band, mostly the corner pub on the ragged fringes of Chelsea near the house where Rick, Cy and Pete lived.

'What's wrong with the name we've got, the Beat Machine?' Simon distributed the brimming beers around the ringmarked table with care.

'Don't like it.' Nasher looked meaningfully over the rim of his glass. He had the most experience as a working musician, and his word carried weight.

'Nah – we've gone off it, 'n' all.' Cy and Rick, friends since childhood, always voted together on band policy.

'We're a different outfit now we've got Nasher – and Simon. When people book us they ought to know it's not the same old Beat Machine, but something better.' Pete handled the bookings. He was the one with a job; he was a clerk in a big engineering company and had access to a telephone.

'Yeah, you're right, we need a new name.' Simon took a small sip from his pint. Beer was not to his taste, but to drink anything else would have been unthinkable. Beer was what the boys drank, so Simon drank it too. 'How about Raw Silk?'

'How about a smack in the kisser?' Cy bared his grey teeth with contempt.

'Atomic Yo-Yo?' Monty put in, claiming the chick's privilege to be dumb.

'Atomic's nice, I like Atomic.' Pete nodded.

'Atomic Pigeon?'

'Atomic Rain?'

'How about the Fall Out?'

'Atomic Fireball?'

'Maybe something like the Explosion?' Simon was almost bouncing in his seat with enthusiasm.

'Shaddup, Simon,' Rick told him kindly. 'We got the balls, you got the juice, remember?'

'Juice.' Cy's speckled eyes glittered.

'I like it,' Nasher considered, his head on one side. 'A little bit rude, short, look great on the van.'

'And on a poster,' said Pete.

'Right, that's it. The Juice.' Rick looked round the table and saw agreement. He raised his glass. 'God bless her and all who sail in her.'

'One more thing.' Nasher put his empty glass down with satisfaction. 'We ain't got a van.' This was important. They needed a van to take their mountain of new equipment on the road. All eyes were on Simon.

'I'll buy a van,' he promised, 'and we can find someone to do one of those far-out paint jobs on it.' Since his legacy had been spent at a rate which was beginning to alarm him, Simon decided to sell his Aston Martin in order to buy the van. It was more of a gesture towards thrift than anything else, since more than half his grandmother's money still lay untouched in the bank.

'I'll miss the Aston,' Simon said as the car's new owner drove it away. 'We had some good times in that car, eh, girl?'

'Yeah,' Monty agreed, wishing he had not put his arm around her. She did not want him to touch her. She did not want to think about the good times they had had before. She did not want to consider the possibility that her love for Simon was dying. She decided to go back to the apartment and roll another joint.

CHAPTER TWELVE

WITH HER blissful honeymoon behind her and her pregnancy confirmed, Cathy expected to be as happy as any woman could possibly be. She had pictured herself and Charlie in a new dimension of intimacy, sharing a home, pursuing their social life and fulfilling the expectations of their families. They would have their ups and downs, of course, but nothing would seriously threaten their union.

Instead, Charlie seemed distracted, and shadows of suspicion began to steal across Cathy's sunny confidence that marriage would put right everything which was wrong with her husband. Soon each day brought some new indication of what Charlie was really doing in the evenings when he had told her he was gambling or taking clients around the clubs.

First the drycleaning came back with a discreet white envelope pinned to the bag in which was a handkerchief, one of Charlie's gold cufflinks and a love-letter signed April. Cathy burned it and determined to say nothing to Charlie. So what if that old bag was still after him? Men hated women who nagged; if she made a scene he'd be angry.

Then one day she reached down to pull the seat in the car forward and felt something soft against her fingertips. Crumpled under the seat was a pair of red, nylon knickers, trimmed with a black silk fringe.

'Aren't they yours?' Charlie asked blandly as he turned the ignition.

'Charlie, do they look like mine?'

'No, not your style at all, now I look at them. Yours are boring old white, aren't they?' He snatched them from her fingers, and sniffed them casually. 'Mmmmmn, Calèche. Must have been before we were married, darling.' And he tossed the scarlet pants out of the car window in Sloane Square.

None of the society columns would dream of ratting on an errant husband, but one gossip writer who often covered Lady Davina's charity functions approached the dowager and remarked, 'I hear Charlie Coseley hasn't let marriage change his way of life.'

Lady Davina directed a piercing glare of enquiry across the journalist's greasy black curls without altering the width of her social smile a centimetre. 'They're blissfully happy according to Catherine. What on earth do you mean?'

'We've been offered half a dozen pictures of Charlie squiring his old flames around town since the honeymoon. I saw to it they were never printed, of course.' The elderly woman bestowed a nod of thanks on him, her long diamond earrings swinging against the swagged wrinkles of her neck. 'But people will talk, of course,' he added, tucking a cigarette into the corner of his blubbery lips. 'And I'd be surprised if the shots haven't been hawked around half Fleet Street by now.'

A few days later, Cathy received a visit of contrived casualness from her grandmother.

'So how are you finding married life?' she enquired. 'Those curtains are simply lovely. Bright, of course, but lovely. The modern style, I suppose, those flowers.'

Cathy passed her a cup of tea. 'Married life is marvellous, Didi, I love every minute of it.'

'Not feeling a little off colour – the baby, perhaps.'

'No, I'm fine.' Cathy patted the modest bulge under her pink smock.

'Well, of course, husbands do tend to play up a tiny bit at times like this. Charlie's pleased, I hope?'

'Absolutely thrilled.'

'I suppose men do feel rather left out when women get interested in babies. Just remember, dear, the best thing in your condition is not to *worry*. Charlie needs you to cosset him, make him feel pampered, let him know he's the most important person in your life. He's still your prince, remember. It would be perfectly natural for Charlie to have a little fling – especially towards the end, you know – and your best course is simply to ignore it. Men need that sort of thing much more than women, in my experience.'

What Cathy needed, quite desperately at the time, was not advice but reassurance.

'Do you love me?' she asked Charlie in bed one night.

'Of course I love you,' he mumbled sleepily. 'I married you, didn't I?'

'But you haven't made love to me for ages, darling. Don't you want me any more?'

'Mmn. Not getting enough? But what about the baby, don't want to hurt the baby, do we?'

'The doctor says it won't hurt the baby.' Cathy was not very good at recognizing her physical needs, but at present there was no mistaking her body's craving. She was tingling with heightened sensuality because of her pregnancy, and yearned for Charlie's caresses more than ever, even though his brief attentions were seldom very satisfying.

He sighed with resignation, rolled over and twisted her right nipple as if it would unscrew.

'Give me a hand, there's a love.' He pulled her hand towards his crotch and she awkwardly kneaded life into his shrivelled penis. The instant he was inside her, however, his reluctant erection failed completely.

'Sorry, darling,' he said, rolling over away from her again. 'What goes up must come down, you know. Try again in the morning, eh?'

But in the morning, he slept late, then ran off to the bank with his tie and a piece of toast and marmalade clutched in one hand, calling over his shoulder, 'Client dinner tonight, darling, don't wait up.'

As she and the baby grew, the physical yearnings of the first months subsided and mental cravings took over. She waited every night in a fever of anxiety until she heard her husband's key jabbing inaccurately at the front door lock; then she closed her eyes and faked sleep.

'Is everything all right with you and Charlie?' Monty asked her sister with a transparent pretence of innocence.

'Perfectly. I've never been happier,' Cathy rejoined in a doubting tone that belied every word. She eyed her sister with envy. They telephoned each other almost every day, but now that Simon and Charlie needed so much of the sisters' attention, they met less often than formerly. Monty was wearing a richly- embroidered Indian blouse and velvet jeans. Her hair was long and curling, her eyes, with their drug-dilated pupils, wide and soft. She looked like some kind of gypsy princess, more exotic than ever.

'You are sure? I mean, he's taking care of you and everything?'

'Well, of course he is, he's my husband isn't he?'

'Husband or not, Swallow says he's always at her gambling parties now, and not on his own, either.'

'He has to entertain the bank's clients, and their wives. Just like Daddy, remember? Of course he's always out, and if they want a bit of a thrill at some chemmy party, he knows where to find it.'

'Swallow says they don't look much like banking types to her.'

Cathy sighed and looked down at her hands, noticing that her fingers were becoming puffy and her wide gold wedding ring was beginning to cut into her flesh uncomfortably. She stole a glance in the mirror, approving of the fresh pink flush which pregnancy had added to her cheeks, set off by her vivid turquoise smock. She looked the picture of happy motherhood, so why was Charlie neglecting her? She knew Monty's anxiety was well founded, but she didn't want to continue the conversation in case her own fears were confirmed. 'Let's talk about something else,' she suggested in a tired voice.

After that, Monty suddenly stopped calling her, and was vague and short if Cathy telephoned her. She doesn't want to talk to me because she knows what Charlie's up to, Cathy surmised, feeling a pang of abandonment, and never guessing that her sister was struggling with her own share of misery.

Charlie was uninterested in the progress of her pregnancy, but Cathy found it exciting and rather frightening.

'I felt the baby move today,' she announced with pride, while they dressed for dinner at Coseley one Saturday. 'It was wonderful, like a little butterfly inside me.'

'Spare me the details,' he joked, opening the closet doors one after another. 'Did you see where the maid put my studs?'

Their sex life evaporated completely as soon as her belly was an appreciable size, and to her horror she began to retain water and bloat around her face, feet and ankles. Their housekeeper timidly suggested she should take off her rings, but the idea was put to her almost too late because she had to rub her fingers with soap, chafing them painfully, to do it. She left her wedding ring on. It sat tightly in the crease of her finger with an unsightly bulge of flesh on either side, but she felt that to take it off would be a bad omen.

Charlie made a number of business trips abroad, seldom bothering to telephone and often staying away over weekends. With Monty mysteriously avoiding her, Cathy felt more and more lonely. Every Friday afternoon she was driven down to Coseley, where she occupied her vacant mind listening to the conversation of Lord Shrewton and his business guests. Should she quit their company, she was instantly prey to the Marchioness's advice about baby clothes, nursery furniture and feeding the infant.

'We'll send you Nanny Bunting,' she said, oozing invasive helpfulness. 'I couldn't have managed my boys without her. *Such* a treasure.'

Back in London during the week, Cathy had little to do except buy baby clothes and attend the exclusive childbirth preparation classes of Miss Betty Parsons.

'It's as if I've become the invisible woman,' she complained to Rosanna. 'You're the only person who ever comes to see me, nobody asks me anywhere. Monty's simply vanished. Just because I'm pregnant I've ceased to exist.'

'I'm sure it's nothing to do with your being pregnant,' Rosanna reassured her. 'Monty's having an awful time herself, Simon's distraught about Daddy being ill. She probably doesn't want to bother you with her problems, that's all. She adores you, Cathy, you know she does.'

'But it isn't only Monty – I thought that when we were married everyone would ask Charlie and me round just like they did when we were engaged. But now Charlie spends his whole time entertaining clients and I'm left on my own.'

'It's just a phase,' Rosanna told her, looking uncomfortable. She suspected that the reason people didn't find Cathy ideal company was because she was wrapped in an invisible cloud of unhappiness. There she was with her serene smile and her brave, little bulge while Charlie was all over town with a string of model girls and low-grade junior socialites, acting more promiscuously than he had even before his marriage. 'Charlie Coseley only got married so he could enjoy committing adultery,' joked his friends, and laughed uproariously.

Cathy was probably the only person in London who did not know where Charlie went, with whom and to do what. No one told her; the women said nothing because they did not want to upset her, and the men said nothing because they did not want to upset Charlie.

Any evidence of infidelity which Cathy acquired, Charlie explained away with sneering irritation. '*Of course* I took Pat Booth to Annabel's – she's looking for finance for a new boutique. Why don't you do something like that, darling, instead of moping around the house all day?'

Finally the florist's account arrived in the morning mail, and, unthinkingly, he tossed it over the bedcover to her with the rest of the bills. When she read it, Cathy could not contain her anguish any more.

'Account 1454, the Earl of Laxford, Miss Annabel Scott, 37 Cheyne Mansions, SW3 Mxd ct fls, £15. Darling Hotpants, see you tonight, all my love, Charlie.'

Cathy's heart sank as she turned over the florist's docket and read the next one in the sheaf of half a dozen stapled to the bill. It was the same message. Only the addresses were different. I suppose, she thought to herself, Charlie calls them all Hotpants so he doesn't have to remember their names.

'Read those,' she said, pushing the papers into his hand. 'Read them and tell me why you're doing this? Why, Charlie?'

'Why do you think?' he snapped back at her, feeling cornered. 'I can hardly fuck you in your condition, can I? You're as fat as a cow, it makes me sick to look at you.'

'But Charlie, I'm having *your* baby. It's for you, for us. Why must you hurt me so when I . . .' she felt tears start in her eyes, 'when I love you so much? Don't you love me any more?'

He finished dressing, lacing his shoes with anger, and stood up. 'Love you? Did I say that? I must have been pissed, or something.'

'What do you mean?' she shouted in disbelief, and grabbed his arm. Angrily he flung her from him.

'Don't do that. Don't touch me or you'll be sorry.'

'But Charlie

'You really are the most stupid woman I've ever met. Can't you see what's in front you? I couldn't love you if you were the last cunt on earth. Christ, you're so boring, and prim and straight – it's like fucking a bloody board. You're a drag. Grow up, darling. No one's going to be eternally grateful just because you opened your legs.'

'But I can change, Charlie, give me a chance.' Cathy was crying now, tears trickling down her cheeks. She wiped them away. He ignored her, looked in the glass to brush invisible specks from the shoulders of his jacket, then walked to the door.

'Charlie!' She thumped the bedcover in desperation. 'Don't go!'

'Goodbye, darling!' he called sarcastically over his shoulder.

She heaved herself out of bed, wincing as her ligaments strained at the violent movement, and ran after him. 'Charlie, please, you can't just go like that.'

'Just watch me!'

Halfway down the elegant curve of the stairway she caught up with him, pulling at his shoulder. He wrenched out of her grasp, a button from his jacket flying off into the stairwell. In the hallway below, the manservant was waiting with his brief-case and umbrella.

'Will you get off me?' Charlie hissed. 'Keep your filthy, common, moneygrabbing little paws to yourself!' He twisted her arm, trying to hurt her.

She had a flash of a vision of him throwing her down the staircase and killing the baby, and in the intimacy of their confrontation he guessed her thoughts at once. '*Oh* no! Oh no – that's just the kind of vulgar, soap-opera stuff you'd like, isn't it?' He began pulling her back towards the bedroom, finally dragging her off her feet, picking her up and carrying her. Once inside he hurled her on to the bed, kicked the door shut and dealt her a vicious back-handed slap across the face.

'Well, this isn't a soap opera, darling, this is real life, and in real life we don't pick fights with our husbands when the servants can hear –' he slapped her again – 'and we don't stage vulgar scenes and scream like a fishwife, and snoop into our husbands' lives. Because if we do . . .' he seized a pillow and she flung her arms over her face, fearing that he was going to smother her. 'If you *ever* behave like this again, I'll smash your stupid face to pulp and I'll go out of that door and I won't come back, and the next you'll see of me will be at the divorce court – OK?'

She was crying too much to speak, so he punched her in the stomach. 'Say, OK, Charlie! Say, I promise I'll be a good girl. Say it, damn you. And stop fucking crying, I can't stand the goddamn noise.' She gasped, trying to control herself enough to say the words, terrified that he would hurt the baby if he punched her again.

'I promise I'll be good, Charlie – *no!*' His arm drew back for another blow and fear snatched at her guts.

'Say it properly, cunt. Say, OK, Charlie, I promise I'll be a good girl.'

'OK, Charlie, I promise I'll be a good girl.'

'That's better. Now was there anything else, my lady?' His eyes were shining with excitement.

'What do you mean?' He hauled her towards him by one leg, twisted it and turned her over on to her stomach. Kneeling, he held her down with an arm-lock. Her nightdress was almost around her shoulders. She heard his zip, felt his penis stabbing between her spread legs.

'I believe you'd like a bit of cock? Can't disappoint you, can I? Marital duty, and all that?' And he rammed into her, jerked once or twice more until he came and then withdrew and walked out of the room. In the doorway, he paused. 'No complaints, I trust? Everything all right now?'

Cathy turned her head away and bit the bedcover to stop herself screaming with rage. As soon as she heard the front door slam behind him she ran for the bathroom, washed, dressed, pulled some dresses into a suitcase and took a taxi to Monty and Simon's apartment. There was no reply to the bell, and she realized that her sister must already be at work. She told the taxi to take her on to Trevor Square.

'My dear, you really could have been more subtle,' Lady Davina spoke with more irritation than sympathy. 'Of course he hit you. Men always hit out when you leave them no alternative. You *must* learn to play your cards more carefully. Charlie would be eating out of your hand if you'd only do what I tell you.'

'But the baby, Didi, he hit the baby.' Cathy's eyes felt sore and she could still taste blood in her mouth from the cuts inside her cheek made by her own teeth.

'Babies are tough little beggars, and I'm sure there's no harm done. Just take care he doesn't do it again, Catherine. Now go back to your home and pretend it never happened. You must *work* at your marriage, dear. Take this as a warning and *try*.'

'But it's not fair. He isn't trying!'

'My dear, this is a man's world, but we can do what we like in our own homes. We may be weak but we've got *all* the advantages in our own territory. A woman should be able to make a man her *slave*.'

By the time Cathy returned to Royal Avenue, Charlie had once again been swamped with remorse. There was a large bouquet waiting for her and he had even had the sensitivity to send them from a different florist.

Charlie came home early from the bank, embraced her tenderly, begged her forgiveness and took her out to dinner at Alvaro's, where they had shared many deliciously romantic evenings before their marriage. He apologized over and over again, calling himself all the names which Cathy had hardly dared imagine, and she forgave him.

The next day purple bruising developed around Cathy's eyes and he cheerfully called her 'Panda'. It was hard to ignore the fact that her wretchedness turned him on. Cathy distracted herself by shopping and so came across the panic-stricken Monty in Harrods.

With her sister once more by her side in life, Cathy's confidence returned. 'I'm going to fight those birds with their own weapons,' she told Monty, her eyes sparkling. 'You'll see – once this baby is born, my poor little husband won't know what's hit him.'

Their son was born ten weeks later, a little earlier than expected, in the middle of a rainy spring evening. Bettina did not bother to leave Brighton, Lady Davina regarded the whole affair with disinterest, and so Monty stoically took on the job of telephoning nightclub after nightclub until Charlie was found.

Half an hour later he swayed into the ward with a small bunch of tulips. Even his mother and father, who arrived a little later, could smell the sickly combination of brandy and marijuana emanating from their son, but he leaned over the little Perspex crib making fond cooing noises and reassured Cathy with hugs and kisses, generally acting the fond father to the satisfaction of them all.

Cathy called the baby James, which was quickly shortened to Jamie. His full name and title was James Charles William Mountclere Coseley, the Viscount Wheynough, but the weight of his lineage did not seem to trouble him. To Cathy's surprise he looked around him with interest, thrashed his limbs with enthusiasm and frequently drifted into a sound peaceful sleep, his long black eyelashes curled on his round red cheeks.

'Doesn't he ever cry?' Monty asked with interest, noticing that overnight her sister seemed to have acquired a lifetime of maternal experience and was holding the tiny body with suddenly practised hands. She never took her eyes off the little being that had so miraculously been created out of her own flesh. Love seemed a feeble description of the emotion which had now transfigured Cathy so that she looked almost like a different person.

'He did cry this morning, when he was hungry.' Cathy smiled softly as she turned the baby's tiny shoulders this way and that to admire his quarter-profiles. 'But he seems quite good-tempered. We're going home tomorrow, aren't we, Gorgeous?' The baby bicycled his tiny legs with enthusiasm. 'Look at his dear little fingernails – do you suppose I should cut them?'

'Let me do it.' Cathy gave Monty the minute pair of blunt baby scissors and one by one uncurled Jamie's fingers and held them still while her sister snipped off the translucent crescents of nail. The baby snuffled at the sensation but did not cry.

Looking thoughtful, Monty replaced the scissors on the night table and went back to the uncomfortable low armchair provided for hospital visitors. The two sisters looked at each other, both thinking of the child Monty had aborted.

'I should feel sad,' Monty said slowly, analysing her feelings. 'I do feel sad. But it isn't important, somehow. He's important; it's like your baby was my baby.' Cathy smiled warmly, but searched her sister's eyes to see if she had really looked into her heart. 'Honestly, that's how I feel,' Monty protested, sensing the question in her sister's look. 'And there's no need to ask how you feel, you haven't stopped smiling all morning.'

It was true; although her skin was drawn with the physical effort of her pregnancy and the baby's birth, Cathy's beauty now had a full-blown quality. Her finely drawn lips, their natural rosewood-red unobscured by lipstick, were relaxed and seemed softer and fuller than before. Although she was breast-feeding the baby, her breasts were scarcely larger in size, but their skin seemed fine and transparent, with blue veins faintly visible inside her ruffled, white lace gown.

A nursery nurse had been engaged for the first month of the baby's life, after which the Coseley family nanny, an elderly, imposing woman with wispy, white hair and a low-slung bosom encased in a grey serge uniform, would take over.

With the weight of the baby off her body, the weight of inertia seemed to lift from her mind as well, and Cathy once more took control of her own life, which meant taking control of her errant husband. The first priority was to repair the damage which her pregnancy had done to her body.

The only problem was that she was not terribly interested in Charlie. He seemed a petulant, demanding creature when his needs were considered in relation to those of her baby. She could think of nothing but little Jamie and it was a supreme effort to turn her attention away from her miraculous, adorable son.

Lady Davina, having observed the dangerous phenomenon of maternal obsession before, paid her granddaughter a special visit.

'Whatever you do, darling, do *not* get wrapped up in your child now.' The advice was so emphatic it was almost an order. 'You'll lose everything if you let yourself wallow in all this baby nonsense. Your husband must be your first priority. Anyone can take care of a baby, after all.'

Since Charlie had scarcely returned home for more than a few hours since his son had been born, Cathy reluctantly took her grandmother's advice. She quenched all her inner misgivings, directed the nurses to bottle-feed Jamie, and booked herself into an expensive health farm the day she was allowed to leave hospital.

The attendants at the health farm scoured her flesh to softness with salt rubs, oiled her face with creams, tightened her slack belly with electric currents and moved her sluggish bowels back to normality with a variety of disgusting but effective treatments. She passed the afternoons reading magazines, devouring articles called 'Your Marriage: Keeping The Excitement' or 'After The Honeymoon – Make Sure He's For Your Eyes Only.'

A fortnight later the size of her body had subsided; her waist was still an inch bigger than it had been before, but she did a hundred sit-ups every morning and was determined it would soon be back to normal.

'Look at Mummy, isn't she beautiful now?' Nanny Bunting demanded, propping the baby up in his enveloping white shawl to gaze at her with his vague blue eyes. The old nanny had travelled up from Coseley and installed herself at Royal Avenue in Cathy's absence. The nursery nurse at once took off in a huff but Cathy, wanting to concentrate all her energies on restoring her marriage, was grateful for the capable way the old woman took charge. A massive black perambulator was parked in the stairwell and piles of snow-white nappies filled the laundry room.

Between 6 pm and 10 pm every evening Cathy heard Jamie crying in his nursery upstairs. 'He's a very wilful little man,' the nanny told her, 'exactly like his father at the same age.'

Her household began to take on the orderly bustle she had envisaged in her engagement days, with the housekeeper tripping up and down stairs with the nursery's meals and Nanny Bunting wheezing down herself in the afternoon when the little Viscount was taken out for a walk in the pram. The servants conducted petty feuds among themselves, squabbling over missing items of laundry and other trivia, until Cathy intervened.

She went shopping, glorying in her restored slenderness and buying the kind of clothes she had seen on some of Charlie's other women – tight velvet jeans, virtually transparent lace blouses worn without a bra, long, figure-hugging chiffon dresses with tiny buttons and puffed sleeves. She cooed and flattered her husband into a malleable mood and coaxed him into taking her out with him for the next evening of entertainment the bank's clientele required.

'You'll be bored silly, darling; just wiggle your tits and take their minds off business,' he instructed her, playfully pinching one of her nipples through its fragile screen of lace.

In fact, Charlie was the one who found business dinners tedious. Cathy discovered that many of his clients were good company; some had been her father's friends, who found it curiously reassuring to meet the daughter of the suicide peer and find her unharmed by the scandal of her father's death. Others were simply charmed by her, ridiculously flattered when she asked them to explain their conversation to her, and delighted to talk to a woman who was neither bored nor frightened by the world of finance.

'See that young man over there,' a senior stockbroker said to her in a Chelsea restaurant one evening. 'Very interesting fellow – sign of the times, in a way. Most of us in banking have always been looking for the best long-term investment – young Mr Slater over there says he isn't interested in long-term investments. Six months is all he's interested in. Wants to take the money and run.'

'So what does he invest in?' Cathy stole a surreptitious glance at the tall figure with protruding ears who was deep in conversation with two other dark-suited men.

'He's an asset stripper. What his company does is buy up companies who're in trouble and undervalued on the stock market. Then he simply scuppers the company and sells off the assets – usually the property's the main thing. Property's going up, you see, but that isn't necessarily reflected in the company's shares, so he can buy them up for less than they're really worth.'

'It sounds rather drastic.' Cathy sipped her claret, swallowing it with displeasure. Charlie's taste in wine was eccentric.

'Drastic – yes. But he's not short of companies to take over. Not enough capital investment over the years – there's a lot of rotten businesses in Britain, resting on their laurels not looking to the future.'

One of the other guests joined the conversation, his eyes fixed glassily on Cathy's breasts, whose subtle exposure he had just noticed.

'Rubbish, rubbish, don't believe a word he says, my dear. You're leading the young lady astray, George. Jim Slater's not cutting the dead wood out of British industry, he's just shuffling worthless paper. Don't forget the man was a financial journalist before he got big in the City – he's got the press in the palm of his hand.'

At the end of the table Charlie sulked and drank steadily. His business dinners were normally all ribald jokes and hard drinking. His guests complimented him on his marvellous little wife as they climbed into their cars, but as soon as he was alone with Cathy in the Jaguar Charlie snapped, 'You stupid cow, why don't you keep your mouth shut? You make me look ridiculous, asking questions like a schoolgirl. It's bloody bad manners to talk business at dinner. If you want to come out with me you can shut up and behave yourself.'

He stamped on the brakes and stopped the car an inch short of a brightly painted Rolls Royce which was blocking half the road. 'Damn!'

'Oh, Charlie, it's John Lennon's car. I saw it in the papers.' Cathy watched with apprehension as Charlie got out and walked towards the psychedelic vehicle, his hands in his pockets. He pulled out a half-crown coin and scored a long wavy line through the paintwork with its milled edge.

'That'll show John Lennon, whoever he thinks he is.' At the far end of the short street, a policeman was watching them.

'Spiv! John Lennon's a spiv! Jim Slater's a spiv! Guttersnipes, the pair of them. They think because they're millionaires on paper that means something. They think they're big men because they've made tin-pot fortunes in a couple of years. They don't understand that making money's easy – keeping it's the trick. John Lennon will go bust before he dies and his sons will be right back in the gutter where he started, you'll see.' And he reversed inaccurately to the end of the street and roared away, still watched by the policeman, who also respected wealth of several centuries' standing.

The more successful Cathy became at holding her own in his world, the more uncomfortable Charlie grew. He had no justification to exclude her from his business life, and decided to scare her away. He arranged a riotous all-male party in a private room with a dozen call girls hired through the notorious Paris madame, Madame Bernard. This proved vastly popular with everyone but his father, who rapidly heard the news.

'That's not our way of doing things, Charlie, I don't want to hear of it happening again,' he told his son at the weekend. 'Your private life is your own affair, but I won't have the name of the bank associated with any kind of scandal whatever.'

'Sometimes he behaves as if our marriage were some kind of contest,' Cathy said, visiting her sister one evening. At this period in their lives they spent many hours discussing their relationships with Simon and Charlie, wondering why love did not make them happy, and how they could turn their romantic yearnings into real life. 'If something happens which I like, he just wriggles around until he finds some way of spoiling it, and then he's happy.' She stretched her legs uncomfortably, stiff from sitting on Monty's Moroccan floor cushions.

'Is he still fucking you?' Monty pulled a cigarette out of the carved soapstone casket from Kashmir which stood on the low brass table.

Cathy smiled with triumph, pushing her glistening curtain of Havana-brown hair back from her face. 'Yes, quite a lot now, thank heavens.' She sighed, drew in a lungful of unaccustomed cigarette smoke and coughed.

'Sorry, I'll open a window.' Monty did this with difficulty, because she rarely opened the apartment's windows. 'You don't sound very happy about it.'

'Well, I try, but it does get boring.'

'Do you have orgasms?' Monty lay back and looked at the ceiling, wondering if a pendant lamp of pierced brass would look good hanging low over the table.

'Well yes, but not very often. He doesn't go on long enough.'

'I don't have them from fucking at all, only if Simon goes down on me,' Monty sighed. She evaded making love now, feeling guilty and cruel every time Simon accepted her flimsy excuses. Cathy also sighed. She had fewer and fewer orgasms now and thought longingly of the days before she was married, when Charlie had tried to arouse her enough to make her forget her tedious addiction to virginity. She went through sex in an oddly detached mood now, as if all the sensations were coming through cottonwool. After every brief coupling with Charlie, she felt a dull ache in the region of her pubic arch.

'I suppose I could ask Charlie to go down on me, but he doesn't like what he calls fiddling about.'

'Maybe you could go in for a bit of 69?' Monty suggested.

Cathy tried this. It was not a success. Her husband's erection subsided in her mouth and he complained that she smelled.

The only aspect of her life which was wholly delightful was her son, a robust, serious child with dark curls who crawled excitedly into her arms at every opportunity, twining his plump, starfish hands in her pearls and pulling himself upright on her lap. Cathy adored him with anxious reserve. It was so easy to love her baby son, but increasingly difficult to love his father. She felt confused. Surely Charlie should be the centre of her world?

Nanny Bunting subtly discouraged her from taking any part in her child's care.

'Clumsy Mummy – Nanny do it,' she would say, taking the bottle or the toy away from Cathy as if she too were a child.

'We would really prefer it if we could bring baby down to Mummy in the afternoon, rather than her coming all the way up to the nursery,' she said one day, and so Cathy received her child every day at 4.30, and somehow the whole house grew to regard the nursery as Nanny's private kingdom.

In the evening she still heard Jamie cry, sometimes for hours on end, and felt vaguely that this was wrong, but she knew nothing about babies and when she asked Nanny Bunting she was told, 'Bless you, Mummy, all babies fret when they're put down for the night. It's nothing to worry about. Crying expands their little lungs.'

One evening when Charlie was out she heard cries which she thought were louder and more desperate than usual, and at last went up to the taboo territory of the nursery to see if anything was wrong.

'Now let that be a lesson to you, not to play with hot things,' Nanny Bunting was saying, standing over the tiny figure of Jamie, who was sitting in front of her by the wall, roaring his heart out.

'Is everything all right, Nanny?' Cathy hesitated in the doorway, feeling that she was intruding but alarmed at her son's uncontrollable distress.

'There, see what you've done, you naughty boy? You've disturbed Mummy and brought her all the way up here in the night. Isn't that a naughty boy?'

'Why is he crying so much?'

'He touched my radiator. Mummy, and burned his little hand, but he won't do that again in a hurry, will he? Clever little man knows it's naughty to touch hot things, doesn't he?'

Cathy firmly picked Jamie up and held him close, murmuring soothing nonsense into his ear and wiping the streaming mucus from his nose and mouth with the hem of her white broderie anglaise peignoir. The baby's frantic screams began to subside. Without a word to Nanny Bunting she took the baby out of the day nursery and walked him up and down the landing until he fell asleep on her shoulder. Clucking with disapproval, Nanny Bunting bustled into the night nursery to tidy the cot, and Cathy heard the old woman muttering angrily to herself as she carried the sleeping infant through the doorway. Oh dear, thought Cathy, I've offended her now.

Next morning she told Charlie about the incident

'My goodness yes, I'll never forget,' he said, tossing aside the *Financial Times*. 'She used to do that to us too. Make us hold something hot so we'd know not to play with fire. She maoe me hold the poker when the end of it was red hot.'

'But isn't that rather cruel?'

'Nonsense. Didn't do me any harm. She's an absolute treasure, Nanny Bunting. For heaven's sake don't rub her up the wrong way, darling. I know you're not accustomed to managing servants, but what on earth would we do without her?'

A few weeks later the old woman had an attack of gout and could not walk. Cathy went up to see her, and found her sitting in state with her swollen foot raised on a stool.

'Can you manage, Nanny? Would you like us to get in a temporary girl to help you?'

'Certainly not!' The old woman glared at her, clearly insulted. 'I'm not in my grave yet, by a long way.' However, the inflammation became so severe that Nanny Bunting was taken away to hospital two days later, and Cathy telephoned an agency for a temporary. A few hours later a very slim girl with hair the colour of her dark-brown uniform arrived, and took Jamie upstairs. Monty arrived at the same time, with a bag full of Tibetan amber beads from Thea Porter to show Cathy.

Half an hour later the sisters were sitting in the drawing room when the temporary nanny appeared in the doorway, with a naked Jamie whimpering and squirming in a cot sheet.

'Mrs, I mean. My Lady, I think you ought to see this,' she said, her voice almost a whisper. She set the child down on the floor and he pulled himself up on the corner of the sofa. The sheet fell away. There were greyish marks on his legs, red weals on his buttocks and a raw rash on his inner thighs.

Cathy and Monty gasped with horrified surprise.

'He's absolutely miserable, My Lady.' The girl timidly turned Jamie around so they could see the bruises on his chest. 'And look at his little hand.' She tenderly turned the fat palm of Jamie's right hand upwards for Cathy to see the suppurating burn at the base of the fingers. 'And just look at his feet . . .' She picked Jamie up and showed them red marks on the soles of his feet.

'Whatever are they?' Monty asked.

'Burns, I think. He's terrified to have me touch him upstairs. He starts screaming the minute I go into his room.'

In the nursery, they were horrified to find that Jamie's cot was cold, wet and stinking.

'It can't have been changed for days.' Monty picked up a sodden blanket with an expression of disgust. 'Nanny Bunting must have just left the bed when he wet it because she couldn't manage to change it.'

'And there's nothing to sterilize the bottles with, and the nappies aren't really clean. No wonder he's a mass of rashes. And look here.' Now emboldened, the temporary nanny pulled open a cupboard, and showed Cathy a dozen brown medicine bottles with old-fashioned handwritten labels.

'That's the gripe water she gets from a special chemist in St James's.' Cathy picked up the nearest bottle with foreboding and uncorked it.

'Beg pardon, My Lady, but it certainly isn't gripe water. I believe it's some old remedy they used for colic, but she's opened all the bottles and not finished any of them.'

'Oh heavens, my poor baby.' Cathy hugged the abused little body as hard as she dared. 'If only I hadn't trusted that old witch. How could I have been so stupid?'

Monty squeezed her sister's shoulders. 'You weren't to know. How could you have known? She was covering up deliberately, afraid you'd fire her if you knew she couldn't cope.'

Suddenly almost weak with guilt, Cathy called the housekeeper and manservant and asked them to move the new nanny and Jamie into one of the spare bedrooms. Next she asked the doctor to call. He was not only her doctor, but Charlie's as well, and the personal physician of the whole Coseley family. He examined Jamie with a frowning face.

'Chronic neglect and ill-treatment,' he announced at last. 'We'll need to get him X-rayed; it looks as if those ribs have been broken. She can't have had the strength to pick the baby up properly.'

'What was the stuff in the medicine bottles?' Monty stood beside her sister and looked at the prosperous physician with mistrust. He seemed to be reacting very calmly.

'It's a sedative mixture, basically. They used it years ago for colic and general fretfulness.'

'What's in it?' Monty pressed him, picking up a sticky bottle and screwing up her eyes to read the label.

'Laudanum, I believe, but not in any harmful concentration, it can't have done him much harm, just stopped him crying.'

Cathy's eyes, normally so serene, were blazing with rage. 'I can't believe anyone could do such terrible things. That wicked, old woman is never going to set foot in my house again. Thank heaven we found out what she was up to before she hurt Jamie any more.'

'Don't be too hard on her.' There was a bland look on the doctor's round face and he made an ineffectual gesture towards covering the naked baby with his large, gold-ringed hand. 'I've seen this kind of thing before, of course. Family brings in the old nanny, not realizing she's past it. Everything's fine for the first six months, but when the baby gets to be a bit of a handful things start to slide.'

'I'm sure they don't realize she's past it,' Cathy said grimly. 'I shall have to speak to my mother-in-law.'

'Yes, the Marchioness. Well, if you need any help, just give me a call.'

'Fat old toad,' sneered Monty as soon as the doctor had left the room. 'He won't offend the Marchioness because he's making a pile out of her. His whole practice depends on him being the Coseley family doctor.'

'Come with me at the weekend,' Cathy asked, her slender fingers deftly fastening the pearl buttons at the back of Jamie's blue, smocked romper-suit. 'I've got to get rid of the old witch and I know the whole-family just won't believe me.'

She was correct. The Marchioness was disbelieving, then insulted, then stubbornly insistent that nothing could be wrong with Nanny Bunting's methods. 'Why, she brought up the entire family virtually single-handed,' she protested.

'And *haven't* they turned out well?' said Monty, alight with gleeful sarcasm. The Marchioness glared at them but prepared to accept defeat. Apart from Charlie's well-publicized escapades, his elder sister had just abandoned her husband and children and was living in Tangier with a nightclub owner; and the haughty cousin Venetia had been arrested in Spain and charged with smuggling marijuana.

Nanny Bunting went back to Coseley as soon as she was fit, and was dispatched to retirement in one of the estate cottages. The slim new girl replaced her in Cathy's household, and stayed for three months; then Cathy woke up in the middle of the night and found Charlie and the nanny in a frenzied clinch on the staircase. The girl squeaked like a frightened rabbit and bolted half-naked downstairs and out of the front door in her nightdress, leaving Charlie with her much-laundered grey-white panties in his hand. Cathy then hired Nanny Barbara, who was a little older, with an air of pious respectability and black hair in a bun which she was always repinning at the nape of her neck. She was Irish, and amusing, full of silly songs and highly-coloured fairy tales which Cathy enjoyed almost as much as Jamie.

Charlie took no interest at all in these domestic dramas. He considered servants to be a lesser race, unworthy of his attention.

Cathy could tell when he was again pursuing another serious affair, because he abruptly stopped making love to her. This time, however, she felt calm and determined. She had discovered quite a lot about her weak, foolish husband's susceptibilities, and curiously, the more she adored her baby son, the easier it was to be detached about managing his father. If Charlie is anybody's, he might as well be mine, she told herself, and set off with Monty for a large lingerie shop in Knightsbridge which had the reputation for supplying all the most expensive call girls in town. They bought a black French bra which was a triumph of engineering, a garter belt and stockings.

'Just think,' Cathy said, as she admired her reflection over her. shoulder in the fitting-room mirror. 'A few years ago at school we couldn't wait to give up wearing stockings.'

'Well, they're a lot more practical for sex than for playing lacrosse in,' Monty sniffed.

The outfit worked on Charlie like a dream. No sooner had Cathy thoughtfully asked him if her stocking seams were straight than he pulled her down on the drawing room floor and started pulling off her clothes with complete disregard for the servants' sensitivities.

Her next problem was April Henessy, who came round one afternoon and announced, 'Charlie's leaving you, Cathy. He just hasn't got the courage to tell you himself. He loves me, he's always loved me, and it's no good pretending any more.'

'Pretending what, exactly?' Cathy felt a rush of cold rage. She had no pity for anyone who threatened her home and happiness. 'Pretending that Charlie's capable of loving anyone, maybe? He may say he loves you, April, he says that to all the girls. I'm his wife, and I'm going to stay his wife.'

'Yeah, but you and Charlie are all finished in bed,' the older woman snapped. 'You don't turn him on, you never did. He says fucking you's like flinging a wet Wellington boot down Oxford Street, since you had the baby.'

'Our sex life is fabulous as always, April. And if I were you, I wouldn't start calling *my* body down. Have you seen yourself in the mirror lately? Good thing the mini-skirt's gone out – your thighs look like waffles from behind.' She marched briskly to the bell push and pressed it. 'Miss Henessy is leaving now,' she told the manservant, whose veneer of non-involvement momentarily cracked with a hearty, '*Yes*, My Lady!' as he pulled wide the door.

Now that she had the enemy on the run, Cathy's confidence blossomed. A few days later she cunningly stage-managed a royal fuck in the shower with her errant husband, after which they slumped happily to the floor and let the warm water continue coursing over their tingling bodies.

'How was that for you, darling?' she murmured.

'Wonderful.'

'Really wonderful?'

'Oh God, now what?'

'Was it like flinging a wet Welly down Oxford Street, by any chance?'

He laughed. 'Thank you, darling. I wish I'd been there.'

'Thank you for what?'

'Getting April off my back. That woman's been such a drag, I just couldn't get rid of her.'

'I believe you – thousands wouldn't.' Cathy skipped out of the shower and flipped the control to cold as she went, deluging Charlie with icy water. As a result, he leapt after her, decided to smack her bottom and they ended up making love again and being an hour late for dinner.

By the time Jamie was an angelic toddler, Cathy had grown quite accustomed to the fluctuation of Charlie's libido, and considered herself well in control of the situation. Lady Davina concurred.

'He's bewitched, the dear boy, simply bewitched,' she exulted, watching Charlie cavort around the dance floor at one of her increasingly ambitious charity balls.

He was rudely ignoring his partner and blowing kisses to Cathy over her head. 'You see how easy it was – all you had to do was keep your head and do exactly as I told you. Men are like puppies, my dear, you simply have to train them. Then they're absolutely *grateful* to you for being firm and keeping them in order. That man's yours for life now, Catherine. Bewitched!'

Cathy smiled in dutiful acknowledgement of her grandmother's praise. In the depths of her heart she now knew the truth about her husband. He was a foolish bag of appetites, the helpless product of overindulgence. She was charmed by him still, but found nothing to respect in him. Cathy would not admit it to herself, but she was struggling to stay the way she thought she ought to be, in love with Charlie.

Rupert Lampeter, Charlie's greatest polo crony and the best man at their wedding, had an airy, grey-stone house on a headland in Antigua, and they went there in February. The party was made up of a dozen or so riotous young hedonists, into whose company a middle-aged American lawyer had plainly been dragged by his girlfriend. Lisa was sixteen, but looked about twelve, even when sunbathing in a tiny leather cache-sexe on a thong, which was all she wore during the daylight hours. Her breasts were tiny, little, brown buds, and her long brown hair fell straight and smooth to her buttocks. She was sweet, clever and adorable, full of games for whiling away the heavy hours of leisure. Her family were apparently wealthy, even by Texas standards.

They were scuba-diving in the next cove when the lawyer, a protruding belly under his mask and air tank, swam up to Cathy in the confusing, blue world below the waves and gestured that he wanted to show her something. They finned away from the others, and he led her to an immense fan coral which was certainly worth the trip. Cathy mimed her appreciation, but sensed other business. When they swam back and surfaced, he had led her to a different cove, and the beach was empty.

'Let's go ashore and get our bearings – we could swim around out there all day,' he suggested, and they waded in and stripped off their gear. Then he suddenly pushed her down clumsily on the sand and started kissing her.

'Hey, stop it!' Cathy protested, scrambling away. 'What on earth do you think you're doing? That's my husband I'm with, you know.'

'And that's my date he's banging hell out of every time I let her out of my sight, so why don't we even up the score a little?' He looked at her with hard, bright grey eyes, a lock of dark hair plastered across his high forehead.

'What, Lisa?'

'Who else? You mean you didn't know?'

'No, of course, I didn't know.' She felt angry and humiliated.

'Hey – don't be offended. Lisa told me that he told her that you have kind of an open marriage, so I thought . . .'

'Well, we don't. Open on Charlie's side, maybe. I just don't think it's very important, that's all. Lots of husbands play around.'

'Yeah, lots of them play around with Lisa, too. She's the nearest thing to a nymphomaniac I've ever met. Got started when she was twelve, she told me. Can you beat that?'

Cathy was unused to the values of sexual sensation-seekers, and gave him a chilling glance. 'No – and I wouldn't want to. Now I'm going back – are you coming or not?'

Ignoring Charlie's new attraction in the claustrophobic atmosphere of the holiday was very hard. Lisa sat topless at lunch, munching vast slices of watermelon and letting the juice drip on to her bare buds until Charlie could not resist leaning over to lick it off. If he went swimming, she went swimming, and what they were doing in the water was obvious to everyone on the beach. Her vivacious conversation turned into a series of private sexy jokes which she shared with Charlie.

On the last evening, Charlie told his wife, 'I'm not coming back with you, Cathy, I'm going to Dallas to stay with Lisa for a while.'

'Be good,' she told him sarcastically.

In London, the days dragged on and on. 'Why do I feel so tired all the time?' she asked Monty, examining her face in the brightly lit mirror in her dressing room and noticing the telltale shadows under her eyes and the barely visible crease of a wrinkle in the tanned skin of her cheek.

'You're worrying about Charlie, that's all . . .' Monty led her sister firmly away from the looking glass. 'You'll get him back, Cathy, you always did before. You're stronger than he is, he *needs* you.'

Cathy sat down heavily on the end of the bed. 'Another fight, another campaign to rescue our marriage – that's what I'm tired of, Monty. I'm not strong enough any more, I just haven't got the stamina to go through it all again.' Two large tears crawled down her coppery cheeks.

'Of course you're strong enough – you love him, don't you?'

Slowly, Cathy shook her head and looked up at her sister with despair in the bronze depths of her eyes. 'No. If I'm honest I don't think I ever loved him, Monty. Not like you loved Simon, anyway. Charlie was just there, that's all. I was supposed to love him so I just talked myself into it. I conned myself, that's all.'

Monty sat beside her sister and were both silent. 'Love's just one big con all round, if you ask me,' Monty looked reflectively at the toes of her pink suede Biba boots. 'It's just a game. I don't think I was ever really in love with Simon, either.'

Cathy jumped up, determined to shake off the gloom that had descended on them like a smothering cloud. 'Well, if love's only a game I'm going to win,' she vowed, running back to the dressing-room mirror and pulling back her long, dark hair. 'Do you think I should cut my hair, Monty?'

Next day a letter from Charlie arrived. 'I'll be back at the end of the month,' she read, 'but not to stay, Cathy. I'm sorry, darling, it just hasn't worked out between us. It's better we split now than later on, don't you think?'

She made herself look as beautiful as she could when he arrived, hung on to her poise like grim death and got him into bed with no trouble at all.

'Home Sweet Home,' he murmured, patting her mound affectionately before he fell asleep.

But two days later, Lisa arrived to rent a house two streets away and Charlie vanished. He vacillated between the two houses for a month, went to Lisa for three months, then returned to Cathy again and bought her a huge collar of diamonds for the heart he had given her when they were courting. He wept like a baby, cursed Lisa, cursed her, went out and got drunk, stayed in and got drunk, started screwing April Henessy again and behaved so erratically at work that his father sent him on an enforced week's vacation.

Anxiously, Cathy asked her grandmother's advice. 'He's just a big baby, remember?' counselled the dowager. 'You smile, you're thrilled to see him, you never mention the other woman, you never make a scene – he'll soon get bored with this stupid little girl and come back to you.'

Cathy lost weight rapidly, and the elegant sweep of her eyebrows flattened out as tension gave her face a permanent frown. The rich bloom of her complexion faded and her skin became dry and prone to ugly rashes. Charlie shuttled from Lisa to Cathy for another six weeks, and every day Cathy sank deeper into depression, becoming more and more desperate and less and less confident.

The matter was decided by his mother, the Marchioness, who had never ceased to resent Cathy as the first woman to come between herself and her beloved son. 'Lisa is a sweet girl, Charlie,' she told him, 'and she obviously adores you. You owe it to her to do the decent thing, dear. You've made every allowance for Catherine but she simply isn't up to being the sort of wife you need. She can't manage servants – that ridiculous nonsense with Nanny – and she's simply lost in your social circle. We should have expected it, of course, looking at the family.'

And so Cathy came back from a shopping trip one afternoon to find another note saying, 'I'm sorry,' and her husband gone. She waited for the inevitable agonized telephone call, but it never came. Instead a letter from a flashy Mayfair law firm arrived, announcing Charlie's intention to divorce her.

'I can't seem to sleep, but I feel as if I'm ready to drop, I'm so tired,' she told the doctor, who gave her some tablets.

'These will help you sleep,' he said, handing her a bottle of large, white pills, 'and these are for the day, in case you need something to keep you going.'

She endured another six weeks with nerves as tight as bowstrings. Monty was concerned; she noticed that Cathy's hair was falling out, and she seemed to have no patience with Jamie whereas before nothing the child did irritated his mother. Cathy had become desperately thin, and Monty saw her hand shake as she poured them tea. Lifting the Georgian silver pot was not easy for her, but then, it was very heavy.

'Are you really OK, Big Sister?'

'Of course I'm OK. Why does everyone keep asking me that?'

Monty realized she would need to be cautious. 'What do you weigh now?'

'Don't nag, please, Monty. I'll never get Charlie back if I lose my figure.'

'But your ribs are sticking out.' Above the deep plunge of her raspberry cashmere sweater, Cathy's collar-bones were sharp as knives.

'I just can't eat very much, that's all. Food makes me sick.'

'Have you told the doctor?'

'No, I only see him for the pills. I'll get well when Charlie comes back, I know I will.' She saw the warning look in her sister's wide, black eyes. 'I'll get him, Monty, in the end. I know it. He's seeing that whore April again. Lisa won't be able to take it when he starts his old tricks.'

'How do you know he's seeing April?' Monty demanded.

'I just know,' Cathy replied, for an instant sounding the note of crazy dismissal that was characteristic of their mother. She had no intention of confiding to her sister that she sometimes sat in her car outside the house where Charlie and Lisa were living, and spent a whole night watching the lights go on and off in the windows and waiting to see if Charlie would come in or go out.

At last the gossip columns discovered that the Earl and Countess of Laxford were living apart, and Cathy saw her name in the newspapers, and pictures of herself alone and Charlie with Lisa. She stared at the newspaper for half an hour, realizing that she had to accept the failure of her marriage.

'Nanny Barbara,' Cathy said the next day, 'why not take Jamie down to the country for a week? His grandparents haven't seen him for ages and they do love him so. I can't go, I've got something on in London.'

She gave the servants the week off, and on Friday went to Elizabeth Arden for a top-to-toe beauty treatment. Back in the empty house, she locked the doors, then went to her dressing room and put on her wedding dress, which lay pristine in white tissue paper, with all its accessories, in a special mahogany chest.

'Alcohol,' she said, 'I must drink something.' She went down to the pantry and found a bottle of champagne, and drew the cork as her father had taught her. Then she went back upstairs.

At three o'clock on the following Monday morning Monty braced herself against the bulk of the Juice's amplifier as Simon swung their van into Sloane Square. The band had played a gig in a distant northern suburb. The Juice were very much a

Monday night band, not big enough to justify the Friday or Saturday gigs, but with enough following to half-fill a bar on a slack evening.

They were all running on speed, and the landlord had given them a bottle of vodka which they were drinking neat. Rick handed it back to Monty from his seat in the front.

'No thanks.' Monty passed the bottle on to Cy.

Rick looked at her at length in the fitful light from the street lamps. Monty had been quiet all evening, which was unusual. Whenever she was upset, she always shook it off when the band went on stage. 'What's up with you tonight? You've hardly said a word all evening.'

With a squeal of tyres, Simon hauled the van out of the square and into King's Road. 'It's her sister – Monty reckons she's cracking up because her old man's run off with some Lolita. She's been moping like a wet hen for days.'

'I have not,' snapped Monty, angry that Simon should intrude on the special bond which she and Cathy shared.

'Don't she live around here, in one of them posh houses?' demanded Rick, taking back the depleted vodka bottle for a final swig.

'We'll pass it any minute,' Monty told him, grateful that Rick at least was taking her anxiety seriously.

'Drive past the house,' Rick ordered Simon suddenly. 'We can't have Monty getting hung-up like this. Let's check things out.'

'Don't be daft, it's the middle of the night.' Simon held his watch out for Rick to see the time.

'Don't matter – we won't stop unless there's lights on. If it's all dark we'll drive on, no harm done. This is it, ain't it, love?'

Gratefully, Monty said yes, and Simon, unwilling to appear callous or to provoke an argument, slowed the van and turned into the narrow side-street which led into Royal Avenue. As soon as they turned the corner they saw Cathy's house, every window ablaze with light. Alarmed, all five of them tumbled out of the vehicle and stood gazing at the bright facade while Monty pressed the bell.

'No answer.'

'Gone away for the weekend, has she?'

'She should be back by now, she's always back by Monday. Anyway, the housekeeper should be there. And all the lights are on.'

Simon strode up the steps and opened the brass letterbox to peer inside. 'There are letters on the mat. No one's picked up the mail.'

Simon, Rick and Monty went down into the basement, where Rick suddenly assumed command. He rattled the handle of the servants' door, which was also locked, then hammered the panels with authority, calling out, 'Anybody there?

Anybody home?' A gust of raw, spring wind blew some dead leaves into the basement area, but there was no sound from the house.

'On holiday, maybe?'

'There's always someone here. And if they were all away, they'd pull the burglar grille down.' Monty looked towards Rick for help, full of fearful premonitions about her sister.

'Good thing housebreaking was part of my education, innit?' In the orange glow of the street lights Rick smiled at her with sympathy. Then he turned and aimed a careful kick at the glass panel of the basement door, reached through the shards, and released the locks. With Monty leading, and Rick and Simon behind, they made their way through the orderly house. In the drawing room Monty pulled the curtains across the naked windows. Simon picked the letters off the doormat and piled them on the marble console in the hallway. Rick kept his eyes intently ahead, scorning to seem impressed by the opulence around him.

In silence they climbed the staircase and Monty pushed open the door of the master bedroom, at once recognizing her sister's wedding dress, apparently flung across the bed. Then she saw Cathy, and instinctively clutched Rick's arm as she stepped back, shocked.

'Oh, my God, look at her.' Inside the crushed silken folds of the dress, Cathy lay half on the bed and half on the floor, her left leg twisted beneath her, her face already bluish where the skin was most delicate. At the same instant Monty and Rick leapt forward to the inert body.

'Like Marilyn Monroe,' said Simon, pointing to the blue patches.

'No.' Monty felt her sister's wrist, Rick's strong fingers probed the neck. How *did* you take someone's pulse? There it was – a pulse, the merest flutter, but it was there. 'Not like Marilyn Monroe. *She's* still alive.'

Chapter Thirteen

ALL SINGAPORE called Philippe's establishment simply 'the French club'. It had an air of prosperous comfort and an anonymous ambience which appealed to Singapore's new élite. They were young, hedonistic and cosmopolitan; the war was already a childhood memory, something their parents used to reproach them for their brazen materialism.

Apart from the exotic beauty of the women who worked there, the French club could have been situated in any big city in the world. At the end of the first year the club had been so successful that Philippe decided to buy the premises next door, combine the two buildings into one complex, and redecorate. Instead of the old, garish plastic, he introduced heavy sofas upholstered in dark red leather, red café curtains dividing the seating into intimate clusters and brass lamps with green shades which cast pools of soft light. Instantly the rooms acquired something of the atmosphere of a European club, but with a bright, contemporary edge that proclaimed a new order.

It proved a little sophisticated for the taste of the older colonial types, who did not care to sink their liquor in the company of Malay princelings or the sons of the Chinese tycoon class, however luxurious the surroundings. For the city's wealthy newcomers, who behaved as if Singapore were the South of France and roared through the new suburbs in open roadsters, it was a perfectly congenial environment.

Ayeshah began to emulate the rich Europeans, who wore white clothes to give themselves the illusion of coolness in the stifling tropical climate. She bought Western fashion magazines at the big hotels, and from them sketched simple, fitted white dresses which she had made by a Chinese dressmaker. She wore her glossy black hair in a fashionable chignon with a single starlike frangipani flower as the only visible reminder to her clientele that they were still in the East.

On the mainland the Communists attacked the British with increasing ferocity. Shortly after Philippe opened his club, the British High Commissioner was killed in an ambush on a mountain road as he was being driven in his Rolls Royce to a hill-station for the weekend. After that more and more British soldiers flooded into Singapore, and British statesmen followed them to begin negotiating independence for the Malay States once the war was over.

In the beginning, the war on the mainland was far away and good for their business, but by 1952 the city itself was full of tension and armed Communists had been flushed out of the villages in the rural parts of Singapore Island. In the daytime there were frequent, angry demonstrations, and when darkness fell to offer cover to an assassin there were killings in the city's thronged alleys. The Malayan police in armoured cars patrolled the streets at night, futilely chasing small groups of rioters who vanished into the deep darkness below the crossed washing poles.

There was an atmosphere of violence and instability which seemed to make everyone want to live for the instant and grab what they could while the going was good. Once again, the port at the crossroads of the world's trade pandered to the momentary perversities of its visitors. Old women sidled through the native quarters with children to sell. Bugis Street became a brightly lit gully of vice, through which swooped flocks of gaudy transves- tites, shrieking in raucous flirtation with the crowds of seamen.

All this Philippe observed with amused detachment. 'I've seen it all before,' he told Ayeshah. 'Saigon went the same way. Every city gets rotten when an army moves in. And they will never defeat the Communists; they have the jungle on their side.'

Ayeshah sensed the changes, but did not see them because she rarely left the club to set foot in the streets at night; Philippe had rented a handsome square bungalow for them in a new suburb, and when they drove home in the pale hours before dawn few people were about. Moreover, she was fiercely singleminded, and no external event concerned her until it affected the flow of clients past her desk.

News of the trouble outside the club's handsome studded doors came to her from Philippe, who spent more and more time at the opium parlour or with his friends, leaving her in charge.

'People come here to see you, not me,' he told her, when she suggested he should spend more time in his club. 'You are a great beauty, *ma chère*, but I am just a *chop chung kwai* and not important. '*Chop chung kwai* was the Cantonese expression for a Eurasian; its literal meaning was 'mixed-up devil'.

There was resentment in what Philippe had said, and in the way he pressed Ayeshah to accept the invitations their regular clients would sometimes extend to her to swim at the Tanglin Club or watch the Maharajah of Jaipur's polo team play the British army officers. With a white man to escort her, she was accepted at these exclusive occasions where he would have been shunned as a half-caste, even though he had been born in Paris.

Philippe was instantly conspicuous in colonial society. His navy-blue blazers, double-breasted and brass buttoned, fitted his narrow hips too well and their colour was slightly too bright; his clothes alone marked him out. Nothing could disguise the Oriental cast of his features, and in his lean, wedge-shaped face his narrow eyes, triangular like those of a Byzantine icon, gleamed with the predatory intelligence of a man who lived on his wits.

The echelon into which Philippe had a guaranteed entree was the topmost social stratum of the drug trade, and it was this business which had bought them their bungalow, their servants and the shining Austin Healey sports car which darted like a dark-green dragonfly around the city. Ayeshah, who had always considered opium the exclusive vice of elderly or simple-minded Chinese, was surprised when she discovered that Philippe was procuring the drug for the fast-living, wealthy socialites of every race. He also dealt in cocaine, which was smuggled into Singapore aboard the huge, rusty freighters that were registered in Panama and brought South American beef to the Orient. His merchandise was of high quality, and his service discreet. In a business in which no one could be trusted, Philippe was a safer contact than most, because he was too much of a snob to exploit his customers. He wanted their social patronage more than money.

He called his customers his friends, and they in turn treated Philippe with as much generosity as they could without drawing attention to their relationship. Ayeshah, at first awestruck by the glamour of this hedonistic cadre, clung to his arm at garden parties and cocktail parties. Soon she was able to see the pleasure-seekers as the colonial élite saw them – wealthy, dissipated and of no consequence. Nevertheless, she was fascinated by their expertise in frivolity. Avid for luxury, she learned to tell natural pearls from dyed, modern jade from antique, Iranian caviar from Russian and a French seam sewn in Paris from a French seam sewn in Hong Kong. Philippe enjoyed developing her taste, but her hunger for fine things had a desperate impatience which puzzled him.

In their third year he decided to observe the French custom of a *fermeture annuelle,* and closed the club in August. He took Ayeshah to an island which had been put at his disposal by a Malay princeling, a pearshaped atoll some three hours by launch from the south-east coast of the peninsula.

Ayeshah was instantly enchanted by this miniature kingdom. They had the run of a tiny pink-stone palace, a little yacht, glorious gardens, brilliant white coral beaches, stables and a private zoo. The bathrooms, opulently panelled in yellowish marble with massive gold fitments, pleased her most.

'Whatever are you doing?' he asked, discovering her seated on the edge of the tub on their first day, her olive-skinned shoulders smooth and bare above the thick white towel. She had been in the bathroom for most of the morning.

'I'm thinking,' she said, with her catlike half-smile, leaning back to trail her fingers in the fragrant, foamy water. She looked satisfied, which was unusual.

'What about?'

'About washing in the river,' she replied.

'When did *you* ever wash in a river?' He sat beside her, full of curiosity. 'Come, tell me. I want to know.'

'It isn't important.' He was irritated. She never talked to him about her past life, her family, or her home; at first, Philippe had thought this was merely delightful, naive reticence, but now, after a few years, he knew Ayeshah was hiding something from him, a secret so large that it was present in her mind all the time, casting a shadow over all her actions.

'It must be something important if you've been thinking about it in here all morning. Why are you always so secretive? I'm tired of all this mystery. Maybe I've taken up with a beautiful ghost.' He smiled, teasing her and stroking the back of her neck lightly with his long ivory fingers.

She shook her head obstinately and stood up. 'I am who I am now. It's none of your business, my life before I met you. I have put it away in a box because I can do nothing about it, and if I ever open that box and look, it will be because it is time for me to do something, and then . . . you will see. You will not like me then.' She turned towards him, pulling the towel with its massive red monogram more tightly around her. 'I'm not interested in the past, Philippe. I want the future, and I want it to be like this.' She looked around the opulent room, full of precious ornaments, kept sweet-smelling and spotless by diligent servants; she paused to admire herself in the pink glass mirror, in which her complexion appeared rose-beige like that of a white woman.

He moved forward to embrace her, but halted. Ayeshah never needed embraces. She never refused them, or showed any distaste, but after months of the most skilful loving of which Philippe was capable he sensed that while her body responded, her soul was inert. The warmth of her passion in his arms had exactly the same quality as the professional friendliness with which she greeted the club's customers.

This knowledge had bred bitterness in Philippe which he had focused elsewhere, on his equivocal racial status. He had begun to reject the city that saw him as irredeemably inferior because of his mixed blood, and had started to talk about Singapore as if it were merely a provincial port in a country whose capital was Paris.

'When we've got enough money in the bank this lousy town won't see us for dust,' he promised her. 'These people are nothing – *nothing.*' He waved his arm around the steamy cool of the bathroom, indicating its owner, his tin-pot court and beyond him their entire acquaintance, British and Asiatic. 'They think they're the most important people in the world but they are just barbarians in smart clothes. When you meet *le tout Paris* then you will know what I'm talking about. In Paris, they wouldn't let men like that clean their shoes, you'll see.'

'When?' she asked him at once. He was taken aback.

'As soon as we've got enough money.'

'Haven't we got enough now?' Her eyes were hard; Ayeshah knew that the bank account stood at over ten thousand dollars, and in addition Philippe had a box of large gold coins buried under the bungalow.

He laughed uneasily. 'Paris is an expensive place, you know. I don't want to crawl back there like a pauper and have my brothers laugh at me.'

'Why don't you write to your brothers, at least, and they can look out for a place for you? Oh please, Philippe. Let's go to Paris. Just think what we can do there. Our club could be famous all over the world; we could entertain film stars and royalty; we could make so much more profit in a really big city. I hate Singapore and all these army people. You're right about them, they're just nobodies in flashy uniforms. Let's go, darling, *please*.'

Her eyes gleamed with ambition and Philippe, who was by and large content to be a minor celebrity in Singapore, was annoyed to find himself levered into action by his own words. He was also unable to refuse Ayeshah anything when she curled her tensile limbs into his arms like a kitten and pressed her warm, sculptured lips into his neck, as she did now. She played ceaselessly on his senses, deliberately keeping him in a permanent state of yearning for the erotic fulfilment of their relationship, and she had only to offer a hint that this ecstasy might be within his grasp to make Philippe her abject slave.

Philippe agreed to write to his two brothers, full-blooded Vietnamese who ran a small restaurant on the Left Bank. A few weeks later they wrote back, full of enthusiasm for his arrival but quoting astronomical prices for the kind of premises he needed. Ayeshah frowned and said nothing. She never nagged him, but her will was like a demon's curse which compelled his obedience.

The day after the letter came from Paris, Singapore city was almost brought to a standstill by the largest anti-British demonstration to date, which swiftly degenerated into a full-scale riot. By nightfall, there were rumours that more than fifteen Europeans had been killed, but the announcements on Radio Malaya referred only to minor disturbances; the area around the club was quiet and people were going about their business as usual.

'Shall I open up?' Ali, the barman, asked Philippe as darkness enveloped the teeming streets. Philippe considered the question, smoothing down his pomaded hair with the palm of his hand. From the next room came some random saxophone phrases and the soft chink of maracas as the Filipino band took their seats.

'Why not? It's quiet enough around here, there won't be any trouble. There's no curfew, is there? Why should we lose business because there was a riot this morning? Who's fighting, anyway?' He took a sip of the tepid black coffee which he always drank throughout the early evening.

'The Malays, they're enraged over this business of the Dutch girl.' Ali flicked imaginary specks of dust from the gleaming array of bottles on the glass shelves.

'The case was in the Supreme Court this morning, and that's where the crowd gathered first.'

'What Dutch girl?'

'Who cares?' Ayeshah was dismissive. 'It's only some boring political nonsense, nothing to do with us – until they're outside throwing stones through our windows.'

She was wearing a tight strapless dress of gathered white silk, and sat awkwardly on a tall stool in front of the bar, a black, high-heeled shoe swinging from the toes of one foot. On the bar in front of her was a day-old copy of the *Straits Times,* which she had been half-heartedly trying to read. Her wide, smooth forehead furrowed as she struggled to follow the type.

Ali went on, proud as always to show off his education, 'It had nothing to do with politics until the authorities screwed things up. Look, here she is.' Ali turned the newspaper over and pointed to a picture of a blonde girl with an open, sun-reddened face. 'The famous Nadya. She was born of Dutch parents who abandoned her when the Japanese invaded, and a Malay family brought her up as a Moslem and married her to a Malay schoolteacher – but now her parents have decided they want her back and brought a petition in the courts.'

Philippe drained his coffee cup. 'It doesn't sound like much of an excuse for a battle to me. There must be a dozen cases like this every year in this crazy place.'

'There wouldn't have been any trouble if the British had not insulted the Malay leaders; now they have taken the side of the foster parents and are stirring up the whole community. There was a very big crowd this morning and the Gurkha soldiers came to break it up, and there was shooting . . .' Ali shrugged again. 'I heard that twenty or thirty people have been killed at least.'

Philippe reached for his creamy panama hat. 'Nonsense. We didn't see any sign of any trouble on our way here; by now everyone will have gone home.'

Ayeshah quickly shook her head. 'The worst fighting is always at night. Once it gets dark people think they can get away with anything, and all the hooligans and looters come out to join in. Let's not open tonight, Philippe. We won't be very busy on a Monday, anyway. Better to lose one evening's business than get involved in any trouble, don't you think?'

He shook his head, glancing down the reservations book by the telephone. 'There's a big party booked in, we can't possibly put them off. Once you do that to people, they never come back. And people stop coming to a club if they are never sure if it's going to be open or not.' He stretched an arm behind the bar and began to snap on the lights. 'Business as usual. I'll be back later, *ma chère.*'

Anxiously Ayeshah watched him leave by the back entrance, while Ali went to open the steel gates at the front. She knew Philippe was paying his usual evening visit to the opium parlour, and would return in an hour or so in a bland good humour. The place was in the middle of the Chinese quarter, but to reach it Philippe would have to pass close to the mosque by North Bridge Road; if Ali was right, the mosque would still be surrounded by crowds listening to speeches broadcast from the loudspeakers.

She was reassured a few hours later, when the club was full of chattering, dancing people and the street outside seemed to have every sports car in Singapore parked in it. Beyond the line of gleaming Jaguars and MGs were half a dozen limousines and a small knot of white-uniformed drivers who stood smoking cigarettes at the street corner.

The event that had filled the club so early in the week was the birthday party of an English girl, the daughter of a senior British army officer. Ayeshah, temporarily idle but poised like a swallow at the corner of the reception desk, watched the girl as she sat demurely between the imposing figure of her father in his dress uniform and her mother in a fluttering, yellow silk gown. She was an ideal European beauty, with golden hair sleek under a velvet head-band and a small, pink mouth drooping in a pout of boredom.

The soothing hum of conversation and the unctuous flow of the dance music obscured the noise from the street until a sudden squeal of tyres penetrated from outside. Two army drivers burst through the club door with pistols in their hands, and an instant later Ayeshah's sharp eyes saw three or four Chinese clients vanish behind the bar, making for the back door.

'Get the shutters down!' one of the drivers ordered. 'There's two hundred people at the end of the road!'

The band faltered into silence and one or two musicians surreptitiously put their instruments into their cases. The few remaining Asian clients made for the back door, and Ayeshah saw some of her girls move sinuously towards the toilets, clutching their purses.

The tall white figure of the British officer stood up.

'Keep calm, everybody. There's nothing to worry about. Just a little local disturbance.'

He signed to the bandleader to continue playing and the music began again, although it sounded thin and uneven because some of the musicians had also left.

One or two couples continued dancing, but the rest shamefacedly quit the floor. There was an air of suppressed panic and Ayeshah heard the clamour of angry voices growing louder as the mob approached in the street outside. Ali ran back through the door; he had succeeded in running down the steel shutters over the windows, but there was no protection for the door. The panels, thin wood under their covering of buttoned, wine-red, imitation leather, soon began to shudder, pounded by boots and sticks.

'Better get down, everybody,' the British officer commanded in an uneasy tone. The rest of the party hesitated. Four sharp pistol shots sounded from the clamouring crowd outside and bullets tore through the door, leaving jagged exit holes in the fabric. The English rose gave a shriek of panic and her mother pulled her down below the edge of their table.

'Everybody under the tables – for heaven's sake get down!' her father shouted again, and this time everyone obeyed.

Ayeshah crouched behind her desk with one of the uniformed army drivers, who drew his gun from the burnished leather holster at his belt. Outside in the street she heard a violent argument break out in the crowd. A group chanted 'Kill the British' over and over again in ritual Arabic, their voices harsh with fanatical hatred. There was a violent rattling noise and she realized that the crowd were trying to tear down the metal shutters protecting the windows.

'The shutters! They're trying to pull down the shutters!' Desperately she turned to the man beside her, her heart leaping with terror inside her chest. 'Shoot back! Stop them! They'll pull the whole wall down!'

The driver raised himself awkwardly so that he was half-leaning against the desk, able to take aim at the window. The crowd gave a roar of triumph as one sheet of hinged metal slats gave way and crashed to the pavement, and the man fired a shot into the air. He was a sturdy corporal in his thirties, whose skin was leathery from the tropical sun.

Stones began to thud on the walls, there was a crash and she saw the men's contorted faces as they began to smash their entry into the club. The pistol was fired again outside and the men at the back of the crowd screamed, 'Kill! Kill! Kill!' The driver fired steadily at the window and hit a man who was already halfway across the window sill. He fell back with a yell, blood spurting across the floor from a wound in his neck.

While the driver was reloading, Ayeshah heard another disturbance behind her, and turned to see a stream of Malay police in khaki and black running through the door at the back, their rifles held ready for action.

'Thank heaven, thank heaven!' she stammered over and over again, 'Thank heaven you got here before they broke in. They're mad! They want to kill everybody!'

The leading constable ignored her, dragged her back from the entry area and took cover behind her desk before opening fire. The rioters fell back in panic, yelling abuse and climbing over each other as they fled down the street.

Then the club was crammed with police and soldiers, orders were shouted and vehicles began to roar up to the splintered door. Within a few minutes all the Europeans had climbed into the police cars or their own vehicles and left, most without even settling their bills.

As the last four police climbed into their jeep and drove away, Ayeshah looked round the club in bitter amazement. None of the officials had taken the slightest notice of her, or of any of the Asiatics in the club. The safety of the Europeans was their sole concern. In their rush to leave, the clients had overturned tables and smashed glasses. The floor was smeared with blood. The door and window were shattered, the protective shutter lay uselessly outside where it had been trampled and she could hear the roar of the mob as they continued fighting a few streets away.

Without waiting to be told, Ali and the bandleader went out to see if the shutter could be fixed, but the stout metal grille had been buckled and the steel fixings bolted to the wall outside were hopelessly twisted.

'We must close the building up somehow,' Ayeshah wailed, feeling close to tears as she stood in the wrecked doorway. 'There's nothing to stop them coming back and burning the place down.'

At the end of the street she saw a familiar slender figure in a pale suit, his panama hat in his hand.

'Philippe! You're all right! Darling, what are we going to do, the place has been absolutely destroyed, they've torn down the shutters . . .' she paused, realizing as he sauntered towards her up the street that he was insulated by the effect of his drug from any real appreciation of the situation. Philippe had strolled back through the riot-racked streets with complete lack of concern, no more anxious than if he had been walking down his precious Champs-Elysées.

Ayeshah, now that she had no immediate cause for fear, was equally without emotion. A woman with less bedrock hatred in her heart would have been dismayed, resentful or panic-stricken; instead, she was calmly practical.

'Ali, go down to Victoria Street and pull some planks off that building site. You know, where they're working on that old, bombed building. Not bamboos, we need good solid wood to nail up the front here. No one will stop you in all this chaos – take a couple of boys from the band with you. Philippe, darling,' she walked forward to greet him and took his arm with a managing air, 'go and get the car, then as soon as the club is closed up safely we can go home.'

But the Austin Healey, which Philippe had prudently parked in a side alley, had been rolled on to its side and set alight, and was now nothing but a burned out shell. This event succeeded in penetrating Philippe's detachment.

'They knew! They must have known my car – everyone in Singapore knows my car! The bastards!' He stood and trembled beside the charred wreck, and for a moment Ayeshah thought he was going to weep.

The next day Philippe willingly withdrew all their money from the bank, bought a money belt for his gold and purchased their passage to Marseilles aboard an Italian liner.

Before she left, Ayeshah secretly made an appointment with a lawyer. He was a sharp young Anglo-Indian, the junior partner in a practice which occupied a floor in a new eight-storey building on Victoria Street, but his eager interest faded rapidly as she explained what she wanted to do. He was not optimistic about her chances of success.

Paris terrified Ayeshah, as Singapore could never have done. The cold, clammy air at once withered her courage. Kilometre after kilometre of macadamed streets, extending further than the eye could see, awed her with the arrogance of their conception. The vast spaces of the Etoile, the Place de la Concorde and the area around the Eiffel Tower made her feel cowed.

She had an immediate sense of the overweening pride of the French, and their contempt for all foreign modes of civilization. At the moment of her arrival the great iron arches of the railway station made her aware that the race who inhabited this land had no fear of natural forces, and saw them only as energy to be harnessed by their omnipotent intellects.

Philippe had taught her a few phrases in French, but the jabber of talk in the streets was incomprehensible. Worse was the dismissive arrogance with which strangers greeted her attempts to talk to them. The French gave shorter shrift to the disadvantaged than even the Chinese.

They lodged first in an apartment of four crowded rooms above the restaurant owned by Philippe's brothers, a dilapidated, ageless building standing crookedly in a winding, medieval alley in the Latin Quarter. In this space lived seven adults, including Philippe's grey-haired grandmother, and a large number of children. The grandmother, sensing at once that Ayeshah's attitude to Philippe was less than ideally loyal and submissive, persecuted her with coldness and shrewish observations about her lack of domestic gifts.

Almost immediately Ayeshah fell ill, with a feverish chest infection the grandmother dismissed as *la grippe*, something all foreigners contracted as soon as they arrived in France. For a few days Ayeshah was smothered with misery, and clung pitifully to Philippe's arms, too proud to ask to go back to the East but nevertheless devastated by the strangeness of their new environment.

Her healthy young constitution soon began to fight off the illness, and at once fortune dealt them an ace.

'Superb! What could be better!' Philippe sat on the edge of their ancient mahogany bed where Ayeshah lay huddled under all the covers she dared appropriate. 'The old shoemender next door is retiring and he has offered my brothers his shop. It's perfect – perfect situation, perfect size, an enormous basement . . .'

'What about the price?' she murmured, pulling the blankets around her as she sat up.

'My brother says it's fair, more than fair, very good. The old boy hasn't any idea of the market value of his premises so we're getting a real bargain. We're on our way again, *ma chère*.'

The news acted like a tonic to Ayeshah who quit her sickbed at once and, dressed in black slacks, woollen stockings and one of Philippe's grey chequered pullovers, accompanied him next door to look over the cobbler's dusty shop.

'I'm going to fit the whole place out in bamboo,' Philippe told her as they stood on the cobbled street outside looking at the building. 'It'll cost almost nothing and we can create a marvellous oriental atmosphere for a few hundred francs.'

Ayeshah looked at him with surprise. 'Can't we make it like our old club, European style?'

He shook his head. 'What you don't understand, little flower, is that a nightclub is a place where people come to perform their dreams. It's a fantasy world where they can take off their inhibitions with their coats at the door. Yes, you must offer comfort, relaxation, luxury – but you must take your client out of his daytime life, so he can become another person for a little while. Here in Paris we have an advantage in being orientals, and we will have a much greater success by offering our clients a few hours in the mysterious East than in trying to compete with the French style of sophistication.'

'But I thought you hated being classed as an oriental?'

'So I do, but one should never confuse business with emotions. And in Paris it's different: the French despise every other race, the Parisians despise everyone else in the world, but it's nothing personal, you see. They think you are inferior but they concede that it's not your fault. But the British think belonging to another race is some kind of insult to them.'

The club was called Le Bambou. Fitting it out took every centime Philippe had, but in its first six weeks it did not do well. It was seldom more than half full, and acquired a forlorn, neglected atmosphere which discouraged new clients.

All the prostitutes in the area, from the streetwalkers who posed half-naked in doorways brazenly tinkling their keys, to the footsore, young waitresses in the cheap restaurants who might occasionally accept a customer's invitation to a party for two, were controlled by a Marseilles pimp known as Bastien. This thickset individual, whose thatch of coarse, curly black hair smelt of violet oil, visited Le Bambou soon after it opened.

'Very nice.' He pursed his lips, setting down his whisky-soda and looking around the empty room. 'Exotic, a little different – I like it. This oriental style is the coming thing, I'm told. Don't worry, my friend, be patient. Soon your club will be packed every night.'

'We need some glamour about the place.' Philippe refilled Bastien's glass with an eagerness that was almost contemptuous. Despite his homily to Ayeshah on the danger of an emotional approach to business, he had taken an instant dislike to this squat satrap of vice who had to be placated before the club could employ hostesses.

'Naturally.' Bastien's thick fingers closed around the neck of the siphon. He shot a small quantity of soda into the whisky and half-emptied his glass in a single gulp. He looked around again, as if evaluating the club for the first time. 'You've got a lot of potential here. I predict a great success for you. Why don't we say five thousand francs? I'll send one of the boys round on Friday.'

'Absolutely impossible,' Philippe spoke fast, half-swallowing the words. 'We don't take that much in a week. I can't do it.'

The Marseillais swallowed the rest of his drink and slipped awkwardly off the high bamboo bar stool to stand up. 'Too bad.' He reached for his black felt hat. 'Perhaps business will improve, anyway – give me a call, huh?'

He left, rolling like a sailor as he walked, and the two youths who had waited by the doorway followed him.

Philippe unconcernedly accepted a loan from his brothers to keep him in business, while Ayeshah became ferociously determined to make the establishment a success.

'Do you think I'm going to stay in that disgusting apartment with your grand-mother one minute longer than I have to? She hates me, she never stops criticizing me and I can't stand being pawed by those smelly children with their snotty noses and sticky fingers. We've got to get out of there, Philippe, or I shall go mad.'

In the daytime, Ayeshah slept late and lounged in the window alcove of their room, smoking cigarettes and staring discontentedly out into the street. She watched the straggling crowd of students, like a tide that washed up and down the pavement twice a day, as they went to and from their classes at the Sorbonne. Every day she was amused by the small groups of tourists, conspicuous with their cameras and foreign clothes, turning their city maps upside down to try to find their way back to the Boulevard St-Michel through the maze of ancient alleys.

'Why don't we offer free entry to students?' she suggested to Philippe. 'That way at least the club will fill up and look alive.'

'Huh. Students haven't got any money to spend. They'll be nothing but trouble.'

'Well, let's try a discount for tourists then?'

'How shall we advertise – put up a poster at the airport?'

'Don't be sarcastic, Philippe, it's a good idea. Come on, let me try. Nothing's worse than this – we're losing more and more money every week.'

He grudgingly agreed to her plan and Ayeshah visited the small printworks where the restaurant menus were done. She ordered one thousand cards and some small posters. Then she systematically visited every hotel on the Left Bank, from the historic to the anonymous, and persuaded them to allow her to put a card in every room. After that, she boldly followed the students into the university annexe and pinned posters on every notice-board. A tiny figure with shining black hair in a ponytail, wearing an overlarge man's sweater and tight, black matador pants, she looked so much like one of the students that no one challenged her.

At once a trickle of hesitant young people came to the club and Ayeshah abandoned her characteristic haughty manner and served them slavishly, allowing couples to sit the whole evening over two Coca-Colas and taking to heart their advice about the kind of music the club should play. Within ten days the word had spread through the Left Bank, and on the second Friday after the posters had gone up the club was crammed with kids.

Both Ayeshah and Philippe retreated behind the bar to help the frenzied barman serve drinks. Philippe grumbled savagely as he ripped the caps off Coca-Cola bottles as fast as he could.

'Your crazy ideas. Why don't you think before rushing out to offer cheap drinks all over town? None of these people will ever come back. All they'll do is tell everyone else that the club's overcrowded and it takes an hour to get served.'

'At least we'll make some money tonight,' she spat back with defiance, then turned with a gesture of mock helplessness to serve a young Italian.

'Money! Five centimes profit on each drink – you call that money?'

Ayeshah decided to ignore him. It was a long, hot, gruelling night and when it was over Philippe had to admit that it had been profitable. By the end of the week he grudgingly acknowledged that the students, although they seemed to drink nothing but Coke, at least filled the club with pretty young girls with whirling petticoats and nodding ponytails, and were enough of a spectacle to amuse the tourists, who had more money to spend. In addition, some of the students were wealthy, especially the foreign ones whose families mistakenly regarded the Sorbonne as some kind of finishing school.

'But we can't survive on this kind of business,' he warned her. 'Where will the students be in vacation-time? And how many tourists are there in Paris in the dead of winter, eh?'

'So – we make a bit of money this way, we pay Bastien, he lets us have some girls and we go for the big money. Simple.'

Philippe scowled and Ayeshah dropped the subject. She appreciated now that her lover was neither a good businessman nor the kind of personality who could fill a nightclub simply with people who enjoyed the ambience around him. Sour complaints were his substitute for enterprise, and opium his response to failure. He had always simply used whatever club he owned as a convenient base for his drug-dealing, but in Paris Philippe had no contacts except his family. He could always find opium for his personal needs; he went more and more often to a foetid top-floor room near the Gare du Nord where a dozen elderly orientals prepared pipes in the traditional way, but most of the drug business was firmly controlled from Marseilles and small operators lived dangerously.

Furthermore, as she grew accustomed to the city that was now her home, Ayeshah realized that Philippe would never achieve the easy access to high society he had enjoyed in Singapore. The film premieres, the jet-set clubs, the glittering balls, the boxes at Longchamp or at the opera were only something to read about in *Paris Match*.

'What do you expect?' he demanded when she wistfully remem-bered cocktails at Raffles Hotel. 'When Singapore was just a fishing village with a handful of pirates across the bay, Paris was the greatest city in the world. It's easy to get to the top in a small town that's still growing, much more difficult in a city that's two thousand years old. Of course we're nothing but small fish in a big pond in Paris. It was your idea to come here, don't forget.'

'I want money, and I want a social position,' she said, her jaw tight with aggression. 'And I don't care how I get them. There must be a way.'

'Maybe I want to fly to the moon,' he replied, putting on his jacket and preparing to go out. 'There must be a way to do that too.

Once more he began to leave the day-to-day running of the establishment to her, but now he realized that she was becoming his enemy. Ayeshah's energy was directed to mastering Paris for her own, undeclared, ambitions and she no longer took the trouble to weave the elaborate dream of eroticism with which she had previously enslaved him. The balance of power in their relationship had shifted. She refused him in bed and, instead of forcing her to submit, Philippe shrugged off his defeat and compensated by keeping a tight grip on the bank accounts, limiting her ultimate control of the club.

Ayeshah countered by cheating him. She rigged the till, watered the drinks and falsified delivery notes. Within six months, she had extracted enough money to pay Bastien's premium for several months, and she went to the pimp behind Philippe's back and frankly explained the situation.

'Lucky man to have a sensible woman to manage him, eh? We shall do good business, you and I, don't worry. And don't worry about Philippe, either. He won't give any trouble, I assure you.' Bastien added the notes she gave him to the fat wad encircled by a rubber band which he kept in his trouser pocket. He was generous to her, sending not only a handful of showy tarts with Italian silk sweaters clinging to their mobile breasts and wings of thick black eyeliner emphasizing their smouldering eyes, but a few groups of businessmen who normally frequented more established clubs in the area.

There followed an unpleasant few weeks in which Le Bambou's clientele changed; the prices soared, the tourists disappeared, the students complained, the new clients confused the prettier girl students with the whores and there was a fight almost every night. Bastien, who at once took to calling in for a whisky-soda at some point in every evening, loaned the club two young toughs in mohair suits who stood idly by the doorway, ostentatiously picking their teeth with flick-knives, and these disturbances gradually ceased.

Philippe, maddeningly, took the credit for the greater profit which they now made with less effort. 'You see, *ma chere*, if you had done as I advised in the first place we would never have had such a struggle. There's no money in students, you can't rely on tourists – business people are the ones with the money.' Ayeshah and Bastien exchanged glances across the corner of the bar.

A waiter rushed to the counter and called for six bottles of the best champagne.

'You see.' Philippe took a satisfied pull at his Gitane and blew pungent smoke into the air. 'Six bottles! That's the way to spend money.'

Ayeshah slipped off her stool and helped the waiter set up the ice-buckets and distribute the new gilt-rimmed champagne goblets around the table which was occupied by a large group of prosperous-looking middle-aged men. Their host seemed to be the youngest of them, a fresh-faced man of Middle Eastern appearance in expensively tailored clothes which made the best of his well-covered figure.

'Who is he?' she asked Bastien, who was personally acquainted with most of their new clientele. 'He was in here last week with a couple of Arabs; they were drinking champagne as if it was going out of style and the girls told me he gave a good tip.'

Bastien nodded, a solemn expression on his heavy features. 'Make a note of that face, *ma petite*. He'll be the most powerful man in France one day, if you want my opinion. Hussain Shahzdeh. He's a fixer. You want it, Hussain can arrange it, whatever it is.'

'I like his style,' Philippe announced in lordly tones.

'Everybody likes his style,' observed Bastien, his shrewd, black eyes watching Ayeshah as she turned away from Philippe with contempt on her beautiful face.

CHAPTER FOURTEEN

J AMES HITCHED his sarong casually around his waist, and tried to keep his
limbs still in the posture of exhaustion appropriate to a labourer slumped on
the palm-thatched bamboo bus-shelter at the end of his day's work. His watch was
rolled into the folds of the sarong around his waist, and he glanced briefly down-
wards to check the time. Thirty seconds to go.

The bus appeared in a cloud of red dust, stopping for the small group of working men standing or squatting around the shelter. James heard the far-off thud
of the first explosion as he climbed aboard, and saw, from the rear of the vehicle,
a dense cloud of black smoke rising from the dockside in the distance. The first
explosion was followed by others, and as the bus left the outskirts of the town
behind, the smoke was rising high in the evening sky.

He jumped off the bus as it began to climb the escarpment. Below him the
town, the river and the Kuala Lumpur road all lay in a broad valley. The hills on
each side rose like waves of foaming green, one upon the other, as far as the eye
could see. The light faded rapidly, and by the time he arrived at the camp he was
finding his way by torchlight through the screeching darkness.

Next morning the fire in the docks was still burning. Twenty-five Japanese had
been killed, two cargo ships damaged and the warehouse full of oil and gasoline
destroyed. The fire had taken hold of latex and copra on the dockside and was raging out of control while shipping waited offshore.

There was no elation. Bill, James, Ibrahim and Lee Kuang Leong had travelled
steadily north up the Malayan peninsula for almost three months, planning and
carrying out sabotage operations with increasing skill and success, moving on swiftly
once each job was completed. Sometimes, when they were lucky enough to steal a
boat, they could be dozens of miles away before any damage was done. The Japanese
announced larger and larger bounties for the capture of white men, dead or alive,
and the Malay police force was almost wholly under their control. The four men
were forced to live in temporary camps in the jungle, and so had been weakened by
illness and poor food, and in place of the schoolboy enthusiasm of their early days
undercover they now shared a sense of living on borrowed time. Their success was
also their enemy; each strike against the Japanese put them in greater danger.

Cunningly, Bill had turned their fears into fuel for their endeavour. He had instituted a system of evaluating each operation and planning the next which kept the small group focused on their task and minimized the damage to their morale when things went wrong. The relentless pressure of activity left no fingerhold for terror in their minds.

Automatically, the four men began to consider their next target, the highway linking the east coast with Kuala Lumpur and the west. The road ran through a succession of mountain gorges where it appeared easy to lay explosives and cause a rockfall. Their stock of explosives, however, was so low that they first needed to find more. Their map showed an area close to Kuala Lumpur where there were two or three quarries, and on this unconfirmed promise they planned to steal dynamite.

'This job will be a real beaut.' Bill traced the slender belt of the road across the map with the earpiece of his spectacles. 'Everything the Japs have got is in the east and this is the only way across to the west of the peninsula. If that road is cut the Japs will have their hands tied, and all their troops will be held back there in the east or down here in Singapore. If only we could radio the Communists, between us we could give the Japs a hell of a beating before they got the road clear.' They had heard that the Chinese Communists had also taken to the jungle, and were gathering strength in several hidden camps in Perak. There were said to be several hundred of them, but with few arms and no radio contact with the outside world.

'If we could knock out the airfield at the same time, the Japs would be paralysed.' Ibrahim pointed to the only airstrip on the east coast. 'If they wanted to send reinforcements they would have to come up from Shonan by train.'

'Shonan.' James pronounced the new Japanese appellation with disdain. 'It won't be Shonan much longer; another six months and we'll be talking about Singapore again.' There was an optimistic silence as Bill folded the map with care. Suddenly, without a word, James got to his feet and ran a few steps down the track leading out of the camp. His acute hearing had detected footsteps. He came back with a Malay girl of about ten years old whom they recognized as the daughter of a village storekeeper who had been supplying them with food, an enchanting little sprite who normally laughed and teased her elders. Now, however, she was silent and lethargic.

'Where's your brother?' Bill asked her. 'He was supposed to be here this morning – where is he?'

She looked blankly at them with her upturned brown eyes and said nothing. They offered her some food, but she made no move to take it.

'Well, she can't hang about here on her own,' Bill unfolded his bony legs and stood up. 'One of you must take her back.'

'For Pete's sake, she's only ten. She's a child. What does it matter – she can take care of herself.' James was eager to move on to the next objective.

'She's our responsibility, old man. Her parents wouldn't let her go anywhere unchaperoned. Maybe there's something wrong. And she could give us away to the Japs. Go on, James, get moving.'

'You don't go – better for me,' suggested Ibrahim, taking the girl's arm. She gave a shriek and clung to James, shaking with the irrational fright of childhood. So James slowly walked her back to the outskirts of the village, and as they approached the site of the family's home he halted by a screen of shrubs.

Something was indeed wrong. The light wind that stirred the palm fronds above them carried the scent of smoke and scorching. The ground was black. The timber-built village store had been burned to the ground, and the neat stacks of dried fish, sacks of rice and tinned goods set out in front of it were reduced to smoking heaps. The fire had spread to the houses on either side, which were half-destroyed; the village seemed deserted. At the back of the gutted building James saw piles of sheeting on the ground. The air smelt of the charred goods and of something worse. James had never before smelt burnt human flesh but the obscene aroma, like roast meat but oddly sugary, was unmistak-able.

He looked down at the child, who was clinging in panic to his leg, and spoke softly in Malay.

'What happened here, Sofiah? You must tell me.'

Very slowly she mumbled the reply. First the Kempeitai, the Japanese secret police, who were already more feared than all the ghosts of the jungle together, had come and taken her father. Then the soldiers had come and killed every-one in the house – her mother, her grandmother, and her sister. They had found her brother hiding under the house, tied him to a tree and gathered all the neighbours to watch as they hacked him to death. Then the Japanese took the cans of kerosene in the store, poured them over the building, and set fire to it.

'They did not find me because I was in my cousin's house,' the girl finished, proud of the good luck which had saved her from the tragedy which was too big for her to understand. 'The Japanese said it was because we helped the white men. They said the time of the white men was finished now and they would be killed like rats and so will anyone who helps them.'

James looked carefully at the quiet houses of the hamlet. Curtains of flowered cotton wavered in the breeze at the empty windows. A brown cow, tethered under a group of palm trees, raised its head and looked at them, flicking flies away with its tail. The stillness and silence of the scene were unnatural; he realized that at his approach the villagers had disappeared into their homes.

'Can you go to your cousin's house now, Sofiah?' She nodded, her lower lip wavering. 'Go on then, and don't tell anyone I was here. You're a brave girl, I won't forget you.'

She looked up at him with coy curiosity. 'What will you do, *tuan?*'

'I don't know. Something. We will take revenge for the death of your family.'

She released her hold on him and shook her head, then ran up the dirt road and vanished into the last dwelling.

As James turned to go a stone fell beside him, then another hit him in the back. He heard angry adult voices raised indoors to stop the stone-throwers. He walked steadily onwards, suddenly feeling a stranger to himself inside his brown skin. His instincts told him that this was the end of their heroic career as saboteurs, but his conscious mind rejected the knowledge and searched desperately for absolution for the death of the storekeeper and his clan.

At the camp, Ibrahim brought the news that the Japanese had done more than massacre one family. They had executed the dockyard foreman and decimated the labour-gangs for failing to inform on the saboteurs. They had launched a senseless attack on a settlement of Chinese smallholders, killing more than a hundred people; the innocent farmers were made to dig their own mass grave, then the entire community was lined up on the edge of the excavation and machine-gunned.

Bill at once ordered the camp to be struck and the traces of it hidden as far as possible. 'We must move out as fast as we can. The Japs will be looking for us with every man they can spare now.'

'Animals! They'll pay for this, we'll make them pay,' James was almost shaking with rage as he began to dig the soft red earth. 'When we do the K. L. road we'll take out half their bloody army.'

'Have you gone raving mad?' The Australian's tone was mal-evolent. James looked at him with surprise, and saw fury in his friend's light-blue eyes.

'We are going to strike back, Bill. For Christ's sake, we can't let them get away with a bloody massacre.'

'Use your head, Jim. Or are you thinking with your dick now you've taken off your trousers?'

'What the hell do you mean?'

'God save us – you really don't know what I'm talking about, do you?' He paused as Ibrahim approached them.

'Shall we leave the stores, sir?' He pointed aloft, to the cache of supplies suspended a hundred feet above the forest floor.

'Get them down and break out all the quinine we've got, but leave the food,' Bill ordered, and then resumed talking to James in a low, fierce voice, not wanting the Malay to hear. 'Now listen, I'm speaking as your commanding officer. There can be no question of us endangering the civilian population by any further activities – right? If we attack the K. L. road, the Japs will torch the town, it's as simple as that.'

'Then what the hell are we doing here?'

'We're doing nothing more, *nothing*. The mere fact that we're at large in the country is a danger to the Malayan people. My orders in this situation are to escape, and make our way to Ceylon if we can.'

'Run away? Like all the rest? I won't do it. I won't betray this country.' James was flinging spadesful of earth aside in fury.

'For Christ's sake, if we stay now we might as well bayonet their children ourselves.' Bill ran his hands through his hair with exasperation. 'Why can't you see that? Which would you rather do – "betray" the people as you call it or fucking murder them?'

James remained silent, standing in the shallow excavation, his eyes cast down. Bill continued in an even lower voice, 'What's the matter with you, James? We're fucked, you can see that. We can't fight any more. The party's over. Our orders are to quit.'

'I know, but . . .' James did not dare continue. He sensed that the lives lost on their account did not weigh as heavily as they should have done with him, and that Bill was outraged by his lack of concern.'. . . It seems too damned cowardly,' he finished.

'Ever heard that discretion was the better part of valour?' Bill stood up, relieved the discussion was over. 'We'll live to fight another day, that's for sure.'

Lee Kuang Leong, their radio operator, finished sweeping the fire's ashes into a banana leaf and tipped the debris into the hole dug by James.

'We take the wireless?' he asked Bill.

'We can't leave it. I grant you it'll slow us down.'

'Can make in two parts, I think.'

'Do it then – good idea.'

In half an hour every trace of their habitation was gone and the ground covered in an innocent mantle of dead leaves and fallen branches. Bill fastened the leather moneybelt which contained their funds – several thousand dollars – around his waist, rolling his sarong over it to hide it.

'OK. Now my orders are to disband this unit in the event of reprisals against the civilian population. James and I will make our way to Port Swettenham and try to get off the peninsula and away to Ceylon. Any ideas, you two?'

'Better I go to Perak, join the Communist army.' Leong spoke without hesitation. 'Many camps in jungle. We can impede the Japanese by peaceful ways, just as we attack imperialists before invasion.' He smiled, testing their tolerance. The Communists' commitment to controlling the country themselves was something he had frequently explained to the whites.

'Fair enough. Ibrahim?'

The Malay seemed undecided. 'I go with him.' he said at last. 'If I go home, it will be bad for my family. Better to stay in the jungle.'

'Right. We'll be going the same road for a few days. Best get started then.'

James walked at the rear of the small column, full of resentful anger. As they marched westwards, James and Bill barely spoke to each other. The Australian was racked with remorse that their adventure had brought tragedy on innocent people. He remembered their schoolboy excitement with a flood of shame, which quenched his spirit and left him vulnerable to a formless despair.

Their physical condition, already debilitated, degenerated further with fearful speed. Within two weeks it was an effort to walk for more than an hour and the thorn-scratches which cross-hatched their arms and legs healed more and more slowly. Bill, with the weakest constitution, began to develop sores on his shins. They all grew thin and their bones seemed to stick through their skin. Lee Kuang Leong was the most distressed by this decline, and began to avoid wounds from the savage jungle foliage with almost girlish hysteria.

The wireless, useless now that the batteries had died, slowed them down considerably but Bill would not sanction its abandonment.

'The one thing we can do, the only function we've got left – is intelligence,' he said. 'As soon as we're among friends we must get a generator rigged somehow.'

At first they avoided the villages, making temporary camps in the jungle at night, which only increased their misery. Day after day there was rain, which soaked their clothes, their equipment and every piece of fire material they found. Soon they were lightheaded with hunger, and risked sending Ibrahim into a *kampong* to buy cooked rice. They stood at the roadside in the lashing rain and ate the food hastily from its wrapping of folded banana leaves, too famished to conceal themselves or seek shelter; they had scarcely swallowed more than a handful of grains when a jeep loaded with Malay police roared past, splattering them with mud. With crazy bravado born of physical weakness, James shouted curses after the vehicle.

'The villagers must have called them,' Ibrahim said with disgust. 'Next time we must choose a *kampong* with no telephone. They were driving too fast to get a close look at us, thanks to God.'

They turned back into the jungle and travelled away from the danger as fast as they could until nightfall, when they halted, rigged a shelter from a waterproof groundsheet and spread another on the sodden earth below it. The rain seemed to be falling harder and faster; since their clothes and packs were already saturated, the shelter was small comfort.

'Do you suppose we can eat the rest of the rice?' James asked Bill, looking hungrily at the squashed parcel of food he had taken from his pack.

'Survival training says never keep cooked food in this climate,' the Australian replied, curling up his long legs as he sat down. His tone was uncertain.

Lee Kuang Leong screwed up his face and spat into the downpour. 'The rice is only cooked a few hours – what harm can it do? I'm going to eat mine.' With deft fingers he unfolded the creased leaf and began to gobble the food. James and Ibrahim copied him at once. Bill paused, silently considering the bad feeling he would engender if he refused to eat and weighing it against the theoretical possibility that the stale food would give him a bellyache. Finally he, too, finished his rice.

In the dead of night they all vomited and lay groaning on the muddy ground while their guts writhed in rejection of the tainted rice. It had begun to ferment during the few hours they had carried it.

'God, it stinks.' James scented the acrid, half-digested mess amid the warm, humus smells of the jungle. 'If the Japs had dogs they could sniff us ten miles away.'

'At least it's stopped bloody raining.'

'That's right, old man, keep looking on the bright side.' James pulled himself shakily upright on the stump of a fallen tree, then sat down hurriedly as his weak knees buckled.

'One more mistake like that and the Japs won't need to look for us any more.' Bill picked his spectacles out of the mud, where they had fallen from his shirt pocket. Now he only wore them to look at the map, and lived in terror that he would lose or break them.

The four men slumped shivering on the wet ground in the darkness, and followed their own thoughts. Bill tried to plan the next day's march from what he remembered of the map, but every train of thought broke like a rotten thread and left his head full of meaningless information. James comforted himself with a reverie of his bed at Bourton, crisp and white with freshly laundered fine, linen sheets and cosy from the warming-pan. Lee thought of a feast he had enjoyed with his comrades when they heard the news of the Japanese invasion, of the sizzling morsels of pork and duck, the fragrant soups and the mounds of sweet, clean rice. Ibrahim dreamed of his home and the young wife he had married only a few months earlier, and the pleasure of sitting on the steps of his house in the cool of the evening with his father-in-law, discussing his new job in the district engineer's department while the women cooked the evening meal.

The strident calls of the night insects faded, and they heard nothing but the drips and trickles of water for a while, until the mournful gibbon whoops announced the dawn. Daylight brought new despair. Ibrahim was too weak to take more than a few steps, and James was hardly stronger. Bill ordered a morning's rest and sat apart from the others, desperately trying to order his thoughts. I'm getting too weak to think, he acknowledged to himself. But if I can't get us out of this, we'll just lie down and die right here.

Steam began to rise from the sticky ground and its thick mantle of vegetation as the heat of the day grew stronger. The Chinese, least affected by the rotten rice, paced slowly to and fro under the tree canopy, craning his neck with its prominent

Adam's apple as he searched the foliage in vain for a bird, a squirrel, or even a frog – anything that could be killed for food.

Suddenly he halted in front of Bill. 'What was the name of that village?' he asked. Bill shook his head to clear it and picked the damp map from his pack. Lee looked intently over his shoulder as he unfolded the tattered document and traced their pitiful progress. The Australian's stained brown finger and the Chinese's spatulate thumb traversed the plan slowly together, then Lee identified a name he evidently knew, and joyfully muttered a stream of curses in his own language.

'Maybe we will be OK,' he announced with total certainty. 'Here is a house I know.' He pointed to a town a few miles further down the road. 'Very rich man, very good comrade. We can ask him for help – I think at least he will give us food, maybe he can give us somewhere dry to sleep.'

'It'll take you half a day to get there,' Bill spoke with dawning hope. 'If you leave now you'll make it by the evening.'

'I can go?' The Chinese, bred to total obedience to authority, looked enquiringly at his commander. Bill nodded. 'Get moving, Lee. I want you back here with all the dry food you can carry by this time tomorrow.'

As Lee's squelching footsteps receded into the background noises of the jungle, James glanced weakly at the Australian, who stood gazing pointlessly in the direction of the Chinese's departure.

'He'll clear off,' James predicted in a peevish voice. 'You're nuts, Bill. We won't see hide or hair of him again.'

Bill shrugged his shoulders, the sharp edges of his shoulder blades clearly visible under his clammy green shirt. 'So what? He was fit, if he saves himself, so much the better for him. No sense him sticking with us now; you won't do the war effort any more good if an able man dies alongside you, eh?'

The three of them sat in silence, too feeble to argue. Ibrahim was feverish and rolled his head weakly from side to side, muttering to himself. James again conjured up the vibrant dream of his childhood home, and slipped away into the world of his imagination. Bill slept fretfully, fighting the desire to give in and resign himself to the hopelessness of their situation.

In the full heat of the next day they heard crashing footsteps approach; James, now a little stronger, stood up and promptly sat down in surprise when he saw Lee tramping towards them, followed by three young Chinese, and with a metal tiffin-carrier in his hand.

'Ha-hah!' the Chinese shouted, his long, hollow-cheeked face radiant with a smile. 'You think you not see Lee any more, heh? Happy to be wrong, sir? We will be all safe now, you see. Our friend makes you all welcome in his house.'

The three-tiered lunch carrier was full of sticky cakes and dry biscuits, and there were bottles of warm fizzy lemonade to wash them down. Half-carrying

Ibrahim, they set off for the friendly house, a square mansion full of high-ceilinged rooms and heavy, dark furniture. Their host was a fat Chinese in a brown suit which creased around his spherical belly and strained at its shiny seams.

The man insisted that they sleep in his house, assured them that they would never be betrayed under his roof, and had his servants conduct them to two enormous box-beds of carved black wood with embroidered curtains.

When they had washed, slept and regained their strength, he gave them a feast so rich and elaborate that they were stuffed after the first three courses and sat, fighting sleep and feeling uncomfortably bloated, while their host made long speeches reviling the Japanese and praising the valiant Communists and the coming revolution.

'And our allies,' Lee Kuang Leong added, raising his bottle of beer to Bill and James, 'who fight with us and share our struggle.'

Later, when Ibrahim had fallen asleep and their host was swaying slowly and belching to himself, Lee leaned towards them again. 'You are surprised I came back for you, heh? You know, we Communists will help you now, and you will help us, but when the Japanese are gone we will be enemies again. Our ambitions are not the same.' He took a slow pull at the bottle. 'But for this moment we want the same thing, to get the Japanese out.'

The food and comfort revived their spirits, and with optimism came a sense of purpose. Their host had a great deal of information. The Japanese had interned thousands of aliens in prison camps all over the country, Indians as well as Europeans.

'I wonder if Gerald got away before the Japs took over Singapore.' James stretched out a lazy hand for his half-finished bowl of soup.

'I can't see him going if he had the chance.' Awkwardly, Bill picked up a few grains of rice with his unaccustomed chopsticks. 'He'll be behind the wire now, if he's still alive. What about undercover groups like us?' He turned enquiringly back to their host, who shook his head. Many Europeans who had been left behind the Japanese lines had given up and escaped by boat in the hope of reaching Ceylon, but a few remained. In the north, an Englishman was living with the Temiar aborigines: in the east three English soldiers were hiding in the house of a Malay Christian missionary; two English planters were living at the main Communist camp in Perak supervising weapon-training.

'Are they attacking the Japanese?' Bill asked, mentally noting everything the fat man said. He kept a journal of their operations, but took care to record nothing in it that would be of use to the Japanese if he were captured.

'No, I think, no. We have no news. Only the bandits attack the Japanese.'

'What bandits?' Eager for action once more, James and Bill heard him with concentrated attention.

'In the hills, at Pulai. Hakka bandits, sons of Kuan-Yin. Very bad men for women, gambling, everything like that, but they are still fighting.'

The news reopened the discussion on their next course of action. Lee was intent on joining the main Communist camp, which was now called the 5th Division of the Malayan People's Liberation Army.

'How many are they?' Bill asked the fat man.

'One hundred, maybe two hundred. Not all in one place, but camps in the hills.'

James saw that Bill was wavering.

'We're the only men trained and left behind with a working knowledge of native languages,' he said slowly. 'I'm the only Englishman I know of who can pass in the Asiatic population. Bill, we can't quit. It'd be madness. We're more good here than sweating over maps in Ceylon, eh?'

The Australian took off his spectacles and polished them on the tail of his fraying shirt. 'You're right,' he agreed at last. 'If some of the other blokes can make out, so can we. Orders are clear that we should remain if there's work we can do in safety. Lee,' he turned to the sleepy Chinese, 'we're with you.' Lee nodded, his eyelids drooping, then slumped gently sideways. 'Now let's figure out a route.'

The map, dimpled with the all-pervading damp, stained and falling apart along its creases, was once more spread before them. Bill took their protector's advice.

'Up the Ipoh road are many friends like me,' he told them with plump self-satisfaction. 'Best you take that road to here,' his manicured finger, smooth and almost creaseless like a yellow sausage, stabbed down on to the faint, red line on the map, 'then the river. Very easy.'

And so it was; with their health restored, they marched easily along the road, until they met a convoy of panic-stricken refugees and saw the distant smoke of a Japanese reprisal party which was massacring and burning its way southwards down the highway.

They quit the road and tramped east, skirting the *padi* fields and the vast pools of slurry around the tin dredges. Much of this part of Perak was already an industrial wasteland, made grey and featureless by the concentration of open mine-workings. Bill then led them higher into the hills, choosing a route round the edges of rubber plantations where he could, because the going was easier although the risk of betrayal was greater. They saw the familiar sight of gangs of Tamil tappers about their work, oblivious of peace or war, uncaring whether the destination of the white juice yielded by the trees was Osaka or Detroit.

'This is it, I hope,' Bill told them at last, 'we'll have to strike off into the jungle and in about a week we should be in the right area.' After a morning spent hacking their way through the dense jungle regrowth, when four hours of back-breaking labour gained them a mere twenty yards, they broke through to the dim, hot calm of the virgin rain-forest and made their way more easily.

In a few days they came to a river bordered by chrome-yellow sandspits, and bathed in the crystal clear water with relief. James washed the mud from his sarong and draped it over the great flanged roots of a tree to dry. It was mid-day, and the forest was paralysed by the heat. A profound stillness and silence, the calm of millions of years of undisturbed vegetable life, held them like an enchanter's spell.

'It's so still you think you can hear the trees growing.' Bill sat on the bank, cleaning his glasses with the clear river water.

'You're whispering,' James whispered back. They grinned at each other.

'You're a good mate, Jim.'

'The best you'll get.'

'Even if you ain't got a conscience.'

'Can't all be perfect, can we?'

'It doesn't even worry you, does it?' Bill had been pondering his friend's peculiar moral deficiency ever since he had argued that they should continue sabotage work in spite of the Japanese reprisals.

'Never thought about it much, to tell you the truth.' James was smiling up at the tree's grey trunk, and the small, almost colourless orchid blooming in a fissure of the bark.

'Would you really have carried on and blown the road?' The question was asked in the spirit of bland intellectual curiosity, but it made James uncomfortable.

'I thought that sabotage was what we were supposed to be doing.' He grinned at his friend, uncertainty dulling his charm. 'I thought it was the right thing to do.'

The Australian put away his spectacles and looked at his friend with genuine concern. Jim wasn't stupid, and he wasn't wicked. He was an honourable man, in many ways one of the best. But when he was enjoying something he was like a child, not wanting anything to spoil his pleasure, unable to tell right from wrong, utterly selfish. Being a soldier, especially in the role of a daring guerrilla fighter, powerfully titillated James's masculine vanity and blinded him to all other considerations. There was no point in arguing with him, Bill realized. He was enamoured of a flawed ideal of manhood, a picture that was all show and violence, with no dimension of responsibility or care. For James, other people were mere objects to be disposed according to his fancy.

'Well, maybe you'll get another chance with the Commies.' Bill lodged his spectacles safely in his shirt pocket once more and glanced downstream', to where Lee was sitting in the shade, rolling a cigarette.

'What do you reckon we'll find up at this camp?' James asked, grateful for the change of subject. He never understood Bill when he got into one of his sermonizing moods.

'I reckon we'll find a couple of dozen peasants who don't know their left foot from their right and a handful of political commissars filling them up with Marx.'

'Can we trust them, Bill?'

'We have to trust them or we'll die. But as your commanding officer my orders are to figure out a way to survive without them as fast as we can.'

Another few hours' march led them to a track that had been freshly trodden, and a few hundred yards down it they were challenged by two young Chinese with guns, who brought them into the guerrilla camp at nightfall.

In a large bamboo house, where twenty or so men and women were eating their evening meal, they were presented to the leader, Chang Hung, and his wife. He treated them like tiresome underlings barely deserving of his dismissal, and they were taken to another, smaller hut where they found two British men eating with a small group of Malays and one Indian.

'Well, this evens up the odds a bit – good to see you, I'm Robertson, this is Evans.' The four men shook hands and Robertson introduced the rest of the party. 'This, as you may gather, is the no-chopsticks mess. They've segregated us so our disgusting eating habits don't offend their revolutionary sensitivities. Tea?'

'Where are these running dogs now, without their money and the trappings of imperialist power? Here in the jungle, where all men are equal, see how pathetic the white men appear! Did they not scatter like fowls when the Japanese came? The time of the white men is over!' The speaker waved his fist, his whole arm trembling with tension, and the audience cheered. This was Chin Peng, a slender Chinese with a bad complexion and spectacles, the political commissar for Perak. James regarded him as the most dangerous of all the Communist leaders. He had a scholarly demeanour which automatically won him respect.

Only James understood the speech, and he translated it for the other Europeans, looking at them as he did so. After six months with the Communists they were a shabby spectacle. Bill was a walking skeleton, with a pot belly and a swelling below his prominent ribs – the enlarged spleen of a malaria sufferer. Evans was not with them in the bamboo meeting-hut; he was dying rapidly of blackwater fever, the consequence of trying to treat malaria with insufficient quinine. James and Robertson, both thin and half-naked, were better off, although Robertson's legs were a mass of suppurating sores. James now wore the moneybelt, which hung loose around his wasted hips. He did not take it off to sleep.

There was prolonged cheering at the end of Chin Peng's speech, followed by a commotion at the back of the hut. A white man wearing only khaki shorts, a gleaming jungle knife thrust through his black cummerbund, entered the hall, accompanied by six bare-chested Temiar braves. Chang Hung greeted him with respect.

'It's Noone!' Bill's lifeless eyes strained to see the newcomer. 'My God, I hope he's brought us some drugs.'

Noone was one of their few links with the outside world. He was a British anthropologist who had been living with the aborigines to study them; full of romantic admiration for their mystical, peaceloving ways, at the onset of the war he had opted to live among them, with a Temiar wife. The aborigines loved him as a brother, and in consequence he could move freely through the deep jungle, guided and fed and defended by them.

As soon as the meeting was over, the British gathered around Noone in the no-chopsticks mess. 'I've got your quinine.' He took a substantial package wrapped in banana leaves from one of his men and dumped it on the floor. 'I've got tobacco, though it's only the native stuff. There's disinfectant, too, and the boys shot you a bird or two.'

They looked hungrily at the two glossy-feathered carcasses. The rations at the camp had dwindled to bad rice and tapioca chips, with tiny amounts of sweet potato for special occasions. It sustained life, but afforded little enjoyment.

Jungle game, James said, was heard but not seen. He himself, the best hunter among them, had bagged nothing but a monkey in six months.

'Thanks, mate.' Bill slapped Noone on the shoulder and shook hands with the Temiars to show his appreciation. 'We've been eating snails for weeks, and there isn't a bamboo shoot for miles.'

'There's no news on batteries for your wireless, though. Chapman sent you his newsletter.' He gave Bill a sheet of ruled paper on which the officer in command of the men remaining in Malaya hand-wrote a jungle newspaper to keep the farflung band informed. 'The worst news isn't in there, though.' He gave them cigarettes rolled the Temiar way, in pungent *nipa* leaves.

'What's that then?'

'Japs are using our men from Changi as slave labour up north. Word is they're dying like flies. I've seen them myself in cattle trucks heading over the Siamese border – living skeletons already. A lot with dysentery, too. You three look fat in comparison.'

They were so low in body and spirit that they barely reacted to the news. There was, after all, nothing they could do to help their comrades-in-arms. Only two things were plentiful in the camp – time and talk. The Chinese were increasingly hostile to all the other races, and in the hours that remained after drilling the surly troops and scavenging for food, James, Bill and Ibrahim ran a desultory education scheme among themselves. James taught Cantonese, Bill taught chess, and Ibrahim instructed them in the Koran – their only printed book.

Next morning the guerrillas put three Malays accused of spying on trial in the large hut. 'You'd better be on parade for this,' Bill told Noone. 'They stage these trials on the bread-and-circuses idea to give their people something to think about. We tried to boycott the last one on principle, but they attacked us for lack of solidarity. Pretty nasty, the whole affair.'

The three accused, two old men and a girl, were charged before a tribunal of the guerrilla leaders, and condemned by a succession of prosecutors. At least one of the men was well advanced in his second childhood; the girl was speechless with terror.

'They're just peasants,' Bill murmured.

Ibrahim nodded. 'Nothing more than rattan-cutters. Harm-less.'

The prosecutors worked themselves into a frenzy of anti-Malay rhetoric. A token defence was woodenly put forward by a young Chinese, then the tribunal made a show of consultation and delivered the verdict of guilty. The three Malays were taken out into the clearing, tied to trees, and bayoneted to death, amid much cheering.

'My job is to mould that rabble into a killing machine,' Bill said with contempt. 'They're so hostile they've even invented a "Chinese" way of firing a goddam rifle. It's like a Mad Hatter's Tea Party – except I wouldn't fancy my chances very long after I left the table.'

'We can't just sit here, starving to death in the middle of a hundred crazy Communists. We've got to get out and do something.' James felt as if frustration instead of hunger were eating his guts.

'For Christ's sake, man, what can we do? We've no equipment, hardly any arms, no wireless, not even enough to keep ourselves alive.' Illness made Bill's normal reasonable tone sound weak and peevish.

'We've enough quinine now for months. Remember your orders, Bill? Find a way to survive without the Communists.'

'So what? We *can't* survive without them. If they think we're betraying them, they'll put us on trial like the other poor bastards. We're trapped. We'll just have to sit it out.'

James flung his hair out of his eyes in angry dismissal of this argument.

'What did you do in the war, Daddy? I *sat it out,* dear, in the jungle, and took lessons in Marxist dialectics. For God's sake, man, what's the matter with you?'

'Are you trying to call me yellow?' Feeble rage gleamed behind Bill's glasses. Ibrahim raised his half-moon eyebrows in amuse-ment.

'Peace, my friends, let the birds do the squawking. What James is trying to tell you, in his heavy-handed European way, is that we have devised a strategy. Do you want to hear it?' Bill nodded grudgingly. 'It is this. In my own state, Pahang, we have two very interesting things. One is the Japanese military HQ; two is a very loyal Malay population, and very few Chinese. We know the Sultan has helped Europeans escape to the jungle, and the police are reluctant to pursue the Japanese orders concerning security.'

Ibrahim spoke with passion instead of with his normal Malay reserve. 'Why do we not leave this place, where, as James says, we can do nothing and our lives may soon be in danger, and travel to Pahang? We should think about organizing a separate Malay resistance. Then we can perhaps recruit agents, start to gather information on the movement of troops and supplies, and pass it back to this camp, maybe to the British headquarters in India or Ceylon?'

Bill thoughtfully fingered his spectacles, which were now wired together where the tiny metal hinges had rusted through. 'But we'll be informed on, for sure.'

Ibrahim shrugged his bony shoulders. 'The jungle will protect us. I am sure the Japanese know the location of this camp, but they know also the difficulties of pursuing guerrillas through this kind of country.'

'And just the three of us?'

James nodded. 'We haven't talked to the others. Evans can't travel in his condition, and one of us must stay here in case they do start sending men in from Ceylon. And I didn't think there was much point in talking to Lee.' Their Chinese companion had become one of the most vociferous Communist officers.

They left the next day with Noone and his Temiars, arousing no immediate suspicion in the Chinese who did not believe the white men could live long in the forest. The aborigines guided them through the deep jungle, using their own tracks which were invisible to the untrained eye. In a week they reached the boundary of the state of Pahang.

'Arthur, my darling,' wrote Jean Anderson, her pencil crawling slowly across the page of damp-roughened paper, 'eighteen years ago today we were married. We never thought, we could never imagine, that we would spend this anniversary in such circumstances as this.' She paused, exhausted by the effort, and looked around the room. The European women interned in Sumatra had been moved to an old prison house, a forbidding square building with heavy double doors and iron-barred cells like animal cages around a central courtyard. These enclosures, which were not locked, served as small dormitories and were furnished with bare platforms of bamboo on which the women slept.

The corner of this grim building which was occupied by Jean and Betty had been decorated with flowers by the other women for Jean's anniversary, and the vivid, succulent pinks of oleanders and the purple-blue of the jungle convolvulus glowed incongruously against the iron grille.

'Today, I think of you all the time,' she continued. It took all her strength to push the pencil across the page. Jean's wiry endurance had been sapped by more than a year of malnutrition and disease. Her legs, once skinny, were now bloated so that her ankles were almost obliterated. Her shoes had long ago disintegrated, and when she walked she wore rough wooden clogs, which were now arranged neatly, side-by-side, at the foot of her sleeping space. 'And I renew my vows to you, Arthur. When this nightmare is over we shall begin our married life anew in such a burst of happiness . . .' The pencil was now blunted and she paused again, looking for Betty. To sharpen the pencil, she needed to borrow a knife, and to borrow a knife she needed to walk to the kitchen, and to get up and walk she needed Betty's help.

There was a burst of giggling from across the dank courtyard. Four or five of the younger women, Betty among them, were amusing themselves by dressing a young Cockney girl as a bride, and now their creation was complete. The scrawny figure wore a veil of ragged mosquito net and carried an elaborate bouquet of wilting blooms and leathery leaves. Her dress was fashioned from an old sheet spotted with rust marks, and she skittishly pulled up the skirt to show a garter created from a perished rubber ring and a few shreds of grey lingerie lace.

'Pity about the bandages, Irene,' Betty laughed, pointing to the ragged dressings covering the tropical ulcers on the girl's ankles. 'Spoil the whole effect.'

'Oh, I don't know – who'll be looking at my feet on my wedding day?'

'Betty,' Jean called out apologetically, and the younger woman turned towards her.

'What is it?' she asked with a trace of irritation. Jean was struggling to get up, and clutching at the iron grille for support, but in her weakened condition she could not manage alone. Reluctantly, Betty left her entertainment and went to help her friend.

'Can you help me to the kitchen, Betty? I need to get the pencil sharpened.'

Betty hesitated. 'Must you, Jean? It's pointless writing to Arthur, they'll never let us send the letters. You won't want to read them at the end of the war, anyway.'

The outlandish bride clattered across to them on her wooden clogs and picked up the two-inch length of pencil with which Jean had been writing. 'I'll go for you,' she offered cheerfully. 'You sit down and take it easy, love. Save your strength.'

Although the women were united in a close, almost cosy, alliance against adversity, and the more robust characters among them were at pains to outlaw pettiness and ill-feeling in the prison community, there was no doubt that every woman in the camp detested Betty. Her furtive, deceitful ways, her selfishness, and above all her conspicuous lack of care for the woman who had saved her life, offended profoundly against their charitable common morality.

Betty, completely obsessed with her own survival, barely noticed their hostility, and they never voiced it. It occasionally puzzled her that the other women did not extend their warm comradeship to her in the same terms as they did to Jean, but she put this down to the snobbery of the middle-class British women who formed the camp's unofficial leadership.

That evening, Jean fell asleep as if the effort of writing had exhausted her. In the middle of the night she began to mutter her husband's name and Betty, suddenly feeling helpless, went to the next-door cell to get help from Irene, the girl who had dressed up.

'Crikey,' she muttered, feeling Jean's forehead wet with sweat. 'She's got a temperature all right. We'd better take her to the hospital straight away. Hope it's not that swamp fever catching up with her.'

They carried Jean round to the hut which acted as a hospital and Betty, because she was no longer sleepy and had nothing else to do, sat and dabbed Jean's face with water for a few hours. She became more and more delirious and her temperature was soaring. Betty knew Jean was going to die. Many of the women with whom they had first been interned had contracted the same fever, and its progress was swift and inevitable. Another day, perhaps two, and Jean would be gone.

Betty slept a few hours before daybreak then woke and queued for her morning cup of rice with a teaspoon of palm oil as a luxury. The Japanese officer in charge of the camp announced that there would be a distribution of mail that day, and most of the two hundred women in the prison eagerly gathered in a long line outside his office, talking excitedly as their captors slowly deciphered the addresses on the small bag of cards.

'Mrs Rawlins?' Betty gave her name without much hope that there would be anything for her.

'Here.' Into her hand was put an envelope addressed to Mrs G. W. Rawlins (British Civilian Internee), Women's Camp, Palembang, Sumatra, c/o Japanese Red Cross, Tokyo, Japan. Up the side was stamped the number of the examiner who had verified that the message was no more than fifty words long and contained no mention of ill-treatment, food shortages or the progress of the war. Betty walked briskly back to her cell.

'Aren't you going to read it?' Next to Betty on the bare bamboo sleeping-platform sat a curious Irene who had no letter of her own. 'Come on, Betty. You stood out there in the sun for an hour to sign for it, you must open it.'

'I can't. I don't know the writing. It might say something awful.'

The girl took the letter from Betty's hand. 'Tell you what we'll do. I'll read it, and if I think you won't like it, I'll keep it for you.'

Betty shook her head. An Englishwoman appeared at the doorway of the bamboo hut, her skeletal form silhouetted against the bright sunlight. 'We need volunteers to bale out the latrines – either of you two?'

'I can't, the sores on my legs haven't healed,' Betty said at once, drawing a contemptuous nod from the older woman. Betty never volunteered for anything unless there was a chance of extra food rations.

'I'll go.' Irene scrambled off the platform and Betty was left alone in the dim heat of the hut. She turned the letter over, looking for a clue to its contents. Then she lay back and surrendered to the mental vacuum which was always waiting for her, narcotic, comforting nothingness.

'Sister Katerina – I didn't see you.' The sweet-faced Dutch nun had entered the hut quietly. She was a respected leader among the camp women and had no doubt been sent to Betty by the others. Deftly she picked up the envelope before Betty could reach it, and without a word opened it and read the card inside. Then she handed it to Betty with a smile.

'Not bad news, I think.'

It was from an officer whose name Betty did not recognize, at Changi internment camp on Singapore Island, informing her that her husband had been alive two months earlier when he had left camp with a party of prisoners 'sent north for an unknown purpose'. 'We shall try to send news of your survival to him. I know he would wish to send you all his love,' the message concluded.

'Happy now?' It was hard to tell. Betty's face was habitually vacant with very little expression. She had suffered, of course, a severe illness after childbirth, but by now they had all suffered as gravely, and many had died.

'Yes, I'm happy. Thank you, Sister. You're so kind.' Betty folded the card in two and tucked it into the old Bakelite soap-dish which contained her remaining precious possessions including the marcasite watch which Gerald had given her on their engagement.

'The kitchen needs another person to pick rice, I think.' The nun held out a hand to help her down from the sleeping-platform.

'What day is it?' Betty asked her. 'I can't keep track of time here.'

'January 24th, today.'

'Good heavens, it's my birthday.' I must tell them in the kitchen, she thought at once, perhaps they'll give me a treat.

'Well, now you can hope with God's help to spend your next birthday with your husband. How many years is it you have been married?'

'Let me count – I can't believe it, but it must be almost four years. My goodness.'

'Congratulations, my dear, and bless you.' To her embarrassment, the nun gave her a firm, clean kiss on each cheek. Even in the enforced intimacy of the internment camp Betty could not learn to like being touched.

'I wonder when that letter was written.' Betty reached out and opened the soap-container to look. 'Where's the date? Oh no!' The nun looked over her shoulder.

'What's the matter now?'

'It's months old. That's no good. Gerald could still be dead and I not know.' With anger, she threw the card down and let the other woman put an arm around her shoulders.

'If God wills it he will be alive. Now, come to do some work and make yourself think of other things. Many women have no news at all, remember. At least, for you, there is still a chance.'

Later, as she sat outside the cooking hut with a wicker-basket, picking out weevils, gravel and woodchippings from the prisoners' meagre rice ration, Betty thought of the marcasite watch. If she sold it, she could buy eggs, or some sugar perhaps. If Gerald was dead, he couldn't mind, could he?

CHAPTER FIFTEEN

THERE WAS a noise in the distance, a low, tired roar that did not rise or fall but ground on remorselessly like a faraway ocean. It was the noise of London traffic. Cathy opened her eyes and dissociated dots of light and colour rushed painfully into her head. She shut her eyes again. She felt weightless, floating, heavy with nothingness.

At her side, something moved. A door opened and closed. The door was somewhere beyond her feet. Her throat was sore and there was a bad taste in her mouth. Her right arm felt awkward, as if it were being bent backwards against the joint. Her foot hurt, her left foot. It was hot and tender, and the blankets were raised over it.

She opened her eyes again and willed the inrush of dots into a picture. A room, a window. She was lying flat and a tube was stuck into her right arm. The door opened and closed again, there was a rustle and a nurse was standing beside her.

'How do you feel?' She picked up the clipboard at the foot of the bed and made some notes on it.

'All right.' Cathy tried to smile.

'Your sister's coming to see you, she'll be here soon, I expect.'

The nurse's manner did not invite conversation. She left the room a few moments later and Cathy tried to sit up. It was difficult. Obviously, she was very weak. There was a large, uncomfortable band of sticking plaster across her throat. Determined, Cathy pulled herself down the bed until she could reach the clipboard, and held it above her eyes to read it. It was Thursday. She had been admitted on Tuesday. Her temperature was normal, but it had been low when she was brought in.

She felt clearheaded but foolish. It was nice to feel so silly. Nothing was important. No one could hurt her. There was nothing to think about.

The door opened violently and Monty rushed to her.

'Darling, darling Cathy!' Monty's hair smelt smoky, reminding her of the world of pain outside the white walls. 'It's all right, darling, I'm here. You're OK, you're going to be OK.' Cathy tried to smile again but her mouth was disobedient. She felt inexpressibly happy to see her sister, but her face was stretching into all sorts of grimaces and as Monty ripped a tissue from the box nearby and dabbed at her eyes, she realized that she was weeping. They hugged each other for a long time.

'Have they told you anything?' Monty asked her at last.

'What anything?'

'No, they haven't, have they, the shits. Your doctor's all right, but the nurses are absolute bitches. I don't think they approve of suicides, somehow.'

The word suicide was puzzling. 'Am I – did I . . . ?' her voice subsided in doubt.

'Don't you remember?'

Cathy tried to remember, and remembered that her husband had left her and wanted to divorce her. She began to cry again. She could remember nothing else. 'Are there any pillows?' she asked. 'I'd like to sit up.'

Monty brought a pile of pillows from a chair and helped her sister upright, moving the cradle over her foot with care.

'Why have they put a tent over my foot? Is there anything to drink? My mouth tastes horrible.'

Monty poured some water. 'You've hurt your foot.'

Slowly, Cathy began to remember. 'But I took pills, I must have been unconscious. How could I have hurt my foot?' She smiled. It was ridiculous. She laughed. She couldn't stop laughing, it was so funny. Her face was wet; she was crying again.

Monty passed her some tissues. 'I'll tell you everything later, when you're more together.'

'No, tell me now.'

'No, Cathy, tomorrow.'

'Don't be silly, you know me – I'll only worry about it.'

'But you're out of your head.'

'Considering the things I do when I'm in my right mind, that's probably as sane as I'll ever be.'

Monty laughed, and Cathy laughed, and they hugged each other; then Cathy started crying again and Monty put the box of tissues by the hand that was not connected to a drip.

'OK, but it's heavy. You're in St George's Hospital, you've been here two days. We found you at home, you'd fallen off the bed. This,' she patted the sticking plaster across Cathy's throat, 'is because they gave you a tracheotomy. You were in intensive care for a day.'

'And that?' Cathy pointed at the hump over her foot.

'Does your foot hurt?'

'Throbs a bit, why?'

'You were lying so the blood supply in your leg was restricted, and no blood was getting through to your foot. They think part of your foot may be dead, because it was deprived of oxygen a long time, and you might be going to get gangrene.'

'My goodness. I thought that only happened in war films when they start amputating people's legs with blunt knives.'

'Don't be silly.' Monty squeezed her hand and tried to sound utterly reassuring. At one point the doctor had mentioned that amputating Cathy's leg was a possibility.

'Does anyone know I'm here?'

'I rang up Lord Shrewton. He was terrific. We agreed he'd tell Charlie, and now you've come round you can see him, if you want.'

'And Jamie? Is Jamie all right?'

'He's fine.'

'Mummy?'

'Yes, I told her. There's some bridge tournament on, so she said she'd only come up if you got worse. Didi went bananas but I told Caroline to tie her down.' They laughed again.

Next day the crazy elation vanished and Cathy felt hopeless. The hospital psychiatrist came to see her, and a doctor.

'The shrink said I was a classic case,' she told Monty. 'His line was I was still grieving for Daddy. I told him he ought to try being married to someone like Charlie. I bet he wouldn't sit there looking so smug if his wife was screwing everything that moved.'

'He's only worried that you'll try it again and get the hospital bad publicity. Did you tell him about the pills the doctor was giving you?'

Cathy shook her head. 'They were only tranquillizers, nothing important.' Her sister looked better, Monty thought. Her cheeks had a vague tinge of colour and her eyes were no longer staring out of her head as if she'd seen a ghost.

'Any news on the foot – how does it feel?'

'Awful. It's agony and they won't give me enough painkillers because they say it's a good sign that it's hurting.'

'Is it infected?'

Cathy nodded. 'They gave me antibiotics, too. If I could walk I'd probably rattle.' They fell into a companionable silence. Cathy reached for the magazine which Monty had brought her and opened it without much interest.

'Did you really want to die?' Monty asked suddenly.

'Yes. It was all I could think about. I just knew it was what I had to do. I'd failed at everything so I had to die.' Cathy spoke slowly, hardly able now to understand how she had felt when she had planned her death with such meticulous care.

'Are you angry with me for stopping you from dying?'

Cathy considered the question. 'No. I'm pleased to be alive now. I feel as if living means everything, when dying meant everything before. I feel awful about Jamie. How could I even think of leaving him?'

'You'd flipped, you didn't know what you were doing. You must have been junked up on tranquillizers for months, too.'

'Do you know what I couldn't make the shrink understand, Monty? I wasn't *trying* anything, I *was* going to kill myself, and I failed and I feel bloody awful. I've failed at everything. I've lost my husband – I did everything I knew to keep him, and I lost.' She snivelled and groped for the tissues.

'He doesn't know you, does he? He's used to seeing hysterical chicks who're trying the old emotional blackmail. He doesn't understand that you weren't just messing about.' Cathy's tears began to burst uncontrollably from behind her closed eyelids. 'You haven't failed,' Monty consoled her. 'You can't win anything if the deck's stacked against you.'

'Other women do.'

'Like who? Mummy? Didi? Mrs Emanuel or the Marchioness? What do you want to be like when you're fifty? Some harpy who fucks up Jamie's life because she hasn't got a life of her own?'

Cathy rubbed tears from her eyes. 'Jamie. Poor little Jamie. How could I have thought of killing myself and leaving him all alone? Are you sure he's OK, Monty? Will you ask them to bring him to see me?'

With long hours in which to think, Cathy soon began to discover the significance of who visited her, and why. Monty came every day and treated the bleak little ward as if it were just another room in her own home, sitting gossiping and watching television. When she was there Cathy forgot that she was injured.

Charlie sent her flowers, with a card promising a visit. His father, Lord Shrewton, visited quite regularly, despite the fact that he was obviously acutely uncomfortable in the presence of a woman who had been so appallingly wronged by his son. Cathy put him at his ease by encouraging him to talk business, and the reserved but sincere affection they held for each other deepened. The Marchioness called once, briefly, twittering inanities.

Her most trying sympathizer was her grandmother, who wafted into the room in her new spring fur, a puff-sleeved chinchilla, and calling, 'Where is the poor, dear girl? My dear, how simply awful for you to be cooped up in this hideous room. You must make them move you at once. Those curtains! Too drab!'

She brought flowers, champagne, and a turquoise silk negligee trimmed with fake *point de Venise* lace. 'Now when Charlie comes you must be sure to look beautiful but fragile. Lie back on the pillows weakly and say almost nothing. Have you got some white make-up? I'll get some sent to you.'

Cathy suddenly saw her grandmother as if she were a creature from another world, incapable of understanding how life on earth was lived. Here I am, she thought, lucky to be alive, lucky to have two legs and facing the possibility that I'll never be able to walk normally again, and Didi's only interested in teaching me to act like a courtesan so I can get Charlie back. If it wasn't for Charlie I wouldn't be in this mess.

Lady Davina at once sensed that her pupil's attention was wandering. 'You've been very, very stupid,' she hissed, her wrinkled, powder-caked face poking forward like a vulture's. 'You've played right into that girl's hands and you'll have to work like a demon to get Charlie back in line now you've behaved like a silly little fool.'

'I thought you said men liked women who acted like silly little fools?' Cathy saw that her sarcasm was completely lost on her grandmother, so she changed the subject. 'Have you seen Jamie, Didi? I miss him so much, but I think the Marchioness wants to keep him down at Coseley so he won't have to see me in hospital.'

The old woman glared at her through beads of blue mascara. 'Have you gone completely mad? There's nothing more likely to put a man off than a snivelling brat about the place.' Her bracelets clashed as she raised her arms in a gesture of despair. 'I never could understand why you allowed Nanny to bring the little horror downstairs all the time and leave toys all over the house. Men can't stand children at any price.'

Cathy sighed and leaned back on the pillows, letting her eyelids droop as if with exhaustion exactly as her grandmother had counselled her to do with Charlie. 'That's it! That's just how you should look!' the old woman exclaimed. 'Now remember to look like that, say nothing, and make him feel guilty. He'll soon come to heel.'

The next day the doctor decided to operate on Cathy's foot and remove the dead tissue. Ten days later he operated again. 'You're going to be with us for some time yet,' he told her and she nodded, too woozy with drugs to take much interest.

Charlie at last came to see her with his usual bedraggled bunch of flowers, bought as an afterthought from the stall in Belgrave Square. 'I love you, Cathy, I'll always love you,' he told her, kissing her hands and fingering the wedding and the engagement ring as he did so. The rings were becoming loose because she was losing weight.

'That's typical,' Monty complained. 'You get skinny when you're miserable and I just get fatter.'

'Well, you must be happy now, then.' Cathy looked at her sister with approval. Monty was decidedly slim. She was wearing a pair of topaz velvet jeans and an antique cream lace blouse that veiled her breasts rather than merely covering them. Her hair cascaded halfway down her back.

'Yeah.' Monty suddenly realized that she was happy, but could not find a reason and did not want to dwell on it in the face of her sister's desolation. 'You'll be back on top of the world once you get out of here.'

Was I ever happy? Cathy wondered when she was alone. She remembered the frothy excitement of her honeymoon and wondered if a feeling based on so much self-delusion could rightly be called happiness.

Charlie was soon appearing around the heavy hospital door almost every day, and she was disturbed to realize that she felt nothing at all for him; no love, no hate, not even contempt. She felt a little sorry for him, because Lisa, the Texan nymphomaniac, was clearly keeping him on his toes.

'She's always giving parties and she expects me to be in time and not get drunk,' he complained. 'God, I miss you, darling.'

When she had been in hospital a month the plastic surgeon came to see her. He was suave and handsome, like a drawing from a woman's magazine romance, with humorous blue eyes and very white teeth.

'What we're going to do,' he explained, patting what was left of her injured foot, 'is realign the bones and put a couple of pins in to hold them straight. Then we'll take a skin graft, and then you should be able to start walking again.' Cathy sighed. She wanted very much to go home and hold Jamie in her arms again. She had begged to see him, but her father-in-law had gently but firmly declined to bring her son to the hospital.

The first operation was a success, but the skin graft did not go so well.

'You've got unusually strong skin for a European. It's healing more as I would expect an Asian or African woman's skin to do,' he told her. 'Eventually I'm hopeful you'll get away with insignificant scars. But your general physical condition is so poor at the moment that you've no resistance to infection. We'll have to try again. I'm going to prescribe some concentrated vitamins and some more iron for you.'

Later that day the surgeon reappeared with a basket of strawberries. 'First of the season,' he announced, putting them on the table beside her bed. 'No sense in missing all the good things in life while you're in here. Plenty of Vitamin C. I've told Sister you're to eat the lot yourself.'

'Do you give all your patients vitamins like this?' she asked him, tempted by the smell of the ripe fruit which filled the overheated hospital air.

'Noonly the beautiful ones.' He kissed her hand in a formal manner.

'You're a plastic surgeon – aren't they all beautiful by the time you've finished with them?'

'No. Not more than they were before I started, anyway. Most women are beautiful, they just won't realize it.' He sighed. He was a man who loved women and wished women loved themselves as much. 'There's nothing I could do to make a woman beautiful if she doesn't see it herself. And there's nothing that could disfigure a woman who believed she was beautiful, whatever she looked like in the mirror. You're that sort. I don't treat many women like you.'

Next day Monty came as usual, and remarked that Cathy looked better.

'I think I've got a crush on the plastic surgeon,' Cathy confided, half-serious.

'Steady on. Don't doctors get struck off the medical register and barred from practising if they start carrying on with their patients? Can I have the last strawberry?' Monty peered into the almost empty basket.

'He gave them to me last night. To be honest, I think he's just trying to cheer me up.'

Monty appraised her sister fondly, and noticed that the drawn look had gone from her face and that her hair, although it was limp and unstyled, now had a hint of its former rich sheen. She was wearing the turquoise silk negligee, but the colour quarrelled with the amber tints of her complexion.

'You look heaps better. What's happening? Are they letting you out?'

'No, I'm going to be in here for weeks and weeks.' Cathy looked despondently at the rise in the blankets where the cradle still protected her foot. 'I'm going to be crippled, Monty. I'm going to have to learn to walk all over again, and I'll never be able to run properly, or dance, or anything.'

'Of course you will.' Monty reached over and squeezed her sister's hand, noticing that the fingernails, which had been bitten to the quick during the anguished period before her suicide attempt, were now a heroic millimetre in length. 'You'll be able to do anything you want to do, just like you always could.'

'There's one thing I'll never do again, and you're to have me committed to an asylum if I look like I'm going to do it.' Cathy held her sister's glance, and her eyes seemed deeper than ever with the shadow of pain behind them. 'I'll never, ever fall in love again, not as long as I live.'

Monty hesitated. Disclaiming love still sounded like a heresy to her. She drew back. 'Famous last words, I bet you,' she said, with all the optimism she could command. She knew that Cathy never committed herself to anything without being prepared to follow it through to the end.

The next day, Charlie called to see Cathy with a bottle of champagne. He tried to make her drink most of it then said, 'I've got a bit of business to sort out – just sign this, will you?' He put a pen in her hand and spread a sheet of paper on the table in front of her.

'What is it?'

'Nothing, just a trust document.'

She started to read the paper.

'You don't have to read it, just sign it.' She ignored him and read the legal paper to the end. It was a consent to a divorce from Charlie, giving him custody of Jamie. Cathy read it again to make sure, struggling to control her emotions. She wanted to kill him, claw out his eyes and trample on the corpse, but hatred, she swiftly realized, would not help her to defend herself.

'I suppose this is Lisa's idea?' she asked him cautiously, pressing the bell for the nurse in case he tried to hit her.

Charlie squirmed and tried to look appealing. 'She wants to get married.'

'More fool her. Why does she want my son as well?'

Charlie looked even more uncomfortable. 'Well, you can't look after him in your condition, can you?'

The nurse came in and Cathy told him to leave. Then she telephoned Pasterns, her solicitors, and the battle commenced. First Charlie's lawyers sent a statement from him alleging that Cathy was mentally unstable and had ill-treated Jamie. Mr Napier from Pasterns came to the hospital, looking most embarrassed.

'I didn't ill-treat Jamie,' Cathy protested. 'It was that awful, senile old Nanny the Coseleys insisted I should have. I've never even smacked him.'

'Can you prove this in any way? Anything written down, any doctor's letters or anything?'

'Well, our doctor will remember, I'm sure. And then there's the girl who came to look after him when Nanny Bunting was ill. And the psychiatrist here will tell you I'm not unstable.'

They wrote to the Coseleys' doctor, who wrote back declining to give evidence. 'It is my policy never to involve myself in the personal affairs of my patients,' his letter said.

'Can't we subpoena him?' Monty asked Mr Napier from her perch on the end of her sister's bed.

'This isn't Perry Mason, my dear. There's no such thing as a sub-poena in English law. We might consider issuing a witness summons, but counsel will probably advise against it. Barristers are always very wary of a hostile witness. Can do more harm than good.'

'How can he just refuse to give evidence, when they're trying to take my child away from me?' Cathy felt as if she were playing a game whose rules had not been explained to her.

'I think he's rather aware of which side his bread is buttered,' Mr Napier said delicately. 'He's the family's doctor, after all.'

Cathy privately carried cynicism even further. Pasterns were sending her bills every two weeks, instead of following their usual sleepy accounting procedure; she rightly took this as a clear indication that they did not anticipate winning her case. She had a distinct impression that to fight the richest noble family in England was considered sheer folly by the superficially attentive professionals in her employ.

Her temporary nanny had already been approached by Charlie's solicitors, who sent her statement to Pasterns. It was very short, and simply said that her impression was that the Countess of Laxford took very little interest in her child.

'No one will believe that girl – she was having an affair with my husband. I found them making love on the stairs in the middle of the night,' Cathy told her lawyer with confidence.

'Do you have any proof?'

'What proof could I possibly have? I saw them with my own eyes and she ran off into the street half-naked.' Her lawyer was being very stupid, Cathy thought.

'My Lady, without proof there's nothing to stop your husband denying it, and then it's just your word against his.' Mr Napier, in his turn, felt his client was being uncharacteristically obtuse.

There was also a statement from Nanny Bunting which stressed her credentials as a child-care expert of forty years' experience and described Cathy as ignorant, immature, a social butterfly and obsessively jealous of her husband.

'The old . . .' Cathy almost bit her tongue, trying to stop herself swearing in front of the prim young man who was once more extracting a document from his bulging black case.

'And I'm afraid the trick-cyclist isn't much help either.' Mr Napier handed her more papers with a warning tone in his voice. 'His opinion is that you're severely depressed, out of touch with reality and generally unable to cope.'

Angry enough to ignore the pain in her foot, Cathy pulled herself up in her bed and scanned the paper. She saw the words 'severe post-natal depression', 'unresolved grief reaction' and 'probability of further attempts' through a mist of rage.

'Don't cry, darling Cathy,' Monty soothed her. 'You'll only get lines around your eyes.'

'Lines around my eyes! Who'll notice them when there's *this* to look at?' Cathy made a despairing gesture to the ugly surgical boot which encased her injured foot. 'And what's the point of looking beautiful if all it gets you is a man like Charlie? I wish I'd been born ugly, then he'd never have fancied me. Why aren't you saying "I told you so"? You saw through him right from the start.'

Monty ignored her, and handed her the walking stick with which she could hobble unevenly along. The boot, heavy and unsightly as it was, at least made it possible to walk after a fashion. Within a few days, Cathy learned to balance well on her damaged foot. She had lost the tips of her first two toes, her muscles were weak from disuse and her foot ached after every effort.

Money was instantly a problem. When she returned to her home she discovered that the bank had allowed Charlie to close their joint account, and requests for maintenance made through Pasterns were left unanswered for weeks. With icy composure Cathy took her jewellery to a well-stocked pawn shop in Victoria, and sold three large silver salvers she found in the pantry cupboard to a dealer in Chancery Lane. Two eighteenth-century French pastoral scenes, her wedding gift from Lady Davina, went to Sotheby's. She had enough to live on, to pay a daily cleaner to keep the echoing house decent, and to settle her lawyers' bills.

There were more distasteful tasks ahead. Cathy swallowed her pride and her contempt and tracked down as many of her husband's lovers as she could – five in all, grubby artificial blondes living on the edges of Chelsea in curiously similar little apartments, with cuddly toys on their beds and the same odour of long-term slovenly housekeeping optimistically smothered with expensive scent, lingering in their hallways.

Her first target was a bit-part actress, younger and more successful than April Henessy, and much less infatuated with Charlie.

'You can count on me,' she said at once, stubbing out a half-smoked cigarette. 'I'll give evidence for you. I'll say whatever you want. I've always said I felt sorry for whoever was married to that flash bastard. He lost me the best part I ever had, you know – blacked my eye the day before we started rehearsals. I'll never forgive him.'

'The case will probably get quite a bit of publicity,' Cathy warned her.

'Right on!' The actress screwed her left eye into a theatrical wink. 'I hope you get a million, love, you deserve it.'

The next day Cathy was amused to see in a gossip column a large picture of the woman in a plunge-necked gown, above the headline 'Earl's Secret Love'. With renewed confidence she visited the remaining four women, but they all instantly refused to make statements confirming their affairs with Charlie. At the last apartment among the out-of-date invitations crowding the dusty mantelpiece, Cathy noticed a Coutts cheque for £1,000 bearing Charlie's vestigial signature.

'I feel as if I'm trying to fight the Mafia,' she told Monty in a weary tone. 'It was the same with the couple who used to keep house for us – Charlie's just paid them all off. None of our friends will help, either. I thought they were my friends, too, but they won't risk losing the Coseley money or the Coseley connections or the Coseley invitations just to help me get my son back.'

'You miss him. don't you?'

'So much, Monty, so much. I hate being in that house. Every night I lie awake and think I can hear him upstairs in the nursery. Whenever the staircase creaks I think it's Jamie coming down to see me.'

'Shall I come and stay with you for a while?' Cathy was thinner than ever now, Monty noticed.

'What about Simon?'

'He doesn't need me – you do.'

By the time her divorce hearing was imminent Cathy could walk almost normally, and the surgical boot had been replaced by a pair of black patent shoes with grosgrain bows made for her with courteous care by her father's former bootmakers, Lobbs of St James's. Her barrister, a jovial man with iron grey hair and a substantial belly which strained at the buttons of his striped waistcoat, eyed her with satisfaction.

'Very attractive, if I may say so. I like to see my clients looking their best. But if you take my advice you'll come to the court looking as plain as you can. Don't try to cover up your limp. Get rid of that Mona Lisa smile, too. Look as miserable as you can.'

'Whatever for?' enquired Cathy, straightening the skirt of the demure navy-blue suit she had bought for the occasion. It had a small lace collar which, she thought, added the ideal touch of fragility and flattered the sallow tint of her neglected complexion.

'Setting aside the question of the custody of your son, any alimony you are awarded will be in a sum fixed by the judge according to his estimation of your prospects of remarriage. Look too pretty, or have a boyfriend waiting in the wings, and you'll get a mere pittance.'

Cathy nodded. 'And what about my son – do you think we'll win?' Jamie was all she cared about. Talking about alimony was a waste of breath.

He answered too quickly to suggest confidence. 'The courts always favour the mother in these affairs but. . . ah . . . I could wish we had more evidence in this case. Of course,' he looked at her with sudden concern, 'you appreciate that this case isn't really about the boy at all, don't you?'

'Then what on earth is it about?'

'The money, My Lady. Your son inherits directly from the Coseley trust, he's a very rich young man, far richer than his father. Whoever gets him gets the loot.'

'But my husband is a wealthy man already, and Lisa's an heiress . . .'

'Nothing rational about greed, in my experience. To him that hath shall more be given – the Good Book says it and it's the way of the world. One can never be too rich or too thin, eh?' He stood up to show her out of his chambers, keeping to himself the opinion that his client was much too thin and had an air of angry, demented bewilderment which was not going to help him demonstrate her mental stability.

Cathy saw Charlie, with Lisa clinging to his arm and a team ol lawyers leafing energetically through their documents, at the far end of the vaulted Gothic corridor outside the court. His barrister was a clean-cut, expansive man whose air of authority immediately made Cathy's lawyers look tentative and shabby.

At the end of the first day of the hearing they were all despondent. The judge clearly accepted the picture of Cathy as a neurotic, unstable woman which Charlie's lawyers painted. There was a purposeful scuffle in the press gallery and next morning the headlines proclaimed: 'Cruelty To Earl's Baby' and carried pictures of Charlie and Lisa looking loving and of Cathy with her bowed head and walking stick, looking like a witch.

The morning mail lay beside the newspaper, and Cathy looked at it without enthusiasm. 'All I ever get is wretched bills, now.' She finished her coffee and stood up.

'What's this?' Monty picked out a thick, grey envelope from among the bills.

'More bad news, I expect. Open it, if you like.'

Inside the envelope was one piece of paper, a page from *Texas Monthly* magazine, part of an article about European aristocracy visiting the state. There was a picture of Charlie playing polo, and beneath it the news that the Earl of Laxford was shortly to take up residence in Dallas with his American wife.

'Who sent it?' Cathy wondered, looking at the envelope. The postmark was smudged beyond interpretation.

'Who cares? It's amazing! That's just what we need – if we can prove they want to take Jamie out of the country the whole situation changes. The judge will see what a shit Charlie really is. We can turn the tables on them!' Monty sprang to her feet and seized the large-brimmed hat of apricot felt which she wore to the court in an attempt to hide her Jimi Hendrix explosion of hair and make her look sane and trustworthy.

Although Cathy now doubted that anything could prevail against the might of the Coseley clan, Monty was proved right. The actress gave evidence on their side and was as good as her word, sturdily accusing Charlie of drinking, drugging and beating her up. When Charlie at last gave evidence and was forced to admit that he planned to live abroad, the judge adjourned the case to his chambers. Charlie began to bluster, as he always did when caught out in deception, and the judge's attitude towards Cathy became sympathetic.

In the small, oak-panelled room, the atmosphere grew tense as the lawyers worked out a compromise. Cathy listened intently and avoided Charlie's eyes. She was too afraid to hope, but with every fibre of her being she willed the judge to give Jamie back to her.

'I am inclined to think that the child will do best where he is, with his paternal grandparents.' The judge at last looked up from his papers at Cathy, who at close quarters did not appear to him to have any potential for sadism or instability at all. She gasped with disappointment and he continued kindly, 'But the court will be able to make another order in time, if you can demonstrate that your life is stable and that you are a fit person to care for your child.'

He gave Cathy access to her son every weekend and for a fortnight in the school holidays, and made an order for £12,000 in lump-sum alimony which, Cathy saw from her barrister's face, was more than had been expected.

Charlie left the court hurriedly with Lisa on his arm.

'The pigs. Charlie never wanted Jamie at all, or the money. It's all that woman.' Monty glared after the couple as they scurried into a taxi.

'That's about the size of it.' Her lawyer took off his wig and smoothed his hair. 'Men who argue about their children in court are usually arguing about money. No one has ever succeeded in putting a price on love.'

'Charlie never cared about money.' Cathy watched her exhusband's taxi pull into the traffic in the Strand.

'I expect he cares enough about spending it and the new wife won't like that at all,' the lawyer told her.

Her ex-father-in-law, Lord Shrewton, took her to lunch at his club the next week. Cathy had felt desolate and aimless for days and was grateful for his invitation.

'I want you to know that you'll always be welcome whenever you want to see little James,' he said, his normal tone of dispassionate reason leaving no doubt that this was the complete truth. 'And I'd also like to say that I don't much admire the way my son has acted over this.'

'I think he had a certain amount of pressure on him,' Cathy chose her words with care.

'That child-woman, yes. Very determined young lady. Of course, Charlie's been bullied by women all his life.' From the Marquess, this was an indiscretion. 'Now, any idea what you're going to do?'

Cathy shook her head, aware that she felt comfortable in this male world of scuffed leather, polished wood and serious talk. The bleak days of anxiety were over, Jamie's future was settled and there was hope that she would one day be able to get him back. Cathy was also aware that by the time she had paid the final bill from Pasterns her money would be barely enough to buy a small apartment. She would need to work, and she had never earned a penny in her life before, or seriously considered doing so.

'Why not come and work for me – for my company, rather? You can type a bit, can't you?' Lord Shrewton sounded sincere, almost eager to employ her.

'I've probably forgotten everything I learned in college,' Cathy admitted.

'Soon pick it up. Nothing to it. You can start whenever you like – on Monday if it suits you?' He was trying to atone for Charlie's behaviour. She agreed. No one else was likely to employ her.

Her divorce settlement was just enough to buy a cramped dark apartment in a huge building south of the Thames in Battersea. Prince of Wales Drive was crammed with every type of person who would have preferred to live across the water in Chelsea but could not afford it; there were many new divorcees like Cathy, fitting furniture meant for more grandiose homes into the narrow rooms, making their new lives with out-of-work actors, secondhand car salesmen and threadbare ex-service families as their neighbours.

At the end of her first week at work, Monty came round with a bottle of claret which she had selected for its pretty label, and they celebrated Cathy's independence. Monty poured the wine into two of the enormous glasses which had been a wedding present from one of Charlie's hard-drinking friends.

'So what's it like?' she asked. Cathy's navy-blue suit looked businesslike and her shoulders, bony as they were, had lost the miserable droop which had crushed them in the past months.

'It's extremely boring,' Cathy said, holding her glass to the light to appreciate the wine's colour. 'But I don't care, I won't be there long. I've made a decision, Monty. I'm going to make money, lots of it. I'm going to get Jamie back and I'm going to get so bloody rich I won't need a penny from the Coseley trust. It's what makes the world go around, money, and now I want my share.'

'But how – what are you going to do?'

'Do? I shall do whatever I have to do.' Cathy kicked off her shoes and put her feet up on the end of the oatmeal tweed sofa that had been too small for Royal Avenue and was now too large for this poky apartment. She had no idea what she was going to do.

CHAPTER SIXTEEN

L ONDON IN 1968 was the worst place in the world in which to fall out of love. The music from every boutique on the King's Road chanted, 'Love, love, love, love is all you need,' at Monty as she made her way to Swallow's office.

Everyone thought that at last there was enough of everything; as much money, freedom, food, drugs, music and love as could possibly be necessary to live a perfect life. The remorseless spirit of the city was sweetened with a sense of abundance. If there was enough for everyone, the right thing to do was to give it away. Kids boarded buses and handed out flowers to the startled, work-weary passengers, wishing them "love and peace". Swallow's clients seldom paid their bills. Girls with pre-Raphaelite hair set up free restaurants at every pop concert. People rolled joints and passed them out into the surrounding crowds to turn on strangers to the simple beauty of co-existence in a world of plenty.

Monty's existence was neither simple nor beautiful, because she could not, no matter how she tried, reawaken her love for Simon. She threw herself into supporting Cathy, finding a purpose for her own life in saving her sister's, but once Cathy was well again and working, Monty looked for something else to quieten her uneasy heart.

'Why aren't *you* playing with this group?' Rosanna Emanuel asked her over lunch one day. She saw Rosanna less and less frequently; their meetings were usually disrupted by her noisy year-old son, and they never seemed to have very much to say to each other.

Monty shrugged. 'What could I do? I'm not really a musician.'

'Yes you are. You're incredibly talented, Monty, you know you are. My parents still talk about you. My mother keeps trying to make me take up singing again, and every time I refuse she says, "Ah, if you had a voice like that Monty your gift would call you to use it." '

Monty shrugged and dug her fork into her *spaghetti alle vongole.* 'I only write songs to amuse myself, I'd be embarrassed to show them to anybody.' What she meant was that she loved her music with a passion that she did not want to share.

'There you are – that's your gift calling you.'

'My voice is useless now, anyway. I smoke too much.'

'Excuses, excuses.' Rosanna decided to drop the subject. She knew Monty well enough to appreciate that she would resist pressure with anger. 'How's the group doing, anyway?'

'Not too bad. They play a couple of gigs a week now, and Simon's getting bigger bookings. He's decided to book some studio time and cut a demo disc.'

The studio had the latest four-track recording equipment, but the walls were cheaply soundproofed with eggboxes. Simon booked it for one night only – the nights were cheaper – and the first hour was wasted in an argument about what they were going to record. Simon wanted the A side to be 'Don't Go Now', the best of their own songs. Rick complained that it was 'doomy' and at last they compromised and decided on an old Chuck Berry number to back it.

At about 3 am, Monty was sitting beside the engineer, watching in fascination as he flipped switches and pulled knobs on the mixing deck, when Simon came out of the studio to get her.

'We need a bit of piano,' he told her, pulling her to her feet. 'Come on, I'll show you what to play.'

On the other side of the glass he sat her down at a scarred old upright piano and gave her a short phrase to play in the song's middle section. They tried it a couple of times, then Rick suggested, 'Do a bit more, Monty – play around with it a bit.' She developed the phrase, and they nodded.

'Maybe a spot of echo . . .' the engineer reached forward for a knob at the far side of his desk.

'Hear it through the cans,' Simon gave her his headphones and she heard her music played back.

'But it sounds awful,' she protested, hating the bouncy, senti-mental sound she had produced. The band shook their heads as one man.

'No, no, it's great,' they reassured her, and Monty shrugged and smiled and played on to the end of the session, feeling embarrassed.

From then onwards they dragged her with them to every gig, sitting her down at a variety of beer-stained, cigarette-burned instruments where she tried her best to hide from the crowd out at the front of the stage. She did not like the packed, passive mass of people who stood waiting for the music to take them out of themselves, and began to take a perverse pleasure in playing with more and more aggression until she could see that she was getting through to them.

Rick insisted that she should sing, too. 'It looks pathetic having someone on stage who isn't singing with the others,' he told her, refusing to argue. Monty sang, and loved it. The sound of her voice, rich, smoky and slightly ragged, complemented Rick's harsh tone to perfection.

'It's good having you with us, Monty,' Rick said one night when they were momentarily on their own by the van. 'It makes things kind of smoother with Simon, you know? It's easier to talk to him sometimes if you're around.'

Before she could respond, Cy and Pete appeared, lugging one of the giant amps in its silver casing, and Rick ran over to help them; but Monty knew what he meant.

There was a permanent awkwardness between Simon and the others. Musically they were perfectly compatible, but socially the fact of Simon's wealth and upbringing was a gulf between them. Simon never walked into a bar expecting to be thrown out or saw a policeman and expected to be stopped and searched.

Simon, like Monty, viewed the new era of love and peace with almost religious feeling as an opportunity to prove that human nature could change for the better. The boys, particularly Rick and Cy, saw it simply as a golden opportunity to score – sex, drugs, or whatever was on offer from people too stupid to look after their own interests. One summer weekend they staged what they called a love-in at their house.

'It was great,' Rick told them afterwards. 'We just went out on the street and stopped everyone we fancied and told them to come and join us. We had about twenty chicks in there at one point.'

'Yeah, it was great,' Cy nodded, his long hair swaying. 'Every time some chick decided to split she'd start looking for her clothes. 'Course, we'd hidden them, hadn't we? Then she couldn't find them, then somebody grabbed hold of her, then that was it for another couple of hours.'

Monty forced a smile. She and Simon still made love occasion-ally, but it was a hypocritical performance on her part. She had grown to detest everything about Simon, from the line of black hairs that grew down the nape of his neck to the way he always started his guitar solos the same way. She was profoundly shocked at the speed with which their love had degenerated to the kind of shell which she recognized as the embryo of her parents' icy sham of marriage. If love was the most important thing in the world, how could it just pop like a balloon, and vanish?

It was a punishing summer for all of them. Simon had twenty copies of their demo disc made, and sent them to every record company in London. There was no response whatsoever and so he patiently called every one of the executives to whom the disc had gone and swallowed dismissal, condescension and rejection with grim good humour as he tried and failed to make them come to hear the band. Monty spent more and more time with the others. The band were like a tribe now, always together, and it was somehow more tactful to go to Rick's filthy room than to invite the boys to Simon's luxurious apartment.

'I can't bear to listen to him,' she told Rick. 'He's so patient and so polite always, and they're such motherfuckers . . .'

'Yeah. He's a trier, old Simon.' Rick tipped sugar into his coffee and stirred it, looking at Monty at length while she, unaware of him, stared at the grimy, rain-streaked window.

The Juice played one or two gigs a week all through the winter, acquiring a group of supporters who crowded to the front of the stage to freak out in Simon's solos or roar at Rick as he baited them. Monty grew more confident on the stage as she realized people liked her; she even had a few fans who were specially her own, who sometimes left flowers on her piano or waited to talk to her at the end of the set.

Although the demo disc was a failure, the Juice's following grew and every call Simon made to book the band into a club was a little easier.

'We're getting through,' Simon told them with reassurance.

'Yeah, but not fast enough. I don't wanna die before I cut my first album,' Cy snarled, spitting out of the van window for emphasis.

Towards the end of the following summer, word went round the pubs in London that there was to be a pop festival on the Isle of Wight, an idyllic fragment of farmland off the south coast of England, a white-cliffed holiday paradise. The summer had seen one or two small festivals already; a few thousand people had discovered the pleasure of sitting together peacefully under the stars to listen to music.

Simon abruptly cancelled the Juice's bookings for the weekend and told them, 'We're going to the Isle of Wight for our holidays – we deserve it.'

From the outset the excursion was not the carefree picnic Simon intended it to be. Cy grumbled ceaselessly in the van. 'Will somebody tell me why we're going to hear a lot of psychedelic garbage with this weekend hippy instead of staying in London to get smashed?' he whined. On the ferry to the island, he found a bottle of whisky and drank most of it in forty minutes.

As they drove to the festival site he suddenly flung open the van door and started throwing out everything he could reach, shouting, 'Free, free!' to the amused villagers at the roadside.

The stage had been erected at the focal point of a natural amphitheatre of green fields, behind which the sea gleamed in the sunlight like polished steel. The narrow lanes, their hedges gay with yellow toadflax and late foxgloves, were crowded with people who walked without haste to the concert ground to merge with the huge carpet of humanity.

Monty felt obscurely hopeful in the middle of the amiable crowd. Her blood tingled in her veins with a premonition of adventure, and as soon as she could she escaped from the ominous atmosphere around Simon and spent a few hours with a group of French hippies who had erected a Red Indian tepee at the edge of the site. They had expensive clothes and some powerful black hash. The children twined starry white camomile flowers in her hair and one of the women pulled off

Monty's T-shirt with distaste and gave her an embroidered voile jacket which tied provocatively under her breasts.

'There you are,' she heard Rick's voice in the crowd as the evening star was beginning to shine through the early shades of dusk. 'Where've you been? Simon's been going frantic.'

'It's so beautiful here – I couldn't stand the hassles any more,' she told him, feeling dreamy from the drugs. 'It's so heavy around Simon at the moment. It really brings me down. Where've you been?'

'Seeing the future' – he jerked his thumb to the stage where a boy in a spangled caftan with a cloud of dark curls was singing something about children with stars in their hair – 'and I don't like it.'

They walked uphill in companionable silence, leaving the huge, peaceful crowd below them. At length they came to the cliff-edge and sat down on the springy turf. The stage was a tiny illuminated picture in the distance, but the sound from the vast banks of speakers floated up to them clearly.

'Look, the chopper!' Rick pointed to a helicopter which floated like a glowing spark over the sea. 'They said the Airplane would be flying in from a yacht. That must be them.' They watched as the helicopter hovered at the rear of the stage, bringing in Jefferson Airplane, the headline band. It set down and became invisible as its lights were extinguished.

'That's what I want. I want to top the bill, make a million and fly-in by helicopter, not be down here, grovelling around in shit.' Rick stubbed his cigarette out in a rabbit hole. 'You know that, don't you? I want it all. I'm hungry, Monty, we're all hungry. That's what all the trouble's about.'

'Simon's not hungry,' she said, lying back and looking up at the indigo sky.

'Nah – he can't be, he's had it too soft all his life. It makes no odds to him whether he makes it this year, next year, sometime or never, but it does to us because making it's all there is for us, you know.' He pulled his cigarettes from his shirtsleeve. He rolled his sleeves neatly about the elbow; like a soldier or a boy scout. He looked at her and tapped out two cigarettes from the crumpled packet.

'You're hungry too, aren't you? It don't make sense, but you are. Sometimes I think you're hungrier than all of us.'

He lit both cigarettes, threw the match away with too much energy and leaned over to put one cigarette between her lips. Then he tore it away again, threw both cigarettes aside and kissed her, almost biting her mouth with a desperate urgency that begged her not to reject him.

At once the rush of passion renewed within her, and she wound her arms around him. Their eagerness made them clumsy as they struggled with their clothes and they were still partly dressed as he thrust into her with cries that sounded half like triumph, half like a whimpering animal.

Afterwards, when the sky was dark and the stars bright, she stroked his hair as he rested his head between her breasts.

'I wanted you for so long,' he murmured. 'You're a great chick. But I thought you were in love with Simon.'

'I thought I was in love with Simon, too. I *was* in love with him once, but it just faded away.' Was that really love? Monty wondered as she watched the moon struggle out from the clouds.

In the morning they slithered down the cliff to the beach and splashed naked in the waves. Then they left the island, hitchhiked back to London and moved Monty's things into Rick's room. Monty left Simon a letter saying goodbye, and felt like a miserable coward.

Soon afterwards Simon called a band meeting in the Wetherby Arms and announced that he was quitting and returning to his job in his father's firm. Monty came to the meeting, but she could not look at Simon, even when she wished him all the luck in the world. Simon accepted her loss fatalistically. He was slowly appreciating that for him, rebellion was useless and that he would, in the end, be forced to conform to the blueprint which his parents had drawn up for his life. Monty, he now realized, was still stubbornly determined to choose her own path; they had arrived at a parting of their destinies.

Monty's life changed dramatically as soon as she moved into the decrepit, grey house where Rick, Cy and Pete lived. The stucco was blistered and the window sills rotted. Inside, Rick's room contained a bed, a table, and two chairs, one of which had no back. There was a gas fire which was connected to a meter, into which shilling coins had to be fed to heat the room.

When the Juice had a gig, they were paid £25. That worked out at £5 each for Monty, Rick, Cy, Pete and Nasher, out of which Rick ran a kitty for petrol for the van. It was not enough to live on, but both Rick and Cy insisted that they were musicians and needed no other job. Every Thursday they went up to the Labour Exchange to sign on for the dole. Monty was paid by Swallow on Friday, which was fortunate, because neither of the boys had any money left by then. After a month, she got a job in a small French restaurant near the office, waiting on tables for one pound an evening and tips. With this, the three of them had just enough money to get through the week, assuming that she stole some food in the restaurant.

One week when the restaurant was shut they went to the pub on Friday night and had 3s 6d between them on Saturday morning, and no food.

'Party-time,' said Rick. They went back to the pub at lunchtime. 'We're having a party at our place tonight – bring a bottle,' he told everyone, not stopping at any table long enough to be obliged to buy a round of drinks.

Towards 11 pm, people began to arrive, most of them already drunk. They brought bottles of beer, wine and whisky. Rick and Cy sat and strummed their guitars, and people drank. The people left and in the morning Rick collected thirty-four empty bottles which he took back to the shop on the corner. There was a deposit of tuppence on each bottle, and they then had enough to buy cornflakes, bread and jam.

This life delighted Monty. Being poor to her was like living in a free zone. There were no expectations, no constraints, no rules except survival. She wore the same pair of jeans every day for a year and got a bigger kick out of doing so than out of all the fabulous dresses which Simon had bought her.

To her surprise, she also felt more loved by Rick than she ever had by Simon. He brought her tea in bed in the morning, and carried shopping for her, and washed up after she cooked meals on the rancid little stove on the landing which the whole house shared. He was easy and relaxed around women, without the edginess inculcated for life by a single-sex boarding school.

'Go away,' she said sleepily one morning as his hands slithered tenderly around her body. 'I'm not fit to fuck this morning – my period's starting.'

'That's nice, I must say. I wake up feeling all randy and you've got the painters in.'

She giggled. 'Have you got a pain?' he asked, closing his hand over her belly protectively.

'No. It's not that, it'll just be a bloody mess, that's all.' He wriggled his erection hopefully against her.

'Tell you what – how about if I take the sheets to the launderette? Can't say fairer than that now, can I?'

'All right, it's a deal.' Rich warm tingles were racing through her flesh. It was extremely messy and he took the sheets to the launderette just as he had promised, making tea for her first.

Rick could hardly believe he had been so lucky as to attract this beautiful, sexy, fantasy creature from another world – because the upper classes were a different world to him. Occasionally Monty would take him to a party given by one of her rich friends, and he would absorb, with resentful amazement, the truth about the lifestyle to which she was accustomed. As a point of pride he refused the champagne, and was overly polite to everyone, at the same time swearing to himself that one day he too would have a big house in Chelsea, with servants and a sunken bath.

'You do love me, don't you?' he said to Monty one night, as they walked home through Chelsea from another of these glittering interludes in their life of squalor.

'Of course I do.' Monty slipped her hand down the back of his jeans.

'I never thought you would, you know. I thought you'd piss off after a weekend or two in that rathole.'

'You don't think much of me, do you?'

'Yeah, I do, that's the trouble. You could have anyone. You could have one of them poncy stockbrokers with pots of money, and drive around in a Mercedes.'

'You'll have a Mercedes, when we get our deal.'

Rick kicked a tin can into the gutter. '*When* we get our deal. When pigs fly, you mean.'

'We'll get it. The band's great now. Someone's bound to sign us.'

'Well, I don't want a fuckin' Mercedes. I'll have a Roller. Got more class.'

They walked on, following the meandering tail of the King's Road. A smell of frying fat from a fish and chip shop wafted towards them on the combination of brewery fumes, gasworks effluent and carbon monoxide which formed the atmosphere of Chelsea's outer limits.

'Got any money?'

Monty felt in her handbag, then in the pockets of her jean jacket. 'Five, six, seven – seven and six. What for?'

'Get some chips, I'm starving.'

'But Rick, we've just been to a party with enough salmon and champagne to sink a battleship. Didn't you eat anything?'

'No. I couldn't.' She didn't ask him why, guessing at the peculiar inversion of pride that had made him refuse the food when he was hungry.

'Get me some – salt, no vinegar,' she yelled after him as he crossed the road.

The Juice was a different band without Simon. Rick took control and they stopped playing the long, complex songs with enigmatic lyrics which Simon had preferred because they showed off his musicianship. Rick liked simple songs with a driving beat that would get the crowd on its feet. He could barely read music, let alone write it, and he relied heavily on Monty.

'Listen to this, love,' he would say, playing a few chords on his guitar. 'I had the next bit yesterday, but I can't remember it.' And she would pick up the cheap acoustic guitar which he seldom used and take the fragment of melody and turn it into a song with all the pulsating, direct power that Rick knew he wanted but could not create for himself.

Words also came very easily to her. The poetry crammed into her head at school as a punishment had trained her mind superbly and, now the ability was needed, the words tumbled out, thrusting and lunging at her listeners' emotions.

Rick was spellbound with admiration. 'The things you know,' he murmured, half-mocking, when she suddenly decided to transpose a song into a different key and made it sound completely different. She made him conscious that he was ill-equipped for his chosen world, capable of striking the pose of a musician but not of understanding his art.

Monty felt as if the working class were not so much another world as another planet. Rick, Cy and Pete had language, folklore and beliefs which were completely alien to her. They even looked different from the solid, well-nourished, upper-class boys she had known before. They were sparrow-boned and skinny. Pete had a slight spinal deformity. Cy's teeth leaned crazily like the tombstones in an old churchyard. All of them smoked heavily and coughed a great deal, especially in the winter. They ate junk food, and drank only at the pub; buying alcohol to drink at home, she discovered, was tantamount to admitting to alcoholism.

While Rick kept his room as neat as a cabin on a ship, Cy's lair was stacked to the ceiling with debris and covered in a thick layer of dust. His bed was a mattress on the floor. His favourite occupation was smashing things, and he was never happier than when he found an abandoned car to wreck or a derelict house to attack as if he could tear it apart with his bare hands.

Next to destruction, Cy liked stealing. Every gig they played gave him the opportunity to steal something. Monty was embarrassed when he walked off with a piece of equipment belonging to another band.

At home, Cy plundered the gas meters with artistry, slowing down the clocks so that they would not register the gas consumed, and making it possible to run the fires all day in winter with a single shilling put through the slot again and again. In supermarkets he stole food. He never paid his fare on the bus. He fiddled his dole money, and was outraged when the Labour Exchange official caught him and threatened to prosecute him.

'It's a fuckin' rip-off,' he yelled, kicking at a corrugated-iron fence around a building site. 'They got no right to say they'll get the law on me. I ain't done nothing.'

'Yes, you have. You cashed your dole cheques and claimed you'd lost them, so they'd give you the money again,' Monty pointed out. 'That's fraud, you know it is.'

'You can fuck off!' Cy shouted. 'Nobody ever ripped you off, did they? What the fuck do you know about it?'

Monty walked on with Rick, leaving Cy pulling down the entire fence. 'He's mad,' she said in wonder. 'Why's he so aggressive?'

'You don't understand.' Rick pulled out his cigarettes and lit two of them, his hands cupped against the biting March wind. 'All Cy knows is being ripped off, and being ripped off begins at home, like charity. If you've been ripped off all your life, well that's all you know how to do, isn't it? So you just go out and do it back.'

Monty took a cigarette from him and inhaled, thinking. 'People can know better. You can learn better. *You* don't rip everyone off all the time, and you and Cy grew up on the same street.'

He looked at her, uncertain. 'You don't know me, love.' She did not react, so he continued, 'Anyway, Cy's got nothing. He's got no way out. I'm his way out, because I can get on stage and act like a monkey and people will pay money to see me. That's the only way out for all of us.'

They waited at the bus stop, cuddled together to keep warm in the raw cold.

Rick's ticket to fortune and fame was his ability to make himself into another person on stage. Without his savage, raw-throated performance, the Juice were nothing but an average bunch of players. Rick was hardly a musician at all, a self-taught guitarist with a few laboriously acquired riffs which he played over and over again in different permutations. But the instant he ran on stage and pulled the microphone from its stand, he became a mad, mocking demon who dominated and excited the audience until they grovelled at his feet, screaming for more.

One night after a gig they were packing up to leave when a man in a white suit, with a boyish face that looked prematurely aged and close-cropped blond hair, came over and spoke to Rick.

'I'd like to buy you a drink,' he said.

'Thanks, mate.' Rick finished coiling up his guitar lead and put it on top of an amplifier.

'Large scotch for me.' Cy sat down at a table at the edge of the half-empty room. Pete and Nasher, the drummer, followed him. Rick sat down last, pulling Monty beside him and putting his arm around her.

'I'm Dennis, Dennis Pointer.' The blond man shook hands with all of them and passed round his cigarettes. 'Anyone managing you?'

'We split with our manager.' It was almost true, since Simon had acted as their manager; Rick allowed the newcomer to light his cigarette.

'Got a deal yet?'

'Not exactly.' Rick shook his head.

'I know you, don't I?' Nasher narrowed his eyes. 'Didn't you have something to do with some horrible bunch of hippies?'

'You mean Yellow Nebula. Yeah, I managed them. Got them an outrageous deal with Virgin and they fucked off to the country to do all the acid they could carry and never came back.' Dennis gave them a speculative look.

'We wouldn't do a thing like that to you.' Rick grinned and blew smoke upwards. 'Pity. Jimmy Booker was a good singer.'

'I'm still handling Jimmy. But I like you lot – I've been following you round a few places.'

'We'll think about it,' Rick told him. The truth was they didn't need to think. They acted cool until the van was round the corner then Rick and Monty shrieked with joy, Nasher beat a tattoo on the wheel arch and Cy put his feet on the dash-board and drummed his heels. They were singing their third chorus of 'She'll Be Coming Round The Mountain' when a police car howled up behind them and they were cautioned for reckless driving.

'Now I'll tell you how to get a deal,' Dennis lectured them all a month later, in a café around the corner from the offices of Excellent Records. 'Don't matter much what you sound like – that's for us to know and keep to ourselves, right? Your music won't cut any ice with that polecat you're going to see. What you gotta do is grab his imagination. You've got to let him know that you're the most filthy, steaming, obscene bunch of lads this side of Sodom and Gomorrah – got it?'

'Nah. What do you want us to do?' Cy screwed up his mouth in an obstinate line.

'Act natural,' Dennis advised him.

The polecat's name was Les Lightfoot; his office was at the end of a long corridor lined with gold discs in gold frames. He had a Julius Caesar haircut and very clean jeans.

'Dennis has played me some of your stuff,' Les began. 'I like your sound. I think the kids'll go for it.'

Cy gave him his most malevolent stare. 'You want to watch your mouth, mate. I could go for you, 'n' all.'

'Tell me about yourselves,' Les invited them.

Cy got up and walked slowly around him, swivelling his high-backed leather chair. 'I don't like you,' he told him. 'I'd consider killing you, if I thought you were alive.'

The polecat swallowed uncomfortably. This was not the way it was supposed to be. The artists were supposed to be respectful and polite, and wear their best gear. This gargoyle with mouldy teeth had a four-inch rip in his jeans, through which the white flesh of his backside was clearly visible.

Pete also stood up and walked to the back of the office, up to a handsome potted palm. He pulled out an aerosol can and sprayed red paint on the fronds. It dripped on to the white shag-pile carpet.

'Looks like blood, don't it?' he remarked.

Nasher appeared to be asleep. 'Don't mind him,' Rick advised the executive amiably. 'He's a narcoleptic. Keeps dropping off. It's a form of epilepsy, apparently.'

'I hope he doesn't do that on stage.' Les Lightfoot loosened the knot in his satin tie.

'It's all right, we just keep on playing. Sometimes he has proper fits, of course. Then one of us has to jam one of his drum sticks between his teeth. Stop him biting his tongue.'

Cy slowly unzipped his fly, and hauled out a semi-inflated pink balloon in the shape of a cock and balls. The balls were tinted an improbable purple. Cy picked a felt pen off the man's desk and began to draw hairs on the balls.

In desperation, the polecat turned to Monty and smiled.

'And what's your name, my dear?' he asked.

Monty had put on a collection of Victorian lace skirts and a camisole which, she knew, made her look gloriously hoydenish. She leaned forward, well aware that she was giving Les a clear view from her clavicle to her waist, down a tunnel of white lace frills.

'My name's Miranda,' she said in her most languid upper-class drawl. 'But actually people usually call me Monty.'

'Pleased to meet you,' the man said foolishly.

Cy pulled out a switchblade knife and stabbed the inflatable penis with it.

Two weeks later Dennis brought them their contracts. Then they had money, but not time to spend it, because Les Lightfoot wanted their first album as soon as possible, and for three months Monty lived in a tunnel between the recording studio and their room. She bought herself a Moog synthesizer but had no time to play with it. They were listening to the first number when Rick said, 'I've been thinking – how about more girls' voices? This sounds OK for the little clubs, but it isn't right for an album. It sounds thin.'

Their producer agreed. 'Monty's voice is terrific, but I think three girls would be better.'

Next day a black girl and a white girl joined them. 'I'm P. J., this is Maggie,' the black girl said. She had enormous eyes and hair cropped flat against her skull. Maggie was squat and messy-looking, with clotted black mascara and a thick Scottish accent.

They were right, Monty thought, as she listened to the playback in the studio; three girls sounded better. It did not occur to her that her status in the group had been eroded, and her individual voice replaced by a mere sound.

Eight songs were recorded one after the other. They represented the best of the Juice's repertoire, but the producer told them they needed at least three more to fill the album. Rick suggested another Chuck Berry standard, which was easily done, but then no one could agree on the final two songs. Les Lightfoot himself came down to the studio and listened to some of the material which the band had often performed, but he at once vetoed its inclusion on the record.

'Old hat stuff,' he announced. 'I'm sorry, boys, you'll have to come up with something new or the deal's off.'

The pressure acted like inspiration on Monty. The same night, as soon as she was alone with Rick, she burrowed into a box of papers and books which she had brought from Simon's apartment and found the little notebook in which she used to write down the songs she composed for fun.

'Maybe we can use some of these.' She seized the old acoustic guitar and began picking out a tune and humming the words.

Rick looked doubtful. 'I dunno – it's a pretty song, all right, but it's not our sort of a song, is it?'

Monty continued to play, developing the melody and changing the words until at last Rick came over and sat on the bed beside her, singing with her and making his own changes. Then they thought of a new idea, and Monty quickly put the outline of it down on paper.

Suddenly it was mid-day, and they stopped for an hour to go to the corner café for tea and bacon sandwiches. By the end of the day the first song was perfect, and Rick called the others to hear it. Everyone was happy with the new song, and they worked on the second one in the studio, with everyone throwing in contributions.

The producer nodded with satisfaction. 'This is the test,' he said to Monty while the boys were running through the final version by themselves. 'The band that gets to the top and stays there is the band that can get its own material together, and be good, and be consistent, and be professional. And there's not a lot of bands like that about.'

By the time they had finished recording the album, all Monty and Rick wanted to do was sleep, but Dennis, their manager, had other plans.

'The real work's only starting,' he told them. 'You'll be doing interviews soon, and we gotta get some photographs done.' Dennis's girlfriend was an assistant on a young fashion magazine, and she took Monty on a very serious shopping expedition. They came back with antique lace knickerbockers, French blue-jean jackets embroidered with coloured glass beads and gloriously sexy, high-heeled sandals of red and silver snakeskin. Merely wearing them made Monty feel excited and apprehensive. She hennaed her hair to a luscious mahogany and had it cut into layers of silky curls.

The interviews started and Rick came into his own. Shrewdly appreciating that his role on the world's stage was to outrage the spectators, he insulted reporters with complete abandon, turning up drunk, stoned, or very late – but never blowing out a press call completely. The Juice was offered one TV show in Newcastle, courtesy of Nasher's link with the area, and Rick and Cy wrecked the set. The *New Musical Express* called them the 'The Terrible Twins of Rock', and Dennis squeezed Rick's shoulder with satisfaction.

'By George,' he said, 'I think he's got it.'

'So now what?' Rick asked him, sitting on Dennis's desk. Dennis had an office now, one room with a telephone at the top of a listing staircase in Soho.

'Excellent ought to give you a tour,' Dennis offered his cigarettes. 'But they're waiting to see how much airplay the album gets. Don't worry, I got a few tricks up my sleeve.'

The tricks, they all knew, were two key disc jockeys for whom Dennis was a convenient supplier of cheap drugs and expensive women. 'Freshly Squeezed', the Juice's first album, entered the charts at number 63. The next week it rose to number 37, because Dennis hired a small army of kids from Swallow's agency to buy it at some of the stores whose sales figured in the charts. At 37, the album automatically went on to the playlists of all the radio stations, and Dennis's influence took it into the top 10.

Excellent Records hastily sent the Juice on a four-week tour of Britain on which they supported the label's biggest name, a psychedelic band called Crimson Lake. Halfway through the itinerary Dennis was called to London for a meeting with the record company, and returned smiling.

'After this, we're going to the States,' he told them. 'We've cracked it.'

By the time they played their final three nights in London, Rick and Monty were lightheaded with exhaustion and Cy had done so much speed that nothing he said made any sense at all, even to Rick.

'I can't handle this,' Rick said suddenly. They were sitting in their room at night. The house seemed cold and neglected, and after a month in hotel rooms the squalor was oppressive. 'One minute I was hustling for a break, the next I'm being treated like I can walk on water. And I don't even know what day of the week it is. Thank God I've got you, love. You're the only thing that's keeping me sane.'

The album's cover showed an oil-streaked man's hand with ragged fingernails squeezing a satin-covered woman's buttock. Its distinctive black-and-white design was soon repeated endlessly in the windows of music stores.

By the time the album was number 3 in the charts, Rick had given so many interviews nothing he said seemed real any more. 'Every time they ask me where I come from, and I tell 'em Croydon, and Cy's mum and my mum worked in the same lightbulb factory, it's like you made it up for me to say, even though it's true,' he told Dennis.

'There's some girl from *Rolling Stone* coming at half past two,' the publicist told him, uncaring.

'But we're going to America today, aren't we?' Monty was becoming wary of Rick after an interview, especially an interview with a girl. He was always hyped-up, arrogant and aggressive, as if his demonic stage personality had temporarily taken control.

'I've ordered a limo to take Rick to the airport and she'll ride out with him,' the publicist countered. 'Sign these, will you?'

Rick looked at the photographs with distaste. 'Why don't you buy a rubber stamp?'

'You're out of date, mate. You sign the print and then we just duplicate the whole thing. Hurry up, the car's waiting.'

In the limousine on the way to the airport, the girl from *Rolling Stone* pulled down all the blinds and took off all her clothes and set about giving Rick a blow job. He wasn't surprised. This sort of thing was happening all the time, the girls seemed to think it was expected and who was he to complain?

There were girls loitering in their hotels, girls hanging around the Excellent offices, girls finagling to get backstage at their gigs. Within a matter of weeks it had become the ambition of every groupie who considered herself worthy of the name to lay Rick Brown of the Juice, and Monty was astonished at their shameless ingenuity. One of them had even dressed herself up in an imitation of Monty's ruffles and denim and tricked a doorman into believing she was the real Monty and giving her a backstage pass.

In America, the girls who tried the interview scam claimed they worked for the BBC; they were much more persistent. Even the stupid ones, instead of hanging around the hotel lobby, gave head to the nearest bellhop, who would then let them into Rick's room. There they waited until they got bored and tried Cy's room instead.

Rick slept with Monty, but few people outside the band realized this.

'Don't tell 'em you live together, for Chrissake,' Les Lightfoot told him. 'We're promoting you as the bad boys par excellence – none of that lovey-dovey crap. Keep the old lady out of sight, please.'

Cy threw a television set off the twenty-second floor balcony of the Hilton in Daytona, Florida. In Memphis, he drove a hired Cadillac into the hotel swimming pool. Somewhere in Wisconsin a chambermaid claimed that he had raped her. The Juice were banned in Kansas.

Cy's room was always where the orgy was, and the mystique took root so fast they seldom needed to do anything more than open the door to a procession of bedraggled girls who wanted only to be able to say that they had laid Rick Brown of the Juice. After them came the small-town jocks, the two-bit rock writers, the passers-by and the hangers-on.

In Dallas, a pair of identical twins took over the scene and immediately sold their story to the *National Enquirer*. Cy read it with relish. 'Right dirty slags they were,' he approved. 'Fucked 'em both flat, and they couldn't get enough. Wanted to do it all again with some spade chick. I told 'em it was all beyond me. I got 'em fuckin' each other's brains out with one of them dildo things. Incredible what some chicks'll do, innit?'

None of them wanted to lay Nasher, who passed blameless evenings trying to phone his wife. Pete picked up a stunning blonde in Pasadena and dropped out of the action.

Monty did not realize that Rick was keeping Cy company with the endless flow of groupies until he leaned over the breakfast trolley in Los Angeles and sleepily scratched his brown curls. Two tiny grey insects, holding each others grippers like square-dancers, fell into his orange juice.

'Ugh,' Monty fished them out with a teaspoon. Rick got up and washed the creatures down the lavatory, muttering something about the hotel being dirty. She did not find out what the insects were until she told P. J. about them.

'Crabs! Yeeuch! Men *are* so disgusting. Hope that's all he's got. You'd better see a doctor.'

The doctor, who was well known on the West Coast as a music business insider, gave Monty a blood test as well. 'You've got the clap,' he told her as if he were telling her the time. 'Better let me take a look at your boyfriend.'

They went home full of penicillin, with orders not to drink alcohol. Cy had downed his first defiant bottle of scotch by the time they were flying over the North Pole.

On the way back to London they agreed that they could not face returning to their rotting house.

'I reckon we should put up at the Savoy,' Rick announced. 'We can afford it, can't we, Dennis?'

'It's not my business how you spend your money. Sure, check into the Savoy and we'll start looking for proper homes next week.' Dennis looked more wrinkled and colourless than ever. They all looked tired and drawn after their weeks on tour, and Monty felt bloated from living on booze, coffee, drugs and hamburgers. She didn't care for the fact that her breasts had enlarged, which Maggie confidently informed her was the inescapable result of singing every night.

In the peach-and-chrome Art Deco calm of the Savoy, Monty let Rick recover for a day and then went on the attack, determined to detach him from Cy and the groupie scene.

'Never, ever, again,' she told him, her voice low and hissing with anger. 'Never. No way. That tour was the most disgusting, humiliating experience of my life. How could you put me through all that, Rick? How could you come and get in my bed when you'd been down the corridor with Cy doing all those revolting things with those revolting groupies?'

He looked small, wretched and ashamed. 'I'm sorry, love, I never realized you'd be hurt.'

'Like hell. What was I supposed to do, join in?'

Rick squirmed unhappily. 'You don't understand.'

'I never do understand, do I? Whenever you and Cy want to wreck everything somehow my understanding just isn't up to the occasion.'

'Look – it's what rock'n'roll is all about, being a big bad boy. Dope and sex groupies, and all that – we've got to have 'em for all the kids who'll never get the chance.'

'Bullshit. You're having them because you want them. It hurts me, it's insulting, and I don't like it.'

'Well, if you don't like it, you know what you can do about it, don't you?' Rick pulled the bathrobe round himself with a defensive gesture. 'I ain't waited all my life to make it to have some jealous chick spoil it all. Go on, fuck off.'

Monty shrugged and walked away. She did not care about his reaction as much as she had expected to; she knew Rick would concede. She was the only stability he had. Without her to reassure him, support him, write his songs and lay down the ground rules of his life, he would simply fall apart in the crazy new world they had entered. She ought to feel sorry for him but two months of continuous exhaustion had left her small capacity for feeling. She got dressed and went for a walk along the Thames Embankment.

When she got back, Rick was dressed, washed, shaved and contrite.

'I'm sorry, darling. I was a right pig.' He put his arms round her. 'I didn't realize how much you'd be hurt, honest, I didn't. Don't go, Monty. I need you, you know.' She saw tears glistening in his eyelashes. 'We mustn't let this happen again,' he said, holding her to him with all his strength. 'We mustn't let all the crap come between us.'

They kissed with real emotion for the first time since they had signed their contracts, and made love like dying people, slow and naked.

They were into the second post-coital cigarette when Rick said, 'Dennis phoned today.'

'Mmn?'

'Just as well he did. I'd forgotten about the next album.'

'What next album?'

'We signed a three-year deal for an album every six months.'

Monty cleared the bliss out of her mind and thought about what he was saying. 'That means we'll have to start recording in a month – shit!'

'Yeah. That's what I thought.'

'We'd better write some songs.'

Rick and Monty sat down, took up a guitar and tried to write new songs, but while Monty began to pick through the bits and pieces of melodies in the bottom of her mind and find words for the half-digested impressions of the last year, Rick kept getting up and walking around the room in agitation, making futile suggestions and getting angry with himself.

'My mind's a blank, I can't think of nothing,' he admitted at last.

'I've got enough to work on here. Why don't you take a break, go and find us somewhere to live?' Monty suggested.

Every two hours room service brought her black coffee, while Rick and Dennis drove round London looking at places to live. Dennis saw an apartment he liked on Knightsbridge and they tried to persuade Monty to come to see it.

'I can't, I've got to finish this song,' she said. People had stopped looking at them in the Savoy Grill now, and the waiter brought her a grilled sole and a green salad every evening without being asked. She was trying to lose weight. The pictures from the American tour had not flattered any part of her body.

'Let's see.' Rick took the notepad she used to write lyrics and looked at what she had written. It was a song about a man trying to call his wife, inspired by Nasher's hopeless battles with the transatlantic telephone cables.

'I can't sing this,' he complained, 'it's crap. All this I-miss-you stuff.'

'No, it's good. You'll like it when you hear it,' she promised him.

'No, I won't – why don't you come up with some good old rockers, eh?'

'You never like anything I do until it's on top of the Hot One Hundred.' Monty meant the single from 'Freshly Squeezed', which was storming up the American charts.

'Oh well, I suppose we can always shove in a few old Chuck Berry numbers to pad it out.' Rick slashed his steak with disdain. He had ordered tournedos Rossini, feeling that this grand name must mean an equally grand slab of meat. The neat little medallion sitting on a circle of soggy toast on his plate looked like some kind of trick played on a jumped-up nobody by a snobbish hotel.

Monty paid no attention to him. Her head was seething with ideas. She finished seven songs in a fortnight, and reworked three of the band's old numbers with some dutiful help from Rick. He had decided to buy a beautiful house in Chelsea very close to Cathy's old home, and was now talking about getting a place in the country and keeping a few horses.

By the time the Juice went into the studios to record their second album, Monty understood what Rosanna Emanuel's mother had said about her talent being something from which she could not escape. Music had claimed her as its willing slave.

CHAPTER SEVENTEEN

WHEN HUSSAIN Shahzdeh was nine years old, his father gave him a hammer and pulled up a brocade *fauteuil* on which he could stand to reach the vast gilt-framed mirror over the marble fire-place of their apartment on the Avenue Foch.

'No Nazi will admire his face in my mirror,' his father said. 'Give it a good whack, my boy.'

Father and son went from room to room, smashing the mirrors as they went. The floors, already dusty and bare of their carpets, were soon covered with silver fragments.

'Whatever are you doing with the boy – have you lost your mind?'

His mother fluttered in like an angry dove and swept him into her arms. He was tall for his age and sturdy. She was small and delicate, and Hussain felt himself to be almost as tall as she was. Her black fox wrap was as richly glossy as her immaculately styled black hair. She moved in a cloud of Mitsouko fragrance.

'Now listen, my darling child, this is very serious.' She held his hands in hers. 'We are going on a long journey, and it will be very dangerous. You may be hungry and cold. There will be no more servants, no amusements, no luxury, at least for a while. You mustn't mind, my darling. I know you won't mind. You'll be a brave soldier, you always are.' She kissed him and hugged him.

'Will there be school?' he asked, seeing some possibilities in the situation.

'No, no school for a while. That will be fun, won't it? We can play together all day.' This sounded much better, not like any kind of deprivation at all.

They each had one suitcase and a gas-mask.

'You can bring a toy, if you like, there's room for Tiger.' Tiger, whiskerless and with half a tail, had slept with him all his life. He shook his head.

His father drove erratically, under a never-ending rain of exclamations and pleadings for care from his mother, down the long roads of the French country-side, through forests and cornfields; sometimes crowds of refugees clogged the highway, sometimes the road was all theirs.

As they travelled southwards the wheat gave way to maize, and the elegant eighteenth-century chateaux of their friends turned into squat grey-stone castles with turrets and moats. Hussain was thrilled.

After four days they arrived at a romantic, little fortress halfway up a Dordogne hillside which was wooded with sweet chestnut trees. Their host, a middle-aged nouveau-riche, was flirting with Hussain's mother on the gravelled terrace when a manservant appeared, empty handed; he coughed for his master's attention, then said something to him in a low voice.

'They've crossed the Loire! Incredible! The filthy Boches have crossed the Loire. Dear God, what have we done that you should punish us this way?'

'We must be on our way immediately,' his mother said, and within minutes they were back in the hot little Lagonda waving goodbye to the regretful industrialist and his wife from inside a cloud of white dust.

By the time Marshal Pétain signed his shameful peace with Hitler they were aboard a sardine fishing-boat on their way to Casablanca where, it was said, some units of the French army were organizing a counter-invasion.

His father at once reported to the office of the commandant of the French regiment which he would have joined earlier had he not obtained an exemption from military service on the grounds of his mental health.

'My health is excellent. It is all a misunderstanding! I want to defend my country,' he announced. He was put in jail while the commandant decided whether he should be prosecuted for desertion or for obtaining false papers.

Then Pétain ordered the army to disband, and after some show of reluctance, the HQ in Algiers enforced the order. His father was released, then re-arrested and taken away in handcuffs.

At this time, Hussain acquired a healthy contempt for authority. He also realized that he was not exactly French. One of the first actions of the collaborationist regime was to set up a committee to review all the naturalizations granted to foreigners in the previous twenty years, with the purpose of stripping 'undesirables' of their French citizenship.

'Don't take any notice of that high-minded nonsense,' his mother instructed him. 'They don't give a damn about the citizenship. What Pétain wants is to strip the Rothschilds of their money to run his stinking little government.'

In consequence, the French community in Casablanca divided into the pure French and the naturalized families. The latter, a group including Russians, Rumanians, Mexicans and a few Iranians like themselves, urgently discussed the best destination if they were made stateless – Switzerland? Portugal? America?

'Your father is a fool,' one of his mother's friends told Hussain, straightening his collar with a gesture of pity. 'He wants to run with the stag and hunt with the hounds at the same time. Of course both will pull him down.'

'You are the man of the family now,' another vivid Persian beauty explained. 'It will be up to you to take care of your mother.'

His father was transferred from prison to prison, and they trailed after him from one fleabitten hotel to another, from Casablanca to Algiers, from Algiers to Marseilles, from Marseilles to Clermont-Ferrand. His parents' naturalization was revoked, their property confiscated and their bank accounts closed. When the military authorities finally released his father from prison, Hussain was twelve years old, a fat boy who was silent and wary with adults and uninterested in children of his own age.

He accompanied his mother as she made new friends in every new town. 'Friends are the greatest asset you have in life,' she said. 'You can have everything you want if you have the right friends.'

The adventure which his mother had promised him began, and' they made their way to the Pyrenees, to a tiny village where the Resistance had guides who would take people across the mountains to Spain. Hitching rides in farm-carts, meeting generosity in one village and treachery in the next, they at last reached Lisbon with nothing in the world but the clothes they had worn for a month and one diamond necklace, which was stitched into the waistband of Hussain's trousers.

'I shall go to London and fight with de Gaulle,' his father announced as soon as his strength returned after the journey.

'You will not,' his mother told his father in fury. 'France has taken everything we have; that lousy country isn't getting my husband as well. You will stay here. We shall go to America. The Americans don't grant citizenship one day and demand it back the next.'

With pitiful self-importance, his father took the diamond neck-lace and exchanged it for three tickets on a liner to America. Hussain looked forward to living in a country which was full of elegant women in satin dresses who sipped cocktails.

When they arrived at the dockside they discovered that the ship on which their passages were booked did not exist, and the agency which had sold the tickets was nothing but a vacant room which, said the *concierge*, no one had ever rented.

Although she screamed and stormed at his father over little things, Hussain's mother did not fly into a rage over this catastrophe. Her liquid brown eyes were alive with thought. It was as if their total destitution was merely an amusing riddle with which she could occupy her mind.

They returned to their shabby hotel. His mother washed and pressed her clothes, pinned up her hair in elegant curls, brushed Hussain's jacket, made him polish his shoes and set out for the house of the wealthiest person of their acquaintance in Lisbon. She told him, 'Never give money to anyone who asks for it like a coward. They don't deserve it. People don't want to see ruin at their door; they want to see courage.'

With the dazzling dignity born of centuries of lineage from the noblest families in Persia, his mother explained to the *marquesa* that they had lost all their money and that she intended to make a living for her family by dressmaking. She mentioned, with a gay little smile, that she was well acquainted with the secrets of Patou, Lanvin and the other giants of *haute couture*. The *marquesa* smiled, too.

'First I will need a sewing machine, of course, and I was wondering if perhaps there is such a thing in your household, an old machine for which your maid no longer has any use?'

They left with a sewing machine and a commission to copy two of the *marquesa*'s favourite costumes in silk. There was a great deal of fine silk in Lisbon at the time; a whole ship's cargo of the glorious fabric had been off-loaded by a captain who preferred to get a bad price for it in Portugal than be sunk by a U-Boat in the Bay of Biscay.

The city was full of such goods and while his mother sat day and night at her sewing machine, Hussain haunted the seamen's bars, finding out where he could procure worsted, linen or crisp cotton at rock bottom prices. The *marquesa* soon became one of the best-dressed women in the city. Her friends sought out Hussain's mother in dozens. By the end of the war she was employing a young Portuguese girl to sew for her, and Hussain had learned all he would ever need to know about buying, selling, marketing and clinching a deal.

His father sat in a café all day with one glass of *fino* in front of him, speaking to no one. His weak mind was dawdling towards insanity. Before they left the city he took his son to a brothel and propelled him into a narrow room which contained a sofa covered in poor-quality pink satin. On it lolled a delicious little whore, hardly older than he was, who wriggled towards him and pounced on his penis as if she were opening a box of chocolates. After half-an-hour of hard work Hussain's penis had not stirred and she withdrew, red in the face and bad-tempered.

Hussain returned to the salon and thanked his father with what he judged to be the appropriate mixture of filial gratitude and manly bonhomie. Privately he assumed that sex was just another of his father's foolish diversions.

The Paris to which they returned was a savage whirlpool of treachery and revenge, where the pickpockets and streetwalkers were being crowded out of the jails by hundreds of distinguished people accused of collaboration with the Nazis. Hundreds more were escaping to the country until the storm died down.

'Why are they doing that?' he asked his mother as they were pushed off the pavement by a crowd who had shaved the heads of two young girls and were spitting on them and tearing their clothes.

'They were whores for the Germans,' she told him. 'Crazy French. They are not denouncing the farmers who fed them or the shopkeepers who served them – oh no. You can't be a traitor if you sell cabbages. That's their idea of honesty.'

'You will see,' she told him later, 'they will give the Rothschilds back everything, but when we ask for our property – well, you will see. There's no advantage to them in dealing fairly with us. French justice is only for the French.'

It was exactly as she predicted. The Avenue Foch apartment belonged to a family of the *haute bourgeoisie* whose deeds were judged to be perfectly legal. Of the Shahzdeh bank accounts there was no trace. In due course a very small sum in compensation was granted to them.

'Give me the money!' his father demanded, swaying as he stood up. i will make us rich again. I feel lucky, I shall go to the casino . . .' His mother simply ignored her husband. Realism had become a conspiracy between her and her son.

In the angry city, there was no sugar, no coffee, no toilet paper, no soap, no petrol, no clothes.

'Naturally, they denounce everybody,' his mother said. 'What else is there to think about? Only hunger. If you can't have a full stomach you can always enjoy the execution of some petty official who used to eat too much.'

Hussain ran into this maze of deceit like a hungry rat. His mother went from the house of one friend to another, drinking bitter coffee and gossiping. Hussain accompanied her and listened. This woman wanted tyres for her automobile, that one needed a bigger apartment for her family, another had a daughter getting married and not so much as a metre of net for the wedding veil.

There was a bar in the Rue St-Antoine where the racketeers gathered. They made a pet of Hussain, now a chubby adolescent with a fat backside and cheerful blackbird eyes. He had an air of trustworthiness which was partly due to his ignorance but increasingly a function of the fact that he *was* trustworthy. What he promised, he delivered. If he could not deliver, he did not promise. There was no side to him, no pretension. Not for him the silk Italian ties and the alligator shoes, the pimplike accoutrements of his profession. He looked almost like a schoolboy, not quite deserving of his long trousers; thus even his sexual deficiency worked to his advantage.

Of course, there were bad types who thought they could put one over on the kid. Hussain sold a car for one of his mother's friends and was attacked in the labyrinthine passages of the St-Germain Metro by two men who stole the money. The same night the man who had bought the car was also attacked, and his face slashed from temple to chin with a cut-throat razor. The scar needed thirty-two stitches, and ever afterwards advertised the loyalty of Hussain's friends.

As well as blackmarket goods, Hussain dealt in influence. A *carte grise* for a stolen vehicle? 'I've heard of a man who might be able to help. Give me twenty-four hours.' A good name for a cabaret dancer who performed for the Nazis? 'Naturally, Mademoiselle did no such thing. People will say anything. I think I know someone who can help . . .' Paris became a vast mosaic of needs and supplies, set in a symmetrical design by his avid memory.

His methods were so subtle he was nicknamed *le p'tit gentil-homme.* To bribe a minor official, he would sit with him in a small bar in a part of town where the man was not known, and explain directly what he wanted. His watch would be on the table in front of him, as if he were timing the conversation. Hussain's watch was the only ostentatious thing about him; its heavy gold bracelet strap winked in the sunlight on a bright day. A few minutes of polite conversation, some enquiries into the man's personal life and his own needs, then Hussain would pay and leave. His watch remained. If the man could not help, he would run after Hussain and return the watch. This happened only once.

Ceaseless activity made him thinner. By the time Hussain celebrated his twentieth birthday he still had a soft-bodied fleshiness, with chubby cheeks and bright eyes, but he had acquired a certain elegance. He looked like what he was – a master fixer.

His father's last refuge from reality was religion and the old man passed his days in the coffee shop by the mosque behind the Jardin des Plantes, sitting at a hammered brass table staring blankly ahead. At last he died, and Hussain bought an elegant apartment on the Quai d'Orsay.

'This is much too grand,' his mother protested. 'Whatever you are doing, it can't be honest. A boy of twenty shouldn't have such money. Hussain, promise me what you are doing, it isn't bad?'

'Of course not. All I do is bring together people who need things with the people who have them. There's nothing wrong, what could be wrong? I'm providing a service.'

'I had no idea you had so much money.' His mother looked in wonder round the empty room, savouring the luxury which she had resigned herself never to enjoy again. The soft blue light from the Seine streamed in at the long windows, highlighting the delicate plaster mouldings around the ceiling.

Hussain now worked with his telephone; his deals were becoming bigger and bigger. In the French colony of Algeria, the communist FLN guerrillas had ambitions beyond bombing banks and assassinating individual administrators. They wanted war, and he spent much time eating couscous and drinking mint tea with men who were looking for guns. He derived the peculiar pleasure of revenge from supplying, through Beirut, French army-surplus arms to the Algerian revolutionaries.

His contacts – it was no longer possible to call all of them friends – were his lifeblood and he socialized relentlessly. In the evenings he would take his mother, always the picture of elegance in black crêpe, to Procope, on the Left Bank, and watch her enjoy seeing Kirk Douglas or Vivien Leigh, or the Aly Khan. He would tell her she was still more beautiful than the Aly's mannequin wife, which was almost true. Then, entertainment over, he would escort her home and begin alone a night-long circuit of clubs and cabarets.

In the small hours of the morning, when the bakers' shops were already perfuming the air with the aroma of the day's first croissants and baguettes, he would reach Le Bambou, a little dive with a fabulously perverse atmosphere which always inspired those of his contacts who nominated sex as the sweetener they preferred.

The entire room was panelled in bamboo, with bamboo stools at the bamboo bar and bamboo mugs for some of the special cocktails. It was a high room, and at one end of it there was a scaffolding of bamboo with cagelike alcoves for the girls. Each girl had a telephone in front of her on a bamboo table. Clients could call up the hostess of their choice from the bar, and she would undulate down to dance with him. The lighting was a mixture of blue and ultraviolet, and some of the girls dressed so that their underwear would glow through their clothes in the ultraviolet beam.

Hussain sometimes bought cocaine or opium from the Bambou's owner, Philippe Thoc, and often brought men there: the Germans and British in particular would sit with popping eyes trying to decide which girl to call. They were mostly Asian or Eurasian, with two obligatory Swedish blondes.

One evening he entered Le Bambou and failed to get his usual delighted greeting from the manageress, Ayeshah. She was sitting at the bar with a face like thunder, a slender figure in a white ribbon-lace dress. The waiters, the barman and the hostesses were shooting nervous glances at her.

Hussain's experience was that other people's trouble was often his business, so he approached her.

'Why are men such idiots?' she demanded. Women often treated Hussain as if he were not really a man at all, sensing his complete lack of sexual interest.

'Which particular man is an idiot?' His eyes were frank and friendly.

'Philippe. Imbecile! You know there's a Chinese proverb – once a man has tasted the poppy he has no use for love? Well, I don't think Philippe has any use for anything. Love, money, his future, *our* future . . .' She glared around the room, her foot in its black velvet shoe twitching with annoyance.

'He can't see what's in front of his nose,' she went on. 'I can't keep these girls long, now. Remember Pan-Pan?'

'The one with the long legs, who wore her hair in a chignon with a long fall?'

She nodded. Hussain always remembered women's looks in detail. 'Well, she's going to strip at the Crazy Horse. And Helga, too, last month. I can't keep a blonde two weeks now. This city's too hot. It's jumping. Paris is the centre of the world – Hollywood-sur-Seine! And Philippe says we are quite happy how we are and why change it? Paris is the centre of the world right now. It's just a great big playground full of film stars and aristocrats, in their furs and their diamonds and their fancy cars. They have everything, they've done everything, they've been everywhere, they've met everyone and they're absolutely bored so they still chase every new thrill they see. How can anyone not want a piece of all that?' She scowled. She was in a vile temper, but instead of diminishing her beauty the malevolence added an unearthly aura of fascination to her features. Her French was heavily accented and inclined to break down completely under emotional stress.

Three men in expensively tailored, grey suits with lapels an inch or so wider than elegance required came into the club and stood at the bar. Hussain raised one eyebrow in their direction. 'Know them?' he asked her.

'Who are they?'

'The one in the middle is an adviser to the Turkish Defence Minister. On his right is Martin, civil servant, develops long-range arms strategy. The other one is with Dassault.' She looked at him with an enquiring expression.

'They make the Mirage fighter, apart from anything else. I can guess what they're talking about.' He gave the men a cheery salute, then turned back to Ayeshah. He had done business with all three men but appreciated that they might not wish to admit in public that they knew a small-time arms dealer.

Ayeshah left him and greeted the men, had the barman mix them complimentary cocktails, then vanished into the offices behind the bar. As she returned to the table, two tiny Thai girls dressed in fuchsia pink came out and negotiated the bamboo steps up to the cages with difficulty in their tight skirts.

'You like my Siamese twins?' She was in a better temper now. 'They really are sisters, you know. Truthfully.'

'I believe you.'

The civil servant reached for the telephone and summoned the two girls to the bar. After some desultory dancing there was an intense conversation and all five left. Ayeshah's richly curved lips gave a small pout of satisfaction.

'I thought he'd go for them.'

'How do you know a thing like that?' Hussain found sex fascinating because everything about it was outside his own experience.

'I don't know.' She shrugged. 'I just know, that's all. I suppose you can read a man's sexuality in his face, if you know what you're looking for. But that's another thing – Philippe! I can't make him understand. There's no future in running a small-time operation like this.' She waved her arm contemptuously around the smoky, noisy *boite*. 'Sure, the club makes a profit, we make a living, but that's nothing compared to what I could do. A nightclub is like the centre of a spider's web. People are attracted, then you catch and hold them, and after that . . . they're yours, you can take what you want from them.'

'What do you mean?' He offered her a cigarette.

She shot him a shrewd glance from below her short, straight eyelashes. 'Listen. I did *that* . . .' she blew disparaging smoke towards the cages, 'two years. I know a lot about men, things you wouldn't believe. And there's one thing I will never believe, that's what they will do for a piece of tail. A man will swim through a river of snot if he thinks there's a friendly pussy on the other side. And as for the bent ones . . .'

she shrugged, indicating that their idiocy was infinite. 'Completely crazy. It's the Achilles heel – sex.' The way she mispronounced Achilles was adorable, even while she was talking with savage cynicism. 'You know, you've seen it too. Even now, my Siamese twins could take photographs and that Turkish pervert would be in big trouble, and he'd pay big money to get out of it. That's better than 200 francs a trick, wouldn't you say?'

Hussain nodded. 'Philippe doesn't agree?'

'Too much trouble, too big a risk . . . he's afraid. No, he's not afraid. He's just nothing.' She folded her arms and sat back.

There had been many advantages for her in Philippe's taste for opium; as their ambitions diverged, she had encouraged him to smoke as much as he liked to get him to the state of dissociated unconcern in which he would let her do what she wanted with the business. Now, however, his personality was beginning to disintegrate and he could no longer be controlled.

'What do you want to do, then? What are these plans for which Philippe has no enthusiasm?'

'Simple. We close this place, buy another, really chic. You see, even now, we're getting some pretty flush clients. I've had Bardot in here with Vadim, Yves Montand . . . but they come here for fun, it's not their style, it's just a curiosity.'

'So, a smart club and . . .'

'The telephone is not a toy, you know. It's the future, I have seen that. Call girls. No more stupid little dolls who just want to shake their asses down at the Crazy Horse. Most of the business my girls do is with tourists, foreigners, out-of-town executives, parties . . . people who don't just want a fuck, they want a whole scene, a performance. They want to feel they've been where the action is, they want to feel they've been to *Paris* – the Paris they all dream of, where *l'amour* is a great art, where women know more about love than anywhere else in the world.'

'So – you want simply to be the most famous madame in the world. Your ambitions aren't modest, are they?'

'Of course not, what would be the point of just a little ambition? No, you're wrong, I don't want to be a great madame. I want more than that.'

'What then?'

'What is there? As much as there is, that's as much as I want.' Again, the look that stabbed his secret thoughts. She was like a panther, he decided. She could switch from kittenish play to the absolute concentration of a killer in the flicker of an eye.

'Does that frighten you?' she asked him.

He considered. 'No. I think you're right. A small ambition isn't worth having.'

'It frightens Philippe.' Philippe almost cowered when she tried to explain her plans to him. 'He thinks I'm going to eat him up.'

'And are you?'

'How should I know? Yes, if it's necessary. He has no right to stand in my way.' They fell silent and watched the dancers and drinkers, the buyers and sellers of flesh, as they circulated under the blue lights like languid fish in an aquarium.

'Shall I show you this place?' Ayeshah was a kitten now, soft and playful. She closed her hand over his wrist.

'Why not – is it far?'

She shook her head. 'Just off the Champs – ten minutes if we go in your car.'

She took him to a four-storey building with graceful wrought-iron balconies that was squeezed between taller buildings in a narrow street between the Champs-Elysees and the Rue St-Honore.

'Wonderful location,' he approved, 'your carriage trade will be gold-plated.'

'The Ritz is one minute away.' She methodically sorted through a large bunch of keys until she found one which opened the door. The pearly dawn light of Paris flowed into a courtyard paved with ancient flagstones.

'I want to make a glass roof here,' she waved both arms skywards, an ineffably beautiful gesture that emphasized the arrogant modelling of her breasts. 'And this can be the dining room, like a conservatory. In the summer we can roll back the roof and eat under the stars. And then here inside, the bar, the dancing, perhaps a room for backgammon – like a library, with a good fire. You can have a lot of people here but, you see, it will still feel intimate, like a private house. I want it all very modern, with leather seating, but not cold, you understand? You can be chic and not intimidate people. No red plush.' She gave a pout of disdain. 'And very nice flowers, looking as if the lady of the house has just done them with her own hands.'

He followed, spellbound, as she led him through the empty building, conjuring up visions which completely blotted out the tired cream paint and cheap partitioning.

'And upstairs – the girls?'

'Absolutely not. The girls somewhere else, maybe not too far. But no connection, no suspicion, ever. Who would come to my club if they thought the beautiful woman they were fortunate enough to meet there would be in the position to destroy their life the next morning?' She raised one perfectly pencilled, black eyebrow as if inviting him to share a huge joke which only they could appreciate.

'Do you love Philippe?' he asked her as he drove her back to Le Bambou in his discreet Peugeot convertible.

'No.'

'Did you ever love him?'

'No. I can't love any man.'

'Do you love anyone?'

'Yes.'

'Women?'

'I am not a lesbian, if that's what you mean. I don't think sex has anything to do with love; that's just stupid nonsense people make up because they feel dirty.'

'Why not answer my question – who do you love?'

She gave him a peculiar stare, for once uncertain how to respond. Then she said, 'I love children, because they are innocent.'

'Do you have any children?' he asked suddenly, prompted by a premonition. He turned to look at her face as she replied, but a young man on a moped a few yards in front of the car suddenly swayed out into the roadway, and Hussain was forced to look back and steer to avoid him.

She ignored the question. 'And you? Who do you love?' she asked him.

'My mother. Don't all men love their mothers?' They cruised over the Pont Neuf and Hussain halted at the crown of the bridge to admire the effect of the dawn on the white façade of the Sainte Chapelle.

'And who else?' she pressed him, as they drove on.

'No one. Passion is a distraction which I have been spared. I love to make deals, that's my great vice.'

In a few minutes they reached the narrow street where Le Bambou was situated. 'What would you say . . .' Hussain paused as he took the keys out of the ignition, 'if I bought that lease for you? It would suit me to have the upper part of the building for my office.'

'You mean, you want to back my club?'

'Yes.'

'I need about half-a-million francs, I think.'

That's what I thought.'

'OK,' she spoke with care, mysteriously calm, 'it's a deal.' She put out her narrow, long-fingered hand and he shook it.

Scarcely a month later Hussain felt as if his destiny had been transferred from the care of one woman to another. His mother had a slight stroke, then a much more serious one which left her partially paralysed. In hospital, X-rays revealed a large tumour of the brain. She began rapidly to decline.

He hired three of the best nurses money could buy, and brought her infusions of verbena tea every two hours, really as an excuse to sit at the end of her bed and have her precious company for a little longer. Even at the door of death she was beautiful, her complexion as pale as a Christmas rose with violet shadows to highlight the proud swell of her cheekbones.

'Promise me something,' she whispered to him one evening. 'Promise me to live a good life, Hussain.'

'Of course. Mother, of course.'

She shook her head, frustrated by her weakness. 'I mean your business. You think I'm foolish, I know, but bad money is the easiest money, I know that. Promise me you will never do anything which would have made me ashamed.'

'I promise.' He pressed her hand and kissed it, noticing tiny bruises where her frail capillaries had burst under the translucent skin.

'Another thing . . .'

'Anything – tell me.'

'Your little Ayeshah, she must go to Givenchy. Tell her,' she paused for breath, her eyes sparkling with fun, 'tell her it is my dying wish. Tell Hubert . . . no, I will tell him.' She made him pass her the writing case and made a supreme effort to control her trembling hand as she wrote to Hubert de Givenchy instructing him to give his personal attention to the new client she was recommending.

That night Hussain's mother died peacefully in her sleep. He cried like an infant for the first time in his life.

Barely a month later, early on a Tuesday evening when Ayeshah was still dressing upstairs and Le Bambou was almost empty, two uniformed *gendarmes* walked into the club and asked to see Philippe. He emerged smiling from his office at the rear of the premises, fearing nothing since he paid the police their graft like a prudent businessman. He was surprised when the *gendarmes* began to question him about his drug-trafficking, since a substantial proportion of his wares was bought directly from the narcotics squad, a favour granted in return for the occasional betrayal of his customers.

When clattering boots resounded on the stairs from the back alley to the rear entrance of the club, and police began swarming through every room, searching with unnecessarily destructive application, Philippe realized that he had fallen prey to a predator bigger than himself. With fatalism that was partly his nature and partly induced by opium, he shrugged his shoulders and allowed handcuffs to be locked around his wrists.

He was led away by the two officers; following them was a third who carried the sack of Moroccan *kif* from his desk. In the office, a police photographer's flashlight illuminated the desk top, the scales, the pharmacist's jar of white powder and the delicately-folded paper packet of cocaine which Philippe had prepared for one of Hussain's acquaintances.

Ayeshah watched her lover's arrest with a curious expression of anticipation. Within an hour Hussain strolled through the door, punctual as ever for his appointment, and he saw at once from the suppressed excitement which was almost making her tremble that Ayeshah understood perfectly how he accomplished the removal of his only possible rival.

He opened his mouth to speak and she instantly pressed two fingers to his lips to silence him.

'Let's talk about something interesting,' she suggested lightly. 'When will you take me to Givenchy?'

He escorted her to the salon the next day, where she was entertained by the great couturier himself and appointed the same fitter who had served Hussain's mother.

'Incredible!' the woman exclaimed, peering at the tape measure pinched between her blood-red fingernails. 'Your measurements are *exactly* the same as the Princess's. Exactly!'

'Was she a princess? I did not know.' Ayeshah was conscious that her slip was not of the best quality silk. It creased unattractively at the waist. There was still so much to learn.

'Why, yes, didn't you know? Very, very old Persian aristocracy, related to the Shah, the old Shah that is. Shahzdeh isn't their real name. The Princess invented it because no one in Paris could pronounce their real name. So considerate. A true aristocrat.'

'If your mother was a princess, you must be a prince?' she asked Hussain that afternoon.

'Yes, that's right. But, believe me, if you're trying to find a home for three ship-loads of contaminated tuna, it is no advantage to be a prince.' He was exasperated. 'Being a prince won't help me get these Nigerians to put their money into escrow. The Africans will buy anything, you know – they just have a little difficulty paying for it.' She smiled. He was confiding in her more and more.

'But if you are backing a nightclub, being a prince would be a help, I think.'

In a few weeks workmen were tearing down the flimsy partitions in Ayeshah's premises and hacking holes in the brickwork to fit the glass roof.

Hussain went to see a doctor. 'As far as I am aware,' he said, 'I have never had any sexual feeling or completed the sexual act. Nevertheless, I would like to get married, and I would like to know if – if anything can be done.'

The doctor sent him on a long pilgrimage to specialists, who did tests to investigate his hormones, his gland functions, his neurological fitness and his potential fertility.

Then the doctor faced him cheerfully across his desk. 'Physically you're in perfect health – well, almost perfect. Your testosterone level could be higher, but we can give you synthetic hormone treatment to counteract that. The major factor in your sexual deficiency is almost certainly psychological, and you would probably find that if you went into analysis for a few years it would be possible to achieve some improvement.'

'Could I have children?'

'You could have children now, if your future wife accepted artificial insemination. Your sperm count is quite normal.'

That evening he called for Ayeshah with a corsage of white orchids and took her to dinner at Procope. Afterwards they strolled in the moonlight by the side of the Seine, as lovers are supposed to do in Paris.

'What would you say . . .' Hussain began, halting opposite the curtains of an ancient creeper by the side of Notre Dame, 'if I asked you to marry me?'

She took his hands but stepped away from him. Tonight the white dress was of a rich brocaded satin, a Givenchy classic which swathed her body like a Greek statue.

'I would make one condition only.' This was the panther speaking; there was no flirtation in her manner.

'What would that be?'

'That you become a prince again.'

'Is that all? What could be simpler? Then will you be my princess, Ayeshah?'

'One more thing – do you want children? Because I can't have them, I think. Anyway, I don't want them.'

He shook his head, the moonlight glinting on the metal buttons of his double-breasted, blue jacket. 'I would not even want you to be my wife in the physical sense, unless you would like to be. The doctors say I can be treated, but I am reluctant to give up an advantage such as sexual disinterest. Unless it would make you happy, of course.'

She smiled, childlike and happy. 'I would not ask that. Let us have a marriage of ambitions.'

'Ambitions and interests.'

They shook hands once more on the deal, and he laughed. 'Of course, we will be the happiest couple in Paris.'

'Why just Paris?'

'All right then, the happiest couple in Europe.'

'Only Europe?'

'The world?'

She shook her head. 'Primitive people are happy, you see. It never occurs to them to be unhappy. All they know is sick or well, old or young, enough to eat or not. We shall be the happiest *civilized* couple in the world.'

They walked on, arm in arm, and Hussain realized that he had no idea where his bride came from. It was not important. She was a citizen of her place and time, just as he was. The rest was just excess baggage.

CHAPTER EIGHTEEN

JAMES, BILL and Ibrahim felt as if their luck changed at the moment they crossed the state line into the smiling green territory of Pahang. After months of frustration, semi-starvation and enduring the obstructive hostility of the Chinese Communists in Perak, they began to revive their hopes of hitting back at the Japanese.

A truck loaded with lumber met them at an appointed place on the road to Kuala Lumpur, and a young Malay flung open the unglazed door.

'*Selamat*!' he said joyfully. The Malay word for peace was the usual greeting. 'What about a real cigarette? I know you want one – no Kensitas in the jungle, eh?' And James filled his lungs voluptuously with fumes of Virginia tobacco.

The driver told them about the loyalty of the Pahang people. The Japanese had requisitioned a royal palace in the old state capital town of Pekan, and made it their headquarters. Their cruelty and ruthlessness were an offence to God. The Sultan himself had issued a secret decree to his people to help the British.

'We are all of one blood,' the driver shouted, hitting the steering wheel for emphasis.

'Drive us through Pekan,' Ibrahim asked him, 'I want to see my enemy.' The red dirt road ran straight and unwavering, like the Roman roads on Salisbury Plain which James's governesses had shown him. At an orderly angle of 90 degrees, it gave on to an equally straight metalled highway which, after an hour's driving, ran across a wide river and into the town of Pekan.

'It's like Cheltenham,' James murmured to himself as they drove through the grid of spacious tree-lined streets along which stood graceful wooden villas washed ice-pink or lime yellow.

Bill said nothing, but craned his neck to admire the immense, ancient trees which bordered the river banks; from each fork or crack in the grey bark sprouted stags' horn ferns. They passed the town mosque, a wooden building elaborately decorated with carvings and painted the cool turquoise-green shade that is considered most pleasing to Allah. Pekan impressed him as a modest, gracious, peaceful settlement, and he recognized its character as being more purely Malay than the striving multi-racial towns of Georgetown or K L. The place was full of the enduring spirit of the people – simple, industrious and harmonizing with both spiritual and earthly authority; it spoke directly to his heart and strengthened his resolve.

'Look there, Japanese HQ, formerly royal palace,' the driver pointed to an imposing stone building in the heavy neo-Victorian style of Anglo-Malay architecture. Its bulk dominated the tranquil elegance of the rest of the town. Around it a fine garden had evidently been razed to deny cover to any attacker. The red-and-white rising sun flag flapped idly above the devastation, and a squad of soldiers, marching raggedly like marionettes, guarded the entrance.

Their rendez-vous was at a coffee shop on the outskirts of the town, by a single-storey suburban mosque whose minaret, crescent and star were silhouetted against the failing evening light. With Bill seated far back in the shadows, they talked with the stall-owner, their driver, the man who owned the lumber company, a police inspector and a local lawyer. By the time the stall owner judged it prudent to put out the lamp they had crystallized their plan.

Bill left the next day with the driver and the lumber lorry, to hide out on a remote *kampong* at the apex of an inland lake three or four hours away. The Japanese had not even bothered to penetrate this poor rural area. He could operate a wireless without fear and train the volunteers the others recruited in safety.

James and Ibrahim rented a small *kampong* house from an elderly widow in a village an hour's drive away. It was the last of the houses which dotted a strip of fertile land between the river and the valley road. Their cover was driving trucks for the lumber company which dominated the area economically, an occupation which allowed them freely to ply the roads between Pekan, the port, Kuala Lumpur and the distant jungle tracts where the trees were felled.

At once men began to seek them out. The first time a figure stepped out of the shadows of his balcony James hurled himself behind the single palm standing at the front of the house, expecting shots or an attack by jungle knife.

James paused in bewilderment for a moment, then recognized their own password, suggested by Ibrahim. Tentatively he called back, 'The road will be clear again by morning.'

There was an awkward, distrustful pause, then James boldly left the cover of the tree and walked forward. The youth waiting for him had been a student in peacetime and was now eager to fight the Japanese. James hid him in the house for two days, then drove him to Bill.

'Our first recruit,' he announced in exultation, 'first of many, you'll see.'

They laundered their money a few hundred dollars at a time, exchanging the old bills issued under the British for the new ones printed by the Japanese. Bill sent a messenger to the house of the fat Chinese who had feasted and sheltered them on their journey to Perak. The house was a charred ruin and their former host and his family were dead; they had been betrayed to the Japanese very soon after the four men had left to find the Communists. By night, Bill's emissary dug into the earth below the ashes where he had been told to search, and retrieved the precious but cumbersome wireless which they had buried before leaving. A few weeks later James discovered a battery in a palm-leaf bag, stuffed under a tarpaulin on his truck by an anonymous well-wisher.

Bill assiduously practised Morse Code. They picked up weather forecasts from American warships and rejoiced. It was their first contact with the real war.

By Christmas 1943, they had fifteen agents in training, and ten in the field. James appeared the picture of a cheery Malay truck-driver, with a smooth skin the colour of strong tea. He found he now needed to take only one Trisoralen tablet a day to maintain the colour, if he kept in the sun. He drove his loads of timber the length and breadth of the state with messages and supplies concealed in hollowed-out billets of wood.

In the village, under Ibrahim's direction, he had been accepted along with all the other disruptive features of the occupation. Kampong Kechil was a village which hardly merited the name, a widely-separated line of simple wooden houses, strung out along the valley road and distanced from each other by *padi* fields, open spaces or vegetable gardens. In consequence it lacked the intimate street life of villages where the houses were grouped closely around one or two wells.

James and Ibrahim spoke Malay all the time, even when alone. When Ibrahim talked to the villagers he derided James as a soft-living, Westernized 'town boy', and made fun of his supposedly degenerate, irreligious ways.

'That way they won't care to get to know you,' he laughed, 'and if you forget your prayers no one will be surprised.' He need not have worried. James's mutable nature adapted to the village ways with a naturalness which astonished his companion; the only aspect of his new life which he could not master was the mechanics of the truck.

'It's good of Allah to spare me from punctures,' he remarked, looking perplexedly at the grimy engine. 'I'd never manage to change a wheel.'

'Allah in his mercy has given you me for a mechanic.' Ibrahim delicately picked up a loose electrical lead which he reconnected to the starter motor. 'Try if it will start now.'

Their house was a simple building of old wood weathered to a reddish grey, with a tin roof. It was built in the traditional style on piles about two feet high, with some ornamental carving decorating the steps and the shuttered window-openings. Bamboo guttering funnelled rainwater into a large earthenware jar by the entrance.

A bridge, five planks wide, spanned the stream which flowed slowly between the house and the road. In the clear grassy space in front of the building their landlady, Maimunah, sometimes sent her cow to graze. Her house lay across the road, some twenty yards farther down, next to a long tin roof under which the villagers processed their latex. Every day Maimunah, a stately woman whose grey hair was bound up in a flower-printed, scarf-like turban, set off for her small plantation of trees, and returned in the late morning with two full tins of latex bouncing on a bamboo pole over her shoulder.

She decanted the white sap into a rectangular trough and added formic acid to it, then sat in the shade for a quarter of an hour waiting for the mixture to harden. After that she tipped out the oblong of coagulated rubber on to a cloth and stamped on it to flatten it, before feeding it through an ancient iron mangle which still bore the gleaming brass plate of its manufacturer in Sheffield.

The result of this procedure was a dirty, yellowish-white blanket of latex which was draped over the fence to dry. Every week a Chinese dealer would visit the *kampong* with his truck, to buy what they produced.

Maimunah had one daughter living in the village with her husband, and their youngest child, a boy of about four years old, sometimes helped her tread the latex, jumping on the stinking mat of resin with excitement. He was a mischievous child whose other delight was to sit in the cab of James's lorry pretending to drive it.

Frequently Maimunah's voice, calling, 'Yusof! Yusof! Where are you? Stop teasing me! Come home now!' would float into the sleepy air, and perhaps later the old woman herself would saunter over the plank bridge to the house to ask James or Ibrahim if they had seen her grandson.

James was sitting on the steps one day when he saw the graceful form of a girl cross the bridge and approach him, hesitantly fumbling with her white scarf to veil her face. She was about fifteen years old. Few of the village women bothered with the traditional Moslem ideals of modesty. The young unmarried girls were the only ones who covered their heads, and in their shyness often made the business of hiding their faces from male eyes delightfully seductive.

'Peace,' she greeted him hesitantly.

'Peace.'

'I am looking for little Yusof. Is he in your truck? I know he likes playing there.' She darted a quick look at James from wide, round eyes, then looked at the ground, embarrassed. As James walked to the truck she followed him a respectful few paces behind. There was no sign of the child.

'I am sorry to disturb you.' She turned to go.

'Wait – I'll see if he's hiding round the back.' James jumped down from the cab and walked round to the tailgate. He heard a splutter under one of the canvas sheets on the platform; he flipped it back and Yusof leapt happily out and ran away down the road. The girl smiled, the whole of her pale, heartshaped face relaxing with relief.

'Khatijah is my oldest granddaughter,' Maimunah told him a few days later. 'She has been living in Malacca where the people have poor manners, I think.'

James realized that she was apologizing for the girl's boldness. 'Khatijah is a widow now,' she added, as if in further mitigation. 'The Japanese killed her husband before her own eyes because he was accused of helping the Communists. Less than a year, they had been married.' She clicked her tongue as if reproving fate for its harshness. 'But all young people must get used to hard times sooner or later.'

In a few days, it became evident that Maimunah had more to be concerned about than her granddaughter's over-familiar manner. The peace of the *kampong* was disrupted by savage argument between Maimunah and her daughter, an overweight woman with a perpetually self-satisfied smile above her double chins. The slight figure of Khatijah soon afterwards carried her small bag of belongings out of her mother's house and walked with some defiance down the road to Maimunah's home.

The two men watched with interest as the girl passed in front of their house. Ibrahim had been ordered by Bill to move south and set up a new centre for the resistance; he finished crushing his clothes into a small, brown fibre suitcase and knotted a loop of string around it tightly, shaking his head as he thought about Khatijah. 'A young widow is as headstrong as a horse which has thrown its rider,' he said, quoting a familiar proverb. 'There'll be nothing but trouble on account of that girl, you'll see.'

'She seemed quiet enough to me.' James was taking Ibrahim's bicycle pump apart and preparing to hide the precious sheet of paper on which their codes were written out inside it.

'The women won't trust her; she won't be able to do anything right now her own mother's thrown her out.'

James pulled the rusty spring out of the body of the pump. 'What has she done?'

'It isn't a question of what she has done, my friend, but what she is. Women are the family's honour, after all. Her husband is dead, so she's come running back to her mother – that's natural. Where else could she go? But it's also natural that the village women will see her as a scarlet woman, all set to take away their own husbands now she has none of her own. She will bring shame on her family if they can't get her married again soon.'

'Hardly her fault that her husband's dead, is it? She's so young.' James realized that his British ideas of fairness would betray him if he questioned these customs publicly, but he felt sympathy for the persecuted girl and dislike for the villagers' narrow-minded callousness towards her. 'What about her father, shouldn't he take care of her until she's married again? That's what the Koran says, isn't it?'

'Ah, there you have it, my friend. Her father was a foreigner, he ran off and left her mother. Already a stain on the family's honour. And now her mother has a new husband and a new life and she doesn't want any living reminders of the mistakes of her wild youth around – understand?'

James nodded, folding up the code sheet and sliding it into the body of the bicycle pump. 'Thank God we weren't born women, eh?' Ibrahim laughed to hear him use this colloquial platitude, giving James a playful punch in the ribs.

'You'll have no trouble without me around, I think.'

'Except with the damn truck.'

'I'll see if I can service it before I leave. My father would weep if he saw me doing that, after paying so much for my education.' Ibrahim's father kept a garage the other side of the state, but had intended his son to become an engineer.

'You'll be building bridges again when the war's over,' James told him.

After Ibrahim left, Maimunah became more friendly, taking a maternal interest in her lonely tenant. Khatijah appeared often to do James's washing for him or bring gifts of food. Sometimes he ate with the two women. As Ibrahim had predicted, Khatijah was shunned by the other villagers; when she was not helping her grandmother she stayed indoors.

Bill designated their force the Liberation Army of Malaya. They were almost a hundred strong, but still had no contact with the British Army commanders in Ceylon. Nevertheless, their optimism strengthened daily. When he was away from their headquarters at the head of the lake, James felt as if cast adrift. He missed the excitement of making plans, the sense of purpose and the companionship. Accustomed to having Bill to take decisions for him or to engage him in rigorous arguments over his actions, he had a sense of his own incompetence when he operated independently.

Desire crept up on James so slowly he was taken by surprise. It was eighteen months since he had had a woman, but poor health and the sense of failure had lowered his libido. Now he was fit again, and lived in a state of periodic elation as the resistance operation gathered momentum. But there was, in truth, very little action he could take, beyond travelling around to recruit men and keeping those already trained in contact with headquarters. Most of his time was unstructured. He was a man ready for obsession.

He began to anticipate the sight of Khatijah's slender, tightly wrapped shape sauntering at the roadside as he approached the village. He saw her once at the riverbank, her wet sarong clinging to her body and accentuating every curve as she poured water over her bare shoulders; and afterwards he looked for her every time he passed the gap in the vegetation that gave him a view of the river.

When James awoke sweating and aroused from a hectic dream of lips and breasts and cascading black hair, he could no longer deny his desire to himself. A few days later he made the seven-hour trip to Kuala Lumpur with a load of timber, and he went to Mary's, anxious to slake this inconvenient appetite before it led him into danger. But Mary's was crammed with Japanese officers, and he dared not enter. Instead he found a slatternly Chinese streetwalker, but as she squabbled over her price he was overcome with self-disgust and ran away.

He took terrible risks at the *kampong*, talking openly to Khatijah as she worked and offering her rides down the road in his truck when she was loaded with latex. Then he took fright at his own rashness, and stayed away for days, prolonging a trip to Bill's headquarters.

'Marvellous news, Jim, bloody marvellous–Ceylon are sending men in at last.' In the damp cool of the early morning, the tall Australian ducked out from under the low bamboo lintel of his hut. 'They've dropped five blokes off the coast of Perak and they've met up with the Communists. It's happening, mate, it's happening at last.' The Australian was also restored to fitness, and his jungle pallor again roasted to Anglo-Saxon ruddiness.

'About bloody time.' English came out of James's mouth awkwardly now, and he had to struggle for the words. 'Listen, do you need me in Kechil? Wouldn't I be more use over the other side, back in Perak, now?'

'I thought you loved the *kampong* life?'

'There's a problem.'

'What kind of problem, for Christ's sake? Are they on to you?'

James shook his head. 'There's a girl.'

'So what. There's girls all over the place.' Bill spoke with irritation.

'Bloody hell, man, you know what I mean. I'm fucking dreaming about her.' He smiled involuntarily at his choice of words. Bill did not smile.

'I'm not going to blow this operation for the sake of your cock. Use a bit of self-control, can't you?'

'It's not so easy, Bill.' But he knew it was useless to go on. The Australian lived a life of cerebral pleasures that was virtually chaste. He had no understanding of the passion that was engulfing James's entire being.

'I've got to have a base near the Jap HQ, and you're the only man who can do it. You've said so yourself.'

James drove angrily back to the *kampong*, thinking through the situation with as much calmness as he could. If he took the girl, the village would turn against him, especially if she got pregnant. He was not at all confident that the villagers believed his native disguise; he sensed that they had rapidly recognized him as British but chose not to acknowledge it openly, partly from loyalty to their cause and partly from natural reticence. He was at least certain that they suspected that he and Ibrahim were involved in anti-Japanese activities. If the village people turned against him the whole operation would be in immediate danger of betrayal.

'I must move out,' he said to himself in Malay as he slowed down along the rutted river road. 'This can't be the only *kampong* where I can hide away. Tomorrow I'll go into Pekan and start asking around.'

Even in the torrential rain he recognized the shape of the body walking along the roadside, holding a banana leaf over her head as an ineffectual umbrella. In the midst of planning his way out of danger, James stopped and leaned across to open the door of the truck. Khatijah climbed in with difficulty in her drenched clothes, smiling shy thanks.

I could do it now, James thought, and no one would know. You can't see twenty yards in this downpour. He felt breathless. Resolutely, he slammed the truck into gear and drove on as fast as he dared, nearly running down a group of water buffalo in his distraction. Neither of them spoke.

They reached the village and he stopped the truck on the area reinforced with stones where he usually parked it. I could do it here, he thought, seeing that the blinding rain still screened them.

Desire was like a hot pain squeezing his genitals. He drew the wide-eyed girl towards him and tugged at her sarong where it was folded above her breasts. He could feel her flesh warm and firm beneath the clammy fabric. The wetness of the cloth made it hard to unfold, and in that instant of difficulty James came to his senses. He threw himself out of the cab in panic and Khatijah scrambled out at her side and ran away in the sluicing rain.

Next morning he prepared to drive to Pekan as soon as he awoke, but Maimunah was watching for him and appeared at the foot of his steps. Her excuse for the visit was a dish of little cakes. Her greeting was friendly and her manner grave.

'The war has brought trouble into many people's lives,' she began. 'In times such as these, what can we do? Our destiny is changed by events just as the sands of the riverbed are shaped by deep waters.'

James lit a cigarette to conceal his anxiety.

She rambled on through a tortuous series of observations about family life until James at last realized she had come to suggest that he married Khatijah. The solution had not occurred to him before. It was simple, perfect. When she mentioned a sum suitable for bridewealth he agreed to it at once.

The occupation was made the excuse for dispensing with most of the wedding formalities. Maimunah decorated her house with a few paper flowers, and as he sat beside Khatijah on the sacred carpet, his status of king-for-a-day perfunctorily indicated by a borrowed strip of gold-embroidered cloth and a hat similarly decorated, James realized that he was at least as satisfied with the marriage as most of Khatijah's relations. Her mother beamed with pleasure; her stepfather, a massively fat and self-important man, grinned like a buddha.

That night, James realized something else which had not crossed his mind before – Khatijah herself worshipped him, if only for restoring her status in the community. She clung to him with kittenish sensuality, giving him delicate caresses then withdrawing, shocked by her own avidity. Naked, she was more beautiful than he had imagined in his most fervid dreams. Her breasts were high and round like pomegranates and her legs sinewy and slender.

He found he could not put her out of his mind by day, as he had been able to do with his Tamil woman. His flesh yearned for her unbearably every night he spent away from her, and at the *kampong* he idled away hours merely watching her prepare their food or cultivate her little plot of vegetables. He spent as much money as he dared buying her jewellery and clothes. When they had been married almost a year she told him she was pregnant, and he was childishly delighted.

He drove to the lakeside camp; there was a dazzling carpet of pink flowers on the pellucid water and Bill was alive with a new optimism.

'They've got through to Ceylon on the radio,' he explained. 'We're in business at last, Jim. Get me everything you can on troop movements, shipping, cargoes, communications, the lot. Spread the word. They're going to start to airdrop ammunition next week. Perak reckons they can raise a thousand men already.'

He led James into his wood and bamboo hut and took away the back wall of woven palm leaves panel by panel; behind it was a secret room stacked with journals, papers, charts, the wireless and a map of Malaya showing the strength of the resistance. James looked at it, unmoved. Bill followed his thoughts at once.

'They'll come over to us in hundreds once the Japs are on the run in Burma,' he said, rapidly assembling the false wall once more. 'Shall we celebrate Christmas?'

'Is it Christmas now?'

'What's the matter, Jim? Can't you even count in English any more?'

James grinned. Bill led him to the end of a listing jetty of planks where the fishermen tied up their small boats, and pulled up a string to which a bottle of champagne was attached.

'Best I could do to chill it.' Bill slapped the label in appreciation and, loosened by its long soak in the water, it peeled away in his hand.

James had not touched alcohol for two years, and his tolerance had vanished. After two tiny glasses he was quite drunk.

'Congratulate me, old man,' he invited Bill, 'I'm going to be a father.'

The blue eyes glared at him in cold perplexity.

'Perfect cover – what could be better?' James was grinning like an idiot.

'You'll be finished if it's born white.'

'Won't be – just a lighter shade of brown, I should think. Mother's half-caste anyway.'

The Australian shook his head. 'For Christ's sake, man, there's a war on. You've got more important things to think about.'

James's gaiety promptly deflated. 'You're right. I'm sorry, Bill,' he raised his glass. 'Here's to victory.'

By the time the child was due they had the news from Europe of Germany's surrender. In Burma, the Japanese were falling back. British aircraft could now reach

Malaya, and were dropping thousands of tons of arms and supplies, with more and more soldiers, to secret airstrips in Perak. Bill's concealed map showed that almost four thousand Malayan citizens could be called up and armed the instant a rebellion against the Japanese was ordered.

The signs that the Japanese were suffering on other fronts were everywhere. In the towns food was scarce, and Khatijah's little vegetable garden was feeding dozens of men in the field. Japanese requisition parties periodically raided the *kampong*, and the cattle, goats and chickens were sent to graze in jungle clearings far away from the road where there was less chance that they would be discovered.

On the docksides of the east and west coast ports the bales of latex piled up; no shipping could get through to pick them up. The price Maimunah got for her latex dropped each week, and James advised her to stockpile the pressed sheets rather than sell them for next-to-nothing. He gave her money.

Supplies of petrol dwindled, and James was forced to run his truck on a crude alcohol distilled from rubber, on which the gallant vehicle spluttered like a bronchitic pensioner.

The Japanese bounty for allied undercover agents was increased, but in the *kampong* James became aware of a subtle shift of loyalty towards him. The villagers' reserve warmed. His father-in-law, Osman, praised him openly before the other men, and ventured a few words of English. James's suspicion that the villagers had never been deceived by his false identity was confirmed when Maimunah presented him with his newborn daughter. The baby had large, round black eyes, and a faint down of black hair on her head. Her skin, James was relieved to notice, was a pleasant olive shade, and her tiny rosebud lips were cinnamon-pink.

He knew that what he had to do was whisper the Moslem call-to-prayer in the newborn infant's ear, but as he prepared to do so Osman took the quiet bundle and said the words for him. The baby snuffled, Osman gave a proprietorial smile and there was a murmur of surprise and approval in the small knot of people standing in the house to see the infant.

'What will you do when the war ends?' Khatijah asked him a few weeks later, swinging the baby in a cradle made from a sarong suspended from the roof by two strings.

'I don't know,' he said. With all his energy directed to the coming uprising, he had not thought beyond the struggle for liberation.

'Will there be fighting again?' she pressed him, curling her lips in the feline smile he could not resist.

'Yes, I think so. And we shall win, the Japanese will go.'

'Will you leave?' She left the swinging cradle and nestled close to him.

'I may have to. I will have orders.' Should he tell her just a little bit of the truth? Would she be able to understand it? She was pitifully young and ignorant, only a peasant for all the intuitive cunning she used to give him pleasure.

'If you leave, will you take us? Say you will, please. I don't want to be left here without you. My stepfather hates me and my mother's always mean to me when he's around.' She was warm and yielding in his arms and the faint vanilla smell of frangipani clung to her hair. No, he must not tell: he had said too much already.

'You mean you want to have an easy life in town and spend all day gossiping with other women instead of working, eh?' She lowered her eyes and pouted, and he leaned over and kissed the warm hollow of her neck, feeling the delicate pulse of the artery under his lips. 'Don't worry,' he murmured. 'If I go back to the town you will come with me – you are my wife.' She giggled and teased him as he played with the braided-thread buttons of her tight blouse, caressing her breasts lovingly.

A few days later a distant, mechanical whine cut into the heavy silence of a cloudless noon, and James looked up to see three aircraft, like silver bullets, flying high overhead in the blue sky. Quickly the news came that the Americans were bombing Singapore, and Bill sent a message calling James to headquarters.

James told Khatijah that he might be away for some time, and set off for the lakeside in a state of high excitement, wondering what more news awaited him. As he jumped down from his cab in the clearing he saw the Australian, with Ibrahim, three Chinese and two unfamiliar British men, sitting in the shade under the palm-thatched shelter beside the hut. Their poses were apathetic, and James at once sensed a peculiar atmosphere of shock.

Ibrahim looked up as he approached.

'It's all over,' he said, his voice flat.

James looked from one face to another.

'What do you mean, it's all over? What's happened? Why all the gloom?'

'The Japanese have surrendered. The Americans dropped some big bombs on Nagasaki. The war's all finished.'

James could think of nothing to say. He was shocked, and disappointed, so were they all, bitterly downcast and feeling they had striven for nothing. But the enemy was vanquished, the war was over, and they knew they should be rejoicing.

'Just like that?' he asked at last.

They nodded. 'They told us this morning.'

'Have we got any orders?'

Bill unfolded his bony height and stood aimlessly, his hands in his pockets. 'Yes, we have orders. Special Operations Division are to join forces with American strategic services and the prisoner-of-war escape liaison to begin recovering our men in captivity. We are,' he picked the paper on which the message had been taken down out of his shirt pocket, unfolded his spectacles, and read, 'to make no move at all until HQ are satisfied that the surrender is holding, but we should set about identifying POW camps in our area. Under no circumstances must we approach a camp until we receive a signal.'

'What about our men?'

'Stay in the jungle, do not engage the enemy, await orders to disband.'

'*What?*'

Ibrahim nodded, his round, humorous face for once grim. 'We've spent two years teaching them how to fight and now we've got to tell them the show's over before it started.'

'Bad luck to sheath a knife before it has tasted blood,' James quoted the Malay proverb with a weak smile, not expecting a response. The situation was beyond the power of charm to lighten it.

'What's the truck running on? Jungle juice?' Bill straightened his shoulders and shook off his despondency, preparing to plan their next actions.

James nodded. 'There's no gas for miles around Kechil.'

'How much can you get hold of? I'll ask for supplies, but they'll be a while coming.'

'As much as you want. Some guys from the *kampong* brew it up.'

'Right. We'll get the map out and see if we can pinpoint locations for any camps we've heard about, then since we've got transport we might as well reconnoitre as much of the state as we can and find out exactly where they are.'

They had a new map, printed in vivid green, blue and brown on a thick silk scarf. The two newly-arrived Englishmen had brought it with them. During the Burmese campaign, the British had discovered that a map made of silk would not rot in the tropical climate, and could be concealed far more easily and put to many more uses than a conventional linen-backed paper chart.

In the next few days the skies filled with aircraft. Over Pekan leaflets were dropped announcing the Allied victory. Japanese troops paraded in front of the palace under their commanding officers and surrendered with no incident, beyond some suicides. In the country, the story was different, and there were many stories of Japanese attacks and Communist reprisals which Bill refused to commit to his journal.

They found three hundred Tamils in an internment camp in the south, hungry and diseased but not seriously debilitated. Another camp inland, whose existence they had not suspected, contained over a thousand workers of mixed Asiatic races, mostly suffering from chronic malnutrition.

A detachment of Gurkha troops was sent to supplement their strength, followed by five Americans commanded by a major whose speech was brisk and clipped and who appeared about thirty-five years old. He had close-cropped, colourless hair and no sense of humour. James asked him his age, and discovered that he was twenty-four.

'You're younger than both of us,' James told him.

'I guess if fighting your way across the Pacific an inch at a time doesn't make a man of you, nothing ever will,' the major responded, blinking rapidly.

Now that they were working alongside seasoned troops, James and Bill had an uncomfortable sense of being amateurs. For three years they had lived in isolation, with no contact with the fighting which had, it seemed, engulfed the whole of the rest of the world. The task to which they had devoted themselves, of raising an underground army of resistance, now seemed of marginal importance.

The war was over, and they had neither of them fired a shot. They were not even versed in the requirements of army bureaucracy, and the mass of conventions, regulations and military practices which they had to assimilate dazed them in its complexity. Neither man shared his feelings with the other. Instead, they applied themselves to their new task with ferocious energy, trying to make up for wasted time. James eradicated every thought of Khatijah and his undercover life on the *kampong* from his mind.

The Americans in particular made them feel like boys. They were spare, scarred and brawny. They knew exactly where to stick a bayonet in a Japanese and twist it so that the man would not die at once but would recall enough pidgin English to give them information. By this method they learned of another camp, not twenty miles from Kuala Lumpur, where Europeans were held.

Bill ordered the wireless operator to send a signal requesting permission to enter the camp.

'What the hell are you doing that for?' the American major demanded.

'Orders – HQ has to send us a signal before we can go in.'

'To hell with that. Men could be dying while you ask your CO's permission. Those guys in Changi looked like the living dead – we weren't a moment too soon. Get going.'

With reluctance, Bill ordered James to take twenty men, find the camp and liberate it and he set off in a Japanese truck whose markings had been obliterated with paint that was still wet.

They drove on dirt roads for half a day looking for the camp, finding it at last at the end of the afternoon, a stone's throw from the main Kuala Lumpur to Singapore railway line. James ordered his men to form a column and they advanced on the raw concrete perimeter fence, the Gurkhas' footsteps resounding behind him with emphatic, parade-ground precision.

The gate opened at their approach, and the stocky Japanese commandant marched out, his sword already held before him. Drawn up behind him were sixteen soldiers. By his side was a skeletal Englishman, wearing only wire-rimmed spectacles and ragged shorts that had once been white.

'Captain Twyford, Royal Navy.' They saluted.

'Captain Bourton. How many men are there here?'

'One hundred and eighty-two British, seventy-five other Euro-peans, two hundred and eleven Asiatics.'

The sun was obliterated by low, dark clouds, which produced a lowering, premature twilight. It had already rained heavily that day, and a thick stratum of white steam was rising from the jungle-covered hillsides. James ordered the Japanese to be confined in one of the featureless, tin-roofed buildings, posted guards and set about assessing the camp's requirements.

'This was a transit camp,' Twyford explained. 'Men were billeted here on their way north to the labour-camps, or on their way back. The only ones who stayed behind were so far gone the medics reckoned they wouldn't finish the journey. They didn't last long, most of them. After a while the Japs agreed to let us have a permanent medical team, which is how I ended up here. MO, you see.'

They found a room which contained unopened Red Cross mail dating back to 1942; beneath the pile of cards was a cache of medical and food supplies, which James ordered to be distributed at once. He radioed Bill, giving him the numbers of internees and Japanese, and requesting more food and disinfectant. 'And quicklime, if you can get it,' he said. 'They've been cremating the dead but it's rained so much there's no dry fuel. We've got half-a-dozen to bury, I've got the men digging graves, but there's only about four feet of earth before we reach bedrock.'

Twyford brought him the list of internees who had passed through the camp, methodically divided into army and civilian, British, European and Asiatic, living and dead. In every division the list of the dead was four or five times longer than that of the living.

'We checked our list against the records in the main camps,' he explained. 'It was damn difficult to keep track. You'd see a division on the way north come through in eight trains, then a few months later they'd only need two trains to take what was left of them back. If a camp was hit by cholera, men would be dying so fast there'd be no one to record their names. Unless a man's mates survived to remember him, we'd lose all trace of him.' He talked on, explaining the minutiae of the sad task with which he had filled his time for two years. When Twyford had gone, James started to read through the list, written in pencil in Twyford's meticulous, clerk's handwriting on several different qualities of paper.

'Rawlins, G. A., Capt.,' he read at last. The record showed that Gerald had travelled north with his battalion in April 1943. The only other observation beside his name read: 'Dec'd Burma railway? 1944.' In his mind's eye James tried to imagine Gerald, emaciated, half-naked, his honest eyes staring in his fleshless face like those of the other men in this isolated pocket of hell. His own robust limbs reproached him. He felt ashamed.

'Douglas Lovell, C. Major.' That name was a recent entry. The old estate manager had travelled north with the last group of prisoners to be sent from Changi. James gathered up the papers and went to find Twyford in his makeshift dispensary, sorting through the newly opened Red Cross supplies of drugs with the help of two Indians.

'I know this man – I worked under him before the war. Is he still here? There's nothing written against his name.'

'He'll be next door.' Twyford handed one of his orderlies a large, blue paper packet of lint dressings. 'The last lot who came through were in terrible shape – all old and sick. They weren't fit to travel, but the Japs were getting desperate and sending out anyone who could hold a shovel. Here,' he indicated to the Indians that they should continue the unpacking, 'I'll show you.'

They found the old man in the adjoining hospital building, lying on the rusty remains of an iron bed without a mattress. The once vigorous, commanding figure was a shrivelled carcass whose breath came slowly and noisily from its sunken mouth. Twyford left him; James, now accustomed to squat instead of sit, watched beside the dying man in silence.

'Can you do anything for him?' he asked one of the Indians who appeared with some of the new supplies and began dabbing red sulphonamide on another patient's ulcerated legs.

'There would be no point, sir. We were very surprised he did not die last night.'

'What's he dying of?'

'Everything, sir. It's no good for a man of his age to do hard work and eat bad food. They had no drugs also. We needed this,' he gestured with the swab of antiseptic, 'months ago but there was nothing. Nothing to buy even if we had money. He was a strong man, sir. Very strong heart. His men told us he had cholera and survived. This is a malarial seizure, Captain Twyford says.'

'I knew him, before the war. I'd like to sit with him for a little while.'

'Yes, sir.'

James put his hand on the wrist, as thin as a bundle of sticks, and felt for a pulse. It was weak and halting. Tears pricked painfully at James's eyes and he let them fall.

Later it grew dark; the orderly brought in a hissing kerosene lamp and James watched the cloud of insects circulate around it, making faint sounds as they collided with the hot glass. In the deep stillness of night, he registered the moment at which the faint breath and the fluttering pulse stopped. James leaned over to listen for the heartbeat, retching with disgust at the smell of the body. The old man was dead.

James got up and left the building. He walked out of the camp gates, his mind numb. In the deepest night the jungle was nearly silent. All he could hear was a few churring insects and water dripping quietly from a million leaves, trickling in a thousand hidden channels.

That was all he ought to have heard. James's acute sense of hearing registered something else, he hardly knew what, something stealthy and metallic. Into his mind flashed the equation a more experienced man would have computed instantly – five hundred internees, hundreds more in transit, and they had found only a handful of Japanese.

James ran back to the gates, yelling to the guards to close them as the first shots rang out. The firing settled quickly into a regular pattern and bullets ricocheted off the camp's blank concrete walls.

Part of his mind registered with relief that he could hear only rifle fire, no heavy guns or even a machine gun. In a blind panic James tore into the hut where his men were billeted and roused them. The Gurkhas had slept in their clothes and, as the small, round-faced men snatched up their weapons and darted into positions along the concrete perimeter fence, he blessed the fact that they were seasoned troops from the finest fighting race in the world.

'Lights!' he ordered. 'Get the generator going!' Within a few moments there was a groan as the camp's primitive dynamo began to turn, and weak yellow illumination flooded the railway track. Half a dozen Japanese soldiers on the far side of the line hit the ground and crawled rapidly back into the cover of the vegetation beyond the embankment.

The Japanese outside the gates fired a ragged crackle of shots which died away as the defenders turned on the powerful searchlights mounted on the camp's two watchtowers. Without being ordered, the radio operator was calling their base.

'They're sending up reinforcements, sir,' he told James, who nodded, thinking with dismay of the hours it had taken him to find the camp in daylight, and wondering how long the relief force would take to trace them, travelling along the winding jungle tracks in the dark.

Twyford appeared at the door of his dispensary, a puzzled expression on his hollow-cheeked face.

James barked, 'Get the arms store open and issue weapons to every man who's fit to fire a gun. Hurry, man!'

'What's happening?' The Medical Officer was plainly confused. 'The Japanese can't attack us, they've surrendered.'

'Go out there and tell 'em, why don't you?' In panic and desperation, James was looking for a scapegoat for his own inexperience. He pushed Twyford's gaunt frame backwards with an accusing finger. 'You let us march into an ambush, you bloody fool,' he snarled. 'Why didn't you tell me the Japanese numbers? Didn't you realize what they were up to?'

'They all marched off yesterday,' Twyford made a feeble gesture with his stick-like arms. 'There were a couple of hundred of them. We thought they'd be going into K. L. to lay down their arms.'

'Well that was the last thing on their minds, by the sounds of it. What arms have they got?'

The exhausted man shook his head helplessly. 'I don't know, rifles . . . small arms. We've seen nothing big. Maybe they've got some explosives.'

'Let's hope you're right – then we can hold them off for a few hours.'

They could see nothing beyond the harsh glare of the camp lights, beyond which the jungle lay in darkness. There was no more shooting and the handful of soldiers waiting with weapons ready and fingers on their triggers shifted nervously in silence.

James decided to order the lights to be shut down, hoping to draw the enemy out into the open. Clouds covered the moon, and in the darkness he strained his ears to catch the smallest sound of men moving outside the camp's walls.

Suddenly there was screaming and some gunfire from the Japanese. Immediately light flooded the area once more and James's men fired rapidly, killing two of the enemy who had been tempted out under cover of the dark. One Japanese succeeded in hurling a grenade over the wall, but it fell in the centre of the parade-ground and exploded harmlessly.

Silence returned and they waited. James ordered the lights to be kept on, knowing the enemy would not fall for the same trick twice. There was a sudden crash of breaking wood, and an uproar of voices as the seventeen Japanese imprisoned in the camp broke out of the building where they were held and ran howling forward across the parade ground to attack the soldiers with their bare hands. His Gurkhas shot them down before James could even take aim with his pistol.

An hour later, the noise of a vehicle engine ripped apart the quietness and an armoured car tore down the road, skidding and floundering on the irregular muddy surface, firing rapidly as it accelerated towards the gate. James's men opened fire. The vehicle began to weave crazily from side to side, bucking over the deep ruts until the driver lost control and it shot off the roadway and overturned. An instant later it exploded, and shreds of metal sliced the air.

'Suicide squad,' James muttered to himself, blinking to keep his eyes straining past the glare of the burning car and into the dark jungle, searching for signs of another attack. He tried to put himself in the Japanese commander's position and guess what his enemy would do next, but his mind was crazed with fear and exhaustion, and could produce no coherent idea.

The night wore on, the silence filled by the mechanical pounding of the generator. James barely moved. At length he heard the jungle insects begin their insistent chorus, and the first rounded notes of the gibbons calling in the forest canopy fell like bubbles of soft sound through the shrill cacophony. The black sky lightened imperceptibly to the east.

As dawn approached there were new sounds, a distant, muffled thud of gunfire which grew louder and closer, then ceased. There was a far-away roar of vehicles. Then there was silence. At last, to his immense relief, James saw a truck like his own bumping slowly towards the camp on the rutted dirt road. There were others behind it, and as they advanced James saw that they were crammed with armed men.

'Thank God, you got here in time,' he said to the American major.

'We've been on the road all night. I knew you had trouble the minute you told us there were only a few Japs in this place. There must have been more. They had to be planning an ambush. We tried to raise you on the radio, but there was no answer, so we figured they'd attacked you already. You did well to hold them off, boy.'

'What . . . was that . . .' James suddenly felt a blanket of exhaustion envelop him.

The American clapped his shoulder in reassurance. 'We got them, sure. Just as the sun came up we ran straight into them back on the road there. They weren't expecting anything to come down that track. A few of them tried to put up a fight but when they realized how many of us there were they just threw down their arms. It's all over.'

James was suddenly aware of a pain like a bruise in his chest, and a dry taste in his mouth reminding him of the dentist. His tongue was sticky with blood.

'Is there a doctor can take a look at you?' He heard the American ask, then sinewy arms caught him as he fell forwards into blackness.

Although it always seemed to him afterwards that the night had been a confusing, inconsequential sequence of events, which had made no more sense than a hallucination, the citation for his decoration insisted that Captain James Bourton had courageously remained at his post and commanded his men with two broken ribs and a punctured lung. He had held off two hundred attacking Japanese, with a loss of only one of his own men.

Inwardly, James felt himself to be a sham. He recalled his panic and disorientation clearly and they did not correspond to his idea of heroic behaviour. He had no recollection whatsoever of the shot that wounded him. But when Bill came to his hospital bedside in Singapore with news of the decoration, he did not voice his doubts, judging it better to be a phoney hero than an outright failure.

'We're going to London,' Bill told him, looking out of the hospital window at what had once been a garden; the muddy ground was covered with row upon row of tents where sick and wounded men had been treated. The troops were moving out now, and the rain-streaked canvas flapped heavily in the wind over deserted ground. 'Then we'll be demobbed. Jesus, you look strange now you're a white man again.'

James nodded and grinned as he rubbed his pale face from which all trace of the drug's brown tint had faded. In the hospital he had even lost his normal weatherbeaten suntan. 'It gives me a shock when I look in the mirror,' he admitted. 'What are you going to do when the army's finished with you, Bill?'

'What am *I* going to do? Come back, quick as I can. No offence, but I don't want to stay in good old England longer than I have to. Can't stand the climate. I'll see if I can get my old job in Perak again, or something else. There's bound to be a use for a guy with my background somewhere in this country. More important, what are *you* going to do?'

'Live off the family for a bit, I suppose.' James was never in the habit of thinking very far ahead, and had passed his weeks in the hospital in a pleasant mental limbo. 'It'll be strange to come home after all these years.'

The Australian eyed him with anger and resignation through his new, steel-framed spectacles. 'What about the woman, Jim?'

'What woman?'

'The woman you married. You remember you married some woman in Kechil? You remember you've got a kid?'

'Of course I remember.' James fidgeted, feeling uncomfortable under his friend's hard stare. The truth was that he had not thought of Khatijah or their child at all for weeks. 'I'll send her some money, she'll have nothing to worry about. That sort of native girl can always get herself a new husband when it suits her.'

'Suppose she's sitting there pining, waiting for you to come marching back down the road to take her away with you.'

'Don't talk soft – more likely she's got a new boyfriend and they've already been down to the mosque to get her divorce all fixed.' James propped the telegram containing the news of his decoration against the empty waterglass on the table beside his bed and looked at it with satisfaction. 'We never fooled those peasants for a minute, you know. They only helped us because they wanted to come out on the winning side and they knew they were on to a good thing. And they were right – the whole village would have starved if it hadn't been for our money. They knew we'd leave when the war ended.'

A month later the ribs were still painful. James lowered himself into the narrow seat in the Dakota and winced. Out of the window, he saw the jungle-covered hills of Malaya slipping away below, the crown of each forest tree distinct even from the aeroplane's height. The sea sparkled in shades of turquoise, then the black expanse of Sumatra appeared and he sat back.

'Where are you going?' Beside him, a Flight Lieutenant held out a cigarette case.

'London. Thanks. And you?'

'Colombo. Looking forward to going home?'

James nodded uncertainly. 'Haven't really thought about it.'

'Wish I was in your shoes.' His companion put away his cigarettes and brought out a wallet. From it he took a photograph, neatly wrapped in cellophane, of a woman and a boy. 'Haven't seen Junior here since I took that. He's in long trousers now, the wife says. You got family?'

'My father's very ill. I got a letter just a couple of days ago.'

'Sorry to hear that. And kids?'

'No – I'm not married.' James spoke the truth, as he saw it. He did not regard a liaison with a woman of another race, contracted under a heathen religion, as having any genuine status.

'Well, you'll be able to take your pick now, old boy.' The other man gave the photograph a last look before replacing it in his worn, black leather wallet. James suddenly felt lonely. Ahead of him lay England, his family, his social position and the emotional desert laid waste by his mother. Behind him, although he had stifled the memory, he knew he was leaving a woman to whom he meant the whole world. And a child – nothing but an inanimate bundle, but a new life which he had created. When he thought of them he had an awesome sense that the child, the accidental product of his gratified carnal appetite, was the finest creation of his life.

CHAPTER NINETEEN

'IKNOW I should *not* be saying this, My Lady.' In the nursery at Coseley, a spacious low-ceilinged room with a view out to the park which was half-obscured by the grey-stone colonnade which decorated the upper storey of the house, Nanny Barbara spoke to Cathy with embarrassment, as she finished getting Jamie ready for his pony ride. 'I do think it's a terrible shame you can't have Jamie with you. The poor mite just pines for you all the week. And your face is a sight to behold on a Friday when you go up to kiss him goodnight. I think that judge was very hard on the both of you.'

Cathy sighed. 'I know, Nanny. But at least Jamie's here and I can see him at weekends – his father might have wanted to take him off to New York now that he's married again.'

'I suppose it is a mercy that he didn't. My Lady.' She brushed the child's glossy dark hair, which was cut very short in an old-fashioned style, and carefully put on his hard, black velvet riding hat. 'But Jamie cries as if his little heart was breaking every single week after you've gone.'

'No I don't, Mummy. I'm very brave, I never cry. Nanny's telling fibs.' Jamie turned and hugged Cathy around the knees, his vivid blue eyes pleading for her to believe him. 'Nanny, you're horrible. You promised you'd never tell.'

Cathy picked up her son and hugged him, feeling a miserable wrench of frustration. The truth was that she also wept at every parting, and struggled through week after dreary week behind her typewriter at the Migatto Group offices living for the moment when she would again be able to feel Jamie's small arms clutching her happily around the neck.

'I'm glad Nanny told me, darling. I miss you, too, you know. Come on, let's go and find your pony now – he must have been waiting for ages.'

'But can I come and live with you soon, Mummy?'

'I hope so, darling. But you wouldn't be able to have your pony in London, would you?'

'Yes I would.'

'But where would you keep him?'

'I'd keep him . . .' the sooty smudges of his eyebrows raised as the little boy tried to think. 'I know where – I'd keep him in my room with my toys. I'd get a special big box for him and he could have breakfast with me every morning.' He chattered on eagerly as Cathy exchanged a sad smile with Nanny Barbara and led her son downstairs and off to the stables, where his black Shetland pony was irritably trying to chew its halter.

She lifted him on to the felt child's saddle, settled his legs in their diminutive jodhpurs around the pony's barrel-shaped sides, shortened the stirrup leathers and led the pony and rider off for a lonely walk around the estate. The splendour of the house and grounds oppressed her, and made her feel hopeless. How could she ever hope to give her son a good life when he was accustomed to so much luxury and all she could claim in the way of wealth were a puny salary and an apartment so small and grim that she felt as if she were living in a pair of upended coffins.

It was February and the grass had a greyish, exhausted look. A cutting wind swept across the Coseley estate from the chalk downs to the west. Cathy wondered if she would ever stop feeling guilty for the few moments of weakness that had made it possible for the divorce court to take her son away from her. She hated to feel guilty, not only because it was painful, but because it was a waste of her emotional energy.

Encouraged by Lord Shrewton, she spent every weekend at Coseley with Jamie. The Marchioness was charming to her now that she no longer had a place in Charlie's affections, and since Cathy had never discovered that the scheming woman had played a part in breaking up her marriage, she enjoyed a pleasant friendship with both the parents of her former husband. Charlie seemed to have no plans to return to England.

Monday morning was always the worst, because after spending the weekend at Coseley with Jamie the pain of parting was still fresh. The joy of loving her son was the only happiness she had and every time she had to leave him she felt as if she were leaving her whole self behind with him.

The hard facts were that Cathy's apartment consisted of only two rooms, and, as a secretary, Cathy hardly earned more than Nanny Barbara, given that the nanny's board and lodging were free.

'I've got to get them to promote me,' she told Monty, as she finished basting the hem of a blue-and-white print dress she was making. She stabbed her needle into the fabric and snatched it out again so angrily that it made little clicking noises at every stitch. 'It's maddening to work with all those men, and know that they aren't any smarter than me, and know that they're earning ten times what I make, even though Lord Shrewton's overpaying me for what I do.'

'What have these guys got that you haven't?' Monty asked, handing her the scissors. Seeing her sister once more making her own dresses out of necessity, she felt awkward in her own lavish clothes. It was so easy to forget how other people lived now that Rick was a big star and they never seemed to go anywhere except by Rolls

Royce or private jet. She twitched the wide lapels of her kingfisher-blue St Laurent satin blazer and wished she'd chosen something less ostentatious.

'The guys have got exams, degrees, old school ties . . . though, now I think of it, some of them haven't got any of those things. My boss is always saying that some of the traders are nothing but East End barrowboys.' She finished stitching and moved to the ironing board to press the garment. 'Clever old Monty – you're quite right. If they can do it, I can.'

'But why the City, Cathy? Wouldn't it be easier doing something like private catering, cooking boardroom lunches and all that?'

'Oh yes, it would be *easier*,' Cathy's voice was harsh as she shook out the finished dress and held it up against her shoulders to show Monty how it looked. 'It would be as easy as anything to make a living cooking, or sewing, or looking after children – but that's all I'd make, a living. This apartment block's full of gallant little divorcees like me, scraping together a few pounds every week out of cooking boardroom lunches and hoping they'll get married again pretty damn quick. Don't you understand, Monty, I need to make *money*, real money, big money, because that's what it will cost to make a home for Jamie. And the place to make real money is the City. All I need is the first break.'

Cathy spoke with more confidence than she felt. The City, she knew well, was like a very large gentlemen's club which took pride in having no plans to admit women members. Thanks to her father, Cathy understood the unwritten rules very well, but changing them seemed an awesome task.

Everything about the building occupied by the Migatto Group impressed three cardinal qualities upon the visitor – prosperity, stability and masculinity. The hallway through which Cathy walked four or more times every day had massive porphyry columns, a marble floor checkered in black and grey and dark oak panelling with carved fruit embellishments by Grinling Gibbons.

The commissionaire attended to a large board telling visitors whether the director and executives in the Migatto companies were in or not. The names had one of three prefixes – Lord, Sir or Mr.

Over the unused fireplace in the hallway hung a portrait of the founder, Samuel Migatto, in a beaver coat and a close-fitting black bonnet with flaps over his ears. He had a white beard, a shrewd eye and a hooked nose which the artist had highlighted.

The portrait dated from the late seventeenth century, when Solomon Migatto first appeared in the meticulous records of London trade. Below his portrait was a facsimile of the page of the Cash and Commerce Journal of the East India Company which registered his debut. Transaction number 309 at the end of *Januarie, Anno 1690*, showed that Samuel paid £7 for the privilege of importing 80 ounces of gold into London.

More portraits of men lined the grey-stone staircase. The higher Cathy climbed, the shabbier the building became. Carved oak gave way to mahogany, which in turn was replaced by teak-veneer doors and polystyrene ceiling-tiles at the top floor, where Cathy shared an office with one other secretary. Miss Finch. Miss Finch was a brisk little spinster with protruding teeth and white hair who reminded Cathy of a West Highland terrier. She worked for a senior director on the second floor.

Cathy's boss, Mr M. J. Gibson-Wright, had an office next to hers, indicating his lowly position in the pecking order.

'My dear, you have been sent to work for a dinosaur,' he told her on her first day. 'By rights I should have faded away three or four years ago, after the last take-over. I frequently leave my brains in my hip pocket, as you will discover. I'm still here because it will be cheaper to let me die than to sack me. Now, where shall we go for lunch – do you like fish?'

His hair was white at the temples and grey over the top, so he looked like a dapper seagull. Mr Gibson-Wright had the perceptible flush of good living, and a combination of age, obesity and arthritis caused him to waddle as he walked. He looked at Cathy and saw a thin, intense girl with haunted eyes and a slight limp, who could, he thought, have been quite a beauty if she were not so steeped in unhappiness.

'I want you to call me G. W. – everybody else does.' He smiled at her approvingly over the silver-plated cruets. The restaurant was decorated in exactly the same ponderous style as the Migatto building, with a lot of dark wood and gilt-framed portraiture. 'What would you say to the potted shrimps?'

'I'm afraid my typing's a little rusty.' Cathy told him with anxiety. 'But I've been practising my shorthand and I'm sure I'll be able . . .'

He waved a glass of pale sherry at her to silence her. 'As far as I am concerned, my dear, your abilities are of no consequence. What I need is someone to buy my cigars, show me which bit of the paper to read, book my table for lunch and put me in my car at the end of the day – if not sooner. Apart from that, your most important duty is to allow no one to disturb me when I am asleep. I take a little nap in the afternoons.'

Cathy's face fell as she realized that there was no hope whatever that these trivial duties would lead her on to better things. Dutifully, she bought his cigars, made his bookings and marked his *Financial Times* every morning, highlighting the passages she thought he ought to read. G. W. took her to lunch several times a week, and told her indiscreet stories about the other men in the restaurant. There were no other women in the restaurants at all, except the waitresses.

Another burden from which Cathy could not escape was her grandmother, who relentlessly put her on the committees of her charity balls and pushed her into the arms of one prospective husband after another, while nagging her endlessly about her deteriorating appearance.

'You can't pine over Charlie for the rest of your life,' advised Lady Davina, oblivious of the fact that Cathy never spoke of her former husband because the only thing she could think of to say about him was that he was a pitiful apology for a human being and, but for Jamie, she wished she had never set eyes on him. 'It's the same for all of us, you know. Girls become women but every man remains a little boy. He was simply bound to lose interest in you once you were married. That's the trick of marriage, you see, dear. Keeping the mystery. Next time, remember that.'

'There isn't going to be a next time, Didi.'

'Nonsense!' the old woman dismissed Cathy's opinion with a wave of her arm and a clash of her bracelets. 'You say that now but you'll soon find life is quite impossible without a husband.'

As much to deflect Lady Davina's interest as to please herself, Cathy began to date Rupert Lampeter, Charlie's one-time polo buddy and best man, the most personable of the small herd of her ex-husband's friends who gathered around her, as soon as she was divorced, hoping to be infected with the Coseley glamour.

Rupert entertained her. He was completely frivolous and largely uninterested in the boutique, the record company, the three restaurants and the property company in which his inheritance was rapidly trickling away. Tall, athletic, beautifully dressed, well-mannered, with wavy, pale blond hair and grey eyes, Rupert was also convinced that no scheming woman would ever entrap him into matrimony, which Cathy found reassuring. He flirted with her exuberantly and she felt herself bloom with his admiration.

Confidently, Rupert drove her home to Battersea one night, parked his little blue Mercedes under the leafy canopy of the plane trees, put his arm delicately around her shoulders and brushed her lips with his. Cathy instantly felt a wave of revulsion so violent that she thought she was going to be sick. Her body seemed to turn icy cold. A clammy film of sweat coated her skin and her arms, which were tentatively returning Rupert's embrace, started to tremble.

'Steady,' he murmured, sensing her strange reaction. 'Poor little girl, you *are* in a state, aren't you? Better take it easy, eh?'

After two weeks, however, things were no better. Rupert was gentle, patient, humorous and desirable, but Cathy could feel nothing but acute physical distress in his arms. Sometimes it seemed as if every individual cell of her body was struggling to escape from the touch of a man.

'It's as if someone's playing some awful joke on me,' she confided to Monty in despair. Rick and Monty had moved into a stucco-fronted house close to the Thames in Chelsea, and Cathy was helping her sister hang her cases full of multicoloured clothes in the dressing room. 'Rupert's perfect, everything I could want in a man; he's far, far kinder than Charlie.' She handed Monty a chamois-leather

Minnehaha dress embroidered with beads. 'I can't tell you how sweet and patient he's been. But as soon as he touches me, I freeze. It's horrible.'

'Do you fancy him?' Monty demanded, stepping over five pairs of high-heeled boots which she had bought but never worn.

'Yes. I think I fancy him, anyway; he's good-looking and funny and I like his aftershave. What else is there?' Perhaps it was the bad light in the cramped room, but Cathy's speckled brown eyes seemed dull and unresponsive.

'Oh not much – feeling your heart jump when you see him, and your insides melt when you touch him and not being able to think about anything else for hours . . . you can *think* you fancy someone, you know.'

Cathy's mobile upper lip twisted with contempt. 'That's little girl hearts-and-flowers stuff. Do you feel that way about Rick?'

Monty paused with her arms full of her vivid chiffon stage dresses, trying to decide whether to hang them apart from her street clothes or not. The truth was that she cared for Rick, she felt fiercely protective of his vulnerability and insecurity, she liked making love with him, and sometimes it felt as if they fitted together like two halves of a single being, but she never felt on Rick's account any of the sensations she had described to Cathy.

'Yes, maybe you're right. Maybe it's only like that the first time and after that, everything else is just . . . toothpaste. 'Monty sighed, feeling much more than her twenty-two years. 'Perhaps your body's being wiser than your mind,' Monty suggested to her sister, finally closing the closet doors on her wardrobe. 'Charlie must have really fucked up your head – perhaps you just aren't ready to love anyone else yet.'

'Yes, perhaps,' Cathy answered doubtfully. 'Do you think I've become frigid, Monty?' She could hardly say the word. Being frigid somehow meant being disqualified from being a woman.

'No, of course not,' Monty reassured her sister at once with a warm hug. 'You just need time to adjust, time to heal, that's all.'

Within herself, Cathy was not reassured. Now that she had experienced sexual repulsion, she noticed how many other areas of her life no longer gave her joy. She was uninterested in clothes, unable to taste food very well, unmoved by beauty in man, woman or art, easily bored and almost unable to laugh at things she knew she ought to have found funny. Every sensual faculty she possessed seemed to be frozen.

The man who finally rescued her from this bleak emotional prison was her boss. Although Cathy presumed that she had been assigned a valetudinarian failure on account of her lack of secretarial skill, Lord Shrewton had deliberately sent her to Mr Gibson-Wright's office in the hope that the old man's ingrained benevolence would find a way to revive her wounded spirit.

'You seem quite intelligent to me,' he told her one day in tones of mild amazement. 'Your father-in-law warned me you'd lost your marbles when young Charlie kicked over the traces. I thought any woman who took on young Coseley would need her head examined. Whatever did you do it for?'

'I was in love with him,' she said.

'Next best thing to being out of your mind, I suppose.'

She giggled, feeling the muscles in her cheeks, long accustomed to disuse, stretch around her smile.

'Don't laugh at my jokes, for heaven's sake. They'll all think you're the new popsy and I'll get no peace at home after that.'

In her first three months at work Cathy typed just seven letters for G. W. Miss Finch suggested that she reorganize the filing room. Cathy suggested that she should instead relieve Miss Finch of the job of taking the minutes of the company's board meetings, but the older woman angrily refused. However, she then fell ill. Cathy was asked to take over her work, and when Miss Finch recovered and returned she found that Cathy had laid a firm claim to her most important function, and negotiated a small raise in salary in consequence.

Every Thursday, a woman identical to Miss Finch came up from the Accounts Department with a tray full of brown-paper envelopes and handed both of them a pay packet. Miss Finch snickered with disapproval at this point, making it clear she did not think Cathy deserved her pay.

'Wages!' G. W. trundled into the office as the accounts clerk was leaving. 'Let's see what they're paying you for putting up with me – hmph! How long will it take you to get a new frock out of *that,* I wonder? Come into my office.'

She followed him along the threadbare carpet.

'I wish they'd give you a decent office,' she said, looking round at the plain little room.

'Badge of rank, dear girl. They've demoted me, this is all I'm entitled to. When it's your turn, never be humble about the inessentials. Women always think status symbols are pretentious – they're not. Badge of rank.'

'What do you mean, when it's my turn?' Cathy sat on the ragged leather couch where G. W. took his afternoon siesta. The room had no chair for a visitor.

G. W. plumped down in his chair. 'You've got twice the guts of most of the men in this building, and twice the brains. You may be hibernating now, young lady, but the day is at hand when you are going to want to use your abilities – and I'm going to show you how to start. Now give me your wages.'

Cathy handed over the envelope and he tore it open with clumsy, old fingers. 'Twenty-four pounds, eh? And two shillings. There's the four pounds, that's your bus fares.' He shoved the notes into her hand, then picked up a telephone.

'We can't open an account for you at my brokers until you've got a bit more to play with, so I'll do your buying for you at first. Now what we want, if we're going to make money by Tuesday, is something fairly lively . . .' He glanced keenly down the list of share prices.

'But that's playing the stock market – I can't do that with my wages,' Cathy protested.

'You don't *play* the stock market,' he corrected her, mimicking her disapproving tone. 'You *play* Monopoly, which is much more risky. You *invest* in the stock market. Now take this . . .' he put a coin in her hand, 'and toss it. Heads we'll go for gold, tails for Fraser's Hill.' The coin came down tails and G. W. telephoned his broker.

That weekend she impatiently scanned the share prices in the newspapers. Fraser's Hill, an Australian mining company, leapt up almost two shillings in two days.

'You've made just over £7,' G. W. told her on Tuesday morning. 'So here's your wages back,' more notes fluttered across his desk. 'Now, shall we take your profit, stick with it, or what?'

Cathy considered. 'If we'd put it in gold we'd have done better . . .' she ventured, picking at the hem of her navy-blue crêpe dress; years with Charlie had made her wary of the consequences of questioning a man's judgement.

'Well done. Yes, we would. Want to switch?'

'Yes,' she decided. 'Fraser's Hill is really overpriced.'

'Broker's commission will knock your profit down, of course . . .'

G. W. made a tent with his fingertips and watched her indulgently.

'Shall we stay where we are, then?'

'It's your money, my dear.'

'OK, let's stay.' Cathy looked more happy than she had at any time in the months since she had first entered the Migatto building. G. W. thought it odd that a young girl should bloom because she was making money, and only look wretched if she were wined, dined and paid compliments, but in the weeks that followed there was no denying the lightness of her step and the smile on her lips, the way the sheen on her hair returned and her complexion became ripe olive instead of a dull yellow, the fact that she grew bored with her demure print dresses and bought a bright-red wool frock instead. Little by little he introduced her to other markets – commodities, currencies and metals – and she almost always made a profit, except when she decided on a property company which immediately went bust.

'Could you have told me it was going to do that?' she asked G. W.

'Yes, my dear, I could. I got a whisper at the bar in the Athenaeum last week. That'll be a problem for you, of course. It's not only who you know that's important in the City, it's what you know, who tells you, how close they are to the action and how up-to-date the information is. Never forget, money is only information in motion. I've made thousands over lunch when things were moving fast. *You*, my dear, can't stand at the bar at the Athenaeum,' he said in tones of gentle regret. Then he looked at the gold watch which lived in his waistcoat pocket, its thick Georgian chain festooned across his stomach. 'Now where shall we go for lunch?'

Miss Finch was by now in a permanent, hostile sulk.

'She thinks I'm gambling my money away,' Cathy told G. W. as she helped him into his car as they returned from lunch. 'She keeps saying "a penny saved is a penny earned" and telling me about her pension.'

'Typical female attitude. Can't see beyond the end of the housekeeping money. Vision! Imagination! Courage! That's the stuff millionaires are made of!'

This seemed the perfect moment to show her hand. 'G. W., will you help me?' He beamed at her with satisfaction.

'What with, my dear?'

'To leave you?'

'Ah, women – they always leave me in the end,' he joked.

'I'm sick of being a secretary. I desperately need to make money, G. W., so I can apply for custody of my son. I need a real job, a career.'

His watery eyes looked startled. 'What – you mean, a career in the City?'

'Yes.' Cathy smiled hopefully.

'Good heavens. Well, why not? A few women have done it. But why ask me? Why not ask Lord Shrewton?'

'Of course I could, and he'd probably find me something, but he'd be doing it out of kindness and feeling guilty and because it would be embarrassing for him to have to refuse me. And everyone would resent me, and I'd never get promoted on my own merit because they'd think I was just the boss's daughter-in-law.'

'I see you've given it some thought. Well now, let's see. You're quick-thinking, good with numbers, cool in a crisis – maybe they should try you down in Metals. These young metal traders make a pile if they're any good. But it's a gift, having the right temperament. You'll soon find out if you aren't any good. But if you want quick money, the Metal Exchange is the place.' He appraised her thoughtfully, getting accustomed to the idea that she was serious. 'I'll have word with Henry Rose who runs the dealing room tomorrow.'

They walked back to their office around the handsome sweep of Finsbury Circus, enjoying the summer sunshine. In the little white-painted bandstand in the gardens a brass ensemble was playing a cheerful medley of tunes from *The Mikado*. For the first time in a very long while, Cathy felt happy.

As usual after lunch, G. W. was pleasantly drunk but not quite so far gone that he needed help up the stairs. He waved his cigar at the portrait of Samuel Migatto. 'He never had a pension, did he? In his day, you could buy your gold and never

know if you'd lose it to the Spanish Armada or the Barbary pirates the next week!'
His free hand grabbed inaccurately at the banister rail.

'Make no mistake, my girl. If it weren't for Jewish bankers, there'd be no English
history to learn!' He paused for breath on the second-floor landing. 'Bonnie Prince
Charlie was seen off by a British army paid by a Migatto loan. Napoleon cost this country 400 million pounds, most of it found right here in the City by Jews and Quakers!'

With a sigh of relief G. W. reached the top floor and headed for his office.
Cathy opened the door and helped him take off his jacket. 'Money's nothing to do
with housekeeping and your pension. If you'd been taught history properly, dear
girl, you'd have realized that. Money's about power and freedom and the future.'
His eyelids closed blissfully and in a few seconds he was asleep. Cathy took off his
shoes and tiptoed back to her office to while away the time until 4.30, when she
would make G. W. his tea and call his chauffeur to take him home.

The next day she arrived at the Migatto building to find Miss Finch bustling in
and out of G. W.'s office.

'It's all over,' she announced, 'he died at home last night. Merciful release.
You're to help me clear the room and then you'll be working downstairs for young
Mr Migatto and Mr Mainwaring.'

Sadly, Cathy collected her belongings from her desk, and packed the small collection of Mr Gibson-Wright's personal things into a crate ready to be taken away
by his family. She felt sad again, not only because she had lost the amiable, kind-
hearted old man who she had hoped would be her mentor, but because she knew
that without him it would be that much more difficult to break out from behind
her typewriter.

Mr Migatto, a fifteenth-generation descendant of Samuel, was a Conservative
Member of Parliament who very seldom appeared in the office. Mr Mainwaring
was bald and self- important. He patted her bottom on every possible occasion and
Cathy started opening doors for herself whenever she could, to avoid giving him an
excuse to get close enough to touch her.

Like G. W., Mr Mainwaring did very little work. He also took her to lunch.

'My wife and I have led separate lives for some years,' he announced on the
first occasion.

'My position involves a considerable amount of entertaining,' he said the second time. 'Do you go out much at all, in the evening?'

'Quite a lot.' This was a lie, told to repel the man. Since Rupert had regretfully
drifted away, Cathy seldom went out except to keep Monty company on evenings
when Rick was out raising hell with Cy.

'The gay divorcee, eh?' She moved her knee just in time to avoid his hand.
Vengefully, Cathy ordered the most expensive dish on the menu. He took this as a
sign of encouragement.

'I'll be off to Brussels on Thursday,' he said, during their third lunch. 'Might stay over the weekend. Nice trip – perhaps you'd care to come?'

'No, thank you,' said Cathy.

'I suppose you think that because you were once married to Lord Shrewton's heir, you can behave how you please.' He glared at her through his heavy spectacles.

'I don't see what my marriage has to do with it,' she said. 'Surely, I can behave how I please whoever I am?'

'If I were you, I wouldn't rely too heavily on your connection with your former husband's family. In my experience such connections mean very little.'

Cathy sipped her wine and tried to think of a way of making Mr Mainwaring leave her alone without making him into an implacable enemy. She wanted very much to tip her bowl of *moules mariniére* down his detestable shirt-front, but restrained the impulse, reminding herself that she intended, somehow or another, to be his equal around a boardroom table one day and it would be foolish to earn his hostility now by humiliating him in public. Already the men at the next table had stopped talking about the prospects for a Conservative victory in the imminent general election and were making small talk while they waited for the confrontation between her and her attacker.

'Tell me something,' she turned the wine bottle round and looked at the label, 'why did you choose this? '62 was the worst year they had since the war. And St Eustache is always on the thin side – that's why it's so cheap.'

Mr Mainwaring looked thunderous. 'You'll find it doesn't pay to get clever with me, young lady. What are you, one of those women's libbers? Burned your bra, have you?'

There was a splutter of smothered laughter from the next table. 'Take care, old boy, this animal bites!' advised a bibulous voice. Its owner was a tall plump man with a young face belied by his sober grey suit and shirt with wide blue stripes. From the many hours she had spent demurely taking minutes in Migatto's boardroom, Cathy recognized him as Henry Rose, a junior director of the firm in the Group which traded in metals and oil, and the man to whom G. W. had promised to speak about a job for her.

Giving Cathy an amiable wink, Rose whistled up a waiter and had the two tables amalgamated, putting an end to the persecution of Cathy for the rest of lunch. They split the bill four ways and Mr Mainwaring slunk away to an appointment which Cathy knew was fictitious, leaving Henry to walk back with her through the narrow City streets.

'Good line, that, about St Eustache. Must remember that. How do you come to know so much about wine?'

'My father taught me.'

'Lucky girl. You must teach me, all I know is how to drink it. You used to work for old G. W. on the top floor, didn't you? Terrible shame – we shall all miss him.'

It's now or never, Cathy told herself. 'I'll miss him, too. As a matter of fact, he promised me he was going to come and see you about me, but I don't suppose he had the chance before he died.'

'Oh? Tell me more.' The expression on his face was frank and friendly. Cathy noticed that he was happy to let her walk on the outside of the pavement, a technical discourtesy to a lady which none of the older men would have permitted themselves. Somehow it made her feel more comfortable. She felt that she was at last out of Lady Davina's sham world where men ruled and women manipulated.

Cathy took a deep breath. 'I'd like to try my luck on the Metal Exchange,' she told him as they approached Migatto's pillared entrance.

He stopped and looked at her in silence for a few moments. 'There's never been a woman on the Metal Exchange before,' he said lightly, 'but why not? It's a pretty tough place – do you think you're up to it?'

'Of course I do, or I wouldn't have asked you.' Damn, Cathy thought, now I've blown it. Why couldn't I have been more tactful? But he did not seem offended.

'Tell me,' he looked her carefully up and down without a hint of lechery, 'were you listening to my conversation in that restaurant while Mainwaring was making an ass of himself?'

Cathy nodded. 'You were talking about the election and you said that if Harold Wilson wasn't thrown out, inflation would hit the sky and the country would be totally washed up.'

He threw back his head and laughed, an uninhibited bellow of jocularity which echoed from the curved facade of Finsbury Circus. 'You didn't miss much, did you?'

'I couldn't help . . .' began Cathy awkwardly as they entered the building and headed for the staircase.

'Don't apologize, that's just what I hoped. You've got the right ear, and the ability to concentrate on two things at once. At least two things at once. That's excellent. The ability to do that's the first thing you need to survive on the Metal Exchange. And you gotta be loud, sharp, quick and confident, good with figures . . .' His voice had slight Cockney nuances, and from other details of his manner and clothing, which for English people amount to an encoded system of class recognition, Cathy placed him socially higher than the barrow boys G. W. spoke about but definitely not from the upper classes, although his gold signet ring and solid gold cufflinks indicated his aspirations.

They paused on the first floor by the double doors to Migatto's dealing-room. Inside she could hear the cacophony of fifty men shouting numbers into telephones.

'And you've got to be super-cool in that mad-house, and that's it, that's all you need.' Henry Rose pushed the dealing-room door open a few inches to let her hear the frantic voices and clatter of activity. 'You don't need breeding or education on the London Metal Exchange. Most of 'em burn out before they're thirty. But there's no rule says you have to be wearing trousers before you go on the floor. Anyone who can do that job, can have it – but if you can't cut it, I'll fire you so fast you won't touch the sides on the way out. What d'you think? Still interested?'

'You're not trying very hard to discourage me.' Cathy tried not to smile too widely, but it was difficult. Henry Rose was appealingly direct. She liked his cynicism, his energy and the fact that he was looking her over in a totally different way to the way any man had appraised her before. She felt herself standing straighter as she talked to him, and sensed the door to her future opening wide.

'Well you've got the primary requirements, including brass bloody nerve,' he told her bluntly. 'Mainwaring won't let you out of his sweaty hands so easily, and he outranks me, as it were, so you'll have to have a word with that ex-father-in-law of yours, get him to lean on the old creep from a great height.'

He was correct. Mr Mainwaring protested in the nastiest terms.

'You girls today, you'll chase anything in trousers. Certainly not. I won't allow it. A girl on the Metal Exchange – ridiculous. Oh, there are a few that've tried it, not a nice sort of girl at all. I know you're just dying to get down there with all those boys and have a good time, aren't you? It's out of the question, my dear. You'll thank me one day.'

So Cathy spoke to Lord Shrewton at Coseley that weekend.

'Young Rose has already had a word with me,' he told her, his pale eyes behind their spectacles glinting with approval. 'One of his better ideas, if you ask me.' This was his idea of a witticism. Lord Shrewton had many fine qualities, but his sense of humour was vestigial.

'Mr Mainwaring says it's out of the question,' Cathy told him.

'It's none of Mr Mainwaring's business, is it?' Lord Shrewton stood with his back to the drawing-room fire, enjoying the heat. 'If Rose has offered you a job you can take it, can't you?'

The next week Henry Rose took her up to Whittington Avenue and into the Metal Exchange building, to the Visitors' Gallery. They looked down on a square, pillared room with a grimy skylight above a circle of worn, red leather benches which was pierced by four gangways.

'That's the Ring,' he explained. 'Thirty-six places, one for a dealer from each of the member firms. We trade the base metals – copper, tin, lead, zinc, silver, aluminium, and nickel. Each metal is traded for five minutes at a time. You can tell which metal is being traded by the symbol on the board up there.' He pointed to a display of signs above the calendar on the wall opposite them. 'The mid-day session is just starting.'

With a quiet bustle the room began to fill up with men – young men, mostly, wearing light-grey suits or dark-grey suits. Some had wide ties, some had narrow ties. Some had long hair, one or two were balding. Most of them had small note-books, and all had an air of intense concentration.

Some of the men took seats around the Ring, the others manned the tele-phones against the walls, and a large proportion of them stood behind the seats. There was a lively buzz of conversation which died away the instant the crescent moon symbol on the signboard glowed with a red light.

There was intense activity at the telephones, and the men standing at the back of the chairs began gesturing like bookmakers in fast, idiosyncratic deaf-and-dumb language. The seated men leaned forward, calling out numbers in loud, urgent voices.

They spoke louder and faster until they were shouting, and the clerks behind them gesticulated as if they were going mad. Finally the dealers were yelling against each other at the tops of their voices. Then a bell rang, the red light died, the shouting stopped, and the men started making notes in their books.

'It's called dealing by open outcry,' Henry told Cathy.

'I can see why. It sounds like a riot in a lunatic asylum. How on earth do they hear what they're saying to each other?'

'You just pick it up – you tune into the guy you're interested in, tune out the others. This is a quiet day – it's usually twice as loud. There'll be a break now and then they'll start the next metal – aluminium. They go right through twice, then there's a free-for-all when you trade the lot together. That's *really* noisy.'

Cathy considered the possibility that she had made an error of judgement. She could already imagine her ladylike voice being drowned by the frenzied yelling of the other dealers.

'Of course, this is a tea-party compared to what goes on in America,' Henry Rose was saying. 'In Chicago, where the traders all stand jam-packed together in a small room, a man died of a heart attack in the middle of a session and nobody even noticed until they'd finished.'

Cathy at once recognized his strategy. 'Are you trying to scare me, Henry?' she asked with her sweetest smile.

'Of course I am,' he announced, giving her a hearty slap on the shoulder which almost knocked her over. 'If you can't take a little kidding from me, the guys down there will shred you. Seriously, you'll have plenty of time to get used to it. I'll start you on the telephone. Just listen to what the client wants and pass it on to the tic-tac man – you *can* count your fingers, I presume?'

Despite the startled looks of the men in the Ring, Cathy's hesitancy left her as soon as she stood at the wall, surrounded by the peeling, ineffectual soundproofing of the Migatto booth with the telephone in her hand, waiting for the red light.

If I blow this I'll lose them thousands, she realized – so I can't possibly blow it.

By her second day she was starting to enjoy the rhythm of the Ring and gaining confidence in her ability. Both her ears were sore from the telephone, and her shoes pinched unbearably by the afternoon, but as Henry had told her there was little difficulty in the job as long as you could think quickly and clearly and not get flustered.

'It's a bit like skiing,' she told Monty at the end of her first week. 'You just have to let go and do it, and trust that you'll still be standing five minutes later.'

'What are the blokes like with you?' Monty looked with envy round Cathy's apartment; with the cool white furnishings, most of which Cathy had made herself, it had a soothing elegance and a homeliness which was missing in the house where she and Rick lived. Luxurious as it was, Monty's own home still looked both bare and untidy. The Juice were touring twice a year and spending six months in recording studios. There never seemed to be time for Monty to get anything done about the house.

'The guys are OK.' Cathy considered. 'We all go to the pub at the end of the day and I buy my round just like they do and it seems fine. They all look at me as if I were something from outer space, of course. I'm not the first woman to do the clerking jobs, but there's never been a woman trader before.'

Monty's eyes widened. 'Is that what you'll be?'

'Well, why not? Since I *can* do it, why shouldn't I?' Cathy was still uncomfortable with knowing how much of a thrill she got out of joining the stream of purposeful men who crowded the City's pavements, each one taking part in running the world. She tried to explain.

'Suppose I was the first woman trader? They'd remember me, I'd have really done something, something important. And I'm making money, Monty. Not a pile, not yet, but more, and I'll be coining it when I'm a trader. Three or four years, I reckon, and I'll be able to get Jamie back.' Cathy, in her red wool dress, lay flat on the sofa; she had kicked off her hand-made, black patent shoes, something she only ever did when she was alone or with Monty because she was conscious of her sad shortened toes.

'Then what?' Monty looked in the mirror, a Georgian relic of her sister's married days, and teased her hair absent-mindedly with an Afro comb. She saw one square of pasteboard tucked into the frame. 'The Belgravia Symphonia,' she read. 'Is this from Rosanna?' Rosanna Emanuel, who now had three children, was also a tireless promoter of her husband's career, and organized the lavish functions which were connected with the work of his firm's charitable trust.

'Yes, she's always asking me to things, but I'm too tired to go most of the time.'

Monty sighed. 'It's crazy, isn't it? I feel as if I've hardly touched the ground on some days. We're still doing two albums a year and two tours a year, and it's killing me. Do you know, they nearly cut our electricity off last week, because I hadn't had time to open the bill and send it to Dennis to get it paid? Isn't it absurd that we're supposed to be making millions and still can't pay our bills? I sometimes think it was easier when we were broke and Cy just fiddled the meters.'

'What's happening to your money?'

'Dennis takes care of everything. If we need money for anything we just ask him.'

'Who does your accounts?'

'Oh, some accountants.' Monty noticed her sister's serene expression curdling with exasperation. 'Honestly, Cathy, don't worry, it's all being taken care of.'

'I think you ought to check up and see some balance sheets. Do you know the Rolling Stones are leaving the country because there's *no way* they can pay their tax bill, even if they stay at the top the rest of their lives?'

'Well, when you're fed up with the Metal Exchange, you can go into business and manage money for superstars, starting with the Juice – OK?'

Cathy sat up and pushed a stray wisp of hair out of her face with impatience. 'That's a great idea, Monty. That's just what I'll do. People like you and Rick will never get on with a straight City type who can't speak your language, and you're in real danger of getting ripped off because of it – not to mention the fact that you don't make the best use of your money. You need a financial consultant who'll take proper care of you.'

Monty yawned, indifferent to her sister's criticism. Money did not interest her, and now that she had, she believed, more money than she could begin to count, even spending it seemed unexciting. 'I think making money is the only thing that really turns you on,' she told Cathy without malice.

Her sister smiled. 'You could be right. Now I want you to teach me something. All the other women on the Metal Exchange didn't make it as traders because no one could hear them in all the shouting. Teach me how to develop my voice, Monty. There must be some exercises I can do.'

Monty made her sister lie on the white wool rug on the floor.

'Now take a deep breath.' Cathy gulped in as much air as she could. 'Now let it out, and do it again, and feel yourself *here*.' She put Cathy's hands over her ribs. 'Feel your ribcage go in and out? That's what you don't want. You want to feel *this* go in and out.' She prodded her sister's concave stomach.

Cathy breathed in and out again. 'That's it,' Monty approved. 'Now practise that. You can't make a good sound if you don't breathe deeply. It calms you down too. Men breathe that way naturally. Women usually just breathe from the upper chest.'

'*Vive la différence.*'

'Louder – say it louder.'

Six months later, Cathy moved up to doing the tic-tac signs which transmitted the message to buy or sell from the telephone to the clerk, who in turn shouted into the trader's ear from behind the red leather bench. At the day's end she had aching arms and an intoxicating sense that she was getting closer to the real action.

Her life, apart from Jamie, was lived between the Metal Exchange and the long, narrow Migatto dealing room where two banks of positions faced each other in the centre of the room and Henry Rose's cheerful bellow occasionally sounded above the hubbub from his desk at the far end. High on the wall opposite him were four brass clocks which recorded the time in London, New York, Tokyo and Penang. A Reuters printer chattered to itself in a corner, spewing out reams of paper printed with the world's news and prices. The long windows were obscured by vertical strips of a white synthetic material which allowed in light but obscured the view outside.

Sometimes Cathy felt as if the dealing room were a noisy, overcrowded, untidy space-ship thousands of miles away from the everyday life of planet Earth. In her wounded emotional condition the all-consuming, high-pressure work was a relief.

Cathy was in the dealing room every morning at 7.00 am, for an hour of relative calm in which to catch up with the paperwork. Every transaction was recorded on a sheet of thin paper, colour-coded according to the metal involved, from white for aluminium to yellow for zinc, and a heavy day's trading would generate a small mountain of multicoloured paper. At around 8 am the pre-market trading would begin and the fifty telephone switchboards became a mass of urgently winking lights. Shortly after eleven the traders and their clerks would hustle down the windswept pavements of London Wall and stream across Gracechurch Street and into Whittington Avenue in time to take their places for the morning market at 11.45.

Shortly after one o'clock, after the last session on silver and the announcement of the official metal prices for the day, Cathy would join the stream of men leaving the Ring and concluding 'kerb' deals as they emerged from the Metal Exchange building. In thirsty crowds they dispersed to the restaurants and drinking clubs in the adjoining streets of the City's Square Mile. Most of the Migatto people favoured the Black Cat, a club which was almost an extension of the Metal Exchange. It was an establishment with no pretensions, existing simply to cool the throats of men who had been yelling themselves hoarse, while successfully meeting the idiosyncratic criteria necessary to escape the tyranny of the British licensing laws.

The Black Cat was one of those rare enclaves where class did not count. Its wines were unremarkable, its food was hearty and its decor smoke-stained and dilapidated. Every new member went through a ritual in which the club committee cut off his tie and pinned it to the wall with a card on which he had to write a joke. Here the golden-haired sons of the great banking dynasties rubbed shoulders with boys from East End dockers' families. Savile Row stood at the bar with Carnaby Street, and pure Cockney ordered at the same time as voices like cut glass.

'Once you've been in the markets it's hard to keep out,' Henry told her, clutching a glass of claret in one fist and looking round the crowded basement room with satisfaction. 'There's a camaraderie between the guys who do this job which is like nothing else. It's a killer, the Metal Exchange, we all know that. It's something you can do when you're young and tough, something we'll all get out of in a few years – then everyone goes their separate ways.'

Cathy enjoyed relaxing with the men for an hour or so after work, but was mystified by their liking for drinking contests and infantile mock fights. She felt accepted now, and was enjoying making friends, especially with Henry whose acute ambition she admired. It was, she discovered, pleasant to keep company with a man and feel no need to seduce him; and it was enjoyable not to have to pretend she knew nothing about money or politics.

Lord Shrewton noted with approval that she thrived in this harsh but rewarding milieu, and for the first time in his life felt somewhat consoled for the disappointment which his son's inadequacy had caused him. At first tentatively, then with greater confidence as Cathy showed enthusiasm, he began to talk business with her at the weekends and show her, as he had once hoped to show Charlie, her way forward in the Group.

These developments flummoxed Lady Davina, who could conceive of no man who would invite a woman into his world and no woman who would welcome such an invitation. For Christmas, she gave Cathy a box of embroidered lace-edged handkerchiefs and a blue Delft vase.

'If you're determined to stay at work, darling, you ought to have some little *feminine* touches about your office,' she advised, trying to invoke Cathy's gratitude in place of the steely question in her granddaughter's chestnut eyes. 'Why not have fresh flowers on your desk – the boys will soon get the idea and start bringing you little bouquets. And you can just drench a little hanky with scent and tuck it into your sleeve so the teeniest scrap of lace peeps out – never let them forget that you're a woman, darling.'

'Lovely, Didi, super idea,' Cathy said quickly, trying not to laugh as she imagined the vase being smashed in the first ten seconds of panic trading and the handkerchiefs engulfed in the jetsam of the dealing room. The old woman glowered, bitterly angry that her granddaughter was now beyond her influence forever and jealous that the young woman had opportunities which had been denied to her.

'Your father would have died of shame if he could see you now,' she said in a low, vicious voice. 'You and your sister. You think you're very clever, don't you? I suppose it's the modern way but it's not what he would have wanted for his daughters, all this running around the world making fools of yourselves.'

'Surely our father died of shame anyway?' Cathy returned calmly, suddenly hating the old woman and her insatiable need to make pawns of all her offspring. She wished Monty were there to side with her, but Monty now had endless excuses why she could never come to family gatherings at Bourton. Cathy gave the vase to Jamie, who broke it at once, and the handkerchiefs to Nanny Barbara.

Henry moved Cathy up to the clerk's station behind the red leather bench, and then, two years after she first set foot in the noisy room, Henry said, 'Ready to go into the Ring, are you?'

'I thought you'd never ask me.'

'There'll be quite a fracas, I should imagine. Press, and so forth.'

By now, she knew his mind in intimate detail. Henry Rose was an accomplished self-publicist who was blatantly encouraging the press to paint him as a bright, dynamic operator who was oriented fearlessly to the future and not afraid to make waves in a traditional City establishment. That very week he had achieved a few lines in the *Financial Times* by announcing formally that men would no longer be required to wear jackets in his dealing room, an innovation which had alarmed the older Migatto directors.

'You mean you've called up a few of your friends in Fleet Street?' she enquired.

'I might have done.'

'Maybe I should get my hair done?' For the past three years, Cathy had worn her hair long, but held back at the nape of her neck with a bow. She had ceased to be concerned with how it looked, and was mostly interested in keeping it out of the way. She decided, with a pang of guilt, to stay in London on Saturday and get her hair cut into a short, severe bob – which, perversely, made her look more beautiful and almost girlish.

Cathy did Monty's deep breathing exercises as she waited for her first session to begin. You can do this, she repeated over and over, it's easy, if those guys can do it, you can do it. She smoothed out the skirt of her clinging dress of burgundy crêpe, which she had selected for its discreetly slit skirt, knowing that when she sat on the red leather bench it would reveal a tantalizing glimpse of thigh.

She was trading tin. There was a hierarchy, even among the metals; the traders started with tin and moved up until they were seniors and could trade the most prestigious metal, copper. Feeling calm, Cathy walked into the circle of red leather and sat down at seat number 27, Migatto's position. Thirty-three men also sat down. The red light glowed around the alchemist's symbol for tin, and one or two of the men spoke at once.

The nasal voice of Maurice, the clerk, sounded in Cathy's ear.

'Three hundred thousand at five.'

Cathy drew a deep breath and opened her mouth to speak.

'Th . . . !' she got no further. Instantly there was a storm of cheering, shouting, stamping, and cat-calls. Men twirled football rattles, rang bells and blew whistles. Someone had a toy trumpet and somebody else was sounding calls on a beagling horn.

Cathy froze with shock. She felt paralysed with embarrassment, straightened her shoulders, looked around the Ring, and smiled. The noise died away to a few cheers, and then, as if nothing had happened, the men carried on trading.

Maurice was speaking again. 'Buy three hundred thousand,' he said.

It was a put-on, another test. *Nobody* could possibly be looking for such a colossal quantity of tin, or any other metal. They were trying to kid her. It was another of their infantile, all-boys-together jokes. Cathy smiled and kept her mouth shut.

'Three hundred thousand,' Maurice said, his voice rising with panic. Cathy did not respond. I'll show them they can't fool me, she thought with satisfaction.

'You s-s-s-stupid bitch – *three hundred thousand!*' Maurice, stammering in agitation, spoke loud enough for his voice to carry into the ring. Several of the men looked at her with alarm and Cathy realized that she had made a mistake, this was not a joke.

Two men offered fifty thousand at six.

'Five,' she said, almost whispering with relief and dismay that she had wasted precious minutes ignoring an order. I've got forty-two seconds to get the deal, she realized. Just before the bell rang, she bought her last fifty thousand to make up the three hundred, at five. She felt ten pounds lighter and ten years older as she got up and walked out of the Ring. As she stood on the pavement outside finishing a couple of kerb deals she was blinded by a flash of light as a press photographer took her photograph.

In the Black Cat, when the afternoon market had finished, Henry poured champagne over her head and the men slapped her on the back, shook her hand, kissed her. The club committee decided to make her a member.

'But I haven't got a tie for the wall,' she protested.

'We'll find one for you.'

'No, wait. Give me a card.' She drew the outline of a tie in a dotted line on the card and wrote beside it, 'You don't miss what you've never had.' Then she signed underneath, 'The Invisible Man.' There was more cheering.

'Better drink some of that champagne,' Henry suggested. 'I don't want you catching cold in wet clothes. You'll lose your voice.'

The next day, Cathy woke at 5 am with a thundering hangover and an irritating idea which would not leave her mind. In spite of knowing the other traders like friends – almost the only true friends she had now – she had been shocked by the noisy outcry with which they had welcomed her into the Ring. The catcalls, the hunting horns and the football rattles – it had seemed like innocent horseplay, but underneath she sensed real hostility to a stranger who had dared to penetrate the group. Suddenly Cathy remembered Rosanna Emanuel's first dinner at Benenden, when another girl had called out something about all Jews having horns. She remembered seeing her friend at first stunned then defending herself with a submissive, placatory smile. That incident had the same scent of mob prejudice, of people swayed by an emotion so violent that they had broken their own rules of behaviour in order to express it.

Cathy deprived Jamie of her company for another Saturday and went shopping. She bought herself a grey suit with a faint white stripe, a blue shirt and a bow tie. Thereafter her flowered dresses and colourful sweaters hung in the back of the wardrobe all week, as she tried to look as much as possible like the men with whom she worked. She traded her handbag for an Asprey briefcase and started drinking scotch – with a lot of water.

'It worked for Rosanna, it'll work for me,' she told herself. 'I'll just blend in, until people forget I'm different.'

Cathy had been trading for a year when she knew she had nothing more to prove to the men of the City of London. As she came up to the Visitors' Gallery before the morning market, she heard her old boss, Mr Mainwaring, showing some guests the Metal Exchange. 'Of course,' he boasted, 'Migatto have always been the most forward-looking of the Metal Exchange's members. Why, just recently we put the first woman trader in the Ring down there. Bright girl. Used to work for me, as a matter of fact.'

Cathy smiled and wished him a pleasant good-morning.

CHAPTER TWENTY

'CHRIST ALMIGHTY – look at the state of that!' A girl with no eyebrows, hair teased into vertical spikes and a black lightning- flash painted down her face walked across King's Road in front of Rick's willow-green Rolls Royce. She was wearing a torn black T-shirt, shiny, black rubber tights which coated her legs like liquid, and a small padlock in her right earlobe.

'Get a move on, darlin'!' Rick shouted out of the car window. The girl paused in the centre of the crossing and scraped her stilettos as if she had trodden in some dog shit.

'Don't wind her up, Rick, or we'll never get there.' They were already half an hour late for the awards ceremony and Monty knew that the strutting apparition in front of them was quite capable of spinning out the confrontation for another half-hour. 'Give her a grin and let's go,' she urged Rick. 'It's that girl from the punk shop – she'll piss about forever if she recognizes you.'

She spoke too late. The girl had recognized the great Rick Brown of the Juice. He was old, rich and successful – everything that she despised. For the punks Rick was a symbol of exploitation. He had made his millions from kids like them, peddling songs about their anger, their pain and their yearnings. But once the royalties had started flowing, Rick and the Juice had sold out the great underclass of youth for whom they claimed to speak, and gone for all the trappings of privilege – the swanky cars, the country estates, the flashy women and the private jets. They had hired bodyguards and big dogs to keep away the kids who had put them at the top.

By 1976, the fat years were finished for Britain. Industries were collapsing like mushrooms rotting in autumn fields, leaving stinking pools of unemployment and deprivation. Kids finished school and signed on the dole, knowing that the odds were that some of them would never be able to work in their lives. The future offered them nothing. They were angry.

The punk girl looked with loathing at the gleaming Rolls Royce carrying people in evening clothes somewhere she could not follow. She raised a finger, gave them the stick-it-up-yer-ass sign, and glowered, deliberately blocking the road. Behind Rick's Rolls a tail of cars began to form along the winding length of King's Road.

Just as their driver was opening his door to move the punk girl out of the way, a pair of uniformed policemen strolled up and hustled her out of the road.

'Thanks, mate,' Rick called to them.

The elder of the two constables reached into his tunic pocket for his notebook, walked up to the car and leaned down to talk to Rick. 'Any chance of an autograph, Rick? The old lady's a real fan of yours.'

Rick wrote his name swiftly with the proffered pen and they drove on. From the pavement, the punk girl again gestured obscenely.

'Filthy scrubber. Who'd want to fuck a thing like that?' Rick settled back in his seat and the car's tinted window rolled smoothly shut.

'She doesn't want to get fucked – that's the point. Why should a girl have to look attractive for men all the time?' The speaker was Cindy Moon, a columnist with *Hit Maker* magazine, who was hosting the awards ceremony. Cindy was given to mouthing women's lib cliches but her own appearance belied her words. Her tinted blond curls were spun into a cloud of gold candyfloss around her shoulders, and her green chiffon dress, tightly cinched at the waist with a gold belt, revealed every feature of her anatomy. She looked like a Barbie doll with added nipples.

'Dunno why we're going to this party, anyway. We aren't nominated for anything, are we?' Rick ran his fingers through his floppy brown hair with a petulant gesture.

'Dennis says you've got to keep in the public eye,' Monty reminded him.

'And they want you to present the award for best new vocalist,' added Cindy, crossing her thin white legs.

'Oh, yeah. Who is it?'

'Bruce Springsteen.'

'Fucking hell – not that one-hit wonder? Still, I suppose it could have been worse, they could've given it to some bunch of punks.'

'They will, next year.' Cindy had been one of the first of the rock establishment to take the new punk bands seriously. Rick gave her an angry look. 'You can't fight it, Rick,' she told him. 'Things don't stand still anywhere, least of all in this business. Hits turn into has-beens quicker than beer turns to piss. The kids who're buying records now were spending their pocket money on penny sweets when you and the Juice had your first hits. They don't want the same old sounds.'

Monty saw a fresh opportunity to talk Rick into taking the band in a new direction. In the beginning, when he had been insecure, he had always taken her advice. When the pressure had been on them to make two albums a year, he had relied on Monty's musical ability with a desperate gratitude. Then Dennis had got them a better deal with Excellent Records, and Rick's attitude had changed. He seemed to resent her talent, and avoided asking for her help.

Instead, he had fallen back into the safe, easy, rock'n'roll style he had given the band at the beginning. Monty realized that he felt threatened when he had to rely on her, but she wanted to record her own songs: she was bored with the Juice's output now, and so were the kids, who bought fewer of their records every year. Rick refused to change the band's style. Maybe, Monty thought, he'd listen to her if Cindy frightened him a little.

'Were we nominated for anything, Cindy?' she asked. 'You were on the judging panel – what happened?'

Cindy's narrow, heavily-glossed lips pouted as she thought. She knew at once why Monty was asking. Monty and Rick had had so many screaming rows in public that everyone in London knew what the tensions in their relationship were. 'You want me to tell you the truth?'

'Of course, that's why I'm asking.'

'I don't believe anyone ever mentioned the Juice. There's so many new bands now . . .' Cindy fell into a studied silence of embarrassment and stared at her long red fingernails. Monty looked covertly at Rick. He was staring out of the car's dark window as if he were not listening.

The awards ceremony at the Savoy was an ordeal. Monty and Rick were not seated together; Dennis still insisted that their relationship should not be stressed in public. Instead, Rick and the rest of the band went around like a street gang of brawling boys and Monty had to find her own level among the second league of friends, engineers, roadies, go-fers, publicists and lig-gers.

From her table at the back of the hall she watched Rick in his old blue denim jacket standing with Cy, Pete and Nasher, reading the nominations for Best New Vocalist. Cy had discovered heroin in the first year of the Juice's success. Now he looked a little more gaunt every year, and one or two of his teeth had dropped out. Pete was getting a distinct belly which bulged over the top of his jeans. Nasher hardly seemed to change, except his hair was thinning and he had taken to wearing a denim cap to disguise his bald spot. The Juice looked middle-aged.

'Talk about the night of the living dead,' sneered a boy sitting opposite her, as Rick mumbled the explanation about Bruce Springsteen being unable to accept his award in person. The boy had a round bullet head covered with black hair which was shaved to half an inch in length, and he wore a small silver ring through one of his nostrils.

'I thought Rick Brown was dead,' his companion drawled, peering at the stage through wraparound dark glasses an inch wide.

'Be better for him if he was,' the first speaker announced, turning his back on the presentation ceremony. 'Did you see their last album didn't even make the top thirty? Ageing savages, that's what they are. Best argument for euthanasia I've seen for years. Excellent will be dumping them at the end of their contract, that's for sure.'

The man with dark glasses flicked them up and down like Groucho Marx as he looked at Monty. 'What's a place like this doing in a girl like you? Don't I know you?'

Monty gave him a withering stare from below half-lowered eyelids.

'Don't be stupid,' the stubble-headed boy told his friend. 'She's one of them. You sing with the Juice, don't you?'

'Yeah. I expect you saw me on TV when you were a baby.' Monty offered her cigarettes to show she wasn't offended by what they had said about the Juice.

'That's your old man we're slagging off, innit?' the crop-haired one challenged her.

'That's right.'

'You don't seem too excited about him, neither.'

Monty shrugged. 'Nothing's exciting after seven years, is it?'

'Dunno – I'll tell you when I'm old. Didn't someone tell me you wrote some of their songs?'

'A lot of the early ones. I don't write the stuff they're doing now.'

'Pity. They could do with some decent material, instead of doing all this plastic American crap. It's bad enough having people waste good money on Eagles albums without getting all that garbage from over here as well.'

'Tell me about it. I think Rick wants to be the next Frank Sinatra or something.'

He blew thick plumes of smoke from his wide nostrils and looked at her directly. 'What about you, what do you want to do? Given up writing songs, or what?'

Monty shook her head, feeling the luxuriant, glistening mass of mahogany-tinted curls stir around her shoulders. Her black silk sweater embroidered with diamanté slipped off her shoulder and she pulled it back casually.

'I write stuff all the time,' she told him.

'Good for you,' he rejoined with a wink.

On stage, Cindy Moon was breathlessly thanking everyone involved in the ceremony and saying goodnight to the TV audience. The floor manager waved his arms, everyone applauded and at last the TV lights dimmed.

Monty stood up to leave with the two young men, who were dressed entirely in black with straps bound around their trouser legs.

'Tell you what,' the short-haired one said to Monty as they left the overheated room, 'when you get fed up with Frank Sinatra there, gimme a bell.' He reached into the pocket of his studded leather jacket and gave her a card. 'Sig Bear: Biffo Records' it said.

'I think you got great tits, 'n'all,' he shouted to her outside the Savoy, as he walked away with his friend. Monty put the card in her silver snakeskin evening purse and forgot about it. She'd had the same conversation a dozen times in the past three years.

I wonder if Rick's having a scene with Cindy, she thought, watching him put his arm around the slender figure in green chiffon and face the TV camera with a smile for an interview. The idea of Rick with another woman – yet *another* woman – barely moved Monty now. Apart from the orgiastic style of the Juice's tours, Rick seemed to feel duty-bound to jump every woman who came near him. What worried Monty far more was the fact that, although she cared for Rick still, it was the vulnerable, hungry, insecure Rick she loved, not the arrogant monster he chose to become in public. Every now and then, when they were exhausted after one of their fights or wrecked at the end of a tour, they would find each other again, but then he would withdraw from her, turn into the taunting sadist he played on stage, and be lost to her. He did not want intimacy. It scared him.

Monty had learned a lot about men in the past seven years. She had begun with tit-for-tat affairs to kill the pain of Rick's unfaithfulness. Then she discovered that some men would come on to her to get at Rick; some – like Nasher – would make a pass out of sympathy for her; some – like Dennis – would attack out of pure, greedy lust and some – like Les Lightfoot, Excellent's A & R man – would try to lay her because they thought they deserved her as a perk of the job.

She had left Rick for three months, and gone to Marrakesh with the effete lead singer of a glam-rock band, but he treated her like another accessory to his pose of ineffable style. Rick, suddenly abject, had pleaded with her so passionately and abased himself so totally over the echoing Moroccan telephone line that she had gone back to him.

Monty watched as a couple of girls came up and asked Rick for his autograph. They tossed their blond hair and swung their hips as he talked to them, turned-on just to be at the edge of a great star's sexual aura. If only they knew, Monty thought, what he's really like in bed. All the tenderness had gone; after seven years of non-stop promiscuity Rick fucked like a robot, giving no pleasure and probably getting none.

Next day there was a meeting with Dennis, their manager, who came to the graceful, white stucco house near the river in Chelsea where Rick and Monty lived when they were in London. Of all of them, he had aged most dramatically. His face was deeply lined and fleshless, like a monkey's, and his blond hair, now cut short, was almost white. With him came a fleshy young man in denims with long brown hair and an unshaven chin.

'This is Keith – he's going to direct our video,' Dennis explained. 'Excellent are gonna spend big money promoting the new album.' He paused to take the gold toot-tube passed to him by Monty and snort a line of coke from the matching gold plate which was being passed around the table.

'D'you think Excellent are going to offer us another contract when this one ends?' Nasher was always the most practical member of the Juice.

'Could be. Could be they just want to get back what they lost on the last album.'

'What do you mean, they lost?' Rick was roaming angrily around the room. 'The album sold OK, didn't it?'

'It sold OK, Rick, but not great. And the tour was fucking expensive.'

'Look, we don't wanna stay with Excellent, do we?' Rick leaned forward on the massive Odeon-style table of blond burrwalnut and looked from one person to another. 'They're old men, they're finished. We wanna move on, right?'

'I never wanted to sign a second deal with Excellent anyway.' Cy gazed at the ceiling, his feet in their green boots propped against the mantelpiece. It was a beautiful, white alabaster mantelpiece, and Cy had already smashed off a corner with his habit of swinging up his legs and bringing his feet down against it with a careless crash. The eighteenth-century chandelier was also looking a little worse for wear. One afternoon Rick and Cy had passed the time shooting at the crystal drops with air pistols.

'If you want my opinion, Excellent are looking to save them-selves money by spending thirty thousand on a video and then making the tour much shorter – just a couple of big gigs here and in the States, no crazy sets or anything.' Dennis closed one nostril and sniffed hard to encourage the last crystals of coke into his bloodstream. 'We can make that work to our advantage. All we gotta do is some-thing that'll cause a bit of a sensation. That shouldn't be too difficult, now should it?'

Keith, the plump young director, spoke for the first time, clearing his throat nervously. 'I've had a few ideas and I thought maybe we could talk them through a bit and then I'll get a storyboard done and we can go into more detail.'

'All right, Keith, tell us how you see us.' There was a dangerous edge of sarcasm in Rick's voice.

'Well, it's a very alienated sort of feel, so I thought we'd maybe try a sort of urban landscape, lots of litter, brick walls, graffiti, trash in the gutters, weird kind of lighting . . .'

The Juice, to a man, looked uninspired. Keith cleared his throat again. 'Or perhaps some bizarre sort of sci-fi scenario, with you all as extra-terrestrials walking through the city, seeing it in all its freakiness . . .'

'The earthlings won't understand,' Nasher said, folding his arms.

There was an awkward pause. What none of them cared to admit was that they were scared of doing a video. Videos were very new; only a few of the biggest stars, like Bowie and the Stones had done one – but Bowie was a performing artist any-way, and Jagger still looked young.

Cy pulled his legs down the mantelpiece, scraping the fragile stone with his boots. 'How about a Roman orgy?' he suggested, running his pallid tongue over his sunken lips. 'I could do with a few dancing girls and grapes and that.'

'Ah – great – yes, a Roman orgy, mmmmmm . . .' Keith fingered his stubble thoughtfully. Monty's heart sank.

They flew to Los Angeles to shoot the video, at the Bel-Air home of a TV talk-show host who was extremely proud of his classical-style pool. It was surrounded by white pillars, with a pediment at one end and a huge gold dolphin spouting water from its mouth at the other. The poolside area was covered in mosaics carefully copied from Pompeii, and a swing on gold ropes dangled over the semi-circular flight of steps leading down into the water.

They started work at about 3 pm. It had taken the rest of the day to dress the set as Keith wanted it, with garlands of roses wound around the swing, rose petals scattered ankle-deep on the ground and gilt couches lined up at the poolside. He had the blue water tinted a glowing purple by the addition of some pink dye. There were ten dancers to shoot first, one with a python and one with a leopard on a gold chain. There was a cage full of doves. As the twi-light approached, flaming torches were fixed to the walls and there was a long pause for re-lighting.

Monty, Rick and the others sat watching with interest, occasionally dipping into the bowl of cocaine which Keith had thoughtfully ordered for them along with four bottles of Jack Daniels and some sandwiches.

'I hope nobody comes near me with that snake,' Nasher shuddered. 'I hate fuckin' snakes.'

'Nobody's asked you to fuck it, Nasher,' Rick told him. The feeble joke indicated how nervous Rick was. He got up and walked away; Monty followed, and he put his arm around her without speaking. They walked along the gravel path at the side of the house. It was the mellow end of the day and the scent of the new-mown lawn and blooming lavender mingled in the gentle air.

They paused at the crest of a slope of manicured turf which led away to a group of palms. The focus of the vista was a floodlit statue of Diana with a fawn and from the distance it was impossible to tell that it was made of fibreglass.

'What d'you reckon to all this?' Rick asked her suddenly.

'The video, you mean?'

'Yeah – are we right to do it, or what?'

'Rick, of course we're right to do it. It's the future. The band's *got* to change, we can't go on doing the same old stuff the same old way forever. The kids who used to buy our records are grown-up now, there's a new audience coming along and they want something different.'

They sat down on the warm grass. Monty folded her arms around her knees like a little girl, watching her loose red silk dress ripple as she moved. Her hair was a wild mass of dark tendrils into which the hairdresser had plaited some red silk thread. Rick wrapped a curl around his finger, admiring its sheen.

'Tell the truth, I don't like what we're doing now,' he admitted. 'We really need you, Monty. You've just got a way with music that I haven't. Oh sure, I can leap around the stage and make a lot of noise and cause a lot of aggravation, but I can't just hear a tune in my head and play it like you can. There were some fabulous songs on those first albums, eh?'

'Yes,' she said simply, not daring to say more in case years of resentment sounded in her voice.

'When all this is over, how would you fancy doing your own album?' he asked suddenly.

'Sending the old lady out to work?' she teased him, delighted.

'Yeah, why not? You've got a better voice than I have, girl, and you know it. That's what I don't like, though. It's not how good you are, it's how big you're hyped. We'll just have to think of something to make 'em sit up and remember who's the boss, that's all.'

'It'll be OK, Rick. It's always OK.'

'I'm sick of it all, if you want the truth.' He patted his pockets, looking for cigarettes. Monty had some in her bag, and gave them to him, but he continued, talking in a low, urgent voice. 'I'm sick of doing it all for them – making money for them, crashing the cars for them, fucking the chicks for them, being photographed for them, dressing up in fancy clothes for them, going round the clubs for them – I want to live my own life, not the life two hundred million people think I ought to live for their benefit.' He shook a cigarette out of the pack, then offered her one, which she did not take. 'You're what I really care about, Monty, if you want the truth.' He looked at her, his speckled grey eyes full of emotion. 'You do love me, girl?' Discarding the unlit cigarette, he reached out for her hand and took hold of it.

'Oh, Rick, of course I love you. I'll always love you.'

'I haven't been very good to you, I know that.'

'You couldn't help it. It seems like we've both been out of control ever since the band made it. Suddenly it wasn't you and me any more. It was the tours and the albums and the TV shows and the money and – oh, I don't know, everything.'

She thought of the endless days in anonymous rooms, of the nights in recording studios when she felt like just one more piece of technology in a high-powered machine for making money and pleasure – pleasure for other people, money they spent just to keep the horrors away long enough for the whole cycle to start all over again.

'What I want to know is – where was it? *It*, you know, The Business, the real thing, the big O – whatever it is you're supposed to have made when you've made it.' Rick stretched out his legs in their bleached jeans. 'It's like it was always coming tomorrow and if we could just do another gig or another couple of songs, then they'd give it us. Everything's just hollow in the centre, somehow.'

He looked at Monty; she was real all right, as real as life. Those huge, black eyes, that velvet skin with its own rich, musky scent that he loved. He remembered how the skin scent changed around her body, how rich and sweet it was down there between her legs, how delicate in the warm hollows of her neck. Rick knew every inch of her body, and wanted it now more than ever. It was the only prize he had won. He stretched out and held the warm heaviness of her breasts, savouring their texture, soft and firm together, the nipples hardening with desire under the fragile silk.

'Rick! Come on, we need you now . . .' the voice of the director's assistant broke into the private world of their intimacy.

'Can't it wait ten minutes?' Rick yelled over Monty's head, his hands warm around her breasts. There was silence. He leaned over to kiss her, but the mood was gone and the nerves had come back. They got up and returned to the set.

An hour later they were all dressed in shimmering tunics tied up with gold ribbons. Monty's was a soft turquoise, the other girls were in pink and white. Rick was in black with a gold key pattern around the hem. The hairdressers put plaits of gold braid round their heads and loaded Monty's wrists and ankles with wide brass bracelets. The make-up girl painted her eyes with sweeps of soft blue and grey, and dusted her golden shoulders with sparkling powder.

'Cocktail time,' Keith announced, and his assistant appeared with a tray of champagne glasses filled with fizzing amber liquid. In the bottom of each glass a few crystals were dissolving.

'Heavens, real champagne cocktails,' Monty muttered nervously. She gulped down the first one, took another, then a third.

A dry-ice machine spouted mist over the surface of the purple water. First Keith ordered shots of the band miming to the playback of their new single, 'Heart's Desire', which had a raunchy, almost disco beat. Three of the dancers crawled around their feet, lasciviously caressing the boys' legs, while two more dancers stood thigh-high in the water and embraced.

Keith shot the boys lolling on the couches drinking whisky and champagne, eating grapes (Cy insisted) and fondling the dancing girls.

'Now, you girls,' Keith pointed to Monty, P. J. and Maggie. 'The swing.' They lifted Monty on to the swing while the other two stood in the water pulling her to and fro. Keith ordered a hand-held camera to come in close on her face. It felt wonderful, swooping to and fro in the warm, steamy air, a little drunk, a little high and full of the sense of love and security she had from getting close to Rick.

'Fabulous, love, fabulous,' Keith grunted. 'Head back – further further – don't worry, love, you're quite safe. Really let go and get into it.' To and fro, back and forth she swung. The music pounded on, louder and louder. Rick and Keith talked intently.

'This is great – I want to do more of you looking really blissed-out and spacy,' Keith told her, helping her off the swing. 'Take this – it'll make your eyes wider.' He gave her a white tablet from a tiny silver pillbox.

Suddenly one of the dancers in the water jumped out on to the poolside and ran towards the choreographer, complaining that the dye in the water was irritating her skin. Keith and the choreographer wrangled at length and the girls in the water were sent away to have cream smeared on their legs to protect their skin. Monty began to feel hot and dreamy. She wanted to lie down somewhere.

At last they were ready to go again, and two of the girl dancers came forward, black girls with braided hair. Keith made Monty lie at the end of the water on her back. The music started again and the girls undulated their bodies over hers, shaking their shoulders frenetically until the gold ribbons holding their tunics unravelled and the light fabric fell away. Monty felt tingling excitement course through her and she writhed her body as Keith directed. A boy dancer held her feet to stop her slipping towards the water; from the corners of her eyes she thought she could see Pete lying on a couch with a naked girl astride him.

It was misty and the light seemed to be growing dimmer. The trembling flames accentuated the dancers' movements. Monty felt her blood race in her limbs with the mixture of drugs and drink. The music thundered on. A hand tore away the top half of her tunic and one of the girls bent over her, her red tongue flickering over her breasts. A shower of rose petals fell on them, caressing her skin, arousing her still further. The set was full of dancing bodies, mist, noise, flowers and flames.

Someone pulled her upright; two of the boys held her against their naked chests, tossing her from one to the other. Monty relaxed in their muscular arms – there was nothing else she could do. She realized, without concern, that she couldn't control her body. She felt like a swallow, swooping weightless through the air. Lips pressed her flesh, teeth nuzzled the softest parts of her body, teasing and toying and now and then threatening with a bite. Somewhere to her left she saw a white boy in a leopard skin kneel before a naked black boy and take his swelling erection in his mouth. They moved slowly together; everything was slow now, even the music.

She was carried, whirled around, thrown from one man to another. Her tunic unravelled, and became nothing more than a drape of diaphanous silk which trailed between her thighs, around her waist, across one of her breasts. There was a girl eating fire, putting lighted brands in her mouth and closing her lips to extinguish them, then exhaling streams of flame.

Splashes. More people were in the water, dancing in the water, churning up the mist, sprinkling rainbow droplets through the air. Wet bodies were dancing together, moving together, hands cupping breasts, fingers sinking into buttocks. There were thighs on thighs, arms around arms.

Monty was lying on a couch on black velvet cushions, raging desire in every atom of her body. Desire for what, for who? She couldn't remember. She wanted, wanted, wanted. She would die if she didn't get. People were leaving the poolside and walking away. The light dimmed further, until the flickering flames from the torches were all that remained. The music died away, and she could hear the cicadas in the palm trees and the small liquid noises of the pool.

Rick was beside her, naked, with the gold fillet still holding back his hair. His arms reached under her and picked her up. He carried her to a pile of cushions in a warm, dim corner, laid her down and began to kiss her body.

'Beautiful, beautiful, so beautiful,' he was murmuring as his hands pushed away the wisps of drapery. She reached towards him but he pushed her back, laughing. 'We're on our own now, darling, and this is your treat. Don't do anything. Nothing. Lie back and enjoy yourself.'

She wanted him like a searing pain. Tremors as light as moths' wings ran over her skin as he touched her. She stroked his cheek as he sucked first one nipple then the other, holding her breasts like precious fruit to his mouth.

'Please, Rick, now – now, darling Rick, *please*,' she begged him, wriggling under his hard, narrow body. But he made her wait, still laughing; finally, sharp shudders of pleasure began before he had even entered her.

It was not enough. It was a stinging pleasure which lashed her senses like a whip, stirring them higher. He knelt between her legs and teased her with his mouth, his tongue stabbing, his lips stroking her taut, wet flesh, lapping in the sweet moisture, avoiding, with cruel cunning, the one touch that would release her from the prison of passion. She writhed beneath him, abandoned, uncaring, wanting nothing but the vortex of hot darkness, and him within her as it whirled her away.

With demonic strength, his hands held her still, and then at last she felt him, hot and avid as she was, but moving into her flesh slowly, so slowly. She screamed as suddenly he withdrew and she clawed at his chest, and saw tracks of blood appear from her nails. Then he was on her, and in her, and they rolled over and over on the cushions, their faces wet with tears, but whose tears? They were on hard tiles, then grass, then half in the warm water. The darkness opened for her and she surrendered to it, wanting to melt or shatter or be destroyed utterly in a cataclysm of love.

'I love you, darling, I love you,' were the last words she heard.

Rick disengaged; he stood up, holding out a hand for the towel which Keith's assistant ran forward to give him. He wrapped it around his waist.

'I hope you got all that,' he said to the director. 'I don't think I could do it again.'

'I got it, don't worry.' Keith patted the camera casing. 'Do that every night, do you?'

Rick grinned and gave him a kidding punch in the ribs. 'Can't beat the old home cooking. Will she be all right?'

'Yeah, don't worry about it. They often zonk out on 'ludes. Take her home and put her to bed and she'll be fine in the morning. With any luck she won't remember anything.'

'You *sure* she's all right?' Rick walked over to Monty's still body and felt her wrist. He hardly needed to. Her heartbeat was visible through her chest wall, like a flutter under the skin between her breasts where the distended artery was pumping.

'Quite sure, trust me. Don't worry about a thing. She won't remember what happened, most like. And by the time I've finished cutting it all together she won't even recognize herself.'

'They're great, aren't they, them qaaludes.' Cy had been standing with the rest of the spectators behind the camera. 'Got any spare?' Keith tipped the contents of his pillbox into his hand.

'Don't give 'em to anyone you don't like,' he advised.

Rick looked at the young director curiously. 'What's this to be, then – the first hardcore rock video?'

Keith shook his head. 'Maybe I'll do you a special tape for private consumption only. But the one I do for Excellent will be OK. Trust me. I'll cut around the naughty bits. But it'll be quite clear what's going on, all the same. The look on your old lady's face will be enough. Those eyes – incredible!'

When Monty regained consciousness the following afternoon she felt thirsty, she had a terrible headache, the skin of her legs and back had come up in a rash in reaction to the dye in the pool water, and she remembered nothing of what had happened. Rick told her that the video was to be edited in New York, and that there would be no time for a private viewing of it by the band before it was rushed out to coincide with the release of 'Heart's Desire'. He was quiet, and very attentive to her, feeling guilty for what he had done.

Monty was taking a taxi home from her hairdresser in London one afternoon when a flickering screen in the window of a record store caught her attention. She made the driver stop, paid him and got out of the cab.

'That must be it, the "Heart's Desire" promo,' she thought, joining the small group of people watching the screen in the store window. She saw Rick's face below the gold headband, his jaw gaping with the mimed effort of singing. Then she saw one of the black girl dancers wriggling up his naked calf, then the snake, then herself singing with P. J. and Maggie. 'Heavens, I look so fat,' she wailed inwardly. The next shot was her own face, eyes languorously half-closed.

She ran eagerly into the store and asked the man at the counter for a copy of the video.

'D'you want the regular version?' he asked her in a low voice.

'What regular version?'

'This one's a bit notorious. We've got the regular version you'll see on the TV, twenty-five quid; and just one or two copies of the special somebody put together from the out-takes. That's a bit pricey, of course.'

'What's in it?' Suddenly it worried Monty that she had no memory at all of the shoot. She could usually remember something, no matter how smashed she got. Instinctively, she knew what the boy was going to say.

'Rick Brown getting it on with some chick. Hot stuff – there's life in the old dog yet. Take a look if you like – I think the lads are running it in the stockroom. Can't get 'em out here serving customers, anyway.'

Monty opened the door he indicated at the back of the store, went down a short concrete corridor and peeked into a room at the end. One glance was enough. Three kids were sitting round the TV on crates, jacking off like monkeys. Monty just had time to glimpse the screen before she withdrew, but the split-second view was enough for her to recognize her own body thrashing as Rick impaled her.

Numb and breathless with shock, she ran out of the store and blundered through the crowds of shoppers looking for a payphone. The first one she found had been vandalized. The second was out of order, and whined in her ear. The frustration made her angry, and the anger made her calm. From the third telephone she called Cathy's office.

'It's horrible, so horrible, Cathy. I can't tell you what they've done, the bastards . . .' Monty gulped, choked and started to cry.

Cathy's voice was firm and soothing. 'Where are you calling from? Tell me where you are and I'll be right over.'

Monty told her, then went to wait in a coffee shop. Twenty minutes later Cathy's steel-blue BMW swooped out of the traffic. The nearside wheels mounted the kerb and it stopped with a jerk. Cathy's slim figure in a black-and-white tweed suit darted through the crowds and Monty flung herself into her sister's arms.

'The most awful thing, Cathy.' Monty started shaking as she told Cathy about the video.

As soon as she understood why her sister was so upset, Cathy said,' O K. Now come and sit in the car and stop the cops covering it in tickets while I go and see how many copies of it I can find. It won't take long to check out Tottenham Court Road – will there be any more anywhere else, do you think?'

Monty shook her head and sniffed, still on the verge of tears. 'This is the place for hot tapes – let's hope they haven't sold too many of them.'

After she had settled her sister in the BMW's passenger seat, Cathy calmly walked into one shop after another up the length of the road where London's principal hi-fi shops clustered. With her smart City suit and her commanding upper-class voice she was an impressive figure, although the shop assistants were taken aback when she firmly asked outright for the bootleg version of the 'Heart's Desire' video.

'What bootleg version? There ain't no bootleg version, and if there were I wouldn't sell it,' blustered one greasy-haired, thickset man in shirtsleeves.

Cathy, cool and pleasant with the merest hint of a persuasive smile on her immaculate red lips, looked directly into his bloodshot eyes. 'Either you sell them to me and make your profit now, or you keep them until tomorrow when we get our court injunction and get stuck with a load of hot tapes you'll never be able to sell at all. I know which I'd prefer.' Within half an hour she had bought every copy of the pornographic tape that she could find.

'Seventeen of them,' she announced, dumping two bags full of tapes on the back seat. 'And I got a copy of the official version too. Now let's get rid of them, shall we?' The powerful engine purred into life and the tyres squealed as she pulled out into the traffic, heading north to Regent's Park. Cathy pulled up beside the canal close to the Zoo, and the two sisters climbed out of the car with the bags which bulged awkwardly with the plastic cassette cases.

'I'll have to keep one,' Monty said with resignation. 'Rick won't be able to wriggle out of this if he has the evidence in front of his eyes.' She took one tape out of her bag, then hurled the remainder over the wrought-iron railings into the water. Cathy threw her bag after it with both hands, and they watched the small pile of plastic evil vanish in the scummy green water.

'How could he do that to you? I could kill him, the filthy little creep.' Cathy's voice was honed with anger and cut like a knife. 'What's happened to him, Monty? He was always good to you, wasn't he? Or was he always a pile of shit, and now that he's rich and famous he can afford to act like one?'

They walked back to the car and Monty paused, her hand on the door. 'He's desperate, Cathy, that's all. Desperate, frightened and weak. He had to do something scandalous just to promote the band, get it back on top again. Of course he cares for me; he loves me in his way. But when he gets with the boys it's suddenly as if I don't exist. He just has to prove he's the boss. He'll do anything to stay in control.'

'Pathetic.' Cathy drove away fast. The trees were just on the point of changing from the dry green of late summer to the gold of early autumn. The peaks of the huge aviary in the Zoo towered above the foliage, and as they passed they saw a heron with a vast wingspan sail through the air inside the wire enclosure.

'It's a cage, in spite of everything, isn't it? It may be very big and very flash, but it's still a cage.' Monty looked tired now, and dejected.

'Time to break out, don't you think?' her sister suggested. 'You're a big bird now.'

'*What me, a swan?*' Monty squawked in imitation of the Ugly Duckling song, and gave a bitter, little smile. 'Yes, I know, I'm a swan and it's time I flew solo. Rick

was going to do that, you know. He said he'd get me my own contract for my own album.'

The car stopped at a red traffic light and Cathy turned to her sister and caressed her cheek. 'Do you need Rick's permission or something?' she asked in a gentle voice.

When Monty got home, she ran the broadcast version of the video and noted with grim fury that although no sexual organs were visible and the action conformed to the laws on indecency, the TV viewers were to be treated to the sight of most of her naked body and – which was much the worst – her naked soul as well. She cringed with embarrassment at the sight of herself grovelling for Rick.

He came in with Dennis just as the tape finished. Monty was afraid that the two men together would shout her down, but she didn't care. Misery had wrung out her mind, leaving it dry of judgement.

'You bastard, you filthy bastard!' she shouted, tearing down the staircase to attack him. 'Is there anything you won't do – tell me? Why not just rip out my guts and eat them? That'll be a good stunt, eh? Coast-to-coast cannibalism, live by satellite?'

Rick looked at her, cold and domineering. 'What in the world are you on about?'

'Don't act the innocent, Rick, not this time. I'm talking about the video.'

She saw the flash of guilt in his eyes before he pulled back his shoulders and began to raise his voice. 'So, there's a bit of skin in the video. So what?'

'So I don't exactly get off on the idea of a million little tykes all around the world wanking over the bit of skin in the video. It's *my* skin, Rick. And I don't care for the world to know how I look when I'm coming, or how you look when you're coming – although I don't suppose you care. And I don't want to know that you and Keith got me out of it on some dope, and you went right ahead and got it on for the cameras while I was out of my head. *Now* do you know what I'm on about?'

'Oh Jesus.' To her surprise, Rick's aggressive tone disappeared and he suddenly looked very small and crushed. He came forward and put his arms around her. 'Look, darlin', I won't blame you if you don't believe this, but I didn't know what I was doing either, truly I didn't. I was as out of it as you were. I don't remember anything, honest. All I can remember is sitting doing coke and booze all day, and . . .' he looked into her eyes, a twisted, painful stare '. . . and the way you looked,' he finished. 'That's all I remember.'

Monty wanted to believe him, but she wanted to hurt him too. 'Well come upstairs and let me refresh your memory,' she hissed. She grabbed his arm, pinching with spite, and pulled him up to the sitting room. Dennis padded after them, embarrassed and self-effacing in his sneakers. Fingers shaking with rage, she slammed the bootleg tape into the machine.

'*What?*' Rick sat down as if stunned, and Monty looked at him intently. Was he telling the truth? He watched in silence as their coupling filled the screen, cut to the music and lovingly interspersed with some extraordinary shots of a tumescent penis against the night panorama of Los Angeles.

'Scorpio rising,' Dennis muttered.

'*Get out of here,*' Rick ordered him in fury.

When the tape was finished Rick fumbled in the pocket of his jeans jacket for his cigarettes, lit two with automatic movements and passed one to her. She looked down at him without pity.

'Don't lie to me, Rick. You knew exactly what you were doing. Don't try to kid me.'

'I swear to God I didn't know, Monty. For Chrissake, what do you think I'm made of?' He reached forward and ran the tape back to a close shot of her body with the flame-light flickering over her golden skin. Shaded by the drifting cloud of her hair, her eyes were half-closed and the lashes cast long shadows on her high, wide cheekbones. Her lips glistened and trembled; she was saying his name over and over again. Her arms were folded to cradle her breasts and the firm honey-smooth globes with their hard dark nipples gleamed in the hazy light. 'Take a look at yourself,' he pleaded, his voice faltering. 'What could I do? I couldn't help myself, I had to do it. You were begging me to fuck you and you're so fuckin' beautiful . . .' He was hanging his head like a shamed child.

'But you didn't have to let them film you.'

'Keith said he'd do a private tape, just for us. I never thought . . . some bastard must have pirated it. Oh God, darlin', I'm sorry.' Suddenly he flung himself into her arms and she held him, feeling his irregular breathing as he haltingly begged her forgiveness.

'We've got to stop it,' he said at last. 'Where did you find this?'

'Tottenham Court Road – Cathy came and bought all she could find. A hundred quid each.'

Rick called Dennis back into the room. 'OK – what do we do now? How do we get these tapes off the streets?'

'Don't worry about it. I'll get some boys on to it right now and buy every one in the city, and we'll call the lawyers and do an injunction. Do you want to stop the regular video as well?'

Rick turned to Monty, implying that the decision was completely hers. She sighed, knowing that she was trapped. If she got the promotional video withdrawn, the record would lose TV exposure and they would have to write off a mint of money.

'No, it's too late now. At least nobody will know it's my bum. 'Monty herself had only recognized the buttock in question by her birthmark, and in the pile of unclothed bodies it had not seemed unduly prominent.

Dennis got on the telephone and gave orders, then left them to spend a sad evening together. The next day the newspapers were full of the story. They made the front pages of the two cheapest tabloids, and even *The Times* carried a report of the court application for an injunction. That afternoon, the BBC banned the 'Heart's Desire' video, announcing that it contravened normal standards of public decency and could not be shown without cuts. There were incessant telephone calls from newspapers and Rick was invited to go on half a dozen main-stream talk-shows as well as the rock shows for which the Juice were already booked. One show even wanted him to debate modern morality with a bishop.

Monty felt icy and detached. She wanted very much to be able to believe Rick, but it was impossible to ignore the chirruping confidence which he now acquired as his old status of mouthpiece of the nation's youth was temporarily restored. Cathy condemned him outright.

'He used you, 'she said flatly. 'You know he did, Monty, you must know. Why won't you accept it? It's not exactly a new situation, is it? He had a straight choice between protecting you and capitalizing on the fact that you care for him, and when it came to the crunch you weren't as important as success.'

Monty said nothing. She knew Cathy was right, but nonetheless yearned to believe that she was wrong. Cindy Moon offered her no comfort.

'It's typical of Rick – he didn't get to be one of the biggest rock stars in the world by taking care of everybody else, did he? He just saw his chance and took it. He's always had a genius for this kind of hype – the whole Juice mystique is built on that rape-and-pillage image.'

Monty nodded, feeling miserable. 'What I can't stand is everyone knowing.' She shivered inside her thin, white T-shirt. 'Every time I meet anyone I'm wondering if they've seen me like that. I just want to hide under a stone until it's all forgotten. I'll die when I have to go out on stage.'

Cindy looked at her with a speculative frown corrugating the arcs of pencil that signified her eyebrows. 'Has Rick told you anything about the tour?'

'What's to tell – thirty-six gigs in forty-three days, starting next week. Then the States after that. If it's Tuesday it must be Oshgosh, Wisconsin.' She shrugged.

'There's a rumour that Rick's changing the whole show.'

'What do you mean?' Again, Monty half-knew the answer.

'Just ask him,' Cindy advised.

Monty asked him, and again Rick put his arms around her and started to talk in tones of desperate sincerity. 'We're dumping Excellent and we're dumping Dennis,' he began. 'It's all been coming for a long time, you know that, and this video business was just the end. He really fouled up. He's out. We're getting a new manager – and a new deal.'

Monty pulled away from him and sat down on the edge of their king-size bed, a sleazy expanse of creased black satin. 'Thanks for asking me how I felt about it. I'm surprised you think the video business was such a wipe-out. I thought it had come off rather well, myself.'

'Oh, don't come the old acid-drop, Monty.' Petulantly, he turned away from her, pretending to look out of the window at the distant tourists flowing towards the punk quarter. In ten years the nerve centre of Chelsea had shifted from the plush squares in the east to the tawdry new shops full of fetishist leather in the west, only a few blocks from the run-down house where Rick and Monty had first lived.

'And what's all this about you changing the stage act?'

'What about it?'

'That's all I've heard.'

'You've been on at me to change for years. I thought you'd be happy.'

'Why not cut the crap and tell me what all this is about?'

'All right, I'll tell you.' Mean and dangerous, he turned towards her, shoving his hair out of his eyes. 'What it's about is – I'm not going down the tubes yet. None of us are. All those creeps like your *dear* friend Cindy, who've been trying so hard to bury the Juice, haven't reckoned with the fact that we aren't dead yet. I'm sick of being measured for my coffin.'

'Fair enough. What else?'

'Nothing else – except don't bother packing for the tour because you ain't coming. We're dumping all you girls. We're hard boys, always have been, and we're not having any more oohs and aahs and sha-la-las in the future. And I'm not having you on my back whining all the time for me to be good and act nice.'

Monty felt both angry and relieved. She had been dreading the tour, and despite the graceless way Rick had chosen to drop her she had a distinct, intoxicating sense of freedom.

'That's fine by me,' she said, getting up and shaking out her hair as she thought through her next move. 'I'll be much happier here in London working on my own songs than trailing round watching you on your Jack-the-lad trip every night.'

'You'd better not be expecting me to have anything to do with them songs of yours either,' he told her at once. 'I'm not getting into anything you do, understand? What do you think you know about how the kids feel – born with a silver spoon in your mouth, talking in that cut-glass voice? It's all down to street credibility now. I can't afford to get involved with your music.'

'Anything else you'd like to say? Like "so long, it's been good to know you" maybe?'

'Don't be daft, Monty. This has got nothing to do with us, it's business, music business, that's all. Don't take it so personal. I love you, girl, I'll always love you.' He moved to take her in his arms again. 'You've got the tape to prove it, eh?'

A fireball of rage exploded in Monty's mind. 'What the fuck do *you* think you know about how the kids feel – you with your Roller and your big house in the country and your designer drugs and your go-fers and your groupies and your hangers-on? Street credibility? Don't make me laugh. You're not even a human being. You're just some robot that's built to sell records. You're a walking, talking rip-off machine, Rick – and you know it.'

He slapped her face, a quick, open-handed blow that barely hurt, a token of violence intended to remind her that he was the boss. 'You're getting hysterical,' he announced. 'Shut up if you can't talk sense.'

Suddenly Monty felt very tired, too tired to hit him, too tired to reach for the Lalique vase on the night table and throw it at him, although the thought crossed her mind. Cathy was right, and Cindy was right. Rick cared for her, but he cared for himself so much more that his love was no longer worth having. And he was doomed, just like a vanishing species. He had lost touch with reality, even the reality of his own feelings, and he would not survive now that his environment was changing.

She pushed him away, went into the dressing room and found her new, red acrylic-pile coat and a bag into which she pulled a haphazard selection of clothes.

'Oh, Monty, don't be stupid,' his tone was wheedling as he followed her. 'Come on, darlin' – now what are you doing?'

'I'm leaving.'

He pulled his hands out of his jeans pockets and took the bag out of her hand. 'Don't be crazy. You're not going, you can't go. I need you. You're the only person I've ever loved, you know that.'

'Heaven help the others then'

He tried to kiss her but she pushed him away, suddenly sickened by the smell of his breath. 'I'll throw up if you touch me. I swear I will,' she snarled. 'You don't know what love means, Rick.'

'That's not fair. That's a mean thing to say.' He was playing the hurt little boy again, but this time Monty's heart did not warm to him.

'Well, think of all the mean, unfair things you've done to me and think about how you'd feel in my place. I've had it with you. I'm only doing what you'd do if you were me.'

Hearing at last that she was serious, he dropped his pose of humility and a venomous glare darkened his grey eyes. 'Suit yourself,' his voice was cold. He dropped her bag at her feet and flung himself out of the room.

Without another word, Monty threw her notebooks, some tapes and a tape recorder into the bag and left, walking out into the exhausted warmth of a late September day. The early fallen leaves from the plane trees littered the ground. She hailed a taxi and drove to Cathy's immaculate white apartment in the Barbican where the telephones made burring noises through the evening like strange electronic birds.

Cathy opened a bottle of champagne and came to sit in the bathroom while her sister luxuriated in the warm tub scented with Floris lime.

'How do you feel?'

'Marvellous, Cathy. I feel as high as I did the day I ran out of the house when Mummy sold my piano, remember? I'm free again.'

Cathy sipped the icy, golden liquid thoughtfully. 'What are you going to do now?'

'Call Cindy, because she'll tell the papers and then everyone will know I've split from Rick. Otherwise, knowing him, he'll be on the phone to his bloody publicist telling the world that *he* dumped *me*. Then I'm going to buy some studio time and make a brilliant tape of some of my songs, and get myself a deal.'

'Can I help? What are you going to use for money?'

'Oh, I'll manage.' Monty stretched luxuriously in the scented water, accidentally soaking some of her hair which was twisted into an untidy knot on top of her head. 'And I might as well get my hair cut – one of those sexy *coupe sauvage* jobs, don't you think?'

'I think you should go round to Dennis first thing tomorrow and get your money situation straight,' Cathy told her firmly, retying the sash of her indigo silk robe.

'It is straight, darling. Our accountant took care of everything. My royalties always went straight into my bank account, my tax was deducted every year, it's all handled. Why should splitting with Rick make a difference?'

'You'd be surprised.' Her sister stood up and reached for a thick, white lavender-scented towel from the stack on the glass shelf, then wrapped it around Monty's dripping body as she splashed out of the bath. 'Whenever some man says he's taken care of everything it usually means he's done bugger-all.'

As soon as the word was out that Monty and Rick had split, Cathy's telephones redoubled their insistent warbling as friends and acquaintances began to call – some to gossip, some to bitch, some to congratulate and some, the most gratifying of all, who wanted to work with her.

Monty recorded five new songs for her demo tape, plus one of the Juice's old hits to remind people of her credentials. Then, with a sense of devilment, she decided to add an old classic, 'Can't Get Used To Losing You', which she sang in a sarcastic whine with a maddening, incessant computer drumbeat which sounded, the engineer said, like someone banging his head against a wall.

When the tape was finished, Monty took Cindy and went shopping to the new boutiques at the World's End, where she bought a leather dress with a strapless top which laced tightly down the back, and was cut so low that it dipped almost to the crease of her buttocks.

'You look like a walking wet-dream,' Cindy told her, admiring the dress in the cracked mirror.

'Let's face it, I *am* a walking wet-dream for half the kids in town,' Monty replied. 'Do you think I should cut my hair?'

'No, men like long hair.'

Monty considered. It seemed a sound argument – the business of peddling your talent seemed to be largely the business of pleasing men. Cindy suggested she add a pair of red plastic stilettoes to the outfit, and some shiny black gloves that reached over her elbows.

'That ought to grab their imagination.' Monty pouted with satisfaction and pulled down the top of the leather dress to exhibit a dangerous depth of bosom. I'd better buy an eye-pencil tomorrow, she thought. Nothing looks more sixties than the old arched eyebrows just a couple of hairs thick.

Sig Bear at Biffo Records never noticed her eyebrows. 'Here she is, the body gorgeous!' he shouted, bursting out of his office into the dank corridor which was Biffo's reception area. His office had no furniture at all, only two telephones on the floor and a black 1950s statue of an Egyptian cat. I suppose, Monty thought, as she sat on the stained carpet, he's going to want to lay me on this at some point.

'Wash your mind out with soap and water,' Sig suggested, ripping open a can of beer and offering it to her. He smiled like a frog, a wide, fat, self-satisfied grin.

'The bottom line,' he told her, 'is that I've been wanting to sign you ever since we set this label up, but we ain't got too much loot to chuck around. In six months I reckon one of the big fish'll swim along and buy us out if we look tasty enough. I'd like to whack out a single from you straight away, then maybe another, then follow up with the album. So what I suggest is a two-year contract, with an option after that. We've got it drawn up somewhere – I'll get the girl to look for it.'

'Did you know I'd be round, then?'

'No, but there's no harm in wishing, is there? That's the power of positive thinking. There's only one thing I don't like about you, to tell the truth.'

'What's that?'

'The name. It's too real. We want a fantasy kind of a name.'

To Monty's surprise, it was Christmas Eve before she got laid on the floor of Sig's office. Apart from the fact that they both skinned their knees on the harsh pile of the carpet, it was thoroughly satisfying. After a decade of sexual liberation, boys were a lot wiser about girls' intimate geography. Afterwards they sat on the floor sharing a beer, watching *The Wizard of Oz* on television. Judy Garland was putting on the ruby slippers. Suddenly Sig gulped down the mouthful of beer which he had just swigged and gestured at the screen with the can.

'That's it,' he announced.

'What's it?'

'Your name – Ruby Slippers.'

'*Great!* I love it!' I'd never be able to think of anything clever like that, she thought. It's perfect. I'm so lucky I've got Sig to take care of all that stuff.

'Follow the yellow brick road,' he gurgled, pushing up the leather skirt she had only just put on.

'Follow the yellow brick road . . .' Luckily, he had not had time to put his trousers back on.

'Follow, follow, follow, follow . . .' There was some snuffling, then silence, then a few grunts. The sightless ceramic eyes of the Egyptian cat looked disapproving. 'Ah Ruby,' he breathed in Monty's ear. 'I always wanted to fuck a chick called Ruby.'

The rest of the winter was much less satisfactory. Because Cathy bullied her every day, Monty at last met Dennis to check out her financial position, and discovered that Rick had copyrighted all the Juice's songs in his name alone. She could claim no royalties, and since a new version of her old telephone song was climbing the Hot 100, and there were two disco versions of other songs doing well in Germany, this was a serious loss.

'You must sue him,' Cathy told her. 'Don't worry about whether you can afford to – you can't afford not do it for your own self-respect. I'll handle the bills.'

Monty hired a slick law firm with offices in Mayfair, but within a few months all her signing money from Biffo had been spent, and she was embarrassed at the amount Cathy was having to find to meet the lawyers' bills when it was plain that the case could drag on for years before coming to court. She also felt increasingly uncomfortable living in Cathy's apartment. She felt as if her big sister were taking over her life completely and so she moved into Cindy Moon's small apartment at the top of a big house in Notting Hill Gate. As Sig was quick to point out, this also gave her the advantage of an association with Cindy's neo-punk public profile.

Biffo released Ruby Slippers' first single, a fast, angry song called 'Lies'. Sig insisted that 'Can't Get Used To Losing You' should be the B side, and Monty realized he was right when it tore up to No. 3 in the British charts. There was a lot of publicity and Monty gave endless interviews about her split with Rick and the video scandal.

She sat with Cindy watching herself on TV. The camera started at the red shoes and moved unsteadily up her body. The studio audience were trying to look animated.

'You've made it, kid. Congratulations.' Cindy patted her ankle. 'What's the matter, why aren't you jumping around being happy? You're a *star!*'

'I don't know.' Monty saw herself on the TV, swinging her leather-swathed hips, her pouting lips jammy with gloss as she mimed to the sound of her own voice. 'It doesn't feel like me, I guess. Not yet, anyway.'

CHAPTER TWENTY-ONE

T HE WINTER of 1945 was one of the bitterest that Britain had ever endured. The cold was no worse than in many other years; the wind blew no more meanly through the streets of London than it had before. What made the winter at the end of the war so cruel was the climate of hopeless disappointment. There was to be no reward for the years of suffering; instead there was to be greater deprivation than ever – no food, no clothes, no fuel, no homes, no work, no end to the brutalizing queues for rations and the making do. Victory had left Britain bankrupt, with nothing to take for comfort but illusions of glory.

The Bourton family's London home had been requisitioned by the War Office, so James and Bill had no option but to take the quarters to which they were ordered, in a shabby Pimlico terrace where an assortment of officers from the less glamorous, more unorthodox outfits in all three services were billeted. It was a cold, dingy, sour-smelling building with dog-eared exhortations to economy stuck to every wall. Over the meagre fire in the lounge was a poem in pokerwork on a piece of packing-case, which was intended to prevent the occupants using too much coal. It read:

> *If it's warmth that you desire,*
> *Poke the wife and not the fire,*
> *And if you lead a single life,*
> *Poke some other bugger's wife.*

Since the trappings of grandeur were all that remained, their value was exaggerated. James, now Captain Lord James Bourton, DSO, quailed under the hearty praise for his supposed grit and courage, and tried to bury the memory of the chaotic fear-filled night in which he had been transformed from a failure to a hero. By the time he stood with Bill Treadwell on a windy street-corner by the side of Buckingham Palace, James was angry that so many people were anxious to make him a hero. He thought the heroes were the men who had died in Malaya, not the lucky ones like himself. The hideous memory of the charnel house by the railway track mocked him, but he could no more repudiate it than give back the medal he now held to his side in a cheap, black mock-leather case. To do either would have been to declare himself a traitor.

'How's your father?' Bill asked as they walked cautiously round the edge of the crowd. A pack of photographers was taking snapshots of the newly decorated men, who posed proudly in their uniforms with their medal-cases open and their families around them. James paused and forced his own case into his coat pocket.

'He's slipping away. They thought he'd die last night, but he hung on. At least it means my mother couldn't come here with me – be grateful for small mercies, at least.'

Lady Davina had been the most vociferous barker of his valour. She proudly annexed to herself the admiration directed to her son, the triumphant warrior.

'What'll you do when he goes? Are you coming back to Malaya?' They turned into St James's Park.

'Yes, I want to. My job's there, if I want it, though the company wants to run the estate now with as few Europeans as they can. Still, that'll be more to my taste than lurking around at Bourton as the second son, and having to touch my brother for money. You're still set to go back?'

'For sure.' The Australian stalked, heronlike, by the side of the concrete lake-basin. The water in the ornamental pools had been drained to prevent German bombers taking bearings from such prominent landmarks. 'Heaven knows what will happen now, Jim. I went to a briefing at the Colonial Office yesterday and these Whitehall types haven't a clue. It's as plain as day to you and me that the Commies will just stay in the jungle and fight us instead of the Japs, but they can't see it. They think they can just ask for the guns they dropped to the Communists to be surrendered, and that'll be that. My guess is there are thousands of arms hidden away in the jungle and the comrades are just waiting for the moment to use them.' He squinted up at the bleak sky. 'My heart's in that country, somewhere, Jim. I feel I belong there. I certainly don't feel that this is home.'

James did not feel that London was home either. He scarcely remembered anything about it, and the alien cityscape of bombed buildings and empty streets only reminded him more forcefully that his war had been a nursery game of make-believe in comparison with the ordeals of others.

At Bourton there were further reminders. The house had been requisitioned as a convalescent hospital, and although most of the wounded men had left already there were enough wrecked bodies to shuffle across the neglected lawns and taunt him with their misfortune. The park was ploughed with ambulance tyre-tracks; many of the great trees which had been the familiar friends of his boyhood had been felled, and the deer had gone.

The Duke of Witheram was dying by inches, his blood struggling through arteries silted with the fat of his own land. He had been barely conscious for several months, and three nurses attended him day and night.

James whiled away the grey days shooting, but there was not much game, since the gamekeepers had been called up to fight and every able man in the village had poached a bird when he could. Shooting was James's cover for taking a walk and enjoying the domesticated contours of the English landscape, in which every tree that flourished did so with a landowner's approval and every field conformed to a farmer's imperative. Only among the immense beech trees of the West Wood did James feel the arcane force of free nature that animated the jungle. James had a sensitivity which would have equipped him to be an artist had he been born into a milieu which recognized art; he enjoyed the docile beauty of his ancestral land but felt confined by it. It was a claustrophobic world in which everything was limited, regulated and ordered, including himself.

At last the night nurse noticed that the old Duke was no longer breathing and, at a decent hour in the early morning, tapped on Hugo's door to announce that his father was dead.

'I do not wish to be known as Dowager,' the widowed Davina told her family as they gathered for a subdued breakfast. 'I shall revert to the title I had before my marriage – so much more attractive. I intend to put an announcement in *The Times* immediately.'

'Mother, I think you should wait a few days. We haven't announced Father's death yet, after all.' Hugo's brown bullock's eyes quelled his mother with reproach.

'Of course, Hugo, you are the head of the family now, I shall do whatever you say,' she conceded. 'Will you be talking to Pasterns about the will?'

'Naturally.'

The new Duke did more than anyone expected him to do. In the greatest display of dynamism he was to give in his lifetime, Hugo took the reins of the estate firmly from his mother's hands and applied himself to mastering the facts of the family's situation. Even his unimpressionable nature was moved by what he discovered. 'We're bust, as near as dammit,' he confided to James in their father's study. 'Mother's run through a fortune without the slightest regard for the future of the estate, and there's no evidence that Father took much interest. He said as much to me himself: "There's enough to see me out; after that you can sink or swim on your own, " that was his line. There's been no maintenance, no investment, no planning of any kind.'

'What are you going to do?' James was relieved that the inflexible law of primogeniture had absolved him of the responsibility for salvaging the family fortune.

'Sit down with some chap from Pasterns who's supposed to be an expert and see if we can cut our losses.'

A few weeks later the team of lawyers arrived, curious to poke around the estate which most of them knew only through the bundles of documents which related to its disposition. Hugo announced a conference on the family's future.

'I want you to know, darling, that it's *all arranged*,' Lady Davina hissed in James's ear as they made their way to the room set aside for the occasion.

'What's arranged?' James pulled away his arm with irritation. He hated his mother's possessive caresses.

'Before your dear Papa went completely ga-ga, I had a word with him about you, and he agreed to something special for you,' she told him, nodding with satisfaction at her own foresight. 'You'll see how clever I've been. You're a very lucky boy.'

When the will was read there was an audible gasp from Hugo as the lawyer read out the codicil to which she referred. The Duke had set up a trust for his younger son to provide a handsome endowment 'in the event that he should see fit to marry and sire issue'. The bequest was in cash, and James knew enough to appreciate that it would be hard to find the money from the diminished estate.

Hugo passed the next two days with the lawyers. Lady Davina bustled about the North Wing, harassing the hospital authorities to quit the main part of the house, so that she could repossess her kingdom, and outlining to James their delectable future as she saw it. She replaced the Red Cross uniform which she had affected during the war with a smart, blue costume made up from black-market wool crêpe, with stylish velvet revers.

'I thought you could have the London house, and I shall spend the winters there with you and the summer down here with Hugo. It'll be such fun, won't it, darling, when this dreary, old rationing is over? You've missed some marvellous parties, of course, but there'll be so many more. London is simply crawling with pretty widows: you'll be able to take your pick.'

Hugo took visible pleasure in dashing her plans; discomfiting his mother's vain ambitions was now the only pleasurable aspect of his task. 'The best we can do is offer the house to the National Trust,' he told them. 'They'll want an endowment with it, and to raise that I propose to sell the farms. The village will revert to the Rural District Council. The London house will have to go, though I'm advised to keep some stake up there so we may buy something smaller. All the property will have to be sold. Assuming that the Trust do buy the house, we'll be allowed to remain in a part of it, and we can retain ownership of the home farm and some of the commercial holdings.'

'Hugo, this is outrageous! I will not allow it! This is my home. I can't possibly have charabancs and daytrippers in my home.'

'Mother, you have no choice. I think you should know that the opinion of our advisers is that we would be in a considerably better position if you had not been determined to play the lady of the manor in quite such extravagant style.'

'You forget, Hugo darling, that if I had not refitted this dismal barn, it wouldn't be the showpiece it is today and you would have precious little chance of interesting the National Trust in it.'

Later she told James, 'See how lucky you are – you'll be living better than Hugo once you're married. Darling, do hurry up. I can't stand another minute in this place knowing I've got to lose it.'

Could she have known what the state of the family's affairs was? Of course she must have known better than anyone. James was haunted by the conviction that his mother had finagled his bequest only to assure her own future standard of living. He was terrified of the prospect of living forever in thrall to her insatiable ego, with a wife whom she would no doubt pick out for him and children who would be her cowed playthings just as he and Hugo had been. The image of a woman rocking a contented infant in a sarong cradle flashed into his mind, trailing with it the faint memory of spiritual peace.

What he craved now was the sturdy sense of self-determination he had enjoyed in Malaya. What he feared was the humiliating role of his mother's pawn. James made up his mind. This bizarre legacy changed nothing. He would never claim it; instead, he would take the first passage he could get to Penang.

Within a month he was gone, and his last sight of England was a crowd of about five hundred dockers at Southampton, fighting among themselves at the end of a demonstration against plans to close down half the dockyard and take away the jobs to which they had only just returned from the war.

James nearly cried with emotion as the train glided to a halt and the familiar, red dirt-road through the jungle opened up before him. There was a small black car waiting at the levelled area beside the railway track, and beside it a figure he recognized with joy.

'Selambaram! I can't believe it – you still here?'

'Where else, *tuan?*' The round eyes of his old conductor gleamed with happiness.

'My God, it's good to see you! How are things?'

'Pretty good, I think you will find. Bukit Helang was a lucky place because it was so difficult to reach that the Japanese mostly left us alone. You will see nothing much has changed, although with so few people to work we could keep only a small area of the estate properly cultivated.'

James beamed with pleasure as they drove through the *kampong*. The dark hardwood houses with elaborately carved eaves seemed far more prosperous than the simpler houses of the Pahang village. Instead of the light green of the *padi* fields, the background was the rich emerald of half-tamed vegetation – palms, glossy banana trees, durians and fruit bushes.

He noticed that the road was rutted, and as they approached the uphill sweep which led to the coolie lines and the estate buildings there were more definite signs of neglect. The jungle grass had invaded the old rubber, and the young plantings were completely overgrown. Half the coolie shacks were derelict and the handsome square pillars of the estate house were no longer as white as cricket flannels, but stained with the red dust. Many of the shutters at the windows were hanging loose and the signs of care upon which Douglas Lovell had insisted – the orchid pots, the well-swept steps, the furled bamboo blinds – had gone.

As the only conductor who had remained during the Japanese occupation, Selambaram had run the estate by giving priority to the clerkly observances of administration, which he understood, while holding blind faith that the forces of nature would cooperate. As a result, James found an immaculate record of chaos. Getting things to rights was to be a long, hard slog.

The rubber trees which had not been tapped had benefited from the rest, and yielded generously. Labour began to return, old workers and new appearing daily, as the word spread that the estate manager was hiring once more. James had the telephone lines and electricity cables restored. For a while he would be the only European on the estate, and he elected to lodge in the estate house rather than go to the trouble of setting up home in a bungalow. His former residence was now roofless, with creepers probing the wooden shingles of the walls. Gerald's bungalow was occupied by a new Malay assistant, and the house used by Anderson, the doctor, was now Selambaram's home.

The greatest change was not in the overgrowth and decay which had seized the estate in three years, but the subtle shift in James's status – in the status of all white men – in the same period. The day the *tuans* ran, the years of rule by another Asian race, had cracked belief in white superiority. The colonial government was making grudging moves to Malaya's independence and James found that although his authority was accepted and he himself viewed with affection and respect, he was no longer looked upon as a permanent feature of the scene.

For the first time in his life he suffered loneliness. Not only was he isolated and exhausted at the end of each day by his work, but the growing uncertainty about the country's future distressed him. Needing always a mould in which to shape his responsive character, he found it difficult to be in such fluid circumstances. His visitors were few. Dr Anderson, who was now responsible for the health of the workers on nine adjoining estates, came once a month to hold a clinic. He was thinner, with sunburned skin wrinkled at his knees and elbows, and the horseshoe of hair around his bald crown was no longer brown but grey. James welcomed his company, and kept the doctor's old Gilbert and Sullivan records and his wind-up gramophone, which had survived the war with only one breakage, in the sitting room to entertain him.

Occasionally a company inspector would appear to tell James he did not need another assistant. Bill Treadwell came, when his new duties as adviser to a state ruler allowed. 'I'm not sure what I'm supposed to be advising him on exactly. Seems to be everything from diseases of oil palms to the likelihood of war with the Communists.'

'How bad is it?' James asked him, narrowing his eyes in the brilliant sunlight as they drove up the road from the railway.

'As bad as it could be. Our old friend Chin Peng has been off to China to train with Mao Tse-tung and he's stirring his boys up like hornets. I never thought that all these months we wasted listening to him indoctrinate his men would be so useful. Once you've a few lessons on Lenin from Chin Peng it's quite clear what they're going to do. Attack the British. Start terrorizing the country the minute they're in a position of enough strength.' He looked with approval around the estate.

'You did get off lightly, and no mistake. Business as usual already.'

'The Malays have taken over the tennis court for badminton, but I've no one to play against anyway.'

'Have you got any sandbags?' James looked at his friend with surprise. 'I'm serious, Jim. You blokes on the isolated estates are going to be very easy targets. I'd think about digging in and defence, if I were you.'

The Times arrived, as it had always done, three weeks late. It brought the news, before his brother's letter, of the sale of Bourton House to the National Trust. The *Straits Times* also arrived every day, discussing in its awkward English the demands for the Malayanization of key industries, for national independence and for action against the Chinese bandits who were terrorizing rural areas.

Seeking action to cure his unease, James wrote to Pasterns asking for clarification of his father's will. Their reply did little more than restate the document's words. In the same post came a letter from the rubber company announcing that the widow of Gerald Rawlins would be visiting the estate with Dr Anderson in the near future.

At the quayside in Georgetown, Betty recalled her first sight of Penang. She felt a lifetime older than the girl who, seven years before, had stood beside an elderly missionary and scanned the multicoloured crowd on shore for the half-forgotten face of her fiancé.

Now she was looking for another barely remembered face, the round, sun-reddened face of Dr Anderson, which at first she overlooked in the throng because he was so changed by his years as a prisoner-of-war. He was thin and stooping, no longer robust, but at the sight of him she felt a warm, enveloping rush of security. Changed as he was, his presence reassured her with an impression of continuity.

'Good trip?' he asked as his driver held open the door of his Rover.

'Not too bad. I'm not a very good sailor, I'm afraid. No sea legs at all.'

'Good to be back to dry land again, eh?'

They continued in pleasant, trivial conversation until they reached the E & O Hotel, and took tea on the terrace in the shade of a pink-and-white awning. They were both coming to terms with the horror of the past and the uncertainty of the future, and the only way to begin this work was with meaningless pleasantry.

Neither wanted to discuss what they would be obliged to discuss, sooner or later. In the women's internment camp in Sumatra, Betty had sat by Jean Anderson through long days in which she had talked distractedly for hours of her husband before she died of swamp fever; under a canvas canopy in the area called Cholera Hill in the labour camp on the Burma railway, the doctor had seen Gerald lose half his remaining weight in a day and then die in violent convulsions as his emaciated body hurled out all its fluid in vomiting and diarrhoea.

They ate together in the crowded dining room, while a Chinese string trio played Franz Lehar waltzes very slowly. Neither of them was hungry. Betty's pink and white bloom of freshness had subtly changed into overall pallor with patches of high colour on her cheeks. She wore a simple, blue crêpe dress. Her hair curled crisply, gilded with a strong, new permanent wave and her blue eyes were more misty than ever.

At last the doctor decided to breach the wall of silence. 'Tell me about Jean,' he asked simply.

'She was terribly, terribly brave,' Betty began in a rush of embarrassment. 'I'm sure she saved my life half a dozen times. I was dreadfully ill after I had the baby. It didn't live, you know. And she . . .' she paused, groping in the emptiness of her memory. Betty dealt with trauma by erasing it from her mind, and now she could recall very little of what had taken place in the women's camp, although it was only a short time ago. It was beyond her emotional strength to remember that she had sold Jean's wedding ring for three eggs and a pair of wooden pattens, and so the incident had been edited from her memory. 'She was always so cheery,' she finished vaguely. 'She talked of you a lot . . . Arthur.' It seemed unduly intimate to use his Christian name.

'I thought of her too, of course.' There was a heavy silence. 'Gerald . . .' he began, but Betty interrupted at once.

'Don't tell me. I can't bear it, please. Don't tell me anything. I know that he's dead, that's all I need to know.'

He nodded with understanding, touched by her frailty. 'Have you any plans?'

'Not really. I must sort out our things, of course, that's why I'm here. But I've no home now, you see. Nothing to go back to in England. Our house was bombed, a direct hit.' She looked wistfully away across the dance floor where two or three couples circulated below the languid ceiling-fans.

He intended to pat her hand in sympathy, but found himself holding it, a small, soft thing that lay limply in his palm like a sick bird, with the wrist pulse fluttering under the pale skin. Betty was comforted by his touch. It reminded her of the early days of her pregnancy, when the doctor alone had understood her fears.

'You're so good to me,' she murmured. 'I feel so lost without my husband. I just don't know what to do. Gerald was my whole life, you see.' She had returned to Malaya for one very simple reason. She not only felt lost without a man in her life, she also felt poor, and the prospect of returning to a life of genteel destitution on a small army pension dismayed her. It had seemed as if Britain were full of brassy, striding women who were thoroughly accustomed to competing for male attention. In the Crown Colony, Betty knew, women were more than ever in the minority and a husband should be easy to catch.

'It's been a rough time for us all,' he consoled her, wanting very much to make sure that this dear, timid creature should never suffer again in her blameless life. She gave him a small grateful smile, sensing that she had secured a suitor.

The next day they began the day's journey to Bukit Helang, and Arthur Anderson escorted her on to the ferry to Port Swettenham, the mainline train to Kuala Lumpur and the smaller train upcountry, from which they were driven to the estate in Gerald's old Model T Ford.

'Welcome, Betty, my dear, welcome. How very good to see you,' James greeted them, noting the doctor's protective stance at once. 'Isn't the old car magnificent? She started at the first turn of the handle when we got her going again.' He patted the vehicle's dusty black roof.

'What has happened to our bungalow?' she asked him, anxiety pinching two vertical lines between her eyebrows. 'I must arrange for all Gerald's things to go back to Georgetown. If there is anything left, of course. There's been so much theft and vandalism, hasn't there, even on the estates the Japanese didn't bother with.'

'We've got off lightly here. Selambaram says the Japs came, ordered him to continue production, then vanished. They shot a couple of men for show, that's all. We were very lucky.'

'You're always lucky, aren't you, James?' It was a guileless observation. 'You must have been born under a lucky star.'

The three of them dined together, with a cluster of oleander blooms in a jampot on the table and a new boy to bring out the soup, the curry and the icecream.

'Your silver!' Betty exclaimed. 'Dear Ahmed buried your silver. I can see him in my mind's eye now, I know exactly where it is. We'll go to find it tomorrow.'

'It'll be gone by now, sure as eggs is eggs,' Anderson observed, stretching his legs in the rattan lounger. 'If you saw the hiding place, plenty of other people probably did, too.'

Betty and James fell easily into something like their old relationship, he courtly and charming, she happy in the security of his care. She mentally compared the doctor with the runaway aristocrat; Arthur would mean quietness and security, which she craved, but James, although the war had taken the edge off his fine youthful confidence, could still dazzle her with his charm. He still had about him the glow imparted by a wealthy background. Above all, perversely, she wanted James more because he seemed less interested in her.

Next morning Betty demanded a boy and set off in the direction of James's old home. A mere half-hour later she burst in on him in the bare stone-floored estate office. 'There!' she cried, dropping a canvas bundle caked with moist, red clay on his blotter. 'Absolutely untouched. Please open it, James, I can't wait. It'll be like having all the lovely days of the past to look at.'

Amused at her enthusiasm, he called for scissors and cut the half-rotted covering. Insects streamed away from their adopted home. 'Watch those red ants,' he cautioned, pulling her back with his arm. 'They bite like fury.'

The sugar-caster, the salt, pepper and mustard pots, the coasters and the napkin rings and cutlery were all tarnished blue-black.

'I shall clean them myself!' she announced. 'You've got some methylated spirit, haven't you? They'll be shining like new by supper time.' And so they were, though it took her the whole afternoon to rub off the discoloration which clung stubbornly to the decoration and the engraved Witheram crests.

'It must be so nice to have a real family.' Wistfully, she ran her rounded fingertips, grey with polish, over the heraldic device on a knife-handle. 'You know I have no one now, James? There's Gerald's family of course, but it isn't the same as your own kin, is it?'

'I suppose not.' He felt tenderness as he leaned over her bent head, watching the humble, stained hands put the finishing polish on their work. He was unaware that she had come to this house because of a shrewd female instinct for finding a provider, and had determined to ensure her future by fanning the ashes of their former closeness. James was also, for once, unaware of his own vulnerability. He never suspected that this little brown mouse of a woman had developed a capacity for selfish artifice quite comparable with that of his mother.

As the days of her visit passed, James lay awake at night, reasoning at random. If he stayed in Malaya, who better for a companion than Betty? If he returned to England, a wife would ensure his fortune, and Betty, dear, little Betty, would never be the sort of managing minx he loathed. He would like to take care of Gerald's widow, as a kindness to his dead friend. He would like an outlet for his betraying sexuality, which had so often endangered his security in the past. The only obstacle was Arthur Anderson, who had grown irritable with jealousy as soon as he sensed that he had lost his place in Betty's affections. However, the doctor had to continue his round of clinics elsewhere in the state, and within a few days he would be gone.

At the other end of the building, Betty also postponed sleep. Betty Bourton, she said to herself. Lady Betty Bourton – no, that would not do. Lady Bettina Bourton – much better. He will just have to call me Bettina, she resolved.

They were married three months later in the Register Office at Kuala Lumpur with Anderson, who appeared to have accepted defeat gracefully, as a witness. James wrote at once to Pasterns advising them of the marriage and anticipating his legacy.

In due course the reply was delivered. 'As you are no doubt aware, the codicil relating to his bequest was drafted in your father's individual style rather than the legal form which is always preferable in such documents in the interests of precision. Taking into account that the will as a whole is drawn up in keeping with the trust documents existing in your family, it is our opinion that the true beneficiaries of this bequest are intended to be your offspring, rather than yourself. It also appears to us that your father intended this provision to apply only to your own natural children, since the wording precludes inheritance by any adopted heir.' The writer then offered James congratulations on his marriage and assured him of the firm's best attentions.

They moved from the estate house into a large, newly built bungalow, with a room for a nursery and an *amah* to care for the child for which James now hoped. Bettina, as it amused him to call her, bustled around arranging the furniture and drilling Ah Ching, the new boy, in the use of their new luxury, an electric stove. She clung to James as she had clung to Gerald, wanting him back in the bungalow for every meal and interpreting every absence as a deliberate unkindness.

To James's dismay their sex life degenerated swiftly through a spiral of misunderstanding to the status of a disaster. Every element in his life combined to render him impotent. His work exhausted him. The clear fact that he needed to conceive a child to assure their future frightened him. Bettina's manipulative dependence angered him. Worst of all, the memory of sweet, golden flesh, of kittenish sensuality and artless pleasing welled up in the darkness and he felt distaste for Bettina's passive white body and pursed-lipped tolerance of his attempts on it.

He drank too much, which made his flesh yet more wayward. He went to bed with dread in his bowels, frightened that he would not be able to achieve an erection, which was more and more often the case. Worse was to come. If he mastered his tiredness and distaste, and achieved ejaculation, a fierce pain flared up in his loins, and persisted for some hours afterwards.

On Anderson's next visit to Bukit Helang, James consulted the doctor about his sexual difficulties. Anderson reacted with swift embarrassment. 'Pain of that kind is very unusual in men,' he said, as if he doubted James's word. 'In women, it's quite common of course. Any trouble with your water, at all?'

'No.'

'Ever had any – ah – venereal disease?'

'No.'

'What about during the occupation, when you and Treadwell were living rough in the jungle – anything with the waterworks then?'

'Heavens, I couldn't begin to remember. We were going down with one illness after another in the beginning. We had no drugs, you see, and we had to eat whatever we could get. I'm a tough specimen and I got off lightly, but I was unconscious for three days once with one of the fevers that hit us.'

'Mmn.' The doctor examined him as if he could hardly bear to handle another man's body, putting on a thin rubber glove to feel the inside of his rectum with one finger. 'Prostate seems a little enlarged.' He was plainly puzzled. 'But it shouldn't be serious. There are no nodules, nothing. This may just be the result of an old urinary infection. Tell you what I'll do – we'll assume that this is another of these damn tropical bugs the boffins haven't caught up with yet and see how it likes some penicillin. Wonderful stuff, penicillin. Takes care of the clap too, you know.' Anderson was not by nature a tactful man, but he would not have dreamed of telling James outright that he suspected that chronic, untreated gonorrhea was the major cause of his problem.

Anderson came to dinner with them and stayed overnight, for which James was grateful since his presence diluted the tense atmosphere between himself and his wife. James's characteristic charm was waning; it was hard to radiate merriment with sexual failure, poverty, and insecurity staring him in the face. He saw no reason to confide his problems to Bettina. She was already whimpering, 'Don't you love me any more?' and following him with reproachful eyes. They were squabbling with more frequency. 'You only married me for Gerald's sake,' she would say, or, 'You married me because you felt sorry for me, didn't you?' She was terrified that he would divorce her; she felt as if the shame of that would kill her, that anything would be better than the misery of living as a stigmatized divorcee on a pittance – she was no longer entitled even to her widow's pension.

James at first argued, swearing with the fluency of lifelong practice that he loved her, but she began to be obsessed with her own inferiority and retreated beyond the reach of flattery. 'I'm no good,' she told him, 'I'm not your class, your family will laugh at me. They must be wondering what on earth possessed you to marry some common little woman with no money or family of her own.'

The doctor returned in a week. 'Thought it best to pop by,' he told James, his bald head gleaming with a film of perspiration. 'Penicillin doesn't agree with everyone. Besides, I'd like to see how it acts on your condition – very interesting, never come across anything like it before.'

Anderson continued to make weekly trips to the estate for four or five months, eventually changing James's treatment to another drug, and always happy to stay the night. James was more glad of his company than anything else. Nothing seemed to affect his body one way or another. He never felt any sexual stirring towards his wife now, and she behaved to him with such coldness he seldom dared to make a move towards her.

One morning James left the bungalow in darkness as usual to take muster, then realized that he had forgotten to put on his wristwatch. Rather than risk turning the car on the pitch-dark narrow track, he left it and ran back through the silence that preceded the jungle dawn, when life seemed suspended as if a thousand creatures were holding their breath in anticipation.

James saw two figures in silhouette against the bamboo blinds and realized that his bedroom door was open and light from the kerosene lamp was streaming across the verandah outside. As he approached, he heard his wife's voice. 'I can't bear it when you're not here, Arthur, I feel so safe with you,' she was saying. 'I know I've made such a terrible mistake. You're the only person I can talk to. I just don't know what to do.' The rattan lounger creaked as she sat down in a tense ball of distress.

'You mustn't blame yourself, Betty. He swept you off your feet, that's all. He's a good-looking chap, a real ladies' man. No girl could resist if he made up his mind to charm her.'

'But he's so different now. He's . . .'

'He's seen me about it, you know.'

'No, I didn't know.' Her voice sank to an embarrassed whisper and James saw his wife bow her head.

'He and Gerald used to go down to that place called Mary's in K. L. before the war. Did you know that?' The shadowy head was shaken and the face appeared in profile as Betty locked up. 'I think he – ah – picked up something there that's the cause of some of this trouble. So you see, my dear, it's nothing to do with you.'

'You mean, some disease?' James smiled grimly to himself at her horrified tone.

The doctor put a reassuring hand on her shoulder. 'No danger from it now, I'm certain. Cleared up long ago but there's probably some scarring. But there's something else, my dear. I should have spotted it at once after all these years out East. Occasionally a man gets accustomed to native women and can't . . . well, if he takes up with a white woman afterwards it's never very successful. There's some fancy psychological explanation. I've seen quite a few men like that in my time and I'm afraid I think James is another one.'

'But he says he *must* have children, Arthur.'

'I'm afraid he has precious little hope of that at the moment.'

'I'm so glad you're here, Arthur. I couldn't go through all this on my own.'

'Would you object if I suggested you should see a colleague of mine in K. L. for some tests? There's just a possibility that there's something which can be done, but we would need to know that everything was all right with you, too.'

'If I must,' Bettina said slowly. 'I suppose I owe it to him to try everything.'

To James's surprise the doctor sat down beside his wife, his arm around her shoulders, and slowly kissed the top of her head. Then Ah Ching appeared at the front of the bungalow and began climbing the steps, and the two people drew apart.

James decided to send a boy to fetch his watch later and returned to his office, his mind in turmoil. Jealousy was the mildest of the emotions he felt. Uppermost was outrage: Anderson had obviously deliberately prolonged his useless treatment in order to have the excuse to meet Betty, and had deceived him about his sexual difficulties. Beyond his anger, however, James saw that the situation could be turned to his advantage. For the first time since the end of the war he allowed himself to think of Khatijah and their child. He pulled out the letters from the lawyers in London and read them again.

Betty found that there were more and more occasions when James could not be with her and suggested she should choose Anderson's company instead. Swiftly her trust in the doctor grew into a passionate affection, which he returned. She began to make shopping trips to Kuala Lumpur whose real purpose was to meet Anderson in the tearoom of Robinson's department store.

She was an easy victim of romance. Impelled by the instinct to find a protector, and with any sensuality she might have achieved blighted by the puritanical ignorance of her upbringing, Betty could adeptly arrange her emotions to suit her circumstances. Genuine passion was beyond her, but instead she felt an equally powerful sensation, an artificial attachment created from equal parts of expediency and fantasy.

James watched the couple carefully during the doctor's visits, feeling contempt for their love affair which seemed to him as banal and sentimental as a cheap Hollywood romance. He took a perverse satisfaction in their shared looks and the furtive fingertip touches they exchanged behind his back.

He invited Anderson to spend the Christmas of 1946 at Bukit Helang. Bill Treadwell also joined them, and at once remarked James's grim, withdrawn mood. 'Not much goodwill to all men about you, Jim,' he said with characteristic directness.

James rejected the invitation to confide his troubles. 'Tell me about the prospects for peace on earth,' he countered. 'Have the Communists disbanded? I heard on Radio Malaya . . .'

The Australian made an expression of contempt. 'Surely you're not still believing everything you hear on Radio Malaya?' They fell into a familiar discussion about the authorities' blindness to the Communist threat and it was not until many hours later that Bill wondered why James was being so reticent about whatever was preying on his mind.

There were electric lights now to hang with the Chinese lanterns and Indian paper flowers on the young casuarina tree which was felled for the celebration, and a frozen turkey from the cold-store in Kuala Lumpur instead of the sucking pig which had graced the board in Douglas Lovell's day.

Knowing that the lovers had formed the habit of meeting on the verandah in the morning after he had left for the muster ground, James set off in darkness as usual the day that work resumed on the estate; then turned back to spy on his wife. Again he saw her with Anderson, two shadows on the blinds, which this time embraced and kissed awkwardly.

'I can't bear it, Arthur,' Betty spoke in a low, hopeless voice. 'I've never known such happiness and I can't stand stealing it this way. I want to be with you for always.'

'Leave him, darling, leave him, why ever won't you leave?'

Little as he cared for Betty now, James felt a stab of jealousy. The two figures sat down side by side and were evidently holding hands. James strained his ears to hear the rest of the conversation.

'I daren't run off, darling, I daren't,' Betty was saying. 'Don't you see what he'd do? He'd finish you. I'm your patient, too, don't forget, Arthur. If it was ever known that you had a love affair with a patient, and with the wife of one of your patients, there'd be a terrible scandal. The Medical Council would bar you from practising ever again. You'd be struck off, and then what?'

'I could still practise out here – no one enquires too deeply into a fellow's credentials in the East.'

'But we'd never be able to go *home*, Arthur,' Bettina spoke with anguish. 'I don't want us to be one of those awful, shady colonial couples. I want to be your wife, and to live with you in England, and have nothing to hide from anybody. I hate this beastly place, I've always hated it.' They sighed and were silent and unhappy for a while.

James felt a surge of contempt. Like most aristocrats, he considered himself above snobbery, but the *petit bourgeois* tone of his wife's love affair disgusted him. The craven preoccupation with professional status, respectability and appearances was anathema to his own values. Much as he despised the lovers' suburban dilemma, however, he appreciated its power to paralyse them.

'I've got to make him divorce me,' his wife said at last. 'Or catch him out with one of his native women. Then I'll be free. It won't be long now, I'm sure of it. If only he doesn't decide to go home with me. I couldn't bear to leave you.'

'He won't go home until he's got his legacy, never fear. And he won't get that until he gets his child, which is impossible. So that's that. We're safe for a while.'

Bettina gave a laugh, the cruel expression of a weak spirit's resentment which ignited hatred in James's heart. 'You're quite sure I can't get pregnant?' she asked the doctor. 'Even if he could – do something?'

The man nodded. 'I've seen the results of those tests you had in K. L. myself and it's exactly as I thought. When you were ill after your child was born there was a lot of abdominal infection and, of course, in those circumstances with no treatment it probably continued unchecked for a long time. There's no chance of the two of you ever having a child. So he'll never get his legacy, unless he settles for a native wife and a brood of half-castes – hardly the thing for the son of a duke, eh?'

'But don't you mind about me, Arthur? I wouldn't mind giving you children if you wanted them.'

'I don't want them. I faced that a long time ago with Jean. All I want is you, my darling, and for us to be together always.'

James drew back to avoid seeing their embrace. His head spun with the implications of what he had heard, and he walked back to his car in a trance. Once the morning's business was underway, he went into his office to consider. Then he called up Selambaram to announce that he would be going away for a few days, and telephoned an acquaintance in Kuala Lumpur to ask for a loan of his car.

He drove slowly down the straight, level road, red dust billowing from the tyre-tracks. It was like driving into a dream. The wooden houses slipped past, half-hidden by thickets of bamboo. In the fields he could see people cutting rice. Was she with them? He half expected Khatijah's graceful form to appear at the roadside and walk towards him, the steps confined to a seductive undulation by the tight dark-red sarong. He was afraid of seeing her, afraid of her reaction when he proposed taking possession of their child. Better hope that she was harvesting rice with the others.

The cindery area of the roadside, where he had so often parked his truck, was waiting for the car. He walked to the house of his father-in-law, conscious of his stiff shorts and sturdy shoes. They did not know him at once, because of his pale skin and Western clothes, but he smiled and joked and reminded them of incidents during the war and at length they saw that he was the same person as the man who had married Khatijah, and greeted him with a mixture of pride and wariness. Here, too, he realized, he had the name of a war hero.

'Your wife is well,' Osman told him as they sat down on the wooden floor. Little Yusof fetched Maimunah, who arrived with a baby in her arms. Behind her trailed a watchful infant with fine, brown hair, dressed in a length of checked cotton which was tucked around her plump stomach. James noticed with relief that his daughter's skin tone was no more than olive, that her hair was not black but several shades of tobacco-brown, that her eyes were oval but not slanting.

'And you have another daughter,' Maimunah was offering him the firmly swaddled bundle in her arms. With disbelief he took it, and looked down on the small face; a pair of dancing, dark eyes scanned him with curiosity. The baby opened its tiny, toothless mouth and yawned. This child was also olive-skinned. He fancied that the eyes turned up at the corners, but could not be sure.

'Born six months ago,' the grandmother told him. Mentally, he counted the months. Yes, it was just possible. They must have conceived this child just before he left the village. 'Very strong baby, laughing all the time.' The tiny limbs struggled in their white wrapping and the baby gave a cooing gurgle.

He handed back the bundle and began negotiations, impatient with the delicate circumlocutions he knew he must use in order to persuade. He wished to return to his own country with his children, and would make a gift of money to Khatijah and another to Osman. He proposed divorcing Khatijah under Moslem law. Their marriage in any case was not valid under the laws of Great Britain. They had certainly expected something like this, and from the eagerness with which Osman began to discuss the terms of the deal James deduced that Khatijah had once more sunk to the status of an outcast in her family. 'Of course,' Osman observed pompously, 'the Holy Koran decrees that children are the property of their father beyond the age of six. Of course, these circumstances are special, because their father wishes to travel so far away.'

Maimunah, on the other hand, wrangled with unfeminine obduracy. 'Khatijah's children are her only happiness, the only wealth she possesses. She will never give them up. She will fight like a tigress for her cubs.' She glared around the dim, stuffy interior of the house. 'Children as young as this need their mother. And besides, no honourable family would entertain such a suggestion.'

Then there was a commotion among the crowd which had assembled on the ground below, and Khatijah herself appeared, her red and brown skirts still wet from the *padi* fields. Obviously one of the children had run to tell her that her husband had reappeared at last and wanted the babies. His heart turned over at the sight of her, vibrant with anguish, all modesty forgotten as her headcovering slipped off her braided black hair.

She flew at him, eyes as wild and staring as those of an angry cat. 'You shall never have them!' she screamed, clawing at his shirt. 'I will die rather than give my babies to you! No other woman is going to bring up my children. They belong to me. I love them. My children are all the world to me. If you take away my children, I will die!'

Uncontrollable sobs tore at her lungs and she began to scream. She hurled herself at her stepfather, begging incoherently to keep the girls, and Maimunah spoke up again, arguing with Osman: 'It's not right to take such tiny children away from their mother. It's cruelty. How will the baby live happily without its mother? Khatijah should be able to bring up her own children.'

The women's opposition made up Osman's mind at once. He had no wish to cut the foolish figure of a family head whose womenfolk disregarded his authority.

'Be quiet, both of you. This man risked his life with the Japanese for us, are we now going to deny him what is rightfully his? I don't need two more mouths to feed, Khatijah – did you think of that?'

'No!' she screamed in fury, hammering her fists on the bare, wooden floor. 'No! No! I won't let you take my babies.' She leapt up, snatched the swaddled baby from her grandmother's arms and ran to the steps, but at once two uncles restrained her and James flinched inwardly as he saw his child torn from its mother's arms.

The older girl, understanding what was to happen, began to scream and clutch Khatijah's skirts, but she, too, was pulled away.

'Take your granddaughter away,' Osman told Maimunah. 'This is best for everyone, and she will realize that when she has calmed herself.' Khatijah's mother stepped forward, eager to remove the embarrassment of her disobedient girl from her husband's sight, but Khatijah halted at the head of the stairs and snarled at James.

'Never forget what you have done today – never! There is nowhere in the world you can take my children that I will not find them and come for them! And I will make you suffer.'

After that, the affair was finished with the same furtive lack of ceremony that had characterized his wedding to Khatijah. With Khatijah's mother and one of her uncles, James drove with the infants to Kuala Lumpur, where he sent the villagers back. Then, he telephoned the estate and ordered his houseboy to bring the *amah* and meet him.

'What on earth is all this?' Bettina demanded as the *amah* carried the baby into the bungalow and James followed carrying the older child, who had at last screamed herself into an exhausted sleep.

'These are my children,' he told her harshly.

She quickly crossed the room and inspected the baby, drawing back the cotton cloth in which it was wrapped with her fingertips. 'What children? What are they? Native brats! I should have known! Not in there,' she commanded the servant as she walked towards the room they had intended as a nursery. 'They can live in the servants' quarters. I won't have you . . . I won't have them near me.'

'Yes, you will, Bettina, my dear.' Wearily, James motioned her to sit down. She remained standing, arms folded, rigid with anger. 'Yes, Ah Ching, that's the right room. The Mem made a mistake.' She opened her mouth to protest but he silenced her with a gesture. 'Now tell me, Bettina – do you want your divorce?'

She stepped back as if he had hit her.

'What!'

'I'm too tired for any lies, Betty. I've known what was going on between you and Anderson for a long time, so there's nothing you can deny. No need to panic.' He smiled at her, summoning the remnants of his old charm to impose his will, and she approached as if drawn by a spell and sat down opposite him. 'We can both have exactly what we want. I can have my inheritance if I have children, and I *have* children. You can have Anderson if I divorce you, and I will divorce you. All that's necessary is for you all to cooperate.'

He got up and took a cheroot from the box on the black, wooden sideboard, then lit it himself. Ah Ching and the *amah* were bustling to and fro with hot water and bed linen. He could hear the sleepy voice of the older child asking in Malay for its mother.

'Cooperate with what, James?' His wife was watching him with suspicion, torn between hope of a way out of the bleak emotional labyrinth in which she was trapped, and fear of her husband.

'Making absolutely sure that there's no question about the legacy business, that's all. I can't take the chance that there'll be any question about the children's legitimacy.'

'Have you taken leave of your senses?' she snapped, her voice almost cracking in fright. 'They're your bastards, James, your *native* bastards. You can't make them any more than that. You don't seriously expect me to pass them off as my own children! You're mad! Two little niggers like that. It's absurd.'

'That's where you're quite wrong. I've thought it out in great detail, Bettina, I'm not a fool. They're three-quarters white, and since my whole family are dark-haired I don't suppose they'll be in the least conspicuous. All I need are birth cer-tificates, and all I need to get birth certificates are a couple of chits from the good doctor – do you see? No one will know any better by the time I get back to England. I'll leave it a few years, of course.'

'You've gone mad, James. You'll never pass them off as white children.' He saw that her hands were shaking, and she clasped them together in the lap of her mauve print dress. She felt weak with tension.

'I don't see why not. They're no darker than I am. The older one's lighter, actually. You'll see tomorrow, she's got brown hair. Darker than you, lighter than me – what would be more likely?'

She looked at him in silence with hope and anxiety mingled in her misty blue eyes. 'And you'll really let me go?'

'Yes.'

'And you won't make any trouble for us?'

'Considering that you would be in a position to make trouble for me, I'd be foolish to even think of it. Of course, if Arthur didn't agree I would have to write to the Medical Council pointing out that he'd alienated my wife's affections, commit-ted adultery with a patient, that sort of thing. You *are* my wife, Bettina. You haven't been a very good wife either, I should say.'

A deep flush of shame darkened her pale face and her expression became anguished. 'I didn't mean to, James, I swear it. I never intended to look at another man. I don't know what happened. The whole thing just grew and grew, day by day, until . . .'

'Until it was bigger than both of you?' He had intended to sneer, but checked himself. Like a horse, Bettina was uncontrollable when she was frightened. He would have to calm her to win her obedience. 'I think we both made a mistake,' he put as much kindness in his voice as he could. 'And we won't be the only ones. A lot of people were unsettled by the war. But there'll be no harm done if we keep our heads, I promise you.' He took her hands and held them, looking into her eyes with a pleading expression which seldom failed to get him what he wanted. 'Of course, I was hurt, dreadfully hurt when I discovered . . .' She began to cry and he released one hand and gave her his handkerchief. 'But when I thought about it, I realized that you're suited to Arthur, he's more your kind of chap than I am. Believe me, I don't want to stand in your way. But I must have my inheritance, don't you see? There's no future for any of us in this country. There'll be all-out war with the Communists soon, it's inevitable. And I'm damned if I'm going to go home to sponge off my brother for the rest of my life.'

'We'd all go to jail if they found out,' she protested, half-convinced.

'Nonsense. They don't send people to jail for this sort of thing. And we'll never be found out, I promise you. The country's still in confusion, a few irregularities in paperwork aren't going to attract any attention. Why not talk to Arthur about it? Sleep on the idea, eh?' he suggested, patting her shoulder. 'I'll take the guest room, shall I?'

The next morning, she agreed. By the end of the week Anderson had accepted the proposition with extremely bad grace, and filled in two dockets confirming the birth of girl babies to James and his wife. James chose the names Catherine and Miranda as a vain homage to Khatijah and Maimunah; he selected birth dates which cut months off the children's real ages, in order that the births should not predate the wedding and that Pasterns should suspect nothing. For the same reason James also insisted that the divorce proceedings should wait a few months.

James decided to remain in Malaya for as long as he could, despite the news that some isolated rubber estates had been attacked by the Communists. They agreed that Bettina would leave as soon as Anderson found a temporary home for them. He and Bettina planned to leave for Britain as soon as another doctor came out to replace him.

Bettina at once became sweet-tempered and friendly towards James; the log-jam of their hostility had been breached. There was an atmosphere of good humour about the bungalow for the first time. James found it charming to return for his lunch and find the two infants sitting in the shade with their *amah*. He acknowledged with pride that, in their white romper-suits and sunbonnets, they were extraordinarily attractive children. The older girl was becoming sweetly attached to him and frequently toddled up to offer him a hibiscus flower, or a snail shell, or whatever treasure had most recently caught her fancy.

Bettina was surprised when he roused her one afternoon from her lie-off. 'Wake up, my dear, you must wake up. It's important.'

Puzzled, she sat up and he passed her the silk wrapper she wore over her nightdress.

'Come into the other room. 'He did not want to tell her this in her bedroom.

'What is it – the Communists?'

'Yes, my dear, the Communists. There's been another attack I'm afraid.'

'Someone we know?'

'Up at Amblehurst.' This was the English name of a rubber plantation almost as remote as theirs, further up in North Perak. 'They killed the manager and his wife, and someone else who was with them.' James paused, wrenched in spite of his disdain for his wife's attachment, because he knew the news he had to give her would remove the only kind of happiness she had. 'Be brave, my dear. It was Arthur. Arthur Anderson is dead.'

She gave him a narrow, cringing look and said at once, 'He can't be. It wasn't his week to go to Amblehurst. It was someone else.'

He mixed a strong gin pahit and put it in her hand. 'I'm sorry, Bettina. My poor Bettina. There isn't any mistake. He's gone.'

Bettina did not cry. She was numbed with shock. 'It isn't fair,' she said, almost crossly. 'I loved him. It isn't fair.' As finally as if she had walked out of a door in real life, she retreated into a distant interior world and behaved like a sleepwalker for weeks. She never mentioned Arthur Anderson again, and never again exhibited any real cheerfulness or energy.

She stayed with James, because she had nowhere else to go. They rubbed along together amiably enough for a year or so, although she was unable to feel anything at all towards the two little girls. She drank a little more with each month that passed, and formed a bridge circle with three other planters' wives who relieved their fearful isolation with a day in Kuala Lumpur once a fortnight.

The Communist guerrillas, led by Chin Peng, picked off more and more of the Europeans who lived in isolation in the jungle, supervising the plunder of the country's resources. Five hundred Europeans died in the same year as Dr Anderson. The Communists attacked in other ways as well: three hundred strikes hit the rubber estates and the tin-mines. The British administration responded slowly, playing down the situation and gagging the press.

James found notices tacked to the trees on his plantation, proclaiming 'Death to the Running Dogs'. Their bungalow was fortified with sandbags, they were given a police guard and James toured the state in an armoured car with a shotgun at the ready.

In 1950, when James's eldest daughter was officially almost four years old, the British High Commissioner, Sir Henry Gurney, was assassinated beside his bullet-riddled Rolls Royce en route to a hill-station for the weekend. James decided it was time to take his wife and children home and claim his inheritance.

The war with the Communists in Malaya continued for twelve years, involving a hundred thousand British citizens. For the National Service conscripts in the fifties it was the posting they most feared because the fight was against two enemies, the Communists and the jungle; of these the jungle proved the more implacable enemy.

Malaya was granted independence in 1957; the war, which was always referred to as 'the Emergency' by the British, ended in 1960 with a victory parade in Kuala Lumpur, and the British military commander sat on the dignitaries' dais next to the American President of Pacific Tin. In London, James turned down invitations to the celebration cocktail parties and dinners. Malaya was now a part of his life which he did not wish to emphasize.

In Penang, Bill Treadwell applied for citizenship of the new country.

CHAPTER TWENTY-TWO

'*GONNA SPEND my whole life through –*' Monty reached forward to the audience, stuck out one hip as far as the tight, leather dress would allow, and marked the beat. The stage lights flashed. '*Lovin' you-u-u-u-u!*'

There was some desultory applause, and Monty and her band made brief bows. A whine of feedback hurt their ears, as it had done periodically right through the performance. The lights died. Three or four beercans sailed through the air and fell short of the small stage.

'Thank you, Ruby Slippers. Thank you, everybody. The DJ spun the new single by the Clash and the crowd pogo-ed into life. Monty stumbled back to the cupboard-like dressing room on shaking legs.

'Christ! That was awful.' She slumped on to a hard chair and looked at her face in the mirror. 'And I look so vile. They hated us, just hated us.' Her new band trailed after her – Winston, who'd done sessions with the Juice when they'd wanted an extra drummer, Stas, who had been playing with another of Biffo Records' hopeful signings when that band had split up, and Tony, who was really doing her a favour, because he was one of the most sought-after session guitarists in town. Monty admired Tony's effortless musicianship so fiercely that she felt overawed by his willingness to follow her into the succession of sleazy punk clubs which they had played over the past few weeks.

They all looked defeated. One of the flying beercans had caught Stas on the temple and he searched for a tissue to mop up the trickle of blood. There were no tissues. The dressing room at Dingwalls club was not equipped with such luxuries.

Sig shouldered through the door, full of energy. 'Great, fuckin' great,' he enthused, giving them all Cokes. 'Isn't she lovely?' He squeezed Monty's ass and the leather dress squeaked under his sweaty hand.

'C'mon, Sig, it was a disaster. All these poxy clubs are disasters. We're not building a following doing this, we're just dying on our feet.'

Sig picked Monty's coat off the hook on the wall, put his arm around her and led her out of the club into the damp night. Dingwalls was built on a cobbled courtyard by the side of a canal, and he supported her firmly as she stumbled over the uneven surface in her red stilettos.

'Now get this straight, girl. You talk like a loser, you will *be* a loser. Nobody does great when they're starting out. You gotta give it time.'

'There's a difference between doing great and having beercans raining down from the ceiling, Sig.'

'Ferchrissake, these kids throw beercans at all the bands they see. They also spit, yell and throw bricks if there are any bricks around. They want to be cool and be punks and stick safety-pins through their noses, that's all. Don't mean nothin'. Not a thing. They liked you, you were good.'

Monty squirmed inwardly; she was frightened of Sig. He was tough, physically strong and completely ruthless. He was also as stubborn as a pig and never conceded an inch when she argued with him. Instead, he would hit her if that was what would get her to do what he wanted, or bully her verbally, or, which was the most likely, simply argue her into a corner so that she obeyed him of her own free will but with fear seeping through her tissues.

The problem was that Monty was not only afraid of Sig. She was also afraid of every one of the boys in studded dog-collars and girls with green hair who stood in a sullen mass on the other side of the microphone. Without the Juice to hide behind, without Rick to blame if they should fail, Monty was getting a chronic case of stage fright.

'I can't stand it much longer,' she told Cindy Moon when Sig allowed her to return home. It was high summer, and the faint pulse of reggae music from the West Indian club in the next street throbbed in the dusty air.

'He's a bastard.' Cindy was sitting cross-legged in front of her typewriter. 'Sig Bear has a heart of solid dirt. How can he push you so hard? If you crack up he'll never get his money out of you. Men are stupid.' She uncoiled and put her arm around Monty. 'You're good. You're a star. Keep hold of that and forget Sig.'

'I'm not good though. I can write pretty songs, sure, and I can play well, but it takes more than that. I should never have let go in front of the band the way I did. I just don't know how to manage people. That was what Rick was so good at. OK, he was arrogant, but he knew how to put on a front for the rest of us, and how to talk people into things.'

'He was just another dominating bastard.' Cindy squeezed Monty's shoulders in a gesture of protection. 'Men are all on total power trips. You don't have to grind other people down in order to get on top of them.'

Monty sat down on the black, plastic-covered divan which was both their sofa and Cindy's bed. She felt as if she were being torn in two between Cindy and Sig, both of whom praised her talent but tried to push her into doing what they wanted.

At least Sig was easy to understand. He wanted her to finish the album and make him money. He did not pretend that he loved her – the word never crossed his thin red lips. Cindy, on the other hand, smothered her with compliments and caresses, wrote her poetry and bought her presents. It was balm to her affection-starved soul. Monty had thought at first that Cindy was gay: there were plenty of rumours that she was.

She soon discovered that Cindy got her kicks going down to the reggae clubs and picking up young black boys. Every month or so she would vanish for a few days of degradation with these contemptuous kids who felt sexually exploited and abused her accordingly. Then Cindy would reappear in the apartment with a witchy, lop-sided smile, show Monty her bruises and announce that white men didn't know the first think about fucking. She had some surprising white boyfriends, too – wealthy, straight business types, but Cindy seldom had a good word to say about any man, whatever his race or proclivity.

She would usually return with some cheap brown heroin powder as well, which she burned on a strip of silver foil to inhale the smoke. Smack was something else of which Monty was terrified. Cy had used it a lot, and it fitted with the nihilistic, destructive surrender to despair in his personality which frightened her because she sensed the same chasm of nothingness in herself. Cindy sometimes offered her some of the drug, but she always refused.

'Tell you what,' Cindy proposed suddenly, 'come and see the Joe Jones Band with me tonight. That'll teach you everything you need to know about men on power trips.'

'Aren't they big in Japan?' Monty enquired with a faint sneer. The British rock élite tended to look on bands which were big in Japan as soulless and commercial.

'Colossal. They're huge in the States, too. I liked a lot of their early stuff, it was sort of Dylanish, country rock. But now all they do is make a lot of noise and flash their equipment about.'

Monty decided to go. She had nothing else to do except sit in the apartment in the heat, fighting the fear in her heart. Cindy took an hour and a half to get ready, at the end of which she looked stunning in another of her diaphanous chiffon dresses, this time striped electric blue and pink. She wore gilt stiletto-heeled sandals and a 1940s fox wrap with the animal's muzzle and paws worked into the design. Monty felt hopelessly dowdy in her leather dress, which was creasing and falling out of shape.

The Joe Jones Band took the stage between two mountains of speakers. With the first crashing chord they played, Monty felt as if she were lifted off her feet and dashed against the wall by a gigantic wave of sound. The volume made her bowels vibrate and her mind empty completely. It was impossible to do anything but give herself wholly to the ocean of noise and let it sweep her away. They were lanky, long-haired American boys. Joe Jones was a mesmeric figure with raven-black hair which whipped about his naked torso. He wore nothing but a pair of skintight, white satin trousers, which revealed every line of his magnificent thigh muscles, and a silver-buckled belt. He leapt around the stage, howling into the hand-mike like a Red Indian warrior.

Cindy had backstage passes and insisted that they should be presented to the performers in their dressing room when the set was finished. She always took advantage of her position as a minor London celebrity to meet the top bands in town, but Monty hated the whole business of standing in a tiny concrete room wondering what to say next to people in whom she was not interested.

Raucous laughter greeted them from behind the dressing-room door. Joe Jones's legs seemed to fill half the room. He was sprawled in the only chair, a half-empty bottle of Bourbon in his fist, his heaving chest mantled with sweat.

'Hi, I'm Cindy Moon from *Hit Maker*, and this is Ruby Slippers. How do you like London?' Cindy always introduced herself the same way. The legs contracted, and Joe Jones shook Cindy's small hand, putting down the bottle in order to do so. At the intrusion of women the boys fell silent.

'I'd say "sit down" but we're a little short of chairs. They showed me the review you gave our last album – you said some very nice things.'

They continued to exchange pleasantries while Monty wished she were somewhere else. The problem was that there was nowhere Monty could look in the mirrored cell without her eyes being drawn to Joe's crotch. The white satin outlined his cock, and he clearly found performing exciting. Even though the erection was subsiding slowly the satin was so tight she could see the ridge of his penis. As if he were aware of her attention, Joe Jones pulled a towel from around his neck and let it fall into his lap, modestly hiding everything. After another ten minutes of small talk Cindy said goodbye and left, with Monty trailing after her.

'See what I mean?' Cindy said as they hailed a cab. 'They think they're so great, making all that noise, drinking all that whisky, having all those chicks scream for them; they're just little boys, that's all. They were just dying for us to come back to their hotel with them. Thank goodness we got out when we did.'

'It might have been fun.'

'You can't seriously *like* all that macho crap.'

Monty said nothing; she was not quite sure how she felt. Of course she was repelled by all that aggressive sexuality. It was the same swaggering sham of maleness that she had hated so much in Rick.

'I've got a headache,' she recognized at last.

'Poor, poor Monty. I'm so sorry.'

At the apartment, Cindy insisted that she should not take an aspirin – 'it makes your stomach bleed' – but instead put a dab of Tiger Balm on Monty's forehead. This did nothing. The pain spread down the left side of her face and settled in her teeth. The next day was a Sunday and the pain in Monty's teeth became so bad that she felt as if she could hardly see.

'I know what would fix it,' Cindy said with a curious reserve.

'What?'

'You won't take it.'

'I'll take anything to stop this agony.'

Cindy's lips twitched. 'A whiff of smack would make the pain go away, I promise.'

Monty shook her head. She went into her own room and telephoned her dentist, but the number did not answer. By the afternoon all she could do was lie down and moan.

'I can't bear seeing you like this,' Cindy said, bringing her some camomile tea. 'Just a tiny bit of smack and you'd be fine.' Monty pushed the mug away, nauseated by the idea of drinking anything.

'You're not thinking you'll get hooked on one hit, are you? It's not the same, inhaling. Look at me, I do it all the time and it's no big deal. You don't see me crawling round the room if I can't get any gear, do you? And believe me, Monty, the pain would just go – it'd be there, but it'd be far away, where you could handle it.'

Monty held out until the evening, then allowed Cindy to sprinkle some of the brown granules into a piece of foil and let her breathe in the smoke. It was a little sickly and acrid, but Monty was accustomed to bizarre chemical tastes.

'Now you'll know what it's all about,' Cindy told her. 'All the kids do smack now. It's nothing, just a good feeling.'

Monty's stomach heaved and she dived for the bathroom to be sick. Then relief came, sweet and calming. As Cindy had predicted the pain was still there, but it was not like pain, just a distant signal that she could ignore. The fear was far away too. Until the drug banished it, Monty had not realized how she had lived every day with terror disseminated throughout her being.

Three weeks later Ruby Slippers had another gig, and Monty asked Cindy for a hit to calm her the day before. It had worn off by the time she had to leave the apartment for the club, so Cindy gave her another. She took the stage in complete confidence, performed well, kept a brave face in front of the band and let Sig say and do what he liked with no sensation of involvement at all.

They began recording the first Ruby Slippers album, and Monty found that she could get a faster hit by embedding a grain of smack into a cigarette. She still vomited every time and as she felt like using the stuff more frequently this was becoming a real inconvenience – and worse.

'I'm terrified Sig'll find out,' she told Cindy. 'He caught me throwing up yesterday and I told him it was food poisoning, but he's too smart to believe that again. What'll I do? He'll kill me if he susses'

'Use a needle,' Cindy advised. This did not seem nearly as alarming to Monty as it would have done three months earlier. True, she hated needles. But she hated the fear more. She allowed Cindy to inject her. 'You'd better lay off this Chinese stuff, though,' her friend said as the lovely calm spread through her. 'It's not very pure. I'll see if I can find you some of the old white stuff. Pharmaceutical grade, that's what you need. Keep to your leg veins, if you can, then your arms will be clean.'

White heroin cost her about five times what the brown stuff did, but it was worth it. Monty had the money which Cathy had lent her for the lawyers' bills, and it slowly found its way into the pocket of the dealer whom Cindy met two or three times a week in a coffeeshop near the *Hit Maker* office. Eventually, the money was gone.

'Can't you ask your sister for more?' Cindy asked.

Monty shook her head. 'I can't lie to her. We're too close, we can practically read each other's thoughts.' The truth was that Monty had been deliberately avoiding Cathy, and this had become sadly easy to do. The days of long, girlish telephone calls were past. In Monty's years with the Juice she had been away on tour for months at a stretch; Cathy, too, travelled on business a great deal. No lapse of time or distance could diminish their closeness, but Monty, privately ashamed and fearing failure, could stay away from her bright confident sister with little effort now.

Cindy gave a pout of disapproval. 'I'm skint until the end of the month,' she hinted.

'We'll just have to do without dope for a bit until I finish the album and Sig pays me some more of what's due from the single,' Monty told her, offended that anyone should suggest she deceive her sister.

The next night, when Monty returned late from the recording studio with Tony and Stas, intending to sit and talk for a while in the apartment, she found the door open.

'Cindy must have left it open,' she said uncertainly. 'That's odd. She's always telling me to be careful to lock up.'

'Could be someone kicked it in.' Tony showed her the lock, which seemed to have been loosened on its screws. 'Anything missing?'

At once Monty noticed that her tape-recorder was gone, and almost all her expensive clothes. She opened the leather-covered case in which she kept her jewellery. It was empty. She felt behind the mirror where she kept a pair of flashy diamond-and-emerald earrings which Rick had given her, rolled up in a scrap of chamois leather. They too had gone.

'Oh God, a break-in. That's all I need.' She collapsed despondently on the black divan. 'Isn't it great the way life always hits you when you're down?' The boys were sympathetic, and stayed with her until Cindy came home a few hours later. Cindy grew viciously angry when they told her that the apartment had been burgled, but Monty watched her with detachment. Cindy had suggested the hiding-place behind the mirror for her precious earrings and Monty could not help reflecting that someone who had not known there was jewellery there would not have thought of looking for valuables in such an odd place.

Early the following morning, Cathy telephoned. 'We've got to go down to Bourton at once – Didi's dying,' she told her sister. 'And I'm going to pick up Mummy first. Do you want to come with me?'

Monty had not seen her mother for years, and did not want to. Neither did she feel any compulsion to pay her last respects to her grandmother. 'No – I don't want to come,' she said. 'It'll only bring me down. And the old bat, too, I shouldn't wonder.' There was a pause at the end of the telephone, and Monty suddenly felt guilty that she always dumped on Cathy the whole responsibility for their unlovable family. 'Unless you'd like me to come, of course, 'she added.

'Please, Monty – I need you. It won't be a great day out, but I think it's something we should do together. Didi's part of our lives, after all.'

Cathy's BMW hurtled like a silver bullet down to Brighton and drew quietly to the kerbside by the tall white house where their mother lived. Bettina seemed to have shrunk in stature, Monty thought. Her hair was inaccurately tinted honey-blonde, with several inches of grey regrowth visible. The whites of her eyes were yellow, her skin was greyish and waxy, and the sisters noticed with horror that the backs of their mother's hands were spotted with small ulcers, the result of self-neglect and malnutrition aggravated by alcoholism.

Without the care of servants, Bettina's apartment was filthy. Piles of unwashed clothes and linen stank on the dusty floors and the kitchen was sticky with grease and crammed with putrid rubbish. Monty opened the bedroom door and recoiled at the stink. Their mother glared at them in mute defiance, challenging them to disapprove of the squalor.

At Bourton there was a peculiar air of furtive relief in the household. The servants were grave but lively. Hugo, their uncle, seemed to be taller; their cousins' children were quiet and cheerful; everyone in the house was trying to ignore the sense of festival that stole upon them as the tyrant lay dying.

'Darlings! So good of you to come to see an old woman,' their grandmother called from the depths of her faded chintz-curtained bed. 'Forgive me, the doctor won't let me get up. But I've fixed him.' She arranged her bedraggled, pink satin bedjacket trimmed with marabou. 'I just happen to know the best man in London for my kind of cancer and he's coming down tomorrow to tell the old quack not to be so ridiculous. I'm remarkably fit for my age.'

Dutifully they sat on the uncomfortable Louis XV gilt chairs and attempted to hold a conversation with the dying woman. Her hair was nothing but a few wisps of dull, greyish-brown tucked under a girlish velvet band. Her sagging eyelids were crusted with blue mascara and a coating of rouge clogged the fissures in her cheeks.

'I wondered, Catherine, when you are thinking of getting married again.' She spoke with a conspiratorial gleam in her watery eyes, her hands with their joints knobbed by arthritis clutching at the satin quilt. 'You must be quick, dear, before you lose your looks completely. Of course, you can't hope to compete with the young beauties of today, but you can always make a man fall in love with you if you know how it's done, dear.'

'Of course, Didi,' murmured Cathy, stealing a glance in the shadowy, ormolu-overhung looking-glass to reassure herself that the creamy perfection of her complexion was still intact, that her hair still gleamed like burnished bronze, and that her black chalk-stripe suit did indeed enhance the delicacy of her build in the way she intended that it should.

'Don't say "of course" to me like that!' The deformed hands clutched more convulsively as if to draw support from the exhausted glamour of the fabric. 'The only point in this work nonsense is that you can meet the right kind of man. Otherwise you'll just end up on the shelf like your sister.'

Monty and Cathy exchanged glances of resignation, and Cathy steered the conversation back to Lady Davina's cleverness in seducing London's leading cancer specialist into attending her. This man appeared the next day, flustered and embarrassed, and spent an hour with the old woman after which he briskly took Hugo aside and advised him, 'Nothing to be done, I doubt she'll last the night. She's having all sorts of delusions, don't take any notice of them.' It was difficult to ignore the demanding shrieks that soon sent the nurse scurrying downstairs to ask the family's advice.

'She wants to come down and make telephone calls,' the alarmed woman explained. 'She says she's got to telephone the Prince of Wales and heaven knows who else. She says she can't stay in bed all day like a slut. She says she's organizing a ball and she simply must have royalty there.'

Hugo stumped upstairs and persuaded his mother to write letters instead of telephoning, and the old woman covered many pages of her rich blue writing paper with scrawled lines which tailed off midway down each page, until the bed was covered with half-written notes and she fell back into her pillows in a doze.

In the evening, Lady Davina awoke and said in apparently lucid tones, 'I want to see my sons. My darling boys, I must see them.' Hugo left the dinner table and went up to his mother again. 'Where's James?' she demanded in anger, as if she suspected Hugo of hiding his brother.

'James isn't here, Mother,' he sighed.

'Poor boy,' she murmured. 'He must miss all the fun we had at the Embassy. He must be so desperately lonely out in the East. We must make him come home, darling, fix something up for him so he'll be able to stay, eh?' The cajoling inflexions of the rasping, old voice were almost obscene.

Later she demanded her jewel box; she spent the last of her strength raking through the jumbled trophies, occasionally holding up some glittering article to the spectral light of her chandelier, reflecting in silence on the hard-won attachment which it had symbolized. At midnight the nurse gently removed a diamond bracelet from her patient's feeble grasp, rearranged the creased pillows and gave the semi-conscious woman her medication. Lady Davina died quietly in her sleep a few hours later.

No one had thought to ask the Trust for permission to use the chapel for the funeral, so Lady Davina received her last respects in the village church before the burial. The sisters looked with interest around the little grey-stone nave. There were few guests. Three elderly women who had outlived Didi, and one old man, one of those on whom she had never ceased to exercise her seductive skills, who left the graveyard with an unsteady step, deluded to the last that he had known a great lady.

As they walked back through the rain-sodden churchyard to their car, Monty asked, 'Are you sorry she's gone, Cathy?' They paused and watched the rest of their family as they dispersed.

'No. She should have died at thirty, for her own sake.' Cathy spoke with surprising harshness. 'I'm just sorry she made me waste so much time.'

Caroline and Edward, with their stout spouses and beefy children in velvet-collared coats, moved slowly down the mossy path. They were sinking into the quagmire of small salaries and dying professions, led by the will-o-the-wisp of land-gentry lifestyle which would eventually lure them as if blindfolded into the anonymous middle classes. Caroline was married to an unprofitable farmer. Edward was the sales director of a small agricultural machinery firm. They were stolid, weatherbeaten and ignorant of any world that did not revolve around shooting seasons and bloodstock lineage.

Cathy suddenly gave an irritated sigh. 'Wherever did we come from, Monty? We're not part of this tribe, are we? We want to change the world, not keep it as it is, pickled in vintage port and old school ties.'

'Now you know how I've felt all my life.' Monty walked briskly to the car and pulled open the door. There was never any need to lock a car in Bourton village. 'We must have a rogue gene or something.'

'Maybe Daddy was the same. It's hard to imagine what he would be like if he were still alive.'

'I think he would have been a wonderful, wicked old man by now.'

Sadness settled on them and they were silent as Cathy drove the short distance back to the big house. They both felt that death had moved one generation closer to them. There was only Bettina ahead of them now, and they were both appalled at her rapid physical deterioration.

That evening Monty sank into black apathy and Cathy looked at her with concern as she sat on the high brass fender by the drawing-room fire staring into the distance. She noticed that her sister had lost weight, and was wearing a cheap army-surplus sweater over an old leather skirt.

'How's the court case going?' Cathy asked, hoping to draw Monty into a more cheerful mood.

'Great. We've got a fabulous barrister, a real shark. He looks as if he trains by biting the heads off live chickens before breakfast. I hope he's as good as the solicitor says he is – he's costing enough.'

'What about the money?'

Monty gave a short, hard laugh. 'That's going great, too. Don't worry about it, I'll cope.'

'You're looking really slim.' It was a sincere compliment and Monty nodded, smiling. 'It must be the worry – look.' She pulled up her sweater and showed Cathy that she could put two hands between the waistband of her skirt and her body.

'Are you sure you're eating enough?'

'Cindy's always on a diet, so we don't eat much.'

'What was the last thing you ate?'

'Cut it out, Cathy.'

She watched in hurt surprise as Monty jumped off the fender and walked out of the room. When they got back to London, Cathy took Monty to lunch at a hearty, oak-panelled City carvery and gave her a cheque for five thousand pounds. Monty hugged her in guilty gratitude. She had not intended to ask Cathy for money, but now she and Cindy had debts and the gift would pay them off as well as buying them a substantial period of chemical peace-of-mind.

Monty became quite certain that Cindy herself had staged the 'burglary'. She also realized that her roommate was making money herself on their deals, and that the heroin she bought was far from being pharmaceutical grade; but these things no longer seemed important. Everything which had disturbed Monty now seemed gloriously unimportant. She was indifferent to the hostility of the band when she strolled into recording sessions an hour late or worse. Doing the publicity photographs was no cause for concern, although she used to feel absurd in the fetishist outfits which Sig ordered her to wear. Even though she had a crop of ugly pimples around her mouth, Monty faced the camera with no anxiety. She grew wonderfully thin.

Sig himself lost the power to scare her. She no longer launched herself into fucking with the desperate dread that if she did not please him she would be finished because he would dump her. She was just active enough to stop him getting suspicious. But Monty's judgement was getting weak, and one night Sig suddenly rolled off her and sat up. He groped for his cigarettes and lit one with an angry gesture.

'What's the matter with you?' His voice was quiet but not friendly.

'Nothing. I just feel a bit weird tonight. I'll be OK in the morning.'

'No, you won't. You'll be sniffing and strung-out in the morning.'

'No I won't. I'll be fine.'

'Sit up,' he ordered. She did so. In the darkness she did not see him raise his arm and the blow was a shock. He knocked her off the bed. Her mouth filled with blood; she had bitten her tongue.

'Listen, you stupid bitch. I don't care if you fucking slit your wrists. You can jump off the Empire State Building for all you mean to me. But we've got a contract, you and I, I've paid you money, and I want my album, and it pisses me off that you ain't giving me an album because you're smacked out all the time.'

'We've nearly finished the album.'

'No you ain't. It's crap, what you've done. I heard the tapes yesterday. You'll have to start again.'

She crawled to the far side of the room swallowing the blood in her mouth. 'That's not true,' she protested, wondering where her clothes were. She heard him get up, walk over to the door and lock it. Then the lights snapped on and she blinked. He stabbed a blunt accusing finger at her as he got back into the bed.

'If I say it's true, it's true. Now come here. We've got unfinished business.' She did not move. 'I'm not coming to get you. I don't give a fuck either way.'

She knew if she challenged him any further he would beat her up thoroughly. Hesitantly, she walked back to the bed and lay inert beside him. He killed his cigarette and pounced on her with furious violence, holding her to him like a doll. His penis was broad rather than long, and distended her delicate tissues painfully even when he was gentle. Sig was in no mood to be gentle now. Her weakness infuriated him because he knew it was her last hiding place. Open defiance he could fight, passive resistance he could not; he rammed at her brutally as if his rage could spark the fight in her.

He paused and she. felt a finger probing clumsily at her anus.

'No please, Sig, that hurts,' she whispered.

'It'll hurt a lot more if you don't get off the stuff,' he answered. 'Relax, stop fighting me. You'll get into it.' He flipped her over as easily as if she were an insect, pulled apart her buttocks and crammed himself into her body. With his weight pinning her down she was powerless and lay unresisting as the vicious strokes tore her flesh. In the end she decided the quickest way to end the agony was to make him come, so she began to respond, faking all the passion she could. He was not fooled. She raked his flesh with her nails, gasped, purred in pretended ecstasy, her hips eagerly grinding, but she could almost feel his sarcastic smile.

After that calculated violation, heroin became as much a way of taking revenge on Sig as anything else. The problem of the album took care of itself when Tony was offered two weeks with a big American producer in Los Angeles and found a loophole in his contract which meant that he could be released.

To Monty's surprise, Tony came to see her before he left, with a bunch of white chrysanthemums and a bottle of wine. He was a slim, quiet, blond man with a self-effacing manner despite his honoured status in the music business, and Monty was even more surprised when he told her: 'Don't think we can't see what's happening with you and Sig, Monty. He's trying to make you over into some punk sex-symbol, and that's just not your style. I've always liked your songs – they come right from the gut, they're honest, emotional. And you've got a fantastic gift for melody. Your music is grown-up music, not this gimmicky, get-rich-quick crap. Stas and Winston feel the same, we've all talked about it. You're dead right about doing the clubs – those kids aren't your audience at all.'

Monty looked at him uncertainly, flattered but anxious. 'I don't know. Sig's very smart about marketing, all of that. I just don't know any more.'

'Well, I know.' Tony refilled their glasses. 'I've had twelve years playing with the best, and I'd rather play with you smacked-out than any other chick that's supposed to be together. Or most other blokes, come to think of it. In your place I'd run out on this album, and get another label to buy out your contract. Go for a producer who's into a really big slick sound, that's what you need.'

It was good advice, but Monty was unable to act on it. She felt powerless, a piece of flotsam carried along by a flood of events. Her money ran out, and she made a deliberate attempt to play on Cathy's sympathy and get more, but Cathy looked shamefaced and shook her head. 'It's a bad time, Monty. I've got a nasty few months ahead of me. You'll have to stall the bills for a bit. I wish I could help you but right now I'm in a jam myself.'

Monty was so focused on her immediate problem of getting cash for drugs that she failed to notice an unaccustomed, haunted look in her sister's eyes, and the fact that she drank more Scotch than usual, throwing down the liquor with a desperation that was quite unlike her characteristic serenity.

The rent was due, and the telephone bill came in. 'It's easy to get money if you know how,' Cindy reassured Monty. 'I'll ask some of my friends.' She reached for the telephone and called someone named Roger who worked in a stockbroking firm. To Monty's amazement Cindy cajoled him into a dinner date, put on one of her alluring dresses and reappeared the next morning with a fistful of ten pound notes.

'You can always get money from men like that,' she told Monty. 'Either they're bent or their wives are frigid little straights obsessed with the children. They're rich, and they're quite happy to pay for a bit of glamour and a few thrills.' Roger took Cindy to Frankfurt on a business trip the following week, and she returned with more money, but made it clear that she was not going to buy Monty's drugs with her earnings, or pay Monty's share of the rent and the bills which were mounting up.

'If I can do it, you can,' she told Monty. 'You're looking so beautiful, any man would get out his chequebook. All you have to do is a bit of the old voodoo – know what I mean?'

Monty knew exactly what she meant: the elaborate game of tease and make-believe which Lady Davina had taught Cathy, and which she herself had used on Sig in the days when she had kidded herself that she was using him, not the other way around. Monty now had a permanent sense of degradation which she partly relished. There was a perverse kick to be had out of abasing herself. It was the only pleasure which remained to her. The drug was no longer enjoyable; it just kept her from feeling vile.

'They like double-dates, 'Cindy told her. 'It's less embarrassing for the blokes if they've got each other for company – means they don't have to make the effort to talk to the women. I'll see if Roger's got a friend.'

Roger was short and thin, with sparse brown hair and very pale blue eyes. He wore the uniform Monty recognized from her voyages to the City with Cathy – a striped shirt, a diagonally-striped tie and a dark-blue suit. The tie was tightly knotted. His friend was a little fatter, a little fairer in colouring and a little more nervous. The four of them went to a very expensive restaurant in Mayfair.

'Check it out,' Cindy told her while they were in the ladies' room. 'Every woman in this place is on the game, except the owner.' Monty looked around the restaurant as she went back to the table. It was full of sober-suited men, some of them famous politicians or film stars. Most of the women were past the first bloom of youth, dressed very discreetly in dull, good-taste silk pant-suits, with a lot of gold jewellery. There was about them a telltale air of disinterest; it was the only difference which Monty could detect between these women and any others.

'Roger's a real drag,' Cindy had confided. 'He just wants everything he's ever read about in Harold Robbins. Let's blow their minds, shall we?'

Blowing the guys' minds meant going to a hotel around the corner and staging an elaborate pretence of lesbianism while the men sat awkwardly on the bed drinking vodka. Cindy kept the act going with a repertoire of outraged shrieks, protestations and compliments to Roger and his friend which flattered them so lavishly that Monty nearly spoiled everything by laughing. Roger gave them £150 in clean ten-pound notes and seemed highly satisfied.

'You see?' Cindy laughed in the cab home. They're perfectly happy, so where's the harm? They can tell all their mates about the two hot chicks who gave them a show last night, and feel like Genghis Khan – and we'll be OK for another three days.'

Monty wondered uneasily about living beyond the three-day limit and was both relieved and dismayed when the telephone rang the next day and Cindy announced, 'Roger wants to see you again – you're in business, kid.'

'I don't want to go, Cindy. You go instead, if you like.'

'Don't be stupid – where else are you going to get a hundred quid for practically nothing? And dinner.'

'I feel I'm using them, Cindy, and I feel I'm being used, and I don't like it.'

'But that's what it's all about, honey – trying to have sex without using somebody is like trying to eat without chewing.'

'Come on, Cindy, suppose it's someone you love.'

'Love? What's *that?*' She spoke as if she had seen a cockroach. 'What's love about, except people getting their needs met? You are a hopeless old hippy, Monty.'

'OK, so I'm a hippy. Right on, peace and love – bury me in my tie-dyed T-shirt. I still don't feel like fucking Roger or anyone else for money. The idea makes me want to throw up. Tell him I'm ill or something.' Privately, Monty decided it was time to pull herself out of this dangerous situation. She would cut down on smack, maybe just do it at the weekends, and find herself a job. Swallow Lamotte's company was still in business; maybe she could go back there. But cutting down made her feel ill – weak, tired, groggy and nauseous. Her gums ached and her eyes were sore.

She went to bed with a mug of sugary tea and tried to watch television to take her mind away from the craving for a hit. The doorbell rang and she did not answer it. Cindy was out, but she had her keys, Monty was sure of that. It might be someone coming to cut off the electricity. The bell rang incessantly, and someone began pounding the door.

'Monty! I know you're up there, I can hear the TV. Open up!' It was Sig, and he was angry. Fear grabbed Monty's guts. He can't get in, she told herself, he can't; the door is strong, he can't break it.

Sig yelled again from the street. 'I'll get you, you slag. You owe me, don't forget. You owe me and I'll collect, if it fucking kills you.' He was throwing stones, but could not throw high enough to reach their windows. Instead, Monty heard a tinkle as a window in the floor below broke.

Eventually Sig went away. Monty was bathed in sweat, her heart leaping in her chest with terror. When Cindy came back she begged her for some gear, but Cindy would not agree to find some for her until Monty had herself telephoned Roger and made a date. After all, Monty told herself, it can't be worse than doing it with Sig. This turned out to be true. Roger was easily satisfied with a straight fuck which barely made the two-minute mark. The hardest part was laughing at his jokes.

'Wowee!' rejoiced Cindy a few days later. 'Roger wants to take you to Paris with him. You're a real hit!'

Not the sort of hit I ought to be, Monty mourned in silence. Cindy loaned her a chiffon dress – now Monty was thin enough to wear her friend's clothes – and a suitably dull skirt and sweater. 'You won't have any trouble with the customs if you look straight,' she advised. 'Just hang on Roger's arm and smile sweetly.'

She took a pretty Art Deco compact for loose powder and washed it. Into the reservoir she tipped Monty's remaining packet of heroin, which was coarse enough to be held down by the small circle of stiff gauze which closed over it. She cut a circle of cellophane from a cigarette packet to fit inside the gauze. Then she dusted a green ostrich-feather puff with face-powder and put it on top.

'Blow away as much of the powder as you can,' she told Monty. 'It's so fine it'll fly away easily and you'll be left with the stuff underneath practically untouched.' She snapped shut the blue enamel casing with a flourish. 'Even if they do search you, which they won't, so much powder will come out of the compact when they open it, they won't bother examining it any further. You can buy some disposable syringes in a *pharmacie*.'

Monty waited at the airline check-in desk, hoping she would not meet anyone she knew, and wondered if anyone would recognize her now, thickly made-up in conventional tones, her hair tamed into balsam-conditioned curls, wearing a neat beige skirt and a simple angora sweater to match.

'Hello, Roger. My, you look great. I'm longing to see Paris. You are a darling to take me,' she gushed, wishing she could spiel out this nonsense as easily as Cindy could. 'I can't wait to get to the hotel,' she breathed, pressing her thigh into his when they were seated.

'Why wait?' he asked. 'Ever joined the mile-high club?' They fastened their seatbelts.

'You wicked man,' she giggled, trying to forget that she and Rick used to watch airline passengers from the sanctuary of the VIP lounge, trying to pick out from the shuffling herds at the boarding gates those who looked so incurably banal that they would find it exciting to screw in an aircraft toilet.

I mustn't think about all that, she told herself as she hurried up the aisle to the john. The days of private planes and being protected are finished forever. Rick really did love me, he just couldn't let himself show it, she thought, as Roger squeezed through the folding door, unzipping his fly and breathing hard. Cindy had suggested that she should leave off her briefs, so there was nothing more to do than slide up the dismal skirt, find a way of propping one leg above the small wash-basin, throw back her head and moan, 'Baby, baby, my God, it's beautiful, Roger, darling Roger,' until he had had enough.

Sex was becoming very uncomfortable. As Sig had predicted, she now had permanent constipation. It felt as if someone had poured cement into her intestines, and she was less inclined to eat than ever.

In Paris, she was careful not to utter one word of her excellent French, although it was very hard not to intervene when he mispronounced the name of their hotel so disastrously that the taxi-driver took them to the wrong side of the city. Luckily Roger had business meetings all the next day, so Monty took a very thorough bath and strolled around aimlessly. She felt alienated to the point of mental paralysis. She could recognize that the city, leafless in the dead of winter, was beautiful, but the beauty could not touch her. It was just another irrelevance.

Monty had developed the druguser's sixth sense for recognizing others. She shadowed two girls she saw meet by the St Michel Metro and exchange a fold of paper for money. They separated and the one with the paper disappeared under the green cross sign of a *pharmacie*. Monty waited for an hour, then went into the shop to get her syringes. She was ready for Roger by the time he returned, and listened with a decent show of attention while he explained what wankers his French clients were. Although her mind was insulated by the smack, it exhausted her to be charming and acquiescent continuously, and she began to understand why call girls acquired that definable air of apathy. She recognized it again in one or two of the women in the restaurant to which they went for dinner. The aggressive stylishness of French women was blunted in them; why bother to be chic for a trick?

'Your heart's not really in this, is it?' Roger sounded peevish. 'Something on your mind? Worried about anything?' He thinks I'm angling for more money, she thought. Cindy had explained that the way to turn a date into a trick was to go moody, tell him you were worried about a specific money problem like your telephone bill, then be deliciously grateful when he offered to take care of it.

'There's nothing on my mind, darling.' She tried to smile and look seductive.

'Do you know who that is?' he asked her, indicating a spruce, dark man with heavy features sitting with an aristocratic-looking blonde in a peach silk shirtwaist dress.

'Isn't he some sort of financier?'

'Some sort of financier? Isn't she cute? Darling, that's Giuseppe Ecole; he's in the middle of the biggest bribery scandal in Europe in the last ten years. If he goes back to Italy they'll clap him in jail the minute he gets off the plane.'

'Heavens. Who's the girl?'

'Who knows – one of Madame Bernard's whores, I suppose.'

A glow of animation entered Monty's lacklustre eyes. 'She really exists then, Madame Bernard?'

'Certainly she does. Not my cup of tea, of course.' One of Roger's most irritating foibles was pretending that he was a man who did not need to pay for sex but was merely generous to his women. 'But I know a few chaps who've been to her little parties and they're apparently pretty memorable occasions.'

Monty watched the couple under her eyelashes. They gossiped like an affectionate husband and wife. She looked at Roger, his chin greasy with butter from his asparagus, his eyes shining with the self-importance which she was there to enhance. If I'm going to do this, she decided, I'll go the whole hog. If I'm going to be patronized I'd rather it was by a bigger shit than Roger and if I'm going to sell my body I'd like it to be to the highest bidder, not for just enough to get me another couple of fifty-quid deals.

She shook off her depression and turned her attention to Roger, getting him bouncing with anticipation of the delights to come. Then, when the blonde with Giuseppe Ecole went to the ladies room, she followed.

They were the only two women in there and there was no time to be diplomatic. 'Are you one of Madame Bernard's girls?' she asked quickly. The woman looked startled, then smiled.

'Do you want to go home and say you've met a real live call girl?' she asked with amusement.

'No,' Monty declared with all the calmness she could command. 'I want to *be* a real live call girl. I think,' she tossed her head with contempt towards the door, indicating her opinion of Roger, 'that if something is worth doing, it's worth doing well.'

'Are you staying in Paris?' the other woman asked, removing a smudge of lipstick from the corner of her mouth with a precise touch. Monty gave her the name of the hotel, her own name and the name in which the room was booked. Then she steeled herself and returned to Roger.

She stayed in the room the next day and the call came at twelve. They met in the Drugstore on the Champs-Elysees, the blonde, Monty, and another, older, blonde woman who weighed, Monty judged, at least two hundred and fifty pounds. Her fat fingers were crowded with wide, gold rings. Her name was Véronique. They asked to see her passport, then chatted pleasantly about Monty's life, her family, her boyfriends and her interests. Monty effortlessly fabricated most of the information which she gave them.

'Let me see your hand,' said fat Véronique, reaching for it with a motherly gesture. 'Ah yes, excellent, a very long lifeline; the other hand, if you please.' In the pretence of reading her palms, Véronique pushed back Monty's sleeves and checked her arms for needle marks. Thanks to Cindy, there were none.

After an hour, Véronique gave her a level stare and said, 'You realize much of this work is extremely tedious? You will be good if you look clean and arrive on time, first of all. In this business we don't like gypsies who are unreliable.'

Monty nodded and smiled, relieved. I've done it, she thought.

'We have to check you out, of course. How long will you be at this number?'

'We're supposed to be going home tomorrow.'

'So, ask him for your money and stay over a day or two.'

Véronique telephoned at noon again the next day and gave Monty an address in the exclusive Marais district. 'We have an apartment where you can stay until you are set up,' she told her, 'then this afternoon we will do some shopping.'

The apartment was in a tall, half-timbered building with a steeply pitched roof. Constructed in the seventeenth century, it now leaned back a few degrees from the quiet street. The ground floor was occupied by a discreetly tawdry *bijouterie* whose windows were half-obscured with credit-card signs. The apartment was on the first and second floors, a slightly awkward assembly of spacious rooms decorated in white, glass and gilt – or perhaps it was gold-plate, Monty speculated as she put her unused syringes in the mirrored cabinet. She decided to celebrate her new success with a hit – a small one, just to settle her nerves.

Véronique called half an hour later and took her to an Yves St Laurent boutique, where she opened an account in Monty's name. Systematically she asked the manageress to bring out dresses, suits, two coats and innumerable accessories, working from memory of the current collection and disdaining to look through the racks. Monty suggested a ravishing, gypsy-style dress in purple lame, with a laced bodice. Véronique shook her head. 'Yves makes clothes for two types of woman, the good and the bad,' she chuckled, 'but you will find the bad women wear the quiet clothes and the good women dress like whores. I think he does it on purpose – it amuses him.'

'What's she like, Madame Bernard?' Monty asked, as their taxi waited in a queue of vehicles. The narrow street was lined with food shops, whose wares, in oval plywood baskets, were arranged in a fabulous display of colour and texture along the crowded sidewalk.

'Nobody knows. No one. No one has ever met her.' Véronique was gazing thoughtfully at heaps of oysters arranged on seaweed an arm's length from the car window.

'You must have met her,' Monty insisted. The shop owner, seeing the fat woman's hungry glance and the beauty of her companion, called out to them and opened a pair of long, pale brown shells with his knife, passing them, one after the other, through the taxi window. '*Mes compliments, mesdemoiselles,*' he called cheerfully as the taxi advanced a few metres.

'Never. Only one woman, in the beginning, spoke to her face to face. One day that woman disappeared, and now Madame Bernard speaks only on the telephone, with a disguised voice. Some electronic invention which makes her sound like Mickey Mouse.' She threw back her head, displaying a plump, powdery pile of extra chins, and gulped down her oyster.

Monty, who hated oysters, offered Véronique hers as well, full of curiosity about her new employer. 'You must be able to guess what she's like,' she persisted. 'You must have got some idea of her, if you've worked with her a long time.'

'Certainly.' Véronique slugged back the second oyster. 'She's a very curious personality, I think. She has an extraordinary understanding of people, of personalities. She can always predict how someone will behave. But she is absolutely without pity. If you betray her, she will never forgive. Sometimes, if I have to give her bad news about somebody, I tremble, really tremble, because I know her reaction will be extreme and something terrible will happen.' The older woman gave Monty a direct stare, making sure her point had been taken.

She's just trying to frighten me, Monty told herself with a defiant sniff. 'Surely you have to be tough in this kind of business?'

'Naturally, but there is a difference between tough and cruel, *n'est-ce pas?* I think it's very strange, because a woman with so much understanding is usually tender. Madame Bernard is tough, yes; she's ruthless. At times the only thing one can say is that she is completely sadistic.' The well-upholstered shoulders in their beige angora sweater shrugged and the long, twisted rope of pearls over Véronique's vast bosom rattled as she gave a sigh of incomprehension.

The next day Monty began to panic. The assurance of the whole operation intimidated her, and what had seemed like a fine adventure now appeared as the final step towards self-destruction. What am I doing to myself, she wondered. I'm already doing smack, now I want to be a prostitute. It's time I got out before I'm in too deep. She never doubted that Véronique would be sympathetic, and was shocked by the explosion that followed her confession that she had changed her mind.

'You don't play games with Madame Bernard, miss! All the trouble we've taken with you! Ungrateful piece of filth!'

'I'll give the clothes back, of course.'

'Impossible! They will not accept them back! You must pay for them.'

'But I don't want them. Of course they'll take them back, most of them are still in their bags, not even unpacked. I've returned clothes to St Laurent dozens of times and they never make a fuss.' Monty was angry now; she had been accustomed to treat the St Laurent boutiques like chain stores during her days with Rick and they had always served her courteously, no matter how many times she had changed her mind. 'You're just trying to trick me, that's all.' Tingling with anger and a fearful foreboding that she had already got in over her head, Monty folded the garments back into their gleaming red and purple boxes and took them back to the boutique. The manageress was absolutely charming and regretted that it was a rule of the house that no clothes could be returned.

'You didn't have that rule when I shopped here before,' Monty challenged her, praying that the woman might recognize her face.

'It is a rule for all Mademoiselle Véronique's friends,' the girl replied with emphasis. From a drawer, she produced a bill for several thousand francs and trusted Monty would settle it soon. The friends of Mademoiselle Véronique always paid promptly, she said.

Monty considered simply leaving the clothes and taking a taxi to the airport. She opened her purse and checked that she had the air ticket which Roger had bought for her in her wallet.

'That's stupid,' the shop assistant put a confidential hand on her arm and spoke in a low voice. 'They won't let you run away. You'll wind up floating down the Seine, just another "suicide". Paris is a serious place for a young woman, and these are serious people, do you understand? Thousands of girls come here every year and no one ever hears of them again.' Monty then remembered that Véronique had not given her back her passport. Grimly she returned to the apartment.

'What do you think I'm doing, lying to you?' Véronique folded her bloated arms over her chest. 'It's you who have lied to us, isn't it? You thought you would amuse yourself by playing at being wicked. You wanted to see if you were good-looking enough to be a top-class hooker, was that it? You thought we wouldn't see what you were the minute we laid eyes on you, eh? Don't you think I know what a junkie looks like? You stupid girls . . . you make me want to puke.'

'I am not a junkie,' Monty said with dignity. The late afternoon light was fading and she made a show of switching on the table lamps. Moving with surprising speed for such a fat woman, Véronique snatched Monty's black leather bag and tipped its contents out on the low glass table. Her pudgy hand pounced on the blue enamel powder compact and opened it with care, evidently knowing what was inside. She picked up the powder puff between finger and thumb and discarded it, flipped up the gauze circle, snatched away the cellophane and waved the half empty container of heroin under Monty's nose.

'What's this then? Sweet-and-Low? You haven't got much left, have you? What were you planning to do when you ran out?'

'It doesn't matter – I don't really need it. I just do a bit for fun now and then.' How the hell did she know where to look, Monty wondered fearfully. She tried hard to think of a way to escape from the trap into which she had so stupidly walked, but her mind was blank.

An imperious ring sounded from the gilt-trimmed fake antique telephone, and Monty jumped with alarm, wondering who could possibly know where she was. Véronique waddled across the room to answer and her whole body mass seemed to shrink as she listened. Monty's acute hearing detected a nasal twitter from the telephone line. That must be Madame Bernard, she told herself, folding her arms to stop herself shivering. Véronique replaced the telephone's earpiece and turned to Monty; her face had blanched under its thick beige make-up and her skin seemed almost green. She was obviously very frightened.

'Someone is coming to deal with you,' she announced, gathering up her coat, gloves and bag with some agitation. 'You are to wait here alone. Give me the apartment keys.'

The fat woman unplugged the telephone and left the apartment clutching it to her chest. Monty heard her turn the keys in the mortice locks at the top and bottom of the door. She ran at once from one window to another, hoping perhaps to find a way out on to a roof or a fire-escape, but every window was sealed. The window in the kitchen overlooked a lead-covered ledge about four feet wide, and although it was now almost dark, she could see beyond it a typical Paris roofscape of parapets and flat-topped buildings over which it would be easy to climb. Monty resolved to smash the window and get away. She could go to the British Embassy, she would be safe there, and she could telephone Cathy to come and fetch her.

As she ran back into the kitchen with a gilt-legged, velvet-covered stool from the bedroom, the lights in the apartment went out. She put down the stool and flipped the switches in desperation, but they were dead.

In the deep twilight, she saw the door of a tall kitchen cupboard open, and a small woman stepped through it. She wore a dark mink jacket and a black tailored suit; on her head was a round hat with a penny-spotted veil which almost obscured her face. In the half light, Monty saw a face of masklike stillness, with heavy-lidded eyes which widened with shock as they saw her. With a movement as swift as a lizard's, the small woman closed the door behind her. Monty had just enough time to see the *escatier de service* beyond the thick wooden panels, and sense that there was at least one other person waiting out there.

'Who are you?' Monty demanded, frightened into truculence.

'Who I am is not important,' the woman said, 'what I want to talk about is who *you* are.' She spoke in English, with a curious, clipped accent that gave her voice a metallic timbre. Slowly, the small, dark woman advanced into the room. She was slim but her figure was rounded, and under the veil Monty could distinguish a heart-shaped, high-cheekboned face and a flat nose like a cat's. She could have been any age between twenty-five and fifty.

'You've no right to keep me here,' Monty continued, stepping back unconsciously as the woman advanced. 'I want my passport back and I want to go home.'

With another movement so quick it seemed like a sleight of hand, the woman opened her black crocodile handbag and gave Monty her passport with a black gloved hand.

'You can go when we've finished our little talk,' she said, gesturing Monty into the drawing room. They sat face to face on the white sofas and Monty felt the woman's eyes scanning her face intently, probing every pore. Monty stared back, trying to see into the woman's face, feeling more and more intimidated.

'Who are you? Are you Madame Bernard?' Monty demanded.

'Madame Bernard does not exist.'

'You would not be able to say that unless you knew who she was.'

A brief smile, like a gleam of winter sunshine, touched the perfectly painted, cyclamen-pink lips.

'In your passport you call yourself a singer. Why do you want to be a whore?' The question was pitched in the kind of even, reasonable tone Monty had heard Cathy use when she was negotiating a difficult deal.

'I don't want to be a whore, I've changed my mind. Anyway, it didn't seem to be too different from what I was doing already.'

To her surprise, the woman picked a malachite case from her bag and offered Monty a cigarette. There was a brief struggle over the stiff table-lighter. 'Do you know what will happen to you if you live that way? Let me tell you.' The cigarette was smouldering, unsmoked, between fingers tightly swathed in black suede. 'You cannot sell love, and you cannot buy it either. It is not a commodity which can be traded. When you love, you give *yourself*. If you try to trade yourself for money – or for security, or social position, whatever it may be – soon you can't love any more.'

Monty gave a short, hard laugh. 'Anything for a quiet life.'

Suddenly the woman was very still, as immobile as a reptile on a rock. Monty sensed that she was very angry. 'When you can't love it's like death in life,' she said slowly.

'A quick fuck's got nothing to do with love, anyway,' Monty argued, confused by the intense emotional atmosphere. The woman made no reply and the words echoed in the silence and mocked Monty with their truth.

'Why did you want money so much that you would do that to get it? You have talent, I think? You have a career, don't you?'

'No. Yes. The thing is . . . I just couldn't handle it. Everyone wanted me to do something I couldn't or be someone I wasn't and . . .' Monty suddenly found her tongue loosened and she talked, pouring out all the terror and pain and struggle of the last year. The woman sat as still as a statue, occasionally asking a short question in her strange, ugly voice.

'So, the drug made you forget how difficult your life was?' she said at last. Monty nodded. 'What about the past – has life been that hard before?'

'A few times, not quite the same. Why are you asking?'

'Because I want to know. Continue, please, tell me what happened.'

Now Monty was mesmerized by this steely personality and she talked on as if she had been hypnotized, about her songs, about Rick and the Juice, about Simon, about her father. When she began to relate the story of her abortion she felt tears begin to run down her cheeks and wiped them away with her sleeve.

Finally she faltered into silence, her heart stripped and raw, feeling drained and feeble. The apartment was completely dark and she could not see the woman's face or her reaction.

'Why don't you stop taking this drug?' the woman asked in a neutral tone.

'I can stop easily,' Monty said, believing this to be true with at least half of her mind.

'Then why don't you? You're throwing your life away.'

'No I'm not.'

'I think you are, my dear.'

'You don't understand.'

'I understand better than you. I hope you never need to understand the things which I have to know.' The voice was suddenly as soft as silk. 'Let me make you a proposition. I know a place in California where I can send you for treatment, and if you are prepared to accept their help you will be able to stop.'

Violently, Monty shook her head. 'That's not necessary. That's ridiculous. Why would you do something like that? It'll cost thousands.'

The voice changed, indicating a smile. 'Let's just say I have made a lot of money and I can choose how I spend it.'

'I'm not going to be your private charity.' A tumult of old and new emotions was raging inside her. Monty felt exhausted, panic-stricken and ready to succumb to the sheer force of the woman's will.

The small, silhouetted figure stood up, walked to the apartment door and unlocked it. 'You have no alternative,' she announced, pulling the door open wide and admitting a dim light from the hallway. 'Except to leave now, in which case you will not get as far as the end of the street. There are so many accidents just here.'

The last shred of Monty's resistance parted. 'But I don't understand,' she protested in a weak voice. 'Why would you want to do this? What am I to you?'

She did not reply. Then, as quickly as she had appeared, the woman left, and Monty heard her quick, light footfalls on the stairs. A few moments later the lights flickered into life, and she blinked in the brightness. She sat on the sofa in miserable apprehension until a heavy tread sounded outside and Véronique came through the door carrying a small Vuitton case.

'Come along,' she said sternly, 'get your things. We must not miss the flight.'

This isn't happening to me, I don't believe this, Monty thought, as she was steered out of the apartment, into a car, through the airport and into the first-class cabin of a Tri-Star. They were offered champagne, and she drank a lot of it and went to sleep.

The smoggy sprawl of Los Angeles behind the square airport tower seemed like a scene from a dream. Monty felt passive and controlled. Her deepest emotions were in turmoil after her conversation with the woman she was more and more convinced must have been Madame Bernard, and throughout the long, dull, uncomfortable flight the curious metallic voice asking the questions Monty had evaded for so long echoed without ceasing in her head.

There was a limousine, chilly with air-conditioning, at the airport, and after hours of driving they arrived at a substantial white-pillared mansion set in the centre of a vivid green lawn. Royal palms cast long shadows in the rich sunlight of the afternoon.

Véronique sat beside her like a watchful toad as she was interviewed by a young man with a dark curling moustache.

'When did you last drink any alcohol?' he enquired.

'On the plane, champagne.'

'Any idea how much? It's difficult, I know . . . ?'

'I suppose about a bottle.' Her nose was running and she was starting to feel the lousiness of withdrawal.

'And your drug of choice is heroin, is that right?'

'Well, I use it sometimes.' She did not like the routine way he used that expression, as if she were obviously just another junkie.

'When was the last time?'

'Heavens . . .' She tried to work out the time changes, and finally judged by how bad she was feeling.

'The day before yesterday. You want to know how much?' He nodded. 'I'm not really sure,' she lied, 'I don't pay much attention.'

She was to share a room with Véronique. They were directed to the laundry store to collect linen to make up the beds. Then Monty was allowed to telephone Cathy in London and tell her sister where she was. Monty looked at the other people in the Centre with curiosity; this was what addicts and alkies looked like. They seemed to be a mixed bunch, old and young, some obviously very wealthy. One of the women, tall with fair hair drawn severely back and a ravaged face, looked faintly familiar.

The next morning Monty attended her first therapy group. They had given her a shot to make the cramps stop, but she still felt shaky and sick as she looked around the people taking their places in the circle of cheap plastic chairs.

'I'm John, and I'm an alcoholic,' began a curly-haired young man.

'I'm Darren, and I'm an alcoholic and chemically dependent,' followed a barrel-chested man in denims.

'I'm Mary-Louise and I'm chemically dependent,' said the matron in a pantsuit beside him.

'I'm Camilla, and I'm an alcoholic and chemically dependent,' said the woman with the ravaged face and fair hair. Monty stifled a gasp as she heard the assured English voice. It was Camilla Carstairs, the daughter of the judge, the lacrosse captain, the prettiest and most perfect of all the irreproachable girls in Benenden School. The last anyone had heard of her she had been married to an ambassador.

Monty suddenly lost the sense that this reality too was something from which she could escape.

Camilla looked at her with a weak but encouraging smile. The rest of the group had introduced themselves and now it was her turn.

'I'm . . .' she hesitated on her name; she seemed to have had so many names. 'I'm Miranda, and I'm chemically dependent,' she said at last.

Chapter Twenty-Three

'WE'RE PART of a revolution, do you realize that?' Henry Rose and Cathy were standing at the corner of St Mary Axe and Leadenhall Street at 7 pm, waiting for a taxi to take them to their dinner meeting at Trader Vic's.

'I never saw you as the Fidel Castro of Finsbury Circus,' Cathy kidded him. They were both distinctly mellowed by early-evening drinking. Henry had been appointed to the board of Migatto's banking division, and they had been celebrating with the Black Cat's best champagne.

'You know what I mean,' he said, sighting a taxi in the distance. Across the road two elderly men, caricatures of the City gentleman with furled umbrellas and pinstriped suits, had also sighted the taxi. 'We've got where we are on ability and nothing else: we didn't go to Eton, we don't belong to the right clubs, nobody pulled strings for us.'

'Not for you, maybe, but I married the boss's son, don't forget.'

The taxi cruised past them and they hailed it, sprinting across the street to get to the vehicle before the slowmoving, pinstriped pair who glowered resentfully as they climbed into the vehicle.

'Shrewton hasn't given you any breaks you don't deserve, you know that. If you couldn't hack it you'd be back in the typing-pool tomorrow.' Henry settled into the corner of the cab, waving cheerily at their disappointed rivals, one of whom made a threatening gesture with his furled umbrella as they drove away. 'In ten years' time, they'll be laughing at the way the old City types did business, with their old-boy networks, their deals done on a handshake, their alcoholic lunches and their chauffeurs taking them home at four o'clock.' Henry, normally the soul of good humour, could not keep an edge of malice out of his voice. A few years older than Cathy, he relished the prospect of his own success at the expense of men who considered themselves his social superiors.

'If my father were still alive he'd never believe it. He spent his life telling me not to get ideas above my station. He was as fossilized as the nobs, in his way. Deep down he hated them, but it was all covered over with a veneer of respect.' Henry's father had been a cutter in a Savile Row tailor's shop, a stooped, obsequious man who was ill-paid for his skill and who took refuge in a pedantic devotion to his craft.

This allowed him to look down on the customers and disparage them for their inability to tell one weight of worsted cloth from another, however noble their lineage, weighty their influence or long their credit might have been.

They sped past the new white Stock Exchange building, the symbol of the switched-on seventies, where women had been admitted to the floor a few weeks earlier. The optimistic sunshine of the springtime glinted on the gothic weathervanes and heraldic symbols which for centuries had shone above the Square Mile's grey temples of commerce. The medieval courts were lost in the evening shadows, and hundreds of feet above the time-scarred stonework of the ancient churches towered the new scaffolding around the City's first skyscraper, fifty-two storeys of steel and glass which would house the headquarters of the National Westminster Bank.

Cathy rearranged the long rope of pearls which gleamed creamily in the folds of pink-striped silk between the lapels of her tailored grey jacket. She got a kick out of the oblique compliment which Henry had paid her, but thought he was right for the wrong reasons.

'It's not because of us, is it, though? The real change is that the world's getting smaller, communications are getting better: the old boys can't adapt, that's all. You tell them we'll be trading in a twenty-four-hour market in ten years' time and it gives them a coronary just thinking about it.'

He laughed, showing an expensive mouthful of dentistry. 'Go on, take some credit, Cathy. Modesty's out of fashion too, you know.'

'I'm not being modest, I'm being accurate.'

'You're being dumb. If someone gives you the chance to brag a bit you should never turn it down. I didn't get where I am today by being accurate, I did it by making damn sure I grabbed all the glory that was going, whether I deserved it or not.'

In the dealing room at Migatto Metals the revolution they were talking about was clearly in progress. It was scarcely a year since Cathy had first stepped into the Ring at the Metal Exchange, but already the Reuters teleprinter had disappeared from the dealing room, and been replaced by a VDU on which the news was transmitted in luminous green. The sheaves of paper to which the traders had to refer grew smaller, as more and more information was electronically conveyed. People now sent telexes instead of written orders.

The pace of business was increasing too, and the more frantic it became the more Cathy loved it. The metals market was responding to the throes of the world's economy; when the dollar was devalued, when civil war broke out in Africa, or another major strike paralysed Britain itself, prices soared or sank and a huge volume of metal changed hands. On those days the dealing room was a madhouse and the Ring complete pandemonium.

Cathy traded without a pause, wildly exhilarated by the pace, her mind a stream of figures, her ears burning from the telephone, her throat sore with incessant talking, barely pausing to eat or drink until the pressure shifted to New York at the end of the day. Then the priority was alcohol, a stiff drink – often several – before she went out to dinner, usually with clients, to massage contacts, sell Migatto's services and generally continue the social side of the business. Her mastery of her new profession delighted her, although it had startled some of Migatto's clients at first.

Only a few months earlier she had snapped, 'Migatto Metal,' into a telephone one afternoon and heard a splutter at the other end of the line.

'Can I speak with the trader please?' She recognized the voice by its Swiss accent.

'This is the trader, Herr Feuer.'

'No, I would like to speak with the trader, please.'

'Herr Feuer, I *am* the trader. What can I do for you?'

The line went dead. Half a minute later she saw Henry leave his desk at the end of the room, throwing down his telephone with a gesture of anger. He bustled down the room to within earshot of her and yelled, 'I'm putting Feuer back to you – he's having a fit because he's got to speak to a woman.'

'I know,' she shouted back, 'he just hung up on me.'

'Fucking Swiss. I told him to stuff it up his *Lederhosen* and join the twentieth century.' There was a surge of amusement from the men around her and the light on Cathy's switchboard winked once more.

'Yes, Herr Feuer. Certainly, Herr Feuer. No trouble at all. I'll be right back to you.' She sold Herr Feuer's aluminium for him and thought no more about it.

That had been six months ago, and now Herr Feuer liked her to call him Heinz and had come round so much to the idea of doing business with a woman that he had invited Cathy to dinner. Since she was a minor celebrity, clients were often eager to meet her, but this time she had insisted that Henry come too because the flirtatious tone in the Swiss-accented voice was quite unmistakable.

Trader Vic's always made Cathy want to smile. The restaurant was the top favourite among young City types and she had to admit the food was delicious; but the idea was ridiculous – a phoney Polynesian paradise with bamboo walls and a palm-thatched roof created in the basement of the Park Lane Hilton a few yards from the concrete, the tarmac and the carbon monoxide of central London.

Heinz Feuer was much younger than she had expected, a slim, tall man in his middle twenties with hair the colour of butterscotch which flopped into his clear green eyes.

'You look much nicer than you sound on the telephone.' The words were out of Cathy's mouth before she could stop them and once more she cursed herself for her unthinking rudeness.

'So do you,' he returned with untroubled candour. 'I thought you'd be an old witch of fifty who smoked cheroots.'

'I thought *you'd* be at least sixty.'

'A real gnome of Zurich, *ja?*'

He wore the kind of clothes that were almost a uniform among the young, rich Europeans who used the markets as just a more exciting way of gambling – brown Cerruti slacks and shirt, a plaid V-necked sweater in muted lovat green, Gucci loafers. Cathy was not at all surprised when he suggested that they accompany him to Crockfords to play roulette after dinner. She weighed the value of his business against the tedium of watching roulette and decided she should accept.

'Heinz is OK, really,' Henry said as they waited while he claimed his car from the Hilton's parking jockey. 'Less of an android than the average Swiss, anyway.'

Cathy yawned, then noticed that Feuer was waving to them from the depths of a white Lamborghini Espada. 'Nice quiet taste in cars, too,' she said with amiable sarcasm.

Since the night with Rupert Lampeter when her body had reacted so violently against a man's touch, Cathy had gradually lost the sensation of icy physical detachment. She felt alive now, sensual and physical. She got a dizzying high from the thrill of the market, she felt melting tenderness towards her son, but she had not felt attracted to a man. The truth was that romance now had a very low priority in Cathy's life. She was making good money now, and had thankfully sold her apartment in Battersea and bought a much bigger and more luxurious home in the new Barbican development, a ten-minute walk from the Migatto office.

As soon as she moved in she realized that she had solved one problem and created another. She was working a fourteen-hour day, and although she now had the space and the means for Jamie to live with her, she would barely have seen him during the week. Passionately as she adored her son, she could see that it would be cruel to uproot him from the familiar comfort of his life at Coseley, where he now attended the village school and ran riot all summer around the estate with a gang of local children, and expect him to flourish in the loneliness of a London apartment.

Lord Shrewton, thinner, greyer and wiser than ever, proposed a compromise as they drove down to Coseley together one Friday evening. 'I expect you'd like to have young James to yourself a bit more now you're – ah – settled. Why don't we send him up to you sometimes for the weekend? No need to tamper with the custody arrangements and let Charlie know what's going on, just arrange things between ourselves, eh?'

'I think that would be ideal,' she agreed at once. She had not seen her former husband since the miserable day at the divorce court when the judge had directed that Jamie should live with his grandparents. Charlie was working for an advertising agency which his new wife's father owned in Dallas, but every now and then she would hear, through Nanny Barbara or one of her old friends, that his affections were straying once more. It was not difficult to imagine that, when Charlie's current meal ticket threw him out, he would scuttle back to England and set about claiming Jamie and the money in trust for him. If she applied outright for custody of her son, she might just precipitate such an action. It seemed better to have Lord Shrewton firmly on her side than to have his loyalty once again split by a legal battle between herself and his son.

Lord Shrewton's solid, unostentatious Rover picked up speed as the river of vehicles leaving the city flowed more freely once it passed the last junction on the Oxford road. The only sign that her former father-in-law was nearing his seventieth birthday was that he invariably fell asleep during the journey home, but Cathy decided to press her advantage while he was in the mood to talk family business.

'I'll be trading copper next week,' she told him. The copper traders were considered the most senior.

'Excellent. I hope Rose gave you a decent raise before he moved on. Certainly deserve it.'

'Thank you. Yes, he did.'

'Nothing to beat the markets – great life if you don't weaken. You seem to thrive on all the ballyhoo. More than most, it strikes me. A lot of traders are just in it for the money, but you've got a taste for the job.'

'I love it, but I don't want to do it forever.'

'Got your eye on young Rose's desk, I suppose. Well, why not? Remind me when you've had enough of trading copper, eh? You'll have more time for the boy too, when you're a director. Good idea.' She heard the gratification in his voice and realized he had been planning to promote her all the time.

In another year Cathy moved up to the position of junior director. She had gained the reputation of a baby tycoon in the making, and was amused to acknowledge that what her colleagues most resented about her was neither her ability nor her connections, but the mystery she preserved about her private life. The fact that the beautiful Miss Bourton gracefully rejected all the approaches which were made to her, and yet seemed to have no man in her life, seemed to imply an insult to most of the male sex. This attitude was not very logical, but after a few years of watching the markets soar and plummet on waves of male emotion, she had realized that there was nothing very logical about the world of high finance.

Even her sister was mildly disbelieving. 'Don't you get lonely?' Monty asked, sitting cross-legged on the oatmeal carpet in Cathy's Barbican apartment, playing dominoes with Jamie one rainy Sunday afternoon. Cathy was curled on the sofa in a red velour tracksuit, absorbed in reams of computer print-out, analysing the past quarter's business.

'No,' she replied truthfully. 'I'm totally blitzed with social life, I've got great mates who I work with all day, I hardly have time to see my old friends and I don't have a lot to say to them in any case. Jamie keeps me sane at weekends, and I don't get enough time with him anyway. You're the only person I'd like to see whom I don't see enough.'

'But don't you yearn to be crushed in someone's manly arms?' asked Monty in a vague tone, giving her sister a meaningful wink over the child's glossy dark head.

'No. I only yearn for the years and the energy I wasted thinking that being crushed in someone's manly arms was all there was to life. If you want the truth, Monty, I'm almost glad I walk with a limp because every step I take reminds me that I nearly lost everything I care about because I listened to Didi and believed all that junk.'

'I can crush you, Mummy,' Jamie announced, rolling happily towards her across the floor. 'I'm stronger than King Kong and I can crush you to bits.'

'Why not crush your aunt instead?' Cathy swiftly pulled the computer sheets away from his trampling feet as he climbed the sofa to embrace her. 'She's letting you win, I can see she is.'

'No she isn't, she's just stupid. Will you play with me now?'

'What is all that stuff anyway?' Monty asked, indicating the printed columns of numbers.

'Sales figures, that sort of thing. Didn't you go to Japan with the Juice?'

'Uh-huh. Three nights at the Budokan.'

'What was it like?'

'Can't remember – booze, dope and jetlag. Story of my life. Why?'

'We're not doing enough business over there and I was thinking of setting up a trip,' she answered, putting aside the print-outs. 'Do we have to play dominoes, Jamie? Louis XIV was playing chess with grown-ups at your age.'

'Well he was French,' her son replied in a dismissive tone before somersaulting over the back of the sofa. 'And I bet they let him win, anyway.'

Later, when Jamie had gone to bed, Monty returned to the subject of her sister's lack of love-life. 'There must be someone you fancy, surely? Just a tiny bit?'

'No. I walk into the City every day knowing that there are thousands of men all around me and I don't fancy any of them.' Cathy wished Monty would stop nagging her. It was not quite true that she felt no attraction for any man. She was aware that now, when Heinz Feuer called, she felt a tiny but distinct thrill. But he was just a playboy, not the kind of man she wanted in her life at all.

On Monday Cathy approached the senior director for whom she worked, Nigel Fairwell. 'I think we ought to plan a trip to Tokyo,' she said. 'The Japanese traders don't make use of half what we can offer them, and since we need to establish ourselves in the options market now, before the competition gets really hot, someone ought to go over and sell them positively. I don't think options have been marketed as well as they could have been.'

'Very well,' Nigel said without enthusiasm. 'Go ahead and set it up.' He was a square-faced, blue-jowled man of about fifty, with broad shoulders and greying black hair.

'The Japanese will never accept you,' Lord Shrewton told Cathy with amusement as she set off for her first trip to Tokyo. 'You'll just have to sit back and let the men do the talking. Japanese won't do business with a woman.'

In Tokyo, she found that her chairman and former father-in-law had less faith in her than the men with whom she worked. The Migatto party comprised herself, Nigel and her former clerk, now her assistant, Maurice. The day began with a breakfast meeting at 8am, with the men smelling powerfully of aftershave and everybody damp-haired from their showers. They sat around the hotel table with Mr Shimura, Mr Matsuyama and Mr Kodo, and Nigel, who had been to Tokyo before, introduced them all to each other. Everybody bowed.

'We're here to talk to you about options, a new product we've introduced at Migatto. This is Miss Bourton, who's our expert. She'll tell you all about them.'

While Nigel, in silence, attacked his eggs and bacon, Cathy went to work. 'Buying options allows you to limit your risk at times when the market is subject to short-term price fluctuations,' she explained. 'The idea is that instead of buying a metal itself, you buy the right to buy it in the future – say in three months' time – but at today's quoted price. Now obviously, if the price rises in the three months . . .' Mr Shimura, Mr Matsuyama and Mr Kodo listened intently.

Their next meeting was at 9.30 am, at a medium-sized brokerage house. Nigel again made the introductions. Everybody bowed. Their host led them to the boardroom, where twelve men sat around the table. At the head of the table stood a blackboard. Their host looked at Nigel with expectation.

'Miss Bourton is our expert – I'll hand you over to her,' he said, taking a seat. Thank God I had a flip-chart prepared, Cathy thought, and she picked up the chalk and wrote OPTIONS across the top of the board, then asked Maurice for a separate stand for the chart. She talked for half an hour, at the end of which the twelve Japanese executives bowed again.

Their next meeting was at eleven, followed by lunch. Cathy's voice was starting to sound rough, so she talked little while Nigel explained how to order a combination of raw fish that would be acceptable to a Western palate. The first afternoon meeting was at the Hayasaka Corporation, who placed more business with Migatto than all the other Tokyo clients together. This time their host led them into a lecture hall where two hundred men were assembled. Everybody bowed.

'Off you go, Cathy,' said Nigel, waving her towards the podium.

'Good afternoon,' she began, noticing the interpreter in a glass booth at the back of the auditorium. Two hundred men reached for their headsets. 'I'm Catherine Bourton from the Migatto Metals Company in London, and I'm here to talk to you about . . .' The interpreter was gesticulating. She tapped the head of the microphone in front of her; it made no sound. At once their host rushed on to the platform to apologize, and there was a five-minute break while a technician was found to restore the sound. Then she began again.

By seven o'clock, the three of them were in a whisky bar with the last two clients of the day, men whom Nigel evidently knew well. A board of raw fish snacks was in front of them, and a bottle of Japanese whisky beside it. Cathy was the only woman in the bar apart from the waitresses, a situation to which she was now completely accustomed in London, but here it was different, although she could not quite put her finger on the change.

She said her piece on options for the last time that day, answered the questions, then leaned back on the bar stool in relief as Nigel saw the clients to the door.

'Jolly well done,' he said when he returned. 'First class, Cathy.'

'I thought they'd never go.' She held out her glass and he poured the last round of whisky. It tasted slightly tainted, but at least it was alcohol and put some kind of energy into her exhausted body. The mathematical facility in her mind, which never seemed to falter no matter how tired she was, calculated that she had now gone two full days and nights without sleep.

'They were a bit confused, I think. Normally the form is to drag us off to one of their god-awful love hotels that they're so proud of. With you in charge they didn't quite know how to play it.'

Cathy laughed. 'Good heavens, I'm sorry if I've deprived you of a good time, Nigel. Don't mind me. I can always go back to the hotel and read a book.'

'Please, you're our excuse! Those places are so tacky you've no idea – all fur-fabric love-seats and heart-shaped jacuzzis.' He ordered another bottle and the barman brought it with a bad grace, slamming it down on the bar in front of them.

'What's got into him?' Maurice, her assistant, a skinny, dark young man with greasy black hair, picked up the bottle to pour the next round. The barman bustled back and took the bottle from him, replacing it on the bar with a crash.

'Very bad!' he announced in barely comprehensible English. 'Very bad! Woman make drink for man, no man make for woman.'

'Oh – he's saying *you* ought to be serving us. Their women always pour the drinks. The geisha bit, you know,' Nigel told her. He picked up the bottle himself. 'Not to worry, old boy, we're English, don't you know – foreign devils, don't know the native customs.'

The barman screeched with fury and seized the bottle before Nigel could pour it. He made a long speech in Japanese, then screwed the cap back on the bottle with an air of finality and pointed to the door. Nigel shrugged and led them out of the bar. They were all embarrassed by the incident.

'I'm awfully sorry,' Cathy began, then stopped, wondering what she had to be sorry about.

'No, it's our fault, we should have slugged it out. We're paying, after all. The customer is always right.' Maurice was looking intently at his feet as they threaded their way through the crowds on the pavement.

'Let's find an honourable Nippon hamburger,' Nigel suggested, leading them away through the crush of people in the neon-harsh streets.

The following four days were exactly the same, except that they kept out of whisky bars as much as they could. Nigel did nothing except make introductions, Cathy did all the talking and Maurice took care of the flip-chart.

They flew back through Athens, where Cathy had learned to anticipate a perpetual air-traffic foul-up. The plane was delayed four hours, and they wearily collected their briefcases and trailed into the transit lounge.

'Miz Caterina Button to information desk, pliz,' the PA mumbled.

'That's you, Cathy,' Nigel said, in a peevish tone which made it clear that he felt that if anyone from the Migatto party had been paged it should have been him. 'Must be the office.'

At the information desk they directed her to the VIP lounge, and at the VIP lounge the receptionist called a steward who led her to a side room, a square, concrete cell containing one table, four chairs and a telephone. She picked up the telephone and heard, through the whistling and hissing of a very bad line, the clipped tones of Lord Shrewton.

'I want you to break your journey and take a trip to one of the Aegean islands. There's a plane waiting to take you on, and I'll be joining you in three or four hours. I'm having a weekend meeting with Prince Hussain Shahzdeh at his wife's new place and she's apparently asked particularly for you to come along.'

'Why me?' Cathy shouted into the receiver. She knew that the Prince dealt with Migatto's banking subsidiary occasionally, but was sure he had nothing to do with her side of the business.

'Your celebrity value, I expect.' Lord Shrewton's dry laugh crackled in her ear. 'The Princess collects interesting people, they're her stock-in-trade.'

Cathy hesitated. She was exhausted, she wanted to write the report on the Tokyo trip for Nigel to sign as soon as possible, and she did not feel very much inclined to indulge the vulgar curiosity of a nightclub owner, albeit the most successful in the world.

'Can't you manage without me?' she asked.

'Absolutely not. This is an order. The place is being called L'Equipe Kalispera – you know her Paris club, L'Equipe? They're sending a courtesy plane, I expect the pilot will be paging you any moment. I'll see you later.' There was a distant click and the line went dead.

An hour later, Cathy, who detested flying in small planes, bit her lips with alarm as the tiny Piper skimmed the ultramarine sea and swooped over the island, a kidney-shaped pile of brown-black rock fringed with white foam. On the convex side the waves lapped at a sweeping, silvery beach which, Cathy deduced at once, had been artificially created from imported sand. The plane hit the tiny runway at a sharp angle and slewed crazily to a halt. White uniformed men ran forward to take her luggage and help her into a white mini-jeep.

L'Equipe Kalispera was an exquisite miniature paradise, rocky and bare with spectacular cliffs which plunged into the crystal sea. There was a white monastery building at the apex of the bare, rocky hills and the meandering but newly surfaced perimeter road was dotted with the small shrines built by Greek islanders to thank heaven for saintly protection from shipwreck.

Cathy was driven to the village, a higgledy-piggledy pile of whitewashed buildings and stepped, cobbled alleys clustered around a circular harbour containing two very large yachts and a flotilla of pleasure boats. Cathy had omitted to reset her watch on the way back from Tokyo, but she judged the time to be around six o'clock in the evening. The sky behind the rim of the rocky hills was tinged with lilac pink. She had the impression that the air was very clear and still; as the jeep drew up in front of a massive studded door of dark wood a single bell began to ring and the sound echoed back and forth across the harbour.

The village turned out to be a very carefully built fake, which was in fact a vast, rambling hotel, furnished with massive pieces of dark antique furniture. Cathy was taken to a suite of white-walled rooms with low, beamed ceilings; the tall windows led out to a small balcony overlooking the water.

She began to unwind, feeling the luxurious tranquillity smooth over her tiredness. The huge, dark wood *armoire* contained a wardrobe of blue and white silk resort clothes which, Cathy was surprised to see, bore the Valentino label. They were exactly the right size, even the delicately tailored bikini and the wide-brimmed hat of plaited natural straw. In the drawers beneath she found ivory crêpe-de-chine underwear and some very plain, gold Cartier jewellery.

On the floor of the closet was a pair of slingback beach shoes of woven brown leather which caused her a pang of disappointment, because she still had to wear custom-made shoes. She saw that these had been made by Lobb. Full of curiosity she slipped one on to her maimed foot, and found that it was a perfect fit.

'They must have been made on my own last,' she muttered aloud in astonishment.

A waiter appeared with a pitcher of a cold, frothy pink beverage which she judged to be a cocktail based on champagne and natural pomegranate juice. She sipped it from a chilled flute of paper-thin silver and felt deliciously refreshed. A maid arrived and drew her a bath which foamed with a milky essence and smelt very strongly of pure rose oil. She had just emerged from the fragrant water and put on a white robe of soft handwoven Greek cotton when the telephone buzzed and Lord Shrewton announced that he had arrived and would call to take her to dinner in an hour.

They dined on a sheltered terrace, enjoying the glimmering semicircle of lights reflected in the harbour water. There was a dish of golden Iranian caviar, some slim-shelled clams steamed with herbs and *noisettes* of tender, pink lamb.

'I'm so glad you ordered me on this trip,' she told him. 'I feel like a new woman.'

'Thought you'd come around to the idea – first trip to Tokyo is always a killer,' he commented. The change of environment had not altered his bearing in the slightest. He had replaced his London uniform of a sober grey suit which always fitted rather badly with an identical lightweight ensemble and his stiffly braced shoulders and tense jaw showed no sign of relaxation.

'Hasn't the Princess got another resort somewhere?' Cathy vaguely remembered reading of a gala launch to the new chain of developments in a magazine, but she only had time to read magazines at the hairdresser's and her sleek, simple bob took barely half an hour to snip into shape every month.

'This is her second venture,' he explained. 'The first was off the coast of Sardinia, L'Equipe Falcone. She's a clever woman. She picks the best architects and creates a first-class leisure complex in a completely natural environment. Then she makes sure she gets the best people to come to it – none of the sort of night-club aristocracy. Exiled royalty doesn't impress her either. The Princess only invites the *crime de la crème.*'

'Such as ourselves.'

'Such as ourselves. I wasn't surprised she asked me to bring you. She likes beautiful women, but she likes them best if they're not making a career out of their looks.'

The next day the Prince and Princess formally welcomed their guests at a reception on the yacht, which slowly backed out of the tiny harbour and cruised around the island, anchoring in a rocky bay below high, steep cliffs, a natural cauldron where the waves churned white on the black rocks and the sea was so clear it was possible to see the sunlight playing on the pebbles of the seabed dozens of metres below the surface.

'She's like a mink,' Cathy murmured as she watched the Princess's small, white-clad figure moving among the throng of people. 'She looks glossy and beautiful but sort of savage.'

Shrewton nodded. 'She can be a dangerous woman,' he muttered from the side of his mouth. 'The French papers call her "The Queen of Darkness". Some of the things that happen to people who've stood in her way cause some unpleasant gossip. The old woman who owned this island, for instance. She didn't want to sell, and one day she just went for a walk in the hills and didn't come back. They never found the body.'

The Princess was moving towards them through the crowd, pausing to exchange a few words with each group of guests, her white silk dress rippling round her firm, slender body. Even in the deep shade of the yacht's canvas canopy the sun caught her diamond earrings and made them blaze. Her black hair was dressed in a simple chignon, revealing perfect bone structure and an unwrinkled olive complexion.

In a short time she reached them and Cathy immediately complimented her on the island. 'This is the most exquisite place I've ever seen – and the clothes in my suite, and the *shoes* – they were such a wonderful surprise . . .' she heard herself becoming almost incoherent with enthusiasm. The Princess's heart-shaped face was at once illuminated with satisfaction and Cathy was touched by the fact that this professional hostess, so full of hard, contrived graciousness, should have remained emotionally accessible.

'I was sure that you would have only business clothes with you, and would prefer to relax this weekend in something more appropriate.' The full lips, painted fuchsia-pink, smiled widely but the Princess's black eyes were scanning Cathy's face. 'You have done me a great honour by coming here. I wanted so much to meet you, I have heard a great deal about you. I know, of course, that you have to leave tomorrow, but would you care to come to have tea with me before you go? It would be nice to talk quietly alone together, don't you think?'

'Of course,' Cathy agreed at once. She spent most of the intervening period with the Prince and Lord Shrewton, listening and watching as they went through the pile of documentation prepared for a consortium which Migatto was forming with one of the Prince's companies. As her chairman had predicted, she found she liked the Prince. He was direct, unpretentious and carried his wealth lightly; as he systematically explored every area of potential weakness in the proposed deal his patient courtesy never faltered.

Cathy sensed that the Prince liked her, too; he made sure she was able to follow the discussions by skilfully setting every decision in its context, and asked her opinion with genuine interest on several points. Cathy, who was accustomed to the way most Middle Eastern businessmen simply ignored any woman until she asserted herself, and then fell into confusion when they realized that they had to deal with her, decided that Prince Hussain was exceptionally astute.

The following afternoon a sparkling launch took her to meet the Princess aboard the yacht. Tea was served in a spacious salon furnished entirely in subtle off-white shades which somehow took the heat from the burning sun outside. Cathy and the Princess sat facing each other in a pair of deep-sided sofas, with the pale expanse of a silk Persian rug between them.

'Lord Shrewton tells me you are an ambitious woman,' the Princess began, sipping her tea from a white bone china cup that was almost translucent. 'Is this not unusual for a woman from your background?'

'Yes, I suppose it is. But I don't think I had very many alternatives . . . I love my work.'

'But you come from a wealthy family, surely?'

'My people were wealthy once, but not any more. When my father died there was nothing left but debts.'

There was a pause and the Princess carefully put down her teacup, pursing her ripe lips in a momentary pout. 'I heard something about your father, I think – some . . . was it . . .' she seemed unable to find the words, but Cathy had half a lifetime of experience in setting people at ease on the issue of her father, the Suicide Peer.

'There was a bit of a scandal at the time, perhaps you heard something about that. He committed suicide, you see. Then we found that he'd lost an awful lot of money, which was the reason. In the City in those days people set so much store on names and reputations.'

The Princess sat back, looking reassured. Cathy had expected that reaction, because she always tried to lighten the atmosphere when she was forced to talk about her father. She shivered slightly. The yacht's air-conditioning was ferocious and she was wearing only a light blue silk shift from the Valentino wardrobe.

'But it must have been a terrible tragedy in your life. You seem to have come to terms with it very well,' the Princess prompted Cathy.

'There was nothing else to do but to come to terms with it. I loved my father very much but he was so full of vitality himself that he would never have wanted me to let the shadow of his death hang over me forever.'

A soft-footed steward in a white uniform came to pour fresh tea. Reflectively, Cathy's gaze strayed across the glittering water to the hazy horizon beyond the harbour mouth. She was thinking of Daddy more and more, she admitted suddenly to herself. Maybe Monty was right, maybe she was lonely. What welled up in her mind increasingly was the echoing emptiness her father had left in her heart. The intense bond between them, that mixture of care and protectiveness, encouragement, spiritual closeness, the sense that the two of them were in a thrilling conspiracy against the entire world – she would never find it again with any man.

It had been different to the warm attachment she shared with Monty; the magical element of sexual polarity had been there with her father. Their love had been the synthesis of two opposing life forces, strong, invincible, able, she had felt, to overcome anything. It should have been strong enough to overcome death.

She shook her head quickly, dismissing the notion that Daddy would have lived if she had loved him more. With the unwavering clarity of vision that was pitiless even towards herself, Cathy recognized that her guilt stemmed from a different source. She had been a mere girl when her father had died. Now she was a woman, and she looked back to him with adult eyes, and recognized that if her father were still living he would have been a man whom she held in slight regard, just as the rest of his business friends had done. She too would have considered him a foolish, charming man of little consequence.

'But you must think of your father sometimes?' the Princess insisted gently.

'Not very much. I don't have much time for reflection nowadays,' Cathy returned at once, unwilling to open her heart to a stranger when, after so many years of pushing her emotions aside, she herself had barely discovered how she really felt.

The Princess asked her about Jamie of whom, she said, Lord Shrewton often spoke, and Cathy talked about her son freely, with a sense of relief. Eventually she sensed that the Princess was restless, and remembering that her hostess was childless, she switched the conversation to the subject of the resort and the Princess's future business plans.

'And what about you, what do you see for yourself in the future?' the older woman asked, crossing her exquisitely modelled legs and rearranging the narrow pleats of her cream silk skirt.

Cathy looked at her frankly and decided that there might be some percentage in flying a kite. 'I'm not sure,' she said. 'I'm a junior director now and although Migatto have the reputation of being a dynamic outfit it is rare for anyone to make it to senior director under the age of forty. I'm not sure I want to wait that long.'

A sweetly humorous smile puckered the Princess's cheeks. 'But Lord Shrewton thinks very highly of you, he's told me so . . .'

'I've never known Lord Shrewton act against his own judgement, and he's got the rest of the group directors to consider. In any case, I think I'd prefer to be independent. In a few years I'd like to put my own team together and set up a financial consultancy.' Cathy saw that the Princess was absorbing what she said with close attention and was encouraged to continue. 'I plan to offer comprehensive advice across the whole financial spectrum. I want a base of business clients, but I'd like to specialize in high-profile private clients. My experience has been that the private client, because the volume of business is often small, is neglected by big institutions. I understood that very well when I thought about the tragedy of my father's death. He wasn't advised, he was exploited by people who were pretending to advise him, and it's a common experience among people with substantial personal wealth. No one's really geared to looking at finance in relation to individuals and their lives. Don't you agree, Princess?'

'Most certainly,' the older woman said at once. 'And when do you plan to make this move?'

'When I'm confident I've got the necessary expertise – three or four years, maybe.'

'Well I hope you will pay me the compliment of accepting me as your very first client? I am a wealthy woman in my own right, independently of the Prince, and I always feel as if I'm a nuisance to his people, someone they deal with as a favour to him, that's all. Promise me that you'll come to me when you are ready?'

'Of course, I should like that very much indeed.' Cathy smiled with delight and congratulated herself on a successful sale. She also was really interested in doing business with the Prince, but to deal with a man of such stupendous wealth would be out of the question for a young, unproven consultancy – unless, of course, there were a special reason why she should come to his attention.

A few moments later the steward announced that the launch was ready to take her back to the shore, and Cathy bade the Princess a warm farewell. She joined Lord Shrewton at the airstrip, and as their plane soared away into the rose-tinted dusk she felt a curious mixture of elation and sadness.

She had confided her ambition to only two people – to Monty who had inspired her, and to Henry Rose who she hoped would join her. In retrospect, she was surprised that she had opened up so readily to the Princess. She was rich, of course, but she was also more than a little sinister. It was not entirely the kind of involvement Cathy had wanted, even for the sake of a good platform from which to approach the Prince. She was surprised also at the force of the feelings which had been unlocked in that casual conversation. Maybe she had been lulled by the Princess's thoughtful welcome, maybe softened by the impressive completeness of L'Equipe Kalispera's conception. Her father would have loved the place, she thought. She would have loved to have gone there with him. A light blanket of sorrow wrapped itself around her as Cathy confronted the enduring pain of her father's loss.

When she returned to London things began to happen which made Cathy wonder if it were not already time for her next move. First of all she sat down at a board meeting and listened in open-mouthed astonishment as Nigel Fairwell announced that the Japanese were now buying options as if they were going out of style, a phenomenon for which he smoothly took all the credit.

'Nigel – I did all the selling in Tokyo,' she protested to him afterwards.

All he said was, 'Don't make a scene, Cathy. You did very well, but it was your first trip to Tokyo after all. Experience counts. You can't expect the Japs to take much notice of a woman.'

'But they *did* take notice – if they're getting into options they must have done. The only man we had any trouble with in the whole week was that barman.'

Nigel put his heavy hand on her shoulder with a paternal gesture. 'I'm sorry if that's your reading of the situation, Cathy. It certainly wasn't mine, or Maurice's, I'm sure.'

Maurice was shortly afterwards made a director, of equal status to Cathy, and given most of her areas of responsibility. She was sent to Geneva for six months to work with the banking subsidiary there, then moved on to New York for another six months where she was given a position in the bank's research department which was valuable experience for her but quite definitely a demotion.

The New York posting was doubly traumatic because that autumn Jamie, who was eight years old, was sent away to the boarding preparatory school which would precede his entry to Eton at the age of thirteen. The fact that she could not be with her son at this, his first important life passage, wrenched her emotions unbearably. She felt she had missed most of the golden years of his childhood, and that soon he would be on the threshold of maturity, ready to leave just as she was ready to have him with her.

She flew back for several weekends to see Jamie, which her colleagues treated as further proof of her lack of commitment. Cathy did not care. Jamie needed her, and as she watched his carefree childishness develop in a matter of weeks into a serious, almost calculating, new wisdom, she did not regret investing in his security for an instant.

Back in London, Cathy was asked to work with the senior marketing director, taking special responsibility for public relations and administration. She was sent on a management course, a seminar on computer technology and another trip to Japan, this time to examine alternative corporate structures. These assignments were all tangential to the group's real business and Cathy realized at once that she was being moved sideways.

'Formally speaking, I'm supposed to be preparing a report on ways in which the group can be reorganized to meet the challenges of the future,' she told Monty, sprawled on her old cream sofa at the end of another slow day. 'But I know, and so does everybody else, that Migatto isn't the slightest bit interested in anything except plodding along in the same old way. So what the new job effectively means is that at the ripe old age of thirty I'm being put out to grass.'

'I thought they were all patting each other on the back for having the first woman on the board?' Monty, Cathy thought, was looking thinner than she ever had in her life, but also rather grey and unhealthy.

'They just stuck me on the top of their crumbling outfit for decoration, like a cherry on a cake. I can see now that that's the only concession to change they're going to make. Lord Shrewton's the only one who can see beyond the end of tomorrow's lunchtime, but he's getting old, Monty, and he hasn't the energy to take them on like he used to.'

'Maybe that's why he likes having you around? Have you talked to him?'

'I'm sure that's why he likes having me around. Of course I've talked to him, but he's a chairman, Monty, not a dictator. He needs more than just me to drag that group into the twentieth century. The majority of the group directors aren't prepared to take me seriously at their level. And I'm not prepared to be shunted round the world, and separated from Jamie, because I'm slightly too famous to be fired without the group getting bad publicity out of it. It's time for me to move on, Monty.'

Cathy spent the next six months discreetly sounding out three men who she knew shared her way of thinking, having long discussions with Henry, and getting to know a useful number of financial journalists. She also rewrote most of Migatto's brochures and planned a new corporate structure which, she judged, would take care of most of the sources of inefficiency in the company and allow the employees to work together with better motivation and communication.

She presented this plan at another board meeting. 'What I am proposing,' she concluded, 'is a system of network management in which all employees will be expected to participate in decision-making processes as equals. I want to institute a structure which will allow information to circulate from the front line in the dealing room back to the board as freely as possible. At present, half the human potential of this company is frustrated by a bureaucratic, hierarchical structure. '

'But you're asking for a radical change, a long-term commitment to a new management style,' Nigel Fairwell protested in tones of shocked disbelief.

'Of course I am,' she said. 'At present we're not growing fast enough and we're wasting our resources. I think that's a problem which needs a radical, long-term solution, don't you?'

There was an awkward pause and a lot of throat-clearing.

'Should never have sent her to Japan,' one of the men muttered under his breath.

The meeting broke up with no commitment other than to read her proposal again. Four or five of the men, including Maurice, went through the dark oak door to the directors' washroom. They came out ten minutes later, laughing together.

When the minutes of the meeting were circulated, Cathy read with astonishment that the board had voted to reject her proposal.

'You were *there*,' she said to Maurice, 'they decided no such thing. They decided to keep it under consideration.'

'Oh, maybe they decided to turn it down later,' he said.

'*But the meeting was over.*'

'I don't know. Maybe they talked about it in the john. I don't remember. You didn't seriously expect them to go for it, did you?' She looked at him with dislike; Maurice was getting unbearably self-important. The mere idea of a sprat like him laughing and joining with the rest of the men in flushing six months of her work down the lavatory made her boil with rage.

'I'm never going to get any further at Migatto,' she said to Monty that evening. 'Sure, I can run off to Lord Shrewton and whine, but it won't crack the real problem. They treat me just like they used to treat my father, you know. Like someone of limited capabilities but a certain value, who has to be kidded that they're of some real consequence. They tolerate me, that's all.'

She had a sad meeting with Lord Shrewton, which she deliberately arranged in his office to indicate that from now on, business and family should be separate.

She sat opposite him at the enormous Jacobean table which he used instead of a desk and made her proposal.

'I'm very angry,' she said with calculated weariness. 'I should resign, I know, but there'll be a rumpus and the papers will want to know why.'

'And you'll be severely tempted to tell them, I shouldn't wonder,' he put in quickly, amusement glowing behind his spectacles. 'That would never do, would it?'

'I see you're way ahead of me,' she smiled.

'Damn shame. You're the best man among them if you want my opinion. I've been very pleased with our association. What shall we do, then? Let you go with a decent pay-off? I suppose you've another job lined up. Headhunter taken you up to a high place and showed you the world?'

'Not exactly – Henry and I want to set up on our own.'

'Pinch all Migatto's business, I suppose. Serve us right.' Her chairman now looked thoroughly pleased with himself, as if her cleverness was entirely to his own credit. 'What sort of figure did you have in mind?'

She told him, and he agreed it after a token show of hesitation.

In addition to her handshake from Migatto, Cathy funded her company with a loan from Henry's bank and mortgages raised on her apartment and his house. They wanted offices which were equipped with the most modern technology, knowing that the faster they could get information and react to it, the more effective they would be. They also needed a full complement of staff from the outset. Their clients would soon take their business elsewhere if there was any delay in processing instructions or drawing contracts.

Henry found the Pall Mall office, which he had redecorated in a severe modern style. The scheme was black and white, with classic, Italian leather chairs, big black leather sofas, black marble tables and a vivid abstract painting which Cathy privately disliked.

'I can see what you're thinking,' he said as she helped him to hang the vast canvas. 'You're thinking we ought to have a nice set of sporting prints or maybe a few ancestral portraits. Shame on you. This company's a tough, fast-moving outfit geared for the twenty-first century, and I'm not having any gentlemanly British junk around the place.'

Princess Ayeshah was true to her word, and within a week of Cathy's approach switched a portfolio of several million francs to the company. She did not, however, achieve her ambition to be CBC's first private client. That privilege was claimed by Heinz Feuer, whose portfolio was even larger than the Princess's, though the Zurich bank who had invested it had done so much more cautiously than the Geneva firm which the Princess had patronized. He also sent Cathy a huge bouquet of lilies, highly scented trumpets with fantastically curled tips and crimson spots on the creamy petals blending to dark red throats.

'A man of taste after all,' Henry approved as their new secretary put them on her desk under the abstract.

'I'm surprised he's got any money left, the way he throws it away at roulette.' Cathy was aware that she sounded unnecessarily priggish.

'He doesn't bet more than he can afford, you know that.'

'Hmn.'

'And what does "hmn" mean? I know what I think it means – it means you think Heinz is a little bit sweet on you and that's why he's given you the business, and that makes you feel all prickly and insulted because he ought to be dealing only from the purest commercial motives.'

'Rubbish.' Cathy folded her arms defensively and glared at Henry.

'Or it could mean that you're just a little bit sweet on Heinz . . .'

'Absolute rubbish. He's a brat – immature, spoiled, too much money, too little sense. Yes, I think he's cute, of course I do. He's very amusing sometimes in a puppy-dog kind of way . . .'

'He's good-looking, too.'

'Yes, he is. So what?'

'Good family. Wall-to-wall Almanach de Gotha on both sides.'

'Oh really, I didn't know. Are you sure you're not sweet on him yourself, Henry? You seem to have taken a lot of interest . . .' At this point her business partner took a swipe at her with a rolled-up copy of the *Financial Times*. She dodged him and knocked the flower vase off the reception desk, and the issue of Heinz Feuer was dropped while CBC's two senior directors discovered that their impeccably equipped office did not yet possess any cleaning cloths or a dustpan and brush.

In the next six months they discovered some more serious deficiencies. They were busy, and they should have been extremely successful. They did such an unexpectedly large volume of business that their computer system, which the salesman had assured them was more than adequate for their needs, could not cope with it. Three of their secretaries resigned in one week because they could not stand the pressure. Even their telephone installation proved inadequate. Soon the inevitable happened and one of their most important commercial clients, a small pension fund, regretfully announced that they planned to take their business elsewhere.

'We've got to get the office re-equipped,' Henry said with desperation as they sat alone together in the office on a stormy Friday evening. 'The fact is we underestimated our success, and if we can't gear up almost immediately we're going to lose a lot of business – and the best clients, too, they'll be the first to go.'

'The computer salesman came today. We can instal a new system over a weekend, but it won't be cheap.'

'Better figure out how much we need.' Henry began scrawling figures on a pad, drumming his plump fingers nervously on his black ash table. Cathy produced her calculator, tapped in the figures and showed him the total. He whistled. 'That much?'

'I think we should reckon on having to spend more than that – our start-up budget was well padded, but obviously not well enough.'

'This is far more than our contingency fund, Cathy. I'm fully extended – so are you. We both raised every penny we could to get this company off the ground. Where are we going to find the money?'

'We've *got* to find it, Henry. For heaven's sake, how can we call ourselves financial consultants if we can't get our own act together?' For an instant Cathy bitterly regretted the fact that she had lent Monty almost all her own savings for her lawsuit against Rick, but she at once realized that such a small sum would have been of no use in their present situation.

'It won't be difficult to get a loan, Cathy, you know that. Even though there's a credit squeeze right now there'd be plenty of people queuing up to back us. But they'd want a piece of the action – we'd lose our independence.'

Cathy shook her head. 'We'd be swallowed up in a year. I've thought it through already. My first reaction was to approach Migatto, because Lord Shrewton would swing a deal like this for me, I'm sure of it. But we'd become just another Migatto subsidiary: in two years both you and I would be eased out of our own company – pfft! We'd be right back where we started.'

'Yeah, that's how I read it, too.' Henry tipped back his black leather chair, put his hands behind his head and stared at the ceiling. He had lost weight in the hectic early days of the company, and was wearing loud, yellow brocade braces to hold up the trousers of his navy-blue suit.

'We could try another way.' Cathy pushed back her hair, which was overdue for a cut – she had had no time for hairdressers lately. 'Look for private finance.'

'Mmn – that's the way my mind was working, too.'

'We'd have to be pretty stealthy about it. If word got out, our clients would start leaving in droves.'

'Any ideas?'

'D'you know a guy called Samir, Jason Samir?'

'You're not serious, Cathy? Samir Holdings? It's a house of cards, the whole group's based on overvalued property. Not exactly the model of a modern venture capitalist, is he? Now Slater Walker's crashed he'll be the next, if you ask me.' Henry looked at Cathy's face and realized that she had already put her idea into practice. 'Did he approach you?'

'Yes. Don't worry, I didn't tell him anything. I didn't tell him he was wasting his time, either. I was just neutral. I know you're right, Henry, but he's the best hope we've got. Let's think about it over the weekend – we'll have to make a move on Monday, one way or the other.'

She drove furiously across London to her apartment through lashing gusts of wind and rain, angry with herself for risking her success by making the classic mistake of undercapitalization. It's pride, she admitted to herself bitterly, I just wanted to do everything all by myself, do it my way, without any help – if I'd been smart enough to ask for help in the beginning I wouldn't be in this mess.

Monty came over as she often did on Friday evenings; she looked strained and depressed, which intensified Cathy's gloom. She rambled on, talking about her problems with her new band, with her new manager and with Rick, and Cathy realized that her sister was hinting that she needed more money. Brusquely she refused, hating herself for doing it and for taking out her own bad temper on her sister.

'I'm sorry, Monty,' she said, 'it's a really bad time right now. I'm in a jam myself, and I've no one else to blame for it.'

'Forget it,' Monty reassured her. 'I shouldn't have asked, I didn't really want to. Don't worry about me, I'll handle it somehow.'

To Cathy's surprise, Lord Shrewton telephoned on Saturday. His normal telephone style was almost monosyllabic but now he made a distinct effort to be chatty. 'Just thought I'd give you a call to see how things were,' he said, not able to sound in the least casual.

'Things are terrific,' Cathy lied, at once alerted and wondering what lay behind his enquiry.

'That Samir fella's been putting it about he's going to move in and take you over.' The dry old voice carried a trace of concern despite its owner's cool emotional temperature.

'Oh is he?' Cathy felt angry and disappointed at the same time. Henry had been right about Samir; it had been a mistake ever to meet him.

'Heard you've parted company with that little pension fund . . .'

'They decided they needed a different kind of service. We weren't really geared for their needs. It was all quite amicable.'

'Bad news travels fast in the City, Cathy.' She sensed that he was more than a little offended by her refusal to confide in him. 'I hope that if you do have a problem of any kind you'll come to me first. I regard you as family, you know that.'

Even Jamie could not raise a smile from his mother when she took him out from school for the day on Sunday. She slept badly and on Monday she drove to the office early with a leaden heart and looked around the empty, luxurious suite of rooms without any sense of pride of ownership, only a grim appreciation of her own folly.

The telex was clattering, printing a message in its little room at the end of the corridor, and she went down to read it. To her surprise, she saw it was from Prince

Hussain Shahzdeh, urgently requesting a meeting in Paris as soon as possible. The tone of the message was emphatic and her mood lifted at once. With quick, deft fingers she acknowledged the communication, then tore off the printed slip of paper and considered her options. It was still two hours before Henry would be arriving, and if the Prince saw her that morning she could be back in the office in the afternoon.

Obeying a mad impulse to leave her problems behind her for half a day, she scrawled a note to Henry, grabbed her dark-blue wide-shouldered cashmere coat and ran out of the office and down to the street. She reclaimed her car from the startled attendant at the carpark and drove to Heathrow airport. The early morning flights to Paris were always fully booked, she knew, but there were always cancellations and with luck she would be able to walk on to a plane. Luck was with her, and from the departure lounge she rang asking her secretary to telephone the Prince and let him know she was on her way.

'This is magnificent, I never expected you to get here so quickly.' The square, dark-suited figure of the Prince burst through the heavy oak doors of his office in a quiet street between the Opera and the Bourse. He spoke in English and shook her hand in his fleshy, firm grip. A middle-aged, quietly elegant, ash-blonde secretary brought them tea with a suppressed flutter of excitement.

'What can I do for you?' Cathy asked, hoping that she still projected the serene confidence which had always been one of her greatest assets. She smoothed the skirt of her navy-blue suit, feeling crumpled after the short flight.

'This is more a question of what I can do for *you.*' His plump face with its thick, black eyebrows bore a pleasant expression but he did not smile. Cathy was startled. This was not what she had been expecting.

'I've been paying close attention to the way you've been running my wife's money and I have to admit I'm most impressed,' he continued. 'You've had a very successful few months. It strikes me that just at the moment you could expand very fast if you had the necessary capitalization.'

'There's no question about that,' Cathy agreed. They had both seen through each other immediately. This conversation, Cathy understood with mingled relief and suspicion, was a formal minuet staged to save her face. He had heard of her trouble, in the same way that Lord Shrewton had – maybe even from Lord Shrewton himself – and was going to offer her the finance she needed. The only question that remained to be answered was – why?

'How would you respond if I offered you a loan which would allow you to expand your operation right now?'

'I would be curious to know why you would do such a thing.'

'In my wife's interest – she feels She has an emotional investment in your success.'

Cathy believed him. Apart from knowing the Prince to be a sincere man, she had sensed the peculiar quality of his relationship with the Princess. She fascinated him and seemed to have the ability to dominate him when she needed to, tough and astute as he was. Cathy had also perceived that the Prince had a moral firmness which his wife did not; while she struck Cathy as the kind of woman who would give nothing without expecting a return of some kind, her husband would be unlikely to strike a deal with hidden strings attached to it.

'I'm flattered that the Princess should feel that way.'

'We talked about you yesterday, and agreed that I should make an offer to you, since my business has rather more liquidity than hers at the moment.' As if he had all the time in the world, the Prince continued a leisurely conversation, in which the exact sum of the loan was never discussed – the implication being that no sum would be beyond his means. Cathy accepted an invitation to lunch with him and the Princess in their apartment. She returned to the office to collect the loan documents which had been drawn up in the interim, and the Prince's car took her to Charles de Gaulle airport.

Before the end of the day she was back in her office, her feet crossed jubilantly on the black marble top of her desk.

'We're saved,' she told Henry, who stood in front of her looking anxious. 'I found a fairy godmother. Or godfather. Both really. The Shahzdehs offered me a loan – look.' She passed him the loan agreement and he looked at it for a few seconds but could not concentrate on it.

'There's got to be a catch somewhere. There's nothing in it for them.'

'They're charging a fair rate of interest.'

'You could think of a hundred better uses for the money.'

'Well, if there's a catch, Henry, I can't see it. It's a perfectly simple deal, it's watertight, unsinkable and copper-bottomed. Now are you going to stand there like a dying duck in a thunderstorm all evening or are we going round to the Ritz for some champagne?'

They closed the office over a weekend for the new computer to be installed, and hired ten more staff to handle their business. Cathy sighed with relief as the first fortnight passed with only minor problems.

A slight figure marched into her office one blazing July morning as she was preparing to go out for lunch.

'Jamie! Of course, it's the school holidays already. But I thought you were going to Coseley first?'

He was ten now, but in his grey school trousers and dark-green blazer he looked older. Jamie was not tall for his age; he was small and slender compared to his friends, but he had a self-possession which made him seem far more mature than they were.

'I got to Coseley and there was nobody there except Nanny Barbara,' he told her. 'There never is, and I'm tired of wandering around all by myself. I want to come and live with you.'

'Darling.' Cathy walked round the black marble desk to sit beside him, using the wheedling tone all mothers adopt towards dangerous preteens. 'You *can't* stay with me, there's nothing for you to do here either. It'll all be different when you go to Eton.'

'I don't want to go to Eton.' His vibrant blue eyes gazed calmly into hers.

'We'd better talk about this.' She reached for the telephone console. 'Can you call the Dorchester and tell them I've been delayed but I'm on my way. And hold all my calls, please. Now Jamie, why don't you want to go to Eton?'

'Because I won't learn anything useful at Eton; you can't deny that, Mummy, you've told me so enough times yourself.'

'But . . .' She was searching her distracted mind for arguments, and not finding any because she knew he was right, and that this was what she wanted, what she had longed for all these years. There was, in truth, no reason at all why he could not live with her full time now. Starting the business had simply wiped everything else from her mind.

'I want to come and live with you, Mum, and go to an ordinary school in London. I'll get my exams, I'm quite clever enough. Then I want to go to Oxford, then a business school in America.'

'You've got it all figured out, haven't you?'

'And I want to be like you, not like my father,' he went on. 'You've really made a mark, Mum. And you've done it all the way you wanted.'

Cathy knew he was deliberately hitting the right buttons, and admired that too.

'Very well, you've convinced me. But I won't have much time for you – you'll have to take care of yourself.'

'That's OK.'

'You'd better speak to your grandfather,' she suggested. 'Just tell him exactly as you've told me, and I think he'll agree.'

She was correct. Lord Shrewton, one of the few men she knew who always put common sense and his duty to his heritage before all other considerations, accepted Jamie's proposal with restrained but obvious pleasure. Charlie, who had been divorced by Lisa and was now living in Los Angeles with a new American wife, made no objection, and Cathy was at last granted legal custody of her son.

Chapter Twenty-Four

T HE CALIFORNIA sunshine was as thick as syrup on the emerald velvet lawn. The driver put Véronique's Vuitton case and Monty's Turkish carpet-bag into the boot of his car.

'We make only one promise to you here at the Centre. What you have to deal with now, Miranda, is living a normal life. We can only guarantee that if you don't go to your aftercare you will go back to using drugs, or something else which alters your relationship to reality.' The Director with the curly moustache shook her hand. They climbed into the car and drove away.

Véronique opened her purse and hunted in it. 'Here's your ticket.' She handed the airline folder to Monty. 'And what was left of your money when we were in Paris. I'll say goodbye to you at the airport.'

Monty flipped open the air ticket and saw that it was for a one-way flight to London. 'But you're sending me home. Why?'

'Madame Bernard has no further wish to deal with you.'

'But I owe her for the clothes. All those St Laurent clothes you bought me – what about them?'

'They are of no consequence. Madame Bernard wishes you to return to your own life now. She has instructed me to tell you never to attempt to contact her again.'

Monty was stunned. The only shadow that had been hanging over her three months at the Centre was the knowledge that she had to deal with her debt to the notorious Paris madame. She dreaded another encounter with the shadowy, ruthless woman who had stripped bare her soul, but she was grateful too and curious about the reasons why Madame Bernard had taken the trouble to be so cruel to her in order to be so kind. Monty knew now that she was the only person who could save her own life, but Madame Bernard had forced her to discover that.

'Perhaps you will tell her I'm truly grateful,' she said, feeling that the words were much too weak for the profound emotion behind them. 'I can't thank her enough. I feel I've been given the chance to start my life over again. Can't I even write to her?'

Véronique nodded. 'You can give a letter to me. I'll see it reaches the woman you met. That's who you mean, isn't it?'

'Oh stop pretending, Véronique. That was Madame Bernard, wasn't it?'

'Who knows? I have worked for her for twenty-five years and I've never met her. I never met the woman who talked to you either. I can tell you nothing. But I can tell you you are absolutely unique in the history of this organization, miss. Anyone who tried what you did would have been taught a lesson she would never have forgotten. You're much luckier than you deserve to be.'

Monty felt reborn after her weeks of therapy. For the first time in her life she had seen herself as she really was, faced herself honestly, reviewed her life and acknowledged that so far her only strategy for dealing with pain had been to blot it out with drugs or drink.

Cathy was waiting for her at Heathrow, looking deliciously severe in a black suit with white silk shirt and a bootlace tie.

'How did it go? Are you OK?' she asked with concern as she hugged her sister.

'More OK than I've ever been in my life,' Monty assured her. 'But it's so good to see you. I've missed you so much.'

'What kind of place was it? You just said it was something to do with drugs?' Cathy gave her sister a keen glance, aware that she had been deceived.

'It was a treatment centre for addicts,' Monty said bluntly.

'But you're not an addict – I mean, you've always taken things, I've known that, but . . .'

'Yes I am an addict, Cathy. Always have been and always will be. The only thing that's different is now I know how to live with it.' Realizing that her sister would be anguished if she knew the whole truth of how she had been living for the past few months, Monty told her only the barest details.

As she anticipated, Cathy was full of remorseful sympathy. 'How terrible! Oh, Monty, I'm so glad you're all right. If only I'd known what was going on. If only I hadn't been so obsessed with my business. Why on earth didn't you tell me?' Suddenly she hated herself for her single-minded ambition. The signs had been there – Monty's pallor, her thinness, the behaviour that seemed confident but had an undertone of lost hope. Why hadn't she noticed, why had she failed the person she loved so much?

'I didn't want to tell you, Cathy. It was just something else I couldn't deal with. I was ashamed, I guess, I was sure you'd disapprove. I think I wanted to kill myself, too. You know when *you* wanted to kill yourself, you didn't tell me because you knew I'd have stopped you. I was determined to go over the edge.'

Cathy held Monty to her, ignoring the crush of the crowded airport around them. 'We must never, ever, do that to each other again. You're right, we're each other's lifelines. We keep each other afloat. If you ever let go of me again, I'll know what's going on.'

They walked to Cathy's car. 'I was in a different world, too,' Monty continued, not wanting to hurt her sister any more. 'I lied to everyone and most of all I lied to myself. I had no real idea how serious things were until I got to the Centre and had to do without the stuff. Then I realized I was just totally dependent.'

'I should have known. I'll never forgive myself.'

'There's no way you could have known, Cathy. When it comes to people who're going down, it takes one to know one. That woman, Madame Bernard, knew where I was at because I suspect she's hit the bottom herself a few times. And I sensed it. If you'd tried to pack me off on a cure I'd have resisted like fury. Coming from her, though, I could accept it.'

'It just doesn't make sense. Why would anyone do something like that for a total stranger?' Cathy shook her head, her thick brown hair swinging heavily as she did so. 'Nothing is for nothing, Monty. That woman wants something from you and she'll call in the favour one day.'

In London, Monty found that a lot had changed in twelve weeks. At the apartment she shared with Cindy, she found a note saying, 'Dear Miss Bourton, please telephone this number when you return.' It was signed with a man's name which she did not recognize. Monty steeled herself and called the number, and a man's voice answered. 'I'm Cindy's brother,' he explained.

'I didn't know she had a brother.'

'She didn't talk about her family much, I gather.' He sounded reserved, upper-class. Why was he using the past tense?

'Were you very close to my sister?' the man asked her. Monty thought about the question. It was quite obvious, now that her reasoning faculty was no longer hiding behind a drug-induced indifference, that Cindy had waited with the deadly patience of a predator to catch her at a weak moment and get her using heroin; then she had become her supplier and financed her own habit that way. How fond could one be of a friend who did something like that?

'I didn't really know her very well,' Monty told him.

'I hope this won't distress you too much, then. My sister was found dead a couple of months ago. She had accidentally injected herself with too much of some drug – you knew she was an addict, I take it?'

Monty made all the appropriate noises of sympathy. It seemed her brother cared very little about Cindy. Cruel and calculating as Cindy had been, Monty felt grief for her dead friend and at the back of her mind the conviction persisted that Cindy's death had been no accident. She had always had her habit so well under control; Cindy just wasn't the type to make a mistake about a dose, or get drunk and forget how much stuff she'd done.

She decided that she did not want to stay at the apartment. She could go to her sister, if she was in town, but staying with Cathy would be fine for only for a couple of days. Then the fact that Monty usually went to bed at 3 am and Cathy usually got up at 5 am would become more than ties of blood could stand.

Instead Monty called Swallow Lamotte, who at once suggested she stay with her and take up her old job. Since 1965 Swallow had rechristened the company three times, sold it twice and liquidated it once; its present title was Urban Survival Services. Everyone had white T-shirts with USS printed on them in red.

Swallow had also transformed herself, from a coltish good-time blonde to a dynamic woman with bright-red hennaed hair and the silhouette of an African fertility goddess. She still had fabulous legs and ripe, soft lips; obesity had not quieted her dress sense – she wore a purple boiler suit, a pink poncho and red cowboy boots.

'You're just in time,' she announced to Monty. 'We've got five people wanting punk waitresses for parties, and we have to find a tank for a David Bowie concert in Battersea Park next week. And you're not staying with me, because we've got to look after the house Jack Nicholson's renting while he's away on location, so you're staying there. And next week the Joe Jones Band are flying in; the joint'll really be jumping then.'

'I bet.' Monty was depressed to find herself on the fringe of the music business, once more a kid outside the shop window of success looking wistfully at the good things which she could not have.

'What are the Joe Jones Band here for – not another tour?'

'No, another album – they've decided to record at Paleward Priory. Now here's the card-index . . .' Swallow dumped a plastic box of file cards in front of Monty. 'Find me six punks for Lady Swabo tonight, blondes if possible.'

Already, the defiant punks had been swallowed up by the British propensity for absorbing dissidents into the social structure.

Tourists were starting to penetrate outer Chelsea, looking for the weird creatures with safety-pins through their noses who obligingly dressed up on Saturday and left their homes in the suburbs for an outrageous *paseo* at the end of the King's Road.

Biffo Records had been taken over by a big American company and Sig Bear was being talked about as the first punk tycoon.

Swallow kept Monty so busy she had little time to think about anything but answering the telephones and getting out the mail. Once a week she went to a meeting in a room behind an Italian café, where for a couple of hours Monty again became Miranda who was chemically dependent, and derived strength from knowing her own weakness. She needed strength to pick up the gift of her new life.

'Have a drink?' Swallow invited her, uncorking her daily bottle of Liebfraumilch.

'No, thank you. I don't drink alcohol any more.'

'Cigarette?' The pack passed under her nose twenty times a day, the smoke permeated the tiny red-and-white office next to the punk leatherwear boutique.

'I've stopped smoking.'

'Fancy a line?' Swallow's friends were always borrowing her make-up mirror to chop up their cocaine.

'Girl, you come at just the right time, we just skin up right now,' Winston greeted her with a joint the size of a half-corona in his hand.

Monty decided to look up some old friends. 'Let's meet for lunch,' suggested Rosanna, and they went to San Lorenzo in Beauchamp Place, a choice Monty immediately regretted when she was greeted by half a dozen music business types to whom she had to explain that, contrary to what Sig Bear had told them the week before, she had not just finished recording her album for Biffo in the South of France.

'You know the children and I are on our own now?' Rosanna mournfully tucked a shred of radiccio into her mouth and tore her eyes away from the sweet trolley. 'Jonathan left us. I found out he'd been staying over with his secretary half the time when he was supposed to be abroad on business. Could anything so corny happen to me?'

'It seems to happen to all of us, sooner or later.' Rosanna was distinctly plump, in a deliciously appetizing way. She wore a Karl Lagerfeld grey suit with a pink crêpe-de-chine ruffled blouse.

'I've got the house, of course, and he's been very generous, but I'm not going to be another alimony drone, Monty. I've got an agent and he thinks he can get me some opera work.'

'Terrific. You always had a better voice than I did.'

'It's just a pity I didn't start using it when you did. I have to lie about my age, you know. My agent says none of the European opera houses will look at a singer under thirty. Do you think I look thirty, Monty? Tell me honestly.'

'No, of course not,' Monty lied. Rosanna sighed as she finished her salad.

'You're so lucky. You've got talent, Monty. I wish I had. And you've got a proper career, I'm just messing about amusing myself.' The sweet trolley passed their table again. 'How many calories do you think there are in a chocolate profiterole?'

'Millions. Let's have some.' Monty waved to the waiter. She felt uncomfortable having Rosanna envy her when her career was becalmed and her talent seemed like a responsibility that it was impossible to fulfil.

'What did they do with you at that Centre?' Swallow demanded when Monty came back from the office completely sober after lunch.

'We just sat around and talked. I've never felt so loved, Swallow. It was wonderful just to be with people and show them who you really are, and have them accept you.'

'Well at least your skin doesn't look like cold potatoes any more. What about your clothes?'

Monty wore the USS T-shirt and jeans everyday, with her old acrylic fur coat if it was cold.

'They're all at Cindy's, unless her brother's got rid of them. I don't want my old clothes any more, Swallow. They weren't anything to do with me, only with the people I was posing as.'

'That leather dress was fabulous.'

'It made me feel like a whore.'

'Fucking hell. I can't stand all this bloody purity. Why not join a convent?'

'Well, I felt ridiculous vamping around with my tits falling out everywhere.'

'And what are you going to do – change your image?'

'I don't *know*, Swallow. I don't want to be Ruby Slippers any more, that's for sure. That was just a bad dream.'

'What are you going to tell Sig?'

'I don't know, I'll have to think about it.'

'Well you'd better hurry up, he's outside right now.'

Monty gasped with fright, then made a determined effort to calm herself. She knew that she had been avoiding dealing with Sig. Sig never avoided dealing with anything; his style was the pre-emptive strike. That was probably why he was a tycoon and she was a mess.

'Baby!' He stood in the doorway, fat and smiling, his black hair now cut with a Mohican scalp-lock, wearing a very expensive-looking black leather jacket. He held out his arms to her.

'Hello, Sig.'

'Baby! Is that all – hello? No kiss for Siggy? Where've you been all this time? Not even a postcard! I missed you.' He gave her a kiss on the cheek.

'I'll leave you two lovebirds together,' Swallow told them, stomping out of the office. 'I'll be in the pub.'

This is a confrontation, Monty told herself. She tried to remember all the role-plays she had done at the Centre, learning to be assertive in situations like this. First, check the body language. Why was she cowering behind her desk, allowing Sig to stand over her?

'What's this I hear – you're off the stuff?' Monty nodded. 'Great, girl, just great. Now we'll really be back in business.'

'Have a chair,' she invited him, pulling out Swallow's seat for him and walking across the office to sit opposite. That was better. Now the eye contact. Monty wanted to look Sig in the eye like she wanted to kiss a cobra, but it had to be done, and she did it. His eyes were rather bloodshot, she noticed.

Now, say what you want in nice, cool language that isn't giving him a whole lot of emotive subtext.

'Sig, I don't want to be Ruby Slippers any more. I felt that it wasn't working and I think I made a mistake about the direction I ought to go in. I know we have a contract, and I'm willing to fulfil it, but not like that.' Now a touch of negative enquiry, just to top the whole thing off with a bit of style. 'I expect that isn't what you wanted to hear?'

'You're dead right, it isn't.' He stood up and shoved his hands into his pockets with aggression. 'I wanted to hear that you'd had the sense to sort yourself out, get off the stuff and come back to reality, and you were gonna get down and finish my album.'

'I will finish your album, but not if it costs my identity.'

'Your fucking identity! Don't give me that shit!'

Monty felt very much like throwing the card-index at him, or lacerating him with sarcasm, or screaming. In an effort to stick to her game plan, she took a deep breath and told him.

'I feel frightened when you shout, Sig.'

'God, you're pathetic,' he spat, walking around the office with stiff, angry strides. 'All right then, have it your own way. I can't get blood out of a stone, I know that. You want to fuck up a brilliant career, it's your business. You won't be so lucky again, you know.'

Monty said nothing; she felt better, not frightened any more.

'You're definitely not coming back, then?' he asked her, leaning on his knuckles like a gorilla.

'I don't want to come back,' she told him.

He flung round and grabbed the door handle. 'I love you, girl,' he said, 'remember that.'

Then he was gone, and the door slammed behind him. A few minutes later Swallow reappeared.

'I saw him go – he didn't look too pleased,' she announced.

'He said he loved me.' Monty sounded doubtful.

'Obviously he loves you, it's written all over him. Why else would he come crawling round?'

Monty stood up and fluffed out her hair. 'Well, if he loves me, he sure had a funny way of showing it. He did a fairly good job of wrecking me, after all. All he wanted was a custom-built artist to make him some money.'

'All men have a funny way of showing it,' Swallow said, locking up the office and leading Monty off to the pub. 'They just don't want to make themselves vulnerable. They don't trust women. Sex is all down to power in the end, haven't you sussed that yet?'

It was a beautiful early evening in May, one of those evenings when London seems like a clean new city. Monty squared her shoulders as she crossed the road, feeling hopeful for no good reason other than that the air was fresh and she was free.

Next day, Swallow took a telephone call which made her give a low, dirty chuckle as she took notes.

'Here you are,' she said to Monty, tearing off a page of her notepad. 'We want a boss vehicle for Joe Jones.' The note said 'US car, big, customized???? Red pref.' Monty picked up her handset and called London's custom car king, who lived in a house behind the gasworks in Fulham.

'I might know where I can get my hands on just the thing,' he told her. 'Is the guy renting or buying?'

'Buying,' called Swallow. 'Up to fifteen thousand.'

That afternoon the car arrived, a gleaming 1950s Chevrolet encrusted with chrome and with so many fins it looked like a pirated space shuttle. It was painted a glowing metallic variant of Chevrolet red, which would have been fine for a lipstick but was excessively vibrant for the ordinary London traffic jam. The price was £16,500.

Swallow and Monty had long ago perfected their car-buying act. Monty crawled inside, taking care not to scuff the white leather seats.

'The stereo doesn't work,' she called out.

Swallow eyed the custom car king bleakly. Monty opened one of the back doors.

'The other door doesn't open,' she shouted.

'It's a beautiful job,' the car king said, licking his lips. 'Mechanically immaculate. Does 110, steady as a rock.'

Monty tried the starter. The vehicle's response was sluggish. 'Reckon it could stand a new battery,' she announced.

'Tell you what.' Swallow said to the fidgeting customizer. 'Get all that seen to, have it back here by this time tomorrow and let's say fifteen thousand.' She turned away with finality. 'Then you can drive it down to Paleward Priory,' she told Monty.

The Priory was a massive grey-stone house which had been built in the fourteenth century, then added to over the generations until it was a comfortable L-shaped mass of masonry with gothic windows and a fine view over a lush river valley. Behind the house was woodland, the tame, luxuriant forestry of the Home Counties in which the trees looked as if they might be made of plastic.

The Priory had belonged to three major rock stars in the past decade, all of whom had embellished it according to their own taste. The first rock star had built the recording studio at the back of the house; the second had landscaped the garden to add a swimming pool, in which it was always too cold to swim; the third had filled the park with fibre-glass statues of African big game. Monty was startled to steer the red Chewy into the driveway and see a family of giraffes frozen under the chestnut trees.

The Joe Jones Band looked as boisterous and hairy as she remembered them. Even with his shirt on, Joe himself had a physical presence that made the air crackle. Contemptuous as she was of the big boys' delight in their new toy, Monty had to admit that the guy was *built*.

'How are you getting back to London?' he asked her. 'Can I drive you to the station?' It would have been absurd to refuse, so Monty climbed in at the passenger door and Joe inched the oversprung, overcharged red monster out into the narrow country lane.

The car had a bench front seat, the kind that made Monty think about people petting at drive-in movies. How long before some dumb groupie gets another notch in her holster right here, Monty thought, stealing a sideways glance at Joe. He took the car out to a major highway and howled along in the fast lane, steering with two fingers. I suppose he thinks he's going to turn me on by scaring me to death, Monty told herself, shifting uncomfortably on the seat.

'I'm sorry, am I going too fast?' Joe swooped the car across to the slow lane and cut its speed to well below the limit. 'I just wanted to see if it would go round the clock. I didn't intend to frighten you.'

'What a patronizing *creep!*' she said to Swallow the next day. 'Why are men so *infantile* ? You should have seen them, crawling all over the stupid car, feeling mucho macho just because they had a hot rod in the driveway.'

'How do you fancy keeping them in order for a few weeks?' Swallow had three telephone lines on hold and a handset in the hollow of each shoulder.

'Mussolini couldn't keep that lot in order, they're so into the old hot and nasty number.'

Swallow snarled down one telephone, cut the other off and kept three lines flashing on hold.

'Well, they want a housekeeper and you're the best I've got.'

Monty realized that she was being asked to spend the summer living at the Priory with five brawling studs.

'No, Swallow. Absolutely not.'

'Absolutely yes. I can't trust this to anyone else. Jack Nicholson's raving about the way you watered his potted palms. '

'I do not wish to spend the best summer of my life fending off passes from five oversexed morons who think they're God's gift to women.'

'Oh come on, Monty, you should be so lucky. What are you afraid of – getting raped?'

Swallow had shrewdly identified the source of Monty's unease. She did feel sexually threatened by the aggressive masculinity of the Joe Jones set-up.

'Is there really no one else you can send?' she asked Swallow with resignation.

Monty had been in Paleward Priory half a day when she realized that the Joe Jones Band was splitting up; the house was permeated with the atmosphere of recrimination. Joe and Al, the keyboards player, spent all day locked in the studio, while the other three members of the band floated around the house drinking and killing time with games of billiards.

She filled the icebox with the beer that made Milwaukee famous and went to the village stores to order steak, bacon and beans. Chilli con carne, bacon sandwiches and barbecues usually took care of these he-man carnivores. The state of the house was not too bad, thanks to a cleaning woman who came in from the village daily.

There was a Blüthner grand piano in the music room, black and shiny, its surface like a mirror. Monty opened it and played a few chords, feeling that the keys were stiff. It had a glorious tone, particularly in the lower registers. Monty ran through a half-remembered piece of Chopin, then tried 'Are You Lonesome Tonight?' which was easier but sounded ludicrous on this well-bred instrument. Then she started picking out some of her own songs, listening to the way they sounded in the piano's rich, sweet texture. It was not quite in tune. The dissonance was almost an enhancement, rather like her sister's limp – the tiny flaw in a perfect beauty. A few phrases of melody floated into her mind and she sighed inwardly. Here it was again. No matter which road she chose, she ended up face-to-face with her own music at the end of it.

'I think the piano in the music room needs tuning,' she told the boys at dinner. 'Would it be OK if I called London for someone to come and fix it?'

Dinner was a most uncomfortable meal. Joe, Al, their engineer and Monty ate in the kitchen, the rest of the band took their food into another room.

'Sure, get the piano tuned,' Joe agreed, reaching for the salad. She watched as he ignored her vat of chilli and ate a heap of lettuce with most of the chopped egg and onion. There was an awkward silence.

'I guess I should tell you what's going on,' he said at last, chewing rapidly. 'This is the last album to which we're committed, and we were hoping to keep it together until it was finished but, ah, it isn't working out that way. We want to go different routes.'

How arrogant of him to say 'we' when he means himself, Monty observed in silence.

'So we've decided to give our record company a *fait accompli*. Al here is cutting a solo album, and I'm producing it for him.'

Monty started clearing the plates and they got up to help her.

'Won't they go bananas when they find out what you're doing?'

'Yeah. But I think they'll come around when they hear the tapes. I'll take a day out next week to meet some of the guys – they'll be in London then. I reckon we can square them.'

She made coffee and the other two men drank theirs quickly and left the kitchen. Joe stayed; he put his feet on the table and picked his teeth, watching Monty as she finished stacking the dishwasher. She felt uncomfortable under his gaze.

'You must have a very good ear to know that the piano was out of tune,' he told her. She did not reply. 'I heard you playing this afternoon,' he continued. 'I'm sure I've heard you some place before. Aren't you . . . didn't you have a record out some time?'

'Yes, I did.' She flicked the drying-up cloths as she folded them, wishing he would stop asking questions.

'Weren't you Rick Brown's old lady for a while?'

'Seven or eight years.'

'Didn't we meet before, when we were playing in London?'

Monty wanted more and more to evade this interrogation. Why doesn't he just make a play for me and get on with it, she wondered. Joe's question lay in the air, a gauntlet she had to pick up.

'Yes. I was introduced to you with Cindy Moon.'

His full, defined lips had the suggestion of a smile about them. He leaned forward, took his feet off the table and threw away the toothpick.

'Why didn't you say? I was sure I knew you.'

'I was another person then. All that was nothing to do with who I am now.' Why was she wasting her hard-learned honesty on this trash? Why didn't he shut up and get out of her kitchen? She felt she had to escape from the conversation, so she said, 'If you've got everything you need, I'll go to bed.'

'Sure.' He stood up. 'I'm sorry if I was keeping you up. That was a beautiful dinner you made.'

'You didn't eat very much of it.'

'I'm more or less vegetarian,' he told her. 'I guess I should have mentioned it.'

She could not get to sleep. Her mind was full of disconnected thoughts that would not be calm, and her body felt uncomfortable. She stripped off the blankets and opened the windows, letting in the sweet air and the scent of the honeysuckle. She sank into a restless unconsciousness, but woke again in the dead of night, soaked in sweat, her skin burning. She had been dreaming about something, but could not remember what.

She turned over, and felt the old, familiar juiciness between her legs. So that was it. Monty ran her hands experimentally over her own body, feeling her breasts tingle and her skin come alive. It had been a long time since she made love, rather than submitting herself to sex.

The next day a familiar face appeared around the kitchen door. It was Tony, the guitarist who had played in her band when she was Ruby Slippers.

'Whatever are you doing here?' she asked, making him a cup of coffee.

'Joe called me, he wants me to do some sessions on this album.' Tony hadn't changed. He was still neat, clean, albino-pale and matter-of-fact. Monty found that she was very happy to see him.

'Joe's off riding some horse,' she said. 'He's usually back by now. He won't be long.'

'Do you like him?' Tony asked, direct as ever.

Monty gave a pout of indecision. 'I can't figure him out,' she told him. 'I can't stand all that macho crap.'

'Joe's nothing like that. He's been there and back. Fascinating bloke – I was sure you'd fall for him.' Tony shook his head, implying that women's sexual preferences were chief among the great mysteries of the universe. 'He was an orphan,' Tony continued, 'his mother abandoned him on an Indian reservation when he was a kid. He was an alcoholic when he was fourteen years old. Dried himself out and went into the Marines, got thrown out. Drifted off to New York, fell into a band, the rest is history.'

'How old is he?' Monty asked, suddenly concerned that he might be older than she was.

'Thirty-ish.'

'Has he ever been married?' OK, she admitted to herself, I care. I want to know.

'Yes, I think so. But, he's never really with anyone now. He knows too much about women, I reckon. It's amazing the way they come on to him.'

There was a scrape of riding boots outside the door and Joe appeared, his jeans ripped at both knees. There were mud stains on his T-shirt. 'This is what happens when your horse takes a unilateral decision to jump a fence,' he explained. 'I've busted my hand. Is there anything to strap it up with?'

He took a shower and sat on the" rim of the bath-tub while Monty ran a taut bandage around his swelling hand. She could no longer deny the message her body was giving her. She was aching with desire; just being close to that half-naked man, watching the water drip from his long, wet hair down the muscular ridges of his abdomen, made her breathless. She was captivated by the thought of his broad, bony hands, with long fingers and nails, holding her and caressing her and dipping into the hot centre of her body where her flesh was streaming wet with anticipation.

'What am I going to *do?*' she demanded of Swallow over the telephone. 'My heart stops every time he comes into the room.'

'Fuck him?' Swallow suggested in practical tones.

'What – and get hung up on another all-action superstud like Rick? Sign on for another term of abuse, like I did with Sig? Come on, Swallow, I need that like I need a hole in the head.'

'So, don't get hung up on him. Fuck him and run,' Swallow counselled.

'I can't.'

'Why not, everybody else does? Joe Jones has had more stray pussy than the Blue Cross. With any luck he won't even notice.'

'Thanks, Swallow, I really needed to hear that.'

'Only trying to be helpful.'

'For heaven's sake, this is *serious*.'

Inactivity, the food of lust, fanned the flames. Monty found herself imagining what Joe was doing every idle minute of her day, tracking him through the mansion with sonar waves of erotic yearning. If he came near her, she felt a visceral lurch which made her knees go weak and her mind a blank. In a desperate attempt to stop him permeating every cell in her body she started spending afternoons at the piano, trying to write a song. It was miserably hard work, which dismayed her; was it possible that she might have lost her talent, the gift which she had always undervalued because it came so readily whenever she called it, which she had almost begun to hate because it demanded so much from her?

She wanted to write a song about the misery of living with a brutal, dominating man, and feeling the pain of subjugation to his selfish needs. She heard it in her head as something very down, bitter and Billie Holiday-like, but the beautiful piano simply couldn't produce the sound of suffering that she wanted.

Swallow's right, she decided at last. I've got to have Joe. Monty knew every trick of inviting sexual approach and she began to use them unashamedly. She stood too close to Joe, touched him and let her hand linger with unmistakable emphasis on his sinewy arm. She held contact with his deep, black eyes longer than was proper, feeling thrilling palpitations as she dropped her gaze to his mouth and ran her eyes caressingly over his lips.

She flirted outrageously, until every conversation became a minefield of suggestive *double-entendres*. Joe was very polite, and she suspected with dismay that he tried to avoid being alone with her. She took a walk in the rain, and came in breathless and bedraggled with her T-shirt clinging to her breasts and her erect nipples clearly revealed; in this irresistible condition she contrived to bump into Joe in a doorway, so she was held in his arms – or would have been, if Joe had not stepped back as if she were going to bite him, his hands held away from her. It was tantalizing to be within the warm aura of the body she craved for a few seconds. Monty was considering more radical measures when Joe unexpectedly sought her out in the kitchen.

He avoided her eyes and said, 'The goddam car's cracking up. Half the exhaust fell off this morning. Can you get it fixed for us?'

The custom car king told Monty to take the Chevrolet to a garage in a north London mews where they specialized in American cars. The garage also specialized in reggae music, which pounded down the street from a colossal ghetto blaster. Two mechanics in Rastafarian hats and blue overalls elevated the Chewy on a hydraulic platform and ripped out the old exhaust, moving in time to the beat. A third stood by and watched, a fat joint smouldering in his hand.

'Hey man, don't stand around. Get the torch over here,' one of them called as they carried a new silencer out of the store and began to fit it, their spanners tinkling as they dropped them on the oil-stained concrete floor.

'*Could you be, could you be, could you be loved?*' sang Bob Marley and Monty lounged by the doorway, swinging her hips with the music. The mechanic put out his joint and turned on the welding torch, laughing as he set an exuberant fall of sparks through the air. One of the other men made a joke and they all roared and fell about, the white flame wavering carelessly across the underside of the car. I hope they know where the petrol tank is, Monty thought.

At the instant the premonition crossed her mind there was a massive explosion. Jagged fragments of metal clattered on the ground all around her. The men screamed, their hair and clothes in flames, blood pouring from wounds cut by flying metal. All over the workshop floor, pools of oil were burning. Monty whirled round, searching frantically for a fire extinguisher. It was too heavy for her, but a man ran out of the office to help her and they began putting out the flames. One mechanic was yelling in agony, his back ablaze.

When all the fires were out, Monty stood up and looked at the scene. The red Chevrolet was nothing but a mass of metal. Joe will be so angry, she thought in fear, putting her hands to her face.

Her face hurt. Her eyebrows rubbed off under her fingers, crisp crumbs of fried hair. Her hair smelt and was falling off in charred lumps. Her body hurt too. She was burnt all over. As she looked at her hands, Monty saw they were as red as steaks. Someone put a blanket around her. 'Come on girl, we're takin' you to hospital,' he said. Monty fell sideways, pain searing her body from the waist upwards. 'Joe's going to be so mad,' she said.

CHAPTER TWENTY-FIVE

PRINCESS AYESHAH chose to call her night club L'Equipe after weeks of turn-ing names over and over in her mind, trying to decide on a single word which would have the right resonance. The name had to suggest exclusivity and elegance which were beyond the power of money to command. It had to have dignity, so that no taint of undue frivolity could attach to a head of state who included the club in his itinerary; at the same time the name of the club had to indicate that no woman to be found there would be less than memorably chic. Above all, the name had to embody the idea of an élite, an enclosed gathering of people with only one thing in common – their position in the highest international social echelon. L'Equipe meant 'the team'; it had the right overtone of exclusivity.

She found her inspiration in the game of polo, which had been a symbol of wealthy amusement familiar to her from childhood; although she had crossed the world and attained a standing far higher than anything of which she could have dreamed in the beginning, polo, she had remarked, always meant the same the world over – the most thrilling, beautiful and expensive pastime imaginable, in which horses so carefully bred and schooled that they were like living works of art were mastered by men with the wealth, the leisure and the athleticism to become superb horsemen.

The club's symbol was a polo pony, a tiny, prancing silhouette which was woven into the carpet, embossed on the menus, embroidered on the linen and engraved on the glasses. Beyond that, the motif was carried through with crossed mallets hung on the walls, and wooden balls arranged in the foyer in a pyramid, like the cannon balls stacked at the Ecole Militaire. The interconnecting rooms were deco-rated in neutral shades of wild silk woven in imitation of the chessboard patterns traditionally groomed into the ponies' coats. There were wing chairs of muted, grey-gold velvet and couches upholstered in leather which was exactly the mature, glowing shade of brown of a well-cared-for saddle.

Hussain, whose aesthetic sense had been honed for life during his childhood, added a collection of eighteenth-century French watercolours which he accepted as a payment from a family who had supported the Pétain government during the Occupation and been rewarded in kind. The delicate, misty paintings, in their plain gold frames, assembled to please one individual eye, added to the impression that L'Equipe was nothing so vulgar as a nightclub, but a luxurious private home.

They compiled a guest list from a mixture of Hussain's mother's old friends, Ayeshah's most glamorous clients from Le Bambou and a selection made from Givenchy's address book. Ayeshah had plunged fearlessly into the new sphere of influence which a gilt chair at the Givenchy shows had opened up for her. The bitterness and frustration, of her years with Philippe lifted from her, and she once more became capable of warm but expedient charm. She exclaimed, she flattered, she alternated vibrant sympathy with effortless poise, she spent money lavishly and she made friends.

As she watched her secretary address the invitations to L'Equipe's opening by hand in her even, cultured script, with every title and decoration meticulously correct, Ayeshah was simultaneously thrilled and appalled by her own audacity. Her life seemed to have been a dizzying roller-coaster of fortune which was now gathering speed for its final impact. She had begun as a barefoot peasant girl dressed in a single strip of mud-spattered cloth, fit for nothing but the eternal chore of planting, harvesting and cooking rice; she had been betrayed, victimized and brutalized, she had endured a life of degradation; now she was a Princess, dressed in couture clothes and planning confidently to impress the most elegant, the most snobbish and the most powerful people in the world. She, who was barely literate, was watching her secretary write invitations to members of half the royal houses of Europe.

She counted the years, and at once felt sad. Ten years had passed in her progress from nothing to everything, and it was too long. She had wasted time, and soon it would be too late for her to achieve her only remaining aim, the most important ambition of all. Ayeshah left the girl to finish the pile of thick cream cards and did what she always did now whenever she felt the shadow of unhappiness; she went shopping. Hussain adored her to spend money, and if a week went by in which no uniformed messenger boy delivered a stack of couturier's boxes to their apartment he would seriously suggest that she had been neglecting her health.

Rumours – skilfully created by Hussain who was adept at conjuring intriguing ideas in his listener's minds with barely spoken hints – filled the city before the new club opened, and in consequence not one member of that self-appointed governing body of style, *le tout Paris,* felt it advisable to refuse an invitation. Two leopards, restrained by jewelled black leather collars and gold chains, patrolled outside at L'Equipe's opening, keeping order as well as any squad of security guards among the glittering crowd which clamoured for entry.

From that spectacular beginning, there were never less than three photographers lurking with their Rolleiflexes under the spindly young plane trees outside the club, waiting patiently for famous faces. They never had to wait long. Sometimes the shy young Yves St Laurent, Marc Bohan's assistant at Dior, would call in with a posy of models. Romy Schneider and Alain Delon, inseparable young lovers, came often. Princess Margaret, a tiny, erect young woman with eyes which flashed like fire opals, found she could sit down and play the piano for her friends in the back-gammon room as easily as she could at Balmoral.

One evening the manager called Ayeshah at the apartment in a flurry of excite-ment. 'Guess who we have a booking for tonight?'

'Margaret again?'

'No, better.'

'Rainier and Grace?'

'Next week, maybe, the way we're going.'

'Well *who*, for heaven's sake?'

'Edward Hardacre.'

'Who the hell is Edward Hardacre?'

'Jackie Kennedy's detective, that's who.'

'*Jackie's* coming to my nightclub?' She knew that the President and his young wife were paying their first official visit. For days the newspapers had talked of nothing else except Jackie's elegance, Jackie's pillbox hats and Jackie's political dilemma in patronizing the Paris fashion houses when she had worked so hard to demonstrate to the world that Washington also could lay a claim to elegance. The Kennedys seemed so much like demi-gods from a distant Olympus that Ayeshah had hardly dared dream that one of them would descend to the door of L'Equipe. She almost shrieked with delight at the news.

Hussain overheard her. As soon as she rang off, he made some telephone calls. In consequence, no paparazzi loitered outside L'Equipe that night, and the President's wife was very grateful for this thoughtfulness.

'This is nearly as good as being seventeen again,' she said wistfully as she left.

The day after that, *France-Soir* had a large picture of Jackie at L'Equipe, taken from across the street with a telephoto lens, but by that time the victim was in Rome, innocently recommending the club to all her friends.

No one ever connected the exquisite Princess Ayeshah with Madame Bernard, whose name swiftly came to stand for the most beautiful women that money could buy. Those men who kept the Reaumur telephone number in their address books under the letter B, most of whom had the discretion to choose not to write any name against that number, were never entirely sure that they were calling Madame Bernard, or that such a person really existed. Ayeshah herself never intended to be known by that name. It simply attached itself to the operation, a consensus nomi-nation from her clientele.

The men who called Madame Bernard's number were answered by a woman's voice which said 'Locations Landon' in a pleasant, neutral tone. The entire trans-action was disguised as an enquiry about an apartment to rent. One room meant one girl, two rooms meant a pair, seven a small party; a north aspect meant a blonde, east a brunette, south a negress. The price structure was encoded in the floor on which the fictitious apartment was to be located, with the first floor denoting the most expensive services. The clients' special requirements were ingeniously expressed in requests for particular features such as security locks, leather furniture or a view of a church. The code was passed on by word of mouth, along with the telephone number.

Agnès, the woman who answered the telephone lived in a small room with a sloping ceiling on the top floor of an undistinguished apartment building. She had worked as a bookkeeper at Le Bambou, and Ayeshah valued her for her meticulous accounts and her complete avarice. Agnès had worn the same grey flannel skirt, winter and summer, for three years. Her long brown hair was coiled around her head in braids and once a month Agnès allowed herself the luxury of shampoo. Agnès rode to work on a moped and complained incessantly about its consumption of petrol. She was ever alert to an opportunity to eat, drink or travel at someone else's expense. The only topic which she discussed with any sign of pleasure was the bank account in which her savings accumulated. She regarded every extra half per cent of interest as a personal victory over the Credit Lyonnais.

Ayeshah explained to Agnès how she was to run the call girl agency and then allowed the prim, sexless creature to name her salary, knowing that Agnès would not have the vision, let alone the courage, to ask for an unreasonable sum. She instructed her to keep two sets of books, one recording the fictitious business of Locations Landon, on which taxes were to be duly paid, and the other containing the true names of the clients and the women they hired, although the exact nature of the transactions was still to be disguised. The records, detailed as they were, would mean nothing to anyone except Agnès and Ayeshah.

The only remaining connection with her old life was Bastien the pimp, to whom Ayeshah directed that a generous monthly payment be made.

'That's not necessary,' he protested when she outlined her plans to him, sitting at the scarred metal table in the depths of a street-corner *tabac* where he normally conducted his business during the daytime. Bastien had an expression of puzzled discomfort in his hard, black eyes. 'You don't want to forget your old friends, of course, but this is too much. I've no doubt we will be able to do business from time to time, naturally we will have interests in common, but we can always come to some arrangement. You know I've always been a reasonable man, Princess,' he used her new title with ironic emphasis.

'I want to pay for more than your blessing and your support – I want silence, *absolute* silence,' she told him. 'There must never, ever be the smallest breath of suspicion about me, do you understand? I've made it look as if this agency is entirely Agnès's business, and I want you to make sure that is exactly what the girls take it to be. As far as the people who knew Ayeshah when she ran Le Bambou are concerned, she struck lucky with Hussain Shahzdeh, broke into the big time and now the arrogant bitch doesn't recognize her old associates on the street. Do you understand?'

He gave her a nod and a smile which revealed his uneven, yellow teeth, noticing that for this meeting she was wearing a cheap blue suit and a wholly uncharacteristic, blue velveteen hat, an outfit so unstylish that she would scarcely be recognized by anyone who had encountered her at Givenchy. 'And besides,' she continued in an earnest tone, 'there is something else I will need you to arrange for me – but not yet.'

Before long, Agnès began to begrudge the hundreds of francs of excessive graft which she paid out each month. She was the kind of employee who was as mean with her employer's money as she was with her own, and the waste implied in every envelope stuffed with hundred-franc bills which she handed to Bastien began to gnaw at her soul.

Only one girl connected with Le Bambou was accepted by Agnès – Pan-Pan, who had become a stripper at the Crazy Horse and who nightly wrapped her magnificent limbs in the rope meshes of a hammock for that establishment's most famous routine. Ayeshah decided to take a risk with Pan-Pan because she would undoubtedly attract other girls of the same calibre to the work. No one else who had known Ayeshah at Le Bambou was employed, but there was no lack of enquiries. When a woman's voice sounded on the telephone line it might come from a haughty, high-class whore, a student who could not pay her book bill, a debutante looking for a thrill or a housewife who merely coveted a washing machine.

Within six months, Agnès complained that there was so much work she could not cope with it by herself any longer, and Ayeshah readily agreed to hire an assistant, choosing one of the poverty-stricken students, a round-eyed Canadian girl with a permanently startled expression. Shortly afterwards, Agnès told Bastien, with inept insolence, that she intended to pay him less. Bastien informed Ayeshah, who made up the shortfall. Four weeks later, on her way home after making another payment to Bastien, Agnès was knocked off her moped on the Boulevard Sebastopol and killed outright by a lorry loaded with concrete slabs whose steering was apparently defective.

The former student knew her employer only as a voice on the telephone, a woman's voice with a curious, unplaceable accent and a distinct, metallic quality. She was joined in the office by Véronique, a former house mannequin at Givenchy who had been dismissed because she could not control her weight. The timid young Canadian had only just shown Véronique how the dual bookkeeping system worked when the voice on the telephone offered her several thousand francs plus her air-ticket to go home. She agreed. Thereafter, none of Ayeshah's employees was ever to meet her. The little attic room was used only as an office. Money was paid into a bank account in the name of Locations Landon. Every week several ruled sheets of paper on which the agency's transactions were recorded with the clients' real names were posted to an address in the suburbs, from which they were posted again to addresses which were changed every few weeks. An elderly Iranian woman, who had once been a maid in Hussain's parents' household, was paid a small pension for the duty of collecting the large manilla envelope each week and placing it personally in the Princess's hands.

His wife's secret empire of vice troubled Hussain's conscience. He considered that the men – many of them eminent, powerful and in positions of considerable public trust – whose names she recorded were incomprehensibly foolish, but when he noticed the unnatural pleasure which Ayeshah took in her potential dominion over them he was disturbed.

'Don't you think this business could prove a danger to us, after all?' he suggested quietly one afternoon, as he watched her at the tiny Empire writing-desk that had been his mother's, scanning the week's delivery of names.

'Of course not. Whatever makes you say that?' She turned swiftly towards him, the colour rushing into her face, her black eyes glittering with alarm. The triple necklace of graduated pearls around her throat rose and fell as she took a sharp breath. Hussain's cooperation was important and the idea that he might change his mind disturbed her.

'You're forced to deal with bad types like Bastien, you're making yourself vulnerable to scandal . . .' he continued in tones of reasonable practicality.

'Nonsense. I know what I'm doing. No one will ever find out, I've made sure of that. And it's far better to have Bastien on our side than to try to cut him out. I've seen how those Marseillais operate, so have you. We've no choice but to involve him. Once you're operating outside the law, the only people you can trust are those who have as much to lose as you do.' Nervously she patted her hair, making sure that the pins which held her immaculate chignon were secure. 'Besides, Hussain, think of the money – the girls make more than the club.'

'But you don't need money. L'Equipe is an enormous success, you're planning to open another club in St Tropez next year and that will be an enormous success too. Speaking as your major backer, I'm delighted. Money isn't what you need now as much as prestige. If anyone ever connected you with Madame Bernard you would be ruined. You can achieve everything you want with clean hands, I'm sure of it. Why take such a risk?'

'But Hussain, I thought you agreed!' She jumped up and crossed the room, moving sinuously in her clinging, cream wool dress, to where her husband stood, leaning against the blue-white marble fireplace with one hand on the mantelpiece. She clung to his arm, pleading for understanding. 'What about the things you want to do? Don't you see that the information we have will give you power? With what we know we will hold every institution in France in the palms of our hands. We could almost bring down the government if we wanted to. And not only France – we've had calls from all over Europe already. How can you tell me to back out when you will need the agency more than I do?'

He broke away from her with an irritated gesture, angry with himself as much as with her. He had never looked for the emotion which other people called love from Ayeshah. Hussain considered love to be nothing more than self-deception, a waste of energy, a weakness. She fascinated him in a way that was beyond senti- ment, and she saw the world from the same perspective. Now, however, he was beginning to suspect that her life was directed to a point beyond their relationship. Could it be that she was attempting to use him in the way she had undoubtedly used Philippe?

'Don't try to make me responsible for what you're doing.' He turned to face her, his face grave, the normal brightness of his glance extinguished. 'I've told you my opinion, if you don't accept it there's nothing I can do about that. The fact remains I think you're being foolish, I think the agency is a weapon which can be used against you much too easily, and I think you should reconsider. That's all.'

'Very well. I think you're wrong and think time will prove me right.' She fol- lowed him and caught hold of both his large, square hands in hers, the firm grip of her slim fingers almost pinching him. 'Don't you realize that there are only two ways to do business, Hussain? Fine, if you can keep everything straight and above board, if you can trade on your spotless reputation and never touch one dirty centime; but if you start on the wrong side of the tracks, if you have to flirt with criminals and accommodate corruption, then you have to go on that way. I might be able to forget Bastien, but he will never forget me, don't you see? We can't break out. I'm trapped, and so are you. The only thing to do is be the biggest gangsters of them all. That's the only freedom we have, don't you understand?'

He smoothed her hair affectionately, hoping she was wrong; his mother's injunction to live a good life never left him, although, like Ayeshah, Hussain's per- sonal morality had been warped by the way in which he had been forced to survive. But Hussain had to admit that his own ambitions were maturing only slowly. He could always find a market for doubtful commodities, there were always desperate men who sought him out for his contacts in the arms trade, but the big business, the business which was legitimate, never came his way no matter what efforts he made to attract it.

The following year his persistent search for the deal that would open the door was at last successful. He was approached by the defence attaché of the embassy of the Central Sahara Republic, who wanted aircraft for Air-Sahara, the new national airline. It was a natural development, the reward of years of discreet, successful trading. Sahara's defence minister had dealt with Hussain a few years earlier, when, as a guerrilla leader, he had bought guns and tanks for the revolution which finally ousted the French.

Hussain had talks with one French and one German aircraft manufacturer, and the French finally offered to pay him the larger fee for introducing the Sahara business. It took months of hard bargaining to get an agreement on a spare-parts contract, a period in which Hussain dropped eight kilos in weight and slept badly.

'Why not just take the Germans? They were prepared to play ball,' Ayeshah asked him.

'There's more in it for us with the French, and I want to set a benchmark,' he replied, 'but if I can't get a good spare-parts agreement, I'll go back to the Germans, certainly. But if I sell Air-Sahara short now, the phone won't ring again on this kind of deal. The time to be truly greedy is when I can afford it.'

The French at last agreed, the contracts were drawn up, and then the storm broke. A disgruntled retired colonel on the aircraft firm's board denounced the deal as aid to the enemies of France and ruinous for the company itself. He also named Hussain, calling him a parasite. He accused Hussain of supplying the anti-French revolution with arms, and of a secret clause in this deal to sell fighter planes to the new government, bombers which would be used against French interests in the rest of Africa.

'The filthy little liar!' Hussain raged, beside himself with both anger and fear that success would be snatched away from him at the last moment. 'I wouldn't sell their lousy Rapier bomber even if I could. It's nothing but a jet-propelled coffin!'

The scandal exploded in August, the worst possible month, when there was no political news and all the politicians were at leisure to give the press sanctimonious statements. The story raged across the front pages of all the national newspapers and soon the most influential was calling for an official enquiry.

Ayeshah calmly took down the small, oblong black box which housed the index cards on which the names of Madame Bernard's clients were noted. Her slender fingers, tipped with cyclamen- pink nails, flicked through the cards and she withdrew two of them and held them out to Hussain with an expression of enquiry. 'Here is your enemy,' she told him, showing him the name of the colonel, 'and this man, I think, is on the board of the newspaper. Now it's your choice, Hussain – what's it to be? A good life and a failed one, or the success which you want, which you have worked for and which you deserve?'

He made a gesture of assent at once and with good grace. 'You were right. I hoped not, but this proves it. How shall we handle it? Shall we start with the newspaper man; the old colonel is a complete fanatic and that type is always unpredictable.'

'Leave it to me,' Ayeshah said, giving her husband a smile which was intended to be reassuring, but which had precisely the opposite effect on him.

Within three days, the newspaper which had demanded an enquiry carried a lengthy statement of retraction from the colonel including a personal apology to Hussain. Beside it was a story from the paper's chief defence correspondent confirming that he had seen the Air-Sahara contract with his own eyes, that it was a superb confirmation of France's superiority in aviation and that it contained no clause in any way prejudicial to the national interest.

'Perfect,' Hussain congratulated Ayeshah. 'If I'd written it myself I couldn't have had a better vindication.'

'It's only the truth, after all,' she reminded him. 'Do you understand what I mean now? In our situation we can't talk about right or wrong. There is no natural justice for us – we were wronged once, and we had to defend ourselves. Now it's impossible for either of us to leave our past behind – all we can do is go on in the same way.'

That week the manilla envelope brought to Ayeshah by the aged domestic contained a spool of recording tape. Hussain awoke at 3 am to hear a faint twitter of voices from the sitting room and reached for his black foulard robe. He and Ayeshah shared separate but adjoining bedrooms, and he went first into his wife's room, where he found that the bed, with its ivory satin quilt and white silk sheets which were changed every day, bore no imprint of her body.

He walked quickly and silently down the corridor and listened for a few moments outside the double doors of the sitting room. He heard a woman's voice, harsh and threatening, and a man's voice, arrogant and aggressive at first, then cracking with emotion as it began to plead. The conversation at last concluded with mumbled words of agreement from the man. There was silence for an instant, then the chattering of reversed voices as the tape was rewound.

Hussain pushed open the door and saw his wife, a tiny, tense figure in her tightly-sashed negligee of oyster satin, intently watching the tape-recorder as the spools revolved. When the tape was completely rewound she touched the switch to play it again, sinking back in her chair to listen and reaching for a cigarette from the silver box on the table beside her. She caught sight of Hussain, gasped with shock, then jumped up to draw him into the room.

'Listen,' she said, 'it's priceless. Listen to this miserable little liar trying to deny everything. Then, when she starts giving him the dates and the times and the money, the girl's names, what they did – everything – he just goes to pieces. I swear he's almost crying. Listen . . .'

'I don't want to hear it.' Hussain gently made her sit down and turned off the tape, inwardly appalled at the enjoyment which had gleamed from her eyes as she described the colonel's collapse.

'Why not? Don't you want at least to hear your enemy surrender?' She squared her shoulders defensively, sensing his disapproval. 'Isn't this the moment you've been waiting for, Hussain?'

'Not I. You. You've been waiting for this, surely? This is the point to which your whole life has been leading you: all this time what you've wanted was to see someone destroyed. You were craving it.'

'No, of course not, how could you suggest such a thing? It's natural to enjoy one's little victories, isn't it?' She smiled coquettishly and sat down, curling her legs under her, aware that she sounded evasive. His manner was not threatening, but Hussain was as cunning, as sensitive and as implacable as she was, and he was asking for an explanation. Ayeshah bit her lip and looked up at him, playing for time.

He looked down at her sadly, then slowly sat beside her and took her hands, making her turn to face him. 'It isn't this man you really want to destroy, is it?' He gestured towards the tape-recorder. 'He was my enemy – but who is yours? Do you know what I think, Ayeshah? I have the sense that this whole operation is something you have created to attack one man, a man whose only vulnerable point is his sexuality, isn't that right?'

She swallowed, weighing up the possible answers. She knew she could not lie to him, because he knew her too well to be deceived; to lie would be to undermine their relationship, perhaps beyond repair, and she needed him. If she told him the truth, perhaps he would help her. She decided to unfold for him the story which for so long she had hardly dared repeat to herself, fearing that the pain and bitterness which she had buried in her memory would once more engulf her.

When she had finished talking, Hussain continued to hold her hands in silence for a long while, understanding at last the weight of hatred which aligned her energies like a lodestone towards the annihilation of the man who had betrayed her. She did not cry. The pain was so keen, so strong, so close to the core of her spirit, that tears would not have eased it.

'You're still afraid of him, aren't you?' he said quietly, stroking her head over and over again.

It was true, although she had not recognized her fear before. She nodded. 'He has everything, after all – wealth, position, power. He can't give me what I want without losing those things.'

Hussain stood up and walked to and fro across the pool of light shed by the single lamp which illuminated the room. He ran his fingers through his short, curly, black hair. 'There's no point whatever in going to lawyers,' he said at last, 'my guess is that you could spend thousands and get nowhere. We'll ask him directly, and if he doesn't agree – yes, we'll destroy him. He'll be finished, I promise you.'

On a fine spring morning, the slight, spruce figure of an Englishman strode across the cobbles of the Place Vendôme, raising his hat to a pair of pretty shopgirls who pranced across his path clutching each other tightly for support as they walked awkwardly over the uneven stones in their high-heeled shoes.

Any Parisian could have identified his nationality at once; the immaculate camel-hair overcoat covered his shoulders like a second skin – only a Savile Row tailor could have moulded cloth to flesh so exactly, without a wrinkle; his black leather briefcase was ostentatiously scuffed, and the stitching was split at one corner – only an English gentleman would advertise his contempt for commerce so blatantly; there were the unmistakable, quasi-military features of his appearance, the severely cropped and parted black hair, the black shoes polished until they gleamed like mirrors; above all, there was the arrogant spring in his stride, the proprietorial width of his smile, the condescending courtesy of his gestures – in 1960, only an Englishman could have been so secure in the delusion that he was superior to the whole of the rest of the world.

Lord James Bourton left the Ritz behind him, crossed the Rue St-Honoré and strolled through the Tuileries gardens, smiling benevolently at the children who scrambled on to the gaily painted merry-go-round under the watchful eyes of their nurses. The trees were mantled with the misty, pale green of their new foliage and beneath his feet the fine gravel was clotted with mud from the frequent squalls of the past few days. The rainy spell had passed now, and the sky was the identical, clear carefree blue of a sky painted by Watteau. He allowed himself a moment's unpatriotic reflection as he strolled across the Pont de la Concorde, acknowledging that the Seine embankment, with its heroic vistas of palaces and monuments, presented a far more inspiring landscape than the grimy borders of the Thames. But then, he reassured himself at once, the French only excelled at inessentials.

He reminded himself of the address from the deep blue pages of his pocket diary. The manservant who opened the door to him was absurdly well-dressed, he remarked, smiling to himself at this typical sign of nouveau-riche ostentation. Still, he could find no fault with the room into which he was shown to wait. He had expected a vulgar riot of Rococo, gilded, overdecorated and uncomfortable; instead the furniture was mostly from the Directoire period, heavy and dark with severe, neo-classical lines. A Greek amphora, subtly illuminated in an alcove, emphasized the atmosphere of homage to antiquity. The heavy fringed curtains of pale grey moire enhanced the room's beautiful, watery radiance.

Curiosity had brought him to Paris this time. He was perfectly certain that his bank would not wish to be involved in any way with Prince Shahzdeh – or his wife. They were not the kind of people with whom a reputable City firm would wish to do business. The Prince was by all accounts an astute businessman, but his background was disreputable in the extreme. And the nightclub business, even at the exalted level of L'Equipe, was notoriously unstable and inseparable from the criminal element. However, when the Prince's letter had arrived at his office, describing a proposed resort development for which he was seeking finance, and suggesting an exploratory meeting, James Bourton decided to agree simply because he wanted to take a look at the Shahzdeh couple.

There were so many rumours about them, about their origins, their wealth, their bizarre relationship. They were both presumed to be of Middle Eastern origin, and Hussain's title was often guessed by Europeans to be false. Many people who encountered the Prince and Princess sensed something unnatural about their liaison but could only express their suspicion in gossip and conjecture. James had heard that the Princess had been nothing but a cabaret dancer in Beirut when her husband had discovered her and fallen under the spell of her extraordinary beauty; he had been told that their bedroom was entirely panelled in mirrors, that the Princess hoarded clothes and owned three thousand pairs of shoes alone, that her exquisite face was entirely the creation of a famous Brazilian plastic surgeon. Naturally, no one would decline the opportunity to meet this legendary creature.

Time passed. A maid brought him the French interpretation of English tea, a watery, scented brew which was undrinkable. The room was very quiet, and James noticed that the continual roar of traffic was muffled by double windows. He looked at his watch and realized he had been waiting almost forty minutes. Still, discourtesy was to be expected from these marginal types. The wait only confirmed his opinion of them.

In her bedroom, Ayeshah wiped a smudge of lipstick from the corner of her mouth and redrew the line with a carmine pencil. With a tremendous effort of will she stilled the tremor of her hand, completed her makeup and rose to her feet, smoothing the tight skirt of her fawn and cream tweed suit and brushing imaginary grains of powder from the *jabot* of her white silk blouse. The glistening, dark sweep of her hair was furled immaculately into a pleat, revealing her small ears with their plain pearl studs. She twisted, checking in the mirror that the seams of her pale beige stockings were straight.

Hussain kissed the top of her head. 'He'll be at a disadvantage now, because he is not on his own ground. Never fear, he can do nothing to hurt you now. Don't forget that I will be directly outside the door. If you need me all you have to do is call. Are you sure that half an hour alone with him will be enough?'

'I don't know. It will be as much as I can stand, I'm sure.' Her face was completely drained of colour under its masklike maquillage. Together they walked down the long corridor. The manservant opened the double doors of the salon and closed them softly behind her. Hussain slowly lowered himself into an armchair beside the doorway.

James turned as he heard the doors open, and stood up as he saw the woman enter the room. She was as stunning as he had expected, a perfect beauty made awesome by her aura of power. The slender but rounded body, the exquisitely delicate legs, the full, sensual mouth and the flawless complexion would have made her irresistible, but her round black eyes with their heavy lids held a warning for anyone who dared to desire her. The Princess's beauty held the traces of corruption, like flaws in a jewel, which James recognized at once.

Ayeshah controlled herself with every ounce of strength she could summon. In the intervening years since their parting she had trained herself to imagine him with a white skin, but the shock of seeing him, standing here in her own home, a pale, privileged Englishman, made her feel faint. She crossed the room and sat down in the dark leather chair which Hussain usually chose; its massive solidity reassured her.

She tried to speak, but for a few instants her mouth would not open. Instead James spoke as he walked towards her. 'Have I the honour of addressing Princess Ayeshah herself?' he enquired in French, expecting her to extend her hand. Realizing that he would touch her, she fixed him with a forbidding stare.

'Do you recognize me?' she asked, feeling herself gain control of the situation.

'Why of course; who could fail to recognize you, Princess? You're famous. Even in England everyone has heard of L'Equipe and its beautiful owner.' James was disconcerted, sensing a peculiar electricity between the woman and himself.

'We met many years before L'Equipe ever existed. Look at me carefully. You ought to remember.'

'I'm sure I would never have forgotten such a charming personality . . .'

'Think carefully,' she warned, a cold, flat note in her voice. He did as she asked with increasing guilty unease. He certainly recognized the tone of her question, it was the kind of reproach which a few women had made to him before, always as a prelude to a clumsy attempt at blackmail.

What her question suggested was, of course, possible. In his forty-odd years James had experienced sexual encounters with more women than he could possibly remember, most of them of Asian or African origin. His youthful libido had survived the brief trauma of his marriage and matured into a voracious sensual appetite. Were it not for her imperious aura, the Princess would have been precisely the exotic type which he most enjoyed. But he had no recollection of her.

Besides, he reasoned swiftly, this woman was wealthy, successful and protected. She would have no need to resort to blackmail. Nevertheless, he followed the precepts of his class for avoiding the possibility of embarrassment, and began courteously to negate her statements.

'Princess, I am quite certain you are mistaken,' he told her, returning to his seat. 'I never forget a face, especially not a beautiful face. Will your husband be joining us shortly? Or perhaps you would care to tell me a little about this development that you are planning in London?'

'I'd prefer to wait for my husband, he will not be long.' Fury began to roar through her mind like a fire. Now Ayeshah knew what his reaction would be; he would look down on her from the unassailable height of his race and standing, and dismiss her. She was sure that for the moment he genuinely did not remember her, and sure that when she forced him to recall everything he would flatly deny it. She racked her brains for a way in which to trap him.

'Tell me about your family, Lord Bourton.' He was momentarily puzzled, then relieved.

'My family? Yes, well –' he coughed, 'I'm a great family man of course. I've got two daughters, lovely girls, at school most of the time . . .'

'May I ask what their names are?'

'The elder one is Catherine, and the younger one was christened Miranda although at home she's usually called by a sort of nickname.' He smiled and there was an awkward silence.

Ayeshah walked to the writing-desk and opened one of its small mahogany drawers. From the drawer she took a photograph, a curled monochrome print measuring two inches by two-and-a-half. It was blurry, having been taken in sunlight too bright for the speed of the equipment, but it was possible to make out two infants in sun-bonnets. One stood upright, the other, a mere baby, was held in the arms of a Chinese girl who wore a blouse and black trousers. They were posed in front of a single-storey wooden building raised on piles.

'Then perhaps, if you do not remember me, you can at least tell me who these children are?'

He examined the indistinct photograph, screwing up his eyes. 'Why, those are my girls, aren't they – with their *amah*? That looks very much like the house I used to have out in . . .' The word 'Malaya' died on his lips as a realization struck like lightning. He looked up at her with the fixed gaze of a doomed animal, terror curdling his blood.

She smiled, and he saw what he had not seen at first, the sweet, kittenish features of Khatijah, the wife he had married in the *kampong* in wartime. In mere appearance she had hardly changed at all, although her skin was pale, her clothes were European, and she wore make-up; but innocence had disappeared from her face and the yielding softness from her movements, affecting a chilling perversion of her allure. It was a spiritual change that had transformed her completely.

'No, I don't look quite the same, do I? Perhaps I shouldn't blame you – I'm hardly a little native girl in a sarong any more, am I? And you don't look much like my handsome, brown-skinned husband either. But appearance isn't everything, is it?'

James had never considered the possibility that he would ever see the woman who had borne his children again. It had been unthinkable, and now that it had happened, and she was standing an arm's length away from him, he was paralysed by fear. Some of his fear was rational: he was afraid for his rich comfortable life, for his impeccable reputation, for the love of his daughters, for his freedom, for his future. Deeper than these was an irrational fear, his old, eternal fear of the female, personified in this angry woman.

She saw his fear and it gave her courage. 'Don't you want to know what I want? Don't you want to know why I've brought you here?'

He could not answer, so she continued. 'You've stolen so much from me, haven't you? My love, my happiness, my honour, my family, my home – everything that I had. When you took away my babies you took my whole life. This . . .' she indicated the room, and beyond it her existence in Paris, 'this is nothing. It's just something that fills up the empty space, that's all.'

She walked slowly around him as if looking for the place to deliver the *coup de grace*. 'I know everything about you. I know much more about you now than when we were married. Don't you think that's curious? Your Australian friend used to tell me your news. Until you left Malaya, of course. He didn't think you'd treated me very well, but I expect you knew that. And I've paid people to watch you, the last few years. Lord James Bourton. And the little Misses Bourton. They're lovely girls, you're right. And I'm their mother, and I want them back.'

'Never.' The double shock unlocked his tongue and James spoke almost before she had finished. 'Never.' The sound of his own voice emboldened him. 'I love my daughters and I'll never let you have them. What kind of a life would you give them, anyway? If you dare . . .'

'Do you love them? Do you love them the way you loved me? Or do you just love the life they brought you? That's all you wanted them for, your inheritance, wasn't it? My God, you'd never even seen the little one before you snatched her away.' She was still and tense, like a snake about to strike, hatred glittering in her black eyes. 'I'd have done anything, you know. I'd have been my own children's *amah* for the sake of being with them.'

He stood up, suddenly desperate to shatter the emotional web in which she was binding him. 'I'm sure you would. You'd have done anything to get out of your little village, as I remember. You thought I was your ticket to a soft life and you still do. You don't love the girls, you don't know them, you've never known them – not the way I do, as people. They wouldn't even recognize you, if they saw you. And if they knew what their mother was . . .'

She drew a sharp breath and he knew that he had found a weapon that was potent against her. He was sure, now, that her elegant façade overlay some evil of which, at the bottom of her heart, she was ashamed. The impression of vice he had read in her face was correct. It had been enough merely to allude to it.

The doors opened with a slight hesitation and a burly, olive-skinned man entered the room, taking command of the situation by his authoritative presence. He advanced towards James with a hand outstretched.

'Allow me to introduce myself – Hussain Shahzdeh.' Dumbly James extended his own hand to meet the Prince's fleshy grasp. Despite the gesture of friendly greeting, he had a momentary impression that the other man was going to hit him. 'Shall we sit down and discuss this situation like reasonable people?'

The three antagonists sat, the Prince and Princess side by side on a long, grey sofa and James facing them, seated in the centre of a black leather couch. Ayeshah, desperately grateful that her husband had arrived to strengthen her attack just as she was faltering, slipped her arm through his.

'I'm sure you will agree that my wife's desire for her children is quite natural.' James nodded. In the presence of another man his attitude was completely different, calculating and devoid of emotion.

'Your concern, naturally, is that you acquired your inheritance, in accordance with a codicil to your father's will, when you acquired your children. Of course, the children were legitimately conceived in wedlock and there is nothing at all to disqualify you from the bequest.'

James nodded again, only partly reassured by the man's amiable tone. Hussain was a type he detested, a cheap market-trader masquerading as a gentleman, a greasy Arab trying to ape European ways while at the same time eating away the fabric of the country which had given him shelter. James was not afraid of him, as he had been of Ayeshah. He had been lifted out of the quicksand of sexual guilt into which she had pushed him. Now that the whole affair was assuming the tenor of an irregular business deal, his concern was to find the most effective way to walk out.

'That's completely correct,' he announced. 'My concern is not financial, it is for the welfare of my daughters. If they were to learn, at this stage in their lives, that my wife, whom they have looked upon as their mother, was not in fact their mother at all, it would be a devastating blow. Absolutely devastating.'

Equally, Hussain loathed James from the depths of his soul for being a threadbare, decadent aristocrat whose fine sentiments disguised emotional bankruptcy. He swallowed his dislike and continued, 'Naturally. So how shall we resolve this situation?'

'There is nothing to resolve. I shall not permit any degree of interference in my children's lives, on any pretext whatever. That's all I have to say.' He stood up, preparing to leave, but Hussain made no move.

'As my wife mentioned, we have made some enquiries, Lord James, and it seems to me that there might be certain advantages to you in coming to an agreement with us.'

'What advantages?'

'You have a few small debts, I believe. Some of the arrangements which you have made with the trustees of your father's estates are perhaps what might be called . . .'

'Absolute nonsense.' James was outraged that a man he considered to be little better than a racketeer was criticizing the probity of his own dealings. 'I've never heard anything so absurd. You've no right to pry into my legal arrangements and when I find out who is responsible, who you've been dealing with, there'll be hell to pay. Good God, do you think you can stand there and try to buy your way into my family?'

He advanced to the door as fast as he could without appearing to flee from the room. 'As you yourself have pointed out, I've nothing to fear, from you or from anyone. If you were ever foolish enough to try to embarrass me with this fantastic story you'd get nowhere, precisely nowhere. You've no proof, I've done nothing wrong. If you have any love at all for those children,' he looked directly at Ayeshah as he spoke and saw with satisfaction that her face was drawn with terrible distress, 'you'll stay away from them, leave them as they are, for your own sake as well as theirs. They've been brought up as two nice, normal English girls; I'm sorry to speak bluntly, but a woman like you is everything they have been taught to despise. Good morning to you.'

While his words still echoed in the room, James snatched his coat and hat from the hands of the startled servant and bolted through the door, out into the sweet, fresh air and the safety of the street. His heart was hammering in his chest. At the street corner he hailed a taxi, suddenly feeling that he had no strength to walk any longer.

Anger and grief broke over Ayeshah like a wave. 'I'll kill him,' she screamed, 'I'll kill him, kill him, kill him.' Her face was skull-like and her eyes seemed to protrude with the force of the emotion which animated her. Protectively, her husband soothed her.

They had already discussed what they would do if James rejected their approach, but Hussain rehearsed the plan to her one last time. 'Now I want you to think about one thing,' he said, with the deepest gravity. 'Which do you want – your children or to destroy their father? Because you must realize that if we succeed now – which we will – and if they ever discover what you have done – which they may – they will hate you.'

'I'll make them love me,' she answered.

CHAPTER TWENTY-SIX

MONTY LOOKED at herself in the mirror; she was not an alluring vision. Her hair was still long at the back, but scorched and frazzled, and it was mere stubble at the front. It had a revolting singed smell. Her eyebrows were gone, and her eyelashes were less than a millimetre long. Her face, neck, breasts and arms were smeared with orange ointment. Her hands were bandaged. To deal with the agony of her burns she had accepted four-hourly pain killers, which made her feel half-stoned. This filled her with fretful anxiety – there had been a substantial proportion of addicts at the Centre who had become dependent on substances prescribed by their doctors for the purest of motives.

'OK – that's enough bad news for one day,' she said to Cathy, who helped her put the hospital gown on and get back into bed.

'When will they let you out?' her sister asked, plumping up the pillows.

'When I've got some skin on my tits, the doctor says. They think I may get away with no scars at all, as long as my hands don't get infected. They got the worst of it. I've got a few little cuts from bits of metal, but I was lucky. You should have seen the car, Cathy: it was a total wreck. Joe will go bananas when he finds out his darling Chewy is in bits all over Paddington.'

Cathy shook her head, half exasperated and half sympathetic. 'Once upon a time I had a sister who stood up, talked back and hit out when she was angry. She was a pain in the ass a lot of the time, but she used to get her own way. Now I've got a sister who crumples like a paper bag whenever fate deals her a dud card. What happened to you, Monty? Where did all the fight go? Now you're so frightened all the time. Why should you care about Joe's darling Chewy? What about your hands, your voice, your face, your career?'

'It was the dope,' Monty told her bleakly. 'It was easier to find some drugs to make life bearable than to go out and fight for what I wanted. And it was easy for me to make a lot of noise when I was a kid and didn't have any real problems, but when the going got tough I got scared. Now I'll have to start again from the beginning.' Monty sighed and looked at her bandaged hands. 'I'm just not as strong as you are, Cathy. And I can't work the same way. I need people, to be with me, to support me, to share my life, to love me. I can't thrive on fighting everyone the way you can.'

Cathy tipped grapes into a bowl. 'I'm sorry. I shouldn't bully you, darling. You're right, I know you are: we have to do things our own different ways. Look,' she put a stack of paperbacks on the night table, 'I brought you the complete works of Jilly Cooper – that should keep your spirits up. I'll come again tomorrow. Will you need a nurse or anything when they let you out?'

'I don't know – I might. My hands won't be any good for at least two weeks.'

As Cathy left, Swallow arrived, and they squeezed past each other in the doorway, Swallow almost spherical in her purple jumpsuit and Cathy slender as ever in her new brown Armani.

'Christ, you look a mess.' Swallow sat awkwardly on the end of the bed. 'Joe Jones wants to come and pay his respects to the body. Is that OK?'

'Oh, Lord. Is he very angry, Swallow?'

'He sounded absolutely choked when I told him.'

Monty looked listlessly at the dingy ceiling. She was going to have to face Joe sometime and take whatever was coming; she didn't want anyone to see her looking the way she was, but maybe he wouldn't be too angry if he saw her looking pitiful. Monty smiled and winced with pain as her traumatized skin was stretched by the movement.

'Tell him he can come whenever he wants,' she said to Swallow. 'Isn't life rich? To think I was trying to make a pass at the guy and instead I went straight out and got his car blown up and ended up looking like Mrs Munster.'

Joe came the next day, his face set. He brought a bunch of flowers and her tape-player with some tapes.

'How bad is it?' he asked, speaking low and fast as if he wanted to get the politeness over with as quickly as possible.

'Oh, not too bad,' Monty lied. 'I'll be fine as soon as my eyebrows grow back.'

'You look like a Japanese mask,' he told her. 'Your eyes really turn up at the corners, don't they?'

OK, time to bite the bullet, Monty thought. 'Joe, I'm so sorry about the car,' she said, trembling inwardly. 'There was nothing I could do about it . . .'

He smiled, which he didn't do very often. 'You hated that car, didn't you?'

'That doesn't matter, what matters is that it was yours, you liked it, I got it wrecked and I'm sorry.'

'Why doesn't it matter – how *you* felt about it?'

'Well . . .' Monty was puzzled. This wasn't what was supposed to happen. He was supposed to call her an idiot, make some general observation about the incompetence of women in general, then zap her with a mighty verbal punch designed to lay out her ego for the next six weeks. 'Well, it wasn't my car, was it?' she offered uncertainly.

'It wasn't mine either. The boys wanted it, the record company paid for it, I only drove it. You're not lying here thinking about the goddam car, are you?' Now she felt stupid.

'There's nothing else I can do,' she told him. 'I can't read those books Swallow brought me because they make me laugh and it hurts to laugh. I can't even make phonecalls because of my hands. Thanks for bringing the tapes, Joe, they'll be the main event of the day.'

'As a matter of fact, I wanted to ask you if you'd do something for me. I've brought a tape of some of the songs I've been doing with Al,' he reached out to the table beside her bed and showed her an unmarked cassette. 'Will you listen to it and tell me what you think of it? I'd particularly like to have your opinion of the third track. We've done it over and over again, and we can't seem to get it right. I know I've approached it wrong, somehow. I just can't put my finger on it.'

She was surprised. The amazing Joe Jones, big in Japan, colossal in the States, seldom out of the top thirty the world over, was asking her advice. 'Sure,' she said, wary. Was this another rip-off in the making?

'Can I come to see you tomorrow?' he asked, taking his weight off the end of her bed. 'Is there anything you need?'

'No, I'm fine,' she told him.

'What's the food like in here?'

'Garbage. And I can't feed myself because of my hands, so I have to have some bloody nurse telling me to eat it all up.'

'OK – why don't I invite you for dinner tomorrow?'

He arrived with more flowers, and some candles, and soon the room was transformed into a private world, flickering and fragrant. A waiter arrived from Mr Chow bringing them a banquet packed in foil trays. Joe poured a tiny cup of transparent tea and held it to her lips.

'This is chrysanthemum,' he told her. 'I hope you like it. I thought it was right for you, more delicate than jasmine.' He picked up the chopsticks, broke the gold paper seal, and selected a morsel from one of the trays. 'This is melon stuffed with dreams.' With the delicacy of a tiny bird feeding its chicks, he popped the food in her mouth.

When the meal was finished, she felt luxuriously drowsy. 'Do you want to know what's wrong with your song?' she asked, looking up at his shadowed face as he rearranged her pillows.

'Not now,' he said, pulling the sheet straight and tucking it under the hard hospital mattress. 'Sing for your supper tomorrow.'

Monty sighed as he blew out the candles and said goodbye. It seemed like the ultimate cruelty of fate to look like a nightmare and feel like hell and be cared for so tenderly by a man who could make her and several million other women melt with desire.

A powerful mood of what-the-hell settled on her the next day, inspired by the doctor who signed her discharge form and told her she could leave.

'The trouble with that song,' she told Joe, recklessly tactless, 'is that you've fucked it up; it's quarrelling with itself. It's got a really strong melody but there's so much else going on you can't hear it. You don't need to dress up those harmonies with all that keyboard stuff you've put underneath. It'll speak for itself if you let it.'

'Less is more, huh?'

'Right.'

'Thanks, I'll do that.' He was sitting on the end of her bed, his jeans stretched taut over the massive quadriceps muscles of his thighs. 'Why don't you help me?'

Monty looked at him with suspicion. Was Joe just another man who wanted to make use of her talent? 'Will you credit me on the album and pay me a fee?'

'Of course. I'll get a contract drawn up for you at once if you agree.' He looked quite hurt that she should make such conditions, but Monty knew now that one of the tricks of a great exploiter is to create a world of upside-down values in which the victim is persuaded that whatever the predator wants is worthless. She had resolved in future to fix her price first.

'I'm not going to be much use around the house until my hands are healed.' She held up her bandaged mitts to remind him.

'Don't worry about that, we'll take care of you. Now, what are you going to wear to come home in? Your clothes must have been burned up.'

'I told the nurse to throw them away. I'll get Swallow to buy some for me later.'

'Let me buy them. Tell me what you want.'

'Anything – jeans or something.' There didn't seem much point in dreaming about lovely clothes when she hardly had any skin to wear underneath them.

'There are only two things a man can't do for a woman,' Swallow predicted ominously, when Monty telephoned her. 'Have a baby and buy her jeans. Why doesn't he just bring up something from the Priory?'

'I think he wants to buy me a present and needs a good excuse,' Monty told her. 'Will you get someone to come and cut my hair? I'll scare the yokels to death looking like this.'

The hairdresser cut her hair as short as a schoolboy's and showed her the effect in the mirror. Monty thought she looked younger and thinner. She had the impression of seeing her face properly for the first time, and she liked it. Joe brought the new jeans, which were two sizes too small.

'Do you really think my ass is that little?' she asked him, gesturing with her bandages.

'Isn't it?' he asked her with concern. 'I reckoned it was about this size,' he made a gesture in the air with his hands; it was unmistakably caressing and Monty began to smile but the pain stopped her.

'Damn you, Joe, will you stop making me laugh? Now get on the telephone and I'll talk to the shop.'

All the shop had was a pair of black trousers that were severely tailored, with a jacket to match which Monty couldn't get on over her bandages. Joe helped her into the clothes and fastened the trousers for her.

'You're much more careful than the nurses,' she told him. Monty was beginning to realize that she had been seriously wrong in assessing his character. He was gentle and thoughtful, nothing like the savage she had seen on stage. He could even change the dressings on her hands without hurting her, which was more than most of the nurses could.

At the Priory, she set to work at once in the studio, directing Joe and Al as they remixed the song on which he'd asked her help; then they went on to finish the remaining three tracks on the album. Her hands were still bandaged, but Joe was quick and subtle about doing what she told him. He was also full of cunning strategies to draw out her ideas and build her confidence.

Joe did all this in his own interest. 'Love' was a word he used very cautiously, never entirely sure that he knew what it meant, but on considering very carefully he thought he loved Monty. He was grateful that she was attracted to him, but most women responded the same way; he sensed that her heart had been broken so often it was mostly scar tissue; he knew with complete certainty that she would only be able to love him if she also found the strength to handle the rest of her life.

Joe was a good teacher, and to his delight Monty grabbed every opportunity he gave her. It was true that they complemented each other artistically: she was a much more sophisticated musician than Joe, but he had a raw power of expression which she did not.

'Aren't we a terrific team?' she asked as they listened to the last track when it finished. 'Fred and Ginger, Tracy and Hepburn, you and me. We're magic.'

He gave her a look that was startled but warm, and the little room seemed even smaller as their intimacy suddenly leapt into a new dimension. Monty felt light-headed and skittish. She trusted him now, and she trusted herself with him – after all, with half her skin still missing, what else could they do but talk? Al, the other musicians, and the engineer had already left. They were alone.

'Why do you always play so loud?' she demanded boldly, leaning back against the mixing deck.

He ran his hand through his silky black hair, thinking. 'When I started out I used to feel this incredible *rage*. I just wanted to kill everything and everyone. The place it really came out was in my music. All I wanted to do was attack, destroy with noise, you know.'

'Don't you feel like that now?'

'No. That's really why the band is splitting up. I'm interested in music that's a whole lot more expressive now. I've had it for communication on the Tarzan level. To tell the truth, I think the boys feel the same. But what we've gotten known for is that megaton fireball noise, and that's what our company wants us to go on doing so they can go on selling the records. You can't blame them. They're in business to make money. People have got a lot of rage inside them and they're willing to pay to have it let out.'

'It was exciting, that killer sound.' She wondered if he remembered just how excited he had been when they first met, and she hadn't been able to do anything but stare at his crotch. He dropped his eyes from her face at once, and she realized that he did remember, and was embarrassed.

'What's excitement all about, though?' He still couldn't look at her, she noticed. 'Let me tell you something. I don't know if you'll understand but I'll try to explain.' Now he looked up, appealing to her. 'I've had all the excitement I can stand, more than most people have in a lifetime. Thrillsville USA, that's my home town. I've done dope, I've done booze, I've done jumping out of aeroplanes . . . and God knows what it is that I've got, but women have come on to me all my life. Once I was a big star and all, it was just ridiculous. It was like every chick in the world wanted my scalp. I know I laid 427 chicks in our first year, because we kept count, but after that I couldn't tell you. It got to be a game, seeing what I could get them to do.'

She nodded, remembering how Rick and Cy used to amuse themselves the same way.

'I was doing the same thing I was doing on stage – hitting back,' he continued. 'I realized I had to break the circle; OK, so women had used me, my mother had abandoned me, my wife had left me – so what? I couldn't stay on a revenge trip for ever. I was the one who was suffering, I was the one who felt degraded. And I realized I was using fucking just the way I'd used alcohol, to cover up. It was something I could do to distract myself from everything I didn't like in my life. So I decided I'd let it go.'

'You mean you gave up fucking?' Monty looked at him in amusement. A man who didn't fuck seemed an idea as bizarre as water that wasn't wet.

He nodded, searching her face to see if she understood. 'It wasn't at all difficult. I didn't give up for ever, I just wanted it to mean something. I felt it was time to take responsibility for my life. One day you have to admit that the buck stops with you.'

Monty nodded. 'I learned that at the Centre. I'm an addict, did you know that?' They talked on, trading secrets. She told him about her relationship with Rick, and with Sig Bear. 'What I can't understand is that they both said they loved me, and they *did* love me, in their way, but all they did was take what they needed from me, and never think that they were destroying me.'

He shook his head with emphasis. 'They didn't love you, Monty. Nobody who loved you could ever use you.'

She shrugged, wishing she could believe it were true.

After that they talked all the time, until it felt as if they knew each other like brother and sister. Somehow it became clear that they loved each other; they desired each other, too – at least, Monty was almost sure Joe wanted her as much as she wanted him. He didn't flirt with her and he would not touch her, but their bodies were bonded mysteriously together.

Monty's new skin grew fast and flawless as she healed. Her face and body were as good as new – although rather pink – in a month. The bandages came off her hands and that skin too regenerated, at first as fine as poppy petals, then thicker. By the beginning of August, only a slight puckering and discoloration on one hand remained to show that she'd been burned.

One by one the disaffected members of the band had left the Priory, and then when the album was finished the technicians departed. Al was the last to go and Joe and Monty waved him goodbye from the driveway, like parents seeing off the last child to fly the nest. It was an uncertain summer evening, with towering columns of black cloud building up in the sky and the swallows flying very low above the lawn in front of the music room windows.

They went into the empty house, made tea and took it into the sitting room. Joe sprawled on the chintz sofa that was so vast and shapeless, it was like an ocean of printed roses. Monty walked to and fro in front of the narrow stone-framed windows, watching the unearthly dusk light in the valley. Their silence was as heavy as the stormy air. The question 'what now?' hung between them like a sword poised to part them. Monty could feel Joe's eyes follow her as she paced the carpet.

'Can I play you something?' she asked him, desperate to cut the tension.

'Of course.' He pulled in his legs and stood up, and she led him into the music room, which was tall and narrow with french windows open to the garden and the valley below it. The eighteenth-century tapestry curtains stirred as a warm wind began to gust.

'I haven't got any words for this yet,' she opened the piano and sat down, 'but I think I've got the tune all figured out. Anyway . . .' She raised her hands to the keys and began to play, finding the melody which had been lying at the back of her mind for a week. The notes seemed to arrange themselves by magic, until they were a tune that seemed a simple flowing line of sound with delicate harmonies reflected within it. She played it through three times, until she was sure it was perfect.

'What do you think?' she asked him. Joe was sitting on a hard, black leather couch by the window.

'It's pretty,' he nodded, approving.

'No, it isn't,' she told him calmly, wondering why he was being so obtuse. 'It's beautiful. It's the most beautiful thing I've ever written. If I never write anything better than that I'll die happy.'

Of course. This was another of his games, a test to discover her true feelings, to see how sure of herself she was. He was sitting there, relaxed and expressionless, creating a climate of emotional neutrality in which she could express herself freely.

Monty walked across to Joe and stood looking down at his great, sprawled body. His arms were spread out across the back of the couch, and she could see a sinew flickering in his left bicep.

'What I'd like to do is go into the studio tomorrow and record this. When my contract with Biffo ends I want to start singing again, but this time the way I want, and I'd love it if you produced me, like you did Al.' She looked him squarely in the eyes. Inside her a chasm of fear opened. Suppose he said no? Suppose she had read him wrong? Suppose he made some slimy excuse and rejected her – now, when she had opened up to him and dared to say what she needed?

'OK,' said Joe. 'Let's do it.' The flicker of nervous tension had moved to his lips. 'Why start tomorrow?' he asked, knowing the answer. 'Why not now?'

Outside big drops of rain were beginning to fall, leaving spots of moisture the size of pennies on the flagstones.

'We have something else to do now,' she said, and stood astride him. Slowly, she sank down to sit across his lap. To her joy and relief, first one arm then the other left the back of the couch and he embraced her, his face pressed between her breasts. She felt the heat from his thighs strike up into her body, and hugged her knees around him.

Joe raised his face to hers and she took his lips, shutting her eyes to savour their harshness and the pleasure of the months of yearning coming to fruition at last. Lust as keen as anguish twisted inside her. She plunged her hands into his thick, black hair and strained him to her, feeling her blood catch fire. Their lips parted and their tongues met, flickering and darting around their mouths.

Monty felt fear again, knowing she was going to be vulnerable to this man as she had never been before, that he would possess her completely, but also make her the gift of himself. Soon there would be nowhere to hide, no escape from the demands of the life they would create together.

He sensed her fear and held her to him with as much strength as he thought she could bear. 'It's all right,' he murmured, his lips brushing her ear. 'We'll make it. We love each other. We'll always love each other.'

She kissed his forehead, his eyelids, the sharp bridge of his nose, tasting the salt film of perspiration on his skin. Her lips explored the sinewy warmth of his neck, the firm swell of the shoulder muscles, the hollows behind the sharp collar bones, the tender membrane of his throat. With careful hands she pulled at the thin fabric of his T-shirt and pressed her mouth to the ridges of his chest.

'Can I touch you?' he asked her in a soft voice. 'Is your skin strong enough?'

'I think so.' She pulled her own shirt over her head and threw aside the two garments together, offering him her breasts. This was the moment for which she had craved. His hands held her and his mouth closed over her flesh, trying the texture of the new skin with pressure as delicate as a falling leaf. His tongue, narrow and red, teased the swelling nipples and she heard a soft moan rise in her throat.

Outside the rain began to fall hard and fast, and the wind whipped wavelets in the sheets of water on the stones. A fierce gust blew back the glass doors and whipped the curtains. 'Let's go upstairs,' he whispered.

She shut the french windows, seeing the storm clouds circling above as if the sky were boiling. With their arms around each other's naked waists they walked slowly to the staircase and began to climb. Joe was a full twelve inches taller than she and to walk this way was awkward. She slipped on the polished oak tread and he snatched her up protectively. The contact of their skin was electric; restraint abandoned them. Joe took off her jeans, then his own, and they stood clasped together below the stained glass window at the half-landing, glorying in their nakedness and wanting this first time to last for ever.

It seemed to Monty that they stayed a lifetime on the staircase below the streaming window. Kneeling between his thighs she made love to him with her mouth, caressing the beautiful shaft of flesh that would soon be enveloped in the centre of her. At last he asked her to stop, curled his long body between her legs and began to part the folds of her flesh with his fingers and tease with his tongue, coaxing the petals to swell and unfold and the sweet-smelling moisture to run. The small liquid noises echoed in the empty mansion.

Finally he drew her across him and their bodies locked slowly together. Monty curled her arms around his neck and let her pelvis rock gently. His hands on her hips slowed her almost to stillness and they rested together, listening to the rain and holding on to the moments of closeness as long as they could.

At last Joe said, 'Darling, you're freezing. Let's go to bed,' and they separated and ran up to his room where they dived under the tangled quilt like romping children.

Their jeans lay discarded on the stairs, the sloughed-off skins of their old selves. In the warmth of the bed they set about the next phase of their union, acting like what they were, two sensual sophisticates showing off their skills.

At last they grew tired and fell asleep, while outside the storm continued in the darkness. Monty woke some hours later, and lay still in Joe's arms listening to the thunder, which rolled like the balls in a giant's skittle-alley behind the distant Chiltern Hills. Lightning flickered at the far side of the valley, its blue radiance glowing briefly in their room.

She realized that Joe also was awake.

'I love you,' she whispered, twisting towards him. 'I feel like I've never loved anyone before.'

'You never have loved anyone before,' he told her, drawing her close. 'And nobody has ever loved you.'

The thunder sounded louder and closer, Monty counted the seconds between the noise and the light.

'Twelve,' she said. 'It's twelve miles away.' As if to mock her, a deafening clap sounded above the house, rattling the windows and shaking the floor below them. The lightning tore open the sky at the next instant, filling the room with white glare.

Obeying a primitive instinct to seek comfort, they searched for each other's lips and felt warm and moist and strong in their humanity under the tumult of angry elements continued outside. She saw the whites of Joe's eyes gleam in the darkness and felt his hair fall around her face as he leaned over her, his breath coming faster than before. She sensed that now he was struggling to tame an impulse that was searing all his senses, and slid her hands under his, linking their fingers.

'Do it,' she told him, 'whatever it is, do it. I can take it.'

He paused an instant, then fell upon her like a demon in the darkness, a mad spirit of the storm wanting to smash their bodies to atoms and let them recombine. With his strength unchecked, he held her, turned her, picked her up like a plaything, steadied her against his thrusts. At last he collapsed with an animal cry shuddering with the violence of release.

They slept again, and in the morning she took what she wanted from him, passing the dreamy dawn in a mist of ecstasy. The sky was clear and the sunlight seemed fresh-washed like the landscape. Chuckling rivers of rainwater ran down the pathways in the hillside and in the chestnut wood a pigeon called.

For the rest of the day, everything seemed like an intrusion between them. They did not want to get dressed, because it diminished their intimacy. When the telephone rang, they did not answer it. The mail lay untouched on the mat in the hallway. They walked through the rainwashed garden, picking currants from the bush trained against the wall and dipped their feet in the cold pool to wash off the mud. They made love when, where and how their bodies craved each other, prisoners of desire who did not want their freedom.

The next day, they were ready to admit the world into their own universe. Joe made telephone calls, and at midday the engineer appeared, followed by Tony, her old guitarist. Winston arrived in the afternoon, by which time Monty had found words for her song. They began recording, and when it was finished the five of them listened to the playback in silence.

Winston laughed and slapped Monty's hand. 'That is *the* most beautiful song I ever heard in my entire life, girl.'

Joe rewound the tape and picked up a marker to label it. 'What are we calling this?' he asked her.

'Broken Wings,' she told him. 'Now, shall I play you what I want to back it with?'

Eager to try her new plans out, Monty asked Sig Bear to release her from her Biffo contract.

'Not a chance,' he told her. 'Just because you've run off with some Hiawatha, don't think you can come round here threatening to zap me with the old thunder-mittens and get everything you fancy. Any song you write now belongs to me, and don't you forget it.'

So Joe took Monty to Arizona and they spent six months finding a site for their house and working with the architect to build it. His recording company offered her a new contract. The day her contract with Biffo expired, they went to Los Angeles to prepare her first album, and then make the video to promote it. It was a very simple film, with Monty in a black suit and white shirt, her hair cut short, and the band in their normal clothes, playing against a plain, white background.

The company were nervous of 'Broken Wings', saying it was too downbeat; instead they released 'Man Beats Woman' as her first single. It climbed quickly to number three, and stayed in the top thirty for six weeks. In Britain, 'Broken Wings' was a smash. Monty was called the new Joan Armatrading, the new Carly Simon, the new Annie Lennox and a great new rock original. When the Grammy awards were announced, she won the category of the Best New Artist. The following year she won the Best Vocal Performance by a Female Artist; then it was Best Contemporary Female Solo Vocal Performance.

The next year, she was accused of dominating the award categories for female artists. Two years later she was asked to host the awards ceremony, but declined because she was expecting her baby. That year also she won her copyright action against Rick, the Juice and Excellent Music, and got her songs back at last.

Three months after Paloma was born, Monty telephoned her sister in London.

'Hello,' said Cathy's voice, 'CBC Investment Corporation.'

'What's the matter, Cathy – switchboard operator got the sack already?'

'*Monty!* What are you doing on the line?'

'Calling you, dummy, what do you think I'm doing?'

'Do you know what time it is?'

'Oh no – have I fouled up again? I'm sorry, Cathy, I never can remember all the time changes.' Cathy smiled to herself. Monty could remember the most complex musical notations but the implications of time zones were beyond her.

'Good thing I was working late, huh? So how are you?'

'Terrific – why aren't you coming over to see your niece?'

'I meant to, Monty, honestly I did. I'll be over at the weekend, OK? It's just been so hectic lately, the dollar's gone mad, and . . .'

Monty smiled to herself. Cathy always seemed to be busy. She had mailed Cathy articles from magazines about overcommitment and overwork being characteristic of the female tycoon, but it didn't do any good. Cathy only said they were characteristic of male tycoons as well. Monty had begun to suspect her sister must be happy working.

She arrived for the weekend as promised, and admired Paloma, who was three months old, feeling with a pang of regret all the long-forgotten emotions of early motherhood as she coaxed a wavering smile from the tiny red mouth, and watched the big, blue eyes focus slowly on her face.

What was the right thing to say about babies at this age – ah, yes, Cathy remembered. 'How is she at night?' she asked.

'Not too bad,' Monty said with caution. 'She sleeps about six hours, then wakes at five or six. '

At 5.30 the next morning Monty was sitting up in bed feeding Paloma, the pair of them pillowed comfortably against Joe's chest. She shifted uncomfortably. 'Something's fallen into the bed, darling,' she told Joe. 'It feels like one of her toys or something. Can you get it? It's digging into me.'

He slipped his hand over the surface of the sheet and pulled out the antique silver rattle attached to an ivory ring which Cathy had brought as a gift for the baby. 'Just a minute, there's something else.' He felt under the pillow, and withdrew a small, white leather jewel-box, which he put on the shelf by the bedside.

When Paloma was asleep again, Monty noticed the box. 'What's this?' she asked. 'Isn't it yours?'

'You know it isn't. I don't have any jewels except the ones you gave me.' She looked at him with curiosity. He had already given her a huge heart-shaped diamond ring to mark Paloma's birth. 'It's not from me,' he said.

Monty opened the box. On a nest of black velvet sat an immense pink pearl.

At 6 am, Cathy stretched out like a starfish under the white comforter, and the fingertips of her right hand encountered a hard object under her pillow. It was a white leather box, lined with black velvet, containing another very large pink pearl.

CHAPTER TWENTY-SEVEN

CATHY FLEW to Singapore at the beginning of September, for a conference called by the International Tin Federation. It was an exhausting three days of seminars in a featureless modern hotel, at which the four hundred delegates addressed the likelihood that the tin cartel would shortly collapse and the world price of the metal would fall drastically, a catastrophe for both its producers and the traders.

The seminars had been tiring, and the knowledge that nothing could be done to avert the disaster gave her a sense of frustration. It should have been a relief to fly north to Penang to begin exploring her father's past, but Cathy could not shake her sense of foreboding as the small 350-seater Fokker left the white skyscrapers of Singapore below and flew out of Changi airport. In less than an hour they would be in Kuala Lumpur.

Cathy was always intrigued that within so short a distance two cities could be so different. Singapore was a place with no memory, only a future. Among the mountain ranges of highrise development only Raffles Hotel had retained an aroma of the past. The fanshaped traveller's palms and the pleasing, white- pillared balconies were dwarfed by the sixty-storey towers at either side. Now Raffles, too, was unhurriedly preparing for the twenty-first century, and the shabby suites, which had reminded Cathy of the dank boxrooms at Bourton, were being refurbished by David Hicks.

Forty minutes away from this anonymous international trade centre, Kuala Lumpur had a sturdy sense of continuous time; respect for the past was part of the Malay national character. The city was dusty and chaotic, a sprawl of harsh modernity and Hollywood-Moorish monuments surrounded by endless green jungle.

Night fell quickly as she arrived, and there was nothing to do but check into the Hilton and plan the next day. She called her offices in New York and London, feeling restless and anxious. Finally she put through a call to Monty in Arizona where it was early in the morning. 'What's the matter?' her sister asked at once, sensing a note of agitation in her voice. 'Are you all right, Cathy?'

'I'm OK,' she said slowly, listening to her voice echo on the line. 'I'm just not sure what we're doing here. Do you think we're going about this the right way?'

'Who knows? We've got to do whatever we can. I wish I was with you, Cathy.'

'Paloma needs you more than I do right now.' She could hear the baby cooing in the background and guessed that Monty was holding her while she talked.

Cathy hung up and turned over in her mind the reasoning behind the trip, but felt the logic of it crumble. How could the pearls be connected with her father? She tried to talk herself into a more positive frame of mind. You're on your own, thousands of miles from home, dealing with the kind of problem you hate because it's formless and smells of irrationality: you're bound to feel anxious, she told herself.

Finding Treadwell had been simplicity itself. Her mother, as she expected, had been unable, or unwilling, to help. Bettina's physical and mental deterioration was accelerating, and Cathy now paid for a nurse to visit her every day, to keep her and the flat tidy and clean, and to insist that her ulcers were dressed and the prescribed tablets were taken. She still visited the bridge club two or three times a week, apparently retaining enough mental clarity to play the game and enough self-control not to appear drunk in front of her companions. The rest of the time, however, she lived in a state of complete alcoholic oblivion. Cathy occasionally tried to persuade her to move to a nursing home, but the old woman stubbornly refused.

When Cathy asked her about William Treadwell, all her mother said was, 'We knew nobody of that name in Malaya.'

'But Daddy told me about him.'

'You were a child, you must be mistaken,' her mother replied, screwing up her colourless mouth in defiance. 'No one of that name, I told you.'

In her London office, Cathy's secretary acquired a set of Malaysian telephone directories in which she had no trouble finding a William Treadwell listed in Penang with the title *Haji* added to his name, which Cathy knew indicated a Moslem who had made a pilgrimage to Mecca. Feeling that there could not be too many Moslems with Anglo-Saxon names on the island, Cathy had dictated a letter, which had been answered at once, and then had arranged a meeting for the day following the end of the Singapore conference.

The next day she took another small plane to Penang, flying over the tops of the jungle trees, then the glistening aquamarine sea of the Straits of Malacca, until they touched down on Penang Island.

Treadwell met her at his office in Georgetown, an anonymous stone box in a stuffy Victorian building on King Street. The faint scent of cloves emanated from his lightweight fawn suit: he was now the proprietor of a small spice-trading business. The gold lettering on the door announced the Oriental Spice Company. He was a thin, stooped man with spectacles who looked more like a professor than a businessman. His hair was white, his face and neck red from the tropic sun. The hand which shook hers was bony, but its grip was strong.

'So it's not just your father that brings you out East?' he asked her.

'I had to come for a conference on the tin crisis in Singapore. It seemed a good opportunity.'

'Mn. That'll be a bad business for Malaysia. You're in that world are you?'

'I'm in finance, yes. It's going to be a bad business for all of us, by the looks of things, but the producers are the ones who'll suffer most, you're right. The world's very small; you can't pretend we aren't interdependent.'

His faded blue eyes looked at her keenly. 'Some things never change do they? Here I am exporting spices just like the young men from the East India Company who came this way in the 1860s. In your father's day, of course, it was the price of rubber everyone got excited about down at the club. Now rubber's on the way out and they want everyone to produce palm oil, diversify the economy a bit.' There was a silence and Cathy knew she had to smooth the way for a conversation about her father.

'I expect you heard about my father's death,' she began. 'I was seventeen when it happened. There was a terrible fuss, because he'd left so many debts. And we felt terrible, my sister and I, because we simply couldn't understand why a parent would commit suicide. It took us a long time to get over it. I still can't believe it was more than twenty years ago.'

An elderly Chinese secretary brought in a tray set with a garish tea set, and poured them two cups of strong Indian tea. Bill looked at the woman sitting across his scarred wooden desk and saw both strength and beauty. She had, he recognized, none of her father's weakness and all of her mother's beauty; he had not expected this. He had prepared himself for a typical, upper-class Englishwoman in early middle age, perhaps with finer features than the norm, but with only the blundering force of the British temperament, not this clear-eyed, intellectual toughness which he sensed like a core of steel in her character.

The Australian had anticipated this day for almost forty years, and had turned over and over in his mind the moral imperatives which ought to direct his conduct. He had at last resolved that he would assess the character of the woman who sought him out – if she ever did so – and then decide how to act. It would be wrong to ruin two good but limited lives, if that was what they proved to be, with truths which time had made irrelevant.

'I've always felt as if I hardly knew my father, because he died when I was so young. Now I feel the time is right to get to know him, as much as I can.'

'He was remarkable.' Bill took her lead gratefully. 'A remarkable man in every way. A cut above most of the fellahs who came out East. Marvellous mind he had, when he chose to use it. Very amusing, a lot of charm, extraordinary gift for the Oriental languages. Never met anyone quite like him.'

So far, just a standard eulogy. She couldn't expect more over a cup of tea from a perfect stranger.

'He said you taught him to play chess?'

'When we were guests of the Chinese Communists in the occupation. We used to play on a board scratched in the dirt, with the tops of beer bottles and little bits of bamboo for the pieces.'

'Who won?'

'He did, when he put his mind to it.'

'He taught me to play, when I was a little girl. He could never concentrate though, so he always lost.'

'That was about the size of it, yes. Always alert, you see, so he was easily distracted.' Bill's hands, the fingers crooked with age, carefully removed his horn-rimmed spectacles, which he put down on the desk-top in front of him.

'And is the rubber estate he worked on still producing? I'd love to see it.'

He hesitated, looking at her with curiosity, collecting his thoughts. 'We could drive out there tomorrow, if you like. I wouldn't mind seeing the place again myself. I'm told there's a road now, it'll be a day trip.'

'Terrific.'

She offered to drive and hired a car, then checked into the E & O Hotel, now much less than the finest hostelry in town, but, like Raffles, full of evocative atmosphere. My father came here, she told herself, following the porter across the cool, chequered marble floor. On the terrace where her father had inadvertently become engaged to foolish Lucy Kennedy, she looked out over the grey-blue waves and watched a fisherman in a narrow wooden skiff pull in his nets.

They drove aboard the slow iron ferry the next morning, and took a route south over a narrow but well-metalled highway, through a landscape ravaged by tin-mining, a succession of dreary grey workings interspersed with a harsh tangle of secondary jungle.

'This is Ipoh – they called it the town that tin built,' Bill explained as they drove down the straight main street lined with shop-houses, slowly negotiating a throng of bicycles and trishaws. 'Government housing,' he waved his hand at an orderly estate of rectangular bungalows with zigzag ironwork balconies. 'This was the first of their cheap housing schemes, designed to help people get off the land and into the industrial centres where there was work.'

They sped on through village after village of ornate dark-wood bungalows. Bill explained to her what the daily routine of the estate would have been, how the planters' wives passed their days, and how hazardous life was during the Emergency. She realized that this gaunt, old man was withholding the kind of information about her father which she wanted, and wondered why.

'When did you become a Moslem?' she asked him.

'When the country became independent. After that you couldn't hold a position of responsibility unless you were a Malayan citizen. I was working as a development officer in the state of Perak, helping to build the new country, give it a sound infrastructure. I loved the place, always have, and I decided to apply for citizenship so I could stay on. Quite a few Europeans did. I decided to take the religion, too. I'm an all-or-nothing type: it appeals to me. There's nothing left to chance in Islam. And I thought it was not enough just to say you love a country. You have to commit yourself to it.'

'How did my father react?'

'He thought I was mad, of course. Going native, he called it. The British thought that was the worst thing a man could do.'

'I suppose if you believed all that God-is-an-Englishman stuff, you wouldn't understand.'

He watched her covertly as she reacted to his statement and was satisfied. 'You don't buy that line, I take it.'

'That kind of thinking took the great out of Britain.' Cathy swerved to avoid a truck full of oil palm kernels which was driving down the centre of the road. Treadwell gave a dry chuckle.

'Nothing in the Koran about the way a man's supposed to drive, of course.'

After four hours the road began to climb through low, wooded hills. It followed a narrow railway line up a valley, then Treadwell directed her down a fork to the right. They drove through a village, slowing down for a group of brown cows being driven down the road by a little girl in a cotton frock who idly tapped their rumps with a bamboo pole. In time, the walls of shimmering green jungle foliage gave way to orderly rows of grey-trunked rubber trees.

'This was just a beaten track in your father's day,' he told her. The rubber used to come down here on ox-carts to be loaded on to the train.'

'Who owns the estate now?'

'Fella called Choy. Lives in Penang, great big house on Burmah Road. The manager will be a Chinese, too, I expect.' They drove slowly past tin-roofed, hardwood houses where the estate workers lived, pausing to let a man wheeling a bicycle loaded with cans of latex cross in front of them. The old estate house still dominated the landscape from the brow of the hill, although its stucco was peeling and the shutters, bare of paint, had lost some of their slats.

The estate manager was an Indian, a fleshy man of about thirty with heavy-framed spectacles, who told them to take their time and look around at their leisure. He had one of his assistants fetch a yellowed photograph album, and showed them pictures of the estate staff in the early days of the Emergency. Cathy had no trouble picking out her father by his beaming smile and energetic posture.

'I suppose that's my mother,' she said, pointing to the figure in a cotton frock beside him, but standing apart.

'She's still alive, I take it?' Treadwell asked.

'She's very ill,' Cathy told him, and although he expressed regret she felt there was something in his manner which suggested he had not cared for her mother particularly.

The old bungalows had long since been razed, and a plantation of oil palms waved feathery fronds where Cathy and Monty had played as babies under their *amah's* watchful eye.

'Your father was a good manager, got on well with everybody.' Bill stood awkwardly on the broken ground beside the track. 'After the war, of course, he was a great hero to the Europeans out here. Not many of us stayed behind when the Japanese came and lived to tell the tale.'

As they retraced their steps to the estate house, he told her about the days of the occupation, carefully testing her attitudes. 'I can't think of any other man – who could have done what your father did. He passed himself off as a Malay, lived in a *kampong*, took some drug we'd been given to darken our skins. He blended in perfectly. In the turmoil of the occupation people got used to strangers, even in the villages. That was his nature, you see. Mercurial temperament, adapt to anything. The local people knew, I think, but by the time their suspicions had grown they were in danger themselves for harbouring a European and the disguise was enough to deceive the Japanese. We all had a price on our heads in those days.'

Cathy turned the car and drove them back, feeling empty. She did not know what she had expected to find, but she was disappointed that she had felt no sense of recognition in this place at all, even though she had been born here. There was nothing more to see. It was as if her eyes had never looked down this gentle slope of obedient vegetation before. She had no recollection of the place at all.

'My father didn't talk about the past much.' She let the car run smoothly over the bumpy track, then drove faster down the road to the railway. 'He never even told us what he got his decoration for.'

'I expect he was keen to get on with his life in England and put the war behind him. Our war didn't turn out as we planned it, you see. When the Americans dropped the bomb, it set everything we'd done here, recruiting and training men to overthrow the Japanese, at nothing. We risked our lives as well as any other man – more so, given the jungle. Quite a lot of fellas just lay down and died of typhus or blackwater fever or some other tropical disease.'

'Daddy was always very strong. He never seemed to get ill.'

'He was a survivor. We both were. He was decorated for an incident after the war was officially over – there were quite a few isolated Japanese units in the jungle who chose not to hear the news. He went to open up a prison camp down south somewhere, and they attacked in the night. Your father was quite badly wounded, but I don't believe he even knew it. Just fought them all off until we got there to relieve him. Oh yes, he was a brave man – didn't know what fear was.'

On the long drive back he fell asleep, but woke as they approached the thronged streets of Butterworth, where they halted to wait for the ferry.

'It's curious,' Cathy told him as they stood by the iron wall of the ferry looking out over the dark waves. 'I feel as if I know my father less now, rather than more. None of this seems to be connected with him at all, and yet it must have been so important to him.'

After years of practice in negotiation, she had a sixth sense of withheld information, and was sure that this man had chosen not to tell her something material about her father's past. Treadwell impressed her. He was thoughtful and intelligent, not at all the florid boon-companion she had anticipated. But the man he had described to her was not her father. Cathy was too honest to have avoided the impression that her father had been a flawed man, and Treadwell had described a paragon. Perhaps if she appealed to him he would decide to be open with her.

'I always had the impression that you fell out with my father, or he fell out with you,' she said with caution, wondering if he would choose to disinter a painful memory after so many years. They were walking back to the car.

'I think it's fair to say that I fell out with him,' the old man said, picking his way on unsteady legs across the metal deck.

'What did you argue about?'

'If he never told you, then it isn't my place to fill you in.' He opened the car door and sank wearily into the seat. 'You're a tough young lady, aren't you?' he asked in a pleasant tone as the car bumped over the ferry gangway.

'Not so young anymore,' she corrected him.

'Your sister, what's she like?'

'Absolutely different from me. She's more emotional than I am, more open to people. And she's always testing, questioning, trying to find better ways to do things, better ways to live. More adventurous than me, but more vulnerable too. She's a singer, you might have heard of her: Monty's her name.'

'Just Monty? I don't know much about singers, I'm afraid. What I mean is – is she tough?'

'She's got a different kind of strength.'

'Where is she?'

'America, she lives there. She's just had her first child, a little girl.'

'Would she come out here?'

Now Cathy knew that she had been right. There was more to tell, much more, and Treadwell had been sounding her out all day, seeing if it would be right to unlock the past.

'If it was important,' she said.

'You'd better ask her, then.'

Cathy delivered him to the door of his modern bungalow in a small village on the undeveloped side of Penang Island at 10 pm. She drove back past the garish hotels along Batu Feringgi beach, slowing down near the souvenir shops and restaurants which were decorated with strings of coloured lights and thronged with wandering herds of tourists who strayed into the road. The highway twisted along the shoreline overlooked by condominium towers, the milky sea lapping the large rocks below. Now, at last, she had a sense of momentum.

Telephoning Monty was difficult. The line was cut several times and it was three hours before Cathy could get a connection. Her sister's voice was faint and almost inaudible.

'You've got to come out here right away,' Cathy shouted. 'I don't know what it is but he says it's important. I'm at the E & O Hotel in Georgetown. Cable me your flight time and I'll meet you.'

'OK,' she heard the indistinct voice say.

'She wants me to come,' Monty told Joe, the telephone still in her hand. 'I knew she would. I should have gone with her in the first place. Paloma will be fine with you.'

'Are you sure you want to go alone?' He held her close, feeling protective but also disturbed. Although he tried not to be, Joe felt jealous of Monty's bond with her sister. It was more than a mere emotion, it was an affinity of spirit which seemed as eternally strong as the force which held the earth in its orbit, and his own love could not compete with it.

'I feel I must,' she said slowly. 'It'll be awful without you, but whatever this is, it's something Cathy and I have to do together.'

He nodded. They had not slept apart since the beginning of their relationship. 'I'll miss you. We'll miss you. Don't worry about Paloma, she'll be OK.'

When she arrived at the small, hot, crowded airport twenty hours later, Cathy was waiting, a still figure in a black silk dress, and, as she kissed her sister, Monty suddenly felt as if they were children again, facing the unknown world together.

The next day they drove to Treadwell's house, and sat side by side on the cushions of the sagging teak-framed sofa in his hot, dim sitting room, where the warm breeze from the sea a few hundred yards away barely stirred the curtains of blue and white flowered cotton. At home, Cathy noticed, Bill wore a *songkok*, the oval Malay fez, which contrasted with his craggy Anglo-Saxon features.

His Malay wife, a thin yellow-skinned woman in a white blouse and blue skirt, brought them tea in thick, white china cups, then withdrew to the rear of the building.

'What I'm going to tell you is going to shock you,' he said, looking severe. 'I've thought very carefully about whether I should do this, because it may not be for the best as far as your happiness is concerned. I'm not one of those who thinks we're put on earth to suffer, but I believe that there's more to life than happiness, and I suspect you may feel the same way.' He looked from one woman to the other, absorbing their faces. Now that he saw the younger one he was astonished that no one had ever questioned her origins before. The strong, curling black hair, the slightly flattened nose, the slanted eyes – the story was all there to be read.

'When we met the other day, I hadn't made up my mind what was the best course,' he continued, talking to Cathy. 'But I felt you'd come here with some kind of understanding already. My impression of you is almost that you're the man your father should have been. Maybe you've had a harder life than he did, in the beginning. Jim was my friend, I was attached to him as if he were my brother. But he'd been spoiled, somehow. Not indulged so much, but set on the wrong path, as it were. It was as if he saw the world the other way up. You're right, we fell out in the end. You've got all of his charm and none of his weakness. He would have been a terrible ladies' man, if he'd been inclined that way.'

'And he wasn't?' Cathy heard her voice sound uncertain. She had never considered the question of her father's sexuality.

'Not in the modern way, no. Quite a few of the old colonial types preferred native women – I think your father was one of them.' He looked at them carefully to see if they were shocked, but met the steady gaze of two brown and two black eyes.

'Are you telling us that he had a mistress?' Cathy prompted gently.

'Several, I shouldn't be surprised. He also had a wife. During the war, when we lived undercover, he married a Malay girl. He was completely crazy about her. I didn't understand it. She was a beautiful girl, but I thought he was mad, told him so. Of course it helped his cover, no doubt about that. It was a lot harder for the people he hid with to turn in one of their own.'

'What happened to her?' Monty felt hot, despite her loose, red silk dress; she tried to imagine her father making love, but no image would come to her mind. It was as if they were talking about another person.

'He left her flat at the end of the war, never gave her a second thought. I went to see them a few times, gave them some money.' He paused, wondering if he had chosen the best way to unfold the story. Now that the two women were sitting in his house he could hardly believe it was true himself. 'There were children,' he said at last, looking from one to another with fierce intensity.

'You mean we've got brothers and sisters somewhere?' Cathy felt her pleated white skirt sticking to the backs of her thighs in the heat, and shifted uncomfortably on the low sofa.

'No.' His pale tongue moistened his lips and she saw his Adam's apple bob as he swallowed. 'He had two girl children with this Malay woman. When he came back after the war he married – that woman in the photograph.' Plainly, he could hardly speak Bettina's name. 'Do you know very much about your family's financial arrangements?'

'We know that the money he lost was really ours, intended to be in trust for us,' Cathy told him.

'That was all the money your father had. He needed to marry and start a family before it would be released. When it was clear that our old life here was finished, your father was desperate. And he found he couldn't have children with that woman – so he went looking for his Malay wife.'

Monty's dark, velvet eyes widened in surprise. '*You mean Cathy and I . . .*'

'He brought you back to the estate and passed you off as the children of his new marriage. False birth certificates, the lot. I never thought he'd get away with it. Obviously, he did.'

'So we aren't . . . we aren't Bettina's children, his wife's children, at all?' They looked at one other at the same instant and drew together, clutching each other's arms; then they looked back at him, questioningly.

'British law didn't recognize his first marriage. There'll be a record at the mosque, perhaps. Did you ever . . . did no one ever say anything about it?'

They shook their heads. 'I don't believe the rest of the family knew. My grandmother was a very difficult woman, but my father was her favourite and she could never keep any kind of secret. If she knew anything, she'd have let it out one day.'

'Your mother – Betty, the woman you thought was your mother . . .'

'She never told us anything. She never even told us where babies come from, let alone anything about ourselves.' Monty had never stopped hating Bettina, and now she felt an enormous sense of release. 'I didn't get on with her, you see. I used to dream of something like this.'

Cathy nodded agreement. 'All we ever had was this feeling that we didn't belong, that we were different somehow.'

'Well.' He gave a gentle smile, looking from one face to the other, seeing that they had not yet fully absorbed the impact of what he had told them. 'Now you know that you really are different.'

'So what was she like, our real mother?' asked Monty.

'Sweet little thing. Worshipped the ground below his feet. Enchanting. Like a little cat.' She saw that Treadwell's red-rimmed eyes were glistening. 'She used to break my heart, asking me when he was going to come back. And she loved you so – of course, all the Malays love children, but she adored you, just adored you.' He looked away through the window at the sparkling sea and the misty horizon.

'I hit him when I found out what he'd done. I'll never forget coming up to the bungalow and there you both were, in all the little white togs they used to do up their babies in in those days. And you,' again he spoke to Cathy, 'at that age you were the image of him. I realized at once. Went straight in and floored him, broke one of his teeth. I couldn't have anything to do with him, after that. I went straight down to see her and she was in a terrible state. The whole family was arguing about whether to get the doctor for her – not a real doctor, the medicine man they call in to deal with evil spirits. She was just lying there, eyes open, not seeing anything, as if she was in a trance. She was ill, just skin and bone, she had a fever of some sort, but they weren't interested in that, they were afraid some ghost had taken possession of her. Only the grandmother was prepared to accept she was ill.'

He sighed and took a mouthful of his tea, which was almost cold. The sisters sat in silence as he continued, 'It wasn't the best situation for her. Her mother was a selfish woman, she'd been left by the girl's father – incidentally, they said he was a white man, English-speaking but not from England – and frankly she just wanted to get rid of her however she could. I took the girl to a hospital, and the grandmother with her. And I made sure she got the money, or what was left of it: your father had paid them off. It took about three months before she was better, and then she decided to go and seek her fortune in Singapore. She had some idea of being an *amah* in an English family and then getting him to take her on in his household so that she could be with you that way.'

Cathy sat in silence, oddly aware of the waves splashing on the distant, purple rocks. She remembered the anguish she had felt at being parted from Jamie when he was a baby, and tears of sympathy for the mother she had never known pricked her eyelids.

'Don't blame him,' Treadwell said suddenly. 'I blamed him, but really he couldn't help himself. In some things your father just couldn't tell right from wrong. I don't think he ever really knew what a terrible thing he'd done. He was like a coolie, you know. You couldn't ever get through to the coolies not to lie, or steal or cheat on their quotas or do their work right. That kind of morality was a luxury to them, a luxury they couldn't afford. No sense in being a fine individual if someone else owns you, is there? Your father was just the same about women. He'd been made use of, I guess, by his family, somehow. I'd argue with him, but he couldn't see what I was on about.'

He blew his nose in a large white handkerchief, then reached for a worn document-case on the chequered cloth that covered the table, and handed it to them. Cathy took the heavy leather folder from him. 'That's the journal I kept during the occupation. You might be interested to read it.'

'What happened to her when she went to Singapore? Where is she now?' Monty pressed him. He looked away, unwilling to continue and afraid of their reaction.

'We should know,' Cathy urged him in even tones. 'Even if you think we might not thank you for telling us.'

'Well, you may not thank me, but there it is. You're right, you must know. She was tricked, trapped by a few Chinese who ran a cheap dance hall, and she became what they called a taxi-dancer. Little better than a prostitute really. A lot of the girls who were abandoned by Europeans drifted to the towns and ended up that way – the Malays are very strait-laced and their families wouldn't take them back. Then she began to change, she got hard, eaten up with hatred, obsessed with getting money from the British soldiers – there were thousands of them in Singapore then.'

'You kept in touch?' Cathy enquired.

'For as long as I could. She used to ask me for news of you, she'd lap up any little detail I could tell her. I brought her photographs. He never knew, or he'd have tried to stop me. Then she took up with a Eurasian boyfriend, regular lounge-lizard, and started running with the fast set in Singapore. Your father left when the Emergency started, took you back to England, and shortly afterwards she persuaded this man to take her to France. They planned to open a nightclub in Paris.'

There was a worn manilla folder on the table, and he opened it, sorting through the few scraps of paper it contained. Slowly he selected a narrow, blue card and passed it to Cathy. It bore the name 'Le Bambou' in white pseudo-Chinese lettering. She turned it over and saw some smudged, barely legible writing. 'We are a great suces. Soon I can get my children. My thank to you for everthing,' it read, above an elaborately scrawled signature.

'She could barely write,' he said. 'That was the last I heard of her.'

'How terrible,' Cathy turned the card over again then passed it to Monty. 'She must have suffered terribly. How could our father have done such a thing?'

'He didn't really believe she was an ordinary human being, with real human feelings – finer feelings than his own, as it turned out. The British Empire was built on the belief that the natives weren't full members of the human race, don't forget.'

He could see that the older one was taking it harder than her sister. She was looking dazed now, gazing round the room as if she were seeing it for the first time.

'The village is still there of course. I'll take you to it, if you like. But the family left. The grandmother died, the mother and her husband moved out to Malacca where his people were, then they moved again and I lost track of them. This was, oh, twenty years ago.'

'I'd like to see the village,' Cathy said, her voice suddenly sounding far away.

'Tomorrow, if you like. Best plan would be to fly over to Kuantan, on the far side of the peninsula, the east coast. From there it's a couple of hours' drive.'

As they drove back to Georgetown Monty felt as if she had been released from a prison which had confined her all her life. 'Of course, of course.' She shook her head as she drove. 'Didn't you always feel it? Of course, Bettina couldn't care for us – my God, I feel almost sorry for her. Keeping a secret like that all those years, no wonder she hit the bottle. She never loved us, why should she? And do you think Daddy died because the secret was going to come out?'

'Please, Monty, please, don't let's think about it too much, not yet.' Cathy slid wearily from the car outside the hotel and they walked into the empty hallway which mysteriously retained the scent of old wood and polish characteristic of an English country house. She felt unreal, as if she were watching herself in a film. 'Don't you want to telephone Joe?' she asked Monty, suddenly wanting to be alone with the turmoil of her emotions.

Her sister spent an hour reassuring herself that Paloma had accepted her absence with insulting lack of distress, then appeared in Cathy's room. 'You're really turned-over, aren't you?' Monty said, noticing that Cathy was still sitting in the same dejected pose by her window. Her sister nodded.

'I don't know how I feel, to be honest, Monty. I'm just all confused. Will you sleep in here tonight? I don't want to be alone.'

They woke early and drank some coffee which had an unpleasant chicory after-taste. Treadwell arrived as soon as they had finished, in his own battered Morris, and drove them to the airport. The small plane rose swiftly above the mantle of cloud which blotted out the endless treetops below, and was buffeted by turbulence above the mountainous spine of the peninsula. As it made its descent, Monty peered through the window and saw that the country was almost empty of buildings, an endless expanse of vivid green with a few roads, like gleaming threads, winding through it. There were none of the deep, grey wounds in the jungle made by the tin-workings in the West, and no large, sprawling towns.

From the airport they rented a Datsun, and Treadwell directed Monty, who was at the wheel, along a wide trunk road crowded with trucks and cars. At the outskirts of Kuantan itself they turned along the arterial road to Kuala Lumpur, then branched off after an hour's driving. The road they followed was absolutely straight and barely wide enough for one vehicle. It ran across low hills, between plantations of young rubber and oil palms, and they encountered only one car coming in the opposite direction in forty minutes of fast driving.

'Here – turn right,' Treadwell directed as they crossed a wide iron bridge over a muddy brown river. Monty obediently swung the wheel, and drove slowly along a wide, rutted track fringed with gleaming foliage which rose to a height of eight or nine feet. There were deep ditches on either side of the road, full of rushes whose leaves reflected the bright sunlight like sword-blades. They stopped for a group of half-a-dozen water buffalo who loitered across the road, their grey muzzles lifted and horns swept back as they gazed curiously at the car. One truck, weighed down with massive tree trunks, rolled slowly past them, leaving a choking cloud of red dust behind.

The natural hedge of vegetation gave way to *padi* fields, small enclosures of bright green young rice, with a few bungalows grouped at the far side. 'This is the beginning of the village,' he told them. 'Your house is a little further along.'

Two or three chickens strayed into the road, and again Monty stopped to let them run to safety. They passed the rubber processing plant, where three old cast-iron mangles stood under a rusting tin roof and dirty blankets of latex hung drying on the fence.

'Has it changed?' Monty asked their guide.

He shook his head. 'Hardly at all. People have left, houses have fallen down, the village is smaller than it was, but this kina of life never changes. It's gone on the same way for hundreds of years. The rubber came, about the turn of the century, that was a change, I suppose. Pull in here,' he indicated a place where there was a gravel bay at the roadside.

There was a broad stream beside the road, and some houses, with fifty yards or so between them, which were reached by bridges made of wooden planks. Treadwell approached a woman in a tight-fitting yellow blouse and a turquoise and gold sarong, who was draping freshly-washed shirts on a low, wire line. After a short conversation, he returned to them.

'The house is empty, has been for a few years. Come on, I'll show you.'

All the houses on this side of the peninsula were simpler than those in the west, Cathy noticed. They were square bungalows of weathered wood, mostly undecorated, built on piles, with unglazed windows and roofs of corrugated iron streaked with rust. There was a straggling, half-dead pomegranate bush in front of the house to which Bill led them.

The interior was bare and empty. Monty, oblivious of the dust which might stain her white cotton dress, sat in the doorway and looked down the short flight of steps and away to the plank bridge, sensing the tranquil spirit of the place. Simple people living simple lives had, she thought, created an air of peace there. She tried to imagine herself like the woman Bill had spoken to, hanging out the clothes she had washed in the river.

Cathy's uneven footsteps on the board floor echoed in the deep silence of the clearing around the house. To her this village represented the beginning of the long chain of trade, industry and finance. She herself was placed at the far end of the chain, the rich end, the end that controlled the whole length below it. Here in the village most of the people were trapped in subsistence agriculture, their whole lives given over to mere survival. They had nothing to bargain with in their dealings with the rest of the world. They were powerless and expendable.

'The house where we were born,' she said to Monty, feeling unable to relate anything she saw to herself, or to the memory of her father.

'Did she ever have any other children?' Monty asked Treadwell suddenly.

'No, not as far as I know. I don't think she wanted any, she was so absorbed with you, with the loss of you, her memories of you, her dreams about you. And most of the taxi-dance girls got infections of one sort or another.'

They decided to stay in the area for a few days, and drove back to Kuantan. Treadwell returned to Penang, leaving them with the folder containing a few hazy snapshots of themselves as infants, some old addresses and one or two scrawled notes from their mother. They checked into the Hyatt and spent most of the evening sitting side by side on the long silver beach, watching the waves of the South China Sea, strong and eerily phosphorescent, rolling in and crashing against the steep bank of sand.

'I was happy the way I was,' Cathy said, her chin resting on her knees like a little girl. 'I don't want to be someone else now, and I feel that I'm becoming someone else. It's as if someone were digging up my foundations; I feel as if I'm going to crumble.'

'You'll be all right, Cathy. I'm with you, I'm always with you. You aren't going to crumble, you're going to be stronger when you've taken this in, and happier, too.'

Cathy had obtained the number of a detective agency in Singapore, and when Monty phoned, a Chinese woman with a reassuringly unemotional manner flew up to meet them. Monty gave her the manilla folder and she agreed to start work tracing their mother's family.

After a week, visiting the village every day seemed futile. They decided they had absorbed as much as they could of the atmosphere of their birthplace, and together they travelled to London.

'So, the return of the prodigal boss. What's the news on the pearls?' Henry greeted Cathy with a hug and a kiss on both cheeks as she walked into her office. He was surprised to see that she did not look in the least refreshed by her break but seemed instead to be tense and distracted.

'The pearls?' She had almost forgotten about them. 'Oh, the pearls. Nothing, Henry, unless something's come in while I was away. We discovered something much more serious, I can't tell you anything about it yet. I've got to see Jamie, first. I must drive to Oxford this afternoon.'

Her son, as she expected, was boyishly excited by the idea that his mother had acquired a secret identity. She did not tell him what had become of his newly discovered grandmother, and played down James's actions in the process to reassure herself. That's what I can't accept, she mused as she drove back to London, I can't believe my father did those terrible things. I know he was the sort of man who could be foolish and who lacked judgement, but I can't believe he would be so callous as to rob a mother of her children.

When she told Henry he gave her a penetrating, startled look and at once said, 'Take another week off, Cathy. This is too big for you to handle while you're working. Leave everything to me, I'll cancel my meetings and cover yours.'

She shook her head emphatically. 'No. I'd rather work, it's a relief to have something else to think about. Do you know what the hardest part is? Feeling I don't know my father, that I never knew him, that he conned me into loving him, almost. I was so young when he died, it's maddening to think he was gone before I had a chance to understand him.'

The next day Henry gave her a dusty brown envelope about nine inches square, stuffed with yellowed scraps of newspaper. Stamped across it was the order 'Do not remove from library'. 'That's your father's file from the *Daily Telegraph,*' he told her. 'I asked a friend to get hold of it for me. Maybe that'll be some use – there are a lot of stories about him.'

The file made sad reading. Cathy stayed late in the office smoothing out the crumpled scraps of paper and reading reports of her father's failed business ventures and visits to race meetings.

When she began to read the reports of her father's death and the inquest which followed, Cathy at last found something to add to her new understanding of her father. All the cuttings mentioned his debts. The *Telegraph,* in addition, carried a paragraph which read: *Speculation in the Continental press has continued for some months about Lord James Bourton's connection with the Paris call girl known as Nadine, who is believed to have been murdered at the beginning of October last year.*

Cathy had moved again, to a penthouse apartment in the Barbican, where Monty was waiting for her. They had agreed to tell Treadwell's story only to Joe and Jamie, for the moment.

'There's more to this, I'm sure of it now,' Cathy said, showing Monty the press cuttings. 'I still don't think he told us everything, you know. He was afraid to. Maybe it's only something he suspects.'

'Daddy went to Paris all the time,' Monty said, puzzled by the passion in her sister's manner. 'The European scandal sheets are always printing stories about me, too. There's never anything in them. They said I was dying of leukaemia last year.'

'Well, I'm going to fly over and get someone to go through the newspaper archives anyway. Something may come up, who knows. I can't stand not knowing about Daddy, Monty. Don't you understand, it's suddenly as if we've got no parents. We can't remember our real mother at all, and our father was a totally different person to the man we thought we knew.'

'We're supposed to be going to the Shahzdeh's new resort in two days, had you forgotten?'

'Damn. Yes, I had forgotten.' Cathy was suddenly irritated because, lovely as she anticipated that the new L'Equipe Creole would be, she had no desire to fret away a long weekend on business entertaining when she had been seized by a sense that her life was being turned inside-out. She sighed. She would have to go. Both the Prince and the Princess were important clients, and the Princess had particularly asked Cathy to introduce her sister.

The resort was an island in the Caribbean near Martinique; Joe and Paloma flew out to join them there, which lightened the atmosphere. A gulf was opening between Cathy and Monty: they both sensed it and were the more distressed because the discovery of their birth seemed to be separating them, when it should have united them. Cathy's attitude was opposed to Monty's in every respect. She could not stop thinking about her father, while Monty was impatient for news of her mother. Before leaving London, she had briefed a second detective to search for the woman in Paris, and at the same time to pursue the rumours which had obviously troubled their father before his death. Joe made things easier. He took the weight of Monty's impetuous curiosity, and soothed Cathy's distress.

L'Equipe Creole was the sixth of Princess Ayeshah's resorts and one of the most beautiful. It was a large coral island fringed with natural beaches of pink and white sand which ran gently into clear water thronged with electric-bright coloured fish. The central buildings, of local grey-brown honeycomb stone, were at the crest of the island's central hill, and the Princess's guests were accommodated in bunga-lows in the traditional Caribbean style, with soaring steep-pitched roofs of pale pickled pine.

A thicket of frangipani had been planted downwind of the central hall, and as the guests assembled for the welcoming reception, its sweet vanilla fragrance was carried to them on the warm breeze. Despite the beauty and luxury around them, both sisters were oppressed rather than soothed by the island. Monty had a sense that she was" wasting time on a diversion, and Cathy was unable to relax, and felt her exhausted emotions assaulted by the hedonistic atmosphere.

Princess Ayeshah was not accompanied by her husband, who had been detained in Paris on business. She wore a high-necked, long-sleeved gown of ruched white crêpe-de-chine, and her hair, as always, was styled in a chignon which had grown fuller and more shapely in response to changing fashion. She gave Cathy a warm welcome.

'May I introduce my sister?' Cathy stepped back to present Monty, who shook the Princess's hand with no more than social politeness. She saw a small, hard, elegant woman with the pallor and brittle sociability which Monty associated with the nightclub world. It was not these days a way of life which Monty admired.

'I'm delighted you could come, I have wanted to meet you for so long,' said the Princess, giving Monty a formal embrace of welcome. 'I was hoping we would have time for a private talk before you leave?'

'Yes, of course,' Monty said. After all, she had come here as a favour to Cathy, to meet a client of her sister's who was curious about her. For Cathy's sake she would accept the Princess's overtures gracefully. They agreed to meet the next morning. Monty then attached herself to the Princess and followed her as she made her way graciously around the room. Cathy felt tired, unnaturally so, and she soon left the party to go back to her bungalow. There she lay on the bed but could not sleep, tossing and turning unhappily for a couple of hours until Monty appeared.

'Oh Cathy, I'm sorry – I was enjoying myself. I didn't think that you might not be up to it.'

'I can't stop thinking about it all.' Cathy sat up against the cool, white linen pillows. 'I keep thinking about Mummy and Daddy, the people we called Mummy and Daddy, anyway. Who knows what they really are to us?'

'Cheer up, Cathy, please. Aren't you just a very little bit glad that you aren't Bettina's daughter? She wasn't exactly the best of mothers, was she?'

'You don't understand!' Cathy, who scarcely raised her voice usually, almost shouted at her sister. 'We can't say that, we've no right to make that kind of judgement, we don't know anything about her. But Bettina isn't important to me, it's Daddy I care about. I can't accept that he lied to us all those years. How could he look at me every day of his life and *know* and never tell us? I just can't take it in.'

She fretted sleeplessly for most of the night. At last she slept; she dreamed vividly but could remember nothing, and woke as the birds were calling at the beginning of the sudden Caribbean dawn.

She called for coffee, and was surprised when the telephone rang almost as soon as she put it down. 'We have a telex for you, Miss Bourton. It came in overnight. Would you like us to send it round with the coffee?'

'Yes, of course.'

The telex was from Mr Phillips at Garrard's, BINGO, it read, PEARLS ANSWERING DESCRIPTION OF YOURS FISHED JANUARY SMALL INDONESIA COMPANY SAWA TRADING FLORES SUNDA. LAST SEEN IN POSSESSION OF COMPANY OWNER. PURSUING FURTHER ENQUIRIES. PHILLIPS.

Cathy had again almost forgotten about the pearls, but now her interest revived. She and Monty had tried to unravel a trivial mystery and discovered something far more serious, perhaps fatal to her own inner serenity. The question of the pearls was something which would drive away the brooding clouds of self-doubt in her mind, for a while at least. Her new toy, her portable telex, invited her to action. She sent a message to Henry in London asking for everything he could find out about the Sawa Trading Company, then paced her terrace with impatience, planning to wait until Paloma was awake and she could decently invade the intimacy of her sister's family.

To calm her nerves, she put on her new white bikini and the white, crushed silk robe, checking the effect approvingly in the mirror before setting out to stroll to the pool for a swim. A hummingbird, like a flying emerald, was breakfasting among the yellow alamanda flowers.

The island's chief success was the swimming pool, a gleaming blue-green lake landscaped to resemble a jungle rock basin, with a high waterfall at one end and ferns gushing from hollows in the grey-black boulders. Someone else was already in the water and, vast as the inviting expanse of aquamarine was, Cathy had wanted it all to herself. She paused, irritated. A woman, also in a white bikini, was swimming lazily where the water was deepest.

Cathy recognized the Princess, and was at once intrigued. The Princess was so elusive, so protective of her own privacy, that the opportunity to watch her like this was like the chance of watching a cheetah at a watering hole. How extraordinary her body was, Cathy noticed. The Princess's age was another of the great mysteries about her. She was as firm-fleshed and graceful as a polo pony although she must be in her fifties. Cathy watched in admiration as the high-breasted figure pulled itself out of the water and walked, with an indefinable, seductive waver, to the springboard at Cathy's side of the pool.

The Princess made a showy swallow dive, then swam around to the poolside and began to walk towards the board a second time. Cathy had the overpowering impression of watching herself, just as she had in the disturbing dream when she stayed with Monty in Arizona. All that seemed very long ago, now.

This time the Princess stood poised at the end of the board, an erect figure full of energy like an Art Deco statuette. Cathy noticed that there was a dark shadow just above the back of the right knee, and her hand unconsciously strayed to her own birthmark. I must remember to point out to Monty that the Princess has a mark like that, she told herself. She'll stop worrying about Paloma then.

At length she grew tired of spying on her hostess, and took a buggy down to a cove where the sea swimming was not impeded by the coral close to the surface. She swam for almost an hour. enjoying the physical and mental relaxation, then showered, changed and went to find her sister.

The atmosphere in Monty's bungalow was electric. From the way that Joe looked sharply up as she entered, Cathy knew that they had been talking about her, and at once felt resentment. Monty looked ravishing this morning, somehow vibrant and more than just alive, but she was anxious as well. She wore a loose white dress with white leggings, and was cradling Paloma against one hip.

'You needn't worry about Paloma's birthmark because Princess Ayeshah has one just the same,' Cathy told her in a cheerful tone. The words were like bullets. As soon as she had said them, Cathy realized the implication. Both Joe and Monty looked at her intently, then Monty, without speaking, put Paloma down on the floor and passed two slips of perforated paper to her sister, a pair of telexes – the one from Garrard's and the one she had not seen, from Henry in London.

'I came to find you this morning and met the boy delivering that. I opened it to see if it was important.' Monty indicated the new message. 'And then I read the other one.'

The telex was from Henry. NO PROBLEM RE SAWA TRADING PART OF SHAHZDEH GROUP SUBSIDIARY OF QUADRANT HOLDINGS STOP

SMALL IMPORT EXPORT OUTFIT ACTIVITIES INCLUDE FISHING PEARLS, TORTOISESHELL, ETC REGISTERED UK 1980. A list of directors followed and the message ended 'what gives henry.'

Cathy raised her eyes to her sister's, all at once feeling cold and weak. 'She couldn't possibly be. Impossible. *Impossible.* No, Monty, I won't believe it. Anyway she's Iranian.'

'The Prince is Iranian,' Joe pointed out. 'She could be anything. Does she ever talk about Iran?'

'We've got to see her, ask her. At least, there isn't much doubt that we have her to thank for the pearls,' Monty said, 'But there's something else, Cathy.'

'What?' She saw the sombre look in her sister's eyes and felt afraid.

'I talked to the Princess for a long time last night. The minute she spoke to me, I knew there was something I recognized about her. I thought it was just the sort of recognition you get from seeing a face in the papers. But it wasn't. It was her voice. I know it, I'd know it anywhere, I'll never forget it. That woman may have given us the pearls, and that woman may be our mother, but she's also Madame Bernard – or whoever that woman was who for some reason decided to save a perfect stranger's life when she met me in Paris.'

Cathy leaned back against the wooden rail of the balcony, the brilliant sea glittering behind her, and rubbed her eyes as if she were tired. Rapidly her quick, analytical mind assembled the new information alongside what she already knew, and she began to see the shape of the secret which was yet to be discovered. It was indistinct and deceptive, like a face seen among clouds, but the terrible form of it was unmistakable.

'We must be sure,' she said.

'I *am* sure, Cathy. I could never forget that voice. It sounds like metal.'

'No, no, we need proof, absolute proof.'

'I think you're right,' Joe said. 'You've uncovered so much already, you need to know the whole truth now, before you do anything.'

'But I want to see her, I want to go to her now – think of all the time we've already wasted . . .'

'Yes, think of it,' snapped Cathy suddenly, 'and ask yourself why? She's known me for years now, and never said anything. She knew you, too, and never said anything. Oh, maybe she hinted, but she didn't come out with it. There must be a reason for that, and it can't be a pleasant one.'

'But look what she did for us – my life, your business – she saved them both. Doesn't that prove that she loved us all along?'

Cathy shook her head violently, her wet hair swinging against her cheeks. 'No, all it proves to me is that she wanted us to love her.'

'You're frightened of her,' Monty accused.

'No, I'm not. I'm only frightened for us.' Cathy walked into the cool of the room, away from the harsh morning sunlight. 'I want to leave here now, go back to London, and find out everything else, until I'm satisfied that the whole thing is out in the open.'

Monty followed her sister, feeling bewildered and angry. 'But why don't we simply meet her and ask her?'

'For the same reason that she never met us, and told us – twenty years ago, when our father died.'

'I think you need to know more, Monty.' Joe swept Paloma into his arms as she marched unsteadily towards the balcony. 'The way this woman has acted to you is ambivalent, like she wants one thing but her nerve fails her when she goes for it.' Reluctantly, Monty agreed to go back to London. They prepared to leave immediately, and Monty sat down to write the Princess a note explaining why she could not keep her appointment.

'What shall I say?' she asked Cathy, her mind blank.

'Urgent family business,' Cathy suggested, her face hard.

CHAPTER TWENTY-EIGHT

S UNDAY, 6TH October 1963 was a dull, overcast and humid day. At Longchamp racecourse, the glittering crowd assembled for the Prix de l'Arc de Triomphe sweated slightly in their formal dress. The dazzling gaiety which normally pervaded the world's most brilliant race meeting seemed to be subdued by the sulky climate. The towering figure of President de Gaulle was, unusually, absent from the scene, as was his dapper Foreign Minister who was in Washington enduring a distinctly cool reception from President Kennedy.

There was no British horse in the race, which was also unusual, and in consequence very few British voices were to be heard among the crowd's excited clamour. The British had another reason for staying away besides their lack of national interest in the race. An immense scandal, involving prostitutes, politicians, aristocrats and a Russian spy, had almost toppled the Conservative Government. A display of hedonistic behaviour a few months after the Profumo affair was considered by most of Longchamp's British devotees to be in bad taste.

One Englishman remained oblivious to the sensitive moral climate in his country.

'Time to take a look at the runners, don't you think?' Lord James Bourton put down his champagne and reached for his fieldglasses, indicating to the twelve men who had accepted his invitation to share his bank's box at Longchamp that he intended to move down to the paddock and watch the horses parade before the race.

'Good idea,' assented a clipped voice, and the narrow frame of Eddie Shrewton appeared between the glass doors which separated the box's seats from the hospitality area behind.

'Right – anyone else?' James beamed his jagged smile, disguising his resentment at having to waste his talents as a host on a man so difficult to amuse. Shrewton had come to Paris with three other directors from the old-established Migatto group whom James knew well. He was more than ten years older than James and was being spoken of as the group's next chairman. James already knew him, of course, in the distant manner in which every British aristocrat knew the others, as a name, a title, a face and a set of connections. After twenty-four hours of close personal acquaintanceship, however, James disliked the man; not seriously, because James did nothing seriously, but distinctly. Eddie Shrewton was joyless, earnest and reserved. He seemed older than he was, not only because his hair was prematurely grey but also because his tall, thin body was ungainly, his morning suit hung badly from his stiff shoulders, and he rarely smiled.

He had not placed a bet on the race, barely entered into the lengthy discussions about the riders' ability, the horses' form, the going on the course and the hopes of the owners, and was only now showing enthusiasm for the stroll to the paddock because, James plainly recognized, he was bored by the entire proceedings. The man had no gift for frivolity; furthermore – and this was the nub of James's distaste – he had an air of substance and consequence which James knew he himself would never be able to acquire. Most of the time, James was able to distract himself from the knowledge that he was a failure, but it was a difficult trick to pull off in the presence of a man like Eddie Shrewton.

As they joined the crowd which streamed through the starkly graceful interior of the new grandstand James did his best to make conversation.

'Nasty business with Relko after the Derby,' he said. A startled look flashed behind Shrewton's spectacles.

'Was there? I didn't know.'

'Devil of a fuss about it – dope test was positive. Jockey Club enquiry only finished last week.'

'Oh really.' James gave up. The man knew nothing of the sport of kings, and showed no inclination to learn. The only course left was elementary instruction. 'There he is now,' he said, indicating Relko on the far side of the white-railed enclosure. The horse was dancing nervously sideways as if on tiptoe, his gleaming, brown sides already darkened with sweat. 'Brilliant horse on his day, made a very good showing at the Prix Royal Oak here a few weeks ago. Crowd cheered him all the way to the unsaddling enclosure. Not surprising he's the favourite today.'

James watched with interest as the horses were led into the ring one by one. His passion for the turf had begun to wane recently, since two of his London bookmakers had refused him credit. However, he found the Arc, as the British called France's most important international race, impossible to miss. The whole of Paris seemed to stream into the Bois de Boulogne and gather in the hope, often rewarded, of celebrating the supremacy of French bloodstock. The women were impeccably elegant; the course in its light woodland setting made such a charming picture; the *turfistes* were so passionately partisan as they told each other that Relko was the finest horse ever ridden; even the jockeys' silks seemed to have a clarity of colour which was missing at the English meetings. Longchamp seemed more than ever the scene of beauty, breeding and high emotion which Raoul Dufy had delighted to paint. Even if no British horse was running this year, James could not stay away from the Arc.

Since that unpleasant day three years ago when he had been tricked into a meeting with the Princess Ayeshah, James had avoided Paris, but the lure of the Arc was irresistible. Nevertheless, he looked around with unease, fearing the sight of his enemy among the ferociously chic women who preened like fabulous birds of paradise beside their dark-garbed escorts. The custom at Longchamp was that while the horses paraded inside the paddock, a parallel display of impeccably groomed, highly-bred and savagely competitive animals took place outside the rails.

Lord James Bourton was so unassailably secure in his sense of social and racial superiority to the woman who had borne his children that he had dealt with her threat by ignoring it. The notion that a peasant woman could possibly cause him damage seemed quite impossible. He could not believe it; he could barely acknowledge the facts of their distant association. His confidence was a quicksand which swallowed up the truth and left no trace of it to disturb his mental equilibrium.

Only a deeply buried core of guilt remained to undermine his pleasure, and it produced merely a momentary tremor of discomfort which passed as soon as James noticed that the horse on which he had placed a substantial sum, Le Mesnil, was being led into the paddock. He had had a tip that the three-year-old had recovered his form after losing badly at Chantilly in the spring, and had put three bets of a thousand pounds on him to win with separate bookmakers. With odds of 10 to 1, Le Mesnil could make him a useful sum.

In the sixteen years since he had claimed his inheritance, James had sunk rapidly into debt. His spending on pleasure and debauchery had been high and his business judgement poor. After Ayeshah and Hussain had indicated that they knew of his precarious financial position he had been sufficiently frightened to take the final step of mortgaging his home and consolidating his debts with a single loan company. Money had no real significance for James, and he would apply his mind to his finances only when forced.

Recently he had found a more attractive way to redeem his position and that had added to his desire to visit Paris again this year. Through his racing friends he had met a young Frenchman whose family were trapped in Algeria by the new government's vicious restrictions on foreign exchange. A French national who wished to leave the new-hatched Communist state could take only the equivalent of thirty US dollars with him. All the French bank accounts in Algeria had been frozen. James had spent a long night drinking with the anguished young man, consoling him for the fact that his family, after seventy years of planting olive groves and growing oranges in the colony they had loved, were now to be trapped in poverty in a hostile new country. At last the Frenchman had asked for his help, and James had agreed to import a succession of Berber carpets, which would make their way to Casablanca from the family's most southerly estate in Algeria. Stitched into the centre of each tightly-rolled bundle would be a long paper-wrapped cylinder, a cache of gold napoleons.

James opened an account in a false name at a small private bank in London, and stored the gold in the vault, ready for the *pieds-noirs* whenever they chose to quit Algeria, and far from the scrutiny of the French or Algerian authorities. In the meantime, he took a handsome rake-off from each consignment. The transaction allowed him to service his debts and enjoy his normal lavish lifestyle without extending his attenuated credit any further.

Le Mesnil sauntered gracefully around the paddock, swishing his tail and mouthing his bit, showing in every step the confident, settled air of a winner. His groom had sensibly separated him from his bay stablemate Sanctus, who was playing up nervously as usual. Behind Sanctus walked Baron Guy de Rothschild's Exbury, a small, light-framed chestnut with three white socks, calmly ignoring the restless prancing ahead of him. James smiled to himself, reminded of his daughters by the contrasting demeanour of the two colts: Sanctus full of ability which his jockey could barely control, was like Monty, while Exbury, a pretty animal, ostentatiously cool, with a steady, level gaze, had exactly Cathy's temperament.

'They'll be off down the course soon – last chance to put some money on,' James prompted his prim companion. Eddie Shrewton was gazing at the horses with little interest. 'See anything you fancy, Eddie?'

'Little chestnut looks useful,' he answered, indicating Exbury who was standing quietly while his jockey mounted.

'Rothschild hasn't had a winner since 1934, but Exbury's beaten last year's champion so I'd say he's a likely contender,' James advised. 'He ran very well in the Coronation Cup, too. Whether he's got the quality to pass Relko's another matter, but you could back worse, I'd say.' They returned to the box and Shrewton telephoned a modest bet on Exbury.

Sanctus had to be led down to the start, and Relko tore past him in a lather of sweat. Exbury, James noticed with irritation, strode out well as he passed the *moulin*. He considered a last- minute bet on Rothschild's chestnut, but his dislike of Eddie Shrewton held him back.

'They'll be starting them in stalls next year,' he informed his party as the race began. 'The French will try anything new.'

'Makes sense to improve the course as much as possible. Why not, if they've the money to invest in the sport? The stand is superb – makes Longchamp a lot more pleasant than Ascot,' Shrewton observed as the runners, led by Relko, approached the gentle hill near the beginning of the course. James did not answer him but followed the horses intently with his binoculars. Relko dropped back and another horse, a pacemaker rather than a serious contender, took the lead as they crested the hill. Sanctus faltered on the downhill run, and as they approached the straight Le Mesnil took the lead and the crowd gave a roar.

'He's well on his way home now,' shouted James in delight as Le Mesnil drew away from the tightly grouped horses behind him.

Two furlongs from the finish Relko's jockey asked his mount for a final effort, but the favourite had spent his force too early in the race and had nothing left to give. Le Mesnil led by a clear distance of eight lengths. With an unfaltering, strong stride, his head up, his nostrils" flared and his jockey barely needing to encourage him with an occasional sight of the whip, he bore down on the finish.

Exbury's jockey at last gave his horse a back-handed tap which set the little chestnut alight. The horse running alongside him also surged ahead, but Exbury, as if moving into an extra gear, pulled away from the rest, with an astonishing surge of acceleration. He reached the darker horse a hundred metres from the line, amid hysterical cheering from the crowd. James sat down in silence as Exbury streaked past the winning post, a clear two lengths ahead of his horse, Le Mesnil.

'Good show,' he said to Shrewton, shaking his hand and disguising his own keen disappointment with the ease of a lifetime's training. 'Damn good show. Genuine champion, magnificent race. I'll take your lead in future, Eddie.' A pink flush of embarrassed pleasure coloured Eddie Shrewton's monochrome complexion as he accepted the rest of the party's congratulations. Relko, the favourite, who had lost his backers millions of francs, galloped home to jeers and catcalls from the crowd.

'Bloody Frogs, no sense of sportsmanship,' said James. 'Come on, let's go and see Guy in his moment of glory.'

That evening James led his party to a hostelry close to the Bois which was celebrated for its discretion rather than its cuisine. It was an ugly Belle Epoque mansion with a large, ill-kempt garden. Kitchen aromas percolated into the high-ceilinged dining room, which echoed with the clatter of plates and cutlery, while upstairs the bedrooms were furnished with massive four-poster beds whose once opulent hangings never lost their odour of damp, moth and stale cigar smoke. James's custom was to finish the Longchamp weekend with a dinner in the private salon, a room with french doors to the garden and a high vaulted ceiling.

His guests would be joined around the oval table by a dozen of Madame Bernard's girls; after supper the waiters would withdraw leaving them alone; there would be more drinking, teasing, shrieks of laughter, perhaps a little performance if one of the girls had a speciality, and then the party would disperse according to their individual tastes. The only rule James imposed was that no one should lapse so far from decency as to try to take one of the hookers back to the Ritz; James liked to be known at the Ritz, and did not care to risk his standing by inviting a scandal.

The girls arrived in four low-riding black Citroëns. They had been taking benzedrine and were raucously gay, swooping on the men with cries of delight, winding their slender arms around their necks and demanding their names while they nibbled earlobes and loosened ties. Madame Bernard's people knew James's tastes and the last one out of the cars was a tall lissom girl in a gold-lame sheath dress, carrying a white leather bandbox. She had a matt brown skin and aquiline features which proclaimed her North African origin as clearly as the harsh intonations of her accent. She had evidently been told to pay him particular attention, and took no interest in the other men.

'Nadine is superb at the *danse du ventre*,' the brunette hanging on Shrewton's arm whispered through scarlet lips. 'It's something you should not miss. I'm sure she has brought her costume.'

'No doubt she has.' James smiled into Nadine's sloe eyes and gave her slim waist a squeeze, but he felt boredom steal upon him like the autumn mist he could see rising from the cold dew-pearled lawn outside. The evening would be entirely predictable and he found that he had little appetite for any of it.

The truth was that James had aged since his encounter with the Princess; it was as if a decade or more had caught up with him all at once. The change was barely visible in his springy black hair or his dark eyes which sparkled in their network of deepening wrinkles. The force of his charm was undimmed. Inside, however, his spirit was faltering. The sustained mental effort of cancelling the aggressively renewed memory of Khatijah was draining him. His voluptuous enthusiasm had waned; sexual gratification seemed barely worth the effort and he could be turned off by the merest unpleasant detail of an encounter – cheap scent, the impression that he was being watched, or a woman's offhand manner.

For the past eighteen months James had been keeping a West Indian prostitute in Bayswater, for comfort as much as for sex. She was a cheerful woman who amused him with her down-to-earth manner and was so plump she made him think of a dark-brown Michelin man. His mistrust of women was increasing with age; more and more he preferred the familiar, if coarse, pleasure of the whore he knew to the more refined delights which might be only promised by a stranger.

He had drunk champagne all day and had a strong thirst. Instead of wine he drank brandy and soda with the meal, finally emptying the siphon. He handed the empty container in its wire-mesh covering to a waiter and demanded another, but it was slow to arrive and he continued to drink the cognac neat, telling himself it was fine vintage spirit and not as injurious to his constitution as cheap brandy would have been. Before long he had an ugly headache.

He noticed Eddie Shrewton at the far end of the expanse of white damask that was now stained with claret and littered with cigar ash. He was as withdrawn and disinterested as ever and would no doubt shortly slip away back to the hotel. James pursed his lips with contempt for the thin-blooded creature whose favour he was required to court.

Nadine emerged through the service door, and was greeted with whoops of enthusiasm from the diners. She had exchanged her gold sheath for her dance costume, a lurid wrapping of chiffon veils over a green sequinned girdle, and her wrists and ankles clashed with heavy brass bracelets. Two waiters swiftly removed the tablecloth, and she climbed on to the scarred oak surface beneath and began to undulate slowly from one man to another, twisting her wrists and twitching her pelvis rhythmically. Whining Arab music sounded from the walnut gramophone cabinet. James leaned back in his chair, an uncomfortable carved Gothic affair upholstered in red plush, and gazed vacantly towards the gyrating body through the dense pall of blue smoke that hung above the table. He realized that he was very drunk. He closed his eyes and had the sensation that the room was swinging to and fro, so he snapped his eyes open again.

Two or three of the men were on their feet now, tucking hundred-franc notes beneath the slight overhang of taut brown flesh at the rim of the sequinned girdle. Not to be outdone, James flourished a thousand francs and she advanced upon him. He crushed the money against her shimmering belly and the girl sank to her knees on the table in front of him, her supple brown body shuddering lasciviously as she leaned backwards. Her small high breasts shivered in the confines of their sequinned harness.

The tempo of the music increased and another whisper of transparent fabric dropped from the girl's coral-tipped fingers. Now there were only three left, two tied in loose knots over her hip bones to accentuate their movement, and one draped between them. The dance was probably as old as lust itself, and James had seen it too many times to be moved, even by this accomplished and nubile artist. He closed his eyes once more and let boredom and brandy submerge his consciousness.

He came round to feel the cool, damp night air in his face and his feet dragging awkwardly across the gravel of the driveway. Concerned not to scratch his black patent shoes he coordinated his legs sufficiently to stumble between the two men who, with his arms around their shoulders, were half-carrying him. A car door was opened and he fell into the rear seat of the vehicle. His legs were inert again, but someone lifted them inside the car and shut the door. There were voices, then two men got into the front of the car. He heard the staccato voice of Eddie Shrewton telling the driver to take them to the Ritz, then lost consciousness once more.

The distinctive sound of the Paris traffic can be heard even in the hushed depths of the Ritz, and James knew where he was before he opened his eyes. He decided to keep his eyes closed for a while. He could tell, by the rosy glow of blood through his eyelids, that it was daytime. He felt as if his skull were being crushed in a red-hot vice. That was the brandy. He had been a fool to drink so much of it. He was getting too old to drink as he used to do.

He became aware of two other sources of discomfort: his mouth was hideously dry so that his desiccated lips stuck to his teeth, and his bladder was full. James lay still as long as he could, trying to summon some saliva to moisten his lips. At last he decided he must move, and rolled off the bed on to his hands and knees on the thick carpet. He gained his feet shakily and walked to the bathroom. When he had urinated and drunk some water, he decided to clean his teeth. That done he felt better and walked back to the bedroom, where the girl on his bed lay spreadeagled on her stomach in a pose of abandoned relaxation, her arms flung out above her head. Her naked body was completely uncovered except for her face which was smothered in a tumult of black curls. With automatic thoughtfulness, he tucked the gold satin quilt around her; the girl was quite chilled. She must have kicked the cover off hours ago.

He sat for a long time on the chaise-longue at the foot of the bed, sipping water and collecting his devastated wits. At length he checked his watch. It was 1.15 in the afternoon. There was no particular need to hurry, he had chartered a private plane for his party, but they would need to be on their way by the end of the afternoon.

There was a knock at the door, an imperious double-rap which commanded James to rise to his feet and cross the small, oval sitting room of his suite to answer it.

'Ah – you're up and about at last.' Eddie Shrewton, in a dark blue suit, which fitted no better than his morning dress, swayed awkwardly from one foot to another outside the door. 'How are you feeling?'

'Bloody awful.' James smiled broadly. 'Feels like a pneumatic drill in my head. Come in, come in. I was just going to order some coffee.'

'I'll do it.' The older man called room service with an air of authority, then turned to the pitiful creature he had brought home unconscious the previous night. Lord Shrewton had no more admiration for James than James had for him, but expended less energy on such emotional considerations. Bourton was an amusing fellow, he could see that, but he made an ass of himself so often over women, drink or money that Shrewton's sense of humour was unequal to the task of appreciating him. Worse, there was something unsound about him. The older man's instinct was that James was not to be trusted but, since he had no facts to support the hunch, he kept it strictly to himself.

'If you tell me what the orders of the day are, I'll start getting things moving,' Shrewton said, seeing that James was unshaven and still in his evening clothes. 'The other fellas are downstairs having a spot of lunch.'

'Not to worry, old man. We've all the time in the world.' Now that his senses were returning to normal, James felt nauseous. He was aware that his hands were shaking. Eddie Shrewton was ill. Bourton was certainly in no state to cope with the travel arrangements and although he clearly had no work of any consequence to be doing in London, that was not the case with most of his guests.

James felt that he was being discourteous and collected what strength remained. 'I'll get the cars laid on for two hours' time.' He stood up and looked distractedly round the room for his itinerary. 'Damn. I know I put it down somewhere.'

Briskly, Shrewton began to lift cushions and open drawers. They moved into the bedroom, and James again saw the sleeping girl. Bewilderment halted him in his search for the travel documents: he had no recollection of taking the girl back to the hotel, indeed he could remember very little about the previous night, but one of the iron rules of his life was that he never took girls back to the Ritz. He did not care to court Eddie Shrewton's disapproval by asking him if the girl had ridden back with them in the car. However she had got there, getting her out of the hotel unseen was an important priority. She had slept enough.

James sat heavily on the bed and shook the girl's shoulder. 'Nadine. Nadine, my dear. Wake up, Nadine. Time to go home now.'

She did not stir.

'Nadine. Come along, dear. Wake up, now. Nadine.'

Eddie Shrewton overcame his distaste and embarrassment and crossed the room to stand over James and the sleeping woman. 'Didn't you give us some sermon about not taking girls back to the hotel?' he asked, trying not to phrase the question as an accusation.

'Damn right. It's just not done, in my book.'

'Well she wasn't with us when I brought you back, you know. She was still shimmying all over the table and the fellas were howling for her to take the last of those veils off.' The older man's pale hand reached out and pulled the tangle of hair off the girl's face. He touched her cheek with his fingertips, then her neck.

'You fool, Bourton. You bloody fool. She's dead – can't you see?'

James jumped off the bed and stared in horror at the body. 'But I didn't . . . But I was . . . Oh God, I never . . . I couldn't . . . Eddie, I hope you don't think . . .'

'No. I don't. You were blind drunk. I put you to bed myself. You couldn't lift a finger. You couldn't have screwed a rat in that condition, much less done this.' With a gesture that was so careful it was almost tender, he swept the girl's waterfall of dark hair to one side and tried to turn her over, but her left arm, which was hanging over the edge of the bed, would not move. When he investigated, Shrewton found that it was fixed to the iron frame of the bed by a pair of steel handcuffs. Around her neck, tightly embedded in the horribly contused flesh, was James's black satin tie, which he removed and put in his pocket.

There was a discreet tap at the door of the suite and Shrewton sprinted to it immediately, closing the bedroom door deftly as he went. He took the tray with coffee from the waiter. He glanced at the bill, then said in English, raising his voice to impress his meaning upon the foreigner, 'This is charged to the wrong room.

I asked you to charge it to my room – change the number on the bill, will you? Here,' he gave the number, and watched while the man altered the figure on the top righthand corner of the slip of paper, gave him a tip of exactly 15 per cent and shut the door without undue haste.

'Where did those girls come from? D'you call someone, know someone?'

James was standing against the wall by the bedroom door, as if trying to get as far away as possible from the dead girl. 'What?' He screwed up his eyes as if looking into bright light.

'Don't you see what this is?' James looked at him with a dull expression, and Shrewton realized that between his hangover and the shock he was completely stupefied. With firm gentleness, he led the younger man out of the bedroom, shut the door, and made him sit on the grey sofa in the little salon.

'You didn't touch that woman, but we'll have a devil of a job proving it. This is a set-up. Someone wants to blackmail you, or maybe me, or maybe all of us. They killed the girl and put her in bed with you. Now – where did she come from?'

'That's it – Madame Bernard.' James's slumped body straightened. 'I'll call her number, they'll know what to do, they must have got out of this kind of jam before, or worse, I shouldn't wonder.'

He tried to stand up and reached towards the telephone on a side table, but Shrewton pushed him firmly back into the depths of the sofa. 'Don't be a complete ass, Bourton. That Madame, whoever she is, must be involved in this, don't you see? Her or someone she's working with. Have you – ah – have you had dealings with her in the past?'

James nodded.

'Any trouble? A grudge, a vendetta, some kind of deal that didn't work out . . . ?' His voice tailed off. Eddie Shrewton could not imagine what kind of transaction with a call-girl agency could have gone so sour that the guilty party would be framed for murder. He could imagine that there was no degree of stupidity of which James would be incapable.

James shook his head. 'Nothing. Always a very amicable association. Absolutely confidential, never a whisper. Not cheap of course . . .' The other man made a gesture of impatience. Shrewton knew there was only one thing he could do, and it must be done quickly before the hotel staff became aware of the situation. He left James with instructions not to open the door to anyone except him, ran down the corridor to his own suite and made one telephone call, to the ambassador's private line at the British Embassy. The ambassador, his contemporary at Eton, understood instantly the implications of the call. 'I'd better get round there now,' he said, as calmly as if agreeing to an impromptu game of tennis.

'Is there an embassy physician – trustworthy sort?'

'Certainly. I'll hunt him out and be over within the hour.'

The two men were announced forty minutes later, and Shrewton took them to James's suite. The ambassador was small, plump and neatly made; the doctor, who was French, was older than Shrewton had expected, white-haired, slow-moving and hesitant.

With difficulty because the corpse was stiffening, they turned the girl on to her back and the four men instantly averted their eyes as her torn, bloody stomach was revealed. The smooth-skinned belly that had rippled sensuously twelve hours earlier was a mass of thin, precise cuts.

'Ritual murder,' the doctor explained as he carefully patted the shredded flesh with febrile fingers. 'Very common among the Algerians, Tunisians, a lot of the Africans. But it wasn't done here, there isn't enough blood. There's an artery nicked, she'd have poured blood when it was done. But you see the sheets?' He spread the crumpled linen flat, showing them the extent of the bloodstains. 'They'd be soaked if that had been done here.'

'She died from being strangled?' enquired Shrewton, his voice hushed.

'Hard to say definitely without a post-mortem, but I should imagine so. And she was moved quickly. I can tell that because the body fat changes after a certain time and retains the traces of pressure from the way the body was lying at the time of death. She was killed somewhere else, then brought here. A very clever job, but it won't stand up in a court.'

'Whose name is the suite booked in?' The ambassador stood up and walked to the windows to draw the curtain, then dropped his short arms to his sides, realizing that there was no point.

'Bourton here. He was with me all night.'

'In your suite?'

'Eventually. We were out drinking until late. He keeled over in the corridor and I put him to bed on the couch in my room.' James, still stunned by the shock, stared dumbly at his feet to cover his amazement. He had expected Eddie Shrewton to be pedantically, faithfully and maliciously truthful about the entire affair.

'So he was with you the whole time?'

'Until we came here this morning and found her.'

'All night?'

'I couldn't sleep so I was pretty much awake all the time. I give you my word, he was under my eyes the entire period.'

The ambassador nodded, apparently satisfied. 'I'll call the Minister, see what we can do. Don't touch anything and stay where I can get you on the telephone at once.'

Shrewton led James back to his own suite and began patiently to telephone London, calling his own office, his home and James's office with news of their delayed return. Cars were organized and the rest of the party were sent home, knowing nothing of what had taken place. By the end of the afternoon half a dozen men in white overalls arrived with a stretcher, an ambulance and a hacksaw, and removed the body of the girl under the doctor's direction.

The two men spent a sombre evening together. James, still numb with shock, was moved to a room connected to his companion's suite and fell into a deep sleep just after nine o'clock. In the morning the ambassador's car called for them, and they had a meeting at the Embassy with an unsmiling civil servant, who regretted, at length but without much sincerity, that such a crime could have been committed against a foreigner on French soil.

By the following afternoon they were on their way to the airport. 'Eddie, you saved me. You don't know what kind of mess . . .'

'I can guess. I don't want you to tell me. And don't thank me, I was in as much trouble as you were and anything I did was for myself as much as you. From what I hear, you haven't got much more to lose, but I'm not quite in the same position.' The man was so lacking in humour that when he did make an attempt at levity it passed almost unnoticed. James fell silent in the corner of the car and forced himself to look at the grey streets. Whenever he shut his eyes the ghastly sight of the girl's lacerated flesh seemed to be projected into his mind. He could not banish the image.

The doctor had been wrong. The tracery of cuts was not an indication of an Arab ritual murder. The sliced skin had fallen into a pattern which James had recognized instantly, a pattern which he had seen every day of his life; the Bourton coat of arms had been carved into the woman's body. For the next few months James was overpowered by the certainty that a vengeful destiny was pursuing him. The girl he had thoughtlessly abandoned seventeen years ago had transformed herself into a pitiless Nemesis. The deepest terror of his subconscious, the female destroyer seeking to consume him, had become flesh. His years of carefree, forgetful pleasure were at an end and the final reckoning was inescapable. James had no doubt at all that Ayeshah had procured the girl's murder, that she had tried to frame him and would then perhaps have offered to procure his liberty in exchange for her children. He had escaped her only by the good fortune of Eddie Shrewton's concern, but he was still in danger.

Two days after his return to England the French papers reported that the mutilated body of a prostitute had been found on waste ground on the outskirts of Paris. This was such a common occurrence that it merited only a few lines in *Le Monde*. The rumours began immediately, however, and they were accurate, specific and aimed at James. An English *milord* had been involved in the prostitute's murder; she had been killed at a debauched private party attended by a dozen prominent Englishmen at the end of the Longchamp weekend, and he had carved his armorial bearings on her body. Coming so soon after the Profumo scandal, the stories confirmed the long-established European conception of a degenerate British aristocracy, and the Continental newspapers took them up with enthusiasm.

Then a photograph appeared, a blurred but recognizable shot of a dishevelled James brandishing a thousand-franc note under the dancing girl's bare stomach. Clippings from the scandal-sheets began to arrive in the mail at James's office, and he ordered his secretary not to open his letters. He tried to telephone Eddie Shrewton, but could not get through; the secretary was embarrassed, but had clearly been told to block James's calls.

James lived every day on the edge of panic. His heart beat irregularly, shuddering in painful palpitations which left him breathless. He felt constantly cold and tired, but sweaty flushes would strike him without warning. He lost weight and his complexion grew waxy and bloated. He tried to drink to blot out his anxiety, but his tolerance for alcohol vanished and he began to black out whenever he drank to excess.

In November, two officers of the City Police Fraud Squad asked him for a meeting. Their manner was diffident and professionally neutral. They were pursuing investigations at the request of Interpol into an alleged violation of the Algerian exchange control regulations. James felt crushed by the heavy yoke of destiny.

Only his daughters had the ability to mitigate his distress and when he collected them from school at the end of the winter term it was with a wave of relief. The mere sight of them running eagerly towards him, their young faces full of pure emotion, their limbs innocently graceful, warmed his heart. He hugged them, wrapped in their heavy winter clothes, and felt restored. He soon noticed how in a few weeks they had both moved so much closer to womanhood. Monty already had a bosom of mature proportions, and Cathy's demure beauty had lost its girlishness. James told himself that even in loving his daughters he had lived in a fool's paradise; before long other men would take possession of them, leaving him bereft of love completely.

For Christmas he bought them each a string of pearls, perfect, creamy jewels as flawless as their clear young complexions. He wanted to give his girls jewellery now to be sure of being the first man to pay that tribute to their maturing femininity. A resigned, defeated peace replaced his earlier distress and he found emotional sanctuary in the family festival at Bourton, tainted as it was by his mother's dominating presence and the waspish coldness of his wife. Guilt, like a vampire, had sucked him dry of every emotion except love for his daughters.

In May the Fraud Squad visited him again, accompanied by a French detective. Now they had traced the bank account he had opened in a false name, and although James wearily denied any knowledge of it, or of the gold allegedly smuggled out of Algeria in the carpets he had imported, all four men knew that the case was proved and that a prosecution would follow in a few weeks.

He brought the girls to London at half-term, and heaped them with presents on the pretext that they needed summer clothes. 'Your father must love you very much,' the saleswoman at Fortnum and Mason remarked as she folded two slim evening purses of black patent leather in sheets of crackling tissue. 'There's not many men would take such an interest in what their daughters wear.'

'I suppose he does,' Cathy replied, wondering if she dared ask for some new shoes. She was used to people remarking on the rapport between her father and herself, but never understood why. Her father's love was like the air she breathed, invisible all around her. She would not appreciate how vital it was until she had to live without it.

He took them back to school, kissed them and said goodbye, resolving that it would be for the last time. His own life was ruined, but he could still save theirs. He could save them from his own selfish stupidity and from Ayeshah's mad desire to possess them.

He flew to Paris and met the Princess once more at her apartment. This time there was no delay before the double doors opened and she appeared. A cold, echoing calm, like the icy silence of the high Alps, had settled on James and he felt nothing as she approached him. He was at an emotional altitude above fear. Nothing could now distress him.

She wore a white Chanel suit trimmed with gold braid which, for the first time that James could recall, gave a slight impression of vulgarity to her appearance. Her eyes glittered under their heavy lids.

'You have delayed much too long,' she said to him at once. 'You should have come to me last year, then I could have done something. Now things have gone too far.'

'Yes, they have. You've finished me, you can congratulate yourself.'

The secrets which they shared were so grave that the atmosphere between them became almost intimate. Ayeshah was disconcerted; she had not expected this feeling of a bond with the man she hated. James, his sensibilities blunted by trauma, felt nothing.

'Last time I was here you invited me on a false pretext.' He had difficulty focusing his eyes and he looked at her as if he were not seeing her. 'Now 1 must apologize, because I am here under false pretences. I have nothing to discuss with you. I'm not asking you for anything. I have come only to tell you that you will never get the children. Never.'

'Are you going to keep me away from them when you are in jail?' Complacently, she crossed her legs and reached to the silver cigarette box on a side table.

'If you had any notion of love, you would have gone to them long ago. But I don't think you do.' He screwed up his eyes as if looking at a bright light, the deep wrinkles spreading across his face. '"Queen of Darkness" is the right name for you.

You don't understand love. You can go to your children, and you can stand before them as their mother, but they'll never love you. I've made sure of that.' With deliberate absence of chivalry, he allowed her to light her own cigarette.

'You're so confident, *Lord* James Bourton. You think you can make the world and everything in it exactly how you want it to be, as if you were God. You think that if you can't see me, I don't exist, and that if you can't understand me, I must be evil. And you think you can create your children exactly as you want them to be, as if they have no will, no characters of their own.' She stood up and walked to the mantelpiece, blowing cigarette smoke sharply upwards. 'In a sense you are right, of course. Whatever I am, that's what you made me. It's not I who have destroyed you. You've destroyed yourself.'

'You're still a peasant, aren't you? Nothing's your responsibility, nothing's your fault, you're just the innocent victim of it all.' Anger was slowly penetrating James's anaesthetized senses and he felt lightheaded with the force of the emotion. 'I didn't make you what you are. That was your choice. But I've made damn sure my daughters won't follow you. They'll be fine young women soon, and when they find out that you're their mother – if they find out – they'll have more contempt for you than I do.'

'I don't think so.' Ayeshah was suddenly anxious. This was not how she had envisaged the final encounter with the man who had stolen her children. She had wanted to see his ineffable pride devastated, to watch him wallow in humiliation, to hear him beg her to save him from ruin; this half-insane state of defiance was something she had not imagined, and his words hurt her. 'Anyway, how will you know? When I am together with my children, you will be in prison.'

'That's another thing you're wrong about,' he told her in a quiet voice. 'I'll be somewhere where you can't reach me, when you meet – if you're ever misguided enough to make yourself known to them. In a way I wish I could be there. You will lose them twice. I did you wrong in the beginning, I admit that. But you've betrayed yourself just as much as I betrayed you. That's what they won't accept.' She stared at him angrily, unable to find the words to reply. James stood up, paused for an instant because he felt dizzy, then walked to the door. 'I've said everything I have to say to you,' he said, authority at last returning to his voice. 'You've made too many mistakes. It's too late to win your daughters' love now. It was all for nothing, Princess. You'll realize that soon.'

He strolled back to the Ritz feeling physically weak but mentally euphoric. The account was square now. There would be a scandal, of course, but not a big one – his brother and Eddie Shrewton between them would see to that. And then his fight with Ayeshah would be taken up by Cathy and Monty, his beloved daughters, in whom he had perfect confidence.

CHAPTER TWENTY-NINE

ONTY TRIED not to sulk, but she felt as if Cathy had dragged her down
from a sublime emotional peak, and she was full of resentment. She was full
of passionate impatience for the solution to the mystery of her life, and could not
bear to be forced to wait. The idea of her real mother, a new and important force
in her life, filled her with deep joy and she was afraid that the delay, and the information which they were seeking, would somehow mar the perfect pleasure which
lay ahead of her. When they returned to London she was rough with Paloma, and
withdrew from Joe, who immediately flared into such uncharacteristic anger that
she was startled.

'I'm sorry,' she said, 'it's Cathy, she's the one who's upset me, not you. Let's do
something, get out of here. I can't stand being in her apartment when I feel like
this.' They took Paloma to the zoo, but it was windswept and bleak, the sight of the
confined animals depressed them both and Paloma screamed with terror when
one of the goats in the children's enclosure tried to nibble her sleeve. They left
and walked down to the rose garden in Regent's Park, where the last of the season's
blooms hung limply from their stems.

'Why are you angry?' he asked her quietly, drawing her to a wooden bench
where they sat down.

'I don't know. I feel that something's been snatched away from me, something
important. I think Cathy's being selfish. I hate her when she's being the almighty
older sister who's always right about everything. I suppose it's the world she works
in, but she's so dominating sometimes, her way has to be the only way . . .' Monty
was aware that she sounded weak. 'Oh, I don't know. What's the matter with me,
Joe? I did very well without a mother for so long. Why am I so attracted to this
woman I hardly know?'

'What is it that draws you to her?' Joe asked, putting his arm around her and
running his fingers through the pile of her spotted fur coat.

'I didn't like her when I met her as Madame Bernard,' Monty told him. 'I was
grateful, of course, but she made my blood freeze, she was so sinister. I didn't want
to meet her when I knew her as Princess Ayeshah. Cathy had to persuade me. You
know I hate those glittery, night-time people.'

He nodded, the gusting autumn wind blowing a strand of his long black hair across his face. 'I remember, you said you'd meet her for Cathy's sake but you wouldn't have crossed the street for her if anyone else had asked you.'

Monty laughed. 'Oh dear, did I really? But you're right, what's the difference now I know that she's my mother? Maybe I'm being romantic, idealizing her in my mind already?'

'What do you think?'

She knew he had once again talked her into seeing herself clearly, but just for once she wanted him to order her around. 'You're a man, you're supposed to tell me what I think,' she kidded him. 'Anyway, stop hiding behind being a guru as usual. What do *you* think?'

'I think you're a wicked, immoral woman.' His full lips curled in a smile and he ruffled her fur collar.

'Why?'

'What are you doing wearing a coat like this? Don't you know that the acrylic is a protected species?'

'Why, that's sentimental garbage, Mr Jones. The acrylic is a nasty, ratlike little animal, no better than vermin, and anyway, this one's ranched.' They laughed into the wind together and felt reunited.

'You know what?' Monty continued as they walked back through the light scattering of yellow early-autumn leaves on the pathway. 'She isn't real to me, even though I know her. I can't imagine my real mother, or her being my real mother. It's just too big for me to get my head around. But all the time, when I was a kid, I had this feeling that there was something missing in my life, like a lost piece of the puzzle. When I fell in love for the first time I felt complete, somehow, like I'd found the missing piece. Then when the love died, there was that great hole again.'

'I know. I used to feel that way, too.' Joe paused to fasten the studs on Paloma's pink, quilted babysuit. 'I never knew my mother, couldn't remember anything about her, and I used to think if only I could find her I'd be OK, like the other kids. Then one day I just decided that was dumb, I didn't want to be like the other kids . . .'

'. . . and they weren't the way you thought they were anyway,' Monty finished, as they walked on. 'I realized that when Cathy's marriage broke up and she wasn't my perfect sister any more, but just as weak as I was in her way. But now I've got that stupid feeling again, that maybe this time there *is* a missing piece after all and now I've finally found it. I just think my real mother is going to make everything I don't like about myself OK, but when I think about who she really is and what she really is . . . Oh, Joe, why is life so damn difficult?'

Cathy ordered the man who was investigating the European press coverage of her father's death to send whatever he had discovered to London immediately, and as an afterthought asked if he could get a copy of the marriage certificate of Prince Hussain Shahzdeh. The next day a courier delivered a bulky packet to her apartment, and she and Monty sat down at the round Georgian table, which was used for work more than entertaining and began to spread out the copies of long-forgotten newspaper articles. There had been no time to translate them, and as neither of them spoke German, Dutch or more than a few words of Italian they concentrated on the French stories.

Cathy's face was set as she read over and over again the accusation that her father had been found in bed with a dead call girl beside him. 'I don't believe it,' she said at once. 'It's a lie. Someone tried to frame him.'

'There's dozens of them, this must have gone on for months,' Monty said in a small voice, stunned by the lurid implications of the rumours.

'Now you see why I wanted to wait.' Cathy pulled a large sheet of paper towards her. It was folded in half. As she opened it she saw the smudged but unmistakable picture of her father waving money against a woman's half-naked body. She gasped, and Monty snatched the page from her and spread it out.

'Jesus.' She gulped with the shock of the image, violently repelled by it. Nevertheless, Monty forced herself to look, and to absorb every detail of her father's face. He looked drunk and dishevelled, and there was something so redolent of habitual corruption in the gesture of the outstretched arm that the picture branded Monty's mind. She suddenly connected her father with the men she had courted when she too had tried to sell herself, imagining him as another of those contemptible lechers whom she had despised so much.

Cathy's mind relentlessly imposed a pattern on the confusion of vile information in front of her. Somehow it all seemed so much more horrifying in French. The passionate, precise language, well-adapted for sexual innuendo, conjured up visions of debauchery far worse than the evidence of the poorly focused photograph.

She began to stack the reports in date order. 'You're right, there are too many of them,' she said to Monty. 'Look, here are two from the same rag, saying almost the same thing, within two weeks of each other. And there, the same thing again . . . and look, his name is the only one mentioned but there are half a dozen other men in this picture. This isn't genuine reporting, this is an orchestrated campaign.' She sat back from the table and made a tent out of her fingers while she thought, a pompous gesture which she usually tried to avoid. 'If you're right and she is also this Madame Bernard . . .'

'And I am right, Cathy.'

'I think you are. It makes sense, though it's horrible to think about. Then she must be mixed up in this somehow. I cannot, I just cannot, believe our father would kill someone like that.'

Monty was studying the photograph, trying to make out the other men's faces. 'Does he look familiar to you?' she pointed to the most distant figure, a blurred shape wearing spectacles.

'No. It could be anyone. Let's look through the other stories, see if there are any names.'

At last Monty found a whole page from a German magazine which contained, next to a story that the Queen was divorcing Prince Philip, a small update on the scandal with three names in addition to their father's. Two of them Cathy recognized, but knew that the men were dead. The third was 'Shroeton'.

'Shrewton?' Monty enquired. 'That's probably how they'd write it in German.'

'If it *is* him . . .' Cathy began, and then checked herself. 'Why am I pretending? It *is* him. As a matter of fact, I'm glad. It looks as if Lord Shrewton's almost the only man in my life who hasn't lied to me for years. Whatever the bottom line is, he'll give it to me, and he'll make it quick and clean.'

Cathy telephoned her former father-in-law and calmly pressed him into seeing them that afternoon in his office. He worked in the Migatto building only two days a week now, and was preparing to retire the following year.

'You remember my sister?' Monty, sleek in a wide-shouldered black jacket and tapered trousers, shook the old man's soft hand, and they sat on the hard Jacobean chairs beside his table.

'This must be very important,' he said, offering them drinks, which his secretary poured. When the woman had left the room, Cathy came directly to the point. 'This isn't going to be easy for you, but you've always paid me the compliment of being direct with me, and I hope you'll be able to do that now. Monty and I took a decision to investigate the circumstances surrounding our father's death. We became aware that because we were so young at the time we hadn't been told the whole truth.'

Lord Shrewton drew a breath of anticipation, and Cathy continued. 'We've discovered that there was a scandal involving him with the killing of a prostitute in Paris a few months before he died. I wondered if you knew anything about it?'

'You've a good idea that I do know something or you wouldn't be here.' He sipped pale malt whisky neat from a crystal tumbler. 'You've a right to the truth, now you've read all the lies. I was with your father right through the night that it happened. He was unconscious. He'd been drinking. We found the girl in his room the next morning. She'd been horribly cut up and strangled.' He paused, giving the two women time to take in what he was saying. Now completely white-haired, Lord Shrewton seemed as pale as death itself, but he was as incorruptible as a diamond and Cathy felt relief that she was at last getting a full account of her father's affairs.

'It was a set-up,' he announced, his voice crackling with outrage still, more than twenty years after the event. 'Someone wanted to blackmail him, and I stopped them. I got our embassy in and had the whole affair hushed up. For my own good as much as his, I have to admit. '

'I don't suppose you got on with him very well,' Cathy prompted.

'You have to get on with all sorts of people in business, but yes, you're right, your father wasn't my type. Not that I didn't have sympathy for him. Second son – that's a hard row to hoe. He'd done better than many of 'em.'

'If you hushed it up, where did these rumours come from?'

'From her, from the woman who was after him. The woman he used to find all these party girls for his private celebrations. At least, I presumed it was her and he thought it likely. Lord knows what he'd done to deserve it.'

'So you were never really certain who was behind it?' Monty asked, disappointed that there was still so much uncertainty.

'Not at the time, but later I found out because she tried to blackmail me as well. She telephoned me, but we never met. I told her to get lost. That's the only way to deal with these people.' Behind his spectacles, which were dusty and needed polishing, the astute old eyes flickered from one face to another. 'I don't suppose you think too much of your father now, eh? Natural, of course. It's not a pretty story, even though he was absolutely innocent.'

'But apart from the fact that it was the woman who sent him the girls, you never knew who she was?'

'Never gave a name, of course not. The only thing I remember that was distinctive was the funny nasal voice she had.'

'What did she want from him? Did you ever discover?' Cathy was fitting together the final pieces of the jigsaw.

'No, I didn't even enquire. Nothing to do with me, the less I knew the better. But he had other troubles as well, I think it was the combination that brought him down. Debts, as you know, and he was mixed up in an exchange control fraud of some kind. He was desperate, you see.'

'And what did she want from you?' Monty demanded, and Cathy turned towards her sister as she spoke, astonished that she had not thought to ask the question herself.

'Curious. Extraordinarily curious, considering the way things turned out. She said she didn't want two innocent girls to suffer for their father's wickedness, and wanted me to promise that I'd take care of you two if anything happened to him.'

'*What?*' the two women spoke in unison, amazement on their faces.

'Yes. Cathy, my dear, I hope you know me well enough to trust me in this. Of course, when my son brought you to our house barely a year later I was suspicious, highly suspicious, but I saw at once that you were as innocent as a newborn lamb and that Charlie was mad about you – and no one could order my son's affections, whatever was at stake. I don't have to tell you, you know it well enough I dare say.'

He slowly rose to his feet and walked around the table to take a chair close to her. 'I expect you'll go away now and feel that everything I've done for you I did because someone was twisting my arm. It's very important that you shouldn't think that. After that first attempt, this woman never got in touch with me again. I think she knew that she'd met her match. I was, as you know, disgusted with the way my son treated you, and after the divorce I was sorry for you and I felt it would be right to offer you a chance to rebuild the life he had destroyed. But after that, my dear, you were on your own. I gave you nothing but what you thoroughly deserved, you must believe me when I tell you that.'

Cathy nodded, feeling the prickling rush of tears again. She reached out and squeezed the pale hands which were spotted with the brown marks of age. 'And you are absolutely certain you don't know who this woman was, apart from having something to do with the girls? Did he ever give you a name?'

'The girls came through that organization – Madame Bernard. He talked about her as if she were one woman; she might have been a whole business. Everyone knew about her in those days.'

'And did you ever think all of this might possibly have had any connection with the Princess Ayeshah?'

He gave her a quick, hard look of enquiry, then shook his head. 'The Princess? No. Never occurred to me. She knows all sorts, the Princess, no doubt some of them not very savoury people, but I never had any reason to believe she was mixed up in this business. Her husband started doing business with me two or three years later, and . . .' he paused, searching for words.

'And what?' Cathy urged, tingling with anticipation. Now she could see everything clearly, and her way ahead was open.

'It always puzzled me, our association. He'd have been far better off with some of the other merchant banks. We weren't really in his line, I was surprised when he approached us. But it was a happy business relationship, as long as it lasted.'

'One last question.' Cathy remembered that she had two fingers of whisky waiting to be drunk, and drained half of it in one gulp, thankful for the fiery spirit's warmth in her throat which was dry and tight with tension. 'You hushed up this affair at the time . . .'

'I was about to become chairman here, last thing I needed . . .'

'Of course. But now, if I tried to revive the investigation, how would you feel?'

'Are you thinking of doing that?'

'We haven't discussed it together.' Cathy looked at Monty, who stared back at her with unmistakable anger in her black eyes.

'You'd be taking a perfectly right and proper course if you did,' he rapped with something like his old severity. 'I can't say I'd welcome it, raking over old coals, but I'd support you, give whatever evidence was necessary. Ambassador's dead now, so are most of the other fellahs. To some extent I suppose it's been on my conscience.'

They thanked him and left, walking back to the Barbican in a stunned silence. The apartment was quiet and empty, because Joe had taken Paloma out. They sat at opposite ends of the square black leather sofa.

'I can see why you like him – he's a fine man,' Monty said at last, running her hands through her short hair.

'There aren't enough like him,' Cathy replied, easing her shoulders out of the jacket of her dark red suit. It was tightly fitted, in the new season's style, with a long, narrow skirt that flared below her knees. She kicked off her plain, black leather pumps and smoothed her stockings, black with a scattering of tiny dots, over her tired feet. 'Do you realize what it all means, Monty?'

'She must have been trying to get us back somehow.' Monty propped her head in her hand and looked at her sister. Cathy was very white, but her characteristic serenity had returned and, with her perpetually smiling mouth, she looked almost contented.

'Was she? Or was she simply trying to blackmail him for her own reasons?'

Monty shook her head emphatically. 'What reasons? Hussain must have been loaded, even in those days. She can't have needed money.'

'I'd guess Hussain's business was still semi-covert in those days, maybe she was trying to get Daddy's support for one of his deals . . .' While she was speaking, thinking aloud, Cathy regretfully admitted that her father's support in business would scarcely have been worth such an effort. 'No, it can't have been blackmail, you're right. But if she had wanted us, wanted to see us or meet us, she could have done that at any time. She could have just driven to the ferry and been on our doorstep in a few hours, if that was all she wanted.'

'Maybe she was afraid. She was nothing when he left her, don't forget. OK, she'd come a long way from that village, but she must have felt intimidated by the power and the money all around him.' Monty gave a short, bitter laugh. 'She wasn't to know our father was broke.'

'Wasn't she? My guess is she had a damn good idea. She was trying to finish him. She wanted to kill him, she just didn't have the nerve to do it herself. Do you know why I think he killed himself?'

'Poor Daddy, he must have been so miserable. He knew he was going to hit the bottom. He had to lose us or lose everything else. No one can make a choice like that.'

'Uh-huh.' Cathy shook her head with maddening certainty. 'That wasn't it. He'd have found something to enjoy in being poor, you know. His friends would have rallied round and paid his debts, people always do in that situation. A scandal wouldn't have killed him, he'd almost have enjoyed it for the grief it would have caused Didi and our . . . and Bettina. No, he didn't just give up hope, despair and die. You remember Treadwell called him a survivor – he should have known if anyone did. I think Treadwell did know.'

'Know what?' Irritably, Monty crossed her legs, pinching the creases in her trousers to have an excuse not to look at Cathy. She was beginning to feel very angry with her sister.

'He killed himself for our sake.' Cathy reached across and took Monty's hand, which held hers with distinct reserve. 'He wanted to make absolutely sure that that woman would never have any claim to us. He wanted to make sure that we'd hate her, that even if she tried to deceive us we'd be able to find out, put two and two together, and realize what she was. She's pure evil, Monty.'

'You can't say that, she's our mother. Look what he did to her, look what they all did to her. What chance did she have? Wouldn't you have hated any man who did that to you?'

'Would you make those excuses for yourself? We've had some bad breaks, too. They took Jamie away from me, you were nearly put on the game yourself – and by Madame Bernard. How many other girls do you think she trapped that way, sending them down to St Laurent to run up a bill they couldn't pay? And you didn't have to pull your life around, she only gave you the opportunity, it was your strength, your motivation. We've both suffered but we made different choices.'

'But she did save me, Cathy, and you too, when you'd just started and you needed money. She was there when we needed her, she was trying to be a mother to us.'

Cathy released Monty's hand. She felt absolutely calm, as if she were high above the world looking down on the meaningless affairs of people below her. 'No she wasn't. She was trying to buy us, trying to buy our love.'

'You're very hard,' Monty told her. 'Harder than she was. Can't you find any sympathy for her?'

Cathy shook her head. 'Hard yes, cruel no. Monty, she's killed people, she killed that girl, she had her cut up, sliced like salami and put in bed next to our father. She's probably killed dozens of other people. She's a criminal, a psychopath. She's played with us for years, deceived us, lied to us, spied on us, manipulated us, tried to draw us into her web, make us grateful, force our love – can't you see that? Sympathy? No, I haven't any sympathy. She's a monster, and that's what she's made herself.'

Monty gave her sister a stony look. 'You just don't like to admit that you might owe her a few things – like the great success that you're so proud of. Suddenly there's a possibility that you had a little help with your life and you can't take it.' Swept by a wave of anger, Monty jumped up and stood over her sister. 'Why don't you examine your own motives before you start judging other people? You're still in love with Daddy, you won't blame him for anything. Instead you're trying to blame her.'

'Why are you always so stupid and emotional? It's all there, Monty, as plain as the nose on your face. You're the one who can't face the truth, not me!'

Like a brushfire after a drought, fury set their exhausted emotions blazing. Suddenly they were arguing, shouting at each other as they had never done in their lives before, saying things that they knew were untrue only in order to wound.

'You're just a frigid, dominating bitch, Cathy! All you care about is money and power, so you can't understand anyone who doesn't think the same way. You're wrong, you're wrong. Why can't you accept it?'

'Don't scream at me as if I was one of your bloody entourage. You're on a total ego-trip, you've been on it for years, you want everyone to obey you instantly, believe whatever you believe, do whatever you say. Well, I'm your sister, I'm the one you can't fool. Don't forget that! You'll never be a big star to me, just a snivelling brat who's always in trouble.'

The terrible tension of the past few weeks was breaking at last and rage swept through them, destroying everything in its path. Like children they were terrified by the power of their own anger, but unable to stop.

'You can't handle this because it's about fucking, and that's something you don't like because in that area you're a total *failure*,' Monty snarled. 'But fucking was all there was between our mother and father; and she made her fortune from it and he died because of it. What's the matter, Cathy – can't you face the facts of life?'

Cathy jumped up, shoving her sister furiously away from her. 'What facts can't I handle? I'm pretty damn clear on the fact that that woman killed our father.'

'Yes, but she's our mother too, don't forget, our own flesh and blood. Whatever she is, she's part of us, flesh of our flesh. Now I think about it you look quite like her . . .' There was a sharp crack as Cathy hit Monty full in the face, then hit her again, grabbing her by the lapel of her jacket to stop her moving away. Monty seized Cathy's wrists and wrenched them furiously. 'You don't want to know – you can't take it, can you? You want to be little Miss Perfect, all your life as tidy as your school cupboard, no dirt in any of the corners? We came from dirt, we were born in it, our whole lives are down to nothing but the worst things two people could ever do to each other . . .'

Viciously Monty pulled Cathy's hair and Cathy struck out again. The two of them were standing face to face, flushed scarlet with anger and trembling with the force of the emotion, when there was a rattle of keys and the noise of the front door opening at the lowest level of the duplex, announcing Joe's return. Suddenly Cathy's face crumpled in tears and she collapsed in a miserable heap on the floor. Monty, at once full of horror at her sister's pain, flew downstairs to ask Joe to leave them alone for a while, and ran back to Cathy, quivering with remorse.

'I'm sorry, I'm sorry, darling Cathy,' she murmured, her arms around the heaving shoulders, feeling their warmth through the thin, grey satin blouse. 'I didn't mean it, any of it, I didn't mean to be so cruel.'

'No, no, Monty, you're right really. So am I. Neither of us can bear it, now we know the truth.' A suppressed sob tore her throat, and Cathy cried until her face ached, but still more tears came and she could not stop them. She cried for the tragedy of both their parents' lives, for the pain of her father's loss which she suppressed every day, and most of all for the fear of losing Monty, who held her until at last the storm of weeping was ended.

They were silent for a long while, then at last Monty said, 'I didn't mean it. I can't handle this either. It's too much.'

'We can do anything if we do it together.' Cathy wiped her wet cheeks with her sleeves, oblivious of the marks on the silk.

'Did you mean that about reopening the inquest?' Monty helped her to get up.

'I don't know, I can't decide. Yes, she ought to be charged with murder, for killing that girl if not for killing our father. But that's not why I want to call in the police. I want revenge for what she did to Daddy, just like she wanted revenge for what he did to her. And I don't want revenge for Daddy's sake, either, I can't pretend that. I want it for me, because I can't believe in him any more as my wonderful, adorable father. I'm no better than she is, am I? And I'm frightened, I just want to stop her, Monty. I'm so scared that she'll destroy our lives like she did his – she's so full of hate.'

'What do we do – call Scotland Yard?'

'I couldn't do it, Monty, could you?'

'No. I couldn't turn her in, she's our mother, whatever else she might be. And we can't be absolutely certain, either. We're guessing, that's all. We need to be sure.'

'Lord Shrewton's the only one who's acted decently, I'd like to have his advice,' Cathy decided at last. As she had anticipated, her former father-in-law declined to take any decisions for them but calmly suggested that they first assemble all the evidence against the Princess and take the advice of lawyers before proceeding any further.

At Pasterns Mr Napier, now a portly, balding man with a red face and pin-striped trousers, tried to talk them out of taking any official action. 'It'll be a beastly affair, a stain on your own children's lives . . .'

'No, it won't,' Monty told him with irritation. 'Our children's lives are their own to create as they choose. They'll be responsible for what they are, just as we are.'

'What about the stains on our lives, Mr Napier?' Cathy asked in her most reasonable voice. 'It wasn't very pleasant, coming out as the daughter of the Suicide

Peer, hearing everybody whispering every time I came into a room. I loved my father, Mr Napier, and this woman took him away from me just when I needed him most. I can't put that right, I can't turn the clock back and have my life over again.' Until she spoke those painful words, Cathy had never admitted, even to herself, how painful it had been to face publicly the scandal of her father's death. She had been brave, and thought only of making good his loss by marrying gloriously. Now at last she acknowledged the pain she had felt.

'You certainly have an immense volume of evidence here, but the final connection between the murder, this Madame person – if she exists – and the Princess is not, in my opinion, proved at all. Without an admission from her you would really have no case,' he announced with finality, dismissing the stack of grey document boxes which contained sworn statements by Bill Treadwell in Penang, Lord Shrewton, and the sisters themselves, as well as reports from the two investigators they had briefed. Feeling almost superstitiously afraid, Cathy had copied the entire file and lodged a duplicate volume in a bank vault.

Mr Napier's condescending professional superiority had the effect of making both Cathy and Monty more positively determined to bring their mother to justice.

'He's being cautious, that's a lawyer's job,' Lord Shrewton observed. 'And he's right, you'll need concrete evidence if you're hoping to reopen the inquest and then proceed to a prosecution. I think we should hear what the police have to say, don't you?'

The City Police are a species which considers itself separate from the drab run of average British officers of the law. Their responsibility is restricted to London's ancient heart, the square mile and three-quarters which is now the city's business district, and the crimes which concern them are almost exclusively minor parking offences and major frauds. This latter category attracts officers of far keener intelligence than most branches of police work, and requires them to maintain close and friendly relations with the people who control the nation's wealth.

In consequence, Chief Inspector Kitchener was more like a business associate of Lord Shrewton than a police detective, and when the sisters agreed to consult him they were reassured by his relaxed, practical manner. He was a small, wiry man with keen blue eyes who listened to them courteously and said at length, 'You're right to approach this cautiously. I can understand that you're in two minds about the whole business, it must have been quite a lot to take in.' Cathy and Monty nodded at once, grateful for his sympathy.

'She's not unknown to us, the Madame figure – that side of her operations at least. We've investigated two or three other cases, similar in that there was an intention to blackmail. She's a very dangerous woman. We can pursue this with our colleagues in the Sûreté in Paris, but I've little doubt that she has very highly placed contacts and probably we won't get very far. It'll be much more satisfactory if we can handle this in London. Do you think there's any chance we can get her to come here? If we do that, and if our suspicions are correct, I can hold her on a passport offence while we make our own investigations. From the documents you've got here, it's clear that she didn't produce her own birth certificate when she was married, or when she applied for her passport either. With her out of the way here, we'll be able to proceed more easily.'

'I can invite her over on a business matter. She won't be able to resist, I suspect.' Cathy felt a thrill of apprehension. She knew that the Princess must have been suspicious of their sudden departure from L'Equipe Creole, so soon after her first official meeting with Monty. But she had no reason to fear a meeting with her daughters, particularly if it were possible that they had at last discovered that she was their mother.

They arranged the meeting exactly as Cathy always fixed meetings with her most important clients. Her secretary telephoned the Princess's secretary and asked for the earliest possible date on which the Princess could come to London on an urgent matter. The reply came within half an hour, and the Princess arranged to come two days later and asked for a car to meet her private plane at Lydd Airport and bring her to London.

'Don't go,' Hussain advised her at once. 'Ayeshah, think. We know they know almost everything now. You've had them followed out to Penang, you know they've seen Treadwell, they found the scent of the Nadine affair, followed that up. The older one at least is a very intelligent woman, and she has a high moral character, I think. They know who you are, what you are, to them as well as what you are in yourself. This meeting can't bring you any good.'

'The younger one is different – warmer, more emotional. She may have persuaded her sister, who knows? She can't wish me any harm. Don't forget I know a few things about her.' Ayeshah was perfectly composed, although her elation was so strong that he saw her hands were trembling. Nothing, he realized, would stop her pursuing this final victory; she would not be checked even by the knowledge of almost certain danger to herself.

Hussain shook his greying head with exasperation. A hundred times in the past two decades he had wished that the tie which bound him to his wife could be severed, but now that he sensed the possibility that she might be in danger he found the loneliness of life without her impossible to contemplate.

'For the last time, I implore you, Ayeshah, don't go. It's a trap.'

She laughed, a bitter, joyless sound which grated on his heart. 'They couldn't trap me, Hussain. How, what could they do? Nothing without blackening their own names, and that of their father, and giving their own children a scandal to live down the rest of their lives.'

'Maybe they are brave enough to do that.'

'Brave! Don't talk like a child. Stupid is what it would be and you say yourself they're not stupid. You will see that I'm right. I shall have my girls at last. They are my children, they love me.'

'I'll give you full security cover,' Inspector Kitchener told the sisters.

'Is that really necessary?' Monty demanded. 'She's only one tiny woman, after all.'

'There's no way of knowing what kind of back-up she'll arrange for herself and I'm taking no chances,' he replied.

'We're in your hands, of course,' Cathy reassured him. 'But could I ask just one thing? If things should turn out as badly as we suspect they may, and she is involved in the murder, and you decide to arrest her . . . I'd rather it wasn't done in my office.'

'Certainly, certainly.' The Inspector shuffled his feet, for the first time embarrassed by the emotional dilemma in which the two women were caught.

The police planned the operation carefully, and as the golden Rolls Royce which met the Princess left the tiny airfield and began its journey to London across the flat grey expanse of Romney Marsh, an anonymous blue Ford fell into the line of traffic a few cars behind it. As the road meandered northwards the two cars followed the same route, the Ford maintaining a discreet distance between them.

In an hour the vehicles were proceeding slowly through the grimy wasteland of the city's south-eastern fringes. Their progress was halting, from one queue of traffic to the next, until they crossed the Thames at Westminster and quit the main flow of traffic to speed along Horseguards Parade. It was a keen, cold morning a few days before Christmas and London was packed with shoppers. The streets were jammed with slow-moving traffic, and in Regent Street and Oxford Street the illuminated decorations were reflected in the plate-glass windows of the busy stores. In St James's Park the trees raised leafless branches to the gunmetal sky, and office workers walked hurriedly to lunchtime destinations, their arms folded over their coats for warmth.

Cathy stood by the window in her office, looking down at the traffic-clogged street below. She felt fearful, a sensation to which she was not accustomed. Apprehension was like a pain under her ribs, burning intensely and spreading out through her limbs. The more she tried to suppress her fear, the stronger it grew.

'Are you scared?' Monty asked, from her perch on the edge of Cathy's marble-topped table. She was dressed unusually smartly, with a crisp, white pique shirt under her black suit and a small diamond brooch at the collar.

'Yes. I'm terrified of her, isn't it strange? I know that I've got the right to do this, that this is what we ought to do, but I can't get rid of the feeling that it's wrong too.'

'I'm scared too, scared that when I see her I won't be able to go through with it. How can we do this to our own mother?'

'By thinking of what she's done to us, to our father, and to heaven knows how many other people.' Resolutely, Cathy turned away from the window, the skirt of her dark grey suit swinging with each decisive step. 'I've seen the car at the end of the street – she'll be here in a minute.' The golden Rolls Royce at last crawled to the kerb outside the building's entrance below, and the doorman went to open the door.

Rapidly, Cathy crossed the room and pressed a button on the console of a black telephone in the conversation area of her office. 'Can you hear OK?' she asked.

From the next room she heard Lord Shrewton's voice, un-emotional as ever. 'Loud and clear,' he reassured her.

'Have you seen her yet?' asked Joe's rich American voice.

'Outside right now. I'm leaving the phone switched through now, you'll hear everything.' Cathy had removed the tiny lightbulb in the console which indicated that the microphone was activated, and when she replaced the receiver, the telephone looked as if it were not in use.

Monty was at the window. In the street below the small figure of the Princess, moving with its characteristic reptilian quickness and half-buried in a close-fitting pale mink coat, stepped out of the car.

A few minutes later the Princess Ayeshah was standing in front of them, the force of her personality filling the room. She was plainly in the grip of high emotion which was held in check by her uncertainty. She did not know what to expect, and was unable to take control of the situation. Cathy at once seized the initiative. Cool out, she told herself, make it normal, get this crazy situation mastered before it explodes in our faces.

'Good morning, Princess, I hope you had a pleasant journey?' Cathy herself took the blond mink coat and handed it to her secretary. In a severe, white gaberdine dress which tapered from wide shoulders to a narrow skirt, the Princess relaxed a little, and greeted Cathy with dry kisses on both cheeks, exclaiming at the pleasure of meeting Monty again.

They sat at the end of Cathy's office, around a low, black lacquer table on which the telephone stood behind a small, sweet-scented gardenia bush, a large black ashtray and copies of the *Financial Times* and the *Wall Street Journal*. The Princess at once lit a cigarette which Cathy took as an encouraging sign of her nervousness.

'I must apologize,' she said pleasantly. 'I've nothing to discuss with you in the way of business. This is a personal affair, that's why we're both here. I'm sure you can guess what it's about.'

The Princess's tense mask of a face at once blossomed into a smile and she put down the cigarette. 'You know who I am.' She looked at the two sisters and tried, as she had tried many times before when one or other of them was with her, not knowing of their relationship, to feel love. Nothing happened. She felt nothing at all.

'We think that you are our mother, our real mother,' Monty took up the conversation, ignoring the Princess's stare and the peculiar flat quality of her eyes. They should have been alive with animation, which was what the rest of her tense, mobile body suggested, but they seemed to be opaque, with no light in them. 'We know that we are the children of a woman my father married in Malaya during the war, whose name was Khatijah binti Ahmad, and we think that you are the same person.' Monty, too, searched her heart for emotion but found none.

'Yes, I am Khatijah. I am your mother. You have found me at last.' The words sounded very large now that they had finally been spoken. Monty was suddenly frightened that the older woman was going to embrace her, and she pulled back. The three women looked at each other as if surprised by their own frankness.

'You found us a long time ago, didn't you? Why didn't you ever tell us you were our mother?' Cathy tried to keep the telltale note of concern from her voice. She was touched by the sight of the Princess in a way which she had not anticipated. The spectacle of Ayeshah's glacial serenity crumbling under the force of her emotions stirred a sense of recognition in her elder daughter.

'I was afraid you would laugh at me, or turn away from me. You were already quite old by the time I came to Europe, you know. Tell me honestly, if a strange half-oriental woman had come to you when you were twelve years old and said she was your mother, what do you think you would have done?'

She's trying to play on my prejudices, Cathy realized with a sudden shudder of contempt. As her mother talked, she analysed her features, trying to find herself in the heart-shaped, olive-skinned face and the perfectly painted bow of the mouth. She looked across to Monty, and saw more likeness there, in the straight, broad, catlike nose and the sensual modelling of the face. But, Cathy saw as she crossed her knees under the pleated grey skirt, she herself had her mother's legs.

'I don't suppose we would have believed you.' Monty smiled.

'Even up to now I was never certain that you would want me. That's why I sent you the pearls. I know how clever you are,' she smiled at Cathy, 'and I knew you would soon find me, and put the whole story together. Then it was up to you, what you wanted to do. But then your father would have done everything he could to prevent it,' she continued, blowing cigarette smoke fiercely from her pursed lips.

'Did he ever try?' asked Cathy in the supremely disinterested tone she employed for extracting vital information.

'He told me you would never accept me, that you were proper little English ladies and that I was everything you had been taught to despise.' The bitter emotion behind her words was unmistakable, but Cathy, with a poignant vision of her father in her mind, was not moved. She led her mother onwards, probing deeper and deeper into her heart.

By instinct, Monty moved the conversation to the subject of Bettina and confided her own feelings of alienation from the woman she had believed was her mother.

'How I hated that woman,' Ayeshah almost spat. 'I used to dream that I would cut off her hands for daring to touch my children. Can you imagine how I wanted to touch you both, all those years?'

'She didn't like us at all, she almost never touched us,' Monty remembered sadly. Now, as she said the words, the feelings no longer seemed important. 'I don't think our father even noticed us very much until we were old enough to answer him back.'

'Such a waste, such a waste of love.' Ayeshah looked down, feeling she should weep, but she had no tears.

Cathy forced herself to pursue the conversation's predetermined course. 'When did you contact him after you had made your way to Europe?'

'In 1959. I remember it as if it were yesterday. His face – you could not imagine the expression. He thought he had left me in the mud of the *padi* field, that he was completely safe, that a little peasant woman could never, ever, follow him across the world to take her revenge.'

'I can imagine he would have been surprised. But what did you ask him for?'

'Why, for you, of course. I wanted you with me, I wanted us to be together, I wanted at least for you to know me as your mother.'

Monty felt as if she were taking part in a dream. Now that her real mother was in front of her the fear that some overpowering, natural emotion would overwhelm her seemed ridiculous. With the insight acquired in exploring her own weaknesses, Monty recognized the sly justifications, the maze of self-deceptions, the elaborate tapestry of lies which the Princess had woven in order to rationalize her own impulse towards evil. She saw her mother as nothing but a weak, wicked woman who had taken the easy route through life at the expense of her own character.

'Tell me,' the Princess continued, 'didn't you always know in some part of you that you were different?'

'Oh yes,' Monty agreed, grateful for an opportunity to disguise her growing contempt. 'I used to think I was a changeling, you know, a fairy child who'd been exchanged in the cradle.'

'What did our father say when you asked for us?' Cathy was anxious that the conversation should not wander. Now she did not want to find anything more to pity in the Princess. She wanted this traumatic meeting over with as soon as possible.

'He laughed. He threatened me, and then he began to pretend I did not exist. He always did that. When we were married he would start to think about his war, the fighting he imagined would come, and then he would not even know I was with him. He did the same thing. He thought about you, about his life, his business, his money, his social position – pfft! I disappeared, he made me vanish, just like smoke.' She ground out her cigarette with unmistakable anger, leaving the butt, stained with cyclamen-pink lipstick, crushed almost flat in the ashtray.

'You must have been very angry?' Monty prompted.

'I have never been so angry in my life, never. Not even in the beginning. You,' she pointed at Monty with a stabbing gesture, 'you were a tiny baby, just a few months old, and you were taken right out of my arms, but even then I was not as angry as I was when I saw he was denying everything to himself.'

'So what did you do?'

'What I had to do. It was so easy. Men are so weak, aren't they? They can never resist . . .' She looked from one face to another and Cathy tried hard to forget that this contemptuous opinion was being expressed of her father. She smiled with all the warmth she could summon at the Princess.

'So that story about the call girl who was found dead in bed . . .'

'He walked right into the whole thing. He had those tastes you know, your father. He always liked those exotic girls. He might just as well have hanged himself with his own hands. And then of course the shame of it was more than he could bear. That was something he could not deny, he could not hide from.'

Both sisters suddenly sat back, instinctively repelled by Aye-shah's suggestion. 'You mean our father really killed that woman?' Cathy, too, could see that the Princess was a woman who found it easy to believe her own lies.

The Princess hesitated, suddenly aware of the snare which James had laid for her. She heard his voice, harsh and accusing, echoing in her head, telling her that she was everything her daughters despised, that they would never accept her. Now that they were beside her, she saw that it was true. She felt disoriented, confused and panic-stricken, like a cornered animal. The trap was so intricate, so precise, so carefully framed, so inescapable that she could admire its workmanship even as she twisted within it. She had walked into it because it was constructed of love and loyalty, feelings which she no longer had and could no longer recognize. The camouflage had deceived her perfectly.

Cathy and Monty both saw the Princess falter and willed themselves to stay calm and not alarm her on the brink of confession.

'Did he really kill her?' Monty asked the question again as softly as she could.

Ayeshah saw with terrifying clarity that the whole of her life was at the point of implosion. Within a few seconds everything would fall in on itself in a useless, ugly mass, like an overripe fruit which has been eaten from within by insects. She felt powerless to stop the inevitable collapse. If she lied to her daughters, these two women who were judging her implacably by their own standards, the deceit would bar them from her, would block their relationship at once; if she told them the truth, they might reject her. Suddenly she bowed her head and her shoulders slumped. It would be best to risk the truth, after all, she decided.

'No. No, he didn't kill her; she was dead when she was put there. They told me he was so drunk he would not have woken up if the Ritz had burned down around him.' She looked up, making her final appeal. 'But you realize that I did it for you? Everything I've done, I did for you. I wanted you so much . . .'

'You did it all for yourself. You didn't want us, you wanted revenge.' Cathy stood up, feeling icy calm in place of fear like a cold chasm around her heart.

'You don't understand,' Ayeshah countered quickly, her voice weak.

'We do understand.' Monty stood up, suddenly hating this woman for being so much less than the perfectly fulfilling mother figure of her fantasies. 'You hated our father more than you loved us – if you ever loved us.'

'How can you say that to me? I am your mother, your mother! I've suffered for you all these years, hoping and wishing for the day when you will finally come to find me . . . and now . . .' She looked in disbelief at the two women.

'It's no good,' Monty told her, wishing she could summon the strength to be gentle as she heard herself speak harshly. 'We can't – well, I can't – accept you as my mother. I don't want to.'

The Princess's eyes at last flashed with animation. 'Don't you think you owe me something, then? Think of what I did for you. Think of what you might have become if I hadn't done what any mother would have done, and helped you when you were in trouble.'

'You saved me from destroying myself and I'll always owe you for that,' Monty answered, looking down at the small, white figure without emotion. 'But don't you remember what you told me then – that you can't buy love? That's what you're trying to do. And you're doing it because you want the final victory over our father. Even though you've killed him you still want to kill the love for him that we have in our hearts, too. You can't do it.'

'I did not kill him. He killed himself because he was a pathetic, stupid man and he knew he had to pay for his cruelty to me . . .' Ayeshah stopped, realizing that she was condemning herself further out of her own mouth. She stood up, a pitifully small figure in the room of large, solid furniture. 'You are upset, both of you. The discoveries you have made must have unsettled you terribly. I will leave you now and you can think about what we have said. Then, perhaps, we can meet again and talk more calmly.'

Cathy at once reached for the telephone and called her secretary, asking for the Princess's coat. 'She's leaving now, it's all finished,' she said, feeling tired.

At the window, Monty saw that the street below was cordoned off with the white tape which the police use to close streets during dangerous operations. In a side road waited a police transporter with a dozen uniformed officers waiting outside it, one of them listening to his radio. It seemed an unnecessary army to capture one little woman.

The Princess lifted her face to be kissed, and they both obediently pressed their lips to her smooth cheeks. Monty saw she had left a smudge of her rose-pink lipstick behind, and wiped it off with her fingertips, a gesture that should have been tender but was not.

After she had gone Cathy and Monty fell into each others arms, shaking with relief.

'Do you want to watch?' Monty asked, gesturing to the window.

'No.' Cathy shook her head. 'I know we've done the right thing but I don't want to see the police take her.'

Monty pulled herself away and looked at Cathy, searching her bronze-brown eyes for recognition and finding it at once. 'All that time, when I was growing up, thinking I wanted another mother –' she smiled bitterly, 'if only I'd known.'

The next day Cathy returned to her office as usual, feeling strangely fresh and young. The great weight of fear which had oppressed her for months had lifted and she felt so lighthearted that it seemed as if she could bounce.

'How do you feel?' Henry Rose enquired anxiously, suspicious of her ability to cover up her emotions.

'Fine, Henry, honestly, I feel terrific,' she replied.

'Heinz Feuer's flying in today. He wants to talk about our advice that he's holding too much gold, but I can easily see him for you . . .'

'Heinz Feuer doesn't want to talk about our advice, he's quite bright enough to know he's holding too much gold without us telling him. He's come to see me, Henry, and that's who he will see.' The idea of an evening with the humorous young Swiss seemed suddenly appealing. He had grown up a lot in the ten years she had known him. He was younger than she was, of course, but that was part of his charm. 'I like Heinz Feuer, he makes me laugh, Henry.'

'But don't you want me to . .'

'To make sure he knows that business is business and everything else is off limits? No, Henry. Not tonight. You may go home early, if you like.' Now more than ever, Cathy could not stop herself smiling. Suddenly she felt ready to accept Heinz Feuer's romantic admiration. She wondered why she had resisted it for so long.

Monty and Joe sent Paloma out with her nurse that morning, and went back to bed to make love. Afterwards, Monty was very quiet. Joe stroked her hair, twisting the fleecy dark curls around his strong fingers.

'How do you feel?' he asked her, kissing her olive-skinned shoulder.

'Weird. I can't work it all out in my mind, Joe. I knew she was my mother, but I couldn't feel anything. She was just another person to me. It makes me feel – I don't know – kind of serious.'

'You're entitled to that, don't you think? Yesterday was a hell of a day for you.'

'Joe?'

'Yes?'

'I'd like us to get married.'

'Why?'

'For the reason people climb a mountain – because it's there.'

'OK,' he said at once, 'I'll buy that.'

29741404R00302

F Volume 7

The World Book Encyclopedia

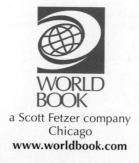

WORLD
BOOK

a Scott Fetzer company
Chicago
www.worldbook.com

The World Book Encyclopedia

For information on other World Book publications, visit our website at **www.worldbook.com** or call **1-800-WORLDBK (967-5325)**. For information about sales to schools and libraries, call **1-800-975-3250 (United States); 1-800-837-5365 (Canada).**

World Book, Inc.
233 North Michigan Avenue
Chicago, IL 60601
U.S.A.

Beyond the Page
Use your smartphone or tablet to scan this QR code and see a chronology of events, activities, and other special material prepared by World Book editors. (You will need to download a QR code reader to your device if you have not already done so.) If you do not have a mobile device, simply type this URL into your browser: http://www.worldbook.com/current

About the SPINESCAPE®

The SPINESCAPE design for the 2014 edition—*Vibrant World of Facts*—represents, through the image of layers of colorful fabric, the beauty of discovery of the rich tapestry that is the world of knowledge. An important part of learning is the recognition that individual facts acquire relevance and meaning when they are understood to be part of a larger whole. *The World Book Encyclopedia,* as a comprehensive, general reference work, presents and places in context information that spans all areas of knowledge, enabling users to explore a broad spectrum of facts and uncover the nature of their relationships.

Photo credit:
© SIME/eStock Photo; © Bruno Morandi, Hemis/Corbis Images; © Bruno Morandi, Getty Images

Library of Congress Cataloging-in-Publication Data

The World Book encyclopedia.
   volumes cm
   Includes index.
   Summary: "A 22-volume, highly illustrated, A-Z general encyclopedia for all ages, featuring sections on how to use World Book, other research aids, pronunciation key, a student guide to better writing, speaking, and research skills, and comprehensive index"--Provided by publisher.
   ISBN 978-0-7166-0114-2
   1. Encyclopedias and dictionaries. I. World Book, Inc.
AE5.W55 2014
030--dc23

2013023368

Printed in the United States of America by RR Donnelley, Willard, Ohio
1st printing November 2013

SUSTAINABLE FORESTRY INITIATIVE
Certified Chain of Custody
At Least 20% Certified Forest Content

www.sfiprogram.org
SFI-01042

Logo applies to text stock

Ff

F is the sixth letter of the alphabet used for the modern English language. It is also used in a number of other languages, including French, German, and Spanish. The sound of the letter *F* occurs in such words as *free, soft, half, coffee,* and *off.* The word *of* is the only instance in English in which *F* is pronounced like *V.*

Scholars believe the letter *F* evolved from an Egyptian *hieroglyph* (pictorial symbol) that represented a mace, a club with a heavy head. By around 1500 B.C., hieroglyphs had been adapted into an alphabet—the earliest known alphabet—known as Proto-Sinaitic. By 1100 B.C., an alphabet for the Phoenician language had evolved from Proto-Sinaitic. See **Semitic languages.**

The Phoenician letter that can be traced to the Egyptian mace hieroglyph is the sixth letter of the Phoenician alphabet, *waw.* The Phoenicians used the letter to repre-

sent the beginning *W* sound of *waw,* their word for *peg.*

Around 800 B.C., when the Greeks adapted the Phoenician alphabet, the letter *waw* evolved into two new letters, *digamma* and *upsilon. Digamma* resembled a modern capital *F,* and the ancient Greeks used it for the *W* sound. By around 400 B.C., *digamma* had dropped out of the alphabet used for classical Greek texts. But by then, *digamma* had passed to the Etruscans, who adopted the Greek alphabet around 700 B.C. The Etruscan language had an *F* sound. The Etruscans represented this sound by different letters over time—using, for example, their letters for *W* and *H.* The Etruscan letter for *W,* adapted from *digamma,* looked somewhat like a capital *F.* When the Romans adapted Etruscan letters, they simplified the letter to *F.*   Peter T. Daniels

See also **Alphabet; Greek language.**

WORLD BOOK map and illustrations

Development of the letter *F*

Seafarers and traders aided the transmission of letters along the coast of the Mediterranean Sea.

The Latin alphabet was adopted from the Etruscan alphabet by the Romans around 650 B.C. The Romans simplified the Etruscan way of representing the sound of *F,* using just one letter.

The Etruscan alphabet was adopted from the Greek about 700 B.C. Etruscan had an *F* sound. The Etruscans represented the *F* sound with a pair of letters—*digamma* and the Etruscan letter for *H.*

Faster ways of writing letters developed during Roman times. Curved, connected lines were faster to write than imitations of the *inscriptional* (carved) Roman letters. The inscriptional forms of the letters developed into capital letters. The curved forms developed into small letters. The form of most small letters, including *f,* was set by around A.D. 800.

ϝ   *f*   f
A.D. 300   1500   Today

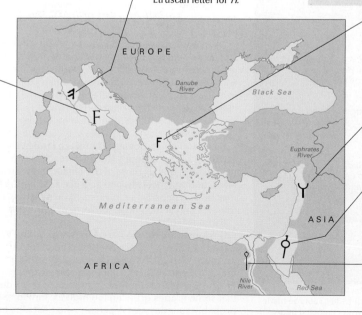

The Greek alphabet evolved from the Phoenician by around 800 B.C. The Greek letter *digamma,* used for the sound of *W,* was one of many letters that evolved from *waw. Digamma* was used in some dialects of ancient Greek, but not in the writings of classical ancient Greek.

The Phoenician alphabet had evolved from the Proto-Sinaitic by around 1100 B.C. The Phoenician letter *waw* looked something like a capital *Y.*

A Proto-Sinaitic alphabet for a Semitic language evolved from Egyptian hieroglyphs by around 1500 B.C. The Proto-Sinaitic letter that came from the mace hieroglyph was the letter *waw.*

The Egyptians, about 3000 B.C., drew a hieroglyph representing a mace.

Faber, *FAY buhr,* **Eberhard,** *EHB ur hahrd* (1822-1879), an American businessman born in Bavaria, built the first mass-production pencil factory in the United States. His great-grandfather had started making pencils in Bavaria in 1761. Faber moved to New York City in 1848 and opened a branch of the family firm there the next year. He sold pencils from Bavaria and exported cedar boards from Florida to European pencil manufacturers.

Faber had to pay a tariff on the pencils he imported, and so he decided it would be cheaper to make them himself. He developed labor-saving machinery to avoid high production costs and, in 1861, built a pencil factory in New York City. Faber later also made pens, erasers, and other stationery products. Faber was born in Stein, near Nuremberg, Germany.   Barry W. Poulson

Fabergé, *FAB uhr ZHAY,* **Peter Carl** (1846-1920), was a Russian goldsmith and jeweler who won international fame for his design of decorative objects. His imaginative creations included cigarette cases, picture frames, parasol handles, and miniature flowers and animals, as well as clocks and other traditional items.

Fabergé's objects were made from gold, silver, and various gemstones native to Russia. He decorated many items with a brilliantly colored enamel that was characteristic of his work. Fabergé's most famous pieces are the beautifully crafted Easter eggs he made for Czars Alexander III and Nicholas II. See **Decorative arts** (picture).

The Resurrection Egg: The Forbes Magazine Collection

A Fabergé Easter egg was created about 1889. Fabergé made the egg of gold, diamonds, and pearls, with enameled figures.

Fabergé was born in St. Petersburg. He received his first training from his father, a successful jeweler, and inherited the small family business at the age of 24. He expanded the business into a company with workshops in the Russian cities of Kiev, Moscow, Odessa, and St. Petersburg, and eventually in London. Czar Alexander III appointed him imperial jeweler in 1884. The Soviet government took over Fabergé's firm after the Bolshevik Revolution of 1917. Fabergé fled to Switzerland, where he died.   Marilyn Pfeifer Swezey

Fabian Society, *FAY bee uhn,* is a group of British socialists. The society was founded in 1884. It was named for Quintus Fabius Maximus, a Roman general who avoided defeat by refusing to fight any decisive battles against Hannibal. The Fabians teach that socialism can be achieved gradually, through a series of reforms (see **Socialism**). They differ from the Communists, who believe that the people can gain ownership of the means of production only through revolution. Noted Fabians have included George Bernard Shaw, H. G. Wells, and Sidney and Beatrice Webb. Fabian ideas became the basis of the British Labour Party (see **Labour Party**). Today, the society sponsors and publishes research on political and social issues.   Chris Cook

See also **Fabius Maximus, Quintus; Webb, Sidney and Beatrice.**

Fabius Maximus, *FAH bee uhs MAK suh muhs,* **Quintus,** *KWIHN tuhs* (275?-203 B.C.), was a Roman military leader known for his strategy of wearing down the enemy but avoiding any decisive conflict. He was a hero of the Second Punic War (218-201 B.C.) between ancient Rome and Carthage, a city in northern Africa.

In 217 B.C., the great Carthaginian general Hannibal won a major victory over the Romans at Lake Trasimene, in northern Italy. In response to this military emergency, the people appointed Fabius, who had already held several high Roman offices, to the powerful temporary office of dictator. As dictator, Fabius followed a strategy of avoiding full-scale battles with Hannibal. Instead, he tried to slowly wear down the Carthaginian army in small raids and skirmishes. This strategy earned Fabius the nickname *Cunctator* (The Delayer).

Many Romans opposed Fabius's tactics. After Fabius stepped down as dictator at the end of 217 B.C., Roman leaders reversed his policy and sought a major battle with Hannibal. However, the new Roman policy resulted in a disastrous Roman defeat at Cannae, in southern Italy. The Romans then returned to Fabius's cautious strategy, which laid the foundation for Rome's eventual victory over Carthage.   Arthur M. Eckstein

See also **Fabian Society; Hannibal; Punic Wars.**

Fable is a brief fictitious story that teaches a moral. In most fables, one or more of the characters is an animal, plant, or thing that talks and acts like a person. A fable may be told in prose or in verse. In many fables, the moral is told at the end in the form of a proverb.

Famous fables include "The Fox and the Grapes," "The City Mouse and the Country Mouse," and "The Wolf in Sheep's Clothing." These tales have been told and retold for more than 2,000 years. They remain popular because they illustrate truths that almost anyone can recognize. In "The Fox and the Grapes," for example, a fox decides that some grapes growing too high for him to reach are probably sour anyway. A person who hears the tale rec-

Engraving (1879) by William Salter Herrick (Bettmann Archive)

The fable "The Fox and the Grapes" tells of a fox who wants to eat a bunch of grapes on a vine. After he finds he can't reach the grapes, he decides that they were probably sour anyway.

ognizes the fox's attitude as a common human failing. The moral of the fable—that people often express a dislike for what they cannot have—is summed up in the expression "sour grapes."

Nearly all ancient peoples invented folk tales in which animals had human traits. The fox was often pictured as sly, and the owl as wise. In time, people began to tell the stories to teach morals. The tales thus became fables.

Most of the fables that are popular in Western countries can be traced back to ancient Greece and India. The majority of the Greek fables are credited to Aesop, a Greek slave who lived about 600 B.C. Aesop had a reputation for telling wise, witty tales about animals, but scholars know little else about him. The fables known as "Aesop's fables" probably came from several ancient sources. Some of the stories originated in India.

The fables of the people of India were influenced by their belief that after death, human beings might be reborn as animals. Indian storytellers made up many tales of such rebirths and used them to teach a variety of morals. Some of these fables had reached the West by the start of the Christian era and were included in early collections of Aesop's fables. During the 200's B.C. or after, the Indians collected their best-known fables in a work called the *Panchatantra.*

Through the centuries, many writers have retold the ancient fables. The most famous such writer was Jean de La Fontaine, a French poet of the 1600's. He retold Aesop's fables in elegant verse and expanded their meanings. Fables always made fun of human follies, but La Fontaine turned such satire into biting social criticism.

In La Fontaine's version of "The Fox and the Crow," for example, a fox robs a crow of some cheese by telling him what a fine singing voice he must have. As the flattered crow opens his mouth to caw, the cheese drops from his beak. Earlier versions of the fable poked fun at

the crow for being fooled by the fox's flattery. La Fontaine's version includes the fox's trickery and ends with a moral: "Every flatterer lives at the expense of his listeners." La Fontaine wrote his fables mainly for adults, but they have long been favorites of French children.

La Fontaine has had many imitators. One of the most successful was Ivan Krylov, a Russian poet of the early 1800's. Krylov translated La Fontaine's fables into Russian and also wrote many of his own. Krylov intended his stories mainly for adults. But they have become the most popular children's stories in Russia.

During the 1900's, writers continued to develop the fable as a literary form. The Irish novelist James Joyce wove "The Fox and the Grapes" and "The Ant and the Grasshopper" into his *Finnegans Wake* (1939). The fables help create the mood of fantasy that characterizes this novel. The American humorist James Thurber revived the fable as a form of social criticism. His fables are noted for their stinging portrayal of the anxieties of modern life.   Mark E. Workman

See also **Aesop's fables; Allegory; Folklore; La Fontaine, Jean de; Literature for children** (Traditional literature).

Fabre, *FAH buhr,* **Jean Henri Casimir,** *zhahn ahn REE ka zee MEER* (1823-1915), a French naturalist, spent his life observing insects and spiders. He wrote simply of what he saw in the gardens and fields near his home. He received the ribbon of the Legion of Honor but was fired from his teaching position because he allowed girls to attend his science classes. Fabre was almost unknown outside of France until he was nearly 80. Then the great scientific societies recognized his work. He wrote a 10-volume *Souvenirs Entomologiques.* Fabre was born on Dec. 22, 1823, in St. Léon. He died on Oct. 11, 1915.   Carolyn Merchant

Fabric. See Textile.

Face is the front part of a person's head. It consists of the forehead, eyes, nose, mouth, cheeks, and chin. Muscles and skin cover the face. Eyelids, lashes, and eyebrows protect the eyes from glare and dust. The tip of the nose is made up of cartilage and skin, which act as a flexible cushion. The channels of the nose are covered with tiny hairs that strain out dust and dirt in the air. The mouth includes the roof, teeth, lips, and tongue, and is lined with *mucous membrane,* a layer of tissue that produces mucous to keep itself moist. The lower jaw is the only bony part of the face that moves.

The facial skeleton is made up of 14 bones and 32 teeth. The *frontal bone* forms part of the forehead. The *nasal bones* and *lacrimal bones* combine to support the bridge and base of the nose. The middle portion of the face, including the cheekbones and upper jawbones, is formed by the *zygomatic bones* and *maxillae.* The *mandible* forms the jaw. The *vomer bones, ethmoid bones,* and *palatine bones* lie deeper in the face. There are also a number of muscles in the face. There is a circular muscle around the mouth and one around each eye. Other muscles spread out over the face from the edges of the circular muscles.

The face is the most distinctive part of a person. It differs in each person because of variations in the nose, eyes, and other features. These variations enable us to recognize each other and tell one another apart. The face expresses much of what goes on in our mind. Our facial muscles often show the emotions we feel. We cannot always control our expression.   Charles W. Cummings

See also **Bell's palsy; Head.**

Face fly is an annoying pest for livestock. Groups of adult face flies feed on the fluid around the eyes, noses, and mouths of livestock, especially cattle. They also feed on blood from the wounds that other flies make on cattle. Face flies do not bite and are not known to carry germs that cause human diseases. But they can transmit diseases to horses, donkeys, and cattle. The face fly looks like the common house fly, but the two insects differ in their habits.

The female face fly lays eggs in fresh cow manure. Face fly *larvae* (maggots) develop faster than house fly larvae. Mature face fly larvae are yellowish instead of white, but otherwise resemble house fly maggots. Face flies hibernate in barns, houses, and other shelters.

WORLD BOOK illustration by Shirley Hooper, Oxford Illustrators Limited

Face fly

The first known face flies in North America were discovered in Nova Scotia in 1952. They probably came from Europe. The flies soon spread throughout most of the United States.   E. W. Cupp

Scientific classification. The scientific name of the face fly is *Musca autumnalis.*

Facebook is a social networking website that connects people with common interests. Facebook enables its users to keep up to date on one another's activities. Users can send messages to one another and share pictures, videos, and interesting websites or articles. They can also join networks set up by such organizations as schools, businesses, and charities. Millions of people around the world use Facebook in over 60 languages.

Uses. Facebook users create *profiles* that typically include photographs and information about themselves. Much activity on Facebook revolves around a process known as *friending.* Users can send other people or organizations "friend requests." If the other party accepts, the two users become *friends.* Friends can see information on each other's profiles and interact more easily.

Some Facebook users have hundreds or thousands of such friends. By enabling communication over vast networks of friends, Facebook helps ideas spread quickly through online "word of mouth." Facebook has reshaped the way advertisers, charities, news organizations, and political campaigns spread their messages.

History. Mark Zuckerberg, a student at Harvard University, founded Facebook in his dorm room in 2004. Four other students—Chris Hughes, Andrew McCollum, Dustin Moskovitz, and Eduardo Saverin—also helped. The name *Facebook* refers to the books of student names and photographs distributed by some colleges and universities. The website, like such books, was designed to help students connect and make new friends.

Originally, only Harvard students could use Facebook. Facebook's founders soon made the website available to other colleges in the Boston area. Interest continued to

grow, and the website eventually became open to any university or high school student. In September 2006, Facebook opened to anyone over the age of 13 with an e-mail address.

Facebook's headquarters are in Palo Alto, California. It also operates out of Dublin, Ireland; and Seoul, South Korea.   Mary Ann Allison

See also **Zuckerberg, Mark.**

Facet. See **Diamond** (How diamonds are cut to make jewels; pictures).

Facsimile. See **Fax machine.**

Factor. Factors of a number are numbers which, when multiplied together, give the original number. For example, the numbers 3 and 4 are factors of 12 because $3 \times 4 = 12$. The other whole number factors of 12 are 2 and 6, and 1 and 12. *Factoring* (determining factors) provides insight into one of the many relationships among numbers.

Every whole number, except 1, can be expressed as the product of at least two factors. A number that has exactly two different factors, itself and 1, is called a *prime number.* The number 7 is prime because 1 and 7 are its only factors. The eight smallest primes are 2, 3, 5, 7, 11, 13, 17, and 19. A number that has more than two factors is called a *composite number.* The number 4 is composite because it has three factors, 1, 2, and 4. The eight smallest composite numbers are 4, 6, 8, 9, 10, 12, 14, and 15. The number 1 is neither composite nor prime.

Prime factors of a number are those prime numbers which, when multiplied together, equal the number. Each composite number is a product of only one set of prime numbers. For example, 24 can only be expressed as a product of prime numbers as $2 \times 2 \times 2 \times 3$ (in any order). The *prime factorization* of 24 is $2 \times 2 \times 2 \times 3$, and the *prime factors* of 24 are 2 and 3.

To find the prime factors of a number, divide the number by any prime number that divides it evenly. It is usually easiest to use the smallest prime number that divides the number evenly. For example, to find the prime factors of 220, begin by dividing by 2 ($220 \div 2 = 110$). Continue dividing the *quotient* (number obtained) by 2 until it is no longer divisible by 2 ($110 \div 2 = 55$). But 55 cannot be divided by 2 without leaving a remainder. The next prime, 3, does not divide 55 without a remainder either. But the next greater prime, 5, does divide 55 equally ($55 \div 5 = 11$). The number 11, like 2 and 5, is a prime number. Therefore the prime factorization of 220 is $2 \times 2 \times 5 \times 11$, and the prime factors are 2, 5, and 11. The product $2 \times 2 \times 5 \times 11$ (in any order) is the only way 220 can be expressed as the product of prime numbers. The process may be written like this:

$$2 \underline{\smash{)220}}$$
$$2 \underline{\smash{)110}}$$
$$2 \underline{\smash{)55}}$$

(leaves a remainder)

$$3 \underline{\smash{)55}}$$

(leaves a remainder)

$$5 \underline{\smash{)55}}$$
$$11 \quad \text{(prime)}$$

Common factors. If a number is a factor of two or more numbers, it is called a *common factor* of those numbers. For example, 1, 3, 5, and 15 are the factors of 15; and 1, 2, 4, 5, 10, and 20 are the factors of 20. The numbers 1 and 5 are common to both these sets of factors. The numbers 30 and 45 have four common factors: 1, 3, 5, and 15.

If two numbers have more than one common factor, the greatest one is called the *greatest common factor.* It is also the *greatest common divisor* because a factor of a number is also a divisor of that number. To find the greatest common factor of two or more numbers, first find the set of all the factors for each number. Then select the largest factor that is in all the sets. The greatest common factor of 18, 30, and 42 is in this example:

Number	Set of factors
18	1, 2, 3, 6, 9, 18
30	1, 2, 3, 5, 6, 10, 15, 30
42	1, 2, 3, 6, 7, 14, 21, 42

The number 6 is the greatest factor common to all the sets, so 6 is the greatest common factor of 18, 30, and 42.

Relative primes. Two numbers that have no common factors other than 1 are *relatively prime* or *prime in relation to each other.* For example, the factors of 12 are 1, 2, 3, 4, 6, and 12. The factors of 35 are 1, 5, 7, and 35. Twelve and 35 have no common factors other than 1. They are relatively prime.

Algebraic factors. *Algebraic expressions,* which use letters to represent unknown numbers, also have factors. The factors of $3ab$, for example, are 1, 3, a, b, $3a$, $3b$, ab, and $3ab$. The factors of a^2b are 1, a, b, a^2, ab, and a^2b.

Factoring can help simplify more complicated algebraic expressions, such as $5x + 5$. This expression is a product of two factors: 5 and $(x + 1)$. Such an expression might be easier to work with when written as $5(x + 1)$ instead of $5x + 5$. Likewise, the expression $2a^2 + 4ab$ can be written as the product of two of its factors: $2a$ and $(a + 2b)$. Robert M. Vancko

See also **Algebra; Multiplication; Number theory; Sieve of Eratosthenes.**

Factory is a building or group of buildings in which products are manufactured. Factories range in size from home garages to groups of buildings covering whole city blocks. Inside, workers and machines turn raw materials into parts and then assemble parts into finished products. Factories, also called *plants,* employ about one-fourth of the world's labor force.

Before the development of factories, workers made most manufactured products in homes or small workshops. The development of power-driven machines in the 1700's and 1800's made the modern factory system possible in many countries (see **Industrial Revolution**).

Kinds of factories. Factories use the principle of *division of labor*—that is, they divide the work into a number of separate operations. There are four main manufacturing methods used in factories: (1) repetitive, (2) process, (3) fixed-position, and (4) cellular.

A factory uses *repetitive manufacturing* to make many units of the same product. Automobile makers use a repetitive approach called the *assembly-line* method, in which the auto frame moves on a conveyor through the factory. As the frame moves, parts arrive on other conveyors and get attached to the frame.

Process manufacturing is used for a wide variety of products, such as specialized tools or complex mechanical parts that are made to order. Machines are grouped by the types of operations they perform. Each job moves through the factory visiting only the machine groups needed. Skilled operators must set up the machines for each job. Factories that do process manufacturing are often called *job shops.*

A factory uses *fixed-position manufacturing* to make only a small number of units of the same product. In aircraft factories, the product cannot be moved because of its size. Instead, workers and equipment must come to the product. Completing one unit may take months.

Cellular manufacturing combines repetitive and process methods. Machines are set up in a linear or U-shaped *cell* to make a family of similar products. The factory may have many cells, each making a different product family. Cells may be set up to make a certain number of units of a product. Once that number is finished, the cells are changed to make another product.

Location and design. Manufacturers try to build their factories in areas where land and employees are available at low cost. The chosen locations also must have good access to highways, railroads, or ports to allow for receiving materials and shipping finished products. Many plants have a one-story structure, which permits materials to move easily through them.

Manufacturers often use computers to link factories to customers and suppliers. As customers use products, the factory plans which products to produce and automatically orders the needed materials from suppliers. In many factories, computers control the operations of machines and the flow of work through the plant. The computers enable a few technicians to survey and operate the entire factory efficiently. Such factories may use robots and computer-controlled machine tools to perform complex, tiring, or dangerous tasks. Ronald G. Askin

Related articles in *World Book* include:

Automation	Industry	Mass production
Electricity (In industry)	Invention	Sweatshop
	Labor force	Technology
Industrial relations	Manufacturing	

Factory farming is a term that people often apply to highly mechanized systems for raising large numbers of livestock, usually many thousands. Livestock producers raise the animals in confinement so that they can more easily manage the large numbers of animals. Livestock producers commonly raise hogs and poultry in a building and keep them from roaming outside. The building's ventilation, heating, cooling, feeding, and watering systems are mechanically controlled. Each animal is referred to by an individual identification number rather than by name. Operators of small farms have difficulty competing in the livestock market with factory farms. Factory farming is also called *corporate farming.*

Some people claim that factory farming results in indifference and even brutality toward livestock. They believe that animals in factory farms are abused and diseased. However, other people believe that factory farms provide healthful conditions. They point out that poor conditions produce unhealthy animals that are stunted or unable to reproduce, resulting in no profit for the farm operators. Many people are concerned that animal wastes from large operations are polluting the land and water. Most states that have large factory farms have laws or are enacting laws dealing with the environmental aspects of these operations. John Carlson

See also **Livestock.**

Faeroe Islands. See Faroe Islands.

Fafnir, *FAHV nihr,* in Scandinavian mythology, was a man who turned himself into a dragon. Poems and stories from medieval Iceland describe him as a powerful, greedy, and violent man with magical powers. He killed his father, Hreidmar, and stole his family's gold. He then turned himself into a dragon and spent the rest of his life guarding the gold. His brother Regin tried to reclaim the gold and asked the hero Sigurd to kill Fafnir. Regin planned to betray and kill Sigurd after Fafnir's death.

Fafnir sometimes left his lair to drink from a nearby river. Sigurd dug a hole in the path that led to the river. He hid in the hole until Fafnir crawled over it, and then used his sword to stab Fafnir in the heart. Sigurd roasted the heart, and by tasting its magic juice was able to understand the language of birds. The birds warned Sigurd that Regin wanted to kill him, so Sigurd killed Regin.

The German composer Richard Wagner told a version of this story in his opera *Siegfried* (1876). In the opera, Fafnir is slain by the Germanic hero Siegfried.

Carl Lindahl

Fahd (1921?-2005) ruled as king and prime minister of Saudi Arabia from 1982 until his death in 2005. He came to power following the death of his half-brother King Khalid. When Khalid became king in 1975, Fahd was named next in line to the throne and first deputy prime minister of Saudi Arabia. Fahd ran the daily affairs of the government because Khalid was not in good health and he lacked Fahd's detailed knowledge of government functions. Fahd tried to maintain the traditional Islamic moral values of Saudi Arabia while continuing the rapid modernization made possible by the country's great oil wealth.

In August 1990, Iraqi forces invaded and occupied oil-rich Kuwait. Many people feared Iraq would next invade Saudi Arabia. Fahd invited foreign troops, including those from the United States, to come to Saudi Arabia to defend that country. The Saudis and foreign nations formed an alliance. In February 1991, under U.S. military leadership, these allies drove the Iraqis out of Kuwait. See **Persian Gulf War of 1991.**

Saudi Arabian Information Service, Washington, D.C.

Fahd

In the mid-1990's, King Fahd's health began to decline. His half brother Abdullah, next in line to the throne, became increasingly responsible for running the Saudi government. Fahd died on Aug. 1, 2005, and Abdullah then became king and prime minister.

Fahd ibn Abd al-Aziz Al Saud was born in Riyadh. His father was King Abd al-Aziz ibn Saud, known as Ibn Saud, the founder of Saudi Arabia.   Malcolm C. Peck

Fahrenheit, Gabriel Daniel (1686-1736), sometimes called Daniel Gabriel Fahrenheit, a German physicist, developed the Fahrenheit temperature scale. He also made the thermometer more accurate by using mercury instead of mixtures of alcohol and water in the thermometer tube (see **Thermometer**).

Fahrenheit determined three fixed temperatures: 0 °F for the freezing point of ice, salt, and water; 32 °F for the freezing point of pure water; and 212 °F for the boiling point of water. These three temperatures, from lowest to highest, are equal to −18 °C, 0 °C, and 100 °C on the Celsius temperature scale.

Fahrenheit was born on May 24, 1686, in Danzig (now Gdańsk, Poland). He died on Sept. 16, 1736.

Margaret J. Osler

See also **Fahrenheit scale.**

Fahrenheit scale is the scale for measuring temperature commonly used in the United States. It is also used in a few other countries, such as Belize and the Bahamas. Elsewhere, the Celsius scale has replaced the Fahrenheit scale (see **Celsius scale**). The Celsius and the Kelvin scales are both used for scientific applications.

The German physicist Gabriel Daniel Fahrenheit, sometimes called Daniel Gabriel Fahrenheit, developed the scale. He assigned 0 °F to the temperature at which a mixture of water, ice, and ammonium chloride, a type of salt, are in *equilibrium*. In this case, equilibrium occurs when the solution neither freezes nor melts further. Fahrenheit then assigned three other reference points to his scale: the freezing point of water, the boiling point of water, and the average internal temperature of the human body. After adjustments by both Fahrenheit and later scientists, these temperatures became set at 32 °F, 212 °F, and 98.6 °F, respectively. Air temperatures across Earth vary over 200 Fahrenheit degrees. For example, temperatures in Antarctica can fall below –100 °F. Temperatures can exceed 130 °F in the Sahara.

To convert a Fahrenheit temperature to Celsius, subtract 32 from the Fahrenheit temperature. Then multiply by $\frac{5}{9}$:
$$°C = \frac{5}{9} (°F - 32).$$
To change a Celsius temperature to Fahrenheit, multiply the Celsius temperature by $\frac{9}{5}$. Then add 32:
$$°F = \frac{9}{5} °C + 32.$$ Robert M. Rauber

Faïence, *fy AHNS* or *fay AHNS,* is a kind of earthenware. Faïence is glazed with tin oxide to produce a creamy white color. The ware can be decorated with other metallic oxides that turn various colors when the pottery is *fired* (baked).

Faïence is related to two other types of earthenware, majolica and delft. But the three have different forms of decoration and assumed their styles in different countries. Faïence came from France, majolica from Italy, and delft from the Netherlands.

The French named faïence for Faenza, Italy, which was the center for the production of tin oxide-glazed pottery during the 1500's. Today, potters in Germany, the Scandinavian countries, and Spain produce tin oxide-glazed wares known as faïence.   William C. Gates, Jr.

Fainting is a temporary loss of consciousness. A fainting person becomes pale, begins to perspire, and then loses consciousness and collapses. The person also has a weak pulse and breathes irregularly.

Fainting usually lasts only a few minutes. As the person regains consciousness, the muscles become firm, the pulse becomes stronger, and breathing becomes regular.

Fainting occurs when there is an insufficient supply of blood to the brain for a short time. This results from a *dilation* (widening) of blood vessels in the body followed by a drop in heart rate and blood pressure. It is often

A fainting spell can be relieved by having the person lie on the floor with the legs slightly elevated, as shown here. The person should be given plenty of room and air.

triggered by emotional shock. Other common causes of fainting include overexertion, standing for long periods, and certain medical conditions, such as heart disease.

A person who has fainted should be placed flat on the back. Raise the legs slightly if the person shows no signs of injury. Get medical assistance in all cases of fainting. A person who feels weak or dizzy may avoid fainting by lying down or sitting with the head level with the knees.

Carlotta M. Rinke

Critically reviewed by the American Red Cross

See also **First aid** (Fainting).

Fair is an event held for the presenting or viewing of exhibits. Depending on the theme of the fair, the exhibits may be agricultural, commercial, industrial, or artistic.

Some fairs are called *expositions* or *exhibitions.* Small fairs last just a few days and involve exhibitors and visitors from a local area. The largest fairs run for months. They attract exhibitors and visitors from a large number of nations. Fairs are a major industry in the United States and Canada.

There are three basic types of fairs—agricultural fairs, trade fairs, and world's fairs. This article discusses agricultural and trade fairs. For information on world's fairs, see the **World's fair** article.

Agricultural fairs are the most common type of fair in the United States and Canada. Such fairs hold contests for the best examples of crops, livestock, poultry, and other farm products. Most agricultural fairs organize competitions for various home-prepared foods. Companies exhibit and demonstrate agricultural machinery and other equipment. Farm youth groups and adult organizations also participate.

Agricultural fairs provide amusements and entertainment for visitors. For example, many agricultural fairs provide a carnival midway with rides and games. At large fairs, famous entertainers perform before large audiences in a grandstand or coliseum. Visitors can purchase many kinds of food and souvenirs at concession stands. Sports events are also popular at some fairs. These events include harness racing, horse racing, automobile racing, and rodeos. Each day's activities may end with a fireworks display.

Agricultural fairs can be divided into three general categories, primarily based on their size. These categories are, from smallest to largest, county fairs, regional or district fairs, and state fairs. Some regional fairs, however, are larger than state fairs. The smallest fairs may cover only a few acres or hectares of open space

© michael rubin / Shutterstock.com

State fairs are held every summer and fall throughout the United States. Exhibits, games, and exciting rides attract large crowds to a state fair midway, shown here.

near a town. The biggest fairs are held at permanent fairgrounds. The fairgrounds include large buildings and such special facilities as grandstands and race tracks.

County fairs normally last from two to five days and are operated by a volunteer staff. County fairs mainly attract exhibitors and visitors from the local area.

Regional fairs serve a larger geographical area than county fairs. They have a permanent staff and may last as long as two weeks. The fair is usually held in the late summer or autumn and is generally the major fair or exhibition in the area.

State fairs are sometimes operated by a department of the state government. However, a number of state fairs are operated by nonprofit organizations.

Trade fairs normally center on a specific product or industry. For example, a trade fair may confine itself to the computer industry or to book publishing. Generally, trade fairs are intended to provide commercial exposure for the products of the exhibitors. Some of these fairs limit admission only to people within the field covered by the fair. Other trade fairs encourage attendance by the general public.

Most trade fairs are held in large exhibition halls in major cities. Fairs are often held in a different city each year. Guest performers may entertain visitors at special shows, but the fair has no carnival midway.

History. Fairs date back to Biblical times. The book of Ezekiel, which was written in the 500's B.C., has several references to fairs. During the early centuries of Christianity, the church took an active part in sponsoring fairs as part of the observance of religious holidays and seasons. During the mid-1500's, the church stopped participating in and promoting fairs. As a result, fairs lost their religious associations and became events devoted to commercial exhibits and entertainment.

In 1641, the government of New Netherland authorized the first annual fair in the American colonies, to be held in New Amsterdam (now New York City). By the mid-1700's, fairs had become common throughout the colonies. They were primarily agricultural and served as an important showcase for the farm products of the local area. The first state fairs were held in New Jersey and New York about 1840.   John E. Findling

See also **City** (picture: Trade fairs); **Toronto** (The city); **World's fair.**

Fair Deal is the name United States President Harry S. Truman gave to his domestic legislative program in 1949. He said it offered the American people "the promise of equal rights and equal opportunities." See also **Truman, Harry S.** (Problems at home).   Alonzo L. Hamby

Fair employment practices. See Equal Employment Opportunity Commission.

Fair Labor Standards Act is a United States law that sets the *minimum* (least possible) wage and the length of the standard workweek for most employees in the country. It applies to employees of firms that do business in more than one state and have annual sales of at least $500,000. It also sets minimum age requirements for all workers. The act was passed in 1938 and has been *amended* (changed) many times. A 1963 amendment, the Equal Pay Act, requires that men and women be paid equally for equal work. The Wage and Hour Division (WHD) of the U.S. Department of Labor enforces the act.

Congress passed the Fair Labor Standards Act as part of the New Deal, which was President Franklin D. Roosevelt's program to end the Great Depression. The act originally set a minimum wage of 25 cents an hour. Amendments have raised the wage repeatedly.

The act at first limited the standard workweek to 44 hours. The workweek was reduced to 40 hours—the current length—by 1940. Time worked beyond the 40-hour limit is called *overtime.* Employees are entitled to be paid at a rate of 1 ½ times their regular rate for overtime.

The Fair Labor Standards Act bans the employment of children less than 14 years old, except for certain types of jobs. Children under 14 can deliver papers, baby-sit, work in a business owned solely by their parents, or work in limited employment in certain agricultural jobs. Jobs as actors or performers have no age limitation for children. Children 14 or 15 years old are prohibited from working in factories or during school hours. People less than 18 years old may not work in jobs declared hazardous by the U.S. secretary of labor. Such occupations include mining and certain factory jobs.   James G. Scoville

See also **Child labor; Minimum wage; Wages and hours.**

Fair-trade laws were designed to prevent large retail stores from selling certain merchandise at extremely low prices in attempts to drive their smaller competitors out of business. Such laws are also called *resale price maintenance laws.* Many states in the United States once had such laws. However, fair-trade laws have been illegal in the United States since 1975.

In some states, if any retailer agreed with a manufacturer to sell an item at a particular price, the state's fair-trade laws required all retailers to sell the item at that price. Other states allowed merchants to sell an item either at a price specified by the manufacturer or at a higher price. Goods covered by fair-trade laws included television sets, clothing, watches, bicycles, and jewelry.

In 1931, California became the first state to pass a fair-trade law. By 1950, 45 states had such laws. Ordinarily, price fixing would violate federal antitrust laws (see **Antitrust laws**). But two federal laws, the Miller-Tydings Act of 1937 and the McGuire Act of 1952, made such price fixing legal. Opponents of fair-trade laws argued that the laws cost consumers millions of dollars in higher prices. In time, many states repealed such laws. The U.S. Congress abolished the remaining ones in 1975 by repealing the Miller-Tydings and McGuire acts.   Jay Diamond

Fairbanks (pop. 31,535; met. area pop. 97,581) is the second largest city in Alaska. Only Anchorage has more people. Fairbanks lies in east-central Alaska, about 115 miles (185 kilometers) south of the Arctic Circle. It is a transportation and supply center for central and northern Alaska and is the northernmost city on the state's system of paved roads (see **Alaska** [political map]).

Fairbanks lies on the Chena River, near where the Chena joins the Tanana River. The city lies midway along the Trans-Alaska Pipeline, which transports oil 800 miles (1,300 kilometers) from Prudhoe Bay on Alaska's north coast to Valdez on the south coast. The main employers are local, state, and federal government agencies; military bases; and the University of Alaska Fairbanks. Mining, agriculture, forestry, and tourism also provide some jobs. The architecture of Fairbanks ranges from modern office buildings to log cabins and plywood shacks.

© AccentAlaska.com/Alamy Images

Fairbanks, Alaska, the chief financial and trade center of the interior of Alaska, lies on the banks of the Chena River, *center.* Fairbanks is in the heart of a great gold-mining region.

Douglas Fairbanks, Sr., was a famous motion-picture actor of the 1920's. In 1929, he starred with his wife, Mary Pickford, in William Shakespeare's comedy *The Taming of the Shrew*.

Bettmann Archive

Temperatures in the city reach as high as 95 °F (35 °C) in summer and as low as –60 °F (–51 °C) in winter. Winters last from mid-October to mid-April. Fairbanks receives an average of about 65 inches (165 centimeters) of snow yearly. It has about 22 hours of daylight on the longest day of the year, on or near June 21, and less than 4 hours on the shortest day, on or near December 21.

Fairbanks was founded in 1901 by E. T. Barnette, a trader whose steamboat ran aground on its way up the Tanana River. Felix Pedro, an Italian immigrant, found gold near Fairbanks in 1902, and Barnette's trading post became a supply center for miners in the area. The city was named after Charles W. Fairbanks, a United States senator from Indiana who became vice president of the United States in 1905. The discovery of oil at Prudhoe Bay in 1968 and the construction of the Trans-Alaska Pipeline between 1974 and 1977 led to the growth of jobs and population in the area. Cary W. de Wit

Fairbanks, Charles Warren (1852-1918), served as vice president of the United States from 1905 to 1909 under President Theodore Roosevelt. Fairbanks hoped to be the Republican presidential candidate in 1908. But Fairbanks was too conservative for Roosevelt, and the president helped William Howard Taft win the nomination. Fairbanks again was the Republican vice presidential candidate in 1916. However, Fairbanks and presidential candidate Charles Evans Hughes lost the 1916 election to the Democratic candidates, Woodrow Wilson and his running mate, Thomas R. Marshall.

Culver

Charles W. Fairbanks

Fairbanks was born on May 11, 1852, on a farm near Unionville Center, Ohio, and graduated from Ohio Wesleyan University. Fairbanks became a successful railroad lawyer in Indianapolis.

Fairbanks served as a U.S. senator from Indiana from 1897 to 1905. He led the American delegation to the Joint High Commission that tried to settle all outstanding difficulties with Canada in 1898. He died on June 4, 1918.
Robert W. Cherny

Fairbanks, Douglas, Sr. (1883-1939), was an American motion-picture actor who became famous for his acrobatic acting in colorful adventure films. All of Fairbanks's notable movies were silent films. They included *The Mark of Zorro* (1920), *Robin Hood* (1922), *The Thief of Baghdad* (1924), and *The Black Pirate* (1926). Fairbanks's name is still associated with the exaggerated, romantic style of such motion pictures.

Fairbanks was born on May 23, 1883, in Denver. His real name was Douglas Elton Ullman. For several years, he starred in comedies on Broadway. Fairbanks made his movie debut in 1915.

Fairbanks helped found the United Artists studio in 1919 with the early Hollywood film stars Charlie Chaplin and Mary Pickford, and the motion-picture director D. W. Griffith.

Fairbanks married Pickford in 1920. He died on Dec. 12, 1939. James MacKillop

Fairchild, Sherman Mills (1896-1971), was an American inventor and businessman who pioneered in aircraft design and aerial photography. In 1918, he invented a camera with a special shutter that increased the accuracy of aerial photographs.

In the 1920's, Fairchild founded the first of many companies he would run throughout his life. His companies developed aerial cameras, conducted aerial surveys, and designed and built airplanes. In 1926, he introduced the Fairchild FC-2 plane, the first with folding wings and an enclosed cabin instead of the usual open cockpit. The cabin protected photographers from wind and cold. During World War II (1939-1945), the United States Army used the Fairchild 71 for transport and aerial photography. Fairchild was born on April 7, 1896, in Oneonta, New York. He died on March 28, 1971. Anne Millbrooke

Fairfield, Cicily Isabel. See West, Rebecca.

Fairless, Benjamin Franklin (1890-1962), was an American industrialist. He was president of U.S. Steel Corporation from 1938 to 1953 and chairman of the board from 1952 to 1955. He held several positions with the American Iron and Steel Institute and served as its president from 1955 until his death. Fairless received the Bessemer Medal in 1951 for distinguished service to the iron and steel industry.

Fairless was born Benjamin F. Williams on May 3, 1890, in Pigeon Run, Ohio. He took the name Fairless from an uncle who adopted him. He graduated from Ohio Northern University. Fairless died on Jan. 1, 1962.
Robert E. Wright

Fairy, according to tradition, is a humanlike supernatural creature that lives alongside human beings but is seldom seen by them. Fairies appear often in the folklore of western Europe, particularly that of the Celtic cultures of the United Kingdom and Ireland. Legends hold that fairies have magic powers. Fairies are sometimes helpful but can be mischievous and even cruel.

© Mary Evans Picture Library/Alamy Images

The king and queen of the fairies were named Oberon and Titania in many tales. William Shakespeare featured them in his comedy *A Midsummer Night's Dream.*

© Shutterstock

Rumpelstiltskin was a wicked fairy in German folklore. He spun gold from straw to get a poor young woman to give him her first-born child. However, the young woman tricks Rumpelstiltskin so he cannot collect his debt.

Different cultures have many terms for fairies and fairylike creatures. These include *brownie; pixie; bucca, púca,* or *pwca; bogey, bug-a-boo,* or *bogeyman;* and *hob* or *hobgoblin.* People once thought it was risky to talk about fairies by name. Instead, they referred to fairies as "the wee folk" or "the good neighbors."

No one knows how the belief in fairies began. In some stories, fairies were angels who were forced to leave heaven because of some wrongdoing. In other stories, fairies were spirits of the dead. Some scholars think that fairies began as ancient nature spirits, such as the spirits of mountains, streams, and trees. Even today, people in some communities avoid removing certain rocks or trees when building roads, for fear of offending the fairies believed to live in them.

Fairies appear in many folk stories and legends. People often told such stories to explain things that they did not understand. For example, people walking at night through marshes and swamplands sometimes noticed strange lights. A person who left the path to follow such a light could become hopelessly lost in the darkness. Stories held that these lights were fairies trying to trick people to leave the safety of the path. Today, scientists understand that these lights, called *will-o-the-wisp* or *fox fires,* are caused by the natural burning of *methane* (marsh gas) produced by decaying plants.

Types of fairies. Folklorists describe fairies as either *solitary* or *trooping.* Solitary fairies always appear alone, while trooping fairies live together.

Solitary fairies. The *leprechaun* of Ireland is a solitary fairy sometimes spotted in a field, often working at making shoes. If captured, a leprechaun must reveal where he has hidden his pot of gold. However, the leprechaun usually manages to escape through some clever trick. The *banshee,* another solitary fairy, foretells death. In Scotland, the banshee can be heard wailing by a river as she washes the clothes of the person who soon will die. In Ireland, many people believe that if they hear the sound of a wailing banshee, someone in their family will soon perish.

Trooping fairies live together in a society often called *fairyland.* Fairyland may be under the ground, inside a hollow hill called a *fairy mound,* or beneath a lake. The entrance may be a door in a hill or under the roots of trees. In most stories, a king and queen rule fairyland. Queen Mab is a famous fairy queen in Irish folklore. Oberon is king of the fairies in many legends.

Life in fairyland resembles life in the human world. Fairies work, marry, and have children. Time passes slowly in fairyland, so there is no old age or death. However, it is dangerous for human beings to enter the world of fairies. Many legends describe the difference between time in fairyland and in the human world. In one legend, a man spends what he believes is one night in fairyland. But after he returns home, he finds that hundreds of years have passed and no one remembers him.

Magic powers. Fairies have many magic powers. The most important is the ability to make themselves invisible to people. They use this power to steal items that they need from people. However, some people possess *fairy sight.* They can see fairies as they move to and from their underground homes. Sometimes fairies become visible to a person who plucks a four-leaf clover or steps into a *fairy ring.* A fairy ring is a circle of mushrooms around greener grass or bare soil in a field or meadow. Fairies are said to dance in fairy rings.

Many fairies can fly and travel great distances quickly. Small whirlwinds called *dust devils* were thought by some people to be caused by groups of fairies flying from place to place.

Appearance. Older traditions describe fairies as similar in size and appearance to human beings. But fairies always have some distinguishing feature. They may have greenish skin, for example, or a squinting eye. Later traditions hold that fairies are smaller than human beings— sometimes the size of insects. These fairies often have transparent wings. Some fairies, including pixies, have great beauty. Other traditions describe fairies as old men with deformed bodies. Many fairies wear green or white clothing with red caps. Brownies usually wear shabby brown cloaks and hoods.

Fairies and people sometimes marry. A man might go to fairyland to live with his bride, or he might bring his fairy wife back to his home. In many stories, a person must follow strict rules to marry a fairy. For example, a human husband must never scold or strike his fairy wife or refer to her being a fairy. If he does, she immediately returns to fairyland.

Fairies sometimes reward people for doing them a favor. According to one story, a farmer who mends a fairy shovel or chair will receive delicious food in return. Grateful fairies also may leave money for people who have treated them well.

In fairyland, fairies often have trouble giving birth. A common type of fairy legend tells how fairies kidnap a human woman and take her to fairyland to help deliver a baby. The fairies blindfold the woman before she enters and leaves fairyland so that the entrance to the fairy world will remain secret.

Fairies nearly always reward the woman well for her help, but they can be cruel if she gives away their secrets. In one legend, a woman puts some magic ointment on a newborn fairy's eye and accidentally rubs some on one of her own eyes. The ointment enables her to see fairies who are normally invisible to human beings. Later, the woman sees a fairy in a marketplace and speaks to him. The fairy asks which eye the woman sees him with. After she tells him, he blinds her in that eye.

Fairies sometimes try to trick women into caring for fairy babies. The fairies may exchange their babies, called *changelings,* for healthy newborn human infants. Usually, a human mother can see that a changeling has been substituted for her child because the fairy baby has some ugly physical feature or habit. If the mother threatens to harm the changeling, it may leave and give back the woman's own child. Folklore scholars think that some kinds of birth defects may have inspired this belief in changelings.

People who believe in fairies have developed many customs to win the favor of fairies or to protect themselves from evil ones. Fairies love milk, and so people may leave bowls of cream outside to please them. To prevent fairies from stealing milk, they might protect stalls holding milk cows with a magical charm, usually a piece of iron, such as an old horseshoe. Parents might hang an open pair of scissors over a child's crib as a charm to prevent fairies from stealing the infant. If travelers lose their way due to a fairy's trick, they can break the spell by turning a piece of their clothing inside out.

Fairy tales are children's fantasy stories that occur in some imaginary land and time. They sometimes—but not always—include fairies or fairylike creatures.

The French writer Charles Perrault collected a book of folk stories called *Tales of Mother Goose* (1697). In one tale, Cinderella's fairy godmother changes a pumpkin into a carriage and mice into horses. In another story, an evil fairy condemns Sleeping Beauty to death. But a good fairy changes the curse from death to a long sleep, so a handsome prince can awaken the girl with a kiss.

In the early 1800's, two German scholars, the brothers Jakob and Wilhelm Grimm, published a collection of folk stories that became known in English as *Grimm's Fairy Tales.* One tale, "Rumpelstiltskin," tells of a strange creature who spins gold from straw to get a young woman to give him her first-born child.

Some authors have made up their own stories about fairies. The Danish writer Hans Christian Andersen wrote several volumes of stories from 1835 until his death in 1875. In one tale, "Thumbelina," a fairylike girl springs from the heart of a magic flower and later meets and marries a fairy prince.

The Italian author Carlo Collodi wrote *Pinocchio* (1883), a children's novel where a fairy character brings a wooden doll to life. These stories have been told and retold in many different ways, so that now children around the world know them.

Fairies in literature. For hundreds of years, authors have written about fairies in novels, plays, and stories. Geoffrey Chaucer's *Wife of Bath's Tale,* written in the 1300's, concerns a fairy woman who marries a knight.

The English playwright William Shakespeare used fairies as major characters in his comedy *A Midsummer Night's Dream* (about 1595). This play includes Oberon and Titania, the king and queen of the fairies, and the mischievous fairy Puck. A fairy named Ariel appears in Shakespeare's *The Tempest* (about 1611).

Fairies and other imaginary creatures inspired the works of the English author J. R. R. Tolkien. In *The Hobbit* (1937) and the three-volume *The Lord of the Rings* (1954-1955), Tolkien described a race of wise and gifted elves that share many characteristics with trooping fairies.

Fairies appear in the Harry Potter series of novels written by the British author J. K. Rowling. Published in the late 1990's and early 2000's, these books introduced readers to many new fairylike characters.   Bill Ellis

Related articles in *World Book* include:

Andersen, Hans Christian	Gremlin
Banshee	Grimm's Fairy Tales
Elf	Puck
Folklore	

For a list of collections of fairy tales, see **Literature for children** (Books to read [Traditional literature/fairy tales, folk tales, and myths]).

Fairy tale. See Fairy.

Faisal, *FY suhl* (1906?-1975), was king of Saudi Arabia from 1964 to 1975. Faisal's name is sometimes spelled *Faysal* or *Feisal.* He restored harmony within the Al Saud ruling family and thus made the country's government more stable. He also became an important world leader. On March 25, 1975, Faisal was assassinated by one of his nephews.

Faisal controlled Saudi Arabia's vast oil resources. He used oil profits for industrialization, school and hospital construction, and many other public projects. In 1973, he authorized an Arab oil embargo against the United States and the Netherlands, nations that supported Israel in the 1973 Arab-Israeli war.

Faisal ibn Abd al-Aziz al Faisal Al Saud was born in Riyadh. He was next in line to the throne from 1953 to 1964, and he served as prime minister from 1953 to 1960 and from 1962 to 1964, when his brother Saud was king of Saudi Arabia.   Joseph A. Kechichian

See also **Saudi Arabia** (History).

Faisal I, *FY suhl* (1885-1933), was king of Iraq from 1921 to 1933. He also reigned as king of Syria in 1920. His name is sometimes spelled *Faysal* or *Feisal.*

Faisal was born on May 20, 1885. He was a son of Sharîf Hussein of Hejaz, whom the government of the Ottoman Empire appointed *emir* (ruler) of the city of Mecca in 1908. Today, Mecca is in Saudi Arabia. During World War I (1914-1918), with help from the United Kingdom, Faisal led an Arab revolt against the Ottomans. In 1918, as part of the Allied forces, he and his army helped capture the Ottoman-controlled city of Damascus in Syria. Faisal became Syria's ruler. In March 1920, a nationalist, Arab-Syrian Congress under Allied supervision declared Faisal Syria's king. In July 1920, he was expelled by the French, who took full control of Syria.

Also in 1920, the British gained control of Iraq. They chose Faisal as Iraq's king in 1921. As king, Faisal worked to balance the interests of Iraq's political factions, including a group that called for Iraqi independence from the United Kingdom. Iraq gained independence in 1932. Faisal died on Sept. 8, 1933, and was succeeded by his son Ghazi. See **Iraq** (History).   Michel Le Gall

Faith. See **Religion.**

Faith healing involves the belief that trust in God's power can cure sickness and other physical problems. Faith healing and praying for the sick presuppose a connection between physical health and spiritual well-being. Faith healing is performed mainly through prayer and by faith healers who lay hands on the ill person.

In Christianity, the doctrine of faith healing has its roots in New Testament stories of miraculous healings performed by Jesus Christ. Mark 16:18 and 1 Corinthians 12:9 mention believers with the gift of healing. James 5:14-15 describe laying hands on, praying for, and putting oil on the forehead of the sick.

In the late 1800's and early 1900's, some leaders of the Holiness and Pentecostal religious movements in the United States began to claim that prayer, not medicine, could heal the sick. Others did not reject medicine but believed that faith healing and medicine should be used together. Some Pentecostals thought the Holy Spirit gave them the power to heal others.

The American evangelist Aimee Semple McPherson was among the best-known faith healers of the early 1900's. The healing movement gained popularity following World War II (1939-1945), especially because of Pentecostal evangelist Oral Roberts. He held many tent revivals that included faith healing. At first, most people who attended healing revivals were poor and lacked the money to pay for medical care. Today, people who seek faith healing come from all social and economic classes.

Critics have charged that faith healers are frauds, and that reported cures are faked. Even faith healers acknowledge that not everyone who seeks their help experiences a cure. Some healers believe that a lack of faith on the part of the sick person may prevent healing.

Believers in faith healing differ from Christian Scientists, who consider sickness a mental state. Because of the interest in faith healing, many Christian churches offer prayers for the sick at their services. These services generally do not promise cures.   Charles H. Lippy

See also **McPherson, Aimee Semple; Pentecostal churches.**

Fakir, *fuh KIHR* or *FAY kuhr,* is a Muslim or Hindu man who practices extreme self-denial as part of his religion. *Fakir* is an Arabic word meaning *poor,* especially *poor in the sight of God.* Fakirs usually live on charity and spend most of their lives in religious contemplation. Some can actually perform such feats of will power as walking on hot coals. But they also frequently practice deception. Some fakirs live in religious communities. Others wander about alone. People whose way of life resembles that of fakirs include Muslim *dervishes* and Hindu *yogis.*   Richard C. Martin

See also **Dervish; Yoga.**

Falange Española, *FAY lanj,* or *fah LAHNG hay, ehs pahn YOH lah,* also called Spanish Phalanx, was the only legal political party in Spain under dictator Francisco Franco. The Falange Española was founded in 1933 as a fascist group that attempted to overthrow the republic through violence. José Antonio Primo de Rivera, son of former dictator Miguel Primo de Rivera, founded the party. Falangists supported Franco during the Spanish Civil War (1936-1939). In 1937, Franco took control of the party. After 1945, the party was known as the National Movement. In 1977, after Franco's death, the democratic government of Spain abolished it.   Stanley G. Payne

Falcon is a kind of small bird of prey. Falcons are found in various habitats around the world. They live in grasslands, forests, deserts, and Arctic tundras, and along seacoasts. Falcons probably first appeared thousands of years ago in the grasslands of Africa. Today, there are about 40 species, about half of them found in Africa. The best-known North American species include the *American kestrel,* the *peregrine falcon,* and the *gyrfalcon.*

Like hawks, falcons have a hooked beak and powerful feet with strong claws. Falcons differ from hawks in having dark eyes; long, pointed wings that curve back in a sickle shape; and beaks that have a "tooth" on each side. Most falcons measure from 8 to 24 inches (20 to 60 centimeters) long. Females are larger than males.

Falcons are exceptionally powerful fliers. They often make spectacular *stoops* (steep descents) from great heights to capture prey. They use their feet to either grasp or strike at their prey. Unlike hawks, falcons kill the prey with a powerful bite to the head or neck. Hawks normally kill prey with their claws.

Falcons do not build nests. Females lay their eggs on the ground, on rocky ledges, in abandoned nests, or in holes in trees, cliffs, or even buildings. They usually lay three to five eggs that are buff or whitish in color with brown, red, or purple spots or blotches. In most species, the female *incubates* (sits on and warms) the eggs, with regular help from the male. Most eggs require about 30 days of incubation. For the first few weeks after the young have hatched, the male provides nearly all the food. Many falcons die in the first year of life. Those that survive typically live for 10 years or more.

Merlin
Falco columbarius
Nests in northern North
America, winters in South
America, Mexico, and the
southern United States
Body length: 12 inches
(30 centimeters)

WORLD BOOK illustration
by John F. Eggert

Aplomado falcon
Falco femoralis
Found in Central and South America
and the extreme southwestern United
States
Body length: 16 inches
(41 centimeters)

American kestrel
Falco sparverius
Found throughout the
Western Hemisphere
Body length: 10 inches
(25 centimeters)

Gyrfalcon
Falco rusticolus
Found near the Arctic Circle
Body length: 24 inches
(61 centimeters)

WORLD BOOK illustrations,
except for the Merlin, by Walter Linsenmaier

© Ron Austing, Photo Researchers

Peregrine-gyrfalcon hybrids such as this one are bred for the sport of falconry. Both peregrines and gyrfalcons are prized for their speed and their breathtaking dives after prey.

The American kestrel is the smallest and most common North American falcon. The adult measures about 8 inches (20 centimeters) long. American kestrels range from Alaska through South America. They live in grasslands, woodlands, and even cities. The male kestrel has a reddish-brown back and tail and grayish-blue wings. The female's wings are brown. American kestrels prey on insects, lizards, and mice, and on other birds. They typically hunt from perches. But on windy days, they may *hover* (stay in one place) in the air while hunting. In

© Thinkstock

The peregrine falcon dives at speeds of more than 200 miles (320 kilometers) per hour. This photo shows a peregrine falcon that has been trained to hunt. The trainer keeps the bird from escaping by holding the *jesses* (straps) hanging from its legs.

some areas, they migrate south for the winter.

The peregrine falcon is one of nature's flying marvels. It can stoop for prey at a speed of over 200 miles (320 kilometers) per hour. This falcon measures up to 20 inches (50 centimeters) long. It is dark blue or bluish-gray above and has white to reddish underparts marked with blackish-brown bars. Peregrine falcons live along cliffs near seacoasts, rivers, and lakes, or in the mountains. They once were found throughout most of the world but are now rare or absent in many areas. Scientists have reintroduced them into many present and former habitats, including a number of large cities. These falcons feed chiefly on other birds. In North America, the peregrine falcon is sometimes called *duck hawk.*

The gyrfalcon is the largest species of falcon. The gyrfalcon grows to a length of 2 feet (60 centimeters). It lives in Arctic regions of North America, Europe, and Asia. Most gyrfalcons have white or gray feathers.

Other North American falcons include the *merlin,* the *prairie falcon,* and the *Aplomado falcon.* The merlin lives in open woodlands and other open areas, and along coastal areas, of northern North America. It migrates to the southern United States, Mexico, and South America for the winter. The prairie falcon inhabits deserts or dry grasslands in western North America. The Aplomado falcon is found in high deserts and tropical lowlands. Its range extends from South America north to the extreme southwestern United States, where it is extremely rare.   James W. Grier

Scientific classification. True falcons belong to the family Falconidae. They make up the genus *Falco.* The American kestrel is *F. sparverius;* the peregrine falcon, *F. peregrinus;* and the gyrfalcon, *F. rusticolus.*

Related articles in *World Book* include:
Bird (picture: Interesting facts   Hawk
   about birds; How birds see)   Kestrel
Bird of prey (picture)   Peregrine falcon
Falconry

Falconer, Ian (1959-   ), is an American artist and author known for his children's books about a pig named Olivia. The 3-year-old Olivia is lively, intelligent, and filled with curiosity and self-confidence. Falconer has created a distinctive visual style for the books. He draws the illustrations in black and white with splashes of bright red. He also writes the stories. He introduced Olivia in *Olivia* (2000), his first children's book. The book was inspired by Falconer's niece, also named Olivia.

Falconer was born in 1959 in Connecticut. He studied art history at New York University and painting at the Parsons School of Design (now Parsons the New School for Design) and the Otis Art Institute (now Otis College of Art and Design). He has also designed costumes and sets for ballets and operas and created covers for *The New Yorker* magazine.   John Cech

Falconry, once the "sport of kings," is the art of training falcons, hawks, or eagles to hunt game. A *falconer* is a person who hunts with trained birds of prey.

Training the birds requires patience and persistence. Basically, a hunting bird must be tamed, or "manned," and taught to return to the falconer's fist or to a lure. Special devices aid the falconer. A hood covers the eyes of the bird, keeping it calm. Small bells or radio transmitters are placed on the bird to help locate it when lost. Leg straps called *jesses* restrict the bird's movement when it is on the falconer's hand or perch. A heavy glove protects the falconer's hand from the bird's claws.

The ancient Chinese and the ancient Persians independently began the sport of falconry more than 3,000 years ago. Falconry flourished in Europe during the Middle Ages. Each social class was assigned a certain falcon or hawk to fly as a symbol of rank. Kings flew majestic gyrfalcons, and serfs flew goshawks. In the 1700's, the wide use of firearms nearly brought an end to falconry. The sport, however, continues to attract many followers, especially in North America, Europe, and the Middle East.   Thomas G. Balgooyen

Falkland Islands, *FAWK lund,* make up an overseas territory of the United Kingdom. The islands lie in the South Atlantic Ocean about 320 miles (515 kilometers) east of the southern coast of Argentina (see **South America** [political map]). They form the southernmost British overseas territory outside the British Antarctic Territory. Argentina also claims ownership of the Falkland Islands. Argentina calls them the Islas Malvinas.

The territory includes two large islands, East and West Falkland, and hundreds of smaller ones. East Falkland covers 2,550 square miles (6,605 square kilometers), and West Falkland covers 1,750 square miles (4,533 square kilometers). The remaining islands have a combined area of about 400 square miles (1,035 square kilometers). All the islands together have a coastline of 800 miles (1,288 kilometers). The climate is damp and cool. Strong winds limit the growth of trees on the islands.

Most of the approximately 3,000 inhabitants are of British origin. About three-fourths of the people live in Stanley, the capital and chief town. Stanley is on East Falkland Island. The Falkland Islands' main source of income comes from the sale of fishing licenses to foreign fishing fleets. Many of the islanders raise sheep and export wool. The sale of postage stamps and coins, primarily to collectors, also contributes to the economy.

A governor, chief executive, and Executive Council (cabinet) administer the Falkland Islands. The British monarch appoints the governor, who appoints the chief executive. A partly elected Legislative Assembly makes the islands' laws. The government provides free elementary and secondary education.

The British explorer John Davis sighted the Falklands in 1592. British Captain John Strong first landed on the islands in 1690. He named them for Viscount Falkland, the treasurer of the Royal Navy. France, Spain, and Argentina later claimed the Falklands, but British rule was established in 1833. The British won a naval victory over Germany near the islands in 1914, during World War I.

In April 1982, Argentine troops occupied the islands. The United Kingdom then sent military forces to the Falklands. Air, land, and sea battles broke out. Argentina surrendered in June 1982. After the conflict, the British built an air force base on East Falkland.

In the early 2000's, Argentina's government began pressing the British government anew to hold negotiations about who should control the Falklands. In 2010, British companies began exploring for oil in waters near the islands. In 2013, Falkland Islanders voted almost unanimously in a local *referendum* (direct vote by the people) to remain under British rule. Argentina discredited the vote.   Richard W. Wilkie

Fall. See Autumn.

Fall, Albert Bacon (1861-1944), served as United States secretary of the interior from 1921 to 1923 under President Warren G. Harding. As interior secretary, Fall participated in the events that became known as the Teapot Dome scandal, an illegal lease of government oil reserves to private oil companies. As a result, Fall became the first U.S. Cabinet member to be convicted of a felony committed while in office.

In 1921, Fall persuaded Harding and Secretary of the Navy Edwin Denby to transfer control of three naval oil reserves from the Navy Department to the Department of the Interior. The reserves were in Teapot Dome, Wyoming, and Elk Hills, California. In 1922, Fall leased the reserves in Teapot Dome to oilman Harry F. Sinclair and those in Elk Hills to oilman Edward L. Doheny, without competitive bidding. Fall resigned in 1923 and joined Sinclair's company. In 1924, a Senate investigation revealed Fall had accepted a $100,000 "loan" from Doheny and more than $300,000 in cash, bonds, and livestock from Sinclair for helping arrange the leases. In 1929, Fall was convicted of receiving a bribe. He was sentenced to a year in prison and fined $100,000.

Fall was born in Frankfort, Kentucky, on Nov. 26, 1861. From 1912 to 1921, he served as a U.S. senator from New Mexico. He died on Nov. 30, 1944.   Robert D. Parmet

See also **Teapot Dome.**

Fall line is a series of waterfalls and rapids formed where hard rock meets softer rock. The falls and rapids develop as a river or stream erodes some of the softer rock, creating a ledge over which the water flows. In the eastern United States, a Fall Line stretches from southern New York to Alabama. It formed as water carried

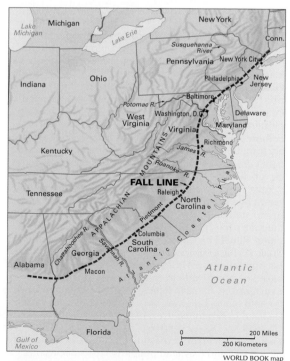

WORLD BOOK map

The Fall Line in the eastern United States extends from New York to Alabama. A series of waterfalls lies along the Fall Line and provides electric power to many cities on the line.

away some of the soft sediments of the Atlantic Coastal Plain, leaving behind the harder rocks of the Piedmont—the plateau east of the Appalachian Mountains. Nearly every stream on the Fall Line has rapids or waterfalls.

The Fall Line of the eastern United States is a great source of electric power. The falling water can be used to turn turbines to generate electric power. Also, the Fall Line generally marks the farthest point inland a ship can go. For these reasons, many important cities have grown up along the Fall Line.   Michael E. Ritter

See also **Piedmont Region; Plain; Waterfall.**

Fall River (pop. 88,857) is an industrial city in southeastern Massachusetts. It lies in a hilly area where the Taunton River flows into Mount Hope Bay (see **Massachusetts** [political map]). The Quequechan River flows through the city. The city's name comes from *Falling Water,* the translation of Quequechan, an Indian name.

From the 1870's until the 1920's, Fall River was the largest center in the United States for the manufacture of cotton textiles. The number of mills declined sharply after 1929. But garment making and the finishing of textile fabrics are still important industries. Other industries include the manufacture of bakery products, commercial dryers, lighting fixtures, plastics, and rubber gloves.

Many granite buildings along the Quequechan River are former cotton mills that now house various industries. The battleship USS *Massachusetts,* which fought in World War II (1939-1945), is docked in Battleship Cove in Mount Hope Bay. The ship is a tourist attraction.

Settlers from Plymouth Colony purchased part of what is now Fall River from the Wampanoag Indians in 1659. In the Battle of Fall River, fought in 1778 during the American Revolution (1775-1783), the townspeople put up a strong defense against a British force. The settlement was incorporated as a town in 1803. From 1804 to 1834, it was called Troy. The name was changed to Fall River in 1834. It was the site of the famous Lizzie Borden murder trial in 1893 (see **Borden, Lizzie**). Fall River has a mayor-council form of government.   Laurence A. Lewis

Falla, *FAH yuh* or *FAH lyah,* **Manuel de,** *mah NWEHL deh* (1876-1946), was a Spanish composer who gained international recognition for his success in developing a modern Spanish style of music. He based many of his compositions on Spanish folklore, folk music, and literary traditions. His best-known work, the music for the ballet *The Three-Cornered Hat* (1919), is based on popular folk music.

Falla's opera *La Vida Breve* won a contest for the best opera by a Spanish composer in 1905, but it was not performed until 1913. His other important works include the music for the ballet *El Amor Brujo* (1915), with its famous "Ritual Fire Dance," and *Nights in the Gardens of Spain* (1916), a composition for piano and orchestra. Falla's puppet opera *Master Peter's Puppet Show* (1923) was based on an episode from the famous Spanish novel *Don Quixote. Fantasia Bética* (1920) is Falla's major work for solo piano. Falla was born on Nov. 23, 1876, in Cádiz. He lived in Argentina from 1939 until his death on Nov. 14, 1946.   Vincent McDermott

Fallacy is an error in reasoning. Many fallacies appear persuasive and may lead people to false conclusions. *Logicians* (people who study logic) divide fallacies into two main groups, *formal* and *informal.*

A formal fallacy is an argument containing a faulty structure or form. The following incorrect argument is an example of a formal fallacy: Because only seniors have their pictures in the book, and because John is a senior, then John's picture is in the book.

Informal fallacies are errors other than violations of the rules of formal logic. One informal fallacy, called *hasty generalization,* is the assumption that what is true of a few cases is true in general. The assumption that what is true of parts is also true of the whole is a fallacy based on a *presumption* or *silent assumption.* A fallacy of *relevance* is an argument in which the truth of the conclusion does not depend on the claims made by the *premises* (beginning statements).   Morton L. Schagrin

See also **Logic.**

Fallen Timbers, Battle of. See **Indian wars** (Conflicts in the Midwest); **Indiana** (Territorial days); **Wayne, Anthony.**

Falling bodies, Law of. Several laws, or rules, tell what an object does when it is allowed to fall to the ground without anything stopping it. These are called the laws of falling bodies. From the time of Aristotle to the end of the 1500's, people believed that if two bodies of different mass were dropped from the same height at the same time, the heavier one would hit the ground first. The great Italian scientist Galileo did not believe this was true. He reasoned that if two bricks of the same mass fall at the same speed, side by side, they ought to fall at the same speed even when cemented together. Therefore, a single brick would fall just as fast as the heavier two bricks cemented together.

Other scientists disagreed with Galileo. According to a story that probably is not true, he proved his theory about 1590 in an experiment at the famous Leaning Tower of Pisa. Galileo is supposed to have gone to the top of the tower with two cannon balls, one large and the other small. He dropped them both at the same instant, and they reached the ground at nearly the same time. There was a small difference, but not nearly so great as the difference between their weights. Galileo concluded that it was the resistance of the air which caused the difference in time of fall. Whether or not Galileo actually conducted this experiment, his reasoning was correct.

The dispute was not finally settled until the air pump

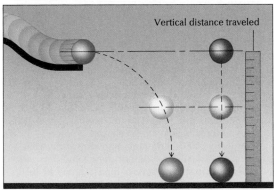

Vertical distance traveled

WORLD BOOK diagram by Laura Lee Lizak

Falling bodies descend at the same rate, regardless of horizontal motion, when their fall is caused by gravity. Although the blue ball travels farther than the red ball, they both hit the ground at the same time. The blue ball's horizontal motion, caused by the chute, does not affect its vertical speed.

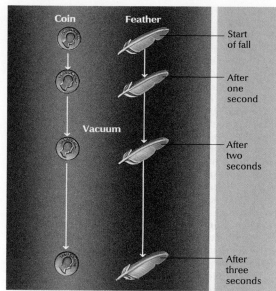

Coin Feather

Start of fall

After one second

Vacuum

After two seconds

After three seconds

WORLD BOOK diagram by Laura Lee Lizak

Bodies falling freely in a vacuum descend at the same speed regardless of their size, shape, or weight. But different objects falling through air may descend at different speeds. This is because objects of different shape meet different amounts of air resistance as they fall.

was invented about 1650. Then it was shown that if the air were pumped from a long tube, and a feather and a coin were dropped down the tube at the same instant, they would fall side by side and reach the bottom together. The force which draws bodies toward Earth is called *gravity* (see **Gravitation**).

It has been found that the force of gravity acts on all bodies alike, regardless of shape, size, composition, or density. Earth attracts bodies toward its center, so all bodies on Earth tend to fall in a direct line toward that point. This is the direction called *down,* and it is exactly perpendicular to the surface of still water.

There are three things to consider in studying the laws of falling bodies. One is the *distance* the body travels when it falls. The second is its *velocity,* or speed in a given direction. The third is its *acceleration,* the rate at which its speed increases as it falls (see **Motion** [Describing motion]). The abbreviations of these three terms are *d, v,* and *a.*

The longer a freely falling body falls, the faster it travels. The first law of falling bodies says that, under the influence of gravity alone, all bodies fall with the same acceleration. If the bodies start from rest, and their velocities increase at the same rate, their velocities will remain equal as they fall.

Actually, when various kinds of bodies fall through the air, they fall at different velocities. The air resists the falling bodies, so they are not falling under the influence of gravity alone. You can test this resistance by dropping two sheets of newspaper, one unfolded and the other crushed into a ball. Both pieces have the same weight, so they give a perfect illustration that the difference of shape and not of mass causes the difference in the speed at which various kinds of bodies fall.

The acceleration of a falling body is the same for each

second during which the body falls. There are no spurts in its "pickup," and its fall is described as *uniformly accelerated* motion. This is true if gravity is the only force acting on the body. Gravity acting on a body that falls from rest increases its velocity during each second of fall by the same amount of velocity that the body had at the end of its first second of fall. The velocity at the end of the first second is 32.16 feet (9.802 meters) per second (at the latitude of New York City). The speed of the body increases at a rate of 32.16 feet per second for each second it falls. The body's acceleration is expressed as *32.16 feet per second per second.* This figure is used in most calculations.

At the end of the 1st second $v = (0 \text{ [rest]} + 32.16) =$ 32.16 feet per second.
At the end of the 2nd second $v = (32.16 + 32.16) =$ 64.32 feet per second.
At the end of the 3rd second $v = (64.32 + 32.16) =$ 96.48 feet per second.
At the end of the 4th second $v = (96.48 + 32.16) =$ 128.64 feet per second.

A simple formula to get the velocity of a falling body at the end of any second is to multiply the body's acceleration, *a,* or 32.16 feet per second per second, by the time the body has fallen in seconds, *t.* This can be written in the form of an equation as:

$$v = a \times t = 32.16 \times t$$

There is also a simple formula to find the distance a body falls in a given second. Multiply the distance it falls the first second by twice the total number of seconds, minus 1. The distance fallen during the first second is always 16.08 feet (4.901 meters), which comes from the value of the acceleration, *a,* divided by 2. Thus, the distance fallen during the third second is 16.08 feet $\times [(2 \times 3) - 1]$ = 80.40 feet. The distance fallen during the fourth second equals 16.08 feet $\times [(2 \times 4) - 1] = 112.56$ feet. In equation form, the distance traveled in any second is:

$$d = \left(\frac{a}{2}\right) \times (2t-1) = \left(\frac{32.16}{2}\right) \times (2t-1) = 16.08 \times (2t-1)$$

By adding the distance fallen during any given second to the distances for all the preceding seconds, you can find the total distance traveled at the end of that given second. For instance, at the end of the third second, a body has fallen $16.08 + 48.24 + 80.40$ feet, which adds up to 144.72 feet. Now 144.72 can also be divided up this way: $3 \times 3 \times 16.08$. The total distance fallen in 4 seconds, 257.28 feet, can be divided this way: $4 \times 4 \times 16.08$. So a shorter formula has been worked out which says that the distance a falling body travels in a given time equals the value of its acceleration divided by 2 and then multiplied by the square of the number of seconds, or 16.08 times the square of the number of seconds.

$$d = \left(\frac{a}{2}\right) \times t^2 = \left(\frac{32.16}{2}\right) \times t^2 = 16.08 \times t^2$$

The above three equations are true not only for falling bodies, but for any bodies that have uniformly accelerated motion. Any acceleration, *a,* can be used instead of 32.16 feet per second per second.   Michael Dine

Fallopian tube, also called *oviduct* or *uterine tube,* is either of a pair of female reproductive organs through which eggs from the ovaries pass to the uterus. The fallopian tube is the site where an egg is usually fertilized by the male's sperm. See **Reproduction, Human** (The human reproductive system; picture).

In women, each fallopian tube is about 4 inches (10 centimeters) long. The tubes are lined with two types of cells, *ciliated cells* and *secretory cells.* The ciliated cells have *cilia* (hairlike structures) on their surface that help carry the egg into and through the tube. The secretory cells produce secretions that nourish the egg.

After entering the tube, an egg must be fertilized by sperm within about 24 hours or it dies. Sperm enter the tube through the uterus, and contractions of the tube help move the sperm toward the ovary. The egg remains in the fallopian tube for about 72 hours before passing into the uterus. An *ectopic pregnancy* occurs when a fertilized egg does not pass to the uterus, but attaches and begins to grow inside the fallopian tube. The baby cannot survive such a pregnancy, which may also be fatal to the mother if untreated.

Blockages in the fallopian tube may result from diseases or birth defects and can cause infertility. In some cases, the blockage can be removed surgically. A woman with blocked tubes may become pregnant through a procedure called *in vitro fertilization.* In this procedure, eggs collected from the ovaries are fertilized in a laboratory dish with sperm and then inserted back into the uterus.   Lynn J. Romrell

Fallout is radioactive material that settles over Earth's surface following a nuclear explosion. Fallout can also be released by a nuclear reactor as part of an accident. Some of the material consists of atoms known as *radioactive isotopes* or *radioisotopes.* These isotopes form from the *fission* (splitting) of uranium or plutonium in a nuclear weapon or reactor. Radioisotopes also form when radiation that results from an explosion causes other atoms nearby to become radioactive.

After an explosion or accident, the radioisotopes in the air, on the ground, and in the bodies of living things *decay* (break down) into more stable isotopes. They do so by emitting radiation in the form of alpha particles, beta particles, and gamma rays. Exposure to large amounts of this radiation can result in immediate sickness and even death. Exposure to this radiation over longer periods can cause cancer and damage genes.

The testing of nuclear weapons in the atmosphere once produced large amounts of fallout. Today, fallout from aboveground testing has been eliminated by underground testing. However, a serious accident in a nuclear reactor can also create fallout.

How fallout is produced. Nuclear explosions produce a giant fireball of intensely hot gases and dust. Everything inside the fireball or in contact with it is *vaporized* (turned into a gas). When an explosion occurs close to Earth's surface, the fireball vaporizes soil, vegetation, and buildings. The intensely hot gases of the fireball also draw in dirt, dust, and other small particles as the fireball rises into the atmosphere. The radioisotopes formed during fission then combine with the vaporized materials. As the vaporized materials rise and cool, some of them condense into solid particles ranging in size from fine invisible dust to ashes the size of snowflakes. These particles, to which radioisotopes have become attached, fall to Earth—thus the term *fallout.*

How fallout is distributed. The time it takes fallout particles to settle out of the atmosphere and reach Earth and the distance they travel from the point of origin depend on several factors: (1) the force of the explosion, (2) the particles' size and composition, (3) the altitude they reach before they start to fall, (4) the pattern of winds that carry them, (5) the latitude at which the release of radioisotopes occurs, and (6) the time of year.

The larger or heavier fallout particles settle near where they are released in an irregularly shaped area, depending on the winds that carry them. In general, the intensity of radiation decreases as the distance from the point of origin increases. But areas of intense radioactivity called *hot spots* may be scattered within the zone of fallout. Hot spots occur when rain, snow, or other precipitation washes fallout particles out of the atmosphere.

The smaller particles of fallout may be scattered by winds to distant parts of the world. Winds traveling

Fallout from an April 1986 accident at the Chernobyl nuclear power plant in eastern Europe covered large parts of Ukraine, Belarus, and Russia. This map shows ground contamination by cesium-137, a radioactive form of the chemical element cesium. Amounts of contamination are given in units of radioactivity called curies.

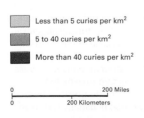

Less than 5 curies per km²

5 to 40 curies per km²

More than 40 curies per km²

0   200 Miles
0   200 Kilometers

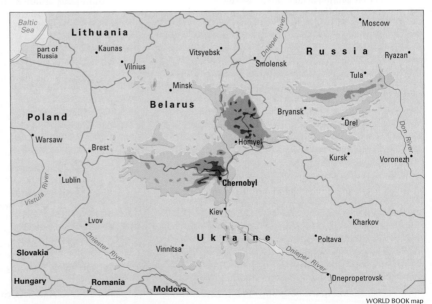

through the *troposphere,* the lowest layer of the atmosphere, carry some fallout for a few days to a few weeks. Winds near Earth's surface often change their direction. But in the upper troposphere, winds generally blow in an eastward direction. Fallout carried to this height circles Earth within a week or two. Most of the fallout drops in a band around Earth near the latitude of the fallout's origin.

In the most powerful nuclear explosions, much of the fallout may rise to the *stratosphere,* which is the layer of atmosphere above the troposphere. In the stratosphere, fallout becomes widely scattered. As a result, it may take from several months to several years to return to Earth's surface.

The fallout hazard. Fallout can be dangerous to plants, animals, and people because of the radioactive elements it contains (see **Radiation sickness**). These radioactive elements include about 200 isotopes of more than 30 chemical elements produced by a nuclear explosion.

Different radioisotopes in fallout give off radiation for different periods. Most fallout decays into more stable isotopes in a matter of hours or days. As a result, the radioactivity at the end of two weeks is only one-thousandth as strong as the radioactivity one hour after the nuclear explosion. A few of the fallout elements continue to give off radiation over a long period. For example, the radioisotope strontium 90 loses half its radioactive strength every 28 years, and the radioisotope cesium 137 loses half its strength every 30 years. See **Radiation** (Radiation and radioactivity).

Exposure to radiation created by fallout occurs mainly in two ways. The first type of exposure results from radioactive particles and debris on the ground. People can protect themselves from this direct radiation by taking refuge in underground fallout shelters or by staying indoors. A covering of soil or the walls of a building provide protection from fallout.

Second, fallout can enter the body through air, food, or drinking water contaminated by radioisotopes. Normally, radioactive particles do not remain airborne long. Thus, contaminated air is only hazardous for a short time. The transfer of radiation through food occurs over longer periods. A common pathway for the transfer of radioisotopes is through milk. This transfer begins when fallout settles on grass and cows eat the grass. Some of the radioisotopes are then transferred to the cow's milk. Anyone who drinks the contaminated milk takes in iodine 131, which collects in the thyroid; strontium 90, which is absorbed by the bones; or cesium 137, which is retained in muscle or other tissues. Foods are also contaminated by the direct deposit of fallout on plants and by the slow uptake of radioisotopes in soil by the roots of plants.

History. From the mid-1940's to the early 1960's, the United States, the Soviet Union, and a few other nations exploded numerous experimental nuclear weapons. As a result of these explosions, fallout increased to alarming levels. In 1963, more than 100 nations, including the United States and the Soviet Union, signed a treaty that banned the testing of nuclear weapons everywhere but underground. Fallout then decreased greatly. China and France did not sign the treaty. But they later stopped testing nuclear weapons aboveground.

Today, accidents at nuclear reactors pose the greatest risk of fallout. In 1986, an accident at the Chernobyl nuclear power plant in Ukraine, then part of the Soviet Union, created fallout consisting mainly of the radioisotopes iodine 131 and cesium 137. A power surge caused fuel in the nuclear reactor to overheat, resulting in a steam explosion and fire. The radioisotopes created by nuclear fission in the reactor escaped into the atmosphere through the smoke from the fire, which burned for 10 days.

The fallout from the Chernobyl accident was distributed by winds. However, the majority of the debris remained in the troposphere. Areas that sustained the highest levels of radioactive deposits were in northwest Ukraine, southeast Belarus, and southwest Russia. In addition, precipitation created hot spots throughout the zone of fallout. Radioactive isotopes were carried into northern and central Europe. Traces of radioactivity were eventually measurable throughout the Northern Hemisphere. The explosion at Chernobyl was the worst nuclear accident in history.

However, other serious accidents have also occurred. One of the worst accidents happened at the Windscale plutonium production plant in northern England in 1957. Fallout from a fire in a reactor at the Windscale plant contaminated about 200 square miles (520 square kilometers) of surrounding countryside.

In the United States, an accident occurred at the Three Mile Island nuclear power plant near Harrisburg, Pennsylvania, in 1979. Overheating caused by an interruption in the reactor's cooling system resulted in severe damage to a reactor core. However, a protective building that contained the reactor largely prevented the radioactive debris from being released into the environment. In 2011, the Fukushima Daiichi Nuclear Power Station in Japan released about 10 to 20 percent as much fallout as did the Chernobyl disaster. A tsunami wave produced by an earthquake had damaged the complex, resulting in overheating and steam explosions.   Steven L. Simon

See also **Chernobyl disaster; Civil defense; Isotope; Nuclear energy** (Safety concerns); **Nuclear weapon; Radiation** (Effects of radiation).

Fallout shelter. See Civil defense.

Falls. See Waterfall.

False imprisonment is any unlawful restraint of a person, whether by confinement in a jail or elsewhere, by threats, or by force. An unlawful arrest, called a *false arrest,* is a form of false imprisonment. However, false imprisonment may also follow a legal arrest.

False imprisonment is an offense against both the victim and the state. The victim may sue for damages, charge the offender with a crime, or both.

James O. Finckenauer

False teeth. See Dentistry (Prosthodontics).

Family, in biology, is a unit of scientific classification. Scientists have developed an orderly arrangement of all living things to show certain relationships among them. Organisms are classified in seven major groups. These groups are called kingdoms, phyla or divisions, classes, orders, families, genera, and species. Members of a family are more closely related than members of an order, but not so closely related as members of a genus.

Theodore J. Crovello

See also **Classification, Scientific** (table).

A nuclear Russian family

© Jonathan T. Wright, Bruce Coleman Inc.

An extended Indian family

© Gottlieb, Monkmeyer

A single-parent American family

© David R. Frazier

A childless Chinese couple

© Todd Gipstein, Corbis

People of all cultures live in families. These groups range from two people to *extended families,* in which grandparents, parents, and children may share a home. The most common family type in many nations, the *nuclear family,* consists of a mother, a father, and their children.

Family

Family is the basic unit of social organization in all human societies. Since prehistoric times, families have served as the primary institution responsible for raising children and for providing people with food and shelter. Families also serve to satisfy people's need for love and support.

The term *family* generally refers to a group of people related to one another by birth, marriage, or adoption. In contemporary society, people often apply the word *family* to any group that feels a sense of *kinship* (family connection).

Varieties of families

Family types vary in different countries and among different cultures. In Western, industrialized societies, the *nuclear family* ranks as the most common family type. A nuclear family consists of a father, a mother, and their children.

Nuclear families exist alongside many other types of family units. In the *single-parent family,* for example, a mother or a father heads the family alone. A family

known as a *blended family* is formed when a divorced or widowed parent remarries. As divorce rates have risen, the number of single-parent and blended families has increased.

An increasingly common family form in Western societies is the *consensual union,* in which couples live together but remain unmarried. When a homosexual couple decides to live together as a family, they form a *same-sex union.* Although such unions have become more common, most countries do not recognize them as legal families. People often call a married couple whose children have grown up and left home an *empty-nest family.*

In many parts of the world, parents and children live together with other family members under the same roof. These *complex families* usually contain several generations of family members, including grandparents, parents, and children. They may also include brothers or sisters and their families, uncles, aunts, and cousins. Even when relatives do not live together, they still consider themselves members of the same *extended family.*

In Latin American and Hispanic American cultures, the extended family, called *la familia,* includes grandparents, uncles, aunts, and cousins.

Some cultures follow a traditional practice called *polygamy,* in which a person can have more than one *spouse* (husband or wife). The two chief forms of polygamy are *polygyny* and *polyandry.* In *polygyny,* a man marries more than one woman. In *polyandry,* a woman has more than one husband.

Since the early 1800's, various *utopian communities* have attempted to create substitutes for the nuclear family. Utopian communities are groups of people who want to create an ideal society in which everyone will be happy. The Oneida community, which flourished in rural New York state from the 1840's to the late 1870's, considered all its adult citizens married to one another. Oneida children were raised by the community as a whole. One of the aims of such utopian communities was to modify the rigid family roles of husband and wife so that women could participate more equally in society.

Family relationships

Family members can be related to one another by *blood*—that is, by birth; by *affinity*—that is, through marriage; or through adoption. Most nuclear families consist of a father, a mother, and their *biological children* (children born to them). When a couple adopt a child, the child becomes a member of their family. Brothers and sisters who share the same parents are *siblings.* Half *brothers* and *half sisters* share either the same biological mother or biological father. When divorced or widowed parents remarry, the parent's new spouse becomes the children's *stepfather* or *stepmother.* Children from the couple's previous marriages become *stepbrothers* and *stepsisters* to one another.

When people marry, they gain a new set of relatives called *in-laws.* The mother of a person's spouse is called a *mother-in-law,* the brother is called a *brother-in-law,* and so on throughout the rest of the family.

The parents of a person's mother or father are that person's *grandparents. Great-grandparents* are the parents of a person's grandparents. An *aunt* is the sister of a person's mother or father. An *uncle* is the brother of a parent. An uncle's wife is also called aunt, and an aunt's husband is also called uncle. A *first cousin* is the child of a person's aunt or uncle. The child of a first cousin is a person's *first cousin once removed*—that is, removed by one generation. Children of first cousins are *second cousins* to each other.

Some people consider certain friends as part of their family because they feel special affection for them. Although these friends are not true family members, such friends are called *fictive kin,* and family members might call them "aunts" or "uncles." Relatives or close friends of a parent may become *godparents* to that parent's children. Godparents, as sponsors to a Christian baptism, often play more vital roles in the lives of families than other fictive kin. In Latin American and Hispanic American families, godparents, called *compadres,* provide advice, emotional support, and assistance in times of need.

Importance of the family

Family functions. Families perform many necessary functions, both for individual family members and for society as a whole. In virtually all cultures, the family serves as the basic institution for bearing children, caring for them during their early years, and preparing them to function effectively in society. Families around the world must also provide food and clothing to their members. In addition, families meet important psychological needs, such as the need for love, support, and companionship.

The family's duties have changed over time. In the past, families not only cared for the young but also grew their own food, made their own clothing, and provided services for themselves that modern families generally do not provide. Parents taught reading, writing, and craft skills to their children. Families also cared for sick and elderly relatives and often provided financial support for members in need. Since the 1800's, many of these traditional responsibilities have shifted to such institutions as schools, hospitals, insurance companies, and nursing homes.

Roles within the family have also changed. Traditionally, the father was expected to take up an occupation to support his wife and children. The mother, in turn, ran the home and cared for the children. Today, however, both parents commonly work outside the home, and fathers often perform household duties formerly expected of women.

Home life. The home is the center of family activities. These activities include raising children, eating meals, playing games, watching television, keeping house, and entertaining friends. In the home, children learn basic social skills, such as how to talk and get along with others. They also learn health and safety habits there.

A family's home life is influenced by which members live in the home and by the roles each member plays. Home life can also be affected by relatives who live outside the family's home. Traditions, laws, and social conditions help determine who lives in a home and the place each family member holds.

Traditions, which are customs or beliefs that people have followed for a long time, strongly influence family life. For example, some Americans have little contact with relatives outside the nuclear family. But many Chinese families feel strong ties to such relatives and see them often. Aunts, uncles, and cousins traditionally play important roles in the lives of these people.

Laws affect family behavior in various ways. Some laws set forth the legal rights and responsibilities people have as husbands, wives, parents, and children. In many Western nations, laws forbid abuse of children by parents, and of one spouse by the other. Laws also deal with marriage, divorce, and adoption.

Social conditions can also influence family life. For example, in cultures that discourage women from working outside the home, mothers become full-time homemakers, while men act as the sole wage earners.

Development of the family

Ancient families. Most ancient societies had no term exactly the same as our modern word for family. This was because ancient families varied widely in their size and structure depending on social class. The wealthiest households contained dozens of kinsfolk, servants, and slaves. At the same time, slaves and poor free people had no opportunity to establish independent homes.

Ancient families had strict arrangements of higher- and lower-ranking persons. In ancient Roman society, which flourished about 2,000 years ago, the male head of the family, the *paterfamilias,* had absolute authority. Under Roman law, he could sell his children, abandon them, or even put them to death. Male heads of families arranged marriages in most ancient societies. Fathers often contracted daughters to marry at young ages. In ancient Greek culture, which reached its height during the mid-400's B.C., the average marriage age of women ranged from 12 to 15, while many men married at about age 30.

The ancient world permitted a variety of family practices that most people would condemn today. In ancient Greece and Rome, for example, parents could leave handicapped or sickly infants outdoors to die, a practice called *exposure*. In ancient Egypt, which arose about 5,000 years ago, men could marry their sisters. Most cultures today consider such marriages *incest* and prohibit them by law.

Ancient cultures also permitted easy divorce and often practiced polygyny and *concubinage* (the practice of a husband living with a woman who was not his legal wife). Polygyny and concubinage enabled a powerful or wealthy family to have children when the man's first wife failed to produce an *heir*, a child who could inherit the family's wealth.

Development of the Western family. Christianity played a critical role in the emergence of new family patterns. At the beginning of the Christian era, as early as the A.D. 300's, family patterns in Western Europe began to diverge from those in the non-Western world. Western European families placed an emphasis on the bond between husband and wife, as opposed to broader kinship relationships.

The Christian church encouraged young people to remain *celibate* (unmarried) and to enter religious orders. During the early Christian era, a growing number of women in Western Europe never married or bore children. The church also condemned the exposure of infants and opposed concubinage, polygyny, arranged marriages, marriages with close kin, and divorce. The church insisted that marriages could not be dissolved by divorce, helping make the nuclear family more important than in the past.

During the Middle Ages in Europe, which lasted from about the A.D. 400's through the 1400's, the wealthiest households could contain 40 or more people. These inhabitants included such nonrelatives as *pages* (boys from wealthy families in training to become knights) and servants. But the average medieval household was much smaller, containing about four or five members. Most families lived in cramped houses that lacked privacy. Relatives often shared beds and used the same rooms for working, entertaining, cooking, eating, storage, and sleeping.

Medieval households were productive units. Wives cooked, preserved food, made textiles and clothing, tended gardens, and brewed beer. In addition to farming, many husbands engaged in such crafts as carpentry, ironworking, and barrel-making.

Family life in medieval Europe was unstable. Famine, plagues, and other calamities caused a radical decline in population. Because most parents worked much of the

© Thinkstock

Touring places of interest is a popular family activity throughout the world. This photograph shows a family visiting a temple in Bali.

day, young children received little supervision from adults. Economic pressures forced many parents to send their children away from home at young ages, often before the age of 8. Numerous children became servants in private homes, apprentices in business, or workers for the church. Because of the high death rate, many people remarried. A large number of marriages involved partners who had been married before. Consequently, numerous medieval families contained stepparents and stepchildren.

During the 1500's, Protestant reformers often criticized the Roman Catholic Church for permitting certain family practices. These practices included allowing young people to marry without parental consent, forbidding clergy to marry, and prohibiting divorce and remarriage when marriages broke down. Many Protestant societies, including those in Puritan New England, required parental consent to make a marriage valid and instituted laws against wife beating and adultery. Protestant countries recognized a right to divorce with remarriage in cases of abandonment, adultery, and extreme physical cruelty.

Early Western families in America. During America's colonial period, which lasted from the 1500's to 1775, the family served many functions. It educated children, cared for the elderly and sick, taught job skills to the young, and functioned as the economic center of production. Every person was strongly urged to live in a family. In some parts of New England, the government taxed bachelors and imposed other penalties on those who did not marry. Married couples who lived apart from each other had to show good reason.

American families in the 1600's were led by the father. He had to give his legal consent before his children could marry. His control over inheritance kept his grown sons and daughters dependent upon him for years, while they waited for his permission to marry and to establish a separate household.

Early Americans did not consider love a requirement for marriage, and couples assumed that love would follow marriage. Relations between spouses tended to be formal. Husbands and wives treated each other with correct, serious manners rather than the relaxed, friendly way families interact today.

African American families under slavery faced unique problems in early America. Many states refused to recognize slave marriages as legal. Moreover, about a third of all slave marriages were broken by sale, and about half of all slave children were sold from their parents. Even when sale did not break the marriage, slave spouses often resided on separate plantations. On large plantations, a slave father might have a different owner than his wife had, and he could visit his wife and family only with his master's permission.

Despite all these obstacles, enslaved African Americans forged strong family and kinship ties. Most slaves married and lived with the same spouse until death. To sustain a sense of family identity, slaves named their children after parents, grandparents, and other kin. Enslaved African Americans also passed down family names to their children, usually the name of an ancestor's owner rather than that of the current owner. Ties to an immediate family stretched outward to an involved network of extended kin. Whenever children were sold to neighboring plantations, grandparents, aunts, uncles, and cousins took on the functions of parents. Strangers cared for and protected children who had lost their blood relatives.

Changes. During the mid-1700's, family life in colonial America and parts of Europe underwent far-reaching changes. Parents gave children more freedom in selecting their own spouse. This freedom led people to view marriage increasingly as an emotional bond involving love and affection. Spouses displayed affection for each other more openly. In addition, parents became more interested in their children's development. Instead of viewing children as miniature adults, parents regarded children as people with special needs and began to buy them children's books, games, and toys.

During the early 1800's, many middle-class families became able to rely on a single wage-earner, where the husband worked outside the home and the wife served as a full-time homemaker and mother. Many of these families could afford to keep their children home into their late teens, instead of sending them out as servants or apprentices. By the mid-1800's, such family events as the vacation and the birthday party had appeared.

For many working-class families, however, low wages and a lack of year-round employment meant that all family members had to work. All members of a working-class family had to help earn a living. Wives did piecework in the home, took in laundry, or rented rooms to boarders. Many working-class families depended on the labor of children.

By the end of the 1800's, many people in Western societies had become worried about what was happening to the family. The divorce rate was rising. Infant and child death rates were high, with as many as a third of children dying by the age of 15. Meanwhile, more Western women never married, and the birth rate had fallen sharply during the 1800's. Instead of bearing seven or more children, as women had in 1800, a typical middle-class woman in the United States bore only three.

At the beginning of the 1900's, groups of people fought to improve the well-being of families and children. To reduce children's death rate, these reformers lobbied for an end to child labor. They also fought for special *pensions* (government payments) to enable widows to raise their children at home, instead of sending them to orphanages.

As more people grew concerned about strengthening families, a new family ideal became popular by the 1920's. This ideal, called the *companionate family,* held that husbands and wives should be "friends and lovers" and that parents and children should be "pals."

During the Great Depression of the 1930's, unemployment, lower wages, and the demands of needy relatives tore at the fabric of family life. Many people had to share living quarters with relatives, delay marriage, and put off having children. The divorce rate fell because fewer people could afford it, but many fathers deserted their families. Families sought to cope by planting gardens,

Photograph (1908) by Lewis Wickes Hine; International Museum of Photography, Rochester, N.Y.

A family of the early 1900's made artificial flowers in their home to sell. Working as a group to earn a living was an important function of the family everywhere before the Industrial Revolution began in the 1700's. But by the time this photograph was taken, few families in industrial societies still worked together at home to support themselves.

canning food, and making clothing. Children worked in part-time jobs, and wives worked outside the home or took in sewing or laundry. Many families housed lodgers, and some set up a small grocery store in a front parlor.

World War II (1939-1945) also subjected families to severe strain. During the war, families faced a great shortage of housing, a lack of schools and child-care facilities, and prolonged separation from loved ones. When fathers went to war, mothers ran their homes and cared for their children alone, and women went to work in war industries. The stresses of wartime contributed to an increase in the divorce rate. Many young people became unsupervised "latchkey children," returning from school each day to an empty home, and rates of juvenile delinquency rose.

The late 1940's and 1950's witnessed a sharp reaction to the stresses of the Great Depression and World War II. The divorce rate slowed, and couples married earlier than their parents had. Women bore more children at younger ages and closer together than in the past. The result was a "baby boom."

Since the mid-1900's, families in all Western countries have undergone far-reaching changes. From the 1960's to the 1980's, birth rates dropped and divorce rates rose considerably. In addition, mothers entered the labor force in record numbers, and a growing proportion of children were born to unmarried mothers. The pace of familial change slowed during the late 1900's and early 2000's, but family life remains considerably altered from what it was before the 1960's.

Non-Western families. Traditionally, non-Western societies have attached less importance to the nuclear family than to the larger family network. People in this network, which is often called the *lineage, clan,* or *tribe,* trace their descent to a common ancestor. In many parts of the world, kinship ties determine whom one can and cannot marry and where one lives after marriage. Different kinds of societies have produced different extended family traditions. The three major kinds of societies are known as *patrilineal, matrilineal,* and *bilateral kinship.*

In patrilineal societies, including many in India, China, and various African countries, a husband and wife commonly reside with the husband's father and his kin after marriage. In matrilineal cultures, such as the Navajo and the Pueblo of the American Southwest, a husband joins his wife's mother's household. Within matrilineal societies, a mother's older brother often has responsibility for disciplining children and offering advice about marriage. In cultures with a bilateral kinship system, such as that of the Inuit (Eskimos), a couple might join either the husband's father's family or the wife's mother's family, or form an independent household.

Forms of marriage have also differed across cultures. Some societies, including many African cultures, allow men to take more than one wife. In such societies, only the wealthiest males can afford polygyny. Many societies, such as those of China and India, also practiced arranged marriages and *child marriage* (marriage at or before puberty). In addition, numerous non-Western cultures permitted divorce and remarriage long before Western countries legalized such practices. A number of predominantly Catholic countries did not permit divorce and remarriage until the late 1900's.

© chiakto / Shutterstock

A Mongolian family blends modern technology with the traditional way of life of nomadic herders. The family lives in a felt tent called a *ger* that is fitted with solar panels for heating.

Since the mid-1900's, families around the world have become more similar. Birth rates are dropping, divorce rates are rising, increasing numbers of homes are headed by women, and more births are taking place outside of marriage. As societies allow more personal choice, such practices as child marriage, arranged marriages, polygyny, and concubinage have become less common.

Challenges and opportunities

Public concern about the family remains high for many reasons. High rates of teenage pregnancy and births to unmarried mothers force many young women to leave school or abandon career plans. Children from such families often grow up in poverty and will more likely turn to crime. Drug and alcohol use and domestic violence also plague many families and lead to developmental disorders in children.

With both mothers and fathers in many families working, parents struggle to find enough time to spend with their children. Working parents who can afford to may send their children to day care, but such parents often feel guilty that they do not spend enough time with their children. Those who cannot afford to or do not choose to use day care often have to leave their jobs or take cuts in pay. The resulting loss of income makes it harder for them to keep up their standard of living. For poorer parents, such a cut in earnings can be devastating.

Although not a new problem, divorce remains an important challenge for families to overcome. Most men and women who seek a divorce do so because they cannot solve certain problems in their marriage. Such problems may include differences in goals or financial difficulty. If such problems remain unsolved, the marriage often breaks down. Divorce can affect every member of the family deeply. Children, for example, may grow up in a fatherless or motherless home. If one or both of the parents remarry, the children may fail to develop loving relationships with their new stepparents.

Despite the challenges of today's society, however, the family is not a dying institution. In many respects, family life today is stronger than it was in the past. Most people marry and have children. Although divorce rates are higher than in the past, most individuals who do divorce eventually remarry.

Because of declining death rates, more couples now grow into old age together, and more children have living grandparents. These relatives generally live much farther away from each other than they did in the past. However, e-mail and other communications technology may promote greater contact between separated family members.

Meanwhile, parents now make greater emotional and economic investment in their children. Lower birth rates mean that parents can devote more attention and greater financial resources to each child. Fathers especially have become more involved in child rearing.

More than ever before, families in trouble can receive help from outside sources, such as a family counselor, a social worker, or a psychologist. Such specialists often meet with the entire family to help its members work out problems together. Public welfare agencies and other organizations provide economic aid to poor families and assistance to abused spouses or children.

In the future, families will continue to face many challenges, especially the need to balance the demands of work and family life. Working parents must not only care for their young children, but, because of increasing life spans, tend to aging parents as well.   Steven Mintz

Related articles. See the *Way of life* or *Family life* section of various country articles, such as **Mexico** (Way of life). See also the articles on groups of people, such as **Inuit** and **Indian, American.** Other related articles in *World Book* include:

Children

Adolescent	Child	Children's home
Adoption	Child welfare	Day care
Baby	Children's Bureau	Growth

Parents

Divorce	Marriage	Parents Without
Foster care	Parent	Partners
Guardian	Parent education	

Family life in ancient times

Egypt, Ancient (Family life)	Rome, Ancient (Family life)
Greece, Ancient (Family life)	

Other related articles

Birth control	Latin America (picture: Family
Children and Families,	ties)
Administration for	Planned Parenthood Federa-
Civil union	tion of America
Clan	Polygamy
Community	Tribe
Cousin	Women's movement (Impact
Domestic violence	of women's movements)
Genealogy	

Outline

I. **Varieties of families**
II. **Family relationships**
III. **Importance of the family**
    A. Family functions   B. Home life
IV. **Development of the family**
    A. Ancient families
    B. Development of the Western family
    C. Early Western families in America
    D. Changes
    E. Non-Western families
V. **Challenges and opportunities**

Questions

What are the three major kinds of extended families?
What responsibilities do parents have toward their children?
How was family life affected as Western nations became increasingly industrialized in the 1700's and 1800's?
How are second cousins related to each other?
What are some functions the family fulfills in society?
What are some reasons for the changes in traditional family patterns?
What was a companionate family?
How did Christianity affect the development of the Western family?

Family and consumer sciences is a field of study that focuses on improving the well-being of individuals, families, and communities. The field is still mostly known internationally as *home economics.* But since the 1960's, a variety of names, including *human ecology, human sciences,* and *human environmental science* have come into use in the United States. These changes in names have reflected changes in society, universities, and the profession.

Family and consumer science professionals emphasize the interconnections and interactions among different systems. For example, these systems could include the family system and the community system or consumers and the economic system. Professionals trained in the field may work as researchers, scientists, designers, teachers, human service professionals, writers, consultants, administrators, or entrepreneurs.

Areas of study

Because the lives of individuals and families are interconnected, the specializations in family and consumer sciences are also connected. They include (1) human development and family studies; (2) design, production of consumer goods and services, and retailing; (3) hospitality management; (4) nutrition, dietetics, and food science; (5) family and consumer sciences education and communications; and (6) consumer economics and family resource management. Programs in these areas connect and join courses from other specialized areas and use knowledge of these relationships to address many concerns of everyday life.

Human development and family studies focuses on the physical, emotional, psychological, and social development of individuals of all ages. It also covers interactions between family members. Students in these studies learn to teach such topics as cooperation, parenting, family relationships, development throughout the life cycle, group decision making and problem solving, and conflict and crisis prevention and management. Students may become day-care managers for children or vulnerable adults, teachers of young children and youth, marriage and family counselors, or community service professionals.

Design, production of consumer goods and services, and retailing aims to increase human well-being by providing resources for daily living. Programs in this area focus on the design of apparel and home furnishings. Programs also concentrate on the development and sale of *consumer goods* (items produced for use by individuals and families) and *services* (activities performed that have value, such as legal advice). Some programs focus on the interior design of homes, offices, stores, hotels, and other buildings. Graduates may have careers as interior or apparel designers, fiber artists, sales or advertising specialists, or managers and buyers for retail companies.

Hospitality management focuses on providing for people's needs away from home. Courses include hotel and motel management; restaurant, beverage, and food service management; food preparation; nutrition; human relations; marketing; and finance. Graduates can manage hotels, restaurants, and rental housing, or plan conventions and recreational activities.

Nutrition, dietetics, and food science focuses on the knowledge and skills needed to ensure that individuals get adequate nutrition and enjoy food. Students in this area study the body's nutritional requirements, the nutritional value of various foods, food safety, the relationship of diet to disease and its prevention, the development of food products, and food service management. Study in this area can lead to a career as a dietitian, public health nutritionist, fitness consultant, or food or nutrition scientist.

Family and consumer sciences education and communications prepares teachers and other communicators for work in schools, businesses, government agencies, or television and other media. Some graduates work as teachers in schools, universities, or community-based programs. Others find careers in advertising, journalism, and broadcasting.

Consumer economics and family resource management examines how individuals and families manage money, time, energy, talent, and other resources. Students in this area focus on family financial planning, family and consumer economics, and protecting the interests of consumers.

History

The field of family and consumer sciences—originally called home economics—developed largely in response to the Industrial Revolution, a period of rapid industrialization that began in the 1700's. The Industrial Revolution had a large impact on individual and family life by the 1800's.

In the 1800's, educated women were not allowed to enter many male-dominated careers, so they created their own profession of home economics. They used this new profession to address such social problems as unsanitary, overcrowded housing with inadequate plumbing and ventilation; inadequate city sanitary services and water systems; infectious diseases (the main cause of death); unhealthy diets; the drudgery of housework; and deteriorating home life. Professional home economists applied science to improving the safety and wholesomeness of food and water and taught sanitary practices.

In the mid-1800's, Catharine E. Beecher established schools for young women that taught cooking, child care, home management, and other skills under the name *domestic economy.* Her efforts led to the founding of a home economics movement. In the late 1800's, Ellen Richards, a chemist and the first woman admitted to the Massachusetts Institute of Technology, promoted science applied to the practical problems of the home. She led the transition of the movement into a profession during 10 annual conferences in Lake Placid, New York, that were held from 1899 to 1909. Richards and others

founded the American Home Economics Association (now the American Association of Family and Consumer Sciences) and the *Journal of Home Economics* in 1909.

Over the years, new specializations emerged, and universities and other institutions adopted a variety of names for their home economics programs, creating confusion. In 1993, in Scottsdale, Arizona, representatives of five home economics-related organizations recommended that the profession change its name to family and consumer sciences.

The field of family and consumer sciences has changed greatly in response to U.S. and global developments. These developments included new knowledge, changes in the roles of men and women, fewer families with full-time homemakers, diminishing natural resources, more pollution and waste problems, and technological advances.

Career requirements

Professionals in family and consumer sciences have at least a bachelor's degree. Many positions require advanced degrees. Students may be required to take courses in the biological, physical, and social sciences. Other studies include courses that teach students to work across specializations as a way to solve real problems of daily life. Some specializations require courses in the arts and humanities.

The American Association of Family and Consumer Sciences accredits U.S. college and university programs and certifies professionals in family and consumer sciences and various specializations. Other professional associations certify other specialized programs and people within the field.   Virginia B. Vincenti

See also **Beecher, Catharine Esther.**

Family planning. See Birth control; Planned Parenthood Federation of America.

Famine is a prolonged food shortage that causes widespread hunger and death. Throughout history, famine has struck at least one area of the world every few years. Many of the less developed countries of Africa, Asia, and Latin America have barely enough food for their people. Roughly a half billion people on Earth are seriously malnourished. They either have too little food, or they eat the wrong food. When food production or imports drop, famine may strike. Thousands or millions of people may die.

Causes of famine

Many famines have more than one cause. For example, the great Bengal famine of 1943 in eastern India was caused by both historical and natural events. World War II (1939-1945) created a general food shortage. The war also led to the cutoff of rice imports from Burma (now Myanmar), which was occupied by the Japanese. Then a cyclone destroyed much farmland. Famine struck, and more than 1 ½ million people died.

Nearly all famines result from crop failures. The chief causes of crop failure include *drought* (prolonged lack of rain), too much rainfall and flooding, and plant diseases and pests. Many other factors may also help create a famine.

Drought ranks as the chief cause of famine. Certain regions of Africa, China, and India have always been hardest hit by famine. All have large areas near deserts, where the rainfall is light and variable. In a dry year, crops in those areas fail. Famine may strike. In the 1870's, for example, dry weather in the Deccan Plateau of southern India caused a famine. The famine took about 5 million lives. During the same period, a famine in China killed more than 9 million people.

In the late 1960's and early 1970's, lack of rain produced widespread famine in a region of Africa called the Sahel. The Sahel lies just south of the Sahara. Famine again struck the Sahel and parts of eastern and southern Africa during the mid-1980's. The famine was especially devastating in Ethiopia. A civil war in that country hampered relief efforts. Since the late 1960's, millions of Africans have died of malnutrition or hunger-related causes. But many have been saved by international assistance.

Too much rainfall may also bring famine. Rivers swollen by heavy rains overflow their banks and destroy farmland. Other crops rot in the field because of the excess water. In the 1300's, several years of heavy rains created widespread famine in western Europe. The Huang He River in northern China is called *China's Sorrow* because it often floods. When it floods, it ruins crops and brings famine. In 1929 and 1930, flooding along this river caused a famine that killed about 2 million people.

Plant diseases and pests sometimes produce famine. During the 1840's, a plant disease destroyed most of Ireland's potato crop. As a result, about 1 million people died from starvation or disease. Millions emigrated. Occasionally, swarms of locusts cause widespread destruction of crops and vegetation in the Sahel and other areas of Africa.

Other causes of famine include both natural and human ones. Such natural disasters as cyclones, earthquakes, early frosts, and *tsunamis* (sequences of huge, destructive ocean waves) may strike. If they affect a large area, they destroy enough crops to create a famine. War may result in a famine if many farmers leave their fields and join the armed forces. Sometimes, an army deliberately creates a famine to starve an enemy into surrender. The army may destroy stored food and growing crops. It also may set up a blockade to cut off the enemy's food supply. Blockades prevented food shipments from reaching the Biafra region in the Nigerian civil war (1967-1970). A famine resulted. Over a million Biafrans probably starved.

Poor transportation may also contribute to a famine because of the difficulty of shipping food where it is most needed. Many famines result largely from primitive transportation. A famine in what is now the state of Uttar Pradesh in northern India killed about 800,000 people in 1837 and 1838. Lack of transportation prevented the shipment of grain from other areas of India.

Effects of famine

The chief effects of famine include death and disease, destruction of livestock and seed, crime and other social disorders, and migration.

Death and disease are the main and most immediate effects of famine. People who lack sufficient food lose weight and grow weak. Many famine victims become so feeble that they die from diarrhea or some other ailment. The weakened condition of a starvation victim is called *marasmus.* Old people and young children usually are the first to die.

Children who have some food but lack sufficient protein develop a condition called *kwashiorkor.* One symptom is *edema* (puffy swelling of the face, forearms, and ankles). Changes in the color and texture of the hair and skin also may occur. Young victims who do not die from kwashiorkor or starvation may grow up with severe mental and physical disabilities.

Famines also increase the possibility of epidemics. Cholera, typhus, and other diseases take many lives because people weakened by hunger do not recover easily from disease. Large numbers of the victims flee from their homes and live in crowded refugee camps. In such conditions, disease spreads quickly.

Destruction of livestock and seed during a famine prolongs the disaster. Many farm animals die or are killed for food. Farmers, to avoid starvation, may have to eat all their seed before planting begins. Such losses hinder them from returning to a normal life and may lower production levels.

Crime and other social disorders increase during a famine. Such crimes as looting, prostitution, and theft multiply. Desperate people steal food and other items they could not otherwise get. They may sell stolen goods to buy food. There may be outbreaks of violence, particularly near food distribution centers.

Migration. Large numbers of famine victims leave their homes. Many people from rural areas flock to cities or refugee camps where food may be available. In the confusion, parents and children may be separated.

Prolonged famine may result in emigration. The potato famine in Ireland caused millions of people to settle in other countries, chiefly the United States.

Fighting famine

The United Nations (UN) and several other international organizations provide emergency help for famine vic-

© Time & Life Pictures/Getty Images

Famine has been a major cause of death and disease in many parts of the world. During the mid-1900's in China, many families suffered from severe food shortages.

Famine victims may receive food, medical care, or other assistance from international organizations. This child, with his mother, is receiving treatment at an emergency center in Iriba, Chad.

tims. Various agencies also work to increase the world's food supply and thus prevent future famines. Many nations hope to prevent famine by increasing their food production. If a nation can build up a large enough reserve of food, regional crop failures will not cause disastrous shortages. For additional information about world food programs and methods of producing more food, see the *World Book* articles on **Food supply** (Increasing the food supply; Food supply programs) and **United Nations** (Fighting hunger).

If a nation's population grows as fast as its food production, little food will be left over to build up a reserve. For this reason, many nations have promoted birth control programs to limit their population growth (see **Birth control** [In other countries]). However, such programs have had limited success in areas where large numbers of people remain poor. Many poor people want large families so the children can help with the work and, later, care for the parents.

John A. Harrington, Jr.

See also **Great Irish Famine.**

Famous Five was a group of Canadian feminists of the late 1800's and early 1900's. The group consisted of Henrietta Muir Edwards, Nellie McClung, Louise McKinney, Emily Murphy, and Irene Parlby. The five reformers met in the province of Alberta, where they campaigned for various social causes. Such causes included *temperance* (limiting alcohol consumption), *dower rights* (widows' rights to some of their husbands' property), *suffrage* (the right to vote), and the creation of special law courts for women. The group became famous as a result of the Persons Case, a groundbreaking legal case of the late 1920's.

The Persons Case began in 1927. That year, the five women petitioned the government of Canada to direct a question to the Supreme Court of Canada. The question concerned whether it was constitutional to appoint women to Canada's Senate, the upper house of the Canadian legislature. The government then asked the Supreme Court to examine the meaning of the word *persons* in the British North America Act. The act, passed in 1867, was Canada's basic governing document. On April 24, 1928, the Supreme Court ruled that the word *persons* referred only to men. Therefore, women could not serve in the Canadian Senate.

The women next appealed to the Judicial Committee of the Privy Council of the United Kingdom, which at that time served as the highest court of appeal for Canada. On Oct. 18, 1929, the committee ruled that the word *persons* included both males and females. In February 1930, Canadian Prime Minister W. L. Mackenzie King appointed Cairine Wilson as the country's first woman senator.

The Persons Case made the five reformers national heroines. They became known as the Alberta Five, and later as the Famous Five. In 1938, Canada's government put up a plaque honoring the Famous Five in the lobby of the national Senate chamber in Ottawa. In 1999, a monument featuring the women was installed in Olympic Park in Calgary. A replica of the monument stands on Parliament Hill in Ottawa.

Kelly L. Mitchell

See also **McClung, Nellie; Murphy, Emily Gowan.**

Fan is a device people use to create an artificial breeze. By moving air around, a fan makes it easier for the air to evaporate sweat from a person's skin or to *dissipate* (disperse) heat from an electrical or electronic device.

Many early cultures in Mesopotamia, the Mediterranean, and Asia used hand fans. Some such fans were as simple as palm leaves. Beginning in ancient Egyptian times, fans served as fashion accessories and status symbols. Many fans were crafted from expensive materials. Wealthy and important people could display their rank by having servants fan them with large ceremonial fans.

Folding fans probably originated in Japan by the 800's. The Portuguese brought them to Europe during the 1500's. Fans soon became an important fashion accessory for European women. For several hundred years, correct handling of fans was a social skill, and women used fans to accent the grace of their hands and the beauty of their eyes. Skilled craftworkers made fans from such ele-

The Metropolitan Museum of Art, New York City, Gift of Ella Mabel Clark, 1948

A French fan from the 1800's is decorated with a winter scene. It is made of paper, silk, lace, and mother-of-pearl.

gant materials as feathers, lace, parchment, and silk. Commissioned artists decorated many paper and fabric fans with delicate paintings. Fans were often mounted on sticks of bone, ivory, mother-of-pearl, or other fine substances, decorated with carving or gilding.

Electric fans have largely replaced hand fans for cooling. Most electric fans move the air using a rotating set of curved blades. Many types of electrical and electronic equipment have built-in fans that help prevent components from overheating. H. Kristina Haugland

Faneuil, *FAN uhl* or *FAN yuhl,* **Peter** (1700-1743), a Boston merchant, built Faneuil Hall for Boston as a public market and meeting place. It was completed in 1742. Fire gutted the hall in 1761, and repairs were completed in 1763. Faneuil Hall now has historical paintings and a military museum. A huge grasshopper weather vane on top of the building has become a Boston landmark. The hall became known as the *Cradle of Liberty* because of the historic meetings there in the years leading up to the American Revolution (1775-1783).

Faneuil was born on June 20, 1700, in New Rochelle, New York. He moved to Boston at age 12 to live with an uncle. He inherited his uncle's fortune in 1738. Faneuil died on March 3, 1743. John W. Ifkovic

See also **Boston** (Downtown Boston; picture: Historic Faneuil Hall).

Fang. See **Snake** (Fangs and venom glands; diagram); **Spider** (Chelicerae).

Fannie Mae. See **Federal National Mortgage Association.**

Fanon, *fah NAWN,* **Frantz Omar** (1925-1961), was a political theorist who became a leader of Algeria's struggle to gain independence from France. A black, he also supported other African independence movements and helped strengthen ties between Arabs and black nationalists of Africa.

Fanon was born on July 20, 1925, in the French colony of Martinique, in the French West Indies. As a young man, he studied psychiatry and medicine in France. He later worked in a hospital in Blida, Algeria. In 1956, he joined Algeria's independence movement. For a time, he represented the movement as a diplomat in Ghana. Fanon's first book, *Black Skin, White Masks* (1952), is a psychological study of problems blacks face because of racism. In *L´An V de la révolution algérienne* (1959)—published in English in 1965 as *Studies in a Dying Colonialism*—Fanon described the Algerians' struggle for independence as both a social revolution and a nationalist movement. Fanon's book *The Wretched of the Earth* (1961) made him famous. In it, he argued that Algerians could achieve independence only through violent revolution. Fanon died on Dec. 6, 1961. William I. Shorrock

Fantasia, *fan TAY zhee uh,* is an instrumental musical composition that has no fixed form or style. Instead, it depends on the composer's imagination.

Some fantasias are written in such a free style that they sound as though the performer is making up the composition as he or she plays. Such fantasias are composed mainly for organ or piano. In the 1700's, the German composer Johann Sebastian Bach and his son Carl Philipp Emanuel were masters of this type of fantasia. Another type, called a *fantasy piece,* is a short, dreamlike composition. The German composer Robert Schumann wrote many fantasy pieces. Longer fantasias resemble a

sonata, but they are much freer in form. Schumann, Franz Schubert of Austria, and the Polish-born composer Frédéric Chopin composed a number of longer fantasias in the 1800's. In England during the 1500's and 1600's, composers wrote pieces for instrumental ensembles that were called fantasias or *fancies.* R. M. Longyear

Fantasy. See **Literature for children** (Fiction).

FAO. See **Food and Agriculture Organization.**

Far East is a term that is sometimes used for the easternmost part of Asia. Traditionally, the term Far East has been used to refer to China, Japan, Korea, Taiwan, and eastern Siberia in Russia. This region, excluding eastern Siberia, is now often called East Asia. The meaning of the term *Far East* is sometimes extended to include Southeast Asia. The countries of Southeast Asia are Brunei, Cambodia, Indonesia, Laos, Malaysia, Myanmar, the Philippines, Singapore, Thailand, and Vietnam. Europeans created the term Far East. The region lies far to the east of Europe. See also **Asia.** Grant Hardy

Farad, *FAR uhd,* is a unit used to measure electrical capacitance. It is named for the English physicist Michael Faraday, and its symbol is F.

The electric charge in a capacitor is directly proportional to the *potential difference* (voltage) applied to it. If 1 coulomb of charge gives a capacitor a potential difference of 1 volt, the capacitance is a farad. In electronics, the *microfarad* and the *picofarad* are usually used to measure capacitance. A microfarad (µF) is one-millionth of a farad, and a picofarad (pF) is one-millionth of a microfarad. Michael Dine

See also **Capacitor; Coulomb; Volt.**

Faraday, *FAIR uh day,* **Michael** (1791-1867), one of the greatest English chemists and physicists, discovered the principle of electromagnetic induction in 1831 (see **Electromagnetism**). He found that moving a magnet through a coil of copper wire caused an electric current to flow in the wire. The electric generator and the electric motor are based on this principle. Joseph Henry, an American physicist, discovered induction shortly before Faraday but did not publish his findings (see **Henry, Joseph**).

Faraday's work in electrochemistry led him to discover a mathematical relationship between electricity and the *valence* (combining power) of a chemical element. Faraday's law states this relationship. It gave the first clue to the existence of electrons (see **Electron**). Faraday introduced ideas that would become the basis of field theory in physics. He maintained that magnetic, electric, and gravitational forces are passed from one body to another through *lines of force,* or strains in the area between the two bodies.

Faraday was born near London on Sept. 22, 1791. He was first apprenticed to a bookbinder. He became Sir Humphry Davy's assistant at the Royal Institution in London in 1813 and remained there for 54 years. Although never formally educated, he received an honorary doctorate degree from the University of Oxford in 1832. The next year, he became the Fullerian Professor of Chemistry at the Royal Institution, a post he kept until his death. Faraday was a popular lecturer. He gave scientific lectures for children every Christmas. The most famous one is called "The Chemical History of a Candle" (1860). Faraday died on Aug. 25, 1867. Julia Borst Brazas

See also **Electricity** (Electricity and magnetism).

Farce. See **Comedy; Drama** (Comedy).

Fargo (pop. 105,549; met. area pop. 208,777), is the largest city in North Dakota. It lies in the valley of the Red River of the North, one of the nation's great farming regions (see **North Dakota** [political map]). The Fargo metropolitan area includes Cass County in North Dakota and Clay County in Minnesota. The city is the seat of Cass County and has a commission form of government. For Fargo's rainfall and monthly temperatures, see **North Dakota** (Climate).

Fargo's products include computer software, dairy and other food products, furniture and cabinets, metal products, sugar beet harvesters and cultivators, and tractors. The city is a regional medical center and a center for shopping and entertainment. It is the home of the Fargodome events and convention center. Fargo is also a wholesale distribution center and is known as the *Transportation Hub of the Northwest.* Railroad passenger trains and freight lines, airlines, and bus lines serve the city. North Dakota State University is in Fargo.

Fargo was founded in 1871 and was named for William G. Fargo of the famed Wells, Fargo & Company express. A combination of factors, including ice jams, spring thawing, and the area's geology, have led to frequent spring floods in the Fargo area. The city experienced historic flooding when the Red River overran its banks in 1897, 1997, and 2009.   Douglas C. Munski

See also **North Dakota** (picture).

Fargo-Moorhead Convention & Visitors Bureau

A minor league baseball game in Fargo draws many spectators. Fargo, North Dakota's largest city, is a regional center for entertainment, medicine, trade, and transportation.

Fargo, William George (1818-1881), was a partner in the gold rush express company of Wells, Fargo & Company (see **Wells, Fargo & Company**). His company's stagecoaches provided the best and fastest transportation between the East and the West in the mid-1800's. The city of Fargo, North Dakota, is named after him.

As a young man in Buffalo, New York, Fargo was a messenger with Wells and Company, the first express company to go west of Buffalo. Later, he became part owner. After the California Gold Rush began in 1848, demand grew for the transport of goods to and from California. As a result, in 1852, Fargo and other investors formed Wells, Fargo & Company, an express service that carried goods across the country to San Francisco. Wells, Fargo operated in most parts of the United States. When the transcontinental rail line was completed in

1869, the railroad took most of the express business.

Fargo was born on May 20, 1818, in Pompey, New York. He served as mayor of Buffalo from 1862 to 1866. He died on Aug. 3, 1881.   Jerome O. Steffen

Farjeon, *FAHR juhn,* **Eleanor** (1881-1965), was a British author who became famous for her stories and poems for children. Her best-known works are noted for their combination of humor and fantasy.

Farjeon's popular collection *The Little Bookroom* (1955) contains her personal choices from among the many stories she wrote for children. The title refers to a special small room where the author read as a child. Farjeon's other collections of stories include *Jim at the Corner and Other Stories* (1934) and *Martin Pippin in the Daisy-Field* (1937).

Farjeon selected a number of favorite poems from her works for the collection *The Children's Bells* (1934). The book includes poems on fairies, the seasons, and the experiences of childhood. Many of her poems were also published in *Eleanor Farjeon's Poems for Children* (1951).

Farjeon was born on Feb. 13, 1881, in London. She wrote more than 100 books and plays, including a few for adults. She died on June 5, 1965.   Marilyn Fain Apseloff

Farley, *FAHR lee,* **James Aloysius,** *jaymz AL oh IHSH uhs* (1888-1976), a politician and businessman, served as postmaster general of the United States from 1933 to 1940. During his term as postmaster general, which was then a Cabinet post, Farley greatly improved airmail service. From 1932 to 1940, he was chairman of the Democratic National Committee, and he managed the national presidential campaigns of Franklin D. Roosevelt during the elections of 1932 and 1936. In 1940, Farley resigned his Cabinet and party positions because he opposed a third presidential term for Roosevelt. Farley also served as chairman of the New York State Democratic Committee from 1930 until he resigned in 1944.

Farley was born on May 30, 1888, in Grassy Point, New York, and entered the building supply business. He became chairman of the Coca-Cola Export Corporation in 1940. He died on June 9, 1976.   Alonzo L. Hamby

Farley, Walter (1915-1989), an American children's author, became known for his *Black Stallion* series of novels. The series began with *The Black Stallion* (1941). In this book, a teenager named Alec Ramsey rescues and tames the Black Stallion, a half-wild Arabian horse. The series of 21 novels also features the Black Stallion's offspring as well as Ramsey's friend Steve Duncan and horse trainer Henry Dailey, a retired jockey. In addition, it includes *Man o' War* (1962), a fictionalized biography of the great American race horse.

Farley wrote his last book, *The Young Black Stallion* (1989), with his son Steven. Critics and readers have praised the series for its authentic information about horses, exciting adventures, and rich character portraits. In addition to the *Black Stallion* series, Farley wrote several books for younger readers, including a series about a pony, with such titles as *Little Black, a Pony* (1961) and *The Little Black Pony Races* (1968).

Walter Lorimer Farley was born on June 26, 1915, in Syracuse, New York. He began writing the story that would become *The Black Stallion* in high school. He bred Arabian horses from 1946 to 1965. Farley died on Oct. 16, 1989. Steven Farley continued the *Black Stallion* series after his father's death.   Ann D. Carlson

© Montgomery Martin, Alamy Images

© Jacques Jangoux, Alamy Images

Farming techniques and resources vary greatly around the world. In a developed country such as the United States, *left,* farmers use powered machines to harvest vast fields of crops. In a developing region such as western Africa, *above,* farmers may rely on handheld tools to raise crops on small plots of cleared forestland.

Farm and farming

Farm and farming. Farming is the use of land and other resources to raise crops and livestock. The lands and facilities in which crops and livestock are raised are called farms.

The practice of farming began long before written history. The ability to manage farmland played a role in the rise and fall of ancient civilizations. And for most of history, farming was by far the world's primary occupation. As recently as 1700, more than 90 percent of the world's people worked as farmers. Even so, farms covered only 7 percent of Earth's land.

By the 2000's, farms had spread dramatically to cover about 40 percent of Earth's land. But through the use of modern technology, far fewer people were required to operate them. Today, less than half of the world's people are farmers. In some less developed countries, the majority of people still work as farmers. In developed countries, farmers may represent as little as 2 percent of the population, despite vast areas of farmland.

Farms differ greatly from place to place. Some farms are small plots of cleared forestland that supply only enough food for the farmer's family. Other farms are huge fields of crops that are harvested by machines and sold on global markets. Some farms grow or raise mostly one crop or animal. Others produce a variety of crops and livestock. Some farms rely on rain to water the crops, and other farms water crops through the use of irrigation systems. An increasing number of farmers grow crops in cities rather than in the countryside.

Wherever and however they are raised, crops need water and soil. Crops also need protection from such pests as insects and weeds. Farming crops involves sev-

eral steps. The soil must be prepared. Seeds are then planted. Farmers must protect the crops as they grow. Finally, they must harvest crops and process them for use or storage.

Livestock farmers must supply their animals' basic needs. Animals must be given adequate shelter, food, and water, and protection from disease. Some animals, such as cattle and sheep, are raised for part of their lives

Outline

I. Kinds of farms
  A. Farm size
  B. Commercialization
  C. Farm specialization
  D. Farm inputs and technologies
  E. Farm location

II. Crops and their needs
  A. Soil management
  B. Water management
  C. Pest control

III. Farming crops
  A. Preparing the soil
  B. Planting
  C. Cultivating
  D. Harvesting
  E. Processing and storage

IV. The needs of livestock
  A. Livestock care
  B. Livestock breeding

V. Raising livestock
  A. Livestock grazing
  B. Livestock finishing
  C. Confinement operations

VI. Farm management
  A. Managing risk
  B. Financing
  C. Marketing

VII. Challenges and resources for farmers
  A. Resources for farmers
  B. Farm organizations
  C. Farming and hunger

on open pastures. Others, such as chickens and hogs, may be raised their entire lives in buildings, where machines feed them and dispose of their waste.

As an occupation, farming presents many challenges and risks. Farmers generally receive income only after their crops are harvested and sold. Changes in the weather and the markets can thus greatly affect their livelihood. In developed countries, government programs may help to provide a safety net for farmers. In less developed countries, many farmers are extremely poor. They may have little access to government assistance programs or advanced farming technology.

This article describes the many kinds of farms that exist around the world today. It discusses techniques for growing crops and raising livestock. It also discusses the business of farming, the challenges that farmers face, and the resources available to them. For information on the history of farming and its relation to human society and the environment, see **Agriculture**. See **Food supply** for more information about how farms feed the world's people. The **Gardening** and **Horticulture** articles cover the growing of plants on a smaller scale.

Kinds of farms

Farms vary widely in terms of size, use of technology, and kinds of crops and livestock produced. These characteristics and others can be used to classify farms into different types.

Farm size varies considerably around the world. In the 2010's, the average farm size was about 420 acres (170 hectares) in the United States and 30 acres (12 hectares) in Europe. In Asia and Africa, typical farms are *small farms,* generally defined as being less than 5 acres (2 hectares) in size.

Asia and Africa are home to the vast majority of the world's small farmers. In the poorest Asian and African nations, farming may constitute a third or more of the *gross domestic product* (GDP), the total economic value of a country's goods and services. In these countries, small farmers are often extremely poor, despite their contribution to GDP. Many of them suffer from hunger and malnutrition.

One method used by the United States Department of Agriculture (USDA) classifies farm size in terms of sales. According to this USDA assessment, small farms are those that sell between $1,000 and $250,000 worth of produce per year. About 90 percent of U.S. farms meet this description. However, most U.S. farm produce—and profit—comes from large farms. Many U.S. small farmers rely on nonfarm-based sources to supplement their income. The distribution of farm size and profit follows a similar pattern in many other developed countries.

Commercialization. A farm's degree of commercialization—that is, the extent to which it sells its produce on the market—serves as another means of classification. In less developed countries, many small farmers practice *subsistence farming.* In this system, the farm basically produces just enough food to feed the farmer's family. Other small farmers are *semisubsistence farmers,* growing small amounts of extra food for sale to others. In contrast, farms in developed countries are almost always commercial enterprises, regardless of size. On such farms, all crops and livestock are grown for sale.

Subsistence farms. Subsistence farming has been the main form of farming for most of human history. One form of subsistence farming is called *shifting agriculture* or *slash-and-burn agriculture.* This method involves cutting down and burning small areas of forest to use as farmland. The burned material fertilizes the soil. After a few years of farming, the soil becomes exhausted of *nutrients* (nourishing substances), so the farmers move to a new area and begin the process again. Given enough time, the soil may recover its fertility to be used again.

In many subsistence farming systems, men and women share some of the work, while other responsibilities are divided by gender and age. For example, in the farms of sub-Saharan Africa—the part of Africa south of the Sahara—men are usually responsible for clearing the land and preparing the soil. Women typically provide fuel and water for the farm, manage weeds, and process crops during and after harvest. Despite their many contributions to managing daily farm work, women rarely have control over farm resources and income. Male farmers enjoy better access to land, credit,

Mississippi Agricultural and Industrial Board

A mechanical cotton picker can harvest as much cotton as 80 workers picking the crop by hand. Farms in the southern half of the United States grow this important crop.

© AgStock Images, Inc./Alamy Images

Vegetable farming uses both machines and hand labor. This machine on a California farm cuts and gathers tomato plants. Workers then remove the tomatoes from the stems by hand.

Poultry farming involves raising birds for their meat or eggs. Poultry farms usually require relatively little land. This farm in Oregon raises turkeys, which are sold for their meat.

farming necessities, and educational opportunities.

Despite a relative lack of technological and economic sophistication, subsistence and semisubsistence farms can be complex and resilient. Such farms may grow a wide diversity of crops. Thus, if one crop fails, the farmers will still have enough food. Crop diversity can also help maintain water and nutrient balance in the soil and enable farmers to harvest food and eat a balanced diet during all seasons.

Population growth and the reduction of available land have made subsistence and semisubsistence farming more difficult In many areas. Land cleared and farmed in shifting agriculture is often not given enough time to regenerate. As a result, the soil may become permanently damaged—and additional land might have to be cleared to grow enough food. Many small subsistence and semisubsistence farmers are moving from farming a variety of crops to growing *monocultures*—that is, large

areas of a single crop—and selling crops for cash.

Commercial farms. In industrialized countries, farming has shifted from a prominent way of life to an important business. The term *agribusiness* describes all business activities involved in food production, including food processing, food distribution, and the development of resources and equipment used on farms. Agribusiness is a huge industry that ultimately depends on farms. But farmers form a small percentage of the people employed in agribusiness. Other agribusiness professionals include agricultural scientists, manufacturers, and marketers.

Like other businesses, farms must be profitable and sustainable in the long term. Successful farmers are experts not only in agriculture but also in accounting, marketing, and financing. Farmers earn their income primarily from what they sell. They also must protect their resources to ensure the farm will remain profitable in future years. Many farmers receive some money from government farm programs intended to reduce the risks involved in farming.

In the United States, about 90 percent of farms are owned by individuals or families. Most of the time, the owners also operate the farm. But sometimes, they rent all or some of the land in an arrangement called *tenant farming*. Less than 10 percent of U.S. farms are *partnerships* of two or more owners. Farms owned by corporations make up an even smaller portion of U.S. farms. Such *corporate farms* receive certain tax benefits that individual or partnership farms do not. Family-owned farms are not necessarily small farms. Likewise, not all corporate farms are giant operations owned by multinational corporations. In fact, most corporate farms are run by families.

Farms in Canada are generally similar to those in the United States. European farms are typically smaller and raise higher-value products than most farms of North America, but their business practices are similar. In other countries, farms may be organized differently. In China, for example, farms are owned by local organizations called *collectives* and leased to family farmers. The farmers must supply a given amount of food to the Chinese

Cattle ranching is the main type of farming on the Western grasslands of the United States. This Montana ranch has fairly rich grazing land. Many other ranches are in dry regions of the West. They must cover a huge area to provide enough grass for large numbers of cattle.

Machines milk cows in a dairy farm's milking parlor, *left*. Dairy farms in developed countries typically make use of milking machines and other labor-saving technologies.

© Thinkstock

government, but they can keep and sell any additional produce.

Farm specialization. Another classification, often used in the United States, divides farms into two main groups: (1) *specialized farms* and (2) *mixed farms*. A specialized farm primarily produces one particular type of crop or livestock. A mixed farm raises a variety of crops and livestock.

Specialized farms often grow monocultures on huge fields. These monoculture crops tend to be those best suited for the farm's region. For example, corn is often the most profitable crop to grow in regions that have level land, fertile soil, and a warm, moist growing season. Wheat grows best in a drier and somewhat cooler climate. Dairy farming is often the most profitable kind of farming in regions with rolling land, rich pastures, and a short growing season. For such monoculture

© Caro/Alamy Images

Workers on a plantation, such as this coffee farm, often raise and harvest a single crop for export. Many plantations are supported by foreign investment.

crops as bananas, sugar cane, and tobacco, the farms are sometimes called *plantations*. In Central and South America and in Africa, many plantations raise specialized crops for export. Such plantations are often supported by foreign investment.

Though specialized farms typically rely on one particular crop or livestock species, many of them have additional products. Some specialized crop farms, for example, also raise livestock. They may use their livestock's manure as fertilizer. The difference between a specialized farm and a mixed farm is a matter of degree. In the United States, for example, a farm is considered a specialized farm if it earns more than half its income from the sale of one kind of crop or livestock.

Farm inputs and technologies. Farms vary in their technological sophistication and in their use of fertilizers, pesticides, livestock medicines, and other *inputs*. Many subsistence farmers are low-input farmers. They rely on simple technology that has been in use for thousands of years, and they mainly use resources that come from the farm itself. Commercial farms in developed countries, by contrast, often rely on such technological advances as engine-powered machinery, computer systems, and genetic engineering. Such technologies may be too expensive for poor farmers to afford. Other farms in developed countries deliberately do not use certain types of controversial technologies and inputs.

Industrialized agriculture, sometimes called *conventional agriculture,* relies on technologies first developed during the 1800's. Powered machines do much of the physical labor on such farms, greatly reducing labor costs. Industrialized agriculture relies on synthetic fertilizers—mostly mixtures of nitrogen, phosphorous, and potassium—to enrich the soil. Such farms also use a variety of pesticides. *Insecticides* are pesticides that kill insect pests that eat or damage crops. *Fungicides* kill harmful fungi. *Herbicides* kill weeds that compete with crops for resources.

In industrialized agriculture, livestock producers also make use of synthetic chemicals, most of which are added to animal feed. *Antibiotics* protect animals against disease and infection. Other chemicals, called *hormones*, speed up animals' growth and their rate of milk or egg production. Such livestock as chickens and hogs can be raised entirely in buildings with automated feeding and controlled temperatures.

The widespread use of industrialized farming techniques has greatly increased the food supply around the world. It has also decreased the number of people needed to manage farms. Industrialized farms are highly productive. But industrialized farming relies on large inputs of energy and synthetic chemicals. Many of these inputs are derived from fossil fuels, such as coal, oil, and natural gas, which exist in limited and dwindling supplies. In addition, chemical runoff and waste products from industrialized farms can cause environmental damage and health problems.

Breeding and genetic engineering. Before humans could farm, they had to change wild plants and animals to make them suitable for agriculture. For example, early humans selected and planted seeds from the largest, tastiest plants. Thus, those plants survived and reproduced more often, passing their traits on to their offspring. This process, called *selective breeding,* is still used in agriculture today.

Later, farmers developed the practice of selectively *cross-pollinating* plants of the same species. This process involves causing one specific plant to pollinate another, producing offspring that combine desirable features from each parent. During the 1960's, this technique led to the development of extremely productive varieties of rice, wheat, and corn. The use of these crop varieties, along with industrialized farming techniques, greatly increased agricultural production around the world in what became known as the Green Revolution.

Genetic engineering, in contrast to older breeding techniques, involves altering the patterns of a living thing's *genes* (hereditary material) directly (see **Genetic engineering**). Plants and animals altered by genetic engineering are called *genetically modified organisms* (GMO's). GMO's can be developed with a number of desirable traits, such as longer shelf life or higher nutritional content. Some GMO's are developed for resistance to insects, fungi, and other pests, reducing the need for chemical pesticides. GMO's may require less water or have a higher tolerance for bad soil, and so can be planted in areas that would otherwise be difficult to farm.

The use of GMO's remains controversial. Some GMO critics focus on the unknown health and environmental consequences of the new organisms. Other critics charge that GMO's are not sufficiently regulated, citing the potential for abuse by powerful, profit-driven GMO developers. In Canada and the United States, many crops grown on industrialized farms and sold in grocery stores are GMO's. The law in these countries requires no special labeling of GMO products. The use of GMO's is much more limited in countries with stricter regulation and labeling requirements, including Australia, China, India, most of Europe, and parts of Africa.

Organic farming involves restricting the use of a number of controversial inputs and technologies, including synthetic fertilizers and pesticides. Organically raised livestock are not given hormones, antibiotics, or other synthetic food additives. In addition, organic farmers do not use GMO's.

Organic producers use a variety of techniques to maximize the efficiency of their operations. Some apply *compost* (decayed plant and animal matter) to the soil instead of synthetic fertilizers. Organic farmers may rely

Technological advances have made modern farms extremely productive and efficient. This farmer uses a tractor with Global Positioning System (GPS) navigation to precisely prepare a field.

© Lou Linwei, Alamy Images

Urban farming operations, such as this vegetable garden in Guangdong, China, have gained importance as a source of agricultural income and food for city dwellers around the world.

on natural predators instead of pesticides to control pest populations.

In the United States, farms must be certified by the USDA in order to label their produce "organic." Other countries have their own organic certification processes. The certification process can be lengthy and expensive. But demand is high for organic products, enabling farmers to sell them at premium prices. Farmers in less developed countries often cannot afford such inputs as fertilizers, pesticides, or GMO's, and thus use organic farming methods by necessity.

Other specialized technologies include (1) hydroponics and (2) greenhouses. Hydroponic farming involves growing crops in canals or large tanks filled either with water or with sand, gravel, or other materials covered with water. The nutrients that the plant needs are added to the water. The water usually circulates to assure that the roots get air. Greenhouses are structures of plastic, glass, or other translucent materials that help protect the plants inside from extreme temperatures, wind, and pests. Hydroponics and greenhouses enable farmers to grow certain crops throughout the year, regardless of outside conditions.

Farm location. Farms can be classified based on the unique features of their surrounding land, soil, and climate. A farm's location determines which methods must be used to grow crops. It also may limit which crops can be grown on the farm.

Access to water greatly limits where farms can develop. *Rainfed farms* rely on natural rainfall for their water supply. In some cases, farms in rainy areas may suffer from too much water. Farmers may use drainage systems to ensure crops are not at risk from drowning.

Irrigated farms, by contrast, rely on water from distant sources, such as rivers or reservoirs. Farmers have long relied on irrigation systems. Ancient civilizations built canals and aqueducts to transport water to farmland. Wells and cisterns were created to store water for farms during dry seasons. Irrigation systems enable widespread farming in dry regions, such as the western United States and many places in the Middle East.

Urban farming. In 1800, only a small percentage of people lived in cities. The vast majority of people lived where they worked—on rural farms. By 2010, about half of the world's people lived in cities. Though most farms today are still in rural areas, an increasing number of city dwellers grow plants in urban environments.

Examples of urban farming include community and school gardens and "green roof" farms on top of buildings. In less developed countries, where many city dwellers suffer from extreme poverty and lack of access to markets, urban farms can save families from starvation. In parts of Africa, Asia, and Latin America, more than 50 percent of urban households practice urban farming. However, some places restrict or even outlaw urban farming. Concerns over food safety and threats to human health from livestock diseases and wastes often motivate such restrictions.

Crops and their needs

Tens of thousands of edible plants grow on Earth. But only 150 or so are grown widely as food crops. Nearly all of the plant-based calories people consume come from just a few dozen crops. And just three crops—corn, rice, and wheat—make up more than half of those calories. Other important plant-based sources of calories include cassava, millet, potatoes, sorghum, and soybeans.

All crops require nutrients and water to grow. Soil supplies most of the nutrients. It also stores the water that the crops need. Crops take root in the soil and absorb the nutrients and water through their roots.

Crops differ in the amount of nutrients and water they need. Farmers must make sure that the soil and water resources meet the needs of each crop. Farmers must also plan measures to control pests, which could damage or ruin a crop.

The science of field crop production is called *agronomy*. In many cases, farmers must use different methods to grow fruits, vegetables, and nuts. The science of growing these types of crops is called *horticulture*. For much more information on horticultural methods, see the articles **Fruit** and **Gardening.** Fruits and vegetables grown in large fields, such as pineapples and potatoes, are raised in much the same way as any other field crop.

Soil management. Soil consists chiefly of mineral particles mixed with decaying *organic* (once living) matter. Chemical reactions involving these substances release most of the nutrients that crops need. Some of the most important reactions—notably, the decay of organic matter—require certain microorganisms. To be fertile, therefore, soil must consist of the right mixture of minerals, organic matter, and helpful microorganisms.

Soil must also hold proper amounts of air and water. A plant's roots need air to function properly, and some microorganisms need air to survive. Too much moisture in the soil reduces the supply of air, drowning plant roots and destroying helpful microorganisms. Too little moisture deprives crops of needed water.

Plants need 17 chemical elements for healthy growth. The elements needed in the largest quantities are calcium, carbon, hydrogen, magnesium, nitrogen, oxygen, phosphorus, potassium, and sulfur. Most crops require relatively large amounts of these elements. Elements needed in lesser amounts are called *trace elements*. They are boron, chlorine, copper, iron, manganese, molybdenum, nickel, and zinc. Certain types of plants also require small amounts of cobalt and silicon. Water and air supply all the necessary carbon, hydrogen, and oxygen. The other elements must come from the soil.

After deciding which crops to grow, farmers may analyze the soil to determine if the nutrient levels are adequate. Farmers can send soil samples to a soil-testing laboratory for an accurate analysis. The test results help the farmer plan a scientific program of fertilizer use. Chemical companies provide fertilizers to supply almost any crop requirement. Most crops absorb much nitrogen, phosphorus, and potassium. Thus, most commercial fertilizers consist chiefly of these elements.

The richest soil, called *topsoil,* lies at and just below the surface. If this topsoil is not protected, it may be blown away by strong winds or washed away by heavy rains—a process called *erosion.* Effective soil management, therefore, also includes methods of soil conservation. These methods are discussed in detail in the *Farming crops* section of this article.

Water management. In most cases, farmers rely entirely on rainfall to water crops. In some cases, however, farmers irrigate their crops. Where rainfall is light or uncertain, many farmers practice *dryland farming.* In dryland farming, part of the cropland is left *fallow* (unplanted) each year. The fallow soil can store moisture for a crop the following year. Wheat is the main crop grown by dryland farming.

Some farms have too much water rather than too little. An excess of water prevents roots from taking in air. In most instances, excess water occurs on low-lying land and on land crossed by streams or rivers. Fields that tend to have too much water require a drainage system. One common drainage system consists of lengths of tile pipe buried 3 to 4 feet (0.9 to 1.2 meters) below the surface of the field. Excess water in the soil filters through cracks in the pipe and then flows to open drainage ditches at the edge of the field.

Pest control. Agronomists use the word *pest* in referring to weeds, insects, and plant diseases—including those caused by fungi, bacteria, and viruses—that threaten crops. In industrialized agriculture, the most common way of controlling pests is through the use of chemical pesticides. Scientists have developed thousands of pesticides for use on farms. Each one is designed to fight certain types of weeds, plant diseases, or harmful insects. All pesticides must be used with extreme care. If used improperly, they may pollute the environment or the food supply, endangering the health of people and animals. To help prevent such problems, many governments set and enforce standards for the manufacture, sale, and use of pesticides.

Farmers also use other methods of pest control in addition to pesticides. For example, turning the soil with a plow or mechanical cultivator kills most weeds. However, herbicides control weeds more thoroughly than does soil turning. Some herbicides remain active in the soil for long periods and so kill weed seedlings as they develop. Scientists have also developed pest-resistant crops through the use of crossbreeding and of genetic engineering.

Farmers may use a system known as *integrated pest management* to control pests. This system can include a combination of several methods. One method involves *crop rotation,* the planting of the same field with differ-

ent crops from year to year. Rotating the crop can disrupt the spread of pests that damage a particular crop. Another method involves spraying a synthetic *pheromone* on a crop. A pheromone acts as a chemical signal, triggering special behavior in certain organisms. For example, a pheromone may prevent certain pest insects from mating (see **Pheromone**). In yet another method, farmers may increase the population of a pest's natural predator in the area where a crop is planted. Another management technique, known as *soil solarization,* involves covering the soil with a black tarp before planting. The cover absorbs heat from sunlight and greatly increases the soil's temperature, killing weeds and pests. Other techniques include changing planting seasons, increasing the distance between plants, and manually pulling weeds.

Farming crops

Field crop farming involves at least five separate operations: (1) preparing the soil, (2) planting, (3) cultivating, (4) harvesting, and (5) processing and storage. Tractors, which can pull or push other specialized farm machinery, can help in performing each of these operations easily and quickly. However, most small farmers in developing countries cannot afford such machinery. They perform farming tasks with small handheld tools or, in

© Shutterstock

Irrigation systems enable farmers to grow crops in regions with insufficient rainfall. A center-pivot system gives these fields their characteristic round shape. A central well supplies water to a series of sprinklers on a long arm. The arm rotates around the well, distributing water throughout the field.

some cases, with instruments pulled by animals.

Preparing the soil primarily involves establishing a *seedbed*—that is, an area of soil in which seeds can be planted and in which they will sprout, take root, and grow. Many farmers make the seedbed using an ancient process called *tillage*. Tillage involves digging into the soil and mixing it. Other farmers do not till the soil, or they till it only to a limited extent.

Tillage loosens the soil, kills weeds, and improves the circulation of water and air in the soil. Plows serve as the chief tillage devices. One of the most common types of plow is the *moldboard plow.* The bottom of a moldboard plow turns over about the top 6 to 10 inches (15 to 25 centimeters) of soil. This method of plowing, called *clean plowing,* buries most weeds and other plant material that were on the surface.

At plowing time, some fields have *cover crops,* whereas others may be scattered with dead stalks and leaves and other *plant residues.* Both cover crops and plant residues help the soil maintain humidity and help reduce erosion. Plowing buries this material, adding more organic matter and nutrients to the soil.

In many areas, the topsoil is too thin or too fragile for clean plowing. Farmers in these areas use such implements as a *chisel plow,* a *harrow,* or a *cultivator* to break up the soil without turning it over completely. This method, called *conservation tillage,* kills fewer weeds than does clean plowing. But it leaves more plant matter on the surface and helps reduce erosion. Other plowing methods also help conserve soil. On sloping land, for example, farmers plow across, rather than up and down, the slope. The plowed soil forms ridges across the

Tillage and planting equipment

These drawings show some of the equipment that farmers use to *till* (work) the soil and to plant crops. A *moldboard plow* turns over a layer of soil, burying any weeds or plant materials that were on the surface. *Chisel plows, harrows,* and *cultivators,* on the other hand, break up the soil without turning it over completely. A machine called a *planter* cuts *furrows* (grooves) into soil, drops seeds into the furrows, and buries the seeds—all in one operation.

WORLD BOOK illustrations by Robert Keys

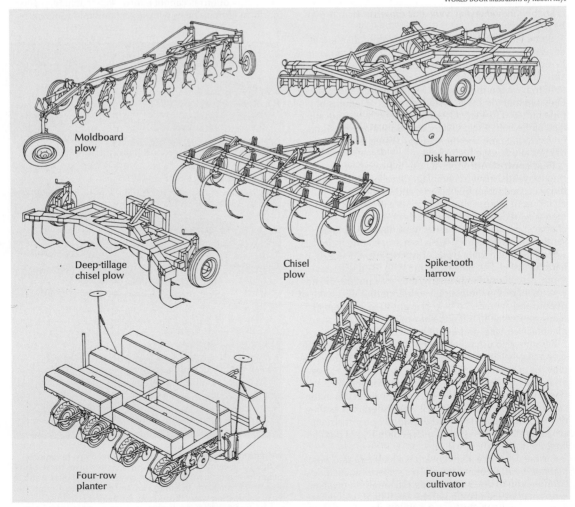

Moldboard plow

Disk harrow

Deep-tillage chisel plow

Chisel plow

Spike-tooth harrow

Four-row planter

Four-row cultivator

© Shutterstock

A special method of plowing called *conservation tillage* leaves some of the residues from the previous crop on the surface of the soil. The residues help prevent soil erosion. This tractor is pulling a chisel plow, a chief tool of conservation tillage.

© Shutterstock

A seed drill plants seeds. It cuts furrows, drops seeds into them, and then covers the seeds with soil. Large seed drills may be 30 feet (9.1 meters) wide or even wider. They can plant 24 or more rows at a time. Some drills also apply fertilizer and a herbicide.

slope, helping to prevent erosion by rainwater. Such plowing is called *contour plowing*.

No-till and reduced tillage methods involve preparing a seedbed with little tilling or no tilling at all. In the no-till system, residues from the prior growing season, called *mulch*, are left covering the field. The mulch protects the soil against erosion and helps maintain moisture. Without tilling, weeds remain in the soil. Farmers thus typically use herbicides in place of tilling to kill weeds. Fertilizers are applied on the surface, where they dissolve in water and soak through the mulch. In most cases, no further soil preparation is necessary, and the seedbed is ready for planting.

Many farmers have adopted no-till or a reduced or conservation tillage system. The no-till method has many advantages compared with traditional tilling. For example, the mulch helps prevent erosion and helps keep moisture in the soil. By eliminating the mechanical turning of the soil, the method saves labor, time, and fuel. There is also less risk of compacting the soil and damaging its structure, because heavy machinery passes through the field fewer times. However, no-till has some disadvantages. For example, reliance on herbicides costs money and can have harmful effects on the environment. In addition, herbicides do not kill some weeds. Planting may also be delayed because mulch tends to keep fields cooler and moister.

Planting. In areas of the Northern Hemisphere with mild winters, farmers typically plant certain types of barley, oats, and wheat in the fall. The plants begin to develop before the growing season ends and then rest during the winter. The young plants start to grow again in the spring and are ready to be harvested by midsummer. Where the winters are exceptionally cold, on the other hand, farmers plant most crops in the spring—after the danger of frost has passed.

Most field crops grown on large farms are planted by machines called *planters* or *drills*. These machines cut *furrows* (narrow grooves) in the soil, drop seeds into each furrow, and cover the seeds with soil—all in one operation. On the other hand, poor, small farmers usually plant seeds in three distinct steps—digging holes, dropping seeds in, and covering the seeds—with hand-held equipment.

Farmers can use special planting methods to help conserve soil. On sloping land, for example, different crops are often planted in long, alternating strips. For example, corn may be planted between bands of alfalfa. The alfalfa helps slow the flow of rain water down the slope. This method of planting is called *strip cropping*.

Farmers may apply some fertilizers and pesticides to the soil during planting. These chemicals may be distributed by equipment attached to the seed drill.

Cultivating. Herbicides applied before or during planting kill many kinds of weeds, but not all of them. Some weeds may therefore develop with the crops. Weeds are usually not a significant problem in small-grain fields because the plants grow close together, leaving little room for weeds. In fields where row crops are grown, however, weeds can multiply rapidly between rows. Farmers often control such weeds with cultivators. These devices stir the soil between rows, uprooting and burying any weeds. Farmers who are poor may spend several hours a week uprooting weeds by hand or with a hand hoe.

Harvesting. Nearly all large farms harvest field crops using machines. *Combines* are used to harvest most grain and seed crops, including barley, corn, rice, soy-

J. C. Allen and Son

A cultivator, *shown here,* stirs the soil between rows of corn. This process, used on crops planted in broadly spaced rows, uproots any weeds that herbicides have not controlled.

© Shutterstock

A combine cuts and threshes grain in one operation. Combines replaced machinery that only cut or only threshed a grain crop. This combine is harvesting wheat.

beans, and wheat. A combine performs several tasks. First, it cuts the plant stalks. Then, it *threshes* the cuttings—that is, it separates the grain or seeds from the straw and other residues. The combine returns the residues to the ground and collects the grain or seeds in a tank or bin.

Some farmers harvest corn with special machines. The machines pick the ears from the stalks but do not remove the grain from the ears. The grain is removed later. The grain is then processed to make livestock feed. In the case of sweet corn, the ears are left whole and sold for human consumption. Special machines are also used to harvest other field crops, including peanuts, potatoes, and sugar beets. Some machines mow such crops as alfalfa and clover. The machines leave the mowed crops on the ground, where they dry and become hay. Machines called *hay balers* gather the hay and bind it into bales.

Some farmers harvest green grain or grass to make a kind of livestock feed called *silage.* To make silage, farmers harvest the entire plant and then chop it up. Some silage machines harvest the crop and chop it in one operation.

Processing and storage. Crops raised to supply food for human consumption are called *food crops.* Many food crops tend to spoil quickly, so farmers ship these crops to market as soon as possible. Food grains, however, can be stored for months on farms with proper facilities. Before grain is stored, it must be dried. Most farms that store large amounts of grain have special grain-drying equipment and large storage bins.

Crops raised to supply feed for livestock are called *feed crops.* Some crops, such as corn and soybeans, are

used for both human food and livestock feed. Various grass crops are used to make hay and silage. Hay must be kept dry until it is used, so it is usually stored in barns. Unlike hay, silage must be kept moist. Most farmers store it in airtight structures called *silos.* Soybeans must be specially processed to be used for livestock feed. Most farmers buy soybean meal ready-made from commercial suppliers. Such suppliers have removed the oil from the soybeans to use for food products and other purposes. Many farmers have equipment for milling feed grains other than soybeans. Farmers often feed corn to hogs without any processing.

The needs of livestock

To raise livestock successfully, farmers must provide the animals with proper daily care. They must also purchase new animals or select certain animals for breeding to replace those that are slaughtered for market or that outgrow their usefulness.

Livestock care consists of providing feed and shelter for the animals and safeguarding their health. The success of a livestock farm largely depends on how skillfully the farmer manages each of these jobs.

Feed can be divided into two main types: (1) *forage* and (2) *feed concentrates.* Forage consists of plants that livestock graze on or that have been cut to make hay or silage. Forage supplies livestock mainly with *roughage* (fiber). Feed concentrates consist chiefly of feed grains, such as corn and sorghum, and soybean meal. They mainly serve as a source of food energy and contain little roughage. In most cases, the grain is milled and mixed with vitamins and minerals. Some farmers also add antibiotics and synthetic hormones to feed concentrates to promote the animals' health and growth. Some farmers produce their own concentrates. Other farmers buy feed concentrates from commercial suppliers.

Cattle and sheep can live mainly on forage. Their digestive systems enable them to break down forage. Both sheep and cattle consume forage by grazing in pastures. However, cattle and sheep that are confined, either indoors or outdoors, are fed hay or silage. Although these animals can live on forage, farmers also feed them concentrates to ensure a balanced diet. Cattle and sheep that are being prepared for slaughter are usually fed large amounts of concentrates. The high-energy content of such a diet helps *finish* (fatten) the animals quickly. Unlike cattle and sheep, hogs and poultry cannot digest large quantities of forage. Most farmers therefore raise them primarily on concentrates.

Most livestock farms require substantial quantities of prepared feed. An egg-laying hen, for example, needs about ½ to 4 pounds (0.2 to 1.8 kilograms) of feed each week. A dairy cow eats about 300 to 700 pounds (135 to 315 kilograms) of feed each week.

Shelter. Most kinds of livestock need protection against extremely cold weather. Mature beef cattle and sheep, however, are less affected by the cold than are the majority of livestock. This resilience is due to the cattle's hide and the sheep's thick pelt. Ranchers may keep these animals on open rangeland throughout the year. Most other farmers provide shelter for their animals at least part of the time. Some livestock, including most poultry and swine, may be raised entirely indoors.

Health care for livestock has become much more effective through the development of vaccines and other drugs. Before these drugs were available, such diseases as anthrax and hog cholera killed large numbers of livestock. Farmers now prevent many kinds of diseases by having their animals vaccinated. Animals with infectious diseases can be treated with penicillin and other germ-killing antibiotics. Farmers sometimes add low levels of antibiotics to livestock feed as a preventive measure, especially in the case of young animals.

Livestock breeding. Most farm animals are raised to provide livestock products. However, some farmers also raise *breeding stock*—that is, animals of superior quality that are used mainly to make offspring. The offspring may inherit a combination of their parents' desirable qualities, such as large size and weight or exceptional ability to produce milk or eggs. Farmers select animals to become breeding stock on the basis of their qualities and those of their offspring. For example, a cow that produces much milk and whose daughter does the same may be removed from the milk herd and placed in the breeding herd. After a number of years, such selective breeding can significantly improve the quality of all the animals on a farm.

The development of *artificial insemination* and *embryo transfers* has greatly sped up the process of selective breeding. Artificial insemination technology enables farmers to extract *sperm* (male reproductive cells) from a superior bull, freeze it, and ship it to many different farms. The sperm can then be inserted into a large num-

An automated grain storage system

Grain can be stored for months after harvesting if it has been dried to prevent spoilage. Many farms that store large quantities of grain have an automated system for drying the grain and for transferring it to and from storage bins. These drawings show how such a system works.

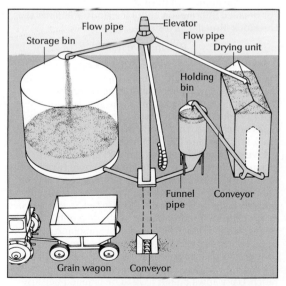

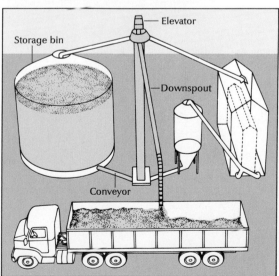

WORLD BOOK diagrams by Robert Keys

Drying and storage. Grain is brought from the fields by grain wagon and dumped on a conveyor, which carries it to an elevator. The elevator lifts the grain and releases it through a flow pipe into the drying unit. Here, hot forced air dries the grain. The dried grain, represented by the gold-colored areas, is moved by a conveyor to a holding bin. The grain funnels from the bin onto the elevator, which lifts it to a flow pipe at the top of the elevator. The grain then flows into the storage bin.

Unloading from storage. Farmers often store grain in hopes that the market price will rise. An automated storage system enables a farmer to ship stored grain to market quickly in case of a sudden increase in prices. To ship the stored grain, the farmer activates a conveyor at the foot of the storage bin. The conveyor removes grain from the bin and carries it to the elevator. The elevator lifts the grain and releases it into a downspout. The grain flows through the spout and into a waiting truck.

Rugged grazing land, such as this pasture in New Zealand, is well suited to raising sheep. Sheep can survive by grazing on grasses and shrubs.

J. C. Allen and Son

A modern egg farm raises hundreds or thousands of hens in a *confinement building*. The birds are kept in small cages to conserve their energy and to make egg-gathering easier.

© Thinkstock

Baby hogs depend on their mother's milk. Many hog farmers keep the babies partially separated from the mother while they are nursing to prevent them from being crushed.

ber of cows, which will give birth to desirable offspring. Additionally, farmers can take fertilized eggs from cows with superior traits and insert them into a number of additional cows. This technique, called embryo transfer, increases the number of offspring with the superior traits. For detailed information about livestock breeding, see **Livestock** (Breeding livestock).

Raising livestock

Many small farmers integrate livestock animals with the rest of their farming system. They may use the animals to pull farm equipment or supply manure for fertilizer. Other livestock farms are more specialized. Livestock production on such farms involves three main types of activities. They are (1) livestock grazing, (2) livestock finishing, and (3) confinement operations.

Livestock grazing takes place on about a fourth of all land on Earth. In the United States, about two-thirds of farmland is used for livestock grazing, especially for beef cattle and sheep. Most of this land is grassland on ranches in the western half of the United States. However, ranches do not produce enough grain or other high-energy feed to finish the animals for slaughter. In developed countries, ranchers often ship their meat animals to specialized farms for finishing. Sheep raised for wool live mainly on grass, so these animals remain on the ranch. Dairy cows do not have to be fattened because their main purpose is to produce milk. However, after cows have *calved* (given birth), dairy farmers typically supply them with a rich diet of silage and concentrate to help them produce the optimum amount of milk.

Livestock finishing, or fattening, relies on the large-scale use of feed concentrates. Livestock finishing often takes place in major grain-producing areas. For example, in the United States, the majority of hog farms are in the chief corn-producing states, such as Illinois, Iowa, Minnesota, and Nebraska. Some farmers finish beef cattle, hogs, or sheep that they have raised from birth. Many others sell their young animals for finishing, either to farmers who have excess feed grain or to *feed lots*. Feed lots specialize in finishing young beef cattle or sheep. The animals are kept in pens and fed large amounts of feed concentrates. The largest feed lots finish thousands of animals at a time.

Confinement operations mass-produce certain kinds of livestock and livestock products. The largest operations produce poultry and eggs. Feed lots are a form of a confinement operation. Many feed lots are simply areas of open land that have been fenced in and divided into large pens. The animals are confined inside the pens, but they can still move relatively freely. In a full confinement operation, the animals are kept inside a building in pens or individual cages that greatly limit their motion. These animals use less energy by moving

little and not fighting or competing for mates. As a result, they can produce more meat or other products.

Many confinement buildings have enclosures for hundreds or even thousands of animals. Most of these buildings are equipped with automatic machinery that brings feed to the animals and clears away their waste. In the United States, nearly all broiler chickens and a large share of laying hens are raised in confinement. A large number of American farmers also use confinement techniques to raise hogs, beef cattle, and dairy cattle. The technique is used to increase production efficiency and maximize the use of land.

The use of confinement on organic farms is somewhat restricted. By law, organic farms must allow their livestock some access to the outdoors, though the access may simply be a small fenced-in area outside the building. Some farmers raise livestock largely on pastures or in outdoor environments, marketing their products as more humane than those raised on industrialized farms.

An automated livestock farm The farm in this drawing uses a variety of automatic machinery to help raise large numbers of beef cattle. The farm also grows corn, hay, and other crops to feed the animals. After feed crops are harvested, they are loaded into the tall storage structures at the left through blower pipes. Conveyors remove them from storage as they are needed and carry them to a feed preparation room in the livestock building. Here, machinery mixes the feed and sends it by conveyor to the feeding trough in the main livestock room. The cattle remain in this room most of the time. Machinery scrapes their manure from the floor and pumps it into the outdoor storage tank at the right. The manure is used as fertilizer. As the cattle grow fat enough for slaughter, they are shipped to market in trucks.

WORLD BOOK diagram by Robert Addison; with technical assistance of A. O. Smith Harvestore Products, Inc.

Farm management

Farm management is the process by which farmers maximize their efficiency and use of resources to receive the highest possible profits while sustaining the future livelihood of their farms. Farm management involves all aspects of farming, including selecting inputs, managing production, protecting soil and water resources, and seeking out ideal markets for farm products. Some farm owners hire dedicated farm managers to run their farms.

Managing risk. Farms face unique business risks. A farm's success depends heavily on factors out of farmers' control, such as weather and the behavior of global markets. As a result, farm income can vary greatly between farms and from year to year.

Farmers must identify risks and prepare accordingly. They must be prepared to keep costs low and to absorb unexpected crop losses and changes in the cost of such inputs as seeds, fertilizers, and fuel. The prices of farm products also tend to fluctuate greatly, introducing more uncertainty. Farmers must be prepared to financially survive an unexpected disaster, such as a sudden freeze, drought, or pest infestation. For farmers in developing countries, a weather disaster could mean the loss of their farms or even starvation. In developed countries, on the other hand, many commercial farmers can purchase *crop insurance,* which may cover a portion of their loss in such circumstances (see **Crop insurance**). Farmers may also take advantage of government disas-

ter assistance programs.

Financing. Unlike many workers, farmers do not receive a steady weekly or monthly income. Farmers get paid only after production, when they sell their crops or livestock products. Thus, farmers must make a significant initial investment in inputs, followed by a long period of labor, before they actually make money. During this time, farmers often must seek financial assistance. This assistance may include farm loan programs, agricultural subsidies, and price supports. These methods of assistance are discussed in a later section.

Marketing. Most farm products are *commodities.* A commodity is a raw, unprocessed good—such as grain or milk—that can easily be bought and sold in large amounts around the world. In general, a commodity produced in one place sells for about the same price as a commodity produced in another.

Some farmers sell directly to food-processing companies, stores, or customers. However, farmers may have difficulty finding or reaching high-paying buyers—or, in some cases, any buyers at all. Many farmers thus belong to *marketing cooperatives.* A marketing cooperative tries to find the best markets for its members' products. Cooperatives generally assure farmers of a market, but they may not guarantee a specific selling price. If the supply of a product exceeds the demand, the price normally falls.

Some commercial farmers can nearly eliminate marketing risks by an arrangement called *contract farming.* In contract farming, a farmer signs a contract with a

Changes in U.S. farming between 1900 and 2000

	1900	1925	1950	1975	2000
Farm population	29,875,000	31,190,000	23,048,000	8,864,000	2,988,000
Total land in farms (in acres)	838,591,000	924,319,000	1,202,019,000	1,059,420,000	945,080,000
Number of farms	5,737,000	6,470,600	5,647,800	2,521,400	2,166,800
Average size of farms (in acres)	146	143	213	420	436
Average assets per farm†	unknown	unknown	$23,815	$205,241	$555,202
Average crop production per acre (index numbers‡)	50	62	71	126	197
Average annual gross income per farm	$1,306	$2,120	$5,714	$39,898	$111,548

*One acre equals 0.4047 hectare.
†Includes value of land, buildings, livestock, motor vehicles, machinery, and stored crops.
‡The index numbers show changes in relation to the base year of 1967, which equals 100.
Source: U.S. Department of Agriculture.

WORLD BOOK graph by Precision Graphics

Nicholas deVore III, Bruce Coleman Inc.

A grain dealer buys truckloads of wheat from local farmers. The wheat is stored in elevators, *background.* It is later resold through a grain exchange or directly to a milling company.

© Tom Lindsey, Alamy Images

Bidding at a cattle auction determines the price of animals offered for sale. The cattle are sold to the highest bidder. Farmers often sell hogs and sheep, as well as cattle, at auctions.

food-processing or food-distributing firm. In most cases, the firm agrees to pay a certain price for a specified amount of the farmer's product. Crops and livestock for processing or export are often produced under such agreements. However, not all farmers support contract farming. Such arrangements can give buyers a great deal of power, potentially enabling them to take advantage of farmers. In addition, farmers who sell on contract generally cannot benefit if market prices rise.

Some farmers sell beef cattle, hogs, and sheep at *auction markets.* The buyers at a livestock auction bid on the animals, and the animals are sold to the highest bidder.

If farmers can add value to a product and distinguish it from other commodities, they may be able to charge higher prices. For example, some farmers produce a subset of goods for alternative or high-demand markets. These products, such as organic foods, may sell for higher prices. Farmers may also market their products directly to local urban or suburban consumers. Such consumers may be willing to pay a premium for locally produced farm goods. In *community-supported agriculture,* local consumers pay farmers a set price for a season's worth of farm goods. Such programs enable farmers to gain income before harvest.

Challenges and resources for farmers

Farms in developed countries today are the most productive in history by far. Farmers today can take advantage of a wide array of labor-saving technology. Farmers also benefit from communication technology, which helps them learn about the latest agricultural advances and monitor global markets.

But farmers continue to face many challenges. Earth's increasing population—and rising standards of living in

J. C. Allen and Son

Keeping farm equipment in working condition is a major task on today's highly mechanized farms. This farmer is servicing his combine, *right,* and its special corn-picking attachment, *left.*

many countries—puts pressure on farmers to produce enough food to meet demand. Meanwhile, rising costs of fuel, fertilizer, and other petroleum-based inputs also put pressure on farmers. Although farms have greatly expanded in the last century, much of their expansion has involved cutting down forests or disrupting areas with poor soil and fragile ecosystems. Such *marginal lands* are difficult to protect against degradation. Much modern agricultural research involves balancing the production of an adequate food supply with protecting Earth's environment.

In developed countries, farmers benefit from a number of government programs that provide them with a measure of financial security. But such security does not always extend to farmworkers. Many farms employ migrant laborers. Such workers move into an area temporarily to harvest time-sensitive crops, such as ripe fruit. Migrant workers generally receive low wages. In many developed countries, especially the United States, migrant workers often come from poorer, developing countries. Such workers have few of the protections offered to the developed countries' citizens.

In less developed countries, many farmers are too poor to afford labor-saving or communications technology. In addition, few, if any, government programs exist to help these farmers. Such farmers have great difficulty escaping poverty and hunger.

Resources for farmers. Farmers in developed countries benefit from a number of government resources. Farm subsidies include direct payments to farmers. Various other government programs offer assistance to farmers in the form of loans or disaster relief.

Farm subsidies help stabilize farm income and influence overall agricultural production. Many countries offer farm subsidies. They can support farmers when prices for farm products are low. They also may encourage the production—or lack of production—of certain crops. In the United States, common farm commodities supported by subsidies are corn, wheat, feed grains, barley, rice, oats, cotton, milk, peanuts, sugar, tobacco, and oilseeds. Additionally, farmers may receive subsidies for conservation efforts, for help after disasters, and for research.

Subsidies were originally created to protect farmers from the inherent risks in agricultural production. But subsidies are often controversial. From an economic perspective, subsidies can cause distortions in agricultural markets. For example, a subsidy may encourage the widespread growing of a crop, creating an unnecessarily large surplus. In addition, many beneficiaries of government subsidies are large, profitable farms. Subsidies may also be poorly targeted or mismanaged. During the 2000's, for example, more than $1 billion in U.S. subsidies went to landowners who no longer actually used their land for farming.

Other programs. Many government programs help farmers in various ways. They include farm loan programs, energy programs, and disaster assistance programs. In the United States, these programs are funded through the Farm Service Agency (FSA) of the USDA. Similar programs exist in other developed countries.

Farm loan programs aid farmers in securing money for farming and ranching needs. *Farm ownership loans* help farmers purchase or enlarge their farms or ranches.

Operating loans help pay for agricultural equipment, livestock, repairs, and other operating expenses. *Emergency loans* are available to farmers who have suffered agricultural losses caused by such natural disasters as droughts, floods, or tornadoes. *Conservation loans* assist farmers to implement conservation practices. In the awarding of loans, special consideration may be given to support inexperienced, socially disadvantaged, minority, or women farmers.

Energy programs assist producers of renewable energy sources, such as crops that are used to make *biofuels.* Biofuels are fuels derived from materials in plants. They contrast with *fossil fuels,* which are derived from limited and dwindling supplies of coal, oil, and natural gas.

Disaster assistance programs provide aid to farmers in the event of agricultural losses due to natural disaster. The Conservation Reserve Program (CRP) is a voluntary program for those who own agricultural land. The CRP pays incentives or provides assistance to farmers who participate in efforts to help preserve farmland, soil, wetlands, grasslands, forests, and source waters or engage in other environmentally beneficial activities.

Farm organizations. In the United States, the USDA supports agriculture in many ways. For example, the USDA helps to support farmers by supporting rural communities in general, through grants, loans, insurance programs, technological and disaster assistance, and education and research programs. The agency also heads conservation efforts and works to ensure *food security* in both the United States and the rest of the world. Food security is the reliable access of households to a healthy diet of food. The USDA works with and funds many other organizations that support farming.

Also in the United States, schools called *land-grant universities* and their colleges of agriculture, food, and environmental sciences support farming. They conduct research at experimental stations and spread new knowledge to farmers through Cooperative Extension offices in counties throughout the country.

Many farmers are members of organizations concerned with the growing of a particular commodity. Farmers pay annual fees, which support adult education within the group. Often, commodity organizations work with land-grant universities. United States farmers also benefit from other nongovernmental organizations, notably the American Farm Bureau Federation. Farm-oriented youth organizations in the United States include 4-H, the Young Farmers Association, and the National FFA Organization.

The Food and Agriculture Organization (FAO) of the United Nations and the Consultative Group on International Agricultural Research (CGIAR) are major international farm organizations. They work to eliminate hunger around the world by improving nutrition and farm production. They also offer technical assistance and advice on agricultural policy and planning.

Farming and hunger. In the 2010's, nearly 1 billion people suffered from hunger and malnutrition. Nearly all of them lived in less developed countries, and many were small farmers in rural areas. Such farmers usually live on land with marginal growing potential. They often lack access to such resources as water for irrigation, productive varieties of crops, fertilizer, farming machinery, and scientific knowledge. Farmers who are poor also tend to be especially vulnerable to loss from environmental damage. *Global warming,* the observed rise in Earth's average temperature, is forecast to change the climate in many of the places where poor small farmers live, introducing more challenges to their livelihoods.

Farm-based economic growth has been shown to be more effective in fighting poverty than is growth in any other industrial sector. Increasing access to agricultural education—particularly for female farmers—has been identified as a source of many potential benefits to farming systems in less developed countries.

Maria Navarro

Related articles in *World Book.* See **Agriculture** and its list of *Related articles.* See also the *Agriculture* section of the state, province, country, and continent articles. See also:

Kinds of farming

Aquaculture	Gardening	Plantation
Dairying	Horticulture	Ranching
Factory farming	Hydroponics	Tree farming
Floriculture	Nursery	Truck farming
Fur (Fur ranching)		

Major crops

Alfalfa	Corn	Peanut	Sorghum	Tobacco
Banana	Cotton	Potato	Soybean	Vegetable
Barley	Fruit	Rice	Sugar	Wheat
Bean	Oats	Rye		

Chief kinds of livestock

Cattle	Duck	Hog	Poultry	Sheep
Chicken	Goat	Horse	Rabbit	Turkey

Farm buildings and equipment

Barn	Plow	Threshing
Combine	Pump	machine
Greenhouse	Rake	Tractor
Harness	Reaper	Truck
Harrow	Silo	Windmill
Milking machine		

Methods and problems

Breeding	Fungicide
Cloud seeding	Herbicide
Conservation	Hybrid
Cropping system	Insecticide
Drainage	Irrigation
Drought	Migrant labor
Dryland farming	Pest control
Erosion	Weed
Fertilizer	Windbreak
Fumigation	

Government agencies and programs

Agricultural Stabilization and Conservation Service
Agriculture, Department of
Commodity Credit Corporation
Cooperative Extension System
Farm Credit System
Farmers Home Administration
Land Management, Bureau of
Reclamation, Bureau of
Rural Electrification Administration

Farm organizations

Cooperative
FFA
4-H
Grange, National
National Farmers Union
United Farm Workers of America

Other related articles

Agribusiness
Agricultural education
Agricultural experiment station
Agronomy
Airplane (Special-purpose planes)
Food
Food supply
Grain
Land-grant university
Livestock
Pet (Farm pets)
Soil
Tenant farming

Additional resources

Level I
Dumas, Philippe. *A Farm.* Creative Education, 1999.
Peterson, Cris. *Century Farm: One Hundred Years on a Family Farm.* Boyds Mills, 1999.
Wilkes, Angela. *A Farm Through Time.* Dorling Kindersley, 2001.
Willard, Nancy. *Cracked Corn and Snow Ice Cream: A Family Almanac.* 1997. Reprint. Harcourt, 2005.

Level II
Bell, Michael M. *Farming for Us All.* Penn. State Univ. Pr., 2004.
Danbom, David B. *Born in the Country: A History of Rural America.* Johns Hopkins, 1995.
Heiney, Paul. *Country Life.* DK Pub., 1998. Discusses home farming.
Imhoff, Dan. *Farming with the Wild: A New Vision for Conservation-Based Agriculture.* Sierra Club, 2003.
Ivanko, John D., and Kivirist, Lisa. *Rural Renaissance: Renewing the Quest for the Good Life.* New Soc., 2004.

Farm Credit System is a nationwide system of cooperatively owned banks and associations in the United States. The system is the nation's largest agricultural lender. It provides loans to farmers and ranchers and their marketing, purchasing, and business service cooperatives in the United States and Puerto Rico. It also provides loans to people with aquatic operations, such as fishing or aquatic farming.

The United States government supplied the original capital for the system. However, farmers gradually replaced the government's capital, and they now own all the stock in the system's cooperatives. The system obtains most of its loan funds from the sales of securities to the public.

The Farm Credit System is supervised and regulated by the Farm Credit Administration (FCA), an independent United States government agency. A three-member board of directors sets FCA policies. Members are appointed by the president. One member serves as chief executive officer of the agency.

Organization. The Farm Credit System consists of five regional banks and approximately 90 local lending associations. The local associations are in all 50 states and Puerto Rico. The regional banks lend funds to the local associations, which in turn lend money directly to farmers, ranchers, rural homeowners, and rural businesses. One of the regional banks—CoBank, based in suburban Denver—also lends funds to large *agribusinesses, agricultural cooperatives,* and rural energy, communications, and water companies throughout the United States. An agribusiness is a company that produces, processes, markets, or distributes farm products, or that supplies goods or services to farmers. An agricultural cooperative is an association in which farmers work with one another to market farm products, purchase supplies, or furnish farm services.

Each regional bank and local association is owned and controlled by its borrowers. To receive a loan, a borrower must purchase stock in the bank or association. Each bank and association has a board of directors elected by the borrowers.

The Federal Farm Credit Banks Funding Corporation manages the sale of Farm Credit System securities. It is the main source of funds to the five system banks. The Funding Corporation is owned and operated by the banks. It is headed by a 10-member board.

The Farm Credit System Insurance Corporation (FCSIC) provides insurance to investors in system securities. System banks pay annual premiums into the insurance fund. The three members of the FCA board of directors also make up the FCSIC board of directors.

History. Congress authorized Federal Land Banks in 1916. By 1947, government capital invested in these banks was repaid. Federal Intermediate Credit Banks were authorized in 1923. The FCA was established in 1933. Production Credit Associations and Banks for Cooperatives were authorized that same year.

In the early 1980's, many farmers experienced serious financial difficulties due to high interest rates, a loss of international markets, and related problems. As a result, the Farm Credit System had record losses. Because of these losses, Congress restructured parts of the Farm Credit System through the Agricultural Credit Act of 1987. The act's passage resulted in a large-scale reorganization of the Farm Credit System, which included the establishment of Farm Credit Banks.   Raymond J. Miller, Jr.

Farmer. See Agriculture; Farm and farming.

Farmer, James Leonard (1920-1999), an American civil rights leader, was assistant secretary of the Department of Health, Education, and Welfare in 1969 and 1970. He helped set up the Congress of Racial Equality (CORE) in 1942 and served as its national director until 1966. Farmer guided CORE through marches, sit-ins, and *freedom rides* (bus rides to test the enforcement of desegregation) (see **Congress of Racial Equality**). Farmer was one of several black leaders who helped organize the 1963 March on Washington.

Farmer served as program director of the National Association for the Advancement of Colored People (NAACP) from 1959 to 1961. He was a professor of social welfare at Lincoln (Pennsylvania) University in 1966 and 1967.

Wide World
James L. Farmer

In 1968, Farmer ran unsuccessfully for a seat in the United States House of Representatives from Brooklyn, a section of New York City. In 1976, he became associate director of the Coalition of American Public Employees, a group of labor and professional organizations.

Farmer was born Jan. 20, 1920, in Marshall, Texas. He graduated from Wiley College in 1938 and the Howard University School of Religion in 1941. Farmer died on July 9, 1999.   Robert A. Pratt

Farmer-Labor Party was a leading Minnesota political party. It was founded in 1918 and later took over the work of the Nonpartisan League. Its platform included government ownership of some industries, social security laws, and protection for farmers and labor union members. The party's outstanding leader was Floyd B. Olson, Minnesota governor from 1931 to 1936. The party elected candidates to state and national offices. In 1944, the party merged with the Minnesota Democratic Party to form the Democratic-Farmer-Labor Party. The Farmer-Labor Party was also the name of an organization formed in Chicago in 1919. It lasted until 1924.

Donald R. McCoy

Farmers Home Administration was an agency of the United States Department of Agriculture from 1946 to 1994. The agency coordinated a nationwide rural development program and promoted cooperation between the federal government and state and local rural development projects. It offered loans to small-farm owners for agricultural supplies, land purchases, living needs, and disaster relief. It also provided financing for business and industrial development, community facilities, and housing in rural areas. Community loans were made for fire protection, medical facilities, and waste disposal systems. The agency was dissolved in 1994, and its farm loan programs were transferred to the Agriculture Department's Farm Service Agency. The rural housing programs became part of the department's rural and community development programs.

Critically reviewed by the Department of Agriculture

Farmers organizations. See Farm and farming and its list of *Related articles.*

Farming. See Agriculture; Farm and farming.

Farnese Bull, *fahr NAY say,* is a famous ancient group sculpture that portrays an episode in Greek mythology. Its name comes from the Farnese Palace in Rome, where the sculpture was once kept. The *Farnese Bull* is a striking marble copy of a lost sculpture made in the 100's B.C. by the Greek sculptors Apollonios and Tauriskos of Tralles. Unknown Roman sculptors made the copy in the A.D. 200's, adding their own elements to the original plan of the sculpture. The copy was discovered during an excavation in Rome in the 1500's, and lost portions of it were restored by Renaissance artists.

The sculpture shows two young men tying Dirce, the wife of King Lycus of Thebes, to a bull. Dirce had cruelly mistreated and imprisoned Antiope, who was Lycus's niece and, according to some stories, had been his first wife. Dirce planned to kill Antiope by binding her to a bull's horns. But Antiope's twin sons tied Dirce to the bull instead.   Marjorie S. Venit

Farnsworth, Philo Taylor, *FY loh* (1906-1971), an American inventor, was a pioneer in television technology. While still a teenager, he created an electronic television system that was superior to the mechanical discs then used experimentally. At age 20, Farnsworth applied for a patent for an electronic television camera tube that became known as an *image dissector.* It created an image by producing an electronic signal that corresponded to the brightness of the objects being televised. Farnsworth demonstrated the image dissector in 1927.

In 1939, Radio Corporation of America (RCA) obtained a license from Farnsworth to produce electronic television transmission systems that combined his technology with theirs. Farnsworth later studied nuclear energy and radar. He was born on Aug. 19, 1906, in Beaver, Utah. A statue of him represents Utah in Statuary Hall in Washington, D.C. He died March 11, 1971. *Joseph H. Udelson*

Faroe Islands, *FAIR oh,* also spelled *Faeroe* and *Føroyar,* are a group of 18 islands and some reefs in the North Atlantic Ocean. They lie between Iceland and the Shetland Islands. The group has an area of 538 square miles (1,393 square kilometers) and a population of about 50,000. The major islands are Streymoy, Eysturoy, Vágar, Sudhuroy, and Sandoy.

The 687 miles (1,106 kilometers) of coastline are steep and deeply indented. Treacherous currents along the shores of the islands make navigation difficult. The islanders are a people of Norse origin who mainly fish and raise sheep. They also sell the eggs and feathers of the many sea birds that nest on the cliffs. The islanders do little farming.

Norway ruled over the Faroe Islands from the 800's until 1380, when they came under the control of Denmark. British forces occupied the islands during World War II (1939-1945), but the civil government remained the same. In 1948, Denmark granted the Faroes self-government. The islanders have their own parliament, or *Løgting,* and send representatives to the Danish parliament in Copenhagen. The seat of government is Tórshavn on Streymoy. *M. Donald Hancock*

WORLD BOOK map

Location of Faroe Islands

National Archaeological Museum, Naples, Italy (Alinari/Art Resource)

The *Farnese Bull* is a marble copy made in the A.D. 200's of the original Greek sculpture—now lost—carved in the 100's B.C.

Farouk I. See Faruk I.

Farquhar, *FAHR kwuhr,* **George** (1678-1707), is a transitional figure in the history of English drama. His plays contain the wit found in Restoration comedy of the late 1600's and the emphasis on character and plot found in English plays of the 1700's.

Farquhar wrote eight comedies in his brief life and is best known for two of them. In *The Beaux' Stratagem* (1707), two young Londoners visit a country town seeking rich wives. Both have comic adventures, and one wins an heiress. *The Recruiting Officer* (1706) describes the adventures of army recruiters in a country town.

Farquhar was born in Londonderry, Ireland, in 1678. He worked as an actor in Dublin before going to London to write comedy. A careless young man, he lived in constant need. He died on April 29, 1707. *Jack D. Durant*

Farragut, *FAR uh guht,* **David Glasgow,** *DAY vihd GLAS goh* (1801-1870), a United States naval officer, won fame at the American Civil War battle of Mobile Bay in 1864. At that battle, Farragut declared: "Damn the torpedoes! Full speed ahead!" Congress created the rank of full admiral for him in 1866.

Farragut showed his loyalty to the Union when he gave up his home in Norfolk, Virginia, at the start of the Civil War to fight on the Northern side. He took command of the important Western Gulf Blockading Squadron and cooperated brilliantly with General B. F. Butler and General E. R. S. Canby in operations against New Orleans and the forts at Mobile Bay. He won the nickname of *Old Salamander* when he ran his boats under heavy gunfire between the New Orleans forts on April 24, 1862, and the Mobile Bay forts on Aug. 5, 1864.

Farragut sailed up the Mississippi River with his heavy seagoing ships to bombard Vicksburg in 1862, a year before General Ulysses S. Grant captured the city by land. Farragut led a fleet to attack Mobile in 1864. His sailors fought their way into Mobile Bay, captured or destroyed enemy ships, and occupied the forts.

Farragut was born near Knoxville, Tennessee, on July 5, 1801. He took the name David after his adoption in 1810 by Captain David Porter, a U.S. naval officer noted for his service in the War of 1812 (1812-1815). David Dixon Porter, Farragut's adoptive brother, also gained fame as a Union naval officer in the Civil War.

The Smithsonian Institution

David G. Farragut

Before the Civil War, Farragut battled pirates in the Caribbean and fought in the war with Mexico. In 1867 and 1868, he commanded U.S. naval forces in European waters. He died on Aug. 14, 1870. *John F. Marszalek*

See also **Civil War, American** (Battle of Mobile Bay); **Porter, David; Porter, David Dixon.**

Farrakhan, *FAHR uh kahn,* **Louis** (1933-), became the leader of the Nation of Islam in 1977. This religious organization favors racial separation, black nationalism, and economic independence for African Americans.

A powerful speaker, Farrakhan is admired by many

blacks both inside and outside the Nation of Islam. He is also controversial. Many people have accused Farrakhan of prejudiced statements against Jews and other whites. However, he has argued that news reports have misrepresented his remarks.

AP/Wide World
Louis Farrakhan

Farrakhan was born Louis Eugene Walcott in New York City on May 11, 1933. He grew up in Boston. In 1955, Black Muslim minister Malcolm X recruited him to join the Nation of Islam. Walcott changed his name to Louis X. He adopted the name Louis Haleem Abdul Farrakhan in 1965.

In 1975, the leader of the Nation of Islam, Elijah Muhammad, died. To succeed him as leader, the Black Muslims chose one of his sons, Warith (formerly Wallace) Deen Mohammed (sometimes spelled Muhammad). Farrakhan disagreed with Mohammed's teachings, which involved the abandonment of radical black nationalism and the adoption of orthodox Sunni Islam. In 1977, Farrakhan broke away from Mohammed's group and formed his own Nation of Islam. Today, only Farrakhan's group uses the name Nation of Islam.

In 1995, Farrakhan became the chief organizer—and a leader—of a large rally of African American men in Washington, D.C. Known as the Million Man March, the event was designed to encourage black men to take personal responsibility for improving conditions in black communities. Crowd estimates ranged from 400,000 to more than a million. Farrakhan has led a number of other events, including the Million Family March in 2000 and the Millions More Movement in 2005.

In 1997, Farrakhan began to move closer to orthodox Sunni Islam. He adopted the orthodox Friday worship service, prayer posture, and fasting. These measures helped end 25 years of separation between Farrakhan and Mohammed. The two declared their unity at the International Islamic Conference in 2000. But they continued to lead separate movements. Mohammed died in 2008.   Lawrence H. Mamiya

See also **Black Muslims; Malcolm X; Muhammad, Elijah; Nation of Islam.**

Farrell, *FAIR uhl,* **James T.** (1904-1979), was an American writer known for his novels about lower middle-class life in a decaying neighborhood of a large city. Farrell followed the theory of Naturalism in his early works, believing that people are strongly influenced by their environment (see **Naturalism**). Farrell's best-known work is the *Studs Lonigan* trilogy—*Young Lonigan* (1932), *The Young Manhood of Studs Lonigan* (1934), and *Judgment Day* (1935). These three controversial novels are written largely in the language of Lonigan, the title character, a young tough. They explore the impact of urban industrial life on a boy growing up in a poor neighborhood in Chicago.

James Thomas Farrell was born on Feb. 27, 1904, in Chicago. After the Lonigan series, he wrote five novels featuring Danny O'Neill, a stronger, more sensitive hero than Lonigan. These stories show Farrell's newly found faith in people's ability to deal with their circumstances. Farrell died on Aug. 22, 1979.   Samuel Chase Coale

Farsightedness, also called *longsightedness,* is a visual defect in which a person can see distant objects clearly, but near vision may be blurred. Doctors call this condition *hyperopia.* In most cases of farsightedness, the eyes are too short from front to back. As a result, light rays from an object reach the retina before they can be brought into focus.

The eye may be able to correct its own farsightedness through a process called *accommodation.* In accommodation, certain eye muscles contract, making the lens of the eye rounder and thicker. The lens then has a greater ability to focus. The lens of a normal eye accommodates only to bring nearby objects into focus. However, the lens of a farsighted eye must also accommodate for sharp distance vision. Although a farsighted eye receives sharp images of distant objects, the excessive accommodation may cause eyestrain and headaches. In addition, the lens may not accommodate enough for sharp near vision.

Young people and mildly farsighted people can accommodate enough for sharp vision at both near and far distances. But, as a person grows older, the lens loses its ability to accommodate. Many farsighted people first notice the condition at that time. Farsightedness is easily corrected with eyeglasses or contact lenses. As an alternative, doctors may use high-frequency radio waves to change the shape of the cornea in a technique called *conductive keratoplasty.* Laser surgery also may be used to reshape the cornea.   Ronald A. Krefman

See also **Eye** (Farsightedness); **Glasses** (Prescription glasses); **LASIK surgery.**

Farthing was a coin of the lowest value in British currency. It was worth one-fourth of a penny, or the 960th part of a pound sterling (see **Pound**). The farthing was first issued in the 1220's, during the reign of King Henry III (1216-1272). It was a silver coin until 1613. The metal for a farthing was then usually copper until 1860, when the metal was changed to bronze. The British government withdrew the farthing from circulation on Jan. 1, 1961.   R. G. Doty

Faruk I, *fah ROOK* (1920-1965), also spelled *Farouk,* was the last king of Egypt. He became king in 1936, succeeding his father, Fuad I. Faruk was popular at the beginning of his reign. But he symbolized traditions that had been discredited by British occupation of Egypt. In 1952, rebels directed by General Muhammad Naguib forced Faruk to give up his throne. The rebels charged that there was corruption in the government. Faruk went into exile in Europe. He died on March 18, 1965, in Rome. He was born on Feb. 11, 1920, in Cairo.

Justin McCarthy

See also **Egypt** (History); **Nasser, Gamal Abdel.**

Fasces, *FAS eez,* were a symbol of power during the days of the Roman

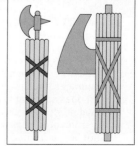

WORLD BOOK illustration by Lisa Wilkinson
Fasces

Republic, of the Roman Empire, and, later, of the Fascist government of dictator Benito Mussolini in Italy. Fasces consisted of a bundle of birch or elm rods bound together by a strap. The blade of an ax projected from the bundle. Servants called *lictors* carried these bundles ahead of such officials as magistrates, governors, and emperors. The fasces stood for the official's power to punish people or put them to death, and also symbolized unity. Fasces appear on the back of some American dimes. Alexander J. Groth

Fascism, *FASH ihz uhm,* is an extreme form of *authoritarian* government. An authoritarian government allows a few people to run a country. The rest of the population takes little part in decision making. Fascism involves total government control of political, economic, cultural, religious, and social activities.

Fascism resembles Communism. Communism, however, calls for the government to own all industry. Fascism allows industry to remain in private ownership, though under government control. Other important features of fascism include extreme *nationalism*—not just loving one's own country, but believing other countries to be inferior. This belief often causes fascist governments to persecute minority groups within their country. Fascist governments often pursue aggressive policies toward other nations.

Fascism has varied from country to country. This article discusses fascism mainly as it existed in Italy under Benito Mussolini from 1922 to 1943 and in Germany under Adolf Hitler from 1933 to 1945.

Life under fascism

Political life. In most cases, fascists rise to power after a nation has suffered an economic collapse, a military defeat, or some other disaster. The fascists win mass support by promising to revive the economy and to restore national pride. They may also appeal to a fear of Communism or a hatred of minorities. In time, the fascists may gain control of the government—through peaceful elections or by force.

After the fascist party takes power, its members replace the officials who run the government. In most cases, one individual—usually a dictator with great popular appeal—becomes the leader of the government. Fascists permit no other political party and no opposition to their policies.

The fascist desire for national glory leads to an increase in military spirit and a build-up of the armed forces. The military build-up can be used to put down opposition from within the fascist nation. It also allows a fascist government to seize land from, or gain influence over, foreign nations.

Economic life. A fascist government permits and even encourages private enterprise—as long as such activity serves the government's goals. However, the government maintains strict control of industry to make sure it produces what the nation needs. The government discourages or bans imports of certain essential products. It does not want to depend on other countries for such vital products as oil and steel.

The government also forbids strikes so that production will not be interrupted. Fascism outlaws labor unions and replaces them with a network of organizations in the major industries. These organizations, which consist of both workers and employers, are called *corporations.* They differ from the organizations called corporations in other countries. Through the fascist corporations, the government determines wages, hours, and production goals. A fascist country is sometimes called a *corporative state.*

Personal liberty is severely limited under a fascist government. For example, the government limits travel to other countries and restricts any contact with people from those countries. In addition, the government controls information. Newspapers, radio, and other means of communication are used for state *propaganda.* Propaganda is one-sided communication designed to influence people's thinking and actions. Fascist governments use strict *censorship* (control of information) to silence opposing views. A secret police force crushes any resistance. Opposition may lead to imprisonment, torture, and death.

Fascists consider other peoples inferior to their own nationality group. As a result, a fascist government may persecute or even kill Roma (sometimes called Gypsies), Jews, or members of other minority groups.

History

The word *fascism* comes from ancient Roman symbols of authority called *fasces* (see **Fasces**). Many historians trace the start of modern fascism to Napoleon I, who ruled France as a dictator during the early 1800's. Napoleon was not a true fascist, but fascists later adopted many of his methods. Napoleon promised his people that he would restore the glory of France through military conquest. To prevent opposition, he established one of the first secret police systems. Napoleon also controlled the French press and used propaganda and strict censorship to win support of his programs.

Fascism in Italy. Italy was on the winning side of World War I (1914-1918), but the war left the nation's economy in poor condition. In addition, the peace treaties gave Italy far less territory than it had expected.

Benito Mussolini's Fascist Party promised to give Italians prosperity. Mussolini vowed to restore Italy to the glory it had enjoyed during the days of the Roman Empire. The party gained the support of many landowners, business and military leaders, and members of the middle class. By 1922, the Fascists had become powerful enough to force the king of Italy to make Mussolini prime minister. Mussolini, who became known as *Il Duce* (The Leader), began to create a dictatorship. He abolished all political parties in Italy except the Fascist Party and seized control of industries, newspapers, police, and schools.

In 1940, under Mussolini's leadership, Italy entered World War II (1939-1945) on the side of Nazi Germany. The Fascist government was overthrown in 1943, when Italy surrendered to the Allies.

Fascism in Germany. Germany was defeated in World War I and lost much of its territory under the peace treaties. The treaties also forced Germany to *disarm* (give up its weapons of war) and to pay heavy penalties for war damages.

The German economy was damaged by severe *inflation* (a continual increase in prices throughout the economy) in the 1920's. This inflation, followed by a worldwide *depression* (deep, extended slump in total business activity) in the early 1930's, ruined the German economy.

A fascist party called the National Socialist German Workers' Party, or Nazi Party, gained strength rapidly during Germany's economic crisis. By 1933, the Nazis were the strongest party in Germany. Their leader, Adolf Hitler, became the head of the government. Hitler soon overthrew the constitution and began to transform himself into a dictator and make Germany a fascist state. His secret police wiped out opposition.

Hitler, who was called *der Führer* (the leader), preached that Germans were superior people and that Jews, Slavs, Roma, and other minorities were inferior. His followers used these beliefs to justify the brutal Nazi persecution of Jews and other groups. The Nazis eventually killed about 6 million Jews. Hitler vowed to extend Germany's borders and to avenge the nation's humiliation in World War I. He built up the armed forces and prepared for war. In 1939, World War II began when German armies invaded Poland. The Allies defeated Germany in 1945, and the Nazi government crumbled.

Fascism in other countries. In Hungary, a fascist party called the Arrow Cross gained much support in the late 1930's. During the same period, a fascist organization called the Iron Guard became the strongest political party in Romania. Fascist groups also gained considerable strength in Japan in the 1930's. All these fascist movements disappeared after the Nazi defeat in 1945.

Today, the rulers of many developing nations are following fascist policies in an effort to promote industrial growth and national unity. But because of the association of fascism with racism—and with Mussolini and Hitler—these leaders deny any similarity to fascist dictators.   Thomas S. Vontz

Related articles in *World Book* include:
Fasces
Hitler, Adolf
Mussolini, Benito
Nationalism
Nazism
Police state
Romania (Depression and fascism)
Totalitarianism
World War II (The rise of dictatorships)

Additional resources

Downing, David. *Fascism.* Heinemann Lib., 2003.
Paxton, Robert O. *The Anatomy of Fascism.* Knopf, 2004.
Payne, Stanley G. *A History of Fascism, 1914-1945.* Univ. of Wis. Pr., 1995.
Tames, Richard L. *Fascism.* Raintree, 2001.

Fashion, in its broadest sense, is a particular style that is popular for a short time and then replaced by another. Fashions may last just a few months or several years. We speak of fashions in automobiles, furniture, or interior design, as well as in music, literature, and art. But most commonly, fashion refers to a style of clothing that is worn at a given time but is expected to change.

Often, fashions in several areas are linked, giving rise to a period style. During the 1920's, for example, clothing, interiors, and architecture all featured straight, simple lines and bold colors. In addition, they reflected a fascination with modern technology, such as the automobile and electric power. This period style is known as *Art Deco.*

Although *fashion* usually refers to dress, it does not mean the same thing as *clothing.* People have worn clothing since prehistoric times, but people have only been concerned with fashion since the Middle Ages (about the A.D. 400's through the 1400's). Before then, people wore clothes that reflected the long-standing customs of their communities, and clothing styles changed extremely slowly.

Fashion, however, causes styles to change rapidly for a variety of historical, psychological, and sociological reasons. A clothing style may be introduced as a fashion, but the style becomes a *custom* if it is handed down from generation to generation. A fashion that quickly comes and goes is called a *fad.* See **Custom.**

The origins of fashion. Fashion develops in areas where people compete with one another for social status. Scholars believe that fashions began to appear in northern Europe and Italy when a system of social classes developed in the late Middle Ages. At that time, the people of Europe began to classify one another into groups based on such factors as wealth, ancestry, and occupation. The clothes people wore helped identify them as members of a particular social class. Before, only wealthy and powerful individuals concerned themselves with the style of their clothes. As the class system developed, more people began to compete for positions within society. Fashion was one means by which people competed with one another.

Regional differences became common. During the Renaissance (about 1300 to 1600), fashionable dress in Northern Europe differed greatly from Italian fashions. Italian cities, such as Venice and Florence, had developed styles that incorporated the influence of their trade with Asia and the Middle East.

Before the 1800's, many countries controlled fashion with regulations called *sumptuary laws.* Sumptuary laws limited the amount of money people could spend on private luxuries. Many such laws were designed to preserve divisions among the classes and regulated fashion according to a person's rank in society. In some countries, only the ruling class could legally wear silk, fur, and the colors red and purple. In Paris in the 1300's, middle-class women were forbidden by law to wear high headdresses, wide sleeves, and fur trimmings.

Other sumptuary laws forced people to buy products manufactured in their own country to help the country's economy. For example, an English law in the 1700's prohibited people of all classes from wearing cotton cloth produced outside of England. But the lure of fashion caused many people to break this law. The cloth was so popular that people risked arrest to wear it.

Why people follow fashion. People follow fashion for many reasons. Often people imitate the style of a person or group with whom they identify. In the past, most fashions originated in the upper classes and trickled down to the lower ones. Ordinary people sometimes hoped to raise their social position by following the fashions of privileged people. In a way, this process still happens. Modern celebrities, such as film stars, singers, and athletes—rather than aristocrats—now set fashions.

Fashion is also a form of nonverbal communication that provides a way for people to express their identities and values. For example, in the 1960's, many young people adopted an international youth style that included miniskirts and mod jackets. The fashions likely appealed to young people because, at first, many adults disapproved of them. Eventually, adults began copying them.

People also follow fashion to make themselves more attractive. When the standard of beauty changes, fashion changes with it. For example, as physical fitness became a popular standard of good looks in the 1980's, people began to wear athletic clothing more often.

Why fashions change. Fashions considered appropriate for men and women have changed as standards of masculinity and femininity have changed. Until the late 1700's, upper-class European men dressed as elaborately as women. It was acceptable for men to wear bright-colored or pastel suits trimmed with gold and lace, hats decorated with feathers, high-heeled shoes, and fancy jewelry. But by the mid-1800's, men had abandoned color and decoration in favor of plain, dark-colored wool suits. People considered this new fashion democratic, businesslike, and masculine. Until the early 1900's, European and American women rarely wore trousers, and their skirts almost always covered their ankles. By the 1920's, however, standards of feminine modesty had changed to the point that women began to wear both trousers and shorter skirts.

A clothing style may become fashionable over time with many different groups. For example, people began wearing blue jeans during the mid-1800's as ordinary work clothes. For decades, they were worn chiefly by outdoor laborers, such as farmers and cowboys. In the 1940's and 1950's, American teen-agers adopted blue jeans as a comfortable, casual youth fashion. Young people during the 1960's wore blue jeans as a symbol of rebellious political and social beliefs. By the 1970's, people no longer considered jeans rebellious, and expensive designer jeans had become fashionable.

Contrary to popular belief, political events seldom cause fashions to change. However, they may speed up changes that have already begun. For example, during the French Revolution (1789-1799), simple clothing replaced the extravagant costumes made fashionable by French aristocrats. But simple styles had become popular years earlier when men in England started wearing practical, dark suits instead of elegant, colorful clothes. English people identified these plain suits with political and personal liberty. Because many French people admired English liberty, this style was already becoming fashionable in France before the revolution.

Foreign wars or voyages of exploration have also introduced people to new styles of clothing. During the 1100's and the 1200's, European soldiers who traveled to the Middle East as part of the Crusades brought back silks and other rich fabrics. They incorporated the patterns of these textiles into their own designs as well. A number of traditional Asian garments later became fashionable in Europe. For example, cotton pajamas and the Kashmir shawl originated in India, and folding fans were introduced from Japan.

The Industrial Revolution during the 1700's and 1800's caused rapid changes in the development of fashion. The invention of mechanical looms, chemical dyes, artificial fabrics, and methods of mass production made fashions affordable to more people. In addition, new means of mass communication spread European and American fashions throughout the world. The Industrial

Fashions of the 1890's featured intricate decoration, such as richly carved furniture and latticework in interior design. Clothing was often adorned with embroidery, lace, frills, and ribbons.

Fashions of the 1950's emphasized simple designs with few decorations. Mass production made fashionable styles of clothing and furniture affordable for most families.

Revolution caused people throughout the world to dress more and more alike. Today, fashions are similar all over the world.

The fashion industry. Since the 1800's, the fashion industry has operated on two levels: *couture* and *ready-to-wear.* Couture refers to expensive, one-of-a-kind clothes created for rich consumers by high-fashion designers called *couturiers.* Couturiers often try to guess which styles will be popular in the future. Successful couture designs are later copied by manufacturers of ready-to-wear. Ready-to-wear clothing is produced in large quantities and sold for lower prices. In addition to greater fashion availability because of ready-to-wear clothing, fashion has also become accessible to more people because of the Internet and a market in second-hand fashions.   Clare Sauro

Related articles in *World Book* include:

Armani, Giorgio	Hairdressing	Lagerfeld, Karl
Body art	Hat	Lauren, Ralph
Chanel, Coco	Jeans	Modeling
Clothing	Karan, Donna	Saint Laurent, Yves
Dior, Christian	Klein, Calvin	Shoe

Additional resources

Cumming, Valerie. *Understanding Fashion History.* Costume & Fashion Pr., 2004.
Pendergast, Sara, and others. *Fashion, Costume, and Culture.* 5 vols. UXL, 2004.
Steele, Valerie, ed. *Encyclopedia of Clothing and Fashion.* 3 vols. Scribner, 2005.

Fast is abstinence from food, or certain kinds of food, for a time. The custom of fasting has played a part in the practices of every major religious group at some time.

There are many purposes for fasting. It has often been a way in which people have sought pardon for their misdeeds. In some religions, people fast during times of mourning. In others, the people believe that fasting will take their minds away from physical things, and produce a state of spiritual joy and happiness.

There are important fast days in Judaism, Christianity, and Islam. Jewish law orders a fast on Yom Kippur, the Day of Atonement. Many Orthodox Jews follow the custom of having the bride and groom fast on the day before their wedding. Many Christians fast during Lent, the period of 40 days, excluding Sundays, from Ash Wednesday, commemorating the 40 days that Jesus spent fasting in the wilderness. In general, for Christians, fasting seldom means doing without all food for an entire day. People who are not well can usually receive permission from their religious leaders not to fast.

Muslims fast from dawn to sunset every day during Ramadan, the ninth month of their year. During these hours, Muslims abstain from food and beverage, even though this month often comes during the hottest season of the year. Buddhists and Hindus also fast.

Most people have fasted at some time during their lives, either for religious reasons, for initiation ceremonies, or for help in developing magical powers or control over the body. In some religions, such as Zoroastrianism, religious leaders have protested against fasting from food. They claim that the food fast actually has no moral value, when compared with "fasting from evil" with eyes, hands, tongue, or feet.

Sometimes, personal or political goals are sought through fasting. Mohandas Gandhi of India used fasting both as a penance and as a means of political protest (see **Gandhi, Mohandas Karamchand**).

People have also fasted for health reasons. Scientists have studied the effects of fasting on the body and found that food intake increases the body's metabolism (see **Metabolism**). After fasting, metabolism can become as much as 22 percent lower than the normal rate. But research has also shown that, after long periods of fasting, the body tends to adjust by lowering the rate of metabolism itself. After fasting, a person should gradually resume eating. Religious groups do not intend fasting to be harmful. They believe it promotes self-control and strengthens the will.   Jonathan Z. Smith

See also **Lent; Ramadan; Yom Kippur.**

Fat is one of three main classes of nutrients that provide energy to the body. The other two classes are carbohydrates and proteins. Fats are found in animals and plants. An animal fat or plant fat that is liquid at room temperature is called an *oil.* A processed type of beef fat called *tallow* and some other fats are hard at room temperature. Such fats as butter, lard, and margarine are soft at room temperature.

Fat has many important uses. It is a concentrated source of food energy for animals and plants. Fat is stored under the surface of the skin of many kinds of animals, including human beings. These fat deposits provide energy reserves and act as insulation against heat loss. Deposits of fat around the eyeballs and other organs of animals serve as cushions against injury. Women need a certain amount of fat in their bodies to have normal menstrual cycles. Most of the fat in plants is stored in seeds, where it provides the first food for young seedlings as they grow. Many industries use animal or plant fats in manufacturing various products.

Structure. Fats consist primarily of compounds called *triglycerides.* Triglycerides contain one molecule of an alcohol called *glycerol,* also called *glycerin,* which is made up of atoms of carbon, hydrogen, and oxygen. The glycerol combines with three molecules of substances called *fatty acids.* Each of these fatty acids consists of a long chain of carbon atoms that have hydrogen atoms attached. The fatty acid chains are linked to the glycerol molecule to form a molecule of triglyceride.

Fatty acids occur in two forms called *saturated* and *unsaturated.* A saturated fatty acid has a chemical structure in which as many hydrogen atoms as possible are linked to its carbon chain. When all three of the fatty acids in a triglyceride are saturated, it is called a *saturated fat.* Most fats from animal sources contain a large proportion of saturated fats and are said to be *highly saturated.* For example, butter contains about 60 percent saturated fat.

An unsaturated fatty acid contains at least two fewer hydrogen atoms than a saturated fatty acid containing the same number of carbons. A triglyceride that contains one or more unsaturated fatty acids is known as an *unsaturated fat.* A fat with one unsaturated fatty acid is called a *monounsaturated fat.* A fat that contains more than one is called *polyunsaturated.* Most—but not all—fats from vegetable sources are unsaturated.

The most highly saturated fats tend to be hardest at room temperature. The hardness of a fat is also affected by the length of the carbon chains in its fatty acids. Most oils are polyunsaturated. The hardness of an unsaturated fat can be increased by *hydrogenation,* a process that artificially adds hydrogen to the fatty acids. Hydrogenation of such vegetable oils as corn, cottonseed, and soybean produces margarines and shortenings.

Biological and nutritional importance. The chemical structure of fats gives them certain important biological properties. For example, fats and oils do not dissolve in water, which makes up most of the body. Their insolubility in water enables fats to form membranes that surround all the body's cells. These membranes help cells maintain an environment within their borders that differs from the environment outside them. Some of the body's most important processes occur in this environment inside cells.

The structure of fats

A molecule of fat includes three fatty acid chains, each of which consists of a chain of carbon atoms with hydrogen atoms attached. The chemical diagram at the top shows one molecule of a *saturated fat.* Its fatty acid chains are saturated with hydrogen—that is, each gray carbon atom is linked to as many blue hydrogen atoms as possible. The bottom diagram shows 1 of the 3 chains of an *unsaturated fat.* This type of fat contains fewer than the maximum possible number of hydrogen atoms.

One molecule of a saturated fat

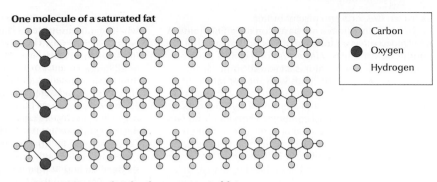

Carbon
Oxygen
Hydrogen

One fatty acid in a molecule of an unsaturated fat

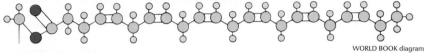

WORLD BOOK diagram

Fat is a more efficient fuel than either carbohydrates or proteins. Fat can produce about 4,000 calories of energy per pound (9 calories per gram). Carbohydrates and proteins can each produce about 1,800 calories per pound (4 calories per gram), less than half the energy produced by fat. Fat is also the body's most efficient form of stored fuel. The body converts carbohydrates and proteins into fat for storage and draws on this fat when extra fuel is needed.

Certain fatty acids, called *essential fatty acids,* are needed for growth and maintenance of the body. The body cannot make essential fatty acids, so they must be obtained from the diet. Essential fatty acids are building blocks for the membranes around cells. They also help form many of the complicated structures inside cells. Essential fatty acids are a main part of the membranes of the *retina,* the part of the eye that turns light into nerve impulses. *Synapses,* the junctions between the body's individual nerve cells, are also rich in essential fatty acids. All essential fatty acids are polyunsaturated.

Fats and disease. Many scientists believe that limiting the amount and types of fats eaten can help reduce the risk of developing certain diseases, including *coronary artery disease*. This disease results when deposits of *plaque* build up on the inner walls of the arteries that nourish the heart. Plaque consists of fat, calcium, and dead cells. The deposits may eventually make artery walls hard, rough, and narrow. Many heart attacks result from a blood clot that blocks such a narrowed artery.

A fatty compound called *cholesterol* is one of the main substances involved in formation of plaque. Cholesterol is found in many foods, including egg yolks, butter, and red meat. Eating both cholesterol and saturated fats seems to increase the amount of cholesterol in the blood. Most scientists recommend eating a diet low in overall fat, with cholesterol and saturated fats eaten most sparingly of all. Many scientists think that limiting the amount of fat eaten—especially saturated fat— may also help people avoid certain types of cancer.

Eating a high-fat diet can contribute to excess consumption of calories, which can lead to *obesity.* Obesity is overweight severe enough to pose a medical risk. People with obesity have an increased likelihood of many health problems, including diabetes, coronary

artery disease, and a liver disorder called *cirrhosis.* In the United States, all processed foods must carry a label that states the amount of total fat and the amount of cholesterol and saturated fat in a serving. This information is provided to help people control the amount of fat and calories in their diets.

Industrial uses. Fats from a wide variety of plants and animals supply many of the raw materials used in manufacturing. Linseed oil is used in making paints that have an oil base. Manufacturers use coconut oil in making such products as hydraulic brake fluid, lipstick, soap, and chocolate coating for ice cream bars. Tallow is an important ingredient in soaps, cosmetics, and lubricants.

Cliffe D. Joel

Related articles in *World Book* include:

Blubber	Glycerol	Stearic acid
Butter	Lard	Suet
Cholesterol	Margarine	Tallow
Detergent and soap	Nutrition (Fats)	Triglyceride
Fat substitute	Oil	Vegetable oil
	Perfume	

Fat substitute is a substance used in foods in place of fats and oils. Fats and oils are types of *lipids,* a class of substances found in all living things. Lipids are essential for good health. However, consuming fats and oils at more than about one-third of calories in a diet can lead to undesirable weight gain. It can also increase risk of certain kinds of cancer and of diseases of the heart and arteries. Fat substitutes are used to help reduce the amount of fats and oils people consume in foods.

Some fat substitutes are based on *carbohydrates* or *proteins,* two other classes of substances found in living things. Starches, which are types of carbohydrates, and proteins can serve as fat substitutes without being modified. In addition, carbohydrates and proteins can bond with water to form gels that mimic the consistency and smoothness of lipids in foods. Such fat substitutes can be made from egg and milk proteins or from natural fruit bases that contain *pectin,* a material that forms jellies. Most carbohydrate-based fat substitutes can be used in such foods as baked goods, salad dressings, cheese, and frozen desserts. Gels made with proteins break down when heated. These substitutes are used primarily in products that do not require heating, such as frozen desserts and peanut butter.

Other fat substitutes are based on modified lipids. A fat molecule has a molecule of *glycerol,* an alcohol, combined with three *fatty acids,* long chains of carbon atoms with hydrogen atoms attached. Some fat substitutes use lower-calorie lipids with shorter fatty-acid chains. These lipids occur as liquids and are used primarily in sports drinks and nutritional supplements. Another lower-calorie lipid combines short and long fatty-acid chains to produce solid or semisolid substitutes. These are mostly used in baked goods and chocolate.

Another type of modified lipid is made by attaching long fatty-acid chains to other molecules, usually *sucrose* (sugar). Such fat substitutes add no calories because they cannot be digested, but they also reduce the body's absorption of several vitamins. These substitutes can withstand heat, and so can be used to fry foods. The Food and Drug Administration of the United States approved a fat substitute of this type, called *olestra,* in 1996 for limited use in fried snack foods.   K. M. Schaich

Fatah, *FAH tah* or *fah TAH,* also called al-Fatah or Fateh, is one of the largest groups within the Palestine Liberation Organization (PLO). The PLO is a political body that represents the Palestinians, an Arab group native to the historic region of Palestine. This region today consists of Israel, the West Bank, and the Gaza Strip. *Fatah* is an Arabic term meaning *victory, conquest,* or *opening.* The name *Fatah* also is derived from the initials—in reverse order—of the Arabic phrase that means Palestine National Liberation Movement. Fatah calls for using both violent and political means to achieve an independent Palestinian state in Palestine.

Fatah began in the late 1950's as a secret movement of a small number of Palestinians, including Yasir Arafat. In 1959, they started publishing a magazine that promoted taking up arms to free Palestine from Israeli control. Fatah grew into a centrally controlled organization with Arafat as leader. In 1965, Fatah began guerrilla attacks and raids in Israel. These operations continued into the 1970's. After the 1967 war in which Israel gained control of the West Bank and Gaza Strip, Fatah and other guerrilla groups took over the PLO. In 1969, Arafat became chairman of the PLO Executive Committee. In 1993, the PLO signed an agreement with Israel to establish the Palestinian Authority (PA) for parts of the West Bank and Gaza. In 1996, Arafat was elected PA president, and Fatah members won most PA legislative seats. Arafat died in 2004. Mahmoud Abbas replaced him as head of the PLO, and Farouk Kaddoumi replaced him as head of Fatah. In 2005, Abbas, the Fatah candidate, was elected to succeed Arafat as president of the PA.   Jamal R. Nassar

See also **Arafat, Yasir; Palestine Liberation Organization; Palestinian Authority.**

Fatalism, *FAY tuh lihz uhm,* is the belief that events are determined by forces that human beings cannot control. Although all fatalists accept this general belief, they hold different views about the kinds of forces that determine events. In Greek mythology, for example, three goddesses called the Fates controlled human destiny. Theological fatalists believe God determines events. Scientific fatalists, generally called *determinists,* believe events are caused by physical, chemical, and biological forces described in scientific theories.

Fatalists may hold differing views about whether all events are predetermined as part of a universal plan, or whether only some events are destined to occur. Those who base their fatalism on science generally hold the universal form of fatalism. Because fatalists believe some or all future events are as unchangeable as past events, they often believe it is possible to predict the future. See also **Fates; Free will; Predestination.**   Stephen Nathanson

Fates were three goddesses who ruled people's lives. According to Greek and Roman mythology, the goddesses spun and cut the thread of life. They were called *Parcae* among the Romans and *Moirai* among the Greeks. Clotho was the spinner of the thread, and Lachesis decided how long it was to be. Atropos cut the thread. They were the daughters of Zeus and Themis.

The Fates were usually described as stern, gloomy, elderly goddesses. But in ancient Greece, the Moirai were also worshiped sometimes as goddesses who helped with childbirth and a successful harvest.

Ancient artists represented Clotho holding the spindle of thread. Lachesis carries rods, which she shakes to decide a person's fate. Atropos holds a tablet on which she writes the decision. See also **Norns.**   Justin M. Glenn

Father's Day is a day on which the people of many countries express appreciation for their fathers by giving them gifts or greeting cards. In the United States and Canada, Father's Day falls on the third Sunday in June.

Sonora Louise Smart Dodd of Spokane, Washington, got the idea to set aside a special day to honor fathers in 1909, after listening to a sermon on Mother's Day. She wanted to honor her father, William Jackson Smart. Smart's wife died in 1898, and he raised their six children on his own. Dodd drew up a petition recommending adoption of a national father's day. The Spokane Ministerial Association and the local Young Men's Christian Association (YMCA) supported it. Through Sonora Dodd's efforts, Spokane celebrated the first Father's Day on June 19, 1910. Over the years, many resolutions to make the day an official national holiday were introduced. Finally, in 1972, President Richard M. Nixon signed Father's Day into law.   Sharron G. Uhler

Fathers of Confederation. See Confederation of Canada (table; picture).

Fathom, *FATH uhm,* is a unit of length used to measure ropes or cables and the depths of water. One fathom is equal to 6 feet (1.829 meters). Navigators mark a rope in fathoms and drop it into the water to measure the depth.   Richard S. Davis

Fathometer, *fa THAHM uh tuhr,* is an instrument used on ships to measure the depth of the water. It sends a pulse or wave of sound down through the water to be echoed back from the bottom. Navigators can measure the depth below the ship by measuring the time it takes the sound to return. Continuous soundings of this kind can be taken throughout a voyage. A fathometer has two main parts: (1) an underwater generator that produces sound and (2) a *hydrophone* that receives the echo. The echo is amplified and sent to a device called a *depth indicator* and to a recorder. The reliability of a fathometer depends on a number of factors, such as the depth, temperature, and saltiness of the water. See also **Sonar.**

Daniel G. Jablonski

Fatigue, *fuh TEEG,* is another name for tiredness. We know from experience that fatigue will usually disappear after we rest. However, sometimes fatigue is a symptom of illness. Physically ill people often become fatigued after even a slight amount of work or exertion. Such people need a great deal of rest, often much more than they would need if they were well. Doctors have found that fatigue occurs frequently during many kinds of illnesses.

Fatigue may be one of the symptoms of a physical illness. Fatigue may also accompany such mental illnesses as *panic disorder* and *depression* (see **Mental illness** [Anxiety disorders; Mood disorders]). In either case, rest helps a person feel less tired. But no amount of rest will cure the tendency to become tired easily. This tendency will disappear or improve only if the physical or mental illness that causes the fatigue in a person is improved or cured.

Doctors do not know exactly what causes fatigue. They do not know why a person feels tired after exertion or mental effort. However, they do know that psychological as well as physical factors contribute to fatigue. The effect of fatigue has been closely studied. Researchers have shown that people who spend long hours at things that bore them or at tasks they do not want to do soon develop fatigue. If the person's *morale* (general attitude) and *incentive* (promise of reward) are good, it takes longer for fatigue to develop. But, no matter how good morale or incentive might be, a person who works or plays long enough or hard enough will develop a feeling of fatigue. Paula J. Clayton

See also **Chronic fatigue syndrome; Health.**

Fátima, *FAT uh muh,* **Our Lady of,** refers to the Virgin Mary, who reportedly appeared near Fátima, Portugal, in 1917. On May 13 of that year, three children told of seeing a vision of a lady while they were tending sheep. They said that the lady, brighter than the sun and standing on a cloud, told them to come there on the 13th day of each month until the following October, when she would tell them who she was. On October 13, she said that she was Our Lady of the Rosary and told the children to say the rosary every day. She called for people to reform their lives and asked that a chapel be built in her honor. The Basilica of Our Lady of Fátima stands on the site of the visions.

In 1930, the Roman Catholic Church authorized devotion to Our Lady of Fátima. Since then, millions of people have made pilgrimages to Fátima. For the location of Fátima, see **Portugal** (political map). Robert P. Imbelli

Fātimid dynasty, *FAT uh mihd,* was a line of Muslim rulers who held power from A.D. 909 to 1171. The rulers claimed descent from Fātimah, a daughter of the Prophet Muhammad, and her husband, Alī ibn Abī Tālib, a cousin of the Prophet. The dynasty and its followers belonged to the Shī'ah branch of Islam and to a sect called the Seveners. In 909, they gained control over land that had been held by the larger group of rival Sunni Muslims and rose to power in northern Africa. At various times, the Fātimid empire included Sicily, Syria, and parts of Arabia and Palestine.

For many years, the Fātimids made their capitals in what are now the cities of Al Qayrawan and Al Mahdiyah, Tunisia. But after winning control of Egypt in 969, they founded a new capital, Cairo. There, they built many beautiful buildings and established al-Azhar University. Today, this university is one of the oldest universities in the world and the most influential religious school in Islam. The Fātimids also established great libraries in Cairo and in Tripoli, Lebanon.

The Fātimid rulers were good leaders, but internal conflict eventually broke the dynasty apart. Members of the court struggled for power in the 1160's, and Nūr al-Dīn, a Syrian leader, became involved. The last Cairo ruler asked Nūr al-Dīn for protection against an invasion in 1168. Nūr al-Dīn sent a strong force that included Saladin, a soldier who overthrew the Fātimid dynasty in 1171. Today, followers of Shī'ah Islam who remain loyal to the Fātimids are known as Ismā'īlīs. Richard C. Martin

See also **Cairo** (History); **Muhammad; Saladin; Shī'ites.**

Faulkner, *FAWK nuhr,* **William** (1897-1962), ranks among the leading authors in American literature. He gained fame for his novels about the fictional "Yoknapatawpha County" and its county seat of Jefferson. Faulkner patterned the county after the area around his hometown, Oxford, Mississippi. He explored the county's geography, history, economy, and social and moral life. Faulkner received the 1949 Nobel Prize in literature. He won Pulitzer Prizes in 1955 for *A Fable* and in 1963 for *The Reivers.*

Faulkner's work is characterized by a remarkable range of technique, theme, and tone. In *The Sound and the Fury* (1929) and *As I Lay Dying* (1930), he used stream-of-consciousness, in which the story is told through the seemingly chaotic thoughts of a character. In *Requiem for a Nun* (1951), Faulkner alternated sections of prose fiction with sections of a play. In *A Fable* (1954), he created a World War I soldier whose experiences parallel the Passion of Jesus Christ. Faulkner was skillful in creating complicated situations that involve a variety of characters, each with a different reaction to the situation. He used this technique to dramatize the complexity of life and the difficulty of arriving at truth.

The traditions and history of the South were a favorite Faulkner theme. *Sartoris* (1929) and *The Unvanquished* (1938) tell the story of several generations of the Sartoris family. *The Reivers* (1962) is a humorous story of a young boy's adventures during a trip from Mississippi to Memphis. Faulkner examined the relationship between blacks and whites in several works, including *Light in August* (1932); *Absalom, Absalom!* (1936); and *Go Down, Moses* (1942). Here, Faulkner was especially concerned with people of mixed racial background and their problems in establishing an identity.

Most of Faulkner's novels have a serious, even tragic, tone. But in nearly all of them, tragedy is profoundly mixed with comedy. Faulkner's comic sense was the legacy of Mark Twain and other writers. Twain was a direct influence on him. *The Hamlet* (1940), *The Town* (1957), and *The Mansion* (1959) make up the Snopes Trilogy. These novels form a tragicomic chronicle of the Snopes family and their impact on Yoknapatawpha County. Faulkner's short stories have the same range of technique, theme, and tone as his novels. Faulk-

Wide World
William Faulkner

ner's stories appear in *The Collected Stories of William Faulkner* (1950) and *The Uncollected Stories of William Faulkner* (published in 1979, after his death). The Library of America published an authoritative edition of all of Faulkner's novels in five volumes (1985-2006).

Faulkner was born on Sept. 25, 1897, in New Albany, Mississippi. He spent most of his life in Oxford. Faulkner worked occasionally in Hollywood as a motion-picture scriptwriter from 1932 to 1954. He died on July 6, 1962.

Many early critics of Faulkner denounced his books for their emphasis on violence and abnormality. *Sanctuary* (1931), a story involving rape and murder, drew the most severe criticism. Later, many critics recognized that Faulkner had been criticizing the faults in society by showing them in contrast to what he called the "eternal verities." These verities are universal values such as love, honor, pity, pride, compassion, and sacrifice. Faulkner said it is the writer's duty to remind readers of these values.   Noel Polk

Fault. See Earthquake; Plate tectonics; San Andreas Fault.

Faun, *fawn,* was a half-human and half-animal spirit of the woods and herds in Roman mythology. The fauns corresponded to Greek satyrs. Like the satyrs, they enjoyed drinking, playing tricks, and chasing lovely young women called *nymphs.* Fauns were followers of Bacchus, the god of wine. The name *faun* comes from Faunus, whom the Romans identified with Pan, the Greek god of fields and woods.   Elaine Fantham

See also **Satyr.**

Fauna, *FAW nuh,* is the name given to the animal life of a certain period or part of the world. It corresponds to the word *flora,* which means the plant life of a certain place or time. Thus we may speak of the fauna and flora (animals and plants) of North America or of a past geological period. The term *fauna* comes from the name of a Roman goddess of fields and flocks.   George B. Johnson

Fauré, *foh RAY,* **Gabriel Urbain,** *ga bree EHL oor BAN* (1845-1924), was a French composer. He was an important composer of French songs and *song cycles* (series of songs). Fauré also composed extensively for solo piano and for chamber groups. Fauré's style is characterized by his adventurous use of harmony.

Fauré's major compositions include *Requiem* (1900), a work for chorus and orchestra; and two song cycles, *La Bonne Chanson* (1894) and *La Chanson d'Eve* (1906-1910). Fauré also wrote the orchestral suite *Pelléas et Melisande* (1898) and two operas, *Prométhée* (1900) and *Pénélope* (1913).

Fauré was born on May 12, 1845, in Pamiers, near Toulouse. He worked primarily as a church organist until 1896, when he was appointed professor of composition at the Paris Conservatory. He served as director of the conservatory from 1905 to 1920. Fauré died on Nov. 4, 1924.   Vincent McDermott

Faust, *fowst,* more correctly called Faustus, *FOWS tuhs,* was a German astrologer and magician who became an important figure in legend and literature. The historical figure was Georg Faustus, who probably lived from about 1480 to 1540. Germans considered him a fraud and criminal. Martin Luther, the founder of Protestantism, believed Faust had devilish powers.

In 1587, a crude legendary biography appeared, called *The History of Johann Faust,* or the *Faustbook.* The unknown author borrowed many sensational legends about other magicians. In the *Faustbook,* Faust sells his soul to the devil Mephistopheles for 24 years in exchange for whatever he wishes. Faust flies throughout Europe performing magic, and finally goes to hell, horrified by his damnation. The book was widely translated and rewritten three times in the next 125 years.

The first artistic version of the *Faustbook* was *The Tragical History of Doctor Faustus* (about 1588), a verse tragedy by the English playwright Christopher Marlowe. In the play, Faustus is a scholar who yearns to know all human experience. He often wavers about his bargain with the devil and finally wants to repent, but he cannot.

Many popular plays and puppet shows about Faust appeared during the 1600's and 1700's, mainly in Germany. These works were influenced by Marlowe's play but were gruesome and silly with little literary merit.

The greatest literary version of the Faust story was a poetic drama by the German writer Johann Wolfgang von Goethe. He wrote *Faust* in two parts (published in 1808 and 1832), changing the story radically. In this version, Faust's magic and his pact with the devil are seen as part of a quest for knowledge and experience that is good in the end. Goethe's Faust is finally saved by God.

There have been many later versions of the Faust story. Dorothy Sayers of England, Thomas Mann of Germany, and Paul Valéry of France were among the writers who adapted the legend of Faust in their works during the 1900's.   Tina Boyer

See also **Goethe, Johann Wolfgang von; Marlowe, Christopher; Mephistopheles; Opera** *(Faust).*

Fauves, *fohvz,* were a group of French artists who painted in a style that emphasized intense color and rapid, vigorous brushstrokes. Fauvism flourished from 1905 to 1907. Henri Matisse led the movement, and members included André Derain, Raoul Dufy, and Maurice de Vlaminck.

The Fauves tried to express as directly as possible the vividness and excitement of nature. The group was influenced by the bright colors, bold patterns, and brushwork of such artists of the 1880's and 1890's as Paul Cézanne, Paul Gauguin, Georges Seurat, and Vincent van Gogh.

The word *fauves* means *wild beasts* in French. An art critic gave the painters this name because of the unusual boldness of their style. Most of the Fauves changed their style of painting by about 1907. But the movement had great influence throughout Europe, especially on German Expressionism.

David Cateforis

Each artist mentioned in this article has a biography in *World Book.* See also **Painting** (The Fauves).

Favre, *fahrv,* **Brett** (1969-   ), ranks among the greatest quarterbacks in National Football League (NFL) history. Favre, who played most of his career with the Green Bay Packers, was noted for guiding his team to last-minute victories through dramatic scoring drives. Favre holds the NFL records for career pass completions (6,300), yards passing (71,838), touchdown passes (508), and consecutive games started (297).

In 2005, Favre became only the third NFL quarterback, along with Dan Marino of the Miami Dolphins and John Elway of the Denver Broncos, to pass for 50,000 yards during his career. Favre was named the NFL's Most

Valuable Player for the 1995, 1996, and 1997 seasons. He helped lead the Packers to victory in the 1997 Super Bowl. In 2006, Favre joined Marino as one of only two National Football League quarterbacks to throw 400 touchdown passes in his career. In 2007, Favre won his 149th game as a quarterback, breaking the record of 148 victories set by Elway.

Brett Lorenzo Favre was born on Oct. 10, 1969, in Gulfport, Mississippi. He was a star quarterback at the University of Southern Mississippi from 1987 to 1990.

Favre was drafted by the Atlanta Falcons in 1991 and played two games for Atlanta before being traded to Green Bay in 1992. Green Bay traded him to the New York Jets in 2008. Favre played for the Minnesota Vikings in 2009 and 2010 before retiring. Favre and his mother, Bonita, and sportswriter Chris Havel are coauthors of an illustrated account of the quarterback's personal life and football career called *Favre* (2004).

Neil Milbert

Fawkes, *fawks,* **Guy** (1570-1606), participated in a conspiracy to blow up King James I and the Parliament on Nov. 5, 1605, to stop the persecution of Roman Catholics in England (see **Gunpowder Plot**). Fawkes is the person most closely identified with the plot because he was discovered in the cellar beneath Parliament, waiting to set off the explosion. Fawkes and the other conspirators were tortured and hanged. Fawkes died on Jan. 31, 1606. Parliament proclaimed November 5 an annual day of thanksgiving shortly after Fawkes's arrest. The United Kingdom still celebrates Guy Fawkes Day by burning him in effigy.   Robert Bucholz

Fawn. See Deer.

Fax machine is an electronic device that sends and receives written words and pictures over the telephone network. The word *fax* comes from the word *facsimile* (pronounced *fak SIHM uh lee*), which means an exact copy or likeness. A fax machine resembles a small copying machine but is equipped with a telephone or connected to one. Most modern fax machines can fit on a desktop.

Fax machines enable people throughout the world to exchange business documents and other printed material in seconds. The cost of sending a fax is based on telephone rates. Cheaper, faster Internet communication methods have replaced fax machines for many purposes.

How a fax machine works. Both the sender and the receiver must have a fax machine. The sender inserts the document into a feeder and dials the phone number of the fax machine to which the message is being sent. Once the phone connection is made, a light-sensitive device scans each page and creates an electric signal corresponding to the light and dark spots on the page. This signal is coded and sent over telephone lines to the receiving fax machine. That machine uses the signal to create an exact duplicate of the original page, and prints it out.

Multifunction fax machines. Many fax machines can make photocopies, scan documents into a computer, or print computer documents. Fax machines designed for home use may also offer telephone and telephone answering machine features.

Oil painting; the Museum of Modern Art, New York City

Fauve paintings show the emphasis of this group of painters on intense color and bold brushstrokes. André Derain, a leader of the Fauves, painted *London Bridge* in 1906.

Some fax machines can send faxes directly from a connected computer's files, without printing them first. A computer can also send and receive faxes if it is equipped with a special electronic circuit board called a *fax board*.

History. The first primitive fax machine was built in 1842 by Alexander Bain, a Scottish physicist. Many inventors in Europe and the United States worked on facsimile devices in the late 1800's and early 1900's. In the 1930's, news services began using fax machines to transmit photographs. This method of sending pictures was referred to by the trade name Wirephoto or the generic term *telephoto*. Fax machines became increasingly popular in business in the 1980's after manufacturers developed machines that were smaller, cheaper, and faster.

In the past, fax machines printed onto heat-sensitive paper. The paper tended to curl and fade, and it was hard to read and write on. Most modern machines print onto ordinary paper. Modern fax machines can transmit a page in a few seconds. Some fax machines can store hundreds of documents in memory and transmit them to 100 or more destinations at specified times.

Lynda Perini

See also **Communication** (picture).

FBI. See Federal Bureau of Investigation.

FCC. See Federal Communications Commission.

FDA. See Food and Drug Administration.

FDIC. See Federal Deposit Insurance Corporation.

FDR Memorial. See Franklin Delano Roosevelt Memorial.

Fear. See Emotion; Phobia.

Feast of Weeks. See Shavuot.

Feasts and festivals are special times of celebration. Most of them take place once a year and may last for one or more days. Many feasts and festivals honor great leaders, saints, or gods or spirits. Others celebrate a harvest, the beginning of a season or of a year, or the anniversary of a historical event. Most are joyous occasions, but some involve mourning and repentance.

During some feasts and festivals, adults stay away from their jobs, and children stay home from school. Some people celebrate happy events by decorating their homes and their streets, wearing special clothes, and exchanging gifts. Many of these celebrations include special meals, dancing, and parades. Solemn occasions may be observed with fasts, meditation, and prayer. In the past, nearly all feasts and festivals were religious. Today, many of them celebrate nonreligious events. This article discusses feasts and festivals in five major religions. For a discussion of nonreligious celebrations, see **Holiday.**

In Christianity, the most important festivals recall major events in the life of Jesus Christ. These festivals include Christmas, which celebrates his birth; and Easter, his Resurrection. Other Christian festivals honor the Virgin Mary, various saints, and the founding of the church.

Christians celebrate feasts and festivals both in church and at home. Celebrations vary widely among different groups. Many Protestants and Roman Catholics consider Christmas the most joyous and elaborate festival. Members of the Eastern Orthodox Churches regard Easter as their most important celebration. Some feasts and festivals are celebrated only in certain parts of the world. For example, a town may hold a festival for its patron saint.

In Judaism, the most sacred festivals are Rosh Ha-Shanah, the Jewish New Year; and Yom Kippur, the Day of Atonement. According to Jewish tradition, people are judged on Rosh Ha-Shanah for their deeds of the past year. On Yom Kippur, Jews fast, express their regret for past sins, and declare their hope to perform good deeds during the coming year.

Many Jewish festivals commemorate major events in Jewish history. For example, Passover celebrates the Exodus of the Jews from Egypt. Hanukkah is a celebration of a Jewish victory over the Syrians in 165 B.C. Purim honors the rescue of the Jews of Persia (now Iran) from a plot to kill them. Jews celebrate these festivals both in synagogues and at home.

In Islam. All followers of Islam, called Muslims, observe two celebrations—'Id al-Ad-hā (also spelled *Eid al-Adha*), the Feast of Sacrifice, and 'Id al-Fitr, the Feast of Fast-Breaking. The Feast of Sacrifice occurs on the last day of the annual pilgrimage to Mecca, in the 12th month of the Islamic calendar. Animals are sacrificed to commemorate the Biblical prophet Abraham, whose faithfulness to God prevented the sacrifice of his older son, Ishmael (Abraham's younger son, Isaac, in the Bible). The joyous Feast of Fast-Breaking is held on the first day after Ramadan. During Ramadan, Muslims do not eat or drink from dawn to sunset.

Many Muslims celebrate the birthday of the Prophet Muhammad, born in about 570. Muslims who belong to the Shī'ah division of Islam set aside a day to mourn the death of Husayn ibn Alī, a grandson of Muhammad.

In Buddhism. Buddhists hold two principal kinds of festivals. The first type commemorates several key events in the life of Buddha—chiefly his birth, enlightenment, and death. Buddhists in different parts of the world observe these events in a variety of ways. In Japan, for example, Buddhists celebrate Buddha's birthday by decorating their temples with flowers and pouring sweet tea over statues of the infant Buddha.

The second type of Buddhist festival honors the community of Buddhist monks. One such festival marks the end of the monks' annual retreat. During this celebration, groups of villagers perform a ceremony called the *kathina,* in which they give robes to the monks.

In Hinduism. Hindus hold festivals to honor each of the hundreds of Hindu gods and goddesses. Most of these festivals are local celebrations at the temples and honor specific divinities.

A few festivals are observed by all Hindus, chiefly in their homes and villages. These festivals, which include Holi and Diwali (also called Dipivali), combine religious ceremonies with feasts, fireworks, parades, and other traditional amusements. Holi, the spring festival, is a boisterous celebration in which people throw colored water at one another. During the festival of Diwali, which honors several Hindu gods, including the goddess of wealth and beauty, Hindus decorate houses and streets with lights.   Robert J. Myers

Related articles in *World Book* include:

All Saints' Day	Diwali
Ash Wednesday	Doll (Doll festivals and customs)
Assumption	
Candlemas Day	Easter
Chinese New Year	Epiphany
Christmas	Fair
Día de los muertos	Good Friday

Guadalupe Day
Halloween
Hanukkah
Holi
Holiday
'Id al-Ad-hā
'Id al-Fitr
Islam (Holidays and celebrations)
Judaism (Holy days and festivals)
Mardi Gras
Maundy Thursday
May Day
Michaelmas
New Year's Day

Oktoberfest
Olympic Games
Palm Sunday
Passover
Pentecost
Purim
Ramadan
Rosh Ha-Shanah
Sabbath
Saturnalia
Shavuot
Simhat Torah
Sukkot
Tishah be-Av
Yom Kippur

Additional resources

Bellenir, Karen, ed. *Religious Holidays and Calendars.* 3rd ed. Omnigraphics, 2004.

Ganeri, Anita. *A Year of Festivals.* Smart Apple Media, 2004. Younger readers. Series includes separate books on major religions, such as *Buddhist Festivals Throughout the Year.*

Roy, Christian. *Traditional Festivals: A Multicultural Encyclopedia.* 2 vols. ABC-CLIO, 2005.

Feather is one of the light, thin growths that cover a bird's body. Feathers consist chiefly of a tough substance called *beta keratin.* A similar substance called *alpha keratin* occurs in the hair of mammals and the scales of fish and reptiles. Unlike hair and scales, feathers have a complicated branching pattern.

Kinds and parts of feathers. Birds can have two chief kinds of feathers: (1) contour and (2) down. The parts of a feather vary, depending on the feather.

Contour feathers grow only in special areas called *pterylae.* From the pterylae, the relatively large contour feathers fan out to cover the bird almost completely.

A typical contour feather has a broad, flat *vane* attached to a long central *shaft.* The shaft consists of two parts. A hollow, rounded base, called the *calamus* or *quill,* extends from the vane into the bird's skin. The solid, tapering upper part of the shaft, called the *rachis,* runs through the vane. The vane is formed by *barbs* that branch from the sides of the rachis and *barbules* that branch from the barbs. Hooks on the barbules link neighboring barbs, giving the vane both strength and flexibility. A sudden blow to the vane is more likely to separate the hooks from neighboring barbs than to tear or break the feather. The bird can refasten the hooks by pressing the barbs together with its beak.

Down feathers, unlike contour feathers, grow on all parts of a bird's body. They have an extremely short rachis, so the barbs branch from almost the same point on the shaft. The barbules of a down feather have no hooks, making the vane appear fluffy.

Functions of feathers. Feathers help enable most birds to fly, partially by making it easier for them to flap their wings in the air. Feathers also help birds maintain a constant body temperature. For example, down feathers keep birds warm by trapping warm air next to the body. In addition, feathers provide coloring that helps birds hide from enemies or attract mates. Although feathers are remarkably durable, they gradually wear out. Most birds shed their feathers and grow a new set at least once a year. This process is called *molting.*

How people use feathers. People have used feathers for a variety of purposes. For hundreds of years, American Indians used feathers to make arrows and

Parts of a contour feather

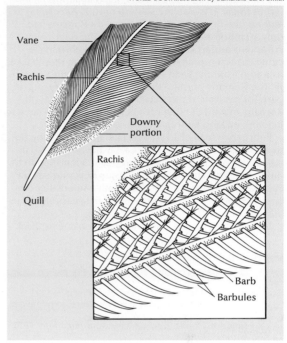

WORLD BOOK illustration by Samantha Carol Smith

Vane
Rachis
Downy portion
Quill
Rachis
Barb
Barbules

headdresses. Until the mid-1800's, when pens with steel points became popular, most people wrote with quill pens. Today, manufacturers use feathers as stuffing in pillows and furniture. Down feathers provide excellent insulation in jackets, quilts, and sleeping bags. Designers decorate hats and other garments with feathers.

Some uses of feathers, however, have come under heavy criticism. For example, the overuse of feathers for women's hats has endangered the survival of many kinds of birds. Laws forbid the importation of bird feathers into many countries.   Edward H. Burtt, Jr.

Related articles in *World Book* include:

Bird (Feathers; illustration: How a bird flies)
Bird-of-paradise
Egret
Molting
Ostrich
Peacock
Pen
Pheasant

Feather star. See Sea lily.

Feboldson, *FEE bohld suhn,* **Febold,** *FEE bohld,* is a giant Swedish hero of many tall tales of Kansas and Nebraska. Feboldson performed fantastic feats that reflect the clever ways in which the American pioneers solved various problems. In one story, Feboldson started tree planting in the Great Plains region by tossing handfuls of cottonwood seeds into prairie dog holes. Another tale tells how he devised a way of digging postholes by using a creature called the happy auger. When the happy auger sat down, it spun around on its drill-like tail, forming a perfect posthole.

Feboldson may be based on an actual Swedish pioneer of the 1800's. The character was developed in the late 1920's by two Nebraska journalists, Don Holmes and Wayne T. Carroll. Paul R. Beath, a Nebraska lawyer, compiled *Febold Feboldson: Tall Tales from the Great Plains* (1948, 1962).   Ellen J. Stekert

February is the second month of the year according to the Gregorian calendar, which is used in almost all the world today. It is also the shortest month. According to legend, the first calendar of the ancient Romans had only 10 months. But in about 700 B.C., the ruler Numa Pompilius added January and February. February became the last month of the Roman year. The month takes its name from the Latin word *februare*, meaning *to purify*. The Romans purified themselves in February to prepare for festivals at the start of the new year. Later, the Romans moved the beginning of the year from March to January, making February the second month.

February usually had 28 days until the time of the Roman statesman Julius Caesar. Caesar gave it 29 days in standard years and 30 every four years. According to tradition, the Roman emperor Augustus took one day off February to add to August, the month named after him. Today, February has 28 days in standard years and 29 in leap years.

In the United States, February is designated as Black History Month, a time to honor the accomplishments of African Americans and their contributions to society. Washington's Birthday, celebrated on the third Monday in February, is a U.S. federal holiday that honors George Washington, the first president of the United States. However, many people call the holiday Presidents' Day, especially honoring Abraham Lincoln (born on February 12) and George Washington (born on February 22).

Candlemas is a Christian festival celebrated on February 2. The holiday's name comes from a traditional custom of blessing candles in church and distributing the candles to worshipers. February 2 is recognized in a more whimsical fashion in the United States as Ground-Hog Day. On this day, everyone listens for reports of Punxsutawney Phil, the nation's "official" groundhog. According to tradition, if the groundhog sees his shadow on the morning of February 2, he will be frightened back into his burrow and six more weeks of winter can be expected. If he does not see his shadow, spring will arrive early that year.

Important February events

1　Supreme Court of the United States first met, 1790.
　—Louis S. St. Laurent, second French Canadian prime minister of Canada, born 1882.
　—Langston Hughes, African American author, born 1902.
2　Ground-Hog Day.
　—Talleyrand, French statesman, born 1754.
　—By the Treaty of Guadalupe Hidalgo, Mexico gave New Mexico and California to the United States, 1848.
　—James Joyce, Irish novelist and poet, born 1882.
　—Jascha Heifetz, Lithuanian American violinist, born 1901.
　—The last German troops surrendered at Stalingrad during World War II, 1943.
3　Felix Mendelssohn, German composer, born 1809.
　—Horace Greeley, American publisher, born 1811.
4　Ceylon (now Sri Lanka) became independent in 1948.
　—Confederate States of America organized, 1861.
　—Philippine Rebellion against the United States began, 1899.
　—Charles A. Lindbergh, American aviator, born 1902.
　—Yalta Conference began, 1945.
　—Amendment 24 to the U.S. Constitution, banning poll tax, proclaimed, 1964.
5　Sir Robert Peel, British statesman, born 1788.
　—Dwight L. Moody, American evangelist, born 1837.
6　Waitangi Day, New Zealand. In recognition of the Treaty of Waitangi signed in 1840 between the native Maori and European settlers.
　—Queen Anne of England born 1665.
　—Aaron Burr, American political leader, born 1756.
　—Massachusetts ratified the U.S. Constitution, 1788.

　—Babe Ruth, American home run king, born 1895.
　—The United States Senate ratified the peace treaty ending the Spanish-American War, 1899.
　—Ronald Reagan, 40th U.S. president, born 1911.
　—Elizabeth II became queen of the United Kingdom, 1952.
7　Charles Dickens, British novelist, born 1812.
　—Sinclair Lewis, American novelist, born 1885.
8　Mary, Queen of Scots, executed in 1587.
　—College of William and Mary, second oldest college in the United States, chartered in 1693.
　—John Ruskin, English essayist and critic, born 1819.
　—William T. Sherman, Union Army general in the American Civil War, born 1820.
　—Jules Verne, French novelist, born 1828.
　—Russo-Japanese War began, 1904.
　—Boy Scouts of America incorporated, 1910.
9　William Henry Harrison, ninth U.S. president, born 1773.
10　Treaty of Paris ended the French and Indian War, also known as the Seven Years' War, 1763.
　—Charles Lamb, English essayist and critic, born 1775.
11　National Foundation Day, Japan.
　—Thomas A. Edison, American inventor, born 1847.
12　Lady Jane Grey, the "nine-day queen" of England, executed 1554.
　—Tadeusz Kościuszko, Polish patriot, born 1746.
　—Charles Darwin, British naturalist, born 1809.
　—Abraham Lincoln, 16th U.S. president, born 1809.
　—John L. Lewis, American labor leader, born 1880.
13　Grant Wood, American painter, born 1891.
14　Valentine's Day.

Feb. birthstone—
amethyst

Feb. flower—
primrose

Four U.S. presidents born in February—Washington, Feb. 22;
W. H. Harrison, Feb. 9; Lincoln, Feb. 12; Reagan, Feb. 6

In Japan, people celebrate a holiday called Setsubun on February 3 or 4. According to the lunar calendar used in the past, this date marks the changing of the seasons and the end of winter. Another holiday observed in Japan is National Foundation Day, celebrated on February 11. According to tradition, Jimmu founded the imperial dynasty and the empire of Japan on that day in 660 B.C.

People in most Western countries celebrate Valentine's Day on February 14. The custom of exchanging greetings on this day goes back hundreds of years.

February 21 is Shaheed Dibash (Martyrs' Day) in Bangladesh. On this day, people remember those who died during demonstrations that called for the Bengali language to have an equal status with the Urdu language in 1952, when Bangladesh was still part of Pakistan.

The flowers associated with February are the primrose and the violet. The amethyst is the birthstone for February.   Carole S. Angell

Quotations

I crown thee king of intimate delights,
Fireside enjoyments, home-born happiness,
And all the comforts that the lowly roof
Of undisturb'd retirement, and the hours
Of long uninterrupted evening know.

William Cowper

The February sunshine steeps your boughs,
And tints the buds and swells the leaves within

William Cullen Bryant

Hail to thy returning festival, old Bishop Valentine!
Like unto thee, assuredly, there is no other mitred father in the calendar.

Charles Lamb

Related articles in *World Book* include:

Amethyst	Chinese New Year	Presidents' Day
Calendar	Groundhog Day	Primrose
Candlemas Day	Leap year	Valentine's Day

Important February events

14 Oregon became the 33rd U.S. state, 1859.
 —John Barrymore, American actor, born 1882.
 —Arizona became the 48th U.S. state, 1912.
15 Galileo, Italian astronomer and physicist, born 1564.
 —Cyrus McCormick, American inventor, born 1809.
 —Susan B. Anthony, American women's suffrage leader, born 1820.
 —Elihu Root, U.S. statesman and lawyer, born 1845.
16 Henry Adams, American historian, born 1838.
17 Thomas Robert Malthus, British economist, born 1766.
18 Democracy Day, Nepal.
 —Mary I, first reigning queen of England, born 1516.
 —John Bunyan's *Pilgrim's Progress* was licensed for publication, 1678.
 —Jefferson Davis took the oath as provisional president of the Confederate States of America, 1861.
 —Wendell Willkie, American political leader, born 1892.
 —San Francisco's Golden Gate International Exposition opened, 1939.
 —Gambia became independent in 1965.
19 Nicolaus Copernicus, Polish astronomer, born 1473.
 —David Garrick, English actor, born 1717.
 —Thomas A. Edison patented the phonograph, 1878.
20 John H. Glenn, Jr., astronaut, became the first American to orbit Earth in 1962.
21 Shaheed Dibash (Martyrs' Day), Bangladesh.
22 George Washington, first U.S. president, born 1732.
 —Arthur Schopenhauer, German philosopher, born 1788.
 —The United States acquired the Florida territory from Spain, 1819.

 —James Russell Lowell, American poet, born 1819.
 —Robert Baden-Powell, founder of the Scout movement, born 1857.
23 Samuel Pepys, English diarist, born 1633.
 —George Frideric Handel, German composer, born 1685.
 —W. E. B. Du Bois, American civil rights leader, historian, and sociologist, born 1868.
 —Amendment 25 to the U.S. Constitution, on presidential succession, proclaimed in 1967.
24 Winslow Homer, American painter, born 1836.
25 National Day, Kuwait
 —José de San Martín, liberator of Argentina, Chile, and Peru, born 1778.
 —Enrico Caruso, Italian singer, born 1873.
 —Amendment 16 to the U.S. Constitution, authorizing the income tax, proclaimed in 1913.
 —President Ferdinand Marcos of the Philippines resigned from office and fled the country, 1986.
26 Victor Hugo, French poet and novelist, born 1802.
 —Napoleon escaped from the island of Elba, 1815.
 —William Frederick Cody (better known as Buffalo Bill), American frontiersman, born 1846.
27 Henry Wadsworth Longfellow, American poet, born 1807.
 —Marian Anderson, American singer, born 1897.
27 Vincent Massey took the oath as the first Canadian-born governor general of Canada, 1952.
28 Marquis de Montcalm, French commander in Quebec, born 1712.
29 Gioacchino Antonio Rossini, Italian composer, born 1792.

WORLD BOOK illustrations by Mike Hagel

Feb. 6—Elizabeth II becomes queen of the United Kingdom

Feb. 14—Valentine's Day

Feb. 20—John Glenn orbits Earth

Feb. 23—W. E. B. Du Bois born

Federal Aviation Administration (FAA) is an agency in the United States Department of Transportation. It controls air traffic; certifies aircraft, airports, and pilots and other personnel; and operates air navigation aids. The FAA announces and enforces air traffic procedures. Its research and development services deal with air traffic and air navigation and landing aids.

The FAA was founded in 1958. An administrator appointed by the president directs the FAA.

Critically reviewed by the Federal Aviation Administration

Federal Bureau of Investigation (FBI) is the primary investigating branch of the United States Department of Justice. The FBI investigates a wide variety of crimes that deal with the safety and security of the United States and its citizens. In addition, the bureau gathers *intelligence* (information) about individuals and groups that it considers dangerous to national security. The prevention of terrorism is a central goal of the FBI. The FBI also collects evidence in lawsuits that involve the federal government. Bureau investigators are called *special agents.*

Laws passed by the U.S. Congress provide the basic framework for many of the FBI's powers and procedures. A director, appointed by the president with the approval of the Senate, supervises the FBI from headquarters in Washington, D.C. The FBI has about 60 field offices in the United States and Puerto Rico and about 60 posts in other countries.

FBI operations

Criminal investigation. The FBI investigates such federal crimes as assault on the president, bank robbery, bombing, hijacking, and kidnapping. It handles cases involving stolen money, property, or vehicles that have been taken from one state to another. The bureau fights organized crime groups and investigates financial crimes, such as counterfeiting and check fraud. The FBI investigates computer-related crimes involving criminal acts and national security issues.

At the request of state or local authorities, the FBI helps capture fleeing criminals. The FBI also examines violations of civil rights laws and violations of laws concerning toxic wastes. In addition, it works with the federal Drug Enforcement Administration to investigate violations of criminal drug laws.

The FBI has several programs that specialize in handling investigations of specific crimes. In all criminal investigations, the FBI presents its findings to the Department of Justice, which decides whether to prosecute.

Intelligence operations of the FBI consist of gathering information about individuals or organizations engaged in activities that may be dangerous to national security. These operations include the investigation of terrorist groups, riots, spy activities, treason, and threats to overthrow the government. The bureau is responsible for detecting and counteracting the actions of foreign intelligence operations that seek to gather sensitive information about the United States. The FBI reports to the president, Congress, or the Justice Department for action.

Other services. The FBI provides various services to law enforcement agencies throughout the United States and in other countries. Such agencies may request help from the FBI Criminal Justice Information Services Divi-

sion (CJIS) or the FBI Laboratory. The bureau also trains selected police officials.

CJIS has the world's largest fingerprint collections. Its files contain prints of both criminals and civilians. CJIS also maintains the National Crime Information Center, a computerized system that stores records on criminal suspects and stolen property. The FBI Laboratory is widely regarded as one of the world's finest crime laboratories. FBI scientists examine pieces of evidence there and often testify in court.

The FBI issues an annual publication called *Crime in the United States,* which includes a record of rates and trends in major crimes. The bureau also distributes descriptions of its *Ten Most Wanted Fugitives.* The FBI Academy in Quantico, Virginia, provides training in advanced methods of fighting crime.

FBI agents

Men and women who wish to be special agents must be U.S. citizens between 23 and 37 years old and in excellent physical condition. They must also have a college degree. Future agents go through a 17-week training program at the FBI Academy. They study crime detection, evidence, constitutional and criminal law, and methods of investigation. They also learn self-defense and how to use firearms. Agents later receive periodic refresher training to keep them up to date.

History

In 1908, Attorney General Charles J. Bonaparte organized a group of special investigators in the Justice Department. This group, called the Bureau of Investigation, investigated such offenses as illegal business practices and land sales. Its first director was Stanley W. Finch, an attorney. J. Edgar Hoover, a Justice Department lawyer, became its director in 1924 and headed it until his death in 1972. Congress named the bureau the FBI in 1935.

A wave of bank robberies, kidnappings, and other violent crimes broke out in the United States during the 1930's. Congress passed laws giving the FBI increased authority to combat this lawlessness. FBI agents, who were nicknamed *G-Men,* or *Government Men,* became admired for tracking down such gangsters as John Dillinger and George "Machine Gun" Kelly.

During World War II (1939-1945), the FBI broke up enemy spy rings in the United States. In the 1950's and 1960's, special agents arrested Communist spies who had stolen secret atomic and military information. The bureau also investigated protest organizations in the 1960's and early 1970's. Clarence M. Kelley, a former special agent, became director of the FBI in 1973.

In 1975, a Senate committee revealed that FBI agents had committed burglaries and spied illegally on U.S. citizens during some domestic security investigations. The Senate investigators also charged that Hoover had given certain presidents damaging personal information about some of their political opponents. The Justice Department set up guidelines to prevent further abuses.

In 1976, Congress limited the term of the FBI director to 10 years. William H. Webster, a federal judge, became director of the bureau in 1978. In 1987, William S. Sessions, also a federal judge, became head of the FBI. In 1993, the Justice Department accused Sessions of taking personal trips at government expense and of other unethical conduct. That year, President Bill Clinton dismissed him, and Louis J. Freeh, a federal judge and former FBI agent, became the agency's director.

In 2001, the FBI arrested one of its agents for providing classified information to Russia. He confessed and was convicted. Later in 2001, the FBI revealed that agents had mishandled documents relating to the 1995 terrorist bombing of the Alfred P. Murrah Federal Building in Oklahoma City. Freeh resigned as director in 2001, and Robert S. Mueller III, a Justice Department lawyer, succeeded him.

On Sept. 11, 2001, terrorists crashed hijacked commercial airplanes into the World Trade Center in New York City and into the Pentagon Building near Washington, D.C. A fourth hijacked plane crashed in Pennsylvania. The FBI and other government agencies received criticism for failing to detect the terrorists' activity in the months leading up to the September 11 attacks. In 2002, Mueller announced plans to reorganize the FBI with an increased focus on the prevention of terrorism.

In 2004, Congress passed the Intelligence Reform and Terrorism Prevention Act, which included many antiterrorism measures affecting the FBI. The act created the Office of the Director of National Intelligence to oversee the intelligence-gathering operations of various federal agencies.

The U.S. government introduced additional reforms in 2005, including the creation of a new organization called the National Security Branch within the FBI. The National Security Branch is responsible for intelligence operations within the United States. The Federal Bureau of Investigation website at http://www.fbi.gov gives more information on FBI activities.   Robert W. Taylor

See also **Crime; Hoover, J. Edgar.**

Federal Communications Commission (FCC) is an independent agency of the United States government. The FCC is responsible for the regulation of U.S. interstate and foreign communication by radio, television, wire, satellite, and cable. The agency develops, implements, and enforces a wide variety of federal rules and standards. It seeks to promote the fair, safe, and efficient operation of the nation's communications systems. The FCC was established in 1934.

The FCC performs several functions. These functions include approving or disapproving interstate rate increases for telephone systems; allocating bands of frequencies for different types of radio and television operations; issuing licenses to stations and station operators; monitoring broadcasts to detect unlicensed operations and technical violations; and enforcing broadcasting standards relating to obscenity and indecency. AM and FM radio, television broadcast services, and telephone systems all use transmitters licensed by the FCC.

The FCC has five commissioners. The president, with the approval of the Senate, appoints them for five-year terms. The president selects one commissioner to be the chairperson.

Critically reviewed by the Federal Communications Commission

See also **Monitoring station; Radio** (Government regulation of radio); **Television** (Government regulations).

Federal Deposit Insurance Corporation (FDIC) is an independent United States government agency that insures deposits at almost all U.S. banks and savings and loan associations, or *thrifts.* The FDIC insures indi-

vidual accounts in banks and thrifts for up to $250,000. It pays off the accounts if an insured institution fails and is not bought by another institution. The FDIC also provides financial assistance to problem institutions to keep them from failing. In addition, it regulates and examines banks and thrifts to promote safe business practices.

A five-member board of directors manages the FDIC. The president appoints three of the directors for terms of six years. The other two are the comptroller of the currency and the director of the Bureau of Consumer Financial Protection. The FDIC is funded by fees paid by insured institutions and from earnings on U.S. government securities.

The FDIC was created in 1933 to help end a banking crisis during the Great Depression. In 1989, Congress gave the FDIC responsibility for insuring thrifts after a crisis in the industry led to the bankruptcy of the Federal Savings and Loan Insurance Corporation.

Critically reviewed by the Federal Deposit Insurance Corporation

Federal district is a tract of land that a country sets apart as the seat of its national capital. The United States District of Columbia is a federal district. Other countries with a federal district include Australia, Brazil, Malaysia, Mexico, and Venezuela.

Federal Election Commission is an independent regulatory agency of the United States government. The commission enforces the Federal Election Campaign Act, which governs campaign financing in connection with elections to federal offices. The act includes requirements to disclose campaign contributions and expenses, restrictions on the amounts a person or group may contribute to a candidate, and prohibitions on the use of corporation and labor union funds to influence federal elections.

The commission also administers the public financing of presidential campaigns and national nominating conventions. It has the power to conduct investigations and audits of campaign funds. The agency serves as a national clearinghouse for information and research about the administration of elections.

Congress established the commission in 1974. Its six members are appointed by the president, subject to the Senate's approval. No more than three members may belong to the same political party.

Critically reviewed by the Federal Election Commission

Federal Emergency Management Agency (FEMA) is a United States government agency that helps communities prepare for and recover from natural and human-made disasters. It seeks to minimize loss of life and property from such events as earthquakes, fires, tornadoes, hurricanes, hazardous spills, nuclear explosions, and terrorist acts.

In the case of a severely destructive event, the president may declare a location to be a *federal disaster area.* At that point, FEMA provides funding for such needs as temporary housing and home repairs. It also offers assistance for the repairs of roads, buildings, and utilities. In addition, FEMA works to distribute information, lend support, and offer training so that communities may be prepared for future disasters.

President Jimmy Carter established FEMA in 1979 as an independent agency of the U.S. government. In the 1980's, a time of great tension between the United States and the Soviet Union, FEMA devoted much of its effort to readiness for nuclear attack. Its chief responsibility at this time was the preparation of emergency shelters for political and military leaders in the case of nuclear war. In the 1990's, FEMA's focus shifted to hurricanes, earthquakes, and other disasters. In the early 2000's, terrorist attacks became a top priority. In 2003, FEMA became part of the new Department of Homeland Security.

In 2005, Hurricane Katrina, one of the most destructive storms in U.S. history, struck New Orleans and other parts of the Gulf Coast. About 1,800 people died, and numerous others were left without food, water, shelter, and other basic needs. Many people charged that the federal government, and FEMA in particular, acted slowly in providing aid to the areas hit by the storm. In 2006, a Senate panel recommended that FEMA be abolished and replaced with a new agency that would prepare for and respond to emergencies.   Dee Garrison

See also **Civil defense.**

Federal government. See Federalism.

Federal government debt. See National debt.

Federal Hall, in New York City, was the first Capitol of the United States under the Constitution. City Hall, the original building on the site, was finished in 1703. It also housed the Stamp Act Congress in 1765 and of the Congress of the Confederation from 1785 to 1789. On April 30, 1789, George Washington took the oath as president there. The present structure was built in 1842. Federal Hall became a national memorial in 1955. See also L'Enfant, Pierre C.   Critically reviewed by the National Park Service

Federal Highway Administration (FHWA) is an agency within the United States Department of Transportation. The agency provides billions of dollars in federal aid annually to the states to fund highway research, planning, design, and construction. It coordinates highways with public transit and rail and air travel to achieve the most effective balance of transportation systems and facilities. The FHWA works to improve the total operation and safety of the nation's highway systems. It also works to lessen the environmental impact of highways and regulates truck and bus travel.

Congress established the FHWA in 1967. It replaced the Bureau of Public Roads. The U.S. president appoints the head of the agency. Headquarters are in Washington, D.C.   Critically reviewed by the Federal Highway Administration

Federal Home Loan Mortgage Corporation is a government-sponsored enterprise (GSE) controlled by the United States government. It is commonly referred to as Freddie Mac. The organization helps assure that enough money is available for home mortgages.

Freddie Mac does not loan money directly to buyers purchasing a home. Instead, Freddie Mac purchases mortgages from the banks, savings and loan associations, mortgage companies, and other financial institutions that make these loans. Freddie Mac bundles mortgages together and sells them to investors in the form of financial assets called *mortgage-backed securities.* The investors who own these securities receive principal and interest from the homeowners' mortgage payments on the loans purchased by Freddie Mac.

Congress created Freddie Mac in 1970 as a private corporation. In 2008, the organization faltered after it had heavily invested in risky mortgages. A credit and financial crisis had begun in 2007, leading to an increase in home *foreclosures,* the legal procedure by which

lenders take over mortgaged properties from borrowers unable to afford their mortgage payments. Freddie Mac owned or guaranteed so many mortgages in the United States that it could not meet its financial obligations. In 2008, U.S. Secretary of the Treasury Henry M. Paulson, Jr., signed an agreement that the government would cover future losses for Freddie Mac, and the organization became government-owned.   Ken Rebeck

Federal Housing Administration (FHA) is a United States government agency that works with private industry to provide good housing. The FHA insures mortgages on private homes, multifamily rental housing projects, cooperative and condominium housing, nursing homes, and hospitals. The FHA also insures loans to improve property and provides special programs for elderly people, military veterans, and disaster victims.

The loans are made by banks, building associations, mortgage firms, and other approved lending institutions. The borrower applies to the lender for the loans. Most FHA operations are paid for by the agency's income from fees, insurance premiums on loans, and interest on investment of insurance reserves.

The FHA also sets the minimum property standards for housing, analyzes local housing markets, and makes appraisals and technical studies. The FHA was established in 1934 and is part of the Department of Housing and Urban Development. A commissioner heads the FHA.   Critically reviewed by the Federal Housing Administration

Federal Maritime Commission is an independent agency of the United States government. The commission administers the nation's shipping laws that apply to cargo shipments between the continental United States and foreign locations or offshore domestic territories. It regulates the rates, services, and agreements of shipping firms and terminal operators. It also regulates and licenses ocean freight forwarders.

The commission requires evidence of financial responsibility from owners and charterers of vessels that carry 50 or more passengers and that sail from U.S. ports. This policy ensures that the owners and charterers can pay claims involving accidental death and injury and can refund fares in the case of a canceled voyage.

The Federal Maritime Commission was established in 1961. The president appoints the commission's five members with the Senate's approval. The president also names one of the commissioners to serve as its chairperson.   Critically reviewed by the Federal Maritime Commission

Federal National Mortgage Association is a government-sponsored enterprise (GSE) controlled by the United States government. It is commonly referred to as Fannie Mae. The organization helps assure that enough money is available for home mortgages.

Fannie Mae does not loan money directly to buyers purchasing a home. Instead, Fannie Mae purchases mortgages from the banks, savings and loan associations, mortgage companies, and other financial institutions that make these loans. Fannie Mae bundles mortgages together and sells them to investors in the form of financial assets called *mortgage-backed securities.* The investors who own these securities receive principal and interest from the homeowners' mortgage payments on the loans purchased by Fannie Mae.

Fannie Mae was established in 1938 as a government-owned corporation with the aim of making home mort-

The Federal Reserve System is the central banking system of the United States. The nation is divided into 12 districts, each with a Federal Reserve Bank. These banks issue Federal Reserve Notes, which make up nearly all the paper money in circulation. A number on each note identifies the bank that issued it. The system also includes Federal Reserve branch banks throughout the country.

★ Federal Reserve Bank

• Federal Reserve Branch Bank

— Federal Reserve district boundary

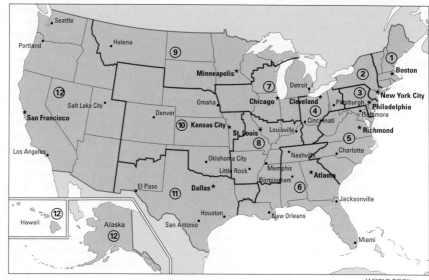

WORLD BOOK maps

gages more readily available. The organization was placed under the Housing and Home Finance Agency in 1950. In 1954, Fannie Mae was reorganized as a corporation owned jointly by the government and private stockholders. It became a private corporation in 1968.

In 2008, the corporation faltered after it had heavily invested in risky mortgages. A credit and financial crisis had begun in 2007, leading to an increase in home *foreclosures,* the legal procedure by which lenders take over mortgaged properties from borrowers unable to afford their mortgage payments. Fannie Mae owned or guaranteed so many of the mortgages that it could not meet its financial obligations. In 2008, U.S. Secretary of the Treasury Henry M. Paulson, Jr., signed an agreement that the government would cover future losses for Fannie Mae, and Fannie Mae once again became government-owned.   Ken Rebeck

Federal Reserve System, an independent agency of the United States government, is the central banking system of the United States. As the central bank, the Federal Reserve, often called the Fed, has many jobs. These include issuing currency and managing the *money supply* (the total amount of U.S. currency and bank deposits held by people and by private financial institutions). The Fed also makes loans to commercial banks and supervises the U.S. financial system. The Fed is most often in the news when it conducts *monetary policy*—altering the money supply to influence economic activity and the overall health of the economy.

Organization. The Federal Reserve System consists of a seven-member Board of Governors in Washington, D.C., and 12 Federal Reserve Banks across the United States. Each Federal Reserve Bank has a president and its own district. Most districts have from one to five Federal Reserve Bank branches. The Board of Governors administers the system. The U.S. president appoints each of its members to a 14-year term. The president names one member to serve as chairman for four years. A chairman is often reappointed for more than one term.

The Federal Open Market Committee of the Fed decides the direction of U.S. monetary policy. The committee consists of the Board of Governors, the president of the New York district Federal Reserve Bank, and the presidents of four other Federal Reserve Banks. The presidents of the Federal Reserve Banks outside the New York district serve on a rotating basis.

The Fed operates more independently of the president and Congress than do typical government agencies. Because the governors serve 14-year terms, each president appoints no more than a few. As a result, the president cannot fill the board with governors who favor a particular political policy. The Fed also has far more financial independence than most agencies because it raises all its operating expenses from investment income and service fees. The Fed reports to Congress about its proposed policies, but it is legally free to make its own policy decisions.

Many economists support the independence of the Fed—and other central banks. They believe that executive and legislative branches of government have less motivation than central banks do to reduce *inflation* when necessary. Inflation is a continual increase in prices throughout a nation's economy. The independence of the Fed, however, is not absolute. Congress created the agency, and Congress can abolish it.

Monetary policy. The Fed controls the U.S. money supply to support a stable, healthy economy. A healthy economy is one in which output grows over time, people looking for jobs can find them, and prices for things people buy do not rise quickly (that is, inflation is kept in check). By changing the money supply, the Fed can increase or decrease the average rate of interest lenders charge borrowers, which influences borrowing and spending by consumers and businesses, or *economic activity.* The Fed slows economic activity by raising interest rates if it believes prices are rising too quickly. It lowers interest rates if it hopes to reduce the level of unemployment. The Fed changes the money supply by (1) using open market operations, (2) changing the discount rate, and (3) changing reserve requirements.

Open market operations are the primary tool the Fed uses to carry out its monetary policy. They involve the sale or purchase of *government securities,* including Treasury bills (T-bills), bonds, and notes. When the Federal Open Market Committee wants to increase interest rates, it can direct the New York district Federal Reserve Bank to sell government securities in the "open market." When private banks purchase the securities, they have fewer reserves (see *Reserve requirements* below) to loan out. As loans decrease, demand deposits (checking accounts) decrease, reducing the money supply. Interest rates rise as borrowers compete for loans. If the Fed wants to reduce interest rates, it buys back government securities on the open market.

The discount rate is the interest rate banks pay when they borrow money from a Federal Reserve Bank. By raising the discount rate, the Fed can increase the cost to banks for making loans. As a result, banks raise interest rates, which leads to a decrease in the money supply. Lowering the discount rate has the opposite effect.

Reserve requirements are percentages of deposits that deposit-taking institutions must set aside either as currency in their vaults or as deposits in their district Federal Reserve Bank. An institution can use the rest of its deposits to make loans. Raising the reserve requirement reduces the amount of reserves banks have available for loans, reducing the money supply and causing interest rates to rise. Lowering the reserve requirement has the opposite effect.

Other Fed activities. The Fed has other responsibilities as well. It acts as the bank for the government by holding deposits for the Treasury and other federal agencies. It also holds reserves for private banks and processes checks between these banks. During financial crises, the Fed often becomes the "lender of last resort," making loans to banks and other financial institutions that have serious financial difficulties. Along with other federal agencies, the Fed also oversees and regulates commercial banks and financial institutions to ensure the stability of the U.S. financial system.

History. During the 1800's and early 1900's, financial panics occasionally rocked the banking system in the United States. These panics were often accompanied by *runs on banks,* in which many depositors would attempt to withdraw their money from a bank at the same time. During most of this period, the United States did not have a central bank to help stabilize its banking system and prevent panics.

Two early attempts to form a central bank for the United States failed. The First Bank of the United States operated from 1791 to 1811, and the Second Bank of the United States operated from 1816 to 1836. A financial crisis in the early 1900's led Congress to pass the Federal Reserve Act of 1913. This act established the Federal Reserve System as the nation's central bank.

The Banking Act of 1933 created the Federal Open Market Committee. With this act, the Banking Act of 1935, and provisions in the Employment Act of 1946, Congress gave all authority over U.S. monetary policy to the Fed.   Ken Rebeck

See also **Bank; Greenspan, Alan; Inflation** (Monetary policy); **Money** (Federal Reserve Notes; The money supply; Monetary policy).

Federal system. See Federalism.

Federal Trade Commission (FTC) is an independent U.S. government agency that works to (1) maintain free and fair competition in the economy and (2) protect consumers from unfair or misleading practices. The FTC issues *cease and desist orders* against companies or individuals that it believes engage in unlawful practices. The firms or people must then stop such practices unless a court sets aside the orders. The FTC also issues trade regulation guides for business and industry and conducts a variety of consumer-protection activities. Congress created the FTC in 1914. The president appoints the five FTC commissioners, subject to Senate approval, to seven-year terms. See also **Advertising** (Regulation of advertising); **Monopoly and competition** (History).   Critically reviewed by the Federal Trade Commission

Federalism is a system of government in which political power is divided between a *central* (national) government and smaller governmental units. The central government is often called the *federal government,* and the smaller units, *states* or *provinces.* In a federal system, the division of powers is usually defined in a constitution. The United States, Canada, Australia, and Switzerland have federal systems.

Federal systems differ from *unitary* systems. In a unitary system, all political power legally derives from the central government. States or provinces have only the powers the central government grants them.

In a true federal system, some powers are constitutionally reserved for the states or provinces. Also in a federal system, the central government has some clearly stated powers to act directly on the people. This feature distinguishes a federal system from a loose grouping of states, commonly called a *confederation.* A confederation can act only through its individual member states.   Thomas S. Vontz

See also **Canada, Government of; Devolution; Government; State government; United States, Government of the;** and the *Government* section of the countries mentioned in this article.

Federalist, The, is a series of 85 letters that urged ratification of the United States Constitution. The letters were written to newspapers by the American statesmen Alexander Hamilton, James Madison, and John Jay. The letters sought primarily to influence the New York ratifying convention, and they were printed in several New York newspapers. All except eight essays appeared in 1787 and 1788 under the signature "Publius." Hamilton wrote 51 of the essays, Madison 29, and Jay 5. The collected essays appeared in book form as *The Federalist.*

The Federalist authors used both logical argument and appeal to prejudice. They emphasized the weaknesses in the Articles of Confederation, the dangers in British sea power and Spanish intrigue, the desirability and need of a stronger central government, and the safeguards of the new Constitution.

The authors did not defend every point in the proposed Constitution. But they argued that it was the best document on which agreement could be reached. They asserted that the checks and balances system of the Constitution would create a strong government and still protect the states' rights. The Federalist papers greatly influenced acceptance of the Constitution, and they are still important in interpreting it.   Donna J. Spindel

Federalist Party was one of the first political organizations in the United States. The Federalists controlled the nation's government from 1789 to 1801. They favored a strong central government, a large peacetime army and navy, and a stable financial system.

After George Washington became president in 1789, a political division appeared between those who favored a strong federal government and those who opposed it. The Federalist Party developed under the leadership of Alexander Hamilton, Washington's secretary of the treasury. Hamilton believed that the Constitution should be loosely interpreted to build up federal power. He favored the interests of commerce and manufacturing over agriculture. Hamilton also wanted the new government to be on a sound financial basis. He proposed tax increases and the establishment of a national bank.

Thomas Jefferson and James Madison opposed Hamilton. Their followers became known as Democratic-Republicans. They believed that the Constitution should be strictly interpreted, and that the states and the citizens should retain as many of their powers and rights as possible. John Adams, a Federalist, succeeded Washington as president in 1797. The Federalists lost control of the national government when Jefferson became president in 1801. Their party ceased to exist as a national organization after the election of 1816. But it remained influential in many states until it disappeared in the 1820's.

The term *Federalists* also refers to the group of people who fought for the adoption of the Constitution in 1787 and 1788. This group was a loose alliance, not an organized political party.   Donald R. Hickey

See also **Adams, John** (Vice president; Adams' administration); **Anti-Federalists; Democratic-Republican Party; Hamilton, Alexander; Political party** (Development of parties in the United States).

Federer, Roger (1981-   ), a Swiss tennis star, became dominant in men's professional tennis in the early 2000's. He won his 15th grand slam tournament in 2009, breaking the record of 14 held by Pete Sampras of the United States. Federer won three of the four grand slam events in 2004—Wimbledon, the Australian Open, and the US Open. He also won the Wimbledon championship in 2003, 2005, 2006, 2007, 2009, and 2012; the US Open in 2005, 2006, 2007, and 2008; and the French Open in 2009, becoming the sixth man to win all four grand slam titles during his career. Federer won the Australian Open again in 2006, 2007, and 2010. In 2007, he broke American star Jimmy Connors's record of 160 consecutive weeks ranked as the number-one player in the world. Federer's record ended at 238 weeks in 2008. Since then, he has held the number-one ranking again more than once. Federer also won the gold medal in men's doubles for Switzerland with partner Stanislas Wawrinka at the 2008 Summer Olympic Games.

Federer is noted for his complete game, including a strong serve and powerful forehand and backhand strokes. He is effective on all surfaces—clay, hard-court, and grass, and in both indoor and outdoor matches.

Federer was born on Aug. 8, 1981, in Basel, Switzerland. He dominated junior tennis in 1997 and 1998, winning the Wimbledon singles and doubles junior titles in 1998. He turned professional in that year.   Tony Lance

Fee, in modern property law, describes the kind of ownership that may pass to an owner's heirs on his or her death. A *fee simple absolute* is complete ownership of land. A *fee simple determinable* is ownership that is automatically lost if the property is used in a way pro-

hibited by the previous owner. A *fee simple conditional* gives the previous owner a choice of whether to retake land used in a certain way. A *fee tail* is ownership that must pass in a certain way, as from father to eldest son. The term *fee,* or *fief,* also referred to land ownership under the English feudal system. A fief was also the piece of land that a lord granted to a servant in return for certain services (see **Feudalism**).   Sherman L. Cohn

Feed is a term for food given to farm animals. *Roughage feeds* are coarse. They include pasture grasses and *legumes* (plants of the pea family), as well as the remains of crops such as corn and wheat. Some grasses and legumes are dried and fed to livestock as hay. Farmers often preserve whole corn plants and other crops to produce a feed called *silage.* Such grains as barley, corn, or grain sorghum are called *concentrates* when ground and mixed with other ingredients as feed.

Livestock also eat by-products of milling, brewing, food processing, and other industries. Crops used to produce oils yield by-product feeds known as *oilseed meals.*   Elisabeth Huff-Lonergan

Related articles in *World Book* include:

Alfalfa	Dairying (Feeding)	Grass
Cattle (Feeding)	Farm and farming	Hay
Corn (Livestock feed)	(Processing and storage; Live-	Hog (Raising hogs) Livestock
Cotton (Uses of cotton)	stock care) Grain	Silo Soybean

Feet. See **Foot.**

Feininger, *FY nihng uhr,* **Lyonel** (1871-1956), was an American painter whose works combine qualities of Cubism and Expressionism. In his mature work, he uses flat planes of color and thin straight lines. Feininger was born on July 17, 1871, in New York City. His parents

Oil painting (1930); Neue Staatsgalerie, Munich, Germany

Feininger's *The Market Church in Halle* shows how the artist used straight lines to divide forms and space into flat planes.

were musicians. In 1887, he went to Germany to join his parents, who were on tour. Feininger stayed in Europe and worked as a political and satirical cartoonist in Berlin and Paris from 1894 to 1908. He then turned to painting and soon earned an international reputation. In 1919, Feininger became the first professor chosen by Walter Gropius for the Bauhaus school of art and design in Germany. Feininger did not return to the United States until 1937, after the Nazis labeled him a "degenerate artist." He died on Jan. 13, 1956.   Charles C. Eldredge

See also **Bauhaus.**

Feinstein, *FYN styn,* **Dianne** (1933-   ), is one of the most prominent women in American politics. A Democrat, she has represented California in the United States Senate since 1992. She was mayor of San Francisco from 1978 to 1988.

Dianne Goldman was born in San Francisco on June 22, 1933. She graduated from Stanford University in 1955. In 1962, she married Bertram Feinstein, a neurosurgeon. From 1969 to 1978, she served on the San Francisco Board of Supervisors. She succeeded to the office of mayor in 1978, when Mayor George R. Moscone was assassinated. Feinstein was elected mayor in 1979 and reelected in 1983.

U.S. Senate

Dianne Feinstein

In April 1983, before the end of her first term, Feinstein won a *recall election* (a vote to decide whether she should be removed from office). Feinstein's sponsorship of a ban on handguns had led to a petition for the recall. Her accomplishments as mayor included redeveloping downtown San Francisco, rebuilding the city's cable car system, and eliminating a deficit in the city budget.

Feinstein was first elected to the U.S. Senate in 1992 to fill the final two years in the term of Pete Wilson. He had resigned to become governor of California after narrowly defeating Feinstein in a 1990 election for governor. Feinstein was elected to her first full term in the Senate in 1994. As a senator, she became known for her efforts to protect wilderness lands from development. Feinstein has served on the Senate Judiciary Committee and the Appropriations Committee. She has also chaired the Senate Select Committee on Intelligence.   June Sochen

Feisal. See Faisal.

Feke, *feek,* **Robert** (1707?-1752?), was the earliest noteworthy American-born painter. His *Portrait of Isaac Royall and His Family* (1741) combines a knowledge of English portrait poses and the clear outlines of American primitive painting. The portrait is reproduced in **Colonial life in America** (Arts). Feke was born in Oyster Bay, Long Island, New York. Little is known about his life. By 1741, he was painting portraits in Boston. Feke traveled frequently in search of commissions.   Elizabeth Garrity Ellis

Feldspar is the name of a group of minerals that make up about 60 percent of Earth's crust. Feldspars occur in most *igneous rocks* and in many *metamorphic* and *sedimentary rocks* (see **Rock**). Extremely large feldspar crystals are found in a coarse-grained igneous rock called

pegmatite. Feldspars rank among the hard minerals (see **Hardness**). Feldspars range in color from clear white or gray to shades of blue, green, or pink.

All feldspars contain alumina and silica. Feldspars may be classified into two general groups, *alkali feldspars* and *plagioclase feldspars,* according to the other elements they contain. All alkali feldspars contain potassium, and most contain sodium. The most common minerals in this group are *microcline, orthoclase,* and *sanidine.* Most plagioclase feldspars, such as *andesine* and *labradorite,* contain both sodium and calcium. Some feldspar crystals, called *perthites,* consist of alkali and plagioclase feldspars.

Feldspar is used in making glass and ceramics. Some feldspar crystals are used as gemstones, ornaments, and architectural decorations. The most popular of these crystals are *moonstone* (milky-white perthite), *Amazon stone* (green microcline), and labradorite, which is *iridescent* (displaying changing colors). A process called *weathering* changes feldspars into other minerals, chiefly clay minerals and salts. *Kaolin,* the most important of these clay minerals, is used in making fine chinaware.   Mark A. Helper

See also **Crystal** (picture); **Granite; Moonstone.**

Feller, Bob (1918-2010), became the strikeout king of baseball while pitching for the Cleveland Indians. Feller was a right-handed pitcher with a dominating fast ball. He struck out 2,581 batters while winning 266 games from 1936 through 1956. Feller led the American League seven times in strikeouts and five times in the number of innings pitched. On Oct. 2, 1938, Feller set a modern major league record by striking out 18 batters in a single game. He won 20 or more games in six seasons, leading the American League in victories each time. In 1940, his best season, Feller won 27 games and lost 11. He struck out a career-high 348 batters in 1946.

Robert William Andrew Feller was born on Feb. 3, 1918, in Van Meter, Iowa. He joined the Indians at the age of 17 after graduating from high school. Feller missed nearly four seasons at the height of his career, from 1942 until late 1945, after enlisting in the United States Navy during World War II (1939-1945). In 1962, Feller was elected to the National Baseball Hall of Fame. He died on Dec. 15, 2010.   Neil Milbert

Fellini, Federico (1920-1993), was a famous Italian motion-picture director. He originated his own ideas for his movies, usually developing the story as the film was being made. Many of his films blend realism and social satire with fantasy. They rely heavily on the use of symbolism and imagery, which create dreamlike sequences that are sometimes deliberately obscure.

Fellini was born in Rimini, Italy, on Jan. 20, 1920. As a child, he ran away to the circus for a few days, and the experience inspired much of his work. He collaborated with Alberto Lattuada on his first motion picture, *Variety Lights* (1950). Fellini's first international success, *La Strada* (1954), won an Academy Award as best foreign film and made his wife, Julietta Masina, a star. This grimly realistic, yet poetic film describes the relationship between a brutal circus strongman and a half-witted young woman. *Nights of Cabiria* (1957), *8½* (1963), and *Amarcord* (1973) also won Academy Awards as best foreign films.

Fellini's *La Dolce Vita* (1960) is an autobiographical and complex study of moral corruption in Italian society of the day. He also used autobiographical material in *8½*. Fellini's other major motion pictures include *I Vitelloni* (1953), *Juliet of the Spirits* (1965), *Fellini's Roma* (1972), and *City of Women* (1980). He was married to Masina from 1943 until his death on Oct. 31, 1993. Rachel Gallagher

Fellowship is a sum of money given to scholars so they can continue their studies. Some fellowships are for specified periods of time, but others are for life. Fellowships have been made since the Middle Ages.

Fellowships are usually given by universities, foundations, learned societies, corporations, and governments. Universities give fellowships for graduate work. Sometimes fellows teach classes. Foundations and learned societies give fellowships for graduate study and individual research in such areas as education, medicine, and international relations. Large foundation and learned society fellowship programs in the United States include those of the Alfred P. Sloan Foundation, the American Council of Learned Societies, the John D. and Catherine T. MacArthur Foundation, the John Simon Guggenheim Memorial Foundation, and the Social Science Research Council. Corporation fellowships often encourage research in fields of interest to the sponsoring firm. The U.S. government conducts fellowship programs in the arts, humanities, and sciences through the National Endowment for the Arts, the National Endowment for the Humanities, and the National Science Foundation.

In the United States, most fellowships last for one or two years and provide from a few hundred to several thousand dollars. In the United Kingdom, the grants are often given for three to five years. C. Kiger

See also **Foundation; Scholarship.**

Fellowship of Christian Athletes is a nondenominational organization mainly of athletes and coaches that promotes Christian ideals. The Fellowship, often called FCA, conducts summer camps at campsites and college campuses. Student athletes in junior high school, high school, and college meet in groups called Huddles. Adult chapters provide personal and financial support to the Huddles and fellowship for adults and coaches. The organization publishes a magazine called *Sharing the Victory.*

The FCA was founded in 1954. It is a nonprofit organization supervised by a national board of trustees. The home office is in Kansas City, Missouri.

Critically reviewed by the Fellowship of Christian Athletes

Felony, *FEHL uh nee,* is a crime for which punishment is death or imprisonment for a year or more. Felonies include murder, robbery, burglary, kidnapping, treason, and certain other serious crimes. A violation of law less serious is called a *misdemeanor* and is punishable by a fine or jail sentence (see **Misdemeanor).**

A person directly injured by a felony may agree not to prosecute in return for some payment or other valuable consideration. For example, a person may promise not to prosecute a thief who returns the stolen goods. Making such an agreement is called *compounding a felony* and is a crime punishable by fine or imprisonment.

Charles F. Wellford

See also **Burglary; Robbery.**

Felt is a fabric made of wool fibers or animal hair matted together by heat, moisture, and pressure. Felt varies greatly in weight, thickness, and value. Manufacturers use felt to make hats, slippers, chalkboard erasers, rug

pads, and padding used in pianos and other musical instruments. Felt is usually made 72 inches (183 centimeters) wide. Keith Slater

FEMA. See Federal Emergency Management Agency.

Female. See Reproduction; Sexuality.

Feminine gender. See Gender.

Feminism, *FEHM uh nihz uhm,* is the belief that women should have economic, political, and social equality with men. The specific ideas of feminism vary depending on time, place, culture, and other factors. Many feminists challenge traditional gender roles and demand increased educational and employment opportunities. Feminists may call for greater involvement of women in politics. They may also focus on issues related to sex and reproductive rights, the prevention of violence against women, and the well-being of women throughout the world.

Many people regard the emergence of feminism— and the resulting changes in the status of women—as a turning point in the history of society. Until the early 1900's, women in most countries were denied the right to vote and to pursue their educational or career goals. Many societies expected women to devote their time to raising children, preparing food, and cleaning.

In the late 1600's, the British author Mary Astell presented one of the first major arguments supporting improved education for women. Her work, *A Serious Proposal to the Ladies,* was published in two volumes, in 1694 and 1697. In *A Vindication of the Rights of Woman* (1792), the British writer Mary Wollstonecraft criticized the "state of degradation" in which society kept women and demanded better educational opportunities.

In the 1800's, many women became active in social and political reform efforts, including antislavery movements. Such activity led many women to demand higher social status. The American antislavery leader Sarah M. Grimké wrote *Letters on the Equality of the Sexes and the Condition of Woman* (1838). She argued against religious leaders who claimed that the Bible supported the inferior position of women.

The word *feminism* comes from the French term

Culver

Feminism concentrated at first on winning *suffrage,* the right to vote. In 1915, women marched in a suffrage parade in New York City, *shown here.*

fèminisme, which was first used by French social reformers of the 1800's. During the late 1800's, the central goal of feminism was the right to vote, called *suffrage.* The International Council of Women, established in 1888, helped coordinate feminist efforts throughout the world. In 1893, New Zealand granted women the right to vote. Australia and many European countries followed during the early 1900's. Women in the United States gained suffrage in 1920. See **Woman suffrage.**

After winning the right to vote, feminists began focusing on other issues. Margaret Sanger of the United States and Marie Stopes of the United Kingdom helped lead campaigns for birth control. Other feminists focused on job discrimination, wages, and other issues affecting women in the workplace. In the 1960's, the civil rights movement and student protests led to increased political activism among a younger generation of women. The efforts of these women became known as the *women's liberation movement,* or the "second wave" of feminism.

In 1966, the American feminist Betty Friedan helped found the National Organization for Women (NOW), an organization dedicated to achieving equality between women and men. A similar organization, the National Action Committee on the Status of Women, was founded in Canada in 1971. In the late 1900's, feminist publications such as *Ms.* magazine, cofounded in 1972 by Gloria Steinem, helped raise awareness of women's issues. Many high schools, colleges, and universities began offering *women's studies* courses that examined the achievements and experiences of women in various fields.

Since the late 1900's, many activists have become known as "third wave" feminists, because their aims differ somewhat from those of earlier feminists. These activists increasingly apply feminist beliefs to issues relating to race and ethnicity, sexual orientation, social class, and role in government.   Melanie S. Gustafson

See also **Sex discrimination; Women's movement.**

Additional resources

Boles, Janet K., and Hoeveler, D. L. *The A to Z of Feminism.* Scarecrow, 2006.
Hawkesworth, Mary E. *Globalization and Feminist Activism.* Rowman & Littlefield, 2006.
Heywood, Leslie L, ed. *The Women's Movement Today.* 2 vols. Greenwood, 2006.
Johnson, Allan G. *The Gender Knot: Unraveling Our Patriarchal Legacy.* Rev. ed. Temple Univ. Pr., 2005.
Snodgrass, Mary E. *Encyclopedia of Feminist Literature.* Facts on File, 2006.

Femur. See Leg.

Fencing is the art and sport of swordsmanship using blunted weapons. Fencers use one of three types of weapons—the foil, the epee, or the sabre. Fencing meets are conducted as individual or team events. But even in team events, only two fencers compete against each other at one time. Fencing is open to both men and women, but they do not compete against each other.

There is evidence that fencing competitions date back at least 5,000 years to ancient Egypt and Japan. In Europe, modern swordsmanship dates back to about 1400. Fencing schools became popular in Italy, and traveling Italian fencing masters spread the technique of swordsmanship to England, France, and Spain. By the late

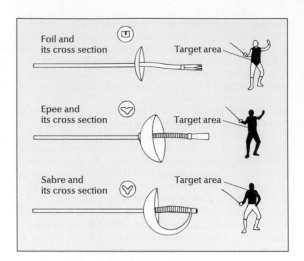

Fencing weapons and their target areas

1800's, fencing had become part of the education of a gentleman. Fencing was one of the original sports included in the modern Olympic Games.

Fencers wear heavy wire-mesh masks with thick canvas bibs to protect the head and neck. They also wear thick canvas or nylon jackets and knickers and a padded glove on the hand holding the weapon.

The foil has a slender, flexible quadrilateral blade and a small, circular guard. The blade is 90 centimeters (3 feet) long. Foil fencers try to score touches or hits by touching their opponent's torso with the point.

Foil fencers must follow a certain sequence of moves, called *conventions.* The fencer who first *attacks* has the *right of way* or *priority* in scoring until the defender *par-*

WORLD BOOK illustrations by David Cunningham

Fencing moves follow a sequence. Competition begins with fencers *on guard.* One fencer uses a *lunge* to *attack.* The defender blocks the attack with a *parry.* A *touch* ends the action.

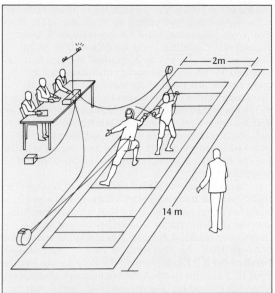

WORLD BOOK illustration by David Cunningham

The fencing area is 2 meters (6 feet 7 inches) wide and 14 meters (46 feet) long. An electronic device activates a light when a fencer scores a touch. A scorekeeper, timekeeper, and signaling apparatus operator sit at a table. The chief official, called the *referee,* stands while observing the action.

ries (blocks) the attack or the attack is unsuccessful. The defender is then allowed to *riposte* (counterattack). Action continues until a fencer scores a touch or the action becomes too confused for the chief official, the referee, to follow.

If the fencer touches the opponent outside the torso area, no touch is scored and action resumes. If a fencer touches the opponent on the torso, then a touch is scored. If both fencers touch each other and the referee cannot determine who had the right of way, there is no score. Most foil bouts have a 5-minute time limit. The first fencer to score five touches wins.

The epee has a rigid triangular blade with a bell-shaped guard. The blade is 90 centimeters long. Epee fencing has no conventions of right of way. Touches on any part of the body count. However, touches must be scored with the point of the weapon. If both fencers touch each other at the same time, both touches count. Most epee bouts have a 5-minute time limit. Five touches win the bout. Epee fencing for one touch is part of a five-sport competition called the modern pentathlon (see **Pentathlon, Modern**).

The sabre has a flexible triangular blade with a guard that curves around the knuckles. The blade is 88 centimeters (2 feet 11 inches) long. In sabre fencing, touches may be scored on any part of the body above the hips, including the head and arms, either with the point or with one of the two cutting edges. Sabre fencing follows the same conventions of right of way as foil fencing. Most sabre bouts have a 5-minute time limit. Five touches win the bout.

Fencing organizations. The United States Fencing Association (USFA) administers fencing in the United States. The USFA is the U.S. member of the International Fencing Federation (FIE). The FIE conducts the world championships and the fencing events of the Olympic Games. In addition, the FIE establishes the official rules of the sport.

Critically reviewed by the United States Fencing Association

See also **Olympic Games** (table: Fencing); **Sword.**

Additional resources

Cohen, Richard A. *By the Sword: A History of Gladiators, Musketeers, Samurai, Swashbucklers, and Olympic Champions.* Random Hse., 2002.
Evangelista, Nick. *The Art and Science of Fencing.* 1996. Reprint. McGraw, 1999. *The Encyclopedia of the Sword.* Greenwood, 1995.

Fénelon, *fayn LAWN,* **François de Salignac de la Mothe-,** *frahn SWAH duh sa lee NYAK duh la MAWT* (1651-1715), was a French author and a Roman Catholic archbishop. He became known for his advanced political, social, and educational ideas.

Fénelon's *Treatise on the Education of Girls* (1687) shows his keen understanding of child psychology. His best-known work is *Telemachus* (1695-1699), a novel written to instruct the Duke of Burgundy, grandson of King Louis XIV. The book is about a young man who observes the governments of many countries. It was intended to teach the duke the duties of high office. Fénelon's criticism of absolute monarchy was implied in *Telemachus* and clearly stated in a *Letter to Louis XIV,* published after Fénelon's death. The main ideas described in *Telemachus* had been foreshadowed by his *Dialogs of the Dead* (1692). In *Maxims of the Saints* (1697), Fénelon favored *quietism,* a religious movement that denied the value of conventional religious practices. The church condemned the *Maxims,* and Fénelon lost his influence in religious life and court life.

Fénelon was born on Aug. 6, 1651, at Périgord. He was ordained about 1675 and was appointed archbishop of Cambrai in 1695. Fénelon died on Jan. 7, 1715.

Robert B. Griffin

Fenian movement, *FEE nee uhn,* was a struggle by Irish nationalists to free Ireland from English rule. In the late 1850's, a group of Irish patriots called *Fenians* began to plan a revolution. The Fenians took their name from the *Fianna,* a band of mythical Irish warriors (see **Irish literature** [Heroic tales, romances, and sagas]).

Most Fenians belonged to a secret society called the Irish Republican Brotherhood (IRB), which was founded in Dublin on St. Patrick's Day, March 17, 1858. In 1866 and 1867, the Fenians attacked police stations in Ireland and set off bombs in England. But the English authorities put down the rebellion and imprisoned hundreds of suspected rebels.

Many people who had emigrated from Ireland to the United States supported the Fenian movement. In the late 1860's, Irish American Fenians staged three unsuccessful raids on Canada, then a member of the British Empire.

The Fenian goal of independence through revolution was adopted by later Irish republican movements. Ireland became independent in 1921, after several years of guerrilla warfare. Mary Daly

Fennec, *FEHN ehk,* is the smallest kind of fox. It stands about 8 inches (20 centimeters) tall at the shoulders and weighs about 3 pounds (1.35 kilograms). Its enormous ears grow about 5 inches (13 centimeters) long. The animal ranges in color from white to pale reddish-orange and has a bushy, black-tipped tail.

Fennecs live in the deserts of northern Africa and the Arabian Peninsula. They are well adapted to desert life. Their light coloring keeps them cool in the daytime heat and helps them blend into the sand to avoid enemies. Their fur provides protection from the hot sun and warmth during cold nights. The hair on the soles of their feet enables them to run quickly over hot sand. Because their bodies lose water slowly, fennecs can go for days without drinking.

Fennecs dig burrows deep in the sand and rest in them during the daytime. Up to 12 animals may share one burrow. Female fennecs give birth to two to five young each spring. At night, fennecs hunt such food as locusts, lizards, or small mammals. They also forage for birds' eggs, plant bulbs, and fruits.   Anne Innis Dagg

Scientific classification. The fennec belongs to the family Canidae. Its scientific name is *Vulpes zerda.*

See also **Fox** (Fennecs).

Fennel, *FEHN uhl,* is an herb related to parsley. It grows wild as a perennial plant in southern Europe. Fennel is cultivated annually or every two years in the United States, India, and Japan and in parts of Europe.

The fennel plant has fragrant, finely divided leaves and yellow flowers. Its seeds also are fragrant, and they have a licorice taste. The leaves and seeds are used to flavor candy, liqueurs, medicines, and fish and other foods. Oil of fennel, which is made from the seeds, gives soaps and perfumes a pleasing fragrance. One variety of fennel, *Florence fennel* or *finocchio,* has a bulblike base that is eaten as a vegetable. It is sweet and crisp and has a licorice taste.

WORLD BOOK illustration
by Lorraine Epstein

Fennel

Spanish fennel is related to the buttercup and is not a true fennel. It grows in western Asia and in the region of the Mediterranean Sea.   Albert Liptay

Scientific classification. Fennel is a member of the parsley family, Apiaceae or Umbelliferae. It is *Foeniculum vulgare.* Spanish fennel belongs to the crowfoot family, Ranunculaceae. It is *Nigella hispanica.*

Fer-de-lance, *FAIR duh LAHNS,* is one of the largest and deadliest of the poisonous snakes. It lives in tropical America and on some islands in the Caribbean. It has velvety scales, marks of rich brown and gray, and a yellowish throat. The fer-de-lance lives in both wet and dry places, in forests as well as open country. Young snakes eat lizards and frogs. Adults feed on birds and small mammals. There may be more than 70 young in a brood. The baby snakes have fully formed fangs and can give a poisonous bite. A fer-de-lance strikes swiftly. It may grow to 8 feet (2.4 meters) in length. Its name is French and means *lance blade.* See also **Viper.**   Albert F. Bennett

Scientific classification. The fer-de-lance belongs to the viper family, Viperidae. Its scientific name is *Bothrops atrox.*

Ferber, Edna (1885-1968), an American novelist and playwright, wrote many books about the colorful Ameri-

can life of the 1800's. She won the 1925 Pulitzer Prize for fiction for her first best-selling novel, *So Big* (1924). She also wrote *Show Boat* (1926), *Cimarron* (1930), *Saratoga Trunk* (1941), *Giant* (1952), and *Ice Palace* (1958). *Show Boat* was made into a popular musical. She said that she intended her books to be social criticism as well as good stories. She often wrote about strong women characters. Ferber's other novels include *Dawn O'Hara* (1911), her first book; *The Girls* (1921); and *Come and Get It* (1935). *Roast Beef, Medium* (1913) is a collection of stories. She had considerable success with the plays she wrote with George S. Kaufman. The best known of these are *The Royal Family* (1927), *Dinner at Eight* (1932), and *Stage Door* (1936).

Ferber was born in Kalamazoo, Michigan, on Aug. 15, 1885. She grew up in Appleton, Wisconsin. At age 17, when her father went blind, she took a newspaper job with the *Appleton Daily Crescent.* Ferber told her life story in two books, *A Peculiar Treasure* (1939) and *A Kind of Magic* (1963). She died April 16, 1968.   Bert Hitchcock

Ferdinand II (1578-1637) ruled the Holy Roman Empire from 1619 until his death. A devout Roman Catholic, Ferdinand dedicated his reign to restoring Catholicism to its former dominant position in the Protestant German states of the empire.

Ferdinand was born on July 9, 1578. He was the son of Archduke Charles of Styria, a province in what is now Austria. Ferdinand belonged to the Habsburg (or Hapsburg) family, which had long controlled the empire. He became emperor during the Thirty Years' War (1618-1648). The war had begun as a conflict between Protestants and Catholics, and Ferdinand defeated many rebel Protestant nobles.

To limit Ferdinand's power, leaders from several European countries began to help the rebels. Catholic nobles in the empire also grew to fear Ferdinand's power. In 1635, he forced Catholic and Protestant nobles to sign the Peace of Prague, increasing his authority over them. But expansion of the war quickly ended his dominance. Ferdinand died on Feb. 15, 1637.   Jonathan W. Zophy

Ferdinand III (1608-1657) ruled the Holy Roman Empire from 1637 until his death. Ferdinand tried to promote his authority over the German states of the empire and to strengthen the Roman Catholic Church in them.

Ferdinand was born on July 13, 1608. He was a member of the House of Habsburg (or Hapsburg), a Catholic family that had long dominated the empire. He succeed-

WORLD BOOK illustration by Richard Lewington, The Garden Studio

The fer-de-lance is a large, poisonous snake that lives in tropical regions of North and South America.

ed his father, Ferdinand II, as emperor and continued his father's policies in the Thirty Years' War (1618-1648). During this war, Ferdinand III sought to increase his authority over the German states, promote Catholicism in Germany, and expand Habsburg power in Europe. But the war exhausted his resources. Following several military defeats, he signed the Peace of Westphalia in 1648. This agreement ended the war. It weakened Ferdinand's authority in the empire, but strengthened his control over the Habsburg family's lands. Ferdinand died on April 2, 1657.   Jonathan W. Zophy

Ferdinand V (1452-1516) ruled the kingdom of Castile in what is now Spain. He helped unify various Spanish kingdoms into one country. He also ruled the Spanish kingdom of Aragon, and Sicily, as Ferdinand II. He ruled Naples as Ferdinand III.

Ferdinand was born on March 10, 1452, in Sos, Aragon. He was prince of Aragon when he married his cousin Princess Isabella of Castile in 1469. She became Queen Isabella I of Castile in 1474, and he became King Ferdinand V of Castile. He became King Ferdinand II of Aragon in 1479. Thus, most of what is now Spain came under their rule. They added to Spain's power by conquering the Moors (North African Muslims) of the kingdom of Granada in 1492. That same year, they sent the Italian navigator Christopher Columbus on his first voyage of discovery to North America. After Isabella died in 1504, Ferdinand added the kingdom of Navarre to Castile. He died on Jan. 23, 1516.

Carla Rahn Phillips and William D. Phillips, Jr.

See also **Castile and Aragon; Columbus, Christopher; Spain** (Union of the Spanish kingdoms).

Ferdinand, Archduke. See **World War I** (The assassination of an archduke).

Ferlinghetti, *fur lihn GEHT ee,* **Lawrence** (1919-   ), is an American poet best known as a leader of the Beat movement of the 1950's. The Beats were writers who condemned commercialism and middle-class American values. Ferlinghetti writes in colloquial free verse. His poetry describes the need to release literature and life from conformity and timidity. He believes drugs, Zen Buddhism, and emotional and physical love can open the soul to truth and beauty. The grotesque and a feeling of euphoria are closely interwoven in his work, especially in his most famous poem, *A Coney Island of the Mind* (1958). The poem is also a satiric criticism of American culture. Ferlinghetti wrote *Endless Life: Selected Poems* in 1981 and *Love in the Days of Rage* in 1988. He has also composed *oral messages*—poems to be spoken to jazz accompaniment. Ferlinghetti was born on March 24, 1919, in Yonkers, New York. See also **Beat movement.**   Bonnie Costello

Fermat, *fehr MAH,* **Pierre de** (1601-1665), a French mathematician, founded modern number theory. He also helped invent analytic geometry and lay the foundation for calculus. He proved mathematically that the law for the *refraction* (bending) of light results from light's following the path that takes the shortest time. Fermat and the French philosopher and mathematician Blaise Pascal invented the theory of probability.

The ancient Greeks knew there are many whole-number solutions of the equation $x^2+y^2=z^2$ (for example, $3^2+4^2=5^2$). But in 1637 Fermat wrote in the margin of a book that there is no positive whole-number solution

of $x^n+y^n=z^n$ if n is greater than 2. Fermat noted that he had found a wonderful proof of this fact, but that there was not enough room to write it down. No proof of "Fermat's last theorem" was found for more than 350 years. But in 1993, British mathematician Andrew Wiles announced that he had proved the theorem. Wiles published his complete proof, with corrections, in 1995.

Fermat was born on Aug. 17, 1601, in Beaumont-de-Lomagne, near Toulouse. He practiced law in Toulouse and studied mathematics for pleasure. Fermat died on Jan. 12, 1665.   Judith V. Grabiner

Fermentation, *FUR mehn TAY shuhn,* is a biological process that breaks down organic materials in the absence of oxygen. Fermentation is carried out by microbes, such as bacteria, molds, and yeasts. Fermentation has many practical uses. For example, certain molds ferment mixtures of sugars and other chemicals to produce penicillin. In beer brewing, yeast consumes sugar from malted grain, turning it into carbon dioxide gas, heat, ethyl alcohol, and small amounts of other compounds. Fermentation by bacteria serves as an essential step in the production of cheese and yogurt. Fermentation can also be harmful. For example, fermentation in meat can cause the deadly food poisoning *botulism.*

Manufacturers make a variety of food and beverage products through fermentation. Most such products use the same basic methods. First, workers fill stainless steel tanks with carbohydrates and other nutrients. Then, they allow microbes to ferment the nutrients over a period of days. When fermentation is complete, the manufacturer may further refine the product. For instance, spirits manufacturers distill the liquid to separate the ethyl alcohol.

People also use fermentation to grow and produce microorganisms, such as yeast and *Lactobacillus.* Dairy food makers use *Lactobacillus* in the making of cheese and yogurt. Fermentation is also used to make pharmaceuticals, vitamins, and industrial chemicals. Some wastewater systems use bacteria to ferment sewage water, producing methane gas.

People have used fermentation to make alcoholic beverages since ancient times. But scientists did not discover how microbes cause fermentation until the 1800's. At that time, the French biologist Louis Pasteur studied fermentation in wine. His work advanced the French wine industry and led to a better understanding of food-borne illness.   Karl Ockert

Related articles in *World Book* include:

Alcoholic beverage	Lactic acid	Yeast
Food preservation	Pasteur, Louis	Yogurt
(Acid; History)	Silo	

Fermi, *FUR mee* or *FEHR mee,* **Enrico,** *ehn REE koh* (1901-1954), an Italian-born American physicist, designed the first nuclear reactor and produced the first nuclear chain reaction in 1942. He later worked on the atomic bomb project at Los Alamos, New Mexico.

Fermi won the 1938 Nobel Prize in physics for his work on nuclear processes. He made important contributions to radioactivity, quantum theory, and other areas of physics.

Fermi began bombarding many chemical elements with neutrons in 1934. He proved that slow neutrons are very effective in producing radioactive atoms. As a result of these experiments, Fermi announced in 1934 what he thought were elements weighing more than uranium, not realizing that he had actually split the atom. Otto Hahn and Fritz Strassmann of Germany performed a similar experiment in 1938. Lise Meitner and Otto Frisch showed that these experiments had split the uranium atom and named the process *nuclear fission.* Fermi and other scientists used nuclear fission to power the first atomic bombs in 1945.

Fermi was born on Sept. 29, 1901, in Rome. He earned a doctor's degree from the University of Pisa in 1922. He then returned to Rome, where he became professor of theoretical physics at the University of Rome in 1927. Fermi left Italy in 1938 to escape the Fascist regime and settled in the United States. He became a professor of physics at Columbia University in 1939. Fermi moved to the University of Chicago as a professor of physics in 1942. He became an American citizen in 1944. After World War II (1939-1945), Fermi pioneered research on high-energy particles. He died on Nov. 28, 1954.

Matthew Stanley

See also **Meitner, Lise; Nuclear energy** (The development of nuclear weapons).

Fermi National Accelerator Laboratory, *FUR mee* or *FEHR mee,* is a high-energy physics laboratory in Batavia, Illinois. Scientists from all over the world go to the laboratory to study subatomic particles. The laboratory is commonly called *Fermilab.*

Fermilab scientists study data collected by telescopes, observatories, and particle accelerators around the world. The Tevatron, a type of particle accelerator called a *synchrotron,* was the laboratory's main instrument from 1972 to 2011. After the Tevatron shut down, scientists at Fermilab began using data collected by the more powerful Large Hadron Collider (LHC), outside Geneva, Switzerland. A type of particle called a *neutrino* is created and studied at Fermilab using special particle accelerators much smaller than the Tevatron or LHC.

The laboratory's name honors Italian-born American physicist Enrico Fermi, the first person to produce a nuclear chain reaction. Fermi Research Alliance, LLC—a corporation owned by the University of Chicago and Universities Research Association, Inc., a group of universities in the United States, Canada, Italy, and Japan—manages the laboratory. The Department of Energy pays for its operation.

Critically reviewed by Fermi National Accelerator Laboratory

See also **Particle accelerator; Particle detector** (picture); **Synchrotron.**

Fermion, *FEHR mee ahn* or *FUR mee ahn,* is any member of a certain class of atomic and subatomic particles. Every particle is classified as either a fermion or a *boson.* The simplest fermions are *leptons* and *quarks.* These are *elementary particles*—that is, they have no known smaller parts. The electron is one of six types of leptons. There are also six types of quarks. Fermions also include *composite objects* that are made up of an odd number of fermions. Neutrons and protons are such fermions. Each is composed of three quarks. Other composite fermions include certain nuclei, atoms, and molecules.

Every type of fermion has an antimatter opposite, an *antifermion,* which is identical in mass but opposite in electric charge or certain other properties. A fermion can be created only in a pair with a corresponding antifermion and can be destroyed only by encountering such an antifermion. However, certain types of fermions may decay into other fermions.

Fermions differ from bosons in *spin,* a measure of internal rotation. Fermions have half-integer values of spin ($\frac{1}{2}$, $\frac{3}{2}$, $\frac{5}{2}$, and so forth). Bosons have whole-integer values (0, 1, 2, and so forth). Fermions were named after Italian-born physicist Enrico Fermi, who proposed a theory of their behavior in the 1920's.   Robert H. March

Fermium, *FUR mee uhm,* is an artificially created radioactive element. Its chemical symbol is Fm. Its *atomic number* (number of protons in its nucleus) is 100. Fermium has more than a dozen known *isotopes,* forms with the same number of protons but different numbers of neutrons. The most stable isotope has an *atomic mass number* (total number of protons and neutrons) of 257. That isotope has a *half-life* of 100.5 days—that is, due to radioactive decay, only half the atoms in a sample of isotope 257 would still be atoms of that isotope after 100.5 days.

A team of American scientists led by Albert Ghiorso discovered fermium in 1953. They found it in radioactive debris produced by the first hydrogen bomb explosion in 1952. Fermium was named for Enrico Fermi, the Italian-born physicist who produced the first controlled nuclear chain reaction (see **Fermi, Enrico**). Small amounts of fermium are produced in nuclear reactors for scientific research.   Richard L. Hahn

See also **Einsteinium; Element, Chemical; Supersymmetry; Transuranium element.**

Fern is a type of green, nonflowering plant that grows in most parts of the world. Ferns vary widely in size and form. Some ferns look like mosses and measure about 1 inch (2.5 centimeters) in length. Others resemble palm trees and grow more than 65 feet (20 meters) tall. Ferns have some of the most beautiful and varied leaves among all plants. The leaves of many ferns are long and lacy and consist of hundreds of tiny leaflets. Other ferns have simple, rounded leaves. The leaves of the mosquito fern measure only about $\frac{1}{10}$ inch (2 millimeters) long. There are thousands of *species* (kinds) of ferns.

Ferns can be found in all parts of the world except the driest deserts and coldest regions. However, most ferns live in tropical regions. Ferns typically grow in damp, shady areas. In the tropics, many ferns grow on the trunks and branches of trees. In milder climates, ferns may be found growing along streams in woods and in the cracks and overhangs of rock cliffs.

Ferns rank among the oldest types of plants that live on land. Scientists believe that ferns first appeared from 350 million to 400 million years ago. Like mosses and other nonseed plants, ferns reproduce by releasing tiny, thick-walled cells called *spores.* Ferns do not produce flowers or seeds.

People enjoy ferns mainly for their beauty. Ferns are grown in many gardens, especially as background in shady areas. Several fern species are popular as house plants.

Parts of a fern. Ferns have well-developed stems, roots, and leaves. The stem of a fern stores food that the plant needs to grow. As long as the stem is alive, the fern will continue to grow and make new leaves and roots. The stem may grow upright above the ground, horizontally along the ground, or even underground. The stems of ferns often form branches. A large clump of ferns forms if a stem branches many times. Fern

O. Franken, Stock, Boston

L. West, Bruce Coleman Inc.

Ferns grow in a variety of habitats. Tree ferns, such as the one shown at the top, grow in the tropics. Bracken, *above,* is found in fields throughout most of the world.

um, a structure that covers and protects the sorus.

Life cycle of a fern. Ferns grow and reproduce in two stages—sexual and asexual. Each stage has its own unique form. This kind of life cycle is called *alternation of generations.*

During the asexual stage, the fern is called a *sporophyte.* The sporophyte produces spores. It is the form commonly recognized as a fern. A sporophyte may produce millions of spores. But only some of the spores land in places suitable for growth. A fern spore develops into a small, heart-shaped plant called a *gametophyte.*

The growth of the gametophyte begins the sexual stage of the fern's life cycle. The gametophyte produces *gametes,* the male and female sex cells known as sperm and eggs. Fern gametophytes are usually called *prothallia.* After a few weeks, prothallia develop sex organs. Male sex organs are called *antheridia.* Female sex organs are called *archegonia.* In most ferns, antheridia and archegonia are produced on separate prothallia. When the sperm are mature and the prothallia are wet, the antheridia split open and the sperm swim out. The sperm usually swim into the archegonia of other prothallia. A sperm that reaches an egg joins with it to form a single cell, called a *zygote.*

The zygote grows into a mass of cells called an *embryo.* Part of the embryo absorbs food from the prothallium. Other parts develop into the first leaf, the first root, and the stem of a new sporophyte. The embryo draws its energy from the prothallium until the root enters the soil and the sporophyte can live on its own. At this point, the prothallium shrivels and dies.

Kinds of ferns. Thousands of fern species grow around the world. Among the best known are (1) bracken, (2) the royal fern, and (3) the Western sword fern.

Bracken is one of the most common ferns worldwide. It has large, triangular fronds that grow from a cordlike underground *rhizome.* Its sori occur along the edges of the frond, protected by the rolled edge of the leaf. Bracken lives in open areas, especially along roadside woodlands and in abandoned fields. People consider it a nuisance in pastures because it can poison livestock. Bracken is hard to get rid of because its rhizome

stems usually grow slowly and may live for 100 years or more.

The roots also may live a long time. They anchor the stem to the ground and absorb water and nutrients.

Unlike the stem and roots, the leaves of a fern usually live only one or two years. A new set of leaves grows from the tip of the stem every year. A young fern leaf is coiled like the top of a violin and is called a *fiddlehead.* It uncurls as it grows. The leaf is attached to the stem by a stalk called the *stipe.* The fern leaf is often called a *frond.*

Fern leaves make food for the plant through *photosynthesis* (see **Photosynthesis**). Many fern leaves also carry the *sporangia,* the tiny structures that produce spores. These structures have a stalk and a capsule filled with spores. Sporangia are typically found in clusters on the underside of fern leaves. Each cluster of sporangia is called a *sorus,* and all the clusters on a fern are the *sori.* Ferns are the only plants that have sori. Biologists identify and classify ferns based in part on how the sori are arranged. Also important is the presence of the *indusi-*

Bill Tronca, Tom Stack & Assoc.   Robert and Linda Mitchell

Reproduction in ferns involves two forms of the fern plant. The mature plant, called a *sporophyte,* bears tiny *sporangia* on its leaves, *left.* The sporangia release spores, which grow into *gametophytes, right.* Gametophytes produce male and female sex cells that unite and develop into sporophytes.

reaches deep underground.

The royal fern is a particularly beautiful species found in swampy forests of Asia, Europe, and eastern North America. It has a short, thick stem, with many fronds growing around the top of the stem like a basket. The fronds may grow up to 6 feet (2 meters) long and are divided into many narrow leaflets. The spore-producing part of this fern is at the tip of the frond.

The Western sword fern lives in forests of the North American Pacific Coast. Its sori are round and protected by circular indusia. Like the royal fern, the Western sword fern has fronds that grow in a circle from a short stem. Each year's fronds last until late in the following season. As a result, this fern is green throughout the year. Florists use the Western sword fern as greenery because fronds cut from the plant last a long time in cold storage.   Robbin C. Moran

Scientific classification. Ferns make up the class Polypodiopsida, which is sometimes called Pteridopsida. The scientific name for bracken is *Pteridium aquilinum;* the royal fern is *Osmunda regalis;* and the Western sword fern is *Polystichum munitum.*

See also **Fossil** (picture: A carbonized fossil); **Plant** (pictures).

Fernando Po. See Equatorial Guinea.

Ferraro, *fuhr RAH roh,* **Geraldine Anne** (1935-2011), was the first woman chosen as a vice presidential candidate by a major American political party. She became the Democratic nominee for vice president of the United States in 1984. Ferraro and her presidential running mate, former Vice President Walter F. Mondale, lost to their Republican opponents, President Ronald Reagan and Vice President George H. W. Bush. Previously, Ferraro had served three terms in the United States House of Representatives.

Ferraro was born on Aug. 26, 1935, in Newburgh, New York. She received a Bachelor of Arts degree from Marymount Manhattan College in 1956 and a law degree from Fordham University in 1960. Also in 1960, she married John A. Zaccaro. She and her husband had three children. From 1961 to 1974, Ferraro occasionally handled legal matters for her husband's real estate business. She started her career in government service in 1974, when she became an assistant district attorney in Queens County, New York.

In 1978, Ferraro was elected to the U.S. House of Representatives. She represented a district in Queens, from which she won reelection in 1980 and 1982. Ferraro served on the House committees on post office and civil service, public works and transportation, and budget. In 1981, she became a member of the Democratic Steering and Policy Committee, which controls committee assignments for Democrats in the House. In Congress, she was known for her liberal views on domestic issues. She regularly voted for bills designed to benefit workers, women, and elderly people, and she

© AP Images
Geraldine A. Ferraro

opposed efforts to ban abortion. In 1992 and 1998, she tried unsuccessfully to win the Democratic nomination for one of New York's U.S. Senate seats. Ferraro died on March 26, 2011.   Lee Thornton

Ferre, *feh REH,* **Maurice** (1935-   ), became the first Hispanic mayor of a large United States city when he took office as mayor of Miami in 1973. He was appointed to the office after Mayor David Kennedy had been charged with planning to offer and receive bribes. Later that year, Ferre was elected to the office. He was reelected to five additional terms, beginning in 1975. Ferre failed to win reelection in 1985. As mayor, he became a major force in extensive development of Miami's downtown area. In 2001, Ferre ran again for mayor of Miami but lost the election.

Maurice Antonio Ferre was born on June 23, 1935, in Ponce, Puerto Rico. The son of a wealthy businessman, he earned a bachelor's degree in architectur-

© Ken Hawkins, Sygma
Maurice Ferre

al engineering from the University of Miami. He then worked in Miami in his family's concrete and real estate business. In 1967, Ferre was elected to Florida's House of Representatives, where he served until 1968. In 1967, he was appointed to the Miami City Commission. In 1993, Ferre was elected to the Dade County (now Miami-Dade County) Board of Commissioners. Miami covers much of Miami-Dade County.   Rick Hirsch

Ferret is a small mammal with a long, slim body and short legs. Ferrets are weasels. If frightened, these animals can discharge a strong-smelling fluid from scent glands under their tails.

People often keep the *domestic ferret* as a pet. The animal was originally bred in ancient times to hunt rats and rabbits, but it is seldom used for hunting today. The domestic ferret is a descendant of the *European polecat,* which was once found throughout Europe. The terms *ferret* and *polecat* are often used interchangeably. See **Polecat.**

Male domestic ferrets grow up to 25 inches (64 centimeters) long, including the tail. Females are smaller. Domestic ferrets vary in color from nearly white to nearly black. Most have creamy-colored fur with dark hair tips, feet, and tail, and a "mask" of dark fur around the eyes. Some owners have the scent glands of pet ferrets removed, but the animals still give off a musky odor from other skin glands.

The *black-footed ferret* is native to western North America. It resembles the domestic ferret, but it is slightly smaller. Black-footed ferrets have mostly dull yellow fur that is slightly darker on the back. They also have black feet, a black tail tip, and black fur around the eyes.

In the past, black-footed ferrets inhabited much of the Great Plains. The ferrets depended on prairie dogs for food and lived in underground burrows made by prairie dogs. But since the late 1800's, ranchers have eliminated prairie dogs from much of the Great Plains because they consider the animals pests. The black-footed ferret

WORLD BOOK illustration by John F. Eggert

The black-footed ferret has a mostly dull yellow body with black feet, a black tail tip, and black fur around the eyes.

has become rare as a result of this decrease in the number of prairie dogs as well as the spread of disease and the loss of the ferret's rangeland to agriculture. The ferrets are classified as an endangered species in the United States.

Scientists once thought black-footed ferrets were extinct. In 1981, however, a population of more than 125 black-footed ferrets was discovered in Wyoming. Over the next several years, many of these animals died of a disease called distemper. Because scientists were concerned that all the wild ferrets would die from the disease, the remaining animals were captured. Since then, scientists have successfully bred the ferrets in captivity. In 1991, they began releasing these ferrets into western grasslands that contained prairie dog populations. The ferrets are again reproducing in the wild.

Barbara L. Clauson and Robert M. Timm

Scientific classification. The scientific name of the domestic ferret is *Mustela putorius*. The black-footed ferret is *M. nigripes*.

Ferris wheel is an entertainment device used at fairs, carnivals, and amusement and theme parks. A Ferris wheel is a power-driven vertical wheel with a steel frame. Passenger cabs are mounted on the rim of the wheel. Today's Ferris wheels stand about 40 to 45 feet (12 to 14 meters) high and carry 12 to 16 passenger cabs. Ferris wheels were originally called *pleasure wheels*.

© Thinkstock

A ferry can carry people, vehicles, and freight across rivers, lakes, bays, and other bodies of water.

The first wheel was built by George W. Gale Ferris, a mechanical engineer in Galesburg, Illinois. Ferris built it for the World's Columbian Exposition in Chicago in 1893. The wheel was 250 feet (76 meters) in diameter. Each of its 36 cabs could hold 60 people. This Ferris wheel was used at the Louisiana Purchase Exposition in St. Louis,

Chicago History Museum

The Ferris wheel at the World's Columbian Exposition in Chicago in 1893 was the first one built. Its 36 passenger cabs could carry 2,160 people.

Missouri, in 1904 and then was sold for scrap metal.

In 1900, William E. Sullivan began making portable versions of the Ferris wheel in Jacksonville, Illinois, for the Eli Bridge Co. In England, a Ferris wheel is called an *Eli wheel* or a *big wheel.* Don B. Wilmeth

Ferrous sulfate, *FEHR uhs SUHL fayt* (chemical formula, $FeSO_4 \cdot 7H_2O$), is a substance that occurs in light-green crystals. The crystals turn rusty brown when they react with oxygen in moist air. Ferrous sulfate is an iron salt of sulfuric acid. It can be made by combining iron with sulfuric acid or by oxidizing *iron pyrites,* a compound of iron and sulfur. Ferrous sulfate is used to dye fabrics and leather and to make ink. It is also used to purify water, and as a disinfectant, wood preservative, and weedkiller. Marianna A. Busch

Ferry is a boat used to carry people, vehicles, and cargo across narrow bodies of water. Most large ferries have a large opening at each end so they can be loaded and unloaded without being turned around.

People have used ferries for thousands of years. Early ferries included rafts and small boats that were rowed, sailed, paddled, or moved by poles across water. Many ferries were guided by cables stretched between shores, and were pulled by ferry workers on the shore of destination.

Some cable-guided ferries are pushed by motorboats. Most large ferries in use today are powered by their own engines.

Bridges and tunnels have replaced many ferries. But ferries still operate in the Baltic and Mediterranean seas, between Manhattan and Staten islands in the New York area, and in other places around the world.

Paul F. Johnston

Fertile Crescent is an arc-shaped region in western Asia. This historic region extends between the Mediterranean Sea, to the west, and the Persian Gulf, to the east. Mountains stand to the north and the Syrian Desert lies to the south. The Tigris and Euphrates rivers flow

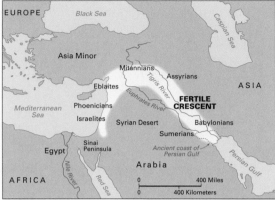

WORLD BOOK map

The Fertile Crescent is a historic region that curves above the Syrian Desert from the Mediterranean Sea to the Persian Gulf.

through the region. James H. Breasted, an American historian, made up the term *Fertile Crescent* in 1916 to describe the fertile northern border of the Syrian desert. The Sumerians developed the world's first civilization on the flood plain of the Tigris and Euphrates rivers at the southeastern end of the Fertile Crescent around 3500 B.C. The Akkadians, Assyrians, Babylonians, Canaanites, Eblaites, Israelites, and Phoenicians also lived in the Fertile Crescent.   Richard L. Zettler

See also **Asia** (History).

Fertility drug. See Fertilization; Multiple birth.

Fertilization, *FUR tuh luh ZAY shuhn,* is the process by which male and female sex cells unite to form a new individual. It is the first step in sexual reproduction. The male reproductive system produces sex cells called *spermatozoa,* or *sperm.* The female reproductive system produces sex cells called *eggs,* or *ova.* A fertilized egg, which results from the union of a sperm and an egg, is called a *zygote.* As the zygote develops further, it becomes an *embryo.* This article discusses fertilization among animals. For information about fertilization among plants, see **Plant** (How plants reproduce).

Among animals, fertilization may be external or internal. During external fertilization, male and female sex cells unite outside the female's body. The male releases sperm into water at about the same time the female releases eggs. Some sperm come into contact with eggs and fertilize them. Almost all aquatic invertebrates and some vertebrates, including the majority of fish and amphibians, reproduce in this way.

Internal fertilization occurs when the male deposits sperm directly into the female's body. Most land animals, including insects, reptiles, birds, and mammals, reproduce in this way. In almost all mammals and some reptiles, the embryo develops inside the female's body

after fertilization. However, in birds and most reptiles, the female lays an egg in which the embryo develops. The egg is protected by a shell and contains material that nourishes the growing embryo.

Scientists have developed methods of promoting fertilization in mammals, including human beings. For example, *fertility drugs* increase a female's chances of becoming pregnant. In addition, eggs may be fertilized by a process called *artificial insemination.* In this process, sperm are collected from the male and later injected into the female by artificial methods.

Scientists have also united mammalian sperm and eggs *in vitro*—that is, in an artificial environment outside the body. The zygote must then be transferred into the female reproductive system to develop. The human infants that have resulted from in vitro fertilization are sometimes called "test-tube babies."   Kelly Selman

Related articles in *World Book* include:

Breeding	Infertility	Reproduction,
Embryo	Pollen	Human
In vitro fertilization	Reproduction	

Fertilizer is a substance that is added to soil to help plants grow. Farmers use various fertilizers to help produce abundant crops. Home gardeners use fertilizers to raise large, healthy flowers and vegetables. Landscapers spread fertilizers on lawns and golf courses to help grow thick, green grass.

Fertilizers contain *nutrients* (nourishing substances) that are essential for plant growth. Some fertilizers are made from such organic materials as manure or sewage sludge. Others are manufactured from certain minerals or are produced as synthetic compounds.

People have used fertilizers for thousands of years— even though at one time they did not know why it was beneficial for plants. Long before they understood plant nutrition, people noticed that animal droppings, wood ashes, and certain minerals helped plants thrive. During the 1800's and early 1900's, scientists identified 16 chemical elements that are essential for plant nutrition.

Today, farmers throughout the world use billions of dollars worth of fertilizers annually. Increased production resulting from the use of fertilizers accounts for about a fourth of all crop production. Without fertilizers, greater amounts of land and labor would be needed to produce the same quantity of food and fiber.

The importance of fertilizer

Green plants produce the food they use. They produce it by means of the process of photosynthesis (see **Photosynthesis**). This process requires large amounts of nine chemical elements—carbon, hydrogen, oxygen, nitrogen, phosphorus, potassium, calcium, magnesium, and sulfur. It also requires smaller amounts of several other elements. These elements, called *micronutrients* because so little of each is needed, include boron, chlorine, copper, iron, manganese, molybdenum, and zinc.

Air and water provide most of the carbon, hydrogen, and oxygen that green plants need for growth. The other elements must come chiefly from the soil.

The elements plants receive from soil are normally provided by decaying plant and animal matter and dissolved minerals. But sometimes soil does not have enough of the substances, resulting in a need for fertilizer. The harvest of crops, for example, involves removing plants from the soil before they decay. The mineral elements contained in the harvested portions of the crops do not return to the soil. As a result, fertilizer must be added to replace the elements. Nitrogen, phosphorus, and potassium are the elements that soil most often lacks.

Kinds of fertilizers

There are two chief kinds of fertilizers, *inorganic* and *organic.* Manufacturers produce inorganic fertilizers from certain minerals or synthetic substances. Organic fertilizers come from decayed plant or animal matter.

Inorganic fertilizers are the most widely used fertilizers. They supply three main elements: nitrogen, phosphorus, and potassium.

Nitrogen fertilizers are the most widely used inorganic fertilizers. They are produced mainly from ammonia gas. Manufacturers convert the gas into liquid forms. Both gas and liquid forms may be applied directly to the soil. Manufacturers also use ammonia in producing solid fertilizers. Solid fertilizers include ammonium sulfate, ammonium nitrate, ammonium phosphate, and an organic compound called *urea.* Each of these fertilizers provides the soil with large amounts of nitrogen. Some, including ammonium sulfate and ammonium phosphate, furnish the soil with other elements in addition to nitrogen.

Phosphorus fertilizers are also called *phosphates.* Finely ground apatite may be applied to soil as a solid fertilizer called *rock phosphate.* Apatite also may be treated with sulfuric acid or phosphoric acid to make liquid fertilizers called *superphosphates.*

Potassium fertilizers come largely from deposits of potassium chloride. Manufacturers mine the deposits or extract them with water. The manufacturers then produce such fertilizers as potassium chloride, potassium nitrate, and potassium sulfate.

Other inorganic fertilizers provide soil with various elements. Those containing gypsum, for example, supply sulfur. Manufacturers also produce fertilizers that provide specific micronutrients.

Organic fertilizers are made from a variety of substances. They include manure, plant matter, sewage sludge, and wastes from meat-packing plants. These fertilizers contain a smaller percentage of nutrients than do inorganic fertilizers. Therefore, they must be used in larger quantities to obtain the same results. Some organic fertilizers may also cost more. However, they solve a disposal problem, because much organic waste has little use other than as fertilizer. Plant matter is used as fertilizer in two main ways: after treatment in a compost pile or as green manure.

A compost pile consists of various types of plant matter mixed together in proportions designed to speed up *decomposition* (decay). Soil, fertilizer, or lime may also be added to the compost pile. The pile is allowed to decay for several months before being used as fertilizer. See **Compost.**

Green manure consists of certain crops that farmers use as fertilizer. For example, some plants have bacteria in *nodules* (knotlike growths) on their roots. These bacteria take nitrogen out of the air and convert it into a form that plants can use. Such plants, called *legumes,* include alfalfa, beans, and clover. Farmers may plant a crop of legumes and then plow the young plants into the soil. As the plants decay, nitrogen and other elements are released into the soil. They enrich the soil so it can nourish other crops.

Commercial fertilizer containing nitrogen, phosphorus, and potassium helped produce the healthy green corn on the left. The weak, brown corn on the right received no fertilizer.

The fertilizer industry

The majority of the fertilizers produced in the world are used on farm crops. China, India, Russia, and the United States are the world's leading producers of fertilizers. Other leading fertilizer producers include Belarus, Canada, Germany, and Indonesia.

Raw materials for fertilizers come from several sources. Ammonia, the basic source of nitrogen fertilizers, is formed by combining nitrogen from the air with hydrogen from natural gas. Many petroleum companies produce ammonia because they have large supplies of natural gas.

The leading producers of phosphate rock include China, Morocco, and the United States. China and Morocco have the largest reserves of phosphate rock. Florida is the leading U.S. state in phosphate rock production.

Large deposits of potassium chloride, the major source of potassium fertilizer, occur in Canada. Saskatchewan is the leading Canadian province in potassium chloride production, and New Mexico is the leading U.S. state.

Production and sale. Fertilizer is produced in four basic forms. *Straight goods fertilizer* is any chemical compound that contains one or two fertilizer elements. *Bulk blend fertilizer* is a mixture of straight goods fertilizers. *Manufactured fertilizer* consists of two or more chemicals that are mixed and then formed into small pellets. Each pellet may contain nitrogen, phosphorus, and potassium and perhaps certain micronutrients. *Liquid fertilizer* consists of one or more fertilizer materials dissolved in water. It may be sprayed on plants or soil, injected into soil, or added to irrigation water.

Most fertilizers release their plant nutrients into the soil almost immediately. Manufacturers also produce a special type of fertilizer, called *controlled-release fertilizer,* that gives up its nutrients gradually. This type has been found useful when plants need a constant supply of nutrients over a long period.

Problems of the fertilizer industry. Every year, large amounts of fertilizer must be produced to meet the world's growing need for food. The fertilizer industry tries to match its production with this need. If it does not do so, severe food shortages might result.

A shortage of raw materials could cause a low supply of fertilizer. Some materials, such as natural gas and phosphorus, have uses other than in making fertilizer. Their use by other industries could cause a shortage for fertilizer manufacturers.

The mining and processing of the raw materials needed to make fertilizer may damage the environment. Many minerals used in making fertilizer come from open-pit mines, which leave large unproductive areas unless properly landscaped. In addition, the excessive use of fertilizer can contribute to water pollution. For example, erosion may carry fertilized soil into lakes and streams. The nutrient elements in the soil then increase the growth of *algae* (simple plantlike organisms) in water. When the algae die, they decay and use up the oxygen supply in the water.   Richard T. Koenig

Related articles in *World Book* include:

Fertilizer materials

Ammonia	Anhydrous ammonia
Ash	Nitrate
Calcium	Nitrogen
Compost	Phosphate
Guano	Phosphoric acid
Lime	Phosphorus
Limestone	Potassium
Manure	Sulfur
Mulch	Urea

Other related articles

Agricultural education
Agriculture (Agricultural practices; Agriculture and the environment)
Agronomy
Eutrophication
Soil (Characteristics of soils)
Water pollution

Fès. See Fez (city).

Fescue, *FEHS kyoo,* is a group of grasses that grow in *temperate* regions, where summers are hot and winters are cool or cold. Most fescue grasses grow in bunches called *tufts.* Fescue may grow to a height of 6 to 48 inches (15 to 122 centimeters) or more.

Many fescues are important as *forage* (feed for livestock). In the western United States, these grasses include *Arizona fescue, Idaho fescue,* and *green fescue. Alpine fescue* grows at high elevations from the Rocky Mountains westward.

Tall fescue is a popular forage grass in humid regions of the United States, particularly in Kentucky, Missouri, and Tennessee. Gardeners and homeowners also use it in lawns in these areas. Fine-leaved fescues, such as *sheep fescue* and *red fescue,* grow in a mat ideal for lawns.   Kay H. Asay

Scientific classification. Fescue makes up the genus *Festuca.* Arizona fescue is *Festuca arizonica.* Idaho fescue is *F. idahoensis;* green fescue, *F. viridula;* tall fescue, *F. arundinacea;* and red fescue, *F. rubra.* Both Alpine fescue and sheep fescue are *F. ovina.*

Festival. See Feasts and festivals.
Festival of Lights. See Hanukkah.
Fetal alcohol syndrome (FAS) is a severe developmental disorder caused by exposure to alcohol before birth. It is characterized by a pattern of physical and mental disorders that include growth deficiencies, facial abnormalities, and brain damage. The highest risk of FAS occurs in the babies of women who drink alcohol several days a week while pregnant and have many drinks on each occasion. Health experts recommend that women avoid all alcohol use during pregnancy.

Physicians diagnose FAS if they observe a pattern of abnormalities in association with known or suspected exposure to alcohol before birth. Symptoms of FAS include small body size and low birth weight. Babies born with FAS also have characteristic facial features. These facial features include small eyes, a thin upper lip, and an absent or indistinct *philtrum* (groove on the upper lip).

Brain damage is usually the most critical feature of FAS. The damage often results in intellectual disability, which generally ranges from mild to moderate but may be severe. Fetal alcohol exposure is associated with a wide range of behavioral problems, including delayed behavioral development, sleep disturbances, attention deficit disorder, hyperactivity, learning disabilities, and vision and hearing disorders.

There is no cure for FAS. However, FAS can be prevented by avoiding alcohol during pregnancy and encouraging others to do so. Treatment for FAS depends on the patient's age and individual disorders. Many people with FAS can achieve a normal life with proper medical care and family support.   Larry Burd

See also **Intellectual disability** (Environmental factors).

Fetish, *FEE tihsh* or *FEHT ihsh,* is an object that is believed to have magical powers or to embody or contain a powerful spirit. The term is sometimes spelled *fetich.* The objects that are treated as fetishes differ from one society to another. But many fetishes are bones, carved statues, or unusual stones. Fetishes also include a rabbit's foot or a coin believed to bring good luck.

The supposed powers of fetishes also vary among societies. For example, a people may believe that a fetish

© Odyssey Productions

Fetishes can take the form of such common objects as stones and bones. These fetishes belong to a Kikuyu shaman of Kenya. The Kikuyu believe that spirits control the fetishes and that a shaman can predict the future by tossing them.

has the power to make its owner invisible or to cure a certain type of illness. In parts of Africa, *fetishism* (the belief in fetishes) plays an important part in many traditional religions.

Psychiatrists use the term *fetish* to describe a normally nonsexual object that causes a sexual response in a certain individual. Such an object might be a lock of hair or a piece of clothing.   Edward O. Henry

See also **Superstition.**

Fetus. See **Baby** (The developing baby).

Feud is a long and sometimes murderous conflict between individuals, families, or groups. Feuds often occur in societies that lack a police force, other government law enforcement agency, or other form of central authority. They are also common in regions far from the center of authority or where central authority is hard to enforce because of rugged terrain or harsh climate. In addition, people inclined to take the law into their own hands frequently become involved in feuds. For example, feuds often occur among city youth gangs. Feuds that feature repeated bouts of violence for revenge are known as *blood feuds.*

Most feuds begin when a member of one group or family insults or harms a member of another group or family. Then members of the victim's group seek revenge. If members seek to avenge a murder, they may kill the murderer or a member of the murderer's family. One such attack leads to another, and the feud continues. Families may keep fighting for years. New acts of violence keep the feud alive. Feuding only ceases when both sides can agree on blame and forgiveness.

Many feuds have occurred in the mountains of Afghanistan; on the islands of Corsica and Sicily; and among such isolated African herding societies as the Maasai and the Nuer. Anthropologists have written about famous blood feuds among Albanians of the Balkans and Chechens of the Caucasus Mountains region. Feuds also have frequently occurred in the Appalachian Mountains of the United States. The bloody quarrel between the Hatfield and McCoy families was the most famous Appalachian feud. At least 20 people died in this conflict, which began in the 1860's and lasted about 30 years.   Russell Zanca

Feudalism is the general term used to describe the political and military system of western Europe during the Middle Ages. At that time, there was no strong central government and little security, but feudalism fulfilled the basic need for justice and protection.

Feudalism is often confused with *manorialism.* Manorialism was the system of organizing agricultural labor. Manorialism refers to the economic relationship between the lord of a manor and his peasant tenants (see **Manorialism**). But feudalism was mainly a political and military system. Both the lord and his subjects, called *vassals,* were aristocrats. The lord gave vassals land in return for military and other services. The lord and the vassals were bound through ceremonies and oaths.

The word *feudal* comes from a Latin term for *fief.* The fief was the estate or land granted by a lord in return for a vassal's loyalty and service. Some fiefs were large enough to support one knight. Others were great provinces of a kingdom, such as the province of Normandy in France. The church, which owned large fiefs, was also part of the feudal system.

In the A.D. 400's, Germanic tribes conquered the West Roman Empire and divided it into many kingdoms. The Germanic peoples were loyal only to their tribal chiefs or to their families. Their customs replaced many Roman laws, and the strong central and local governments of the Romans disappeared. Such changes and further invasions resulted in general disorder and constant warfare in the years following the fall of the West Roman Empire. Feudalism helped establish order in Europe under these conditions.

Feudalism reached its height between the 800's and 1200's, spreading from France into England, Spain, and other parts of the Christian world. But by the 1400's, it was disappearing or becoming an outdated system.

The beginnings of feudalism. Feudalism had two main roots. One was the relationship of honor among the Germanic war bands that wandered over much of Europe in the early Middle Ages. Pledging their loyalty, warriors fought for the honor of their leader and were expected to remain with him even to death. In turn, the leader was responsible for his men and rewarded them with treasures and glory.

Archives Générales du Royaume, Brussels

A knight armed for battle in the 1200's carried a cross-hilted sword and a kite-shaped shield. His helmet completely covered his head. Other knights could identify him only by his heraldic symbol. The symbol of the Flemish lion that appears on the shield and horse's coverlet in this seal identifies the knight as Guy de Dampierre, the Count of Flanders.

The second main root of feudalism was the system of *tenure* (landholding). Under this system, a lord would grant land to a person on certain conditions or in return for services other than rent or payment. People who owned land might turn it over to a lord in return for protection. The lord allowed peasants to stay on the land as tenants. Although the peasants lost their independence, the protection of a powerful local lord was more important. The system of tenure was already in use in the former provinces of the Roman Empire when the Germanic invaders settled there in the A.D. 400's.

By the 700's, the Islamic Empire had spread from Africa to Spain, and it threatened parts of Europe. Kings and important nobles began giving fiefs to free and noble warriors in return for military service. These fiefs included land, the buildings on it, and the peasants who lived and worked on it. The warriors who received the fiefs were called *vassals,* from a Latin word meaning *military retainer.* By the 800's, the relationship of honor and loyalty that existed between leader and warrior in the Germanic war bands was combined with a system for holding land and providing services in exchange. This combination was feudalism.

The principles of feudalism. Only noblemen or aristocratic warriors could take part in feudal practices. A saying of the time stated, "No land without a lord, and no lord without land." A man became a vassal of the lord in a ceremony called *homage.* The future vassal promised to be loyal, fight for the lord, and become the lord's man *(homo* in Latin). The lord promised to treat the vassal with honor. See **Homage.**

After performing homage, the new vassal was *invested with* (given the rights to) his fief. This was done in an *investiture* ceremony. At the ceremony, the lord often gave his vassal a clod of dirt, a stick, or some other such object as a symbol of the fief.

The vassal received only the use or possession of the fief, not ownership of it. He held the fief in return for services he had promised. As long as the vassal held the fief, he received what the land—and the peasants—produced, collected taxes, held court, administered justice, and managed the peasants' labor. When the vassal died, his son usually took over the fief. The son provided the same services as his father.

By 1100, it had become the custom for a man's oldest son to inherit the fief. This custom was called *primogeniture* (the right of the first-born). Primogeniture ensured that the fief would not be broken up among many sons and that one heir would assume responsibility for the services to the lord. See **Primogeniture.**

If a vassal died without heirs, the fief *escheated* (went back) to the lord. The lord could then grant it to another person as he wished. If the dead vassal's heir was a young child, the lord had the right of *wardship* and became the protector of the *ward* (child). The lord could grant the wardship to another vassal, who held the fief and its profits until the young heir came of age. In many cases, the lord also had a right to choose marriage partners for his wards and for the daughters or widows of his vassal. If a woman inherited a fief, her husband performed homage and became the lord's vassal. Such rights of the lord were called feudal *incidents.* They were sources of power and profit for the lord.

The lord had other rights called *aids.* All vassals had to make a special payment when the lord's oldest son was knighted and when his oldest daughter married. If the lord was captured and held for ransom, the vassals had to pay the ransom. But feudal aids and rights were limited. For example, a lord could not require new conditions or levy higher taxes on his vassals. The lord also was supposed to consult his vassals before making major decisions, such as whether or not to go to war.

Knighthood under feudalism. A vassal's main service to his lord was military. By the 700's, vassals had to supply a certain number of knights to serve the lord for a certain number of days, usually 40. Knights were armored warriors on war horses. The larger the fief held by a vassal, the more knights the vassal had to provide.

It became the custom for a vassal to divide his own fief and distribute parts of it to his knights. The knights then became his vassals. This practice of dividing fiefs was called *subinfeudation.* By the 1200's, it had developed so far that several layers of feudal relations might separate a knight at the bottom from a baron or a king. At each level, a noble was both lord and vassal.

Justice under feudalism. Quarrels among vassals were settled at the lord's *court,* which consisted of all the vassals. Many of the legal customs developed at the feudal court have become part of the legal systems of the United Kingdom and the United States. For example, the lord presided over feudal courts. In courts today, a judge presides. A vassal received judgment from other vassals who were his *peers* (social equals). Today, citizens receive judgment from their peers on a jury. Other judicial customs of feudal days have disappeared. One such custom was *trial by combat,* which involved a fight between the vassals involved in a dispute. The winner of the fight was also declared the winner of the case. It was accepted that God gave victory to the honest vassal or correct side.

A vassal had to answer the *summons* (order to appear) of a feudal court. If the vassal failed to appear or did not obey the court's decision, the lord could take back the vassal's fief. A rebellious vassal was declared a *felon.*

The lord was expected to seek the advice and consent of his vassals before making laws. In time, this practice led to the idea that no ruler can make laws without the consent of the people being governed. Modern parliaments in Europe developed from the meetings of vassals summoned by a lord or a king.

The decline of feudalism. By the 1200's, several events in Europe led to the decline of feudalism. An economic revival put more money back into use. Because soldiers could be paid, fewer lords relied on vassals to provide the services of knights. The invention of gunpowder and of such weapons as the longbow and the cannon lessened the dominance of knights. Stone castles occupied by feudal lords no longer could stand against cannons. Cities grew wealthier and became more important, and rulers had less need of the aristocracy. People trained in government service took over the functions that vassals had performed on their fiefs.

Joel T. Rosenthal

Related articles in *World Book* include:

Castle	Manorialism
Freedom (The Middle Ages)	Middle Ages
Homage	Primogeniture
Knights and knighthood	Serf
Law (The Middle Ages)	

Feuerbach, *FOY uhr bahk,* **Ludwig Andreas,** *LOOT vihk ahn DRAY uhs* (1804-1872), was a German philosopher. He studied under the German philosopher G. W. F. Hegel. He later turned away from Hegel's philosophical idealism and stressed the scientific study of humanity.

In *Thoughts on Death and Immortality* (1830), Feuerbach challenged Christian teachings. But he actually placed a high value on religion. He thought it expressed humanity's idea of its true essence. Feuerbach presented this idea in his major work, *The Essence of Christianity* (1841). He argued that although religion portrays human creativity as if it depends on God, God is really the projection of an ideal image of humanity's capacities.

Feuerbach also believed that philosophers, such as Hegel, had an excessively abstract view of human nature. He believed that they had missed the significance of concrete physical experience. Feuerbach's ideas influenced Karl Marx, the German social philosopher who founded revolutionary Communism. But Marx attacked him for merely criticizing views of the human condition, rather than acting directly to improve it. Feuerbach was born on July 28, 1804, in Landshut. He died on Sept. 13, 1872.   Karl Ameriks

Fever is a condition in which the brain maintains the body temperature at a higher than normal level. Fever is one of the most common symptoms of disease. When fever is the primary symptom, it may be part of the disease's name, such as in *scarlet fever* or *yellow fever.*

Not every rise in body temperature is a fever. For example, sitting in a sauna can produce an above-normal body temperature. But in this case, unlike what happens in a fever, the brain instructs the body to lower its temperature by sweating and increasing skin blood flow,

and the individual feels the urge to be in a cool place.

Fever results when an infection or an allergic or toxic reaction causes the brain's temperature setting to rise. For example, after a flu virus enters the human body, the body releases proteins called *endogenous pyrogens* or *leukocyte pyrogens.* These proteins trigger the release of certain chemicals in the *hypothalamus,* the part of the brain mainly responsible for regulating body temperature. The chemicals, called *prostaglandins,* act on nerve cells to produce a sensation of coldness. This sensation causes the hypothalamus to raise body temperature by making the body burn fat, decrease skin blood flow, shiver, and develop an urge to stay warm. *Antipyretic drugs,* such as aspirin and acetaminophen, reduce fever by slowing prostaglandin production.

Research has shown that fevers speed up the body's defenses against invading viruses and bacteria. Because fever can help fight infection, some medical experts advise against reducing a moderate fever. In human beings, normal body temperature ranges from about 98 to 99 °F (36.7 to 37.2 °C), depending on the individual and the time of day. A moderate fever generally ranges from 100 to 102 °F (37.7 to 38.9 °C). Most experts agree that fevers probably should be reduced if they rise above 102 °F (38.9 °C), or if they occur in pregnant women, people with heart disease, or the elderly. It is wise to consult a doctor when deciding how to handle a fever.

Fever occurs in all *vertebrates* (animals with backbones) and in many *invertebrates* (animals without backbones). It first appeared at least 300 million years ago as a way to fight disease. In warm-blooded vertebrates—that is, birds and mammals—fever results from physiological and behavioral changes. Cold-blooded vertebrates, such as fish and reptiles—and such invertebrates as grasshoppers and scorpions—achieve fevers by moving into the heat, where they can maintain a high body temperature.   Matthew J. Kluger

Fever blister. See Cold sore; Herpes, Genital.

Feverfew is a bushy plant native to Europe. It can grow 3 feet (90 centimeters) high. Its leaves have a strong scent when crushed. Small, white, daisylike flowers come up in late summer. People once used the flowers to cure fever and other ailments.   James E. Simon

Scientific classification. The feverfew's scientific name is *Tanacetum parthenium.*

Few, William (1748-1828), a lawyer, judge, and banker, was a Georgia signer of the Constitution of the United States. At the Constitutional Convention of 1787, Few supported the establishment of a strong national government. He later helped win *ratification* (approval) of the Constitution by Georgia.

Few was born on June 8, 1748, near Baltimore. He was largely self-educated. In 1776, Few moved to Georgia and became a lawyer. He was elected to the Georgia General Assembly in 1777, 1779, 1783, and 1793. Few was a member of the Second Continental Congress and the Congress of the Confederation from 1780 to 1788. He served in the U.S. Senate from 1789 to 1793. From 1796 to 1799, Few was a judge of the U.S. Circuit Court. He served in the New York State Legislature from 1802 to 1805. Few later became president of City Bank of New York. He died on July 16, 1828.   Joan R. Gundersen

Feynman, *FYN muhn,* **Richard Phillips** (1918-1988), an American physicist, shared the 1965 Nobel Prize in

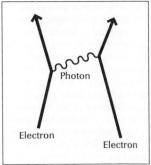

A Feynman diagram provides a simple way to picture complex interactions between elementary particles. In this diagram, two negatively charged *electrons* push away from each other by exchanging a *photon,* a particle of light.

WORLD BOOK illustration

physics with Julian S. Schwinger of the United States and Sin-Itiro Tomonaga of Japan. Working independently, the three men developed an improved theory of *quantum electrodynamics* (QED) in the late 1940's. QED is the study of the interaction of electrically charged *subatomic particles* (pieces of matter smaller than atoms) and electromagnetic radiation, such as light. Feynman also developed a method of using diagrams to picture elementary particle interactions. *Feynman diagrams* became a standard calculation tool in physics because they simplify the difficult calculations of a field of study called *quantum field theory.* See **Quantum field theory.**

Feynman was born on May 11, 1918, in Far Rockaway, a suburb of New York City. He earned a Ph.D. degree from Princeton University in New Jersey in 1942. From 1942 to 1945, he worked on the atomic bomb project, first at Princeton and then at Los Alamos, New Mexico. Feynman became a professor of theoretical physics at Cornell University in Ithaca, New York, in 1945. He served on the faculty of the California Institute of Technology in Pasadena from 1950 until his death in 1988. Feynman told of his experiences in *Surely You're Joking, Mr. Feynman!* (1985). Feynman served on the presidential commission that investigated the 1986 accident that destroyed the space shuttle Challenger. He died on Feb. 15, 1988. Matthew Stanley

Fez, also spelled *Fès* (pop. 946,815), is the religious center of Morocco and one of its traditional capitals. It boasts the Mosque of Mulai Idrīs, a noted Muslim shrine. Karaouiyine University, one of the world's oldest universities, was founded in Fez in 859.

Fez lies in the deep valley of the Fez River in northern Morocco (see **Morocco** [map]). Railroads connect it with other cities in North Africa. Fez is noted for its silk, woolen, and leather goods. The Arab ruler Idrīs II founded Fez as his capital in 808. The city declined in the 1600's, when Sultan Ismail built his palace in Meknès. But it again became the capital from 1728 until the French occupation of Morocco in 1912.

Kenneth J. Perkins

Fez is a tall, red, brimless cap with a colored tassel of silk or wool. It is worn in Egypt and in North Africa, where it is sometimes called a *tarboosh.* All fezzes were once colored with a dye made from the juice of red berries found only in Morocco. This same color can now be produced by chemical dyes. The fez was first made in Fez, Morocco. Lois M. Gurel

FFA is a youth organization that promotes agricultural education in the United States. The organization helps students in grades 7 through 12 prepare for careers in farming, agricultural science, *agribusiness* (business involving agriculture), and other fields. In addition, it trains them to become responsible citizens and leaders. FFA forms part of the agricultural education program in a number of U.S. public schools. The organization was established in 1928 as Future Farmers of America. In 1988, it changed its name to the National FFA Organization.

FFA has thousands of school chapters in the United States, Puerto Rico, and the Virgin Islands. A school must have a full-time agriculture teacher before it can form an FFA chapter. Only students who are studying agriculture may become members of the organization. Students may continue their membership for three years after they leave high school, or until they reach the age of 21, whichever is longer.

The FFA emblem features an owl, a plow, and a rising sun within the cross section of an ear of corn. An American eagle appears above the design. The owl represents wisdom and knowledge, and the plow stands for labor and tilling the soil. The rising sun symbolizes each new day of progress in agriculture. The corn stands for the agricultural interests of all FFA members. The eagle is a symbol of national freedom and the ability to explore new horizons.

FFA members wear distinctive blue corduroy jackets. The emblems and names on the jackets are embroidered in gold and blue, the FFA colors. FFA operates a merchandising unit that sells FFA clothing, jewelry, and other items. The organization also publishes *New Horizons,* a quarterly magazine for its members. In addition, FFA releases *Making a Difference,* a monthly e-mail newsletter for agriculture teachers.

The National FFA Organization has headquarters in Alexandria, Virginia. Its business center is in Indianapolis. The organization's website at http://www.ffa.org presents information on its activities.

What FFA members do

Training. Each FFA member carries out a project over several years called a *supervised agricultural experience* (SAE) program. Through SAE programs, members put into practice the knowledge gained in agriculture classes. Members usually begin with a small program and then increase the scope of the program as they advance in their classroom work. An FFA adviser works with each student to supervise and help with the program. Members pursue programs in such areas as agricultural production, food science, forestry, agriculture sales and service, and *horticulture* (the science of growing flowers, fruits, vegetables, and plants).

FFA chapters often help members launch their programs. In some areas, an FFA chapter or a school may own a farm or greenhouse where members can work on their

FFA emblem

FFA activities help students prepare for careers in farming, agricultural science, and other fields. FFA members may visit a greenhouse, *shown here,* to examine plants and work on special projects.

National FFA Organization

programs. The organization encourages members to expand their programs so that, by the time they complete high school, they will be prepared to enter the work force or to pursue further education.

FFA members investigate career opportunities in various fields related to agriculture. They study such subjects as farm economics, marketing, computer science, and biotechnology. In addition, they learn how to keep accurate financial records. With their teachers, members visit agribusinesses and agricultural experiment stations to observe the development of new agricultural methods. FFA also teaches members how to select, use, care for, and repair various types of equipment.

Through participation in chapter meetings, FFA members develop public speaking skills and learn to work with others for the benefit of the community. FFA officials recommend that chapters meet at least once a month.

Activities. FFA members compete in local, state, and national contests and award programs. National contests are held in such fields as public speaking, agricultural mechanics, dairy cattle judging, livestock judging, poultry judging, dairy foods evaluation, meat evaluation, farm business management, forestry, and nursery skills and landscaping. Students also participate in competitions involving business and marketing skills.

Local FFA chapters sponsor recreational activities, organize educational tours, and conduct safety campaigns and home-improvement projects. They sometimes organize and manage community fairs. The chapters also hold annual parent-member banquets.

Degrees. FFA awards its members various degrees for their achievements in agricultural projects, community service, cooperation, leadership, and scholarship. The *Discovery* degree may be granted to students based

on knowledge gained in seventh- and eighth-grade agricultural education programs. The *Greenhand* degree is for FFA members in their first year of high school. To earn the degree, members must demonstrate knowledge of FFA, its goals, and its history. After completing at least two semesters of agricultural course work, students become eligible to receive the *Chapter FFA* degree. Most FFA members receive the Chapter FFA degree. Once they earn it, they may wear a silver FFA pin.

The *State FFA* degree is much more difficult to attain. State FFA associations award this degree for outstanding achievement in agricultural career development, leadership, and scholarship. They present it at annual state conventions. A person who receives the degree

Purposes of FFA

1. To develop competent and assertive agricultural leadership.
2. To increase awareness of the global and technological importance of agriculture and its contribution to our well-being.
3. To strengthen the confidence of agriculture students in themselves and their work.
4. To promote the intelligent choice and establishment of an agricultural career.
5. To encourage achievement in supervised agricultural experience programs.
6. To encourage wise management of economic, environmental, and human resources of the community.
7. To develop interpersonal skills in teamwork, communications, human relations, and social interaction.
8. To build character and promote citizenship, volunteerism, and patriotism.
9. To promote cooperation and cooperative attitudes among all people.
10. To promote healthy lifestyles.
11. To encourage excellence in scholarship.

must have worked at least 300 unpaid hours, or earned a specified amount of money and invested it productively. Members who have earned the State FFA degree wear a gold emblem pin.

The *American FFA* degree is the highest FFA degree. The National FFA Organization presents it each year to members nominated by the state associations. To qualify for the degree, a person must have earned a certain amount of money through SAE programs or earned a smaller amount and worked 2,250 hours outside class. In addition, the person must demonstrate outstanding leadership and community involvement. To encourage students to maintain their interest in agriculture, only FFA members who have been out of high school for at least one year may be nominated. Each person who earns the American FFA degree receives a gold key and partial travel expenses to the national convention.

FFA also presents honorary degrees to men and women who perform exceptional service to the organization. These individuals receive *Honorary Chapter, State,* or *American FFA* degrees and pins.

Awards encourage FFA members to do better work in areas ranging from farm business management to computer technology. The National FFA Foundation, Inc., sponsors numerous proficiency awards for FFA members, including awards for agricultural mechanics, agricultural processing, agricultural sales and service, horticulture, natural resources, and production agriculture. The foundation presents four Star Farmer and four Star Agribusiness awards each year to outstanding candidates for the American FFA degree. Other national awards are made for group achievements in chapter activities and to winners of the national FFA public speaking contest.

State FFA associations present awards at state conventions. Local chapters award medals to outstanding members during parent-member banquets or at special school assemblies. Chapters offer awards in such fields as agricultural communications, food science and technology, horticulture, wildlife management, and safety.

Organization

FFA operates on local, state, and national levels. Student members belong to chapters organized at local schools. Agricultural instructors serve as chapter advisers. Chapters are organized under state associations. Each state association is headed by a state adviser and an executive secretary. The state associations are chartered by the National FFA Organization.

The National FFA Organization provides direction, materials, and support for the state associations. It also hosts a national convention every year. Delegates at the convention elect a president, a secretary, and four vice presidents. The four vice presidents represent the Central region, the Eastern region, the Southern region, and the Western region of FFA. The main governing body of the National FFA Organization is the board of directors. The board consists of the national FFA adviser, who serves as chairperson; state supervisors of agricultural education; and staff members of the U.S. Department of Education.

The National FFA Foundation, Inc., organized in 1944, collects donations from businesses to support FFA programs and activities. The National Alumni Association,

formed in 1971, coordinates volunteer activities and promotes the development of FFA programs.

History

In 1917, Congress passed the Smith-Hughes Act, which gave the federal government the power to establish a national program of vocational education. It also permitted the government to pay half the cost of a vocational agriculture program in each state. The government now pays only about a sixth of the cost. The states and local communities pay the rest. A Federal Board for Vocational Education administered the Smith-Hughes Act at first. Later, the Department of Health, Education, and Welfare took over the management of the program. In 1980, the program was transferred to the newly created Department of Education.

In the early 1920's, vocational agriculture students formed clubs in many communities around the country. In some states, local clubs joined in statewide associations. One of these state associations—the Future Farmers of Virginia, founded in 1925—became the model for FFA. In November 1928, 33 representatives from 18 state associations met in Kansas City, Missouri. They adopted a constitution and founded Future Farmers of America, which would later become known as FFA. Congress granted the organization a federal charter in 1950.

In 1955, FFA began a program to promote international understanding. Since then, it has offered international exchange programs and helped promote agricultural education in a number of countries. In 1965, FFA joined with the New Farmers of America, an organization for African American agriculture students. In 1969, FFA delegates voted to allow girls to become FFA members. Formerly, only boys could join.

Critically reviewed by the National FFA Organization

Related articles in *World Book* include:

Agricultural education	Agricultural experiment station	Fair
	Agriculture	Farm and farming
		4-H

FHA. See Federal Housing Administration.

Fiat, *FY uht, FY at,* or *FEE aht,* in government, is an executive order or decree that requires obedience but is not a law. Many legal scholars consider a fiat to be an order that is issued for purposes other than to carry out legislation. Such orders sometimes come into conflict with one or more laws. In many cases, these conflicts are resolved by the courts. The term *fiat* comes from Latin. Its Latin meaning is *let it be done.*   Anthony D'Amato

See also Executive order.

Fiber is a hairlike strand of a substance that is extremely long in relation to its width. A fiber is at least 100 times longer than it is wide. Fibers are flexible and may be spun into yarn and made into fabrics. A fiber is the smallest visible unit of any textile product. Manufacturers use fibers in clothing and in such home furnishings as carpets, drapes, and upholstery. They also use fibers in many industrial products, including parachutes, fire hoses, insulation, and tires. In medicine, fibers are used to make artificial arteries and tendons.

Some fibers occur in nature, and others are manufactured. Most natural fibers come from plants and animals. These fibers include cotton, flax, silk, and wool. There are two types of manufactured fibers. *Regenerated fibers* come from natural materials, but manufacturers must process the materials to form a fiber structure. *Synthetic fibers* are made entirely from chemicals.

No one knows when human beings learned to spin natural fibers into yarn to make fabrics. The earliest evidence of fabric is a fragment of linen found in what is now southern Turkey, dated between 8000 and 7000 B.C. Wool fabrics date from about 6000 B.C. Cotton was first used about 3000 B.C. The Chinese discovered silk about 2640 B.C. Rayon, the first practical manufactured fiber, was developed in 1884. See **Textile** (History).

All natural fibers but silk range from about ½ inch to 8 inches (1.3 to 20 centimeters) long. A silk fiber's length depends on the size of the silkworm's cocoon. Fibers of limited length are called *staple fibers*. Textile mills spin these fibers into yarn. Manufactured fibers have no limit in length. Machines produce them in long, continuous strands called *continuous filaments*. Manufacturers may use a single filament to make a *monofilament* yarn. They may also *draw* (pull) many filaments together to produce one *multifilament* yarn. When manufacturers blend synthetic fibers with natural ones, they must first cut the synthetic fibers into staple lengths.

The properties of a fiber depend on its chemical composition and physical structure. Manufacturers use fibers that have properties suited to their products. For example, fibers used in clothing must feel pleasant to the touch, be water absorbent, have a good luster, and drape to fit the body. For industrial use, a fiber's strength and durability are important. One fiber, SPECTRA-900, is 10 times stronger than steel. Another class of fibers, *spandex,* can stretch like rubber.

Natural fibers

Natural fibers come mainly from plants and animals. They account for more than half the fibers produced in the world yearly.

Plant fibers. *Cotton* is the most widely used natural fiber. Cotton mills spin staple fibers from cotton *bolls* (seed pods) into yarns for clothing, and for household and industrial fabrics. Cotton cloth is absorbent, soft, and comfortable to wear. *Flax,* a strong fiber from the stems of flax plants, is used to make clothing and linen products. *Hemp, jute,* and *sisal* are coarse plant fibers used in cords, ropes, and rough fabrics.

Science Photo Library from Photo Researchers © Michael Abbey, Photo Researchers

Wool and nylon fibers show the difference between organic and synthetic fibers. Organic wool fibers, *left,* have a scaly structure similar to human hair. Synthetic nylon fibers, *right,* have a smooth surface that makes them resistant to wear.

Animal fibers include fur and hair. *Wool,* the hair of sheep and certain other animals, is popular in clothing and home furnishings. Wool fibers have a scalelike surface that resembles shingles on a roof. Manufacturers mat wool fibers together in a process known as *felting.* This process produces air pockets within the matted fibers. Air trapped in these pockets acts as an insulator that helps keep the wearer warm. Silk is the strongest natural fiber. Manufacturers unwind silk filaments from silkworm cocoons and make silk yarn for clothing and decorative fabrics.

Manufactured fibers

The study of plastics has helped chemists learn how to combine chemicals to create synthetic *polymers* (long, chainlike molecules) with specific properties, including the ability to be shaped into fibers. The variety and qualities of manufactured fibers make them popular with consumers and manufacturers. See **Textile** (Manufactured fibers).

Machines melt synthetic polymers or mix them in *solvents* (substances that dissolve other substances) to create a liquid. The machines then force streams of the liquid through tiny holes in a device called a *spinneret.* The streams harden into filament fibers that are drawn and wound onto spools or cut into staple lengths.

Regenerated fibers are also known as *cellulosics* because they are derived from *cellulose,* a polymer in plant cells. Manufacturers process wood pulp to make such cellulosics as rayon. Rayon has many properties that resemble those of cotton. Using a production method called *acetylation,* manufacturers chemically convert cellulose to produce *acetate,* a fiber silkier than rayon. Rayon and acetate are used in clothing. Manufacturers use industrial versions of rayon to make yarns for tires.

Synthetic fibers are manufactured from chemicals. Most are stronger than either natural or regenerated fibers. Synthetic fibers, as well as the regenerated fiber acetate, are *thermoplastic* (softened by heat). Manufacturers shape these fibers at high temperatures, adding such features as pleats and creases. These fibers will melt if touched with too hot an iron. The most widely used kinds of synthetic fibers are (1) nylon fibers, (2) polyester fibers, (3) acrylic fibers, and (4) olefin fibers.

Nylon fibers, or *polyamide* fibers, were the first synthetic fibers. Fabrics made from strong, lightweight nylon fibers are used in such products as windbreakers and tents. Nylon fibers are also widely used in carpets, hosiery, and ropes.

Polyester fibers are durable and quickly regain their shape after being stretched or wrinkled. They are used in clothing and bedding. Many garments contain a blend of polyester and cotton fibers. The polyester fibers provide wash-and-wear characteristics, and the cotton fibers make the fabrics comfortable to wear. Manufacturers also use polyester fibers in filters, sails, tires, and other industrial fabrics.

Acrylic fibers are soft and durable. A number of acrylic yarns resemble wool and are used in clothing, especially sweaters. Many artificial furs also are made from acrylic fibers.

Olefin fibers are strong and resist stains. These properties make olefin fibers useful in carpets, upholstery, and ropes.

Other synthetic fibers. Yarns called *Lastex* are made from synthetic elastic fibers wrapped in cotton, nylon, or other fibers. Lastex and spandex enable garments to hold their shape and return to their original size after being stretched. Special metal treatments produce *metallic fibers,* such as gold and silver filaments, that can be used to decorate fabrics.   Richard Kotek

Related articles in *World Book* include:

Natural fibers

Abacá	Flax	Kapok	Sisal
Asbestos	Hemp	Ramie	Wool
Cotton	Jute	Silk	

Manufactured fibers

Acetate	Fiberglass	Nylon	Rayon
Acrylic	Microfiber	Polyester	Spandex
Aramid			

Other related articles

Agriculture	Cellulose	Palm	Thread
(Raw ma-	Linen	Plastics	Wallboard
terials)	Mohair	Textile	

Fiber, Dietary, refers to a variety of edible plant materials that normally pass undigested through the body. Fiber, sometimes called *roughage,* helps in the healthy functioning of the stomach and intestines. Good sources of fiber include beans, bran, cabbage and other leafy vegetables, fruits, nuts, and whole-grain bread.

Dietary fibers are mainly complex carbohydrates, such as cellulose and pectin. These substances regulate the time it takes for food to empty from the stomach and pass through the intestines. Fiber increases the weight of *stools* (solid waste matter) by absorbing and retaining water. The increase in stool bulk can help relieve constipation and diarrhea.

Researchers believe that a high-fiber diet can help prevent *diverticulosis,* a common disorder of the *colon* (part of the large intestine). In this disorder, small pouches called *diverticula* stick out along the surface of the colon. Diverticulosis may lead to *diverticulitis,* a disease in which the pouches become inflamed and cause pain, infection, and bleeding. Diverticula often develop when waste material becomes hard and compact and cannot move easily through the colon. The resulting pressure can force the inner membrane of the colon to bulge out through the organ's lining. Fiber softens waste material and thus prevents diverticula from forming. Evidence also indicates that fruits and vegetables, which are good sources of fiber in the diet, may reduce the risk of cancer of the colon.   John A. Schaffner

See also **Diverticulitis.**

Fiber optics is a branch of physics based on the transmission of light through transparent fibers of glass or plastic. These *optical fibers* can carry light over distances ranging from a few inches or centimeters to more than 100 miles (160 kilometers). Such fibers work individually or in bundles. Some individual fibers measure less than 0.00015 inch (0.004 millimeter) in diameter —thinner than a human hair.

Optical fibers have a highly transparent core of glass or plastic surrounded by a covering called a *cladding.* Light impulses from a laser, a light bulb, or some other source enter one end of the optical fiber. As light travels through the core, the cladding typically keeps it inside. The cladding is designed to bend or reflect—inward—

light rays that strike its inside surface. At the other end of the fiber, a detector, such as a photosensitive device or the human eye, receives the light.

Kinds of optical fibers. The two basic kinds of optical fibers are *single-mode fibers* and *multi-mode fibers.* Single-mode fibers are used for high-speed long-distance transmissions. They have extremely small cores, and they accept light only along the axis of the fibers. Tiny lasers send light directly into the fiber. Low-loss connectors may be used to join fibers within the system without significantly degrading the light signal. Such connectors also join fibers to the detector. Multi-mode fibers have much larger cores than those of single-mode fibers, and they accept light from a variety of angles. Multi-mode fibers can use more types of light sources and cheaper connectors than can single-mode fibers, but they cannot be used over long distances.

Uses of optical fibers. Optical fibers have a number of uses. Industries use them to measure temperature, pressure, acceleration, and voltage. In fiber-optic communication systems, lasers transmit messages in *digital* (numeric) code by flashing on and off at high speeds. Such a code may represent a voice, or an electronic file containing text, numbers, or illustrations. The light from many lasers can be added together onto a single fiber. This enables thousands of "streams" of data to pass through a single fiber-optic cable at one time. The data travel to interpreting devices that convert the messages back into the form of the original signals.

Corning Glass Works

An optical fiber thin enough to hold between two fingers can transmit several times as much data as a large cable of wires.

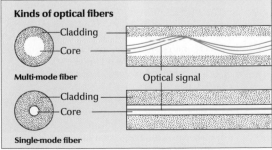

WORLD BOOK diagram by Zorica Dabich

The two kinds of optical fibers are *multi-mode fiber,* which has a big core and lets light travel along many paths, and *single-mode fiber,* which has a small core and provides only one path.

Fiber-optic communication systems have a number of features that make them superior to systems that use traditional copper cables. Besides having a much larger information-carrying capacity, they are not bothered by electrical interference and require fewer amplifiers than copper-cable systems of equal length. Many communication companies have installed large networks of fiber-optic cables across the continents and under the oceans.

Optical fibers are well-suited for medical use. They can be made in extremely thin, flexible strands for insertion into the blood vessels, lungs, and other hollow parts of the body. Optical fibers enable physicians to look and work inside the body through tiny incisions. Instruments called *endoscopes* carry two bundles of optical fibers inside a long tube. One bundle directs light at the tissue being examined. The other transmits light reflected from the tissue, producing a detailed image. Endoscopes may be designed to look into specific areas. For example, physicians use an *arthroscope* to examine knees, shoulders, and other joints (see **Arthroscopy**).

Optical fibers also can be used to measure temperature and other bodily properties. They can be inserted into blood vessels to give a quick, accurate analysis of blood chemistry. Another medical use is to direct intense laser light that stops bleeding or burns away abnormal tissue.   Nathan M. Denkin

See also **Communication** (picture: Fiber-optic communication); **Laser; Telecommunications; Telephone** (How a telephone call travels).

Fiberboard. See Wallboard.

Fiberglass, also called *fibrous glass,* is glass in the form of fine *fibers* (threads). The fibers may be many times finer than human hair, and may look and feel like silk. The flexible glass fibers are stronger than steel, and will not burn, stretch, rot, or fade.

Uses. Manufacturers use fiberglass to make a variety of products. It is woven into cloth for such products as curtains and tablecloths. The cloth will not wrinkle or soil easily, and it needs no ironing. Fiberglass textiles are also used for electrical insulation. In bulk form, it is used for air filters and for heat and sound insulation. Air trapped between the fibers makes it a good insulator.

Fiberglass reinforced plastics are extremely strong and light in weight. They can be molded, shaped, twisted, and poured for many different uses. Manufacturers use them to make automobile bodies, boat hulls, building panels, fishing rods, and aircraft parts. The fibers used to strengthen plastic may be woven or matted together, or they may be individual strands.

How fiberglass is made. Fiberglass is made from sand and other raw materials used to make ordinary glass (see **Glass** [Composition of glass]). Strands of fiberglass may be made in different ways. In one method, the raw materials are heated and formed into small glass marbles so workers can examine them for impurities. The marbles are then melted in special electric furnaces. The melted glass runs down through tiny holes at the bottom of the furnace. A spinning drum catches the fibers of hot glass and winds them on bobbins, like threads on spools. Because the drum revolves much faster than the glass flows, tension pulls the fibers and draws them out into still finer strands. The drum can pull out 2 miles (3.2 kilometers) of fibers in a minute. Up

to 95 miles (153 kilometers) of fiber can be drawn from one marble ⅝ inch (16 millimeters) in diameter. The fiber can be twisted together into yarns and cords. The yarns may be woven into cloth, tape, and other kinds of fabrics. In another method, called the *direct melt process,* the marble-making steps are omitted.

Bulk fiberglass, also called *fiberglass wool,* is made somewhat differently. Sand and other raw materials are melted in a furnace. The melted glass flows from tiny holes in the furnace. Then high-pressure jets of steam catch it and draw it into fine fibers from 8 to 15 inches (20 to 38 centimeters) long. The fibers are gathered on a conveyor belt in the form of a white woollike mass.

History. The Egyptians used coarse glass fibers for decorative purposes before the time of Christ. Edward Drummond Libbey, an American glass manufacturer, exhibited a dress made of fiberglass and silk at the Columbian Exposition in Chicago in 1893. During World War I (1914-1918), fiberglass was made in Germany as a substitute for asbestos. During the 1930's, the Owens Illinois Glass Company (now called Owens-Illinois, Inc.) and the Corning Glass Works developed practical methods of making fiberglass commercially.   Richard F. Blewitt

Fibonacci, *FEE boh NAHT chee,* **Leonardo,** *LAY oh NAHR doh* (1170?- ?), an Italian mathematician, helped introduce into Western Europe the system of numerals still widely used today. This system is known as the *Hindu-Arabic numeral system* (see **Arabic numerals**). He was known during his time as Leonardo of Pisa.

Around 1192, Fibonacci went to northern Africa with his father, a merchant from Pisa. There, he learned Arabic and studied the mathematical knowledge of the Islamic world, which in many ways surpassed that of Europe. In 1202, after returning to Pisa, he wrote *Liber Abbaci,* often translated as *Book of Calculation.* The book explained Hindu-Arabic numerals and Islamic algebra to Europeans. Around 1225, Fibonacci wrote *Liber Quadratorum,* often translated as *Book of Squares.* It deals with number theory and the properties of *squares,* numbers equal to another number multiplied by itself.

Fibonacci is best known today for a famous sequence of numbers—1, 1, 2, 3, 5, 8, 13, and so on—in which each number equals the sum of the two numbers before it. Fibonacci introduced this sequence in a problem involving rabbits, but mathematicians have found use for it in many branches of mathematics.   Victor J. Katz

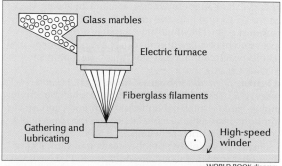

WORLD BOOK diagram

Fiberglass is often made by melting glass marbles in a furnace. The melted glass flows through tiny holes at the bottom of the furnace and comes out as fine filaments. The filaments are then gathered together, lubricated, and wound around a reel.

Fibrillation. See Heart (Abnormal heart rhythms).

Fibrin, FY bruhn, is a white, fibrous protein substance that makes up the most important part of a blood clot. Fibrin is formed from *fibrinogen,* a protein found in the blood. When a blood vessel is damaged, a series of chemical reactions causes fibrinogen to *coagulate* (thicken) into strings of fibrin that form a mesh at the site of the damage. Red blood cells and cells called *platelets* combine with the fibrin to form a clot. In addition, clots may form inside a blood vessel and stop the flow of blood through it. Such clots can lead to heart attacks, strokes, and other life-endangering conditions.

Richard H. Dean

Fibromyalgia, FY broh my AL jee uh, is a condition in which people experience long-lasting, severe pain in muscles and other soft tissues throughout their bodies. Patients with fibromyalgia also have places on their bodies called *tender points* that are unusually sensitive. Physicians test for tender points by pressing firmly where the points are known to occur. Fibromyalgia patients feel pain from an amount of pressure that would not seem uncomfortable to people without the disorder.

In addition to pain and tenderness, most fibromyalgia patients experience fatigue and sleep problems. Headaches and abdominal pain are also common symptoms. Many patients report feeling anxious, depressed, or stressed. The disorder usually occurs in people in their 30's or 40's. It affects more women than men.

There is no laboratory test, X ray, or other procedure that proves conclusively that a person has fibromyalgia. Doctors usually diagnose the condition by taking a careful history of symptoms and determining that a patient has tender points.

Experts disagree about the cause of fibromyalgia. Some doctors believe that the condition arises chiefly due to mood disorders. These experts think that stress, depression, or worries disturb sleep. Troubled sleep then increases sensitivity to pain, possibly by changing the balance of messenger chemicals in the brain and nervous system. Two messenger chemicals that may be involved are *serotonin* and *norepinephrine.* Other doctors think that an imbalance of messenger chemicals occurs first. The imbalance then leads to altered moods, sleeplessness, pain, tenderness, and other symptoms.

Treatment of fibromyalgia almost always includes an exercise program. Exercise decreases pain sensitivity and improves physical fitness. Doctors often prescribe drugs called *antidepressants*, which reduce pain, restore sleep, and improve mood. Physicians may also suggest pain-relieving drugs. Because stress and depression may cause fibromyalgia or make it worse, psychological treatment may help relieve symptoms.

David S. Pisetsky

Fichte, FIHK tuh, **Johann Gottlieb,** YOH hahn GAWT leep (1762-1814), was a German philosopher. He strongly influenced German metaphysics, aesthetics, and social thought. In addition, Fichte influenced the ideas of philosophers Friedrich Schelling and G. W. F. Hegel.

Fichte was a follower of the idealism of German philosopher Immanuel Kant. Fichte believed that the mind is the essence of the universe. Our ideas, he maintained, do not come from experience of the material world. Instead, our minds are part of the universal creative mind. Fichte dealt with these ideas in his *Foundation of the Complete Theory of Knowledge* (1794). His chief political work is the patriotic *Addresses to the German Nation* (1808). In it, Fichte expressed his faith in German culture and national spirit. The book had a major impact on German nationalism.

Fichte was born on May 19, 1762, in Rammenau, near Bautzen. He taught at the University of Jena from 1794 to 1799. Fichte was a popular lecturer but lost his position after being accused of atheism. He served on the faculty of the University of Berlin from 1810 until his death on Jan. 27, 1814. Karl Ameriks

Fiction is a story created from an author's imagination. It may be written in prose or verse. Novels and short stories are the most popular forms of fiction. Other forms of fiction include dramas and *narrative poems* (poems that tell a story). Fiction differs from biographies, histories, and other *nonfiction,* which is created entirely from facts. The word *fiction* comes from the Latin word *fictio,* which means *a making* or *a fashioning.*

Characteristics of fiction. All fiction contains elements that are partly or entirely imaginary. Such elements include characters and settings. In some fiction, the imaginary elements are obvious. For example, *Alice's Adventures in Wonderland* (1865), by the English author Lewis Carroll, has wildly unrealistic characters and events. But fiction does not necessarily differ much from reality. Many fictional works feature true-to-life characters and realistic settings, and some fiction is based on real people and real events. For example, Napoleon's invasion of Russia in 1812 is the background of *War and Peace* (1869), a novel by the Russian writer Leo Tolstoy. The factual elements in fiction are always combined with imaginary situations and incidents.

The chief purpose of most fiction is to entertain. But a serious work of fiction also stimulates the mind. By creating characters, placing them in specific situations, and establishing a point of view, writers of serious fiction set forth judgments. These judgments may involve moral, philosophical, psychological, or social problems. They may also concern the relationship between imagination and reality.

History. Storytelling is as old as humanity. Prehistoric people passed on legends and myths from generation to generation by word of mouth. Fiction has appeared in a wide variety of forms since the development of writing about 5,500 years ago. But certain general forms have been dominant during various eras.

The most popular forms of fiction in ancient times included the *epic* and the *fable.* Epics are long narrative poems about heroes or gods. Two of the most famous epics, the *Iliad* and the *Odyssey,* were probably composed by the Greek poet Homer in the 700's B.C. Fables are brief tales with a moral. Among the best-known fables are the animal stories attributed to the Greek slave Aesop, who lived about 600 B.C. See **Epic; Fable.**

From the 1100's to the 1400's, during the Middle Ages, the *romance* became the leading form of fiction. Most medieval romances tell about adventures of knights or other court figures. Many of these stories feature supernatural characters and events. See **Romance.**

Since the mid-1700's, the chief forms of fiction have been the novel and the short story (see **Novel; Short story**). The novel flourished in England during the 1700's and 1800's. Henry Fielding wrote such satirical novels as

Tom Jones (1749). In the 1800's, Charles Dickens wrote sentimental novels that still criticized society. In some modern works of fiction, the authors have abandoned traditional storytelling devices, such as oversized plots and clear-cut characters and settings. The American writer Gertrude Stein used fiction to try to capture the workings of the unconscious mind. The Argentine writer Jorge Luis Borges probed the nature of fiction itself in such collections of stories as *Ficciones* (1944, 1962).   H. George Hahn

Related articles. See the articles on national literatures, such as **American literature** and **French literature.** See also:

Detective story	Literature for chil-	Pulitzer Prizes
Drama	dren (Fiction)	(table: Fiction)
Ghost story	Novel	Science fiction
	Poetry	Writing (Fiction)

Fiddler crab is the name of a group of small crabs that live along temperate and tropical seacoasts. These crabs burrow into sand and mud on beaches, salt marshes,

WORLD BOOK illustration by James Teason

A fiddler crab lives along sandy or muddy seacoasts. The male, *shown here*, uses its large front *chela* (claw) to attract females.

and mangrove swamps. Like all crabs, a fiddler crab has two claws called *chelae*. In the male, one chela is much larger than the other. The male waves the large chela to threaten other males or to attract females. The waves somewhat resemble the movements of a person playing a violin, and give fiddler crabs their name.

Fiddler crabs eat water organisms called *algae*. The crabs feed by picking up small balls of sand and mud with their claws. They scrape algae from the sand grains. Males cannot use the large chela for feeding because it is too large to maneuver to their mouth.

Some fiddler crabs change in color from light to dark during the day. This occurs because of the movement of *pigment* (coloring matter) within special cells in the skin. See **Biological clock** (Other rhythms).   Jonathan Green

Scientific classification. Fiddler crabs belong to the subphylum Crustacea and the order Decapoda.

See also **Crab.**

Fiedler, *FEED luhr,* **Arthur** (1894-1979), conducted the Boston Pops Orchestra from 1930 to 1979. He organized and conducted the Boston Sinfonietta, later known as the Arthur Fiedler Sinfonietta, and the Boston Esplanade Concerts.

Fiedler was born on May 17, 1894, in Boston, and studied at the Royal Academy of Music in Berlin. He taught at Boston University. Fiedler died on July 10, 1979.
          John H. Baron

Field, Cyrus West (1819-1892), was an American financier who promoted the first telegraph cable across the Atlantic (see **Cable**). The first fully successful cable was laid in 1866, after four previous attempts. The first cable, laid in 1857, broke 360 miles (579 kilometers) from shore. An attempt in June 1858 also failed. Field promoted a successful effort to lay a cable between Ireland and Newfoundland in August 1858. Technical carelessness ruined the cable's insulation, and it failed four weeks later. In 1865, Field attempted to lay a new cable. The cable broke when the project was almost done. The project succeeded in 1866, with the laying of a new cable and the repair of the old. Field later promoted the New York elevated railroad. He also wanted to lay a cable across the Pacific.

Field was born on Nov. 30, 1819, in Stockbridge, Massachusetts. He made his fortune initially as a paper merchant. He had three well-known brothers. David Dudley Field, Jr., a lawyer, won recognition for reforming legal procedure. Stephen Johnson Field served as an associate justice of the Supreme Court of the United States. Henry Martyn Field was a clergyman and historian. Cyrus Field died on July 12, 1892.   George H. Daniels

Field, David Dudley, Jr. (1805-1894), was a prominent lawyer and legal reformer. He wrote a code of legal procedure that the state of New York adopted in 1848. This code served as a model for legal reform in many other states in the United States.

Field was born on Feb. 13, 1805, in Haddam, Connecticut. He studied law in New York City and became successful there. In 1872, Field wrote an important code to reform international law. In addition, he founded an organization for legal reform now known as the International Law Association.

Field also helped form the Republican Party. In 1860, he helped Abraham Lincoln win the Republican nomination for president of the United States. Field died on April 13, 1894. His brother Stephen Johnson Field became an associate justice of the Supreme Court of the United States. Another brother, Cyrus West Field, promoted the first telegraph cable across the Atlantic.
          David M. O'Brien

Field, Eugene (1850-1895), was a popular American author and journalist who is best known today as a writer of children's literature. Many of his poems and stories are highly fanciful and sentimental. Field's most famous works are probably "Wynken, Blynken, and Nod," a whimsical lullaby; and "Little Boy Blue," a poem about the death of a child.

Besides writing for children, Field worked as a newspaper columnist in Kansas City, Missouri, and in Denver, Colorado. In 1883, he moved to Chicago to write a humorous column called "Sharps and Flats" for the *Chicago Daily News*. Field's writings influenced the development of humorous newspaper columns in the United States. They also introduced poetry and other literary material to thousands of poorly educated people who read newspapers.

Field was born on Sept. 2, 1850, in St. Louis. He attended Williams College, Knox College, and the University of Missouri but never graduated.

Many of Field's poems and stories for children were collected in *A Little Book of Western Verse* (1889), *With Trumpet and Drum* (1892), *The Holy Cross and Other*

Tales (1893), and *Lullaby-land,* which was published in 1897, after his death. Field died on Nov. 4, 1895.

Eugene K. Garber

Field, Marshall, I (1834-1906), an American merchant, established Marshall Field and Company (now Macy's), a famous Chicago department store. Field's family became prominent in merchandising, publishing, and philanthropy.

His life. Marshall Field I was born in Conway Township, Massachusetts, probably on Sept. 18, 1834. He came to Chicago in 1856 and obtained a job with a dry goods firm. In 1865, Field bought an interest in a rival business. By 1881, he gained control of the firm, and it became known as Marshall Field and Company.

Field introduced many new merchandising strategies. For instance, he marked prices on the merchandise and let customers exchange goods if they were dissatisfied with their purchases. Field's slogan was "Give the Lady What She Wants," and he made an effort to attract women to his store. Marshall Field and Company developed new advertising methods and window displays to attract customers. It was the first store to sell bargain goods in its basement.

Field's philanthropic activities included a gift of land as a site for a new University of Chicago. He also contributed about $9 million to establish the Field Museum in Chicago, one of the world's largest natural history museums. Field died on Jan. 16, 1906.

His family. Marshall Field II, the son of Marshall Field I, did not take part in the family enterprises because of poor health and a lack of interest in the business.

Marshall Field III, the son of Marshall Field II, began the family publishing business. In 1940, he helped found *PM,* a New York City daily newspaper. He founded *The Chicago Sun* in 1941 and purchased control of another Chicago paper, the *Daily Times,* in 1947. The next year, he merged the two papers into the *Chicago Sun-Times.* Field's other communications activities included World Book and Childcraft, which became Field Enterprises Educational Corporation (now World Book, Inc.); the book-publishing houses of Simon & Schuster and Pocket Books; and several radio stations. Field established Field Enterprises, Inc., to consolidate his business activities. In 1940, he established the Field Foundation, which focused on solving social problems. Field was born on Sept. 28, 1893, in Chicago and died on Nov. 8, 1956.

Marshall Field IV, the son of Marshall Field III, expanded the Field publishing enterprises. He became editor and publisher of the *Chicago Sun-Times* in 1950 and was named president of Field Enterprises in 1956. He later became chairman of the board of Field Enterprises. In 1959, Field bought the *Chicago Daily News.* In 1963, he formed Publishers Newspaper Syndicate. Field was born on June 15, 1916, in New York City and died on Sept. 18, 1965.

Marshall Field V, son of Marshall Field IV, served as chairman of the board of Field Enterprises from 1972 to 1984. Field served as publisher of the *Sun-Times* and of the *Daily News.* In 1978, Field Enterprises sold World Book, Inc., to the Scott & Fetzer (now Scott Fetzer) Company. In 1984, Field Enterprises sold the *Sun-Times.* That same year, Field and his half brother, Frederick W. Field, who co-owned Field Enterprises, dissolved the company. Marshall Field V then founded the Field Corporation

to manage his businesses. Field was born on May 13, 1941, in Charlottesville, Virginia.   Robert E. Wright

Field, Rachel (1894-1942), was an American author. She is best known for her books for children.

Field won a Newbery Medal in 1930 for *Hitty, Her First Hundred Years* (1929), a story of a doll's adventures. *Hitty* is based on an antique doll that Field and the book's illustrator, Dorothy P. Lathrop, found in a shop in New York City.

Field also wrote *Calico Bush* (1931), a children's novel about pioneer life. Her books of poetry include *Taxis and Toadstools* (1926). In addition, she wrote several plays for children. Among the novels that Field wrote for adults are *All This and Heaven Too* (1938) and *And Now Tomorrow* (1942). Field was born on Sept. 19, 1894, in New York City. She died on March 15, 1942.

Kathryn Pierson Jennings

Field, Stephen Johnson (1816-1899), was an associate justice of the Supreme Court of the United States from 1863 to 1897. On the court, Field worked to protect capitalism and property rights of individuals.

Field was born on Nov. 4, 1816, in Haddam, Connecticut. He graduated from Williams College in 1837. In 1841, he formed a law practice in New York City with his brother David Dudley Field, Jr., who later became a prominent legal reformer. In 1849, Stephen moved to California. He was elected to the State Legislature in 1850 and served until 1857. Field won election to California's Supreme Court in 1857. He served on the California court until 1863. Field died on April 9, 1899. Field's brother Cyrus West Field promoted the first telegraph cable across the Atlantic Ocean.   David M. O'Brien

Field artillery. Artillery (Kinds of artillery; pictures).

Field event. See Track and field.

Field glasses. See Binoculars.

Field hockey is a fast and exciting team sport in which players use sticks to try to hit a ball into their opponents' goal. In the United States, field hockey is played primarily by girls and women, but it is a popular male sport in many other countries.

The field and equipment. The teams compete on a smooth grass or artificial turf field 100 yards (91 meters) long and 60 yards (55 meters) wide. Various lines divide the field into sections. A *goal line* runs along the width of the field at each end. A wide arc called a *striking circle* extends from each goal line. A center line, also called a *midfield line,* parallel to the goal lines divides the field in half.

A goal cage stands in the center of each goal line. The cage has two goal posts 7 feet (2.13 meters) high and 12 feet (3.66 meters) apart. The posts are connected by a crossbar. A net is attached to the posts and crossbar. A backboard 18 inches (46 centimeters) high and 12 feet (3.66 meters) long is placed inside the net. Sideboards the height of the backboard are attached to the backs of the goal posts at right angles to the goal line.

Each player carries a stick with a curved end that is flat on its left side and rounded on its right. Only the flat side may be used to hit the ball. Most players use sticks that vary from 34 to 37 inches (86 to 94 centimeters) in length. The ball is about 9 inches (23 centimeters) in circumference and weighs about 5 ½ ounces (160 grams). The outer surface is smooth. The inside may be either solid or hollow.

David Madison, Bruce Coleman Inc.

Field hockey is a fast-moving team sport. Players try to hit a ball toward their opponents' goal, using sticks curved at one end. A goalkeeper tries to block shots before they go into the goal.

The game is divided into two halves and varies in length from 50 to 70 minutes. Older and more skillful players compete in the longer games. Each team has 11 players. The most common setup consists of three forwards, four midfielders, three backs, and a goalkeeper. Two umpires supervise the game. The umpires are sometimes aided by one or two timekeepers.

Players try to move the ball using only their sticks until they are in a position to shoot it into the other team's goal. Each goal counts 1 point. A goal is scored each time an offensive player hits the ball from within the striking circle so it crosses the goal line between the goal posts.

The game starts with a *center pass*. A player from one team hits or pushes the ball with the stick from the center line to a teammate. At the time of the center pass, no players of the opposing team may be within 5 yards (4.6 meters) of the ball. All players except the one executing the center pass must remain in their own half of the field. The ball may be played in any direction once the game begins. Play resumes with a center pass after each goal.

The rules allow no body contact or dangerous hitting and prohibit a player from playing a ball above shoulder height with any part of the stick except when stopping a shot on goal. The goalkeeper may kick the ball or stop it with any part of the body, including the hand, but only when the ball is inside the striking circle.

History. The origin of field hockey is unknown. Ancient Greek carvings show players using crooked sticks to hit a small object. Only men played field hockey for many years. In 1889, the All England Women's Hockey Association was established. Constance M. K. Applebee of the British College of Physical Education promoted field hockey in the United States during the early 1900's. The United States Field Hockey Association (USFHA) for women was organized in 1922. The Field Hockey Association of America (FHAA) for men was formed in 1928. The USFHA and the FHAA merged in 1993 under the USFHA name.

Men's field hockey has been part of the Summer Olympics since 1908. Women's field hockey became an Olympic sport in 1980. Rules are made by the International Hockey Federation's Rules Board and are the same for men and women.

Critically reviewed by USA Field Hockey

See also **Hockey.**

Field Museum, in Chicago, is one of the world's largest and best-known natural history museums. It serves as a center for public education and for scientific study of environments and cultures. The museum's collections include more than 20 million items, including both *artifacts* (things made by people) and natural objects.

The Field Museum's department of education provides lectures, short courses, and workshops. The museum also conducts natural history tours and sends traveling exhibits to schools. Its library has thousands of volumes for the use of scientists and the general public. Its Rapid Biological Inventory program conducts studies of threatened wilderness areas, among other activities. The museum is privately supported but receives funds from the city, state, and federal governments.

Exhibits. The museum collections are organized into anthropology, botany, geology, and zoology. The Field Museum is widely known for its dinosaur fossils, espe-

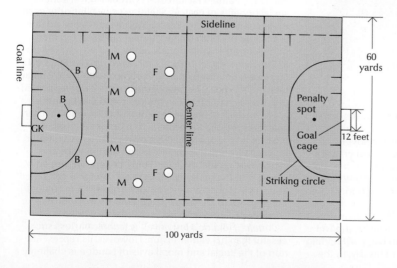

A field hockey field is divided into two halves by a solid center line. Two broken lines run parallel to the center line and to a goal line at each end of the field. A broken line runs the length of the field near each sideline. In a game, goals must be scored from within the striking circle. This diagram shows a typical formation during a center pass, with three forwards, four midfielders, three backs, and a goalkeeper.

WORLD BOOK diagram

cially "Sue," a *Tyrannosaurus rex* skeleton measuring 42 feet (13 meters) in length. The museum's resource center provides further opportunities for in-depth learning. The center has books, computer programs, museum samples, and other materials. The museum also presents exhibits on the Internet.

History. The Chicago merchant and philanthropist Marshall Field I founded the museum in 1893 and gave it more than $9 million during his lifetime. The museum was first called the Columbian Museum of Chicago. Within a year of its founding, its name was changed to the Field Columbian Museum. The current building was designed by the famous Chicago architect Daniel Burnham and opened in 1921. During most of the period from 1905 to 1994, the museum was known as the Field Museum of Natural History. From 1943 to 1966, it was called the Chicago Natural History Museum. In 1994, it became known simply as the Field Museum.

Critically reviewed by the Field Museum

See also **Dinosaur** (picture: A museum display).

Field spaniel is a hunting dog. It has a flat, glossy coat that may be black, liver-colored, or roan. The dog also may have tan markings under its tail, and on its eyebrows, mouth, and feet. The field spaniel stands about 18 inches (46 centimeters) high at the shoulder and weighs from 35 to 50 pounds (16 to 23 kilograms). The breed originated in England in the mid-1800's and is gaining in popularity in the United States. The field spaniel is intelligent and has great perseverance.

Critically reviewed by the Field Spaniel Society of America

J. Ralph and Helga Alderfer

The field spaniel originated in England.

Fielding, Henry (1707-1754), an English author, helped raise the novel to the status of high literature and shaped it as a literary form. He was the first novelist to merge comedy with satire and morality and to create a panoramic and realistic view of society. He satirized corruption ruthlessly, but he was a conservative who saw traditional social and moral institutions as sound with no need of uprooting.

His life. Fielding was born on April 22, 1707, near Glastonbury. He studied at Eton College and at the University of Leyden in Holland. Settling in London, Fielding became the most popular playwright of his day. In the

1730's, he wrote about 20 satires and comic revues, notably *The Tragedy of Tragedies; or, The Life and Death of Tom Thumb the Great* (1731). Many of his plays ridiculed the corrupt government of Prime Minister Robert Walpole. One of these, *The Historical Register for the Year 1736* (1737), helped inspire the Licensing Act of 1737, a censorship law that ended Fielding's playwriting career.

Detail of an engraving by William Hogarth; The British Museum, London

Henry Fielding

Fielding then studied law, but finding it hard to support himself as a lawyer, he worked as an essayist and an editor of several journals. He also began writing novels during this period. In the late 1740's, Fielding served as a judge in London. He worked hard to fight crime, founding the *Bow Street Runners,* who became the model for the London police force (see **Police** [History]). Fielding suffered from poor health and sought a milder climate. On a trip to Portugal, he wrote his last book, *The Journal of a Voyage to Lisbon* (published in 1755, after his death). He died near Lisbon on Oct. 8, 1754.

His novels. Fielding is most remembered for his three major novels, *Joseph Andrews* (1742), *Tom Jones* (1749), and *Amelia* (1751). To them, he brought all his training in classical literature, playwriting, the law, and journalism. He enlivened these elements with his comic temperament sharpened by a satiric and ethical aim.

In his novels, Fielding used elements of the classical epic. These elements include unified plots, eloquent language, episodes of love and adventure, a wide range of action, and firm narrative control. He also used conventions of the epic to satirize character types. For example, by presenting lowly people as heroic and trivial actions as mighty, he made fun of human faults, such as hypocrisy and vanity. All his main characters reflect two of his major themes, the importance of good will and charity.

Joseph Andrews is a *parody* (mock imitation) of *Pamela* (1740), Samuel Richardson's popular novel about the social benefits of chastity. Fielding's novel introduces the great comic character Parson Abraham Adams. Adams is a tangle of contradicting human qualities, but thoroughly good and hilariously funny.

The History of Tom Jones, a Foundling, Fielding's masterpiece, contains numerous subplots with many characters and themes. The novel consists of 18 *books* divided into 6 in the country, 6 on the road, and 6 in London.

The main plot features a group of unforgettable characters, especially the orphan Tom Jones who pursues his true love, Sophia, and his own maturity. A symbolic journey through life, the novel reveals the traps and vices awaiting the innocent Tom—deception, sex, envy, greed, and hypocrisy. With its great variety of settings and its vivid characters, the story provides a portrait of the England of Fielding's day. Fielding's own voice as narrator provides a humorous and ethical tone.

Amelia, Fielding's last novel, is technically less successful than his earlier fiction. However, its representation of the social and moral evils of London is chillingly realistic. Like Fielding's other novels, *Amelia* ends happily in the golden world of rural England, with the traditional social order intact and undamaged.

Fielding wrote two other works of fiction. *An Apology for the Life of Mrs. Shamela Andrews* (1741) begins the parody of *Pamela* that he continued in *Joseph Andrews*. In *The Life of Mr. Jonathan Wild the Great* (1743), Fielding satirized an actual notorious London criminal and the corrupt prime minister Sir Robert Walpole. Through them, the author arrived at ironic definitions of greatness and goodness.   H. George Hahn

Additional resources

Battestin, Martin C. *Henry Fielding*. 1989. Reprint. Routledge, 1993. *A Henry Fielding Companion*. Greenwood, 2000.
Bertelsen, Lance. *Henry Fielding at Work*. Palgrave, 2000.
Rivero, Albert J., ed. *Critical Essays on Henry Fielding*. G. K. Hall, 1998.

Fields, W. C. (1880?-1946), was an American motion-picture comedian. Fields incorporated his personal prejudices into his films, and it became difficult to separate his real personality from his film characters. In his movies, Fields often played swindling characters. He was at war with the world, battling both people and objects. He hated children, and they hated him. Fields's trademarks included a top hat, a monstrous nose, and a distinctive side-of-the-mouth manner of speaking.

Fields made his film debut in 1915 in a brief role in a comedy. He was in several silent films but did not win fame until the emergence of sound films. His major movies include *The Old-Fashioned Way* (1934), *It's a Gift* (1934), *The Man on the Flying Trapeze* (1935), *David Copperfield* (1935), *Poppy* (1936), *The Big Broadcast of 1938* (1937), *You Can't Cheat an Honest Man* (1939), *My Little Chickadee* (1940), *The Bank Dick* (1940), and *Never Give a Sucker an Even Break* (1941).

Fields was born in Philadelphia, probably on Jan. 29, 1880. His real name was William Claude Dukenfield. He began his show business career at the age of 14. He died on Dec. 25, 1946.   Rachel Gallagher

Additional resources

Curtis, James. *W. C. Fields*. Knopf, 2003.
Fields, Ronald J. *W. C. Fields*. St. Martin's, 1984.
Gehring, Wes D. *Groucho and W. C. Fields*. Univ. Pr. of Miss., 1994.
Louvish, Simon. *Man on the Flying Trapeze: The Life and Times of W. C. Fields*. 1997. Reprint. Norton, 1999.

Penguin Photo

W. C. Fields was a popular motion-picture comedian. He and Mae West starred in the film *My Little Chickadee, shown here.*

Fiesta. See **Mexico** (Holidays).

Fife is a small woodwind instrument that belongs to the flute family. It consists of a wooden tube that has from six to eight finger holes along its length and a mouth hole near one end.

A player holds the fife in a horizontal position and blows across the mouth hole. The fife produces a shrill, penetrating sound. The player covers and uncovers the finger holes to produce different notes.

The fife originated in Switzerland in the 1500's. It was later used throughout western Europe and in the United States. Traditionally, fifes were played with drums in military units and were associated with patriotic groups. They are now played primarily in ceremonial fife and drum corps.   André P. Larson

© Wally McNamee, Corbis

Mouth hole   Finger holes

WORLD BOOK illustration by Jay Bensen

The fife is a small, flutelike woodwind instrument that produces a high-pitched sound. The musician blows into a *mouth hole* and opens and closes *finger holes* to produce different notes.

Fifteenth Amendment to the United States Constitution guarantees that an American citizen shall not be discriminated against in exercising the right to vote. It states that the federal and state governments cannot bar a citizen from voting because the person had been a slave or because of race.

Amendment 15 was ratified on Feb. 3, 1870. Seven Southern states tried to bypass it by adding *grandfather clauses* to their constitutions. One such clause gave the right to vote to people who could vote on Jan. 1, 1867, and to their family descendants. In 1915 and 1939, the Supreme Court of the United States declared grandfather clauses unconstitutional. For information on recent legislation protecting the right to vote, see **Voting** (Restrictions on voting).   Charles V. Hamilton

See also **Grandfather clause; Constitution of the United States.**

Fifth Amendment to the United States Constitution guarantees that people cannot be forced to testify against themselves in a criminal case. It also provides that a person cannot be placed in jeopardy twice for the same offense. Amendment 5 also guarantees that (1) a person cannot be deprived of life, liberty, or property without due process of law; (2) a person cannot be held to answer for a "capital, or otherwise infamous crime" unless he or she has been indicted by a grand jury, except that military personnel are subject to court-martial; (3) property cannot be taken from a person without just compensation. Amendment 5 is a part of the Bill of Rights that was ratified on Dec. 15, 1791. See also **Bill of rights; Due process of law; Constitution of the United States.**   James O. Finckenauer

Fifth column refers to undercover agents operating within the ranks of an enemy to undermine its cause. The agents pave the way for military or political invasion. They may work in an army, political party, or industry. Their activities include spying, sabotage, economic subversion, propaganda, agitation, infiltration, and even assassination, terror, and revolt. The term *fifth column* was first used during the Spanish Civil War (1936-1939) to describe the work of Francisco Franco's followers in Loyalist Madrid. Emilio Mola, a general under Franco, said, "I have four columns moving against Madrid, and a fifth will rise up inside the city itself."   Douglas L. Wheeler

Fifty-Four Forty or Fight was a slogan used during a boundary dispute between the United States and the United Kingdom. An 1818 treaty allowed both nations to occupy the Oregon Country, lying between 42° and 54°40′ north latitude. In the 1830's and 1840's, American expansionists wanted to take the whole area, by force if necessary. In 1846, during James K. Polk's presidency, the United States made a new treaty that set 49° as a boundary, except for Vancouver Island. The United States secured the land south of the line, and the United Kingdom obtained the land to the north. See also **British Columbia** (The border dispute); **Polk, James Knox** ("Oregon fever").   Jerome O. Steffen

Fig is a fruit that has probably been cultivated for more than 10,000 years. It originated in the Mediterranean region, and ancient Greek, Roman, and Egyptian documents describe its popularity as a food. Figs are small and round or pear-shaped. They have green, yellow, pink, purple, brown, or black skins, depending on the variety. They have a high sugar content, and people eat them fresh, dried, canned, or preserved in sugar.

Figs grow on trees of the same name. Fig trees thrive in climates with hot, dry summers and cool, moist winters. Important fig-producing countries include Portugal, Italy, Greece, and Turkey. California produces most of the figs grown in the United States.

Most fig trees grow to less than 33 feet (10 meters) tall and have a trunk about 3 ¼ feet (1 meter) in diameter. The trees have deeply lobed leaves. The fruit develops from podlike structures that grow on the branches and that contain hundreds of tiny flowers. As the fruits develop, these structures enlarge and become fleshy. Fig trees bear two or three crops of fruit each year.

There are four main types of figs: (1) caprifigs, (2) Smyrna figs, (3) common figs, and (4) San Pedro figs. The wild caprifig trees seldom produce edible fruit. Small fig wasps live inside the caprifigs. When the wasps leave the figs, they carry pollen from the flowers. The Smyrna fig depends on these pollen-carrying wasps to pollinate its flowers. All varieties of Smyrna figs require pollen from caprifigs to bear fruit. The common fig does not require pollination to produce fruit. The San Pedro fig produces two types of fig crops each year. The first crop, harvested in early summer, develops without pollination, like the common fig. The second crop, which matures in late summer, must be pollinated by the fig wasp like the Smyrna fig.

Growers produce new fig trees from branches cut from other fig trees. In most cases, the new trees bear fruit two to four years later. Mediterranean fruit flies and tiny worms called *nematodes* are among the fig tree's most troublesome pests. Ripe figs spoil easily and cannot be shipped long distances to market. Therefore, most growers dry their crop—either in the sun or in ovens—before shipping.   Michael G. Barbour

Scientific classification. Fig trees belong to the mulberry family, Moraceae. They are *Ficus carica.*

Figaro. See **Beaumarchais, Pierre de.**

Fightingfish is a small, quarrelsome fish that lives in the waters around the Malay Archipelago. It is often called the *Betta* or *Siamese fightingfish.* It has been bred to develop long, waving tails and fins. When the male is excited, it becomes colored with reds, greens, purples, and blues. Most fighting occurs between males, though females will occasionally attack males. Fightingfish dash at each other, biting the opponent's fins until one of the fish is exhausted. One fightingfish will even attack its own image in a mirror. Watching fights between male

WORLD BOOK illustration by Kate Lloyd-Jones, Linden Artists Ltd.
Figs are the fruit of the fig tree, which generally grows in warm climates. The plant's flowers grow inside the fruit.

© Heather Angel, Biophotos
Fightingfish grow about 2 ½ inches (6.4 cm) long. The male, *bottom,* displays its beautiful tail and fins to the female, *top.*

fightingfish is a popular spectator sport in Thailand.

John E. McCosker

Scientific classification. The scientific name of the fightingfish is *Betta splendens.*

See also **Fish** (pictures: Fish of tropical fresh waters; A male Siamese fightingfish).

Figure of speech is the use of words in certain conventional patterns of thought and expression. For example, we might read that "The spy was cornered *like a rat* . . . The crowd *surged* forward . . . The *redcoats* withdrew . . . Justice *hung her head* . . . Here was *mercy* indeed! . . . The *entire nation* screamed vengeance."

Each of these figures of speech has its own name. The first is *simile,* when the spy is compared with a rat, using the connective word *like.* The second is *metaphor,* when the author compares the movement of the crowd to that of an oncoming wave without using the connective words *like* or *as.* The third is *metonymy,* when the word *redcoats* stands for the soldiers who wear them. The fourth, *personification,* speaks of justice as though it were a person. The fifth is *irony,* because the author means the opposite of mercy. The sixth is *hyperbole,* or exaggeration for special effect.

Figures of speech are the flowers of rhetoric. They give to poetry much of its beauty and power. The English poet John Milton wrote, in "On His Being Arrived at the Age of Twenty-Three" (1631),

How soon hath Time, the subtle thief of youth,
Stolen on his wing my three and twentieth year!
My hasting days fly on with full career,
But my late spring no bud or blossom shew'th.

Without consciously analyzing the personification, metonymy, and metaphor used, the reader still senses the richness of imagery and poetic thought. Everyday speech also uses many such figures. Marianne Cooley

See also **Irony; Metaphor; Simile.**

Figure skating. See **Ice skating.**

Figwort family is a large group of herbs, shrubs, and small trees. The scientific name for this family is Scrophulariaceae (pronounced *SKRAHF yuh LAIR ee AY see ee).* Some plants in this family are used in medicines. They have bell-shaped flowers that are divided into two lips. The flowers grow atop a slender stem, while the leaves often grow in pairs on the stem.

The figwort family flourishes especially in *temperate* regions, which have hot summers and cool or cold winters. It includes wildflowers and weeds, such as mullein, butter-and-eggs, speedwell, and lousewort. The cultivated varieties include butterfly bushes and Cape fuchsias. Certain figworts live partially as parasites on other plants. Scrophularia, from which the family is named, is a medicinal figwort. People at one time believed that it would cure scrofula (see **Scrofula**). Kenneth A. Nicely

See also **Mullein.**

Fiji, *FEE jee,* is a country in the South Pacific Ocean. It is made up of about 330 islands and about 500 more tiny atolls, islets, and reefs. The island of Viti Levu (Big Fiji) covers about half of Fiji's area, and Vanua Levu (Big Land) about a third. Many of Fiji's other islands are merely piles of sand on coral reefs. Suva is the capital and largest city (see **Suva**). The country's official name is Republic of the Fiji Islands.

More than half of Fiji's people are native Fijians of

Fiji

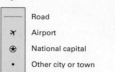

——	Road
✈	Airport
⊛	National capital
•	Other city or town
+	Elevation above sea level

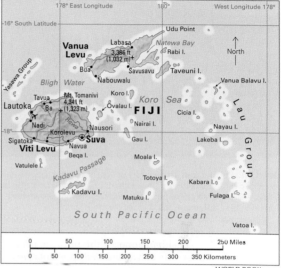

WORLD BOOK maps

chiefly Melanesian descent. About one-third are descendants of laborers imported from India. The remainder have Chinese, European, Micronesian, or Polynesian ancestry. Fiji became independent in 1970 after being a British crown colony since 1874.

Government. According to Fiji's Constitution, the prime minister is head of the government. The prime minister selects a Cabinet to help carry out the functions of government. In addition, Fiji has a president, who is head of state. The president is appointed to a five-year term by the Great Council of Chiefs, a traditional body of

Facts in brief

Capital: Suva.
Official languages: English, Fijian, and Hindustani.
Area: 7,055 mi² (18,272 km²). *Greatest distances*—north-south, 364 mi (586 km); east-west, 334 mi (538 km). *Coastline*—925 mi (1,489 km).
Elevation: *Highest*—Mount Tomanivi, on Viti Levu, 4,341 ft (1,323 m) above sea level. *Lowest*—sea level.
Population: *Estimated 2014 population*—889,000; density, 126 per mi² (49 per km²); distribution, 52 percent urban, 48 percent rural. *2007 census*—837,271.
Chief products: *Agriculture*—cattle, coconuts, sugar cane. *Manufacturing*—cement, cigarettes, clothing. *Mining*—gold.
National anthem: "God Bless Fiji."
Flag: The British Union Jack appears in the upper left on a light blue field. On the right is the shield from Fiji's coat of arms with a British lion, a dove, coconut palms, and such agricultural products as bananas and sugar cane. Adopted on Oct. 10, 1970. See **Flag** (picture: Flags of Asia and the Pacific).
Money: *Basic unit*—Fiji dollar. One hundred cents equal one Fiji dollar.

Cal Harbert, DPI

Suva, the capital and largest city of Fiji, is also the nation's chief port and commercial center. Suva lies on the southern coast of Viti Levu, the largest of Fiji's islands. Many government buildings, such as the one shown here, which once housed Fiji's Parliament, stand along the city's shoreline.

Cal Harbert, DPI

Sugar cane is one of Fiji's chief agricultural products. Workers load sugar cane stalks onto a wagon. Bananas and coconuts also grow well in Fiji's tropical climate.

Fijian chiefs. The president appoints the prime minister. Fiji's Parliament consists of a House of Representatives and a Senate.

In 2006, Fiji's military chief seized control of the government. Since 2007, he has been interim prime minister. In 2009, the president suspended the Constitution.

People. About half of Fijians live in rural areas. Native Fijians follow such traditional customs as the ceremonial drinking of *kava,* a beverage made from the roots of the kava plant. Kava is called *yaqona* in Fiji. The men wear skirts called *sulus,* and the women wear cotton dresses. On ceremonial occasions, the women may wear grass skirts. Most native Fijians are Christians.

Most of the Indians are descendants of about 60,000 laborers brought from India between 1879 and 1916 to work on Fiji's sugar plantations. Many Indians still work in the cane fields, but others have become prosperous shopkeepers or business people. Indians control much of Fiji's business and industry. The Indian women wear the *sari,* the traditional dress of India. Most of the Indians are Muslims or Hindus.

Fijians speak three main languages: English, Fijian, and Hindustani, the spoken form of Hindi. English is used in the schools. Most children from ages 6 to 17 attend school. Most Fijian and Indian youngsters attend separate schools. The University of the South Pacific, the only university in the country, serves students from Fiji and other South Pacific islands. The main campus is in Suva.

Land. Most of the Fiji islands were formed by volcanoes. Coral reefs surround nearly all the islands. The larger islands have high volcanic peaks, rolling hills, rivers, and grasslands. Tropical rain forests cover over half of Fiji's total area. The islands have fertile coastal plains and river valleys. Cool winds make Fiji's tropical climate relatively comfortable. Temperatures range from about 60 to 90 °F (16 to 32 °C). Heavy rains and tropical storms occur frequently between November and April.

Economy. Agriculture is important to the economy of Fiji. Fijians raise cattle and chickens and grow such crops as coconuts and sugar cane. Gold is the country's chief mineral. Tourism is a major economic activity, and it employs many islanders. Fiji exports clothing, fish, and sugar. The country imports food, machinery, motor vehicles, and petroleum products. Products manufactured in Fiji include cement, cigarettes, clothing, and food and beverages.

Fiji has been called the "crossroads of the South Pacific." The airport at Nadi, on Viti Levu, is a busy terminal for planes flying the Pacific. Fiji also lies on major shipping routes and has several excellent harbors.

History. Melanesians migrated to Fiji thousands of years ago, probably from Indonesia. A small group of Polynesians settled there during the A.D. 100's. In 1643, Abel Tasman, a Dutch navigator, became the first European to see Fiji. Captain James Cook, a British explorer, visited Vatoa, one of the southern islands, in 1774. During the 1800's, traders, Methodist missionaries, and escaped Australian convicts came to visit or settle there.

Fijian tribes fought one another until 1871, when a chief named Cakobau extended his influence over much of Fiji. With the help of King George Tupou I of nearby Tonga, Cakobau brought peace to Fiji. To protect the country from outside interference, Cakobau asked the United Kingdom to make Fiji a crown colony. The United Kingdom did so on Oct. 10, 1874. Fiji remained a colony until, at its own request, it became an independent nation on Oct. 10, 1970, with Ratu Sir Kamisese Mara as prime minister. Since independence, Fiji's government has encouraged tourism and the development of manufacturing and forestry. Fiji's government has also promoted the production of new crops to reduce Fiji's dependence on sugar cane and coconuts.

Ethnic Fijians traditionally have held the most political power in Fiji. In April 1987, an Indian-backed coalition won a majority in parliament. The coalition leader, Timoci Bavadra, a Fijian, replaced Mara as prime minister. Bavadra appointed a multiracial Cabinet. Many Fijians resented Bavadra's action because they wanted power to stay in Fijian hands. Military officers led by Sitiveni Rabuka overthrew Bavadra and declared the right of Fijians to govern Fiji. In December 1987, Rabuka returned Fiji to civilian rule. In 1990, Fiji adopted a Constitution designed to ensure that power remained with the Fijians. But in 1997, the Constitution was amended to grant political power to all races. In 1999, Mahendra Chaudhry became Fiji's first prime minister of Indian descent.

In May 2000, rebels claiming to represent the interests of native Fijians seized Chaudhry and most Cabinet members and held them hostage. The Fijian military took charge of the government and revoked the 1997 Constitution. In July, the hostages were released. Fijian courts later reinstated the 1997 Constitution, and an interim government was established. In parliamentary elections held in 2001 and 2006, a party dominated by ethnic Fijians won the most seats. However, in December 2006, Frank Bainimarama, Fiji's military chief, seized control of the government. Bainimarama repeatedly refused international pressure to set a date for new elections.

Bainimarama agreed to a "roadmap" to democracy. An independent commission created a draft constitution based on suggestions received from the Fijian public. The commission presented the draft to the government, and it was intended to be reviewed by an expert panel. However, Bainimarama rejected the draft constitution, canceled the expert panel, and replaced the draft constitution with a new one drawn up by his government.

Brij V. Lal

Filaria, *fih LAIR ee uh,* is a long, threadlike roundworm that lives as a parasite in human beings and animals. Filariae are commonly found in tropical and subtropical countries. The male worm is shorter than the female, and it has a curved tail.

The *larvae* (young worms) are born alive. They live in the blood near the body surface of the *host* (the animal in which they live). When a bloodsucking fly or mosquito bites an infected person, it takes up larvae with the blood. The larvae develop in the mosquito's or fly's head near the mouth. Then when the insect bites another animal, the larvae enter the wound and infect a new host.

Wuchereria bancrofti is a filaria harmful to human beings. It is found in Africa, South America, and the Far East. The adult worms live in the *lymph,* a body fluid (see **Lymphatic system**). When they block the flow of lymph, a disease called *elephantiasis, or lymphatic fi-*

E. R. Degginger

Filaria, shown here under a microscope, is a parasite common in tropical countries.

lariasis, results. This disease is characterized by severe swelling of the limbs, usually the legs (see **Elephantiasis**). *Wuchereria bancrofti* can be eliminated by controlling the mosquitoes that carry the larvae. Other kinds of filariae infect such animals as cattle and dogs.

David F. Oetinger

Scientific classification. Filariae are members of the roundworm phylum, Nematoda.

See also **Manson, Sir Patrick; Roundworm.**

Filbert is the name for the nut and the plant of a group of trees and shrubs closely related to the birches. The nuts are also called hazelnuts and cobnuts (see **Hazel**). Some filberts grow 60 feet (18 meters) tall. Others are shrubs that normally grow 2 to 30 feet (0.6 to 9 meters) high. Filberts are native to North America, Europe, and Asia. Larger filbert nuts grow best on cultivated trees. The seeds taste better roasted than raw. The nuts form in compact clusters, with each nut encased within its own husk. The nuts have smooth and hard but thin and brittle shells. The kernels are single.

Richard A. Jaynes

Filibustering, *FIHL uh BUHS tuhr ihng,* is the practice by which a minority in a legislature uses extended debate to block or delay action on a proposed bill. Members of the minority make long speeches, demand roll calls, propose useless motions, and use other tactics to delay or kill a bill. If the minority prevents a vote on a bill, the bill cannot become law.

In the United States, the Senate has a tradition of unlimited debate. A senator who holds the floor may speak without interruption. The Senate can end a filibuster by reaching informal compromise with the filibusterers, or by invoking the *cloture rule* to end debate (see **Cloture**). This rule was adopted in 1917 and strengthened in later years. Under the rule, a vote of 60 senators, three-fifths of the Senate, can limit each senator to one hour of debate on most bills. Final action on a bill is required within 30 hours after the rule has been invoked. Today, many senators seek agreement of 60 of their colleagues to avoid a filibuster of controversial legislation.

From 1917 to 1962, Southerners opposed to civil rights bills staged many filibusters. During these years, cloture was invoked only four times. Today, filibusters and clotures occur routinely on a wide range of bills.

Collectively, the longest filibuster since the cloture rule was adopted lasted 75 days and involved the Civil Rights Bill of 1964. Individually, Senator Strom Thurmond of South Carolina filibustered 24 hours and 18 minutes in a debate over a different civil rights bill in 1957.

The word *filibuster* originally meant *pirate.* Some members of Congress charged that the use of delaying tactics to block the will of the majority was like *filibustering* (piracy).

Canada's parliament has time limitations for a member to debate a bill. Filibusters still can occur when an entire party permits each of its members to debate an issue for his or her allotted time. The parliaments of Australia and New Zealand also have time limits upon debates by members. Filibusters can still be accomplished in other ways. For example, opposition members can add on thousands of unimportant amendments to a bill to delay voting. Thomas S. Vontz

Filipinos. See Philippines (introduction; The people).

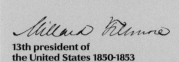

**13th president of
the United States 1850-1853**

Taylor
12th president
1849-1850
Whig

Fillmore
13th president
1850-1853
Whig

Pierce
14th president
1853-1857
Democrat

National Portrait Gallery, Smithsonian Institution, Washington, D.C.

Fillmore, Millard (1800-1874), the second vice president of the United States to inherit the nation's highest office, became president when Zachary Taylor died. During Fillmore's 32 months in office as president, his most important action was his approval of the Compromise of 1850. This series of laws helped delay the Civil War for more than 10 years.

A self-made man, Fillmore had been a poor boy who was once a clothmaker's apprentice. He studied law, then won election to the New York state legislature and to Congress. He became known nationally only after the Whig Party chose him to be Taylor's vice presidential running mate in 1848.

As vice president, Fillmore presided coolly over the heated Senate debates between slavery and antislavery forces. The Compromise of 1850, which he helped achieve, had been opposed by President Taylor because of its concessions to the South. But when Taylor died, Fillmore urged passage of the compromise and quickly signed it into law. Fillmore personally did not approve of slavery. But he loved the Union and preferred compromise to the risk of war.

Important dates in Fillmore's life

1800	(Jan. 7) Born in Locke, N.Y.
1826	(Feb. 5) Married Abigail Powers.
1832	Elected to U.S. House of Representatives.
1848	Elected vice president of the United States.
1850	(July 10) Sworn in as president.
1852	Defeated in bid for presidential nomination.
1853	Mrs. Abigail Fillmore died.
1856	Defeated in presidential election.
1858	(Feb. 10) Married Mrs. Caroline McIntosh.
1874	(March 8) Died in Buffalo, N.Y.

Fillmore faithfully enforced the compromise, including its provision for the return of runaway slaves. This policy lost him the support of most Northerners, and he was not nominated for president in 1852.

A conservative dresser, Fillmore always wore a dark frock coat and a high-collared shirt with a black silk neckcloth tied in a bow in front. He had kindly blue eyes and a gracious, courteous manner. People admired his modesty. When Great Britain's Oxford University offered him an honorary degree, Fillmore replied that he had done nothing to deserve the honor and would not accept the degree.

Early life

Millard Fillmore was born in Locke, N.Y., on Jan. 7, 1800. He was the second child in a family of three girls and six boys. His parents, Nathaniel and Phoebe Millard Fillmore, had moved to the frontier from Bennington, Vt. The elder Fillmore had hoped to improve his fortune, but he lost his farm through a faulty title. He then moved to another part of Cayuga County, where he rented a heavily wooded piece of land. Millard helped his father clear timber and work the farm.

Education. Millard attended school for only short periods, but he learned reading, spelling, arithmetic, and geography. His father owned two books, the Bible and a hymnbook.

At the age of 14, Millard was apprenticed to a clothmaker. His master treated Millard so badly that the boy once threatened him with an ax. He found a new master, but he bought his freedom from the apprenticeship in 1819 for $30. In the same year, he also purchased the first book he had ever owned, a dictionary. Fillmore decided to become a lawyer. He taught school while he

	Existing state
	New state
	Existing territory
	New territory

California became the 31st state in 1850. Three new territories were formed during Fillmore's presidency—New Mexico and Utah in 1850 and Washington in 1853.

The United States flag had 31 stars during most of Fillmore's presidency. California became the 31st state on Sept. 9, 1850, two months after Fillmore took office.

The world of President Fillmore

The "underground railroad" enabled many slaves to escape to the Northern States or to Canada during the mid-1800's. The underground railroad—neither underground nor a railroad—was an informal system of routes to freedom. Many people who opposed slavery provided hiding places and other assistance to slaves traveling along these routes.

Uncle Tom's Cabin, a novel about slavery by Harriet Beecher Stowe, was first published in serial form in 1851 and 1852, then in book form in 1852. The novel aroused Northern sentiment against the South and angered many Southerners, who considered it an unjust portrayal of slavery.

Swedish soprano Jenny Lind made a triumphant tour of the United States from 1850 to 1852. She was known as the *Swedish Nightingale.*

Herman Melville's *Moby-Dick* was published in 1851. This highly symbolic novel was poorly received by critics and the public, but later was recognized as a literary masterpiece.

The Taiping Rebellion erupted in China in 1850 and threatened the power of the Qing dynasty. Millions of people died during the revolt, which lasted until 1864.

"Go West, young man" was a phrase made popular by Horace Greeley, editor of the *New York Tribune,* around 1851. Greeley used the phrase as advice to the unemployed of New York City.

Expanding railroads encouraged settlement of the Midwest. Direct rail lines linked New York and Chicago in 1852.

Louis Napoleon proclaimed himself emperor of France in 1852 and ruled as a dictator until he was overthrown in 1870.

WORLD BOOK map

studied with a local judge. In 1823, he opened a law office in East Aurora, New York.

Fillmore's family. Millard Fillmore met Abigail Powers (March 13, 1798-March 30, 1853) in 1819, when they attended the same school. She was the daughter of a Baptist minister. He was then 19 years old, and she was 21. They fell in love and were married in 1826. Mrs. Fillmore was a teacher, and she continued to teach until 1828. The couple had two children, Millard Powers Fillmore (1828-1889) and Mary Abigail Fillmore (1832-1854). In 1830, the family moved to Buffalo, New York.

Political and public career

Fillmore won election to the New York House of Representatives in 1828 with the help of Thurlow Weed, an Albany publisher who helped form the Whig Party. Fillmore was twice reelected.

Congressman. In 1832, Fillmore was elected to the U.S. House of Representatives. He served from 1833 to 1835 and from 1837 to 1843. He generally favored the nationalistic policies of Henry Clay. As chairman of the Ways and Means Committee, Fillmore was the chief author of the tariff of 1842, which raised duties on manufactured goods. He ran for governor of New York in 1844 but was defeated and returned to his law practice. In 1846, he became the first chancellor of the University of Buffalo. The next year, he was elected comptroller of New York.

Vice president. The Whigs nominated Fillmore for vice president in 1848 on a ticket headed by General Zachary Taylor, the hero of the Mexican War. The Democrats nominated Senator Lewis Cass of Michigan for president and former Congressman William O. Butler of Kentucky for vice president. During the campaign, the

Democrats split over the slavery issue, and many voted for the Free Soil ticket (see **Free Soil Party**). Taylor and Fillmore won the election by a margin of 36 electoral votes.

Fillmore presided over the Senate debate on the

Buffalo and Erie County Historical Society

Abigail Powers Fillmore, the president's first wife, met Millard when they attended the same school. She was two years older than he. Poor health restricted her activities as first lady.

As vice president, Fillmore presided over major Senate debates on slavery. This picture shows him seated on the upper center platform while Daniel Webster addresses the chamber.

Library of Congress

Compromise of 1850 (see **Compromise of 1850**). Before the issue was settled, President Taylor died on July 9, 1850. Fillmore was sworn in as the new president the next day.

Fillmore's Administration (1850-1853)

Accomplishments. After becoming president, Fillmore came forth strongly in favor of compromise on slavery. As his first act, he replaced Taylor's Cabinet with men who had led the fight for compromise.

In September, Congress passed the series of laws that made up the Compromise of 1850. Fillmore promptly signed them. The compromise admitted California as a free state and organized territorial governments for Utah and New Mexico. These territories could decide for themselves whether or not to allow slavery. The compromise also settled a Texas boundary dispute, abolished the slave trade in the District of Columbia, and established a stricter fugitive slave law (see **Fugitive slave laws**).

Also during Fillmore's Administration, Congress reduced the basic postal rate from 5 to 3 cents. Later in 1852, the president sent Commodore Matthew C. Perry on an expedition to the Far East. Two years later, after Fillmore had left the presidency, this voyage resulted in the first trade treaty with Japan.

Life in the White House. Abigail Fillmore found her responsibilities as first lady a heavy burden on her health. Her 18-year-old daughter, Mary, took over many official tasks. Mrs. Fillmore arranged for the purchase of the first cooking stove in the White House. She also set up the first White House library. When the Library of

Congress burned in 1851, Fillmore and his Cabinet helped fight the blaze.

Election of 1852. When the Whigs met to nominate a presidential candidate in 1852, they were divided between friends and foes of the Compromise of 1850. Southerners supported Fillmore. But most Northerners rejected him, and a small group of pro-Compromise delegates from New England supported Secretary of State Daniel Webster. General Winfield Scott, an antislavery candidate, was finally nominated. He lost the election.

Later years

Mrs. Fillmore died less than a month after her husband left office. She was buried in Washington, D.C.

Fillmore returned to Buffalo and resumed his law practice. The Know-Nothing and the Whig parties nominated him for president in 1856. But the Republicans, who nominated General John C. Frémont, cut into his support. Democrat James Buchanan won. Fillmore ran third, carrying only Maryland.

In 1858, Fillmore married Mrs. Caroline Carmichael McIntosh (Oct. 21, 1813-Aug. 11, 1881), a widow. During the Civil War, he opposed many of Abraham Lincoln's policies. After the war, he favored the Reconstruction program of President Andrew Johnson. Fillmore died on March 8, 1874, and was buried in Forest Lawn Cemetery in Buffalo.   Michael F. Holt

Related articles in *World Book* include:

Clay, Henry	Perry, Matthew C.	Taylor, Zachary
Know-Nothings	President of the U.S.	Whig Party

Outline

I. **Early life**
    A. Education   B. Fillmore's family
II. **Political and public career**
    A. Congressman   B. Vice president
III. **Fillmore's Administration (1850-1853)**
    A. Accomplishments   B. Life in the White House
    C. Election of 1852
IV. **Later years**

Questions

What did Fillmore do that is credited with delaying the Civil War for 10 years?
How did Fillmore meet his first wife?
Why did Fillmore support some proslavery measures even though he opposed slavery?

Fillmore's Cabinet

Secretary of state . . . .* Daniel Webster
	* Edward Everett (1852)
Secretary of the treasury	Thomas Corwin
Secretary of war	Charles M. Conrad
Attorney general	John J. Crittenden
Postmaster general	Nathan K. Hall
	Samuel D. Hubbard (1852)
Secretary of the Navy	William A. Graham
	John P. Kennedy (1852)
Secretary of the interior	Thomas M. T. McKennan
	Alexander H. H. Stuart (1850)

*Has a separate biography in *World Book.*

Why did he refuse a degree from Oxford University?
How did the argument over slavery help Zachary Taylor and Fillmore win office in 1848?

Additional resources

Joseph, Paul. *Millard Fillmore.* ABDO, 1999. Younger readers.
Rayback, Robert J. *Millard Fillmore.* 1959. Reprint. Am. Political Biography Pr., 1992. A standard source.
Santow, Dan. *Millard Fillmore.* Children's Pr., 2004. Younger readers.
Scarry, Robert J. *Millard Fillmore.* McFarland, 2001.
Smith, Elbert B. *The Presidencies of Zachary Taylor and Millard Fillmore.* Univ. Pr. of Kans., 1988.
Souter, Gerry and Janet. *Millard Fillmore.* Child's World, 2002. Younger readers.

Film. See Motion picture (The film); **Photography** (Film photography).

Filmstrip was a related series of still pictures on 35-millimeter film. A projector flashed one after another of these pictures on a screen. From about the 1940's to the 1980's, teachers used filmstrips for instruction. They were easier to use, could be stored in less space, and cost less than slides.

Filmstrips were black and white or in color. A record player or tape recorder attached to the projector provided sound for some filmstrips. The recording explained the film and sometimes had music. Some recordings changed pictures automatically by transmitting a silent signal to the projector. Other types gave a beep when the operator should change pictures. But teachers often preferred to explain the picture themselves or to have a pupil do it. In this way, the picture could be changed whenever desired. Students could ask questions immediately instead of waiting until the end of the picture.

Robert A. Sobieszek

Filter is a device that removes unwanted quantities from the flow of liquids or gases, or from the transmission of electric currents, beams of light, and sound waves. Filters that remove solid particles or other impurities from liquids or gases are made from paper, cloth, charcoal, porcelain, fiberglass, or some other porous material. Glass or gelatin filters are used on cameras to filter out certain light rays (see **Photography** [Filters]).

Internal-combustion engines use various types of filters to remove impurities from air, lubricating oils, or fuel. Dry-paper filters on carburetors remove impurities from air before it enters the engine. Most oil filters also are made of fibrous paper. Many fuel filters have a stack of ceramic or metal disks separated by narrow spaces, but a few consist of wire screen. Some high-temperature engines also use magnetic filters. The filters attract metallic particles smaller than 1 micron (0.001 millimeter, or $\frac{1}{25,400}$ inch).

Cigarette filters, usually made of cellulose acetate, remove some of the tar and nicotine particles from cigarette smoke. Air conditioners use filters made of fiberglass or metal, coated with an adhesive, to remove dust and pollen from the air. Almost all large cities have filtration plants to filter water.   Evan Powell

See also **Air conditioning** (Cleaning the air); **Aquarium, Home** (picture).

Filtration. See Water (City water systems).

Fin whale is the second-largest animal on Earth. Only the closely related blue whale is larger. Female fin whales may reach 88 feet (27 meters) in length and weigh as much as 80 tons (70 metric tons). Males are slightly smaller. Fin whales are dark gray on top and light gray or whitish below. The right side of a fin whale's lower jaw is bright white. The whale has a *dorsal fin* on the rear half of the back. The head looks pointed as seen from the side and V-shaped as seen from above.

The fin whale has wide plates called *baleen* hanging from its upper jaw. The whale uses the baleen to strain food, such as tiny shellfish called *krill,* from the water. The whale feeds by lunging into masses of krill or other prey, taking in huge amounts of food and water. It then closes its mouth and forces the water out through the baleen, trapping the food inside. Two or more fin whales often lunge together in apparent attempts to corral the prey.

Fin whales live in all oceans. They migrate to cooler waters to feed in summer and to warmer waters to breed in winter. Fin whales were hunted heavily in the mid-1900's. International Whaling Commission restrictions now protect fin whales.   Bernd Würsig

Scientific classification. The scientific name of the fin whale is *Balaenoptera physalus.*

See also **Whale** (picture).

Finance. See Bank; Budget; Economics; Money.

Finance company is a firm that loans money to people who promise to repay the loan with interest in a specified period of time. Borrowers must offer some guarantee that they will repay the loan, such as a lien on their salary or personal possessions (see Lien).

Some finance companies also offer credit card services that let the holder buy merchandise. They also make loans to merchants and manufacturers. A merchant may offer the finance company a purchaser's contract to buy goods on installment payments as security for cash loans (see Installment plan). Some finance companies buy these contracts. Business people who need a loan can offer property, merchandise, or unpaid bills due to them as security. See also **Loan company.**

Joanna H. Frodin

Finch is a general term applied to any small seed-eating songbird. Finches include towhees, goldfinches, buntings, and grosbeaks. They live on all of the continents except Antarctica and on most ocean islands. Their stout cone-shaped bills, strong skulls, large jaw muscles, and grinding gizzards enable these birds to eat hard seeds.

In North America, the term *finch* usually refers to members of the family Fringillidae. Many of these finches have striking red and yellow colors. These birds also sing beautifully, often while in flight. Finches build closely woven, cup-shaped nests in the branches of trees and shrubs. The female lays three to six bluish eggs that are usually streaked or spotted. She sits on and warms the eggs until they hatch, and the male finds food. Both the male and female care for the young.

Edward H. Burtt, Jr.

Scientific classification. Finches belong to five families: Emberizidae, Fringillidae, Passeridae, Ploceidae, and Estrildidae.

Related articles in *World Book* include:

Bird (pictures)	Crossbill	Linnet
Bullfinch	Goldfinch	Pine siskin
Bunting	Grosbeak	Sparrow
Canary	Junco	Towhee
Cardinal		

Fine is a payment of money ordered by a court from a person who has been found guilty of violating a law. The word comes from the Latin *finem facere,* which means *to put an end to.* The term originated in England in 1275, when the courts began to permit convicts to be released from prison when they paid a required amount of money. A fine is often the punishment for a *misdemeanor* (minor crime). But a fine and a prison sentence can be the penalty for a major crime. People who cannot pay a fine assessed against them are usually ordered to serve a prison sentence.   James O. Finckenauer

Fine arts is a term that refers in its broadest modern sense to architecture, ballet, concert music, literature, opera, painting, and sculpture. The adjective *fine* is meant to emphasize the beautiful in art, as distinguished from art that is primarily intended to be useful, morally uplifting, or merely pleasing.

The term *fine arts* has been defined differently in various historical periods. For example, during most of the Middle Ages, which lasted from about the 400's through the 1400's, there were seven fine arts or branches of learning. They were called the *liberal arts* and consisted of arithmetic, astronomy, *dialectic* (a form of logic), geometry, grammar, music, and rhetoric. It was not until the Renaissance, which began in the early 1300's, that painting, sculpture, and the performing arts came to be considered legitimate branches of the arts.

In modern times, there have been different definitions of the fine arts and different philosophies concerning what varieties of art should properly be called *fine.* For example, many people today believe that only those arts that appeal to the sense of sight belong to the fine arts. According to this view, painting and sculpture rank as the primary fine arts, followed by architecture and landscape architecture.

Fine arts are sometimes contrasted with the *decorative arts.* The term decorative arts is generally reserved for works of art produced for actual use. Decorative arts are often called *applied arts* or industrial arts. They include woodwork (especially furniture), metalwork, ceramics, glass, and sometimes textiles. The use of such contrasting categories reflect the concept that the fine arts exist only for their beauty while the decorative arts exist mainly for their usefulness.

Some authorities have combined the traditional fine and decorative arts under the term *visual arts,* and they group music, opera, and drama under the term *auditory arts.* Still others group music, dance, film, and the theater arts as the *performing arts.* These works must be performed by people or by the mechanical means of the camera or phonograph.

Increasingly, distinctions between the fine arts and decorative arts are being discarded. Today, people tend to regard ceramics and furniture as fine arts in spite of their functional aspects and place them with literature, painting, and sculpture. Whenever artists employ good design and produce works satisfying to the eye, mind, and ear, modern thought tends to classify these works as fine art.   John W. Keefe

Related articles in *World Book* include:

Aesthetics	Classical music
Architecture	Dance
Art and the arts	Design
Ballet	Drama
Drawing	Novel
Furniture	Opera
Glass	Painting
Graphic arts	Philosophy (Aesthetics)
Jewelry	Photography
Landscape architecture	Poetry
Literature	Pottery
Mosaic	Sculpture
Motion picture	Theater
Music	

Finger. See Hand.

Finger, Charles Joseph (1869?-1941), an American adventure writer, won the 1925 Newbery Medal for his children's book *Tales from Silver Lands* (1924). This work is a retelling of 19 fairy tales from the Indians of South America.

Finger's colorful adventures as a young man furnished him with rich background material for the 35 books he wrote during his life. His fiction includes *Courageous Companions* (1929), *A Dog at His Heel* (1936), and *Give a Man a Horse* (1938). He also wrote *Seven Horizons* (1930), an autobiography.

Finger left home when he was 16. He roamed Africa, Alaska, and the Antarctic, and explored much of the United States. He spent 10 years in South America, hunting gold, herding sheep, and living with Indians, sailors, miners, and *gauchos* (cowboys). When he was past 50, he bought a farm in the Ozark hills of Arkansas and began to write stories.

Finger was born in Willesden, England. He studied in England and Germany. Finger became a United States citizen in 1896. He died on Jan. 7, 1941, at Gayeta Lodge in Fayetteville.   Kathryn Pierson Jennings

Finger alphabet. See Sign language (picture).

Finger Lakes are a group of long, narrow lakes in west-central New York. They received their name because they are shaped somewhat like the fingers of a hand. For the location of the lakes, see **New York** (physical map).

Most geographers include 11 lakes in the group. The lakes are, from east to west, Otisco, Skaneateles, Owasco, Cayuga, Seneca, Keuka, Canandaigua, Honeoye, Canadice, Hemlock, and Conesus. All the lakes lie generally in a north-south direction.

The most common explanation for how the lakes were formed is that glacial ice sheets deepened valleys that already existed in the area. Water from melting glaciers filled the valleys, which were dammed at their southern ends by glacial deposits of soil and rock.

Seneca is the largest of the Finger Lakes. It is 37 miles (60 kilometers) long and 3 miles (4.8 kilometers) wide at its broadest point. This lake lies 446 feet (136 meters) above sea level and is 600 feet (180 meters) deep at some points. Watkins Glen, a famous summer resort, is at the head of Seneca Lake.

Cayuga Lake is 40 miles (64 kilometers) long, 1 to 3 miles (1.6 to 4.8 kilometers) wide, 435 feet (133 meters) deep, and lies 380 feet (116 meters) above sea level. Taughannock Falls (215 feet, or 66 meters), near the head of Cayuga Lake, is one of the highest waterfalls east of the Rocky Mountains. Seneca Lake and Cayuga Lake are connected at their northern ends by the Cayuga and Seneca Canal, which is part of the New York State Canal System.

The Finger Lakes lie in rolling country, with rounded

hills from 60 to 800 feet (18 to 240 meters) above the level of the lakes. Thick woods, vineyards, orchards, and dairy farms cover most of the lake shores. Streams that run through many gorges and glens empty into the lakes.   Ray Bromley

Finger painting is a method of painting pictures using the fingers, hands, and arms to apply the paint. A finger painter works with a thick, pasty paint and, in most cases, a wet piece of paper. The painter spreads, rolls, or pats the paint on the paper. The surfaces of the fingers, hands, and arms produce different designs.

Finger painting is enjoyed by both children and adults. The activity appeals especially to youngsters because it is easy and fun. Finger painting provides many adults with a relaxing hobby. It is used as a form of therapy for people with mental illnesses because it helps them express their feelings. It is also a practical activity for partially sighted people because it stresses movement and does not require attention to visual details.

The standard paper used in finger painting is large and has a glazed side, on which the paint is applied. The paper should be soaked in water and then placed on a smooth, hard surface made of plastic or another material that can be washed easily. The painter smooths out all wrinkles and air bubbles from the paper and puts about two tablespoons of paint in the center of the paper. Beginners should work with one or two colors until they learn the techniques of finger painting. If the paint is too thick or begins to dry, it may be mixed with a few drops of water. Paint can be removed from the paper and hands with a wet sponge or cloth. If a second color of paint is used, it should be mixed with water to give it the same consistency as the first color.

Most finger painters work from a standing position, which allows them to move freely. The artist can spread the paint on the paper any way he or she chooses. Some

WORLD BOOK photo

A young artist applies finger paint to a piece of damp paper. Children enjoy finger painting because it is easy to learn and allows them to use their imagination to create countless designs.

finger painters work in rhythm with music. Artists may create abstract designs, or realistic pictures of birds, flowers, mountains, trees, or other subjects.

After the painting is finished, it should be lifted by the corners and placed on a newspaper to dry. Drying takes about an hour. If the painting wrinkles, press a warm iron against the back to flatten it out. Some artists paint on waterproofed canvas, glass, or other materials that last longer than paper.

No one knows for certain when finger painting began. As early as A.D. 750, Chinese artists created finger paintings.   Margaret A. Wolff

Finger spelling. See Deafness (Special language techniques); Sign language.

Finger painting by Margaret A. Wolff (WORLD BOOK photo)

A finger painting shows an arrangement of plantlike forms. The picture is an example of the detailed designs that a skilled finger painter can create. The artist used the fingertips, palm, and other parts of the hand and arm to paint this picture.

Fingernail. See Nail (finger).

Fingerprinting is a method of identifying people using impressions made by the fingers, thumb, and palm of the hand. These impressions show patterns formed by small ridges on the skin. Each person has a unique pattern of ridges. Experts believe that no two people have identical fingerprints. Fingerprints generally remain the same throughout a person's life. They only change in cases of certain diseases or injuries.

Law enforcement officers use fingerprints to investigate crime. Expert witnesses often present fingerprints as evidence in criminal trials. Prints may also help identify victims of wars, natural disasters, epidemics, accidents, and other circumstances that make other identification methods impossible. Some government agencies and corporations use fingerprinting to prevent crime. For example, many airports, banks, and military bases check fingerprints before allowing access to certain areas and computer systems.

Today, organizations and individuals increasingly identify people through examination of *genetic* (hereditary) material. This is called *DNA analysis* or *DNA fingerprinting.* DNA identification is a more scientifically advanced process. But it is not always as specific. For example, identical twins have identical DNA but different fingerprints. See **DNA fingerprinting.**

Types of fingerprints. There are four main types of fingerprints. They are (1) *known prints* (also called *exemplar prints*), (2) *latent prints;* (3) *patent prints;* and (4) *plastic prints.* Known prints are intentionally recorded from a person for the purpose of identification. Traditionally, known prints are recorded by applying ink to a person's fingers. The fingers are then pressed or rolled onto paper. Today, many known fingerprints are recorded electronically and stored in computer databases. Investigators may collect latent prints from a crime scene. The prints do not become visible until exposed by some method. Patent prints are prints easily visible to the unaided eye. Plastic prints are three-dimensional impressions in a soft or flexible surface, such as wax.

Most latent fingerprints are formed by residue of per-

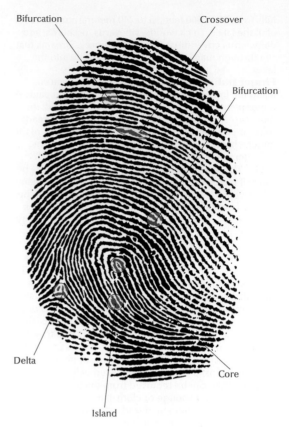

Fingerprint characteristics enable a trained examiner to compare prints. The characteristics are patterns formed by ridges and furrows on the skin of each fingertip. Examiners compare characteristics around the center or *core* of the print. A point where a ridge diverges is called a *bifurcation.* An *island* is a small isolated portion of a ridge. A *crossover* is a point where two ridges appear to cross. A triangular *delta* occurs where two or more ridges come together. Each person has a unique pattern of characteristics. A trained examiner decides whether two prints share enough characteristics for a positive identification.

spiration and oils from human skin and other substances picked up from the environment. These prints must be *developed* (made visible) to be photographed. Development methods vary depending on the type of surface being examined. Examiners may use powders or chemicals to make latent prints visible. These substances stick to the invisible residues, making the fingerprint visible. Some fingerprints are clearly visible and do not need to be developed. These often include fingerprints made by soiled fingers. They may also include those found on such surfaces as blood, dust, or powder.

Fingerprint identification. Trained fingerprint examiners compare collected fingerprints with known standards to determine if they came from the same person. Many countries require that prints have a certain number of matched characteristics. These are points where ridges in the skin end or branch. In other countries, however, the examiner decides independently whether the prints have enough detail for an identification.

Computer fingerprint systems can record fingerprints and compare them with prints in an electronic database. This type of system can be used at police departments, airports, military bases, and border checkpoints.

Mike Fink was a colorful American folk hero. He gained fame for his exploits as an Indian fighter on the Pennsylvania frontier and as a keelboater on the Ohio and Mississippi rivers. A famous story tells how Fink shot the scalp lock off an Indian named Proud Joe as a prank, *shown here.* Later, Proud Joe tried to get revenge on Fink, but he killed one of Fink's companions by mistake. Fink killed Proud Joe during the fight.

Bettmann Archive

People often use computers to aid in fingerprint identification. Computers can sort through huge fingerprint databases, producing lists of possible matches to a collected print. A trained examiner then decides whether two prints share enough unique characteristics for a positive identification.

There are two main purposes for taking and examining fingerprints. They are *archival fingerprint identification* and *forensic fingerprint identification.* In archival fingerprint identification, examiners compare new known prints with known fingerprints collected earlier. Archival fingerprint identification is often used to verify or disprove claims of identity. Security officials often use archival fingerprint identification to check people's identity during international travel. During this process, they may compare a person's fingerprints with an electronic database of known criminals or terrorists.

In forensic fingerprint identification, examiners compare latent fingerprints with known prints collected from suspects or victims. The main goal is to help identify or eliminate suspects in a criminal investigation. However, latent fingerprints are often distorted or incomplete. As a result, they may appear different from known prints, even if they are from the same person. Forensic examiners disagree over the exact number and types of similarities needed for an accurate identification.

History. In the 1860's, Sir William J. Herschel, a British colonial administrator, began using archival fingerprint identification to prevent fraud in India. In 1880, Henry Faulds, a Scottish doctor, proposed the use of forensic fingerprint identification to help solve crimes. During the 1880's and 1890's, Francis Galton, a British scientist and statistician, worked to develop the scientific foundations for fingerprint identification.   Jason H. Byrd

See also **Biometrics; Footprinting.**

Fink, Mike (1770?-1823), was an American frontier fighter and boatman whose adventures became the subject of many stories and legends. Fink's great strength, boastful nature, and skill with his rifle and his fists made him a hero on the frontier. He also was notorious for playing cruel pranks. One story tells how Fink punished his wife for flirting with another man by making her lie in a pile of dry leaves, which he then set on fire.

Fink was born at or near Fort Pitt (now Pittsburgh), Pennsylvania. As a youth, he gained fame for his expert marksmanship while fighting the British and Indians on the Pennsylvania frontier. During the early 1800's, Fink became the most famous of the rugged keelboaters who worked on the Ohio and Mississippi rivers. After steamboats replaced keelboats, Fink joined the Rocky Mountain Fur Company as a boatman and trapper. On his first expedition, he was killed by a companion.

Many stories have been told about how Fink died. But nearly all the tales agree that he died as a result of a shooting match. Fink and a friend named Carpenter were taking turns shooting a cup off each other's head. According to one story, Carpenter shot first and accidentally grazed Fink's scalp. Fink became enraged and shot his friend through the forehead. In revenge, one of Carpenter's friends shot Fink in the heart.   Harry Oster

© Hannu Vallas, Lehtikuva Oy

Helsinki, Finland's capital and largest city, stands at the southern tip of the country on the Gulf of Finland. The city is also one of the nation's chief ports and its commercial and cultural center. The Lutheran Cathedral, *upper right,* rises above Senate Square in the city's historic district.

Finland

Finland is a country in northern Europe famous for its scenic beauty. Thousands of lovely lakes dot Finland's landscape, and thick forests cover over 70 percent of the land. The country has a long, deeply indented coast, marked by colorful red and gray granite rocks. Thousands of scenic islands lie offshore.

Sweden lies to the west of Finland, northern Norway lies to the north, and Russia lies to the east. The Gulf of Finland and the Gulf of Bothnia, two extensions of the Baltic Sea, border Finland on the south and southwest. The northernmost part of the country lies inside the Arctic Circle in a region called the *Land of the Midnight Sun.* In this region of Finland, the sun shines 24 hours a day for long periods each summer. Helsinki, the country's capital and largest city, is in the south on the Gulf of Finland.

Most of Finland's people live in the southern part of the country, where the climate is mildest. Finns love outdoor activities and the arts. They have a high standard of living and receive many welfare benefits from the national government.

Much of Finland's wealth comes from its huge forests. They form the basis of the country's thriving forest-products industry, which includes woodworking and the manufacture of paper and pulp.

Finland's location between Russia on the east and Sweden on the west has played an important role in the country's history. In the 1000's, Sweden and Russia began to battle for possession of Finland. Sweden gradual-ly gained control in the 1100's and 1200's, but conflict between Sweden and Russia over Finland continued for hundreds of years.

Today, Swedish remains equal with Finnish as an official language of Finland. Russia had control of the country from 1809 until 1917, when Finland declared itself independent. The nation then became a republic with a president and parliament. During World War II

Facts in brief

Capital: Helsinki (in Swedish, Helsingfors).
Official languages: Finnish and Swedish.
Official name: Republic of Finland. Finland's name in Finnish is Suomi.
Area: 130,669 mi² (338,432 km²), including 12,943 mi² (33,522 km²) of inland water. *Greatest distances*—east west, 320 ml (515 km); north-south, 640 mi (1,030 km). *Coastline*—1,462 mi (2,353 km).
Elevation: *Highest*—Mount Haltia, 4,344 ft (1,324 m) above sea level. *Lowest*—sea level.
Population: *Estimated 2014 population*—5,437,000; density, 42 per mi² (16 per km²); distribution, 68 percent urban, 32 percent rural. *2011 official government estimate*—5,401,267.
Chief products: *Agriculture*—barley, beef, milk, oats, pork, potatoes, poultry, sugar beets, wheat. *Forestry*—birch, pine, spruce. *Manufacturing*—electronics, machinery, paper products, ships, wood products. *Mining*—copper, nickel, zinc.
National anthem: "Maamme" (in Finnish) or "Vårt Land" (in Swedish), meaning "Our Land."
Money: *Basic unit*—euro. One hundred cents equal one euro. The markka was taken out of circulation in 2002.

(1939-1945), Finland fought two wars with the Soviet Union, which was formed under Russia's leadership in 1922 and existed until 1991.

Government

Finland is a democratic republic. Its Constitution went into force in 2000, replacing the original constitution adopted in 1919. The Constitution guarantees the people such rights as freedom of speech, freedom of worship, and equality before the law. All Finns who are 18 and older may vote.

The president is Finland's head of state and chief executive. The president is elected to a six-year term by the people of Finland. If no candidate wins more than half of the votes cast, a runoff is held between the two most popular candidates. No president may serve more than two terms in a row.

The president may issue orders that do not violate existing laws, *veto* (reject) bills passed by the parliament, and dissolve the parliament and call for new elections. The president handles foreign relations and acts as head of the armed forces. The president makes decisions concerning war and peace, but the parliament must approve these decisions.

The prime minister and Cabinet. With the advice of parliament, the president appoints the prime minister, who is head of government. The prime minister, with the president's approval, forms a Cabinet made up of members of several political parties. The political parties involved must agree on the Cabinet selections. Cabinet members head the government departments. The prime minister presides over the Cabinet and works with it in setting government programs, which must be acceptable to the parliament.

The parliament of Finland is a one-house legislature called the Eduskunta (in Swedish, the Riksdag). The people elect its 200 members to four-year terms. The parliament creates the country's laws and makes important decisions on the government budget and taxes. If the president vetoes a bill, the Eduskunta can override the veto and pass the bill by a simple majority vote.

Local government. For purposes of local government, Finland is divided into 19 regions, plus the autonomous Aland Islands. The regions are subdivided into hundreds of municipalities. They range in size from thinly populated rural areas to large cities. A council elected by the people governs each municipality. Municipalities collect their own taxes to support hospitals, schools, and other local institutions.

Political parties. Election to the Eduskunta is based on a system called *proportional representation.* This system gives a political party a share of seats in the parliament according to its share of the total votes cast in an election. The system encourages small parties to put up candidates and makes it hard for any one party to win a majority. As a result of proportional representation, a number of parties usually have seats in the Eduskunta.

The parties that generally receive the most votes are the Social Democratic Party, supported mostly by working-class and lower-middle-class voters; the centrist Center Party; and the conservative National Coalition Party. Other parties include the Christian Democrats, Green League, Left Alliance, Swedish People's Party, and True Finns.

© Superstock

Parliament Building in Helsinki is the meeting place of Finland's one-house legislature, the Eduskunta. The building was completed in 1931.

Finland's civil flag, *shown here,* was adopted in 1918. The state flag includes the coat of arms.

The Finnish coat of arms was adopted in its present form in 1918. But its basic design dates back to the 1500's.

WORLD BOOK map

Finland is a northern European nation bordering Sweden, Norway, and Russia. Its coast stretches along gulfs of the Baltic Sea.

Finland
political map

WORLD BOOK map

International boundary
Expressway
Road
Railroad
Ferry
Canal
National capital
Other city or town

Cities and towns

Äänekoski	13,758	.F	3
Alavus (Alavo)	9,930	.F	3
Anjalankoski	17,631	.G	4
Borgå (Porvoo)	44,969	.H	3
Ekenäs (Tammi- saari)	14,632	.H	3
Espoo (Esbo)	213,271	.H	3
Forssa	18,506	.G	3
Haapajärvi	8,236	.E	3
Hämeenlinna	46,108	.G	3
Hamina	9,832	.G	4
Hangö (Hanko)	10,044	.H	3
Harjavalta*	7,877	.G	2
Heinola	21,178	.G	4
Helsinki (Helsingfors)	555,474		
	†1,027,305	.H	3
Hollola*	20,378	.G	3
Hyvinkää	42,545	.G	3
Iisalmi	23,113	.E	4
Ikaalinen	7,744	.G	2
Imatra	30,663	.G	4
Inari	7,360	.B	4
Jakobstad (Pietarsaari)	19,636	.E	3
Jämsä	15,537	.G	3
Järvenpää	35,915	.G	3
Joensuu	51,758	.F	5
Jyväskylä	78,996	.F	3
Kajaani	36,088	.E	4
Kangasala*	22,276	.G	3
Kankaanpää	13,018	.G	2
Karis (Karjaa)	8,877	.H	3
Karkkila	8,753	.G	3
Kemi	23,689	.D	3
Kemijärvi	10,484	.C	4
Kerava	30,270	.H	3
Kirkkonummi*	29,694	.H	3
Kokemäki (Kumo)	8,714	.G	2
Kokkola (Karleby)	35,539	.E	3
Kotka	54,846	.G	4
Kouvola	31,364	.G	4
Kristinestad (Kristiinan- kaupunki)	8,084	.F	2
Kuopio	86,651	.F	4
Kurikka	10,708	.F	2
Kuusamo	17,729	.D	4
Kuusankoski	20,656	.G	4
Lahti	96,921		
	†110,160	.G	3
Lappeenranta	58,041	.G	4
Lapua	14,055	.F	3
Laukaa	16,548	.F	3
Lieksa	15,208	.E	5
Lohja (Lojo)	35,243	.H	3
Loimaa	7,184	.G	3
Mariehamn (Maarian- hamina)	10,488	.H	2
Mikkeli	46,727	.G	4
Naantali	13,133	.G	2
Nokia	26,905	.G	3
Nurmes	9,781	.E	5
Nurmijärvi	33,104	.G	3
Nykarleby (Uusi- kaarlepyy)	7,492	.E	2
Oulainen	8,203	.E	3
Oulu	120,753		
	†157,605	.D	3
Outokumpu	8,155	.F	4
Pargas (Parainen)	11,943	.H	2
Parkano	7,807	.F	3
Pieksämäki	12,918	.F	4
Pori	75,994	.G	2
Raahe	17,076	.E	3
Raisio	23,149	.G	2
Rauma	37,190	.G	2
Riihimäki	26,173	.G	3
Rovaniemi	35,427	.C	3
Salo	24,561	.H	3
Savonlinna	27,796	.F	5
Seinäjoki	30,290	.F	3
Siilinjärvi*	19,742	.F	4
Suolahti	5,624	.F	3
Suomussalmi	11,003	.D	4
Suonenjoki	8,048	.F	4
Taivalkoski	5,127	.D	4
Tampere	195,468		
	†270,753	.G	3
Tornio	22,617	.D	3
Turku (Åbo)	172,561		
	†239,018	.G	2
Tuusula*	31,957	.H	3
Utsjoki	1,394	.A	4
Uusikaupunki	17,019	.G	2
Vaasa (Vasa)	56,737	.F	2
Valkeakoski	20,493	.G	3
Vammala	15,450	.G	3
Vantaa (Vanda)	178,471	.H	3
Varkaus	23,246	.F	4
Vihti*	23,858	.H	3
Viitasaari	7,915	.F	3
Virrat (Virdois)	8,236	.F	3
Ylitornio	5,535	.C	3
Ylivieska	13,248	.E	3
Ylöjärvi	20,518	.G	3

*Does not appear on map: key shows general location.
†Population of locality (metro- politan area equivalent).
Source: 2000 census.

The Aura River winds through Turku, Finland's oldest city. Turku was founded in the mid-1200's. This photograph shows people enjoying a summer festival along the banks of the river. Turku Cathedral rises in the background.

© Matti Kolho, Lehtikuva Oy

Courts. Finland's highest court of appeal is the Supreme Court. Six regional courts hear appeals from lower courts. Special courts handle such matters as impeachment of government officials and labor disputes.

Armed forces. Finland has an army, navy, and air force. Healthy men between 18 and 60 must serve 6 to 12 months in the armed forces.

People

Ancestry and population. More than 90 percent of Finland's people are Finnish by descent, and most of the rest are Swedish. Russians compose about 1 percent of the population.

Most of Finland's people live in the south, where the climate is less harsh. About two-thirds of all Finns live in cities and towns. Helsinki, Finland's capital and largest city, has more than 500,000 people. Roughly a fifth of the nation's people live in Helsinki and its suburbs. See **Helsinki.**

Several thousand Sami (also called Lapps) live in Finland. Most of them live in the far northern part of the country. The Sami's homeland, called Sapmi (also known as Lapland), stretches across much of far northern Finland, Norway, and Sweden. The ancestors of the Sami lived in Finland long before the first Finns arrived thousands of years ago. See **Sami.**

Languages. Finland has two official languages—Finnish and Swedish. Most of the people speak Finnish, and many speak Swedish. Most of the Swedish-speaking people live on the south and west coasts and on the offshore Aland Islands. Finnish and Swedish belong to different language families. The Sami speak a language related to Finnish. See **Language** (Language families).

Way of life. In Finland's cities, most people own or rent apartments. Most people in rural areas live in one-family homes on farms or in villages.

The Finns enjoy fish, especially herring, perch, pike, and salmon. Popular meats include beef, veal, pork, and sausage. Smoked reindeer is a special treat. Boiled potatoes covered with butter and dill sprigs make up a favorite side dish. Butter and milk are important parts of the Finnish diet.

The most famous feature of Finnish life is a special kind of bath called a *sauna*. Most Finns take a sauna at least once a week for cleansing and relaxation. In a sauna room or bathhouse, stones are heated over a stove or furnace. The temperature in the sauna rises to between 176 and 212 °F (80 and 100 °C). Bathers sit or lie on wooden benches until they begin to perspire freely. They may throw water on the stones to produce vapor and make the sauna feel even hotter. They may beat themselves gently with leafy birch twigs to stimulate circulation. While taking a sauna, Finns relax and talk quietly. Typically, newspapers, televisions, and other distractions are not allowed.

© Dave G. Houser

In a sauna, heat causes the body to perspire and relax. Bathers then take a cold shower or swim in cold water. They may repeat the process. Saunas have long been a part of Finnish life.

After heating up in the sauna, bathers take a cold shower or plunge into a lake. They may repeat the cycle of heating and cooling several times. When they are finished, they rest until their body returns to normal temperature.

Social welfare. The government of Finland provides the people with many welfare services. Since the 1920's, maternity and child welfare centers have given free health care to pregnant women, mothers, and children. Since 1948, families have received an allowance every time they have had a new baby as well as a yearly allowance for each child under the age of 16.

In 1939, Finland began an old-age and disability insurance program. This program guarantees monthly pensions to people 65 years and older and to permanently disabled citizens. In 1963, Finland set up a health insurance program for all citizens.

The government began to guarantee workers annual holidays in the 1920's. Today, workers who remain in the same job for one year receive a 26-day annual vacation. After 10 years, they receive 36 days.

Recreation. The Finns love outdoor sports. In winter, they enjoy ice hockey, ice skating, ski-jumping, cross-country skiing, and downhill skiing. Popular summer sports include *pesäpallo* (a Finnish form of baseball), swimming, boating, and hiking. In summer, thousands of city families flock to their cottages and saunas on lakes, the seacoast, or the offshore islands. Favorite spectator sports include track-and-field events and ice hockey matches. The Finns also enjoy ballets, concerts, motion pictures, plays, and operas.

Education. Almost all adult Finns can read and write. All elementary school students and most other students go to public schools. The rest attend private schools, which may charge a small tuition fee. Elementary school students receive one meal a day, books, and medical and dental care, all free of charge.

Finland has a *comprehensive school system.* Under this system, children are required to attend elementary schools called *basic schools* for nine years. They begin at the age of 7. They attend the lower level of the schools for six years and the upper level for three years.

After completing basic school, students may choose to enter an *upper secondary school* or a *vocational school.* Upper secondary schools, which offer three-year courses, emphasize academic subjects. Vocational schools, most of which offer two-year courses, emphasize education in skilled manual work.

Most vocational school students enter the job market after graduating. Graduates of upper secondary schools may apply to a *polytechnical institute* or a university. Polytechnical institutes chiefly prepare students for careers in business. The universities offer a wide variety of higher-education programs.

Finland has numerous universities and polytechnical institutes. The University of Helsinki is the country's largest university.

Religion. The Evangelical Lutheran Church is the state church of Finland, and the national government has supreme authority over it. However, the people have complete freedom of worship. Most Finns are Evangelical Lutherans.

Many people do not belong to any religious group. Religions with small followings in Finland include various other Protestant churches and the Eastern Orthodox Church.

The Forging of the Sampo (1893), an oil painting on canvas by Akseli Gallen-Kallela; Ateneum Art Museum; with permission of Matti Sirén (photo © Central Art Archives/Antti Kuivalainen)

The *Kalevala,* Finland's national epic, is a collection of peasant songs, poems, and chants. This illustration is by Akseli Gallen-Kallela, who created many famous illustrations of the epic.

The arts. Finland has a rich folk culture, which is reflected in the country's crafts, literature, music, and painting. The person most responsible for preserving Finland's oral folklore was Elias Lönnrot, a country doctor. He collected the centuries-old songs, poems, and chants of the Finnish peasants and assembled them into a collection published in 1835. This huge collection, called the *Kalevala,* became Finland's national epic.

During the 1800's and 1900's, the *Kalevala* inspired many artists. Akseli Gallen-Kallela used its themes in many paintings. Composer Jean Sibelius based most of his symphonic poems on the work. American poet Henry Wadsworth Longfellow patterned the rhythm of his poem *The Song of Hiawatha* on the *Kalevala.*

In the early 1800's, Johan Ludvig Runeberg became known as Finland's national poet. His poem "Vårt Land" is the country's national anthem. Other writers of the 1800's include the novelist Aleksis Kivi and the playwright Minna Canth, an early champion of women's rights. In the 1900's, the novelists Frans Eemil Sillanpää and Mika Waltari gained international fame. Sillanpää won the Nobel Prize for literature in 1939.

Finnish glassware, ceramics, furniture, and textiles are world famous for the simple beauty of their design. This same simplicity of line and shape can be seen in the works of Finland's best-known architects—Eliel Saarinen and Alvar Aalto. Saarinen's famous designs include the railroad station and the National Museum in Helsinki. Aalto gained fame not only as an architect, but also as a town planner and furniture designer.

The land

Finland is largely a plateau broken by small hills and valleys and low ridges and hollows. The land rises gradually from south-southwest to north-northeast, but the average altitude is only 400 to 600 feet (120 to 180 meters) above sea level. Mount Haltia, the country's highest point, stands 4,344 feet (1,324 meters) above sea level in the far northwestern region of Finland. About 60,000 lakes are scattered throughout the country, and forests cover almost two-thirds of the land.

Land regions. Finland has four main land regions: (1) the Coastal Lowlands, (2) the Lake District, (3) the Upland District, and (4) the Coastal Islands.

The Coastal Lowlands lie along the Gulf of Bothnia and Gulf of Finland. Finland's coastline is 1,462 miles (2,353 kilometers) long. Many small lakes lie in the Coastal Lowlands. The region has less forestland and a milder climate than the Lake and Upland districts have. The lowlands also have some of the country's most fertile soil. As a result, the region offers the best conditions for farming. The Coastal Lowlands of the south have the mildest climate and the most productive farms. Most of Finland's people live in this area.

The Lake District occupies central Finland north and east of the Coastal Lowlands. The region has thousands of island-dotted lakes. The lakes cover about half the to-

tal area of the district. Narrow channels or short rivers connect many of the lakes. Saimaa, the largest lake in Finland, covers about 680 square miles (1,760 square kilometers) in the southeastern part of the region. The Saimaa Lake System, which is about 185 miles (298 kilometers) long, links several lakes in the area. A fleet of steamers travels the system, stopping at towns on the shores of the lakes. Forests of birch, pine, and spruce cover most of the land in the Lake District. Most farmlands in the region lie in the southwestern part of the Lake District.

The Upland District is Finland's northernmost and least densely populated region. It covers about 40 percent of the country. The Upland District has a harsher climate and less fertile soil than the other regions have. As one travels north through the Upland District, plant life becomes increasingly scarce. Stunted pines and arctic birches grow in parts of the district. However, the northernmost part of the region is a *tundra*—a frozen, treeless plain.

Most of Finland's hills rise in the Upland District. Swamps and marshlands separate the hills. Several rivers in the region provide energy for hydroelectric power stations.

The Coastal Islands consist of thousands of islands in the Gulf of Bothnia and Gulf of Finland. The great majori-

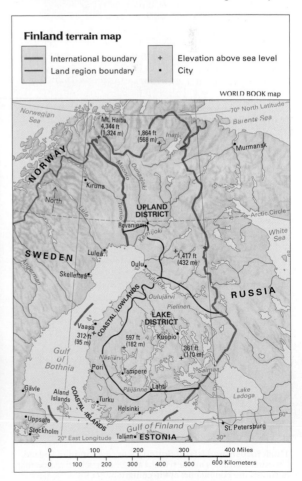

Finland terrain map

⎯⎯ International boundary	+ Elevation above sea level
⎯⎯ Land region boundary	• City

WORLD BOOK map

© Matti Kolho, Kuvasuomi Ky

Sami reindeer herders work in the Upland District in northern Finland. Much of the Upland District is part of Sapmi, the homeland of the Sami.

ty of these islands are small and uninhabited. The thin, rocky soil on many of Finland's islands cannot support much plant life, but many kinds of plants thrive on a few of the larger islands. People who fish for a living reside on some of the islands. However, Finland's islands serve chiefly as summer recreation areas. Many Finns have cottages or saunas on them.

The most important islands are the Aland group, which consists of about 6,500 islands off Finland's southwest coast. People, almost all of whom speak Swedish, live on about 80 of these islands. The land area of the Aland Islands totals 572 square miles (1,481 square kilometers). The main island, also called Aland, is Finland's largest island. Aland covers 285 square miles (738 square kilometers) and is an important tourist and shipping center.

Embassy of Finland

Thick forests and island-dotted lakes cover most of Finland. This small farm lies in the scenic Lake District, a land region that occupies the central part of the country.

Rivers. Finland's longest river is the Kemijoki. It rises in the Upland District near the Russian border and winds southwestward 340 miles (547 kilometers) to the Gulf of Bothnia. The Kemijoki and its chief branch, the Ounasjoki, provide important logging routes and rich salmon catches. Several hydroelectric stations have been built along both rivers.

The Muonio River begins about 60 miles (97 kilometers) southeast of the point where the Norwegian, Swedish, and Finnish borders meet. The river flows south about 110 miles (177 kilometers), forming part of the border between Sweden and Finland. The Muonio provides a logging route.

The Oulujoki River rises in the northern part of the Lake District and empties into the Gulf of Bothnia. The river is only about 80 miles (130 kilometers) long. But it serves as an important logging route. Its 105-foot (32-meter) Pyhä Falls provides power for a major hydroelectric plant.

Climate

Finland has a much milder climate than most other regions of the world that lie as far north. In January, for example, Helsinki's temperatures often average 25 to 35 °F (14 to 18 °C) higher than the temperatures in parts of Canada at the same latitude. Finland's climate is influenced chiefly by the Gulf Stream, a warm ocean current that flows off Norway's west coast. Finland's many lakes and the gulfs of Bothnia and Finland help give the country a relatively mild climate.

July temperatures in Finland average 55 to 63 °F (13° to 17 °C). The temperature reaches 50 °F (10 °C) or higher on 110 to 122 days a year in the south and on 50 to 85 days a year in the north. February is usually Finland's coldest month, with temperatures averaging from −7 to 26 °F (−22 to −3 °C). In northern Finland, winter temperatures sometimes drop as low as −60 °F (−51 °C).

The amount of *precipitation* (rain, melted snow, and other forms of moisture) varies between southern and northern Finland. The south receives about 27 inches (69 centimeters) a year, and the north only about 16 inches (41 centimeters). August usually has the heaviest amount of rainfall.

Snow covers the ground in southern Finland from December to April, and northern Finland is snowbound from October to April. Most of the country is icebound in winter, but special icebreaking boats keep the major Finnish ports open so passenger traffic and shipping can continue.

Northern Finland lies in the *Land of the Midnight Sun,* and so has continuous daylight during part of the summer (see **Midnight sun**). At the country's northernmost point, constant daylight lasts for about $2\frac{1}{2}$ months. The period of midnight sun decreases southward. Southern Finland never has continuous daylight, but it averages 19 hours of daylight a day in midsummer.

In winter, Finland has similar periods of continuous darkness. The sun never rises above the horizon in the northernmost areas of Finland for about 2 months in the winter. Southern areas only receive about 6 hours of sunlight a day in midwinter. The winter night sky—especially in northern Finland—often becomes glorious with bright displays of the aurora borealis, or northern lights (see **Aurora**).

Economy

Finland has a strong economy based mostly on private ownership. However, the national government has a monopoly in a few businesses, such as the railway and postal systems. In forestry and certain other industries, government-owned businesses compete with private companies.

Service industries account for nearly 65 percent of Finland's *gross domestic product* (GDP). The GDP is the total value of goods and services produced within a country in a year. Manufacturing, construction, utilities, and mining together account for nearly 35 percent. Agriculture, forestry, and fishing—taken together—account for less than 5 percent of the GDP.

Natural resources. Finland's greatest natural resource is its widespread forests. They cover over 70 percent of the land—a higher percentage than in any other European country. But Finland's other resources are limited. Its soil is poor, and the growing season short. The country has no reserves of natural gas or oil. Water power produces much of the country's electric power. Finland mines chalk, coal, copper, gold, nickel, silver, stone, talc, and zinc.

Forestry plays a leading role in Finland's economy. Although forestry by itself accounts for less than 5 percent of the GDP, much of Finland's industry is forest-based. Forestry and forest-products industries provide about one-sixth of Finland's exports. The government owns about a third of Finland's forests, chiefly in the north. But these northern forests make up a small percentage of the country's annual forest growth because of the short growing season in the north. Most private forests are owned by individual farmers. They work their farmland in summer and cut trees in their forests throughout the year. Pine, spruce, and birch trees cover much of the forestland.

Service industries are those economic activities that provide services rather than produce goods. Service in-

© Nokia, Inc.

A mobile communications device is inspected at a plant in Salo, Finland. Mobile communications technology and other electronic products are among Finland's leading exports.

Finland's gross domestic product

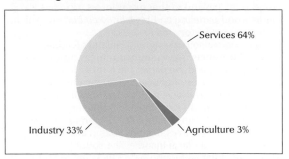

Services 64%

Industry 33%

Agriculture 3%

Finland's gross domestic product (GDP) was $244,676,000,000 in 2007. The GDP is the total value of goods and services produced within a country in a year. *Services* include community, government, and personal services; finance, insurance, real estate, and business services; trade, restaurants, and hotels; and transportation and communication. *Industry* includes construction, manufacturing, mining, and utilities. *Agriculture* includes agriculture, forestry, and fishing.

Production and workers by economic activities

Economic activities	Percent of GDP produced	Employed workers	
		Number of persons	Percent of total
Manufacturing	24	445,000	18
Community, government, & personal services	21	824,000	33
Finance, insurance, real estate, & business services	21	358,000	14
Trade, restaurants, & hotels	12	395,000	16
Transportation & communication	10	175,000	7
Construction	6	174,000	7
Agriculture, forestry, & fishing	3	113,000	5
Utilities	2	16,000	1
Mining	*	5,000	*
Total†	100	2,505,000	100

*Less than one-half of 1 percent.
†Figures do not add up to 100 percent due to rounding.
Figures are for 2007.
Sources: Statistics Finland; International Labour Organization; International Monetary Fund.

dustries account for nearly 65 percent of Finland's GDP and employ about 70 percent of its workers. The leading categories of service industry in Finland are community, government, and personal services and also finance, insurance, real estate, and business services. The government controls several large companies in Finland. The country's hotels, restaurants, and shops are aided by the millions of tourists who visit Finland each year. Many of these tourists come from Germany, Russia, Sweden, and the United Kingdom.

Manufacturing. Electrical equipment ranks as Finland's leading manufactured product. Telecommunications equipment is a major contributor to this sector. Nokia, the world's largest mobile telephone producer, has its headquarters in Espoo, near Helsinki.

Woodworking, pulp and paper production, and other forest-based industries traditionally have been among Finland's chief manufacturing industries. Finland is one of the world's top producers of plywood. The country is also a leading producer of paper and paperboard and wood pulp. Finland's other major forest products include wood paneling and *prefabricated houses*, which are erected in factory-made sections.

Machinery also ranks among Finland's leading manufactured products. The country produces machinery for use in farming and the paper and lumber industries. Finland also produces chemicals, metal products, printed items, processed foods, and transportation equipment.

Agriculture. Most of Finland's farmland lies in the south and west. The country's farms tend to be small. Dairy farming and livestock production account for much of Finland's farm income. The country's farmers raise many beef and dairy cattle, chickens, and hogs. Horses, reindeer, and sheep are also raised. Barley, oats, rye, and wheat are the main grain crops. Other crops include potatoes, rapeseed, and sugar beets. Finland's farmers produce all the cereals, eggs, meat, and milk needed by the people.

Foreign trade. Finland depends heavily on foreign trade. It imports large quantities of food products, iron and steel, machinery, petroleum and petroleum products, and transportation equipment. Electronics, such as cellular telephones, account for about 25 percent of Finland's exports. Wood, wood products, paper, and pulp also make up much of the country's exports. Other exports include cars, chemicals, machinery, and ships.

Finland's major trading partners include China, Germany, Russia, Sweden, the United Kingdom, and the United States. In 1995, Finland became a member of the European Union (EU), an economic and political organization of European nations. The EU has removed almost all tariffs and other restrictions on trade between member countries. See **European Union.**

Transportation. The government owns almost all of Finland's railroads. The country has a good network of roads and highways. Helsinki Airport is the country's busiest airport. The Finnish airline, Finnair, is partially owned by the government. It offers international and domestic flights. As a result of the great distances between many major Finnish communities and the difficulties of travel by land, Finland has one of Europe's busiest and most extensive domestic air networks. A system of inland waterways connects various lakes and seaports. Sköldvik, near Helsinki, is Finland's busiest port.

Communication. Finland's daily newspapers are privately owned. The largest dailies are *Helsingin Sanomat, Ilta Sanomat,* and *Iltalehti,* all of Helsinki; *Aamulehti* of Tampere; and *Turun Sanomat* of Turku. *Hufvudstadsbladet,* a large Swedish-language newspaper, is published in Helsinki.

The government operates the main radio and television networks. Much of the radio and television programming is in Finnish or Swedish. Commercial stations and cable television became popular in the late 1900's. Finland has high rates of mobile telephone and computer use, ranking among the leading nations in the use of such equipment.

History

Early years. The ancestors of the Finns and the Sami arrived in what is now Finland more than 5,000 years ago. At first, they lived as *nomadic* (traveling) hunters and gatherers. The ancestors of the Sami lived in the in-

© Matti Bjorkman, Lehtikuva Oy

Forestry and forest-products industries play an important role in Finland's economy. Forests cover over 70 percent of the country. A majority of the forests are privately owned.

land and more northerly areas. The ancestors of the Finns moved into the country from the southern shores of the Gulf of Finland. Their original homeland may have been between the Volga River and the Ural Mountains in what is now Russia. They eventually adopted agriculture and the raising of animals. The Finns gradually pushed the Sami—who continued to rely on hunting, gathering, and fishing—farther and farther north. The early Finns were divided into three loosely organized tribes that often fought one another.

In the 1000's, Sweden and Russia began a struggle for control of Finland. Both nations wanted to extend their boundaries. In addition, Sweden wanted to convert the Finns to Roman Catholicism, and Russia wanted to convert them to Eastern Orthodoxy.

Swedish rule. In the 1100's and 1200's, Sweden gradually conquered all Finland and established Catholicism as the official religion. Many Swedes settled in Finland, and Swedish became the official language. But Finns shared equal rights with Swedes. In 1593, a general church council held in Sweden made Lutheranism the official religion.

From the 1500's through the 1700's, Sweden and Russia fought several wars over Finland. Russia won the Finnish province of Vyborg after the Great Northern War (1700-1721), known in Finland as the Great Wrath. For several years of that war and from 1741 to 1743, Russia occupied all Finland. Sweden and Russia fought over Finland again from 1788 to 1790. After the 1788-1790 war, some Finns began to think Sweden could not protect their land. But a plot to create an independent Finland under Russian protection failed to win wide support.

Control by Russia. In 1808, Russia again invaded Finland. It conquered the country in 1809 and made it an independent grand duchy, but with the czar as grand duke. The duchy had local self-rule based on government systems developed during Swedish control. Russia returned Vyborg to the duchy.

During the 1800's, Finns began to develop feelings of nationalism as they took increasing pride in their country and its culture. In 1835, Elias Lönnrot collected and edited the *Kalevala,* whose heroic themes strengthened the growing sense of nationalism. Many Finnish leaders began to urge that Finnish be made an official language equal with Swedish. But Finnish did not become a fully equal official language until 1902.

In 1899, Czar Nicholas II began a program to force the Finns to accept Russian government and culture. He took away most of Finland's powers of self-rule and disbanded the Finnish national army. Russian was made the official language. In 1903, the Russian governor suspended Finland's constitution and became dictator. Finnish resistance reached a peak in 1905 with a six-day nationwide strike. The czar then restored much of Finland's self-government. In 1906, the Finns created their first parliament elected by all adult citizens, women as well as men. During the next several years, Russia again tried to Russianize Finland.

Finland stayed out of World War I (1914-1918). But its merchant ships were blockaded in the Gulf of Bothnia, and the country suffered food shortages and unemployment. In 1917, a revolution in Russia overthrew the czar. Finland then decided to declare its freedom.

The new republic. Finland declared its independence from Russia on Dec. 6, 1917. Russia's new Bolshevik (Communist) government recognized the new nation, but some Russian troops remained in Finland. In preparing for independence, the Finns had become divided into two groups—socialists, who formed armed units called the Red Guard, and nonsocialists, who formed armed units called the White Guard. Both groups had demanded Finnish independence, but the socialists also wanted revolutionary social changes.

In January 1918, the White Guard, led by Carl Gustaf Mannerheim, began operations in western Finland to expel the Russian troops. Meanwhile, the Red Guard attempted to take over the Finnish government in Helsinki. A bloody civil war broke out between the two groups. The Whites received aid from Germany, and the Reds from Russia. The war ended in a White victory in May 1918.

In 1919, Finland adopted a republican constitution, and Kaarlo Juho Ståhlberg became the first president. But Finland's relations with Sweden and Russia re-

Important dates in Finland

1100's-1200's Sweden gradually conquered all of Finland.
1500's-1700's Sweden and Russia fought several wars for possession of Finland.
1809 Finland became a grand duchy of the Russian Empire.
1917 Finland declared its independence from Russia.
1918 Finnish socialists and nonsocialists fought a civil war.
1919 Finland adopted a republican constitution.
1939-1940 The Soviet Union defeated Finland in the Winter War.
1941-1944 The Soviet Union defeated Finland in the Continuation War.
1946 Finland established a policy of neutrality in international politics.
1955 Finland joined the United Nations (UN) and the Nordic Council.
1981 President Urho Kekkonen resigned from office because of poor health. He had served as president since 1956.
1995 Finland joined the European Union, an economic and political organization of European nations.

mained unsettled. Finland and Sweden quarreled over possession of the Aland Islands. In 1921, the League of Nations awarded the islands to Finland. Disputes with Russia centered on Karelia, a large region east of present-day Finland. Finland demanded that the eastern part of Karelia be made part of Finland, like the rest of Karelia, or that it be made independent of Russia. Russia did not accept either of these demands, and relations between the two countries remained tense for years.

World War II (1939-1945). Although Finland never officially allied itself with any nation in World War II, the Soviet Union invaded the country twice. (The Soviet Union had been formed under Russia's leadership in 1922, and it existed until 1991.) The *Winter War* began on Nov. 30, 1939, when Soviet troops marched into Finland. Mannerheim led the strong Finnish resistance, which included troops on skis. But Finland had to agree to a peace treaty in March 1940. Under the peace treaty, Finland was forced to give up the southern part of Karelia, where 12 percent of the Finnish people lived. The

© Hulton Getty from Liaison

Finnish infantry troops on skis fought the invading Soviet army during the Winter War (1939-1940). The Finns were well-equipped for fighting in the winter weather, but they were vastly outnumbered by the Soviet troops.

area made up a tenth of Finland's territory and included Lake Ladoga and Finland's second largest city, Viipuri (now Vyborg). The Soviet Union also received a naval base at Hangö in the southwestern part of Finland.

In 1941, Finland allowed Germany to station troops in northern Finland and to move them through the region to attack the Soviet Union. The Soviet Union then bombed Finland, beginning the *Continuation War.* Finnish troops recaptured southern Karelia. But in 1944, Soviet troops pushed farther and farther into Finland, and the country had to give up. On Sept. 19, 1944, Finland and the Soviet Union signed an armistice. As the German troops retreated from northern Finland, they burned towns, villages, and forests behind them.

The destruction by the Germans was only part of Finland's heavy war losses. About 100,000 Finns died, and about 50,000 were permanently disabled. The Soviet Union regained southern Karelia and won other Finnish territories as well. The Soviet Union also leased a military base at Porkkala, near Helsinki, but gave up its base at Hangö. About 420,000 Karelians fled to Finland, where the government gave them new land. Finland also had to pay the Soviet Union large *reparations* (payment for damages). See **Russo-Finnish wars.**

Postwar developments. Mannerheim became Finland's president in 1944, but he retired in 1946 because of poor health. Juho K. Paasikivi finished Mannerheim's term and was elected to a full term in 1950. Paasikivi set a policy of Finnish neutrality in international politics. Under him, Finland also developed close economic and cultural ties with the Soviet Union, Denmark, Norway, and Sweden. In 1955, the Soviet Union returned Porkkala to Finland, and the two nations renewed a 1948 treaty of friendship and assistance.

Also in 1955, Finland joined both the United Nations and the Nordic Council, which includes Denmark, Iceland, Norway, and Sweden. Citizens of Nordic Council countries may work and receive social benefits in any member nation, and they may travel among member nations without a passport or visa. As a result, many Finns have moved to Sweden, which has a more developed economy and more welfare benefits than Finland has.

In 1956, Urho Kekkonen was elected president. He continued to emphasize neutrality in international affairs and was reelected in 1962 and 1968. Finland joined the European Free Trade Association (EFTA), an economic organization, as an associate member in 1961 and became a full member in 1986.

The late 1900's. During the late 1970's and early 1980's, Finland completed construction of four nuclear power plants. These plants supply about a third of the nation's energy needs. Finland hoped to improve the economy in the underdeveloped north and so relieve overcrowding in the booming south.

In January 1973, Finland's parliament passed a bill to extend Kekkonen's term from 1974 to 1978. Kekkonen was reelected in 1978. In September 1981, he took a medical leave from office, and Prime Minister Mauno Koivisto became acting president. Kekkonen resigned from office in October 1981 because of poor health. Koivisto was elected president in January 1982. Kekkonen died in 1986. Koivisto was reelected in 1988. In 1994, Martti Ahtisaari was elected to succeed him.

Recent developments. In 1995, Finland withdrew

from EFTA and joined the European Union (EU). The EU works for economic and political cooperation among its member nations. In 1999, Finland began using the euro, the EU's basic monetary unit. In 2000, Finland elected its first woman president, Tarja Halonen. In 2003, Matti Vanhanen became head of the ruling Center Party and prime minister of Finland. Mari Kiviniemi replaced Vanhanen in 2010, becoming Finland's second woman prime minister. The first woman prime minister, Anneli Jäätteenmäki, served briefly in 2003.

The conservative National Coalition Party won parliamentary elections in 2011, and Jyrki Katainen became prime minister. In 2012, Sauli Niinistö became the first National Coalition Party president since 1956.

John Lindow

Related articles in *World Book* include:

Biographies

Aalto, Alvar	Saarinen, Eero
Nurmi, Paavo	Sibelius, Jean

Other related articles

Helsinki
Lapland
Russo-Finnish wars
Sami
Sauna
Tampere
Tapiola

Outline

I. Government	
A. The president	D. Local government
B. The prime minister and Cabinet	E. Political parties
C. The parliament	F. Courts
	G. Armed forces
II. People	
A. Ancestry and population	E. Recreation
B. Languages	F. Education
C. Way of life	G. Religion
D. Social welfare	H. The arts
III. The land	
A. Land regions	B. Rivers
IV. Climate	
V. Economy	
A. Natural resources	E. Agriculture
B. Forestry	F. Foreign trade
C. Service industries	G. Transportation
D. Manufacturing	H. Communication
VI. History	

Finlay, Carlos Juan (1833-1915), a Cuban physician, was the first person to suggest that yellow fever might be transmitted by the bite of a mosquito now known as the yellow fever mosquito *(Aedes aegypti).* The American Yellow Fever Commission, which went to Havana, Cuba, in 1900, conducted experiments using mosquitoes provided by Finlay. The experiments supported Finlay's theory. Finlay was born on Dec. 3, 1833, in Puerto Principe (now Camagüey). He graduated from Jefferson Medical College in Philadelphia in 1855. He was chief sanitary officer of Cuba from 1902 to 1909. Finlay died on Aug. 20, 1915.   Matthew Ramsey

See also **Yellow fever.**

Finn MacCool, *FIHN muh KOOL,* was the leader of the Fianna, an Irish band of warriors who appear in the Fionn cycle, also known as the Fenian cycle, of ancient Irish tales. His name is also spelled *MacCumhal* or *Mac Cumhaill.* The tales are set in the province of Leinster about A.D. 200. Finn is also a familiar figure in Irish folk tales, which sometimes portray him as a giant. Several tales tell how Finn burned his thumb while cooking the salmon of knowledge. He put his thumb in his mouth to ease the pain. From that day, he had only to put his thumb in his mouth when he was perplexed to discover the solution to a problem.

Fionn tales focus not only on Finn but also on his son Oisin and his grandson Oscar. Finn and Oisin appear as Fingal and Ossian in the Ossianic poems published by the Scottish poet James Macpherson from 1760 to 1765. Macpherson claimed he had translated the poems from originals written by Ossian, but Macpherson was revealed as the actual author of at least some of them. Finn and Oisin also appear in the work of writers of the Irish Literary Renaissance of the late 1800's, notably in the poem *The Wanderings of Oisin* (1889) by William Butler Yeats. Finn as a giant is also the model for the character of Finn in James Joyce's experimental novel *Finnegans Wake* (1939).   James E. Doan

See also **Giant's Causeway; Irish literature** (Heroic tales, romances, and sagas); **Mythology** (Celtic mythology [The Fionn cycle]).

Finnish spitz is a strong, sturdy dog related to the Siberian husky, the Samoyed, and other Arctic dogs. A Finnish spitz looks somewhat like a fox. The dog has a thick, red-gold coat; erect, pointed ears; and brown eyes. Its bushy, curled tail falls over its hindquarters. The male Finnish spitz stands from 17 ½ to 20 inches (44.5 to 51 centimeters) tall at the shoulder and weighs about 30 pounds (14 kilograms). The female is slightly smaller.

The Finnish spitz is the national dog of Finland.

The Finnish spitz is the national dog of Finland. It is descended from dogs used for hunting by the early Finns. Finns still use the dog to hunt game birds. Outside Finland, however, the Finnish spitz is kept primarily as a pet. The dog is intelligent and good-tempered.

Critically reviewed by the Finnish Spitz Club of America

Finns. See Finland (People).

Fiord, *fyawrd,* also spelled *fjord,* is a long, narrow, winding inlet or arm of the sea. *Fiord* is a Norwegian word, first applied to the deep bays and inlets along the ragged and mountainous coastline of Norway. Geolo-

gists debate the origin of fiords. Some believe that rivers cut valleys that were then deepened by glaciers millions of years ago. Others think that fiords sit upon *faults* (cracks in Earth's crust), where the rock was weaker and more easily eroded by glaciers. Most fiords have steep, rocky walls. Some have foaming, roaring waterfalls. Most fiords also have shallow *sills* (underwater ridges) at their mouths that become more deeply submerged further inland. Small stretches of fertile farmland lie below some of the fiord walls.

The coasts of Alaska, British Columbia, Maine, Newfoundland and Labrador, Greenland, and New Zealand contain inlets like Norway's fiords. *Sea loch* or *firth* is the name for such an inlet in the United Kingdom.

Paul R. Bierman

See also **Norway** (Coast and islands; picture).

Fir is a common name for a number of handsome evergreen trees that belong to the pine family. Nine species of firs grow in the United States. Most of them grow in the mountains of the West. The *Douglas-fir,* a valuable timber tree, is not a true fir. It belongs to a separate *genus* (group) in the pine family (see **Douglas-fir**).

When a fir tree grows in the open, it is shaped somewhat like a pyramid. It has dense foliage. Its needle-shaped leaves do not grow in clusters like pine needles

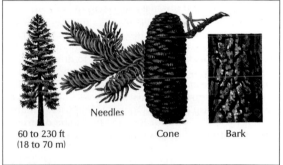

60 to 230 ft
(18 to 70 m)

Needles

Cone

Bark

The California red fir grows in the mountains of California and southern Oregon.

but occur evenly all around the branch. They are usually soft, blunt, and fragrant. In many species, the needles are dark green above, with light-colored lines on the bottom surface. Firs have distinctive cylinder-shaped cones that grow upright on the branches. When the cones mature, they shed their scales, leaving a bare, spinelike axis. The bark of young firs contains blisters filled with a sticky substance called *resin.* Resin helps protect firs from wood-boring insects.

Because of their shape and fragrance, true firs are widely used as Christmas trees. Especially popular for this use are the *balsam fir* and *Fraser fir.* The balsam fir grows in the northern United States and much of Canada. It may reach 60 feet (18 meters) tall. The Fraser fir grows in the mountains of North Carolina, Tennessee, and Virginia. It stands 30 to 50 feet (9 to 15 meters) tall.

The firs of western North America become much larger than balsam and Fraser firs. Most western firs are used for timber and for paper pulp. The *noble fir* is the largest true fir. This tree stands up to 250 feet (76 meters) tall, and its trunk measures up to 8 feet (2.4 meters) in diameter. The noble fir grows only in the Cascade Mountains in Oregon and southern Washington. Its wood is stronger and more valuable than that of other true firs. The *grand fir* grows in British Columbia, in western Washington and Oregon, and in the northern Rocky Mountains. Its nearly odorless white wood is often used for food containers. The *California red fir* grows in the mountains of California and southern Oregon. The *Pacific silver fir* is common in Oregon, Washington, and British Columbia. The *subalpine fir,* the most widespread western fir, grows from central Alaska to southern Arizona. It can live at higher elevations than other firs.   Douglas G. Sprugel

Scientific classification. Firs belong to the pine family, Pinaceae, and make up the genus *Abies.* The scientific name for the balsam fir is *A. balsamea;* the Fraser fir is *A. fraseri;* the grand fir, *A. grandis;* the noble fir, *A. procera;* the California red fir, *A. magnifica;* the Pacific silver fir, *A. amabilis;* and the subalpine fir, *A. lasiocarpa.*

See also **Balsam fir; Conifer; Tree** (Broadleaf and needleleaf trees [picture]).

Fire. The earliest use people made of fire was to keep warm. As civilizations advanced, people learned to use fire in many other ways. People learned to use fire to cook food, to shape weapons and tools, to change clay into pottery, and to furnish light. But early peoples had extremely slow and unsatisfactory ways of kindling fires. Today, we have not only improved the methods of kindling fires, but we also use fire in many more ways. Fire furnishes the energy to drive machines, and it keeps industries running. It supplies the power to drive trains, ships, and planes, and it generates electricity. Fire is also used to remove and destroy waste materials. In addition, fire is used in separating most metals from their ores, as well as in forging and shaping metals into useful things.

Controlled fire is useful. But fire can also be destructive. Uncontrolled fire kills thousands of people and destroys billions of dollars worth of property each year. Fires burned down large parts of London in 1666, Chicago in 1871, and Tokyo in 1923. Fires also destroy large areas of trees and brush every year.

What is fire?

Fire is the heat and light that comes from burning substances. In 1777, Antoine Lavoisier, a French chemist, proved that burning is the result of the rapid union of oxygen with other substances (see **Lavoisier, Antoine L.**). As a substance burns, heat and light are produced. Burning is also called *combustion.* Often oxygen unites with other substances at such a slow rate that little heat and no light are given off. When this happens, we call the process *oxidation,* rather than *burning* or *combustion.* Oxidation takes place whenever oxygen unites with other substances either rapidly or slowly. For example, when oxygen unites with gasoline, the action takes place rapidly and heat and light are given off. This process may be described by any of the three words, burning, combustion, or oxidation. When oxygen unites with iron and causes it to rust, burning, or combustion, does not take place, but oxidation does.

Kinds of fire. All substances do not burn in the same manner. Charcoal, for example, gives off heat with a faint glow. But other substances, such as coal, gas, magnesium, oil, and wood, give off heat with a flame. The color of the flame depends chiefly on the kind of material being burned and on the temperature.

Substances may burn in different ways, but they all require oxygen to burn. Sometimes old rags soaked with oil or paint are thrown aside and forgotten. Oxygen from the air may slowly unite with the oil in the rags. At first, there will not be a fire. But as oxidation gradually takes place, enough heat accumulates to set the rags on fire. This type of burning, called *spontaneous combustion,* causes many fires.

Very rapid burning may cause explosions like those produced by gunpowder and dynamite. Here, oxidation takes place so rapidly that great volumes of gases are produced. These require many hundreds of times the

Jones & Laughlin Steel Corp.

Controlled fire is essential in various industrial processes, especially in the manufacture of steel, *shown here.* Intense flames melt scrap iron, iron ore, and other raw materials in an open-hearth furnace to produce molten steel.

© Chuck O'Rear, West Light

Uncontrolled fire, such as this house fire, can be extremely destructive. Such fire kills thousands of people and destroys billions of dollars of property every year. Water puts out fire by cooling the burning materials.

space that was formerly occupied by the gunpowder or dynamite before it was oxidized. These gases expand so rapidly and violently that they produce an explosion.

How fire is produced. Three conditions must exist before a fire can be made. There must be a fuel or a substance that will burn. The fuel must be heated to its *ignition temperature*. This is the lowest temperature at which combustion can begin and continue. Finally, there must be plenty of oxygen, which usually comes from the surrounding air.

Fuels are of three classes, solids, liquids, and gases. Coal and wood are examples of solids. Oil and gasoline are liquid fuels. Natural gas and hydrogen are gaseous fuels.

The burning of a solid fuel often depends on the form of the fuel. For example, you may not be able to light a large log with a match, but a small twig from the same tree may catch fire easily with the same match. This is because heat flows to the inside of the log, and the log cannot maintain a high enough temperature to keep burning. But when several logs are burned together, heat also flows from each log to the others and keeps the fire going. This explains why it is easy to start a fire with splinters or shavings.

The ignition temperatures of fuels differ. For a solid or liquid fuel to ignite, some of the fuel must first be heated to the temperature at which it *vaporizes* (turns to a gas). Solids generally have higher ignition temperatures than liquids because they vaporize at higher temperatures. For example, the ignition temperatures of most woods and plastics range from about 500 to 900 °F (260 to 480 °C). A liquid fuel such as gasoline can ignite at a temperature as low as –36 °F (–38 °C).

How fires behave. A candle burning in a room without drafts produces a steady flame. The flame's heat vaporizes just enough candle wax to keep the flame burning at the same height.

Uncontrolled fires, on the other hand, fuel themselves by vaporizing the solid or liquid materials they find in their path. A house fire or forest fire may begin with easily ignitable materials. As the fire grows, it radiates more heat. The heat contributes to further growth, and the process accelerates as long as fuel and oxygen remain available.

In a house fire, a phenomenon known as *flashover* occurs when all the surfaces in a room reach their ignition temperature. At this point, a relatively small fire suddenly ignites the remaining materials, filling the room with flames. Because fires in structures can grow quickly and suddenly, professional fire fighters should immediately be called to control them.

In a forest fire, leaves, twigs, and other materials along the ground usually make up the fuel. But wind and certain types of terrain may cause a forest fire to spread rapidly through the crowns of trees. In some forests, if a fire has not occurred for a long time, fuel materials may build up. People sometimes intentionally set *prescribed fires* to reduce fuels and prevent dangerous crown fires. Wildfires occur naturally in most places on Earth. Some species and ecological processes depend on them. Natural wildfires are a problem only if they threaten buildings or public safety.

We can control the fire in a furnace by regulating the supply of fuel and oxygen it receives. But only winds and the flow of air created by the fire regulate the rate of burning of an uncontrolled fire.

Fireproof materials. The term *fireproof* suggests that a material has been treated with a substance that will prevent it from burning. However, no material is truly fireproof. Even such noncombustible materials as concrete and stone can become damaged by an intense fire.

Materials can, however, be treated with a *fire retardant* to reduce their ability to burn. Most fire retardants act to raise the ignition temperature of a material or to reduce the heat produced by combustion. Such treatments can slow combustion but they do not eliminate it. See **Fireproofing.**

Methods of starting fires. There are several methods of starting a fire, but in each of them the three necessary conditions for a fire must be present. Before matches were invented, the flint and steel method was used. This method required a piece of steel, a flint (hard rock), and a tinder. The tinder was generally made from cotton or linen cloth, or from dried, powdered bark from certain trees. It was heated in an oven until it was nearly ready to burn. It was then placed in a tinderbox to keep it perfectly dry. When the fire was to be started, tinder was placed on the ground and the flint struck against the steel. Some of the sparks made by the flint and steel would fly into the tinder and light it.

Another early method of starting fires was by friction. This method consisted of whirling a stick in a notch in a board until the wood powder that was produced began to glow. Enough oxygen to turn the glow into a blaze was supplied by blowing carefully on the glowing powder.

The first match was invented in 1827 by the English pharmacist John Walker. The tip of this match was coated with a mixture of antimony sulfide and potassium chlorate that was held on the wooden matchstick by gum arabic and starch. When this tip was rubbed on a rough surface, friction produced enough heat to ignite the chemicals. The burning chemicals then produced enough heat to ignite the matchstick. Safer and more efficient matches were developed later. See **Match** (History).

What fire produces

An entire piece of wood or coal will not burn, even if there is sufficient oxygen present. Most of us have taken the ashes from a charcoal grill or fireplace. The ash, generally a mixture of minerals, is present in the fuel, but will not unite with the oxygen. Some fuels have a lower ash content than others. This is important to remember when buying charcoal or wood because you want the fuel with the lowest ash content, provided that it is good in other respects.

Often the bottom of a pan or a skillet becomes black when it is placed over a fire. This discoloration occurs because of soot. Soot is primarily unburned carbon. The skillet becomes coated because it cools the flame, preventing the temperature from getting high enough to burn the fuel completely. If a furnace produces great quantities of soot, some of the carbon of the fuel is not being burned, and is wasted. This problem can be remedied by seeing that sufficient air is supplied to burn all the carbon in the fuel.

Gases. Substances that burn in air are nearly always composed of two elements, carbon and hydrogen, or their compounds. For example, coal, coke, and charcoal are mostly carbon. Natural gas, gasoline, and fuel oils consist of many compounds of hydrogen and carbon. When these fuels burn, the oxygen of the air unites with the carbon and hydrogen to form carbon dioxide gas and water vapor. These gases usually mix with the air and disappear. The uniting of the oxygen with the hydrogen and the carbon is what produces the heat and flame of the fire.

Often, a deadly gas called carbon monoxide forms when there is not enough oxygen to burn the fuel completely. For example, when gasoline burns in an automobile engine, some of this gas forms and comes out the exhaust pipe. If you are in a closed garage when this happens, you are in danger of breathing this gas. Death may result. A person should never run the engine of an automobile in a closed garage.

Most people who are killed in fires in buildings die from inhaling carbon monoxide. Both smoldering fires and too little oxygen following flashover can promote the production of this gas.

Smoke is a mixture of soot and other particles with the gases produced by combustion. Smoke from fires can contain carbon monoxide and other poisonous gases. The soot and particles hamper vision and thus can make it difficult to escape from fires. In general, smoke results from incomplete combustion, which wastes energy and pollutes the environment.

Light. Most of the energy caused by a fire goes into heat, but some of it goes into light. The light results either because the carbon particles in the flame become so hot that they give off light energy, or because the gas that is burning is a type that gives off light.

Ever since fire was discovered, people have been trying to convert more energy from heat into light energy. People first used flaming pieces of wood as torches. They later discovered that if the wood was dipped into pitch before lighting it, the light lasted longer and was much brighter.

Years afterward, people poured oil in a dish, placed a wick in it, and lighted the wick. This approach gave a better light. Later, the tallow candle, which people could conveniently carry around, was invented. The kerosene lamp, with its chimney to help control the air currents, was a big improvement over the candle. After electric energy was made usable, the American inventor Thomas A. Edison sent an electric current through a carbon *filament* (wire) until the filament became so hot that it gave off light.

Fire in legend and religion

We can only guess that prehistoric people may have gained a knowledge of fire from observing things in nature, such as the fire of volcanoes and the heat of the sun. Prehistoric people also must have noticed that sparks fly when stones are struck upon one another, or when the hoofs or claws of an animal strike some hard substance.

In Persian literature, there is a story of the discovery of fire in a fight with a dragon. A stone that the hero used as a weapon missed the monster and struck a rock. Light shone forth, and human beings saw fire for the

first time. The mythology of nearly all early peoples contains some account of accidental or supernatural events that first revealed fire to human beings. Early peoples regarded fire as a true gift of the gods. Fire was considered sacred because it was so essential to the welfare of people. Fire worship and sun worship have existed since early times.

Because fire was so hard to produce, the custom soon became common of keeping a public fire, which was never allowed to die out. These fires were kept in every village among the Egyptians, Persians, Greeks, and Romans. They were often in the civic center of the community.

The Temple of Vesta in Rome was an outstanding example of the importance of fire to the Romans. Vesta was originally the goddess of the hearth, and her shrine was in every home. But when religion became an affair of state, a temple was erected in which the sacred fire was kept burning at all times. See **Vesta**.

David L. Peterson

Related articles in *World Book* include:
Camping (Building a campfire)
Chicago Fire
Combustion
Fire department
Fire extinguisher
Fire prevention
Fireproofing
Match
Prometheus

Fire, Ring of. See Ring of Fire.

Fire alarm. See Fire department.

Fire ant is an ant known for its painful, burning stings. There are hundreds of *species* (kinds). One of these, the *red imported fire ant,* is a major pest in the southeastern United States. This species builds large dirt mounds that measure up to 2 feet (0.6 meter) high. The mounds are so hard they can damage farm machinery. Hundreds of thousands of fire ants may inhabit one mound, and some areas have more than 200 mounds per acre. If a person or animal disturbs a mound, the ants swarm out to attack the intruder. The ant's sting leaves a small, pus-filled, itchy bump that is easily infected. Some people experience severe—in rare cases, fatal—reactions to fire ant venom.

Red imported fire ants range in color from red to brown and measure about ¼ inch (6 millimeters) long. This species is native to South America. It probably entered the United States by accident aboard freight shipped through Mobile, Alabama, during the 1930's. It has since spread rapidly and now inhabits an area that stretches from North Carolina to central Texas. In the 1980's, scientists developed special insecticides that contain soybean oil, which attracts fire ants. The use of such insecticides as fire ant baits may help control the population of fire ants.

Native species of fire ants in the southeastern United States do not pose major agricultural or health problems. An additional foreign species—the *black imported fire ant*—probably entered the United States from South America in 1918.

S. Bradleigh Vinson

Scientific classification. Fire ants make up the genus *Solenopsis*. The red imported fire ant is *Solenopsis invicta.*

Fire blight. See Blight; Pear (Diseases).

© Jerry Sharp, Shutterstock

Fighting fires is one of the most important tasks of a fire department. Many firefighters and a variety of equipment are needed to put out a large building fire, such as the one shown here.

Fire department

Fire department is one of the most important organizations in a community. Every year, fires kill thousands of people, injure thousands more, and destroy billions of dollars worth of property. The firefighters who work for fire departments risk their lives to save people and protect property from fires. Firefighters battle fires that break out in homes, factories, office buildings, stores, forests, and many other places.

Fire department members strive just as hard to prevent fires as they do to put them out. They inspect buildings to enforce fire safety laws. They conduct safety programs about smoke detectors. They teach people about possible fire dangers in their homes and places of work.

The men and women who work for fire departments also help people who are involved in emergencies other than fires. For example, firefighters rescue people who may be trapped in cars, planes, or trains after a crash. They aid victims of such emergencies as earthquakes, floods, hurricanes, and tornadoes. They also help victims of terrorist actions, such as bombings.

The work of a fire department

Firefighting. A fire department is sometimes called a fire *brigade.* Smaller units within a brigade, or department, are sometimes called *companies.*

The two basic units of most fire departments are *engine companies* and *ladder companies.* Engine companies operate large trucks called engines that carry a wa-

ter pump and hoses to direct water onto a fire. Ladder companies operate large trucks that carry a variety of ladders of different sizes and lengths. Some ladder trucks also have a ladder or platform that can be extended to higher floors. This allows firefighters to reach people and fires on those floors. Both engines and ladder trucks carry many tools and pieces of equipment for fighting fires, as well as rescue equipment. At a fire or emergency, the engine and ladder companies work together under the direction of an officer of the department.

After the fire department is notified of an alarm, the engine and ladder companies drive to the location of

Outline
I. **The work of a fire department**
   A. Firefighting
   B. Emergency rescue operations
   C. Emergency medical operations
   D. Additional operations
   E. Fire cause and arson investigations
   F. Fire prevention and fire safety
II. **Fire department equipment and resources**
   A. Dispatch and communication centers
   B. Water systems
   C. Trucks and vehicles
   D. Protective clothing
III. **History**
   A. Fire protection in Europe
   B. Fire protection in North America
IV. **Careers**

the emergency. They often arrive within minutes of receiving the alarm. The first officer that arrives sizes up the fire and then directs the firefighters into action. Their first task is to search for and rescue people who are trapped by the fire. Their next task is to put out the fire as quickly and safely as possible. They must also stop the fire from spreading to the surrounding buildings. This last step is called *protecting exposures.*

In most city locations, engine companies depend on fire hydrants to get the water they need to fight a fire. A firefighter connects a hose from the nearest fire hydrant to the engine. Firefighters then stretch hoses from the engine toward the fire. The engine pumps water through the connected hoses under pressure. The pressurized water allows firefighters to direct their hose streams on the fire and put it out.

Ladder company members sometimes break windows and cut holes in the roof of the structure to allow the gases, smoke, and heat to escape. This process is called *ventilation.* If a building is not ventilated, the heat and pressure from the gases created by the fire can overcome the firefighters inside and they could be hurt or killed. Ventilation also reduces the chance of the gases in the burning building exploding.

After the fire is put out and all the people who were rescued have been treated, the firefighters work at *salvage* and *overhaul.* Salvage involves moving or covering any property or valuables in the building to prevent, or at least significantly reduce, smoke and water damage.

As a final step, firefighters perform overhaul operations. They check the building for evidence of a fire's cause and search for remaining heat or smoldering material that may cause a fire to flare up. Such a fire is known as a *rekindle.*

Emergency rescue operations. Many fire departments have rescue companies that respond to nonfire emergencies. For example, rescue workers may be called to free people trapped under the wreckage of a fallen building or in a car after an accident. Rescue teams have special equipment to cut open walls, doors, and vehicles so they can safely remove the injured. Then victims can be taken to the hospital for more advanced treatment and care. Many large fire departments also

have specialized teams to rescue people who are stranded underwater or in swift-flowing water, or on cliffs or other high places.

Rescue companies may also go to major fires. At a building fire, for example, the rescue workers help the ladder company get people out of the building. They give first aid to people overcome by smoke or suffering from burns.

Emergency medical operations. A large number of fire departments provide Emergency Medical Services (EMS) as part of their operations. EMS units operate ambulances and provide initial emergency medical care for the ill and injured. The levels and types of EMS workers depend upon the state or region in which they serve. First responders and basic- and intermediate-level emergency medical technicians (EMT's) may provide a wide range of intermediate care from first aid to cardiopulmonary resuscitation (CPR), depending on their level of training. Paramedics are the most highly trained EMS workers and may use more complex equipment and procedures to provide advanced life support. In the United States, EMS workers must pass exams to be licensed by the state in which they work. See **Emergency Medical Services; Paramedic.**

Additional operations. Specialized companies are formed to fight specific types of fires. For example, *fireboat companies* are common in ports where there are many ships. Fireboats pump water from the lake or ocean they sail on and create a pressurized stream to put out fires. These boats can pump thousands of gallons per minute.

Brush companies put out grass fires and fires in *wildland* areas (places with land in its natural state). These companies also protect buildings in such areas. Such companies might include *smoke jumpers*—firefighters who parachute from airplanes into burning wildlands to fight fires. Forest fires can be difficult to fight. Brush companies often fight such fires from the air, using helicopters and airplanes to drop tanks of water or fire retardant on a fire.

Fire cause and arson investigations are conducted by fire departments in cooperation with local or state law enforcement agencies. When investigating a fire, a

© TFoxFoto/Shutterstock

Firefighters ventilate a burning building by making a hole in the roof of the structure. Ventilation may be necessary to release a build-up of smoke and gases that could cause an explosion.

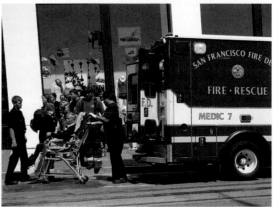

© Glenn Walker, Shutterstock

Fire department paramedics treat people needing emergency medical care. The paramedics operate various vehicles that carry medical equipment and drugs.

fire department is first concerned with what caused the fire. Whether or not a crime was committed is a secondary consideration. The most common crime in fire investigations is arson—the crime of purposely setting fire to a building or other property. See **Arson.**

Fire prevention and fire safety. To help prevent fires and reduce fire losses, local fire departments inspect public buildings. They also teach people about fire safety. Many fire departments have a separate division that handles fire prevention and fire safety programs in their community.

Public building inspections. Most cities have a fire safety code that applies to a wide range of buildings, including apartments, hospitals, schools, day-care centers, department stores, and factories. These codes include a variety of requirements. For example, they specify what materials should be used to construct buildings and how and where sprinklers and fire alarm systems should be installed. They also set requirements for where exit signs and exits should be located and how large exit signs should be. In addition, they specify where and how fire extinguishers and safety lighting systems should be installed.

Fire department officials inspect public buildings to enforce the local code. The officials check the operating condition of the fire protection systems, such as alarms. They note the number and location of exits and fire extinguishers. The inspection also covers housekeeping practices and many other matters that affect fire safety. Fire department inspectors may also review plans for a new building to make sure it meets the safety code.

Public education programs. Because a large number of people die in home fires, home fire safety is an important issue for fire departments. Many home fires are caused by leaving the kitchen when food is cooking, disposing of cigarettes improperly, misusing portable heating equipment, and placing flammable or combustible items too close to heat sources. Many fire departments work with other local agencies to teach people how to prevent fires and what to do during a fire. See the table *What to do in case of fire* in this article.

Fire departments urge people to install smoke alarms in their homes. Smoke alarms detect smoke at the start of a fire. They sound a loud buzzer that warns people to leave immediately. Smoke alarms are attached to the ceilings or walls. At least one working smoke alarm should be installed in each level of a home, typically near sleeping areas. See **Smoke alarm.**

Fire departments also encourage people to install residential fire sprinkler systems in their homes. Sprinklers may extinguish and contain a fire until the fire department can arrive.

Fire department equipment and resources

Fire departments have many resources and kinds of equipment to help them fight fires. Some key elements include the dispatch and communication centers, water supply systems, and the trucks and special fire vehicles used by departments. In addition, the firefighters themselves require special protective clothing that is an important part of fire equipment.

Dispatch and communication centers are where most emergency calls are first answered. Dispatchers send fire, police, and EMS vehicles to an emergency as

What to do in case of fire

1. **Leave the building immediately.** Children should not attempt to fight fires. They should leave the building calmly and quickly. Adults may try to put out a small fire if it seems safe to do so. However, if the fire has begun to spread, civilians should exit the structure that is on fire and contact emergency services. Go outside and, in the United States, call 911.
2. **Never open a door that feels hot.** Before opening any door, touch it briefly with the back of your hand. If the door feels hot, the fire on the other side may be blazing fiercely. You could be killed by the heat and smoke if you opened the door. Try another escape route or wait for help.
3. **Crawl on the floor when going through a smoky area.** Smoke and heated gases tend to rise, and so they will be thinnest near the floor.
4. **Do not run if your clothes catch fire.** Running fans and spreads flames. Stop-Drop-and-Roll if you are on fire—that is, stop moving, drop to the ground, and roll over and over on the ground to put out the fire. Cover your face with your hands while you do this.
5. **Do not return to the building.** After you have escaped, call the fire department. If people are trapped inside, wait for the fire department to rescue them.

needed. Emergency vehicles have radios that allow them to communicate with the dispatch center.

The emergency number for reaching a dispatcher in the United States and Canada is usually 9-1-1. In the United Kingdom, it is 9-9-9; in Australia, it is 0-0-0; and in New Zealand, it is 1-1-1. After reaching an emergency number, callers should inform the emergency dispatcher of their location. This is especially important when calling from a cell phone. Callers should also tell the dispatcher what type of emergency they are calling about. Callers should answer the dispatcher's questions as

© Mike McMillan, Spotfire Images
Smoke jumpers parachute into burning wildland areas to fight fires. These firefighters are able to reach fires in remote areas that would be difficult to access by other means.

carefully as possible. No one should hang up on an emergency call until the dispatcher instructs the caller to do so.

Water systems used for firefighting in cities and towns are normally made up of fire hydrants and water pipes. The pipes that supply hydrants are buried underground throughout the city. Fire departments check hydrants periodically to make sure they are working.

Trucks and vehicles. Many fire departments have several types of fire trucks. The main types are engines (also known as pumpers), ladder trucks, and rescue trucks. There are also several other special fire vehicles.

Engines have a large pump that takes water from a fire hydrant or other source. The pump boosts the pressure of the water and forces it through hoses. Engines used for fighting grass or brush fires carry a tank of water and such tools as shovels and rakes.

Ladder trucks. There are generally two kinds of ladder trucks—aerial ladder trucks and elevating-platform trucks. An aerial ladder truck has a metal extension lad-

der mounted on a turntable. The ladder can be raised as high as 135 feet (41 meters). An elevating-platform truck has a cagelike platform that can hold several people. The platform is attached to a lifting device that is mounted on a turntable. The lifting device consists of either a hinged *boom* (long metal arm) or an extendable boom made of several sections that fit inside each other. The boom on the largest trucks can extend 150 feet (46 meters). A built-in hose runs the length of the boom. The hose is used to direct water on a fire. In most cases, a pump in a nearby engine generates the pressure needed to spray the water. Some trucks carry an aerial ladder platform, a combination device that features a platform mounted atop a ladder.

Ladder trucks have portable ladders of various types and sizes. They also carry *forcible-entry* tools. Common forcible-entry tools include axes, power saws, and sledge hammers. These tools allow firefighters to gain entry into a building and to ventilate it to let out smoke.

Rescue trucks are enclosed vehicles equipped with

Three kinds of fire trucks   The illustrations below show a rescue truck, an engine, and an aerial ladder truck. Rescue trucks carry tools for unusual rescues. The other two kinds of trucks are used to spray water on a fire. An aerial ladder truck can also be used to rescue people through the windows of a burning building.

WORLD BOOK illustrations by Greg Maxson, Precision Graphics

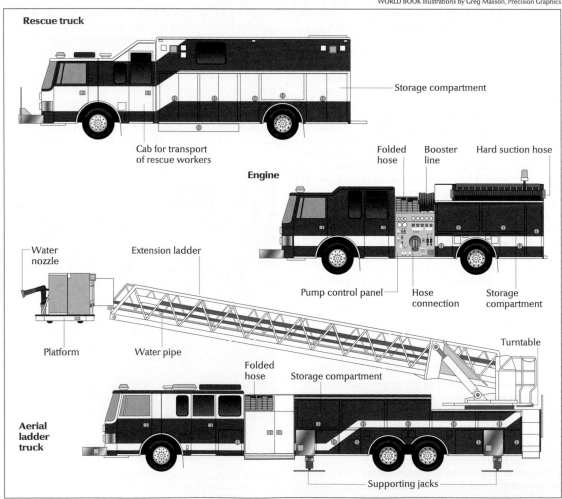

Rescue truck

Storage compartment

Cab for transport of rescue workers

Folded hose   Booster line   Hard suction hose

Engine

Water nozzle

Extension ladder

Pump control panel   Hose connection   Storage compartment

Platform   Water pipe

Turntable

Folded hose   Storage compartment

Aerial ladder truck

Supporting jacks

A firefighter's clothing

Firefighters wear special clothing to protect themselves from fire and other hazards. The clothing includes such garments as fire-resistant pants and coat, heavy leather gloves, and a helmet. An air supply may be carried in a tank strapped to the back.

Austin Fire Department

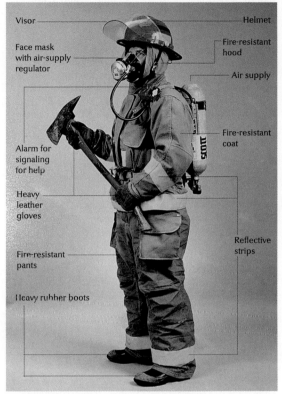

- Visor
- Helmet
- Face mask with air-supply regulator
- Fire-resistant hood
- Air supply
- Alarm for signaling for help
- Fire-resistant coat
- Heavy leather gloves
- Reflective strips
- Fire-resistant pants
- Heavy rubber boots

Some equipment carried on fire trucks

Fire trucks carry a variety of *forcible entry tools,* such as axes, sledge hammers, and crowbars, which are used to gain entry into a building or room. Other equipment on fire trucks includes ropes, bolt cutters, smoke ejectors, and hydraulic rescue tools.

WORLD BOOK illustrations by Yoshi Miyake

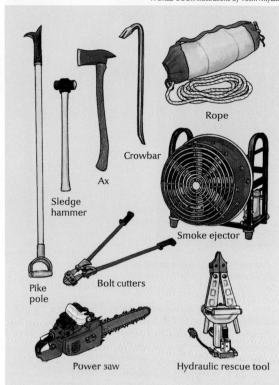

- Rope
- Crowbar
- Ax
- Sledge hammer
- Smoke ejector
- Pike pole
- Bolt cutters
- Power saw
- Hydraulic rescue tool

many of the same kinds of forcible-entry tools that ladder trucks carry. But rescue trucks also carry additional equipment for unusual rescues. Such tools include blowtorches for cutting through metal. Jacks that use *hydraulics* (pressurized liquid for power) to lift heavy objects are also common on rescue trucks.

Rescue trucks may also carry other hydraulic tools. With a hydraulic tool commonly known by the trade name Jaws of Life, firefighters can apply a large amount of pressure to two objects to squeeze them together or pry them apart. The tool is often used to free people trapped in vehicles after an accident. Rescue trucks also carry small hand tools, such as crowbars and saws, as well as ropes and harnesses for rescuing people from water or high places. In addition, they carry medical supplies and equipment.

Special fire vehicles include airport crash trucks and *hazmat* (hazardous materials) trucks. Airport crash trucks are engines that spray foam or dry chemicals on burning aircraft. Water is ineffective against many aircraft fires, such as those that involve jet fuel.

Many hazmat emergencies involve truck or train wrecks in which a dangerous substance is accidentally spilled. Dangerous materials include pesticides, fertilizers, and other chemicals, as well as explosives, gasoline, natural gas, and other fuels. Hazmat trucks carry tools to

stop gas leaks and supplies to absorb or clean up spills of dangerous liquids or solids. Hazmat trucks may include small laboratories used to analyze hazardous materials at the site. These trucks may also carry computers and high-tech communications equipment to consult with experts and authorities about hazmat emergencies.

Protective clothing. Firefighters require special clothing for protection against flames, smoke, falling objects, and other hazards. They wear clothing made of fire-resistant material. Other protective clothing includes special boots and gloves. Firefighters wear helmets designed to protect their head from heat and from falling objects. They also use breathing equipment to avoid inhaling smoke and toxic gases. The equipment consists of a face piece connected to a small air tank strapped on the firefighter's back.

Hazmat trucks may carry suits to protect firefighters from dangerous chemicals. Such one-piece suits cover everything the firefighter wears, including footwear and breathing equipment.

History

Fire protection in Europe. One of the earliest firefighting organizations was established in ancient Rome. Augustus, who became emperor of Rome in 27 B.C., formed a group called the Vigiles in A.D. 6. The Vigiles

© SHOUT/Alamy Images

A *hazmat* (hazardous materials) suit provides special protection for firefighters who handle dangerous chemicals. When finished, firefighters shower to remove chemicals from the suit.

patrolled the streets to watch for and fight fires. To put out a fire, the Vigiles formed lines called *bucket brigades* to pass buckets of water from nearby wells or fountains. Another row of workers passed back the empty buckets.

Scholars know little else about the development of firefighting organizations in Europe until after the Great Fire of London, which occurred in 1666. At that time, most London houses were made of wood and *pitch* (tar) and roofed with thatch. Houses were also closely crowded together. The Great Fire spread quickly through London and reached riverside warehouses and wharves on the River Thames. These buildings held highly flammable materials, including oil, timber, and coal. The citizen firefighting brigades had little success in containing the fire with their buckets of water from the river. The Great Fire burned for about five days, destroyed much of the city, and left thousands of people homeless.

Before the fire, London had no organized fire protection system. After the fire, insurance companies in the city formed private fire brigades to protect their clients' property. Insurance company brigades would fight fires only at buildings the company insured. A sign identified these buildings.

Experts often credit the French emperor Napoleon Bonaparte with creating the first professional fire department to serve the community and not just subscribers. In 1801, Napoleon began making the Paris fire department a more military-type force. He expanded and improved this force, known as the Sapeurs-Pompiers, after he witnessed a fire in 1810 at which the group was ineffective.

Fire protection in North America. When colonists came to North America in the 1600's, they brought their

countries' building construction and firefighting methods with them. Fire protection in North America developed within a tradition of communities helping themselves. Citizens organized volunteer fire companies, even in the largest cities. Volunteer fire departments are staffed by people who serve part time. When a fire breaks out, the volunteers leave their jobs or homes and go to the fire station. They pick up their equipment there and take it to the emergency.

Early fire services. In New Netherland, a Dutch colony in the area of present-day New York, governor Peter Stuyvesant established a fire prevention system in 1648. He appointed four fire wardens to inspect homes and check chimneys for fire hazards. In 1658, he began one of the first community fire alarm systems. He appointed men to patrol the streets at night and watch for fires. These men were called the *rattle watch* because they shook wooden rattles to alert the people when a fire was discovered. The rattle watch then helped organize bucket brigades. A few other colonial cities also had such a fire watch system.

As early as 1678, Boston had some firefighting equipment. A paid crew maintained the equipment and responded to fires.

The 1700's. By the early 1700's, Boston had organizations resembling firefighting "clubs," known as "Mutual Fire Societies." Such societies aided only members.

The American statesman and inventor Benjamin Franklin helped create one of the first American fire departments. He established it in Philadelphia about 1736. His company began as a club for protecting one another's homes in the event of a fire. But it soon became a fire brigade that would protect the entire community. Actual fire companies and departments were also active in Boston, New York City, and Philadelphia in the 1700's.

The first fire safety regulations in Canada were adopted in 1734 in Montreal and Quebec, which were then ruled by France. In 1763, Montreal established the first firefighting organization in Canada, called the Fire Club.

Fire companies in North America acquired their first practical fire pumps, which were made in Europe, in the mid-1700's. Firefighters had to fill the pumps with pails of water and operate and haul them by hand. However, the pumps enabled crews to fight a fire by shooting a steady stream of water from a safe distance.

The 1800's. By the early 1800's, most U.S. and Canadian cities and towns had volunteer fire companies. The companies required large numbers of volunteers to haul the hand pumps and hose carts to fires. In many cities, prominent citizens belonged to the volunteer companies, which became powerful social and political organizations.

By the mid-1800's, volunteer fire departments in larger cities in the United States had reached their peak. They were well organized and, for the most part, effective firefighting forces. But the numerous fire companies competed against each other, sometimes violently. In addition, many were unwilling to adopt the new technology of the steam engine, which was beginning to replace hand pumps. Steam-powered pumping engines pulled by horses required fewer people to operate them. This resistance to change and pressure from insurance companies and influential citizens eventually led to the end of the volunteer system in large cities.

Brown Brothers

Steam pumpers pulled by horses were used by fire departments from the mid-1800's to the early 1900's. They were a major improvement over the hand pumps formerly used.

In 1853, Cincinnati instituted the first professional fire department in the United States. New York City followed in 1865 and Philadelphia in 1871. A professional department did not guarantee that major fires could be quickly and successfully controlled. Devastating fires occurred in Chicago in 1871, in Boston in 1872, in Baltimore in 1904, and in San Francisco in 1906. Nevertheless, professional departments did offer the advantages of a constant labor force, modern equipment, and greater discipline and efficiency. See **Chicago Fire; San Francisco earthquake of 1906.**

The 1900's. From 1910 to 1930, gasoline-powered vehicles replaced horse-drawn fire engines. Some of these early engines, though propelled by a gas engine, still used steam to power their pumps.

In the 1970's, fire departments began to put greater emphasis on preventing fires and educating the public about fire safety. In 1974, the U.S. government established the National Fire Prevention and Control Administration in the Department of Commerce. The agency became the United States Fire Administration (USFA) in 1978. The USFA is now part of the Federal Emergency Management Agency (FEMA) of the Department of Homeland Security. The USFA works to improve fire prevention and education, firefighting technology, and firefighter health and safety. It also operates the National Fire Academy in Emmitsburg, Maryland. The academy gives training programs for firefighters and others in the field of fire prevention and control.

During the 1980's and 1990's, fire departments became more involved in providing emergency medical care, highway accident rescue, hazardous materials handling, and other emergency services. The change of focus coincided with a reduction in the number and size of fires. This reduction resulted from improved public education and better fire safety codes.

Recent developments. The attacks on the United States by terrorists on Sept. 11, 2001, had a major impact on fire safety. More than 300 New York City firefighters and paramedics died in the collapse of the World Trade Center on that day. The September 11 attacks led to the greatest loss of life ever experienced by a department in a single day.

The threat of terrorist attacks in the 2000's created new challenges for firefighters. Firefighters received training in how to work with biological hazards, such as infectious diseases used as weapons. They also trained for events that would create huge numbers of casualties. Departments also invested in communication equipment that allowed them to contact other agencies, such as police departments, in catastrophic attacks.

Careers

The requirements for becoming a paid firefighter vary among fire departments. In general, an applicant must be at least 18 years old with a high school diploma or its equivalent. Some departments will not accept candidates above a certain age, such as 30 or 35. Applicants must be in excellent physical and mental condition.

Some departments require beginning firefighters to have already taken courses or hold certification as an emergency medical technician (EMT) or firefighter. It is an advantage for applicants to have studied fire science or fire engineering at a college or university as well.

After being accepted by a fire department, a trial firefighter takes a training program that may last weeks or months. The program covers such subjects as fire behavior, firefighting strategy, forcible-entry rescue techniques, and emergency medical skills. The entire trial period usually lasts one year. After this period, a firefighter may receive more advanced training in such areas as rescue work and fire prevention. Ken Farmer

Related articles in *World Book* include:

Federal Emergency
  Management Agency
Fire
Fire drill
Fire extinguisher

Fire prevention
Fireproofing
Forestry (Fire and forests)
Safety
Thermography

Fire drill is an activity that is used to teach people how to leave any place safely and quickly if fire breaks out. By practicing a fire drill, people know how to act in a real emergency. They are able to exit a building with less fear and confusion. Fire drills are an important exercise for schools, businesses, and homes.

Most schools hold fire drills regularly so that students learn the fastest and safest way to leave the building. The teacher leads the class outside in an orderly manner. When the students are a safe distance from the school, the teacher makes sure everyone is accounted for. Schools also have classroom directional signs and red lights in hallways that show the nearest exit.

Most other public buildings also have posted signs that direct occupants to fire exits. Some buildings use warning lights, safety officials, and public address systems to guide people to safety.

Home fire safety drills are equally important. A home safety drill includes practicing how to quickly leave the home, gathering outside at an agreed-upon location, and accounting for all family members. Ken Farmer

Fire engine. See Fire department (Trucks and vehicles).

Fire extinguisher is a metal container filled with water or chemicals used to put out fires. Fire extinguishers are portable and easy to operate and can be used to put out small fires before the flames spread.

In the United States, state and local fire laws require that extinguishers be installed in easily seen places in public buildings. Such buildings include factories, schools, stores, and theaters. School buses, boats, and most public vehicles also must have extinguishers.

There are many kinds of fire extinguishers. The kind used depends on the type of fire involved. Fire prevention experts divide fires into four classes—A, B, C, and D—depending on the burning material. *Class A* fires involve such materials as cloth, paper, rubber, or wood. *Class B* fires involve flammable gases or such flammable liquids as cooking grease, gasoline, or oil. *Class C* fires involve motors, switches, or other electrical equipment through which electric current is flowing. *Class D* fires involve combustible metals, such as magnesium chips or shavings. Most extinguishers are labeled with the class, or classes, of fire for which they can be used.

Class D fires require special extinguishers designed for specific metals. But most other fire extinguishers can be classified, by their contents, as one of four types: (1) water, (2) foam, (3) liquefied gas, and (4) dry chemical.

Water extinguishers are used to fight only class A fires. Water conducts electric current, and so it must never be used on a fire involving electrical equipment. A water extinguisher is operated by a lever or a hand pump that shoots the water through an attached hose.

Foam extinguishers are used for class A and class B fires. They contain water and a foaming agent. One type of foam puts out fires that involve combustible liquids by depositing a film between the liquid and the flame.

Liquefied gas extinguishers may be used on class B and C fires. There are three main kinds—*carbon dioxide extinguishers,* which contain carbon dioxide gas; *halon extinguishers,* which contain a gas called *halon;* and *halocarbon extinguishers,* which contain any one of four gases called *halocarbons.* All of these extinguishers have the gas in liquid form under pressure in the container. When the operator squeezes a handle, the liquid flows out of the container and becomes a gas that covers the fire. Liquefied gas extinguishers leave no water or powder. Thus they are the most suitable for class C fires in-

volving delicate electrical equipment that could be damaged by other extinguishers. Large halon or halocarbon extinguishers can also be used to fight class A fires.

Halon harms the ozone layer in Earth's upper atmosphere. This layer protects living things from most of the sun's ultraviolet rays. A 1992 agreement among the major halon-producing nations resulted in a plan for the industrialized countries to stop producing halon by 2000. But the plan also allowed for the continued use of stored or recycled halon. Halon extinguishers are serviced in a closed recovery system, which prevents the release of halon into the atmosphere. Halocarbon extinguishers were developed to replace those with halon.

Dry chemical extinguishers are used on class B and C fires. One type, the *multipurpose dry chemical extinguisher,* also can be used against class A fires. A *stored pressure* dry chemical extinguisher has a cylinder containing a chemical powder and a gas under pressure. Another type of dry chemical extinguisher stores the gas in a cylinder or cartridge separate from the powder. Before using it, users must enable the gas to flow into the main compartment by turning a valve or operating a lever that punctures the gas compartment.

Critically reviewed by the National Fire Protection Association

Fire fighting. See Fire department (Firefighting).

Fire prevention is a term for the many safety measures and programs used to keep harmful fires from starting and to reduce injuries to people and damage to property. Each year, fires cause thousands of deaths throughout the world.

Many individuals, groups, and communities work to prevent fires and reduce injuries to people. They use three main methods: (1) laws and regulations, (2) inspection of buildings and other property, and (3) public education about fire safety. Education includes providing information on safety products such as smoke alarms, automatic sprinkler systems, safety lighting, and other new technology.

Most cities and other local government authorities have codes and standards that require smoke alarms and certain types of fire retardant materials and electric wiring to be used in buildings. Most fire departments and other public agencies inspect public buildings for fire code compliance, fire hazards, and safety risks. In

---

Kinds of fire extinguishers

The chief kinds of fire extinguishers are *water, foam, liquefied gas,* and *dry chemical.* To operate most extinguishers, a person pulls the locking pin and squeezes the operating lever while aiming the nozzle at the base of the fire and moving the nozzle with a sweeping motion across the fire's base.

Water extinguishers are filled with water. They are used to fight class A fires, which involve wood, paper, cloth, or other combustible solids. Water extinguishers must never be used for fires that involve electrical equipment.

Foam extinguishers contain water and a foaming agent. They are used for class A fires and for class B fires. Class B fires involve flammable gases or such flammable liquids as gasoline.

Liquefied gas extinguishers contain carbon dioxide gas, a gas called *halon,* or one of four gases called *halocarbons.* They are used for class B fires and for class C fires, which involve electrical equipment through which electric current is flowing. Larger halon and halocarbon extinguishers are also used for class A fires.

Dry chemical extinguishers contain a chemical powder. They are used on class B or C fires. A type called multipurpose dry chemical can also be used on class A fires.

Parts of a fire extinguisher

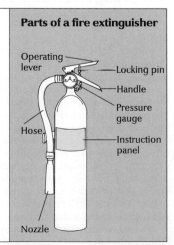

Operating lever
Locking pin
Handle
Pressure gauge
Instruction panel
Hose
Nozzle

some communities, homeowners may request home safety inspections by their local fire department.

Fire safety education is a key factor in fire prevention. Fire departments, community groups, schools, and others teach children and adults about fire hazards and work to reduce fires throughout the community.

In homes and schools. Home fires cause the largest loss of life and the most injuries from fires. The leading causes of fires in the home are cooking, heating equipment, arson, electrical equipment, and smoking. Since the 1980's, both the number of home fires and deaths related to them have been in decline. The decrease is the result of such initiatives as fire prevention programs; regulations requiring furniture to be less easily ignited; and the use of smoke alarms and sprinkler systems, and safer smoking materials such as fire-safe cigarettes.

To prevent cooking-related fires, do not leave food cooking on the stove unattended. A pan of hot cooking oil can quickly become a blazing grease fire. Do not try to move a blazing pan. Instead, put a lid on the pan or use a fire extinguisher to put out the fire. Do not pour water on a grease fire. It will cause the fire to spread.

Limit the amount of trash, old clothing, and other materials stored in attics, basements, or closets in your home. They could quickly catch fire in those places. Flammable liquids such as gasoline, charcoal lighter, propane tanks, and other dangerous items should be stored in a safe place outside the home. Such materials should be stored in a separate storage area, if possible, or at least in the garage. Make sure there is a working smoke alarm in the home and consider installing a residential sprinkler system.

In old homes and schools, have a qualified electrician regularly check electric wiring and replace any that appears weak or worn. Limit the use of extension cords. A fire can also result from overloading one outlet with appliances. See **Safety** (Safety at home; Safety at school).

Many types of fabrics burn easily. Parents should teach children not to stand near heaters, candles, lighted stoves, bonfires, or other sources of high heat. Children should also be taught not to play with matches or cigarette lighters. Playing with matches causes loss of life and thousands of dollars in damage yearly in the United States.

If fabrics or similar materials catch fire, use a fire extinguisher to put out the blaze. Call the fire department quickly, after exiting the house, if the fire is beyond control. This call should be made from outside the house.

Many school programs educate children about fire hazards. Young children may learn about these dangers through the use of coloring books, rhymes, slogans, or videos and movies about fire prevention. Sometimes children will visit a fire station. Firefighters and teachers also may give children talks and demonstrations about the risks of fire and other hazards.

In the community, fire departments and other public agencies work to improve fire safety through laws, inspections, and educational programs. They promote fire prevention and fire safety through billboards, newspapers, pamphlets, posters, radio and television, and social media and the Internet.

In industry, fire prevention is especially important because fire must be used for so many jobs. Fire is used to perform such tasks as melting metals, heating chemicals, and generating electric power. Machines and furnaces used for these and other manufacturing jobs are at risk due to fires. Inspectors check these machines and other areas of a factory for potential fire hazards and

Fire hazards in the home

Many fires start at home, and most are caused by carelessness. Home fires cause the largest loss of life and the most injuries from fires. These pictures show careless habits that can result in fire.

An overloaded electrical outlet can cause overheated wires to burn.

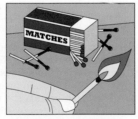

Playing with matches can result in rugs, clothing, and other items being set aflame.

Storing flammable liquids near a furnace can cause escaping fumes to catch fire.

Gasoline should not be used to start fires. It is too flammable and uncontrollable.

A grease fire can quickly ignite from a pan of hot cooking oil that is left unattended.

Throwing away cigarettes that are still burning can start a wastebasket fire.

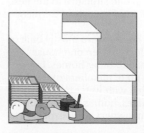

Stored rags soaked with grease, oil, or paint can quickly burst into flame.

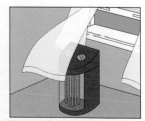

WORLD BOOK illustrations by Matt Carrington

Space heaters located too close to blowing curtains can cause the fabric to catch fire.

© Southwest Research Institute

A flammability test determines how fast a substance burns. These scientists are observing how a car's plastic fuel tank holds up during a fire.

risks to protect workers and reduce the chance of fire. Employers train workers to operate machines safely and to report any problems that could cause fire.

In the event of a fire in a business, there are additional losses beyond the building and its contents. Most businesses have insurance that covers at least some of the costs of replacing equipment and inventory, as well as repairing or replacing the building. However, such businesses also face indirect costs such as the loss of business during the repairs, potential loss of employees due to temporary or permanent job loss, and the possible loss of investors due to lack of confidence in the company. Recovery actions for a business often take a long time after a fire. In many cases, the business does not survive a serious fire loss.

Some businesses have workers that are trained and properly equipped to fight small fires at their jobs. Factory notices, pamphlets, and other methods also promote fire safety.

Fire prevention laws have been commonplace since ancient times. These laws normally were passed to protect the citizens and their homes in the event of a fire. About 18 B.C., the Roman Emperor Augustus set maximum heights for houses and minimum thicknesses for their walls to reduce the spread of fires. Later laws required minimum separations between buildings to prevent fires from spreading from one structure to the next. Some of these laws were still used in parts of Germany and Italy as late as the 1600's.

In the American Colonies, homes were mostly built of wood and other natural products. When one house caught on fire, it quickly spread to other homes. Early fire departments were made up of members of the community who used buckets filled with water to extinguish the flames. In many communities, homes were required to have fire buckets, and homeowners were expected to use them to help fight fires.

In 1896, the National Fire Protection Association was formed to develop national fire codes and standards for homes, buildings, and businesses. The first Fire

Prevention Day was observed in the United States in 1911. In 1922, the United States and Canada observed National Fire Prevention Week, the first campaign to educate the public in fire safety. Each year, both countries observe National Fire Prevention Week during the week of October 9, the anniversary of the great Chicago Fire of 1871.

Australia, the Netherlands, Sweden, and the United Kingdom also stress public education in fire prevention. But most industrialized nations rely more on laws, inspections, and worker training. In many countries, insurance requirements form the basis of fire prevention programs.

Forest fires. Tens of thousands of wildfires are reported each year in the United States. Most of these fires are caused by people. Wildfires destroy homes and damage wildlife habitat and watersheds that provide drinking water for millions of people. The U.S. Forest Service makes major efforts nationwide to reduce fire danger through fire prevention programs. The Forest Service works with homeowners and public and private land owners to reduce the risk of fire. In recent years, managing fires has become riskier and more complex due to climate change, suburbs sprawling into forest lands, and the increase in flammable vegetation.

Ken Farmer

Related articles in *World Book* include:
Combustion
Electricity (Electrical fire)
Fire department
Fire drill
Fire extinguisher
Fireproofing
Forestry (Fire and forests)
National park (Management of fire and wildlife)

Additional resources

Crawford, Jim A. *Fire Prevention*. Prentice Hall, 2002.
Della-Giustina, Daniel E. *The Fire Safety Management Handbook*. 3rd ed. Am. Soc. of Safety Engineers, 2003.
Nolan, Dennis P. *Encyclopedia of Fire Protection*. 2nd ed. Thomson Delmar Learning, 2006.
Todd, Colin S. *Fire Precautions*. 2nd ed. Gower, 2000.

Fire worship is an ancient religious practice based on the idea that fire is sacred. Since early times, people have worshiped fire because it destroys, purifies, and gives heat and light. Some equate a god or spirit with fire. The Parsis of India and other followers of a religion called Zoroastrianism use fire as a divine symbol. The ancient Greeks and Romans considered fire one of the major elements that made up the world. Today, people build bonfires for various occasions. This practice probably developed from the tradition of fire worship. See also **Vesta**. Sarah M. Pike

Firearm is any device that uses gunpowder to fire a bullet or shell. Generally, the term is used for light firearms, such as rifles, machine guns, shotguns, and pistols. They are often called *small arms*. Heavier firearms are generally referred to as *artillery*.

Mechanism. Any firearm, large or small, has four essential parts: (1) the barrel, (2) the chamber, (3) the breech mechanism, and (4) the firing mechanism. The *barrel* is a long tube. Its interior may be smooth, as in a shotgun, or it may have *rifling* (spiral grooves), as in most handguns and rifles. The *chamber* is a widened hole at the *breech* (rear) end of the barrel. It holds the *cartridge* (explosive

Parts of a double-barreled shotgun

A hinge-action double-barreled shotgun is fired by first moving the release handle to one side and pulling the barrels downward to open the firing chambers. New shells are inserted into the chambers by hand. The gun is closed by moving the barrels upward until they lock into position. When the trigger is pulled, the firing pin strikes and ignites the cartridge's primer.

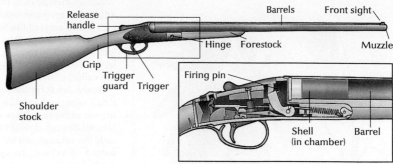

WORLD BOOK diagrams by Oxford Illustrators Limited

charge). The *breech mechanism* closes the rear end of the barrel, holding the cartridge in the chamber. The breech of every modern firearm can be opened for loading and locked for safety in firing. Small arms usually have a metal cylinder, or *bolt,* that is locked when the gun is fired. After firing, the bolt draws back to *eject* (force out) the empty cartridge case and to reload. Artillery uses screw plugs or breechblocks.

The *firing mechanism* ignites the powder in a firearm. In some large artillery pieces, it is an electric device. In small arms, a spring drives a pointed *firing pin* through the breech bolt against a *primer* (tiny explosive charge) in the cartridge. The firing pin is *cocked* (drawn back) against a hook called the *sear.* When the trigger is pulled, the sear releases the pin, which in turn snaps

Types of firearms

WORLD BOOK illustrations by Oxford Illustrators Limited

Revolver

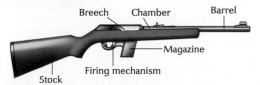

Semiautomatic rifle

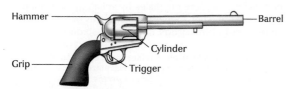

50-millimeter howitzer

forward to strike the primer. A jet of flame from the primer ignites the rest of the powder, creating a gas. Pressure caused by rapid expansion of the gas propels the bullet from the barrel.

A device called a *safety* is intended to prevent a firearm from firing accidentally if it is dropped or if it snags on an object. However, safeties on most long guns, such as rifles and shotguns, block the trigger but not the hammer or firing pin. Thus, such guns can fire when dropped.

History. The Chinese invented gunpowder before A.D. 900. As early as the first half of the 1100's, they may have used a handheld firearm that resembled a small cannon. Travelers brought gunpowder from Asia to Europe in the 1200's. Beginning in the 1300's, Europeans developed cannons and then smaller handheld firearms. See **Gunpowder.**

The invention of firearms led to great changes in warfare. Bullets could penetrate armor. Powerful, accurate cannons could destroy castle walls. However, early handheld weapons were heavy and clumsy, and soldiers had to load the firearms from the muzzle.

The rifle was invented about 1500. The spiral grooves in its barrel made it more accurate than any previous firearm. Smokeless powder was developed in the 1800's. Breechloading systems replaced dangerous muzzle loading. Many improvements since have resulted in high-powered firearms. Jeffrey Scott Doyle

Related articles in *World Book* include:

Ammunition	Cannon	Gun	Mortar
Armor	Carbine	Gunpowder	Musket
Artillery	Explosive	Handgun	Rifle
Bazooka	Flintlock	Harquebus	Shotgun
Blunderbuss	Garand rifle	Machine gun	

Additional resources

Chase, Kenneth. *Firearms: A Global History to 1700.* Cambridge, 2003.
Pauly, Roger. *Firearms.* Greenwood, 2004.
Shooter's Bible. Stoeger, published annually.

Fireball is a meteor that burns brightly as it plunges through Earth's atmosphere. If the fireball explodes at the end of its path, it is generally called a *bolide.* Some pieces may survive the explosion and fall to Earth. Only brightness makes a fireball different from an ordinary meteor. A fireball is as bright as Jupiter or Venus. In rare cases, it may be as bright as a full moon. A sound like thunder occasionally accompanies the passage of a fireball. See also **Meteor.** Lee J. Rickard

Firebird. See **Baltimore oriole.**

WORLD BOOK illustration by Christabel King

The firecracker flower has long, slender leaves and a long stem that ends in a cluster of bright flowers.

Firecracker flower is a plant with colorful tubelike flowers. The plant grows to 3 feet (91 centimeters) tall and has long, grasslike leaves that arise from its base. The flowers form a cluster at the tip of the stem. They are mostly bright red, with green tips that curve back. The firecracker flower grows in southwestern Oregon and northern California. It is a *perennial*—that is, it can live for more than two years.

Laurent Penet

Scientific classification. The firecracker flower's scientific name is *Dichelostemma ida-maia.*

Firedamp. See Damp.

Firefly is any member of a family of soft-bodied beetles known for producing glowing or flashing light. Fireflies are also called *lightning bugs.* There are about 1,900 *species* (kinds) of fireflies. Members of the firefly family live on all the continents except Antarctica. In the United States and Canada, there are about 200 species. The *pyralis firefly,* also called the *big dipper firefly,* is one of the most familiar North American species found east of the Rocky Mountains. These fireflies are active in the early evening and can be seen floating silently over meadows and lawns, flashing their yellow lights.

James E. Lloyd,
University of Florida

Fireflies have a flat, oblong body, and most have light organs on the underside of the abdomen. The species shown here are *Photinus pyralis, above,* and *Pyractomena ecostata, right.*

Not all members of the firefly family give off light as adults. For example, adults of most North American species found west of the Rocky Mountains do not produce light. However, the *larvae* (young) of all firefly species and the eggs of some species give off light. The glowing larvae and the flightless females of some species are often called *glowworms.*

Body. Adult fireflies are flattish, oblong insects about ¼ to ¾ of an inch (5 to 20 millimeters) long. Most are dull brown or black, with red, orange, or yellow markings. Like all beetles, fireflies have two pairs of wings but use only the second pair for flying. The first pair, the *elytra,* form a cover over the second pair. The females of some firefly species do not fly, and their wings and elytra are extremely short or absent.

Firefly light organs are usually on the underside of the *abdomen*—the last section of an insect's body. A chemical reaction that takes place in the light organs produces the firefly's light. This kind of heatless light is known as *bioluminescence.*

Life. Fireflies use their lights to find mates. Each firefly species has its own light signal. Female fireflies perch on the ground or in the bushes and wait until a male flies nearby flashing the correct signal. She then answers him with her own light.

Fireflies lay their eggs in moist places on or in the ground. The eggs hatch into flightless larvae that are often seen glowing on damp lawns and along streams. The larvae take one or two years to develop. They then pass through a brief *pupal* state, during which they change into adults. The adults live for 5 to 30 days. Firefly larvae eat snails, earthworms, and other insect larvae. They kill their prey by injecting poison into them. Adult fireflies may feed on nectar or eat nothing. However, the females of some firefly species prey on the males of other species. They lure the males by imitating the mating signals of the other species. The enemies of fireflies include various birds, frogs, lizards, and spiders.

James E. Lloyd

Scientific classification. Fireflies make up the family Lampyridae in the order Coleoptera, class Insecta. The scientific name for the pyralis firefly is *Photinus pyralis.*

See also **Beetle** (picture); **Bioluminescence.**

Fireproofing is the popular name for the coatings and methods used to protect paper, plastic, textiles, wood, and other materials against fire. Fire prevention experts, however, consider the term *fireproofing* misleading because even such noncombustible materials as steel and concrete are affected to some degree by intense fire. Steel can weaken or melt, and concrete can crack. Experts instead refer to materials that have been protected against fire as *fire resistant* or *fire retarded.* They call the substances that are used to protect such materials *fire retardants.*

Fire retardants help prevent materials from burning or being severely damaged when exposed to fire. Some fire retardants increase the time it takes for treated articles to ignite. Others cause a material to extinguish itself if it is ignited by a brief fire, thereby preventing the fire from spreading to surrounding objects.

Fire results from the combination of fuel, heat, and oxygen. When solid materials are heated to a high enough temperature, their molecules break down to produce flammable vapors that can chemically react with the oxygen in air. Fire retardants help materials resist fire by interfering with these reactions. For example, a combustible surface may be protected against fire by being covered with a special fire-retardant *intumescent coating.* Upon exposure to fire, an intumescent coating swells up to form a thick layer of insulating foam between the surface (the fuel) and the fire (the heat).

Many fire retardants produce physical or chemical changes in a material to make it less flammable. Some, for example, cause a material, when exposed to fire, to become coated with a fire-resistant layer of charred carbon. Retardants that alter the flammability of materials are applied in a number of ways. For example, textile manufacturers obtain nearly permanent fire resistance in fabrics used in carpets, clothing, draperies, and upholstery through processes that molecularly bond retardant compounds to the fabric. Temporary fire retardation can be obtained by soaking fabrics in solutions of such chemicals as borax, boric acid, diammonium phosphate, and ammonium sulfate. Paper makers often add similar chemicals to paper and cardboard.

In many countries, materials used to build houses, schools, and other buildings must meet fire-resistance standards. These standards are typically set by local governments. Other regulations require that certain types of clothing, such as children's sleepwear, be treated with fire retardants.　　　R. Craig Schroll

Firestone, Harvey Samuel (1868-1938), was an American industrial leader who pioneered in the field of automobile tires. He founded the Firestone Tire & Rubber Company (now Bridgestone/Firestone, Inc.) in Akron, Ohio, in 1900. He served as president of this company from 1903 to 1926, and was chairman of the board of directors until his death on Feb. 7, 1938. Firestone had close relationships with the automaker Henry Ford and the inventor Thomas Edison.

Firestone was born on Dec. 20, 1868, on a farm in Columbiana County, Ohio, and grew up there. After working as a bookkeeper and a patent medicine salesman, in 1895 he began work at his uncle's Columbus Buggy Company. Later he became a manager at the Consolidated Rubber Tire Company, a top manufacturer of carriage tires. Firestone started his own company and became an expert in *pneumatic* (air-filled) tire design. The company flourished when it began supplying such tires for vehicles produced by the Ford Motor Company.

Firestone was a competitive businessman who cut prices whenever possible and shunned industry agreements. His keen interest in technical progress caused his company to lead in many improvements, especially in the area of truck tires. In 1931, Firestone became the first to market a practical air-filled tire for farm machinery.

In 1926, Firestone signed an agreement with the Liberian government to lease 1 million acres (400,000 hectares) of land for the development of rubber plantations. He made large loans to Liberia and built a new and improved harbor for the country. Firestone also led in investigating the rubber resources of the Philippines and South America, and he promoted a search for alternative sources for natural rubber in the United States.

　　　John A. Heitmann

Fireweed, also called *willow herb,* is a plant that looks like a long wand. It is native to North America, Europe, and Asia. It grows from 3 to 6 feet (0.9 to 1.8 meters) high.

Narrow leaves up to 6 inches (15 centimeters) long grow along the stem. In summer, clusters of rose-purple flowers bloom on the stem. The fruits are slender, four-sided pods. The plant is called *fireweed* because it springs up quickly after forest fires. It is the official flower of the Canadian territory of Yukon.　　　William G. D'Arcy

Scientific classification. The fireweed's scientific name is *Chamerion angustifolium.*

Fireworks are combinations of gunpowder and other ingredients that explode with loud noises and colorful sparks and flames when they burn. They are also called *pyrotechnics.* Fireworks that only make a loud noise are called *firecrackers.* Fireworks are dangerous because they contain gunpowder. They should be handled only by experts. Fireworks handled improperly can explode and cause serious injury to the untrained user. Many states prohibit the use of fireworks by the general public. The federal government limits the explosive power of fireworks that can be used by nonprofessional users.

Most fireworks are made by packing gunpowder in hollow paper tubes. A coarse gunpowder tightly packed is used to *propel* (drive) rockets into the air. A finer and more loosely packed gunpowder explodes the rocket once it is in the air. See **Gunpowder.**

Manufacturers add small amounts of special chemicals to the gunpowder to create colors. They add sodium compounds to produce yellow, strontium compounds for red, and copper and barium compounds for blue and green. Charcoal is another substance that can be added. It gives the rocket a sparkling, flaming tail.

How fireworks work. Fireworks rockets, also called *skyrockets,* operate on a principle close to that used in large military rockets. A *fuse,* which may be made of rolled paper soaked with saltpeter, ignites the coarse gunpowder charge, forming gases that stream out of the end of the paper tube. This propels the rocket into the air. When the rocket is near its highest point of flight, the coarse gunpowder ignites the finer charge, and the finer charge explodes. The explosion breaks up the rocket and ignites many small firecrackers in the *nose* (forward section) of the rocket.

Roman candles have gunpowder charges separated by inactive material. They shoot out a series of separate groups of sparks and flaming projectiles, which often explode with booming noises. *Flowers* have many small bursting charges that send out petals and threadlike pistils of different colors. *Lances* are paper tubes filled with color-producing fireworks. They are arranged on a wooden frame so that when set afire they outline a scene, a portrait, or a flag.

Other uses of fireworks. Fireworks also have serious uses. A device called a *fusee* burns with a bright red flame and is used as a danger signal on highways and railroads. Railroads use giant firecrackers called *torpedoes.* The torpedoes explode while the train is passing over them to warn the engineer of danger ahead.

People can signal for help by using a *Very* pistol. The pistol shoots a flare into the air that can be seen far away. *Parachute flares* are used to light up landing areas. A kind of fireworks rocket shoots lifelines to shipwrecks. Another kind has been used to scatter silver iodide in clouds to produce rain. *Star shells* are used in wartime to light up battlefields.　　　Paul Worsey

See also **Explosive; Independence Day.**

First aid

First aid is the immediate care given to a victim of an accident, sudden illness, or other medical emergency. Proper first aid can save a victim's life, especially if the victim is bleeding heavily, has stopped breathing, or has been poisoned. First aid also can prevent the development of additional medical problems that might result from an injury or illness.

Emergency treatment should be administered by the person on the scene who has the best knowledge of first aid. The treatment should be continued until professional medical help is available. First aid also involves reassuring a victim, relieving the pain, and moving the victim, if necessary, to a hospital or clinic.

This article describes some basic first-aid techniques. But even the best descriptions are not a substitute for a course in which experts demonstrate procedures. People interested in taking a first-aid training course should contact their local chapter of the American Red Cross.

General rules for first aid

Analyze the situation quickly and decide whether you can help the victim. If you decide to treat the victim, begin at once. But if you are confused or unsure of yourself, do not attempt to give treatment. In many cases, the wrong treatment causes more damage than no treatment at all. For professional help in giving first aid, call a hospital, an emergency medical service, the fire department, or the police.

The general steps to take in any situation requiring first aid include the following: (1) call a local emergency medical service or a physician for help, (2) provide urgent care for life-threatening emergencies, (3) examine the victim for injuries, and (4) treat the victim for shock.

Call for assistance. Send someone else to call for a doctor, an ambulance, or other help while you care for the victim. If you are alone with the victim, you must decide when you can safely leave to call for assistance. Always treat the victim for any life-threatening conditions before leaving to summon aid.

When telephoning for help, be ready to describe the nature of the victim's illness or injury, the first aid measures you have taken, and the exact location of the victim. Also be prepared to write down any instructions a physician may give you. Repeat the instructions and ask questions to clarify orders you do not understand.

If you decide to take the victim to a hospital emergency room, first telephone the hospital to say you are coming. The hospital staff will then be better prepared to treat the victim's particular problems.

Every home should have a list of emergency phone numbers posted on or near the telephone. However, if such numbers are not available, the operator can assist you in contacting the proper person or emergency unit.

Provide urgent care. Certain medical emergencies require immediate care to save the victim's life. If the victim is bleeding severely, has been poisoned, or has

stopped breathing, treatment must begin at once. A delay of even a few minutes can be fatal in these cases. The treatments for these emergencies are discussed in this article in the sections on *First aid for bleeding, Treatment for poisoning,* and *Restoring breathing.*

Do not move a victim who may have a broken bone, internal injuries, or damage to the neck or spine, unless absolutely necessary to prevent further injury. If the victim is lying down, keep the person in that position. Do not allow the victim to get up and walk about. Never give food or liquid to a person who may need surgery.

If the victim is unconscious, turn the head to one side to help prevent the person from choking on blood, saliva, or vomit. But do not move the head of a person who may have a broken neck or a spinal injury. Never pour a liquid into the mouth of an unconscious person.

Make sure that the victim has an open airway. The *airway* consists of the nose, mouth, and upper throat. These passages must stay open for the victim to breathe. For information on opening the airway, see the section of this article on *Giving artificial respiration.*

Examine the victim for injuries only after treating the person for any life-threatening emergencies. Then treat the individual injuries. The victim may suffer from diabetes, heart trouble, or some other disease that can cause sudden illness. Many persons with such medical problems carry a medical tag or card. The tag or card lists instructions for care that should be followed exactly. If you must examine the victim's identification papers to look for a medical card, you should do so in the presence of a witness, if possible.

Make the victim comfortable, but touch the person as little as possible. If necessary, shade the victim from the sun or cover the victim to prevent chilling. Loosen the person's clothing. But do not pull on the victim's belt, because this pressure could damage an injured spine.

Remain calm and reassure the victim. Explain what has happened and what is being done. Ask any spectators to stand back.

Treat for shock. Shock results from the body's failure to circulate blood properly. Any serious injury or illness can cause shock. It most often occurs after an injury that causes blood loss, when there is a probability of heart attack, or during overwhelming infection. When a person is in shock, the blood fails to supply enough oxygen and food to the brain and other organs. The most serious form of shock may result in death.

A victim in shock may appear fearful, light-headed, confused, weak, and extremely thirsty. In some cases, the victim may feel nauseated. The skin appears pale and feels cold and damp. The pulse is rapid, and breathing is quick and shallow or deep and irregular. It is best to treat a seriously injured person for shock even if these signs are not present. The treatment will help prevent a person from going into shock.

To treat shock, place the victim on his or her back, with the legs raised slightly. If the victim has trouble breathing in this position, place the person in a half-sitting, half-lying position. Warm the victim by placing blankets over and under the body.

First aid for bleeding

Severe *hemorrhage* (bleeding) can cause death in minutes. Bleeding from most small wounds stops by it

Carlotta M. Rinke, the contributor of this article, is a physician in private practice and a Clinical Assistant Professor of Medicine at Loyola University of Chicago.

self in a short time, after the blood begins to *clot* (thicken). But clotting alone cannot stop the flow of blood from large wounds. When treating a bleeding victim, you should attempt to stop the bleeding, protect the victim from further injury, and prevent shock. As with any situation involving first aid, medical assistance should be called for immediately. Emergency treatments for severe bleeding include such techniques as (1) direct pressure on the wound and (2) pressure on arteries carrying blood to the wound.

Direct pressure. The most effective way of controlling heavy bleeding is to press directly on the wound itself. If possible, have the victim lie down and elevate the bleeding part above the rest of the body. Then place a sterile dressing over the wound and press firmly on it with your hand. If you do not have a sterile dressing, use a clean towel or other cloth folded to make a pad. If no cloth is available, press your hand directly on the wound while someone else obtains the necessary material. Apply constant pressure to the wound for about 10 to 15 minutes, or until professional help arrives.

If the victim bleeds through the first dressing, add another on top of it and apply firmer pressure. Do not remove the first dressing from the wound. After the hemorrhage has stopped, secure the dressing with a bandage.

Pressure on arteries. Sometimes, direct pressure and elevation fail to stop severe bleeding. If such bleeding is from an arm or leg, you may be able to stop it by applying pressure to the artery that supplies blood to the injured limb. The illustrations in this article on *How to control bleeding* show the points at which pressure should be applied to these arteries. Pressure on arteries should be used in addition to—not instead of—direct pressure and elevation.

Treatment for poisoning

There are four ways in which a victim may become poisoned. The poison may be swallowed, inhaled, injected, or absorbed through the skin.

If a poison victim is unconscious, having difficulty breathing, or having seizures, call for an ambulance immediately. If necessary, perform artificial respiration. If the victim has become poisoned by injection, keep the affected area lower than the level of the heart to slow the spread of the poison.

If a person has been poisoned by taking a drug, keep the person's breathing passage open. Quickly try to identify the drug, and then immediately call a physician or emergency medical service for help.

Swallowed poisons. A person who has swallowed a poisonous substance may die within minutes if not treated. The first step in treating the victim is to identify the poison. Identification of the poison helps determine the proper procedure for treating the victim. Immediately call a poison control center or a physician and follow the center's or the physician's instructions carefully. If the victim has swallowed a commercial product, take the container to the phone when you make the call so that you can provide information about the product. The poison control center or physician will tell you what to do. Do not put anything in the victim's mouth unless you have been told to do so by medical professionals.

Inhaled poisons. If the victim has inhaled a poison, such as carbon monoxide or chlorine gas, move the person to fresh air immediately. Open all windows and doors to ventilate the area. Then call a poison control center or a physician for advice.

Injected poisons include those transmitted by insect stings or bites and snakebite. For information on the

How to control bleeding

These photographs show how to stop bleeding from an arm or leg. The person giving the treatment applies pressure directly to the wound and raises it above the rest of the body. With his other hand, he helps control the bleeding by pressing on the arteries that supply blood to the affected limb. The diagram indicates the pressure points for the arteries of the arms and legs.

WORLD BOOK photos by Ralph Brunke

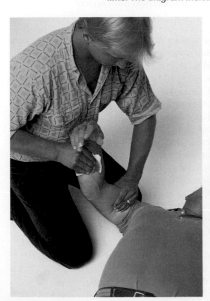 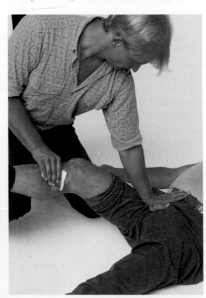 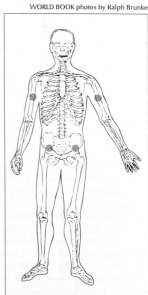

treatment of snakebite, see the section on *Snakebite* in this article.

To treat a spider bite, apply cold compresses to the affected area. Afterward, apply a soothing lotion, such as calamine lotion, to the area.

When a person is bitten by a tick, the tick often adheres to the skin or scalp. Remove the tick at once. Pull the tick out steadily and firmly, not suddenly. Do not use your bare hands. Use a glove, a piece of plastic wrap or paper, or even a leaf. If you have tweezers, grasp the tick's mouthparts as close to the skin as possible. Do not attempt to remove the tick by burning it off, by coating it with petroleum jelly, or by putting oil on it. Clean the bite area with soap and water. Save the tick in a small, sealed container for possible identification. If a rash or flulike symptoms develop within the next several weeks, contact your physician.

When a bee stings a person, the insect's stinger remains in the wound. The person should scrape the stinger off immediately, taking care not to pinch or squeeze the sting. This action reduces the amount of poison that enters the wound.

A victim may experience a severe allergic reaction to a bite or sting. You should either call a physician for advice or take the victim to the nearest location that provides emergency medical treatment.

Poisons on the skin. Poisons can be absorbed through the skin as a result of contact with poisonous plants or chemical substances, such as insecticides. If a victim's skin has been exposed to a poison, remove all contaminated clothing and flush the skin with water for about 10 minutes. Afterward, wash the affected area with soap and water and then rinse it. Wear protective gloves to avoid exposing yourself to the poison.

Restoring breathing

Begin artificial respiration as soon as possible for any victim whose breathing has stopped. Two or three minutes without breathing can cause permanent brain damage, and six minutes can be fatal. Signs of breath stoppage include the lack of regular chest movements and a blue color in lips, tongue, or fingernails.

Removing the cause of breathing failure. The steps you take before administering artificial respiration depend on the cause of breathing failure. For example, if the victim's airway is blocked, you must remove the obstruction before beginning artificial respiration.

Electric shock also can cause respiratory failure. In cases of electric shock, free the victim from contact with the current before attempting artificial respiration. Turn off the current if possible. Do not touch the victim with your bare hands or with a wet or metal object until the contact has been broken. If you cannot turn off the current, free the victim from contact by using a dry stick, rope, or cloth. Be sure to stand on a dry surface that will not conduct electric current.

Respiratory failure can also result from breathing air that lacks sufficient oxygen. Such air may be present in storage bins, poorly ventilated mines, and closed vaults. Breathing also may stop because the victim has inhaled large quantities of carbon monoxide, a substance that interferes with the blood's ability to carry oxygen. In any of these cases, move the victim into fresh air before beginning artificial respiration.

Giving artificial respiration. The most efficient method of artificial respiration is *mouth-to-mouth resuscitation*. To administer mouth-to-mouth resuscitation, place the victim on his or her back, on a firm surface if possible. Kneel down near the head and, using your fingers or a handkerchief, quickly remove such objects as dentures, food, or vomit from the mouth. Place one of your hands under the victim's chin and the other on the forehead. Tilt the victim's head back by lifting with the hand under the chin and pressing down with the one on the forehead. This position—with the chin pointing upward and the neck arched—opens the airway.

To treat an infant or small child, take a breath and place your mouth over both the mouth and nose. Blow gently into the child's mouth and nose. Then remove your mouth and listen for air to flow back out of the child's lungs. Take a breath and blow again. Repeat this procedure every three seconds.

If the victim is an older child or an adult, pinch the nostrils shut with the hand you have placed on the forehead. Take a deep breath, cover the mouth tightly with your own, and blow hard enough to make the chest rise. Then remove your mouth and listen for the return air flow. Repeat this procedure every five seconds.

If the victim's mouth is too large for you to make a tight seal over it with your own, or if the victim has suffered a severe mouth injury, use mouth-to-nose resuscitation. Maintain the head-tilt position, and use the hand under the victim's chin to hold the mouth tightly shut. Then blow into the victim's nose.

If the victim's chest does not rise when you blow in, check the mouth again to be sure that there is nothing in it. Also make certain that the head is tilted back far enough and that the lower jaw is pulled upward. If you still cannot make the victim's chest expand, it may mean that an object is blocking the airway. The recommended technique for removing an object from the throat is the *Heimlich maneuver*. This technique is described in the *Choking* section of this article. After the throat has been cleared, continue artificial respiration until the victim starts to breathe or until expert help arrives.

Other first-aid procedures

Animal bites or stings. Bites made by nonpoisonous animals can result in serious infections and diseases if left untreated. Wash the area of the bite thoroughly with soap and water. Rinse the wound and cover it with a gauze dressing. Call a physician. If possible, the animal should be kept under observation by a veterinarian to determine if it has rabies.

Bites by poisonous animals include those of some spiders, insects, and snakes. Such bites require medical attention. For information about treatment, see the sections in this article on *Injected poisons* and *Snakebite*.

Burns. The first-aid treatment of burns depends on the severity of the injury. Burns are classified, in order of increasing severity, as first-, second-, or third-degree. *First-degree burns* produce a reddening of the top layer of skin. *Second-degree burns* damage deeper skin layers. These burns give the injured skin a red or spotted appearance and cause blisters. *Third-degree burns* destroy tissues in the deepest layer of skin. The injury has a white or charred appearance.

To treat first- and second-degree burns, apply dress-

How to give artificial respiration

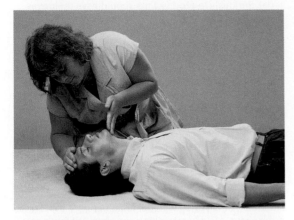

Open the airway. Place one hand on the victim's forehead and the other under the chin. Then tilt the victim's head back and lift the lower jaw.

For the mouth-to-mouth method, pinch the victim's nostrils shut. Take a deep breath, place your mouth tightly over the victim's mouth, and blow until the victim's chest rises.

WORLD BOOK photos by Steven Spicer

Listen for air being exhaled. Remove your mouth and release the victim's nose to allow the victim to breathe out. Repeat the procedure every five seconds for an adult.

ings soaked in iced, sterile solution to the injured area for about 20 or 30 minutes. Then dress the area with sterile bandages. Victims suffering first- or second-degree burns on the face or over an area larger than the size of the hand should receive professional attention.

A person who receives third-degree burns should not be treated at home. The person should instead be treated by a physician immediately. Large burns may be wrapped in a clean sheet or towel, or in plastic bags or kitchen wrap. Plastic bags or wrap should never be placed over the face. Clothing stuck to the wound should not be pulled away.

In treating any kind of burn, do not open blisters, and do not smear the injury with petroleum ointment, butter, or any greasy substance. If the victim has suffered burns around the face or has been exposed to smoke, watch for respiratory difficulties. If the victim has trouble breathing, give artificial respiration. Severe burns cause much pain and a loss of body fluids and may send the victim into shock. In such cases, take the first-aid measures to prevent or treat shock.

Chemical burns should be flushed with large amounts of water. Use a hose, shower, or bucket. Wash the injury for at least 10 minutes. Remove any clothing that has been covered by the chemical and cover the burn with a sterile dressing. Take the victim to a physician immediately.

Sunburn, in most cases, is a first-degree burn. Extremely deep sunburn may cause second-degree burns, with blistering. Do not open any blisters. Apply cool compresses to relieve pain. Consult a physician in cases of severe sunburn.

Choking occurs when food or some other object blocks the *trachea* (windpipe). A person who is choking cannot breathe or speak. After a short time, the victim's skin turns blue and he or she collapses. If the object is not removed in 4 to 6 minutes, death can occur.

An effective way to remove an object blocking the windpipe is a technique called the *Heimlich maneuver.* To perform this maneuver, stand behind the victim and place your arms around the victim's waist. Make a fist and place it so that the thumb is against the victim's abdomen, slightly above the navel and below the ribcage. Grasp your fist with your other hand and then press your fist into the victim's abdomen with a quick upward thrust. This thrusting action forces air out of the victim's lungs and blows the object from the trachea.

If the victim has collapsed or is too large for you to support or place your arms around, lay the person on his or her back. Then face the victim and kneel straddling the hips. Place one of your hands over the other, with the heel of the bottom hand on the victim's abdomen, slightly above the navel and below the ribcage. Then press your hands into the victim's abdomen with a quick upward thrust.

When applying the Heimlich maneuver, be careful not to apply pressure on the victim's ribs. Such pressure may break the ribs of a child or an adult.

Concussion is a head injury caused by a violent blow or shock. If the victim has been knocked unconscious, place the victim flat on his or her back, taking care not to move the neck. Give artificial respiration if the breathing stops. Get medical help as soon as possible.

Victims of a violent head blow might not lose consciousness at the time of the injury. However, they should be watched closely for the next 12 to 24 hours. They may develop delayed symptoms that should be treated by a physician. Such delayed symptoms include loss of consciousness, repeated vomiting, severe headache, pale appearance, weakness in the arms or legs, unsteady walking, convulsions, unusual behavior, difficulty in talking, pupils of unequal size, double vision, watery discharge from the ears or nose, and excessive drowsiness. Check the victim for alertness every 15 minutes immediately following the injury and awaken him or her every 3 hours during that night. If signs of a concussion appear, consult a physician.

Convulsion and epileptic seizure. A person who is suffering a convulsion experiences violent, completely involuntary contractions of the muscles. Major convulsions, particularly those that are associated with epileptic seizures, also involve loss of consciousness. The victim falls to the ground. The muscles twitch and jerk, or they become rigid. Most attacks last a few minutes.

Try to prevent the victim from being injured during the attack. Leave the victim in the position in which he or she falls, but move aside objects that the victim might strike during the seizure. Do not attempt to restrain the victim, and do not attempt to move the head. You may, however, loosen the victim's clothing. Put a folded handkerchief between the teeth to prevent the victim from biting his or her tongue. But be careful not to place your fingers in the victim's mouth because the person could bite them. After the attack, if there is no evidence that the victim may have fallen or may have injured the spine, turn the victim's head to one side to prevent choking in case vomiting occurs.

Eye injury. If acids or alkalis have been splashed into the eye, immediately flush the eye with water. Flush continuously at least 10 minutes for acids and 20 minutes for alkalis. Use a continuous stream of water from a tap or a hose, or pour the water from a cup or other container. Flush the eye from the inside corner outward, to avoid washing the chemical into the other eye. Cover the eye with sterile gauze or a clean pad and take the victim to an eye doctor.

Dust particles or other foreign objects can be removed from the eye by gently flushing with water. Or they can be removed with the corner of a clean hand-

kerchief. However, do not wipe across the *cornea* (clear central part of the eye) with a handkerchief or other material. Seriously injured victims should have their eyes examined at the emergency department of a hospital.

Fainting is a brief, sudden period of unconsciousness. It occurs when blood pressure falls to the point where the brain does not receive enough oxygen. Typically, it occurs when a person is standing. The victim falls to the ground while losing consciousness. Leave the victim lying down. Loosen the clothing and raise the feet slightly. Blood will flow back into the head, and the victim should regain consciousness promptly. Should the victim fail to do so, lay the person on his or her side and make sure the airway stays open. Call a physician.

Just before fainting, a person may feel weak or numb. Other symptoms include nausea, light-headedness, blurred vision, pale appearance, sweating, or excessive yawning. A person experiencing these symptoms should lie down or sit with the head between the knees. If the victim has a heart or lung problem, fainting may be a serious condition related to the ailment. The conditions of such patients should be evaluated in a hospital's emergency department.

Fractures and dislocations. A *fracture* is a break in a bone. A *dislocation* occurs when the end of a bone is forced out of its normal position in a joint. Fractures and dislocations frequently result from automobile and sports accidents.

Signs of fractures and dislocations include pain, an unusual position of a joint or bone, and tenderness and swelling around the injury. The victim may also experience a grating sensation, caused by fragments of broken bone rubbing together. The victim may be unable to use a hand or a foot.

Keep the victim quiet and treat for shock. If possible, do not move the person until expert help arrives. Improper handling of an injured bone or joint may seriously damage arteries, muscles, or nerves. It may also increase the severity of the fracture or dislocation.

If you must move the victim before help arrives, apply a splint to the injured area. The splint prevents broken or dislocated bones from moving. You can make a splint from any material that will support the injured part without bending. For fractures of the arm or leg, the splint should be long enough to prevent movement of joints

WORLD BOOK photos by Dan Miller

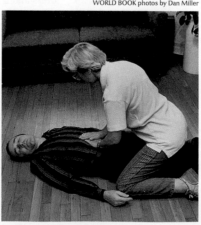

A treatment for choking on an object stuck in the trachea can be applied to a standing victim, *left,* or one who is lying down, *right.* In this technique, called the *Heimlich maneuver,* the person giving the treatment presses sharply on the victim's abdomen. The pressure forces air out of the victim's lungs and blows the blockage from the trachea.

above and below the injury. Pad the splint surfaces that touch the body. Do not try to correct any deformities before splinting. Do not push bone fragments back into an open wound.

Use strips of cloth to tie the splint above and below the point of injury. Do not tie the splint so tightly that it interferes with circulation. Blueness or swelling in fingers, for example, indicates that a splint has been tied too tightly to an arm.

Do not move a person who may have suffered a broken neck or other spinal injury. A person may receive such an injury by diving into shallow water, falling from a considerable height, or striking the head in an auto accident. Moving such an accident victim may cause permanent paralysis or death.

Frostbite may occur when the skin is exposed to extreme cold. It most frequently affects the skin of the ears, fingers, nose, or toes.

Frostbitten skin appears very pale or grayish-blue and feels numb. It should be handled gently. Never massage frostbitten skin, and do not rub it with snow or bathe it in cold water. Warm the affected area with the heat of your hand or cover it with a heavy cloth until you can get the victim indoors. Thaw the affected skin by soaking it in lukewarm water. The temperature of this water should be between 102 and 105 °F (39 and 41 °C). Keep the temperature in this range by adding more warm water as needed. Never use water hotter than 105 °F (41 °C). If warm water is not available, wrap the frostbitten area with blankets. Obtain medical assistance as quickly as possible. If a victim of frostbite must be moved, protect the person from additional exposure.

Never treat frostbite with heat from a stove or with a heating pad, hot water bottle, or heat lamp. Such treatment may produce temperatures that can damage frostbitten tissue. If frostbite blisters occur, do not break them. Bandage them to prevent infection.

Heart attack. Most heart attacks begin with a crushing tightness or intense pressure behind the *sternum* (breastbone). This pain may spread across the chest, affecting the arms, the neck, the jaw, or the pit of the stomach. In most cases, it lasts more than five minutes. The victim appears worried, has difficulty breathing, and may perspire heavily and experience feelings of weakness and nausea. He or she may vomit.

Call a physician or summon an ambulance that has oxygen equipment. Stay calm and reassure the victim that help is on the way. The victim should not be picked up or allowed to move. Place him or her in the most comfortable sitting or half-sitting, half-lying position. Do not give the victim liquids without a doctor's orders.

In severe heart attacks and serious accidents, the victim's heart may stop beating. An effective method of treatment in such cases is *cardiopulmonary resuscitation,* commonly called *CPR.* CPR consists of artificial respiration and artificial circulation of the blood. Anyone can learn to perform CPR. See **Cardiopulmonary resuscitation.**

Heatstroke and heat exhaustion can occur when the body becomes overheated. Heatstroke is the more serious of the two conditions. A person suffering heatstroke feels hot but cannot sweat. The skin becomes hot, dry, and red. The body temperature rises so high that it can cause brain damage if not lowered quickly. Undress

the victim. Either place the victim in a tub of cool water or apply cold, wet towels to the entire body. Get medical attention as quickly as possible.

A person suffering heat exhaustion, also called *heat prostration,* displays many of the symptoms of shock. These symptoms include faintness, headache, and nausea. The skin is cold, gray, and wet with perspiration. In most cases, the body temperature remains about normal. Treat the victim as if he or she were in shock. Place the victim on his or her back, with the legs raised slightly. If the victim has trouble breathing in this position, place the person in a half-sitting, half-lying position. Take the victim to a hospital, in an air-conditioned vehicle if possible.

Nosebleed. To control a nosebleed, have the victim sit up and lean forward. Then press the nostrils firmly together for 5 to 10 minutes. Consult a physician if the bleeding does not stop within 10 to 15 minutes.

Snakebite. The treatment of a snakebite depends on whether or not the snake is poisonous. If the snake is nonpoisonous, the bite should be washed thoroughly with soap and water. A person bitten by a poisonous snake requires medical attention. Most poisonous snakebites cause deep, burning pain along with swelling and discoloration. Within minutes, the victim may begin to feel numb and have difficulty breathing. Call a physician or take the victim to a hospital. If possible, kill the snake and bring it along for identification.

Keep the victim motionless and quiet, because activity increases the poison's spread. If the bite is on an arm or a leg, tie a band above the wound, between it and the heart. The band should be loose enough for you to slip your finger under it. Do not loosen the band until professional help is obtained. For more information on emergency treatment of snakebite, see **Snakebite.**

Transporting the victim

Moving a seriously injured person to a medical facility requires great care. Rough or careless handling can make the victim's injuries even more serious. If a victim must be moved, call for an ambulance.

If you must transport the victim yourself, be sure that you have thoroughly examined the person to determine the full extent of the injuries. All bleeding should be under control, and breathing should be satisfactory and comfortable. Treat the victim for shock and splint any fractures and dislocations. If the victim must be lifted, get someone to help you, in order to avoid rough handling. Whenever possible, use a stretcher to carry a seriously injured person.

If a person may have suffered a back or neck injury, wait for professional help. Move such a victim only if it is necessary to save the person's life. Take great care not to bend or twist the body or neck. Carry the victim on a wide, hard surface, such as a lightweight door.

During transport, drive safely. If possible, two people should transport the victim. One can ensure that the victim's airway remains open and give comfort while the other drives.   Carlotta M. Rinke

Related articles in *World Book* include:

Conditions requiring first aid

Asphyxiation	Bleeding
Bee (Sting)	Blister

Bruise	Fracture	Nosebleed	Shock
Burn	Frostbite	Poison	Snakebite
Dislocation	Hemorrhage	Poison ivy	Stroke
Drowning	Hyperthermia	Rabies	Sunburn
Fainting	Hypothermia		

Other related articles

Ambulance	Emergency Medical Services
Antidote	Emetic
Antiseptic	Red Cross
Bandage	Respirator
Cardiopulmonary	Safety
resuscitation	Tourniquet
Defibrillator	

Outline

I. General rules for first aid
   A. Call for assistance   C. Examine the victim
   B. Provide urgent care   D. Treat for shock
II. First aid for bleeding
   A. Direct pressure   B. Pressure on arteries
III. Treatment for poisoning
   A. Swallowed poisons   C. Injected poisons
   B. Inhaled poisons   D. Poisons on the skin
IV. Restoring breathing
   A. Removing the cause of breathing failure
   B. Giving artificial respiration
V. Other first-aid procedures
   A. Animal bites or stings   H. Fractures and dislocations
   B. Burns   I. Frostbite
   C. Choking   J. Heart attack
   D. Concussion   K. Heatstroke and heat
   E. Convulsion and   exhaustion
      epileptic seizure   L. Nosebleed
   F. Eye injury   M.Snakebite
   G. Fainting
VI. Transporting the victim

Questions

What should be done if a poisoning victim is unconscious?
Why should an animal that has bitten a person be kept under observation by a veterinarian?
What is the purpose of a splint?
What information should a person administering first aid tell a doctor called in an emergency?
Why is it important to keep a snakebite victim motionless?
Why should a victim be examined for a medical tag or medical identification card?
What are the three types of burns? Which type should always be treated by a physician immediately?
What techniques should be used to stop severe bleeding in an arm or leg?
What are some of the signs that indicate a person may have suffered a concussion?
What kinds of injuries may cause the condition called *shock?*

Additional resources

Auerbach, Paul S. *Medicine for the Outdoors.* Lyons Pr., 1999.
Gale, Karen B. *The Kids' Guide to First Aid.* Williamson, 2002. Younger readers.
Krohmer, Jon R., ed. *American College of Emergency Physicians First Aid Manual.* Dorling Kindersley, 2001.
National Safety Council staff. *First Aid and CPR.* 4th ed. Jones & Bartlett, 2001. *First Aid and CPR Essentials.* 4th ed. 2001.
Zand, Janet, and others. *A Parent's Guide to Medical Emergencies: First Aid for Your Child.* Avery Pub., 1997.

First Amendment. See Constitution of the United States (Amendment 1).

First Continental Congress. See Continental Congress.

First ladies of the United States are the wives of the presidents of the United States. Women other than wives who handle social functions for presidents are called *White House hostesses.* Most of the hostesses

have assisted a president whose wife was deceased or too ill to serve as an official hostess.

The duties of most of the first ladies have centered around social activities, such as receptions and dinners at the White House. However, some first ladies have taken on much larger responsibilities. Abigail Adams was an early supporter of women's rights. In 1776, before her husband—John Adams—became president, he was involved in helping establish the new nation of the United States. Abigail urged John to "remember the ladies"

First ladies of the United States

The first ladies of the United States are listed below. The second column provides the years the women held the position, and the third lists their husbands. See also the list of presidents and hostesses in the **White House hostesses** article in *World Book.*

Name	Years	President
* Martha Custis Washington	1789-1797	George Washington
* Abigail Smith Adams	1797-1801	John Adams
* Dolley Payne Madison	1809-1817	James Madison
Elizabeth Kortright Monroe	1817-1825	James Monroe
Louisa Johnson Adams	1825-1829	John Quincy Adams
Anna Symmes Harrison	1841	William H. Harrison
Letitia Christian Tyler	1841-1842	John Tyler
Julia Gardiner Tyler	1844-1845	John Tyler
Sarah Childress Polk	1845-1849	James K. Polk
Margaret Smith Taylor	1849-1850	Zachary Taylor
Abigail Powers Fillmore	1850-1853	Millard Fillmore
Jane Appleton Pierce	1853-1857	Franklin Pierce
* Mary Todd Lincoln	1861-1865	Abraham Lincoln
Eliza McCardle Johnson	1865-1869	Andrew Johnson
Julia Dent Grant	1869-1877	Ulysses S. Grant
Lucy Webb Hayes	1877-1881	Rutherford B. Hayes
Lucretia Rudolph Garfield	1881	James A. Garfield
Frances Folsom Cleveland	1886-1889	Grover Cleveland
Caroline Scott Harrison	1889-1892	Benjamin Harrison
Frances Folsom Cleveland	1893-1897	Grover Cleveland
Ida Saxton McKinley	1897-1901	William McKinley
Edith Carow Roosevelt	1901-1909	Theodore Roosevelt
Helen Herron Taft	1909-1913	William H. Taft
Ellen Axson Wilson	1913-1914	Woodrow Wilson
* Edith Bolling Wilson	1915-1921	Woodrow Wilson
Florence Kling Harding	1921-1923	Warren G. Harding
Grace Goodhue Coolidge	1923-1929	Calvin Coolidge
Lou Henry Hoover	1929-1933	Herbert Hoover
* Eleanor Roosevelt	1933-1945	Franklin D. Roosevelt
Elizabeth (Bess) Wallace Truman	1945-1953	Harry S. Truman
Mamie Doud Eisenhower	1953-1961	Dwight D. Eisenhower
* Jacqueline Bouvier Kennedy	1961-1963	John F. Kennedy
Claudia (Lady Bird) Taylor Johnson	1963-1969	Lyndon B. Johnson
Thelma (Pat) Ryan Nixon	1969-1974	Richard M. Nixon
Elizabeth (Betty) Bloomer Ford	1974-1977	Gerald R. Ford
Rosalynn Smith Carter	1977-1981	Jimmy Carter
Nancy Davis Reagan	1981-1989	Ronald W. Reagan
Barbara Pierce Bush	1989-1993	George H. W. Bush
* Hillary Rodham Clinton	1993-2001	Bill Clinton
Laura Welch Bush	2001-2009	George W. Bush
*Michelle Robinson Obama	2009-	Barack Obama

*Has a separate biography in *World Book.* Mrs. Kennedy's biography is entered as **Onassis, Jacqueline Kennedy.**

The Granger Collection   UPI/Corbis-Bettmann   © Brad Markel, Gamma/Liaison

First ladies of the United States have had many roles. These pictures, *left to right,* show Dolley Madison saving a portrait of George Washington during a British invasion; Eleanor Roosevelt visiting coal miners; and Nancy Reagan urging children to avoid the use of illegal drugs.

when making the nation's laws. In the early 1800's, Dolley Madison became known for her popular social events as first lady of James Madison and as a White House hostess of Thomas Jefferson. But she is also famous for saving many state papers and a portrait of George Washington after the British invaded Washington, D.C., during the War of 1812 (1812-1815). Lucy Webb Hayes, the wife of Rutherford B. Hayes, was the first president's wife with a college degree. She promoted such social causes as aid to the poor and the prohibition of alcohol.

After President Woodrow Wilson became severely ill in 1919, First Lady Edith Wilson screened his incoming work and visitors. Lou Henry Hoover, Herbert Hoover's wife, learned several languages and became a scholar. While first lady, she wrote articles for scientific and historical publications. Eleanor Roosevelt was a public figure in her own right during and after the long presidency of Franklin D. Roosevelt (1933-1945). She is famous for her humanitarian work. Nancy Reagan, wife of Ronald Reagan, led efforts in the 1980's to combat abuse of illegal drugs. In 2000, Hillary Rodham Clinton, wife of Bill Clinton, was elected to the U.S. Senate from New York. Her election marked the first time that the wife of a U.S. president was elected to public office. In 2009, Michelle Robinson Obama, the wife of Barack Obama, became the first African American first lady.   Kathryn Kish Sklar

Related articles. In the table with this article, each first lady of the United States whose entry is marked with an asterisk (*) has a separate article in *World Book.* Also, each article on a U.S. president includes information on first ladies and White House hostesses, as well as one or more pictures of a first lady or a hostess. See also **White house hostesses.**

Firth of Forth is the large mouth of the River Forth on the east coast of Scotland. The baylike firth connects with the North Sea (see **United Kingdom** [terrain map]). The Firth of Forth is 50 miles (80 kilometers) long and 30 miles (48 kilometers) wide at its widest point.

One of the world's longest suspension bridges spans the firth at Queensferry. The bridge was finished in 1964. It is 8,244 feet (2,513 meters) long and has a 3,300-foot (1,006-meter) center span. A cantilever railroad bridge

1.5 miles (2.5 kilometers) long also crosses the firth at Queensferry. It was completed in 1890.   A. S. Mather

Fischer, Bobby (1943-2008), became the first American to win the official world chess championship. He won the title in 1972 by defeating defending world chess champion Boris Spassky of the Soviet Union in the most publicized chess match ever. In 1975, the World Chess Federation took away his title after he refused to defend it by playing Soviet challenger Anatoly Karpov under federation rules. Fischer never played another tournament game. He did not play again in public until 1992, when he defeated Spassky in an exhibition match in Yugoslavia. Fischer's participation in the match violated United States sanctions against Yugoslavia, and the U.S. government issued a warrant for his arrest. Fischer eventually fled to Japan, where he was imprisoned for nine months in 2004 and 2005. He then left Japan for Iceland, which had granted him citizenship.

Robert James Fischer was born March 9, 1943, in Chicago. He was raised in New York City. In 1958, at age 14, he won his first U.S. chess championship. Later in 1958, at age 15 years and 6 months, he became the youngest international grandmaster in chess history to that time. His *My Sixty Memorable Games* (1969) is regarded as a chess classic. Fischer died on Jan. 17, 2008.   Larry Evans

Fischer-Dieskau, *FIHSH uhr DEE skow,* **Dietrich** (1925-2012), a German baritone, was one of the finest singers of *lieder* (German art songs) of his time (see **Lieder**). Fischer-Dieskau won fame for his concerts and his many recordings. He sang with many top conductors and often performed with the noted piano accompanist Gerald Moore. Fischer-Dieskau also performed with the world's leading opera companies.

Fischer-Dieskau was born on May 28, 1925, in Berlin, Germany, and studied music there. He made his debut in 1947 in the German composer Johannes Brahms's *A German Requiem* (1869). He retired as a performer in 1993.

Fischer-Dieskau collected and introduced over 750 songs in *The Fischer-Dieskau Book of Lieder* (1977). He also wrote *Schubert's Songs* (1977). Fischer-Dieskau died on May 18, 2012.   Charles H. Webb

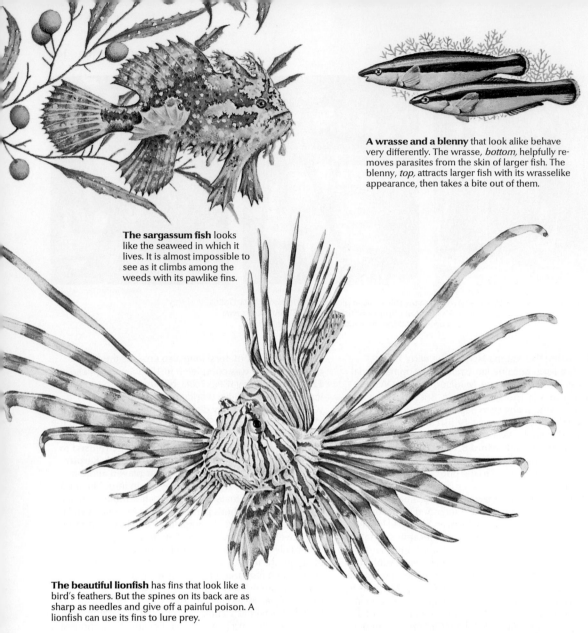

A wrasse and a blenny that look alike behave very differently. The wrasse, *bottom,* helpfully removes parasites from the skin of larger fish. The blenny, *top,* attracts larger fish with its wrasselike appearance, then takes a bite out of them.

The sargassum fish looks like the seaweed in which it lives. It is almost impossible to see as it climbs among the weeds with its pawlike fins.

The beautiful lionfish has fins that look like a bird's feathers. But the spines on its back are as sharp as needles and give off a painful poison. A lionfish can use its fins to lure prey.

Fish

Fish are *vertebrates* (backboned animals) that live in water. There are more kinds of fish than all other kinds of water and land vertebrates put together. The various kinds of fish differ so greatly in shape, color, and size that it is hard to believe they all belong to the same group of animals. For example, some fish look like lumpy rocks, and others like wriggly worms. Some fish are nearly as flat as pancakes, and others can blow themselves up like balloons. Fish have all the colors of the rainbow. Many have colors as bright as the most

John E. McCosker, the contributor of this article, is a Senior Scientist at the California Academy of Sciences.

brightly colored birds. Their rich reds, yellows, blues, and purples form hundreds of beautiful patterns, from stripes and lacelike designs to polka dots.

One of the world's smallest fishes, the stout infantfish of Australia's Great Barrier Reef, grows only about ¼ inch (7 millimeters) long. The largest fish is the whale shark, which may grow more than 40 feet (12 meters) long and weigh over 15 tons (14 metric tons). It feeds on tiny, drifting aquatic organisms called *plankton* and is completely harmless to most other fish and to human beings. The most dangerous fish weigh only a few pounds or kilograms. They include the deadly stonefish, whose poisonous spines may kill a human being.

Fish live almost anywhere there is water. They are found in the near-freezing waters of the Arctic and in the warm waters of tropical jungles. Other fish live in roaring mountain streams and in peaceful underground

The porcupinefish is covered with protective spines. For added protection, the fish fills itself with water to change from its normal appearance, *bottom,* to that of a prickly balloon, *top.*

Roy Pinney, Globe

An archerfish catches an insect resting above the surface by spitting drops of water at it. The drops strike with enough force to knock the insect into the water, where the fish can eat it.

Interesting facts about fish

One of the smallest fishes is the stout infantfish of Australia's Great Barrier Reef. It grows only about ¼ inch (7 millimeters) long.

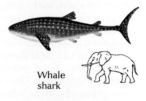

The largest fish is the whale shark. It may weigh more than 15 tons (14 metric tons) —over twice as much as an average African elephant. This fish is harmless to people. It eats mainly small floating organisms.

Whale shark

A four-eyed fish, the anableps, has eyes divided in two. When the fish swims just below the surface, the top half of each eye sees above the surface and the bottom half sees underwater.

Anableps

The black swallower can swallow fish twice its own size. Its jaws have "hinges" that enable them to open wide, and its stomach can stretch to several times its normal size. A fish swallowed whole is gradually digested.

Black swallower

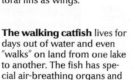

The flying hatchetfish is one of the few fish that can really fly. A hatchetfish can take off from the water's surface and fly as far as 10 feet (3 meters). The fish uses its pectoral fins as wings.

Flying hatchetfish

The walking catfish lives for days out of water and even "walks" on land from one lake to another. The fish has special air-breathing organs and uses its side fins and tail to help it crawl on the ground.

Walking catfish

The most numerous fishes in the world are bristlemouths, a kind of tiny saltwater fish. Scientists believe that bristlemouths number in the billions of billions.

rivers. Some fish make long journeys across the ocean. Others spend most of their life buried in sand on the bottom of the ocean. Most fish never leave water. Yet some fish are able to survive for months in dried-up riverbeds.

Fish have enormous importance to human beings. They provide food for millions of people. Fishing enthusiasts catch them for sport, and people keep them as pets. In addition, fish are important in the *balance of nature.* They eat plants and animals and, in turn, become food for other animals and provide nutrients for plants. Fish thus help keep in balance the total number of plants and animals on Earth.

All fish have two main features in common. (1) They have a backbone, and so they are vertebrates. (2) They breathe mainly by means of gills. Nearly all fish are also *cold-blooded* animals—that is, they cannot regulate their body temperature, which changes with the temperature of their surroundings. In addition, almost all fish have fins, which they use for swimming. All other water animals differ from fish in at least one of these ways. Dol-

phins, porpoises, and whales look like fish and have a backbone and fins, but they are *mammals* (animals that feed their young with the mother's milk). Mammals breathe with lungs rather than gills. They are also *warm-blooded*—their body temperature remains about the same when the air or water temperature changes. Some water animals are called *fish,* but they do not have a backbone and so are not fish. These animals include jellyfish and starfish. Clams, crabs, lobsters, oysters, scallops, and shrimps are called *shellfish.* But they also lack a backbone.

The first fish appeared on Earth about 500 million years ago. They were the first animals to have a backbone. Most scientists believe that these early fish became the ancestors of all other vertebrates.

Fish benefit people in many ways. Fish make up a major part of the people's diet in Japan and Norway. In other countries, the people eat fish to add variety to their meals. For thousands of years, people have also enjoyed fishing for sport. Many people keep fish as pets. Fish are also important in the balance of nature.

Food and game fish. Fish rank among the most nourishing of all foods. Fish flesh contains about as much protein as meat does. Each year, millions of tons of cod, herring, tuna, and other ocean food fish are caught commercially. Commercial fishing also takes place in inland waters, where such freshwater food fish as perch and trout are caught. The *World Book* article on **Fishing industry** discusses commercial fishing throughout the world.

Businesses called *fish farms* raise certain types of fish for food. Fish farms in the United States raise catfish, salmon, and trout. In other countries, they raise carp and milkfish. Fish farmers raise the fish in ponds and use special feeding methods to make the fish grow larger and faster than they grow in the wild.

Some persons enjoy fishing simply for fun. Many of these people like to go after *game fish.* Game fish are noted for their fighting spirit or some other quality that adds to the excitement of fishing. They include such giant ocean fish as marlin and sailfish and such fresh water fish as black bass and rainbow trout. Most game fish are also food fish. See the article on **Fishing** for detailed information on sport fishing.

Other useful fish. Certain fish, such as anchovettas and menhaden, are caught commercially but are not good to eat. Industries process these fish to make glue, livestock feed, and other products. Scientists often

Fish in the balance of nature

Fish help keep the number of organisms on Earth in balance. Fish feed on some aquatic organisms and themselves become food for others. This process is called a *food chain.* Fish are part of many food chains, as shown in the diagram below. The blue symbols represent various aquatic organisms that fish eat. The red symbols represent living things that eat fish or are nourished by the matter that remains after fish die and decay.

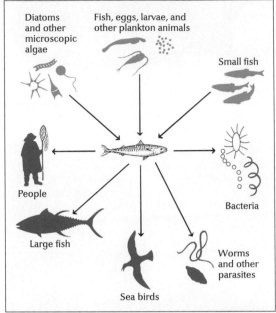

Diatoms and other microscopic algae

Fish, eggs, larvae, and other plankton animals

Small fish

People

Bacteria

Large fish

Worms and other parasites

Sea birds

WORLD BOOK diagram

Jen & Des Bartlett, Bruce Coleman Inc.

Fish hatcheries raise fish that are used to stock rivers. The workers at the left are removing the eggs from a female salmon. The eggs are then fertilized with *milt* from a male salmon, *center.* The fertilized eggs are kept in an *incubator, right,* until they hatch into baby salmon.

use goldfish and other small fish as experimental animals in medical research. They require less space and care than other experimental animals. Some fish produce substances used as medicines. For example, a chemical produced by puffers is used to treat asthma. Many people enjoy keeping fish as pets in home aquariums (see **Aquarium, Home; Aquarium, Public**). Popular aquarium fish include goldfish, guppies, and tetras.

Harmful fish. Few species of fish will attack a human being. They include certain sharks, especially tiger sharks and white sharks, which occasionally attack swimmers. Barracudas and moray eels may also attack a swimmer if provoked. Certain types of piranhas are bloodthirsty fish with razor-sharp teeth. A group of them can strip the flesh from a large mammal in minutes. Some other fish, including sting rays and stonefish, have poisonous spines that can injure or kill anything that tries to eat them. The flesh of filefish, puffers, and some other fish is poisonous and can cause sickness or death if eaten.

Many species of fish have become pests after being introduced into certain waters. For example, sea lampreys that entered the Great Lakes and Asian catfish introduced into inland waters of Florida have become threats to native fish.

Fish in the balance of nature. All the fish in a particular environment, such as a lake or a certain area of the ocean, make up a *fish community.* The fish in a community are part of a system in which energy is transferred from one living thing to another in the form of food. Such a system is called a *food chain.*

Nearly all food chains begin with the energy from sunlight. Plants and other photosynthetic organisms use this energy to make their food. In the ocean and in fresh water, the most important kinds of life are part of the *plankton*—the great mass of tiny organisms that drifts near the surface. Certain fish eat plankton and are in turn eaten by other fish. These fish may then be eaten by still other fish. Some of these fish may also be eaten by people or by birds or other animals. Many fish die naturally. Their bodies then sink and decay. The decayed matter provides nourishment for water plants, animals, and other organisms.

Every fish community forms part of a larger natural community made up of all the organisms in an area. A natural community includes numerous food chains, which together are called a *food web.* The complicated feeding patterns involved in a food web keep any one form of life from becoming too numerous and so preserve the balance of nature.

The balance of a community may be upset if large numbers of one species in the community are destroyed. People may upset the balance in this way by catching too many fish of a particular kind. Or they may pollute the water so badly that certain kinds of aquatic life, including certain fish, can no longer live in it. To learn how people conserve fish, see **Fishing industry** (Fishery conservation).

Kinds of fish

Scientists have named and described more than 24,000 kinds of fishes. Each year, they discover new species, and so the total increases continually. Fish make up more than half of all known species of vertebrates.

Scientists who study fish are called *ichthyologists* (pronounced *IHK thee AHL uh jihsts*). They divide fish into two main groups: (1) *jawed* and (2) *jawless.* Almost all fish have jaws. The only jawless species are lampreys and hagfish. Jawed fish are further divided into two groups according to the composition of their skeletons. One group has a skeleton composed of a tough, elastic substance called *cartilage.* Sharks, rays, and chimaeras make up this group. The other group has a skeleton composed largely or partly of bone. Members of this group, called *bony fish,* make up by far the largest group of fish in the world.

The section of this article called *A classification of fish* lists the major subgroups into which bony fish are divided. This section discusses the chief characteristics of (1) bony fish; (2) sharks, rays, and chimaeras; and (3) lampreys and hagfish.

Bony fish

Bony fish can be divided into two main groups. One group has bony rays to support their fins. These fish, called *spiny-finned fish,* include most modern species. The other group, the *fleshy-finned fish,* have more fleshy fins than do spiny-finned fish.

Spiny-finned fish include about 23,000 species. They make up about 95 percent of all known kinds of fish. Some have bony skeletons. They are called *teleosts,* which comes from two Greek words meaning *complete* and *bone.* Nearly all food fish, game fish, and aquarium fish are teleosts. They include such well-known groups of fish as bass, catfish, cod, herring, minnows, perch, trout, and tuna. Each group of fish consists of a number of species. For example, Johnny darters, walleyes, and yellow perch are all kinds of perch.

Thousands of species of teleosts are not so well known. A large number live in jungle rivers or coral reefs. Some are deep-sea species seldom seen by human beings. They include more than 150 kinds of deep-sea anglers. These small, fierce-looking fish have fanglike teeth and glowing light organs. Deep-sea anglers live in the ocean depths and seldom if ever come to the surface.

Many teleosts have unusual names and are as strange and colorful as their names. For example, the elephant-nose mormyrid has a snout shaped much like an elephant's trunk. The fish uses its snout to hunt for food along river bottoms. Another strange fish, the upside-down catfish, regularly swims on its back.

Many millions of years ago, there were only a few species of teleosts. They were greatly outnumbered by sharks and the ancestors of certain present-day bony fish. The early teleosts looked much alike and lived in only a few parts of the world. Yet they became the most numerous, varied, and widespread of all fish mainly be-

Bill Noel Kleeman, Tom Stack & Associates

A leaping trout is a sight familiar to many people. But some species of fish are seldom seen. Many kinds of fish live in such places as jungle rivers or deep parts of the ocean.

cause they were better able than other fish to *adapt* (adjust) to changes in their environment. In adapting to these changes, their bodies and body organs changed in various ways. Such changes are called *adaptations*.

Today, the various species of teleosts differ from one another in so many ways that they seem to have little in common. For example, many teleosts have flexible, highly efficient fins, which have helped them become excellent swimmers. Sailfish and tuna can swim long distances at high speed. Many teleosts that live among coral reefs are expert at darting in and out of the coral. But a number of other teleosts swim hardly at all. Some anglerfish spend most of their adult life lying on the ocean floor. Certain eellike teleosts are finless and so are poor swimmers. They burrow into mud on the bottom and remain there much of the time. A large number of teleosts have fins that are adapted to uses other than swimming. For example, flyingfish have winglike fins that help them glide above the surface of the water. The mudskipper has muscular fins that it uses to hop about on land.

Other bony fish include sturgeons, paddlefish, gars, and bowfins. Sturgeons rank as the largest of all freshwater fish. The largest sturgeon ever caught weighed more than 4,500 pounds (2,040 kilograms). Instead of scales, sturgeons have an armorlike covering consisting of five rows of thick, bony plates. Some sturgeons live in salt water but return to fresh water to lay their eggs. Paddlefish are strange-looking fish found only in China and the Mississippi Valley of the United States. They have

huge snouts shaped somewhat like canoe paddles. Bowfins and gars are extremely fierce fish of eastern North America. They have unusually strong jaws and sharp teeth.

Fleshy-finned fish include the coelacanth and six species of lungfish. They make up less than 1 percent of all fish species. These odd-looking fish are related to fish that lived many millions of years ago.

All the fleshy-finned bony fish except the coelacanth live in fresh water. Coelacanths live off the southeastern coast of Africa. Coelacanths are not closely related to any other living fish, and there is only one known species of coelacanth.

Lungfish live in Africa, Australia, and South America. They breathe with lunglike organs as well as gills. The African and South American species can go without food and water longer than any other vertebrates. They live buried in dry mud for months at a time, during which they neither eat nor drink.

Sharks, rays, and chimaeras

Sharks, rays, and chimaeras total about 965 species, or about 4 percent of all known fish. All of these species have jaws and a skeleton of cartilage rather than bone. Almost all live in salt water. Sharks and rays are the most important members of the group and make up about 925 species.

Most sharks have a torpedo-shaped body. The bodies of most rays are shaped somewhat like pancakes. A large, winglike fin extends outward from each side of a ray's flattened head and body. But the angel shark has a flattened body, and the sawfish and a few other rays are torpedo shaped. As a result, the best way to tell a shark from a ray is by the position of the *gill slits*. In sharks and rays, gill slits are slotlike openings on the outside of the body, leading from the gills. A shark's gill slits are on the sides of its head just back of the eyes. A ray's are underneath its side fins.

Chimaeras, or ratfish, include about 40 species. They are medium-sized fish with large eyes and a long, slender, pointed tail. They live near the ocean bottom. Several species have long, pointed snouts.

Lampreys and hagfish

Lampreys and hagfish are the most primitive of all fish. There are about 40 species of lampreys and about 50 species of hagfish. They make up less than 1 percent of all fish species. Lampreys live in both salt water and fresh water. Hagfish live only in the ocean.

Lampreys and hagfish have slimy, scaleless bodies shaped somewhat like the bodies of eels. But they are not closely related to eels, which are teleosts. Like sharks, rays, and chimaeras, lampreys and hagfish have a skeleton made of cartilage. But unlike all other fish, lampreys and hagfish lack jaws. A lamprey's mouth consists mainly of a round sucking organ and a toothed tongue. Certain types of lampreys use their sucking organ to attach themselves to other fish. They use their toothed tongue to cut into their victim and feed on its blood (see **Lamprey** [picture: A parasitic lamprey's mouth]). Hagfish have a slitlike mouth with sharp teeth but no sucking organ. They eat the insides of dead fish.

The chief kinds of fish

WORLD BOOK illustration by Marion Pahl

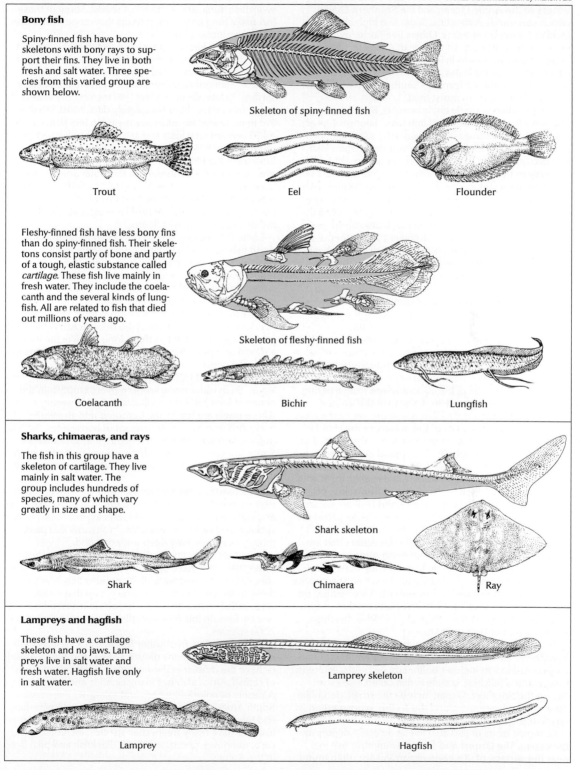

Bony fish

Spiny-finned fish have bony skeletons with bony rays to support their fins. They live in both fresh and salt water. Three species from this varied group are shown below.

Skeleton of spiny-finned fish

Trout

Eel

Flounder

Fleshy-finned fish have less bony fins than do spiny-finned fish. Their skeletons consist partly of bone and partly of a tough, elastic substance called *cartilage*. These fish live mainly in fresh water. They include the coelacanth and the several kinds of lungfish. All are related to fish that died out millions of years ago.

Skeleton of fleshy-finned fish

Coelacanth

Bichir

Lungfish

Sharks, chimaeras, and rays

The fish in this group have a skeleton of cartilage. They live mainly in salt water. The group includes hundreds of species, many of which vary greatly in size and shape.

Shark skeleton

Shark

Chimaera

Ray

Lampreys and hagfish

These fish have a cartilage skeleton and no jaws. Lampreys live in salt water and fresh water. Hagfish live only in salt water.

Lamprey skeleton

Lamprey

Hagfish

Fish live almost anywhere there is water. They thrive in the warm waters of the South Pacific and in the icy waters of the Arctic Ocean and the Southern Ocean, which surrounds Antarctica. Some live high above sea level in mountain streams. Others live far below sea level in the deepest parts of the ocean. Many fish have adapted themselves to living in such unusual places as caves, desert water holes, marshes, and swamps. A few fish, including the African and South American lungfish, can live for months in moist mud.

Fish thus live in many environments. But all these environments can be classified into two major groups according to the saltiness of the water: (1) saltwater environments and (2) freshwater environments. Some fish can live only in the salty waters of the ocean. Others can live only in fresh water. Still others can live in either salt water or fresh water. The sections on *The bodies of fish* and *How fish live* discuss how fish adjust to their environment. This section describes some of the main saltwater and freshwater environments. It also discusses fish migrations from one environment to another. A series of color illustrations shows the kinds of fish that live in the various environments. The illustration for each fish gives the fish's common and scientific names and the average or maximum length of an adult fish.

Saltwater environments. About 14,400 species—or about three-fifths of all known fish—live in the ocean. These saltwater, or *marine,* fish live in an almost endless variety of ocean environments. Most of them are suited to a particular type of environment and cannot survive in one much different from it. Water temperature is one of the chief factors in determining where a fish can live. Water temperatures at the surface range from freezing in polar regions to about 86 °F (30 °C) in the tropics.

Many saltwater species live where the water is always warm. The warmest parts of the ocean are the shallow tropical waters around coral reefs. More than a third of all known saltwater species live around coral reefs in the Indian and Pacific oceans. Many other species live around reefs in the West Indies. Coral reefs swarm with angelfish, butterflyfish, parrotfish, and thousands of other species with fantastic shapes and brilliant colors. Barracudas, groupers, moray eels, and sharks prowl the clear coral waters in search of prey.

Many kinds of fish also live in ocean waters that are neither very warm nor very cold. Such *temperate* waters occur north and south of the tropics. They make excellent fishing grounds, especially off the western coasts of continents. In these areas, nutrient-rich water comes up from the depths and supports the plankton that, in turn, supports enormous quantities of anchovies, herrings, sardines, and other food fish.

The cold waters of the Arctic and Southern oceans have fewer kinds of fish than do tropical and temperate waters. Arctic fish include bullheads, eelpouts, sculpins, skates, and a jellylike, scaleless fish called a sea snail. Fish of the Southern Ocean include the small, perchlike Antarctic cod, eelpouts, and the icefish, whose blood is nearly transparent rather than red.

Different kinds of fish also live at different depths in the ocean. The largest and fastest-swimming fish live near the surface of the *open ocean* and are often found great distances from shore. Fish that live near the surface of the open ocean include bonito, mackerel, marlin, swordfish, tuna, and a variety of sharks. Some of these fish make long annual migrations that range from tropical to near-polar waters.

Many more kinds of ocean fish live in midwater and in the depths than near the surface. Their environment differs greatly from that of species which live near the surface. Sunlight cannot reach far beneath the ocean's surface. Below about 600 feet (180 meters), the waters range from dimly lit to completely dark. Most fish that live in midwater far out at sea measure less than 6 inches (15 centimeters) long and are black, black-violet, or reddish-brown. Most of them have light organs that flash on and off in the darkness. Many also have large eyes and mouths. A number of midwater species are related to the herring. One such group includes the tiny bristlemouths. Scientists believe that bristlemouths outnumber all other kinds of fish. They estimate that bristlemouths number in the billions.

Some fish species live on the ocean bottom. Many of these fish, such as eels, flounders, puffers, seahorses, and soles, live in shallow coastal waters. But many others live at the bottom far from shore. They include rattails and many other fish with large heads and eyes and long, slender, pointed tails. Many species of rattails grow 1 foot (30 centimeters) or more long. One of the strangest bottom dwellers of the deep ocean is the tripod, or spider, fish. It has three long fins like the legs of a tripod or a three-legged stool. The fish uses its fins to sit on the ocean bottom.

Some kinds of fish live in *brackish* (slightly salty) water. Such water occurs where rivers empty into the ocean, where salt water collects in coastal swamps, and where pools are left by the outgoing tide. Brackish-water fish include certain species of barracudas, flatfish, gobies, herring, killifish, silversides, and sticklebacks. Some saltwater fish, including various kinds of herring, lampreys, salmon, smelt, and sticklebacks, can also live in fresh water.

Freshwater environments. Fish live on every continent except Antarctica. They are found in most lakes, rivers, and streams and in brooks, creeks, marshes, ponds, springs, and swamps. Some live in streams that pass through caves or flow deep underground.

Scientists have classified about 9,600 kinds of freshwater fish. They make up about two-fifths of all fish species. Almost all freshwater fish are bony fish. Many of these bony fish belong to a large group that includes carp, catfish, characins, electric eels, loaches, minnows, and suckers. In this group, catfish alone total more than 2,500 species.

Like ocean fish, freshwater fish live in a variety of climates. Tropical regions of Africa, Asia, and South America have the most species, including hundreds of kinds of catfish. Africa also has many cichlids and mormyrids. A variety of colorful loaches and minnows live in Asia. South American species include electric eels, piranhas, and tetras. Temperate regions, especially in North America, also have many freshwater species, including bass, carp, minnows, perch, and trout. Blackfish and pike live in the Arctic.

In every climate, certain kinds of freshwater fish require a particular kind of environment. Some species, including many kinds of graylings, minnows, and trout, live mainly in cool, clear, fast-moving streams. Many species of carp and catfish thrive in warm, muddy, slow-moving rivers. Some fish, such as bluegills, lake trout, white bass, and whitefish, live chiefly in lakes. Black bullheads, largemouth bass, muskellunge, northern pike, rainbow trout, yellow perch, and many other species are found both in lakes and in streams and rivers.

Like marine fish, freshwater fish live at different levels in the water. For example, many cave, spring, and swamp fish live near the surface. Gars, muskellunge, and whitefish ordinarily live in midwater. Bottom dwellers include darters, sturgeon, and many kinds of catfish and suckers.

Some freshwater species live in unusual environments. For example, some live in mountain streams so swift and violent that few other forms of life can survive in them. These fish cling to rocks with their mouth or some special suction organ. A number of species live in caves and underground streams. These fish never see daylight. Most of them have pale or white skin, and many of them are blind. A few kinds of freshwater fish live in hot springs where the temperature rises as high as 104 °F (40 °C).

Fish migrations. Relatively few kinds of fish can travel freely between fresh water and salt water. They make such migrations to *spawn* (lay eggs). Saltwater fish that swim to fresh water for spawning are called *anadromous* fish. They include alewives, blueback herring, sea lampreys, smelt, and most species of salmon and shad. Freshwater fish that spawn in salt water are called *catadromous* fish. They include North American and European eels and certain kinds of gobies. Some normally anadromous fish, including large numbers of certain species of alewives, lampreys, salmon, and smelt, have become *landlocked*—that is, they have become freshwater natives. After hatching, the young do not migrate to the ocean. The section *How fish adjust to change* explains why most fish cannot travel freely between salt water and fresh water.

Many saltwater species migrate from one part of the ocean to another at certain times of the year. For example, many kinds of mackerel and certain other fish of the open ocean move toward shore to spawn. Each summer, many species of haddock and other cold-water fish migrate from coastal waters to cooler waters farther out at sea. Some freshwater fish make similar migrations. For example, some trout swim from lakes into rivers to spawn. Some other fish of temperate lakes and streams, such as bass, bluegills, and perch, live near the warm surface during summer. When winter comes, the waters freeze at the surface but remain slightly warmer beneath the ice. The fish then migrate toward the bottom and remain there until warm weather returns.

Where ocean fish live   Many kinds of saltwater fish live far from shore. There, the sea can be divided into three main levels according to the amount of sunlight that reaches various depths, *below left.* Different kinds of fish live at each level.

WORLD BOOK illustration by Marion Pahl

Upper waters (brightest sunlight)

600 feet (180 meters)

Fish of the upper waters include such fast swimmers as the marlin and tuna. The largest kinds of fish, including the giant manta ray, also live in this region. Many upper-water fish travel great distances and range from tropical to arctic waters. Some often swim close to shore.

Bluefin Tuna
Blue Marlin
Manta Ray

Midwaters (dim sunlight)

3,000 feet (900 meters)

Fish of the midwaters include the oarfish, which grows as long as 55 feet (17 meters). But most midwater fish grow less than 6 inches (15 centimeters) long. The lanternfish and hatchetfish have light-producing organs, as do most midwater fish. Some kinds of midwater fish swim into upper waters to feed or lay eggs.

Oarfish
Lanternfish
Hatchetfish

Depths (little or no sunlight)

Fish of the depths live in waters that are always cold and almost totally dark. Such waters extend from lower midwaters to the bottom. Lower-midwater fish include anglerfish and other species with large mouths and sharp teeth. The rattail and the tripod fish live near the ocean bottom.

Deep-Sea Angler
Tripod Fish
Rattail

Fish of coastal waters and the open ocean

Some saltwater fish live along the coasts of continents. Others live far from shore in the open ocean, though many of these fish also swim close to shore from time to time. Both coastal and open-ocean species are pictured in these drawings. Fish of the open ocean shown here include dolphinfish, flyingfish, herring, mackerel, manta rays, marlin, ocean sunfish, sailfish, swordfish, and tuna. Most of the other fish pictured live mainly in coastal waters. Some coastal fish, such as bull sharks and sawfish, always stay close to land. Others, such as bluefish and great barracuda, sometimes swim far out to sea.

© Shutterstock

Exciting game fish, such as this sailfish, live throughout upper ocean waters. Many saltwater game fish are also important food fish. Fishing fleets catch many far out at sea.

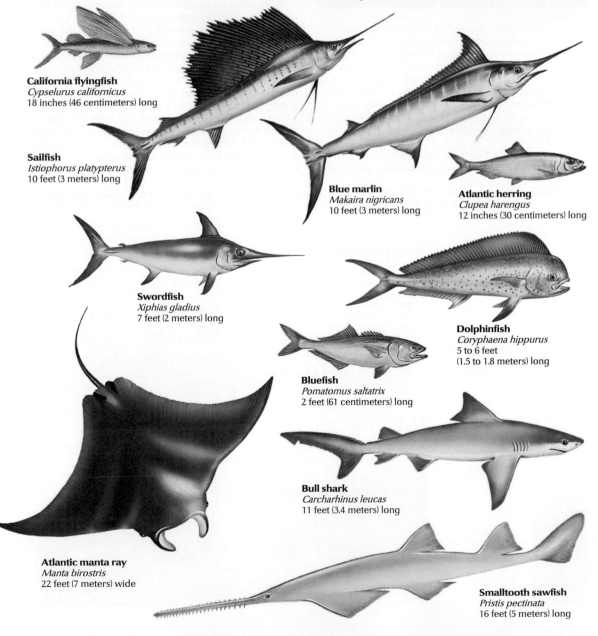

California flyingfish
Cypselurus californicus
18 inches (46 centimeters) long

Sailfish
Istiophorus platypterus
10 feet (3 meters) long

Blue marlin
Makaira nigricans
10 feet (3 meters) long

Atlantic herring
Clupea harengus
12 inches (30 centimeters) long

Swordfish
Xiphias gladius
7 feet (2 meters) long

Dolphinfish
Coryphaena hippurus
5 to 6 feet
(1.5 to 1.8 meters) long

Bluefish
Pomatomus saltatrix
2 feet (61 centimeters) long

Bull shark
Carcharhinus leucas
11 feet (3.4 meters) long

Atlantic manta ray
Manta birostris
22 feet (7 meters) wide

Smalltooth sawfish
Pristis pectinata
16 feet (5 meters) long

© Shutterstock

© Shutterstock

A slow swimmer, the enormous goliath grouper keeps close to the bottom in coastal waters. Many fish move slowly unless stirred to fast action by an approaching prey or predator.

A spotted eagle ray glides swiftly through coastal waters in search of prey. This fish has poisonous spines in its tail that can injure a human swimmer.

WORLD BOOK illustrations by Donald Moss

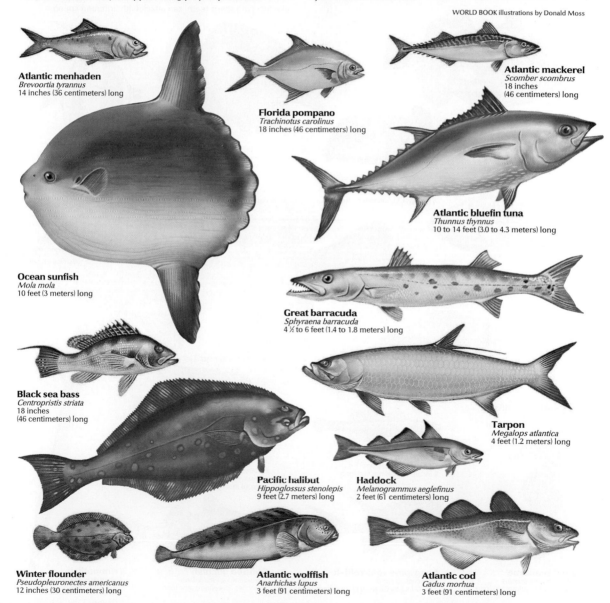

Atlantic menhaden
Brevoortia tyrannus
14 inches (36 centimeters) long

Florida pompano
Trachinotus carolinus
18 inches (46 centimeters) long

Atlantic mackerel
Scomber scombrus
18 inches
(46 centimeters) long

Ocean sunfish
Mola mola
10 feet (3 meters) long

Atlantic bluefin tuna
Thunnus thynnus
10 to 14 feet (3.0 to 4.3 meters) long

Great barracuda
Sphyraena barracuda
4 ½ to 6 feet (1.4 to 1.8 meters) long

Black sea bass
Centropristis striata
18 inches
(46 centimeters) long

Tarpon
Megalops atlantica
4 feet (1.2 meters) long

Pacific halibut
Hippoglossus stenolepis
9 feet (2.7 meters) long

Haddock
Melanogrammus aeglefinus
2 feet (61 centimeters) long

Winter flounder
Pseudopleuronectes americanus
12 inches (30 centimeters) long

Atlantic wolffish
Anarhichas lupus
3 feet (91 centimeters) long

Atlantic cod
Gadus morhua
3 feet (91 centimeters) long

Fish of coral reefs

Hundreds of kinds of saltwater fish live in the warm, shallow waters around coral reefs. Most of these reefs are in the Indian and Pacific oceans and around the West Indies. A reef's clear, sunlit waters swarm with fish that dart in and out of the coral. Many of them are among the most beautiful in the world. Reef fish differ greatly in appearance and in many other ways. For example, some are mainly plant eaters, such as parrotfish and surgeonfish. Others, including triggerfish and trunkfish, eat small water animals as well as plants. Still others are *predators* that hunt smaller fish. Such fish include groupers and moray eels.

Ben Cropp, Tom Stack & Associates

A fierce hunter, this speckled moray eel lives in and around coral reefs and catches smaller fish as prey. The moray, a snake-like fish with sharp teeth, can attack with lightning speed.

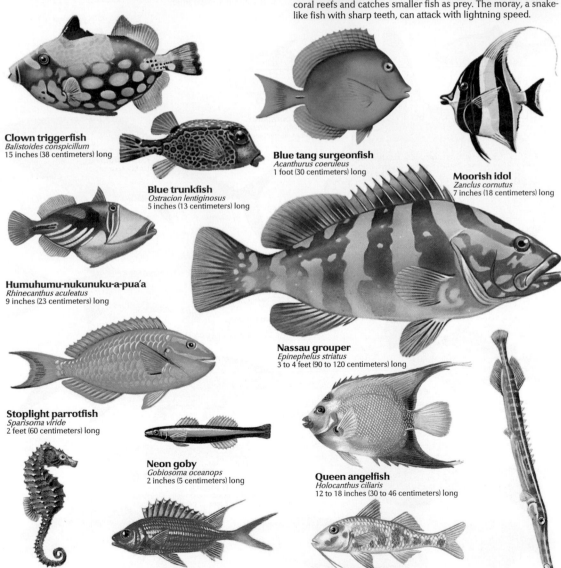

Clown triggerfish
Balistoides conspicillum
15 inches (38 centimeters) long

Blue trunkfish
Ostracion lentiginosus
5 inches (13 centimeters) long

Blue tang surgeonfish
Acanthurus coeruleus
1 foot (30 centimeters) long

Moorish idol
Zanclus cornutus
7 inches (18 centimeters) long

Humuhumu-nukunuku-a-pua'a
Rhinecanthus aculeatus
9 inches (23 centimeters) long

Nassau grouper
Epinephelus striatus
3 to 4 feet (90 to 120 centimeters) long

Stoplight parrotfish
Sparisoma viride
2 feet (60 centimeters) long

Neon goby
Gobiosoma oceanops
2 inches (5 centimeters) long

Queen angelfish
Holocanthus ciliaris
12 to 18 inches (30 to 46 centimeters) long

Lined seahorse
Hippocampus erectus
5 inches (13 centimeters) long

Longspine squirrelfish
Holocentrus rufus
7 to 12 inches (18 to 30 centimeters) long

Spotted goatfish
Pseudupeneus maculatus
10 inches (25 centimeters) long

Trumpetfish
Aulostomus maculatus
2 feet (60 centimeters) long

© Shutterstock

Small, lively swimmers, such as this school of French grunts, create almost constant movement around a reef. Some swim about hunting for food during the day, and others do so at night.

Allan Power, Bruce Coleman Ltd.

The harlequin tuskfish is one of the many brilliantly colored species that live among the coral. Dazzling colors or color patterns may help protect these fish by confusing their enemies.

WORLD BOOK illustrations by Donald Moss

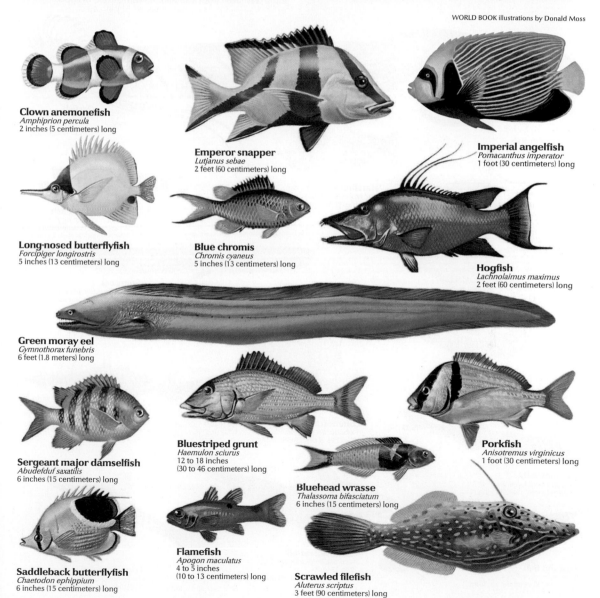

Clown anemonefish
Amphiprion percula
2 inches (5 centimeters) long

Emperor snapper
Lutjanus sebae
2 feet (60 centimeters) long

Imperial angelfish
Pomacanthus imperator
1 foot (30 centimeters) long

Long-nosed butterflyfish
Forcipiger longirostris
5 inches (13 centimeters) long

Blue chromis
Chromis cyaneus
5 inches (13 centimeters) long

Hogfish
Lachnolaimus maximus
2 feet (60 centimeters) long

Green moray eel
Gymnothorax funebris
6 feet (1.8 meters) long

Sergeant major damselfish
Abudefduf saxatilis
6 inches (15 centimeters) long

Bluestriped grunt
Haemulon sciurus
12 to 18 inches
(30 to 46 centimeters) long

Porkfish
Anisotremus virginicus
1 foot (30 centimeters) long

Bluehead wrasse
Thalassoma bifasciatum
6 inches (15 centimeters) long

Saddleback butterflyfish
Chaetodon ephippium
6 inches (15 centimeters) long

Flamefish
Apogon maculatus
4 to 5 inches
(10 to 13 centimeters) long

Scrawled filefish
Aluterus scriptus
3 feet (90 centimeters) long

Fish of the deep ocean

Fish of the deep ocean include some of the most unusual and least-known fish in the world. Many of them have large eyes, huge mouths, fanglike teeth, and light organs that flash on and off in the dark waters of the depths. Most deep-ocean fish seldom, if ever, come to the surface. Oarfish, however, sometimes swim up from the lower midwaters and create the strange appearance of a "sea serpent" as they break the surface. A number of species of deepwater fish are familiar only to scientists and have been given only scientific names. These fish include various brotulids and stomiatoids and certain species of anglers.

Ron Church, Tom Stack & Associates

A channel rockfish rests on the ocean bottom, 4,000 feet (1,200 meters) down. There, the ocean is almost totally dark. This photograph was taken from a submarine with the aid of lights.

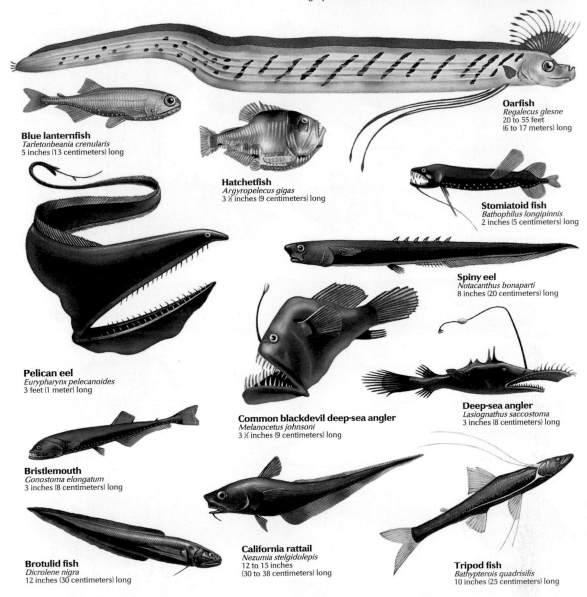

Blue lanternfish
Tarletonbeania crenularis
5 inches (13 centimeters) long

Hatchetfish
Argyropelecus gigas
3 ½ inches (9 centimeters) long

Oarfish
Regalecus glesne
20 to 55 feet
(6 to 17 meters) long

Stomiatoid fish
Bathophilus longipinnis
2 inches (5 centimeters) long

Spiny eel
Notacanthus bonaparti
8 inches (20 centimeters) long

Pelican eel
Eurypharynx pelecanoides
3 feet (1 meter) long

Common blackdevil deep-sea angler
Melanocetus johnsoni
3 ½ inches (9 centimeters) long

Deep-sea angler
Lasiognathus saccostoma
3 inches (8 centimeters) long

Bristlemouth
Gonostoma elongatum
3 inches (8 centimeters) long

Brotulid fish
Dicrolene nigra
12 inches (30 centimeters) long

California rattail
Nezumia stelgidolepis
12 to 15 inches
(30 to 38 centimeters) long

Tripod fish
Bathypterois quadrisilis
10 inches (25 centimeters) long

Fish of tropical fresh waters

Tropical regions of Africa, Asia, and South America have a tremendous variety of freshwater fish. Many of the smaller species are popular aquarium fish. These fish include the guppies, mollies, and swordtails of North and South America and the Siamese fightingfish of Asia. Large tropical freshwater fish include the giant arapaima, which lives in jungle rivers of South America. The arapaima is one of the largest freshwater fish in the world. Some arapaimas weigh more than 200 pounds (91 kilograms). The elephant-nose mormyrid of tropical Africa uses its long snout to hunt for food under stones and in mud on river bottoms.

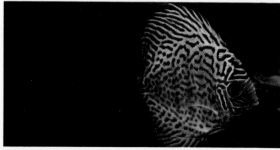

© Thinkstock

The South American discus fish is one of many colorful species that live in tropical fresh waters. Tropical fish are popular in home aquariums, partly because of their relative ease of care.

WORLD BOOK illustrations by Donald Moss and Colin Newman, Bernard Thornton Artists

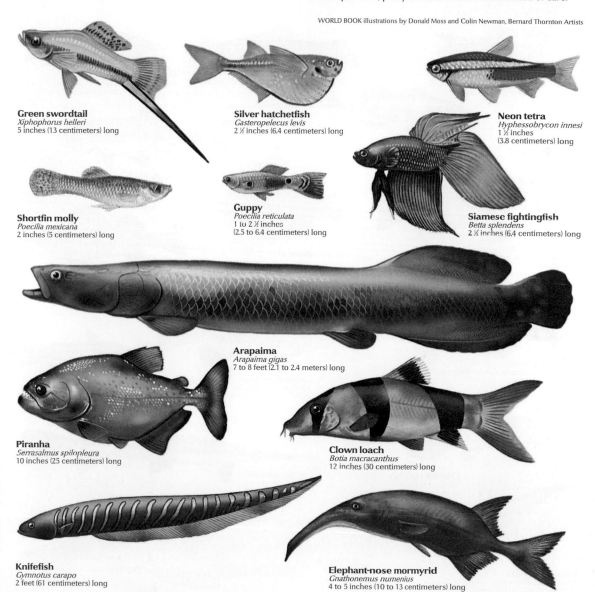

Green swordtail
Xiphophorus helleri
5 inches (13 centimeters) long

Silver hatchetfish
Gasteropelecus levis
2 ½ inches (6.4 centimeters) long

Neon tetra
Hyphessobrycon innesi
1 ½ inches
(3.8 centimeters) long

Shortfin molly
Poecilia mexicana
2 inches (5 centimeters) long

Guppy
Poecilia reticulata
1 to 2 ½ inches
(2.5 to 6.4 centimeters) long

Siamese fightingfish
Betta splendens
2 ½ inches (6.4 centimeters) long

Arapaima
Arapaima gigas
7 to 8 feet (2.1 to 2.4 meters) long

Piranha
Serrasalmus spilopleura
10 inches (25 centimeters) long

Clown loach
Botia macracanthus
12 inches (30 centimeters) long

Knifefish
Gymnotus carapo
2 feet (61 centimeters) long

Elephant-nose mormyrid
Gnathonemus numenius
4 to 5 inches (10 to 13 centimeters) long

Fish of temperate fresh waters

Unlike tropical waters, temperate waters become cold during part of the year. Fish that live in such waters must adjust their living habits to changes in water temperature. For example, in lakes that freeze over during winter, most fish move down to warmer water near the bottom and remain there until spring. The fish pictured here live in temperate lakes, rivers, and streams of North America. Many alewives, coho salmon, rainbow trout, and white sturgeon live in salt water but swim into fresh water to lay their eggs. American eels live in fresh water but swim to the ocean to lay their eggs.

Ron Church, Tom Stack & Associates

Cavefish live without seeing in the dark waters of caves and underground rivers. These Ozark cavefish have small, sightless eyes, but some other cavefish have no eyes at all.

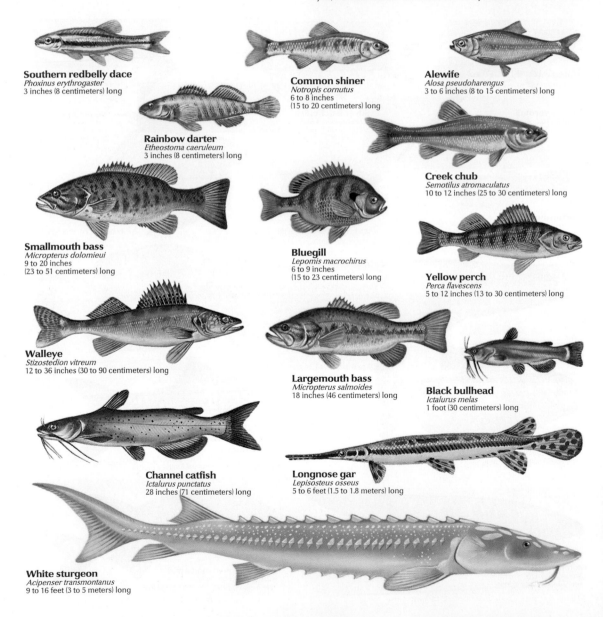

Southern redbelly dace
Phoxinus erythrogaster
3 inches (8 centimeters) long

Common shiner
Notropis cornutus
6 to 8 inches
(15 to 20 centimeters) long

Alewife
Alosa pseudoharengus
3 to 6 inches (8 to 15 centimeters) long

Rainbow darter
Etheostoma caeruleum
3 inches (8 centimeters) long

Creek chub
Semotilus atromaculatus
10 to 12 inches (25 to 30 centimeters) long

Smallmouth bass
Micropterus dolomieui
9 to 20 inches
(23 to 51 centimeters) long

Bluegill
Lepomis macrochirus
6 to 9 inches
(15 to 23 centimeters) long

Yellow perch
Perca flavescens
5 to 12 inches (13 to 30 centimeters) long

Walleye
Stizostedion vitreum
12 to 36 inches (30 to 90 centimeters) long

Largemouth bass
Micropterus salmoides
18 inches (46 centimeters) long

Black bullhead
Ictalurus melas
1 foot (30 centimeters) long

Channel catfish
Ictalurus punctatus
28 inches (71 centimeters) long

Longnose gar
Lepisosteus osseus
5 to 6 feet (1.5 to 1.8 meters) long

White sturgeon
Acipenser transmontanus
9 to 16 feet (3 to 5 meters) long

Jay Schmidt, FPG

Fighting foaming rapids, a steelhead swims from the ocean to fresh water, where it will lay its eggs. This yearly trip makes the steelhead a popular freshwater game fish.

Tom Myers, FPG

Kokanee salmon are a *landlocked* form of sockeye salmon. They live entirely in fresh water, unlike most other sockeye salmon, which live in the ocean but lay their eggs in fresh water.

WORLD BOOK illustrations by Donald Moss

Grass pickerel
Esox americanus vermiculatus
6 to 10 inches
(15 to 25 centimeters) long

Pumpkinseed
Lepomis gibbosus
4 to 8 inches (10 to 20 centimeters) long

Brook trout
Salvelinus fontinalis
10 inches
(25 centimeters) long

Rainbow trout
Oncorhynchus mykiss
14 inches
(36 centimeters) long

Northern pike
Esox lucius
28 to 52 inches
(71 to 132 centimeters) long

Lake whitefish
Coregonus clupeaformis
20 to 24 inches (51 to 61 centimeters) long

Coho salmon
Oncorhynchus kisutch
2 to 3 feet
(61 to 91 centimeters) long

Muskellunge
Esox masquinongy
$2\frac{1}{3}$ to 6 feet (0.7 to 1.8 meters) long

Carp
Cyprinus carpio
12 to 30 inches (30 to 76 centimeters) long

Black crappie
Pomoxis nigromaculatus
10 to 12 inches
(25 to 30 centimeters) long

Paddlefish
Polyodon spathula
4 feet (1.2 meters) long

Smallmouth buffalo
Ictiobus bubalus
15 to 26 inches (38 to 66 centimeters) long

American eel
Anguilla rostrata
$1\frac{1}{2}$ to 5 feet (46 to 152 centimeters) long

In some ways, a fish's body resembles that of other vertebrates. For example, fish, like other vertebrates, have an internal skeleton, an outer skin, and such internal organs as a heart, intestines, and a brain. But in a number of ways, a fish's body differs from that of other vertebrates. For example, fish have fins instead of legs, and gills instead of lungs. Lampreys and hagfish differ from all other vertebrates—and from all other fish—in many ways. Their body characteristics are discussed in an earlier section on *Lampreys and hagfish*. This section deals with the physical features that most other fish have in common.

External anatomy

Shape. Most fish have a streamlined body. The head is somewhat rounded at the front. Fish have no neck, and so the head blends smoothly into the trunk. The trunk, in turn, narrows into the tail. Aside from this basic similarity, fish have a variety of shapes. Tuna and many other fast swimmers have a torpedolike shape. Herring, freshwater sunfish, and some other species are flattened from side to side. Many bottom-dwelling fish, including most rays, are flattened from top to bottom. A number of species are shaped like things in their surroundings. For example, anglerfish and stonefish resemble rocks, and pipefish look like long, slender weeds. This camouflage, called *protective resemblance,* helps a fish escape the notice of its enemies and its prey.

Skin and color. Most fish have a fairly tough skin. It contains blood vessels, nerves, and connective tissue. It also contains certain special cells. Some of these cells produce a slimy *mucus.* This mucus makes fish slippery. Other special cells, called *chromatophores* or *pigment cells,* give fish many of their colors. A chromatophore contains red, yellow, or brownish-black pigments. These colors may combine and produce other colors, such as orange and green. Some species have more chromatophores of a particular color than other species have or have their chromatophores grouped differently. Such differences cause many variations in coloring among species. Besides chromatophores, many fish also have whitish or silvery pigments in their skin and scales. In sunlight, these pigments produce a variety of bright rainbow colors.

The color of most fish matches that of their surroundings. For example, most fish that live near the surface of the open ocean have a blue back, which matches the color of the ocean surface. This type of camouflage is called *protective coloration.* But certain brightly colored fish, including some that have poisonous spines, do not blend with their surroundings. Bright colors may protect a fish by confusing its enemies or by warning them that it has poisonous spines or flesh.

Many fish can change their color to match color changes that are present in their surroundings. Flatfish and some other fish that have two or more colors can also change the pattern formed by their colors. A fish receives the impulse to make such changes through its eyes. Signals from a fish's nerves then rearrange the pigments in the chromatophores to make them darker or lighter. The darkening or lightening of the chromatophores produces the different color patterns.

Scales. Most jawed fish have a protective covering of scales. Teleost fish have thin, bony scales that are rounded at the edge. There are two main types of teleost scales—*ctenoid* and *cycloid.* Ctenoid scales have tiny points on their surface. Fish that feel rough to the touch, such as bass and perch, have ctenoid scales. Cycloid scales have a smooth surface. They are found on such fish as carp and salmon. Some bony fish, including bichirs and gars, have thick, heavy *ganoid* scales. Sharks and most rays are covered with *placoid* scales, which resemble tiny, closely spaced teeth. Some fish, including certain kinds of eels and fresh-water catfish, are scaleless.

Fins are movable structures that help a fish swim and keep its balance. A fish moves its fins by means of muscles. Except for a few finless species, all spiny-finned bony fish have *rayed fins.* These fins consist of a web of skin supported by a skeleton of rods called *rays.* Some ray-finned fish have soft rays. Others have both soft rays and rays which are stiff and sharp to the touch. Fleshy-finned bony fish commonly have *lobed fins,* which consist of a fleshy base fringed with rays. Lobed fins are less flexible than rayed fins. Sharks, rays, and chimaeras have fleshy, skin-covered fins supported by numerous fine rays made of a tough material called *keratin.*

Fish fins are classified according to their position on

Kinds of fish scales

These drawings show examples of the four main types of fish scales and the pattern each type forms on the fish's body. Most modern bony fish have ctenoid or cycloid scales. Some catfish and a few other species have no scales at all.

WORLD BOOK illustration by Marion Pahl

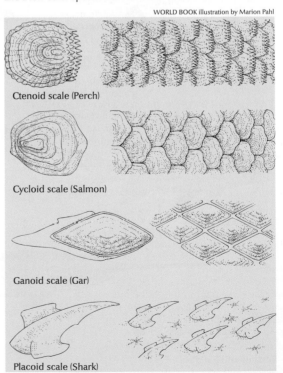

Ctenoid scale (Perch)

Cycloid scale (Salmon)

Ganoid scale (Gar)

Placoid scale (Shark)

External anatomy of a fish

This drawing of a yellow perch shows the external features most fish have in common. Many kinds of fish do not have all the fins shown here, or they lack such features as gill covers or scales. For example, lampreys and hagfish have no scales and no pelvic or pectoral fins.

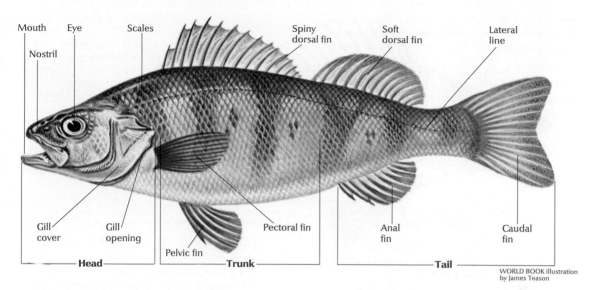

Mouth Eye Scales Spiny dorsal fin Soft dorsal fin Lateral line
Nostril
Gill cover Gill opening Pectoral fin Anal fin Caudal fin
Pelvic fin
Head **Trunk** **Tail**

WORLD BOOK illustration by James Teason

the body as well as according to their structure. Classified in this way, a fin is either *median* or *paired.*

Median fins are vertical fins on a fish's back, underside, or tail. They include *dorsal, anal,* and *caudal* fins. The dorsal fin grows along the back and helps a fish keep upright. Almost all fish have at least one dorsal fin, and many have two or three. The anal fin grows on the underside. Like a dorsal fin, it helps a fish remain upright. Some fish have two anal fins. The caudal fin is at the end of the tail. A fish swings its caudal fin from side to side to propel itself through the water and to help in steering.

Paired fins are two identical fins, one on each side of the body. Most fish have both *pectoral* and *pelvic* paired fins. The pectoral, or shoulder, fins of most fish grow on the sides, just back of the head. Most fish have their pelvic, or leg, fins just below and behind their pectoral fins. But some have their pelvic fins as far forward as the throat or nearly as far back as the anal fin. Pelvic fins are also called *ventral* fins. Most fish use their paired fins mainly to turn, stop, and make other maneuvers.

Skeleton and muscles

A fish's skeleton provides a framework for the head, trunk, tail, and fins. The central framework for the trunk and tail is the backbone. It consists of many separate segments of bone or cartilage called *vertebrae.* In bony fish, each vertebra has a spine at the top, and each tail vertebra also has a spine at the bottom. Ribs are attached to the vertebrae. The skull consists chiefly of the brain case and supports for the mouth and gills. The pectoral fins of most fish are attached to the back of the skull by a structure called a *pectoral girdle.* The pelvic fins are supported by a structure called a *pelvic girdle,* which is attached to the pectoral girdle or supported by

muscular tissue in the abdomen. The dorsal fins are supported by structures of bone or cartilage, which are rooted in tissue above the backbone. The caudal fin is supported by the tail, and the anal fin by structures of bone or cartilage below the backbone.

Like all vertebrates, fish have three kinds of muscles: (1) *skeletal muscles,* (2) *smooth muscles,* and (3) *heart muscles.* Fish use their skeletal muscles to move their bones and fins. A fish's flesh consists almost entirely of skeletal muscles. They are arranged one behind the other in broad vertical bands called *myomeres.* The myomeres can easily be seen in a skinned fish. Each myomere is controlled by a separate nerve. As a result, a fish can bend the front part of its body in one direction while bending its tail in the opposite direction. Most fish make such movements with their bodies to swim. A fish's smooth muscles and heart muscles work automatically. The smooth muscles are responsible for operating such internal organs as the stomach and intestines. Heart muscles form and operate the heart.

Systems of the body

The internal organs of fish, like those of other vertebrates, are grouped into various systems according to the function they serve. The major systems include the respiratory, digestive, circulatory, nervous, and reproductive systems. Some of these systems resemble those of other vertebrates, but others differ in many ways.

Respiratory system. Unlike land animals, almost all fish get their oxygen from water. Water contains a certain amount of dissolved oxygen. To get oxygen, fish gulp water through the mouth and pump it over the gills. Most fish have four pairs of gills enclosed in a *gill chamber* on each side of the head. Each gill consists of two rows of fleshy *filaments* attached to a *gill arch.*

The skeleton of a fish

The skeletons of most fish consist mainly of (1) a skull, (2) a backbone, (3) ribs, (4) fin rays, and (5) supports for fin rays or fins. The skeleton of a yellow perch is shown below.

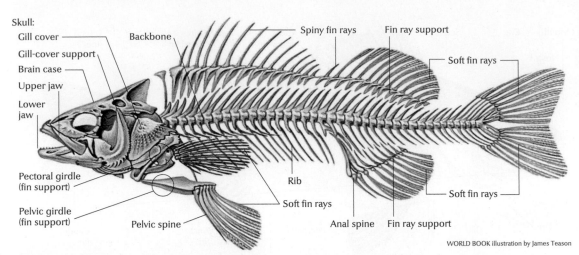

Skull:
Gill cover
Gill-cover support
Brain case
Upper jaw
Lower jaw
Pectoral girdle (fin support)
Pelvic girdle (fin support)
Pelvic spine
Backbone
Soft fin rays
Rib
Spiny fin rays
Fin ray support
Soft fin rays
Soft fin rays
Anal spine
Fin ray support

WORLD BOOK illustration by James Teason

Water passes into the gill chambers through *gill slits.* A flap of bone called a *gill cover* protects the gills of bony fish. Sharks and rays do not have gill covers. Their gill slits form visible openings on the outside of the body.

In a bony fish, the breathing process begins when the gill covers close and the mouth opens. At the same time, the walls of the mouth expand outward, drawing water into the mouth. The walls of the mouth then move inward, the mouth closes, and the gill covers open. This action forces the water from the mouth into the gill chambers. In each chamber, the water passes over the gill filaments. They absorb oxygen from the water and replace it with carbon dioxide formed during the breathing process. The water then passes out through the gill openings, and the process is repeated.

Digestive system, or *digestive tract,* changes food into materials that nourish the body cells. It eliminates materials that are not used. In fish, this system leads from the mouth to the *anus,* an opening in front of the anal fin. Most fish have a jawed mouth with a tongue and teeth. A fish cannot move its tongue. Most fish have their teeth rooted in the jaws. They use their teeth to seize prey or to tear off pieces of their victim's flesh. Some of them also have teeth on the roof of the mouth or on the tongue. Most fish also have teeth in the *pharynx,* a short tube behind the mouth. They use these teeth to crush or grind food.

In all fish, food passes through the pharynx on the way to the *esophagus,* another tubelike organ. A fish's esophagus expands easily, which allows the fish to swallow its food whole. From the esophagus, food passes into the *stomach,* where it is partly digested. Some fish have their esophagus or stomach enlarged into a *gizzard.* The gizzard grinds food into small pieces before it passes into the intestines. The digestive process is completed in the intestines. The digested food enters the blood stream. Waste products and undigested food pass out through the anus.

How a fish's gills work

Like all animals, fish need oxygen to change food into body energy. These drawings show how a fish's gills enable it to get oxygen from the water and to get rid of carbon dioxide, a body waste.

WORLD BOOK illustration by Margaret Ann Moran

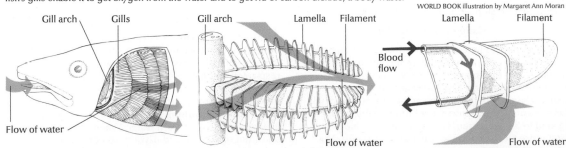

Gill arch
Gills
Flow of water

Gill arch
Lamella
Filament
Flow of water

Lamella
Filament
Blood flow
Flow of water

Most fish have four gills on each side of the head. Water enters the mouth and flows out through the gills. Each gill is made up of fleshy, threadlike *filaments.*

Water from the mouth passes over the filaments, which are closely spaced along a *gill arch* in two rows. Three of the many filaments of a gill are shown above.

Each filament has many tiny extensions called *lamellae.* Blood flowing through a lamella takes oxygen from the water and releases carbon dioxide into the water.

Internal organs of a fish

This view of a yellow perch shows the chief internal organs found in most fish. These organs are parts of the systems that perform such body processes as breathing and digestion.

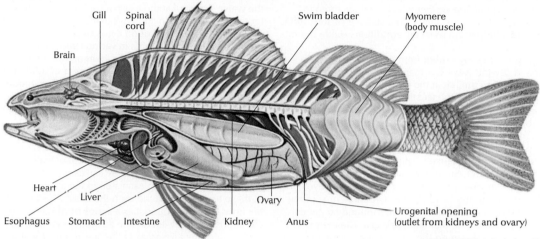

Gill   Spinal cord   Brain   Swim bladder   Myomere (body muscle)   Heart   Liver   Esophagus   Stomach   Intestine   Kidney   Ovary   Anus   Urogenital opening (outlet from kidneys and ovary)

WORLD BOOK illustration by James Teason

Circulatory system distributes blood to all parts of the body. It includes the heart and blood vessels. A fish's heart consists of two main chambers—the *atrium* and the *ventricle.* The blood flows through *veins* to the atrium. It then passes to the ventricle. Muscles in the ventricle pump the blood through *arteries* to the gills, where the blood receives oxygen and gives off carbon dioxide. Arteries then carry the blood throughout the body. The blood carries food from the intestines and oxygen from the gills to the body cells. It also carries away waste products from the cells. A fish's kidneys remove the waste products from the blood, which returns to the heart through the veins.

Nervous system of fish, like that of other vertebrates, consists of a *spinal cord, brain,* and *nerves.* However, a fish's nervous system is not so complex as that of mammals and other higher vertebrates. The spinal cord, which consists of soft nerve tissue, runs from the brain through the backbone. The brain is an enlargement of the spinal cord and is enclosed in the skull. The nerves extend from the brain and spinal cord to every part of the body. Some nerves, called *sensory* nerves, carry messages from the sense organs to the spinal cord and brain. Other nerves, called *motor* nerves, carry messages from the brain and spinal cord to the muscles. A fish can consciously control its skeletal muscles. But it has no conscious control over the smooth muscles and heart muscles. These muscles work automatically.

Reproductive system. As in all vertebrates, the reproductive organs of fish are *testes* in males and *ovaries* in females. The testes produce male sex cells, or *sperm.* The sperm is contained in a fluid called *milt.* The ovaries produce female sex cells, or *eggs.* Fish eggs are also called *roe* or *spawn.* Most fish release their sex cells into the water through an opening near the anus. The males of some species have special structures for transferring sperm directly into the females. Male sharks, for example, have such a structure, called a *clasper,* on each pelvic fin. The claspers are used to insert sperm into the female's body.

Special organs

Most bony fish have a swim bladder below the backbone. This baglike organ is also called a gas bladder. In most fish, the swim bladder provides *buoyancy,* which enables the fish to remain at a particular depth in the water. In lungfish and a few other fish, the swim bladder serves as an air-breathing lung. Still other fish, including many catfish, use their swim bladders to produce sounds as well as to provide buoyancy. Some species communicate by means of such sounds.

A fish would sink to the bottom if it did not have a way of keeping buoyant. Most fish gain buoyancy by inflating their swim bladder with gases produced by their blood. But water pressure increases with depth. As a fish swims deeper, the increased water pressure makes its swim bladder smaller and so reduces the fish's buoyancy. The amount of gas in the bladder must be increased so that the bladder remains large enough to maintain buoyancy. A fish's nervous system automatically regulates the amount of gas in the bladder so that it is kept properly filled. Sharks and rays do not have a swim bladder. To keep buoyant, most of these fish must swim constantly. When they rest, they stop swimming and so sink toward the bottom. Many bottom-dwelling bony fish also lack a swim bladder.

Many fish have organs that produce light or electricity. But these organs are simply adaptations of structures found in all or most fish. For example, many deep-sea fish have light-producing organs developed from parts of their skin or digestive tract. Some species use these organs to attract prey or possibly to communicate with others of their species. Various other fish have electricity-producing organs developed from muscles in their eyes, gills, or trunk. Some species use these organs to communicate or to stun or kill enemies or prey.

Like all vertebrates, fish have sense organs that tell them what is happening in their environment. The organs enable them to see, hear, smell, taste, and touch. In addition, almost all fish have a special sense organ called the *lateral line system,* which enables them to "touch" objects at a distance. Fish also have various other senses that help them meet the conditions of life underwater.

Sight. A fish's eyes differ from those of land vertebrates in several ways. For example, most fish can see to the right and to the left at the same time. This ability makes up in part for the fact that a fish has no neck and so cannot turn its head. Fish also lack eyelids. In land vertebrates, eyelids help moisten the eyes and shield them from sunlight. A fish's eyes are kept moist by the flow of water over them. They do not need to be shielded from sunlight because sunlight is seldom extremely bright underwater. Some fish have unusual adaptations of the eye. For example, adult flatfish have both eyes on the same side of the head. A flatfish spends most of the time lying on its side on the ocean floor and so needs eyes only on the side that faces upward. The eyes of certain deep-sea fish are on the ends of short structures that stick out from the head. These structures can be raised upward, allowing the fish to see overhead as well as to the sides and front.

A few kinds of fish are born blind. They include certain species of catfish that live in total darkness in the waters of caves and a species of whalefish, which lives in the ocean depths. Some of these fish have eyes but no vision. Others lack eyes completely.

Hearing. All fish can probably hear sounds produced in the water. Fish can also hear sounds made on shore or above the water if they are loud enough. Catfish and certain other fish have a keen sense of hearing.

Fish have an inner ear enclosed in a chamber on each side of the head. Each ear consists of a group of pouches and tubelike canals. Fish have no outer ears or eardrums to receive sound vibrations. Sound vibrations are carried to the inner ears by the body tissues.

Smell and taste. All fish have a sense of smell. It is highly developed in many species, including catfish, salmon, and sharks. In most fish, the *olfactory organs* (organs of smell) consist of two pouches, one on each side of the snout. The pouches are lined with nerve tissue that is highly sensitive to odors from substances in the water. A nostril at the front of each pouch allows water to enter the pouch and pass over the tissue. The water leaves the pouch through a nostril at the back.

Most fish have taste buds in various parts of the mouth. Some species also have them on other parts of the body. Catfish, sturgeon, and a number of other fish have whiskerlike feelers called *barbels* near the mouth. They use the barbels both to taste and to touch.

Touch and the lateral line system are closely related. Most fish have a well-developed sense of touch. Nerve endings throughout the skin react to the slightest pressure and change of temperature. The lateral line system senses changes in the movement of water. It consists mainly of a series of tiny canals under the skin. A main canal runs along each side of the trunk. Branches of these two canals extend onto the head. A fish senses the flow of water around it as a series of vibrations. The vibrations enter the lateral line through pores and activate certain sensitive areas in the line. If the flow of water around a fish changes, the pattern of vibrations sensed through the lateral line also changes. Nerves relay this information to the brain. Changes in the pattern of vibrations may warn a fish of approaching danger or indicate the location of objects outside its range of vision.

Other senses include those that help a fish keep its balance and avoid unfavorable waters. The inner ears help a fish keep its balance. They contain a fluid and several hard, free-moving *otoliths* (ear stones). Whenever a fish begins to swim in other than an upright, level position, the fluid and otoliths move over sensitive nerve endings in the ears. The nerves signal the brain about the changes in the position of the body. The brain then sends messages to the fin muscles, which move to restore the fish's balance. Fish can also sense any changes in the pressure, salt content, or temperature of the water. As a result, they can avoid swimming very far into unfavorable waters.

The lateral line system

The lateral line system makes a fish sensitive to vibrations in the water. It consists of a series of tubelike *canals* in a fish's skin. Vibrations enter the canals through *pores* (openings in the skin) and travel to sensory organs in the canals. Nerves connect these organs to the brain.

WORLD BOOK illustrations by Marion Pahl and Zorica Dabich

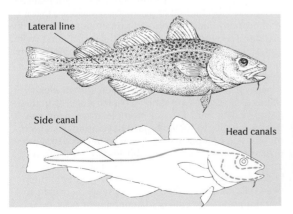

Lateral line

Side canal

Head canals

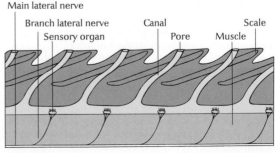

Main lateral nerve

Branch lateral nerve   Canal   Scale

Sensory organ   Pore   Muscle

Every fish begins life in an egg. In the egg, the undeveloped fish, called an *embryo,* feeds on the yolk until ready to hatch. The section *How fish reproduce* discusses where and how fish lay their eggs. After a fish hatches, it is called a *larva* or *fry.* The fish reaches adulthood when it begins to produce sperm or eggs. Most small fish, such as guppies and many minnows, become adults within a few months after hatching. But some small fish become adults only a few minutes after hatching. Large fish require several years. Many of these fish pass through one or more *juvenile* stages before becoming adults. Almost all fish continue to grow as long as they live. During its lifetime, a fish may increase several thousand times in size. The longest-lived fish are probably certain sturgeon, some of which have lived in aquariums more than 50 years. For the life spans of various other fish in captivity, see **Animal** (table: Length of life of animals).

How fish get food. Most fish are *carnivores* (meat-eaters). They eat shellfish, worms, and other kinds of water animals. Above all, they eat other fish. They sometimes eat their own young. Some fish are mainly *herbivores* (plant-eaters). They chiefly eat water plants and algae. Most of these fish probably also eat animals. Some fish live mainly on plankton. They include many kinds of flyingfish and herring and the three largest fish of all—the whale shark, giant manta ray, and basking shark. Some fish are *scavengers.* They feed mainly on waste products and on the dead bodies of animals that sink to the bottom.

Many fish have body organs specially adapted for capturing food. Certain fish of the ocean depths attract their prey with flashing lures. The dorsal fin of some anglerfish dangles above their mouth and serves as a bait for other fish. Such species as gars and swordfish have long, beaklike jaws, which they use for spearing or slashing their prey. Barracudas and certain piranhas and sharks are well known for their razor-sharp teeth, with which they tear the flesh from their victims. Electric eels and some other fish with electricity-producing organs stun their prey with an electric shock. Many fish have comblike *gill rakers.* These structures strain plankton from the water pumped through the gills.

How fish swim. Most fish gain *thrust* (power for forward movement) by swinging the tail fin from side to side while curving the rest of the body alternately to the left and to the right. Some fish, such as marlin and tuna, depend mainly on tail motion for thrust. Other fish, including many kinds of eels, rely chiefly on the curving motion of the body. Fish maneuver by moving their fins. To make a left turn, for example, a fish extends its left pectoral fin. To stop, a fish extends both of its pectoral fins.

A fish's swimming ability is affected by the shape and location of its fins. Most fast, powerful swimmers, such as swordfish and tuna, have a deeply forked or crescent-shaped tail fin and sickle-shaped pectorals. All their fins are relatively large. At the other extreme, most slow swimmers, such as bowfins and bullheads, have a squared or rounded tail fin and rounded pectorals.

How fish protect themselves. All fish, except the largest ones, live in constant danger of being attacked

How a fish develops

Most fish develop from egg to adult in stages. These photographs show three stages in the development of brook trout.

These tiny trout eggs lie among grains of sand. Curled inside each egg is an undeveloped fish called an *embryo.* The large dots are the embryo's eyes. The egg yolk nourishes the embryo.

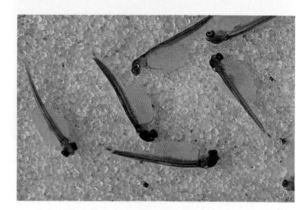

A newly hatched fish, called a *larva* or *fry,* continues to draw nourishment from the egg yolk by means of blood vessels that extend through the yolk. The yolk is contained in a *yolk sac.*

Treat Davidson, NAS

This 3-month-old trout has used its supply of yolk and now hunts for food. As it grows, it will take on the appearance of an adult trout. Most trout become adults in 2 to 5 years.

and eaten by other fish or other animals. To survive, fish must be able to defend themselves against predators. If a species loses more individuals each generation than it gains, it will in time die out.

Protective coloration and protective resemblance are the most common methods of self-defense. A fish that blends with its surroundings is more likely to escape from its enemies than one whose color or shape is extremely noticeable. Many fish that do not blend with their surroundings depend on swimming speed or maneuvering ability to escape from their enemies.

Fish also have other kinds of defense. Some fish, such as gars, pipefish, and seahorses, are protected by a covering of thick, heavy scales or bony plates. Other species have sharp spines that are difficult for predators to swallow. In many of these species, including scorpionfish, sting rays, and stonefish, one or more of the spines are poisonous. When threatened, the porcupinefish inflates its spine-covered body with water until it is shaped like a balloon. The fish's larger size and erect spines may discourage an enemy. Many eels that live on the bottom dig holes in which they hide from their enemies. Razor fish dive into sand on the bottom. A few fish do the opposite. For example, flyingfish and needlefish escape danger by propelling themselves out of the water.

How fish rest. Like all animals, fish need rest. Many species have periods of what might be called sleep. Others simply remain inactive for short periods. But even at rest, many fish continue to move their fins to keep their position in the water.

Fish have no eyelids, and so they cannot close their eyes when sleeping. But while asleep, a fish is probably unaware of the impressions received by its eyes. Some fish sleep on the bottom, resting on their belly or side. Other species sleep in midwater, in a horizontal position. The slippery dick, a coral-reef fish, sleeps on the bottom under a covering of sand. The striped parrot-

© Shutterstock

A flounder, which has both eyes on one side of its body, lies on the ocean bottom with both eyes facing up. Flounders change their color pattern to match the background.

© Andre Seale, Alamy Images

The electric eel stuns its enemies and prey with a powerful electric shock. The electricity-producing organs take up most of the body. The other inner organs lie just back of the head.

How fish swim

The dogfish and most other fish swim by swinging their tail from side to side, while curving the rest of their body in the opposite direction. Some fish, such as tuna, move the front of their body little in swimming. Eels and some other fish bend their body in snakelike curves.

WORLD BOOK illustration by Marion Pahl

Dogfish

Tuna

Eel

A fleshy bait grows from the head of an anglerfish, *above left,* and out of the mouth of a stargazer, *above right.* The wormlike bait attracts smaller fish. Anglerfish and stargazers snap up small fish with astonishing speed, but they move slowly at most other times.

fish, another coral-reef fish, encloses itself in an "envelope" of mucus before going to sleep. The fish secretes the mucus from special glands in its gill chambers.

Certain air-breathing fish, such as the African and South American lungfish, sleep out of water for months at a time. These fish live in rivers or ponds that dry up during periods of drought. The fish lie buried in hardened mud until the return of the rainy season. This kind of long sleep during dry periods is called *estivation.* During estivation, a fish breathes little and lives off the protein and fat stored in its body.

How fish live together. Among many species, the individual fish that make up the species live mainly by themselves. Such fish include most predatory fish. Many sharks, for example, hunt and feed by themselves and join other sharks only for mating.

Among many other species, the fish live together in closely knit groups called *schools.* About a fifth of all fish species are schooling species. A school may have few or many fish. A school of tuna, for example, may consist of fewer than 25 individuals. Many schools of herring number in the hundreds of millions. All the fish in a school are about the same size. Baby fish and adult fish are never in the same school. In some schooling species, the fish become part of a school when they are young and remain with it throughout their lives. Other species form schools for only a few weeks after they hatch. The fish in a school usually travel in close formation as a defense against predators. But a school often breaks up at night to feed and then regroups the next morning. The approach of a predator brings the fish quickly back together.

Fish protected by spines include the demon stinger, *above left,* and the stonefish, *above right.* Both fish give off poison through their spines. The stonefish's poison is the deadliest of all fish poisons. It can kill a human being in minutes.

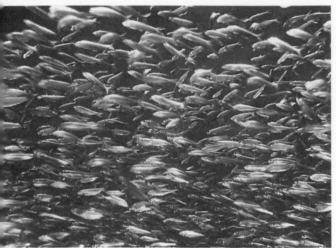

Ron Church, Tom Stack & Associates

Thousands of sardines make up this school. They live together most of the time but may separate at night to feed. They swim quickly back together when threatened by an enemy.

Ben Cropp, Tom Stack & Associates

A coral trout and a wrasse help each other. The small wrasse is removing parasites from the gills of the coral trout. The wrasse thus obtains food and the coral trout is cleaned.

Marineland of Florida

Three remoras ride on a lemon shark. The remoras use a sucking disk on their head to hold on to the shark. They also eat scraps of the shark's food.

Fish also form other types of relationships. Among cod, perch, and many other species, a number of individuals may gather in the same area for feeding, resting, or spawning. Such a group is only temporary and is not so closely knit as a school. Some fish, including certain angelfish and wrasses, form unusual relationships with larger fish of other species. In many such relationships, the smaller fish removes parasites or dead tissue from the larger fish. The smaller fish thus obtains food, and the other is cleaned.

How fish adjust to change. Fish sometimes need to adjust to changes in their environment. The two most common changes are (1) changes in water temperature and (2) changes in the salt content of water.

In general, the body temperature of each species of fish equals that of the water in which the species lives. If the water temperature rises or falls, a fish can adjust to the change because its body temperature changes accordingly. But the change in the water temperature must not be too great and must occur gradually. Most fish can adjust to a change in the water temperature of up to 15 °F. (8 °C)—if the change is not sudden. Water temperatures usually change slowly, and so there is time for a fish's body to make the necessary adjustment. But occasionally, the temperature drops suddenly and severely, killing many fish. In addition, freshwater fish are sometimes endangered by *thermal pollution,* which occurs when factories and electric power plants release hot water into rivers or lakes. The resulting increase in water temperature may be greater than most fish can adjust to.

Both fresh water and ocean water contain various salts, many of which fish need in their diet. But ocean water is far saltier than fresh water. Fish that migrate between the two must adjust to changes in the salt content of the water. Relatively few fish can make such an adjustment.

Both freshwater and saltwater fish have about the same amount of dissolved salts in their body fluids. But the body fluids of ocean fish are not so salty as the water in which the fish live. Under certain circumstances, water from a weak solution will flow into a strong solution. This natural process, called *osmosis,* takes place if the two solutions are separated by a *membrane* (thin layer) through which only the water can pass (see **Osmosis**). The skin and gill membranes of fish are of this type. For this reason, marine fish constantly lose water from their body fluids into the stronger salt solution of the sea water. To make up for this loss, they drink much water. But ocean water contains more salt than marine fish need. The fish pass the extra salt out through their gills and through their digestive tract. Saltwater fish need all the water they drink. As a result, these fish produce only small amounts of urine.

Freshwater fish have the opposite problem with osmosis. Their body fluids are saltier than fresh water. As a result, the fish constantly absorb water through their membranes. In fact, freshwater fish absorb so much water that they do not need to drink any. Instead, the fish must get rid of the extra water that their bodies absorb. As a result, freshwater fish produce great quantities of urine.

All fish reproduce sexually. In sexual reproduction, a sperm unites with an egg in a process called *fertilization*. The fertilized egg develops into a new individual. Males produce sperm and females produce eggs in almost all fish species. But in a few species, the same individual produces both sperm and eggs. In many species, fish change sex during their lifetime. Fish born as males may later become females, and fish born as females may later become males.

The eggs of most fish are fertilized outside the female's body. A female releases her eggs into the water at the same time that a male releases his sperm. Some sperm come in contact with some eggs, and fertilization takes place. This process is called *external fertilization*. The entire process during which eggs and sperm are released into the water and the eggs are fertilized is called *spawning*. Almost all bony fish reproduce in this way.

Sharks, rays, chimaeras, and a few bony fish, such as guppies and mosquito fish, reproduce in a different manner. The eggs of these fish are fertilized inside the female, a process called *internal fertilization*. For internal fertilization to occur, males and females must mate. The males have special organs for transferring sperm into the females. After fertilization, the females of some species release their eggs into the water before they hatch. Other females hatch the eggs inside their bodies and so give birth to living young. Fish that bear living young include many sharks and rays, guppies, and some halfbeaks and scorpionfish.

This section discusses spawning, the method by which most fish reproduce.

Preparation for spawning. Most fish have a *spawning season* each year, during which they may spawn several times. But some tropical species breed throughout the year. The majority of fish spawn in spring or early summer, when the water is warm and the days are long. But certain cold-water fish, such as brook trout and Atlantic cod, spawn in fall or winter.

Most fish return to particular *spawning grounds* year after year. Many freshwater fish travel only a short distance to their spawning grounds. They may simply move from the deeper parts of a river or lake to shallow waters near shore. But other fish may migrate tremendous distances to spawn. For example, European freshwater eels cross 3,000 miles (4,800 kilometers) of ocean to reach their spawning grounds in the western Atlantic.

At their spawning grounds, the males and females of some species swim off in pairs to spawn. Among other species, the males and females spawn in groups. Many males and females tell each other apart by differences in appearance. The females of some species are larger than the males. Among other species, the males develop unusually bright colors during spawning season. During the rest of the year, they look much like the females of their species. In some species, males and females look so different that for many years scientists thought they belonged to different species. Among other fish, the sexes look so much alike that they can be told apart only by differences in behavior. For example, many males adopt a special type of *courting* behavior to attract females. A courting male may swim round and round a female or perform a lively "dance" to attract her attention.

How fish reproduce

Fish reproduce *sexually*—by uniting a *sperm* (male sex cell) with an *egg* (female sex cell). In most species, the union of sex cells takes place in the water. Trout reproduction is shown below.

The female trout, *above center,* makes a nest for her eggs. She uses her tail to scoop the nest out on the gravelly bottom. The male trout, *left,* does not help make the nest.

After the nest has been made, the male moves alongside the female. As the female releases her eggs, the male releases his sperm. The sperm cells unite with the eggs in the nest.

WORLD BOOK illustration by Harry McNaught

The female then covers the nest to protect the eggs. She heads into the current and swishes her tail in the gravel to stir it up. The current carries the loosened gravel back over the eggs.

Among some species, including cod, Siamese fighting fish, and certain gobies and sticklebacks, a male claims a territory for spawning and fights off any male intruders. Many fish, especially those that live in fresh water, build nests for their eggs. A male freshwater bass, for example, uses its tail fin to scoop out a nest on the bottom of a lake or stream.

Spawning and care of the eggs. After the preparations have been made, the males and females touch in a certain way or make certain signals with their fins or body. Depending on the species, a female may lay a few eggs or many eggs—even millions—during the spawning season. Most fish eggs measure $\frac{1}{8}$ inch (3 millimeters) in diameter or less.

Some fish, such as cod and herring, abandon their eggs after spawning. A female cod may lay as many as 9 million eggs during a spawning season. Cod eggs, like those of many other ocean fish, float near the surface and scatter as soon as they are laid. Predators eat many of the eggs. Others drift into waters too cold for hatching. Only a few cod eggs out of millions develop into adult fish. A female herring lays about 50,000 eggs in a season. But herring eggs, like those of certain other marine fish, sink to the bottom and have an adhesive covering that helps them stick there. As a result, herring eggs are less likely to be eaten by predators or to drift into waters unfavorable for hatching.

A number of fish protect their eggs. They include many freshwater nest builders, such as bass, salmon, certain sticklebacks, and trouts. The females of these species lay far fewer eggs than do the females of the cod and herring groups. Like herring eggs, the eggs of many of the freshwater nest builders sink to the bottom and have an adhesive covering. But they have an even better chance of surviving than herring eggs because they receive some protection.

The amount and kind of protection given by fish to their eggs vary greatly. Salmon and trout cover their fertilized eggs with gravel but abandon them soon after. Male freshwater bass guard the eggs fiercely until they hatch. Among ocean fish, female seahorses and pipefish lay their eggs in a pouch on the underside of the male. The eggs hatch inside the male's pouch. Some fish, including certain ocean catfish and cardinal fish, carry their eggs in their mouth during the hatching period. In some species, the male carries the eggs. In other species, the female carries them.

Hatching and care of the young. The eggs of most fish species hatch in less than two months. Eggs laid in warm water hatch faster than those laid in cold water. The eggs of some tropical fish hatch in less than 24 hours. On the other hand, the eggs of certain cold-water fish require four or five months to hatch. The males of a few species guard their young for a short time after they hatch. These fish include freshwater bass, bowfins, brown bullheads, Siamese fightingfish, and some sticklebacks. But most other fish provide no protection for their offspring.

© NaturePL/SuperStock

A male Siamese fightingfish blows bubbles that stick together to make a nest for eggs laid by the female. He then collects the eggs in his mouth and blows them into the nest.

© Doug Perrine, Nature Picture Library

Some fish bear live young instead of laying eggs. In this photograph, a well-developed baby lemon shark (pale tail showing at bottom) emerges from its mother.

William M. Stevens, Tom Stack & Assoc.

Mouthbreeding fish hold their eggs in their mouth before hatching. This male jawfish has a mouthful of eggs. Females of some species and males of others hold the eggs.

A fish that lived 58 million years ago left its "picture" in this fossil. Such fossil imprints reveal many details about fish that once swam in prehistoric oceans but are now extinct. Scientists study fossils to discover how fish developed through the ages.

Scientists learn how fish evolved by studying the fossils of fish that are now extinct. The fossils show the changes that occurred in the anatomy of fish down through the ages.

The first fish appeared on Earth about 500 million years ago. These fish are called *ostracoderms.* They were slow, bottom-dwelling animals that were covered from head to tail with a heavy armor of thick bony plates and scales. Like today's lampreys and hagfish, ostracoderms had no jaws and had poorly formed fins. For this reason, scientists group lampreys, hagfish, and ostracoderms together. Ostracoderms were not only the first fish, but they were also the first animals to have a backbone. Most scientists believe that the history of all other vertebrates can be traced back to the ostracoderms. The ostracoderms gave rise to jawed fish with backbones, and they in turn gave rise to *tetrapods* (vertebrates with four legs). These tetrapods spent part of their lives on land. They became the ancestors of all land vertebrates.

Ostracoderms probably reached the peak of their development about 400 million years ago. About the same time, two other groups of fish were developing—*acanthodians* and *placoderms.* The acanthodians became the first known jawed fish. The placoderms were the largest fish up to that time. Some members of the placoderm group called *Dunkleosteus* grew up to 23 feet (7 meters) long and had powerful jaws and sharp bony plates that served as teeth.

The Age of Fishes was a period in Earth's history when fish developed remarkably. Scientists call this age the Devonian Period. It began about 416 million years ago and lasted about 57 million years. During much of this time, *Dunkleosteus* and other large placoderms ruled the seas.

The first bony fish appeared early in the Devonian Period. They were mostly small or medium-sized and, like all fish of that time, were heavily armored. These early bony fish belonged to two main groups—*sarcopterygians* and *actinopterygians.*

The sarcopterygians had fleshy or lobed fins. Few fish today are even distantly related to this group. The coelacanth and the lungfish are the only surviving sarcopterygians. Some scientists believe that among fish, lungfish are the nearest living relatives of land vertebrates. The actinopterygians had rayed fins without fleshy lobes at the base. Among the first actinopterygians were the *chondrosteans,* which differed in many ways from modern ray-finned fish. The chondrosteans were the ancestors of today's ray-finned fish, which make up about 95 percent of all the world's fish species. The paddlefish and sturgeons are the only surviving chondrosteans, and most scientists believe the bichirs are their nearest relatives.

The first sharks appeared during the Devonian Period. They looked much like certain sharks that exist today. The first rays appeared approximately 200 million years after the first sharks. By the end of the Devonian Period, nearly all jawless fish had become extinct. The only exceptions were the ancestors of today's lampreys and hagfish. Some acanthodians and placoderms remained through the Devonian Period, but these fish also died out in time.

The first modern fish appeared during the Mesozoic Era, which began about 251 million years ago. The chondrosteans of the Devonian Period had given rise to the first *neopterygians,* the group from which most of today's fish species developed. Modern bowfin and freshwater gars resemble the earliest forms of neopterygians. From fish such as these arose the teleosts, the advanced modern fishes.

The teleosts lost the heavy armor that covered the bodies of most earlier fish. At first, all teleosts had soft-rayed fins. These fish gave rise to present-day catfish, eels, minnows, and other soft-finned fish. The first spiny-finned fish appeared during the Cretaceous Period, which began about 145 million years ago. These fish were the ancestors of such highly developed present-day fish as perch and tuna. Since the Cretaceous Period, teleosts have been by far the most important group of fish. John E. McCosker

A classification of fish

Ichthyologists classify fish into various groups according to the body characteristics they have in common. They divide all fish into two superclasses: (1) *Agnatha,* meaning *jawless,* and (2) *Gnathostomata,* meaning *jawed.* The superclass *Agnatha* consists of two classes of living species that are grouped into two orders. The much larger superclass *Gnathostomata* is divided into classes, subclasses, and orders. The orders are further divided into families, the families into genera, and the genera into species.

Superclass Agnatha. Mouth jawless; skeleton of cartilage; no paired fins, air bladder, or scales; about 90 species in 2 orders:

Order Petromyzoniformes—lampreys. Large sucking mouth; 7 pairs of external gill openings; some species parasitic; live in salt and fresh water.

Order Myxiniformes—hagfish. Small nonsucking mouth; 1 to 16 pairs of external gill openings; nonparasitic; salt water.

Lamprey
(Petromyzoniformes)

Superclass Gnathostomata. Mouth jawed; most species have paired fins and scales; about 24,000 species in 2 classes:

Class Chondrichthyes. Skeleton of cartilage; no air bladder; about 965 species commonly grouped into 3 orders. However, scientists believe this class should be divided into 9 to 14 orders.

Order Squaliformes—sharks. Most have torpedo shape; upturned tail; 5 to 7 pairs of gill slits; no gill covers; placoid scales; mostly salt water.

Order Rajiformes—rays. Most have body flattened from top to bottom; whiplike tail; 5 pairs of gill slits under pectorals rather than on sides; no gill covers; placoid scales; mostly salt water.

Order Chimaeriformes—chimaeras. Short-, long-, and elephant-nosed species; pointed tail; 4 pairs of gill slits; gill covers; scaleless; salt water.

Blue shark
(Squaliformes)

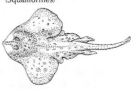

Little skate
(Rajiformes)

Class Osteichthyes. Skeleton largely or partly bone; most species have 5 pairs of gill slits, gill covers, air bladder, and cycloid or ctenoid scales; about 23,000 species in 2 subclasses:

Subclass Sarcopterygii. Fleshy fins; skeleton partly cartilage and partly bone (primitive bony); 7 species in 3 orders:

Order Ceratodontiformes—Australian lungfish. Single gas bladder acts as an air-breathing lung; fresh water.

Order Lepidosireniformes—African and South American lungfish. Pair of gas bladders act as air-breathing lungs; fresh water.

Order Coelacanthiformes—coelacanth. Single ancient species; salt water.

Australian lungfish
(Ceratodontiformes)

Subclass Actinopterygii. Rayed fins; skeleton largely or partly bone; single dorsal and anal fins in most orders; about 23,000 species in 34 orders.

Order Polypteriformes—bichirs. Slender body; thick ganoid scales; long dorsal fin composed of separate finlets; lunglike gas bladder; fresh water.

Order Acipenseriformes—paddlefish, sturgeon. Heavy body; paddlefish nearly scaleless; sturgeon have bony plates instead of scales; fresh water; some sturgeon anadromous.

Order Semionotiformes—gars. Long, slender body and jaws; short, far-back dorsal fin; diamond-shaped ganoid scales; lunglike air bladder.

Order Amiiformes—bowfin. Stout body, rounded tail fin; long, wavy dorsal fin; cycloid scales; bony plate under chin; single species.

Order Elopiformes—bonefish, tarpon, ten-pounders. Soft fin rays; low pectorals; abdominal pelvics; deeply forked tail; silvery body; mostly salt water.

Order Anguilliformes—eels. Soft fin rays; many species lack pectorals; no pelvics; most species scaleless; snakelike; mostly salt water; some catadromous.

Order Notacanthiformes—spiny eels. Soft and spiny fin rays; low pectorals; abdominal pelvics; no tail fin; long, tapering body; salt water, on bottom.

Order Clupeiformes—anchovies, herring, sardines, shad. Soft fin rays; low pectorals; abdominal pelvics; deeply forked tail; silvery body flattened from side to side; travel in large schools; mostly salt water.

Order Mormyriformes—mormyrids. Soft fin rays; low pectorals; abdominal pelvics; many have long snout; electric charge-producing organs; fresh water.

Order Osteoglossiformes—bonytongues, freshwater butterflyfish, mooneyes. Soft fin rays; low pectorals; abdominal pelvics; many have large scales and rounded tail fins; extremely varied body forms; fresh water.

Order Cypriniformes—characins, gymnotid eels, loaches, minnows, suckers. Soft fin rays; most characins have a second, adipose dorsal; most species have low pectorals, abdominal pelvics; air bladder connected to inner ear by series of bones called *Weberian apparatus;* extremely varied body forms; fresh water.

Order Salmoniformes—dragonfish, mudminnows, pike, salmon, viperfish. Soft fin rays; salmon have a second, *adipose* (fatty and rayless) dorsal fin; most have low pectorals; abdominal pelvics; salt and fresh water.

Order Myctophiformes—lanternfish. Soft fin rays; many species have a second, adipose dorsal; fairly low pectorals; abdominal pelvics; light-producing organs; mostly deep salt water.

Sturgeon
(Acipenseriformes)

Longnose gar
(Semionotiformes)

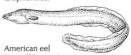

Bonefish
(Elopiformes)

American eel
(Anguilliformes)

American shad
(Clupeiformes)

Mormyrid
(Mormyriformes)

This table lists the major groups down through orders into which fish are classified. The groups are arranged according to their probable evolutionary development. One or more representative families are listed after the name of each order, along with important characteristics of the fish in the order. The table lists 42 orders. But some ichthyologists list fewer than 42, and others list more. Ichthyologists also disagree on the names of some orders, the way the orders should be arranged, and the species included in each.

Superclass Gnathostomata (continued)

Blue catfish
(Siluriformes)

Order Siluriformes—catfish. Soft fin rays, but some species have dorsal and pectoral spines; some have a second, adipose dorsal; low pectorals; abdominal pelvics; most scaleless; all have Weberian apparatus and barbels; mostly fresh water.

Order Gonorhynchiformes—sandfish. Soft fin rays; low pectorals; pelvics behind abdomen; slender body; beaked snout; primitive Weberian apparatus; salt water.

Order Percopsiformes—cavefish, pirate perch, trout perch. Soft fin rays except for a few spiny rays in pirate perch and trout perch; trout perch have a second, adipose dorsal; low pectorals; pelvics far forward but lacking in most cavefish; large lateral line canals in head; fresh water.

Trout perch
(Percopsiformes)

Order Batrachoidiformes—toadfish. Spiny and soft fin rays; two dorsal fins—one spiny, one soft; pectorals midway up sides; pelvics under throat; some have light-producing organs; many have poisonous spines; mostly salt water.

Order Gobiesociformes—clingfish. Soft fin rays except for single spines in pelvics; pectorals midway up sides; pelvics, under throat, form sucking disk that enables fish to cling to rocks; scaleless; small body; mostly salt water.

Order Lophiiformes—anglers, batfish, frogfish, goosefish. Spiny and soft fin rays; dorsal fin has spiny ray at front, forming dangling lure; pectorals midway up sides, forming fleshy flaps; pelvics under throat or lacking; broad, flat body; many species have light-producing organs; salt water.

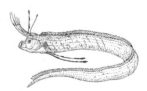

Goosefish
(Lophiiformes)

Order Gadiformes—cod, hakes, pearlfish. Most have soft fin rays; some cod have three dorsals, two anals; high pectorals; pelvics far forward; mostly salt water.

Order Atheriniformes—flyingfish, halfbeaks, killifish, needlefish, live-bearing topminnows. Most have soft fin rays; pectorals high or midway up sides; abdominal pelvics; near surface of salt, fresh, and brackish water.

Flyingfish
(Atheriniformes)

Order Polymixiformes—beardfish. Spiny and soft fin rays; pectorals midway up sides; pelvics under chest; forked tail; two chin whiskers; salt water.

Order Beryciformes—pinecone fish, squirrelfish. Spiny and soft fin rays; pectorals midway up sides; pelvics under chest; brilliantly colored; salt water.

Order Zeiformes—boarfish, dories. Spiny and soft fin rays; pectorals midway up sides; pelvics under chest; body extremely flattened from side to side; upturned mouth; salt water.

Order Lampridiformes—crestfish, oarfish, opahs, ribbonfish. Soft fin rays; many species have unusually long dorsal and anal fins; pectorals midway up sides; pelvics under chest or lacking; varied body forms; salt water.

Oarfish
(Lampridiformes)

Order Gasterosteiformes—pipefish, seahorses, sticklebacks, trumpetfish. Spiny and soft fin rays; pectorals midway up sides; pelvics under chest; slender body; tubular snout; many encased in bony plates or rings; salt and fresh water.

Order Channiformes—snakeheads. Soft fin rays; low pectorals; pelvics under chest or lacking; special air-breathing organs; fresh water.

Order Scorpaeniformes—scorpionfish, sculpins. Spiny and soft fin rays; usually two dorsals—one spiny, one soft; pectorals midway up sides; pelvics under chest; cheek covered by bony plate; many have extremely sharp, poisonous spines; varied body forms; salt and fresh water.

Snakehead
(Channiformes)

Order Pegasiformes—sea moths. Spiny and soft fin rays; large, spiny, winglike pectorals high on sides; small pelvics between chest and abdomen; small body encased in bony plates and rings; extended snout; salt water.

Order Dactylopteriformes—flying gurnards. Spiny and soft fin rays; two dorsal fins—one spiny, one soft; huge, winglike pectorals midway up sides; pelvics under chest; head encased in heavy bone; salt water.

Order Synbranchiformes—swamp eels. Soft fin rays; dorsal and anal fins rayless; no pectorals; pelvics under throat or lacking; gill openings under head; special air-breathing organs; eel-shaped body; fresh and brackish water.

Common jack
(Perciformes)

Order Perciformes—bass, blennies, gobies, jacks, mackerel, perch. Spiny and soft fin rays; many have two dorsal fins—one spiny, one soft; pectorals midway up sides; pelvics under chest and composed of one spine and five soft rays in most species; extremely varied body forms; largest fish order, with 8,000 to 10,000 species; salt and fresh water.

Order Pleuronectiformes—flounders, soles, tonguefish. Most have soft fin rays; long dorsal and anal fins; pectorals and pelvics small or lacking; flattened body; adults have both eyes on same side of head; mostly salt water.

Order Tetraodontiformes—boxfish, ocean sunfish, puffers, triggerfish. Spiny and soft fin rays; pectorals midway up sides; pelvics under chest or lacking; scaleless or covered with spines, bony plates, or hard scales; many are poisonous to eat; varied body forms; mostly salt water.

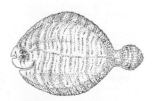

Naked sole
(Pleuronectiformes)

Study aids

Related articles in *World Book* include:

Freshwater fish

Alewife	Loach
Anableps	Lungfish
Archerfish	Minnow
Bass	Molly
Bowfin	Muskellunge
Buffalo	Pacu
Bullhead	Paddlefish
Carp	Perch
Catfish	Pickerel
Cavefish	Pike
Chub	Piranha
Climbing perch	Pupfish
Crappie	Roach
Darter	Ruffe
Drum	Salmon
Eel	Sculpin
Electric eel	Smelt
Electric fish	Stickleback
Fightingfish	Sturgeon
Gar	Sucker
Goldfish	Sunfish
Grayling	Trout
Lamprey	Whitefish

Saltwater fish

Alewife	Mullet
Amberjack	Oarfish
Anchovy	Parrotfish
Angelfish	Pilotfish
Barracuda	Pipefish
Bass	Pollock
Blackfish	Pompano
Bluefish	Porcupinefish
Bonefish	Porgy
Bonito	Puffer
Bream	Ray
Butterfish	Redfish
Butterflyfish	Remora
Capelin	Roughy
Catfish	Sailfish
Clownfish	Salmon
Cod	Sardine
Coelacanth	Sawfish
Doctorfish	Sculpin
Dogfish	Seadragon
Dolphinfish	Seahorse
Drum	Shad
Eel	Shark
Electric fish	Skate
Electric ray	Smelt
Flatfish	Snapper
Flounder	Sole
Flyingfish	Spot
Goby	Sprat
Goliath grouper	Stickleback
Grouper	Stingray
Grunion	Stonefish
Grunt	Sturgeon
Gurnard	Swordfish
Haddock	Tarpon
Hagfish	Tilefish
Hake	Toadfish
Halibut	Triggerfish
Herring	Tripod fish
Kingfish	Trout
Lamprey	Tuna
Lanternfish	Turbot
Lumpfish	Wahoo
Mackerel	Weakfish
Marlin	Wolffish
Menhaden	Wrasse

Other related articles

Animal (pictures)
Aquaculture
Aquarium, Home
Aquarium, Public
Deep sea (Vertebrates)
Evolution
Fish and Wildlife Service
Fishing
Fishing industry
Food supply (Livestock and fish)
Grand Banks
Heart (Fish)
Ichthyology
Ocean (Life in the ocean; pictures)
Plankton
Prehistoric animal
Sea serpent
Seafood
Sound (Animal sounds)
Spawn
Tropical fish

Outline

I. **The importance of fish**
    A. Food and game fish
    B. Other useful fish
    C. Harmful fish
    D. Fish in the balance of nature

II. **Kinds of fish**
    A. Bony fish
    B. Sharks, rays, and chimaeras
    C. Lampreys and hagfish

III. **Where fish live**
    A. Saltwater environments
    B. Freshwater environments
    C. Fish migrations

IV. **The bodies of fish**
    A. External anatomy   C. Systems of the body
    B. Skeleton and muscles   D. Special organs

V. **The senses of fish**
    A. Sight
    B. Hearing
    C. Smell and taste
    D. Touch and the lateral line system
    E. Other senses

VI. **How fish live**
    A. How fish get food
    B. How fish swim
    C. How fish protect themselves
    D. How fish rest
    E. How fish live together
    F. How fish adjust to change

VII. **How fish reproduce**
    A. Preparation for spawning
    B. Spawning and care of the eggs
    C. Hatching and care of the young

VIII. **The development of fish**
    A. The first fish   C. The first modern fish
    B. The Age of Fishes

IX. **A classification of fish**

Questions

What kind of food do most fish eat?
How are lampreys and hagfish different from other fish?
What are *median fins?* What are *paired fins?* What are *chromatophores?*
How much change in water temperature can most fish survive?
What are *fish farms?*
What is the process by which most fish eggs are fertilized?
Which parts of the world have the most kinds of freshwater fish?
What were *ostracoderms?*
How do fish turn and make other swimming maneuvers?
What are the two main groups of jawed fish? How do they differ?

Additional resources

Level I

Buttfield, Helen. *The Secret Life of Fishes: From Angels to Zebras on the Coral Reef.* Abrams, 1999.

Filisky, Michael. *Peterson First Guide to Fishes of North America.* 1989. Reprint. Houghton, 1998.

Spilsbury, Louise and Richard. *Classifying Fish.* Heinemann Lib., 2003. *The Life Cycle of Fish.* 2003.

Stewart, Melissa. *Fishes.* Children's Pr., 2001.

Level II

Berra, Tim M. *Freshwater Fish Distribution.* Academic Pr., 2001.

Dipper, Frances A. *Extraordinary Fish.* Dorling Kindersley, 2001.

Moyle, Peter B., and Cech, J. J., Jr. *Fishes: An Introduction to Ichthyology.* 5th ed. Prentice Hall, 2004.

Nelson, Joseph S. *Fishes of the World.* 3rd ed. Wiley, 1994.

Reebs, Stéphan. *Fish Behavior in the Aquarium and in the Wild.* Cornell Univ. Pr., 2001.

Fish, Hamilton (1808-1893), was an American statesman. Fish served as United States secretary of state from 1869 to 1877, during the presidency of Ulysses S. Grant.

As secretary of state, Fish negotiated the Treaty of Washington, signed in 1871 by the United States and the United Kingdom. Under this treaty, the two countries agreed to refer the *Alabama* Claims to a special court for arbitration. The *Alabama* Claims were U.S. demands for British payment for damage done by British-built Confederate warships during the American Civil War (1861-1865). The ships, the most famous of which was the *Alabama,* had destroyed many Union ships.

Fish was born on Aug. 3, 1808, in New York City. He graduated from Columbia College (now part of Columbia University) in 1827. He became a lawyer in 1830. From 1843 to 1845, Fish represented New York in the United States House of Representatives. In 1849 and 1850, he served as governor of New York. He served in the United States Senate from 1851 to 1857. As senator, Fish opposed the spread of slavery to new territories. He died on Sept. 7, 1893. Robert D. Parmet

Fish and Wildlife Service is an agency of the United States government that helps conserve the nation's birds, mammals, fish, and other wildlife. It operates more than 500 wildlife refuges. In addition, the agency runs many other field stations, including national fish hatcheries, habitat resources field offices, and research laboratories.

The service regulates the hunting of migratory birds and conducts programs to conserve fisheries. It also studies the effects of development projects on fish and wildlife and recommends ways to prevent or minimize harmful effects. The agency runs programs to restore endangered and threatened species and works to enforce the Endangered Species Act of 1973. It also cooperates with other organizations devoted to conserving wildlife.

The Fish and Wildlife Service allocates funds to the states and territories for fish and wildlife conservation. It also publishes scientific reports on wildlife. The agency was established in 1940 as part of the Department of the Interior.

Critically reviewed by the United States Fish and Wildlife Service

See also **Bird** (Birdbanding); **Endangered species** (Protecting endangered species); **National Wildlife Refuge System; Wildlife conservation.**

Fish farm. See Fishing industry.

Fish hawk. See Osprey.

Fisher. See Marten.

Fisher, Saint John (1469?-1535), was a Roman Catholic bishop of Rochester, England. He was beheaded for saying that King Henry VIII was not the supreme head of the church in England.

Fisher was born in Beverley, near Hull, and was educated at Cambridge University. He later founded St. John's College at Cambridge. Fisher was also a learned theologian who wrote a number of important books. While Fisher was awaiting death in prison, Pope Paul III made him a cardinal. Fisher died on June 22, 1535. His feast day is July 9. Marvin R. O'Connell

Fisher, Vardis (1895-1968), an American author, became best known for his fictional history of the Mormons, *The Children of God* (1939). Fisher's 12-volume novel series, *The Testament of Man,* traced human thought from its beginnings to the present. The first novel in this series, *Darkness and the Deep,* was published in 1943.

Fisher was born on March 31, 1895, in Annis, Idaho. He graduated from the University of Utah and received a Ph.D. degree from the University of Chicago. Fisher died on July 9, 1968. Bernard Duffey

Fishery. See Fishing industry.

Fishes, Age of. See Devonian Period.

Fishing is one of the most popular, relaxing, and rewarding forms of outdoor recreation. People enjoy fishing in a wide variety of fresh, saltwater, and *brackish* (slightly salty) bays, lakes, oceans, rivers, and streams.

Some people fish with simple bamboo or cane poles. Others use modern rods, reels, and other equipment that require greater skill to operate. People who use the combination of a rod, reel, and line to catch fish are called *anglers.* The challenge of angling involves outsmarting, hooking, *playing* (tiring out), and finally landing the fish. Some anglers catch fish only for enjoyment and release the fish after landing them, while other anglers catch fish either to eat or to preserve as trophies. Fishing derbies and contests are popular, with participants competing for prizes of money or merchandise. For example, in bass fishing, competitors can make a living from prize money along with endorsement money from companies that manufacture fishing equipment and clothing.

Some common methods of fishing include *casting, still fishing, drift fishing, trolling,* and *ice fishing.* In casting, anglers use rods to throw a line with natural or artificial bait into the water. Then they retrieve the line by hand or by turning the handle of a reel to tempt the fish to bite the bait. In still fishing, the angler casts the bait from a bank or an anchored boat and waits for the fish to bite. In drift fishing, the angler allows the bait to trail the boat, which drifts freely with the current. In trolling, the bait is dragged, at or below the surface, behind a moving boat. In ice fishing, a popular winter sport in cold regions, the angler fishes through a hole chopped in the ice.

This article discusses recreational fishing. For information on commercial fishing, see the article **Fishing industry.**

Fishing equipment

Manufacturers produce a wide variety of *tackle* (equipment) designed for every type of fishing. Fishing tackle includes rods, reels, lines, leaders, sinkers, floats, hooks, and bait. The choice of equipment depends chiefly on the kinds of fish sought.

The three most basic fishing tools are the rod, reel, and line. They can be obtained in a wide range of sizes, types, and styles, from those designed for small species of fish to the larger, more hard-fighting species. Small freshwater fish, such as bluegill, crappie, perch, and sunfish, are sometimes called *pan fish* because they are small enough to fit in a frying pan. Some of the large, hard-fighting saltwater game fish include marlin, sailfish, swordfish, and tuna.

Rods are tapered poles of various thicknesses and lengths. The most basic rod, often called a fishing pole and popular with children, consists of a tree branch with a piece of string tied at the end to serve as the line. Many rods are made from such materials as aluminum, bamboo, and steel. Modern materials, such as boron, fiberglass, and graphite, also have become popular for making rods because they are strong yet lightweight and flexible.

Most rods include a handle, a *reel seat,* and *guides.* The reel seat is the area near the handle where the reel is attached. Guides are ring-shaped attachments along the shaft that permit the line to flow easily. Some rods consist of two or more sections joined by *ferrules* (sockets and plugs), which allow the pole to be taken apart and stored easily.

Rods come in many lengths, weights, diameters, and designs to complement various methods of fishing and types of fish sought. Each rod is designed for use with a particular type of reel and line. The *action* (flexibility) of fishing rods also varies, ranging from limber to stiff. Stronger, longer, and more flexible rods often are needed to catch larger species of fish.

Reels store unused line, release line in casting, and retrieve line as the reel's handle is turned. Most reels have a *drag-setting device* that controls the tension of the line on the spool while catching the fish. There are four basic types of reels: (1) spinning, (2) spin-casting, (3) bait-casting, and (4) fly. Each is manufactured in varying sizes and designs. Spinning and spin-casting reels are the easiest to use and the most popular. Generally, the larger the reel, the more line it will hold. Reels that hold strong line must be large because the size of the line increases along with its *lifting strength* (weight it can lift before breaking).

Spinning reels have an open-faced spool mounted on the seat of the reel in a position that is parallel to the rod. The spool does not turn when the line is cast or retrieved. When cast, the line merely peels off the open end of the spool. Spinning reels have a handle and a *bail* for retrieving line or for allowing line to be played off the spool. The bail is a semicircular device that winds the line evenly around the spool. The spool turns only when the fish pulls on the line hard enough to overcome the drag.

Spin-casting reels resemble spinning reels, but the spool is enclosed within a cylindrical hood or cap. Line coming off the spool passes through a hole in the hood or cap. A push-button releases line freely from the spool during casting. This reel also has a turning handle to retrieve line. A device winds the line evenly onto the spool and prevents it from tangling.

Rods and reels

Parts of a spinning rod

Tip section

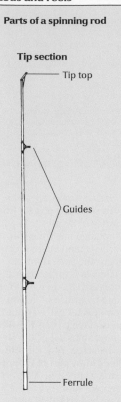

- Tip top
- Guides
- Ferrule

Butt section

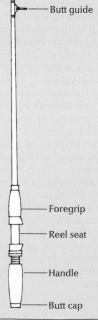

- Ferrule
- Butt guide
- Foregrip
- Reel seat
- Handle
- Butt cap

Bait-casting reel

Spin-casting reel

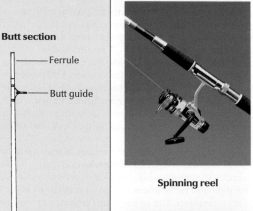

Spinning reel

WORLD BOOK photos by Steve Spicer

Fly reel

Some basic types of lures

A popping plug floats on top of the water. When the rod is jerked, the plug's hollowed mouth goes underwater and makes popping sounds that attract fish.

A spinner has a metal blade that spins as it is drawn through the water. Spinners attract fish by their motion, vibration, and bright flashing colors.

Flies are made of feathers, hair, or other materials. A wet fly, *left*, sinks below the surface of the water. A dry fly, *right*, floats on the surface.

A floating and diving plug floats on the surface of the water until the line is *retrieved* (gathered in). The plug then dives below the surface.

A plastic worm can be made to slide or hop along the bottom of the water by slowly retrieving the line. It does not catch on weeds as easily as other lures.

A streamer fly has a long wing made of feathers or hair. It is designed to imitate a small bait fish. Most streamer flies sink below the surface.

WORLD BOOK illustrations by James Teason

A deep diver plug dives quickly while the line is being retrieved. It may dive to a depth of 10 to 20 feet (3 to 6 meters) or more.

A jig sinks quickly after hitting the water. As the rod is jerked, a jig attracts fish by making short, rapid hops along the bottom of the water.

A spoon flutters or wobbles when pulled through the water. The action of this type of lure is designed to imitate that of a wounded bait fish.

Bait-casting reels have a wide spool that lies across the reel seat perpendicular to the rod. In addition, the reel has a handle that turns to retrieve line as well as a button to release the spool for casting. The spool revolves several turns for each turn of the reel handle. Most bait-casting reels have a *level-wind device* that winds line evenly across the spool. These reels, which are called *free spool bait-casting reels,* allow longer, smoother casts.

Fly reels. In fly fishing, the angler pulls the line off the fly reel and then casts the lines using the rod. There are two basic types of fly reels, *single-action* and *automatic.* The single-action fly reel has a handle that turns a spool and retrieves line. The automatic reel has a spring mechanism that gathers line onto the spool with a push of a lever or trigger.

Lines consist of such natural fibers as cotton, linen, or silk; or such synthetic fibers as rayon, nylon, or dacron. *Monofilament lines* are single strands of plastic fibers. They are the most popular and are used on spinning, spin-casting, and bait-casting reels. These lines are strong for their tiny diameter and, because they are clear or tinted to the color of water, they are almost invisible to fish. Some lines are made of many fibers braided or twisted together for strength.

Specially coated braided lines are used on fly reels. These lines are designed to float or suspend, or to sink to different depths. They are also heavier than monofilament lines. In fly fishing, the extra weight of a braided line is needed to carry the line smoothly through the air when it is cast.

Lines are made in a variety of thicknesses and lengths. They are rated in *pounds test,* which measures their lifting strength. Most lines range in lifting strength from ¼ pound (0.1 kilogram) test to approximately 200 pounds (90 kilograms) test. Fly lines are rated with density and size ratios.

Leaders are short pieces of line connected to the end of the line and attached to a hook. Some are made of synthetics, such as monofilament materials, and others are made of wire. Wire leaders are used to catch sharp-toothed or rough-scaled fish that may cut monofilament leaders. Monofilament leaders are transparent and therefore less visible to fish. They are not needed with monofilament lines that are themselves transparent. Leaders range in length from 12 inches (30 centimeters) to 12 feet (3.7 meters) or longer. A leader may be attached to a line with a device called a *swivel.* A swivel allows the bait attached to the leader to rotate freely and thus prevents twisting of the line.

Sinkers are weights generally made of cast or molded lead. They are attached to a leader or line and serve many functions. Sinkers hold the bait at or near the bottom of the water. They provide the needed weight to cast bait great distances. Sinkers additionally can be used to move with the currents, as in trolling or drifting. Anglers select the type and size of sinker that is just heavy enough to hold the bait at the desired depth. Lead sinkers are molded into various sizes and shapes designed for waters with muddy, rocky, or sandy bottoms. Sinkers weigh from ⅟₁₆ ounce (1.8 grams) to 3 pounds (1.4 kilograms).

Floats suspend the bait in water or allow the bait to drift along at desired depths in moving water. They are made of plastic, plastic foam, cork, or other materials that float. Floats are frequently called *bobbers* because they bob or wiggle whenever a fish strikes or nibbles at the bait. Like sinkers, floats also provide additional weight for casting.

Hooks are made of strong metals that maintain their shape and sharpness. They come in hundreds of styles.

Bait used to catch fish may be either natural substances or artificial items.

Natural bait. Most fresh and saltwater fish feed on a variety of smaller fish or other aquatic organisms. Therefore, small fish or other water creatures placed on a hook alive serve as the best kinds of natural bait. Fish used as bait include freshwater minnows and saltwater anchovies, herring, and smelt.

Freshwater fish eat insects, frogs, and worms. Saltwater fish also eat worms, along with clams and crabs. Fish that feed on dead animals and plants will eat *cut bait* (pieces of dead fish or animals) or prepared bait. Some freshwater fish will eat bread dough, cheese, fish eggs, marshmallows, and popcorn.

Artificial bait consists of a wide variety of items called *lures.* Most lures are designed in shape, color, and movement to represent natural bait. Examples of lures include *flies, plugs, spinners, spoons,* and *jigs.* Lures, unlike natural bait, can be used over and over. Some lures can be cast great distances.

Flies are lightweight lures made of feathers, fur, hair, and yarn tied onto a hook. There are two types of flies, *dry* (floating) and *wet* (sinking). Some flies look like insects, small fish, or frogs to attract fish that feed on these animals.

However, fish do not always feed out of hunger. For this reason, many flies have strange colors and shapes that appeal to the fish's other senses, such as anger and territorial aggression. Such fish as salmon and steelhead feed on flies of this type.

Plugs are made of wood or plastic materials and are designed to look like small fish, frogs, or other natural food sources. There are two kinds of plugs—floating and sinking. Floating plugs lie on the surface of the water, and sinking plugs remain underwater. Some plugs are equipped with a diving plane or bill in front. Plugs with this feature dive to certain depths when retrieved at certain speeds. Plugs are designed to make noise, vibrate, roll, spin, wiggle, twirl, or flash to tempt gamefish to strike them.

Spinners have a revolving blade in front of the hook that spins and refracts light as the lure is retrieved through water. Spinners may be used alone or with other lures. The noise, vibration, and motion of spinners help direct fish toward them in either cloudy or deep, dark water.

Spoons are rounded, oblong, or dished-out metal lures that flutter when they are pulled through the water. The action of a spoon resembles that of a wounded baitfish. This similarity helps attract fish because some species instinctively feed on wounded prey whether they are hungry or not. Spoons that weigh only 1/16 ounce (1.8 grams) may be used for small panfish. Spoons weighing 2 ounces (57 grams) may be used for larger game fish.

Some popular bait hooks

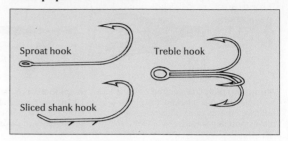

Parts of a fishhook

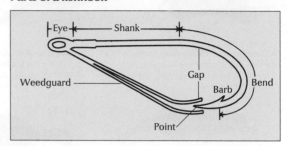

Some fishing tackle

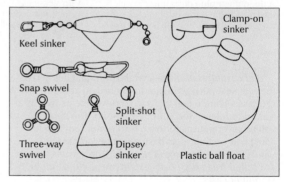

Two basic fishing knots

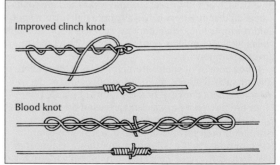

WORLD BOOK illustrations by David Cunningham

Fishing knots are used for a variety of purposes. Two important fishing knots are the *improved clinch knot* and the *blood knot.* An improved clinch knot is used to tie lines or leaders to hooks, lures, or *swivels.* Swivels are attachments that allow a line or leader to rotate freely and thus prevent twisting of the line or leader. A blood knot is used to join two lines or two leaders together.

Five ways to rig a fishing line
This illustration shows five of the many ways of rigging a fishing line. For fly fishing, the line may be rigged with a long leader. For bottom fishing, drift fishing, and *trolling* (fishing from a moving boat), sinkers are used to hold the bait or lure at the proper depth. In *still fishing* (fishing from a shore or anchored boat), a float may be used to suspend the bait in the water.

WORLD BOOK illustration by David Cunningham

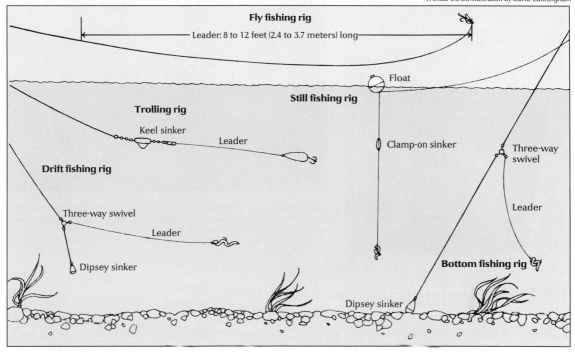

Jigs are weighted tubelike lures with feathers or hair attached. When placed at the bottom of the water, jigs make short hops when the rod is jerked.

Other equipment for anglers includes nets, tackle boxes, *gaffs, stringers, creels,* and electronic devices. Gaffs are barbed spears or long-handled hooks used to pull large fish from the water. Stringers are cords and chains used to keep fish alive in the water but restrained. A creel is a container made of canvas, wicker, rattan, or willow that holds fish out of water. Damp vegetation placed in the creels helps keep fish fresh and permits anglers to carry this catch while they continue fishing. Some electronic devices, such as sonar, are helpful in locating schools of fish. Other electronic devices measure water temperature and *salinity* (salt content).

Fishing tips

Anglers must learn how fish react differently to each given situation. Fish can be moody, aggressive, cooperative, stubborn, shy, and cunning. Anglers' chances of outsmarting fish will increase as they learn more about the character of each species and its feeding habits. However, fish also learn, which makes sportfishing a great challenge. Anglers need to exercise patience and be willing to change strategies as well as bait to outwit game fish.

The habits of various species of fish influence the choice of bait that anglers use and how they present the bait to the fish. Some species of fish are *benthic* (bottom dwelling), while other species feed or swim near the surface. Some fish are held to a boundary, such as a pond or reservoir. Other fish can travel freely between lakes and river systems. *Anadromous* species can move from fresh water to salt water. These fish include salmon and sturgeon.

Water temperature greatly influences the hunger and activity of fish. If possible, a fish will move to other levels or areas to find its preferred temperature range. Salmon and trout are examples of fish that dwell in cold water. Fish that dwell in warm water include crappies, sunfish, and catfish.

Fish are more active during low light periods of the early morning and the late evening. Some fish are *nocturnal* species. These types of fish feed mostly at night. Most species of fish behave according to a general pattern. However, the behavior of fish is never completely predictable.

In the United States and Canada, state and provincial fishing laws regulate the seasons of the year that fish may be caught. Some areas of the United States and Canada are set aside specifically for catching and releasing live fish. Many states and provinces issue fishing licenses and limit how many fish may be caught.

Lew Freedman

See the articles on the game fish that are mentioned in this article. See also **Fish; Indian, American** (Hunting, gathering, and fishing); **Inuit** (picture: Ice fishing); **Spearfishing.**

Fishing banks. See Grand Banks.

Various types of fishing gear and vessels are used to catch fish. Much of the world's commercial catch is harvested with huge nets like the one being used at the left to haul in tuna. Many fishing vessels, such as the Egyptian *stern trawler* above, also carry equipment on board to process fish after they have been caught.

Fishing industry

Fishing industry is an important economic activity that provides food and jobs for millions of people. The fishing industry includes all the activities involved in the commercial and recreational capture of fish and shellfish. The catching, processing, marketing, and conservation of fish and shellfish are all parts of the industry. The industry also provides various other products from the sea, such as seaweeds.

Fish are an excellent source of protein, one of the chief *nutrients* (nourishing substances) that people need for a good diet. As the world's population has grown, so has the demand for food—especially food rich in protein. The fishing industry has increased its annual catch to help meet this demand. The industry markets food fish in a variety of forms. The fish are sold fresh, canned, cured, or frozen. In addition, about a third of the world's fish catch is used to produce high-quality animal feed and various industrial products.

The oceans are by far the main source of fish. Only a small portion of the world's commercial fish catch comes from such inland waters as lakes and rivers. Much of the inland water catch comes from *aquaculture* (fish farming). Fish farms are enclosures built on land, or areas in natural bodies of water, where fish and shellfish are raised for food. Fish farms may be inland or off ocean shores.

The fishing industry catches many kinds of fish. Such fish as anchovies, capelin, herring, mackerel, salmon, sardines, and tuna are caught near the surface of oceans and seas. Such fish as cod, flounder, hake, and pollock are harvested near the ocean floor. Freshwater fish, such as carp, catfish, and whitefish, are caught in inland waters or raised on fish farms.

The worldwide annual fish catch totals about 155 million tons (140 million metric tons). China is, by far, the leading fishing nation in the world. The country accounts for about a third of the world's total fish catch. Other leading fishing countries include Chile, India, Indonesia, Japan, Peru, Thailand, the United States, and Vietnam.

The fishing industry employs millions of people worldwide. Many people work on oceangoing fishing boats, coastal craft, or small boats. Other areas of the fishing industry include the processing, packaging, and distribution of fish products. People who work in these areas of the industry perform such tasks as purchasing fish, filleting fish, *shucking* (opening and cutting) oysters, operating canning machines, and inspecting fish markets to enforce pure-food laws.

People have fished for thousands of years. Through the centuries, they have used hooks, spears, nets, and traps to capture fish. People still use such equipment. However, commercial fishing crews now harvest the majority of their catch with huge nets. In addition, modern fishing vessels have a variety of devices that make fishing more efficient. For example, advanced navigational aids and fish-finding equipment enable fishing crews to range far from their home ports and to precisely locate schools of fish. Refrigeration systems aboard the vessels help keep the catch fresh during long voyages at sea.

During the mid-1900's, many countries expanded their fishing fleets. These fleets increased their fish catch along their home coasts as well as in distant waters. As a result, the fish harvest generally increased each year. But at the same time, overfishing severely reduced stocks in some fishing areas. Disputes also arose among countries over the ownership of fish resources. Traditionally, fish have been considered common property—that is, no one owned them until they were caught. The fish then became the property of whoever caught them. After the development of long-range fishing fleets, many nations wanted to protect the fish resources along their coasts from fleets of other countries. As a result, a number of international commissions were formed to promote fish conservation and to help settle disputes over fishing rights.

During the 1970's, almost all nations bordering the sea established *fishery conservation zones,* also known as *exclusive economic zones,* in further efforts to conserve and protect their fish resources. These zones extend 200 *nautical miles* from a nation's coast. A nautical mile equals 1.15 statute miles, or 1.85 kilometers. Countries that have adopted such zones claim authority over all fishing—and ownership of all fish and other natural resources—within the zones.

Where fish are caught

Areas where fish are caught commercially or recreationally are called *fisheries.* In many cases, fishing crews harvest more than one species of fish from a particular fishery. A fishery may be a small lake. Or it may extend across an enormous section of an ocean. For example, the tuna fishery that lies off the west coast of Central and South America covers about 5 million square miles (13 million square kilometers).

Ocean fisheries provide about three-fourths of the world's commercial fish catch. This figure includes the production from marine fish farms. Almost all the ocean catch comes from waters near seacoasts, especially the

shallow waters over the *continental shelf.* The continental shelf consists of submerged land along the coasts of the continents. In some places, the shelf extends great distances out into the sea.

Many of the fish caught in waters over the continental shelf are taken from regions of *upwelling.* Upwelling occurs during certain seasons when winds blow surface waters near the coast offshore. The colder bottom wa-

Worldwide fish and shellfish catch

Chief kinds	Annual catch	
	In tons	In metric tons
Carp, barbel, cyprinid	23,649,000	21,454,000
Herring, sardine, anchovy	22,173,000	20,115,000
Cod, hake, haddock	8,495,000	7,707,000
Shrimp, prawn	7,187,000	6,520,000
Tuna, bonito, billfish	6,960,000	6,314,000
Clam, cockles, arkshell	5,701,000	5,172,000
Squid, cuttlefish, octopus	4,755,000	4,314,000
Oyster	4,731,000	4,291,000
Tilapia, cichlid	3,917,000	3,553,000
Salmon, trout, smelt	3,448,000	3,128,000
Scallop	2,397,000	2,174,000
Mussel	1,886,000	1,711,000
Crab	1,720,000	1,561,000
Flounder, halibut, sole	1,205,000	1,094,000
Shark, ray, chimaera	812,000	736,000
Shad	651,000	590,000
Abalone, winkle, conch	542,000	492,000
Eel	303,000	275,000
Lobster	275,000	250,000
Krill, plankton	173,000	157,000

Figures are for 2008. Figures do not include the catch of the jack, bass, or mackerel groups, which were not reported separately for 2008.
Source: FAOSTAT, Statistics Division, Food and Agriculture Organization of the United Nations. http://www.faostat.fao.org. Data accessed in 2010.

Chief commercial fishing areas This map shows the world's major commercial fishing areas. Most lie along the *continental shelf,* the submerged land around the continents. Inland fishing areas include rivers and lakes. The map also shows the chief fish and shellfish, with the most valuable catches in boldface type.

WORLD BOOK map

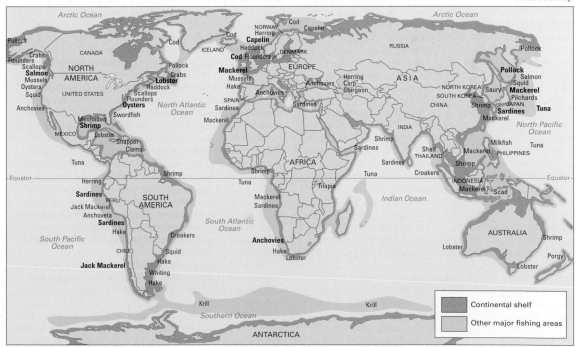

Leading fishing countries

Tons of fish and shellfish caught in a year

China	50,097,000 tons (45,447,000 metric tons)
Peru	7,972,000 tons (7,232,000 metric tons)
India	7,928,000 tons (7,192,000 metric tons)
Indonesia	7,040,000 tons (6,386,000 metric tons)
United States	5,689,000 tons (5,161,000 metric tons)
Japan	5,480,000 tons (4,972,000 metric tons)
Chile	5,084,000 tons (4,612,000 metric tons)
Vietnam	4,513,000 tons (4,094,000 metric tons)
Thailand	4,199,000 tons (3,809,000 metric tons)
Russia	3,832,000 tons (3,476,000 metric tons)

Figures are for a three-year average, 2006-2008.
Source: FAOSTAT, Statistics Division, Food and Agriculture Organization of the UN.
http://www.faostat.fao.org. Data accessed in 2010.

Leading fishing states and provinces

Tons of fish and shellfish caught in a year

Alaska	2,318,000 tons (2,103,000 metric tons)
Louisiana	486,000 tons (441,000 metric tons)
Newfoundland and Labrador	371,000 tons (336,000 metric tons)
Nova Scotia	280,000 tons (254,000 metric tons)
Washington	227,000 tons (206,000 metric tons)
Virginia	220,000 tons (199,000 metric tons)
California	183,000 tons (166,000 metric tons)
British Columbia	175,000 tons (159,000 metric tons)
Massachusetts	165,000 tons (149,000 metric tons)
New Brunswick	114,000 tons (103,000 metric tons)

Figures are for a three-year average, 2007-2009.
Sources: Fisheries and Oceans Canada; U.S. National Marine Fisheries Service.

ters, which are rich in nutrients, then rise to the surface near the coast. This upwelling provides nutrients for the growth of tiny organisms that fish feed on, thus promoting growth of the fish population. Upwelling takes place chiefly along the coasts of Peru, western North America, northwest and southwest Africa, Somalia, the Arabian Peninsula, and Antarctica.

Atlantic Ocean fisheries. About 15 percent of the world's annual fish catch comes from the Atlantic Ocean. The northern Atlantic is the most productive area. The coast of North America from Newfoundland and Labrador to New England is an important fishing area. Leading fishing catches in this region include cod, flounder, herring, lobsters, and scallops. The Gulf of Mexico, an arm of the Atlantic Ocean, is a productive area for the United States fishing industry. It supports the nation's main menhaden fishery. The Gulf of Mexico also provides large quantities of crabs, lobsters, and shrimp.

The Atlantic Ocean has several other rich fishing areas. They include the northeast Atlantic near Iceland and the United Kingdom and the southwest Atlantic near Argentina and Brazil. Crews from a number of nations—including Denmark, Iceland, Norway, Russia, and the United Kingdom—fish the waters of the northeast Atlantic. They catch herring, capelin, mackerel, sand lances, and many other types of fish. The major catches in the southwest Atlantic include hake, squid, and whiting.

Pacific Ocean fisheries. About 50 percent of the world's fish catch comes from the Pacific Ocean. The northern Pacific is the most productive fishing area. The chief fish caught in the Bering Sea, the Gulf of Alaska, and other areas of the northern Pacific include anchovies, mackerel, and pollock. Salmon are also an important catch. Leading shellfish harvested from the northern Pacific include crabs, oysters, and scallops.

Other important fisheries of the Pacific Ocean include the waters of the southeast Pacific off the coast of South America and the coastal seas of the western Pacific from Indonesia to Japan. The chief fish caught in the waters off the west coast of South America include anchovetas and jack mackerel. The leading fishing countries in this area are Peru and Chile. Important catches in the western Pacific include mackerel, scad, and tuna. Indonesia, the Philippines, Thailand, and Vietnam are the leading fishing countries of this area.

Indian Ocean fisheries. About 7 percent of the world's fish catch comes from the Indian Ocean. Leading catches in the Indian Ocean include croakers, shad, tuna, and shrimp. The leading fishing countries of this region are India, Indonesia, Myanmar, and Thailand.

Inland fisheries. About 25 percent of the commercial catch worldwide is harvested yearly from ponds, lakes, rivers, streams, and fish farms in inland waters. China and India lead all other countries in the fish catch from inland waters. China's annual inland-water catch accounts for about 50 percent of the world total, and India's is about 10 percent of the total. Both countries chiefly harvest carp, tilapia, and other plant-eating fish. Other leading inland-water fishing countries include Bangladesh, Egypt, Indonesia, Myanmar, the Philippines, Thailand, and Vietnam.

The major freshwater fisheries of the United States include the inland waters of the Southern States and the Great Lakes. The inland waters of the South are fished for buffalo fish, carp, catfish, and crayfish. The Great Lakes are fished chiefly for carp, chub, smelt, whitefish, and yellow perch.

The primary fish caught in Canada's inland waters include smelt, trout, walleye, whitefish, and yellow perch. The Great Lakes are the center of the freshwater fishing industry in Canada.

Fish farms. Each year, the world's fish farms produce more than 70 million tons (64 million metric tons) of fish, shellfish, and *aquatic plants* (plants that live in water).

Fish farms range from simple ponds or flooded rice fields to highly engineered hatcheries in which the environment is almost completely controlled. Fish farmers try to eliminate pollutants and other harmful environmental conditions so that fish can flourish. However, production can be severely affected by the spread of an infectious disease. Farmers provide fish with proper nutrients and protect them from animals that prey on them. Aquaculture is commonly used to rebuild salmon and trout stocks that have been severely reduced.

The main fish raised on fish farms throughout the world include carp, catfish, salmon, tilapia, and trout. China leads all countries in aquaculture production. In terms of quantity produced, China harvests over three-fifths of the world total. Other leading aquaculture countries include Bangladesh, Chile, India, Indonesia, Japan, Norway, South Korea, Thailand, and Vietnam. The main fish and shellfish raised on fish farms in the United States include catfish, clams, crayfish, oysters, salmon, and trout.

How fish are caught

Fishing vessels vary greatly in size and in the number of crew members they carry. Vessels in coastal fishing fleets are 25 to 130 feet (8 to 40 meters) long. Their crews consist of as many as 20 to 25 people or as few as 1 or 2, depending on the fishing method being used. Coastal vessels can remain at sea for several days or weeks. The ships store their fish catch in holds chilled either by ice or by refrigeration systems.

Long-range fishing fleets stay at sea for months at a time and travel great distances from their home ports. Many modern fleets include *processing-catcher vessels,* as well as processors, refrigerated transporters, and supply ships. Processing-catcher vessels, which measure about 260 feet (80 meters) in length, both catch fish and process the harvest into various products. Their crews have from 50 to 100 members and in most cases include a number of women. Many processing-catcher vessels can process and freeze more than 100 tons (90 metric tons) of fish daily.

Fishing crews use a variety of gear to catch fish. The equipment used depends on the behavior of the fish be-ing sought and the nature of the fishing area. The chief types of gear include (1) nets, (2) hooks, (3) traps, and (4) harpoons.

Nets. Most of the world's commercial fish catch is taken by huge nets. There are three main types of nets: (1) seines, (2) trawls, and (3) gill nets.

Seines (pronounced *saynz)* account for more than a third of the world's fish catch. Fishing crews use seines chiefly to catch anchovies, capelin, herring, mackerel, menhaden, sardines, tuna, and other *pelagic,* schooling fish. Pelagic fish swim near the surface of the water.

The most widely used seine is the rectangular *purse seine.* Purse seines range from about 660 to 6,600 feet (200 to 2,000 meters) long. They have floats along the top and weights and rings along the bottom edge. A rope or cable called a *purse line* runs through the rings.

A purse seine is set into the water from a large vessel called a *seiner* with the aid of a small, high-powered boat called a *skiff.* After the crew spots a school of fish, they launch the skiff from the seiner with one end of the net attached. The seiner speeds ahead, encircling the school and playing out the net as it goes. The bottom of the seine is then closed off with the purse line, capturing the school. Seiners vary from about 30 to 230 feet (10 to 70 meters) in length and carry 12 to 20 people.

Trawls are funnel-shaped nets that are closed off at the tail end, where the fish collect, and open at the mouth. The most commonly used trawl is the *otter trawl.* The net has floats along the top edge of the mouth and weights on the bottom edge. The net is attached by two long towing cables to the back of a vessel called a *stern trawler* or *trawler.* A large doorlike *otter board* is attached to each towing cable near the open end of the net. As the trawler tows the net, the water forces the otter boards to spread apart, holding the net open to capture the fish. The mouths of otter trawls used in midwater can spread out to a width of about 300 feet (90 meters). Those used on the ocean bottom spread to a width of about 120 feet (37 meters).

Trawls catch cod, flounder, hake, pollock, red snapper, scallops, shrimp, and other fish and shellfish that live on or near the ocean floor. Most trawling is done over the continental shelf in waters less than 660 feet

© Shutterstock

A fish farm, such as this one on the coast of Italy, is a place where fish are raised in enclosed pens. The farmers supply the fish with the food and nutrients that the fish need to grow quickly.

(200 meters) deep. But some stern trawlers fish in waters as deep as 3,300 feet (1,000 meters). Trawlers use sonar and other equipment to locate concentrations of fish (see **Sonar**). A small trawler needs a crew of at least four members. Most trawlers more than 150 feet (45 meters) long carry processing equipment and require larger crews.

Trawling accounts for about a third of the world's fish harvest. The otter trawl is the chief fishing gear of distant-water fleets of European and Asian nations that harvest fish from the ocean bottom.

Gill nets are long rectangular nets with floats on top and weights on the bottom. They range from 50 to 1,200 feet (15 to 370 meters) in length. The nets hang in the water near the surface or close to the ocean floor. A gill net is made of thin twine and is nearly invisible in the water. The net hangs in the path of migrating fish and forms a wall of webbing that entangles the fish. The open spaces of a gill net allow fish to thrust only their heads into the net. The fish try to swim through the net, thrashing about and becoming more entangled.

Common types of fishing nets

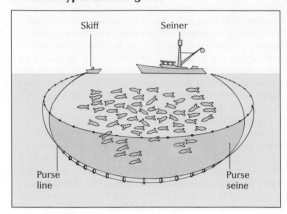

A **purse seine** is set from a vessel called a *seiner* by a *skiff* (small boat). Fish are caught by surrounding them with the net and then closing off its bottom with a *purse line* (rope or cable).

© Natureworld/Alamy Images

A **long-liner** is shown in this photograph, processing fish caught in the Mediterranean Sea. Such ships use a long main line with many attached *dropper lines* that lure fish with baited hooks.

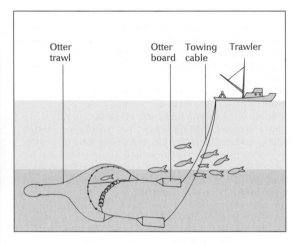

An **otter trawl** is towed by a vessel called a *trawler* or *stern trawler*. The towing causes two doorlike *otter boards* near the mouth of the net to hold the net open to capture fish.

© Shutterstock

A **small U.S. shrimp boat,** *shown here,* drags nets over the sea bottom to harvest shrimp. The catch is quickly frozen or canned on the boat or onshore to prevent the shrimp from spoiling.

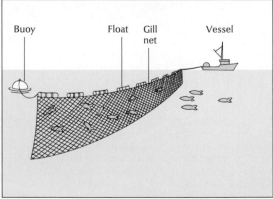

WORLD BOOK illustrations by Bill and Judie Anderson

A **gill net** forms a wall of webbing that entangles fish when they swim into it. The size of the open spaces of gill nets varies according to the type of fish being sought.

Gill nets catch billfish, herring, salmon, sharks, and bottom fish. However, all these fish can be caught with other types of gear. As a result, the total catch with gill nets is less than 5 percent of the world harvest. Most vessels equipped with gill nets are less than 50 feet (15 meters) long and have crews of one or two.

Drift nets are long gill nets of nylon webbing. They are used mainly in open waters by distant-water fleets. A single net measures about 3 nautical miles long. One vessel can set out 8 to 10 drift nets, stretching a total of about 30 nautical miles. Fishing crews set out drift nets at night and pull them in during the day. The nets catch billfish, salmon, and tuna.

Drift nets accidentally catch animals besides the target fish. They often entangle dolphins, marine birds, seals, turtles, and whales. In addition, large drift-net fisheries in the open ocean create hazards to ships whose propellers can become tangled in the nets. Fishing groups and environmental organizations have called for a halt to drift-net fishing. In 1989, the United Nations (UN) passed a resolution banning the use of drift nets in the South Pacific after June 1991. In November 1991, the UN passed a *moratorium* (temporary halt) on drift nets in *international waters* (bodies of water that lie outside the authority of any nation). The moratorium, which took effect on Jan. 1, 1993, banned the use of all drift nets at least $1\frac{1}{2}$ nautical miles long in international waters. Most nations have complied with the moratorium.

Hooks take advantage of the feeding behavior of fish. Bait or lures attached to a hook tempt fish to bite the hook. Hooks account for only a small percentage of the world's fish catch. The most common hooking methods used by commercial fishing crews are (1) bait fishing, (2) trolling, and (3) long-lining.

Bait fishing. In bait fishing, after the crew sights a school of fish, they throw live bait or ground-up fish into the water from the boat. The bait attracts schools of tuna or other species that feed on smaller fish to the surface near the boat. As the fish feed excitedly on the bait, the crew uses poles with bare hooks to haul them in. Most bait boats have a walkway around the stern from which a crew of as many as 20 people pull in the fish.

Trolling involves towing as many as six fishing lines from two long poles. One pole extends from each side of a vessel. In many cases, metal flashers or feather lures attached to the lines attract fish. A large fleet of trolling vessels, called trollers, fishes for albacore and salmon off the coasts of British Columbia and the western United States. Billfish and tuna are also caught by trolling. Most trollers have crews of only two people.

Long-lining involves using a long *main line* with attached short *dropper lines*. The main line may be stretched across the water's surface to catch such pelagic fish as billfish, sharks, and tuna, or near the ocean floor to catch such bottom fish as cod and halibut. Thousands of dropper lines with baited hooks may hang from the main line. Pelagic long-lines may be as long as 60 nautical miles. Bottom lines are much shorter. A small long-line vessel needs a crew of only 3 or 4 members. Large Japanese tuna vessels carry crews of 20 to 45.

Traps depend on the migratory or feeding habits of fish. Most traps contain bait to attract fish. Only a small fraction of the worldwide fish harvest is taken by means of traps. A fish trap has an entry consisting of a funnel-

Common methods of hooking and trapping

Terry Domico, Earth Images

Long-lining involves using a long *main line* like those coiled inside the buckets. Short *dropper lines* with hooks, shown around the rims of the buckets, are attached to the main line.

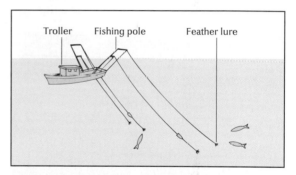

Trolling involves towing fishing lines from poles that extend from the sides of a *troller* (trolling vessel). Feather lures are often attached to the ends of the lines to attract fish.

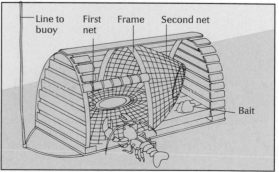

WORLD BOOK illustrations by Bill and Judie Anderson

Trapping is often used to catch lobsters and other shellfish. Traps are designed so that once a fish or shellfish reaches the bait, it has little chance of escaping.

like tunnel or ramp. This entry directs fish through a small opening in the side of the trap. Once inside the trap, the fish have little chance of escaping.

Small, baited, boxlike traps capture chiefly shellfish, such as crabs and lobsters. These traps lie on the bottom of the ocean or a lake or stream and are tethered to a buoy on the surface. Larger, stationary traps float near shore in the path of migrating fish. These traps are anchored in place or fastened to wooden pilings driven into the seabed. They have been used mainly to catch herring and salmon but are not often used today.

Harpoons are barbed spears connected by a line to a vessel or large float. They may be shot from a cannon or hurled by a crew member. Harpoons have been used mainly to harvest whales and large game fish that swim near the ocean surface, such as swordfish and marlin. For more information on whaling and the use of harpoons, see **Whale** (Whaling).

How fish are processed and marketed

Methods of processing. The quality of fish declines rapidly after they die. Bacteria that can cause spoilage immediately begin to attack the fish, and enzymes start to break down the protein in fish tissues. As a result, a number of processing methods have been developed through the years to prolong the freshness of fish.

Drying, salt curing, and smoking have been used to process fish for thousands of years. All three methods reduce the moisture content of fish and thus slow the growth of bacteria and the breakdown of protein.

Drying fish in the open air for six weeks or more removes most of the water from them. Drying is generally used along with salt curing or smoking.

In salt curing, processors first cut open the fish and remove the head and backbone. They then cover the fish with salt, which draws out the moisture and produces a salty solution called *brine.* Next, the fish are *dry-salted* or *pickled.* In dry-salting, workers drain off the brine and hang the fish up to dry. In pickling, the fish are stored in the brine.

To smoke fish, processors first cut up the fish and soak them in brine. They then place the fish in a large oven, where smoke and heat from smoldering wood chips dries the fish. Processors use this method chiefly to improve the flavor of fish.

Canning involves sealing cut-up fish in metal or glass containers and then cooking the contents under pressure. The high temperature and pressure kill bacteria and halt protein breakdown.

Freezing also prevents the growth of bacteria and protein breakdown. The quickly frozen fish are packaged in airtight wrappers or covered with a thin layer of ice. They are stored at −20 °F (−29 °C) or lower. Much of the catch of such fish as cod and flounder is *filleted* (deboned) and frozen. Often, the individual fillets are frozen together in large blocks of fish. These blocks may then be made into fish sticks and meal-sized portions of breaded fish.

Processing fish aboard ship helps keep the catch from spoiling. The fishermen in this photograph are cleaning freshly caught fish on a Bulgarian ship.

Packing fish in ice prevents spoilage. Many fish and shellfish caught at sea are quickly processed and frozen. This worker is packing fish on a fishing boat.

Ted Spiegel, Black Star

Onshore processing of fish is done in fishing ports. These workers at a plant in Prince Rupert, Canada, are preparing deboned, meal-sized portions of fish for shipment to markets.

Fish may be minced and blended before freezing to make *surimi,* a fish paste with a high protein content. In Japan, surimi is used mainly to make fish cakes. Surimi is used in other countries to make imitation shellfish products, including imitation crab legs and shrimp.

Other processing methods are used to produce meal and oil from fish. These industrial products are made from such species as anchovies, capelin, herring, menhaden, and sardines, and from scraps left over after fileting. To produce fish meal and fish oil, processors first cook the fish with steam. They then squeeze out most of the water and oil. The remaining material, a high-protein meal, is then dried. Fish oil is obtained by separating the oil from the water in a whirling device called a *centrifuge.*

Feed companies add fish meal to livestock feed and dry pet food. Hatchery managers also feed the meal to trout and salmon raised in hatcheries. Manufacturers use fish oil to make a number of products, including glue, paint, lubricants, and ink.

Marketing. Fresh fish may be sold daily in fishing ports near fishing areas. However, fish and fish products to be sold in distant markets must first be processed to prevent spoilage.

Most fish processors operate in fishing ports. Many fishing crews sell their catches to processors at set prices or at auctions after fishing trips. The price a catch brings at auction depends on the supply of fish at the market and the demand for it. A fishing crew may not know in advance what a harvest will earn—if it sells at all. The uncertainty of the auction market has led some fishing crews to form *marketing cooperatives,* groups that

collect the catch of their members and sell it to processors. Cooperatives enable their members to know, before they leave port, how much fish to catch and how much the harvest will earn. Processors place orders with the cooperative for a specific quantity of fish before a fishing trip. At the same time, both sides agree on the price to be paid for the catch.

Processors sell most of their fish products to fish brokers in large cities. The brokers, in turn, sell the products to restaurants and food stores.

Fishery conservation

The world demand for food continues to grow as the human population increases. The harvest of ocean fish continues to expand to meet world food demands. Overfishing has greatly reduced some fish stocks in many of the world's fisheries. Although fish resources are considered renewable, scientists believe that the oceans can produce only a limited quantity of fish over time.

In addition to overfishing, *bycatch* poses a tremendous challenge to fishery conservation. Bycatch includes fish and other marine animals that are inadvertently captured along with target fish species. Often, such creatures cannot be captured legally in a particular fishery or cannot be marketed. Some animals caught as bycatch are returned to the sea alive, but many die and are discarded. Bycatch occurs in practically all fisheries. It cannot be avoided because most fishing areas are inhabited by a variety of fish and other marine animals, and fishing gear is not selective enough to capture only the target species. Scientists estimate that about 25 percent of the world commercial fish harvest is discarded as bycatch.

Government regulation. Most major fishing nations have laws to conserve and protect their fish resources. Almost all nations that border the sea have established authority over fishery conservation zones extending 200 nautical miles from their shores. These zones are intended to protect the nations' coastal fishing industries by controlling the harvest by fleets from other countries. Nations may also pass conservation laws to manage and safeguard marine life in local coastal fisheries.

Many regulations try to curb the impact of fishing and its associated bycatch on the overall ecology of fisheries. Some regulations set quotas that limit the total catch of certain species in a fishery and in a few cases limit the number of fishing vessels permitted in an area. Others restrict the areas and the time of year in which crews may fish. The size and type of fishing gear that may be used in a fishery are also regulated.

Water pollution controls also aid in fishery conservation. Such controls limit the amount of harmful materials that may be released into inland and coastal waters. These materials can kill fish or the plants and animals on which fish feed.

International commissions and treaties. Through the years, fishing nations have agreed to work together in managing fishery resources in international waters. A number of commissions have been established to protect a particular species of fish or all species in a certain area. For example, the International Pacific Halibut Commission helps regulate halibut fishing off the west coasts of Canada and the United States. The International Council for the Exploration of the Sea promotes the conservation of all fish species in the North Atlantic Ocean.

Most international commissions devoted to fishery conservation operate in a similar manner. Scientists from the member nations or from the organization itself gather statistics on the size of the catch and conduct other research regarding a particular fishery or species of fish. The commissions meet annually to review the results of these studies and to recommend ways of managing fishery resources. Each member nation then has the responsibility of passing and enforcing laws based on the recommendations.

Many nations also make *bilateral treaties* to manage fishery resources in international waters. Under such treaties, two nations agree to meet periodically to exchange information on fisheries of interest to both countries and to discuss conservation measures.

National agencies and international commissions are developing codes of conduct for responsible fishing. These guidelines are designed to ensure that no fish population falls too low to maintain diversity of species in a fishery. The rules also take into account environmental factors that can affect stocks of various species.

Scientific research involves many activities to improve fishery management. Researchers determine the maximum number or weight of fish that can be harvested annually without severely damaging the stock. Researchers often rely on records of the harvest from a fishery to check changes in the abundance of stocks from year to year. They also conduct fishery resource surveys. By analyzing information provided by such activities, they determine what quantity of a species can be harvested in a particular area. However, collapses of fish stocks often occur in spite of such determinations. Such collapses can occur because changing environmental conditions can affect the growth and survival of marine animals over short periods as well as long ones.

Scientists study the effects of the environment on changes in fish abundance and the effects of fishing on other species. Most fish feed on other fish. Dolphins, seals, and marine birds also prey on fish. Overfishing of prey species, such as anchovies, herring, and sardines, reduces the food supply of predator species. However, overfishing of predator species, such as cod, salmon, and tuna, increases the supply of prey species. Thus, scientists are working to develop management techniques that help conserve a fishery's entire *ecosystem*—that is, all the living and nonliving things in the fishery and the relationships among them—rather than just an individual species. To help reduce bycatch, scientists study ways of modifying fishing gear to reduce the capture of nontarget species.

Some researchers work to increase the rates of survival and growth of fish. Such research especially helps fish farmers. Commercially raised fish have greatly increased fish production, chiefly in Asia and Europe. In addition, some researchers are studying unharvested types of fish to develop new products and markets. Such efforts seek to both increase the world's food supply and promote fish conservation. Through the development of new fish resources, the world's total catch can remain constant—or even be increased—without overfishing individual stocks.   James Sulikowski

Related articles in *World Book*. Many articles on countries, states, and provinces have a section on fishing industry. See, for example, **Japan** (Fishing industry); **Alabama** (Fishing industry). See also:

Some food fishes

Anchovy	Pompano
Bass	Redfish
Carp	Roughy
Catfish	Salmon
Cod	Sardine
Dogfish	Shad
Drum	Smelt
Flounder	Snapper
Grouper	Sole
Haddock	Sprat
Hake	Sturgeon
Halibut	Swordfish
Herring	Trout
Mackerel	Tuna
Menhaden	Turbot
Mullet	Weakfish
Perch	Whitefish
Pollock	

Other seafoods

Abalone	Lobster	Scallop
Clam	Mussel	Shrimp
Crab	Oyster	Squid
Crayfish		

Other related articles

Aquaculture	Krill
Cormorant	Net
Fish	Ocean (Fisheries)
Fishing	Pearl
Food preservation	Seafood
Grand Banks	Sponge
Gulf Stream	Whale

Outline

I. Where fish are caught
   A. Ocean fisheries   C. Fish farms
   B. Inland fisheries
II. How fish are caught
   A. Nets   C. Traps
   B. Hooks   D. Harpoons
III. How fish are processed and marketed
   A. Methods of processing
   B. Marketing
IV. Fishery conservation
   A. Government regulation
   B. International commissions and treaties
   C. Scientific research

Questions

What types of fisheries provide most of the world's commercial fish catch?

Why are fish a valuable food?

What is *upwelling?* How does it help the fish population in an area grow?

How does the marketing cooperative method of selling a fish catch differ from the auction method?

What are *fish farms?*

Which are the world's leading fishing countries?

What is a *purse seine?* How does it work?

How may overfishing of one species of fish affect the populations of other species?

What are fish meal and fish oil? What are these products used for?

How do fishery conservation zones aid in fish conservation?

Fishing laws. See Fishing industry (Fishery conservation).

Fishworm. See Earthworm.

Fisk, James (1834-1872), was an American financier who was involved in several business scandals in the late 1800's. Fisk helped cause the collapse of the gold market on Sept. 24, 1869, known as *Black Friday.* He and industrialist Jay Gould had tried to monopolize the market by buying all the gold in New York City. The United States Treasury intervened, and the price of gold fell. Fisk and Gould, however, made $11 million in profit.

Fisk was born on April 1, 1834, in Bennington, Vermont. During the American Civil War (1861-1865), he became rich by selling cotton from areas of the South controlled by Union forces. After the war, Fisk, Gould, and Daniel Drew made huge profits by manipulating the stock of the Erie Railroad. Fisk bought an opera house in New York City and held many parties there, earning the nickname "Jubilee Jim." At the age of 37, Fisk was fatally shot by Edward Stokes, a rival for his mistress, the actress Josie Mansfield. Fisk died on Jan. 7, 1872.

Peter d'A. Jones

Fiske, John (1842-1901), was an American philosopher and historian who helped promote the theory of evolution. According to this theory, all living things have *evolved* (developed gradually) from a few common ancestors. Fiske sought to bring the ideas of evolution and religion into harmony. Critics of evolution charged that it conflicted with the belief that God created all living things. Fiske rejected that argument and saw evolution simply as God's way of doing things. He developed this idea in *The Outlines of Cosmic Philosophy* (1874).

Fiske also became a popular lecturer and writer on early American history. He applied the theory of evolutionary change to history. In his book *The Beginnings of New England* (1889), Fiske stressed the European origins of United States institutions. Fiske was born on March 30, 1842, in Hartford, Connecticut. He died on July 4, 1901.   Robert C. Sims

Fiske, Minnie Maddern (1865-1932), was a leading American stage actress during the late 1800's and early 1900's. She was an early supporter of a natural style of acting in the United States, departing from the more exaggerated romantic style popular in the 1800's. Fiske was the chief promoter in the United States of the realistic dramas of the Norwegian playwright Henrik Ibsen. She performed in several Ibsen plays, including *A Doll's House* in 1894 and *Hedda Gabler* in 1903.

Fiske was born on Dec. 19, 1865, in New Orleans into a family of actors and actresses. Her given and family name was Marie Augusta Davey. In 1890, she married Harrison Grey Fiske, a newspaper editor and playwright, who wrote several plays for her. After her marriage, she performed under the name Mrs. Fiske. She died on Feb. 15, 1932.   Don B. Wilmeth

Fission, in physics, is the splitting of the nucleus of an atom into two nearly equal lighter nuclei. This process occurs most readily in such heavy elements as uranium and plutonium. Fission can take place naturally or it can be produced artificially by striking a fissionable nucleus with a neutron or some other nuclear particle. In addition, neutrons and gamma-ray photons are often released during fission.

When a nucleus splits into two *fission fragments,* a large amount of energy is released. This energy comes from a decrease in the mass of the original fissionable nucleus. The energy can be calculated using the physicist Albert Einstein's equation: $E=mc^2$ (energy=mass × the speed of light squared). To calculate the energy re-

leased, m equals the difference in mass between the original nucleus and the mass of the fission fragments. The fission of 2.2 pounds (1 kilogram) of uranium releases more energy than the burning of 6.6 million pounds (3 million kilograms) of coal.

A fissioning nucleus also releases several neutrons. These free neutrons may strike other nuclei and cause them to fission. A continuous series of such fissions, called a *chain reaction,* produces the energy in atomic bombs and nuclear reactors.   Robert B. Prigo

See also **Nuclear energy; Plutonium; Radiation** (diagram: Nuclear fission); **Uranium.**

Fitch, Clyde (1865-1909), was one of the most productive and successful American playwrights of his time. His works include farces, problem plays, historical plays, and plays about high society. Several of Fitch's plays are notable for their realistic presentation of familiar scenes from life in his day. Fitch was stage manager for his plays, controlling every detail of their production.

William Clyde Fitch was born on May 2, 1865, in Elmira, New York. From *Beau Brummell* (1890) to *The City* (1909), he wrote more than 30 original plays and 22 adaptations of novels and foreign plays. In 1901, Fitch had four plays running in New York City at the same time, *Barbara Frietchie* (1899) and *Lovers' Lane, Captain Jinks of the Horse Marines,* and *The Climbers* (all 1901). His other plays include *The Girl with the Green Eyes* (1902), *Her Great Match* (1905), and *The Truth* (1907). He died on Sept. 4, 1909.   Frederick C. Wilkins

Fitch, John (1743-1798), was an American inventor. He designed the first workable steamboat in the United States. Fitch demonstrated this boat on the Delaware River near Philadelphia on Aug. 22, 1787. A steam engine powered six paddles on each side of the 45-foot (14-meter) boat. The steamboat reached a speed of about 3 miles (4.8 kilometers) per hour.

Fitch launched a 60-foot (18-meter) boat in 1788. It was propelled by paddles at the stern. A more powerful boat, launched in 1790, reached a speed of about 8 miles (13 kilometers) per hour. It operated in regular passenger service between Philadelphia and Trenton, New Jersey. But there was not enough demand for passage to make this boat financially successful.

Fitch was born on Jan. 21, 1743, on a farm near Windsor, Connecticut. After trying out a number of trades, he became a successful brass worker and silversmith in Trenton. He gave up this business during the American

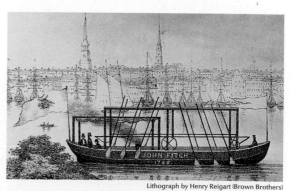

Lithograph by Henry Reigart (Brown Brothers)

One of John Fitch's earliest steamboats sailed on the Delaware River. Philadelphia can be seen on the opposite shore.

Revolution (1775-1783). Fitch turned his attention to the construction of a steamboat in 1785. He obtained patents on his work in the United States and France in 1791. However, he had constant trouble with his financial affairs and never succeeded in making his boats profitable. He died in poverty in July 1798.   J. P. Hartman

See also **Fulton, Robert; Ship** (The first steamboats); Steamboat.

FitzGerald, Edward (1809-1883), was an English writer famous for compiling and translating *The Rubaiyat of Omar Khayyam,* a collection of short poems attributed to the Persian poet, astronomer, and mathematician Omar Khayyam. The collection's melancholy theme of "drink and be merry for tomorrow we die" described the mood of many people in England in the late 1800's.

FitzGerald's translation was first published anonymously in 1859. The translation was ignored until 1860, when the famous English poet Dante Gabriel Rossetti and his circle discovered the work and helped popularize it. FitzGerald prepared three revised editions that were published in 1868, 1872, and 1879. In addition to the *Rubaiyat,* FitzGerald was known for his translations of Greek and Spanish literature and for his charming letters. FitzGerald was born on March 31, 1809, in Suffolk. He died on June 14, 1883.   Jerome Bump

See also **Rubaiyat.**

Fitzgerald, Ella (1917-1996), ranked among the best and most popular singers in jazz history. She became known for her pure and beautiful tone, extended range, flawless intonation, and strong sense of jazz feeling. She also became famous for her ability to improvise through *scat singing.* In this style, rhythmic wordless syllables are sung instead of lyrics.

Pablo Records

Ella Fitzgerald

Fitzgerald was born on April 25, 1917, in Newport News, Virginia. Her father died when she was a child, and she moved to Yonkers, New York, with her mother. In 1935, she won an amateur talent contest at the Apollo Theatre in Harlem. This led to an engagement with the big band of drummer Chick Webb. She became the band's featured vocalist and recorded her first hit, "A-Tisket, A-Tasket," with the band in 1938.

Upon Webb's death in 1939, Fitzgerald took over the band, leading it until 1942, when she began a career as a soloist and with vocal groups. She increased her fame while working with the "Jazz at the Philharmonic" touring group of musicians and singers beginning in 1948. She died on June 15, 1996.   Eddie Cook

Fitzgerald, F. Scott (1896-1940), was the leading writer of America's Jazz Age, the Roaring Twenties, and one of its glittering heroes. The chief quality of his talent was his ability to be both a leading participant in the high life he described, and a detached observer of it. Few readers saw the serious side of Fitzgerald, and he was not generally recognized as a gifted writer during his lifetime. Most readers then considered his stories a chronicle and even a celebration of moral decline. But

later readers realized that Fitzgerald's works contained a deeper moral theme.

Bettmann Archive

F. Scott Fitzgerald

Francis Scott Key Fitzgerald was born in St. Paul, Minnesota, on Sept. 24, 1896. He attended Princeton University, where he wrote amateur musical comedies. He left Princeton in 1917 without a degree. Years later, Fitzgerald remarked that perhaps he should have continued writing musicals, but he said, "I am too much a moralist at heart, and really want to preach at people in some acceptable form, rather than entertain them."

Fitzgerald won fame and fortune for his first novel, *This Side of Paradise* (1920). It is an immature work but was the first novel to anticipate the pleasure-seeking generation of the Roaring Twenties. A similar novel, *The Beautiful and Damned* (1921), and two collections of short stories, *Flappers and Philosophers* (1920) and *Tales of the Jazz Age* (1922), helped increase his popularity.

The Great Gatsby (1925) was less popular than Fitzgerald's earlier works, but it was his masterpiece and the first of three successive novels that earned him lasting literary importance. The lively yet deeply moral novel centers around Jay Gatsby, a wealthy bootlegger. It presents a penetrating criticism of the moral emptiness that Fitzgerald saw in wealthy American society of the 1920's.

Fitzgerald's next novel, *Tender Is the Night* (1934, revised edition by Malcolm Cowley, 1951), is a beautifully written but disjointed account of the general decline of a few glamorous Americans in Europe. The book failed because readers during the Great Depression of the 1930's were not interested in Jazz Age "parties." Fitzgerald died before he completed *The Last Tycoon* (1941), a novel about Hollywood life.

Critics generally agree that Fitzgerald's early success damaged his personal life and marred his literary production. This success led to extravagant living and a need for a large income. It probably contributed to Fitzgerald's alcoholism and the mental breakdown of his wife, Zelda. The success also probably led to his physical and spiritual collapse, which he described frankly in the long essay *The Crack-Up* (1936). Fitzgerald spent his last years as a scriptwriter in Hollywood and died there on Dec. 21, 1940. A few years after his death, his books won him the recognition he had desired while alive.

Samuel Chase Coale

See also **American literature** (The Lost Generation); **Lost Generation; Roaring Twenties.**

Fitzpatrick, Thomas (1799?-1854), was a trapper and guide in the American West. He also served as an Indian agent. Indian agents represented the United States government in its dealings with American Indians.

Fitzpatrick was born in County Cavan, Ireland. He moved to the United States when he was about 16. In the early 1820's, he became a leader of fur-trapping expeditions. He spent much time in the Rocky Mountains searching for fur-bearing animals. In 1824, Fitzpatrick was second in command to Jedediah S. Smith in an early expedition that crossed the South Pass of the Rockies. The pass became the route of many travelers.

In the 1840's, Fitzpatrick became a major guide on the American frontier. He helped lead settlers, missionaries, explorers, and military units to destinations in the West. In 1846, the government appointed him an Indian agent. In 1851 and 1853, Fitzpatrick negotiated treaties with Indians for the government. He died on Feb. 7, 1854.

Jerome O. Steffen

Fitzsimmons, Bob (1863-1917), held the world's heavyweight boxing championship from 1897 to 1899. He also held the world's middleweight title from 1891 until he won the heavyweight championship in 1897. He was the light heavyweight champion of the world from 1903 until 1905, becoming boxing's first three-time champion. Fitzsimmons gained the heavyweight title by knocking out James J. Corbett in 14 rounds. He is credited with originating the solar plexus punch in this fight (see **Solar plexus**). Fitzsimmons lost the heavyweight title to James J. Jeffries on a knockout in the 11th round.

Robert James Fitzsimmons was born on May 26, 1863, in Helston, Cornwall, England. He grew up in New Zealand and did his early fighting in Australia. Fitzsimmons moved to the United States in 1890. He died on Oct. 22, 1917.   Bert Randolph Sugar

Fitzsimmons, Frank Edward (1908-1981), served as president of the Teamsters Union from 1971 to 1981. At that time, it was the largest labor union in the United States. Most of the union's members are truckdrivers.

Fitzsimmons was born on April 7, 1908, in Jeannette, Pennsylvania. He began his union career in 1937 as business agent of the Teamsters local in Detroit. In 1940, he became vice president of the local. The international union appointed him to a vice presidency in 1961. He became acting head of the Teamsters after union president James R. Hoffa was imprisoned in 1967. Fitzsimmons succeeded Hoffa as president after Hoffa resigned in June 1971. The union elected Fitzsimmons to a full term the next month and to another five-year term in 1976. He died on May 6, 1981.   Mark Anner

FitzSimons, Thomas (1741-1811), was a Pennsylvanian signer of the Constitution of the United States. His name is also spelled Fitzsimmons. At the Constitutional Convention of 1787, FitzSimons favored a strong central government with the power to tax imports and exports.

FitzSimons was born in Ireland. By 1760, he had immigrated to Philadelphia, where he soon became a leading merchant specializing in trade with the West Indies. During the American Revolution (1775-1783), he raised and commanded a company of militia.

FitzSimons served in the Congress of the Confederation in 1782 and 1783. He was later elected to several terms in the Pennsylvania legislature. As a Federalist Party member of the U.S. House of Representatives from 1789 to 1795, he supported protective tariffs to promote American manufacturing. FitzSimons was one of the founders of the Bank of North America and the Insurance Company of North America. He lost much of his political influence after personal difficulties caused him to declare bankruptcy in 1805. FitzSimons died on Aug. 26, 1811.   Richard D. Brown

Five Civilized Tribes is a name for the Chickasaw, Choctaw, Cherokee, Creek, and Seminole Indians. White settlers gave the tribes this name in the 1800's, after the tribes had adopted a number of European customs. Many settlers considered European ways more civilized than Indian ones. The tribes once farmed and hunted in what is now the Southeastern United States. Most of these Indians lived in towns. Europeans, who began to explore the area in the 1500's, brought diseases that killed thousands of Indians. By the early 1700's, the Indian population had dropped by about 75 percent.

Meanwhile, the Indians and three European powers— Britain, France, and Spain—fought for the land, sometimes forming alliances with one another. Britain (later also called the United Kingdom) won the struggle, but the United States took over after the American Revolution (1775-1783).

The tribes began to realize that they could not defeat the whites or continue living in traditional ways. Many Indians started to attend churches and send their children to schools run by missionaries. Some Indians acquired cotton plantations and slaves.

But white settlers wanted the tribes' land. Between 1830 and 1842, the government forced most of these Indians to move to the Indian Territory, in what is now Oklahoma. Thousands died on the journey. The Cherokee called their trip the Trail of Tears. This term is sometimes used to refer to the removal of the other tribes as well. A small number of Indians stayed in the Southeast.

The United States pledged to uphold forever the Indians' land rights in the Indian Territory. However, Congress took away the western part of the Indians' land after the American Civil War (1861-1865), partly to punish the tribes for helping the South fight the North. Congress began to dissolve the tribal governments gradually in 1898 and, in 1901, granted citizenship to all Indians in the territory. Today, most members of the tribes live much as other Oklahomans do. Many prefer to be known as members of the Five Nations.   Charles Hudson

See the separate articles on each tribe. See also **Indian Territory; Oklahoma** (History); **Trail of Tears.**

Five-year plan is a program to increase a country's standard of living in a five-year period. The Soviet Union also used such plans to organize the production and distribution of goods and services. It began its first five-year plan in 1928. In 1958, it replaced the five-year plan with a seven-year plan (1959-1965) that was aimed at surpassing the industrial progress of the United States. The Soviet five-year plans were reinstated in 1966 and used until 1990. The Soviet Union was dissolved in 1991. China, India, and other countries have adopted five-year plans. See also **China** (The beginning of Communist rule; The Great Leap Forward); **India** (India in the 1950's and early 1960's); **Union of Soviet Socialist Republics** (Stalin's policies).   Richard C. Wiles

Fivepins. See **Bowling** (Canadian fivepins).

Fixture, in law, refers to personal property that has been affixed to houses, land, or other real estate. A fixture becomes part of the real estate to which it is attached. Key factors in determining whether property is a fixture are the method of attachment and the parties' intention to make the property a permanent part of the real estate. For example, if a tenant installs electric wiring in rented property, the wiring may become part of the landlord's real estate unless the tenant and landlord agree otherwise before installation.   Linda Henry Elrod

Fjord. See **Fiord.**

National flags are perhaps the most important group of flags. A nation's flag stands for its land, its people, its government, and its ideals. When the flags of several countries are displayed, they are flown at the same height from separate staffs of equal size.

© Spencer Grant, Photo Researchers

Flag

Flag is a piece of cloth, usually with a picture or design on it, that stands for something. A flag may represent a nation, person, or organization; it may symbolize a belief or idea; or it may transmit information. The most important group of flags are probably national flags. A nation's flag is a stirring sight as it flies in the wind. Its bright colors and striking design stand for the country's land, its people, its government, and its ideals. A country's flag can stir people to joy, to courage, and to sacrifice. Spe-

Whitney Smith, the contributor of this article, is Director of the Flag Research Center (Winchester, Massachusetts), editor of The Flag Bulletin, and author of The Flag Book of the United States and Flags Through the Ages and Across the World. Colors, sizes, proportions, and designs are all based on information supplied by official sources and checked by the Flag Research Center. Text information on the flags of countries, states, and provinces can be found in the separate articles in World Book.

cial rules for display and care have grown up around people's wish to honor their nation's flag.

Nations use many kinds of flags besides national flags. Some countries fly a special *state* flag over embassies and other government buildings at home and abroad. Presidents, kings, queens, and other government leaders may have their own flags. States, provinces, and cities are represented by flags. Some flags stand for international organizations, such as the United Nations (UN) and the Red Cross. Such regional groups as the Organization of American States and the European Union have flags. Other organizational flags include those of youth groups, like the Boy Scouts and the Girl Scouts, and hobby societies. Many religions and churches have their own flags. Flags also may be used to send messages.

Such peoples as the Egyptians, Persians, Greeks, and Romans carried flaglike objects thousands of years ago.

These "flags," called *standards,* consisted of symbols attached to the tops of poles. The symbols, which might include cloth, wood, metal, and other materials, usually stood for the people's gods or rulers. Soldiers carried the symbols into battle, hoping that their gods would help them win.

Flags became important during battles for a variety of reasons. Soldiers of the Egyptians and other ancient peoples sometimes tied streamers to the poles they carried. The streamers—like later cloth flags—showed which way the wind blew, and helped soldiers see the direction to aim their arrows. Flags stood for each side in a battle, and generals watched them to see where their soldiers were. Fighting often centered around the flag, and defending the flag was regarded as the chief duty of a soldier. If the soldier carrying the flag was killed or wounded, others would "rally round the flag" to prevent the enemy from capturing it. If the flag was captured, many soldiers would give up the fight.

The symbols used in flags may go back thousands of years. The Shield of David, an ancient symbol of the Jews popularly known as the "Star of David," appears on the flag of Israel. The cross, a symbol of Christianity, is displayed on the flags of many Christian nations. The crescent and star in the flags of many Muslim countries are symbols of peace and life. Stars on flags often stand for unity. The number of stars on a nation's flag may show how many states are united in the country.

Interesting facts about flags

The first "flags" consisted of symbols attached to the tops of poles. Such flaglike objects appear in Egyptian art of the mid-3000's B.C.

Cloth flags are thought by some historians to have first been used in China. Made of silk, these flags were in use before 1500 B.C.

Knights in the Middle Ages carried square flags with a streamer called a *Schwenkel.* A knight's promotion to higher rank was symbolized by having the Schwenkel cut off. The resulting flag was called a *banner,* and the knight became a *knight-banneret.*

National flags are among the most recent kinds of flags. They were first used in the 1700's in Europe and North America. Until then, most flags stood for the personal authority of rulers.

Flags at sea. Before the days of radio, a complicated system of flag design and display grew up around the need for communication at sea. Flag codes enabled the sending of messages between ships or from a ship to shore. A ship would salute another vessel by *dipping,* or lowering, its flag. Such salutes played a major role in international diplomacy.

Flag colors. Most national flags use one or more of only seven basic colors. These colors are red, white, blue, green, yellow, black, and orange.

Flag symbols often reflect historical events. The cross that appears in many European flags originated in the flags carried by Crusaders to the Holy Land. Some flags used in Arab countries show the eagle of Saladin, a Muslim warrior who fought the Crusaders in the 1100's.

Burning is considered the most dignified way to destroy a flag that is no longer fit for display. But burning a usable flag often signifies political protest.

Flag terms

Badge is an emblem or design, usually on the fly.

Battle flag is carried by armed forces on land.

Battle streamer, attached to the flag of a military unit, names battles or campaigns where the unit served with distinction.

Bend on means to attach signal flags to a halyard.

Breadth, a British measurement for flags, is 9 inches (23 centimeters) wide. A four-breadth flag is 36 inches (91 centimeters) wide. The term originated when flag cloth was made in 9-inch (23-centimeter) strips.

Bunting is cloth decorated with the national colors. The term is also used for the woolen cloth used in making flags.

Burgee is a flag or pennant that ends in a swallowtail of two points.

Canton is the upper corner of a flag next to the staff where a special design, such as a union, appears.

Color is a special flag carried by a military unit or officer. In the armed forces of many countries, regiments and larger units often carry two colors—the national flag and a unit flag.

Courtesy flag is the national flag of the country a merchant ship or yacht visits, hoisted as the ship enters port.

Device is an emblem or design, usually on the fly.

Ensign is a national flag flown by a naval ship. Some countries also have ensigns for other armed services.

Ensign staff is the staff at the stern of a ship.

Field is the background of a flag.

Fimbriation is a narrow line separating two other colors in a flag.

Flag hoist is a group of signal flags attached to the same halyard and hoisted as a unit.

Fly is the free end of a flag, farthest from the staff. The term is also used for the horizontal length of the flag.

Garrison flag, in the United States Army, flies over military posts on holidays and special days. A garrison flag is 20 feet (6 meters) wide by 38 feet (12 meters) long, more than twice as wide and long as a post flag.

Ground is the background of a flag.

Guidon is a small flag carried at the front or right of a military unit to guide the marchers.

Halyard is a rope used to hoist and lower a flag.

Hoist is the part of the flag closest to the staff. The term is also used for the vertical width of a flag.

House flag is flown by a merchant ship to identify the company that owns it.

Jack is a small flag flown at the bow of a ship.

Jackstaff is the staff at the bow of a ship.

Merchant flag is a flag flown by a merchant ship.

National flag is the flag of a country.

Pennant is a small triangular or tapering flag.

Pilot flag is flown from a ship that wants the aid of a pilot when entering port.

Post flag, in the U.S. Army, flies regularly over every Army base. It is 8 feet 11 ⅜ inches (2.73 meters) wide by 17 feet (5.18 meters) long.

Reeve means to pull the halyard through the truck, raising or lowering a flag.

Staff is the pole a flag hangs on.

Standard is a flag around which people rally. Today, the term usually refers to the personal flag of a ruler, such as the *Royal Standard* of the British monarch.

State flag is the flag flown by the government of a country. Many state flags are the same as national flags but with the country's coat of arms added.

Storm flag, in the U.S. Army, flies over an Army base in stormy weather. It is 5 feet (1.5 meters) wide by 9 feet 6 inches (2.9 meters) long, half as wide and half as long as a post flag.

Truck is the wooden or metal block at the top of a flagpole below the *finial* (staff ornament). It includes a pulley or holes for the halyards.

Union is a design that symbolizes unity. It may appear in the canton, as the stars do in the U.S. flag. Or it may be the entire flag, as in the *Union Flag* of the United Kingdom.

Vexillology is the study of flag history and symbolism. The name comes from the Latin word *vexillum,* which means *flag.*

Most national flags use one or more of only seven basic colors. These colors are red, white, blue, green, yellow, black, and orange. The colors were all used in *heraldry*, a system of designs that grew up during the Middle Ages (see **Heraldry**). Designs on many flags follow rules of heraldry. Such designs include, for example, a strip of white or yellow separating two colors. The Mexican flag, with white between red and green bands, follows this rule.

Popular stories often explain why flags have certain colors and designs. For example, the Austrian flag supposedly dates from an event in 1191, during the Third Crusade, a military expedition attempting to regain the Holy Land from the Muslims. When Duke Leopold V removed his blood-stained cloak after a battle, he found that his belt had kept a band of the cloth white. From

then on, he used a red flag with a white stripe across it. Austria adopted this design in 1919. Denmark's national flag—a white cross on red—is said to have originated more than 750 years ago. During a great battle in 1219, according to tradition, a red flag bearing a white cross fell from heaven and inspired the Danes to victory.

Nations that have a common history or culture may use the same colors in their flags. Blue and white appear in the flags of Costa Rica, El Salvador, Guatemala, Honduras, and Nicaragua. These nations were once joined in the United Provinces of Central America, which had a blue-and-white flag. Four colors—black, green, red, and white—stand for Arab unity. Some or all of these colors appear in the flags of Egypt, Iraq, Jordan, Kuwait, Oman, Sudan, Syria, the United Arab Emirates, and Yemen.

The study of the history and symbolism of flags is

Parts of a flag

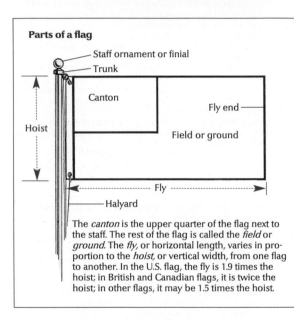

The *canton* is the upper quarter of the flag next to the staff. The rest of the flag is called the *field* or *ground*. The *fly*, or horizontal length, varies in proportion to the *hoist*, or vertical width, from one flag to another. In the U.S. flag, the fly is 1.9 times the hoist; in British and Canadian flags, it is twice the hoist; in other flags, it may be 1.5 times the hoist.

Staff ornaments or finials

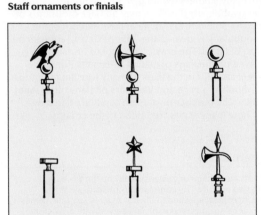

Ornaments called *finials* decorate the tops of flagstaffs. Popular finials include, *clockwise from top left,* the spread eagle, halberd, ball, guidon, star, and flat truck.

The shapes of flags   Flags may have many shapes, including oblong, square, and tapering. The tapering flags include triangular ones called *pennants* and ones that end in two points called *swallowtails*. Swallowtail flags may be broad or long and narrow.

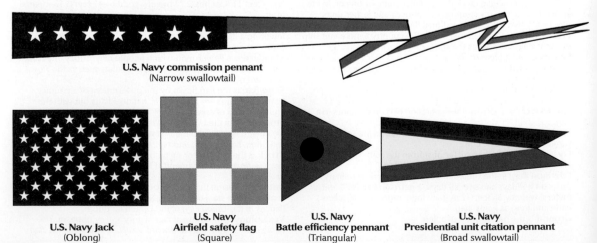

U.S. Navy commission pennant
(Narrow swallowtail)

U.S. Navy Jack
(Oblong)

**U.S. Navy
Airfield safety flag**
(Square)

**U.S. Navy
Battle efficiency pennant**
(Triangular)

**U.S. Navy
Presidential unit citation pennant**
(Broad swallowtail)

A family of flags

Many governments have flags for various purposes. For example, the British have a family of flags. The queen has two flags she can use: the Royal Standard, as queen, and her own standard, as head of the Commonwealth.

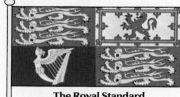

The Royal Standard
The queen's flag

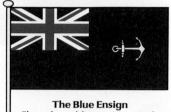

The queen's standard
The queen's personal flag

The Union Flag
The national flag

The Red Ensign
Flown by privately owned ships

The Blue Ensign
Flown by public service vessels

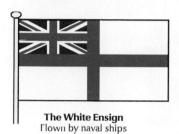

The White Ensign
Flown by naval ships

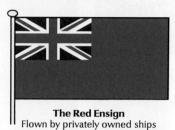

The army flag
Flown at army bases

The Royal Air Force ensign
Flown at RAF bases

called *vexillology.* The name comes from the Latin word *vexillum,* meaning a square flag or banner. Roman cavalry units carried the vexillum, which hung from a crossbar fastened to a staff.

Kinds of flags

National flags are in many ways the most important flags in the world. They stand for all the people in a country, just as state and city flags stand for the people in smaller areas. But there are many other kinds of flags. Some flags stand for only one person, and others for one part of the government. Some flags are used only by the armed forces, and others only at sea. Some flags are used only to send messages.

Many government agencies have their own flags. Such United States units as the Foreign Service have special flags. Many British agencies fly the Blue Ensign, usually with a badge in the fly.

Civil and state flags. Some countries have a special *state flag* that only the government uses. It flies on public buildings within that country. Usually, a state flag is a national flag with a coat of arms added to it. When a country has a state flag, the national flag flown by individuals is known as a *civil flag.* Each country decides whether its civil or state flag will be flown at United Nations (UN) Headquarters. Generally, the flag that flies at the UN is the one used abroad for other purposes. The country flags that appear in this article are the ones that fly at the UN.

Flags of individuals. Many rulers and important government leaders have personal flags. For example, the President and Vice President of the United States and

members of the Cabinet have special flags. The British monarch and members of the royal family have special flags. The queen's flag, called the *Royal Standard,* is raised over a building as she enters it and is lowered when she leaves. The queen also has a *personal standard* for use in the countries of the Commonwealth—an organization of former British colonies—that have become republics. In Canada and some other Commonwealth countries, the queen uses a special personal standard designed for each particular country. The governor general of Canada, as the queen's personal representative, also has a special flag.

Flags such as the Royal Standard, the President's flag, or the governor general's flag are called personal flags. But these flags stand for the authority of the office—for example, of the presidency or monarchy—and not of the officeholder. For this reason, these flags usually do not change when the individual is replaced. The queen's personal standard, in contrast, stands for her alone, and may never be used by anyone else.

Many personal flags are older than national ones. They developed during the Middle Ages and became especially important in battle. Members of the nobility flew banners of various sizes, depending on their rank. With the development of national unity in Europe, flags symbolizing the personal authority of a ruler became less important. National flags representing all the people developed.

Military flags. Flags have always been important in the armed forces. Most countries have special flags for individual military units. In addition, some countries have separate flags for each branch of their armed

PH3 West, U.S. Navy

JO1 Marc Boyd, U.S. Navy

Ships use the international flag code to aid communication at sea. Flags are stored by letter and numeral, *top,* and hoisted to send messages to other ships or to shore, *above.* The ship at the right is participating in a signaling drill.

Phan Paul Hawthorne, U.S. Navy

forces and for top-ranking officers.

    Army flags. Armies once went into combat carrying *battle flags.* Some of these army flags were quite different from the national flags of the times. However, soldiers now carry flags mostly for parades and ceremonies. Large units, such as regiments, have special

flags known as *colors.* These flags often bear the names of the battles or campaigns where the unit served with distinction. United States Army units attach pennants called *battle streamers* to their flags to show where they have fought. Smaller units of the Army carry small flags known as *guidons* in parades. The guidon serves as a

Text continues on page 208.

International flag code includes a code and answering pennant flown beneath the national flag, *above,* as well as flags for letters and numerals and substitutes, *right.* A ship receiving a signal raises its answering pennant to show that the message—or *hoist*—has been understood. Substitutes repeat any flag that precedes them.

International alphabet flags

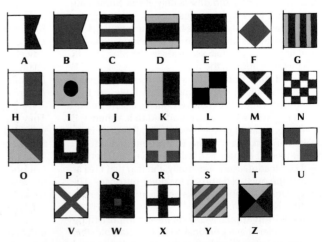

A B C D E F G

H I J K L M N

O P Q R S T U

V W X Y Z

Storm warning flags fly at shore stations to warn boats of hazardous wind and sea conditions. The red or red-and-black flags are designed to be visible even from a distance.

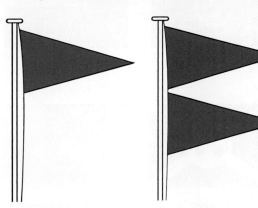

Small craft advisory
Winds up to 38 mph
(61 kph)

Gale warning
Winds from 39 to 54 mph
(63 to 87 kph)

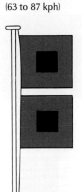

Storm warning
Winds from 55 to 73 mph
(89 to 117 kph)

Hurricane warning
Winds at least 74 mph
(119 kph)

PH2 Charles W. Moore, U.S. Navy

A U.S. Navy signalman uses semaphore flags to send a message to the crew of another ship. The signalman holds the flags in various positions to indicate letters and numbers.

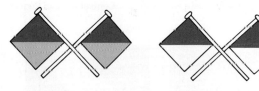

Semaphore flags are used to send messages between ships or between a ship and shore. Red-and-yellow flags are used at sea, and red-and-white ones are used on land.

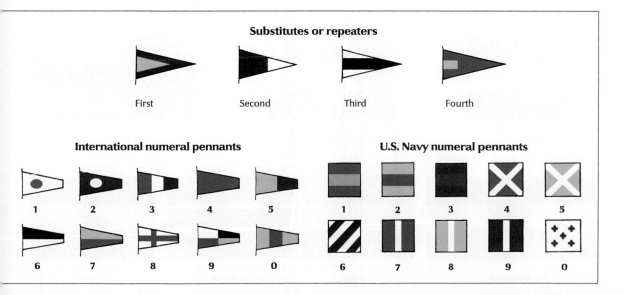

Substitutes or repeaters

First

Second

Third

Fourth

International numeral pennants

1
2
3
4
5

6
7
8
9
0

U.S. Navy numeral pennants

1
2
3
4
5

6
7
8
9
0

Flags of Africa

The ratio that appears below each flag represents the relation between the hoist (vertical width) and the fly (horizontal length). For example, Algeria's flag is two units vertically for every three units horizontally.

Algeria 2:3

Angola 2:3

Benin 2:3

Botswana 2:3

Burkina Faso 2:3

Burundi 3:5

Cameroon 2:3

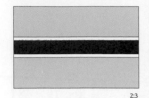

Cape Verde 10:17

Central African Republic 3:5

Chad 2:3

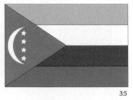

Comoros 3:5

Congo, Democratic Republic of the 3:4

Congo, Republic of the 2:3

Côte d'Ivoire 2:3

Djibouti 21:38

Egypt 2:3

Equatorial Guinea 2:3

Eritrea 1:2

Ethiopia 1:2

Gabon 3:4

Gambia 2:3

Ghana 2:3

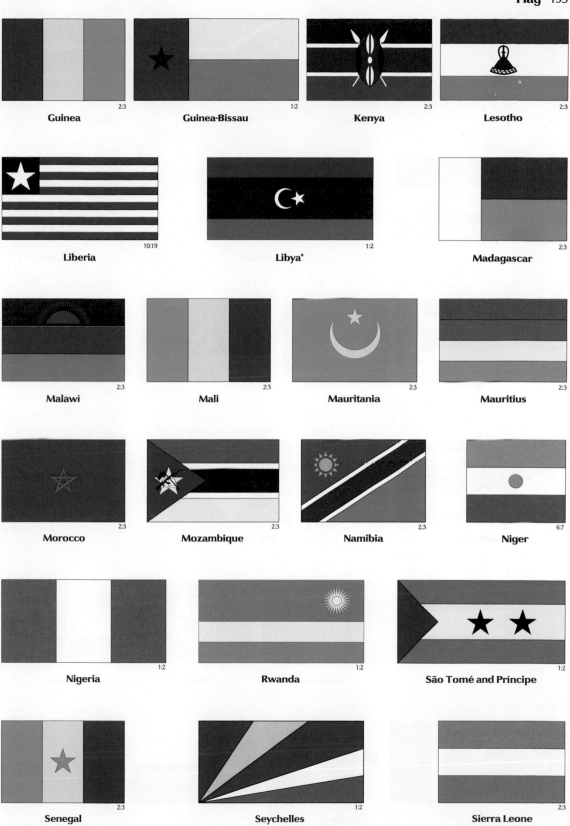

Guinea 2:3

Guinea-Bissau 1:2

Kenya 2:3

Lesotho 2:3

Liberia 10:19

Libya* 1:2

Madagascar 2:3

Malawi 2:3

Mali 2:3

Mauritania 2:3

Mauritius 2:3

Morocco 2:3

Mozambique 2:3

Namibia 2:3

Niger 6:7

Nigeria 1:2

Rwanda 1:2

São Tomé and Príncipe 1:2

Senegal 2:3

Seychelles 1:2

Sierra Leone 2:3

* Flag used by the interim government of Libya beginning in 2011.

Flags of Africa

continued

Somalia

South Africa

South Sudan

Sudan

Swaziland

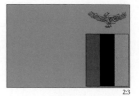

Tanzania

Togo

Tunisia

Uganda

Zambia

Zimbabwe

Flags of the Americas

Antigua and Barbuda

Argentina

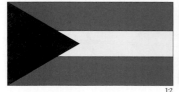

Bahamas

Barbados

Belize

Bolivia*

Brazil

Canada

Chile

Colombia

* State flag shown; civil flag does not have coat of arms.

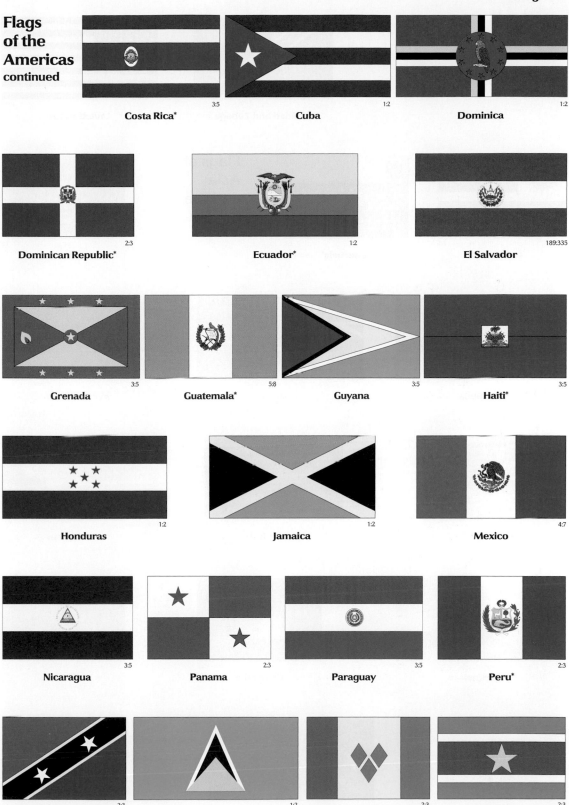

**Flags
of the
Americas**
continued

Costa Rica*   3:5

Cuba   1:2

Dominica   1:2

Dominican Republic*   2:3

Ecuador*   1:2

El Salvador   189:335

Grenada   3:5

Guatemala*   5:8

Guyana   3:5

Haiti*   3:5

Honduras   1:2

Jamaica   1:2

Mexico   4:7

Nicaragua   3:5

Panama   2:3

Paraguay   3:5

Peru*   2:3

St. Kitts and Nevis   2:3

St. Lucia   1:2

St. Vincent and the
Grenadines   2:3

Suriname   2:3

* State flag shown; civil flag does not have coat of arms.

Flags
of the Americas

continued

3:5

Trinidad and Tobago

10:19

United States

2:3

Uruguay

2:3

Venezuela*

Flags of
Asia
and the
Pacific

2:3

Afghanistan

1:2

Armenia

1:2

Australia

1:2

Azerbaijan

3:5

Bahrain

3:5

Bangladesh

2:3

Bhutan

1:2

Brunei

2:3

Cambodia

2:3

China

3:5

Cyprus

1:2

East Timor

1:2

Fiji

* State flag shown; civil flag does not have coat of arms.

Flags of Asia and the Pacific

continued

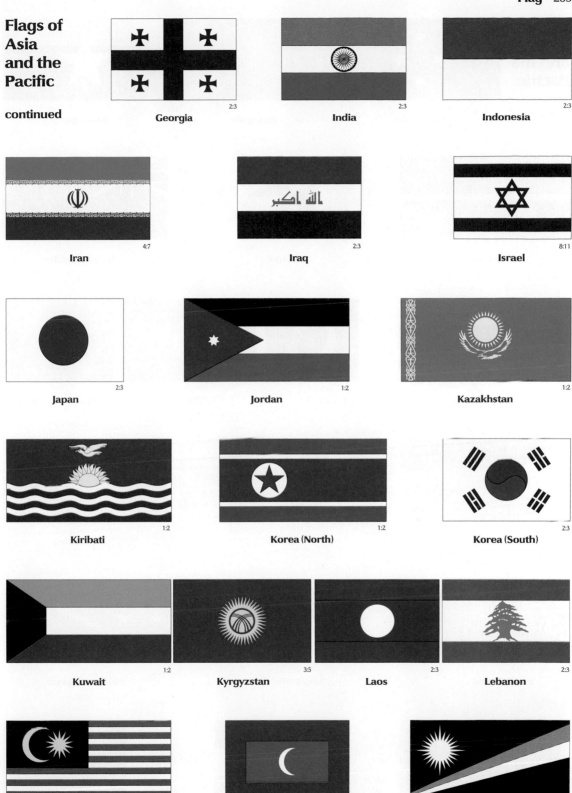

Georgia 2:3

India 2:3

Indonesia 2:3

Iran 4:7

Iraq 2:3

Israel 8:11

Japan 2:3

Jordan 1:2

Kazakhstan 1:2

Kiribati 1:2

Korea (North) 1:2

Korea (South) 2:3

Kuwait 1:2

Kyrgyzstan 3:5

Laos 2:3

Lebanon 2:3

Malaysia 1:2

Maldives 2:3

Marshall Islands 100:190

Flags of Asia and the Pacific

continued

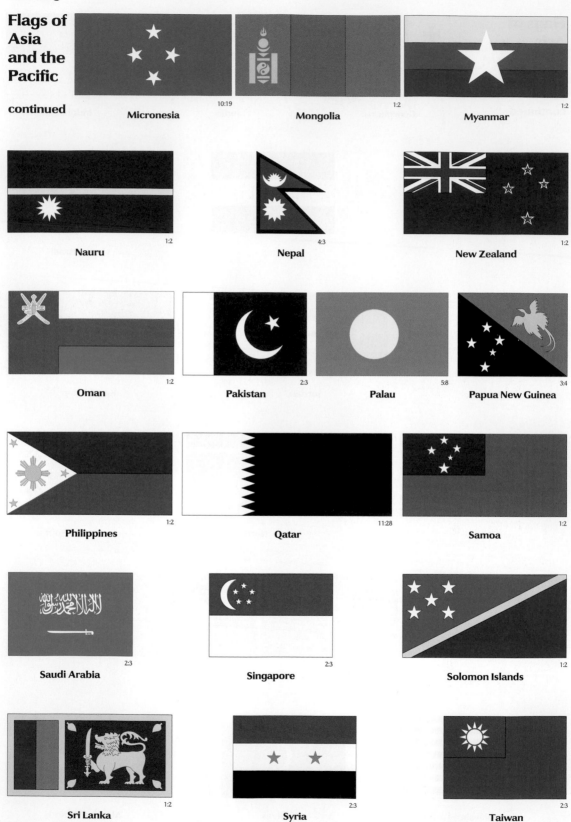

Micronesia 10:19

Mongolia 1:2

Myanmar 1:2

Nauru 1:2

Nepal 4:3

New Zealand 1:2

Oman 1:2

Pakistan 2:3

Palau 5:8

Papua New Guinea 3:4

Philippines 1:2

Qatar 11:28

Samoa 1:2

Saudi Arabia 2:3

Singapore 2:3

Solomon Islands 1:2

Sri Lanka 1:2

Syria 2:3

Taiwan 2:3

Flags of Asia and the Pacific

continued

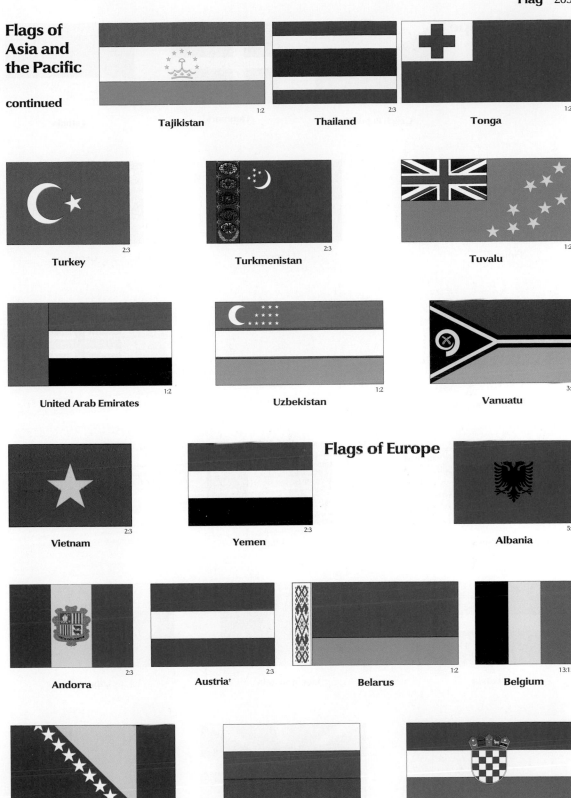

Tajikistan 1:2

Thailand 2:3

Tonga 1:2

Turkey 2:3

Turkmenistan 2:3

Tuvalu 1:2

United Arab Emirates 1:2

Uzbekistan 1:2

Vanuatu 3:5

Vietnam 2:3

Yemen 2:3

Flags of Europe

Albania 5:7

Andorra 2:3

Austria† 2:3

Belarus 1:2

Belgium 13:15

Bosnia-Herzegovina 1:2

Bulgaria 3:5

Croatia 1:2

† Civil flag shown; state flag includes coat of arms.

Flags of Europe

continued

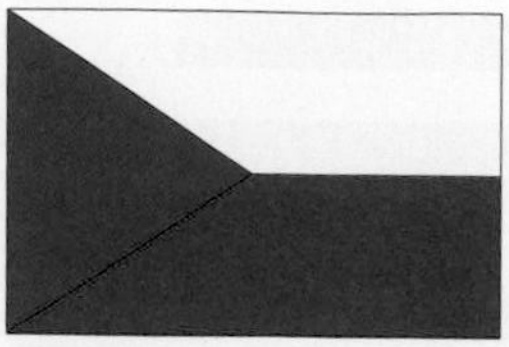

Czech Republic   2:3

Denmark‡   28:37

Estonia   7:11

Finland†   11:18

France   2:3

Germany†   3:5

Greece   2:3

Hungary   2:3

Iceland‡   18:25

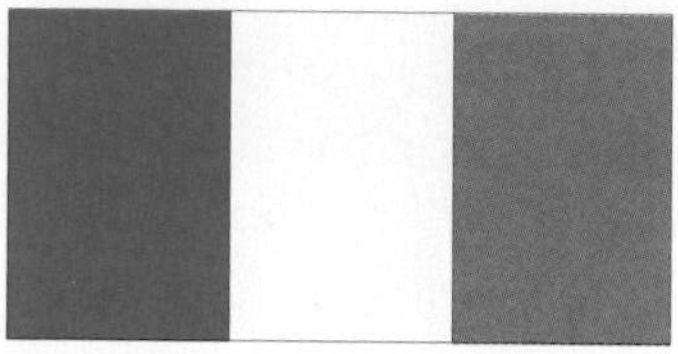

Ireland   1:2

Italy   2:3

Kosovo   2:3

Latvia   1:2

Liechtenstein   3:5

Lithuania   1:2

Luxembourg   3:5

Macedonia   1:2

Malta   2:3

† Civil flag shown; state flag includes coat of arms.

‡ Civil flag shown; state flag is swallowtailed.

Flags of Europe

continued

Moldova 1:2

Monaco† 4:5

Montenegro 1:2

Netherlands 2:3

Norway‡ 8:11

Poland 5:8

Portugal 2:3

Romania 2:3

Russia 2:3

San Marino* 3:4

Serbia 2:3

Slovakia 2:3

Slovenia 1:2

Spain* 2:3

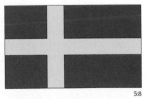
Sweden 5:8

Switzerland 1:1

Ukraine 2:3

United Kingdom 1:2

Vatican City 1:1

* State flag shown; civil flag does not have coat of arms.
† Civil flag shown; state flag has an all-white field with a coat of arms in the center.
‡ Civil flag shown; state flag is swallowtailed.

guide for the soldiers marching in the parade.

Navy flags. Navy ships usually fly several types of flags. An *ensign*—a national flag flown by the navy or other armed services—is displayed when a ship is at sea. The ensign is usually flown from a flagstaff at the stern or from a crossbar on the mast of the ship. In peacetime, the ensign need not be displayed if the ship is out of sight of land and no other ships are nearby. In wartime, the ensign is always displayed to show the ship's nationality.

When a navy ship is in port or at anchor, a small flag called the *jack* flies from the *jackstaff*—a short flagpole at the bow—and the ensign is flown from the flagstaff at the stern. Ships of most navies fly *command flags* to show the title or command of any flag officer on board. If no officer higher than the commanding officer is on board, a flag called a *commission pennant* is flown to show the ship is in active service.

Air force flags often are flown over air bases. For example, the British Air Force flies a pale blue ensign with the aircraft recognition emblem used on planes in the ensign's *fly,* the part of the flag farthest from the staff. Air force units also have their own flags and guidons.

Flags of the sea. A merchant ship flies a *house flag* of the company that owns it. At the stern, it also flies the national flag of the country in which it is registered. Instead of the national flag, the ships of some countries fly a *merchant flag* that differs from the national flag used on land. Canadian and U.S. ships fly their national flags, but British vessels fly the Red Ensign. When a ship's captain wants a pilot to help the ship enter port, the captain may hoist a *pilot flag.* As a courtesy, a ship also flies the flag of any country it visits.

Flags that talk. Flags are often used for signaling. Sailors may use special flags to relay orders to other ships. The U.S. Coast Guard uses *storm warning flags* to provide weather warnings.

Hand signal flags. In signaling, a *wigwag flag* is used to indicate the dots and dashes of the Morse code (see **Morse code**). A signaler uses two *semaphore flags* to spell out a message, holding them in various positions to indicate letters and numerals. The U.S. Navy uses semaphore flags for short-range signaling. Sailors use red-and-yellow flags to send messages between ships. Red-and-white flags are used on land.

The international flag code, the most complete flag signaling system, has more than 40 flags. A flag stands for each letter of the alphabet, and pennants stand for zero and the numerals 1 through 9. To send messages, sailors fly *hoists* of one to five flags that have code meanings or spell out words.

Each ship carries a code book that explains the flags of the international code in nine languages—English, French, German, Greek, Italian, Japanese, Norwegian, Russian, and Spanish. With the code book, any captain can understand messages sent to the ship. Warships fly the *code and answering pennant* when they use the international code, so other ships will know that they are not using a secret code.

Sailors use certain flags from the international code for warnings or announcements. A ship in harbor that is about to sail hoists the flag for the letter *P,* a flag once known as the *blue peter.* A ship flies the *D* if it is having difficulty steering, and the *O* if it has lost someone over-

board. Flying the flags for the letters *I* and *T* together warns that a ship is on fire; and the signal *MAA* requests urgent medical advice.

Flags of the United States and Canada

The *Stars and Stripes* is the most popular name for the red, white, and blue national flag of the United States. No one knows where this name came from, but we do know the origin of several other names. Francis Scott Key first called the United States flag the *Star-Spangled Banner* in 1814, when he wrote the poem that became the national anthem. William Driver, a sea captain from Salem, Massachusetts, gave the name *Old Glory* to the U.S. flag in 1824.

The Stars and Stripes stands for the land, the people, the government, and the ideals of the United States, no matter when or where it is displayed. Some other flags also stand for the United States, or its government, in certain situations. The *Navy Jack,* a blue flag with white stars, stands for the United States whenever it flies from a United States Navy ship. The stars, stripes, and colors of the United States flag appear in many federal and state flags.

Canada's flag, with its maple leaf design, was adopted in 1964—more than 30 years after the country became independent. Before that, Canada had used the British flag and versions of the British Red Ensign. Today, Canada continues to fly the British flag—known in Canada as the Royal Union—as a symbol of its membership in the Commonwealth.

The design of the British flag appears on the flags of several Canadian provinces. The French-speaking province of Quebec has four *fleurs-de-lis,* symbols of France, on its flag.

Canada's coat of arms appears on the personal standard used by Queen Elizabeth II of the United Kingdom, who is also queen of Canada, when she visits Canada. Other Canadian government flags include the flag of the governor general and the Canadian Armed Forces flag.

First United States flags. At the beginning of the American Revolution (1775-1783), the colonists fought under many flags. The first flag to represent all the colo-

The Stars and Stripes first flew...

...**on a U.S. Navy ship** on Nov. 1, 1777, when John Paul Jones left Portsmouth, New Hampshire, in the *Ranger.*

...**in a foreign port** on Dec. 2, 1777, when Jones sailed into Nantes, France, on the *Ranger.*

...**over foreign land** on Jan. 28, 1778, when John Rathbone of the sloop *Providence* captured Fort Nassau in the Bahamas.

...**in the Pacific Ocean** in 1784 when John Green and the *Empress of China* sailed to Macau, near Hong Kong.

...**around the world** from Sept. 30, 1787, to Aug. 10, 1790, on the ship *Columbia* of Boston.

...**in a naval battle in the Pacific** on March 25, 1813, when the frigate *Essex,* commanded by David Porter, captured the Peruvian cruiser *Nereyda.*

...**in Antarctica** in 1840 on the pilot boat *Flying Fish* of the Charles Wilkes expedition.

...**in a Flag Day celebration** in 1861 throughout Connecticut. An editorial in *The Hartford Courant* suggested the statewide observance.

...**on the moon** on July 20, 1969, after U.S. astronauts Neil A. Armstrong and Buzz Aldrin landed there in their Apollo 11 spacecraft.

Flags in United States history

The Viking flag of Leif Eriksson was the first flag in North America, in the 1000's.

The Spanish flag carried by Columbus in 1492, *left,* combined the arms of Castile and Leon. Columbus's own flag, *right,* bore the initials F and Y for Ferdinand and Isabella (Ysabel).

This French flag was one of many flown in North America between 1604 and 1763.

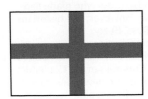

Flags in the British colonies. Britain's North American colonies began with Jamestown in 1607. At the left is a flag of England. The British flag, *right,* was adopted in 1606.

Dutch-East India Company flag of Henry Hudson flew in the New York area in 1609.

Russian-American Company flag flew at Russian settlements in Alaska in 1806.

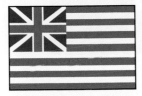

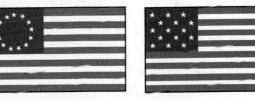

The Continental Colors served as America's first national flag from 1775 to 1777.

The flag of 1777 had no official arrangement for the stars. The most popular design had alternating rows of 3, 2, 3, 2, and 3 stars. Another flag with 13 stars in a circle was rarely used.

The flag of 1795 had 15 stripes, as well as 15 stars, to stand for the 15 states.

The flag of 1818 went back to 13 stripes and had 20 stars for the 20 states. One design had four rows of five stars each. The Great Star Flag, *right,* formed the 20 stars in a large star.

The flag of 1861, used in the Civil War, had stars for 34 states, including the South.

The 48-star flag served as the national flag of the United States from 1912 to 1959.

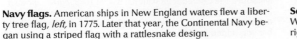

Navy flags. American ships in New England waters flew a liberty tree flag, *left,* in 1775. Later that year, the Continental Navy began using a striped flag with a rattlesnake design.

Southern flags include those flown during the Revolutionary War period. The flag at left was flown by a Virginia regiment. At right is a flag flown by defenders of Charleston, S.C., in 1776.

Today's 50-star United States flag has the following dimensions: hoist (width) of flag, 1.0 unit; fly (length) of flag, 1.9; hoist of union, .5385 (⅓); fly of union, .76; width of each stripe, .0769 (⅓); and diameter of each star, .0616.

nies was the *Continental Colors,* also called the *Cambridge,* or *Grand Union, Flag.* This flag, on which the British flag appeared at the upper left, served as the unofficial American flag from 1775 to 1777. It was also the first American flag to be saluted by another country.

After the Declaration of Independence on July 4, 1776, the British flag was no longer appropriate as part of the U.S. flag. On June 14, 1777, the Continental Congress resolved that "the Flag of the united states be 13 stripes alternate red and white," and that "the Union be 13 stars white in a blue field representing a new constellation." This American flag received its first salute from another country on Feb. 14, 1778, when French vessels in Quiberon Bay, France, saluted American naval officer John Paul Jones and his ship *Ranger.*

No one knows for sure who designed this flag, or who made the first one. Francis Hopkinson, a delegate to the Continental Congress, claimed that he had designed it. Most scholars accept this claim.

In 1870, William J. Canby claimed that his grandmother, Betsy Ross, had made the first United States flag. Betsy Ross was a Philadelphia seamstress who made flags during the Revolutionary War. However, few historians support Canby's claim. See **Ross, Betsy.**

The colors. The Continental Congress left no record to show why it chose red, white, and blue as the colors for the flag. But, in 1782, the Congress of the Confederation chose these same colors for the newly designed Great Seal of the United States. The resolution on the seal listed meanings for the colors. *Red* is for hardiness

(Text continues on page 214.)

 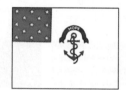 

New England flags. Shown from left to right, the Taunton Flag was raised at Taunton, Massachusetts, in 1774. The Bedford Flag, flown in 1775, bears the Latin words *vince aut morire,* meaning *conquer or die.* The Rhode Island Flag was carried in battle until 1781. A flag representing New England flew from 1686 to 1707. It was the first regional American flag.

Perry's flag in 1813 bore the last words of James Lawrence, a hero of the War of 1812.

Texas flags. A Texas flag that flew when Texas was part of Mexico, *left,* bore the date of Mexico's Constitution. The Texas Navy Flag, *right,* had a lone star.

The Bear Flag flew over an independent California republic for one month in 1846.

Confederate flags. The Stars and Bars, *above left,* adopted in 1861, had stars for 7 seceding states. It looked too much like the U.S. flag, so troops carried a battle flag, *above right.* It had stars for 11 states and for secession governments in Kentucky and

Missouri. The Confederate national flag of 1863, *above left,* also had stars for 11 states and for the secession governments in Kentucky and Missouri. The flag resembled a flag of truce, so a red bar was added in 1865, *above right.*

Flags of the United States government

President

Vice president

Secretary of state

Secretary of the treasury

Secretary of defense

Attorney general

Secretary of the interior

Secretary of agriculture

Secretary of commerce

Secretary of labor*

Secretary of health and human services

Secretary of housing and urban development

Secretary of transportation

Secretary of energy*

Secretary of education*

Flags of the armed forces

U.S. Air Force

U.S. Navy

Secretary of veterans affairs

Secretary of homeland security*

U.S. Army

U.S. Coast Guard

U.S. Marine Corps

*Secretary does not have a personal flag; flies the flag of the department.

Flags of the U.S. states, territories, and District of Columbia

Alabama 2:3*

Alaska 125:177

Arizona 2:3

Arkansas 2:3*

California 2:3

Colorado 2:3†

Connecticut 26:33

Delaware 2:3*

Florida 2:3*

Georgia 2:3*

Hawaii 1:2

Idaho 26:33

Illinois 3:5††

Indiana 3:5§

Iowa 2:3*

Kansas 3:5

Kentucky 10:19

Louisiana 2:3

Maine 26:33

Maryland 2:3*

Massachusetts 3:5

Michigan 2:3*

Minnesota 3:5*

Mississippi 2:3

Missouri 7:12

Montana 5:8§

Nebraska 3:5*

Nevada 2:3*

* State uses any of the standard commercial ratios of 2:3, 3:5, or 5:8.
† State also uses ratios of 3:5 and 10:19.

Louisiana flag image provided by Louisiana Secretary of State.

†† State also uses ratios of 2:3, 5:8, and 10:19.
§ State also uses a ratio of 2:3.

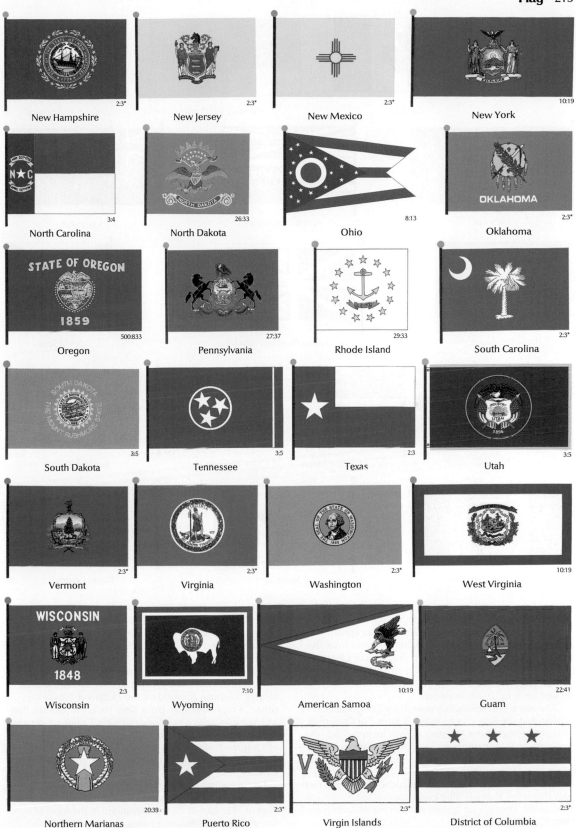

New Hampshire 2:3*

New Jersey 2:3*

New Mexico 2:3*

New York 10:19

North Carolina 3:4

North Dakota 26:33

Ohio 8:13

Oklahoma 2:3*

Oregon 500:833

Pennsylvania 27:37

Rhode Island 29:33

South Carolina 2:3*

South Dakota 3:5

Tennessee 3:5

Texas 2:3

Utah 3:5

Vermont 2:3*

Virginia 2:3*

Washington 2:3*

West Virginia 10:19

Wisconsin 2:3

Wyoming 7:10

American Samoa 10:19

Guam 22:41

Northern Marianas 20:39

Puerto Rico 2:3*

Virgin Islands 2:3*

District of Columbia 2:3*

* State or territory uses any of the standard commercial ratios of 2:3, 3:5, or 5:8.

Flags of Canada

Government, provinces, and territories

Canada 1:2

Queen's standard 8:13

Governor general 3:5

Alberta 1:2

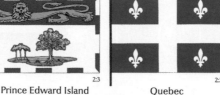

British Columbia 3:5

Manitoba 1:2

New Brunswick 5:8

Newfoundland and Labrador 1:2

Nova Scotia 3:4

Ontario 1:2

Prince Edward Island 2:3

Quebec 2:3

Saskatchewan 1:2

Northwest Territories 1:2

Nunavut 26:47

Yukon Territory 1:2

and courage, *white* for purity and innocence, and *blue* for vigilance, perseverance, and justice.

The stripes in the flag stand for the 13 original colonies. The stripes were probably adopted from the flag of the colonial patriot group the Sons of Liberty, which had five red and four white stripes. The British Union Jack was added to show that the colonists did not at first seek full independence.

The stars. The resolution passed by Congress in 1777 stated that the flag should have 13 stars. But Congress did not indicate how the stars should be arranged. The most popular arrangement showed the stars in alternating rows of 3, 2, 3, 2, and 3 stars. Another version had 12 stars in a circle with the 13th star in the center. A flag with 13 stars in a circle is often associated with the period. However, there is little evidence that such a design was used. There is no historical basis for assigning each star to a particular state.

Changes in the United States flag. By 1794, two new states had joined the Union. Congress decided to add two stars and two stripes to the flag. It ordered a 15-stripe flag used after May 1, 1795. The stars appeared in five rows, three in a row.

Five more states had come into the Union by 1817. Congress did not want the flag to have 20 stars and 20 stripes, because it would be too cluttered. Peter Wendover, a representative from New York, proposed a flag of 13 stripes, with a star for each state. Congress accepted the idea. On April 4, 1818, it set the number of stripes at 13 again. It also ordered that a new star be added to the flag on the July 4th after each new state joined the Union.

Congress still did not say how the stars should be arranged, so flags used various designs. The *Great Star Flag* of 1818 had its 20 stars arranged in the form of a five-pointed star. In some cases, the Army and Navy

Flags in Canadian history

The Royal Banner of England was carried by the explorer John Cabot when he arrived at the eastern coast of what is now Canada in 1497. Cabot claimed the land he found for King Henry VII, but he did not establish a permanent settlement there.

This British Union Flag, adopted by Britain (now also called the United Kingdom) in 1606, began flying in Canada in the 1600's. It shows two British symbols—the red cross of St. George, symbolizing England, and the white cross of St. Andrew, representing Scotland.

This French flag was used in New France—the French empire in North America—between 1604 and 1763. It is based on the French Royal Banner first used in the late 1300's. White was the French royal color beginning about 1600.

This Canadian Red Ensign came into use in 1957. It featured a form of the British Union Flag adopted in 1801 and the Canadian coat of arms, first used in 1921. But the British Union Flag remained the chief flag flown in Canada.

worked out the new designs for the stars when a new state entered the Union. But in some cases, no official action was ever taken. During the American Civil War (1861-1865), President Abraham Lincoln refused to have the stars for Southern States taken from the flag. Union troops fought under a 33-star flag the first three months of the war, a 34-star flag until 1863, and a 35-star flag until the war's end. No design was officially set for the 46-star flag used from 1908 to 1912. Presidential orders fixed the positions of the stars in 1912 (for 48 stars) and in 1959 (for 49 and, later in the year, for 50). The 50th star officially became part of the flag on July 4, 1960.

History of the Canadian flag. In 1867, the United Kingdom passed an act uniting four of its Canadian colonies as the Dominion of Canada. The British Union Flag thus became the official flag of Canada. But many Canadians wanted a flag that represented their own country. Some Canadians began to use the British Red Ensign with a symbol of Canada in the fly. The first such flag displayed the Canadian coat of arms, which then consisted of the coats of arms of the four original provinces. After additional provinces joined the Dominion, a popular version of the Red Ensign included the arms of all the

provinces. Such symbols of Canada as the beaver and the maple leaf also appeared on some of these flags.

At first, the United Kingdom officially permitted Canadian versions of the Red Ensign to be flown only at sea. Nevertheless, Canadians flew these flags on land as well. However, in the early 1900's, British opposition to the use of the Red Ensign in Canada grew. In 1924, a government decision allowed the Canadian Red Ensign to be flown on Canadian government buildings outside Canada. This flag displayed Canada's official coat of arms, which had been granted in 1921. But the British flag remained the chief flag flown within Canada.

Canada gained independence from the United Kingdom in 1931. But the British monarch remained Canada's head of state, and the British flag continued to be Canada's official flag. In the 1940's, Canadians began flying the Red Ensign with Canada's coat of arms within Canada, but they did not adopt it as their national flag. For the next 20 years, Canadians continued to argue about the flag. Some Canadians wished to retain the British flag. Others wanted to use the Canadian Red Ensign. Still others wanted to create a new, distinctively Canadian, flag.

In 1964, the Canadian Parliament finally decided to

Flags of world organizations

United Nations

North Atlantic Treaty Organization (NATO)

African Union (AU)

European Union and Council of Europe

Arab League

Organization of American States

International Olympic Committee

Red Cross   Red Crescent   Red Crystal

Flags of relief organizations. The International Red Cross and Red Crescent Movement has three flags: the Red Cross, the Red Crescent, and the Red Crystal.

Historical flags of the world

The earliest flags, or *standards,* consisted of symbols attached to poles. Egyptian soldiers of the 3000's B.C. carried standards like the one at the left (a falcon perched on a pole). The first cloth flags were probably from China. By 1500 B.C., the Chinese military used such flags as the red-and-white banner shown below.

Roman flags included the *vexillum, left,* a cavalry battle standard. At right is the *labarum* (imperial standard) of Constantine the Great, who adopted Christianity in the A.D. 300's. The letters *XP* on the staff mean *Christ.*

Religious flags. A Shī'ite Muslim flag, *left,* shows the sword of Alī ibn Abī Tālib, the first leader of the Shī'ah division of Islam. The crusader's flag, *right,* was used in the 1100's by Christians seeking to conquer the Holy Land.

English and French flags. King Richard I of England adopted the three lions, *left,* in 1198. This French Royal Banner, *right,* was used from the late 1300's to the 1600's.

Traders' flags. Ships from Venice flew the symbol of Saint Mark, the city's patron, beginning in the 1300's, *left.* The flag of the Hanseatic League, *right,* dates to about the same time.

Holy Roman Empire flag flew in what is now Germany from the 1200's until 1806.

Crosses in the British flag. The British Union Flag, *far left,* combines symbols of England, Scotland, and Ireland. The cross of St. George, *above left,* was a national symbol of England as early as the 1200's. The cross of St. Andrew, *above right,* had long been a symbol of Scotland, and the cross of St. Patrick, *far right,* of Ireland. The United Kingdom first flew this Union Flag in 1801.

Latin American flags. Simón Bolívar flew this flag, *left,* in Venezuela and Colombia in 1819. The Army of the Andes raised José de San Martín's flag, *center,* in Argentina in 1817. The flag of the United Provinces of Central America, *right,* flew from 1823 to 1839.

Flags of four empires disappeared in the early 1900's. The flag of the Chinese Empire, *far left,* came down when the empire collapsed in 1912. That of the Russian Empire, *above left,* fell during the Russian Revolution of 1917. The imperial flags of Austria-Hungary, *above right,* and Germany, *far right,* were replaced by flags of republics at the end of World War I in 1918.

Spain's Republican Flag flew from 1931 to the end of the Spanish Civil War in 1939.

Flags of three dictatorships. Germany used the Nazi swastika, *left,* from 1933 to 1945. Japan's navy flew the rising sun, *center,* during World War II (1939-1945). It readopted the flag in 1952. The flag of the Soviet Union, *right,* flew from 1923 until the country was dissolved in 1991.

Ethnic flags

Ethnic flags represent a cultural group. Some ethnic flags stand for a group no matter where its members may live. The Romani flag represents Roma throughout the world, but the Franco-Ontarian flag stands for only the French-speaking people who live in Canada's province of Ontario.

WORLD BOOK illustration

The Romani flag features a red *chakra* (wheel) at the center. The symbol, which is similar to the emblem on the flag of India, celebrates the Indian ancestry of the Roma. The blue of the flag's field symbolizes the sky, and the green, the land.

Office of Francophone Affairs, Ontario, Canada (WORLD BOOK illustration)

The Franco-Ontarian flag of Ontario's French-speaking people shows a white fleur-de-lis on the green segment of the flag's field. The green emblem on the white segment of the field is a trillium, Ontario's provincial flower.

create an official national flag. Toward the end of that year, after several months of debate, it adopted the flag in use today. A historian named George F. G. Stanley designed the flag, in which a red maple leaf appeared on a white square between two red bands. The maple leaf had been a symbol of Canada since the early 1800's. Red and white had been Canada's official colors since the creation of the country's coat of arms in 1921. On Jan. 28, 1965, the queen officially proclaimed the Maple Leaf Flag to be Canada's national flag. The flag was raised for the first time on Feb. 15, 1965.

Honoring a national flag

Some countries have *flag codes,* or sets of rules for displaying and honoring national flags. The UN also has a flag code. Most countries do not have such codes. They simply expect their citizens to treat their flags with respect. Congress first passed a U.S. flag code in 1942 and has amended it a number of times. The president may proclaim changes in the flag code. The following sections give basic rules for honoring *any* national flag.

Displaying the flag. Most countries agree that one national flag may not be flown above another. However, the United Nations flag flies above all other flags at UN Headquarters in New York City. In addition, some nations permit a church pennant to be flown above the national flag while naval chaplains conduct services at sea.

Flag customs vary from one country to another. For example, the U.S. flag flies over the White House whether or not the president is in Washington, D.C. But the personal flag of the queen of the United Kingdom flies only from the building she is in at the time. The United States flag flies over the Capitol every day. The U.S. flag also flies over the House of Representatives wing of the Capitol when the House is in session and over the Senate wing when the Senate is in session. The British flag flies over the Houses of Parliament in London only when Parliament is meeting, or on holidays and special days. The same rule applies to the Canadian flag.

In the United States, the national flag should be displayed every day except when weather conditions are severe enough to damage the flag. The flag is customarily displayed from sunrise to sunset, but it is not illegal to fly the flag 24 hours a day. When flown at night, it should be spotlighted.

The United States flag should be flown at polling places on election days. Legal public holidays and other special days for flying the United States flag include the following:

New Year's Day, January 1
Presidential Inauguration Day, January 20 (every fourth year)
Presidents' Day, the third Monday in February
Easter Sunday, no fixed date
Mother's Day, the second Sunday in May
Armed Forces Day, the third Saturday in May
Memorial Day, the last Monday in May
Flag Day, June 14
Independence Day, July 4
Labor Day, the first Monday in September
Constitution Day and Citizenship Day, September 17
Columbus Day, the second Monday in October
Veterans Day, November 11
Thanksgiving Day, the fourth Thursday in November
Christmas Day, December 25

In Canada, the national flag may fly from government buildings from sunrise to sunset. It also flies on holidays and special days, including the following:

New Year's Day, January 1
Good Friday, no fixed date
Easter Monday, no fixed date
Victoria Day and *the Queen's Birthday,* the Monday before May 25
Canada Day, July 1
Labour Day, the first Monday in September
Thanksgiving Day, the second Monday in October
Remembrance Day, November 11
Christmas Day, December 25

Hanging the flag outdoors. When the flags of several countries are displayed, they should be flown from separate staffs of equal size. The flags should also be about the same size. Almost every country requires that its own flag be given the position of honor among the flags. In most countries, this position is to the left of observers as they face the main entrance to a building. The national flag may also be placed in the center of the group of flags, or at each end of a line of flags. At headquarters of international organizations, such as the UN, flags are flown in the alphabetical order of their country names in English.

From a building, a national flag should be hoisted, top first, either on a staff or on a rope suspended over the sidewalk.

Over a street, a national flag should be suspended vertically with its top to the north on an east-west street, or to the east on a north-south street.

Hanging the flag indoors. A national flag should have a prominent place on a speaker's platform, but it should not be used to decorate the platform. Instead, bunting in the national colors should be used for decoration. In the United States, the red, white, and blue bunting should be arranged with the blue at the top. In the United States, the national flag must hang free, either flat against a wall or from a staff. In Canada, the national flag may be gathered up like bunting in a display.

When a national flag is displayed flat on a wall on a speaker's platform, it should be above and behind the speaker. When hung from a staff, the flag should be at the speaker's right. Any other flag should be to the right of the national flag from the standpoint of the observer. If a national flag is displayed with another flag from crossed staffs against a wall, it should be on the observer's left. When a number of flags are grouped on staffs, the national flag should be in the center and at the highest point of the group.

Raising and lowering the flag. A national flag should be *hoisted* (run up) briskly. It is lowered slowly, and should be gathered and folded before it touches the ground. When displayed with other flags from several staffs, the national flag should be raised first and lowered last.

Breaking the flag means unfurling it dramatically at the top of the staff. The flag is folded or rolled loosely. Before it is hoisted, the *halyard* (hoisting rope) is tied loosely around it. When the halyard is pulled sharply, the flag unfolds.

Striking the flag means lowering it at sea, or taking it down in battle as a sign of surrender.

Dipping the flag means lowering it slightly, then immediately raising it again as a salute. In Canada and Great Britain, certain flags may be *trailed* (lowered until the peaks of their staffs touch the ground) as a salute to the queen. The U.S. flag should not be dipped to any person or thing, and it should never be trailed. But when a ship from a country recognized by the United States dips its flag to a U.S. Navy ship, the naval vessel returns the salute. Most other navies follow this rule.

Flying upside down, a national flag is traditionally a signal of distress. However, it is often displayed upside down as a political protest.

Flying at half-mast, usually halfway up the staff, a national flag is a signal of mourning. The flag should be hoisted to the top of the staff for an instant before being lowered to half-mast. It should be hoisted to the peak again before being lowered for the day or night. By tradition, the national flag flies at half-mast only when the entire country mourns. If local flags are flown at half-mast for occasions of local mourning, the national flag may be flown at full mast with them. Citizens may salute and pledge allegiance to the flag when it flies at half-mast.

In the United States, the U.S. flag flies at half-mast (1) for 30 days after the death of the President or a former President; (2) for 10 days after the death of the Vice President, the chief justice of the United States or a retired chief justice, or the Speaker of the House of Representatives; and (3) from the day of death until burial of an associate justice, a Cabinet member, or the governor of a state, territory, or possession. The flag also flies at half-mast in Washington, D.C., on the day of death and the following day for a U.S. senator or representative, a territorial delegate, or the resident commissioner of Puerto Rico. The U.S. flag flies at half-mast in a state from the day the governor or one of the state's U.S. senators dies until burial. The same practice is followed in (1) a congressional district for a representative, (2) a territory for a territorial governor or delegate, and (3) Puerto Rico for the governor or resident commissioner.

In Canada, the national flag flies at half-mast only on occasions of national mourning, such as the death of the sovereign. However, the flag on the Parliament buildings in Ottawa is lowered to half-mast on certain occasions. These occasions include the day of the funeral of a member of the Senate, the House of Commons, or the Privy Council.

Carrying the flag. A national flag should always be held aloft and free, never flat or horizontal. The person who carries the flag is called the *colorbearer.*

A color guard, in military and patriotic organizations, usually includes the colorbearer, two escorts, and a bearer of an organizational flag or other flag. The colorbearer with the national flag must be on the marching right of the other colorbearer. The escorts march on each side of the bearers. Nonmilitary color guards often include only one colorbearer and two escorts.

When a national flag is carried into a meeting hall, everyone in the hall should stand facing the platform. The colorbearer marches to the front and faces the audience, followed by the escorts. They stand on each side as the colorbearer puts the flag into its stand.

In a parade, when a national flag is carried with other flags, it should be on the marching right. If there is a line of other flags, the colorbearer with the national flag marches alone in front of the center of the line.

On a float, a national flag should be hung from a staff with its folds falling free, or it should be hung flat.

On an automobile, a national flag should hang free and not drape over the car. It may also be tied to the antenna or to a staff fixed firmly to the chassis or to the right fender.

Saluting the flag. When a national flag is raised or lowered as part of a ceremony, or when it passes by in a parade or in review, everyone present should face it and stand at attention. A man or woman in a military uniform should give a hand salute. Men and women not in uniform salute by placing the right hand over the heart. A man wearing a hat should remove his hat with his right hand and hold it at his left shoulder, with his palm facing his heart. The flag should be saluted at the moment it passes by in a parade or in review. Citizens of other

Displaying a nation's flag

The flag should be honored as a symbol of the nation it represents. These pictures illustrate points to remember in displaying the flag.

WORLD BOOK illustrations by Paul D. Turnbaugh

Salute the flag at the moment it passes in a parade. Put your hand over your heart or give the military salute. Never use the flag for patriotic decorations. Use bunting instead.

When marching, always carry the flag to the right of any other flag in a procession.

When marching in front, be sure to carry the flag alone in front of the center of the line if there are many other flags.

As a color guard, keep in a straight line, with your escorts on the outside and the flag always to the right of your organizational banner.

As a colorbearer, hold the staff at a slight angle from your body. Or carry it with one hand, resting the staff on your right shoulder.

On an automobile, tie the flag to the antenna or clamp the flagstaff to the right fender. Do not drape the flag over the vehicle.

From a building, hang the flag on a staff or on a rope over the sidewalk, with its canton away from the building.

During periods of mourning, hoist the flag to the peak before you lower it to half-mast as a symbol of mourning. Raise it to the peak again before lowering it at the end of the day.

In a window, hang the flag vertically with its canton to the left of a person who is seeing it from outside the building.

Over the street, hang the flag with its canton to the east on a north-south street or to the north on an east-west one.

On the same flagpole, hang the flag above other flags or pennants. Never hang one national flag above another in a time of peace.

Upside down. Never hang the flag upside down except as a signal of some serious emergency. It is a recognized distress signal.

With other flags. Hang the flags of several nations on equal staffs. Hang the flag to the left facing the viewer, hoisting it first and lowering it last.

Behind a speaker, hang the flag flat against the wall. Do not gather or drape it on the platform. Use bunting for such decoration.

Beside a speaker, put the flag in the position of honor on the person's right. At a religious service, the flag should go to the right of the minister, priest, or rabbi.

In a corridor or lobby, hang the flag vertically opposite the main entrance with its canton to the left of a person coming in the door.

With grouped staffs, place the flag at the center and highest point. With crossed staffs, put the flag on the viewer's left, its staff on top.

On a casket, drape the flag with its canton at the head and over the left shoulder of the body. Do not lower the flag into the grave.

countries should stand at attention, but they need not salute.

United States citizens give the Pledge of Allegiance to the flag by holding the right hand over the heart. If civilians hear the pledge recited, they should stand at attention and men should remove their hats. People in uniform should salute. If the national anthem is played while the U.S. flag is displayed, everyone present should face the flag and salute. If it is not displayed, everyone should face toward the music and show respect in the same way as when hearing the Pledge of Allegiance.

Permitted and prohibited uses. Certain traditions have developed about the uses of national flags. This section describes some of them.

At funerals, a national flag may be used to cover the casket. An armed color guard may accompany the flag-draped casket of a person who served in the armed forces, but not into the church or chapel. The flag should be removed before the color guard fires a salute. The flag should not be lowered into the grave or allowed to touch the ground. It may be used again after the funeral.

At an unveiling of a statue or monument, a national flag should have a prominent place. But the U.S. flag should never be used as part of the covering for the monument. The Canadian flag may be used in the covering but must be lifted off the statue.

A national flag should never be used for receiving, carrying, holding, or delivering anything. It should never be used as bedding, drapery, or wearing apparel. But a flag patch may be attached to such uniforms as those of athletes, fire fighters, police officers, and members of patriotic organizations. A flag lapel pin should be worn on the left lapel near the heart. The national flag should not be printed on paper napkins, boxes, or other items that will be discarded. The U.S. flag should not be used

for advertising purposes. It should not be marked or have anything attached to it. Advertising signs should not be fastened to the staff or halyards.

Caring for the flag. A national flag should be folded carefully and put away when not in use. The U.S. flag may be given a special *military fold*. It should first be folded twice lengthwise to form a long strip. Then, starting at the stripe end, it should be given a series of triangular folds to form a compact triangle. If the flag is permanently attached to its staff, it should be *furled* (wrapped around the staff). It should then be *cased* (wrapped with a cover).

A national flag may be mended, dry-cleaned, or washed. An old flag, or one with an out-of-date design, may be displayed as long as it is in a respectable condition. When a flag is no longer fit for display, it should be destroyed in some dignified way, preferably by burning.

Manufacturing flags

Some governments issue specifications for the design, proportions, and colors of their official flags. However, flags are subject to variations as manufacturers standardize common colors and proportions to reduce their costs.

Almost all flags are made of cloth. Most flags that fly outdoors are made with synthetic fabrics. The most commonly used fabrics include nylon, polyester, and acrylics. All of these fabrics are light, strong, and color-fast. For many years, flag makers used *bunting* in flags. This woolen cloth came in long strips called *breadths,* which were 9 inches (23 centimeters) wide. Some inexpensive flags are made of cotton, and the cotton fabric is sometimes also called bunting. Special ceremonial flags are made of rayon, which looks richer than cotton or nylon.

Sewing is a common method of making flags. Strips

Manufacturing U.S. flags   Flag manufacturers in the United States use skilled workers and modern equipment to produce flags of high quality. New high-speed machinery has increased the efficiency and precision of flag making. Greater use of synthetic materials has resulted in stronger, more wear-resistant flags.

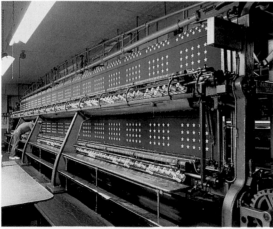

Annin & Co.

Sewing white stars onto blue fabric, a huge machine produces hundreds of star fields at the same time. The modern machine embroidery is of especially high quality and precision. In the past, workers had to sew each star in place.

Annin & Co.

Sewing the stripes in long panels, automatic sewing machines join strips of red and white cloth. A worker oversees the operation and makes necessary adjustments. These high-speed machines produce stripes for thousands of flags every day.

Annin & Co.

Annin & Co.

Assembly and packaging. After the stars and stripes have been prepared by machine, a worker sews the stripes in place on the star field. Finished flags are packaged along with a booklet outlining rules for displaying and honoring the flag.

of flag material are sewn together in the proper positions and sizes to create the flag. Elaborate designs, such as complicated seals, may be printed on cloth and then *appliquéd,* or sewn, onto the background fabric. They may also be embroidered on the flag by hand. Especially complicated flags, such as the United Kingdom's Royal Standard, may be painted or embroidered entirely by hand.

Many flags are printed, sometimes on paper or plastic materials, but usually on cloth. Flags and pennants are often printed on cloth by the silk-screen process. A separate silk-screen stencil is used for each color in the flag (see **Screen printing**).

In making a United States flag, workers use machines to cut stars from white cloth and then to embroider them to the blue field of the *canton* (upper corner). The huge machines produce hundreds of star fields at the same time. Other machines sew together long strips of red and white fabric to form the stripes. Many flag makers sew panels of six stripes for the area below the blue field and seven stripes for the area beside it, then cut the panels into the proper lengths. The blue field and panels of stripes of the flag are then sewn together. A strip of strong *heading* material is sewn along the *hoist,* the part of the flag closest to the staff, for strength. A machine punches holes at the top and bottom of the heading and inserts *grommets* (metal rings) in them for clipping the flag to the halyard.

In making small Canadian flags, workers use silk-screen printing. With the maple leaf and red stripes as a stencil, they paint the red areas on rolls of white cloth. Then they cut up the cloth into individual flags. For large flags, three pieces of cloth, two red and one white, are sewn together and the maple leaf is appliquéd on each side of the white material.

In most countries, private firms make all the flags, though some governments make their own. Millions of flags are made each year worldwide.   Whitney Smith

Related articles in *World Book* include:

Flag Day	Jones, John Paul	Semaphore
Flag officer	Key, Francis Scott	Star-Spangled
Heraldry	Pledge of	Banner
Hopkinson,	Allegiance	Union Jack
Francis	Ross, Betsy	United States flag

Outline

I. **Kinds of flags**
  A. Civil and state flags
  B. Flags of individuals
  C. Military flags
  D. Flags of the sea
  E. Flags that talk
II. **Flags of the world**
III. **Flags of the United States and Canada**
  A. First United States flags
  B. Changes in the United States flag
  C. History of the Canadian flag
IV. **Honoring a national flag**
  A. Displaying the flag
  B. Hanging the flag outdoors
  C. Hanging the flag indoors
  D. Raising and lowering the flag
  E. Carrying the flag
  F. Saluting the flag
  G. Permitted and prohibited uses
  H. Caring for the flag
V. **Manufacturing flags**

Flag Day is celebrated on June 14 in memory of the day in 1777 when the Continental Congress adopted the Stars and Stripes as the official flag of the United States. It is not an official national holiday, but the president proclaims a public Flag Day observance every year. In Pennsylvania, Flag Day is a legal holiday.

On Flag Day, people display the flag on their homes, businesses, and public buildings. Some schools honor the flag with special programs that may feature discussions of the flag's origin and meaning. Many patriotic organizations hold parades and other observances.

Flag Day was first widely observed in 1877 to celebrate the 100th anniversary of the selection of the flag. Some people suggested that Flag Day be observed each year. Early leaders of campaigns to establish Flag Day as an annual national celebration included William T. Kerr of Pittsburgh and Bernard J. Cigrand of Waubeka, Wisconsin. In 1897, the governor of New York proclaimed a Flag Day celebration for the first time as an annual event in that state. President Woodrow Wilson established Flag Day as an annual national celebration in his proclamation issued on May 30, 1916. In 1949, President Harry S. Truman officially recognized June 14 as Flag Day by signing the National Flag Day Bill.   Jack Santino

See also **Flag** (First United States flags).

Flag officer is the rank of the five highest officer grades in the United States Navy. These are fleet admiral, admiral, vice admiral, rear admiral (upper half), and rear admiral (lower half). A flag officer usually commands a fleet or squadron. A flag officer's ship flies a flag that indicates the officer's rank. See also **Admiral; Rank, Military.**　　Whitney Smith

Flagellate. See Protozoan (Kinds).

Flagellum, plural *flagella,* is a tiny, whiplike structure certain cells use to move. A cell can propel itself through liquid by moving its flagella.

A cell may have several flagella, only one flagellum, or none. The arrangement of flagella on the surface of the cell also varies. For example, some bacteria have several flagella in the same spot. Others have flagella on opposite ends of the cell. Still others have flagella spread around the cell surface.

Flagella are found among many *prokaryotes*—a group of organisms made up of archaea and bacteria. Flagella also are found in certain cells of *eukaryotes*—a group of organisms that includes animals, plants, and single-celled *protozoans.* For example, sperm move using flagella. However, while the flagella appear similar, they differ in structure. The flagella of eukaryotes are made of structures called *microtubules.* The flagella of prokaryotes lack microtubules. Eukaryotic flagella move by a flicking motion, but prokaryotic flagella rotate. The flagella of archaea and bacteria also differ. For instance, the flagella of both groups are powered by a molecular "motor" within the cell. But the motors in archaeal flagella work differently than those in bacterial flagella.

Scientists have shown that flagella *evolved* (developed over many generations) independently in archaea, bacteria, and eukaryotes. Research suggests they evolved in a series of steps from simpler structures.　　Mark J. Pallen

See also **Bacteria** (How bacteria move); **Protozoan** (Flagellates).

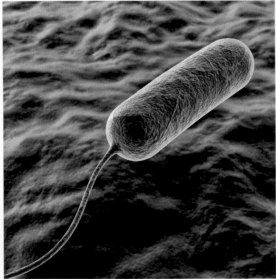

© BioMedical/Shutterstock

The flagellum is a whiplike structure that a cell uses to move. The flagellum of this bacterium spins somewhat like a propeller to move the cell through liquid.

The Metropolitan Museum of Art, New York City, Crosby Brown Collection

The flageolet is played by blowing through one end and opening and closing finger and thumb holes.

Flageolet, *FLAJ uh LEHT,* is a small woodwind instrument that belongs to the flute family. It consists of an ivory, wooden, or metal tube with a mouthpiece at one end. The tube has four finger holes on top and two thumb holes underneath. A player holds the flageolet vertically and blows through the mouthpiece. The flageolet has a high sound similar to that of the piccolo, but softer. The flageolet gained its greatest popularity in the 1600's.　　André P. Larson

Flagler, Henry Morrison (1830-1913), was an American businessman. He became a partner of the industrialist John D. Rockefeller and helped him organize the Standard Oil Company in 1870. Flagler remained a top executive at Standard Oil until 1911. But after the early 1880's, his main business activity was in Florida. In 1886, he helped organize what became the Florida East Coast Railroad. He later extended the railroad so that by 1912, it stretched from Jacksonville to Key West. Flagler built luxurious resort hotels in St. Augustine, Palm Beach, Miami, and other cities.

Flagler was born on Jan. 2, 1830, in Hopewell, near Canandaigua, New York. He died on May 20, 1913.

Roger M. Olien

Flagstad, *FLAG stad* or *FLAHG stah,* **Kirsten,** *KUR stuhn* or *KIHSH tuhn* (1895-1962), a Norwegian operatic soprano, became famous as an interpreter of the heroines in the German composer Richard Wagner's operas. Previously unknown to American audiences, she debuted in 1935 as Sieglinde in *Die Walküre* at the Metropolitan Opera House in New York City. Her debut was a storybook triumph. Flagstad achieved her greatest fame in the heavier Wagner roles, such as Brünnhilde and Isolde. She overwhelmed audiences with the power and ease of her singing. Flagstad retired from the operatic stage in 1954, but she continued to sing in concerts and to record opera and songs. She directed the new Norwegian State Opera from 1958 to 1960.

Flagstad was born on July 12, 1895, in Oslo. She made her operatic debut there when she was 18 years old. Flagstad died on Dec. 7, 1962.　　Martin Bernheimer

Flagstaff (pop. 65,870; met. area pop. 134,421) is a retail and transportation center near the San Francisco Mountains in Arizona (see **Arizona** [political map]). It is a gateway city to the Grand Canyon. Flagstaff is the home of Northern Arizona University, the Museum of Northern Arizona, and Lowell Observatory, from which an as-

© Lowell Observatory

Flagstaff is the site of Lowell Observatory, from which astronomer Clyde W. Tombaugh discovered Pluto.

FourByFive

A flame thrower can hurl a tongue of flame 150 feet (46 meters). The operator carries two tanks of fuel and a tank of compressed air to provide the pressure needed to squirt the fuel through the gun. When ready to fire, the portable flame thrower weighs about 50 pounds (23 kilograms).

tronomer discovered Pluto. The city is the headquarters of a United States Geological Survey science center and the Office of Navajo and Hopi Indian Relocation. Walnut Canyon, Sunset Crater Volcano, and Wupatki national monuments are nearby. In 1876, the U.S. centennial, settlers made a flagstaff from a pine tree and flew the U.S. flag from it. The city's name is said to have come from this incident. Flagstaff has a council-manager government. It is the seat of Coconino County.   Randy Wilson

See also **Radar** (picture: Radar mapping).

Flaherty, *FLAH uhr tee,* **Robert Joseph** (1884-1951), was a pioneer American filmmaker. He is considered the father of documentary motion pictures. Flaherty became noted for his treatment of the lives of isolated peoples in the silent films *Nanook of the North* (1922) and *Moana* (1926) and in the sound film *Man of Aran* (1934). His short film *The Land* (1942) showed the effects of erosion. *Louisiana Story* (1948) portrayed the impact of the discovery of oil on a poor family in the bayous of Louisiana.

Flaherty was born on Feb. 16, 1884, in Iron Mountain, Michigan. He codirected the feature films *White Shadows of the South Seas* (1927) with W. S. Van Dyke, *Tabu* (1931) with F. W. Murnau, and *Elephant Boy* (1937) with Zoltan Korda. Flaherty's wife, Frances Hubbard Flaherty, worked on several of his documentaries. Robert Flaherty died on July 23, 1951.   Rachel Gallagher

Flame thrower is a device that shoots a stream of burning fuel, much as a fire hose shoots water. A flexible tube connects the flame gun to fuel tanks on the operator's back. A tank of compressed air between the fuel tanks provides the pressure to squirt the fuel through the gun. Portable flame throwers weigh a total of about 50 pounds (23 kilograms) when they are ready to fire.

The Germans introduced flame throwers during World War I (1914-1918). But the weapons were not widely used until World War II (1939-1945), when United States soldiers used them against the Japanese. Soldiers used flame throwers against fortifications that could not be captured with rifles alone. The weapons terrified enemy soldiers. Soldiers often panicked and fled at the

sight of long, searing tongues of flame coming toward them. American soldiers called the weapon the *GI hotfoot.*

During World War I, flame thrower fuel was a mixture of gasoline and oil. During World War II, a jellied gasoline called *napalm* was developed (see **Napalm**). By using napalm, soldiers could shoot portable flame throwers 150 feet (46 meters). Flame throwers that were mounted on tanks could reach targets 750 feet (230 meters) away. When the jellied fuel hit a target, it scattered into sticky blobs. These blobs bounced through small openings into fortifications. The napalm stuck to the target and was very difficult to extinguish.

Since the 1940's, flame throwers have served several functions in civilian life. Flame throwers can be used by farmers to burn away tough weeds and to destroy such harmful insects as tent caterpillars. They can also be used to break rocks and melt snow.   Frances M. Lussier

Flamenco, *fluh MEHNG koh,* is a type of dance and music originally associated with the Roma (sometimes called Gypsies) of southern Spain. Flamenco dance and music are now performed on the stage with guitars and castanets, but they are also performed at small gatherings of families and friends.

Performers of flamenco dance and music are expected to improvise and add passionate and spirited personal interpretations to create intense and energetic performances. Flamenco dancing, often in colorful costumes, may be performed by a single person, a couple, or a larger group. A performance includes skillful footwork, forceful but flowing arm movements, hand clapping, and finger snapping. Sometimes the dancers use castanets to complement the musicians' steady yet ornamented rhythms.

Flamenco music includes singing *(cante flamenco)*

Flamenco is a type of dance that originated in southern Spain. The professional flamenco dancers shown at the left are performing in a Spanish club. The colorful costumes, energetic performances, and accompaniment by guitars and hand clapping are typical of flamenco dancing.

and guitar playing *(toque flamenco)*. Sometimes the music is performed without dancing.   Patricia W. Rader

See also **Spain** (picture: Flamenco dancers).

Flamingo, *fluh MIHNG goh,* is any of several birds with long, stiltlike legs and a curved bill and neck. Flamingos live in many parts of the world and spend their entire life near lakes, marshes, and seas.

Most flamingos stand from 3 to 5 feet (91 to 150 centimeters) tall. The color of a flamingo's feathers—except for some black wing feathers—varies from bright red to pale pink. For example, flamingos of the Caribbean area have coral-red feathers, and South American flamingos have pinkish-white feathers. Most flamingos eat shellfish and small, plantlike water organisms called *algae.* They use hairlike "combs" along the edges of the bill to strain food from mud and sand. Flamingos, like ducks, have webbed feet.

Flamingos live in colonies, some of which have thousands of members. They mate once a year. Flamingos build a nest that consists of a mound of mud. Most of the females lay a single egg in a shallow hole at the top of the nest. The parents take turns sitting on the egg to keep it warm. The egg hatches after about 30 days.

Lesser flamingos, like other flamingo species, live in colonies. These flamingos live mostly in eastern and southern Africa.

Young flamingos leave the nest after about 5 days and form small groups. But the young flamingos return to the nest to feed on a fluid produced in the digestive system of the parents. The adults dribble this fluid from their mouth into the youngster's bill. After about two weeks, the young are herded into a group called a *crèche* and start to find their own food. Flamingos live from 20 to 30 years in their natural surroundings. They can survive even longer in captivity.

There are several *species* (kinds) of flamingos. The greater flamingo ranks as the most widespread species. It lives in various parts of Africa, southern Asia, and southern Europe. The American flamingo lives in the Caribbean, as well as in parts of Central and South America. The lesser flamingo makes its home mostly in eastern and southern Africa. Other flamingo species live in South America.   James J. Dinsmore

Scientific classification. The scientific name of the greater flamingo is *Phoenicopterus roseus.* The American flamingo is *P. ruber.* The Chilean flamingo is *P. chilensis.* The lesser flamingo is *Phoeniconaias minor.* The Andean flamingo is *Phoenicoparrus andinus.* The James's flamingo is *Phoenicoparrus jamesi.*

See also **Bird** (How birds feed [picture: A flamingo]).

Flamingos live in marshy areas in many parts of the world. These graceful birds feed on small organisms that they find in muddy water.

Flanagan, *FLAN uh guhn,* **Edward Joseph** (1886-1948), a Roman Catholic priest, founded Boys Town near Omaha, Nebraska, in 1917. He opened the community to boys of all races and religions. Flanagan's work there was featured in the popular motion picture *Boys Town* (1938). Numerous institutions similar to Boys Town were founded in the United States and Canada, but they did not all succeed.

Boys Town Hall of History

Father Flanagan

Flanagan was born on July 13, 1886, in Ballymoe, near Roscommon, Ireland. He came to the United States in 1904 and studied for the priesthood. Flanagan finished his education at the Gregorian University in Rome and at the University of Innsbruck in Austria. Then he became a parish priest in O'Neill, Nebraska.

Flanagan's first social service was with a Workingmen's Hostel in Omaha. But he became interested in the treatment of boys who were homeless or had broken the law. He died on May 15, 1948.   Alan Keith-Lucas

See also **Boys Town.**

Flanders is one of three official regions of Belgium (see **Belgium** [political map]). Flanders covers the northern part of the country, where the people speak Dutch. Belgium's other two regions are the French-speaking Wallonia region and the national capital district of Brussels. Flanders includes the provinces of Antwerp, East Flanders, Limburg, Vlaams-Brabant, and West Flanders. The people of Flanders are called Flemings.

Like Belgium's other regions, Flanders has its own prime minister and parliament. The region's government is based in Brussels. It has authority over most of the region's domestic matters—such as the economy, education, and health care—and some foreign affairs. The flag of Flanders pictures a black lion on a gold background.

The boundaries of Flanders have changed over time. During much of its history, the historical region of Flanders covered lands that are now northwestern Belgium, northern France, and a small part of the Netherlands. Starting in the 800's, a series of nobles, each known as the Count of Flanders, ruled the area. From the 1500's to

1830, control of the region shifted to rulers of various countries, including Spain, Austria, France, and the Netherlands. In 1830, Belgium won its independence. The Belgian parliament passed a series of constitutional reforms from 1970 to 2001 that established the current political region of Flanders.

The people of Flanders have made numerous contributions to art and culture. Famous Flemish painters of the 1400's through the 1600's include Jan Van Eyck, Hans Memling, Pieter Bruegel the Elder, Sir Anthony Van Dyck, and Peter Paul Rubens. James Ensor was an important Flemish painter of the late 1800's and early 1900's. Guido Gezelle was a great Flemish poet of the 1800's. In the mid-1800's, the author Hendrik Conscience played a leading role in developing the Flemish novel. The Catholic University of Louvain, founded in 1425, is one of the oldest universities in Europe.

Flanders has long been an important trading area for the nations of Europe. Antwerp, in northern Flanders, is Belgium's largest city and one of Europe's chief ports. The Flemish cities of Bruges, Ghent, and Ypres also developed into active trading centers. Flanders is one of the leading European regions for high-tech industrial development. Major products of Flanders include automobiles, chemicals, cut diamonds, metals, and textiles. The region's many farms grow potatoes, sugar beets, wheat, and other crops. Such livestock as cattle, chicken, and pigs are raised in Flanders.   Janet L. Polasky

See also **Flemings.**

Flanders Field is a United States military cemetery near Waregem, Belgium. Buried in this cemetery are the bodies of 368 members of the armed forces who died in World War I (1914-1918). Canadian poet John McCrae wrote the famous poem "In Flanders Fields" (see **McCrae, John**).

Flannel is a soft, warm fabric. It is made from wool and from blends that consist of wool and cotton or rayon. Manufacturers usually brush flannel to give it a *napped* (raised) surface. Most kinds of flannel are produced in the *twill weave*—that is, they have a pattern of raised, diagonal lines woven into them. Some flannels have a flat texture made by using a *plain weave.* Flannel is used chiefly in suits and coats. In the United Kingdom, a washcloth is referred to as a flannel.

A soft fabric called *flannelette* resembles flannel and is often confused with it. Flannelette is normally made entirely from cotton.   Keith Slater

Flare, Solar. See **Sun** (Particle radiation; Flares).

Flash flood is a sudden, often unexpected accumulation of water on normally dry land. Flash floods develop more rapidly than other floods and occur chiefly near small rivers or streams. Most flash floods result from storms that produce heavy rains over short periods. Occasionally, a flash flood may result from another event, such as a dam break, the sudden breakup of an ice jam along a river, or rapid snowmelt caused by a volcanic eruption. Flash floods can cause injury or death because they generally occur without warning, leaving little time for escape.

The majority of flash floods happen during warm months, when thunderstorms are most frequent. Flash floods occur commonly in mountainous and hilly areas. Typically, heavy rain from a thunderstorm falls on a mountain or hill and is channeled into narrow valleys

Flanders is a region in northern Belgium.

WORLD BOOK maps

and canyons below. The water collects in these areas, overflowing small rivers or streams or causing dry streambeds to flood.

A flash flood can catch people by surprise because the flooding may take place far from its cause. Deaths often result from drivers trying to maneuver vehicles through or out of flooded areas. As little as 2 feet (0.6 meter) of rapidly moving floodwater can carry away most automobiles. Flash floods can also trigger deadly landslides. Experts recommend that people move to high ground at the first sign of a flash flood and wait for floodwaters to recede.   Robert M. Rauber

See also **Flood** (River floods).

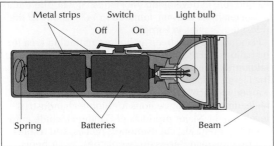

WORLD BOOK diagram by Arthur Grebetz

A flashlight shines as electric current is carried from the batteries to the light bulb through metal strips and a spring.

Flashlight is a portable electric light in a metal, fiber, or plastic case. A typical flashlight consists of a light source, power source, case, and on-off switch. The light source is a *lamp* (light bulb). A reflector and a lens help focus the light into a beam. Most flashlight lamps are incandescent, but small fluorescent lamps are sometimes used (see **Electric light**). Dry-cell batteries provide the power for most flashlights. The first dry-cell flashlight was made about 1898 in New York City. See also **Battery** (Types of batteries).   William Hand Allen

Flat-coated retriever is a breed of medium-sized dog often used for hunting, flushing, and retrieving game from land and water. It is black or brown and has a long, strong head and a thick, flat-lying, glossy coat of

© Thinkstock

The flat-coated retriever has a thick coat.

medium length. It weighs from 60 to 75 pounds (27 to 34 kilograms) and stands from 22 to 24 inches (56 to 61 centimeters) tall at the shoulder. The flat-coated retriever is intelligent, playful, and good-natured. It makes an active, affectionate house pet.

Critically reviewed by the Flat-coated Retriever Society of America

Flat tax is a term used to describe any proposal that would flatten tax rates and eliminate most tax exemptions. The term was first used to describe a proposal to reform and simplify the United States income tax. The original proposal was made by Stanford University economists Robert E. Hall and Alvin Rabushka in their book *The Flat Tax* (1985).

Hall and Rabushka's flat-tax plan would create a *basic exemption* (amount of income excluded from taxation) for each household. It would eliminate all deductions for personal expenditures, such as mortgage interest and charitable contributions. It would tax the *labor income* (wages, salaries, and pensions) of individuals and the *tax base* (difference between taxable receipts and deductible expenses) of businesses at a single ("flat") rate. This rate would be approximately 20 percent—about half the highest current rates.

Other changes would include revised rules regarding capital, interest, and dividends. Under the flat tax, businesses could deduct the entire expense of *capital investments* (purchases of physical assets, such as buildings or machinery) immediately. Currently, U.S. businesses may deduct only *depreciation* (loss in value) over the life of an asset. The immediate deduction of an asset's entire purchase price would be simpler, and flat-tax supporters say it would encourage saving, investment, and economic growth. Also under the flat tax, interest, dividends, and *capital gains* (profits from the sale of assets) would be exempt from taxation, and interest would not be a deductible business expense. Exemption of capital gains and other capital income, and the elimination of deductions, would greatly simplify the tax returns of many individuals.

Opponents of the flat tax argue that the plan would shift tax burdens dramatically from the wealthy to the middle class. They also point out that current tax exemptions serve useful purposes, such as encouraging home ownership and charitable contributions. In addition, such a fundamental change in tax policy would raise complex questions about how to treat current investments and debt.   Charles E. McLure, Jr.

See also **Income tax.**

Flatboat is a large, raftlike barge used to haul freight and passengers on such inland waterways as lakes, rivers, and canals. Historically, a flatboat had a flat bottom, vertical sides, and usually square ends. A *keelboat,* sometimes called a flatboat, was a long, narrow craft, sharp at one or both ends. It was built on a simple *keel* (central fin) and ribs. These boats carried goods and people during the westward movement in the United States. Pioneers put their furniture and livestock on flatboats. The boats were moved by the current and by long oars also used for steering. After reaching their destination, flatboats were often taken apart, and the hull planks and other timbers were reused for other purposes. A vast flatboat freight business grew on the Mississippi River and its tributaries in the 1800's.   Paul F. Johnston

Flatfish is the name of a large group of valuable food

fishes that include the halibut, flounder, and sole. Flat-fishes live in salt water worldwide. There are hundreds of *species* (kinds). Flatfishes have a body that appears to be flattened horizontally. The fish actually lies on its side, with both eyes on the same side of the head. When the flatfish is first hatched, it looks like any other kind of fish. But after it has grown from ½ to ¾ inch (13 to 19 millimeters) long, one eye begins to move closer to the eye on the opposite side of the head, and the mouth becomes twisted. The eyeless side of the fish stays under and loses its color. The upper side becomes darker. The fish then changes color to blend with its surroundings. See also **Flounder; Halibut; Sole; Turbot.**   Tomio Iwamoto

Flatfoot is an inherited condition in which the long arch of the foot appears to be flat or collapsed. The condition results from weak ligaments that are unable to support the arch. Many people think flat feet cause pain. However, this is not true because the height of the arch does not affect how the foot functions.   John F. Waller

Flatworm is a type of worm known for the flat body shape of many *species* (kinds)—especially larger ones. Some flatworms live freely on land or in water. Others live as parasites in human beings or other animals.

Flatworms have a simple body structure. A layer of cells called the *epidermis* covers the animal's body. In most flatworms, a mouth on the head, rear, or underside opens into a simple, sacklike intestine. A tightly packed mass of cells called *parenchyma* fills the body between the epidermis and intestine and contains the reproductive organs. Muscles, glands, and major nerves lie under the epidermis near the parenchyma.

Many flatworms have a smooth, soft body. Some flatworms have suckers or other projections on the body. Parasitic species use them to attach to their *host,* the organism on which they live. Some flatworms have spines and tiny, needlelike *spicules* that serve as a kind of skeleton. Most flatworms measure less than 1 inch (2.5 centimeters) long. But the largest flatworms, called *tapeworms,* may grow up to 100 feet (30 meters) long.

There are tens of thousands of species of flatworms.

The largest group of species, called Neodermata, includes monogeneans, trematodes, and tapeworms. These parasitic flatworms live in a wide variety of hosts, usually *vertebrates* (animals with backbones). The rest of the flatworms are turbellarians, mostly free-living species found in sand or mud or on underwater plants. A few species live on land in moist soil.

Almost all flatworms are *hermaphroditic*—that is, the same individual has both male and female reproductive organs. Most turbellarians lay eggs that hatch into young resembling tiny adults. In other turbellarians, and in all parasitic flatworms, the young—called *larvae*—look different from adults and live in different habitats. For example, the larva of a monogenean has hairlike *cilia* that enable it to swim. The larva swims until it finds an appropriate fish for a host. The larva attaches to the fish and develops into an adult. The adult, which lives on the skin and gills of the fish, lacks cilia and cannot swim.

Parasitic flatworms cause disease in their hosts. Schistosomiasis, for example, is a tropical disease caused by trematodes called *schistosomes* or *blood flukes* living in the blood vessels of the abdomen. Adult tapeworms that live in the intestine of human beings do not usually

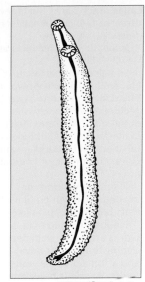

WORLD BOOK illustration by Zorica Dabich

The blood fluke may inhabit the blood vessels of the abdomen of human beings. This flatworm causes schistosomiasis, a disabling disease common in tropical regions.

© North Wind Picture Archives/Alamy Images

Flatboats on the Ohio River carried thousands of immigrants to new settlements in the Midwest during the early 1800's.

cause much harm. But tapeworm larvae cause serious diseases that can be fatal if not treated.

Seth Tyler

Scientific classification. Flatworms make up the phylum Platyhelminthes.

See also **Animal** (picture: Animals of the oceans); Fluke; Planarian; Tapeworm; Worm.

Flaubert, *floh BAIR,* **Gustave,** *goos TAHV* (1821-1880), was a French writer whose novels contain some of the most vivid and lifelike characters and descriptions in literature. He blended precise observation with careful attention to language and form. Flaubert's *Madame Bovary* is considered perhaps the most perfect French novel.

Flaubert was born on Dec. 12, 1821, in Rouen. He lived in solitude, devoting himself to literature. His love of artistic beauty was paralleled by his hatred of materialism.

Flaubert tended to be a skeptic and a pessimist. His works are never sentimental or soft, but they are always deeply human. His novels show he was both a realist and a romantic. The realism can be seen in his attention to detail and his objective description of characters and events. The romanticism appears in the exotic subject matter that Flaubert chose. *Madame Bovary* (1856) is a poetically realistic treatment of a case of adultery in a village in Normandy. *Salammbô* (1862) is a colorful historical novel about ancient Carthage. *A Sentimental Education* (1869), a kind of autobiographical novel, is an example of strict literary realism. *The Temptation of St. Anthony* (1874) is a marvelous fantasy. *Three Tales* (1877) examines religious experience through three small masterpieces that take

Bettmann Archive

Gustave Flaubert

place in different historical periods: "A Simple Heart" (modern), "The Legend of St. Julian the Hospitaller" (medieval), and "Herodias" (Biblical). Flaubert died on May 8, 1880.   Thomas H. Goetz

Flavian Amphitheater. See Colosseum.

Flavonoid, *FLAY vuh NOYD,* is any of a number of chemicals made by plants. Flavonoids have many important roles in the life cycle of plants. For example, some flavonoids protect leaves from being damaged by ultraviolet light. Others provide the color of flowers, fruits, and leaves. There are more than 4,000 naturally occurring flavonoids. A single plant does not make all of the flavonoids, only certain ones. Each plant species may produce a particular combination of the chemicals.

Because much of our food comes from plants, scientists are studying how the flavonoids in fruits and vegetables may affect human health and nutrition. Some flavonoids act as *antioxidants,* chemical compounds that may prevent some types of cell damage. These flavonoids may help protect against heart disease by preventing blood clots and keeping cholesterol from building up inside arteries. Scientists have also found that some flavonoids can prevent the formation of certain types of tumors. Since almost all fruits and vegeta-

bles contain beneficial flavonoids, experts recommend eating at least five servings each day.

Cecilia A. McIntosh

Flax is a plant raised for its fiber and seed. The fiber is made into linen fabric and a variety of other products, including rope, thread, and high-quality paper. The seeds contain *linseed oil,* which is used primarily in the production of paints and varnishes.

There are about 230 species of flax. Only one species, *Linum usitatissimum,* is grown commercially. Different varieties of this species are grown for fiber and for seed.

The flax plant stands from 3 to 4 feet (0.9 to 1.2 meters) high and has either white or blue flowers. The variety grown for fiber has a slender stem that branches near the top. Seed flax is bushier than fiber flax and bears more seeds.

Flax may be attacked by a number of fungus diseases, including *rust, wilt,* and *pasmo.* Before planting flax, farmers treat the seeds with chemicals called *fungicides* to protect them against these diseases. Farmers also plant varieties of flax that are resistant to disease.

World production of fiber flax amounts to about 880,000 tons (800,000 metric tons) annually. China and France are the leading countries in fiber flax production. Other leading growers include Belarus, Russia, and the United Kingdom. The United States and Canada do not raise fiber flax. World flaxseed production totals about 80 million bushels, or 2,200,000 tons (2,000,000 metric tons) yearly. Leading flaxseed-producing countries include Canada, China, India, and the United States.

Growing and processing fiber flax. Fiber flax grows best in cool, moist climates with rainy summers. It is planted in the spring after the danger of frost has passed. It is generally grown in rotation with other crops. Rotation helps reduce the effects of diseases.

Fiber flax is harvested three to four months after planting. If the plants are harvested too early, the fibers will be fine and silky, but weak. If the plants become too ripe, the fibers will be stiff and rough and difficult to spin into yarn. Farmers harvest fiber flax with a machine that pulls the stalks from the ground. On some farms, workers harvest flax by hand.

After the plants have been harvested, the flax stems are soaked in water. This process, which is called *ret-*

Leading flaxseed-growing countries

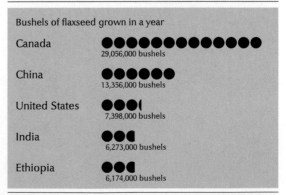

Bushels of flaxseed grown in a year

Canada
29,056,000 bushels

China
13,356,000 bushels

United States
7,398,000 bushels

India
6,273,000 bushels

Ethiopia
6,174,000 bushels

One bushel equals 56 pounds (25 kilograms).
Figures are for a three-year average, 2008-2010.
Source: FAOSTAT, Statistics Division, Food and Agriculture Organization of the UN.
http://www.faostat.fao.org. Data accessed in 2012.

WORLD BOOK illustrations by Lorraine Epstein   © Nigel Cattlin, Holt Studios

Flax is valued for its seeds and its fibers. Seed flax, *left,* produces linseed oil. Fiber flax, *center,* is used to make linen. Farmers use a machine to harvest flaxseed, *right.*

ting, rots the stalk and exposes the fibers that lie under the woody part of the stem. There are two methods of retting—*dew-retting* and *water-retting.* In dew-retting, farmers spread the flax in the field and allow the dew to rot the plants for several weeks. During the dew-retting process, the stems are turned several times and the seeds are removed. In water-retting, the seeds are removed first and the stems are then soaked in large tanks of warm water for four to eight days.

After retting, the flax stems are dried and sent through a machine that breaks them into small pieces called *shives.* Next, in a process called *scutching,* the machine separates the shives from the fibers by beating the stems with a whirling paddle or blade. In the next step, called *hackling,* the *tow* (short) and *line* (long) fibers are straightened out and separated from each other by combing.

After combing, the fibers are baled and sent to mills for processing. The seeds that were removed from the plants are processed for oil.

Growing and processing seed flax. Seed flax grows best in areas with cool climates and dry summers. Most seed flax is planted in early spring. In the fall, combines harvest the flax and separate the seeds from the rest of the plant. The seeds are then shipped to mills to be processed.

In the mill, the flaxseeds are ground into a meal and steamed. The oil is then removed either by squeezing the meal in a hydraulic press or by treating the meal with chemicals called *solvents.* Flaxseeds consist of about 40 percent oil and 60 percent water and solid matter. One bushel of seeds produces about 2 ½ gallons (9.5 liters) of linseed oil. The meal that remains after processing is used as a high-protein feed for livestock. People also use ground flaxseed to make breads and other foods.

In the United States, the unused portions of the seed flax plant are processed to remove the tow fibers. The fibers are made into yarn and into paper for cigarettes, Bibles, and other products.

History. Flax is one of the oldest cultivated crops. Flaxseeds that have been found in Syria and Turkey indi-

cate that the plant might have been grown as early as 7000 B.C. The Egyptians began cultivating flax about 5000 B.C. By about 1000 B.C., the cultivation of flax had spread to Western Europe. In the A.D. 700's, the areas that are now Belgium and France became leading producers of fine linen.

The first settlers in the United States and Canada planted fiber flax to make linen. But the invention of a cotton gin by Eli Whitney in 1793 made cotton yarn more economical than linen yarn. As a result, the two countries eventually abandoned fiber flax production. Flaxseed production declined in the United States and Canada in the 1950's because of the increasing popularity of latex paints over oil-based paints.   David S. Seigler

Scientific classification. Flax belongs to the family Linaceae and makes up the genus *Linum.*

See also **Linen; Linseed oil.**

Flea, *flee,* is a small, wingless insect that lives on mammals and birds and sucks blood for food. Fleas are dangerous pests because they can carry the germs that cause plague and typhus. They get the disease germs by biting infected rats and ground squirrels. See **Plague; Typhus.**

A flea has flat sides and a head much smaller than the rest of the body. The flea's shape and its strong, spiny legs help it glide quickly and easily through the hairs or feathers of its host. Fleas puncture the skin with their beaks to get blood.

Fleas live on human beings, cats, dogs, rats, birds, horses, poultry, rabbits, and many wild ani-

WORLD BOOK illustration by Shirley Hooper, Oxford Illustrators Limited

Common European flea

mals. A few kinds live only on certain types of animals. But most kinds pass readily from animal to human beings and from animal to animal. They leave the host as soon as it dies because they must have blood for food.

Fleas are strong and have great leaping ability for their size. Scientists have found that the flea that lives on people can jump 13 inches (33 centimeters). Fleas can be made to perform tricks such as pulling tiny wagons. *Flea circuses* feature troupes of fleas that have been "trained" to do such tricks.

Kinds of fleas. The common *European,* or *human, flea* is about ⅛ inch (3 millimeters) long. It lives in the folds of clothing. It drops its eggs about the house instead of attaching them to clothing. The larvae look like maggots. When they become adults, they seek a host. Some people attract fleas more than others do, and some become sensitive to the bites. The skin around the bite becomes inflamed in such people.

The *chigoe,* another kind of flea, is native to South America. But it has spread to Africa and many temperate regions. The female chigoe burrows into the skin to lay eggs. These insects cause ulcers to form on the skin. The flea must be removed before the ulcer will heal.

Rat, cat, and dog fleas also may be serious pests. They lay many tiny oval white eggs on the animals or in their sleeping places. When the eggs hatch, the larvae crawl into bedding and floor cracks. They spin their cocoons in dust and appear as adults about two weeks later.

Controlling fleas. Cleanliness and proper care of pets are the best protection against fleas. Dogs that have fleas should be scrubbed with soaps that contain an appropriate insecticide. Periodically treating pets with such soaps kills the insects. Owners can guard against fleas by changing their pets' bedding often. Also, pet owners can destroy the larvae by spraying or dusting the pets' quarters with an insecticide. David L. Denlinger

Scientific classification. Fleas make up the order Siphonaptera. The scientific name of the common European, or human, flea is *Pulex irritans.*

Fleabane is a group of plants that people once thought could kill fleas. Lotions used to drive away insects may still contain fleabane oil. Fleabanes are found throughout the world. There are hundreds of *species* (kinds).

The *daisy fleabane,* an annual, is cultivated in North America. Its white, daisylike flowers tend to grow in

WORLD BOOK illustration by Lorraine Epstein

Fleabane got its name because people once thought the plant could kill fleas. The fleabane above has violet flowers.

clusters. Long, pointed leaves grow along the stem, which can reach a height of 5 feet (1.5 meters). The bright orange flowers of the *double orange daisy,* a perennial, usually stand alone. This plant may grow 10 inches (25 centimeters) high. Most fleabanes bloom in spring or early summer.

Some species have been used medicinally. The plant was gathered while in flower and then dried. Druggists sold it as *erigeron,* a drug used to treat diarrhea and dropsy and to stop the flow of blood. James E. Simon

Scientific classification. Fleabanes make up the genus *Erigeron.* The daisy fleabane is *Erigeron annuus.* The double orange daisy is *E. aurantiacus.* The best-known medicinal fleabane is *E. canadensis.*

Fleet Prison, a historic London jail, took its name from its location near the River Fleet. As early as the 1100's, it was the king's prison. In the 1500's and 1600's, it housed Puritans and victims of the Court of the Star Chamber (see **Star Chamber**). Later, it was a debtor's prison. In the 1700's, it became noted for cruelty. From the early 1600's until 1753, members of the clergy performed secret marriages in the prison. These ceremonies were called "Fleet marriages." The prison was abandoned in 1842, and it was later torn down. Basil D. Henning

Fleming, Sir Alexander (1881-1955), was a British bacteriologist at St. Mary's Hospital at the University of London. In 1928, he discovered the germ-killing power of the green mold, *Penicillium notatum,* from which the lifesaving antibiotic called penicillin was first purified (see **Antibiotic; Penicillin**).

For his discovery, Fleming shared the 1945 Nobel Prize in medicine with British scientists Howard Florey and Ernst B. Chain. Florey and Chain helped develop the use of this drug (see **Florey, Lord; Chain, Ernst Boris**).

The discovery and development of penicillin opened a new era for medicine, and World War II (1939-1945) provided an opportune field trial for

Max Ehlert, Miller Services

Sir Alexander Fleming

the drug. Fleming discovered penicillin accidentally when he saw that a bit of mold growing in a culture plate in his laboratory had destroyed bacteria around it. Fleming also discovered lysozyme, a substance found in human tears. Even when diluted, this agent can dissolve certain germs. Fleming was born on Aug. 6, 1881, near Darvel, Scotland. He attended St. Mary's Medical School in London. He died on March 11, 1955. Audrey B. Davis

Additional resources

Bankston, John. *Alexander Fleming and the Story of Penicillin.* Mitchell Lane, 2002. Younger readers.
Hantula, Richard. *Alexander Fleming.* World Almanac, 2003. Younger readers.
Tocci, Salvatore. *Alexander Fleming.* Enslow, 2002. Younger readers.

Fleming, Ian (1908-1964), was an English novelist who became one of the most popular authors of the mid-1900's. Fleming won fame for his creation of James Bond, a British secret service agent who attracts both danger and beautiful women in his series of fantastic adventures. The sophisticated Bond, also known by the code name 007, is one of three British agents who use a double-0 code number. The double-0 means these secret service agents are licensed to kill at their discretion.

Bond first appeared in *Casino Royale* (1953) and then in 11 other novels and two collections of short stories. The books attracted many types of readers. *Diamonds Are Forever* (1956) was a favorite of the more sophisticated readers, while *Doctor No* (1958) had a general appeal like the thrillers of the 1800's. A popular series of movies based on the Bond novels helped spread the character's fame. Fleming also wrote *Chitty Chitty Bang Bang* (1964), which was a children's story about an old racing car that could fly. After Fleming's death on Aug. 12, 1964, the English author John Gardner continued the Bond series.

Ian Lancaster Fleming was born on May 28, 1908, in London. During World War II (1939-1945), he did espionage work as the personal assistant to the director of British Naval Intelligence.   David Geherin

Fleming, Renée (1959-   ), an American soprano, is one of the outstanding opera singers of her time. Fleming became noted for the beauty of her voice and the charm of her acting. She has excelled in classical operatic roles and has also won praise for her performances in modern operas. Fleming has sung a broad vocal repertoire that includes American pop songs, German *lieder* (art songs), and jazz. She has gained recognition for her concert performances and for her recordings.

Fleming was born on Feb. 14, 1959, in Indiana, Pennsylvania, and grew up in Rochester, New York.

© Harry How, Corbis

Renée Fleming

She first planned a career in music education but took up singing while studying at the State University of New York at Potsdam, where she received a bachelor's degree in music in 1981. Fleming earned a master's degree from the Eastman School of Music in 1983. She won the Metropolitan Opera National Council Auditions, an annual award designed to encourage young singers, in 1988.

Fleming began singing professionally in 1988 and made her debut at the Metropolitan Opera in 1991 as Countess Almaviva in the opera *The Marriage of Figaro* by the Austrian composer Wolfgang Amadeus Mozart. She later won acclaim as the Marschallin in the opera *Der Rosenkavalier* by Richard Strauss of Germany and in the title roles in *Manon* by the French composer Jules Massenet and *Rusalka* by the Czech composer Antonín Dvořák. Fleming has also starred in modern operas by such American composers as John Corigliano, Carlisle Floyd, and André Previn.   Thomas A. Bauman

Fleming, Sir Sandford (1827-1915), a Canadian civil engineer, built the Intercolonial Railway, which connected New Brunswick and Nova Scotia with Quebec. He also made surveys for the main line of the Canadian Pacific Railway. After 1876, he played a prominent role in establishing standard time zones (see **Standard time**).

Fleming proposed the use of the 24-hour system of keeping time. In addition, he persuaded the Canadian, Australian, and British governments to cooperate in laying the Pacific cable between Australia and Vancouver in 1902, in an attempt to have a system of communication connecting the entire British Empire.

Fleming was born on Jan. 7, 1827, in Kirkcaldy, Scotland. He moved to Canada when he was 18. He joined the engineering staff of the Ontario, Simcoe and Huron Railway and in 1857 became its chief engineer. He was important in railway development for all Canada. An advocate of transcontinental railroads, he became engineer in chief of the government railroads and a director of the Canadian Pacific Railway. He also paid the expense of locating a railway line in Newfoundland. He retired from active engineering in 1880.

Fleming served as chancellor of Queen's University at Kingston, Ontario, from 1880 to 1915. He died on July 22, 1915.   George H. Drury

Flemings are a group of people who live in northern Belgium. The region they inhabit is called Flanders. It consists of the provinces of Antwerp, East Flanders, West Flanders, Limburg, and the northern half of Brabant (see **Belgium** [political map]). Historically, Flanders had different boundaries and included parts of France and the Netherlands. The Flemings make up about 55 percent of the Belgian population.

The Flemish language and culture developed after the Franks, a Germanic tribe, settled in what is now Flanders in the A.D. 200's to 400's. In southern Belgium, now called Wallonia, the local Celtic population was denser and the Roman influence stronger. Frankish invaders there were largely absorbed by the local culture.

During the Middle Ages, from about A.D. 400 through the 1400's, the Flemings dominated European trade. Agriculture, fishing, and textiles also became thriving industries in Flanders. Between the 1400's and 1600's, the region produced some of the world's greatest painters, including Jan van Eyck, Pieter Bruegel the Elder, and Peter Paul Rubens.

Language differences have long led to conflict between the Flemings and Walloons. The Flemings speak Dutch, and the Walloons speak French. When Belgium gained independence in 1830, French became its only official language. Flemings protested and demanded the right to be educated and govern in Dutch, rather than French. Dutch finally gained official recognition in the late 1800's. The Belgian government and most businesses now use both languages. Flemings have also won the right to schools and universities that teach in Dutch. However, the conflicts between the Flemings and Walloons have continued. Constitutional changes made from 1970 to 2001 granted extensive self-rule to Flanders and Wallonia.   Janet L. Polasky

See also **Belgium** (People [Languages; The arts]); **Flanders; Walloons.**

Flesh is the name given to the soft tissues or parts of the body of human beings and of most animals with backbones. It is made up chiefly of muscle and connective tissue but also includes some fat. The flesh is the meaty part of the body that surrounds the skeleton and body cavity. It does not include the organs in the body cavity or the bony and liquid tissues of the body. Animal flesh, or meat, is high in essential nutrients such as fat, protein, and minerals. The word *flesh* also refers to the pulpy parts of fruits and vegetables.   Paul R. Bergstresser

Flesh-eating animal. See Carnivore.

Flesh-eating plant. See Carnivorous plant.

Fletcher, John (1579-1625), was an English playwright. For many years, Fletcher's plays were as highly praised as William Shakespeare's and Ben Jonson's. Fletcher wrote many kinds of drama, but his fame centers on his skillful tragicomedies and such comedies of manners as *The Wild Goose-Chase* (1621). Like similar Restoration plays written later, this play was meant to please a pleasure-loving, sophisticated upper-class audience.

Fletcher was born in Sussex. His success began with his famous collaboration with Francis Beaumont (about 1608-1613). But he wrote before and after this association. Many of the so-called "Beaumont and Fletcher" plays belong to Fletcher only or to Fletcher working with others (see **Beaumont, Francis**). Shakespeare probably wrote *The Two Noble Kinsmen* and *Henry VIII* with Fletcher. Fletcher died on Aug. 29, 1625.   Albert Wertheim

Fletcher v. Peck, an 1810 Supreme Court case, marked the first time the Supreme Court of the United States interpreted the contract clause of the U.S. Constitution. The clause prohibits states from passing any law that impairs the obligation of contracts. In 1795, members of the Georgia state legislature took bribes to grant land to several companies. The next legislature *revoked* (took back) the grants, but some of the land had already been sold by the companies. The new owners of the land argued that by revoking the grants, Georgia had interfered with a lawful contract. The Supreme Court agreed with the landowners and declared the original sale legal. By voiding the Georgia law, the court extended its power of *judicial review* (authority to declare laws unconstitutional) to include state laws.   Gregg Ivers

Fleur-de-lis, *FLUR duh LEE,* is a French name that literally means *flower of the lily* but actually refers to the iris.

The kings of France used an irislike design in heraldry. Some historians think this design originally represented an iris. Other historians believe the iris was once known as a lily, and so the design was called *flower of the lily.* Others claim that the name originally meant *flower of Louis.* According to legend, the Frankish king Clovis I used the fleur-de-lis in the early 500's after an angel gave him an iris for accepting Christianity. *Clovis* is an early form of the name *Louis.* King Louis VI, who ruled France from 1108 to 1137, first used fleurs-de-lis for his coat of arms.   Whitney Smith

See also **Flag** (picture: Historical flags of the world); **Heraldry; Iris** (picture).

Flexner, Abraham (1866-1959), was a leading authority on higher education, especially in the field of medicine. In 1930, he organized and became the first director of the Institute for Advanced Study at Princeton, New Jersey (see **Institute for Advanced Study**). His study of American medical colleges, published in 1910, caused sweeping changes in curriculum and teaching methods. He was secretary of the General Education Board, an organization that provided financial assistance to United States education, from 1912 to 1928. Flexner was born on Nov. 13, 1866, in Louisville, Kentucky. He died on Sept. 21, 1959.   Glenn Smith

Flextime. See Wages and hours (Hours).

Flicker is the name of several species of woodpeckers that live in North America and South America. The *red-shafted flicker* and the *yellow-shafted flicker* are commonly found in wooded regions of Canada and the United States. Both are subspecies of the *northern flicker.* The red-shafted flicker is brown and black, with a gray neck and throat and a creamy-white breast marked with black. The male has a red mark on each cheek, and both sexes have bright red underwings. The bird is 12 to 14 inches (30 to 36 centimeters) long. The yellow-shafted flicker resembles the red-shafted flicker, but the throat

Detail of an illuminated French manuscript (1400's); Musée Condé, Chantilly, France (Laurie Platt Winfrey, Inc.)

The fleur-de-lis is an irislike design used in heraldry. The fleur-de-lis is especially associated with French royalty. The kings of France began using the design in the early Middle Ages. A pattern of gold fleur-de-lis forms a background to this scene showing the baptism of Clovis I, king of the Franks, who converted to Christianity sometime around A.D. 500.

WORLD BOOK illustration by Trevor Boyer, Linden Artists Ltd.

The red-shafted flicker has red markings on its head and underwings. Flickers live in forests throughout North America.

is brown, the red mark is on the back of the head, and the underwings are golden-yellow. This bird is also called the *golden-winged woodpecker* and the *yellowhammer.*

Flickers build their nests in holes they dig in trees with their bills. Because of this habit, some people call the bird the *highhole* or *highholder.* Females lay 3 to 10 white eggs. Both parents care for the eggs and young.

Flickers find much of their food on the ground. They feed chiefly on ants. They also eat worms, insects, and berries.   Fred J. Alsop III

Scientific classification. Flickers are in the genus *Coloptes.* The red-shafted flicker is *Coloptes auratus cafer.* The yellow-shafted flicker is *C. auratus auratus.*

See also **Bird** (picture: Birds of forests and woodlands); **Woodpecker; Yellowhammer.**

Flickertail State. See North Dakota.

Flight. See Airplane (Principles of flight); **Bird** (How birds move).

Flightless bird. See Bird (Birds of Australia and New Zealand; Birds of the Pacific Islands; How birds move).

Flin Flon is a town on the border of Manitoba and Saskatchewan. Most of it is in Manitoba. Flin Flon has a population of 5,592—with 5,363 in Manitoba and 229 in Saskatchewan. Flin Flon is an important mining center. The town sprawls over bare, rocky hills around Ross Lake. For the location of Flin Flon, see **Manitoba** (political map).

Flin Flon was founded in 1914. Copper and zinc deposits and deposits of gold and other precious metals were discovered there in 1915, but they were not fully developed until 1930. In the older part of Flin Flon, water mains and sewers lie aboveground because digging through the rock terrain is too expensive.   Rich Billy

Flint (pop. 102,434; met. area pop. 425,790) is one of the largest cities in Michigan. Flint is a leading producer of automotive parts. General Motors Corporation, one of the world's largest automakers, was founded in Flint. The city lies on the Flint River, about 60 miles (100 kilometers) northwest of Detroit. For location, see **Michigan** (political map).

The Flint Cultural Center campus near downtown is home to a number of attractions. They include an art school and museum, a history museum, a music school, a performing arts center, a planetarium, a theater, and the main public library. Educational institutions in the city include Baker College of Flint, Kettering University, and the University of Michigan-Flint.

Flint is the county seat of Genesee County. The city has a mayor-council form of government.

Chippewa Indians lived in what is now the Flint area when Jacob Smith, the first white settler there, arrived in 1819. Smith, a fur trader from Detroit, built a trading post at a spot where Indians crossed the Flint River. During the 1830's, the Flint River settlement developed in the area. Flint was incorporated as a city in 1855.

Vast white pine forests near Flint attracted lumber companies during the mid-1800's, and the city became a center of lumber milling. By 1900, Flint's factories were making more than 100,000 wooden road carts and carriages a year, and Flint became known as the *Vehicle City.* The Charles Stewart Mott Foundation was founded in Flint in 1926. It has helped finance many civic improvements in the city (see **Mott Foundation**).

Flint's automobile industry began to grow rapidly after 1903, when the Buick Motor Company moved from Detroit to Flint. William C. Durant, a Flint carriage manufacturer, took control of Buick in 1904. He founded General Motors in Flint in 1908 and moved the Chevrolet Motor Company's manufacturing operations from Detroit to Flint in 1912.

The automobile industry drew thousands of workers to the city, and Flint's population rose from 13,000 in 1900 to 156,000 in 1930. Flint continued to grow as the automobile industry expanded in the mid-1900's. But

Flint Convention & Visitors Bureau

The Robert T. Longway Planetarium in Flint, Michigan, is part of an educational and cultural center in the city.

Flint experienced high unemployment during periods of decline in automobile sales.

A major renewal program that began in the late 1970's helped modernize the downtown area. The program included construction of a large hotel and a park.

In the 1980's, GM began closing many of its factories in Flint as American automobile makers faced strong international competition. In 1998, GM moved Buick's headquarters back to Detroit and, in 1999, closed the huge Buick assembly center in Flint. The reduction of the GM presence in the city led to high unemployment and a shrinking tax base. By the beginning of the 2000's, the municipal government was deeply in debt. In early 2002, Flint recalled its mayor, in part for financial mismanagement. In July, the state of Michigan appointed a financial manager to take control of Flint's government. The financial manager returned control to the city in mid-2004.   Lawrence R. Gustin

Flint is a hard rock that ranges in color from brown to dark gray to black. It consists of tiny crystals of the mineral quartz. In most cases, flint occurs as small masses embedded in chalk, limestone, and other rocks. Lighter colored deposits that occur as continuous layers are called *chert.*

Flint sometimes forms from microscopic organisms

Field Museum, Chicago

Flint is a hard, even-grained rock. Prehistoric people used flint to make such sharp tools or weapons as this spearpoint.

that live in water and have shells that contain *silica.* Silica is a compound of silicon and oxygen, the two elements that make up the mineral quartz. After these organisms die, their shells sink to the bottom of the sea. As time passes, silica dissolves and resolidifies to form flint.

Most flint is so even grained that it can be chipped into smooth, curved flakes. During prehistoric times, people fashioned flint into sharp tools and weapons, such as knives, spears, and arrowheads. Later, people discovered that striking flint against iron or steel produces a spark, and so used flint to start fires. The flintlock firearms that were manufactured from the 1600's to the mid-1800's made use of this property of flint.

Mark A. Helper

See also **Arrowhead** (picture); **Fire** (Methods of starting fires).

Garry James Collection (WORLD BOOK photo by Roger Fuhr)

A flintlock pistol was effective only at close range.

Flintlock was a firing mechanism used in pistols, muskets, and other firearms from about 1620 to the mid-1800's. Flintlock weapons had a piece of flint clamped in a piece called a *cock.* When the trigger was pulled, the cock snapped forward and the flint struck a piece of steel on a pivot, creating sparks. At the same time, a small pan filled with gunpowder was exposed. The sparks caused the gunpowder to explode and ignite the main charge in the barrel. Flintlocks could be *half-cocked*—that is, in a safety position—or *fully cocked* and ready for firing. Flintlock weapons were eventually replaced by firearms that used percussion caps.

Walter J. Karcheski, Jr.

See also **Firearm; Musket; Revolution, American** (Weapons and tactics; picture).

Floe. See **Iceberg.**

Flood is a body of water temporarily covering what is normally dry land. Floods most commonly occur along rivers. In addition, they can occur around lakes, wetlands, and seacoasts. Floods occur naturally and can benefit certain ecosystems. However, human activities can change the frequency and severity of floods, contributing to destruction. In developed areas, floods can cause great damage to property. Floods consistently rank among the costliest natural disasters around the world. They cause billions of dollars in damage each year.

River floods. Most rivers overflow their channels with small floods about once every two years. Larger floods occur less frequently. For example, moderate floods might occur once every 5 to 10 years on a particular river. Exceptionally large floods might occur only once in a hundred years. The period over which a flood of a particular magnitude will occur is called that flood's *recurrence interval.* For example, an exceptionally large flood that only occurs once in a hundred years has a 100-year recurrence interval. It is called a *100-year flood.*

Common causes of river floods include excessive rainfall and the sudden melting of snow and ice. Heavy rains can produce *flash floods.* In such floods, a small river or stream rises suddenly and overflows. Flash floods occur chiefly in mountainous areas and often with little warning.

In 1993, several months of heavy rains in the United States Midwest resulted in flooding along the upper Mississippi and the Missouri river systems. The floods caused about $15 billion to $20 billion in damage. They forced tens of thousands of people from their homes. Heavy rains, strong winds, and storm surges from Hurricane Irene in 2011 caused approximately $16 billion in damage throughout the Caribbean and the eastern United States. Relatively few people were killed in each flood, however, due to effective emergency response and regulations that limit development in flood-prone areas. Excessive rainfall from Tropical Storm Washi in 2011 caused flash floods in the Philippines that killed more than 1,200 people. The floods caused tens of millions of dollars in damage.

Rivers that cannot carry their load of *sediments* (sand and gravel) pose a particular flood risk. For example, the Huang He (Yellow River) in China receives more sediment than it can carry to the ocean. The sediment settles out in the riverbed. The added sediment makes the river channel more shallow, increasing the chance of flooding. One of the worst Huang He floods ever recorded was in 1887. Up to a million people were killed in the flood. Possibly millions more died from the starvation and disease that followed. The Huang He has been called *China's Sorrow* because its floods cause such great destruction.

The land next to a river that can become covered with water during a flood is called the *flood plain*. Floods enable an important natural exchange of water, sediment, and nutrients between a river and its flood plain. In ancient Egypt, for example, yearly floods of the Nile River deposited fresh, nutrient-rich soil in the Nile Valley. This yearly replenishment enabled the early Egyptians to grow crops, helping their civilization to thrive for thousands of years. However, the severity of the floods was somewhat unpredictable, and large floods could cause significant damage. In the mid-1900's, therefore, the Egyptians constructed a dam on the Nile River to control floodwaters. The Nile Valley no longer floods. The use of irrigation and fertilizer has replaced the water and nutrients once delivered by flooding.

Seacoast floods. Most seacoast floods result from storms. Hurricanes and other powerful storms create gi-

Artstreet

A flash flood may occur when a river or stream rises suddenly and overflows. This picture shows water rushing across a road during a flash flood.

ant rushes of seawater called *storm surges* that can travel far inland. In 1970, a cyclone and storm surge in the Bay of Bengal caused huge waves that struck the coast of Bangladesh (then called East Pakistan) and possibly killed from 300,000 to 500,000 people. The flood also destroyed the cattle, crops, or homes of millions of other victims. In 2005, Hurricane Katrina caused a storm surge and severe flooding in the U.S. Gulf Coast. These floods contributed to the storm's more than 1,800 deaths and estimated $100 billion in damage. The most severe destruction occurred in New Orleans.

Seacoast flooding can also result from a *tsunami*. A tsunami is a series of powerful ocean waves generated by an earthquake, landslide, volcanic eruption, or asteroid impact. The giant waves of a tsunami can travel long distances, flooding vast stretches of coastline. Tsunamis are most common along coasts of the Pacific and Indian oceans and of the Mediterranean Sea. These regions undergo frequent earthquakes and volcanic eruptions. In 2004, an undersea earthquake near the island of Sumatra, Indonesia, caused a tsunami that rose up to 100 feet (30 meters) high as it reached shore. The waves flooded coastal areas in many countries bordering the Indian Ocean. About 228,000 people were killed.

Other floods. A *megaflood* is a sudden and enormous flood. Megafloods result from catastrophic releases of water, often from large lakes or glaciers. One such flood occurred about 14,500 years ago at Lake Bonneville (now the Great Salt Lake) in Utah. The lake overflowed and then washed away a natural dam at its northern end. The resulting megaflood released a volume of water comparable to that of Lake Michigan. Similarly, a natural ice dam containing glacial Lake Missoula in Montana periodically ruptured between about 15,000 and 13,000 years ago. The ruptures caused megafloods that sculpted the Channeled Scablands in the state of Washington.

Lakes can also flood. For example, Tonle Sap Lake in Cambodia floods each year when the Mekong River

© Randy Taylor, Sygma

Floodwaters can cause great damage. They have often destroyed entire communities. Floods that occur in the spring often result from melting snow and heavy rains, which combine to raise the level of rivers above their banks.

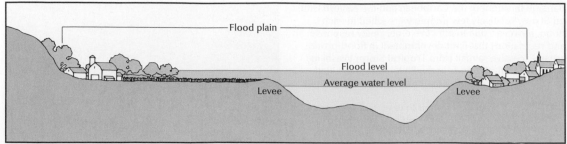

Flood plain

Flood level

Average water level

Levee

Levee

WORLD BOOK diagram by David Cunningham

A flood occurs when a river rises above its normal level and overflows its banks. People have built *levees* (dikes) along some rivers to hold back the high water, but a river may overflow even such barriers. Floodwaters generally cover only a river's *flood plain,* the nearby low-lying land. But sometimes extremely high waters flood a much larger area.

overflows to fill its basin. The lake's waters can rise more than 30 feet (9 meters). Entire towns within the lake basin are built on stilts or floats to accommodate the flooding. Storms and high winds can cause floods along lakeshores. Some floods occur when the water of a lake rocks suddenly from side to side. Such a movement is called a *seiche.*

Flood control involves constructing dams and retention basins to store water. It also involves building levees, dikes, and flood walls to confine floodwaters.

Some of the most extensive flood control systems in the world include the floodway diversions on the Red River of the North, which crosses the border between the United States and Canada, and the system of levees, spillways, and wetlands maintained along the Mississippi River system. Adjustable gates called *floodgates* are commonly used to control storm surges in places near or below sea level. Such places include the Netherlands, New Orleans, and Venice, Italy.

Reducing flood losses. The losses that result from floods can be reduced in many ways. In many places, for example, regulations limit the construction of permanent buildings on flood plains. Emergency response programs help by warning and evacuating people in flood-prone areas. They also provide relief aid for flood victims. In some places, flood insurance can be purchased to help cover the costs of flood damage.

Government agencies in many countries identify flood-prone areas. They use this information to set forth regulations for managing flood plains. Many of these regulations require that a small strip of land along a waterway be left vacant. Such a strip is called a *floodway.* Numerous communities reserve a wider area along the floodway for use as farmland or parkland. In the United States, floodway maps are available from the Federal Emergency Management Agency (FEMA).

Scientists called *hydrologists* forecast floods using complex mathematical models. The models depend on radar and satellite images to estimate rainfall and snowmelt. They also make use of live measurements of the flow of rivers. In the United States, the National Weather Service maintains a network of river forecast centers and hydrologic service areas. This network provides flood warnings that can greatly reduce loss of life and damage to property.

The World Health Organization (WHO) documents the most significant floods in its Emergency Events Database. The database resides at the Collaborating Centre for Research on the Epidemiology of Disasters in Brussels, Belgium. The center studies the effects of floods and other disasters on public health. It also helps emergency aid workers.   Patrick Belmont

Related articles in *World Book* include:

Conservation
Dam
Deluge
Disaster
Flash flood
Huang He
Johnstown Flood
Levee
Mississippi River
Missouri River
Ohio River
Reclamation, Bureau of
Tennessee Valley Authority
Tsunami

© Joe Traver, Gamma/Liaison

Flood control is often achieved through such temporary measures as sandbagging. These workers are placing sandbags along the shore of Lake Ontario to prevent its steadily rising waters from overflowing. Sandbagging is also used to control lake flooding caused by storms and high winds.

Flooring is the general name given to all materials used to cover floors. The main purposes of flooring are to keep rooms clean, dry, and warm, and to provide decoration. Common floorings include concrete, linoleum, stone, sheet vinyl, wall-to-wall carpeting, wood, and tile. Tile may be made of carpet, ceramics, cork, rubber, vinyl or other plastics, or *vinyl composite* (vinyl embedded within reinforcing material). Another popular floor covering is *laminate flooring*. This flooring begins with a fiberboard or particleboard core. The top side is covered with a layer of paper printed with a woodgrain or other design pattern. The paper is then coated with a clear, durable layer of plastic composite.

The first floors were probably only the leveled dirt of the land over which early shelters were built. Ancient temples and large public buildings had floors of stone and baked clay. The Greeks used marble in floors. The Romans learned how to make cement. Stone was the most common flooring of public buildings and churches during the Middle Ages, from the A.D. 400's through the 1400's. In the 1500's, the Venetians developed *terrazzo,* flooring made of granulated marble mixed with gray or white cement. Wood was first used as flooring in the Middle Ages. *Parquet* floors of different colored woods arranged in designs decorated early palaces. Linoleum was invented in England about 1860.   Paul Bianchina

See also **House** (Floors); **Interior design** (Floor coverings); **Linoleum; Tile.**

Flora is the name given to the plant life of a particular period of time or part of the world. It corresponds to the word *fauna,* which is the term for the animal life of a certain place or time. The term *flora* is taken from the name of the mythological Roman goddess of flowers and spring.   David H. Wagner

Florence (pop. 358,079) is an Italian city that became famous as the birthplace of the Renaissance. During the Renaissance, from about 1300 to 1600, some of the greatest painters, sculptors, and writers in history lived and worked in Florence.

The city lies on both banks of the Arno River in central Italy, at the foot of the Apennines mountain range. For location, see **Italy** (political map). Florence is the capital of both the province of Florence and the region of Tuscany. Its name in Italian is *Firenze.*

Such great artists as Leonardo da Vinci, Fra Angelico,

Santa Maria Novella in Florence is a leading example of Italian Renaissance architecture. The church's facade was designed by Leon Battista Alberti in the mid-1400's.

Giotto, and Michelangelo produced many of Florence's splendid paintings and sculptures. Great writers who lived in the city included Giovanni Boccaccio, Dante, and Petrarch.

Florentines also won fame in other fields. The architect Filippo Brunelleschi and the political analyst Niccolò Machiavelli were born in Florence, and the astronomer Galileo did some of his work there.

Today, about a million tourists visit Florence yearly to see its magnificent art galleries, churches, and museums. Florentines consider Michelangelo's famous marble statue, *David,* as the symbol of their city's artistic spirit.

The city covers about 40 square miles (104 square kilometers) in the middle of a rich farming area. The oldest part of Florence lies in a small area divided by the Arno. Most of the city's famous buildings are on the right bank, north of the river. A broad public square called the Piazza della Signoria is a major public gather-

The Ponte Vecchio (Old Bridge) spans the Arno River in Florence. Shops line both sides of the bridge, a historic landmark built in 1345.

World Film Enterprises, Black Star

Art treasures of Florence include many statues in the Piazza della Signoria, a square in the heart of the city.

ing spot and tourist attraction on the right bank. Towering over the piazza is the Palazzo Vecchio, or Palazzo della Signoria, a palace that has been the center of local government since the Middle Ages.

Many old, impressive churches stand on the right bank of the Arno. The Cathedral of Florence, called the Duomo, is in the Piazza del Duomo. The eight-sided Baptistery, with its beautifully decorated bronze doors by Lorenzo Ghiberti and Andrea Pisano, is part of this piazza. The piazza also features a *campanile* (bell tower) built by Giotto and Pisano.

The tombs of Galileo, Machiavelli, Michelangelo, and other famous Florentines are in the Church of Santa Croce. This church also has frescoes by Giotto. The Church of San Marco and an adjacent museum display a collection of paintings by Fra Angelico and other artists of the 1400's. The chapel of the Church of San Lorenzo has the large stone figures carved by Michelangelo for the tombs of the powerful Medici family.

Many outstanding art galleries and museums are also on the right bank. The famous Uffizi Palace, which once housed government offices, is now an art gallery. It owns one of the world's finest collections of paintings and statues. The National Museum of the Bargello exhibits many masterpieces of Renaissance sculpture. The Galleria dell' Accademia displays medieval and Renaissance sculpture, including Michelangelo's *David.*

Florence's most elegant shopping area lies along the Via Tornabuoni, a street in the western part of the old section of the city. Some shops on this street display the kinds of clothing and leather goods that have made Florence famous for fashion.

Six bridges connect the right bank with the Oltrarno, the section of Florence south of the river. Goldsmith and jewelry shops line one of these bridges, the Ponte Vecchio, which was built in 1345. The other bridges replaced bridges destroyed during World War II (1939-1945) by retreating German troops. The present Ponte Santa Trinita is an exact reconstruction of the original

bridge, which had stood since 1570.

The Oltrarno includes many antique, silver, and woodcarving shops, but its most famous attraction is the Pitti Palace. This palace—the largest in Florence—was begun in 1458 as a home for Luca Pitti, a wealthy merchant. It now displays an excellent collection of paintings. The Boboli Gardens, behind the palace, are among the most beautiful gardens in Italy.

Modern apartment buildings stand in Florence's suburbs, which have developed since the 1950's. Industry is concentrated north of the city.

The people. Almost all Florentines are Roman Catholic. The language spoken by the medieval Florentines became the basis of modern Italian.

Most of the families in the oldest part of the city live in old stone buildings that lack central heating. Many of the families in the suburbs make their homes in modern apartment buildings.

Florentines, like most Italians, traditionally eat their largest meal at lunchtime. This meal may include fruit, meat, vegetables, and one of several kinds of noodles called *pasta,* such as spaghetti or ravioli. Local specialties include *ribollito* (vegetable soup), Chianti wine, and beefsteak.

Florence has many public markets. Shoppers meet daily in the marketplaces and chat as they shop. The Mercato Nuovo, a merchandising square in the heart of Florence, attracts thousands of tourists each day.

© SCALA, Art Resource

Bronze doors known as the *Gates of Paradise* stand at the east entrance of the baptistery in Florence. Lorenzo Ghiberti, an Italian sculptor and goldsmith, created the doors in the 1400's.

Education and cultural life. Florence is the home of the University of Florence and several research institutes. The Academy of Fine Arts and the Luigi Cherubini Conservatory of Music are also in the city. Operas are presented at the Teatro Comunale and the Teatro Verdi. Florence has some of Italy's oldest and most valuable public libraries. For example, the Biblioteca Laurenziana, which opened to the public in 1571, contains several famous ancient texts. Other notable public libraries include the Marucelliana and the Riccardiana.

Economy. Florentines have made fine handicrafts since the days of the Renaissance. Many of the people make or sell such handicrafts as leather products, jewelry, mosaics, pottery, and articles made of straw. Tourism is an important economic activity of Florence.

Factories in the city produce clothing, drugs, foods, glass, and plastics. Florence is a major communications and railroad center of Italy.

History. The Etruscans, a tribe that migrated to Italy from Asia, first settled in what is now Florence. They arrived there about 200 B.C., but their settlement was destroyed in 82 B.C. following a Roman civil war. In 59 B.C., the Roman ruler Julius Caesar set up a colony on the Arno. He named the colony *Florentia,* a Latin word meaning *blossoming.* The name later became *Florence.*

Florence remained a small, unimportant town until about A.D. 1000. It then began to develop into a self-governing area called a *city-state.* Its population grew from perhaps 5,000 in A.D. 900 to about 30,000 in 1200.

The people of Florence developed new processes for refining wool, and the city gained importance for its woolen textiles. Florentine bankers became successful and brought much wealth to the city. The population reached about 100,000 in the early 1300's. Florence fought many wars during the 1300's and early 1400's, gaining and losing territory at various times. Plagues killed many of its people during this period.

During the 1300's, four Florentines introduced new styles of painting and writing that grew into great achievements of the Renaissance. Giotto painted pictures with realistic figures instead of stiff, formal subjects. In literature, Dante, Petrarch, and Boccaccio developed Italian as a literary language and helped renew interest in the classics. For the next 300 years, Florence was a center of one of the greatest periods of cultural achievement in history.

The wealthy Medici family gained control of Florence in the early 1400's. By that time, Florence had become a strong and almost independent city-state. It controlled part of what is now central Italy. The city achieved its greatest splendor under the most famous Medici, Lorenzo the Magnificent, who ruled from 1469 to 1492. Except for brief periods, members of the Medici family governed until 1737. During their rule, Florentine literature, theater, and opera thrived in Florence and were imitated throughout Europe.

Florence was the capital of Italy from 1865 to 1870, when the government moved to Rome. Many improvements were carried out in Florence during its period as the capital. For example, the tree-lined boulevards and large piazzas just outside the historic center of Florence were built at that time.

During World War II (1939-1945), several ancient palaces were destroyed during the fighting for Florence. But most of the city's art treasures escaped harm.

In 1966, a flood damaged books, manuscripts, valuable works of art, and museums and other buildings in Florence. Many nations aided in the restoration of the artworks. Most of the paintings and manuscripts were saved, though some required years of careful work. The city has become a world center for the study of art preservation.

Population growth in Florence led to such problems as that of traffic crowding the narrow streets of the old section. In 1970, private cars were banned from the historic center of the city.

Art restoration was an important focus during the 1980's and 1990's. A number of Renaissance masterpieces were cleaned and restored.   David I. Kertzer

Related articles in *World Book* include:
Architecture (Renaissance; picture: The dome of the Cathedral of Florence)
Florin
Painting (The Renaissance)
Renaissance (The Italian Renaissance)
Savonarola, Girolamo
Sculpture (Italian Renaissance sculpture; pictures)

Flores Island, *FLOH ruhs* (pop. 3,816), known for its abundant foliage, is the westernmost island of the Portuguese Azores. It covers 55 square miles (143 square kilometers). The main occupations are dairying and raising cattle. Most of the island's people live in Santa Cruz, the largest town, or in Lajes. See also **Azores.**

Florey, *FLOHR ee,* **Lord** (1898-1968), a British bacteriologist, helped develop with Ernst B. Chain the antibiotic penicillin (see **Antibiotic; Penicillin**). Alexander Fleming discovered penicillin in 1928. Florey shared the 1945 Nobel Prize in physiology or medicine with Fleming and Chain (see **Fleming, Sir Alexander; Chain, Ernst Boris**). In 1940 and 1941, Florey's research team at the University of Oxford isolated penicillin in relatively pure form and tested it.

Howard Walter Florey was born on Sept. 24, 1898, in Adelaide, Australia. He studied at the University of Adelaide and, as a Rhodes scholar, at Magdalen College at Oxford. Florey died on Feb. 21, 1968.   Audrey B. Davis

Floriculture, *FLAWR uh kuhl chuhr,* is the art, science, and business of growing ornamental plants such as flowers and leafy foliage plants. People use these plants for decoration and give them as gifts.

Raising and marketing cut flowers and decorative plants ranks as a large industry. In mild climates, people grow cut flowers and potted plants outdoors, even in winter. But in cold climates, such plants are grown in greenhouses that can be heated during cold weather.

Floriculturists can control the blooming of flowers by various techniques. These techniques include planting the flowers on certain dates, removing the tips of the plants, and regulating the growing temperature and the periods of darkness. Sometimes, growers artificially lengthen or shorten the period of light the plant receives each day. These methods increase the value of ornamental plants. For example, floriculturists can cause poinsettias to be ready for Christmas. Researchers in floriculture also have developed long-stemmed carnations, thornless roses, and double snapdragons. Floriculturists work in nurseries, florist shops, seed companies, public and private gardens, zoos, and environmental planning companies.   Gerry Moore

See also **Greenhouse; Horticulture.**

© Shutterstock

The Florida Everglades is a fascinating region of natural beauty. Thousands of islands are scattered throughout the vast wetlands, serving as home to a wide variety of plant and animal life.

Florida *The Sunshine State*

Florida is one of the leading tourist states in the United States. This land of swaying palm trees and warm ocean breezes attracts tens of millions of visitors from throughout the world the year around. Many of these vacationers enjoy Walt Disney World Resort and other theme parks in and around Orlando. Miami Beach, a seaside suburb of Miami, is one of the state's many famous resort centers. Other popular seaside resorts include Clearwater, Daytona Beach, Fort Lauderdale, Fort Myers Beach, Key West, Naples, Palm Beach, Panama City, Sanibel Island, and Sarasota.

Florida has been nicknamed the *Sunshine State* because it has many sunny days. Partly as a result of the warm, sunny climate, millions of older people spend their retirement years in the state. Tallahassee is the cap-

ital of Florida. Jacksonville is the state's largest city.

Florida is the southernmost state on the U.S. mainland. A large part of the state consists of a peninsula that juts south about 400 miles (640 kilometers) into the sea. The state's northwestern part, called the Panhandle, extends along the northern shore of the Gulf of Mexico. Florida faces the Atlantic Ocean on the east and the Gulf of Mexico on the west. The state's southern tip is less than 100 miles (160 kilometers) from Cuba. Florida's coastline is longer than that of any other state except Alaska.

Florida's population is growing faster than that of all but a few other states. Its economy is also expanding rapidly, especially in banking, business services, and the manufacture of computers and other electronic equipment. Florida farmers grow about 70 percent of the nation's orange and grapefruit crops. Almost all the frozen orange juice produced in the United States is processed in Florida.

In 1513, the Spanish explorer Juan Ponce de León claimed the Florida region for Spain. He called the

The contributors of this article are Peter O. Muller, Professor of Geography at the University of Miami, and Irvin D. S. Winsboro, Professor of History at Florida Gulf Coast University.

Interesting facts about Florida

WORLD BOOK illustrations by Kevin Chadwick

The first federal wildlife refuge in the United States was established by President Theodore Roosevelt in 1903 at Pelican Island. The island, in the Indian River near Sebastian, was set aside for the protection of native birds, such as brown pelicans, herons, and egrets. The refuge has since been enlarged, and it now covers about 4,400 acres (1,780 hectares).

Pelican Island

The first federal savings and loan association was the First Federal Savings and Loan Association of Miami, which received its charter on Aug. 8, 1933.

The first training center for Navy pilots, the U.S. Navy Aeronautic Station, was established in Pensacola in 1914. The facility is now known as Naval Air Station Pensacola. Today, all U.S. Navy aviators begin their training there.

U.S. Navy Aeronautic Station

© Superstock

Downtown Jacksonville lies on the St. Johns River in northeastern Florida. Jacksonville is the state's largest city and its center of finance and insurance. The city is also a busy port.

region La Florida, probably because he arrived there a few days after Easter, which the Spanish called Pascua Florida (Easter of the Flowers). In 1565, the Spaniards established St. Augustine, the first permanent European settlement in what became the United States. Britain gained control of Florida in 1763 but ceded it back to Spain in 1783. After the American Revolution (1775-1783), the United States controlled all the land it now occupies from the Atlantic Ocean to the Mississippi River except for Spanish Florida.

The United States formally obtained Florida from Spain in 1821, and Congress established the Territory of Florida the next year. Florida became a state in 1845. Shortly before the American Civil War began in 1861, Florida left the Union and then joined the Confederacy. Tallahassee was the only Confederate state capital east of the Mississippi River that Union forces did not capture during the war. Florida was readmitted to the Union in 1868. The population of Florida started to swell during the early 1900's and has been growing ever since.

Bob Glander, Shostal

Sandy beaches along the Gulf of Mexico, such as this one at Clearwater Beach, attract many swimmers and sunbathers. Florida's warm, sunny climate makes it a popular vacationland.

Florida in brief

Symbols of Florida

The state flag, adopted in 1899, bears the state seal. Diagonal red bars extend from the corners of the flag over a white field. The seal was adopted in 1985. It reflects minor changes that corrected inaccuracies in the 1868 seal. The revised seal depicts a Seminole Indian woman strewing flowers. A sabal palm, the state tree, rises in the center. A Florida steamboat sails in the background before the rising sun.

State flag

State of Florida
State seal

Florida (brown) ranks 21st in size among all the states and is the largest of the Southern States (yellow).

General information

Statehood: March 3, 1845, the 27th state.
State abbreviations: Fla. (traditional); FL (postal).
State motto: *In God We Trust* (unofficial).
State song: "Old Folks at Home" ("Swanee River"). Words and music by Stephen Foster.
State anthem: "Florida (Where the Sawgrass Meets the Sky)." Words and music by Jan Hinton.

The State Capitol is in Tallahassee, the capital of Florida since 1824—two years after the U.S. Congress established the Territory of Florida.

Land and climate

Area: 58,976 mi² (152,747 km²), including 5,373 mi² (13,916 km²) of inland water but excluding 1,128 mi² (2,923 km²) of coastal water.
Elevation: *Highest*—345 ft (105 m) above sea level in Walton County. *Lowest*—sea level.
Coastline: 1,350 mi (2,172 km)—580 mi (933 km) along the Atlantic Ocean; 770 mi (1,239 km) along the Gulf of Mexico.
Record high temperature: 109 °F (43 °C) at Monticello on June 29, 1931.
Record low temperature: -2 °F (-19 °C) at Tallahassee on Feb. 13, 1899.
Average July temperature: 81 °F (27 °C).
Average January temperature: 59 °F (15 °C).
Average yearly precipitation: 54 in (137 cm).

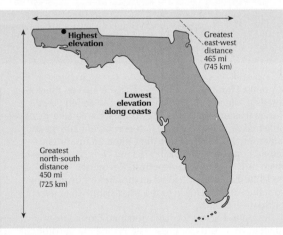

Highest elevation

Greatest east-west distance 465 mi (745 km)

Lowest elevation along coasts

Greatest north-south distance 450 mi (725 km)

Important dates

Pedro Menéndez de Avilés founded St. Augustine, the first permanent European settlement in what is now the United States.

Spain regained control of Florida.

| 1513 | 1565 | 1763 | 1783 | 1821 |

Juan Ponce de León landed on the Florida coast and claimed the region for Spain.

Spain ceded Florida to Britain.

Florida formally came under United States control.

State bird
Northern mockingbird

State flower
Orange blossom

State tree
Sabal palmetto
(Cabbage palmetto)

People

Population: 18,801,310
Rank among the states: 4th
Density: 319 per mi² (123 per km²), U.S. average 85 per mi² (33 per km²)
Distribution: 91 percent urban, 9 percent rural
Largest cities in Florida

Jacksonville	821,784
Miami	399,457
Tampa	335,709
St. Petersburg	244,769
Orlando	238,300
Hialeah	224,669

Source: 2010 census.

Population trend

Millions

Source: U.S. Census Bureau.

Year	Population
2010	18,801,310
2000	15,982,378
1990	12,937,926
1980	9,746,324
1970	6,791,443
1960	4,951,560
1950	2,771,305
1940	1,897,414
1930	1,468,211
1920	968,470
1910	752,619
1900	528,542
1890	391,422
1880	269,493
1870	187,748
1860	140,424
1850	87,445
1840	54,477
1830	34,730

Economy

Chief products

Agriculture: beef cattle, greenhouse and nursery products, milk, oranges, sugar cane, tomatoes.
Manufacturing: chemicals, computer and electronic products, medical equipment, processed foods and beverages, transportation equipment.
Mining: limestone, petroleum, phosphate rock, portland cement.

Gross domestic product

Value of goods and services produced in 2010: $727,972,000,000. *Services* include community, business, and personal services; finance; government; trade; and transportation and communication. *Industry* includes construction, manufacturing, mining, and utilities. *Agriculture* includes agriculture, fishing, and forestry.
Source: U.S. Bureau of Economic Analysis.

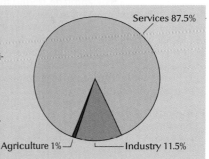

Services 87.5%
Agriculture 1%
Industry 11.5%

Government

State government

Governor: 4-year term
State senators: 40; 4-year terms
State representatives: 120; 2-year terms
Counties: 67

Federal government

United States senators: 2
United States representatives: 27
Electoral votes: 29

Sources of information

Florida's official website at http://www.myflorida.com provides a gateway to much information on the state's government, history, and economy.

In addition, the website at http://www.visitflorida.com provides information about tourism.

Florida became the 27th state on March 3.

The Walt Disney World entertainment complex opened near Orlando.

Florida's electoral votes were the deciding factor in the U.S. presidential election.

1845 — **1961** — **1971** — **1992** — **2000**

The first United States astronaut flights were launched from Cape Canaveral.

Hurricane Andrew killed 44 people in Florida and caused much property damage.

Population. The 2010 United States census reported that Florida had 18,801,310 people. The population had increased about 18 percent over the 2000 figure of 15,982,378. Of states east of the Mississippi River, only Georgia and North Carolina had a higher percentage of growth during the first decade of the 2000's. Florida ranks fourth in population among the 50 states.

About 94 percent of Florida's people live in metropolitan areas. Florida has 20 metropolitan areas entirely within the borders of the state (see **Metropolitan area**). Over half of the state's population lives in the Miami-Fort Lauderdale-Pompano Beach, Orlando-Kissimmee-Sanford, and Tampa-St. Petersburg-Clearwater metropolitan areas. For the names and populations of Florida's metropolitan areas, see the *Index* to Florida's political map.

Jacksonville is Florida's largest city, with a population of more than 820,000. Other cities over 150,000, in order of population, are Miami, Tampa, St. Petersburg, Orlando, Hialeah, Tallahassee, Fort Lauderdale, Port St. Lucie, Pembroke Pines, and Cape Coral. Most of Florida's largest cities lie on or near the Atlantic or Gulf coasts.

Many older people move to Florida from other parts of the country after they retire. About 15 percent of the state's population are African Americans. Hispanics, who may be of any race, make up over 20 percent of Florida's population. Many Floridians are of Cuban, English, German, Irish, or Italian ancestry.

Schools. Spanish priests ran Florida's earliest schools in the 1600's. Spanish and Indian children studied religion and the Spanish language. During the mid-1700's, English colonists provided education for the children of wealthier families. A formal system of public education in Florida began with the Constitution of 1868. Public education was well established by the early 1900's.

Today, the governor appoints a Board of Education. The board has authority over elementary through postsecondary education. The Department of Education

Population density

About 94 percent of Floridians live in metropolitan areas. Most of the biggest cities lie on or near the Atlantic or Gulf coasts. Jacksonville, Miami, and Tampa are the state's largest cities.

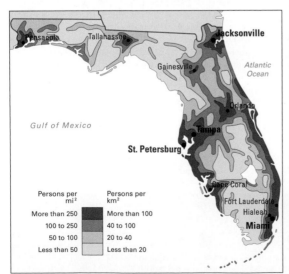

Persons per mi²
- More than 250
- 100 to 250
- 50 to 100
- Less than 50

Persons per km²
- More than 100
- 40 to 100
- 20 to 40
- Less than 20

WORLD BOOK map; based on U.S. Census Bureau data.

© AP/Wide World

The Orange Bowl Parade in Miami is a colorful annual event. The parade takes place before the Orange Bowl football game, which is played on or near New Year's Day.

Wendell Metzen, Southern Stock

Baseball spring training is a major tourist attraction in Florida. Many major league teams take advantage of the state's warm, sunny climate to get ready for competition.

Ned Haines, Photo Researchers

Florida Southern College, in Lakeland, was founded in 1885. The college chapel, *shown here,* is a distinctive building designed by the famous American architect Frank Lloyd Wright.

The John and Mable Ringling Museum of Art in Sarasota has a fine collection of paintings. Beautiful sculptures decorate the courtyard of the museum.

Photri

Universities and colleges

This table lists the nonprofit universities and colleges in Florida that grant bachelor's or advanced degrees and are accredited by the Southern Association of Colleges and Schools.

Name	Mailing address	Name	Mailing address	Name	Mailing address
Adventist University of Health Sciences	Orlando	Florida Institute of Technology	Melbourne	Polk State College	Winter Haven
Ave Maria University	Ave Maria	Florida International University	Miami	Ringling College of Art and Design	Sarasota
Baptist College of Florida	Graceville	Florida Memorial University	Miami	Rollins College	Winter Park
Barry University	Miami Shores	Florida Southern College	Lakeland	St. John Vianney College Seminary	Miami
Beacon College	Leesburg	Florida State College at Jacksonville	Jacksonville	St. Johns River State College	Palatka
Bethune-Cookman University	Daytona Beach	Florida State University	Tallahassee	St. Leo University	St. Leo
Broward College	Fort Lauderdale	Gulf Coast State College	Panama City	St. Petersburg College	St. Petersburg
Central Florida, College of	Ocala	Hodges University	Naples	St. Thomas University	Miami Gardens
Central Florida, University of	Orlando	Indian River State College	Fort Pierce	St. Vincent de Paul Regional Seminary	Boynton Beach
Chipola College	Marianna	Jacksonville University	Jacksonville	Santa Fe College	Gainesville
Clearwater Christian College	Clearwater	Johnson & Wales University	North Miami	Seminole State College of Florida	*
Daytona State College	Daytona Beach	Keiser University	Fort Lauderdale	South Florida, University of	Tampa
Eckerd College	St. Petersburg	Lake Sumter State College	Leesburg	South Florida Sarasota-Manatee, University of	Sarasota
Edison State College	Fort Myers	Lynn University	Boca Raton	South Florida St. Petersburg, University of	St. Petersburg
Edward Waters College	Jacksonville	Miami, University of	Coral Gables	Southeastern University	Lakeland
Embry-Riddle Aeronautical University	Daytona Beach	Miami Dade College	Miami	State College of Florida, Manatee-Sarasota	Bradenton
Everglades University	Boca Raton	New College of Florida	Sarasota	Stetson University	De Land
Flagler College	St. Augustine	North Florida, University of	Jacksonville	Tampa, University of	Tampa
Florida, University of	Gainesville	Northwest Florida State College	Niceville	Valencia College	Orlando
Florida Agricultural and Mechanical University	Tallahassee	Nova Southeastern University	Fort Lauderdale	Warner University	Lake Wales
Florida Atlantic University	Boca Raton	Palm Beach Atlantic University	West Palm Beach	Webber International University	Babson Park
Florida Christian College	Kissimmee	Palm Beach State College	Lake Worth	West Florida, University of	Pensacola
Florida College	Temple Terrace	Pensacola Junior College	Pensacola		
Florida Gateway College	Lake City				
Florida Gulf Coast University	Fort Myers				

*Campuses in Altamonte Springs, Heathrow, Oviedo, and Sanford.

administers the policies of the board. A commissioner of education leads the department. The commissioner is appointed by the governor. The Department of Education supervises public schools and public community colleges and universities. The department also supervises state-supported vocational education programs. Children from age 6 through 15 must attend school. For the number of students and teachers in Florida, see **Education** (table).

Libraries. The Walton-DeFuniak Library in DeFuniak Springs, established in 1886, is the oldest library in Florida still serving the public. The state's first free, tax-supported library opened in Jacksonville in 1905. The state administers the State Library of Florida in Tallahassee. The Florida Historical Society maintains the Library of Florida History in Cocoa. The P. K. Yonge Library of Florida History, at the University of Florida, has an extensive collection of books about the state.

Museums. The John and Mable Ringling Museum of Art in Sarasota is noted for its Baroque art collection. Also on the grounds are the Ringling mansion and the Circus Museums. History museums in Florida include the Museum of Florida History in Tallahassee and HistoryMiami in Miami. The state's art museums include the Cummer Museum of Art and Gardens in Jacksonville; the Museum of Fine Arts and the Salvador Dalí Museum in St. Petersburg; and the Norton Museum of Art in West Palm Beach. Other important museums are the Florida Museum of Natural History in Gainesville and the Vizcaya Museum and Gardens in Miami.

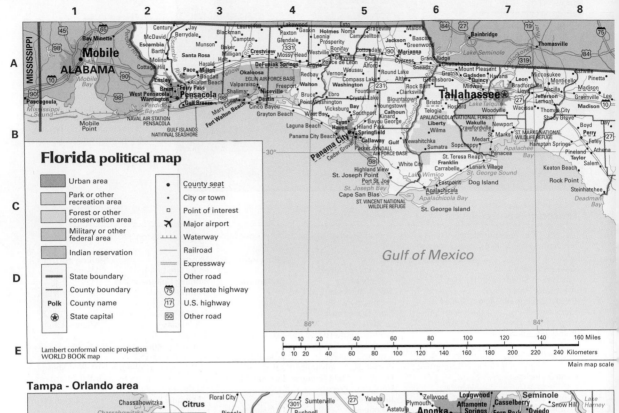

Florida political map

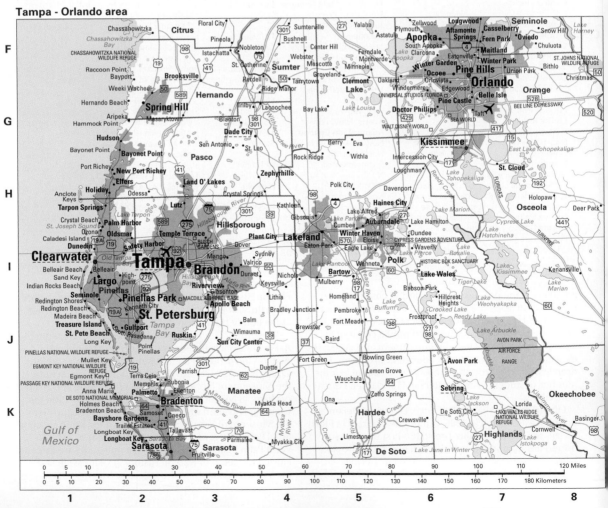

Tampa - Orlando area

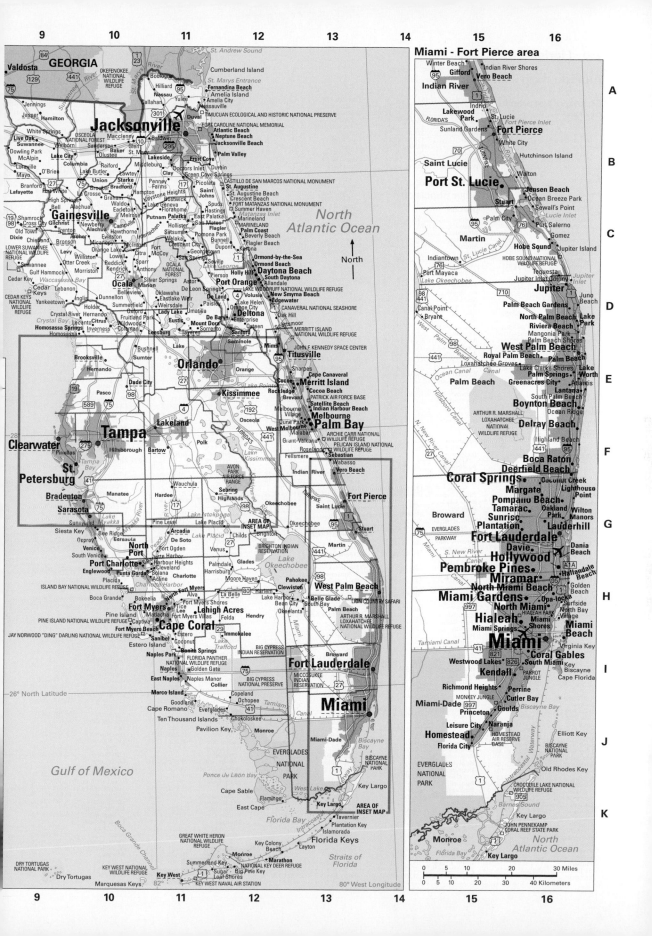

Florida map index

Metropolitan areas

Cape Coral-Fort Myers ... 618,754
Crestview-Fort Walton Beach-Destin ... 180,822
Deltona-Daytona Beach-Ormond Beach ... 494,593
Gainesville ... 264,275
Jacksonville ... 1,345,596
Lakeland-Winter Haven ... 602,095
Miami-Fort Lauderdale-Pompano Beach ... 5,564,635
Naples-Marco Island ... 321,520
North Port-Bradenton-Sarasota ... 702,281
Ocala ... 331,298
Orlando-Kissimmee-Sanford ... 2,134,411
Palm Bay-Melbourne-Titusville ... 543,376
Palm Coast ... 95,696
Panama City-Lynn Haven-Panama City Beach ... 168,852
Pensacola-Ferry Pass-Brent ... 448,991
Port St. Lucie ... 424,107
Punta Gorda ... 159,978
Sebastian-Vero Beach ... 138,028
Tallahassee ... 367,413
Tampa-St. Petersburg-Clearwater ... 2,783,243

Metropolitan divisions

Fort Lauderdale-Pompano Beach-Deerfield Beach ... 1,748,066
Miami-Miami Beach-Kendall ... 2,496,435
West Palm Beach-Boca Raton-Boynton Beach ... 1,320,134

Counties

Alachua ... 247,336 .. C 10
Baker ... 27,115 .. B 10
Bay ... 168,852 .. B 5
Bradford ... 28,520 .. B 10
Brevard ... 543,376 .. E 12
Broward ... 1,748,066 .. I 13
Calhoun ... 14,625 .. B 5
Charlotte ... 159,978 .. H 11
Citrus ... 141,236 .. D 10
Clay ... 190,865 .. B 11
Collier ... 321,520 .. I 11
Columbia ... 67,531 .. C 9
De Soto ... 34,862 .. G 11
Dixie ... 16,422 .. C 9
Duval ... 864,263 .. A 11
Escambia ... 297,619 .. A 2
Flagler ... 95,696 .. C 11
Franklin ... 11,549 .. B 6
Gadsden ... 46,389 .. B 6
Gilchrist ... 16,939 .. C 9
Glades ... 12,884 .. H 12
Gulf ... 15,863 .. B 5
Hamilton ... 14,799 .. A 9
Hardee ... 27,731 .. G 11
Hendry ... 39,140 .. H 12
Hernando ... 172,778 .. E 10
Highlands ... 98,786 .. G 12
Hillsborough ... 1,229,226 .. F 10
Holmes ... 19,927 .. A 4
Indian River ... 138,028 .. F 13
Jackson ... 49,746 .. A 5
Jefferson ... 14,761 .. A 7
Lafayette ... 8,870 .. B 9
Lake ... 297,052 .. D 11
Lee ... 618,754 .. H 11
Leon ... 275,487 .. A 7
Levy ... 40,801 .. C 9
Liberty ... 8,365 .. B 6
Madison ... 19,224 .. B 8
Manatee ... 322,833 .. G 10
Marion ... 331,298 .. D 10
Martin ... 146,318 .. G 13
Miami-Dade ... 2,496,435 .. J 13
Monroe ... 73,090 .. J 12
Nassau ... 73,314 .. A 11
Okaloosa ... 180,822 .. A 3
Okeechobee ... 39,996 .. G 12
Orange ... 1,145,956 .. E 12
Osceola ... 268,685 .. F 12
Palm Beach ... 1,320,134 .. H 13
Pasco ... 464,697 .. E 10
Pinellas ... 916,542 .. F 9
Polk ... 602,095 .. F 11
Putnam ... 74,364 .. C 11
St. Johns ... 190,039 .. B 11
St. Lucie ... 277,789 .. G 13
Santa Rosa ... 151,372 .. A 3
Sarasota ... 379,448 .. H 10
Seminole ... 422,718 .. D 12
Sumter ... 93,420 .. E 10
Suwannee ... 41,551 .. B 9
Taylor ... 22,570 .. C 8
Union ... 15,535 .. B 10
Volusia ... 494,593 .. D 12
Wakulla ... 30,776 .. B 7
Walton ... 55,043 .. A 4
Washington ... 24,896 .. A 5

Cities, towns, and other populated places

Alachua ... 9,059 .. C 10
Alafaya*† ... 78,113 .. F 7
Altamonte Springs ... 41,496 .. F 7
Alturas*† ... 4,185 .. I 5
Alva† ... 2,596 .. H 11
Anna Maria ... 1,503 .. K 2
Apalachicola° ... 2,231 .. C 6
Apollo Beach† ... 14,055 .. I 3
Apopka ... 41,542 .. F 6
Arcadia° ... 7,637 .. G 11
Archer ... 1,118 .. C 10
Asbury Lake*† ... 8,700 .. B 11
Astatula ... 1,810 .. D 11
Astor† ... 1,556 .. D 11
Atlantic Beach ... 12,655 .. B 11
Atlantis ... 2,005 .. E 16
Auburndale ... 13,507 .. H 5
Aventura* ... 35,762 .. H 16
Avon Park ... 8,836 .. J 6
Azalea Park*† ... 12,556 .. G 7
Babson Park† ... 1,356 .. I 6
Bagdad† ... 3,761 .. A 3
Bal Harbour* ... 2,513 .. H 16
Baldwin ... 1,425 .. B 11
Bartow° ... 17,298 .. F 11
Bay Harbor Islands* ... 5,628 .. H 16
Bay Hill*† ... 4,884 .. G 6
Bay Pines*† ... 2,931 .. I 2
Bayonet Point† ... 23,467 .. G 2
Bayshore Gardens† ... 16,323 .. K 2
Beacon Square† ... 7,224 .. H 2
Bee Ridge† ... 9,598 .. G 10
Bellair [-Meadowbrook Terrace]*† ... 13,343 .. B 11
Belle Glade ... 17,467 .. H 13
Belle Isle ... 5,988 .. G 7
Belleair ... 3,869 .. I 1
Belleair Beach ... 1,560 .. I 1
Belleair Bluffs* ... 2,031 .. I 1
Belleview ... 4,492 .. D 10
Bellview*† ... 23,355 .. A 2
Beverly Hills*† ... 8,445 .. B 11
Big Coppitt Key*† ... 2,458 .. K 11
Big Cypress Indian Reservation ... 591 .. I 12
Big Pine Key† ... 4,252 .. K 12
Biscayne Park* ... 3,055 .. H 16
Bithlo† ... 8,268 .. F 8
Bloomingdale*† ... 22,711 .. I 3
Blountstown° ... 2,514 .. B 6
Boca Raton ... 84,392 .. F 16
Bonifay° ... 2,793 .. A 5
Bonita Springs ... 43,914 .. I 11
Bowling Green ... 2,930 .. J 5
Boynton Beach ... 68,217 .. E 16
Bradenton° ... 49,546 .. G 10
Bradenton Beach ... 1,171 .. K 2
Brandon† ... 103,483 .. I 3
Brent† ... 21,804 .. A 2
Brighton Indian Reservation ... 694 .. G 12
Bristol° ... 996 .. B 6
Broadview Park*† ... 7,125 .. G 16
Bronson° ... 1,113 .. C 9
Brookridge*† ... 4,420 .. F 3
Brooksville° ... 7,719 .. E 10
Brownsville*† ... 15,313 .. H 16
Buckingham*† ... 4,036 .. H 11
Buenaventura Lakes*† ... 26,079 .. G 7
Bunnell° ... 2,676 .. C 12
Bushnell° ... 2,418 .. E 10
Butler Beach*† ... 4,951 .. B 12
Callahan ... 1,123 .. A 11
Callaway ... 14,405 .. B 5
Campbell*† ... 2,479 .. G 6
Cape Canaveral ... 9,912 .. E 13
Cape Coral ... 154,305 .. H 11
Carrabelle ... 2,778 .. C 6
Carrollwood*† ... 33,365 .. I 2
Casselberry ... 26,241 .. F 7
Cedar Grove ... 3,397 .. B 5
Celebration*† ... 7,427 .. H 6
Century ... 1,698 .. A 2
Charlotte Harbor† ... 3,714 .. G 11
Charlotte Park*† ... 2,325 .. H 11
Chattahoochee ... 3,652 .. A 6
Cheval*† ... 10,702 .. H 2
Chiefland ... 2,245 .. C 9
Chipley° ... 3,605 .. A 5
Chuluota† ... 2,483 .. F 8
Citrus Hills*† ... 7,470 .. D 10
Citrus Park*† ... 24,252 .. I 2
Citrus Springs*† ... 8,622 .. D 10
Clair Mel, see Palm River [-Clair Mel]
Clarcona† ... 2,990 .. F 6
Clearwater° ... 107,865 .. F 9
Clermont ... 28,742 .. F 5
Cleveland† ... 2,990 .. H 11
Clewiston ... 7,155 .. H 12
Cocoa ... 17,140 .. E 12
Cocoa Beach ... 11,231 .. E 13
Cocoa West*† ... 5,925 .. E 12
Coconut Creek ... 52,909 .. F 16
Coleman ... 703 .. D 10
Combee Settlement*† ... 5,577 .. I 4
Conway*† ... 13,467 .. F 7
Cooper City* ... 28,547 .. G 16
Coral Gables ... 46,780 .. I 16
Coral Springs ... 121,096 .. F 16
Coral Terrace*† ... 24,376 .. I 16
Cortez*† ... 4,241 .. K 2
Country Club*† ... 47,105 .. H 16
Crawfordville†° ... 3,702 .. B 7
Crescent Beach† ... 931 .. C 12
Crescent City ... 1,577 .. C 11
Crestview° ... 20,978 .. A 3
Crooked Lake Park*† ... 1,722 .. I 6
Cross City° ... 1,728 .. C 9
Crystal Lake*† ... 5,514 .. I 5
Crystal River ... 3,108 .. D 10
Cudjoe Key*† ... 1,763 .. K 12
Cutler Bay ... 40,286 .. I 15
Cypress Gardens*† ... 8,917 .. I 5
Cypress Lake*† ... 11,846 .. H 11
Cypress Quarters*† ... 1,215 .. G 12
Dade City° ... 6,437 .. E 10
Dade City North*† ... 3,113 .. G 4
Dania Beach ... 29,639 .. G 16
Davenport ... 2,888 .. H 6
Davie ... 91,992 .. G 16
Daytona Beach ... 61,005 .. D 12
Daytona Beach Shores* ... 4,247 .. D 12
De Bary† ... 19,320 .. D 12
Deerfield Beach ... 75,018 .. F 16
DeFuniak Springs° ... 5,177 .. B 4
De Land° ... 27,031 .. D 12
De Land Southwest*† ... 1,052 .. D 12
De Leon Springs† ... 2,614 .. D 11
Delray Beach ... 60,522 .. F 16
Deltona† ... 85,182 .. D 12
Desoto Lakes*† ... 3,646 .. K 3
Destin ... 12,305 .. B 4
Doctor Phillips† ... 10,981 .. G 6
Doral*† ... 45,704 .. H 15
Dover† ... 3,702 .. I 3
Dundee ... 3,717 .. I 6
Dunedin ... 35,321 .. I 1
Dunnellon ... 1,733 .. D 10
Eagle Lake ... 2,255 .. I 5
East Lake [-Orient Park]*† ... 22,753 .. I 3
East Palatka† ... 1,654 .. C 11
Eastpoint† ... 2,337 .. C 6
Eatonville ... 2,159 .. F 7
Edgewater ... 20,750 .. D 12
Edgewood ... 2,503 .. G 7
Eglin AFB† ... 2,274 .. A 4
Egypt Lake-Leto*† ... 35,282 .. I 2
Elfers† ... 13,986 .. H 2
Ellenton† ... 4,275 .. K 2
El Portal* ... 2,325 .. H 16
Englewood† ... 14,863 .. H 10
Ensley† ... 20,602 .. A 2
Estero† ... 22,612 .. I 11
Eustis ... 18,558 .. D 11
Fairview Shores*† ... 10,239 .. F 7
Feather Sound*† ... 3,420 .. I 2
Fellsmere ... 5,197 .. F 13
Fern Park† ... 7,704 .. F 7
Fernandina Beach° ... 11,487 .. A 11
Ferry Pass† ... 28,921 .. A 2
Fish Hawk*† ... 14,087 .. I 4
Flagler Beach ... 4,484 .. C 12
Fleming Island*† ... 27,126 .. B 11
Floral City† ... 5,217 .. F 3
Florida City ... 11,245 .. J 15
Florida Ridge*† ... 18,164 .. A 15
Forest City*† ... 13,854 .. F 7
Fort Lauderdale° ... 165,521 .. I 13
Fort Meade ... 5,626 .. J 5
Fort Myers° ... 62,298 .. H 11
Fort Myers Beach† ... 6,277 .. H 11
Fort Myers Shores† ... 5,487 .. H 11
Fort Pierce° ... 41,590 .. G 13
Fort Pierce North† ... 6,474 .. A 15
Fort Pierce South*† ... 5,062 .. B 15
Fort Walton Beach ... 19,507 .. B 3
Fountainbleau*† ... 59,764 .. I 15
Four Corners*† ... 26,116 .. H 6
Frostproof ... 2,992 .. J 6
Fruit Cove† ... 29,362 .. B 11
Fruitland Park ... 4,078 .. E 11
Fruitville† ... 13,224 .. K 3
Fussels Corner*† ... 5,561 .. H 5
Gainesville° ... 124,354 .. C 10
Gateway*† ... 8,401 .. H 11
Geneva*† ... 2,940 .. E 12
Gibsonton† ... 14,234 .. I 3
Gifford† ... 9,590 .. A 15
Gladeview*† ... 11,535 .. H 16
Glencoe*† ... 2,582 .. D 12
Glenvar Heights*† ... 16,898 .. I 16
Golden Gate† ... 23,961 .. I 11
Golden Glades*† ... 33,145 .. H 16
Goldenrod*† ... 12,039 .. F 7
Gonzalez*† ... 13,273 .. A 2
Goulding*† ... 4,102 .. B 2
Goulds† ... 10,103 .. I 15
Graceville ... 2,278 .. A 5
Grant-Valkaria ... 3,850 .. F 13
Green Cove Springs° ... 6,908 .. B 11
Greenacres City ... 37,573 .. E 16
Greenville ... 843 .. B 8
Gretna ... 1,460 .. A 6
Grove City*† ... 1,804 .. H 10
Groveland ... 8,729 .. F 5
Gulf Breeze ... 5,763 .. B 3
Gulf Gate Estates*† ... 10,911 .. G 10
Gulfport ... 12,029 .. J 2
Haines City ... 20,535 .. H 6
Hallandale Beach ... 37,113 .. H 16
Harbor Bluffs*† ... 2,860 .. I 1
Harbour Heights† ... 2,987 .. H 10
Harlem† ... 2,658 .. H 12
Harlem Heights*† ... 1,975 .. H 11
Havana ... 1,754 .. A 7
Haverhill* ... 1,873 .. E 16
Hawthorne ... 1,417 .. C 10
Heathrow*† ... 5,896 .. D 11
Hernando† ... 9,054 .. D 10
Hernando Beach† ... 2,299 .. G 2
Hialeah ... 224,669 .. H 16
Hialeah Gardens* ... 21,744 .. H 16
High Point*† ... 3,686 .. F 3
High Springs ... 5,350 .. B 9
Highland Beach ... 3,539 .. F 16
Highland City† ... 10,834 .. I 5
Hilliard ... 3,086 .. A 11
Hillsboro Beach* ... 1,875 .. F 16
Hobe Sound† ... 11,521 .. C 16
Holden Heights*† ... 3,679 .. F 6
Holiday† ... 22,403 .. H 1
Holly Hill ... 11,659 .. D 12
Hollywood ... 140,768 .. G 16
Hollywood Indian Reservation* ... 1,742 .. G 16
Holmes Beach ... 3,836 .. K 2
Homestead ... 60,512 .. J 15
Homestead AFB† ... 964 .. J 15
Homosassa† ... 2,578 .. D 9
Homosassa Springs† ... 13,791 .. D 10
Hudson† ... 12,158 .. G 2
Hunters Creek*† ... 14,321 .. G 6
Hutchinson Island South*† ... 5,201 .. B 15
Immokalee† ... 24,154 .. I 12
Indialantic* ... 2,720 .. F 13
Indian Harbour Beach ... 8,225 .. E 13
Indian River Estates*† ... 6,220 .. B 15
Indian River Shores ... 3,901 .. A 15
Indian Rocks Beach ... 4,113 .. I 1
Indian Shores* ... 1,420 .. I 1
Indiantown† ... 6,083 .. C 15
Inglis ... 1,325 .. D 9
Interlachen ... 1,403 .. C 11
Inverness° ... 7,210 .. D 10
Inwood*† ... 6,403 .. I 5
Iona*† ... 15,369 .. H 11
Islamorada ... 6,119 .. K 13
Ives Estates*† ... 19,525 .. H 16
Jacksonville° ... 821,784 .. B 11
Jacksonville Beach ... 21,362 .. B 11
Jan Phyl Village*† ... 5,573 .. I 5
Jasmine Estates*† ... 18,989 .. H 2
Jasper° ... 4,546 .. A 9
Jennings ... 878 .. A 9
Jensen Beach† ... 11,707 .. B 16
June Park† ... 4,094 .. F 13
Juno Beach ... 3,176 .. D 16
Jupiter ... 55,156 .. D 16
Kathleen† ... 6,332 .. H 4
Kendale Lakes*† ... 56,148 .. I 15
Kendall† ... 75,371 .. I 15
Kendall West*† ... 36,154 .. I 15
Kenneth City ... 4,980 .. J 2
Kensington Park*† ... 3,901 .. K 3
Key Biscayne*† ... 12,344 .. I 16
Key Largo† ... 10,433 .. K 13
Key West° ... 24,649 .. K 11
Keystone*† ... 24,039 .. H 2
Keystone Heights ... 1,350 .. C 10
Kissimmee° ... 59,682 .. E 12
La Belle° ... 4,640 .. H 12
Lacoochee† ... 1,714 .. G 4
Lady Lake ... 13,926 .. D 11
Laguna Beach† ... 3,932 .. B 4
Lake Alfred ... 5,015 .. H 5
Lake Buena Vista* ... 10 .. G 6
Lake Butler° ... 1,897 .. B 10
Lake City° ... 12,046 .. B 9
Lake Clarke Shores ... 3,376 .. E 16
Lake Hamilton ... 1,231 .. H 6
Lake Helen ... 2,624 .. D 12
Lake Lorraine*† ... 7,010 .. A 3
Lake Magdalene*† ... 28,509 .. I 3
Lake Mary* ... 13,822 .. D 12
Lake Panasoffkee*† ... 3,551 .. D 10
Lake Park ... 8,155 .. D 16
Lake Placid ... 2,223 .. G 12
Lake Sarasota*† ... 4,679 .. G 10
Lake Wales ... 14,225 .. I 6
Lake Worth ... 34,910 .. E 16
Lakeland ... 97,422 .. F 11
Lakeland Highlands*† ... 11,056 .. I 4
Lakeside† ... 30,943 .. B 11
Lakewood Park† ... 11,323 .. A 15
Land O'Lakes† ... 31,996 .. H 2
Lantana ... 10,423 .. E 16
Largo ... 77,648 .. I 1
Lauderdale-by-the-Sea ... 6,056 .. G 16
Lauderdale Lakes* ... 32,593 .. G 16
Lauderhill ... 66,887 .. G 16
Laurel*† ... 8,171 .. G 10
Lealman* ... 19,879 .. I 1
Lecanto† ... 5,882 .. D 10
Leesburg ... 20,117 .. D 11
Lehigh Acres† ... 86,784 .. H 11
Leisure City† ... 22,655 .. J 15
Lely*† ... 3,451 .. I 11
Lely Resort*† ... 4,646 .. I 11
Lighthouse Point ... 10,344 .. F 16
Live Oak° ... 6,850 .. B 9
Lochmoor Waterway Estates*† ... 4,204 .. H 11
Lockhart*† ... 13,060 .. F 6
Longboat Key ... 6,888 .. K 2
Longwood ... 13,657 .. F 7
Loughman† ... 2,680 .. H 6
Lower Grand Lagoon*† ... 3,881 .. B 5
Loxahatchee Groves ... 3,180 .. E 16
Lutz† ... 19,344 .. H 3
Lynn Haven ... 18,493 .. B 5
Macclenny° ... 6,374 .. B 10
Madeira Beach ... 4,263 .. J 1
Madison° ... 2,843 .. B 8
Maitland ... 15,751 .. F 7

Malabar ....2,757 ..F 13
Malone ....2,088 ..A 6
Manasota Key*† ..1,229 ..H 11
Manatee
  Road*† ....2,244 ..C 9
Mango† ....11,313 ..I 3
Mangonia Park ..1,888 ..D 16
Marathon† ....8,297 ..K 12
Marco Island ...16,413 ..J 11
Margate ....53,284 ..F 16
Marianna ....6,102 ..A 6
Mascotte* ....5,101 ..F 5
Meadow
  Woods*† ......19,879 ..G 7
Meadows,
  The*† ....3,994 ..K 3
Medulla*† ....8,892 ..J 4
Melbourne .....76,068 ..F 13
Melbourne
  Beach* ....3,101 ..F 13
Memphis† ....7,848 ..K 2
Merritt
  Island* ....34,743 ..J 13
Miami° ....399,457 ..J 13
Miami Beach ...87,779 ..H 16
Miami
  Gardens .....107,167 ..H 16
Miami Lakes* ..29,361 ..H 16
Miami Shores ..10,493 ..H 16
Miami Springs ..13,809 ..H 16
Micco*† ....9,052 ..F 13
Miccosukee
  Indian
  Reservation .....406 ..I 13
Middleburg† ....13,008 ..B 11
Midway° ....3,004 ..A 7
Milton° ....8,826 ..A 3
Mims† ....7,058 ..E 12
Minneola ....9,403 ..F 5
Miramar ......122,041 ..H 16
Miramar
  Beach*† ....6,146 ..B 3
Molino† ....1,277 ..A 2
Monticello° .....2,506 ..A 8
Monteverde .....1,463 ..F 5
Moore Haven° ..1,680 ..H 12
Mount Dora ....12,370 ..D 11
Mount
  Plymouth*† ....4,011 ..D 11
Mulberry ....3,817 ..H 4
Myrtle
  Grove*† ....15,870 ..A 2
Naples° ....19,537 ..J 11
Naples
  Manor*† ....5,562 ..J 11
Naples Park† ....5,967 ..J 11
Naranja† ....8,303 ..J 15
Nassau Village
  [-Ratliff]*† .....5,337 ..A 11
Neptune Beach ..7,037 ..B 11
New Port
  Richey ....14,911 ..H 2
New Port Richey
  East*† ....10,036 ..H 2
New Smyrna
  Beach ....22,464 ..D 12
Newberry ....4,950 ..C 10
Niceville ....12,749 ..A 4
Nokomis*† ....3,167 ..G 10
North Bay
  Village ....7,137 ..H 16
North
  Brooksville*† ..3,544 ..F 3
North
  DeLand* ......1,450 ..D 12
North Fort
  Myers* ....39,407 ..H 11
North Key
  Largo*† ....1,244 ..K 16
North
  Lauderdale* ..41,023 ..G 16
North Miami ...58,786 ..H 16
North Miami
  Beach ....41,523 ..H 16
North Palm
  Beach ....12,015 ..D 16
North Port .....57,357 ..G 10
North River
  Shores*† ......3,079 ..B 15
North
  Sarasota*† ....6,982 ..K 2
North Weeki
  Wachee*† ......8,524 ..F 2
Oak Hill ....1,792 ..D 13
Oak Ridge*† ...22,685 ..G 6
Oakland ....2,538 ..F 6
Oakland Park ..41,363 ..G 16
Ocala° ....56,315 ..D 10
Ocean City*† ...5,550 ..A 3
Ocean Ridge ...1,786 ..E 16
Ocoee ....35,579 ..F 6
Ojus*† ....18,036 ..H 16
Okeechobee° ...5,621 ..G 12
Oldsmar ....13,591 ..I 2
Olympia
  Heights*† .....13,488 ..I 15
Opa-locka ......15,219 ..H 16
Orange City ....10,599 ..D 12
Orange Park* ...8,412 ..B 11
Orient Park, see
  East Lake
  [-Orient Park]
Orlando° ......238,300 ..E 11
Orlovista*† ......6,123 ..F 6

Ormond
  Beach ....38,137 ..C 12
Ormond- by-
  the-Sea† ....7,406 ..C 12
Osprey† ....6,100 ..G 10
Oviedo ....33,342 ..F 7
Pace† ....20,039 ..A 3
Page Park*† ....514 ..H 11
Pahokee ....5,649 ..H 13
Palatka° ....10,558 ..C 11
Palm Bay ......103,190 ..F 13
Palm Beach ......8,348 ..E 16
Palm Beach
  Gardens ......48,452 ..D 16
Palm Beach
  Shores ....1,142 ..D 16
Palm City† .....23,120 ..C 15
Palm Coast° ...75,180 ..C 12
Palm Harbor† ..57,439 ..H 2
Palm River
  [-Clair
  Mel]*† ....21,024 ..I 2
Palm Springs ..18,928 ..E 16
Palm Springs
  North*† ....5,253 ..H 16
Palm Valley*† ..20,019 ..B 11
Palmetto ....12,606 ..K 2
Palmetto Bay* ..23,410 ..I 16
Palmetto
  Estates*† ......13,535 ..J 15
Panama City° ..36,484 ..B 5
Panama City
  Beach ....12,018 ..B 5
Parker ....4,317 ..B 5
Parkland* ......23,962 ..F 16
Pebble
  Creek*† ....7,622 ..H 3
Pelican Bay*† ...6,346 ..J 11
Pembroke
  Park* ....6,102 ..G 16
Pembroke
  Pines ....154,750 ..G 16
Pensacola° .....51,923 ..A 2
Perry° ....7,017 ..B 8
Pierson ....1,736 ..D 11
Pine Castle† ...10,805 ..G 7
Pine Hills† .....60,076 ..F 6
Pine Island
  Center*† ......1,854 ..H 10
Pine Manor*† ...3,428 ..H 11
Pinecrest* ......18,223 ..I 16
Pinellas Park ..49,079 ..J 2
Pinewood*† .....16,520 ..H 16
Plant City ......34,721 ..I 4
Plantation .....84,955 ..G 16
Plantation*† ....4,919 ..K 13
Poinciana*† .....53,193 ..H 7
Polk City ....1,562 ..H 5
Pompano
  Beach ....99,845 ..F 16
Ponce Inlet*† ...3,032 ..D 12
Port
  Charlotte† ....54,392 ..H 10
Port La Belle*† ..3,530 ..H 12
Port Orange ....56,048 ..D 12
Port Richey .....2,671 ..H 2
Port St. Joe° ...3,445 ..C 5
Port St. John* ..12,267 ..E 12
Port St. Lucie .164,603 ..B 15
Port Salerno*† .10,091 ..C 16
Pretty Bayou*† ..3,206 ..B 5
Princeton† .....22,038 ..I 15
Progress
  Village*† ....5,392 ..I 3
Punta Gorda° ..16,641 ..H 10
Punta Rassa*† ..1,750 ..H 11
Quincy° ....7,972 ..B 6
Ratliff, see Nassau
  Village [-Ratliff]
Redington
  Beach ....1,427 ..I 1
Redington
  Shores ....2,121 ..I 1
Richmond
  Heights† ......8,541 ..I 15
Richmond
  West*† ....31,973 ..I 15
Ridge Manor† ...4,513 ..G 4
Ridge Wood
  Heights*† ......4,795 ..G 10
Ridgecrest*† ...2,558 ..I 11
Rio*† ....965 ..B 16
River Ridge*† ..4,702 ..D 12
Riverview† .....71,050 ..I 3
Riviera Beach ..32,488 ..D 16
Rockledge ......24,926 ..F 12
Roosevelt
  Gardens*† .....2,456 ..G 16
Roseland*† .....1,472 ..F 13
Rotonda*† ....8,759 ..H 11
Royal Palm
  Beach ....34,140 ..D 16
Ruskin† ....17,208 ..J 3
Safety Harbor ..16,884 ..I 2
St. Augustine° .12,975 ..B 12
St. Augustine
  Beach ....6,176 ..B 12
St. Augustine
  Shores*† ....7,359 ..C 12
St. Augustine
  South*† ....4,998 ..C 12
St. Cloud ....35,183 ..H 7
St. James City*† .3,784 ..H 10
St. Leo ....1,340 ..G 3

St. Pete Beach ...9,346 ..I 2
St. Peters-
  burg ....244,769 ..F 9
Samoset† ....3,854 ..K 2
Samsula
  [-Spruce
  Creek]† ....5,047 ..D 12
San Antonio ...1,138 ..G 3
San Carlos
  Park*† ....16,824 ..H 11
Sanford° ....53,570 ..D 12
Sanibel ....6,469 ..J 11
Sarasota° ......51,917 ..G 10
Sarasota
  Springs*† .....14,395 ..K 3
Satellite
  Beach ....10,109 ..E 13
Sawgrass*† ......4,880 ..B 11
Sebastian ......21,929 ..F 13
Sebring° ....10,491 ..G 11
Seffner*† ....7,579 ..I 3
Seminole ....17,233 ..I 1
Sewall's Point ..1,996 ..B 16
Shady Hills*† ..11,523 ..G 2
Sharpes† ....3,411 ..E 12
Siesta Key*† ....6,565 ..G 10
Silver Lake*† ...1,879 ..D 11
Silver Springs
  Shores*† ....6,539 ..D 10
Sky Lake*† ......6,153 ..G 6
Sneads ....1,849 ..A 6
Solana† ....742 ..H 11
South
  Apopka† ....5,728 ..F 6
South Bay ....4,876 ..H 13
South Beach*† ..3,501 ..A 15
South Braden-
  ton*† ....22,178 ..K 2
South
  Brooksville*† ..4,007 ..F 3
South
  Daytona ......12,252 ..D 12
South Gate
  Ridge*† ....5,688 ..G 10
South
  Highpoint*† ...5,195 ..I 2
South Miami ...11,657 ..I 16
South Miami
  Heights*† .....35,696 ..I 15
South Palm
  Beach ....1,171 ..E 16
South
  Pasadena ......4,964 ..J 2
South Patrick
  Shores*† ....5,875 ..E 13
South
  Sarasota*† ....4,950 ..G 10
South Venice* .13,949 ..G 10
Southchase*† ..15,921 ..G 7
Southeast
  Arcadia*† ......6,554 ..G 11
Southgate*† ....7,173 ..G 10
Southwest
  Ranches* ......7,345 ..G 16
Spring Hill† ...98,621 ..G 2
Springfield ......8,903 ..B 5

Spruce Creek,
  see Samsula
  [-Spruce Creek]
Starke° ....5,449 ..B 10
Stock Island*† ..3,919 ..K 11
Stuart° ....15,593 ..G 13
Sugarmill
  Woods*† ....8,287 ..F 2
Sun City
  Center† ....19,258 ..J 3
Suncoast
  Estates*† ....4,384 ..H 11
Sunny Isles
  Beach*† ....20,832 ..H 16
Sunrise ....84,439 ..G 16
Sunset*† ....16,389 ..I 15
Surfside ....5,744 ..H 16
Sweetwater* ..13,499 ..H 15
Tallahassee° .181,376 ..B 7
Tamarac* ......60,427 ..G 16
Tamiami*† ......55,271 ..H 16
Tampa° ....335,709 ..F 10
Tangelo Park*† ..2,231 ..G 6
Tarpon
  Springs ......23,484 ..H 1
Tavares° ....13,951 ..D 11
Tavernier† ......2,136 ..K 13
Taylor Creek*† ..4,348 ..G 12
Temple
  Terrace ....24,541 ..I 3
Tequesta ....5,629 ..C 16
The Meadows, see
  Meadows, The
Tice*† ....4,470 ..H 11
Timber
  Pines*† ....5,386 ..G 2
Titusville° .....43,761 ..E 12
Town 'n'
  Country*† .....78,442 ..I 2
Treasure
  Island ....6,705 ..J 1
Trenton° ....1,999 ..C 9
Trinity*† ....10,907 ..H 2
Tyndall AFB*† ..2,994 ..B 5
Umatilla ....3,456 ..E 11
Union Park† .....9,765 ..F 7
University*† ....41,163 ..I 3
Upper Grand
  Lagoon*† ......13,963 ..B 5
Valparaiso ......5,036 ..A 3
Valrico*† ....35,545 ..I 3
Vamo*† ....4,727 ..G 10
Venice ....20,748 ..G 10
Venice
  Gardens*† ......7,104 ..G 10
Vero Beach° ...15,220 ..F 13
Vero Beach
  South*† ....23,092 ..A 15
Villano
  Beach*† ....2,678 ..B 12
Villas*† ....11,569 ..H 11
Virginia
  Gardens* ......2,375 ..H 16
Wabasso† ....609 ..F 13
Wahneta† ....5,091 ..I 5
Waldo ....1,015 ..C 10

Warm Mineral
  Springs*† ......5,061 ..G 10
Warrington† ....14,531 ..B 2
Washington
  Park*† ....1,672 ..G 16
Watertown*† ....2,829 ..B 10
Wauchula° ......5,001 ..F 11
Waverly*† ....767 ..I 6
Wedgefield*† ....6,705 ..G 8
Wekiva
  Springs*† ......21,998 ..F 6
Wellington*† ...56,500 ..H 13
Wesley
  Chapel*† ......44,092 ..H 3
West
  Bradenton*† ...4,192 ..J 2
West DeLand*† ..3,535 ..D 11
West Little
  River*† ....34,699 ..J 13
West
  Melbourne ....18,355 ..F 13
West Miami* ...5,965 ..I 16
West Palm
  Beach° ....99,919 ..H 14
West
  Pensacola*† ..21,339 ..A 2
West
  Samoset*† .....5,583 ..K 2
Westchase*† ...21,747 ..I 2
Westchester† ..29,862 ..I 16
Westgate*† ......7,975 ..E 16
Weston* ....65,333 ..G 15
Westview*† ......9,650 ..J 13
Westwood
  Lakes† ....11,838 ..I 15
Wewahitchka ...1,981 ..B 6
Whiskey
  Creek*† ....4,655 ..H 11
White City*† ...3,719 ..A 15
Whitfield*† .....2,882 ..K 2
Wildwood ....6,709 ..D 10
Williamsburg*† ..7,646 ..G 6
Williston ....2,768 ..C 10
Willow Oak*† ...6,732 ..I 4
Wilton
  Manors ....11,632 ..G 16
Wimauma† ....6,373 ..I 3
Windermere ...2,462 ..G 6
Winter
  Garden ....34,568 ..F 6
Winter Haven ..33,874 ..I 5
Winter Park ...27,852 ..F 7
Winter
  Springs* ......33,282 ..F 7
Woodville† ......2,978 ..B 7
Wright*† ....23,127 ..A 3
Yalaha† ....1,364 ..F 5
Yulee† ....11,491 ..A 11
Zephyrhills ....13,288 ..H 4
Zephyrhills
  North*† ....2,600 ..H 4
Zephyrhills
  South*† ....5,276 ..H 4
Zephyrhills
  West*† ....5,865 ..H 3
Zolfo Springs ..1,827 ..K 5

© Alan Schein, Corbis Stock Market

Miami Beach is one of Florida's famous resort centers. Its hotels, beaches, and recreational areas attract many visitors. The city lies on an island just east of Miami in the southern part of the state.

*Does not appear on the map; key shows general location.
†Census designated place—unincorporated, but recognized as a significant settled community by the U.S. Census Bureau.
°County seat.
Source: 2010 census.

Great stretches of sandy beaches and a warm, sunny climate make Florida a year-round vacationland. Southern Florida is one of the world's most beautiful resort areas. Its attractions include Everglades National Park and the Florida Keys. The keys are a chain of small islands that extends into the Gulf of Mexico. People enjoy swimming, fishing, and water-skiing in the inland and coastal waters. Visitors may see historic sites that date back to the early Indian inhabitants and to the Spanish explorers. The Orange Bowl football game in Miami Gardens on or near New Year's Day is one of Florida's leading annual events. The state has professional baseball, basketball, football, and hockey teams. Horse racing, greyhound racing, and jai alai games are popular.

Joachim Messerschmidt, Bruce Coleman Inc.

Epcot in Walt Disney World Resort near Orlando

© Superstock

Castillo de San Marcos in St. Augustine

Places to visit

Busch Gardens Tampa Bay, in Tampa, is a family adventure park with African-themed attractions. The park offers roller coasters and other rides, animal habitats featuring more than 2,700 animals, live entertainment, and restaurants.

Everglades National Park, in southern Florida, covers 1,506,539 acres (609,675 hectares) and forms the largest subtropical wilderness in the United States.

John Pennekamp Coral Reef State Park, near Key Largo, was the first undersea park in the continental United States. Visitors can see the living reef formations from glass-bottom boats or by snorkeling.

Kennedy Space Center Visitor Complex, in Cape Canaveral, is the visitor center for the John F. Kennedy Space Center. It offers bus tours of the space center and also features exhibits that deal with space travel.

Key West, at the southern end of U.S. 1, is an old seaport and resort city. It offers a wide variety of water activities.

Lion Country Safari, near West Palm Beach, is an animal preserve where lions and other wild animals roam free. Visitors may drive through the area in cars.

Marineland Dolphin Adventure, the world's first oceanarium, is between St. Augustine and Daytona Beach on Florida's Atlantic coast. Built in 1938, Marineland includes more than 100 kinds of marine creatures in their natural surroundings.

Ormond-Daytona Beach stretches for about 23 miles (37 kilometers) along the Atlantic coastline. Tides have beaten the beach to the hardness and smoothness of a highway. During the day, tourists can drive their cars along the beach.

St. Augustine is the oldest permanent European settlement in the United States. Visitors may tour restored Spanish and British colonial homes and visit the Castillo de San Marcos, a fort built by the Spanish in the 1600's.

Sanibel Island, near Fort Myers, has one of the world's finest beaches for collecting seashells. Captiva Island, a luxury resort, is nearby.

SeaWorld Orlando features dolphin and killer whale shows. The marine center also has a water-skiing show.

Stephen Foster Folk Culture Center State Park, in north-central Florida, offers tours of the Stephen Foster Museum and Carillon Tower, the opportunity to see working artists in Craft Square, and canoe and kayak rides on the Suwannee River.

Universal Orlando features two theme parks, Universal Studios Florida and Islands of Adventure. Visitors can also enjoy live entertainment, fine dining, dancing, and shopping at Universal Studios CityWalk.

Walt Disney World Resort, near Orlando, has an amusement park, a recreational center, a storybook castle, a movie studio complex, and other attractions. It includes Epcot (Experimental Prototype Community of Tomorrow), which features displays about future technology. Epcot has re-creations of historical landmarks of the United States and other countries.

Zoo Miami is a large zoo that displays animals in settings modeled after different parts of the world. It also features a monorail and an aviary where exotic birds fly freely.

National parklands. In addition to Everglades National Park, Florida parklands managed by the National Park Service include Biscayne National Park, Dry Tortugas National Park, and a number of national memorials and national monuments. For more information, see the map and tables in the *World Book* article on **National Park System.**

National forests. Florida has three national forests. The largest, Apalachicola National Forest, spreads across northwestern Florida. The other two are Ocala National Forest and Osceola National Forest.

State parks. For information on Florida's many state parks and historic memorials, visit http://www.dep.state.fl.us/parks.

A performing whale
at SeaWorld Orlando

© Joachim Messerschmidt, Bruce Coleman Inc.

© Martin Bennett, Alamy Images

Roller coaster at Busch Gardens Tampa Bay

© Stephen Frink, Southern Stock

John Pennekamp Coral Reef State Park near Key Largo

Land regions. Florida is part of the Atlantic-Gulf Coastal Plain, a large land region that extends along the coast from New Jersey to southern Texas. Within Florida, there are three main land regions: (1) the Atlantic Coastal Plain, (2) the East Gulf Coastal Plain, and (3) the Florida Uplands.

The Atlantic Coastal Plain of Florida covers the entire eastern part of the state. It is a low, level plain ranging in width from 30 to 100 miles (48 to 160 kilometers). A narrow ribbon of sand bars, coral reefs, and barrier islands lies in the Atlantic Ocean, just offshore from the mainland. Lagoons, rivers, bays, and long, shallow lakes lie between much of this ribbon and the mainland.

Big Cypress Swamp and the Everglades cover most of southern Florida. Water covers much of this region, especially during the rainy months.

The Florida Keys make up the southernmost part of the state. These small islands curve southwestward for about 150 miles (241 kilometers) off the mainland from Miami. Key Largo is the largest island.

The East Gulf Coastal Plain of Florida has two main sections. One section covers the southwestern part of the peninsula, including Tampa Bay and part of the Everglades and Big Cypress Swamp. The other section of Florida's East Gulf Coastal Plain curves around the northern edge of the Gulf of Mexico across the panhandle to Florida's western border.

The East Gulf Coastal Plain is similar to the Atlantic Coastal Plain. Long, narrow barrier islands extend along the Gulf of Mexico coastline. Coastal swamps stretch inland in places. Much swampland in the region has been drained, and the land used for farming or urban development, especially in southwestern Florida.

The Florida Uplands is shaped somewhat like a giant arm and hand. A finger of the hand points down the center of the state toward the southern tip of the peninsula. The uplands separate the two sections of the East Gulf Coastal Plain from each other and separate the northern section from the Atlantic Coastal Plain.

The uplands region is higher than Florida's other land regions. However, its average elevation is only between 200 and 300 feet (61 and 91 meters) above sea level. Lakes are common in the Florida Uplands. Many of these lakes were formed in *sinkholes*—cave-ins where a limestone bed near the surface has been dissolved by water action. Pine forests grow in the northern section of the uplands.

The northern part of the Florida Uplands extends from the northwestern corner of the state along the northern border for about 275 miles (443 kilometers). Its width varies from about 30 to 50 miles (48 to 80 kilometers). This section has fertile valleys and rolling hills of red clay. Many hardwood and softwood forests are found there. The southern part of the Florida Uplands is a region of low hills and lakes. It covers an area about 100 miles (160 kilometers) wide and about 160 miles (257 kilometers) long.

Coastline of Florida is 1,350 miles (2,173 kilometers) long. The Atlantic coast has 580 miles (933 kilometers) of shoreline. The Gulf coast is 770 miles (1,240 kilometers) long. When lagoons, bays, and barrier islands are included, the Atlantic coastline is 3,331 miles (5,361 kilometers) long and the Gulf coast is 5,095 miles (8,200 kilometers) long. Biscayne Bay, extending south from

© Matt Bradley, Tom Stack & Associates

The Florida Keys are a chain of islands that stretch from the southern tip of the state into the Gulf of Mexico. Bridges over the Gulf, such as Seven Mile Bridge, *shown here,* link the islands.

WORLD BOOK map

Land regions of Florida

Map index

Apalachee Bay	.........B	5
Apalachicola Bay	.......B	4
Apalachicola R.	........A	4
Aucilla R.	................A	5
Big Cypress Swamp	...E	7
Biscayne Bay	...........E	8
Blackwater R.	...........A	2
Caloosahatchee R.	......D	7
Cape Canaveral	C	8
Cape Romano	..........E	7
Cape Sable	..............F	7
Cape San Blas	...........B	3
Castillo de San Marcos Natl. Mon.	...........B	7
Cedar Keys	.............B	5
Charlotte Harbor	........D	6
Choctawhatchee Bay	..A	3
Choctawhatchee R.	.....A	3
Deadman Bay	..........B	5
East Lake Tohopekaliga	C	7
Everglades Natl. Park	...F	8
Everglades, The	........E	7
Florida Bay	.............F	7
Florida Keys	............F	7
Florida, Straits of	.......F	8
Fort Matanzas Natl. Mon.	...............B	7
Highest point in Florida	...............A	3
Hillsboro Canal	.........E	8
Hillsborough R.	C	6
Horseshoe Cove	.......B	5
Horseshoe Pt.	...........B	5
Indian Prairie Canal	.....D	7
Indian R.	C	8
Key Largo	..............F	8
Kissimmee R.	..........D	7
Lake Apopka	C	7
Lake George	...........B	7
Lake Istokpoga	........D	7
Lake Kissimmee	C	7
Lake Okeechobee	.......D	7
Lake Seminole	.........A	4
Lake Tohopekaliga	C	7
Lake Trafford	...........E	7
Lake Weohyakapka	C	7
Manatee R.	..............D	6
Marquesas Keys	.......F	6
Miami Canal	............E	8
North New River Canal	...............E	8
Ochlockonee R.	........A	5
Peace R.	................D	7
Perdido R.	..............A	2
Ponce de Leon Bay	.....F	7
Saddlebunch Keys	.....F	7
St. Andrew Bay	........A	3
St. George I.	............B	4
St. Johns R.	.............B	7
St. Lucie Canal	..........D	8
St. Marys Entrance	......A	7
St. Marys R.	.............A	7
Santa Rosa I.	.............A	2
Suwannee R.	............B	6
Suwannee Sound	.......B	5
Tamiami Canal	..........E	8
Tampa Bay	..............D	6
Ten Thousand Is.	........E	7
Tsala Apopka Lake	C	6
Waccasassa Bay	........B	6
Whitewater Bay	........F	7
Withlacoochee R.	.......B	6
Yellow R.	................A	2

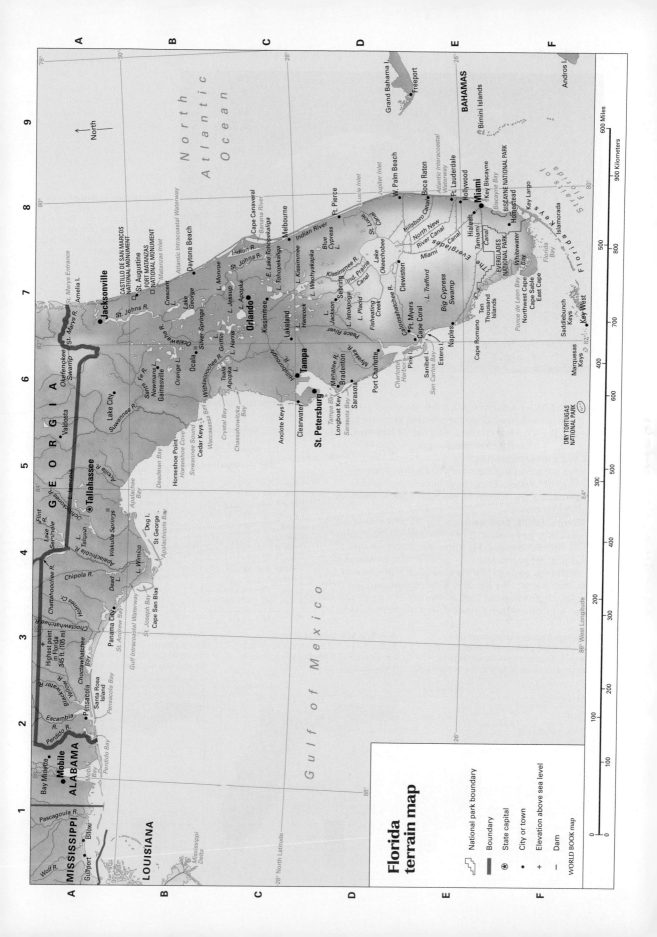

Florida
terrain map

	National park boundary
	Boundary
⊛	State capital
•	City or town
+	Elevation above sea level
—	Dam

WORLD BOOK map

North

North Atlantic Ocean

Gulf of Mexico

MISSISSIPPI

ALABAMA

LOUISIANA

GEORGIA

BAHAMAS

Tallahassee

Jacksonville

Orlando

Tampa

St. Petersburg

Clearwater

Lakeland

Ft. Myers

Cape Coral

Naples

Miami

Hialeah

Ft. Lauderdale

Hollywood

Boca Raton

W. Palm Beach

Ft. Pierce

Melbourne

Daytona Beach

St. Augustine

Key West

Key Largo

Islamorada

Homestead

Freeport

Mobile

Bay Minette

Pascagoula R.

Biloxi

Gulfport

Wolf R.

Pensacola

Santa Rosa Island

Panama City

Lake City

Valdosta

Gainesville

Ocala

Sarasota

Bradenton

Port Charlotte

Clewiston

Sebring

Kissimmee

Indian River

Cape Canaveral

Okefenokee Swamp

Everglades

The

EVERGLADES NATIONAL PARK

BISCAYNE NATIONAL PARK

DRY TORTUGAS NATIONAL PARK

CASTILLO DE SAN MARCOS NATIONAL MONUMENT

FORT MATANZAS NATIONAL MONUMENT

Highest point in Florida 345 ft. (105 m)

Florida Keys

Florida Bay

Biscayne Bay

Straits of Florida

Bimini Islands

Grand Bahama I.

Andros I.

Ten Thousand Islands

Big Cypress Swamp

Lake Okeechobee

Blue Cypress L.

L. Kissimmee

L. Istokpoga

L. Placid

L. Trafford

Caloosahatchee R.

Peace River

Withlacoochee R.

Ocklawaha R.

St. Johns R.

Kissimmee R.

Ind. Prairie Canal

Fisheating Creek

Tamiami Canal

Miami Canal

North New River Canal

Hillsboro Canal

St. Lucie Canal

Apalachicola R.

Choctawhatchee R.

Chipola R.

Yellow R.

Blackwater R.

Escambia R.

Perdido R.

Suwannee R.

Santa Fe R.

Aucilla R.

Ochlockonee R.

Chattahoochee R.

Flint R.

Holmes Cr.

Choctawhatchee

L. Seminole

L. Talquin

L. Wimico

Dead L.

Wakulla Springs

St. Marks

Cedar Keys

Anclote Keys

Longboat Key

Sanibel I.

Pine I.

Estero I.

Marquesas Keys

Saddlebunch Keys

Cape Romano

Cape Sable

Northwest Cape

East Cape

Whitewater Bay

Ponce de Leon Bay

Key Biscayne

Banana River

Indian R.

L. George

L. Monroe

L. Jessup

L. Apopka

Silver Springs

L. Griffin

L. Harris

Orange L.

Apopka

Tsala L.

Crescent L.

E. Lake Tohopekaliga

L. Tohopekaliga

Wewahyakapka

Hancock

L. Jackson

Manatee R.

Myakka R.

Hillsborough R.

Newmans L.

St. Johns R.

St. Marys R.

St. Marys Entrance

Amelia I.

Atlantic Intracoastal Waterway

Matanzas Inlet

Lucie Inlet

Jupiter Inlet

Atlantic Intracoastal Waterway

Horseshoe Cove

Horseshoe Point

Waccasassa Bay

Crystal Bay

Chassahowitzka Bay

Deadman Bay

Sewanee Sound

Apalachee Bay

Charlotte Harbor

Pine I.

San Carlos Bay

Estero Bay

Tampa Bay

Sarasota Bay

Gulf Intracoastal Waterway

St. Joseph Bay

St. Andrew Bay

Choctawhatchee Bay

Pensacola Bay

Perdido Bay

Mobile Bay

Mississippi Delta

Cape San Blas

St. George I.

Dog I.

30°

28°

26°

88°

86° West Longitude

84°

82°

80°

78°

28° North Latitude

26° North Latitude

| 0 | 100 | 200 | 300 | 400 | 500 | 600 Miles |
| 0 | 100 | 200 | 300 | 400 | 500 | 600 | 700 | 800 | 900 Kilometers |

A | B | C | D | E | F

Everglades National Park includes large areas of wetlands that provide a home for wildlife. In this picture, two roseate spoonbills wade near a young alligator.

© Shutterstock

Miami, is the one major bay on the Atlantic coast. The most important bays along the western coast include Tampa Bay, Charlotte Harbor, San Carlos Bay, and Sarasota Bay. Florida Bay, beyond the peninsula's southern tip, separates the Florida Keys from the mainland. Several bays stretch along the northern Florida shoreline of the Gulf of Mexico. These bays include Apalachee, Apalachicola, St. Joseph, St. Andrew, Choctawhatchee, and Pensacola.

Rivers, lakes, and springs. The St. Johns River is the largest river in the state. It begins near Melbourne and flows about 275 miles (443 kilometers) north. It runs almost parallel to the Atlantic coastline. The St. Marys River, along the eastern Florida-Georgia border, flows east into the Atlantic. The Perdido River, on the northwestern border, drains into the Gulf of Mexico. The Apalachicola River is northwestern Florida's most important river. It

Average monthly weather

	Tallahassee						Miami				
	Temperatures				**Days of rain or snow**		**Temperatures**				**Days of rain or snow**
	°F		**°C**				**°F**		**°C**		
	High	**Low**	**High**	**Low**			**High**	**Low**	**High**	**Low**	
Jan.	64	40	18	4	10	Jan.	77	60	25	16	7
Feb.	67	42	19	6	9	Feb.	78	61	26	16	6
Mar.	74	48	23	9	9	Mar.	81	64	27	18	6
Apr.	80	53	27	12	6	Apr.	84	68	29	20	6
May	87	62	31	17	8	May	87	72	31	22	10
June	91	70	33	21	13	June	90	75	32	24	15
July	92	73	33	23	17	July	91	77	33	25	16
Aug.	92	73	33	23	14	Aug.	91	77	33	25	18
Sept.	89	69	32	21	9	Sept.	89	76	32	24	18
Oct.	81	57	27	14	5	Oct.	85	72	29	22	14
Nov.	73	48	23	9	7	Nov.	81	68	27	20	8
Dec.	66	42	19	6	8	Dec.	78	62	26	17	7

Average January temperatures
The southern portion of Florida has the warmest temperatures in wintertime. Temperatures steadily decline northward.

Average July temperatures
Florida has a hot summertime climate. Temperatures differ by only a few degrees throughout the state.

Average yearly precipitation
Florida has a rainy climate. The heaviest precipitation falls in the southeastern and northwestern portions of the state.

WORLD BOOK map based on the ATLAS OF FLORIDA ©1992 University Press of Florida. By permission of the publisher.

WORLD BOOK map

Degrees Fahrenheit	Degrees Celsius
Above 64	Above 18
58 to 64	14 to 18
52 to 58	11 to 14
Below 52	Below 11

WORLD BOOK map

Degrees Fahrenheit	Degrees Celsius
Above 83	Above 29
82 to 83	28 to 29
81 to 82	27 to 28
Below 81	Below 27

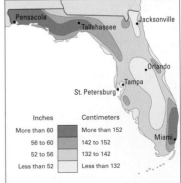

Inches	Centimeters
More than 60	More than 152
56 to 60	142 to 152
52 to 56	132 to 142
Less than 52	Less than 132

forms where the Chattahoochee and Flint rivers join at the northern boundary of the state. It flows south to the Gulf of Mexico. The Suwannee River flows southwest from the Florida-Georgia border. It also empties into the Gulf. Stephen Foster made this river famous in his song "Old Folks at Home" (1851), also called "Swanee River." Other rivers connect many of the lakes of the uplands.

Lake Okeechobee is Florida's largest lake. It covers about 680 square miles (1,760 square kilometers). The lake is the second largest natural body of fresh water wholly within the United States. Only Lake Michigan covers a larger area. About 30,000 shallow lakes lie throughout central Florida.

Florida has 17 large springs and countless smaller ones. Many of the springs contain healthful mineral waters. Wakulla Springs, near Tallahassee, is one of the nation's deepest springs. Its depth is 185 feet (56 meters). Silver Springs, southeast of Ocala, is the state's largest spring. Many of the springs are so clear that plant life on the bottom may be seen as deep as 80 feet (24 meters).

Plant and animal life. Forests cover about half of Florida. Common trees in the state include ashes, beeches, baldcypresses, sweet gums, hickories, magnolias, mangroves, maples, oaks, palms, and pines.

Common wildflowers of Florida include irises, lilies, lupines, orchids, and sunflowers. The state also has such climbing vines as Carolina yellow jasmine, Cherokee rose, morning-glory, and trumpet creeper. Other flowers that grow throughout Florida include azaleas, camellias, gardenias, hibiscus, oleanders, and poinsettias. The bougainvillea and the flame vine (also called golden bignonia) brighten many southern Florida gardens. Dogwoods, magnolias, and redbuds flourish in the north.

Black bears, deer, gray foxes, and wild cats live in many parts of the state. Smaller animals, such as opossums, otters, raccoons, and squirrels, are also common. Florida has the largest colonies of anhinga, egrets, herons, ibises, and pelicans north of the Caribbean Sea. Alligators live in the swamps.

More kinds of fishes may be found in Florida's waters than in any other part of the world. The freshwater lakes and rivers support bass, bream, catfish, and crappies. Florida's ocean waters hold bluefish, grouper, mackerel, marlin, menhaden, pompano, red snapper, sailfish, sea trout, and tarpon. Clams, conchs, crabs, crayfish, oysters, scallops, and shrimp live in Florida's coastal waters. Mullets inhabit salt water and *brackish* (salty) marshes.

Climate. Most of Florida has a warm, humid climate similar to that of the other Southern States. The southern tip has a tropical wet and dry climate like that of Central America and large parts of Africa and South America.

Atlantic and Gulf breezes relieve some of the summer heat near the coasts. Winters are usually mild, even in northern Florida. July temperatures are much the same in the northern and southern parts of the state. Jacksonville, in the north, has an average July temperature of 82 °F (28 °C). Miami, in the south, averages 84 °F (29 °C) in July. But in January, Miami averages 68 °F (20 °C). Jacksonville's average temperature drops to 53 °F (12 °C). The coastal areas have slightly cooler summers and warmer winters than do inland areas. Destructive frosts rarely occur in southern Florida. But occasional cold waves damage crops as far south as the Everglades.

Florida's highest and lowest temperatures occurred within 30 miles (48 kilometers) of each other. Tallahassee recorded the lowest temperature, –2 °F (–19 °C), on Feb. 13, 1899. Nearby Monticello recorded the highest temperature, 109 °F (43 °C), on June 29, 1931.

Nearly all of Florida's precipitation falls in the form of rain. The state's average yearly precipitation is 54 inches (137 centimeters). An average of 32 inches (81 centimeters) falls in the rainy season, from May to October.

Florida lies along the path of many of the hurricanes that sweep across the Atlantic Ocean every summer and fall. Destructive hurricanes have struck Florida several times. Tornadoes and waterspouts also affect the state. Droughts and wildfires have become increasingly frequent occurrences.

Economy

The economy of Florida has become more diverse. However, traditional industries, such as the tourist trade and the growing of citrus fruits, remain important. Companies have been attracted to the state by its warm climate and business-friendly reputation. Manufacturing in central Florida has benefited from the growth of high-technology industries, especially computer-related and electronics industries.

Service industries, taken together, account for the largest portion of Florida's *gross domestic product.* Gross domestic product is the total value of all goods and services produced in the state in a year. Florida agriculture is famous for growing citrus fruits. About 70 percent of both the orange and grapefruit crops of the United States are grown in Florida. The state also receives much income from the mining of phosphate rock. Phosphate is used to make fertilizer.

Natural resources. Florida's natural resources include sandy beaches and a sunny climate. In addition, the state has thick forests and phosphate and mineral sands deposits.

Soil. Most of Florida's soils are sandy, especially in the coastal plains. The most fertile soils are in the south. Much of the area's rich wetland has been drained and used for farming. The soils of the Florida Uplands are chiefly sandy loams and clays.

Minerals. Most of Florida lies on huge beds of limestone, the state's most plentiful mineral. Florida has the country's largest phosphate deposits. Most of the state's phosphate comes from mines in west-central Florida. Large stores of peat, sand and gravel, and *fuller's earth,* a clay used in filters, are found throughout the state. Florida's sandy areas have mineral sands, including ilmenite, rutile, and zircon. Brick clays and kaolin, a pottery clay, are found in Putnam County. Natural gas and oil are mined in northwestern and southern Florida.

Forests cover about half of the state. Florida has hundreds of kinds of trees. Slash pines are a valuable tree in Florida. The most common hardwood trees are baldcypress, black tupelo, magnolia, oak, and sweet gum. Other common trees include ash, beech, hickory, maple, and yellow pines (loblolly and longleaf). Hardwoods and

Florida economy

General economy

Gross domestic product (GDP)* (2011) $754,255,000,000
  Rank among U.S. states   4th
Unemployment rate (2012)   8.7% (U.S. avg: 8.1%)

*Gross domestic product is the total value of goods and services produced in a year.
Sources: U.S. Bureau of Economic Analysis and U.S. Bureau of Labor Statistics.

Production and workers by economic activities

Economic activities	Percent of GDP produced	Employed workers	
		Number of people	Percent of total
Community, business, & personal services	25	3,710,700	38
Finance, insurance, & real estate	25	1,222,300	12
Trade, restaurants, & hotels	18	2,227,000	23
Government	13	1,206,200	12
Transportation & communication	7	462,500	5
Manufacturing	5	340,100	3
Construction	4	506,900	5
Utilities	2	24,400	*
Agriculture	1	145,700	1
Mining	*	20,300	*
Total†	100	9,866,100	100

*Less than one-half of 1 percent.
†Figures may not add up to 100 percent due to rounding.
Figures are for 2010; employment figures include full- and part-time workers.
Source: *World Book* estimates based on data from U.S. Bureau of Economic Analysis.

Agriculture

Cash receipts $8,262,486,000
  Rank among U.S. states   17th
Distribution   82% crops, 18% livestock
Farms   47,500
Farm acres (hectares)   9,250,000 (3,740,000)
  Rank among U.S. states   30th
Farmland   25% of Florida

Leading products

1. Greenhouse and nursery products   (ranks 2nd in U.S.)
2. Oranges   (ranks 1st in U.S.)
3. Tomatoes   (ranks 2nd in U.S.)
4. Dairy products
5. Sugar cane   (ranks 2nd in U.S.)
6. Cattle and calves
Other products: broilers, eggs, grapefruit, green peppers, potatoes, strawberries, sweet corn, watermelon.

Manufacturing

Value added by manufacture* $44,876,500,000
  Rank among U.S. states   19th

Leading products

1. Computer and electronic products
2. Food and beverages
3. Chemicals
4. Medical equipment
5. Transportation equipment
Other products: fabricated metals, nonmetallic minerals.

*Value added by manufacture is the increase in value of raw materials after they become finished products.

Figures are for 2010, except for the agricultural figures, which are for 2011.
Sources: U.S. Census Bureau, U.S. Department of Agriculture.

continued on page 259

Economy of Florida

This map shows the economic uses of land in Florida and where the state's leading farm, mineral, and forest products are produced. The major urban areas (shown in red) are the state's important manufacturing centers.

Mostly cropland

Woodland mixed with cropland and grazing

Forest land

Marsh and swampland

Urban area

• Manufacturing center

• Mineral deposit

WORLD BOOK map

Mining

Nonfuel mineral production	$2,680,000,000
Rank among U.S. states	8th
Coal (tons)	*
Crude oil (barrels†)	1,664,000
Rank among U.S. states	24th
Natural gas (cubic feet‡)	12,409,000,000
Rank among U.S. states	23rd

*No significant mining of this product in Florida.
†One barrel equals 42 gallons (159 liters).
‡One cubic foot equals 0.0283 cubic meter.

Leading products

1. Phosphate rock (ranks 1st in U.S.)
2. Limestone (ranks 4th in U.S.)
3. Portland cement
4. Petroleum
5. Sand and gravel
Other products: clays, masonry cement, peat.

Fishing

Commercial catch	$184,376,000
Rank among U.S. states	9th

Leading catches

1. Shrimp (ranks 3rd in U.S.)
2. Lobsters (ranks 3rd in U.S.)
3. Crabs (ranks 5th in U.S.)
4. Snapper (ranks 1st in U.S.)
Other catches: grouper, mackerel, mullet, oysters, tuna.

Electric power

Natural gas	56.1%
Coal	26.1%
Nuclear	10.4%
Petroleum	4.0%
Other	3.4%

Figures are for 2010.
Sources: U.S. Energy Information Administration, U.S. Geological Survey, U.S. National Marine Fisheries Service.

pines are plentiful in the northern half of the state. Mangrove and gumbo limbo trees are found in southern Florida's coastal marshlands.

Service industries provide about 90 percent of both Florida's employment and its gross domestic product. Service industries chiefly operate in the Jacksonville, Miami, Orlando, and Tampa-St. Petersburg areas.

Florida's restaurants and hotels benefit from the tens of millions of tourists who visit each year. Many hotels and resorts line the coastal areas. Walt Disney World Resort, a theme park and entertainment complex near Orlando, is one of the world's leading tourist attractions.

Florida's leading financial centers are the Jacksonville, Miami, Orlando, and Tampa-St. Petersburg areas. Real estate companies have brought in much income by developing retirement communities and vacation resorts. Investment firms operating in Florida receive much business from retired people.

Tallahassee, the state capital, is the center of government activities. The federal government operates the John F. Kennedy Space Center on Cape Canaveral, Eglin Air Force Base in the Panhandle, and Naval Air Station Pensacola. Two of the nation's largest supermarket chains, Publix Super Markets, Inc., and Winn-Dixie Stores, Inc., have their headquarters in Florida. Several shipping and cruise lines are based in Florida.

Manufacturing. Computer and electronic products lead Florida's manufactured products. Communications equipment, computer microchips and components, and search and navigational, medical, and measuring equipment are this sector's leading products. Many of these high-tech jobs are in the Orlando and Tampa areas. Many Internet companies are based in South Florida.

Food and beverage processing is also important. Citrus fruit processing is one of the largest industries in the state. Processing plants, mostly in central Florida, produce fresh citrus fruit juices, canned juices, canned fruit, and citrus by-products. Florida also produces baked goods, dairy products, meat, seafood, soft drinks, and sugar products.

Other leading products include chemicals, fabricated metal products, medical equipment, nonmetallic minerals, and transportation equipment. Fertilizer and *pharmaceuticals* (medicinal drugs) are the leading chemical products. Machine shop products and metal doors and windows are key parts of the fabricated metal products sector. Medical equipment is made chiefly in the Jacksonville, Miami, and Tampa-St. Petersburg areas. Cement and concrete products are the leading nonmetallic mineral products. Aircraft parts, airplanes, and ships are also made in Florida.

Agriculture. Farmland covers about one-fourth of Florida's land area. Crops account for about four-fifths of Florida's total farm income. Oranges are the state's single most important farm product. Other citrus fruits grown in the state include grapefruit and tangerines. Florida is the nation's largest producer of grapefruit and oranges. The state's chief citrus groves lie in south-central Florida. The state also grows blueberries, strawberries, and watermelons.

Tomatoes are Florida's most important vegetable crop. Most of the tomatoes come from southern Florida,

Wendell Metzen, Bruce Coleman Inc.

Workers harvest oranges in a citrus grove in southern Florida. The state produces about 70 percent of both the orange and the grapefruit crops grown in the United States.

the main vegetable-growing region. Other vegetables produced in Florida include cabbage, cucumbers, peppers, potatoes, snap beans, squash, and sweet corn. Many northern states rely on Florida for fresh vegetables during cold months.

Sugar cane is another important crop. Florida is one of the nation's leading sugar cane producers. The region just south of Lake Okeechobee is the center of sugar cane growing. Other field crops cultivated in Florida include corn, cotton, hay, and peanuts. Florida ranks second to California in the production of greenhouse and nursery products. Most of the greenhouse and nursery products are grown in central and southern Florida.

Livestock and livestock products account for about one-fifth of Florida's farm income. Beef cattle and milk rank among the state's major livestock products. Many cattle are raised in central Florida. Poultry and egg production is also important. Farms in Marion County raise thoroughbred race horses. Florida is also an important state for *aquaculture* (fish farming).

Mining. Limestone and phosphate rock are Florida's most valuable mined products. The state is a leading producer of both products. Counties in west-central Florida produce phosphate rock. Quarries throughout the state provide limestone.

Natural gas and petroleum are mined chiefly in northwestern and southern Florida. Mines in Gadsden and Marion counties supply fuller's earth, a clay used to filter petroleum. Putnam County produces large amounts of kaolin, a pottery clay. Ilmenite, monazite, thorium, and zircon are taken from sands near the St. Johns River.

Fishing industry. Crab, lobster, shrimp, and snapper are Florida's leading catches. They account for about two-thirds of the total fishing value. Other fishes include clams, grouper, mackerel, mullet, oysters, sharks, swordfish, and tuna. The waters off Monroe and Pinellas counties are major sponge-fishing centers.

Electric power and utilities. FPL Group of Juno Beach is Florida's largest utility company. Plants that burn coal and plants that burn natural gas are the leading producers of Florida's power. Nuclear power plants and petroleum-burning plants supply most of the remaining electric power.

Transportation. Miami International Airport handles much of the air passenger and air freight travel to and from Latin America. Thus, Miami is often called the gateway to Latin America. Miami International and Orlando International rank among the country's busiest airports. Tampa and Fort Lauderdale also have major airports.

Rail lines provide freight service throughout the state. Florida has an extensive system of roads and highways. Florida's Turnpike connects many of the major cities. Four major interstate highways cross Florida.

Jacksonville, Miami, Port Everglades, and Tampa have major ports. Florida has more of the Atlantic Intracoastal Waterway than any other state. Florida's section of the Gulf Intracoastal Waterway winds along its Gulf Coast.

Communication. The first newspaper in Florida was the *East Florida Gazette* of St. Augustine. William Charles Wells, a Scottish physician, published the *Gazette* in 1783. He established the paper to support the British side in the American Revolution (1775-1783). Wells stopped publishing the *Gazette* and returned to England after the Spanish regained control of Florida in 1783. Florida's oldest newspaper is *The Florida Times-Union.* It was established in 1864 and is still published daily in Jacksonville. The state's other newspapers include the South Florida *Sun Sentinel,* published in Fort Lauderdale; *The Miami Herald;* the *Orlando Sentinel;* the *St. Petersburg Times;* and *The Tampa Tribune.*

Government

Constitution of Florida went into effect in 1969. Earlier constitutions went into effect in 1839 (before Florida became a state), 1861, 1865, 1868, and 1887.

Constitutional *amendments* (changes) must be approved by a majority of people voting on them in a general or special election. Amendments may be proposed by the Legislature. Three-fifths of each legislative house must approve the proposed amendment. In addition, citizens may propose amendments through the *initiative* process by presenting a petition signed by a specified number of voters. The people may also petition to call a constitutional convention. The petition must then be approved by the voters.

Executive. Florida's governor and lieutenant governor are elected as a team. The state's voters cast one vote for the governor and lieutenant governor. The governor and lieutenant governor serve four-year terms. The state's term limits prevent them from serving more than two terms in a row.

The governor of Florida appoints the state's public service commissioners and many of its judges. Members of the Cabinet are elected to four-year terms. Under the state's term limits, Cabinet members may not serve more than eight years in a row. The Cabinet consists of three members: the attorney general, the chief financial officer, and the commissioner of agriculture.

Legislature consists of a 40-member Senate and a 120-member House of Representatives. Senators serve four-year terms, and representatives serve two-year terms. Under the state's term limits, senators and representatives may not serve more than eight years in a row. The Legislature's regular 60-day session usually opens on the first Tuesday after the first Monday in March each year.

Special sessions may be called by the governor. Special sessions may also be called by joint agreement of the leaders of each legislative house, or by a three-fifths vote of all members of the Legislature. Regular or special sessions of the Legislature may be extended by a three-fifths vote of each house.

In 1965, a federal court ordered Florida to *reapportion* (redivide) its Legislature to provide equal representation based on population. The Legislature drew up a reapportionment plan. But the Supreme Court of the United States ruled it unconstitutional. In 1967, a federal court devised its own reapportionment plan. Since 1969, the state Constitution has required reapportionment every 10 years, after each federal census.

Courts. The Florida Supreme Court has seven justices. All of them are appointed by the governor to six-

The governors of Florida

	Party	Term		Party	Term
William D. Moseley	Democratic	1845-1849	John W. Martin	Democratic	1925-1929
Thomas Brown	Whig	1849-1853	Doyle E. Carlton	Democratic	1929-1933
James E. Broome	Democratic	1853-1857	David Sholtz	Democratic	1933-1937
Madison S. Perry	Democratic	1857-1861	Fred P. Cone	Democratic	1937-1941
John Milton	Democratic	1861-1865	Spessard L. Holland	Democratic	1941-1945
Abraham K. Allison	Democratic	1865	Millard F. Caldwell	Democratic	1945-1949
William Marvin	None	1865	Fuller Warren	Democratic	1949-1953
David S. Walker	Conservative	1865-1868	Daniel T. McCarty	Democratic	1953
Harrison Reed	Republican	1868-1873	Charley E. Johns	Democratic	1953-1955
Ossian B. Hart	Republican	1873-1874	LeRoy Collins	Democratic	1955-1961
Marcellus L. Stearns	Republican	1874-1877	C. Farris Bryant	Democratic	1961-1965
George F. Drew	Democratic	1877-1881	W. Haydon Burns	Democratic	1965-1967
William D. Bloxham	Democratic	1881-1885	Claude R. Kirk, Jr.	Republican	1967-1971
Edward A. Perry	Democratic	1885-1889	Reubin O'D. Askew	Democratic	1971-1979
Francis P. Fleming	Democratic	1889-1893	Bob Graham	Democratic	1979-1987
Henry L. Mitchell	Democratic	1893-1897	Wayne Mixson	Democratic	1987
William D. Bloxham	Democratic	1897-1901	Bob Martinez	Republican	1987-1991
William S. Jennings	Democratic	1901-1905	Lawton Chiles	Democratic	1991-1998
Napoleon B. Broward	Democratic	1905-1909	Buddy MacKay	Democratic	1998-1999
Albert W. Gilchrist	Democratic	1909-1913	Jeb Bush	Republican	1999-2007
Park Trammell	Democratic	1913-1917	Charlie Crist	Republican	2007-2011
Sidney J. Catts	Prohibition	1917-1921	Rick Scott	Republican	2011-
Cary A. Hardee	Democratic	1921-1925			

year terms. The justices elect one of their members to a two-year term as chief justice. Florida has five district courts of appeals. The governor appoints judges of these courts to six-year terms. In making appointments to the Supreme Court and courts of appeals, the governor chooses from among candidates selected by judicial nominating committees. Florida has 20 circuit courts and 67 county courts. Circuit and county court judges are elected to six-year terms.

Local government. Florida's 67 counties can vary their form of government by adopting special county charters approved by the Legislature and the people of the county. Most of the counties are governed by a board of five commissioners and are divided into five districts. County voters elect a resident from each district to serve on the county commission. Other elected county officers may include the circuit court clerk, sheriff, supervisor of elections, property appraiser, and tax collector. County officials serve four-year terms. Most counties also have an appointed county administrator.

Chartered counties and municipalities have *home rule* (self-government) to the extent that they may make laws. Counties and municipalities also have the power to *consolidate* (combine) and work as a single government.

Revenue. Taxation provides about half of the state government's *general revenue* (income). Most of the rest comes from federal grants and other United States government programs. A general sales tax generates more than half of all tax revenue. Other taxes include those on motor fuels, motor vehicle licenses, and utilities, and a corporate income tax. Florida levies no tax on personal income.

Politics. Since the Reconstruction period ended in 1877, most of Florida's governors have been Democrats (see **Reconstruction**). From 1880 through 1948, Democratic presidential candidates lost the state's electoral votes only in 1928. But since the 1952 election, Republican candidates have won the votes most of the time. For Florida's voting record in presidential elections, see **Electoral College** (table).

History

Early days. Burial mounds found along Florida's western coast show that Indians lived in the region about 12,000 years ago. Major tribes included the Calusa and the Tequesta in the south and the Ais on the Atlantic coast. The Indians hunted and fished for a living. The Timucua in the central and northeast regions and the Apalachee in the northwest were farmers and hunters. Other Indians included the Tocobaga of the Tampa Bay area and the Matecumbe in the keys region.

Exploration and Spanish settlement. The Spanish explorer Juan Ponce de León reached Florida in 1513, a few days after Easter. He had been searching for the island of Bimini, which the Spanish thought lay north of Cuba. Some stories said Bimini was the site of the Fountain of Youth. Ponce de León claimed the region for Spain. He named it La Florida, probably in honor of Pas-

cua Florida (Spanish for Easter). He returned to Florida in 1521 to start a colony but was wounded in a battle with the Calusa Indians and soon died.

In 1528, a Spaniard named Pánfilo de Narváez led an expedition of several hundred men to Florida's southwestern coast. He traveled northward searching for wealth. But hostile Indians, disease, starvation, and storms at sea eventually killed Narváez and almost all of his men. Another Spaniard, Hernando de Soto, landed an expedition in the Tampa Bay area in 1539. He led his men beyond the Florida region. In 1541, de Soto became the first European to reach the Mississippi River.

In 1564, a group of Huguenots (French Protestants) established a colony on the St. Johns River. They built Fort Caroline near what is now Jacksonville. King Philip II of Spain sent a sea captain named Pedro Menéndez de

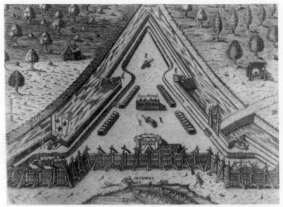

Engraving (1591) by Theodor de Bry
(Library of Congress)

Fort Caroline was built by *Huguenots* (French Protestants) in 1564 near the site of present-day Jacksonville. Spanish forces drove the French out of the Florida region in 1565.

Avilés to drive the French from Florida. Menéndez and his men arrived in Florida in 1565. They founded St. Augustine, the first permanent European settlement in what is now the United States. They destroyed the French forces and ended French attempts to settle in eastern Florida.

The Spaniards spent much of the next 200 years trying to teach their way of life to the Indians. Meanwhile, British colonists established settlements to the north, and France started colonies to the west. In the mid-1700's, wars broke out between the British and French colonists. Spain sided with the French. In 1762, British forces captured the port of Havana, Cuba. In 1763, Spain gave Florida to Britain in exchange for Havana.

The British period. Britain divided the Florida region into two separate colonies—East Florida and West Florida. West Florida included the part of the region west of the Apalachicola River. It also included parts of what are now Alabama, Mississippi, and Louisiana. East Florida included the rest of the Florida region. British control of Florida lasted until Spanish forces marched into West Florida in 1779, during the Revolutionary War in America (1775-1783). The British, already weakened by war, surrendered West Florida to Spain in 1781. Spain regained control of all Florida in 1783.

The second Spanish period. After the Revolutionary War ended in 1783, the United States controlled all the land it now occupies from the Atlantic Ocean to the Mississippi River except for Spanish Florida. Indians and escaped slaves and prisoners took refuge in the Florida region. In 1812, a group of eastern Florida settlers rebelled and declared their independence from Spain. But the Spaniards stopped the rebellion.

During the War of 1812 (1812-1814), Spain let the United Kingdom use Pensacola as a naval base. In 1814, American troops led by General Andrew Jackson stormed into Florida and seized Pensacola. During the First Seminole War (1817-1818), Jackson captured Fort St. Marks on the Gulf of Mexico and then took Pensacola once again. Finally, in the Adams-Onís Treaty of 1819, Spain agreed to turn Florida over to the United States. The United States did not actually pay any money to

Spain for Florida. However, it agreed to pay $5 million to U.S. citizens for property damages.

Territorial days. Florida formally came under U.S. control in 1821. Andrew Jackson served as temporary governor until November of that year. In 1822, Congress organized the Territory of Florida, and William P. Duval became the first territorial governor.

Thousands of American settlers poured into Florida. One of the major problems they faced was finding enough land for settlement. Seminole Indians lived in some of the territory's richest farmland. The U.S. government offered land west of the Mississippi River to the Seminole if they would leave Florida territory. Some of the Seminole accepted the offer, but others refused to leave their homes. In the Second Seminole War (1835-1842), most of the band was defeated. This war and the Third Seminole War (1855-1858) resulted in the forced resettlement of more Seminole, but a few hundred of the band fled into the swamps and remained in Florida.

Statehood. In 1839, Florida drew up a constitution in preparation for statehood, but it had to wait for admission to the Union. Florida would be a slave state, and Congress wanted to maintain a balance between slave and free states. Florida was admitted to the Union as a slave state on March 3, 1845. The following year, Iowa was admitted as a free state.

The Civil War and Reconstruction. In 1860, Abraham Lincoln was elected president. Florida and most of the other slave states regarded Lincoln as a threat to their way of life. On Jan. 10, 1861, Florida *seceded* (withdrew) from the Union and later joined the Confederacy.

Union forces captured most of Florida's coastal towns and Key West early in the American Civil War (1861-1865). But Confederate forces won the Battle of Olustee on Feb. 20, 1864, thereby keeping control of the interior region. This region's farmers shipped cattle, hogs, salt and other foodstuffs to the rest of the Confederacy. In the Battle of Natural Bridge in March 1865, a small band of Confederate troops, helped by young boys and old men, successfully defended Tallahassee against Union forces. Tallahassee and Austin, Texas, were the only Confederate state capitals that federal troops did not capture.

During the Reconstruction period after the Civil War, Florida and the other Confederate states came under federal military rule. The defeated states had to meet certain requirements before they could be readmitted to the Union. Florida abolished slavery, but it refused to accept some of the other requirements. Republicans gained control of the Florida state government in 1868. In that year, the Legislature ratified the 14th Amendment to the Constitution of the United States, guaranteeing civil rights, and Florida was readmitted to the Union.

Progress as a state. Florida developed rapidly during the 1880's. Geologists discovered large phosphate deposits. The state government and private investors renewed attempts to drain the swamplands. Railroad lines built by tycoons Henry M. Flagler and Henry B. Plant led to the opening of new land for development. Citrus groves were planted in north-central Florida. Resort cities sprang up. People and money from northern states poured into Florida.

A severe freeze during the winter of 1894-1895 damaged much of the state's citrus crops. Citrus growers

Historic Florida

Juan Ponce de León of Spain landed on the Florida coast in 1513 and explored parts of the region. Ponce de León claimed the Florida region for Spain.

WORLD BOOK map

Florida was ceded to the United States by Spain in 1819. The British had controlled the area for part of the late 1700's. Florida became a U.S. territory in 1822 and a state in 1845.

Apollo 11, the first spacecraft to land astronauts on the moon, lifted off from Cape Canaveral (then called Cape Kennedy) on July 16, 1969.

Important dates in Florida

WORLD BOOK illustrations by Richard Bonson, The Art Agency

1513	Juan Ponce de León landed on the Florida coast and claimed the region for Spain.
1528	Pánfilo de Narváez led an expedition into Florida.
1539	Hernando de Soto led an expedition through Florida.
1564	French Huguenot settlers built Fort Caroline on the St. Johns River.
1565	Pedro Menéndez de Avilés founded St. Augustine, the first permanent European settlement in what is now the United States.
1763	Spain ceded Florida to Britain.
1783	Spain regained control of Florida.
1819	The United States obtained Florida from Spain.
1821	Florida formally came under U.S. control.
1822	The U.S. Congress established the Territory of Florida.
1835-1842	During the Second Seminole War, many of the Seminole who had refused to move out of the territory lost their land.
1845	Florida became the 27th U.S. state on March 3.
1861	Florida seceded from the Union and joined the Confederacy.
1868	Florida was readmitted to the Union.

1896	Henry M. Flagler's Florida East Coast Railroad reached Miami.
1920-1925	Land speculators poured into the state. The population increased at a tremendous rate.
1947	Everglades National Park was established.
1958	The United States launched its first satellite from Cape Canaveral.
1961	The first U.S. space flights carrying astronauts were launched from Cape Canaveral.
1969	Apollo 11, the first spacecraft to land astronauts on the moon, was launched from Cape Canaveral.
1971	The Walt Disney World entertainment complex opened near Orlando.
1992	Hurricane Andrew killed 44 people in Florida and caused about $25 billion in property damage there.
2000	Florida's electoral votes decided the U.S. presidential election, giving Texas Governor George W. Bush a victory over Vice President Al Gore.
2011	The space shuttle Atlantis landed at Kennedy Space Center near Cape Canaveral, marking the end of the U.S. space shuttle program.

planted new groves in the south-central part of the state. This move contributed to the development of southern Florida. In 1896, Flagler extended his Florida East Coast Railroad line south to Miami.

The early 1900's. In 1906, the state began draining the swampland near Fort Lauderdale. This development opened up new land for farms and resorts.

Reports of fantastic profits to be made in Florida real estate swept the country. Hundreds of thousands of land speculators flocked to the state. Florida's population soared. Seven new counties were formed in 1921. By 1925, Florida's economy had become a swelling bubble of progress and prosperity. The bubble burst in 1926, when a severe depression hit Florida. Banks closed. Wealthy people suddenly lost their money. Two destructive hurricanes struck Florida's Atlantic coast in 1926 and 1928, killing hundreds of people. The state had partly recovered from these disasters by the late 1920's. Then, in 1929, the Great Depression struck the nation.

Federal and state welfare measures helped the people of Florida fight the depression. The state created jobs to develop its natural resources. The construction of paper mills by private industries led to forest conservation programs. Cooling plants were built to preserve perishable fruits and vegetables. Farmers established cooperative farm groups and cooperative markets. The state suffered setbacks in 1935 and in 1941, when severe hurricanes swept across southern Florida.

The mid-1900's. Florida's location along the Atlantic Ocean and near the Panama Canal made the state vital to the defense of the Western Hemisphere during World War II (1939-1945). Land, sea, and air bases were established in many parts of the state.

After the war, Florida's population grew rapidly. Tourism boomed and remained the state's leading source of income. But industrial expansion helped give Florida a more balanced economy. Development of industries in such fields as chemicals, electronics, paper and paper products, and ocean and space exploration provided jobs for Florida's swelling labor force.

In the 1950's, Cape Canaveral became a space and rocket center. The United States launched its first satellite from Cape Canaveral in 1958, its first human space flights in 1961, and its first spaceship carrying astronauts to the moon in 1969.

In the early 1960's, Cuba fell under Communist control. Many Cubans who opposed the Communists fled to Florida, settling mainly in Miami and Hialeah.

Like many other states, Florida faced serious racial problems during the 1950's and 1960's. In 1954, the Supreme Court of the United States ruled that compulsory segregation in public schools was unconstitutional. The Florida Constitution at that time did not permit black children and white children to attend the same schools. Integration of the state's public schools began in Dade County (now Miami-Dade County) in 1959. By the early 1970's, every county had integrated all or most of its public schools.

In the 1960's, Florida began an ambitious program to expand its facilities for higher education. This program was partly designed to serve the future demands for personnel in the oceanographic and aerospace industries. During the 1960's, 4 new state university campuses, several new private colleges and universities, and 15

NASA

A space shuttle is transported to the launch facility at Cape Canaveral. The space shuttle Columbia, the first reusable spacecraft, was launched from Cape Canaveral in 1981.

new public community colleges were established in Florida. An additional state university campus and a public community college opened in the early 1970's.

The late 1900's. Florida grew rapidly during the 1970's and 1980's. Its population increased by 44 percent from 1970 to 1980, and by 33 percent from 1980 to 1990. In 1971, the Walt Disney World entertainment center opened near Orlando. The Orlando area became the fastest-growing region of the state. Other booming areas included the suburbs of a number of cities—Miami, Tampa, Jacksonville, Fort Lauderdale, and West Palm Beach. In 1977, a new state capitol was completed in Tallahassee. The building rises 22 stories.

During the first half of the 1980's, the number of jobs in Florida rose by 24 percent. Many of these jobs were in electronics, manufacturing, and skilled services. Florida's economy continued to rely heavily on tourism and the citrus industry. But the expansion of trade, financial, and other service industries greatly strengthened the state's prospects for stable growth.

Florida's spectacular growth brought problems. The increasing population required more homes, roads, schools, sewage- and water-treatment plants, and health and social services. More than 100,000 Cuban and Haitian refugees settled in Florida in the late 1900's. Many of them were poor and had few job skills, and they caused increased demands upon social service agencies.

Uncontrolled development also led to growing concern for protecting and improving Florida's environment. During the 1970's, protests led to the cancellation of work on a jetport near the Everglades and a canal across northern Florida. Conservationists argued that these projects would endanger wildlife and destroy much natural beauty. In the 1960's, a canal was built to shorten the course of the Kissimmee River, which empties into Lake Okeechobee. By the mid-1980's, excess nutrients carried by the canal were causing *algae* (simple plantlike organisms) to thrive in the lake. This situation threatened other forms of life in Lake Okeechobee. In 1992, Congress approved a project to restore the Kissimmee to its former course. Work began in 1999 and is expected to be done in the second decade of the 2000's.

From 1983 through 1985, Florida's citrus industry suffered serious setbacks. Freezing weather and a fungal disease called *citrus canker* destroyed many central Florida citrus groves. In 1992, Hurricane Andrew struck. The hurricane killed 65 people directly or indirectly, 44 of them in Florida. It caused about $25 billion in property damage in the state, most of it in Dade County (now Miami-Dade County) in southeastern Florida. In Homestead, south of Miami, about 90 percent of the city's buildings were destroyed or damaged.

In 1998, some of the worst wildfires in U.S. history swept through Florida. More than 500,000 acres (200,000 hectares) were burned. Northern and central Florida were the hardest hit. In all, more than 2,300 blazes broke out between late May and late July.

The early 2000's. Florida became a focus of attention in the 2000 presidential election. The outcome of the race between Texas Governor George W. Bush and Vice President Al Gore depended upon who won Florida's 25 electoral votes. The vote in Florida was so close that the state did a recount. Gore requested hand recounts in certain counties. Bush challenged in court the need for those recounts. Five weeks after the election, the U.S. Supreme Court ruled to halt the recounts. Gore conceded to Bush. See **Election of 2000.**

Hurricane Charley struck Florida's west coast and tore across the state in August 2004. It caused 35 deaths and $14 billion in property damage. By the end of September, three more hurricanes had battered the state.

In August 2005, Hurricane Katrina struck southern Florida on its path toward the Gulf Coast. Katrina caused many deaths and widespread damage. Hurricane Wilma struck Florida's southwest coast in October and proceeded northeast, causing more death and destruction.

In 2010, an explosion on an offshore oil rig caused millions of gallons of oil to pour from an underwater well into the Gulf of Mexico. Within weeks, oil began appearing along Florida's coast. The spill ranked as one of the worst environmental disasters in U.S. history. Also in 2010, Republican Governor Charlie Crist ran for the U.S. Senate as an independent but lost the race.

In 2011, the United States ended the space shuttle program. Florida officials feared the state could lose several thousand jobs at the Kennedy Space Center and elsewhere.　　　　Peter O. Muller and Irvin D. S. Winsboro

Related articles in *World Book* include:

Biographies

Bethune, Mary M.
De Soto, Hernando
Ferre, Maurice
Mallory, Stephen R.
Menéndez de Avilés, Pedro
Narváez, Pánfilo de
Osceola
Ponce de León, Juan
Rawlings, Marjorie Kinnan
Reno, Janet
Smith, Edmund Kirby

Cities

Fort Lauderdale
Jacksonville
Key West
Miami
Miami Beach
Orlando
Pensacola
Saint Augustine
Saint Petersburg
Sarasota
Tallahassee
Tampa

History

Confederate States of America
Election of 2000
Fort Pickens
Fountain of Youth
Seminole Indians

National parks and monuments

Biscayne National Park
Castillo de San Marcos National Monument
Dry Tortugas National Park
Everglades National Park
Fort Matanzas National Monument

Physical features

Everglades
Florida Keys
Gulf of Mexico
Lake Okeechobee
Okefenokee Swamp
Suwannee River

Other related articles

Atlantic Intracoastal Waterway
Cape Canaveral
Gulf Intracoastal Waterway
Kennedy Space Center
Patrick Air Force Base

Outline

I. **People**
　A. Population
　B. Schools
　C. Libraries
　D. Museums
II. **Visitor's guide**
III. **Land and climate**
　A. Land regions
　B. Coastline
　C. Rivers, lakes, and springs
　D. Plant and animal life
　E. Climate
IV. **Economy**
　A. Natural resources
　B. Service industries
　C. Manufacturing
　D. Agriculture
　E. Mining
　F Fishing industry
　G. Electric power and utilities
　H. Transportation
　I. Communication
V. **Government**
　A. Constitution
　B. Executive
　C. Legislature
　D. Courts
　E. Local government
　F. Revenue
　G. Politics
VI. **History**

Additional resources

Level I

Cannavale, Matthew C. *Florida, 1513-1821.* National Geographic Children's Bks., 2006.
Hess, Debra, and Wiesenfeld, L. P. *Florida.* 2nd ed. Marshall Cavendish Benchmark, 2011.
Marx, Trish. *Everglades Forever.* 2004. Reprint. Lee & Low, 2008.
Mountjoy, Shane. *St. Augustine.* Chelsea Hse., 2007.
Orr, Tamra B. *Florida.* Children's Pr., 2008.

Level II

Bryan, Jonathan R., and others. *Roadside Geology of Florida.* Mountain Pr. Pub. Co., 2008.
Gannon, Michael. *Florida.* Rev. ed. Univ. Pr. of Fla., 2003.
Grunwald, Michael. *The Swamp: The Everglades, Florida, and the Politics of Paradise.* Simon & Schuster, 2006.
Hoffman, Paul E. *Florida's Frontiers.* Ind. Univ. Pr., 2002.
Milanich, Jerald T. *Florida's Indians from Ancient Times to the Present.* Univ. Pr. of Fla., 1998.
Mormino, Gary R. *Land of Sunshine, State of Dreams: A Social History of Modern Florida.* 2005. Reprint. Univ. Pr. of Fla., 2008.
Purdy, Barbara A. *Florida's People During the Last Ice Age.* Univ. Pr. of Fla., 2008.
Rivers, Larry E. *Slavery in Florida.* 2000. Reprint. Univ. Pr. of Fla., 2009.
Tebeau, Charlton W., and Marina, William. *A History of Florida.* 3rd ed. Univ. of Miami Pr., 1999.

Florida, University of, is a combined state and land-grant university in Gainesville, Florida. It was founded in 1853 and is the state's largest university. The university also operates the Institute of Food and Agricultural Sciences, the Florida Museum of Natural History, and several research centers. The University of Florida's athletic teams are called the Gators. The university's website at http://www.ufl.edu offers additional information.

Critically reviewed by the University of Florida

Florida Keys are a group of small islands or reefs that stretch in a curved line about 150 miles (241 kilometers) long from Biscayne Bay at Miami southwest into the Gulf of Mexico. The word *keys* comes from the Spanish word *cayos,* which means *small islands.*

The Florida Keys are remarkable examples of coral formation. The islands attract a large tourist trade. Leading tourist activities include boating, scuba diving, and sport fishing. Commercial fishing also is important to the area's economy. Key West, farthest from the mainland, has the most important harbor. It is joined to the mainland by U.S. Route 1, an overseas highway 128 miles (206 kilometers) long.

Peter O. Muller

See also **Florida** (physical map; picture: The Florida Keys); **Key West.**

© James Blank, The Stock Market

The Florida Keys offer a variety of water activities. In this photo, visitors relax on a beach in Key West.

Florida panther is a large, wild cat that lives in the forests and swamps of southern Florida. The Florida panther is a subspecies of the mountain lion (also known as cougar or puma). Mountain lions once roamed throughout the United States, Mexico, and southern Canada. However, settlers destroyed most of the mountain lions and much of their habitat east of the Rocky Mountains. By the late 1800's, most of the remaining mountain lions east of the Rocky Mountains lived in Texas and Florida. As a result of this separation, Florida panthers became genetically distinct from their western relatives. Today, only about 100 to 160 Florida panthers survive in the wild.

Adult Florida panthers tend to live alone, except when

Michael Dunbar, Florida Game and Fresh Water Fish Commission

The Florida panther lives in the forests and swamps of southern Florida. It spends some of its time in trees. Only about 100 to 160 Florida panthers survive in the wild.

mating. They prey chiefly on white-tailed deer. They also eat raccoons and other small mammals.

Human expansion in southern Florida continues to reduce the habitat of the panther and endangers its survival in the wild. Mercury and pesticide contamination in the animal's habitat also pose threats. In addition, inbreeding within the small population has reduced genetic diversity among the panthers, making them more vulnerable to disease.   Charles F. Facemire

Scientific classification. The scientific name of the Florida panther is *Puma concolor coryi.*

See also **Mountain lion.**

Florida State University is a public institution of higher education in Tallahassee, Florida. It is part of the Florida State University system. Florida State University was founded in 1851. The university's athletic teams are called the Seminoles. The university's website at http://www.fsu.edu offers additional information.

Critically reviewed by Florida State University

Florin, *FLAWR uhn,* is a coin first made in the Italian city of Florence in 1252. Made of gold, the florin weighed about an eighth of an ounce (3.5 grams). Florins became popular for trade during the economic expansion of Europe from the 1200's to the 1400's. The coin's name comes from an Italian word meaning *little flower.* It refers to a lily, the symbol of Florence. A lily appears on one side of the coin. The other side has a figure of Saint John the Baptist, the guardian saint of Florence.

Florence stopped making florins in the early 1500's. But many European countries produced their own versions of the florin. In 1849, the United Kingdom issued its first silver florin, worth 2 shillings, or a 10th of a pound. In 1971, the United Kingdom switched to *decimal currency,* a system of money based on multiples of 10. The florin continued to circulate with a value of 10 pence until 1993. *Florin* was also another name for the *guilder,* a unit of money used in the Netherlands until the country replaced it with the euro, the European Union currency, in 2002.   R. G. Doty

Florissant Fossil Beds National Monument, *FLAWR uh suhnt,* is near Florissant, Colorado. The monument features fossil insects, leaves, seeds, and tree stumps that date back roughly 35 million years. Congress authorized Florissant Fossil Beds National Monument in 1969. For the area of Florissant Fossil Beds National Monument, see **National Park System** (table: National monuments). For location, see **Colorado** (political map).   Critically reviewed by the National Park Service

Florist. See Floriculture; Flower (As decoration).

Flotation process, *floh TAY shuhn,* is used to separate valuable minerals from each other or from other minerals with which they are mixed. In this process, the material that contains the minerals is first crushed and ground fine. It is then put into a tank called a *flotation cell* that contains water and certain chemicals called *flotation reagents.* These chemicals form a water-repellent film around the particles of one of the minerals, but not around the others.

To separate the minerals, the liquid in the flotation cell is stirred and air is piped in. Air bubbles cling to the water-repellent particles, causing them to rise to the top and float. For collection, the bubbles carrying the minerals must be trapped in a froth on the surface. A frothing agent, such as pine oil or eucalyptus oil, is added to create the froth. The froth with the mineral-laden bubbles can then be skimmed off. The other minerals or materials remain in the liquid.   William Hustrulid

See also **Copper** (Milling).

Flotsam, *FLAHT suhm,* **jetsam,** *JEHT suhm,* **and lagan,** *LAG uhn,* are terms used to describe goods in the sea. Goods found floating in the sea are called *flotsam.* The term includes both goods cast from a vessel in distress and goods that float when a ship sinks. *Jetsam* is goods voluntarily cast overboard in an emergency, usually to lighten the vessel. Jetsam sinks and remains underwater. *Lagan,* or *ligan,* is cargo that someone has sunk with the intention of recovering it later. The person usually ties a buoy to lagan to mark its location.

Flotsam, jetsam, and lagan are not abandoned or derelict property. That is, the owner or master of the ship does not intend to give up the goods permanently. The owner intends to recover the goods at some later date. Under the maritime law, flotsam, jetsam, and lagan remain the property of their original owner, no matter how long they lie in the sea. The finder may only hold them for salvage, which is a legal reward the owner pays to the finder. Many courts rule that the owner must claim the goods within a year after someone else has recovered them.   George P. Smith II

See also **Salvage.**

Flounder is the name of a variety of saltwater flatfishes. Flounders live on the sandy and muddy bottoms of bays and along the shores of most seas. There are hundreds of *species* (kinds) of flounders. The *winter flounder,* or *blackback,* can be found from Labrador to Cape Hatteras, and is an important food fish. The *summer flounder,* a popular game fish, ranges from Cape Cod to Flori-

WORLD BOOK illustration by Colin Newman, Linden Artists Ltd.

The starry flounder is a popular game fish along the California coast. This fish can be identified by the colored bands on its fins. Its body is covered with sharp, thornlike spines in its skin.

da. It also is known as the *fluke* or the *plaice.*

The flounder has a greatly compressed body with both eyes on the same side of the head. The side of the flounder facing up takes on the color of the bottom of the sea where the fish lives. The side toward the bottom is nearly white. When the flounder first hatches, it looks like a typical fish. After it grows to be about ½ inch (13 millimeters) long, the body becomes flattened, and both eyes move to one side of the head. The side of the head on which the eyes appear depends on the species of flounder. Flounders have markings that blend with their surroundings. The fish can lie camouflaged on the ocean floor. This makes it easier for them to catch the shrimp and small fish that form their basic diet. The dab, halibut, and European turbot are in the flounder group. Flounders also are related to soles.   David W. Greenfield

Scientific classification. Flounders belong to several families of fish. The starry flounder is *Platichthys stellatus.* The winter flounder is *Pseudopleuronectes americanus.* The summer flounder is *Paralichthys dentatus.*

See also **Flatfish; Halibut; Sole; Turbot.**

Flour is the ground powder of grains or other crops that serves as a basic ingredient in many important foods. Flour made from ground wheat is used to bake

© Stewart M. Green, Tom Stack & Assoc.

Florissant Fossil Beds National Monument is in central Colorado. Its attractions include fossilized tree stumps, *above,* that date from about 35 million years ago.

bread. Wheat flour is also the main ingredient in such foods as cakes, cookies, crackers, pancakes, and pasta. Other grains that are ground into flour include barley, corn, millet, oats, rice, and rye. Still other kinds of flour are produced by grinding beans, nuts, seeds, or such *tubers* (underground stems) as potatoes and cassava.

Bread ranks as the world's most widely eaten food, and people in many countries receive much of their nourishment from foods made with flour. Each person in the United States eats an average of about 120 pounds (54 kilograms) of flour from wheat and other grains annually. Canadians eat an average of about 135 pounds (61 kilograms) of flour per person each year.

By the 9000's B.C., prehistoric people were grinding crude flour from wild grain by crushing the grain between rocks. Later, the ancient Greeks and Romans used water wheels to power flour mills.

The chemistry of flour. Flour consists mostly of molecules called *carbohydrates,* an important source of nutrition. The carbohydrates in flour are chiefly starches. When heated, starches absorb water and swell. Cooks thus use the starches in flour to thicken sauces, stews, puddings, and pie fillings.

Wheat flour contains special molecules that, when moistened, form a sticky, stretchy substance called *gluten.* Along with starches, gluten gives structure to baked goods. In a batter or dough, sheets of gluten hold in expanding bubbles of carbon dioxide gas created by such *leavening agents* as yeast or baking powder. Gluten thus helps baked products rise, rather than remain flat and dense. However, some people's digestive systems cannot tolerate gluten. They must avoid foods made with wheat flour.

Types of flour. In the United States, Canada, and Europe, most of the flour people use is called *white flour.* It is ground only from the inner parts of wheat kernels. *Whole-wheat flour* is made by grinding entire wheat kernels. Whole-wheat flour does not form gluten as readily as white flour does. Whole-wheat flour also gives foods a rougher texture and stronger flavor than does white flour alone.

There are three main types of white wheat flour: (1) bread flour, (2) cake flour, and (3) all-purpose flour. The three types of flour differ primarily in their protein content. Bread flour contains at least 11 percent protein. Cake flour contains less than 8 ½ percent protein. All-purpose flour generally has a protein content of about 10 ½ percent.

The more protein flour has, the stronger the gluten it forms. Bakers use high-protein bread flour to make

How flour is milled

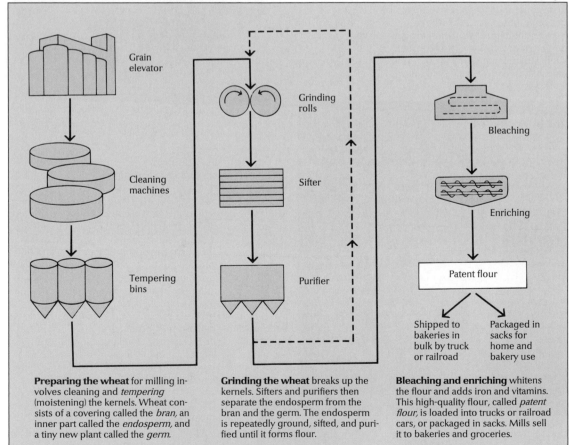

Grain elevator

Cleaning machines

Tempering bins

Grinding rolls

Sifter

Purifier

Bleaching

Enriching

Patent flour

Shipped to bakeries in bulk by truck or railroad

Packaged in sacks for home and bakery use

Preparing the wheat for milling involves cleaning and *tempering* (moistening) the kernels. Wheat consists of a covering called the *bran,* an inner part called the *endosperm,* and a tiny new plant called the *germ.*

Grinding the wheat breaks up the kernels. Sifters and purifiers then separate the endosperm from the bran and the germ. The endosperm is repeatedly ground, sifted, and purified until it forms flour.

Bleaching and enriching whitens the flour and adds iron and vitamins. This high-quality flour, called *patent flour,* is loaded into trucks or railroad cars, or packaged in sacks. Mills sell it to bakeries and groceries.

Chemists test samples of bread made from flour from different varieties of wheat. Seeds from the varieties that produce high-quality bread are distributed to farmers for planting.

breads with a sturdy, chewy texture. Cake flour, with its low protein content, results in baked goods with a more tender texture. All-purpose flour is often used in cookies, pie crusts, dinner rolls, biscuits, and other baked goods that require a balance between sturdiness and tenderness.

Other types of flour have different uses in cooking and baking. Flours made from barley and rye form smaller amounts of gluten than does wheat flour. Other flours do not form gluten at all. Buckwheat and rice flour are used to make certain kinds of Asian noodles. Cornmeal, made from grinding corn kernels, is an important ingredient in corn bread and tortillas.

How white flour is milled. Wheat kernels form the raw material for white flour. They consist of a tough covering called the *bran,* a mellow inner part called the *endosperm,* and a tiny new wheat plant called the *germ.* To make white flour, millers separate the endosperm from the bran and germ and then grind the endosperm into flour.

Various cleaning machines first remove dirt, straw, and other impurities from the grain. Next, the wheat is *tempered* (moistened). The moisture makes the endosperm more mellow and the bran tougher.

The tempered wheat passes between a series of rough steel rollers that crush the endosperm into chunks. Pieces of bran and germ cling to the chunks of endosperm or form separate flakes. Then the crushed grain is sifted. The tiniest bits of endosperm, which have become flour, pass through the sifter into a bin. Larger particles collect in the sifter. Next, these larger particles are put into a machine called a *purifier.* There, currents of air blow flakes of bran away from the endosperm particles. The endosperm particles are then repeatedly ground between smooth rollers, sifted, and purified until they form flour. In most mills, about 72 percent of the wheat eventually becomes flour. The rest is sold chiefly as livestock feed.

Newly milled white flour is cream-colored, but some mills bleach it to make it white. They may also add chemicals that strengthen the gluten. Some chemicals both bleach the flour and strengthen the gluten. Such treatments must be carefully controlled because the addition of too much of a chemical ruins the flour.

Wheat is rich in starch, protein, B vitamins, and such minerals as iron and phosphorus. However, the vitamins and some of the minerals are chiefly in the bran and germ, which milling removes from white flour. Most millers in the United States and many other countries enrich their product by adding iron and vitamins to white flour made for home use. Before enriched white flour became widely available in the 1940's, many people who relied on foods baked with white flour suffered from malnutrition.

History. People probably began to make crude flour between 15,000 B.C. and 9000 B.C. They used rocks to crush wild grain on other rocks. After farming began to develop, people made flour from such cultivated grains as barley, millet, rice, rye, and wheat.

By the 1000's B.C., millers ground grain between two large, flat millstones. Later, domestic animals or slaves rotated the top stone to crush the grain. By the A.D. 1100's, windmills were powering flour mills in Europe.

Few further advances in milling occurred until 1780. That year, in England, a Scottish engineer named James Watt built the first steam-powered flour mill. In 1802, Oliver Evans, a Philadelphia miller, opened the first such mill in the United States. During the late 1800's, metal rollers replaced millstones in many American and European mills. Edmund La Croix and other millers in Minneapolis, Minnesota, perfected the purifier in the 1870's. By the early 1900's, automation had made flour mills more productive than ever.   Mary E. Zahik

See also **Baking; Bread; Corn** (The dry-milling industry); **Gluten; Pasta; Wheat** (Food for people).

Flour beetle is any of several small, reddish, flattened beetles that breed in flour, meal, and other grain prod-

Flour beetles breed in flour, meal, and other grain products. They often cause the food to spoil.

ucts. They often spoil the food. Adult flour beetles are about ⅙ inch (4 millimeters) long. Flour beetles are found in all parts of the world, and all year long, in warm buildings.   Ellis W. Huddleston

Scientific classification. Flour beetles belong to the family Tenebrionidae. Common species are *Tribolium confusum* and *T. castaneum.*

Flow chart. See **Computer** (Preparing a program).

© Minden Pictures/Masterfile

Colorful wildflowers grow along the Alsek River in Glacier Bay National Park in Alaska. Wildflower blossoms appear on the ground when spring comes to colder climates. The flowers have only a brief summer in which to grow and produce seed.

Flower

Flower is a blossom, or it may be an entire plant that is known for its blossoms. People admire flowers for their beauty. But flowers also have a vital function: they are the means by which most plants reproduce. Flowers usually produce pollen and seeds.

People may think of flowers as being brightly colored and showy. Common examples of such flowers include buttercups, orchids, roses, tulips, violets, and hundreds of other garden flowers and wildflowers. In some plants, such as grasses and oaks, however, the flowers are so small and plain that few people recognize them

The contributor of this article, Gerry Moore, is Director of the Department of Science at the Brooklyn Botanic Garden in New York.

as flowers. Some trees, such as catalpas and horse chestnuts, have beautiful blossoms. But the trees themselves are never referred to as flowers. All the plants classified as either garden flowers or wildflowers are smaller than trees. Also, most of these flowering plants have soft stems rather than woody stems.

People prize flowers for their gorgeous colors, delightful fragrances, and attractive shapes. Because of their beauty, flowers are a favorite form of decoration. People also use flowers to express their feelings. For more than 50,000 years, people have placed flowers on the graves of loved ones as a sign of remembrance and respect. Flowers at weddings symbolize love, happiness, and *fertility* (the ability to produce children). Certain flowers also have a religious meaning. Among Christians, for example, the white Easter lily stands for

Outline

I. The uses of flowers
A. As decoration
B. In landscaping
C. Other uses
II. Garden flowers
A. Garden annuals
B. Garden biennials
C. Garden perennials
D. Garden perennials grown from bulbs
E. Flowering shrubs
III. Wildflowers
A. Flowers of the Arctic tundra
B. Flowers of woodlands and forests
C. Flowers of prairies and dry plains
D. Flowers of summer-dry regions
E. Flowers of alpine tundras
F. Flowers of the desert
G. Flowers of the tropics and subtropics

IV. The parts of a flower
A. The calyx
B. The corolla
C. The stamens
D. The carpels
E. Variations in flower structure
V. The role of flowers in reproduction
A. Cross-pollination
B. Self-pollination
C. Fertilization
VI. Flower hobbies
A. Studying wildflowers
B. Flower arranging
C. Flower breeding
VII. How flowers are named and classified
A. The naming of flowers
B. The classifying of flowers
VIII. The evolution of flowering plants

purity. Buddhists and Hindus regard the lotus as sacred, perhaps because its lovely flower rises above the mud in which it grows.

Originally, all flowers were wildflowers. Prehistoric people found wildflowers growing nearly everywhere, from the cold plains of the Arctic to the humid rain forests of the tropics. In time, people learned to grow plants from seeds. They could then raise the prettiest and sweetest-smelling flowers in gardens. By 3000 B.C., the Egyptians and other peoples of the Middle East had begun to cultivate a variety of garden flowers, including jasmines, poppies, and water lilies.

Today, people in every country raise a variety of cultivated flowers. Breeders have developed many new kinds of flowers that are not found in the wild. Thousands of *species* (kinds) of flowering plants still grow in the wild throughout the world. But many of them are becoming rare as people destroy wilderness areas to make room for farms and cities.

The function of flowers is to make pollen and seeds. Every blossom has male or female parts—or both. The male parts of a flower produce pollen. The pollen contains male sex cells. Female sex cells are found in the *ovary,* a structure at the base of a flower. In most cases, seeds can develop only after male sex cells in the pollen fertilize female sex cells in the ovary. The seeds then develop in the ovary.

The transfer of pollen from the male parts of a flower to the female parts is called *pollination.* In many flowering plants, the pollen is carried from the male parts of one flower to the female parts of another. The wind pollinates some kinds of flowers, blowing pollen from the male parts to the female parts. Such flowers often have small, plain, odorless blossoms. Showy or sweet-smelling blossoms attract insects, birds, or other animals. These animals serve as *pollinators,* helping to transfer pollen from one flower to another. Many kinds of flowering plants also pollinate themselves.

Plants that produce flowers are called *angiosperms.* The word *angiosperm* comes from two Greek words meaning *vessel* and *seed.* Before the seeds are fertilized, they are protected in the ovary. After the seeds are fertilized, the ovary grows into a structure called a fruit. The

fruit encloses and protects the ripening seeds. The rest of the blossom gradually dies.

Scientists believe that there are hundreds of thousands of species of angiosperms around the world. All garden flowers and wildflowers belong to this group. So do nearly all other familiar plants, including cattails, grasses, and palms. One major exception is the *gymnosperms.* Like angiosperms, gymnosperms reproduce by means of seeds. However, gymnosperms produce their seeds not within fruits but rather in cones or cone-like structures. These cones develop from structures that resemble plain flowers. But scientists do not consider them to be flowers in the strict sense of the word. Examples of gymnosperms include ancient plants called *cycads,* a shrub called *ephedra,* ginkgo, and pine trees.

For detailed information about plants in general, see **Plant.** *World Book* also has hundreds of articles on individual flowers and flowering shrubs. See the list of *Related articles* at the end of this article.

The uses of flowers

The blossoms of most flowering plants have little food value compared with other plant parts, such as the leaves and fruit. Most blossoms also lack chemicals or

Lotus flowers pile around a statue of Buddha during a religious festival in Thailand. The lotus is sacred to Buddhists and Hindus.

Interesting facts about flowers

Robert W. Mitchell,
Tom Stack & Associates

Yucca flowers are pollinated
only by female yucca moths,
which lay their eggs in the
flowers' seed-producing organs. The eggs hatch into
caterpillars, which feed on
some of the seeds.

Werner Stoy,
Camera Hawaii

The night-blooming cereus
is a climbing cactus with
large, fragrant, white flowers
that open only at night. The
plants are native to Central
America and are grown in
areas with tropical climates.

M. Fogden, Bruce Coleman Inc.

Red-hot pokers have long,
slender stems topped by
spikes of small, brilliantly
colored flowers. They belong
to the lily family and may
reach a height of 5 feet (1.5
meters). Red-hot pokers
grow wild in Africa.

Stone plants of South Africa
have leaves that look like the
stones among which the
plants grow. Each plant has
two fleshy leaves. A white or
yellow flower grows in a slit
between the tops of the
leaves.

© Blickwinkel/Alamy Images

The bee orchid of Europe resembles a female bee. The resemblance attracts male bees,
which pollinate the orchids as
they travel between blossoms.

© Shutterstock

Gloriosa lilies have long,
graceful *stamens* (male
reproductive parts). The stems
may measure up to 6 feet
(1.8 meters) tall. The flowers
grow in Asia and Africa.

Diana & Rick Sullivan, Bruce Coleman Ltd.

The titan arum has the
largest *inflorescence* (cluster
of blossoms) of any flower in
the world. The inflorescence
can reach more than 7 feet (2.1
meters) tall. It gives off the
odor of rotting flesh to attract
beetles and flies. These
insects carry the plant's
pollen. The titan arum is
native to Sumatra.

AP Photo

© Shutterstock

The rafflesia is the world's largest flower. It can measure over 3
feet (90 centimeters) across. Rafflesias grow in Southeast Asia.
They have no stems or leaves and are parasites on other plants.

other materials that are useful for manufacturing. As a
result, people use flowers mainly as decoration and in
landscaping. The production and marketing of flowers is
a major industry in many countries.

As decoration. People use flowers as table decorations in homes and restaurants. Flowers often decorate
the altars in churches and other places of worship.
Women may wear flowers in their hair or pinned to
their clothing. Hawaiians often string flowers together to
make necklaces called *leis*. Flowers add beauty and col-
or to many public festivals. One of the most famous is
the Rose Parade. It is part of the Tournament of Roses
held every New Year's Day in Pasadena, California. The
parade features floats decorated with hundreds of thousands of roses and other flowers.

Flowers used as decoration may be either cut flowers
or flowering house plants. Cut flowers are garden flowers that were harvested while in bloom. They stay fresh
several days if their stems are kept in water. Popular cut
flowers include daisies, gladioluses, irises, and roses.
Flowering house plants can be grown indoors in containers. Such plants include African violets, azaleas, and
wax begonias. Unlike cut flowers, flowering house
plants may last almost indefinitely.

Many home gardeners grow their own cut flowers.
Greenhouses and flower farms raise them commercially.
Greenhouses also grow flowering house plants commercially, as do nurseries. Commercial producers sell
their flowers to retail florists. The florists resell them to
the public. Many florists are trained in the art of flower

© Picture Contact/Alamy Images

A flower auction in the Netherlands offers flowers from all around the world. This photograph shows batches of flowers available for sale at the Aalsmeer flower auction. Each day, millions of flowers are sold at Aalsmeer. The Netherlands has long been a center of the flower trade.

arranging. Such florists may supply flowers for such occasions as funerals and weddings. The section *Flower hobbies* discusses flower arranging.

In landscaping. Flowers add greatly to the beauty of gardens, parks, yards, and other landscaped areas. The flowers may be planted in beds or borders. They may be arranged according to color, shape, and size. Spring, summer, and autumn varieties may be planted to provide a continuous display of blooms. Some of the most popular plants used in landscaping are flowering shrubs. Such plants include bridal wreaths, forsythias, hydrangeas, and lilacs. Flowering shrubs bloom year after year and require little care.

Many public gardens and parks have beautiful displays of flowers. The Missouri Botanical Garden in St. Louis is famous for its water lilies. The Royal Botanical Gardens in Ontario is famous for its lilacs. The Royal Botanic Gardens, Kew, in the United Kingdom, has one of the world's largest collections of living plants. Kirstenbosch National Botanical Garden in Cape Town, South Africa, cultivates only native plant life, including many endangered wildflowers. The Australian National Botanic Gardens, in Canberra, displays a large collection of plants native to Australia, including many wildflowers.

Other uses. In most cases, people do not eat flower buds or blossoms. There are some exceptions, however. The flower buds of broccoli, cauliflower, and globe artichoke plants are widely used as vegetables. Broccoli and cauliflower buds grow in thick clusters called *heads*. The heads are eaten with the stems. Artichoke buds grow singly. Only the bud is eaten. Certain seasonings additionally come from flower buds or flower parts.

Werner Stoy, Camera Hawaii

Colorful leis, which often consist of flowers strung together, are worn as necklaces in Hawaii and other Pacific islands. This lei is made of frangipani blossoms.

A flower-covered float carries a child during the Battle of Flowers Parade in Laredo, Spain. Parades around the world feature floats decorated with blossoms.

For example, cloves are the dried flower buds of the clove tree. Saffron comes from female parts of purple autumn crocuses. The petals of some flowers, such as roses and marigolds, have a sweet or spicy taste. They are sometimes used to flavor soups and salads, especially in Europe and Asia. Some people use dandelion and elderberry blossoms to make wine. Many people consider lightly battered and fried squash blossoms a delicacy.

Bees make honey from *nectar,* a sugary liquid produced by flowers. The bees gather nectar. They eat some of it and store the rest in their hives. The nectar in the hives gradually turns into honey. Some of the most common honey plants include alfalfa, buckwheat, clover, orange, and sage.

The petals of certain flowers contain sweet-smelling oils. Such flowers include jasmines, mimosas, and roses. The oils obtained from these flowers supply the fragrances for many high-quality perfumes. However, most perfumes today are made synthetically from chemicals.

Garden flowers

Some kinds of garden flowers resemble their wild relatives. Other kinds have been bred so that their blooms are more attractive than those of their wild relatives. Garden flowers are grown on farms, in nurseries, in greenhouses, and in gardens. Some kinds of garden flowers also make excellent house plants.

Garden flowers can be divided into three main groups based on how long they live. They are (1) annuals, (2) biennials, and (3) perennials. *Annuals* sprout from seed, grow to full size, bloom, produce seeds, and die—all within one growing season or year. *Biennials* live for two growing seasons or years. They do not produce flowers and seeds until their second growing season. After that, they die. Perennials live for three growing seasons or longer. They may or may not bloom during their first year of growth. But after perennials have begun to bloom, they may do so every year almost indefinitely, depending on the species.

All annuals and biennials are *herbs*—that is, they have soft stems. Some perennials, called *herbaceous perenni-*

als, are also herbs. The stems of herbaceous perennials wither and die at the end of each summer in *temperate* regions. Temperate regions have warm summers and cool or cold winters. However, the roots of herbaceous perennials survive through the winter. They grow new stems in spring. Some kinds of herbaceous perennials grow from *bulbs* (underground stems). Still others grow from bulblike structures, such as *corms* or *rhizomes.* Other perennials, called *woody perennials,* have woody stems. These plants include shrubs and trees. Their stems do not wither at the end of summer. In temperate regions, however, most woody perennials shed their leaves in autumn. They then go through a period of reduced activity in winter called *dormancy.*

The great majority of garden flowers are annuals or perennials. Only a few are biennials. However, the classification of flowers as annuals, biennials, or perennials is not always precise. For example, most perennials that are native to warm climates cannot survive cold winters. These flowers therefore cannot be grown as perennials in such places as Canada. But some warm-weather perennials bloom during their first year of growth. They can thus be grown as annuals in northern climates. Such flowers include gloxinias and wax begonias.

Saffron crocus flowers are collected by workers near Srinagar in Kashmir, close to the border of India and Pakistan. Saffron, an orange-yellow spice and dye, is made from parts of the flower.

Botanical gardens display collections of flowering plants, shrubs, and trees, often from many parts of the world. Canada's beautiful Butchart Gardens, *shown here,* near Victoria, British Columbia, include an English rose garden and Italian and Japanese gardens.

© Shutterstock

State flowers of the United States

Alabama
Common camellia
Camellia japonica

Alaska
Alpine forget-me-not
Myosotis alpestris

Arizona
Saguaro cactus blossom
Carnegiea gigantea

Arkansas
Apple blossom*

California
California poppy
Eschscholzia californica

Colorado
Colorado blue columbine (white-and-lavender columbine)
Aquilegia cocrulea

Connecticut
Mountain laurel
Kalmia latifolia

Delaware
Peach blossom
Prunus persica

District of Columbia
American Beauty rose
Rosa "American Beauty"

Florida
Orange blossom
Citrus sinensis

Georgia
Cherokee rose
Rosa laevigata

Hawaii
Yellow hibiscus
Hibiscus brackenridgei

Idaho
Syringa (Lewis's mock orange)
Philadelphus lewisii

Illinois
Native purple violet*

Indiana
Peony*

Iowa
Wild rose*

Kansas
Common sunflower
Helianthus annuus

Kentucky
Goldenrod*

Louisiana
Southern magnolia
Magnolia grandiflora

Maine
Eastern white pine cone and tassel
Pinus strobus

Maryland
Black-eyed Susan
Rudbeckia hirta

Massachusetts
Trailing arbutus (mayflower)
Epigaea repens

Michigan
Apple blossom*

Minnesota
Showy lady's-slipper (pink-and-white lady's-slipper)
Cypripedium reginae

Mississippi
Southern magnolia
Magnolia grandiflora

Missouri
Hawthorn*

Montana
Bitter root
Lewisia rediviva

Nebraska
Giant goldenrod
Solidago gigantea

Nevada
Common sagebrush (big sagebrush)
Artemisia tridentata

New Hampshire
Common lilac
Syringa vulgaris

New Jersey
Common blue violet
Viola sororia

New Mexico
Yucca flower*

New York
Rose*

North Carolina
Flowering dogwood
Cornus florida

North Dakota
Wild rose
Rosa arkansana and *Rosa blanda*

Ohio
Scarlet carnation
Dianthus caryophyllus

Oklahoma
Oklahoma rose
Rosa odorata "Oklahoma"

Oregon
Oregon grape
Mahonia aquifolium

Pennsylvania
Mountain laurel
Kalmia latifolia

Rhode Island
Common blue violet
Viola sororia

South Carolina
Yellow jessamine
Gelsemium sempervirens

South Dakota
Eastern pasqueflower
Pulsatilla patens

Tennessee
Iris*

Texas
Bluebonnet*

Utah
Sego lily
Calochortus nuttallii

Vermont
Red clover
Trifolium pratense

Virginia
Flowering dogwood
Cornus florida

Washington
Pacific rhododendron (coast rhododendron)
Rhododendron macrophyllum

West Virginia
Great rhododendron (giant laurel or rosebay)
Rhododendron maximum

Wisconsin
Wood violet
Viola papilionacea

Wyoming
Wyoming Indian paintbrush
Castilleja linariifolia

Floral emblems of the Canadian provinces and territories

Alberta
Prickly rose (prickly wild rose)
Rosa acicularis

British Columbia
Pacific dogwood
Cornus nuttalli

Manitoba
Eastern pasqueflower
Pulsatilla patens

New Brunswick
Early blue violet
Viola palmata

Newfoundland and Labrador
Purple pitcher plant
Sarracenia purpurea

Northwest Territories
White mountain avens (eight-petaled mountain avens)
Dryas octopetala

Nova Scotia
Trailing arbutus (mayflower)
Epigaea repens

Nunavut
Purple saxifrage
Saxifraga oppositifolia

Ontario
White trillium
Trillium grandiflorum

Prince Edward Island
Pink lady's-slipper
Cypripedium acaule

Quebec
Blue flag iris
Iris versicolor

Saskatchewan
Wood lily (Western red lily)
Lilium philadelphicum

Yukon
Fireweed
Epilobium angustifolium

*No species designated.

Garden annuals

Most annuals bloom about 8 to 10 weeks after the seeds are planted. In warm climates, annuals can be planted outdoors at any time of the year. In areas with cold winters, gardeners usually plant them in spring. Certain species can survive a light frost. These plants, called *hardy annuals,* may be started outdoors from seed as soon as the ground has thawed completely. They include bachelor's buttons, morning-glories, pansies, petunias, sunflowers, sweet alyssum, and sweet peas. However, some hardy annuals, such as pansies and petunias, grow slowly. Gardeners give these flowers a head start by planting them as seedlings. Some gardeners grow their own seedlings. Others buy them from commercial greenhouses. In either case, the seeds are planted indoors in late winter or early spring. The seedlings can be transplanted outdoors as soon as the ground has completely thawed.

Some annuals, such as garden balsams and marigolds, cannot survive even a light frost. These *tender annuals* should not be planted outdoors until all danger of frost has passed. In northern regions, frosts may occur for a month or more after the ground has thawed. Gardeners in these regions almost always give tender annuals a head start by sowing the seeds indoors before the growing season begins. They then plant the seedlings outdoors in spring.

Sweet pea
Lathyrus odoratus

Morning-glory
Ipomoea purpurea

Petunia
Petunia hybrida

Garden nasturtium
Tropaeolum majus

Snapdragon
Antirrhinum majus

Zinnia
Zinnia elegans

Bachelor's button
Centaurea cyanus

French marigold
Tagetes patula

Garden balsam
Impatiens balsamina

Pansy
Viola tricolor

Common sunflower
Helianthus annuus

Larkspur
Consolida ambigua

Cosmos
Cosmos bipinnatus

Garden biennials

Gardeners who wish to start biennials outdoors usually plant the seeds in midsummer. The plants grow a few leaves by autumn. The leaves may then die. However, the roots survive through the winter. In the next growing season, the plants grow a new stem, bloom, produce seeds, and die. Instead of starting biennials outdoors, many gardeners buy them as seedlings in spring and raise them as annuals.

Hollyhock
Althaea rosea

Canterbury bells
Campanula medium

Iceland poppy
Papaver nudicaule

Foxglove
Digitalis purpurea

Sweet William
Dianthus barbatus

Garden perennials

Popular garden perennials include asters, bleeding hearts, chrysanthemums, columbines, day lilies, delphiniums, irises, lupines, peonies, poppies, primroses, and violets. Most of these flowers need an annual cold season for the growth of new buds. They therefore do not grow well in tropical climates. On the other hand, warm-weather perennials may be raised indoors in northern climates. Many of them are favorite house plants. Some of these perennials are illustrated in this article under the heading *Flowers of the tropics and subtropics.* They include African violets, gloxinias, ivy geraniums, and wax begonias.

Some perennials, such as columbines and delphiniums, bloom vigorously only three or four years. Most gardeners start these plants from seeds and replace them when necessary. In many cases, perennials are started from *cuttings.* Cuttings are pieces cut from the stems or roots of adult plants. When planted in water or soil, a cutting develops into a plant identical to the parent. Like seedlings, cuttings should be started indoors. Some gardeners start cuttings taken from their own plants. Others buy cuttings that have already rooted.

In general, spring is the best time to plant perennials outdoors in climates with harsh winters. Early autumn is usually the best time in warmer climates.

Most perennials spread by sending out shoots from their roots. The shoots develop into new stems. Most species produce new shoots soon after they have bloomed each year. Over several years, the offshoots from only one plant may cover a wide area. But in most cases, the plants bloom better if they are dug up, divided, and replanted every few years.

Lily of the valley
Convallaria majalis

New York aster
Aster novi-belgii

Tall bearded iris
Iris germanica

Peony
Paeonia officinalis

Garden perennial lupine
Lupinus polyphyllus

Polyanthus primrose
Primula polyantha

Sweet violet
Viola odorata

Hardy chrysanthemum
Chrysanthemum morifolium

Christmas rose
Helleborus niger

Himalayan blue poppy
Meconopsis betonicifolia

Oriental poppy
Papaver bracteatum

Chinese delphinium
Delphinium grandiflorum

Phlox
Phlox paniculata

Tawny-orange day lily
Hemerocallis fulva

Common garden canna
Canna generalis

Bleeding heart
Dicentra spectabilis

Balloon flower
Platycodon grandiflorus

Garden perennials grown from bulbs

A bulb is an underground stem with a large bud, wrapped in starchy tissue. The bud develops into a new plant when the weather becomes favorable. The starchy tissue provides the developing plant with food.

Flowers that grow from bulbs or bulblike structures include crocuses, daffodils, fritillaries, gladioluses, hyacinths, Madonna lilies, tuberous begonias, and tulips. Such plants as crocuses and tulips grow better in cool climates than in warm ones. The bulbs of daffodils, hyacinths, and some other flowers can be left in the ground through the winter in colder climates. Certain other flowers, such as gladioluses, cannot survive in extremely cold weather. Gardeners in colder regions dig up these tender bulbs or rootlike parts in autumn. They store them indoors and replant them outdoors in spring.

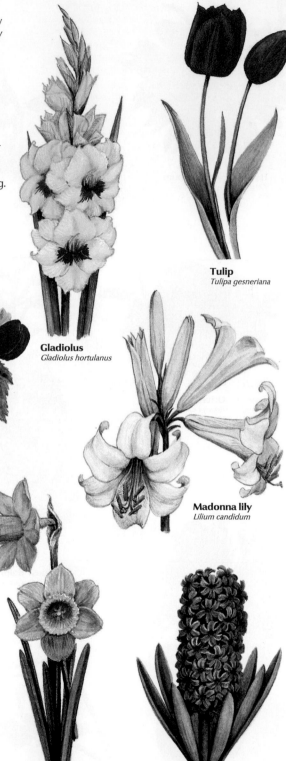

Tulip
Tulipa gesneriana

Cloth-of-gold crocus
Crocus angustifolius

Gladiolus
Gladiolus hortulanus

Tuberous begonia
Begonia tuberhybrida

Madonna lily
Lilium candidum

Dahlia
Dahlia pinnata

Crown imperial
Fritillaria imperialis

Daffodil
Narcissus pseudonarcissus

Hyacinth
Hyacinthus orientalis

Flowering shrubs

Shrubs, like trees, have woody stems. But shrubs do not grow as tall as trees. Most shrubs also have two or more thin stems, rather than a single thick one. As a rule, flowering shrubs grow best in areas with fairly long summers and cool winters. Some species cannot stand cold weather. Popular kinds of flowering shrubs include azaleas, flowering quinces, forsythias, honeysuckles, hydrangeas, lilacs, redbuds, roses, and spireas.

Most beginning gardeners buy shrubs as young plants that are ready to set into the garden. However, gardeners can easily produce their own plants from mature shrubbery. Like herbaceous perennials, many shrubs spread by sending out shoots from their roots. Such shoots will develop into new plants if they are dug up with part of the root and replanted. Shrubs that do not send out shoots can be reproduced from cuttings.

Hybrid tea rose
Rosa dilecta

Flame azalea
Rhododendron calendulaceum

Tatarian honeysuckle
Lonicera tatarica

Rose of Sharon
Hibiscus syriacus

Bridal wreath
Spiraea prunifolia

Border forsythia
Forsythia intermedia

Big-leaved hydrangea
Hydrangea macrophylla

Common lilac
Syringa vulgaris

WORLD BOOK illustrations by Allianora Rosse

A carpet of wildflowers brightens a mountain meadow. Wildflowers grow almost everywhere—in woods, fields, deserts, jungles, and swamps; on mountains and prairies; and along rivers and seacoasts. Each environment promotes the growth of different kinds of flowers.

Wildflowers

Each species of flowering plant grows best in a particular type of environment called a *habitat.* The species may be unable to grow at all in a much hotter, cooler, wetter, or drier location. Gardeners can control a plant's environment to some extent. They can therefore grow certain flowers in otherwise unfavorable locations. For example, flowers that need ample moisture can be raised in dry climates if the gardener supplies the necessary water. When flowers grow in the wild, they do not receive such special treatment. Each species can survive only in the habitat to which it is naturally suited.

There are hundreds of thousands of kinds of flowering plants in the world. The majority are native to the tropics. The remaining species are native to Europe, North America, and other nontropical regions.

Different species of wildflowers grow in seven major wildflower habitats. These habitats are (1) the Arctic tundra, (2) woodlands and forests, (3) prairies and dry plains, (4) summer-dry regions (regions with mild climates and dry summers), (5) alpine tundras, (6) deserts, and (7) tropical and subtropical regions. In addition, a major wildflower habitat may include various special environments, such as wetlands and shorelines. These special environments have their own types of wildflowers. For example, some varieties of woodland flowers grow

mainly in woodland swamps. *Aquatic* flowers are specially adapted to live in water. They may be found in any environment that has lakes or rivers.

Many wildflowers have spread from their native home to other parts of the world with similar habitats. In some cases, people have introduced the flowers into new areas, either accidentally or on purpose. In other cases, the wind or animals have carried the seeds. Certain seeds easily stick to the bodies of animals. They may be carried long distances by animals that migrate. Wildflowers introduced into North America from other parts of the world include bindweed, chicory, dandelions, furze, mullein, mustard, oxeye daisies, and Queen Anne's lace. Most of these plants now grow widely throughout North America. Wildflowers native to North America have also been introduced to other parts of the world. They include Canada goldenrod, false indigo, large-leaved beggars ticks, and water pennywort. In many cases, these introduced species become *invasive species*. Invasive species spread so quickly that they threaten native species (see **Invasive species**).

The drawings in this section illustrate typical flowers of each major wildflower habitat. Except for the tropical and subtropical flowers, most of the species pictured are native to North America. In many cases, however, flowers closely related to these species grow in similar environments in other parts of the world.

Flowers of the Arctic tundra

The Arctic tundra extends across the extreme northern parts of North America, Europe, and Asia. It is a cold, dry, treeless grassland. Most of the region has an annual frost-free period of less than two months. The ground remains frozen all year except at the surface. The surface thaws in spring. It remains soggy throughout most of the summer. The tundra has few annuals. However, a variety of herbaceous perennials thrive there. These hardy plants include cinquefoils, fireweeds, louseworts, poppies, and saxifrages. They come to life suddenly in spring and brighten the brief Arctic summers with their colorful blossoms.

© Anthony Hathaway, Dreamstime

WORLD BOOK illustrations by James Teason

Lapland rosebay
Rhododendron lapponicum

Four-angled mountain heather
Cassiope tetragona

Dwarf fireweed
Epilobium latifolium

White mountain avens
Dryas octopetala

Arctic lupine
Lupinus arcticus

Shrubby cinquefoil
Potentilla fruticosa

Purple saxifrage
Saxifraga oppositifolia

Arctic poppy
Papaver radicatum

Woolly lousewort
Pedicularis lanata

Flowers of woodlands and forests

Trees need considerable moisture and a yearly frost-free period of more than two months to reach full size. Forests grow only in regions that meet these needs. Seedlings have difficulty competing with established plants in wooded areas. As a result, such areas have few annuals. Nearly all the flowers are perennials.

There are two main types of forests: (1) needleleaf and (2) broadleaf. Needleleaf forests stretch south from the Arctic tundra across most of Canada, northern Europe, and northern Asia. The trees in these forests are mainly gymnosperms rather than flowering plants. However, these forests contain the same kinds of flowers as the tundra. They also have such species as bog orchids, columbines, and pitcher plants.

The largest broadleaf forests outside the tropics are in the eastern half of the United States, in eastern Asia, and in western and central Europe. The growth of flowers in these forests is regulated largely by the amount of shade. Many woodland flowers bloom in early spring, before the trees develop leaves, heavily shading the woods. These early-blooming species are called *spring ephemerals.* They include bloodroots, toothworts, trilliums, and trout lilies. After the woods become shaded, flowers bloom mainly in clearings and in meadows at the edge of the woods. Such species as spiderworts and touch-me-nots blossom in late spring or early summer. Others, such as asters and goldenrods, bloom in late summer or autumn.

© Christina Richards, Shutterstock

Needleleaf forest

Fairy slipper
Calypso bulbosa

Indian pipe
Monotropa uniflora

Vermilion Indian paintbrush
Castilleja miniata

Bunchberry
Cornus canadensis

Colorado blue columbine
Aquilegia coerulea

Labrador tea
Ledum groenlandicum

Broadleaf forest

WORLD BOOK illustrations by James Teason

Tuberous water lily
Nymphaea tuberosa

Yellow dogtooth violet
Erythronium americanum

Trailing arbutus
Epigaea repens

Bloodroot
Sanguinaria canadensis

Fringed gentian
Gentianopsis crinita

Dutchman's-breeches
Dicentra cucullaria

Spotted touch-me-not
Impatiens capensis

Round-lobed hepatica
Hepatica americana

Marsh marigold
Caltha palustris

Mayapple
Podophyllum peltatum

Gary goldenrod
Solidago nemoralis

White trillium
Trillium grandiflorum

Flowers of prairies and dry plains

Prairies and dry plains are grasslands. They receive less rainfall than do woodlands. Prairies have hot summers and cold winters. They once covered much of central North America as well as large areas of Argentina, central Asia, and South Africa. Today, people have turned most of these areas into farmland. However, some prairies remain in their natural state. These areas produce tall grasses and traditional spring, summer, and fall flowers. Most prairie flowers are perennials. Grasses grow so thick on prairies that few seeds can penetrate the sod. As a result, annuals have difficulty surviving. Typical North American prairie flowers include blazing stars, pasqueflowers, coneflowers, rattlesnake masters, sunflowers, tickseeds, and wild indigo.

The prairies of the United States and Canada give way to dry plains in the west. These plains, called *steppes,* receive less moisture than prairies. Because the plains are so dry, short grasses grow better than tall grasses do. Steppes also adjoin the prairies of Argentina, central Asia, and South Africa. The moister areas of the steppes have many of the same kinds of flowers as the prairies. The drier sections have drought-resistant species and more annuals. Typical flowers of the North American dry plains include prickly pear cactuses, low townsendias, scarlet globe mallows, and sunflowers.

© Fallsview/Dreamstime

White evening primrose
Oenothera nuttallii

Smooth fleabane
Erigeron glabellus

Tall sunflower
Helianthus giganteus

Scarlet globe mallow
Sphaeralcea coccinea

Dotted blazing star
Liatris punctata

WORLD BOOK illustrations by Christabel King

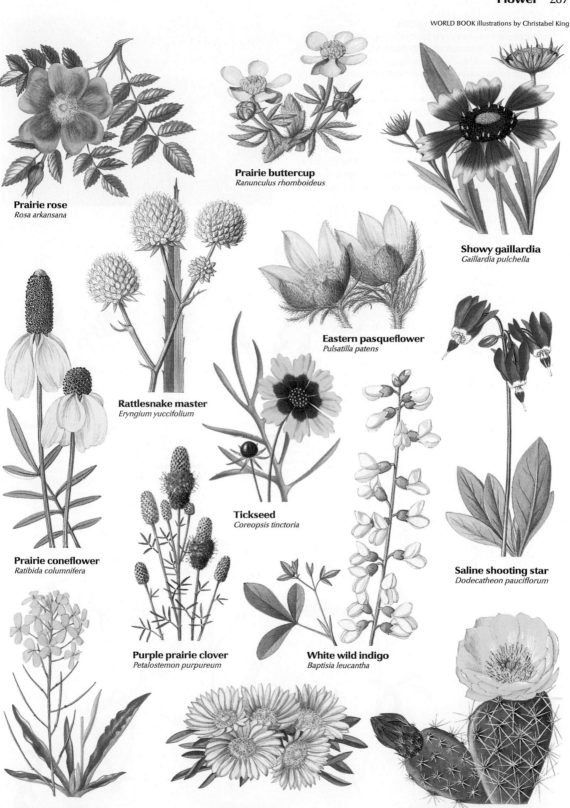

Prairie rose
Rosa arkansana

Prairie buttercup
Ranunculus rhomboideus

Showy gaillardia
Gaillardia pulchella

Rattlesnake master
Eryngium yuccifolium

Eastern pasqueflower
Pulsatilla patens

Prairie coneflower
Ratibida columnifera

Tickseed
Coreopsis tinctoria

Saline shooting star
Dodecatheon pauciflorum

Purple prairie clover
Petalostemon purpureum

White wild indigo
Baptisia leucantha

Western wallflower
Erysimum asperum

Low townsendia
Townsendia sericea

Plains prickly pear cactus
Opuntia polyacantha

Flowers of summer-dry regions

Summer-dry regions are found along the Mediterranean Sea, in California, and in parts of Australia, Chile, and South Africa. The mild, moderately dry climate of these regions provides an ideal environment for the growth of wildflowers. A high percentage of these flowers are annuals. Most of these annuals flower in spring. Summer-dry regions include grasslands, woodlands, and *chaparrals* (regions of shrubs and undersized trees). A tremendous variety of wildflowers thrives in the California chaparral and its neighboring grasslands and oak woodlands. Some of these flowers, such as fiddlenecks and fire poppies, are California natives. Others, such as black mustard and star thistles, originated in the Mediterranean region.

© Sarah Scott, Shutterstock

Yellow-and-white monkey flower
Mimulus bicolor

Purple owl's clover
Orthocarpus purpurascens

Common fiddleneck
Amsinckia menziesii var.
intermedia

Yellow star thistle
Centaurea solstitialis

Red-stemmed storksbill
Erodium cicutarium

California poppy
Eschscholzia californica

Fire poppy
Papaver californicum

Goldfields
Lasthenia chrysostoma

Five-spot
Nemophila maculata

Flowers of alpine tundras

Alpine tundras lie at high elevations in mountains throughout the world. Like the Arctic, these areas are too cold and dry for trees to grow. But grasses, low shrubs, and a variety of wildflowers thrive. The chief alpine tundras are in the European Alps, the Himalaya of Asia, and the Rocky Mountains of North America. Most alpine flowers grow in mountain meadows. But some species are suited to rocky places. As in the Arctic, the yearly frost-free period is usually less than two months. As a result, nearly all the flowers are perennials. Most are small and grow slowly. Some do not bloom until they are 10 years old or older. Many alpine flowers are the same as those of the Arctic or are close relatives.

© Julia Britvich, Dreamstime

WORLD BOOK illustrations by Kate Lloyd-Jones, Linden Artists Ltd.

Club-moss ivesia
Ivesia lycopodioides

Alpine forget-me-not
Myosotis alpestris

Tolmie's saxifrage
Saxifraga tolmiei

Alpine lewisia
Lewisia pygmaea

Moss campion
Silene acaulis

Arctic gentian
Gentiana algida

Alpine avens
Geum rossii

Alpine phacelia
Phacelia sericea

Sticky polemonium
Polemonium viscosum

Flowers of the desert

Deserts are extremely dry regions with a generally warm climate. Most deserts receive less than 10 inches (25 centimeters) of rainfall a year. In some cases, all the rain falls in one or two tremendous cloudbursts. Desert flowers must therefore be able to survive for many months without rain.

Some desert flowers are shrubs. These plants have vast networks of roots that absorb all available moisture in the soil. Other desert flowers are herbaceous perennials with thick, spongy stems. The stems store water, which the plants use during the long dry spells. Cactuses are the best-known examples of this type of plant. Still other flowers are annuals. Annuals thrive in deserts because they compete with relatively few perennials. In addition, the seeds of many annuals can survive even the longest dry periods. The seeds lie buried until the rains return. Then they sprout, and the plants complete their entire life cycle within only a few weeks.

The deserts of southwestern North America have a wide variety of flowers, including most of the familiar kinds of cactuses. Many of the cactuses have beautiful blossoms. Cactuses are common in deserts in North and South America. But they are absent, except where introduced, elsewhere. The North American deserts also have numerous flowering shrubs and hundreds of annuals. The shrubs include such species as brittlebushes and desert mallows. Desert marigolds, devil's claws, evening primroses, ghost flowers, and sand verbenas are only a few of the many colorful annuals.

© Anton Foltin, Shutterstock

Claret-cup cactus
Echinocereus triglochidiatus

Woolly daisy
Eriophyllum wallacei

Kennedy's mariposa lily
Calochortus kennedyi

Brittlebush
Encelia farinosa

Desert sand verbena
Abronia villosa

Mojave desert star
Monoptilon bellioides

Desert marigold
Baileya multiradiata

WORLD BOOK illustrations by Kate Lloyd-Jones, Linden Artists Ltd.

Desert bluebell
Phacelia campanularia

Ghost flower
Mohavea confertiflora

Arizona poppy
Kallstroemia grandiflora

Giant four-o'clock
Mirabilis froebelii

Teddy bear cholla
Opuntia bigelovii

Desert chicory
Rafinesquia neo-mexicana

Beaver-tail cactus
Opuntia basilaris

Soapweed
Yucca glauca

Birdcage evening primrose
Oenothera deltoides

Desert mallow
Sphaeralcea ambigua

Desert lily
Hesperocallis undulata

Flowers of the tropics and subtropics

Thousands of species of wildflowers grow in the humid and warm to hot climate of the tropics and subtropics. The tropical rain forests of Central and South America have the greatest variety of tropical flowers. These plants include thousands of kinds of rare and beautiful orchids. Hundreds of species of flowering plants are native to Hawaii. However, many have become extinct or extremely rare as a result of land development and overpicking. Southern regions of China and South Africa have the richest assortment of subtropical flowers. Southern Florida also has many species. Some of them, such as clamshell orchids, are Florida natives. Others, such as bougainvilleas, are introduced species.

© Melissa Burtram, istockphoto

WORLD BOOK illustrations by James Teason

African violet
Saintpaulia ionantha
Tropical East Africa

Ivy geranium
Pelargonium peltatum
South Africa

Bird-of-paradise
Strelitzia reginae
South Africa

Clamshell orchid
Epidendrum cochleatum
Subtropical and tropical America

Wax begonia
Begonia semperflorens
Brazil

East Indian lotus
Nelumbo nucifera
Tropical Asia and Australia

Gloxinia
Sinningia speciosa
Brazil

Cape jasmine gardenia
Gardenia jasminoides
China

Torch ginger
Nicolaia elatior
Indonesia

The parts of a flower

The typical flower develops at the tip of a flower stalk. The tip of the stalk is somewhat enlarged, forming a structure called a *receptacle.* A bud grows from the receptacle and develops into a flower.

Most flowers have four main parts: (1) the calyx, (2) the corolla, (3) the stamens, and (4) the carpels. The calyx is the outermost part of a flower. It consists of a set of leaflike or petallike structures called *sepals.* The corolla consists of a flower's petals. The stamens and carpels make up the reproductive parts of flowers. The stamens are the male parts, and the carpels are the female parts. Every flower has either stamens or carpels—or both. Flowers that have all four main parts are called *complete flowers.* Flowers that lack one or more of the parts are called *incomplete flowers.* In many wind-pollinated flowers, the calyx and corolla are greatly reduced or absent. In addition to the main parts, many flowers have glands that produce nectar to attract pollinators. These glands, called *nectaries,* lie near the base of the flower.

In most flowers, each main part consists of three, four, or five elements or of multiples of three, four, or five elements. In a trillium, for example, three sepals form the calyx, and three petals form the corolla. The flower has six stamens, and the female part consists of three carpels. The elements may be separate from one another, such as the petals of a poppy or a rose. Or the elements may be *fused* (joined together), such as the carpels in trillium. In flowers with fused petals, for example, the corolla is shaped like a tube, bell, trumpet, pouch, or saucer. Flowers with such corollas include morning-glories, daffodils, and petunias. In such species as primroses and verbenas, the petals are fused at the base and free at the tip. The corolla thus has a tubelike or bell-like base and a fringed edge.

In buttercups, morning-glories, and most other flowers, all the main parts are arranged around the center of the flower in a circular fashion. If we divide the flower in half in any direction, the halves will be alike. Such flowers are considered to be *radially symmetrical.* Orchids, snapdragons, and certain other flowers can be divided into identical halves only lengthwise. Such flowers are *bilaterally symmetrical.*

The calyx. The sepals, which make up the calyx, are the first parts to form among most flowers. They protect the flower's developing inner parts. The sepals usually remain attached to the rest of the flower after it opens.

In many flowers, such as buttercups and magnolias, the sepals are greenish, leaflike structures. Other flowers have sepals that look like petals. Among many members of the iris, lily, and orchid families, the sepals and the petals look so much alike that they cannot be told apart. Botanists call these petallike structures *tepals.* Certain kinds of flowers have colorful sepals in place of petals. These flowers include anemones, hepaticas, larkspurs, and marsh marigolds.

The corolla consists of a flower's petals. It is the showy, brightly colored part of most flowers. The colors of the petals—and of colored sepals—attract insects or birds that help spread pollen. The colors come from chemicals in the plant's tissues. These chemicals are often present in all parts of the plant, not only the petals or sepals. But large amounts of green or brown pigments mask the bright colors in other parts of the plant. Many flowers also have spots, stripes, or other markings on their petals that attract insects or birds. In most cases, the odors of flowers come from oily substances in the petals. Strong odors, like bright colors, attract animals, including insects.

The stamens are the male, pollen-producing parts of a flower. They are hard to see in some flowers. In other flowers, the stamens are the most attractive part. For example, male acacia flowers consist mainly of a large feathery tuft of colorful stamens.

In most flowers, each stamen has two parts—a *filament* and an *anther.* The filament is a threadlike or ribbonlike stalk. The anther is at the tip of the filaments. It is usually an enlarged part that consists of four tiny baglike structures that produce pollen. After the pollen is ripe,

Parts of a flower   A typical flower has four main parts. They are (1) the calyx, (2) the corolla, (3) the stamens, and (4) the carpels. The calyx forms the outermost part and consists of leaflike *sepals.* The corolla consists of the petals. The stamens and carpels make up a flower's reproductive parts.

WORLD BOOK illustration by James Teason

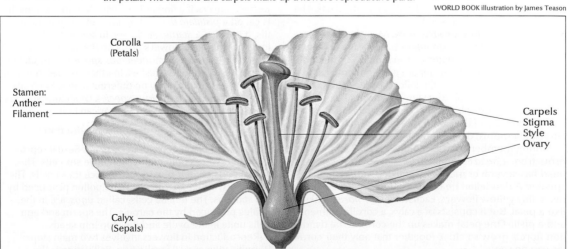

Corolla (Petals)

Stamen:
Anther
Filament

Carpels
Stigma
Style
Ovary

Calyx (Sepals)

Variations in flower structure

Flowers vary in the shape, number, and color of their main parts. In addition, some species lack one or more of these parts. The examples shown here illustrate four variations in flower form.

WORLD BOOK illustrations by James Teason

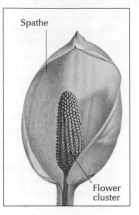

A composite flower is many small flowers. The daisy has tiny *disk flowers* in the center and individual *ray flowers* that look like petals.

A leaflike spathe surrounds the tiny flowers of the skunk cabbage. The flowers grow in a cluster on a stalk. Some spathes have bright colors.

Large white bracts encircle the flowers of the dogwood. Many people mistakenly think that the attractive bracts are part of the flower.

Long red stamens make up the showiest part of bottle-brush blossoms. The blossoms form a spike that resembles a brush used to wash bottles.

these structures split open and release the pollen.

The stamens are separate from one another in many flowers. But in such species as hollyhocks and sweet peas, some or all of the filaments are fused and form a tube around the carpels. In some flowers, the stamens are fused with other flower parts. For example, the stamens of gentians are fused to the petals, and the stamens of most orchids are fused to the carpels.

The carpels are the female, seed-bearing parts of a flower. Some flowers, including all members of the pea family, have only one carpel. But most flowers have two or more. In many species, the carpels are fused into one compound structure, often referred to as a *pistil.*

Among most flowers, each pistil or carpel has three parts—a *stigma,* a *style,* and an *ovary.* The stigma is a sticky area at the top. The style consists of a slender tube that leads from the stigma to the ovary. The ovary is the part at the base that contains one or more structures called *ovules.* The ovary will develop into the fruits. The ovules will become the seeds.

Variations in flower structure. Many kinds of flowers grow in clusters called *inflorescences.* In some species, such as bridal wreaths and snapdragons, the individual flowers in each cluster are easy to identify as flowers. In other species, the inflorescence looks like a single flower. The individual flowers that make up the inflorescence look like petals. These species include the many members of the composite family, such as asters, chrysanthemums, dandelions, and sunflowers.

Among members of the composite family, the flowers grow from a *head* at the tip of the flower stalk. Each head has several or many flowers, depending on the species. A dandelion head, for example, may have 100 or more tiny yellow flowers. Each flower, or *floret,* looks like a petal. But it consists of a calyx, a corolla, stamens, and a pistil. One petal makes up the corolla. The dandelion florets grow so close together that only their corollas can be seen.

The flowers of some plants grow in plain, tassellike inflorescences called *catkins.* A catkin is composed of *naked flowers*—that is, flowers that lack both petals and sepals. Plants that have catkins include alders, poplars, and willows.

Many plants that have inflorescences also have leaflike structures called *bracts* just beneath each flower cluster. Most bracts are small and green. But in a few species, they are so large and showy that most people mistake them for part of the flower. The showy "petals" of bougainvilleas, dogwoods, and poinsettias are bracts. The flowers themselves are small, plain-looking inflorescences at the center of the bracts.

Among most species of flowering plants, each plant bears flowers that have both stamens and pistils. Such flowers are called *perfect flowers.* In some species, however, each plant bears flowers that have either pistils or stamens, but not both. Such flowers are called *imperfect flowers.* If a flower has pistils but no stamens, it is called a *pistillate flower.* If it has stamens but no pistils, it is called a *staminate flower.* In some species, staminate and pistillate flowers grow on the same plant. Such species are known as *monoecious species.* They include begonias, oaks, and squashes. In other species, the male and female flowers grow on different plants. Such species are known as *dioecious species.* Dioecious species include poplars, willows, and American holly.

The role of flowers in reproduction

Flowering plants reproduce *sexually.* Sexual reproduction requires both male and female sex cells. The sexual parts of their blossoms produce these cells. The male cells, called *sperm,* are in the pollen produced by the stamens. The female cells, called *eggs,* are in the ovules produced by the carpels. The sperm and egg cells unite in the ovule and develop into seeds.

Reproduction in flowers involves two main steps: (1) pollination and (2) fertilization. Pollination is the transfer of pollen from a stamen to the stigma of a carpel. Fertilization is the union of a sperm cell with an egg cell. Fertilization occurs in much the same way in all flowering plants. However, there are two methods of pollination: (1) cross-pollination and (2) self-pollination. Cross-pollination involves the transfer of pollen from a stamen on one plant to a pistil on another plant. In self-pollination, pollen is transferred from a stamen of one flower to a pistil of the same flower or to a pistil of another blossom on the same plant.

Cross-pollination is the method of pollination in most flowering plants. This method requires an agent to carry the pollen from flower to flower. Insects are the most common agents of cross-pollination.

Many insects depend on flowers for food. Bees live on nectar and pollen. Certain beetles and flies also feed on both nectar and pollen. Butterflies and moths live on nectar. As an insect travels from flower to flower in search of food, pollen grains stick to its body. Some or all of these grains may brush off onto the stigmas of some flowers that the insect visits. One or more of these flowers may thus become cross-pollinated.

When searching for food, an insect could easily fail to visit a particular kind of flower unless the flower attracted it. Most flowers that depend on insects for pollination are brightly colored or strongly scented. Each kind of pollinating insect is attracted by certain colors or odors. It thus visits certain flowers rather than others. However, most insect-pollinated flowers are pollinated by more than one kind of insect. For example, moths and butterflies visit many of the same flowers. A few kinds of insects and flowers have developed highly specialized relationships with each other. Such flowers are pollinated only by a particular kind of insect. For example, yucca moths are the only insects that pollinate yucca plants.

Bees. More kinds of flowers are pollinated by bees than by any other kind of insect. Bees cannot see the color red. Otherwise, they have a keen sense of sight. They also have a well-developed sense of smell. Bees are strongly attracted by yellow and blue blossoms, especially those with a sweet odor. Bees can see *ultraviolet light,* a kind of light invisible to human beings. Many flowers, particularly yellow ones, have elaborate ultraviolet markings. These markings attract bees to the flowers and even pinpoint the location of the nectaries.

Many of the flowers pollinated by bees have a highly complicated structure to encourage cross-pollination and discourage self-pollination. For example, a bee can reach the nectar of a snapdragon only after brushing against the stigma. It then cannot leave the flower without touching the pollen. Furthermore, the bee cannot touch the stigma after it touches the pollen.

Butterflies and moths are attracted to flowers that produce abundant nectar. In many such flowers, the nectaries are long and tube-shaped or lie at the base of a long tube-shaped corolla. Butterflies and moths have exceptionally long, tubelike mouthparts. They use them to reach into these structures and suck up the nectar. Butterflies prefer flowers with sweet-smelling yellow or blue blossoms.

Unlike most bees and butterflies, many moths rest during the day and search for food at night. Many of the flowers that attract moths open only at night. Most of these flowers are pale-colored or white. The light colors make them easier to see at night than dark blossoms. Many of the flowers are also strongly scented and give off their scent only at night. Flowering tobacco and various kinds of evening primroses and honeysuckles are among the plants commonly pollinated by moths.

Beetles and flies. Beetles visit flowers in which both nectar and pollen are plentiful. They prefer white or dull-colored flowers with spicy odors, such as magnolias and wild roses.

The mouthparts of most flies are too short to suck nectar from tube-shaped flowers. These flies usually visit flowers with flat corollas, such as hawthorn blossoms and buttercups. Some flowers, such as carrion flowers and skunk cabbages, have a foul odor that attracts flies.

Other agents. Some birds feed on nectar and so help pollinate flowers. Unlike most pollinating insects, birds have a weak sense of smell. But birds have sharp vision. They also see red as well as other colors. Most odorless red flowers are pollinated by birds. In North America,

Yellow flowers have ultraviolet markings that attract bees and indicate where nectar is produced. The human eye cannot see these markings, *left.* But when the flowers are photographed in ultraviolet light, *right,* dark areas appear that resemble the markings seen by bees.

A bee covered in pollen sips nectar from a flower. The bee will leave some of the yellow pollen grains at other flowers it visits, pollinating them. Many flowers rely on insects for pollination.

The structure of hibiscus helps avoid self-pollination. The yellow pollen grains on the anthers are beneath the reddish stigmas, making it unlikely that the flower will pollinate itself.

hummingbirds are the chief bird pollinators. Hummingbirds are particularly attracted to red, orange, and yellow flowers. Such flowers include cardinal flowers, columbines, fuchsias, and Indian paintbrushes. Bats and wind are also agents of pollination. Bats pollinate certain strongly scented flowers of the tropics. Wind spreads the pollen of most plants with flowers that lack petals and sepals. These plants include grasses, oaks, ragweeds, and sedges.

Self-pollination. Many species of plants normally pollinate themselves. Such plants include barley, oats, peas, and wheat. However, self-pollination also occurs frequently in many species that depend on cross-pollination. In such cases, pollen may simply fall onto a stigma of the same plant.

Self-pollination is impossible in dioecious species because the male and female flowers grow on different plants. In addition, many other plants have characteristics that discourage or prevent self-pollination. In such flowers as hibiscuses and lilies, for example, the stamens are much shorter than the pistils. Any pollen that drops from the stamens is therefore unlikely to reach a stigma of a pistil on the same plant. In some plants, the stamens and carpels mature at slightly different times, preventing self-pollination. Many kinds of plants, such as flowering tobacco and rye, have chemicals in their cells that prevent self-pollination.

Fertilization. In flowering plants, a unique type of fertilization known as *double fertilization* occurs. A pollen grain that lands on a stigma may grow a *pollen tube.* The tube pushes its way down the style to an ovule in the ovary. Sperm from the pollen grain travels down the tube to the ovule. Fertilization occurs when a sperm unites with an egg cell in the ovule. The fertilized egg cell develops into an *embryo* (partly developed plant).

Simultaneously, another fertilization takes place. This fertilization gives rise to *endosperm tissue.* Endosperm tissue provides energy and nutrients for the embryo. A seed then begins to develop that includes the embryo and endosperm. The ovary itself develops into a fruit that encloses the seed. For an illustration of this process, see **Plant** (The reproduction of plants).

An ovary may be penetrated by many pollen tubes. The number of seeds that develop depends on the number of ovules. An ovary that has only one ovule develops into a single-seed fruit, such as an acorn or cherry. An ovary that has many ovules develops into a fruit with many seeds, such as an apple or watermelon.

Flower hobbies

Two of the most popular flower hobbies are outdoor and indoor gardening. They are discussed in the article **Gardening.** This section deals with three other flower hobbies. They are (1) studying wildflowers, (2) flower arranging, and (3) flower breeding.

Studying wildflowers. To study wildflowers scientifically, you must be able to identify them. Handbooks help provide such identification. Most of these books deal with the flowers of a particular region.

One way to learn about wildflowers is to study them in their natural surroundings. For example, you might try to identify all the species in a particular area, such as a meadow. By taking careful notes and revisiting the location at various times of the year, you can produce a "biography" of the flowering plants there. Another way of studying wildflowers is by collecting them. However, you must follow certain rules in picking wildflowers.

Rules for picking wildflowers. As many as one-third of the world's native flowering plants are threatened with extinction. Most countries and local governments have laws or regulations that prohibit picking wildflowers in public parks and forests. Such laws help conserve the species. But they also help preserve the blossoms so that more people can enjoy them.

In an area not protected by conservation laws, do not pick a flower unless that species is plentiful in the area. As a general rule, never dig up the roots of wildflowers.

Preserving wildflower specimens. The easiest way to preserve flower specimens is by pressing them. This method can preserve not only the blossoms of wildflowers but also the entire plant, including the roots. While a specimen is still fresh, arrange it between two sheets of newspaper. Then place the newspaper between two stacks of blotting paper or between the pages of an old phone book. Apply pressure by tying the blotting paper or phone book into a tight bundle or by using a weight. The pressure flattens the specimen. It also squeezes out the moisture. Change the newspaper wrapping daily and move the specimen to a dry part of the blotting paper or phone book. After 7 to 10 days, the specimen should be dried out, unless it was especially juicy. The preserved specimen will last almost indefinitely if protected from moisture and insects.

Tape or glue each finished specimen to a sheet of heavy paper. Then label the mounted specimen. Include its common and scientific names, the place where the flower was found, the date it was picked, and any interesting facts about its growing habits. An organized collection of mounted pressed flowers is called a *herbarium.* See **Herbarium.**

Flower arranging. The ancient Egyptians, Greeks, and Romans all practiced the art of making decorative arrangements of cut flowers. However, the art developed to its fullest in Japan. The Japanese tradition of flower arranging dates from the 500's. At that time, Japanese Buddhists began to make floral arrangements in an elaborate style for the altars of their temples. Over time, the Japanese refined and simplified this style and worked out its artistic principles. These Japanese principles had a strong influence on flower arranging in many other countries.

The Japanese style tries above all to make each floral arrangement look natural, as if it were growing outdoors. Flower arrangers follow carefully worked out principles of design and color to achieve this natural effect. They use leaves and stems as major elements in many arrangements. In Europe and the Americas, on the other hand, traditional styles of flower arranging tend to emphasize only the blossoms.

Most flower arrangements are made of fresh flowers. However, you can use dried flowers. You can dry flowers by hanging the blossoms head downward in a dark, dry, well-ventilated room for about three weeks. You can also dry grasses and leaves in this way. Then, you can add them to the flower arrangement.

Flower breeding has become an increasingly popular hobby among gardeners. Each year, amateur gardeners in many countries produce hundreds of new varieties of flowers. Roses are especially popular for breeding. But many gardeners also work with such flowers as chrysanthemums, irises, orchids, and water lilies. Most new varieties introduce changes in the color, fragrance, shape, or size of the blossoms. Flower breeding has also produced such improvements as greater hardi-

© Andreas Von Einsiedel, DK Images/Getty Images

Pressing flowers requires blotting paper or newspaper. The flowers are tied up between the pages of a large book or pressed beneath a heavy object. The pressure flattens the flowers and squeezes out moisture. After two to four weeks, the flowers should be completely dry. Pressed flowers will last almost indefinitely if protected from insects and moisture.

ness and greater resistance to diseases and insects.

Gardeners breed flowers by crossing two related species or two varieties of the same species. Each parent is selected for a desired characteristic, such as the color or size of its blossoms. The breeder takes pollen from one parent and places it on a stigma of the other parent. Some of the resulting offspring may have the desired characteristics of both parents. Such offspring are called *hybrids.* By repeating experiments with many parents and many varieties, gardeners can produce hybrids of greater vigor and beauty.

How flowers are named and classified

The naming of flowers. Flowers have both common names and scientific names. Many common names can be traced back hundreds or even thousands of years. The practice of giving plants modern scientific names began during the mid-1700's.

Common names. The common names of many wildflowers originated in folklore. In numerous cases, a plant's name comes from a traditional belief concerning the plant. For example, people believed that agueweed cured a fever called the *ague.* They believed that colicroot cured abdominal cramps called *colic.* In other cases, a plant's common name simply describes a characteristic of the plant. For example, the leaves of pitcher

© Photo Japan/Alamy Images

Flower arranging is a celebrated art in Japan. This arrangement of spring buds in a bamboo vase exemplifies the Japanese emphasis on simplicity and natural arrangements.

plants form a pitcherlike shape. Skunk cabbages are named for their unpleasant odor.

The common names of many wildflowers end in *-wort,* such as birthwort, liverwort, milkwort, ragwort, and soapwort. The ending *-wort* comes from the Old English word *wyrt,* meaning *root* or *plant.* The first part of each name refers to some special characteristic of the plant, such as its appearance or supposed healing powers. For example, birthworts provided a medicine that was believed to help women during childbirth.

The common names of many poisonous or supposedly poisonous wildflowers end in *-bane.* These flowers include cowbane, dogbane, and fleabane. The word ending comes from the Old English word *bana,* meaning *murderer.* The animal mentioned in each case was supposedly the one most affected by the poison. Some of the plants, including fleabane, are actually harmless.

The common names for many garden flowers can be traced back to Latin or ancient Greek. For example, the English name *lily* comes from the Latin name *lilium.* Hyacinths are named after Hyacinthus, a youth in Greek mythology famed for his beauty. The names of some garden flowers come from languages other than Latin and Greek. For example, the name *tulip* comes from the Turkish word *tülbent,* meaning *turban.* Some tulips are shaped somewhat like turbans. People brought tulips to Europe from Turkey.

A number of flowers have been named after people. For example, begonias were named in honor of Michel Begon, a governor of French Canada and an amateur botanist.

Scientific names. The common names of flowers are not suitable for scientific purposes. In many cases, the same flower has more than one common name. For example, in the United States, a marsh marigold is also called a cowslip, kingcup, and May blob. In other cases, people use the same name for entirely different flowers. For example, several different species of flowers are called bluebells in various English-speaking countries. To avoid confusion, botanists thus refer to each species of flower by its scientific name.

A scientific name consists of a two-part Latin name, called a *binomial.* The first part of the binomial refers to the *genus* (group of species) to which the species belongs. The second part of the name is called the *specific epithet.* For example, the flower known as a cowslip, kingcup, marsh marigold, or May blob has the scientific name *Caltha palustris.* The genus name, *Caltha,* is the Latin word for *marsh marigold.* The second part of the name, *palustris,* is a Latin word meaning *marsh loving.* No other species of plant in the world is named *Caltha palustris.* By using scientific names, botanists can identify every species of plant precisely.

The classifying of flowers. Flowering plants make up a *division* (major group) of plants called Anthophyta. This division is split up into two major classes: (1) *eudicotyledons,* also called *eudicots,* and (2) *monocotyledons,* also known as *monocots.* The pollen of eudicots has a structure distinct from that of other flowering plants. Also, the seeds of eudicots and other flowering plants have two tiny leaves called *cotyledons.* The seeds of monocots have only one cotyledon. The petals and other flower parts of most monocots usually grow in threes or in multiples of three, and the veins in their

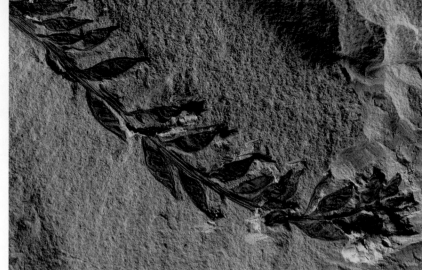

Archaefructus is among the earliest known flowering plants. The plant lived about 125 million years ago in what is now China. *Archaefructus* probably grew in shallow water, with its flowers extending above the water's surface. This fossil of the extinct plant was discovered in China's Liaoning Province.

© Jonathan Blair, National Geographic/Getty Images

leaves usually parallel one another. The flower parts of eudicots typically grow in fours or fives or in multiples of four or five, and the veins in their leaves are usually branched rather than parallel. There are many more species of eudicots than monocots.

A small number of flowering plants, including magnolias and water lilies, also have two cotyledons, but they are not eudicots. They are placed in separate, smaller classes.

Each class of flowering plants is divided into *orders,* each order into *families,* and each family into *genera* (the plural of *genus)*. The table at the end of this article lists families that include many familiar garden flowers and wildflowers. The table gives (1) typical characteristics of most flowers in the family; and (2) the common names of representative flowers.

The evolution of flowering plants

Flowering plants make up the vast majority of plant species today. But angiosperms appeared relatively recently in the history of plant life. Plants first colonized the land more than 430 million years ago. The oldest known angiosperm fossils are only about 130 million years old.

A number of unique traits distinguish angiosperms. These include the development of flowers and fruits. Scientists disagree on when exactly the first plant with all the characteristic traits of angiosperms appeared. Experts also debate which nonflowering seed plants gave rise to the first angiosperms.

Angiosperms developed during the time of the dinosaurs. Prior to the appearance of the angiosperms, gymnosperms were the only seed plants. Among the most abundant plants were early forms of such trees as conifers, cycads, and ginkgoes.

One of the earliest examples of a fossil angiosperm is *Archaefructus.* It lived in China about 125 million years ago. *Archaefructus* probably grew in shallow water, with its flowers extending above the water's surface. Its flowers lacked the showy petals seen in many modern flowering plants.

Angiosperms became much more diverse soon after they first appeared. Early angiosperm groups included the water lilies and the magnolias. By about 120 million years ago, monocots and eudicots had both developed. By the end of the Cretaceous Period about 65 million years ago, angiosperms had begun to replace gymnosperms as the most common seed plants.

Angiosperms had a number of characteristics that enabled them to compete successfully against other plants. For example, most gymnosperms rely on the wind for pollination. Many angiosperms developed adaptations, such as showy flowers and nectar, to encourage pollination by insects and other animals. Pollination by animals is more successful than wind pollination in many environments. In addition, angiosperms develop seeds more rapidly after fertilization than do gymnosperms. This rapid seed development enables angiosperms to colonize open areas more quickly. Angiosperms also are the only plants that develop fruit. Animals that eat fruit often pass the seeds in their waste, leaving the seeds unharmed. In this way, animals carry angiosperm seeds far from the parent plants. By contrast, most gymnosperms rely on wind to disperse their seeds. The wind seldom carries seeds far.

The evolution of flowering plants made possible the appearance of thousands of new species. For example, the advent of pollination encouraged tremendous diversity among insects, which specialized to visit particular angiosperm species. Many new species of bees, beetles, butterflies, and other insect pollinators evolved in this way. At the same time, flowering plants became more diverse, as species developed adaptations to attract particular pollinators. This relationship—in which the evolution of one species drives the evolution of another and vice versa—is called *coevolution.*

The development of fruits also led to coevolution. The dinosaurs became extinct about 65 million years ago. At that time, many new species of birds and mammals appeared. These new species consumed the fruits of angiosperms. Angiosperms became more diverse as they developed fruits to appeal to particular animal species.

Great forests of angiosperms came to cover much of Earth during the Cenozoic Era, which began about 65 million years ago and continues today. Angiosperm trees were slower to spread to areas with cold climates and high elevations. In these areas, conifers and other gymnosperms remain common. At the beginning of the Pleistocene Epoch, about 2.6 million years ago, Earth became colder and drier. At this time, large areas of forest were replaced by angiosperm herbs, including grasses.

Gerry Moore

Representative families of flowers

Eudicotyledons

Balsam or forget-me-not family (Balsaminaceae)
Hundreds of species of mostly annual or perennial herbs. The flowers are bilaterally symmetrical and have three to five sepals, five petals, and five stamens. One of the sepals forms a long, spur-shaped nectary. Garden balsams, touch-me-nots.

Begonia family (Begoniaceae)
Hundreds of species of mostly perennial herbs and shrubs, with staminate and pistillate flowers on the same plant. The staminate flowers have two or more tepals and many stamens. The pistillate flowers have two or more tepals and a compound pistil. Begonias.

Bellflower family (Campanulaceae)
Hundreds of species of mostly annual or perennial herbs; some shrubs, trees, and vines. The flowers of most species have five sepals, five petals, and five stamens. In most species, the petals are fused along most of their length, forming a bell-shaped corolla. Bellflowers.

Borage family (Boraginaceae)
Hundreds of species of mostly annual or perennial herbs; some shrubs, small trees, and vines. The flowers of most species have five sepals fused at the base, five petals fused into a tubular shape at the base, and five stamens. Forget-me-nots, heliotropes, lungworts.

Buttercup or crowfoot family (Ranunculaceae)
Hundreds of species of mostly annual or perennial herbs; some shrubs and vines. The majority have many stamens and carpels. Petal and sepal number varies. Anemones, bugbanes, buttercups, columbines, crowfoots, hepaticas, larkspurs.

Cactus family (Cactaceae)
Hundreds of species of perennial herbs, shrubs, trees, and vines. Most species have numerous petals, petallike sepals, and many stamens. The petals and sepals are fused at the base. Cactuses.

Composite family (Asteraceae or Compositae)
Thousands of species of herbs, shrubs, trees, and vines. The flowers consist of several to many small flowers arranged in a head. Ageratums, arnicas, asters, black-eyed Susans, blazing stars, bonesets, calendulas, chicories, chrysanthemums, compass plants, coneflowers, cosmos, dahlias, daisies, dandelions, fleabanes, gaillardias, goldenrods, marigolds, sunflowers, thistles, tickseeds, zinnias.

Evening primrose family (Onagraceae)
Hundreds of species of mostly annual or perennial herbs; some shrubs, trees, and vines. The majority have four sepals, four petals, and four or eight stamens. The sepals can be fused, often forming a long tube. Evening primroses, fuchsias, godetias.

Gentian family (Gentianaceae)
Hundreds of species of mostly herbs; some shrubs, trees, and vines. Most species have four or five sepals, four or five petals, and four or five stamens. The sepals are often fused to form a cup-shaped calyx. The petals are often fused into a tubular shape. Gentians.

Geranium family (Geraniaceae)
Hundreds of species of mostly herbs. Most species have five sepals, five petals, and 5 or 10 stamens. Crane's-bills, geraniums, pelargoniums, stork's-bills.

Mallow family (Malvaceae)
Hundreds of species of herbs; some shrubs and trees. The flowers have five sepals, five petals, and many stamens. The filaments of the stamens are fused, forming a tube around the pistil. Hibiscuses, hollyhocks, mallows.

Morning-glory family (Convolvulaceae)
Hundreds of species of mostly annual or perennial herbaceous vines; some shrubs, trees, and woody vines. The flowers have five sepals, five petals, and five stamens. In most species, the petals are fused into a bell- or funnel-shaped corolla. Bindweeds, dodders, moonflowers, morning-glories.

Mustard or cabbage family (Brassicaceae or Cruciferae)
Thousands of species of mostly herbs. The flowers have four sepals and four petals in the shape of a cross. Most species have six stamens. Candytufts, cresses, mustards, rockets, stocks, wallflowers.

Nasturtium family (Tropaeolaceae)
Dozens of species of annual or perennial herbs. The flowers of most species have five sepals, five petals, and eight stamens. One or more of the sepals form a spur at the back of the flower. Nasturtiums.

Spotted touch-me-not

Wax begonia

Clustered bellflower

Spring forget-me-not

Prickly pear

Upland boneset

Common buttercup

Common evening primrose

Wild geranium

Pine-barren gentian

Common morning-glory

Marsh mallow

White mustard

Nasturtium

Nightshade or potato family (Solanaceae)
Thousands of species of herbs, shrubs, trees, and vines. Most have flowers with five fused sepals, five petals fused into such shapes as funnels and tubes, and five stamens. Capsicums, flowering tobaccos, mandrakes, nightshades, petunias.

Parsley or carrot family (Apiaceae or Umbelliferae)
Thousands of species of mostly herbs; some shrubs and trees. In most species, the flowers are small and arranged in clusters. The florets usually have five sepals, five petals, and five stamens. Queen Anne's lace, rattlesnake master, sweet cicely.

Pea or legume family (Fabaceae or Leguminosae)
Thousands of species of herbs, shrubs, trees, and vines. Many flowers in this family have 5 petals, 5 sepals, and 10 stamens. Acacias, brooms, clovers, locoweeds, lupines, mimosas, redbuds, sweet pea, wild indigos, wisterias.

Phlox family (Polemoniaceae)
Hundreds of species of mostly perennial herbs; some annual herbs, some shrubs and vines. The flowers usually have five fused sepals, five petals, and five stamens. The petals are fused at the base. Jacob's-ladders, phloxes.

Pink or carnation family (Caryophyllaceae)
Hundreds of species of mostly herbs. The flowers of most species have five sepals, five petals, and 5 or 10 stamens. Baby's-breath, campions, carnations, pinks.

Plantain family (Plantaginaceae)
Hundreds of species of mostly herbs and shrubs. The majority have four or five petals, four or five sepals, and two or four stamens. Foxgloves, plantains, snapdragons, toadflaxes.

Poppy family (Papaveraceae)
Hundreds of species of mostly annual or perennial herbs. The flowers generally have two or three sepals, twice as many petals as stamens. Bloodroot, poppies.

Primrose family (Primulaceae)
Hundreds of species of annual or perennial herbs. Most species have five sepals, five petals, and five stamens. The petals are generally fused into a tubular shape at the base. The sepals are fused into a cuplike shape. Loosestrifes, pimpernels, primroses.

Rose family (Rosaceae)
Thousands of species of herbs, shrubs, and trees; some vines. The flowers of most species have five sepals, five petals, and numerous stamens. Agrimonies, cinquefoils, cotoneasters, hawthorns, pyracanthas, roses, spiraeas.

Saxifrage family (Saxifragaceae)
Hundreds of species of perennial herbs. The flowers of most species have five sepals, five petals, and up to 10 stamens. Coralbells, saxifrages.

Violet family (Violaceae)
Hundreds of species of herbs, shrubs, and trees; some vines. The flowers have five sepals, five petals, and five stamens. In many species, the petal nearest the stem is larger than the others and has a hollow sac or spur at the back. Pansies, violets.

Monocotyledons

Amaryllis family (Amaryllidaceae)
Hundreds of species of mostly bulbous perennial herbs. The flowers have six tepals and usually six stamens. All the floral parts, including the carpels, are often fused at the base of the flower. Amaryllises, daffodils, snowdrops.

Iris family (Iridaceae)
Hundreds of species of mostly perennial herbs. The flowers have six tepals and three stamens. All the floral parts are often fused at the base, forming a tube. Crocuses, freesias, gladioluses, irises.

Lily family (Liliaceae)
Hundreds of species of mostly perennial herbs. The flowers of most species have six tepals and six stamens. In some species, the tepals are fused at the base. Dogtooth violets, fritillaries, lilies, tulips.

Orchid family (Orchidaceae)
Thousands of species of perennial herbs with bilaterally symmetrical flowers. The flowers of most species have three petallike sepals; three petals; and one or two stamens, which are fused with the style and stigma to form a column. Fairy-slippers, lady's-slippers, pogonias.

Queen Anne's lace

Petunia

Phlox

Garden pea

Snapdragon

Maiden pink

California poppy

Scarlet pimpernel

Smooth rose

Early saxifrage

Round-leafed yellow violet

Blue flag iris

Daffodil

Lily of the valley

Showy lady's-slipper

WORLD BOOK
illustrations by
Patricia J. Wynne

Related articles in *World Book* include:

Articles on individual flowers

World Book has hundreds of separate articles on flowering plants. Those that have showy blossoms and are not trees are listed below:

Garden flowers

Ageratum	Lily of the valley
Amaryllis	Lobelia
Anemone	Lotus
Aster	Lupine
Baby's-breath	Marigold
Bachelor's-button	Moonflower
Begonia	Morning-glory
Belladonna	Narcissus
Bird's-foot trefoil	Nasturtium
Bleeding heart	Oxalis
Calendula	Painted-tongue
Candytuft	Pansy
Canna	Peony
Canterbury bell	Petunia
Carnation	Phlox
Chrysanthemum	Pink
Cineraria	Plumbago
Cockscomb	Poppy
Cosmos	Portulaca
Crocus	Primrose
Daffodil	Pyrethrum
Day lily	Salvia
Easter lily	Snapdragon
Echinacea	Star-of-Bethlehem
Feverfew	Statice
Firecracker flower	Stock
Flowering tobacco	Strawflower
Four-o'clock	Sunflower
Foxglove	Sweet alyssum
Geranium	Sweet pea
Gladiolus	Sweet William
Godetia	Tansy
Heliotrope	Tiger lily
Hibiscus	Tuberose
Hollyhock	Tulip
Hyacinth	Verbena
Ice plant	Violet
Impatiens	Viper's bugloss
Iris	Wallflower
Jonquil	Wisteria
Larkspur	Zinnia

Wildflowers

Aconite
Adonis
Agrimony
Amaranth
Arnica
Bedstraw
Beggarweed
Bellflower
Bindweed
Bitter root
Black-eyed Susan
Bladderwort
Blazing star
Bloodroot
Bluebell
Bluebonnet
Boneset
Buckwheat
Bugbane
Bunchberry
Buttercup
Butterwort
Cactus
Calla

Canada thistle
Cardinal flower
Chicory
Cinquefoil
Clematis
Clover
Cocklebur
Colchicum
Coltsfoot
Columbine
Compass plant
Coreopsis
Cowslip
Daisy
Dandelion
Devil's paintbrush
Dodder
Dogbane
Dogtooth violet
Dutchman's-breeches
Edelweiss
Evening primrose
Fireweed
Fleabane
Forget-me-not
Fritillary
Gaillardia
Gentian
Glasswort
Goldenrod
Heath
Hellebore
Henbane
Hepatica
Immortelle
Indian paintbrush
Indian pipe
Jack-in-the-pulpit
Jimson weed
Lady's-slipper
Lamb's-quarters
Lily

Locoweed
Loosestrife
Lungwort
Mallow
Mariposa lily
Mayapple
Milkweed
Monkey flower
Mountain avens
Mullein
Mustard
Oregon grape
Pasqueflower
Pitcher plant
Pokeweed
Prickly pear
Purslane
Pussy willow
Ragweed
Saint-John's-wort
Saxifrage
Scarlet pimpernel
Skunk cabbage
Smartweed
Snakeroot
Snowdrop
Soap plant
Solomon's-seal
Spring-beauty
Sundew
Thistle
Toadflax
Trailing arbutus
Trillium
Valerian
Velvetleaf
Venus's-flytrap
Vetch
Water lily
Wild carrot
Yellow jessamine

Tropical and subtropical flowers

Acacia
African violet
Aloe
Anthurium
Bird-of-paradise
  flower
Bougainvillea
Freesia
Fuchsia
Gardenia
Gloxinia
Orchid
Passion-flower
Pelican flower
Poinsettia
Rafflesia
Slipperwort
Water hyacinth

Flowering shrubs

Azalea
Bridal wreath
Broom
Camellia
Cherry laurel
Dogwood
Eglantine
Forsythia
Furze

Hawthorn
Honeysuckle
Hydrangea
Jasmine
Lilac
Mock orange
Myrtle
Ocotillo
Redbud
Rhododendron
Rose
Rose of Sharon
Snowball
Spirea
Twinflower
Yucca

Other related articles

Angiosperm
Botany
Breeding
Broccoli
Bulb
Caper
Cauliflower
Dicotyledon
Duckweed
Floriculture
Fruit
Gardening
Inflorescence
Monocotyledon
Perfume
Plant
Pollen
Seed
Shrub
Spice
Tree
Trefoil
Vine
Weed

Flower arranging. See Flower (Flower hobbies; picture).

Flowering maple is the common name for dozens of *species* (kinds) of herbs and shrubs that grow in temper-

A-Z Botanical Collection Ltd.

Bright red-and-yellow blossoms of a flowering maple contrast with the plant's dark green leaves.

ate regions of Africa, Asia, and North and South America. Flowering maples usually have heart-shaped leaves. The flowers may be a wide variety of colors. They grow singly or in clusters.   Walter S. Judd

Scientific classification. Flowering maples belong to the genus *Abutilon*. A common species is *Abutilon hybridum*.

Flowering tobacco is any of a group of plants that produce colorful flowers with a five-pointed star shape. Flowering tobacco is grown for its sweet-scented flowers. It grows wild primarily in the tropics of the Western Hemisphere. But it is cultivated in the United States. The leaves of flowering tobacco are hairy and sticky. The flowers are yellow, purple, red, or white, and shaped

WORLD BOOK illustration by Christabel King

Flowering tobacco is grown for its sweet-scented flowers. It grows wild in warm climates but is also cultivated.

like long tubes that flare open at the end. Flowering tobacco is sensitive to cold and should be sheltered. It can be grown from seed in rich, light soil. The seeds should be planted in a hotbed or greenhouse in the early spring and later transplanted outdoors.   Jerry M. Baskin

Scientific classification. Flowering tobaccos belong to the genus *Nicotiana*. A common species is *Nicotiana alata*.

Flowerpecker is the name of a group of small birds with short legs and tails. Flowerpeckers live from southern Asia to the Philippines and from Australia eastward to the Solomon Islands. Many *species* (kinds) have dark, often brown, coloring. However, males of some species are brightly colored. Flowerpeckers feed mainly on small berries, but they also eat insects and nectar.

James J. Dinsmore

Scientific classification. Flowerpeckers make up the flowerpecker family, Dicaeidae.

Floyd, William (1734-1821), an American statesman, was a New York signer of the Declaration of Independence in 1776. He served in the Continental Congress almost continuously from 1774 to 1781. He then served in the Congress of the Confederation from 1781 to 1783 and the United States Congress from 1789 to 1791. Floyd performed his most useful work in congressional committees. He later supported the movement to make Thomas Jefferson president. Floyd was born on Dec. 17,

1734, in Suffolk County, New York. He died on Aug. 4, 1821.   Jack N. Rakove

FLQ. See Canada, History of (The Quebec separatist movement; The separatist threat).

Flu. See Influenza.

Flügelhorn is a brass musical instrument that resembles a large cornet and has the same general range of about 2 ½ octaves. However, the flügelhorn is actually a member of the bugle family. A musician produces tones by blowing into the flügelhorn's cup-shaped mouthpiece and vibrating the lips. The player changes notes by fingering the instrument's three valves and changing lip tension. The flügelhorn has a mellow tone and a rich lower range. This makes it useful both as a solo instrument and as a link between the trumpet and trombone when played in ensembles. The flügelhorn is used in popular music and jazz and occasionally in concert bands.   Stewart L. Ross

Fluid is any substance that flows easily. A slight pressure or force will change the form of a fluid. But fluids are also elastic, so they tend to return to their former size when the pressure is removed. Fluids include all liquids and gases. Water at ordinary temperature is a fluid and a liquid. Air is a fluid and a gas. A liquid tends always to occupy the same volume. A gas, however, readily changes its volume by expanding or contracting to fill, or fit into, any container in which it is placed.

Gases are compressible fluids, and liquids are incompressible fluids. Pressure changes generally do not affect the density of a liquid (see **Density**). But in practice no liquid is completely incompressible.

A *perfect fluid* is frictionless—that is, it offers no resistance to flow except that of inertia (see **Inertia**). An *elastic fluid* has greater forces resisting changes to size or shape than forces resisting flow. A thicker, *viscous fluid,* such as molasses, is slow-flowing because of the fluid's internal friction.   Raymond E. Davis

See also Fluid mechanics; Hydraulics.

Fluid mechanics is the study of how fluids—liquids and gases—behave at rest and in motion. Scientists and engineers use fluid mechanics to analyze how a fluid affects a vehicle moving through it, a structure covered by it, or a pipe or channel through which it flows. Other uses include analyses of river flows, ocean waves, and weather systems. The main branches of fluid mechanics are (1) *fluid statics,* (2) *external fluid mechanics,* and (3) *internal fluid mechanics.*

Fluid statics describes the balance between gravity and pressure in fluids at rest. An important law of fluid statics is *Archimedes' principle,* which explains the forces that keep ships afloat (see **Hydraulics** [Archimedes' principle]). Fluid statics helps engineers design ships, submarines, and dams.

External fluid mechanics is the study of forces acting on a stationary object in a moving fluid—a skyscraper in the wind, for example—or a moving object in a stationary fluid, such as an airplane flying through the air. *Aerodynamics* deals with forces produced by air and other gases; *hydrodynamics,* with forces produced by water and other liquids.

Internal fluid mechanics describes fluid flow through pipes or tubes. Engineers use internal fluid mechanics in the design of pipelines for the transport of oil or water. They also apply it to the design of such machinery as fans, pumps, turbines, and compressors.   Allen Plotkin

See also Aerodynamics; Mechanics.

Fluidic engine. See Hydraulic engine.

Fluke, a fish. See Flounder.

Fluke is any one of a large group of parasitic flatworms (see **Flatworm**). Flukes live in nearly every organ—including the intestine, liver, and lungs—of human beings and other animals. They also live in the blood. Most adult flukes are flat and leaflike, but some are round or long and wormlike. They have one or two suckers that hold them to body tissue in the *host* (animal in which they live). Most flukes have both male and female reproductive organs.

Flukes have complicated life cycles involving different stages of development and from two to four hosts. The first host is usually a snail, in which the young flukes multiply. Later stages of the fluke enter fish, crabs, insects, or other animals. Some attach to plants.

If a person eats an improperly cooked animal infected by flukes in their early developmental stages, the flukes may infect the person's body. The early stages of schistosomes (blood flukes) swim in water and burrow through the skin to reach blood vessels. The flukes that infect human beings are common in the Far East, tropical parts of the Western Hemisphere, and Africa.   Seth Tyler

Scientific classification. Flukes make up the class Trematoda. The liver fluke of human beings is *Clonorchis sinensis,* the lung fluke is *Paragonimus westermani,* and a common type of blood fluke is *Schistosoma mansoni.*

See also **Animal** (picture: Fluke).

Fluorescence, *FLOO uh REHS uhns,* is a process by which a variety of substances give off light or another form of electromagnetic radiation when they absorb energy. The term *fluorescence* also refers to the light emitted by these substances. Many gases, liquids, and solids become fluorescent when exposed to radiation or to electrically charged particles.

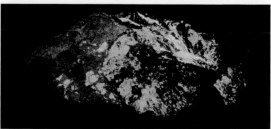

E. R. Degginger

Fluorescence occurs when certain substances absorb energy and give off electromagnetic radiation. Ultraviolet rays cause the mineral, *top,* to give off blue and green light, *above.*

Fluorescent lighting is widely used in factories, offices, schools, and in some homes. Many electron microscopes have fluorescent screens. Biologists stain cells and tissues with fluorescent dyes to observe biological processes. Chemists detect certain air and water pollutants by using fluorescence. It also is used to detect lead poisoning and to identify minerals.

The color of fluorescing light depends on the substance involved and on the type of energy absorbed. In the majority of cases, the wavelengths of fluorescing light are longer than those of the absorbed radiation. However, fluorescence has been observed throughout the visible portion of the electromagnetic spectrum and also in its ultraviolet and infrared regions (see **Electromagnetic waves** [The electromagnetic spectrum]).

Many kinds of energy cause fluorescence. For example, electric current produces fluorescence in neon signs. Ultraviolet rays, visible light, X rays, and various other forms of radiation also cause fluorescence.

When a fluorescent substance absorbs energy, electrons in its atoms become *excited*—that is, their energy level increases. In some cases, the electrons remain excited for only 1 trillionth of a second. The excess energy is emitted as electromagnetic radiation. The process stops when the energy source is removed.

Scientists observed fluorescence as early as the mid-1500's. George G. Stokes, a British physicist, first explained it in 1852 and named the light.

Robert B. Prigo

See also **Fluorescent lamp; Fluoroscopy; Light** (Luminescence and fluorescence); **Luminescence; Phosphorescence.**

Fluorescent lamp, *FLUU REHS uhnt,* is a device that produces light by passing electric current through a gas enclosed in a tube instead of through a filament. A fluorescent lamp uses less power than an incandescent lamp uses to produce the same amount of light. It also produces only a fifth as much heat. Fluorescent lamps last much longer than incandescent lamps and can be coiled into light-bulb shapes, called *compact fluorescent lamps* or *lights* (CFL's). The first commercial fluorescent lamp was introduced in 1938 by the General Electric Company.

A fluorescent lamp consists of a glass tube containing, under pressure, a small amount of mercury vapor and an *inert* (chemically inactive) gas, typically argon. The tubes are made in a variety of shapes, including circular, straight, spiral, and U-shaped. Electric current flowing through the tube causes the mercury vapor to give off invisible ultraviolet light. The inside of the tube is coated with chemicals called *phosphors* that give off visible light when struck by ultraviolet rays. The color of the light depends on the phosphors. Because fluorescent lamps contain mercury, an environmentally harmful metal, they must be disposed of carefully.

There are three main kinds of fluorescent lamp circuits: (1) preheat, (2) rapid-start, and (3) instant-start. Fixtures using a preheat circuit cost the least but tend to flicker on starting and have the shortest lamp life. Lamps last longest in rapid-start fixtures, which are thus the cheapest to operate and maintain. Instant-start fixtures start more quickly but tend to have a shorter lamp life.

A fluorescent circuit includes a device called a *ballast.* The ballast provides voltage to start the lamp and also regulates the flow of electric current in the lamp circuit. There are two main types of ballasts: (1) magnetic and (2) electronic. In a magnetic ballast, a coil of wire acts as an *inductor,* opposing any increase or decrease in the flow of current (see **Inductance**). Electronic ballasts regulate current flow using components made from solid *semiconductor* materials. Such materials conduct current better than insulators but not as well as conductors. Electronic ballasts are more expensive than magnetic ones, but they are also more efficient.

At each end of the lamp is an *electrode,* a coil of tungsten wire coated with substances called *lanthanide oxides.* When a preheat or rapid-start lamp is turned on, electric current flows through the wire. The wire becomes heated, and the lanthanide oxides give off electrons. Some electrons strike the argon atoms and *ionize* them—that is, give the atoms a positive or negative electric charge. When ionized, the argon can conduct electric current. Current flows through the gas from electrode to electrode, forming an *arc* (stream of electrons). Instant-start lamps start at such high voltage that the arc forms immediately. When an electron in the arc strikes a mercury atom, it raises the energy level of an electron in the atom. As this electron returns to its normal state, it emits ultraviolet energy.   William Hand Allen

See also **Electric light; Fluorescence; Light bulb; Lighting.**

Fluoridation is the addition of a chemical called *fluoride* to water supplies to help teeth resist decay. In the 1930's, researchers discovered that people who grew up

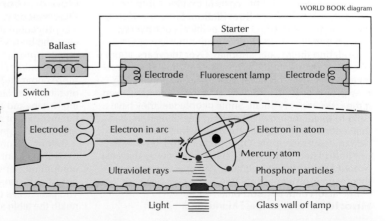

WORLD BOOK diagram

How a fluorescent lamp works

A preheat fluorescent lamp needs a *starter* and a *ballast* to operate. The starter switches electric current through the electrodes at each end of the lamp. The current heats the electrodes so they can give off electrons. Then the ballast sends a surge of current between the electrodes to form an *arc* (stream of electrons) in the lamp. The lamp contains mercury vapor. The arc knocks electrons in the mercury atoms out of their normal position. When the electrons return to their position, the atoms give off invisible ultraviolet rays. These rays strike phosphor particles on the walls of the lamp and cause them to glow.

Starter

Ballast

Switch

Electrode   Fluorescent lamp   Electrode

Electrode   Electron in arc   Electron in atom

Mercury atom

Ultraviolet rays

Phosphor particles

Light   Glass wall of lamp

where water naturally contained fluoride had up to two-thirds fewer cavities than people living in areas without fluoride in the water. Newburgh, New York, and Grand Rapids, Michigan, began to fluoridate their water in 1945, as an experiment. By the 1950's, the tests showed that the incidence of tooth decay had decreased in these cities, and United States public health officials recommended fluoridation for all communities.

Today, about half the people of the United States drink fluoridated water. In most other countries, fluoridation is not used as widely as it is in the United States. The use of fluoride tablets and toothpastes and the application of strong fluoride solutions to the teeth by dentists can also help prevent tooth decay.

Local governments or the people of a community often must decide whether the water supply should be fluoridated. This means balancing the benefits, risks, and costs of fluoridation, as well as moral questions about its widespread use. People disagree over these issues, and fluoridation has always been controversial.

Benefits, risks, and costs. Many studies have shown that fluoridation reduces tooth decay substantially. However, rates of tooth decay also have declined in areas without fluoridated water, perhaps chiefly because of the widespread use of fluoride toothpastes.

Excessive fluoride intake can be harmful, especially to the bones and teeth. In India and other countries, for example, bone damage has occurred in people whose drinking water contained fluoride levels from 2 to 3 parts per million (ppm) or more. The level most commonly used in fluoridated water is 1 ppm. In the United States and elsewhere, *mottling* (discoloration) of the teeth becomes more common as the level of fluoride in drinking water increases. Even at the fluoride level recommended for fluoridation, some people develop white flecks or patches on their teeth.

Some scientists believe that fluoridation involves special risks for people with kidney disease and for those particularly sensitive to toxic substances. However, ill effects from fluoridation have never been shown to be widespread. Most experts believe that the risk of harm from fluoridation is quite small.

Most U.S. public health officials and dentists favor fluoridation. They believe that it provides important benefits and involves little or no health risk. Supporters also argue that fluoridation gives the whole community fluoride protection simply, effectively, and at a small expense compared with the costs of treating tooth decay.

Controversies over fluoridation. Since the 1950's, fluoridation has sparked much political controversy. Heated debates erupt when communities consider fluoridating their water supplies. Over the years, about 6 of every 10 communities voting on fluoridation have rejected it. Many people object to fluoridation because they prefer not to take any risks associated with it, even if the risks are very small. Some people feel they have a right to make their own choices in health matters, and that a community violates this right when it adds fluoride to its water supply. On the other hand, if water is not fluoridated, people may suffer tooth decay that easily could have been prevented. Many people feel that this result is also unacceptable.   Edward Groth III

See also **Teeth** (A good diet).

Fluoride. See Fluorine; Fluoridation.

Fluorine, *FLOO uh reen,* is a chemical element. At ordinary temperatures, it is a pale yellow gas. Fluorine combines with other elements more readily than does any other element. Compounds that contain fluorine are called *fluorides.*

The principal source of fluorine is the mineral *fluorite,* also called *fluorspar.* Fluorite consists of the compound calcium fluoride. Steelmakers use fluorite to purify steel. Chemical companies treat fluorite with sulfuric acid to produce hydrogen fluoride, which is used to make aluminum and to produce compounds called *chlorofluorocarbons* (see **Chlorofluorocarbon**). Small amounts of fluorides applied to the teeth greatly reduce tooth decay. For this reason, fluorides are added to toothpaste, and many communities add fluorides to their drinking water.

Fluorine is the lightest of the elements known as *halogens* (see **Halogen**). It has the chemical symbol F. Fluorine's *atomic number* (number of protons in its nucleus) is 9. Its *relative atomic mass* is 18.9984032. An element's relative atomic mass equals its *mass* (amount of matter) divided by $\frac{1}{12}$ of the mass of carbon 12, the most abundant form of carbon. Fluorine may be condensed to a liquid that boils at -188.14 °C and freezes at -219.62 °C. Fluorine was first isolated in 1886 by the French chemist Henri Moissan.   Marianna A. Busch

See also **Element, Chemical** (tables); **Fluoridation.**

Fluorite, *FLOO uh ryt,* also called *fluorspar* or *fluor,* is a common mineral composed of calcium and fluorine. Its chemical formula is CaF_2. In rare cases, other elements may substitute for the calcium in fluorite.

Fluorite is important in the production of aluminum, steel, and hydrofluoric acid, a chemical used in manufacturing fluorine. Some lenses and prisms used in optical instruments consist of fluorite.

Fluorite crystals have a glassy luster and are cubic or eight-sided in shape. Fluorite may be transparent and colorless when pure. It also can occur in many colors due to defects in crystal structure or to impurities. Fluorite will often *fluoresce* (give off light) when exposed to ultraviolet radiation.

Fluorite occurs widely in such rocks as granite, granitic pegmatite, and syenite, and in ore veins. Fluorite crystals may also line the cavity of spherically shaped, hollow stones called *geodes.* Major deposits of fluorite are found in Canada, England, Germany, Mexico, and the United States.   Mark A. Helper

See also **Fluorescence; Fluorine; Mineral** (picture).

Fluorocarbon. See Chlorofluorocarbon.

Fluoroscopy, *flu RAHS kuh pee,* is a diagnostic medical procedure that uses X rays. It enables a physician to view the body's internal structure and processes. Fluoroscopy produces an X-ray image of body organs actually functioning. Fluoroscopy differs from *radiography,* a more common X-ray process that produces still images on film. Physicians use fluoroscopy to view malfunctioning organs and to observe such medical procedures as the insertion of a *catheter* (tube) in an artery and the removal of foreign objects from the lungs or stomach.

Before a fluoroscopic examination of the digestive tract, the patient drinks a liquid containing a barium compound. Barium strongly absorbs X rays, and so the digestive organs show up more clearly in the image. The patient lies on a table. An X-ray tube is mounted beneath the table and a device called an *image intensifier*

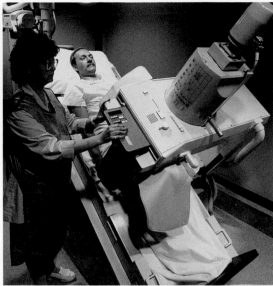

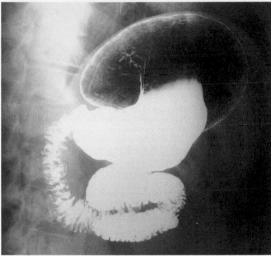

A fluoroscope, *top,* enables doctors to view internal organs of the body while they function. The patient rests on a table with an X-ray tube beneath it. A large device called an *image intensifier* converts the X rays passing through the patient into an image that a physician can view on a TV monitor. A physician may also obtain a still picture, such as the fluoroscopic image of the stomach, *bottom.* The patient drinks a solution that causes the stomach and other organs to appear white in the image.

is suspended above the patient. X rays passing through the patient form an invisible image in the image intensifier. The image intensifier converts the X rays into a visible image that is recorded by a television camera. The physician views this image on a TV monitor.

Fluoroscopy uses relatively low doses of X rays. As a result, the risk of undesirable effects is small. The American inventor Thomas A. Edison developed the first practical fluoroscope in 1896.   Raymond L. Tanner

See also **Fluorescence; X rays.**

Fluorspar. See Fluorite.
Fluothane. See Halothane.
Flute is a woodwind instrument that serves as a soprano voice in many bands, orchestras, and woodwind groups. Most flutes are metal. They consist chiefly of a tube with a mouthpiece near one end. A musician holds the flute in a horizontal position and blows across an oval hole in the mouthpiece. At the same time, the player presses levers called *keys* along the tube. The keys open and close *tone holes* to produce different notes.

The *concert flute in C* is the most popular. It has a range of three octaves. Other flutes include the *piccolo, alto flute,* and *bass flute.* The piccolo resembles a small concert flute but is pitched one octave higher (see **Piccolo**). The alto flute is pitched a fourth lower, and the bass flute an octave lower, than the concert flute.

Bone and wooden flutes were played in such countries as ancient Egypt, China, and Greece. Wooden flutes became widely used in Europe during the mid-1700's. In the mid-1800's, Theobald Böhm, a German musician, developed the first cylindrical metal flute. Böhm also developed the system of keys and tone holes used in today's flutes.   André P. Larson

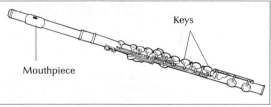

The flute is a woodwind instrument popular in bands and orchestras. A musician plays the flute by blowing across a hole in the mouthpiece and pressing keys that cover the tone holes.

Flux, *fluhks,* in chemistry and metallurgy, is a substance that lowers the melting point of a substance to which it is added. A flux added to ore before melting helps to separate the impurities from the metal. In smelting iron, the flux used is generally limestone. The flux combines readily with the impurities to form slag, which can then be easily removed. Fluxes made of borax, soda, and potash are used to separate base metal from gold and silver. The term *flux* also refers to the rate of flow of matter or energy across a given surface.   Simon Lekakh

See also **Smelting.**

Fran Hall, N.A.S.

A horse fly's eyes act as prisms, breaking light into bands of color.

Jane Burton

Grace A. Thompson, N.A.S.

A house fly searches for food on a crust of bread. The stiff bristles on the fly's body and legs may carry many disease germs that brush off on anything the insect touches.

The greenbottle fly is named for the color of its shiny coat.

Fly

Fly is an insect with one pair of well-developed wings. The common house fly is one of the best-known kinds of flies. Other kinds include black flies, blow flies, bot flies, crane flies, deer flies, fruit flies, gnats, horse flies, leaf miners, midges, mosquitoes, robber flies, sand flies, tsetse flies, and warble flies.

A number of other insects are often called flies, but they have four wings and are not true flies. These insects include butterflies, caddisflies, damselflies, dragonflies, mayflies, scorpionflies, and stoneflies.

Flies live throughout most of the world. Among the smallest are the midges called *no-see-ums,* which inhabit forests and coastal marshes. They measure about 1/20 inch (1.3 millimeters) long. One of the largest flies, a kind of *mydas fly,* occurs in South America. It grows 3 inches (7.6 centimeters) long and also measures 3 inches from the tip of one wing to the tip of the other.

Flies are among the fastest flying insects. The buzzing of a fly is the sound of its wings beating. A house fly's wings beat about 200 times a second, and some midges move their wings 1,000 times a second. House flies fly at an average speed of 4 ½ miles (7.2 kilometers) per hour. They can fly even faster for short distances to escape enemies, which include people and many birds.

Some flies rank among the most dangerous pests known. They carry germs inside their bodies, on the tip of their mouthparts, or in the hair on their bodies. When a fly "bites," or when it touches any object, the insect may leave some of these germs behind. Flies carry germs that cause serious diseases in people and other animals. Such diseases include malaria, sleeping sickness, and dysentery. Flies also cause diseases that affect plants.

People have developed many ways to control flies in places where the insects can become too abundant. Some swamps are drained or covered with oil. People also spray chemical *insecticides* in swamps and rivers to kill newly hatched flies. Other helpful control practices include the proper disposal of garbage, decaying plants, and animal wastes.

Flies also can prove helpful to people and the environment. Some types carry pollen from one plant to another, much as bees do. Others eat insect pests. Scien-

Facts in brief

Names: *Male,* none; *female,* none; *young,* maggots or wrigglers; *group,* swarm.
Number of newborn: 1 to 250 at a time, depending on species. As many as 1,000 a year for each female.
Length of life: Average 21 days in summer for house flies.
Where found: Throughout most of the world.
Scientific classification: Flies belong to the class Insecta, and they make up the order Diptera.

tists use fruit flies in the study of *heredity*. These flies have provided valuable information on how traits are passed on from one generation to the next.

There are thousands of *species* (kinds) of flies. They make up an *order* (chief group) of insects. The scientific name of the order is *Diptera*, which comes from Greek words that mean *two wings*. This article provides general information about flies. To learn more about various kinds of flies, see the separate *World Book* articles listed in the *Related articles* at the end of this article.

The body of a fly

A fly's body has three main parts: (1) the head, (2) the thorax, and (3) the abdomen. The body wall consists of three layers and is covered with fine hair. Many kinds of flies have dull black, brown, gray, or yellowish bodies. A few kinds, including soldier flies and hover flies, may have bright orange, white, or yellow markings. Some kinds, such as bluebottle flies and greenbottle flies, are shiny blue or green. They seem to sparkle with brassy, coppery, or golden lights.

Head. A fly has two large eyes that cover most of its head. The males of some species have eyes so large that they squeeze against each other. The eyes of most female flies are farther apart.

Like most other kinds of insects, a fly has *compound* eyes made up of thousands of six-sided lenses. A house fly has about 4,000 lenses in each eye. No two lenses point in exactly the same direction, and each lens works independently. Everything a fly sees seems to be broken up into small bits. The insect does not have sharp vision, but it can quickly see any movement.

A fly has two antennae that warn it of danger and help it find food. The antennae grow near the center of the head between the eyes. The size and shape of the antennae vary widely among different species of flies, and even between males and females of the same species. A house fly's antennae are short and thick; a female mosquito's are long and covered with soft hair; and a male mosquito's are long and feathery. The antennae can feel changes in the movement of the air, which may warn of an approaching enemy. Flies also smell with their antennae. The odor of the chemicals in rotting meat and garbage attracts house flies. The odors of certain chemicals bring vinegar flies to wine cellars.

The mouth of a fly looks somewhat like a funnel. The broadest part is nearest the head, and tubelike part called the *proboscis* extends downward. A fly uses its proboscis as a straw to sip liquids, its only food.

Flies do not bite or chew because they cannot open their jaws. Mosquitoes, sand flies, stable flies, and other kinds of "biting" flies have sharp mouthparts hidden in the proboscis. They stab these sharp points into a victim's skin and inject saliva to keep the blood from clotting. Then the flies sip the blood. Blow flies, fruit flies, and house flies do not have piercing mouthparts. Instead, they have two soft, oval-shaped parts called *labella* at the tip of the proboscis. The flies use these parts somewhat like sponges to lap up liquids, which they then suck into the proboscis. They sip liquids, or turn solid foods such as sugar or starch into liquids by dropping saliva on them.

Thorax. A fly's muscles are attached to the inside wall of the thorax. These strong muscles move the insect's legs and wings. A fly has six legs. It uses all its legs when it walks but often stands on only four legs. The legs of most kinds of flies end in claws that help them cling to such flat surfaces as walls or ceilings. House flies and certain other flies also have hairy, sticky pads called *pulvilli* on their feet. These pads help the insects walk on the smooth, slippery surfaces of windows and mirrors.

A fly's wings are so thin that the veins show through. The veins not only carry blood to the wings, but they also help stiffen and support the wings. Instead of hind wings, a fly has a pair of thick, rodlike parts with knobs at the tips. These parts are called *halteres*. The halteres give the fly its sense of balance. Halteres vibrate at the same rate as the wings beat when the insect is flying.

A fly is airborne as soon as it beats its wings. It does not have to run or jump to take off. In the air, the halteres keep the insect in balance and guide it so it can dart quickly and easily in any direction. A fly does not glide in the air or to a landing as do butterflies, moths, and most other flying insects. A fly beats its wings until its feet touch something to land on. If you pick up a fly, but leave the legs and wings free, the wings begin to beat immediately. Scientists sometimes do this with flies when studying wing movements.

Abdomen. A fly breathes through air holes called *spiracles* along the sides of its body. The abdomen has

WORLD BOOK illustration by Tom Dolan

Body of a house fly

External — Compound eye, Antenna, Palpi, Mouthparts, Thorax, Halter, Wing, Legs, Abdomen, Pulvilli, Claws

Internal — Nerve center, Stomach, Muscles, Salivary gland, Esophagus, Pharynx, Salivary duct, Nerve center, Intestine, Crop, Rectum

Kinds of mouthparts

Lapping and sucking (house fly) — Compound eye, Antennae, Palpi, Proboscis, Labellum

Biting (stable fly) — Compound eye, Antenna, Palpus, Proboscis

Life cycle of the house fly

Eggs

Larvae

Pupae

Newly emerged adult

Avril Ramage, Oxford Scientific Films

eight pairs of spiracles, and the thorax has two pairs. Air flows through the holes into tubes that carry it to all parts of the fly's body.

The life of a fly

A fly's life is divided into four stages: (1) egg, (2) larva, (3) pupa, and (4) adult. At each stage, the fly's appearance changes completely.

Egg. A female fly lays from 1 to about 250 eggs at a time, depending on the species. During her lifetime, one female may produce as many as a thousand eggs. The females of many species simply drop their eggs on water, on the ground, or on other animals. Some species stack the eggs in neat bundles.

At the tip of a female fly's abdomen is an organ called the *ovipositor,* through which the eggs are laid. The house fly usually places her ovipositor onto soft masses of decaying plant or animal material and lays her eggs there. One kind of mosquito arranges its eggs in groups that look somewhat like rafts. The eggs float on water until the larvae hatch.

The eggs of many kinds of flies are white or pale yellow, and they resemble grains of rice. A house fly's eggs hatch in 8 to 30 hours, but the time depends on the species of fly. Some mosquitoes lay their eggs during late autumn. But the eggs do not hatch until spring.

Larva. People refer to most fly larvae as *maggots.* Mosquito larvae are called *wrigglers* because of the way they move in water. The larvae of most kinds of flies look like worms or small caterpillars. They often live in food, garbage, sewage, soil, water, and in living or dead plants and animals. A tsetse fly larva grows inside its mother's body and receives nourishment from her.

Fly larvae spend all their time eating and growing. They *molt* (shed their skin and grow a new one) several times as they grow. The larval stage lasts from a few days to two years, depending on the species. The larvae then change into pupae.

Pupa is the stage of final growth before a fly becomes an adult. The pupae of mosquitoes and some other kinds of flies that develop in water are active swimmers. Most pupae that live on land remain quiet. The larvae of some flies build a strong oval-shaped case called a *puparium* around their bodies. Black fly larvae spin a cocoon for protection. Inside, the larva gradually loses its wormlike look and takes on the shape of the adult fly. Then the adult fly bursts one end of the pupal case or splits the pupal skin down the back and crawls out. The pupal stage of a house fly lasts from three to six days in hot weather, and longer in cool weather. The length of time varies among the different species.

Adult. When the adult emerges from the pupal case, its wings are still moist and soft. The air dries the wings quickly, and blood flows into the wing veins and stiffens them. The thin wing tissue hardens in a few hours or a few days, depending on the species, and the adult flies away to find a mate.

A fly has reached full size when it comes out of the pupal case. A small fly grows no larger as it gets older, even though its abdomen may swell with food or eggs.

Adult house flies live about 21 days in summer. They survive longer in cool weather but are less active. Most adult flies die when the weather gets cold, but some hibernate. Many larvae and pupae stay alive during the winter. They develop into adults in spring.   E. W. Cupp

Some flies that spread disease

Fly	Disease	Host
Apple maggots	Bacterial rot	Apples
Black flies	Onchocerciasis (river blindness)	Human beings
Deer flies	Tularemia (rabbit fever)	Human beings, rodents
Fly maggots	Bacterial soft rot	Potato, cabbage, other vegetables
Horse flies	Anthrax	Human beings, animals
House flies	Amebic dysentery	Human beings, animals
	Typhoid fever	Human beings
	Bacillary dysentery	Human beings
	Cholera	Human beings
Mosquitoes	Filariasis	Human beings, animals
	Malaria	Human beings, animals
	Yellow fever	Human beings, monkeys
	Dengue	Human beings, monkeys
	Encephalitis	Human beings, animals
Olive fruit fly	Olive knot	Olives
Sand flies	Kala-azar	Human beings, animals
Tsetse flies	Sleeping sickness	Human beings, animals

Related articles in *World Book* include:

Apple maggot	Gnat	Mediterranean
Bee fly	Hessian fly	fruit fly
Bot fly	Horse fly	Midge
Caddisfly	Insect	Mosquito
DDT	Insecticide	Sand fly
Deer fly	Leafminer	Tsetse fly
Face fly	Leishmaniasis	Warble fly
Filaria	Maggot	
Fruit fly		

Fly, Artificial. See Fishing (Bait).

Flycatcher is the name of several groups of birds that catch insects in the air. Flycatchers perch quietly until an insect flies past. Then they dart out quickly and seize their prey. The birds close their bills with a sharp, clicking sound. Flycatchers live throughout the world. Those found in North and South America are known as *tyrant flycatchers.*

Flycatchers have a wide range of calls and songs, both musical and harsh. The loud call of the *great-crested flycatcher* sounds like "wheep" or "creep." The noisy *sulfur-bellied flycatcher* calls "kip, kip, kip, squeelya, squeelya." The nesting habits of these birds also vary greatly. Some nest in holes in trees. Others build nests of mud or of plant materials.

WORLD BOOK illustration by Trevor Boyer, Linden Artists Ltd.
The Acadian flycatcher lives in the United States.

Most American flycatchers live in wooded regions with warm, tropical climates. They are generally dull in color, ranging from brown or gray to olive-green above and white to yellow below. Their wide bills help the birds catch flying insects. Some species have a crest at the top of the head. The tail usually ends in the shape of a square or a shallow fork.

Nearly 35 *species* (kinds) of flycatchers live in the United States. One species, the *vermilion flycatcher,* is dark brown above and bright red on the head and underparts. It is about 6 inches (15 centimeters) long. This bird makes its nest out of twigs and grasses bound with spider webs. It lives in woodlands, grasslands, and desert areas from the southern United States to Argentina. The *scissor-tailed flycatcher* measures 13 inches (33 centimeters) in length. It has a long, deeply forked tail. The head and throat are silvery-gray, the underparts are salmon-colored, and the wings and tail are black. This bird ranges from the central part of the United States to Central America. Other species of flycatcher found in the United States include the *Acadian, alder,* and *yellow-bellied flycatchers. Kingbirds, phoebes,* and *wood pewees* also are in the family of American flycatchers.

Fred J. Alsop, III

Scientific classification. American flycatchers belong to the tyrant flycatcher family, Tyrannidae. The scientific name for the great-crested flycatcher is *Myiarchus crinitus.* The sulfur-bellied

flycatcher is *Myiodynastes luteiventris;* the vermilion, *Pyrocephalus rubinus;* and the scissor-tailed, *Tyrannus forficatus.* Non-American flycatchers belong to the Old World flycatcher family, Muscicapidae.

See also **Bird** (pictures: Birds of grasslands; Birds' eggs); **Kingbird; Pewee; Phoebe.**

Flying, in aircraft. See Aviation.

Flying buttress. See Architecture (Gothic).

Flying dragon is the name commonly given to the so-called flying lizards of southeastern Asia and the East Indies. They grow to a length of about 8 inches (20 centimeters). They do not really fly but glide by means of folds of skin stretched over their ribs.

Flying dragons live in trees and glide from tree to tree to search for food or to avoid their enemies. When resting, the lizards fold their "wings" against the sides of their bodies. During the mating season, male flying dragons spread their brightly colored "wings" to attract females.   Raymond B. Huey

Scientific classification. Flying dragons make up the genus *Draco.*

© Tom McHugh, Photo Researchers
A flying dragon glides by spreading folds of skin.

Flying Dutchman is a ghost ship in folklore. There are many versions of the legend of the *Flying Dutchman.* The most common story involves the sighting of a phantom ship as it attempts to sail around the Cape of Good Hope in Africa. However, the captain has been cursed and his crew consists of dead men. The ship never reaches port and is doomed to sail on eternally. According to some versions of the legend, the curse resulted from an act of cruelty by the captain, perhaps aboard a ship carrying slaves. Other versions say he bargained with the Devil and lost.

The theme of the *Flying Dutchman* has been used in a number of literary and musical works. The English poet Samuel Taylor Coleridge based his poem "The Rime of the Ancient Mariner" (1798) on the legend. The German composer Richard Wagner adapted the story into his opera *The Flying Dutchman* (1843).   David J. Winslow

Flying fish. See Flyingfish.

Flying fox is a group of large bats. They are not closely related to foxes. There are dozens of *species* (kinds) of flying foxes. They live in most tropical regions except South America. They are especially common in regions of the South Pacific. Flying foxes are the largest bats in the world. The head and body are about 1 foot (30 centimeters) long, and the wingspread can be up to 6 ½ feet (2 meters). The name *flying fox* comes from the bat's face, which resembles that of a fox. Flying foxes eat mostly fruit and are more properly known as *fruit bats*. They also feed on flower buds, nectar, and pollen. They typically spend the day hanging in trees, often with other fruit bats. Some kinds of flying foxes are in danger of dying out completely. They are threatened by habitat destruction and hunting.   Clyde Jones

Scientific classification. Flying foxes make up the genus *Pteropus*.

Flying lemur, or colugo, is a mammal of Southeast Asia. It is about the size of a cat. A flying lemur is not a true lemur (see **Lemur**). Flying lemurs can glide as far as 100 yards (91 meters) from tree to tree, but they do not actually fly. Large folds of skin on the animal's sides connect its neck, legs, and tail. When it spreads its legs, this skin forms "wings" used in gliding. Flying lemurs have a pointed face, large eyes, and brown or gray fur with white spots. They live in rain forests and eat tropical flowers, fruits, and leaves. Most females give birth to

John Mackinnon, Bruce Coleman Ltd.

The flying lemur does not actually fly. It has large folds of skin along its sides that connect its neck, legs, and tail. When the animal spreads its legs, this skin forms "wings" that are used in gliding from tree to tree, as shown here.

one baby every year. There are two *species* (kinds), called the Philippine flying lemur and the Sunda flying lemur. See also **Mammal** (picture).   Bruce A. Brewer

Scientific classification. The scientific name of the Philippine flying lemur is *Cynocephalus volans*. The Sunda flying lemur is *Galeopterus variegates*.

Flying lizard. See Flying dragon.
Flying saucer. See Unidentified flying object.
Flying squirrel is a squirrel that can glide through the air. A fold of skin on each side of its body connects the front and back legs. When a flying squirrel stretches out its legs, the folds of skin form "wings." It glides from tree to tree, using its broad, flat tail to guide its flight. The squirrel's path is downward, then straight, and finally upward. Glides of more than 150 feet (46 meters) have been recorded. Flying squirrels always finish lower than

© J. Alsop, Bruce Coleman Inc.

The flying squirrel glides through the air by spreading its legs. Folded skin that grows between the legs stretches out to form "wings." The animal can glide more than 150 feet (46 meters).

where they started. A high starting point makes a long glide possible. Flying squirrels live in the forests of Asia, Europe, and North America. American flying squirrels are 8 to 12 inches (20 to 30 centimeters) long, including the tail. Their coat is gray or brownish-red on the upper parts of the body and white or cream-colored on the underparts. Some Asian flying squirrels grow 4 feet (1.2 meters) long.

Flying squirrels nest in the hollows of trees. They hunt for food only at night. Other squirrels hunt by day. Flying squirrels eat berries, birds' eggs, fungi, insects, and nuts. They also eat young birds and the meat of any *carcasses* (dead animals) they can find. Female flying squirrels have from two to three young twice a year. By six weeks of age, the young are "flying" on their own.   Clark E. Adams

Scientific classification. Flying squirrels make up the subfamily Pteromyinae of the squirrel family, Sciuridae. The common flying squirrel of the United States is *Glaucomys volans*. The larger *G. sabrinus* lives in Canada and the northern United States.

Flying Tigers was the nickname for the American Volunteer Group (AVG), a small force of pilots from the United States who fought for the Chinese Air Force against Japan during World War II (1939-1945). The noses of the AVG's P-40 Tomahawk fighter planes were painted with the mouth of a tiger shark.

Japan invaded China in 1937. Retired U.S. Army Air Corps Captain Claire L. Chennault formed the AVG in 1941. President Franklin Roosevelt gave 100 Army, Navy, and Marine pilots permission to resign their commissions and join the AVG in an effort to help the Chinese defend themselves from Japanese bombing. Three squadrons of Flying Tigers fought in the skies above China and Burma (now Myanmar) until July 1942, when they were incorporated into the U.S. Army Air Force. In its 28 weeks of combat, the AVG was credited with the destruction of nearly 300 Japanese planes. Fourteen Flying Tiger pilots were killed in action.   Adrian R. Lewis

See also **Chennault, Claire Lee; World War II** (The China-Burma-India theater).
Flyingfish is a type of fish that throws itself from the water with the motion of its strong tail. In the air, it glides by spreading its large fins, which act like wings.

Body muscles and the tail fin help the fish turn in flight. The flight often covers 150 to 1,000 feet (46 to 300 meters). Flyingfish live in all warm seas. There are dozens of *species* (kinds). The California flyingfish grows about 18 inches (46 centimeters) long. The sharp-nosed flyingfish lives off both coasts of tropical America. Flyingfish are excellent food. See also **Gurnard; Fish** (picture: Fish of coastal waters and the open ocean). John E. McCosker

Scientific classification. Flyingfish make up the family Exocoetidae. The California flyingfish is *Cypselurus californicus* or *Cheilopogon pinnatibarbatus*. The sharp-nosed flyingfish is *Fodiator acutus*.

Flynn, Elizabeth Gurley (1890-1964), was an American labor leader. In 1961, she became the first woman to head the Communist Party of the United States of America (CPUSA).

Flynn was born on Aug. 7, 1890, in Concord, New Hampshire. Her parents often took her to socialist meetings after the family moved to New York City in 1900. By the time she was 15, Flynn had begun speaking on street corners for workers' rights. In 1906, she joined the Industrial Workers of the World (IWW), an early labor union (see **Industrial Workers of the World**). She remained active in the IWW for 10 years, during which time she led several strikes.

Many of the people who opposed U.S. involvement in World War I (1914-1918) were accused of disloyalty and sent to prison under the Espionage Act of 1917 and the Sedition Act of 1918. In 1919, Flynn turned her attention toward the legal and political defense of such individuals. Flynn's experiences with these cases led her to help form the American Civil Liberties Union (ACLU) in 1920.

Flynn joined the Communist Party in 1937. After World War II (1939-1945), anti-Communist feeling was high in the United States. Many members, and especially the leaders, of the Communist Party were jailed for violating the Smith Act. Similar to the Espionage and Sedition acts, the U.S. government used the Smith Act in the early years of the Cold War to target opponents of U.S. policy (see **Cold War**). Flynn organized and raised money for the defense of these party members. She herself was charged with violating the Smith Act in the early 1950's and was convicted in 1953. Flynn spent from January 1955 to May 1957 in prison. After her release, Flynn became head of the Communist Party of the United States. She died in Moscow on Sept. 5, 1964, during a visit to the Soviet Union. Lisa Phillips

Flytrap. See **Pitcher plant; Venus's-flytrap.**

Flyway. See **Bird** (Where birds migrate).

Flywheel is a heavy disc attached to an engine or motor that helps maintain a stable speed. It is used where the forces driving the engine shaft are not constant. The driving forces in a gasoline engine, for example, occur in cycles in which a piston moves back and forth in the engine's cylinder. The driving forces produce the power needed by the engine's load. Sometimes, the driving forces grow momentarily larger than necessary for the engine's load, and the engine speed increases. Then the flywheel absorbs the excess energy and prevents the speed from increasing rapidly. At other times, the driving forces from the piston become momentarily smaller than necessary. Then the flywheel's *inertia*—that is, its tendency to stay in motion—keeps the speed from decreasing quickly. The action of a flywheel decreases as the number of cylinders of a gasoline engine increases. See also **Gasoline engine; Starter; Steam engine** (picture). William H. Haverdink

FM. See **Frequency modulation.**

Foam rubber. See **Rubber** (Sponge rubber).

Foch, *fawsh,* **Ferdinand,** *fehr dee NAHN* (1851-1929), a French military leader, commanded the Allies in the final months of World War I (1914-1918). His offensive campaigns helped defeat Germany and end the war.

Foch was born in Tarbes, France, on Oct. 2, 1851. He served in the Franco-Prussian War (1870-1871), and he joined the French artillery in 1874. Foch became a professor at the École Supérieure de Guerre, the French war college, in 1895, and head of the college in 1908. His lectures and publications emphasized offensive warfare.

At the start of World War I, Foch led a French army corps, but he soon became an army commander. In the fall of 1914, he played a prominent role in the First Battle of the Marne and coordinated Allied forces in the First Battle of Ypres. He directed Allied offensives in Artois in 1915 and French forces in the Battle of the Somme in 1916. These operations failed, and Foch was relieved of his com-

United Press Int.
Ferdinand Foch

mand in late 1916. In 1917, however, he was appointed chief of the War Ministry's general staff and sent to the Italian front to oversee Allied assistance to the Italian army. He then became France's representative on the Allied Supreme War Council.

In 1918, great German offensives in France caused a crisis for the Allies. Owing to his experience, Foch was chosen as commander in chief of the British, French, and United States armies on the Western Front. From July to November, he directed counteroffensives that freed much of northern France and Belgium from German control. On August 6, Foch achieved the army's highest rank—marshal of France. Foch led the delegation that signed the armistice with Germany on November 11. On November 21, he was elected to the French Academy, a body of distinguished intellectuals and statesmen.

At the Paris Peace Conference in 1919, Foch argued that France should maintain a military frontier on the Rhine River and that Germany should lose control of areas west of the Rhine. When French Premier Georges Clemenceau yielded to American and British opposition to these demands, Foch predicted another war within 20 years. He died March 20, 1929, in Paris. David Stevenson

See also **World War I** (The last campaigns).

Foehn, *fayn,* is a warm, dry wind that blows down a mountainside. The air loses its moisture as it rises to the mountaintop. It is heated by compression as it comes down the other side of the mountain. Foehns occur in mountainous regions throughout the world. They blow frequently in the Alps, where the warm wind received its name. In the Rocky Mountains, a foehn is called a *chinook* (see **Chinook**). These winds often bring rapid temperature changes. For example, the temperature at Havre, Montana, rose 33 °F (18 °C) in one hour when a chinook suddenly arrived on Feb. 15, 1948. Foehns or chinooks cause snow to melt rapidly. The winds often make the climate of areas in which they occur much warmer than neighboring areas.   Richard A. Dirks

Fog is a collection of tiny water droplets that float in the air. Fog is similar to clouds, except that clouds do not touch the earth's surface, as fog does.

Fog forms from water that has evaporated from lakes, oceans, and rivers, or from moist soil and plants. This evaporated water, called *water vapor,* expands and cools as it rises into the air. Air can hold only a certain amount of water vapor at any given temperature. This amount is called the *holding capacity.* As the temperature of the air decreases, so does its holding capacity. When the temperature drops so that the amount of water vapor in the air exceeds the holding capacity, some of the water vapor begins to *condense* (change into small droplets of water). Fog disappears when the air temperature rises and the holding capacity increases. According to international definition, fog is any condensation that reduces visibility to less than 3,281 feet (1 kilometer). Fog that does not greatly reduce visibility is called *mist* or *haze.*

There are four main kinds of fog: (1) *advection fog,* (2) *frontal fog,* (3) *radiation fog,* and (4) *upslope fog.*

Advection fog develops from air traveling over a surface of a different temperature. One kind of advection fog, called *sea fog,* occurs when warm, moist air travels over a cold surface. Sea fog is most common along seacoasts and lakeshores. Another kind of advection fog,

called *steam fog,* results from cold air passing over warm water. Water vapor, evaporating continuously from the water surface, comes into contact with the cold air. When the air reaches its holding capacity, the excess water vapor condenses quickly into fog droplets that steam up from the water surface. Steam fog commonly appears on cold winter days over the Great Lakes and over warm lakes in Florida.

Frontal fog forms along a *front.* A front is a boundary between two air masses of different temperatures. Frontal fog is produced when raindrops fall from the warmer air mass into the colder one, where they evaporate. They thereby cause the water vapor in the cold air to exceed the air's holding capacity.

Radiation fog occurs on calm, clear nights as the ground loses warmth through radiation into the air. A layer of fog forms along the ground, gradually becoming denser. Radiation fog is most common in the San Joaquin Valley in California and in other deep valleys.

Upslope fog develops when moist air moves upward along sloping terrain. The air cools as it moves up the slope until it can no longer hold the water vapor. Fog droplets then form along the slope.   T. Theodore Fujita

See also **Cloud; Dew; Smog; Water.**

FOIA. See Freedom of Information Act.

Foil. See Fencing.

Fokine, *faw KEEN,* **Michel,** *mih SHEHL* (1880-1942), was a great Russian *choreographer* (dance creator). Fokine invented the one-act ballet based on music by a first-rate composer. The dance and scenery in his ballets merge with the mood and drama of the music to create a powerful theater event. Fokine composed more than

Kinds of fog   Fog is a mass of tiny water droplets that are suspended in the air at or near the earth's surface. Fog, which reduces visibility, forms when water vapor in the air *condenses* (returns to liquid form). The four main kinds of fog are advection fog, frontal fog, radiation fog, and upslope fog.

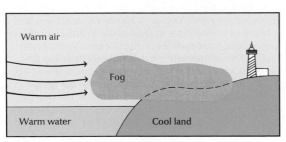

Advection fog occurs when warm, moist air travels over a cool surface, such as a seacoast or a lakeshore. It also may form when cold air passes over bodies of warm water.

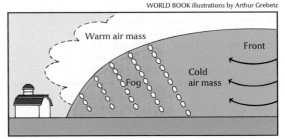

Frontal fog develops on the boundary between two air masses of different temperatures. Raindrops fall from the warmer air mass into the colder one, evaporate, and turn into fog.

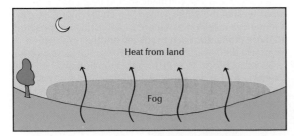

Radiation fog occurs at night, when the ground gives off heat through radiation. As the land cools, so does the air above it. Because this cooler air can hold less water vapor, fog is formed.

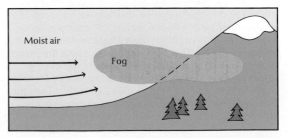

Upslope fog forms when moist air flows upward over a sloping land surface. As the air travels up the slope, it grows cooler. This cooling of the moist air produces fog.

Photo by Emil Otto Hoppé (The Dance Collection, N.Y. Public Library)

Michel Fokine and his wife, Vera, danced in a 1921 revival of his ballet *Daphnis and Chloë,* based on an ancient Greek story.

60 one-act ballets between 1905 and 1942. The best known include *The Dying Swan, Les Sylphides, Prince Igor, Scheherazade, Le Spectre de la Rose, Petrouchka, L'Épreuve d'Amour,* and *The Firebird.*

Fokine was born on April 23, 1880, in St. Petersburg. There he became soloist with the Maryinsky Ballet (now the Kirov Ballet). He left Russia for Western Europe with Sergei Diaghilev's Ballets Russes in 1909. His early work with the Ballets Russes in Paris marked the beginning of his career as a choreographer. He became a U.S. citizen in 1932. Fokine died on Aug. 22, 1942.   Katy Matheson

See also **Ballet** (Ballet in Russia).

Fokker, *FAHK uhr,* **Anthony Herman Gerard** (1890-1939), was a Dutch engineer, pilot, and aircraft manufacturer. He moved to Germany at age 20 and set up a manufacturing plant near Berlin at age 22. Fokker designed monoplanes, biplanes, and triplanes. His factories supplied airplanes for Germany in World War I (1914-1918). After the war, he set up plants in the Netherlands and the United States in which he made successful transport aircraft. Fokker was born on April 6, 1890, in Kediri, Java. He died on Dec. 23, 1939.   Ronald J. Ferrara

Folate. See Folic acid.

Foley, Thomas Stephen (1929-2013), a Democrat from the state of Washington, served in the United States House of Representatives from 1965 to 1995. Foley was speaker of the House from 1989 to 1995. He was majority leader of the House from 1987 until he became speaker. Foley served as majority *whip* (assistant leader) of the House from 1981 to 1987. He was United States ambassador to Japan from 1997 to 2001.

Bruce Hoertel, Gamma/Liaison

Thomas Foley

Foley was born May 6, 1929, in Spokane, Washington. He graduated from the University of Washington in 1951 and the University of Washington Law School in 1957. He soon became deputy prosecutor in the Spokane County attorney's office and, later, the assistant state attorney general for Spokane. He won election to the U.S. House in 1964. He was chairman of the House's Agriculture Committee from 1975 to 1981 and of the House Democratic Caucus from 1976 to 1981. In the mid-1980's, he helped form House Democrats' positions on such issues as arms control, the budget, and military aid to rebels in Nicaragua. Foley died on Oct. 18, 2013.   Guy Halverson

Folger Shakespeare Library, *FOHL juhr,* an independent library in Washington, D.C., houses one of the world's most important collections of books by and about William Shakespeare. The library also holds collections on Britain (now the United Kingdom) for the period from the mid-1400's to the mid-1700's. In addition to research functions, the library also provides a large number of interpretive programs for the public.

Henry Clay Folger, a former president of the Standard Oil Company of New York, founded the library in 1930. He left his fortune for the trustees of Amherst College to administer toward the development of a great research library. Scholars from all parts of the world come to the Folger Shakespeare Library for research in Shakespeare studies, history, and literature. The library building, a magnificent marble structure, was completed in 1932.

Critically reviewed by the Folger Shakespeare Library

See also **Washington, D.C.** (picture: The Folger Shakespeare Library's theater).

Folic acid is one of the B-complex vitamins necessary for good health. A lack of folic acid in the diet can lead to anemia. In pregnant women, folic acid deficiency can cause a group of serious birth defects called *neural tube defects,* including the spinal disorder *spina bifida (SPY nuh BIHF uh duh).* Neural tube defects result when the brain, spinal cord, or other parts of the central nervous system do not form properly during fetal development. Physicians advise all women who may become pregnant or who are pregnant to add folic acid to their diet to prevent such birth defects.

The recommended dietary allowance (RDA) of folic acid for an adult is 400 micrograms daily. Folic acid occurs naturally in small amounts in green leafy vegetables, citrus fruits and juices, dried beans, nuts, and milk. Other sources include fortified grain products and vitamin supplements. Folic acid helps break down a substance called *homocysteine (HOH muh SIHS tee ihn)* in blood. High levels of homocysteine have been linked with increased risk of heart disease.   Bonita L. Marks

See also **Spina bifida; Vitamin** (Water-soluble vitamins).

Folicin. See Folic acid.

Folio, *FOH lee oh,* is the name printers and publishers use for a sheet of paper folded once, making four pages, front and back. The word *folio* may also mean the page number of a book. Even-numbered pages, or folios, are always on the left. Odd-numbered folios are on the right. A *quarto* is a sheet folded twice, making four leaves or eight pages. An *octavo* is a sheet folded into eight leaves or 16 pages. The octavo format, or shape of the book, is the one in most common use. See also **Shakespeare, William** (Folios).   Charles F. Sieger

A folk painting by Edward Hicks called *The Peaceable Kingdom, shown here,* is based on an Old Testament prophecy. The prophecy proclaims that in God's kingdom, the lion would lie down with the lamb and a little child would lead all creatures. The background shows the American colonial leader William Penn signing a treaty with the Indians. Hicks painted dozens of versions of this subject.

Oil painting on canvas (about 1840-1845); New York State Historical Association, Cooperstown, New York

Folk art is a term that refers to the work of craft workers who have received little or no formal training. Folk art is intended for use by common people rather than by the educated classes who are the audience for mainstream "fine art." Most folk art is functional or utilitarian—that is, it consists of art for daily use and sometimes for special occasions, such as weddings and funerals.

Folk arts often flourish in particular geographical regions among people who share a common language, religion, or other unifying characteristics. Folk artists generally use traditional tools, materials, and craft techniques. Their work rarely shows an awareness of current movements and other developments in the arts. Folk art is not created for museums, though many galleries and museums show folk art and collectors pay high prices for prized examples.

Folk art has been produced in many countries for hundreds of years. This article deals with American folk art, especially during its most productive period, from about 1780 to about 1860. Most of the folk artists who worked in small towns in Illinois, New England, New York, Ohio, and Pennsylvania have been identified.

American folk artists created a wide variety of works, including paintings, sculptures, and such household objects as dishes, pots, and quilts. They also produced store signs, weather vanes, and other everyday objects. During the 1800's, sailors carved whalebone and sharks' teeth into a special kind of folk sculpture called *scrimshaw.*

By 1875, the demand for folk art had declined in America because of the widespread use of machines. The machines could manufacture more goods in less time—and with fewer mistakes—than could human

hands. But folk art continued in isolated rural areas, and some is still created today.

For many years, scholars and art collectors paid little attention to folk art. The first real interest in American folk art occurred in the late 1920's. At that time, a group of professional artists on vacation in Maine noticed folk art on sale in junk shops. They began to buy it because they admired its fresh, simple quality and its freedom from formal rules.

Today, much folk art is enjoyed simply for its beauty and for its skillful craftwork. In addition, folk art reflects everyday life. Much of it shows the social attitudes, political views, religious feelings, and routine habits of the people of a certain period and place. These elements make folk art a valuable source of information to historians and others interested in ordinary people of the past.

Kinds of folk art

Painting. Folk artists painted some subjects from memory and others from life. In many cases, folk artists copied or adapted engravings and various other kinds of prints originally created by trained artists.

Many American folk painters began by making business signs. Until about 1870, many Americans could not read, and so shopkeepers used pictorial signs to advertise their products. For example, a sign showing a pig represented a butcher shop. A picture of a boot advertised a shoemaker. Most signs had bright colors and bold designs to catch the eye of passers-by.

The influence of sign painting can be seen in much early American portrait painting. Portraits were the most common type of folk painting. Artists called *limners* traveled throughout a region, painting likenesses of local residents. These portraits, like store signs, had vivid colors and simple but bold compositions.

In addition to signs and portraits, folk artists painted pictures of houses, landscapes, and ships. Many landscapes showed scenes of life on farms or in small towns. These scenes tell much about now-forgotten activities that once were so common that nobody bothered to write about them.

Sculpture. One of the earliest types of folk sculpture was the *figurehead* of a ship. A figurehead is a statue that decorates the bow of a vessel. In most cases, the statue is of a woman. Early folk carving also included gravestones.

The so-called cigar store Indian was a popular subject for some carvers. A life-sized wooden figure of an Indian warrior stood outside many shops that sold tobacco products. The Indian figures were first displayed by English merchants of the late 1600's. The merchants used this form of advertisement because Indians had introduced tobacco to the Virginia settlers.

Folk sculptors made animals and other figures for merry-go-rounds. Folk sculptors also carved and decorated toys and *decoys.* Decoys are wooden figures of ducks and geese that are used by hunters to attract game birds.

Weather vanes ranked among the most important kinds of folk sculpture. Farmers and sailors needed to know about changes in the weather, and so farm build-

The Talcott Family (1832), a water color on paper

Portraits were painted by folk artists called *limners.* While in her early 20's, Deborah Goldsmith traveled throughout northern New York, painting local residents. This family ranks among her best-known compositions. The painting provides a valuable record of American clothing and furnishings of the time.

Metal weather vanes of the late 1800's were made from wood patterns carved by experienced craftworkers. A folk sculptor designed the weather vane at the right in the form of the Statue of Liberty.

Copper weather vane (after 1886)

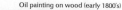

Advertisements featured several kinds of folk art. Sculptors carved wooden Indians, *left,* which stood outside tobacco shops. Painters designed colorful signs, *below,* to advertise a store's products.

Painted wood (1800's); Virginia Museum of Fine Arts, Richmond

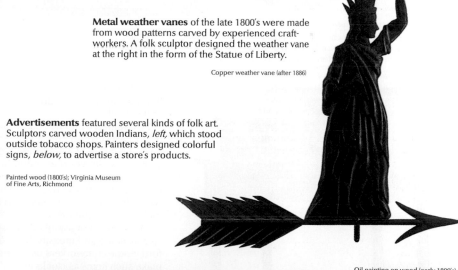

Oil painting on wood (early 1800's)

Metal coffeepot
(about 1820)

Wooden hatbox
(late 1700's)

Wooden butter
mold (1800's)

Wooden scoop
(late 1700's)
Private collection

Stoneware jugs
(late 1800's/early 1900's)
© Decorative Arts/Alamy
Images

Earthenware pie plate (1814)
Philadelphia Museum of Art, purchased by E. A. Barber

Cotton and wool woven coverlet (1835) Private collection

Household objects were carefully carved and vividly decorated to make them as attractive as possible. Craftworkers used colorful designs in painting the hatbox and kitchen utensils shown on the left. A weaver chose bold patterns for the coverlet on the right and added an unusual border.

A dressing table, built in 1835 by a New England craftworker, was made of cheap wood. The artist painted and decorated the table in imitation of an expensive rosewood piece.

ings and ships had weather vanes to show the direction of the wind.

Household objects. Folk art included many decorative objects used at home. Some of these objects brightened the inside of a home, and others seemed to make daily chores less boring. A number of folk artists made colorful kitchen utensils of earthenware and tin. Some homemakers specialized in sewing quilts, many of which featured bright colors and lively designs of animals, flowers, and trees.

Many pieces of useful folk art substituted for expensive furniture and utensils that most people could not afford. Some craftworkers used poor-quality wood to make such items as clocks and tables. Folk artists then painted and decorated such pieces to imitate stylish furniture made from expensive woods such as mahogany or rosewood.

Scrimshaw. During long voyages, many sailors made small carvings and engravings from sperm whale teeth, whalebone, or tortoise or sea shells. Such carvings and engravings became known as *scrimshaw.*

Engravings made by American sailors during the 1800's rank as the finest examples of scrimshaw. First, the sailor smoothed and polished the object. Then he scratched a picture or design into the surface with a sharp instrument. Finally, he filled in the engraved lines with colored inks. Some sailors engraved accurate scenes of activities at sea, such as naval battles and whale hunts. Sailors also copied illustrations from books and magazines.

Many pieces of scrimshaw were useful objects, such as knitting needles and corset stays. Sailors sometimes decorated coconut shells, ostrich eggs, and other objects from nature as souvenirs of their travels.

Folk artists

Most American folk artists probably considered themselves craftworkers rather than artists. They would have used the word *artist* for those who studied and followed traditions of art created through the centuries by Europeans.

The names of most American folk artists have been lost. However, a few are known because they wrote their name on their works, developed a recognizable style, or created a large number of items. The best-known of these artists include Erastus Salisbury Field, Edward Hicks, Ammi Phillips, Eunice Pinney, and Wilhelm Schimmel.

Many folk artists were skilled craftworkers who could build houses and ships as well as paint or carve. Edward Hicks, for example, was born in Bucks County, Pennsylvania, and served a seven-year apprenticeship to a local coachmaker as a painter. Then, at the age of 21, Hicks decided to work for himself. He earned his living by lettering signs, but he is best known today for his many versions of a painting he called *The Peaceable Kingdom*.

Some folk artists were amateurs who created folk art for fun, to pass the time, or to impress their neighbors.

Still others were students, most of them teenagers. They painted water colors, made drawings, or embroidered pieces of cloth as classroom assignments. Sometimes such schoolwork produced objects that today are valued as important pieces of folk art.

A number of folk artists had a regular job and used their artistic talent to increase their income. Schoolteachers, shopkeepers, and even physicians and lawyers earned extra money by selling objects they had created.

Some folk artists traveled throughout a region, trading pieces of their art for food and lodging. During the 1880's, Wilhelm Schimmel wandered through Cumberland County, Pennsylvania, seeking work and begging for food. In exchange for meals, Schimmel gave people animal figures he had carved and then colored with bits of paint. Today, his figures rank among the most prized American folk sculpture.

Folk art collections

Several museums in the United States exhibit only folk art or have large folk art collections. Most are in the East, where the majority of folk artists lived.

In New England, folk art can be seen at the Old Sturbridge Village in Sturbridge, Massachusetts; and at the Shelburne Museum in Shelburne, Vermont. The Museum of Fine Arts in Boston also has a large collection.

The Pennsylvania Dutch region of southeastern Pennsylvania was an important center of folk art, and several museums there exhibit such art today. They include the Landis Valley Museum in Lancaster and the Schwenk-

A figurehead of a giant eagle decorated the bow of the warship *Lancaster*. The sculptor designed the eagle to symbolize the power and authority of the United States wherever the *Lancaster* sailed.

Painted wood figurehead (about 1875) by John Haley Bellamy; The Mariners' Museum, Newport News, Virginia

Whaling Museum, New Bedford, Mass.

Scrimshaw consisted of carvings and engravings made by sailors during long voyages. The engraving on the sperm whale tooth, *above,* shows whalers towing a dead whale to their ship.

African American folk art shows the influence of the African heritage of American slaves. A former slave probably carved this wooden figure of a boy with a bucket about 1860. The expressionless face and seated position are features of African sculpture.

Boy with Bucket, pinewood sculpture by an unknown American artist; Abby Aldrich Rockefeller Folk Art Collection, Williamsburg, Virginia

felder Library & Heritage Center in Pennsburg. The Museum of Art in Philadelphia and the Bucks County Historical Society in Doylestown, Pennsylvania, also have notable folk art collections.

The New York State Historical Association in Cooperstown exhibits folk art. The Metropolitan Museum of Art, in New York City, has an important collection. Another collection may be seen at the Winterthur Museum and Country Estate in Winterthur, Delaware.

The Abby Aldrich Rockefeller Folk Art Museum in Williamsburg, Virginia, is one of the world's largest museums devoted only to folk art. In Washington, D.C., folk art can be seen at the National Gallery of Art and the Smithsonian Institution. In the Midwest, the Henry Ford Museum in Dearborn, Michigan, has an outstanding folk art collection.   Michael Plante

Related articles in *World Book* include:
Colonial life in America (Arts)
Feke, Robert
Hicks, Edward
Latin America (The arts; pictures)
Moses, Grandma
Pennsylvania Dutch (picture)
Pickett, Joseph
Sampler

Additional resources

Artisans Around the World. 6 vols. Raintree Steck-Vaughn, 1999-2000. Younger readers.
Panchyk, Richard. *American Folk Art for Kids.* Chicago Review Pr., 2004.
Russell, Charles, ed. *Self-Taught Art: The Culture and Aesthetics of American Vernacular Art.* Univ. Pr. of Miss., 2001.
Wertkin, Gerard C., ed. *Encyclopedia of American Folk Art.* Routledge, 2004.

Folk costume. See Clothing.

Folk dancing is the traditional form of social dancing of a nation or ethnic group. Throughout history, almost every culture has developed its own folk dances. These dances have been passed down from generation to generation. People have composed *dance songs,* a type of folk music, to accompany many of the dances.

Most folk dances originated as a form of celebration or religious worship or as a method of controlling mysterious forces. The form and movements of many of these dances were based on community-held beliefs. For example, some early folk dances were performed in a circle because people believed this shape had magical powers. In some early cultures, circular motion was thought to bring good luck or drive away evil.

Early peoples had dances to celebrate such events as birth, marriage, and even death. In some societies, young people conducted courtship through dances. The *Ländler* of Austria and the *fandango* of Spain are pantomime dances based on gestures of courtship.

Other folk dances were originally performed to cure disease, to obtain such favors as plentiful crops, or to celebrate success in battle. The *tarantella* of Italy originated as a method of curing the bite of the tarantula. The Scots once celebrated victories in battle by dancing the *sword dance.*

The meanings of most folk dances change with the

J. Kankel, Bavaria-Verlag

Folk dancing is an important event at folk festivals throughout the world. These dancers in traditional costumes are performing a German folk dance on Bavarian Folk Costume Day. This annual festival is held in Bad Wiessee, Germany, near Munich.

passage of time. Sometimes dances that originally had religious or ritual purposes came to be danced chiefly for recreation.

Today, the *square dance* is perhaps the most popular folk dance in the United States. The square dance is usually danced by four couples in a square formation. The dancers swing about, bow, change partners, and perform other lively movements as directed by a caller. Popular European folk dances include the *Irish jig,* the *flamenco* of Spain, and the *polka* of Bohemia, a region in what is now the Czech Republic. Among black African and American Indian groups, traditional dances remain a vital part of religious ceremonies, as well as a form of entertainment. Selma Landen Odom

See the pictures of dancers in the following articles: **Hispanic Americans; Indonesia; Jews; Lithuania; Romania; and Spain.** See also **Dance; Latin America** (Dance); **Square dancing.**

Additional resources

Harris, Jane A., and others. *Dance A While.* 8th ed. Allyn & Bacon, 2000.
Lane, Christy, and Langhout, Susan. *Multicultural Folk Dance Guide.* 2 vols. Human Kinetics, 1998.
Weikart, Phyllis S. *Teaching Folk Dance.* High/Scope Pr., 1997.

Folk literature. See Folklore; Literature for children (Traditional literature).

Folk music consists of a people's traditional songs and melodies. Folk songs deal with almost every kind of human activity. Many of these songs express the political or religious beliefs of a people or describe their social relationships or history. Other folk songs simply provide amusement.

Characteristics of folk music. Folk music usually is learned by listening to it rather than by reading the notes or words. The music is passed from person to person, from place to place, and from generation to generation.

The melody and words of a song may develop over a long time. Over the years, a song may change a great deal, either by accident or from a desire for change. A tune may be shortened or lengthened, or its pitches and rhythms altered. Part of one song may be combined with part of another. In these ways, families of tunes are created. The words of a song also may change over time. In addition, one set of words may be sung with different melodies, or different words may be sung to a single melody.

Folk music usually is composed and performed by nonprofessional musicians. In many cases, the composer of a song or melody cannot be identified. Songs by professional composers may be considered folk music if they become part of a people's traditional music. For example, the American composer Stephen Foster wrote such songs as "Oh! Susanna" and "Old Folks at Home," which are accepted widely as folk music.

Folk music is known and accepted by a large number of people in a society. It may be thought of as expressing the character of a nation or of an ethnic or social group. In some sense, folk music is the music of the people.

Kinds of folk music. The *ballad* is one of the main types of European and American folk songs. A ballad tells a story, usually based on actual events. Ballads have a stanza form, in which a melody is repeated for each of several verses. There may also be a refrain that is sung several times during the song.

Some ballads relate legendary incidents that occurred a long time ago. For example, "Barbara Allen" is a tragic love story that dates from at least the 1600's. Many versions of the song exist, some of which originated in England and others in Scotland. Some ballads are based on more recent events. "Peat Bog Soldiers" describes the plight of prisoners in Nazi concentration camps during the 1930's and 1940's. Many ballads tell about the deeds of heroes. For example, "Casey Jones" praises a brave railroad engineer, and "John Brown's Body" honors a famous abolitionist.

Some folk songs deal with a particular activity, occupation, or set of circumstances. American soldiers sang "Gee, but I Want to Go Home" during World War I (1914-1918) and World War II (1939-1945). "Midnight Special" describes the loneliness of prison life.

Laborers create *work songs* to coordinate their movements, to help their long days pass more quickly, or to sing after work. Popular work songs include "Old Chisholm Trail," sung by cowboys, and "Drunken Sailor," sung by sailors. Some *union songs* call for better conditions for workers. The execution of a famous labor organizer in 1915 inspired the union song "Joe Hill." Slaves sang about their suffering, and to encourage one another, in *spirituals* such as "Go Down, Moses" and "Joshua Fought the Battle of Jericho." In the mid-1900's, African Americans sang "We Shall Overcome" and "Ain't Gonna Let Nobody Turn Me Around" to further their struggle for civil rights. There are also such religious folk songs as "Amazing Grace," children's songs, and songs that mark the changing seasons or the stages of a person's life.

Some folk songs are meant only to entertain. People dance to "Buffalo Gals" and other *dance songs. Game songs,* such as "Ring-Around-the-Rosy," give instructions on how to play a certain game. Some songs, including "Arkansas Traveler" and "Froggie Went a Courting," are intended to make people laugh.

Instruments used to accompany folk songs include the guitar, banjo, dulcimer, harmonica, and violin. There is also a large body of dance music for instruments. Complex versions of folk tunes are played in modern fiddle contests and folk festivals. The best-known fiddle tunes include "Soldier's Joy," "Sailor's Hornpipe," and "Grey Eagle."

American folk music is noted for its energy, humor, and emotional impact. The major influences on American folk music came from the United Kingdom and other European countries, and from Africa. Various national and ethnic groups preserve the folk music of their ancestors. For example, Americans of Greek ancestry hold festivals during which traditional Greek songs and dances are performed.

The traditional songs of Native Americans are also an important part of the American folk heritage. Some tribes believed that the gods gave them all the songs at the beginning of time and that new songs could not be composed. Other tribes thought that songs came to them in dreams or in other mystical ways. A number of tribes have folk songs designed to control the weather or to cure illness. They believe the songs must be sung correctly because errors could rob the songs of their power.

The early American colonists from the United Kingdom brought their folk music traditions with them, especially ballads and instrumental dance melodies. Later settlers from other countries also brought their own folk music, which interacted and combined with the British music in various ways. For example, country music, which developed in the United States in the early 1900's, combined elements of folk music from the United Kingdom with blues, popular songs, and religious music.

The slaves who were brought to America from Africa had their own musical traditions. Many slaveowners did not allow the slaves to sing or play their native music. But the slaves created new songs that combined African and European traditions. Many of these songs follow the *call and response* pattern, in which a leader sings a line and the group answers. Drums and other percussion instruments may play a complex rhythmic accompaniment.

During the folk revival of the mid-1900's, a number of singers gained great popularity performing American folk songs. Some of these singers also wrote songs that have become part of the American folk tradition. The best known of these songs were concerned with social problems, such as poverty and racial prejudice, or they protested against war. The leading singer-composers included Joan Baez, Bob Dylan, Woody Guthrie, Huddie Ledbetter (known as Leadbelly), and Pete Seeger.

Valerie Woodring Goertzen

Related articles in *World Book* include:

Baez, Joan	Guthrie, Woody
Ballad	Ladysmith Black Mambazo
Blues	Latin America (Music)
Burleigh, Harry Thacker	Popular music (The folk music
Calypso	revival)
Country music	Reggae
Dylan, Bob	Rock music (New styles and
Folk dancing	sounds)
Folklore	Seeger, Pete
Foster, Stephen Collins	Spiritual

Additional resources

Lornell, Kip. *Introducing American Folk Music.* 2nd ed. McGraw, 2002.
Nettl, Bruno, and others, eds. *The Garland Encyclopedia of World Music.* 10 vols. Garland, 1997-2002.

Folklore is any of the beliefs, customs, and traditions practiced by and passed among a group of people who share some connection. Such a group, called a *folk,* may consist of people of a certain ethnicity, people who live in a certain region, an extended family, or even a small group of friends. People often think of folklore as old stories and songs. But it can also include architecture, arts and crafts, dances, games, holiday and religious celebrations, jokes, proverbs, and slang. Scholars today recognize folklore as an important means of sharing learning or knowledge. Folklore also serves other purposes, such as promoting unity within a group or providing entertainment.

Much folklore passes orally from person to person. When written, folklore can be transmitted through rhymes, proverbs, or stories, or even as graffiti or e-mail messages. Some folklore is learned and passed down by imitation and custom. For centuries, for example, children have learned games, such as jump rope and

tic-tac-toe, by watching and imitating other youngsters. Customary greetings, such as shaking hands in Western culture or bowing in Asian countries, are also learned by observing others rather than from books or school.

As people move from one land to another, they carry their folklore to new areas and adapt it to new surroundings. From the 1500's to the 1800's, for example, European and American slave traders brought thousands of West Africans to the Western Hemisphere as slaves. Many slaves shared with one another West African folk tales about a sly spider named Anansi. Through the years, the slaves continued to tell tales of Anansi, though the stories gradually changed to reflect life in the New World. In the southern United States, for example, the spider's name was often changed to Miss Nancy.

Origins of folklore

Scholars once associated folklore with uneducated people who could not read or write, or with people in isolated rural societies whose ways of life had changed little for hundreds of years. The scholars thought that after people moved to cities, they gradually lost touch with "authentic" folk traditions. However, modern scholars realize that the transition to city life did not displace folklore. In fact, new folklore traditions developed with city life, including urban legends and e-mail jokes.

Modern scholars consider a folk to be any group of people who share at least one common linking factor. This factor may be geography, as in the folklore of the Ozark Mountains region; religious heritage, as in Jewish folklore; a shared occupation, as in military folklore; or ethnic background, as in Irish American folklore. Even a family or a group of friends can have a folklore made up of its own traditions and stories.

Many scholars have noticed common themes in folklore from around the world. Two German brothers, Jakob and Wilhelm Grimm, were among the first folklore scholars to point out such themes. From 1807 to 1814, they collected folk tales from peasants who lived near Kassel, Germany. The stories they collected became famous as *Grimm's Fairy Tales.* The Grimms be-

Coyote Changing the Moon by Eating It by Daniel Stolpe, Native Images Gallery

The trickster is a central figure in the folklore of many cultures. Coyote, a popular trickster in American Indian folklore, tries to eat the moon in this woodcut based on a Maidu Indian myth.

Elements of folklore often appear in regional arts and crafts. The *hex signs* on this barn, for example, show the influence of the Pennsylvania Dutch, German immigrants who came to Pennsylvania in the 1600's and 1700's. They painted the sign of a star in a circle to protect against evil spirits. Today, the symbols serve mainly as decorations.

© J. Irwin, Robertstock

lieved that by collecting the tales, they were preserving the heritage of all Germans. But they realized that similar versions of their tales existed throughout Europe, the Middle East, and Asia.

Characteristics of folklore

Folklore can be short and simple or long and complicated. Brief proverbs, such as "Time flies" and "Money talks," are short examples of folklore. Some Indonesian folk plays, on the other hand, begin at sundown and end at dawn. Many types of folklore are spoken or sung, but others consist of behavior or gestures. For instance, Americans usually point to their chest when referring to themselves, while Japanese point to their nose. Folklore may also include everyday arts and crafts, buildings, and household objects. For example, people in many cultures make scarecrows, a common folk craft, to keep birds out of gardens.

To be considered authentic folklore, an item must exist in more than one version. Typically, the item also has existed in more than one period and place. For example, scholars have identified more than 1,000 versions of the fairy tale about Cinderella. These versions developed through hundreds of years in many countries, including China, France, Germany, and Turkey.

Changes in folklore often occur as it passes from person to person. These changes, called *variations,* are one of the surest indications that the item is true folklore. Variations frequently appear in both the words and music of folk songs. The same lyrics may be used with different tunes, or different words may be set to the same music. The nursery rhymes "Baa, Baa Black Sheep" and "Twinkle, Twinkle Little Star" have the same melody. Some people use the folk saying "As slow as molasses," others "As slow as molasses in January," and still others "As slow as molasses in January running uphill."

Kinds of folklore

Myths are religious stories that explain how the world and humanity developed into their present form. Myths differ from most types of folk stories because myths are considered to be true among the people who develop them.

Many myths describe the creation of Earth. In some of these stories, a figure creates Earth out of dust or mud. In others, Earth emerges from a flood or mist. A number of myths describe the creation of life and the origin of death.

Folk tales are fictional stories about animals or human beings. Most of these tales are not set in any particular time or place, and they begin and end in a certain way. For example, many English folk tales begin with the phrase "Once upon a time" and end with "They lived happily ever after."

Fables are a popular type of folk tale. They are animal stories that try to teach people how to behave. One fable describes a race between a tortoise and a hare. The tor-

Miniature (early 1300's) from the *Manesse Song Manuscript* by an unknown Swiss painter; Heidelberg University Library

Medieval folk musicians traveled throughout France and Germany. They often entertained royalty with long, elaborate songs that celebrated the heroic deeds of legendary kings and knights.

Fairy tales from around the world often share common themes. This illustration comes from a Korean folk tale similar to the story of Cinderella. In both of the stories, a poor girl's hard work is rewarded with the help of a motherly figure with magical powers. Scholars have identified more than 1,000 versions of the Cinderella story. To be considered true folklore, a story must have at least two versions.

Korean Cinderella ©1982 Seoul International Publishing House/deGrummond Children's
Literature Collection, McCain Library, University of Southern Mississippi

toise, though it is a far slower animal, wins because the hare foolishly stops to sleep. This story teaches the lesson that someone who works steadily can come out ahead of a person who is faster or has a head start.

In many European fairy tales, the hero or heroine leaves home to seek some goal. After various adventures, he or she wins a prize or a marriage partner, in many cases a prince or princess.

One popular kind of folk tale has a trickster as the hero. Each culture has its own trickster figure. Most tricksters are animals who act like human beings. In Africa, tricksters include the tortoise; the hare; and Anansi, the spider. The coyote is a popular trickster in North American Indian folklore. Jokes that consist of short funny stories are another type of folk tale.

Folk tales have inspired many famous works of literature. The English poet Geoffrey Chaucer used a number of folk tales in his *Canterbury Tales.* William Shakespeare based the plots of several of his plays on folk tales. These plays include *King Lear, The Merchant of Venice,* and *The Taming of the Shrew.*

Legends, like myths, are stories told as though they were true. However, legends are set in the real world and in relatively recent times. Certain legends have attracted artists, composers, and writers for centuries. One legend tells about a medieval German scholar named Faust who sold his soul to the devil. This legend has been the basis of many novels, plays, operas, and orchestral works.

Folklore includes many legendary heroes. Robin Hood was a legendary English hero who stole from the rich and gave to the poor. In Swiss legends, William Tell was an expert with a crossbow who resisted tyranny. Davy Crockett was a famous American frontiersman who was elected to the U.S. Congress from Tennessee in 1827. After Crockett died in the battle of the Alamo in 1836, he became a popular figure in American folklore. John Henry is the African American hero of many legends in the South. A famous ballad describes how he competed against a steam drill in a race to see whether

a man or a machine could dig a tunnel faster. Using only a hammer, John Henry won, but he died of exhaustion.

Many legends tell about human beings who meet supernatural creatures, such as fairies, ghosts, vampires, and witches. Others tell of holy persons and religious leaders. Some legends describe how saints work miracles or bless places or things.

The action in myths and folk tales ends at the conclusion of the story. But the action in many legends has not been completed by the story's end. For example, a legend about a buried treasure may end by saying that the treasure has not yet been found. A legend about a haunted house may suggest that the house is still haunted. A number of legends tell of creatures that may exist but are rarely seen, such as the Loch Ness monster, a sea serpent in Scotland; and the Yeti, a hairy beast in the Himalaya. From time to time, scientific expeditions have tried to find evidence that these creatures actually exist.

Legends also develop about the present day. Just before 2000, for example, legends predicted that widespread disasters would result from the *millennium bug,* a problem that caused some computers to malfunction starting on Jan. 1, 2000.

Folk songs have been created for almost every human activity. Many are associated with work. For example, sailors sing songs called *chanteys* while pulling in their lines. Folk songs may deal with birth, childhood, courtship, marriage, or death. Parents sing folk lullabies to babies. Children sing traditional songs as part of games and share funny imitations of commercial jingles.

Some folk songs are related to seasonal activities, such as planting and harvesting. Many are sung on certain holidays and festivals. The folk song "The Twelve Days of Christmas" is a well-known carol. Other folk songs are sung at weddings and funerals. Some folk songs celebrate the deeds of real or imaginary heroes, or build a sense of community through singing.

Superstitions and customs are involved largely in marking a person's advancement from one stage of life to another. For example, many cultures include a custom

Black folk dances in America developed from West African religious dances. From the early 1600's to the mid-1800's, thousands of West Africans were transported to the Western Hemisphere as slaves. This water-color painting of the late 1700's shows Southern plantation slaves performing a folk dance. Their musical instruments also originated in West Africa.

Abby Aldrich Rockefeller Folk Art Center (Colonial Williamsburg)

called *couvade* to protect unborn babies. In couvade, husbands pretend that they are about to give birth. They may avoid eating certain foods considered harmful to the expected baby or avoid working because such activity could cause injury to the unborn child.

A wedding custom called *charivari* is widespread in some European societies. On the wedding night, friends of the bride and groom provide a noisy serenade by banging on pots and pans outside the couple's bedroom. The desire to avoid charivari led to the practice of leaving on a honeymoon immediately after a wedding.

Many superstitions and customs supposedly help affect or predict the future. The people of fishing communities may hold elaborate ceremonies that are designed to ensure a good catch. Astrologers try to foretell future events by analyzing the relationships among the planets and stars. Children may also make folded paper "fortune tellers" to playfully predict the future.

Holidays are special occasions celebrated by a group, and almost all of them include folklore. Christmas is especially rich in folklore. A group may celebrate this holiday with its own special foods and costumes. Many groups have variations of the same folk custom. In a number of countries, for example, children receive presents on Christmas. In the United States, Santa Claus brings the presents. In Italy, an old woman named La Befana distributes the gifts. In some countries of Europe, the gifts come from the Christ child. In others, the Three Wise Men bring them.   Simon J. Bronner

Related articles in *World Book* include:

Kinds of folklore

Ballad	Folk art	Mythology	Riddle
Dance (Folk dances)	Folk dancing	Nursery rhyme	Romance
	Folk music		Saga
Epic	Legend	Proverb	Superstition
Fable	Limerick		

American folklore and legends

Appleseed, Johnny	Crockett, Davy
Blackbeard	Feboldson, Febold
Bunyan, Paul	Fink, Mike
Frietchie, Barbara	Laffite, Jean
Henry, John	Magarac, Joe
Jones, Casey	Pecos Bill
Kidd, William	Rip Van Winkle

British folklore and legends

Arthur, King	Lancelot, Sir
Beowulf	Launfal, Sir
Bruce, Robert	Loch Ness
Brut	monster
Excalibur	Peter Pan
Galahad, Sir	Rob Roy
Godiva, Lady	Robin Hood
Guy of Warwick	Round Table
Holy Grail	Turpin, Dick
Jones, Davy	

German folklore and legends

Brunhild	Munchausen, Baron
Fafnir	Nibelungenlied
Faust	Pied Piper of Hamelin
Grimm's Fairy Tales	Siegfried
Lorelei	Tannhauser
Mephistopheles	

Irish folklore and legends

Banshee	Finn MacCool
Blarney Stone	Giant's Causeway
Cuchulainn	Shamrock

Other folklore and legends

Aesop's fables	Literature for children (Traditional literature; Fractured folklore)
Amadis of Gaul	
Arabian Nights	
Cid, The	Mother Goose
Don Juan	Roland
Dragon	Santa Claus
Edda	Storytelling
Fairy	Tell, William
Flying Dutchman	Vampire
Fountain of Youth	Werewolf
Gilgamesh, Epic of	Winkelried, Arnold von
Gnome	Witchcraft (Witchcraft as sorcery)
Jack Frost	
Jinni	Yeti

Folkway. See Mores.

Folsom point, a type of prehistoric spearhead, was the first evidence that human beings lived in North America during the Ice Age. A cowboy first discovered the stone points near Folsom, New Mexico, during the early 1900's. In 1926, scientists found the spearheads mingled with the bones of an extinct species of bison and identified the points as prehistoric weapons. The ancient bison disappeared about 10,000 years ago, following the end of the last ice age. The discovery of weapons with the bison bones proved that people had migrated to North America by about 8000 B.C.

P. Hollembeak and J. Beckett,
American Museum of Natural History

A Folsom point is a long, thin, prehistoric spearhead.

Before the discovery of the Folsom point, most scientists had believed that the first people had come to the Americas more recently. Most scientists today think the spearheads are 10,000 to 11,000 years old. Researchers have also discovered Folsom points in New Mexico, Colorado, and Texas.

Folsom points differ from later spearheads in that they have a long, thin shape rather than a triangular one. Folsom points also have a long flake of rock removed down the center of one or both faces. The groove created by removing the flake is called a *flute,* and this type of stone point is called a *fluted* point. Dean Snow

See also **Indian, American** (The first Americans [picture: Spear points]).

Fonda, Henry (1905-1982), was an American stage and motion-picture actor. He became famous for his portrayals of leading men of integrity and for his seemingly effortless acting style. Fonda appeared in more than 80 films. His most famous role was the title character in the comedy *Mr. Roberts,* which he played on both stage (1948) and screen (1955).

Fonda won the 1981 Academy Award as best actor for his performance in *On Golden Pond,* in which he co-starred with his daughter, Jane. He also received acclaim for his performances in *The Trail of the Lonesome Pine* (1936), *Young Mr. Lincoln* (1939), *The Grapes of Wrath* (1940), *The Lady Eve* (1941), *The Ox-Bow Incident* (1943), and *Twelve Angry Men* (1957). His son, Peter, is a film actor and director.

Henry Jaynes Fonda was born on May 16, 1905, in

Indelible, Inc.

Henry Fonda

Grand Island, Nebraska. He first gained recognition for his performance in the Broadway revue *New Faces* (1934). Fonda made his film debut in *The Farmer Takes a Wife* (1935). *Fonda: My Life* (1981) is his autobiography. He died on Aug. 12, 1982. Rachel Gallagher

Fonda, Jane (1937-   ), an American motion-picture actress, won Academy Awards as best actress for her performances in *Klute* (1971) and *Coming Home* (1978). She has appeared in more than 45 films, many of which she co-produced through her own company.

Jane Seymour Fonda was born on Dec. 21, 1937, in New York City. She is the daughter of the actor Henry Fonda. She made her film debut in *Tall Story* (1960). Her other films include *A Walk on the Wild Side* (1962), *Cat Ballou* (1965), *Barbarella* (1968), *They Shoot Horses, Don't They?* (1969), *Julia* (1977), *The China Syndrome* (1979), and *The Morning After* (1987). In 1981, she co-starred with her father in *On Golden Pond.* After appearing in *Stanley and Iris* in 1990, Jane Fonda did not make another film until *Monster-in-Law* in 2005. She also starred in *Peace, Love, and Misunderstanding* (2012) and *Lee Daniels' The Butler* (2013).

Fonda became noted for her antiwar views during American participation in the Vietnam War from 1965 to 1973 and for her work as a political activist. She is also known for her physical fitness workout programs. Fonda was married to French motion-picture director Roger

AP/Wide World

Jane Fonda

Vadim from 1965 to 1973, American political activist and politician Tom Hayden from 1973 to 1990, and American broadcasting executive Ted Turner from 1991 to 2001. Her brother, Peter Fonda, is also an actor. She wrote an autobiography, *My Life So Far* (2005), and a memoir and self-help book, *Prime Time* (2011). Rachel Gallagher

Fong, Hiram Leong (1906-2004), a Republican from Hawaii, was the first Asian American to serve in the United States Senate. He held office from 1959 to 1977. As a political leader, he worked to promote harmony among Hawaii's various ethnic groups.

The son of Chinese immigrants, Fong was born on Oct. 15, 1906, in Honolulu. He went to work at an early age to help his family, which included 10 brothers and sisters. He put himself through college, earning a doctorate from Harvard Law School in 1935. In 1942, Fong founded a law firm. Later in 1942, Fong joined the Army Air Forces and served as a major until 1944. He became wealthy by buying real estate and a banana plantation.

Fong served in Hawaii's territorial House of Representatives from 1938 to 1954. In 1959, when Hawaii became a state, he was elected to one of its two U.S. Senate seats. He was reelected in 1964 and 1970. Fong was considered a liberal Republican early in his Senate career, but he supported the conservative policies of President Richard M. Nixon in the late 1960's and early 1970's. Fong died on Aug. 18, 2004. Jackie Koszczuk

Fontainebleau, *FAHN tihn BLOH* or *fawn tehn BLOH* (pop. 15,688), a small city in northern France, is famous

The château of Fontainebleau is a famous French Renaissance palace. The structure is known for its diverse architectural styles, beautifully decorated interiors, and magnificent gardens.

for a magnificent *château* (castle) that stands in a nearby forest. The city lies about 35 miles (56 kilometers) southeast of Paris. For the location of Fontainebleau, see **France** (political map).

King Francis I transformed a medieval castle into the château of Fontainebleau in the early 1500's. King Louis XIII, who reigned from 1610 to 1643, was responsible for much of its construction. French kings continued to add to and remodel the château as late as the 1700's. As a result, the structure displays various architectural and decorative styles. It has many paintings and elegant carvings by the Italian artists Francesco Primaticcio and Rosso Fiorentino. The ballroom and the Francis I gallery feature especially impressive works of art. The château also has a small museum of Chinese art objects collected by Empress Eugénie, the wife of Emperor Napoleon III.

Many French kings used the château of Fontainebleau as a summer home. In 1814, Emperor Napoleon I gave up the throne of France at the château.   William M. Reddy

Fontane, Theodor (1819-1898), a German author, became known for his realistic and critical novels about Prussian society during the 1800's. Many of his works vividly portray the manners, morals, and social activities of the upper classes in Prussia. In his portrayal of characters and society, Fontane blends precise observation with humor, compassion, and irony.

Most of Fontane's stories take place in Berlin and the surrounding countryside. Most of his novels deal with personal conflicts of the chief characters, many of whom are women. Fontane's masterpiece, *Effi Briest* (1895), is a realistic yet sympathetic account of marital estrangement, adultery, and divorce. Several of his other novels also deal with love and marriage in a traditional, class-conscious society, including *Trials and Tribulations* (1888), *Beyond Recall* (1891), and *Jenny Treibel* (1892). He depicts the decline of the Prussian aristocracy in *A Man of Honor* (1883) and *The Poggenpuhl Family* (1896).

Fontane was born in the province of Brandenburg. He was almost 60 years old when his first novel was published. Before that time, Fontane was known as an author of ballads and travel books.   Werner Hoffmeister

Fontanne, *fahn TAN,* **Lynn** (1887-1983), was an American actress. She and her husband, Alfred Lunt, became the most celebrated acting team of their time. Fontanne was a sophisticated, glamorous, and accomplished performer. She was best known for her leading roles in *The*

Guardsman (1924), *Strange Interlude* (1928), *Elizabeth the Queen* (1930), *Reunion in Vienna* (1931), *Design for Living* (1933), *The Great Sebastians* (1956), and *The Visit* (1958). Lunt was her co-star in all these plays except *Strange Interlude.* See **Lunt, Alfred.**

Fontanne was born near London, England. Her given first and middle names were Lillie Louise. She made her acting debut in 1905. She first visited America in 1910 and settled in the United States in 1916. She achieved her first major success in 1921 in *Dulcy.* In 1922, she married Alfred Lunt.   Daniel J. Watermeier

Fonteyn, *fahn TAYN,* **Margot** (1919-1991), is generally considered the greatest British ballerina of the 1900's. Critics praised her precise technique and the warmth and delicacy of her style. Sir Frederick Ashton, a great English *choreographer* (dance creator), created many ballets for her, including *Daphnis and Chloë* and *Symphonic Variations.* Fonteyn gave perhaps her greatest performances in Ashton's *Ondine.* She and Ashton established a refined form of dancing that became known as the *British style.*

Fonteyn was born in Reigate, England. Her real name

Margot Fonteyn is often considered the greatest British ballerina of all time. In 1962, Fonteyn formed a partnership with Russian-born dancer Rudolf Nureyev, *shown with her in this photo.*

was Margaret Hookham. At age 14, Fonteyn began dancing with the Vic-Wells Ballet (now the Royal Ballet) in London. In 1962, she began her partnership with the Russian-born dancer Rudolf Nureyev. Queen Elizabeth II named her a Dame Commander in the Order of the British Empire in 1956, and she became known as Dame Margot Fonteyn.   Joan Brock Pikula

Foochow. See Fuzhou.

An American family eating at a fast-food restaurant

WORLD BOOK photo

A family in Senegal eating from a common bowl

Owen Franken, Stock, Boston

Saudi Arabian men feasting on camel meat and rice

© Tor Eigeland, Alamy Images

A French couple lunching on cheeses and cold cuts

Owen Franken, Stock, Boston

Food is a basic necessity of life. In addition, people everywhere enjoy eating. However, the kinds of food that people eat and how much food they have differ greatly around the world. There are also wide differences in the ways that people of various cultures prepare, serve, and eat food.

Food

Food is one of our most basic needs. We cannot live without it. Food gives us the energy for everything we do—walking, talking, working, playing, reading, and even thinking and breathing. Food also provides the energy our nerves, muscles, heart, and glands need to work. In addition, food supplies the nourishing substances our bodies require to build and repair tissues and to regulate body organs and systems.

All living things must have food to live. Green plants use the energy of sunlight to make food out of *carbon dioxide* (a gas in the air) and water and other substances from the soil. Other living things depend on the food made by green plants. The food that people and other animals eat comes chiefly from plants or from animals that eat plants.

Food does more than help keep us alive, strong, and healthy. Food also adds pleasure to living. We enjoy the flavors, odors, colors, and textures of foods. We celebrate special occasions with our favorite meals and feasts.

Although most of the food we eat comes from plants or animals, the variety of foods is remarkable. Plants provide such basic foods as grains, fruits, and vegetables. Animals provide meat, eggs, and milk. These basic foods may require little or no preparation before they are eaten. Or they may be greatly changed by processing. For example, milk may be made into such foods as butter, cheese, ice cream, and yogurt.

The chief foods that people eat differ widely throughout the world. People in Asia commonly eat rice with their meals. In the Pacific Islands, people depend heavily on fish. People in Turkey eat cracked-wheat bread and yogurt. In Argentina and Uruguay, beef forms an important part of people's diets.

What people eat depends chiefly on where they live and on how much money they have. It also depends on their customs, health, lifestyle, and religious beliefs. Children learn many eating habits from their parents. However, each person develops individual food preferences and prejudices. Eating habits are also influenced by how much time people have to buy, prepare, and eat food.

In developing countries, many families must produce all their food themselves. In the United States, Canada, and other developed countries, however, most people rely on the *food industry* for their food. The food industry includes farmers, food-processing companies, researchers, shipping companies, and food stores. The

© Chad Ehlers, Alamy Images

A Japanese family dining at home

© Borderlands/Alamy Images

Bolivian women eating potatoes during a festival

growth of the food industry has greatly increased the amount and kinds of foods available in developed countries.

The supply of food is a major concern of the human race. In many areas of the world, millions of people go hungry and many die of starvation. Food shortages and famine result from crop failures, natural disasters, overpopulation, wars, and other causes. For detailed information about food supply problems, see the articles **Food supply** and **Famine.**

Sources of food

Plants supply most of the food people eat. In many African, Asian, and Latin American countries, the people depend on plants for more than two-thirds of their food. In Australia, Europe, North America, and parts of South America, the people eat much meat. But even in these areas, over half the diet consists of food from plants.

Consumers commonly buy some basic foods, including eggs, fruits, and vegetables, in their natural form. But basic foods are also processed before they reach the market. Most other foods, such as meat and milk, are processed.

All canned, dried, frozen, and pickled foods have been processed. Processors also produce baked goods, frozen dinners, and many other *convenience foods,*

which save work for the cook when preparing a meal.

Food from plants. The most important foods obtained from plants are (1) grains and (2) fruits and vegetables.

Grains, also called *cereals,* are the seeds of such plants as barley, corn, millet, oats, rice, rye, sorghum, and wheat. The human diet has been based on grains for thousands of years. Rice or a grain product, particularly bread, is the main food in many cultures. Millers grind much of the world's grain, especially wheat, into flour. Wheat flour is used in almost all breads, in pastries, and in macaroni and other kinds of noodles. Processors also make breakfast cereals from grains.

Fruits and vegetables add a variety of colors, flavors, and textures to the diet. Popular fruits include apples, bananas, cherries, melons, oranges, peaches, pineapples, and strawberries. Most fruits are eaten as snacks or in a salad or dessert.

Favorite vegetables include beans, broccoli, cabbage, carrots, celery, lettuce, onions, peas, potatoes, and sweet corn. Vegetables are commonly eaten during the main part of a meal. They may be served raw in a salad, cooked and served with a sauce, or added to a soup.

Other foods from plants include nuts, herbs and spices, and beverages. Coffee, cocoa, tea, and many other drinks are made from plants. Nuts are popular snacks and can be used as flavorings in other foods. Cooks also use herbs and spices to flavor foods.

Food manufacturers use plant materials to make cooking oils, sugar, and syrups. They also use plants to

Interesting facts about food

Dumplings are eaten In various forms around the world. Chinese *won ton,* Italian *ravioli,* Jewish *kreplach,* and Polish *pierogi* are types of dumplings filled with meat, cheese, or vegetables.

Frankfurters, also known as *hot dogs,* were named after Frankfurt (am Main), Germany. Experts believe these sausages were first made in Germany during the Middle Ages. About 1900, an American vendor selling cooked frankfurters supposedly called them "hot dachshund sausages" because they resembled the long-bodied dog.

Hamburger was originally called *Hamburg steak.* It was named after Hamburg, Germany.

Hundred-year-old eggs, a delicacy in China, are preserved duck eggs. They are cured in the shell for about six months in a mixture of ashes, lime, salt, and tea. The curing makes the eggs taste like cheese.

Ice cream cones were first served at the St. Louis World's Fair in 1904. A thin, crisp waffle was rolled into a handy holder for a scoop of ice cream.

Pancakes are probably the oldest prepared food. The first pancakes were a mixture of pounded grain and water spread on a hot stone. Today, people enjoy such pancake variations as French *crepes,* Hungarian *palacintas,* Indian *dosai,* Jewish *blintzes,* and Russian *blini.*

Pizza, as we know it today, originated in Italy. The first modern pizza was topped with green basil, white mozzarella cheese, and red tomato sauce to reflect the colors of Italy's flag.

Pretzels, according to tradition, were first made in the 600's by European monks as a reward for children who learned their prayers. The crossed ends of a pretzel represent praying hands.

Raw fish is a favorite food of many people. The Japanese enjoy *sashimi,* thin slices of raw seafood. *Ceviche* is a popular Latin-American appetizer of raw fish in lime juice. Swedes prepare *gravlax,* cured salmon with dill.

Sandwiches were named after the Earl of Sandwich, an English nobleman of the 1700's. While playing cards, he ordered a servant to bring him two slices of bread with a piece of roast meat between them.

WORLD BOOK photo

The variety of foods is amazing. This picture shows a few of the products—breads, breakfast cereals, pastas, pancakes, pastries, and snack foods—that can be made from wheat.

make imitation foods. For example, they make foods that look and taste like meats from soybeans. They make nondairy creamers from vegetable fats.

Food from animals includes (1) meat, (2) eggs, and (3) dairy products. These foods cost more to produce than do foods from plants. As a result, foods from animals are eaten more in developed countries than in developing ones.

Meat consists mainly of the muscle, fat, and other parts of an animal's body. The word *meat* most commonly means the red meat of cattle, hogs, sheep, and game animals. However, the flesh of fish and poultry is also considered meat.

In the United States and Canada, popular red meats include beef and veal from cattle, pork from hogs, and lamb and mutton from sheep. Many Americans and Canadians also enjoy kidney, liver, tongue, and other *variety meats.* Favorite fish include cod, perch, salmon, trout, and tuna. Clams, crabs, lobsters, oysters, scallops, and shrimp are favorite shellfish. The most popular kinds of poultry are chicken, duck, goose, and turkey. In some countries, people enjoy the meat of caribou, goats, horses, monkeys, rabbits, or snakes. They might also eat ants, grasshoppers, snails, or turtles.

Much poultry is marketed as the whole animal. Many other meats are sold as *cuts,* such as chops and steaks. Meat usually is heated before it is eaten. Heating develops the flavor and destroys microbes that may cause illness if present in the meat. Ham and corned beef are *cured* (preserved) before being marketed. Meats also are processed into such products as frankfurters and cold cuts. Meat is commonly eaten during the main part of a meal.

Eggs. Farmers raise poultry, especially chickens, for their eggs as well as for their meat. Chicken eggs are popular as a breakfast or supper dish, or they can be used in custards and other cooked dishes. The eggs of certain kinds of fish are used to make a delicacy called *caviar.* In some countries, people enjoy the eggs of such birds as emus, gulls, or penguins. People of various countries also eat the eggs of alligators, crocodiles, or certain other reptiles.

Dairy products are important foods in many cultures. Cows provide most of the milk used in the United States and Canada. But such animals as camels, goats, reindeer, and sheep supply milk in other parts of the world. Milk and milk products reach the market in many forms. In addition to whole milk, people can buy buttermilk, skim milk, low-fat milk, and condensed, dried, and evaporated milk. Other products include butter, cheese, cream, ice cream, sour cream, and yogurt.

How the body uses food

Food supplies the *nutrients* (nourishing substances) that the body needs for (1) producing energy, (2) building and repairing tissues, and (3) regulating body processes. The main kinds of nutrients are water, carbohydrates, fats, proteins, minerals, and vitamins. Each kind of nutrient plays an important role in keeping the body healthy. Many foods are highly nourishing, but no one food supplies every necessary nutrient.

As the body digests food, the food is broken down into the various nutrients. The food eventually enters the small intestine, and the nutrients pass through the intestinal wall into the bloodstream. The blood distributes the nutrients to cells throughout the body.

In addition to nutrients, food supplies other important substances, especially water and fiber. Every living thing must maintain a certain water supply, or it will die. Fiber adds bulk to food and keeps waste products moving through the intestine.

People who do not get enough food to eat suffer from *undernutrition.* A person whose diet seriously lacks any nutrient is said to be *malnourished.* Some malnourished people have plenty of food, but they choose to eat foods that do not supply all the necessary nutrients. Some people develop health problems because they eat too much and become overweight.

A moderate, well-balanced diet can help ensure good health. For detailed information about the foods that contribute to a healthful diet, see **Nutrition.**

Producing energy. One of the most important ways in which the body uses food is to produce energy. The proteins in food can be used to provide energy. But carbohydrates and fats serve as the major energy sources. Carbohydrates are the starches and sugars in food. Grains and potatoes are good sources of starch. Sugars include table sugar, found in candy and other sweets, and the sugars in fruits and milk. Fats are found in eggs, meats, milk, nuts, certain vegetables, and other foods.

During digestion, carbohydrates are broken down into *simple sugars,* and fats are broken down into *fatty acids* and *glycerol.* In the body's cells, these materials, along with oxygen and other substances, take part in chemical reactions. Some of these reactions assemble molecules into new materials. Other reactions then break down the new materials to release energy. See **Cell** (Producing energy).

Some of this energy enables us to perform our daily

activities and powers the heart, lungs, and other organs. The remainder is heat, which helps keep the body temperature at about 98.6 °F (37 °C). Without this heat, the body would be unable to function properly.

Building and repairing tissues. Bones, muscles, and other body tissues constantly wear out and need to be repaired or replaced. In addition, growth depends on the formation of new tissues. The body uses the proteins in food to build and repair tissue.

All body tissues consist mainly of proteins. Proteins, in turn, are made up of chemical units called *amino acids.* The human body must obtain certain amino acids from the proteins in foods to make the proteins it needs. Digestion breaks down the proteins in foods into amino acids. The body then combines the amino acids into the kinds of proteins it requires.

Animal foods, such as meat, eggs, and dairy products, are especially rich in proteins. In addition, these proteins have all the amino acids the body needs. Grains, nuts, peanuts, and dried beans and peas are also high in protein. But many plant foods lack one or more essential amino acids.

Some minerals help build body tissues. For example, calcium, phosphorus, and magnesium help build bones and teeth. Milk and other dairy products are good sources of these minerals. Iron is required for normal red blood cells. Red meat is an excellent source of iron and other minerals that the body needs in small amounts.

Regulating body processes. The body uses proteins not only to build and repair tissues but also to help regulate various body processes. Certain proteins called *enzymes* speed up chemical reactions in the body. Enzymes help the body produce energy, digest food, and build other proteins. Many *hormones,* which regulate chemical activities throughout the body, are proteins. The *antibodies* that the body makes to fight infection are also proteins. All these proteins, like the proteins in body tissues, are made in the body from the amino acids in the food we eat.

The minerals and vitamins in food also play a major role in many body processes. People need only small amounts of minerals and vitamins. But these nutrients are just as important for good health as are water, carbohydrates, fats, and proteins.

Minerals aid in numerous body processes. For example, iron and copper help build red blood cells. Sodium and other minerals regulate the amount of water in the body's cells. Calcium is necessary for blood clotting. Other important minerals are chlorine, cobalt, fluorine, iodine, magnesium, manganese, tin, and zinc.

Vitamins perform a variety of functions. They aid growth and help protect the body from disease. Vitamin A helps us see at night and promotes healthy bones, skin, and teeth. Various B vitamins help the body use carbohydrates, fats, and proteins for energy. Vitamin C is necessary for healthy blood vessels and sound bones and teeth. Vitamin D helps the body use calcium and phosphorus.

Vitamins and minerals are found in a variety of foods. A well-balanced diet provides an adequate supply of all the vitamins and minerals a person needs. A shortage of certain vitamins can cause disease. For example, too little vitamin C causes scurvy, which is marked by sore gums and bleeding under the skin. Too little vitamin D can lead to rickets, a bone disease.

Why diets differ around the world

The kinds of food that people eat vary from one country to another and even within countries. In some countries, for example, the people eat much meat. In some other countries, meat is served only on special occasions. People who are *vegetarians* eat no meat at all. Many people like certain foods that other people find very unappetizing. The Chinese use the nests of birds called swifts to make bird's-nest soup. The birds build the nests with their saliva.

People of various cultures also prepare foods differently. In many cases, the fuel resources and cooking equipment available determine how foods are prepared. Thus, some people cook foods over an open fire. Others may use a microwave oven. Still others may eat most of their foods raw. Some people add fiery spices to their dishes. Others prefer little seasoning. Some people eat only natural, or unprocessed, foods. Others eat foods that have been highly processed.

Diets differ for a number of reasons, including (1) geographic reasons, (2) economic reasons, (3) religious reasons, and (4) customs. But differences in diet are not as great as they once were. The growth of tourism and the development of modern transportation and communication systems have led to an exchange of foods and eating habits among people throughout the world.

Geographic reasons. The location, climate, and physical features of a region help determine what the people of that region eat. In general, people who live on islands or along seacoasts depend heavily on foods from the ocean. People who live far from the sea rely mainly on livestock or grains for food. People of tropical areas can grow a variety of fruits and vegetables the year around. People who live in cool regions, which have a short growing season, depend on such crops as grains or potatoes. Terrain and soil also help determine what crops the people of a region can grow. For example, corn grows best on level, open fields with rich, well-drained soil. Rice grows best in lowland areas where the soil holds water well.

Although geography still strongly influences what people in many parts of the world eat, its importance has declined—especially in industrial countries. The development of faster transportation and of modern methods of food preservation enables many people to eat foods produced in distant lands. For example, people in numerous countries enjoy bananas from Ecuador, olives and oranges from Spain, dairy products from New Zealand, and sardines from Norway. In addition, many farmers have learned how to grow crops in unfavorable areas. Where land is hilly, for example, they might carve strips of land out of the hillsides. In dry areas, farmers might use irrigation. In areas with cold winters, they might grow certain fruits and vegetables in greenhouses during the winter.

Economic reasons. The variety and amount of food that people have to eat depend largely on their country's economy. But even in the richest countries, some people cannot afford a good diet. Others simply choose to eat foods that are not nourishing. But some people in the poorest countries have a well-balanced diet.

© Shutterstock

© Travel Pictures/Alamy Images

Where people live influences what foods they eat. Indonesian workers harvest seaweed, *above left.* It forms an important part of the diet in east Asia. A northern African woman gathers and dries dates for food, *above right.* The date palm grows easily in the region's hot, dry climate.

Most developed countries can produce all the food their people need, or the countries can afford to import the extra necessary supplies. The farmers use modern machinery and scientific methods to increase their production. Developed countries also have modern facilities to process, transport, and store food.

In highly developed countries, most families can afford to buy a variety of foods, and they are more likely to have a well-balanced diet. Their diet is rich in meat, eggs, and dairy products. They also eat large amounts of grain products and of fresh and preserved fruits and vegetables. They also enjoy the convenience of prepared or ready-to-cook foods. They often dine at restaurants or buy take-out food to eat at home.

Most developing countries seldom produce enough food for all their people. In addition, the countries cannot afford to import the extra supplies they need. Many farmers are too poor to buy fertilizers, machinery, and other materials that would increase their output. Developing countries also lack modern facilities for processing, transporting, and storing food.

In some developing nations, many people suffer from an inadequate diet. They are too poor to buy all the food they need or a wide variety of foods. Millions of families depend on the foods they can produce themselves on small plots of land. Grains and other carbohydrates are the main foods of the majority of people in most developing countries. These foods are the least costly to produce or buy, and they require no refrigeration or other special storage. Meat, milk, and eggs are too expensive for most people. Many families bake their own bread and make most other foods from the basic ingredients. They might even grind grain into flour to make bread.

Religious reasons. Many religions have rules that deal with food. Some religions do not permit their members to eat certain foods. Hindus do not eat beef be-

cause cattle are considered sacred. Some groups of Hindus are forbidden to eat any meat. Orthodox Jews do not eat pork, shellfish, and certain other foods. They also follow strict dietary laws regarding the storing, preparing, and serving of food.

Some religions set aside certain days for fasting and feasting. Muslims may not eat or drink from dawn to sunset during Ramadan, the ninth month of the Islamic year. They celebrate Ramadan's end with a feast.

Customs influence what people eat and how they prepare, serve, and eat foods. Many countries and regions have traditional dishes, most of which are based on locally produced foods. In many cases, the dishes of various cultures include the same basic ingredients. But different seasonings and cooking methods give the dish a special regional or national flavor. In the United States, for example, people enjoy such distinctively different chicken dishes as Southern-fried chicken, Louisiana chicken creole, and Texas-style barbecued chicken.

Many people consider France to be the world center of fine foods and cookery. French chefs are especially known for their elaborate dishes with rich sauces and for their fancy pastries. Perhaps the most famous English dish is roast beef and *Yorkshire pudding,* a batter pudding baked in beef juices. Italy is known for its spaghetti, macaroni, and other *pastas* and for its sauces made with tomatoes, garlic, and olive oil. Sausages, potatoes, cabbage, and beer are common in the German diet. Scandinavians enjoy herring and other fish. They also make excellent cheeses and many kinds of breads.

The Spanish and Portuguese also eat much fish. Their use of onions and garlic for seasoning influenced cookery in the Caribbean islands, Mexico, and other parts of Latin America that they colonized. Caribbean cooking features such local fruits and vegetables as *plantains* (a kind of banana) and *cassava* (a starchy root). Mexican food is noted for its use of a variety of peppers. Mexicans enjoy flat breads, called *tortillas,* made from corn or wheat flour. They may eat the tortillas plain or wrapped around cheese, meat, and beans to form *tacos.*

The main food of many people in the Middle East is *pita bread,* a flat bread made from wheat. For celebrations, people of the region often prepare *shish kebab.* This dish consists of cubes of lamb, tomatoes, peppers, and onions roasted on a spikelike skewer.

Rice is the main dish of many people in Japan, southern China, India, and Southeast Asia. Japanese meals commonly include vegetables, *tofu* (soybean curd), and raw or cooked fish. Chinese cookery varies by region. Cooks in southern China stir-fry chopped vegetables and meat, which they serve with a mild sauce and rice. In northern regions, people enjoy spicy fried foods served with noodles. Indians and many Southeast Asians enjoy *curry.* This stewlike dish is made of eggs, fish, meat, or vegetables and cooked in a spicy sauce.

Corn, rice, and other grains are the basic foods of many people in Africa. In Nigeria, food is often cooked in palm oil or peanut oil, and it may be sharply seasoned with red peppers. The people of Congo (Kinshasa) serve corn and rice as a thick porridge. If they can afford it, they add meat or fish to the porridge. Many Ethiopians enjoy raw meat in a red pepper sauce.

In some cultures, the way food is served is almost as important as how it is prepared. For example, French and Japanese chefs carefully arrange food to make each dish look beautiful. In Sweden, *smörgåsbord* is a popular way to serve guests. Smörgåsbord consists of a long table set with a dazzling selection of breads, cheeses, fish, salads, and hot and cold meats.

Customs also can affect the times when people eat. In most Western cultures, for example, people commonly eat three meals a day. These meals are breakfast, lunch, and dinner. The British add a light, extra meal called *tea* late in the afternoon. At this meal, they serve strong tea and such foods as biscuits, cakes, or sandwiches.

In most Western cultures, people eat from individual plates and use knives, forks, and spoons. In China and Japan, the people use chopsticks. In many societies, the people eat from a common serving dish and use few utensils. Some people scoop up their food with bread or with their fingers.

The food industry

In developing countries, many families produce their own food or buy food from local farmers. In developed countries, however, most people depend on the food industry. This section describes the food industry in the United States. However, much of the information also applies to the food industries in Australia, Canada, the United Kingdom, and other developed countries.

The food industry consists of all the activities involved in producing food and getting it to consumers. The main branches of the industry include (1) production, (2) processing, (3) packaging, (4) transportation, and (5) marketing. Government regulations cover each branch and help assure consumers of safe, good-quality products. In addition, food companies and other organizations conduct research to increase the food supply and to improve food products.

The food industry is one of the largest industries in the United States. About 3 million Americans, including self-employed farmers, work on farms to produce basic foods. Food-processing plants employ more than $1\frac{1}{2}$ million workers to prepare and package foods for the market. Millions of other workers are involved in the transporting and marketing of food.

Each branch of the food industry contributes to the prices of foods in the market place. The prices reflect the cost of producing the basic food as well as the processing, packaging, transportation, and marketing costs. All these costs, plus the profits of each branch of the industry, are paid by consumers.

The human diet differs greatly in rich and poor nations. In rich nations, most homemakers, such as the American woman at the left, can afford to buy a wide variety of foods. In poor countries, many families, such as the one in Nepal at the right, must produce their own food.

Production. American farmers use modern equipment and scientific methods to produce the enormous quantities of raw materials used by food processors. The great majority of farmers specialize in raising one kind of crop or one kind of livestock.

Most U.S. farmers who specialize in crops raise a *field crop.* Field crops require a fairly large amount of land to be profitable. The chief field crops are grains, especially corn and wheat; peanuts; potatoes; soybeans; and sugar beets. Some farmers grow such produce as celery, green beans, lettuce, onions, or tomatoes. Others raise berries, grapes, nuts, or such tree fruits as apples, cherries, oranges, peaches, or pears.

Livestock farmers who raise beef cattle, hogs, and sheep produce most of the nation's meat. Many other livestock farmers keep dairy cattle or raise poultry. Some farmers raise bees, fish, goats, or rabbits.

The production of basic foods also includes the activities of commercial fishing fleets. These fleets catch huge quantities of fish and shellfish. In addition, about 10 percent of the world's annual fish harvest comes from *fish farms,* enclosures built on land, or areas in natural bodies of water.

Processing. Most foods we eat have been processed. Processing changes the raw farm product into a form people can consume. Many processes—such as pasteurization, canning, drying, and freezing—are done to preserve the food product. Food can also be preserved by a process called *irradiation* that uses radiation to kill bacteria. Some processes improve the quality of food. For example, homogenized milk does not separate, and tenderized beef steaks are easier to eat.

Fresh eggs, fruits, and vegetables may be only washed and sorted before they reach the market. Or they may be dried or frozen. Fruits and vegetables also may be canned or pickled or used to make juice.

Meat packers slaughter cattle, hogs, and sheep. They then prepare the fresh meat for shipment to market. Meat packers also can, cure, freeze, and smoke meat, and they make it into sausages. Processors also slaughter and prepare chickens, turkeys, and other poultry for market. Large amounts of fish and shellfish are cleaned and marketed fresh. Processors also can, freeze, or pickle certain kinds of fish and shellfish. Dairy plants pasteurize and homogenize milk. Most dairies also add vitamins to milk. In addition, dairies make butter, cheese, ice cream, and yogurt from milk.

Processors manufacture many foods from basic plant and animal materials. For example, they make sugar from sugar beets and sugar cane, syrup from corn, and cooking oil from peanuts, soybeans, and various other plants. Other manufactured foods include synthetic and convenience foods. Processors developed margarine — which generally is made from corn, cottonseed, safflower, or soybean oil—as imitation butter. They make egg substitutes from egg whites and other ingredients. Processors use cooked meats and vegetables in canned and dried soups, frozen dinners, and canned and frozen casseroles. They combine dried eggs, flour, sugar, and other foods in packaged dessert mixes.

Jim Wood, *Cuisine* magazine

An attractive food display appeals to the eye and stimulates the appetite. This colorful assortment of dishes for an Easter celebration includes a cheese-covered ham, *center,* and red caviar, *foreground.* For many people, the way that food is served is almost as important as how it is prepared.

Many processors add chemicals called *additives* to foods. Various kinds of additives may be used in foods to improve or retain some quality, such as its color, flavor, nutritional value, or storage life. Additives require approval by the Food and Drug Administration (FDA). For detailed information about these chemicals, see Food additive.

Packaging makes foods easy to handle and identify. It also helps protect them from spilling and from being bruised or broken. In addition, special packaging materials and methods protect foods from air, bacteria, insects, light, moisture, and odors—all of which might spoil the food. Attractive packaging also helps promote the sale of foods. The majority of foods, especially processed ones, are packaged. In most cases, machines pack the food into containers. Packaging is usually the last step in the processing of food.

Food companies use the kinds of packaging that best suit the needs and uses of their products. For example, eggs are packed in thick, sturdy cardboard or plastic cartons to protect them from breaking. Some foods, such as coffee, jelly, and peanut butter, are used a little at a time. They are packed in cans or jars that have a resealable lid. Plastic bags and wrap keep air away from meat, bread, potato chips, and many other foods. Such dairy products as milk and cottage cheese are packed in plastic containers that protect them from air and light.

In *vacuum packing,* a pump removes almost all the air from a package. Sometimes, a gas such as nitrogen or carbon dioxide is then pumped into the package to flush away any remaining air. Then the package is sealed.

Packaging may also make the home preparation or use of food easier. For example, many frozen foods can be cooked in boil-in plastic bags, in microwave-usable containers, or in aluminum trays. Aerosol cans dispense whipped cream, and plastic squeeze bottles dispense ketchup or mustard.

Transportation. Commercial shipping companies transport most of the food from producers to processors and from processors to market. Nearly all fresh foods are perishable, and must be shipped quickly. Many vegetable farmers haul their produce to nearby markets soon after it is harvested. Over longer distances, however, refrigerated trucks, railroad cars, and ships help keep perishable produce fresh. Refrigerated vehicles also haul dairy products and frozen foods. In some cases, airplanes transport highly perishable foods, such as fish, or expensive foods, such as live lobsters. Specially designed trucks and trains haul livestock.

Marketing. Some farmers take their produce to a *farmers' market* in a nearby city. There, consumers can purchase their food directly from the farmer who grew it. Some restaurants also purchase food from farmers' markets.

Numerous grain, dairy, and other farmers sell their products directly to a food processor. Many other farmers belong to a *marketing cooperative.* A marketing cooperative collects the products of member farmers. It then sells the products to processors. Farmers sell their livestock to meat packers at large centers called *terminal markets* or at smaller *auction markets.*

Most food-processing companies and a number of farmers sell their products to a *wholesaler.* Wholesalers buy large quantities of a product and then sell smaller

WORLD BOOK photo

Wholesale produce firms, *shown here,* buy large quantities of fruits and vegetables from farmers. The firms then sell smaller amounts to restaurants, supermarkets, and other retailers.

amounts to *retailers.* Food retailers include supermarkets, grocery stores, convenience stores, delicatessens, butcher shops, restaurants, and other businesses that sell food to consumers.

Supermarkets and groceries sell a variety of foods. Other stores sell only one line of food, such as baked goods, fish, or meat. Consumers can buy prepared meals at restaurants and cafeterias. In many office and public buildings, vending machines dispense foods.

Government regulations. In the United States, federal, state, and local government agencies supervise the food industry. These agencies help protect the health of consumers by ensuring the quality, cleanliness, and purity of foods. They also prevent food companies from making false claims about the foods they sell. Federal and state laws regulate weights, measures, and container sizes to protect buyers from being cheated.

The FDA enforces standards for the food industry in general and for the truthful labeling of food products. The Department of Agriculture inspects and grades poultry, red meats, and fresh produce. The Department of Commerce supervises the production of foods made with fish. Regulations of the U.S. Postal Service and the Federal Trade Commission (FTC) guard against false or misleading food advertisements. The Environmental Protection Agency (EPA) establishes acceptable levels for pesticide residue on plants grown for food. Local health departments set standards of sanitation for dairy farms and dairy plants and for stores, restaurants, and other establishments that sell or serve food.

Food research is conducted by food companies, food growers' associations, food institutes, government agencies, research foundations, and universities. Their efforts have led to a tremendous increase in the quantity, quality, and variety of foods available.

Agricultural researchers work to increase the food supply by developing more productive varieties of plants and livestock and more effective fertilizers and pesticides. Other researchers seek ways to improve the flavor, appearance, or nutritional value of food products. Still others study the effects of preservatives and packaging on the storage life of food. Researchers in food safety study the health risks to consumers due to microbes, impurities, and additives found in food.

Many food company researchers work to develop new foods, and they seek ways to make the home preparation of processed foods easier. Home economists develop new recipes, and dietitians and nutritionists look for ways in which to improve the human diet. Agricultural economists study farm management and crop and livestock production.

Food through the ages

Prehistoric times. The earliest people ate whatever plant food they could find, including wild fruits, mushrooms, nuts, roots, and seeds. They caught fish and small land animals and ate the meat of dead animals they found. In time, people developed weapons to hunt large animals, such as bears, bison, deer, and wild cattle. Early people probably spent much time searching for food. If the food supply in an area ran out, they moved on. The earliest people probably roasted some of their food over burning wood from fires that had started naturally. After people discovered how to make fire, they could roast food more often. After they learned how to make pots, they could also boil and stew food.

By about 8000 B.C., people in several areas around the world had begun to raise plants and animals for food. Farming assured people of a steadier food supply. It also meant settling in one area instead of traveling about in search of food. Grains were especially important crops. Farmers also raised cattle, goats, sheep, and other animals for meat and milk.

Some groups of prehistoric people were nomadic shepherds. These groups traveled across the countryside in well-established patterns. They raised such animals as camels, goats, and sheep. Much of the nomads' diet consisted of meat and milk from their livestock.

Ancient times. Between 3500 and 1500 B.C., the first great civilizations developed in river valleys. These valleys were the Nile Valley in Egypt, the Tigris-Euphrates Valley in what is now Iraq, the Indus Valley in what is now Pakistan and northwestern India, and the Huang He Valley in China. All these valleys had fertile soil and a favorable climate, which enabled farmers to produce abundant yields. In ancient Egypt, for example, farmers along the Nile could raise two or three crops a year on the same fields. They grew barley and wheat and such vegetables as beans, lettuce, and peas. The Egyptians also raised such fruits as grapes and melons. Their livestock included cattle, goats, and sheep.

Ancient Greece and later ancient Rome could not produce enough food for their growing populations. They thus had to import large quantities of food from other countries. They also conquered and colonized lands that had plentiful food supplies. The Greeks and Romans thus enjoyed cherries from Persia; apricots, peaches, and spices from Asia; and, most important, wheat from Egypt. By the A.D. 200's, the Roman Empire covered much of Europe, most of the Middle East, and the Mediterranean coast of Africa. Most of the empire's large farms specialized in raising wheat, which formed the basis of the Roman diet.

The Middle Ages. After the Roman Empire split apart in the A.D. 400's, international trade dropped sharply. In time, much of the land of Europe was divided into *manors.* A manor was a large estate controlled by a lord and worked by peasants. Manors provided all the foods needed by the lords and the peasants. These foods included grains; grapes and other fruits; such vegetables as beans, cabbages, and turnips; and poultry, cattle, and other livestock.

Between 1000 and 1300, thousands of Europeans went to the Middle East to fight in the Crusades. The crusaders acquired a taste for spices and Middle Eastern foods. After the crusaders returned to Europe, their desire for different foods helped to renew international trade. It also helped stimulate the exploration of new lands.

Foods of the New World. In 1492, the Italian navigator Christopher Columbus sailed west from Spain. He was seeking a short sea route to the spice lands of the Indies. But he landed in the New World, America, not the Indies. Although Columbus did not find spices, his voyage led to a new world of food for Europeans. American Indians introduced Europeans to avocados, chocolate, corn, peanuts, peppers, pineapples, sweet and

Illustration from the Très Riches Heures du Duc de Berry (1412-16), illuminated manuscript on vellum by the Limbourg brothers; Musée Condé, Chantilly (Art Resource)

During the Middle Ages, food was produced on *manors,* large estates controlled by lords. The peasants who lived on a manor raised livestock and grew crops.

white potatoes, squashes, and tomatoes.

The American colonists enjoyed many of the Indian foods. In fact, the Indians taught them how to raise corn, which became their most important crop.

Recent developments. As trade continued to expand, so did consumers' ability to get foods raised far away. Advances in food preservation gave consumers in developed countries access to virtually all foods grown in distant lands. Such advances were canning, which began in the early 1800's, and mechanical refrigeration, which became widespread by the 1920's.

In the United States today, most people can obtain all the food they need to maintain a healthy body. Furthermore, special foods have been developed to meet specific health needs of certain groups of people. One such group consists of those who are *obese* (extremely fat). Studies show that about one-fourth of U.S. adults are obese. Obesity can increase the risk of getting various life-threatening ailments, such as heart disease. Eating large amounts of sugar and fat can contribute to obesity. To help control their weight, many people use artificial sweeteners, such as aspartame and saccharin, and food products formulated with fat replacers.

Another group consists of individuals who have been advised by their doctors to reduce their intake of sodium. Some studies indicate that too much sodium can lead to high blood pressure. Food-processing companies have developed salt-free versions of crackers, certain salad dressings, and other food products that traditionally have contained much salt.

In addition, many Americans believe that additives and other chemicals used in food production and processing harm the body. They are also concerned that important nutrients are lost in processing. As a result, so-called *health foods* have become popular. These foods include unprocessed foods and foods grown without fertilizers and pesticides.   Jane Ann Raymond Bowers

Related articles. See various country articles in *World Book* in which local foods are discussed, such as **Mexico** (Food and drink). See also the following articles:

Kinds of food

Bread	Fish	Meat	Seafood
Candy	Fruit	Milk	Spice
Cereal	Grain	Nut	Sugar
Cheese	Herb	Poultry	Vegetable
Egg			

Nutrition

Antioxidant	Fat substitute	Nutrition
Carbohydrate	Fiber, Dietary	Organic food
Cholesterol	Health	Protein
Diet	Health food	Trans fats
Digestive system	Lipid	Vitamin
Fat		Weight control

Preparation and processing

Artificial sweetener	Fishing industry	Freeze-drying
	Food, Frozen	Meat packing
Cold storage	Food additive	Packaging
Cooking	Food preservation	Refrigeration
Dehydrated food		

Special food dishes

Barbecue	Pizza
Bird's-nest soup	Sushi
Caviar	Trepang
Pemmican	

Beverages

Alcoholic beverage	Coffee Maguey	Maté Soft drink	Tea

Other related articles

Agriculture	Food and Drug Administration
Animal (Adaptations for eating; Providing food)	Food poisoning
Center for Science in the Public Interest	Food supply
	Inuit (Food)
Christmas (Christmas feasting)	Kosher
Easter (The lamb; Other foods)	Marketing
Eating disorder	Plant
Family and consumer sciences	Prehistoric people (The rise of agriculture)
Fast	Restaurant
Flower (Other uses)	Salt
Food and Agriculture Organization	Space exploration (Eating and drinking)
	Thanksgiving Day

Outline

I. Sources of food
  A. Food from plants   B. Food from animals
II. How the body uses food
  A. Producing energy
  B. Building and repairing tissues
  C. Regulating body processes
III. Why diets differ around the world
  A. Geographic reasons
  B. Economic reasons
  C. Religious reasons
  D. Customs
IV. The food industry
  A. Production
  B. Processing
  C. Packaging
  D. Transportation
  E. Marketing
  F. Government regulations
  G. Food research
IV. Food through the ages

Questions

What were some foods that the American Indians introduced to Europeans?

How does the physical environment help determine what the people of a region eat?

What are the most important foods from plants? From animals?

What are *food additives?* What do they do?

How does packaging help keep food from spoiling?

What is *curry? Shish kebab? Smörgåsbord?*

Why is it important to have a well-balanced diet?

Why do diets differ in developed and developing countries?

How are people's food habits changing?

Why are proteins essential to good health?

Additional resources

Level I

Haduch, Bill. *Food Rules!* Dutton, 2001. Assorted facts about food.

Meltzer, Milton. *Food.* Copper Beech, 1998. A history of food in culture.

Tames, Richard. *Food: Feasts, Cooks, and Kitchens.* Watts, 1994.

Ventura, Piero. *Food: Its Evolution Through the Ages.* Houghton, 1994.

Level II

Barer-Stein, Thelma. *You Eat What You Are: People, Culture and Food Traditions.* 2nd ed. Firefly Bks., 1999.

Davidson, Alan, ed. *The Oxford Companion to Food.* Oxford, 1999.

Trager, James. *The Food Chronology.* 1995. Reprint. Henry Holt, 1997.

Ward, Susie, and others. *The Gourmet Atlas.* Macmillan, 1997.

Food, Frozen. Freezing is one of the best ways to preserve foods. Food-processing companies freeze such foods as baked goods, orange juice, pizzas, vegetables, and complete precooked meals. Freezing preserves food by preventing the growth of microbes that spoil food and by slowing food-spoiling chemical reactions. Frozen foods should be stored at temperatures of 0 °F (–18 °C) or below.

Almost all foods frozen commercially are quickly frozen, whereas food frozen at home is slowly frozen. Quick freezing preserves most foods better than slow freezing. Slow freezing changes the structure of some foods in such a way that the foods leak fluids when they are later defrosted. This leakage results in undesirable changes in the food's texture. For example, leakage can cause vegetables to become mushy, and meat tough. During slow freezing, the food may not cool quickly enough to prevent spoilage by microbes or by chemical reactions.

Commercial freezing of food began in the United States before 1865. Food-processing companies originally froze food by using ice cut from ponds or rivers. In the late 1850's, such companies began making ice by using a process that involved the mechanical compression of ammonia (see **Refrigeration** [Mechanical refrigeration]). The ice was used to freeze meat and vegetables for international distribution.

These early methods of freezing allowed only for slow freezing. But in the mid-1920's, Clarence Birdseye, an American inventor, developed a quick-freezing process for fish and vegetables. In 1929, the Postum Company (now General Foods Corporation) purchased his patents and began to produce frozen foods. Frozen foods became popular in the United States in the 1950's, when freezers became widely available.

Commercial methods of quick-freezing

There are several commercial methods of freezing foods quickly. These methods include (1) air-blast freezing, (2) indirect-contact freezing, (3) cryogenic freezing, and (4) liquid immersion freezing.

Air-blast freezing uses a steady flow of cold air at 0 to –40 °F (–18 to –40 °C). The cold air is produced by passing air over coils cooled by a mechanical ammonia-compression system. The cold air is then blown into an insulated tunnel. In many arrangements, the food passes through the tunnel on a conveyor belt. In most cases, processing firms package the food before sending it through the tunnel. But for faster freezing, some processors freeze foods before packaging them.

Air-blast freezing is quick and efficient, but it can partially dehydrate unpackaged foods. A type of air-blast freezing called *fluidized bed freezing* forces air upward through a bed of food pieces. Strawberries, peas, and other kinds of fruits and vegetables are *individually quick frozen* (IQF) by this method.

Indirect-contact freezing, also called *plate freezing,* uses adjustable metal plates that have hollow walls. A *refrigerant* (cooling substance) inside the plate walls cools the plate surfaces to temperatures as low as –40 °F (–40 °C). Packaged foods are placed between the plates, which are then adjusted to make contact with the upper and lower surfaces of the packages. As the plates absorb heat, the food freezes.

Ron Sherman, Bruce Coleman Inc.

Concentrated orange juice is frozen in cans. First, the juice is poured into the cans, *shown here.* Then the cans are sealed and immersed in a refrigerated alcohol or salt solution.

Cryogenic freezing uses a *cryogen* (liquefied gas), such as liquid nitrogen under pressure at –280 °F (–173 °C). Carbon dioxide may also be used, either as a liquid or in a solid form called *dry ice.* The cryogen or dry ice is first *vaporized* (turned into a misty gas). The cold vapor then flows into a chamber, where it freezes the food. The cryogenic freezing method is expensive, but it freezes food faster and results in better products than the air-blast and indirect-contact methods do.

Liquid immersion freezing uses a refrigerated solution of salt or of a type of alcohol called *glycol.* A mechanical conveyor moves food in cans or other packages through the solution. Processing companies use salt or glycol solutions to freeze such products as canned fruit juices and poultry that is sealed in plastic film.

In the past, food companies used a method where unpackaged foods were sprayed with, or dipped in, liquid *chlorofluorocarbons* (CFC's) at –21 °F (–29 °C). CFC's are chemicals that contain carbon, chlorine, and fluorine. Because CFC's harm the environment, many countries have restricted their production. As a result, processing companies switched to other methods in place of liquid-CFC freezing, which had been used to freeze such foods as shrimp and corn on the cob.

Freezing food at home

People freeze foods at home by placing them in cabinet deep-freezers or in the freezer compartments of refrigerators. Both of these kinds of freezers operate at about 0 °F (–18 °C).

Freezer capacities vary considerably. A 10-cubic-foot (0.28-cubic-meter) freezer can hold up to about 25 pounds (11 kilograms) of food. Some large cabinet units hold as much as 150 pounds (68 kilograms). But regardless of a freezer's size, it is important not to overload the unit. Overloading prevents the freezer from maintaining the temperature at or below 0 °F (–18 °C). In addition, a freezer should not be completely filled with unfrozen food, because the food will freeze too slowly.

Home freezers freeze food more slowly than do commercial freezing systems. As a result, freezing food at home results in lower food quality than does commercial freezing. However, many foods make acceptable products when frozen at home. Such foods can be stored for a year at 0 °F (–18 °C) if properly prepared, packaged, and frozen.

Preparing foods for freezing involves several steps. First, the foods should be washed, trimmed, and cut to the desired size. Vegetables and certain kinds of fruits should then be *blanched*—that is, steamed or boiled for one to three minutes. Blanching destroys chemicals called *enzymes* that can give the food a disagreeable odor, flavor, or color. Even in a freezer, enzymes may remain active.

Fruits may or may not be blanched, depending on their intended use. Fruits intended for cooking should be blanched. But blanching gives food a cooked flavor, and so fruits that are to be eaten uncooked should not be blanched. Fruits that are not blanched lose quality more rapidly in a freezer than do blanched fruits.

Meats need little preparation for freezing. In general, meat, including poultry and fish, should be frozen uncooked. Cooked meat, when frozen, spoils two or three times faster than meat frozen raw.

In general, thawed foods should not be refrozen. Refreezing food and thawing it again reduces the food's quality. Unless the food was previously thawed in a refrigerator or microwave oven, refreezing and thawing it again may make it unsafe.

Packaging is an important part of freezing food at home. Proper packaging protects the food while it is stored in the freezer. The food should be packed tightly in an airtight container to prevent evaporation. Evaporation can dry the food out. It also can cause snow called *package ice* to form inside containers that have too much air space. In addition, evaporation results in a dull or dried-out appearance called *freezer burn*. To speed freezing and thawing, food should be placed in small packages.

Problems with frozen foods

Frozen foods can cause food poisoning if they are not frozen soon enough or if they are not cooked soon enough after thawing. Food-poisoning organisms can grow in food if its temperature exceeds 45 to 50 °F (7 to 10 °C) for only a few hours. If the food is cooked before it is frozen, it should immediately be put in a refrigerator or freezer. Allowing warm food to cool at room temperature permits the growth of food-poisoning microbes that may survive the freezing process.

Foods should be thawed in a microwave oven or, if such an oven is not available, in a refrigerator. Both methods prevent the growth of food-poisoning organisms. However, refrigerator thawing allows physical and chemical changes that reduce food quality.

To help prevent the loss of quality that occurs in vegetables as a result of slow thawing, processing firms package many vegetables in sealed plastic pouches. Consumers can thaw the vegetables rapidly—and cook them—by transferring the unopened pouch from a freezer into boiling water. The tightly packed pouches also prevent freezer burn and the formation of package ice. Many frozen foods can be cooked in a microwave oven as soon as they are removed from the freezer.

Most states of the United States require that frozen foods be stored at or below 0 °F (–18 °C). However, supermarket freezer shelves are often overstocked, and many supermarket and home freezers have automatic defrost cycles that raise and lower the temperature repeatedly. The temperature of commercially frozen food also may repeatedly rise and fall as the food is moved from one freezer to another during distribution. As a result, some frozen foods often exceed 0 °F. The repeated temperature changes lead to loss of food quality. For example, they cause ice crystals to form in ice cream, giving it a grainy texture. They also promote freezer burn and the formation of ice.   Gregory R. Ziegler

See also **Birdseye, Clarence; Food preservation; Refrigeration.**

Food additive is any substance that a food manufacturer adds to a food. Some additives increase a food's nutritional value. Others improve the color, flavor, or texture of foods. Still others keep foods from spoiling.

Some food additives come from other foods. Scientists create other additives in the laboratory. Some people consider food additives dangerous to their health. But many of these substances occur naturally in foods that people have eaten for centuries.

Kinds of additives. There are thousands of food additives. They can be classified into six major groups: (1) nutrients; (2) flavoring agents; (3) coloring agents; (4) preservatives; (5) emulsifiers, stabilizers, and thickeners; and (6) acids and alkalis.

Nutrients, such as minerals and vitamins, make foods more nourishing. The addition of the B-complex vitamins folic acid and niacin to flour, pasta, and rice has helped reduce the incidence of a serious spinal defect called spina bifida and has virtually eliminated the nutrient deficiency disease pellagra. Addition of the mineral iodine to table salt has made incidence of goiter rare.

Flavoring agents include all spices and natural flavors, as well as such artificial flavors as vanillin, which is used in place of natural vanilla. Most flavors are added in tiny quantities. Some flavoring agents, such as monosodium glutamate (MSG), enhance a food's natural flavor. *Sweeteners* add sweetness. Natural sweeteners include sucrose, fructose, dextrose, and corn syrup. Artificial sweeteners include acesulfame-K, aspartame, saccharin, and sucralose.

Coloring agents help make foods look appealing. For example, canned cherry pie filling may have red color added to replace color lost during processing. Colas would be clear without the addition of caramel coloring.

Emulsifiers, stabilizers, and thickeners help the ingredients in a food to mix and hold together. Lecithin is an *emulsifier,* an additive that keeps one substance evenly dispersed in another. It helps prevent the fat in chocolate from separating and forming *bloom,* a white discoloration. The emulsifiers stearoyl-2-lactylate and polysorbate 60 keep bread soft. Carrageenin, a stabilizer, keeps the chocolate particles in chocolate milk from settling. Xanthan gum is used to thicken salad dressings.

Preservatives extend the shelf life of foods. Chemical compounds called *antimicrobial agents* destroy or inhibit the growth of microbes, allowing foods to be safely kept for a longer time. Nitrite added to cured meats prevents the growth of the bacteria that cause a kind of food poisoning called *botulism* (see **Botulism**). Calcium propionate retards the growth of mold in bread. Such *antioxidants* as BHA and BHT help to maintain flavor by slowing down *oxidation,* a chemical reaction. EDTA and other *sequestrants* prevent metal ions in foods from promoting oxidation by binding the ions together.

Acids and alkalis change the pH of some foods, a measure of whether the food is acidic or alkaline (see pH). Acids help prevent the growth of certain bacteria. They can also add flavor. Citric acid added to drinks gives them a tart taste. In *Dutch-processing,* alkalis are added to cocoa to reduce its natural acidity and bitterness. Alkalis can also darken the color of food products.

Government regulations. Government committees and regulatory bodies define the maximum amounts of additives permitted in food. In the United States, the Federal Food, Drug, and Cosmetic Act prohibits the use of any food additive shown, by appropriate tests, to cause cancer in people or animals. It also requires a manufacturer to prove a new food additive safe and effective before using it. The Food and Drug Administration (FDA) enforces the act.   Grady W. Chism

See also **Artificial sweetener; Fat substitute; Monosodium glutamate; Pure food and drug laws.**

Food and Agriculture Organization (FAO) is a specialized agency of the United Nations. Its full name is the Food and Agriculture Organization of the United Nations. The agency works to improve the production, distribution, and use of food and other products of the world's farms, forests, and fisheries. Its goals include raising the level of nutrition and the standard of living of all people, especially the rural poor. Most member countries of the UN belong to the FAO.

The FAO and the United Nations co-sponsor the World Food Programme. This program uses food surpluses and cash from donor nations to provide emergency relief and to stimulate development. The FAO was set up in 1945. It has headquarters in Rome.

Critically reviewed by the Food and Agriculture Organization

See also **Food supply** (Food supply programs); **United Nations** (Fighting hunger).

Food and Drug Administration (FDA) is an agency in the United States Department of Health and Human Services. It seeks to protect the public health by ensuring the purity and security of foods; the safety and effectiveness of drugs, medical devices, biological products, and radiation-emitting products; and the safety of cosmetics. The FDA oversees the review and approval of new medicines and medical devices. It also monitors the safety of dietary supplements, though it does not review and approve the supplements before they are sold.

The FDA helps to ensure that people receive accurate information about the foods and drugs that they use. The agency calls for the truthful description of product benefits and risks and for safety and honesty in packaging. The FDA designed the "nutrition facts" panel that appears on packaged foods in the United States.

The FDA originated in the late 1800's as the Division of Chemistry (later called the Bureau of Chemistry). The agency adopted its present name in 1930. Laws administered by the agency include the Federal Food, Drug, and Cosmetic Act of 1938, the Drug Amendments of 1962, and the Medical Devices Amendments of 1976.

In the 1990's, the FDA accelerated its review and approval processes for new drugs. In the years that followed, a number of widely used drugs were withdrawn from the market for safety reasons. Many people argued that in speeding up its review process the FDA failed to protect the public from unsafe drugs. The Food Safety

Modernization Act of 2010 gave the FDA increased authority to inspect food processing facilities more often, to enforce stricter standards, and to recall contaminated foods.   Mary K. Olson

See also **Pure food and drug laws.**

Food chain. See Ecology; **Animal** (Adaptations for eating); **Fish** (Fish in the balance of nature).

Food coloring. See Food additive (Kinds of additives).

Food for Peace is a United States government program that gives food assistance to other countries. The goals of Food for Peace include combating hunger and malnutrition and promoting agricultural and other economic development.

Food for Peace is administered by the Agency for International Development (USAID), an independent agency of the U.S. government. Through USAID, agricultural products from the United States are shipped to the countries that need aid. USAID contracts with *nongovernmental organizations* (NGO's) to distribute the food to needy people. Food for Peace also works to develop projects that will improve the agricultural capabilities of nations in need. The U.S. Congress established Food for Peace in 1954.

Critically reviewed by the Department of Agriculture

Food groups. See Nutrition.

Food poisoning is illness that results from eating food that is contaminated by microorganisms or chemicals, or that is poisonous in itself. Food can be contaminated by such chemicals as lead or zinc, leading to food poisoning. Several varieties of mushrooms and certain species of fish are poisonous if eaten. More often, food poisoning is caused by microorganisms, such as bacteria, molds, viruses, and parasites.

Some food-poisoning agents are already in food at the time the game or livestock is killed or the plants are harvested. Many microorganisms cause food to spoil but are otherwise harmless. Certain bacteria that grow in food, however, produce *toxins* (poisons) that cause illness. The bacterium *Staphylococcus* (STAF uh luh KAHK uhs) produces toxins that cause vomiting and diarrhea a few hours after the contaminated food is eaten. The bacterium *Clostridium botulinum* (klahs TRIHD ee uhm BAHCH uh LIHN uhm) causes a far more serious, often fatal, type of food poisoning called *botulism.*

Many instances of food poisoning are really infections by bacteria, viruses, or parasites that multiply in the body and cause illness. The most common foodborne bacteria are *Salmonella* and *Campylobacter* (KAM pih loh BAK tuhr). These bacteria affect the stomach and intestines, causing nausea and diarrhea. A variety of the common bacterium *Escherichia coli* (EHSH uh RIHK ee uh KOH ly) called *E. coli O157:H7* causes severe illness and kidney failure, particularly in children. The virus that causes hepatitis A, a serious liver disease, is often transmitted to people through contaminated food or water. Disease-causing parasites, such as *Cryptosporidium* (KRIHP toh spaw RIHD ee uhm) and *Giardia* (jeh AHR dee uh), often contaminate uncooked vegetables.

Food-poisoning illnesses are usually brief and mild, and cause no permanent harm in healthy people. The elderly, the very young, pregnant women, and people whose immune systems are weakened by illness or medication are most susceptible to food poisoning.

Proper processing and preparation of food destroy

most food-poisoning agents and prevent most illness. Food preparers should wash their hands often and not work if they are ill. People should always thoroughly wash foods before eating them, especially if the food is eaten raw. Refrigerating, freezing, or holding cooked foods at temperatures too high for bacteria to grow are also important for keeping foods safe.   Dean O. Cliver

Related articles in *World Book* include:

Botulism	Hepatitis
Campylobacter	Listeria
E. coli	Salmonellosis
Food preservation	Staphylococcus
Giardiasis	

Food preservation

Food preservation is any technique used to slow the normal decay of food. There are many methods of food preservation. Some methods, such as drying and fermenting, were first used thousands of years ago. Other methods of preservation, such as canning, rely on technology and processes first developed in the 1800's. Still other methods, such as irradiation, have developed even more recently.

Food preservation has long been necessary because the availability of food varies with the seasons. In the past, for example, many people were farmers and grew their own food. But many farm products can only be harvested during certain times of year. To ensure a steady supply of food throughout the year, people learned ways to preserve foods. In modern times, preservation methods enable the food industry to process, transport, and distribute food products around the world. In all developed countries, government agencies highly regulate the food industry to ensure that food is safely preserved.

How food spoils

All food will eventually spoil if not preserved. Some foods, such as nuts and grains, can be stored for months with almost no treatment. Other foods, such as milk and meat, stay fresh only one or two days without preservation. The time that a particular food can be maintained in edible condition is called its *shelf life*. Preservation can extend a food's shelf life, but not indefinitely.

Food is subject to three predominant kinds of deterioration or spoilage. They are (1) biological, (2) chemical, and (3) physical deterioration.

Biological deterioration results from harmful microorganisms that grow in food. Microorganisms include bacteria, molds, and yeasts. Harmful microorganisms exist everywhere in the environment. They grow on virtually any surface, including on animal skins and vegetable peels. But such protective coverings generally stop harmful microorganisms from getting inside healthy living tissue. Thus, most cases of biological deterioration occur because of *contamination*—that is, the introduction of microorganisms into healthy food through a break in skin or weakened tissue.

Food spoils when harmful microorganisms multiply in the food. Bacteria multiply rapidly, producing acids, gases, and other chemicals in the process. Some chemicals produced by bacteria may be poisonous to human beings. For example, the bacteria *Clostridium botulinum* produces a dangerous toxin that causes a type of food poisoning called *botulism*. Botulism is often fatal to humans. Yeast and mold, which are larger and more complex than bacteria, can also multiply rapidly in food.

Seedlike structures called *spores* are of special concern in food preservation. All molds—and some bacteria and yeast—produce spores. Under proper conditions, spores can *germinate* (activate) and become full-sized cells. Spores can survive high temperatures, poisonous chemicals, and other extreme conditions. Food preservation methods are designed to inactivate bacterial spores, which are especially resistant.

Microorganisms are among the top causes of food loss. But not all microorganisms cause disease or food spoilage. In fact, some microorganisms are actually used to make and preserve foods. For example, yeast is used to make bread. Bacteria and molds are important in cheese making. Bacteria also create acids used to preserve pickled foods.

Chemical deterioration is caused by reactions that change the molecular arrangement of food. Such chemical reactions may not be harmful in every circumstance. For example, chemical reactions involving molecules called *enzymes* ripen fruit after harvest. But beyond a certain point, enzymatic reactions cause fruit to become overripe and spoil. The weakened tissues enable microorganisms to penetrate and cause further damage. Foods can also deteriorate from chemical reactions involving light or oxygen.

Physical deterioration involves large-scale damage to food products, such as being crushed, broken apart, or melted. Storing food at improper temperatures causes physical deterioration. In addition, such pests as insects and rodents cause physical deterioration.

How foods are preserved

A number of methods are used to preserve food. Preservation methods make use of heat, cold, drying, acid, salt and sugar, smoke, added chemicals, controlled air, and high-energy radiation. Any of these methods will cause deterioration of the food if used in excess. For instance, high heat over a long period will kill all microorganisms. However, too much heat ruins food's flavor and texture. Often, food is preserved with a number of less extreme methods used in combination.

Heat is effective for food preservation because most microorganisms grow best in the temperature range of

Campbell Soup Company

Food preservation helps prevent food spoilage. Canning, freezing, and a number of other methods are used to preserve a wide variety of foods, such as those shown here.

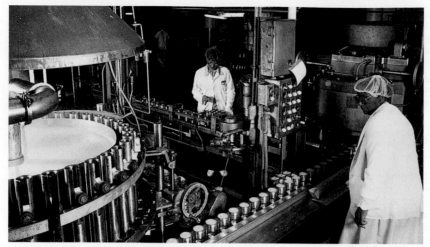

Campbell Soup Company

Canning preserves food by heating it in airtight containers. Before any food is canned, inspectors make sure the food is properly cleaned and prepared.

40 to 140 °F (4 to 60 °C). Most bacteria are killed in the temperature range of 170 to 200 °F (77 to 93 °C) if they are held at such temperatures for a long enough time. Some heat-resistant spores may require temperatures greater than 212 °F (100 °C), the boiling temperature of water.

Heat treatments range in severity. *Blanching* is a mild heat treatment in which food is briefly boiled or steamed. Blanching deactivates enzymes and reduces the number of microorganisms. Fruits and vegetables are frequently blanched prior to freezing.

Pasteurization is a more severe heat treatment. In pasteurization, food is held at a constant high temperature—typically below the boiling point of water—for a certain period. Pasteurization kills many dangerous microorganisms. But pasteurization is usually combined with other preservation methods, such as refrigeration, because pasteurized products still contain many living microorganisms.

The most severe heat treatment commonly used in food preservation is *commercial sterilization*. In commercial sterilization, all microorganisms that might spoil food under typical storage and handling conditions have been destroyed and will not grow in the food. Unlike medical equipment, however, commercially sterilized food is not completely sterile.

Canning is a common method of food preservation in developed countries. The process ensures commercial sterilization. In canning, foods are sealed in airtight containers and are heated to destroy microorganisms that may cause spoilage. A wide variety of foods are canned. They include fruits, vegetables, fish, meat, poultry, and soups.

Before food is canned, it is thoroughly cleaned. Many foods, such as fruits and vegetables, are cut, sliced, or peeled before canning. After the raw food is prepared, the canning process follows five basic steps: (1) filling, (2) exhausting, (3) sealing, (4) processing, and (5) cooling.

Filling. Food is placed in containers, typically metal cans or glass jars. Machines can fill more than a thousand containers in a minute. The empty space above the food in the container is called *headspace*. Headspace is carefully controlled. Too little headspace may cause

cans to bulge during heating. Too much headspace results in underweight cans and shorter shelf life.

Exhausting involves the removal of air in the headspace to form a partial vacuum in the container. Exhausting removes oxygen and thus slows the growth of many microorganisms that cause decay.

Sealing. Machines seal several hundred metal cans per minute. Glass containers are sealed at a somewhat slower rate. Sealed containers are airtight.

Processing. In processing, containers are heated to a carefully controlled temperature for a certain time. The time and temperature vary with the product being canned and the size of the container. During processing, microorganisms that may cause spoilage are destroyed. Containers are heated in cookers called *retorts*.

Cooling follows processing to prevent overcooking. Containers may be cooled by transferring them from the retort into cold water. They may also be sprayed with cold water. Some canned products are first cooled partially by water and then fully cooled by air.

One of the disadvantages of canning is that the heat

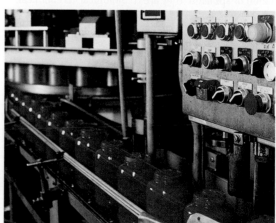

Campbell Soup Company

Filling is generally done by machines. Some machines fill up to 1,200 containers a minute. The glass containers shown here are being filled with spaghetti sauce before they are sealed.

required for sterilization changes the food's texture, color, and flavor. In addition, some nutrients are lost in the canning process. However, canned foods are popular with consumers because of their low cost, convenience, variety, and relatively long shelf life.

Cold storage, including refrigeration and freezing, is used to control microorganisms and enzyme activity. Refrigeration keeps food fresh at temperatures above 32 °F (0 °C). Storage at or near that temperature largely prevents the growth and activity of most microorganisms that cause food spoilage. It also decreases enzyme activity that causes changes in the color, flavor, and texture of foods. Foods requiring refrigeration include eggs, fish, fruits, meats, milk, and vegetables.

Frozen storage maintains the food in the frozen state. Freezing prevents microbial activity and slows down enzymatic deterioration. Though most foods contain large amounts of water, food freezes differently than pure water. The *solutes* (dissolved sugars and salts) in foods reduce the initial freezing point to lower than 32 °F (0 °C). Typically, foods begin to freeze at around 31 to 28 °F (–0.5 to –2 °C). Frozen foods are stored at or below 0 °F (–18 °C).

Vegetables are among the main foods preserved by freezing. Before freezing, vegetables are first blanched. Blanching prevents enzymes from changing the flavor and texture of vegetables during frozen storage. Other foods preserved by freezing include fish, juices, meat, and poultry. Before freezing, food may be cleaned, peeled, or prepared in other ways. Some foods, such as frozen entrees, are cooked before freezing.

Some common commercial equipment freezes food with cold air. Such freezers ensure that cold air is constantly moving around the food product. Moving air carries heat away from food much more quickly than does still air. *Air-blast freezers* use a fan to create a strong wind. This wind, combined with temperatures as low as –40 °F (–40 °C), causes rapid freezing of foods. In many air-blast freezers, packages of food travel slowly through the unit on a conveyor belt until frozen.

Other commercial equipment freezes food through the use of solid surfaces or liquids. In *plate freezers,* food is frozen through contact with cold surfaces. Such freezers are cabinets with shelves that contain refrigerants. Food is placed on or in between the shelves. The cabinet is then closed until the food freezes. *Cryogenic freezers* use liquid nitrogen, liquid carbon dioxide, or solid carbon dioxide to freeze foods. These substances form at extremely low temperatures and rapidly freeze food. Food products that take several hours to freeze in an air-blast freezer may require only minutes in a cryogenic freezer.

Drying is the removal of water from food. Although there are a number of ways to remove water, usually "drying" means *thermal drying.* Thermal drying uses heat to remove moisture from food. The microorganisms that cause food spoilage require moisture to survive. After much of the water is removed from foods, microorganisms cannot grow or cause food to spoil. Hundreds of foods are dried, including eggs, milk, mushrooms, peas, raisins, and soups.

Some thermal drying methods make use of hot air. In *sun drying* or *solar drying,* food is spread out in thin layers in hot, sunny weather. The sun's heat dries the food.

Fruits and grains are often dried in this manner. *Convection air drying* uses moving hot air to dry food. A fan may blow air around food that is put in a sealed cabinet. Alternately, the food may move on conveyor belts through hot air. *Spray drying* involves spraying droplets of liquid foods or *slurries* (mixtures of liquids and finely ground solid particles) into a large, heated chamber. Hot air is also blown into the chamber. The hot air dries the food droplets to form powders. Milk is often dried by this method.

Freeze-drying is typically done in a low air environment. Under partial vacuum conditions, ice can change directly from a solid to a gas, without first becoming a liquid. This process, called *sublimation,* is the basis of freeze-drying. As the ice vaporizes, the food maintains its shape, but becomes a *porous* (spongelike) dry solid. Freeze-drying is a more expensive process than air drying methods, so it is used for fewer types of foods. These foods are often heat-sensitive, such as coffee and tea, or highly valued and perishable items, such as mushrooms, shrimp, and strawberries.

Acid can preserve foods by creating an environment in which spoilage microorganisms will not grow. The acid may be present in the food naturally, such as in berries, apples, and citrus fruits. Otherwise, food makers may add acids to the product. Such added acids include citric acid and acetic acid. Some pickled vegetables are preserved by acetic acid added as vinegar.

Acid may also be produced in foods by acid-making bacteria. This process is called *fermentation.* In contrast to other preservation methods, fermentation encourages the growth of certain kinds of bacteria. The bacteria most often used in fermented foods produce acetic acid or lactic acid. These two groups of bacteria are used in the production of many foods, including kimchi, salami, sauerkraut, sour cream, vinegar, and many cheeses.

Salt and sugar are solutes that dissolve in water. The solutes draw water out of bacteria, yeast, and mold present in food. The microorganisms become dehydrated and cannot grow or multiply. The high sugar content in fruit jams, for example, enables them to last much longer than fresh fruits. Meats and fish are preserved with salt in a process called *curing.* Often curing also involves chemicals called nitrates and nitrites, as well as sugar and spices for flavoring.

In general, yeasts and molds are more tolerant of high solute conditions than are bacteria. For this reason, yeasts and molds may grow on such foods as jam.

Smoking foods can preserve them through both heat and chemicals in the smoke. For example, wood smoke contains small amounts of formaldehyde and other chemicals that preserve food. Smoked products, such as many types of ham and bacon, are often cured first. The smoking is primarily done for flavor, rather than for preservation.

Additives include chemicals added to food to prevent spoilage. There are many chemicals that can kill microorganisms or inhibit their growth. But most of these chemicals are not permitted as food additives. When a chemical is permitted for use, it is added at low levels to control microorganisms and to maintain quality. Additives generally require approval by the government before they can be used. Common preservatives include sodium benzoate, sorbic acid, and sulfur dioxide.

Controlled air, used in controlled-atmosphere storage, changes the composition of air in order to preserve food. The normal composition of air is 21 percent oxygen and 79 percent nitrogen. In a controlled atmosphere, the gas mixture is much lower in oxygen and higher in carbon dioxide than normal. The rest of the air is typically made up of nitrogen, which has no effect on food. The exact mix of gases depends on the product being preserved.

Fresh fruits and vegetables are stored in controlled atmospheres. Harvested fruits and vegetables are living tissues that *respire*. Respiration is the reaction of oxygen and sugars to produce carbon dioxide, water, and heat. During storage, it is important to reduce the rate of respiration to maintain the quality of fruits and vegetables. Air with less oxygen and more carbon dioxide helps slow respiration. Lower air temperatures also help reduce the rate of respiration.

Irradiation makes use of *ionizing radiation* to kill or deactivate microorganisms in food. Ionizing radiation includes such high-energy forms of electromagnetic radiation as X rays and gamma rays. It also includes beams of electrons. Ionizing radiation can change the structure of atoms by stripping away the electrons that normally surround an atom's *nucleus* (core). These changes can destroy genetic material in cells, killing bacteria and other organisms that grow in food. Low doses of such radiation cause little or no chemical change in the food itself.

Food irradiation is used in dozens of countries. Commonly irradiated foods include red meat, poultry, various grains, spices, and many kinds of fruits and vegetables. However, the specific foods allowed to be treated by radiation vary by country. Consumer safety concerns have led many countries to require labeling on irradiated food.

History

Prehistoric people probably dried grains, nuts, fruits, roots, and other plant products in the sun. People who lived in cold climates likely kept food outside their caves or huts in the winter to prevent spoilage. In warmer climates, people probably stored foods in caves and other cooler places.

Early preservation. After fire was discovered, people probably dried fish and meat over a fire. Drying by fire may have led to the development of smoking as a method of preservation. Salt curing and fermentation are two other early methods of preservation. Ancient people salted meat or fish to prevent spoiling. Nomadic peoples in Asia used fermentation to make cheese. Fermentation of fruit juice to make wine also dates back to ancient times.

Modern food preservation began in the 1700's. Lazzaro Spallanzani, an Italian naturalist, sealed broth in glass flasks and heated them for an hour or more. The broth remained sterile as long as the flasks remained sealed.

By the early 1800's, Nicolas Appert, a candy maker from Paris, had worked out a canning process in which food was packed in glass jars. The jars were tightly sealed with corks and then heated in boiling water. Appert also published the first book on canning, which

gave specific canning methods for more than 50 foods. Although Appert had made a major contribution to canning, he did not understand why his process worked. This understanding came 50 years later when the French chemist Louis Pasteur discovered that heat kills harmful microorganisms (see **Pasteur, Louis**).

Cold storage had long been used to preserve foods. But special techniques were required to keep food cold in hot weather. At first, people cut ice from ponds and lakes during the winter, storing it in insulated buildings called *ice houses*. The insulation slowed its melting in the summer. In 1851, the first commercial machine for making ice was patented by John Gorrie, an American physician. Although Gorrie's business was a commercial failure, the large-scale use of refrigeration became important over the next several decades. By the early 1900's, there were about 2,000 ice plants in the United States.

Advances in refrigeration made possible frozen foods. In the mid-1920's, Clarence Birdseye, an American inventor, developed the first modern quick-freezing process. He used moving, chilled metal belts to quick-freeze fish.

Food was not dried in great volume in the United States until World War I (1914-1918), when dried food became important to feed soldiers. World War II (1939-1945) created further demand for dried food.

Scientists began experimenting with food irradiation in the early 1900's. In 1953, the United States formed the National Food Irradiation Program. Since that time, the FDA has approved a number of irradiation methods for various food products. In 2000, for example, the FDA approved irradiating fresh eggs to control salmonella bacteria.   Kathryn L. McCarthy

Related articles in *World Book* include:

Methods of preserving food

Cold storage	Irradiation
Dehydrated food	Meat packing
Fermentation	Pasteurization
Food, Frozen	Refrigeration
Freeze-drying	Sterilization
Fumigation	

Preservatives

Antibiotic	Salt
Dry ice	Spice
Food additive	Sugar
Nitrate	Sulfur dioxide
Nitrite	Vinegar

Other related articles

Bacteria
Birdseye, Clarence
Botulism
Enzyme
Evaporated milk
Fishing industry (Methods of processing)
Food and Drug Administration
Food poisoning
Jelly and jam
Mold
Pasteur, Louis
Pure food and drug laws
Spallanzani, Lazzaro
Yeast

Food service industry. See Restaurant.
Food Stamp Program. See Supplemental Nutrition Assistance Program.

© Stock Asylum/Alamy Images

© Mike Goldwater, Alamy Images

The food supply in developed and developing countries differs greatly. Farmers produce enough food to feed the world's people, but it is not distributed evenly. *Above left,* a United States farmer harvests a huge crop of corn. *Above right,* food aid is distributed to Ethiopian farmers.

Food supply

Food supply is the total amount of food available to all the world's people. No one can live without food. As a result, the supply of food has always ranked among humanity's chief concerns. The food supply depends mainly on the world's farmers. Farmers raise the crops and livestock that provide most of our food. As the world's population has grown, so too has the demand for food. Farmers and other food producers have faced a major challenge in meeting this demand.

The availability of food can vary from year to year and from country to country. World food production has increased steadily since 1970. Modern farmers produce enough food to feed the world's population. Yet hundreds of millions of people suffer from hunger and malnutrition. These people lack *food security*—that is, reliable access to sufficient food and nutrition. Producing enough food is not sufficient on its own to ensure food security. In most places, food is a *commodity* that is bought and sold on the market. Thus, even if enough food is produced to feed everyone, many people may lack the money to afford it. Problems with the distribution of food can also undermine food security.

Without food security, people and countries remain more vulnerable to *food crises*. A food crisis may be caused by a sudden disruption to food production. Such a disruption may result from widespread damage to crops from such natural causes as drought, flooding, and insect infestation. Human activities, such as warfare, can also lead to food crises. In addition, food crises may result from changes in market prices or trade patterns.

Experts use the term *food sovereignty* to describe the degree to which local groups control their own supply of food, apart from global market trends. Movements for increased food sovereignty have become popular in less developed regions such as Latin America, Africa, and Asia. Food sovereignty involves not only controlling the overall supply of food but also preserving local traditions of food and diet.

This article discusses basic food needs, major sources of food, and conditions that affect the food supply. It also discusses efforts to improve the food supply and food security. For more information, see the articles **Agriculture, Farm and farming, Food,** and **Nutrition.**

Outline

I. **Basic human food needs**
   A. Calories   B. Protein
II. **Major sources of food**
   A. Cereal grains
   B. Other crops
   C. Livestock and seafood
III. **Conditions that affect the food supply**
   A. Limited agricultural resources
   B. Increased demand for food
   C. Distribution problems
   D. National agriculture policies
   E. The economy and agriculture
IV. **Increasing the food supply**
   A. Developing new farmland
   B. Making farmland more productive
   C. Reducing the demand for feed grain
   D. Developing new sources of food
V. **Food supply programs**
   A. Technical and financial programs
   B. Food aid programs
   C. Research programs
   D. Food reserves

Basic human food needs

Food contains a number of *nutrients* (nourishing substances) that humans need to live. Food supplies energy that human bodies use for daily activities. This energy can be measured in units called *calories*. Food also supplies human bodies with a nutrient called *protein*. The body uses protein for energy and also for building, repairing, and maintaining its cells and tissues. In addition, the body depends on small amounts of *micronutrients*, such as vitamins and minerals, to maintain health. No single food contains all the nutrients the body needs. Thus, food security depends on access to a varied and balanced supply of foods.

More than 800 million people worldwide suffer from hunger or malnutrition. Most of these people live in less developed countries, particularly in sub-Saharan Africa (the part of Africa south of the Sahara) and South Asia. Young children and women—especially pregnant or nursing women—are particularly vulnerable to hunger and malnutrition. The rural poor and people who belong to ethnic or racial minorities within their countries are also vulnerable to these problems.

Calories. Two types of nutrients—*carbohydrates* and fats—normally provide most of the calories in the human diet. Carbohydrates include starches and sugars. *Cereal grains,* the most widely grown type of food, are rich in carbohydrates. The main cereal grains are barley, corn, millet, oats, rice, rye, sorghum, and wheat.

The number of calories a person needs each day depends on the person's sex, age, body build, and degree of physical activity. Larger and more active people require more calories. Children and young people who are still growing need more calories than their size would indicate.

Daily calorie *consumption* (intake) in the poorest countries is below 2,000—far fewer than most active people require. In some developed countries, daily calorie consumption averages over 3,300—far more than most people need. The body stores most excess calories as fat.

Protein, like carbohydrates and fat, can provide energy. But protein also serves as an important building block for cells. Animal-based sources of protein include dairy products, eggs, fish, and meat. The best plant-based sources of protein are *legumes* or *pulses*, including beans and peas. Cereal grains also supply some protein.

Proteins consist of smaller units called *amino acids*. Most animal proteins supply all the amino acids the body needs. A given plant source may lack certain amino acids. But certain combinations of plants, such as beans and rice, supply all the necessary amino acids.

Daily protein consumption in some developed countries averages 100 or more grams per day. In the poorest countries, people consume less than 50 grams of protein per day on average. Because many people in these countries have too few calories in their diet, much of the protein they consume is used to meet their energy needs, leaving less protein to build and maintain body cells.

Major sources of food

Certain crops, called *staples*, provide much of the world's nutrition and so are grown in huge quantities. Cereal grains serve as the most important staple crop. In

Per capita distribution of the world's calorie supply

This graph shows the number of calories that would be available daily *per capita* (for each person) in the world's major regions if the calories were divided equally among all the people in the region.

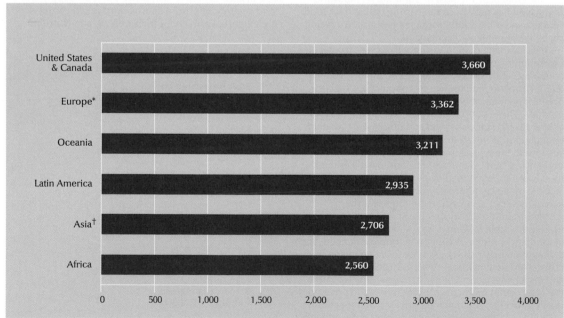

Region	Calories
United States & Canada	3,660
Europe*	3,362
Oceania	3,211
Latin America	2,935
Asia†	2,706
Africa	2,560

*Including Asian part of Russia.   †Excluding Asian part of Russia.
Figures are for 2009. Source: FAOSTAT, Statistics Division, Food and Agriculture Organization of the UN. http://www.faostat.fao.org. Data accessed in 2013.

some regions, such crops as potatoes and yams are staples.

Cereal grains rank as the world's most important food source. Worldwide, they supply about half the calories and much of the protein that people consume.

Almost all the grain grown in less developed countries is *food grain*—that is, grain consumed directly by people as food. The people may simply cook the grain as a main dish. Or they may use it to make bread, noodles, or some other food. People in developed countries also consume grain directly. But they also use much of it as *feed grain,* which is fed to livestock. People consume this grain indirectly in the form of such livestock products as meat, eggs, and dairy.

Certain grains used chiefly as feed in some countries are used chiefly as food in other countries. For example, most of the corn grown in the United States becomes livestock feed. But in some African and Latin American countries, corn serves as an important food grain.

Other crops. Soybeans and other legumes rank second only to rice as a source of food in many Asian countries. Potatoes serve as a staple food in parts of Europe and South America. People in some tropical areas rely largely on such local foods as bananas, *cassava* (a starchy root), and sweet potatoes or yams.

Livestock and seafood are the main sources of animal protein. On a worldwide basis, meat, eggs, and dairy products supply about 80 percent of the animal protein in the human diet. Seafood supplies about 20 percent of the animal protein people consume. In certain countries, however, fish provide a much larger percentage of the animal protein. Such countries include Japan, Norway, and the Philippines. Many people worry that the worldwide fish supply is being drastically diminished by overfishing. As a result, international commissions and some national governments are actively seeking to conserve fishing areas.

Conditions that affect the food supply

The food supply consists mainly of food produced during the current year. But it also includes *reserves*, also called *stocks*, left over from previous years. Food reserves are necessary to help prevent shortages after poor farming years. To build up reserves, the countries of the world overall must produce more food in a year than they consume. But few countries produce a surplus. The United States produces by far the largest surplus. Argentina, Australia, Brazil, Canada, and New Zealand also regularly produce a food surplus.

Most countries produce some food and then import additional supplies. Most developed countries that do not produce sufficient food can afford to import the extra supplies they need. The United Kingdom and Japan are examples of such countries. But less developed countries may lack enough money to import all the food they need, especially during food crises. For example, during global economic turmoil in 2007 and 2008, prices of staple grains and other foods rose significantly. The increase made it difficult for less developed countries to import a sufficient amount of food.

The amount of food produced by a country depends partly on the country's agricultural resources, such as land and water. No country has an unlimited supply of these resources. The worldwide food supply thus depends on limited agricultural resources and the ever-increasing demand for food. The supply of food within a

Per capita distribution of the world's protein supply

This graph shows the grams of protein that would be available daily *per capita* (for each person) in the world's major regions if each region's protein supply was divided equally among its people.

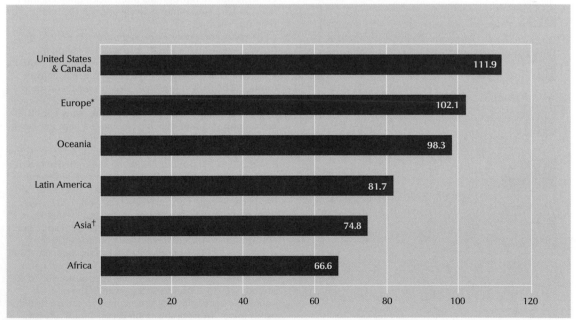

Region	grams
United States & Canada	111.9
Europe*	102.1
Oceania	98.3
Latin America	81.7
Asia†	74.8
Africa	66.6

*Including Asian part of Russia.   †Excluding Asian part of Russia.
Figures are for 2009. Source: FAOSTAT, Statistics Division, Food and Agriculture Organization of the UN.   http://www.faostat.fao.org. Data accessed in 2013.

certain country can also be affected by problems of distribution, national agricultural policy, and the economy.

Limited agricultural resources. Farming requires resources, especially land, water, energy, and fertilizer. Land serves as the chief agricultural resource. Land used for growing crops must be level and fertile. But most of the world's good cropland is already in use. Most of the unused farmable land lies in remote areas, far from markets and transportation.

All crops require water to grow—some more than others—but rainfall is distributed unevenly over Earth's surface. Some farmers can depend on rainfall for all the water they need. In other areas, the rainfall is too light or uncertain. Farmers in these areas must use irrigation water, if it is available. The supply of irrigation water is limited, and farmers in some countries use nearly all the available supply.

Many farmers depend heavily on energy resources—particularly petroleum fuels—to operate tractors, irrigation pumps, and other equipment. They use fertilizers to enrich the soil. Most fertilizers are nitrogen-based and are made from natural gas. But supplies of petroleum and natural gas are limited. Thus, farms will someday

The relation between food production and population

This graph shows the percentage contributions to world food production and world population of each major world region.

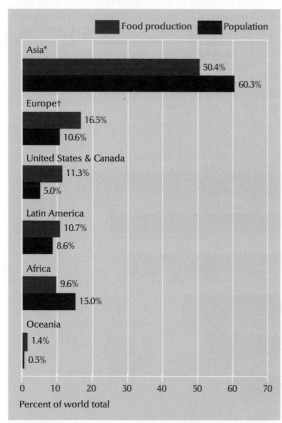

*Excluding Asian part of Russia.   †Including Asian part of Russia.
Figures are for 2009 and may not add up to 100 percent due to rounding.
Source: FAOSTAT, Statistics Division, Food and Agriculture Organization of the UN.
http://www.faostat.fao.org. Data accessed in 2013.

need other sources of energy and nitrogen fertilizers. Meanwhile, the energy needs of farmers have greatly increased. Since 1950, the amount of energy used to produce a ton of grain has more than doubled. In some countries, the energy used to produce fertilizer exceeds that used to power tractors. In every country, rising prices for energy and fertilizer add to the cost of food.

Increased use of agricultural resources can help farmers produce more food. But it can also cause environmental problems. For example, increased use of nitrogen fertilizers sometimes creates a build-up of nitrogen compounds in the soil. Rain water eventually washes these compounds into rivers and streams. There the compounds contribute to an overgrowth of algae, serving as a major source of water pollution.

Increased demand for food chiefly results from the growth in world population. To a lesser extent, it also comes from rising standards of living. Higher living standards enable people to afford both bigger meals and higher quality foods.

The effect of population growth. Experts measure a country's food supply by the amount of food *per capita.* The per capita amount is how much food would be available for each person if the food were distributed equally among all. The food supply thus depends not only on the total amount of food but also on the number of people who must be fed.

World food production is increasing at a rate slightly higher than world population growth. The changes vary from place to place, however. In Europe and many parts of Asia, people have relatively few children, and food production has outpaced population growth. But in other regions, especially Africa, population continues to grow faster than food production.

In an attempt to avoid disastrous food shortages, many less developed countries have promoted birth control programs to curb population growth (see **Birth control**). But such programs often lack significant influence and are sometimes actively opposed for cultural or religious reasons.

The effect of higher living standards. As people improve their living standards, especially through increased personal income, they usually eat more food. In time, they also generally begin to eat more expensive foods, particularly more meat. Greater meat consumption typically requires an increase in the amount of grain used for livestock feed. For this reason, many countries with a high standard of living also have a high per capita consumption of grain.

In developed countries, people may directly consume about 200 to 300 pounds (90 to 135 kilograms) of grain per person annually. In many such countries, several times that amount of grain per person is fed to livestock each year. People consume this grain indirectly in the form of meat, eggs, and dairy products. In addition, grain is also used to make alcohol. Total per capita grain consumption in some developed countries can thus reach about 2,000 pounds (900 kilograms) annually. Total per capita grain consumption in less developed countries, on the other hand, often averages about 400 to 600 pounds (180 to 270 kilograms) a year. In the poorest countries, per capita grain consumption can be significantly lower. Most of this grain is consumed directly.

Distribution problems. Less developed countries

High-yield crops, such as this hybrid rice under development in the Philippines, can increase the food supply. During the Green Revolution of the 1960's, many farmers in less developed countries began using high-yield crops.

© Joerg Boethling, Alamy Images

are more likely to lack adequate forms of *infrastructure,* such as modern facilities for the transportation and storage of food. In many cases, food supplies cannot be delivered immediately where they are needed. They also cannot be safely stored to await shipment. As a result, large quantities of food spoil or are eaten by rodents and insects. Thus, food waste in such countries is likely to occur between farmers and food *retailers* (sellers).

In developed countries, food waste more often occurs among retailers and consumers. Such countries have adequate transportation and storage infrastructures. But retailers and consumers there throw away much food through strictly following expiration dates. Much prepared food in homes and in restaurants also ends up being thrown away.

National agricultural policies. Many countries fund agricultural research and farmer education. Such policies can greatly increase the food supply.

Many nations also influence the food supply by actively managing the agricultural industry. For much of the 1900's, many countries—including the United States—adopted a policy of *supply management.* The primary goal of the policy was to maintain a stable supply of certain agricultural products, while at the same time avoiding too great a surplus. Supply management policy relied on income *subsidies* to farmers. These subsidies, often money paid directly to farmers, guaranteed high prices for agricultural products, even if the market value of such products was low. Supply management also relied on *production controls,* measures that limit the acreage of a commodity that can be harvested.

One effect of supply management policy was to help stabilize a country's economy for agriculture, limiting price fluctuations and protecting the overall food supply. The policy, however, also encouraged farmers to overproduce some commodities—such as wheat—for which they received subsidies. The surplus that resulted was often sent to less developed countries as food aid. As a result, some less developed countries became more dependent on imported food aid and invested less in their own food systems.

The economy and agriculture. Since the 1980's and 1990's, most countries have weakened or eliminated supply management policy. While the United States continues to provide subsidies to farmers, for example, it has eliminated production controls. The market econ-

omy now exerts a stronger influence in agriculture. This influence has helped make agriculture less stable. Annual prices *fluctuate* (vary up and down) more markedly than they did during the era of supply management.

Increased fluctuation in prices affects both farmers and consumers, especially in less developed countries. Fluctuating annual prices, especially sharp declines in price, can hurt farmers' incomes. For example, coffee prices were once kept artificially high through a worldwide supply management policy called the International Coffee Agreement. When the agreement collapsed in 1989, world coffee prices dropped by about 50 percent in a few years. The price collapse led to a "coffee crisis" in which coffee farmers saw their incomes drop dramatically, and many of them could no longer support themselves. Coffee prices have remained extremely unpredictable since the collapse of the agreement.

Sharp increases in food prices can make it difficult for consumers to afford adequate food. In developed countries, most people spend only a small fraction of their income on food and so can better absorb price increases. In less developed countries, on the other hand, consumers may spend more than half of their incomes on food. They have little additional income to accommodate a large spike in staple prices. From mid-2007 to early 2008, for example, wheat prices increased by more than 200 percent. The jump harmed the ability of poorer households to support themselves.

Increasing the food supply

Most increases in food supply result from greater output by farms. Farm output can be increased in two main ways: by developing new farmland and by making existing farmland more productive. Two other methods of increasing the food supply involve reducing the demand for feed grain and developing new sources of food.

Developing new farmland is difficult and costly. The largest areas of land that could be developed for farming are in sub-Saharan Africa and in the Amazon River Basin of South America. Dense forests cover much of this land. The tropical soil and climate are also not ideal for many kinds of farming.

Nations often establish expensive programs to encourage farmers to clear land and plant crops. However, forest soils lack many important plant nutrients and are quickly depleted by farming. Scientists are working to develop farming methods that preserve forest soils.

In addition, the expansion of farmlands can threaten tropical rain forests and other valuable natural areas. Scientists fear that continued destruction of forests and other habitats will lead to the extinction of thousands of species of plants and animals.

Making farmland more productive. Farmers have two main methods of making the land more productive. They may increase their use of irrigation, energy, and fertilizer. Or they may use improved varieties of grains and livestock. Improved varieties produce higher crop yields and larger amounts of livestock products. Farmers in developed countries have used both methods for many years. In the 1960's, farmers in some less developed countries also adopted both methods to increase their production of wheat and rice. This effort proved so successful that it has become known as the Green Revolution.

The development of high-yield varieties of rice and wheat made the Green Revolution possible. But the revolution also required greater use of irrigation water, energy, and fertilizer. Many farmers took water from wells, installing electric or diesel-powered pumps to bring it to the surface. To get the highest yields, farmers had to enrich the soil with fertilizers. During the 1960's and 1970's, these methods helped such countries as India and Mexico more than double their wheat production.

The Green Revolution can continue to make farmland more productive. If farmers in the tropics have enough water, fertilizer, and other essential resources, for example, they can grow multiple crops a year on the same land. But the Green Revolution's ability to increase the food supply is limited. Many farmers in less developed countries cannot afford the additional resources that the Green Revolution requires. In any case, greater use of these resources makes land more productive only to a point. Farmers in the 2010's used roughly 10 times as much fertilizer as they did in 1950. However, grain yields

© Neil Palmer, CIAT
Agricultural research seeks to increase the quantity and quality of the food supply. This researcher in Colombia handles plant samples stored at a facility called a *gene bank.*

in the 2010's were only about three times as large—and the rates of increase are slowing.

Much agricultural research is being done to further increase farmland productivity. For example, scientists are working to develop varieties of grain that not only produce higher yields but also have other improved characteristics. Such grain might supply more complete nutrition, make more efficient use of water and fertilizer, and grow with better resistance to insects and disease. However, it is difficult to develop a plant variety with so many different positive characteristics. The necessary research therefore takes much time and money.

In some instances, less developed countries have benefited from the introduction of large-scale agriculture. This practice has often been promoted as a way to generate income through export of crops. However, small-scale farming can make more efficient use of land than large-scale farming does. Many experts now encourage small-scale farming over large-scale farming to increase food supplies for local people in less developed countries.

Reducing the demand for feed grain would increase the amount of calories and plant-based protein available for human consumption. This increase would occur because livestock consume more calories and protein than they produce. Grain-fed beef cattle are especially inefficient in this respect. By some measures, it takes roughly 10 pounds (4.5 kilograms) of grain to produce only 1 pound (0.5 kilogram) of boneless beef. But 10 pounds of grain supplies several times as many calories as does 1 pound of beef, and more protein as well.

In the past, almost all beef cattle grazed on grass and other forage up to the time of slaughter. But since the mid-1900's, cattle-fattening establishments called *feed lots* have become popular in the United States, Canada, and other developed countries. A feed lot fattens cattle on grain. Today, most U.S. beef cattle are fattened on feed lots, consuming enormous quantities of grain, especially corn. The demand for feed grain would lessen if the cattle industry returned to raising cattle chiefly on forage. But relying on forage would not produce enough beef to satisfy U.S. demand. In addition, many people in the United States prefer the flavor of beef from grain-fed cattle. The demand for feed grain would also decline if people in developed countries ate less meat.

Developing new sources of food. Such oilseed crops as coconuts, cottonseed, peanuts, and soybeans can all serve as valuable sources of protein. Soybeans have an especially high protein content. Soy-based foods, such as tofu, have long been important in Asia, where soybeans originated. But with this exception, none of these oilseed crops ranks as a major, widespread food source. Instead, farmers grow the crops mainly for their oils. These oils are used to make such products as margarine, salad dressing, and many kinds of prepared dishes and snacks. The protein, however, remains in the *meal,* the part of the seed that is left after the oil has been removed. Most of the meal is used for livestock feed.

Since the mid-1900's, food scientists have been working to make the protein in soybean meal available for human consumption. They have developed a variety of inexpensive, specially flavored foods from soybean meal. Some of these products have been successfully marketed in various parts of the world, often as meat and dairy substitutes. Food scientists are also working to convert other oilseed crop meal into foods that will have a broad appeal. Such crops are widely grown in the tropics. They could provide millions of people in less developed countries with inexpensive protein.

Scientists and manufacturers of food products have also developed methods of enriching food. For example, manufacturers often add micronutrients to bread and to other grain products to improve nutritional value.

Food supply programs

Various organizations sponsor programs to increase and improve the world's food supply. The chief international organizations include two United Nations (UN) agencies: the Food and Agriculture Organization (FAO) and the World Bank. The World Food Council, a group of food experts appointed by the United Nations, helps coordinate the work of the various international organizations. Many developed nations have set up their own agencies to help increase the world's food supply.

Private groups sponsor a number of important food supply programs. For example, the Rockefeller Foundation has long been one of the biggest contributors to agricultural research in less developed countries. The foundation is a philanthropic organization founded in the United States by the Rockefeller family.

Technical and financial programs work to expand farm output in less developed countries. The Food and Agriculture Organization sponsors the chief technical assistance programs. These programs seek mainly to train farmers in modern agricultural methods. The United Nations Development Programme also sponsors technical aid programs.

Most financial help for agriculture in less developed countries takes the form of low-interest loans. The World Bank and regional banks associated with the World Bank provide most of these loans. In 1976, the United Nations established the International Fund for Agricultural Development to obtain additional loan funds from prosperous UN member nations. The United States offers technical aid and loans chiefly through its Agency for International Development.

Food aid programs provide shipments of food to countries that need emergency aid. Industrialized countries in Europe and the Americas, along with Japan, contribute most of this aid. The United States ranks as the largest contributor. Most of the assistance given by the United States is administered through the federal government's Food for Peace program. The World Food Programme, sponsored by the UN and the FAO, channels donations from individual countries to nations in need of aid. The Food Assistance Convention, an international treaty signed by many developed countries, directs grain donations and other forms of assistance from individual countries to nations in need. Many private charitable organizations also supply food aid.

Research programs. Scientific research programs seek to increase both the quantity and the quality of the food supply. Researchers are constantly trying to develop cereal grains that can provide higher amounts of protein while also giving high enough yields.

Research scientists are also seeking ways to conserve

AP

A food crisis in Somalia in 2011, started by drought and political instability, threatened millions with starvation. In this photograph, children line up for emergency food aid in Mogadishu.

agricultural resources. Some of this research is aimed at developing varieties of grain that make more efficient use of water and fertilizer. Animal scientists are conducting similar experiments to develop varieties of cattle that produce more meat for the same amount of feed. International organizations and national governments have placed controls on the harvesting of many types of fish to prevent excessive depletion of stocks. In addition, more of the world's fish supply is being produced through *aquaculture,* the controlled farming of fish and aquatic plants.

Many research projects take place at agricultural research institutes sponsored by the Consultative Group on International Agricultural Research (CGIAR). CGIAR is funded by a mix of governments, international agencies, and private foundations. These institutes have been established in less developed countries. Each specializes in a particular type of research. In Mexico, for example, the International Center for the Improvement of Maize and Wheat focuses on producing improved varieties of corn, wheat, and other grains. Some of the institutes, such as the International Institute of Tropical Agriculture, in Nigeria, focus on improving agriculture specifically in places with tropical climates.

Food reserves. The world's food reserves consist of the individual reserves of the major exporting countries. Each country administers its own reserves. Some food from these reserves is supplied to nations in need of aid through programs conducted separately by each government. Another part of the reserves is pledged by governments to international organizations, such as the World Food Programme.   Bill Winders

Related articles in *World Book* include:

Agency for International
  Development

Birth control

Famine

Fishing industry
Food and Agriculture Organization
Food for Peace
Foreign aid
Great Irish Famine
Hunger
Population
Standard of living
Technical assistances
United Nations (Fighting hunger)
World Bank

Questions

Why do most developing countries seldom have enough food?
What are four methods to increase the food supply?
What plants are the most important source of food?
Which country produces the most surplus food?
How do higher living standards affect the food supply?
What is the Green Revolution?
How would a reduction in the demand for feed grain increase the food supply? Why?

Additional resources

Fridell, Ron. *The War on Hunger: Dealing with Dictators, Deserts, and Debt.* 21st Century Bks., 2003. Younger readers.
Goldberg, Jake. *Food: The Struggle to Sustain the Human Community.* Watts, 1999.
Hunger. Bread for the World Inst., published annually.
McGovern, George S. The Third Freedom: Ending Hunger in Our Time. Simon & Schuster, 2001.
Smil, Vaclav. *Feeding the World.* MIT Pr., 2000.
Wild, Alan. *Soils, Land, and Food: Managing the Land During the 21st Century.* Cambridge, 2003.

Food value. See Nutrition.

Food web. See Ecology (Ecosystems); **Fish** (Fish in the balance of nature).

Fool's gold. See Pyrite; Mineral (picture).

Foot, in poetry. See **Poetry** (Rhythm and meter).

Foot is a unit of length in the inch-pound system of measurement customarily used in the United States. It is equal to one-third of a yard, and contains 12 inches. A 1959 international agreement defines the yard in a way that makes the foot equal to exactly 0.3048 meter. See **Weights and measures** (Conversion factors).

A *square foot* is a unit of area. It is equal to the area of a square whose sides are 1 foot long. It contains 12 × 12, or 144, square inches (about 929 square centimeters). A *cubic foot* is a unit of volume. It is equal to the volume of a cube 1 foot high, 1 foot wide, and 1 foot deep. It contains 12 × 12 × 12, or 1,728, cubic inches (about 28,317 cubic centimeters). The symbol for foot is ´.

The foot measurement began in ancient times based on the length of the human foot. By the Middle Ages, the foot as defined by different European countries ranged from 10 to 20 inches. In 1305, England set the foot equal to 12 inches, where 1 inch equaled the length of "three grains of barley dry and round."   Bruce F. Field

Foot is the structure at the end of the leg, on which humans and some animals stand. In animals that walk on all four legs, the ends of the front and hind limbs, or feet, are much the same. In humans, birds, and animals such as the kangaroo that walk on their hind limbs, the foot is heavier and stronger than its counterpart on the forelimb, the hand.

The bones. The human foot has 26 bones. They are (1) the seven *tarsals,* or anklebones; (2) the five *metatarsals,* or instep bones; and (3) the 14 *phalanges,* or toe bones. The tarsal bones are the *talus, calcaneus, navicular, cuboid,* and the three *cuneiform* bones. They

form the heel and back part of the instep. The metatarsal bones connect the cuneiforms and the cuboid with the phalanges, and form the front part of the instep. The big toe has two phalanges. Each of the other toes has three. The ends of the phalanges meet the underside of the metatarsals to form the *ball of the foot.*

The arches. The bones of the foot form three arches, two running lengthwise and one running across the instep. The arches provide the natural elastic spring of the foot in walking or jumping. The main arch reaches from the heel bone to the ball of the foot. It is called the *long medial* or *plantar* arch. This arch touches the ground only at the heel and ball of the foot and thus acts as a shock absorber for the leg and spinal column. A thick layer of flexible cartilage covers the ends of the bones of the arch (see **Cartilage**). The cartilage helps make the arch shock-absorbent. The *lateral* arch runs along the outside of the foot, and the *transverse* or *metatarsal* arch lies across the ball of the foot. The condition known as *flatfoot* may be caused by the breakdown of the arches of the foot (see **Flatfoot**).

Ligaments and muscles support the arches of the foot. The long plantar ligament, called the *plantar fascia,* is very strong. It keeps the bones of the foot in place and protects the nerves, muscles, and blood vessels in the hollow of the foot. The foot has as many muscles as the hand. But its structure permits less flexibility and freedom of movement than does that of the hand.

Tough, thick skin covers the *sole,* or bottom, of the foot. A thick pad of fatty tissue lies between the skin and the bones and the plantar ligament. This layer of fat acts like an air cushion to protect the inner parts of the foot from pressure on the foot and from jarring. Disorders of the foot, such as corns, may result from wearing badly fitted shoes.   Leslie S. Matthews

Related articles in *World Book* include:

Achilles tendon	Chilblain
Animal (Adaptations for moving about)	Clubfoot
	Corn
Ankle	Footprinting
Athlete's foot	Immersion foot
Bunion	Podiatry
Callus	

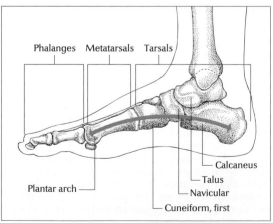

WORLD BOOK illustration by Patricia Wynne

The foot has three sets of bones—the *tarsals,* or anklebones; *metatarsals,* or instep bones; and *phalanges,* or toe bones. The *plantar arch* extends from the heel to the ball of the foot.

Foot, Michael (1913-2010), served as the leader of the United Kingdom's Labour Party from 1980 to 1983. He was a member of the party's left wing. The left wing supports government-sponsored social welfare programs and government ownership of some businesses.

Foot was born on July 23, 1913, in Plymouth, England, and attended Oxford University. He became a newspaper columnist and editor and a forceful left-wing critic of British government policies. From 1945 to 1955, Foot represented a district of Plymouth in the House of Commons. He represented the Ebbw Vale district of Wales from 1960 to 1983 and Blaenau Gwent from 1983 to 1992.

AP/Wide World
Michael Foot

In 1976, James Callaghan was elected as Labour Party leader and prime minister. Foot received the second largest number of votes and became deputy prime minister and leader of the House of Commons. His term in the offices ended in 1979, when the Conservative Party won control of the government. Callaghan resigned as Labour Party leader in 1980, and party members elected Foot to succeed him. Foot resigned as leader in 1983 after the Labour Party suffered its worst election defeat since 1918. Foot died on March 3, 2010.   Richard Rose

Foot-and-mouth disease is a highly contagious viral disease of cattle, sheep, hogs, and other animals with *cloven* (divided) hoofs. It is also known as *hoof-and-mouth disease.* The infection does not actually affect the hard structures of the hoof, but rather the soft tissues around it. Foot-and-mouth disease occurs among livestock in many regions of the world, particularly in Africa, Asia, and South America. The disease is rare in Australia, much of Europe, and North America.

Cause and symptoms. A small, ball-shaped virus causes foot-and-mouth disease. Healthy livestock may acquire the disease through contact with infected animals or with objects that have been contaminated by saliva, other body fluids, or wastes from infected animals. Winds may spread the virus, as may animals that are not themselves affected by foot-and-mouth-disease, such as birds, cats, and rats. People may also spread the virus if they have been in direct contact with it. It is possible for people to develop a mild, temporary infection.

The virus produces painful, fluid-filled blisters on the lips, tongue, gums, nostrils, and upper part of the foot. In animals, blisters also develop in the tissue between the two parts of the hoof. The blisters break open after a few days and become raw sores. Infected animals also develop a high fever, *salivate* (drool) excessively, have difficulty walking, and lose weight. In female animals, the virus also affects the milk-producing glands, decreasing their yield. Foot-and-mouth disease rarely kills adult animals, but it causes a higher death rate among the young. The disease hurts farmers economically by reducing their livestock's meat and milk production.

Control. There are no specific cures or treatments for foot-and-mouth disease, but farmers use a variety of methods to control or prevent it. In the African, Asian, and South American countries where the disease is *endemic* (found regularly), livestock owners control it chiefly through the use of vaccines. Veterinarians must administer vaccines at regular intervals because most protect the animals for only a short period.

In the United States and most other countries where the disease is not endemic, it is controlled chiefly through import restrictions and quarantine procedures. Such measures normally prevent the introduction of the virus. In addition, these countries have policies for eliminating the virus if an outbreak occurs. Most such policies call for slaughtering infected animals, burying or burning their carcasses, and decontaminating the area where they lived. In 2001, a rare outbreak of the disease in Europe led to the slaughter of hundreds of thousands of cattle, sheep, and pigs. Imports of meat from Europe were banned in the United States and other countries in an attempt to control the spread of the disease.

Max Brugh

Foot-candle is a unit of measurement of *illumination,* the amount of light that falls on an object. The foot-candle is part of the customary system of measurement.

Two factors determine the amount of light an object receives: (1) the *luminous intensity* (the amount of light a light source produces) and (2) the distance between the light source and the object. As the luminous intensity increases, illumination also increases. As the distance increases, illumination decreases by the distance squared.

To calculate in foot-candles the illumination *(E)* on a surface perpendicular to a light ray, scientists use the formula

$$E = \frac{I}{D^2}$$

I is the luminous intensity in *candelas* (see **Candela**). *D* is the distance in feet between the light source and the object.

In the metric system, illumination is measured in a unit called the *lux.* Distance is measured in meters. One foot-candle equals 10.764 lux.   Ronald N. Helms

See also **Lighting** (Quantity of light).

Foot-pound is a unit of work and energy in the inch-pound system of measurement customarily used in the United States. Physicists define *work* as the arithmetical product of a force that acts on an object and the distance through which the object moves. In other words, the amount of work done equals the force times the distance. Thus, 1 foot-pound of work is done when a force of 1 pound acts on an object that moves 1 foot. When the force is 2 pounds and the object moves 3 feet, 6 foot-pounds of work are done.

Energy is the ability to do work. One foot-pound is the energy needed to move an object 1 foot against the opposition of 1 pound of force. Thus, it takes 1 foot-pound of energy to raise an object that weighs 1 pound a distance of 1 foot. In this case, the opposing force is the weight of the object. When a 2-pound object is raised 3 feet, 6 foot-pounds of energy are used. These are examples of mechanical energy. The foot-pound can also be used to measure any other form of energy, such as chemical energy.

In the metric system, work and energy are measured in *joules.* One foot-pound equals 1.356 joules. Foot-pound is abbreviated as *ft-lb.*   Hugh D. Young

See also **Energy** (Units of work and energy); **Joule; Work.**

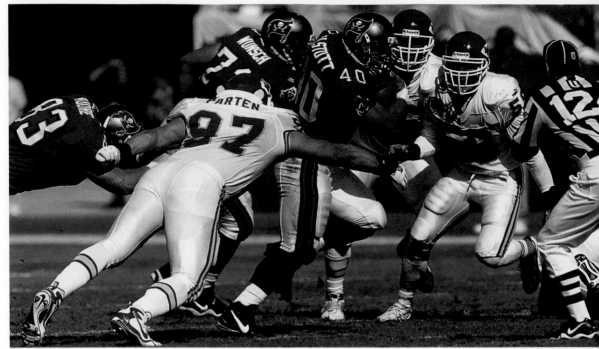

Action-packed plays make football an exciting game. In the play shown here, the defensive team, wearing white uniforms, tries to stop the ball carrier, wearing red, from advancing the ball. His teammates block for him. An official, wearing a striped shirt, watches for rules violations.

Football

Football, also called *American football,* is an exciting team sport played chiefly in the United States and Canada. The term *football* is also used for team sports played in other parts of the world. For example, the game called *soccer* in the United States is called *association football,* or simply *football,* in most other countries. A game resembling American football, called *rugby,* is also played in many countries as either *rugby union* or *rugby league.* Other types of football include *Gaelic football,* played in Ireland, and *Australian rules football,* played in Australia. This article discusses American football. For information on other sports called football, see **Soccer** and **Rugby football.**

American football is played by elementary school, high school, college, and professional teams. Millions of people crowd stadiums each football season to watch their favorite teams. Millions of people also watch games on television between college football teams as well as televised competition in the two major professional leagues, the National Football League (NFL) of the United States and the Canadian Football League (CFL).

In the United States, football is played by two teams of 11 players each. Canadian teams have 12 players. Each team tries to score points, mainly by running or passing plays that move an oval ball across the opposing team's goal line. Such a run or pass scores a touchdown. During a game, possession of the ball shifts from team to team. The team with the ball is the *offensive team* or *of-*

fense. The other team is the *defensive team* or *defense.* It tries to prevent the offense from scoring.

A good football team combines strength and speed. Physical contact, especially involving blocking and tackling, is a basic part of football. The sport also requires quick reactions and thorough preparation for each game. In addition, split-second teamwork is essential.

There are several variations of football. Two variations—touch football and flag football—eliminate much of the physical contact. In touch football, a play ends when a defensive player merely touches, rather than tackles, the ball carrier. In flag football, a play ends when a defender pulls a piece of cloth, called a *flag,* from the belt or back pocket of the ball carrier.

Touch and flag football are popular in high school and college *intramural* programs. In such programs, teams from the same school compete against one another. Some high schools with small enrollments have football teams with six, eight, or nine players. A few professional women's football teams have formed leagues, and a few high schools have teams for girls. The game is played almost entirely by men and boys, however, and this article concerns male football only.

This article deals chiefly with football in the United States. The game differs slightly in Canada. The section *Canadian football* describes some of the differences.

The field and equipment

The field. Most distances in football are measured in yards. One yard equals 0.91 meter. Football is played on a level area 120 yards long and 53 ⅓ yards wide. The field may have a surface of natural grass or of a synthetic material. All indoor stadiums and many outdoor stadiums use green synthetic surfaces that look like grass.

The football field is marked with white lines. It is often called a *gridiron* because the pattern of lines resembles the cooking utensil used to broil foods. A *sideline* borders each of the two long sides of the field. Any player who touches or crosses a sideline is out of bounds. *Yard lines* cross the field every 5 yards. Near each end of the field is a *goal line*. The goal lines are 100 yards apart. An area called an *end zone* extends 10 yards beyond each goal line. The yard lines are numbered from each goal line to the 50-yard line, also called *midfield*.

Two rows of lines, called *hash marks,* parallel the sidelines. All plays start with the ball between or on the hash marks. If a play ends out of bounds or between hash marks and the sideline, the ball is placed on the nearest hash mark for the next play.

In high school and college football, two *goal posts* stand on the end line 10 yards behind each goal line. A crossbar connects the posts 10 feet (3 meters) above the ground. In the NFL, a single post 6 feet (1.8 meters) behind the end line curves forward and supports the crossbar directly over the end line. In high school games, the goal posts are each 20 feet (6 meters) high and 23 feet 4 inches (7 meters) apart. In college and NFL football games, the goal posts are each 30 feet (9 meters) high and 18 feet 6 inches (5.6 meters) apart.

The ball is oval. It is about 11 inches (28 centimeters) long and about 7 inches (18 centimeters) in diameter at the center. Balls used in high school, college, and professional games are made of four pieces of leather stitched together. Footballs used in recreation may be made of rubber or plastic. A football has a rubber lining, which is inflated to an air pressure of $12\frac{1}{2}$ to $13\frac{1}{2}$ pounds per square inch (0.88 to 0.95 kilogram per square cen-

MacGregor® Sporting Goods

The football is oval. Balls used in high school, college, and professional games have a pebble-grained leather covering. Laces along one seam provide a grip for passers and ball carriers.

timeter). The ball weighs 14 to 15 ounces (397 to 425 grams). Leather laces along one seam provide a grip for holding and passing the ball.

The uniform. A football player's uniform is made of cotton or nylon and consists of a shirt and pants. The shirt, which is called a *jersey,* has the player's number—and sometimes his name—sewn on the back and front for identification by the officials and spectators. The uniforms fit tightly so that opposing players cannot easily grasp them when trying to block or tackle.

Protective equipment helps prevent injuries. The amount of equipment a player wears depends on his position. The section called *The players and coaches* describes the duties of the various players. Linemen wear more protective equipment than other players because they are involved in the most physical contact through

Diagram of a U.S. football field

The football field is marked with white lines. Yard lines cross the field every 5 yards (4.6 meters). Hash marks run down the field across the yard lines, dividing the field into three unequal sections. The hash marks for college games are shown in red. Hash marks for the National Football League are shown in blue. Goal posts stand on the end lines behind the goal lines.

WORLD BOOK diagram

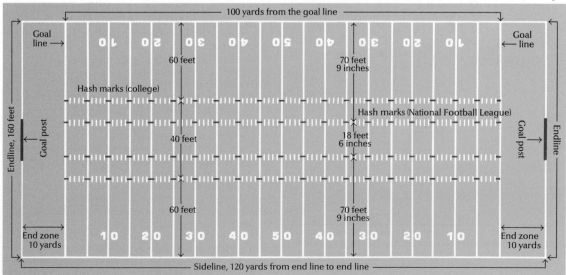

Football terms

Blitz is a defensive maneuver in which one or more linebackers and defensive backs charge through the offensive line and try to tackle the quarterback before he can pass or hand off the ball.

Draw is a running play in which the quarterback fakes a pass to get the defensive linemen to pursue him. He then hands the ball to a running back who attempts to advance through the gap vacated by the defensive linemen.

Fair catch can be made by a player receiving a punt or kickoff. The player cannot run with the ball or be tackled. The ball is put into play where it is caught. A raised hand means the player who receives the ball is requesting a fair catch.

Field position refers to the location of the ball on the field. If the offense has the ball near its opponent's goal line, it has good field position. If the offense has the ball near its own goal line, it has poor field position.

Option is an offensive play in which the quarterback runs along the line of scrimmage with the choice of keeping the ball or tossing it to a running back.

Prevent defense refers to a defensive formation that includes extra defensive backs to guard against an expected long pass.

Roll-out is a passing play in which the passer runs toward a sideline before throwing the ball. This play helps the passer avoid tacklers, giving him more time to find a receiver.

Sack is the tackle of a quarterback before he can throw a pass.

Screen pass is a play in which the quarterback retreats behind the line of scrimmage and then tosses a short pass to a receiver waiting behind several blockers.

Sweep means a running play around either end.

Trap is a running play in which the offensive line allows a defensive lineman into the backfield and blocks him from the side. The ball carrier then runs through the hole left by the lineman.

Shoulder pad

Shoulder pad extension

Elbow pad

Rib pad

Helmet

Face mask

Chin guard

Hip pad

Arm guard

Thigh pad

Knee pad

Liner

WORLD BOOK illustration by Bill and Judie Anderson

Protective equipment helps prevent injuries. The amount and type of padding depend on a player's position. Linemen wear the most padding because they do the most blocking and tackling. Backs and ends wear less so they can move more easily.

blocking and tackling. Backs and ends wear less equipment so that they can run at top speed.

Each player wears a helmet held in place with a chin guard. The helmet has a face mask. Most players also wear a mouthpiece to help prevent injuries to their teeth. Under their uniforms, the players wear shoulder, hip, thigh, and knee pads. In many cases, the thigh pads and knee pads are sewn into the pants. Some players also use arm guards, elbow pads, rib pads, and liners to protect the shins.

Football players wear shoes that help prevent slipping and provide good traction for running. When the game is played on grass, players wear shoes with cleats. On synthetic surfaces, they wear shoes with specially designed soles for better traction. Some players wear high-top shoes that lace up to their ankles. The lacing gives the ankles more support and helps prevent sprains. Most backs and ends prefer low-cut shoes that enable them to make quick *cuts* (changes in direction).

The players and coaches

Most football teams have players who specialize in offense and others who play defense. Before each play, the offense from one team and the opponents' defense face each other along the *line of scrimmage.* This imaginary line aligns with the spot where the preceding play ended. The line of scrimmage parallels the yard lines and passes through the tip of the ball nearest each team's goal. Thus, each team has its own line of scrimmage, separated by the length of the football. The area between the two lines is called the *neutral zone.*

The offensive team consists of seven players called *linemen* and four called *backs.* The team must have at least seven players on the line of scrimmage when the play begins. The five linemen in the middle are known as *interior linemen.* They are the *center,* two *guards*, and two *tackles.* The center *snaps* (tosses or hands) the ball between his legs to a back to begin a play. All five interior linemen block for the ball carriers, the passers, and the pass receivers.

The two linemen farthest from the center on either side are *ends.* In addition to blocking, they are eligible to catch passes. In most offensive strategies, the end called the *tight end* is used more as a blocker than a pass receiver. He lines up close to the tackle to be in a better position to block. The other end is the more important pass receiver. He usually splits away from the other linemen to improve his opportunity to run downfield to catch passes. He is normally called a *wide receiver,* though the older term *split end* is sometimes used.

The four backs make up the *backfield.* The team's arrangements of players, called *offensive formations* or simply *offenses,* receive their names from the various positions of the backs. For example, in the T-formation, the *quarterback* receives the snap close to the center. The *fullback* lines up 5 yards directly behind the quarterback, and two *halfbacks* line up on either side of the fullback. A line drawn from the quarterback to the fullback makes the stem of a T, and a line from one halfback to the other is the top bar.

Although the T-formation is seldom used today, the most popular offenses are variations of the T. The quarterback still lines up behind the center for the snap. He hands off to one of the backs and also throws most of

Offensive and defensive formations

Before each play, the teams line up in offensive and defensive formations on the line of scrimmage. Some offensive formations are more effective for passing, and others are more effective for running. The defense selects a formation that will likely stop the play it believes the offense will try.

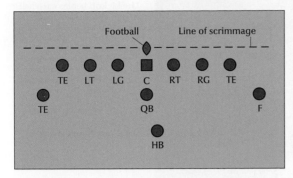

The single back is a popular offensive formation. Only one running back lines up behind the quarterback. The other back moves to a flanker position to block or become a pass receiver.

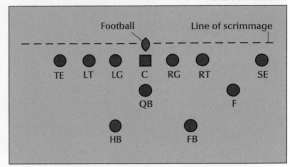

The pro-set formation is an offensive formation that has two running backs split behind the quarterback and two wide receivers, one in the backfield and one on the line of scrimmage.

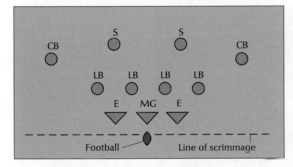

The three-four defense is often used when the defense expects a pass. It has only three linemen. The four linebackers and four defensive backs provide extra coverage of receivers.

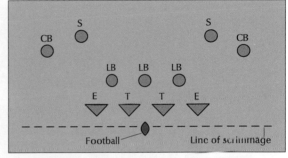

The four-three defense is the basic defense in professional football. The four linemen, three linebackers, and four defensive backs can defend well against both passing and running plays.

Key to positions   C=center; CB=cornerback; E=end; F=flanker; FB=fullback; HB=halfback; LB=linebacker; LG=left guard; LT=left tackle; MG= middle guard; QB=quarterback; RG=right guard; RT=right tackle; S=safety; SE= split end; T=tackle; TE=tight end

the passes. One halfback lines up a yard or two off the line of scrimmage and is called a *flanker.* Sometimes both halfbacks will become flankers. In one variation, a back goes *in motion.* This means that before the ball is snapped, the man in motion will move left or right. He cannot move forward. This maneuver forces the defense to shift and often leave a weak spot.

The remaining backs who are neither flankers nor in motion do most of the running and are thus called *running backs.* If one of the running backs is primarily a blocker, he may be called a *blocking back.* Another variation of the T-formation has only one running back. The blocking back moves to a flanker position to improve his blocking angle or to enable him to break down-field to receive a pass. Sometimes the back goes in motion from the flanker position. A back used in this way may be called an *H-back.* Every back who lines up behind the center is eligible to catch a pass, including the quarterback in certain circumstances. A *pro-set formation* has two running backs split apart and two wide receivers, one in the backfield and one on the line of scrimmage.

The defensive team is divided into three units: the

line, the linebackers, and the secondary.

The line may have as many players as the defensive team chooses. But most teams use three, four, or five players. A three-man line consists of a *middle guard,* also called a *nose guard* or *nose tackle,* and two *ends.* A four-man line, called the *front four,* consists of two tackles and two ends. A five-man line consists of a *middle guard,* two tackles, and two ends. The defensive linemen use their size and strength against offensive blockers.

The linebackers position themselves two or three yards behind the linemen. A team that uses a four-man line will normally have three linebackers. The player who lines up facing the center is the *middle linebacker.* The two other players, called *outside linebackers,* stand outside the defensive ends. Four linebackers are used with a three-man line, and two are used with a five-man line. In certain defensive formations, the linebackers will move up to the line of scrimmage with the linemen.

Linebackers, especially middle linebackers, make many tackles. They must combine strength with the ability to move quickly to wherever the ball carrier is running. They must also be good pass defenders.

AP

The kickoff begins each half. A team also kicks off after scoring a touchdown or a field goal. The receiving team places two players near its goal line. The player nearest the ball catches it and runs back the kick. His teammates block for him. The kicking team lines up in a row across the field. The kicker kicks the ball from a tee, and his teammates run down the field to tackle the runner.

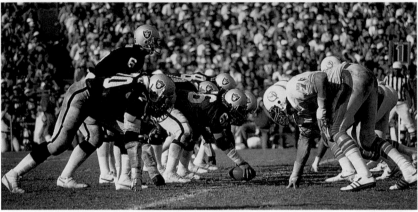

Focus on Sports

The line of scrimmage is an imaginary line that extends from the forward tip of the ball to both sidelines. Offensive and defensive players must stay on their side of the line until the center snap begins the play. If any part of a player's body is beyond the line of scrimmage when the ball is snapped, an official calls an *offside* penalty on that player's team.

The secondary is made up of two *cornerbacks* and two *safeties*. They are often called *defensive backs*. Their chief task is to defend against the offensive team's passing attacks. They also try to tackle ball carriers who have gotten by the linemen and linebackers. Defensive backs must be fast enough to cover speedy pass receivers, and they must be especially sure tacklers.

The cornerbacks stand 8 to 10 yards behind the line of scrimmage at the corners of the defensive formation. They defend against short passes thrown toward the sidelines. Safeties play 8 to 12 yards behind the line of scrimmage and defend against long passes. Sometimes, secondaries use *double coverage,* in which two defensive backs cover an especially dangerous receiver.

Many defensive teams favor *zone coverage* in the secondary, and others prefer *man-to-man coverage.* In zone coverage, each defensive back is responsible for a certain area. In man-to-man coverage, a defensive back is assigned to cover a particular receiver.

The coaches. Every team has a coaching staff made up of a *head coach* and a number of *assistant coaches.* The head coach decides which players play which positions and, often, what plays are used during a game. Most assistant coaches work with particular players on the offensive and defensive teams. Some assistant coaches may perform other duties, such as scouting opposing teams for their strengths and weaknesses.

Between games, the coaches conduct practices to correct players' mistakes and to oversee their physical conditioning. The coaches also prepare for the next game by developing a *game plan.* A game plan is a list of offensive plays and defensive formations that the coaches believe will work against the opponent. A few coaches discuss the game plan with the quarterback and then allow him to select his own plays during the game. However, most coaches prefer to choose the plays themselves. During a game, they send in their instructions for each play with a substitute player, by hand signals from the sidelines, or by transmitting messages to a tiny radio receiver in the quarterback's helmet.

How football is played

The playing time in college and professional football games is 60 minutes. High school games last 48 minutes. A game is divided into halves. Each half, in turn, consists of two quarters. An intermission, called *half-time,* lasts about 20 minutes between halves. There are 1-minute or 2-minute rest periods after the first and third quarters.

At the end of each quarter, teams change goals.

The official time clock is stopped only (1) after an incomplete pass, (2) if a player is injured, (3) after a team scores, (4) if a ball carrier goes out of bounds, (5) if a player on either team or an official calls a time out before the ball is snapped, or (6) after an official calls a penalty. Each team may call up to three time outs each half. Time outs last 90 seconds in high school and college games and 2 minutes in NFL games. In college games, the clock is also stopped briefly after each first down to move the first down markers. During the final 2 minutes of NFL games, the clock is stopped after some plays while the ball is put in position for the next play.

The kickoff starts each half of a game. A team also kicks off after it scores a touchdown or a field goal.

The team that kicks off to begin the game is decided by a coin toss at midfield. The team that wins the toss may make the kickoff, receive the kickoff, or select the goal it wishes to defend. The team that loses the toss gets the choice of kicking, receiving, or defending either goal when the second half begins. The team winning the coin toss may defer its choice to the second half. The other team then chooses.

Pete Miller, National Football League Properties, Inc.

A head coach discusses a play with his quarterback. The coach gets suggestions on strategy through headphones from assistants watching the game from a press box above the field.

WORLD BOOK Illustrations

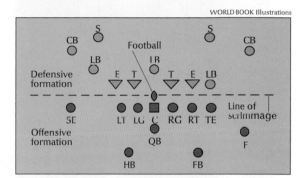

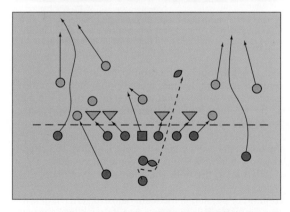

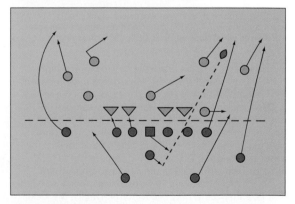

A running play combines various movements. The play shown here calls for the fullback to run the ball between his right guard and right tackle. The fullback gets the handoff from the quarterback and cuts to his right. The linemen and halfback block the defensive linemen and linebackers. The flanker and split end run down-field to decoy the defensive backs into expecting a pass.

A passing play requires split-second timing. The play shown here calls for the linemen and halfbacks to block while the quarterback passes to the tight end. If the tight end is covered, the quarterback can pass to the split end or the flanker. Even if his blockers give him good protection from the defense, the passer has only a few seconds to select a receiver and throw the ball.

Key to positions C=center; CB=cornerback; E=end; F=flanker; FB=fullback; HB=halfback; LB=linebacker; LG=left guard; LT=left tackle; MG= middle guard; QB=quarterback; RG=right guard; RT=right tackle; S=safety; SE= split end; T=tackle; TE=tight end

© Carl Skalak, Jr., OPTICOM

A pitchout is a play in which the quarterback *pitches* (tosses) the ball underhand to a back who runs around end. In the play shown here, another back runs ahead of the ball carrier to block.

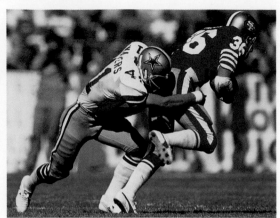

Focus on Sports

Tackling is the chief defensive skill. The tackler usually hits with his shoulders and wraps his arms around the ball carrier, *shown here.* He must hold tight so the runner cannot squirm away.

Michael Yada, National Football League Properties, Inc.

Passing combined with a good running attack produces a well-balanced offense. A good passer can throw the football accurately even when he is about to be tackled, *shown here.*

Pete Miller, National Football League Properties, Inc.

A pass receiver makes a difficult catch after maneuvering away from the defense. A good pass receiver can catch the football while running swiftly and hold onto it while being tackled.

The kickoff is made from the 40-yard line in high school games and from the 35-yard line in college and NFL games. Most kickers prop the ball on a tee to kick it.

The kicker's teammates stand in a line across the field until the ball is kicked. Generally, the receiving team places two fast runners near its goal line. The runner nearest the ball catches it and runs it back toward the other team's goal. The opposing players run to tackle him, and the runner's teammates try to block them.

After a kickoff travels 10 yards, it becomes a *free ball*—that is, either team may recover it. Normally, the kicker tries to kick the ball as far down the field as possible. Sometimes, he will kick it only a short distance to give his team a chance to recover the ball before the receiving team does. This maneuver is called an *onside kick.*

The ball is ruled *dead* if it is kicked beyond the end zone or if the kick returner catches it in the end zone and touches the ground with his knee. The officials then call a *touchback* and put the ball in play on the receiving team's 20-yard line. The kick returner is ruled *down* if he goes out of bounds or if any part of his body except his feet or hands touches the ground. In the NFL, the kick returner must be downed by an opponent. If the returner slips and falls but is not touched by an opposing player, he may get up and advance the ball until he is tackled or goes out of bounds.

After the kick returner is downed, the officials place the ball at the point where the return ended. The offensive and defensive teams then come on the field.

Advancing the ball. The offense has four plays, called *downs,* to advance the ball at least 10 yards by running or passing. If the team gains 10 yards, it gets a *first down.* If it fails to make a first down, it loses possession of the ball. Each time a team gets a first down, it receives another four downs to gain 10 yards.

In college games, when a player is tackled in bounds or does not get a first down, the offense has 40 seconds to put the ball in play after the referee has signaled to begin. If the player goes out of bounds or gets a first down, the offense has 25 seconds after the ball is spotted. In the NFL, the offense has 40 seconds in all cases.

Before a play begins, each team usually gathers in a

huddle behind its side of the line of scrimmage. In the offensive huddle, the quarterback names his team's next play, the formation to be used, and the number or color he will call out to signal the center to snap the ball. In the defensive huddle, a formation is called that the team hopes will stop the offensive play.

After the teams have huddled, they line up facing each other along the line of scrimmage. The center begins the play by snapping the ball to the quarterback. The quarterback then hands or *pitches* (tosses) the ball to a running back, runs with it himself, or throws a pass. The offense directs running plays around either of the ends, between an end and a tackle, between a tackle and a guard, or between a guard and the center.

On a passing play, the passer is usually the quarterback. Occasionally, another back or even an end will throw the ball. The passer must throw from behind the line of scrimmage. Only the ends and backs may catch a pass. The tackles, guards, and center must stay behind the line of scrimmage until the ball is thrown. They may then run down-field and block for the pass receiver.

If a defensive player catches a pass, it is called an *interception*. The defensive player may return the ball toward the opponent's goal until he is downed or goes out of bounds. His team's offensive players then come on the field and try to score.

Official signals Officials use a variety of hand signals during a football game. The referee usually gives the signals for various fouls. Other signals may be given by any of the officials.

WORLD BOOK illustrations by David Cunningham

First down

Touchdown, successful field goal, successful extra point

Safety

Penalty refused, incomplete pass, missed field goal, missed extra point

Time out

Personal foul

Holding

Roughing the kicker

Illegal use of hands

Clipping

Illegal forward pass

Interference

Ineligible receiver

Illegal contact

Facemasking

Offside

Illegal motion

Unsportsmanlike conduct

Illegal cut

Delay of game

Focus on Sports

© Dale Zanine, Icon Sports Media Inc.

Kicking consists of punting, *left,* and place kicking, *above*. For a punt, the center snaps the ball back to the kicker, who drops it and kicks it before the ball hits the ground. For a place kick, the center snaps the ball back to a holder kneeling on the ground. The holder catches the ball and places it on one end. Players from the opposing team try to block both punts and place kicks.

The defense may also gain possession of the ball by recovering a *fumble*. A fumble occurs if an offensive player drops the ball. Interceptions and fumbles are also called *turnovers*. A defensive player may run with a fumble if he catches the ball before it hits the ground or if he picks the ball off the ground while he is on his feet. In college games, if the player recovers the ball while he is on the ground, the ball is dead and his team gets the ball at that spot. In the NFL, the player may get up and run with the ball after recovering it while on the ground.

If the offensive team does not make a first down in three plays, it usually punts the ball on fourth down. A punt gives possession of the ball to the other team. The kicker stands 10 to 12 yards behind the center, who snaps the ball to him for the punt. A long or well-aimed punt can force the other team to start its offense deep on its own side of the field. If, instead of punting, the offense tries to make a first down on fourth down and fails, the other team gets the ball where the play ends.

Scoring. A team earns points by scoring a touchdown, a conversion, a field goal, or a safety.

Touchdown. A touchdown earns 6 points. The offense scores nearly all touchdowns. It does so by running the ball or catching a pass over the opposing team's goal line. Occasionally, the defense scores a touchdown through an interception or a fumble recovery or by recovering a blocked punt in the end zone. A team can also score a touchdown on a kickoff or punt return.

Conversion. After a touchdown, the scoring team tries for a conversion, also called the *extra point* or *point after touchdown*. Before a conversion attempt, the ball is placed on the 2-yard line in the NFL and on the 3-yard line in high school and college games. A kicker scores 1 point by place-kicking the football over the crossbar and between the goal posts. The offense can score a 2-point conversion by running or passing the ball over the goal line. In college games, the defensive team scores 2 points if it blocks the conversion kick, recovers a fumble, or intercepts a pass and then advances the ball into the opponent's end zone at the opposite end of the field. In the NFL, the defense cannot score on a blocked conversion, a fumble recovery, or a pass interception. The ball is dead as soon as the conversion fails.

Field goal. A field goal is worth 3 points. It is scored by place-kicking the ball over the crossbar and between the goal posts. The kick may be made from anywhere on the field. If the field goal is missed, the defensive team gets possession of the ball. In high school games, the ball is placed on the 20-yard line. In college games, the ball is returned to the line of scrimmage or to the 20-yard line if the line of scrimmage was inside the 20. In the NFL, the ball is placed where the kick was tried, usually about 7 yards behind the line of scrimmage.

Safety. Only the defense can score a safety, which is worth 2 points. The defense earns a safety if it tackles the ball carrier in his own end zone, if the ball carrier steps out of the back or side of his end zone, or if a blocked punt goes out of the end zone.

The officials supervise the football game and enforce the rules. Each official has particular duties, but any of the officials may call a rule violation.

The chief official is the *referee,* who has general charge of the game. He has the final word on all rulings. The referee stands behind the offensive backfield. The *umpire* is positioned behind the defensive line and watches for violations in the line. The *head linesman* stands at one end of the line of scrimmage. He marks the forward progress of the ball and supervises the sidelines crew, which keeps track of the downs and the yardage needed for a first down. The *field judge* stands behind the defensive secondary in the middle of the field. He watches for violations on punt returns and pass plays down-field. The *back judge* is positioned behind the defensive secondary near a sideline. His job is to spot violations between the defensive backs and the offensive pass receivers. The *line judge* stands opposite the head linesman and, like the umpire, watches for violations in the line. The line judge is also the official timekeeper. The NFL also uses a *side judge*. He stands opposite the back judge and on the same side of the field as the head linesman. The side judge has the same responsibilities as those of the back judge.

Violations and penalties are called when players break the rules. An official signals a violation by throwing a flag in the air. In most cases, a violation occurs during a play, and the officials allow the play to be completed. The referee then explains the violation to the captain of the team that was fouled. The captain may accept the penalty to be imposed on the other team. Or he may refuse the penalty and keep the completed play. If he accepts the penalty, the down is usually replayed. A team is penalized for a violation with a loss of yardage and, in some cases, also the loss of a down. Common violations include clipping, holding, offside, interference, roughing, and illegal procedure.

Clipping is committed if an offensive player blocks a defensive player from behind, beyond the line of scrimmage. The penalty is 15 yards.

Holding is called against an offensive player who uses his hands to block a defensive player. In high school and college, a defensive player is penalized for holding if he uses his hands except to tackle a ball carrier. In the NFL, a defensive player may use his hands under certain conditions. The penalty is 10 yards for offensive holding. In the NFL, defensive holding includes a 5-yard penalty plus an automatic first down for the offense.

Offside is called if any part of a player's body is beyond the line of scrimmage when the ball is snapped. The penalty is 5 yards.

Interference is ruled if the pass receiver or pass defender is blocked, tackled, or shoved while the ball is in the air. In defensive interference in the NFL, the offense gets the ball at the spot of the foul and receives a first down. In college football, the defense is penalized from the line of scrimmage and the offense receives a first down. In offensive interference, the offense is penalized 15 yards and loss of the down.

Roughing is a foul committed against a kicker or passer. The defense may not tackle or bump a kicker while he is punting or place-kicking. The defense may tackle a passer only while he has the ball. The player may not be hit after he throws the pass. The penalty for roughing a kicker or passer is 15 yards and an automatic first down.

Illegal procedure is called if the offense does not have seven players on the line of scrimmage or if an offensive player moves forward before the ball is snapped. It is also called if the offense or defense has more than 11 players on the field. The penalty is 5 yards.

Heisman Trophy winners

Year	Player	School	Position	Year	Player	School	Position
1935	Jay Berwanger	Chicago	Quarterback	1977	Earl Campbell	Texas	Running back
1936	Larry Kelley	Yale	End	1978	Billy Sims	Oklahoma	Running back
1937	Clint Frank	Yale	Running back	1979	Charles White	Southern California	Running back
1938	Davey O'Brien	Texas Christian	Running back	1980	George Rogers	South Carolina	Running back
1939	Nile Kinnick	Iowa	Running back	1981	Marcus Allen	Southern California	Running back
1940	Tom Harmon	Michigan	Running back	1982	Herschel Walker	Georgia	Running back
1941	Bruce Smith	Minnesota	Running back	1983	Mike Rozier	Nebraska	Running back
1942	Frank Sinkwich	Georgia	Running back	1984	Doug Flutie	Boston College	Quarterback
1943	Angelo Bertelli	Notre Dame	Quarterback	1985	Bo Jackson	Auburn	Running back
1944	Les Horvath	Ohio State	Running back	1986	Vinny Testaverde	Miami	Quarterback
1945	Doc Blanchard	Army	Running back	1987	Tim Brown	Notre Dame	Running back
1946	Glenn Davis	Army	Running back	1988	Barry Sanders	Oklahoma State	Running back
1947	Johnny Lujack	Notre Dame	Quarterback	1989	Andre Ware	Houston	Quarterback
1948	Doak Walker	Southern Methodist	Running back	1990	Ty Detmer	Brigham Young	Quarterback
				1991	Desmond Howard	Michigan	Wide receiver
1949	Leon Hart	Notre Dame	End				
1950	Vic Janowicz	Ohio State	Running back	1992	Gino Torretta	Miami	Quarterback
1951	Dick Kazmaier	Princeton	Running back	1993	Charlie Ward	Florida State	Quarterback
1952	Billy Vessels	Oklahoma	Running back	1994	Rashaan Salaam	Colorado	Running back
1953	Johnny Lattner	Notre Dame	Running back	1995	Eddie George	Ohio State	Running back
1954	Alan Ameche	Wisconsin	Running back	1996	Danny Wuerffel	Florida	Quarterback
1955	Howard Cassady	Ohio State	Running back	1997	Charles Woodson	Michigan	Defensive back
1956	Paul Hornung	Notre Dame	Running back				
1957	John Crow	Texas A&M	Running back	1998	Ricky Williams	Texas	Running back
1958	Pete Dawkins	Army	Running back	1999	Ron Dayne	Wisconsin	Running back
1959	Billy Cannon	Louisiana State	Running back	2000	Chris Weinke	Florida State	Quarterback
1960	Joe Bellino	Navy	Running back	2001	Eric Crouch	Nebraska	Quarterback
1961	Ernie Davis	Syracuse	Running back	2002	Carson Palmer	Southern California	Quarterback
1962	Terry Baker	Oregon State	Quarterback	2003	Jason White	Oklahoma	Quarterback
1963	Roger Staubach	Navy	Quarterback	2004	Matt Leinart	Southern California	Quarterback
1964	John Huarte	Notre Dame	Quarterback	2005	Vacant*		
1965	Mike Garrett	Southern California	Running back	2006	Troy Smith	Ohio State	Quarterback
1966	Steve Spurrier	Florida	Quarterback	2007	Tim Tebow	Florida	Quarterback
1967	Gary Beban	UCLA	Quarterback	2008	Sam Bradford	Oklahoma	Quarterback
1968	O. J. Simpson	Southern California	Running back	2009	Mark Ingram	Alabama	Running back
1969	Steve Owens	Oklahoma	Running back	2010	Cam Newton	Auburn	Quarterback
1970	Jim Plunkett	Stanford	Quarterback	2011	Robert Griffin III	Baylor	Quarterback
1971	Pat Sullivan	Auburn	Quarterback	2012	Johnny Manziel	Texas A&M	Quarterback
1972	Johnny Rodgers	Nebraska	Running back				
1973	John Cappelletti	Penn State	Running back				
1974	Archie Griffin	Ohio State	Running back				
1975	Archie Griffin	Ohio State	Running back				
1976	Tony Dorsett	Pittsburgh	Running back				

*Reggie Bush, a running back from the University of Southern California, received the award in 2005. Bush returned the trophy in 2010, and the award was declared vacant.

Football competition

Most organized football games in the United States are played by high school, college, and professional teams. There are also programs for young players not organized by schools. These include "pee wee" programs of the Pop Warner league for children aged 5 to 16. The league is organized according to players' ages.

High school competition. Thousands of U.S. high schools have football teams. The National Federation of State High School Associations oversees most athletic programs, including football. Each state also has an organization that sets rules and policies for high school sports teams. Most teams compete in classifications determined by school enrollment and location. Most states have a play-off schedule that ends with two teams competing for the state championship in their classification.

College competition. Hundreds of U.S. colleges and universities sponsor football teams. Most of the schools belong to a conference. Each conference sets standards and rules for competition. Every season, teams play one another for the conference championship. Some teams, called *independents,* do not belong to a conference. They play other independents and conference teams.

Conference and independent teams belong to the National Collegiate Athletic Association (NCAA) or the National Association of Intercollegiate Athletics (NAIA). These organizations set rules and supervise competition among member teams. Teams from two-year schools, called junior colleges or community colleges, also compete against one another. They are governed by the National Junior College Athletic Association.

Most college teams play 12-game regular seasons. After each season, some of the teams with the best records are invited to play in bowl games. Most bowl games occur in late December or early January. Beginning in 2014, four teams will be selected to compete in the College Football Playoff. The two semi-final games and the championship game of the play-off will rotate among six bowls. There are also postseason all-star games. Players who have ended their college careers may be invited to play in one or more of these games.

Professional competition. The National Football League has been in operation as a professional league since 1920. The NFL consists of 32 teams. The teams are divided into the American Football Conference and the National Football Conference, each with four divisions.

Teams in the NFL play a regular season schedule of 16 games. The division champions and the next two teams in each conference with the best won-lost records advance to the play-offs. A series of play-off games deter-

Canadian Football League

East Division	West Division
Hamilton Tiger-Cats	British Columbia Lions
Montreal Alouettes	Calgary Stampeders
Ottawa RedBlacks	Edmonton Eskimos
Toronto Argonauts	Saskatchewan Roughriders
Winnipeg Blue Bombers	

mines the two conference champions. These teams then play for the NFL title in a game called the Super Bowl.

Each year, NFL teams obtain college football players through a system known as a *draft.* The teams choose mostly seniors who have completed their college playing careers. But juniors and underclassmen who declare their eligibility for the draft may be picked. The first choice goes to the team that ended the preceding season with the worst record, unless that team trades the draft choice. The Super Bowl winner picks last. No team may sign a player drafted by another team unless the player is released by the drafting team. A college player who is not drafted may sign with any professional team.

Canadian football

Although hockey ranks as Canada's favorite team sport, football is gaining popularity. Football is played in Canada by high schools, colleges and universities, and the nine professional teams of the Canadian Football League (CFL). The CFL playing field is 130 yards long and 65 yards wide, and the goal posts are on the goal line.

Most Canadian football is played by 12-member teams. Eleven of the positions resemble those in U.S. football. On offense, the 12th player usually lines up in the backfield but may also be used as an end. On defense, the 12th player usually plays in the secondary. The offense has only three downs to make a first down.

Scoring in Canadian football differs from that in U.S. football in only one way. The Canadian field has a dead-line 20 yards behind each goal line. On a kickoff, the receiving team must advance the ball out of the area between the dead-line and the goal line. If it fails, the kicking team scores 1 point, called a *single.* The same rule applies to a punt.

Nearly all Canadian colleges and universities compete in four regional conferences. The champions of each conference meet in postseason play-offs. The team that wins the play-offs is the national collegiate champion and receives the Vanier Cup.

The CFL is divided into an East Division and a West Division. Teams play 18-game regular season schedules. The division champions compete for the league title. The winning team receives the Grey Cup. For a table of cup winners, see **Grey Cup.**

National Football League

American Football Conference		National Football Conference	
North Division	**East Division**	**North Division**	**East Division**
Baltimore Ravens	Buffalo Bills	Chicago Bears	Dallas Cowboys
Cincinnati Bengals	Miami Dolphins	Detroit Lions	New York Giants
Cleveland Browns	New England Patriots	Green Bay Packers	Philadelphia Eagles
Pittsburgh Steelers	New York Jets	Minnesota Vikings	Washington Redskins
South Division	**West Division**	**South Division**	**West Division**
Houston Texans	Denver Broncos	Atlanta Falcons	Arizona Cardinals
Indianapolis Colts	Kansas City Chiefs	Carolina Panthers	St. Louis Rams
Jacksonville Jaguars	Oakland Raiders	New Orleans Saints	San Francisco 49ers
Tennessee Titans	San Diego Chargers	Tampa Bay Buccaneers	Seattle Seahawks

The history of football

Beginnings. Football began to develop during the mid-1800's, when a game similar to soccer was played in the eastern United States. The object of the game was simply to kick a round ball across the other team's goal line. The teams sometimes had 30 or more players. As the soccerlike game became popular, stricter rules were adopted and schools began to organize teams. The first college game was played on Nov. 6, 1869, in New Brunswick, New Jersey. In that game, Rutgers defeated the College of New Jersey (now Princeton University), 6-4.

The first game resembling present-day football was played in 1874, when a team from McGill University in Montreal, Canada, visited Harvard University. The Canadian team wanted to play the English game of rugby, which permitted running with the ball and tackling. Harvard preferred to play its soccerlike game, in which players advanced the ball mainly by kicking. The teams agreed to play two games, the first under Harvard rules and the second under McGill rules. Harvard liked McGill's rugby game so much that it introduced the sport to other colleges. Running and tackling soon became as important as kicking in the U.S. game.

Shortly after colleges took up rugby-style football, they began to change and improve the game. The most influential figure in modernizing football was Walter Camp, who had played for Yale University from 1876 to 1882. During the 1880's, Camp led colleges to adopt rules that increased the game's action and competition. Camp was largely responsible for establishing the system of downs and yards to gain and for introducing the center snap to the quarterback. He also helped set up the scoring system in which touchdowns, conversions, field goals, and safeties were worth different numbers of points. In 1889, he and sportswriter Caspar Whitney began the tradition of picking an annual all-American team to honor the best college players in the country.

U.S. professional football champions

National Football League (NFL)*

1920	Akron Pros	1932	Chicago Bears	1944	Green Bay Packers	1956	New York Giants
1921	Chicago Staleys	1933	Chicago Bears	1945	Cleveland Rams	1957	Detroit Lions
1922	Canton Bulldogs	1934	New York Giants	1946	Chicago Bears	1958	Baltimore Colts
1923	Canton Bulldogs	1935	Detroit Lions	1947	Chicago Cardinals	1959	Baltimore Colts
1924	Cleveland Bulldogs	1936	Green Bay Packers	1948	Philadelphia Eagles	1960	Philadelphia Eagles
1925	Chicago Cardinals	1937	Washington Redskins	1949	Philadelphia Eagles	1961	Green Bay Packers
1926	Frankford Yellow Jackets	1938	New York Giants	1950	Cleveland Browns	1962	Green Bay Packers
1927	New York Giants	1939	Green Bay Packers	1951	Los Angeles Rams	1963	Chicago Bears
1928	Providence Steam Roller	1940	Chicago Bears	1952	Detroit Lions	1964	Cleveland Browns
1929	Green Bay Packers	1941	Chicago Bears	1953	Detroit Lions	1965	Green Bay Packers
1930	Green Bay Packers	1942	Washington Redskins	1954	Cleveland Browns		
1931	Green Bay Packers	1943	Chicago Bears	1955	Cleveland Browns		

American Football League (AFL)

1960	Houston Oilers	1962	Dallas Texans	1964	Buffalo Bills
1961	Houston Oilers	1963	San Diego Chargers	1965	Buffalo Bills

Super Bowl**

1967	Green Bay Packers (NFL) 35, Kansas City Chiefs (AFL) 10
1968	Green Bay Packers (NFL) 33, Oakland Raiders (AFL) 14
1969	New York Jets (AFL) 16, Baltimore Colts (NFL) 7
1970	Kansas City Chiefs (AFL) 23, Minnesota Vikings (NFL) 7
1971	Baltimore Colts (AFC) 16, Dallas Cowboys (NFC) 13
1972	Dallas Cowboys (NFC) 24, Miami Dolphins (AFC) 3
1973	Miami Dolphins (AFC) 14, Washington Redskins (NFC) 7
1974	Miami Dolphins (AFC) 24, Minnesota Vikings (NFC) 7
1975	Pittsburgh Steelers (AFC) 16, Minnesota Vikings (NFC) 6
1976	Pittsburgh Steelers (AFC) 21, Dallas Cowboys (NFC) 17
1977	Oakland Raiders (AFC) 32, Minnesota Vikings (NFC) 14
1978	Dallas Cowboys (NFC) 27, Denver Broncos (AFC) 10
1979	Pittsburgh Steelers (AFC) 35, Dallas Cowboys (NFC) 31
1980	Pittsburgh Steelers (AFC) 31, Los Angeles Rams (NFC) 19
1981	Oakland Raiders (AFC) 27, Philadelphia Eagles (NFC) 10
1982	San Francisco 49ers (NFC) 26, Cincinnati Bengals (AFC) 21
1983	Washington Redskins (NFC) 27, Miami Dolphins (AFC) 17
1984	Los Angeles Raiders (AFC) 38, Washington Redskins (NFC) 9
1985	San Francisco 49ers (NFC) 38, Miami Dolphins (AFC) 16
1986	Chicago Bears (NFC) 46, New England Patriots (AFC) 10
1987	New York Giants (NFC) 39, Denver Broncos (AFC) 20
1988	Washington Redskins (NFC) 42, Denver Broncos (AFC) 10
1989	San Francisco 49ers (NFC) 20, Cincinnati Bengals (AFC) 16
1990	San Francisco 49ers (NFC) 55, Denver Broncos (AFC) 10
1991	New York Giants (NFC) 20, Buffalo Bills (AFC) 19
1992	Washington Redskins (NFC) 37, Buffalo Bills (AFC) 24
1993	Dallas Cowboys (NFC) 52, Buffalo Bills (AFC) 17
1994	Dallas Cowboys (NFC) 30, Buffalo Bills (AFC) 13
1995	San Francisco 49ers (NFC) 49, San Diego Chargers (AFC) 26
1996	Dallas Cowboys (NFC) 27, Pittsburgh Steelers (AFC) 17
1997	Green Bay Packers (NFC) 35, New England Patriots (AFC) 21
1998	Denver Broncos (AFC) 31, Green Bay Packers (NFC) 24
1999	Denver Broncos (AFC) 34, Atlanta Falcons (NFC) 19
2000	St. Louis Rams (NFC) 23, Tennessee Titans (AFC) 16
2001	Baltimore Ravens (AFC) 34, New York Giants (NFC) 7
2002	New England Patriots (AFC) 20, St. Louis Rams (NFC) 17
2003	Tampa Bay Buccaneers (NFC) 48, Oakland Raiders (AFC) 21
2004	New England Patriots (AFC) 32, Carolina Panthers (NFC) 29
2005	New England Patriots (AFC) 24, Philadelphia Eagles (NFC) 21
2006	Pittsburgh Steelers (AFC) 21, Seattle Seahawks (NFC) 10
2007	Indianapolis Colts (AFC) 29, Chicago Bears (NFC) 17
2008	New York Giants (NFC) 17, New England Patriots (AFC) 14
2009	Pittsburgh Steelers (AFC) 27, Arizona Cardinals (NFC) 23
2010	New Orleans Saints (NFC) 31, Indianapolis Colts (AFC) 17
2011	Green Bay Packers (NFC) 31, Pittsburgh Steelers (AFC) 25
2012	New York Giants (NFC) 21, New England Patriots (AFC) 17
2013	Baltimore Ravens (AFC) 34, San Francisco 49ers (NFC) 31

*American Professional Football Association in 1920 and 1921.   **The NFL and AFL champions played in the Super Bowl through 1970, when the leagues merged into one league consisting of the National Football Conference (NFC) and the American Football Conference (AFC). Starting in 1971, the NFC and AFC champions played in the Super Bowl for the NFL title.

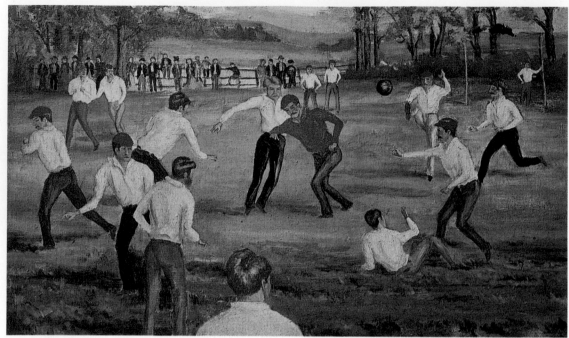

Painting by William Boyd; collection of William Boyd (WORLD BOOK photo by Tom Morton)

The first college game was played between Rutgers and what is now Princeton in 1869. The contest resembled soccer rather than modern football. Teams could advance the ball only by kicking.

During the 1880's, football gained in popularity. More colleges played the sport, and many high schools formed teams. Numerous towns organized teams of players who were not in high school or college. Rivalries grew between teams from neighboring towns.

Changes in the game. By 1900, football consisted mostly of running, blocking, and tackling. The blocking and tackling became increasingly violent, and many players suffered serious injuries. The uniforms provided little protection. Players did not even wear helmets. Many games were organized fights rather than athletic contests. In 1905, President Theodore Roosevelt urged changes in the rules to make the game safer.

In 1906, college coaches and faculty members tried to find ways to eliminate some of the violence in football. One new rule permitted a back to throw the ball forward to another back or to one of the ends. According to many historians, the first forward pass was thrown in 1906 by Wesleyan University in a game against Yale.

At first, teams ignored the forward pass. They did not consider it a logical way to advance the ball. Passing finally became popular in 1913 as a result of a game that

AP/Wide World

Football games from 1906 to 1910 were played on fields marked with a checkerboard pattern of lines. The squares measured 5 yards on each side and helped officials spot rule violations. For example, an offensive player could not throw a pass within 5 yards of the center.

year between Notre Dame and Army. The stronger, heavier Army team was favored to defeat the Notre Dame team. But Notre Dame quarterback Gus Dorais led his team to a 35-13 victory by throwing the ball several times to his end Knute Rockne. Rockne later became a famous head coach at Notre Dame. By the 1920's, the forward pass had become a basic part of football and helped make the game more exciting. Meanwhile, most other basic rules had been adopted. In 1912, for example, a touchdown's value was set at 6 points, and the number of downs was set at four.

The rise of professional football. On Nov. 12, 1892, William "Pudge" Heffelfinger was paid $500 to play football for the Allegheny Athletic Association in a game against the Pittsburgh Athletic Club. Sports historians mark this game as the start of professional football. In the early days of football, many college players played with their school teams on Saturdays and with profes-

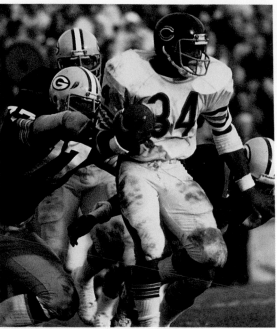

Focus on Sports

Walter Payton was one of the greatest running backs in football history. During his career from 1975 to 1987, Payton rushed for 16,726 yards, the second highest total in NFL history.

sional teams on Sundays. They usually performed professionally under assumed names because of rules permitting only amateurs in college football.

Professional football had little organization until 1920, when the American Professional Football Association was founded. In 1922, the organization was renamed the National Football League (NFL).

Professional football began to win wide support in 1925. That year, Red Grange, a famous all-American halfback from the University of Illinois, signed to play with the Chicago Bears. He played in a series of games that drew more than 350,000 fans. In 1933, the NFL split into two divisions. Later that year, the Bears, Western Division champions, defeated the New York Giants, Eastern Division champions, for the first world professional football title. The league held its first draft in 1936.

In 1944, an eight-team league called the All-America Football Conference was formed. The league began competition in 1946. The All-America Football Conference and the NFL merged in 1950 into a 13-team league.

During the 1950's, professional football began to gain great popularity throughout the United States. Under the leadership of Pete Rozelle, NFL commissioner from 1960 to 1989, the league added several teams and enormously increased its income from television.

In 1960, another professional league, the American Football League (AFL), was formed. The AFL competed with the NFL for fans and players. The 1966 NFL and AFL champions played in the first Super Bowl in January 1967. The Super Bowl became the most popular annual televised sports event in the United States. After years of rivalry, the two leagues merged in 1970 into one league consisting of the American Football Conference and the National Football Conference.

© UPI/Archive Photos

The Four Horsemen formed a famous Notre Dame backfield from 1922 to 1924. The four players were, *left to right,* Don Miller, Elmer Layden, Jim Crowley, and Harry Stuhldreher.

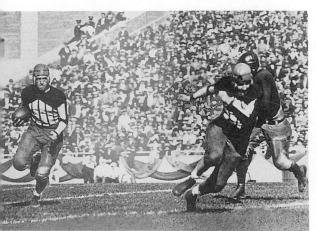

University of Illinois Athletic Association

Red Grange was a star running back at the University of Illinois. In a game against Michigan in 1924, *shown here,* Grange scored a touchdown on each of the first four times he carried the ball.

© Andy Lyons, Getty Images

Peyton Manning ranks among the finest quarterbacks in National Football League history. Manning became known for his passing accuracy and his arm strength.

AP Photo

Ray Lewis ranks among the greatest linebackers in National Football League (NFL) history. He became known as a fierce competitor, a team leader, and one of the league's hardest tacklers.

New professional leagues. A new professional league, the World Football League, played in 1974 and part of 1975 before financial losses put it out of business. Another professional league, the United States Football League, began play in 1983 but suspended play after the 1985 season.

In 1987, the indoor Arena Football League was established. After canceling the 2009 season, the league resumed play in 2010. Games are played on an indoor padded surface 50 yards long and 85 feet wide. The crossbar is 10 feet above the playing surface, and the goal posts are 9 feet apart. Eight players are on the field for each team. Scoring is the same as in conventional football with two exceptions. Teams receive four points for drop kicking field goals instead of using a player to hold the ball, and teams receive two points for drop kicking the point after touchdown instead of using a player as holder.

In 1991, competition began in the 10-team World League of American Football, an international professional league sponsored by the National Football League. The league consisted of three European teams, one in Canada, and six in the United States. In 1998, the league was renamed NFL Europe and reorganized into a six-team league of European teams. The name of the league changed again in 2006 to NFL Europa. However, in 2007, the NFL disbanded the league.

Violence issues. Excessive violence in games and the injuries the violence produces have become major issues in football, especially in the NFL in the early 2000's. Numerous former NFL players have sued the NFL, claiming that the league had been aware for decades that concussions from playing football cause brain damage but concealed that information from players. In another violence matter, the NFL charged that members of the New Orleans Saints defense maintained a bounty program for three seasons starting in 2009 that paid cash rewards to players who inflicted injuries that forced opposing players to leave the game. There were allegations that other NFL teams also offered bounty incentives for injuring opponents.   Neil Milbert

Related articles in *World Book* include:

Bradshaw, Terry	Manning, Peyton	Shula, Don
Brady, Tom	Marino, Dan	Simpson, O. J.
Brown, Jim	Montana, Joe	Smith, Emmitt
Bryant, Paul	Namath, Joe	Soccer
Favre, Brett	Payton, Walter	Stagg, Amos
Grange, Red	Rice, Jerry	Alonzo
Grey Cup	Robinson, Eddie	Tarkenton, Fran
Halas, George S.	Rockne, Knute	Thorpe, Jim
Heisman Memori-	Rugby football	Tomlinson,
al Trophy	Sanders, Barry	LaDainian
Kemp, Jack F.	Sanders, Deion	Unitas, Johnny
Lombardi, Vince		Warner, Pop

Outline

I. The field and equipment
   A. The field   C. The uniform
   B. The ball   D. Protective equipment

II. The players and coaches
   A. The offensive team   C. The coaches
   B. The defensive team

III. How football is played
   A. The playing time   D. Scoring
   B. The kickoff   E. The officials
   C. Advancing the ball   F. Violations and penalties

IV. Football competition
   A. High school competition
   B. College competition
   C. Professional competition

V. Canadian football

VI. The history of football

Foote, Andrew Hull (1806-1863), was a Union Navy officer during the American Civil War (1861-1865). He became the first United States naval officer to command a flotilla of ironclad gunboats in battle. His fleet joined the Army in attacks on Fort Henry on the Tennessee River and on Fort Donelson on the Cumberland River in February 1862. He helped break the Confederate line of defense in the area. He became a rear admiral in July 1862.

A wound he received in the attack on Fort Donelson led to his death on June 26, 1863.

Foote was born in New Haven, Connecticut, on Sept. 12, 1806. He joined the Navy at the age of 16. From 1849 to 1851, he commanded the USS *Perry* along the coast of Africa in operations against the African slave trade.

John F. Marszalek

Footnote is a note in smaller type at the bottom of a page. When such notes are printed at the end of a chapter or book, they are known as *endnotes.* Authors can use notes to *cite* (refer to) the sources or authority for what the author says. Notes may give information or make comments that are not suitable for including in the text. Notes can also refer a reader to other opinions, or send a reader to other pages or sections of a work.

A number in small type is commonly used to draw attention to a footnote or an endnote. The numbers should run consecutively. An asterisk (*), dagger (†), or double dagger (‡) may be used instead of a number.

Authors rely on footnotes to help keep a text free of excess information. For example, a student writing a composition about the aardvark might want to tell some fact about this animal that had been learned from *The World Book Encyclopedia.* The following sentence would be awkward:

> In an article entitled Aardvark on page 2 of Volume A of *The World Book Encyclopedia*, it is stated that in the 1600's Dutch settlers in southern Africa gave the aardvark its name.

When a footnote is used, however, the sentence can be quickly and easily read:

> In the 1600's, Dutch settlers in southern Africa gave the aardvark its name.[1]

_____
[1]"Aardvark," *The World Book Encyclopedia*, Vol. A, p. 2.

There are several ways to write footnotes and endnotes that cite sources. Be sure to ask you teacher or librarian how footnotes and endnotes should be written at your school. One of the most common citation styles is the MLA style, published by the Modern Language Association. For information on that style, see the section *A Guide to Writing Skills* in the Research Guide/Index, Volume 22.
William E. Coles, Jr.

Footprinting is a system of identification similar to fingerprinting. Footprints are the impressions made by ridges on the soles of the feet. Like fingerprints, footprints remain unchanged throughout a person's lifetime. No individual's footprints have been found to be identical to those of another person. Footprints found at the scene of a crime may help identify suspects. Footprints also provide a means of identification when fingerprints cannot be obtained because of severe burns or other injuries. Many hospitals footprint newborn infants for identification shortly after birth and keep the prints on file for future reference. See also **Fingerprinting.**

John I. Thornton

Forbes, Esther (1891-1967), was an American author. She won the 1943 Pulitzer Prize in American history for her brilliant historical biography, *Paul Revere and the World He Lived In.* While writing this book, she became interested in the apprentice boys of Boston, and the part they played in the American Revolution. After finishing the adult biography, Forbes wrote for young people the novel *Johnny Tremain,* about an apprentice in the exciting days of the Boston Tea Party. This book won the Newbery Medal in 1944. She also wrote such American historical novels as *A Mirror for Witches* (1928), *Paradise* (1937), *The General's Lady* (1938), *The Running of the Tide* (1948), and *Rainbow on the Road* (1954).

Forbes was born in Westborough, Massachusetts. She studied at the University of Wisconsin. Jill P. May

Forbidden City. See Beijing (The city); Lhasa.

Force is a push or a pull. In your everyday life, you experience a variety of forces. You apply a force to a ball when you throw it up in the air. As the ball rises, the force of gravity slows it down. As the ball descends, gravity makes it fall more rapidly. When you catch the ball, it applies a downward force to your hands. But your hands apply an upward force to the ball to stop it.

Characteristics of force

Size and direction are two essential characteristics of force. You might push a box across the floor with a force that has a size of 45 pounds (200 newtons) and is directed toward the south. Because force has both a size and a direction, scientists call it a *vector quantity.* Physicists usually indicate a vector quantity by a letter with an arrow over it. Thus, $\vec{F}$ stands for force. Scientists also refer to the motion of a body in terms of a vector quantity—a combination of speed and direction known as *velocity.* An automobile might have a velocity of 60 miles (100 kilometers) per hour eastward.

Overcoming inertia. A force acts by overcoming *inertia,* which is a property of all matter. The English scientist Isaac Newton described inertia in 1687, in the first of three laws of motion. He said that, due to inertia, a body in motion continues to move with a constant velocity, while a motionless object tends to remain still.

Acceleration. Physicists refer to any change in motion—whether the change involves speed, direction, or both—as an *acceleration.* The force necessary to accelerate an object by a given amount depends on the object's

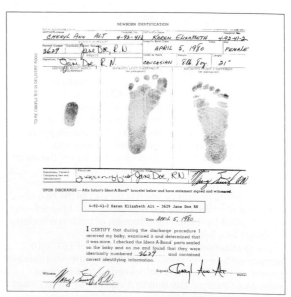

University of Illinois Hospital

Footprints of a newborn baby are recorded by many hospitals for identification purposes. The baby's footprints appear on a certificate along with the mother's fingerprint.

mass (amount of matter). The greater the mass, the greater the force must be.

Newton described the relationship between force, mass, and acceleration in his second law of motion. This law can be expressed as $\vec{F} = m\vec{a}$, where $\vec{F}$ is force, m is mass, and $\vec{a}$ is acceleration. In the International System of Units (SI), the modern metric system used by scientists, force can be given in newtons, mass in kilograms, and acceleration in meters per second per second.

Concurrent forces. In most changes of velocity that we observe, more than one force is acting on the accelerated object. Such *concurrent forces* produce a single *net force,* also called a *resultant force.* Suppose you are part of a tug-of-war team. If your team pulls harder on the rope than the opposing team does, there will be a net force in your direction, so the rope will accelerate in your direction. But if both teams pull equally hard, the forces will be in *equilibrium.* The rope will not move.

Kinds of force

All known forces are forms of four *fundamental forces*—(1) gravitation, (2) the *electromagnetic force,* (3) the *strong force,* and (4) the *weak force.*

Gravitation was the first of the fundamental forces to be understood scientifically. Isaac Newton explained this force in his law of gravitation, which was published in 1687. Scientists accepted Newton's law until 1915, when German-born physicist Albert Einstein proposed the general theory of relativity. Einstein's theory did not totally contradict Newton's law, but expanded upon it.

Newton's law of gravitation was a result of Newton's thinking about the planets' orbits. He reasoned that the planets move in their orbits because a force is applied to them. If there were no force, the planets' inertia would make them move in straight lines and fly off into space. Newton showed that what keeps the planets in orbit is the force of gravity. He also showed that gravitation is *universal.* That is, it acts in the same way between any two objects that have mass—between Earth and the sun as well as between an apple and Earth.

The force of gravity between objects arises from the attraction between the particles of matter that make up the objects. These particles—unknown in Newton's time—include atoms and the *subatomic particles* of which the atoms are composed. All but the simplest atoms have a nucleus of protons and neutrons, with electrons whirling about the nucleus. Protons and neutrons, in turn, consist of particles called *quarks;* each proton or neutron is composed of three quarks.

Newton's law of gravitation gives the size of the force of gravity as $F = G_N m_1 m_2 \div d^2$, where F is the force, G_N is a number known as the *gravitational constant* or *Newton's constant,* m_1 and m_2 are the masses of the two objects, and d^2 is the distance between them *squared*—that is, multiplied by itself. The direction of the force is along a straight line between the objects.

The gravitational constant has a value of 6.67×10^{-11} newton-meters^2 per kilogram^2. If the number were written out, the first 6 would be preceded by a decimal point and 10 zeros. The unit of measure for the constant, newton-meters^2 per kilogram^2, makes the answer come out in newtons when mass is given in kilograms and distance in meters.

The equation shows that gravity becomes weaker as the distance between the two objects increases. The force weakens as the square of this distance. Thus, if the distance triples, the force becomes one-ninth of its original size. The equation also shows that the force becomes larger as the mass of either object gets larger. So, if the mass of one of the objects triples, the force becomes three times as large.

Einstein's theory of general relativity overcomes faults in Newton's law. One fault is an incorrect description of the acceleration of objects at velocities close to the speed of light. But for most calculations involving slow objects, it is not necessary to consider relativity.

Einstein's theory is difficult to understand because it describes processes that we cannot observe in daily life. The theory states, for example, that matter and energy modify both space and time, and that this modification is the origin of the gravitational force. According to a simplified explanation, any object that has mass "curves" or "warps" the space near itself. If another body travels past this object, the body will follow the curvature, thereby moving toward the object. Newton's law—which does not allow for a curvature of space—would say that the traveling body will change direction due to a force.

The electromagnetic force consists of two parts: (1) the electric force and (2) the magnetic force.

The electric force is an attraction or repulsion between objects that carry an electric charge. Electric forces between subatomic particles play a major role in our everyday lives. For example, these forces create *chemical bonds,* attractions that hold atoms together in molecules. In addition, electric forces between molecules hold objects together.

The equation for the size of the electric force is $F = k q_1 q_2 \div d^2$, where F is the force in newtons, d is the distance in meters, and q_1 and q_2 are the charges in *coulombs.* One coulomb is the amount of charge flowing through a cross section of wire in a current of one ampere. The k represents a number that makes the answer come out in newtons. Its value is roughly 9 billion newton-meters^2 per coulomb^2. The direction of the force is along a straight line between the two objects.

The electric force is similar to the gravitational force. Both forces weaken as the square of the distance between the objects. In addition, the force becomes larger as the charge of either object gets larger.

There is a major difference, however, between the gravitational and electric forces. Gravity is always *attractive*—that is, it always pulls objects together. The electric force does not. Objects that have opposite charges attract each other, while objects with like charges repel each other. So a proton, which carries a positive charge, attracts an electron, which is negatively charged. But protons repel one another, and so do electrons.

There is another major difference between the two forces: The electric force between two oppositely charged subatomic particles is much larger than the gravitational force between them. For example, the electric force between two electrons is about 10^{35} times as large as the gravitational force between them. The number 10^{35} is scientific notation for a 1 followed by 35 zeros.

What is true on the tiny scale of atoms and molecules is not true, however, on the huge scale of the sun and planets. The electric force between Earth and the sun is much smaller than the gravitational force between them.

The gravitational attractions between the particles that make up Earth and those that make up the sun simply add up to equal the attraction between the two bodies. But the electric forces between the particles do not add up because each of those bodies has almost exactly the same number of protons and electrons. Thus, the sun's protons attract Earth's electrons, and the sun's electrons attract Earth's protons. But these attractions are offset by the repulsion between the sun's protons and Earth's protons and the repulsion between the sun's electrons and those of Earth.

The magnetic force that is used in everyday objects arises from two sources: (1) the combined magnetic forces of "miniature magnets" and (2) the movement of electrons through wires as electric current.

Electrons, protons, and neutrons are miniature magnets—and so are many kinds of atoms. Such objects act together in a refrigerator magnet to produce a large enough force to hold a photograph against the refrigerator. In an electric motor, electric current in wire coils creates a magnetic force that drives the motor. Each coil is part of an *electromagnet,* a device that becomes a magnet when the current flows.

A magnet applies force by means of a *magnetic field.* Physicists define a magnetic field as a region of space in which a moving, electrically charged object would experience a magnetic force. The magnet creates the field, and the field, in turn, applies the force to the object.

The size of the force depends on the amount of charge carried by the object, the velocity of the object, and the strength of the field. If any of these three factors changes by a given amount, the force will change by a proportional amount. For example, if velocity is tripled, force also will triple.

The direction of the force depends on whether the object has a positive or a negative charge, the direction in which the object is moving, and the direction of the magnetic field. Scientists define the direction of the field as the direction of lines of force flowing out of the north pole and into the south pole of the magnet (see **Magnetism** [diagram: A magnetic field]).

The directions of motion, field, and force are at right angles to one another. For example, if a positively charged object is moving northward and the direction of the field is toward the east, the field will accelerate the particle vertically downward. If the object is negatively charged, the field will accelerate it vertically upward.

The strong force holds protons and neutrons together in atomic nuclei. The protons are so close to one another that there is a huge electric repulsion between them. The strong force overcomes this repulsion. If there were no strong force, only one chemical element could exist—hydrogen, with one proton in its nucleus.

The strong force holds quarks together in protons and neutrons much as the electric force holds electrons and protons together in atoms. The strong force holds protons and neutrons together in nuclei much as the electric force holds atoms together in molecules.

The weak force can change one type of particle into another. For example, in the main process by which the sun produces energy, the weak force changes a proton into a neutron. It does this by *emitting* (sending out) a particle called a W^+. This particle carries off the proton's positive charge, then breaks apart into a positively charged *positron* and an electrically neutral *neutrino.*

The weak force also takes part in a kind of radioactivity known as *beta decay.* In the most common form of this process, a neutron in a nucleus changes into a proton. The neutron emits a W^- particle, which then breaks apart into an electron and an antineutrino.   Michael Dine

Related articles in *World Book* include:

Centrifugal force	Gravitation	Pressure
Centripetal force	Gyroscope	Radiation
Dynamics	Inertia	Relativity
Electricity	Magnetism	Statics
Electromotive	Newton	Subatomic particle
force	Newton, Sir Isaac	Torque
Energy	Physics	Weight
Friction	Power	Work

Force bill was any of several measures passed or considered by the United States Congress that authorized the use of military power to enforce federal law. The first force bill was sometimes called the "Bloody Bill." It became a law on March 2, 1833, after South Carolina had declared the protective tariff laws of 1828 and 1832 "null, void, and no law" within the borders of the state (see **Nullification**). The bill authorized the president to use U.S. armed forces to collect the duties. A compromise tariff was passed, and bloodshed was averted.

During the period of Reconstruction (1865-1877), three other force bills were passed. Two of them (one signed on May 31, 1870, and another on Feb. 28, 1871) were designed to enforce the 15th Amendment (voting rights for blacks). An act of April 20, 1871, known as the Ku Klux Klan Act, was meant to enforce the 14th Amendment (civil rights).

The Lodge Federal Elections Bill of 1890, which passed the House of Representatives but not the Senate, was also called a force bill. Its purpose was to use federal authority to prevent discrimination against black voters in the Southern States. It was denounced in the South as an attempt to bring back the methods of Reconstruction (see **Reconstruction**).   H. Wayne Morgan

Ford is a place where a stream or river can be crossed. During early times, people had to cross a waterway by wading through or swimming across its shallow part. During wartime, soldiers must often *ford* (cross) water where bridges have been blown up. They sometimes do this by placing *pontoons* (portable floats) in a line across the water. See also **Pontoon bridge.**   Paul R. Bierman

Ford, Ford Madox (1873-1939), was an English author of complex and symbolic novels that show the influence of the psychological novels of Henry James. In *The Good Soldier* (1915), his best-known work, Ford revealed with keen irony the declining influence of the upper class in English life. This novel was followed by the series called *Parade's End,* which consists of *Some Do Not* (1924), *No More Parades* (1925), *A Man Could Stand Up* (1926), and *The Last Post* (1928). The series traces changes in English society during and after World War I (1914-1918). Ford and Joseph Conrad wrote two novels together, *The Inheritors* (1901) and *Romance* (1903).

Ford was born Ford Madox Hueffer on Dec. 17, 1873, in Merton, England. He edited two famous literary magazines, the *English Review* and the *Transatlantic Review,* and was writer-in-residence at Olivet College in Michigan from 1937 until his death on June 26, 1939.
      Garrett Stewart

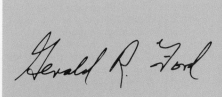

**38th president of the
United States 1974-1977**

Nixon
37th president
1969-1974
Republican

Ford
38th president
1974-1977
Republican

Carter
39th president
1977-1981
Democrat

**Nelson A.
Rockefeller**
Vice president
1974-1977

Gerald R. Ford Library

Ford, Gerald Rudolph (1913-2006), was the only vice president of the United States to become president upon the resignation of a chief executive. Richard M. Nixon resigned as president on Aug. 9, 1974, and Ford took office that same day. When Nixon left the presidency, he faced almost certain impeachment because of his role in the Watergate political scandal.

Ford had been vice president for only eight months when he became president. Nixon had appointed him to succeed Vice President Spiro T. Agnew, who resigned while under criminal investigation for graft. Ford was the first person to be appointed to fill a vacancy in the vice presidency. In addition, he was the only person to serve as both vice president and president who did not win election to either office. In the 1976 election, Ford was defeated in his bid for a full term as president by former Governor Jimmy Carter of Georgia, his Democratic opponent.

Ford, a Michigan Republican, had been elected to the U.S. House of Representatives 13 straight times before he replaced Agnew. He also had served as House minority leader.

Americans warmly welcomed Ford to the presidency. He had a calm, friendly manner and a reputation for honesty. But Ford's popularity dropped sharply just one month into his term after he pardoned Nixon for all federal crimes that Nixon might have committed as president. Many Americans felt that Nixon should have been brought to trial in the Watergate scandal. Others be-

Yanek Mieczkowski, the contributor of this article, is Associate Professor of History at Dowling College and the author of Gerald Ford and the Challenges of the 1970s.

lieved that Nixon should not have been pardoned until he admitted his role in the scandal.

Ford faced major economic problems, including a recession, double-digit inflation, and high unemployment. The economy began to recover in 1975, though the unemployment rate remained high. U.S. foreign policy suffered a major defeat in 1975, when the Vietnam War ended with a Communist victory.

Ford stood 6 feet 1 inch (185 centimeters) tall and loved sports. He often turned to the sports section of his newspaper before reading any other news. Ford starred as a football player in high school and college, and football had a major influence on his life. "Thanks to my football experience," he once said, "I know the value of team play. It is, I believe, one of the most important lessons to be learned and practiced in our lives." Ford swam regularly and also enjoyed golf and skiing.

Early life

Family background. Ford was born on July 14, 1913, in Omaha, Nebraska. He was named Leslie Lynch King, Jr. His father, Leslie Lynch King, Sr., operated a family wool business there. Leslie's parents were divorced two years after his birth. His mother, Dorothy Gardner King, then took him to Grand Rapids, Michigan, where her parents lived. In 1916, she married Gerald R. Ford, a paint salesman, who adopted the boy and gave him his name. Ford was the only U.S. president to have undergone a complete name change. The stocky, blond youth, who became known as "Jerry," grew up with three younger half brothers, James, Richard, and Thomas.

Boyhood. Jerry's parents encouraged him to develop pride in civic responsibility. His stepfather participated in programs to aid needy youths in Grand Rapids and

Sorrow and celebration characterized two events that took place during the Ford administration. The Vietnam War ended in a Communist victory in 1975. Thousands of South Vietnamese refugees fled from their homeland in a U.S.-sponsored airlift, *left.* In 1976, a fleet of tall ships from various nations, *below,* sailed toward New York City harbor to take part in festivities marking the bicentennial of the founding of the United States.

The world of President Ford

Ethiopian Emperor Haile Selassie was deposed by military leaders in 1974 after a 44-year reign.

The Soviet Union deported Alexander Solzhenitsyn, a Nobel Prize-winning novelist, in 1974. He later settled in the United States.

The continuing drama of the Watergate scandal reached a climax in 1975, when top members of the Nixon administration were found guilty of perjury, conspiracy, and obstruction of justice. Former Attorney General John Mitchell and presidential aides John Ehrlichman and H. R. Haldeman were among the people sentenced to prison.

Portugal's colonial rule in Africa ended in 1975, when it granted independence to Angola, Cape Verde, Mozambique, and São Tomé and Príncipe.

Juan Carlos I became king of Spain in 1975, following the death of Francisco Franco, Spain's dictator since 1939.

The Apollo-Soyuz Test Project accomplished its goal of cooperation in space in July 1975. A U.S. spacecraft docked with a Soviet spacecraft in space, and crew members from both vehicles conducted joint scientific experiments.

Women were admitted to the military academies of the United States Army, Air Force, and Navy for the first time in 1976.

The deaths of Chinese Communist leaders Mao Zedong and Zhou Enlai in 1976 marked the end of an era. The two men had led China since 1949.

The movement for an independent Quebec gained strength in Canada in 1976, when a separatist political party won control of the provincial government.

Jean-Claude Francolon, Gamma/Liaison; Ted Hardin, Black Star

took an active interest in local politics. His mother devoted much of her time to charity projects and other activities of the Grace Episcopal Church, where the Fords worshiped. Jerry joined the Boy Scouts and achieved the rank of Eagle Scout, the highest level in Scouting. He later proudly referred to himself as the nation's "first Eagle Scout vice president."

Jerry was a strong, husky boy who excelled in sports. He first gained public attention as the star center of the South High School football team. He was selected to the all-city high school football team three times and was named to the all-state team as a high school senior.

At school, Jerry usually wore a suit and tie, though most boys in those days wore a sport shirt, slacks, and a sweater. He studied hard and received good grades. He also won a contest in which he was chosen the most popular high school senior in Grand Rapids.

As a teen-ager, Jerry waited on tables and washed dishes at a small restaurant across the street from South High School. One day, his real father came in and introduced himself to the startled youth. Jerry knew about his

natural father but had no recollection of him. King asked Jerry if he would like to live with the King family. Jerry told King that he considered the Fords his family.

College student. In 1931, Ford entered the University of Michigan. He earned good grades and played center on the undefeated Michigan football teams of 1932 and 1933. In 1934, his teammates named him the team's most valuable player. He played center on the college team that lost to the Chicago Bears, 5 to 0, in the 1935 All-Star Football Game.

Ford graduated from Michigan in 1935. The Detroit Lions and the Green Bay Packers offered him contracts to play professional football, but Ford had decided to study law. He accepted a job as assistant football coach

Important dates in Ford's life

1913	(July 14) Born in Omaha, Nebraska.
1935	Graduated from the University of Michigan.
1942-1946	Served in the U.S. Navy during World War II.
1948	(Oct. 15) Married Elizabeth (Betty) Bloomer.
1948	Elected to the first of 13 successive terms in the U.S. House of Representatives.
1965	Became House minority leader.
1973	(Dec. 6) Became vice president of the United States.
1974	(Aug. 9) Succeeded to the presidency.
1976	Lost presidential election to Jimmy Carter.
2006	(Dec. 26) Died in Rancho Mirage, California.

Gerald R. Ford Library

Ford's birthplace was this house in Omaha, Nebraska. His parents divorced when he was 2. Ford and his mother moved to Grand Rapids, Michigan, where she remarried and he spent his boyhood.

Young Jerry, shown at the age of 2 ½, liked to play with his dog, Spot. He developed into a strong, husky child who enjoyed sports and became active in the Boy Scouts.

and boxing coach at Yale University, hoping he could also study law there. Ford coached full-time at Yale from 1935 until 1938, taking law classes part-time. In 1938, when Yale Law School accepted him for full-time study, he continued to coach full-time. Ford received his law degree from Yale in 1941. He ranked in the top third of his graduating class.

Grand Rapids lawyer

In June 1941, Ford was admitted to the Michigan bar. Shortly afterward, he and Philip W. Buchen, a former roommate at the University of Michigan, opened a law office in Grand Rapids. The United States entered World War II in December 1941, and Ford soon volunteered for the United States Navy.

Naval officer. Ford entered the Navy as an ensign in April 1942. He taught physical training at a base in Chapel Hill, North Carolina, for a year. Then he became the physical-training director and assistant navigation officer of the USS *Monterey,* an aircraft carrier. In 1943 and 1944, the *Monterey* took part in every big naval battle in the Pacific Ocean. A scary moment for Ford came in late 1944, when he almost fell off the carrier's deck during a violent typhoon. In January 1946, Ford was discharged as a lieutenant commander.

Entry into politics. Ford resumed his law career in Grand Rapids and became active in a local Republican reform group. Leaders of the organization, called the Home Front, included U.S. Senator Arthur H. Vandenberg of Michigan and Ford's stepfather. The two men urged Ford to challenge U.S. Representative Bartel J. Jonkman of Michigan's fifth congressional district in the 1948 Republican primary.

An *isolationist,* Jonkman believed that the United States should stay out of foreign affairs as much as possible. Ford had supported that policy before World War II, but the war changed his views. He now supported an active international role for the United States. Ford defeated Jonkman in the primary and then beat Fred Barr, his Democratic opponent in the November election.

Marriage. In 1947, Ford met Elizabeth (Betty) Bloomer (April 8, 1918-July 8, 2011). She was born in Chicago and moved to Grand Rapids with her family when she was 3 years old. Her father, William S. Bloomer, was a machinery salesman. Her mother, Hortense, took an active interest in Grand Rapids community affairs.

As a child, Betty became interested in dancing. She continued to study dance and, during the 1930's, joined a New York City group directed by the noted dancer

Ford starred as center on the University of Michigan football team. His teammates named him most valuable player in 1934. He later coached football and boxing at Yale University.

The Ford family in 1948. Seated are, *left to right,* Gerald's half brother James; his mother, Dorothy; and Gerald. Standing are half brother Thomas; Gerald Ford, Sr.; and half brother Richard.

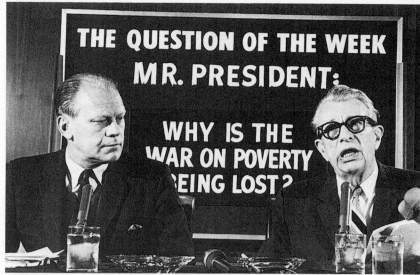

THE QUESTION OF THE WEEK
MR. PRESIDENT:

WHY IS THE
WAR ON POVERTY
EING LOST?

As House minority leader, Ford appeared with Senate Minority Leader Everett M. Dirksen in a series of televised press conferences in the late 1960's.

United Press Int.

Martha Graham. In 1942, she returned to Grand Rapids and married William Warren, a local furniture salesman. They were divorced in 1947.

When Ford met Betty, she was working as a fashion coordinator for a Grand Rapids department store. They married on Oct. 15, 1948, just before Ford's first election to the U.S. House of Representatives. Ford campaigned on the day of his wedding and arrived late for the ceremony. The Fords had four children, Michael Gerald (1950-   ), John Gardner (1952-   ), Steven Meigs (1956-   ), and Susan Elizabeth (1957-   ). The family lived in a four-bedroom house in Alexandria, Virginia.

Career in Congress

Rise to power. Ford gained a reputation as a loyal Republican and a hard worker during his early terms in Congress. In 1950, he won a seat on the House Appropriations Committee and became an expert on the federal budget.

During the early 1960's, Ford became increasingly popular among young Republican members of Congress. In 1963, they helped elect him chairman of the Republican Conference of the House. In this position, his first leadership role in the House, Ford presided at meetings of the Republican representatives.

In November 1963, President Lyndon B. Johnson established the Warren Commission to investigate the assassination of President John F. Kennedy. Johnson appointed Ford as one of the seven members of the commission. Ford and a member of his staff, John R. Stiles, later wrote a book about Lee Harvey Oswald, *Portrait of the Assassin* (1965).

House minority leader. In 1965, Ford was chosen House minority leader. As minority leader, he urged House Republicans to do more than just criticize the proposals of Democrats, who held a majority in the House. Ford worked for Republican alternatives to Democratic programs.

Ford attracted national attention when he appeared with Senate Minority Leader Everett M. Dirksen on a series of televised Republican press conferences. The se-

ries, which reporters called the "Ev and Jerry Show," drew increased attention to Republican views.

Ford supported President Johnson's early policies in the Vietnam War. But by 1967, with no end of the war in sight, Ford began to criticize U.S. military strategy in Vietnam. That year, he gave a speech entitled "Why Are We Pulling Our Punches in Vietnam?" The speech encouraged Republicans to oppose Johnson's war policies. In addition, Republicans and Southern Democrats joined under Ford's leadership in opposing many of Johnson's social programs. Ford considered these programs either too costly or unnecessary.

In 1968, Richard M. Nixon was elected president. The Democrats kept control of both houses of Congress, but Ford helped win approval of a number of Nixon's policies concerning the Vietnam War and inflation.

The resignation of Agnew. In 1972, Nixon and Vice President Spiro T. Agnew won reelection in a landslide. Early in 1973, federal investigators uncovered evidence that Agnew had accepted bribes while serving as Maryland's governor and later as vice president. Because of the charges against him, Agnew resigned from the vice presidency on Oct. 10, 1973. Nixon nominated Ford to replace Agnew. The nomination required the approval of both houses of Congress under procedures established in 1967 by the 25th Amendment to the U.S. Constitution. Previously, vice presidential vacancies had remained unfilled until the next presidential election.

The Senate approved Ford's nomination by a 92 to 3 vote on November 27. The House approved it, 387 to 35, on December 6, and Ford was sworn in as the 40th vice president later that day. He became the first appointed vice president in the nation's history.

Vice president (1973-1974)

When Ford became vice president, Congress was investigating Nixon's role in the Watergate scandal, which had begun in June 1972. Some members of Congress believed that Nixon was hiding evidence. The scandal arose after Nixon's reelection committee became involved in a burglary at Democratic national headquarters in the Watergate building complex in Washington, D.C. Later, evidence linked several top White House aides with the burglary or with an effort to conceal information about it.

Speaking tour. The Watergate scandal shook public confidence in Nixon, even though he insisted he had no part in it. As vice president, Ford went on a nationwide speaking tour and expressed his faith in Nixon. He addressed business, civic, and youth groups in cities throughout the country. Ford also took part in many Republican fund-raising activities and campaigned for Republican candidates. By mid-1974, the vice president had visited about 40 states and made about 500 public appearances.

The resignation of Nixon. In July 1974, the House Judiciary Committee recommended that Nixon be impeached. It voted to adopt three articles of impeachment for consideration by the full House of Representatives. The first article accused the president of interfering with justice by acting to hide evidence about the Watergate burglary from federal law-enforcement officials. The other articles charged that Nixon had abused presidential powers and illegally withheld evidence from the judiciary committee.

Ford continued to defend Nixon, arguing that the president had committed no impeachable offense. Ford predicted that the House of Representatives would not impeach Nixon.

Then, on August 5, Nixon released transcripts of taped White House conversations that clearly supported the first proposed article of impeachment. Almost all of Nixon's remaining support in Congress collapsed. The Republican leaders of both the House and Senate warned Nixon that he faced certain impeachment and removal from office.

Nixon resigned as president on the morning of August 9. At noon that day, Ford took the oath of office as the 38th president of the United States. Warren E. Burger, chief justice of the United States, administered the presidential oath of office to Ford in the East Room of the White House. Ford's inaugural address contained one of the most famous lines from his presidency, as he reassured scandal-weary Americans that "our long national nightmare is over."

Ford's administration (1974-1977)

Ford kept all of Nixon's Cabinet officers at the start of his administration. He nominated Nelson A. Rockefeller, former governor of New York, as vice president. Rockefeller took office in December 1974, after both the Senate and the House confirmed his nomination.

Political philosophy. Ford described himself as a conservative in fiscal matters, a moderate on social policy, and an internationalist in foreign affairs. As president, one of his top priorities was to limit government spending and decrease the federal budget deficit. A large deficit, he feared, would increase inflation and harm the economy. Ford also believed in cutting taxes and reducing government regulations that he felt hurt business activity.

Early problems. Once in office, Ford confronted soaring inflation and a loss of public confidence in the government. Inflation created hardships among many Americans, especially the poor and the elderly. Sharp rises in prices also threatened to cause a severe business slump.

Public faith in government had plunged to its lowest level in years, largely because of the Watergate scandal. In addition, Nixon had devoted so much time to defending himself during the investigations that he had been unable to concentrate on government policy.

Fighting on the Mediterranean island of Cyprus provided the first foreign crisis for the new president. In August 1974, Turkish troops invaded Cyprus and took control of a large part of the island. The take-over occurred after Turkish Cypriots strongly protested the formation of a new government by Greek Cypriots. Angry Greeks, Greek Cypriots, and Americans of Greek ancestry charged that the United States should have used its influence to stop the Turks. Over Ford's objections, Congress passed a ban on military aid to Turkey. The measure remained in effect until Jimmy Carter's presidency.

The national scene. Democrats won many seats in Congress during the November 1974 midterm elections, and the new 94th Congress had a large Democratic majority. Although Ford remained personally popular on Capitol Hill, he had political battles with the Democratic-controlled Congress, which opposed many of his poli-

J.P. Laffont, Sygma

Ford became vice president in 1973, after Spiro Agnew resigned. Nixon and Mrs. Ford watched as Chief Justice Warren Burger administered the oath of office.

Ford was sworn in as president on Aug. 9, 1974, in the East Room of the White House. Betty Ford watched Chief Justice Warren Burger administer the oath of office.

Dirck Halstead, *Time* Magazine

cies. Ford vetoed 66 bills. He believed most of these bills would have increased the federal budget deficit.

The Nixon pardon severely hurt Ford's early popularity. On Sept. 8, 1974, he pardoned Nixon for all federal crimes the former president might have committed as chief executive. Ford said he took the action to end divisions within the nation and to refocus the country's attention on domestic and diplomatic problems. But the pardon angered millions of Americans. Many of them believed that the government should have brought Nixon to trial. Others felt that Ford should not have granted the pardon until Nixon had admitted his involvement in the Watergate scandal.

The amnesty program. Eight days after he pardoned Nixon, Ford offered amnesty to draft dodgers and deserters of the Vietnam War period. The program required most of these men to work in a public service job for up to two years. About 22,000 of the approximately 106,000 eligible men applied for amnesty under the program. Most of the rest objected to the work requirement and refused to apply.

The economy. At the beginning of his administration, Ford called inflation the nation's "public enemy Number One." He established the Council on Wage and Price Stability to expose inflationary wage and price increases.

To slow inflation, Ford proposed small tax increases for corporations, families, and individuals. But he dropped these plans later in 1974 after a recession struck the nation. Ford proposed a tax cut to stimulate the economy. Congress passed the measure, and Ford signed it in March 1975.

By mid-1975, inflation slowed, and the economy began to recover from the recession. But in May that year, nearly 9 percent of the nation's labor force had no jobs—the highest level of unemployment since 1941. The unemployment rate dropped slowly during the recovery. In October 1976, unemployment still stood at about 8 percent, which hurt Ford politically. His record on inflation was much better, however. During 1976, the inflation rate ran below 6 percent.

Energy policy. During the 1970's, the nation suffered energy shortages. To end the energy crisis, Ford proposed eliminating price controls on oil, which created shortages. Congress resisted Ford's proposals, but he signed legislation that gradually reduced controls and encouraged energy conservation. He also emphasized

David Rubinger, *Time* Magazine

The Turkish invasion of the island of Cyprus was Ford's first foreign crisis. Critics thought he should have used United States influence to stop the Turks.

Vice president and Cabinet

Vice president	*Nelson A. Rockefeller
Secretary of state	*Henry A. Kissinger
Secretary of the treasury	William E. Simon
Secretary of defense	James R. Schlesinger
	*Donald H. Rumsfeld (1975)
Attorney general	William B. Saxbe
	Edward H. Levi (1975)
Secretary of the interior	Rogers C. B. Morton
	Stanley K. Hathaway (1975)
	Thomas S. Kleppe (1975)
Secretary of agriculture	Earl L. Butz
	John A. Knebel (1976)
Secretary of commerce	Frederick B. Dent
	Rogers C. B. Morton (1975)
	*Elliot L. Richardson (1975)
Secretary of labor	Peter J. Brennan
	John T. Dunlop (1975)
	W. J. Usery, Jr. (1976)
Secretary of health, education, and welfare	*Caspar Weinberger
	F. David Mathews (1975)
Secretary of housing and urban development	James T. Lynn
	Carla A. Hills (1975)
Secretary of transportation	Claude S. Brinegar
	William T. Coleman, Jr. (1975)

*Has a biography in *World Book.*

the use of energy sources such as coal instead of oil.

Two attempted assassinations of Ford occurred in California during September 1975. The first attempt, by Lynette Alice Fromme, a follower of a convicted murderer named Charles Manson, took place on September 5 in Sacramento. A Secret Service agent saw Fromme pointing a pistol at Ford and grabbed the gun before it was fired. On September 22, Sara Jane Moore, who had been associated with groups protesting U.S. government policies, shot at Ford in San Francisco but missed. Both women were convicted of attempted assassination of a president and sentenced to life imprisonment. Moore was released in 2007.

Foreign affairs. Ford relied heavily on the guidance of Secretary of State Henry A. Kissinger, who had also been Nixon's chief adviser on foreign policy. In 1975, Ford and Kissinger helped Egypt and Israel settle a territorial dispute that had resulted from a 1973 war between the two countries. Ford continued Nixon's program to improve U.S. relations with China and the Soviet Union. He visited both countries, and he also became the first U.S. president to visit Japan.

The Vietnam War ended in April 1975, after Communist North Vietnam conquered South Vietnam. Shortly before South Vietnam fell, Ford asked Congress to give that nation $722 million in emergency military aid. But Congress rejected the request. Ford arranged to evacuate refugees from South Vietnam. About 100,000 of them came to the United States.

The Mayagüez seizure. In May 1975, Cambodian Communist troops seized the *Mayagüez,* a U.S. merchant ship, in the Gulf of Thailand. Ford sent 200 U.S. Marines to the area, and they quickly recaptured the ship and rescued its 39 crew members.

Meetings with foreign leaders. In July 1975, Ford traveled to Helsinki, Finland, to participate in the Conference on Security and Cooperation in Europe. The Hel-

sinki Accords, signed by Ford and the leaders of 34 other nations, promoted human rights and greater freedom in Eastern Europe and the Soviet Union. Ford regarded this agreement as his most important foreign policy achievement. In 1975 and 1976, Ford also met with the leaders of the key U.S. allies. The meetings marked the start of annual Group of Seven (G-7) summits.

Life in the White House was relaxed during Ford's presidency. Ford tried to improve presidential relations with reporters and granted many interviews. The Fords impressed visitors with their warmth and friendliness. They liked to entertain and invited over 900 guests to a White House Christmas party for members of Congress in 1974. The Fords especially enjoyed dancing. A highlight of Ford's presidency was the 1976 Bicentennial, when the United States observed the 200th anniversary of its independence. As part of the celebrations, Ford visited Philadelphia and rang the Liberty Bell.

Susan Ford was the only one of the four Ford children who lived in the White House during most of Ford's presidency. As a gift, Susan gave her father a pet dog, a golden retriever named Liberty. For vacations, the Fords often went to Vail, Colorado.

Betty Ford underwent surgery for breast cancer two months after Ford became president. She won the admiration of millions when she resumed her busy schedule of activities after recovering from the operation. Mrs. Ford also became noted for her support of women's rights. She campaigned for adoption of the Equal Rights Amendment to the U.S. Constitution. This amendment was designed to give women the same rights men had in business and other fields.

The 1976 election. Former Governor Ronald Reagan of California challenged Ford for the 1976 Republican

Gerald R. Ford Library

The president's family poses in the White House. Behind President and Mrs. Ford are, *left to right,* daughter Susan, sons Steven, John, and Michael, and Michael's wife, Gayle.

presidential nomination. Ford and Reagan fought a close, bitter contest in the state primary elections. Ford narrowly won the nomination on the first ballot at the Republican National Convention in Kansas City, Missouri. At Ford's request, the convention nominated Senator Robert J. Dole of Kansas for vice president. Their Democratic opponents were former Governor Jimmy Carter of Georgia and Senator Walter F. Mondale of Minnesota.

During his campaign against Carter, Ford pledged to continue policies that he believed had brought about economic recovery and lower inflation. Carter charged that Ford's policies had contributed to the continuing high rate of unemployment. Reminding voters of the Watergate scandal, Carter also promised, "I will never lie to you." The campaign included the second series of nationally televised debates between presidential candidates in U.S. history. The first series took place in 1960. In the 1976 election, Carter defeated Ford by 1,678,069 popular votes out of more than 81 ½ million. Ford carried 27 states, while Carter carried 23 states and the District of Columbia. But Carter got 297 electoral votes compared to Ford's 240. See **Electoral College** (table).

Later years

After Ford left the White House, he moved to Rancho Mirage, California. He also had a summer home in Beaver Creek, Colorado. He served on the board of directors of several U.S. companies and lectured at colleges and universities. In 1979, he wrote his autobiography, *A Time to Heal*. The book's title reflected what Ford viewed as his role in history—a president who "healed" the nation after the Watergate scandal, the Vietnam War, and economic troubles. At the 1980 Republican National Convention, Republican presidential nominee Ronald Reagan asked Ford to be his running mate, but Ford declined. In 1981, the Gerald R. Ford Museum opened in Grand Rapids, and the Gerald R. Ford Library opened in Ann Arbor, Michigan.

Ford and his wife became known for their support of charitable causes in their California and Colorado communities. In 1982, Betty Ford helped found the Betty Ford Center in Rancho Mirage. The center treats alcoholism and drug abuse. She helped open the center after seeking treatment in 1978 for her own addiction to alcohol and prescription drugs. The Fords also helped establish and fund a domestic violence center, a children's museum, and other nonprofit facilities.

Ford died on Dec. 26, 2006, at his home in Rancho Mirage. He is buried on the grounds of the Gerald R. Ford Museum in Grand Rapids.   Yanek Mieczkowski

Related articles in *World Book* include:

Agnew, Spiro T.	Republican Party
Constitution of the United States (Amendment 25)	Rockefeller, Nelson A.
	United States, History of the
Nixon, Richard M.	Vice president of the United
President of the United States	States
Presidential succession	Watergate

Outline

I. Early life
 A. Family background
 B. Boyhood
 C. College student
II. Grand Rapids lawyer
 A. Naval officer
 B. Entry into politics
 C. Marriage
III. Career in Congress
 A. Rise to power
 B. House minority leader
 C. The resignation of Agnew
IV. Vice president (1973-1974)
 A. Speaking tour
 B. The resignation of Nixon
V. Ford's administration (1974-1977)
 A. Political philosophy
 B. Early problems
 C. The national scene
 D. Foreign affairs
 E. Life in the White House
 F. The 1976 election
VI. Later years

Additional resources

Cannon, James M. *Time and Chance: Gerald Ford's Appointment with History.* 1994. Reprint. Univ. of Mich. Pr., 1998.
Firestone, Bernard J., and Ugrinsky, Alexej, eds. *Gerald R. Ford and the Politics of Post-Watergate America.* 2 vols. Greenwood, 1993.
Francis, Sandra. *Gerald R. Ford.* Child's World, 2002. Younger readers.
Greene, John R. *The Limits of Power: The Nixon and Ford Administrations.* Ind. Univ. Pr., 1992. *The Presidency of Gerald R. Ford.* Univ. Pr. of Kans., 1995.

Ford, Hannibal Choate (1877-1955), an American inventor and engineer, developed equipment to control the range and accuracy of gunfire. He perfected the method that allowed guns to aim accurately from the rolling decks of a ship at sea.

Ford formed the Ford Instrument Company in 1915 and was its first president. Later, the company became a division of the Sperry Rand Corporation (now part of Unisys Corporation). He helped make many improvements on typewriters and also invented an automatic bombsight. Ford was born on May 8, 1877, in Dryden, New York, and died on March 12, 1955.   Jack Sweetman

Ford, Harrison (1942-   ), is an American actor best known as a rugged man of integrity in action films. Ford starred in some of the most popular motion pictures in history. By the late 1980's, he ranked among the most successful movie stars in the world.

Ford was born July 13, 1942, in Chicago. He played minor roles in television and motion pictures in Hollywood in the late 1960's. He left acting due to the slow progress of his career and became a carpenter. Ford returned to movies in 1973 in a supporting role in *American Graffiti,* written and directed by George Lucas. Ford became a star with his performance as the cocky starship captain Han Solo in the science-fiction film *Star Wars* (1977), also directed by Lucas. Ford continued the character in the sequels *The Empire Strikes Back* (1980) and *Return of the Jedi* (1983). Ford increased his international reputation as the archaeologist and adventurer Indiana Jones in *Raiders of the Lost Ark* (1981), followed by *Indiana Jones and the Temple of Doom* (1984), *Indiana Jones and the Last Crusade* (1989), and *Indiana Jones and the Kingdom of the Crystal Skull* (2008), all directed by Steven Spielberg. Among Ford's other important films of the 1980's are *Blade Runner* (1982), *Witness* (1985), *The Mosquito Coast* (1986), and *Working Girl* (1988).

AP/Wide World
Harrison Ford

Ford's other notable films include *Patriot Games* (1992), *The Fugitive* (1993), *Clear and Present Danger* (1994), *The Devil's Own* and *Air Force One* (both 1997), *What Lies Beneath* (2000), *K-19: The Widowmaker* (2002), *Extraordinary Measures* and *Morning Glory* (both 2010), *Cowboys and Aliens* (2011), and *42* (2013).   Louis Giannetti

Ford, Henry (1863-1947), was the leading manufacturer of American automobiles in the early 1900's. He established the Ford Motor Company, which revolutionized the automobile industry with its assembly line method of production. The savings from this technique helped Ford sell automobiles at a lower price than anyone else. From 1908 to 1927, more than half the cars sold in the United States were Fords.

Early life. Ford was born on July 30, 1863, on a farm in what is now Dearborn, Michigan. He became a machinist at the age of 16 and later worked as an engineer at a Detroit electric company. As a young man, Ford became interested in a new invention, automobiles. He built his first successful gasoline engine in 1893 and his first automobile in 1896.

Industrial accomplishments. In 1903, Ford organized the Ford Motor Company. Like other automobile companies, Ford produced only expensive cars. But Ford soon began working to make a simple, sturdy car that large numbers of people could afford. He achieved one of the first such automobiles with the Model T, which appeared in 1908. In 1909, Ford decided to produce only Model T's. The original price of $850 for a Model T car was too high for many customers. To lower the price, Ford and his executives tried new ways to reduce production costs. For example, the company created an assembly line method in which conveyor belts brought automobile parts to workers. Each worker performed a particular task, such as adding or tightening a part. This system helped reduce the assembly time of a Ford automobile from about 12 ½ worker-hours in 1912 to about 1 ½ worker-hours in 1914.

Oil painting on canvas (early 1950's) by Norman Rockwell; Henry Ford Museum and Greenfield Village, Dearborn, Mich.

Henry Ford's first automobile was built in a workshop in Detroit. The automobile, completed in 1896, is now on display at the Henry Ford Museum in Dearborn, Michigan.

Ford Motor Company

Henry Ford

Ford Motor Company began to produce its own parts instead of buying them from independent suppliers at a higher price. Ford also shipped automobile parts, rather than assembled automobiles, to market areas, where assembly plants put the parts together. Parts cost less to ship than whole automobiles did. The company also began to make its own glass and steel.

As the company's production costs fell, Ford passed much of the savings on to his customers. The price of a Model T touring car dropped to $550 in 1913, $440 in 1915, and $290 in 1924, putting the automobile within reach of the average family.

In 1914, Ford raised the minimum wage to $5 a day for his employees 22 years of age and older, more than twice what most wage earners received. Ford also reduced the workday from 9 to 8 hours. Workers flocked to Ford plants seeking jobs, and Ford could choose the hardest-working and smartest ones. To encourage productivity, Ford introduced a profit-sharing plan, which set aside part of the company's profits for its employees.

During the mid-1920's, Ford continued to produce the Model T even though its popularity had declined. Meanwhile, the General Motors Corporation (GM) gained an increasing share of the U.S. automobile market. GM offered a wide variety of models equipped with many luxuries. GM also introduced new designs yearly and advertised its cars as symbols of wealth and taste. Ford, however, continued to offer only basic transportation at a low cost. The Model T changed little from year to year, and from 1914 to 1925, it came in only one color: black.

Ford finally introduced a new automobile design, the Model A, in 1927, after more than 15 million Model T's had been sold. In 1932, Ford introduced the first low-priced car with a *V-8 engine,* a powerful engine that had eight cylinders arranged in a V-shaped pattern. By that time, however, GM had taken the lead from Ford Motor in U.S. auto sales. Ford Motor declined throughout the 1930's, and some people began to question Henry Ford's management skills. In 1945, Henry Ford II, one of Ford's grandsons, took over the company.

Political and charitable activities. Ford had long taken an interest in political affairs. In 1915, during World War I, he and about 170 other people traveled to Europe at his expense to seek peace. The group, which lacked approval by the U.S. government, failed to persuade the warring nations to settle their differences.

In 1918, the year the war ended, Ford ran as a Democrat for a Senate seat from Michigan. He lost the election and did not seek public office again, but he continued to speak on political issues. Ford was *anti-Semitic* (prejudiced against Jews). He published newspapers and books that attacked Jews. He also opposed labor unions. He fought attempts by the United Automobile Workers (UAW) to organize his employees.

Ford devoted much time and money to educational and charitable works. He established Greenfield Village

An assembly line in 1913 was used to build Model T automobiles in Highland Park, Michigan.

and the Henry Ford Museum, both in Dearborn. The village is a group of restored historical buildings. The museum includes exhibits in science, industry, and art. In 1936, Ford and his son, Edsel, set up the Ford Foundation, one of the world's largest foundations, which gives grants for education, research, and development. Ford died on April 7, 1947.

Ford wrote four books with author Samuel Crowther. They are *My Life and Work* (1922), *Today and Tomorrow* (1926), *Edison As I Know Him* (1930), and *Moving Forward* (1931). Tamra S. Davis

See also **Automobile** (Mass production); **Ford, Henry, II; Ford Foundation; Ford Motor Company.**

Ford, Henry, II (1917-1987), was an American automobile manufacturer who reorganized the Ford Motor Company during the 1940's and rescued it from near bankruptcy. He was a grandson of Henry Ford, who organized the company in 1903.

Henry Ford II was born on Sept. 4, 1917, in Detroit. During World War II (1939-1945), he served in the United States Navy at Great Lakes Naval Training Center. In 1943, his father, Edsel Ford, then president of Ford Motor Company, died. Henry Ford II was released from the Navy to work at his grandfather's company, which produced military vehicles and other supplies needed for the war effort.

Ford became vice president of the company in 1943 and took over the presidency from his grandfather in 1945. At that time, the company was losing about $9 million a month. Ford hired a team of expert managers to help him reorganize the company. He also introduced new marketing methods and automobile designs to meet the changing tastes of the American public. In 1949, after the reorganization, the company earned about $177 million. Ford's leadership was responsible for the company's return to profitability.

During the 1950's and 1960's, such successful models as the Thunderbird, Falcon, Mustang, and Maverick helped keep the company strong. In 1960, Ford became chairman of the board and chief executive officer of Ford Motor. He retired as chief executive officer in 1979 and as chairman in 1980. He died on Sept. 29, 1987.

Ford helped establish a number of social welfare organizations. In 1967, for example, he helped found the Urban Coalition, which worked to solve problems in large cities. This organization became the National Urban Coalition in 1970. In 1968, Ford helped organize the National Alliance of Business to find jobs for the unemployed. Tamra S. Davis

See also **Ford, Henry; Ford Motor Company.**

Ford, John (1586-1640?), was an English playwright. Such critics of the 1900's as T. S. Eliot have ranked Ford as the finest English playwright in the period after the death of William Shakespeare.

Ford wrote in collaboration with other playwrights but created several distinguished plays of his own. The most famous are two sensational tragedies, *The Broken Heart* (1629) and *'Tis Pity She's a Whore* (1632?); and the historical drama *Perkin Warbeck* (1633), about a man who claims to be the rightful heir to the English throne.

Ford was strongly influenced by the idea of *melancholy,* a name given in his time to a disease of the mind. Individuals afflicted with melancholy in modern times might be called *neurotic.* This psychological aspect of Ford's plays has contributed greatly to their success with modern audiences and readers. Ford was born in Devonshire. Albert Wertheim

Ford, John (1895-1973), became the first motion-picture director to win Academy Awards for four movies. He won the awards for *The Informer* (1935), *The Grapes of Wrath* (1940), *How Green Was My Valley*

(1941), and *The Quiet Man* (1952). Ford became famous for staging outdoor action films with a keen sense of background and deep feeling for people. His major outdoor and Western movies include *The Iron Horse* (1924), *The Hurricane* (1937), *Stagecoach* (1939), *My Darling Clementine* (1946), *Fort Apache* (1948), *She Wore a Yellow Ribbon* (1949), *Mogambo* (1952), *The Searchers* (1956), *The Man Who Shot Liberty Valance* (1962), and *Cheyenne Autumn* (1964).

Ford was born on Feb. 1, 1895, in Portland, Maine. His real name was Sean Aloysius O'Feeney. Ford began his directing career in 1914 and directed more than 200 movies. He died on Aug. 31, 1973.

Gene D. Phillips

Ford, Wendell Hampton (1924-   ), a Democrat from Kentucky, was a member of the United States Senate from 1974 to 1999. He served as majority *whip* (assistant leader) of the Senate from 1990 to 1995, while his party held the Senate majority. He was minority whip from 1995 to 1999. Ford served as governor of Kentucky from 1971 to 1974.

As a senator, Ford became known as a moderate who favored backroom bargaining and quiet compromise rather than open confrontation on the Senate floor. He served as chairman of the Senate Committee on Rules and Administration from 1987 to 1995. As chairman, he became a strong supporter of campaign-finance reform.

Ford was born on Sept. 8, 1924, in Thruston, Kentucky, near Owensboro. He attended the University of Kentucky in 1942 and 1943. In 1945 and 1946, he served in the U.S. Army. He later worked as an executive in the insurance industry. Ford served in the Kentucky Senate from 1965 to 1967 and as lieutenant governor of Kentucky from 1967 to 1971.   Guy Halverson

Ford Foundation is an independent nonprofit organization that provides money for projects to advance human well-being. The foundation has four main goals: (1) to strengthen democratic values, (2) to reduce poverty and injustice, (3) to promote international cooperation, and (4) to advance human achievement. It grants funds primarily to institutions—both in the United States and in other countries—that help advance these goals.

The Ford Foundation has headquarters in New York City and field offices in Africa, Asia, and Latin America. The foundation was established in 1936.

Programs. The Ford Foundation supports projects and activities that seek to improve human welfare in nine primary issue areas. These areas are: (1) making government more democratic and accountable, (2) ensuring human rights, (3) strengthening the role of philanthropy on issues of social justice, (4) working toward economic fairness and security for low-income people, (5) promoting opportunity through equitable development of metropolitan areas, (6) promoting sustainable development of natural resources for the benefit of poor communities, (7) expanding educational opportunity and scholarship, (8) supporting freedom of expression, and (9) strengthening sexual and reproductive health and rights. The Ford Foundation also supports a number of special initiatives and partnerships throughout the world.

Leadership. A 15-member board of trustees governs the Ford Foundation. The board includes members from the United States and from other countries. It deter-

mines policies related to spending and management, sets organizational standards, and selects the foundation's president. The president and other staff members are responsible for approving and administering individual grants.

History. Edsel Ford, the son of the American automobile manufacturer Henry Ford, chartered the Ford Foundation in 1936. Its purpose was to "receive and administer funds for scientific, educational, and charitable purposes, all for the public welfare." In its early years, most of the foundation's grants went to charitable and educational institutions in Michigan. The wills of Edsel and Henry, both of whom died in the 1940's, left nearly $500 million to the foundation. Under the leadership of Henry Ford II, Edsel's son, the foundation broadened its programs to address national and international challenges. For assets, see **Foundation** (table).

Critically reviewed by the Ford Foundation

See also **Ford, Henry; Ford, Henry, II; Ford Motor Company.**

Ford Motor Company is one of the world's largest automotive manufacturers. Each year, Ford builds millions of cars and trucks throughout the world. It employs hundreds of thousands of people.

Ford produces cars under the brands Ford and Lincoln. Ford also owns shares in Aston Martin and in the Mazda Motor Corporation. Ford's corporate headquarters are in Dearborn, Michigan.

The company has assembly and manufacturing plants worldwide. Ford's Rouge Manufacturing Complex near Detroit is an important site in industrial history. At its peak in the 1930's, the complex covered 1,100 acres (450 hectares) and employed 100,000 workers. In 2000, a restoration project began on the plant.

Henry Ford, an American machinist and engineer, organized the company in 1903. The success of the Ford Model N, brought out in 1906, led to the company's introduction of its famous Model T in 1908. Affectionately known as the "Tin Lizzie," this simple and inexpensive car outsold all other cars for almost 20 years. The model changed little from year to year, and from 1914 to 1925, it came in only one color, black.

The Ford company established the first moving assembly line at its factory in Highland Park, Michigan, in 1913. Using this method, all but the body of the Model T could be assembled in 93 minutes. The assembly line enabled Ford to cut prices, making cars affordable for average families. The Model T gave way to the Model A in 1927. In 1932, Ford mass-produced the V-8 engine, a powerful engine with eight cylinders arranged in a V.

Ford family interests controlled the company until 1956. That year, the Ford Foundation sold 10,200,000 shares of its Ford stock to the public in what was at the time the largest single stock issue ever offered to the public. With this sale, the Ford Motor Company became a publicly owned company.

Famous Ford models include the Model T, Thunderbird, Mustang, and the Ford F-150 pickup truck. Famous models made under the Lincoln brand include the Continental and the Town Car. Well-known Mercury models include the Cougar, Grand Marquis, and Sable.

Barry Winfield

See also **Ford, Henry; Manufacturing** (table: World's leading manufacturers).

Fordham, *FAWR duhm,* **University** is a private, independent institution of higher education in New York. Its two main campuses are in New York City—Rose Hill in the Bronx and Lincoln Center in Manhattan. It also has a branch campus in West Harrison, New York. John Hughes, the Roman Catholic archbishop of New York, founded the institution in 1841 as St. John's College at Rose Hill. The college's teachings followed the tradition of the Society of Jesus, also known as the Jesuits, a Roman Catholic religious order for men. The college was renamed Fordham University in 1907. In 1974, Thomas More College for women merged with Fordham, and the university began to admit women. The school's sports teams are called the Rams.

Fordham's website at http://www.fordham.edu presents information about the university.

Critically reviewed by Fordham University

Ford's Theatre. See Lincoln, Abraham (Assassination).

Forearm. See Arm.

Forecasting, Weather. See Meteorology; Weather (with pictures); Weather Service, National.

Foreclosure. See Mortgage.

Foreign aid refers to the money, goods, or services that governments and private organizations give to assist other nations and their people. Both private groups and governments give aid to help less developed countries fight poverty, disease, and other problems. Since the end of World War II in 1945, foreign aid has been an important part of foreign policy for a large number of nations.

Governments give foreign aid for three main purposes: (1) to promote security and stability; (2) to improve economic conditions; and (3) to achieve political objectives, including humanitarian goals.

Nations giving foreign aid may try to strengthen their own national defenses by strengthening friendly or neutral governments. They may also give aid to create or maintain trade and investment ties with other nations. And when they give aid, they usually expect the receiving nations to support, or at least not oppose, their political policies.

Kinds of foreign aid

Foreign aid takes many forms. It may be packages of food or clothing for needy people, or volunteers working in villages. It could be technicians who teach others such things as modern farming methods or how to operate heavy construction machinery. Foreign aid could also take the form of long-term loans to help less developed countries build roads and power plants.

Foreign aid includes money, supplies, and technical assistance aimed at helping another country build up its economic or military power. However, foreign aid does not include military forces sent to help another country. Nor does it include international trade, private international investment, or diplomatic efforts to help other countries.

Private aid is offered by voluntary nongovernment organizations, such as CARE and the Red Cross. Governments give *official* aid. Official aid given by one country to another is called *bilateral* aid. Aid given by a group of countries through the United Nations (UN) or other institutions is called *multilateral* aid.

© Tracing Tea / Shutterstock

Aid in solving water supply issues includes technical assistance. Afghanaid, a private humanitarian organization from the United Kingdom, installed the equipment needed to bring clean water into the center of the small Afghan village of Nechem.

United States aid programs

Large-scale foreign aid began during World War II (1939-1945). From the early 1940's to the mid-1960's, the United States gave or lent about $140 billion in foreign aid. At one time or another, almost every country in the world has received U.S. aid. Since World War II, about a third of all U.S. aid has gone to help other nations build up their armed forces. The rest has gone to teach people new skills, to provide emergency aid for people who lacked food or homes, and to build up national wealth and income in poor countries. Changes in types of aid and in the countries receiving aid reflect changes in U.S. national interests since 1940.

World War II aid. From 1940 through 1945, the United States gave more than $50 billion in supplies and equipment to its allies, especially the United Kingdom and the Soviet Union. It gave much of this aid through the Lend-Lease Program. The United States also started a technical and development assistance program for Latin America and gave funds to war relief programs.

Relief and reconstruction. One of the most pressing needs at the end of World War II was to provide food and shelter for millions of people in Europe and Asia. Another was to help the people rebuild their war-torn countries. The United Nations Relief and Rehabilitation Administration (UNRRA), an organization financed largely by U.S. grants, helped meet these needs. So did U.S. loans to the United Kingdom and other nations. But these were only temporary measures. In 1948, the United States began the first broad reconstruction program, the Marshall Plan (European Recovery Program). The plan gave the countries of Western Europe about $13 billion for rebuilding over a period of four years.

Economic development and mutual security. After the Marshall Plan, U.S. interests turned to promoting the economic development and military security of developing countries in Africa, Asia, and Latin America. In 1950, the U.S. Congress authorized $35 million for President Harry S. Truman's proposed Point Four Program to give technical assistance to these countries.

The threat of Communism changed the emphasis in foreign aid. Americans were concerned about the Com-

Aid to education provides funds and teachers for schools and universities in many countries, including Ethiopia, *shown here*. The Agency for International Development administers most of the economic and foreign aid programs sponsored by the U.S. government.

© Abbas, Gamma/Liaison

munist take-over in China in 1949, the Korean War in the 1950's, and increasing Cold War tensions between the United States and the Soviet Union. To stop the spread of Communism, the United States helped found the North Atlantic Treaty Organization (NATO) and pledged military aid to NATO members. It gave military and economic aid to developing countries facing Soviet or Chinese pressure. These countries included Greece, Laos, South Korea, South Vietnam, Taiwan, and Turkey. The United States also gave mutual security aid to India, Pakistan, and other less developed countries it considered to be of major political importance.

In the 1960's, Presidents John F. Kennedy and Lyndon B. Johnson strongly supported technical assistance and economic development programs. In 1961, Congress established the Agency for International Development (AID) to administer all U.S. bilateral aid programs, and Kennedy established the Peace Corps. Thousands of Peace Corps volunteers have lived and worked with people in various countries to help them improve their living conditions. In 1961, the United States and 19 Latin American countries formed the Alliance for Progress to promote economic development and social reform in Latin America.

But in the early 1970's, the United States reduced its foreign aid program. Public support for foreign aid had weakened, and the United States felt it needed the money more for military and domestic programs. In the mid-1970's, U.S. foreign aid began to rise again, especially to Egypt and Israel. But it declined again in the 1990's, following the breakup of the Soviet Union.

Recent developments. In the early 2000's, the United States continued to provide aid to Egypt and Israel. It also assisted many nations in their efforts to fight terrorism and to stop the flow of illegal drugs. Since the U.S. invasion of Iraq and the fall of the government of Saddam Hussein in 2003, the United States has contributed large amounts of aid for the rebuilding of Iraq.

Other countries' aid programs

Other nations besides the United States give economic aid to less developed countries. Japan gives much of its aid to other Asian nations. It lends money to China, Myanmar, Vietnam, and other countries for development projects. Japan also supplies money and technical aid to such Pacific Island nations as Fiji, Papua New Guinea, and Samoa. France has given much to French overseas territories and to its former colonies in Africa. Belgium, the United Kingdom, and other former colonial powers also give aid to their former colonies.

Leading contributors of foreign aid

Contributor	Aid (in millions of U.S. dollars)	Aid (as percentage of GNI*)
United States	$30,353	0.21%
United Kingdom	13,053	0.57
Germany	12,985	0.39
France	12,915	0.50
Japan	11,054	0.20
Netherlands	6,357	0.81
Spain	5,949	0.43
Canada	5,202	0.34
Norway	4,580	1.10
Sweden	4,533	0.97

Leading recipients of foreign aid

Recipient	Aid (in millions of U.S. dollars)	Aid (as percentage of GNI*†)
Afghanistan	$6,374	44.70%
Ethiopia	3,529	11.91
Democratic Republic of the Congo	3,413	27.84
Haiti	3,076	45.69
Pakistan	3,021	1.66
Tanzania	2,961	12.87
Vietnam	2,945	3.06
India	2,807	0.16
Palestinian Administered Areas	2,519	40.93
Iraq	2,192	2.82

*GNI = gross national income. The gross national income is the total value of goods and services produced by the firms of a country in a year.
†Foreign aid is not counted as part of a recipient country's GNI. These figures represent the percentage of the GNI to which the aid would be equivalent.
Figures are for 2010.
Sources: *World Book* estimates based on data from the Organisation for Economic Co-operation and Development and the United Nations.

The Soviet Union, before it broke up in 1991, gave large amounts of military and economic aid to several countries, including Afghanistan, Cuba, Egypt, North Korea, India, and Vietnam. Because of Cold War tensions, the Soviet Union used the aid largely for security purposes. The aid declined in the 1970's and was cut drastically in the 1980's, as the Soviet Union experienced economic problems.

Many countries use foreign aid to promote international trade and to foster cultural or diplomatic ties. France has been a major source of technical assistance, particularly to countries in Africa. Belgium, the United Kingdom, Germany, and Italy also have supplied much technical assistance.

A number of countries coordinate their bilateral aid through the Organisation for Economic Co-operation and Development (OECD). The countries providing aid often negotiate as a group with aid-receiving countries to determine the size and use of aid programs.

Multilateral aid programs

About a fourth of all official foreign aid is multilateral. A large part of this aid is channeled through the United Nations and various UN agencies. Most multilateral aid goes for development and technical assistance, and disaster relief. Multilateral agencies do not offer military aid. However, the aid they do offer may release for military use funds that had been reserved for other projects.

Technical assistance and relief. UN technical assistance, refugee, and relief programs are financed mostly by contributions from UN member governments. A large share of these contributions goes to the United Nations Development Programme (UNDP). The UNDP is responsible for selecting aid projects and distributing funds to agencies to carry out the projects. Each agency also receives funds directly from member countries.

A number of agencies carry out much of the UN's technical assistance work in less developed countries. The Food and Agriculture Organization of the United Nations (FAO) promotes agricultural development. The United Nations Educational, Scientific and Cultural Organization (UNESCO) gives educational and scientific assistance. The World Health Organization (WHO) helps countries improve their health services. The United Nations Children's Fund (UNICEF) helps fight children's diseases and assists needy children and mothers. The International Labour Organization (ILO) conducts labor training programs. Other agencies also give technical assistance to less developed countries. The United Nations Industrial Development Organization (UNIDO) was formed in 1966 to give advice on industrial development. Other agencies aid refugees.

The United Nations Conference on Trade and Development (UNCTAD) does not give aid. But it serves as a forum for its members to frame aid and trade policies to benefit less developed countries. For more information on most of the UN's specialized agencies, see **United Nations** (Specialized agencies).

Worldwide lending programs help less developed countries finance development projects. The International Bank for Reconstruction and Development—commonly called the World Bank—makes long-term loans to member governments at reasonable interest rates. The International Development Association (IDA), a World Bank affiliate, makes loans to the least developed member countries, allowing 50 years to repay with no interest. Another World Bank affiliate, the International Finance Corporation (IFC), invests in private enterprises in less developed countries.

Regional development programs aid poor countries in particular areas. There are four major regional development banks. The Inter-American Development Bank (IDB), established in 1959, makes development loans to governments and private firms in Latin America. The African Development Bank (AfDB), established in 1964, lends money to promote development in Africa. The Asian Development Bank (ADB), established in 1966, makes development loans in Asia and the Pacific. The European Bank for Reconstruction and Development (EBRD), established in 1991, lends funds mainly to private firms in eastern Europe and central Asia, with the goal of building market economies in those regions.

Each of the four major regional development banks is owned and financed by dozens of member countries. The members include the poor nations that borrow from the bank as well as wealthy donor nations within and outside the region. The banks fund their loans by borrowing on international capital markets and by collecting direct contributions from donor nations.

Several other multilateral banks and funds lend to poor countries. These institutions include the European Investment Bank, which is the European Union's long-term lending arm; the Islamic Development Bank, which finances projects in Islamic countries; and the OPEC Fund for International Development, which is overseen by the Organization of the Petroleum Exporting Countries (OPEC). In addition, there are smaller development banks that serve the Andean region, the Caribbean, Central America, and regions within Africa.   Tom Mockaitis

Related articles in *World Book* include:
Agency for International Development
Alliance for Progress
Asian Development Bank
Developing country
Economics (Distribution of income)
European Union
Food and Agriculture Organization
Food for Peace
Foreign policy
International Finance Corporation
International Labour Organization
International trade
Lend-Lease
Marshall Plan
Peace Corps
Technical assistance
UNESCO
UNICEF
United Nations (Specialized agencies; Working for progress)
World Bank
World Health Organization

Additional resources

Arvin, B. Mak, ed. *New Perspectives on Foreign Aid and Economic Development.* Praeger, 2002.
Cracknell, Basil E. *Evaluating Development Aid: Issues, Problems, and Solutions.* Sage, 2000.
Degnbol-Martinussen, John, and Engberg-Pedersen, Poul. *Aid: Understanding International Development Cooperation.* Zed Bks., 2003.
Lancaster, Carol. *Transforming Foreign Aid.* Inst. for International Economics, 2000.
Neumayer, Eric. *The Pattern of Aid Giving.* Routledge, 2003.

Foreign bill of exchange. See Bill of exchange.

Foreign correspondent reports the news from important places in other countries. Such reporters may work for a newspaper, magazine, news service, or radio or television network in their own country.

Increasing interest in international affairs has assured foreign correspondents a permanent place in journalism. Their stories provide the most reliable public report of affairs in other nations. The Associated Press and other news services, as well as major newspapers such as *The New York Times,* employ many of the foreign correspondents who report to United States readers. Others are heard through major radio and TV networks.

The foreign correspondents who have become best known are those who served during wars. Richard Harding Davis covered the Spanish-American War (1898), the Anglo-Boer War of 1899-1902, the Russo-Japanese War (1904-1905), and the early part of World War I (1914-1918). During World War II (1939-1945), Ernie Pyle's columns from the United Kingdom, Africa, and Europe appeared in numerous papers. His columns were written in a simple, folksy style and became highly popular. See **Davis, Richard Harding; Pyle, Ernie.**

In early American newspapers, foreign news was copied from papers brought from other countries, mostly the United Kingdom. But there was little opportunity for really effective foreign correspondence until ocean cables became available after 1858. The development of radio broadcasting in the 1920's increased the demand for fast reporting of events abroad. The launching of communications satellites in the 1960's led to the instantaneous transmission of television news stories from other countries.   Maurine H. Beasley

See also **War correspondent.**

Foreign exchange. See Balance of payments (Balance of payments and exchange rates).

Foreign Legion is a distinguished branch of the French Army. Called *Légion étrangère* in French, it consists of foreign volunteers commanded by French officers. The Legion is an elite fighting force, and its members are among the finest soldiers in the world. It has a romantic image that has increased over the years because of the Legion's fierceness in battle.

Service in the Legion. The Legion has headquarters in Aubagne, France. Those who apply for duty in the Legion must be single men between 17 and 40 years old. They must pass a strict physical examination to be accepted. The Legion accepts only about 10 percent of all applicants. Legionnaires enlist for an initial contract of five years and are allowed to join under an assumed name if they wish. The Legion has traditionally been a haven for adventurers and men seeking escape from a troubled past or even from the law. Today, however, the force runs a strict background check of all applicants, and it will not accept former criminals or men fleeing from serious criminal charges.

Uniform and traditions of the Legion. The full dress uniform of Legionnaires consists of khaki trousers, a khaki shirt with green shoulder boards and red *epaulets* (shoulder decorations), and a blue sash worn around the waist. The Legionnaire's dress hat is a white *kepi,* a cap with a round, flat top and a visor. Officers wear a black kepi. Legion *pionniers* (engineers) have beards, and their dress uniforms include a leather apron and an ax, which

is a symbol of their branch of service. The Legion's official colors are red and green. Its insignia is a grenade with seven flames. Legion battle uniforms consist of camouflage fatigues and a green beret or helmet. The Legion's traditional motto is *Honneur et Fidélité* (Honor and Fidelity), but it also uses the motto *Legio Patria Nostra* (The Legion Is Our Country).

History. King Louis Philippe created the Legion in 1831 to make use of foreign adventurers who had flocked to France during the revolution of 1830. The Legion played an important role in the French conquest of Algeria, which began in 1830, and it soon emerged as an elite force in the French Army. Legionnaires fought in Europe in the Crimean War (1854-1856), a war of independence in Italy (1859), and the Franco-Prussian War (1870-1871). The Legion also fought overseas as the French sought to establish a global empire.

In 1862, the French sent troops to try to seize control of Mexico. On April 30, 1863, 65 Legionnaires serving in Mexico were attacked by 2,000 Mexican revolutionaries at the Battle of Camerone. Led by Captain Jean Danjou, the Legionnaires held out all day, and the last survivors made a wild bayonet charge. The battle is sacred to the Legion, and the name *Camerone* is inscribed on every Legion flag. Legionnaires around the world mark the battle's anniversary each year.

From 1871 to 1914, the Legion fought throughout the world to expand and defend the French empire. During this period, Legionnaires served in Dahomey (now Benin), Formosa (now Taiwan), Indochina (now Cambodia, Laos, and Vietnam), Madagascar, Morocco, and Sudan.

During World War I (1914-1918), thousands of foreigners rushed to defend France against German invaders. These men enlisted in the Legion and fought fiercely in some of the largest battles in history. Many Legionnaires were killed. By the end of the war, the Legion was one of the most decorated units in the French Army.

In World War II (1939-1945), Legionnaires served in the opening battles in Norway and France. After France surrendered in 1940, most Legionnaires joined Charles de Gaulle's Free French and continued to fight the Germans. Others supported Vichy France, the French administration that largely cooperated with the Germans. In Syria in 1941, Vichy and Free French Legionnaires fought against each other. The Free French Legionnaires fought gallantly against the Germans at the Battle of Bir Hakeim (also spelled Bir Hacheim and Bi'r al Hukayyim) in North Africa in 1942. In 1944 and 1945, they participated in the campaigns that liberated France and defeated Germany.

From 1946 to 1954, the Legion was stationed in Indochina, where it fought against Vietminh Communist rebels. At the siege of Dien Bien Phu in 1954, the Legionnaires added further luster to their reputation when they fought to nearly the last man. The Legion was rebuilt and sent to Algeria, where it served during a revolutionary war from 1954 to 1962. In April 1961, when President Charles de Gaulle's negotiations with Algerian nationalist leaders made it appear that he might withdraw French troops, Legionnaires in Algeria participated in a failed attempt to overthrow him. As a result, the Legion fell into disfavor.

By the 1970's, the Legion's reputation had recovered, and it had become an elite force ready for rapid assignment around the world. In 1978, the Legion went to Zaire—now Congo (Kinshasa)—in the midst of a civil war and rescued foreigners trapped there. During the 1970's and 1980's, Legion forces were sent to Chad several times during that nation's civil wars and conflict with Libya.

The Legion served in the Persian Gulf War of 1991 and in the campaign against terrorism in Afghanistan that began in 2001. Beginning in 2002, it was assigned to protect foreigners and restore order in Côte d'Ivoire during a civil war there.   Robert B. Bruce

Foreign office. See Diplomacy.

Foreign policy refers to the ways in which nations advance their interests and objectives in world politics. Countries ordinarily pursue their objectives through *diplomacy* (official negotiations) with other countries and through participation in international organizations. However, in certain cases, governments use military force to protect or promote their interests.

Areas of foreign policy commonly include environmental protection, human rights issues, international trade, and the prevention or resolution of armed conflict. Most nations have several broad foreign policy aims that remain the same, even if their political leadership changes. For instance, nearly all democracies list peace, security, and justice among their chief foreign policy goals. In addition, certain vital interests—such as economic well-being and safety from foreign attack—are common for all governments throughout the world.

A number of factors directly or indirectly affect foreign policy. Such factors include features of government, the education, beliefs, and opinions of the general population; relations with other countries and international organizations; and economic and military strength. No government can maintain a foreign policy that does not fit the nation's resources and capabilities.

Influences on foreign policy

A nation's foreign policy is influenced by conditions within the nation itself, as well as by interactions with other countries and international bodies. Foreign policy is a continuous process, because each new step depends on past actions and the reactions of the global community.

Domestic policy—that is, laws and regulations in effect within the nation's borders—sometimes affects, or interferes with, foreign policy. For instance, if one nation's domestic policy violates the human rights of its citizens, other nations may pressure the government to change its practices. Another example involves the large *subsidies* (payments) that some national governments use to support their farming industries. The subsidies are a matter of domestic policy, yet they also influence trading relationships with other countries. Such policies may cause friction with nations who depend on the free trade of agricultural goods.

Historical and social traditions in a country play a large part in its foreign policy. For example, Canadian foreign policy differs from that of the United States, even though both are democracies with a long record as good neighbors. Until 1931, Canada was part of the British Empire. Therefore, Canadians have traditionally been more concerned with European affairs, and less interested in East Asia, than have Americans. Social relations between cultural groups within a country may also affect foreign policy.

Alliances. All countries rely on the good will and cooperation of other nations. Governments continually modify their own policies to obtain and preserve allies. Many nations belong to alliances and organizations—such as the European Union (EU) or the North Atlantic Treaty Organization (NATO)—that help increase their influence and protect their interests. In addition, governments may enter into agreements with other countries to cooperate for economic, environmental, military, or other purposes. For example, two or more national governments may sign a treaty to eliminate trade barriers, or to provide military assistance for one another in times of war.

Economic factors have a major impact on foreign policy. National economies throughout the world depend heavily on international trade and the export of products from their domestic industries. Governments closely follow economic conditions and develop policies to promote their business interests. Many nations take part in *reciprocal trade agreements,* in which two or more governments agree to lower tariffs or other trade barriers on certain goods or services.

Most nations belong to the World Trade Organization (WTO), an international organization that promotes trade among nations. Some governments alter their economic policies to meet the WTO's guidelines. China, for instance, attained WTO membership in 2001, but only after many years of negotiations and reforms.

Military strength also plays an important role in foreign policy. Governments pay close attention to the military capabilities and resources of nations throughout the world. Because the United States possesses more military power than any other nation, many governments consider the possible reactions of the U.S. government when they develop their foreign policy. In some cases, governments and international organizations take action to prevent other nations from building or acquiring *weapons of mass destruction*—that is, biological, chemical, or nuclear weapons.

Shaping foreign policy

The development of foreign policy involves a series of choices from among a variety of possible courses. These choices are traditionally shaped by a nation's political leaders, lawmakers, and general population.

The executive. The primary responsibility for the design and execution of foreign policy belongs to the nation's chief executive. Most presidents and prime ministers have the power to advance policies, negotiate international agreements, and authorize the use of military force. The chief executive usually has the support of a number of government agencies and institutions. For instance, the Department of State aids the president of the United States in foreign policy matters. The Ministry of Foreign Affairs in Canada and the Foreign and Commonwealth Office in the United Kingdom serve similar functions. Other government departments and agencies—in such areas as defense and intelligence—also help the chief executive shape foreign policy.

The legislature. In most democracies, the legislative branch of government has authority to debate foreign policy strategies, to monitor the policies of the executive branch, and to provide or restrict funding for various purposes. However, during times of crisis—such as when a nation is at war—the foreign policy role of the legislature is sometimes limited. In nondemocratic governments, lawmaking bodies usually have substantially less impact on foreign policy.

Public opinion. In democratic societies, the nation's people play a major role in shaping government policy. Political leaders pay close attention to public opinion and work to build and maintain support for foreign policy strategies. This effort usually involves educating people on central issues and providing arguments in support of the government's positions. If a nation's foreign policy lacks public support, the government may have difficulty carrying it out. For instance, declining public support for the Vietnam War (1957-1975) was a major factor in the U.S. government's decision to withdraw its troops. Public opinion has significantly less impact in nondemocratic societies.   Richard E. Rupp

Related articles. See the *History* section of country articles, such as **France** (History). See also **Canada, History of; United States, History of the.** See also:

Diplomacy
Foreign aid
Foreign Service
International law
International relations
International trade

Foreign relations. See Foreign policy; International relations.

Foreign Service is an organization through which the international affairs of the United States government are conducted. Members of the Foreign Service hold posts throughout the world and represent the people of the United States. The Foreign Service is administered by the U.S. Department of State and other government agencies that are directly involved in foreign affairs. The service provides trained personnel for U.S. offices in other countries. Members of the Foreign Service also fill numerous positions within the United States.

Foreign Service careers

Many members of the Foreign Service work at the Department of State in Washington, D.C., or at such U.S. government agencies as the Agency for International Development, the Department of Agriculture, and the Department of Commerce. All other Foreign Service members serve in foreign countries. Most Foreign Service employees serve overseas for periods of 5 to 7 years out of every 10 years.

Members of the Foreign Service carry out a variety of tasks. Many have *diplomatic* posts that require them to carry on day-to-day relationships between the United States and other countries. Others have *consular* posts, in which they assist U.S. citizens abroad and handle U.S. business and commercial affairs overseas. Foreign Service members perform administrative work in U.S. embassies, missions, and consulates; negotiate with government officials of other countries; report on economic, political, and social conditions; issue passports and visas; and interpret U.S. policies to governments and citizens of other countries. Some members of the Foreign Service perform specialized tasks in economics, international labor affairs, and other areas.

The Department of State attempts to assign Foreign

Service members to posts consistent with the members' individual and family needs. But Foreign Service members must be willing to work in any post that is assigned to them. Members are also expected to publicly support the policies of the U.S. government, regardless of the members' own personal views. Foreign Service members serve at some personal risk, and a number of members have been killed in the line of duty over the years. On the other hand, careers in the Foreign Service offer many benefits and advantages. During overseas assignments, for example, employees may receive allowances for living expenses, travel, official entertainment, and other expenses associated with their work. They also receive a salary, health insurance, and other benefits.

Most newly appointed Foreign Service members receive orientation at the Foreign Service Institute in Washington, D.C., before they are sent abroad. The institute teaches the languages and customs of other countries, gives advanced instruction in foreign affairs, and provides training in specialized activities of the Foreign Service. The institute also offers courses for the spouses and dependents of Foreign Service officers and other government officials who work overseas.

Personnel

There are two main classifications of Foreign Service personnel: (1) Foreign Service officers and (2) Foreign Service specialists.

Foreign Service officers (FSO's) are assigned positions both in the United States and abroad. Their responsibilities include promoting U.S. foreign policy, protecting U.S. citizens, and helping U.S. businesses throughout the world. Each Foreign Service officer chooses one of five career tracks: (1) consular, (2) economic, (3) management, (4) political, or (5) public diplomacy. The career track determines the type of assignments an officer will likely receive.

People who wish to become Foreign Service officers must be U.S. citizens between the ages of 21 and 59. They must pass both a written examination and an oral *assessment* (evaluation). During the written examination, applicants must answer questions on a wide range of topics, including U.S. culture and government, management and finance, and English language skills. During the assessment, applicants are judged on their creativity and communication skills, and on their ability to work with others and analyze ideas and problems. Applicants must also go through a background investigation, a medical examination, and a final review.

Foreign Service specialists provide support in a specific area of expertise. They include workers in such fields as medicine, information management, diplomatic security, human resources, and office management. Applicants who wish to become specialists must first select a specific job category. During the evaluation process, they must participate in a writing exercise and a structured interview, as well as a background investigation, a medical examination, and a final review.

History

Beginnings. In the early years of the United States, many people opposed having any representation abroad. This opposition was so great that even the highest-ranking U.S. diplomats sent abroad held only the rank of minister, instead of ambassador. Such a diplomat often carried only the title of *chargé d'affaires.*

Early diplomats of the United States included John Adams, Benjamin Franklin, John Jay, Thomas Jefferson, and James Monroe. In those early years, ministers had to pay their own travel expenses, provide their own living quarters, and hire their own secretaries. However, despite the low esteem diplomats received, four of the first six U.S. presidents—Adams, Jefferson, Monroe, and John Quincy Adams—had a diplomatic background.

The *spoils system,* or appointment and promotion on a political basis, dominated the Foreign Service throughout the 1800's and the early 1900's. As a result, U.S. representation abroad consisted mainly of untrained personnel. Diplomatic positions served as rewards for service and frequently went to unqualified political associates and wealthy people who were campaign contributors.

The Rogers Act. World War I (1914-1918) imposed new responsibilities on the Foreign Service and brought about substantial reforms. In 1924, the Rogers Act—introduced by Massachusetts Congressman John Jacob Rogers—brought about significant improvements in the Foreign Service. The act combined the consular and diplomatic responsibilities of the service and established the basis of the organization as it exists today. The act also established difficult competitive examinations for Foreign Service officers.

Additional changes occurred in the Foreign Service in the middle and late 1900's. Many stemmed from the Foreign Service Act of 1946. This legislation gave ambassadors and ministers their first pay raises in nearly 100 years. It raised pay levels generally and set up a new class system for the Foreign Service.

The Foreign Service Act of 1980 led to other significant changes. It increased Foreign Service salaries, set up an office for the job placement of spouses of Foreign Service members, and improved retirement and survivors benefits for such spouses.

Many top-ranking ambassadors still receive appointments on political grounds. But most of the chiefs of overseas posts have advanced through the Foreign Service ranks.   Richard E. Rupp

See also **Ambassador; Consul; Diplomacy; State, Department of.**

Foreign trade. See **International trade.**

Foreign trade zone is an area in the United States where importers may store, exhibit, and process foreign goods without paying *customs duties* (import taxes). The zones are policed by U.S. Customs and Border Protection. Customs officials collect duty only if the goods entering the country are to be used or sold. If the goods are exported directly from the foreign trade zones, no duty is paid. In other countries, foreign trade zones are sometimes called *free trade zones* or *free ports* (see **Free trade zone**).

There are two types of foreign trade zones. *General-purpose zones,* most of which are at ports or industrial parks, are open for use by multiple importers. *Subzones,* most of which are at manufacturing plants, are for a single importer. The Foreign-Trade Zones Board—made up of the secretaries of commerce and the treasury—licenses the zones and monitors activity within them. The board was created in 1934.   Robert M. Stern

Foreman, George

(1949-   ), an American boxer, became the oldest fighter to win the heavyweight championship. On Nov. 5, 1994, Foreman knocked out champion Michael Moorer to win the World Boxing Association and International Boxing Federation versions of the heavyweight title. Foreman was 45 years and 10 months old when he won the fight, more than 7

A. Berliner, Gamma/Liaison
George Foreman

years older than the previous oldest champion, Joe Walcott. Foreman previously held the heavyweight title from January 1973 to October 1974. He won it with an upset victory over champion Joe Frazier. Foreman lost the heavyweight title when he was knocked out by Muhammad Ali. The defeat was the first since Foreman turned professional in 1969.

George Edward Foreman was born on Jan. 10, 1949, in Marshall, Texas. He first became famous for winning the heavyweight championship at the 1968 Olympic Games. He retired from boxing in 1977 but resumed his fighting career in 1987. Foreman failed to regain the heavyweight title in 1991, losing a decision to champion Evander Holyfield. In 1997, Foreman again announced his retirement. He had a career record of 76 victories, 68 by knockouts, and 5 defeats. Beginning in the late 1980's, Foreman became a popular television personality.

Nigel Collins

Forensic pathology is the study of disease and injury as it applies to legal matters. Forensic pathologists often conduct their studies through a procedure called *autopsy.* An autopsy is an external and internal examination of a dead body.

There are two main branches of forensic pathology. They are *anatomic pathology* and *clinical pathology.* Anatomic pathology deals with the study of tissues obtained from living or dead people. A forensic pathologist may perform an autopsy on a body to determine the cause of death. This procedure is usually done in cases where a death cannot be otherwise explained. Clinical pathology involves the collection and study of body fluids, such as blood or saliva. Laboratory analysis of these materials can help determine the cause of a death.

Legal officials may insist on an autopsy when a person's death results from suicide, homicide, or unknown causes. Forensic pathologists may also gather other kinds of evidence from a crime scene to help determine the cause of a death. In some cases, experts can learn why someone died from a detailed review of medical records.

In the United States, the American Board of Pathology first recognized forensic pathology as a separate branch of medical pathology in 1959. Today, many countries require that a medical examiner or coroner be trained in forensic pathology.   Jason H. Byrd

See also **Autopsy; Forensic science; Medical examiner; Pathology.**

Forensic science is the use of scientific principles and methods to analyze material connected with a

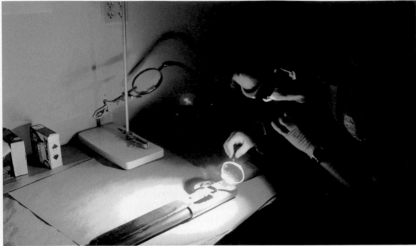

© Jennifer Simonson, Star Tribune/ZUMA Press

A forensic scientist may use a variety of sophisticated scientific tools and methods to analyze evidence connected with a crime. This forensic scientist is using laser technology to examine a gun that has been stained with dye. The laser causes fingerprints to become more visible.

crime. Such material is called *physical evidence*. It may include documents, drugs, fibers, fingerprints, hair, and soil. For example, a forensic scientist may connect glass splinters or a gun found on a suspect to broken glass or a bullet taken from the scene of a crime.

For much of the history of law, criminal trials depended upon evidence given by people who witnessed the crime. Rarely was an attempt made to find physical evidence at the crime scene or from the criminal. Beginning in the 1800's, a small number of scientists began using physical evidence in criminal cases.

In the early 1900's, the French physician Edmond Locard developed the principle that would become central to forensic science. In what is known today as the *Locard exchange principle,* he stated that every contact, no matter how slight, causes a transfer of material. Thus, a criminal always leaves some amount of material at a crime scene. In addition, some amount of material from a crime scene will remain, for a time at least, on a criminal. Forensic scientists examine this transferred material.

Forensic science is largely based on comparisons. Characteristics of items are compared to link them to a common source. The strength, or value, of the evidence depends on the certainty of the match. For example, forensic scientists may compare a piece of paint from the scene of a hit-and-run accident with the paint from a suspect's vehicle. They try to determine how many characteristics of the paint chip are the same as the paint from the vehicle. The scientists examine and compare the size and shape of the chip, its color and chemical composition, and the number of layers of paint. The more characteristics that match, the stronger the evidence is.

Forensic scientists most often work at crime laboratories. There are thousands of crime labs around the world. They range from those run by a government—such as the large, well-equipped lab of the United States Federal Bureau of Investigation (FBI) in Quantico, Virginia—to smaller local laboratories. Some labs specialize. The U.S. Internal Revenue Service crime lab in Chicago concentrates on the examination of documents. The U.S. Fish and Wildlife Service Forensics Laboratory

in Ashland, Oregon, works only on crimes against endangered wildlife.

Crime scene investigations

After a crime, police officers *secure* (seal off) the crime scene as quickly as possible. They establish the boundaries of the scene and mark them with special tape or barriers. After enclosing the area, the officers permit only authorized people access. Investigators then systematically search the scene for evidence. They collect and package any object that might be related to the crime and transport it to the crime lab. They take precautions to avoid disturbing or contaminating the evidence, which would harm the investigation.

Generally, trained law enforcement officers or crime scene investigators gather evidence at a crime scene. Forensic scientists seldom go to the crime scene unless an unusual type of evidence is involved that requires special handling.

General kinds of evidence

Evidence can be classified into several general categories. They include direct and indirect evidence and class and individual evidence.

Direct and indirect evidence. Direct evidence, also called *testimonial evidence,* is a verbal description of a crime by a witness. For example, a witness may observe a stabbing and describe the incident.

Indirect evidence may lead someone to conclude that an event occurred or that a fact is true, but the evidence does not conclusively prove the event or fact. Indirect evidence linking an accused person to a crime might include fingerprints on a weapon or a victim's blood on the clothing of the accused.

Indirect evidence is also called *circumstantial evidence.* It describes a circumstance, or event. The more circumstantial evidence confirms the event, the stronger the case against the accused.

Class and individual evidence. There are two main types of physical evidence, *class evidence* and *individual evidence.* Most physical evidence is class evidence—material common to a group of similar objects that cannot be linked to one particular source. A paint chip from a hit-and-run accident would likely be class evidence. However, a chip that exactly fit a hole in the paint on the suspect's vehicle could be individual evidence.

Individual evidence is physical evidence that can be related to only one source. For example, most scientists consider DNA (deoxyribonucleic acid) to be individual evidence. DNA is genetic material found in all living cells. Experts can match some samples of DNA to a particular person with a mathematical certainty of billions to one. It is extremely unlikely that any two unrelated individuals possess identical DNA. Investigators may compare DNA found at the crime scene with DNA from a suspected criminal. On the basis of this comparison, the suspect can be included or excluded as a possible source of the DNA found at the scene of the crime.

What a forensic scientist analyzes

Forensic scientists analyze various kinds of physical evidence. They may use biology, chemistry, computer science, earth sciences, mathematics, and physics in their work.

Fingerprints. Humans have designs on the skin of the fingertips formed by small ridges. These designs are called *friction ridges*. The impressions made by such ridges are fingerprints. Fingerprints were used for identification in China about 3,000 years ago, but their scientific study began in the mid-1800's. Scientists believe that no two people have the same fingerprints. Thus, fingerprints are classified as individual evidence.

Many of the fingerprints at a crime scene are *latent* (not visible to the eye). Investigators use special types of powders or chemicals to discover and develop latent prints. Then they *digitize* the prints—that is, they translate the prints from their original form into a form that a computer can read. Digitizing prints enables scientists to enter them into a database that other scientists can search to find matches. The FBI's Integrated Automated Fingerprint Identification System database, for example, contains millions of fingerprint records. It can compare prints so rapidly that a preliminary match can be made in minutes.

Impressions occur when an object is pressed against or into a surface. Tires and footwear, for example, may leave impressions that can be developed and compared with a known source. Law enforcement experts have created large databases of tire and footwear impressions from nearly all manufacturers. Most impressions are considered class evidence. For example, a number of cars may have the same type of tire. The more worn and damaged the tire is, however, the more it will show unique features that can change it from class to individual evidence.

Firearms. By examining a bullet and cartridge, forensic scientists can often identify the type and manufacturer of the weapon. Identification of the type of gun that fired a cartridge provides class evidence. Marks inside the gun barrel can, however, cause markings on a bullet as it is fired. Comparing a bullet from a crime scene with one fired from a known weapon can sometimes provide a match that is considered unique, and therefore individual evidence.

Controlled substances are drugs or other chemicals whose possession and use is restricted by law. Law en-

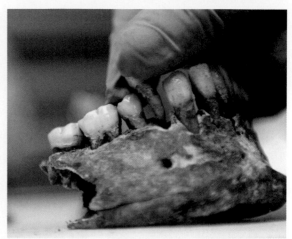
© AFP/Getty Images
Examining bones from a murder victim is a job of a forensic anthropologist. This jawbone is being analyzed by a forensic anthropologist in an effort to identify a murder victim in Colombia.

forcement officials at the scene of an arrest can administer initial tests for such drugs as cocaine and marijuana. If the test is positive, officials deliver the material to the crime lab, where a forensic scientist confirms the initial identification.

Poisons have been a common method of murder for centuries. In a crime lab, experts in poisons, called *toxicologists,* analyze substances to try to identify poisons. This analysis can be complex, requiring a knowledge of chemistry and medicine.

Blood is often a by-product of violent crime. Sophisticated tests are needed to determine if a stain is blood and, if so, whether it is human or animal blood. The pattern of bloodstains may also aid in the reconstruction of a crime scene and provide key evidence.

Trace evidence may include tiny amounts of fibers, glass and metal particles, hair, paint, plant material, or plastics. Sophisticated and expensive instruments may be required to identify trace evidence.

Careers in forensic science

Beginning forensic scientists should have at least a bachelor's degree in biology, chemistry, physics, or a related natural science. A graduate degree in forensic science is also helpful.

Most forensic scientists are civilians who do not carry a weapon or have the power to arrest people. They seldom search for clues at a crime scene. Instead, they work in laboratories, carefully and systematically examining material. A forensic scientist must often appear as an expert witness in the courtroom to justify his or her results.   John G. Funkhouser

Related articles in *World Book* include:
Ballistics (Forensic ballistics)
Crime scene investigation
DNA fingerprinting
Evidence
Fingerprinting
Footprinting
Forensic pathology

Foreordination. See Predestination.

Jerry Frank, DPI
Robert Frerck, Dimensions
© Shutterstock

Tropical rain forest   **Tropical dry forest**   **Savanna**

Different kinds of forests grow in different parts of the world. Many scientists divide the world's forests into the six main *formations* (types) shown in the photographs above and on the next page. The forests that make up each formation have similar plant and animal life.

Forest

Forest is a large area of land covered with trees. But a forest is much more than just trees. It also includes smaller plants, such as mosses, shrubs, and wildflowers. In addition, many kinds of birds, insects, and other animals make their home in the forest. Millions upon millions of living things that can only be seen under a microscope also live in the forest.

Climate, soil, and water determine the kinds of plants and animals that can live in a forest. The living things and their environment together make up the forest *ecosystem*. An ecosystem consists of all the living and nonliving things in a particular area and the relationships among them.

The forest ecosystem is highly complicated. The trees and other green plants use sunlight to make their own food from the air and from water and minerals in the soil. The plants themselves serve as food for certain animals. These animals, in turn, are eaten by other animals. After plants and animals die, their remains are broken down by bacteria and other organisms, such as protozoans and fungi. This process returns minerals to the soil, where they can again be used by plants to make food.

Although individual members of the ecosystem die, the forest itself lives on. If the forest is wisely managed, it provides us with a continuous source of wood and many other products.

Before people began to clear the forests for farms and cities, great stretches of forestland covered about 60 percent of Earth's land area. Today, forests occupy about 30 percent of the land. The forests differ greatly from one part of the world to another. For example, the steamy, vine-choked rain forests of central Africa are far different from the cool, towering spruce and fir forests of northern Canada.

This article provides general information on the importance of forests and describes their structure. It discusses the major kinds of forests in the world and in the United States and Canada. It also tells how forests function as an ecosystem and how they have changed and developed through the ages. Finally, the article describes how human activities have destroyed many forested areas. For detailed information on forest products and forest management, see the articles **Forest products** and **Forestry.**

The importance of forests

Forests have always had great importance to people. Prehistoric people obtained their food mainly by hunting and by gathering wild plants. Many of these people lived in the forest and were a natural part of it. With the development of civilization, people settled in cities. However, they still went to the forest to get timber and to hunt.

Today, people depend on forests more than ever, especially for their (1) economic value, (2) environmental value, and (3) enjoyment value. The science of forestry is

Jen and Des Bartlett, Bruce Coleman Inc.

Ray Atkeson, DPI

© Shutterstock

Temperate deciduous forest   **Temperate evergreen forest**   **Boreal forest**

concerned with increasing and preserving these values by careful management of forestland

Economic value. Forests supply many products. Wood from forest trees provides lumber, plywood, railroad ties, and shingles. It is also used in making furniture, tool handles, and thousands of other products. In many parts of the world, wood serves as the chief fuel for cooking and heating.

Various manufacturing processes change wood into a great number of different products. Paper is one of the most valuable products made from wood. Other processed wood products include cellophane, plastics, and such fibers as rayon and acetate.

Forests provide many important products besides wood. Latex, which is used in making rubber, and turpentine come from forest trees. Various fats, gums, oils, and waxes used in manufacturing also come from trees. In some primitive societies, forest plants and animals make up a large part of the people's diet.

Unlike most other natural resources, such as coal, oil, and mineral deposits, forest resources are renewable. As long as there are forests, people can count on a steady supply of forest products.

Environmental value. Forests help conserve and enrich the environment in several ways. For example, forest soil soaks up large amounts of rainfall. It thus prevents the rapid runoff of water that can cause erosion and flooding. In addition, rain is filtered as it passes through the soil and becomes *ground water*. This ground water flows through the ground and provides a clean, fresh source of water for streams, lakes, and wells.

Forest plants, like all green plants, help renew the atmosphere. As the trees and other green plants make food, they give off oxygen. They also remove carbon dioxide from the air. People and nearly all other living things require oxygen. If green plants did not continuously renew the oxygen supply, almost all life would soon stop. If carbon dioxide increases in the atmosphere, it could severely alter Earth's climate.

Forests also provide a home for many plants and animals that can live nowhere else. Without the forest, many kinds of wildlife could not exist.

Enjoyment value. The natural beauty and peace of the forest offer a special source of enjoyment. In the United States, Canada, and many other countries, huge forestlands have been set aside for people's enjoyment. Many people use these forests for such activities as camping, hiking, and hunting. Others visit them simply to enjoy the scenery and relax in the quiet beauty.

The structure of forests

Every forest has various *strata* (layers) of plants. The five basic forest strata, from highest to lowest, are (1) the canopy, (2) the understory, (3) the shrub layer, (4) the herb layer, and (5) the forest floor.

The canopy consists mainly of the *crowns* (branches and leaves) of the tallest trees. The most common trees in the canopy are called the *dominant* trees of the forest. Certain plants, especially climbing vines and epiphytes, may grow in the canopy. *Epiphytes* are plants that grow on other plants for support but absorb from the air the water and other materials they need to make food.

The canopy receives full sunlight. As a result, it produces more food than does any other layer. In some forests, the canopy is so dense it almost forms a roof over the forest. Fruit-eating birds, and insects and mammals that eat leaves or fruit, live in the canopy.

The understory is made up of trees shorter than those of the canopy. Some of these trees are smaller species that grow well in the shade of the canopy. Others are young trees that may in time join the canopy layer. Because the understory grows in shade, it is not as productive as the canopy. However, the understory provides food and shelter for many forest animals.

The shrub layer consists mainly of shrubs. Shrubs, like trees, have woody stems. But unlike trees, they have more than one stem, and none of the stems grows as tall as a tree. Forests with a dense canopy and understory may have only a spotty shrub layer. The trees in such forests filter out so much light that few shrubs can grow beneath them. Most forests with a more open canopy and understory have heavy shrub growth. Many birds and insects live in the shrub layer.

The herb layer consists of ferns, grasses, wildflowers, and other soft-stemmed plants. Tree seedlings also make up part of this layer. Like the shrub layer, the herb layer grows thickest in forests with a more open canopy and understory. Yet even in forests with dense tree layers, enough sunlight reaches the ground to support some herb growth. The herb layer is the home of forest animals that live on the ground. They include such small animals as insects, mice, snakes, turtles, and ground-nesting birds and such large animals as bears and deer.

The forest floor is covered with mats of moss and with various objects that have fallen from the upper layers. Leaves, twigs, and animal droppings—as well as dead animals and plants—build up on the forest floor. Among these objects, an incredible number of small organisms can be found. They include earthworms, fungi, insects, and spiders, plus countless bacteria and other microscopic life. All these organisms break down the waste materials into the basic chemical elements necessary for new plant growth.

Kinds of forests

Many systems are used to classify the world's forests. Some systems classify a forest according to the characteristics of its dominant trees. A *needleleaf forest,* for example, consists of a forest in which the dominant trees have long, narrow, needlelike leaves. Such forests are also called *coniferous* (cone-bearing) because the trees bear cones. The seeds grow in these cones. A *broadleaf forest* is made up mainly of trees with broad, flat leaves. Forests in which the dominant trees shed all their leaves during certain seasons of the year, and then grow new ones, are classed as *deciduous forests.* In an *evergreen forest,* the dominant trees grow new leaves before shedding the old ones. Thus they remain green throughout the year.

In some other systems, forests are classified according to the usable qualities of the trees. A forest of broadleaf trees may be classed as a *hardwood forest* because most broadleaf trees have hard wood, which makes fine furniture. A forest of needleleaf trees may be classed as a *softwood forest* because most needleleaf trees have softer wood than broadleaf trees have.

Many scientists classify forests according to various *ecological systems.* Under such systems, forests with similar climate, soil, and amounts of moisture are grouped into *formations.* Climate, soil, and moisture determine the kinds of trees found in a forest formation.

The structure of the forest

Every forest has various *strata* (layers) of plants. The five basic strata, from highest to lowest, are (1) the canopy, (2) the understory, (3) the shrub layer, (4) the herb layer, and (5) the forest floor. This illustration shows the strata as they might appear in a temperate deciduous forest.

WORLD BOOK illustration by Jean Helmer

Canopy

Understory

Shrub layer

Herb layer

Forest floor

One common ecological system groups the world's forests into six major formations. They are (1) tropical rain forests, (2) tropical dry forests, (3) temperate deciduous forests, (4) temperate evergreen forests, (5) boreal forests, and (6) savannas.

Tropical rain forests grow near the equator, where the climate is warm and wet the year around. The largest of these forests grow in the Amazon River Basin of South America, the Congo River Basin of Africa, and throughout much of Southeast Asia.

Of the six forest formations, tropical rain forests have the greatest variety of trees. As many as 100 species—none of which is dominant—may grow in 1 square mile (2.6 square kilometers) of land. Nearly all the trees of tropical rain forests are broadleaf evergreens, though some palm trees and tree ferns can also be found. In most of the forests, the trees form three canopies. The upper canopy may reach more than 165 feet (50 meters) high. A few exceptionally tall trees, called *emergents,* tower above the upper canopy. The understory trees form the two lower canopies.

The shrub and herb layers are sparse because little sunlight penetrates the dense canopies. However, many climbing plants and epiphytes crowd the branches of the canopies, where the sunlight is fullest.

Most of the animals of the tropical rain forests also live in the canopies, where they can find plentiful food. These animals include such flying or climbing creatures as bats, birds, insects, lizards, mice, monkeys, opossums, sloths, and snakes.

Tropical dry forests grow in warm areas that have wet and dry seasons. Such conditions occur in tropical to subtropical regions in many parts of the world. Tropical dry forests also are known as *tropical seasonal forests* or *seasonally dry tropical forests.*

Tropical dry forests have a great variety of tree species, though not nearly as many as the rain forests. They also have fewer climbing plants and epiphytes. Unlike the trees of the rain forest, many tropical dry species are deciduous. The deciduous trees are found in regions with especially distinct wet and dry seasons. The trees shed their leaves in the dry season.

Tropical dry forests have a canopy about 100 feet (30 meters) high. One understory grows beneath the canopy. Bamboos and palms may form a dense shrub layer, and a thick herb layer blankets the ground. The animal life resembles that of the rain forest.

Temperate deciduous forests grow in eastern North America, western Europe, and eastern Asia. These regions have a *temperate* climate, with warm summers and cold winters.

The canopy of temperate deciduous forests is about 100 feet (30 meters) high. Two or more kinds of trees dominate the canopy and another 15 to 25 kinds may be present. Most trees in these forests are broadleaf and deciduous. They shed their leaves in fall. The understory, shrub, and herb layers may be dense. The herb layer has two growing periods each year. Plants of the first growth appear in early spring, before the trees develop new leaves. These plants die by summer and are replaced by plants that grow in the shade of the canopy.

Large animals of the temperate deciduous forests include bears, deer, and, rarely, wolves. These forests are also the home of hundreds of smaller mammals and birds. Many of the birds migrate south in fall, and some of the mammals hibernate during the winter.

Some temperate areas support mixed deciduous and evergreen forests. In the Great Lakes region of North America, for example, the cold winters promote the growth of heavily mixed forests of deciduous and evergreen trees. Forests of evergreen pine and deciduous oak and hickory grow on the dry coastal plains of the southeastern United States.

Temperate evergreen forests. In some temperate regions, the environment favors the growth of evergreen forests. Such forests grow along coastal areas that have mild winters with heavy rainfall. These areas include the northwest coast of North America, the south coast of Chile, the west coast of New Zealand, and the southeast coast of Australia. Temperate evergreen forests also cover the lower mountain slopes in Asia, Europe, and western North America. In these regions, the cool climate favors the growth of evergreen trees.

The strata and the plant and animal life vary greatly from one temperate evergreen forest to another. For ex-

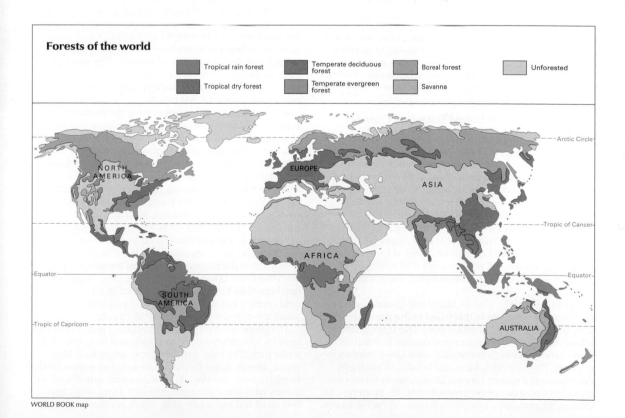

Forests of the world

Tropical rain forest
Tropical dry forest
Temperate deciduous forest
Temperate evergreen forest
Boreal forest
Savanna
Unforested

WORLD BOOK map

ample, the mountainous evergreen forests of Asia, Europe, and North America are made up of conifers. The coastal forests of Australia and New Zealand, on the other hand, consist of broadleaf evergreen trees.

Boreal forests, also called *taiga,* are found in regions that have an extremely cold winter and a short growing season. The word *boreal* means *northern.* Vast boreal forests stretch across northern Europe, Asia, and North America. Similar forests also cover the higher mountain slopes on these continents.

Boreal forests have the simplest structure of all forest formations. They have only one uneven layer of trees, which reaches up to about 75 feet (23 meters) high. In most of the boreal forests, the dominant trees are needleleaf evergreens—either spruce and fir or spruce and pine. The shrub layer is spotty. However, mosses and lichens form a thick layer on the forest floor and also grow on the tree trunks and branches. There are few herbs.

Many small mammals, such as beavers, mice, porcupines, and snowshoe hares, live in the boreal forests. Larger mammals include bears, caribou, foxes, moose, and wolves. Birds of the boreal forests include ducks, loons, owls, warblers, and woodpeckers.

Savannas are areas of widely spaced trees. In some savannas, the trees grow in clumps. In others, individual trees grow throughout the area, forming an uneven, widely open canopy. In either case, most of the ground is covered by shrubs and herbs, especially grasses. As a result, some biologists classify savannas as grasslands. Savannas are found in regions where low rainfall, poor soil, frequent fires, or other environmental features limit tree growth.

The largest savannas are tropical savannas. They grow throughout much of Central America, Brazil, Africa, India, Southeast Asia, and Australia. Animals of the tropical savannas include giraffes, lions, tigers, and zebras.

Temperate savannas, also called *woodlands,* grow in the United States, Canada, Mexico, and Cuba. They have such animals as bears, deer, elk, and pumas.

Forests of the United States and Canada

The United States and Canada are rich in forests. Before the first white settlers arrived in the 1600's, forests covered most of the land from the Atlantic Ocean to the Mississippi River. Altogether, nearly 40 percent of the land north of Mexico was forested at that time. More than half this forestland was in Canada and Alaska, where only a small portion has been cleared. Even in the lower United States, forests still grow on much of the original forestland. Today, the United States has about 755 million acres (305 million hectares) of forests, and Canada has about 765 million acres (310 million hectares). In both countries, forests cover about a third of the land area.

The forests of the United States and Canada include all the major formations discussed in the previous section, except for tropical rain forests. The U.S.-Canadian forests can be divided into many smaller formations. One common system recognizes nine U.S.-Canadian formations. They are (1) subtropical forests, (2) southern deciduous-evergreen forests, (3) deciduous forests, (4) northern deciduous-evergreen forests, (5) temperate savannas, (6) mountain evergreen forests, (7) Pacific coastal forests, (8) boreal forests, and (9) subarctic woodlands.

Subtropical forests thrive along the coasts of the Atlantic Ocean and the Gulf of Mexico in the Southeastern United States. In these regions, the climate stays hot and humid throughout the year.

In southern Florida, raised areas of the swampy Everglades support forests of live oak, mahogany, and sabal palm. These forests have a dense undergrowth of ferns, shrubs, and small trees. Epiphytes and vines crowd the branches of the taller trees. Broadleaf-evergreen forests grow farther north, along the edges of the Atlantic and Gulf coasts. The dominant trees in these forests are bay, holly, live oak, and magnolia. Thick growths of Spanish moss, an epiphyte that looks like long gray hair, hang from the branches.

Southern deciduous-evergreen forests grow on the flat, sandy coastal plains of the Southeastern United States. The forests extend along the Atlantic Coastal Plain from New Jersey to Florida and along the Gulf Coastal Plain from Florida to Texas. These regions have long, hot summers and short winters.

Most of the forests consist of evergreen pine and deciduous oak. Pitch pine is the most common evergreen in the northern part of these forests. Going southward, pitch pine is replaced, in order, by loblolly, longleaf, and slash pine.

Deciduous forests occupy a region bounded by the coastal plains on the south and east, the Great Lakes on the north, and the Great Plains on the west. This region has dependable rainfall and distinct seasons. Severe frosts and heavy snows occur during winter in the northern parts of this formation.

The northern part of the deciduous forest region was once covered by glaciers. But the glaciers did not reach the southern portion, which has the oldest and richest deciduous forest in North America. This forest lies in the central Appalachian Mountains region. The dominant trees of the forest include ash, basswood, beech, buckeye, cucumber magnolia, hickory, sugar maple, yellow-poplar, and several kinds of oaks.

In most deciduous forests outside the central Appalachians, fewer species of trees dominate. For example, various kinds of oaks dominate the forests from southern New England to northwestern Georgia. Hickory and yellow-poplars—and in drier areas several species of pine—grow among the oak trees. Beech and sugar maple trees dominate the northeastern and north-central deciduous forests. However, these forests also have many other kinds of trees, such as black cherry, red maple, red oak, and white elm. The northwestern deciduous forests are dominated by basswood and maple. Some oak trees also grow in these forests.

Northern deciduous-evergreen forests stretch from the Great Lakes across southeastern Canada and northern New York and New England. In this region of cold winters and warm summers, deciduous trees of the south are mixed with conifers of the north.

The dominant evergreens throughout much of this region include white-cedar, hemlock, and jack, red, and white pine. The chief broadleaf species include basswood, beech, sugar maple, white ash, and yellow birch. In moist areas, hemlock and white-cedar grow in mixed stands with black ash and white elm. Drier areas have forests of red and white pine, which is mixed with some

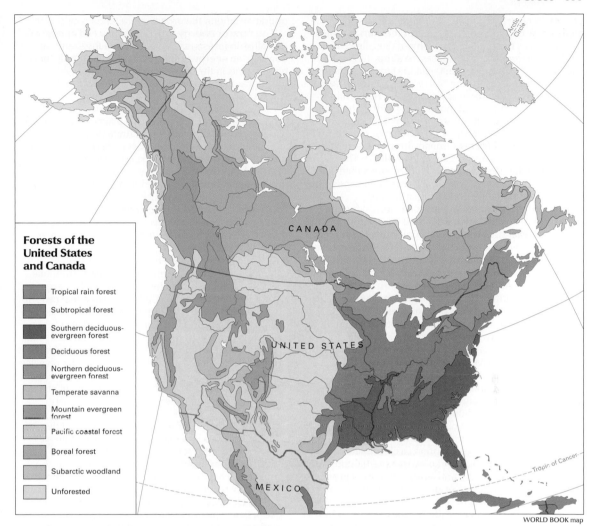

Forests of the United States and Canada

- Tropical rain forest
- Subtropical forest
- Southern deciduous-evergreen forest
- Deciduous forest
- Northern deciduous-evergreen forest
- Temperate savanna
- Mountain evergreen forest
- Pacific coastal forest
- Boreal forest
- Subarctic woodland
- Unforested

WORLD BOOK map

ironwood and red oak. Areas that are neither especially dry nor moist support maple or beech forests. The region's swamps are covered with black spruce and larch.

Temperate savannas are found in areas of Canada and the United States that have lower annual rainfall and a long season of dryness. Temperate savannas dominated by aspen grow in North Dakota, Manitoba, Saskatchewan, and Alberta. Outside this region, oak, pine, or both oak and pine dominate the temperate savannas of North America. Savannas of bur oak, mixed in some areas with other oaks or hickory, extend in a belt from Manitoba through Texas. Coniferous savannas of juniper and piñon pine cover the dry foothills of the mountainous regions of the southwestern United States from Texas to Arizona, and the southern half of Mexico. In California, the foothills of the Sierra Nevada have similar savannas of blue oak and digger pine. Along the coast of southern California, the climate supports a broadleaf savanna of various species of oaks.

Mountain evergreen forests grow above the foothill savannas of the mountains of the western United States and Canada. In general, the climate in the mountains becomes colder, wetter, and windier with increas-

ing altitude. The forests of the lower and middle slopes are called *montane forests*. Those of the upper slopes are known as *subalpine forests*.

In the Rockies, the lower montane forests consist of unmixed stands of ponderosa pine. At higher elevations, Douglas-fir becomes dominant. Douglas-fir is mixed with grand fir in the northern Rockies and with blue spruce and white fir in the southern Rockies. Above this zone lie the cold, snowy subalpine forests, which are dominated by Engelmann spruce and subalpine fir. Lodgepole pine is also common in both the montane and subalpine zones, especially in areas that have been affected by fire. The highest elevation at which trees can grow is called the *timber line*. Beyond this point, the climate is too severe for tree growth. At the timber line, the trees grow in a scattered, savannalike way. The timber-line regions are dominated by bristlecone pine in the southern Rockies, by limber pine in the central Rockies, and by Lyall's larch and whitebark pine in the northern Rockies.

In the Sierra Nevada, incense-cedar grows in moist areas of the lower montane forests. Douglas-fir, Jeffrey pine, ponderosa pine, and sugar pine thrive on drier slopes. In central California, magnificent giant sequoia trees grow on the western slopes of the Sierra Nevada. Sequoias are the bulkiest, though not the tallest, of all trees. The largest sequoias measure about 100 feet (30 meters) around at the base. White fir dominates the upper montane forests of the Sierra Nevada. At subalpine elevations, mountains support forests of red fir mixed with lodgepole pine and mountain hemlock. These subalpine forests thin out into savannas of bristlecone and whitebark pine at elevations near the timber line.

Pacific coastal forests extend along the Pacific Ocean from west-central California to Alaska. The warm currents of the Pacific help give this region a mild climate the year around. Warm, moisture-filled winds from the ocean bring heavy annual precipitation.

Huge conifers dominate the Pacific coastal forests. Forests of redwood, the tallest living trees, grow along a narrow coastal strip from central California to southern Oregon. Many tower more than 300 feet (91 meters). Inland from the redwoods and to the north grow forests of Douglas-fir, Sitka spruce, western hemlock, and western redcedar. Along the coast of northern Washington and southern British Columbia, high annual precipitation supports thick temperate rain forests. These forests, with their moss-covered Douglas-fir, western hemlock, Sitka spruce, and western redcedar, make up a damp, green wilderness found nowhere else in North America.

Boreal forests sweep across northern North America from northwestern Alaska to the island of Newfoundland. In this region of severe cold and heavy snowfall, winter lasts seven to eight months. But the short growing season has dependable rainfall and many daylight hours. Boreal forests are dominated by coniferous evergreens, chiefly balsam fir, black spruce, jack pine, and white spruce. Some areas support larch, a deciduous conifer. Such deciduous broadleaf trees as balsam poplar, trembling aspen, and white birch grow in areas that have been burned over by forest fires. These forests have many *bogs* (areas of wet, spongy ground). Some bogs are treeless. Others, called *muskegs,* are covered by a deep mat of moss on which dwarfed conifers grow.

Subarctic woodlands lie along the northern edge of the boreal forests. The climate in this region is bitterly cold, with low precipitation and an extremely brief growing season. These conditions force the trees to grow in a widely spaced, savannalike fashion. Black spruce dominates most of the region. Other boreal trees, such as aspen, larch, white birch, and white spruce, grow in some places. North of the woodlands lies the Arctic tundra, where trees cannot survive.

The life of the forest

Forests are filled with an incredible variety of plant and animal life. For example, scientists recorded nearly 10,500 kinds of organisms in a deciduous forest in Switzerland. The number of individual plants and animals in a forest is enormous.

All life in the forest is part of a complex ecosystem, which also includes the physical environment. Ecologists study forest life by examining the ways in which the organisms interact with one another and their environment. Such interactions involve (1) the flow of energy through the ecosystem, (2) the cycling of essential chemicals within the ecosystem, and (3) competition and cooperation among the organisms.

The flow of energy. All organisms need energy to stay alive. In forests, as in most other ecosystems, life depends on energy from the sun. However, only the green plants in the forest use the sun's energy directly. Through a process called *photosynthesis,* they use sunlight to produce food.

All other forest organisms rely on green plants to capture the energy of sunlight. Green plants are thus the *primary producers* in the forest. Animals that eat plants are known as *primary consumers* or *herbivores.* Animals that eat herbivores are called *secondary consumers* or *predators.* Secondary consumers themselves may fall prey to other predators, called *tertiary* (third) *consumers.* This series of primary producers and various levels of consumers is known as a *food chain.*

In a typical forest food chain, tree leaves (primary producers) are eaten by caterpillars (primary consumers). The caterpillars, in turn, are eaten by shrews (secondary consumers), which are then eaten by owls (tertiary consumers). Energy, in the form of food, passes from one level of the food chain to the next. But much energy is lost at each level. Therefore, a forest ecosystem can support, in terms of weight, far more green plants than herbivores and far more herbivores than predators.

The cycling of chemicals. All living things are made up of certain basic chemical elements. The supply of these chemicals is limited, and so they must be recycled for life to continue.

The *decomposers* of the forest floor promote chemical recycling. Decomposers include bacteria, earthworms, fungi, and some insects. They obtain food by breaking down dead plants and the wastes and dead bodies of animals into their basic chemicals. The elements pass into the soil, where they are absorbed by the roots of growing plants. Without decomposition, the supply of such essential elements as nitrogen, phosphorus, and potassium would soon be exhausted.

Some chemical recycling does not involve decomposers. Green plants, for example, release oxygen during photosynthesis. Animals—and plants as well—need this chemical to *oxidize* (burn) food and so release energy. In the oxidation process, animals and plants give off carbon dioxide, which the green plants need for photosynthesis. Thus the cycling of oxygen and carbon dioxide works together and maintains a steady supply of the two chemicals.

Competition and cooperation. Every forest animal and plant must compete with individuals of its own and similar species for such necessities as nutrients, space, and water. For example, red squirrels in a boreal forest must compete with one another—and with certain other herbivores—for conifer seeds, their chief food. Similarly, the conifers compete with one another and with other types of plants for water and sunlight. This competition helps ensure that the organisms best adapted to the forest will survive and reproduce.

Cooperation among the organisms of the forest is common. For many species, cooperation is necessary for survival. For example, birds and mammals that eat fruit rely on plants for food. But the plants, in turn, may depend on these animals to help spread their seeds. Similarly, certain microscopic fungi grow on roots of trees. The fungi obtain food from the tree, but they also

How a forest develops   A forest develops through a series of changes in the kinds of plants and animals that live in an area. This process is called *ecological succession.* The pictures below show how a forest might develop and succession occur on abandoned farmland in the Southeastern United States.

WORLD BOOK illustrations by Jean Helmer

A grassy meadow develops during the first few years. Pine seedlings appear throughout the meadow.

An evergreen forest gradually develops. Young pines need full sun, so deciduous trees form the understory.

A deciduous-evergreen forest develops as the old pines die. Deciduous trees fill in the gaps in the canopy.

A wholly deciduous forest finally develops. This forest is the *climax* (final) stage in the succession.

help the tree absorb needed water and nutrients.

For a diagram of a forest ecosystem, see **Ecology.**

Forest succession

In forests and other natural areas, a series of orderly changes may occur in the kinds of plants and animals that live in the area. This series of changes is called *ecological succession.* Areas undergoing succession pass through one or more *intermediate* stages until a final *climax* stage is reached. Forests exist in intermediate or climax stages of ecological succession in many places.

To illustrate how a forest develops and succession occurs, let us imagine an area of abandoned farmland in the Southeastern United States. The abandoned land will first support communities of low-growing weeds, insects, and mice. The land then gradually becomes a meadow as grasses and larger herbs and shrubs begin to appear. At the same time, rabbits, snakes, and ground-nesting birds begin to move into the area.

In a few years, young pine trees stand throughout the meadow. As the trees mature, the meadow becomes an intermediate forest of pines. The meadow herbs and shrubs die and are replaced by plants that grow better in the shade of the pine canopy. As the meadow plants disappear, so do the food chains based on them. New herbivores and predators enter the area, forming food chains based on the plant life of the pine forest.

Years pass, and the pines grow old and large. But few young pines grow beneath them because pine seedlings need direct sunlight. Instead, broadleaf trees— particularly oaks—form the understory. As the old pines die, oaks fill the openings in the canopy. Gradually, a mixed deciduous-evergreen forest develops.

But the succession is still not complete. Young oaks grow well in the shade of the canopy, but pines do not. Thus a climax oak forest may eventually replace the mixed forest. However, pine wood is more valuable than oak wood. For this reason, foresters in the Southeastern United States use controlled fires to check the growth of oaks and so prevent climax forests from developing.

Different successional series occur in different areas. In southern boreal regions, for instance, balsam fir and white spruce dominate the climax forests. If fire, disease, or windstorms destroy a coniferous forest, an intermediate forest of trembling aspen and white birch may develop in its place. These deciduous trees grow better in direct sunlight and on unprotected, bare ground than do fir and spruce.

The aspen-birch forest provides the protection young boreal conifers need, and soon spruce and fir seedlings make up most of the understory. In time, these conifers grow taller than the aspen and birch trees. Deciduous species cannot reproduce in the shade of the new canopy, and eventually the climax forest of fir and spruce trees is reestablished.

The history of forests

The first forests developed in marshlands about 365 million years ago, toward the end of the Devonian Period. They consisted of tree-sized club mosses and ferns,

Early forests   Forests evolved throughout the various periods of Earth's history. At the beginning of the Carboniferous Period, about 359 million years ago, tree-sized club mosses and horsetails were dominant forest plants. By the start of the Jurassic Period, about 200 million years ago, conifers had become widespread. During the Paleogene Period, which began about 65 million years ago, flowering broadleaf trees started to become common.

WORLD BOOK illustrations by Paul D. Turnbaugh

Carboniferous forest   **Jurassic forest**   **Paleogene forest**

some of which had trunks nearly 40 feet (12 meters) tall and about 3 feet (1 meter) thick. These forests became the home of early amphibians and insects.

By the beginning of the Carboniferous Period—about 359 million years ago—vast swamps covered much of North America. Forests of giant club mosses and horsetails up to 125 feet (38 meters) tall grew in these warm swamps. Ferns about 10 feet (3 meters) tall formed a thick undergrowth that sheltered huge cockroaches, dragonflies, scorpions, and spiders. In time, seed ferns and primitive conifers developed in the swamp forests. When plants of the swamp forests died, they fell into the mud and water that covered the forest floor. The mud and water did not contain enough oxygen to support decomposers. As a result, the plants did not decay but became buried under layer after layer of mud. Over millions of years, the weight and pressure on the plants turned them into great coal deposits.

Later forests. As the Mesozoic Era began, about 251 million years ago, severe changes in climate and in Earth's surface wiped out the swamp forests. In the new, drier environment, gymnosperm trees became dominant. *Gymnosperms* are plants whose seeds are not enclosed in a fruit or seedcase. Such trees included seed ferns and primitive conifers like those that grew in the swamp forests. They also included cycad and ginkgo trees, which became widespread. Gymnosperm trees formed forests that covered much of Earth. Amphibians, insects, and large reptiles lived in these forests.

The oldest known fossils of flowering plants date to the early part of the Cretaceous Period, about 130 million years ago. Flowering plants, called *angiosperms,* produce seeds enclosed in a fruit or seedcase. Many angiosperm trees became prominent in the forests. They included magnolias, maples, and willows. Flowering

shrubs and herbs became common undergrowth plants.

At the start of the Cenozoic Era, about 65 million years ago, Earth's climate turned cooler. Magnificent temperate forests then spread across North America, Europe, and Asia. The forests included flowering broadleaf trees and needleleaf conifers. Many birds and mammals lived in these forests.

Modern forests. Earth's climate continued to turn colder. By about 2.4 million years ago, the first of several great waves of glaciers had begun to advance over much of North America, Europe, and Asia. By the time the last of these glaciers had retreated—about 11,500 years ago—the ice sheets had destroyed large areas of the temperate forests in North America and Europe. Only the temperate forests of southeastern Asia remained largely untouched.

The forests of the world took on their modern distribution after the last of the glaciers retreated. For example, the great boreal forests developed across northern Europe and North America. But the world's forest regions are not permanent. Today, for instance, temperate forests are invading the southern edge of the boreal region. Another ice age or other dramatic environmental changes could greatly alter the world's forests.

Deforestation

Human activities have had tremendous impact on modern forests. For at least 10,000 years, people have cut down forests to clear areas for farmland. Starting in the 1800's, great expanses of forest have been eliminated due to logging and industrial pollution. The destruction and degrading of forests is called *deforestation.*

Severe deforestation now occurs around the world. Until the late 1940's, rain forests covered about 8.7 million square miles (22.5 million square kilometers) of

Earth's land. Today, they cover less than half that area. Millions of acres or hectares of rain forests are destroyed each year. Since 1800, huge areas of temperate forests have also been cleared. Many parts of eastern North America, for example, have less than 2 percent of even degraded forests remaining.

Industrial pollution is a chief cause of deforestation. Factories often release poisonous gases into the air and dangerous wastes into lakes and rivers. Air pollutants may combine with rain or other precipitation and fall to earth as *acid rain* (see **Acid rain**). Acid rain and polluted bodies of water can restrict plant growth or even kill most plants in a forest.

Massive deforestation has made many remaining forest tracts small, isolated islands. As forests become smaller, their ability to sustain the full variety of plant species decreases. Many forests are so seriously degraded by logging activities that they fail to regenerate replacement forests.

Loss of forests has helped create many ecological problems. For example, rain water normally trapped by the forests is causing more floods around the world. In addition, as forest areas decrease or degrade, the production of oxygen from photosynthesis also decreases. Oxygen renewal is vital to the survival of oxygen-breathing organisms. At the same time, as less carbon dioxide is taken up by photosynthesis, the amounts of carbon dioxide released into the air increases. Thus more heat from the sun is trapped near Earth's surface instead of being reflected back into space. Many scientists believe that this *greenhouse effect* is causing a steady warming that could lead to threatening climatic conditions. See **Greenhouse effect.**

The destruction of forest ecosystems also destroys

© Glyn Davies, International Centre for Conservation Education
Deforestation of a tropical rain forest destroys the habitat of many plants and animals. This photograph shows loggers clearing part of a rain forest in Malaysia.

the habitats of many living creatures. Countless species of animals and plants have been wiped out by deforestation, and more are killed each year at an increasing rate.

To combat these problems, people and governments have been seeking out and protecting old growth forests that remain undisturbed by human beings.

http://bit.ly/11FT7SM

Such protection enables scientists to conduct long-term research on how old growth forests sustain the variety of plants and animals that live there.   Paul F. Maycock

Related articles in *World Book.* See **Tree** and its list of *Related articles.* See also the *Economy* section of the various country, state, and province articles. Other related articles include:

Amazon rain forest	Forest Service
Animal (Where animals live)	Forestry
Conservation	Jungle
Deforestation	National forest
Ecology	Petrified forest
Forest products	Rain forest

Outline

I. **The importance of forests**
   A. Economic value
   B. Environmental value
   C. Enjoyment value
II. **The structure of forests**
   A. The canopy
   B. The understory
   C. The shrub layer
   D. The herb layer
   E. The forest floor
III. **Kinds of forests**
   A. Tropical rain forests
   B. Tropical seasonal forests
   C. Temperate deciduous forests
   D. Temperate evergreen forests
   E. Boreal forests
   F. Savannas
IV. **Forests of the United States and Canada**
   A. Subtropical forests
   B. Southern deciduous-evergreen forests
   C. Deciduous forests
   D. Northern deciduous-evergreen forests
   E. Temperate savannas
   F. Mountain evergreen forests
   G. Pacific coastal forests
   H. Boreal forests
   I. Subarctic woodlands
V. **The life of the forest**
   A. The flow of energy
   B. The cycling of chemicals
   C. Competition and cooperation
VI. **Forest succession**
VII. **The history of forests**
VIII. **Deforestation**

Additional resources

Level I
Johansson, Philip. *The Temperate Forest: A Web of Life.* Enslow, 2004.
Staub, Frank J. *America's Forests.* Carolrhoda, 1998.

Level II
Kricher, John C. *A Field Guide to California and Pacific Northwest Forests.* Houghton, 1998. *A Field Guide to Eastern Forests, North America.* 1988. Reprint. 1998. *A Field Guide to Rocky Mountain and Southwest Forests.* 1998.
Walker, Laurence C. *The North American Forests.* CRC Pr., 1999.

Forest conservation. See Conservation (Forest conservation); Forestry.
Forest fire. See Forestry (Fire and forests).

Forest products have long provided people with food, shelter, clothing, and fuel. Prehistoric people ate berries and nuts that grew in forests. They built shelters from the branches of trees and wore clothing made of plant materials. About 1 $\frac{1}{2}$ million years ago, they began using wood as a fuel to make fire.

Today, wood is one of our most important raw materials. It is used in making thousands of products, from building materials, to paper, to photographic film. Despite its usefulness as a raw material, the chief use of wood throughout the world is as a fuel.

There are thousands of forest products. Most can be classified into one of five main groups: (1) wood products, (2) wood-based composite products, (3) fiber products, (4) chemical products, and (5) fuel products. Wood products are made from solid wood. Wood-based composite products contain wood and at least one other material. Manufacturers use wood fibers to produce fiber products. Chemical products are made by breaking down wood and wood fibers and chemically treating them. Such chemical products as cellophane, lacquer, and rayon are made from wood but do not feel or look like wood. Fuel products include logs, wood pellets, and charcoal. Other forest products come from the bark, fruit, gum, leaves, and sap of trees.

This article describes different forest products. For information about logging, see **Lumber**.

Wood products

Wood has many characteristics that make it an important construction material. Carpenters and woodworkers can easily shape it with tools and fasten it with nails, screws, staples, and adhesives. It is light but strong. Wood provides insulation against electric current, heat, cold, and sound. It can hold paint and other finishes, and it does not rust. Unlike metal, cement-based, or plastic construction materials, wood is a *renewable resource*—that is, a new supply grows after the timber has been harvested. Some of the chief wood structural materials are round timbers, lumber, and veneer products.

Round timbers include pilings, poles, and posts. Pilings driven into the ground provide foundations for buildings, wharves, and other heavy structures. Poles link overhead telephone wires and power lines. People use posts chiefly to build fences. Round timbers are simply trees that have been stripped of their branches and bark, and cut into logs. The logs are dried and treated for protection against decay and insect attack.

Lumber includes boards and larger pieces of wood that have been sawed from logs. In the United States, the construction industry uses about 50 percent of the lumber production. The rest goes to make crates, furniture, railroad ties, sporting goods, toys, and thousands of other products. See **Lumber**.

Wood scientists classify lumber as *softwood* or *hardwood,* depending on the kind of tree. This classification does not always indicate the hardness of the wood. Various softwoods produce harder lumber than do some hardwoods. Softwood lumber comes from needleleaf trees that are also called *evergreens* or *conifers.* Builders use this type of lumber for most structural work because of its straightness and length. Softwoods include

Some kinds of forest products

Trees provide thousands of products. Wood products include various types of lumber. Wood-based composite products include plywood and particleboard. Rayon, cellophane, and turpentine are made from wood by chemical processes. Other forest products include charcoal and nuts.

WORLD BOOK illustrations by David Cunningham

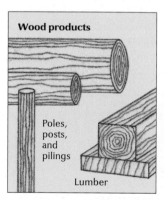

Wood products

Poles, posts, and pilings

Lumber

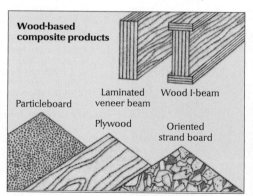

Wood-based composite products

Particleboard

Laminated veneer beam

Wood I-beam

Plywood

Oriented strand board

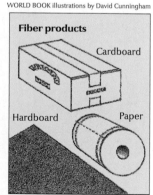

Fiber products

Cardboard

Hardboard

Paper

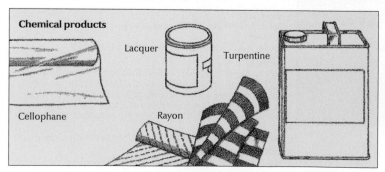

Chemical products

Lacquer

Turpentine

Cellophane

Rayon

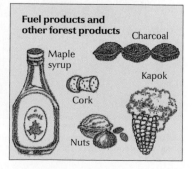

Fuel products and other forest products

Charcoal

Maple syrup

Kapok

Cork

Nuts

pine, larch, fir, hemlock, redwood, cypress, cedar, and Douglas-fir.

Hardwood lumber comes from trees that lose their leaves every autumn. Many hardwoods have beautiful grain patterns. For this reason, builders and furniture makers use hardwoods for cabinets, flooring, furniture, and paneling. Popular hardwoods include birch, mahogany, maple, oak, sweet gum, and walnut.

Veneer products are made of thin sheets of wood called *veneers.* These veneers may be cut into long strips or other shapes. Veneer products include baskets, matches, tongue depressors, and toothpicks.

Wood-based composite products

Manufacturers produce many products using wood together with at least one other material. By combining materials, they can take advantage of the best properties of each. Wood-based composite products include plywood and particleboard, which are made by combining wood with adhesive resins.

Plywood consists of a number of veneers that are glued together. The veneers are arranged so that the grain direction in each layer is at a right angle to the grain direction of the next layer. This arrangement gives plywood several advantages over lumber. For example, plywood shrinks and swells less than lumber, and it can be easily nailed near the edges without splitting. The construction and furniture industries use large amounts of plywood.

Particleboard is made from wood shavings, flakes, wafers, splinters, or sawdust. Some of these materials come from scrap left over in sawmills and paper mills. Particleboard makers mix the wood with an adhesive and press it at a high temperature and pressure to form large sheets or panels. Particleboard shrinks and swells little in length and width. It may be used as a base for flooring and furniture. One type of particleboard, called *oriented strand board* (OSB), has the strength of plywood and many of the same uses. To make OSB, manufacturers use waxes and resins to bond layers of wood flakes positioned with their grains running in alternating directions.

Other wood-based composite products are made by combining wood with such materials as fiberglass, metals, polyvinyl chloride, polypropylene, and Portland cement. Wood-based composites commonly substitute for lumber. For example, laminated veneer lumber is made of parallel laminated sheets of veneer manufactured to standard lumber dimensions.

Fiber products

Wood is made up of many tiny fibers. Manufacturers produce paper and paperboard, hardboard, and insulation board from wood fibers. Wood fiber is also used as attic insulation, as a protective soil covering called *mulch,* and even as a dietary fiber in breakfast cereals.

Paper and paperboard are made from wood chips that have been reduced to a fiber pulp by chemicals,

Some uses of forest products

Wood products

Lumber

Barrels	Furniture
Baseball bats	Laminated beams
Boats	Mine timbers
Bowling pins	Moldings
Boxes	Pallets
Cabinets	Paneling
Caskets	Pencils
Crates	Railroad ties
Doors	Shingles
Fencing	Structural timber
Flooring	Window frames

Round timbers

Bridges	Pilings
Fence posts	Utility poles
Log homes	

Veneer products

Baskets	Tongue
Boxes	depressors
Matches	Toothpicks

Wood-based composite products

Particle board

Cabinet tops	Furniture
Door cores	Paneling
Drawer sides	Roof decking
Floor under-	Sheathing
layment	Siding

Plywood

Boats	Furniture
Cabinets	House foundations
Concrete forms	Paneling
Containers	Roof decking
Floor under-	Sheathing
layment	Siding

Other wood-based composite products

Cement-bonded	Laminated veneer
panels	lumber
Extruded	Parallel strand
wood/plastic	lumber
products	Plastic lumber
	Wood I-beams

Fiber products

Hardboard

Automobile	Garage doors
interiors	Paneling
Cabinets	Siding
Furniture	Signs

Insulation board

Ceiling tile	Sheathing

Medium density fiberboard

Drawer sides	Paneling
Dresser tops	
and tabletops	

Paper and paperboard

Bags	Newspaper
Books	Packaging
Cartons	Tissue

Chemical products

Cellulose products

Acetate	Lacquers
Adhesives	Photographic film
Cellophane	Plastics
Ceramics	Rayon
Detergent addi-	Tire cords
tives	

Lignin products

Animal feeds	Ceramics
Artificial vanilla	Cement

Dyes	Printing inks
Plastics	Textile binder

Naval stores

Adhesives	Printing inks
Cleaners	Rosin
Disinfectants	Synthetic rubber
Linoleum	Turpentine
flooring	Varnishes
Lubricants	

Fuel products

Charcoal	Sawdust
Fireplace logs	Wood chips
Pulverized fuel	Wood pellets

Other forest products

Bark

Adhesives	Fuel
Cork	Soil mulch
Dyes	Tannic acid

Fruit and seeds

Beechnuts	Hickory nuts
Black walnuts	Kapok
Blueberries	Pecans
Cranberries	Pine nuts

Gum

Pine oil	Tall oil
Rosin	Turpentine

Leaves

Holly	Pharmaceuticals
Household	Soap
cleaner	Wreaths
Perfumes	

Sap

Maple sugar	Maple syrup

heat, or mechanical treatment. The pulp is then formed into a mat, filtered, drained, and pressed. Paper products include bags, books, cartons, packaging materials, and tissue.

Medium density fiberboard (MDF) is made from wood that has been reduced to individual fibers or fiber bundles and then been bonded with adhesive. MDF is used primarily to make tops with molded edges for tables or other furniture.

Hardboard is made by pressing wood fibers into sheets at a high temperature and pressure. The fibers are held together primarily by *lignin,* a substance that naturally occurs in and between wood fibers. Hardboard is used chiefly in furniture, siding, and paneling.

Insulation board is manufactured from wood fibers that are formed into a mat, pressed lightly, and dried. It weighs less than hardboard. Insulation board is used for acoustical tile and under siding in construction.

Chemical products

Many wood products are made from wood or bark that has been broken down into such basic chemical parts as cellulose and lignin. Cellulose is the main ingredient of wood fibers.

Cellulose products. Cellulose may be chemically treated to change its properties and to produce such compounds as *cellulose acetate* and *cellulose nitrate.* Both of these compounds are used in adhesives, lacquers, and plastics. Plastic items molded from cellulose compounds include piano keys, tool handles, and table tennis balls. Cellulose nitrate is also an ingredient in explosives. Other cellulose compounds have specialized uses in such products as paint, foods, and textiles.

Textile manufacturers process cellulose to produce rayon and acetate fibers, which are used for clothing, draperies, and upholstery. Rayon cords strengthen tires. Other materials made from cellulose include cellophane and photographic film. See **Cellulose; Rayon.**

Lignin products. Lignin has far fewer uses than cellulose. It is used in making printing inks, dyes, and concrete. Manufacturers use it to *bind* (hold together) animal food pellets and textiles. Artificial vanilla, a flavoring used in many foods, is also made from lignin.

Naval stores include turpentine and rosin—materials once essential to the operation of wooden sailing ships. Almost all naval stores come from the processing of pine pulp.

Fuel products

In many developing countries, wood has long served as the primary fuel for cooking and heating. In industrialized countries, wood has been burned mainly in fireplaces and charcoal grills. After petroleum prices rose in the 1970's, wood became a popular fuel in communities near forested areas. Fuel products made from wood include split, dried logs; compressed wood pellets; charcoal; and sawmill by-products. In addition, the forest products industry burns the thick liquid that results from pulping wood.

Other forest products

Although most forest products are made from wood, some come from the bark, fruit and seeds, gum, leaves, and sap of trees. By-products from sawmills include wood chips, shavings, and sawdust. These by-products may be used in making particleboard and other products, in bedding for animals, and in floor-sweeping compounds.

The bark from the cork oak tree provides cork for such products as bottle stoppers, bulletin boards, and insulation. The bark of the hemlock and other trees furnishes tannic acid used in processing animal hides. Bark is sometimes used as fuel, ground cover, or mulch.

Fruit and seeds harvested from forest trees include

Leading countries in forest products

Wood removed from forests in a year

United States	●●●●●●●●●●●●●●●●●● 618,160,000 cubic yards (472,620,000 m³)	
India	●●●●●●●●●●●● 429,890,000 cubic yards (328,680,000 m³)	
China	●●●●●●●●●(374,210,000 cubic yards (286,100,000 m³)	
Brazil	●●●●●●●●(334,680,000 cubic yards (255,880,000 m³)	
Canada	●●●●●●● 269,300,000 cubic yards (205,890,000 m³)	
Russia	●●●●●●(249,300,000 cubic yards (190,600,000 m³)	
Indonesia	●●● 133,170,000 cubic yards (101,820,000 m³)	
Ethiopia	●●● 127,410,000 cubic yards (97,410,000 m³)	
Congo (Kinshasa)	●●(97,730,000 cubic yards (74,720,000 m³)	
Nigeria	●● 92,460,000 cubic yards (70,690,000 m³)	

Figures are for 2006.
Source: Food and Agriculture Organization of the United Nations.

Leading states and provinces in forest products

Wood removed from forests in a year

British Columbia*	●●●●●●●●●●●●●● 113,810,000 cubic yards (87,010,000 m³)	
Quebec*	●●●●●●(50,310,000 cubic yards (38,460,000 m³)	
Georgia	●●●●●● 49,650,000 cubic yards (37,960,000 m³)	
Alabama	●●●●●(42,860,000 cubic yards (32,770,000 m³)	
Mississippi	●●●●● 40,520,000 cubic yards (30,980,000 m³)	
North Carolina	●●●●● 39,810,000 cubic yards (30,440,000 m³)	
Oregon	●●●●(38,510,000 cubic yards (29,450,000 m³)	
Alberta*	●●●●(36,030,000 cubic yards (27,550,000 m³)	
Washington	●●●● 33,300,000 cubic yards (25,460,000 m³)	
Louisiana	●●●● 31,770,000 cubic yards (24,290,000 m³)	

Figures are for 2006, except for *, where figures are for 2005.
Sources: U.S. Forest Service; Canadian Council of Forest Ministers.

Plywood is a widely used wood product. Workers in this manufacturing plant in Vancouver, Canada, are stacking sheets of glued wood that will be joined together under a hot press to make plywood.

© Bill Staley, West Stock

many kinds of nuts. The seedpods of the kapok, or silk-cotton, tree provide kapok fibers, widely used as a filler in jackets and sleeping bags. Latex is a milky substance produced by plants and trees of the sapodilla family. It is the source of natural rubber, which is used to make balloons, hoses, rubber gloves, tires, and other items.

The leaves of some forest trees furnish ornamental greenery for Christmas wreaths and similar products. Certain evergreen and eucalyptus leaves are distilled to produce oil used in perfumes, household cleaners, soaps, and certain drugs. Sap from certain kinds of maple trees is made into maple syrup and maple sugar.

The forest products industry

The manufacture of forest products is a major industry in many countries. The United States, India, and China are the world's leading producers of forest products. Canada is also an important producer of forest products.

In the United States, the forest products industry employs more than 1 million people and produces hundreds of billions of dollars worth of goods annually. United States forest products companies own about 70 million acres (28 million hectares) of commercially valuable forestland. They harvest timber in state and national forests under government contracts. They also buy logs from the owners of small wooded areas.

In China, economic reforms that began in 1980 have led to a greater demand for private housing. This demand has, in turn, brought a huge increase in the production of forest products for use as construction materials. In India, millions of people depend on gathering and selling forest products for cash.

Canada's forest products industry is a leading source of export income. About 340,000 Canadians work for companies that make forest products. Each year, these firms produce goods worth tens of billions of dollars. Canada is the world's top producer of *newsprint,* the paper on which newspapers are printed. It makes about a fifth of the world's supply each year. Much of this newsprint is exported to the United States.   Jim L. Bowyer

Related articles in *World Book.* See **Wood** and its list of *Related articles.* See also the following articles:

Bark	Lacquer	Resin	Tannic acid
Charcoal	Lumber	Rosin	Tar
Cork	Paper	Rubber	Turpentine
Gum	Rayon	Sap	

Forest ranger. See Forestry; Forest Service.

Forest Service is an agency of the United States Department of Agriculture. Its task is promoting the best use of forestland. It manages about 190 million acres (77 million hectares) of national forests and other lands.

Forest Service rangers try to protect these forests against insects, disease, and fire. The rangers preserve wildlife and supervise grazing. They see that no more timber is cut in any one year than a single year's growth can replace. They keep a cover of plants on sloping land to guard against rapid soil erosion and floods. The rangers also supervise camping and picnic areas, and keep up a system of lookout stations, telephone lines, two-way radio communication, and roads and trails. They often help rescue people who are lost or injured.

The Forest Service cooperates with state and local governments and private landowners. For example, it advises and assists them in protecting and planting forests. The agency carries on research programs at five regional experimental stations and at the Forest Products Laboratory in Madison, Wisconsin. It conducts research on tropical forests at an institute in Puerto Rico. It also conducts research projects at sites throughout the United States. Founded as the Bureau of Forestry, the agency became the Forest Service in 1905.

Critically reviewed by the Forest Service

See also **National forest.**

Forester, Cecil Scott (1899-1966), was an English novelist who won fame for his fictional creation of Horatio Hornblower, a British naval hero of the 1800's. Hornblower's exciting adventures, his coolness and inventiveness under stress, and his weakness for women endeared him to a large reading public. Hornblower rises from midshipman to admiral in a series of 12 novels that begins with *The Happy Return* (published in the United States as *Beat to Quarters,* 1937). Other novels in the series include *Flying Colours* (1938), *A Ship of the Line* (1939), and *Lord Hornblower* (1946). Forester's adventure novel *The African Queen* (1935) was made into a popular motion picture in 1951.

Forester believed his other novels, especially *The General* (1936), equal to the Hornblower books. But his readers overwhelmingly favored the naval hero. Forester was born on Aug. 27, 1899, in Cairo, Egypt, and was educated in England. He lived in the United States from 1945 until his death on April 2, 1966.   Garrett Stewart

Risley Equipment Ltd.   Georgia-Pacific Corp.

Harvesting and planting trees mechanically contributes to efficient management of timber resources. A tree-felling sawhead, *left,* cuts a tree down in a few seconds with its powerful blade. A
planting gun, *right,* digs a hole, inserts a seedling, and pats down the soil in one operation.

Forestry is the science and art of managing forest resources for human benefit. The practice of forestry sus-
tains forest *ecosystems*—that is, the living things in an
area and the relationships between them. Forestry also
helps people take timber for the manufacture of lumber,
plywood, paper, and other wood products. Forestry includes the management not only of trees, but also of
other valuable forest resources. These resources include a forest's water, its wildlife, its rare and endangered plants and animals, and the plants that grow beneath the trees.

In general, forests are managed with the goal of providing several benefits at once. This concept is called
multiple use forest management. In the United States,
this concept is applied in national forests, most state
forests, and many private forests. In addition to furnishing timber, these forests may provide water for communities; food and shelter for wildlife; grazing land for livestock; and recreation areas for campers, hikers, and pic-
nickers.

In some forests, however, the importance of one resource may outweigh that of others. For example, companies that manufacture wood products manage their
forests primarily for maximum timber production. Other
forests may be protected as parks or as wilderness or
recreation areas.

This article discusses the scientific management of

forest ecosystems. For information on the various products made from trees, see **Forest products.** For a discussion of forest ecology, see **Forest.**

Managing timber resources

One goal of managing timber resources is to achieve
an approximate balance between the annual harvest and
growth of wood. This balance, called a *sustained yield,*
ensures a continuous supply of timber. Sustained yield
is achieved by managing forests so they have areas of
trees in each of several age groups, from seedlings to
mature trees. The science of establishing, growing, and
harvesting *stands* (large groups) of trees for sustained
yield is called *silviculture.* Silviculture also focuses on
growing and using trees for wildlife habitat, watershed
protection, and other uses. Foresters study how various
species (kinds) of trees grow in different climates and
soils, and how much sunlight and water the trees need.
Foresters also breed trees that have improved growth
rates and greater resistance to diseases and pests.

Harvesting. There are four silvicultural methods
used in the harvest of timber: (1) clearcutting, (2) seed
tree cutting, (3) shelterwood cutting, and (4) selection
cutting. Each method is designed to provide an environment that favors the establishment of certain kinds of
trees. New trees grow from seeds produced by the remaining or surrounding trees, from sprouting stumps or

roots, or from seeds or seedlings that foresters plant.

Clearcutting is the removal of all the trees in a certain area of a forest. It is generally used to quickly reestablish a stand. Regrowth after clearcutting may involve planting seeds or sprouting from stumps. Clearcut areas must be large enough to prevent surrounding forests from affecting the young trees growing within the clearcut opening. Aspen, jack pine, lodgepole pine, and paper birch are examples of commonly clearcut trees. Such trees regenerate quickly.

Seed tree cutting resembles clearcutting, but foresters leave a few trees widely scattered in the harvested area to provide a natural source of seeds. These seed trees may be removed after a few years when the new stand is established. Seed tree cutting can be used with various conifer trees, including longleaf pine, western larch, and white pine.

Shelterwood cutting involves harvesting timber in several stages over 10 to 20 years. Foresters establish a new stand as the old one is removed. Shelterwood cutting can be used to regenerate Douglas-fir, oak, ponderosa pine, and white pine, which require shade during their first few years of growth. It also allows the growth of some trees in a stand to continue after the majority of the trees have ceased growing well.

Selection cutting is the harvesting of individual or small patches of mature trees to make room for new and younger trees. The trees are removed on the basis of their size, health, quality, and nearness to other trees. However, foresters leave most larger trees standing to produce seeds. Selection cutting leaves only small openings in a forest. It thus works best with trees that grow well in shade. Such trees include American beech, fir, hemlock, and sugar maple. Forests may be harvested by selection cutting every 10 to 30 years.

Planting. Foresters may plant new trees in an area from seeds, or they may plant *seedlings* (young trees) that have been raised in a nursery. When foresters plant trees on harvested land or in an existing forest, the process is called *artificial regeneration*. When foresters plant trees in an area that was never covered by a forest, the process is called *afforestation*.

Seeds can be planted in various ways. In large areas that have been destroyed by wildfire, seeds can be spread across sites by hand, by machine, or even by airplanes and helicopters. Depending on the method, foresters usually sow up to 30,000 seeds per acre (75,000 per hectare) to ensure adequate tree growth.

Forests are planted with seedlings in late winter or early spring, before the buds of the seedlings have opened for the growing season. Seedlings grow in a nursery for one to four years before being transplanted to the forest. Depending on the seedlings' sizes, foresters generally plant between 500 trees and 2,000 trees per acre (1,250 and 6,250 trees per hectare). They use hand tools or planting machines. A person can plant between 1 and 3 acres (0.4 and 1.2 hectares) a day by hand. Machines can plant much faster, but they only work well on level ground.

Tree improvement involves breeding trees for superior growth rates and increased resistance to diseases and pests. Foresters begin this process by searching forests for the straightest and fastest-growing trees of the species. These trees must also have high-quality wood and be healthy and free of harmful insects and other pests. Tree improvement programs have been used for black walnut, Douglas-fir, loblolly pine, and several other species.

After foresters find a superior tree, they take cuttings, called *scions,* from its branches. The scions are brought to a nursery and *grafted* (joined) to the roots of very young trees (see **Grafting**). The scions receive nutrients through the roots of the trees but keep the characteristics of the tree from which they were cut. Foresters may use the grafted scions in reforestation. They may also take pollen from the male flowers to pollinate female flowers of scions from other superior trees. The foresters keep careful records of the scions used for each pollination.

After pollination, the female flowers yield seeds that are planted in the nursery to produce seedlings. Foresters transplant the seedlings into special planta-

How timber is harvested

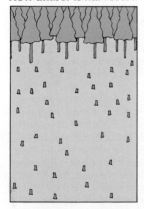   

WORLD BOOK illustrations by David Cunningham

Clearcutting removes all the trees in a large area. It provides full sunlight in which new seedlings can develop.

Seed tree cutting leaves a few scattered trees in the area to provide a source of seeds for a new crop.

Shelterwood cutting, which is used for trees that require shade to develop, removes trees in several stages.

Selection cutting involves harvesting small patches of mature trees to make room for new and younger trees.

tions and closely measure the growth of the trees. If the trees from a particular set of parents appear to grow quickly with superior characteristics, the seeds from those parents may be produced commercially for reforestation.

Community forestry, also called *social forestry*, is a system of forest management that treats woodlands as a communal resource. In some regions, including parts of North America and northwestern Europe, forests have been set aside for community use for hundreds of years. Rural communities in many developing countries practice community forestry to provide themselves with fuel wood and timber and with food from forest plants and animals.

Community forestry takes many forms. In *village woodlots,* trees are grown for firewood on any spare patches of land. *Agroforestry* involves techniques that produce trees in combination with crops, animals, or other products. In *intercropping*, cereals, vegetables, and fruit are grown between rows of newly planted trees until the trees grow too tall and overshadow them. *Silvipasture* involves managing tree growth through controlled forest grazing by animals. *Multiple-product forestry* utilizes techniques designed to increase the yield of fruit, wild game, honey, and many other forest commodities in addition to timber.

Managing other forest resources

Water. All forests grow within *watersheds*—that is, regions that supply water for rivers and streams. Forest soils collect water by soaking up rain and melted snow. The soil of a forest is covered by a spongy layer of leaves and twigs, called *litter.* The action of earthworms,

© Shutterstock

A forest campground may provide cooking facilities, electrical outlets, and plumbing. Foresters plan recreation areas to meet the needs of campers without harming the environment.

insects, rodents, and decaying roots creates open spaces within the soil. When rain or snow falls, the water fills these spaces and is absorbed by the litter. Much of the water is used by plants, and some flows underground and then into rivers, streams, and wells.

Watershed management largely involves keeping forest soil *porous* (filled with open spaces) so it can absorb a large amount of water. Proper forest harvesting reduces the water lost and so increases the underground supply and flow of water. If forest soils are not managed carefully, the soil will become hard and nonporous. Water flows over the surface of such ground, carrying mud and other materials into nearby streams and lakes. This runoff damages other soil, pollutes the water of the streams, and may even cause flooding.

Foresters help keep soil porous in several ways. They reforest harvested areas quickly to assure a continuous supply of litter. They ensure that roads built for logging operations are carefully designed to prevent soil erosion. Foresters also regulate livestock grazing to maintain a good cover of grass and to prevent the animals from packing down the earth.

Wildlife. Forests provide homes for a wide variety of wildlife, including bears, birds, fish, and rodents. Forest wildlife management involves maintaining a balance between the number of animals in a forest and the supply of food, water, and shelter.

Dense forests of old, tall trees provide good homes for birds, insects, and such climbing mammals as raccoons and squirrels. But the shade in such forests prevents the growth of enough herbs, shrubs, and small trees to feed large animals that live on the ground. However, openings made in the forest during the timber harvest allow more sunlight to reach the forest floor. New plants sprout in the clearings, providing food for wildlife. Hollow trees may be left in large openings to serve as dens and nesting places.

Wildlife management also involves controlling animal populations by regulating hunting. Hunting can help control large populations of deer, elk, and other animals

© John Running, Stock, Boston

Artificial regeneration involves planting new trees in ground covered—or once covered—by forest. This forester is planting pine seedlings where trees were burned out in a forest fire.

that can degrade forest ecosystems by damaging trees and reducing ground cover.

Rangeland. Many forests in dry regions have widely spaced trees with heavy undergrowth of grass and shrubs. Ranchers often graze livestock in such areas. The use of such rangeland must be carefully regulated to prevent overgrazing, which can damage tree roots and erode the soil. Foresters manage grasslands by controlling the number of livestock in a given area. Foresters may require ranchers to move livestock away from land that is heavily grazed to new pastures. These actions prevent the animals from eating too much grass in any one area.

Recreation areas. The scenic beauty and natural resources of forests provide opportunities for many recreational activities, including camping, fishing, hiking, and hunting. Millions of people visit state and national forests annually. Forest-products companies and private landowners also may open areas of their woodlands to the public.

Many areas of national and regional forests are managed primarily for recreation. Foresters carefully plan these areas to provide benefits to visitors with minimum harm to the forests. For example, before developing a campground, foresters study such factors as the terrain, the amount of shade, and the availability of water in the area. They can then install picnic tables, cooking equipment, electrical outlets, plumbing, roads and trails, and parking areas without seriously upsetting the ecological balance of the forest.

Fire and forests

Most scientists consider forest fires an essential natural process. Although fire can cause great destruction, it produces great ecological benefits. Fires recycle *nutrients*—that is, substances that plants need for growth. Fires clear trees and other vegetation that can prevent new tree growth. In fact, some pine and oak species actually grow best when forest fires occur. To take advantage of such benefits, foresters permit certain types of

© Liane Enkelis, Stock, Boston

Fighting a forest fire involves removing the fuel from the path of the flames. Firefighters may clear leaves, wood, and other material from the forest floor with axes and shovels, *as shown here.*

fires to burn. *Prescribed fires* are set by fire crews in safe conditions with low winds and high humidity, far from human dwellings.

Other fires, especially those that endanger lives or property, are referred to as *wildfires.* Wildfires are generally fought quickly and aggressively. Some wildfires are caused by lightning strikes. But most are caused by human beings. The fires may be started accidentally or deliberately. During dry seasons, when fires can easily start, foresters may restrict open campfires or even close a forest to the public to reduce the danger of fire. Foresters may watch for fires from lookout towers, or they may patrol forests by airplane.

To extinguish a wildfire, firefighters must remove the blanket of litter and dead wood from the forest floor. These materials serve as fuel for fire. Firefighting crews spray water or chemicals on the burning area to cool the fire and slow its progress. They then can get close enough to the flames to dig a *fireline,* also called a *firebreak.* Firefighters start a fireline by clearing all logs, brush, and trees from a wide strip around the fire. They then scrape away the litter and some of the soil with axes, shovels, or bulldozers. Highly trained firefighters called *smoke jumpers* may parachute from airplanes or helicopters to dig a fireline in an area that is difficult to reach by land.

After creating a fireline, the firefighters may set *backfires* to burn the area between the line and the forest fire itself. Backfires remove additional fuel and widen the fireline to help stop the spread of the flames. After a fire dies, the firefighters clear any flammable material from the edge of the burned area. This action prevents the material from smoldering and starting new fires.

Protecting forest ecosystems

The full benefits of forest ecosystems can be obtained only if they are protected from diseases, insect pests, and invasive species. Many countries have passed legislation designed to protect forest resources in other ways. Such laws control how roads, buildings, and industrial facilities are built in forests. They also give governments powers and funds to fight forest fires, pests, and diseases, and to regulate timber production.

Diseases and pests. Most tree diseases are caused by fungal infections. Such infections may enter the tree directly, or they may enter through an insect carrier. Diseases attack trees chiefly by clogging the flow of sap, killing the leaves, or rotting the roots or wood. Insects damage trees either by feeding on inner bark, by sucking the fluid from the leaves or stems, or by eating the leaves. Insects that eat tree leaves are called *defoliators.* Most native diseases and pests only occasionally become problems, usually when stands are old or unhealthy.

Foresters control diseases and pests by three chief methods: (1) biological controls, (2) silvicultural controls, and (3) direct controls. Biological controls fight diseases and pests with their natural enemies. For example, foresters might control an insect pest by spraying a forest with a disease organism which affects that particular species of insect. Silvicultural controls use methods of timber management to make a forest undesirable for diseases and pests. For example, foresters may remove old, weak trees that are easy prey for fungi and insects.

Direct controls include the use of chemical pesticides to kill fungi and insects. Such chemicals can kill nontarget plants and animals, and so pesticides are generally used only if other controls fail.

Invasive species pose one of the most substantial threats to forests. Invasive species include nonnative plants, animals, and microbes that cause environmental and economic harm to ecosystems. These species are often accidentally transported between countries in nursery and horticultural products or undetected in overseas shipping containers. Many of the most severe forest diseases and insects are invasive. Invasive diseases include beech bark disease, chestnut blight, Dutch elm disease, sudden oak death, and white pine blister rust. Invasive insects include the Asian long-horned beetle, emerald ash borer, gypsy moth, and hemlock woolly adelgid. Each of these invasive species has caused or could potentially cause the loss of a tree species from forests in large parts of North America.

Invasive plant and animal species also can cause significant damage, although the damage may occur more slowly. For example, invasive wild boars have caused significant damage to forest floor plants throughout Hawaii and much of the southeastern United States. Bush honeysuckle, garlic mustard, kudzu, multiflora rose, and salt cedar are several of the many invasive plant species that have displaced native forest plants and dramatically changed forest ecosystems.

Foresters deal with invasive species in many ways. Often, they use pesticides to control their spread because invasive species can be difficult to control with other methods. Foresters may use prescribed fire or biological controls. Foresters also try to prevent invasive species from being introduced and spread in the first place. This prevention includes banning the transport of seeds, firewood, and other plant material from region to region.

History

People have relied on forests since prehistoric times. Many scientists believe deforestation led to the decline of many early civilizations. But throughout history, cultures learned to regulate the use of forests to prevent shortages of timber. During the Middle Ages, from about the A.D. 400's through the 1400's, forest wildlife was protected to ensure a sufficient supply of game for the nobility to hunt. In the 1500's, people in France and some German states began setting aside forest plantations for timber cutting and other areas for growing new trees to replace those being harvested. Forest management methods soon spread throughout Europe. In the 1700's and 1800's, the first colleges teaching forestry subjects opened in France and Germany.

In North America, the early settlers treated the vast timber resources as though they would last forever. They cleared much more land than they needed for their homes and crops and destroyed large areas of forestland by using wasteful logging methods. By 1891, a conservation movement had started, and the United States Congress authorized the president to set aside wooded areas called *forest reserves.* The United States Forest Service was established in 1905. The service was given control of the forest reserves. In 1907, the forest reserves became known as national forests. The Canadi-

an Forest Service was established in 1899.

Since the mid-1900's, logging and the expansion of agriculture have damaged or cleared vast areas of the world's rain forests. Deforestation has largely occurred in less developed nations as they have sought to secure short-term economic benefits. Deforestation continues in many such places today. Worldwide conservation organizations have begun working with local governments to promote sound management of tropical forests by the people who use them. Conservationists have also sought to include large areas of intact tropical forest in parks and reserves that will protect such ecosystems for future generations.   Mike R. Saunders

Related articles in *World Book.* See **Forest** and **Forest products** and their lists of *Related articles.* See also:

Aphid	Nursery
Conservation	Pinchot, Gifford
Deforestation	Scale insect
Dutch elm disease	Spotted owl
Forest Service	Tree farming
Gypsy moth	Tussock moth
National forest	Wildlife conservation

Forfeiture, *FAWR fuh chuhr,* is a legal punishment or penalty by which a person who is guilty of wrongdoing or who has breached a contract or condition loses some right or possession. People who drive too fast may have their licenses taken away and thus *forfeit* the right to drive. A corporation may forfeit its charter if it abuses its privileges. Ordinarily, in the United States, forfeitures of this type can be made only by court action or by administrative action which is later subject to a court's review. *Civil,* or *contractual,* forfeiture may occur when a person fails to perform certain duties required under a contract. For example, if a person fails to make payment for an automobile that was purchased on credit, he or she may forfeit ownership of the automobile.

Joel C. Dobris

Forge. See **Forging** (Hand forging; picture).

Forgery, *FAWR juhr ee,* is deliberately tampering with a written paper for the purpose of deceit or fraud. Common forgeries include fraudulently signing another person's name to a check or document, changing the figures on a check to alter its amount, and making changes in a will or contract. The punishment for forgery is usually imprisonment. Intent to defraud must be proved before a person can be convicted of forgery. Literary forgers have tried to pass off forged documents as rare manuscripts. See also **Counterfeiting.**   Charles F. Wellford

Forget-me-not is a group of plants that are known for their light blue flowers. Many forget-me-nots are European varieties that are grown as garden flowers. These forget-me-nots have hairy stems and soft, hairy leaves. The small flowers are light blue with yellow centers and grow in clusters. Several kinds of forget-me-nots have white or pink flowers. Almost all kinds have pink flower buds. Forget-me-nots grow wild or as garden flowers in *temperate* regions, where there are hot summers and cool or cold winters.

Most forget-me-nots grow best in shady, moist places. The most popular kinds are *perennials,* which live for more than one growing season. Gardeners grow them by breaking up clumps of existing plants and transplanting them. Several common varieties are *annuals* that live only one growing season. They are grown from seed and bloom in autumn.

The common forget-me-not, *shown here,* grows clusters of light-blue flowers.

The forget-me-not is a symbol of friendship and of true love. The flower appears in many legends. In German legend, *forget me not* were the last words a lover spoke before he drowned trying to get the flower for his sweetheart. According to another legend, all the plants and animals shrank away from Adam and Eve when the two were expelled from the Garden of Eden, except for one tiny blue flower that said, "Forget me not!"

James S. Miller

Scientific classification. Forget-me-nots make up the genus *Myosotis. Myosotis* means *mouse ear* and refers to the leaves.

See also **Flower** (picture: Flowers of Alpine tundras).

Forging is a process in which metal is shaped by being heated and then hammered or pressed. Almost any metal can be forged. The most commonly forged metals include steel and aluminum, and alloys of nickel and titanium. *Forgings* (objects made by forging) range in size from small hand tools to huge engine shafts weighing hundreds of tons. They include such products as wrenches, crankshafts, axles, and supports for aircraft landing gear.

Metals are composed of crystals. The hammering or pressing of metal bends the crystals and makes their structure less stable. But the heat used in forging enables new crystals to form in place of the deformed ones. In most cases, this process, called *recrystallization,* toughens the metal. For this reason, manufacturers forge many metal products that must withstand great stress.

Metal can be forged either by hand, using a handheld hammer, or by machine. Hand forging, which is probably the oldest method of shaping metal, has been practiced since prehistoric times. Today, however, nearly all forging is done by machine.

Hand forging is used primarily for small forgings and in repair work. It is practiced by blacksmiths, who forge horseshoes and other small iron objects. Blacksmiths first heat iron in a *forge* (open furnace) until it becomes red-hot. Then they remove the iron with tongs and hammer it into shape while holding it against an anvil.

Machine forging enables forgings to be mass-produced. Forging machines vary greatly in size and can handle objects that are far too heavy to forge by hand. Large cranes must be used to turn some of the heaviest forgings on the anvils.

There are two kinds of forging machines, *forging hammers* and *forging presses.* Both use hollow tools called *dies* to help shape metal. The metal is forced into the die and takes the shape of the die's cavity.

Forging hammers shape metal by striking it repeatedly in rapid succession. The power to raise the hammer is provided by steam, hydraulic energy, or electric energy. In some forging hammers, the power also lowers the hammer. In other machines, called *drop hammers,* the hammer falls of its own weight. Forging hammers are used to shape most small forgings.

Forging presses squeeze metal into shape. Pressing is

A blacksmith forges small iron objects by hand. Blacksmiths heat a piece of iron to a red glow in a *forge* (open furnace) before they shape it using a handheld hammer.

A huge steel forging emerges from a forging press at a steel mill. Forging presses squeeze red-hot metal into a desired shape by forcing it into a die.

a much slower process than hammering, but only a press can provide the force necessary to make the most massive forgings. Pressing also causes less shock to the machine and the building that houses it than hammering does. Most forging presses are powered by hydraulic energy.

Dies that help shape forgings may be paired or single. Paired dies are used to make tools, engine parts, and other forgings that have complex shapes. The upper die is attached to the hammer or the moving part of the press, and the lower die to the anvil. Items produced by paired dies are called *closed die forgings* or, if a drop hammer is used, *drop forgings.*   Thomas J. Misa

See also **Die and diemaking; Machine tool; Steam hammer.**

Formaldehyde is probably most familiar as the active ingredient in the solution used to preserve insects and other biological specimens. This solution, called *formalin,* is a water solution containing 35 to 40 percent formaldehyde by weight. Formaldehyde itself is a colorless gas which is the simplest member of the class of organic chemicals called *aldehydes.*

Formaldehyde was discovered in 1867 by August Wilhelm von Hofmann, a German chemist. It is made commercially by the oxidation of methanol (methyl alcohol). Formaldehyde is used for disinfecting, for embalming, and for preserving grains and vegetables. It is also used in the manufacture of *pharmaceuticals* (medicinal drugs), urea resins, and dyes. The plastics industry prepares Bakelite from formaldehyde and phenol.

Formaldehyde has a stifling odor and can irritate membranes of the eyes, nose, and throat. In addition, laboratory tests have shown that formaldehyde probably causes cancer. The chemical formula of formaldehyde is CH_2O. It boils at −21 °C.   Robert C. Gadwood

See also **Methanol.**

Formalin. See Formaldehyde.

Formic acid is an important industrial chemical. It is used as a preservative and antibacterial additive in animal feed. It is also used in the manufacture of dyes, rubber, leather items, and many other products.

Formic acid has the chemical formula CH_2O_2. In its pure form, the acid is a strong-smelling, colorless liquid. It is highly corrosive and can cause severe burns if it comes in contact with a person's skin.

Formic acid gets its name from *Formica rufa,* the scientific name for a species of red ants. The acid was originally obtained by the destruction and distillation of these ants. Today, formic acid is produced in a number of industrial processes. Formic acid mixes completely with water. It boils at 100.5 °C.

Marianna A. Busch

Formosa. See Taiwan.

Formula. See Baby (Feeding procedures); in science, see Algebra (Writing formulas); **Chemistry.**

Formula One racing. See Automobile racing (Formula One racing).

Forrest, Edwin (1806-1872), was probably the first important actor in the history of American theater. Forrest was the most popular actor of his time. He dominated the American stage from the mid-1820's until his death.

Forrest's style reflected the romantic school of acting, which was vigorous, passionate, and seemingly unrestrained. Forrest's muscular physique made him an im-

pressive figure on stage. Although some people considered his acting coarse and excessively emotional, Forrest was a disciplined, conscientious performer. He earned his early reputation in such plays by William Shakespeare as *King Lear, Othello,* and *Richard III.* But he also encouraged native drama in the United States by offering prizes for new plays written by Americans. Forrest was born in Philadelphia on March 9, 1806. He died on Dec. 12, 1872.   Stanley L. Glenn

Culver Pictures
Edwin Forrest

Forrest, Nathan Bedford (1821-1877), was a Confederate general in the American Civil War. He was a brilliant cavalry leader. He enlisted as a private in the Confederate Army in June 1861 and became a lieutenant colonel in command of a battalion of cavalry by October. Forrest had no military education. However, he achieved amazing success as a strategist and tactician. When asked the secret of his military victories, Forrest is said to have replied, "To get there first with the most men."

Forrest escaped with his troops from the Battle of Fort Donelson and fought at Shiloh in 1862 (see **Civil War, American** [Raids]). Forrest then developed raiding tactics that made his cavalry a fearsome striking force. At Brice's Cross Roads, Mississippi, in June 1864, Forrest won a battle that was a model for cavalry warfare.

Forrest became a lieutenant general in February 1865. He was beaten by the Union Army at Selma, Alabama, in April 1865. After the war, Forrest served as the first leader of the Ku Klux Klan, a white-supremacist organization that attempted to deny blacks their civil rights. Forrest was born in Bedford County, Tennessee, on July 13, 1821. He died on Oct. 29, 1877.   Steven E. Woodworth

Forrestal, *FAWR ihst uhl,* **James Vincent** (1892-1949), was the first United States secretary of defense. He served from September 1947 until March 1949. He also served as secretary of the Navy from 1944 to 1947 and helped build the U.S. fleet into the largest in the world. In 1954, the Navy named a class of aircraft carriers the *Forrestal* in his honor.

When Congress passed the National Security Act in 1947 to unify the armed forces, it created a civilian secretary of defense. President Harry S. Truman appointed Forrestal to the post. Forrestal resigned in 1949 due to mental and physical exhaustion. The strain of his job was blamed by many for his suicide two months later.

Forrestal was born in Beacon, New York, on Feb. 15, 1892. In World War I (1914-1918), he was a naval aviator and then turned to a financial career in New York City. Forrestal died on May 22, 1949.

Alonzo L. Hamby

Forster, E. M. (1879-1970), was an English novelist, essayist, and literary critic. His novels show his interest in personal relationships and in the social, psychological, and racial obstacles to such relationships. His fiction stresses the value of following generous impulses.

Forster's most highly praised novels are *Howards End* (1910) and *A Passage to India* (1924). *Howards End* is a social comedy with tragic overtones about several English middle-class characters. It reflects Forster's ideal of an "aristocracy of the sensitive, the considerate, and the plucky." *A Passage to India* describes the clash between English and traditional Indian cultures in India. Forster's other four novels are *Where Angels Fear to Tread* (1905), *The Longest Journey* (1907), *A Room with a View* (1908), and *Maurice* (completed in 1914, published in 1971, after the author's death).

For the last 46 years of his life, Forster produced only nonfiction. But he wrote his essays, biographies, and literary criticism in a masterly style with the grace, polish, and elegant wit that characterized his novels. Edward Morgan Forster was born on Jan. 1, 1879, in London. He died on June 7, 1970.   Garrett Stewart

See also **Bloomsbury Group**.

Forsythia, *fawr SIHTH ee uh,* is a group of shrubs that produce abundant yellow flowers. They grow as high as 9 feet (2.7 meters) and have spreading, arched branches. People sometimes call forsythias *golden bells* because they have yellow flowers that look like tiny golden bells. One to six flowers grow in clusters. Forsythias produce many blossoms, which open in early spring before the leaves appear. The leaves grow 3 to 5 inches (8 to 13

W. Atlee Burpee Co.

Forsythias are hardy, spreading shrubs. They bloom in early spring and have tiny, bell-shaped yellow flowers.

centimeters) long and are egg-shaped. They usually have jagged edges. Forsythias grow well in any garden soil and can withstand cold temperatures. Forsythias are named for the British botanist William Forsyth.

Fred T. Davies, Jr.

Scientific classification. Forsythias make up the genus *Forsythia.* Two types are *Forsythia suspensa* and *F. viridissima.*

See also **Flower** (picture: Garden perennials).

Fort originally was a fortified building or place that provided defense against attack. On the American frontier, many forts also served as trading posts. Many cities that grew up around forts bear their names, including Fort Wayne, Indiana. The term *fort* now applies to permanent United States Army posts. For information on various forts, see the articles and cross-references on forts following this article. See also **Castle**.   Hugh M. Cole

Fort Belvoir, *BEHL vawr,* Virginia, is the site of numerous administrative, research, academic, and logistical

Department of Defense and Army agencies. Fort Belvoir also houses National Guard and Army reserve units. The fort covers about 8,700 acres (3,500 hectares) along the Potomac River 18 miles (29 kilometers) south of Washington, D.C. The Army's Engineer School began using the site for training exercises in 1915. Camp construction began in 1918. Fort Belvoir was named for Belvoir, the home of Colonel George William Fairfax, a friend and neighbor of George Washington. The fort once housed the United States Army Engineer Center and the Army Materiel Command.   Erik B. Villard

Fort Benning, Georgia, is the site of the United States Army Maneuver Center of Excellence. The Maneuver Center includes the Army Infantry School and the Army Armor School. Also at Fort Benning is the Western Hemisphere Institute for Security Cooperation. The post covers 182,000 acres (73,650 hectares). It lies 9 miles (14 kilometers) south of Columbus on the Chattahoochee River. The Army established Camp Benning in 1918. The facility was named for Brigadier General Henry L. Benning, who served in the Confederate Army in the American Civil War (1861-1865).   Erik B. Villard

Bill C. Walton, U.S. Army

Paratroop trainees practice parachute jumping at Fort Benning, the chief training center for U.S. airborne troops.

Fort Bliss, Texas, is a major post of the United States Army. Since the 1940's, Fort Bliss has served as a center for air defense training. The post's training areas, missile firing ranges, and facilities cover about 1,100,000 acres (445,000 hectares) in Texas and New Mexico. The base was founded in 1848 as an infantry post. In 1854, it was named Fort Bliss for Lieutenant Colonel William W. S. Bliss, an aide to the future U.S. President Zachary Taylor during the Mexican War (1846-1848).   Erik B. Villard

Fort Bragg, North Carolina, is the headquarters of the United States Army Forces Command. This command supervises the combat readiness of the Army's active and reserve forces. Fort Bragg serves as the home of the

Army's Special Operations Command, which oversees Special Forces, Rangers, and other units. The fort also houses airborne combat units of the Army, and the John F. Kennedy Special Warfare Center and School, which trains troops in psychological and guerrilla warfare. The post lies 9 miles (14 kilometers) northwest of Fayetteville, and it occupies about 161,000 acres (65,000 hectares).

Fort Bragg was founded in 1918, and named for Braxton Bragg, a Confederate Army general in the American Civil War (1861-1865). The U.S. Army trained its first two airborne divisions, the 82nd and the 101st, at Fort Bragg during World War II (1939-1945). After the war, the post became the headquarters of the 82nd Airborne Division and the XVIII Airborne Corps. Erik B. Villard

Fort Dearborn, a famous American fort, was built near the mouth of the Chicago River, close to Chicago's present Michigan Avenue Bridge (officially DuSable Bridge). Soldiers led by Captain John Whistler built the fort in 1803. It was named for General Henry Dearborn. The double stockade had blockhouses on two corners, log barracks, stables, and an American Indian agency.

A garrison of soldiers at Fort Dearborn protected the few Americans on the frontier from attacks by Indians. Soon after the beginning of the War of 1812 (1812-1815), the troops and settlers were ordered to move to Fort Wayne for greater safety. The soldiers feared Indian attacks on the way and urged Captain Nathan Heald to stay within the stockade. The captain insisted on obeying orders. He destroyed all of the ammunition that could not be carried and left the post with about 100 troops and settlers on Aug. 15, 1812.

That day, a force of 500 Potawatomi and allied Indians attacked the Americans near the fort (at the eastern end of Chicago's present 18th Street). They killed more than half of the Americans, captured the rest, and burned the fort the next day. Fort Dearborn was rebuilt about 1816

and torn down in 1836. By then, the danger of Indian attack in the area had passed. Richard D. Brown

See also **Dearborn, Henry.**

Fort-de-France, *FAWR duh FRAHNS* (pop. 90,347), is the capital of Martinique, an island in the Caribbean region. Martinique is an overseas *region* and an overseas *department* of France. French regions are administrative divisions that resemble states in the United States, and each region has one or more departments. Fort-de-France lies on the west coast of Martinique (see **West Indies** [map]). Fort-de-France has palm-lined streets and colorful buildings. La Savane, a large waterfront park, lies along the Baie des Flamands, which is south of the city. Fort-de-France is a shipping center for sugar, rum, fruit, and other products of Martinique. The city attracts many tourists. Fort Saint-Louis, a French naval base that dates back to the 1600's, is there. Fort-de-France was founded in 1675. It was called Fort Royal until the late 1700's, when it received its present name. The city has been the capital of Martinique since 1692. The city was partly destroyed by an earthquake in 1839 and by a fire in 1890. See also **Martinique.** Gustavo A. Antonini

Fort Donelson. See Civil War, American (Battles of Fort Henry and Fort Donelson).

Fort Duquesne, *doo KAYN,* was built by the French in 1754 at the headwaters of the Ohio River near what is now Pittsburgh. French forces had driven Virginian fur traders from this site. The French named the fort after the Marquis Michel-Ange Duquesne, governor general of Canada. The Battle of the Great Meadows, in which Lieutenant Colonel George Washington and a band of Virginia militia defeated a small band of French troops, took place near the fort in 1754. This battle marked the beginning of the French and Indian War (1754-1763).

In 1755, the French ambushed and defeated British and colonial American troops under General Edward

Chicago Park District

A replica of Fort Dearborn was built in 1933 for Chicago's Century of Progress Exposition and later dismantled. It contained articles used by settlers at the time the original fort was built.

Braddock near Fort Duquesne. Three years later, the French burned the fort and fled northward when they learned that a superior British force under General John Forbes was approaching.   Edward K. Muller

See also **French and Indian wars.**

Fort Eustis, *YOO stihs,* Virginia, is the headquarters of the United States Army Training and Doctrine Command. This command controls all Army individual schooling and training and manages the Army Reserve Officers Training Corps (ROTC) program. It covers about 8,300 acres (3,360 hectares) and lies 11 miles (18 kilometers) south of Williamsburg. Fort Eustis has the nation's only all-military-operated railway system. The post was set up as a Coast Artillery training area in 1918 and named for Brigadier General Abraham Eustis, an artillery officer of the early 1800's. In 2011, the Army Training and Doctrine Command headquarters moved from Fort Monroe, Virginia, to Fort Eustis.

Erik B. Villard

Fort Frederica National Monument, *frehd uh REE kuh,* is on Saint Simons Island in Georgia. The monument contains the ruins of a town built in the 1700's. James Edward Oglethorpe, founder of the colony of Georgia, had the fort built as a defense against the Spaniards. For the fort's area, see **National Park System** (table: National monuments).

Critically reviewed by the National Park Service

Fort George G. Meade, Maryland, is a United States Army base. It houses the headquarters of the National Security Agency/Central Security Service and the U.S. Cyber Command. The fort covers about 5,400 acres (2,200 hectares) and lies about 15 miles (24 kilometers) northeast of Washington, D.C.

The post was established in 1917 to house troops drafted during World War I (1914-1918). It was originally named Camp Meade for Major General George Gordon Meade, a Union Army commander during the American Civil War (1861-1865). In 1928, the post was renamed Fort Leonard Wood. The Army gave the post its current name in 1929.   Erik B. Villard

Fort Gordon, Georgia, is the home of the United States Army Signal Center and the Dwight D. Eisenhower Army Medical Center. It lies 15 miles (24 kilometers) southwest of Augusta and covers about 56,000 acres (23,000 hectares). It was founded in 1941 as an infantry training center and named for Lieutenant General John B. Gordon, a Confederate Army officer and former governor of Georgia. The Signal Corps Training Center was established at the post in 1948.   Erik B. Villard

Fort Henry, Battle of. See Civil War, American (Battles of Fort Henry and Fort Donelson).

Fort Hood, Texas, is a large active-duty United States military post. It houses tens of thousands of military personnel and their family members, as well as civilian support staff. Fort Hood lies 2 miles (3 kilometers) west of Killeen, and covers about 214,000 acres (87,000 hectares). The post was founded in 1942 as Camp Hood and named for John B. Hood, a Confederate Army general who commanded the Texas Brigade. It became a permanent fort in 1950. North Fort Hood lies 17 miles (27 kilometers) to the north.

In 2009, Fort Hood was the site of a mass shooting. The gunman, an Army psychiatrist stationed at the fort, shot dozens of people, killing 13.   Erik B. Villard

Karl Kummels, Shostal

The gold depository at Fort Knox stores gold reserves owned by the United States government.

Fort Knox, Kentucky, is the home of the United States Army Human Resource Center of Excellence and Army Accessions Command. It covers 110,000 acres (44,500 hectares) and lies 35 miles (56 kilometers) south of Louisville. Members of the U.S. Army and Marine Corps train at Fort Knox to serve in armored units. The post's General George Patton Museum holds displays of military equipment, vehicles, and artifacts. In addition, the U.S. Mint operates a depository at Fort Knox for storage of gold reserves.

The United States government took over part of the present post for Army maneuvers in 1918. Camp Knox was established that same year and named for Major General Henry Knox, the first U.S. secretary of war. Its name became Fort Knox in 1932. The Treasury Department completed the gold depository in 1936. Fort Knox has been called "the Home of Armor," because the Army created its first armored force there in 1940. In 2011, the Army Armor Center and School moved from Fort Knox to Fort Benning in Georgia.   Critically reviewed by Fort Knox

Fort-Lamy. See N'Djamena.

Fort Lauderdale, *LAW duhr DAYL* (pop. 165,521), is a major resort city in Florida. It lies on the Atlantic Ocean in the southeastern part of the state, approximately 25 miles (40 kilometers) north of Miami. For the location, see **Florida** (political map). Fort Lauderdale's location and warm climate have made it a leading vacation and retirement center.

During the 1800's, Seminole Indians lived in what is now Fort Lauderdale. White settlers, most of whom farmed and fished for a living, first arrived in the area in the 1890's. They named their settlement after a fort that Major William Lauderdale had built there in 1838, during the Second Seminole War (1835-1842).

Description. Fort Lauderdale, the county seat of Broward County, covers about 32 square miles (83 square kilometers). This area includes 3 square miles (8 square kilometers) of inland water. Fort Lauderdale has about 85 miles (137 kilometers) of navigable canals and waterways. The city also has about 6 miles (10 kilometers) of ocean beaches, where people can go boating, fishing, and swimming.

Fort Lauderdale is part of the Miami-Fort Lauderdale-Pompano Beach metropolitan area. This area has a population of 5,564,635 and consists of Broward, Miami-Dade, and Palm Beach counties. Fort Lauderdale is also part of the Fort Lauderdale-Pompano Beach-Deerfield Beach metropolitan division, which covers Broward County and has 1,748,066 people.

Cultural attractions in the city include the Broward Center for the Performing Arts, the Museum of Art, and the Parker Playhouse. In addition, Fort Lauderdale has a ballet company. Nova Southeastern University and a few campuses of Florida Atlantic University are in or near the city.

Marine commerce and tourism are important industries in the city. Port Everglades, at the south end of Fort Lauderdale, serves as a major port for cargo ships and passenger cruisers. Major airlines use Fort Lauderdale-Hollywood International Airport.

Government and history. Fort Lauderdale has a commission-manager form of government. The voters in the city elect a mayor and four commissioners to a three-year term. The commissioners hire a city manager to serve as the chief administrator of Fort Lauderdale's local government.

The city had a population of only about 150 when it was incorporated in 1911. After World War II ended in 1945, a tourist boom resulted in a rapid population growth. Fort Lauderdale received national attention during the 1960's, when thousands of college students began to spend their spring vacation there.

During the last half of the 1900's, Fort Lauderdale's continued population growth made it one of the fastest-growing cities in the United States. The city's population rose from about 18,000 in 1940 to about 150,000 in 1990.

Fort Lauderdale's population growth slowed during the 1990's and the first decade of the 2000's. But the population of the metropolitan area increased greatly.

In 1990, a gigantic outlet shopping mall called Sawgrass Mills opened in Sunrise, west of Fort Lauderdale. By 2000, Sawgrass Mills was attracting more than 25 million visitors a year. In 2001, Sawgrass Mills completed the addition of a large entertainment complex.

Peter O. Muller

Fort Leavenworth, *LEHV uhn wurth,* Kansas, is the home of the United States Army Combined Arms Center. It also houses the Army Command and General Staff College, the Army's senior tactical school. The fort covers about 5,600 acres (2,300 hectares) on the Missouri River, about 30 miles (50 kilometers) northwest of Kansas City. The Army operates a military prison there, the U.S. Disciplinary Barracks. The fort was named for Brigadier General Henry Leavenworth, who founded it in 1827.

Erik B. Villard

See also **Kansas** (Places to visit).

Fort Lee, Virginia, is the home of the United States Army Combined Arms Support Command, the Army Quartermaster Center and School, the Army Logistics University, the Defense Commissary Agency, and the Army Transportation Corps and School. It lies 3 miles (5 kilometers) east of Petersburg and covers about 5,600 acres (2,300 hectares). The post was founded in 1917 and named for Confederate General Robert E. Lee. After

World War I (1914-1918), it served as a wildlife sanctuary until it reopened during World War II (1939-1945). It became a permanent fort in 1950.   Erik B. Villard

Fort Leonard Wood, Missouri, is the home of the United States Army's Engineer School; its Military Police School; and its Chemical, Biological, Radiological, and Nuclear School. The fort covers about 63,000 acres (25,500 hectares) and is in the Mark Twain National Forest, 135 miles (215 kilometers) southwest of St. Louis (see **Missouri** [political map]). The post was established in 1940 and named for Major General Leonard Wood, who was Army chief of staff from 1910 to 1914. Fort Leonard Wood provides basic and advanced training for Army recruits in the midwestern United States.   Erik B. Villard

See also **Wood, Leonard.**

Fort Marion National Monument. See Castillo de San Marcos National Monument.

Fort Matanzas National Monument, *muh TAN zuhs,* is near St. Augustine, Florida. The Spanish built the fort in the early 1740's. It served as a defense for St. Augustine against British colonizers. St. Augustine is the oldest permanent settlement established in the United States by Europeans. Fort Matanzas National Monument was established in 1924. For area, see **National Park System** (table: National monuments).

Critically reviewed by the National Park Service

Fort McHenry National Monument and Historic Shrine is in Baltimore. Francis Scott Key composed "The Star-Spangled Banner" as he watched a battle at the fort during the War of 1812 (1812-1815). The fort was named for James McHenry, a signer of the Constitution of the United States from Maryland. The fort became a national park in 1925 and was designated a national monument in 1939. For area, see **National Park System** (table: National monuments).

Critically reviewed by the National Park Service

See also **Maryland** (picture: The Fort McHenry National Monument).

Fort McPherson, *muhk FUHR suhn,* Georgia, served as the headquarters of the United States Army Forces Command. This command supervises the combat readiness of all the Army's active and reserve forces. The fort covered about 480 acres (190 hectares) within the city limits of Atlanta. The Army made it a post in 1889 and named it in honor of Major General James B. McPherson, a Union Army commander killed in the American Civil War (1861-1865). Fort McPherson closed in 2011. The headquarters of the United States Army Forces Command then moved to Fort Bragg, North Carolina.

Erik B. Villard

Fort Monmouth, *MAHN muhth,* New Jersey, was the headquarters of the United States Army Communications-Electronics Command. It also housed the U.S. Military Academy Preparatory School and electronics research and development laboratories. The fort stood about 40 miles (65 kilometers) south of New York City. The post was established in 1917. It received the name of Fort Monmouth in 1925 to honor the soldiers who fought on the fields of Monmouth during the American Revolution (1775-1783). Fort Monmouth closed in 2011. The U.S. Military Academy Preparatory School moved to West Point, New York. Most of the communications and electronics activities at Fort Monmouth moved to Aberdeen Proving Ground in Maryland.   Erik B. Villard

Fort Monroe National Monument is in Hampton, Virginia. Fort Monroe served as a United States Army post from about 1820 to 2011. The historic fort stands on Old Point Comfort at the mouth of the James River, about 11 miles (18 kilometers) north of Norfolk. It overlooks the entrance to Hampton Roads, a channel that empties into Chesapeake Bay.

Engineers began building a fort there in 1819, although the site had been fortified as early as 1609. In 1832, the post was named Fort Monroe, in honor of President James Monroe. The American poet Edgar Allan Poe served at Fort Monroe before he entered West Point. Robert E. Lee supervised construction of the walled fort in the early 1830's. Jefferson Davis, president of the Confederacy, was imprisoned at Fort Monroe for two years after the American Civil War ended in 1865. In the late 1900's, the fort became the home of a command that trained soldiers and developed weapons systems. The original fort is still surrounded by a moat. After Fort Monroe closed in 2011, President Barack Obama declared the site a national monument. For the area of Fort Monroe National Monument, see **National Park System** (table: National monuments).   Erik B. Villard

Fort Moultrie, *MOOL tree* or *MOHL tree,* is an American fort on Sullivan's Island at the main entrance to Charleston Harbor, South Carolina. Settlers first called it Fort Sullivan. In 1776, during the American Revolution, the fort withstood a British attack designed to capture Charleston and make it a base of British operations in the South. The American forces at Charleston were commanded by Colonel William Moultrie, for whom the fort was renamed. This defense saved the South temporarily from invasion. Later in the war, British troops under General Sir Henry Clinton attacked again, and Fort Moultrie fell on May 7, 1780.

Just before the American Civil War began in 1861, a United States garrison occupied Fort Moultrie. It was abandoned by its commander, Major Robert Anderson, who moved his troops to Fort Sumter on Dec. 26, 1860. During the bombardment of Sumter the following April, Fort Moultrie served as Confederate headquarters.

The American author Edgar Allan Poe was once a sergeant major at Fort Moultrie. The Seminole Indian leader Osceola, who was imprisoned in the fort during the Second Seminole War (1835-1842), is buried there. Fort Moultrie is now part of the Fort Sumter National Monument.   Robert A. Becker

See also **Fort Sumter; Moultrie, William.**

Fort Necessity was a small, circular log stockade built by George Washington in 1754 in southwestern Pennsylvania. Washington surrendered it to the French in 1754. The French allowed his army to march out of the fort and return home. The site became a national battlefield site in 1931 and a national battlefield in 1961. For area, see **National Park System** (table: National battlefields). See also **Washington, George** (Surrender of Fort Necessity).   Fred W. Anderson

Fort Niagara was built by the French in 1726 on land bought from the Seneca Indians. It stood on the eastern shore of the Niagara River and guarded a narrow passage that led to the rich fur lands west of the river. British forces captured the fort in 1759 during the French and Indian War (1754-1763). They used it during the American Revolution (1775-1783) as a starting point for

raids against western settlers. Fort Niagara remained in British hands until 1796, when the Jay Treaty finally gave it to the United States. The British captured the fort again during the War of 1812 (1812-1815). It remained in British hands until 1815.

Fort Little Niagara was the name of another fort in the same region. The French built this fort in 1751, and destroyed it during the French and Indian War to prevent the British from taking it.   Richard D. Brown

Fort Peck Dam, on the Missouri River in northeastern Montana, is one of the largest earth-fill dams in the world. It contains about 125,600,000 cubic yards (96,100,000 cubic meters) of earth. Fort Peck Dam was completed in 1940. It stretches for nearly 4 miles (6 kilometers) across the Missouri. The main section is 10,578 feet (3,224 meters) long, and a dike section on the west riverbank is 10,448 feet (3,185 meters) long. The dam is 250 feet (76 meters) high. Its reservoir, Fort Peck Lake, holds 15.4 million acre-feet (19 billion cubic meters) of water. See also **Dam** (picture).   Edward C. Pritchett

Fort Pickens was a United States military post on Santa Rosa Island near Pensacola, Florida. It remained under federal control throughout the American Civil War (1861-1865). After Florida *seceded* (withdrew) from the Union in January 1861, Lieutenant Adam J. Slemmer moved a small body of federal soldiers into Fort Pickens. Union and Confederate authorities agreed that the Union would not reinforce the fort, and that the Confederate States would not attack it. But after Confederate forces fired on Fort Sumter, South Carolina, on April 12, 1861, and the war began, the Union rushed reinforcements to Fort Pickens. The fort's defenders withstood a surprise attack on Oct. 9, 1861.   James M. McPherson

Fort Pulaski National Monument, *puh LAS kee* or *pyoo LAS kee,* is on the coast of Georgia. It includes a brick fort which Union forces captured in 1862. The fort could not withstand the Union Army's cannon attack. The monument was established in 1924. For the area of Fort Pulaski National Monument, see **National Park System** (table: National monuments).
      Critically reviewed by the National Park Service

Fort Randall Dam is part of a large-scale federal program for the development of the Missouri River basin. The dam lies in south-central South Dakota near Lake Andes above old Fort Randall. United States Army engineers began building this electric-power and navigation project in 1946. They completed it in 1956. The dam is 165 feet (50 meters) high and 10,700 feet (3,260 meters) long. The earth-fill dam contains 50 million cubic yards (38 million cubic meters) of earth. Its reservoir, Lake Francis Case, holds 3.8 million acre-feet (4.7 billion cubic meters) of water. The power plant has a capacity of 320,000 kilowatts and began operating in 1954.
      Edward C. Pritchett

Fort Riley, Kansas, is the home of the United States Army's First Infantry Division. It lies about 100 miles (160 kilometers) west of Kansas City and covers about 100,000 acres (40,000 hectares). The Army set up the post in 1853 and later named it for Major General Bennett C. Riley, who fought in the Mexican War (1846-1848). Fort Riley is known as "the cradle of the cavalry" because many cavalry regiments were organized there, including Lieutenant Colonel George A. Custer's Seventh Cavalry. See also **Kansas** (Places to visit).   Erik B. Villard

Fort Rucker, Alabama, houses the United States Army Aviation Center of Excellence. The center trains pilots and maintenance workers for the Army's own air force of small fixed-wing airplanes and helicopters. Also at the post are the Army Combat Readiness/Safety Center, the Army Aviation Technical Test Center, and the Army Aeromedical Center. The post lies about 20 miles (32 kilometers) northwest of Dothan and covers about 64,000 acres (26,000 hectares). It was set up in 1942 and named for Colonel Edmund W. Rucker, a Confederate Army cavalry leader.   Erik B. Villard

Fort Sam Houston, Texas, houses the headquarters of United States Army North, also called the Fifth U.S. Army; U.S. Army South; and the U.S. Army Medical Command. The fort covers 3,160 acres (1,280 hectares) in San Antonio and about 28,000 acres (11,300 hectares) at Camp Bullis, 20 miles (32 kilometers) northwest of the city. The post was established in 1876 as the Military Post of San Antonio. In 1890, its name was changed to honor Sam Houston, the first president of the Republic of Texas. In 2010, Fort Sam Houston—along with Lackland Air Force Base and Randolph Air Force Base—became part of Joint Base San Antonio.   Erik B. Villard

Fort Shafter, Hawaii, serves as the headquarters of United States Army, Pacific. It covers 589 acres (238 hectares) north of Honolulu's main urban area. The post was set up as Kahauiki Military Reservation in 1899. In 1907, it was named for Major General William R. Shafter, who fought in the American Civil War (1861-1865) and the Spanish-American War (1898).   Erik B. Villard

Fort Sill, Oklahoma, is the site of the United States Army Field Artillery Center and School. The post covers 94,220 acres (38,000 hectares) near Lawton. The Army established the post in 1869 to keep watch over the Comanche and Kiowa tribes. The post was named after Brigadier General Joshua W. Sill, a Union commander killed at the Battle of Stones River during the American Civil War (1861-1865). The grave of the Apache leader Geronimo is at Fort Sill.   Erik B. Villard

Fort Smith (pop. 86,209; met. area pop. 298,592) is a manufacturing and transportation center in western Arkansas and the state's second largest city. Only Little Rock has more people. Fort Smith lies at the foot of the Boston Mountains (see **Arkansas** [political map]). Part of its metropolitan area lies in Oklahoma. The Fort Smith area includes coal and natural gas deposits. National forests lie to the city's north, southwest, and south. Fort Smith factories produce foods, furniture, heating and air-conditioning units, home refrigerators, and steel.

Downtown Fort Smith has a national historic site that includes the courtroom of the famous frontier "hanging judge," Isaac C. Parker. The area also includes a historical museum, a trolley-railway museum, an art center-community theater complex, and a civic center.

Fort Smith began as a fort that was established by the United States Army in 1817 to keep peace between the Osage and Cherokee Indians. The fort was named for General Thomas A. Smith, commander of the military district in which the fort stood. Fort Smith grew into a town, which was incorporated in 1842. It was incorporated as a city in 1885. The discovery of natural gas near the city in about 1900 gave the growing Fort Smith industries a cheap source of power. In 1969, a federal navigation project on the Arkansas River made it possible for barges to reach Fort Smith from New Orleans. Fort Smith became an important river port.   Jerome J. Huff, Jr.

See also **Arkansas** (Interesting facts about Arkansas).

Fort Stanwix National Monument, in Rome, New York, was authorized in 1935 as a memorial to United States colonial history. In 1758, during the French and Indian War (1754-1763), British and American colonial troops built the fort along an important transportation route in New York's Mohawk Valley. The fort was abandoned after the war. In 1776, at the urging of the allied Oneida Indians, the Americans claimed and repaired the fort. In August 1777, the fort's defenders held off a 21-day siege by British-led forces. For area, see **National Park System** (table: National monuments).

Fort Sumter was the site of the first shot fired in the American Civil War (1861-1865). On April 12, 1861, Confederate forces fired on the fort, which stood on an island in the harbor of Charleston, South Carolina. The following day, after heavy bombardment, United States troops under Major Robert Anderson surrendered to Confederate forces led by General Pierre G. T. Beauregard. On April 14, the U.S. troops withdrew from the fort. Not a single person was killed in the battle.

Fort Sumter had been a symbol of federal authority for the North and the South since December 1860, when South Carolina became the first state to *secede* (withdraw) from the Union. After South Carolina's secession, the two sides turned their guns toward each other. The crisis reached its peak when President Abraham Lincoln ordered that supplies be sent to the fort. The Confederacy fired on the fort rather than allow it to be resupplied. The Union sought to retake the fort several times but did not succeed until February 1865.   Gabor S. Boritt

See also **Civil War, American** (Secession; picture); **Ruffin, Edmund; South Carolina** (picture).

Fort Sumter National Monument lies in Charleston Harbor, South Carolina. It was authorized in 1948 as a Civil War memorial. For area, see **National Park System** (table: National monuments). See also **Fort Sumter.**

Fort Supply Dam is a federal flood-control project in northwestern Oklahoma. It is on Wolf Creek near its junction with the North Canadian River. The dam is an earth-fill dam 11,865 feet (3,616 meters) long and 85 feet (26 meters) high. It was finished in 1942. The reservoir holds about 13,900 acre-feet (17 million cubic meters) of water. It has a maximum capacity of about 100,700 acre-feet (124 million cubic meters).   Edward C. Pritchett

Fort Ticonderoga, on the western shore of Lake Champlain in New York state, was a stronghold during the American Revolution (1775-1783). It controlled an invasion route from Canada to the American Colonies. The fort was originally a British post. After the war began, a group of Americans organized an attempt to seize the fort. The group included Ethan Allen, leader of a group of Vermont soldiers called the Green Mountain Boys. On May 10, 1775, Allen and Colonel Benedict Arnold led a force of 83 men in an attack on Fort Ticonderoga. They surprised the unprepared British troops and seized the fort without firing a shot. The British recaptured the fort in 1777 but abandoned it in 1780. In 1908, the fort was rebuilt, and a museum opened there.   Richard D. Brown

Fort Union National Monument is near Watrous, New Mexico. The fort was built in 1851 as a defensive point on the Santa Fe Trail. The monument was authorized in 1954 and established in 1956. For area, see **National Park System** (table: National monuments).

Critically reviewed by the National Park Service

Fort Wayne (pop. 253,691; met. area pop. 416,257) is a commercial and industrial center in northeastern Indiana. It is the state's second largest city. Only Indianapolis has more people. Fort Wayne lies about 130 miles (209 kilometers) northeast of Indianapolis. For location, see **Indiana** (political map). Fort Wayne, the county seat of Allen County, covers about 110 square miles (285 square kilometers). The St. Marys and St. Joseph rivers join within the city to form the Maumee River.

Cultural attractions in Fort Wayne include the Fort Wayne Philharmonic. The Arts United Center is home to the Fort Wayne Ballet, the Civic Theatre, the Fort Wayne Youtheatre, and other performing arts groups. Museums include the History Center of the Allen County-Fort Wayne Historical Society, the Fort Wayne Museum of Art, and the Jack D. Diehm Museum of Natural History.

A campus of Indiana University-Purdue University is in Fort Wayne. Other institutions of higher education include the Indiana Institute of Technology, the University of St. Francis, and a campus of Taylor University. Fort Wayne's biggest tourist attraction, the Three Rivers Festival, is held in July. The festival includes a parade, historical displays, and other events.

The area has hundreds of manufacturing plants. The chief products include electronic parts and equipment, machinery, trucks, and transportation equipment. Major airlines and freight trains serve the city.

The Miami Indians settled in what is now the Fort Wayne area before white settlers arrived. A United States Army officer, Major General "Mad Anthony" Wayne, built a fort there in 1794. The fort and the town that grew up around it were named in his honor. Fort Wayne was incorporated as a city in 1840.

Fort Wayne was a fur-trading center until the 1830's. In 1832, construction began at Fort Wayne on the Wabash

Fort Ticonderoga, a military stronghold on Lake Champlain during the American Revolution, has been rebuilt as a museum.

and Erie Canal, which linked Lake Erie with the Wabash River. Fort Wayne was nicknamed *The Summit City* because it stands on the highest point between the waterways leading to the Atlantic Ocean and those leading to the Gulf of Mexico. The city's population grew as Irish and German immigrants came to work on the canal and in related industries. A railroad built through the city in 1854 helped attract industry. By 1900, the population had grown to more than 45,000.

In the 1990's, new developments in the downtown area included Headwaters Park, a public park and festival center, and Courthouse Green, a plaza east of the Allen County Courthouse that provides a pedestrian link to the downtown commercial buildings. Annexations in the early 2000's contributed to population growth. Fort Wayne has a mayor-council form of government.

Carolyn M. DiPaolo

See also **Indiana** (picture: Historic Fort Wayne).

Fort William, Ontario. See **Thunder Bay.**

Fort Worth, Texas (pop. 741,206), is a major industrial city and one of the nation's chief aircraft producers. It is a leading Southwestern market for oil and grain. Fort Worth lies about 30 miles (50 kilometers) west of Dallas in north-central Texas (see **Texas** [political map]).

Major Ripley A. Arnold founded Fort Worth in 1849 as an Army post to protect settlers from Indian attacks. The post was named for Major General William J. Worth, a hero of the Mexican War (1846-1848). Fort Worth is occasionally called "Cowtown." The city got this early nickname because of its history as a cattle-marketing center.

The city occupies about 350 square miles (906 square kilometers) in the center of Tarrant County. Fort Worth is part of the Dallas-Fort Worth-Arlington metropolitan area. This area has a population of 6,371,773 and covers 8,991 square miles (23,287 square kilometers). The city is also part of the Fort Worth-Arlington metropolitan division. The division covers Johnson, Parker, Tarrant, and Wise counties and has a population of 2,136,022.

Fort Worth's main business district lies on the south bank of the Trinity River, which runs through the center of the city. The tallest buildings in the city include Burnett Plaza, D. R. Horton Tower, and 777 Main (formerly Carter Burgess Plaza). At the southeast end of the downtown area, the Fort Worth Convention Center covers 14 city blocks between Houston and Commerce streets. South of the Convention Center are the Fort Worth Water Gardens, designed by architect Philip Johnson.

About 35 percent of the city's people are Hispanic Americans. African Americans make up about 20 percent of the population.

Economy of Fort Worth is based on tourism, trade, transportation, and manufacturing. Major attractions include downtown, the Stockyards, the Cultural District, and the zoo. Fort Worth serves the Southwest as a center for finance and wholesale trade. The airline industry is also an important employer in the Fort Worth area.

The city is home to hundreds of manufacturing firms. Fort Worth's largest industries make airplanes, helicopters, and electronic equipment. Other products include food products, mobile homes, and oil-well equipment. The city is also one of the region's leading grain-milling and storage centers. The Naval Air Station Joint Reserve Base Fort Worth is a major employer in the city.

Fort Worth lies in the center of a rich oil-producing

region, and dozens of oil companies have offices in the city. It is served by freight and passenger rail lines, and bus and truck lines. Two interstate highways intersect in the downtown area. The Dallas-Fort Worth International Airport lies about midway between the two cities.

Education and cultural life. Fort Worth is the home of the Southwestern Baptist Theological Seminary, Texas Christian University, Texas Wesleyan University, and the University of North Texas Health Science Center. A campus of the University of Texas is in nearby Arlington. The Fort Worth Independent School District manages and operates the city's public schools, supervised by an elected Board of Education Trustees. Fort Worth also has a number of private schools, many of which are supported by religious groups. The *Fort Worth Star-Telegram* is the only daily newspaper in Fort Worth.

Fort Worth's symphony orchestra and ballet and opera companies use the downtown Bass Performance Hall. Many people enjoy summer musicals at the Casa Mañana. The Fort Worth Stock Show & Rodeo is one of the nation's largest livestock shows. The city is home to minor league baseball and hockey teams. The Texas Rangers of the American League play their home baseball games in Arlington. The Texas Motor Speedway, north of the city, features automobile races.

A number of Fort Worth's museums are in the Cultural District, near the downtown area. The district is home to the Modern Art Museum of Fort Worth, the Kimbell Art Museum, and the Amon Carter Museum of American Art. Other museums in the district include the Fort Worth Museum of Science and History, which is one of the largest children's museums in the United States, and the National Cowgirl Museum and Hall of Fame, which honors pioneering women of the American West.

In Forest Park, 3 miles (5 kilometers) west of downtown, the Fort Worth Zoo has hundreds of kinds of animals. The park also has the actual homes of early Fort Worth settlers in a log cabin village. The nearby Botanic Garden, the oldest in Texas, features over 2,500 native and exotic plants.

Government. Fort Worth has a council-manager form of government. Voters elect the mayor and eight council members to two-year terms. The mayor and council members all serve without salary. The council employs a city manager as the administrative head of the government. The city manager carries out policies set by the council, prepares the budget, and appoints and dismisses department heads. The government gets most of its income from property and sales taxes.

History. On June 6, 1849, Major Ripley A. Arnold established an Army post called Fort Worth to protect settlers from attacks by Indians. The soldiers left in 1853, and many settlers moved into the Army buildings. Fort Worth became the county seat of Tarrant County in 1860. During the 1860's and 1870's, the people traded with cowboys driving cattle to markets in Kansas. Fort Worth was incorporated as a city in 1873.

In 1876, the Texas and Pacific Railway reached Fort Worth, allowing cattle to be shipped directly from the city. As the railroad and cattle industries developed, the city's population increased from 500 in 1870 to 26,688 in 1900.

In 1902, the Swift and Armour companies built large meat-packing plants in Fort Worth. The meat industry helped Fort Worth's population reach 73,312 by 1910. The discovery of several oil fields in West Texas about 1915 brought more people to Fort Worth. By 1930, the city's population had climbed to 163,447. The Great Depression almost stopped Fort Worth's growth during the 1930's. Only 14,000 new residents settled there between 1930 and 1940.

During World War II (1939-1945), Fort Worth became a center for the manufacture of airplanes, helicopters, and other military products. Jobs created by defense industries caused a sharp population rise during and after the war. The city had 356,268 people by 1960.

Fort Worth's growth slowed during the 1960's, and its population declined in the 1970's as many people moved to the suburbs. Unemployment in the defense and oil industries and the closure of meat-packing plants contributed to the population slowdown and decline.

Fort Worth's development has been affected by a traditional rivalry with Dallas, which has a larger population and a stronger economy. Efforts toward greater cooperation led to construction of the Dallas-Fort Worth International Airport, which opened in 1974.

To help slow and offset the movement of people and trade away from the city into the suburbs, city leaders

Fort Worth Convention & Visitors Bureau

Fort Worth is a manufacturing center and a grain and oil market in north-central Texas. The downtown area, *shown here,* includes a mix of modern high-rises and historic buildings.

began a major downtown revitalization program in the late 1970's. New office towers were built and a group of small historic buildings was restored, creating a shopping and entertainment area known as Sundance Square.

In the 1980's, Fort Worth's population began to grow, largely because of an increase in national defense spending in the area. The city still depends heavily on jobs in defense plants, even though its economy has broadened. Fort Worth grew dramatically during the early 2000's. Between 2000 and 2010, the city added more than 200,000 people.   Carol Roark

Fortaleza, *FAWR tuh LAY zuh,* is a city on the northeast coast of Brazil. The municipality of Fortaleza has a population of 2,452,185. A municipality may include rural areas as well as the urban center. For location, see **Brazil** (political map). Fortaleza is the capital of the state of Ceará. The Metropolitan Cathedral, a large Gothic church, is a major city landmark. Fortaleza's economy depends largely on the activities of the state and city governments and on the processing and export of such products as cotton and carnauba wax.

Fortaleza was first settled in the early 1600's, when the Portuguese built a fort there. Fortaleza received the status of a town in 1711. In 1799, it became the capital of Ceará. Fortaleza experienced rapid growth in the middle and late 1900's. Today, it is one of Brazil's largest cities by population.   J. H. Galloway

Fortas, Abe (1910-1982), served as an associate justice of the Supreme Court of the United States from 1965 to 1969. He was appointed to the court by President Lyndon B. Johnson. During his time on the court, Fortas became one of its most liberal members. He supported civil rights, free speech, and personal privacy. He also worked to expand the rights of criminal defendants.

In 1968, President Johnson nominated Fortas for the position of chief justice to replace the retiring Earl Warren. Johnson withdrew the nomination at Fortas's request after a Senate *filibuster* (extended debate) prevented a vote on the nomination. Many legal scholars attributed the filibuster to election-year politics and opposition from conservatives (see **Filibustering**).

In 1969, Fortas resigned from the court after receiving widespread criticism for his association with the Wolfson Family Foundation. Financier Louis E. Wolfson had been convicted of stock manipulation in 1967. At a time when Wolfson was under federal investigation, Fortas had agreed to consult on developing Wolfson Family Foundation programs involving juvenile civil rights in Florida. The foundation was to pay $20,000 a year for life to Fortas and, if she outlived him, to his wife. But Fortas soon canceled the agreement.

Fortas was born on June 19, 1910, in Memphis. He graduated from Southwestern College and Yale Law School. From 1933 to 1937, he was an assistant professor of law at Yale. Fortas also held a number of government posts. He became undersecretary of the interior in 1942. He entered private law practice in Washington, D.C., in 1947. He became known as one of the city's most powerful political attorneys before his appointment to the Supreme Court. After his resignation from the court, he returned to private practice in Washington, but not with the visibility of his earlier career. Fortas died on April 5, 1982.   Bruce Allen Murphy

Forten, James (1766-1842), was an African American businessman who won fame as an abolitionist during the early 1800's. He believed that most American blacks wanted to live as free people in the United States. He opposed efforts at the time to help blacks move to Africa.

Forten was born on Sept. 2, 1766, in Philadelphia, the son of free parents. He was a powder boy on an American ship during the Revolutionary War in America (1775-1783). Forten was captured in the war at the age of 15 and spent seven months on a British prison ship. In 1786, he worked in a Philadelphia sailmaking shop. Forten rose to the position of foreman two years later and became owner of the business in 1798. About that time, he invented a device that helped crew members handle heavy sails. The invention greatly aided his business, and Forten became wealthy.

During the War of 1812, Forten helped recruit about 2,500 blacks as part of a force to defend Philadelphia against a British invasion. In 1817, he presided over a meeting of Philadelphia blacks who protested the American Colonization Society's attempts to resettle free blacks in Africa. During the 1830's, he contributed much money to the noted abolitionist William Lloyd Garrison and to Garrison's antislavery newspaper, *The Liberator.* Forten also helped runaway slaves seeking freedom in the North. He died on March 4, 1842.   Otey M. Scruggs

See also **Abolition movement.**

Fortress of Louisbourg. See Canada (National historic sites).

Fortuna, *fawr TOO nuh* or *fawr TYOO nuh,* was the goddess of luck in Roman mythology. Fortuna was associated only with good fortune in early Roman religion. But after she became identified with Tyche, the Greek goddess of chance, she was also considered a giver of bad luck. Fortuna often is shown with a wheel that she turned to bring success or failure. She also appears with a rudder, symbolizing her power to steer people's lives. The word *fortune* comes from her name.   Elaine Fantham

Fortunetelling is the practice of predicting future events using special techniques that include astrology and palmistry and such ritual objects as tarot cards and crystal balls. People who claim to foretell the future are called *fortunetellers, psychics,* or *readers.* Some of these techniques of prediction are complex, and fortunetellers often claim they are scientific. But most scientists do not consider them to be scientific.

Some fortunetellers say they have a form of *clairvoyance* that makes them aware of events before they occur. Clairvoyance is the knowledge of events, objects, or people without using any known senses. Scientists do not know whether clairvoyance actually exists. However, most fortunetellers do not claim clairvoyant powers.

Fortunetelling has been especially popular during certain periods of history. For example, the ancient Greeks and Romans believed the gods spoke to them through prophets called *oracles.* Many people went to oracles for advice about the future. In later times, the Christian church discouraged fortunetelling. However, astrology, an ancient type of fortunetelling, became extremely popular in Europe during the Renaissance, the period from about 1300 to about 1600. Some forms of fortunetelling remain popular today in modern Western cultures as well as in more isolated societies and less-developed countries. Most Americans regard fortunetelling as a form of amusement, but many people believe in it sincerely.

Methods of fortunetelling. Throughout history, hundreds of different fortunetelling methods have been used. One of the most famous methods involves gazing into a crystal ball. Many methods of fortunetelling seem to depend entirely on chance. For example, fortunetellers have made predictions based on the order in which a rooster ate grains of wheat placed on letters drawn on the ground. Predictions also have been based on the shape taken by oil poured on water, or on segments of writing chosen from a book at random.

However, fortunetellers claim that mysterious causes and relationships, not chance, make their predictions possible. For example, astrology is based on the belief that the sun, moon, planets, and stars control people's lives. Therefore, astrologers claim that the positions and movements of these bodies supposedly can be used to predict the future.

Other fortunetelling systems include numerology and palmistry. In numerology, a fortuneteller makes predictions through numbers based on a person's name and birth date. In palmistry, a fortuneteller tries to foresee an individual's future by studying the lines, markings, shape, and the size of the person's hand.

Risks of fortunetelling. Today, fortunetellers may be genuinely committed to helping people or mainly concerned with making money. Fraud committed by some fortunetellers has resulted in legal restrictions on fortunetelling in many cities and states. Some fortunetellers only pretend to rely on the various methods they use. These fraudulent fortunetellers may actually rely more on a broad range of knowledge about human behavior. For example, some fortunetellers know what most people prefer to hear and thus make statements about the future that fit those expectations. They may also make general statements about the future that are unclear and can apply to almost anyone.

Americans spend millions of dollars annually on fortunetelling. People may visit fortunetellers on a whim, for entertainment, or out of a genuine need for psychological help or to help find meaning in their lives. Many of them find their visits to fortunetellers therapeutic and helpful. Some people may use the information they receive from the fortuneteller to help them make decisions about relationships and careers.   Sarah M. Pike

Related articles in *World Book* include:

Astrology	Nostradamus
Augur	Numerology
Clairvoyance	Occultism
Divination	Omen
Graphology	Oracle
Halloween (Fortunetelling)	Palmistry
Magic	Superstition

Forty-Niners were gold seekers who rushed to California after gold was discovered there in 1848. The first Forty-Niners reached San Francisco on the steamer *California* on Feb. 28, 1849. Ships from all parts of the world carried other gold seekers there. But most arrived in covered wagons by way of the Oregon Trail and the California Trail. Gold seekers increased California's population from about 15,000 early in 1848 to nearly 100,000 by the end of 1849. The Forty-Niners made up the first of a series of migrations to California that became even heavier during the following years.   Duane A. Smith

See also **California** (The gold rush); **Gold rush** (picture).

Forum, Roman, was the section of ancient Rome that served as the center of government. It was the administrative, legislative, and legal center of the Republic and of the Roman Empire. Many important buildings and

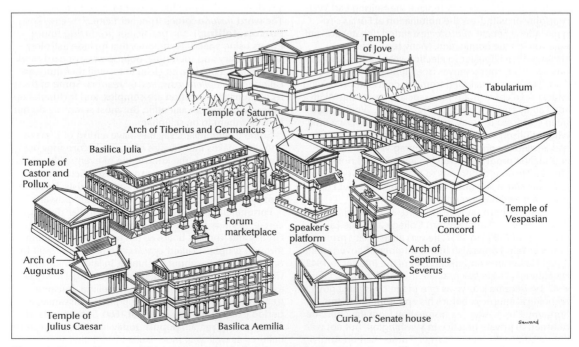

The early Roman Forum had this arrangement during the period of its greatest magnificence.

monuments stood there, including the Curia (Senate house), the temples of Concord and Saturn, the Basilica Julia and Basilica Aemilia, the Arch of Septimius Severus, and the Tabularium (Hall of Records).

Events in the Roman Forum often affected the rest of the known world. Marcus Tullius Cicero's stirring speeches on the floor of the Curia in the 60's B.C. saved the Republic from a rebellion led by Catiline. Also at the Forum, in 27 B.C., the senate gave Augustus the powers that made him the first emperor of Rome. Romans went to the Forum to hear famous orators speak and to see the valuables seized after distant battles.

In Rome's earliest days, the Forum area was a swamp used as a cemetery by the people of surrounding villages. The Etruscans turned these villages into the city of Rome and drained the marshes, probably during the 500's B.C. Residents built shops and temples around the edges of the Forum area. The Forum became the civic and legal center of Rome by the mid-100's B.C., and the merchants moved their shops to other parts of the city.

The Germanic peoples who invaded Rome in the A.D. 400's did not destroy the Forum. But its buildings gradually crumbled after the fall of Rome, and people came to call it *Cow Plain* because it had become so desolate. Excavations have since uncovered many of the ancient columns and arches. Rome had other forums, some with architecture as outstanding as that of the Roman Forum. Several emperors named forums in their own honor. But only the first forum was called *Forum Romanum* (Roman Forum). D. Brendan Nagle

See also **Rome** (Forums; picture: Roman Forum); **Rome, Ancient** (picture).

Foscolo, Ugo (1778-1827), was an Italian author whose *Le ultime lettere di Jacopo Ortis* (1802, revised in 1817) is sometimes considered the first modern Italian novel. It is the tragic story of a young student's love for Teresa, a woman whose hand has been promised to another man, Odoardo. The story is told in the form of letters and shows the influence of the German writer Johann Wolfgang von Goethe's *The Sorrows of Young Werther.* Many of Foscolo's odes and sonnets tell in a lyrical yet classical style about his personal sufferings and disappointments. His best-known poem, *The Sepulchers* (1806-1807), is an ode that stresses the importance of graves as living reminders of one's ancestors.

Foscolo was born on Feb. 6, 1778, on the island of Zákinthos in the Ionian Sea. His early poetry is filled with his desire to see Italy unified. In 1815, Foscolo left Italy for England, where he spent the rest of his life teaching Italian and writing essays for periodicals and newspapers. He died on Sept. 10, 1827. Richard H. Lansing

Fosdick, Harry Emerson (1878-1969), became one of the best-known Protestant preachers in the United States. He devoted his entire career as a preacher, professor, and author to the conflict between modern life and religion. He preached the right of science to its place in the world. Fosdick opposed the views held by the fundamentalists (see **Fundamentalism**).

Fosdick was pastor of the First Baptist Church in Montclair, New Jersey; and the First Presbyterian Church, Park Avenue Baptist Church, and the nondenominational Riverside Church, all in New York City. He was professor of preaching at Union Theological Seminary in New York City from 1915 to 1946. He served with

the Young Men's Christian Association (YMCA) in England, Scotland, and France during World War I (1914-1918). Fosdick's many books include *The Manhood of the Master* (1913), *The Meaning of Prayer* (1915), *The Modern Use of the Bible* (1924), *On Being a Real Person* (1943), and an autobiography, *The Living of These Days* (1956).

Fosdick was born on May 24, 1878, in Buffalo, New York. He graduated from Colgate University. Fosdick also studied at Union Theological Seminary and Columbia University. He died on Oct. 9, 1969. Charles H. Lippy

Fossey, Dian (1932-1985), was an American zoologist who studied the mountain gorillas of the Virunga Mountains in east-central Africa. She founded the Karisoke Research Center in Rwanda and lived there in

© Veit/Watkins from Sipa

Dian Fossey studied and photographed mountain gorillas in Africa. She won their trust by imitating their sounds and habits.

near isolation for almost 18 years. Fossey's research on wild mountain gorillas led to efforts to protect this rare and endangered species. She was mysteriously murdered at her camp in Rwanda in December 1985.

Fossey was born on Jan. 16, 1932, in San Francisco. She received a bachelor's degree in occupational therapy from San Jose State College (now San Jose State University) in 1954. In 1963, inspired by a book about mountain gorillas by American zoologist George Schaller, Fossey borrowed money and traveled to Africa to see the animals. There, Fossey visited the camp of British anthropologist Louis Leakey. In 1966, Leakey picked Fossey to begin a long-term field study of the animals. Fossey received a doctorate for her gorilla research from Cambridge University in Cambridge, England, in 1974.

To gain acceptance by the mountain gorillas, Fossey imitated their habits and sounds. She studied them daily and came to know each animal individually. After several of her favorite mountain gorillas were killed, Fossey focused on protecting the animals from poachers and from the destruction of their mountain habitat. Some United States officials believe Fossey may have been murdered by poachers angered by her strong attempts to protect the animals. Fossey described her research in the book *Gorillas in the Mist* (1983). A motion picture about her with the same title was released in 1988. Randall L. Susman

A fossil skeleton can serve as a popular museum exhibit. This *Tyrannosaurus rex* fossil, known as "Sue," ranks among the world's best-preserved dinosaur skeletons. Such fossils help people visualize ancient species and help scientists learn more about the ways of life of prehistoric creatures.

Fossil

Fossil is the mark or remains of an organism that lived thousands or millions of years ago. Some of the best-known fossils include leaves, shells, or skeletons that were preserved after a plant or animal died. Other fossils include tracks, trails, or burrows left by moving animals.

Most fossils occur in *sedimentary rocks*. Such fossils formed from plant or animal remains that were quickly buried in *sediments*—the mud or sand that collects at the bottom of rivers, lakes, swamps, and oceans. Over time, these sediments became buried under other sediments. The upper sediments pressed down on the layers of mud and squeezed them into compact rock layers. Water that traveled slowly through the layers of sand deposited mineral cement around these particles, cementing the layers together to form rocks.

A few fossils formed in other ways. For example, whole plants or animals became preserved in ice, tar, or hardened sap.

The oldest fossils are microscopic traces of bacteria that probably lived about 3 ½ billion years ago. The oldest animal fossils are remains of *invertebrates* (animals without a backbone) about 600 million years old. The oldest fossils of *vertebrates* (animals with a backbone) are fossil fish about 450 million years old.

Fossils occur more commonly than many people realize. Even so, only a small portion of the countless organisms that have lived on Earth have been preserved as fossils. Many *species* (kinds) of organisms lived and died without leaving any trace in the fossil record.

Although the fossil record is incomplete, many important groups of organisms have left fossil remains. These fossils help scientists discover what forms of life existed at various periods in the past and how these prehistoric species lived. Fossils also indicate how life on Earth has gradually changed over time. This article explains how fossils provide information on ancient life. For a description of ancient animals, see **Prehistoric animal;** for a description of early human beings, see **Prehistoric people.**

How fossils reveal the past

In the distant past, when most fossils formed, the world was different from today. Plants and animals that have long since vanished inhabited the waters and land. A region now elevated to form high mountains may have been the floor of an ancient sea. Where a lush tropical forest thrived millions of years ago, there may now be a cool, dry plain. Even the continents have drifted far from the positions they occupied hundreds of millions of years ago. No human beings were present to record these changes. But *paleontologists* (scientists who study prehistoric life) have pieced together much of the story of Earth's past by examining its fossil record.

Understanding ancient plants and animals. By studying fossils, paleontologists can learn much about the appearance and ways of life of prehistoric organisms. One way scientists learn about a fossil animal or plant is by comparing it to living species. In many cases the comparisons show that the fossil species has close living relatives. Similarities and differences between the fossil species and its living relatives can provide important information. For example, according to anthropologists, fossils show that *Homo erectus*—a species that lived from about 1,800,000 to 300,000 years ago—was an ancient ancestor of modern human beings. Its fossilized pelvis, leg, and foot bones are similar in structure to modern human bones. Paleontologists know that modern human bones are designed for walking upright. From this evidence, they have determined that *Homo erectus* also walked upright (see **Homo erectus**).

Fossil plants and animals that do not have close living relatives prove more difficult to understand. One way to learn how they lived is to compare their fossils to unrelated living species that have similarly shaped structures. For example, fossils show that about 240 million to 65 million years ago there lived a group of reptiles with one long, slender finger extending from each front limb. This bone structure does not resemble that of any living reptile. It appears, however, similar to the wings of modern birds and bats. Since modern birds and bats use their wings for flying, paleontologists conclude that these ancient creatures also flew. Paleontologists call them *pterosaurs,* which means *winged lizards.*

The conditions under which fossil creatures died can also reveal how they lived. Paleontologists have found fossil nests of partially grown baby dinosaurs. These fossils indicate certain species of dinosaurs fed and cared for their young in nests, much as today's birds do.

Fossils of tracks, trails, or burrows—called *trace fos-* *sils*—provide information on the behavior of prehistoric animals. Groups of dinosaur tracks, for example, suggest that some species of dinosaurs traveled in herds. Other trace fossils show that primitive worms lived in simple tubes dug in the sea floor.

Tracing the development of life. The fossil record provides important evidence of the history of life. Fossils indicate that over hundreds of millions of years life on Earth has *evolved* (developed gradually) from simple, one-celled bacteria and algae into a tremendous variety of complex organisms. Fossils also indicate that certain species changed dramatically, giving rise to entirely new forms of life.

The location of fossils in the *strata* (layers) of sedimentary rock can show how living things increased in complexity through time. As sediment was deposited, new layers settled on top of older ones. When the sediment turned to stone, these layers were preserved in the order in which they were laid down. In undisturbed strata, fossils in the lower—and thus older—layers are more primitive than those in younger strata nearer the surface.

The fossils preserved in the strata of the Grand Canyon in Arizona provide a good example of the increasing complexity of living things. Strata near the bottom are about 1 billion years old and contain only primitive fossil algae. Strata dating from about 500 million years ago contain fossils of invertebrates, including those of extinct sea animals called *trilobites.* Remains of fish first appear in strata about 400 million years old. Some of the upper strata, which formed between 330 million and 260 million years ago, contain tracks of the first land animals.

Certain fossils indicate that particular groups of plants or animals evolved from others. These *transition fossils* combine characteristics of two major groups. For example, fossil skeletons of *Ichthyostega,* a creature that lived about 360 million years ago, provide evidence that *tetra pods* (four-legged animals) evolved from fish. *Ichthyostega* had legs, enabling it to live on land. *Ichthyostega's* leg bones, however, were similar to the fin bones of fish. It

Donald Baird

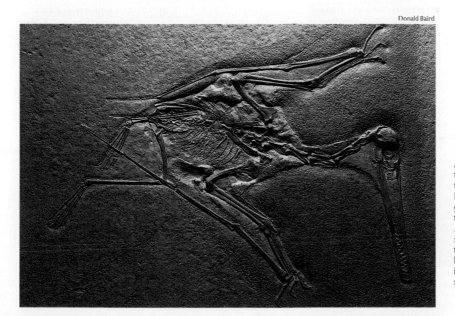

http://bit.ly/1OqOykg

A fossil *Pterodactylus,* a type of pterosaur, provides information on the animal's behavior. The long, slender finger bones, which are similar to birds' wings, indicate that *Pterodactylus* flew. Its tapered snout and sharp teeth suggest that it fed on worms and other burrowing creatures, plucking them out of the earth as some modern birds do.

also had fishlike teeth and a broad, finned tail for swimming. Fossils indicate that later tetrapods lost these fishlike traits and became better adapted to life on land.

Fossils also show how groups of plants and animals became more diverse after they originated. Fossil leaves and pollen grains of the first flowering plants date from the early Cretaceous Period, sometime after 138 million years ago. These fossils record only a small number of species. Fossils from later in the Cretaceous, about 90 million years ago, include a wide variety of flowering plants from many different environments.

Recording Earth's changes. Paleontologists use fossils to determine how Earth's climate and landscape have changed over millions of years. For instance, they have found fossils of tropical palm trees in Wyoming, an area that has a cool climate today. These fossils indicate that the climate in that area has cooled. Paleontologists have found fossil oysters in Kansas and other areas that lie far inland today. Such fossils reveal that a shallow sea once spread over these areas.

Fossils also provide evidence supporting the theory of *continental drift*—the idea that the positions of the continents have changed over hundreds of millions of years. Paleontologists have found similar kinds of fossil

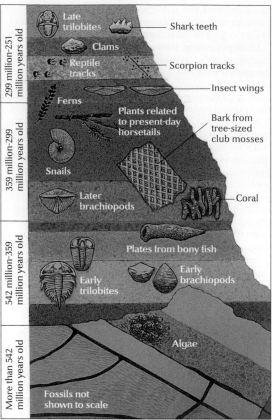

WORLD BOOK diagram by Paul D. Turnbaugh

Fossils embedded in different layers of rock or *strata* record a history of living things. The deep strata shown here are from Precambrian times. They contain fossils of such early life forms as algae. The shallow strata are from the Permian Period. They contain fossils of later forms, such as plants and reptiles.

© David McNew, Getty Images

Layers of rock called *strata* can be exposed by erosion, as seen here on the shores of Arizona's Lake Powell. The strata hold fossils of different ages, with older fossils closer to the bottom.

dinosaurs on all of the modern continents. These similar species could not have evolved on separate continents. Because of such evidence, Earth scientists now recognize that when dinosaurs first appeared—about 230 million years ago—nearly all of Earth's land mass was united as a single supercontinent. In contrast, fossils of mammals show complex differences from continent to continent. Thus scientists know that, by the time the Age of Mammals began about 65 million years ago, Earth's land

© Shutterstock

© Shutterstock

Fossils reveal ancient environments. A fossil leaf, *above left,* suggests Wyoming once had a tropical climate. A fossil oyster, *above right,* indicates a sea once covered part of Argentina.

mass had divided into many continents. See **Plate tectonics.**

How fossils form

The great majority of plants and animals die and decay without leaving any trace in the fossil record. Bacteria and other microorganisms break down such soft tissues as leaves or flesh. As a result, these tissues rarely leave fossil records. Even most hard parts, such as bones, teeth, shells, or wood, are eventually worn away by moving water or dissolved by chemicals. But when plant or animal remains have been buried in sediment, they may become fossilized. These remains are occasionally preserved without much change. Most, however, become altered after burial. Many disappear completely, but still leave a fossil record in the sediment.

Fossils may be preserved in several ways. The main ways are: (1) the formation of impressions, molds, and casts; (2) carbonization; and (3) the action of minerals.

Formation of impressions, molds, and casts. Some fossils consist of the preserved form or outline of animal or plant remains. Impressions, also called *prints* or *imprints,* are shallow fossil depressions in rock. They form when thin plant or animal parts become buried in sediment and then decay. After the sediment has turned to stone, only the outline of the plant or animal remains preserved. Many impressions consist of small grooves left by the bones of fish or the thick-walled veins found inside leaves. Sometimes even delicate soft parts, such as feathers or leaves, are preserved as impressions.

Molds form after hard parts become buried in mud, clay, or other material that turns to stone. Later, water dissolves the buried hard part, leaving a mold—a hollow space in the shape of the original hard part—inside the rock. A cast forms when water containing dissolved minerals and other fine particles later drains through a mold. The water deposits these substances, which eventually fill the mold, forming a copy of the original hard part. Many seashells are preserved as molds or casts.

Carbonization results when decaying tissues leave behind traces of carbon. Living tissues consist of compounds of carbon and other chemical elements. As decaying tissues break down into their chemical parts, most of the chemicals disappear. In carbonization, a thin, black film of carbon remains in the shape of the organism. Plants, fish, and soft-bodied creatures have been preserved in precise detail by carbonization.

The action of minerals. Many plants and animals became fossilized after water that contained minerals soaked into the pores of the original hard parts. This action is called *petrifaction.* In many such fossils, some or all of the original material remains, but it has been strengthened and preserved by the minerals. This process is called *permineralization.* The huge tree trunks in petrified forests were preserved by permineralization.

In other cases, the minerals in the water totally replaced the original plant or animal part. This process, called *replacement,* involves two events that happen at the same time: The water dissolves the compounds that make up the original material, while the minerals are deposited in their place. Replacement can duplicate even microscopic details of the original hard part.

Other processes. Occasionally, animal and plant structures are fossilized with little or no change. In

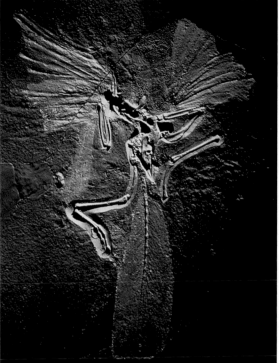

American Museum of Natural History

An impression of an *Archaeopteryx* began to form when the bird was buried in soft silt. The silt turned to limestone, preserving the delicate outlines of the bird's wing and tail feathers.

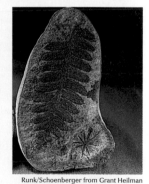

American Museum of Natural History

A mold preserved the three-dimensional form of a trilobite after its body decayed.

Runk/Schoenberger from Grant Heilman

A carbonized fossil of a fern consists of traces of carbon in the shape of the leaf.

mummification, an animal's skin and other tissues are preserved by drying or by the action of chemicals. Mummification may occur when a dead animal is buried in a dry place, such as a desert, or in asphalt or some other oily substance.

Some processes fossilize whole animals. Insects sometimes are preserved whole in *amber,* the hardened sap of ancient pines or other trees. Such insects were trapped in the sticky sap and then sealed when it turned to amber. In Alaska and in Siberia, a region in northern Asia, woolly mammoths thousands of years old have

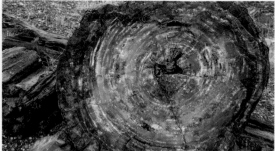

© Shutterstock

Petrified wood formed after dissolved minerals were deposited in the pores of dead tree trunks. The structure of the wood, including bark and growth rings, is visible in this specimen.

survived frozen in the ground. Their hair, skin, flesh, and internal organs have been preserved as they were when the mammoths died. Food preserved in their stomachs even reveals what they ate.

Studying fossils

Discovering fossils. Fossils can occur wherever sedimentary rocks lie exposed. In moist regions, these rocks are usually buried under a layer of soil and plant life, but they become exposed by water erosion along

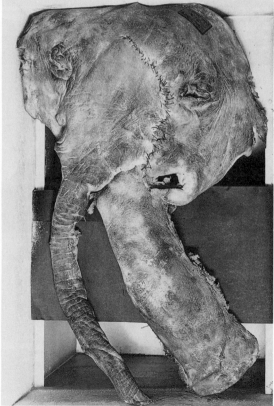

American Museum of Natural History

A baby woolly mammoth was unearthed from the frozen ground in Alaska. Scientists can learn a great deal from such frozen fossils because much of their tissue has survived intact.

the sides of river valleys. Sedimentary layers also become uncovered during highway construction and other building projects. In deserts and other arid regions, erosion exposes sedimentary rocks over broad areas. And oil-well drilling often brings up fossil-bearing sedimentary rocks from deep under the ground.

Paleontologists search in specific areas for particular types of fossils. For example, Mongolia provides a rich source of dinosaur fossils. Paleontologists hunt for fossil ancestors of human beings in eastern and southern Africa. All continents have numerous deposits containing well-preserved ancient marine invertebrates and microscopic organisms.

Collecting fossils. Different fossils require different collecting techniques. Fossils of shells, teeth, and bones preserved in soft sand or mud prove easiest to collect. Paleontologists can dig out these fossils with a trowel or shovel or remove them by hand. They also can use a *sieve* (strainer) to remove small fossils from the sediment. Fossils preserved in hard rock are most easily found and collected when they have become exposed by natural *weathering.* Weathering refers to the chemical and physical processes that break down rock at Earth's surface. Fossils that are more resistant to weathering than the surrounding rocks stand out on exposed rocky surfaces. Most such fossils can be collected by breaking loose the rock with a chisel, hammer, or pick. Paleontologists also expose and collect fossils that are hidden in solid rock by breaking the rock with a sledge hammer or a hammer and chisel. Rocks containing fossils often break along the surfaces of the fossils.

Scientists must protect fragile fossils before breaking them out of the rock. Paleontologists wrap the exposed parts of such fossils in layers of cloth soaked with wet plaster. After the plaster hardens, the fossils can be safely chipped from the rock and transported to a laboratory, where the plaster is removed.

In the laboratory, paleontologists use electric grinding tools, fine picks, or even needles to remove any remaining rock. Acid-resistant fossils that contain limestone may be soaked in a weak acid solution, which dissolves the limestone but not the fossils. Paleontologists may decide to leave a fossil attractively exposed but still partly hidden in the rock.

Working with fragments. Many fossils are collected in fragments, which scientists must assemble like pieces of a jigsaw puzzle. In general, the first time a fossil species is reconstructed in this manner, the fragments must represent the complete specimen. Scientists can make later reconstructions from incomplete fragments by comparing them to the complete fossil and replacing the missing parts with artificial materials.

Some fossils are so small that paleontologists can discover and study them only with a microscope. Such fossils typically occur in loose sediment or hard rock. For fossils preserved in loose sediment, scientists must sort them from the sediment grains under a microscope. For fossils in hard rock, researchers often grind the rock so thin that it becomes transparent. Sections of fossils in transparent rock become visible under a microscope.

Paleontologists can reconstruct vertebrate fossils as *free mounts,* in which the skeleton seems to stand by itself. Scientists first make a small model of the finished skeleton. They then construct a framework of steel, plas-

© Shutterstock

© Shutterstock

Preparing fossils requires patience and the proper tools. In these photographs, a paleon-tologist carefully brushes sediment away from a delicate trilobite fossil, and a lab technician uses an air drill to clean a mammoth tooth.

tic, or other strong material to support the skeleton. Finally, they fasten the bones to the outside of the framework to hide it. Scientists sometimes construct mounts using plaster replicas of fossil bones.

Classifying fossils. As with living things, fossil species are classified according to how closely related they are to one another. Scientists generally determine how closely related various species are by comparing their biological features (see **Classification, Scientific**). With fossil groups, most of these features are the shapes of more commonly fossilized hard parts, such as shells, teeth, and skeletons. For example, paleontologists may look at skull shape and tooth size when determining the different species of saber-toothed cats.

Dating fossils. Through many decades of research, paleontologists have learned the order in which most kinds of fossils occur in the geological record. When a fossil species is first discovered, it usually occurs along with other species. If paleontologists know the position of the other species in the history of life, they can determine the position of the new species. This type of dating only indicates whether one fossil is older or younger than another. It does not provide a fossil's age in years.

Paleontologists determine the age of a fossil by measuring *radioactive isotopes* in the rocks that contain the fossil. Radioactive isotopes are forms of chemical elements that break down, or *decay,* to form other materials. Scientists know the rates of decay for various such isotopes. By comparing the amount of a radioactive isotope in a rock to the amount of the material produced by its decay, scientists can calculate how long the decay has been taking place. This length of time represents the age of the rock and the fossils it contains.

Steven M. Stanley

Related articles in *World Book* include:

Andrews, Roy Chapman
Ant (picture: Fossils of ants)
Broom, Robert
Coal (picture: Fossil ferns)
Cuvier, Baron
Dinosaur
Earth
Evolution

Florissant Fossil Beds National
    Monument
Geology
Insect (picture: Fossil insects)
Olduvai Gorge
Osborn, Henry F.
Paleobotany
Paleontology

Plant (The evolution of plants)
Rock (Organic sediments)

Teilhard de Chardin, Pierre
Tree (Fossil trees)

Outline

I. **How fossils reveal the past**
    A. Understanding ancient plants and animals
    B. Tracing the development of life
    C. Recording Earth's changes
II. **How fossils form**
    A. Formation of impressions, molds, and casts
    B. Carbonization
    C. The action of minerals
    D. Other processes
III. **Studying fossils**
    A. Discovering fossils   D. Classifying fossils
    B. Collecting fossils   E. Dating fossils
    C. Working with fragments

Fossil Butte National Monument, *byoot,* an area of rare plant and animal fossils, is in southwestern Wyoming. The fossils date from the Paleocene Epoch and the Eocene Epoch, which together lasted from about 65 million to 34 million years ago. The site became a national monument in 1972. For its area, see **National Park System** (table: National monuments).

Critically reviewed by the National Park Service

Fossil fuel is an energy-providing material formed from the long-dead remains of living things. Fossil fuels include coal, natural gas, and petroleum. Manufacturers use chemicals from fossil fuels to make many products, including plastics, steel, and agricultural fertilizers. The gasoline in cars comes from petroleum. Natural gas provides heat for homes. Many power plants burn coal to create electric power. Fossil fuels provide a tremendous amount of energy. In fact, most of the energy modern people use comes from burning fossil fuels.

Formation. Geologists believe fossil fuels come from living things that died millions of years ago. The remains eventually became buried with layers of sand and mud. Over time, the weight of these layers pressed down on the remains. The resulting pressure and heat, along with other natural processes, transformed the remains into the various fossil fuels.

Concerns. There is a limited amount of fossil fuels. In addition, fossil fuels are formed by processes that take millions of years. As a result, fossil fuels are considered *nonrenewable resources*—that is, resources that cannot be replaced. Developed and developing countries use vast amounts of energy, rapidly depleting the supply of fossil fuels. Society's dependence on fossil fuels has been blamed for global economic problems and wars.

Burning fossil fuels also causes environmental problems, including air pollution and acid rain. Such burning also releases large amounts of carbon dioxide and other *greenhouse gases.* The gases trap heat in Earth's atmosphere, contributing to global warming.

C.-Y. Cynthia Lin

See also **Coal; Gas; Global warming; Petroleum.**

Foster, Sir George Eulas (1847-1931), was an outstanding Canadian statesman. He was minister of trade and commerce from 1911 to 1921 during the administrations of Sir Robert L. Borden and Arthur Meighen. From 1882 to 1900 and from 1904 to 1921, Foster served in the Canadian House of Commons. He served in the Canadian Senate from 1921 until his death on Dec. 30, 1931.

Foster was born on Sept. 3, 1847, in Carleton County, New Brunswick. He attended the University of New Brunswick and was a professor of classics there from 1873 to 1879. Foster was knighted in 1914. He was on the Canadian delegation to the Paris Peace Conference in 1919. He also served as a delegate to the League of Nations in 1920, 1921, 1926, and 1929.   Robert Craig Brown

Foster, Jodie (1962-   ), is an American film actress and director known for the keen intelligence she brings to many roles. Foster became a star as a young girl in *Taxi Driver* (1976). She won praise for her performance in that film as a young, drug-addicted prostitute. She continued her success as an adult actress and also distinguished herself as a director. She won two Academy Awards as best actress, for her roles in *The Accused* (1988) and *The Silence of the Lambs* (1991).

Alicia Christian Foster, nicknamed Jodie as a girl, was born on Nov. 19, 1962, in Los Angeles. She began appearing in television commercials at age 3 and soon played in TV movies. She made her film debut in 1972 in the Walt Disney adventure film *Napoleon and Samantha.* Her other films include *Bugsy Malone* (1976), *Freaky Friday* (1976), *Foxes* (1980), *The Hotel New Hampshire* (1984), *Sommersby* (1993), *Maverick* and *Nell* (both 1994), *Contact* (1997), *Anna and the King* (1999), *Panic Room* (2002), *Flightplan* (2005), *Inside Man* (2006), *The Brave One* (2007), *Nim's Island* (2008), *Carnage* (2011), and *Elysium* (2013). She made her debut as a film director in *Little Man Tate* (1991), in which she also starred. She also directed *Home for the Holidays* (1995). She directed and starred in *The Beaver* (2011).

While Foster was building her film career, she attended Yale University. In 1981, while she was a college student, a fan of hers named John W. Hinckley, Jr., wounded President Ronald Reagan in an assassination attempt. Hinckley did it, he said, to "impress" Foster. She graduated with honors from Yale in 1985 with a degree in literature.   Louis Giannetti

Foster, Stephen Collins (1826-1864), was one of America's best-loved songwriters. The best of Foster's songs have become part of the American cultural heritage. Some of them became so popular during Foster's lifetime that they were adapted (with suitable words) for Sunday school use. Foster's songs are frequently mov-

ing in their sincerity and simplicity. His most popular works include "Old Folks at Home," which he wrote in 1851 (also known as "Swanee River," see **Suwannee River**); "Massa's in de Cold, Cold Ground" (1852); and "My Old Kentucky Home, Good Night" (1853). He also wrote such rollicking songs as "Oh! Susanna" (1848) and "Camptown Races" (1850), and such romantic songs as "Jeanie with the Light Brown Hair" (1854) and "Beautiful Dreamer" (1864). He wrote more than 200 songs, and

University of Pittsburgh

Stephen Foster

wrote the words and the music for most of them.

Foster was born on July 4, 1826, near Lawrenceville, Pennsylvania (now part of Pittsburgh). He had little musical training, but he had a great gift of melody. At the age of 6, he taught himself to play the clarinet, and he could pick up any tune by ear. He composed "The Tioga Waltz" (1841) for piano at 14. Three years later, his first song, "Open Thy Lattice, Love," was published.

Foster wrote his first minstrel melodies, called "Ethiopian songs," in the 1840's. These were "Lou'siana Belle" (1847) and "Old Uncle Ned" (1848). Blackface minstrel shows, in which white entertainers blackened their faces, were becoming popular in the United States (see **Minstrel show**). Foster decided to write songs for the minstrels and to improve the quality of their music.

Foster went to Cincinnati in 1846 to work as a bookkeeper for his brother. That year, he wrote "Oh! Susanna." Soon it became the favorite song of the "Forty-Niners" in the California gold rush of 1849. He married Jane McDowell in 1850 and settled in Pittsburgh to work as a composer. He arranged with the minstrel leader E. P. Christy to have his new songs performed on the minstrel stage. Foster was a poor businessman, and he sold many of his most famous songs for little money. He lived in New York City from 1860 until his death on Jan. 13, 1864, struggling against illness, poverty, and alcoholism.   Don Wilmeth

Foster care provides children, youth, or adults with supervision and a place to live outside of their usual home setting. People are placed in foster care because they must leave their homes for their own safety or well-being, and they are unable to live on their own.

Children, youth, or adults in foster care live in family homes, group homes, or special institutions. In a *family home,* a couple or a single adult cares for one or more individuals living in their home. The couple or adult serves as the foster parents or parent of the person in care. In a *group home,* a staff or live-in couple cares for 6 to 12 children, youth, or adults in a single household.

Institutions have larger staffs and care for more individuals than group homes do. However, many institutions provide care in small cottages or other homelike settings. Most institutions are *residential treatment centers.* In such facilities, individuals receive help in dealing with their psychological and behavioral challenges or substance abuse issues.

Individuals may be placed in foster care if it is found

that a parent or others in their home have abused them. Foster care is also provided for children, youth, or adults whose caregivers have abandoned or neglected them or are no longer able to care for them. Most adults who live in foster care are unable to completely care for themselves on a daily basis because of physical, mental, or emotional challenges or advanced age. Those who need more specialized care may live in a skilled nursing facility instead of receiving foster care.

Most individuals in foster care are *wards* (protected persons) of a court of law. The court places the person under the supervision of a public or private agency. In many cases, this is a social service agency. In many countries, the agency is a state, provincial, territorial, or local government department. The agency provides or finds foster care for the child or adult and is accountable to the court for the welfare of the individual.

The agencies that run foster care programs select, train, and supervise the people who provide foster care. The provider may be a relative of the foster person. Such an arrangement is called *kinship care.*

People who provide foster care often need special skills to help the children or adults they care for live healthy and enjoyable lives. Professional foster care associations, social service agency workers, and others train foster care providers and help them deal with difficult situations. Most people who provide foster care as private individuals receive financial payment or reimbursement from their state, province, or territory. Most states, provinces, and territories inspect foster care institutions, group homes, and family homes. They license or approve the homes before placing individuals in their care, as well as on an ongoing basis.

Most programs try to establish a more permanent home for individuals in foster care by providing counseling, treatment, or other assistance to help their families care for them at home. If children or youth are not able to return to their birth families, they may go to live with other relatives or be adopted by their foster parents or another family.

Some adults and older adolescents in foster care attend *independent living programs.* These programs teach individuals in foster care skills that prepare them to care for themselves.

Foster care continues for as long as the child or adult needs support or supervision and until a permanent living arrangement has been found. Most children placed in foster care do not spend their entire childhood there.

Susan Cutler Egbert

Foucault, *foo KOH,* **Jean Bernard Léon,** *zhahn behr NAR lay AWN* (1819-1868), a French physicist, used a revolving mirror to measure the speed of light. Some types of measuring apparatus still use adaptations of his method. Foucault proved in 1850 that light travels more slowly in water than in air, and that the speed varies inversely with the index of refraction. He also made improvements in the mirrors of reflecting telescopes.

Foucault demonstrated the rotation of Earth on its axis with a pendulum experiment, and also by using a gyroscope that maintained its axis in a fixed direction while Earth turned relative to that direction (see **Gyroscope; Pendulum** [Other pendulums]). Foucault also discovered the existence of *eddy currents.* These currents are produced in a conductor moving in a magnetic field. Foucault was born on Sept. 18, 1819, in Paris. He died on Feb. 11, 1868. Naomi Pasachoff

Foucault, *foo KOH,* **Michel,** *mee SHEHL* (1926-1984), was a French philosopher and historian. His theories have been widely influential in the study of culture, literature, history, and related fields.

In *The Order of Things* (1966), Foucault divided the history of European culture since 1500 into three eras separated by intervals of disruptive change. The eras were the late Renaissance (1500's), the classical era (mid-1600's to late 1700's), and the modern era (early 1800's to the present). He defined each era by a distinct *episteme,* meaning a set of relations that organize and produce whatever counts as knowledge in that era. Each episteme follows others in no logical sequence.

In *The Archaeology of Knowledge* (1969), Foucault describes *discursive practices,* by which he means the language and ideas used by a particular profession or that define a particular field of knowledge. He wrote several books about the role of discursive practices in the development of medical clinics, mental hospitals, and prisons. He wanted to show how discursive practices emerged and changed. He also wanted to reveal the way they enabled some groups to exert power over society and individuals. Foucault's final work was the three-volume *The History of Sexuality* (1976, 1984), in which he traced the ways of talking about sexuality and of attempts to channel, control, or regulate it. Foucault was born on Oct. 15, 1926, in Poitiers. He died on June 25, 1984. Donald G. Marshall

Foundation. See Building construction; House.

Foundation is a nongovernmental, nonprofit organization that aids educational, social, charitable, religious, or other activities. Gifts of money from wealthy individuals and groups help establish and finance most foundations. Foundations are usually governed by one or more legally appointed administrators called *trustees* or *directors.* The trustees may administer the foundation by themselves or hire executives to manage the foundation's work. Many foundations are called *endowments, funds, nonprofit corporations,* or *trusts.*

Foundations vary in the ways they manage and spend their funds. They may support programs in a wide range of fields or only in a specific area. Some foundations are designed to spend all their money within a specified period, such as a certain number of years following a donor's death. Others operate *in perpetuity* (without time limit). Foundations that operate in perpetuity try to preserve their assets—such as stocks and bonds—while spending only as much money as the law requires. The legal requirement is sometimes called a *payout rate.*

Foundations are more common and influential in the United States than they are in most other countries. Major U.S. foundations include the Ford Foundation, the Bill & Melinda Gates Foundation, the J. Paul Getty Trust, and the Robert Wood Johnson Foundation. Other prominent foundations include the Lucie and André Chagnon Foundation and the Vancouver Foundation in Canada; the Ian Potter Foundation in Australia; the Gatsby Charitable Foundation and the Wellcome Trust in the United Kingdom; the Compagnia di San Paolo in Italy; and the Robert Bosch Foundation in Germany.

The Foundation Center, an independent organization headquartered in New York City, is the leading source of information about United States foundations. It maintains a directory of thousands of U.S. foundations and their grants. The directory is available online and in print form. The Canadian counterpart of the Foundation Center is Imagine Canada, with headquarters in Toronto. Philanthropy UK, headquartered in London, performs similar functions in the United Kingdom.

Kinds of foundations

Foundations differ in the ways that they are funded, organized, and managed. The two main categories are *privately supported* foundations and *publicly supported* foundations. Privately supported foundations receive funding from a single source, such as an individual, family, or business. Publicly supported foundations receive funding from a variety of sources. Private foundations include *independent* foundations, *company-sponsored* foundations, and *operating* foundations. The most common type of publicly supported foundation is the *community* foundation.

Independent foundations are established by individuals or families and often bear their founders' names. Examples of independent foundations include the Carnegie Corporation of New York, the Chagnon and Ford foundations, and the Lilly Endowment. The charters of many independent foundations allow them to make grants in a variety of fields, such as education, health, and social welfare.

Company-sponsored foundations receive funds from profit-making businesses. The foundations are legally separate from the businesses, but usually operate under their control. The foundations are also separate from charitable giving programs administered directly by the businesses. Major company-sponsored foundations include the Alcoa Foundation, Fidelity

Foundation, General Motors Foundation, and Merck Company Foundation.

Operating foundations directly run programs determined by their charter or governing body. Operating foundations award few or no grants to outside organizations. For example, the J. Paul Getty Trust runs art museums and related programs.

Community foundations, sometimes called *community trusts,* operate much like private foundations. However, their funds come from many donors rather than from a single individual, family, or corporation. These foundations make grants for social, educational, or other charitable purposes in a specific community or region. Their boards of directors tend to represent the community served. Large community foundations include the Cleveland Foundation, the Marin Community Foundation, the New York Community Trust, and the Vancouver Foundation.

The work of foundations

Foundations support organizations and programs in a variety of fields. These fields include education, human services, health, arts and humanities, public and society benefit, environment and animals, science and technology, and international affairs. Most foundations define their purposes broadly, to allow trustees some degree of flexibility in how they distribute funds. For example, the charter of the Rockefeller Foundation states that its purpose is "to promote the well-being of mankind throughout the world."

Education is historically the largest category of foundation giving. Many foundation grants go to elementary schools, high schools, institutions of higher education, and libraries.

The Gates Foundation and the Lilly Endowment are

Major foundations throughout the world

Name	Assets†	Founded	Headquarters
Annenberg Foundation	1,602,000,000	1989	Los Angeles
Atlantic Philanthropies	2,292,000,000	1982	Hamilton, Bermuda
Bertelsmann Foundation	1,200,000,000	1977	Gütersloh, Germany
Bosch Foundation, Robert	6,955,000,000	1964	Stuttgart, Germany
Chagnon Foundation, Lucie and André	1,115,000,000	2000	Montreal, Canada
Compagnia di San Paolo	8,205,000,000	1563	Turin, Italy
Ford Foundation*	10,882,000,000	1936	New York City
Gates Foundation, Bill & Melinda*	33,912,000,000	2000	Seattle
Gatsby Charitable Foundation	712,000,000	1967	London
Getty Trust, J. Paul	9,339,000,000	1953	Los Angeles
Hewlett Foundation, William and Flora	6,869,000,000	1966	Menlo Park, California
Johnson Foundation, Robert Wood	8,490,000,000	1936	Princeton, New Jersey
Kellogg Foundation, W. K.*	7,238,000,000	1930	Battle Creek, Michigan
Lilly Endowment*	5,150,000,000	1937	Indianapolis
MacArthur Foundation, John D. and Catherine T.	5,238,000,000	1970	Chicago
McConnell Family Foundation, J. W.*	401,000,000	1937	Montreal, Canada
Mellon Foundation, Andrew W.*	5,052,000,000	1969	New York City
Nobel Foundation	437,000,000	1900	Stockholm, Sweden
Packard Foundation, David and Lucile	5,699,000,000	1964	Los Altos, California
Rhodes Trust	173,000,000	1902	Oxford, United Kingdom
Rockefeller Foundation*	3,317,000,000	1913	New York City
Vancouver Foundation*	726,000,000	1943	Vancouver, Canada
Vehbi Koç Foundation	1,200,000,000	1969	Istanbul, Turkey
Wallenberg Foundation, Knut and Alice	6,891,000,000	1917	Stockholm, Sweden
Wellcome Trust*	19,692,000,000	1936	London

*Has a separate article in *World Book.*
†In U.S. dollars.
Figures are for 2009 or more recent years.
Sources: *World Book* estimates based on data from the Foundation Center, Canada Revenue Agency, and individual foundation websites.

prominent foundations in this field. In the 1950's, the Ford Foundation and the Carnegie Corporation of New York collaborated to establish the National Merit Scholarship Corporation, which awards scholarships to outstanding high school students in the United States. The Carnegie Corporation also helped launch the educational television program "Sesame Street" in the 1960's. Other important foundations that support education include the Annenberg Foundation, J. W. McConnell Family Foundation, and Walton Family Foundation.

Human services covers youth development; legal, justice, and anticrime programs; housing and shelter; recreation and sports; food, nutrition, and agriculture; employment; and safety and disaster relief. The Annie E. Casey Foundation, the Chagnon Foundation, the W. K. Kellogg Foundation, the Lilly Endowment, and the Harry and Jeanette Weinberg Foundation rank among the leading foundations in this area.

Health has traditionally been a major area of foundation giving. Most grants go to organizations involved with hospitals and medical care; medical research; mental health; and specific diseases, such as cancer or AIDS. Beginning in 1915, the Rockefeller Foundation led a successful 30-year effort to develop and administer a vaccine to prevent yellow fever. In the 1970's, the Johnson Foundation played an important role in developing the 911 emergency medical service system throughout the United States. Other major contributors to health causes include the Duke Endowment, the Gates Foundation, the Kellogg Foundation, the Albert and Mary Lasker Foundation, the Robert W. Woodruff Foundation, Canada's SickKids Foundation, and Australia's Heart Foundation.

Arts and humanities. Foundations play a leading role in supporting the arts and humanities. Most grants go to performing arts groups, museums, and organizations involved with media and with historic preservation. Funding provided by foundations associated with financier and art collector Andrew W. Mellon helped build and maintain the National Gallery of Art in Washington, D.C. Foundations active in the field of arts and humanities include the Annenberg Foundation, the Ford Foundation, the J. Paul Getty Trust, the Andrew W. Mellon Foundation, and the Wallace Foundation.

Public and society benefit, sometimes known as *social welfare,* includes civil rights, social action, community improvement, and public affairs. It also includes grants to promote philanthropy and volunteerism. Many foundations grant money to federated giving programs, such as the United Way, the Jewish Federation, and the Catholic Appeal. Important foundations in this field include the Ford Foundation, the Kellogg Foundation, the John D. and Catherine T. MacArthur Foundation, the Charles Stewart Mott Foundation, and the Pew Charitable Trusts.

Environment and animals programs promote the protection of natural resources, botanical and horticultural projects, pollution control, and wildlife preservation. Foundations that fund efforts to conserve natural resources include the McConnell Family Foundation, the Gordon and Betty Moore Foundation, the David and Lucile Packard Foundation, and the Turner Foundation.

Science and technology receive a relatively small percentage of foundation grants. But some science-related grants—for example, in engineering education or biomedical research—may be included in other categories. The W. M. Keck Foundation funded Hawaii's Keck Observatory and created the Keck Graduate Institute of Applied Life Sciences in California. The Packard Foundation established and funded the Monterey Bay Aquarium Research Institute, a marine research facility in California. The Gates Foundation has funded research on the human *genome* (complete set of genes in a cell).

International affairs usually interest a relatively small percentage of foundations. But certain world events—such as a natural disaster or a major political change—can have a dramatic effect on the amount of support they provide. The principal funding areas include economic development and relief services; security and arms control; educational and cultural exchanges; foreign policy issues; and human rights.

In the 1940's, the Rockefeller Foundation—later joined by the Ford Foundation and others—began funding research centers in Mexico and, in the 1960's, in the Philippines and elsewhere. Scientists at these centers developed much better-yielding rice and wheat varieties. Widespread use of these varieties led to the "green revolution," a huge increase in the capacity of poor nations to feed themselves.

Other foundations concerned with international affairs include the Central European University Foundation and the Open Society Institute. Both are funded by the Hungarian-born American financier George Soros. The Ford Foundation has grant-making programs in many countries throughout the world.

History

Early organizations that resembled foundations emerged in ancient Greece and ancient Rome. The Greek philosopher Plato established a fund to support his academy. Many Roman emperors set up municipal foundations for the relief of the poor. During the Middle Ages, which lasted from about the A.D. 400's through the 1400's, the Roman Catholic Church administered private funds for hospitals, schools, and other charitable causes.

Similar organizations were established in the United States in the late 1700's and early 1800's. In 1790, the will left by the American statesman Benjamin Franklin established funds for the poor in Boston and Philadelphia. In 1846, funds left by the British scientist James Smithson were used to found the Smithsonian Institution "for the increase and diffusion of knowledge among men." The first modern American foundations were the Peabody and Slater funds. George Peabody, an American banker, founded the Peabody Education Fund in 1867 to aid public education in the southern United States after the American Civil War (1861-1865). John Fox Slater, a manufacturer, founded the Slater Fund in New York in 1882 to help educate former slaves in the South.

Andrew Carnegie, one of the greatest steel manufacturers in the United States, spread the idea in the late 1800's that people with large fortunes should give away part of their wealth for the betterment of humanity. Carnegie established several funds, including the Carnegie Endowment for International Peace, the Carnegie Foundation for the Advancement of Teaching, and the Carnegie Corporation of New York. Many other wealthy people—such as John D. Rockefeller, Henry Ford, Andrew

W. Mellon, J. Paul Getty, Julius Rosenwald, David and Lucile Packard, Bill Gates, and Warren Buffett—have worked to follow the example of Carnegie.

Leslie Lenkowsky

Related articles in *World Book* include:

Biographies

Carnegie, Andrew	Kellogg, W. K.
Field, Marshall, I	Mellon, Andrew
Ford, Henry	Rockefeller, John Davison
Gates, Bill	Smithson, James
Getty, J. Paul	Soros, George

Foundations

See the separate articles on some of the major foundations listed in the table with this article. See also:
Carnegie Corporation of New York
Carnegie Foundation for the Advancement of Teaching
Heritage Foundation
Mott Foundation
National Science Foundation
Pew Charitable Trusts

Other related articles

Brookings Institution	Rhodes Scholarship
Endowment	Scholarship
Fellowship	Smithsonian Institution
Philanthropy	United Way Worldwide

Founding Fathers were American statesmen of the revolutionary period (late 1700's), particularly those who wrote the Constitution of the United States. The Founding Fathers included Benjamin Franklin, Alexander Hamilton, James Madison, Gouverneur Morris, George Washington, and other delegates to the Constitutional Convention of 1787.   Donna J. Spindel

See also **Constitution of the United States.**

Foundry is a plant where workers make molded metal products called *castings*. Products made in foundries range from engine blocks to toy soldiers. The process of pouring melted metals into molds is called *founding.* The metals commonly used include aluminum, brass, bronze, iron, lead, magnesium, steel, and zinc (see **Cast and casting**). Dies can also be made in foundries (see **Die and diemaking**).

Foundries that turn out heavy castings often do their founding in large pits in the floor. Overhead cranes ease the work of lifting and carrying the heavy molds and castings from place to place. Some foundries are highly automated. In such foundries, machines are used to make the molds, pour the metal, and clean the castings.

Thomas J. Misa

See also **Forging.**

Fountain is a jet or stream of water that rises naturally or artificially as a result of pressure. In a natural fountain, this pressure comes from the weight of water collected in a reservoir, the water's temperature, or both. The water flows through an underground passage until it can discharge, as in a spring, or shoot out, as in a geyser. In artificial fountains, pumps supply the pressure. This article deals with artificial fountains.

Artificial fountains can be both decorative and practical. They help keep pools and ponds clean and can reduce excess flow of water. Many decorative fountains are in plazas, parks, and malls. In such fountains, water may flow from or over sculptures of people, mythical creatures, or natural objects. People enjoy watching and hearing the water's movement.

Fountains have existed for thousands of years. In ancient Greece, people built fountains above springs thought to have magical powers. The Greeks added beautiful statues of Greek gods and goddesses to the flowing waters. The ancient Romans built hundreds of fountains in Rome, copying Greek designs.

Some of the most complicated and beautiful fountains in Europe were built during the Renaissance and Baroque periods, from the 1500's to the 1700's. Elaborate pumping systems created wide cascades of water, channeled water down steps, or forced it to shoot up in powerful jets. Many famous fountains were built during the 1600's and 1700's. These include the Fountain of the Four Rivers (1651) and the Trevi Fountain (1762), both in Rome. The fountains at the Palace of Versailles (begun in 1661), near Paris, are also well known.

During the late 1800's and early 1900's, many fountains that imitated Classical designs were built in city parks and public squares and on private estates in the United States. Beginning in the 1960's, many U.S. landscape architects introduced fresh ideas into fountain design. Today, architects use computers to control lights and waterflow in public fountains. These fountains are as elaborate and beautiful as those of any previous era.

Robert R. Harvey

See also **Artesian well; Geyser; Rome** (picture: The Fountain of Neptune); **Taft, Lorado** (picture); **Versailles, Palace of** (picture).

A fountain at the Palace of Versailles, near Paris, is one of several beautiful fountains on the palace grounds. Begun in 1661, the Versailles fountains had elaborate pumping systems that were characteristic of many fountains built in Europe from the 1500's to the 1700's.

Fountain of Castalia. See Parnassus.

Fountain of Youth was an imaginary spring. Many legends were told about it in both Europe and America. The waters of the spring were supposed to make old people young.

Early Spanish settlers in the Caribbean region believed that the Fountain of Youth was on an island called Bimini. In 1513, the Spanish explorer Juan Ponce de León set out to find Bimini. During his voyage, he discovered Florida, which since then has been linked to the imaginary fountain.   Helen Delpar

See also **Ponce de León, Juan.**

Four Corners is the only place in the United States where four states meet. Arizona, Colorado, New Mexico, and Utah come together at this point. A monument marks the site, identified during an 1868 federal government survey. The monument includes a granite and brass marker that bears the seals of the four states. In 2009, officials from the National Geodetic Survey said that the 1868 survey had been inaccurate. Legal experts pointed out, however, that the state boundary markers had become legally binding once the four states accepted the 1868 survey. As a result, the location of the monument is correct. For location, see **United States** (political map).   Lay James Gibson

Four-eyed fish. See Anableps.

4-H is a youth organization that helps young people learn skills, serve their communities, and gain real-world experience. 4-H programs operate in more than 70 countries. In the United States, millions of young people participate in 4-H. Hundreds of thousands of adults serve as volunteer leaders. The 4-H emblem is a green four-leaf clover. It has a white *H* on each leaf. The four *H's* stand for *head, heart, hands,* and *health.*

The 4-H movement began in the United States during the early 1900's. At first, 4-H programs revolved around after-school clubs and fairs with an emphasis on agriculture and related activities. Participants worked on projects such as canning, raising livestock and poultry, and growing crops. Today, only about 11 percent of 4-H members in the United States live on farms. The modern organization serves youth in rural, urban, and suburban communities in every state of the United States.

Members of 4-H work on a variety of projects and activities. These projects and activities focus on citizenship, healthy living, and science. 4-H also operates a number of programs, both in and out of schools. The programs educate members in such areas as agriculture, computer science, environmental protection, robotics, rocketry, and sustainable energy.

The Cooperative Extension System guides 4-H work in the United States. The system is a nationwide educational network (see **Cooperative extension system**). The extension system works in cooperation with state *land-grant universities.* Such universities are partly endowed by the U.S. government (see **Land-grant university**). An extension office in nearly every county of the United States employs one or more agents. The agents recruit and assist local 4-H volunteer leaders. They also help members with projects.

National 4-H Council

The 4-H emblem is a four-leaf clover with an *H* on each leaf. The four *H's* stand for *head, heart, hands,* and *health.*

Organization

In the United States, anyone 9 to 19 years old may become a member of 4-H. Some states also have a program—usually called Cloverbuds—for children from 5 to 9 years old. College-aged youths can join a program called Collegiate 4-H. In Canada, the ages for membership vary depending on the province.

Young people may participate in 4-H through a variety

© Linda Stelter, Birmingham News/Landov

Teamwork and leadership are a major emphasis of many 4-H programs. In this photo, 4-H members must work together to lift a hula hoop, using one finger each. 4-H encourages members to plan group activities and become active in their communities.

of programs, including 4-H clubs, 4-H camps, and both afterschool and in-school programs. Youth may also form a 4-H special interest club. Members of a special interest club work on a joint project or workshop. In addition, 4-H offers membership through individual study programs and instructional television programs.

Slogans and symbols. 4-H encourages members to "Join the Revolution of Responsibility." This slogan refers to a movement for positive change in communities. Young people are challenged to make measurable differences wherever they live.

4-H members reinforce their high standards with the motto, "To Make the Best Better," and with this pledge:

I pledge My Head to clearer thinking,
My Heart to greater loyalty,
My Hands to larger service, and
My Health to better living,
For my club, my community, my country, and my world.

There is no official 4-H uniform. However, many members wear 4-H pins or clothing with the 4-H clover emblem or other identification.

Members and volunteers. Young people may join a 4-H program already in their community. Or they may organize a new club or group. In the United States, members join through their county extension office. In Canada, they enroll through the provincial 4-H agencies. Local clubs operate throughout the United States and Canada.

Volunteers are essential to the success of the 4-H program. Most 4-H clubs choose their own adult volunteer leaders. Many select a parent or other relative of a club member. Adult volunteer leaders donate their time, provide transportation, and purchase some teaching materials. They help members with their projects and activities and also may lead a project group.

Teenagers may become junior or teen leaders after several years of 4-H work. They assist adult leaders. They also help younger members with their work and with their project records.

Government organization. County extension agents help organize 4-H programs within the county. They also help train local volunteer leaders.

AP Photo

Farming activities, once the central focus of 4-H, continue to feature in many 4-H programs. In this photograph, a 4-H member works with a llama at a local farm.

Each state has a 4-H leader at the state land-grant university. State leaders and their staff choose the 4-H projects their state will offer. They organize statewide 4-H events. They also help prepare aids and materials for members and volunteer leaders.

On a national level, 4-H in the United States is directed by an assistant deputy director and a staff for 4-H and youth programs in the U.S. Department of Agriculture. In Canada, most 4-H programs are administered by the provincial departments of agriculture.

The National 4-H Council in the United States supports 4-H work on a nationwide basis. The council is a private, not-for-profit partner of 4-H National Headquarters. The council raises funds, organizes 4-H programs and events, manages communications and the 4-H brand, and develops resources for 4-H professionals and volunteers.

The National 4-H Council also operates the 4-H Mall. The mall is an online store that sells 4-H branded items, such as shirts, pens, and mugs. In addition, the council operates the National 4-H Youth Conference Center in Chevy Chase, Maryland. The center offers 4-H members summer courses on leadership and citizenship. The center also offers leader-training and professional development sessions.

The National 4-H Council was established in 1976. The council resulted from the merger of two previous 4-H organizations—the National 4-H Service Committee and the National 4-H Foundation. A board of trustees administers the National 4-H Council. Its work is supported by contributions from corporations, foundations, and individuals. The national 4-H website at www.4-H.org provides additional information.

Canadian groups. Two national groups—the Canadian 4-H Council and the Canadian 4-H Foundation—provide educational support. The council coordinates 4-H programs and events in Canada. The foundation raises funds for 4-H. Members of both groups represent business and nonprofit organizations as well as the national and provincial governments. The council and foundation headquarters are in Ottawa, Ontario.

Projects and activities

Members of 4-H serve their communities with one or more special projects a year. For example, a 4-H club might plant trees or conduct a bicycle safety program. Many clubs and groups prepare educational exhibits for community fairs.

Individual projects. Each 4-H member carries out at least one project a year. In most states, a member may select the project from a list of 50 to 100 choices. Members may also design their own projects. A 4-H project may involve almost any subject that encourages the young person to learn and to use the imagination. Most projects involve working with and improving the local community.

Some subjects have several project levels. Members may continue working in these subject areas over a number of years. Other projects are for certain age groups. For example, projects for older members include studies about possible career choices or health issues such as drug abuse and physical fitness.

Many 4-H members who live in rural areas choose projects that deal with crops and livestock, forestry, and

Community service enables 4-H members to make a positive difference in the world around them. In this photograph, 4-H members work with offenders and their families at a women's correctional center to prepare healthful snacks.

AP Photo

marketing. Both urban and rural members enjoy projects involving clothing, computers, home improvement, nutrition, public speaking, and the conservation of natural resources.

Various 4-H projects that were once limited to farm youngsters have been developed to serve members in cities as well. A rural youth, for example, may choose a project in raising and caring for a horse. A city youth who does not own a horse may select a project in horsemanship. Projects that once helped rural youth learn how to raise crops have also been made more flexible for city members. For example, suburban youths may learn how to plant large community gardens. Inner-city members who have limited space may learn how to tend backyard plots, window boxes, or indoor plants.

Each 4-H member receives a booklet that explains the requirements of the selected project. The booklet also includes information and questions to make the member think and learn about the subject. For example, a booklet for a project involving food, nutrition, and fitness might include information on consumer choices, food groups, and exercise.

The county extension office provides visual aids and other teaching materials to 4-H members. County agents and volunteer leaders visit members at home to review their projects.

Many 4-H members finish a year's project by preparing an educational exhibit about their subject for a local or county fair. Other members finish their project work by taking part in computer demonstrations, public speaking contests, or other special activities related to their projects. Some members prepare talks and demonstrations to share what they have learned. Members may earn medals, certificates, ribbons, trophies, and scholarships for their work.

Group activities. Teenagers interested in a particular subject may organize a joint project or workshop dealing with that subject. Members of such 4-H special interest groups need not belong to a local 4-H club. After completing a project or workshop, the group may start another one. Or the members may join other special interest groups.

Most 4-H clubs and groups carry out community service activities. For example, they may assist blood drives in their neighborhood. Or they may lead community beautification programs. Many 4-H clubs and groups fight such problems as drug abuse and pollution. Members may help people with disabilities, elderly citizens, and impoverished communities.

4-H members often meet in groups for recreation. They hold picnics and sporting events and go on hikes. Some clubs organize music and drama programs. Camping is a favorite 4-H activity. Thousands of members attend 4-H camps each summer.

Older 4-H members may join county senior clubs and councils or county junior leader groups. Members of these organizations are especially active in community service programs. Older 4-H members also develop leadership abilities as they help younger members with their projects.

National, state, and county events

Soon after Thanksgiving each year, hundreds of U.S. 4-H members meet for the National 4-H Congress. Most *delegates* (chosen representatives) receive free trips to the congress as winners of state, sectional, or national 4-H contests. These contests cover such areas as 4-H projects or citizenship. The congress also honors individuals and businesses for their service to 4-H. Delegates discuss problems that affect young people in the United States. They also hear speeches by leaders in agriculture, government, industry, and science.

Each spring, delegates from the United States and Canada attend the weeklong National 4-H Conference in Chevy Chase. These delegates include both young people and adults. They tour the city and attend workshops to discuss contemporary issues and plan future 4-H programs.

Urban activities have grown in importance for 4-H as cities continue to increase in population. This photograph shows a 4-H city gardening project.

AP Photo

The United States observes National 4-H Week each year during the first full week of October. During that same week, the nation celebrates 4-H National Youth Science Day, a rallying event for 4-H science programs. Newspapers, magazines, radio, and television programs showcase the achievements of young 4-H members.

Many states sponsor meetings similar to the national conferences. Other events sponsored by states and counties include fairs, workshops, camps, and exhibitions.

Each November, the Canadian 4-H Council sponsors a weeklong National 4-H Conference in Toronto. Both Canadian and U.S. 4-H members participate in the conference. The members tour Toronto, meet with government and business officials, discuss current social and economic issues, and exchange ideas about 4-H work.

History

The roots of the 4-H movement can be traced back to the late 1800's. Scientific advances at the time held the potential to make farming easier and more efficient. But researchers at public universities noticed that adults in rural communities were often slow to adopt such advances. The researchers found that young people, on the other hand, were more open to new ways of doing things. Researchers believed that they could introduce agricultural advances to farming communities by teaching them to young people. They thought that young people would be more likely to experiment with new technology and would share their discoveries with adults in their communities.

The desire to connect school education to country life led to the development of hands-on learning programs. Early programs used both public and private resources to help rural youth. A number of community-based programs helped youths learn about industrial advances and solve agricultural challenges.

The first 4-H program was an agricultural club in Clark County, Ohio. A. B. Graham, an American educator, began the program in 1902. It was variously called the Tomato Club or the Corn-growing Club. In the same year, the American educator T. A. (Dad) Erikson of Douglas County, Minnesota, organized agricultural clubs and fairs that met after school. An Iowa educator named Jessie Field Shambaugh organized similar clubs. She

also designed the clover symbol in 1910, earning her the nickname "the mother of 4-H."

In 1914, the Smith-Lever Act established what is now the Cooperative Extension System. The Smith-Lever Act also granted states federal funds to organize boys' and girls' agricultural clubs. By the mid-1920's, these clubs were known as 4-H clubs and used the clover emblem.

Agricultural clubs grew more slowly in Canada. The first clubs began in 1913. But they were not organized nationally until 1931, when the government formed the Canadian Council on Boys' and Girls' Clubs (now called the Canadian 4-H Council).

Expansion. 4-H clubs spread throughout the United States, with extension staff at county and state offices supporting the program. Such staff members provided research-based information, informal education, and technical advice directly to individuals, families, and communities. Over time, 4-H programs began focusing on urban and suburban communities in addition to rural communities.

In 1948, the International Farm Youth Exchange began sending young people to experience farming in other countries. The exchange helped expand 4-H's presence around the globe.

In 2010, 4-H launched its "Join the Revolution of Re-

Library of Congress

Early 4-H programs centered on advances in agriculture and related activities. In this photo, taken at a 1921 4-H fair, three prizewinners demonstrate the canning process they developed.

sponsibility" campaign. The campaign showcased 4-H members' positive effects on their local communities.

Critically reviewed by the National 4-H Council

See also **Agricultural education.**

Four Horsemen of the Apocalypse, *uh PAHK uh lihps,* are beings mentioned in the sixth chapter of the Book of Revelation, the final book of the New Testament in the Christian Bible. The chapter tells of a scroll in God's right hand that is sealed with seven seals. When the first four of these seals are opened, four horsemen appear. Their horses are white, red, black, and pale green. The horsemen represent hardships that the human race must endure before the end of the world, specifically conquest, war, famine, and death.

WORLD BOOK illustration by Lorraine Epstein

The four-o'clock has colorful, fragrant flowers.

Woodcut (about 1496) by Albrecht Dürer; the Metropolitan Museum of Art, Gift of Junius S. Morgan, 1919

The Four Horsemen of the Apocalypse symbolize the forces of destruction and war in the New Testament Book of Revelation. They represent Conquest, War, Famine, and Death.

The four horsemen are often featured in art and literature. The German artist Albrecht Dürer included a picture of them in a series of woodcuts illustrating the Book of Revelation.   Terrance D. Callan

Four-o'clock, also called the *marvel-of-Peru,* is an attractive perennial from tropical America. The plant is easy to grow and is cultivated as an annual in North America.

The four-o'clock gets its name because its flowers open late in the afternoon and close in the morning. The plant grows from 2 to 4 feet (61 to 120 centimeters) high. Its fragrant flowers may be white, pink, red, yellow, or a mixture of some of these colors. What appear to be the

flowers are actually colorful *involucres* (modified leaves) surrounding the tiny true flowers. Four-o'clocks grown in warmer regions may have roots that weigh more than 40 pounds (18 kilograms).

The four-o'clock grows well in almost any kind of soil. The plant can be started from seeds, or from its roots, saved for planting in the spring. The four-o'clock makes an attractive, bushy border plant.   Michael J. Tanabe

Scientific classification. The scientific name of the four-o'clock is *Mirabilis jalapa.*

See also **Flower** (picture: Flowers of the desert).

Fourier, *FOO ree ay,* **Charles** (1772-1837), was an important French socialist. He criticized the social conditions of his times and held that society could be improved if private property were eliminated.

Fourier thought society could be improved through an economic and social regrouping of people. He wanted to create small, self-sufficient farm communities of about 1,600 people each. Each person would own a share of the property in these communities. All people in the community would be required to work, but they could choose their own type of work. Fourier's ideas attracted many followers. However, he could not put together enough money to start such a venture. Fourier was born François Marie Charles Fourier in Besançon, France, on April 7, 1772. He died on Oct. 10, 1837.

Stephen Schneck

Fourteen Points were a set of principles proposed by United States President Woodrow Wilson as the basis for ending World War I (1914-1918) and for keeping the peace. On Jan. 8, 1918, in an address before the U.S. Congress, Wilson stated these proposals, which became famous as the *Fourteen Points.* The proposals included "open covenants openly arrived at," removal of barriers to trade among nations, and "adjustment of all colonial claims." The Fourteen Points also proposed arms reductions, the formation of a "general association of nations," and the principle of *self-determination,* under which no ethnic group would have to be governed by a nation or state it opposed.

Wilson never offered any detailed explanation of how the Fourteen Points might work. In spite of this vagueness, millions hailed the principles as the basis for a free, peaceful world. But at the Paris Peace Conference in 1919, Wilson encountered much opposition to the Fourteen Points. Wilson's principles were frequently modified in the compromises he was forced to make in negotiating the peace treaties.   Kendrick A. Clements

For a summary of the text of the Fourteen Points, see **Wilson, Woodrow** (The Fourteen Points).

Fourteenth Amendment to the Constitution of the United States forbids the states to deny any citizen the rights granted by federal law. It also defines how citizenship is acquired and declares that all citizens are entitled to equal protection of the law. The original purpose of the amendment was to provide citizenship for former slaves and give them full civil rights. Amendment 14 took effect on July 9, 1868.

Through the years, the Supreme Court of the United States has interpreted the 14th Amendment in different ways. In 1905, the court used it in *Lochner v. New York* to strike down state laws regulating working hours. Later courts reversed this decision.

The court has applied the equal protection clause many times. In 1954, in *Brown v. Board of Education of Topeka,* the court ruled that racial segregation in public schools is unconstitutional. In 1971, the court declared in *Reed v. Reed* that no person may be denied equality before the law because of sex. In 1973, in *Roe v. Wade,* the court ruled that states may not prohibit a woman, under certain conditions, from having an abortion. In 1978, the court ruled in *Regents of the University of California v. Allan Bakke* that university admissions programs may not use quotas to achieve racial balance.

June Sochen

See also **Bakke case; Brown v. Board of Education of Topeka; Constitution of the United States** (Amendment 14); **Lochner v. New York; Roe v. Wade.**

Fourth dimension. We usually think of space as having three dimensions: length, width, and height. A box that is 6 feet long, 4 feet wide, and 2 feet high can be described by the ordered set of numbers (6,4,2). Such a set may also describe the position of a point in space—for example, the position of an airplane. But three numbers cannot represent the location of a *moving* plane. To indicate when a plane in flight is at a particular location, such as (6,4,2), we need a fourth dimension—time.

The path of a flying plane can be plotted in four dimensions as shown in the graph to the right, where the plane takes off from point *O* and travels southeast. The position on the *x*-axis shows its distance south of point *O;* the position on the *y*-axis, its distance east of point *O;* and the position on the *z*-axis, its altitude. Curve *P* represents the path of the plane through space. The points along curve *P* indicate the location of the plane at four different times, called t_0 to t_4.

The fourth dimension need not always represent time, however. It may represent anything that we can measure, including temperature and weight.

In the early 1900's, the mathematician Hermann Minkowski realized that the special relativity theory proposed by physicist Albert Einstein described a universe with four dimensions. According to Minkowski, time combines with the three dimensions of space to form *space-time.* Mathematicians afterward began to study geometries of four or more dimensions. See **Relativity.**

Thomas J. Brieske

Fourth estate is a name often given to the newspaper profession. Among the members of the fourth estate are those who gather, write, and edit the news for the press. Some people use the term to refer to journalists in all news media.

The phrase *fourth estate* is believed to have first been used in writing by Thomas Babington Macaulay. In 1828, he wrote in an essay that "The gallery in which the reporters sit has become a fourth estate of the realm."

Macaulay was adding a term to those already used for the three estates, or classes, of the English realm. These were lords spiritual, lords temporal, and commons. The three estates later came to stand for government, while reference to a fourth estate described any other influential body in English political life, such as the army or the press.   Rich Gordon

Fourth of July. See Independence Day.

Fourth Republic. See France (History).

Fovea centralis. See Eye (Focusing; diagrams: Parts of the eye; Structure of the retina).

Fowl. See Poultry; Chicken.

Fox is a doglike animal with a bushy tail and a sharp snout. Foxes belong to the same family of animals as coyotes, dogs, jackals, and wolves. True foxes include the Arctic fox, the gray fox, and the red fox. Several foxlike animals are also called foxes. Foxes and foxlike animals live throughout the world, except in Antarctica and Southeast Asia and on some islands. They may be found in farmlands and forests, on deserts, and even in wooded areas of some cities and suburbs.

Foxes are quick, skillful hunters. The red fox can easily catch a dodging rabbit. This fox can also creep silently toward a bird, then rush up and pounce on it.

Some kinds of foxes have long, soft fur that has historically been valued highly. People still trap foxes for their fur and also raise the animals on fur farms, but such practices have declined in many areas. See **Fur.**

Some people hunt the red fox because of its skill in trying to avoid capture. The hunters use hounds to follow the scent of the fox. Many hunters seek only the excitement of the chase and do not kill the fox. However, other hunters kill foxes, and fox hunting remains a controversial pastime. See **Fox hunting.**

Most foxes are about the same size. Gray foxes and red foxes, the most common kinds in the United States and Canada, grow from 23 to 27 inches (58 to 69 cen-

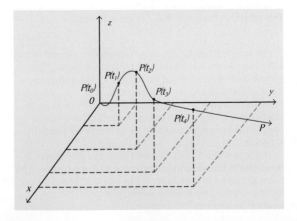

timeters) long. The tail measures an additional 14 to 16 inches (36 to 41 centimeters). Most of these animals weigh from 8 to 11 pounds (3.6 to 5 kilograms).

The body of a fox

Most species of foxes resemble small, slender dogs. But unlike most dogs, foxes have a bushy tail. Foxes also have large, pointed ears and a long, sharp snout.

A fox has keen hearing and an excellent sense of smell. It depends especially on these two senses in locating prey. A red fox can hear a mouse squeak over 100 feet (30 meters) away. Foxes quickly see moving objects, but they might not notice objects that are motionless.

A fox has four toes and a toelike *dewclaw* on each front foot. The animal's dewclaw is actually a nonmovable thumb and does not reach the ground. Each hind foot has only four toes. When a fox walks or trots, its hind paws step into the tracks of the front paws.

Most foxes carry their tails straight backward when running. The tail droops when the animal walks. A fox may sleep with its tail over its nose and front paws. Many foxes have a scent gland on the tail. Scent from this gland gives foxes a distinctive odor.

The life of a fox

Most knowledge about foxes comes from studies of the red fox. The information in this section refers mostly to the red fox, but other species of foxes do not differ greatly.

Foxes live in family groups while the young are growing up. At other times, they live alone or in pairs. They do not form packs as wolves do. A male and a female mate in early winter. They play together and cooperate in hunting. If one of a pair of foxes is chased by an enemy, its mate may dash out of a hiding place and lead the pursuers astray.

Foxes communicate with one another with growls, yelps, and short yapping barks. A fox also makes *scent stations* by urinating at various spots. The scent stations tell foxes in the area that another fox is present.

Young. A female fox gives birth to her young in late winter or early spring. A young fox is usually called a *pup* but may also be called a *cub* or a *kit*. Red foxes have

Facts in brief

Names: *Male,* dog; *female,* vixen; *young,* pup, cub, or kit.
Gestation period: 49 to 79 days, depending on species.
Length of life: Up to 14 years.
Where found: Throughout the world except Antarctica, Southeast Asia, and some islands.
Scientific classification: Foxes belong to the family Canidae. The bat-eared fox is *Otocyon megalotis.* The gray fox is *Urocyon cinereoargenteus.* The kit fox is *Vulpes velox.* The red fox is *Vulpes fulva.* The maned wolf is *Chrysocyon brachyurus.* The raccoon dog is *Nyctereutes procyonoides.*

four to nine pups at a time. Gray foxes have three to five. Both the *vixen* (female) and the *dog* (male) bring their pups food and lead enemies away from them.

A newborn fox weighs about 4 ounces (110 grams) and has a short muzzle and closed eyes. Its eyes open about nine days after birth. Pups drink the mother's milk for about five weeks. Then they begin to eat some solid food and leave their den for short periods. Later, the pups wrestle with one another and pounce on insects, leaves, sticks, and their parents' tails. The adults also bring live mice for the young to pounce on. Later, the adults show the pups how to stalk prey. The pups start to live on their own in late summer and may wander far from their place of birth. The parents may separate then or in early fall and rejoin during the winter.

Dens. Foxes settle in dens after mating. A fox den may be underground, in a cave, among rocks, or in a hollow log or tree. Some red foxes dig their own dens, but most use burrows abandoned by such animals as woodchucks. The foxes may enlarge a burrow if necessary. An underground den may be as long as 75 feet (23 meters) and have several entrances. A main tunnel leads to several chambers that the animals use for nests and for storing food. Two pairs of red foxes may share one burrow. Gray foxes dig less than red foxes. Most gray foxes live in caves, rock piles, logs, or tree holes.

Many kinds of foxes live in dens only while raising pups. When the pups can hunt for themselves, the adults and pups both sleep in the open most of the time.

Food. Foxes eat almost any animal they can catch easily, especially mice and other kinds of rodents. They also

© Thinkstock © Shutterstock

Red foxes live in family groups. An adult male and female, *above left,* stay together after mating until their pups, also called *cubs* or *kits,* mature. Red fox pups, *above right,* stay close to the den when they are young, but they venture farther afield as they grow older.

The skeleton of a fox

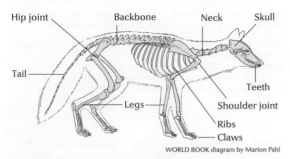

Hip joint — Backbone — Neck — Skull
Tail —
Legs —
Teeth
Shoulder joint
Ribs
Claws

WORLD BOOK diagram by Marion Pahl

hunt birds, frogs, insects, lizards, and rabbits. Foxes also eat many kinds of fruit and the remains of dead animals. Most species hide the uneaten parts of their prey. They dig a hole, drop the meat in, and spread dirt over it.

Foxes may prey on farmers' chickens if the birds roam freely or if the chicken coops are not closed tightly. But foxes help farmers by eating mice and rats. In some areas where foxes had been killed off, rodents increased so much that farmers brought in other foxes.

Hunting. Foxes hunt mostly at night and remain active the year around. They often roam grassy meadows and listen for the squeaks of mice. The grass conceals the mice, but if a fox sees a slight movement of blades of grass, it jumps onto the spot. Foxes sometimes stand on their hind legs to get a better view in tall grass. A fox also may lie in wait and pounce on a ground squirrel or a woodchuck as the victim leaves its burrow.

Kinds of foxes

Red foxes live throughout most of Asia, Europe, and northern North America. They are the most common foxes of Canada and the northern United States.

The majority of red foxes have bright rusty-red or red-orange fur, with whitish fur on the belly. They have blackish legs and a white tip on the tail. But not all red foxes have red coats. Some, called *silver foxes,* have coats of black fur tipped with white. Silver foxes may appear blackish, gray, or frosty silver, depending on the length of the white tips. Silver foxes with black fur are called *black foxes.* Other red foxes, called *cross foxes,* have rusty-red coats with a large black cross at the shoulders. The cross extends down the middle of the back. Silver foxes, cross foxes, and typical red foxes may be born at the same time to the same parents.

Kit foxes, also called *swift foxes,* roam the grasslands and deserts of western North America. The kit fox has sandy yellow-gray fur with a black tip on the tail. This fox, a close relative of the red fox, measures from 15 to 20 inches (38 to 51 centimeters) long, not including a tail 11 inches (28 centimeters) long. It weighs from 4 to 6 pounds (1.8 to 2.7 kilograms). This animal got its name because of its small size. The word *kit* means a young or small furry animal. See **Animal** (Animals of the deserts [picture]).

Gray foxes live throughout most of the United States, Mexico, and Central America, and in part of northern South America. Some live in the far southern parts of Canada. They are the most common foxes of the southern United States. The gray fox's back is the color of salt and pepper mixed together. Its underparts are whitish.

The sides of the neck, shoulders, and legs, and the tail's underside are rust-colored. The tail has a black tip. This fox is also called the *tree fox* because it climbs trees.

Arctic foxes live in the far northern regions of Asia, Europe, and North America. The long fur of the Arctic fox's coat protects the animal from the extreme cold. The Arctic fox has shorter, more rounded ears than most other foxes. These small ears let less body heat escape than larger ears would. Arctic foxes are about the same size as red foxes. See **Arctic fox.**

Fennecs, the smallest kind of foxes, live in the deserts of North Africa and Arabia. A fennec grows only about 16 inches (41 centimeters) long and weighs 2 to 3 pounds (0.9 kilogram to 1.4 kilograms). It has pale sandy fur with whitish underparts. Its ears are 4 to 6 inches (10 to 15 centimeters) long. Fennecs have a large surface area through which they can lose body heat to keep from becoming overheated. See **Fennec.**

Bat-eared foxes, also called *big-eared foxes,* live in dry areas of eastern and southern Africa. A bat-eared fox has large ears that resemble those of a fennec. It has a gray-brown back and sandy underparts. This animal is about the size of a red fox. Bat-eared foxes feed mostly on insects, especially termites. They also eat fruits and such rodents as mice and rats. Bat-eared foxes can change direction sharply while running at full speed, and this ability helps them catch rodents.

Raccoon dogs, which live in eastern Asia, have chunky, grayish bodies and masked faces that make them look like raccoons. But these animals are closely related to foxes, not raccoons. A raccoon dog measures about 22 inches (56 centimeters) long, not including a tail 6 inches (15 centimeters) long. It weighs up to 18 pounds (8 kilograms). Raccoon dogs that live in places with bitter cold winters sleep during much of the winter.

South American "foxes" are not true foxes, but they resemble foxes. They include several grayish or brownish animals of various sizes. The largest one, the *maned wolf,* grows as long as 4 feet (1.2 meters) and may weigh 50 pounds (23 kilograms). It is called a wolf because of its large size, but it looks like a long-legged red fox. It has long, yellowish-orange fur that grows especially

Anthony Mercieca, Photo Researchers

The fennec is a small fox with large ears and a black-tipped tail. The animal rests in a burrow during the day and hunts food at night. Fennecs live in North Africa and Arabia.

E. R. Degginger

The Arctic fox lives in the polar region of the Arctic Ocean. Its long fur coat protects the animal from the extreme cold.

long and manelike along the middle of its back. It feeds on insects, small animals, and fruits.   Clark E. Adams

Fox is one of the four major television networks in the United States. The network's full name is Fox Broadcasting Company. Fox is owned by 21st Century Fox.

Fox was established in 1986 by the Australian-born media executive Rupert Murdoch. In 1985, Murdoch became an American citizen so that he could buy a chain of U.S. TV stations. He then bought the Twentieth Century Fox motion-picture studio in Hollywood. Murdoch used his stations to launch the Fox network. Until 2013, Fox was owned by News Corporation (also called News Corp). That year, News Corp was separated into two companies. The entertainment part of the business, which included Fox, was renamed 21st Century Fox. The name News Corp was retained for newspaper and other publishing ventures.

The new network had early successes with the situation comedy "Married . . . with Children" and the animated series "The Simpsons," which both poke fun at American popular culture and family life. "The Simpsons" is the longest-running series in TV history.

Fox helped pioneer reality television in the late 1980's with the popular crime series "America's Most Wanted" and "Cops." In the early 1990's, Fox introduced prime-time soap operas aimed at teenage and young-adult audiences with "Melrose Place" and "Beverly Hills 90210." It also made a strong pitch to African American viewers with "In Living Color," a variety show featuring a predominantly black cast. The show became a cornerstone for a cluster of Fox shows aimed at black viewers.

In the mid-1990's, Fox sought to expand its reach with shows aimed at mass audiences. The science-fiction series "The X-Files" (1993-2002) gained a wide audience. The singing competition show "American Idol," which began in 2002, has attracted some of the biggest audiences in television history.   Michael Curtin

See also **Murdoch, Rupert.**

Fox, Charles James (1749-1806), a brilliant English statesman and speaker, was a friend of the American Colonies in their fight for freedom. He also defended the French Revolution (1789-1799) when most British leaders, including Edmund Burke, opposed it.

Fox was born on Jan. 24, 1749, in Westminster. In 1768, he entered Parliament as a Tory, but later joined the Whig Party. Because of his support in Parliament of the

American Colonies during the American Revolution (1775-1783), King George III became his enemy. Fox had a major role in the preliminaries of the impeachment of Warren Hastings (see **Hastings, Warren**). Fox also worked for the abolition of the slave trade. Fox became England's secretary for foreign affairs in 1806. He died on Sept. 13, 1806.   James J. Sack

Fox, George (1624-1691), an English religious leader, founded the Society of Friends, or Quakers, about 1647. He taught that the presence of the "Inner Light" in the individual should guide that person's faith and actions. His followers were called Quakers because Fox once told a judge "to tremble at the word of the Lord." See **Quakers.**

As a young man, Fox believed he had received a divine call, and he began traveling to preach his ideas of religion. Missionary work took him through Ireland, Scotland, the Caribbean, North America, and the Netherlands. Fox urged his many followers to give up worldly pleasures. He was imprisoned several times for his teachings. Fox was born in Leicestershire, England, in July 1624. He died on Jan. 13, 1691.   Peter W. Williams

Fox, Paula (1923-   ), an American author, won the 1974 Newbery Medal for her children's novel *The Slave Dancer*. This story describes the experiences of a white boy and a black slave aboard an American ship carrying slaves from Africa in 1840.

Paula Fox was born on April 22, 1923, in New York City. Her other children's books include *How Many Miles to Babylon?* (1967), *The Stone-Faced Boy* (1968), *Portrait of Ivan* (1969), *Blowfish Live in the Sea* (1970), *A Place Apart* (1980), *One-Eyed Cat* (1984), *The Moonlight Man* (1986), and *Lily and the Lost Boy* (1987). She has also written several books for adults.   Virginia L. Wolf

Fox, Terry (1958-1981), was a courageous young Canadian athlete. Fox had only one leg but tried to run across Canada in 1980 to help raise money for cancer research.

Canapress

Terry Fox, a bone cancer victim, raised about $25 million for cancer research during a run across Canada in 1980.

Terrance Stanley Fox was born on July 28, 1958, in Winnipeg, Manitoba. Doctors amputated Fox's right leg above the knee because of bone cancer in 1977 and gave him an artificial leg.

The suffering Fox witnessed in the cancer wards where he was treated inspired him to make his run. He trained for 15 months and began the run in April 1980 at St. John's, Newfoundland. Fox called it the "Marathon of Hope" and averaged nearly a marathon, or about 26 miles (42 kilometers), a day for 143 days. He ran through snow, hail, and intense heat. Fox ran 3,339 miles (5,374 kilometers). He was forced to stop the run near Thunder Bay, Ontario, on September 1 after learning that cancer had spread to his lungs. Fox died on June 28, 1981. His run raised about $25 million for cancer research.

Before Fox died, he was awarded the Order of Canada, the nation's highest civilian honor. In 2005, the Royal Canadian Mint issued a one-dollar coin commemorating Fox. Runs in his memory are held yearly in Canada to raise money for cancer research. Fox's run inspired Steve Fonyo, another Canadian who had lost a leg to cancer. In 1985, Fonyo completed a 14-month, 4,924-mile (7,920-kilometer) run across Canada. Leslie Scrivener

Fox hunting is a sport in which a pack of specially trained hounds track a wild fox in the countryside by using their powers of smell. The most common breeds of dog used in the hunt are the English foxhound, the American foxhound, and the harrier. Historically, fox hunting has been most popular in the United Kingdom, but laws restricting the sport were passed in 2004. However, regular fox hunts have also taken place in many other countries, including Australia, Canada, France, India, Ireland, Italy, Russia, and the United States.

A traditional fox hunt is controlled by one or more supervisors called *masters*. A *huntsman* directs the pack. The huntsman is typically aided by two or three *whippers-in*. The hunters ride horses and wear traditional hunting costumes that include scarlet coats, white neckties called *cravats*, and black velvet caps. The hunt begins with a *meet* where the hunters and hounds gather. The master releases the hounds, who seek the fox. The discovery of the fox is signaled by the barking of the dogs, the sounding of a hunting horn, and a shout of "Tally ho!" The hounds and riders hunt the fox through open countryside, which may include such obstacles as fences, ditches, and streams. The hunt ends when the fox escapes, is killed, or *goes to ground* (hides in a hole). The horses usually are specially trained field hunters.

In the United Kingdom, where foxes are generally considered pests, the goal of the hunt is usually to kill the fox. If the fox is killed, the master awards the animal's *brush* (tail), *mask* (head), and *pads* (feet) to members of the party the master feels contributed most to the success of the hunt. The fox's body is given to the dogs. In the United States, where foxes are not as numerous, the chief purpose of the hunt is the chase. The fox is normally released after being cornered or going to ground.

Fox hunting has aroused much controversy, especially among animal rights activists who consider the sport cruel to the fox. Supporters of fox hunting claim that the hunt is a legitimate sport and helps control the fox population, thus helping farmers protect their livestock. They also say that the hunt is more humane than other methods of killing foxes, such as trapping or poisoning.

In the United Kingdom, supporters also argue that fox hunting represents a significant tradition in rural areas.

Fox hunting originated in ancient times in Assyria, Egypt, and Persia. The modern form of the sport developed in England in the mid-1700's with the red fox as the quarry. In the United States, the gray fox, the coyote, and the lynx are the quarry in different parts of the country.

In 2002, the Scottish Parliament passed a law restricting hunting with dogs in Scotland. The law contained many exemptions, but it did ban some traditional forms of fox hunting. The Parliament of the United Kingdom passed similar restrictions for England and Wales that went into effect in 2005. Supporters of fox hunting have campaigned vigorously against the laws, and the sport continues in the United Kingdom. Neil Milbert

Fox Quesada, Vicente, *fahks kay SAH thah, bee THAYN tay* (1942-   ), served as president of Mexico from 2000 to 2006. Fox represented the Partido Acción Nacional (National Action Party), also known as PAN. He succeeded Ernesto Zedillo Ponce de León of the Partido Revolucionario Institucional (Institutional Revolutionary Party), also known as the PRI. The PRI had ruled Mexico from 1929 to 2000.

Fox was born on July 2, 1942, in Mexico City. He studied business administration at Ibero-American University in Mexico. In 1964, he became a salesman for the Coca-Cola Company in Mexico. He worked his way up to serve as Coke's chief executive in Mexico from 1975 to 1979. In 1979, Fox left Coke to run a family business with his brothers. His business experiences convinced him of the need for political reform.

Fox served in Mexico's Congress from 1988 to 1991. In 1991, he ran for governor of the state of Guanajuato but lost. He won the governorship in 1995 and served until 1999, when he began his presidential campaign.

During his presidency, Fox reinforced the importance of the Mexican judiciary, especially the Supreme Court of Justice, Mexico's highest court. He also enacted a law requiring government agencies to answer questions about their performance. During Fox's presidency, the percentage of Mexicans living in poverty declined for the first time in many years. However, Fox failed to achieve many of his proposed reforms, including reforming the tax system. Despite Fox's personal popularity, many Mexicans were unsatisfied with his performance as president. Roderic A. Camp

Fox terrier. See Smooth fox terrier; Toy fox terrier; Wire fox terrier.

Fox trot. See Ballroom dancing.

Foxglove is a group of plants known for their flowers, which are shaped somewhat like fingers of a glove. Foxgloves are native to Europe, northern Africa, and western and central Asia. The leaves of the purple foxglove and the Grecian foxglove contain a powerful chemical used to make the drug *digitalis*. In rare cases, children and animals have died from this chemical after eating foxgloves. Physicians once used small amounts of digitalis to treat certain heart diseases (see **Digitalis**).

Foxgloves grow 2 to 5 feet (60 to 150 centimeters) tall. Their long oval leaves grow along the stem. The bell-shaped flowers are purple, pink, lilac, yellow, or white—the deeper-colored ones more or less spotted. They grow in clusters along one side of the stem. The plants are biennials or short-lived perennials, usually dying af-

ter the second season. Growers should plant new foxglove seed yearly.   Donna M. Eggers Ware

Scientific classification. Foxgloves make up the genus *Digitalis*. The purple foxglove is *Digitalis purpurea*. The Grecian fox-glove is *D. lanata*.

Foxhound. See American foxhound; English fox-hound.

Foxtail barley is a troublesome weed found through-out North America. It is also called *squirreltail barley* and *wild barley.* The plant has a slender, rounded stem that grows about 2 feet (61 centimeters) tall with narrow, rough leaves. A drooping *spike* (cluster of flowers) grows at the tip of the stem and develops a bristly beard that looks like a fox's tail. Foxtail barley can be a nuisance because it grows rapidly and kills off other plants. Also, its seeds cling to the wool of sheep and irritate their hides. When animals eat the plant, the leaves and flow-ers sometimes stick in their throats and cause them to choke. Foxtail barley may be infected by the toxic fungus ergot (see Ergot).   Harold D. Coble

Scientific classification. The scientific name of foxtail barley is *Hordeum jubatum.*

Foxx, Jimmie (1907-1967), became one of the leading home run hitters in baseball history. A strong righthand-ed batter, Foxx hit 534 home runs during 20 seasons in the major leagues. He won the triple crown of batting in 1933, leading the American League in batting average (.356), home runs (48), and runs batted in (163).

Foxx was used mainly as a catcher and third baseman after breaking into the major leagues with the Philadel-phia Athletics in 1925. He became the team's first base-man in 1929. Foxx remained with the Athletics under manager Connie Mack through 1935. He then played for the Boston Red Sox (1936-1942), the Chicago Cubs (1942 and 1944), and the Philadelphia Phillies (1945). He had a lifetime batting average of .325. In 1932, 1933, and 1938, Foxx was selected the American League's Most Valuable Player. He was elected to the National Baseball Hall of Fame in 1951.

James Emory Foxx was born in Sudlersville, Maryland, on Oct. 22, 1907. He died on July 21, 1967.   Neil Milbert

Foyt, A. J. (1935-   ), became one of the greatest driv-ers in auto racing history. Foyt won the national Indy car championship seven times. He also won 67 Indy car races, more than any other driver. Foyt is one of only three drivers to win the Indianapolis 500 four times. The others are Rick Mears and Al Unser, Sr. Foyt is the only person to win the Indianapolis 500 race, for Indy cars; the Daytona 500 race, for stock cars; and the 24-hour races of Le Mans, France, and Daytona Beach, Florida, for sports cars. In 1993, he retired as a driver but re-mained in racing as a car owner.

Anthony Joseph Foyt, Jr., was born on Jan. 16, 1935, in Houston. Larry Foyt, his son, and A. J. Foyt IV, his grand-son, are also auto racing drivers.   Sylvia Wilkinson

Fra Angelico. See Angelico, Fra.

Fractal, *FRAK tuhl,* is a complex geometric figure made up of patterns that repeat themselves at smaller and smaller scales. Any of its smallest structures is simi-lar in shape to a larger structure, which, in turn, is simi-lar to an even larger one, and so on. The characteristic of looking alike at different scales is called *self-similarity.*

Fractals are actually graphs of simple mathematical equations. Scientists have used fractals to reveal some

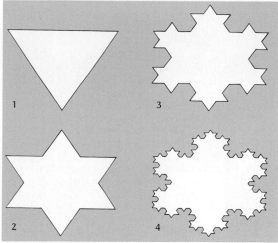

WORLD BOOK diagram by Linda Kinnaman

A Koch snowflake is a fractal that is formed by adding small tri-angles to the sides of larger triangles. This diagram shows the formation of a Koch snowflake in four steps.

of the regularities that occur in natural processes and objects. The branch of a fern plant is an example of a natural fractal. Growing out of the stalk of the branch are leaflets with the same shape as the branch. Each leaflet, in turn, is made up of smaller leaflets that also have the same shape as the branch. Many other plants, including cauliflower and broccoli, have a fractal structure.

There are two main types of fractals—*regular fractals* and *random fractals.* Regular fractals, or *geometric frac-tals,* consist of large and small structures that are exact copies of each other, except for their size. For example, a regular fractal known as the *Koch snowflake* is made up entirely of small triangles added to the sides of larger triangles. In random fractals, the large-scale and small-scale structures may differ in detail. Many irregular pat-terns found in nature, such as the shapes of coastlines, mountains, and clouds, can be represented by random fractals. Other examples include the path of a bolt of lightning and *Brownian motion,* the random movement of a microscopic particle suspended in a fluid.

The study of what became known as fractals began in the late 1800's, when the German mathematicians Georg Cantor and Karl Theodor Wilhelm Weierstrass investi-gated graphs with self-similar properties. Their work re-ceived little attention for many years. Interest increased greatly in the late 1960's, however, especially in the work of Benoît Mandelbrot, a Polish-born American mathe-matician. In 1975, Mandelbrot invented the term *fractal.* He based the term on *fractus,* a Latin word meaning a broken stone with an irregular surface.

In the late 1970's, Mandelbrot and others began to study a particular equation whose graph is a fractal. This equation became known as the *Mandelbrot set.* Scien-tists use computers to produce graphs of the Mandel-brot set because the graphs require a large number of calculations. The computer can "magnify" any section of the fractal by making more and more calculations on the part of the equation represented by that section. The "magnifications" reveal an endless succession of repeat-ing patterns.   Harold M. Hastings

WORLD BOOK photo

Students learn to add fractions. The four basic operations of arithmetic—addition, subtraction, multiplication, and division—can all be performed using fractions.

Fraction

Fraction is a part of something. When objects are measured, often the measurements do not come out in whole units. A book may weigh between 2 and 3 pounds (0.9 and 1.3 kilograms). The amount over 2 pounds is a fraction of a pound. A board may measure between 10 and 11 inches (25 and 28 centimeters) long. It is 10 inches plus a fraction of an inch long. The word *fraction* comes from a Latin word meaning *to break.* Fractions result from breaking a unit up into a number of equal parts. A unit can be broken into any number of parts. If you break a stick into two pieces, however, you do not necessarily have two halves of the stick. To have two halves of the stick, you must break it into two pieces of equal length.

Fractions are written in numerical form as two numerals separated by a line.

$$\text{⅖ or 2/5}$$

In arithmetic, a fraction generally stands for the number of equal parts into which something has been divided and the number of those parts that are being considered. For example, the fraction ⅖ represents two parts of something that has been divided into five equal parts.

The fraction form is also used for (1) expressing division, (2) representing a ratio, and (3) stating a rate. In expressing division, the fraction ⅖ may indicate two divid-

Karen Connors Fuson, the contributor of this article, is Professor of Education at Northwestern University.

ed by five—for example, dividing two candy bars equally among five people. A ratio is a comparison of two quantities that are both measured in the same units. A ratio may compare a part to a whole or a part to another part. For example, if there are two girls and three boys on a debating team, the ratio of girls (a part) to team members (the whole) is two to five (⅖). The ratio of girls (a part) to boys (another part) on the team is two to three (⅔). In mathematics, any number that can be written as the ratio of two whole numbers is called a *rational number* (see **Ratio**). Rate is the relation between two quantities that are measured in different units. For example, a basketball team may score at the rate of two goals per every five minutes of play.

The different uses and meanings of fractions are closely related. Often, understanding one of the meanings of fractions will help make understanding other uses easier. This article concentrates on the meaning of fractions as parts of a whole and examines the use of fractions in arithmetic.

Expressing fractions

In words. The names for fractions come from the number of equal parts into which a whole unit has been divided. In English, there are special names for the fractional parts formed when a unit is divided into two, three, or four equal parts. When a unit is broken into two equal parts, each part is called a half. When it is broken into three equal parts, each part is called a third. And when it is broken into four equal parts, each part is called a quarter or a fourth. The names for other fractional parts are made by adding *-th* to the end of the word that tells the number of equal parts into which the unit has been broken. For example, the fractional parts made by breaking a mile into 10 equal parts are called *tenths* of a mile.

As a unit is broken into more and more equal parts, each part gets smaller and smaller. But the fraction names make it sound as though the parts were getting larger and larger. The *-th* in *sixth,* for instance, means that each part is one of six equal parts of a whole unit. If the same unit were broken into 12 equal parts, each part would be a twelfth. Although a twelfth may sound larger than a sixth, each twelfth actually is only half as big as each sixth. The larger-sounding fraction name means that the original unit has been broken into more—and thus smaller—parts.

The number word before the fraction name tells how many of the fractional parts are being considered. For example, five-sixths represents five of the sixths into which something has been broken. Six-sixths means that a unit has been divided into six equal parts, and all six parts are being considered. Therefore, six-sixths equals one whole unit. Similarly, seven-sevenths, eight-eighths, nine-ninths, and so on all equal one.

In symbols. When fractions are written in numerical form, the bottom, or second, numeral is called the *denominator* (namer). It provides the name of the fraction, telling the number of equal parts into which the unit has been broken. The top, or first, numeral is called the *numerator* (numberer). It tells how many of the fractional parts are being considered. The numerator and the denominator are called the *terms* of a fraction.

Fraction terms

Cancellation involves dividing a numerator and a denominator by the same number.

Common, in arithmetic, means *shared* or *the same.* Fractions with the same denominator, such as ⅓ and ⅔, have a *common denominator.*

Complex fraction has a fraction in its numerator, its denominator, or both. The fraction $7\frac{1}{2}/\frac{5}{6}$ is a complex fraction.

Converting a fraction means changing its form but not its value. For example, ½ can be converted to 6/12 by multiplying both the numerator and the denominator by two: ½ × 6/6 = 6/12. The fraction 6/6 is a form of one.

Decimal fractions have denominators of 10 or of 10 multiplied by itself a number of times.

Denominator is the number written below the line in a fraction. In the fraction ⅔, the denominator is 3. The denominator tells into how many parts a whole has been divided.

Equivalent fractions have different numerators and denominators, but still express the same part of a whole. For example, the fractions ½ and 2/4 are equivalent.

Improper fraction has a numerator that is equal to, or larger than, the denominator. For example, 6/6 and 5/3 are improper fractions.

Mixed number is a combination of a fraction and a whole number. For example, 2 ¼ is a mixed number.

Numerator is the number written above the line in a fraction. In the fraction ⅔, the numerator is 2. The numerator tells how many parts are being considered.

Proper fraction is a fraction whose numerator is smaller than its denominator. For example, ¾ is a proper fraction, because 3 is smaller than 4.

Reducing a fraction means converting it to an equivalent fraction with a smaller numerator and denominator. But the new fraction has the same value as the old.

Term refers to either the numerator or the denominator of a fraction.

Value of a fraction is the number that the fraction stands for. Equivalent fractions, such as ⅔ and 4/6, have the same value and stand for the same number.

Such fractions as 3/10, 7/100, and 3/1,000 are called *decimal fractions.* Decimal fractions have denominators of 10 or 10 multiplied by itself a number of times. Decimal fractions can be written without a denominator by using the decimal system. In this system, the value of each decimal place in a figure is 10 times smaller than that of the place to its left. For example, the first place to the right of the decimal point is the 1/10 's (tenths) place. The second place to the right of the decimal point is the 1/100 's (hundredths) place.

When decimal fractions are written using the decimal system, the number of parts into which the unit has been divided is indicated by the number of decimal places used. The numerals that are in the decimal places used represent the number of parts that are being considered. For example, the fraction 3/10 may be written as

Expressing fractions in words When a unit is divided into two equal parts, each part is called *one-half.* Each of three equal parts of a unit is *one-third.* The names for other fractions are made by adding *-th* to the number of parts.

WORLD BOOK illustration

One unit	
One-*half* of a unit	Broken (divided) into *two* equal parts
One-*third* of a unit	Broken (divided) into *three* equal parts
One-*fourth* of a unit	Broken (divided) into *four* equal parts
One-*fifth* of a unit	Broken (divided) into *five* equal parts
One-*sixth* of a unit	Broken (divided) into *six* equal parts
One-*seventh* of a unit	Broken (divided) into *seven* equal parts
One-*eighth* of a unit	Broken (divided) into *eight* equal parts
One-*ninth* of a unit	Broken (divided) into *nine* equal parts
One-*tenth* of a unit	Broken (divided) into *ten* equal parts
One-*eleventh* of a unit	Broken (divided) into *eleven* equal parts

0.7 in the decimal system. Twenty-seven hundredths is written as 0.27. For information on changing fractions to decimals and changing decimals to fractions, see **Decimal system** (Decimals and fractions).

Equivalent fractions

When two fractions have different numerators and denominators but still express the same part of a whole, they are called *equivalent fractions.* The chart on the following page shows several equivalent fractions.

If you compare the part of the whole unit formed by $\frac{1}{2}$ with the part formed by two $\frac{1}{4}$'s, you can see that they have the same length. When $\frac{1}{2}$ of the original unit is broken into two equal parts, each of those new parts is $\frac{1}{4}$ of the whole unit. The chart also shows that three $\frac{1}{6}$'s are the same as $\frac{1}{2}$ broken into three equal parts, four $\frac{1}{8}$'s are $\frac{1}{2}$ broken into four equal parts, and so on.

Breaking each part of a fraction into more equal parts is the same as multiplying the numerator and the denominator of that fraction by the same number. Multiplying the numerator and denominator of a fraction by the same number produces an equivalent fraction that has larger numbers in both the numerator and denominator.

To make an equivalent fraction with smaller numbers in both numerator and denominator, divide the numerator and denominator by the same number.

$$\frac{6 \div 2}{12 \div 2} = \frac{3}{6} \qquad \frac{5 \div 5}{10 \div 5} = \frac{1}{2}$$

Finding an equivalent fraction with smaller numbers in the numerator and the denominator is called *reducing* the fraction. When no number except 1 can be used to divide both the numerator and denominator evenly, the fraction is said to be *reduced to its lowest terms.*

Comparing fractions

When two fractions have the same denominator, it is easy to tell which fraction is larger. The fraction with the larger number in the numerator is larger, because more parts of the unit are being considered. For instance, $\frac{4}{7}$ of something is larger than $\frac{3}{7}$ of that same thing.

When two fractions have different denominators, it is more difficult to find out which fraction is larger. To compare fractions with different denominators, change the fractions into equivalent fractions. This process is called finding a *common denominator.* An easy way of finding a common denominator is to multiply the two original denominators and use that product as the common denominator. Then, multiply the numerator and denominator of each of the fractions by the number that will give the common denominator. For example, to find out which fraction is larger, $\frac{1}{2}$ or $\frac{3}{7}$, multiply the denominators to find the common denominator: $2 \times 7 = 14$. Fourteen will be the common denominator. To change $\frac{1}{2}$ to an equivalent fraction with 14 in the denominator, multiply both the numerator and the denominator by seven. To change $\frac{3}{7}$ to an equivalent fraction with a denominator of 14, multiply the numerator and the denominator by two, because $7 \times 2 = 14$.

$$\frac{3}{7} \times \frac{}{?} \times \frac{}{14} \quad 7 \times 2 = 14, \quad \frac{3}{7} \times \frac{2}{2} = \frac{6}{14}$$

$$\frac{1}{2} \times \frac{}{?} \times \frac{}{14} \quad 2 \times 7 = 14, \quad \frac{1}{2} \times \frac{7}{7} = \frac{7}{14}$$

So, $\frac{3}{7}$ is equal to $\frac{6}{14}$ and $\frac{1}{2}$ is equal to $\frac{7}{14}$. Because $\frac{7}{14}$ is larger than $\frac{6}{14}$, $\frac{1}{2}$ is larger than $\frac{3}{7}$. This method of finding a common denominator may be thought of as multiplying both the numerator and the denominator of each fraction by the denominator of the other fraction.

Calculations using fractions

Addition and subtraction of fractions can be performed only when the fractions have the same denominator. When the denominators are the same, they name the same sized parts of the whole. You can add sevenths to sevenths to get sevenths. You can subtract thirds from thirds to get thirds. But you cannot add sevenths and thirds, or subtract thirds from sevenths.

To add or subtract fractions that already have the same denominator, add or subtract the numerators but do not change the denominator. The denominator in the answer will be the same as the denominator of the fractions in the problem. When fractions are added or subtracted, the total number of fractional parts changes, but the size of each of those parts does not change.

$$\frac{2}{6} + \frac{3}{6} = \frac{5}{6} \qquad \frac{7}{8} - \frac{5}{8} = \frac{2}{8}$$

To add or subtract fractions that have different denominators, first rename each fraction to an equivalent fraction so that the new fractions have a common denominator. Then add or subtract.

$$\frac{2}{6} - \frac{1}{2} = \frac{2 \times 2}{3 \times 2} - \frac{1 \times 3}{2 \times 3} = \frac{4}{6} - \frac{3}{6} = \frac{1}{6}$$

Multiplication of fractions is similar to multiplication of whole numbers. One meaning for multiplication is that of repeated addition.

3×4 means $4 + 4 + 4$, or three groups of 4.

$3 \times \frac{1}{2}$ means $\frac{1}{2} + \frac{1}{2} + \frac{1}{2}$, or three groups of $\frac{1}{2}$, or three $\frac{1}{2}$'s.

Multiplying to find equivalent fractions is like breaking a fractional part into smaller parts. For example, multiplying both the numerator and denominator of $\frac{1}{2}$ by 3 gives $\frac{3}{6}$, which expresses the same part of the whole as $\frac{1}{2}$. This operation is the same as breaking $\frac{1}{2}$ into three equal parts.

WORLD BOOK illustration

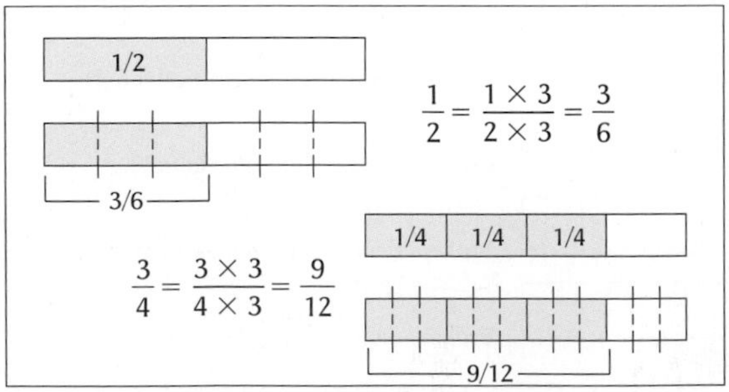

When positive whole numbers are multiplied, the product is *larger* than either of the original numbers. But when a fraction is multiplied by a fraction, the product is *smaller* than the original fraction because you are just taking a part of it.

$\frac{2}{3} \times \frac{4}{5}$ means $\frac{2}{3}$ of $\frac{1}{5}$ + $\frac{2}{3}$ of $\frac{1}{5}$ + $\frac{2}{3}$ of $\frac{1}{5}$ + $\frac{2}{3}$ of $\frac{1}{5}$, or $\frac{2}{3}$ of a group of four $\frac{1}{5}$'s, or $\frac{2}{3}$ of $\frac{4}{5}$.

The fraction $\frac{4}{5}$ stands for four of the parts formed when a unit is divided into five equal parts. The problem $\frac{2}{3} \times \frac{4}{5}$ means taking $\frac{2}{3}$ of each of those four $\frac{1}{5}$'s. We can find $\frac{2}{3}$ of $\frac{1}{5}$ by breaking $\frac{1}{5}$ into three equal parts and taking two of them. When a unit has been divided into five equal parts ($\frac{1}{5}$), and each of these five parts has been further divided into three equal parts ($\frac{1}{3}$), the result is that the original whole unit has been divided into 15 equal parts, or $\frac{1}{15}$'s. Therefore, $\frac{1}{3}$ of $\frac{1}{5}$ is $\frac{1}{15}$. If we take two $\frac{1}{15}$'s from each of four $\frac{1}{5}$'s, we have $\frac{2}{3}$ of $\frac{4}{5}$, or $\frac{8}{15}$.

To multiply two fractions, multiply their two numerators to get the new numerator. Then multiply their two denominators to get the new denominator.

$$\frac{1}{2} \times \frac{1}{4} = \frac{1 \times 1}{2 \times 4} = \frac{1}{8} \qquad \frac{5}{6} \times \frac{3}{4} = \frac{5 \times 3}{6 \times 4} = \frac{15}{24}$$

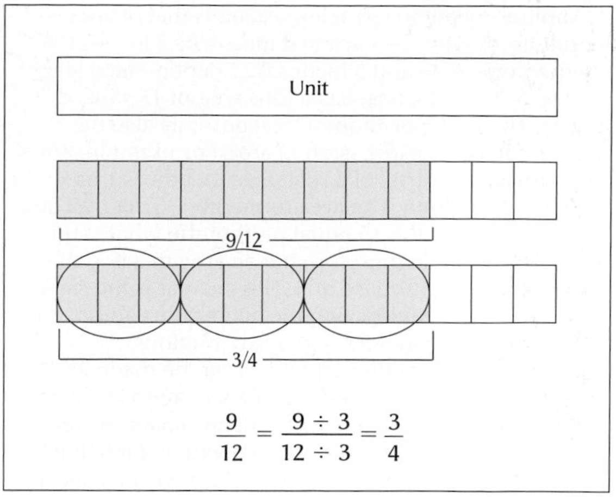
Unit
9/12
3/4
9/12 = 9 ÷ 3 / 12 ÷ 3 = 3/4

WORLD BOOK illustration

Dividing to find equivalent fractions is called *reducing fractions.* For example, dividing the numerator and denominator of $\frac{9}{12}$ by 3 gives $\frac{3}{4}$. This is like grouping nine $\frac{1}{12}$'s into three groups of three $\frac{1}{12}$'s. Each group of three $\frac{1}{12}$'s equals $\frac{1}{4}$.

Equivalent fractions

Fractions may have different numerators and denominators and still express the same part of a whole unit. Such fractions are called *equivalent fractions.* The chart below shows a unit that has been divided into different fractional parts. It also shows several groups of fractional parts that are equivalent to $\frac{1}{2}$, $\frac{1}{3}$, or $\frac{1}{4}$. For example, $\frac{1}{2}$ expresses the same part of the unit as a group of two $\frac{1}{4}$'s ($\frac{2}{4}$) or of five $\frac{1}{10}$'s ($\frac{5}{10}$). For this reason, $\frac{1}{2}$, $\frac{2}{4}$, and $\frac{5}{10}$ are equivalent fractions.

WORLD BOOK chart

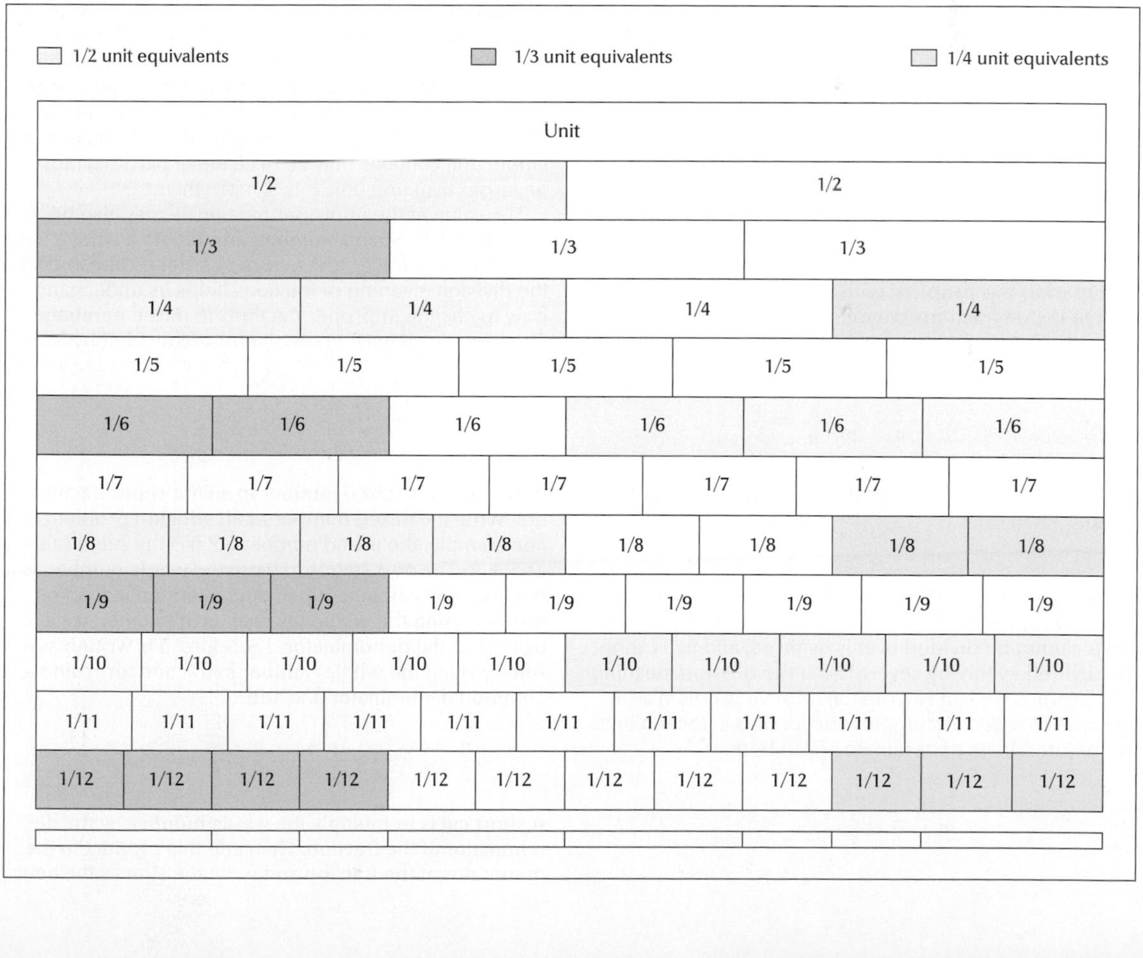
1/2 unit equivalents
1/3 unit equivalents
1/4 unit equivalents
Unit
1/2 1/2
1/3 1/3 1/3
1/4 1/4 1/4 1/4
1/5 1/5 1/5 1/5 1/5
1/6 1/6 1/6 1/6 1/6 1/6
1/7 1/7 1/7 1/7 1/7 1/7 1/7
1/8 1/8 1/8 1/8 1/8 1/8 1/8 1/8
1/9 1/9 1/9 1/9 1/9 1/9 1/9 1/9 1/9
1/10 1/10 1/10 1/10 1/10 1/10 1/10 1/10 1/10 1/10
1/11 1/11 1/11 1/11 1/11 1/11 1/11 1/11 1/11 1/11 1/11
1/12 1/12 1/12 1/12 1/12 1/12 1/12 1/12 1/12 1/12 1/12 1/12

Another meaning of multiplication is that of area—length times width. A card that measures 3 inches (7.6 centimeters) wide and 5 inches (12.7 centimeters) long, or 3 *by* 5 (3 × 5) inches, has a total area of 15 square inches. The multiplication of fractions may also be thought of as the expression of area. For example, $\frac{2}{3} \times \frac{4}{5}$ may indicate the area of a rectangle that measures $\frac{2}{3}$ unit wide by $\frac{4}{5}$ unit long. The area formed by $\frac{2}{3}$ unit by $\frac{4}{5}$ unit includes eight of the 15 equal parts of the whole square unit. The rectangle therefore has an area that is $\frac{8}{15}$ of the area of the whole square unit. This answer is the same as that found by multiplying the numerators and multiplying the denominators of the two fractions.

Often, multiplication of fractions can be made easier by first performing *cancellation*. Cancellation involves dividing both a numerator and a denominator by the same number. This is the same as dividing a fraction by one, and so it does not alter the answer. When canceling, cross out the old terms and write in the new terms. In the following problem, the 7's can be canceled by dividing a numerator and a denominator by 7, and the 6 and the 8 can be canceled by dividing by 2.

$$\frac{\overset{1}{\cancel{7}}}{\underset{4}{\cancel{8}}} \times \frac{\overset{3}{\cancel{6}}}{\underset{1}{\cancel{7}}} = \frac{3}{4}$$

Division. A division problem can be rewritten as a multiplication problem.

$63 \div 9$ means "how many 9's in 63?" or $9 \times ? = 63$.

$\frac{9}{20} \div \frac{3}{4}$ means "how many $\frac{3}{4}$'s in $\frac{9}{20}$?" or $\frac{3 \times ?}{4 \times ?}$? $= \frac{9}{20}$.

The second problem can be rewritten as:

$$\frac{9 \div 3}{20 \div 4} = \frac{?}{?}$$

Comparing this problem with the original one, we see that to divide fractions we must divide the numerators to get the new numerator and divide the denominators to get the new denominator.

$$\frac{9}{20} \div \frac{3}{4} = \frac{9 \div 3}{20 \div 4} = \frac{3}{5}$$

However, many division problems do not come out even.

$$\frac{2}{5} \div \frac{3}{7} = \frac{2 \div 3}{5 \div 7}$$

Two cannot be divided evenly by three, and five cannot be divided evenly by seven. Using the division meaning of fractions, we can rewrite the original problem as a *complex fraction*. A complex fraction has a fraction in its numerator, in its denominator, or in both.

$$\frac{2}{5} \div \frac{3}{7} = \frac{\frac{2}{5}}{\frac{3}{7}}$$

We can simplify this problem by multiplying the fractions in the numerator and the denominator by the *inverse* of the denominator. The inverse of a fraction is formed by putting its numerator in the denominator and its denominator in the numerator. The inverse of $\frac{3}{7}$ is $\frac{7}{3}$. The product of any fraction and its inverse is one.

$$\frac{3}{7} \times \frac{7}{3} = \frac{3 \times 7}{7 \times 3} = \frac{21}{21} = 1$$

Multiplying both the numerator and the denominator of a complex fraction by the inverse of its denominator is the same as multiplying the complex fraction by one. This operation forms a simpler equivalent fraction with a denominator of 1.

$$\frac{2}{5} \div \frac{3}{7} = \frac{\frac{2}{5}}{\frac{3}{7}} = \frac{\frac{2}{5} \times \frac{7}{3}}{\frac{3}{7} \times \frac{7}{3}} = \frac{\frac{2}{5} \times \frac{7}{3}}{\frac{21}{21}} = \frac{2}{5} \times \frac{7}{3}$$

So, $\frac{2}{5} \div \frac{3}{7} = \frac{2}{5} \times \frac{7}{3}$, or $\frac{2}{5}$ times the inverse of $\frac{3}{7}$. Dividing by a fraction is the same as multiplying by the inverse of that fraction.

$$\frac{2}{5} \div \frac{3}{7} = \frac{2}{5} \times \frac{7}{3} = \frac{2 \times 7}{5 \times 3} = \frac{14}{15}$$

Improper fractions

A fraction with a numerator that is smaller than its denominator is called a *proper fraction*. A fraction in which the numerator is equal to or larger than the denominator is called an *improper fraction*. All improper fractions have a value that is equal to or greater than one. For example, the fraction $\frac{27}{20}$ stands for 27 of the parts formed when a unit is divided into 20 equal parts. Because one whole unit contains only 20 of 20 equal parts, $\frac{27}{20}$ must be larger than one unit. It is $\frac{7}{20}$ more than 1.

The value of the improper fraction $\frac{27}{20}$ may also be written as $1\frac{7}{20}$. Such a number, combining a whole number and a fraction, is a *mixed number*. Thinking of the division meaning of fractions helps us understand how to change improper fractions to mixed numbers. For example, $\frac{26}{3}$ may be rewritten as 26 divided by 3.

$$\frac{26}{3} = \begin{array}{r} 8 \\ 3\overline{)26} \\ 24 \\ \hline 2 \end{array} = 8\frac{2}{3}$$

To change a mixed number to an improper fraction, first write the mixed number as an addition problem. For example, the mixed number $5\frac{2}{3}$ has the same value as $5 + \frac{2}{3}$. The next step is to write the whole number as a fraction. Any whole number can be written in fraction form by using the whole number as the numerator and using 1 as the denominator. Therefore, 5 is written as $\frac{5}{1}$. After writing the whole number in fraction form, find a common denominator and add.

$$5\frac{2}{3} = \frac{5}{1} + \frac{2}{3} = \frac{5 \times 3}{1 \times 3} + \frac{2}{3} = \frac{15}{3} + \frac{2}{3} = \frac{17}{3}$$

A short cut is to multiply the whole number by the denominator of the fraction. Then add this product to the numerator of the fraction and write the sum as the new

Two ways of multiplying fractions

The diagram on the left expresses the problem ⅔ × ⅘ by dividing a whole unit into smaller parts and then taking a fraction of those parts. The diagram on the right shows how multiplying fractions can be thought of in terms of area. The blue rectangle represents a fraction of the larger rectangle. One side is ⅔ the length of the large rectangle, and the other is ⅘ of its width.

WORLD BOOK illustrations

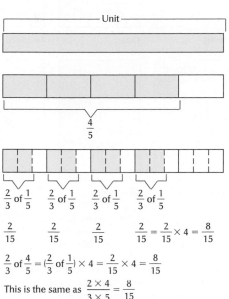

The expression $\frac{2}{3} \times \frac{4}{5}$ can mean dividing 4 of the fifths of a unit into 3 parts each and taking 2 parts of each.

$\frac{2}{3}$ of $\frac{1}{5}$ $\frac{2}{3}$ of $\frac{1}{5}$ $\frac{2}{3}$ of $\frac{1}{5}$ $\frac{2}{3}$ of $\frac{1}{5}$

$\frac{2}{15}$ $\frac{2}{15}$ $\frac{2}{15}$ $\frac{2}{15} = \frac{2}{15} \times 4 = \frac{8}{15}$

$\frac{2}{3}$ of $\frac{4}{5} = (\frac{2}{3}$ of $\frac{1}{5}) \times 4 = \frac{2}{15} \times 4 = \frac{8}{15}$

This is the same as $\frac{2 \times 4}{3 \times 5} = \frac{8}{15}$

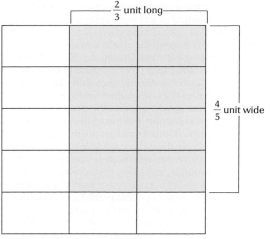

The expression $\frac{2}{3} \times \frac{4}{5}$ has an area meaning of $\frac{2}{3}$ by $\frac{4}{5}$, or the area of a rectangle $\frac{2}{3}$ unit long and $\frac{4}{5}$ unit wide.

$\frac{2}{3}$ unit long

$\frac{4}{5}$ unit wide

length × width = area

$\frac{2}{3}$ unit × $\frac{4}{5}$ unit = $\frac{2 \times 4 \text{ (number of parts in rectangle)}}{3 \times 5 \text{ (number of parts in whole unit)}}$

$= \frac{8}{15}$ of one square unit

numerator. The denominator remains the same.

$$6\frac{7}{8} = \frac{(6 \times 8) + 7}{8} = \frac{48 + 7}{8} = \frac{55}{8}$$

When adding or subtracting mixed numbers, you can write the mixed numbers as addition problems first. Then the whole numbers may be added or subtracted separately from the fractions.

$$9\frac{3}{8} + 4\frac{2}{5} =$$

$$9\frac{3}{8} = 9 + \frac{3}{8} = 9 + \frac{3 \times 5}{8 \times 5} = 9 + \frac{15}{40}$$

$$+ \quad 4\frac{2}{5} = 4 + \frac{2}{5} = 4 + \frac{2 \times 8}{5 \times 8} = 4 + \frac{16}{40}$$

$$= 13 + \frac{31}{40} = 13\frac{31}{40}$$

However, some problems that involve subtraction of mixed numbers are more complicated.

$$8\frac{1}{3} - 4\frac{2}{5} =$$

$$8\frac{1}{3} = 8 + \frac{1}{3} = 8 + \frac{1 \times 5}{3 \times 5} = 8 + \frac{5}{15}$$

$$- \quad 4\frac{2}{5} = 4 + \frac{2}{5} = 4 + \frac{2 \times 3}{5 \times 3} = 4 + \frac{6}{15}$$

Normally, the next step would be to subtract the whole numbers and then subtract the fractions. But ⁶⁄₁₅ cannot be subtracted from ⁵⁄₁₅. To subtract these fractions, we must make the top fraction larger. This can be done by borrowing 1 from the 8. If we do so, the whole number becomes 7. Then we can add the borrowed 1, in the form of ¹⁵⁄₁₅, to ⁵⁄₁₅ and subtract the fractions.

$$8 + \frac{5}{15} = 7 + 1 + \frac{5}{15} = 7 + \frac{15}{15} + \frac{5}{15} = 7 + \frac{20}{15}$$

$$- \quad 4 + \frac{6}{15} = \qquad\qquad\qquad\qquad 4 + \frac{6}{15}$$

$$3 + \frac{14}{15} = 3\frac{14}{15}$$

To multiply or divide mixed numbers, change them to improper fractions. Then multiply or divide as usual.

History

More than 4,000 years ago, ancient Babylonian astronomers used fractions made by dividing a unit into 60 parts, then dividing each of these parts into 60 parts, and so on. This system is still used for telling time and for measuring angles in minutes and seconds. The ancient Chinese developed decimal fractions made by dividing units over and over again by 10.

Egyptian mathematicians who helped build the pyramids more than 4,000 years ago used only fractions with 1 in the numerator. Such fractions are called *unit fractions*. The use of only unit fractions made it necessary to express other fractional parts as sums. For example, ¾ is expressed in unit fractions as ½ + ¼.

About 2,000 years ago, the ancient Greeks wrote fractions with the numerator on the bottom and the denominator on the top. They did not separate the numerator and denominator by a line. Later, they began writing fractions with the numerator on the top and the denominator on the bottom. Hindu mathematicians in India adopted this method of writing fractions.

During the A.D. 700's, Arabs conquered parts of India. There, the Arabs learned the decimal system and this method of writing fractions. During the 300 years that followed, the Arabs spread this knowledge through western Asia, across northern Africa, and into Spain.

During the late 1400's, several arithmetic books that explained the use of fractions and the decimal system were published in Europe. Following the publication of these books, large numbers of Europeans began to use fractions to perform everyday calculations.

Today, fractions are used mostly in connection with inches, cups, pounds, and other measurements in the inch-pound system of measurement customarily used in the United States. However, almost all other countries use the metric system of weights and measures. The metric system of measurement uses decimal fractions that are written with a decimal point rather than with a numerator and a denominator (see **Metric system**).

Also, many problems that were once done with fractions using paper and pencil are now done on electronic calculators. These calculators express fractions in the decimal form. As a result of these changes, there are fewer and fewer uses for the fraction form. However, the fraction form continues to be an important means of expressing rates, ratios, and division. The fraction form also continues to be important in algebra and in other special areas of mathematics as a method of writing rational numbers.   Karen Connors Fuson

Related articles in *World Book* include:

Arithmetic	Proportion
Decimal system	Ratio
Percentage	Rational number

Outline

I. **Expressing fractions**
   A. In words   B. In symbols
II. **Equivalent fractions**
III. **Comparing fractions**
IV. **Calculations using fractions**
   A. Addition and   B. Multiplication
       subtraction   C. Division
V. **Improper fractions**
VI. **History**

Fractional distillation. See Distillation; Petroleum (Refining petroleum).

Fracture is a broken bone. There are many kinds of fractures. Common types include closed, open, multiple, comminuted, greenstick, and spiral fractures. In a *closed,* or *simple, fracture,* a bone breaks, but the skin over it does not. In an *open,* or *compound, fracture,* both the bone and skin break, and there is danger of infection. *Multiple fracture* means there is more than one break in a bone. A *comminuted fracture* occurs when a bone breaks into three or more major fragments or as

Some common kinds of fractures

Closed   Open   Multiple

Comminuted   Greenstick   Spiral

many as hundreds of tiny pieces. In a *greenstick fracture,* the break cuts only part way through the bone. A *spiral fracture* results when a bone is broken by a twisting force.

People of all ages break bones. However, the bones of old people are more fragile than the bones of young people. The bones of older people break more easily and need more time to heal.

A physician can detect a fracture in several ways. Usually, there is pain, soreness, or tenderness in a fracture area. Swelling and discoloration also occur. Sometimes, there is movement of the bone under the skin and obvious deformity. *Crepitus* often signals a broken bone. Crepitus is a harsh grating sound caused when the broken ends of the bone rub together. In some cases, only an X ray will reveal a fracture.

Fractures should be treated only by physicians. The injured part should be kept motionless until a physician arrives.   James A. Hill

See also **First aid** (Fractures and dislocations).

Fragile X syndrome, often called FXS, is the most common inherited form of mental retardation. The condition was first described by two British scientists, the physician James Purdon Martin and the geneticist Julia Bell, in 1943. For many years, it was known as Martin-Bell syndrome. In 1969, Herbert Lubs, an American geneticist, discovered that the syndrome was associated with an unusual narrowing and occasional break at the end of the X chromosome, one of the two chromosomes that determine a person's sex. The other is the Y chromosome. In 1991, scientists discovered the genetic *mutation* that causes FXS. A mutation is a permanent change in a gene's coded chemical instructions.

FXS has a complicated pattern of inheritance, and the risk of a child having the disorder increases across generations of a family that possesses the mutation. The genetic mutation that causes FXS is known as a *trinucleotide repeat expansion disorder.* In FXS, a particular sequence of DNA on the X chromosome known as CGG, composed of the chemical compounds cytosine (C) and guanine (G), is greatly expanded beyond its normal size. This abnormal DNA sequence disrupts the production of a protein called *fragile X mental retardation protein* (FMRP) that is necessary for normal brain development.

Normally, the DNA sequence CGG is repeated between 5 and 50 times on the X chromosome. However, a trinucleotide repeat expansion disorder can cause the CGG sequence to repeat many more times, increase in length, and become unstable or fragile. Individuals who have from 50 to 200 repeats are called *premutation carriers.* These individuals can transmit FXS to their children but may not be affected themselves. Individuals with 200 or more CGG sequence repeats on the X chromosome will have the symptoms that characterize FXS.

Males have one X chromosome and one Y chromosome, and females have two X chromosomes. In general, males are more severely affected by FXS than females are because their only X chromosome carries the mutation. Males with FXS usually have mild to severe mental retardation. They may also seem shy and have problems with social skills, anxiety, and attention. Many also speak rapidly and may repeat favorite words or topics. Some have *autism,* which is a condition characterized by limited ability to communicate and interact with other people. Females generally have milder symptoms because they often have a normal X chromosome to help counteract the effects of the abnormal one. Of affected females, about one-third will have normal development, one-third a mild learning disability, and one-third mental retardation. They may also be shy and have behavioral and emotional problems.

There is no cure for FXS. Physicians often prescribe medications to help behavioral and emotional problems. Individuals with FXS can also benefit from special education and therapy. Scientists are working to learn more about how FMRP works and what treatments can help restore or improve mental function. They are also investigating the use of gene therapy to treat this disorder (see **Gene therapy**). With a supportive family and school or work environment, most individuals with FXS can have a high quality of life despite the challenges they face.   Don Bailey and W. R. Kenan

See also **Autism; Intellectual disability.**

Fragmentation, *FRAG muhn TAY shuhn,* is the breaking of any material into small pieces. The fragmentation bomb or shell is used against troops, trucks, and grounded aircraft. It has a heavy case that breaks into thousands of small *fragments* (pieces) when it explodes.

Some fragmentation bombs are cases containing hundreds of small bombs, or *bomblets.* These bombs vary in size. Fragmentation shells fired from artillery guns have fuses usually set so the shells burst in the air just above the enemy troops.   Norman Polmar

See also **Bomb** (Fragmentation bombs).

Fragonard, *fra gaw NAR,* **Jean Honoré,** *zhahn aw naw RAY* (1732-1806), a French painter, was one of the most versatile artists of the 1700's. Early in his career, he painted in the decorative Rococo style adopted from his teacher, François Boucher. From 1756 to 1761, Fragonard studied in Rome, where Italian art and settings influenced his work. Following his return to Paris, he first tried to make a career with large-scale historical scenes.

He soon found he had more success producing small, charming Rococo works such as *The Swing* (about 1766).

About 1769, Fragonard created a remarkable group of paintings known as *Fantasy Heads.* The paintings are studies of his literary and artistic friends painted in bursts of quick inspiration. Later, he began painting charming scenes of mothers and children, sometimes as religious subjects. In addition, Fragonard painted exuberant landscapes. In the early 1770's, he painted four decorative panels called *The Progress of Love* for Madame du Barry, mistress of King Louis XV, but she rejected them. Fragonard was born on April 5, 1732, in Grasse, France. He died on Aug. 22, 1806.   Eric M. Zafran

See also **Painting** (picture: *Bathers*)*;* **Rococo.**

Frambesia. See Yaws.

Framingham Heart Study is an ongoing medical research project that has yielded important information about heart disease. The study began in 1948, and it has since become the longest-running medical study of its kind in history. Findings from the study have changed the way doctors treat heart disease and have suggested ways to prevent it. The National Heart, Lung and Blood Institute (NHLBI) funds and directs the project.

In 1948, physicians recruited 5,209 adult residents of Framingham, Massachusetts, to participate in the study. Physicians examined the volunteers every two to four years and interviewed them about their diet and lifestyles. They hoped that data gathered over many years would help them learn why certain individuals developed heart disease, while others did not. In 1971, physicians added 5,124 children of the original participants and their spouses to the study.

Researchers analyzing data from the study discovered several *risk factors*—that is, behaviors or conditions that increased a person's chance of developing heart disease. High blood pressure, high cholesterol levels, cigarette smoking, diabetes, obesity, and lack of physical activity have all been identified as risk factors for heart disease through the Framingham Heart Study.

Framingham was the first major heart study to include women as subjects. Earlier studies focused only on men, who seemed more likely to get heart disease. The original volunteers for the study were primarily white, so researchers could not automatically apply their findings to other ethnic groups. In 1995, they began the OMNI Study, made up of volunteers from Framingham's nonwhite population. Researchers use data from the OMNI Study to help determine if risk factors for heart disease differ between ethnic groups.

In 1998, physicians involved in the Framingham study identified a gene associated with high blood pressure in men. The finding established a link between heart disease and the genetic makeup of an individual. Researchers hope that further analysis of data from the study will reveal how genes contribute to the development of certain illnesses. Scientists have also used data from the study to investigate such diseases as Alzheimer's, arthritis, cancer, diabetes, and osteoporosis.

Critically reviewed by the National Heart, Lung and Blood Institute

Franc, *frangk,* was the standard coin of France. The franc was also used in Belgium and Luxembourg. In 2002, Belgium, France, and Luxembourg replaced the franc with euro notes and coins. The franc is still used in Switzerland and many other countries. See also **Euro.**

© Bertrand/Explorer from Photo Researchers

The Arc de Triomphe in Paris is a symbol of French patriotism. Napoleon Bonaparte began the stone arch as a monument to his troops in 1806, and King Louis Philippe completed it in 1836. Under the arch lies the tomb of France's Unknown Soldier of World War I.

France

France is a country in western Europe. It is Europe's third largest country in area. Only Russia and Ukraine have more land. France is also one of Europe's largest countries in population.

France's capital and largest city is Paris, one of the great cities of the world. For hundreds of years, Paris has been a world center of the arts, business, education, and intellectual life. Many great artists have produced their finest masterpieces there. Every year, millions of

Mark Kesselman is the contributor of this article. He is a professor in the Department of Political Science at Columbia University in New York City.

tourists visit such famous Paris landmarks as the Cathedral of Notre Dame, the Eiffel Tower, and the Louvre—one of the largest art museums in the world.

There is much more to France than Paris, however. The snow-capped Alps in the southeastern part of the country form the border between France and Italy. Sunny beaches and steep cliffs stretch along the southern coast on the Mediterranean Sea. Fishing villages dot the Atlantic coast of northwestern France. The peaceful, wooded Loire Valley of central France has many historic *châteaux* (castles). Colorful apple orchards, dairy farms, and vineyards lie throughout much of the countryside. Many regions have fields of wheat.

The French are famous for their enjoyment of life.

Figaro Magazine from Gamma/Liaison

The French countryside has many picturesque villages. This village lies in the Périgord region of southwestern France. Many French villagers farm the land or work in nearby cities.

© Cotton Coulson, Woodfin Camp, Inc.

Mont-St.-Michel is a large rock that juts from the waters off the coast of Lower Normandy. A medieval abbey sits on the top of the rock, and a small village lies at the base.

© Shutterstock

Open-air markets spill out onto the sidewalks of many French cities and towns. These shoppers are selecting fresh fruits and vegetables. The French value good food and skillful cooking.

Good food and good wine are an important part of everyday living for most French people. The delicious breads, appetizers, sauces, soups, and desserts of France are copied by cooks in most parts of the world. The wines of France are considered the world's best.

France has a long and colorful history. Julius Caesar and his Roman soldiers conquered the region more than 2,000 years ago. In the late part of the A.D. 400's, after Rome fell, the Franks and other Germanic tribes invaded the region. France was named for the Franks. By the A.D. 800's, Charlemagne, the king of the Franks, had built the area into a huge kingdom.

In 1792, during the French Revolution, France became one of the first nations to overthrow its king and set up a republic. A few years later, Napoleon Bonaparte seized power. He conquered much of Europe before he finally was defeated. During World War I (1914-1918) and World War II (1939-1945), France was a battleground for Allied armies and invading German forces.

France is one of the world's leading manufacturing nations. It is, for example, one of the largest producers of automobiles in the world. It also has large chemical and steel industries. It is a leader in growing wheat, vegetables, and many other crops. France stands high among the countries of the world in its trade with other nations, as measured by exports. It also has an important role in world politics. Its foreign policies affect millions of people in other countries.

France in brief

General information

Capital: Paris.
Official language: French.
Official name: République Française (French Republic).
National anthem: "La Marseillaise."
National motto: *Liberté, Égalité, Fraternité* (Liberty, Equality, Fraternity).

Largest population centers (2006 official estimates)

Cities	Metropolitan areas
Paris (2,181,371)	Paris (10,142,977)
Marseille (839,043)	Marseille (1,418,481)
Lyon (472,305)	Lyon (1,417,463)
Toulouse (437,715)	Lille (1,016,205)
Nice (347,060)	Nice (940,017)

The French flag is called the *tricolor*. In 1789, King Louis XVI first used its three colors to represent France. France has no official coat of arms.

Land and climate

Land: France lies in western Europe, with coastlines on the Atlantic Ocean and Mediterranean Sea. The country borders Spain, Andorra, Monaco, Italy, Switzerland, Germany, Luxembourg, and Belgium, and lies across the English Channel from the United Kingdom. The Pyrenees Mountains separate France from Spain. The Alps border Italy; the Alps and Jura Mountains border Switzerland. The Central Highlands occupies south-central France. Most of northern, western, and north-central France is flat or has rolling hills. Major rivers include the Loire, Seine, and Rhône.

Area: 212,935 mi² (551,500 km²), including mainland France and Corsica. *Greatest distances*—east-west, 605 mi (974 km); north-south, 590 mi (950 km). *Coastline*—2,300 mi (3,701 km).
Elevation: *Highest*—Mont Blanc, 15,771 ft (4,807 m). *Lowest*—below sea level at the Rhône River delta.
Climate: Warm summers and cool winters, except on the Mediterranean coast, which is warmer in all seasons. Typical daytime summer high about 75 °F (24 °C) in the north; 82 °F (28 °C) on the Mediterranean coast. Winter daytime highs about 43 °F (6 °C) in the north; about 54 °F (12 °C) on the Mediterranean coast. Moderate precipitation all year, except for dry summers along the Mediterranean.

Government

Form of government: Republic.
Head of state: President.
Head of government: Prime minister.
Legislature: Parliament of two houses—the National Assembly (577 members) and the Senate (348 members). The National Assembly is more powerful than the Senate.
Executive: Prime minister and president each have some executive powers.
Judiciary: Highest courts are the Court of Cassation and the Constitutional Council.
Political subdivisions: 27 regions, containing 101 departments. These numbers include both metropolitan and overseas regions and departments.

People

Population: *Estimated 2014 population*—64,097,000; *2009 official government estimate*—62,465,709.
Population density: 301 per mi² (116 per km²).
Distribution: 78 percent urban, 22 percent rural.
Major ethnic/national groups: About 93 percent French (including Basques, Bretons, and others who have long lived in France). About 7 percent recent immigrants and their descendants—mostly from Algeria, Morocco, Tunisia, Italy, Portugal, Spain, Turkey, and Indochina.
Major religions: 85 percent Roman Catholic, 8 percent Muslim, 2 percent Protestant, 1 percent Jewish.

Population trend

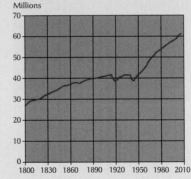

Year	Population
1801	27,349,000
1821	30,462,000
1831	32,569,000
1841	34,230,000
1851	35,783,000
1861	37,386,000
1871	36,103,000
1881	37,406,000
1891	38,133,000
1901	38,451,000
1911	39,192,000
1921	38,798,000
1931	41,228,000
1946	39,848,000
1954	42,781,000
1962	46,500,000
1975	52,544,000
1982	54,335,000
1990	56,634,000
1999	58,518,395
2006	62,817,120

Economy

Chief products: *Agriculture*—beef and dairy cattle, chickens and eggs, corn, grapes, hogs, potatoes, sugar beets, wheat. *Manufacturing*—aerospace equipment, automobiles, chemicals, electronic goods, iron and steel, processed foods and beverages, railway equipment, textiles and clothing.
Money: *Basic unit*—euro. One hundred cents equal one euro. The French franc was taken out of circulation in 2002.
Foreign trade: *Major exports*—automobiles, chemicals, machinery, wine. *Major imports*—automobiles, chemicals, iron and steel products, machinery, petroleum products, pharmaceuticals. *Major trading partners*—Belgium, China, Germany, Italy, Netherlands, Spain, Switzerland, United Kingdom, United States.

The political importance of France today resulted partly from the leadership of Charles de Gaulle, who served as president of the country from 1958 to 1969. De Gaulle looked on France as a world power and followed a policy that was independent of both the United States and the Communist nations. De Gaulle ended France's close military ties with the United States and tried to improve relations with Communist countries. De Gaulle's actions angered many other nations, but to the French people he was a symbol of their nation's greatness.

Government

France is a republic with a strong national government. Its present government, called the Fifth Republic, has been in effect since 1958. The First Republic was established in 1792. Between 1792 and 1958, the structure of the French government changed a number of times.

National government. France's national government has three branches. They are (1) an executive branch headed by a president and a prime minister, (2) a legislative branch consisting of a two-chamber Parliament, and (3) a judicial branch, or system of courts.

The president of France is elected to a five-year term by the voters, who must be 18 or older. The president can serve only two terms. The president appoints the prime minister (also called premier). The prime minister chooses the other ministers who make up the Council of Ministers.

The president of France is considered the head of state, and the prime minister is the head of government. The president manages France's foreign affairs and has a major role in shaping policy. The prime minister directs the day-to-day operations of the government.

France's Parliament consists of two houses, the National Assembly and the Senate. The National Assembly consists of 577 *deputies*, who are elected by the voters for five-year terms, unless an election is called earlier. The president has the power to dissolve the National Assembly and call for new elections. The Senate has 348 members. Senators are elected to six-year terms by regional and city electoral colleges.

The National Assembly is more powerful than the Senate. If the two houses of Parliament disagree on the text of a proposed law, the National Assembly makes the final decision. In addition, the Council of Ministers must have the support of a majority of members in the National Assembly. Without such a majority, the ministers must resign, and the president would then appoint a new prime minister.

Local government. Mainland France and the island of Corsica are referred to as *metropolitan France*. France also has a number of overseas possessions. The inhabited possessions are French Guiana in South America; Guadeloupe, Martinique, Saint-Barthélemy, and Saint-Martin, all in the West Indies; Réunion and Mayotte, both in the Indian Ocean; New Caledonia, French Polynesia, and the Wallis and Futuna Islands, all in the South Pacific Ocean; and Saint-Pierre and Miquelon in the North Atlantic Ocean. These possessions are considered part of France. Their people vote for France's president and send representatives to the French Parliament.

The basic unit of local government in France is the *commune*. Metropolitan France has about 36,500 communes. They vary in size from small villages to large cities. A mayor and a local council govern each commune.

Metropolitan France is divided into 96 *departments*. Locally elected councils administer the departments. In addition, each department has a commissioner who is appointed by the national government and represents the government. Each department is part of one of metropolitan France's 22 *regions*. Each region has a regional council, elected by the people, and a president, who is elected by the council members. The region of Corsica has a special status with more local independence. France also has five overseas departments: French Guiana, Guadeloupe, Martinique, Mayotte, and Réunion. Each of the overseas departments is also a region.

Politics. France's leading conservative party is the Union for a Popular Movement (known by its French initials, UMP). The UMP supports policies similar to those of former French President Charles de Gaulle. It favors a strong national government and an independent foreign policy. Unlike de Gaulle, the UMP also advocates free-market policies and reducing government regulation of business. Another conservative party, the National Front, holds more extreme right-wing beliefs. It opposes immigration and favors the death penalty.

The Socialist Party and the French Communist Party hold liberal or radical views. In theory, both parties support public ownership or control of most of the nation's factories, machines, and other means of production. In practice, though, the Socialists have worked with private business since the 1930's. Both parties, as well as some conservative parties, support government-financed social security and medical benefits.

In 2001, France adopted a new law to increase the number of women in politics. The law requires political parties to nominate as many women as men as candidates in most elections.

Courts operate in each department. Appeals from civil and criminal courts may be taken to Courts of Appeal. The Courts of Assizes hear cases involving murder and other serious crimes. The decisions of the Courts of Appeal and Assizes are generally final. But the Court of Cassation, the highest appeals court of France, may review them. It can return cases to the lower courts for new trials. The Constitutional Council can rule on laws passed by Parliament.

A minister of justice controls the appointments and promotions of judges. Judges are appointed for life.

Armed forces. France has an army, navy, and air force. Military service is voluntary.

People

Among the people of France, there are notable regional differences in language and tradition. As a result, many people have a strong sense of regional identity. In the Basque region, Brittany, and Corsica, some people have sought independence from France. But most people in the various regions feel comfortable having both a regional identity and a national "French" identity.

Ancestry. In ancient times, peoples called Gauls lived in what is now France. The Gauls were a Celtic people related to the Welsh and the Irish. Roman, Germanic, and then Norse invaders came from the south, east, and north. The Romans brought peace to the warring Gallic tribes, and Roman law became the basis of modern French law. The name of France came from Germanic

France map index

Cities and towns

Abbeville ....24,052 ..B 6
Agen ....33,728 ..H 5
Aix-en-Provence ...142,534 ..I 9
Aix-les-Bains ....27,375 ..G 9
Ajaccio ....63,723 ..J 11
Albertville ......18,009 ..F 9
Albi ....48,712 ..I 6
Alençon ....28,458 ..D 5
Alès ....39,943 ..H 8
Alfortville* ......42,743 ..C 7
Amiens ....136,105 †161,311 ..B 6
Angers ....152,337 †227,771 ..E 4
Anglet ....37,646 ..I 3
Angoulême .....42,096 †105,021 ..G 5
Annecy ....51,023 †144,682 ..F 9
Annemasse .....28,572 ..F 9
Annonay ....17,088 ..G 8
Antibes ....75,820 ..I 10
Antony* ....60,552 ..C 6
Argenteuil* ....102,683 ..C 6
Arles ....51,970 ..I 8
Armentières ....24,836 ..A 7
Arras ....42,015 ..A 7
Asnieres-sur-Seine* ....82,351 ..C 6
Aubagne ....44,682 ..I 9
Aubervilliers* ...73,506 ..C 7
Auch ....21,545 ..I 5
Audincourt .....14,637 ..D 10
Aulnay-sous-Bois* ....81,600 ..C 7
Aurillac ....29,477 ..G 7
Autun ....14,806 ..E 8
Auxerre ....37,419 ..D 7
Avignon ....92,454 †273,359 ..H 9
Azay-le-Rideau ...3,337 ..E 5
Bagneux* ....38,936 ..C 6
Bagnolet* ....34,069 ..C 6
Bar-le-Duc ......16,041 ..C 8
Bastia ....43,577 ..I 11
Bayonne ....44,406 †189,836 ..I 4
Beaune ....21,778 ..E 8
Beauvais ....55,481 ..B 6
Belfort ....50,863 ..D 10
Bergerac ....27,716 ..H 5
Besançon ......117,080 †134,951 ..E 9
Béthune ....26,472 †259,293 ..A 7
Béziers ....72,245 ..I 7
Biarritz ....26,690 ..I 3
Blois ....48,487 ..D 6
Bobigny* ....47,806 ..C 6
Bondy* ....53,311 ..C 7
Bordeaux ......232,260 †803,117 ..G 4
Boulogne-Billancourt ..110,251 ..C 6
Boulogne-sur-Mer ......44,273 ..A 6
Bourg-en-Bresse ....40,156 ..F 8
Bourges ....70,828 ..E 7
Brest ....144,548 †206,394 ..C 1
Brétigny-sur-Orge* ....22,753 ..C 6
Brive-la-Gaillarde .....50,009 ..G 6
Bron ....38,919 ..F 8
Bruay-la-Buissière .....23,813 ..A 7
Caen ....110,399 †196,323 ..C 5
Cagnes-sur-Mer ......48,313 ..I 10
Cahors ....20,062 ..H 6
Calais ....74,888 †103,277 ..A 6
Caluire-et-Cuire* ....41,418 ..F 8
Cambrai ....32,594 ..B 7
Cannes ....70,610 ..I 10
Carcassonne ....46,639 ..I 7
Carpentras ......27,451 ..H 9
Castres ....43,141 ..I 6
Cavaillon ....25,819 ..I 9
Cergy* ....56,873 ..C 6
Chalon-sur-Sâone ....46,534 ..E 8
Châlons-en-Champagne ..46,184 ..C 8
Chambéry ......57,543 †119,266 ..G 9
Chamonix [-Mont Blanc] ..9,195 ..F 10
Champigny-sur-Marne* ...74,863 ..C 7
Charenton-le-Pont* ....28,395 ..C 6
Charleville-Mézières .....51,997 ..B 8
Chartres ....40,022 ..D 6
Chateauroux ....47,559 ..E 6
Châtellerault ....34,402 ..E 5
Chaumont ......24,357 ..D 8
Chelles* ....48,616 ..C 7
Chenôve ....14,921 ..E 8
Cherbourg [-Octeville] ...40,838 ..B 4

See footnotes at end of index.

Choisy-le-Roi* ...36,198 ..C 6
Cholet ....54,632 ..E 4
Clamart* ....50,655 ..C 6
Clermont-Ferrand .....138,992 †260,657 ..G 7
Clichy* ....57,162 ..C 6
Cognac ....19,409 ..G 4
Colmar ....65,713 ..D 10
Colombes* ......82,026 ..C 6
Colomiers ......32,110 ..I 6
Compiègne .....42,036 ..B 7
Concarneau ....19,953 ..D 2
Conflans-Ste.-Honorine* ....33,671 ..C 6
Corbeil-Essonnes .....40,929 ..C 6
Courbevoie* ....84,415 ..C 6
Creil ....33,479 †101,100 ..C 6
Créteil ....88,939 ..C 7
Croix ....20,926 ..E 6
Dax ....20,810 ..I 4
Denain ....20,339 ..A 7
Dieppe ....33,618 ..B 5
Dijon ....151,504 †238,088 ..E 9
Dole ....24,606 ..E 9
Douai ....42,766 †‡512,462 ..A 7
Douarnenez ....15,608 ..D 2
Draguignan .....37,088 ..I 10
Drancy* ....66,063 ..C 6
Draveil* ....28,736 ..C 6
Dreux ....32,723 ..C 6
Dunkerque .....69,274 †182,973 ..A 6
Échirolles ....35,687 ..G 9
Elbeuf ....17,277 ..C 5
Épernay ....24,456 ..C 7
Épinal ....34,014 ..D 9
Épinay-sur-Seine* ....51,598 ..C 6
Ermont* ....28,074 ..C 6
Étampes ....22,568 ..D 6
Évreux ....51,239 ..C 6
Évry ....52,651 ..C 6
Fécamp ....19,424 ..B 5
Firminy ....17,975 ..G 8
Flers ....16,094 ..C 4
Fontaine ....22,936 ..G 9
Fontainebleau ..15,688 ..D 7
Fontenay-sous-Bois* ....51,727 ..C 6
Forbach ....21,956 ..C 9
Fougères ....20,941 ..D 4
Franconville* ...32,988 ..C 6
Fréjus ....51,537 ..I 10
Gagny* ....37,729 ..C 7
Gap ....37,332 ..H 9
Garges-lès-Gonesse* .....39,672 ..C 6
Gennevilliers* ..43,054 ..C 6
Givors ....18,454 ..G 8
Grasse ....48,801 ..I 10
Grenoble ......156,107 †427,658 ..G 9
Grigny* ....25,981 ..C 6
Haguenau ......34,891 ..C 10
Hautmont ....15,190 ..B 8
Hazebrouck ....21,101 ..A 6
Houilles* ....30,835 ..C 6
Hyères ....55,077 ..I 10
Issy-les-Moulineaux* ....61,471 ..C 6
Istres ....42,090 ..I 8
Ivry-sur-Seine* ..55,608 ..C 6
Joué-les-Tours ..36,233 ..E 5
La Ciotat ....32,126 ..I 9
La Courneuve* ..37,034 ..C 6
Lambersart* ....28,543 ..A 7
Lanester ....22,627 ..D 2
Laon ....26,522 ..B 7
La Rochelle .....77,196 †119,702 ..F 4
La Roche-sur-Yon ......50,717 ..E 3
La Seyne-sur-Mer ......56,768 ..I 9
Laval ....51,233 ..D 4
Le Blanc-Mesnil* ....51,109 ..C 6
Le Cannet ....42,531 ..I 10
Le Chesnay* .....29,542 ..C 6
Le Creusot ......23,813 ..E 8
Le Havre ....182,580 †238,776 ..B 5
Le Mans ....144,016 †192,910 ..D 5
Lens ....35,583 ..A 7
Le Perreux-sur-Marne* ...32,067 ..C 7
Le Plessis-Robinson* ....23,312 ..C 6
Le Puy-en-Velay ....19,321 ..G 8
Les Abymes* ....60,053 ..E 6
Les Mureaux* ...32,634 ..C 6
Levallois-Perret* ....62,851 ..C 6
L'Haÿ-les-Roses* ....30,428 ..C 6
Libourne ....23,296 ..G 5
Liévin ....32,565 ..A 7
Lille ....226,014 †1,016,205 ..A 7
Limoges ....136,539 †177,439 ..F 6
Lisieux ....23,343 ..C 5

(Index continued on page 458.)

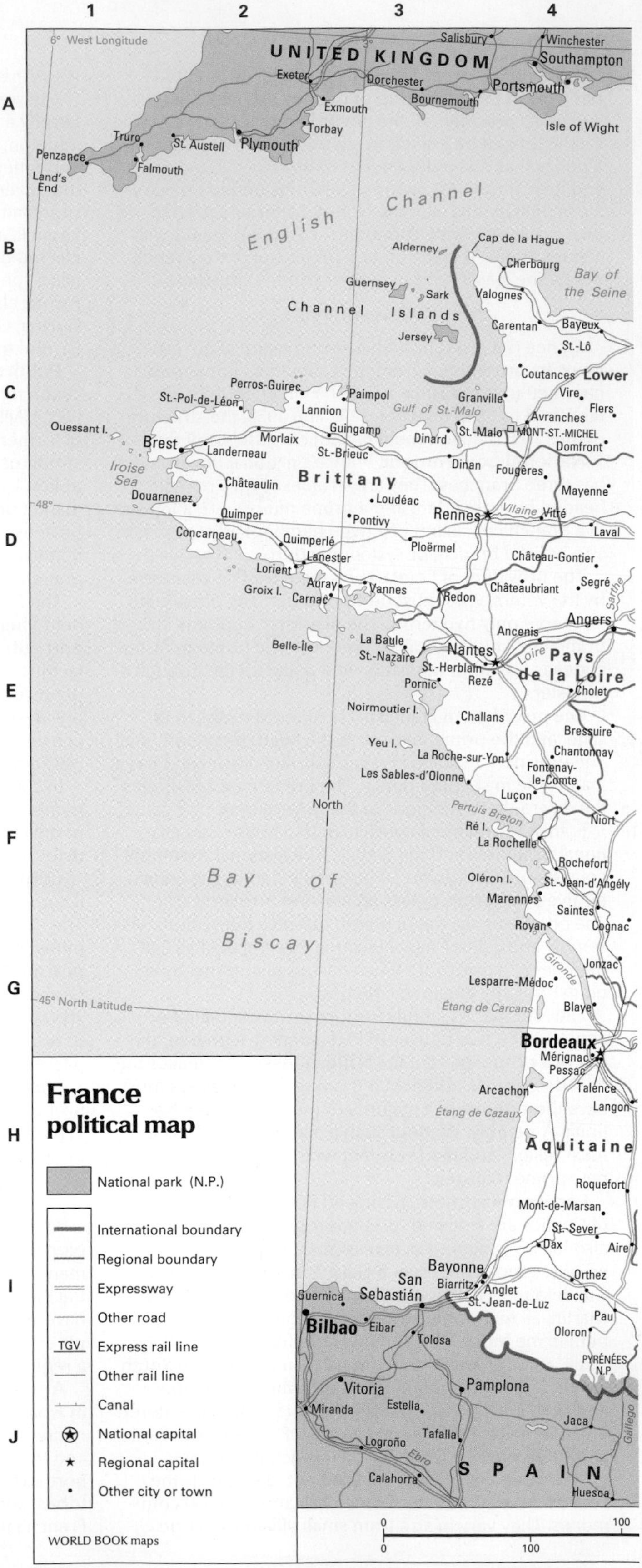

1
2
3
4
A
B
C
D
E
F
G
H
I
J
6° West Longitude
UNITED KINGDOM
Salisbury
Winchester
Southampton
Exeter
Dorchester
Portsmouth
Exmouth
Bournemouth
Torbay
Isle of Wight
Truro
St. Austell
Plymouth
Penzance
Falmouth
Land's End
English Channel
Alderney
Cap de la Hague
Cherbourg
Bay of the Seine
Guernsey
Sark
Valognes
Channel Islands
Jersey
Carentan
Bayeux
St.-Lô
Coutances
Lower
Perros-Guirec
Paimpol
Granville
Vire
Flers
St.-Pol-de-Léon
Lannion
Gulf of St.-Malo
Avranches
Ouessant I.
Guingamp
Dinard
St.-Malo
MONT-ST.-MICHEL
Brest
Morlaix
Domfront
Landerneau
St.-Brieuc
Dinan
Fougères
Iroise Sea
Châteaulin
Brittany
Mayenne
Douarnenez
Loudéac
48°
Quimper
Pontivy
Rennes
Vilaine
Vitré
Laval
Concarneau
Quimperlé
Ploërmel
Lanester
Château-Gontier
Lorient
Auray
Vannes
Châteaubriant
Segré
Groix I.
Carnac
Redon
Sarthe
Angers
Belle-Île
La Baule
Ancenis
St.-Nazaire
Nantes
Loire
Pays de la Loire
St.-Herblain
Rezé
Pornic
Cholet
Noirmoutier I.
Challans
Bressuire
Yeu I.
La Roche-sur-Yon
Chantonnay
Fontenay-le-Comte
Les Sables-d'Olonne
North
Luçon
Pertuis Breton
Ré I.
Niort
La Rochelle
Rochefort
Bay of Biscay
Oléron I.
St.-Jean-d'Angély
Marennes
Saintes
Royan
Cognac
Gironde
Jonzac
Lesparre-Médoc
45° North Latitude
Étang de Carcans
Blaye
Bordeaux
Mérignac
Pessac
Arcachon
Talence
Langon
Étang de Cazaux
France political map
Aquitaine
National park (N.P.)
Roquefort
International boundary
Mont-de-Marsan
Regional boundary
St.-Sever
Dax
Aire
Expressway
Bayonne
Orthez
San Sebastián
Biarritz
Anglet
St.-Jean-de-Luz
Lacq
Other road
Guernica
Pau
Bilbao
Eibar
Oloron
Express rail line
TGV
Tolosa
PYRÉNÉES N.P.
Other rail line
Vitoria
Pamplona
Canal
Miranda
Estella
Jaca
National capital
Tafalla
Gállego
Regional capital
Logroño
Ebro
SPAIN
Other city or town
Calahorra
Huesca
WORLD BOOK maps
0
100
0
100

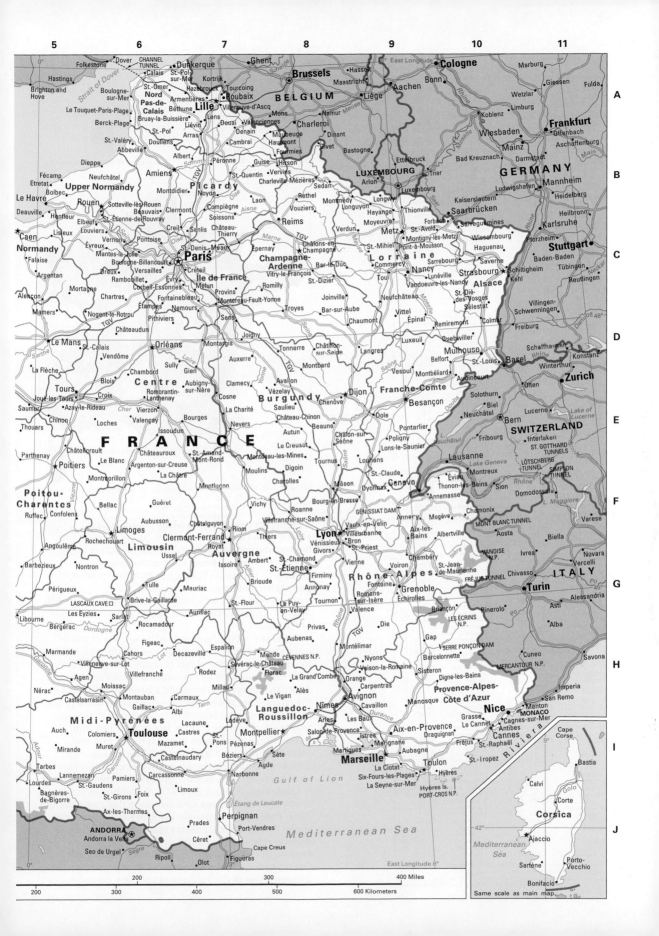

Livry-Gargan* ....41,556 ..C 7
Longwy ....14,317 ..B 9
Lons-le-
　Saunier ....17,879 ..E 9
Lorient 58,547
　　　　†116,764 ..D 2
Lourdes ....15,265 ..I 5
Lunéville ....19,881 ..C 9
Lyon 472,305
　　　　†1,417,463 ..F 8
Mâcon ....34,171 ..F 8
Maisons-
　Alfort* ....53,233 ..C 6
Malakoff* ....30,509 ..C 6
Manosque ....21,162 ..I 9
Mantes-la-Jolie ..41,930 ..C 6
Marcq-en-
　Baroeul* ......38,939 ..A 7
Marignane ......32,921 ..I 9
Marseille 839,043
　　　　†1,418,481 ..I 9
Martigues ......46,318 ..I 9
Massy* ....40,183 ..C 6
Maubeuge ....32,699 ..A 8
Meaux ....48,842 ..C 7
Melun ....37,663 ..C 7
Menton ....27,655 ..I 11
Mérignac ....65,469 ..G 4
Metz 124,435
　　　　†322,946 ..C 9
Meudon* ....44,745 ..C 6
Meyzieu* ....28,738 ..G 9
Millau ....22,133 ..H 7
Montargis ....15,794 ..D 7
Montauban ......53,941 ..H 6
Montbéliard 26,535
　　　　†109,118 ..D 10
Montceau-
　les-Mines ....19,538 ..E 8
Mont-de-
　Marsan ....30,230 ..I 4
Montélimar .....33,924 ..H 8
Montereau-
　Fault-Yonne ..16,768 ..D 7
Montigny-le-
　Bretonneux* ..33,968 ..C 6
Montigny-lès-
　Metz ....22,843 ..C 9
Montluçon ......39,869 ..F 7
Montpellier ...251,634
　　　　†318,225 ..I 8
Montreuil* ....101,587 ..C 7
Montrouge* .....45,178 ..C 6
Morlaix ....15,695 ..C 2
Moulins ....20,519 ..F 7
Mulhouse 110,514
　　　　†238,638 ..D 10
Nancy 105,468
　　　　†331,279 ..C 9
Nanterre* ......88,316 ..C 6
Nantes 282,853
　　　　†568,743 ..E 4
Narbonne ....50,776 ..I 7
Neuilly-sur-
　Marne* ....33,352 ..C 7
Neuilly-sur-
　Seine* ....61,471 ..C 6
Nevers ....38,496 ..E 7
Nice 347,060
　　　　†940,017 ..I 10
Nîmes 144,092
　　　　†161,565 ..I 8
Niort ....58,066 ..F 4
Noisy-le-
　Grand* ....61,341 ..C 7
Noisy-le-Sec* ...38,587 ..C 7
Orange ....29,859 ..H 8
Orléans 113,130
　　　　†269,283 ..D 6
Orly* ....21,197 ..C 6
Orsay* ....16,597 ..C 6
Oullins* ....25,694 ..F 8
Oyonnax ....23,618 ..F 9
Palaiseau* ......30,339 ..C 6
Pantin* ....52,857 ..C 6
Paris 2,181,371
　　　　†10,142,977 ..C 6
Pau 83,903
　　　　†193,991 ..I 4
Périgueux ....29,558 ..G 5
Perpignan 115,326
　　　　†178,501 ..J 7
Pessac ....57,187 ..H 4
Poissy* ....35,860 ..C 6
Poitiers 88,776
　　　　†126,652 ..F 5
Pontoise ....28,674 ..C 6
Puteaux* ....42,981 ..C 6
Quimper ....64,902 ..D 2
Reims 183,837
　　　　†212,021 ..C 8
Rennes 209,613
　　　　†282,550 ..D 4
Rezé ....37,333 ..E 4
Roanne ....36,126 ..F 8
Rochefort ....26,299 ..F 4
Rodez ....24,028 ..H 7
Romans-sur-
　Isère ....33,138 ..G 9
Rosny-sous-
　Bois* ....41,174 ..C 7
Roubaix ....97,952 ..A 7
Rouen 107,904
　　　　†388,798 ..B 5
Royan ....18,202 ..G 4
Rueil-
　Malmaison* ...77,265 ..C 6

St-Brieuc ....46,437 ..C 3
St-Chamond ....35,608 ..G 8
St-Cloud* ....29,385 ..C 6
St-Denis ....97,875 ..C 6
St-Dié-des-
　Vosges ....21,642 ..D 10
St-Dizier ....26,972 ..C 8
St-Étienne 177,480
　　　　†286,400 ..G 8
St-Étienne-du-
　Rouvray ......27,815 ..C 6
St-Germain-
　en-Laye* .....41,312 ..C 6
St-Herblain .....43,901 ..E 3
St-Lô ....19,643 ..C 4
St-Malo ....49,661 ..C 3
St-Martin-
　d'Hères* .....35,217 ..G 9
St-Maur-des-
　Fossés* ......75,214 ..C 6
St-Nazaire 68,838
　　　　†143,106 ..E 3
St-Ouen* ....42,950 ..C 6
St-Pol-sur-
　Mer ....22,100 ..A 6
St-Priest ....40,746 ..G 8
St-Quentin .....56,792 ..B 7
St-Raphaël .....33,804 ..I 10
Ste-Geneviève-
　des-Bois* ....34,024 ..D 6
Saintes ....26,531 ..G 4
Salon-de-
　Provence .....40,147 ..I 9
Sarcelles* ......58,654 ..C 6
Sarre-
　guemines ....21,773 ..C 10
Sartrouville* ...51,600 ..C 6
Saumur ....28,654 ..E 5
Savigny-sur-
　Orge* ....37,259 ..C 6
Schiltigheim ...31,239 ..C 10
Sedan ....19,934 ..B 8
Sens ....26,961 ..D 7
Sète ....43,008 ..I 8
Sevran* ....51,106 ..C 7
Sèvres* ....23,726 ..C 6
Six-Fours-les-
　Plages ......34,325 ..I 9
Soissons ....28,442 ..C 7
Sotteville-lès-
　Rouen ....30,076 ..B 6
Stains* ....34,670 ..C 6
Strasbourg 272,975
　　　　†440,265 ..C 10
Suresnes* ......44,197 ..C 6
Talence ....40,920 ..H 4
Tarbes ....45,433 ..I 5
Thiais* ....29,315 ..C 6
Thionville 41,127
　　　　†130,437 ..B 9
Thonon-les-
　Bains ....31,213 ..F 10
Toulon 167,816
　　　　†543,065 ..I 9
Toulouse 437,715
　　　　†850,873 ..I 6
Tourcoing ......92,357 ..A 7
Tours 136,942
　　　　†306,974 ..E 5
Trappes* ....29,529 ..C 6
Tremblay-en-
　France* ......35,340 ..C 7
Troyes 61,344
　　　　†131,039 ..D 8
Tulle ....15,734 ..G 6
Valence 65,263
　　　　†120,922 ..G 9
Valenciennes ...42,426
　　　　†355,660 ..A 7
Vandoeuvre-
　les-Nancy ....31,447 ..C 9
Vannes ....53,079 ..D 3
Vanves* ....26,878 ..C 6
Vaulx-en-Velin .40,300 ..F 8
Vénissieux .....57,179 ..G 8
Verdun ....19,374 ..C 8
Vernon ....24,018 ..C 6
Versailles ......87,549 ..C 6
Vesoul ....16,370 ..D 9
Vichy ....26,108 ..F 7
Vienne ....30,092 ..G 8
Vierzon ....28,147 ..E 6
Villefranche-
　sur-Saône ....34,188 ..F 8
Villejuif* ....50,571 ..C 6
Villemomble* ...28,339 ..C 6
Villenave-
　d'Ornon* .....29,958 ..H 4
Villeneuve-
　d'Ascq ....61,151 ..A 7
Villeneuve-St-
　Georges* .....30,450 ..C 6
Villeneuve-
　sur-Lot ....23,466 ..H 5
Villepinte* .....35,592 ..C 7
Villeurbanne ..136,473 ..F 8
Villiers-le-Bel* .27,130 ..C 6
Vincennes* .....47,488 ..C 6
Vitrolles* ......37,190 ..I 10
Vitry-le-
　François ......15,086 ..C 8
Vitry-sur-
　Seine* ....82,902 ..C 6
Voiron ....20,672 ..G 9
Wattrelos* .....42,852 ..A 7
Yerres* ....28,572 ..C 6

*Does not appear on map; key shows general location.
†Population of metropolitan area, including suburbs.
‡Figure includes metropolitan area of both Douai and Lens.
Source: 2006 official estimate, considered to be the 2009 legal population.

Population density

The population distribution of mainland France is fairly even. Paris is the most heavily populated urban area. On Corsica, pictured in the bottom right-hand corner of the map, most people live near the coast.

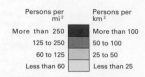

Persons per mi²		Persons per km²
More than 250		More than 100
125 to 250		50 to 100
60 to 125		25 to 50
Less than 60		Less than 25

WORLD BOOK map

conquerors called Franks. Many people of northeastern France have Germanic ancestors. Some people from Normandy, in northwestern France, trace their ancestry back to the Norse people who settled there.

About 7 percent of France's population consists of people from other countries. The largest groups are from Algeria, Cambodia, Italy, Laos, Morocco, Portugal, Spain, Tunisia, Turkey, Vietnam, and African lands south of the Sahara.

In the late 1900's, hundreds of thousands of immigrants from former French colonies in Africa and Asia moved to France. The status of these immigrants and their descendants is a controversial issue. For example, Algerian immigrants represent a large work force that the country has not yet absorbed. Algerian workers are often the first to be laid off during periods of slow economic activity. Many of them live in poor neighborhoods. Some immigrants from Morocco, Portugal, Tunisia, Turkey, and lands south of the Sahara are in similar situations. However, many Vietnamese refugees have become more fully integrated into French society.

Language. Around the 1500's, the language that is now called French was spoken only in the area around Paris. The rest of the people living in what is now France spoke Breton, Dutch, Euskara (Basque), or German, or dialects related to modern French, such as Picard, Provençal, or Walloon. The building of the modern French nation is closely tied to the standardization and increased use of the local dialect of Paris starting in the

1500's. For a detailed discussion of the French language, including its development, see **French language.**

On the island of Corsica, the majority of the population speaks Corsican. Some Basques living along the Pyrenees Mountains speak Euskara. The region of Brittany has a significant number of people who speak Breton. Along the border with Belgium, many people speak the Flemish dialect of Dutch. The region of Alsace has many German-speaking people. In most of these regions, French is taught in the schools, and the number of people who speak the regional tongue has dwindled from one generation to the next. In Corsica, Brittany, and the Pyrenees, people have formed groups to promote the use of the local language.

Way of life

City life. About four-fifths of the French people live in urban areas. In the larger cities, most people live in apartments. Many Parisians live in old apartment buildings. In general, the older a building is, the more prestigious it is. Many French city dwellers tolerate buildings with old plumbing and appliances so that they may enjoy antique fireplaces and ceiling beams.

Strict zoning regulations help protect and enhance the center of many French cities. Such regulations may prohibit traffic on certain city streets or limit high-rise construction in the center of a city. The regulations are designed to ensure a high quality of life for urban residents. Such urban problems as overcrowding and high crime rates are more likely to occur in the outskirts of cities or in nearby suburbs.

While city living is generally pleasant, it is also expensive. Many poor city residents live outside the city centers in run-down apartments or in housing complexes built by the government. Many middle-class people cannot afford to live in Paris and instead live in a suburb as a second choice. Mass transit systems carry people from the suburbs to a variety of jobs and recreational and cultural activities in the city.

© Howard Friedman, Photo Researchers

Villages set amid well-tended fields typify much of rural France. About a fifth of the French live in rural areas. Most enjoy the same comforts and conveniences as city dwellers.

Rural life. Only about a fifth of the French people live in rural areas. But France traditionally has been an agricultural society. The French are thus more familiar with—and more respectful of—such activities as farming and hunting than are people in many urbanized nations.

Most rural residents enjoy the same comforts and conveniences as city dwellers. Most of them live in single-family houses in villages or on farms. They own a car and a television set and have such appliances as a refrigerator and a washing machine.

Farm families make up much of the rural population in France. Most farmers own their land. Some rent all or part of their land. A few French farmers are wealthy. But many farmers require other sources of income to support their families. A spouse or another family member may hold a job as a factory worker, office worker, or teacher. In poorer areas, such as Brittany, some farmers earn barely enough to support themselves.

Food and drink. The French consider cooking an art. French *haute cuisine* (gourmet cooking) has set a standard accepted in many parts of the world since the 1700's. French chefs have created many delicious sauces and fancy appetizers.

French appetizers include *escargots* (snails) in garlic butter sauce, scallops and mushrooms in a creamy wine sauce, and puff pastries filled with chicken in cream sauce. Sausages and *pâtés* (chopped meat cooked with spices) also serve as appetizers. Goose liver pâté with black mushroomlike *truffles* is considered a special delicacy. French cooks put fillings of cheese, vegetables, shrimp, ham, or bacon into omelets, *crêpes* (thin, rolled pancakes), and *quiche* (custard baked in a pastry shell). These dishes are served as appetizers or light meals.

A traditional French main meal has several courses. It starts with an appetizer or soup. Popular main courses include chicken, chops, fish, or steaks. A green salad often follows the main course, then cheese or fresh fruit.

© Guy Marche, FPG

Apartment buildings, such as these in Lyon, are home to many French city dwellers.

Crusty French bread accompanies most meals. A very special meal might add a dessert after the cheese course. Desserts include fancy pastries, fruit tarts, and crêpes filled with whipped cream or cooked fruit.

Such hearty French specialties as *bouillabaisse* and *cassoulet* make a full meal and need few extras. Bouillabaisse is a chunky chowder with six or more kinds of fish and shellfish. Cassoulet is a casserole of beans, sausage, poultry, and pork.

The French eat light breakfasts. A typical breakfast consists of such soft rolls as *croissants* and *brioches,* served with butter and jam, plus coffee.

Some French people drink wine at lunch and dinner, sometimes different wines for different courses. Beer, cider, or mineral water may substitute for wine. Coffee is served at breakfast, and after other meals.

Ethnic cooking is becoming more popular. For example, many restaurants offer Indian, Italian, Mexican, Thai, or Vietnamese dishes.

Recreation. The greatest national sporting event in France is the Tour de France, a bicycle race. Every July, about 200 professional cyclists race around France and sometimes parts of neighboring countries. They ride almost daily for three weeks and finish in Paris. Thousands of spectators line the route and cheer them along.

France's most popular team sport is soccer. Almost every area and region has its own team. The French also enjoy such sports as *boules* (a form of bowling), fishing, ice skating, rugby, skiing, swimming, and tennis. Basketball has also become popular, and a number of professional teams have been set up.

All French workers are entitled to five weeks of paid vacation every year. In July and August, cars filled with vacationers crowd the highways leading south to the Mediterranean Sea and the mountains. To accommodate the vacationers, there are thousands of special camps and resorts that organize activities for children

and adults. Many French people have second homes in the country. Vacation festivals in many cities throughout France feature folk dancing, music, parades, and theater.

Throughout the year, city dwellers take daily walks through public parks. They may stop at one of the sidewalk cafes that dot many city boulevards.

Holidays. Most French holidays and festivals are closely connected with the Roman Catholic Church. Many cities celebrate Shrove Tuesday, the last day before Lent, with a festival called Carnaval. The Carnaval celebration in Nice includes a colorful parade, and it attracts many tourists. Most villages honor their local patron saints with a festival in July.

On *Noël* (Christmas), French families hold reunions, and the children receive gifts. The French people also exchange gifts on *Le Jour de l'An* (New Year's Day). On *Pâques* (Easter), the children receive colored candy eggs and chocolate chickens.

The French national holiday is Bastille Day, July 14. It marks the capture of the Bastille, a fortified prison, by the people of Paris in 1789, during the French Revolution. A large military parade is held in Paris on Bastille Day. At night, the people watch fireworks and dance in the streets until dawn. The French celebrate Labor Day on May 1 and Armistice Day on November 11.

Religion. About 85 percent of the French people are Roman Catholics. About 8 percent are Muslims, and about 2 percent are Protestants. About 1 percent are Jews. From 1801 to 1905, the French government recognized Roman Catholicism as the religion of the majority of the people. Bishops and priests were state officials and were paid by the government. This church-state connection, established by Napoleon and Pope Pius VII, was broken by French law in 1905.

Education. French children from the ages of 6 to 16 must go to school. Most of the children attend public schools. The other children attend private schools, most

© Bernard Hermann, Gamma/Liaison

Sidewalk cafes provide a pleasant place for French people to stop to eat or drink and visit with friends. The cafes are popular spots in most French cities and towns.

AP/Wide World

The Tour de France is the greatest national sporting event in France. Each July, about 200 of the world's top cyclists compete in the three-week race.

of which are operated by the Roman Catholic Church.

Children from ages 2 through 6 may attend free nursery schools. Reading is taught during the last year of these schools. Children from ages 6 through 11 attend elementary schools. Formerly, boys and girls went to separate schools. But since the 1970's, they have attended school together. After five years of elementary school, children enter a *collège.* A collège is a four-year school that resembles a junior high school.

After collège, students enter either a vocational high school or a general high school. Both kinds of high schools are called *lycées.*

Vocational high schools offer job training in business, crafts, farming, and industry. General high schools provide a three-year course that prepares students to enter universities. The last year of general high school is a period of specialized study. Students may specialize in one broad area of study, such as literature, science, economics and social science, or industrial science and technology. A *baccalauréat* examination completes this program. This examination is so difficult that about a third of the students fail to pass it.

France has about 80 universities. Each university selects its courses and teaching methods. Students have a voice in university administration. The government provides financial support to students.

France also has schools of higher education called *grandes écoles* (great schools). They prepare students for high-ranking careers in the civil and military services, commerce, education, industry, and other fields.

Museums and libraries. France has many excellent museums. The best known, the Louvre in Paris, is one of the largest art museums in the world.

Many old castles and palaces, once the homes of kings and emperors, are national historical museums. They include the Palace of Versailles, which was built by King Louis XIV during the 1600's.

© Peter Vadnal, Art Resource

French museums are among the best in the world. The Orsay Museum, *shown here,* occupies a restored former railway station in Paris. It displays art from the 1800's and 1900's.

The Orsay Museum in Paris, located in a beautifully restored former railway station, exhibits paintings from the 1800's and 1900's—including many Impressionist works. The Georges Pompidou National Center of Art and Culture in Paris includes a museum of modern art, a major public reference library, and a music research institute. The Museum of Mankind in Paris has important scientific exhibits.

Public libraries are in all large French cities. France's national library, the Bibliothèque Nationale de France, is one of the largest libraries in Europe. Other important libraries include the Mazarine Library of the Institute of France, the country's major learned society. The University of Paris also has fine libraries.

Arts

Since the Middle Ages, French writers, artists, architects, and composers have been among the cultural leaders of Europe. During many periods of history, French styles in painting, music, drama, and other art forms served as models for other countries. This section discusses only some of France's major contributions to the arts. For more detailed information, see the articles **Architecture, Classical music, Drama, French literature, Motion picture, Painting,** and **Sculpture.**

Literature. Poetry was the most important literary form among medieval French writers. Musician-poets called *troubadours* wrote love songs in the Provençal dialect of southern France. Poets called *trouvères* carried this poetry to northern France. Other poets wrote epic poems and long fictional works called *romances.*

During the Renaissance, François Rabelais was the most important French fiction writer. His satirical *Gar-*

© Claudia Parks, The Stock Market

Bastille Day, July 14, is France's national holiday. The people of France celebrate the holiday with dancing, fireworks, and parades. These dancers are performing at a celebration in Arles.

gantua and Pantagruel (1532-1564) is a masterpiece of Western literature. Pierre de Ronsard and Joachim du Bellay were the major poets of the Pléiade, a group of seven poets whose poetry was based on ancient Greek and Roman models. Michel de Montaigne, the last great writer of the French Renaissance, created the personal essay as a literary form.

French Classical art, which spanned the 1600's and 1700's, stressed order, balance, and harmony, and placed heavy emphasis on the role of the intellect in analyzing human behavior. François de Malherbe was the first and greatest Classical poet. His clear, rational, and sober poems became the basic style for Classical verse. The leading prose writers were two philosophers, René Descartes and Blaise Pascal. The greatest expression of French Classical literature was in drama. The major figures were Pierre Corneille, Jean Racine, and Molière. Corneille and Racine wrote tragedies. Molière ranks as the greatest writer of comedy in French drama.

The Enlightenment, also called the Age of Reason, was a period of intellectual achievement in the 1600's and 1700's. The period was dominated by philosophical literature. Writers emphasized reason and observation as the best methods of learning truth. The crucial figures in this movement were Voltaire, Denis Diderot, and Jean Jacques Rousseau. Rousseau was also an important forerunner of Romanticism because he valued feeling more than reason, and impulse and spontaneity more than self-discipline. He introduced true and passionate love to the French novel, popularized descriptions of nature, and created a lyrical and eloquent prose style.

Romanticism began in the late 1700's and flourished until the mid-1800's. The greatest Romantic writer was Victor Hugo, a novelist, poet, and playwright. Honoré de Balzac, Stendhal, and George Sand were also great Romantic novelists, though the work of these writers was more realistic than that of the typical Romantic novelist.

Realism was a movement of the middle and late 1800's that tried to portray life accurately and objectively. Naturalism was a movement that emerged as an extreme form of Realism. Gustave Flaubert was the major representative of Realism, notably for his novel *Madame Bovary* (1856). Guy de Maupassant gained recognition for his Realistic short stories. The novelist Émile Zola was the leading Naturalistic writer.

Paul Claudel, André Gide, Marcel Proust, and Paul Valéry were the leading French writers of the early 1900's. Claudel wrote works that reflected his deep Roman Catholic faith. Gide and Proust were major novelists. Valéry wrote Classical poetry. Philosophers Jean-Paul Sartre and Albert Camus wrote important drama and essays in the mid-1900's. Simone de Beauvoir, also in the mid-1900's, supported women's rights.

Major French writers of the late 1900's included Alain Robbe-Grillet and Claude Simon. They became known for the New Novel, which moved away from traditional approaches to storytelling. The New Novel concentrated instead on descriptions of events as experienced by the characters. Marguerite Duras was a leading French feminist writer of the late 1900's.

Painting. In the 1600's, the French artist Claude established a tradition of landscape painting that greatly influenced later artists in Europe and America. His landscapes illustrate the Classical admiration for balance, order, and harmony. In the 1700's, François Boucher, Jean Honoré Fragonard, and Antoine Watteau were masters of the elegant, decorative style called Rococo. In the early 1800's, Théodore Géricault and Eugène Delacroix best represented the colorful and dramatic style of the Romantic movement. Gustave Courbet helped found the Realist movement in art in the mid-1800's.

Impressionism was a movement of the late 1800's and early 1900's centered on French painting. The Impressionists tried to capture the immediate impression of an object or event. The leading painters included Édouard Manet, Camille Pissarro, Edgar Degas, Claude Monet, and Pierre Renoir. A movement called Postimpressionism developed out of Impressionism. The key French Postimpressionists were Paul Cézanne, Paul Gauguin, Georges Seurat, and Henri de Toulouse-Lautrec.

In the 1900's, such painters as Georges Braque, Pablo Picasso (who was born in Spain), Henri Matisse, and Fer-

© Tetrel/Explorer from Photo Researchers

Castles called *châteaux* were the high point of French Renaissance architecture. Many of these magnificent castles stand in the Loire Valley. At Chenonceaux, near Tours, a château spans the River Cher, *shown here*. It was built in the 1500's.

Bronze statue (1902-1904); the Rodin Museum, Philadelphia, gift of Jules E. Mastbaum

Auguste Rodin's *The Thinker*, shown here, is one of the French sculptor's most famous works. Several versions of this statue exist. Like many of Rodin's sculptures, *The Thinker* portrays the human figure in an attitude of great emotional intensity.

nand Léger helped shape modern art.

Sculpture. Much of the finest French sculpture of the medieval period was created as decoration for the Gothic cathedrals. Jean Antoine Houdon was one of the greatest sculptors of the 1700's. He was known for his statues of important men and women in Europe and America. Auguste Rodin is often considered the leading sculptor of the 1800's. Aristide Maillol, Jean Arp, and Antoine Pevsner were important sculptors of the 1900's.

Architecture. The abbey at the top of Mont-St.-Michel, off the coast of Lower Normandy, is a fine example of medieval architecture. France also has a number of magnificent Gothic cathedrals that were built from about 1150 to 1300. Examples include the Cathedral of Notre Dame in Paris and cathedrals in the cities of Amiens, Chartres, Reims, and Rouen. The finest French Renaissance architecture appeared during the 1500's in castles called *châteaux.* The best examples include those at Azay-le-Rideau, Chambord, and Fontainebleau. The spectacular Palace at Versailles, begun about 1661, is a monument of French Baroque art.

The Swiss-born French architect Le Corbusier was one of the most important architects of the 1900's. He had a great influence on modern architecture with his International Style.

Music. In the 1600's, composer Jean-Baptiste Lully wrote the first significant French operas. Jean Philippe Rameau, a major French composer of the 1700's, was also known for his operas. François Couperin was an important composer of music for a keyboard instrument called the *harpsichord.*

During the 1800's, Hector Berlioz was the greatest French Romantic composer. He gained fame for his large-scale orchestral works. Georges Bizet wrote the Romantic *Carmen* (1875), probably the most popular opera ever written. The Impressionist movement of the late 1800's produced two great composers, Claude Debussy and Maurice Ravel.

St. John on Patmos, a manuscript painting from *The Hours of Étienne Chevalier* (1450-1455); Musée Conde, Chantilly (Giraudon/Art Resource)

Early French paintings include the richly colored miniature shown here, a work of the 1400's by Jean Fouquet.

The Table (1925), an oil painting on canvas; Tate Gallery, London (Art Resource)

French paintings of the 1900's include this interior scene by Pierre Bonnard, who used vivid colors and rich textures.

Detail of the library of Louis XVI (late 1700's) in the Palace of Versailles; Giraudon/Art Resource

Masterpieces of French decorative art include the elegant furnishings of a room at the Palace of Versailles.

In the 1900's, composers Pierre Boulez and Olivier Messiaen were leaders in experimental music. Boulez became known for his work in electronic music.

Motion pictures. France has had a thriving motion-picture industry since the 1920's, when such important directors as René Clair and Jean Renoir launched their careers. Clair first won acclaim with his silent comedy *An Italian Straw Hat* (1927). Renoir's most admired films include *Grand Illusion* (1937), which attacks the futility of war, and *The Rules of the Game* (1939), which satirizes the relationships of upper-class people at a weekend house party.

In the late 1950's and early 1960's, the French had a profound impact on filmmaking with a movement called the New Wave. The leaders of the New Wave were young French film critics who turned to directing. Their aim was to revive what they saw as a stuffy French film industry. They believed that a film should be the personal artistic expression of the director, whom they called the *auteur* (author). These critics-turned-directors included Claude Chabrol, Jean Luc-Godard, Jacques Rivette, Eric Rohmer, and François Truffaut.

Claude Chabrol is credited with starting the New Wave with *Le Beau Serge* (1958). Louis Malle gained recognition as an important New Wave director with *The Lovers* (1958). Other important New Wave films include *The 400 Blows* (1959), directed by François Truffaut, and *Breathless* (1960), directed by Jean Luc-Godard.

The land

France has wide differences in geography. The northern and western regions consist mainly of flat or rolling plains. Hills and mountains rise in the eastern, central, and southern parts of France.

France has 10 main land regions. They are (1) the Brittany-Normandy Hills, (2) the Northern France Plains, (3) the Northeastern Plateaus, (4) the Rhine Valley, (5) the Aquitanian Lowlands, (6) the Central Highlands, (7) the French Alps and Jura Mountains, (8) the Pyrenees Mountains, (9) the Mediterranean Lowlands and Rhône-Saône Valley, and (10) Corsica.

The Brittany-Normandy Hills have low, rounded hills and rolling plains. This region consists of ancient rock covered by poor soils, with some fertile areas along the coast. Apple orchards, dairy farms, and grasslands crisscross the land. In some areas, thick hedges separate the fields. Many bays indent the rugged coast and have important fishing harbors.

The Northern France Plains have highly fertile soils and productive industries. The plains are flat or rolling and are broken up by forest-covered hills and plateaus. This heavily populated region includes Paris. The Paris Basin, also called the Île-de-France, is a large, circular area drained by the Seine and other major rivers. East of Paris, a series of rocky ridges resembles the upturned edge of a huge saucer.

The Northeastern Plateaus share the Ardennes Mountains with Belgium. This wooded region becomes a little more rugged to the southeast in the Vosges Mountains. The Northeastern Plateaus region has great deposits of iron ore, and it produces iron and steel. Farmers raise livestock and a variety of crops on the lower slopes and in the valleys. Lumber workers operate in the large forests.

The Rhine Valley has steep slopes and flat bottom lands. Trees and vines cover the slopes, and rich farmlands lie along the Rhine River. This river, which forms part of France's boundary with Germany, is the main inland waterway in Europe. Important roads and railways follow its course.

The Aquitanian Lowlands are drained by the Garonne River and the streams that flow into it. Sandy beaches lie along the coast. Inland, the region has pine forests, rolling plains, and sand dunes. Its many vineyards sup-

© Victor Englebert, Photo Researchers

The cliffs of Normandy rise along the English Channel, in the Brittany-Normandy Hills of northwestern France. Most of this region consists of ancient rock covered by poor soils. However, some fertile areas lie near the coast.

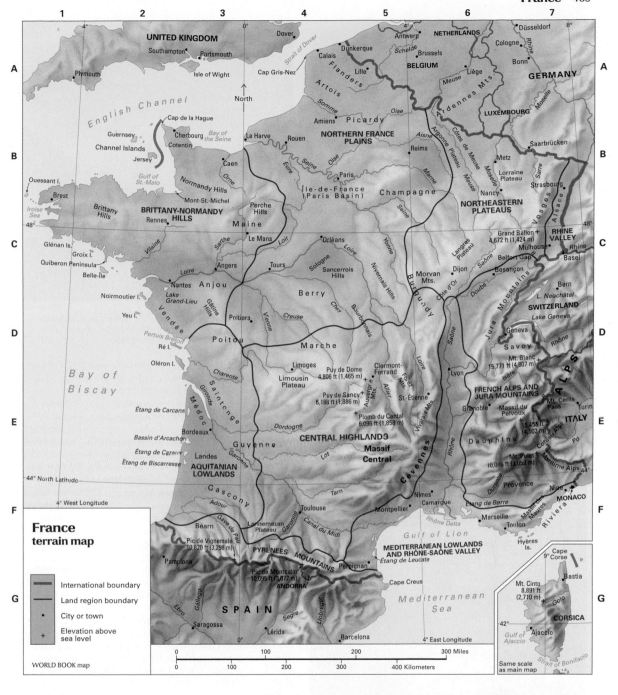

France terrain map

WORLD BOOK map

Legend:
- International boundary
- Land region boundary
- • City or town
- + Elevation above sea level

Physical features

Adour River ....F 3
Aisne River ....B 5
Allier River ....F 5
Alps (mountains) ....E 7
Ardennes Mountains ....B 6
Argonne Plateau ....B 6
Bassin d'Arcachon
  (inlet) ....E 2
Bay of Biscay ....E 1
Bay of the Seine ....B 3
Belfort Gap (pass) .....C 7
Belle-Île (island) ......C 1
Brittany Hills ....C 2
Canal du Midi ....F 4
Cap de la Hague
  (cape) ....B 2

Cap Gris-Nez (cape) ....A 4
Cévennes (mountains) ..E 5
Cher River ....D 4
Côte d'Or (hills) ....C 6
Cotentin (peninsula) ...B 2
Côtes de Meuse
  (hills) ....B 6
Creuse River ....C 4
Dordogne River ....E 4
Doubs River ....C 6
Durance River ....F 6
English Channel ....A 2
étang de Berre
  (lagoon) ....F 6
Eure River ....B 4
Garonne River ....E 3
Gave de Pau (stream) ..F 3
Gironde (estuary) ......E 3

Gulf of Lion ....F 5
Gulf of St.-Malo ....B 2
Hyères Islands ....F 7
Isère River ....E 6
Jura Mountains ....D 6
Lake Grand-Lieu ....D 2
Limousin Plateau ......E 4
Loir River ....C 4
Loire River ....C 5
Lorraine Plateau ......B 6
Lot River ....E 4
Maritime Alps
  (mountains) ....E 7
Marne River ....B 5
Massif Central
  (mountains) ....E 5
Mediterranean Sea .....G 6
Meuse River ....B 6

Mont Blanc
  (mountain) ....D 7
Mont Cenis Pass ....E 7
Mont Cinto (mountain) .G 7
Mont Pelat
  (mountain) ....E 7
Moselle River ....B 6
Nivernais Hills ....C 5
Noirmoutier Island ....D 2
Normandy Hills ....B 3
Oise River ....B 5
Oléron Island ....D 2
Ouessant Island ....B 1
Paris Basin ....B 4
Pertuis Breton
  (strait) ....D 2
Pic de Vignemale
  (mountain) ....F 3

Puy de Sancy
  (mountain) ....E 5
Pyrenees Mountains ...F 4
Ré Island ....D 2
Rhine River ....C 7
Rhône Delta ....F 6
Rhône River ....E 6
Riviera (coast) ....F 7
Saône River ....D 6
Sarthe River ....C 3
Seine River ....A 4
Somme River ....A 4
Strait of Dover ....A 4
Tarn River ....F 4
Vienne River ....D 4
Vilaine River ....C 2
Vosges (mountains) ...C 7
Yonne River ....C 5

© Luis Villota, The Stock Market

In Alsace, on the Northeastern Plateaus, vineyards spread over the rolling valleys and lower slopes of the Vosges Mountains. The region also has large forests and many potash deposits.

© D. Phillipe, FPG

Mont Blanc, in the French Alps, is the highest peak in France, rising 15,771 feet (4,807 meters). A thick blanket of snow always covers most of the top half of the mountain.

© Michele Burges, The Stock Market

The sunny Riviera is warmed by breezes from the Mediterranean Sea. The Alps shield the area from cold north winds. The Riviera's ideal climate attracts vacationers throughout the year.

ply grapes for France's important wine industry. Oil and natural gas fields are in the Landes area, a forested section south of the major seaport of Bordeaux.

The Central Highlands, or *Massif Central,* is thinly populated. The soils in the region are poor, except in some valleys where rye and other crops are grown. Cattle and sheep graze on the lower grasslands, and forests cover the higher slopes. The Loire River, about 650 miles (1,050 kilometers) long, rises in the Cévennes, a mountain range. The Loire is the longest river in France.

The French Alps and Jura Mountains border on Italy and Switzerland. Snow-capped Mont Blanc, the highest point in France, rises 15,771 feet (4,807 meters). Many tourists visit nearby Chamonix and other ski resorts in the mountains. Mountain streams provide much hydroelectric power.

The Pyrenees Mountains extend along France's border with Spain. Many peaks in this range rise more than 10,000 feet (3,000 meters). The rugged mountains have poor soils and are thinly populated.

The Mediterranean Lowlands and Rhône-Saône Valley region has productive farming areas, and irrigation is used widely. Fruits, vegetables, and wine grapes are important products. Marseille, on the Mediterranean Sea, is the leading seaport of France. The coast also includes the Riviera, a famous resort area.

Corsica is a Mediterranean island about 100 miles (160 kilometers) southeast of mainland France. It has hills and mountains similar to those of the Central Highlands. The island has generally poor soils and a steep, rocky coastline. Crops are grown in the valleys, and sheep graze in the mountains.

Climate

The climate varies widely among the various regions of France. The differences in climate are closely related to the distance of the land from the Atlantic Ocean or

Average January temperatures

Inland regions of France have cold winters. The country's coastal regions have milder winters.

Average July temperatures

Along the Atlantic coast and in most inland regions, summers are mild. The Mediterranean coast has hot summers.

Average yearly precipitation

Mountainous regions receive the most precipitation. Inland regions and the Mediterranean coast receive the least.

WORLD BOOK maps

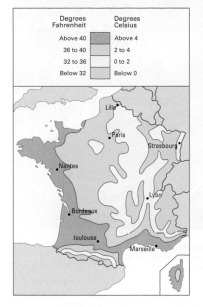

Degrees Fahrenheit	Degrees Celsius
Above 40	Above 4
36 to 40	2 to 4
32 to 36	0 to 2
Below 32	Below 0

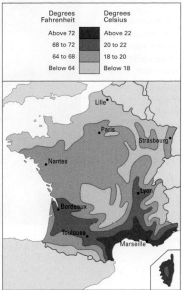

Degrees Fahrenheit	Degrees Celsius
Above 72	Above 22
68 to 72	20 to 22
64 to 68	18 to 20
Below 64	Below 18

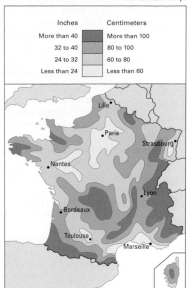

Inches	Centimeters
More than 40	More than 100
32 to 40	80 to 100
24 to 32	60 to 80
Less than 24	Less than 60

Average monthly weather

	Paris					Marseille				
	Temperatures				Days of rain or snow		Temperatures			Days of rain or snow
	°F		°C				°F		°C	
	High	Low	High	Low			High	Low	High	Low
Jan.	42	32	6	0	15	Jan.	53	38	12	3	10
Feb.	45	33	7	1	13	Feb.	52	37	11	3	9
Mar.	52	36	11	2	15	Mar.	55	38	13	3	8
Apr.	60	41	16	5	14	Apr.	59	41	15	5	10
May	67	47	19	8	13	May	65	46	18	8	10
June	73	52	23	11	11	June	72	52	22	11	9
July	76	55	24	13	12	July	78	58	26	14	6
Aug.	75	55	24	13	12	Aug.	83	61	28	16	4
Sept.	69	50	21	10	11	Sept.	82	61	28	16	5
Oct.	59	44	15	7	14	Oct.	76	57	24	14	7
Nov.	49	38	9	3	15	Nov.	67	50	19	10	10
Dec.	43	33	6	1	17	Dec.	59	43	15	6	11

the Mediterranean Sea. Westerly winds that blow in from the Atlantic strongly influence the climate of western France. The coastal regions there have a rainy climate with cool winters and mild summers.

To the east, away from the Atlantic, the climate changes sharply between seasons. These inland regions have hot summers and cold winters, with medium rainfall throughout the year. The mountainous regions receive the most *precipitation* (rain, melted snow, and other forms of moisture), most of it in summer. Heavy winter snows fall in the Alps and the Jura Mountains, and huge glaciers are found in the Alps.

Along the Mediterranean Sea, the lowlands have hot, dry summers and mild winters with some rainfall. Swift, cold north winds called *mistrals* sometimes blow over southern France and cause crop damage. The Alps shield the sunny Riviera from the cold north winds during much of the year.

Economy

France is a prosperous nation, and its people have a high standard of living. The prosperity resulted largely from sweeping economic changes that were made after the 1940's. Before World War II began in 1939, the French economy was based chiefly on small farms and business firms. After the war ended in 1945, the French government worked to modernize the economy. New methods of production and trade were developed through a series of national plans. These improvements brought increased production.

Most French businesses are privately owned. The government owns all or part of certain businesses, including some banks and steel companies. Generally, when the Socialists have controlled the government, they have worked to increase government ownership of business. When conservatives have been in control, they have sought to decrease government ownership.

Natural resources play an important part in France's prosperity. Fertile soils are the country's most important natural resource. Most of France's total land area is fertile. The richest farmlands lie in the north and northeast, where wheat and sugar beets are the chief crops. The rainier northwest consists mainly of grasslands and orchards. Many of the drier areas of southern France have good soils for growing grapes. Soils are generally poor in the Central Highlands and on Corsica.

Service industries are those economic activities that provide services rather than produce goods. They account for about 80 percent of both France's workers and its total economic output. Service industries are especially important to the Paris area.

Community, business, personal, and government services form the most important service industry group. This group employs nearly half of all workers. It includes such economic activities as defense, education, health care, and public administration. Federal government activities are based in Paris.

Trade, restaurants, and hotels make up the second most important service industry group in terms of employment. Paris is a major world center for the wholesale trade of automobiles and chemicals. Marseille, France's main seaport, is the center of the country's foreign trade. Lyon is a leading city in the wholesale trade of textiles. Restaurants, hotels, and shops benefit from the tens of millions of people who visit France each year. Most of these tourists come from other European countries.

Other service industries include finance, insurance, and real estate; and transportation and communication. Transportation and communication are discussed later in this section.

Manufacturing. France ranks as one of the world's leading manufacturing nations. The Paris area is the

© SuperStock

Tourism contributes significantly to the French economy. A *bateau-mouche* (excursion boat) carries tourists along the Seine River in Paris. Millions of tourists visit Paris every year.

France's gross domestic product

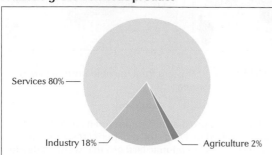

Services 80%

Industry 18%

Agriculture 2%

France's GDP was $2,773,700,000,000 in 2011. The gross domestic product (GDP) is the total value of goods and services produced within a country in a year. *Services* include community, business, and personal services; finance, insurance, and real estate; government; trade; and transportation and communication. *Industry* includes construction and manufacturing, mining, and utilities. *Agriculture* includes agriculture, forestry, and fishing.

Production and workers by economic activities

Economic activities	Percent of GDP produced	Employed workers	
		Number of people	Percent of total
Community, business, personal, & government services	38	13,024,200	48
Finance, insurance, & real estate	18	1,089,100	4
Trade, restaurants, & hotels	14	4,824,400	18
Manufacturing	10	2,905,700	11
Transportation & communication	10	2,149,800	8
Construction	6	1,838,300	7
Agriculture	2	746,300	3
Mining & utilities	2	313,400	1
Total	100	26,891,200	100

Figures are for 2011.
Source: *World Book* estimates based on National Institute for Statistics and Economic Studies.

chief manufacturing center of France, but there are factories in cities and towns throughout the country.

France is one of the largest producers of automobiles in the world. French cars include Renaults and Peugeots. Automobile plants are in the Paris Basin and near Douai, Lyon, and Rennes. France also makes railroad equipment. The country has developed some of the world's fastest trains.

France is a major manufacturer of sophisticated military and commercial airplanes. Toulouse is the center of aircraft production. France has a successful space program, and has launched rockets and several communications satellites. The country also produces aerospace equipment, electronic defense systems, and many kinds of weapons. France has a growing commercial electronics industry that produces computers, radios, telephone equipment, and television sets.

The chemical industry produces a variety of products, from industrial chemicals to medicines and cosmetics. French plants make high-quality glass and tires.

France is an important producer of aluminum and steel. Local and imported wood goes into the production of furniture, lumber, and pulp and paper. The famous French perfume industry, based in Paris, uses flowers that are grown in southeastern France.

France is a major producer of industrial machinery and also ranks as a leader in designing new machines. French firms perform engineering services and construct industrial and transportation projects in many countries. French manufacturers also produce machine tools and *robotic* machines that perform repeated tasks in factories.

Cotton and silk textiles have long been important French products. French plants also produce nylon and other artificial fibers. The Lyon area, long a center for manufacturing silk, also has artificial-fiber factories.

Paris, the fashion capital of the world, produces much of the nation's clothing.

Food processing employs many French people. Famous French foods include breads, fruit preserves, meats, and especially wines and cheeses. France ranks as one of the world's largest wine-producing countries. The wines are aged in deep cellars or caves. France produces butter and hundreds of kinds of cheeses, including Brie, Camembert, and Roquefort. France also is an important producer of sugar.

Agriculture. France is Europe's largest agricultural producer and a leading exporter of farm products. Much of France's farm income comes from meat and dairy. Beef cattle are the chief meat animals. Much of the milk produced on dairy farms is used in making butter and cheese. French farmers have always raised some chickens and hogs, and specialized, large-scale production of these animals is expanding. French farmers also raise ducks, sheep, and turkeys. Most cattle and pigs are raised in western and central France. Many goats and sheep are raised in the southwestern part of the country.

Crops grow on more than a third of France's land. France is one of the world's largest producers of both wheat and grapes. Large farms in the Northern France Plains region grow much of the wheat, France's leading single crop. Most grapes used in making wine are grown in southern France. Grapes for high-quality wines come from several regions, including Alsace, Bordeaux, Burgundy, Champagne, and the Loire Valley. The

© Chip Hires, Gamma/Liaison

Automobile production is one of France's leading industries. Workers build engines in a Renault factory, *shown here*.

Mediterranean region produces grapes used for cheaper wines. Each region produces grapes that have their own special flavor. Grapes from southwestern France are used in brandy.

Apple orchards dot many areas of northern France, especially Normandy. Potatoes, sugar beets, and such livestock-feed crops as barley, corn, oats, and rapeseed are major crops. Other important crops include beans,

Economy of France

This map shows the economic uses of land in France. It also indicates the country's main farm products, its chief mineral deposits, and its most important fishing products. Major manufacturing centers are shown in red.

Mostly cropland

Cropland mixed with grazing land

Mostly grazing land

Forest land

Generally unproductive land

Fishing

● Manufacturing and service industry center

• Mineral deposit

WORLD BOOK map

© Bruce Thomas, The Stock Market

Wine production is a major industry in France. Wooden barrels, *shown here,* hold the wine for aging. A wine tester, at the left, uses a *wine thief* to draw a sample.

carrots, cauliflower, onions, peaches, pears, peas, soybeans, sunflower seeds, and tomatoes.

Forestry. Forests cover about 30 percent of France. Heavily forested sections include the Northeastern Plateaus, the Central Highlands, the southwest coastal areas, and the slopes of the Alps, Juras, Pyrenees, and Vosges. Many forests have been planted in the Landes area of southwestern France for use by the pulp and paper industry. Cork oaks, olive trees, and pine trees grow along the dry Mediterranean coast and on Corsica. Forest fires are common in these regions. Other trees of France include ashes, beeches, and cypresses.

Mining plays a small role in France's economy. Many of France's coal and metal mines have closed. France must import most of its natural gas and petroleum. Discoveries of natural gas at Lacq, in southwestern France, have attracted many industries. French mines also yield gypsum, salt, sulfur, and uranium.

Fishing. Commercial fishing crews work off the French coasts or sail to the waters of Iceland and Newfoundland. Many fleets operate from Brittany and Normandy. Seafood taken includes cod, crabs, hake, herring, lobsters, mackerel, monkfish, pollock, sardines, scallops, tuna, and whiting.

Energy sources. Nuclear power plants provide about three-fourths of France's electric power. France is a world leader in nuclear energy technology and in the production of nuclear fuels. Most of the rest of France's electric power is generated by coal-burning plants or by hydroelectric power. The Alps and the Jura Mountains have many hydroelectric plants.

The world's first tidal power plant began operating in France in 1966. It uses the tides in the mouth of the Rance River in Brittany. These tides are among the highest in the world and may reach a height of 44 feet (13 meters). Solar power is also important.

International trade. France imports more than it exports. It is one of the world's leading trading nations. Its major imports include chemicals, iron and steel products, machinery, petroleum products, *pharmaceuticals*

(medicinal drugs), and vehicles. Its major exports include aircraft, cars, chemical products, machinery, and wine. Over half of its trade is with other members of the European Union (EU), chiefly Germany. The EU is an organization of European nations that works for economic and political cooperation among its members. France's major trade partners outside the EU include China, Switzerland, and the United States.

Transportation. Since the 1700's, France has had more road mileage in relation to its size than any other European country. Its highway system has many multilane expressways. Two of the world's longest highway tunnels link France and Italy. One tunnel, 8 miles (12.9 kilometers) long, cuts through Fréjus Peak. The other, 7.3 miles (11.7 kilometers) long, cuts through Mont Blanc.

The French railroad system, owned and operated by the government, provides both passenger and freight service. In 1981, a high-speed electric train began operating between Paris and Lyon. Called TGV *(train à grande vitesse,* or high-speed train), such trains now serve cities throughout France and link France to cities in other countries. France's TGV's are among the world's fastest passenger trains, traveling at speeds of up to 200 miles (320 kilometers) per hour. In 1994, a tunnel was completed linking France and the United Kingdom by rail. Called the Channel Tunnel or sometimes the Chunnel, it runs beneath the English Channel. A railroad tunnel through Fréjus Peak links France with Italy.

Charles de Gaulle and Orly airports, both near Paris, rank among the world's busiest airports. Lyon, Marseille, and Nice also have major airports. Air France is the national airline. It is part of Air France-KLM, Europe's largest air carrier. Air France-KLM consists of Air France and KLM Royal Dutch Airlines of the Netherlands.

Ships and barges operate on navigable rivers and canals throughout France. These rivers include the Rhine, Rhône, and Seine. Northern and eastern France have well-developed canal systems. Oceangoing ships dock at many fine French seaports. The country's busiest seaports include Bordeaux, Calais, Dunkerque, Le Havre, Marseille, Rouen, and St. Nazaire.

Communication. France has a variety of daily newspapers, representing a wide range of political opinions.

© S. Kanno, FPG

High-speed trains, known in French as *train à grande vitesse* or TGV, carry passengers throughout much of France.

The largest newspaper, *Ouest-France* of Rennes, prints a number of different editions, each with local news. Other major daily newspapers include *Le Figaro, Le Monde, Libération,* and *Le Parisien* of Paris; *Sud Ouest* of Bordeaux; *La Voix du Nord* of Lille; *Le Progrès* of Lyon; *La Provence* of Marseille; and *Le Dauphiné Libéré* of Grenoble. Major weekly news magazines include *L'Express* and *Le Nouvel Observateur.*

France has several television and radio networks. Some are privately owned, and others are operated by independent government agencies. The income of the broadcasting system is largely provided by annual taxes on radios and television sets.

A government agency supervises the motion-picture industry. The agency's activities include giving financial aid to producers, especially of experimental films and movies of serious dramatic value. The Cannes Film Festival, held annually in the city of Cannes on the Riviera, is the world's largest international film event.

History

Early days. In ancient times, tribes of Celts and other peoples lived in what is now France. The Romans called the region Gallia (Gaul). Roman armies began to invade Gaul about 200 B.C. By 121 B.C., Rome controlled the Gallic land along the Mediterranean Sea and in the Rhône Valley. Julius Caesar conquered the entire region between 58 and 51 B.C. The people, called Gauls, soon adopted Roman ways of life. They used the Latin language of the invaders. Gaul prospered under Roman rule for hundreds of years, in spite of foreign invasions during the A.D. 200's and 300's.

Victory of the Franks. The border defenses of the West Roman Empire began to crumble in the A.D. 400's. Germanic tribes from the east, including Burgundians, Franks, and Visigoths, crossed the Rhine River and entered Gaul. They killed many Gauls and drove others west into what is now Brittany.

Clovis, the king of the Salian Franks, defeated the independent Roman governor of Gaul in 486 at Soissons. Clovis then defeated other Germanic tribes in Gaul and extended his kingdom. He founded the Merovingian *dynasty* (series of rulers from the same family), and he adopted orthodox Christianity.

The rise of manorialism and feudalism. From the 600's to the 1000's, during the chaotic years of the early Middle Ages, *manors* covered much of France. Manors were large estates governed by owners called *landlords* or *lords,* who offered military protection to peasants called *serfs. Manorialism* was a system of organizing agricultural labor.

A political and military system called *feudalism* began to appear in the 700's. A feudal lord gave his subjects land in return for military and other services. Both the lord and his subjects, called *vassals,* were aristocrats. The land granted by a lord was called a *fief.* Some small fiefs supported only one vassal. Other fiefs were quite large, such as the province of Normandy. Manorialism and feudalism thrived until the 1100's.

The Carolingian dynasty. By the mid-600's, the Merovingian kings had become weak rulers, interested mainly in personal pleasures. Pepin of Herstal, the chief royal adviser, gradually took over most of the royal powers. His son Charles Martel extended the family's power.

Charles became known as Martel (the Hammer) because he defeated an invading Arab army in 732. The battle began near Tours and ended near Poitiers. Charles Martel became king of the Franks in all but title.

Charles Martel's son Pepin the Short overthrew the last Merovingian ruler and became king of the Franks in 751. He founded the Carolingian dynasty, and enlarged the Frankish kingdom. Pepin also helped develop the political power of the pope by giving Pope Stephen II a large gift of land north of Rome.

Pepin's son Charlemagne was one of the mightiest conquerors of all time. After Charlemagne became king of the Franks, he went on more than 50 military campaigns and expanded his kingdom far beyond the borders of what is now France. He also extended the pope's lands. In 800, Pope Leo III crowned Charlemagne Emperor of the Romans. For the story of Charlemagne and a map of his empire, see **Charlemagne.**

Charlemagne died in 814, and his three grandsons later fought among themselves for control of his huge empire. They divided it into three kingdoms in 843. In the Treaty of Verdun, one grandson, Charles the Bald, received most of what is now France. The second kingdom consisted of much that is now Germany. The third kingdom lay between the other two. It consisted of a strip of land extending from the North Sea to central Italy. The part of the strip that lay north of Italy was divided between the other two kingdoms in 870.

The Capetian dynasty. By the late 900's, the Carolingian kings had lost much power, and the strength of the nobles had increased. The kings became little more than great feudal lords chosen by the other feudal nobles to lead them in war. But in peacetime, most of their authority extended only over their personal estates.

In 987, the nobles ended the Carolingian line of kings. They chose as their king Hugh Capet, who started the Capetian dynasty. Many historians mark the beginning of the French nation from Hugh Capet's coronation.

Kings and emperors of France

Ruler	Reign	Ruler	Reign
* Hugh Capet	987-996	* Louis XI	1461-1483
Robert II	996-1031	* Charles VIII	1483-1498
Henry I	1031-1060	* Louis XII	1498-1515
Philip I	1060-1108	* Francis I	1515-1547
Louis VI	1108-1137	* Henry II	1547-1559
Louis VII	1137-1180	Francis II	1559-1560
* Philip II	1180-1223	* Charles IX	1560-1574
Louis VIII	1223-1226	* Henry III	1574-1589
* Louis IX	1226-1270	* Henry IV	1589-1610
Philip III	1270-1285	* Louis XIII	1610-1643
* Philip IV	1285-1314	* Louis XIV	1643-1715
Louis X	1314-1316	* Louis XV	1715-1774
John I	1316	* Louis XVI	1774-1792
Philip V	1316-1322	* Napoleon I	1804-1814
Charles IV	1322-1328	* Louis XVIII	1814-1815
* Philip VI	1328-1350	* Napoleon I	1815
John II	1350-1364	* Louis XVIII	1815-1824
* Charles V	1364-1380	* Charles X	1824-1830
Charles VI	1380-1422	* Louis Philippe	1830-1848
* Charles VII	1422-1461	* Napoleon III	1852-1870

*Has a separate biography in *World Book.*

Silver and gold statue encrusted with emeralds and rubies by an unknown sculptor (about 1349); Aachen Cathedral (Art Resource)

Charlemagne was the most famous ruler of the Middle Ages. He became king of the Franks in 768. He went on to conquer much of western Europe and unite it under one great empire.

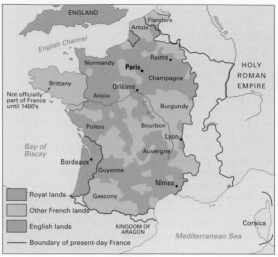

WORLD BOOK map

Capetian France in 1328 consisted of royal lands—those that were the personal holdings of the king—and lands held by French nobles who were vassals of the king.

For many years, the Capetian kings controlled only their royal *domain* (land), between Paris and Orléans. The great feudal nobles ruled their own domains almost independently. The dukes of Normandy were the most powerful of these nobles. Normandy became the most unified and best administered feudal state in Europe. In 1066, the Norman Duke William, later called William the Conqueror, invaded England and became king.

Growth of royal power. The Capetian kings gradually added more territory to their personal lands and became stronger than any of their rivals. In addition, every Capetian king for over 300 years had a son to succeed him on the throne. As a result, the power of the nobles to select kings died out. The nobles were further weak-

Important dates in France

58-51 B.C. Julius Caesar conquered Gaul.
A.D. 486 Clovis, a king of the Franks, defeated the Roman governor of Gaul.
800 Charlemagne became emperor of the Romans.
987 Hugh Capet was crowned king of France.
1302 Philip IV called together the first Estates-General, the ancestor of the French Parliament.
1309-1377 The popes lived in Avignon.
1337-1453 France defeated England during the Hundred Years' War.
1598 Henry IV issued the Edict of Nantes, which gave limited religious freedom to Protestants.
1643-1715 Louis XIV ruled France and consolidated the absolute authority of the French king.
1789-1799 The French Revolution took place. It ended absolute rule by French kings.
1792 The First Republic was established.
1799 Napoleon seized control of France.
1804 Napoleon founded the First Empire.
1814 Napoleon was exiled; Louis XVIII came to power.
1815 Napoleon returned to power but was defeated at Waterloo. Louis XVIII regained the throne.
1848 Revolutionists established the Second Republic.
1852 Napoleon III founded the Second Empire.
1870-1871 Prussia defeated France in the Franco-Prussian War. The Third Republic was begun.

1914-1918 France fought on the Allied side in World War I.
1939-1940 France fought on the Allied side in World War II until defeated by Germany.
1940-1942 Germany occupied northern France.
1942-1944 The Germans occupied all France.
1946 France adopted a new constitution, establishing the Fourth Republic.
1946-1954 A revolution in French Indochina resulted in France's giving up the colony.
1949 France joined the North Atlantic Treaty Organization (NATO).
1954 Revolution broke out in the French territory of Algeria.
1957 France joined the European Economic Community, which led to the country's eventual membership in the European Community and the European Union.
1958 A new constitution was adopted, marking the beginning of the Fifth Republic. Charles de Gaulle was elected president.
1962 France granted independence to Algeria.
1966 De Gaulle withdrew French troops from NATO.
1969 De Gaulle resigned as president.
1994 A railroad tunnel under the English Channel between France and Britain opened.

ened because many of them left France between 1100 and 1300 to join crusades to capture the Holy Land from the Muslims.

Philip II, called Philip Augustus, was one of the most important Capetian kings. After he came to the throne in 1180, he more than doubled the royal domain and tightened his control over the nobles. Philip built up a large body of government officials, many of them from the middle classes in the towns. He also developed Paris as a permanent, expanding capital.

Philip IV, called Philip the Fair, rebelled against the pope's authority. He taxed church officials, arrested a bishop, and even arrested Pope Boniface VIII. Philip won approval for his actions in the first Estates-General, a body of Frenchmen that he called together in 1302. This group was the ancestor of the French Parliament.

In 1305, through Philip's influence, a French archbishop was elected pope and became Pope Clement V. In 1309, Clement moved the pope's court from Rome to Avignon, where it remained until 1377.

Social conditions in Capetian France. By the 1100's, an economic revival in Europe had put money back into use. Towns, which had lost their importance under manorialism and feudalism, sprang up near main trade routes. At first, towns were self-governing. Merchants and craftworkers settled in the towns and formed organizations called *guilds*. Guilds played an important role in town government (see **Guild**). As royal government grew, towns became judicial and administrative centers, as well as manufacturing and trading centers.

Although many people moved to the towns in search of jobs, much of the population stayed in the countryside. Agricultural methods were too primitive to support more than a very small nonagricultural population. Thus, people were still needed on farms to produce food. In both towns and in the country, life expectancy was short.

A period of wars. The last king of the Capetian dynasty, Charles IV, died in 1328 without a male heir. A cousin succeeded him as Philip VI and started the Valois dynasty. In 1337, Philip declared that he would take over lands that King Edward III of England held in France, and Edward, who was a nephew of Charles IV, claimed the French throne. These actions started a series of wars between France and England known as the Hundred Years' War (1337-1453). The English won most of the battles. But the French, after their victory at Orléans under Joan of Arc, drove the English out of most of France.

Louis XI laid the foundations for absolute rule by French kings. During the Hundred Years' War, the kings had lost much of their power to the French nobles. Louis regained this power. His greatest rival was Charles the Bold, Duke of Burgundy. Charles died in battle in 1477 while trying to conquer the city of Nancy, and Louis seized most of his vast lands.

King Francis I invaded northern Italy and captured Milan in 1515. In a later Italian campaign, Francis was defeated by Charles V of the Holy Roman Empire. French wars against the Holy Roman Empire continued into the reign of Henry II. The empire and England were allies. In 1558, this alliance gave Henry an excuse to seize the port city of Calais, England's last possession in France.

Religious wars. During the early 1500's, a religious movement called the Reformation developed Protestantism in Europe. Many French people became Protes-tants. They followed the teachings of John Calvin and were called Huguenots. After 1540, the government persecuted the Huguenots, but they grew in number and political strength. In the late 1500's, French Roman Catholics and the Huguenots fought a series of civil wars that lasted over 30 years. In 1572, thousands of Huguenots were killed in the Massacre of Saint Bartholomew's Day.

Henry III died in 1589 without a male heir. He was followed by Henry of Navarre, who became Henry IV and started the Bourbon dynasty. But Roman Catholic forces prevented him from entering Paris because he was the leader of the Huguenots. In 1593, Henry became a Roman Catholic to achieve peace. He entered Paris in 1594. In 1598, Henry signed the Edict of Nantes, which granted limited freedom of worship to the Huguenots.

The age of absolutism. The power of the kings and their *ministers* (government officials) grew steadily from the 1500's to the 1700's. France became a strong nation, largely through the efforts of these ministers. The first important minister was Maximilien de Béthune, Duke of Sully, who served Henry IV. Sully promoted agriculture and such public works as highways and canals. He reduced the *taille,* the chief tax on the common people.

Louis XIII followed his father, Henry IV, to the throne. But the actual ruler was Louis XIII's prime minister, Armand Jean du Plessis, Cardinal Richelieu. Richelieu increased royal power more than any other individual.

Louis XIII's son Louis XIV was the outstanding example of the absolute French king. He is said to have boasted: "I am the State." After the death of his prime minister, Cardinal Jules Mazarin, in 1661, Louis declared that he would be his own prime minister.

In 1685, Louis canceled the Edict of Nantes and began to persecute the Huguenots savagely. About 200,000 Huguenots fled France. Louis's minister of finance, Jean Baptiste Colbert, promoted a strong economy, but the construction of Louis's grand Palace of Versailles and a series of major wars drained France's finances. Louis tried to rule supreme in Europe. He was stopped by military alliances that included England, Spain, the Holy Roman Empire, and other nations.

The French and Indian wars were four wars fought between France and Great Britain (now called the United Kingdom) in North America between 1689 and 1763. The French and Indian War (1754-1763) was the last of these conflicts. It was called the Seven Years' War in Europe. In the end, France lost nearly all its land in North America. Great Britain gained most of the French territory, and Spain acquired the rest.

The gathering storm. By the 1700's, a government bureaucracy had developed to manage a large standing royal army, as well as to collect taxes. Royal courts upheld law and order. Lawyers and jurists of the courts bought their offices from the king at very high prices. The king allowed those who bought the highest judicial offices to call themselves nobles, and he granted them tax exemptions. This burdensome system worked well enough to allow remarkable economic and population growth in the 1700's. But the population growth exceeded agricultural production capacities, and food shortages and famines became common. Such growth also strained the guild system that governed the activities of merchants and craftworkers in the towns.

Burdened by the needs of the military and unable to

tax nobles or church lands, the government was forced to borrow heavily. In 1786, the government proposed a new land tax in order to avoid bankruptcy. Many urban lawyers, merchants, clerks, and craftworkers, as well as some aristocrats, opposed any new taxes. The French Revolution was born out of this crisis.

The French Revolution. To win support for new taxes, King Louis XVI called a meeting of the Estates-General. The Estates-General was made up of representatives from the three *estates,* or classes—the clergy, the nobility, and the commoners. It opened on May 5, 1789, at Versailles, near Paris. In June 1789, members of the third estate—the commoners—declared themselves a National Assembly, with full power to write a new constitution for France. The third estate had as many representatives as the other two estates combined.

At first, Louis XVI delayed taking action and began gathering troops around Paris to break up the Assembly. However, many French people organized an armed resistance movement in Paris. On July 14, 1789, a huge crowd of Parisians captured the royal fortress called the Bastille. Louis XVI was forced to give in. By September 1791, the Assembly had drafted a new constitution that made France a constitutional, or limited, monarchy, with a one-house legislature.

The new government did not last long. In April 1792, France went to war against Austria and Prussia. These nations wished to restore the king to his position. In the summer of 1792, as foreign armies marched on Paris, revolutionaries imprisoned Louis XVI and his family and overthrew the monarchy. A National Convention, chosen in an election open to nearly all adult French males, began on Sept. 21, 1792, and declared France a republic.

Civil and foreign wars pushed the new republican government to extreme and violent measures. Radical leaders, such as Maximilien Robespierre, gained power. They said that terror was necessary to preserve liberty.

Storming of the Bastille (about 1800), an oil painting on canvas by an unknown artist; Château Versailles (Giraudon/Art Resource)

The storming of the Bastille on July 14, 1789, was an early event in the French Revolution. A huge crowd of Parisians captured the fortress, forcing royal troops to withdraw from Paris.

Thus, while the revolution survived under radical leadership, it also sentenced many "enemies of the republic" to death. Thousands of people were executed. In time, the radicals began to struggle for power among themselves. Robespierre was condemned by his enemies and executed. His death marked the end of the period called the Reign of Terror.

In 1795, a new constitution was adopted that formed a government called the Directory. The Directory, a five-man board, governed France from 1795 to 1799, during the last half of the French Revolution.

Napoleon. During the French Revolution, a young officer named Napoleon Bonaparte rose through the ranks of the army. He was named a general in 1793, and his power grew rapidly. In 1799, Napoleon overthrew the French government and seized control of France.

Napoleon was an excellent administrator. He created a strong, efficient central government and revised and organized French law. He was also a military genius with great ambition. By 1812, Napoleon's forces had conquered most of western and central Europe. But maintaining control over this vast empire eventually overextended French power, and Napoleon was forced to give up his throne in 1814. He returned to rule France again for about three months in 1815 before his final defeat at Waterloo. For the story of Napoleon's life and a map of his empire, see **Napoleon I.**

The revolutions of 1830 and 1848. The Bourbon dynasty returned to power after Napoleon's downfall. Charles X, who became king in 1824, tried to reestablish the total power of the earlier French kings. He was overthrown in the July Revolution of 1830.

The revolutionists placed Louis Philippe on the throne. He belonged to the Orléans branch of the Bourbon family. France was peaceful and prosperous during Louis Philippe's reign. But the poorer classes became dissatisfied because only the wealthy could vote or hold public office. The February Revolution of 1848 overthrew the government and established the Second Republic. All Frenchmen received the right to vote.

The voters elected Louis Napoleon Bonaparte, a nephew of Napoleon, to a four-year term as president in 1848. He seized greater power illegally in 1851 and declared himself president for 10 years. In 1852, he established the Second Empire and declared himself Emperor Napoleon III.

The Franco-Prussian War. During the 1860's, France became alarmed over the growing strength of Prussia. France feared that a united Germany under Prussian leadership would upset Europe's balance of power. In 1870, France declared war on Prussia. Prussia defeated France the next year. In the peace treaty following the war, France was forced to give almost all of Alsace and part of Lorraine to the new German Empire.

The Third Republic. After Prussian victories in 1870, the French revolted against Napoleon III. They established a *provisional* (temporary) republic, which became known as the Third Republic, and in 1871 elected a National Assembly. In March 1871, a revolt called the Paris Commune began against the newly formed government. Participants in the Commune believed that working-class citizens should take control of the government. They opposed the transitional government because it was expected to make France a monarchy again. By May

1871, government forces had crushed the uprising.

In 1875, the Assembly voted to continue the republic and wrote a new constitution. France's strength and prosperity grew through the late 1800's. French explorers and soldiers won a vast colonial empire in Africa and Asia. Only the United Kingdom had a larger overseas empire. France strengthened its army and formed a military alliance with Russia in 1894 and the *Entente Cordiale* (cordial understanding) with the British in 1904. French industries expanded steadily.

By the 1890's, most French people were reconciled to the Third Republic, but few were deeply committed to it. An incident known as the Dreyfus affair finally forced the nation to take sides on the issue. On Oct. 15, 1894, Alfred Dreyfus, a Jewish French army officer, was arrested on suspicion of spying for Germany. In December, a military court found him guilty. However, evidence of his innocence slowly trickled out and eventually attracted much attention. Many people began to rally to Dreyfus's side. They included Socialists representing the French working class and moderate republicans.

Many people believed that the French army had acted arbitrarily in convicting Dreyfus and feared that the republic was endangered. They made Dreyfus a symbol of civil liberties and republican virtues and worked to get him a new trial. Supporters of the army and opponents of republican government came together and denounced Dreyfus and his supporters as unpatriotic. A fight followed that resulted in a strengthening of support for the republic. In 1906, France's highest court reviewed the Dreyfus case and declared Dreyfus innocent.

World War I. During the early 1900's, France and Germany had disagreements over colonial territories, and each country feared an attack by the other. In 1907, France established a diplomatic agreement called the Triple Entente with the United Kingdom and Russia. The French prepared for war.

Soon after the start of World War I (1914-1918), Germany invaded France. The Germans hoped to defeat France quickly. But by late 1914, the French army had halted the German advance. For 3 ½ years, the opposing forces fought from trenches that stretched across northeastern France and Belgium.

The worst fighting faced by the French army during the war took place around the city of Verdun in 1916. In February, the German army launched a major attack to take Verdun. For five months, intense fighting continued, and hundreds of thousands of French and German troops were killed. At first, the Germans made rapid progress. But they were slowly rolled back. In July, the Germans halted their unsuccessful attack.

The Battle of Verdun became a symbol of the French nation's will to resist. But the battle had also drained the nation. From the middle of 1917, France's allies began handling most of the war's major battles. The war produced enormously high casualties, partly as a result of the destructive powers of new weapons, such as the machine gun and poison gas. Millions of French servicemen were killed or wounded. For more on the story of France in the war, see **World War I.**

Between World Wars. In the Treaty of Versailles, signed in 1919, France recovered Alsace and the German part of Lorraine from Germany. France and other Allied nations also were awarded *reparations* (payments for war damages) from Germany. Germany fell behind in making these payments. As a result, French and Belgian troops occupied the Ruhr Valley of Germany in 1923. After Germany agreed to keep up the payments, the troops were withdrawn in 1925.

The French did much to reestablish good relations with Germany. France joined other Allied nations and Germany in the Rhineland Security Pact of 1925. This agreement in part guaranteed the security of the French-German border. France reduced Germany's reparations and dropped various controls over Germany set up by the Treaty of Versailles. Suggestions by Aristide Briand, the French foreign minister, led to the Kellogg-Briand Pact of 1928. The pact was signed by France, Germany, and 13 other nations. But in 1929, France began building the Maginot Line as a fortified defense against Germany.

During the 1930's, a worldwide economic depression and the rise of fascist leader Adolf Hitler in Germany caused serious political unrest in France. In 1936, at a time of widespread labor strikes, a government called the Popular Front came to power in France. It made many promises to striking workers, including annual paid vacations and a 40-hour workweek. It tried to establish a strong position against fascism. But in 1938, the government began to give in to the demands of Nazi Germany. As part of this policy of *appeasement,* France signed the Munich Agreement, which forced Czechoslovakia to give territory to Germany.

World War II began when Germany invaded Poland on Sept. 1, 1939. Two days later, France and the United Kingdom declared war on Germany. On May 10, 1940, the Germans attacked Belgium, Luxembourg, and the Netherlands. They invaded France through Belgium on May 12, passing northwest of the Maginot Line. The Germans launched a major attack to the south on June 5 and entered Paris on June 14. On June 22, France signed an armistice with Germany. The Germans occupied the northern two-thirds of France, and southern France remained under French control. Southern France was governed at Vichy by Marshal Henri Philippe Pétain, who largely cooperated with the Germans.

After France fell, General Charles de Gaulle fled to London. He invited all French patriots to join a movement called Free France and continue fighting the Germans. This *resistance* movement also spread throughout France. Some groups of French people called Maquis hid in hilly areas and fought the Germans. After Allied troops landed in French North Africa in November 1942, German troops also occupied southern France. The Germans tried to seize the French fleet at Toulon. But the French sank most of the fleet's ships to prevent them from being captured by the Germans.

On June 6, 1944, the Allies landed in France at Normandy. They landed in southern France on August 15. After fierce fighting and heavy loss of lives, the Allied troops entered Paris on August 25. De Gaulle soon formed a provisional government and became its president. In 1945, France became a charter member of the United Nations. For the story of France in the war, see **World War II.**

The Fourth Republic. In October 1945, the French people voted to have the National Assembly write a new constitution creating the Fourth Republic. In this election, French women voted for the first time. De Gaulle

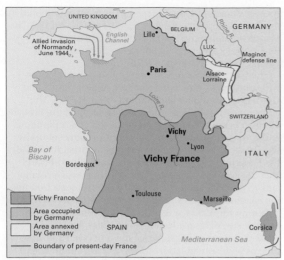

Vichy France

UNITED KINGDOM
BELGIUM
GERMANY
Lille
English Channel
Rhine R.
Allied invasion of Normandy June 1944
LUX.
Maginot defense line
Paris
Alsace-Lorraine
Loire R.
SWITZERLAND
Vichy
Lyon
Bay of Biscay
Vichy France
ITALY
Bordeaux
Toulouse
Marseille
Vichy France
Area occupied by Germany
Area annexed by Germany
SPAIN
Corsica
Boundary of present-day France
Mediterranean Sea

WORLD BOOK map

France in World War II. Germany occupied northern France from 1940 to 1944. Southern France remained under French control, with its capital at Vichy, until 1942, when it was occupied.

AP/Wide World

Allied troops rode through Paris on Aug. 26, 1944, the day after they freed the city from Nazi occupation in World War II. French citizens crowded the streets to welcome the troops.

resigned as president in January 1946 over disagreements with the Assembly. The new Constitution, which was similar to that of the Third Republic, went into effect in October 1946. De Gaulle opposed it because it did not provide strong executive powers.

France received much aid from the United States and rebuilt its cities and industries, which had been badly damaged during the war. But political troubles at home and colonial revolts overseas slowed the nation's economic recovery. France played an important part in the Cold War between the Communist countries and the non-Communist Western nations (see **Cold War**). The Communist Party was one of the largest in France after

the war, and it controlled the chief labor unions. Communist-led strikes in 1947 and 1948 crippled production across the country. But in 1949, France became a charter member of the anti-Communist North Atlantic Treaty Organization (NATO).

The first revolt by a French colony began in Indochina in 1946. Indochina was eventually divided into Cambodia, Laos, and North and South Vietnam. The French withdrew from Indochina in 1954 after heavy losses.

Later in 1954, revolution broke out in the French territory of Algeria. To avoid revolutions in Morocco and Tunisia, France made them independent in 1956. Other French colonies in Africa received independence later. But France refused to give up Algeria, the home of almost a million French settlers. France gradually built up its army in Algeria to about 500,000 men, and the war continued through the 1950's.

In spite of the costly colonial wars, France's economy grew rapidly. By the late 1950's, it had broken all French production records. The boom developed with U.S. aid and a series of national economic plans begun in 1946. French business executives and government officials were determined to prove that France's greatness had not disappeared. Between 1947 and 1958, France helped form several economic organizations that were important steps toward a European confederation. For discussions of these organizations, see **Europe, Council of; European Union** (History).

The Fifth Republic. By 1958, large numbers of French people thought it was useless to continue fighting in Algeria. But the idea of giving up Algeria angered many French army leaders and settlers in the colony. They rebelled in May 1958 and threatened to overthrow the French government by force unless it continued fighting. In a compromise solution, de Gaulle was called back to power as prime minister, with emergency powers for six months. De Gaulle's government prepared a new constitution, which the voters approved on Sept. 28, 1958. This Constitution, which established the Fifth Republic, gave the president greater power than ever before and sharply reduced the power of Parliament. In December, the Electoral College elected de Gaulle to a seven-year term as president.

France under de Gaulle. De Gaulle's government continued the war in Algeria, hoping the Algerians would agree to a compromise settlement that provided some French control. By 1961, however, the government realized that only Algerian independence would end the rebellion. Peace talks began in 1961 and ended with a cease-fire in March 1962. At de Gaulle's urging, French voters approved Algerian independence in April. Algeria became independent on July 3, 1962, and most French settlers there returned to France.

Algerian independence set off a wave of bombings and murders in France and Algeria by the Secret Army Organization (OAS). This group, which included many army officers, accused de Gaulle of betraying France by ending the war. The OAS tried several times to kill de Gaulle. Its leaders were eventually captured and sentenced to prison.

After the Algerian crisis, some French politicians tried to weaken de Gaulle's strong rule. They wanted to reestablish the former power of Parliament and reduce that of the president. But de Gaulle made the presidency even stronger. He declared that the president should have nationwide support and be elected by the people, not by the Electoral College. In 1962, the voters approved a constitutional amendment that provided such elections.

De Gaulle was reelected to a second seven-year term in 1965. French foreign policy became his main interest. De Gaulle declared that the French were "a race created for brilliant deeds," but that they could not achieve greatness with their "destiny in the hands of foreigners." He hoped to make France the leader of an alliance of Western European nations. This alliance would be free of U.S. or Soviet influence.

Instead of relying on American protection through NATO, de Gaulle developed an independent French nuclear weapons program. In 1966, he removed all French troops from NATO. He also declared that all NATO military bases and troops had to be removed from France by April 1967. France withdrew from NATO militarily, but it remained a member politically.

In the 1950's, France had helped form the European Coal and Steel Community, the European Atomic Energy Community, and the European Economic Community (EEC). These agencies later became known as the European Community (EC), which eventually became the European Union (EU).

De Gaulle believed France could work within the EEC to become stronger and more influential in Western Europe. In 1963, he prevented the United Kingdom from joining the EEC. He considered the United Kingdom a rival for leadership in Europe. De Gaulle also believed the United Kingdom's ties with the United States would give America too much influence on Europe's economy.

In the late 1960's, many French people became dissatisfied with de Gaulle's government. This dissatisfaction led to a severe national crisis in May 1968. Students staged demonstrations in Paris, some of which erupted into violent clashes with the police. Additional demonstrations, many accompanied by violence, spread throughout France, and millions of workers joined in by going on strike. The country was paralyzed for more than two weeks, and many people expected the overthrow of de Gaulle's government and possible civil war. But de Gaulle managed to bring the situation under control by the end of May.

De Gaulle called a general election in June, and his supporters won more than 70 percent of the seats in Parliament. However, de Gaulle's reputation as a leader had been seriously damaged by what the French called the "events of May." In April 1969, de Gaulle asked for minor constitutional reforms and said he would resign if the voters did not approve them. The French people voted against the reforms, and de Gaulle resigned.

France after de Gaulle. Georges Pompidou was elected president in June 1969. He had been de Gaulle's prime minister, and he promised to continue de Gaulle's policies. But he changed de Gaulle's foreign policy by cooperating more closely with the United States. He also improved relations with the United Kingdom. In 1971, Pompidou and British Prime Minister Edward Heath agreed on the United Kingdom's entry into the European Community.

At home, Pompidou's government faced economic problems. The nation's industrial growth began to slow, unemployment increased, and inflation rose to a high level. Part of the trouble resulted from the worldwide oil crisis in 1973, when oil-producing countries raised the price of oil sharply. The crisis seriously affected France, which imports most of its petroleum.

Pompidou died in April 1974. The Gaullist Party, which had supported de Gaulle and Pompidou, split into a number of separate groups in the presidential election that followed in May. These groups supported various candidates. As a result, the Gaullist Party was weakened.

France's empire — France's colonial empire spanned two eras. From the early 1600's to the 1760's, France built a vast empire in North America. From the 1800's to the mid-1900's, France held many colonies in Africa and Asia. The names of the remaining French overseas possessions are shown in bold type on the map.

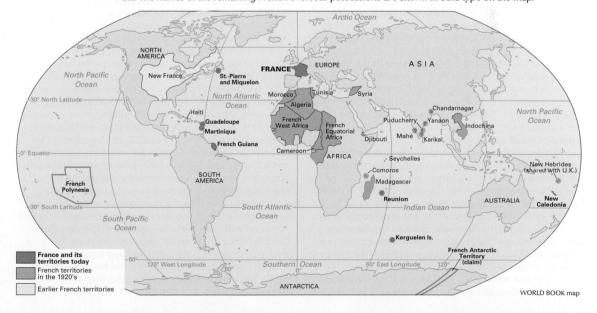

WORLD BOOK map

AP/Wide World

Charles de Gaulle served as president of France from 1958 to 1969. He greatly increased the power of the presidency, particularly in the conduct of foreign policy.

Valéry Giscard d'Estaing, head of the Independent Republican Party, was elected president.

The Gaullists and a group of parties that supported Giscard won a majority of the seats in France's parliamentary elections in 1978. Those parties formed a coalition government. The leftist Socialist and Communist parties were their main opponents.

The loss of most of its colonial empire relieved France of the cost of governing and developing the colonies. But France continued to give economic, technical, and military aid to many of its former colonies. For example, France supported the government of Chad against rebels by supplying military aid and, at times, troops. France also sent troops to Lebanon in 1982 as part of a peacekeeping force. But in 1983, a terrorist bombing killed 54 French soldiers stationed there. France withdrew its troops from Lebanon the following year.

Socialists win power. Politically, France moved sharply to the left in 1981. The voters elected François Mitterrand of the Socialist Party as president. The Socialists also won a majority of the seats in the 1981 parliamentary elections, which gave France its first leftist government since 1958. The new Socialist leaders greatly increased government ownership of businesses. They also increased social spending.

From the time of Napoleon I, France's departments were administered by *prefects*—officials appointed by, and responsible to, the national government. But the Socialist government gave locally elected councils the responsibility for the departments.

The 1981 elections resulted in a sharp decline in the number of parliamentary seats held by Communists. But the Communists had supported Mitterrand in the presidential race. He appointed Communists to four minor cabinet posts, marking the first Communist participation in the cabinet since 1947. In 1984, the Communists resigned after disagreements over economic policies.

The Socialists lost their parliamentary majority to conservatives in the 1986 elections. Mitterrand remained president, but he named Jacques Chirac, a conservative, as prime minister. Chirac ran for president in 1988, but Mitterrand ran against him and won a second term. Mitterrand soon dissolved the National Assembly. In new legislative elections, the Socialists and their allies won a slight majority. Mitterrand then named Michel Rocard, a Socialist, as prime minister. Rocard resigned in 1991, and Socialist Edith Cresson became France's first female prime minister. She resigned in 1992. Mitterrand appointed Socialist Pierre Bérégovoy to succeed her.

In 1993, conservatives won a large majority in parliamentary elections. Mitterrand then appointed a conservative, Edouard Balladur, as prime minister.

Chirac again ran for president in 1995, and this time he was victorious. During his campaign, he promised he would try to reduce France's high unemployment rate. Chirac, the founder of the conservative Rally for the Republic (RPR) party, named RPR member Alain Juppé to serve as prime minister.

Recent developments. In 1997, Chirac called for parliamentary elections to take place earlier than expected. He hoped for a show of support for his government so he could put through economic reforms. In the elections, however, the conservatives lost their majority in Parliament, and the Socialist Party ended up with the most seats. Chirac then appointed Lionel Jospin, the head of the Socialist Party, to serve as prime minister.

Chirac and Jospin ran for president in 2002, but Jospin was eliminated in the first round of voting. Chirac was reelected in the second round. Jospin resigned as prime minister. Parliamentary elections later in 2002 gave the most seats to Chirac's new party, Union for a Presidential Majority (later renamed Union for a Popular Movement or UMP), and its allies. Chirac named Jean-Pierre Raffarin, a conservative, as prime minister.

In 2004, the European Union asked member nations to approve a new constitution. Chirac called on French voters to support the constitution, but they rejected it in a referendum in 2005. In response, Raffarin resigned and Dominique de Villepin became prime minister.

Youths began rioting in some suburbs of Paris in October 2005. Most of the rioters were Muslims of North African ancestry who considered themselves victims of discrimination, especially by the police. The violence continued for about three weeks and spread to other French cities with large immigrant populations. French authorities imposed curfews and took other emergency measures, which helped restore peace.

In 2006, the French government announced a youth employment plan that gave employers permission to dismiss newly hired young workers without cause during a trial period. Student labor unions and other youth groups sponsored demonstrations against the plan. The government eventually withdrew the amendment.

In the 2007 presidential elections, Nicolas Sarkozy, leader of the UMP, defeated Ségolène Royal, the Socialist Party candidate. Sarkozy succeeded Chirac as president in May 2007. Sarkozy appointed François Fillon as prime minister. In 2012, Socialist Party candidate François Hollande defeated Sarkozy's bid for reelection. Hollande became president in May 2012. He named Jean-Marc Ayrault as prime minister.   Mark Kesselman

Related articles in *World Book* include:

Kings and emperors

See the table *Kings and emperors of France* with this article.

Other biographies

Anne of Austria
Briand, Aristide
Catherine de Médicis
Charlemagne
Charles Martel
Chateaubriand, François R. de
Chirac, Jacques René
Claudel, Paul
Clemenceau, Georges
Clovis I
Colbert, Jean B.
Condorcet, Marquis de
Corday, Charlotte
Danton, Georges-Jacques
De Gaulle, Charles A. J. M.
Foch, Ferdinand
Genêt, Edmond C. É.
Giscard d'Estaing, Valery
Joan of Arc, Saint
Lafayette, Marquis de
Lamartine, Alphonse
Laval, Pierre

Marat, Jean-Paul
Marie de Médicis
Mazarin, Jules
Mirabeau, Comte de
Mitterrand, François Maurice
Montcalm, Marquis de
Ney, Michel
Pepin the Short
Pétain, Henri P.
Poincaré, Raymond
Richelieu, Cardinal
Robespierre
Rochambeau, Comte de
Roland de la Platière, Marie Jeanne
Sarkozy, Nicolas
Sieyès, Emmanuel J.
Talleyrand
Talon, Jean B.
Thiers, Louis Adolphe
Tocqueville, Alexis de
William I, the Conqueror

Cities and towns

Amiens
Avignon
Bordeaux
Brest
Calais
Cannes
Carcassonne
Chartres
Cherbourg
Dunkerque

Fontainebleau
Grenoble
La Rochelle
Le Havre
Le Mans
Lille
Lourdes
Lyon
Marseille
Nantes

Nice
Orléans
Paris
Reims
Rouen
Strasbourg
Toulon
Toulouse
Tours
Vichy

History

Agincourt, Battle of
Algeria (The Algerian Revolution)
Austerlitz, Battle of
Bastille
Bourbon
Capetian dynasty
Celts
Continental System
Crécy, Battle of
Crimean War
Crusades
Dauphin
Dreyfus affair
Estates-General
European Union
Feudalism
Franco-Prussian War
Franks
French and Indian wars

French Revolution
Gaul
Grand Alliance
Huguenots
Hundred Years' War
Indochina (French Indochina)
July Revolution
Kellogg-Briand Pact
Louisbourg
Maginot Line
Manorialism
Maquis
Merovingian dynasty
Middle Ages
Mississippi Scheme
Munich Agreement
Nantes, Edict of

Napoleonic Wars
New France
Norman Conquest
Normans
Papal States
Poitiers, Battle of
Reformation
Reign of Terror
Renaissance
Revolution of 1848
Ruhr (History)
Succession wars (The war of the Spanish succession)
Valois
Verdun, Treaty of
Versailles, Treaty of
Waldenses
World War I
World War II
Zouaves

Overseas possessions

French Guiana
French Polynesia
Guadeloupe
Martinique

Mayotte
New Caledonia
Réunion
Saint-Pierre and Miquelon

Physical features

Aisne River

Alps

Ardennes Mountains and Forest
Bay of Biscay
Corsica
Dover, Strait of
English Channel
Lascaux Cave
Loire River

Marne River
Mont Blanc
Mont-Saint-Michel
Pyrenees
Rhône River
Saône River
Seine River

Regions

Alsace-Lorraine
Brittany
Burgundy
Flanders

Gascony
Normandy
Riviera

Other related articles

Air force (The French Air Force)
Army (The French Army)
Basques
Bastille Day
Bibliothèque Nationale de France
Bicycle racing (Road races)
Channel Tunnel
Christmas (In France)
Code Napoléon
Democracy (French contributions to democracy)
Doll (The history of dolls)
École des Beaux-Arts
Eiffel Tower
Fleur-de-lis
Foreign Legion
French Academy

French language
French literature
Furniture
Institute of France
Louvre
Marseillaise
Navy (Major navies of the world)
Paris, University of
Salic law
Sorbonne
Statue of Liberty
Theater (France)
Tour de France
Tuileries
Versailles, Palace of
Wine (Where wine comes from)

Outline

I. **Government**
   A. National government
   B. Local government
   C. Politics
   D. Courts
   E. Armed forces

II. **People**
   A. Ancestry
   B. Language

III. **Way of life**
   A. City life
   B. Rural life
   C. Food and drink
   D. Recreation
   E. Holidays
   F. Religion
   G. Education
   H. Museums and libraries

IV. **Arts**
   A. Literature
   B. Painting
   C. Sculpture
   D. Architecture
   E. Music
   F. Motion pictures

V. **The land**
VI. **Climate**
VII. **Economy**
   A. Natural resources
   B. Service industries
   C. Manufacturing
   D. Agriculture
   E. Forestry
   F. Mining
   G. Fishing
   H. Energy sources
   I. International trade
   J. Transportation
   K. Communication

VIII. **History**

Additional resources

Bailey, Rosemary. *France*. 3rd ed. National Geographic Soc., 2011.
Frommer's France. Wiley, frequently updated. A travel guide.
Kedward, Rod. *France and the French*. Overlook, 2006.
McGregor, James H. S. *Paris from the Ground Up*. Harvard Univ. Pr., 2009.
Moynahan, Brian. *The French Century: An Illustrated History of Modern France*. Flammarion, 2007.
Nardo, Don. *France*. Children's Pr., 2008. Younger readers.
Raymond, Gino. *Historical Dictionary of France*. 2nd ed. Scarecrow, 2008.

France, *frans* or *frahns,* **Anatole,** *a na TAWL* (1844-1924), was the pen name of Jacques Anatole François Thibault, a French novelist and critic. He won the 1921 Nobel Prize in literature.

France was born on April 16, 1844, in Paris, the son of a well-to-do bookseller. His childhood was filled with the magic of literature. In his autobiography, *My Friend's Book* (1885), France recalled the pleasures of those years and the mental stimulation he received from Paris, especially its libraries and bookshops.

France's first successful novel was *The Crime of Sylvester Bonnard* (1881). Beginning in 1886, he wrote a literary column for the newspaper *Le Temps.* His clear and elegant style, the subtlety of his observation, and his disinterested rejection of extreme causes gained him the reputation of being a friendly, easy-going man. France's novel *Thaïs* (1890) seemed to symbolize his ideals of pleasure and wisdom.

The famous Dreyfus affair, which shook the nation, led France to write about political and social issues (see **Dreyfus affair**). His novels of the 1900's reflect his part in the struggle for social justice that took place in the country. He began to ridicule society and its institutions in *Penguin Island* (1908), his most famous novel, and in *The Gods Are Athirst* (1912) and *The Revolt of the Angels* (1914). The irony of these novels has been compared to that of the works of Voltaire. France died on Oct. 12, 1924.   Thomas H. Goetz

Francesca, Piero della. See Piero della Francesca.
Franchise, *FRAN chyz,* is the right to sell certain products or services for a particular period at a specific location. The agreement by which a company, individual, or governmental unit grants such a right is also called a *franchise.* There are two main types of franchise agreements—private and public.

Private franchises. Under a private franchise agreement, a *franchisee* (buyer) normally pays a fee to a *franchisor* (seller) to obtain the franchise. The franchisee may also pay a percentage of the firm's sales to the franchisor. In return, the franchisor provides the franchisee with personnel training, financial assistance, and advertising. In addition, the franchisor often allows the franchisee to use a well-known trade name. Stores, restaurants, hotels, and other businesses operate under private franchise agreements. Businesses that operate in this way include Baskin-Robbins, Burger King, Dunkin' Donuts, Holiday Inn, H & R Block, and Subway.

The use of a well-known trade name can be extremely valuable to the franchisee. For example, suppose a family is traveling through an unfamiliar town and sees three possible places to stop for dinner—Chuck's Chicken, Bill's Burgers, and a Burger King. Because the Burger King trade name is well known, the family may have dinner there instead of at the other establishments. The people who operate franchised businesses usually seek to ensure that the quality of goods and services is consistent from one location to another.

Public franchises are usually between public utilities and a city or other governmental unit. For example, suppose a city and an electric company have reached an agreement about electric service for the city. Under a typical agreement, the city would grant the company the right to run power lines on city land and to be the only electric company in the area. In return, the company

would have to serve all public needs for this service and to have its fees approved by a governmental body such as a public service commission. Other public services that may be franchises include telephone service, garbage collection, and cable television.   V. Ann Paulins

See also **Chain store** (Franchise chain stores); **McDonald's Corporation; Restaurant** (Chains and franchises).
Francis (1936-   ) was elected pope of the Roman Catholic Church in 2013. He succeeded Pope Benedict XVI, the first pope to resign in nearly 600 years. Francis, an Argentine of Italian ancestry, is the first pope from Latin America and the first Jesuit pope. Jesuits are members of a religious order called the Society of Jesus. Francis is known for his commitment to social justice, especially for the poor; his humble lifestyle; and his conservative religious beliefs. He speaks Spanish, Italian, Latin, English, French, German, and Ukrainian.

Francis was born Jorge Mario Bergoglio (pronounced *HAWR hay MAH ree oh bur GOH lee oh)* on Dec. 17, 1936, in Buenos Aires, Argentina. His parents were from Italian immigrant families. In the 1950's, Bergoglio attended the University of Buenos Aires, where he earned a master's degree in chemistry. Bergoglio then entered the Jesuit seminary of Villa Devoto in Buenos Aires and began studying to become a priest. In 1958, he joined the Society of Jesus. He was ordained a priest in 1969. From the late 1950's through the 1980's, Bergoglio pursued further studies in Argentina, Chile, and Germany and received degrees in philosophy and theology. During the 1960's, he taught literature, psychology, and theology at several educational institutions.

From 1973 through 1979, Bergoglio served as the Jesuit *provincial* for Argentina—that is, the head church official in charge of Jesuits. In 1976, military leaders overthrew the country's government and established a dictatorship that lasted until 1983. That period in Argentina's history became known as the "dirty war." Government officials kidnapped, imprisoned, tortured, and executed thousands of people who opposed them, including some priests. Some critics claim that Bergoglio did not do enough to stand up to the military government. However, Vatican officials deny such charges, pointing out that Bergoglio actually protected many people during the dictatorship.

During the 1980's, Bergoglio served as rector of the Philosophical and Theological Faculty of San Miguel, a seminary in Buenos Aires, and as a parish priest. Pope John Paul II appointed Bergoglio as an *auxiliary* (assisting) bishop of Buenos Aires in 1992. Bergoglio became *coadjutor* archbishop of Buenos Aires in 1997, and archbishop in 1998. A coadjutor usually succeeds the archbishop whom he serves. In 2001, Bergoglio was made a cardinal. From 2005 to 2011, he served as president of the Bishops' Conference of Argentina. The College of Cardinals elected him pope on March 13, 2013. He took the name Francis, after Saint Francis of Assisi, who gave up all his possessions to work among the poor.

Chester Gillis

See also **Bishop; Cardinal; Francis of Assisi, Saint; Jesuits; Pope** (pictures).
Francis I (1494-1547) of France became king in 1515. He succeeded Louis XII, who was both his cousin and his father-in-law. Francis began his reign brilliantly with a great victory over Swiss forces in the Battle of Marigna-

no in 1515. This victory allowed him to capture the city-state of Milan in northern Italy. It also enabled him to negotiate the Concordat of Bologna with Pope Leo X in 1516. The Concordat greatly strengthened the king's influence over the Roman Catholic Church in France. The new doctrines of Protestantism entered France during Francis's reign. After a period of hesitant and contradictory policies toward the Protestants, Francis turned to active persecution of them.

During his reign, Francis for years carried on a bitter struggle with Holy Roman Emperor Charles V, who was also King Charles I of Spain (see **Charles V** [Holy Roman emperor]). France lost Milan to Charles in 1522. In 1525, during an attempt to regain this city-state, Francis was captured and imprisoned. But Charles released him the following year. The last war between Francis and Charles ended inconclusively in 1544.

Francis enjoyed beautiful surroundings, took an interest in new art and literature, and spent money lavishly. Such activities gave him a reputation as a supporter of the Renaissance.

Francis was born in Cognac, France, on Sept. 12, 1494, and died on March 31, 1547. He belonged to the Valois family of French kings.   Donald A. Bailey

Francis I, Holy Roman emperor. See **Habsburg, House of; Maria Theresa.**

Francis I, of Austria. See **Francis II.**

Francis II (1768-1835) was the last Holy Roman emperor. He also reigned as Emperor Francis I of Austria. Francis opposed revolutionary movements generated in Europe by the French Revolution (1789-1799).

Francis was born in Florence, Italy, on Feb. 12, 1768, and belonged to the Habsburg (or Hapsburg) family. He succeeded his father, Leopold II, as ruler of Austria in 1792 and was elected Holy Roman emperor that same year. In 1804, Francis adopted the additional title of emperor of Austria. By 1806, Emperor Napoleon I of France had forced Francis to resign as Holy Roman emperor, and the Holy Roman Empire ended. After 1809, Francis allowed his shrewd foreign minister, Prince von Metternich, to direct Austria's foreign affairs. Under Metternich's guidance, Austria in time joined Prussia, Russia, and the United Kingdom to fight Napoleon. The united European powers defeated Napoleon in 1814 and 1815.

As emperor of Austria, Francis blocked all efforts aimed at even modest political reform. He died on March 2, 1835.   Peter N. Stearns

See also **Aix-la-Chapelle, Congress of; Holy Alliance; Marie Louise; Metternich.**

Francis, Dick (1920-2010), was a British author of mystery novels, most with horse-racing backgrounds. Francis's books feature ordinary young men who are called upon to become heroes. They are not detectives but are cast into roles in which they must solve mysteries. Francis's thrillers have won acclaim for their crisp, clear prose and expert handling of character and suspense.

Richard Stanley Francis was born on Oct. 31, 1920, near Tenby, Wales. He was a leading English steeplechase jockey from 1948 to 1957. He was racing correspondent for the London *Sunday Express* from 1957 to 1973. His first mystery novel, *Dead Cert,* appeared in 1962. Some of Francis's later mysteries have explored such subjects as photography *(Reflex,* 1981), banking *(Banker,* 1983), gems *(Straight,* 1989), and glass blowing

(Shattered, 2000). *The Sport of Queens* (1957) deals with Francis's racing career. Prior to her death in 2000, Francis's wife, Mary, collaborated with him on the research and editing of his novels. Francis wrote the thrillers *Dead Heat* (2007), *Silks* (2008), and *Even Money* (2009) with Felix Francis, his son. Dick Francis died on Feb. 14, 2010.   David Geherin

Francis de Sales, *saylz,* **Saint** (1567-1622), was a French nobleman who became a Roman Catholic saint. He attended the College of Clermont in Paris. There Francis became so devoted to the Blessed Virgin Mary that he took a vow of *chastity* (purity) and dedicated himself to her service. After becoming a doctor of law in Padua, Italy, he entered the priesthood in 1593. In 1602, Francis became bishop of Geneva, Switzerland. He and Saint Jane de Chantal established the Visitation Order for the purposes of teaching and caring for the sick. Francis wrote many spiritual books, the most popular of which is *An Introduction to the Devout Life* (1609).

Francis was born on Aug. 21, 1567, in Thorens in Savoy, France. He died on Dec. 28, 1622. His feast day is January 24.   Marvin R. O'Connell

Francis Joseph. See **Franz Joseph.**

Francis of Assisi, *uh SEE zee,* **Saint** (1181 or 1182-1226), founded the Franciscans, a Roman Catholic religious order. The Franciscans devote themselves to preaching and to caring for the poor and the sick. Francis's deep respect for nature and love of animals led Pope John Paul II to name him the patron saint of ecology in 1979.

Francis combined an absolute dedication to poverty with a joyful affirmation of creation. He wrote "Canticle of the Sun" in 1225, while he was in intense physical pain. This poem nevertheless praises God through the gifts of creation, including Brother Sun and Sister Earth.

Francis was born in Assisi, Italy. His real name was Giovanni Bernardone. His father was a wealthy cloth merchant. As a young man, Francis led a happy and frivolous life and dreamed of heroic exploits. In 1202, he joined the young men of Assisi in a battle against the neighboring city of Perugia. He was captured and spent a year in prison. About 1205, Francis began a process of religious conversion. This process was marked by an encounter with a leper and a call Francis believed he heard from God to repair a ruined church near Assisi.

By 1208, Francis had renounced all his belongings, including the clothes he was wearing, and accepted total poverty in imitation of Jesus Christ. Francis's remarkable spirit and commitment to Christ soon attracted followers. In 1209, Francis formulated a *rule* (program of life) for the Franciscan order, which was approved by Pope Innocent III in 1210. In 1212, Francis and his friend Saint Clare founded the Poor Clares, a Franciscan order for women. See **Franciscans.**

Because the Franciscans were not attached to a place or to possessions, they could travel freely as missionaries. Francis himself traveled throughout Italy and to Spain. He even went to Egypt during a military expedition called the Fifth Crusade, to try to convert the Muslim sultan to Christianity.

In 1220, Francis returned to Italy from his missionary travels and resigned as head of the Franciscans. Disappointed that many of his followers were unwilling to practice total poverty, Francis spent his final years in

Saint Francis of Assisi was one of the most popular saints of the Middle Ages. This painting by the Italian artist Giovanni Bellini shows Francis about to receive the *stigmata*—wounds resembling those that Jesus received at the Crucifixion. The gentle animals and peaceful landscape symbolize the saint's love of nature and all living things.

Saint Francis in the Desert (about 1480), a tempera and oil painting on a wood panel; © The Frick Collection, New York City.

prayer and solitude. In 1224, Francis experienced a mystical vision while praying and was said to have received the *stigmata,* five wounds resembling those Christ suffered during the Crucifixion. Francis died on Oct. 3, 1226. He was *canonized* (declared a saint) in 1228. His feast day is October 4. Marilyn J. Harran

See also **Christianity** (picture); **Italian literature** (The Middle Ages); **Roman Catholic Church** (picture: Innocent III).

Francis Xavier. See Xavier, Saint Francis.

Franciscans are members of a variety of Roman Catholic religious *orders* (communities). They take their inspiration and *rule* (program of life) from Saint Francis of Assisi. In 1209, Francis founded the Order of Friars Minor to reform the church around the spirit of poverty based on the Gospels. In 1212, Francis and his friend Saint Clare founded an order for women called the Second Order of St. Francis, or the Poor Clares.

The original order's expansion led to an overly complex organization and a consequent need to revise the rule. A split occurred between the Spirituals or *zelanti* and the main body, later called the Conventuals. The Spirituals wanted strict observance of Francis's original rule. The Conventuals advocated moderation. Pope John XXII settled the dispute in favor of the Conventuals in 1317. In 1415, a reform movement within the Conventuals resulted in the formation of another group called the Observants. In 1897, Pope Leo XIII issued a unification decree that produced today's three independent families of Franciscan orders for men—the Friars Minor, Friars Minor Conventuals, and Friars Minor Capuchins.

The early Franciscans devoted themselves to preaching and to caring for the spiritual needs of the people.

But the order soon branched out into educational, missionary, and social work. David G. Schultenover

Related articles in *World Book* include:
California (History)
Capuchins
Francis of Assisi, Saint
Friar
Mission life in America
Religious life (Religious life in the Middle Ages)

Francium, *FRAN see uhm,* is a radioactive element produced in certain nuclear reactions. It is the heaviest member of the group of elements called the *alkali metals.* The group also includes cesium, lithium, potassium, rubidium, and sodium. Francium's chemical properties closely resemble those of cesium. See **Alkali metal; Cesium.**

The chemical symbol of francium is Fr, and its *atomic number* (number of protons in its nucleus) is 87. Francium has many *isotopes,* forms with the same number of protons but different numbers of neutrons. The most stable isotope has an *atomic mass number* (total number of protons and neutrons) of 223. This isotope has a *half-life* of 22 minutes—that is, due to radioactive decay, only half the atoms in a sample of isotope 223 would still be atoms of that isotope after 22 minutes.

The French scientist Marguerite Perey discovered francium in 1939 as a product of the radioactive decay of actinium. Duward F. Shriver

Franck, *frahngk,* **César** (1822-1890), was a French composer, organist, and teacher. His compositions are a synthesis of the strict Viennese forms of sonata, symphony, and quartet and the late Romantic harmonies of composers Franz Liszt and Richard Wagner.

Franck wrote several oratorios and operas, but he achieved his greatest success with his instrumental works. The Symphony in D minor (1889) is his most frequently performed piece, followed by the Sonata in A major (1887) for violin and piano. Franck's other compositions include the Quintet in F minor (1880) for piano and strings, the String Quartet in D major (1890), the complex *Symphonic Variations* (1886) for piano and orchestra, and the *Prelude, Chorale, and Fugue* (1885) for piano.

César Auguste Jean Guillaume Hubert Franck was born on Dec. 10, 1822, in Liège, Belgium, and moved to Paris with his family in 1835. He was the organist at the Basilica of Ste.-Clotilde from 1858 until his death. Franck gave many acclaimed organ concerts following services at the church. His *Six Pieces* (1868) for organ emerged from those concerts. Franck taught organ at the Paris Conservatory from 1872 until his death, exerting a strong influence on such composers as Paul Dukas, Vincent d'Indy, and Henri Duparc. Franck died on Nov. 8, 1890.

Vincent McDermott

Franco, Francisco (1892-1975), was dictator of Spain from 1939 until his death in 1975. He came to power at the end of the Spanish Civil War (1936-1939). In that war, he led the rebel Nationalist Army to victory over the *Loyalist* (Republican) forces. After the war ended in 1939, Franco held complete control of Spain. His regime was similar to a Fascist dictatorship. He carried out the functions of chief of state, prime minister, commander in chief, and leader of the Falange Española, the only political party permitted (see **Falange Española**). He adopted the title of *El Caudillo* (The Leader). At first, Franco tried to eliminate all opposition. He later eased restrictions.

His early life. Franco was born Francisco Franco Bahamonde on Dec. 4, 1892, in El Ferrol del Caudillo, in the province of La Coruña. His father was a naval officer. Young Franco was trained as an army officer at the Infantry Academy of Toledo. Between 1912 and 1927, he held important command posts in Spanish Morocco. His troops there helped put down a long rebellion against Spanish rule. He was made a general at the age of 34.

In 1931, Spain became a republic. During the next five years, disputes involving Spanish political groups became increasingly severe. At first, Franco avoided becoming involved in the disputes. But when the moderate conservatives won the election of 1933, Franco became identified with them. In 1934, Franco helped put down a revolt by *leftists,* who wanted sweeping changes in Spain's way of life. In 1935, he became army chief of staff. The following year, the leftists won the election and sent Franco to a post in the Canary Islands.

Military leaders plotted to overthrow the leftist government in 1936. Franco delayed taking part in the plot, but he was promised command of the most important part of the army. The revolt began in July 1936 and started a civil war. A few months later, the rebel generals named Franco commander in chief and dictator. Franco's forces, called Nationalists, got strong support from Italy and Germany. On April 1, 1939, after 32 months of bitter fighting, the Nationalists gained complete victory. Franco then became dictator without opposition.

As dictator, Franco kept Spain officially neutral during World War II (1939-1945). But he sent "volunteers" to help Germany fight the Soviet Union. After the war, the victorious Allies would have little to do with Spain because of Franco's pro-Fascist policies.

The Western powers became friendlier toward Franco during the Cold War with the Soviet Union, because he opposed Communism. Franco signed an agreement with the United States in 1953. He permitted the United States to build air and naval bases in Spain in exchange for economic and military aid. This aid helped bring about industrial expansion. Spain's living standard rose dramatically during the 1960's. By the mid-1970's, Spain had become a relatively modern, industrialized country.

In the early 1960's, opposition to Franco became more outspoken. Miners and other workers went on strike, though strikes were illegal. Opposition groups organized in secret. Franco relaxed police controls and economic restriction somewhat. In 1966, strict press censorship was relaxed.

Franco declared, in 1947, that Spain would be ruled by a king after he left office. In 1969, Franco named Prince Juan Carlos to be king and head of state after Franco's death or retirement. Juan Carlos is the grandson of King Alfonso XIII, who left Spain in 1931. Franco died on Nov. 20, 1975, and Juan Carlos became king (see **Juan Carlos I**).   Stanley G. Payne

See also **Spain** (Government; History); **Spanish Civil War.**

Franco-Prussian War (1870-1871) began as a conflict between France and Prussia, a German state. But after other German states joined Prussia's cause, the conflict became one between France and a strong, unified Germany. Germany won the war in less than 10 months.

Background to the war. Prussia's defeat of Austria in the 1866 Seven Weeks' War made Prussia the leading German power. Prussian Prime Minister Otto von Bismarck wanted to create a powerful German empire by merging Prussia with the south German states of Baden, Bavaria, Hesse, and Württemberg. He created military alliances with these states, hoping to unify them by provoking a war with France.

An excuse for war was easily found. Prince Leopold, a relative of Prussian King Wilhelm I, had been offered the Spanish crown. French Emperor Napoleon III objected to the proposal, fearing the spread of German influence. Leopold was withdrawn from consideration, but Napoleon wanted a Prussian guarantee that Leopold would never take the Spanish throne. Wilhelm refused the French demand and sent a telegram to Bismarck telling what had happened. A condensed version of the telegram aroused great fury when it was published in France. Unaware of Prussia's alliance with the south German states, the French declared war on July 19, 1870.

Progress of the war. General Helmuth Karl von Moltke, head of the Prussian Army, had made careful preparations for war with France. The French were largely unprepared. The Germans defeated the French in a series of battles along the Franco-German frontier. Two French armies were then separated and kept apart by the Germans. One of the French armies became surrounded at Metz. The other French army met the Germans in a great battle near Sedan on August 31. The French were overwhelmed, and Napoleon III, who was with the French forces, was taken prisoner. On September 4, the French government in Paris deposed Napoleon and proclaimed the Third Republic. The French army at Metz surrendered in late October.

The siege and Commune of Paris. German forces

encircled Paris in mid-September. Léon Gambetta, a leader in the French government, escaped from Paris in a hot-air balloon. He raised an army at Tours but failed to defeat the German forces. In Paris, German forces repulsed each French attempt to break the siege. Supplies ran low in the city, and people resorted to eating pets, horses, rats, and other animals. Communication with the outside world continued through the use of balloons and carrier pigeons. Frustrated by the Parisians' refusal to surrender, the Germans began shelling Paris in January 1871. Several hundred people were killed. Paris finally surrendered on January 28, 10 days after the creation of the German Empire.

Frustrated with the provisional French government, revolutionaries took over Paris in March. The uprising, known as the Paris Commune, lasted to the end of May. Government troops ended the uprising with bloody battles against the *Communards* (participants in the Paris Commune) in the streets of Paris.

The end and the aftermath. The Treaty of Frankfurt ended the war on May 10, 1871. The treaty forced France to give most of Alsace and part of Lorraine to Germany and pay Germany 5 billion francs.

Some 156,000 French and 28,000 German soldiers died in the Franco-Prussian War. The war ended France's Second Empire and created a new German Empire under Prussian leadership. It led to the creation of France's Third Republic and the bloody Paris Commune. The shelling of Paris and the loss of Alsace-Lorraine created hostility and a desire for revenge among the French. These and other factors led directly to another Franco-German conflict as part of World War I (1914-1918).   Charles W. Ingrao

Related articles in *World Book* include:

Alsace-Lorraine	Moltke, Helmuth Karl von
Balloon (Balloons in war)	Napoleon III
Bismarck, Otto von	Prussia
Germany (The unification of Germany)	Seven Weeks' War
	Wilhelm (I)

Frank, Anne (1929-1945), a German Jewish girl, wrote a vivid, tender diary while hiding from the Nazis during World War II. Annelies Marie Frank was born on June 12, 1929, in Frankfurt (am Main), Germany. She and her family moved to the Netherlands in 1933 after the Nazis began to persecute Jews. In 1942, during the Nazi occupation of the Netherlands, the family hid in a secret annex behind the Amsterdam office and warehouse of her father's food products business. Anne recorded her experiences in a diary. Two years later, the family was betrayed and arrested. Anne died in the Nazis' Bergen-Belsen concentration camp in Germany in March 1945. Her diary was published in 1947 and later was made into a play and a film, both called *The Diary of Anne Frank.*   Alison Leslie Gold

See also **Diary of Anne Frank.**

Anne Frank Fonds, Basel/Anne Frank House, Amsterdam from Hulton/Archive

Anne Frank

Frankenstein is a famous horror novel written by the English author Mary Shelley. The novel was published in 1818 under the title *Frankenstein, or the Modern Prometheus.* It tells the story of Victor Frankenstein, a scientist who tries to create a living being for the good of humanity but instead produces a monster.

Frankenstein creates his monster by assembling parts of dead bodies and activating the creature with electricity. The monster, which has no name in the book, is actually a gentle, intelligent creature. However, everyone fears and mistreats him because of his hideous appearance. Frankenstein himself rejects the monster and refuses to create a mate for him. The monster's terrible loneliness drives him to seek revenge by murdering Frankenstein's wife, brother, and best friend. Frankenstein dies while attempting to find and kill the monster, who disappears into the Arctic at the end of the novel.

A number of horror films have been based on the character of Frankenstein's monster. Most of these films have little to do with the serious themes of the novel. These themes include the possible dangers involved in scientific experimentation with life and the suffering caused by judging people by their appearance.

David Geherin

See also **Science fiction** (The first science fiction); **Shelley, Mary Wollstonecraft.**

Frankenthaler, Helen (1928-2011), was a leading American painter. In the 1950's, working in the Abstract Expressionist style, she developed a painting technique called *soak-stain.* Using this method, Frankenthaler poured thin paint directly onto the raw canvas. As the paint soaked into the canvas, staining it with color, texture was eliminated and the flatness in the canvas surface was emphasized.

The lyrical interaction of forms and colors in Frankenthaler's paintings illustrates the physical process of their creation. Colors run into one another and forms seem to overlap through the different stainings. Some areas of the harmonious, well-balanced compositions remain unstained, which further illustrates the lack of separation between the paint and canvas surface. Most of Frankenthaler's paintings have a narrative title, such as *Mountains and Sea,* which is reproduced in the **Painting** article. She was also a printmaker. Frankenthaler was born on Dec. 12, 1928, in New York City. Frankenthaler died on Dec. 27, 2011.   Deborah Leveton

Frankfort (pop. 25,527) is the capital of Kentucky. The city lies in north-central Kentucky, at the western edge of the state's Bluegrass Region. For the location of Frankfort, see **Kentucky** (political map).

The chief industry of Frankfort is government. The Kentucky state government ranks as the city's largest employer. Whiskey distilling is an important private industry in Frankfort. Other products include motor vehicle parts, fabricated metals, plastics, and electrical equipment.

Landmarks of Frankfort include the State Capitol, which resembles the United States Capitol in design; and the Old State House, now a museum. Many tourists visit the Frankfort Cemetery to see the graves of the American frontiersman Daniel Boone and his wife, Rebecca. Other attractions include tours of historic homes and of distilleries, which produce Kentucky bourbon whiskey. Kentucky State University is in Frankfort.

Like many cities, Frankfort has had to deal with the flow of business to suburban shopping centers. From the late 1950's to the 1980's, urban renewal efforts eliminated slums and restored part of downtown Frankfort. Capital Plaza, a modernistic office, hotel, and retail complex, was completed in the 1980's. In the 1990's and early 2000's, renovations to buildings in the historic business district helped renew interest in downtown as a center for shopping and entertainment.

In 1751, Christopher Gist became the first white person to reach what is now Frankfort. In 1773, Hancock Taylor made the first survey of the land. The Virginia legislature established Frankfort as a town in 1786, before Kentucky became a state. Kentucky achieved statehood in 1792, and Frankfort was selected as its capital. Frankfort is the seat of Franklin County and has a council-manager form of government.   Tracy Campbell

See also **Kentucky** (pictures).

Frankfurt, *FRANGK fuhrt* or *FRAHNGK furt* (pop. 667,925), is the transportation hub of Germany. The full name of the city is Frankfurt am Main. It stands on the Main River. For the location of Frankfurt, see **Germany** (political map). A network of railroads and highways links the city with all parts of western Europe. Frankfurt has one of the largest airports in Europe. A river and canal system links the city with the North Sea. Frankfurt has three harbor areas and ranks as one of the busiest inland ports in Germany.

The city is a world center of banking and commerce. The Rothschild family opened its first bank there in 1798 (see **Rothschild**). The 56-story Commerzbank building, which opened in 1997, is one of Europe's tallest buildings. Frankfurt holds two great trade fairs a year. The fair held in September opened first in 1240, and the February fair started in 1330. Frankfurt also holds many specialized trade fairs, including its famous annual book fair. Factories in Frankfurt produce chemicals, machinery, and electrical equipment.

Frankfurt is an important center of German intellectual and cultural life. The city is the birthplace of the famous German writer Johann Wolfgang von Goethe, whose home is now a museum. Frankfurt's attractions include the Römer town hall, a building that dates from the 1400's. The building contains the Kaisersaal, the meeting room at one time of the German emperors and princes. Also in the city is the Paulskirche, a church where leaders of the unsuccessful Revolution of 1848 met to draft a German national constitution.

Frankfurt's geographical position made it important from the time of the Roman Empire. The shallow ford in the Main River provided the easiest north-south river crossing in all Germany. The Franks forded the river in early times, and the city's name means *ford of the Franks* (see **Franks**). Merchants traveling between Mediterranean countries and northern Europe naturally passed through Frankfurt. In about A.D. 500, the Franks seized a Roman fort at the crossing and founded a settlement. Allied bombers leveled nearly half of Frankfurt during World War II (1939-1945), but the city was rebuilt after the war.   Peter H. Merkl

Frankfurter. See Sausage.

Frankfurter, Felix (1882-1965), served as an associate justice of the Supreme Court of the United States from 1939 until he retired in 1962. Before 1939, he spent 25 years as professor of law at Harvard University and was an influential adviser to President Franklin D. Roosevelt. Roosevelt appointed him to the court.

As a Supreme Court justice, Frankfurter was a leading supporter of *judicial restraint*—that is, he was reluctant to interfere with the policies of the executive or legislative branches of government unless those policies were clearly unconstitutional. Frankfurter's writings include *The Case of Sacco and Vanzetti* and *The Commerce Clause Under Marshall, Taney and Waite.*

Frankfurter was born on Nov. 15, 1882, in Vienna, Austria, and came to the United States in 1894. He learned English quickly, became an American citizen, and graduated from the College of the City of New York and Harvard Law School. Frankfurter died on Feb. 22, 1965.
          Bruce Allen Murphy

Frankincense is a fragrant gum resin used as a raw material for perfumes. Perfumers call it *olibanum.* Since ancient times, people have burned it as an incense in religious services. The ancient Egyptians used it in medicines. The Bible says that one of the wise men brought Jesus a gift of frankincense (Matthew 2). Today, it also serves to mask the unpleasant odors of mixtures used for fumigation.

Frankincense comes from trees of the genus *Boswellia* that grow in the southern Arabian peninsula and northern Somalia. Harvesters cut into the bark of the trees and collect the resin in the form of colorless to pale yellow drops called *tears.* Perfumers extract oil from the tears by dissolving them in alcohol, then passing steam through them. The oil gives perfumes a long-lasting, spicy fragrance.   Patricia Ann Mullen

Franklin, Aretha (1942-   ), an American rhythm and blues singer, ranks among the best-selling female artists in the history of recorded music. Franklin is popularly known as the "Queen of Soul." Her 1967 recording of "Respect" became an inspirational anthem for the civil rights movement and a symbol of black pride.

Aretha Louise Franklin was born on March 25, 1942, in Memphis, and was raised in Detroit. She began her singing career at the age of 12 in the Detroit church of her father, C. L. Franklin, a noted preacher and gospel singer. She later transferred the passion and intensity of her gospel singing to popular songs. Most of Franklin's recordings also feature her piano playing.

Franklin's period of greatest popularity came in the late 1960's and early 1970's. In 1967 alone, she had five top-10 hit recordings—"I Never Loved a Man (The Way I Love You)," "Respect," "Baby, I Love You," "(You Make Me Feel Like) A Natural Woman," and "Chain of Fools." In 1968, she recorded the hits "(Sweet Sweet Baby) Since You've Been Gone," "Think," "The House That Jack Built," and "I Say a Little Prayer." Franklin's other hits include "Share Your Love with Me" (1969), "Call Me" (1970), "Spanish Harlem" and "Rock Steady" (both 1971), "Day Dreaming" (1972), "Until You Come Back to Me (That's What I'm Gonna Do)" (1973), "Freeway of Love" (1985), and "Jimmy Lee" (1986). Franklin recorded gospel music on such albums as *Amazing Grace* (1972) and *One Lord, One Faith, One Baptism* (1987).

In 1987, Franklin became the first woman inducted into the Rock and Roll Hall of Fame. Her autobiography, *Aretha: From These Roots*, was published in 1999.
          Don McLeese

Detail of a pastel portrait (1783) by Joseph-Sifrède Duplessis; New York Public Library (Bettmann Archive)

Franklin served his nation as a statesman, scientist, and public leader.

Benjamin Franklin

Franklin, Benjamin (1706-1790), was a jack-of-all-trades and master of many. No other American, except possibly Thomas Jefferson, has done so many things so well. During his long and useful life, Franklin concerned himself with such different matters as statesmanship and soapmaking, book-printing and cabbage-growing, and the rise of tides and the fall of empires. He also invented an efficient heating stove and proved that lightning is a huge electric spark.

As a statesman, Franklin stood in the front rank of the people who built the United States. He was the only person who signed all four of these key documents in American history: the Declaration of Independence, the Treaty of Alliance with France, the Treaty of Paris that made peace with Great Britain (now also called the United Kingdom), and the Constitution of the United States. Franklin's services as a diplomat in France helped greatly in winning the Revolutionary War in America (1775-1783). Many historians consider him the ablest and most successful diplomat that America has ever sent abroad.

Franklin was a leader of his day in the study of electricity. As an inventor, he was unequaled in the United States until the time of Thomas A. Edison. People still read *The Autobiography of Benjamin Franklin* (1789) and quote sayings from Franklin's *Poor Richard's Almanac* (1733-1758). Franklin also helped establish Pennsylvania's first university and America's first city hospital.

Franklin's fame extended to Europe as well as America. Thomas Jefferson hailed him as "the greatest man and ornament of the age and country in which he lived." A French statesman, Comte de Mirabeau, called Franklin "the sage whom two worlds claimed as their own."

Early life

Benjamin Franklin was born in Boston on Jan. 17, 1706. He was the 15th child, and youngest son, in a family of 17 children. His parents, Josiah and Abiah Franklin, were hard-working and religious. His father made soap and candles in his shop "at the sign of the Blue Ball" on Milk Street, and later in a bigger house on Union Street.

Student and apprentice. Benjamin attended school in Boston for only two years. He proved himself excellent in reading, fair in writing, and poor in arithmetic. Josiah Franklin decided that he could not afford further education for his youngest son. He kept Benjamin home after the age of 10 to help cut wicks and melt tallow in the candle and soap shop.

Franklin's schooling ended, but his education did not. He believed that "the doors of wisdom are never shut," and continued to read every book that he could get. He worked on his own writing style, using a volume of the British journal *The Spectator* as a model. His prose became clear, simple, and effective. The boy also taught himself the basic principles of algebra and geometry, navigation, grammar, logic, and the natural and physical sciences. He studied and partially mastered French, German, Italian, Spanish, and Latin. He eagerly read such books as *Pilgrim's Progress* (1678, 1684), Plutarch's *Lives* (about A.D. 100), Cotton Mather's *Bonifacius* (1710), and Daniel Defoe's *Robinson Crusoe* (1719). Franklin made himself one of the best-educated persons of his time.

Franklin did not care much for the trade of candlemaking. When the boy was 12, his father persuaded him to become an apprentice to his older brother James, a printer. Benjamin soon became a skilled printer himself. He wrote several newspaper articles, signed them "Silence Dogood," and slipped them under the printshop door. James admired the articles and printed several of them. But the brothers quarreled frequently, and Benjamin longed to become his own master. He also wished to escape from his brother's beatings, which Benjamin later called the cause of his "Aversion to arbitrary Power that has stuck to me thro' my whole Life."

At 17, Franklin ran away to Philadelphia. The story of his arrival there, as told in his autobiography, has become a classic of American folklore. Many tales describe the runaway apprentice trudging bravely up Market Street with a Dutch dollar in his pocket, carrying one loaf of bread under each arm and eating a third.

Printer. From 1723 to 1730, Franklin worked for various printers in Philadelphia and in London, England. He became part owner of a print shop in 1728, when he was 22. Two years later, he became sole owner of the business. He began publishing *The Pennsylvania Gazette,* writing much of the material for this newspaper himself. His name gradually became known throughout the colonies. Franklin had a simple formula for business success. He believed that successful people had to work just a little harder than any of their competitors. As one of his neighbors said: "The industry of that Franklin is superior to anything I ever saw … I see him still at work when I go home from the club; and he is at work again before his neighbors are out of bed."

Franklin married Deborah Read (1708-1774), the daughter of his first Philadelphia landlady, in 1730. Deborah was not nearly so well educated as her husband, but her work in the printing shop helped diversify the business. Franklin quickly became a leader in the printing trade. He sent a series of former apprentices to open shops in other locations, from Newport in Rhode Island to the British colony of Antigua in the Caribbean Sea.

The Franklins raised three children, William Franklin (1731?-1813), Francis Folger Franklin (1732-1736), and Sarah Franklin Bache (1743-1808). William Franklin became governor of New Jersey in 1762 and a leading Tory, or Loyalist, when he sided with the British in 1776. Sarah Franklin Bache helped collect funds for American troops during the Revolutionary War. She also raised a large family, including the printer and political activist Benjamin Franklin Bache (1769-1798).

The first citizen of Philadelphia

Publisher. Franklin's printing business prospered from the start. He developed *The Pennsylvania Gazette* into one of the most successful newspapers in the colonies. He published it from 1729 until 1766. Franklin was often on the lookout for new ideas. Historians credit him as the first editor in America to publish a newspaper cartoon, and to illustrate a news story with a map. He laid many of his projects for civic reform before the public in his newspaper.

Franklin achieved even greater financial success with *Poor Richard's Almanac* than with his newspaper. He wrote and published the almanac for every year from 1733 to 1758. The almanac's fame rests mainly on the witty sayings that Franklin scattered through each issue. Many of these sayings preach the virtues of industry and frugality. "Early to bed and early to rise, makes a man healthy, wealthy, and wise." "God helps them that help themselves." "Little strokes fell great oaks." Other sayings reflect his thoughts on human nature. "He's a fool that makes his doctor his heir." "He that falls in love with himself will have no rivals." See **Poor Richard's Almanac.**

Franklin retired from running the print shop in 1748, at the age of 42, so that he could pursue science and politics full time.

Civic leader. Franklin was always interested in public affairs. In 1736, he became clerk of the Pennsylvania Assembly. The poor service of the colonial postal service disturbed him greatly. Hoping to improve matters, he became Philadelphia's postmaster in 1737. He impressed the British government with his efficiency in this posi-

Printer and publisher

As an apprentice, Franklin began his lifelong career in printing and publishing at the age of 12.

Bettmann Archive

As a printer, Franklin bought a press with Hugh Meredith in 1728. He became sole owner two years later.

tion, and in 1753 he became a deputy postmaster general for all the colonies. Franklin worked hard at this job and introduced many needed reforms. He set up the first city delivery system and the first Dead-Mail Office. He speeded foreign mail deliveries by using the fastest packet ships available across the Atlantic Ocean. To speed domestic mail service, he hired more post riders and required his couriers to ride both night and day. Franklin also helped Canada establish its first regular postal service. He opened post offices at Quebec, Montreal, and Trois Rivières in 1763. He also established messenger service between Montreal and New York.

> *Poor Richard, 1733.*
> AN
> **Almanack**
> For the Year of Chrift
> **1733,**
> Being the Firft after LEAP YEAR.
>
> *And makes fince the Creation* Years
> By the Account of the Eaftern Greeks   7241
> By the Latin Church, when ☉ ent. ♈   6932
> By the Computation of *W. W.*   5742
> By the *Roman* Chronology   5682
> By the *Jewifh* Rabbies.   5494
>
> *Wherein is contained*
> The Lunations, Eclipfes, Judgment of the Weather, Spring Tides, Planets Motions & mutual Afpects, Sun and Moon's Rifing and Setting, Length of Days, Time of High Water, Fairs, Courts, and obfervable Days.
> Fitted to the Latitude of Forty Degrees, and a Meridian of Five Hours Weft from *London,* but may without fenfible Error, ferve all the adjacent Places, even from *Newfoundland* to *South-Carolina.*
> By *RICHARD SAUNDERS,* Philom.
> PHILADELPHIA:
> Printed and fold by *B. FRANKLIN,* at the New Printing-Office near the Market.

Bettmann Archive

As an author, Franklin signed the pen name Richard Saunders to his famous *Poor Richard's Almanac.*

Franklin was public-spirited and worked constantly to make Philadelphia a better city. He helped establish the first subscription library in the American Colonies. The members of this library contributed money to buy books, and then used them free of charge. The Library Company of Philadelphia still exists. Fire losses in Philadelphia were alarmingly high, and Franklin organized a fire department. He reformed the city police when he saw that criminals were getting away without punishment. City streets were unpaved, dirty, and dark, so he started a program to pave, clean, and light them. Philadelphia shamefully neglected the sick and people with mental illness during Franklin's time. He raised money to help build a city hospital, the Pennsylvania Hospital, for these people.

Scholars in the American Colonies had no special clubs or professional organizations, so Franklin helped establish the American Philosophical Society, with headquarters in Philadelphia. The city had no school for higher education, so Franklin helped found the academy that grew into the University of Pennsylvania. As a result of such projects, Philadelphia became the most advanced city in the 13 colonies.

The scientist

Experiments with electricity. Franklin was one of the first persons in the world to experiment with electricity. He became famous for his description of an electrical experiment he said he conducted at Philadelphia. In 1752, he described how he flew a homemade kite during a thunderstorm to prove that lightning is a giant electric spark. According to Franklin, a bolt of lightning struck a pointed wire fastened to the kite and traveled down the kite string to a key fastened at the end, where it caused a spark. Franklin also tamed lightning by inventing the lightning rod (see **Lightning rod**). He urged his fellow citizens to use this device as a sure "means of securing the habitations and other buildings from mischief from thunder and lightning." When lightning struck Franklin's own home, his lightning rod saved the building from damage. Franklin's lightning rod demonstrated his saying that "An ounce of prevention is worth a pound of cure." Authorities generally agree that Franklin created such electrical terms as *armature, condenser,* and *battery.* See **Electricity** (History).

Franklin's experiments with electricity involved some personal risk. He knocked himself unconscious at least once. He had been trying to kill a turkey with an electric shock, but something went wrong and Franklin, not the bird, was stunned. Franklin later said: "I meant to kill a turkey, and instead, I nearly killed a goose."

Other studies. Franklin's scientific interests ranged far beyond electricity. He became the first scientist to study the movement of the Gulf Stream in the Atlantic Ocean. He spent much time charting its course and recording its temperature, speed, and depth. He favored daylight saving time in summer. It struck him as silly and wasteful that people should "live much by candle-light and sleep by sunshine."

Franklin gave the world several other valuable inventions in addition to the lightning rod. The Franklin stove proved most useful to the people of his day. By arranging the flues in his own stove in an efficient way, he could make his sitting room twice as warm with one-fourth as much fuel as he had been using. People continue to appreciate his invention of bifocal eyeglasses. This invention allowed both reading and distant lenses to be set in a single frame. Franklin discovered that disease flourishes in poorly ventilated rooms. Franklin also showed how to improve acid soil by using lime. He refused to patent any of his inventions or to use them for profit. He preferred to have them used freely as his contribution to people's comfort and convenience.

Franklin appreciated the inventive efforts of other people. He said that he would like to return to Earth a hundred years later to see what progress humanity had made. The first successful balloon flight took place in 1783, during Franklin's stay in Paris. Many bystanders scoffed at the new device and asked, "What good is it?" Franklin retorted, "What good is a newborn baby?"

Franklin's scientific work won him many high honors. The Royal Society of London elected him a member, a rare honor for a person living in the colonies. Publishers translated his writings on electricity into French, German, and Italian. The great English statesman William Pitt told the House of Lords that Franklin ranked with Isaac Newton as a scientist. He called Franklin "an honor not to the English nation only but to human nature."

The public servant

The Plan of Union. In the spring of 1754, war broke out between the British and French in America (see **French and Indian wars**). Franklin felt that the colonies had to unite for self-defense against the French and Indians. He printed the famous "Join or Die" cartoon in his newspaper. This cartoon showed a snake cut up into pieces that represented the colonies.

Franklin presented his Plan of Union at a conference of seven colonies at Albany, New York. This plan tried to bring the colonies together in "one general government," in part to negotiate better with Native Americans who were joined through the Iroquois Confederacy. The Plan of Union contained some of the ideas that were later included in the Articles of Confederation and the Constitution of the United States. The delegates at the Albany Congress approved Franklin's plan, but the colonies failed to ratify it. Said Franklin: "Everyone cries a union is absolutely necessary, but when it comes to the manner and form of the union, their weak noddles are perfectly distracted." See **Albany Congress**.

The war led Franklin to turn his attention to military

Public-minded citizen

WORLD BOOK illustrations by Robert Addison

A subscription library Franklin helped set up in 1731 was the first of its kind in America.

The academy he helped found, *left,* later became the University of Pennsylvania.

The city hospital he organized, *right,* was the first in America.

Postal service improved when Franklin became a deputy postmaster general in 1753.

matters. During two earlier conflicts, he had urged Philadelphians, including the pacifist Quakers who dominated Pennsylvania politics, to defend the city by supporting a militia company he founded. In 1755, General Edward Braddock and two British regiments arrived in America with orders to capture the French stronghold of Fort Duquesne, at the point where the Allegheny and Monongahela rivers met. The British had trouble finding horses and wagons for the expedition, and Franklin helped provide the necessary equipment. However, the French and Indians ambushed the British on the banks of the Monongahela River. Braddock was killed, and the British army was almost destroyed. In the meantime, Franklin raised volunteer colonial armies to defend frontier towns and supervised construction of a fort at Weissport in Carbon County, Pennsylvania.

A delegate in London. In 1757, the Pennsylvania legislature sent Franklin to London to speak for the colony in a tax dispute with the *proprietors* (descendants of William Penn living in Britain). The proprietors controlled the governor of the colony, and would not allow the

swer a series of 174 questions dealing with "taxation without representation." Members of the House threw questions at him for nearly two hours. He answered briefly and clearly. His knowledge of taxation problems impressed his audience, and his reputation grew throughout Europe. The Stamp Act was repealed a short time later, and Franklin received some of the credit.

Political relations between Britain and the colonies grew steadily worse. Franklin wanted America to remain in the British Empire, but he also wanted the rights of the colonists recognized and protected. Like other patriot leaders, he grew frustrated with the tendency of many Britons to see colonists as inferiors. Franklin pledged his entire fortune to pay for the tea destroyed in the Boston Tea Party if the British government would agree to repeal what the colonists felt was an unjust tax on tea (see **Boston Tea Party**). The British ignored his proposal. Franklin realized that his usefulness in Britain had ended, and he sailed for home on March 21, 1775. He had worked hard to keep the American Colonies in the empire on the basis of mutual respect and good will.

Scientist and inventor

WORLD BOOK illustrations by Robert Addison

Franklin and his kite, *left,* showed the world that lightning is actually an enormous electric spark.

Franklin's glasses. He invented bifocal lenses for distance and reading use.

His lightning rod saved many buildings from fires caused by lightning.

The Franklin stove gave more heat than other stoves, and used much less fuel.

colony to pass any tax bill for defense unless their own estates were left tax-free. In 1760, Franklin finally succeeded in getting the British Parliament to adopt a measure that permitted the taxation of both the colonists and the proprietors. Franklin remained in Britain during most of the next 15 years as a sort of unofficial ambassador and spokesman for the American point of view.

A debate developed in Britain in the early 1760's at the end of the French and Indian War. The French, who lost the war, agreed to give the British either the French province of Canada or the French island of Guadeloupe in the West Indies. At the height of the argument, Franklin published an influential pamphlet that compared the boundless future of Canada with the relative unimportance of Guadeloupe. In this and other writings, Franklin supported the North American colonies and described them as crucial to the British Empire.

Franklin also took part in the fight over the Stamp Act (see **Stamp Act**). He seems to have been rather slow to recognize that the proposed measure threatened the American Colonies, but once he realized its dangers, he joined the struggle for repeal of the act. This fight led to one of the high points of his career. On Feb. 13, 1766, Franklin appeared before the House of Commons to an-

The statesman

Organizing the new nation. Franklin arrived in Philadelphia on May 5, 1775, about two weeks after the Revolutionary War began. The next day, the people of Philadelphia chose him to serve in the Second Continental Congress. Franklin seldom spoke at the Congress, but he became one of its most active and influential members. He submitted a proposed Plan of Union that contained ideas from his earlier Albany Plan of Union. This plan laid the groundwork for the Articles of Confederation. Franklin served on a commission that went to Canada in an unsuccessful attempt to persuade the French Canadians to join the Revolutionary War. He also worked on committees dealing with such varied matters as printing paper money, reorganizing the Continental Army, and finding supplies of powder and lead.

The Continental Congress chose Franklin as postmaster general in 1775 because of his experience as a colonial postmaster. The government directed him to organize a postal system quickly. He soon had mail service from Portland, Maine, to Savannah, Georgia. He gave his salary to the relief of wounded soldiers.

Franklin helped draft the Declaration of Independence and was one of the document's signers. During

Benjamin Franklin served as minister to France from 1778 to 1785. This picture shows Franklin in 1778 at the court of King Louis XVI and Queen Marie Antoinette, *seated right.*

Franklin represented Pennsylvania at the Constitutional Convention in 1787. He supported compromises that held the convention together.

the signing ceremonies, according to tradition, John Hancock warned his fellow delegates, "We must be unanimous; there must be no pulling different ways; we must all hang together." "Yes," Franklin replied, "we must indeed all hang together, or assuredly we shall all hang separately."

Serving in France. Shortly after the Declaration of Independence was adopted in July 1776, Congress appointed Franklin as one of three commissioners sent to represent the United States in France. The war was not going well, and Congress realized an alliance with France might mean the difference between victory and defeat. Late in 1776, at the age of 70, Franklin set forth on the most important task of his life.

Franklin received a tremendous welcome in Paris. The French people were charmed by his kindness, his simple dress and manner, his wise and witty sayings, and his tact and courtesy in greeting the nobility and common people alike. Crowds ran after him in the streets. Poets wrote glowing verses in his honor, and artists made portraits and busts of him.

In spite of Franklin's popularity, the French government hesitated to make a treaty of alliance with the American Colonies. Such a treaty would surely mean war between France and Britain. So Franklin tactfully set out to win the French government to the American cause. His chance came after British General John Burgoyne's army surrendered at Saratoga. The French were impressed by this American victory and agreed to a treaty of alliance. The pact was signed on Feb. 6, 1778. Franklin then arranged transportation to America for French officers, soldiers, and guns. He managed to keep loans and gifts of money flowing to the United States. Many historians believe that without this aid the Americans could not have won their independence.

In 1778, Franklin was appointed minister to France. He helped draft the Treaty of Paris, which ended the Revolutionary War. France, Britain, and Spain all had interests in the American Colonies, and Franklin found it difficult to arrange a treaty that satisfied them all. The treaty gave the new nation territory extending west to the Mississip-

pi River and north to Canada. Franklin was one of the signers of the Treaty of Paris in 1783.

The twilight years

Franklin returned to Philadelphia in 1785. For the next two years, he served as president of the executive council of Pennsylvania. In 1787, Pennsylvania sent Franklin to the Constitutional Convention. The delegates met in Independence Hall and drafted the Constitution of the United States. The 81-year-old Franklin was the oldest delegate at the convention.

Franklin helped the convention settle the bitter dispute between large and small states over representation in Congress. He did this by supporting the so-called Great Compromise. The compromise sought to satisfy both groups by setting up a two-house Congress. It also allowed three-fifths of slaves to be counted for the purpose of taxation and representation. Franklin had not wanted slaves to be counted. However, as in earlier debates during the revolutionary years, he believed that ensuring the survival of the nation was more important than fighting slavery. In his last formal speech to the convention, Franklin appealed to his fellow delegates for unanimous support of the Constitution.

Franklin's attendance at the Constitutional Convention was his last major public service. However, his interest in public affairs continued to the end of his life. He rejoiced in Washington's inauguration as the first president of the United States. He hoped that the example of the new nation would lead to a United States of Europe. In 1787, he was elected president of the Pennsylvania Abolition Society. Franklin's last public act was to sign an appeal to Congress calling for the speedy abolition of slavery. Franklin had owned slaves and defended Americans against charges of hypocrisy on the issue of slavery. Only in private had he supported slavery's critics. But abolitionists later claimed Franklin as an antislavery pioneer because of his final stance on the issue.

Franklin died on the night of April 17, 1790, at the age of 84. About 20,000 people honored him at his funeral. He was buried in the cemetery of Christ Church in

Philadelphia beside his wife, who had died in 1774.

Franklin accomplished much in many fields, but he began his will, "I, Benjamin Franklin, printer ..." Franklin left $5,000 each to Boston and Philadelphia, in trust funds to be loaned out at interest. He directed that part of the accumulated funds be used for public works after 100 years, and the rest after 200 years. Part of the money was used to establish Franklin Union (now the Benjamin Franklin Institute of Technology), a Boston trade school; and the Franklin Institute, an organization in Philadelphia that promotes science education.

His place in history

Franklin became known to future generations for his lifelong concern for the happiness, well-being, and dignity of humanity. George Washington summarized American popular sentiment in a letter to Franklin in 1789: "If to be venerated for benevolence, if to be admired for talents, if to be esteemed for patriotism, if to be beloved for philanthropy, can gratify the human mind, you must have the pleasing consolation to know that you have not lived in vain."

Philadelphia has also revered the memory of its most famous citizen. The University of Pennsylvania named its athletic field in his honor. One of the city's showplaces is the spacious Benjamin Franklin Parkway. Midway along the parkway stands the Franklin Institute Science Museum, dedicated to popularizing the sciences that Franklin loved. This building contains the Benjamin Franklin National Memorial, with a famous statue of Franklin by James Earle Fraser (see **Franklin Institute Science Museum**). Independence National Historical Park includes the site of Franklin's home and many museum exhibits about Franklin and his world.   David Waldstreicher

Related articles in *World Book* include:

Adult education (History)
American literature
  (Philadelphia)
Autobiography
Cartoon (picture: Many early
  cartoons)
Electricity (History)

Harmonica
Kite
Philadelphia
Poor Richard's Almanac
Rebus
Stamp collecting (picture: The
  first stamps)

Outline

I. **Early life**
   A. Student and apprentice B. Printer
II. **The first citizen of Philadelphia**
   A. Publisher   B. Civic leader
III. **The scientist**
   A. Experiments with electricity
   B. Other studies
IV. **The public servant**
   A. The Plan of Union
   B. A delegate in London
V. **The statesman**
   A. Organizing the new nation
   B. Serving in France
VI. **The twilight years**
VII. **His place in history**

Additional resources

Brands, H. W. *The First American: The Life and Times of Benjamin Franklin.* Doubleday, 2000.
Isaacson, Walter. *Benjamin Franklin.* Simon & Schuster, 2004.
Miller, Brandon M. *Benjamin Franklin, American Genius.* Chicago Review Pr., 2010. Younger readers.
Morgan, Edmund S. *Benjamin Franklin.* Yale, 2002.
Mulford, Carla, ed. *The Cambridge Companion to Benjamin Franklin.* Cambridge, 2008.
Pangle, Lorraine S. *The Political Philosophy of Benjamin Franklin.* Johns Hopkins, 2007.

Franklin, Sir John (1786-1847), an English explorer, led several expeditions to the Arctic region. He lost his life during an expedition to find the Northwest Passage, a northern water route across North America.

Franklin was born on April 16, 1786, in Lincolnshire, England, and joined the British Navy at the age of 15. He was a midshipman on Matthew Flinders's voyage around Australia from 1801 to 1803. In 1819, Franklin explored the mouth of the Coppermine River, in what is now northern Canada, while leading his first Arctic expedition. He led his second expedition to the Arctic in 1825 and 1826. In 1845, Franklin led the best-equipped expedition to enter the Arctic up to that time. He discovered a Northwest Passage, but he died on June 11, 1847, during the expedition. His crew died too. When no one returned from the voyage, Lady Franklin sponsored many expeditions to search for her husband. A full exploration of the Arctic resulted. A search party led by Sir Robert McClure crossed the Northwest Passage from 1850 to 1854. Later, explorers found evidence of Franklin's party and reconstructed his voyage.   Barry M. Gough

See also **Northwest Passage**.

Franklin, John Hope (1915-2009), an American historian, wrote many books about African Americans. His book *From Slavery to Freedom* (1947) is a widely praised account of blacks in America.

Franklin was born on Jan. 2, 1915, in Rentiesville, Oklahoma. He earned a bachelor's degree at Fisk University, and master's and doctor's degrees at Harvard University. Franklin taught at colleges in North Carolina from 1939 to 1947, and then at Howard University until 1956. He was a professor at Brooklyn College from 1956 to 1964, at the University of Chicago from 1964 to 1982, and at Duke University from 1982 to 1985.

Franklin's books include *The Free Negro in North Carolina* (1943), *The Militant South* (1956), *Reconstruction After the Civil War* (1961), *The Emancipation Proclamation* (1963), *Race and History: Selected Essays 1938-1988* (1990), and *The Color Line: Legacy for the Twenty-First Century* (1993). He co-wrote a junior high school textbook, *Land of the Free* (1966). Franklin died on March 25, 2009.   Robert A. Pratt

Franklin, Rosalind Elsie (1920-1958), was a British chemist famous for her studies of molecules and crystals. Her work helped determine the structure of *deoxyribonucleic acid* (DNA), a molecule that directs the formation and development of cells and organisms. Franklin also determined the structure of certain viruses, and she advanced *crystallography* (the study of crystals).

Franklin was born in London on July 25, 1920. She received a Ph.D. in physical chemistry from Cambridge University in 1945. She then spent several years in Paris studying crystals. Using *X-ray diffraction* techniques, which show how crystals deflect X rays, she discovered the size, shape, and arrangement of the molecules making up many crystals. In 1951, she moved to London to analyze DNA molecules. She soon produced X-ray diffraction pictures clearly showing that DNA was shaped like a double *helix* (spiral).

Later in 1951, Franklin presented her theory about the DNA double helix at a seminar attended by the American biologist James D. Watson. Watson and the British biologist Francis H. C. Crick were studying the structure of DNA by building three-dimensional models. Watson and Crick combined Franklin's work with their own research to produce a complete DNA model. They presented this model, the first ever published, in 1953. But Franklin did not receive credit for her contributions.

Franklin later determined the complex structure of the tobacco mosaic virus, which attacks tobacco plants. She died of cancer on April 16, 1958.   Alan R. Rushton

See also **DNA; X rays** (In crystal research).

Franklin, State of, was never admitted to the Union. It was organized as a state between 1784 and 1788, and had its own constitution and governor. In 1784, North Carolina ceded part of its western lands to the federal government. Before Congress could vote to accept the region, North Carolina withdrew the offer. The people of the area already governed themselves under the so-called Watauga Association. In August and December

State of Franklin

WORLD BOOK map

1784, they held meetings to create their own state, which they named in honor of Benjamin Franklin. They elected John Sevier governor and formally requested Congress to recognize Franklin as a state. But North Carolina opposed the admission of Franklin to the Union, and Congress decided to refuse Franklin's request.

For four years, the region had two competing governments. Both Franklin and North Carolina established courts and levied taxes. In the confusion, Franklin's government gradually lost its influence. Sevier's term as governor ended in 1788, and the people of Franklin rejoined North Carolina. In 1796, the region became part of the new state of Tennessee, and Sevier became the state's first governor.   Fred W. Anderson

See also **Sevier, John; Watauga Association.**

Franklin Delano Roosevelt Memorial honors Franklin D. Roosevelt, who led the United States through the Great Depression and World War II during his long presidency from 1933 to 1945. It is also called the FDR Memorial or the Roosevelt Memorial. It is one of four major presidential memorials on the National Mall in Washington, D.C. The others are the Jefferson Memorial, Lincoln Memorial, and Washington Monument. The memorial stands along the Tidal Basin, a scenic lagoon encircled by beautiful cherry trees.

The FDR Memorial covers about 7 ½ acres (3 hectares). It includes four partially walled-off areas called *rooms.* The walls and floors are granite. Each room represents one of Roosevelt's terms.

Room One features a bas-relief sculpture of Roosevelt waving from an open car during his first inauguration parade. Inscriptions in the granite include Roosevelt's call for courage during the Depression: "The only thing we have to fear is fear itself." Images of the Depression

AP/Wide World

The Roosevelt Memorial includes representations of many scenes from Franklin D. Roosevelt's presidency. This part of the memorial has a statue of the president and his dog Fala, *far left.*

dominate Room Two. Sculptures show a weary rural couple, people in a bread line, and a man listening to one of Roosevelt's radio broadcasts called "fireside chats." Room Three includes a large statue of Roosevelt with his dog Fala. A wall reduced to rubble symbolizes destruction from World War II. Room Four features a bas-relief sculpture of Roosevelt's funeral procession. The room also has a statue of First Lady Eleanor Roosevelt and a time line of the president's life carved into a series of steps.

Stricken with polio in 1921, Roosevelt used a wheelchair or other mobility aids the rest of his life. Shortly after the FDR Memorial opened, the government authorized an addition to the structure that would depict the president using a wheelchair. A sculpture of Roosevelt in a wheelchair now sits at the entrance to the memorial.

The Roosevelt Memorial was funded by private contributions and Congress. The memorial was dedicated on May 2, 1997. It is administered by the National Park Service.   Critically reviewed by the National Park Service

See also **Washington, D.C.** (picture).

Franklin Institute Science Museum is a science education institution in Philadelphia. It has exhibits on a wide variety of subjects, including machines, the human body, aviation, astronomy, trains, electricity, and Earth. The museum includes the Fels Planetarium, the Tuttleman IMAX Theater, the Franklin Theater, and the Benjamin Franklin National Memorial.

The Franklin Institute Science Museum was one of the first museums to develop exhibits involving the participation of visitors. In some of these exhibits, visitors pull levers and press buttons to learn fundamental scientific principles. In others, a visitor may ride a bike across the museum on a high wire or fly a jet in a flight simulator. Today, the museum also has an interactive computer network that asks visitors questions and explains basic scientific themes.

The museum is part of the Franklin Institute, an organization that promotes science education. The institute was founded in 1824 as the Franklin Institute of the State of Pennsylvania for the Promotion of the Mechanic Arts. It was named after the American statesman Benjamin Franklin. Its *Journal of The Franklin Institute,* first published in 1826, is one of the nation's oldest continuously published scholarly journals. The science museum opened in 1934. Critically reviewed by the Franklin Institute

Franklin stove. See Heating (History).

Franks were among the Germanic peoples who sometimes traded with the Roman Empire and at other times attacked its borders. Roman sources mention the Franks from the A.D. 200's. The two major branches of the Franks were the Salians and the Ripuarians. The Salians settled in the Low Countries on the lower Rhine, near the North Sea. The Ripuarians moved into the region around what are now the cities of Trier and Cologne, Germany, on the middle Rhine.

In 486, Clovis, a king of the Salian Franks, began to take over the regions of Gaul (roughly modern France) that were ruled by the Romans and other Germanic peoples. He replaced Burgundian, Roman, and Visigoth realms with his own kingdom, which stretched from east of the Rhine River to the Pyrenees Mountains. When Clovis died in 511, the Franks, though a small mi-

The Frankish kingdom in A.D. 768

WORLD BOOK map

nority in Gaul, had such a firm hold on the region that it came to be called Francia, or France, after them.

Clovis had belonged to a powerful Frankish family called the Merovingians. His descendants ruled as kings until 751, when another Frankish family, the Carolingians, took over. The most famous Carolingian king was Charlemagne. From 768 to 814, he created an empire far larger than that of Clovis. In 800, Pope Leo III made him emperor of the Romans. Although Charlemagne's descendants ruled until 987, the Frankish empire began to break up soon after his death in 814. Kevin Uhalde

See also Carolingian Empire; Charlemagne; Charles Martel; Clovis I; Merovingian dynasty.

Franz Ferdinand (1863-1914), was the archduke of Austria and heir to the throne of the Habsburg empire of Austria-Hungary. His assassination in 1914 led to the outbreak of World War I (1914-1918).

Franz Ferdinand Karl Ludwig Joseph Maria was born on Dec. 18, 1863, in Graz, Austria. Part of the Habsburg

royal family, he was the oldest son of Archduke Karl Ludwig, a younger brother of Emperor Franz Joseph. On June 28, 1914, Franz Ferdinand was in Sarajevo, the capital of Austria-Hungary's province of Bosnia-Herzegovina. After a bomb attack failed earlier in the day, Gavrilo Princip, a Bosnian Serb nationalist, fired two pistol shots into Franz Ferdinand's car. The shots killed the archduke and his wife, Sophie. On July 28, Austria declared war on Serbia, triggering World War I.

Critically reviewed by the National World War I Museum, Kansas City

See also Austria-Hungary; Franz Joseph; World War I (introduction; Beginning of the war).

Franz Josef Land is a group of about 190 islands in the Arctic Ocean, north of Novaya Zemlya. For location, see Russia (terrain map). Its northernmost islands are the most northerly land in the Eastern Hemisphere. Franz Josef Land has an area of about 8,000 square miles (20,720 square kilometers) and is part of Russia.

The largest islands of Franz Josef Land include Alexandra Land, George Land, Graham Bell Island, and Wilczek Land. Glaciers cover most of Franz Josef Land, which has about 1,000 lakes. Scientific stations are on a few islands.

An Austro-Hungarian expedition discovered the islands in 1873 and named them for Emperor Franz Josef (also spelled Franz Joseph). The Soviet Union claimed the islands in 1926. When the Soviet Union broke up in 1991, the islands became part of Russia. Grigory Ioffe

Franz Joseph (1830-1916), also spelled Franz Josef, was the aged ruler of the dual monarchy of Austria-Hungary at the beginning of World War I (1914-1918). Franz Joseph ruled as emperor of Austria for 68 years. His popularity, as well as military force, held the widely different elements of the dual monarchy together. When his heir and nephew, Archduke Franz Ferdinand, was assassinated in 1914, Franz Joseph declared war on Serbia. This led to World War I (see Serbia; World War I).

Franz Joseph was born on Oct. 18, 1830. He became emperor of Austria in 1848, a year of national revolutions. He was a member of the ancient ruling family of Habsburg (see Habsburg, House of). During his long reign, Austria prospered. But it suffered several military defeats. In the war against Sardinia and France in 1859, Austria lost the province of Lombardy (see Sardinia, Kingdom of). Prussia defeated Austria and three smaller German states in the Seven Weeks' War of 1866. As a result, Austria lost much of its influence in Germany (see Seven Weeks' War). Franz Joseph then adopted more liberal internal policies, granting the Hungarians their own government. This brought about the Austro-Hungarian empire, and Franz Joseph took the additional title of king of Hungary in 1867 (see Austria-Hungary).

Franz Joseph's only son, Archduke Rudolph, committed suicide in 1889. An Italian anarchist killed Franz Joseph's wife, Elisabeth, in 1898. Franz Joseph died on Nov. 21, 1916. A great-nephew, Charles I, succeeded him as emperor (see Charles I). John W. Boyer

Fraser, Simon (1776-1862), was a fur trader and explorer in what is now the Canadian province of British Columbia. He worked for the North West Company, a Montreal fur-trading firm. In 1805, he was put in charge of the company's operations west of the Rocky Mountains. He built that area's first trading posts and explored many of its rivers. In 1808, Fraser explored what is now called the Fraser River. Fraser was born in Bennington,

Vermont. He moved with his family to Canada when he was a child. He died on Aug. 18, 1862.

Jean Barman

Fraser River is a waterway in British Columbia that is famous for its salmon fisheries. It flows across the southern part of the province, from the Rocky Mountains to the Strait of Georgia near Vancouver, British Columbia (see **British Columbia** [physical map]).

The Fraser River is about 850 miles (1,370 kilometers) long. Its chief tributaries include the Chilcotin, Nechako, and Thompson rivers. The river drains about 90,000 square miles (233,100 square kilometers), mostly in southern British Columbia. Highways and railroads follow the Fraser. Sawmills and pulp and paper mills are important in the river valley towns of Prince George, Kamloops, and Quesnel. Sir Alexander Mackenzie, an explorer and fur trader, traveled the middle section of the river in 1793. The river was named for Simon Fraser, a fur trader who followed it to the sea in 1808. The Fraser region was the site of a gold rush in 1858.

Graeme Wynn

Fraternal Order of Eagles. See Eagles, Fraternal Order of.

Fraternal organization is an association set up to provide companionship or economic benefits for its members and, in many cases, to perform community service. There are three main types of fraternal organizations: (1) college fraternities and sororities, (2) social fraternal societies, and (3) fraternal benefit societies.

College fraternities and sororities offer social and educational opportunities to college and university students. For more information on these organizations, see the **Fraternity** and **Sorority** articles.

Social fraternal societies provide social opportunities and, in some cases, a chance to celebrate patriotic ideals. These organizations include the Benevolent and Protective Order of Elks and the American Legion.

Fraternal benefit societies also provide their members with social opportunities. But in addition, they offer life, accident, and health insurance and retirement savings plans. The Knights of Columbus and the Sons of Norway are fraternal benefit societies.

Common characteristics. Many fraternal organizations maintain such traditions as secret passwords, rituals, and initiation rites. Most restrict their membership to maintain the organization's "common bond." Some admit only men or only women. Some limit their membership to people of certain religious denominations, ethnic backgrounds, or trades. Many fraternal organizations for men have auxiliary orders that members' wives, mothers, daughters, or sisters can join. A few fraternal organizations are limited to a single state, but almost all have national or international membership.

Governing methods. In most fraternal organizations, local lodges or chapters elect representatives to serve on a local governing board. The organization may also have state or regional governing bodies. Each fraternal organization holds a national convention of delegates elected by local groups. The delegates vote on the organization's rules and elect the officers who make up the organization's supreme governing body. These officers serve until the next convention is held.

History. Early fraternal organizations resembled English *friendly societies,* which first appeared in the 1500's.

Working people set up these clubs to provide members with social opportunities and sickness and death benefits. Some fraternal organizations founded branches in the United States and Canada in the early 1800's. New fraternal organizations also were established in North America.

The National Fraternal Congress was formed in 1886 to provide state regulation and uniform legislation for fraternal benefit organizations. In 1901, certain fraternal societies formed the rival Associated Fraternities of America. The two associations united in 1913 to form the National Fraternal Congress of America.

Critically reviewed by the National Fraternal Congress of America

Related articles in *World Book* include:
B'nai B'rith
DeMolay International
Eagles, Fraternal Order of
Eastern Star
Elks, Benevolent and Protective Order of
Job's Daughters
Knights of Columbus
Knights of Peter Claver
Knights of Pythias
Masonry
Moose International, Inc.
Odd Fellows, Independent Order of
Rainbow for Girls
Rosicrucian Order
Tammany, Society of

Fraternity is a society of college or university students and graduates. Fraternities are also called *Greek-letter societies* because most fraternities form their names by combining two or three letters of the Greek alphabet. The word *fraternity* comes from the Latin word *frater,* meaning *brother.*

The best-known kind of fraternity is the *general* or *social fraternity. Professional fraternities* are made up of people who are preparing for or working in such professions as education, law, medicine, and science. Fraternities called *honor societies* select their members for their exceptional academic records. *Recognition societies* are for people with superior achievement in a specific undertaking. A student may join only one general fraternity. But a general fraternity member may also join a professional fraternity, an honor society, or both.

Many fraternities admit both men and women, but most general fraternities are for men. Women's organizations for college students are discussed in the **Sorority** article. Most fraternities have *chapters* (local units) throughout the United States and Canada. Intercollegiate, national, and international fraternities have thousands of chapters with millions of members.

The first Greek-letter fraternity, Phi Beta Kappa, was founded in the United States in 1776 at the College of William and Mary in Williamsburg, Virginia. It began as a general fraternity, then later became an honor society. The Kappa Alpha Society, founded in 1825 at Union College in Schenectady, New York, is the oldest ongoing general fraternity.

General fraternities

Membership. To join a social fraternity, a student must receive an invitation approved by the chapter members. This invitation to join is called a *bid.* Bids are issued following a period called *rush.* During rush, students who are interested in joining a fraternity attend events to learn about various fraternities and meet their members. Students who accept bids become trial members called *pledges* or *associates.*

Pledges must prove their ability to live, study, and work with fraternity members before they are accepted into full membership. Many fraternities assign to each pledge an upperclassman called a *big brother* who offers advice, guidance, and support.

Some fraternities subject pledges to a controversial practice called *hazing.* Hazing can sometimes require pledges to demonstrate their commitment to the fraternity by performing embarrassing tasks. Such tasks might include wearing odd clothing or running errands for fraternity members. The most controversial hazing involves cruel or dangerous requirements, such as preventing pledges from sleeping or making them drink too much alcohol. More than 40 U.S. states have passed laws that ban hazing. Some fraternities have replaced hazing with community service projects that give members and pledges an opportunity to work together.

A pledge or associate who fulfills all requirements is initiated and receives a fraternity pin. Pledges who become full members are known as the *brothers* of a fraternity. Brothers promise to keep the organization's ceremonies and mottoes secret.

Activities. Fraternities play an important role in many aspects of college life. Most fraternities maintain a residence called a *fraternity house* where their members live, socialize, and eat. Residential life provides experience in self-government and develops skills in cooperation, leadership, and relationships.

Fraternities participate in a wide variety of social service programs and extend hospitality to students from other countries. Fraternities also contribute scholarship money for fellow students to attend college and for children to go to summer camps. The majority of fraternities have *alumni* (graduate) chapters and associations that advise chapters about financial affairs as well as life after college.

Fraternities are well known for sponsoring such social activities as dances and parties. Some chapters have allowed social events to become occasions on which members drink too much alcohol or abuse other drugs. Other chapters have sometimes encouraged behavior that is disrespectful or sexually aggressive toward female guests. In response to such problems, some campuses have established policies that regulate parties and enforce legal restrictions on drinking. Other campuses have banned alcohol completely.

Organization. Each general fraternity chapter is a self-governing unit. However, fraternities are regulated by college officials and a campus interfraternity council, as well as the national or international headquarters of each fraternity.

Most colleges have an interfraternity council, which consists of representatives from all fraternities on campus. The council promotes the constructive aspects of fraternity life, settles disputes between fraternities, and enforces conduct codes. The North-American Interfraternity Conference (NIC), established in 1909, is a federation of local interfraternity councils. The NIC sponsors a meeting each year for its member fraternities. Most national fraternities have a permanent staff and publish a magazine or maintain a site on the Internet.

Professional fraternities

Professional fraternities are made up of people with a common academic or occupational interest. Some professional groups require higher academic standing than do general fraternities. Members may not pledge other fraternities in the same profession, but they may also belong to a general fraternity. Most professional fraternities participate in the Professional Fraternity Association.

Honor and recognition societies

Honor societies are either *departmental* or *general.* A departmental honor society selects men and women who have excelled in a specific academic field, for example French or mathematics. A general honor society selects members who have exceptional achievement in all fields of study. A recognition society admits members who have done outstanding work in a particular undertaking, such as retailing or community service.

Stephen M. Fain

See also **Phi Beta Kappa.**

Fraud is an intentional untruth or a dishonest scheme used to take deliberate and unfair advantage of another person or group of people. It includes any means—such as surprise, trickery, pressure, or cunning—by which one person or group cheats another. Fraud can involve money, *securities* (stocks and bonds), bank and credit card accounts, insurance plans, real estate, jewelry, and other goods. Countries throughout the world have laws against numerous types of fraud.

Fraud can range from individual schemes to major corporate scandals. For example, *identity theft* is a type of fraud that involves the unauthorized use of an individual's personal information, such as a name or credit card number. *Corporate fraud* includes various misdeeds committed by businesses or professional people. A company that deliberately misrepresents its financial condition may harm its investors and employees, but its executives may benefit illegally from such fraudulent information. Fraud committed by businesses and professional people is sometimes called *white-collar crime.*

Cases of fraud are often categorized as *actual fraud* or *constructive fraud.* Actual fraud involves misrepresentation designed specifically to cheat others, as when a company sells lots in a subdivision that does not exist. Actual fraud includes something intentionally said, done, or omitted with the design of continuing what a person knows to be a cheat or a deception. Constructive fraud includes acts or words that tend to lead others to wrong assumptions or conclusions. For example, a person is committing constructive fraud if he or she sells an automobile without telling the buyer that it often stalls.

In many cases, a victim of fraud may sue the wrongdoer and recover the amount of damages caused by the fraud. However, identifying and locating the wrongdoer is often difficult. For instance, a fraudulent business might close without notice and open a similar business under a new name in a different city.   Randi L. Sims

See also **Business ethics; Crime** (Types of crimes); **Identity theft.**

Frazer, *FRAY zuhr,* **Sir James George** (1854-1941), a Scottish anthropologist, wrote the famous *Golden Bough* (1890). This book traces the development of the world's religions. He also wrote *Psyche's Task* (1909); *To-*

temism and Exogamy (1910); *Folk-Lore in the Old Testament* (1918); and *Anthologia Anthropologica: The Native Races of America* (1938-1939). Frazer was born on Jan. 1, 1854, in Glasgow. He was educated at Glasgow and Cambridge universities. He taught social anthropology at the University of Liverpool. Frazer died on May 7, 1941. See also **Mythology** (Anthropological approaches).

Russell Zanca

Frazier, *FRAY zhuhr,* **Edward Franklin** (1894-1962), a sociologist, was a leading authority on black life in the United States. His writings prompted studies of how such forces as slavery and the prejudices of whites affected the black family. His best-known book is *The Negro Family in the United States* (1939).

Frazier was born on Sept. 24, 1894, in Baltimore. He attended Howard and Clark universities before earning a doctor's degree from the University of Chicago in 1931. He taught at several schools from 1916 to 1934. He headed the sociology department at Howard University from 1934 to 1959. He was president of the American Sociological Society in 1948. Frazier died on May 17, 1962. His books include *The Free Negro Family* (1932), *The Negro in the United States* (1949), *Black Bourgeoisie* (1957), and *The Negro Church in America* (published in 1964, after his death).   Robert A. Pratt

Freckles. See **Skin** (Skin color).

Freddie Mac. See **Federal Home Loan Mortgage Corporation.**

Frederic, *FREHD uhr ihk* or *FREHD rihk,* **Harold** (1856-1898), played an important part in the rise of Realism in American fiction. Frederic believed that writers should describe realistically the life they had experienced. His best novels portray the narrow, grim small-town life of his native upstate New York in the late 1800's. Frederic also was interested in the impact of controversial ideas and of the developing political and industrial forces of the day.

Frederic's best novel, *The Damnation of Theron Ware* (1896), describes the influence of controversial social and religious ideas on a rigid small-town congregation. In *Seth's Brother's Wife* (1887), Frederic portrayed the mingling of politics and journalism in a small town. *The Market Place* (1899) depicts a greedy American inventor whose financial and social successes feed his ambitions for political power in England. Frederic was born on Aug. 19, 1856, in Utica, New York. He died on Oct. 19, 1898.   Alan Gribben

Frederick I (1121?-1190), called *Barbarossa* or *Red Beard,* succeeded his uncle Conrad III as king of Germany in 1152. He became Holy Roman emperor in 1155. The German people admired and respected him as a great national hero. In 1180, he defeated his great rival for power in Germany, Henry the Lion, Duke of Saxony and Bavaria. He enforced his authority in Germany and the Slavic borderlands to the east.

He was less successful in a bitter struggle against Pope Alexander III and the Lombard League of North Italian cities. The league defeated Frederick at the Battle of Legnano in 1176. It was in this battle that foot soldiers recorded their first great victory over feudal cavalry. The Lombard cities forced Frederick to grant them self-government in the Peace of Constance in 1183. He started on the Third Crusade to the Holy Land in 1189, but drowned June 10, 1190, while crossing a river. But a German legend says Barbarossa is not dead but sleeping beside a huge table in the Kyffhäuser Mountains. When his beard grows around the table, he will arise and conquer Germany's enemies.   Charles W. Ingrao

Frederick II (1194-1250), called *Stupor Mundi* (The Amazement of the World), was one of the most brilliant rulers of his time. He was a fine administrator, an able soldier, and a scientist. He knew several languages and encouraged the development of poetry and sculpture. His book on falcons is still consulted by experts.

Frederick was born on Dec. 26, 1194. He belonged to the royal Hohenstaufen family. He was the son of the Holy Roman Emperor Henry VI and grandson of Frederick I. Frederick II was crowned German king when he was 2 years old and king of Italy when he was 4. He became Holy Roman emperor in 1215 and made himself king of Jerusalem in 1229. He established the University of Naples in 1224. Throughout his life, Frederick was in conflict with the popes and the rising towns of Germany and Italy. He died on Dec. 13, 1250. See **Gregory IX.**

Charles W. Ingrao

Frederick II (1712-1786), the third king of Prussia, became known as Frederick the Great. He started his reign in May 1740 and a few months later invaded Silesia, one of the richest provinces of Maria Theresa of Austria. This attack caused the War of the Austrian Succession. It also led to the Seven Years' War, in which Frederick held off the armies of three major powers, Austria, France, and Russia. He kept most of Silesia and expanded Prussia when he joined with Austria and Russia and took a part of Poland (see **Poland** [The partitions]). Frederick built a strong government and army. He encouraged industry and agriculture. He also made Prussia a rival to Austria for control of other German states.

Frederick has been called an "enlightened despot" because he supported the progressive ideas and reforms of the Enlightenment period (see **Enlightenment**). The French writer Voltaire lived at Frederick's court as a guest from 1750 to 1753. The Germans remember Frederick as a strong king and a great military hero. He was born on Jan. 24, 1712, in Berlin. He was the son of Frederick William I of Prussia and Princess Sophia Dorothea of Hanover, the sister of King George II of Britain. Frederick died on Aug. 17, 1786.   Charles W. Ingrao

See also **Frederick William I; Maria Theresa; Prussia** (Frederick II); **Seven Years' War; Succession wars.**

Frederick III (1831-1888), the only son of Wilhelm I, became king of Prussia and German emperor in 1888. He died of cancer on June 15, 1888, just three months after he succeeded his father. He believed in parliamentary government and took an important part in political affairs during his father's reign. Bismarck, chancellor of Imperial Germany, opposed Frederick's liberal views (see **Bismarck, Otto von**). Frederick was born on Oct. 18, 1831, in Potsdam. He married the Princess Royal Victoria, daughter of Queen Victoria of the United Kingdom. Their oldest son was Wilhelm II (see **Wilhelm** [Wilhelm II]). See also **Prussia.**   Charles W. Ingrao

Frederick the Great. See **Frederick II** (of Prussia).

Frederick William (1620-1688), often called the Great Elector, ruled the German state of Brandenburg from 1640 to 1688. Brandenburg later became the heart of the powerful Prussian kingdom.

During his rule, Frederick William laid the foundations for the future military greatness of Prussia. He was only 20 years old when he succeeded his father as *elector* (ruler). He ruled Brandenburg during the last eight years of the Thirty Years' War (1618-1648), which brought great ruin to Brandenburg (see **Thirty Years' War**). After the war ended in 1648, Frederick William began to send people to towns that had been deserted. He also won the power to raise and collect taxes and used money to build a standing army.

Frederick William fought against both King Louis XIV of France and King Charles XI of Sweden. He defeated Swedish troops in an important battle at Fehrbellin, Germany, in 1675.

Throughout his reign, Frederick William devoted much of his time to improving his territory. He encouraged industries, opened canals, and established a postal system. He reorganized the universities of Frankfurt and Königsberg and founded the Royal Library in Berlin. At his death on May 9, 1688, Frederick William left to his son Frederick III of Brandenburg (later King Frederick I of Prussia) a prosperous state and a large army. Frederick William was born on Feb. 16, 1620.   Charles W. Ingrao

Frederick William I (1688-1740) served as king of Prussia from 1713 until his death on May 31, 1740. He developed the most efficient government in Europe and made Prussia a leading military power.

Frederick William I was born on Aug. 15, 1688, in Berlin. He was a member of the Hohenzollern royal family and the son of Frederick I, the first king of Prussia. After becoming king, Frederick William I established a merit system for hiring and promoting government officials and eliminated corruption in the government by placing spies to observe employees at all levels. He also sharply reduced the number of government officials and cut government expenses.

The king used the money saved through his cost-cutting measures to improve the Prussian Army. He doubled the size of the army to over 80,000 troops and made it the best-trained army in Europe. Frederick William I was called the "sergeant king" because he spent much of his time with his soldiers. He paid large sums of money to recruit a "Giants Regiment," made up of soldiers more than 6 feet (180 centimeters) tall. Despite the strength of his army, he was a timid statesman who kept Prussia out of war for almost his entire reign.

Unlike his father and his son, who later became known as Frederick the Great, Frederick William I had little interest in the arts or education. He publicly ridiculed the young Frederick for preferring poetry, music, and philosophy to military affairs.   Charles W. Ingrao

Fredericksburg, Virginia (pop. 24,286), is one of the most historic cities in the United States. It lies on the Rappahannock River, between Richmond, Virginia, and Washington, D.C. (see **Virginia** [political map]). The city grew as a colonial trading post because of its location. Today, interstate highways make the area a distribution center for the East Coast. The former homes of George Washington's mother and sister are in the city. Across the river is Ferry Farm, where Washington spent part of his boyhood. The former law offices of the nation's fifth president, James Monroe, are in Fredericksburg. Four Civil War battlefields lie in or near the city. Fredericksburg is the home of the University of Mary Washington, named for Washington's mother.   Phil Jenkins

Fredericton (pop. 56,224) is the capital of the Canadian province of New Brunswick. The city lies on the Saint John River, in the southwestern part of the province. For location, see **New Brunswick** (political map).

Fredericton's industries include technology, research, education, defense, manufacturing, trade, and various services. The provincial and federal governments are Fredericton's major employers. The city has many craftworkers. The workers' products include jewelry, leather goods, pottery, and wooden toys. Fredericton is the home of the Beaverbrook Art Gallery and Christ Church Cathedral. The cathedral is one of North America's finest examples of architecture in the Gothic style. In addition, the city is the home of the University of New Brunswick and St. Thomas University.

Maliseet (also called Wolastoqiyik) and Mi'kmaq Indians once lived in what is now the Fredericton area. The British founded Fredericton in 1762 on the site of an abandoned French settlement. They named it in honor of Prince Frederick, the second son of King George III. After the American Revolution ended in 1783, about 6,000 people from the United States moved to Fredericton because they wanted to remain British subjects. The city became the capital of New Brunswick in 1785. The provincial legislative building was built in downtown Fredericton in 1880 (see **New Brunswick** [picture: The Legislative Building]).

In 1974, several surrounding communities united with Fredericton, and the city's population rose from 24,254 to about 44,000. An urban renewal project called Kings Place opened in 1974. The project includes business offices and a shopping center. Fredericton has a council-manager form of government.   Sterling Kneebone

Frederik VIII (1843-1912), of the House of Glücksborg, was king of Denmark from 1906 to 1912. Frederik, also spelled Frederick, was born on June 3, 1843. His father was Christian IX. One of Frederik's brothers became King George I of Greece, and several of his sisters married royal heirs. Frederik's second son, Carl, was crowned King Haakon VII of Norway. Frederik died on May 14, 1912, and his oldest son succeeded him as Christian X.   Kirsten Wolf

Free city is an independent or nearly independent city-state with its own government. Many such city-states developed in Germany in the Middle Ages, from about the 400's through the 1400's. In the 1200's, the first German free cities received independence from all authority except the Holy Roman emperor as a reward for helping him against the nobles. In 1871, the free cities Bremen, Hamburg, and Lübeck became states of the German Empire. Danzig (now Gdańsk, Poland) and Fiume (now Rijeka, Croatia) were free cities for a time under the League of Nations, a forerunner of the United Nations. Today, Vatican City may be considered a free city. See also **City-state; Gdańsk; Vatican City.**   Anthony D'Amato

Free enterprise system. See **Business** (Business in a free enterprise system); **Capitalism.**

Free Methodist Church is a Christian religious denomination based in the United States. It follows the Methodist teachings of English clergyman John Wesley and a doctrine of free will. The church was founded in 1860 by ministers and lay members excluded from the Genesee Conference of the Methodist Episcopal Church because they tried to restore historic Wesleyan principles to the church. They believed in simplicity of life and worship; rent-free seats in church; abolition of slavery; and freedom from secret societies. See **Methodists**.

The church has missionaries around the world and a large membership outside the United States. Its headquarters are in Indianapolis. The church's official name is the Free Methodist Church—USA.

Critically reviewed by the Free Methodist Church

Free port. See Free trade zone.

Free school. See Alternative school.

Free silver was a plan to put more money in circulation in the United States by coining silver dollars. The plan was backed chiefly by farmers and silver miners in the late 1800's, when the United States government usually used gold coins to redeem paper money.

Supporters of the free-silver plan wanted all silver that was brought to the mint made into coins on a standard that made 16 ounces (498 grams) of silver equal to 1 ounce (31.1 grams) of gold. The 16-to-1 standard had existed before the U.S. Treasury stopped making silver dollars in 1873.

Farmers believed the plan would help them get higher prices for crops. Miners and silver producers also favored it as a market for their silver. The Populist Party supported the free-silver plan in the 1892 elections, and Democrat William Jennings Bryan urged the adoption of the plan when he ran for president in 1896. The issue died after Alaskan gold discoveries in 1896 increased the supply of money.   H. Wayne Morgan

See also **Bryan, William Jennings; Populism.**

Free Soil Party was a political group organized in Buffalo, New York, in 1848. The party opposed the extension of slavery into the territories and the admission of new slave states to the Union. Many members of the party had once belonged to the Liberty Party (see **Liberty Party**). The Free Soil Party was joined and strengthened by a discontented faction of the Democratic Party in New York that was known as the Barnburners.

Martin Van Buren became the Free Soilers' candidate for president in 1848. Their campaign slogan was "Free Soil, Free Speech, Free Labor, and Free Men." The party did not carry any state, but it polled over 291,000 votes. Thirteen Free Soil candidates were elected to the House of Representatives. A coalition of the Free Soil and Democratic parties elected Salmon P. Chase to the Senate in 1848, and Charles Sumner in 1851.

The Free Soil Party lost the support of the Barnburners before the presidential election of 1852. This loss cut the party strength far below what it had been in the preceding election, but the Free Soil Party candidate for the presidency, John P. Hale, still polled 156,000 votes. Before the election of 1856, the remnants of the Free Soil Party had joined forces with the newly formed Republican Party.   Donald R. McCoy

See also **Barnburners.**

Free trade is the policy of permitting the people of a country to buy and sell where they please without restrictions. A nation that follows the policy of free trade does not prevent its citizens from buying goods made in other countries, or encourage them to buy at home.

The opposite of free trade is *protection,* the policy of protecting home industries from outside competition. This protection may be provided by placing *tariffs,* or special taxes, on foreign goods; by restricting the amounts of goods that people may bring into the country; or by many other practices.

The theory of free trade is based on the same reasoning as the idea that there should be free trade among the sections of a country. Consumers in Indiana gain by buying oranges from California, where the fruit can be grown less expensively. They would also gain by buying woolen goods from the United Kingdom if the goods could be produced there at less cost than in the United States.

Free-trade thinking is based on the principle of *comparative advantage* (see **International trade**). According to this principle, market forces lead producers in each area to specialize in the production of goods on which their costs are lower. Each area imports goods that are costlier for it to produce. This leads to the greatest total worldwide production, so that consumers receive the largest possible supply of goods at the lowest prices.

Objections to free trade. Despite superior efficiency under free trade, most countries favor some protection. One reason is the unsettled state of world affairs. Many people believe that so long as there is risk of war, a nation should not be too dependent on foreign supplies. Another reason is to support the incomes of those workers and firms that may be harmed by cheaper imports. Today, many less developed countries use protection to encourage their "infant" industries, more or less as the United States did in the 1800's.

Those people who favor free trade argue that protection can be harmful to a country's welfare and can lead to national isolation, national jealousies, and threats of war, which in turn necessitate even greater protection. They believe that free trade leads to understanding and world peace.   Robert M. Stern

Related articles in *World Book* include:

Asia-Pacific Economic Cooperation	Exports and imports
Customs union	Free trade zone
European Free Trade Association	North American Free Trade Agreement
European Union	Smith, Adam
	Tariff

Free trade zone is an area in a country where goods can be imported without paying *customs duties* (import taxes). Foreign traders may store, exhibit, assemble, or process products in these zones before shipping them elsewhere for sale or use. Free trade zones are often near such transportation centers as seaports and airports. A free trade zone differs from a *free port,* which is an entire city or territory where no customs duties are collected.

Free trade zones encourage foreign trade by enabling merchants to conduct their trade more cheaply than would otherwise be possible. If goods are imported directly from a free trade zone, traders pay duties only to the country where the goods will be sold or used. No duty is paid to the country in which the zone operates. The zone also enables traders to exhibit their goods at a site near the intended market without paying duties before the items are sold.

There are hundreds of free trade zones in the world. In the United States, such zones are called *foreign trade zones.* In 1934, Congress established the Foreign-Trade Zones Board to authorize and administer the zones. The board is an agency of the U.S. Department of Commerce.   Roma Dauphin

Free verse is a style of poetry that does not follow traditional rules of poetry composition. In writing free verse, poets avoid such usual elements as regular meter or rhyme. Instead, they vary the lengths of lines, use irregular numbers of syllables in lines, and employ odd breaks at the end of each line. They also use irregular accents and rhythms and uneven rhyme schemes. But free verse is not free from all form. It does employ such basic poetic techniques as alliteration and repetition.

Free verse first flourished during the 1800's when the Romantic poets adopted the style. The American poet Walt Whitman is often considered the father of free verse, using the style effectively in his "Song of Myself" (1855). In the early 1900's, a movement in poetry called Imagism began using free verse. Such Imagist poets as the American-born T. S. Eliot and Ezra Pound used free verse to create poetry based on the placement of precise images next to personal commentary. E. E. Cummings, a highly unorthodox American poet, experimented with unusual punctuation and typography. By the mid-1900's, free verse had become the standard verse form in poetry, especially in the works of such American poets as Robert Lowell, Theodore Roethke, and William Carlos Williams.   Samuel Chase Coale

Each poet mentioned in this article has a biography in *World Book*. For an example of free verse, see Theodore Roethke's poem under *Forms* in the **Poetry** article. See also **Meter**.

Free will is a term for the free choice most of us assume we have in making decisions. Our moral and legal systems, which praise, blame, reward, and punish, seem to assume that people have free will. If people lack free will, it seems unreasonable to hold them responsible for their decisions and actions. It would be difficult justifying the rewarding or punishing of people for actions they could not help doing.

The idea that there is free will has been questioned because it seems to conflict with the widely held belief in *determinism.* Determinism is the view that every event is already determined by previously existing conditions or causes. According to this view, the present state of the world determines everything that will happen in the future. Then human decisions and actions, like all other events, would be determined by causes that precede them. Critics of free will maintain that our choices are not really free if they are already determined before we make them.   Ivan Soll

Freebooter. See Pirate.

Freedman, Russell (1929-   ), is an American author of biographies, histories, and other nonfiction books for children and young adults. Freedman has won praise for the factual accuracy of his books and his engaging writing style.

Freedman won the 1988 Newbery Medal for *Lincoln: A Photobiography* (1987). The medal is awarded annually to the best book for children by an American. Freedman's biography of President Abraham Lincoln is more realistic and complex than earlier biographies of Lincoln for children. Freedman enhanced the impact of his story by including more than 80 photographs and reproductions of original documents.

Freedman's other biographies include *The Wright Brothers: How They Invented the Airplane* (1991), *Eleanor Roosevelt: A Life of Discovery* (1993), *The Life and Death of Crazy Horse* (1996), *Martha Graham: A Dancer's Life* (1998), *Babe Didrikson Zaharias: The Making of a Champion* (1999), *The Voice that Challenged a Nation: Marian Anderson and the Struggle for Equal Rights* (2004), and *The Adventures of Marco Polo* (2006). Like the Lincoln book, these biographies include extensive original research, often with authentic photographs and artwork that help illuminate the subjects.

Freedman's first children's book was *Teenagers Who Made History* (1961). Until 1985, he specialized in wildlife books. He wrote more than 20 books about animal behavior, beginning with *How Animals Learn* (1969), written with James E. Morriss, a high-school teacher of life sciences. Freedman then turned to American historical subjects, such as *Indian Chiefs* (1987), *Kids at Work: Lewis Hine and the Crusade Against Child Labor* (1994), *Give Me Liberty!: The Story of the Declaration of Independence* (2000), *In the Days of the Vaqueros: America's First True Cowboys* (2001), *Children of the Great Depression* (2005), *Freedom Walkers: The Story of the Montgomery Bus Boycott* (2006), and *Who Was First? Discovering the Americas* (2007); and *Washington at Valley Forge* (2008). Freedman also wrote *Confucius: The Golden Rule* (2002), a biography of the Chinese philosopher.

Russell Bruce Freedman was born on Oct. 11, 1929, in San Francisco. He received a B.A. degree from the University of California at Berkeley in 1951. He was a reporter and editor for the Associated Press from 1953 to 1956 in San Francisco. Freedman moved to New York City and worked as a publicity writer from 1956 to 1960 and as an editor in educational publishing from 1961 to 1965. He then became a full-time writer. In 1998, Freedman received the Laura Ingalls Wilder Award, presented to an author or illustrator who has made "a lasting and substantial contribution" to children's literature.

Ann D. Carlson

Freedmen's Bureau was an agency created by Congress to help the slaves freed at the end of the American Civil War (1861-1865). It provided food and shelter for poor people and supervised contracts between former slaves and their employers. The bureau protected the rights of blacks, provided opportunities for education, and helped them in many other ways.

In March 1865, Congress created the Bureau of Refugees, Freedmen, and Abandoned Lands. The bureau, better known as the Freedmen's Bureau, was part of the War Department. Its commissioner, General Oliver O. Howard, directed its agents.

Northern missionary and charity groups helped the Freedmen's Bureau finance and set up more than 4,300 schools for blacks. These schools included Atlanta, Fisk, Hampton, and Howard universities. The agency built many hospitals and provided millions of meals for poor blacks and whites. It also supervised the distribution of abandoned lands to former slaves.

President Andrew Johnson criticized the bureau's work as unconstitutional meddling in the affairs of the Southern States. Johnson blocked the agency's distribution of abandoned lands to freed blacks. He vetoed two bills to renew the bureau, but Congress repassed one of them and expanded the powers of the bureau in 1866. Democrats charged that the agency used blacks to gain more power for the Republican Party. The bureau was disbanded in 1872.   Alton Hornsby, Jr.

Freedom is the ability to make choices and to carry them out. The words *freedom* and *liberty* mean much the same thing. For people to have complete freedom, there must be no restrictions on how they think, speak, or act. They must be aware of what their choices are, and they must have the power to decide among those choices. They also must have the means and the opportunity to think, speak, and act without being controlled by anyone else. However, no organized society can actually provide all these conditions at all times.

From a legal point of view, people are free if society imposes no unjust, unnecessary, or unreasonable limits on them. Society must also protect their rights—that is, their basic liberties, powers, and privileges. A free society tries to distribute the conditions of freedom equally among the people.

Today, many societies put a high value on legal freedom. But people have not always considered it so desirable. Through the centuries, for example, many men and women—and even whole societies—have set goals of self-fulfillment or self-perfection. They have believed that achieving those goals would do more to make people "free" than would the legal protection of their rights in society. Many societies have thought it natural and desirable for a few people to restrict the liberty of all others. This article discusses the ways that governments and laws both protect and restrict freedom.

Kinds of freedom

Most legal freedoms can be divided into three main groups: (1) political freedom, (2) social freedom, and (3) economic freedom.

Political freedom gives people a voice in government and an opportunity to take part in its decisions. This freedom includes the right to vote, to choose between rival candidates for public office, and to run for office oneself. Political freedom also includes the right to criticize government policies, which is part of free speech. People who are politically free can also form and join political parties and organizations. This right is part of the freedom of assembly.

In the past, many people considered political freedom the most important freedom. They believed that men and women who were politically free could vote all other freedoms for themselves. But most people now realize that political liberty means little unless economic and social freedom support it. For example, the right to vote does not have much value if people lack the information to vote in their own best interests.

Social freedom includes freedom of speech, of the press, and of religion; freedom of assembly; academic freedom; the right to due process of law; and equal protection of the laws.

Freedom of speech is the right to speak out publicly or privately. Political liberty depends on this right. People need to hold free discussions and to exchange ideas so they can decide wisely on political issues. Free speech also contributes to political freedom by making government officials aware of public opinion. See **Freedom of speech**.

Freedom of the press is the right to publish facts, ideas, and opinions without interference from the government or private groups. This right extends to radio, television, the Internet, and motion pictures as well as to printed material. Freedom of the press may be considered a special type of freedom of speech, and it is important for the same reasons. See **Freedom of the press**.

Freedom of religion means the right to believe in and to practice the faith of one's choice. It also includes the right to have no religion at all. See **Freedom of religion**.

Freedom of assembly is the right to meet together and to form groups with others of similar interests. It also means that people may associate with anyone they wish. On the other hand, no one may be forced to join an association against his or her will. See **Freedom of assembly**.

Academic freedom is a group of freedoms claimed by teachers and students. It includes the right to teach, discuss, research, write, and publish without interference. It promotes the exchange of ideas and the spread of knowledge. See **Academic freedom**.

Due process of law is a group of legal requirements that must be met before a person accused of a crime can be punished. By protecting an individual against unjust imprisonment, due process serves as a safeguard of personal freedom. Due process includes people's right to know the charges against them. The law also guarantees the right to obtain a legal order called a *writ of habeas corpus.* This writ orders the police to free a prisoner if no legal charge can be placed against the person. It protects people from being imprisoned unjustly. See **Due process of law; Habeas corpus.**

Equal protection of the laws is a legal requirement that the laws apply equally to everyone regardless of differences in race, national origin, religion, gender, age, sexual orientation, wealth, or rank. The government cannot treat people unequally unless it has a legally defensible reason for doing so. This requirement seeks to fulfill the promise that no person shall unjustifiably have more freedom than another person.

Economic freedom enables people to make their own economic decisions. This freedom includes the right to own property, to use it, and to profit from it. Workers are free to choose and change jobs. People have the freedom to save money and invest it as they wish. Such freedoms form the basis of an economic system called *capitalism* (see **Capitalism**).

The basic principle of capitalism is the policy of *laissez faire,* which states that government should not interfere in most economic affairs. According to laissez faire, everyone would be best off if allowed to pursue his or her own economic interests without restriction or special treatment from government.

Since the 1930's, economic freedom has come to mean that everyone has the right to a satisfactory standard of living. This concept of economic freedom, sometimes called "freedom from want," often conflicts with the principle of laissez faire. For example, government has imposed minimum-wage laws that limit the smallest amount of money per hour an employer can pay. Laws also protect workers' rights to reasonable hours, holidays with pay, and safe working conditions. And if people cannot earn a living because of disability, old age, or unemployment, they receive special aid.

Limits on freedom

The laws of every organized society form a complicated pattern of balanced freedoms and restrictions. Some people think of laws as the natural enemies of freedom. In fact, people called *anarchists* believe that all systems of government and laws destroy liberty (see **Anarchism**). Actually, the law both limits and protects the freedom of an individual. For example, it forbids people to hit others. But it also guarantees that people will be free from being hit.

Reasons for limits on freedom. The major reason for restricting freedom is to prevent harm to others. To achieve the goal of equal freedom for everyone, a government may have to restrict the liberty of certain individuals or groups to act in certain ways. In the United States, for example, restaurant owners no longer have the freedom to refuse to serve people because of race.

Society also limits personal freedom in order to maintain order and keep things running smoothly. When two cars cannot cross an intersection at the same time without colliding, traffic regulations specify which should go first. Also, every person must accept certain duties and responsibilities to maintain and protect society. Many of these duties limit freedom. For example, a citizen has the duty to pay taxes and to serve on a jury. The idea of personal freedom has nearly always carried with it some amount of duty to society.

Limits on political freedom. Democracies divide political power among the branches of government, between government and the citizens, and between the majority and minority parties. These divisions of power restrict various liberties. For example, citizens have the right to vote. As a result, elected officials must respect voter opinion. They are not free to govern as they please. A system called the *separation of powers* divides authority among the three branches of government—executive, legislative, and judicial. Each branch is limited by the others' power. Majority rule does not give the majority party the liberty to do whatever it wants. No matter how large the majority, it can never take away certain rights and freedoms of the minority.

Limits on social freedom prevent people from using their liberty in ways that would harm the health, safety, or welfare of others. For example, free speech does not include the right to shout "Fire!" in a crowded theater if there is no fire. Freedom of speech and of the press do not allow a person to tell lies that damage another's reputation. Such statements are called *slander* if spoken and *libel* if written.

The law also prohibits speeches or publications that would endanger the nation's peace or security. Under certain conditions, it forbids speeches that call on people to riot. It also outlaws *sedition* (calling for rebellion).

In addition, many governments limit freedom of speech and of the press to protect public morals. For example, many states of the United States have laws against *pornography* (indecent pictures and writings). See **Obscenity and pornography.**

The government limits freedom of religion by forbidding certain religious practices. For example, it prohibits human sacrifice. It also bans *polygamy* (marriage to more than one person at a time), though Islam and other religions permit the practice.

Most other social freedoms can be restricted or set aside to protect other people or to safeguard the nation. For example, people may not use freedom of assembly to disturb the peace or to block public streets or sidewalks. The writ of habeas corpus may be suspended during a rebellion or an invasion.

Limits on economic freedom. In the past, most governments put few limits on economic freedom. They followed a policy of not interfering in economic affairs.

But since the 1800's, the development of large-scale capitalism has concentrated wealth in the hands of relatively few people. This development has convinced many people that government must intervene to protect underprivileged groups and promote equality of economic opportunity. Such beliefs have led to increased restrictions on big business and other powerful economic groups. For example, the Supreme Court of the United States once ruled that minimum-wage laws violated the "freedom of contract" between employer and employee. But today, laws regulate wages, hours, and working conditions; forbid child labor; and even guarantee unemployment insurance. Most people believe these laws protect economic freedom rather than violate it.

Economic freedom is also limited when it conflicts with other people's rights or welfare. For example, no one is free to cheat others. The right of hotelkeepers to do what they choose with their property does not allow them to refuse a room to people of a certain race or religion. The freedom of manufacturers to run their factories as they wish does not allow them to dump industrial wastes into other people's drinking water.

History

In ancient Greece and Rome, only the highest classes had much freedom. By about 500 B.C., Athens and several other Greek city-states had democratic governments. Citizens could vote and hold office, but they made up a minority of the population. Women, slaves, and foreigners did not have these rights.

For many years, the lower classes could not hold public office or marry into upper-class families. Lowest of all were the slaves, who, as a form of property, had no legal rights.

The Middle Ages produced a political and economic system called *feudalism.* Under feudalism, the peasants known as *serfs* had little freedom, but nobles had much. Lower-ranking noblemen furnished troops and paid taxes to a higher-ranking nobleman called their *lord.* The lower-ranking noblemen were known as the lord's *vassals.* Vassals had many important rights. For example, a lord had to call his vassals together and get their permission before he could collect extra taxes. Another custom called for disputes between a vassal and his lord to be settled by a court of the vassal's *peers*—men of the same rank as he.

In 1215, King John of England approved a document called Magna Carta. This document made laws of many customary feudal liberties. For example, it confirmed the tradition that the king could raise no special tax without the consent of his nobles. This provision brought about the development of Parliament. In addition, the document stated that no freeman could be imprisoned, exiled, or deprived of property, except as provided by law. The ideas of due process of law and trial by jury developed from this concept. Most important of all, Magna Carta established the principle that even the king had to obey the law. See **Magna Carta.**

In the Middle Ages, the Christian church restricted freedom of thought in Europe. The church persecuted Jews, Muslims, and others who disagreed with its beliefs. It restricted writings it considered contrary to church teachings. But church teachings also acted as a check on the unreasonable use of political power.

The Renaissance and the Reformation emphasized the importance of the individual. As a result, people began to demand greater personal freedom. Anabaptists and other Protestant groups elected their own ministers and held free and open discussions. These practices carried over into politics and contributed to the growth of democracy and political freedom. In 1620, for example, the Pilgrims who settled in Massachusetts signed a document called the Mayflower Compact, in which they agreed to obey "just and equal laws."

During the Enlightenment, also known as the Age of Reason, many people began to regard freedom as a natural right. Parliament passed the English Bill of Rights in 1689. This bill eliminated many powers of the king and guaranteed the basic rights and liberties of the English people.

At the same time, the English philosopher John Locke declared that every person is born with natural rights that cannot be taken away. These rights include the right to life and to own property; and freedom of opinion, religion, and speech. Locke's book *Two Treatises of Government* (1690) argued that the chief purpose of government was to protect these rights. If a government did not adequately protect the citizens' liberty, they had the right to revolt.

In 1776, the American colonists used many of Locke's ideas in the Declaration of Independence. For example, the declaration stated that people had God-given rights to "life, Liberty and the pursuit of Happiness."

As the Industrial Revolution spread during the 1700's, the free enterprise system became firmly established. The Scottish economist Adam Smith argued for the laissez faire policy in his book *The Wealth of Nations* (1776).

In the 1700's, three major French philosophers—Montesquieu, Jean-Jacques Rousseau, and Voltaire—spoke out for individual rights and freedoms. Montesquieu's book *The Spirit of the Laws* (1748) called for representative government with separation of powers into executive, legislative, and judicial branches. Rousseau declared in his book *The Social Contract* (1762) that government draws its powers from the consent of the people who are governed. Voltaire's many writings opposed government interference with individual rights.

The writings of these three men helped cause the French Revolution, which began in 1789. The revolution was devoted to liberty and equality. It did not succeed in making France a democracy. But it did wipe out many abuses and limit the king's powers.

The American Revolution (1775-1783) won the colonies independence from Great Britain (now called the United Kingdom). In 1788, the Constitution of the United States established a democratic government with powers divided among the president, Congress, and the federal courts. The first 10 amendments to the Constitution took effect in 1791. These amendments, now known as the Bill of Rights, guaranteed such basic liberties as freedom of speech, press, and religion; and the right to trial by jury.

The 1800's brought into practice many beliefs about freedom that had developed during the Enlightenment. In 1830, and again in 1848, revolutionary movements swept over much of Europe. Many European monarchs lost most of their powers. By 1848, the citizens of many nations had won basic civil liberties and at least the beginnings of democratic government. These nations included Belgium, Denmark, and the Netherlands.

Most European nations also ended slavery during the 1800's. In 1865, the 13th Amendment to the Constitution abolished slavery in the United States. The 15th Amendment, adopted in 1870, gave former slaves the right to vote.

Workers also gained many important rights during the 1800's. Many nations, including the United Kingdom and the United States, passed laws that regulated working conditions in factories. Workers in several countries won the right to form labor unions.

The 1900's. After World War I ended in 1918, many European nations established representative democracies. A number of them also gave women the right to vote. The United States did so in 1920 with the 19th Amendment. By 1932, 16 European nations had become republics governed by elected representatives.

By the 1930's, many people no longer believed that the simple absence of restrictions could make them free. Instead, the idea of freedom expanded to include employment, health, and adequate food and housing. In 1941, President Franklin D. Roosevelt reflected this broad view in his "four freedoms" message. He called for four freedoms—freedom of speech, freedom of religion, freedom from want, and freedom from fear—to be spread throughout the world.

In 1948, the United Nations General Assembly adopted the Universal Declaration of Human Rights. This declaration listed rights and freedoms that the UN thought should be the goals of all nations.

In the 1960's, the civil rights struggle by blacks resulted in much important legislation in the United States. The 24th Amendment to the Constitution, adopted in 1964, banned poll taxes in federal elections. The Civil Rights Act of 1964 forbade employers and unions to discriminate on the basis of color, national origin, race, religion, or sex. The act also prohibited hotels and restaurants from such discrimination in serving customers.

In 1972, Congress passed the Equal Rights Amendment to the Constitution. The amendment would have guaranteed equality of rights under the law to all persons regardless of sex. However, it never took effect because it failed to win ratification from the states.

Bruce Allen Murphy

Related articles in *World Book* include:

Academic freedom	Freedom of assembly
Bill of rights	Freedom of religion
Censorship	Freedom of speech
Civil rights	Freedom of the press
Communism (Restrictions on	Human rights
personal freedom)	Privacy, Right of
Democracy	Voting

Freedom, Academic. See Academic freedom.

Freedom Day, National, falls on February 1. It commemorates the day a resolution was signed proposing an amendment to the Constitution to outlaw slavery. Congress adopted the resolution, and President Abraham Lincoln signed it on Feb. 1, 1865. Amendment 13 was ratified by the states and was proclaimed on Dec. 18, 1865 (see **Constitution of the United States**). It freed all slaves in the North. Lincoln's Emancipation Proclamation of Jan. 1, 1863, had freed only the slaves in territories that were in rebellion against the United States (see **Emancipation Proclamation**).

In 1948, Congress authorized the president to proclaim the first day of February in each year as National Freedom Day. President Harry S. Truman made Feb. 1, 1949, the first such day.   Jack Santino

Freedom of assembly is the right of people to gather peacefully to exchange ideas or to protest social, economic, or political conditions and demand reform. Some people believe this freedom also extends to the right to assemble and associate on the Internet. Constitutions and the traditions of democracies throughout the world respect the right of freedom of assembly. But no country, including the United States, claims the right as absolute.

In the United States, the First Amendment to the Constitution guarantees the right of freedom of assembly. It says that the government may make no law that diminishes "the right of the people peaceably to assemble." Almost all state constitutions also ensure freedom of assembly.

Most public gatherings in the United States proceed without active interference by police or other officials. But sometimes law enforcement officers make arrests when political demonstrations are large or controversial, or when the demonstrations threaten to turn violent. Later, courts may be asked to determine whether the police violated the people's right to assemble.

In 1937, the Supreme Court of the United States struck down an attempt by the state of Oregon to limit freedom of assembly. A speaker at a Communist Party rally was convicted under a state law. The law said that citizens of Oregon could not participate in organizations that advocated the violent overthrow of the government. The meeting itself was peaceful. The speaker did not urge anyone to act violently or to commit a crime. The Supreme Court reversed the speaker's conviction. The court ruled that peaceful assembly for lawful discussion could not be made a crime. It also said that those who help conduct such meetings could not be considered criminals.

People do not have an absolute right to gather wherever or whenever they please. A town, city, or county may reasonably regulate the time, place, and manner of assembling. For example, a city might restrict large, noisy demonstrations to a particular area or to certain times of the day. The Supreme Court has ruled that protesters cannot be denied access to public places traditionally open to gatherings, such as parks and public sidewalks. But the government may refuse entrance to other places that have traditionally been off limits to demonstrations. Such places include military bases, prisons, private property, or corporate property, such as shopping malls.

Although the government may regulate gatherings, it may not do so unreasonably. Most cities and towns require demonstrators, strikers, and marchers to obtain a permit before assembling. The Supreme Court has struck down permit systems that give officials absolute authority to deny people the opportunity to meet. In

1939, in the first such case, the court voided a permit plan in Jersey City, New Jersey. This plan had given absolute power to the director of public safety to decide who could assemble in public places and who could not. The court said that no city official may deny the right to assemble because of a personal whim or because of a disagreement with the content of the message. It said laws regulating permits for the use of public property should be based only on safety standards that all groups could know in advance.

In other countries. All democratic governments recognize some form of freedom of assembly. But none of them uphold it to the degree established by the U.S. Constitution. The United Kingdom generally permits peaceful assemblies. But the British police have considerable power to prohibit or disband large gatherings as they think necessary. In several instances in the 1900's, the British government exercised emergency powers to suppress public meetings, even on private premises. For example, the government prevented fascists and others from meeting during World War II (1939-1945). In Canada, the 1982 Charter of Rights and Freedoms specifically guarantees the right of peaceful assembly.

International organizations recognize freedom of assembly as a fundamental human right. The Universal Declaration of Human Rights, adopted in 1948, proclaims that "everyone has the right to freedom of peaceful assembly." The International Labour Organization, a specialized agency of the United Nations, calls for permitting workers to meet and organize free of government interference.

Not every society, however, endorses freedom of assembly. In 1989, the Chinese government brutally disbanded a large, peaceful assembly of students and other citizens in Beijing's Tiananmen Square. Soldiers fired into the crowd and killed many demonstrators. The protesters were calling for more democracy in China and an end to corruption in government.

A mass protest led to a much different outcome in the Soviet Union. In 1991, a huge crowd gathered in Moscow's Red Square. The group defied tanks and troops to protest the temporary imprisonment of Soviet President Mikhail S. Gorbachev by a group of conservative officials of the Communist Party. The coup against Gorbachev failed, and the Soviet Union soon dissolved.

In 2011, mass political protests led to the downfall of dictators in Egypt, Libya, Tunisia, and Yemen. Many activists took advantage of Internet social networks such as Facebook and Twitter that provided them with an effective means of political organization that the dictators had not yet learned to control. However, similar protests in Iran and Syria were met with government crackdowns, killing thousands of protesters and leading to mass imprisonments.

History. Freedom of assembly has been fully recognized only since the late 1600's. Ancient democracies endorsed a more limited right to assemble. At various times in the history of Greece and Rome, a small part of the total population could meet in citizen assemblies to help make government decisions. But the majority of the people could not protest government actions.

In England, people traditionally assembled mainly for the purpose of *petitioning* (making a formal request of) the government. England first recognized this as a right in Magna Carta, a historic charter of liberties, in 1215. A later act stated that if more than 10 people gathered to present a signed appeal to the king or Parliament, even respectfully requesting a change in the law, they were guilty of the crime of "tumultuous petitioning." The English Bill of Rights of 1689 finally recognized an absolute right to petition the king. But assembly still carried risks. In 1715, a statute called the Riot Act banned "riotous assemblies." The act required groups of 12 or more to disband when a government authority told them to do so. The phrase *to read the riot act,* which means *to order a disturbance to stop,* refers to this law.

In the American Colonies, the First Continental Congress, in 1774, demanded a broader right of the people "peaceably to assemble, consider of their grievances, and petition the King." State constitutions and the First Amendment finally incorporated the specific rights of petition and assembly.   Bruce Allen Murphy

See also **Freedom** (Social freedom).

Freedom of Information Act is a law that authorizes anyone to examine most of the records of agencies of the United States government. Records can be obtained by presenting an agency with a written request for specific documents. Congress passed the law, often called the FOIA, in 1966 in an effort to discourage secrecy in government.

The FOIA states that agencies can withhold only certain types of documents. These include records relating to national security, personnel files of government employees, and records of criminal investigations. The FOIA enables a person to challenge the government in court if an agency refuses to release information covered by the act.

The FOIA was strengthened by the Privacy Act Amendments of 1974. One of these amendments provided for disciplinary action against any government official found to be withholding documents illegally. Another amendment required the agencies to answer an FOIA inquiry within 10 working days. A later law, the "Electronic Freedom of Information Act Amendments (E-FOIA) of 1996, increased the time for an agency to respond to an FOIA query to 20 days. It also required most organizations to provide electronic records for most documents created after Nov. 1, 1996. The OPEN Government Act of 2007 extended agency time on an FOIA request to 30 days. The 2007 act also defined representatives of the news media to include bloggers and others working in electronic media.   Jethro K. Lieberman

See also **Sunshine laws.**

Freedom of religion is the right of a person to believe in and practice whatever faith he or she chooses. It also includes the right of an individual to have no religious beliefs at all.

Like most rights, freedom of religion is not absolute. Most countries prohibit religious practices that injure people or that are thought to threaten to destroy society. For example, most governments forbid human sacrifice and *polygamy,* the practice of having more than one wife or husband at the same time.

Throughout most of history, many people have been persecuted for their religious beliefs. The denial of religious liberty probably stems from two major sources—personal and political. Religion touches the deepest feelings of many people. Strong religious views have

led to intolerance among various faiths. Some governments have close ties to one religion and consider people of other faiths to be a threat to political authority. A government also may regard religion as politically dangerous because religions may place allegiance to God above obedience to the state.

The question of morality has caused many conflicts between church and state. Both religion and government are concerned with morality. They work together if the moral goals desired by the state are the same as those sought by the church. But discord may result if they have different views about morality. An example is the disagreement of many religious people with governments that allow abortion.

In the United States. The desire for religious freedom was a major reason Europeans settled in America. The Puritans and many other groups came to the New World to escape religious persecution in Europe.

The First Amendment of the U.S. Constitution guarantees that "Congress shall make no law respecting an establishment of religion, or prohibiting the free exercise thereof … ." This provision originally protected religious groups from unfair treatment by the federal government only. Until the mid-1800's, New Hampshire and other states had laws that prohibited non-Protestants from holding public office. Several states, including Connecticut and Massachusetts, even had official churches. Since the 1940's, however, the Supreme Court of the United States has ruled that all the states must uphold the First Amendment's guarantees of religious freedom.

Today, freedom of religion remains an issue in the United States. Various court rulings have interpreted the First Amendment to mean that the government may not promote or give special treatment to any religion. However, the government may deny certain economic benefits to individuals who violate state or federal laws for religious reasons. The Supreme Court has also allowed the government to give some forms of financial aid to students of religious schools. The courts have also ruled unconstitutional a number of programs to teach the Bible or recite prayers in public schools. These rulings are highly controversial. See **Religious education; School prayer.**

But church and state are not completely separated in the United States. The nation's motto is *In God We Trust.* Sessions of Congress open with prayers, and court witnesses swear oaths on the Bible. Several court decisions support such practices. However, the Supreme Court has ruled that some religious displays on public property are constitutional but others are not.

Christian moral views have had a predominant influence on U.S. laws because most of the nation's people are Christians. In 1878, for example, the Supreme Court upheld a federal law against polygamy, even though this law restricted the religious freedom of one Christian group, the Mormons. At that time, the Mormon faith included belief in polygamy. But the laws and the courts agreed with the view of most Americans that polygamy is harmful to society.

In other countries. Religion has been discouraged or even forbidden in countries ruled by dictators. Before the 1980's, for example, the Communist governments of the Soviet Union and Eastern European countries persecuted religion on a large scale. A person's highest allegiance, they believed, belonged to Communism, not to a Supreme Being. Although they did not forbid religion entirely, they made it difficult for people to practice any faith. Beginning in 1989, the Communist governments of many Eastern European countries were replaced with reform governments that permitted more religious freedom. In 1990, Soviet leaders passed a law that restored religious freedom in the Soviet Union. In 1991, the Communist Party lost control of the Soviet government, and later that year the Soviet Union was dissolved.

In some countries that have an official state church, or where most of the people belong to one church, other faiths do not have religious freedom. For example, many Muslim nations discriminate against Christians and Jews.

Other countries, including Denmark and Norway, have state churches. But the governments of these nations grant freedom of worship to other religious groups. In some countries, the government provides equal support for all religions.

History. Many ancient peoples permitted broad religious freedom. These peoples worshiped many gods and readily accepted groups with new gods. Jews and, later, Christians could not do so because they worshiped only one God. They also believed that allegiance to God was higher than allegiance to any ruler or state. Some ancient peoples did not accept these beliefs, and they persecuted Christians and Jews.

During the Middle Ages, from about the A.D. 400's through the 1400's, the Roman Catholic Church dominated Europe and permitted little religious freedom. The Catholic Church persecuted Jews and Muslims. The church also punished people for any serious disagreement with its teachings. In 1415, the Bohemian religious reformer John Hus was burned at the stake for challenging the authority of the pope.

The Reformation, a religious movement of the 1500's, gave birth to Protestantism. The Catholic Church and Catholic rulers persecuted Protestant groups. Many Protestant denominations persecuted Catholics and other Protestant groups as well.

However, by the 1700's and 1800's the variety of religions that resulted from the Reformation had led to increased tolerance in many countries. These countries included Great Britain, the Netherlands, and the United States. But intolerance remained strong in some countries. Poland and Russia, for example, severely persecuted Jews. One of the most savage examples of religious persecutions in history occurred in the 1930's and 1940's, when Nazi Germany killed about 6 million Jews.

Bruce Allen Murphy

Freedom of speech is the right to speak out publicly or privately. The term covers all forms of expression, including books, newspapers, magazines, radio, television, motion pictures, and electronic documents on computer networks. Many scholars consider freedom of speech a natural right.

In a democracy, freedom of speech is a necessity. Democratic constitutions guarantee people the right to express their opinions freely because democracy is government of, by, and for the people. The people have to have information to help them determine the best political and social policies for their country. Democratic governments need to know what most people believe and

want. The governments also need to know the opinions of various minorities.

Most nondemocratic nations deny freedom of speech to their people. The governments of these countries operate under the theory that the ruler or governing party "knows best" what is good for the people. Such governments believe that freedom of speech would interfere with the conduct of public affairs and would create disorder.

Limitations. All societies, including democratic ones, put various limitations on what people may say. They prohibit certain types of speech that they believe might harm the government or the people. But drawing a line between dangerous and harmless speech can be extremely difficult.

Most democratic nations have five major restrictions on free expression. (1) Laws covering *libel* and *slander* prohibit speech or publication that harms a person's reputation (see Libel; Slander). (2) Some laws forbid speech that offends public decency by using obscenities or by encouraging people to commit acts that are considered to be immoral. (3) Laws against spying, treason, and urging violence prohibit speech that endangers life, property, or national security. (4) Other laws forbid speech that invades the right of people not to listen to it. For example, a city ordinance might limit the times when people may use loudspeakers on public streets. (5) Other laws ban speech that is intended to intimidate or express hatred toward other people or make the target want to fight immediately.

In the United States. Freedom of speech was one of the goals of the American colonists that led to the American Revolution (1775-1783). Since 1791, the First Amendment to the United States Constitution has protected freedom of speech from interference by the federal government.

Since 1925, the Supreme Court of the United States has protected free speech against interference by state or local governments. The court has done this by using the *due process* clause of the 14th Amendment (see **Due process of law**).

The government restricts some speech considered dangerous or immoral. The first major federal law that limited speech was the Sedition Act of 1798 (see **Alien and Sedition Acts**). It provided punishment for speaking or writing against the government. The law expired in 1801 and was not renewed.

In the late 1800's, Congress passed a number of laws against obscenity. But during the 1900's, court decisions generally eased such restrictions. For example, judges lifted the bans on such famous books as *Ulysses* by James Joyce, in 1933, and *Lady Chatterley's Lover* by D. H. Lawrence, in 1960. See **Obscenity and pornography**.

The Espionage Act of 1917 and the Sedition Act of 1918, passed during World War I, forbade speeches and publications that interfered with the war effort. Since 1919, the Supreme Court has suggested that the government can restrict speech if it poses a "clear and present danger" of an evil that the government has a right to prevent. In 1940, Congress passed the Smith Act, which made it a crime to urge the violent overthrow of the United States government. See **Smith Act**.

Most periods of increased restrictions on speech occur when threats to individuals, national security, or social morality seem grave. During such times of stress, the courts have provided little protection for individual freedom. In the early 1950's, for example, fear of Communism was strong in the United States because of the Korean War and the conviction of several Americans as Soviet spies. In 1951, the Supreme Court upheld the Smith Act in the case of 11 leaders of the Communist Party convicted for advocating the overthrow of the government. Since the mid-1950's, however, the courts have become more concerned about personal rights and have provided greater protection for freedom of expression. In 1989 and again in 1990, for example, the Supreme Court ruled that the government cannot punish a person for burning the American flag as a form of political protest. In 2000, the court ruled that the government could not require cable systems to limit sexually explicit channels to late night.

In other countries. The development of freedom of speech in most Western European countries and English-speaking nations has resembled that in the United States. In various other countries, this freedom has grown more slowly or not at all.

The United Kingdom and France have long traditions of protecting freedom of speech. But like the United States, these countries place certain restrictions on free expression in the interests of national security. Smaller Western European countries, such as Denmark and Switzerland, generally have fewer restrictions on free speech. Ireland bases some of its controls over freedom of expression on the moral teachings of the Roman Catholic Church, to which the majority of the Irish people belong.

The rulers of some countries have simply ignored or have taken away constitutional guarantees of freedom of speech. For example, the rulers of China and North Korea severely limit freedom of speech. These dictators believe they alone hold the truth. Therefore, they say, any opposition must be based on falsehood and regarded as dangerous.

History. Throughout history, people have fought for freedom of speech. In the 400's B.C., the city-state of Athens in ancient Greece gave its citizens much freedom of expression. Later, freedom of speech became linked with struggles for political and religious freedom. These struggles took place in the Middle Ages, from about the A.D. 400's through the 1400's. They also played an important part in the Reformation, a religious movement of the 1500's that gave rise to Protestantism.

In the 1600's and 1700's, a period called the Enlightenment, many people began to regard freedom of speech as a natural right. Such philosophers as John Locke of England and Voltaire of France based this idea on their belief in the importance of the individual. Every person, they declared, has a right to speak freely and to have a voice in the government. Thomas Jefferson expressed this idea in the Declaration of Independence.

During the 1800's, democratic ideas grew and increasing numbers of people gained freedom of speech. But at the same time, the growth of cities and industry required more and more people to live and work in large groups. To some people, such as the German philosopher Karl Marx, society's interests became more important than those of the individual. They thought nations could operate best under an intelligent central authority,

rather than with democracy and individual freedom.

In the 1900's, a number of nations came under such totalitarian forms of government as Communism and fascism. These nations abolished or put heavy curbs on freedom of speech. By the late 1980's, however, many of these nations had begun to ease the restrictions.

Technological advances have helped create a centralization of both power and communications in many industrial nations. In such nations, a government can use this power to restrict speech, so that the ordinary person with an idea to express may find it difficult to reach an audience. On the other hand, the same technological advances have produced new methods of communication. These new methods could lead to increased freedom of speech.   Bruce Allen Murphy

See also **Censorship; Freedom; Freedom of the press; Public opinion; Schenck v. United States.**

Freedom of the press is the right to publish facts, ideas, and opinions without interference from the government or from private groups. This right applies to the printed media, including books and newspapers, and to the electronic media, including radio, television, and computer networks.

Freedom of the press has been disputed since modern printing began in the 1400's, because words have great power to influence people. Today, this power is greater than ever because of the many modern methods of communication. A number of governments place limits on the press because they believe the power of words would be used to oppose them. Many governments have taken control of the press to use it in their own interests. Most publishers and writers, on the other hand, fight for as much freedom as possible.

Democratic constitutions grant freedom of the press to encourage the exchange of ideas and to check the power of the government. Citizens of democracies need information to help them decide whether to support the policies of their national and local governments. In a democracy, freedom of the press applies not only to political and social issues but also to business, cultural, religious, and scientific matters.

Most democratic governments limit freedom of the press in three major types of cases. In such cases, these governments believe that press freedom could endanger individuals, national security, or social morality. (1) Laws against *libel* and *invasion of privacy* protect people from writings that could threaten their reputation or privacy (see **Libel**). (2) Laws against *sedition* (urging revolution) and treason work to prevent publication of material that could harm a nation's security. (3) Laws against *obscenity* (offensive language) aim at the protection of the morals of the people.

Dictatorships do not allow freedom of the press. Dictators believe they alone hold the truth—and that opposition to them endangers the nation.

In the United States, freedom of the press is guaranteed by the First Amendment to the Constitution. All state constitutions also include protection for press freedom. Court decisions help make clear both the extent and the limits of this freedom. In general, the First Amendment prohibits censorship by the government before publication.

The U.S. press regulates itself to a great extent. For example, most publishers do not print material that they know is false or that could lead to crime, riot, or revolution. They also avoid publishing libelous material, obscenities, and other matter that might offend a large number of readers. In addition, because the press in the United States depends heavily on advertising income, it sometimes does not publish material that would displease its advertisers.

Freedom of the press was one goal of the American Colonies in their struggle for independence from Great Britain (now called the United Kingdom). The libel trial of John Peter Zenger in 1735 became an important step in the fight for this freedom. Zenger was the publisher of the *New-York Weekly Journal,* which criticized the British government. A jury found Zenger innocent after his attorney argued that Zenger had printed the truth and that truth is not libelous. See **Zenger, John Peter**.

The severest restrictions on the press in the United States—and in all other countries—are imposed during times of crisis, especially wartime. During World War II (1939-1945), for example, Congress passed laws banning the publication of any material that could interfere with the war effort or harm national security.

In the late 1960's and early 1970's, criticism by the U.S. press of the nation's involvement in Vietnam became widespread. This criticism helped broaden public opposition to the Vietnam War (1957-1975) and probably influenced the government's change in policy toward the war. In 1971, the government tried to stop *The New York Times* and *The Washington Post* from publishing parts of a secret study of the war. The government claimed that publication of the so-called Pentagon Papers could harm national security. But the Supreme Court of the United States blocked the government's action.

Also in the 1960's and 1970's, many judges issued rulings frequently referred to as *gag orders.* The orders forbade the press to publish information that judges thought might violate a defendant's right to a fair trial. Such information might include confessions made by defendants or facts about their past. The press argued that gag orders violated the First Amendment. In 1976, the Nebraska Press Association challenged a Nebraska gag order before the Supreme Court. The court ruled that such orders are unconstitutional, except in extraordinary circumstances.

In other countries. Freedom of the press exists largely in the Western European countries, the English-speaking nations, and Japan. It is present to a limited extent in some Latin American countries.

Press restrictions vary greatly from country to country. In Italy, the press restricts itself on what it prints about the pope. Such nations as Australia and Ireland have strict obscenity laws. But the obscenity laws in such countries as Norway and Sweden are relatively lenient. Denmark dropped all its obscenity laws in the 1960's.

The governments of many countries have strict overall controls on the press. A number of nations in Asia, Latin America, and the Middle East have censorship boards that check all publications. The censorship boards make sure that newspapers and other publications follow government guidelines and agree with official policy.

The governments of China and certain other Communist nations own and operate the press themselves. The Communist Party in those countries makes sure that the press follows the policies of the party.

History. Rulers and church leaders restricted the writing and distribution of certain material even before there was a press. In those days, when everything was written by hand, books considered offensive were banned or burned. Since the A.D. 400's, the Roman Catholic Church has restricted material that it considers contrary to church teachings.

Early printers had to obtain a license from the government or from some religious group for any material they wanted to publish. In 1644, the English poet and political writer John Milton criticized such licensing in his pamphlet *Areopagitica.* This essay was one of the earliest arguments for freedom of the press. In time, the United Kingdom and other nations ended the licensing system. By the 1800's, the press of many countries had considerable freedom.

Freedom of the press led to some abuses. In the late 1800's, for example, some newspapers in the United States published false and sensational material to attract the attention of readers. Some people favored government regulation to stop such abuses by the so-called "yellow press." But in most cases, such regulation would have been unconstitutional.

During the 1900's, journalists and other media professionals in the United States became far more careful and conscientious in checking facts and reporting the news. In many other countries, however, the press lost its freedom. For example, the Fascists in Italy and the Nazis in Germany destroyed press freedom before and during World War II and used the press for their own purposes. Civilian or military dictatorships ruled many countries in the middle and late 1900's. All these governments censored the press heavily.   Bruce Allen Murphy

Related articles in *World Book* include:

Censorship	Journalism (Restrictions on
Communism (Restrictions on	freedom of the press)
personal freedom)	Newspaper (Newspapers in
Freedom	other countries)
Freedom of speech	Obscenity and pornography

Freedom riders were civil rights supporters who protested the continued *segregation* of buses and bus terminals in the southern United States. On segregated buses, African Americans were banned from sitting in certain seats reserved for whites only. Segregated terminals had separate facilities for whites and blacks. In 1946, the Supreme Court of the United States had ruled that it was unconstitutional for public buses that crossed state lines to be segregated. The freedom rides took place in 1961. At that time, most Southern States still had laws segregating their buses and bus terminals.

On May 4, 1961, the Congress of Racial Equality (CORE), a civil rights group, organized the freedom rides. These rides were meant to draw attention to the places where the Supreme Court ruling was not being followed. Volunteers included many college students and members of the clergy. They traveled on buses from Northern cities and Washington, D.C., to places in the South. African American and white freedom riders sat together in all parts of the buses. At bus terminals, they ignored the signs that separated "white only" areas from those for "colored," or African American, patrons.

At first, state and local authorities ignored the freedom riders. But as the activists traveled into Alabama and other states of the Deep South, they met with resist-

Freedom riders protested the continued segregation of buses and bus terminals in the southern United States. This photo shows freedom riders, protected by the police and National Guard, arriving in Montgomery, Alabama, in May 1961.

ance. Angry mobs of *segregationists*—people who supported segregation—threw rocks at some buses. When the freedom riders got off the buses, many were injured in conflicts with crowds or the authorities. Hundreds were jailed. In May, a bus bound for New Orleans was attacked and burned in Anniston, Alabama. On May 20, U.S. Attorney General Robert F. Kennedy sent federal marshals to Alabama. He ordered them to keep the peace and protect the freedom riders. By 1962, segregation had ended in nearly all buses and bus terminals in the United States.   Bruce Allen Murphy

Freehold. See Estate.

Freeholder. See Colonial life in America (Economic reasons).

Freeman, Mary Eleanor Wilkins (1852-1930), was an American author. She became known for her short stories, which accurately and sensitively describe New England village life in the late 1800's. Freeman's works reflect her Puritan religious background and often deal with matters of conscience. Her stories also vividly portray the economic hardships of rural New England life. The central character in several stories is an older woman in conflict with her family, village society, or a suitor.

Freeman's best stories were published in the two collections *A Humble Romance* (1887) and *A New England Nun* (1891). In addition to short stories, Freeman wrote children's stories, a play, poems, and 12 novels.

Freeman was born on Oct. 31, 1852, in Randolph, Massachusetts. She died on March 13, 1930.

Bert Hitchcock

Freeman-Thomas, Freeman. See Willingdon, Marquess of.

Freeman's Farm, Battles of. See Revolution, American (Victory at Saratoga; table: Major battles).

Freemasonry. See Masonry.

Freeport Doctrine. See Lincoln, Abraham (The debates with Douglas).

Freer Gallery of Art, in Washington, D.C., is a government museum famous for its collections of Asian art.

These include paintings, sculpture, bronzes, ceramics, glass, jade, lacquer, and metalwork from the Middle East and East Asia. The gallery has important Biblical manuscripts in Greek, Aramaic, and Armenian. It also has many works by James Whistler and other American painters of the late 1800's.

The museum's library has a particularly important collection of works on Chinese and Japanese art. The staff carries on research in the arts and cultures represented in the collections. The Smithsonian Institution administers the building and endowment fund. Charles Lang Freer, a Detroit industrialist, gave his collections and an endowment to the Smithsonian by deed of gift executed in 1906.   Critically reviewed by the Freer Gallery of Art

Freesia, *FREE zhuh,* is the name of more than a dozen *species* (kinds) of plants with fragrant, colorful flowers. Native to South Africa, freesias are cultivated in greenhouses around the world. The plants have long, narrow leaves that grow from the base of the stem. The flowers are tube-shaped with six petals at the end. They are usually white or yellow but may also be shades of pink, red, blue, or purple. In cultivation, freesias may grow 18 inches (46 centimeters) high. Freesias grow from a *corm* (bulblike stem). Gardeners plant the corm indoors in late

The freesia has lovely, fragrant flowers. Gardeners grow freesias in greenhouses because these plants bloom in winter.

summer. Freesias grow best in a cool greenhouse. The flowers appear in winter.   Kenneth A. Nicely

Scientific classification. Freesias make up the genus *Freesia.*

Freestone. See Limestone.

Freethinker is a person who refuses to accept the authority of a church or the Bible. A freethinker insists on the freedom to form religious opinions on the basis of his or her own reasoning powers.

The name *freethinker* dates back to the 1700's. The English philosopher Anthony Collins used the term in his *Discourse of Freethinking* (1713). Collins and his friend John Toland argued against the authority of the Christian Church. Later, Lord Bolingbroke and David Hume were among the leading English freethinkers. In France, Voltaire was the leader of a group of people who argued for "natural" religion, as against revealed religion. Freethinking became fashionable in Germany during the reign of Frederick the Great, from 1740 to 1786. At the present time, few freethinkers belong to organized groups. Modern freedom of religion has made such organized bodies unnecessary.

David E. Klemm

Freetown (pop. 772,873) is the seaport capital of Sierra Leone. It stands on the estuary of the Sierra Leone River and has an excellent harbor. The city has a tropical climate. Temperatures in Freetown average 80 °F (27 °C), and rainfall totals approximately 150 inches (381 centimeters) a year. For the location of the city, see **Sierra Leone** (map).

Industries in Freetown include fish processing and soap factories and ship repair yards. Exports include chromite, diamonds, ginger, gold, kola nuts, palm oil and kernels, and platinum. British philanthropists founded the city in 1787 as a home for freed slaves.

James W. Fernandez

Freeway. See **Road** (Primary highways).

Freeze-drying is a method of preserving substances by removing water from them. The food industry freeze-dries such heat-sensitive products as coffee, tea, shrimp, mushrooms, and strawberries. Biologists use freeze-drying to preserve delicate or small organisms for display or microscopic study. Drug companies use it to prepare many medicines. Freeze-drying is also called *lyophilization* (pronounced *ly AHF uh luh ZAY shuhn*).

In freeze-drying, the item is frozen. Most commonly, the frozen product is placed in a chamber. Air is pumped out to create a vacuum. Then, the product is gently heated. In vacuum conditions, the ice in the substance does not melt into liquid water. Instead, it turns directly into water vapor in a process known as *sublimation*.

As the ice sublimates, the substance dries and becomes *porous*—that is, full of tiny holes. The pores allow easy access to water. *Rehydrating* (adding water to) freeze-dried food can thus restore it nearly to its original form.

Freeze-drying is a gentle drying method. It preserves food's texture, color, and nutrients. However, it is more expensive than other drying methods.

Kathryn L. McCarthy

See also **Coffee** (Instant coffee); **Dehydrated food; Food preservation** (Freeze-drying).

Freezing point is the temperature at which a substance changes from a liquid to a solid. The freezing points of different substances vary greatly. Mercury, for example, freezes at −38.87 °C. However, gold has a freezing point of 1064 °C. The freezing point of any substance depends on the pressure pushing against the substance. All freezing points specified in this article are based on a pressure of *1 atmosphere* (14.696 pounds per square inch [101.325 kilopascals]), the pressure of the atmosphere at average sea level.

The freezing point of a pure substance is identical with its *melting point* (see **Melting point**). For example, water freezes at 0 °C, and its solid form, ice, melts at the same temperature. Thus, at the freezing point, the liquid and solid forms of the substance can exist together in *equilibrium* (a state of balance). Unless heat is added or removed, they will remain in that state indefinitely because for each amount of liquid that freezes, an equal amount of solid melts.

The composition of a substance affects its freezing point. Pure substances, such as a pure element or a simple compound, freeze at one specific temperature. In contrast, mixtures, which consist of several chemically uncombined substances, freeze over a range of temperatures. Bronze, an alloy of copper and tin, solidifies as the temperature falls from 1000 °C to 800 °C.

The freezing point of most liquids can be lowered by adding another substance. This fact is the basis for using antifreeze in automobile radiators during the winter. Antifreeze contains ethylene glycol, which has a freezing point of −13 °C. A mixture of equal parts of ethylene glycol and of water freezes at about −37 °C.

A significant increase in pressure can affect the freezing point. The application of pressure raises the freezing point of gold, mercury, and other substances that contract upon freezing. Pressure promotes this contraction, and so the substances freeze at a temperature above their normal freezing point.

An increase in pressure lowers the freezing point of a few substances, such as antimony, bismuth, and water. These substances expand as they freeze. Added pressure prevents this expansion from occurring at the normal freezing point. As a result, the substances can freeze only at a lower temperature.

Robert B. Prigo

See also **Ice.**

Freight is raw materials or manufactured goods transported from one place to another. In the United States, trucks carry the most freight, and trains carry the second largest amount.

Truck trailers are sometimes *piggybacked*—loaded onto flat railroad cars because rail transportation over long distances is cheaper than trucking. Also, this technique eliminates the need for loading, unloading, and reloading goods. For the same reasons, trailers are often *fishybacked*—loaded onto barges.

Transportation by ship ranks as the least expensive way to send freight. The use of air freight has increased. However, air freight is expensive. Pipelines are used to economically move such substances as natural gas and crude oil.   Jay Diamond

Related articles in *World Book* include:

Barge
Containerization
Interstate commerce
Pipeline
Railroad (What makes up a railroad)
Ship
Transportation
Truck

Freighter. See **Ship** (Kinds of ships).

Fréjus Tunnels, *fray ZHOOS,* are two tunnels—one a railroad tunnel and the other a motor-traffic tunnel—that connect the Italian province of Turin with the French province of Savoy. The tunnels run under Fréjus Peak in the Alps.

The railroad tunnel, which was built between 1857 and 1871, was the first tunnel to be cut through the Alps. The mechanical drill powered by compressed air was used for the first time in building this tunnel. The railroad tunnel is 8.5 miles (13.7 kilometers) long. It was formerly called Mont Cenis Tunnel. The motor-traffic tunnel was finished in 1980 and is 8 miles (12.9 kilometers) long.   Herbert H. Einstein

Frémont, *FREE mahnt,* **John Charles** (1813-1890), sometimes called "The Pathfinder," explored much of the area between the Rocky Mountains and the Pacific Ocean. In 1856, he was the first Republican candidate for president of the United States, but he lost to James Buchanan, a Democrat. Frémont served in the Army and Navy, and as a United States senator.

As a second lieutenant in the Army Topographical Corps, Frémont worked as a surveyor in the Carolina mountains. He made his first important independent survey to the Wind River chain of the Rockies in 1842.On this trip, he met the frontiersman Kit Carson, who became the guide for his expeditions. Frémont's *Report of the Exploring Expedition to the Rocky Mountains* (1845) described this trip and established his reputation.

Frémont explored part of the Oregon region in 1843. He visited Fort Vancouver, moved to the Carson River in Nevada early in 1844, then went to California, a Mexican province. After exploring the Southwest, he returned to St. Louis in August 1844. Frémont helped produce the first scientific map of the American West.

The third expedition, in 1845, was organized with the Mexican War (1846-1848) in prospect. Frémont aroused the suspicions of the Mexican authorities in California, and they ordered him to leave. However, by the summer of 1846 he was inspiring discontented Americans in the Sacramento Valley to organize the Bear Flag Revolt (see **California** [The Mexican War]).

Commodore Robert Stockton of the Navy and General Stephen W. Kearny of the Army became involved in a dispute over conflicting orders, and Frémont sided with Stockton. After Kearny won, he had Frémont court-martialed for insubordination (see **Kearny, Stephen W.**). The Army dismissed Frémont. President James K. Polk overruled the dismissal, but Frémont then resigned. He made a fourth expedition in 1848, searching unsuccessfully for a possible route for a transcontinental railroad. He then settled in California and served as a U.S. senator from September 1850 until March 1851. In a fifth expedition in 1853, he again failed to find a railroad route.

In June 1856, Frémont became the presidential candidate of the newly formed Republican Party. He had been asked to be the Democratic presidential candidate but declined because that party supported slavery. One Republican slogan was "Free Speech, Free Press, Free Soil, Free Men, Frémont, and Victory!" During the campaign, Democrats argued that Frémont's election would cause the Southern States to separate from the Union and possibly lead to civil war. Frémont carried 11 states in the election of 1856. Buchanan, his Democratic rival, carried 19 and won the election.

Early in the American Civil War (1861-1865), President Abraham Lincoln gave Frémont command of the Union Army's Western Department. Frémont issued a proclamation taking over the property of rebelling Missouri slaveowners and freeing their slaves. His act aroused the

Engraving by J. C. Fry;
Chicago History Museum
John Charles Frémont

public and angered Lincoln, who transferred him to western Virginia. From 1878 to 1883, Frémont was territorial governor of Arizona.

Frémont was born on Jan. 21, 1813, in Savannah, Georgia. In 1841, he married Jessie Benton, daughter of powerful Missouri senator Thomas Hart Benton. Jessie Frémont, who had helped her husband write stirring accounts about his Rocky Mountain expeditions, became a regular magazine writer after her husband lost his wealth in the 1870's. She wrote several books describing her experiences. John Frémont died on July 13, 1890.   William H. Goetzmann

See also **Fitzpatrick, Thomas; Lincoln, Abraham** (Election of 1864).

French, language. See **French language.**

French, Daniel Chester (1850-1931), was one of the most famous American sculptors of his time. His best-known works include the large statue of Abraham Lincoln (1922) in the Lincoln Memorial in Washington, D.C., and *The Minute Man* (1875), a Revolutionary War memorial in Concord, Massachusetts. Another important work is *The Angel of Death and the Sculptor* (1892), the Milmore Memorial in Forest Hill Cemetery in Boston. French also did portraits and public sculptures. He was born on April 20, 1850, in Exeter, New Hampshire, and studied in the United States and Italy. He died on Oct. 31, 1931. See also **Lincoln Memorial.**   George Gurney

French Academy is a French organization of intellectuals. It is called *L'Académie Française* in French. Its activities include awarding literary prizes and publishing a dictionary of the French language.

The Academy has 40 members, known as the *Forty Immortals.* Once elected, they are members for life. Most are writers, but others have been scientists, sociologists, philosophers, and doctors. In general, a seat in the Academy becomes vacant only when a member dies. Individuals who wish to be considered for membership contact Academy members to declare their candidacy. The members vote on which person to accept. Until 1894, all members were French-born male citizens of France. Since then, the Academy has included men and women of other nationalities who write in French.

Cardinal Richelieu, a French statesman, founded the French Academy in 1635. It was suppressed in 1793, during the French Revolution (1789-1799). Napoleon I reorganized the Academy in 1803 as part of the Institute of France, a group of learned societies that are supported by the government.   Catharine Savage Brosman

See also **Institute of France.**

French and Indian wars were four wars fought one after another in North America between 1689 and 1763. The wars were fought between France and England, which became part of Britain during the second war. Spain, at times, sided with the French. All fought with the support of Indian allies. In the end, France lost nearly all its land in North America. Britain gained most of the French territory, and Spain acquired the rest.

Causes of the French and Indian wars. In 1689, England's colonies in North America lay along the Atlantic coast. Spain controlled Florida. French settlements lay to the north and west, from what are now Maine and Nova Scotia to the St. Lawrence River Valley. France also had outposts in Newfoundland, the Great Lakes region, and the Mississippi River Valley. Both France and England claimed the inland territory between their settlements. Until about 1750, however, only the Indian tribes who lived in the inland territory actually controlled it. Both the English and the French traded with the Indians for furs. Both, too, had Indian allies, though the French had a greater need for such partnerships. Thinly populated Spanish Florida relied on Indian allies for labor.

Beginning in 1690, the English repeatedly sought to conquer the French settlements. They wanted total control of North America. The French, on the other hand, had little intention of conquering the more numerous English. Instead, they fought to preserve their control of the North American interior, which rested on a vast network of alliances with Indians. The alliances depended on trading furs and fighting each other's enemies.

Access to the fishing waters off the coast of New-foundland provided another source of conflict. In the South, the English and their Indian allies raided Spanish-allied Indians for slaves. Because the French and Spanish empires were officially Roman Catholic and the British Empire officially Protestant, religious hostility added to the tension.

King William's War (1689-1697) was named for King William III of England. It grew out of three separate struggles in Europe, New York, and New England.

In Europe, a union of nations fought against French expansion in the War of the League of Augsburg (see **Grand Alliance**). In New York, Indian allies of the English challenged French control of the fur trade. In New England, Indian allies of the French resisted English expansion. In 1690, the French and their Indian allies attacked Schenectady, New York, and Salmon Falls, New Hampshire. The English responded that same year by seizing Port-Royal, the seat of government in the French region of Acadia (see **Acadia** [map]). They also launched an unsuccessful attempt to conquer Canada. Border raids continued on both sides until the French war with England ended in 1697, with the signing of the Treaty of Ryswick. The 1701 signing of the Great Peace of Montreal ended the French war with the Indians.

Queen Anne's War (1702-1713), named for Queen Anne of Britain, grew out of a conflict in Europe known as the War of the Spanish Succession (see **Succession wars**). It was also a result of continuing Indian resistance to New England's expansion. Spain joined France against the English. The war began in the winter of 1704, when the French and their Indian allies raided the New England frontier, devastating Deerfield, Massachusetts. The English attacked Acadia in 1704 and again in 1707. Also in 1707, England became part of Britain (see **United Kingdom** [History]). In 1710, Britain seized Port-Royal. In the South, the British and their Indian allies devastated the settlements of Spain's Indian allies, enslaving all they captured. They also took the town of St. Augustine, but they did not take the settlement's fort and had to withdraw. Spanish and French forces attacked Charleston, South Carolina, but they failed to capture the city.

Queen Anne's War ended in 1713 with the signing of the Treaty of Utrecht. By the terms of the treaty, France gave Britain Newfoundland, the Nova Scotia peninsula, the tiny islands of St. Pierre and Miquelon, and the territory around Hudson Bay.

King George's War (1744-1748), named for King George II of Britain, grew out of the struggle in Europe known as the War of the Austrian Succession (see **Succession wars**). The fighting in North America began when the French tried to regain Nova Scotia. The greatest battle of the war occurred in 1745, when New England colonial troops under William Pepperrell captured the French fortress of Louisbourg on Cape Breton Island. The Treaty of Aix-la-Chapelle, which ended the war, gave back to Britain and France the territory each side had lost in the war.

The French and Indian War (1754-1763) was the last and most important conflict in North America before the American Revolution (1775-1783). The French and Indian War began in America and then spread to Europe in 1756. It was called the Seven Years' War in Europe and Canada (see **Seven Years' War**).

Territorial rivalries between Britain and France had intensified as their empires expanded into the Ohio River Valley. In 1753, the French built a chain of forts at the

The Battle of Quebec in 1759 ended in victory for Britain. This engraving shows British troops led by General James Wolfe storming the Plains of Abraham, above the city.

The French and Indian War

The French and Indian War led to the end of France's colonial empire in North America. The war also established British dominance over most of the French possessions there. This map shows where the major battles of the war took place.

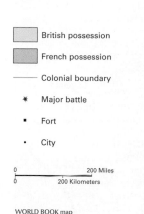

- British possession
- French possession
- Colonial boundary
- * Major battle
- ▪ Fort
- • City

0   200 Miles
0   200 Kilometers

WORLD BOOK map

eastern end of the Ohio region to keep the British out.

The colony of Virginia led the British expansion westward. Virginia's lieutenant governor, Robert Dinwiddie, sent 21-year-old Lieutenant Colonel George Washington to demand that the French abandon their new forts and return to Canada. But the French refused. In 1754, Washington led a band of colonial troops to force the French to withdraw. A French and Indian force defeated Washington at Fort Necessity. Meanwhile, representatives of seven of the British colonies met in Albany, New York, to plan further military action (see **Albany Congress**).

French successes. In 1755, General Edward Braddock led a band of British and colonial soldiers, including George Washington, against Fort Duquesne. A French and Indian force ambushed them shortly before they reached the fort, killing Braddock and many of his men. Washington led the survivors to safety.

The British also failed to take Crown Point or Fort Niagara. But they succeeded in seizing Forts Beauséjour and Gaspereau on the western edge of Nova Scotia. They then expelled the French Acadians and opened their lands to British settlement.

In 1756, the Marquis de Montcalm took charge of the French forces in North America and captured Britain's Fort Oswego. The next year, the French and their Indian allies destroyed Fort William Henry.

British victories. In 1756, William Pitt became the political leader of the British. He devoted tremendous resources to defeating the French in America. In 1758, British forces captured Louisbourg and Forts Frontenac and Duquesne (renamed Pittsburgh in Pitt's honor). In 1759, the British took Crown Point and Forts Niagara and Ticonderoga. They also *besieged* (surrounded and tried to capture) the city of Quebec. After nearly three months, General James Wolfe's army defeated Montcalm's forces on the Plains of Abraham, outside the city

(see **Quebec, Battle of**). British troops under General Jeffery Amherst completed the conquest of Canada with the capture of Montreal in 1760. The British then turned to the Caribbean Sea, conquering the islands of Martinique and Guadeloupe. When Spain allied with France in 1762, the British captured Cuba.

The war ended in 1763 with the signing of the Treaty of Paris. The treaty gave the British all of France's holdings east of the Mississippi River except New Orleans. France had given New Orleans and its lands west of the Mississippi to Spain in 1762. The British received Florida from Spain in exchange for Cuba. France regained Martinique and Guadeloupe as well as St.-Pierre and Miquelon.   Evan P. Haefeli

Related articles in *World Book* include:
Acadia
Amherst, Lord Jeffery
Braddock, Edward
Canada, History of (The colonial wars)
Coureurs de bois
Fort Duquesne
Fort Niagara
Franklin, Benjamin (The Plan of Union)
Montcalm, Marquis de
Pontiac
Rogers's Rangers
Washington, George (Messenger to the French)
Wolfe, James

French bulldog is a strong, heavy little dog. It weighs from 18 to 28 pounds (8 to 13 kilograms). It has a large, square head; rounded ears; and a short nose. Its chunky body is broader in front than in back. It has soft, loose skin that usually is wrinkled on its face and shoulders. The French bulldog has a less wrinkled face than the English one. Its coat may be white, yellowish, or brownish, often with darker-colored patches.

Critically reviewed by the French Bull Dog Club of America

See also **Dog** (picture: Nonsporting dogs).

French Canada. See Canada; Canada, History of; Quebec.

French Canadians. See Canada (People); Canadian literature.

French Equatorial Africa was a federation of French colonies in central Africa. These colonies included four territories that became independent nations in August 1960: the Central African Republic, Chad, Gabon, and the Republic of the Congo. Each nation has a separate article in *World Book.*

The region formerly known as French Equatorial Africa covers 969,114 square miles (2,509,994 square kilometers) and is thinly populated. Most people in the region speak languages in the Niger-Congo family. The Chadian Arabs and Sara peoples in the north and the Bakongo, Banda, Gbaya, and Fang peoples in the south are among the region's largest groups.

The region has vast forest and mineral resources. The richest known mineral deposits lie in Gabon. In addition, Central African Republic has significant deposits of diamonds, and Chad has substantial oil reserves. Chief products include cacao, coffee, cotton, diamonds, manganese, meat, oil, peanuts, rice, and timber.

The first French colonists in the area settled on the Gabon River in the 1840's. In 1910, the French government established French Equatorial Africa as a federation of three (later four) French colonies in the area. The capital was Brazzaville.   Dennis D. Cordell

French Foreign Legion. See Foreign Legion.

French Guiana, *gee AH nuh* or *gee AN uh,* is an overseas possession of France on the northern coast of South America. It lies between Suriname and Brazil. French Guiana covers about 32,253 square miles (83,534 square kilometers). It has a population of about 255,000. Cayenne is the capital and largest city (see **Cayenne**).

The population of French Guiana is diverse. It includes people with African, Amerindian (Native American), Asian, European, and mixed ancestry. French Guiana's land is primarily *old-growth* forest that never has been cut down.

The French settled in what is now French Guiana in the 1600's. Today, French Guiana is an overseas *department* and *region* of France. French regions are administrative divisions that resemble states in the United States. Each region has one or more departments.

Government. French Guiana is governed by French law. The president of France is the head of state. An appointed *prefect* represents the president in French Guiana. French Guianans elect two local governing bodies—the General Council and the Regional Council. French Guiana also sends representatives to the French Parliament. The court system resembles that of France (see **France** [Courts]). Residents of French Guiana with French citizenship may vote in French national elections.

People. French Guiana's diverse population has many Creoles—that is, people of African or mixed African and European descent who were born in French Guiana. Their culture blends French and African influences. It developed over several hundred years among slaves and, later, their free descendants.

Some people of French Guiana are called *metropolitans.* They were born in France, and most have European ancestry. Other population groups include Amerindians, Haitians, Hmong, and Maroons. The

French Guiana

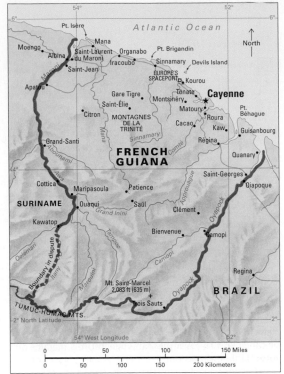

WORLD BOOK maps

Hmong have ancestors from Laos, in Southeast Asia. The Maroons are descended from African slaves who escaped captivity and developed independent societies in forests in French Guiana and Suriname. Many of French Guiana's people were born outside the department, in such foreign countries as Brazil, Haiti, and Suriname. Most of the people live on or near the coast.

Most French Guianans speak French, the official language. A Creole language is commonly spoken as well. French Guiana has a French-style educational system with both public and private schools. Children are required by law to attend school. French Guiana is home to two campuses of the University of the French Antilles and Guiana. Most adults can read and write.

The land and climate. French Guiana's coast and riverbanks are fertile, swampy lowlands. The interior consists mainly of low hills and plateaus. Rain forests cover most of the country. More than 20 rivers flow north through French Guiana to the Atlantic Ocean. The most important rivers are the Maroni and the Oyapock. The Maroni River forms part of French Guiana's border with Suriname, to the west. The Oyapock River divides French Guiana from Brazil, to the east and south.

Cayenne is French Guiana's capital and largest city. This photograph shows a street in the city center. Many of the buildings have balconies and awnings to accommodate the region's tropical climate.

© Jody Amiet, AFP/Getty Images

French Guiana has a tropical climate. Temperatures average about 80 °F (27 °C) throughout the year. About 130 inches (330 centimeters) of rain falls annually. Rainy months include December through February, and April through July.

Economy. French Guiana has a poorly developed economy. It depends heavily on France for financial support. The department has a high unemployment rate.

Manufacturing plays a small role in the economy. French Guiana's leading agricultural products include bananas, cassava, cattle, hogs, pineapples, rice, and sugar cane. Forests cover much of the land, and timber is an important product.

French Guiana imports much more than it exports. Chief imports include food, fuel, *pharmaceuticals* (medicinal drugs), and transportation equipment. Exports include fish, gold, shrimp, and timber. France is by far the department's leading trade partner. Ecotourism is a growing sector of the economy.

France chose French Guiana as its rocket and satellite launch site in 1964 and completed its first launch in 1968. With the founding of the European Space Agency in 1975, France agreed to share the Guiana Space Center, and it became Europe's Spaceport. Rockets lift off from the coastal town of Kourou, an ideal launch site because of its location near the equator and the ocean.

History. French Guiana originally was inhabited by *indigenous* (native) people called Amerindians or Native Americans. The French were the first Europeans to settle in the area, in the 1600's. But Dutch, French, and Spanish traders and explorers had established small trading posts in the region of Cayenne as early as the 1500's. The Treaty of Breda in 1667 gave the territory to France, and French Guiana became a French colony. British and Portuguese forces seized the colony during the Napoleonic Wars (1796-1815) and ruled it for several years before returning it to France.

The young colony of French Guiana was sparsely settled. From the 1600's, the French brought Africans to the

colony to work as slaves on sugar plantations. But the plantation system developed slowly. The colony produced only a small amount of export crops before slavery ended in 1848. In 1763, the French government recruited about 12,000 people from France and several other countries to settle in French Guiana. Most of the settlers died of disease soon after arriving in the colony

In 1852, France established a prison colony on Devil's Island in French Guiana. About 70,000 prisoners were sent to the colony from 1852 to 1938. The prisons closed in 1945, and the prisoners returned to France over the next several years. The discovery of gold in the 1850's at-

© Jody Amiet, AFP/Getty Images

The population of French Guiana is diverse. This picture shows Hmong farmers selling fruit to people with African ancestry in Cayenne. The Hmong have ancestors from Laos, Southeast Asia.

tracted many free people to French Guiana in the late 1800's to early 1900's.

French Guiana became an overseas department of France in 1946. In 1974, it gained regional status and more control over its economy. In a *referendum* (direct popular vote) in 2010, French Guianans voted against increased self-rule.　　Amy B. Wolfson

French Guinea. See French West Africa; Guinea (country).

French horn is a brass musical instrument. It is called a *French horn* to distinguish it from the English horn, a woodwind instrument. Most musicians refer to the French horn simply as the *horn.*

The French horn is a coiled metal tube that ends in a flared bell. A musician uses one hand to press the key levers in various combinations to produce notes. The other hand is placed inside the bell to control the horn's tone.

Northwestern University (WORLD BOOK photo by Ted Nielsen)

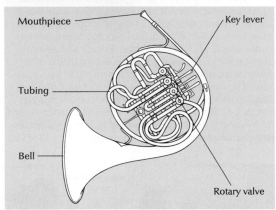

Mouthpiece

Key lever

Tubing

Bell

Rotary valve

WORLD BOOK illustration by Zorica Dabich

The French horn consists largely of a metal tube about 12 feet (3.7 meters) long. The tube is coiled into a circular shape and ends in a large flared bell. The musician produces tones by vibrating the lips in a funnel-shaped mouthpiece. The instrument has three or more valves. The musician fingers the valves with the left hand and places the right hand in the bell to aid the sound quality and for special effects. The player changes notes by moving the valves and changing lip tension. Most professional horn players use a *double horn,* which has different lengths of tubing on each side of the horn. The player can press a lever while performing, choosing which of the two horns will be played.

The French horn is descended from the hunting horn, a coiled valveless instrument sometimes worn around the player's neck.　　Stewart L. Ross

French language is the official language of France and its overseas territories. It is also an official language of Belgium, Canada, Haiti, Luxembourg, Monaco, Switzerland, and many African countries. More people speak such languages as Chinese, English, Russian, or Spanish than speak French. However, French is so widely spoken that it ranks with English as a working language for many international organizations and nonprofit groups.

French is a beautiful and harmonious language. It has served for hundreds of years as the language of diplomats. Its clear style and regular *syntax* (arrangement of words) make it especially suitable for diplomatic, legal, and business use, and for literature.

Many words in English come from French. English began to absorb French words after the Norman conquest of England in 1066. The Normans came from Normandy, a region of what is now France. The king's court and courts of justice used French. However, the common people continued to speak English. French words gradually became part of English. For example, the words *mouton, boeuf,* and *porc,* which the nobility used instead of *sheep, ox,* and *swine,* became *mutton, beef,* and *pork* in English. Thousands of French terms have been adopted, in whole or in part, into English. They include *art, castle, dress, faith, prison,* and *theater.*

French grammar

Nouns and adjectives. All French nouns are either masculine or feminine. The gender of a noun, in turn, affects related pronouns, adjectives, and some participles. For example, *the book (le livre)* is masculine, and *the chair (la chaise)* is feminine. In most cases, adjectives are made feminine by adding *e.* Thus, the feminine of *petit* (small) is *petite.* Plurals are most commonly formed by adding *s* to the singular. The plural of *le petit livre* is *les petits livres.* The plural of *la petite chaise* is *les petites chaises. Le* and *la* are the masculine and feminine singular forms of the definite article *the. Les* is both the masculine plural form and the feminine plural form.

Pronouns. Both older forms of English and French made a distinction between *familiar* (used among family and friends) and polite forms of address. The singular subject pronoun *thou* and the plural subject pronoun *you* in English correspond to *tu* and *vous* in French. *Thou* is no longer used in English. However, the distinction between the familiar *tu* form and the polite or plural *vous* form still exists today in French.

Verbs. French has 14 tenses, 7 simple and 7 compound (see **Tense**). The *simple* tenses are formed by adding endings to the infinitive or to the stem of the verb. The *compound* tenses are made up of the past participle of the verb and an appropriate form of one of the *auxiliary* (helping) verbs *avoir* (to have) or *être* (to be). Included in these tenses is a special French literary past tense (*le passé simple*) that is used in formal writing. French also has a subjunctive case that is often used.

In written French, verbs are classified by the endings of their infinitives. They fall into three groups of regular verbs: *-er* verbs, such as *donner* (to give); *-ir* verbs, such as *finir* (to finish); and *-re* verbs, such as *vendre* (to sell). French also has many irregular verbs.

Word order in French is similar to that in English in many cases. As in English, the normal order is subject-verb-object. A sentence is made negative by placing *ne* before the verb and *pas* after it. A question is formed by inverting the order of the subject and verb or by placing *est-ce que* (is it that) before the sentence. The following are forms of the sentence *John gives the books to my friends:*

Affirmative: *Jean donne les livres à mes amis.*
Negative: *Jean ne donne pas les livres à mes amis.*
Interrogative: *Jean donne-t-il les livres à mes amis?* or *Est-ce que Jean donne les livres à mes amis?*

Pronunciation of French is often difficult for English-speaking people. The French do not pronounce final consonants, except for *c, f, l,* and *r.* For example, *lits* (beds) is pronounced *lee,* and *et* (and) is pronounced *ay.* French vowels are sharp, clear, single sounds. A few do not occur in English. For example, there is no exact equivalent for the *u* of *lune* (moon). It is a sound that combines *ee* and *oo* and is made with the lips rounded. Syllables that end in *n* or *m* have a nasal sound. The French *r* is pronounced by vibrating the *uvula,* a fleshy extension of the roof of the mouth that hangs above the throat. The French *r* sounds harsher than the English *r.*

In French, each syllable of a word usually has the same emphasis. However, the final syllable of a sentence or phrase is sometimes accented. For instance, the expression *comment allez-vous?* (how are you?) is often pronounced *kuhm mawn tah lay VOO.* In addition, the French often link words together. For example, *les enfants* (the children) is pronounced *lay zawn fawn.*

Written French. French uses the same alphabet as English, but its use of *diacritics,* or accents, gives it a distinct appearance on the printed page. Accents in French are used to indicate different sounds or values of a letter. The most common accents in French are the acute accent used over the letter *e* (*é*) and the grave accent, also used over the letter *e* (*è*) or over other vowels such as *a* or *u.* The grave accent helps the reader quickly rec-ognize the meaning of certain *homonyms* (words that sound alike) such as *ou* (or) as opposed to *où* (where).

The other French accents are the diaeresis, the cedilla, and the circumflex. The diaeresis is found in the word *Noël* (Christmas), and the cedilla, in the word *français* (French). The circumflex is generally used to indicate that a letter or letters have been removed from the original Latin word in making the French one, such as *jeûner* (to fast in English, *jejunare* in Latin).

Development

Beginnings. French is one of the Romance languages, which developed from Latin (see **Romance languages**). When Julius Caesar conquered Gaul (now mainly France) in the 50's B.C., he found the people speaking a language called *Gaulish.* The Gauls gradually adopted the language of Caesar's Roman soldiers. This language, called *vernacular* (common) *Latin,* differed from the Latin used by educated people. The Gauls adapted the soldiers' popular Latin. They changed the vocabulary based on the way the words sounded. For example, a Gaul hearing the stressed syllables *bon* and *ta* of the word *bonitatem* (kindness) reduced the word to *bonta.* This word has become *bonté* in modern French.

Only about 350 Gaulish words have become part of modern French. The Franks, who invaded Gaul repeatedly from A.D. 200 to 400, renamed the country France. They contributed about 1,000 words to French. Danish Vikings, who occupied northern France in the 800's, added about 90 words. A number of French words have also come from Greek. As French has developed, its grammar has changed.

Old French. By the 700's, vernacular Latin had evolved so completely into *la langue romane,* also called Romance, that few could read Latin without a dictionary. The new language first appeared in written form in the Oaths of Strasbourg, a treaty signed by two descendants of the Frankish king Charlemagne in 842.

Beginning in the 900's, Romance developed in France into *Old French,* which had two distinct dialects, each with many minor dialects. The *langue d'oc* thrived in the south, and the *langue d'oïl,* in the north. These terms came from the word for *yes,* which was *oc* in the south and *oïl* in the north. The most famous langue d'oc dialect was *Provençal,* the language of the troubadours (see **Troubadour**). A dialect of the langue d'oïl spoken in the area around Paris became the universal tongue in France because of the capital's political influence.

Modern French. During the Renaissance, a period in European history from about 1300 to 1600, more Greek and Latin words were added to French. In the 1500's, the French interacted often with Spaniards and Italians and adopted a number of Spanish and Italian words.

In the 1600's, writers and scholars began to standardize the structure of French. Members of the *Académie française* (French Academy), founded by the French statesman Cardinal Richelieu in 1635, produced a definitive dictionary of the language. Today, the *Académie* is composed of 40 lifetime members who meet regularly to discuss standard usage of French. They also revise definitions and prepare new entries for the next dictionary. Speakers of French consider it one of the most precise languages.   Sandra Elizabeth Miller-Sanchez

See also **French literature; French Academy.**

French words and phrases

(Pronunciations are approximate)

Common words

après, *ah preh,* after	**jaune,** *jhohn,* yellow
aujourd'hui, *oh jhoor dwee,* today	**joli,** *zhaw lee,* pretty
blanc, *blawnk,* white	**madame,** *mah dahm,* madam
bleu, *bluh,* blue	**mademoiselle,** *mahd mwah zehl,* miss
chose, *shohz,* thing	**maison,** *may zawn,* house
court, *koor,* short	**mauvais,** *moh vay,* bad
dans, *dawn,* in, into	**mère,** *mair,* mother
de, *duh,* of, from	**monsieur,** *muh syuh,* Mr., sir
enfant, *awn fawn,* child	**où,** *oo,* where
être, *eh truh,* to be	**père,** *pair,* father
femme, *fahm,* woman	**pour,** *poor,* for
fermer, *fehr may,* to close	**rouge,** *roozh,* red
frère, *frair,* brother	**sans,** *sawn,* without
garçon, *gahr sawn,* boy, waiter	**soeur,** *suhr,* sister
gris, *gree,* gray	**vert,** *vair,* green

Common expressions

au revoir, *oh ruh vwahr,* good-by
bonjour, *bawn zhoor,* hello
comment allez-vous? *kuhm mawn tah lay voo,* how are you?
merci beaucoup, *mehr see boh koo,* thank you very much
parlez-vous français? *pahr lay voo frawn say,* do you speak French?
quelle heure est-il? *kehl ur eh teel,* what time is it?
qu'est-ce que c'est? *kehs kuh say,* what is it?
s'il vous plaît, *seel voo pleh,* please
très bien, *tray byehn,* very well

French literature is one of the world's richest and most influential national literatures. French writers have contributed to every major literary form, excelling in epic poetry, lyric poetry, drama, and fiction and other types of prose.

French literature has strongly influenced the work of writers in many countries. During the 1600's, the French cultural movement called Classicism had a major impact on most European literatures. French writers of the 1700's dominated the intellectual life of Europe. During the 1800's and early 1900's, French literary movements called Realism and Symbolism helped shape the work of writers in many other languages, especially English. In the 1900's, Surrealism and Existentialism moved beyond France to influence the works of writers, thinkers, and other artists throughout Europe and the Americas.

Early French literature

The earliest text dates from the A.D. 800's, during the Middle Ages. Poetry dominated medieval French literature. Much poetry was intended to be sung or recited to largely illiterate audiences by traveling entertainers called *jongleurs*. Gradually, two main kinds of poetry emerged—*lyric* and *narrative*.

Lyric poetry flourished from the 1100's to the 1400's. It began in southern France, where poet-musicians called *troubadours* wrote love songs in the Provençal dialect. Some of this poetry was carried to northern France, where it was imitated by poets called *trouvères*. Both the troubadours and trouvères composed lyric poems that praised women and the ideal of love. These poems were intentionally conventional and repetitive. They concentrated on emotional states, portraying with great subtlety the shifts from joy to despair.

The best-remembered French lyric poet of the Middle Ages was François Villon. He composed many *ballades,* a verse form with three equal stanzas and a shorter concluding stanza. He also wrote long poems that dealt with the themes of love, failure, and death. Villon's verses moved over a wide tonal range, from biting mockery and grotesque imagery to gentler passages on such themes as compassion. His masterpiece is a 2,000-line autobiographical poem, the *Grand Testament* (1461).

Narrative poetry includes four important types: (1) epic poems, (2) romances, (3) lais and contes, and (4) fabliaux. All were written for aristocratic audiences except fabliaux, which were more for the middle class.

Epic poems dealt with warfare and heroic deeds in battle. They were called *chansons de geste* (songs of great deeds). Jongleurs performed the chansons to musical accompaniment. The most famous was *The Song of Roland* (about 1100). It describes an incident during a military campaign led by the famous ruler Charlemagne.

Romances were long fictional works, often full of fantastic adventures. There were several kinds. *Romans antiques* (classical romances) were based on ancient subjects, such as the Trojan War between Greece and Troy, which probably occurred in the 1200's B.C. *Romans bretons* (Breton romances) told stories about King Arthur and his Knights of the Round Table in medieval Britain.

Probably the most widely read and influential French romance is the *Romance of the Rose*. A trouvère named Guillaume de Lorris wrote the first part about 1230. The poet Jean de Meung finished the romance in a darker,

French literature

Masters of French literature from the 1100's to the present rank among the greatest literary figures in the world. This table lists the leading French writers in chronological order. The table also includes a number of works and groups of poets important in the history of French literature during the Middle Ages.

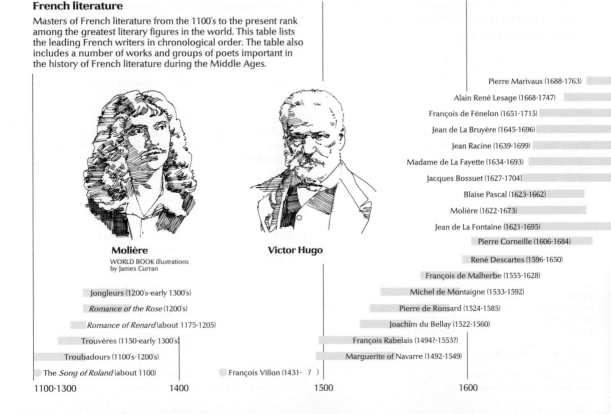

Molière
Victor Hugo
WORLD BOOK illustrations by James Curran

Pierre Marivaux (1688-1763)
Alain René Lesage (1668-1747)
François de Fénelon (1651-1715)
Jean de La Bruyère (1645-1696)
Jean Racine (1639-1699)
Madame de La Fayette (1634-1693)
Jacques Bossuet (1627-1704)
Blaise Pascal (1623-1662)
Molière (1622-1673)
Jean de La Fontaine (1621-1695)
Pierre Corneille (1606-1684)
René Descartes (1596-1650)
François de Malherbe (1555-1628)
Michel de Montaigne (1533-1592)
Pierre de Ronsard (1524-1585)
Joachim du Bellay (1522-1560)
François Rabelais (1494?-1553?)
Marguerite of Navarre (1492-1549)

Jongleurs (1200's-early 1300's)
Romance of the Rose (1200's)
Romance of Renard (about 1175-1205)
Trouvères (1150-early 1300's)
Troubadours (1100's-1200's)
The *Song of Roland* (about 1100)
François Villon (1431- ?)

1100-1300   1400   1500   1600

more cynical vein about 1275 to 1280.

Lais and *contes* were short verse tales about chivalry, love, and the supernatural. Lais were based on Celtic sources. Contes were generally based on Latin sources. The poet Marie de France wrote many important lais in the late 1100's.

Fabliaux were short, usually humorous stories that were often satiric and sometimes coarse. The most famous are found in a collection called *Romance of Renard* (about 1175 to 1205), where animal characters satirize human society.

Early prose included romances that appeared later than verse romances and often told the same stories. Historical chronicles became a major form of prose literature. The best-known historical writers were Philippe de Commines, Jean Froissart, Jean de Joinville, and Geoffroy de Villehardouin.

Early drama was composed primarily in verse and dealt with religious themes. Religious dramas can be grouped into three types. *Mystery plays* dramatized scenes from the Scriptures. *Miracle plays* portrayed the intervention of the Virgin Mary or saints in human affairs. *Morality plays* were symbolic dramas intended to educate. *Secular* (nonreligious) comedies called *farces* developed as interludes during the performance of religious dramas. In the late 1200's, the dramatist Adam de la Halle wrote secular plays that attained high levels of psychological insight and striking effects of realism.

The Renaissance

The Renaissance was a period of European cultural history that began in Italy about 1300 and spread to other parts of Europe. In French literature, the Renaissance extended from the early 1500's to about 1600.

The French Renaissance was a flowering of learning and literature inspired by ancient Greek and Latin models and by developments in Italian art and literature. Writers and scholars called *humanists* played a major role in the Renaissance. Humanists combined learning in a wide range of fields with an increased interest in the individual and in worldly, rather than religious, concerns. See **Humanism.**

From 1494 to 1525, French armies invaded Italy. These invasions led to increased contact with Italian art and literature and with humanist scholars. These contacts helped stimulate the Renaissance in France. During the early 1500's, King Francis I and his sister Marguerite of Navarre served as patrons of humanists and other writers in their courts. Marguerite herself was a learned author. She based her collection of tales called the *Heptaméron* (1558) on *The Decameron* by the Italian Renaissance writer Giovanni Boccaccio in the mid-1300's.

François Rabelais was the most important fiction writer of the French Renaissance and one of the leading medical authorities of his day. His major work is *Gargantua and Pantagruel.* This exuberant, often bawdy, narrative in five parts was published between 1532 and 1564. Rabelais wrote in a quirky style that combined remarkable learning with scenes of crude and often violent physical farce. The work satirizes the legal, political, religious, and social institutions of the time.

The Pléiade was a group of seven poets who wanted to break with tradition to create a new kind of French poetry based on ancient Greek and Roman models.

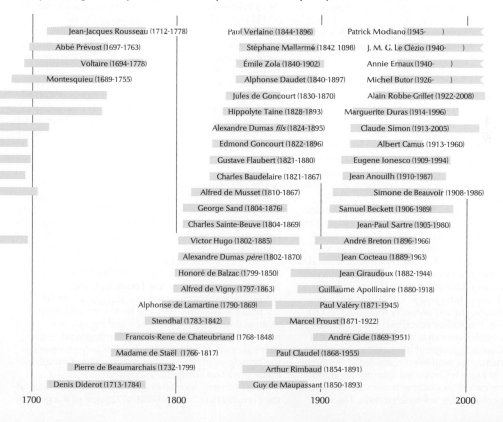

Jean-Jacques Rousseau (1712-1778)
Abbé Prévost (1697-1763)
Voltaire (1694-1778)
Montesquieu (1689-1755)

Paul Verlaine (1844-1896)
Stéphane Mallarmé (1842-1898)
Émile Zola (1840-1902)
Alphonse Daudet (1840-1897)
Jules de Goncourt (1830-1870)
Hippolyte Taine (1828-1893)
Alexandre Dumas *fils* (1824-1895)
Edmond Goncourt (1822-1896)
Gustave Flaubert (1821-1880)
Charles Baudelaire (1821-1867)
Alfred de Musset (1810-1867)
George Sand (1804-1876)
Charles Sainte-Beuve (1804-1869)
Victor Hugo (1802-1885)
Alexandre Dumas *père* (1802-1870)
Honoré de Balzac (1799-1850)
Alfred de Vigny (1797-1863)
Alphonse de Lamartine (1790-1869)
Stendhal (1783-1842)
Francois-Rene de Chateaubriand (1768-1848)
Madame de Staël (1766-1817)
Pierre de Beaumarchais (1732-1799)
Denis Diderot (1713-1784)

Patrick Modiano (1945-)
J. M. G. Le Clézio (1940-)
Annie Ernaux (1940-)
Michel Butor (1926-)
Alain Robbe-Grillet (1922-2008)
Marguerite Duras (1914-1996)
Claude Simon (1913-2005)
Albert Camus (1913-1960)
Eugene Ionesco (1909-1994)
Jean Anouilh (1910-1987)
Simone de Beauvoir (1908-1986)
Samuel Beckett (1906-1989)
Jean-Paul Sartre (1905-1980)
André Breton (1896-1966)
Jean Cocteau (1889-1963)
Jean Giraudoux (1882-1944)
Guillaume Apollinaire (1880-1918)
Paul Valéry (1871-1945)
Marcel Proust (1871-1922)
André Gide (1869-1951)
Paul Claudel (1868-1955)
Arthur Rimbaud (1854-1891)
Guy de Maupassant (1850-1893)

1700   1800   1900   2000

Pierre de Ronsard was the leader of the group. His poetry draws on mythology and ancient forms such as *pastorals* (poems about country life) to depict such themes as love and the passage of youth. His verse reflects an ability to look without flinching at the painful aspects of that experience, such as old age and death.

Joachim du Bellay was another member of the Pléiade. He was the first French poet to extensively use the sonnet form, which he borrowed from Italian Renaissance poets. Du Bellay wrote an important essay called *Defense and Glorification of the French Language* (1549). In the essay, du Bellay "defended" French as a suitable language for poetry against those who favored Latin, the language used not only by Roman poets but also by most writers throughout the Middle Ages.

Étienne Jodelle was a dramatist and a member of the Pléiade. He wrote what has been called the first original French comedy, *Eugène* (1552), and the first tragedy, *Cleopatra Prisoner* (1552).

Lyon. Another group of poets, including Maurice Scève and Pernette du Guillot, arose in the southern city of Lyon. Scève's poetry is remarkable for the complexity of its grammar and images. His major work is a carefully crafted series of 459 *dizaines* (10-line stanzas) titled *Délie* (1544). *Délie* celebrates the poet's love for a woman, sometimes thought to have been the poet Pernette du Guillot. Du Guillot's writings frequently played on the erotic possibilities of a shared language between lovers.

Michel de Montaigne created the personal essay as a literary form. A personal essay is written in an informal, conversational style. Montaigne's essays were shaped by a broad classical education. They were intensely self-examining, loosely organized meditations on such topics as education, travel, death, customs, knowledge, and the author himself. A strong but forgiving skepticism about human nature runs through Montaigne's writings.

The Classical age

The reigns of King Louis XIII and especially King Louis XIV are known as the *Classical age* in French literature. This period, from about 1600 to the early 1700's, is widely considered the high point in French literature.

Classical writers did not reject the ideals of the Renaissance. However, the period developed a greater spirit of order and refinement. French writers especially emphasized reason and the intellect in analyzing ideas and human behavior. See **Classicism.**

Classical poetry. François de Malherbe was the first important Classical poet and the most influential. During the early 1600's, Malherbe wrote clear, rational, sober poetry that laid the basic style for Classical verse. Jean de La Fontaine and Nicolas Boileau-Despreaux were also leading Classical poets. La Fontaine wrote a famous collection of moralizing tales about animal characters in clear, insightful, often biting verse called *Fables* (1668-1694). Boileau wrote *The Art of Poetry* (1674). In this critical work in verse, the author described the principles of moderation and nobility of style that characterized the aspirations of Classical poetry of his time.

Classical drama has long been considered the greatest expression of French Classicism. During this period, a 12-syllable line called *alexandrine* was established as the dominant poetic meter in French drama. The most famous authors of Classical drama were Pierre Corneille, Jean Racine, and Molière.

Corneille was the first great Classical writer of tragedy. His plays present noble characters involved in seemingly insoluble conflicts of duty, loyalty, and love. Corneille stressed the importance of the will, self-control, honor, and freedom. His tragedies include *The Cid* (1636 or 1637), *Horace* (1640), and *Polyeucte* (1642).

Racine was recognized in his own time as the greatest writer of Classical tragedy. His plays show characters in the grip of passions they cannot control. Racine reworked ancient Greek and Roman subjects in such masterpieces as *Andromaque* (1667) and *Phèdre* (1677). He also adapted Biblical themes, as in *Athalie* (1691).

Molière was the leading writer of comedy in French drama. His most effective plays are satires that present strong characters in conflict with social conventions. Molière wrote his finest comedies in the mid-1660's. They include *Tartuffe, Don Juan,* and *The Misanthrope.*

Classical prose. Two philosophers wrote works that rank as masterpieces of French Classical prose. René Descartes wrote *Discourse on Method* (1637), which laid the groundwork for much later French philosophy and esthetics. Initially known as a mathematician, Blaise Pascal wrote influential prose works that reveal his deep Christian faith. Pascal's best-known religious work is a collection of reflections called *Pensées.* The work was first published in 1670, after Pascal's death, but a complete edition did not appear until 1844.

A group of writers called *moralists* described human conduct and manners in letters, sayings called *maxims,* and other prose forms. The *Reflections* (1664) by the Duc de La Rochefoucauld are a particularly strong example of this style, which can be psychologically penetrating, bitterly cynical, and brilliantly concise. The satire *The Characters of Theophrastus* (1688) by Jean de La Bruyère combines maxims with literary portraits of the people and social types of the day.

Madame de La Fayette wrote one of the first important novels in French literature, *The Princess of Clèves* (1678). The novel has been praised for its psychological analysis and skillful construction. Its theme of passionate love held in check would influence later writers, including Jean-Jacques Rousseau.

The Enlightenment

The 1700's in France are often called the Enlightenment, or the Age of Reason. During this century, progressive thinkers emphasized reason as the best way to learn truth. They were inspired by discoveries in the sciences, which indicated that natural events conform to intelligible, underlying laws. Much of the literature of this period was produced by philosophical thinkers called *philosophes,* especially Voltaire, Denis Diderot, and Jean-Jacques Rousseau. See **Enlightenment.**

Voltaire was the most famous and controversial literary figure of his time. He used his talents and reputation as an author to fight intolerance and bigotry and to promote rationalism. Voltaire's most famous work is the satirical novel *Candide* (1759). He also helped develop the principles of modern historical writing through his many works on European and world history.

Denis Diderot is chiefly remembered as the editor of the French *Encyclopédie* (1751-1772), one of the great intellectual achievements of the Enlightenment. The *Ency-clopédie* was a collection of learned articles by writers in many fields. He was also known for his fiction, such as his novel *Jacques the Fatalist and His Master* (1778-1780).

Jean-Jacques Rousseau proposed changes in French society in his novel *The New Heloise* (1761) and in education in the novel *Émile* (1762). Rousseau's autobiographical *Confessions* (published in 1782 and 1789, after his death) helped create the modern literature of self-analysis. Rousseau's sensitivity to nature helped reintroduce a meditative and lyrical feeling into French literature. This sensitivity also influenced his writings on politics and social order, such as *Discourses* (1750 and 1755) and *The Social Contract* (1762).

The Marquis de Sade was little known in his own time and disdained by later generations. But in the 1900's, he came to be considered one of the Enlightenment's great writers. His cruel pornographic novels, such as *Philosophy in the Boudoir* (1795), mock the optimistic visions of nature and social order promoted by writers of his day.

Montesquieu, who was also known for his political writings, wrote witty social criticism in his *Persian Letters* (1721). Alain René Lesage produced a famous satirical novel, *Gil Blas* (1715-1735). The Abbé Prévost composed a popular sentimental novel, *Manon Lescaut* (1731). Pierre de Beaumarchais wrote the satirical comedies *The Barber of Seville* (1775) and *The Marriage of Figaro* (1784). Both plays deal with the irrational nature of aristocratic privilege.

Romanticism

Romanticism was a movement that had its roots in the late 1700's and flourished during the early and mid-1800's. Romanticism was partly a reaction against Classicism and the Enlightenment. Romantic writers rejected what they considered to be the excessive rationalism and lifeless literary forms of previous periods. The Romantics emphasized the emotions and the imagination over reason, and they promoted freer forms of literary expression. The writer's personality was often the most important element in a work. See **Romanticism.**

The Preromantics. French Romanticism was influenced by earlier Romantic movements in England, Spain, and especially Germany. A number of French writers, called Preromantics, also helped shape the movement during the late 1700's and 1800's.

Jean-Jacques Rousseau was also an important forerunner of Romanticism because of his interest in self-examination, his sensitivity to the natural world, and the importance he gave to feeling and spontaneity. Rousseau also influenced the Romantics with his lyrical prose style and his depiction of passionate but frustrated love.

François-René de Chateaubriand exerted a tremendous influence through his fiction. The feelings of boredom, loneliness, and grief that dominate his writings became essential elements of Romantic literature.

Madame de Staël influenced French Romantic critical theory with *On Literature* (1800). She introduced German Romanticism into France in *On Germany* (1810). The poet André Chenier incorporated several technical elements into his verse that were adopted by Romantic poets.

Romantic poetry is generally considered to have begun in France with the 1820 publication of *Poetic Meditations* by Alphonse de Lamartine. His melancholy poems dealt with nature, love, and solitude.

Victor Hugo was considered by the people of his day to be the greatest figure in French Romanticism, excelling as a poet, dramatist, and fiction writer. Hugo's *Odes and Various Poems* (1822) demonstrate a mastery of the 12-syllable alexandrine line combined with unconventional rhythmic effects. Many of his poems have a colorful, exotic quality. Hugo's later collections, such as *Leaves of Autumn* (1831) and *The Contemplations* (1856), are more personal and meditative.

Alfred de Vigny is best known for *Antique and Modern Poems* (1826). The poems are philosophical and often dramatic, stressing human unhappiness and the loneliness of the superior individual.

Alfred de Musset had great lyrical gifts. His melancholy and musical poems concern love, suffering, and solitude. In his lyrics called *Nights* (1835-1837), Musset described the anguish he suffered over a lost love.

Romantic drama dealt with historical subjects and melodramatic situations, often mixing comedy with tragedy. The dramas emphasized color and spectacle, unlike the more controlled dramas of Classicism and the Enlightenment. Victor Hugo wrote the first significant Romantic play, the historical drama *Hernani* (1830). Vigny's *Chatterton* (1835) featured a popular character in Romantic literature, the neglected artist. Musset wrote sophisticated comedies noted for their verbal brilliance.

Romantic fiction. Alexandre Dumas *père* (the elder) wrote the famous historical novel *The Three Musketeers* (1844), set during the reign of King Louis XIII in the 1600's. Victor Hugo's *The Hunchback of Notre Dame* (1831) showed the Romantic taste for the Middle Ages. It also reflects his lifelong attempts to correct social injustices through the power of literature.

Some Romantic writers moved toward a more realistic style of fiction. Such authors as Honoré de Balzac, George Sand, and Stendhal retained many Romantic characteristics in their work. But they modified their Romanticism with attempts to portray objective natural and social conditions of human life.

Beginning in 1829, Balzac wrote almost 100 novels and stories that were collected as *The Human Comedy* (1842-1848). In this series, the author attempted to describe the entire French society of his time.

George Sand was the pen name of a Frenchwoman who began her literary career by writing novels of love and passion, such as *Indiana* (1832) and *Lélia* (1833). Later, she turned to rural subjects, especially in her novel of country life, *The Devil's Pool* (1846).

Stendhal was a master psychologist who liked passionate, strong characters and melodramatic situations. He used a clear and ironic style to portray the struggle between passion and calculating ambition. His two best-known works are *The Red and the Black* (1830) and *The Charterhouse of Parma* (1839).

Gautier and Nerval. Théophile Gautier and Gérard de Nerval stand out among the second generation of Romantic writers. Gautier was distinguished by the verve and dry humor of his prose and the lyricism of his poetry. His fiction includes several supernatural tales and the novel *The Spiritualist* (1866). The collection of poems called *Enamels and Cameos* (1852) represent his mastery of verse technique. Gautier coined the term "Art for art's sake," which would become a rallying cry for

for defending the independent value of artistic creation.

Nerval's early poetry was distinguished by its musical lyricism, while his later poems turned inward onto a personal world of spiritualism. His prose includes a collection of short fiction called *The Daughters of Fire* (1854). Many of these short pieces are based on autobiographical material and create dreamlike effects. Nerval wrote *Aurélia* (1855), one of the most important first-person accounts of madness in the French language.

Realism

Realism was a literary doctrine that emerged partly as a reaction against Romanticism. The Realists believed that art should reproduce life accurately, honestly, and objectively. By the mid-1800's, Realism dominated French literature. See **Realism.**

Gustave Flaubert was the major representative of French Realism. He followed Balzac in his love of detail and his careful observation of human behavior. For his novel *Madame Bovary* (1856), Flaubert deliberately chose an ordinary subject—a dull country doctor and his shallow wife. In spite of its seemingly tedious subject, *Madame Bovary* was condemned as obscene and Flaubert was brought to trial on its account.

Guy de Maupassant became known for his Realistic short stories, which showed him to be a keen observer of human behavior with a cruel streak. Many of his stories portray provincial life in Normandy and the frustrated existence of petty civil servants in Paris.

There were two main types of Realistic drama in France. One was the *well-made play,* which emphasized plot and suspense. The comedies of Eugène Scribe were the best examples. The other type was the *problem play* or *thesis play.* Most dealt with social problems, such as divorce and legal injustice. The leading writers of problem plays were Émile Augier, Eugène Brieux, and Alexandre Dumas *fils* (the younger).

Naturalism

During the late 1800's, a movement called Naturalism developed as an extreme form of Realism. Naturalistic writers emphasized the sordid and coarse aspects of human conduct. The typical Naturalistic work is pessimistic and often criticizes social injustice. See **Naturalism.**

Émile Zola was the leading French Naturalistic writer. He proposed to treat fiction as a "laboratory" in which the laws of human behavior could be discovered. Zola created masterpieces of description and social criticism in his series of 20 novels called *The Rougon-Macquart* (1871-1893). The novels follow the members of a single extended family through extremes of fortune, misery, depravity, and unrelenting struggle.

The brothers Edmond and Jules de Goncourt collaborated on *Germinie Lacerteux* (1864), a somber novel about a servant girl who leads a life of vice. But the brothers were better known for their *Journal,* a record of the literary and social life of Paris from 1851 to 1896.

Henri Becque was the most important Naturalistic playwright. His drama *The Vultures* (1882) is a bitter exploration of ruthless human conduct.

Symbolism

French Symbolism was a literary movement of the late 1800's. The term Symbolism has also been applied to the work of French writers who did not belong to the movement but were associated with it. See **Symbolism.**

The key figures in the Symbolist movement were the poets Charles Baudelaire, Stéphane Mallarmé, Paul Verlaine, and Arthur Rimbaud. They wanted to liberate the techniques of poetry from traditional styles to create freer verse forms. The Symbolists believed poetry should suggest meanings through impressions, intuitions, and sensations rather than attempt to capture an elusive reality through straightforward descriptions. Much of their poetry was personal and obscure.

Charles Baudelaire was the forerunner of Symbolism. His *The Flowers of Evil* (1857) is a collection of about 100 related poems. The work reflects Baudelaire's somber fascination with humanity and its vices. His belief that even the lowest aspects of the human condition could give birth to beauty is captured in the collection's title.

Stéphane Mallarmé was the most influential of the Symbolist poets and theorists. His writings are remarkable for their difficult syntax, which often presents readers with impossible choices among different meanings. The most famous of his poems are "The Afternoon of a Faun" (1876) and "A Throw of the Dice "(1897).

Paul Verlaine wrote simple, melodious verse that is delicate, graceful, and musical. In *Songs Without Words* (1874), he tried to create a sense of music in verse.

Arthur Rimbaud was a boy genius. He was producing highly original poetry at the age of 16. At the age of about 19, Rimbaud composed *A Season in Hell* (1873), an autobiographical collection of prose and verse that describes his tortured spiritual experiences.

The 1900's

The early years. Four authors dominated French literature during the early 1900's. They were Paul Claudel, André Gide, Paul Valéry, and Marcel Proust. All were born about 1870, and all passed through a Symbolist phase in their early careers. By 1920, each was recognized as a significant literary figure.

Claudel wrote drama, poetry, criticism, and religious commentary that reflected his strong Roman Catholic beliefs. Claudel's poetry is filled with bold metaphors, violent emotions, and flowery language. However, his best-known works are his religious plays, notably *Break of Noon* (written in 1906) and *The Tidings Brought to Mary* (1912).

Gide was a novelist who generated controversy because of his unorthodox views on religion, families, sexuality, and morality. His fiction won praise for its stylistic innovations and psychological insights into character. In 1909, Gide helped found *The New French Revue,* the leading French literary journal of the early 1900's.

Proust was perhaps the most respected French novelist of the 1900's. His monumental novel *Remembrance of Things Past* was published in seven parts from 1913 to 1927. The novel is a highly personal and poetic work as well as a brilliant study of character and social manners.

Valéry's poetry shows the influence of the rational tradition in French literature. He stressed emotional control and classical forms. His works include the long poem *The Young Fate* (1917) and lyrics collected in *Charms* (1922). He was also an influential literary critic.

Surrealism was a movement founded in 1924 by a group of writers and painters in Paris. The Surrealists explored unconscious thought processes, especially dreams, which they believed must be integrated into rational, waking existence to create a full human experience (see **Surrealism**). The chief theorist and leader of the Surrealists was André Breton. The leading poets were René Char, Paul Éluard, and Louis Aragon. Their themes tended to focus on love and other subjective states, which they expressed through striking associations of words and visual images.

Existentialism was a philosophy that strongly influenced French literature after World War II (1939-1945). Jean-Paul Sartre, the leading Existential writer, became famous for such plays as *No Exit* (1944) and *Dirty Hands* (1948) as well as for philosophical writings and criticism. His works explore moral and political topics, especially the problems of freedom and responsibility. His novel *Nausea* (1938), for example, examines the disturbing consequences of confronting existence itself. Simone de Beauvoir helped popularize Existentialist ideas in such works as *For a Morality of Ambiguity* (1947). Albert Camus was not strictly an Existentialist. However, Camus explored similar ethical and moral problems in such works as the novels *The Stranger* (1942) and *The Plague* (1947) and the long essay *The Myth of Sisyphus* (1942).

Developments in drama. Several novelists and poets contributed to French drama in the mid-1900's, including Sartre and Camus. Other leading playwrights were Jean Giraudoux, Jean Cocteau, and Jean Genet. Giraudoux wrote in a witty, urbane, artificial style. His best-known plays investigate the nature of love or protest against war and greed. Cocteau became known for reworking mythological subjects. Genet drew on ritual to portray characters who were social outsiders.

A movement called the Theater of the Absurd emerged in France in the 1950's. Playwrights in this movement tried to dramatize what they believed was the essentially meaningless nature of life. The leading Absurdists were Samuel Beckett and Eugene Ionesco. Beckett was Irish and Ionesco was Romanian, but they both wrote in French, and their most significant works were first staged in Paris.

The middle and late 1900's. A major development was the New Novel. Its chief representatives included Alain Robbe-Grillet, Michel Butor, Nathalie Sarraute, and Claude Simon. These writers did not apply an external narrative framework to structure the events in their novels. Instead, they tended to develop their novels out of the characters' perceptions of those events. This led to jarring effects of time and perspective.

In the 1970's, a feminist movement appeared in French literature. It was inspired, in part, by Simone de Beauvoir's *The Second Sex* (1949). Marguerite Duras and Hélène Cixous ranked among the leading French feminist writers of the late 1900's and early 2000's. Monique Wittig, an extreme feminist writer, believed the language of past literature represented chiefly a masculine point of view. She tried to replace the masculine language with a feminine one.

In the 1970's and 1980's, French literary criticism was heavily influenced by the philosophical movement called *deconstruction.* Deconstructionist authors focused on how literary techniques contradict intended meaning in texts. The writers questioned the boundaries between literature and other fields, such as philosophy.

Jacques Derrida was the leading deconstructionist.

Recent French literature

During the 1970's and 1980's, the New Novel became less important. Some novelists turned to other art forms. For example, Sarraute concentrated largely on drama, and Robbe-Grillet wrote and directed motion pictures. Many writers continued to produce fiction, however, and the novel remained the dominant literary form in France at the end of the 1900's, showing great diversity.

J.-M. G. Le Clézio wrote in a powerful, poetic style about people's struggles to understand the world despite the cold, technological nature of modern life. Le Clézio won the 2008 Nobel Prize in literature.

Some novelists, including Michel Tournier and Edmond Jabès, turned to existing myths or created their own mythlike worlds. Tournier often used stories from the Bible and other sources to examine issues of human identity and communication. Jabès was deeply influenced by Jewish mysticism. He examined the experiences and implications of the Holocaust, the systematic murder of the Jews by the Nazis during World War II (1939-1945). He also explored the limits of language.

Other writers used autobiographical material. Late in their careers, both Robbe-Grillet and Marguerite Duras used elements from their early lives in fictionalized autobiographies. In his novels, Patrick Modiano used the experiences of his family and his own past to deal with the topics of memory, Jewish identity, and the Nazi occupation of France during World War II. Jorge Sumprun drew on his experiences as a Spanish immigrant in France, a secret Communist, a resistance fighter, and a prisoner in a Nazi concentration camp to create a literature that explores social injustices. His writing style draws on philosophical speculation and complex narrative structures to investigate the nature of self-identity.

Some writers used fiction to challenge social conventions. Annie Ernaux has written about her own experiences to examine the differences between the working class and the middle class. Her novel *The Event* (2000) focuses on a young woman's secret abortion to describe women's sense of social exclusion, powerlessness, and solidarity with one another.

Some writers have drawn on stylistic experimentation, especially nonliterary writing and speech, to comment on society. Michael Houellebecq, in particular, has examined middle-aged longings and other sexual themes in an unemotional style that often borrows from the language of commerce and publicity. Lydie Salvayre has used grotesque characterizations and extreme situations to portray social oppression. She also incorporates the language of judicial procedures in her writing, which creates an effect that is realistic and alienating.

Poetry continued to be important in the late 1900's and early 2000's. Yves Bonnefoy wrote brief, philosophical poems in a complex, compact language. The powerful, difficult poems of Jean-Claude Renard often reflected almost mystical experiences.   Jonathan Strauss

Related articles in *World Book* include:

Early French literature

Chrétien de Troyes	Roland	Trouvère
	Troubadour	Villon, François
Froissart, Jean		

The Renaissance

Du Bellay, Joachim	Montaigne,	Renaissance
Humanism	Michel de	Ronsard, Pierre de
Marot, Clement	Rabelais, François	

The Classical age

Boileau-Despréaux, Nicolas	La Fayette, Madame de
Classicism	La Fontaine, Jean de
Corneille, Pierre	La Rochefoucauld, Duc de
Cyrano de Bergerac, Savinien	Malherbe, François de
de	Molière
Descartes, René	Pascal, Blaise
Fénelon, François de S.	Perrault, Charles
La Bruyère, Jean de	Racine, Jean

The Enlightenment

Beaumarchais, Pierre de	Philosophes
Diderot, Denis	Rousseau, Jean-Jacques
Enlightenment	Sade, Marquis de
Marivaux, Pierre	Voltaire
Montesquieu	

Romanticism

Balzac, Honoré de	Romanticism
Chateaubriand, François de	Rostand, Edmond
Dumas, Alexandre, *pere*	Rousseau, Jean-Jacques
Gautier, Théophile	Sand, George
Hugo, Victor	Staël, Madame de
Lamartine, Alphonse de	Stendhal
Mérimée, Prosper	Vigny, Alfred
Musset, Alfred de	Villiers de l'Isle-Adam, Comte
Nerval, Gérard de	de

Realism and Naturalism

Brieux, Eugène	Naturalism
Daudet, Alphonse	Realism
De Maupassant, Guy	Sainte-Beuve, Charles
Dumas, Alexandre, *fils*	Scribe, Augustin Eugène
Flaubert, Gustave	Verne, Jules
France, Anatole	Zola, Émile
Mistral, Frédéric	

Symbolism

Baudelaire, Charles	Rimbaud, Arthur
Maeterlinck, Maurice	Symbolism
Mallarmé, Stéphane	Verlaine, Paul

The 1900's

Anouilh, Jean	Gide, André
Apollinaire, Guillaume	Giraudoux, Jean
Beauvoir, Simone de	Ionesco, Eugène
Beckett, Samuel	Malraux, André
Breton, André	Mauriac, François
Camus, Albert	Maurois, André
Céline, Louis-Ferdinand	Prévert, Jacques
Claudel, Paul	Proust, Marcel
Cocteau, Jean	Rolland, Romain
Colette	Saint-Exupéry, Antoine de
Derrida, Jacques	Sartre, Jean-Paul
Existentialism	Surrealism
Foucault, Michel	Valéry, Paul
Genet, Jean	

Other related articles

Drama	French language	Philosophy
Epic	Novel	Poetry
French Academy		

Outline

I. Early French literature
   A. Lyric poetry   C. Early prose
   B. Narrative poetry   D. Early drama
II. The Renaissance
   A. François Rabelais   C. Lyon
   B. The Pléiade   D. Michel de Montaigne

III. The Classical age
   A. Classical poetry   C. Classical prose
   B. Classical drama
IV. The Enlightenment
V. Romanticism
   A. The Preromantics   D. Romantic fiction
   B. Romantic poetry   E. Gautier and Nerval
   C. Romantic drama
VI. Realism
VII. Naturalism
VIII. Symbolism
IX. The 1900's
   A. The early years
   B. Surrealism
   C. Existentialism
   D. Developments in drama
   E. The middle and late 1900's
X. Recent French literature

French Polynesia, *PAHL uh NEE zhuh,* is a French overseas possession that lies in the South Pacific Ocean. For location, see **Pacific Islands** (map). French Polynesia consists of more than 120 islands scattered over an area about the size of Western Europe. These islands consist of the Austral, Gambier, Marquesas, Society, and Tuamotu island groups. Papeete, on Tahiti—one of the Society Islands—is the capital of French Polynesia.

About 70 percent of the islands' people are Polynesians. Tourism, agriculture, and fishing are important economic activities. The chief products include *copra* (dried coconut meat), pearls, fish, and tropical fruits and vegetables.

French Polynesia is a political unit of France called an *overseas collectivity.* In 2004, France also granted the islands the designation of *overseas country.* The islanders elect a territorial assembly, which in turn elects the president of French Polynesia. The islands also send representatives to the French Parliament.   Nancy Davis Lewis

See also **Marquesas Islands; Society Islands; Tahiti; Tuamotu Islands.**

French Quarter. See New Orleans (Downtown New Orleans).

French Revolution brought about great changes in the society and government of France. The revolution, which lasted from 1789 to 1799, also had far-reaching effects on the rest of Europe. It introduced democratic ideals to France but did not make the nation a democracy. However, it ended supreme rule by French kings and strengthened the middle class. After the revolution began, no European kings, nobles, or other privileged groups could ever again take their powers for granted or ignore the ideals of liberty and equality.

The revolution began with a government financial crisis but quickly became a movement of reform and violent change. In one of the early events, a crowd in Paris captured the Bastille, a royal fortress and hated symbol of oppression. A series of elected legislatures then took control of the government. King Louis XVI was executed. Thousands of others, including his wife, Marie Antoinette, met the same fate in a period called the Reign of Terror. The revolution ended when Napoleon Bonaparte, a French general, took over the government.

Background. Various social, political, and economic conditions led to the French Revolution. These conditions included dissatisfaction among the lower and middle classes, interest in new ideas about government, and financial problems caused by the costs of wars.

Legal divisions among social groups that had existed for hundreds of years created much discontent. According to law, French society consisted of three groups called *estates.* Members of the clergy made up the first estate, nobles the second, and the rest of the people the third. The peasants formed the largest group in the third estate. Many of them earned so little that they could barely feed their families. The third estate also included the working people of the cities and a large and prosperous middle class made up chiefly of government officials, lawyers, and merchants.

The third estate resented certain advantages of the first two estates. The clergy and nobles did not have to pay most taxes. The third estate, especially the peasants, had to provide almost all the country's tax revenue. Many members of the middle class also were troubled by their social status. They were among the most important people in French society but were not recognized as such because they belonged to the third estate.

The new ideas about government challenged France's *absolute monarchy.* Under this system, the king had almost unlimited authority. He governed by *divine right*— that is, the monarch's right to rule was thought to come from God. There were some checks on the king, but these came mainly from the *parlements* (high courts). During the 1700's, French writers called *philosophes* and philosophers from other countries raised new ideas about freedom. Some of these thinkers, including Jean-Jacques Rousseau, suggested that the right to govern came from the people.

The financial crisis developed because France had gone deeply into debt to finance fighting in the Seven Years' War (1756-1763) and the American Revolution (1775-1783). By 1788, the government was almost bankrupt. The Parlement of Paris insisted that Louis XVI could borrow more money or raise taxes only by calling a meeting of the Estates-General. This body was made up of representatives of the three estates and had last met in 1614. Unwillingly, the king called the meeting.

The revolution begins. The Estates-General opened on May 5, 1789, at Versailles, near Paris. Most members of the first two estates wanted each of the three estates to take up matters and vote on them separately by estate. The third estate had as many representatives as the other two estates combined. It insisted that all the estates be merged into one national assembly and that each representative have one vote. The third estate also wanted the Estates-General to write a constitution.

Louis XVI and most delegates of the first two estates refused the demands of the third estate. In June 1789, the representatives of the third estate declared themselves the National Assembly of France. They gathered at a tennis court and pledged not to disband until they had written a constitution. This vow became known as the Oath of the Tennis Court. The king allowed the three estates to join together as the National Assembly. But he began to gather troops to break up the Assembly.

Meanwhile, the people of France also took action. On July 14, 1789, a huge crowd of Parisians rushed to the Bastille. They believed they would find arms and ammunition there for use in defending themselves against the king's army. The people captured the Bastille and began to tear it down. At the same time, leaders in Paris formed a revolutionary city government. Massive peasant uprisings against feudal lords also broke out in the countryside. A few nobles decided to flee France, and many more followed in the next five years. These people were called *émigrés* because they emigrated. The uprisings in town and countryside saved the National Assembly from being disbanded by the king.

The National Assembly. In August 1789, the Assembly adopted the Decrees of August 4 and the Declaration of the Rights of Man and of the Citizen. The decrees abolished some feudal dues that the peasants owed their lords, the tax advantages of the clergy and nobles, and regional privileges. The declaration guaranteed the same basic rights to all citizens, including "liberty, property, security, and resistance to oppression" as well as representative government.

The Assembly later drafted a constitution that made France a limited monarchy with a one-house legislature. France was divided into 83 regions called *departments,*

Destruction of the Symbols of the Monarchy, Place de la Concorde, August 10, 1793, an oil painting on canvas by Pierre-Antoine Demachy; Musée Carnavalet, Paris

Hatred of the monarchy in France increased because of King Louis XVI's efforts to end the revolution. Louis was executed on Jan. 21, 1793, and the revolution became more extreme. About seven months later, a crowd in Paris burned a crown and a throne that had belonged to the king, *shown here.*

each with elected councils for local government. But the right to vote and hold public office was limited to citizens who paid a certain amount of taxes.

The Assembly seized the property of the Roman Catholic Church. The church lands amounted to about a tenth of the country's land. Much of the church land was sold to rich peasants and members of the middle class. Money from the land sales was used to pay some of the nation's huge debt. The Assembly then reorganized the Catholic Church in France, required the election of priests and bishops by the voters, and closed the church's monasteries and convents. Complete religious tolerance was extended to Protestants and Jews. The Assembly also reformed the court system by requiring the election of judges. By September 1791, the National Assembly believed that the revolution was over. It disbanded at the end of the month to make way for the newly elected Legislative Assembly.

The Legislative Assembly. The new Assembly, made up mainly of representatives of the middle class, opened on Oct. 1, 1791. It soon faced several challenges. The government's stability depended on cooperation between the king and the legislature. But Louis XVI remained opposed to the revolution. He asked other rulers for help in stopping it, and plotted with aristocrats and émigrés to overthrow the new government. In addition, public opinion became bitterly divided. The revolution's religious policy angered many Catholics. Other people demanded stronger measures against opponents of the revolution.

The new government also faced a foreign threat. In April 1792, it went to war against Austria and Prussia. These nations wished to restore the king and émigrés to their positions. The foreign armies defeated French forces in the early fighting and invaded France. Louis XVI and his supporters clearly hoped that the invaders would win. As a result, angry revolutionaries in Paris and other areas demanded that the king be dethroned.

In August 1792, the people of Paris took custody of Louis XVI and his family and imprisoned them. Louis's removal ended the constitutional monarchy. The Assembly then called for a National Convention to be chosen in an election open to nearly all French males age 21 or older, and for a new constitution.

Meanwhile, French armies suffered more military defeats. Parisians feared that the invading armies would soon reach the city. Parisians also feared an uprising by the large number of people in the city's prisons. In the first week of September 1792, small numbers of Parisians took the law into their own hands and executed more than 1,000 prisoners. These executions, called the September Massacres, turned many people in France and Europe against the revolution. On September 20, French forces defeated a Prussian army in the Battle of Valmy. This victory, which prevented the Prussians from advancing on Paris, helped end the crisis.

The National Convention. The king's removal led to a new stage in the revolution. The first stage had been a liberal middle-class reform movement based on a constitutional monarchy. The second stage was organized around principles of democracy. The National Convention opened on Sept. 21, 1792, and declared France a republic. The republic's official slogan was "Liberty, Equality, Fraternity."

The Death of Marat (1793), an oil painting on canvas by Jacques Louis David; The Royal Museum of Fine Arts, Brussels, Belgium (SCALA/Art Resource)

The death of Jean-Paul Marat was an important event in the French Revolution. Charlotte Corday, a Girondist sympathizer, fatally stabbed the Jacobin leader while he took a bath.

Louis XVI was placed on trial for betraying the country. The National Convention found him guilty of treason, and a slim majority voted for the death penalty. The king was beheaded on the guillotine on Jan. 21, 1793. The revolution gradually grew more radical—that is, more open to extreme and violent change. Radical leaders came into prominence. In the Convention, they were known as the Mountain because they sat on the high benches at the rear of the hall. Leaders of the Mountain were Maximilien Robespierre, Georges-Jacques Danton, and Jean-Paul Marat. Their opponents were known as the Gironde because several came from a department of that name. The majority of the deputies in the Convention, known as the Plain, sat between the two rival groups. The Mountain dominated a powerful political club called the Jacobin Club.

Growing disputes between the Mountain and the Gironde led to a struggle for power, and the Mountain won. In June 1793, the Convention expelled and arrested the leading Girondists. In turn, the Girondists' supporters rebelled against the Convention. Charlotte Corday, a Girondist sympathizer, assassinated Jean-Paul Marat in July 1793. In time, the Convention's forces defeated the Girondists' supporters. The Jacobin leaders created a new citizens' army to fight rebellion in France and a war against other European nations. A military draft provided the troops, and rapid promotion of talented soldiers provided the leadership for this strong army.

Terror and equality. The Jacobin government was dictatorial and democratic. It was dictatorial because it suspended civil rights and political freedom in the emergency. The Convention's Committee of Public Safety took over actual rule of France, controlling local governments, the armed forces, and other institutions.

The Committee of Public Safety governed during the most terrible period of the revolution. Its leaders included Robespierre, Lazare Carnot, and Bertrand Barère. The Convention declared a policy of terror against rebels, supporters of the king or the Gironde, and anyone else who publicly disagreed with official policy. Hundreds of thousands of suspects were jailed. Courts handed down thousands of death sentences in what was called the Reign of Terror. Paris grew accustomed to the rattle of two-wheeled carts called *tumbrels* carrying people to the guillotine. The victims included Marie Antoinette, the widow of King Louis XVI.

The Jacobins, however, also followed democratic principles and extended the benefits of the revolution beyond the middle class. Many workers participated in political life for the first time. The Convention authorized free primary education, public assistance for the poor, price controls to protect consumers from inflation, and taxes based on income. It also called for the abolition of slavery in France's colonies. But most of these reforms were never fully carried out because of later changes in the government.

The revolution ends. In time, the radicals began to struggle for power among themselves. Robespierre succeeded in having Danton and other former leaders executed. Many people in France wished to end the Reign of Terror, the Jacobin dictatorship, and the democratic revolution.

Robespierre's enemies in the Convention finally attacked him as a tyrant on July 27 (9 Thermidor by the French calendar), 1794. He was executed the next day. The Reign of Terror ended after Robespierre's death. Conservatives gained control of the Convention and drove the Jacobins from power. Some of the democratic reforms of the past two years were abolished in what became known as the Thermidorian Reaction.

The Convention replaced the democratic constitution it had adopted in 1793 with a new one in 1795. The government formed under this new constitution was called the Directory, referring to the five-man executive directory that ruled along with a two-house legislature. France was still a republic, but once again only citizens who paid a certain amount of taxes could vote.

Meanwhile, France was winning victories on the battlefield. French armies had pushed back the invaders and crossed into Belgium, Germany, and Italy.

The Directory began meeting in October 1795. But it was troubled by war, economic problems, and opposition from supporters of monarchy and former Jacobins. In October 1799, a number of political leaders plotted to overthrow the Directory. They needed military support and turned to Napoleon Bonaparte, a French general who had become a hero in a military campaign in Italy in 1796 and 1797. Bonaparte seized control of the government on Nov. 9 (18 Brumaire in the revolutionary calendar), 1799, ending the revolution.

The French Revolution brought France into opposition with much of Europe. The monarchs who ruled the other nations feared the spread of democratic ideals. The revolution left the French people in extreme dis-

agreement about the best form of government for their country. By 1799, most were probably weary of political conflict altogether. However, the French Revolution created the long-lasting foundations for a unified state, a strong central government, and a free society dominated by the middle class and the landowners.

Rafe Blaufarb

Related articles in *World Book* include:

Biographies

Corday, Charlotte	Mirabeau, Comte de
Danton, Georges-Jacques	Napoleon I
Lafayette, Marquis de	Robespierre
Louis XVI	Roland de la Platière, M. J.
Marat, Jean-Paul	Sieyès, Emmanuel Joseph
Marie Antoinette	Talleyrand

Background and causes

Bastille	Rights of Man,
Divine right of kings	Declaration of the
Estates-General	Rousseau, Jean-Jacques
	Versailles, Palace of

Other related articles

Clothing (The 1700's)	Reign of Terror
Girondists	Swiss Guard
Guillotine	Terrorism (picture: The Reign
Jacobins	of Terror)
Marseillaise	Tuileries

Additional resources

Anderson, James M. *Daily Life During the French Revolution.* Greenwood, 2007.
Doyle, William. *Origins of the French Revolution.* 3rd ed. Oxford, 1999. *The Oxford History of the French Revolution.* 2nd ed. 2003.
Frey, Linda S. and Marsha L. *The French Revolution.* Greenwood, 2004
Neely, Sylvia. *A Concise History of the French Revolution.* Rowman & Littlefield, 2008.

French Somaliland. See Djibouti (country).

French West Africa was a federation of eight colonies in western Africa. France conquered and controlled the territories from 1895 to 1958. Dakar, now the capital of Senegal, was the capital. The eight colonies that made up French West Africa are now independent countries: Côte d'Ivoire, Dahomey (now Benin), French

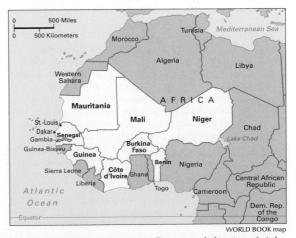

WORLD BOOK map

French West Africa, *shown in yellow,* was a federation of eight territories in western Africa until 1958. But now eight separate and independent countries cover this region.

Guinea (now Guinea), French Sudan (now Mali), Mauritania, Niger, Senegal, and Upper Volta (now Burkina Faso). For more detailed information about these countries, see their separate articles in *World Book.*

The land. French West Africa occupied 1,789,186 square miles (4,633,970 square kilometers), or about one-seventh of the African continent. It included most of the great bulge of Africa that juts into the Atlantic Ocean. An area of rolling plains, it has tropical rain forests along the southern coasts, a belt of thick grasslands across the center, the dry plains of the Sahel farther north, and the barren Sahara in the far north.

History. Before Europeans took control of what became French West Africa, the region's people were divided into many groups. Some were loose associations of families that lived in small areas without centralized authority. Other groups formed more elaborate states, with central governments and large populations.

Several great empires bordered the Sahara. The Ghana Empire was strongest during the A.D. 1000's. The Mali Empire reached its height in the 1300's. The Songhai Empire flourished in the 1500's.

The Portuguese were the first Europeans to explore the west African coast. They arrived in the mid-1400's. Then came the French, the Dutch, and the English. The Europeans were mainly interested in buying slaves they could sell in the Caribbean and America. In 1624, King Louis XIII of France granted a French company a charter to trade in Senegal. The French founded St. Louis, a city in Senegal, as a fortified trading post at the mouth of the Sénégal River in 1658.

Throughout the 1700's, Britain (now also called the United Kingdom) and France competed for control of this area. The French established a trading post at the mouth of the Sénégal River in 1638. In 1658, they built a fort there and founded Saint-Louis, now a city in Senegal. But France did not seriously impose its control in the African interior until the late 1800's. In 1895, France grouped its colonies in western Africa under the authority of a governor general. Dakar became the governor general's headquarters in 1902.

France proclaimed a constitution for the Federation of West Africa in 1904. But many areas remained outside French control. Some remained under military authority until after 1945.

In 1946, French West Africa became a federation of eight overseas territories within the French Union. France extended citizenship rights to the Africans, but gave only some of them the right to vote. In 1956, France gave all Africans in the federation the right to vote.

When France adopted a new constitution in 1958, French Guinea voted to leave the French Union and became an independent country. The other seven territories voted to remain associated with France within the new French Community, an organization that linked France and its overseas territories. But by the end of 1958, these territories had voted to become autonomous republics.

In 1959, French Sudan and Senegal united to form the Federation of Mali. They negotiated with France for full independence but agreed to remain in the French Community. However, the Federation of Mali broke up in August 1960, and French Sudan became the Republic of Mali. The other five republics then asked for complete independence. All of them had received their freedom by the end of 1960.   Dennis D. Cordell

Related articles in *World Book* include:

Arabs	Cote d'Ivoire	Niger
Benin	Guinea	Niger River
Berbers	Mali	Senegal
Burkina Faso	Mauritania	

French West Indies consist of several small islands at the eastern end of the Caribbean Sea (see **West Indies** [map]). They are part of the Lesser Antilles island chain. The French West Indies cover 1,123 square miles (2,908 square kilometers) and have a population of 918,000. They include Guadeloupe and Martinique, each of which is an overseas region and department of France, and St.-Barthélemy and St.-Martin, each of which is an overseas collectivity of France.   Gary Brana-Shute

See also **Guadeloupe; Martinique.**

Freneau, *fruh NOH,* **Philip** (1752-1832), was an American poet and journalist. He became known as the "Poet of the American Revolution" for the poetry he wrote attacking the British during the American Revolution (1775-1783). Freneau also wrote descriptive and imaginative poems about nature, including "The Wild Honey Suckle" (1786) and "The Indian Burying Ground" (1788).

Philip Morin Freneau was born on Jan. 2, 1752, in New York City. He was a sailor during the American Revolution and suffered greatly after being captured by the British. His experiences as a prisoner inspired the poem "The British Prison Ship" (1781).

Freneau was active in politics during much of his life. From 1791 to 1793, he edited the *National Gazette,* a newspaper that opposed the Federalist Party led by Alexander Hamilton. Freneau died on Dec. 18, 1832.   Edward W. Clark

See also **Columbia** (U.S.).

Frequency. See Electric generator (A simple generator); Sound (Frequency and pitch).

Frequency modulation, *FREE kwuhn see MAHJ uh LAY shuhn,* usually called simply FM, is a method of sending sound signals on radio waves. Frequency modulation and *amplitude modulation* (AM) are the two chief means of transmitting music and speech.

A radio wave has a fixed *frequency,* the number of times the wave vibrates per second. It also has a definite *amplitude* (size). In frequency modulation, the frequency of the transmitting radio wave is made higher or lower to correspond with the vibrations of the sound to be sent. But the amplitude of the wave is not varied. In contrast, amplitude modulation keeps the frequency of the transmitting wave constant. But it changes the wave's amplitude in accordance with the vibrations of the sound signal being transmitted.

FM has some advantages over AM. It is relatively free of static from thunderstorms and of other types of interference that affect AM broadcasts. FM also provides a more faithful reproduction of music and speech.

One of the main uses of frequency modulation is FM radio broadcasting. The transmission of stereophonic programs ranks as an important development in this area. In FM stereo broadcasting, sound signals from two microphones or from both *channels* (transmission paths) of a stereo record are sent on the same radio wave. Transmitting a program by this method is called *multi-*

plexing. For the best results, a listener needs a special receiver that can "decode" the sounds from the two channels and send them through two separate speakers.

A commercial FM station can transmit special programs of uninterrupted music in addition to its regular or stereo broadcasts. Such programs provide pleasant background music for offices, restaurants, and stores.

Frequency modulation also has other uses. For example, television stations transmit the audio portion of their programs by this method. Telephone companies also use FM in *microwave radio relaying,* a system designed to send long-distance phone calls.

Edwin H. Armstrong, an American electrical engineer, invented frequency modulation in 1933. FM became widely used in the 1940's.   Richard W. Henry

See also **Radio** (How radio programs are broadcast); **Stereophonic sound system.**

Fresco, *FREHS koh,* is a painting made on damp plaster, using pigments that are mixed with water. *Fresco* is the Italian word for *fresh.* In a true fresco, called *buon fresco,* the artist paints on freshly laid plaster. In a less common type, called *fresco secco* (dry fresco), the artist paints on plaster that has been allowed to dry, and then moistened.

To make *buon fresco,* the artist usually first makes a drawing, called a *cartoon,* that is the exact size of the proposed picture. A smaller sketch in colors is also made. Then, fresh lime plaster—as much as can be painted in one day—is laid on the surface of the wall or ceiling that is to be decorated. The artist places the cartoon on the surface, traces the outline, and then is ready to begin painting.

After mixing the dry pigments with water, the painter brushes them onto the damp plaster. As the plaster sets, it binds the colors permanently to its surface. Work must proceed rapidly because the plaster will not hold colors that are applied after it has dried. At the end of the day, any unpainted plaster is cut away, making a clean edge for the next day's work.

The lime in the plaster bleaches many pigments that are suitable for other painting techniques. Only pigments that can resist the action of the lime can be used in fresco painting. Most are earth colors, whose tones are not as bright as those used in oil painting.

Fresco painting reached its height during the Italian Renaissance of the 1400's and 1500's. Among the most celebrated frescoes of that period are Michelangelo's decorations of the Sistine Chapel in the Vatican. Two Mexican artists, Diego Rivera and José Clemente Orozco, inspired a revival of fresco painting in the United States in the 1930's.   Roger Ward

Related articles in *World Book* include:
Angelico, Fra
Byzantine art (Frescoes and mosaics)
Correggio
Easter (picture: The Resurrection)
Ghirlandajo, Domenico
Giotto
Masaccio
Michelangelo
Mural
Orozco, José C.
Painting
Raphael
Renaissance (pictures)
Rivera, Diego
Simone Martini

Fresno, *FREHZ noh* (pop. 494,665; met. area pop. 930,450), is the main marketing, distribution, and financial center of central California. It lies in Fresno County, in the middle of the fertile San Joaquin Valley. For location, see **California** (political map).

Irrigation from the nearby Kings and San Joaquin rivers helps Fresno County lead the nation's counties in agricultural products sold. Farmers there grow over 200 crops. Grapes and almonds rank as the chief crops. The largest fig orchards in the United States flourish near Fresno. Almost all of the nation's raisins are produced in the Fresno area.

The packing, processing, and shipping of agricultural products is Fresno's chief industry. Other leading economic activities in the Fresno area include construction, retail trade, and the manufacturing of ceramics, chemicals, and farm machinery. Government employment is also an important part of the economy. Spending by tourists and conventioneers also contributes.

Downtown Fresno includes a civic center, a convention center, and the William Saroyan Theatre. The city is the home of the Fresno Art Museum, the Fresno Philharmonic, and the Fresno Grand Opera. Local universities and colleges include California State University, Fresno; Fresno Pacific University; and Fresno Pacific Biblical Seminary.

Yokuts Indians had lived in what is now the Fresno area for at least 8,000 years when Mexican ranchers ac-

Frescoes (1474) in the Ducal Palace of the Gonzaga family (SCALA/Art Resource)
Colorful frescoes decorated many palaces and public buildings of the Italian Renaissance. The Italian painter Andrea Mantegna painted the frescoes shown here in the palace of a duke.

quired land there in the 1840's. The United States captured the California territory from Mexico during the Mexican War (1846-1848).

The gold rush of 1849 attracted thousands of people to California. By 1860, investors were buying land in the Fresno area. Leland Stanford, Collis P. Huntington, Mark Hopkins, and Charles Crocker, the owners of the Central Pacific Railroad, were known as the "Big Four." They realized the area had farm potential. Under their direction, the Central Pacific built a rail line into the San Joaquin Valley. In 1872, the railroad company built the town of Fresno Station (now Fresno). Several irrigation canals were constructed during the 1870's and 1880's, and the town became a booming farm community. Fresno was incorporated as a city in 1885. In the last half of the 1900's, the development of agricultural industries helped create a population boom in Fresno. The city's population increased from 60,685 in 1940 to 494,665 in 2010. Fresno is the county seat of Fresno County and has a mayor-council government.   Robert Phelps

Freud, *froyd,* **Anna** (1895-1982), was an Austrian-born leader in the field of *child psychoanalysis,* the treatment of mental illness in children. Her work was influenced by the psychoanalytic theories of her father, the Austrian physician Sigmund Freud (see **Freud, Sigmund**).

Anna Freud believed that children go through various normal stages of psychological development. She maintained that psychoanalysts must have knowledge of these stages to diagnose and treat mental illness in children. Such knowledge, she believed, can best be obtained through research involving direct observation. Freud also believed that psychoanalytic principles should be applied to all child rearing and child care.

Freud was born in Vienna on Dec. 3, 1895. She did most of her research at the Hampstead Child Therapy Course and Clinic (now called the Anna Freud Centre), which she founded in London in 1947. The clinic's work includes treating children with mental illness and training workers in child therapy. Freud died on Oct. 9, 1982.

Hannah S. Decker

Freud, *froyd,* **Sigmund** (1856-1939), was an Austrian physician who revolutionized ideas on how the human mind works. Freud established the theory that unconscious motives control much behavior. His insights have helped millions of patients with mental illness. Freud's theories have also brought new approaches to child rearing and education and have provided new themes for authors and artists. Most people in Western society view human behavior at least partially in Freudian terms.

His life

Freud was born on May 6, 1856, in Freiberg, Moravia, a region now in the Czech Republic. He was the oldest of eight children, and his father was a wool merchant. When Freud was 4 years old, his family moved to Vienna, the capital of Austria. He graduated from the medical school of the University of Vienna in 1881. Freud later decided to specialize in *neurology,* the study and treatment of disorders of the nervous system.

In 1885, Freud went to Paris to study under Jean Martin Charcot, a famous neurologist. Charcot was working with patients who suffered from a mental illness then called *hysteria.* Some of these people appeared to be blind or paralyzed, but they actually had no physical defects. Charcot found that their physical symptoms could be relieved through hypnosis.

Freud returned to Vienna in 1886 and began to work extensively with hysterical patients. He gradually formed ideas about the origin and treatment of mental illness. Freud used the term *psychoanalysis* for both his theories and his method of treatment. When he first presented his ideas in the 1890's, other physicians reacted with hostility. But Freud eventually attracted followers, and by 1910, he had gained international recognition.

During the following decade, Freud's reputation continued to grow. But two of his early followers, Alfred Adler and Carl Jung, split with Freud and developed their own theories of psychology (see **Adler, Alfred; Jung, Carl G.**). In 1923, Freud published a revised version of many of his earlier theories. That same year, he learned he had cancer of the mouth. He continued his work, though the cancer made working increasingly difficult. In 1938, the Nazis gained control of Austria and began persecuting Jews. Freud, who was Jewish, fled to England with his wife and children. He died there of cancer on Sept. 23, 1939.

Freud's most important writings include *The Interpretation of Dreams* (1900), *Three Essays on the Theory of Sexuality* (1905), *Totem and Taboo* (1913), *Introductory Lectures on Psychoanalysis* (1917), *The Ego and the Id* (1923), and *Civilization and Its Discontents* (1930).

His theories

On behavior. Freud observed that many patients behaved according to drives and experiences of which they were not consciously aware. He thus concluded that the unconscious plays a major role in shaping behavior. He also concluded that the unconscious is full of memories of events from early childhood. Freud noted that if these memories were especially painful, people kept them out of conscious awareness. He used the term *defense mechanisms* for the methods by which individuals handled painful memories. Freud believed that patients used vast amounts of energy in forming defense mechanisms. Tying up energy could affect a person's ability to lead a productive life, causing an illness that Freud called *neurosis.*

Freud also concluded that many childhood memories dealt with sex. He believed that his patients' reports of sexual abuse by a parent were fantasies reflecting unconscious desires. He theorized that sexual functioning begins at birth, and that a person goes through several psychological stages of sexual development. Freud believed the normal pattern of psychosexual development is interrupted in some people. These people become *fixated* at an earlier, immature stage. He felt such fixation could contribute to mental illness in adulthood.

On the mind. Freud divided the mind into three parts: the *id,* the *ego,* and the *superego.* He recognized that each person is born with natural drives

Dr. W. Hoffer

Sigmund Freud

that he called *instincts,* such as sexual desires and the need to be aggressive. The id is the source of instincts, such as the desire for sexual pleasure. The ego resolves conflicts between instincts and external reality. For example, it determines socially appropriate ways to obtain physical satisfaction or to express aggression. The superego is a person's conscience. A person's ideas of right and wrong—learned from parents, teachers, and other people in authority—become part of the person's superego.

All people have some conflict among the three parts of the mind, but certain people have more conflict than others. For example, the superego might oppose angry behavior. In that case, the id and the superego would clash. If the parts of the mind strongly oppose one another, psychological disturbances result.

On treatment. At first, Freud treated neurotic patients by using the hypnotic techniques he had learned from Charcot and the Austrian physician Josef Breuer. But he later modified this approach and simply had patients talk about whatever was on their minds. He called this *free association.* By free associating—that is, by speaking freely—the patient sometimes came upon earlier experiences that contributed to the neurosis.

Often, however, the painful feelings that caused the neurosis were held in the unconscious through defense mechanisms. Freud then analyzed the random thoughts that had been expressed during free association. He did this in an effort to penetrate the patient's defense mechanisms. He also interpreted the patient's dreams, which he believed contained clues to unconscious feelings. Freud talked with the patient about the person's earlier experiences to understand the root of the problem. He paid particular attention to *transference,* the patient's shifting of painful feelings—hostility or love, for example—toward Freud himself. If the psychoanalyst could help the patient understand and deal with unpleasant feelings or painful memories, the symptoms of the neurosis might then disappear.

His influence

Freud was one of the world's most influential thinkers. He showed the crucial importance of unconscious thinking to all human thought and activity. Freud's strongest impact occurred in psychiatry and psychology. His work on the origin and treatment of mental illness helped form the basis of modern psychiatry. In psychology, Freud greatly influenced the field of abnormal psychology and the study of the personality.

Freud's theories on sexual development led to open discussion and treatment of sexual matters and problems. His stress on the importance of childhood helped teach the value of giving children an emotionally nourishing environment. His insights also influenced the fields of anthropology and sociology. Most social scientists accept his concept that an adult's social relationships are patterned after early family relationships.

In art and literature, Freud's theories influenced Surrealism (see **Surrealism**). Like psychoanalysis, Surrealistic painting and writing explore the inner depths of the unconscious mind. Freudian ideas have provided subject matter for authors and artists. Critics often analyze art and literature in Freudian terms.

Since the 1970's, many scholars and mental health professionals have questioned some of Freud's theories. Feminists attacked Freud because he seemed to believe that in some respects women were inferior to men. For example, he thought that women had weaker superegos than men and were driven by envy. Other people challenged the theory that patients' memories of early sexual abuse reflected fantasies rather than actual experiences.

As a result of such criticism, most scholars and psychoanalysts now take a more balanced approach to Freud's theories. They use the ideas and techniques from Freud that they find most useful without strictly following all of his teachings. No one, however, disputes Freud's enormous influence.   Hannah S. Decker

Related articles in *World Book* include:

Dream (The meaning and function of dreams)	Personality (Freud's psychoanalytic theory)
Libido	Phobia
Mythology (Psychological approaches)	Psychoanalysis
Neurosis	Psychotherapy (Psychodynamic-interpersonal psychotherapy)
Oedipus complex	Unconscious

Frey, *fray,* also called Freyr, *frayr,* was the god of agriculture and fertility in Norse mythology. He was the son of the god Njord and the giantess Skadi. Frey's twin sister, Freyja, was the Norse goddess of love and fertility (see **Freyja**). Both belonged to the Vanir, a special group of peace-loving gods.

Myths tell how Frey flew over the earth and water in a chariot pulled by a boar named Golden Bristle. These myths also tell how Frey sailed the seas in a ship large enough to hold all the gods. When Frey was not using his ship, he folded it up and carried it in his pocket.

Before Christianity came to Scandinavia, farmers traveled with an image of Frey in their wagons. They believed that this practice made their crops thrive. Many ancient Scandinavian families claimed to be descended from Frey because they thought his presence guaranteed a plentiful harvest and peace.   Carl Lindahl

Freyja, *FRAY uh,* was a goddess of love and fertility in Norse mythology. She also assisted women in childbirth. Her name is also spelled Freya or Freja. She was the daughter of the god Njord and the giantess Skadi. Her twin brother, Frey, was the Norse god of agriculture and fertility. Both Freyja and Frey belonged to a group of peace-loving gods and goddesses called the Vanir who made the earth fruitful. Freyja had many love affairs. According to Norse myths, Freyja originated a powerful kind of witchcraft called *seithr.* In seithr, certain women communicated with spirits to learn about the future. Freyja sometimes took the form of a bird and sometimes traveled in a wagon pulled by cats.   Carl Lindahl

See also **Frey.**

Friar is a member of a Roman Catholic religious order that originated as a *mendicant* order. Members of these religious communities lived as beggars. The term *friar* comes from a Latin word meaning *brother.* Mendicant orders were founded for active ministry, such as preaching and missionary or social work. Friars are more mobile than members of *monastic* orders, who spend most of their time in monasteries. Friars live in houses called *friaries.*

The church first officially recognized mendicant orders in the early 1200's. The orders multiplied rapidly until the second Council of Lyons (1274) suppressed all but four major ones. They were the Dominicans (called Black Friars or Preaching Friars), Franciscans (Gray Friars or Friars Minor), Carmelites (White Friars or Brothers of the Blessed Virgin Mary of Mount Carmel), and an order of Augustinians (Austin Friars or Hermits of Saint Augustine). A few lesser orders survived the suppression or were founded later. At first, mendicants renounced all possessions held in common and depended on *alms* (charity). But the Council of Trent (1545-1563) authorized the orders to hold goods in common.

David G. Schultenover

See also **Capuchins; Carmelites; Dominicans; Franciscans.**

Frick Collection, in New York City, is one of the world's great art museums. The Frick is especially noted for its masterpieces of European painting from the early Renaissance through the 1800's. It also exhibits outstanding collections of Italian bronzes and decorative arts. The Frick has a permanent collection of more than 1,000 works. In addition, the museum presents special exhibits as well as lectures and chamber music concerts, and it publishes scholarly catalogues and visitor guides. The Frick Art Reference Library is a leading research center for European and American art.

The Frick Collection is in the former mansion of industrialist Henry Clay Frick. The residence was completed in 1914 and bequeathed with its contents to a board of trustees at Frick's death in 1919. It opened to the public in 1935. Critically reviewed by the Frick Collection

Friction is a property that makes objects resist being moved across one another. If two objects with flat surfaces are placed one on top of the other, the top object can be lifted without any resistance except that of gravity. But if one object is pushed or pulled along the surface of the other, friction causes resistance.

Friction has many important uses. It makes the tires of an automobile grip the road. It enables a conveyor belt to turn on pulleys without slipping. You could not walk without friction to keep your shoes from sliding on the sidewalk. It is hard to walk on ice because the smooth surface of the ice produces less friction than a sidewalk, leading shoes to slip.

Friction also has disadvantages. It produces heat that may cause objects to wear. To prevent wear, oil and other lubricants are used to fill spaces between moving machinery parts. The lubricant reduces friction and makes the parts move more easily and produce less heat.

Kinds of friction. There are three chief kinds of friction. *Sliding* or *kinetic* friction is produced when two surfaces slide across each other, as when a book moves across a table. *Rolling friction* is the resistance produced when a body rolls over a surface. The friction between an automobile tire and a street is rolling friction. *Fluid friction* is the friction between a fluid and a solid.

Laws of friction. The basic law of friction says that the force needed to overcome friction is proportional to the total *normal,* or perpendicular, force pressing one surface against the other. That is, when the weight of a box being pulled across a floor is doubled, the force necessary to pull it doubles. When the box weighs four times as much, four times as much force must be used to pull it. The ratio between the force needed to move an object and the force pressing the surfaces together is called the *coefficient of friction* (C.F.).

This ratio can be written with the formula $C.F. = \frac{F}{P}$.

For example, suppose a force of 30 pounds (F) is needed to pull a block weighing 80 pounds (P) across a flat surface. The coefficient of friction (C.F.) equals 30 divided by 80, or 0.375. In the metric system, the force would be measured in units called *newtons*. Suppose a force of 45 newtons is needed to slide a block weighing 12.2 kilograms. The block presses down with a force of 120 newtons. This is because gravity at Earth's surface pulls with a force of 9.8 newtons for every kilogram an object weighs, and 9.8 times 12.2 equals 120. The coefficient of friction equals 45 divided by 120, or 0.375.

The coefficient of friction varies among materials. The C.F. of wood sliding on wood is between 0.25 and 0.50. Metal sliding on metal has a C.F. between 0.15 and 0.20. The frictional force due to rolling friction is about $\frac{1}{100}$ as much as that due to sliding friction. But various conditions, including hardness, smoothness, and diameter of the materials, affect rolling friction. Oil reduces friction. The C.F. for iron rolled on oiled wood, for example, is much less than 0.018. The kind of surface has almost no effect when it is covered with oil or other liquids. The friction then depends on the viscosity of the liquid and the relative speed between the moving surfaces.

Friction between two objects arises from electrical attraction among their molecules. The energy lost to friction is typically transferred to the microscopic motion of the molecules. The resulting increase in motion can be felt as heat. Michael Dine

See also **Bearing; Heat** (Friction).

Friday is the sixth day of the week. The name comes from the Anglo-Saxon word *Frigedaeg,* which means *Frigg's day.* Frigg was a goddess of love in Norse mythology. The Scandinavians considered Friday their luckiest day. But people today associate Friday the 13th with bad luck. One explanation for this belief is that Jesus Christ was crucified on Friday, and 13 men were present at the Last Supper. People have called Friday *hangman's day* because it once was the day for the execution of criminals. In memory of the Crucifixion, some Christians fast on Fridays, except on a feast day, such as Christmas. Christians observe *Good Friday* two days before Easter in memory of Christ's suffering. The Jewish Sabbath begins at sunset on Friday. Friday is also a holy day among Muslims. Muslims also celebrate the creation of Adam on Friday. Jack Santino

See also **Black Friday; Good Friday; Week.**

Friedan, *free DAN,* **Betty** (1921-2006), was an American writer and women's rights activist. She was a founder of the women's liberation movement, or the "second wave" of feminism. Friedan first gained widespread attention for *The Feminine Mystique* (1963). In the book, she examined the effects of societies that encourage women to be homemakers and discourage them from seeking careers outside the home.

In 1966, Friedan helped found the National Organization for Women (NOW) to fight for women's rights. She was a leader of the 1970 Women's Strike for Equality, which marked the 50th anniversary of woman suffrage in the United States. In 1971, she helped found the National Women's Political Caucus, which encourages women to seek political office.

Betty Naomi Goldstein was born on Feb. 4, 1921. She graduated from Smith College in 1942. In 1947, she married Carl Friedman, a theatrical producer, who later dropped the *m* from their last name to make it Friedan. She wrote an autobiography, *Life So Far* (2000). Friedan died on Feb. 4, 2006.

Melanie S. Gustafson

See also National Organization for Women.

Jack Lenahan, *Chicago Sun-Times*
Betty Friedan

Friedman, *FREED muhn,* **Milton** (1912-2006), was an American economist whose controversial theories sparked widespread debate. He was awarded the 1976 Nobel Prize in economics.

Friedman argued against government intervention in the economy, claiming that the forces of a free market will solve most economic problems. He rejected the theories of British economist John Maynard Keynes and his followers, who called for short-term changes in government spending to control the economy. Friedman urged a gradual, continuous increase in the money supply to promote economic growth. He set forth his theories in *A Monetary History of the United States, 1867-1960* (1963). Friedman and other economists who support such theories are *monetarists.* In his book *Capitalism and Freedom* (1962), Friedman proposed a *negative income tax.* Under this plan, families with incomes below a certain level would receive cash payments from the government.

Friedman was born on July 31, 1912, in New York City and received a Ph.D. degree from Columbia University. He taught economics at the University of Chicago from 1946 to 1976. In 1977, he became a senior research fellow at Stanford University's Hoover Institution on War, Revolution, and Peace. Friedman died on Nov. 16, 2006.

Robert E. Wright

Friel, *freel,* **Brian** (1929-   ), is a popular Irish dramatist. Friel's plays are set in Ireland, and they frequently deal with the mixed feelings that the Irish people have about their country and heritage. A large number of Friel's dramas also explore the strength of family ties, or the importance of community for rural people.

Friel's first successful work was *Philadelphia, Here I Come!* (1964). The play portrays a young man, divided

into a public and private self, leaving Ireland for a new life in the United States. He is torn between excitement about his opportunities and guilt about leaving his family and friends. *The Mundy Scheme* (1969) satirizes corrupt politicians and what the author sees as an Irish love for get-rich-quick schemes.

Two of Friel's major plays look at Ireland as a colonized nation. One,*The Freedom of the City* (1973), deals with the tragic conflict between Protestants and Roman Catholics in Northern Ireland. The other, *Translations* (1980), describes how English mapmakers in the 1830's replaced traditional Irish place names with English versions, thus robbing the people of ties to their past.

Dancing at Lughnasa (1990) shows a family overcoming hard times and disappointments with the help of Irish folk music and traditions. *Molly Sweeney* (1994) tells how two men try to restore the sight of a blind Irish girl. His other plays include *Lovers* (1967); *Volunteers* (1975); *Aristocrats* and *Faith Healer* (both 1979); *The Communication Cord* (1982); *Give Me Your Answer, Do!* (1997); *Afterplay* (2002); *Performances* (2003); and *The Home Place* (2005).

Friel was born on Jan. 9, 1929, in Omagh in Northern Ireland. He helped found the Field Day Theatre in Derry.

Thomas P. Adler

Friends, Religious Society of. See Quakers.

Frietchie, *FREECH ee,* **Barbara,** is the name of a woman who supposedly acted bravely to protect the Union flag against Confederate troops in 1862. The incident is known chiefly because it was dramatized in John Greenleaf Whittier's poem "Barbara Frietchie" (1863). It tells of Confederate General Stonewall Jackson leading his troops through Frederick, Maryland, during the American Civil War (1861-1865). When Jackson ordered the Union flag shot down, Frietchie restored it instantly. The 90-year-old woman's patriotic bravery embarrassed Jackson, who replied with the order:

"Who touches a hair of yon grey head,
Dies like a dog! March on!" he said.

The incident may have actually happened, considering that a woman named Barbara Fritchie (1766-1862) lived in Frederick. A reproduction of her home stands on the supposed site of the incident (see Maryland [Places to visit; picture]).

Sargent Bush, Jr.

Frigate, *FRIHG iht,* is a medium-sized warship used by many of the world's larger navies. Frigates chiefly escort other ships. They are also used for patrol duty. Frigates

WORLD BOOK illustration by George Suyeoka

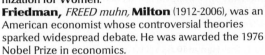

Frigates serve as patrol ships and as escorts for amphibious and merchant ships. The frigate shown here was designed for antisubmarine warfare.

are versatile ships. They can launch rockets and torpedoes against submarines. Some frigates have guided missiles for use against aircraft and surface ships. Some larger frigates can carry one or two antisubmarine helicopters. Frigates use radar and sonar to detect enemy aircraft, surface ships, and submarines.

All active frigates of the United States Navy belong to the *Oliver Hazard Perry* class. Frigates of this class have been *commissioned* (put into active service) since 1977. They can fire various kinds of missiles against ships, aircraft, and land targets. They also carry a 3-inch gun, torpedoes, and at least one helicopter. These ships are 445 feet (136 meters) long, and gas turbines propel them at more than 29 *knots* (nautical miles per hour).

In 1794, frigates became the first warships authorized by the United States Congress. The frigate *Constitution,* nicknamed *Old Ironsides,* ranks as one of the nation's most famous ships. It is docked at the Charlestown Navy Yard in Boston (see **Constitution** [ship]).

During World War II (1939-1945), the U.S. Navy had a class of escort ships called frigates. After the war, the Navy used the term *frigate* for large destroyer-type ships. In 1975, the Navy reclassified most of these ships as *cruisers.* More versatile vessels called *littoral combat ships* have begun to replace the Navy's frigate fleet.

Paul F. Johnston

See also **Cruiser.**

Frigatebird, *FRIHG iht burd,* is a sea bird with a large wingspread and unusually great powers of flight. People sometimes speak of it as the most graceful bird of the seas. It is also called *man-of-war bird.*

Frigatebirds live throughout the tropics. They are about 35 to 40 inches (90 to 100 centimeters) long, but their wings spread to about 8 feet (2.4 meters). Black feathers with a metallic sheen cover the upper part of their bodies. The females, or both sexes of some *species* (kinds), have white feathers on the underside. The young birds have white heads. In nesting season, the male grows a reddish pouch under his bill. He can inflate this pouch like a balloon and uses it in his mating display.

WORLD BOOK illustration by Trevor Boyer, Linden Artists Ltd.

Frigatebirds live in the tropics. The male, *bottom,* grows a reddish pouch during the nesting season.

Frigatebirds breed in colonies and build their nests on rocks, high cliffs, or trees on uninhabited islands. They eat fish, which they catch from the surface of the sea or steal from other birds.   James J. Dinsmore

Scientific classification. Frigatebirds make up the genus *Fregata.* The scientific name for the frigatebird of the coast of the southeastern United States is *Fregata magnificens.* The species *F. minor* and *F. ariel* are most common in the Pacific and Indian oceans.

See also **Bird** (picture: Birds of the ocean and the Antarctic).

Friml, *FRIHM uhl,* **Rudolf** (1879-1972), was one of the most popular composers of operettas of the early 1900's. Friml wrote more than 20 operettas, gaining immediate fame with *The Firefly* (1912), his first show. *Rose-Marie* (1924) became the most popular international hit of the 1920's. It features the ballad "Indian Love Call." Herbert Stothart also contributed to the score, and Otto Harbach and Oscar Hammerstein II wrote the book and lyrics. *The Vagabond King* (1925) contains the well-known "Song of the Vagabonds." Friml composed one of his most popular melodies for *The Ziegfeld Follies of 1923.* After lyrics were added, it became known as "The Donkey Serenade."

Friml was born on Dec. 7, 1879, in Prague, in what is now the Czech Republic, and studied with the famous Czech composer Antonín Dvořák. In 1901, Friml became the piano accompanist for the noted Czech violinist Jan Kubelik. Friml performed in America with Kubelik and as a piano soloist, settling in the United States in 1906. He became a citizen of the United States in 1925. Friml wrote light instrumental pieces for orchestra until he began composing operettas. In the early 1930's, musical tastes changed and the Romantic European style of Friml's compositions seemed outdated. He therefore gave up the theater and spent the rest of his life composing privately and performing piano concerts. Friml died on Nov. 12, 1972.   Ken Bloom

Frisbee, *FRIHZ bee,* is a plastic, saucer-shaped disk that skims through the air when flipped with the hand. It is used both in recreation and in organized sporting events. The word *Frisbee* is a trademark for a popular brand of the disk. Most disks measure from 8.5 to 11 inches (21 to 27 centimeters) in diameter, and weigh between 3.5 and 6.2 ounces (100 to 175 grams).

The disk can be thrown in many different ways to provide both rotational spin and forward motion. By controlling the angle of release, a player can make a disk curve, skip, hover, or travel in a straight line. Skilled players can catch a disk between the legs, behind the back, or on one finger. An experienced player can toss a disk 230 feet (70 meters) or farther. Several events have been developed involving competition in throwing and catching the disk.   Daniel McCulloch Roddick

Frisch, Karl von (1886-1982), an Austrian zoologist, was a pioneer in the field of animal behavior. Frisch and two naturalists—Konrad Lorenz of Austria and Nikolaas Tinbergen, who was born in the Netherlands—won the 1973 Nobel Prize in physiology or medicine.

Frisch's best-known work dealt with the communication system of bees. He discovered that bees "dance" in certain patterns to tell members of their hive where to find food. These patterns can indicate the distance and direction of food from the hive (see **Bee** [Swarming;

Finding food; diagram: Locating food]). Frisch also showed that fish can see colors. Scientists had previously thought fish were color-blind.

Frisch was born in Vienna on Nov. 20, 1886. He studied at the universities of Munich and Vienna and received a Ph.D. degree from the University of Vienna in 1910. From 1910 to 1958, he taught at several European universities. Frisch wrote many books, including *Bees: Their Vision, Chemical Senses, and Language* (1971) and *A Biologist Remembers* (1967), an autobiography. He died on June 12, 1982.   John A. Wiens

Frisch, Max (1911-1991), a Swiss author, became one of the leading writers in the German-speaking world in the last half of the 1900's. His novels and plays concern the problem of identity and the question of how individuals can find their true self.

According to Frisch, the images imposed on us by others, and the images we in turn impose on others, falsify and destroy the authenticity of human personality and individual existence. In his novels *I'm Not Stiller* (1954), *Homo Faber* (1957), and *Wilderness of Mirrors* (1964), Frisch showed the shallowness of how individuals view others and the inability to understand one's own identity. Frisch's plays, notably *Don Juan and the Love for Geometry* (1953), *The Firebugs* (1957-1958), and *Andorra* (1961), deal with the same themes.

Frisch was born on May 15, 1911, in Zurich. He died there on April 4, 1991.   Peter Gontrum

Frisch, Ragnar, *RAHNG nahr* (1895-1973), a Norwegian economist, shared the 1969 Nobel Prize in economics with Jan Tinbergen of the Netherlands. The two men received the award for their work on the development of mathematical models used in *econometrics* (mathematical analysis of economic activity). The Nobel Prize in economics was awarded for the first time in 1969.

Frisch was born in Oslo on March 3, 1895, and graduated from Oslo University. He served as a professor in social economy and statistics at the university from 1925 until his retirement in 1965. He led theoretical investigations concerning production, economic planning, and national accounting. He helped establish the Econometric Society in 1930 and was chief editor of its journal, *Econometrica,* until 1955. Frisch also advised various developing countries, including Egypt and India. He died on Jan. 31, 1973.   William R. Summerhill

Frist, Bill (1952-   ), a Republican politician from Tennessee, was a member of the United States Senate from 1995 to 2007. He served as the leader of the Republicans in the Senate from 2003 to 2007. Frist is also a surgeon.

In the Senate, Frist supported limiting the number of terms a member of Congress may serve. He sponsored legislation to increase funding for fighting AIDS in Africa and the Caribbean. He also supported efforts to eliminate special privileges for senators.

William Harrison Frist was born on Feb. 22, 1952, in Nashville. He earned a bachelor's degree from Princeton University in 1974 and an M.D. degree from Harvard Medical School in 1978. He served his residency at Massachusetts General Hospital from 1978 to 1984. Frist then worked as a heart transplant surgeon at Vanderbilt University. He founded the Vanderbilt Transplant Center in 1989. He is the author of *Transplant* (1989) and *When Every Moment Counts: What You Need to Know About Bioterrorism from the Senate's Only Doctor* (2002). He

also is licensed as a commercial pilot.   Jeremy D. Mayer

Fritillary, *FRIHT uh LEHR ee,* is the common name for a *genus* (group) of herbs that belong to the lily family. This group is made up of about 85 species of plants that grow throughout the North Temperate Zone. Fritillaries have nodding, bell-shaped flowers. All fritillaries bloom in the spring. Many cultivated fritillaries are hardy plants and grow well in good garden soil. Popular kinds of fritillaries include the *crown imperial* and the *checkered lily,* or *snakes-head.* The crown imperial has brick- or yellow-red flowers. The checkered lily has checkered or veined purple-colored flowers.   Kenneth A. Nicely

Scientific classification. Fritillaries belong to the lily family, Liliaceae. The crown imperial fritillary is *Fritillaria imperialis.* The checkered lily is *F. meleagris.*

See also **Flower** (picture: Garden perennials [Bulbs]).

Fröbel, *FRU buhl,* **Friedrich Wilhelm August,** *FREE drihkh VIHL helm OW gust* (1782-1852), was a German educator who founded the kindergarten movement. Fröbel, whose name is also spelled Froebel, started his first kindergarten in 1837. Other educators had established schools for very young children, but he was the first to use the word *kindergarten* for such schools. This word comes from two German words meaning *garden of children.* By 1900, kindergartens had spread throughout Europe, Canada, and the United States.

Fröbel designed the kindergarten to help children learn naturally. His program included free play, games, and such activities as clay modeling, paper cutting, and weaving. Fröbel designed instructional materials that remained standard equipment for many years.

Fröbel believed education should promote the natural development of a person's spiritual being. His book *The Education of Man* (1826) explains his philosophy.

Fröbel was born on April 21, 1782, in Oberweissbach, near Erfurt, Germany. He began to teach in 1805. He opened his first school, an institution for older children, in 1816. He died on June 21, 1852.   Douglas Sloan

See also **Kindergarten** (Early kindergartens).

Frobisher, *FROH bih shuhr,* **Sir Martin** (1535?-1594), was one of the greatest seamen of the reign of Queen Elizabeth I. He fought against the Spanish Armada, the huge Spanish fleet that tried to invade England in 1588, and was knighted for his services.

Frobisher was one of the first English navigators to seek a Northwest Passage to India and eastern Asia. His attempts to reach Asia by sailing west extended geographic knowledge and expanded England's claim to North America. On his first voyage, in 1576, he rounded Greenland's southern end and entered what is now called Frobisher Bay, on Baffin Island's east coast. He thought the bay led to the Pacific Ocean. He took back to England a rock that some people believed was gold ore. On his second trip to North America, in 1577, Frobisher claimed the land for England and returned with 200 tons (180 metric tons) of rock. On his third voyage, in 1578, he took 15 ships and about 400 men, 100 of whom were supposed to start the first English colony in North America. He entered what is now Hudson Strait, but he made no further attempts at discovery and abandoned the plan for a colony. He brought back nearly 1,200 tons (1,090 metric tons) of rock, but it proved worthless.

Frobisher was born in Altofts, Yorkshire. He died on Nov. 22, 1594.   Robert McGhee

E. R. Degginger

© Thinkstock

Frogs vary greatly in color and size. The spotted, brownish-green leopard frog measures from 2 to 3 ½ inches (5 to 9 centimeters) long. The colorful poison dart frog grows from ½ inch to 2 ½ inches (1.3 to 6.4 centimeters). The green tree frog is less than 2 inches long.

© Thinkstock

Frog

Frog is a small, tailless animal with bulging eyes. Almost all frogs also have long back legs. The strong hind legs enable a frog to leap distances far greater than the length of its body. Frogs live on every continent except Antarctica, but tropical regions have the greatest number of *species* (kinds). Frogs are classified as *amphibians.* Most amphibians, including most frogs, spend part of their life as a water animal and part as a land animal. Frogs are related to toads but differ from them in several ways.

The first frogs appeared on Earth during the Jurassic Period, which lasted from about 200 million years ago to about 145 million years ago. Thousands of species of frogs and toads have developed from these early ancestors. Some species spend their entire life in or near water. Others live mainly on land and come to the water only to mate. Still other species never enter the water, not even to mate. Many kinds are climbers that dwell in trees. Others are burrowers that live underground.

Throughout history, frogs have been the source of superstitions. One old myth says that frogs fall from the sky during a rain. Actually, many species that live underground leave their burrows during or after a rain at the start of the mating season. Because people seldom see these frogs the rest of the year, they imagine the animals fell from the sky with the rain.

The body of a frog

The giant, or Goliath, frog of west-central Africa ranks as the largest frog. It can reach more than a foot (30 centimeters) in length. The smallest species of frogs grow only ½ inch (1.3 centimeters) long. Frogs also differ in color. Most kinds are green or brown, but some frogs have colorful markings.

Although different species may vary in size or color, almost all frogs have the same basic body structure. They have large hind legs, short front legs, and a flat head and body with no neck. Adult frogs have no tail, though one North American species has a short, taillike structure. Most frogs have a sticky tongue attached to the front part of the mouth. They can rapidly flip out their tongue to capture prey.

Like higher animals, frogs have such internal organs as a heart, liver, lungs, and kidneys. However, some of the internal organs differ from those of higher animals. For example, a frog's heart has three chambers instead of four. And although adult frogs breathe by means of lungs, they also breathe through their skin.

Legs. A few burrowing species have short hind legs and cannot hop. But all other frogs have long, powerful hind legs, which they use for jumping. Many frogs can leap 20 times their body length on a level surface. Frogs also use their large hind legs for swimming. Most water-dwelling species have webbed toes on their hind feet. The smaller front legs, or arms, prop a frog up when it sits. The front legs also help break the animal's fall when it jumps. Frogs that live in trees have tiny, sticky pads on the ends of their fingers and toes. The pads help the animal cling to the tree trunk as it climbs.

Skin. Most frogs have thin, moist skin. Many species have poison glands in their skin. The poison oozes onto the skin and helps protect the frog. If a predator grabs a frog, the poison irritates the predator's mouth and causes the animal to release the frog. Frogs have no hair, though the males of one African species, the so-called hairy frog, look hairy during the mating season. At that time, tiny, blood-rich growths called *papillae,* which resemble hair, grow from the sides of the frog's body.

Skeleton of a grass frog

Ventral (underside) view

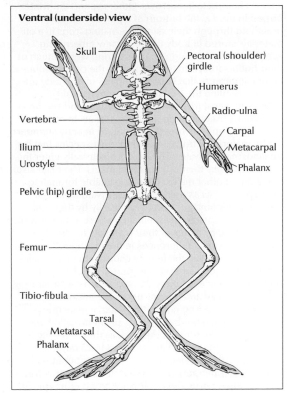

- Skull
- Pectoral (shoulder) girdle
- Humerus
- Radio-ulna
- Carpal
- Metacarpal
- Phalanx
- Vertebra
- Ilium
- Urostyle
- Pelvic (hip) girdle
- Femur
- Tibio-fibula
- Tarsal
- Metatarsal
- Phalanx

These structures provide males with extra oxygen during a period when they are very active.

Some species of frogs change their skin color with changes in the humidity, light, and temperature. Frogs shed the outer layer of their skin many times a year. Using their forelegs, they pull the old skin off over their head. They then usually eat the old skin.

Senses. Frogs have fairly good eyesight, which helps them in capturing food and avoiding enemies. A frog's eyes bulge out, enabling the animal to see in almost all directions. Frogs can close their eyes by pulling the eyeballs deeper into their sockets. This action closes the upper and lower eyelids. Most species also have a thin, partly clear inner eyelid attached to the bottom lid. This inner eyelid, called the *nictitating membrane,* can be moved upward when a frog's eyes are open. It protects the eyes without completely cutting off vision.

Most frogs have a disk of skin behind each eye. Each disk is called a *tympanum,* or eardrum. Sound waves cause the eardrums to vibrate. The vibrations travel to the inner ear, which is connected by nerves to the hearing centers of the brain.

Most frogs have a delicate sense of touch. It is particularly well developed in species that live in water. The tongue and mouth have many taste buds, and frogs often spit out bad-tasting food. The sense of smell varies among species. Frogs that hunt mostly at night or that live underground have the best sense of smell.

Voice. Male frogs of most species have a voice, which they use mainly to call females during the mating season. In some species, the females also have a voice. But the female's voice is not nearly so loud as the male's.

Internal organs of a male grass frog

A frog's internal anatomy resembles that of higher animals in many ways. In addition, frogs are small and easily available. For these reasons, frogs have long been used for dissection in basic biology classes. The drawing at the left shows the organs that are visible when the frog's belly is cut open. The drawing at the right shows the structures behind the first layer of organs.

WORLD BOOK illustrations by Marion Pahl

Ventral views

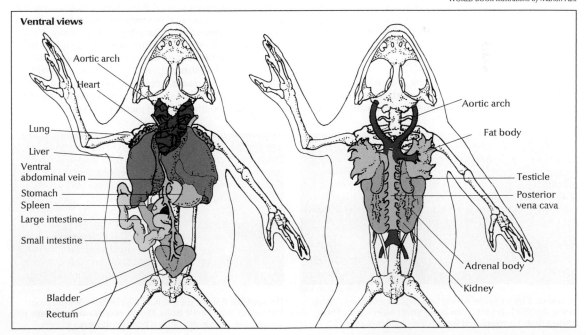

- Aortic arch
- Heart
- Lung
- Liver
- Ventral abdominal vein
- Stomach
- Spleen
- Large intestine
- Small intestine
- Bladder
- Rectum
- Aortic arch
- Fat body
- Testicle
- Posterior vena cava
- Adrenal body
- Kidney

© Shutterstock

© Shutterstock

A male frog sounds a mating call by puffing out its throat and forcing air over its vocal cords. It uses this call to attract a female.

A frog's sticky tongue is used to capture prey. The frog shown at the left is about to eat a fly.

A frog produces sound by means of its *vocal cords.* The vocal cords consist of thin bands of tissue in the *larynx* (voice box), which lies between the mouth and lungs. When a frog forces air from its lungs, the vocal cords vibrate and give off sound.

Among many species, the males have a *vocal sac,* which swells to great size while a call is being made. Species that have a vocal sac produce a much louder call than do similar species that have no sac. Some species have a vocal sac on each side of the head. Others have a single sac in the throat region.

The life of a frog

Frogs, like all other amphibians, are *cold-blooded*—that is, their body temperature tends to be the same as the temperature of the surrounding air or water. Frogs

that live in regions with cold winters hibernate. Some species hibernate in burrows. Others spend the winter buried in mud at the bottom of a pond or stream, breathing through their skin. Hibernating frogs live off materials stored in body tissues. A few hibernating species can live through winters during which much of their bodies freeze. In these species, the cells produce a natural antifreeze that keeps vital parts of the body unfrozen, enabling the frogs to survive bitter cold.

Mating. Most frogs that live in tropical and semitropical regions breed during the rainy season. In other regions, most species breed in spring or in early summer.

The majority of frogs, including most species that live on land, mate in water. The male frogs usually enter the water first. They then call to attract mates. Their call also helps direct other males to a pool suitable for mating. Each species has its own mating call. Naturalists can identify many kinds of frogs more easily by their call than by their appearance. Female frogs respond only to the call made by males of their own species. In certain species, individual differences in the mating call may determine which male the female chooses to mate. Males of some species also have a territorial call. This call warns other males of the same species that a certain area is occupied and that intruders are not welcome.

After a female frog enters the water, a male grasps her and clings to her back. In this position, called *amplexus,* the male fertilizes the eggs as they leave the female's body. The eggs hatch within 3 to 25 days, depending on the species and the water temperature. Higher water temperatures speed up development, and lower temperatures slow it down. Among most species, a tiny, tailed animal known as a *tadpole* or *polliwog* hatches from the egg.

Eggs. The eggs of different species vary in size, color, and shape. A jellylike substance covers frog eggs, providing a protective coating. This jelly also differs from species to species.

Some species lay several thousand eggs at a time. But only a few of these eggs develop into adult frogs. Ducks, fish, insects, and other water creatures eat many of the eggs. Even if the eggs hatch, the tadpoles also face the danger of being eaten by larger water animals. In addition, the pond or stream in which the eggs were laid sometimes dries up. As a result, the tadpoles die.

Certain tropical frogs lay their eggs in rain water that collects among the leaves of plants or in holes in trees.

Treat Davidson, NAS

In water, a frog uses its strong hind legs for swimming. Many water-dwelling species, such as the North American bullfrog, *shown here,* have webbed toes on their hind feet as well.

© Thinkstock

On land, the frog's muscular hind legs are used for jumping. The legs of large edible frogs, like the one shown here, have still another use. People throughout Europe eat them.

The life of a frog A frog's life has three stages: (1) egg, (2) tadpole, and (3) adult frog. Most female frogs lay a clump of several hundred eggs in water. A male frog clings to the female's back and fertilizes the eggs as she lays them. Tiny, fishlike tadpoles hatch from the eggs. As the tadpoles grow, they develop legs and a froglike body. In time, they become adult frogs and can live out of water.

Jahoda, FPG

Newly hatched tadpoles

Jane Burton, Bruce Coleman Inc.

© Shutterstock

© Shutterstock

Frog eggs and egg laying   **Older tadpole, with legs**   **Frog near completion of metamorphosis**

Females in some of these species may return every few days to feed unfertilized eggs to their newly hatched tadpoles. Other tropical species attach their eggs to the underside of leaves that grow over water. When the eggs hatch, the tadpoles fall into the water.

Among some species, one of the parents carries the eggs until they hatch. For example, the females of certain South American tree frogs carry the eggs on their back. Males of another species, Darwin's frog, carry the eggs in their vocal pouch.

Some tropical frogs lay their eggs on land. They lay them under logs or dead leaves. These frogs have no tadpole stage. A young frog hatches from the egg and begins life as a land animal.

Tadpoles are not completely developed when they hatch. At first, the tadpole clings to some support in the water, using its mouth or a tiny sucker. A tadpole has no neck, and so its head and body look like one round form. The animal has a long tail and resembles a little fish. It breathes by means of gills, which are hidden by a covering of skin.

A tadpole's form changes as the animal grows. The tail becomes larger and makes it possible for the animal to swim about to obtain food. Tadpoles eat plants and decaying animal matter. Some tadpoles eat frog eggs and other tadpoles.

In time, the tadpole begins to grow legs. The hind legs appear first. Then the lungs begin to develop and the front legs appear. The digestive system changes, enabling the frog that develops to eat live animals. Just before its *metamorphosis* (change) into a frog, the tadpole loses its gills. Finally, a tiny frog, still bearing a stump of a tail, emerges from the water. Eventually, the animal absorbs its tail and assumes its adult form.

Some tadpoles are so small they can hardly be seen, but tadpoles of a South American species called the paradoxical frog reach more than 10 inches (25 centimeters) in length. A fully developed bullfrog tadpole may measure 6 to 7 inches (15 to 18 centimeters) long. It may

take two or even three years for a bullfrog tadpole to develop into a frog. But among most species, the tadpoles change into adults within a few months. In a few species that breed in temporary ponds, this process may take less than two weeks.

Adult frogs. After a frog becomes an adult, it may take a few months to a few years before the animal is mature enough to breed. The green frog and the pickerel frog mature in about three years. In captivity, a bullfrog may live more than 15 years. But few species of frogs live longer than 6 to 8 years in the wild. Many are eaten by such predators as bats, herons, raccoons, snakes, turtles, and fish.

Adult frogs eat mainly insects and other small animals, including earthworms, minnows, and spiders. Most frogs use their sticky tongue to capture prey. The tongue is flipped out of the mouth in response to movement by the prey. Most frogs have teeth only on their upper jaw. Toads lack teeth altogether. As a result, frogs and toads swallow their prey in one piece. To aid in the swallowing process, the frog's eyes sink through openings in the skull and force the food down the throat.

Kinds of frogs

Frogs and toads make up the order Anura, or Salientia, one of the three main groups of amphibians. Zoologists divide this order into a number of families.

One family of anurans consists of *true frogs.* Toads make up another family. Most toads have a broader, flatter body and darker, drier skin than do most true frogs. Toads are commonly covered with warts, but true frogs have smooth skin. Unlike most true frogs, the majority of toads live on land. The adults go to water only to breed.

Of the other families in the order Anura, some closely resemble true frogs, and others closely resemble toads. Still others have features of both true frogs and toads. Certain frogs have the word *toad* as part of their common name. For example, the spadefoot toad and the midwife toad are frogs.

True frogs rank among the most widespread of all frog families. They include hundreds of species and live on every continent except Antarctica. True frogs are most common in Africa. The majority of these animals live in or near water. They have long hind legs, smooth skin, a narrow waist, and webbed hind feet.

Two well-known species are the North American leopard frog, which is greenish in color, and the European common frog, which has a brownish body. The Goliath frog of Africa ranks as the world's largest living frog. It can grow about 12 to 16 inches (30 to 40 centimeters) long. Another large true frog, the North American bullfrog, may grow up to 8 inches (20 centimeters) in length. One of the most unusual species is the Wallace's flying frog of Southeast Asia. It can glide through the air by using its large webbed feet and flaps of skin fringe on its limbs. When gliding, the frog spreads its limbs, and the webbing and flaps stretch out to form modified "wings."

Tree frogs, like true frogs, live on all continents except Antarctica. Most tree frogs measure less than 2 inches (5 centimeters) long and dwell in trees. These amphibians have greenish or brownish coloring that enables them to blend in with the bushes and trees, thus avoiding predators.

The largest number of tree frogs inhabit tropical areas in Central America and South America. The female marsupial frog of South America carries not only her eggs but also the tadpoles in a pouchlike depression on her back. Some North American tree frogs, called chorus frogs and cricket frogs, live mainly on the ground.

Other frogs include leptodactylid frogs, narrow-mouthed toads, spadefoot toads, and tailed frogs.

Leptodactylid frogs make up a large family of frogs that live mainly in Australia and South America. Their name means *light fingered* and refers to their weakly developed webs and lack of suckers. Many species, such as the South American bullfrog, create a "nest" of foam for their eggs. The frogs make this nest by beating the jelly of some of the eggs into a foam. The barking frog and the cliff frog live on rocky cliffs in Texas. These species lay their eggs under rocks. Tiny frogs hatch from the eggs without going through the tadpole stage.

Narrow-mouthed toads live throughout most tropical and subtropical regions, and are especially common in New Guinea and Madagascar. As their name suggests, the frogs have an extremely narrow mouth. Many species, such as the sheep frog of North America and the termite frog of Africa, live in burrows and eat ants and termites.

Spadefoot toads live in Asia, Europe, North America, and northwestern Africa. The frogs are called spadefoots because most of them have a sharp-edged spadelike growth on each hind foot. They use this growth as a digging tool.

Spadefoot toads dwell underground and are usually active at night. Several species live in dry regions of the United States and Mexico. These spadefoots may remain in their burrows for weeks at a time to stay moist. They breed following heavy rains, often laying eggs in temporary ponds. The tadpoles develop rapidly. If enough food is available, *toadlets* (tiny, developed toads) may emerge in only 12 days. The European spadefoot is known as the "garlic frog" because of its smell.

Tailed frogs live in New Zealand and western North America. The three New Zealand species have muscles that were once used to control a tail. The single North American species has retained a whole taillike structure.

North American tailed frogs inhabit swift mountain streams. Moving water makes external fertilization of the eggs difficult. Instead, the male uses its "tail" to fertilize the eggs while they are inside the female. Tadpoles of these tailed frogs have a large sucker that enables them to hold on to rocks even in the strongest current.

Frogs and people

Frogs benefit people in many ways. They eat numerous kinds of insects, which might otherwise become serious pests. Frogs also provide us with food. The meaty hind legs of larger frogs are considered a delicacy in many countries. Frogs also are used widely in the laboratory. Medical researchers use frogs to test new drugs, and students dissect frogs to learn about anatomy.

Since the 1980's, scientists have noted a worldwide decline of many frog species. People do not know for certain what has caused these declines. Possible factors include pollution, disease, habitat destruction, and acid rain. Another factor may be the thinning of the earth's protective ozone layer, which allows more harmful ultraviolet radiation from the sun to reach the earth. Because frogs have thin, moist skin and an aquatic tadpole stage, they are easily affected by pollution and changes in the environment. Some scientists believe the declining frog population is an early warning of environmental problems that could affect human beings.   Don C. Forester

Scientific classification. True frogs make up the family Ranidae. All North American true frogs are in the genus *Rana*. Tree frogs make up the family Hylidae. Leptodactylid frogs make up the family Leptodactylidae; narrow-mouthed toads, the family Microhylidae; and spadefoot toads, the family Pelobatidae. The tailed frog belongs to the family Leiopelmatidae.

Related articles in *World Book* include:

Amphibian	Metamorphosis (picture:
Bullfrog	Metamorphosis of a frog)
Ear (The ears of animals)	Tadpole
Heart (picture: Animal hearts)	Toad
	Tree frog

Outline

I. **The body of a frog**
   A. Legs   C. Senses
   B. Skin   D. Voice

II. **The life of a frog**
   A. Mating   C. Tadpoles
   B. Eggs   D. Adult frogs

III. **Kinds of frogs**
   A. True frogs   C. Other frogs
   B. Tree frogs

IV. **Frogs and people**

Questions

How many species of frogs are there?
How do tadpoles breathe? How do adult frogs?
In what ways do frogs benefit people?
What do tadpoles eat? What do adult frogs eat?
How did spadefoot toads get their name?
What is the function of a male frog's territorial call?
What are some of the changes a tadpole undergoes during its metamorphosis into a frog?
What is the function of the *nictitating membrane*?
What are some possible reasons for why frog populations have been declining?

Additional resources

Level I

Burns, Diane L. *Frogs, Toads, and Turtles.* Gareth Stevens, 2000.
Greenberg, Daniel A. *Frogs.* Cavendish, 2000.
Pascoe, Elaine. *Tadpoles.* Blackbirch Pr., 1997.

Level II

Behler, John L. and Deborah A. *Frogs.* Sterling Pub., 2005.
Beltz, Ellin. *Frogs.* Firefly Bks., 2005.
Hofrichter, Robert, ed. *Amphibians: The World of Frogs, Toads, Salamanders, and Newts.* Firefly Bks., 2000.

Froissart, *frwah SAHR* or *FROY sahrt,* **Jean,** *zhahn* (1337?-after 1404), was a French historian and poet who is best known for his *Chronicles* (1369-1400?). This four-volume book vividly describes the great events and personalities of western Europe from 1325 to 1400, especially the Hundred Years' War between England and France. Froissart also wrote *Méliador,* a verse romance on the King Arthur legend. His work is considered the finest literary expression of the idea of chivalry and the aristocratic ways of life during his time.

Froissart was born into a middle-class family in Valenciennes. He studied to be a priest but decided to pursue a literary career. From 1361 to 1369, Froissart served as secretary to Queen Philippa of England, the wife of King Edward III. Froissart spent the remainder of his life writing and traveling through Europe. Froissart became a *canon* (church official) of Chimay, Belgium, in 1384.

Jeff Rider

Fromm, *frahm,* **Erich** (1900-1980), was a German-born social philosopher and psychoanalyst. He became a leading supporter of the idea that most human behavior is a learned response to social conditions. In adopting this concept, Fromm rejected much of the theory of the noted Austrian neurologist and psychoanalyst Sigmund Freud. Freud maintained that instincts determine most human behavior.

Fromm applied the ideas of sociology to psychoanalysis. He studied the social and cultural processes by which people come to learn and act out the behavior expected of them by their society.

Fromm wrote numerous books that reflect his many fields of interest, such as philosophy, psychology, religion, and sociology. His major works include *Escape from Freedom* (1941), *Man for Himself* (1947), *The Sane Society* (1955), and *The Art of Loving* (1956).

Fromm was born in Frankfurt (am Main) on March 23, 1900. He earned his Ph.D. degree from the University of Heidelberg in 1922. In 1933, Fromm came to the United States to lecture at the Institute for Psychoanalysis in Chicago. He became a U.S. citizen in 1940. Fromm held positions in psychoanalytical institutions in the United States and taught at universities in the United States and Mexico. He died on March 18, 1980.   Hannah S. Decker

Frond. See **Fern.**

Fronde, *frawnd,* was a series of revolts against the French monarchy. Anne of Austria ruled France from 1643 until her son Louis XIV became king in 1651. The Fronde began in 1648, when Anne and her chief adviser, Cardinal Jules Mazarin, began taxing the French nobility. The rebels protested the tax policies and Mazarin's growing authority. The conclusion of the Fronde in 1653 resulted in a more powerful monarchy.   Janet L. Polasky

Front. See **Weather** (Weather systems).

Frontal bone. See **Head.**

Frontenac, *FRAHN tuh nak* or *frawnt NAHK,* **Comte de,** *kaunt duh* (1620-1698), was governor general of New France, the French empire in North America, in the late 1600's. He helped establish France's power in North America so firmly that it lasted for more than 50 years after his death.

Frontenac was appointed governor general in 1672. His stern, military ways and hot temper often got him into trouble with the civil authorities in New France. But Frontenac knew when to be tactful and when to be masterful with the Indians. The fur trade prospered under his rule.

Frontenac urged exploration of the west and aided the expeditions of Robert Cavelier, Sieur de la Salle; Louis Jolliet; and Father Jacques Marquette. However, he quarreled constantly with Bishop Laval and the priests, mainly about using brandy in the Indian trade. The church objected to its use. Frontenac was recalled to France in 1682.

But in 1689, he was again appointed governor general. The French planned to conquer the English colony of New York and to keep the remaining English colonies along the Atlantic Coast. Frontenac commanded French forces in a combined land and sea attack against the colonies. However, the attack failed. Frontenac then began campaigns against the Iroquois Indians, whom the English encouraged in their attacks on New France. In addition, he sent bands of French fighters and Algonquian Indians to raid English frontier towns in New York and New England. In 1690, Frontenac defended Quebec

Detail of a water color by J. H. de Rinzy; Public Archives of Canada

The Comte de Frontenac served two terms as governor general of New France during the late 1600's. This water color shows Frontenac, seated in a canoe, on his way to Fort Cataraqui, which he built on Lake Ontario in 1673.

against an attacking English fleet. Six years later, Frontenac's forces laid waste the villages and lands of the Iroquois. The Treaty of Ryswick in 1697 stopped the war for
a time. Frontenac died the next year, on Nov. 28, 1698.

Frontenac became a soldier as a boy and was made a
brigadier general at the age of 26. He served in Flanders,
Germany, Italy, Hungary, and Crete before he became
governor general of New France. His given and family
name was Louis de Buade.   John A. Dickinson

See also **Canada, History of** (The royal province).

Frontier. See Pioneer life in America; Western frontier life in America; Westward movement in America.

Frost is a pattern of ice crystals formed from water vapor on grass, windowpanes, and other exposed surfaces near the ground. Frost occurs mainly on cold,
cloudless nights when the air temperature drops below
32 °F (0 °C), which is the freezing point of water.

Frost and dew form in much the same way. During
the day, Earth's surface absorbs heat from the sun. When
the sun sets, Earth begins to cool. The drop in temperature is greater on clear nights than on cloudy nights because there are no clouds to reflect the heat given off
from Earth's surface. As the cooling continues, the water
vapor in the air condenses to form dewdrops on objects. Some of these dewdrops freeze when the temperature falls below 32 °F. The frozen droplets increase in
size, becoming frost crystals when the surrounding

dewdrops evaporate and deposit water vapor on the
crystals. At temperatures below freezing, water vapor
sometimes changes directly into ice crystals without first
forming dewdrops.

Frost crystals, also called *hoarfrost,* occur in two basic
forms—platelike and columnar. The *platelike* crystals are
flat and resemble snow crystals. The *columnar* crystals
are six-sided columns of ice.

The term *frost* also refers to below-freezing temperatures harmful to plants. At such temperatures, the fluids
in plant cells freeze and expand, causing the cell walls to
rupture. Farmers protect crops from this type of frost by
warming cold surface air with heaters. They also use
large fans to mix the surface air with the warmer air
above it. Artificial fog may also be produced to reduce
the loss of heat from the surface.   Margaret A. LeMone

Frost, Robert (1874-1963), became the most popular
American poet of his time. He won the Pulitzer Prize for
poetry in 1924, 1931, 1937, and 1943. In 1960, Congress
voted Frost a gold medal "in recognition of his poetry,
which has enriched the culture of the United States and
the philosophy of the world." Frost's public career
reached a climax in January 1961, when he recited his
poem "The Gift Outright" at the inauguration of President John F. Kennedy.

His life. Robert Lee Frost was born March 26, 1874, in
San Francisco. After his father died in 1885, the family

© George Whiteley, Photo Researchers, Inc.

Platelike frost crystals are flat and closely resemble snow crystals. Frost crystals of this type commonly form delicate, lacy patterns on windowpanes, *shown here.*

© Bill Borsheim, Tom Stack & Associates

Columnar frost crystals are six-sided columns of ice. They may
resemble thick needles when they grow on such exposed objects as blades of grass or leaves of plants, *shown here.*

moved back to New England, the original family home. Frost briefly attended Dartmouth and Harvard colleges but did not earn a degree. In the early 1890's, he worked in New England as a farmer, an editor, and a schoolteacher, absorbing the materials that were to form the themes of many of his most famous poems. In 1912, he moved briefly to England, where his poetry was well received and where he met the poets William Butler Yeats and Ezra Pound. Frost's first volume of poetry, *A Boy's Will,* appeared in 1913. His final collection, *In the Clearing,* appeared in 1962. Frost died on Jan. 29, 1963. *The Notebooks of Robert Frost* was published in 2007.

Wide World
Robert Frost

His poems. Frost's poetry is identified with New England, particularly Vermont and New Hampshire. Frost found inspiration for many of his finest poems in the region's landscapes, folkways, and speech mannerisms. His poetry is noted for its plain language, conventional poetic forms, and graceful style. He was deeply influenced by classical poets, especially Horace. Many of Frost's earliest poems are as richly developed as his later ones.

Frost is sometimes praised for being a direct and straightforward writer. While he is never obscure, he cannot always be read easily. His effects, even at their simplest, depend upon a certain slyness for which the reader must be prepared. In "Precaution," Frost wrote:

> I never dared be radical when young
> For fear it would make me conservative when old.

In his longer, more elaborate poems, Frost writes about complex subjects in a complex style.

Frost tends to restrict himself to New England scenes, but the range of moods in his poetry is rich and varied. He assumes the role of a puckish, homespun philosopher in "Mending Wall." In such poems as "Design" and "Bereft," he responds to the terror and tragedy of life. He writes soberly of vaguely threatening aspects of nature in "Come In" and "Stopping by Woods on a Snowy Evening." In the latter poem, he wrote:

> My little horse must think it queer
> To stop without a farmhouse near
> Between the woods and frozen lake
> The darkest evening of the year.

"Precaution" and the second stanza of "Stopping by Woods on a Snowy Evening" from *The Poetry of Robert Frost* edited by Edward Connery Lathem. Copyright 1936, 1951 by Robert Frost; copyright 1964 by Lesley Frost Ballantine; copyright 1923, 1969 by Henry Holt and Company. Reprinted by permission of Henry Holt and Company, LLC, and Jonathan Cape, an imprint of Random House UK Ltd.

A similar varied pattern can be found in Frost's character studies. "The Witch of Coos" is a comic account of the superstitions of rural New England. In "Home Burial," this same setting is the background of tragedy centering around a child's death. In "The Hill Wife," Frost shows the loneliness and emotional poverty of a rural existence driving a person insane.

By placing people and nature side by side, Frost often appears to write the kind of Romantic poetry associated with England and the United States in the 1800's. There is, however, a crucial difference between his themes and those of the older tradition. The Romantic poets of the 1800's believed people could live in harmony with nature. To Frost, the purposes of people and nature are never the same, and so nature's meanings can never be known. Probing for nature's secrets is futile and foolish. Humanity's best chance for serenity does not come from understanding the natural environment. Serenity comes from working usefully and productively amid the external forces of nature. Frost often used the theme of "significant toil"—toil by which people are nourished and sustained. This theme appears in such famous lyrics as "Birches," "After Apple-Picking," and "Two Tramps in Mud Time." Bonnie Costello

See also **Blank verse.**

Additional resources

Parini, Jay. *Robert Frost.* Henry Holt, 1999.
Richardson, Mark. *The Ordeal of Robert Frost.* 1997. Reprint. Univ. of Ill. Pr., 2000.

Frostbite is an injury that results from overexposure of the skin to extreme cold. It occurs when ice crystals form in body tissues, and blood flow is restricted in the injured area. Frostbite most commonly affects the ears, nose, chin, fingers, and toes. The first sign of frostbite may be a reddening of the skin. The skin of the frostbitten area then becomes pale or turns grayish-blue. Early symptoms include feelings of coldness, tingling, and pain. As frostbite progresses, the pain is replaced by numbness. A victim may not even be aware of the injury. When blood supply to the frostbitten area is lost, *gangrene* (tissue death) may develop (see **Gangrene**).

Frostbite should be cared for by restoring circulation and warmth to the affected area as quickly as possible. Do not rub the frostbitten area with snow or ice because rubbing might remove skin and damage tissue. Get the victim into a warm place and soak the frostbitten body parts in warm, but not hot, water. Loosely bandage the affected area. Place gauze or cloth between fingers or toes before bandaging them. Seek medical attention immediately. Critically reviewed by the American Red Cross

See also **Chilblain; First aid** (Frostbite); **Hypothermia; Immersion foot.**

Frozen food. See Food, Frozen.

FRS. See Federal Reserve System.

Fructose is a sugar produced by nearly all fruits and by many vegetables. Fructose, also known as *levulose* and *fruit sugar,* is nearly twice as sweet as *sucrose* (table sugar). Fructose is used to sweeten such food products as diet foods, gelatin desserts, jellies, soft drinks, and syrups. It is the chief sweetener in honey.

Foods that contain fructose taste as sweet as similar foods made with sucrose, but they may have fewer calories. Fructose gives ice cream and candies a smooth texture. It also absorbs moisture readily and so helps keep baked goods from becoming stale.

Fructose is produced commercially as a liquid, powder, or tablet. Food processing companies use fructose primarily in the form of *high-fructose corn syrup,* which is obtained from cornstarch. Kay Franzen Jamieson

See also **Corn syrup; Sugar** (Kinds of sugar).

Colorful, delicious fruits make up an important food group in a healthful human diet. This fruit market in Barcelona, Spain, sells a variety of fruits from around the world, including apples, cherries, grapes, lemons, mangoes, melons, oranges, papayas, pears, and strawberries.

© San Rostro, age fotostock

Fruit commonly refers to the edible tissue that surrounds the seed or seeds of many flowering plants. People around the world enjoy eating fruits as desserts or snacks. In fact, the word *fruit* comes from a Latin term meaning *enjoy.* Fruit growers worldwide produce hundreds of millions of tons of fruit annually. The most popular kinds include apples, bananas, grapes, oranges, peaches, pears, plums, and strawberries. Fruits make up an important food group in a healthful human diet. They provide rich sources of vitamins and *carbohydrates* (starches and sugars).

The term *fruit* has a somewhat different meaning for *botanists* (scientists who study plants) and for *horticulturists* (experts in growing plants). Botanists define fruit as the part of a flowering plant that contains the seeds. By this definition, fruits also can include acorns, cucumbers, and tomatoes.

Horticulturists describe fruit as an edible seed-bearing structure that (1) consists of fleshy tissue and (2) grows on a *perennial* (plant that lives for more than two growing seasons). This definition excludes nuts, which do not have a fleshy body, and vegetables, which typically grow on *annuals* (plants that live for only one growing season). It also excludes many foods that most people consider fruits. For example, watermelons meet both the botanical and common definitions of fruit. But horticulturists regard them as vegetables because they grow on annual vines. Many people also consider rhubarb a fruit because of its use as a dessert. But people eat the rhubarb leafstalk, not the seed-bearing structure. Thus horticulturists and botanists classify rhubarb as a vegetable.

This article describes the different categories of fruits in botany and in horticulture. It then discusses how people cultivate and market fruit and how they develop new fruit varieties called *cultivars.*

Types of fruits in botany

Fruits grow on flowering plants, which scientists call *angiosperms.* A fruit develops from the plant's *ovary,* the tissue surrounding the seed-bearing structure of the flower. Flowers may have one or more ovaries. Each ovary contains one or more seeds, depending on the plant. Fruits protect the seeds and help them to *disperse* (scatter) to form new plants. Many fruits have three layers after they mature: (1) an outer layer called the *exocarp,* (2) a middle layer called the *mesocarp,* and (3) an inner layer called the *endocarp.* Collectively, the three layers make up the *pericarp.*

Botanists classify fruits into two main groups, *simple fruits* and *compound fruits.* Simple fruits develop from a single ovary. Compound fruits develop from two or more ovaries.

Simple fruits make up by far the largest group of fruits. Many simple fruits have a fleshy pericarp, and others have a dry pericarp. There are three main kinds of fleshy simple fruits: (1) *true berries,* (2) *drupes* (pronounced *droopz),* and (3) *pomes* (pronounced *pohmz).*

True berries include bananas, blueberries, green peppers, grapes, oranges, tomatoes, and watermelons. Some of these fruits, known as *pepos (PEE pohz),* have a firm exocarp. They include muskmelons and watermelons. Berries called *hesperidiums (HEHS puh RIHD ee uhmz)* possess a leathery exocarp. Citrus fruits rank as the best known hesperidiums. Many fruits that have the word *berry* in their common name, such as blackberries, raspberries, and strawberries, are not in fact true berries. Scientists classify them as compound fruits.

Drupes possess a fleshy mesocarp surrounding a hard endocarp called a *stone* or *pit.* A thin exocarp forms the skin. Examples of drupes include apricots, cherries, olives, peaches, and plums.

Pomes have a distinctive core. The core consists of a thin, paperlike endocarp surrounding hollow, seed-bearing cavities. Apples and pears rank among the most popular types of pomes.

Dry simple fruits include beans, milkweed, peas, rice, wheat grains, and true nuts. Botanists regard true nuts as single-seeded fruits with a hard pericarp called a *shell.* People eat the seeds of these plants but not the pericarps. True nuts include acorns, chestnuts, and hazelnuts. Some so-called nuts, almonds for example,

Simple fruits

Simple fruits are classified into two main groups, depending on whether their tissue is fleshy or dry. Fleshy simple fruits include most of the seed-bearing structures that are commonly called fruits. They are divided into three main types: (1) berries, (2) drupes, and (3) pomes. The drawings below show some examples of each of these types and of several dry simple fruits.

Berries consist entirely of fleshy tissue, and most species have many seeds. The seeds are embedded in the flesh. This group includes only a few of the fruits that are commonly known as berries.

Seed · **Orange** Seed · **Grapes** Seed · **Watermelon**

Drupes are fleshy fruits that have a hard inner stone or pit and a single seed. The pit encloses the seed.

Pit · Seed · **Peach** Pit · Seed · **Cherries** Pit · Seed · **Plum**

Pomes have a fleshy outer layer, a paperlike core, and more than one seed. The seeds are enclosed in the core.

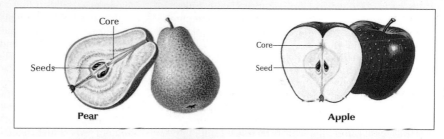

Core · Seeds · **Pear** Core · Seed · **Apple**

Dry simple fruits are produced by many kinds of trees, shrubs, garden plants, and weeds. The seed-bearing structures of nearly all members of the grass family, including corn and wheat, belong to this group.

Seed · **Milkweed pod** Chestnut (encloses the seed) · **Fruit of the chestnut tree** Seed · **Fruit of the maple tree** Seed · **Kernels of corn**

Compound fruits

A compound fruit consists of a cluster of seed-bearing structures, each of which is a complete fruit. Compound fruits are divided into two groups, (1) aggregate fruits and (2) multiple fruits.

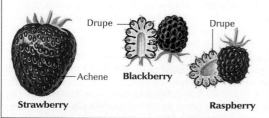

Drupe · Drupe · **Blackberry** Achene · **Strawberry** **Raspberry**

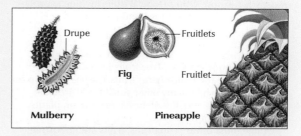

Drupe · **Mulberry** Fruitlets · **Fig** Fruitlet · **Pineapple**

Aggregate fruits include most of the fruits that are commonly called berries. Each fruitlet of a blackberry or raspberry is a small drupe. Each "seed" of a strawberry is a dry fruit called an achene.

Multiple fruits include mulberries, figs, and pineapples. Mulberry fruitlets are small drupes. Each "seed" in a fig and each segment of a pineapple is a fruitlet.

are actually the seeds of drupes. In fact, food processors frequently substitute apricot seeds for almonds in processed foods.

Compound fruits consist of a cluster of ripened ovaries. There are two main types of compound fruits, *aggregate fruits* and *multiple fruits.*

Aggregate fruits develop from single flowers, each of which has many ovaries. The strawberry represents an unusual type of aggregate fruit. Each so-called seed on a strawberry is a true fruit. Botanists call these seedlike fruits *achenes (ay KEENZ)*. The edible fleshy part surrounding the achenes develops from the base of the flower rather than from the ovaries. Other aggregate fruits include blackberries and raspberries.

Multiple fruits grow from a cluster of flowers on a single stem. Figs, mulberries, and pineapples are multiple fruits. Botanists also consider an ear of corn to be a multiple fruit. Each kernel forms a single fruit called a *caryopsis (KAR ee AHP sihs)*.

Types of fruits in horticulture

Farmers have long cultivated various fruits far outside the areas where the plants originally grew. Peaches, for example, once grew only in China but now thrive in many parts of the world. Horticulturists classify fruits into three groups, based on their temperature requirements for growth: (1) temperate fruits, (2) subtropical fruits, and (3) tropical fruits.

Temperate fruits need an annual cold season to grow properly. Farmers raise them chiefly in the *temperate* regions between the tropics and the polar areas. Most temperate fruits thrive in Europe and North America. They also grow in Asia, Australia, and New Zealand. Such temperate fruits as apples, apricots, cherries, peaches, pears, and plums grow on trees. Temperate areas also produce many fruits that grow on plants smaller than trees, including blueberries, cranberries, grapes, kiwis, raspberries, and strawberries.

Subtropical fruits require warm or mild temperatures throughout the year but can survive an occasional light frost. This type of climate characterizes subtropical regions. The most widely grown subtropical fruits, the citrus fruits, consist primarily of grapefruits, lemons, limes, and oranges. Brazil, Israel, Italy, Mexico, Spain, Turkey, and the United States all have important citrus-growing regions. Other subtropical fruits include avocados, figs, and olives.

Tropical fruits cannot tolerate even a light frost. Bananas and pineapples rank as the best-known tropical fruits. Growers cultivate them throughout the tropics, mostly for export. Other tropical fruits include acerolas, cherimoyas, litchis, mangoes, and papayas.

Fruit production

Many fruit *species* (kinds) grow on trees or other long-lived woody plants. Tree fruits include apples, mangoes, and the major citrus fruits. Grapes develop on woody vines, while many other small fruits grow on bushes. Bananas and strawberries develop on plants that have nonwoody stems.

Unlike most other crop plants, fruits are not grown from seeds. Instead, growers develop them from such plant tissues as stems, buds, and roots in a process called *vegetative reproduction.* Plants grown from seeds may vary in many ways from generation to generation. But plants grown vegetatively display similar growth habits and yield fruit of similar quality. Fruit growers strive to *propagate* (reproduce) plants in which such traits remain as consistent as possible over time.

Growers propagate fruit plants in three main ways: (1) by grafting, (2) from cuttings, and (3) from specialized plant structures. Most fruit trees require the grafting method. In this process, the grower joins a bud or piece of stem from a desirable cultivar to a *rootstock* from another plant. A rootstock is a root or a root plus its stem. The resulting tree will produce the desired fruit. Moreover, the rootstock may influence such tree characteristics as size, productivity, and disease resistance.

Farmers propagate some plants by rooted cuttings or specialized structures, such as modified stems called *runners.* Rooted cuttings consist of pieces of stem that have grown roots when placed in water or moist soil. Mature strawberry plants send out long, thin runners that grow along the surface of the soil. Where the runners touch the ground, modified buds called *nodes* form roots that produce *plantlets* (new leaves and stems). These plantlets are actually part of the parent plant but can develop into new plants if separated from the parent.

Most growers buy fruit plants from nurseries that specialize in propagating them. Nurseries produce plants under controlled conditions to reduce or eliminate diseases and insects. They often sell their plants with a guarantee that the plants are pest-free.

A branch of horticulture called *pomology* deals with growing fruit. Pomologists have developed efficient methods of planting, tending, and harvesting fruit.

Planting. Because fruit plants are perennials, growers need not replant them annually. Trees and vines may remain productive for 30 to 50 years or longer. Small fruit plants, including strawberries and raspberries, have a productive life of only a few years. Farmers in mild climates typically plant trees, bushes, and vines in the fall. In cold climates, planting often occurs in spring.

In the past, farmers almost always grew full-sized, free-standing fruit trees. They generally planted the trees from about 20 to 40 feet (6 to 12 meters) apart to allow room for growth. Today, however, most growers prefer specially propagated dwarf trees. Growers space these trees closer together, from about 4 to 20 feet (1.2 to 6 meters) apart. Closer spacing produces a larger crop in the same area. Smaller trees also enable growers to care for and harvest the crop more easily.

Caring for the crop. Most fruit growers use machinery to fertilize, cultivate, and irrigate the plantings. Farmers must fertilize fruit plants at least once a year. Some fertilizers are applied to the soil, while others are sprayed on the plants. Many growers cultivate the soil around young fruit plants periodically. This practice encourages crop growth by controlling weeds and improving the circulation of air and water through the soil. Most fruit plants require considerable moisture. Only a few fruits, such as dates and olives, can grow in dry regions without irrigation. If irrigation is needed, growers use ditches or sprinklers to distribute the water.

Some fruit plants, including blueberry bushes, are free-standing. But growers must train other types, such as grapevines, raspberry bushes, and many young fruit trees, to grow on trellises or other supports. Some trees may even need their trunks propped up so that the trees develop a uniform shape and sturdy structure. Fruits grown on supports receive maximum sunlight, producing a more uniform and better quality product. Supports also make harvesting easier.

Nearly all fruit plants need pruning at least annually. Growers must prune the plants to rid them of unproductive or diseased branches. Most growers also remove some of the crop from trees during the early stages of fruit growth. This practice, called thinning, helps increase the size and quality of the remaining fruit.

Fruit growers often use a system of *integrated pest management* (IPM), which combines natural and chemical controls to fight pests. Farmers usually apply chemical pesticides with tractor-pulled sprayers or specially equipped light airplanes or helicopters.

Sudden spring frosts can endanger fruit crops in temperate or subtropical regions. Growers may use water distributed by sprinklers to protect plants from frost damage. Water releases heat as it freezes. If sprinkled onto the crops continuously, the water protects flowers and young fruit from freezing. Another method of frost protection uses large fans on towers. The fans can mix

naturally occurring warm air 30 to 50 feet (9 to 15 meters) above the ground with the colder air at plant level.

Harvesting. Most fruits ripen quickly after reaching their mature size. Harvesting occurs at different stages of the growth process, depending on the type of fruit and its intended use. Some fruit crops require harvesting when still immature. They include the gooseberries and cherries used to make artificial coloring. For apples, bananas, peaches, and pears, commercial harvesting occurs when the fruits reach full size, but before they ripen. Most fruits taste best if left to ripen on the plant, so home gardeners typically harvest their crops when ripe. Citrus fruits do not go through a distinct ripening process. Thus, harvesting can take place over a long period after they mature.

Fruits bruise more easily than do most other crops, so growers must harvest them with care. Workers pick most fruit crops by hand. However, the increasing cost of hand labor has encouraged the use of fruit-harvesting machines. Some of these machines have arms that shake the fruit loose from the plants. The loosened fruit drops onto outstretched cloths. Other harvesting machines have a rubber fingerlike structure that gently "combs" fruit from the plants.

How horticulturists classify fruits

Any seed-bearing structure produced by a flowering plant is a fruit. But the word *fruit* has a more limited meaning in common usage and in horticulture, the branch of agriculture that includes fruit growing. Thus, the word usually refers to the edible sweet or tart fruits that are popular foods and widely grown farm crops. Horticulturists classify these fruits into three groups, based on temperature requirements for growth: (1) temperate fruits, (2) subtropical fruits, and (3) tropical fruits. Some examples of each of these types are shown below.

WORLD BOOK illustrations by James Teason and Wildlife Art Ltd.

Apricot Cranberries

Blueberries

Apple

Kiwi Plums

Dates Avocado

Grapefruit

Olives

Lemon

Carambola (star fruit)

Mangosteen

Banana Durian

Temperate fruits must have an annual cold season. They are raised mainly in the temperate zones, the regions between the tropics and the polar areas.

Subtropical fruits need warm or mild temperatures throughout the year but can survive occasional light frosts. They are grown chiefly in subtropical regions.

Tropical fruits cannot stand frost. They are raised mainly in the tropics. Large quantities of some species, especially bananas and pineapples, are exported.

Once the fruit has been harvested, farmers usually deliver it immediately to cold storage or controlled-atmosphere storage facilities. There the fruit can finish ripening under controlled conditions. When the fruit becomes ready for market, workers wash it, sort it, and pack it into containers. They then ship the fruit to such buyers as retail stores. Some fruits, including apples, can remain fresh for about a year if stored at temperatures near freezing. But most small fruits or tropical fruits remain fresh for only a few days or weeks in storage. Farmers ship much fruit directly from farms to food processing plants. These plants preserve fruit by such methods as canning, drying, and freezing. Processors often use imperfectly formed fruit in jams, preserves, juices, and other products.

Marketing fruit

The worldwide marketing of fruits has expanded dramatically since the late 1900's. Because of improved transportation and storage techniques, most major food markets now offer fresh fruit grown and shipped from thousands of miles or kilometers away. Such technology enables markets to offer fruits out of season. For example, apples ripen in the fall. But because the Northern Hemisphere and Southern Hemisphere experience fall at opposite times of the year, markets in one hemisphere can sell fresh apples out of season by importing them from the other hemisphere. Thus, markets in the United States can sell apples in spring that they have imported from New Zealand.

Technology also has made more types of fruits available in many countries. Such fruits as carambolas (also called star fruit), durians, and mangosteens once rarely appeared outside the tropics. Today, however, they have become available in much of the world. Human immigration helps further increase the variety of fruit in a particular country. Many immigrants bring unusual fruits with them from their old countries to their new homes. Therefore, nations with large immigrant populations often have especially rich and varied fruit markets.

Developing new fruit cultivars

Horticulturists have modified numerous original fruit species to create improved cultivars. Scientists use several methods to develop new cultivars. In one traditional method, they crossbreed two or more existing cultivars that have different desirable characteristics. Such crossbreeding creates a single new cultivar that exhibits desirable traits from both of its parents. Crossbreeding programs best suit small fruit plants that have short life cycles. Plants with longer life cycles make the process too time-consuming.

Another method for developing cultivars involves using *sports* or *chance seedlings* with desirable characteristics. Sports are *mutations* (random changes) that typically occur on individual branches or buds of plants. In chance seedlings, entire young plants exhibit unusual traits. Fruit plants propagated from sports or chance seedlings can inherit their desirable traits. Horticulturists employed this method to create many of the best-known fruit cultivars, including Delicious apples and varieties of navel oranges.

Since the late 1900's, scientists have increasingly used genetic engineering techniques to develop new culti-

vars. Genetic engineering involves altering a plant's *genes* (units of heredity) to give the plant certain desirable traits. Horticulturists often call such techniques *transgenic technology.*

Transgenic technology enables breeders to focus on precisely the characteristics they want to improve in a cultivar. For example, the first *genetically modified* (GM) food to reach the commercial market was a tomato. Breeders incorporated a gene into this tomato that slowed the ripening process. This genetic modification permitted growers to harvest the fruit at a riper, more flavorful stage. It also enabled the fruit to remain in good condition in the market longer. Other genetic modifications have incorporated vitamins and other nutrients into plants. Still others have improved the plants' resistance to diseases, weed killers, and drought.

Genes used in transgenic technology may come from organisms other than plants. For example, scientists have inserted a gene from a bacterium into several types of crop plants. This gene enables the plants to produce a bacterial protein that kills certain insects when they feed on the plants.

Despite the potential benefits of transgenic technology, there are also potential problems. For example, some people fear that this new technology may produce unintended consequences that cause harm to the environment. Some also fear that the patenting of GM cultivars may give corporations unreasonable monopolies over the production and marketing of such crops. Mainly for these reasons, various governments are considering bans on the sale of GM foods. James E. Pollard

Related articles in *World Book* include:

Temperate fruits

Apple	Cranberry	Nectarine
Apricot	Currant	Oregon grape
Beach plum	Dewberry	Peach
Blackberry	Gooseberry	Pear
Blueberry	Grape	Plum
Boysenberry	Huckleberry	Quince
Casaba	Loganberry	Raspberry
Cherry	Melon	Strawberry
Crab apple	Muskmelon	

Subtropical fruits

Avocado	Kiwi fruit	Orange
Citron	Kumquat	Persimmon
Citrus	Lemon	Pomegranate
Date palm	Lime	Tangelo
Fig	Loquat	Tangerine
Grapefruit	Mandarin	Tangor
	Olive	

Tropical fruits

Acerola	Mango
Banana	Mangosteen
Cherimoya	Papaya
Coconut palm	Pineapple
Guava	Sapodilla
Litchi	Tamarind

Other related articles

Berry	Horticulture	Raisin
Bramble	Hybrid	Rose (The rose
Burbank, Luther	Jelly and jam	family)
Drupe	Nut	Vegetable (Fruits)
Food, Frozen	Pectin	Vitamin
Food preservation	Prune	Wine
Grafting	Pruning	

Additional resources

Blackburne-Maze, Peter. *Fruit: An Illustrated History.* Firefly Bks., 2003.

Green, Aliza. *Field Guide to Produce: How to Identify, Select and Prepare Virtually Every Fruit and Vegetable at the Market.* Quirk Bks., 2004.

Reich, Lee. *Uncommon Fruits for Every Garden.* Timber, 2004.

Ridgwell, Jenny. *Fruits and Vegetables.* Heinemann Lib., 1998. Younger readers.

Fruit bat. See Flying fox.

Fruit fly is any of thousands of kinds of flies whose larvae eat their way through different fruits. Fruit flies include some of the most harmful agricultural pests.

Members of one family of these insects are called *peacock flies* because of their habit of strutting on fruit. They are small insects with many colors and beautiful wings. They lay their eggs in fruits, berries, nuts, and other parts of plants. Larvae that hatch from the eggs are small white maggots that tunnel their way through the fruit. This family of fruit flies includes the destructive *Mediterranean fruit fly, Oriental fruit fly, Mexican fruit fly,* the various cherry fruit flies, and the apple maggot. Control methods include applying chemical sprays and introducing the flies' natural *predators*—that is, animals that hunt the flies. Another control technique involves releasing large numbers of sterilized male flies. A female fly that mates with one of the sterilized males cannot produce fertile eggs.

The *pomace,* or *vinegar, flies* also are called fruit flies. Their maggots feed chiefly on decaying fruit and on crushed grapes in wineries. Scientists often use one species of pomace fly, *Drosophila melanogaster,* in heredity studies. This species is especially useful in such studies because the *chromosomes* (parts of a cell containing hereditary material) of its salivary glands are large. The species also reproduces rapidly.

Sandra J. Glover

Scientific classification. Peacock flies make up the family Tephritidae. The pomace flies form the family Drosophilidae.

See also **Apple maggot; Compound eye** (picture: The compound eye of a fruit fly); **Heredity** (The birth of genetics); **Mediterranean fruit fly.**

WORLD BOOK illustration by Shirley Hooper, Oxford Illustrators Limited

Fruit fly

Frunze. See Bishkek.

Fry, Christopher (1907-2005), was an English playwright. Fry wrote primarily in verse, trying to re-create the beauty and eloquence of Elizabethan drama. Fry achieved his greatest popularity during the late 1940's and early 1950's. However, his attempt to revive drama in verse never became a trend.

Fry's most popular plays were the witty verse comedies *The Lady's Not for Burning* (1948), his best-known play; *A Phoenix Too Frequent* (1946); and *Venus Observed* (1950). He also made adaptations of modern French plays. *The Lark* (1955), based on a drama by Jean Anouilh, deals with Joan of Arc. *Tiger at the Gates* (1955), adapted from a drama by the French playwright Jean Giraudoux, is an antiwar play set during the Trojan War. Fry wrote religious dramas, such as *The Boy with a Cart* (1938) and *The Firstborn* (1948). He also wrote screen-

plays for films, including *Ben-Hur* (1959) and *The Bible* (1966). Fry was born on Dec. 18, 1907, in Bristol and died on June 30, 2005. His real name was Christopher Harris.

Gerald M. Berkowitz

Fry, Elizabeth Gurney (1780-1845), was a British prison reformer. Reflecting her religious and moral views as a strict Quaker, Fry promoted humane care and treatment of prisoners, especially women and their children. From her first visit to London's notorious Newgate Prison in 1813 until her death, Fry worked tirelessly for reform. Many of her ideas, which continue to shape prison policies today, include the establishment of separate facilities for women, religious education, and the training in meaningful work for all inmates. She also argued for the prohibition of alcohol in jails. Elizabeth Gurney Fry was born in Norwich, England, on May 21, 1780. She died on Oct. 12, 1845. Mary Bosworth

Frye, Northrop (1912-1991), was a Canadian literary and social critic. Frye's first book, *Fearful Symmetry: A Study of William Blake* (1947), helped to unlock the mysteries of this English writer's universe. It also showed the important role of human imagination in the creation of the world. From Blake, Frye also learned that all works of literature incorporated similar basic structures. He outlined these forms in *Anatomy of Criticism* (1957).

Although known as a theoretical critic, Frye wrote many books of practical literary criticism, emphasizing William Shakespeare, John Milton, and English Romantic writers. Frye defended the importance of literature in education in *The Educated Imagination* (1963) and *The Well-Tempered Critic* (1963). In *The Great Code: The Bible and Literature* (1982), Frye maintained that the Bible created the basic patterns within which people in the Western world think and act. Frye also contributed to Canadian studies. *The Bush Garden* (1971) was especially influential. Herman Northrop Frye was born on July 14, 1912, in Sherbrooke, Quebec. He died on Jan. 23, 1991.

Ronald B. Hatch

Fu-chou. See Fuzhou.

Fuchs, *fyooks,* **Sir Vivian Ernest** (1908-1999), was a British geologist and Antarctic expert. He headed the British Commonwealth Trans-Antarctic Expedition in 1957 and 1958. Sir Edmund Hillary led the New Zealand party. The expedition, the first known party to cross Antarctica, covered 2,158 miles (3,473 kilometers) in 99 days and made geophysical observations. Fuchs was director of the British Antarctic Survey from 1958 to 1973. Fuchs was born on Feb. 11, 1908, on the Isle of Wight. He died on Nov. 11, 1999. See also **Antarctica** (The International Geophysical Year; map: Antarctica exploration).

Barry M. Gough

Fuchsia, *FYOO shuh,* is a group of tropical plants known for their bright pink and purple flowers. There are more than 100 *species* (kinds). Some grow as shrubs or trees. Others are trailing, climbing, or hanging vinelike plants. Fuchsias are native to Central and South America, Tahiti, and New Zealand. Gardeners around the world cultivate fuchsias.

Fuchsias are sometimes called *lady's eardrops.* The cultivated species have showy hanging flowers. The flower parts are often fleshy and in contrasting bright colors. These fuchsias have trailing stems and are popularly grown in hanging baskets.

Gardeners use cuttings of fuchsias to develop new

WORLD BOOK illustration by Christabel King

Fuchsia flowers resemble dangling earrings. Some fuchsias grow wild. Others are cultivated in gardens and greenhouses.

plants. The cuttings are often stored in cool greenhouses and then planted in the spring. The fuchsia is named after the German botanist Leonhard Fuchs.   Paul E. Berry

Scientific classification. Fuchsias make up the genus *Fuchsia.*

Fuel is a material that provides useful energy. Fuels are used to heat and cool buildings, cook food, power engines, and produce electric power. Some fuels occur naturally, and others are artificially created. Such natural fuels as coal, petroleum, and natural gas are obtained from underground deposits that were formed millions of years ago from the remains of plants and animals. These fuels, called *fossil fuels,* account for about 90 percent of the energy people use today.

Synthetic fuels can be made from fossil fuels, certain types of rock and sand, and *biomass.* Biomass is the name for such replaceable organic matter as garbage, wood, and animal manure that can be used to produce energy. *Biofuels* are made from biological material, such as corn, switchgrass, and other plants. Biofuels, unlike fossil fuels, are a *renewable* form of fuel, because they are regrown each year.

Most fuels release energy by burning with oxygen in the air. But some—especially chemical fuels used in rockets—need special *oxidizers* to burn. Oxidizers are compounds that contain oxygen. Nuclear fuels do not burn but release energy through the *fission* (splitting) or *fusion* (joining together) of atoms.

Since the 1970's, shortages of some fuels and concerns about the environmental effects resulting from the burning of fuels have led people to explore other sources of energy. This article discusses five groups of fuels—(1) solid fuels, (2) liquid fuels, (3) gas fuels, (4) chemical fuels, and (5) nuclear fuels—and their uses. For information on the availability of fuels, their effect on the environment, and alternative energy sources, see **Energy supply** and **Environmental pollution.**

Solid fuels

Coal is used chiefly to produce electric power. It is burned to create heat to turn water into steam. The steam is then used to rotate *turbines,* machines that generate electric power (see **Turbine**). Some coal is made into *coke,* a charcoallike solid that is an essential raw material in the production of iron and steel. Coal is also used to provide energy for industrial machinery and to heat buildings.

There are four types of coal: (1) *lignite,* (2) *subbituminous coal,* (3) *bituminous coal,* and (4) *anthracite.* Bituminous coal is the most plentiful coal used by industry. It contains more carbon and produces more heat than either lignite or subbituminous coal. It is also the coal best suited for making coke. Anthracite is the least plentiful and hardest coal. It contains more carbon and produces more heat than other coals. However, anthracite is difficult to ignite and burns slowly.

Peat is partially decayed plant matter found in swamps called *bogs.* It is used as a fuel chiefly in areas where coal and oil are scarce. Peat can be cut, formed into blocks, and dried. The dried blocks are then burned to heat homes.

Biomass. Wood has been used as a fuel since prehistoric times—longer than any other material. Today, it is an important fuel chiefly in less developed countries, where it is used for cooking and heating. In the United States and other industrialized nations, it is not a major source of energy. But some paper and pulp factories, which make wood products, obtain the energy for their manufacturing processes by burning bark, sawdust, and other wood waste. Wood is also used to make charcoal.

Biomass materials other than wood are also used as fuel. For example, heat produced by burning nutshells, rice and oat hulls, and other by-products of food processing is often used to operate plant equipment.

Liquid fuels

Liquid fuels are made mainly from petroleum, but some synthetic liquid fuels are also produced. Liquid fuels are easy to store and transport. They are the major source of energy for automobiles, airplanes, and other vehicles. Liquid fuels are also used to heat buildings.

Petroleum, also called *crude oil,* ranges from clear yellow-brown oils to thick, black tars. Some crude oil can be burned as fuel in stoves and boilers without processing. However, most petroleum is refined to produce such fuels as *gasoline, diesel oil,* and *kerosene.* Gasoline is used to provide energy for most motor vehicles and piston-engine airplanes. Diesel oil powers most trains, ships, and large trucks. Kerosene provides energy for jet airplanes.

Other fuel oils obtained by refining petroleum include *distillate oils* and *residual oils.* Distillate oils are light oils, which are used chiefly to heat homes and small buildings. Residual oils are heavy, thick oils. They provide energy to power utilities, factories, and large ships. They also are used to heat large buildings.

Synthetic liquid fuels include fuels made from coal, natural gas, biomass, *oil shale,* and *bituminous sands.* Oil shale is a rock that contains *kerogen,* a substance that yields oil when heated. Bituminous sands contain *bitumen,* a substance from which oil can be obtained. Synthetic liquid fuels are processed mainly in areas where one type of fuel is abundant, but other vital fuels are scarce. For example, South Africa has several large plants that make gasoline from coal. In this way, South

Africa—with its abundance of coal and scarcity of petroleum—can provide its own motor fuel.

In the Canadian province of Alberta, plentiful bituminous sands are processed to yield oil. In Brazil, biomass in the form of sugar cane pulp is used to produce biofuel for automobiles.

Gas fuels

Gas fuels include natural and manufactured gases. Such fuels flow easily through pipes and are used to provide energy for homes, businesses, and industries. In many countries, vast networks of pipelines bring gas fuels to millions of consumers.

Natural gas is used to heat buildings, cook food, and provide energy for industries. It consists chiefly of methane, a colorless and odorless gas. A small amount of a foul-smelling chemical compound called *mercaptan* is usually mixed with natural gas so that gas leaks can be promptly detected.

Butane and propane, which make up a small proportion of natural gas, become liquids when placed under large amounts of pressure. When pressure is released, they change back into gas. Such fuels, often called *liquefied petroleum gas* (LPG), are easily stored and shipped as liquids. They provide energy for motor homes and can serve as fuel for people who live far from natural gas pipelines.

Manufactured gas, like synthetic liquid fuels, is used chiefly where certain fuels are abundant and others are scarce. Coal, petroleum, and biomass can all be converted to gas through various engineering processes. Gas can also be produced by treating such biomass as animal manure with bacteria called *anaerobes,* which expel methane as they digest the waste.

Chemical fuels

Chemical fuels, which are produced in solid and liquid form, create great amounts of heat and power. They are used chiefly in rocket engines. Chemical rocket propellants consist of both a fuel and an oxidizer. A common rocket fuel is a chemical compound called *hydrazine.* The oxidizer is a substance, such as nitrogen tetroxide, that contains oxygen. When the propellant is ignited, the oxidizer provides the oxygen the fuel needs to burn. Chemical fuels are also used in some race cars.

Nuclear fuels

Nuclear fuels provide energy through the fission or fusion of their atoms' *nuclei* (cores). Uranium is the most commonly used nuclear fuel, though plutonium also provides nuclear energy. When the nuclei of these elements undergo fission, they release tremendous amounts of heat. Nuclear fuels are used mainly to generate electric power. They also power some submarines and ships. The fusion of hydrogen nuclei can release even more heat than nuclear fission. But scientists have not yet developed the technology needed to harness fusion energy for electric power.   Michael A. Adewumi

Related articles in *World Book* include:

Alcohol	Carbon	Fire
Biomass	Charcoal	Fission
Bituminous sands	Coal	Fusion
Butane and	Coke	Gas
propane	Coke oven gas	Gasoline
Heat	Kerosene	Petroleum
Heating (Sources	Methanol	Plutonium
of heat)	Nuclear energy	Rocket (Kinds of
Hydrocarbon	Oil shale	rocket engines)
Hydrogen	Peat	Uranium

Fuel cell is a device that converts chemical energy to electric energy. In this way, a fuel cell is similar to a battery. However, a battery contains all of the components required to produce electric power. A fuel cell, however, must constantly be fed a fuel and an *oxidizer* to produce power. An oxidizer is a substance that removes electrons in a chemical reaction.

It costs more to produce a given amount of power using a fuel cell than using a battery. However, a fuel cell's *electrodes* (electric terminals) remain largely unchanged during its operation. A battery's electrodes, on the other hand, can be gradually used up. After battery electrodes are consumed, the battery will stop producing power. It must be discarded or recharged. But a fuel cell will continue to produce power as long as the fuel and oxidizer are provided.

The United States Gemini and Apollo space programs of the 1960's used fuel cells to provide electric energy for spacecraft. Today, many scientists are working to produce cost-effective fuel cells to power automobiles.

How a fuel cell works. In a fuel cell, the fuel is fed from outside the cell to one of two electrodes, called the *anode.* There, an *oxidation reaction* releases electrons. The electrons, which are negatively charged, travel outside of the fuel cell through an external circuit. The flow of electrons powers one or more devices, such as motors or lights, that are included in the circuit. The electrons then travel to the other electrode, called the *cathode.* There, they are involved in a *reduction reaction* with the oxidizer, which is fed from outside the cell. In a typical fuel cell, the anode and cathode each contain a *catalyst,* a substance that speeds a chemical reaction. If the catalysts were not present to enable efficient reactions, the fuel cell would produce little or no power. Platinum is commonly used as a catalyst in fuel cells.

Between the anode and the cathode is an *electrolyte.* An electrolyte is a substance that conducts electric current. The electrolyte in a fuel cell may be a solid or a liquid. The electrolyte does not allow electrons to pass through it. However, it acts as an internal circuit by conducting positively charged *ions.* Ions are atoms or molecules that carry a positive or negative electric charge. The ions in a fuel cell are also involved in the oxidation and reduction reactions.

Different devices require different voltages and current to operate. By electrically connecting several fuel cells, voltage and the current may be tuned to satisfy the requirements of various devices. A group of electrically connected fuel cells is called a *fuel cell stack.*

A common fuel cell is the *polymer electrolyte membrane* (PEM) fuel cell. It is also called a *proton exchange membrane* fuel cell. This device is named for the electrolyte it uses. Its electrolyte is a thin, solid membrane composed of long chains of molecules called *polymers.* The two electrodes sit on either side of the membrane. The fuel is hydrogen gas. The oxidizer is either oxygen gas or air. At the anode, hydrogen is oxidized at a platinum catalyst to produce electrons and hydrogen ions. The hydrogen ions pass through the membrane. The

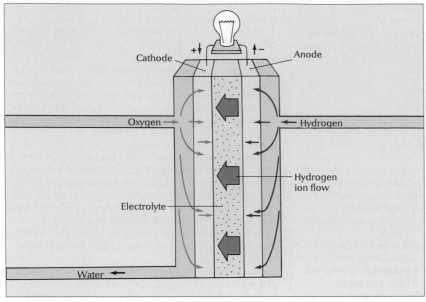

Cathode | Anode
Oxygen | Hydrogen
Hydrogen ion flow
Electrolyte
Water

A fuel cell has two electrical terminals called *electrodes*— the *anode* and the *cathode*. In the fuel cell shown here, hydrogen gas (H_2) is fed to the anode. There, the hydrogen undergoes a process called *oxidation*, which releases hydrogen ions and electrons. The hydrogen ions can pass through the *electrolyte* that separates the electrodes, but the electrons cannot. The electrons instead flow to the cathode through a circuit outside the cell, thus powering the light bulb. At the cathode, oxygen gas (O_2) reacts with these electrons and the hydrogen ions that have passed through the electrolyte, producing water and some heat as by-products.

WORLD BOOK diagram by Linda Kinnaman

electrons are forced through the external circuit. At the cathode, the hydrogen ions and electrons are combined with the oxygen in the presence of platinum. This reaction produces heat, along with water. The water is removed. Matthew M. Fay

Fuel injection is a system for squirting fuel into gasoline and diesel engines. When used on gasoline engines, it replaces the *carburetor,* a device that mixes air and fuel.

Most gasoline engines for cars use *multi-port fuel injection.* In this system, a pump forces fuel under pressure to a nozzle called a *fuel injector* located at each of the engine's cylinders. The injectors then spray the fuel into *intake ports* (chambers) near each cylinder. There

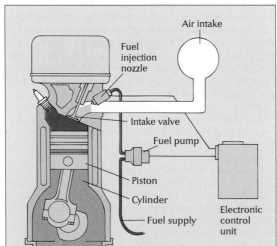

Air intake
Fuel injection nozzle
Intake valve
Fuel pump
Piston
Cylinder
Fuel supply
Electronic control unit

WORLD BOOK diagram by Arthur Grebetz

A fuel injection system pumps gasoline to a nozzle, which sprays the fuel into a chamber. There, the fuel is mixed with air before a valve opens to admit the mixture into the cylinder.

the fuel partially mixes with air before a valve opens to admit the mixture into the cylinder. Some newer cars use *direct fuel injection,* in which fuel is sprayed directly into the cylinder.

Some older gasoline engines use a system called *single point* or *throttle body* fuel injection. This system has only one or two fuel injection nozzles. Each nozzle delivers fuel to several cylinders.

Fuel injection overcomes disadvantages of carburetors. In a carburetor, fuel is drawn into the engine at one location. Poor distribution of the fuel-air mixture can prevent some of the fuel from burning, resulting in lower fuel economy and higher exhaust emissions. The engine also may flood or ice up in cold weather, or develop *vapor lock* in hot weather. Vapor lock interrupts the flow of fuel and can cause the engine to stall (see **Vapor lock**).

Fuel injection includes electronic or mechanical controls to measure the amount of air being drawn into the engine. The controls adjust the amount of time that each injector valve opens to spray fuel, maintaining the proper ratio of fuel to air. The nozzles help break the fuel into a fine spray so that it mixes well with the air and thus burns almost completely. Precise control of the fuel-air mixture also helps control exhaust emissions and enables cold engines to start quickly and run smoothly.

All diesel engines use fuel injection. In most of these engines, the nozzles spray the fuel directly into the cylinder after the piston has compressed the air to high pressures. A diesel pump compresses the fuel to a much higher pressure than for gasoline fuel injection. In some cases, a single pump is located centrally on the engine. In other cases, each of the engine's cylinders has a pump. Gregory W. Davis

See also **Diesel engine** (How a diesel engine works).

Fuentes, *FWEHN tays,* **Carlos** (1928-2012), a Mexican writer, was an important figure in Spanish-American literature. Fuentes wrote imaginative and complex narratives that reflect a keen awareness of history and the workings of power. In his novels, he experimented with shifts in place, time, and the identity of characters.

Fuentes's first novel, *Where the Air Is Clear* (1958), is set in Mexico City and shifts back and forth between the past and present. *The Death of Artemio Cruz* (1962) shifts backward and forward in time as it presents a revolutionary's rise to power and his later moral deterioration. *Change of Skin* (1967) emphasizes the instability of personal identity. Fuentes's most ambitious novel, *Terra Nostra* (1975), goes beyond the facts of history to offer an alternate version of how events might have unfolded.

Fuentes's later work incorporates elements of popular culture. *The Hydra's Head* (1977) resembles a thriller full of political intrigue. *Distant Relations* (1982) is similar to a Gothic novel. *The Old Gringo* (1985) resembles a Western and includes insights into relations between the United States and Mexico. *Christopher Unborn* (1987) is a satirical treatment of modern society. *The Buried Mirror* (1992) is a nonfiction history of Latin America's cultural heritage. *The Years with Laura Díaz* (2000) explores the history of Mexico in the 1900's through a fictional biography of a woman named Laura Díaz. *The Eagle's Throne* (2006) is a political satire set in Mexico in the year 2020. *Destiny and Desire* (2011) combines realism and fantasy in exploring Mexico's culture, politics, and religion. A number of Fuentes's short stories were collected in *Happy Families* (2008). Many of his essays were collected in *This I Believe: An A to Z of a Life* (2005).

Fuentes was born on Nov. 11, 1928, in Panama City, Panama. He was Mexico's ambassador to France from 1975 to 1977. He died on May 15, 2012.   Naomi Lindstrom

Fugard, Athol, *FOO gahrd, ATH uhl* (1932-   ), is a South African playwright. Many of his plays explore the destructive effects of *apartheid,* the policy of racial segregation enforced in South Africa until 1991. Fugard has directed and acted in many of his own plays.

His first play to gain recognition was *The Blood Knot* (1961). It tells the story of two half brothers, one with light skin and the other with dark skin. *Boesman and Lena* (1969) concerns two impoverished people of mixed race and their struggle for survival. Fugard joined black South African actors John Kani and Winston Ntshona in writing the comedy *Sizwe Banzi Is Dead* (1972), in which a black man trades identity papers with a corpse. *"Master Harold" ... and the Boys* (1982) deals with the relationship between a white boy and a black waiter, showing how racism disrupts their friendship. *The Road to Mecca* (1985) examines the role of the artist in the modern world. Fugard's other dramas include *Hello and Goodbye* (1965), *A Lesson from Aloes* (1978), *My Children! My Africa!* (1988), *Playland* (1992), *Valley Song* (1995), and *Exits and Entrances* (2004). Harold Athol Lannigan Fugard, who is white, was born on June 11, 1932, in Middelburg, in what is now Eastern Cape province.   Mardi Valgemae

Fugitive slave laws were laws that provided for the return of runaway slaves who escaped from one state to another. A clause in the Northwest Ordinance of 1787 provided for the return of slaves who had escaped to the free Northwest Territory. The Constitution of the United States, which went into effect in 1788, also provided for the return of fugitive slaves.

In 1793, the U.S. Congress passed a fugitive slave law allowing owners to recover slaves merely by presenting proof of ownership before a magistrate. An order was then issued for the arrest and return of the escaped slaves, who were forbidden a jury trial and the right to give evidence in their own behalf. Under this law, free blacks in the North were sometimes kidnapped and taken South as slaves. For this reason, some Northern states gave orders not to help recover fugitive slaves.

The Compromise of 1850 imposed heavy penalties for aiding the escape or interfering with recovery of a slave. Some Northern states passed *personal liberty laws,* which sometimes forbade state and local officers from obeying national fugitive slave laws.   Robert F. Dalzell, Jr.

Fugue, *fyoog,* is a musical composition in which several voices or instruments repeat a number of melodies with slight variations. A fugue is based on *counterpoint,* a composing technique in which two or more melodies are combined (see **Counterpoint**). The fugue as an independent composition began in the 1600's.

A fugue begins with a section called the *exposition,* in which the melodies are first stated. The basic melody is called the *subject.* It is followed by a melody called the *answer.* The answer resembles the subject, but it is performed in a different but related key. A third melody, the *countersubject,* accompanies the answer. The other melodies then enter in sequence. After all the performers state the subject, the exposition is complete.

After the exposition, the subject is repeated in different but related keys. In most fugues, brief passages called *episodes* link the entrances of the subject. Fugues generally end in *stretto,* in which the subject and answer are performed closer together than in the exposition.   R. M. Longyear

Fuji, Mount. See Mount Fuji.

Fulani, *foo LAH nee,* are a people of the grassland regions of western Africa. The more than 5 million Fulani live as far west as Senegal and as far east as Cameroon. For hundreds of years, most Fulani have been cattle herders and have lived as minority groups among various agricultural peoples. The Fulani are also called *Fula, Fulah, Fulbe, Fulata, Peul,* or *Poul.*

The Fulani originated in what are now Senegal and Guinea. They built a powerful empire there during the A.D. 600's. Some descendants of these Fulani intermarried with people they conquered and became a sepa-

Peter Marlow, Magnum

Fulani girls often wear earrings and necklaces. The Fulani are one of the largest ethnic groups in Nigeria.

rate group, called the Toucouleur (also spelled Tukulor). The Fulani gradually spread eastward and reached Nigeria and Cameroon in the early 1800's.

Many Fulani became Muslims in the early 1700's and conquered a number of their neighbors in holy wars. Between 1804 and 1809, Uthman Dan Fodio, a Muslim religious leader, conquered most of the Hausa states of northern Nigeria. He then established an empire that consisted of several Fulani states. Uthman's empire remained powerful until the British conquered northern Nigeria in 1903. Many Fulani still live in the northern part of Nigeria.   John W. Burton

Fulbright, J. William (1905-1995), an Arkansas Democrat, served in the United States Senate from 1945 to 1974. He was chairman of the Senate Foreign Relations Committee from 1959 to 1974. Fulbright became a leading critic of U.S. involvement in the Vietnam War (1957-1975). During the 1960's and early 1970's, Fulbright was a spokesman for those who wanted Congress to have more control over presidential warmaking powers. He sponsored the Fulbright Act of 1946, which provides funds for the exchange of students between the United States and other countries (see **Fulbright scholarship**).

James William Fulbright was born on April 9, 1905, in Sumner, Missouri, and entered the University of Arkansas at the age of 16. He graduated from Arkansas in 1925 and from the George Washington University Law School in 1934. From 1925 to 1928, he studied at Oxford University in England as a Rhodes scholar. Fulbright served as president of the University of Arkansas from 1939 to 1941 and was elected to the United States House of Representatives in 1942. He criticized U.S. foreign policy in his books, including *Old Myths and New Realities* (1964) and *The Arrogance of Power* (1967). Fulbright died on Feb. 9, 1995.   William J. Eaton

Fulbright scholarship is an award by the United States government for research, teaching, or graduate study. The scholarship program was begun under the Fulbright Act of 1946, named for its sponsor, Senator J. William Fulbright of Arkansas. It seeks to promote better understanding between the peoples of the United States and other countries.

The annual awards allow U.S. citizens to study or work in other lands and permit people of other countries to study or work in the United States. More than 150 countries participate in the program annually.

Money for the awards came at first from the sale of surplus World War II equipment to other countries. The U.S. government and participating countries and universities now fund the program. The Bureau of Educational and Cultural Affairs of the U.S. Department of State oversees the program. The Fulbright Foreign Scholarship Board selects the award winners.

Fulcrum. See Lever.

Fuller, Buckminster (1895-1983), was an American engineer and inventor who sought to express the technology and needs of modern life in buildings and enclosures of space. He had an intense interest in expanding people's ability to control large areas of their environment and still have a close relationship with nature. Fuller believed that solutions should be comprehensive rather than particular. His designs show the influence of such natural molecular structures as the tetrahedron.

Fuller solved many design problems in such diversi-

Dennis Stock, Magnum

Buckminster Fuller became famous for designing large, lightweight prefabricated enclosures called *geodesic domes*.

fied fields as automobiles, buildings, and cities. His influence spread through his lectures, teaching, and writings. A collection of his essays discussing theories and designs was published as *Ideas and Integrities* (1963). The title of Fuller's book *Synergetics* (1975) was the word he used for the cooperation of nature and design.

Richard Buckminster Fuller, Jr., was born in Milton, Massachusetts, on July 12, 1895. He gained international attention in 1927 by designing an all-metal prefabricated home called a *Dymaxion house*. After World War II (1939-1945), Fuller concentrated on designing large, lightweight prefabricated enclosures that he called *geodesic domes*. He died on July 1, 1983.   Nicholas Adams

Fuller, Margaret (1810-1850), was an American journalist and reformer. She became a leader of a philosophical movement called Transcendentalism (see **Transcendentalism**).

Sarah Margaret Fuller was born on May 23, 1810, in Cambridgeport, Massachusetts, near Boston. She began her journalistic career by serving from 1840 to 1842 as editor in chief of the transcendentalist magazine *The Dial*. Under Fuller, *The Dial* became one of the most important periodicals in American literary history. From 1844 to 1846, she wrote literary criticism for the *New York Tribune*. Her book *Papers on Literature and Art* (1846) grew out of her contributions to the *Tribune*.

As a reformer, Fuller campaigned for women's rights. Her most important book, *Woman in the Nineteenth Century* (1845), explores the political, economic, social, and intellectual status of women. She was far ahead of her time in her criticism of discrimination against women because of their sex.

Fuller went to Europe in 1846. In 1848, she gave birth to a child and claimed that she had secretly married the Marchese Angelo Ossoli, a follower of the Italian patriot Giuseppe Mazzini. The couple participated in the Italian revolution of 1848 and 1849. During a voyage to the

United States, they and their son drowned when their ship sank on July 19, 1850.   John Clendenning

Fuller, Melville Weston (1833-1910), served as chief justice of the United States from 1888 to 1910. He was a capable Supreme Court administrator. But he clung to the doctrine of states' rights in a time of problems that required increasing federal regulation. Fuller's best-known decisions declared the national income tax unconstitutional, and, by interpretation, weakened the 1890 Sherman Antitrust Act (see **Antitrust laws**).

Fuller was born in Augusta, Maine, on Feb. 11, 1833. He graduated from Bowdoin College and studied law at Harvard Law School. He was a Chicago corporation lawyer from 1856 to 1888. He served as a member of the Illinois Constitutional Convention in 1862, and later was a member of the Illinois legislature. From 1900 to 1910, Fuller was a member of the Permanent Court of Arbitration at The Hague, which handled legal disputes between nations. He died on July 4, 1910.   Jerre S. Williams

Fuller's earth is a clay-rich material used mainly as a cleaner and purifier. The material consists mostly of *hydrated aluminum silicates*—minerals made up of water and compounds of silicon, oxygen, and aluminum. Often, the material is also rich in compounds of calcium and magnesium. The surface of fuller's earth attracts greasy and oily substances. Factory workers use fuller's earth to soak up oil that has spilled on the floor. Used in litter boxes, fuller's earth soaks up animal wastes. Petroleum companies use it to purify and lighten the color of crude oil.

Fuller's earth also acts as a *catalyst,* a substance that increases the speed of a chemical reaction without being consumed. People once used a form of fuller's earth to remove grease from cloth and wool. Fuller's earth gets its name from this process, called *fulling.*

Ray E. Ferrell, Jr.

Fulmar, *FUL muhr,* is a kind of ocean bird. Fulmars are petrels. They resemble large gulls, with a bill that is nearly as long as the head. The feet are webbed, and the hind toe is reduced to a claw.

Fulmars breed on rocky shores and make shallow nests in high, rocky places. A fulmar lays one egg in the nest. Fulmars feed on any animal matter but prefer fatty substances, such as whale blubber. The bird is valuable for its feathers, down, and oil.

There are two *species* (kinds) of fulmars. The *northern fulmar* lives in far northern seas throughout the Northern Hemisphere. The *southern fulmar* lives in far southern seas throughout the Southern Hemisphere.

James J. Dinsmore

Scientific classification. The scientific name of the northern fulmar is *Fulmarus glacialis.* The southern fulmar's scientific name is *F. glacialoides.*

See also **Petrel.**

Fulton, Robert (1765-1815), was an American inventor, mechanical and civil engineer, and artist. He is best known for designing and building the *Clermont,* the first commercially successful steamboat. The *Clermont* ushered in a new era in the history of transportation. In addition to his work with steamboats, Fulton made important contributions to canal transportation and to the development of the submarine, the torpedo, and steampowered warships.

Early years. Fulton was born Nov. 14, 1765, on a farm near Little Britain in Lancaster County, Pennsylvania. He spent his boyhood in Lancaster and showed inventive talent at an early age. He turned out lead pencils, household utensils for his mother, and skyrockets for a town celebration. Fulton developed a hand-operated paddle wheel for use on a rowboat. He also built a rifle that had sight and bore of original design.

Fulton went to Philadelphia at the age of 17 and was apprenticed to a jeweler. He soon began to win fame as a painter of miniatures and portraits. He saved enough money to buy a farm for his mother.

At the age of 21, Fulton went to England to study with the fashionable American artist Benjamin West. In London, Fulton made a moderate living as an artist. But he became increasingly interested in scientific and engineering developments. After 1793, he gave his full attention to this field and painted only for amusement.

The inventor. Fulton's first enthusiasm was for canal development. He designed new types of canal boats and a system of inclined planes to replace canal locks. Other mechanical problems challenged him. He invented a machine for making rope and one for spinning flax. He made a labor-saving device for cutting marble and invented a dredging machine for cutting canal channels. In 1796, Fulton wrote *A Treatise on the Improvement of Canal Navigation.*

About 1797, Fulton turned his attention to the submarine. In 1800, he built a diving boat, the *Nautilus,* which could descend 25 feet (7.6 meters) underwater. Fulton's work with submarines continued until 1806. He realized the dangers that submarines would bring to naval warfare but thought that they might serve to limit sea war and piracy. Fulton's experimental submarines could dive and surface, and he blew up anchored test craft. But he never found a satisfactory solution to the problem of propulsion underwater. Fulton's ideas interested both the French general Napoleon Bonaparte and the British Admiralty, but neither adopted them wholeheartedly.

In 1802, Robert R. Livingston, the United States minister to France, interested Fulton in turning his attention to the steamboat. Fulton had been interested for many years in the idea of steam propulsion for a boat. An experimental boat, launched on the Seine River in Paris in 1803, sank because the engine was too heavy. But a second boat, built in the same year, operated successfully. Fulton ordered an engine from the British firm of Boulton & Watt and returned to the United States in 1806.

The *Clermont.* Fulton directed the construction of a steamboat in New York in 1807. Registered as the *North River Steamboat of Clermont,* the ship was generally called the *Clermont,* which was also the name of Robert Livingston's home. On Aug. 17, 1807, the steamboat started on its first successful trip, up the Hudson River from New York City to Albany. After some alterations, the boat began to provide regular passenger service on the Hudson.

The *Clermont* was not the first steamboat to be built, but it was the first steamboat to become a practical and financial success. Part of Fulton's success was due to his concern for passenger comfort. His handbills announced: "Dinner will be served at exactly 2 o'clock … Tea with meats … Supper at 8 in the evening" and "A shelf has been added to each berth, on which gentlemen will please put their boots, shoes, and clothes, that

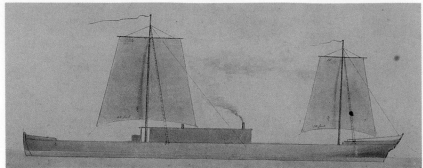

The *Clermont,* invented by Robert Fulton, was the first commercially successful steamboat. The ship made its first successful trip up the Hudson River. Fulton made this water-color sketch of the *Clermont* in 1808.

Courtesy of the New-York Historical Society, New York

the cabin will not be encumbered."

After the success of the *Clermont,* Fulton became occupied with building and operating other boats. He also defended the monopolies that state legislatures had granted to him and Robert Livingston.

Fulton designed and built a steam-powered warship, *Fulton the First,* for the defense of New York harbor in the War of 1812. He died on Feb. 24, 1815. The statue of Fulton in Statuary Hall, in the U.S. Capitol in Washington, D.C., honors his achievements. Paul F. Johnston

See also **Clermont; Fitch, John; Livingston, Robert R.; Ship** (The first steamboats); **Steamboat.**

Fumarole, *FYOO muh rohl,* is a hole or vent in the ground that gives off volcanic gases. Most fumaroles occur in inactive volcanic regions, such as Yellowstone National Park. The gases given off are mainly steam mixed with small amounts of carbon dioxide, hydrogen, hydrogen sulfide, hydrogen chloride, hydrogen fluoride, and sulfuric acid. Some of these gases are poisonous. Others may irritate the throat and lungs and cause choking. Fumaroles that give off sulfurous gases are called *solfataras.* See also **Hot springs.** Paul R. Bierman

Fumigation, *FYOO muh GAY shuhn,* is a method of killing pests that involves the use of toxic gases. It is widely used to eliminate weeds, *nematodes* (roundworms), and other pests from cropland. It is also used to protect such foods as grains and spices from rats and insects during storage. Goods shipped between countries often are fumigated to prevent pests and diseases from spreading from one country to another. Houses, apartments, and other buildings are sometimes fumigated to kill cockroaches, termites, and other insects.

The chemicals used in fumigation are called *fumigants.* They work well only in an enclosed area. For example, stored foods commonly are covered with plastic sheets during fumigation. The sheets trap the gases beneath them, enabling the foods to absorb the fumigants. Some farmland is treated to kill nematodes by injecting fumigants into the soil, which acts as a cover. Plastic sheets are generally used as an additional cover for fields fumigated against weeds, insects, and plant diseases. The sheets are removed about 24 to 48 hours after the fumigants are applied. The fields can be safely planted about one to two weeks later. By then, the gases have been *dissipated* (released) from the soil.

Fumigants are poisonous to people and must be handled with care. They are usually applied by trained, licensed professionals. Commonly used fumigants include cyanide, formaldehyde, and methyl bromide. Foods that have been fumigated are safe to eat only after the fumigant has been dissipated. Walter A. Skroch

See also **Insecticide; Pest control.**

Funafuti, *FYOO nuh FYOOT ee* (pop. 2,800), is the capital of Tuvalu, a small island country in the South Pacific Ocean. Funafuti is one of the smallest and most unusual national capitals. It is the largest islet of an *atoll* that is also called Funafuti. An atoll is a ring-shaped coral reef surrounding a lagoon. The Funafuti atoll consists of 30 islets with a total area of 689 acres (279 hectares). Most of the people live in Fongafale village on the islet of Funafuti. The main government offices of Tuvalu and a hospital, a hotel, a jail, and a wharf are at Vaiaku on the islet. Funafuti was the site of a United States military base during World War II (1939-1945). The base is now an airstrip just east of Vaiaku. See also **Tuvalu.** Michael R. Ogden

Funchal, *fun SHAHL,* is the capital, largest city, and chief port of the Madeira Islands. The municipality of Funchal has a population of 111,892. A municipality may include rural areas as well as the urban center. The Madeira Islands belong to Portugal and lie in the Atlantic Ocean off the northwest coast of Africa. Funchal is on the southern coast of the island of Madeira. The city's pleasant climate makes it a popular resort.

Portuguese settlers founded Funchal in 1421. The city has many beautiful gardens and a cathedral that dates from the 1400's. Funchal's economy is based on the tourist trade and the export of sugar and the famous Madeira wines. The city also produces ceramics and linen embroidery. Funchal has a modern airport, and airlines connect the city with western Europe. Douglas L. Wheeler

Function, in mathematics. See **Algebra** (Functions); **Calculus** (Functions).

Fundamentalism, *FUHN duh MEHN tuh lihz uhm,* commonly refers to a broad movement within Protestantism in the United States. The fundamentalist movement tries to preserve what it considers the basic ideas of Christianity against criticism by liberal theologians.

Development of Protestant fundamentalism. At the end of the 1800's, many liberal religious scholars challenged the accuracy of the Bible. They also used historical research to question previously accepted Christian beliefs. The liberals attempted to adjust Christian theology to then-new discoveries in the sciences, particularly in biology and geology. Many Christians believed the work of the liberals threatened the authenticity and even the survival of Christianity.

From 1910 to 1915, anonymous authors published 12 small volumes titled *The Fundamentals*. Fundamentalism got its name from these booklets. The authors tried to explain what they felt were basic Christian doctrines that should be accepted without question. These doctrines included the *infallibility* (absolute accuracy) of the Bible, including the story of Creation and accounts of miracles. Other doctrines included the virgin birth of Jesus, Christ's atonement for the sins of humanity through his Crucifixion, and his Second Coming.

Fundamentalism began in the North, but it has gained its greatest strength in Southern areas. Baptists and Presbyterians have been most directly affected by the theological debates between liberal and conservative Protestants. Fundamentalism, however, has had an influence on all Protestant denominations, particularly such groups as the Church of God, Assemblies of God, and Pentecostal churches. Conservative fundamentalist beliefs also have influenced television evangelism.

Organizations within a movement called the New Religious Right have adopted social and political positions based on a literal use of Biblical texts. They work to elect candidates whose views reflect their positions. The most controversial positions include those that concern abortion, homosexuality, and the teaching of creationism and intelligent design as opposed to evolution in public schools (see **Evolution** [Acceptance of evolution]).

Fundamentalism in other religions. Beginning in the mid-1900's, the word *fundamentalism* has increasingly been used to describe conservative or extremist movements in non-Christian religious traditions. In Islam, fundamentalist views are often associated with strict interpretations of the sacred book called the Qur'ān and precise obedience to such interpretations. Islamic fundamentalists consider the book as a guide not only to religious faith, but also to civil law. They are generally hostile to any form of *secularism* (nonreligious attitudes) and often suggest that the United States and Western culture in general promote secularism.

In Israel, Jewish fundamentalists have challenged efforts of government leaders to make peace with Palestinians. They have also called for making Jewish religious law binding on all Israelis.

Hindu fundamentalism in India has added to long-standing tension between Hindus and religious minorities, especially Sikhs, Muslims, and Christians. Some disputes have resulted in armed conflict, especially between India and Muslim Pakistan in the region of Kashmir.   Charles H. Lippy

See also **Bob Jones University; Christian Coalition of America; Scopes trial.**

Additional resources

Armstrong, Karen. *The Battle for God.* Knopf, 2000. Examines fundamentalism among several faiths.
Brasher, Brenda E., ed. *Encyclopedia of Fundamentalism.* Routledge, 2001.

Funeral customs are traditions, rituals, rites, and ceremonies that are performed after a person dies. All human societies have such customs, but the practices associated with death vary widely among different cultures. Anthropologists and others who study culture have made efforts to understand the meaning and role of funeral customs in human societies. They observe that funeral customs are deeply rooted in a people's cultural heritage and beliefs about death. Funeral customs may persist long after the cultural beliefs that underlie the funeral customs have faded.

Scholars believe that some funeral customs are intended to ease the dead person's transition to an afterlife. Other practices may have been developed to protect the living from ghosts, evil spirits, or bad luck associated with death. Still other funeral customs are designed to ensure blessings or advice that some cultures believe the dead can provide. Many funeral customs help the living express their grief and honor the dead.

Throughout the world, funeral customs in many different cultures share common elements. These include a public announcement of the death; preparation of the body; ceremonies or other services; a burial or other form of disposal; and mourning.

Preparation of the body varies among peoples. Typically, the corpse is carefully washed, often by a family member. Sometimes, the body is painted or anointed with oils. In some societies, particularly in the United States, an undertaker *embalms* the corpse. In this process, the undertaker removes the blood and injects a chemical solution to slow *decomposition* (decay). In many societies, the corpse may be dressed in special garments or wrapped in a cloth called a *shroud.* The body is then placed in a *coffin,* also called a *casket,* or other container.

In many cultures, people keep watch beside the coffin one or more days in a practice called a *wake*. They may do so in the belief that the wake comforts the spirit of the dead and protects the body from evil spirits. Customs associated with wakes differ among cultures. For example, during a Japanese Buddhist wake, a priest burns incense and reads from a *sutra* (sacred writing). In the United States, a wake may include a photographic display of the dead person's life or a video presentation accompanied by music.

The funeral is a ceremony that may include prayers, hymns, music, and speeches called *eulogies* that recall and praise the dead person. In the United States, many funeral services are held at a place of business called a *funeral home.* After the service, a vehicle called a *hearse* carries the coffin in a procession to the cemetery or crematory. A final brief ceremony is held before the body is buried, placed in a tomb, or cremated. After many funerals, the mourners return home with the dead person's family and share food.

People may place various objects in the coffin or with the burial. These *grave goods* may be possessions that had special meaning to the dead person in life. Some cultures believe that the dead require various items in the afterlife and include them in the burial. Later, the survivors often erect a gravestone or other monument to record the dead person's life and mark the burial site.

Some funeral practices continue long after a person has died. For example, in the African country of Madagascar, people visit the tombs of relatives during the winter. They remove the corpses, wrap them in new shrouds, and hold a party in honor of the dead. They return in the spring to clean the tomb and leave gifts.

Burial is the most common method of disposal of the dead in Christian, Jewish, and Muslim culture. Cremation is customary in Buddhist and Hindu cultures and is increasingly practiced in the United States and Canada.

Traditional Muslims and Orthodox Jews prohibit cremation. Reform Jews and many Protestant religions allow it. The Roman Catholic Church formerly disapproved of the practice. Since 1968, however, the church has allowed Catholics to cremate their dead after holding a funeral with a body and casket.

Some societies dispose of their dead in other ways. For example, the Parsis, a religious group who live mainly in India, take their dead to enclosures called *towers of silence.* There, birds pick the bones clean. The Parsis believe that earth and fire are sacred and must not be violated by burying or burning a corpse.

The Sioux Indians of North America traditionally placed their dead on platforms above the ground. Some Australian Aborigines buried their dead in the hollows of trees. Human sacrifice was a common element in the burial rituals of rulers or wealthy people in many ancient cultures. Typically, wives and servants were killed and buried with the dead person in order to provide services in the afterlife.

Mourning is the expression of grief after a death. People in mourning may deny themselves amusement, avoid certain foods, or wear special clothing. Mourners in many Western cultures wear black, while Armenians and Syrians wear light blue, and Hindus and Chinese wear white. Until the 1940's, Americans and Europeans typically wore black armbands and hung funeral wreaths on their doors while in mourning.

History. Prehistoric people observed special ceremonies when burying their dead. For example, Neandertal burial sites that date to about 60,000 years ago contain tools, weapons, and evidence that flowers were placed in the grave. The ancient Egyptians and other early peoples placed food, jewels, and other goods in tombs. Such provisions showed the belief that a person continued to exist after death and had the same needs as in life. The Egyptians also developed embalming into an advanced technique called *mummification.* They believed the spirit would return someday to inhabit the body, which therefore had to be preserved.

Beginning in the 1900's, as global travel and communication increased, cultures reshaped their traditional funeral customs and created new ones. However, funeral customs remain an important reflection of the cultural heritage and beliefs of a society.   Penny Colman

Related articles in *World Book* include:

Catacombs	Mask (Burial	Mummy	Sarcophagus
Cremation	masks and	Necropolis	Suttee
Death	death	Potter's field	Tomb
Embalming	masks)	Pyramids	Wake
Epitaph			

Additional resources

Pearson, Michael P. *The Archaeology of Death and Burial.* Tex. A&M Univ. Pr., 2000.
Sloan, Christopher. *Bury the Dead.* National Geographic Soc., 2002. Younger readers.

Funeral director. See Embalming (Modern embalming; Funeral customs.

Fungal disease, *FUHNG guhl,* is any sickness caused by fungi. Fungi are simple organisms found almost everywhere in nature. Many kinds of fungi live as *parasites*—that is, they feed on tissues of living plants and animals, including human beings. These fungi often cause diseases in the plants and animals they infect.

In people. The most common fungal diseases in people are skin infections, such as *ringworm* or *athlete's foot.* These conditions can be caused by a number of fungi, including species in the groups *Trichophyton, Microsporum,* and *Epidermophyton.* Other fungi that normally live harmlessly in the body can sometimes cause disease. For example, fungi in the *Candida* group, which commonly inhabit the mouth, bowel, or vagina, can cause a variety of disorders, including a disease of the throat called *thrush.*

Many fungal diseases affect internal organs and organ systems. The most common of these *systemic diseases* include *histoplasmosis, blastomycosis,* and *coccidioidomycosis.* These three diseases attack the lungs and usually are not serious. However, these same disorders can occasionally be deadly in otherwise healthy people, especially those who lack natural resistance because of AIDS or other diseases. In these patients, the fungi may travel through the body to the bones, kidneys, and central nervous system. Some fungal diseases, including *cryptococcosis,* histoplasmosis, and thrush, are associated with AIDS and may indicate infection with HIV, the virus that causes AIDS (see **AIDS**).

Doctors may prescribe antifungal creams or ointments to treat fungal diseases of the skin. One of the main drugs used to treat systemic fungal diseases is *amphotericin B.* Fungal diseases are often cured with medication. In patients without natural resistance, however, these disorders often recur.

In animals. Many fungal diseases of people also occur in animals, particularly mammals. Ringworm is the most common fungal disease that affects animals. Other fungal diseases that affect animals include histoplasmosis and *monoliasis* in mammals and *aspergillosis* in birds.

In plants. Fungi that cause diseases in plants include smuts, rusts, and mildews. These fungi affect many kinds of plants and can seriously damage crops. For example, *black stem rust* harms wheat, *covered smut* attacks barley, and *powdery mildew* damages a wide variety of plants, such as peas and grapes. Fungal diseases that attack trees include *Dutch elm disease* and *chestnut blight.* Farmers use chemicals called *fungicides* to kill fungi (see **Fungicide**). Breeders also try to develop plants resistant to fungal attacks.   Alan A. Harris

Related articles in *World Book* include:

Actinomycosis	Ergot	Rot
Athlete's foot	Fungi	Rust
Blight	Histoplasmosis	Smut
Damping-off	Mildew	Wilt
Dutch elm disease	Ringworm	

Fungi, *FUHN jy,* are organisms that obtain food by absorbing it from other living organisms or from parts of formerly living things. According to *mycologists* (scientists who study fungi), thousands of fungus *species* (types) exist. A number of fungi are too small to be seen without a microscope. But many types can be seen with the unaided eye. Some of the most common fungi include mildews, molds, mushrooms, rusts, and smuts.

Parts of a fungus. Except for yeasts, chytrids, and other one-celled fungi, the main part of a fungus consists of thousands of threadlike cells called *hyphae.* These tiny, branching cells sometimes form a tangled mass called a *mycelium.* In many kinds of fungi, the

Black bread mold Black bread mold ranks as one of the most common fungi. A 10-day growth of this mold covers the slice of bread shown at the left. The tiny fruiting bodies of the mold can be seen in the photograph in the center. The diagram at the right shows the structure of the mold in more detail.

Runk/Schoenberger from
Grant Heilman

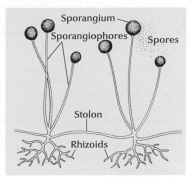

WORLD BOOK illustration
by Sarah Woodward

mycelium grows beneath the surface of the material on which the organism is feeding. For example, the mycelium of a mushroom often grows just beneath the surface of the soil. The umbrella-shaped growth known as a mushroom is actually the *fruiting body* of the fungus. The fruiting body produces cells called *spores,* which develop into new hyphae. Spores are smaller and simpler than the seeds of plants, but both enable an organism to reproduce.

Certain fungi, including some types of molds, bear spores in tiny structures called *sporangia*. In black bread mold, the sporangia form at the tips of upright hyphae called *sporangiophores*. Other hyphae called *stolons* spread over the surface of the bread. They are anchored by *rhizoids* (rootlike structures). Groups of sporangia usually form above the rhizoids. Such fungi as the green mold *Penicillium notatum* produce chains of spores from branched hyphae called *conidiophores*. Still other fungi, including cup fungi, produce spores that they shoot into the air from individual saclike cells.

How a fungus lives. Since fungi cannot produce their own food, they take carbohydrates, proteins, and other nutrients from the living organisms or dead organic matter on which they live. Fungi discharge chemicals called *enzymes* into the material on which they

feed. The enzymes break down complex carbohydrates and proteins into simple compounds that the hyphae can absorb.

Fungi live almost everywhere on land and in water. Mushrooms belong to a large group of fungi called *saprophytes,* which live on dead or decaying matter. Such fungi as mildews and smuts are parasites that feed on living organisms. Some fungi live together with other organisms in ways that are mutually beneficial. For example, a fungus and an organism called an *alga* may live together to form a *lichen* (see **Lichen**). Some fungi also live with the roots of plants in a relationship known as a *mycorrhiza*. The fungus takes carbohydrates from the plant. In return, the fungus helps supply the plant with water and such important minerals as phosphorus, potassium, iron, copper, and zinc. Most trees, shrubs, and herbs have mycorrhizal relationships with fungi.

Fungi generally reproduce by forming spores. Some spores are produced by the union of *gametes* (sex cells). Others, called *asexual* or *imperfect* spores, develop without the union of gametes. Many fungi produce spores both sexually and asexually. Numerous spores are scattered by the wind, and others are transported by water or by animals. Mushrooms, cup fungi, and some other fungi forcefully discharge their spores. A spore that lands in a favorable location *germinates* (starts to grow) and eventually produces a new mycelium.

Yeasts can reproduce by forming sexual spores, but many kinds of yeasts reproduce by *budding*. When a yeast buds, a bulge forms on the cell. A cell wall grows and separates the bud from the original yeast cell. The bud then develops into a new cell. Budding produces a large number of yeast cells rapidly.

The importance of fungi. Many fungi break down complex animal and plant matter into simple compounds. This process of *decomposition* enriches the soil and makes essential substances available to plants and other organisms in a usable form. Through decomposition, fungi also return carbon dioxide to the atmosphere, where green plants can reuse it to make food.

Fungi play a major role in a number of foods. For example, mushrooms and truffles are considered delicacies by many people (see **Truffle**). Cheese manufacturers add molds to Camembert and Roquefort cheeses to ripen them and provide their distinctive flavors. Yeasts

© Shutterstock

Some penicillium molds, such as the one shown here, cause citrus fruits to spoil. Others ripen certain cheeses.

© Thinkstock

Corn smut has infected this corn plant. Smuts and other parasitic fungi cause great damage to grain crops.

cause the *fermentation* that produces alcoholic beverages. In the fermentation process, yeasts break down sugar into carbon dioxide and alcohol. Baker's yeast causes bread to rise by producing carbon dioxide from the carbohydrates in the dough. The carbon dioxide gas bubbles up through the dough, causing the rise. Some people eat yeasts as a rich source of protein and B vitamins.

Some molds produce important drugs called *antibiotics.* Antibiotics weaken or destroy bacteria and other organisms that cause disease. Penicillin, the first and most important antibiotic, was discovered in 1928 by Sir Alexander Fleming, a British bacteriologist. *Penicillium notatum* is one of several green molds that produce penicillin, which physicians use in treating many diseases caused by bacteria. See **Penicillin.**

Some fungi may cause extensive damage. Parasitic fungi destroy many crops and other plants. Important parasitic fungi that attack plants include mildews, rusts, and smuts. Others produce diseases in animals and people. Some mushrooms are poisonous and can cause serious illness or death if eaten. Molds can spoil many kinds of food, and they may also prove poisonous. In damp climates, mildews and other fungi can ruin clothing, bookbindings, and other materials. Fungi may also cause wood to decay or rot.   Joe F. Ammirati

Scientific classification. Fungi make up the kingdom Fungi.

Related articles in *World Book.* See **Fungal disease** and its list of *Related articles.* See also the following articles:

Mold	Parasite	Saprophyte
Mushroom	Puffball	Yeast

Fungicide, *FUHN juh syd,* is a substance used to kill or retard the growth of fungi that are harmful to human beings, other animals, or plants. Diseases caused by fungi can destroy or seriously damage food crops. In the 1840's, a fungal disease destroyed most of the potato crop in Ireland, where people depended heavily on potatoes for food. About 1 million people died from starvation during this disaster, called the Great Irish Famine. A fungus also caused the chestnut blight that killed most of the American chestnut trees in the United States during the early 1900's.

Fungicides are used to protect plants and human beings from fungal diseases. Growers may spray or dust plants with fungicides to control fungal diseases called *rusts, mildews, smuts,* and *molds.* Fungicides also protect potatoes, apples, and other crops from diseases called *blight* and *scab.* Farmers treat many crop seeds with fungicide to prevent *damping off,* a disease that kills young plants. Fruit growers apply fungicides to many fruit crops, including peaches, grapes, and strawberries, to prevent *rotting,* a breakdown of plant tissue or other material caused by fungus.

Human beings use preparations containing a fungicide to prevent such diseases as *athlete's foot* and *ringworm.* Fabrics used for tents and other outdoor purposes may be treated with a fungicide to prevent rotting. Many household cleaning products and some house paints contain a fungicide to prevent mildew.

People have used fungicides for many years. One of the oldest fungicides, powdered sulfur, became common in the late 1800's. It is still used on grapes and other crops to help control mildews. Most fungicides used today are *synthetic* (artificially created) compounds. Chem-

ical companies make them in laboratories and test them extensively for safety and effectiveness before selling them. In the United States, the Environmental Protection Agency (EPA) is responsible for making sure fungicide products are safe for people and the environment.

To be effective, fungicides must be poisonous to fungi. But they must not be harmful to the plants or animals they are supposed to protect. Fungicides must be used with care, because some can harm plants if they are applied too heavily. Some fungicides are poisonous to human beings and animals. Always store such chemicals where children, pets, and livestock cannot reach them. Wash fruits and vegetables treated with fungicides before eating them.   Harold D. Coble

Related articles in *World Book* include:

Fungal disease	Mold
Fungi	Pest control (Pesticides)
Insecticide	Rust
Mildew	

Funj Sultanate, *funj SUHL tuh nayt,* was a Muslim empire in what is now Sudan in northeastern Africa. The empire began in the early 1500's and fell in 1821. It reached its height between 1600 and 1650 when Funj armies conquered neighboring peoples. The Funj became greatly feared in the region between the Red Sea and the Nile River.

The origin of the Funj people is uncertain. They may have descended from Shilluk raiders from the White Nile region. In the early 1500's, the Funj adopted Islam, the Muslim religion. In 1504, they founded their capital, Sennar, south of the present-day city of Wad Madani. The sultanate went on to conquer the northern region of Sudan and nearly all the area between the Blue Nile and White Nile, south of the present-day city of Khartoum. From 1600 to 1650, the Funj used a slave army built by the sultan Badi II Abu Daqn to further extend their empire.

Between 1650 and 1750, the Funj nobles became jealous of the sultans' power and revolted frequently. Finally, in 1761, a group of officers deposed the ruling sultan. A period of decline followed, and the empire fell in 1821 after Egypt invaded it.   Kevin C. MacDonald

Funny bone is not a bone, but a sensitive place at the bend of the elbow. In this area, the *ulnar nerve* lies between the skin and bone. The nerve is relatively unprotected because it lies near the surface. Even a slight blow on this area stimulates the nerve. This stimulation produces pain and a tingling sensation that travels into the ring finger and little finger. Sometimes the funny bone is referred to as "the crazy bone."   Delmas J. Allen

Funston, *FUHN stuhn,* **Frederick** (1865-1917), an American soldier, played an important part in the overseas expansion of the United States in the 1890's and early 1900's. He was nicknamed "Bantam" because he was only 5 feet 5 inches (165 centimeters) tall.

Funston joined the rebel forces in Cuba against Spain in 1896. As a volunteer officer, he commanded U.S. troops in the Philippines during the revolt against U.S. rule that began in 1899. He helped capture Emilio Aguinaldo, the Philippine rebel leader, in 1901. Transferred to the regular Army, Funston restored order in San Francisco after an earthquake in 1906. He commanded U.S. forces at Veracruz, Mexico, in 1914. Funston was born in New Carlisle, Ohio.   Lewis L. Gould

Fur is the thick growth of hair that covers the skin of many kinds of mammals. People make coats and other clothing from fur. They value fur for its beauty as well as the warmth that it provides.

Fur consists of a combination of stiff, oily *guard hair* on top and thick *underfur* beneath. The guard hair sheds moisture, and the underfur acts as an insulating blanket that keeps the animal warm. The fur and skin of an animal are called a *pelt.*

Prehistoric people wore animal skins for warmth and protection. They also used fur for blankets, rugs, and wallhangings. During the 400's B.C., an active fur market opened in Athens, Greece. Fur became a luxury in the Middle Ages (A.D. 400's through the 1400's). During this period, only royalty could afford such expensive furs as ermine and sable.

The desire to profit from furs stimulated much of the early exploration of North America. In the early 1600's, fur trading became the most important industry in Canada. The first fur ranches raised silver foxes in the 1880's in Prince Edward Island, Canada.

Today, the fur industry plays an important role in the economies of a number of nations throughout the world. Most of the world's fur supply comes from fur ranches, also called fur farms, where millions of fur-bearing animals are raised each year. The remainder of the world's fur supply comes from trapping animals in the wild.

The major sources of the most popular furs obtained by trapping are Canada, Russia, and the United States. The United States and many other nations prohibit the import of furs of animals that are in danger of becoming extinct. See **Wildlife conservation.**

Some people object to the killing of animals for their

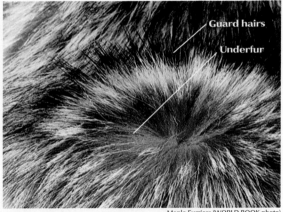

Maple Furriers (WORLD BOOK photo)

Fur consists of long *guard hairs* and thick *underfur.* The guard hairs shed moisture, and the underfur keeps the animal warm.

fur. They especially oppose what they consider inhumane treatment in the trapping and killing of animals or in the animals' confinement on ranches.

Kinds of fur

Natural fur comes from animals. It can vary greatly in color, texture, and value. Natural furs range from jet-black to snow-white, with many shades and combinations of brown, blue, gray, red-orange, and tan. Their textures vary from the velvety softness of sheared beaver to the coarseness of badger.

Artificial fur is manufactured from synthetic fibers. The fibers are processed to resemble real fur. Some-

Some important furs

Fur	Fur family	Animal's natural habitat	Description
*Beaver	Rodent	North America	Dark brown; short, thick fur.
*Chinchilla	Rodent	South America	Blue-gray; long, branched, fine fur.
*Coyote	Dog	North America	Gray, yellow-gray, tan; long, thick fur.
*Ermine	Weasel	Russia, North America	White, black; short, thick fur.
Fisher	Weasel	Canada	Dark brown; short, soft fur.
Fitch	Weasel	Europe	Yellow, beige, brown, black; long, silky fur.
*Fox	Dog	Asia, Europe, North America	Red, blue, silver, white; long, soft fur.
*Lynx	Cat	North America, Finland, Norway, Russia, Sweden	Beige, white; long, silky fur.
*Marten	Weasel	Asia, North America	Blue-brown; soft, thick fur.
*Mink	Weasel	North America, Russia	Brown, gray, white; long, silky fur.
*Mole	Mole	Netherlands, Scotland	Blue, gray; soft, thick fur.
*Muskrat	Rodent	North America, Russia	Brown; long, silky fur.
*Nutria	Rodent	South America	Dark brown; short, soft fur.
*Opossum	Opossum	South America, United States	Creamy; short, rough fur.
*Otter	Weasel	North America, South America	Brown; short, thick fur.
Persian lamb	Sheep	Afghanistan, Kazakhstan, Namibia	Black, brown, gray; woolly, tightly curled fur.
*Rabbit	Rodent	Australia, Europe, Japan, North America	White, brown, gray; short, fluffy fur.
*Raccoon	Raccoon	North America	Silver-gray, dark gray, black; long, coarse fur.
*Sable	Weasel	Canada, Russia	Dark brown; long, silky fur.
*Seal	Seal	Alaska, Canada, Namibia, Russia, Uruguay	Gray, salmon, silver, white; short, silky or stiff fur.
*Skunk	Weasel	North America	Black; long, silky fur.
*Squirrel	Rodent	Asia, Europe, North America	Gray; short, soft fur.

*Has a separate article in *World Book.*

Some kinds of fur

Mink ranges in color from white to many shades of gray and brown.

Fox fur is long and soft. The most popular shades include red, white, and silver.

Muskrat fur is light brown. Some is dyed to resemble other kinds of fur.

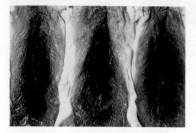

Chinchilla is highly prized for its luxurious softness and unusual coloration.

Sable, one of the most beautiful and expensive furs, has a brown color.

Maple Furriers (WORLD BOOK photos)

Beaver is prized for both its soft underfur, *left,* and its outer guard hair, *right.*

times natural fur fibers are woven into the fabric to make it feel more like genuine fur. Compared with natural fur, artificial fur generally costs less and is not as warm.

How fur is obtained

Fur ranching. Popular furs that are produced on ranches include chinchilla, fox, lamb, mink, and sable. Fur ranchers breed their animals based on the principles of genetics. Ranchers try to produce animals that have the most desirable color and body size, thickness of underfur, length and evenness of guard hair, and overall softness of fur.

Most ranchers breed and raise fur-bearing animals in pens. Once the animals mature, they are usually killed in gas chambers or by an injection of poison.

Trapping. Popular furs obtained from trapped animals include beaver, bobcat, coyote, fisher, fox, lynx, marten, mink, muskrat, nutria, opossum, raccoon, sable, and squirrel. Most trapping is done in the winter months when the animals' furs are thickest, longest, and shiniest.

A trapper sets a series of traps called a *trap line* along riverbanks and other areas the animals visit regularly. The most common type of trap is the *leg-hold trap,* which has metal jaws designed to snap shut, holding an animal by its paw until the trapper arrives to kill it. The *padded trap* has rubber inserts on its jaws. A *Conibear,* also called a *body gripper* or *quick-kill trap,* is designed to stun and kill the animal almost instantly in its scissorlike grip.

Skinning. Ranchers and trappers use two main methods for skinning animals—*cased* and *open.* In the cased method, the rancher or trapper slits a line across the rump from leg to leg and peels the pelt off inside out. Coyotes, ermines, foxes, minks, raccoons, and other small animals are usually skinned by the cased method. In the open method, a line is slit up the animal's belly and the pelt is peeled off from side to side. Such animals as beavers and badgers are skinned by the open method.

After removing the pelts, ranchers and trappers scrape them clean of all fat and tissue. The scraped pelts are then dried.

Marketing fur

Most furs are sold to manufacturers and retailers at large auctions. Trappers sell their furs to a *country collector,* or local buyer, who collects large *lots* (bundles) of similar furs. Country collectors and ranchers then send their furs to auction houses in the world's major fur-trading centers.

The main auction houses in North America are in Seattle and in Toronto, Ontario. Leading European houses are in St. Petersburg, Russia; Copenhagen, Denmark; and Helsinki, Finland. Ranchers' organizations own many major houses.

Representatives of the auction houses visit ranchers and country collectors to arrange shipment of pelts to market. The largest numbers of furs arrive at the houses from November to February.

Buyers may examine several hundred thousand pelts in the warehouse on *inspection days* immediately before the sale. The furs are then auctioned off on *sales days.* Buyers pay for their purchases on or before the *prompt day,* which is usually about a month after the sales days. On the prompt day, furs are shipped according to the buyers' instructions.

Some ranchers and trappers sell their pelts to manufacturers and retailers through a broker. Most brokers work in cities in which large amounts of fur products are made.

Processing fur

Dressing. Pelts are cleaned and made flexible by a process called *dressing*. First, the pelt is softened in a chemical solution that removes all excess tissue and grease. Next, any remaining flesh is scraped from the hide, either by a worker called a *dresser* or by a machine. Then, a dresser applies a special grease to the leather and puts the pelt into a machine called a *kicker*. The kicker has wooden or steel mallets that pound the grease into the pores of the skin. The pelt is then placed into a revolving drum, where it is cleaned and dried with special sawdust. Later, a dresser may pluck out the long guard hairs, leaving the thick underfur. The fur may also be sheared for a plush effect.

Dyeing. Many furs are dyed to achieve a fashionable color or to make them look like a different type of fur. In the past, for example, rabbit fur was dyed to resemble seal fur. Dyers may put pelts into a vat of dye, or they may dye a garment by hand. Sometimes a fur is bleached and then dyed an entirely different color. In a process called *tipping,* only the tips of the guard hairs are dyed. Tipping helps the manufacturer match several pelts to be used in the same garment.

Cutting and sewing. A fur manufacturer first chooses a pattern for a garment and then selects pelts that look very much alike for the garment. A group of such pelts is called a *matched bundle.*

Next, workers stretch the skins and trim off the heads, paws, bellies, rumps, and tails. These parts are used to make cheaper garments. A worker called a *cutter* cuts the pelts into thin strips. An *operator* then sews the strips into long, narrow pieces of fur. These pieces are fit to the pattern and then given to the *blocker.* The blocker applies a small amount of water to the skin to make it stretch just enough to cover the edges of the pattern. Next, the fur is *blocked,* or stapled, to a large paperboard and left to dry. Later, any surplus material is trimmed away and the fur is sewed into a garment. Finally, the garment is cleaned and given to the *finisher,* who sews in a lining.

In the United States, the Fur Products Labeling Act, which was approved in 1951, requires that all fur garments contain a label stating (1) the name in English of the animal that produced the fur, (2) the country of origin of the fur if the fur or the garment is imported, and (3) whether the fur is natural or dyed. If the garment contains fur from paws, bellies, or other scrap parts, the label must so state. In addition, if a garment contains fur products that are secondhand, that fact must be indicated. That is, should a garment be remade or restyled from previously owned fur garments, that must be stated on the label.

Controversy over fur

For the past several decades, there has been a movement against the purchase and wearing of fur garments and other items made from fur. Many are opposed to people wearing fur because they believe that the methods used to obtain pelts cause fur-bearing trapped animals and animals raised on fur ranches to suffer needlessly. Others disagree with this view, and they perceive trapping as a part of regulated wildlife management programs. In addition, the Fur Farm Animal Welfare Coalition, an organization under the Fur Commission USA, monitors practices and conditions on ranches in the United States.   Billie J. Collier

See also **Alaska** (Fur industry); **Animal** (pictures); **Pribilof Islands; Trapping.**

Fur trade was one of the earliest and most important industries in North America. The fur-trading industry played a significant role in the development of the United States and Canada for more than 300 years.

The fur trade began in the 1500's as an exchange be-

David R. Frazier

Fur buyers inspect pelts at a fur merchant's storeroom and decide which ones to purchase. The merchant sells pelts from many parts of the world.

David R. Frazier

Pelts are matched according to color, luster, thickness, and other features. Matched pelts enable a manufacturer to produce a garment that has the same color and texture throughout.

tween American Indians and Europeans. The Indians traded furs for such goods as tools and weapons. Beaver fur, which was used in Europe to make felt hats, became the most valuable of these furs (see **Beaver**). The fur trade prospered until the mid-1800's, when fur-bearing animals became scarce and silk hats became more popular than felt hats made with beaver.

Today, most trappers sell their pelts. But in Canada, some Inuit (formerly called Eskimos) and Indians still trade furs to fur companies for goods.

The early fur trade. The earliest fur traders in North America were French explorers and fishermen who arrived in what is now eastern Canada during the early 1500's. Trade started after the French offered the Indians kettles, knives, and other gifts to establish friendly relations. The Indians, in turn, gave pelts to the French. By the late 1500's, a great demand for fur had developed in Europe. This demand encouraged further exploration of North America. The demand for beaver increased rapidly in the late 1500's, when fashionable European men began to wear felt hats made from beaver fur. Such furs as fox, marten, mink, and otter also were traded.

In 1608, the French explorer Samuel de Champlain established a trading post on the site of the present-day city of Quebec. The city became a fur-trading center. The French expanded their trading activities along the St. Lawrence River and around the Great Lakes. They eventually controlled most of the early fur trade in what became Canada. The French traders obtained furs from the Huron Indians and, later, from the Ottawa. These tribes were not trappers, but they acquired the furs from

other Indians. The French also developed the fur trade along the Mississippi River.

During the early 1600's, English settlers developed a fur trade in what are now New England and Virginia. English traders later formed an alliance with the Iroquois Indians and extended their trading area from Maine down the Atlantic Coast to Georgia.

European business companies handled a large number of the furs shipped from North America during the 1600's and 1700's. The most famous of these firms, the Hudson's Bay Company, was established in 1670. It was founded by a group of English merchants, with the help of two French fur traders, Pierre Esprit Radisson and his brother-in-law, Médard Chouart, Sieur des Groseilliers. The English government gave the company sole trading rights in what is now the Hudson Bay region. See **Hudson's Bay Company; Groseilliers, Médard Chouart, Sieur des; Radisson, Pierre E.**

During the 1700's, French and British fur traders competed bitterly over trading rights in the region between the Allegheny Mountains and the Mississippi River. This competition, plus other conflicts between the two nations, led to the French and Indian War in 1754. Britain (later also called the United Kingdom) won the war and in 1763 took over France's colonies in North America.

During the late 1770's, merchants in Montreal first organized the North West Company to compete with the Hudson's Bay Company. Members of the new firm were called ""Nor'Westers." The company's traders led many daring expeditions in search of fur in far western Canada. However, the company failed financially and, in

The fur trade in North America

The fur trade played an important role in the development of Canada and the United States from the 1500's to the mid-1800's. This map shows the chief areas of the fur trade in North America. The groups that controlled these areas and the periods in which the trade flourished under each group are shown below.

French
1500's to 1763

Colonial American
1600's to late 1700's

Hudson's Bay Company
1670 to 1850's

North West Company
1770's to 1821

Russian
1790's to 1850's

American
1820's to 1850's

→ Fur export route

▪ Trading post

• City

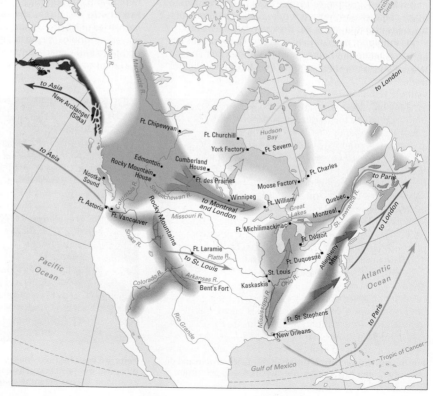

Water color by William Henry Jackson; Denver Public Library, Western History Department

The annual rendezvous, *shown here,* was a center of Western fur trading in the 1800's. Trappers assembled at these gatherings in the Rocky Mountains to trade or sell their pelts to fur companies.

1821, merged with the Hudson's Bay Company.

During the late 1700's, Russia began to develop the fur trade in the area that is now Alaska. The Russian-American Company was established there in 1799.

The 1800's. The Lewis and Clark expedition in 1804 and 1805 led to the development of fur trading in the West. Several companies competed heavily for this trade. They included firms headed by John Jacob Astor, William H. Ashley, Pierre Chouteau, and Manuel Lisa.

Many Indians of the West had little interest in trapping, and so the fur-trading companies hired white frontiersmen to obtain pelts. These trappers became known as "mountain men" because they roamed through wild areas of the Rocky Mountains. Such mountain men as Kit Carson, John Colter, and Jedediah Smith gained fame for their roles in exploring the West.

Ashley, the head of the Rocky Mountain Fur Company, began to hold an annual trappers' gathering in the Rocky Mountains in 1825. At each gathering, called a *rendezvous,* trappers sold their furs and bought supplies for the next year. The rendezvous saved them from traveling long distances to various trading posts.

The fur trade started to decline in the Eastern United States by the late 1700's. The decline resulted chiefly from the clearing of large areas for settlement. As more land was cleared, fur-bearing animals became increasingly scarce. Overtrapping hurt the fur trade in the western United States and western Canada. Also, the value of beaver fur dropped sharply in the 1830's, when European hat manufacturers began to use silk instead of felt. After 1870, the historic fur trade largely ended. But Native Americans and other rural people continue to pro-

duce furs for markets in the United States and Canada.

Effects of the fur trade. The fur trade contributed to the development of British and French empires in North America. During the 1600's, the prospect of wealth from the fur trade attracted many Europeans to the New World. Traders and trappers explored much of North America in search of fur. They built trading posts in the wilderness, and settlements grew up around many of the posts. Some of these settlements later became such major cities as Detroit, New Orleans, and St. Louis in the United States; and Edmonton, Montreal, Quebec, and Winnipeg in Canada.

The fur trade led to conflict between France and Britain in America. Rivalries over trading alliances also arose among Indian tribes that wanted to obtain European goods. The fur trade promoted friendly relations between the Indians and traders. But it also brought Indian hostility toward white settlers because the clearing of land threatened the supply of fur-bearing animals.

The claims of fur traders played a part in establishing the border between the United States and Canada. For example, the areas of trade controlled by U.S. and British traders helped determine the border in the Great Lakes region and in the Pacific Northwest.   Barton H. Barbour

Related articles in *World Book* include:

Astor, John Jacob
Canada, History of
 (Start of the fur
 trade; Explo-
 ration of the
 West)
Chouteau, Pierre,
 Jr.
Fraser, Simon
Fur
Hearne, Samuel
Henry, Alexander
Hudson's Bay
 Company
Mackenzie, Sir
 Alexander
Mackenzie,
 Roderick
North West
 Company
Simpson, Sir
 George
Trading post

Additional resources

Collins, James L. *The Mountain Men.* Watts, 1996. Younger readers.

Hafen, Le Roy R., ed. *French Fur Traders & Voyageurs in the American West.* 1993. Reprint. Univ. of Neb. Pr., 1997. *Fur Traders, Trappers, and Mountain Men of the Upper Missouri.* 1995.

Mackie, Richard S. *Trading Beyond the Mountains: The British Fur Trade on the Pacific, 1793-1843.* UBC Pr., 1997.

Vibert, Elizabeth. *Traders' Tales: Narratives of Cultural Encounters in the Columbian Plateau, 1807-1846.* Univ. of Okla. Pr., 1997.

Furfural, *FUR fuh ral,* is a liquid chemical used in many industries. Manufacturers use it in making nylon, plastics, and other important chemicals. Furfural changes from colorless to yellow and finally dark brown when exposed to air. Its vapor irritates the eyes, nose, and throat.

Many synthetic resins are made using furfural. Manufacturers use these synthetic resins to make plastic products. Furfural is also used in the production of the chemical *furfuryl alcohol.* Furfuryl alcohol is used in making resins that protect metals from *corroding* (being eaten away by chemical action). Furfural is also used in fungicides, germicides, and insecticides—that is, chemicals that kill fungus, germs, or insects.

Chemists call furfural a selective solvent because it will dissolve some materials in a mixture but not others. Petroleum refineries use furfural to dissolve the harmful carbon and sulfur compounds found in impure lubricating oils. Furfural is also used to refine other petroleum products, such as diesel fuel.

Chemical manufacturers prepare furfural by mixing acid with waste plant materials, such as corncobs or the hulls of cottonseeds, oats, or rice. Furfural is also found in some natural oils. Johann Döbereiner, a German chemist, reported his discovery of furfural in 1832. He accidentally obtained the chemical by treating sugar with sulfuric acid and manganese dioxide. American chemists discovered the methods now used to manufacture furfural in the early 1920's.

China, South Africa, and the Dominican Republic are leading producers of furfural. Interest in producing furfural in the United States has increased because the chemical comes from naturally occurring, renewable resources that are not based on petroleum.

Furfural is an organic chemical with the formula C_4H_3OCHO. It belongs to the aldehyde chemical family and is sometimes called *furfuraldehyde.* Furfural freezes at $-37.6\ °F$ ($-38.7\ °C$) and boils at $323\ °F$ ($161.7\ °C$). The chemical is about 1.16 times as dense as water.

Marianna A. Busch

Furies, *FYUR eez,* were the terrible goddesses of vengeance in Roman mythology. The Greeks called them *Erinyes* or *Eumenides.* The Roman poet Virgil wrote of three Furies in his epic poem the *Aeneid.* He called them Alecto, Tisiphone, and Megaera. They carried whips and had snakes in their hair.

The Furies punished people for committing crimes. The Furies were especially vengeful against anyone who had killed a member of his or her family. In his tragedy *The Eumenides,* the Greek playwright Aeschylus describes how they drove Orestes insane for killing his mother, Clytemnestra.   Elaine Fantham

Furlong is a unit of length in the inch-pound system of measurement customarily used in the United States. One furlong equals 40 rods, or ⅛ mile (0.202 kilometer).

Furlong originally meant the length of a furrow in a plowed field. However, this meaning was indefinite because farmers plowed furrows of many different lengths. Gradually, the furlong became a standard length. Among Old English writers, the furlong was ⅛ mile in any of the world's different standards for a mile. Today, the furlong is used mainly to measure distances in horse races.   Bruce F. Field

See also **Weights and measures.**

The Furies were avenging goddesses in classical mythology. This painting shows them in a scene from a Greek tragedy by Aeschylus. They were usually shown with brass wings and snakes on their bodies.

Detail from Greek vase painting of the late 300's B.C.; The British Museum, London

Furnace is a device in which heat is produced. Some furnaces heat the air in people's homes. Others produce steam to run electric power plants. Furnaces are necessary in the manufacture of iron and steel, glass, pottery, and other products. They also are used in petroleum refining. This article deals with both industrial and home heating furnaces. For further information on home heating systems, see the article on **Heating**.

Furnaces range in size from kitchen ovens to the huge furnaces used in steel production. Most industrial furnaces are built of *refractory* (heat-resistant) bricks, which are able to withstand great variation in temperature without weakening. The walls and roofs of some modern furnaces are made of refractory fiberglass cloth that is mounted on metal frames. The combustion chamber in most home heating furnaces is made of steel.

Sources of heat. Most furnaces generate heat by burning fuel. These furnaces are called *combustion furnaces*. Early combustion furnaces burned wood or charcoal. During the 1600's, coal began to replace these fuels. During the mid-1900's, many industrial furnaces were converted to burn oil. Today, most industrial combustion furnaces burn natural gas. This fuel causes almost no air pollution. Natural gas also is easy to control.

A home heating furnace is a type of combustion furnace. Gas piped into a combustion chamber mixes with air drawn in from around the furnace. This gas-air mixture burns. A blower draws in a separate stream of cool air and pushes it around the chamber. Heat from the chamber warms this air before it travels to the rooms. A typical furnace has four combustion chambers.

WORLD BOOK diagram by Arthur Grebetz

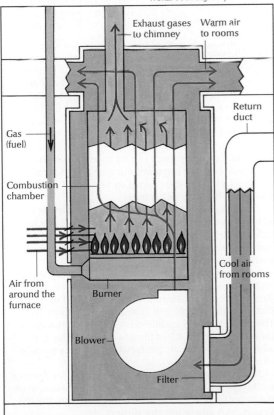

Exhaust gases to chimney

Warm air to rooms

Return duct

Gas (fuel)

Combustion chamber

Cool air from rooms

Air from around the furnace

Burner

Blower

Filter

Most home heating furnaces burn gas or oil.

There are two basic types of combustion furnaces—*direct-fired* and *indirect-fired*. In direct-fired furnaces, the flame is in the same compartment as the *charge* (the material to be heated). In an indirect-fired furnace, also called a *muffle furnace*, the flame is contained in a separate chamber from the charge. This chamber, called a *muffle*, may be a cavity in the furnace wall or a steel tube that runs through the furnace. Indirect-fired furnaces are used when the charge may be harmed by the gases produced during combustion.

Combustion furnaces can be heated to the temperature required to perform a wide variety of jobs simply by burning the fuel. Some jobs, however, such as smelting iron ore or melting glass, need a higher temperature than the combustion of fuel alone can produce. In such cases, the flame is made hotter by burning the fuel with pure oxygen or by heating air before it is mixed with the fuel. For example, air is drawn into a glassmaking furnace through a pile of bricks that has been heated by hot gases leaving the furnace.

Not all furnaces are heated by the combustion of fuel. For example, electric furnaces use electric power to produce heat. Nuclear reactors get their heat from the energy that is released when the nuclei of uranium or plutonium atoms split. Solar furnaces have mirrors that focus the sun's rays on an object that absorbs energy from the rays. See **Nuclear energy**; **Solar energy** (Solar heating).

Heating the charge. There are two basic types of furnaces, based on the way they heat a charge: (1) *batch furnaces* and (2) *continuous furnaces*.

Batch furnaces heat materials singly or a group at a time. Clay pots, for instance, are baked in batches in *kilns* (ovens). After baking, all the pots are removed before the next batch is placed in the kiln.

Handling the hot charges is often a problem in batch processing because of the high temperatures required in industrial furnaces. A number of solutions have been developed. Workers use steel tongs to remove small articles from batch furnaces, and large mechanical arms and cranes handle larger items. In a *car bottom furnace*, a type of batch furnace, the floor and door are on wheels and can be pulled out like a drawer to reach the charge. A *top hat furnace* can be lifted off its base to be loaded or unloaded. Batches of steel and copper are heated in large pot furnaces. Once the materials are melted, the whole furnace is tilted and the glowing hot liquid pours out a spout.

Continuous furnaces heat a steady flow of material that passes through them. This material may be rolled through the furnace on carts, pushed through by hydraulic rams, or carried on conveyor belts. Crude oil and water pass through furnaces in pipes. Some furnaces rely upon gravity to move the material through them. For example, iron ore is fed in at the top of a blast furnace, and molten iron flows out from the bottom. Cement is produced by roasting crushed limestone in a *rotary kiln*, a slightly inclined, long steel tube lined with refractory brick. The pieces of limestone are fed in at the higher end and slowly tumble to the lower end as the kiln rotates.   Larry R. Brand

See also **Boiler**; **Iron and steel** (How iron is made; How steel is made).

Sèvres Room (about 1770); The Metropolitan Museum of Art, Purchase, Mr. and Mrs. Charles Wrightsman Gift, 1976

Beautifully designed furniture can be displayed as works of art. The cabinets, chairs, desks, and tables shown above reflect the elegance of the French rococo style of the late 1700's.

Furniture

Furniture consists of chairs, tables, beds, and other pieces that provide comfort and convenience in our daily lives. Many kinds of furniture are used in homes, schools, and offices. We relax on comfortable couches, and we store various belongings in chests, dressers, and bookcases. Desks provide a place for study and paperwork. Numerous television sets and phonographs have handsome cabinets, and so they also serve as pieces of furniture. In many homes, a piano is an impressive piece of furniture.

In addition to being useful, furniture is attractively designed to make our surroundings more pleasant. Furniture works with other decorative and useful objects to beautify a room. Such items, including rugs and carpets, curtains, draperies, lamps, and pictures, are called *furnishings*.

Most furniture is made of wood or wood products. But furniture makers also use glass, metal, plastics, and a variety of other materials.

Certain pieces of the finest furniture rank among the world's greatest works of art. Over the years, expert designers and *artisans* (skilled craftworkers) have created richly decorated furniture in various styles. Many of these artisans were regarded as artists equal to the most famous painters and sculptors of their day. Today, muse-

ums display examples of their furniture as masterpieces of art.

People who study the history of furniture have given names to the different styles. Some styles are named for important people. For example, Louis XIV furniture is named for King Louis XIV of France. Other styles are named for historical periods. Thus, the Federal style of American furniture recalls the beginning of the federal system of government in the United States. Still other styles, such as art nouveau, take their name from an art movement.

The history of furniture can be seen as a series of styles that become popular for a time and then fall from fashion. Designers then revive earlier styles, adapting them to fit the taste of the time.

The history of furniture is closely related to the history of human culture. For thousands of years, all fine furniture was designed to accommodate the tastes of royalty and the nobility and other wealthy people. These people considered furniture a symbol of their power and rank rather than a practical necessity. Beginning in the A.D. 1500's, a middle class of people gradually developed in Western countries. People of this class wanted furniture that was comfortable and suited to their homes. By the 1800's, the tastes of middle-class buyers set the standard for furniture styles. Most furniture made today is still designed to be practical, comfortable, and easy to maintain.

This article describes the history of furniture from its earliest period to the present time. For a discussion of the importance of furniture in interior design, see the *World Book* article **Interior design.**

John W. Keefe, the contributor of this article, is Principal Curator, Decorative Arts, at the New Orleans Museum of Art.

© Peter Aaron, ESTO

Modern office furniture often emphasizes natural wood and streamlined geometric forms. This furniture is functional and easy to maintain. The style was first popularized by Scandinavian designers in the 1920's.

Henry Francis du Pont Winterthur Museum, Wilmington, Del.

Early U.S. furniture was based on English designs. The American cabinetmaker Duncan Phyfe was a leader in the Federal style, which began in the United States about 1790. Phyfe's furniture, shown on the left, was strongly influenced by English styles of the mid-1700's.

Sofa of laminated rosewood by John Henry Belter; Victoria and Albert Museum, London

Sofa of cherrywood by Wendell Castle; Wendell Castle Studio

Furniture styles have changed dramatically over the years. The elaborate upholstered sofa on the left was made in 1856. The sofa on the right, with its clean, plain design, was created in 1973.

Early furniture

The ancient Egyptians created the first known fine furniture about 3000 B.C. Later, the Greeks and then the Romans developed outstanding furniture in their own characteristic styles. The age of Greek and Roman culture was followed by the Middle Ages, a period that in general produced little important furniture.

Ancient Egypt (3100 B.C.-1070 B.C.). The ancient Egyptians considered the ownership of furniture a mark of social rank. The best-made and most beautiful furniture decorated the palace of the Egyptian king. Members of the nobility, wealthy officials, and landowners also possessed fine furniture. The common people had only one piece of furniture—a three-legged stool—in their simple homes.

Egyptian furniture makers did some of their best work in designing beds. Most beds had legs shaped like the legs of an animal, usually a lion. These beds led to the development of couches in the shape of an animal, such as a lion or a leopard.

Egyptian artisans also made fine chairs. The finest chairs had a seat of woven cord covered with a removable cushion. The development of the armchair was probably the most lasting Egyptian contribution to furniture design. Other Egyptian furniture included boxes, cabinets, and small tables.

Ancient Greece (about 1100 B.C.-A.D. 400). In ancient Greece, as in ancient Egypt, only persons of the highest social rank possessed much furniture. Most Greek citizens owned only a three-legged stool and perhaps a crudely made table.

The Greeks borrowed many furniture forms, including the bed and the couch, from the Egyptians. Beds became major pieces of household decoration in ancient Greece because they were used for dining as well as for sleeping. During a meal, a person would lie on the bed on his or her side, leaning on one elbow for support.

Greek artisans produced a variety of seating furniture. The most important were the thrones made for people of high rank. Some thrones had a low back decorated with one or more carvings of animal heads. Others had a high back with flowerlike carvings. The arm supports were in the form of rams' heads. The most common type of Greek chair, called the *klismos,* had curved legs. The front legs curved forward, and the rear legs curved to the back.

The Greeks used tables more than the Egyptians did. Most Greek tables had three legs that ended in feet shaped like hoofs or paws. Greek artisans decorated the finest furniture with inlaid patterns of fine wood, silver, gold, and gems. They either carved ivory to form the feet or cast them in silver or bronze.

Ancient Rome (700's B.C.-A.D. 400's). The Romans borrowed many furniture forms from the Greeks but gave them a distinctly Roman character. For example, the Romans used more bronze and silver in their furniture than did the Greeks. The Romans used the Greek klismos but made it heavier and larger. They also covered it with upholstery. Roman furniture makers adopted a Greek stool design and developed it into a stool called a *curule.* The curule had two pairs of legs. The delicate,

A common ancient Greek chair was the *klismos, left.* Such chairs had curved legs and a curved back.

A reconstructed Roman stool called a *curule, below,* has curved legs in the shape of an X.

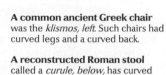

Rijksmuseum, Nijmegen, the Netherlands

Egyptian Museum, Cairo, Egypt
(Metropolitan Museum of Art/Lee Boltin)

An ancient Egyptian throne, *above,* which belonged to King Tutankhamen, is decorated with carvings of lion heads and paws.

Relief from a gravestone
(about 400 B.C.); Archaeological
Museum, Athens, Greece
(Raymond V. Schoder, S.J.)

A simply built chest, *right,* is typical of the furniture of the Middle Ages. Carvings were a common form of furniture decoration during this period.

Church of St. Mary, Stoke D'Abernon,
England (Hanford Photography)

curved legs in each pair crossed in the form of an X.

Tables were very popular among the Romans. Many tables had three or four legs connected by crossbars. The *slab table* was a major Roman contribution to table design. The tabletop consisted of a large slab of marble or wood, which rested on carved upright marble slabs. Artisans sculptured various designs into the upright slabs, including animals, flowers, fruits, and vines.

The Middle Ages. During the period of European history called the Middle Ages, from about the 400's through the 1400's, skillful furniture making generally became a lost art. Most furniture of the Middle Ages was coarse and unrefined by the standards of ancient Greece and Rome. Furniture makers painted or *gilded* (coated with gold) most pieces to disguise their crude construction. As in earlier times, people of high rank owned the best furniture.

Landowners and church officials of the Middle Ages traveled frequently. They usually took their furniture and other possessions with them on their journeys. Much furniture thus was designed to be portable. Large pieces were put together in such a way that they could be taken apart and carried easily. Chests were used for storage as well as for seats.

During the 1200's, a new Western European art style called *Gothic* influenced the design of furniture. Artisans decorated their furniture, especially chests and cupboards, with arches, columns, and other features of Gothic architecture.

Oriental furniture

In the Asian countries, as in Egypt and Europe, only high-ranking officials and wealthy people owned finely crafted furniture. The artisans of China, Japan, and India produced the most noteworthy Oriental furniture. The earliest high-quality Oriental furniture was produced in China during the 200's B.C.

China. By the time of the Han dynasty (206 B.C.-A.D. 220), the Chinese had developed several furniture forms. The most characteristic was the *kang*, a platform on which a person could lie to sleep or rest. The Chinese of this period grouped a variety of small stools and tables around the kang.

Later Chinese furniture falls into two categories: household furniture and the furniture used in royal palaces. Chinese household furniture was simple and practical. Palace furniture was larger, heavier, and more richly decorated than household furniture.

A notable characteristic of all Chinese furniture was the skillful manner in which artisans joined the parts. They used no pegs or nails and seldom used glue. Instead, they carved the edges of parts so expertly that the parts fitted together tightly.

By the early 1400's, the Chinese were using low dining tables supported by gracefully curved legs now known as *cabriole* legs. A cabriole leg has S-shaped curves, and it ends with a decorative foot. Beginning in the 1700's, this design became an important feature of Western furniture and was given the French name *cabriole*. The best-known Chinese chair design had a single vertical *splat*—a piece of wood that formed the center of the chair's back.

Alice Boney Collection, New York City

Chinese dining tables of the 1400's had curved legs that became known as *cabrioles*. This table is 1 foot (30 centimeters) high.

R. Hatfield Ellsworth Collection, New York City (Lee Boltin)

A typical Chinese chair of the 1500's had a single vertical *splat* that formed the center of the chair's back.

Mary and Jackson Burke Collection, New York City (Lee Boltin)

A Japanese cabinet of the early 1600's is made of lacquered wood. The doors and shelves have grapevine designs.

Japan. Japanese architectural styles largely determined that country's furniture styles. Earthquakes occurred frequently in Japan, which resulted in the building of light, one-story buildings. In both homes and palaces, the Japanese used small, lightweight cabinets, chests, and writing tables rather than large, heavy pieces. The Japanese customarily sat and slept on floor mats, and so they used no chairs or beds. Their furniture was simple in shape, but it was beautifully decorated with colorful designs of flowers, animals, and scenes from Japanese literature. Japanese artisans lacquered the furniture to give it a glossy finish. This use of lacquer gave the furniture a distinctive quality. Japanese furniture makers also beautified their work with shell inlays and rich fabrics.

India. The earliest important pieces of Indian furniture were chairs designed to be used by members of the nobility. Such thrones later developed into four-legged platforms on which a person sat with legs folded. Many of these thrones had the shape of a flower blossom. A person sat on cushions and used pillows for a backrest. Indian beds were covered with luxuriously upholstered cushions and mattresses.

© The Frick Collection, New York City

An Italian Renaissance chest called a *cassone, above,* is made of fine wood and beautifully carved. Such chests were the most popular type of furniture in Italy during the Renaissance.

The Renaissance

The Renaissance was a period of European history that lasted from about 1300 to 1600. A major characteristic of the period was a revival of interest in *classical* cultures—that is, the cultures of ancient Greece and Rome. Classical art thus had a strong influence on furniture designed during the Renaissance. Italian artisans created the first important Renaissance furniture. Their work attracted much attention in other European countries, especially France, England, and Spain.

Italy. During the Renaissance, the palaces of Italian nobles became famous for their luxurious interiors, which included fine furniture and magnificent paintings. Actually, these palaces contained few pieces of furniture by today's standards. The best-furnished room in a palace was the *studio,* a library in which the owner kept books, manuscripts, gems, medals, and small sculptures. These items rested on shelves in beautifully ornamented cupboards.

Chests continued to be important articles of furniture, as they were in the Middle Ages. During the early 1500's, a large type of chest called a *cassone* was carved, gilded, and painted with scenes from classical history and mythology. A new form of chest called the *cassapanca* developed from the cassone. The cassapanca had a backrest and arms, and it was used as a sofa as well as a chest. Large cupboards called *sideboards* or *credenzas* became popular pieces of Italian furniture. Artisans decorated them with columns and other features of classical architecture.

France. French Renaissance furniture can be divided into two important styles, called Francis I and Henry II. Each style was named after a French king. Francis I ruled from 1515 to 1547. Henry II ruled from 1547 to 1559.

Before the reign of Francis I, French furniture reflected the Gothic style of the late Middle Ages. A new style developed after Francis brought leading Italian artists to France to remodel the royal *château* (castle) at

Château de Beauregard, Blois, France (P. Hinous, Agence TOP)

A French Renaissance cabinet, *above,* was designed in the Henry II style, which became popular during the mid-1500's. Such cabinets had a small upper section that rested on a larger base. Furniture makers decorated these pieces with carvings of human figures and scenes from Greek and Roman mythology.

English furniture of the Renaissance was solid and sturdy, as this picture indicates. The picture shows the drawing room of Hardwick Hall, an English estate, as it looked in the 1590's. The room has a new and distinctly English furniture form, a dining table called a *draw-table, foreground.* The length of the table could be increased by drawing its halves apart and adding leaves. Carvings of mythical winged beasts support the tabletop.

Fontainebleau. In redesigning the château, the Italian artisans introduced decorative *motifs* (designs) that revolutionized French art of the period. These motifs included the use of columns; carved human heads surrounded by scrolls; carved bands, called *strapwork,* which imitated tooled leather bookbindings; and *niches* (hollowed-out areas in walls).

The Italian-inspired Francis I style of furniture lasted until the mid-1500's. The Henry II style, which was more varied and more identifiably French, then replaced it. Carved human figures still played an important decorative role, as did carved animals. Columns and arches served as supports for tables. But the new style gave furniture a lighter appearance. For example, French artisans refined the traditional cabinet form by placing a small upper section on a larger base.

England. The Italian Renaissance influenced England largely because of the encouragement of King Henry VIII, who ruled England from 1509 to 1547. Henry invited Italian artists and artisans to work in England. English furniture makers then blended the Italian ornamental style with traditional English designs to create an English Renaissance style.

A number of distinctly English furniture forms appeared during the reign of Queen Elizabeth I, who ruled from 1558 to 1603. One of these forms was the *drawtable,* a large oak dining table made in halves that could be drawn apart. The length of this table could be increased by adding one or two top sections called *leaves* after drawing the halves apart. Another fashionable English design was the *court cupboard,* which had open shelves for displaying valuable plates and silverware. The cupboard had legs that were decorated with classical and Italian Renaissance motifs. Perhaps the most impressive pieces of English Renaissance furniture were beds, which featured handsome carvings and expensive fabrics.

Spain developed a Renaissance style that combined Spanish, Italian, and Moorish influences. The Moors were North African Muslims who had invaded Spain in the A.D. 700's. The Moorish impact on Spanish furniture appeared in an emphasis on gilding and the use of geometric designs that were made with ivory and wood inlays.

A major contribution of Spanish artisans was the design of a portable cabinet called a *vargueno.* The vargueno's door was hinged at the lower edge. When opened, the door served as a writing desk. The vargueno had many small drawers and a central cupboard.

A portable cabinet called a *vargueno* was a contribution of Spanish artisans. Varguenos had a door that could serve as a desk. This vargueno, made about 1600, rests on another cabinet.

An Italian tabletop of the 1600's is decorated with semi-precious stones in a technique called *pietre dure.* Other popular tabletops of the period were made of marble or inlaid wood.

Museo dell' Opificio
delle Pietre Dure,
Florence, Italy (SCALA)

The early 1600's were years during which most of Europe was engaged in political and religious wars. This warfare hindered the development of the arts in many European countries. Only Italy and the Netherlands enjoyed peace, and Italian artisans especially became an important source of new furniture design. Dutch furniture makers achieved excellence in creating beautiful floral designs with inlays of tropical woods and *mother-of-pearl* (the lining of certain sea shells).

In France, King Henry IV established royal furniture workshops in the Louvre in Paris. He financed the workshops and brought leading artisans from other countries to work in them.

Italy led in furniture development largely because many rich Italian merchants were building great palaces during the period. The merchants wanted the finest furniture for their palaces, and Italian artisans supplied it.

Many Italian tables had a base modeled on the slab tables of ancient Rome. Other tables had a top made of marble or inlaid wood on a base sculptured in the form of mythical creatures, shells, floral designs, and human figures. Sculptured human figures also supported cabinets, candlestands, and some chairs.

Italian artisans created fashions for chests, cabinets, and cupboards that spread throughout Europe. The cassone of the 1500's developed into a long credenza with a number of doors. The credenza, in turn, gradually

Château of Vaux-le-Vicomte (1661) near Melun, France; (R. Guillemot, Agence TOP)

The Louis XIV style was known for its luxury. Louis Le Vau, the French architect who designed this room, combined beautiful furniture with works of art and architectural decorations to achieve an elegant effect. The sofa and high-backed chairs are typical of the Louis XIV style.

State beds, which featured a carved canopy and luxurious drapings, were important pieces of furniture among the nobility and the wealthy during the late 1600's. Daniel Marot, an influential French furniture maker, designed this state bed for the royal bedroom in Hampton Court Palace, near London.

Queen's Bedroom, Hampton Court Palace; copyright reserved to Her Majesty The Queen

developed into two new forms. One form was a tall two-door cabinet. The other was a tall chest of drawers that rested on a stand.

Many people of the early 1600's considered the quality of upholstery to be a measure of a householder's social rank. As a result, beds—which were richly decorated with silk, velvet, and other luxurious fabrics—became major pieces of furniture. Such large *state beds* were placed in the main room of a palace or large house as well as in the bedrooms.

Louis XIV furniture was the most notable furniture of the late 1600's. Louis XIV had become king of France in 1643, when he was only 4 years old. He took control of the French government in 1661, after the death of France's chief minister, Cardinal Jules Mazarin. Louis, who was then 23 years old, devoted himself to making France the cultural and political center of the Western world. He considered furniture making and the decorative arts to be politically important because he could use them to glorify his position as king. He bought a building on the outskirts of Paris, turned it into workshops, and staffed the shops with expert artisans. He commissioned them to create furnishings for his residences. These furnishings created a new national style of art.

Actually, the artisans worked almost entirely on a single project in Versailles, where they converted a royal hunting lodge into a luxurious royal palace. The noted French architect Charles Le Brun supervised the huge Versailles project and hired artisans from other countries. The decorating and furnishing of the Palace of Versailles became such a large undertaking that many foreign artisans took up permanent residence in France. Many of them married French women and had children who became furniture makers, creating a native French group of artisans.

The remarkable style of the furnishings made for the Palace of Versailles became known as the Louis XIV style. This luxurious style was particularly notable for two characteristics. One was a *veneer* technique invented by a French cabinetmaker, André Charles Boulle. In this technique, artisans "sandwiched" a *veneer* (thin layer of material) between two veneers of a contrasting material. Artisans used such materials as brass, ebony, and a dull silvery metal called pewter. They cut through the layers to create contrasting scrolled patterns. Veneers were applied to Louis XIV cabinets, writing tables, and other furniture. Le Brun and Louis himself were responsible for the second characteristic—furniture of solid silver made for the main rooms at Versailles.

The French influence spreads. The furnishings of the Palace of Versailles set the standard for other royal palaces, and soon French styles were imitated in palaces throughout Europe. But there were also political and religious reasons for the spread of French influence.

The national religion of France was Roman Catholicism, but most French artisans were Protestants. The French Protestants, called Huguenots, enjoyed limited religious freedom under the Edict of Nantes, which was issued by King Henry IV in 1598. In 1685, Louis XIV took away the Huguenots' freedom by canceling the edict. Most of the artisans then fled to the Netherlands or to England. There, they worked among the nobles and wealthy merchants and so established a taste for French design in the two countries.

Daniel Marot became one of the most influential Huguenot artisans both in the Netherlands and in England. Marot worked for William III, who was a Dutch prince before he became king of England in 1689. Marot also designed the interiors and furniture for Hampton Court Palace, near London. His designs created a demand in the late 1600's for high-backed chairs with French-style upholstered seats and backs. Marot's work also led to a fashion for state beds with drapery even more luxurious than that used in France.

Stavros S. Niarchos Collection (Josse)

A low chest of drawers called a *commode* became a popular furniture form of the 1700's. The commode above has curves of bronze. Curved decorations were basic to the *rococo* style of the early 1700's.

The French neoclassical style of the late 1700's, *right,* featured light, graceful furniture with straight lines. The influence of ancient Roman art can be seen in the decorations on the furniture and walls.

Queen's Salon (1781), Versailles, France (Lauros, Giraudon)

Artisans in France and England dominated furniture design during the 1700's. Furniture makers in other countries interpreted the French and English designs and developed them into individual national styles.

French styles

The Régence style of the early 1700's received its name because a *regent* (temporary ruler) governed France during the period. After Louis XIV died in 1715, his 5-year-old great-grandson became King Louis XV. Because of the king's youth, his uncle, the Duke of Orléans, was appointed regent. The duke disliked the formality of Versailles and moved the royal court to Paris. There, a less ceremonial life style developed. People of the court lived in residences called *town houses,* which were smaller and more intimate than the Palace of Versailles. The style of furniture created for these town houses became known as the Régence style.

Régence furniture had a lighter, more graceful quality than Louis XIV furniture, emphasizing curves and delicate floral designs. Perhaps its most important characteristic was the use of the cabriole leg, which was inspired by Chinese furniture.

During the Régence period, the French cabinetmakers André Charles Boulle and Charles Cressent developed a low chest of drawers called a *commode.* This form became one of the most popular of the 1700's and was made with regional variations throughout Europe.

The rococo style. During the 1730's, the Régence style took on the features of a new style called *rococo.* The leading designer of rococo furniture was Juste-Aurèle Meissonnier. His motifs stressed swirling curves, *asymmetrical* (irregular) designs, and carvings in the form of rocks and shells. The name *rococo* came from the word *rocaille,* which was used to describe the rock-

European Room by Mrs. James Ward Thorne, Art Institute of Chicago

French provincial furniture was a comfortable style favored by middle-class people in the French provinces. This bedroom of the 1700's includes a tall cupboard and a bed set into the wall.

and-shell designs. The rococo style was also called the *Louis XV* style.

Rococo furniture was designed to blend with the overall architectural plan of a room. For example, artisans designed tables, mirrors, benches, and beds so that they could be set into wall niches provided by the architect. Oriental furniture styles also influenced rococo design. A style called *chinoiserie,* loosely based on Chinese motifs, became especially popular. Oriental lacquer also became fashionable.

The neoclassical style, called the *Louis XVI* style in France, replaced the rococo style by the late 1750's. The word *neoclassical* is a combination of the prefix *neo,* which means *new,* and the word *classical.* Neoclassical design thus reflected a renewed interest in the furniture motifs of ancient Greece and Rome. Neoclassical designers gradually eliminated the numerous curves of the rococo style in favor of the straight outlines of classical furniture. In place of elaborate rococo decorations, neoclassical artisans used thin pieces of plain wood arranged in geometric designs.

Much neoclassical furniture was inspired by classical motifs that were discovered in the mid-1700's by archaeologists in two ancient Roman cities, Pompeii and Herculaneum. The cities had been buried by an eruption of Mount Vesuvius in A.D. 79.

Art Institute of Chicago

The Queen Anne style of the early 1700's featured splat-backed upholstered chairs and large desks called *secretaries.* The style introduced the cabriole leg into English furniture.

Art Institute of Chicago

The Chippendale style dominated English and American furniture of the mid-1700's. The three chairs in the room shown above have carved mahogany legs, which are characteristic of the style. The influence of Chinese furniture design appears in the splat-backed chair on the left.

Dining room at Osterley Park House (about 1770); the National Trust, London

The English neoclassical style was begun by Robert Adam, a Scottish architect, in the 1760's. His light, harmonious designs can be seen in this dining room. A mirror in a richly carved frame hangs above a table called a *sideboard*. Carved plaster ornaments decorate the walls and ceiling.

English styles

The Palladian style was popular in England during the early 1700's. It was named after Andrea Palladio, an Italian architect of the 1500's. English artisans adopted elements of Palladio's style, which was based on the style of Roman architecture. For example, they decorated chests and cupboards with such architectural features as columns, ornamental moldings called *cornices,* and triangular top sections called *pediments.*

Henry Francis DuPont Winterthur Museum, Wilmington, Del.

Early American furniture was simple and sturdy. Most of the designs were based on English styles. The room at the left dates from about 1670. The cupboard, with its open shelves and a closed cabinet, reflects the influence of a type of English furniture called a *court cupboard.*

The Queen Anne style. The Palladian style was so expensive to produce that only wealthy people could afford it. The English middle class used a less expensive—and more comfortable—style. It was called the Queen Anne style after the queen who ruled England from 1702 to 1714. The Queen Anne style introduced the cabriole leg into English furniture design.

Chippendale furniture. In 1754, the English cabinetmaker and furniture designer Thomas Chippendale published a book of furniture designs called *The Gentleman and the Cabinet-Maker's Director.* It was the first book dealing entirely with furniture to be published in England, and it had a tremendous influence. In the book, Chippendale did not introduce any new styles. But he portrayed existing styles, especially the rococo, with such freedom and vigor that his designs were widely copied. His influence became so widespread that the name Chippendale has come to mean almost any English and American rococo furniture of the mid-1700's.

English neoclassical furniture. Robert Adam, a Scottish architect and furniture designer, introduced the neoclassical style into England in the 1760's. Adam borrowed some of his ideas from the French neoclassical style, but he also contributed many original elements. For decoration, he used delicate floral motifs, ram and ox heads, and other features inspired by ornaments on Roman buildings and tombs. Adam introduced the sideboard, or credenza, into English furniture. He also became known for skillfully blending furniture into the architectural plan of a room.

A number of English furniture makers adopted Adam's neoclassical style during the late 1700's. Two of the best known, George Hepplewhite and Thomas Sheraton, prepared design books that popularized the style. The furniture made according to Adam's original designs was very expensive. Hepplewhite, Sheraton, and other furniture makers simplified the designs to reduce the cost of the furniture for middle-class buyers.

Early American furniture

In the English colonies of North America, furniture design generally reflected the styles that were popular in England at the time. However, colonial artisans developed variations of the English styles. Starting about 1790, the most common early American style was a neoclassical variation called the *Federal* style. This style took its name from the young nation's new federal form of government. Duncan Phyfe, the leading American furniture designer of the period, worked in New York City and helped make it the manufacturing center for the Federal style. High-quality furniture was also produced by artisans in Boston; Philadelphia; and Newport, R.I.

Henry Francis DuPont Winterthur Museum, Wilmington, Del.

The Federal style of American furniture began about 1790. It was influenced by the straight lines of English neoclassical furniture. The pieces in the bedroom shown above were largely based on designs by such English furniture makers as George Hepplewhite and Thomas Sheraton.

Until the early 1800's, furniture fashions were set largely by the tastes of nobles and other wealthy people. But beginning in the early 1800's, the tastes of the middle class set the standard for furniture fashions. People of the middle class wanted variety and novelty in furniture design. As a result, a great number of styles became popular for a short time and were then replaced by new styles.

During the 1800's, many furniture expositions were held in major cities in the United States and Europe. At these expositions, furniture makers from many countries displayed their own designs and viewed the designs of others. These designs greatly influenced public taste. The expositions thus had the effect of establishing international furniture styles. The United States and European countries adopted the same major styles, with some regional differences.

The furniture of the 1800's falls into two categories: (1) furniture based on historical styles and (2) furniture intended to be truly original. Some furniture makers simply copied earlier styles. Others used earlier styles as models but changed them to give them freshness and new vigor. The invention of new furniture-making machines during the 1800's helped designers develop new styles. With these machines, designers could use materials in new ways. For example, they could use cast iron and wire in ways that had been impossible.

The Empire style, the first major style of the 1800's, originated while Emperor Napoleon I ruled the French empire. Like Louis XIV, Napoleon wanted to use furniture as a symbol of political greatness. As a result, Empire furniture was impressive—large and heavy.

Empire artisans borrowed designs from Egyptian, Greek, and Roman furniture. They made chairs with curved rear legs shaped like those on the Greek klismos. They decorated furniture with such classical subjects as lions, sphinxes, and sculptured female figures called *caryatids.* Empire commodes, writing tables, and desks called *secretaries* were designed to fit into the overall plan of a room.

The Regency style, a neoclassical style, was fashionable in England and the United States along with the Empire style. The Regency style was named after the period from 1811 to 1820, when the Prince of Wales served as regent for King George III of England. Most Regency furniture combined Egyptian, Chinese, and Gothic motifs with neoclassical elements. The style featured couches with ends shaped like scrolls, and chairs loosely modeled on the klismos. Stools based on the Roman curule also were popular.

Regency artisans used little carved ornamentation. They often used a decorative technique called *penwork,* in which artists inked designs on light-colored wood or a painted white surface. Regency artisans also decorated furniture with brass inlays.

The Biedermeier and Restauration styles. After the fall of Napoleon I in 1815, two similar yet independent styles developed in Europe. Both were more informal than Empire style furniture and were favored by the middle class.

The Restauration style was popular in France from the restoration of the French monarchy in 1815 to the July Revolution of 1830. Restauration furniture was based on the straight outlines of Empire designs and was heavy in

Fratelli Fabbri Editori, Milan, Italy

An Empire-style dressing table, *above,* features a round mirror and built-in candleholders. The table also has a marble top and curved, crossed legs like the legs of the Roman curule.

Art Institute of Chicago

Biedermeier furniture of the early 1800's had an informal, practical style. The chair and drop-front desk shown above illustrate the appealing simplicity of the style.

Philadelphia Museum of Art, Henry P. McIlhenny Collection in memory of Frances P. McIlhenny

Restauration furniture resembled the French Empire style. This Restauration sofa was made of brightly colored silk and the light maple wood favored by this style of the early 1800's.

Parlor of Lansdowne, Natchez, Miss. (Mrs. George M. Marshall)

Parlor furniture in the rococo revival style, *shown here,* has cabriole legs and oval backs edged with fine wood carvings.

appearance. The furniture was made of a light-colored wood and was often inlaid with darker woods or decorated with classical motifs, such as swans, lyres, and acanthus leaves.

The Biedermeier style was popular in Austria and Germany from 1820 to 1850. The name *Biedermeier* came from a comic character in German popular literature. Like Restauration furniture, it was based on Empire furniture forms and was usually made from light-colored wood. But this style of furniture was lighter, simpler, and more geometric in shape. In addition, some Biedermeier furniture was decorated with classical motifs and inlaid with darker wood. Often the grain of the wood was the chief decoration.

Historical revivals. From the 1830's to the late 1800's, a number of earlier styles were revived. The most important styles, in the order in which they appeared, were the Gothic, rococo, and Renaissance revivals. People used each style in a particular room. They placed Gothic furniture in the library, rococo in the *drawing room* (parlor) and bedroom, and Renaissance in the dining room.

Most Gothic revival furniture consisted of neoclassical forms with Gothic ornaments. These ornaments included pointed arches and decorative patterns called *tracery.* The style was particularly popular in England, where a variation called the *Elizabethan revival* became

Musée de l'Ecole de Nancy, Nancy, France (Gilbert Mangin)

Art Nouveau was a decorative style characterized by a graceful curve known as a *whiplash* curve. This feature appears in both the furniture and the wall and ceiling decorations in the dining room shown here.

fashionable. In France, Gothic revival was known as the *cathedral* or *troubadour* style.

The rococo revival replaced the Gothic revival in the 1840's. Chairs and sofas in this style had cabriole legs and oval backs based upon the Louis XV style of the 1700's. Artisans decorated pieces with rocaille carving and introduced large pieces, such as mirrored wardrobes, sideboards, and display cabinets. Such pieces remained popular throughout the 1800's.

The Renaissance revival began in the court of the French emperor Napoleon III, who ruled from 1852 to 1870. It achieved the greatest popularity in the late 1870's and the 1880's. Artisans of this period tried to reproduce the furniture designs of the 1400's and 1500's. Designers emphasized angular forms and richly upholstered chairs, sofas, and stools.

Art Nouveau was an art movement that developed as a revolt against the historical revival styles. This movement began in the 1800's and lasted until the early 1900's. Art Nouveau furniture featured design elements that were based on natural forms, such as blossoms, roots, stalks, and vines. Artisans combined these forms with a graceful motif called a *whiplash* curve. Art Nouveau decorations also included female heads surrounded by flowing hair.

Middle-class buyers could not afford the handmade and expensive Art Nouveau furniture. After wealthy buyers tired of the style's specialized designs, it fell from fashion. But the popularity of Art Nouveau and its rejection of traditional styles greatly contributed to design developments in furniture of the 1900's.

The 1900's to the present

During the 1900's, many designers rejected traditional furniture styles. The designers of this period made use of new manufacturing methods and new materials to revolutionize both the appearance and the function of furniture.

A variety of modern furniture styles appeared during the 1900's, but most of the styles shared a number of characteristics. The chief characteristic of modern furniture is its *abstract* form—that is, its appearance is not based on recognizable forms, such as animals or human figures. Most modern furniture has little decoration. Designers have used as few materials as possible and have selected materials that are lightweight, hard, and smooth. They have reduced the number of parts in a piece of furniture. For example, modern tables and chairs may have only one support instead of the traditional four legs. Such reductions in materials and parts have made manufacturing simpler and less costly.

Modern designers have also reduced the number of furniture forms used in a room. For example, some designers have eliminated traditional cabinets and cupboards and replaced them with sets of drawers and shelves called *storage units.* Some storage units are built into walls and become part of a room's architecture. Others are *modular units,* which can be moved and combined in various ways to fit a particular setting or to rearrange space in an area.

Early styles

De Stijl (The Style) was an art movement that began in the Netherlands about 1917. Led by the Dutch architect and furniture designer Gerrit Rietveld, the De Stijl movement produced furniture that emphasized abstract, rectangular forms. Rietveld used only the three primary colors—blue, red, and yellow. The pure geometric forms of De Stijl furniture and the lightness and clarity of the design influenced most later styles of the 1900's.

The Bauhaus was an influential school of design founded in 1919 by the German architect and educator Walter Gropius. It made important contributions to furniture design in the 1900's. One such development was

Organic design—a creative technique promoted by the American architect Frank Lloyd Wright—results in furniture that closely matches its architectural setting. This photograph shows the dining room furniture Wright designed for his famous Robie House, which was built in Chicago in 1909.

Classics of modern furniture design

The chairs shown here rank among the furniture masterpieces of the 1900's. Their designs, as in Mies van der Rohe's Barcelona chair and Eero Saarinen's tulip chair, have a light, airy appearance that is typical of most modern furniture. The caption beneath each picture gives the name of the designer, the date the chair was created, and the chair's most important materials.

Atelier International

Gerrit Rietveld (1917)
Painted wood

Knoll International

Marcel Breuer (1928)
Cane and steel tubing

Knoll International

Mies van der Rohe (1929)
Steel and leather

I C F, Inc.

Alvar Aalto (1934)
Molded plywood

Herman Miller, Inc.

Charles Eames (1946)
Plywood and metal

Knoll International

Hans Wegner (1949)
Wood and cane

Knoll International

Harry Bertoia (1952)
Metal rods and wire

Knoll International

Eero Saarinen (1957)
Plastics and aluminum

the use of tubular steel to frame and support chairs, tables, and sofas. Produced by machine, steel tubing could be bent and shaped to form simple, elegant frames that required little hand-finishing and upholstery. Steel tubing thus produced stylish design at a greatly reduced cost.

The Hungarian-born architect Marcel Breuer, a Bauhaus instructor, introduced tubular steel in his light, graceful, comfortable *Wassily chair* of 1925. The Wassily chair had a frame of chrome-plated tubular steel and simple, slinglike canvas or leather upholstery. In 1929, Ludwig Mies van der Rohe, a director of the Bauhaus, created the *Barcelona chair,* which had curved, flat steel struts supporting loose removable leather back and seat cushions. The curved X-shaped legs of this chair resembled those of the ancient Roman curule stool.

The rise of the repressive Nazi government in Germany during the 1930's caused many Bauhaus teachers to emigrate to other countries. They carried with them their advanced ideas in furniture design, thus making the influence of the Bauhaus international.

Organic design is a name frequently given to the furniture of American architect Frank Lloyd Wright and his followers. Wright believed that furniture should fit naturally and easily into its surroundings. To accomplish this, the organic designers reduced their forms to basic geometric outlines. Often these designs were derived from the simple, plain outlines of Japanese furniture and were usually crafted of simple, sturdy oak. Because Wright created his organic designs for a specific setting, they were neither interchangeable, movable, nor inexpensive. They thus differed from the furniture of the De Stijl and Bauhaus, which could be used interchangeably in most homes or working spaces.

Art Deco was the most popular international decorative style in the 1920's and 1930's. The Art Deco style stressed streamlined geometric forms that reflected public interest in images suggesting speed—such as the automobile, the train, and the ocean liner. Brushed steel and other industrial materials were blended with such traditional luxury goods as ivory, gilt-bronze, and exotic woods to produce elegant furniture. Art Deco combined such diverse influences as machine design and ancient Egyptian, Native American, and African art.

Modern Scandinavian design originated in the late 1920's in Denmark, Sweden, and Norway. It became an alternative to the luxury furniture of the Art Deco style and the machine-inspired Bauhaus designs. Kaare Klint,

Designs by Jacques-Emile Ruhlmann; The Metropolitan Museum of Art, New York City

Art Deco emphasized streamlined geometric forms. The desk, chair, and file cabinet shown here were decorated with such luxurious materials as silver, ivory, and sharkskin.

a Danish architect and designer, was one of the first of several leaders of the modern Scandinavian style. The Finnish architect Alvar Aalto also designed innovative furniture in this style. Modern Scandinavian design featured clean, plain design and natural wood and simple fabrics such as cotton, linen, or wool. This style of furniture held wide appeal because it was warm, natural, and easy to maintain, and it fit comfortably into apartments and smaller private homes. By the late 1940's, modern Scandinavian design had become one of the primary branches of furniture design, and it remained popular into the mid-1950's.

The retro style, which gained popularity in the 1950's and 1960's, freely combined elements from the various styles of the early 1900's. Materials and forms became even more simplified. Seating arrangements were composed of *modular units,* which were separate parts that could be combined in various arrangements. Triangular, rhomboid, and boomerang shapes were the most popular shapes in retro design. Supports frequently consisted of "hairpin" bent legs of chrome-plated steel. Some retro furniture had sloping conical brass legs ending in simple coin-shaped pads or similarly formed wooden legs with metal caps.

Popular materials used in the retro style included plastic laminated wood and plywood. In upholstery, polyfoam replaced coil springs and webbing of the previous 100 years. Polyfoam allowed furniture to be both lighter and less costly.

A hallmark of the retro style was a simple chair created by the American designer Charles Eames. The chair had a shieldlike molded plywood seat attached by rubber disks to a thin frame of chromeplated tubular steel rods. The disks permitted the chair seats to shift with the weight of the sitter. Many furniture historians consider Eames the first internationally important American designer of the 1900's.

Retro armchairs took on dramatic body-hugging forms as in the "421" or "butterfly" chair created by the American sculptor and designer Harry Bertoia in 1952.

This chair resembled a woven wire basket set upon a steel rod base and featured a removable polyfoam cushion. The chairs designed by American architect Eero Saarinen for his celebrated "Tulip Suite" of 1957 were formed of molded fiberglass supported on slender aluminum pedestals. The chairs also were equipped with removable upholstered foam cushions.

Recent developments

By the late 1900's, large international furniture-manufacturing companies had generally replaced the privately owned businesses that had dominated furniture design. One of the most prestigious and influential of these companies is Knoll International, founded in New York in 1938 by Hans Knoll. This large firm commissions pieces emphasizing experimental and original concepts from many leading industrial designers and architects.

Another major development in furniture design is the present-day importance of architects as creators of furniture. This development began with such earlier styles as art nouveau and the Bauhaus. The result has been the creation of highly architectural furniture that frequently resembles small-scale buildings or is distinctly related to the building designs of the particular architect.

By the 1930's, starkly glittering pieces in steel, chrome, and glass had become classics of furniture design through the work of Marcel Breuer, Mies van der Rohe, and William Armbruster, among others. Their designs eventually became known as the *International style,* a term that indicated their worldwide popularity. To distinguish this established and frequently expensive style from other modern styles, some historians and critics have named it the *classic modern style.* They also include the furniture of other designers, including

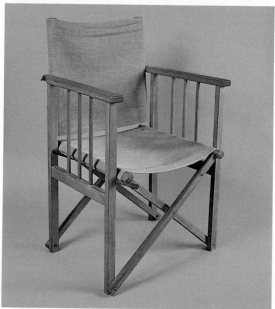

New Orleans Museum of Art, Estate of Robert Gordy (Owen F. Murphy)

Scandinavian furniture emphasized clean designs, natural wood, and simple fabrics. About 1931, Danish designer Kaare Klint created this safari chair of natural birch and linen canvas.

Charles Eames, Harry Bertoia, Finn Juhl, Hans Wegner, and Eero Saarinen, among the classic moderns.

Radical modern design became popular in the late 1960's. Seeking to escape increasingly costly materials, its designers pioneered in the concept of disposable furniture. A famous example of the style was the inflatable plastic "Blow" chair of 1967, designed for the prominent firm of Zanotta in Milan, Italy.

The 1968 "Sacco," or "beanbag" chair, also designed for Zanotta, is another example of this type of furniture. A simple leather or cloth sack was filled with plastic beads that adapted themselves to the movements of the sitter's body.

Postmodern design is a style of the late 1900's that replaced the unadorned forms and surfaces of the classic and radical modern schools with a decorative design. This style often used the materials favored by earlier avant-garde designers but used them in forms borrowed from baroque, traditional Chinese, rococo, and art deco styles. American architect Robert Venturi's bent plywood "Queen Anne," "Sheraton," and "art deco" chairs for Knoll International are examples of postmodern design concepts. Viewed in profile, they appear quite modern. Turned forward, they reveal elaborate cutouts enhanced with historically inspired silk-screen appliqué. The result is an almost whimsical reinterpretation of accepted historical models.

The international firm Memphis has done much to popularize postmodern design in case and seating pieces, clocks, and lighting devices. Colorful speckled surfaces and soft rose, mauve, and blue shades often appear in such designs.

As these factory-produced forms have evolved, there has been a successful return to handcrafted furniture

The beanbag chair was designed in Italy. The example shown here consists of a simple leather sack filled with plastic beads that adapted themselves to the movements of the sitter's body.

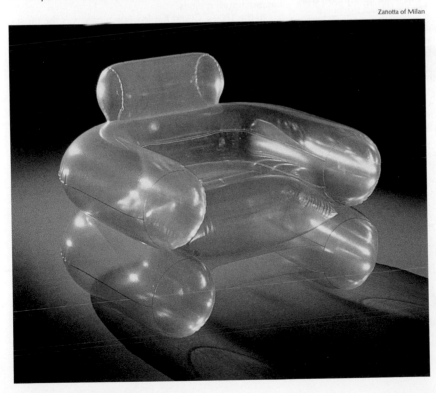

The "Blow" chair was an example of the trend toward inexpensive, disposable furniture during the late 1960's. This Italian-designed chair was made of an inflated plastic shell.

The Brooklyn Museum

Postmodern furniture is a decorative style of the late 1900's. The design firm Memphis was a leader in the postmodern reinterpretation of historical models. The Casablanca sideboard shown here is made of wood covered with laminated plastic.

whose design is based on an antimachine philosophy. Such designer-craftsmen as the American Wendell Castle and Sam Maloof make elaborately sculptural furniture that is deliberately incapable of reproduction by machine. Designers in this school seek to eliminate furniture manufacture as an industrial process and place it on a level with traditional fine arts.

Although the middle and late 1900's have in many ways revolutionized furniture design, most buyers still purchase furniture reproducing earlier period styles. The French and English designs of the late 1700's and early 1800's remain consistently fashionable. Manufacturers making reproductions and interpretations of these styles serve an enormously profitable international market. Despite the scorn in the early 1900's for the mixture of historical styles popular during the Victorian era, current taste prefers a blend of historical and modern furniture styles.

The furniture industry

During the 1700's and early 1800's, furniture making in America was a craft rather than an industry. All the furniture made during this period was produced in small woodworking shops.

The manufacture of furniture became an important industry in the United States in the mid-1800's. Large factories were built to serve the demands of middle-class people, who wanted a wide variety of furniture. The Midwest became the chief furniture-producing region because it had an abundant supply of hardwoods and was close to water transportation routes. Chicago, Cincinnati, and St. Louis became important furniture-manufacturing cities.

In the 1800's, Grand Rapids, Michigan, was the most famous furniture center in the United States. William

KnollStudio, division of Knoll International

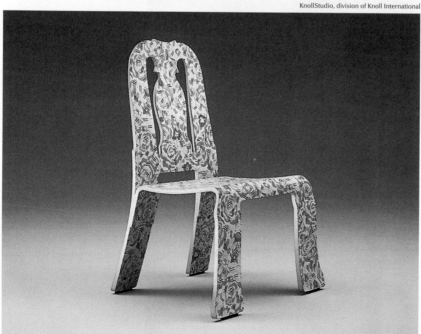

A Robert Venturi chair is the American architect's interpretation of the Queen Anne style of the early 1700's in England. Venturi created the chair of bent plywood in 1984. He designed the piece with historically inspired floral patterns.

Ron Arad Associates (photo © Alberto Piovano)

A clothing store interior features furniture of smooth polished metal. The Israeli designer Ron Arad integrated the counters, racks, lights, and seats to achieve an overall sculptural effect.

Haldane, a cabinetmaker, built the first furniture factory in Grand Rapids in 1848. Later, other furniture factories opened in that city. Artisans and designers from the United Kingdom, the Netherlands, Sweden, and Switzerland settled in Grand Rapids. The expertise and ideas that these Europeans brought with them added to the quality of furniture produced there.

Since the end of World War II in 1945, the southeastern United States has replaced the Midwest as the leading U.S. furniture-making region. The state of California also ranks highly in U.S. furniture production.

Thousands of manufacturers make furniture in the United States. They employ hundreds of thousands of workers. Americans spend billions of dollars annually on commercially produced furniture, making it one of the leading consumer industries in the country.

John W. Keefe

Study aids

Related articles in *World Book* include:

Biographies

Adam (family)	Morris, William
Chippendale, Thomas	Phyfe, Duncan
Eames, Charles	Sheraton, Thomas
Hepplewhite, George	

Styles

Art Deco	Postmodernism
Art Nouveau	Rococo
Bauhaus	

Other related articles

Antique	Mahogany
Architecture	Mount Vernon
Art and the arts (picture: The useful arts)	Museum (picture)
Bed	Pioneer life in America (Furniture and household utensils)
Colonial life in America (Furnishings)	Shakespeare, William (picture: A bedroom in the Birthplace)
Folk art	
Inlay	
Interior design	White House (pictures)
Ironwork, Decorative	Wicker
Lamp	Wood

Knoll Inc.

A chair and footstool by Frank Gehry are made of strips of maple. The 1992 designs were inspired by wooden crates and bushel baskets. The lightweight pieces require no upholstery.

Child's Chair (1964) by Peter Murdoch; Victoria & Albert Museum, London (V & A Picture Library)

A disposable paper chair reflects the influence of the Pop Art movement of the 1960's. The one-piece chair was stamped out of laminated cardboard and decorated with bright polka dots.

Outline

I. Early furniture
  A. Ancient Egypt
  B. Ancient Greece
  C. Ancient Rome
  D. The Middle Ages
II. Oriental furniture
  A. China
  B. Japan
  C. India
III. The Renaissance
  A. Italy   C. England
  B. France   D. Spain
IV. The 1600's
  A. The early 1600's
  B. Louis XIV furniture
  C. The French influence spreads
V. The 1700's
  A. French styles
  B. English styles
  C. Early American furniture
VI. The 1800's
  A. The Empire style
  B. The Regency style
  C. The Biedermeier and Restauration styles
  D. Historical revivals
  E. Art Nouveau
VII. The 1900's to the present
  A. Early styles
  B. Recent developments
VIII. The furniture industry

Questions

Who was the leading designer of the Federal style in American furniture?
What was a *klismos?* A *curule?*
How did the Bauhaus influence furniture design in the 1900's?
What is a *cabriole* leg?
How did Classical art influence Italian Renaissance furniture?
What were the two main characteristics of the Louis XIV style?
How did Japanese architecture influence Japanese furniture?
What were some characteristics of the Regency style?
Who was Kaare Klint? Eero Saarinen?
How did the Rococo style differ from the Neoclassical style?

Additional resources

Boyce, Charles, ed. *Dictionary of Furniture.* 2nd ed. Facts on File, 2001.
Jackson, Albert, and Day, David. *Care and Repair of Furniture.* HarperCollins, 2006.
Keno, Leigh and Leslie. *Hidden Treasures: Searching for Masterpieces of American Furniture.* 2000. Reprint. Warner Bks., 2002.
Miller, Judith. *Furniture.* DK Pub., 2005.
Morley, John. *The History of Furniture.* Little, Brown, 1999.

Furtwängler, *FOORT VEHNG lur,* **Wilhelm,** *VIHL hehlm* (1886-1954), was a noted German orchestra conductor. He was one of the last conductors of the Romantic school, which was known for broad tempos and sweeping emotional interpretations.

Furtwängler was born on Jan. 25, 1886, in Berlin. Beginning in 1905, he led orchestras in Lübeck, Mannheim, Leipzig, and other European cities. Furtwängler became principal conductor of the Berlin Philharmonic Orchestra in 1922 and of the Vienna Philharmonic in 1927. He held both positions for most of the rest of his life. In 1925, he made his American debut at the New York Philharmonic. Furtwängler became a controversial figure after he conducted for the Nazis during World War II (1939-1945). In 1946, American authorities officially cleared him of pro-Nazi activity. Furtwängler died on Nov. 30, 1954.   Martin Bernheimer

Furze is a spiny shrub native to Europe and Africa. It is sometimes called *gorse* or *whin.* The plant has many dark green branches that are covered with spines. It grows to a height of 4 feet (1.2 meters) or more and has

© Carleton Ray, Photo Researchers

A furze shrub has dark green branches covered with spines and fragrant, yellow flowers. Furze is native to Europe and Africa, but gardeners plant it in many parts of the world.

fragrant, yellow flowers. It is used as an ornamental plant or for ground cover in North America and grows wild in some areas.   Ronald L. Jones

Scientific classification. Furze's scientific name is *Ulex europaeus.*

Fuse is a device used to cause—or delay—an explosion. There are two general types, *safety fuse* and *detonating fuse.* The safety fuse allows the person setting off the explosion to reach safety before the blast occurs. A safety fuse is a cord made of black powder enclosed in jute, cotton yarns, and waterproofing materials. When lit, the black powder burns slowly until the flame reaches the explosive. The flame sets off a blasting cap attached to the fuse.

A detonating fuse, also called a *detonating cord,* has a core of high explosive that fires almost instantly over its length. It is used to set off dynamite in quarry blasting, to separate the stages of a rocket, and to release the cargo in space vehicles. It also helps pilots parachute from airplanes in emergencies. A blasting cap is used to explode this fuse. In military use, the word is usually spelled *fuze* and refers to a mechanical device for triggering an explosion by means of electric current, impact, or pressure.   Paul Worsey

See also **Ammunition; Dynamite; Explosive.**

Fuse is a device that protects an electric circuit against damage from excessive current. A fuse contains a short piece of wire made of an alloy that melts readily. The flow of current through a fuse causes the wire to heat up. The wire melts when excessive current passes through the fuse. This action burns out the fuse and breaks the circuit. It also interrupts the flow of electric current because a fuse is always connected *in series* with the circuit it protects (see **Electric circuit** [Series circuits]). A burned-out fuse—commonly called a "blown" fuse—must be replaced for the circuit to function.

Fuses are manufactured in a variety of *current ratings.* The current rating indicates how much electric current the fuse can carry without burning out. The rating is determined by the diameter of the wire used in the device. Some fuses can carry only a fraction of an ampere, but others carry hundreds of amperes.

A type of fuse called a *plug fuse* is used in many homes. A plug fuse has a "window" of glass or mica over its wire. This feature makes it possible to quickly check whether a fuse has burned out. Another type, the *cartridge fuse,* is used in circuits that require large amounts of electric current, such as those for air conditioners and electric ranges. Miniature cartridge fuses are used in automobiles and in amplifiers, television sets, and other electronic equipment. Some fuses are specially

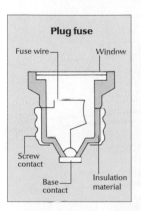

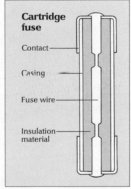

WORLD BOOK illustrations by Arthur Grebetz

Two types of fuses that protect electric circuits in the home are the plug fuse and the cartridge fuse.

designed to withstand a current overload for a limited time. These *time-delay fuses* are useful for electric motors that need a large surge of current during start-up.

Many new homes are equipped with automatic *circuit breakers* instead of fuses (see **Circuit breaker**). These devices can be reset and so they do not have to be replaced after a current overload.   Milton From

Fusion, *FYOO zhuhn,* in physics, is the combining of two atomic nuclei to form the nucleus of a heavier element. Fusion reactions between light nuclei release a great amount of energy. Fusion produces the energy of the sun and other stars and the explosive force of thermonuclear weapons.

Nuclei of hydrogen and other light elements fuse more readily than nuclei of heavier elements do. Scientists conduct most fusion experiments using *deuterium* and *tritium,* two *isotopes* (forms) of hydrogen. A deuteri-

um nucleus and a tritium nucleus fuse to form a helium nucleus. This reaction releases a neutron.

When two light nuclei fuse, a small amount of mass is lost. This mass is converted to energy. Fusion reactions typically release millions of times more energy than chemical reactions do. For example, the fusion of 1 pound (0.45 kilogram) of a mixture of deuterium and tritium releases as much energy as burning 9,000 tons (8,200 metric tons) of coal.

Normally, nuclei repel each other. But if the nuclei are heated many millions of degrees, they begin moving so fast that they may collide and fuse. Fusion reactions typically occur at temperatures higher than 90,000,000 °F (50,000,000 °C).

Scientists often use a device called a *particle accelerator* to give nuclei enough energy to fuse. A particle accelerator uses electric or magnetic force to accelerate the nuclei, causing them to collide at high speeds. Scientists can also use a device called a *magnetic bottle* to achieve fusion. A magnetic bottle confines the nuclei in a strong magnetic field. Scientists then bombard the nuclei with electromagnetic waves or charged particles to increase their temperature. Another device, called an *inertial confinement-system,* rapidly compresses the nuclei to a small point, raising their temperature.

Fusion reactions also occur among nuclei of other elements. For example, nuclei of helium and boron isotopes can fuse with nuclei of hydrogen isotopes. These reactions require even higher temperatures. In the extremely hot cores of stars, light nuclei fuse to form nuclei of such elements as carbon, oxygen, and even iron.

Many scientists believe that fusion occurred on a large scale during a hot, explosive event called the *big bang* at the beginning of the universe. This theory holds that most of the universe's helium was created by the fusion of hydrogen nuclei in the first few minutes of the big bang.   Frank J. Wessel

See also **Nuclear energy** (Nuclear fusion); **Particle accelerator; Radiation** (diagram: Nuclear fusion); **Star** (Fusion in stars).

Future Farmers of America. See **FFA.**

Futures. See **Commodity exchange.**

Futurism was an Italian art movement that flourished from 1909 to about 1916. It was the first of many art movements that tried to break with the past in all areas of life. Futurism glorified the power, speed, and excitement that characterized the machine age. From the French Cubist painters and multiple-exposure photography, the Futurists learned to break up realistic forms into multiple images and overlapping fragments of color. By such means, they tried to portray the energy and speed of modern life. In literature, Futurism demanded the abolition of traditional sentence structures and verse forms.

Futurism was created by the poet Filippo Marinetti. In 1909, Marinetti issued the first of many defiant proclamations published by the Futurists. Marinetti was soon joined by the painters Giacomo Balla, Carlo Carrà, Luigi Russolo, and Gino Severini, and the painter and sculptor Umberto Boccioni. A Futurist sculpture by Boccioni is reproduced in the *World Book* article on **Sculpture.**

By 1916, Futurism had lost most of its vigor. Despite its short life, Futurism influenced the theories and works of such modern art movements as Dadaism, Expression-

Futurist paintings express the energy, speed, and excitement that the movement saw in the machine age. Most of these paintings feature multiple images and overlapping fragments of color.

Red Cross Train (1914), an oil painting by Gino Severini; The Solomon R. Guggenheim Museum, New York City

The Museum of Modern Art, New York City; Aristide Maillol Fund
(photograph © The Museum of Modern Art, New York City)

Oil on canvas; Museum of Modern Art, New York City. Mrs. Simon Guggenheim Fund
(digital image © Museum of Modern Art/Licensed by SCALA/Art Resource)

A Futurist sculpture called *Development of a Bottle in Space* tries to show an object in motion. Umberto Boccioni, the most important Futurist sculptor, created the bronze work in 1912.

A Boccioni painting called *The City Rises* (1910) tries to portray movement and time in a modern city. The painting reflects the style of Futurism, an Italian art movement of the early 1900's.

ism, and Surrealism. Douglas K. S. Hyland

See also **Boccioni, Umberto; Sculpture** (Modern international sculpture).

Additional resources

Apollonio, Umbro, ed. *Futurist Manifestos.* 1973. Reprint. MFA Pubns., 2001.
Humphreys, Richard. *Futurism.* Cambridge, 1999.
Perloff, Marjorie. *The Futurist Moment.* 1986. Reprint. Univ. of Chicago Pr., 2003.

Fuzhou, *foo joh* (pop. 2,124,435), also spelled *Foochow* or *Fu-chou,* is the capital of Fujian Province in China. The city lies on the Min River (see **China** [political map]). Fuzhou was once a center of tea and camphor trade. In 1842, it became a "treaty port" in which the United Kingdom gained special trading rights (see **China** [Clash with the Western powers]). Fuzhou lost importance as a trading center in the late 1800's. Japanese troops occupied the city several times during World War II (1939-1945). Fuzhou is famous for its fine lacquerware. The city's products also include industrial chemicals and electronic products. Mingzheng Shi

FYROM. See Macedonia (country).

INTERSECTIONS

INTERSECTIONS

Readings in the Sciences and Humanities

Second Edition

Steven D. Scott
Brock University

Don Perkins
University of Alberta

Erika Rothwell

PEARSON

Prentice Hall

Toronto

Library and Archives Canada Cataloguing in Publication

Intersections: readings in the sciences and humanities / [compiled by] Steven Scott, Don Perkins, Erika Rothwell. —2nd ed.

Includes bibliographical references and indexes.
ISBN 0-13-124527-9

1. College readers. 2. Essays. 3. Readers—Science. 4. Readers—Humanities. 5. English language—Rhetoric. I. Scott, Steven D. (Steven Douglas), date II. Perkins, Don, date III. Rothwell, Erika, date

PE1417.I57 2005   808.4   C2004-903517-7

0-13-124527-9

Vice-President, Editorial Director: Michael J. Young
Acquisitions Editor: Patty Riediger
Sponsoring Editor: Carolin Sweig
Marketing Manager: Toivo Pajo
Developmental Editor: Jon Maxfield
Production Editor: Cheryl Jackson
Copy Editor: Deborah Viets
Proofreader: Linda Cahill
Production Coordinator: Janis Raisen
Permissions Manager: Susan Wallace-Cox
Permissions Research: Nicola Winstanley
Page Layout: Phyllis Seto
Art Director: Julia Hall
Cover Design: Julia Hall
Cover Image: Photonica

3 4 5 DPC 10 09 08
Printed and bound in Canada.

Table of Contents

ALPHABETICAL BY AUTHOR

Preface   *xiii*

Acknowledgments   *xv*

Honoré de Balzac   **1**
The Pleasures and Pains of Coffee (1830)

Sharon Begley, with Thomas Hayden   **6**
From Both Sides Now (1999)

Laurent Belsie   **10**
The Short, Simple Human Gene Map (2001)

Rachel Carson   **14**
A Fable for Tomorrow (1962)

John Haslett Cuff   **17**
Eat Your Hearts Out Cinephiles, the Tube Is Where It's At (1996)

Charles Darwin   **20**
Excerpt From *The Origin of Species* (1859)

Paul Davies   **24**
Doomsday (1994)

Annie Dillard   **29**
The Writing Life (1989)

Albert Einstein   **33**
How I Created the Theory of Relativity (1922)

Jan Furlong   **38**
Straight Talk at the Parakeet Café (1998)

Alan H. Goodman   **41**
Bred in the Bone? (1997)

Stephen Jay Gould   49
The Monster's Human Nature (1995)

O. B. Hardison, Jr.   57
Charles Darwin's Tree of Life (1989)

Charles E. Harris, Jr.   64
Explaining Disasters: The Case for Preventive Ethics (1995)

Werner Heisenberg   72
What Is an Elementary Particle? (1976)

Michael Ignatieff   83
Myth and Malevolence (1995)

Jay Ingram   87
The Atom's Image Problem (1996)

Axel Kahn   91
Clone Mammals. . . Clone Man? (1997)

Walter Karp   95
Why Johnny Can't Think (1985)

Perri Klass   101
India (1987)

Thomas S. Kuhn   106
The Route to Normal Science (1962)

Lewis H. Lapham   116
Sense and Sensibility (1991)

Stephen Leacock   121
A, B, and C: The Human Element in Mathematics (1911)

Rick McConnell   125
Beginning to Understand the Beginning (1996)

Jessica Mitford   129
Behind the Formaldehyde Curtain (1963)

Joyce Carol Oates   136
"State-of-the-Art Car": The Ferrari Testarossa (1985)

George Orwell   141
Shooting an Elephant (1950)

Cynthia Ozick   **147**
Crocodiled Moats in the Kingdom of Letters (1989)

Henry Petroski   **152**
Lessons from Play; Lessons from Life (1992)

Steven Pinker   **163**
The Official Theory (2002)

Heather Pringle   **172**
The Way We Woo (1993)

John Romano   **182**
Coming Home to Television (1999)

Hilary Rose   **186**
Marie Curie and Mileva Einstein Maríc (1994)

John Ruskin   **193**
The English Villa—Principles of Composition (1838)

Oliver Sacks   **202**
Island Hopping (1996)

Richard Selzer   **218**
A Mask on the Face of Death (1987)

David Suzuki   **228**
The Road from Rio (1992)

Jonathan Swift   **235**
A Modest Proposal (1729)

Henry David Thoreau   **242**
The Ponds (1854)

A. M. Turing   **246**
Computing Machinery and Intelligence (1950)

Sherry Turkle   **267**
Ghosts in the Machine (1995)

Margaret Visser   **273**
Knives, Forks and Spoons (1991)

Gisday Wa and Delgam Uukw   **283**
The Address of the Chiefs (1987)

James D. Watson and Francis H. C. Crick   **287**
Molecular Structure of Nucleic Acids (1953)

**I. Wilmut, A. E. Schnieke, J. McWhir, A. J. Kind, and
K. H. S. Campbell**   **291**
Viable Offspring Derived from Fetal and Adult Mammalian Cells (1997)

Elizabeth K. Wilson   **299**
Bitten by the Space Bug (1996)

Marie Winn   **306**
A Defense of Reading (1977)

Xu Xi   **318**
Don't Rock the Sampan (1999)

Glenn Zorpette   **321**
How Iraq Reverse-Engineered the Bomb (1992)

Appendix A: Joyce Dene   **334**
Waniskâ Nôsim (2003)

Appendix B: Lisa Grekul   **340**
Putting Self-Help "Leviathans" and "Oracles" to Sleep:
A Discussion of Anthony Robbins' *Awaken the Giant Within* and
James Redfield's *The Celestine Prophecy* (1998)

**Appendix C: Robert Gust, Chris Turner, Peter Karl,
and Scott Koehn**   **346**
A Technical Report for a Course in
Mechanical Engineering (1998)

Glossary   *362*

Title Index   *365*

Date Index   *367*

Alternative Table of Contents

THEMATIC

Biology, Natural History, and Nature

Begley, Sharon   6
Belsie, Laurent   10
Carson, Rachel   14
Darwin, Charles   20
Einstein, Albert   33
Goodman, Alan   41
Gould, Stephen Jay   49
Hardison, Jr., O. B.   57
Kahn, Axel   91
Pinker, Steven   163
Suzuki, David   228
Thoreau, Henry David   242
Watson, J. D. and Crick, F. H. C.   287
Wilmut, Ian, et al.   291

Business and Economics

Romano, John   182
Swift, Jonathan   235
Zorpette, Glenn   321

Chemistry

de Balzac, Honoré   1
Carson, Rachel   14
Ingram, Jay   87
Watson, J. D. and Crick, F. H. C.   287
Wilmut, Ian, et al.   291

Computers

Turing, A. M.   246
Turkle, Sherry   267

Cultural Analysis

Begley, Sharon   6
Mitford, Jessica   129
Orwell, George   141
Pringle, Heather   172
Romano, John   182
Sacks, Oliver   202
Visser, Margaret   273
Wa, Gisday and Uukw, Delgam   283
Xi, Xu   318

Education

Karp, Walter   95
Petroski, Henry   152
Romano, John   182
Turing, A. M.   246

Engineering

Harris, Jr., Charles E.   64
Petroski, Henry   152
Wilson, Elizabeth K.   306

Language and Communication

Begley, Sharon   6
Cuff, John Haslett   17
Dillard, Annie   29
Furlong, Jan   38

Ignatieff, Michael   83
McConnell, Rick   125
Romano, John   182
Sacks, Oliver   202
Turkle, Sherry   267
Xi, Xu   318

Manners and Morals

Begley, Sharon   6
Ignatieff, Michael   83
Lapham, Lewis H.   116
Mitford, Jessica   129
Orwell, George   141
Pringle, Heather   172
Visser, Margaret   273
Wa, Gisday and Uukw, Delgam   283
Xi, Xu   318

Medicine

Belsie, Laurent   10
Klass, Perri   101
Sacks, Oliver   202
Selzer, Richard   218
Watson, J. D. and Crick, F. H. C.   287

Myth and Story

Davies, Paul   24
Einstein, Albert   33
Gould, Stephen Jay   49
Ignatieff, Michael   83
Leacock, Stephen   121
Orwell, George   141

Physics

Einstein, Albert   33
Heisenberg, Werner   72
Ingram, Jay   87
Zorpette, Glenn   321

Places

Furlong, Jan   38
Klass, Perri   101
Ruskin, John   193
Selzer, Richard   218
Xi, Xu   318

Race and Racism

Goodman, Alan   41
Sacks, Oliver   202
Wa, Gisday and Uukw,
   Delgam   283
Xi, Xu   318

Science and Ethics/Culture

Begley, Sharon   6
Cuff, John Haslett   17
Harris, Jr., Charles E.   64
Kahn, Axel   91
Klass, Perri   101
Lapham, Lewis H.   116
Mitford, Jessica   129
Pinker, Steven   163
Selzer, Richard   218
Winn, Marie   306
Zorpette, Glenn   321

Scientists

Begley, Sharon   6
Belsie, Laurent   10
Carson, Rachel   14
Darwin, Charles   20
Einstein, Albert   33
Heisenberg, Werner   72

Technology and Inventions

Cuff, John Haslett   17
Harris, Jr., Charles E.   64
Mitford, Jessica   129
Romano, John   182
Ruskin, John   193
Turing, A. M.   246
Turkle, Sherry   267
Visser, Margaret   273
Watson, J. D. and Crick,
   F. H. C.   287
Wilmut, Ian, et al.   291
Wilson, Elizabeth K.
   299
Winn, Marie   306
Zorpette, Glenn   321

Women and Science

Begley, Sharon   6
Rose, Hilary   186

Alternative Table of Contents

STYLISTIC/RHETORICAL

Analogy

Davies, Paul   24
Ingram, Jay   87
Leacock, Stephen   121
Sacks, Oliver   202
Suzuki, David   228
Turing, A. M.   246

Argument/ Persuasion

Gould, Stephen Jay   49
Hardison, Jr., O. B.   57
Harris, Jr., Charles E.   64
Kahn, Axel   91
Karp, Walter   95
Romano, John   182
Swift, Jonathan   235
Turing, A. M.   246
Wa, Gisday, and Uukw, Delgam   283
Watson, J. D. and Crick, F. H. C.   287
Xi, Xu   318

Cause and Effect

Begley, Sharon   6
Harris, Jr., Charles E.   64
Ignatieff, Michael   83
Karp, Walter   95
Orwell, George   141
Swift, Jonathan   235
Wa, Gisday and Uukw, Delgam   283
Winn, Marie   306
Zorpette, Glenn   321

Classification

Begley, Sharon   6
Carson, Rachel   14
Darwin, Charles   20
Goodman, Alan H.   41
Heisenberg, Werner   72
Kuhn, Thomas S.   106
Pinker, Steven   163
Turing, A. M.   246
Visser, Margaret   273
Winn, Marie   306

Collaboration

Begley, Sharon   6
Watson, J. D. and Crick, F. H. C.   287
Wilmut, Ian, et al.   291

Comparison/ Contrast

Cuff, John Haslett   17
Ignatieff, Michael   83
Ingram, Jay   87
Pinker, Steven   163
Romano, John   182
Rose, Hilary   186
Wa, Gisday and Uukw, Delgam   283
Wilson, Elizabeth K.   299

Definition

Belsie, Laurent   10
Goodman, Alan, H.   41
Heisenberg, Werner   72
Ingram, Jay   87
Orwell, George   141
Pinker, Steven   163
Ruskin, John   193
Turing, A. M.   246
Xi, Xu   318

Description

de Balzac, Honoré   1
Furlong, Jan   38
Goodman, Alan, H.   41
Ingram, Jay   87
Mitford, Jessica   129
Oates, Joyce Carol   136
Ruskin, John   193
Sacks, Oliver   202
Thoreau, Henry David   242

Example

Dillard, Annie   29
Harris, Jr., Charles E.   64
Ignatieff, Michael   83
Ingram, Jay   87
Lapham, Lewis H.   116
McConnell, Rick   125
Mitford, Jessica   129
Petroski, Henry   152
Visser, Margaret   273
Wa, Gisday and Uukw, Delgam   283
Xi, Xu   318

Narration

Einstein, Albert   33

Furlong, Jan   38
Leacock, Stephen   121
Orwell, George   141
Sacks, Oliver   202
Wa, Gisday and Uukw,
   Delgam   283
Xi, Xu   318

Process Analysis

Harris, Jr., Charles E.   64
Lapham, Lewis H.   116
Mitford, Jessica   129
Ozick, Cynthia   147
Pinker, Steven   163
Pringle, Heather   172
Romano, John   182
Ruskin, John   193

Swift, Jonathan   235
Turing, A. M.   246
Wa, Gisday and Uukw,
   Delgam   283
Wilson, Elizabeth K.
   299
Zorpette, Glenn   321

Public Address

Romano, John   182
Wa, Gisday and Uukw,
   Delgam   283

Research

Begley, Sharon   6
Belsie, Laurent   10

Goodman, Alan   41
Gould, Stephen Jay   49
Harris, Jr., Charles E.   64
Pinker, Steven   163
Sacks, Oliver   202
Turing, A. M.   246
Turkle, Sherry   267
Watson, J. D. and Crick,
   F. H. C.   287
Wilmut, Ian, et al.   291
Wilson, Elizabeth K.
   299
Zorpette, Glenn   321

Review

Begley, Sharon   6

Preface

Welcome to the second edition of *Intersections*. This collection of readings began as a response to the limitations of the available textbooks used in writing courses that are typically taken by science and technology students, and taught by humanities instructors. We began this project with the premise that rhetoric is a variable and cross-disciplinary concern, and with the awareness that most anthologies are collections of writings in either the humanities *or* the sciences. We wanted to question and cross that boundary. As we began to put this collection together, we proceeded from fairly simple desires. We are all experienced instructors of composition and literature classes, and we decided that we wanted to include readings that we would enjoy, or that we had enjoyed, teaching in the classroom—in particular, but not exclusively, to students whose interests or majors were in the sciences. We wanted a selection that would embrace the range of writing that reflects on technology, in both scientific and cultural fields; a selection that would demonstrate good, clear, emphatic, interesting writing on a variety of topics within those fields; a selection that could serve as models of effective writing and that employed techniques that students could incorporate into their own writing.

We began by looking for pieces by contemporary writers whose works we admire, in periodical publications that we enjoy reading. We searched our sources for appropriate essays and articles, and then began to sort our initial choices and to seek out new pieces for representation across styles, subject matter, genders, and cultures. We collected readings that deal with biology, natural history, chemistry, computers, women's issues, engineering, business, economics, technology, scientific ethics, language, communication, and manners and morals. As our search continued, we began, inevitably, to consider some standard and classic essays by authors whose work has been tested successfully in many classrooms. Our collection soon acquired another characteristic: it spans a wide range of historical periods.

Keeping our mixed sciences/humanities audience in mind, we settled on five principles of selection. First, we have selected readings that provide some historical coverage of the essay as a literary form, without making *Intersections* into an anthology that is devoted solely to the history of the essay. We have included essays as early as Swift's from the beginning of the eighteenth century, but we have also included recently published essays. Second, we have included pieces that we find enjoyable to read. The quality of the writing itself was very important when we were making our choices. We have, therefore, selected essays by long-established writers, but we have also chosen works by newer, sometimes relatively unknown, writers. The authors represented here have widely differing backgrounds, training, and interests, and include scientists, journalists, artists, students, novelists, and sociologists. Third, we wanted this collection to have readings of varying length. Although it is true that students are often asked to write relatively short papers, we thought it was important to include some essays and articles of significant length, to demonstrate that the art of extended exposition is not dead, and to show how to maintain an argument through several thousand words. Fourth, we wanted our collection to incorporate a significant number of Canadian voices without becoming an anthology only of Canadian writing; thus we have included English essays by American, Canadian, and British authors, as well as a few pieces in translation. Finally, we wanted to collect science essays and articles written by women —not only about women in science, but also good scientific writing by women.

Each title we selected is presented in three different tables of contents: alphabetically by author, grouped by theme, and grouped by style/rhetoric. The readings are indexed chronologically according to the date of first publication, and alphabetically by title. Each piece is followed by a brief commentary. These commentaries are meant to aid instructors in conducting classroom discussions, and to aid students in their reading. In addition, we have included questions for discussion and suggestions for writing. These questions address particular aspects and techniques of the individual works, while often making connections to other titles in the collection.

Finally, we have included several appendices: three samples of student writing, and a glossary of basic rhetorical terms to aid students in their comprehension of rhetorical devices and styles. The student writing includes an argumentative and comparative academic paper by a fourth-year English student on two best-selling pieces of popular culture; an award-winning piece from a senior creative non-fiction writing course; and a technical report on the detection of land mines by a group of fourth-year Engineering students. These papers have been included for instructors to use as models for students, and to demonstrate explicitly many of the important features of good student writing: they demonstrate the effective development of a bibliography; the successful embedding of quotations from primary and secondary sources; the appropriate use of information from one field in another setting; and the use of "lively" prose, even in an "academic" assignment.

This is a collection that is designed to cross several boundaries and address several intersections: between genders, among countries, and between science and technology and the humanities. This second edition carries on our tradition of striving for excellence in writing, regardless of discipline. We have added some readings by significant notable authors to our collection, including Oliver Sacks and Albert Einstein, while keeping our losses minimal, we hope. Again, our fondest hope is still that readers, too, will cross boundaries in considering these essays—and that they will enjoy the readings collected here as much as we have enjoyed collecting them.

Acknowledgments

As is true of any project like this one, there are many people who deserve our thanks. First of all, we thank our long-suffering families for their encouragement and sacrifices. We would like to thank the English Department at the University of Alberta for their support in the form of a Graduate Research Assistant. We would also like to thank Sharon Dreger, who was that G.R.A.; Professors Dale Wilkie and Jon C. Stott, for their unflagging enthusiasm and technical advice; Dr. Paul Lumsden, who helped to shape the project into what it has become; and Leonard Swanson, Assistant to the Dean of Engineering, for his prompt, cheerful, and ready supply of Engineering perspectives and materials.

We are grateful to the following reviewers for their thoughtful comments and suggestions: Lorne Daniel, Red Deer College; Linda Dydyk, Dawson College; Amanda Goldrick-Jones, Centre for Academic Writing, University of Winnipeg; Philip Lanthier, Champlain College, Lennoxville Campus; Larry McKill, University of Alberta; Daphne Read, University of Alberta; Jack Robinson, Grant MacEwan Community College; and A.M. Robinson, University of Alberta.

THE PLEASURES AND PAINS OF COFFEE

Honoré de Balzac

BIOGRAPHICAL NOTE

Honoré de Balzac (1799–1850) is considered one of the great French writers. His master-work is a multi-volume novel entitled *La Comédie humaine* (1842–46). This essay appeared as part of an appendix (added after the first edition) to Anthelme Brillat-Savarin's *La Physiologie du goût* (1825). The full appendix deals with the effects of coffee, wine, and tobacco and is entitled *Traité des excitants modernes*. Balzac died while still quite young, probably in part due to the effects of drinking a good deal of very strong coffee.

1   On this subject Brillat-Savarin is far from complete. I can add something to what he has said because coffee is a great power in my life; I have observed its effects on an epic scale. Coffee roasts your insides. Many people claim coffee inspires them; but as everybody likewise knows, coffee only makes boring people even more boring. Think about it: although more grocery stores are staying open in Paris until midnight, few writers are actually becoming more spiritual.

2   But as Brillat-Savarin has correctly observed, coffee sets the blood in motion and stim-ulates the muscles; it accelerates the digestive processes, chases away sleep, and gives us the capacity to engage a little longer in the exercise of our intellects. It is on this last point, in particular, that I want to add my personal experience to Brillat-Savarin's observations, and to add some remarks about coffee from the great sages.

3   Coffee affects the diaphragm and the plexus of the stomach, from which it reaches the brain by barely perceptible radiations which escape complete analysis; that aside, we may surmise that our primary nervous flux conducts an electricity emitted by coffee when we drink it. Coffee's power changes over time. Rossini has personally experienced some of these effects, as, of course, have I.

Translated from the French by Robert Onopa. First published in *The Michigan Quarterly Review*, Spring 1996. Robert Onopa teaches in the Creative Writing Program at the University of Hawaii.

4   "Coffee," Rossini told me, "is an affair of fifteen or twenty days; just the right amount of time, fortunately, to write an opera."

5   This is true. But the length of time during which one can enjoy the benefits of coffee *can* be extended. This knowledge is so useful to so many people that I cannot but confess the secrets of releasing the bean's precious essence.

6   All of you, then you illustrious Human Candles—you who consume your own brilliant selves with the heat and light of your minds—approach and listen to the Gospel of the Watch, of Wakefulness, of Intellectual Travail!

7   1. Coffee completely pulverized in the Turkish manner has a much richer flavor than coffee ground in a coffee mill.

8   In many of the mechanical aspects of pleasure, Orientals are far superior to Europeans. Their particular genius—to observe as carefully as do those toads who spend entire years squatting on their haunches, holding their unblinking eyes open like two suns—has revealed to them what our science has only recently been able to show us through analysis. The principal toxin in coffee is *tannin*, an evil substance which chemists have not yet studied sufficiently. When the stomach membranes have been "tanned," or when the action of the tannin particular to coffee has numbed them by overuse, the membranes become incapable of contracting properly. This becomes the source of the serious disorders affecting the coffee connoisseur. There is a man in London, for example, whose immoderate use of coffee has left him with a stomach twisted in knots. An engraver in Paris I know personally needed five years to recover from the physical state his love of coffee had put him in. Finally, an artist, Chenavard, was burned to death by coffee: all because he went to cafés excessively, as workers go to cabarets, on the flimsiest excuse. Connoisseurs pursue coffee drinking the way they pursue all their passions; they proceed by increments, and, like Nicolet, move from strong to stronger stuff, until consumption becomes abuse. Yet when you pulverize rather than grind coffee, you crush it into a unique form of molecule which retains the harmful tannin and releases only the aroma. That is why Italians, Venetians, Greeks, and Turks can drink coffee incessantly without harm, a coffee the French contemptuously call *cafiot*. Voltaire drank just such coffee.

9   Remember, then. Coffee is composed of two elements: one, the extractable matter, which hot water or cold water dissolves quickly and which conducts the aroma; the other element, the tannin, is less dissolvable in water, and emerges from the surrounding plant tissue only slowly and with more effort. From which follows this axiom: *To brew coffee by contact with boiling water, especially for a long time, is heresy; to brew coffee with water that has already passed through coffee grounds is to subject the stomach and other internal organs to tannin.*

10   2. Using as a benchmark coffee brewed in the immortal coffeepot of my secretary, Auguste de Belloy (the cousin of a Cardinal, and, like him, related to the ancient and illustrious Marquis de Belloy), the very best coffee is made by an infusion of cold rather than boiling water; controlling the water temperature, after pulverizing the beans completely, is a second method of managing its effects.

11   There are, as we have seen, two basic types of coffee which you might brew with hot or cold water: coffee pulverized in the Turkish manner, and coffee that is ground. As we also have seen, when you merely grind coffee in an ordinary grinder, you release the tannin along with the aroma; pulverized coffee flatters the taste even as it stimulates the plexus, which reacts on the thousands of capsules which form your brain.

12　3. The quantity of coffee in the upper receptacle, the way the beans have been crushed, and the amount of water passed through them, determine the strength of the coffee; this three-part formula constitutes the ultimate consideration in dealing with the beverage.

13　Thus, for a while—for a week or two at most—you can obtain the right amount of stimulation with one, then two, cups of coffee brewed from beans which have been crushed with gradually increasing force and infused with hot water.

14　For another week, by decreasing the amount of water in the upper receptacle, by pulverizing the coffee even more finely, and by infusing with cold water, you can continue to obtain the same cerebral power.

15　When you have produced the finest grind with the least water possible, you double the dose by drinking two cups at a time; particularly vigorous constitutions can tolerate three cups. One can continue working this way for several more days.

16　Finally, I have discovered a horrible, rather brutal method that I recommend only to men of excessive vigor, men with thick black hair and skin covered with liver spots, men with big square hands and with legs shaped like bowling pins. It is a question of using finely pulverized, dense coffee, cold and anhydrous (a chemical term meaning without water), consumed on an empty stomach. This coffee *falls* into your stomach, which, as you know from Brillat-Savarin, is a sack whose velvety interior is lined with tapestries of suckers and papillae. The coffee finds nothing else in the sack, and so it attacks these delicate and voluptuous linings; it acts like a food and demands digestive juices; it wrings and twists the stomach for these juices, appealing as a pythoness appeals to her god; it brutalizes these beautiful stomach linings as a wagon master abuses ponies; the plexus becomes inflamed; sparks shoot all the way up to the brain. From that moment on, everything becomes agitated. Ideas quick march into motion like battalions of a grand army to its legendary fighting ground, and the battle rages. Memories charge in, bright flags on high; the cavalry of metaphor deploys with a magnificent gallop; the artillery of logic rushes up with clattering wagons and cartridges; on imagination's orders, sharpshooters sight and fire; forms and shapes and characters rear up; the paper is spread with ink—for the nightly labor begins and ends with torrents of this black water, as a battle opens and concludes with black powder.

17　I recommended this way of drinking coffee to a friend of mine, who absolutely wanted to finish a job promised for the next day: he thought he'd been poisoned and took to his bed, which he guarded like a married man. He was tall, blonde, slender, and had thinning hair; he apparently had a stomach of papier-mâché. There had been, on my part, a failure of observation.

18　When you have reached the point of consuming this kind of coffee, then become exhausted and decide that you really must have more, even though you make it of the finest ingredients and take it perfectly fresh, you will fall into horrible sweats, suffer feebleness of the nerves, and undergo episodes of severe drowsiness. I don't know what would happen if you kept at it then: a sensible nature counseled me to stop at this point, seeing that immediate death was not otherwise my fate. To be restored one must begin with recipes made with milk, and a diet of chicken and other white meats; finally the tension on the harp strings eases, and one returns to the relaxed, meandering, simple-minded, and cryptogamous life of the retired bourgeoisie.

19　The state coffee puts one in when it is drunk on an empty stomach under these magisterial conditions produces a kind of animation that looks like anger: one's voice rises, one's gestures suggest unhealthy impatience; one wants everything to proceed with the speed of ideas; one becomes brusque, ill-tempered about nothing. One actually becomes that fickle character, The Poet, condemned by grocers and their like. One assumes that everyone is equally lucid. A man of spirit must therefore avoid going out in public. I discovered this singular state through a series of accidents which made me lose, without any effort, the ecstasy I had been feeling. Some friends, with whom I had gone out to the country, witnessed me arguing about everything, haranguing with monumental bad faith. The following day I recognized my wrongdoing and we searched the cause. My friends were wise men of the first rank and we found the problem soon enough: coffee wanted its victim.

20   The truth I set down here is subject only to the tiny variations we find among individuals; it is otherwise in complete harmony with the experience of a number of coffee's devotees, among them the celebrated Rossini, a man who has studied the laws of taste, a hero worthy of Brillat-Savarin.

21 OBSERVATION: Among certain weak natures, coffee produces only a kind of harmless congestion of the mind; instead of feeling animated, these people feel drowsy, and they say that coffee makes them sleep. Such individuals may have the legs of serfs and the stomachs of ostriches, but they are badly equipped for the work of thought. Two young travelers, Combes and Tamisier, found the Abyssinians almost universally impotent; the two travelers did not hesitate to regard the misuse of coffee, which the Abyssinians abuse to the last degree, as the cause of this disgrace. If these remarks make it to England, the English government is hereby petitioned to settle this question by experimenting on the first condemned soul at hand, provided that soul is neither female nor too elderly.

22   Tea also contains tannin, but since tea has narcotic qualities, it does not otherwise affect the mind; it stirs the plexus only while its narcotic substances are absorbed rapidly in the intestine. The manner of preparing tea, moreover, is absolute. I am not sure at what point the quantity of water that the tea drinkers pour into their stomachs should be computed in its effects. If the experience of the English is typical, heavy tea-drinking will produce English moral philosophy, a tendency toward a pale complexion, hypocrisy, and backbiting. This much is certain: tea-drinking will not spoil a woman any less morally than physically. Where women drink tea, romance is depraved on its principle; the women are pale, sickly, talkative, boring, and preachy. In certain powerful constitutions, strong tea taken in large doses induces an irritation which overturns the treasures of melancholy; it produces dreams, but less powerful dreams than those of opium, for tea's Phantasmagoria passes in a fog. The ideas are sweet, affable, bland. Your state is not the very deep sleep which distinguishes a noble constitution suffering from fatigue, but an inexpressible drowsiness, rather, which summons up only the daydreams of the morning. An excess of coffee, like that of tea, produces an extensive drying out of the skin, which becomes scorched. Coffee also often induces sweating and makes one violently thirsty. Among those who abuse the bean, saliva becomes as thick and as dry as paper on the tongue.

NOTES AND DISCUSSION

In *The Book of Coffee and Tea* (New York: St. Martin's Press, 1975), Joel, David, and Karl Schapira write that "since its beginning coffee drinking has been associated with scholars, wits, and artists," and that, furthermore, "coffee and coffee houses seem too much an expression of the French sensibility to ever disappear easily, since behind every Parisian there is a wit, a revolutionary, and a gourmand." While in Balzac's time coffee houses may not have been quite as plentiful as they are today, they were, nonetheless, very popular and very important social and political venues. Notice, for instance, the strong social and political distinctions that Balzac draws between himself and Englishmen, who drink tea.

Balzac's account of his coffee preparation and consumption can be summarized with one of his own sentences: "Connoisseurs pursue coffee drinking the way they pursue all their passions; they proceed by increments, and... move from strong to stronger stuff, until consumption becomes abuse." The essay is a personal account of an increasing addiction to caffeine, with precise and strikingly detailed descriptions. While acknowledging that his final suggestion for making coffee is a "horrible, rather brutal method" of extracting the caffeine, Balzac nonetheless seems to have experienced this kind of "coffee"; he once even "recommended this way of drinking coffee to a friend." Balzac describes in detail the physical vigour, on one hand, and accelerated intellectual activity, on the other, that can be derived from strong and frequent enough doses of coffee. Yet, ultimately, Balzac's attitude towards coffee is mixed: he relishes the "sparks [that] shoot all the way up to the brain," but is also aware that his use has become abuse, one side effect of which is rather unsavoury: "saliva becomes as thick and as dry as paper on the tongue."

STUDY QUESTIONS

For Discussion

1. How would you characterize the tone of Balzac's essay? What is the effect of the rather confessional style? Of the name-dropping? Compare the way certain rules and rituals are associated with Balzac's account of coffee consumption.

2. According to Balzac, one of coffee's great benefits is its ability to stimulate intellectual activity, which may partly explain the number of coffee shops on present-day university campuses. In your experience, is Balzac's description of the physiological effects of caffeine accurate?

For Writing

1. Do some research into the physiological and mental benefits and potential dangers of caffeine. Construct a short essay comparing your scientific research with Balzac's personal experiments. Alternatively, observe a physical reaction in yourself—the stress of final exams, perhaps—and try to describe that reaction as it intensifies or weakens over time.

2. Notice the way coffee and tea are connected in Balzac's essay with very different kinds of personalities. Research the way media advertisements portray coffee and tea drinkers and write an analytical essay based on your findings. Do the advertisements match Balzac's observations?

FROM BOTH SIDES NOW

Sharon Begley, with Thomas Hayden

BIOGRAPHICAL NOTE

Sharon Begley (1956–) is a Senior Editor for *Science* and has written many cover stories for *Newsweek*. She is also the co-author of the book *The Mind and the Brain* (2002). Thomas Hayden is a scientific journalist who has written on environmental issues and robotics.

Women do research the same way men do, but the questions they ask nature may be different. Has feminism changed science?

1   One story from the annals of science seems destined to become a minor classic among certain biologists, and it is no coincidence that it concerns sex. Out on the Western plains, biologists were studying herds of mustangs, in which the reigning stallion was believed to have the sole right to procreate. Then a researcher got the bright idea of running DNA tests on the horses. As paternity tests often do, these proved embarrassing: fewer than one third of the herd's foals had been sired by the resident stallions. Instead, mares had snuck over to other herds, mating with males there. Blinded by the "harem" metaphor of mustang social structure, researchers had not even looked for such female behavior.

2   As such examples accumulate, more and more scholars are wondering whether cultural forces such as feminism affect the direction and results of research. In her new book, "Has Feminism Changed Science?" Penn State historian Londa Schiebinger answers with a definite yes. "Science is not value-neutral," she argues. "Getting the right answers—turning the crank—may be gender-free. But it is often in setting priorities about what will and what will not be known that gender has an impact." The claim is inflaming the "science

wars," with their battles over whether science is as isolated and objective as partisans claim.

3   That's the key: it is not that men and women do science differently, but that they choose different questions to pursue, says biologist Patricia Adair Gowaty of the University of Georgia. "The women's movement of the 1960s and 1970s had a huge effect on me," she recalls. "Ideas I was exposed to I have since erected as testable, scientific hypotheses." One hypothesis involves asking under what circumstances female bluebirds have... well, extramarital affairs. "This is how feminism has changed science," says Gowaty. "I'm not doing the science any differently, but I'm asking a question that has not been asked before." Gowaty suspects that a female bluebird risks "extra-pair copulations" if she is healthy and a good forager, which would allow her to support her offspring even if her cuckolded mate left. "By answering this question," says Gowaty, "we'll know more about female biology." And maybe not only the avian kind.

4   Although most scientists dismiss the idea that there is a female "way of knowing"—holistic, nondominating and cooperative—many recognize that the different experiences men and women bring to the lab lead them to scrutinize different aspects of nature. Marine biologist Mary Beth Saffo of the University of Arizona was startled when she looked around a 1989 conference on symbiosis—often beneficial relationships between living things, like the little fish that clean parasites off sharks in return for table scraps. "The majority were women," she says. Was it a coincidence? In the '50s and '60s, says Saffo, biologists tried to understand ecosystems "through a framework of antagonism and competition." "There's more interest in and recognition of mutualism now," or cooperative relationships between species. Although Saffo doesn't go so far as to attribute the shift to feminism, it did coincide with the flood of women into ecology.

5   Something similar happened in the study of humans' primate relatives. From the 1950s to the 1970s primatologists studied savanna baboons. This species is more aggressive, male-dominated and competitive than any other nonhuman primate. "Most of these scientists were men," says primatologist Linda Fedigan of the University of Alberta. The species they chose, she says, reinforced the notion that male dominance and aggression are the norms of primate behavior, including ours, and that it is the males who bring social cohesion to the troop. When feminism and women entered the field, in the 1970s, they upended the stereotype of the passive, dependent female, and questioned the idea that male aggression and alliances are the most powerful shapers of primate society. Instead, it turns out that elderly female baboons determine where the troop will forage each day, and a male's reproductive success depends less on his place in the dominance hierarchy than it does on his relationships with the troop's females. And when women began studying primates other than baboons, they found that females actively pursue males and have loads of extramarital affairs—apparently to get more males to provide and care for the babies. Now females are no longer considered peripheral to primate evolution.

6   Feminism has also changed ideas about how humans evolved from quadrupedal apes to toolmakers, thinkers and talkers. In the 1960s the answer was unquestioned: hunting. The story was that men who learned to cooperate, communicate and make weapons in order to hunt stimulated their brains and drove evolution. Women tagged along and pushed out babies every few years. But female anthropologists now have other ideas. In "Lucy's Legacy," to be published in November, Alison Jolly of Princeton University argues that behavior where females excel (language and forming social bonds) or roles that fall to females (forging links between generations) played the key role in human evolution.

7   But would these insights have come even if feminism never existed? "Because the changes came so quickly after the feminist critique, they must be at least a bit in response," says Linda Fedigan. But have feminists exaggerated their effect? Schiebinger and others claim that it took feminists to overthrow the dogma about active, heroic sperm pursuing the fat, passive egg, and substituting the now standard view that the egg plays an active role in conception by sending out fingerlike microvilli to reel in a sperm. Biologist Paul Gross isn't buying it. "The argument about feminism focusing attention upon the egg is absurd and dishonest," he says, because the egg's active role was noted in textbooks even in the 1960s. "If that's all 'feminist science' can claim as an achievement, then it's a joke." But it does make other claims, in fields from mustang matings to human evolution. If it turns out that the questions science poses, and the answers it seeks, are not walled off from society, maybe that's as it should be.

NOTES AND DISCUSSION

This article explores the current debate about whether or not feminism has influenced the shaping and findings of scientific endeavours. It also functions in part as a review of the book *Has Feminism Changed Science?* by Londa L. Schiebinger (1999). As a review, it seeks to summarize and engage with the thesis of the work without becoming lost in a detailed recounting of the book's content and arguments. Begley opens by suggesting that the research practices of men and women are not different but that the content of their studies may be. She then reiterates the interrogatory title of Schiebinger's book, *Has Feminism Changed Science?*

Having introduced its focus, the article sidesteps into a humorous anecdote designed to demonstrate that cultural assumptions may undermine scientific processes. Begley then quotes what she deems the essential point of Schiebinger's book. The next four body paragraphs present more evidence in support of this idea—the conception that men and women do science differently—by presenting four examples of female scientists whose own research has led them to believe, or at least to suspect, that scientific study is not gender-neutral. The examples cover a fairly wide spectrum: avian biology, marine symbiosis, primatology, and evolutionary anthropology. They were likely chosen to convince readers that the feminist impact on science is wide-reaching and not confined to a single field or line of questioning.

Only in the conclusion is a critic of feminist science introduced. Readers should consider how serious Paul Gross's dismissal of feminist science is and whether including this viewpoint strengthens or weakens the article's apparent support of feminism as an agent of change in science. Has Begley attempted to anticipate and deflate criticism of feminist science to strengthen her support of Schiebinger's position or has she introduced some genuine doubt about its credibility? The conclusion of the paper begins with the word "if," suggesting that the question "Has feminism changed science?" is not completely resolved by Schiebinger's book but that Begley supports a more integrated, intersecting vision of science and society.

STUDY QUESTIONS

For Discussion

1. Discuss Begley's piece as a book review. Do you feel it is effective? How is it similar to and different from book reviews you may have written? Identify three key characteristics

you believe a book review of a non-fictional work should possess. Does Begley's review meet your criteria?

2. All of the examples of "feminist science" deal with biological or anthropological scenarios. Could "feminist science" have an impact on other scientific disciplines, such as physics, chemistry, or engineering?

For Writing

1. Following the criteria set out in discussion question number 1, write a brief review of one of your own textbooks or another non-fiction book you have read recently.

2. Which side do you take in the "science wars" described by Begley? Write a short position paper that articulates your stance and considers how "feminist science" may or may not be considered a new "paradigm," as defined by Thomas Kuhn in his essay "The Route to Normal Science."

THE SHORT, SIMPLE HUMAN GENE MAP

Laurent Belsie

BIOGRAPHICAL NOTE

Laurent Belsie (1959–) was born in Paris, France, but has lived most of his life in the United States. He has a Bachelor's of Science in Journalism from the Medill School of Journalism at Northwestern. For the past 20 years he has worked for the various domestic bureaus of *The Christian Science Monitor*, but has also reported from Europe, Japan, and Haiti. In 2003 he became Editor of two *Monitor* feature sections: Planet and Work & Money.

Humans are complex despite fewer genes than expected, most of them shared with other species

1 Scrambling to unlock the secrets of the human genetic code, researchers stand on the kind of scientific threshold that appears once every century or so. They're poised to understand the forces behind evolution, explode racial myths, change the way doctors diagnose disease, and try to help people live longer.

2 But the first mystery along this long road of scientific discovery boils down to this: If man is so advanced, how come his gene count doesn't look that much different from a weed's or a worm's?

3 The question is forcing scientists to reevaluate their notions of biological complexity and mankind's place in the natural order. "At a basic level, I can assure you we're a lot more complex than worms," says Robert Waterston, director of the genome sequencing center at Washington University... in St. Louis. "The question becomes: How do we account for that complexity?" In this week's issue of *Nature*, Dr. Waterston and his colleagues at the

publicly funded Human Genome Sequencing Consortium reveal that humans possess roughly 32,000 genes. In a separate article to be published in … the journal *Science*, researchers at the privately funded Celera Genomics Corporation also confirmed that the human genome contains between 26,000 and 39,000 genes. That's far fewer than what many scientists were predicting only last year when, in one of science's great rivalries, Celera and the consortium rushed to publish rough drafts of the entire human genome sequence.

4   That string of biological code proved so long — some 3 billion units — scientists had expected it to contain instructions to create anywhere from 50,000 to 140,000 genes. Instead, they have discovered that vast stretches of the code create very few genes.

SO WHAT MAKES US COMPLEX?

5   "It appears that the human genome does indeed contain deserts, or large, gene-poor regions," writes Craig Venter, president of Celera, and 282 other authors in the Science article. Furthermore, just over a third of the human genome contains repetitive sequences that scientists label "junk DNA" because, at the moment, they don't appear to have any function. Researchers will spend coming months taking a deeper look.

6   The lack of human genes poses a conundrum for scientists. If humankind only has 13,000 more genes than Caenorhabditis elegans (a roundworm) or 6,000 more than Arabidopsis thaliana (a weed), what makes people so advanced by comparison?

7   Geneticists have many possible theories. For example, complexity may stem from combinations of genes. Since 30,000 genes can combine in far more ways than 20,000, these combinations alone may be enough to explain human complexity. Also, there's evidence that genes in vertebrates work harder by producing more kinds of proteins than the genes in worms and flies.

8   Then there are parts of genes, known as domains, that get shuffled around into new architectures. Scientists are finding that humans have far more combinations of these architectures than simpler life forms. Finally, there are some genes that humans have that worms and flies don't have. Their presence may account for man's uniqueness.

9   But these are guesses. And if, as suspected, the chimpanzee genome turns out to be stunningly similar to the human genome, then scientists may still be stuck trying to explain how one species has come to so dominate the world in the past 50,000 to 150,000 years while others are still climbing or buzzing around trees.

10   Scientists have also found some 200 genes that humans share with bacteria but not with the higher-order worm or fruit fly. That suggests humans have acquired some genes through other mechanisms than direct inheritance, says Waterston. While scientists understand something about how bacteria can directly transfer genes, how humans acquired them remains a mystery, he adds.

11   "No doubt the genomic view of our place in nature will be both a source of humility and a blow to the idea of human uniqueness," Svante Paabo of Germany's Max Planck Institute of Evolutionary Anthropology writes in a separate article in Science. But, he continues, "the realization that one or a few genetic accidents made human history possible will provide us with a whole new set of philosophical challenges to think about."

12   Human genomic research could also explode popular perceptions about racial differences. For example, the new research suggests that all individuals are 99.99 percent alike. And researchers are finding that the gene pool in Africa, where man is thought to

have originated, remains more diverse than in the rest of the world. These findings under-mine sweeping notions of differences based on skin color, scientists say.

13   "It is often the case that two persons who descend from the same part of the world, and look superficially alike, are less related to each other than to persons from other parts of the world who may look very different," Dr. Paabo writes.

THE DARKER SIDE OF GENETICS

14   But the new science could unwittingly usher in a new era of genetic discrimination. For example, if scientists create diagnostic tests that can determine an individual's predisposi-tion to certain diseases, should that person's insurance company or employer know about it? Many states ban the practice, but no specific national laws exist. And the federal laws that might apply have not yet been tested in the courts.

15   "Without adequate safeguards, the genetic revolution could mean one step forward for science and two steps backwards for civil rights," write United States Sens. James Jeffords (R[epublican) and Tom Daschle (D[emocrat]) in a separate article in this week's Science. "Misuse of genetic information could create a new underclass: the genetically less fortu-nate."

16   On Friday, for the first time ever, the federal Equal Employment Opportunity Commission sued an employer—Burlington Northern Santa Fe Railway—for discrimina-tion based on genetic testing.

17   In a survey of 2,133 employers last year by the American Management Association, seven said they are currently using genetic testing for job applicants or employees, accord-ing to Science.

18   It's not yet clear whether having fewer genes to study—30,000 instead of, say, 100,000—will speed up anticipated medical advances. That's because the new science already gives researchers ways to study thousands of genes at a time. The key will be how easily scientists can turn their enhanced understanding into practical applications.

19   What is clear is that the new approach—looking at systems of genes rather than indi-vidual genes—will transform biologists' view of the human body. "Before we were look-ing through a keyhole," says James Pierce, a professor of genetics at the University of the Sciences in Philadelphia. "Now, the door is open."

NOTES AND DISCUSSION

This article originally appeared in *The Christian Science Monitor* and is an example of scien-tific journalism. It acts as a bridge between the scientific community and the general public by summarizing, simplifying, and discussing leading-edge biological research. Belsie discusses the makeup of the human genome, reports the similarities among human, animal, and plant genomes, explores the work of competing scientists, and speculates upon the effect these new discoveries will have upon medical, ethical, and social practices. The article bears some resemblance to the essay-model prescribed for student writing. In his opening sentence, he offers a general statement that portrays scientists as actively involved in an ongoing competitive race for knowledge that will hold great significance. The second sentence appears to function as the paper's thesis. It has a classic parallel structure that outlines the paper's key points.

The body of the paper is organized around comparisons and contrasts and questions and answers and includes a number of quotations from experts actively engaged in genome research. Belsie carefully and seamlessly introduces the passages and the sources he quotes, giving readers full names, information about places of employment, and positions held, as well as mentioning the source from which the information is drawn—a report, journal, article, etc. The information is introduced in a manner that does not distract from the movement of the paper but that does add weight and credence to the secondary sources cited. Note that much of this paper's content is speculative and the word choice reflects and acknowledges this nature—we are told that "human genomic research *could* also explode popular perceptions about racial differences" and that "the new science *could* unwittingly usher in a new era of genetic discrimination" (emphases added). The paper ends with a (borrowed) image that reinforces this speculative nature, telling readers that looking at systems of genes rather than individual genes is like looking through an open door rather than a keyhole.

STUDY QUESTIONS

For Discussion

1. What sort of impact is created by comparing humanity to a weed or a worm? Why do you think Belsie chose these particular terms? Later he uses Latin terms to restate this point, comparing so-called man to *Caenorhabditis elegans* (roundworm) and *Arabidopsis thaliana* (a weed). How does this comparison differ in nature from the first one?

2. Write a research paragraph on any subject in which you quote at least three secondary sources. Integrate these quotations with care and introduce your experts with detail. Discuss your work with your classmates.

For Writing

1. What do you think of the claim that "misuse of genetic information could create a new underclass—the genetically less fortunate"? Discuss the examples provided by Belsie. Can you think of further instances where genetic discrimination might come into play?

2. Discuss the manner in which this paper's ideas about race relate to the ideas put forth by Alan Goodman in "Bred in the Bone?"

A FABLE FOR

TOMORROW

Rachel Carson

BIOGRAPHICAL NOTE

After receiving a Master's degree in zoology from Johns Hopkins University in 1932, Rachel Carson (1907–64) worked as a marine biologist for the United States Fish and Wildlife Service from 1936–49. In 1951 she wrote *The Sea Around Us*, which warned of the increasing danger of marine pollution. It was followed by *Silent Spring* (1962), which successfully raised public concern over the problems in food chains caused by modern synthetic pesticides. Her work had a tremendous influence on pesticide control in the United States, as well as on the popularization of ecological and conservationist attitudes and activism during the 1970s.

1   There was once a town in the heart of America where all life seemed to live in harmony with its surroundings. The town lay in the midst of a checkerboard of prosperous farms, with fields of grain and hillsides of orchards where, in spring, white clouds of bloom drifted above the green fields. In autumn, oak and maple and birch set up a blaze of color that flamed and flickered across the backdrop of pines. The foxes barked in the hills and deer silently crossed the fields, half hidden in the mists of the fall mornings.

2   Along the roads, laurel, viburnum, and alder, great ferns and wildflowers delighted the traveler's eye through much of the year. Even in winter the roadsides were places of beauty, where countless birds came to feed on the berries and on the seed heads of the dried weeds rising above the snow. The countryside was, in fact, famous for the abundance and variety of its bird life, and when the flood of migrants was pouring through in spring and fall people traveled from great distances to observe them. Others came to fish the streams, which flowed clear and cold out of the hills and contained shady pools where trout lay. So

it had been from the days many years ago when the first settlers raised their houses, sank their wells, and built their barns.

3 Then a strange blight crept over the area and everything began to change. Some evil spell had settled on the community: mysterious maladies swept the flocks of chickens; the cattle and sheep sickened and died. Everywhere was a shadow of death. The farmers spoke of much illness among their families. In the town the doctors had become more and more puzzled by new kinds of sickness appearing among their patients. There had been several sudden and unexplained deaths, not only among adults but even among children, who would be stricken suddenly while at play and die within a few hours.

4 There was a strange stillness. The birds, for example—where had they gone? Many people spoke of them, puzzled and disturbed. The feeding stations in the backyards were deserted. The few birds seen anywhere were moribund; they trembled violently and could not fly. It was a spring without voices. On the mornings that had once throbbed with the dawn chorus of robins, catbirds, doves, jays, wrens, and scores of other bird voices there was no sound; only silence lay over the fields and woods and marsh.

5 On the farms the hens brooded, but no chicks hatched. The farmers complained that they were unable to raise any pigs—the litters were small and the young survived only a few days. The apple trees were coming into bloom but no bees droned among the blossoms, so there was no pollination and there would be no fruit.

6 The roadsides, once so attractive, were now lined with browned and withered vegetation as though swept by fire. These, too, were silent, deserted by all living things. Even the streams were now lifeless. Anglers no longer visited them, for all the fish had died.

7 In the gutters under the eaves and between the shingles of the roofs, a white granular powder still showed a few patches; some weeks before it had fallen like snow upon the roofs and the lawns, the fields and streams. No witchcraft, no enemy action had silenced the rebirth of new life in this stricken world. The people had done it themselves.

8 This town does not actually exist, but it might easily have a thousand counterparts in America or elsewhere in the world. I know of no community that has experienced all the misfortunes I describe. Yet every one of the disasters has actually happened somewhere, and many real communities have already suffered a substantial number of them. A grim specter has crept upon us almost unnoticed, and this imagined tragedy may easily become a stark reality we all shall know.

NOTES AND DISCUSSION

Carson's essay is in the form of a story. Her first line—"There was once a town in the heart of America"—recalls the "once-upon-a-time" opening of many fables and fairy tales. Carson also chooses the simple, easily understood language of such stories. Although she is discussing a modern chemical invention—DDT, or dichlorodiphenyltrichloroethane—and is herself a scientist, she avoids technical or scientific language.

Carson's essay compares and contrasts two scenarios: the town as it used to be, and as it is now. She describes each scenario carefully, detailing the passing of seasons and the interactions of people, landscape, and wildlife. Notice that only two paragraphs describe the town in its ideal state, while five paragraphs describe it after the change. Carson builds suspense by detailing the changes the town endures without revealing the cause until the end of the essay.

Traditionally, fairy tales end happily, but Carson does not disclose any magic remedies at the conclusion of this essay. However, the essay is not the end of Carson's argument, but the beginning. It is the introduction to *Silent Spring*; it is intended to pique readers' interest and draw them into the body of the text where Carson defines the unnamed "white granular powder" and suggests remedies for its use.

STUDY QUESTIONS

For Discussion

1. Carson never identifies the "white granular powder." In your opinion, does this weaken or strengthen her essay and its purpose?

2. Compare and contrast Carson's conclusion with David Suzuki's in "The Road from Rio." How are they similar and dissimilar? What authorial intentions might account for these similarities and differences?

For Writing

1. Identify and examine Carson's use of elements found in traditional fairy tales and myths. How do these elements strengthen or weaken her point?

2. Write an essay that makes its point by describing a person, place, or thing before and after a significant change.

EAT YOUR HEARTS OUT CINEPHILES, THE TUBE IS WHERE IT'S AT

John Haslett Cuff

BIOGRAPHICAL NOTE

John Haslett Cuff wrote this piece about television and popular culture as a column for the newspaper *The Globe and Mail*. He has since become a filmmaker.

---

1 Although film-festival fever is breaking out in Toronto this week, moving west from Montreal and eventually winding up in Vancouver, I could care less, because day in and day out, television is more important and more entertaining than the movies. Even watching summer reruns of *Law & Order*, *ER,* or *The Drew Carey Show* is more appealing to me than a trip to the Cineplex to see the latest megabuck Hollywood bombast, whether it's *Independence Day, The Fan,* or *Courage Under Fire*. But this has not always been the case.

2 Chronologically I am a TV baby. I was born a year after ABC became a "network" of four stations, and I was starting to take my first steps about the same time CBS abandoned its premature commitment to colour and signed the first television superstar, Jackie Gleason. But I was, at first, far more attached to movies, enthralled as a child by the big-screen spectacle of *Quo Vadis* and *War and Peace* and almost any 25-cent double bill that the local Famous Players would let me watch.

3 My passion for films grew, unabated, through the sixties and seventies as I discovered Ingmar Bergman, Akiro Kurosawa, Stanley Kubrick, Martin Scorsese, and Robert Altman. And then, somewhere around the mid-seventies when *Jaws* and *Star Wars* began establishing box office records, the movies began to nosedive into the irrelevance of special effects, even as television began maturing and offering viewers an unparalleled range of entertainments such as *I, Claudius*, and, at the other extreme, *All in the Family*.

4   With the exception of independent and foreign films, still the staple of film festivals and the diet of devoted urban cinephiles, the bloated products of mainstream Hollywood continue to run a poor second to television. The medium has grown up in my lifetime to become the most economical, varied, and influential source of information and entertainment.

5   The obvious advantage television has over movies is its accessibility and the familial intimacy it has established with its audience after decades in the home of virtually every class of person. Even without TV's unquestioned rule as the primary provider of news and information, the culture of television drama and comedy is clearly superior to most of the $30-million-plus (the budget of an average studio movie) offerings available in cinemas.

6   Any five episodes of *Seinfeld*, *Frasier*, or *Roseanne* are arguably funnier and more meticulously crafted than a Jim Carrey, Robin Williams, or Eddie Murphy blockbuster, not to mention more sophisticated and relevant. The same comparison can be made of a top-flight TV drama such as *NYPD Blue* or *ER*. On an ongoing basis, these fine shows deliver more emotional punch and subtlety, as well as character and plot development than almost any $100-million-grossing action flick.

7   While this is true even of some of the most commercial network shows, the quality gap is even more marked when imported and specialty television is brought into the mix. There is simply no equivalent in contemporary, mainstream moviemaking to the oeuvre of a Dennis Potter or Alan Bleasdale, British TV writers who make most movies look like puerile drivel.

8   But these are highly subjective, qualitative comparisons and television is also superior in other significant and quantifiable ways. Most obviously, network television produces more entertainment for much less money than the Hollywood studios. Carrey's payday for a 90-minute movie would almost finance a whole season (22 hours) of prime-time TV drama.

9   Culturally, television is richer in ideas and issues and in its representation of society. Just look at the number and range of roles for women in television, and compare them with the paucity of good parts for women of any age in the movies. There are no film-actress superstars who can open a film and command the money that such muscle-bound hacks as Sly Stallone or Arnold Schwarzenegger routinely earn.

10   Yet television abounds with women stars, young and middle-aged, fat and anorexic. Many of the most enduringly popular sitcoms, such as *Roseanne*, *Murphy Brown*, *Grace Under Fire*, *Ellen,* and *Caroline in the City* dominate the ratings, and TV shows employ award-winning movie actresses such as Christine Lahti, Madeline Kahn, and Mercedes Ruehl in increasing numbers.

11   Television engenders loyalty and empathy with its characters in a way that movies don't, because over the course of a season viewers develop relationships with TV characters, sharing in their development in a way that is impossible in one-off movie fare. Such characters as Dr. Frasier Crane have been visiting us in our homes for years, and we have watched them age through story lines that reflect changes in fashion, society, and even politics.

12   While television has produced a rich mix of exceptional dramas over the past decade, movies have all but abandoned them, preferring high-octane, live-action cartoons instead. Perhaps the most important difference is that TV writers are forced to be more creative with language, plot, and even sex than the creators of movies. Since TV writers are not allowed to use profanity, nudity, or violence with the graphic abandon of their movie peers, the resulting drama is often more powerful, suggestive, and complex.

13   In addition, due to the immediacy of television and the speed with which it is produced, it is more relevant than the movies, more rooted in the social and political news of the day and better able to explore issues that affect the audience and are a vital part of the public dialogue.

14   So, despite the volume of dreck that marks the beginning of any new TV season, I must confess [I always look forward to the new season's offerings]. As for the few movies I really want to see, I'll probably catch them on pay-TV or video. That's a win–win situation.

NOTES AND DISCUSSION

For some time, cultural industries have been rated informally on a scale of relevance and aesthetic and artistic merit. It is not difficult, for instance, to find literary critics who are also fond of and are expert in film studies. Television, however, is different: many people who profess an enduring fondness for literature do not watch (or do not admit to watching) television. Because television is inexpensive and available to most people in North America it is neither exotic nor elitist and, by implication, neither interesting nor sophisticated.

John Haslett Cuff takes a divergent approach in this essay, claiming that television is in fact consistently more "economical, varied, and influential" as well as "more sophisticated and relevant" than Hollywood films. He supplies an abundance of evidence to support his claim and compares and contrasts television with Hollywood films, with television clearly emerging as the superior choice. However, notice the terms on which Cuff constructs his debate: although the opening sentence addresses film festival devotees, Cuff does not single out the festivals' content for criticism. Instead, he compares the "best" of television (the work of Dennis Potter, for instance) with what he considers to be the worst of Hollywood, the big-budget, blockbuster, special-effects-filled movie (like *Independence Day*).

STUDY QUESTIONS

For Discussion

1. Discuss Cuff's argument that the work of Dennis Potter or Alan Bleasdale makes "most movies look like puerile drivel." Do you agree, or has Cuff managed to convince you that most television is superior to most movies?

2. Compare Marie Winn's obvious fear of and dislike for television with Cuff's equally obvious celebration. What do you think Cuff thinks of reading? That is, what unspoken assumptions does Cuff make regarding the responses of television viewers?

For Writing

1. Using some of Cuff's criteria, construct a comparison/contrast essay of your own that examines a recent film and your favourite television shows.

2. Analyze the second-last paragraph of Cuff's argument, which praises the social and political relevance of television over movies. Do you think Cuff's claim is true or justified?

EXCERPT FROM *THE ORIGIN OF SPECIES*

Charles Darwin

BIOGRAPHICAL NOTE

Charles Darwin (1809–92) served as a naturalist on HMS *Beagle* from 1831–36, collecting many natural specimens and obtaining an intimate knowledge of many different landscapes and formations, which he drew on throughout his later career. In 1859 he published his famous *The Origin of Species*, which was violently attacked and vigorously defended in a variety of intellectual circles. Although he was not the first to propose the theory of evolution, Darwin was the first to gain wide acceptance for the idea, through his concept of natural selection.

---

1   Looking to geographical distribution, if we admit that there has been during the long course of ages much migration from one part of the world to another, owing to former climatal and geographical changes and to the many occasional and unknown means of dispersal, then we can understand, on the theory of descent with modification, most of the great leading facts in Distribution. We can see why there should be so striking a parallelism in the distribution of organic beings throughout space, and in their geological succession throughout time; for in both cases the beings have been connected by the bond of ordinary generation, and the means of modification have been the same. We see the full meaning of the wonderful fact, which has struck every traveller, namely, that on the same continent, under the most diverse conditions, under heat and cold, on mountain and lowland, on deserts and marshes, most of the inhabitants within each great class are plainly related; for they are the descendants of the same progenitors and early colonists. On this same principle of former migration, combined in most cases with modification, we can understand, by the aid of the Glacial period, the identity of some few plants, and the close alliance of many others, on the most distant mountains, and in the northern and southern temperate zones; and likewise the close alliance of some of the inhabitants of the sea in the northern and southern temperate latitudes, though separated by the whole intertropical ocean. Although two countries may present physical conditions as closely similar as the same species ever

require, we need feel no surprise at their inhabitants being widely different, if they have been for a long period completely sundered from each other; for as the relation of organism to organism is the most important of all relations, and as the two countries will have received colonists at various periods and in different proportions, from some other country or from each other, the course of modification in the two areas will inevitably have been different.

2   On this view of migration, with subsequent modification, we see why oceanic islands are inhabited by only few species, but of these, why many are peculiar to endemic forms. We clearly see why species belonging to those groups of animals which cannot cross wide spaces of the ocean, as frogs and terrestrial mammals, do not inhabit oceanic islands; and why, on the other hand, new and peculiar species of bats, animals which can traverse the ocean, are found on islands far distant from any continent. Such cases as the presence of peculiar species of bats on oceanic islands and the absence of all other terrestrial mammals, are facts utterly inexplicable on the theory of independent acts of creation.

3   The existence of closely allied or representative species in any two areas, implies, on the theory of descent with modification, that the same parent-forms formerly inhabited both areas; and we almost invariably find that wherever many closely allied species inhabit two areas, some identical species are still common to both. Wherever many closely allied yet distinct species occur, doubtful forms and varieties belonging to the same groups likewise occur. It is a rule of high generality that the inhabitants of each area are related to the inhabitants of the nearest source whence immigrants might have been derived. We see this in the striking relation of nearly all plants and animals of the Galapagos archipelago, of Juan Fernandez, and of the other American islands, to the plants and animals of the neighbouring American mainland; and of those of the Cape de Verde Archipelago, and of the other African islands to the African mainland. It must be admitted that these facts receive no explanation on the theory of creation.

4   The fact, as we have seen, that all past and present organic beings can be arranged within a few great classes, in groups subordinate to groups, and with the extinct groups often falling in between the recent groups, is intelligible on the theory of natural selection with its contingencies of extinction and divergence of character. On these same principles we see how it is, that the mutual affinities of the forms within each class are so complex and circuitous. We see why certain characters are far more serviceable than others for classification; why adaptive characters, though of paramount importance to the beings, are of hardly any importance in classification; why characters derived from rudimentary parts, though of no service to the beings, are often of high classificatory value; and why embryological characters are often the most valuable of all. The real affinities of all organic beings, in contradistinction to their adaptive resemblances, are due to inheritance or community of descent. The Natural System is a genealogical arrangement, with the acquired grades of difference, marked by the terms, varieties, species, genera, families, [etc.]; and we have to discover the lines of descent by the most permanent characters whatever they may be and of however slight vital importance.

5   The similar framework of bones in the hand of a man, wing of a bat, fin of the porpoise, and leg of the horse—the same number of vertebrae forming the neck of the giraffe and of the elephant—and innumerable other such facts, at once explain themselves on the theory of descent with slow and slight successive modifications. The similarity of pattern in the wing and in the leg of a bat, though used for such different purpose, in the jaws and legs of a crab, in the petals, stamens, and pistils of a flower, is likewise, to a large extent, intelligible on the view of the gradual modification of parts or organs, which were

aboriginally alike in an early progenitor in each of these classes. On the principle of successive variations not always supervening at an early age, and being inherited at a corresponding not early period of life, we clearly see why the embryos of mammals, birds, reptiles, and fishes should be so closely similar, and so unlike the adult forms. We may cease marvelling at the embryo of an airbreathing mammal or bird having branchial slits and arteries running in loops, like those of a fish which has to breathe the air dissolved in water by the aid of well-developed branchiae.

6   Disuse, aided sometimes by natural selection, will often have reduced organs when rendered useless under changed habits or conditions of life; and we can understand on this view the meaning of rudimentary organs. But disuse and selection will generally act on each creature, when it has come to maturity and has to play its full part in the struggle for existence, and will thus have little power on an organ during early life; hence the organ will not be reduced or rendered rudimentary at this early age. The calf, for instance, has inherited teeth, which never cut through the gums of the upper jaw, from an early progenitor having well-developed teeth; and we may believe, that the teeth in the mature animal were formerly reduced by disuse, owing to the tongue and palate, or lips, having become excellently fitted through natural selection to browse without their aid; whereas in the calf, the teeth have been left unaffected, and on the principle of inheritance at corresponding ages have been inherited from a remote period to the present day. On the view of each organism with all its separate parts having been specially created, how utterly inexplicable is it that organs bearing the plain stamp of inutility, such as the teeth in the embryonic calf or the shrivelled wings under the soldered wing-covers of many beetles, should so frequently occur. Nature may be said to have taken pains to reveal her scheme of modification, by means of rudimentary organs, of embryological and homologous structures, but we are too blind to understand her meaning.

NOTES AND DISCUSSION

In this passage, excerpted from the fifteenth and final chapter of *The Origin of Species*, Darwin painstakingly recapitulates and summarizes the contents of his book, which he characterizes as "one long argument." The excerpt is typical of Darwin's prose style and rhetorical strategies. Readers will immediately notice that he does not conform to contemporary style conventions for scientific or technical writing. For example, note his use of the pronoun "we" throughout this passage: he includes the reader in his explorations, discoveries, and explanations, making the reader part of the advancing argument, rather than merely an onlooker.

Darwin does not suggest that his observations and ideas are strikingly original, but claims that they are part of humanity's common pursuit of knowledge. He not only carefully establishes a series of cause-and-effect relationships, but also provides some parallel occurrences and then analyzes their meaning. Using these strategies, Darwin argues that evolution and geographical distribution are responsible for the parallels he observes in nature. He draws his examples from a wide variety of biological organisms, creating surprising and interesting comparisons and contrasts. He also deals with locales that are on a global scale, thereby enhancing the scope and impact of his argument. By describing the organisms in near-photographic detail, Darwin also imparts a sense of immediacy and verity to his writing.

STUDY QUESTIONS

For Discussion

1. O. B. Hardison, Jr., writes that Darwin disparaged his own literary style and believed that he was "writing dry scientific prose for scientists." Consider Darwin's audience and the care he takes to anticipate resistance to his argument. After reading this excerpt, what can you deduce about the nature and attitudes of Darwin's readers?

2. Darwin's last sentence begins, "Nature may be said to have taken pains to reveal her scheme of modification...." What literary device is Darwin employing? What effect does this device have on the passage?

For Writing

1. Identify and examine two cause-and-effect relationships that Darwin establishes in this passage. How does he support his contentions?

2. Read more of *The Origin of Species* and then research some current developments in creation theory. How much has the debate between the two theories changed since the publication of *The Origin of Species* in 1859?

DOOMSDAY

Paul Davies

BIOGRAPHICAL NOTE

Paul Davies is a Professor of Natural History at the University of Adelaide, Australia, where he is also Associate Director of the University's Institute of Physics. He has published over one hundred research papers in specialist journals that deal with cosmology, gravitation, and quantum field theory, and over twenty books, including *God and the New Physics* (1983), *Superforce* (1984), *The Cosmic Blueprint* (1987), *The Matter Myth* (1991), and most recently, *About Time* (1995) and *Are We Alone?* (1995). He is also well known as a popular author, broadcaster, and public lecturer. This essay is taken from his 1994 book *The Last Three Minutes*.

---

1   *The date: August 21, 2126. Doomsday.*

2   *The place: Earth. Across the planet a despairing population attempts to hide. For billions there is nowhere to go. Some people flee deep underground, desperately seeking out caves and disused mine shafts, or take to the sea in submarines. Others go on the rampage, murderous and uncaring. Most just sit, sullen and bemused, waiting for the end.*

3   *High in the sky, a huge shaft of light is etched into the fabric of the heavens. What began as a slender pencil of softly radiating nebulosity has swollen day by day to form a maelstrom of gas boiling into the vacuum of space. At the apex of a vapor trail lies a dark, misshapen, menacing lump. The diminutive head of the comet belies its enormous destructive power. It is closing on planet Earth at a staggering 40,000 miles per hour, 10 miles every second—a trillion tons of ice and rock, destined to strike at seventy times the speed of sound.*

4   *Mankind can only watch and wait. The scientists, who have long since abandoned their telescopes in the face of the inevitable, quietly shut down the computers. The endless simulations of disaster are still too uncertain, and their conclusions are too alarming to release to the public anyway. Some scientists have prepared elaborate survival strategies, using their technical knowledge to gain advantage over their fellow citizens. Others plan to observe the cataclysm as carefully as possible, maintaining their role as true scientists to the very end, transmitting data to time capsules buried deep in the Earth. For posterity...*

5   *The moment of impact approaches. All over the world, millions of people nervously check their watches. The last three minutes.*

6   *Directly above ground zero, the sky splits open. A thousand cubic miles of air are blasted aside. A finger of searing flames wider than a city arcs groundward and fifteen seconds later lances the Earth. The planet shudders with the force of ten thousand earthquakes. A shock wave of displaced air sweeps over the surface of the globe, flattening all structures, pulverizing everything in its path. The flat terrain around the impact site rises in a ring of liquid mountains several miles high, exposing the bowels of the Earth in a crater a hundred miles across. The wall of molten rock ripples outward, tossing the landscape about like a blanket flicked in slow motion.*

7   *Within the crater itself, trillions of tons of rock are vaporized. Much more is splashed aloft, some of it flung out into space. Still more is pitched across half a continent to rain down hundreds or even thousands of miles away, wreaking massive destruction on all beneath. Some of the molten ejecta falls into the ocean, raising huge tsunamis that add to the spreading turmoil. A vast column of dusty debris fans out into the atmosphere, blotting out the sun across the whole planet. Now the sunlight is replaced by the sinister, flickering glare of a billion meteors, roasting the ground below with their searing heat, as displaced material plunges back from space into the atmosphere.*

8   The preceding scenario is based on the prediction that comet Swift-Tuttle will hit the earth on August 21, 2126. If it were to, global devastation would undoubtedly follow, destroying human civilization. When this comet paid us a visit in 1993, early calculations suggested that a collision in 2126 was a distinct possibility. Since then, revised calculations indicate that the comet will in fact miss Earth by two weeks: a close shave, but we can breathe easily. However, the danger won't go away entirely. Sooner or later Swift-Tuttle, or an object like it, *will* hit the Earth. Estimates suggest that 10,000 objects half a kilometer or more in diameter move on Earth-intersecting orbits. These astronomical interlopers originate in the frigid outer reaches of the solar system. Some are the remains of comets that have become trapped by the gravitational fields of the planets, others come from the asteroid belt that lies between Mars and Jupiter. Orbital instability causes a continual traffic of these small but lethal bodies into and out of the inner solar system, constituting an ever-present menace to Earth and our sister planets.

9   Many of these objects are capable of causing more damage than all the world's nuclear weapons put together. It is only a matter of time before one strikes. When it does, it will be bad news for people. There will be an abrupt and unprecedented interruption in the history of our species. But for the Earth such an event is more or less routine. Cometary or asteroid impacts of this magnitude occur, on average, every few million years. It is widely believed that one or more such events caused the extinction of the dinosaurs sixty-five million years ago. It could be us next time.

10   Belief in Armageddon is deep-rooted in most religions and cultures. The biblical book of Revelation gives a vivid account of the death and destruction that lie in store for us:

Then there came flashes of lightning, rumblings, peals of thunder, and a severe earthquake. No earthquake like it has ever occurred since man has been on Earth, so tremendous was the quake.... The cities of the nations collapsed.... Every island fled away and the mountains could not be found. From the sky huge hailstones of about a hundred pounds each fell upon men. And they cursed God on account of the plague of hail, because the plague was so terrible.

11   There are certainly lots of nasty things that could happen to Earth, a puny object in a universe pervaded by violent forces, yet our planet has remained hospitable to life for at least three and a half billion years. The secret of our success on planet Earth is space. Lots of it. Our solar system is a tiny island of activity in an ocean of emptiness. The *nearest* star (after the sun) lies more than four light-years away. To get some idea of how far that is, consider that light traverses the ninety-three million miles from the sun in only eight and a half minutes. In four years, it travels more than twenty trillion miles.

12   The sun is a typical dwarf star, lying in a typical region of our galaxy, the Milky Way. The galaxy contains about a hundred billion stars, ranging in mass from a few percent to a hundred times the mass of the sun. These objects, together with a lot of gas clouds and dust and an uncertain number of comets, asteroids, planets, and black holes, slowly orbit the galactic center. Such a huge collection of bodies may give the impression that the galaxy is a very crowded system, until account is taken of the fact that the visible part of the Milky Way measures about a hundred thousand light-years across. It is shaped like a plate, with a central bulge; a few spiral arms made up of stars and gas are strung out around it. Our sun is located in one such spiral arm and is about thirty thousand light-years from the middle.

13   As far as we know, there is nothing very exceptional about the Milky Way. A similar galaxy, called Andromeda, lies about two million light-years away, in the direction of the constellation of that name. It can just be seen with the unaided eye as a fuzzy patch of light. Many billions of galaxies, some spiral, some elliptical, some irregular, adorn the observable universe. The scale of distance is vast. Powerful telescopes can image individual galaxies several *billion* light-years away. In some cases, it has taken their light longer than the age of the Earth (four and a half billion years) to reach us.

14   All this space means that cosmic collisions are rare. The greatest threat to Earth is probably from our own backyard. Asteroids do not normally orbit close to Earth; they are largely confined to the belt between Mars and Jupiter. But the huge mass of Jupiter can disturb the asteroids' orbits, occasionally sending one of them plunging in toward the sun, and thus menacing Earth.

15   Comets pose another threat. These spectacular bodies are believed to originate in an invisible cloud situated about a light year from the sun. Here the threat comes not from Jupiter but from passing stars. The galaxy is not static; it rotates slowly, as its stars orbit the galactic nucleus. The sun and its little retinue of planets take about two hundred million years to complete one circuit of the galaxy, and on the way they have many adventures. Nearby stars may brush the cloud of comets, displacing a few toward the sun. As the comets plunge through the inner solar system, the sun evaporates some of their volatile material, and the solar wind blows it out in a long streamer—the famous cometary tail. Very rarely, a comet will collide with the Earth during its sojourn in the inner solar system. The comet does the damage, but the passing star must bear the responsibility. Fortunately, the huge distances between the stars insulate us against too many such encounters.

16   Other objects can also pass our way on their journey around the galaxy. Giant clouds of gas drift slowly by, and though they are more tenuous even than a laboratory vacuum they can drastically alter the solar wind and may affect the heat flow from the sun. Other, more sinister objects may lurk in the inky depths of space: rogue planets, neutron stars, brown dwarfs, black holes—all these and more could come upon us unseen, without warning, and wreak havoc with the solar system.

17   Or the threat could be more insidious. Some astronomers believe that the sun may belong to a double-star system, in common with a great many other stars in the galaxy. If it exists, our companion star—dubbed Nemesis, or the Death Star—is too dim and too far away to have been discovered yet. But in its slow orbit around the sun it could still make its presence felt gravitationally, by periodically disturbing distant comets and sending some plunging Earthward to produce a series of devastating impacts. Geologists have found that wholesale ecological destruction does indeed occur periodically—about every thirty million years.

18   Looking farther afield, astronomers have observed entire galaxies in apparent collision. What chance is there that the Milky Way will be smashed by another galaxy? There is some evidence, in the very rapid movement of certain stars, that the Milky Way may have already been disrupted by collisions with small nearby galaxies. However, the collision of two galaxies does not necessarily spell disaster for their constituent stars. Galaxies are so sparsely populated that they can merge into one another without individual stellar collisions.

19   Most people are fascinated by the prospect of Doomsday—the sudden, spectacular destruction of the world. But violent death is less of a threat than slow decay. There are many ways in which Earth could gradually become inhospitable. Slow ecological degradation, climatic change, a small variation in the heat output of the sun—all these could threaten our comfort, if not survival, on our fragile planet. Such changes, however, will take place over thousands or even millions of years, and humanity may be able to combat them using advanced technology. The gradual onset of a new ice age, for example, would not spell total disaster for our species, given the time available to reorganize our activities. One can speculate that technology will continue to advance dramatically over the coming millennia; if so, it is tempting to believe that human beings, or their descendants, will gain control over ever-larger physical systems and may eventually be in a position to avert disasters even on an astronomical scale.

20   Can humanity, in principle, survive forever? Possibly. But we shall see that immortality does not come easily and may yet prove to be impossible. The universe itself is subject to physical laws that impose upon it a life cycle of its own: birth, evolution, and—perhaps—death. Our own fate is entangled inextricably with the fate of the stars.

NOTES AND DISCUSSION

Davies begins his essay with a descriptive scenario portraying Doomsday—the end of the world. His evocation of Doomsday is detailed, precise, and compelling. It seems designed to make readers uneasy, like a ghost story told late at night. Consider what effect this opening is likely to have on readers, and think about the essay's appeal.

In the beginning of the essay proper, Davies offers readers only partial reassurance. Much of his essay speculates about how little humanity knows and all the possibilities that surround the unexplained. His specific scenario is based on early predictions that the Swift-Tuttle comet would collide with Earth. Further calculations have shown that Swift-Tuttle will *not* collide with Earth, but Davies argues that the laws of probability ensure that someday some object *will* do so. Next, Davies offers the reader an overview of Earth's position in relation to the sun, the other planets, the galaxy, and other galaxies. He then classifies and discusses the various threats to Earth contained in these schemata: comets, other objects in space, the stars, and galaxies themselves. In the close of his essay, Davies seems to undermine the threat of sudden destruction that he has spent so much time establishing by stating that slow decay is in fact a greater threat to humanity than cataclysmic events. In his conclusion, however, he declares that humanity's fate is entangled with that of the stars and that humanity, like the universe, must be subject to physical laws, which impose life cycles.

STUDY QUESTIONS

For Discussion

1. This essay is about the possible collision of a comet with Earth, as well as the inevitable approach of Doomsday due to slow decline. How would you identify Davies's central topic of discussion? What is the thesis of his essay?
2. What principles and strategies of organization and classification does Davies use in presenting his information?

For Writing

1. Write an alternate Doomsday scenario, based on some observable phenomena in science, as an introduction to an essay in which you agree or disagree with Davies's argument.
2. Write an essay that identifies and classifies technological advances that seem most likely to aid humans in achieving immortality. (You may wish to articulate your system of classification on a separate page.)

THE WRITING LIFE

Annie Dillard

BIOGRAPHICAL NOTE

Annie Dillard won the 1974 Pulitzer Prize for nonfiction for *Pilgrim at Tinker Creek*. She has since written several well-received books of essays, a memoir, and a novel. Dillard is a keen observer of human nature and its connection to the natural world, especially of the ways this connection reflects on human spirituality.

1   Writing every book, the writer must solve two problems: Can it be done? and, Can I do it? Every book has an intrinsic impossibility, which its writer discovers as soon as his first excitement dwindles. The problem is structural; it is insoluble; it is why no one can ever write this book. Complex stories, essays, and poems have this problem, too—the prohibitive structural defect the writer wishes he had never noticed. He writes it in spite of that. He finds ways to minimize the difficulty; he strengthens other virtues; he cantilevers the whole narrative out into thin air, and it holds. And if it can be done, then he can do it, and only he. For there is nothing in the material for this book that suggests to anyone but him alone its possibilities for meaning and feeling.

2   Why are we reading, if not in hope of beauty laid bare, life heightened and its deepest mystery probed? Can the writer isolate and vivify all in experience that most deeply engages our intellects and our hearts? Can the writer renew our hope for literary forms? Why are we reading if not in hope that the writer will magnify and dramatize our days, will illuminate and inspire us with wisdom, courage, and the possibility of meaningfulness, and will press upon our minds the deepest mysteries, so we may feel again their majesty and power? What do we ever know that is higher than that power which, from time to time, seizes our lives, and reveals us startlingly to ourselves as creatures set down here bewildered? Why does death so catch us by surprise, and why love? We still and always want waking. We should amass half dressed in long lines like tribesmen and shake gourds at each other, to wake up; instead we watch television and miss the show.

3   And if we are reading for these things, why would anyone read books with advertising slogans and brand names in them? Why would anyone write such books? Commercial intrusion has overrun and crushed, like the last glaciation, a humane landscape. The new landscape and its climate put metaphysics on the run. Must writers collaborate? Well, in fact, the novel as a form has only rarely been metaphysical; it usually presents society. The novel often aims to fasten down the spirit of its time, to make a heightened simulacrum of our recognizable world in order to present it shaped and analyzed. This has never seemed to me worth doing, but it is certainly one thing literature has always done. (Any writer draws idiosyncratic boundaries in the field.) Writers attracted to metaphysics can simply ignore the commercial blare, as if it were a radio, or use historical settings, or flee to nonfiction or poetry. Writers might even, with their eyes wide open, redeem the commercial claptrap from within the novel, using it not just as a quick, cheap, and perfunctory background but—as Updike did in *Rabbit Is Rich*—as part of the world subject to a broad and sanctifying vision.

4   The sensation of writing a book is the sensation of spinning, blinded by love and daring. It is the sensation of rearing and peering from the bent tip of a grassblade, looking for a route. At its absurd worst, it feels like what mad Jacob Boehme, the German mystic, described in his first book. He was writing, incoherently as usual, about the source of evil. The passage will serve as well for the source of books.

5   "The whole Deity has in its innermost or beginning Birth, in the Pith or Kernel, a very tart, terrible *Sharpness,* in which the astringent Quality is very horrible, tart, hard, dark and cold Attraction or Drawing together, like *Winter,* when there is a fierce, bitter cold Frost, when Water is frozen into Ice, and besides is very intolerable."

6   If you can dissect out the very intolerable, tart, hard, terribly sharp Pith or Kernel, and begin writing the book compressed therein, the sensation changes. Now it feels like alligator wrestling, at the level of the sentence.

7   This is your life. You are a Seminole alligator wrestler. Half naked, with your two bare hands, you hold and fight a sentence's head while its tail tries to knock you over. Several years ago in Florida, an alligator wrestler lost. He was grappling with an alligator in a lagoon in front of a paying crowd. The crowd watched the young Indian and the alligator twist belly to belly in and out of the water; after one plunge, they failed to rise. A young writer named Lorne Ladner described it. Bubbles came up on the water. Then blood came up, and the water stilled. As the minutes elapsed, the people in the crowd exchanged glances; silent, helpless, they quit the stands. It took the Indians a week to find the man's remains.

8   At its best, the sensation of writing is that of any unmerited grace. It is handed to you, but only if you look for it. You search, you break your heart, your back, your brain, and then—and only then—it is handed to you. From the corner of your eye you see motion. Something is moving through the air and headed your way. It is a parcel bound in ribbons and bows; it has two white wings. It flies directly at you; you can read your name on it. If it were a baseball, you would hit it out of the park. It is that one pitch in a thousand you see in slow motion; its wings beat slowly as a hawk's.

9   One line of a poem, the poet said—only one line, but thank God for that one line— drops from the ceiling. Thornton Wilder cited this unnamed writer of sonnets: one line of a sonnet falls from the ceiling, and you tap in the others around it with a jeweler's hammer. Nobody whispers it in your ear. It is like something you memorized once and forgot. Now it comes back and rips away your breath. You find and finger a phrase at a time; you lay it down cautiously, as if with tongs, and wait suspended until the next one finds you: Ah yes, then this; and yes, praise be, then this.

10   Einstein likened the generation of a new idea to a chicken's laying an egg: *"Kieks—auf einmal ist es da."* Cheep—and all at once there it is. Of course, Einstein was not above playing to the crowd.

11   One January day, working alone in that freezing borrowed cabin I used for a study on Puget Sound—heated not at all by the alder I chopped every morning—I wrote one of the final passages of a short, difficult book. It was a wildish passage in which the narrator, I, came upon the baptism of Christ in the water of the bay in front of the house. There was a northeaster on—as I wrote. The stormy salt water I saw from the cabin window looked dark as ink. The parallel rows of breakers made lively, broken lines, closely spaced row on row, moving fast and pulling the eyes; they reproduced the sensation of reading exactly, but without reading's sense. Mostly I shut my eyes. I have never been in so trancelike a state, and in fact I dislike, as romantic, the suggestion that any writer works in any peculiar state. I sat motionless with my eyes shut, like a Greek funerary marble.

12   The writing was simple yet graceless; it surprised me. It was arrhythmical, nonvisual, clunky. It was halting, as if there were no use trying to invoke beauty or power. It was plain and ugly, urgent, like child's talk. "He led him into the water," it said, without antecedents. It read like a translation from the *Gallic Wars*.

13   Once when I opened my eyes the page seemed bright. The windows were steamed and the sun had gone behind the firs on the bluff. I must have had my eyes closed long. I had been repeating to myself, for hours, like a song, "It is the grave of Jesus, where he lay." From Wallace Stevens' poem, "Sunday Morning." It was three o'clock then; I heated some soup. By the time I left, I was scarcely alive. The way home was along the beach. The beach was bright and distinct. The storm still blew. I was light, dizzy, barely there. I remembered some legendary lamas, who wear chains to keep from floating away. Walking itself seemed to be a stunt; I could not tell whether I was walking fast or slowly. My thighs felt as if they had been reamed.

14   And I have remembered it often, later, waking up in that cabin to windows steamed blue and the sun gone around the island; remembered putting down those queer, stark sentences half blind on yellow paper; remembered walking ensorcerized, tethered, down the gray cobble beach like an aisle. Evelyn Underhill describes another life, and a better one, in words that recall to me that day, and many another day, at this queer task: "He goes because he must, as Galahad went towards the Grail: knowing that for those who can live it, this alone is life."

15   Push it. Examine all things intensely and relentlessly. Probe and search each object in a piece of art. Do not leave it, do not course over it, as if it were understood, but instead follow it down until you see it in the mystery of its own specificity and strength. Giacometti's drawings and paintings show his bewilderment and persistence. If he had not acknowledged his bewilderment, he would not have persisted. A twentieth-century master of drawing, Rico Lebrun, taught that "the draftsman must aggress; only by persistent assault will the live image capitulate and give up its secret to an unrelenting line." Who but an artist fierce to know—not fierce to seem to know—would suppose that a live image possessed a secret? The artist is willing to give all his or her strength and life to probing with blunt instruments those same secrets no one can describe in any way but with those instruments' faint tracks.

16   Admire the world for never ending on you—as you would admire an opponent, without taking your eyes from him, or walking away.

17   One of the few things I know about writing is this: spend it all, shoot it, play it, lose it, all, right away, every time. Do not hoard what seems good for a later place in the book,

or for another book; give it, give it all, give it now. The impulse to save something good for a better place later is the signal to spend it now. Something more will arise for later, something better. These things fill from behind, from beneath, like well water. Similarly, the impulse to keep to yourself what you have learned is not only shameful, it is destructive. Anything you do not give freely and abundantly becomes lost to you. You open your safe and find ashes.

18   After Michelangelo died, someone found in his studio a piece of paper on which he had written a note to his apprentice, in the handwriting of his old age: "Draw, Antonio, draw, Antonio, draw and do not waste time."

NOTES AND DISCUSSION

In this piece, taken from her memoir *The Writing Life*, Dillard instructs novice writers to "examine all things intensely and relentlessly." Dillard's own intensity is clearly evident here. With its almost Romantic concern about what nature and specific observation can teach us, Dillard's prose has been compared to Thoreau's, especially to parts of his most famous work, *Walden*.

In another essay, entitled "Transfiguration," Dillard portrays the writer's life as an all-or-nothing endeavour. In this piece, she seems to develop this same sense of the writer as heroic. The writer performs difficult or even impossible tasks: "Every book has an intrinsic impossibility," she writes. Note Dillard's language in this essay, as she seeks to elevate the life of the writer from the realm of ordinary lives. Writers convey "hope" and "beauty" and strive to "isolate and vivify all in experience that most deeply engages our intellects and our hearts."

STUDY QUESTIONS

For Discussion

1. Dillard uses numerous similes and other comparisons in this essay. See, for example, "The sensation of writing a book is the sensation of spinning, blinded by love and daring"; and "I sat motionless with my eyes shut, like a Greek funerary marble." How do these comparisons relate to the specific things described, and to the overall pattern of Dillard's imagery?

2. Does it matter that Dillard "genders" writers male in this essay, though she is a female writer? What cultural associations and assumptions does this gendering have in the essay? Why do you think Dillard made this choice?

For Writing

1. Dillard enjoins writers to "Push it. Examine all things intensely and relentlessly." Write a paragraph in which you try to exhaust the descriptive possibilities of an event that has been important to you. Try to follow Dillard's suggestion. As an alternative, construct an analysis of one of Dillard's paragraphs from this essay.

2. Dillard writes, "One of the few things I know about writing is this: spend it all, shoot it, play it, lose it, all, right away, every time. Do not hoard what seems good for a later place in the book, or for another book; give it, give it all, give it now." Examine and explain Dillard's choice of diction, which recalls, in its intensity and tone, the sports coach. Do you think this tone is intentional? What is its effect?

HOW I CREATED THE THEORY OF RELATIVITY

Albert Einstein
Translated by Yoshimasa A. Ono

BIOGRAPHICAL NOTE

Albert Einstein (1879–1955) is widely considered to have had possibly the greatest scientific and mathematical mind in history. In 1905, at the age of 26, he proposed his special theory of relativity, a theory that discards time and space as absolute entities and views them as relative to moving frames of reference. In 1916, he completed the mathematical formulation of his general theory of relativity, which among other things, represents gravitation as a field rather than a force. In 1921, he won the Nobel Prize for his contributions to theoretical physics. In 1950, he proposed his unified field theory, which attempts to explain gravitation, electromagnetism, and subatomic phenomena in one set of laws. He completed its mathematical formulation in 1953, two years before his death in 1955 at the age of 76.

This translation of a lecture giaven in Kyoto on 14 December 1922 sheds light on Einstein's path to the theory of relativity and offers insights into many other aspects of his work on relativity.

1   I know that when Albert Einstein was awarded the Nobel Prize for Physics in 1922, he was unable to attend the ceremonies in Stockholm in December of that year because of an earlier commitment to visit Japan at the same time. In Japan, Einstein gave a speech entitled "How I Created the Theory of Relativity" at Kyoto University on 14 December 1922. This was an impromptu speech to students and faculty members, made in response to a request by K. Nishida, professor of philosophy at Kyoto University. Einstein himself made no written notes. The talk was delivered in German and a running translation was given to the audience on the spot by J. Ishiwara, who had studied under Arnold Sommerfeld and Einstein from 1912 to 1914 and was a professor of physics at Tohoku University. Ishiwara kept careful notes of the lecture, and published[1] his detailed notes (in Japanese) in the

monthly Japanese periodical *Kaizo* in 1923; Ishiwara's notes are the only existing notes of Einstein's talk. More recently T. Ogawa published[2] a partial translation to English from the Japanese notes in *Japanese Studies in the History of Science*.

2   But Ogawa's translation, as well as the earlier notes by Ishiwara, are not easily accessible to the international physics community. However, the early account by Einstein himself of the origins of his ideas is clearly of great historical interest at the present time. And for this reason, I have prepared a translation of Einstein's entire speech from the Japanese notes by Ishiwara. It is clear that this account of Einstein's throws some light on the current controversy[3] as to whether or not he was aware of the Michelson-Morley experiment when he proposed the special theory of relativity in 1905; the account also offers insight into many other aspects of Einstein's work on relativity.

Y. A. Ono

3   It is not easy to talk about how I reached the idea of the theory of relativity; there were so many hidden complexities to motivate my thought, and the impact of each thought was different at different stages in the development of the idea. I will not mention them all here. Nor will I count the papers I have written on this subject. Instead I will briefly describe the development of my thought directly connected with this problem.

4   It was more than seventeen years ago that I had an idea of developing the theory of relativity for the first time. While I cannot say exactly where that thought came from, I am certain that it was contained in the problem of the optical properties of moving bodies. Light propagates through the sea of ether, in which the Earth is moving. In other words, the ether is moving with respect to the Earth. I tried to find clear experimental evidence for the flow of the ether in the literature of physics, but in vain.

5   Then I myself wanted to verify the flow of the ether with respect to the Earth, in other words, the motion of the Earth. When I first thought about this problem, I did not doubt the existence of the ether or the motion of the Earth through it. I thought of the following experiment using two thermocouples: Set up mirrors so that the light from a single source is to be reflected in two different directions, one parallel to the motion of the Earth and the other antiparallel. If we assume that there is an energy difference between the two reflected beams, we can measure the difference in the generated heat using two thermocouples. Although the idea of this experiment is very similar to that of Michelson, I did not put this experiment to the test.

6   While I was thinking of this problem in my student years, I came to know the strange result of Michelson's experiment. Soon I came to the conclusion that our idea about the motion of the Earth with respect to the ether is incorrect, if we admit Michelson's null result as a fact. This was the first path which led me to the special theory of relativity. Since then I have come to believe that the motion of the Earth cannot be detected by any optical experiment, though the Earth is revolving around the Sun.

7   I had a chance to read Lorentz's monograph of 1895. He discussed and solved completely the problem of electrodynamics within the first [order of] approximation, namely neglecting terms of order higher than v/c, where v is the velocity of a moving body and c is the velocity of light. Then I tried to discuss the Fizeau experiment on the assumption that the Lorentz equations for electrons should hold in the frame of reference of the moving body as well as in the frame of reference of the vacuum as originally discussed by Lorentz. At that time I firmly believed that the electrodynamic equations of Maxwell and Lorentz were correct, Furthermore, the assumption that these equations should hold in the

reference frame of the moving body leads to the concept of the invariance of the velocity of light, which, however, contradicts the addition rule of velocities used in mechanics.

8　　Why do these two concepts contradict each other? I realized that this difficulty was really hard to resolve. I spent almost a year in vain trying to modify the idea of Lorentz in the hope of resolving this problem.

9　　By chance a friend of mine in Bern (Michele Besso) helped me out. It was a beautiful day when I visited him with this problem. I started the conversation with him in the following way: "Recently I have been working on a difficult problem. Today I come here to battle against that problem with you." We discussed every aspect of this problem. Then suddenly I understood where the key to this problem lay. Next day I came back to him again and said to him, without even saying hello, "Thank you. I've completely solved the problem." An analysis of the concept of time was my solution. Time cannot be absolutely defined, and there is an inseparable relation between time and signal velocity. With this new concept, I could resolve all the difficulties completely for the first time.

10　　Within five weeks the special theory of relativity was completed. I did not doubt that the new theory was reasonable from a philosophical point of view. I also found that the new theory was in agreement with Mach's argument. Contrary to the case of the general theory of relativity in which Mach's argument was incorporated in the theory, Mach's analysis had [only] indirect implication in the special theory of relativity.

11　　This is the way the special theory of relativity was created.

12　　My first thought on the general theory of relativity was conceived two years later, in 1907. The idea occurred suddenly. I was dissatisfied with the special theory of relativity, since the theory was restricted to frames of reference moving with constant velocity relative to each other and could not be applied to the general motion of a reference frame. I struggled to remove this restriction and wanted to formulate the problem in the general case.

13　　In 1907 Johannes Stark asked me to write a monograph on the special theory of relativity in the journal Jahrbuch der Radioaktivität. While I was writing this, I came to realize that all the natural laws except the law of gravity could be discussed within the framework of the special theory of relativity. I wanted to find out the reason for this, but I could not attain this goal easily.

14　　The most unsatisfactory point was the following: Although the relationship between inertia and energy was explicitly given by the special theory of relativity, the relationship between inertia and weight, or the energy of the gravitational field, was not clearly elucidated. I felt that this problem could not be resolved within the framework of the special theory of relativity.

15　　The breakthrough came suddenly one day. I was sitting on a chair in my patent office in Bern. Suddenly a thought struck me: If a man falls freely, he would not feel his weight. I was taken aback. This simple thought experiment made a deep impression on me. This led me to the theory of gravity. I continued my thought: A falling man is accelerated. Then what he feels and judges is happening in the accelerated frame of reference. I decided to extend the theory of relativity to the reference frame with acceleration. I felt that in doing so I could solve the problem of gravity at the same time. A falling man does not feel his weight because in his reference frame there is a new gravitational field which cancels the gravitational field due to the Earth. In the accelerated frame of reference, we need a new gravitational field.

16　　I could not solve this problem completely at that time. It took me eight more years until I finally obtained the complete solution. During these years I obtained partial answers to this problem.

17   Ernst Mach was a person who insisted on the idea that systems that have acceleration with respect to each other are equivalent. This idea contradicts Euclidean geometry, since in the frame of reference with acceleration Euclidean geometry cannot be applied. Describing the physical laws without reference to geometry is similar to describing our thought without words. We need words in order to express ourselves. What should we look for to describe our problem? This problem was unsolved until 1912, when I hit upon the idea that the surface theory of Karl Friedrich Gauss might be the key to this mystery. I found that Gauss' surface coordinates were very meaningful for understanding this problem. Until then I did not know that Bernhard Riemann [who was a student of Gauss'] had discussed the foundation of geometry deeply. I happened to remember the lecture on geometry in my student years [in Zurich] by Carl Friedrich Geiser who discussed the Gauss theory. I found that the foundations of geometry had deep physical meaning in this problem.

18   When I came back to Zurich from Prague, my friend the mathematician Marcel Grossman was waiting for me. He had helped me before in supplying me with mathematical literature when I was working at the patent office in Bern and had some difficulties in obtaining mathematical articles. First he taught me the work of Curbastro Gregorio Ricci and later the work of Riemann. I discussed with him whether the problem could be solved using Riemann theory, in other words, by using the concept of the invariance of line elements. We wrote a paper on this subject in 1913, although we could not obtain the correct equations for gravity. I studied Riemann's equations further only to find many reasons why the desired results could not be attained in this way.

19   After two years of struggle, I found that I had made mistakes in my calculations. I went back to the original equation using the invariance theory and tried to construct the correct equations. In two weeks the correct equations appeared in front of me!

20   Concerning my work after 1915, I would like to mention only the problem of cosmology. This problem is related to the geometry of the universe and to time. The foundation of this problem comes from the boundary conditions of the general theory of relativity and the discussion of the problem of inertia by Mach. Although I did not exactly understand Mach's idea about inertia, his influence on my thought was enormous.

21   I solved the problem of cosmology by imposing invariance on the boundary condition for the gravitational equations. I finally eliminated the boundary by considering the Universe to be a closed system. As a result, inertia emerges as a property of interacting matter and it should vanish if there were no other matter to interact with. I believe that with this result the general theory of relativity can be satisfactorily understood epistemologically.

22   This is a short historical survey of my thoughts in creating the theory of relativity.

23   *The translator is grateful to the late Professor E. S. Shankland for encouragement and for informing him of reference 2.*

NOTES

1. J. Ishiwara, *Einstein Ko-en Roku (The Record of Einstein's Addresses),* Tokyo-Tosho, Tokyo (1971), page 78. (Originally published in the periodical Kaizo in 1923.)

2. T. Ogawa, *Japanese Studies in the History of Science* 18, 73 (1979).

3. R. S. Shankland, *Am. J. Phys.* 31, 47 (1963); 41, 895 (1973); 43, 464 (1974). G. Holton, *Am. J. Phys.* 37, 968 (1972); *Isis* 60, 133 (1969); or see *Thematic Origins of Scientific*

Thought, Harvard U. P., Cambridge, Mass. (1973). T. Hiroshige, *Historical Studies in the Physical Sciences,* 7, 3 (1976). A. I. Miller, *Albert Einstein's Special Theory of Relativity,* Addison-Wesley, Reading, Mass. (1981).

NOTES AND DISCUSSION

In this short historical narrative, a translation of a lecture originally given in German in Kyoto, Japan, on 14 December 1922, Einstein explains some of "the development of my thought directly connected with this problem [the special theory of relativity]." He describes the key to the special theory of relativity in this way: "An analysis of the concept of time was my solution. Time cannot be absolutely defined, and there is an inseparable relation between time and signal velocity." The key to the general theory of relativity was gravity: "A falling man does not feel his weight because in his reference frame there is a new gravitational field which cancels the gravitational field due to the Earth. In the accelerated frame of reference, we need a new gravitational field." The essay is a straightforward historical account that is designed to enable the reader to understand the general theory of relativity "epistemologically."

STUDY QUESTIONS

For Discussion

1. Einstein notes that he removed one of his major difficulties with formulating the general theory of relativity "by considering the Universe to be a closed system." What, do you think, are some of the implications of considering the Universe as an open system?

2. Academic pursuits, such as mathematics and physics, are generally taken to be solitary occupations, yet Einstein describes his work as often a very social activity. In your opinion, what are the strengths and drawbacks to doing collaborative work in academic disciplines?

For Writing

1. Do some research in order to discover and define "Michelson's experiment" and "Mach's idea about inertia." Einstein acknowledges using these pieces of information in his own work. Write a short essay in which you discuss whether Einstein's theories support or refute these two sources.

2. Do some research to discover the exact definitions of Einstein's special theory of relativity and his general theory of relativity. Write a short essay in which you discuss the extent to which the historical account given here really does shed light on the theories.

STRAIGHT TALK AT THE PARAKEET CAFÉ

Jan Furlong

BIOGRAPHICAL NOTE

A native Australian and long-time resident of Edmonton, Alberta, Jan Furlong wrote this essay while a student at the University of Alberta.

---

1   The Parakeet Café was packed that night. Diners filled the small room and spilled out onto the pavement and under the frangipane trees along the curb-side. We crushed the fallen flowers underfoot as we entered and carried with us their waxen, sugary scent. The chorus of Van Morrison's "Into the Mystic" filtered through the voices of the crowd: cool-looking people, hip-looking people, in oversized clothing and tethered in leather jewelry. A redhead with a single braid in overalls and velvet slippers tossed something brandied in a pan behind the counter, while the neon parrot flashed on and off even more brightly as evening deepened. Definitely not my sort of place.

2   "No hope of a table, I s'pose?" I ask fatalistically. The redhead turns to face us. He's flushed. Wisps have escaped the braid and straggle forlornly over his face. His overalls are spotted with grease and generously powdered with flour. He is nursing what appears to be an opened vein in his left palm. He looks us up and down, cocks an eyebrow at a pile of fold-up metal furniture propped in a corner, then juts his chin in the direction of the street. With his good hand he thrusts a menu under my arm as I bash and rattle my table through the doorway. BYOB and self-seating, evidently.

3   Wedged between a mailbox and a telephone booth, I scan the menu and brush away moths while Margaret arranges to have our wine chilled. Through the parrot-lit storefront I can see Red give her more of the eyebrow treatment. I brace myself: Margaret is a big woman, even bigger when her feathers are ruffled. But I feel no chill in the air, hear no

sound of breaking glass; with amazing docility she steps behind the counter and lays the bottle harmlessly in the 'fridge. She comes back toward me wiping her hands on a tissue, her nostrils flared. "What this place needs," she snorts, "is a firm hand."

4   Margaret is my best friend. We met fifteen years ago when we were public servants together in Queensland. We agree on most things, and on others—well, I usually come around to her way of thinking eventually. Indeed, the goat cheese and the calamari are better than I'd expected. She expends great time and thought on choosing my dessert, running a critical finger down the list of tortes, regaling me with her culinary triumphs in this field, extolling the virtues of fresh ingredients over packaged, reliving the great dessert experiences of her youth. We love desserts. I raised a toast to her once in one of Sydney's better brasseries: that we would gladly drink our own urine, given the assurance that dessert was to follow.

5   "Not bad plonk, whatd'yer reckon?" I enquire solicitously. I'm a beer drinker myself, but I've chosen a little white that has set me back $6.50 and has come with an actual cork. True, the first gulp gripped one's jaw with an authority amounting to savagery while the second touched off shudders over one's entire frame, but then this was a chablis. Margaret smiles—or is it a tic?—and pats my hand. "Well, of course, you're a beer drinker, aren't you? Let's see, I think you'd probably like the pumpkin cheesecake."

6   We kill the bottle in record time, chewing over Margaret's trips to Africa and the Far East, her job as a technical writer, her pottery classes at Canberra's National University, her tragic affair with a Brisbane chemist. We both know she deserves better. Margaret was a ravishing, voluptuous creature as a girl and even now, despite her bulk, there are resonances of that beauty: in the graceful gestures of her well-kept hands, in the slow and deliberate way she crosses her legs, how she swings her glossy hair in its sleek bob. She speaks clearly and well, choosing her words with that same finicky care that Westerners use eating with chopsticks. And she listens carefully, cradling her chin in one hand, twisting the stem of her wine glass with the other, her narrow green eyes looking deep into mine. I enjoy her immensely; bringing our cheesecakes back to the table I sneak my maraschino cherry onto her plate.

7   We eat in absorbed silence, always a good idea given the texture of pumpkin and cream cheese. We are smiling conspiratorially as we spoon up the froth from our cappuccinos when there is a shrill cry from the next table. I glance across, and find myself unable to look away. He couldn't have been more than seventeen. Slight, tanned, he wore a faded pink sarong knotted at the waist—in front, North Coast style. His lips looked flaked and dry. He had the shoulder-length, white-gold hair that only surfers on the dole can afford. A moth had landed and entangled itself there; he raked his fingers through and through and turned down the corners of his mouth. His companion, a dark, heavy man in a safari jacket, leaned across, picked the moth out by its furry body and threw it onto the road. He had the silky, silvery powder from its wings on his hands; the boy's hair would feel like that, I thought.

8   Margaret leans across the table at me. "Nothing but a bum-boy," she hisses. Where Margaret spits, tall trees wither and die. It's not a gay word, a prison word; it's pure public school—something abject, pimply, furtive. I feel as though I have been bitten by a snake. I see now, yes, he is on the defensive: leaning ever so slightly away from the man at his side, hunching his near shoulder self-protectively, clasping and unclasping his hands between his knees. I catch his eye and try to smile. Maybe he's broke and hungry. The little bastard winks and shows me the underside of his tongue. I've had about enough of the

Parakeet Café. I throw a couple of twenties on the table and as we leave I give the Red the finger.

NOTES AND DISCUSSION

It is difficult to write English—indeed, any language—and remain strictly gender-neutral. This essay is a personal narrative that confronts the difficulties with gender and language. Notice the author's strategy in the construction of the essay's persona: there are many apparently conflicting messages about who the main character is, and what he or she is like. You might want to make a list of characteristics that you know for sure about the main character, and then see how many of those characteristics, even if accurate, are stereotypes. Notice, for instance, that it is impossible to tell the narrator's gender. On the one hand, he could be male: he prefers to drink beer, wrestles tables into place, pays for the meal, and "give[s] the Red the finger" when he and Margaret leave. On the other hand, she could be female: she eats cheesecake (and "love[s] desserts" in general), is Margaret's best friend, defers to Margaret's opinion on "most things," and lets Margaret choose everything they eat from the menu. The essay apparently takes place in Australia, and the narrator is apparently Australian, but examine closely the evidence that tells you even this much. Finally, notice how stereotypes are used in this essay, not only about the main character, but also about the less important characters. For example: think about the picture that is created in your mind when you read about "a redhead with a single braid in overalls and velvet slippers," or about the Brisbane chemist mentioned in paragraph six who had an affair with Margaret.

STUDY QUESTIONS

For Discussion

1. Note the way that language is used in this essay. How would you respond to the suggestion that all language is always already loaded with markers, some referring to gender, some to other cultural considerations, and that those markers often exist at such an unconscious level that we notice them only when they are mentioned specifically or used inappropriately?

2. Compare Furlong's use of gender and stereotypes to Lapham's use of so-called "political correctness" in "Sense and Sensibility." While the two essays have some concerns in common, their strategies are very different from each other. Explain these differences.

For Writing

1. Choose a social situation that you have recently experienced and try to describe that situation in a completely gender-neutral paragraph. Alternatively, write that same paragraph in a way that avoids any gender or cultural stereotypes.

2. Stereotypes are invoked and indirectly critiqued in "Straight Talk." Write a plan for a scientific paper on the dangers of stereotypes. How would your paper's strategy differ from that of "Straight Talk"?

BRED IN THE BONE?

Alan H. Goodman

BIOGRAPHICAL NOTE

Alan H. Goodman is a professor of anthropology at Hampshire College in Amherst, Massachusetts. He delivered a talk on the topic of this essay to the Anthropology Section of the New York Academy of Science on October 28, 1996.

1   On the morning of May 30, 1995, rescue workers in Oklahoma City made a final, melancholy sweep through the ruins of the Alfred P. Murrah Federal Building. In the weeks after the building was bombed, 165 victims had been discovered and removed, but three more bodies had been lodged in places too unstable to reach. Rather than risk more lives in a futile rescue—any survivors of the blast would have long since died of starvation or suffocation—workers simply had marked the three locations with Day-Glo orange paint, before bringing down the rest of the building with dynamite. Now they picked methodically through the rubble, searching for glimpses of orange.

2   Clyde Snow, a forensic anthropologist with a long history of identifying victims of war crimes, was stationed in the state morgue at the time, listening to reports from the bomb site. "Everything was going swimmingly," he later recalled. "When they got down to level zero, people could hear them talking on their mobile phones: 'Okay, we have one, two, three bodies.... Fine, wrap it up, we can all go home.'" The rescue team, events soon showed, was jumping the gun just a bit. Two or three minutes after the third body had been found, a voice suddenly broke back over the airwaves: "Hey wait a minute! We've got a leg down here. A left leg."

3   During the explosion and its aftermath, about twenty-five of the victims had been dismembered. Snow assumed, at first, that the leg must belong to one of those. "In all the

This article is reprinted by permission of *The Sciences* and is from the March/April 1997 issue. Individual subscriptions are US$28 per year. Write to: The Sciences, 2 East 63rd Street, New York, NY 10021.

confusion, with bodies going back and forth for X rays, I thought somebody just over-looked that one body had a left leg missing," he said. "So we'll just match it up." But one recount after another yielded the same number: 168 right legs, 168 left legs; none of the survivors was missing a leg. "We went through autopsy records, pathology reports, body diagrams, and photographs. I did it twice, the pathologist did it twice," Snow said. "It was just a mathematical paradox."

4   Baffled, Snow took a closer look at the leg itself. Sheared off just above the knee by the blast, it still wore the remains of a black, military-style boot, two socks and an olive-drab blousing strap. Its skin, Snow said, suggested "a darkly complected Caucasoid." By measuring the lower leg and plugging the numbers into computer programs that categorize bones by race and sex, Snow confirmed his hunch: the leg probably came from a white male. An attorney for the prime suspect in the bombing, Timothy J. McVeigh, pounced on the news, suggesting that the leg belonged to the "real bomber." Snow wondered if it might belong to one of the transients who hung out on the first floor of the building. Fred B. Jordan, the Chief Medical Examiner for the state of Oklahoma, guessed that the leg belonged to a person walking alongside the truck carrying explosives.

5   As it turned out, the leg belonged to none of the above. Its owner was one Lakesha R. Levy of New Orleans, an Airman First Class, stationed at Tinker Air Force Base in Midwest City, Oklahoma. On April 19 Levy had gone to the Murrah building to get a Social Security card and gotten caught near the epicenter of the blast. Levy was five feet, five inches tall, twenty-one years old and female. She was also, in the words of one forensics expert, "obviously black." With that disclosure, McVeigh's attorney declared, "no one can have confidence in any of the forensic work in this case."

6   Just a few weeks before the leg was found, in the pages of [*The Sciences*] magazine, Snow had said that he could accurately discern a victim's race from its skull 90 percent of the time. True, a skull provides more clues to its owner's identity than a leg does, and Levy's leg was discovered and examined under extremely trying conditions. But the leg was still covered in skin, only partly decomposed, and skin is the most common indicator of "race."

7   In fact, numerous examples suggest that mistakes like the one in Oklahoma City are common. They are common not because forensics experts do shoddy work—they don't, the errors in Oklahoma City notwithstanding—but because their conclusions are based on a deeply flawed premise. As long as race is used as a shorthand to describe human biological variations—variations that blur from one race into the next, and are greatest *within* so-called races rather than among them—misidentifications are inevitable. Whether it is used in police work, medical studies, or countless everyday situations where people are grouped biologically, the answer is the same: race science is bad science.

8   Thirty years ago, the American paleontologist George Gaylord Simpson declared all pre-Darwinian definitions of humanity worthless. "We will be better off," he wrote, "if we ignore them completely." The scientific concept of race—an outgrowth of the Greek idea of a great chain of being and the Platonic notion of ideal types—is anti-evolutionary to its core. It should therefore have been the first relic consigned to the scrap heap.

9   Race should have been discarded at the turn of the [last] century, when the American anthropologist Franz Boas showed that race, language, and culture do not go hand-in-hand, as raciologists had contended. But race persisted. It should have vanished in the 1930s, when the "new evolutionary synthesis" helped explain subtle human variations. Yet between 1899, when William Z. Ripley published *Races of Europe*, and 1939, when the American anthropologist Carleton S. Coon published a book by the same name, the

concept of race as type persisted almost unchanged. (Coon, on the eve of the Second World War, went to some lengths to ponder the essence of Jewishness. "There is a quality of looking Jewish," he wrote, "and its existence cannot be denied.") Race should have disappeared in the 1950s and 1960s, when physical anthropologists switched from studying types to studying variations as responses to evolutionary forces. But race lived on. To Coon, for instance, races just became populations with distinct adaptive problems.

10   Most anthropologists today acknowledge that biological races are a myth. Yet the idea survives, in a variety of forms. A crude typology of world views goes something like this. At one end of the spectrum are the true believers: at the University of Western Ontario in London, for example, the psychologist J. Philippe Rushton asserts that there are three main races—Mongoloid, Negroid, and Caucasoid—and he ranks them according to intelligence and procreative ability. Here, sure enough, the old racial stereotypes leak out: the two traits allegedly appear in inverse proportion. You can have either a large brain or a large... (insert sexual organ of choice). Rushton's Mongoloids rank as the most intelligent; Negroids allegedly have the strongest sexual drive; Caucasoids fit into the comfortable middle.

11   At the other end of the spectrum are two groups who agree that races are a myth, but draw radically different conclusions from that premise. The politically conservative group, known for proclaiming a "color-free society," argues that if races do not exist, sociopolitical policies such as affirmative action ought not to be based on race. Social constructionists, on the other hand, realize that race-as-bad-biology has nothing to do with race-as-lived-experience. Social policy does not need a biological basis, especially when a dark-skinned American is still roughly twice as likely to be denied a mortgage as is a light-skinned person with an equivalent income. True races may not exist, but racism does.

12   A fourth group, the confused, occupies the middle ground. Some do not understand why race biology is such bad science, yet they avoid any appeal to race because they do not want to be politically incorrect. Others apply race as a quasi-biological, quasi-genetic category and cannot figure out what is wrong with it. Still others think the stance against racial biology is political rather than scientific.

13   That middle category of the confused is huge. It includes nearly all public health and medical professionals, as well as most physical anthropologists. Moreover, the continued "soft" use of race by that well-meaning group acts to legitimize the "hard" use by true believers and scientific racists.

14   And if most professionals are confused about race, most of the public is both dazed and confused. There is no single, stable, or monolithic public perception about race, but races are generally thought to be about genes (or blood) and (only slightly less permanent) cultural ties. Regardless, race is considered to be deep, primordial, and constant: in short, indistinguishable from its nineteenth-century definition.

15   In 1992 the forensic anthropologist Norman J. Sauer of Michigan State University in East Lansing published an article in the journal *Social Science and Medicine* provocatively titled, "Forensic Anthropology and the Concept of Race: If Races Don't Exist, Why Are Forensic Anthropologists So Good at Identifying Them?" Race may be unscientific, Sauer argued, but people of one socially constructed racial category still tend to look alike—and different from the people of another "race." The biological anthropologist C. Loring Brace of the University of Michigan in Ann Arbor explains Sauer's paradox in a slightly different way. Forensic scientists are good at estimating race, Brace says, because so-called racial variations are statistically confounded with real regional differences. People do vary in a systematic way depending on their environment.

16   Both arguments make sense, and forensic anthropologists do important work. But how good are they, really, at identifying race? Like Snow, the authors of forensic texts and review articles typically maintain that the race of a skull can be correctly identified between 85 and 90 percent of the time. The scientific reference for those estimates—if cited as anything other than common knowledge—is a single, groundbreaking study by the physical anthropologists Eugene Giles, at the University of Illinois in Urbana-Champaign, and Orville S. Elliot, at the University of Victoria in British Columbia. In the early 1960s Giles and Elliot measured the skulls of modern, adult blacks and whites who had died in Missouri and Ohio, many of them at the turn of [last] century, as well as Native American skulls from a prehistoric site in Indian Knoll, Kentucky. Using a statistical equation known as a discriminant function, they then identified a combination of eight measurements that could determine a skull's "race" once its sex was known.

17   When Giles and Elliot applied the formula to additional skulls from the same collections, it agreed with the race assigned to the deceased at death between 80 and 90 percent of the time. To be useful, however, the formula has to work in places other than Missouri, Ohio, and prehistoric Kentucky. I have found four retests of the Giles and Elliot method, and their results do not inspire confidence. Two of the retests restricted themselves to Native American skulls: in one of them almost two-thirds of the skulls were correctly classified as Native Americans; in the second, only 31 percent were correctly classified. For the two other studies, in which the skulls were of mixed race, skulls were correctly identified as Native American just 18.2 percent and 14.3 percent of the time. Thus in three of the four tests, the formula proved less accurate than a random assignment of races to skulls—not even good enough for government work.

18   Contemporary Native American skulls may be particularly hard to classify because the formula is based on a very old sample. But the four retests were carried out on complete crania that had already been sexed, a necessary prerequisite to determining race. Forensic anthropologists often have much less to go on. Moreover, Native Americans are easier to classify than Hispanics or Southeast Asians, not to mention infants, children, or adolescents of any race. At best, in other words, racial identifications are depressingly inaccurate. At worst, they are completely haphazard. How many bodies and body parts, like Lakesha Levy's leg, are sending investigators down wrong paths because the wrong box was checked off?

19   Forensic anthropologists usually blame such mistakes on the melting pot. Yet distinct racial types have never existed. What changes are social definitions of race—the color line—and human biology. Whites in Cleveland in 1897 were different from whites in Amarillo, Texas, in 1997. Science 101: generalizations ought not to be based on an ill-defined, constantly changing, and contextually loaded variable.

20   Skulls and corpses, one could argue, have ceased to care to which race they belong—though their families and friends might disagree. But when physicians base their actions on perceived racial categories, their patients ought to care a great deal. Does race, however imperfect a category, help physicians diagnose, treat, prevent, or understand the etiology of a disease?

21   Before the Second World War, physicians were often blinded by the conviction that certain races suffered from certain diseases. People who had sickle-cell anemia, for instance, were assumed to have "African blood." In 1927 the American physician J. S. Lawrence discovered a case of the disease in a "white" person. "Special attention was paid to the question of racial admixture of negro blood in the family but no evidence could be obtained," Lawrence wrote in the *Journal of Clinical Investigation*. "There must be some

caution in calling this sickle-cell anemia because no evidence of negro blood could be found."

22   Evelynn M. Hammonds, a historian of science at the Massachusetts Institute of Technology, has brought to my attention some early diagnoses of ovarian cysts that express the same logic. In 1899 the American physician Thomas R. Brown reported that he often heard surgeons say that tumors found in black women had all the features of ovarian cysts, "but inasmuch as the patient is a negress it is certainly not so, as multilocular cysts are unknown in the negress." The following year Daniel H. Williams, the eminent African-American physician and the first American to perform successful heart surgery, quoted a physician from Alabama speculating that: "Possibly the Alabama negro has not evoluted to the cyst-bearing age." Williams went on to show unambiguously, in a study, that ovarian cysts are common in black women including women from Alabama. He noted that white physicians have a history of ignoring black women, then offered examples of black women whose cysts swelled to 100 pounds or more before they were diagnosed.

23   Today the paradigm of racially distinct diseases has been replaced by the more flexible idea of a race as disease risk factor. Yet the medical effects are the same. Some 25 million Americans are said to suffer from osteoporosis, a progressive loss of bone mass that leads to 1.5 million fractures a year. Since the nineteenth century, blacks have been thought to have thicker bones than whites have and to lose bone mass more slowly with age. (A few years ago, when a dentist visited my laboratory, he was shocked to find that neither one of us could tell a black jaw from a white one.) In the journal *Seminars in Nuclear Medicine*, a review titled "Osteoporosis: The State of the Art in 1987" listed race as a major risk factor. The section on race begins: "It is a well-known fact that blacks do not suffer from osteoporosis."

24   That "fact" is backed by a single reference, a seminal paper by the American physical anthropologist Mildred Trotter and her colleagues titled "Densities of Bones of White and Negro Skeletons." Trotter and her colleagues evaluated the bone densities of skeletons from forty adult blacks and forty adult whites. They excluded skeletons with obvious bone diseases, but they did not describe how they chose the cadavers or whether the samples were matched for causes of death, diet, or other known risk factors for osteoporosis. Of the ten bones they studied in each skeleton, Trotter and her colleagues found that six tended to be denser in blacks than in whites; the other four showed no differences by race. Furthermore, the authors wrote, the decline in density took place at "approximately the same rate" for each sex-race group.

25   Trotter and her colleagues may have realized that their data could be overinterpreted. In later publications they present scatterplots with age on one axis and bone density on the other. The scatterplots confirm that bone densities tend to decline with age: the clusters of data points slope downward. It is a challenge, however, to discern any difference between the densities of bones from blacks and those from whites. The six lowest radius densities, for example, were found in bones of blacks.

26   Let me be clear: I am only following citations to see if the data say what the references say they say. But my conclusion is dismaying. If the "well-known fact that blacks do not suffer from osteoporosis" is based on poorly interpreted data, then black women may not be getting enough preventive care, are not targeted in the media, and are underdiagnosed as osteoporotic.

27   In every instance I have cited, a double leap of scientific faith seems to have taken place. First, a serious medical condition (sickle-cell anemia, ovarian cysts, osteoporosis) is regarded as genetic, even though environmental factors have not been adequately exam-

ined. Second, anything genetic is assumed to imply a panracial phenomenon. Thus, what might be true in a statistical sense is assumed true for all members of a so-called race. All blacks are protected from osteoporosis. All blacks are less prone to heart disease. By the same logic, Native Americans have some special predisposition to obesity and diabetes, though, in truth, rates vary wildly among groups and regions.

28   Why are my findings more than idiosyncratic examples? Why does race not work as a shorthand for biological variation? The answer lies in the structure of human variation and in the chameleon-like concept of race.

29 •   Most traits vary in small increments, or clines, across geographic areas. Imagine a merchant walking from Stockholm, Sweden, to Cape Town, South Africa, in the year 1400. He would notice that the skin colors of local people darkened until he reached the equator, then slowly turned lighter again. If he took a different route, perhaps starting in Siberia and wandering all the way to Singapore, he would observe the same phenomenon, though none of the people he passed on this second route would be classified as white or black today: all of them would be "Asian." Race, in other words, does not determine skin color, nor does skin color determine race. As Frank B. Livingstone, an anthropological geneticist at the University of Michigan in Ann Arbor, put it more than thirty years ago: "There are no races, there are only clines."

30 •   Most traits are nonconcordant. That is, traits tend to vary in different and entirely independent ways. If you know a person's height, you can guess weight and shoe size because tall people tend to be heavier and have bigger feet than short people. Those traits are concordant. By the same token, however, you could guess nothing about the person's skin color, facial features, or most genes. Height is nonconcordant with nearly every other trait. If you know skin color, you might be able to guess eye color and perhaps (but surprisingly inaccurately) hair color and form. But that is all. Race, for that reason, is only skin deep.

31 •   As I mentioned earlier, nearly all variations in genetic traits occur within so-called races rather than among them. Some thirty years ago the population geneticist Richard C. Lewontin of Harvard University conducted a statistical study of blood groups with two of the more common forms. On average, he found about 94 percent of the variation in blood forms occurred within perceived races; fewer than 6 percent could be explained by variations among races. Extrapolating from race to individuals is hardly more accurate than extrapolating from the human species to an individual.

32   One could argue that such classifications, however crude, are still useful as first approximations. Here is where one needs to see race as something more that the equivalent of shoe size.

33 •   Racial differences are interpreted differently. Sometimes people consider them genetic, sometimes ethnic or cultural, and sometimes they use the term "race" to mean differences in lived experience. When race is assigned as a risk factor, the meaning is often unclear, and that ambiguity dramatically affects medical treatment. Sometimes race is a proxy for socioeconomic status or even for the effects of racism. If so, a particular racial classification suggests a possible set of actions. But if a racial classification is intended to signal a panracial genetic difference, as in osteoporosis, an entirely different set of actions should be undertaken. The conflation of genetics with culture, class, and lived experience may be the most serious flaw in racial analysis.

34 •   Race is impossible to define in a stable, repeatable way because, to repeat, race as biology varies with time and place, as do social classifications. Color lines change. When the skeletons studied by Giles and Elliot began to be collected in Cleveland at the turn of

the [last] century, the United States Census Bureau classified people not only as white or black, but as mulatto, quadroon, or octoroon. Europe at the time was thought to be home to a dozen or so distinct races. One cannot do predictive science based on a changing and undefinable cause.

35   In studies such as those on osteoporosis—or any other disease—race is either undefined or assigned on the basis of the patient's own self-identification. "Since self-assignments to racial categories are commonly used," the authors of a review of race and nutritional status wrote in 1976, "the problem of racial identification is minimal." Compare that statement with the finding of a recent infant-mortality study by Robert A. Hahn, a medical anthropologist at the Center for Disease Control and Prevention in Atlanta, Georgia. Thirty-seven percent of the babies described as Native American on their birth certificates, Hahn discovered, were described as some other race on their death certificates.

36   When I started out in anthropology in the 1970s, I thought anthropologists would stop using race by the 1990s. Why does it persist? At the very least, on a scientific level, it violates the first law of medicine: Do no harm. For every instance in which knowing race helps an investigator, there is probably another instance in which it leads to a missed diagnosis or the premature closing of a police file. At best, it is a proxy for something else. Why not study that something else?

37   There are good, simple alternatives to classifying by race. In biological studies, from forensics to epidemiology, investigators could focus on traits specific to the problem at hand. If the problem is describing human remains, simply describe those remains as well as possible. In Oklahoma City, for example, the police would have been better off looking for anyone with a dark complexion rather than searching for a "darkly complected Caucasoid." Police officers are used to searching for people with specific traits ("suspect has a smiley-face tattoo on his left bicep"). Why not be equally specific about skin color and other "racial" traits? Epidemiologists, for their part, could focus on likely causal traits. If skin color is a risk factor, classify people by skin color alone. If the risk factor is a genetic trait, such as type A blood, compare individuals with and without type A blood.

38   I do not for a moment think that knowing race is a myth eliminates racism. But as long as well-meaning investigators continue to use the concept of race without clearly defining it, they reify race as biology. In so doing, they mislead the public and encourage racist notions. According to the American sociologist Donal E. Muir, those who continue to see race in biology but mean no harm by it are nothing more than "kind racists." By continuing to legitimize race, they inadvertently aid the "mean racists" who wish to do harm. Far too many scientists, unfortunately, still belong to both categories.

NOTES AND DISCUSSION

In "Bred in the Bone?" Alan Goodman argues that "true races may not exist, but racism does." This essay is an argument against institutional racism, and a hope that, if science moves beyond racism, the rest of society can also get over something that is only a culturally constructed category.

Goodman begins his paper with a striking example of a forensic misdiagnosis, and then continues to build his essay around examples and assumptions concerning race. He shows that, biologically, race is skin deep: it is a cultural myth and has no hard scientific basis or usefulness. It therefore needs finally to be expunged from scientific investigation: "As long as race is used as a shorthand to describe human biological variations—variations that blur from one race into the next, and are greatest *within* so-called races rather than among them — misidentifications are inevitable." Notice the way Goodman acknowledges, only to dismiss, scientists who support "race" as a useful or productive scientific category. If scientists continue to pretend that "race" is a useful category, though all the evidence indicates that it is nothing more than a myth, then they are in fact supporting institutionalized racism. And if scientists continue to be racist, one cannot expect society at large to get over racism.

Goodman's strategy is sound throughout, but the essay is especially striking in its treatment of the opening materials. It begins with a vivid anecdote that most of Goodman's audience will have some familiarity with. The Oklahoma City bombing is also likely to have some significant emotional and intellectual impact. It certainly has metaphoric and symbolic resonance.

STUDY QUESTIONS

For Discussion

1. Discuss Goodman's argument that science and scientists have an important social and cultural responsibility to lead the rest of society in battling racism. Do you agree with Goodman? Why, or why not?

2. Goodman claims that race is culturally constructed, not biologically based — it is founded, in fact, on bias — and that colour is only skin deep: "Distinct racial types have never existed. What changes are social definitions of race — the color line — and human biology." Discuss this claim, and Goodman's support of it.

For Writing

1. Compare the fundamental assumptions and strategies of Goodman's essay, which argues against racism in science, to Furlong's "Straight Talk at the Parakeet Café," which argues against sexism in language. As part of your paper, compile a list of racist tendencies that you detect in language.

2. Write a persuasive paper in which you argue for or against this proposition: since science and reason did not invent racism, though they implicitly supported it for years, science and reason cannot rid society of racism merely by proving that race is a myth.

THE MONSTER'S HUMAN NATURE

Stephen Jay Gould

BIOGRAPHICAL NOTE

Stephen Jay Gould (1941–2002) was a paleontologist and educator at Harvard University. He is known for writing that makes science and scientific concepts entertaining and approachable to a non-specialized public. His essays are collected in several volumes, including *The Flamingo's Smile* (1985), *Bully for Brontosaurus* (1991), and *Eight Little Piggies* (1993). This essay is from his collection *Dinosaur in a Haystack: Reflections in Natural History* (1995).

---

1   An old Latin proverb tells us to "beware the man of one book"—*cave ab homine unius libri*. Yet Hollywood knows only one theme in making monster movies, from the archetypal *Frankenstein* of 1931 to the recent mega-hit *Jurassic Park*. Human technology must not go beyond an intended order decreed by God or set by nature's laws. No matter how benevolent the purposes of the transgressor, such cosmic arrogance can only lead to killer tomatoes, very large rabbits with sharp teeth, giant ants in the Los Angeles sewers, or even larger blobs that swallow entire cities as they grow. Yet these films often use far more subtle books as their sources and, in so doing, distort the originals beyond all thematic recognition.

2   The trend began in 1931 with *Frankenstein*, Hollywood's first great monster "talkie" (though Mr. Karloff only grunted, while Colin Clive, as Henry Frankenstein, emoted). Hollywood decreed its chosen theme by the most "up front" of all conceivable strategies. The film begins with a prologue (even before the titles roll) featuring a well-dressed man standing on stage before a curtain, both to issue a warning about potential fright, and to

announce the film's deeper theme as the story of "a man of science who sought to create a man after his own image without reckoning upon God."

3   In the movie, Dr. Waldman, Henry's old medical school professor, speaks of his pupil's "insane ambition to create life," a diagnosis supported by Frankenstein's own feverish words of enthusiasm: "I created it. I made it with my own hands from the bodies I took from graves, from the gallows, from anywhere."

4   The best of a cartload of sequels, *The Bride of Frankenstein* (1935), makes the favored theme even more explicit in a prologue featuring Mary Wollstonecraft Shelley, who published *Frankenstein* in 1818 when she was only nineteen years old, in conversation with her husband Percy and their buddy Lord Byron. She states: "My purpose was to write a moral lesson of the punishment that befell a mortal man who dared to emulate God."

5   Shelley's original *Frankenstein* is a rich book of many themes, but I can find little therein to support the Hollywood reading. The text is neither a diatribe on the dangers of technology nor a warning about overextended ambition against a natural order. We find no passages about disobeying God—an unlikely subject for Mary Shelley and her free-thinking friends (Percy had been expelled from Oxford in 1811 for publishing a defense of atheism). Victor Frankenstein (I do not know why Hollywood changed him to Henry) is guilty of a great moral failing, as we shall see later, but his crime is not technological transgression against a natural or divine order.

6   We can find a few passages about the awesome power of science, but these words are not negative. Professor Waldman, a sympathetic character in the book, states, for example, "They [scientists] penetrate into the recesses of nature, and show how she works in her hiding places. They ascend into the heavens; they have discovered how the blood circulates, and the nature of the air we breathe. They have acquired new and almost unlimited powers." We do learn that ardor without compassion or moral consideration can lead to trouble, but Shelley applies this argument to any endeavor, not especially to scientific discovery (her examples are, in fact, all political). Victor Frankenstein says:

> A human being in perfection ought always to preserve a calm and peaceful mind, and never to allow passion or a transitory desire to disturb his tranquility. I do not think that the pursuit of knowledge is an exception to this rule. If the study to which you apply yourself has a tendency to weaken your affections... then that study is certainly unlawful, that is to say, not befitting the human mind. If this rule were always observed... Greece had not been enslaved; Caesar would have spared his country; America would have been discovered more gradually, and the empires of Mexico and Peru had not been destroyed.

7   Victor's own motivations are entirely idealistic: "I thought, that if I could bestow animation upon lifeless matter, I might in process of time (although I now found it impossible) renew life where death had apparently devoted the body to corruption." Finally, as Victor lies dying in the Arctic, he makes his most forceful statement on the dangers of scientific ambition, but he only berates himself and his own failures, while stating that others might well succeed. Victor says his dying words to the ship's captain who found him on the polar ice: "Farewell, Walton! Seek happiness in tranquility, and avoid ambition, even if it be only the apparently innocent one of distinguishing yourself in science and discoveries. Yet why do I say this? I have myself been blasted in these hopes, yet another may succeed."

8   But Hollywood dumbed these subtleties down to the easy formula—"man must not go beyond what God and nature intended" (you almost have to use the old gender-biased language for such a simplistic archaism [*sic*])—and has been treading in its own foot-

steps ever since. The latest incarnation, *Jurassic Park*, substitutes a *Velociraptor* re-created from old DNA for Karloff cobbled together from bits and pieces of corpses, but hardly alters the argument an iota.

9   Karloff's *Frankenstein* contains an even more serious and equally prominent distortion of a theme that I regard as the primary lesson of Mary Shelley's book—another lamentable example of Hollywood's sense that the American public cannot tolerate even the slightest exercise in intellectual complexity. Why is the monster evil? Shelley provides a nuanced and subtle answer that, to me, sets the central theme of her book. But Hollywood opted for a simplistic solution, so precisely opposite to Shelley's intent that the movie can no longer claim to be telling a moral fable (despite protestations of the man in front of the curtain, or Mary Shelley herself in the sequel), and becomes instead, as I suppose the makers intended all along, a pure horror film.

10   James Whale, director of the 1931 *Frankenstein*, devoted the movie's long and striking opening scenes to this inversion of Shelley's intent—so the filmmakers obviously viewed this alteration as crucial. The movie opens with a burial at a graveyard. The mourners depart, and Henry with his obedient servant, the evil hunchbacked Fritz, digs up the body and carts it away. They then cut down another dead man from the gallows, but Henry exclaims, "The neck's broken. The brain is useless; we must find another brain."

11   The scene now switches to Goldstadt Medical College, where Professor Waldman is lecturing on cranial anatomy and comparing "one of the most perfect specimens of the normal brain" with "the abnormal brain of a typical criminal." Waldman firmly locates the criminal's depravity in the inherited malformations of his brain; anatomy is destiny. Note, Waldman says, "the scarcity of convolutions on the frontal lobes and the distinct degeneration of the middle frontal lobes. All of these degenerate characteristics check amazingly with the case history of the dead man before us, whose life was one of brutality, of violence, and of murder."

12   Fritz breaks in after the students leave and steals the normal brain, but the sound of a gong startles him and he drops the precious object, shattering its container. Fritz then has to take the criminal brain instead, but he never tells Henry. The monster is evil because Henry unwittingly makes him of evil stuff. Later in the film, Henry expresses his puzzlement at the monster's nasty temperament, for he made his creature of the best materials. But Waldman, finally realizing the source of the monster's behavior, tells Henry, "The brain that was stolen from my laboratory was a criminal brain." Henry then counters with one of cinema's greatest double takes, and finally manages a feeble retort: "Oh, well, after all, it's only a piece of dead tissue." "Only evil will come from it," Waldman replies. "You have created a monster and it will destroy you." True enough, at least until the sequel.

13   Karloff's intrinsically evil monster stands condemned by the same biological determinism that has so tragically, and falsely, restricted the lives of millions who committed no transgression besides membership in a despised race, sex, or social class. Karloff's actions record his internal state. He manages a few grunts and, in *The Bride of Frankenstein*, even learns some words from a blind man who cannot perceive his ugliness, though the monster never gets much beyond "eat," "smoke," "friend," and "good." Shelley's monster, by contrast, is a most remarkably literate fellow. He learns French by assimilation after hiding, for several months, in the hovel of a noble family temporarily in straitened circumstances. His three favorite books would bring joy to the heart of any college English professor who could persuade students to read and enjoy even one: Plutarch's *Lives*, Goethe's *Sorrows of Young Werther*, and Milton's *Paradise Lost* (of which Shelley's novel is an evident parody). The original monster's thundering threat certainly packs more oomph than Karloff's

pitiable grunts: "I will glut the maw of death, until it be satiated with the blood of your remaining friends."

14   Shelley's monster is not evil by inherent constitution. He is born unformed—carrying the predispositions of human nature, but without the specific behaviors that can only be set by upbringing and education. He is the Enlightenment's man of hope, whom learning and compassion might model to goodness and wisdom. But he is also a victim of post-Enlightenment pessimism as the cruel rejection of his natural fellows drives him to fury and revenge. (Even as a murderer, the monster remains fastidious and purposive. Victor Frankenstein is the source of his anger, and he kills only the friends and lovers whose deaths will bring Victor most grief; he does not, like Godzilla or the Blob, rampage through cities.)

15   Mary Shelley chose her words carefully to take a properly nuanced position at a fruitfully intermediate point between nature and nurture—whereas Hollywood opted for nature alone to explain the monster's evil deeds. Frankenstein's creature is not inherently good by internal construction—a benevolent theory of "nature alone," but no different in mode of explanation from Hollywood's opposite version. He is, rather, born *capable* of goodness, even with an *inclination* toward kindness, should circumstances of his upbringing call forth this favored response. In his final confession to Captain Walton, before heading north to immolate himself at the Pole, the monster says:

> My heart was fashioned to be *susceptible of love and sympathy*; and, when wrenched by misery to vice and hatred, it did not endure the violence of the change without torture, such as you cannot even imagine. [My italics to note Shelley's careful phrasing in terms of potentiality or inclination, rather than determinism.]

16   He then adds:

> Once my fancy was soothed with dreams of virtue, of fame, and of enjoyment. Once I falsely hoped to meet with beings who, pardoning my outward form, would love me for the excellent qualities which I was *capable of bringing forth*. I was nourished with high thoughts of honor and devotion. But now vice has degraded me beneath the meanest animal... When I call over the frightful catalogue of my deeds, I cannot believe that I am he whose thoughts were once filled with sublime and transcendent visions of the beauty and the majesty of goodness. But it is even so; the fallen angel becomes a malignant devil.

17   Why, then, does the monster turn to evil against an inherent inclination to goodness? Shelley gives us an interesting answer that seems almost trivial in invoking such a superficial reason, but that emerges as profound when we grasp her general theory of human nature. He becomes evil, of course, because humans reject him so violently and so unjustly. His resulting loneliness becomes unbearable. He states:

> And what was I? Of my creation and creator I was absolutely ignorant; but I knew that I possessed no money, no friends, no kind of property. I was, besides, endowed with a figure hideously deformed and loathsome... When I looked around, I saw and heard none like me. Was I then a monster, a blot upon the earth, from which all men fled, and whom all men disowned?

18   But why is the monster so rejected, if his feelings incline toward benevolence, and his acts to evident goodness? He certainly tries to act kindly, in helping (albeit secretly) the family in the hovel that serves as his hiding place:

I had been accustomed during the night, to steal a part of their store for my own consumption; but when I found that in doing this I inflicted pain on the cottagers, I abstained, and satisfied myself with berries, nuts, and roots, which I gathered from a neighboring wood. I discovered also another means through which I was enabled to assist their labors. I found that the youth spent a great part of each day in collecting wood for the family fire; and, during the night, I often took his tools, the use of which I quickly discovered, and brought home firing sufficient for the consumption of several days.

19   Shelley tells us that all humans reject and even loathe the monster for a visceral reason of literal superficiality: his truly terrifying ugliness—a reason both heartrending in its deep injustice, and profound in its biological accuracy and philosophical insight about the meaning of human nature.

20   The monster, by Shelley's description, could scarcely have been less attractive in appearance. Victor Frankenstein describes the first sight of his creature alive:

How can I describe my emotions at this catastrophe, or how delineate the wretch whom with such infinite pains and care I had endeavored to form? His limbs were in proportion, and I had selected his features as beautiful. Beautiful!—Great God! His yellow skin scarcely covered the work of muscles and arteries beneath; his hair was lustrous black, and flowing; his teeth of a pearly whiteness; but these luxuriances only formed a more horrid contrast with his watery eyes, that seemed almost of the same color as the dun white sockets in which they were set, his shriveled complexion, and straight black lips.

21   Moreover, at his hyper-NBA height of eight feet, the monster scares the bejeezus out of all who cast eyes upon him.

22   The monster quickly grasps this unfair source of human fear and plans a strategy to overcome initial reactions, and to prevail by goodness of soul. He presents himself first to the blind old father in the hovel above his hiding place and makes a good impression. He hopes to win the man's confidence, and thus gain a favorable introduction to the world of sighted people. But, in his joy at acceptance, he stays too long. The man's son returns and drives the monster away—as fear and loathing overwhelm any inclination to hear about inner decency.

23   The monster finally acknowledges his inability to overcome visceral fear at his ugliness; his resulting despair and loneliness drive him to evil deeds:

I am malicious because I am miserable; am I not shunned and hated by all mankind?... Shall I respect man when he condemns me? Let him live with me in the interchange of kindness, and, instead of injury, I would bestow every benefit upon him with tears of gratitude at his acceptance. But that cannot be; the human senses are insurmountable barriers to our union.

24   Our struggle to formulate a humane and accurate idea of human nature focuses on proper positions between the false and sterile poles of nature and nurture. Pure nativism—as in the Hollywood version of the monster's depravity—leads to a cruel and inaccurate theory of biological determinism, the source of so much misery and such pervasive suppression of hope in millions belonging to unfavored races, sexes, or social classes. But pure "nurturism" can be just as cruel, and just as wrong—as in the blame, once heaped upon loving parents in bygone days of rampant Freudianism, for failures in rearing as putative sources of mental illness or retardation that we can now identify as genetically based—for all organs, including brains, are subject to inborn illness.

25   The solution, as all thoughtful people recognize, must lie in properly melding the themes of inborn predisposition and shaping through life's experiences. This fruitful joining cannot

take the false form of percentages adding to 100—as in "intelligence is 80 percent nature and 20 percent nurture," or "homosexuality is 50 percent inborn and 50 percent learned," and a hundred other harmful statements in this foolish format. When two ends of such a spectrum are commingled, the result is not a separable amalgam (like shuffling two decks of cards with different backs), but an entirely new and higher entity that cannot be decomposed (just as adults cannot be separated into maternal and paternal contributions to their totality).

26   The best guide to a proper integration lies in recognizing that nature supplies general ordering rules and predispositions—often strong, to be sure—while nurture shapes specific manifestations over a wide range of potential outcomes. We make classical "category mistakes" when we attribute too much specificity to nature—as in the pop sociobiology of supposed genes for complexly social phenomena like rape and racism; or when we view deep structures as purely social constructs—as in earlier claims that even the most general rules of grammar must be learned contingencies without any universality across cultures. Noam Chomsky's linguistic theories represent the paradigm for modern concepts of proper integration between nature and nurture—principles of universal grammar as inborn learning rules, with peculiarities of any particular language as a product of cultural circumstances and place of upbringing.

27   Frankenstein's creature becomes a monster because he is cruelly ensnared by one of the deepest predispositions of our biological inheritance—our instinctive aversion toward seriously malformed individuals. (Konrad Lorenz, the most famous ethologist of the last generation, based much of his theory on the primacy of this inborn rule.) We are now appalled by the injustice of such a predisposition, but this proper moral feeling is an evolutionary latecomer, imposed by human consciousness upon a much older mammalian pattern.

28   We almost surely inherit such an instinctive aversion to serious malformation, but remember that nature can only supply a predisposition, while culture shapes specific results. And now we can grasp—for Mary Shelley presented the issue to us so wisely—the true tragedy of Frankenstein's monster, and the moral dereliction of Victor himself. The predisposition for aversion toward ugliness can be overcome by learning and understanding. I trust that we have all trained ourselves in this essential form of compassion, and that we all work hard to suppress that frisson of rejection (which in honest moments we all admit we feel), and to judge people by their qualities of soul, not by their external appearances.

29   Frankenstein's monster was a good man in an appallingly ugly body. His countrymen could have been educated to accept him, but the person responsible for that instruction—his creator, Victor Frankenstein—ran away from his foremost duty, and abandoned his creation at first sight. Victor's sin does not lie in misuse of technology, or hubris in emulating God; we cannot find these themes in Mary Shelley's account. Victor failed because he followed a predisposition of human nature—visceral disgust at the monster's appearance—and did not undertake the duty of any creator or parent: to teach his own charge and to educate others in acceptability.

30   He could have schooled his creature (and not left the monster to learn language by eavesdropping and by scrounging for books in a hiding place under a hovel). He could have told the world what he had done. He could have introduced his benevolent and educated monster to people prepared to judge him on merit. But he took one look at his handiwork, and ran away forever. In other words, he bowed to a base aspect of our common nature, and did not accept the particular moral duty of our potential nurture:

> I had worked hard for nearly two years, for the sole purpose of infusing life into an inanimate body. For this I had deprived myself of rest and health. I had desired it with an ardor that far exceeded moderation; but now that I had finished, the beauty of the dream vanished, and breathless horror and disgust filled my heart. Unable to endure the aspect of the being I had created, I rushed out of the room... A mummy again endued with animation could not be so hideous as that wretch. I had gazed on him while unfinished; he was ugly then; but when those muscles and joints were rendered capable of motion, it became a thing such as even Dante could not have conceived.

31   The very first line of the preface of *Frankenstein* has often been misinterpreted: "The event on which this fiction is founded has been supposed, by Dr. Darwin, and some of the physiological writers of Germany, as not of impossible occurrence." People suppose that "Dr. Darwin" must be Charles of evolutionary fame. But Charles Darwin was born on Lincoln's birthday in 1809, and wasn't even ten years old when Mary Shelley wrote her novel. "Dr. Darwin" is Charles's grandfather Erasmus, one of England's most famous physicians, and an atheist who believed in the material basis of life. (Shelley is referring to his idea that such physical forces as electricity might be harnessed to quicken inanimate matter—for life has no inherently spiritual component, and might therefore emerge from nonliving substances infused with enough energy.)

32   I will, however, close with my favorite moral statement from Charles Darwin, who, like Mary Shelley, also emphasized our duty to foster the favorable specificities that nurture and education can control. Mary Shelley wrote a moral tale, not about hubris or technology, but about responsibility to all creatures of feeling and to the products of one's own hand. The monster's misery arose from the moral failure of other humans, not from his own inherent and unchangeable constitution. Charles Darwin later invoked the same theory of human nature to remind us of duties to all people in universal bonds of brotherhood: "If the misery of our poor be caused not by the laws of nature, but by our institutions, great is our sin."

NOTES AND DISCUSSION

Gould's dual thesis is clearly stated in the opening paragraph: Hollywood films distort the thematic subtlety of their sources beyond all recognition, and Hollywood constantly reiterates the theme that disaster can only result from technology exceeding or subverting the laws of God and nature. Gould then narrows his argument and makes the 1931 screen adaptation of Mary Shelley's *Frankenstein* his primary focus; however, he also confronts the old debate over whether nature or nurture is the more influential determinant operating upon humanity.

For the bulk of the essay, Gould supports his argument by comparing and contrasting selected passages from the 1818 edition of Shelley's novel with corresponding scenes from the Hollywood versions. Notice how he creates an informal tone that invites the reader to join him in laughing at the foibles of Hollywood. It is important to note that if you have not read Shelley's novel or seen the film versions, you must depend entirely upon Gould's selection of passages and description of scenes in attempting to weigh and consider his argument. If you have read the novel or seen either or both Frankenstein films discussed, you then have your own readings and recollections to rely upon as well. Part of Gould's purpose may, in fact, be to interest readers in exploring the different tellings of the Frankenstein story and to consider more deeply the relationship between text and film. If you have read the novel, you will no doubt notice that Gould makes no reference to the subtitle of Shelley's novel, "The Modern Prometheus," or to the religious and mythic themes of the original *Frankenstein*.

STUDY QUESTIONS

For Discussion

1. Gould's characterization of Hollywood's portrayal of the scientist as evil echoes an image from popular culture. List some other Hollywood portrayals of scientists. Do your findings match Gould's claims?

2. Why, in Gould's opinion, does Hollywood keep telling the same stories? Gould labels Hollywood stories "simplifications." What simplifications take place in Gould's own essay?

For Writing

1. If you have read Mary Shelley's *Frankenstein*, do you still agree with Gould's central thesis? Alternatively, read a novel that is the basis for a Hollywood film with which you are already familiar. Do you see any of the patterns that Gould identifies emerging?

2. Compare and contrast Heather Pringle's exploration of the "nature vs. nurture" question in "The Way We Woo" with Gould's treatment of the issue. Which essay makes a more convincing argument?

CHARLES DARWIN'S TREE OF LIFE

O. B. Hardison, Jr.

BIOGRAPHICAL NOTE

During a distinguished career, O. B. Hardison, Jr. (1928–90) was director of the Folger Shakespeare Library in Washington, DC, a visiting scholar at many universities, and Professor of English at Georgetown University. He was also a founder of the Quark Club, whose members are scientists and humanists interested in cultural change and exchange. Hardison published two collections of poetry and several books. His last book, *Disappearing Through the Skylight: Culture and Technology in the Twentieth Century* (1989), from which this essay is taken, won the *Los Angeles Times'* Book Prize for 1990.

1   The culmination and—for many Victorians—the vindication of the Baconian tradition in science was Charles Darwin's *The Origin of Species* (1859). Darwin acknowledges his debt to Bacon in his *Autobiography* (1876): "I worked on the true Baconian principles, and without any theory collected facts on a wholesale scale."

2   Wholesale is right. The book brings together twenty years of painstaking, minutely detailed observation ranging over the whole spectrum of organic life. Like Bacon, Darwin made little use of mathematics, although he had attempted (unsuccessfully) to deepen his mathematical knowledge while at Cambridge. Nor was Darwin the sort of scientist whose observations depend on instruments. His four-volume study of barnacles—*Cirripedia* (1851–54)—uses microscopy frequently, but much of his best work could have been written entirely on the basis of direct observation.

3   As soon as it was published, *The Origin of Species* was recognized as one of those books that change history. Its reception was partly a tribute to the overwhelming wealth of detail it offers in support of the theory Darwin finally worked out to hold his enormous

bundle of facts together and partly a case of powder waiting for a spark. Darwin was initially criticized for giving insufficient credit to his predecessors, and the third edition of *The Origin of Species* includes a list of important moments in the earlier history of the theory of evolution. It begins with Jean-Baptiste Lamarck, who proposed a generally evolutionary theory of biology in the *Histoire naturelle des animaux* (1815). Charles Lyell's *Principles of Geology* (1832) is not included in the list because it is not specifically evolutionary, but its analysis of the evidence of geological change over time was indispensable to Darwin. Using Lyell, he could be certain that the variations he observed among animals of the same species in the Galápagos Islands had occurred within a relatively short span of geologic time.

4   Another source mentioned in the list and the immediate stimulus to the publication of *The Origin of Species* was an essay by Alfred Russell Wallace entitled "On the Tendency of Varieties to Depart Indefinitely from the Original Type." Wallace sent this essay to Darwin in 1858, and it convinced Darwin that if he did not publish his own work he risked being anticipated. He acknowledges Wallace's paper in his introduction and admits in the *Autobiography* that it "contained exactly the same theory as mine." Again according to the *Autobiography*, it was Darwin's reading of Malthus that suggested, around 1838, that all species are locked in a remorseless struggle for survival.

5   In spite of these and other anticipations, *The Origin of Species* was an immediate sensation. By ignoring religious dogma and wishful thinking, Darwin was able to buckle and bow his mind to the nature of things and to produce the sort of powerful, overarching concept that reveals coherence in a vast area of experience that had previously seemed chaotic.

6   A modern reader can see a kinship between Darwin's passionate interest in all things living, beginning with his undergraduate hobby of collecting beetles, and the outburst of nature poetry that occurred in the Romantic period.

7   Darwin was unaware of this kinship. In the *Autobiography* he says that "up to the age of thirty, or beyond it, poetry of many kinds, such as the works of Milton, Gray, Byron, Wordsworth, Coleridge, and Shelley... gave me the greatest pleasure.... But now for many years I cannot endure to read a line of poetry." His *Journal of the Voyage of the Beagle* is filled with appreciative comments about tropical landscape and its animals and plants, but he remarks that natural scenery "does not cause me the exquisite delight which it formerly did." He is probably contrasting his own methodical descriptions of landscape with the romanticized landscapes of writers like Byron and painters like Turner. He plays the role of Baconian ascetic collecting "without any theory... facts on a wholesale scale." His mind, he says (again in the *Autobiography*), has become "a kind of machine for grinding laws out of large collections of facts."

8   The idea that the mind is a machine that grinds laws out of facts echoes Bacon's injunction to use reason to "deliver and reduce" the imagination. The same asceticism is evident in Darwin's disparaging comments about his literary style. He believed he was writing dry scientific prose for other scientists, and John Ruskin, among others, agreed. Darwin was astounded, gratified, and a little frightened by his popular success.

9   No one can read Darwin today without recognizing that he was wrong about his style. As Stanley Edgar Hyman observes in *The Tangled Bank* (1962), both *The Voyage of the Beagle* and *The Origin of Species* are filled with passages that are beautiful and sensitive, whatever Darwin may have thought of them. The writing is effective precisely because it does not strain for the gingerbread opulence fashionable in mid-Victorian English prose.

It has a freedom from pretense, a quality of authority, as moving as the natural descriptions in Wordsworth's *Prelude*. It is effective precisely because it stems from direct observation of the things and relationships that nature comprises. In addition to revealing a mind "buckled and bowed" to nature, it reveals a mind that has surrendered to the kaleidoscope of life around it. Consider the following comment on the life-styles of woodpeckers:

> Can a more striking instance of adaptation be given than that of a woodpecker for climbing trees and seizing insects in chinks in the bark? Yet in North America there are woodpeckers which feed largely on fruit, and others with elongated wings which chase insects on the wing. On the plains of La Plata, where hardly a tree grows, there is a woodpecker... which has two toes before and two behind, a long pointed tongue, pointed tail-feathers, sufficiently stiff to support the bird on a post, but not so stiff as in the typical woodpeckers, and a straight strong beak.... Hence this [bird] in all essential parts of its structure is a woodpecker. Even in such trifling characters as the colouring, the harsh tone of the voice, and undulatory flight, its close blood-relationship to our common woodpecker is plainly declared; yet... in certain large districts it does not climb trees, and it makes its nest in holes in banks! In certain other districts, however... this same woodpecker... frequents trees, and bores holes in the trunk for its nest.

10   Darwin was familiar with Audubon's *Birds of America*, and remarks that Audubon "is the only observer to witness the frigate-bird, which has all its four toes webbed, alight on the surface of the ocean." In spite of a possible touch of irony in this remark, the affinity between the two naturalists is striking. Darwin fixes things in the middle distance by means of words. The central device in his description of the La Plata woodpecker is detail: elongated wings, insects caught on the wing, two toes before and two behind, stiff tail, elongated beak, harsh voice, a nest in a hole in a bank. The accumulating details express close observation which is also loving observation. They create a thingly poetry, a poetry of the actual.

11   In a similar way, Audubon fixes in images a nature that flaunts itself palpably and colorfully in the middle distance. In the process both Darwin and Audubon create an art of the actual.

12   A year before *The Origin of Species*, Oliver Wendell Holmes published "The Chambered Nautilus." It is a poem that attempts to fix a thing that is out there in the middle distance in verse:

> Year after year behold the silent toil
> That spread his lustrous coil;
> Still as the spiral grew,
> He left the past year's dwelling for the new,
> Stole with soft step its shining archway through, built up its idle door,
> Stretched in his last-found home, and knew the old no more.

13   Here, instead of the scientist becoming poet, the poet becomes a scientist. The problem is that the poem cannot forget it is art. It is more clumsy, finally, than Darwin's description of the La Plata woodpecker. Closer to Darwin are the photographs of Mathew Brady, the histories of Ranke and Burckhardt, and the novels of Balzac, George Eliot, and Turgenev.

14   Feeling is usually implicit in Darwin's prose but repressed. Facts are facts and poetry is poetry. Occasionally, however, Darwin allowed his feelings to bubble to the surface. The closing paragraph of *The Origin of Species* is a case in point. It describes a scene,

... clothed with many plants of many kinds, with birds singing on the bushes, with various insects flitting about, and with worms crawling through the damp earth, and... these elaborately constructed forms, so different from each other, and dependent upon each other in so complex a manner, have all been produced by laws acting around us.... Thus, from the war of nature, from famine and death, the most exalted object which we are capable of conceiving, namely, the production of the higher animals, directly follows.

15   No passage is more obviously dominated by aesthetic feeling than Darwin's description of the variety of species created by the struggle for existence. The idea of the struggle is central to *The Origin of Species*. It involves a paradox that fascinated Darwin. Out of a silent but deadly struggle comes the infinitely varied and exotically beautiful mosaic of life:

> How have all these exquisite adaptations of one part of the organization to another part, and to the conditions of life, and of one organic being to another being, been perfected? We see these beautiful co-adaptations most plainly in the woodpecker and the mistletoe; and only a little less plainly in the humblest parasite which clings to the hairs of a quadruped or feathers of a bird; in the structure of the beetle which dives through the water; in the plumed seed which is wafted by the gentlest breeze; in short, we see beautiful adaptations everywhere and in every part of the organic world.

16   *Exquisite, perfected, beautiful, humblest, plumed, gentlest.* The world described by these adjectives is not cold, alien, or indifferent. It is a work of art. Nor is Darwin's prose the dispassionate, dry prose of a treatise devoted only to facts. Because it is the work of a naturalist, it pays close attention to detail. The parts are there because they are there in nature in the middle distance: the woodpecker, the mistletoe, the parasite clinging to the quadruped, the feathers of the bird, the water beetle, the plumed seed. They illustrate the harmonious relations created by the struggle for survival—"co-adaptation" is Darwin's word. The prose enacts these harmonies through elegantly controlled rhythms.

17   Darwin's language invites the reader to share experience as well as to understand it. *Exquisite, beautiful,* and *gentle* orient him emotionally at the same time that his attention is focused on the objects that give rise to the emotion—mistletoe, parasite, water beetle, plumed seed.

18   The passage flatly contradicts Darwin's statement in the *Autobiography* that his artistic sensitivity had atrophied by the time he was thirty. That he thought it did shows only that he believed with his contemporaries that science is science and art is art. The problem was in his psyche, not his prose. The tradition that science should be dispassionate and practical, that it is a kind of servitude to nature that demands the banishment of the humanity of the observer, prevented him from understanding that he was, in fact, responding to nature aesthetically and communicating that response in remarkably poetic prose. There is no detectable difference in this passage between a hypothetical figure labeled "scientific observer" and another hypothetical figure named "literary artist."

19   The most striking example of Darwin's artistry occurs in the "summary" of Chapter 3. The passage deals explicitly with the tragic implications of natural selection. It is a sustained meditation on a single image. The image—the Tree of Life—is practical because the branching limbs are a vivid representation of the branching pattern of evolution. However, the image is also mythic, an archetype familiar from Genesis and also from Egyptian, Buddhist, Greek, and other sources. In mythology, the Tree of Life connects the underworld and the heavens. It is the axis on which the spheres turn and the path along which creatures from the invisible world visit and take leave of earth. It is an ever-green

symbol of fertility, bearing fruit in winter. It is the wood of the Cross on which God dies and the wood reborn that announces the return of life by sending out new branches in the spring. All of this symbolism is familiar from studies of archetypal and primitive imagery. Behind it is what Rudolf Otto calls, in *The Idea of the Holy*, the terrifying and fascinating mystery of things: *mysterium tremendum et fascinans*.

20   It is surprising to find a scientist, particularly a preeminent Victorian scientist and a self-avowed disciple of Bacon, using an archetypal image. Yet Darwin's elaboration is both sensitive and remarkably full. Central to it is the paradox of life in death, and throughout, one senses the hovering presence of the *mysterium tremendum et fascinans*:

> The affinities of all the beings of the same class have sometimes been represented by a great tree. I believe this simile largely speaks the truth. The green and budding twigs may represent existing species; and those produced during former years may represent the long succession of extinct species. At each period of growth all the growing twigs have tried to branch out on all sides, and to overtop and kill the surrounding twigs and branches, in the same manner as species and groups of species have at all times overmastered other species in the great battle of life.... Of the many twigs which flourished when the tree was a mere bush, only two or three, now grown into great branches, yet survive and bear the other branches; so with the species which lived during long-past geological periods, very few have left living... descendants.
>
> From the first growth of the tree, many a limb and branch has decayed and dropped off; and all these fallen branches of various sizes may represent those whole orders, families, and genera which have now no living representatives, and which are known to us only in a fossil state. As we here and there see a thin, straggling branch springing from a fork low down in a tree, and which by some chance has been favored and is still alive on its summit, so we occasionally see an animal like the Ornithorhynchus or Lepidosiren, which in some small degree connects by its affinities two large branches of life, and which has apparently been saved from fatal competition by having inhabited a protected station. As buds give rise by growth to fresh buds, and these, if vigorous, branch out and overtop on all sides many a feebler branch, so by generation I believe it has been with the great Tree of Life, which fills with its dead and broken branches the crust of the earth, and covers the surface with its everbranching and beautiful ramifications.

21   Darwin's music here is stately and somber. The central image is established at the beginning: a great tree green at the top but filled with dead branches beneath the crown. The passage becomes an elegy for all the orders of life that have perished since the tree began. Words suggesting death crowd the sentences: *overtopped, kill, the great battle for life, decayed, dropped off, fallen, no living representative, straggling branch, fatal competition*. As the passage moves toward its conclusion, a change, a kind of reversal, can be felt. Words suggesting life become more frequent: *alive, life, saved, fresh buds, vigorous*. The final sentence restates the central paradox in a contrast between universal desolation—"dead and broken branches [filling] the crust of the earth"—with images of eternal fertility—"ever-branching and beautiful ramifications."

22   In spite of the poetic qualities of *The Origin of Species*, the idea of science as the dispassionate observation of things is central to the Darwinian moment. Observation reveals truth; and once revealed, truth can be generalized.

23   The truths discovered by Darwin were applied almost immediately to sociology and political science. Herbert Spencer had coined the phrase "survival of the fittest" in 1852 in an article on the pressures caused by population growth entitled "A Theory of Population." Buttressed by the prestige of *The Origin of Species*, the concept of the

survival of the fittest was used to justify laissez-faire capitalism. Andrew Carnegie remarked in 1900, "A struggle is inevitable [in society] and it is a question of the survival of the fittest." John D. Rockefeller added, "The growth of a large business is merely the survival of the fittest." Capitalism enables the strong to survive while the weak are destroyed. Socialism, conversely, protects the weak and frustrates the strong. Marx turned over the coin: socialism is a later and therefore a higher product of evolution than bourgeois capitalism. Being superior, it will replace capitalism as surely as warm-blooded mammals replaced dinosaurs.

24   Darwin also influenced cultural thought. To say this is to say that he changed not only the way the real was managed but the way it was imagined. The writing of history became evolutionary—so much so that historians often assumed an evolutionary model and tailored their facts to fit. The histories of political systems, national economies, technologies, machinery, literary genres, philosophical systems, and even styles of dress were presented as examples of evolution, usually interpreted to mean examples of progress from simple to complex, with simple considered good, and complex better.

25   And, of course, Darwin's theories were both attacked and supported in the name of religion. Adam Sedgwick, professor of geology at Cambridge, began the long history of attacks on Darwin when he wrote in "Objections to Mr. Darwin's Theory of the Origin of Species" (1860): "I cannot conclude without expressing my detestation of the theory, because of its unflinching materialism." Among the sins for which Darwin was most bitterly attacked was his argument that species are constantly coming into existence and dying, an argument that contradicts the fundamentalist reading of Genesis. He was also attacked for suggesting that struggle, including violent struggle, is ultimately beneficial, and that, by implication, the meek will not inherit the earth. Finally, he was attacked for suggesting that man is an animal sharing a common ancestor with the apes, an idea that is implicit in *The Origin of Species* and stated unequivocally in *The Descent of Man* (1871).

26   Darwin's conclusion to *The Origin of Species* is a summary of his vision. It has a strong emotional coloring even in its initial form. Perhaps because of the attacks, Darwin added the phrase "by the Creator" to the first revised (1860) and later editions of the book: "There is a grandeur in this view of life, with its several powers, having been originally breathed by the Creator into a few forms or into one; and that, whilst this planet has gone cycling on according to the fixed law of gravity, from so simple a beginning endless forms most beautiful and most wonderful have been, and are being evolved."

27   Whether the reference to God represents Darwin's personal view of religion is outside the scope of the present discussion. Probably it does not. At any rate the notion that God is revealed in evolution remains powerfully attractive today both to biologists and, as shown by Teilhard de Chardin's *The Phenomenon of Man* (1955), to those attempting to formulate a scientific theology. More generally, in spite of his literary disclaimers, Darwin initiated a whole genre of writing, typified by the work today of Bertel Bager, Lewis Thomas, and Annie Dillard, which dwells on the intricate beauties of natural design.

28   Many of the applications of Darwin's ideas were, however, patently strained from the beginning. Time revealed the inadequacies of others. Social Darwinism is studied in history classes but is no longer a viable political creed. Evolutionary histories of this and that are still being written, but the approach has been shown to be seriously misleading in many applications. More fundamental, by the middle of the twentieth century Baconian empiricism was no longer adequate to the idea of nature that science had developed. Einstein and Heisenberg made it clear that mind and nature—subject and object—are involved in each other and not separate empires. An objective world that can be "observed"

and "understood" if only the imagination can be held in check simply does not exist. Facts are not observations "collected... on a wholesale scale." They are knots in a net.

NOTES AND DISCUSSION

Hardison's essay explores the nature of science and scientific writing by focusing on the career and publications of the famous English naturalist, Charles Darwin. Hardison builds his essay upon excerpts from Darwin's writing, seamlessly integrating many quotations into his own writing by using a variety of punctuation. Through his presentation and analysis of Darwin's writing, Hardison defines the nature of Darwin's scientific work, but also reveals much about his own definition and vision of science.

Consider, for example, the stress he places on the fact that much of Darwin's four volumes of *Cirripedia* "could have been written entirely on the basis of direct observation," without technical support. Furthermore, Darwin's science is said to have been conducted on a "wholesale scale," encompassing the works of previous naturalists, as well as his travels, his collections of natural specimens, and his interest in poetry. Darwin compared his own mind to a machine designed to grind laws out of a large collection of facts. But Hardison rejects this claim, arguing that Darwin's own conception of his science and writing is flawed, and that in fact Darwin combined the roles of scientist and poet. He then provides specific examples—extended passages of Darwin's prose—which he analyzes closely to support his thesis. Hardison next outlines Darwin's influence on social, political, economic, and cultural thought, as well as on literature, again providing specific examples and quotations to support his point. Hardison thus implies that Darwin's holistic approach to science, as well as the artistry of both his science and his scientific writing, were fundamental to his influence. There is no doubt that Hardison also wishes to influence his readers' understanding of the nature of science.

STUDY QUESTIONS

For Discussion

1. Examine the way Hardison characterizes Darwin's approach to science. What does this characterization imply about the nature and methodology of science in general, and about Hardison's own vision of science, in particular?

2. What does Hardison's final metaphor of "knots in a net" suggest? How does it influence your understanding of the end of the essay?

For Writing

1. Hardison suggests that Darwin influenced the writing of Annie Dillard, among others. A selection from Dillard is included in this anthology. Write an analysis in which you decide whether the qualities that Hardison perceives in Darwin's writing also appear in Dillard's.

2. Analyze Hardison's own style as he analyzes Darwin's, considering the audience he addresses, and the tone he employs.

EXPLAINING DISASTERS: THE CASE FOR PREVENTIVE ETHICS

Charles E. Harris, Jr.

BIOGRAPHICAL NOTE

Charles E. Harris, Jr., is a member of the Department of Philosophy at Texas A & M University, College Station, Texas. His special teaching and research interest is practical ethics. He has published a book on that topic entitled *Applying Moral Theories*.

---

1   In 1986, the space shuttle Challenger exploded during launch, taking the lives of six astronauts and one teacher, Christa McAuliffe. The disaster virtually stopped U.S. space exploration for two years. How should this disaster be explained?

2   Most disasters have multiple explanations. One type or explanation in the Challenger case focuses on the flaws in the design of the field joints in the boosters, or on other engineering failures. Another type locates the problem in improper management practices, either at the National Aeronautics and Space Administration (NASA) or with Morton Thiokol, the manufacturer of the boosters. Another type finds the fault in unethical conduct on the part of NASA or the private contractors. Still other types of explanation might attribute the disaster to an unanticipated convergence of events, or just plain bad luck. I shall confine myself, however, to the first three types of explanation: bad engineering, bad management, and bad ethics.

3   Even though we may know that it is insufficient, there seems to be a natural tendency to focus on a single type of explanation. The result is that these three types of explanation compete with one another in the minds of many people. If an event can be explained in terms of engineering failures, for example, we may think there is no need to look for evidence of improper management or unethical conduct. If there is evidence of incompetent management, why look for engineering problems or ethical improprieties? One reason for this tendency may be that people tend to look for explanations most congruent with their own areas of expertise. Engineers usually look for the explanation of a disaster in bad engineering, most often in faulty design. Managers or management consultants tend to find the explanation in bad management. Ethicists are more likely to look for explanations in terms of ethically improper behavior.

4   Contrary to this approach, there are good reasons to believe that these three types of explanation are not mutually exclusive. The same disaster can be explained in terms of bad engineering, bad management and bad ethics. One consequence of taking this more pluralistic approach to explaining disasters is that the place of ethical considerations in explaining disasters is not neglected. An appreciation of the importance of ethical failures can, in turn, serve to underscore the importance of avoiding these failures in the future. I shall refer to this effort to isolate the ethical failures involved in engineering disasters and to use this knowledge to prevent such failures in the future as *preventive ethics.*

5   Before proceeding further, it is important to point out that there is a distinction between an engineering disaster and an ethically improper use of engineering. The Challenger explosion was an engineering disaster: it involved a technical malfunction that had catastrophic consequences. The employment of German engineers to design the gas valves used at Auschwitz was not an engineering disaster. The valves evidently worked all too well. The problem was that the end to which engineering design was directed was unethical. Few people would question the relevance of ethical categories in explaining the tragedy of Auschwitz: the ends toward which engineering design was directed were unethical. For most of us, however, the goals of engineering work in the Challenger project were not unethical. If ethical categories are relevant, they must be relevant in a different way. I am concerned with this second type of situation, not the first.

THREE TYPES OF EXPLANATION

6   What do we mean by an explanation of a disaster? In explaining a disaster, at least two conditions must be met. First, there must be a failure or impropriety of some sort. Since we are limiting ourselves to three types of explanation, we shall be concerned with three types of failure: in engineering, in management, and in ethics. When we say there has been a failure of some sort, we mean that the rules, standards, or canons appropriate to that area have been violated. Thus, to say that a disaster exhibited improper engineering means that engineering standards were violated. To say that a disaster exhibited improper management means that the canons of good management practice were violated. Similarly, to say that a disaster exhibited unethical conduct means that the canons of proper ethical conduct were violated.

7   A second condition is that the impropriety must have been a contributing cause of the disaster. While there may be times when a single cause is sufficient to explain a disaster, it is more common to find that there are several contributing causes. I shall offer the following as a working account (not a formal definition) of a contributing cause: Event A is a contributing cause of Event B, when Event A is prior to Event B and when the existence of Event A makes Event B more likely to occur. Using these two conditions as tests, we can make a case that the Challenger disaster can be explained in all three ways: it was bad engineering, bad management and bad ethics.

8   The case for explanation in terms of bad engineering is based on the design flaws in the seal between the sections of the boosters. One of the canons of good engineering design is that static and dynamic situations must be carefully distinguished, and the design must

fit the situation. Yet in the case of the Challenger, this canon was violated. The O-ring seal between the sections of the boosters was designed for a static situation, but the flexing to which the seal was subjected in flight meant that it should have been designed for a dynamic situation. This design flaw, along with the unusually cold weather that caused the O-rings to lose some of their resiliency, was perhaps the most obvious engineering explanation of the disaster.[1]

9   Furthermore, the design flaw was a contributing cause to the disaster. The design flaw made the disaster much more probable. Indeed, apart from this design flaw, the disaster might never have occurred. So both of the conditions of explanation in terms of an engineering failure are fulfilled. There were violations of engineering principles, and these violations made the disaster much more likely to happen.

10   There is also a case for an explanation of the Challenger disaster in terms of bad management. To say that an event exhibits bad management is to say that it violates the standards of good management.[2] One of the standards of good management is that managers should establish and maintain effective communication with their employees. The reason for this is that good communication not only enhances employee morale, but also furnishes managers with information that is essential in making sound management decisions. In order to enhance communication, managers must do at least two things. First, they must create an atmosphere in which employees can bring up problems without fear of reprisal. Second, they must respond positively to employees when they utilize this freedom to bring up problems. This does not mean that managers must always follow employees' advice, but they must consider and evaluate it carefully.

11   These requirements of good management practice, which are especially important with regard to professional employees, were evidently violated by Morton Thiokol managers. Roger Boisjoly reports that he alerted Thiokol managers to the problems with the O-ring seal a year or more before the Challenger disaster. He even asked for funding to look for solutions. Not only was his request ignored, but there was evidently an atmosphere of intimidation that inhibited engineers from communicating their concerns freely. On the night before the disastrous launch, Boisjoly and other engineers made their case for a no-launch recommendation to NASA, primarily on the basis of anticipated difficulties with the O-ring seals at the low launch temperatures. After first being accepted by Thiokol managers, this recommendation was later reversed, partially at least as a result of protests from NASA. According to Boisjoly's account, when he objected to the reversal of the original recommendation, his manager (Gerald Mason) looked at him in a way that indicated he was about to be fired.[3]

12   Improper management was also a contributing cause of the disaster. If Thiokol managers had been more responsive to Boisjoly's early warnings, they might have ordered research aimed at improving the O-ring seal, and an improved seal might well have averted the disaster. If Thiokol and NASA managers had listened to the engineers on the night before the launch, they might have recommended against the launch and the launch might not have taken place. So bad management was also an explanation of the disaster, in that

---

[1] I have used two written sources for my account of the Challenger disaster. One source is the commission chaired by William P. Rogers in 1986 [1]. I shall refer to this as the Rogers Commission Report. The other is Roger Boisjoly's, "The Challenger disaster: Moral responsibility and the working engineer" [2].

[2] For further discussion of the engineer/manager relationship, see [3].

[3] Reported in [4].

management principles were violated, and the violations made it more likely that a disaster would occur.

13   Finally, a case can be made that ethically improper conduct was part of the explanation of the disaster. To say that something is unethical is to say that it violates ethical standards. One such standard is the Golden Rule: "Do unto others as you would have them do unto you." One wonders if Thiokol or NASA managers would have been willing to fly in the Challenger themselves, knowing what they did about the problems with the O-rings. I am inclined to say that they would not, and that their action violated the Golden Rule.

14   Perhaps even more telling is the violation of the standard of free and informed consent. People should be informed about unusual dangers to which they might be subjected and given the chance to consent or not consent to the dangers. According to the Rogers Commission, this canon was not fully honored with respect to the problem created by ice formation on the Challenger, due to the sub-freezing temperatures the night before launch. Although they had been consulted about the ice problem, the crew was not fully apprised of its seriousness [1, p. 118]. There is also no record of the crew's having been adequately informed of the O-ring problem, even though it was known to be potentially life-threatening. These deficiencies can only be considered serious violations of the principle of informed consent. Even though the astronauts knew that they were engaged in a high-risk mission, the principle of informed consent was not thereby rendered irrelevant. The astronauts should have been informed of the unusual problems.

15   In addition to the violation of widely-accepted ethical precepts, the events preceding the Challenger disaster exhibit other types of ethical deficiencies. The Rogers Commission concluded that Thiokol management reversed its original decision "contrary to the views of its engineers in order to accommodate a major customer" [1, p. 104]. What explains this reversal? NASA managers expressed extreme displeasure with the original Thiokol decision not to launch, probably due to pressures on them for a quick success.[4] The testimony of Robert Lund, the vice president of engineering at Morton Thiokol, centers around a shift in the burden of proof. Whereas NASA originally adopted a policy that a launch recommendation bore the burden of proof, it had shifted to the position that a no-launch recommendation bore the burden of proof [1, p. 93]. After first agreeing with his engineers, Lund changed his mind, perhaps in response to pressure from Mason. The testimony of Jerry Mason, a senior vice president at Morton Thiokol, centers around the claim that the engineering evidence was inconclusive and that a management decision had to be made [1, p. 773]. There is evidence, then, that both NASA and Thiokol managers may have exhibited ethical deficiencies. One thinks of weakness of will (lack of courage to do what one knows is right), self-deception, and self-interest as likely candidates for these deficiencies.

16   A good case can also be made that ethical failures were a contributing cause to the disaster. If the managers at NASA and Thiokol had put themselves in the place of the astronauts and had never been affected by weakness of will, self-deception, or self-interest, they would almost certainly have taken the O-ring problems more seriously. The managers would probably have paid attention to Boisjoly's early warnings and ordered further testing, which might have led to the correction of the problem. If managers had held consistently to the canon of free and informed consent, they would have fully informed the

---

[4] According to Roger Boisjoly, George Hardy of NASA said he was appalled by Thiokol's no-launch recommendation. See [2, p. 8].

astronauts of the O-ring problem. We do not know, of course, whether the astronauts would have decided to fly if they had been informed about the O-ring problem. There is, however, a significant chance that they would have decided not to fly, especially if the information about the O-ring problem had been added to the information about the danger due to ice. Even if they had decided to fly, the managers and engineers might have been more likely to try to correct the O-ring problem, knowing that they must inform the astronauts about it.

17   Thus, if managers and engineers had avoided unethical conduct, they would have been more likely to have made different decisions. This means that ethical failings were present and could be considered contributing causes of the disaster.

PRIMACY OF THE ENGINEERING EXPLANATION

18   If this analysis is correct, there is nothing wrong with saying that bad engineering, bad management and faulty ethics all play a part in explaining the Challenger disaster. Principles of sound engineering, sound management and sound ethics were violated, and these violations could all be considered contributing causes to the disaster. These three types of explanation are not mutually exclusive. One cannot show that one type of explanation is inapplicable merely by showing that another type of explanation is applicable. One cannot show, for example, that an explanation in terms of ethical failings is irrelevant by showing that an explanation in terms of engineering ineptitude is relevant.

19   But isn't the engineering explanation more fundamental than the others? Even if all three types of explanation are relevant, doesn't the engineering explanation occupy pride of place? The simple answer to this question is, "Yes." The engineering deficiencies seem to be the most crucial, in the sense that the disaster almost certainly would not have occurred if there had been no problem with the O-rings. This cannot be said of the management and ethical failures. Even if management practices and ethical conduct had been exemplary, the disaster might still have occurred. Suppose Thiokol managers had listened to Boisjoly's early warnings about the O-ring deficiencies and ordered further testing and research to resolve the problems. A bad design might still have resulted. Even if NASA and Thiokol managers had listened with an open mind and in a non-intimidating way to the engineers on the night before the launch, they might still have concluded in good faith that the engineering evidence was not compelling. While the managers might have made a mistake, they might not have violated principles of sound management.

20   The situation is similar with regard to the ethical improprieties. Suppose Thiokol managers had attempted to follow the Golden Rule, so that they ordered further research and development on the O-rings. This research and development could still have issued in a bad design. They might even in good faith have been willing to fly themselves. Furthermore, if the astronauts had been fully informed about the problems with ice and the O-rings, so that the requirement of free and informed consent was met, they might have decided to fly anyway. And if engineers and managers had resisted unethical influences on the night before the launch, they still might have made a decision to launch.

21   Of course following sound engineering principles does not guarantee that there will be no design mistakes, but it is still true that the disaster probably would not have occurred if the design mistakes had been corrected. By contrast, the disaster might still have occurred, even if the management and ethical failures *had* been corrected. In this sense, then, the engineering failure can be considered the most fundamental or at least the most direct explanation of the Challenger disaster.

PREVENTIVE ETHICS

22   It does not follow, however, that management and ethical considerations are irrelevant in explaining the disaster. There is good reason to believe that there were management and ethical failures, and that these were contributing causes to the disaster. We cannot say for certain that eliminating these failures would have kept the Challenger disaster from happening, but it would have made the disaster less likely. This is because eliminating the management and ethical failures would have made the engineering failures themselves less likely to have happened. Of course there are other reasons besides preventing disasters for engaging in sound ethical and management practices, but I am concerned here only with this reason.

23   Thus, understanding why a disaster happened puts us in a better position to *prevent* similar disasters in the future. This is one of the reasons engineers want to look for the engineering explanation of a disaster. Engineers, like the rest of us, learn from experience. If they can isolate the engineering factors that explain a disaster, they can do something to prevent similar mistakes in the future. Perhaps we could call this *preventive engineering*.[5]

24   The same thing could be said about management failures. If managers at NASA, Morton Thiokol, and perhaps other private contractors had established a more open and non-intimidating atmosphere for their engineers and had been more adept at listening to the engineers' concerns, remedial measures might have been taken regarding the O-rings and the disaster might not have happened. Perhaps we can call this *preventive management.*

25   By similar reasoning we can say that discovering and attempting to eliminate ethical failures can also aid in preventing similar disasters in the future. As we have seen, if managers had been more attentive to ethical considerations such as the Golden Rule and the principle of informed consent and had not succumbed to self-interest or excessive external pressures, they might have taken stronger measures to correct the O-ring problems. Similarly, greater ethical concern and strength of will might have led more engineers to insist that either the O-ring problem be remedied or the Challenger should not fly. Exposing these problems and attempting to eliminate them can make an important contribution to preventing similar disasters in the future. I have already referred to this as part of preventive ethics.

26   The idea of preventive ethics is not wholly new. Some large health-care organizations employ medical ethicists on the corporate level in order to aid in the formulation of ethically acceptable policies. Management in these organizations apparently believes that operating by ethically acceptable policies may prevent legal and public-image problems and serve as a defense if such problems arise. Promoting codes of ethics and installing ethics officers and procedures for promoting ethical awareness may be a part of this same philosophy.

27   So far I have focused exclusively on the Challenger case in order to illustrate the ethical dimension of explaining disasters and the concept of preventive ethics. But many other famous cases in engineering ethics also exemplify ethical failures and suggest that the elimination of those failures might have prevented the disasters, or at least made them less probable. Engineers and managers were aware, for example, of the problems with the cargo hatch door of the McDonnell Douglas DC-10, but only one engineer appears to have made

---

[5]Steven B. Young and Willem H. Vanderburg develop the concept of "preventive engineering" in [5].

any concerted effort to remedy the problem. If managers and engineers had resisted unethical influences or imaginatively placed themselves in the position of passengers in the DC-10, would they have acted differently? If they had, the crash near Paris, France, which killed all 346 passengers might have been avoided. Ford engineers and managers were aware of the susceptibility of the Ford Pinto to explosion from even low-impact rear-end collisions. Would they have been more inclined to remedy the design defect if they had taken seriously the possibility that they or a family member might have driven the car, or if they had considered informing the public of the danger from rear-end collisions? Similar arguments might be made about the Chevrolet Corvair, the Union Carbide disaster in Bhopal, India, and many other cases not so well known.

28   There is no way of knowing whether greater ethical sensitivity and the absence of impediments to ethically responsible action would have prevented these particular disasters, but it seems almost certain that the presence of these factors can prevent *some* unfortunate and tragic engineering disasters. This is enough to make preventive ethics worthwhile.

NOTES

[1] William P. Rogers, "Report to the President by the Presidential Commission on the Space Shuttle Challenger Accident," Washington, DC, June 6, 1986.

[2] Roger Boisjoly, "The Challenger disaster: Moral responsibility and the working engineer," in *Ethical Issues in Engineering,* Deborah C. Johnson, ed. Englewood Cliffs, NJ: Prentice Hall, 1991, pp. 6–14.

[3] Charles E. Harris, Jr., Michael S. Pritchard, and Michael J. Rabins, *Engineering Ethics.* Belmont, CA: Wadsworth, 1995, pp. 273–277.

[4] Roger Boisjoly, Massachusetts Institute of Technology, Cambridge, MA, Jan. 7, 1987, videotape record of remarks to audience.

[5] Steven B. Young and Willem H. Vanderburg, "A materials life cycle framework for preventive engineering," *IEEE Technol. & Soc. Mag.,* vol. 11, pp. 26–31, Fall 1992.

NOTES AND DISCUSSION

In "Explaining Disasters," Charles E. Harris, Jr., examines the explosion of the space shuttle *Challenger* in 1986 and attempts to explain why the disaster happened. Harris points out that there is a "natural tendency" to look for single explanations for disasters, and that "people tend to look for explanations most congruent with their own areas of expertise." Thus, argues Harris, engineers look for explanations "in bad engineering." However, single explanations are not often enough. Harris's theory is that the *Challenger* disaster, like many events like it, properly has a three-pronged explanation. Harris isolates "bad engineering, bad management, and bad ethics" as the linked problems that all contributed to the catastrophe; he then makes the case that the three explanations are not mutually exclusive.

While he is very willing to admit that if the engineering problems with the *Challenger*'s O-rings had not existed, the explosion would not have happened, Harris is an ethicist, and in his essay argues strongly that more ethically sound behaviour—more ethical sensitivity— might have helped to prevent the *Challenger* disaster, and would almost certainly help to prevent future similar catastrophes. Harris ends his essay by making the case for what he calls "preventive ethics" as having the potential to "prevent *some* unfortunate and tragic engineering disasters."

STUDY QUESTIONS

For Discussion

1. Do you think that Harris makes a convincing case that explanations of disasters typically should have a three-part structure? Why, or why not?

2. Do you think that Harris makes a convincing case that a heightened sense of ethics would help to prevent disasters in the future? If so, what factors helped to convince you? If not, how could Harris strengthen his claim?

For Writing

1. Do some research about an engineering disaster of your choice and write a short essay in which you apply Harris's three-part explanation rubric. Is the ethical part of Harris's rubric an essential part of the explanation you offer for the disaster you have selected?

2. Consider Harris's discussion in the light of Henry Petroski's suggestion that typically more is learned from failures than from consistent success. Write a short essay in which you discuss whether Petroski's position is an ethical one, from Harris's point of view.

WHAT IS AN ELEMENTARY PARTICLE?

Werner Heisenberg

BIOGRAPHICAL NOTE

Werner Heisenberg (1901–1976) was one of the more influential and important theorists of quantum physics of the early twentieth century. He is best known for his writings about quantum uncertainty—that is, the proposition that the position and velocity of subatomic particles cannot be known precisely but can only be calculated in terms of probabilities—and for articulating the "uncertainty principle," the idea that science can neither scrutinize the present nor predict the future with complete exactitude. Heisenberg's universe is, then, very different from Einstein's. He suggests that it is impossible to observe subatomic particles directly: the position of those particles may only be calculated, and even those calculations cannot ever be precise, but are only statistically probable. Einstein greeted Heisenberg's claims with incredulity, declaring that "God does not play dice with the universe."

1　The question "What is an elementary particle?" must naturally be answered above all by experiment. So I shall first summarize briefly the most important experimental findings of elementary particle physics during the last fifty years, and will try to show that, if the experiments are viewed without prejudice, the question alluded to has already been largely answered by these findings, and that there is no longer much for the theoretician to add. In the second part I will then go on to enlarge upon the philosophical problems connected with the concept of an elementary particle. For I believe that certain mistaken developments in the theory of elementary particles—and I fear that there are such—are due to the fact that their authors would claim that they do not wish to trouble about philosophy, but that in reality they unconsciously start out from a bad philosophy, and have therefore fallen

From *Tradition in Science* by Werner Heisenberg. Copyright © 1983 by Werner Heisenberg. Reprinted by permission of HarperCollins Publishers, Inc. Originally from a lecture to the Session of the German Physical Society on March 5, 1975. In *Die Naturwissenschaften*, 63, pp. 1–7 (1976), Spring, 1976.

through prejudice into unreasonable statements of the problem. One may say, with some exaggeration, perhaps, that good physics has been inadvertently spoiled by bad philosophy. Finally I shall say something of these problematic developments themselves, compare them with erroneous developments in the history of quantum mechanics in which I was myself involved, and consider how such wrong turnings can be avoided. The close of the lecture should therefore be more optimistic again.

2   First, then, to the experimental facts. Not quite fifty years ago, Dirac, in his theory of electrons, predicted that in addition to electrons there would also have to exist the appropriate anti-particles, the positrons; and a few years later the existence of positrons, their origin in pair-creation, and hence the existence of so-called anti-matter, was experimentally demonstrated by Anderson and Blackett. It was a discovery of the first order. For till then it had mostly been supposed that there are two kinds of fundamental particle, electrons and protons, which are distinguished above all others by the fact that they can never be changed, so that their number is always constant as well, and which for that very reason had been called elementary particles. All matter was supposed in the end to be made up of electrons and protons. The experimental proof of pair-creation and positrons showed that this idea was false. Electrons can be created and again disappear; so their number is by no means constant; they are not elementary in the sense previously assumed.

3   The next important step was Fermi's discovery of artificial radioactivity. It was learnt from many experiments that one atomic nucleus can turn into another by emission of particles, if the conservation laws for energy, angular momentum, electric charge, etc., allow this. The transformation of energy into matter, which had already been recognized as possible in Einstein's relativity theory, is thus a very commonly observable phenomenon. There is no talk here of any conservation of the number of particles. But there are indeed physical properties, characterizable by quantum numbers—I am thinking, say, of angular momentum or electric charge—in which the quantum numbers can then take on positive and negative values, and for these a conservation law holds.

4   In the thirties there was yet another important experimental discovery. It was found that in cosmic radiation there are very energetic particles, which, on collision with other particles, say a proton, in the emulsion of a photographic plate, can let loose a shower of many secondary particles. Many physicists believed for a time that such showers can originate only through a sort of cascade formation in atomic nuclei; but it later turned out that, even in a collision between a single pair of energetic particles, the theoretically conjectured multiple production of secondary particles does in fact occur. At the end of the forties, Powell discovered the pions, which play the major part in these showers. This showed that in collisions of high-energy particles, the transformation of energy into matter is quite generally the decisive process, so that it obviously no longer makes sense to speak of a splitting of the original particle. The concept of "division" had come, by experiment, to lose its meaning.

5   In the experiments of the fifties and sixties, this new situation was repeatedly confirmed: many new particles were discovered, with long and short lives, and no unambiguous answer could be given any longer to the question about what these particles consisted of, since this question no longer has a rational meaning. A proton, for example, could be made up of neutron and pion, or Λ-hyperon and kaon, or out of two nucleons and an anti-nucleon; it would be simplest of all to say that a proton just consists of continuous matter, and all these statements are equally correct or equally false. The difference between elementary and composite particles has thus basically disappeared. And that is no doubt the most important experimental finding of the last fifty years.

6   As a consequence of this development, the experiments have strongly suggested an analogy: the elementary particles are something like the stationary states of an atom or a molecule. There is a whole spectrum of particles, just as there is a spectrum, say, of the iron atom or a molecule, where we may think, in the latter case, of the various stationary states of molecule, or even of the many different possible molecules of chemistry. Among particles, we shall speak of a spectrum of "matter." In fact, during the sixties and seventies, the experiments with the big accelerators have shown that this analogy fits all the findings so far. Like the stationary states of the atom, the particles, too, can be characterized by quantum numbers, that is, by symmetry- or transformation-properties, and the exact or approximately valid conservation principles associated with them decide as to the possibility of the transformations. Just as the transformation properties of an excited hydrogen atom under spatial rotation decide whether it can fall to a lower state by emission of a photon, so too, the question whether a $\varnothing$-boson, say, can degenerate into a ρ-boson by emission of a pion, is decided by such symmetry properties. Just as the various stationary states of an atom have very different lifetimes, so too with particles. The ground state of an atom is stable, and has an infinitely long lifetime, and the same is true of such particles as the electron, proton, deuteron, etc. But these stable particles are in no way more elementary than the unstable ones. The ground state of the hydrogen atom follows from the same Schrödinger equation as the excited states do. Nor are the electron and photon in any way more elementary than, say, a Λ-hyperon.

7   The experimental particle-physics of recent years has thus fulfilled much the same tasks, in the course of its development, as the spectroscopy of the early twenties. Just as, at that time, a large compilation was brought out, the so-called Paschen-Götze tables, in which the stationary states of all atom shells were collected, so now we have the annually supplemented *Reviews of Particle Properties*, in which the stationary states of matter and its transformation-properties are recorded. The work of compiling such a comprehensive tabulation therefore corresponds, say, to the star-cataloging of the astronomers, and every observer hopes, of course, that he will one day find a particularly interesting object in his chosen area.

8   Yet there are also characteristic differences between particle physics and the physics of atomic shells. In the latter we are dealing with such low energies, that the characteristic features of relativity theory can be neglected, and nonrelativistic quantum mechanics used, therefore, for description. This means that the governing symmetry-groups may differ in atomic-shell physics on the one hand, and in particles on the other. The Galileo group of shell physics is replaced, at the particle level, by the Lorentz-group; and in particle physics we also have new groups, such as the isospin group, which is isomorphic to the SU_2 group, and then the SU_3 group, the group of scaling transformations, and still others. It is an important experimental task to define the governing groups of particle physics, and in the past twenty years it has already been largely accomplished.

9   Here we can learn from shell physics, that in those very groups which manifestly designate only approximately valid symmetrics, two basically different types may be distinguished. Consider, say, among optical spectra, the O_3 group of spatial rotations, and the $O_3 \times O_3$ group, which governs the multiplet-structure in spectra. The basic equations of quantum mechanics are strictly invariant with respect to the group of spatial rotations. The states of atoms having greater angular momenta are therefore severely degenerate, that is, there are numerous states of exactly equal energy. Only if the atom is placed in an external electromagnetic field do the states split up, and the familiar fine structure emerge, as in the Zeeman or Stark effect. This degeneracy can also be abolished if the ground state of

the system is not rotation-invariant, as in the ground states of a crystal or ferro-magnet. In this case there is also a splitting of levels; the two spin-directions of an electron in a ferro-magnet are no longer associated with exactly the same energy. Furthermore, by a well-known theorem of Goldstone, there are bosons whose energy tends to zero with increasing wavelength, and, in the case of the ferro-magnet, Bloch's spin-waves or magnons.

10   It is different with the group $O_3 \times O_3$, from which result the familiar multiplets of optical spectra. Here we are dealing with an approximate symmetry, which comes about in that the spin-path interactions in a specific region are small, so that the spins and paths of electrons can be skewed counter to each other, without producing much change in the interaction. The $O_3 \times O_3$ symmetry is therefore also a useful approximation only in particular parts of the spectrum. Empirically, the two kinds of broken symmetry are most clearly distinguishable in that, for the fundamental symmetry broken by the ground state, there must, by the Goldstone theorem, be associated bosons of zero rest mass, or long-range forces. If we find them, there is reason to believe that the degeneracy of the ground state plays an important role here.

11   Now if these findings are transferred from atomic-shell physics to particle physics, it is very natural, on the basis of the experiments, to interpret the Lorentz group and the SU_2 group, the isospin group, that is, fundamental symmetries of the underlying law of nature. Electromagnetism and gravitation then appear as the long-range forces associated with symmetry broken by the ground state. The higher groups, SU_3, SU_4, SU_6, or $SU_2 \times SU_2$, $SU_3 \times SU_3$ and so on, would then have to rank as dynamic symmetries, just like $O_3 \times O_3$ in atomic-shell physics. Of the dilatation or scaling group, it may be doubted whether it should be counted among the fundamental symmetries; it is perturbed by the existence of particles with finite mass, and by the gravitation due to masses in the universe. Owing to its close relation to the Lorentz group, it certainly ought to be numbered among the fundamental symmetries. The foregoing assignment of perturbed symmetries to the two basic types is made plausible, as I was already saying, by the experimental findings, but it is not yet possible, perhaps, to speak of a final settlement. The most important thing is that, with regard to the symmetry groups that present themselves in the phenomenology of spectra, the question must be asked, and if possible answered, as to which of the two basic types they belong to.

12   Let me point to yet another feature of shell-physics: among optical spectra there are non-combining, or more accurately, weakly combining term-systems, such as the spectra or para- and ortho-helium. In particle physics we can perhaps compare the division of the fermion spectrum into baryons and leptons with features of this type.

13   The analogy between the stationary states of an atom or molecule, and the particles of elementary particle physics, is therefore almost complete, and with this, so it seems to me, I have also given a complete qualitative answer to the initial question "What is an elementary particle?" But only a qualitative answer! The theorist is now confronted with the further question, whether he can also underpin this qualitative understanding by means of quantitative calculations. For this it is first necessary to answer a prior question: What is it, anyway, to understand a spectrum in quantitative terms?

14   For this we have a string of examples, from both classical physics and quantum mechanics alike. Let us consider, say, the spectrum of the elastic vibrations of a steel plate. If we are not to be content with a qualitative understanding, we shall start from the fact that the plate can be characterized by specific elastic properties, which can be mathematically represented. Having achieved this, we still have to append the boundary conditions, adding, for example, that the plate is circular or rectangular, that it is, or is not, under tension, and from this, at least in principle, the spectrum of elastic or acoustic vibrations can be calculated. Owing to the level of complexity, we shall certainly not, indeed, be able to work out all the vibrations exactly, but may yet, perhaps, calculate the lowest, with the smallest number of nodal lines.

15   Thus two elements are necessary for quantitative understanding: the exactly formulated knowledge, in mathematical terms, of the dynamic behavior of the plate, and the boundary conditions, which can be regarded as "contingent," as determined, that is, by local circumstances; the plate, of course, could also be dissected in other ways. It is like this, too, with the electrodynamic oscillations of a cavity resonator. The Maxwellian equations determine the dynamic behavior, and the shape of the cavity defines the boundary conditions. And so it is, also, with the optical spectrum of the iron atom. The Schrödinger equation for a system with a nucleus and 26 electrons determines the dynamic behavior, and to this we add the boundary conditions, which state in this instance that the wavefunction shall vanish at infinity. If the atom were to be enclosed in a small box, a somewhat altered spectrum would result.

16   If we transfer these ideas to particle physics, it becomes a question, therefore, of first ascertaining by experiment the dynamical properties of the matter system, and formulating this in mathematical terms. As the contingent element, we now add the boundary conditions, which here will consist essentially of statements about so-called empty space, i.e., about the cosmos and its symmetry properties. The first step must in any case be the attempt to formulate mathematically a law of nature that lays down the dynamics of matter. For the second step, we have to make statements about the boundary conditions. For without these, the spectrum just cannot be defined. I would guess, for example, that in one of the "black holes" of contemporary astrophysics, the spectrum of elementary particles would look totally different from our own. Unfortunately, we cannot experiment on the point.

17   But now a word more about the decisive first step, namely the formulation of the dynamical law. There are pessimists among particle physicists, who believe that there simply is no such law of nature, defining the dynamic properties of matter. With such a view I confess that I can make no headway at all. For somehow the dynamics of matter has to exist, or else there would be no spectrum; and in that case we should also be able to describe it mathematically. The pessimistic view would mean that the whole of particle physics is directed, eventually, at producing a gigantic tabulation containing the maximum number of stationary states of matter, transition-probabilities, and the like, a "Super-Review of Particle Properties," and thus a compilation in which there is nothing more to understand, and which therefore, no doubt, would no longer be read by anyone. But there is also not the least occasion for such pessimism, and I set particular store by this assertion. For we actually observe a particle spectrum with sharp lines, and so, indirectly, a sharply defined dynamics of matter as well. The experimental findings, briefly sketched above, also contain already very definite indications as to the fundamental invariance properties of this fundamental law of nature, and we know from the dispersion relations a great deal about the level of causality that is formulated in this law. We thus have the essential determinants of the law already to hand, and after so many other spectra in physics have finally been understood to some extent in quantitative terms, it will also be possible here, despite the high degree of complexity involved. At this point—and just because of its complexity—I would sooner not discuss the special proposal that was long ago made by myself, together with Pauli, for a mathematical formulation of the underlying law, and which, even now, I still believe to have the best chances of being the right one. But I would like to point out with all emphasis, that the formulation of such a law is the indispensable

precondition for understanding the spectrum of elementary particles. All else is not understanding; it is hardly more than a start to the tabulation project, and as theorists, at least, we should not be content with that.

18   I now come to the philosophy by which the physics of elementary particles is consciously or unconsciously guided. For two and a half millennia, the question has been debated by philosophers and scientists, as to what happens when we try to keep on dividing up matter. What are the smallest constituent parts of matter? Different philosophers have given very different answers to this question, which have all exerted their influence on the history of natural science. The best known is that of the philosopher Democritus. In attempting to go on dividing, we finally light upon indivisible, immutable objects, the atoms, and all materials are composed of atoms. The position and motions of the atoms determine the quality of the materials. In Aristotle and his medieval successors, the concept of minimal particles is not so sharply defined. There are, indeed, minimal particles here for every kind of material—on further division the parts would no longer display the characteristic properties of the material—but these minimal parts are continuously changeable, like the materials themselves. Mathematically speaking, therefore, materials are infinitely divisible; matter is pictured as continuous.

19   The clearest opposing position to that of Democritus was adopted by Plato. In attempting continual division we ultimately arrive, in Plato's opinion, at mathematical forms: the regular solids of stereometry, which are definable by their symmetry properties, and the triangles from which they can be constructed. These forms are not themselves matter, but they shape it. The element earth, for example, is based on the shape of the cube, the element fire on the shape of the tetrahedron. It is common to all these philosophers, that they wish in some way to dispose of the antinomy of the infinitely small, which, as everyone knows, was discussed in detail by Kant.

20   Of course, there are and have been more naïve attempts at rationalizing this antinomy. Biologists, for example, have developed the notion that the seed of an apple contains an invisibly small apple tree, which in turn bears blossom and fruit; that again in the fruit there are seeds, in which once more a still tinier apple tree is hidden, and so *ad infinitum*. In the same way, in the early days of the Bohr-Rutherford theory of the atom as a miniature planetary system, we developed with some glee the thesis that upon the planets of this system, the electrons, there are again very tiny creatures living, who build houses, cultivate fields and do atomic physics, arriving once more at the thesis of their atoms as miniature planetary systems, and so *ad infinitum*. In the background here, as I said already, there is always lurking the Kantian antinomy, that it is very hard, on the one hand, to think of matter as infinitely divisible, but also difficult, on the other, to imagine this division one day coming to an enforced stop. The antinomy, as we know, is ultimately brought about by our erroneous belief that we can also apply our intuition to situations on the very small scale. The strongest influence on the physics and chemistry of recent centuries has undoubtedly been exerted by the atomism of Democritus. It permits an intuitive description of small-scale chemical processes. The atoms can be compared to the mass-points of Newtonian mechanics, and such a comparison leads to a satisfying statistical theory of heat. The chemist's atoms were not, indeed, mass-points at all, but miniature planetary systems, and the atomic nucleus was composed of protons and neutrons, but electrons, protons, and eventually even neutrons could, it was thought, quite well be regarded as the true atoms, that is, as the ultimate indivisible building-blocks of matter. During the last hundred years, the Democritean idea of the atom had thus become an integrating component of the physicist's view of the material world; it was readily intelligible and to some extent intuitive, and determined physical thinking even among physicists who wanted to have nothing to do with philosophy. At this point I should now like to justify my suggestion, that today in the physics of elementary particles, good physics is unconsciously being spoiled by bad philosophy.

21   We cannot, of course, avoid employing a language that stems from this traditional philosophy. We ask, "What does the proton consist of?" "Can one divide the electron, or is it indivisible?" "Is the light-quantum simple, or is it composite?" But these questions are wrongly put, since the words *divide* or *consist of* have largely lost their meaning. It would thus be our task to adapt our language and thought, and hence also our scientific philosophy, to this new situation engendered by the experiments. But that, unfortunately, is very difficult. The result is that false questions and false ideas repeatedly creep into particle physics, and lead to the erroneous developments of which I am about to speak. But first a further remark about the demand for intuitability.

22   There have been philosophers who have held intuitability to be the precondition for all true understanding. Thus here in Munich, for example, the philosopher Hugo Dingler has championed the view that intuitive Euclidean geometry is the only true geometry, since it is presupposed in the construction of our measuring instruments; and on the latter point, Dingler is quite correct. Hence, he says, the experimental findings which underlie the general theory of relativity should be described in other terms than those of a more general Riemannian geometry, which deviates from the Euclidean; for otherwise we become involved in contradictions. But this demand is obviously extreme. To justify what we do by way of experiment, it is enough that, in the dimensions of our apparatus, the geometry of Euclid holds to a sufficiently good approximation. We must therefore come to agree that the experimental findings on the very small and very large scale no longer provide us with an intuitive picture, and must learn to manage there without intuitions. We then recognize, for example, that the aforementioned antinomy of the infinitely small is resolved, among elementary particles, in a very subtle fashion, in a way that neither Kant nor the ancient philosophers could have thought of, namely inasmuch as the term *divide* loses its meaning.

23   If we wish to compare the findings of contemporary particle physics with any earlier philosophy, it can only be with the philosophy of Plato; for the particles of present-day physics are representations of symmetry groups, so the quantum theory tells us, and to that extent they resemble the symmetrical bodies of the Platonic view.

24   But our purpose here was to occupy ourselves not with philosophy, but with physics, and so I will now go on to discuss that development in theoretical particle physics, which in my view sets out from a false statement of the problem. There is first of all the thesis, that the observed particles, such as protons, pions, hyperons, and many others, are made up of smaller unobserved particles, the quarks, or else from partons, gluons, charmed particles, or whatever these imagined particles may all be called. Here the question has obviously been asked, "What do protons consist of?" But it has been forgotten in the process, that the term *consist of* only has a halfway clear meaning if we are able to dissect the particle in question, with a small expenditure of energy, into constituents whose rest mass is very much greater than this energy-cost; otherwise, the term *consist of* has lost its meaning. And that is the situation with protons. In order to demonstrate this loss of meaning in a seemingly well-defined term, I cannot forebear from telling a story that Niels Bohr was wont to retail on such occasions. A small boy comes into a shop with twopence in his hand, and tells the shopkeeper that he would like twopence-worth of mixed sweets. The shopkeeper hands him two sweets, and says: "You can mix them for yourself." In the case

of the proton, the concept "consist of" has just as much meaning as the concept of "mixing" in the tale of the small boy.

25   Now many will object to this, that the quark hypothesis has been drawn from empirical findings, namely the establishing of the empirical relevance of the SU_3 group; and furthermore, it holds up in the interpretation of many experiments on the application of the SU_3 group as well. This is not to be contested. But I should like to put forward a counter-example from the history of quantum mechanics, in which I myself was involved; a counter-example which clearly displays the weakness of arguments of this type. Prior to the appearance of Bohr's theory, many physicists maintained that an atom must be made up of harmonic oscillators. For the optical spectrum certainly contains sharp lines, and they can only be emitted by harmonic oscillators. The charges on these oscillators would have to correspond to other electromagnetic values than those on the electron, and there would also have to be very many oscillators, since there are very many lines in the spectrum.

26   Regardless of these difficulties, Woldemar Voigt constructed at Göttingen in 1912 a theory of the anomalous Zeeman effect of the D-lines in the optical spectrum of sodium, and did so in the following way: he assumed a pair of coupled oscillators which, in the absence of an external magnetic field, yielded the frequencies of the two D-lines. He was able to arrange a coupling of the oscillators with one another, and with the external field, in such a way that, in weak magnetic fields, the anomalous Zeeman effect came out correct, and that in very strong magnetic fields the Paschen-Back effect was also correctly represented. For the intermediate region of moderate fields, he obtained, for the frequencies and intensities, long and complex quadratic roots; formulae, that is, which were largely incomprehensible, but which obviously reproduced the experiments with great exactness. Fifteen years later, Jordan and I took the trouble to work out the same problem by the methods of the quantum-mechanical theory of perturbation. To our great astonishment, we came out with exactly the old Voigtian formulae, so far as both frequencies and intensities were concerned and this, too, in the complex area of the moderate fields. The reasons for this we were later well able to perceive; it was a purely formal and mathematical one. The quantum-mechanical theory of perturbation leads to a system of coupled linear equations, and the frequencies are determined by the eigen values of the equation-system. A system of coupled harmonic oscillators leads equally, in the classical theory, to such a coupled linear equations-system. Since, in Voigt's theory, the most important parameter had been cancelled out, it was therefore no wonder that the right answer emerged. But the Voigtian theory contributed nothing to the understanding of atomic structure.

27   Why was this attempt of Voigt's so successful on the one hand, and so futile on the other? Because he was only concerned to examine the D-lines, without taking the whole line-spectrum into account. Voigt had made phenomenological use of a certain aspect of the oscillator hypothesis, and had either ignored all the other discrepancies of this model, or deliberately left them in obscurity. Thus he had simply not taken his hypothesis in real earnest. In the same way, I fear that the quark hypothesis is just not taken seriously by its exponents. The questions about the statistics of quarks, about the forces that hold them together, about the particles corresponding to these forces, about the reasons why quarks never appear as free particles, about the pair-creation of quarks in the interior of the elementary particle—all these questions are more or less left in obscurity. If there was a desire to take the quark hypothesis in real earnest, it would be necessary to make a precise mathematical approach to the dynamics of quarks, and the forces that hold them together,

and to show that, qualitatively at least, this approach can reproduce correctly the many different features of particle physics that are known today. There should be no question in particle physics to which this approach could not be applied. Such attempts are not known to me, and I am afraid, also, that every such attempt which is presented in precise mathematical language would be very quickly refutable. I shall therefore formulate my objections in the shape of questions: "Does the quark hypothesis really contribute more to understanding of the particle spectrum, than the Voigtian hypothesis of oscillators contributed, in its day, to understanding of the structure of atomic shells?" "Does there not still lurk behind the quark hypothesis the notion, long ago refuted by experiment, that we are able to distinguish simple and composite particles?"

28   I would now like to take up briefly a few questions of detail. If the SU_3 group plays an important part in the structure of the particle spectrum, and this we must assume on the basis of the experiments, then it is important to decide whether we are dealing with a fundamental symmetry of the underlying natural law, or with a dynamic symmetry, which from the onset can only have approximate validity. If this decision is left unclear, then all further assumptions about the dynamics underlying the spectrum also remain unclear, and then we can no longer understand anything. In the higher symmetrics, such as SU_4, SU_6, SU_{12}, $SU_2 \infty SU_2$ and so on, we are very probably dealing with dynamic symmetries, which can be of use in the phenomenology; but their heuristic value could be compared, in my view, with that of the cycles and epicycles in Ptolemaic astronomy. They permit only very indirect back-inferences to the structure of the underlying natural law.

29   Finally, a word more about the most important experimental findings of recent years. Bosons of relatively high mass, in the region of 3–4 GeV, and of long lifetime, have lately been discovered. Such states are basically quite to be expected, as Dürr in particular has emphasized. Whether, owing to the peculiarity of their long lifetime, they can be regarded to some degree as composed of other already known long-lived particles, is, of course, a difficult dynamical question, in which the whole complexity of many-particle physics becomes operative. To me, however, it would appear a quite needless speculation, to attempt the introduction of further new particles *ad hoc*, of which the objects in question are to consist. For this would again be that misstatement of the question, which makes no contribution to the understanding of the spectrum.

30   Again, in the storage-rings at Geneva, and in the Batavia machine, the total action cross-sections for proton–proton collisions at very high energies have been measured. It has turned out that the cross-sections increase as the square of the logarithm of the energy, an effect already long ago surmised, in theory, for the asymptotic region. These results, which have also been found, meanwhile, in the collision of other particles, make it probable, therefore, that in the big accelerators the asymptotic region has already been reached, and hence that there, too, we no longer have any surprises to expect.

31   Quite generally, in new experiments, we should not hope for a *deus ex machina* that will suddenly make the spectrum of particles intelligible. For the experiments of the last fifty years already give a qualitatively quite satisfying, noncontradictory, and closed answer to the question "What is an elementary particle?" Much as in quantum chemistry, the quantitative details can be clarified, not suddenly, but only by much physical and mathematical precision-work over the years.

32   Hence I can conclude with an optimistic look ahead to developments in particle physics which seem to me to give promise of success. New experimental findings are always valuable, of course, even when at first they merely enlarge the tabulated record; but they are especially interesting when they answer critical questions of theory. In theory, we

shall have to endeavor, without any semi-philosophical preconceptions, to make precise assumptions concerning the underlying dynamics of matter. This must be taken with complete seriousness, and we should not, therefore, be content with vague hypotheses, in which most things are left obscure. For the particle spectrum can be understood only if we know the underlying dynamics of matter; it is the dynamics that count. All else would be merely a sort of word-painting based on the tabulated record, and in that case the record itself would doubtless be more informative than the word-painting.

NOTES AND DISCUSSION

"What Is an Elementary Particle?" is a model of clear writing; Heisenberg is firmly in control of his material from the start. Notice how the first paragraph embodies the elements of the classic opening paragraph by clearly and succinctly identifying and labelling the aims and various sections of the piece. The first section of the essay deals with "the experimental facts" and is marked by a very careful chronological development, ending with the statements, "The difference between elementary and composite particles has thus basically disappeared. And that is no doubt the most important experimental finding of the last fifty years." The second section, as promised, elaborates some of the complications and implications—for both classical and quantum physics—that arise from that finding. The third section specifically addresses "the philosophy by which the physics of elementary particles is consciously or unconsciously guided."

At a pivotal point in the essay, Heisenberg acknowledges that "we cannot... avoid employing a language that stems from... traditional philosophy," which permits and even encourages "an intuitive description of small-scale chemical processes." However, traditional language and philosophy only define, and allow for, a way of thinking that is fundamentally wrong-headed when applied to quantum physics. The very questions that they promote "are wrongly put, since the words *divide* or *consist of* have largely lost their meaning." Science, for Heisenberg, is in some significant ways bounded and defined by language and its limits of expression. One of the essay's more arresting claims is that, for true scientific advances to be possible, "bad philosophy," ungrounded biases, and inadequate language must be overcome: an inadequate philosophy will condemn us to inadequate science.

Heisenberg claims, in part, that our language and therefore our ways of thinking have not really caught up to the experimental findings of particle physics. The essay concludes in this way: "For the particle spectrum can be understood only if we know the underlying dynamics of matter; it is the dynamics that count. All else would be merely a sort of word-painting based on the tabulated record, and in that case the record itself would doubtless be more informative than the word-painting." Heisenberg has thus identified a thorny problem: our language and our philosophy dictate the ways we think; the ways we think dictate our science; and our science has shown clearly that our language and philosophy are no longer adequate to describe where science is leading.

STUDY QUESTIONS

For Discussion

1. Heisenberg claims at the beginning of the essay that he will end on a "positive note," yet he seems to have described a logical circle. Do you see any obvious ways out of the difficulties that Heisenberg suggests we have fallen into?

2. In the course of his discussion, Heisenberg uses some very specific, very technical language and information, from both philosophy and physics. What conclusions can you draw about Heisenberg's assumed audience?

For Writing

1. One of the implications of Heisenberg's theories is that the borders between philosophy and physics, between the humanities and the sciences, have broken down. In a short essay compare and contrast the notions of science presented in this essay with those presented in this collection by one of the following writers: O. B. Hardison, Jay Ingram, Thomas Kuhn, or Cynthia Ozick.

2. Write a short essay, using definition as the principal rhetorical mode, to discuss Heisenberg's suggestion that "today in the physics of elementary particles, good physics is unconsciously being spoiled by bad philosophy." Be sure to offer definitions of both physics and philosophy.

MYTH AND
MALEVOLENCE

Michael Ignatieff

BIOGRAPHICAL NOTE

Michael Ignatieff has been a history professor at the University of British Columbia, and a research fellow of King's College, Cambridge. He is now a writer and broadcaster in London, England. His works include *The Russian Album* (1987), a family memoir that won the Governor General's Award for non-fiction, and *Blood and Belonging: Journeys into the New Nationalism* (1993).

1   In the summer of 1992, when Serbian militias were viciously "cleansing" the Muslim villages of southeastern Bosnia, journalists asked the Serbs of Foca and Goradze why people they had lived with for centuries deserved such treatment. The Serbs seemed surprised by the question. Didn't everybody know that Muslims killed Serbian children and floated their crucified bodies down the river Drina? Several old women, doing their washing by the riverbank, swore they had seen them with their own eyes.

2   No one could persuade these old women otherwise. They were in the grip of one of the oldest atrocity myths in Western culture. The Romans accused the early Christians of just this sort of child sacrifice. When the Christians got a state church of their own, they turned the same myth against the Jews. The earliest recorded accusation occurred in the English town of Norwich in 1144, when the Jewish community was accused of killing a Christian child and draining his blood for use in satanic rituals. In all its apparitions, the tortured or crucified child surfaces, like an image in a nightmare, whenever an ethnic or religious majority has to read into its subconscious to justify the persecution of a minority. As the millennium ends, Muslim Europeans find themselves the target of a myth that, when the millennium began, was a blood libel against the Jews.

3   Myths endure because they offer repertoires of moral justification. Myths turn crime into fate and murder into necessity; they both justify atrocity and perpetuate it. The Balkan wars have been among the most inhuman in an inhuman century. Intrastate wars, the war of village against village, neighbor against neighbor, will usually engender more atrocities than the impersonal wars between states. Small wonder that the three urban communities most thoroughly destroyed by the Balkan conflict—Vukovar, Mostar, and Sarajevo—had the highest rates of ethnic intermarriage.

4   It is as if the very intermingling of the combatants forced these communities into displays of terror and destruction to demarcate the territories and values they were defending. What Serbs once shared with their neighbors had to be defiled, so that sharing would never be possible again. Atrocities draw the innocent bystander into collusion with the guilty perpetrator and engrave the myth of inhuman otherness in the subconscious of both sides.

5   This myth of inhuman otherness does such violence to the facts that it can gain a foothold only if ordinary people on every side can be made to forget that in reality their differences are small. It is nonsense to call the Balkan communities ethnic groups at all. Intermarriage down the centuries has blurred ethnic differences to the vanishing point; religious differences have collapsed in the general secularization of Balkan culture; modernization has converged material aspirations toward the same Mercedes cars and Swiss-style chalets. Nationalism in the Balkans is what Freud called the narcissism of minor difference. Lies, demagoguery, and propaganda have turned permeable identities into bunkered mentalities. Serbs and Croats who once shared the same language are being told that Serbian and Croatian are as distinct as the Cyrillic and Latin scripts in which they are written. Nationalistic narcissism is a hothouse for atrocity myths that blossom forth in order to portray each community as the blameless victim of the motiveless malevolence of the other.

6   In the Balkans these myths collapse time. The past can never safely become the past. It remains immobilized in a neurotic, hysterical present. The very name each group gives the other locks both sides into a past that is a nightmare. Serbs call all Croatian fighters Ustase, the fascist minority of World War II Croatia. Croatians call the Serbs Chetniks, the fascist minority on the other side. The naming process is intended to visit the sins of the fathers upon the sons forever.

7   Renaming enemies rewrites the past so that their very identity can be expunged from history. The Bosnian Serbs assert that the Muslims don't really exist, since they are renegade Serbs who converted to Islam in order to gain land and privileges from their Ottoman overlords. Thorvald Stoltenberg, the former U.N. mediator, has been heard to repeat this preposterous fable. In other ways too the outside world ignorantly colludes in Balkan mythmaking. The Western fantasy that all Muslims are fanatics and all Islam is fundamentalist underwrites the Serbs' myth that they, like the Christian host turning back the Turks at the gates of Vienna in 1683, are holding the Islamic tide from Europe's southern flank.

8   There is no easy awakening from the nightmare of their history. But outsiders can do something to break the demonic hold of myth. War-crimes tribunals and human-rights commissions are not the irrelevance they seem. Their function is to plunge the burning coals of myth into the icy bath of evidence; to hold the remaining ember of truth aloft for all to see; to show that history never justifies crime; and to teach people that they need truth as much as they need peace, and can't hope to get one without the other.

NOTES AND DISCUSSION

Michael Ignatieff illustrates in grotesque detail the abuse of language that groups in power may resort to in order to stay in power; he also demonstrates the effects of this abuse. Ignatieff opens with an example of euphemism: the word "cleansing," which substitutes for "genocide." Later, he discusses the purposes and effects of name-calling in human affairs. Interestingly, he himself seems to use the word "myth" euphemistically, sometimes to mean "fantasy," sometimes to mean "legend," and frequently to mean "lies and propaganda."

Ignatieff's primary focus is a recent example of one particular atrocity myth that has been a propaganda tool throughout Western history. He uses the cause-and-effect and process analysis methods to explain how myths become "necessary" and are employed to "justify" atrocity, particularly in the "narcissistic" realm of modern nationalism. As language, such myths are a form of violence in themselves, and can lead to violence of a bloodier kind.

Note as well the intense figurative language Ignatieff uses in his conclusion. In a piece that looks at how some language never gets a chance to become stale, Ignatieff's metaphors might seem flamboyant and sensational; but then, maybe a plea such as his for truth and sanity in such extreme circumstances needs to be made in extreme language.

STUDY QUESTIONS

For Discussion

1. Ignatieff calls on outsiders to intervene to settle bloody local feuds, since they are uncontaminated by local myths. Are outsiders necessarily less contaminated? Might not imported myths become just as dangerous in such emotionally charged conflicts? For example, what role might the religion of a "peace-keeping" force play?

2. Look up Freud's analysis of the Narcissus myth, as well as the classical account of the myth (from Ovid's *Metamorphoses*). Note in particular Freud's use of "narcissism of minor differences." Think about the ways Freud has adapted the classical myth of Narcissus, which is itself a cautionary tale. How has Ignatieff further adapted the myth through his appropriation of Freud?

For Writing

1. One of the practices Ignatieff alludes to is the use of euphemism—replacing an ugly word with a prettier one to hide or to glorify reality. He draws attention to the word "cleansing" when used to refer to genocide. Euphemism is part of the job of "renaming" that precedes and accompanies atrocities, or, in a less violent situation, an unpopular or risky political decision. Discuss this practice in relation to those that Orwell describes in "Shooting An Elephant," and look for some examples of these practices in the "political" vocabulary of your own local or national government.

2. Are you aware of other myths that are used to excuse the persecution of unwanted members of a population, or to define another group of people as less than human or as unworthy of humane treatment? Relate one or two such myths, and explain how they make the unpleasant and irresponsible seem "natural." Be specific, both about the myth itself and about its ramifications.

(This analysis need not refer to "society" in general, but could refer to a myth or story circulating within a group you are part of, or excluded from. For example, numerous "urban myths" of random violence caution us against various criminal elements. These are myths because they are not borne out by crime statistics, but serve to keep people on edge and on the defensive.)

THE ATOM'S IMAGE PROBLEM

Jay Ingram

BIOGRAPHICAL NOTE

Jay Ingram is a science writer and broadcaster. He may be best known to Canadians as the former host of CBC Radio's science program "Quirks and Quarks." He is the author of several books on science and everyday life and the co-host of *@discovery.ca*, a daily science news magazine on television's Discovery Channel. He also writes a column for *Equinox* magazine, from which this essay is taken.

---

1 What do you envision when you hear the word *atom*? I bet if you see anything at all it is a miniature solar system, with the nucleus of the atom as the sun, and tiny electrons whirling planetlike around it. And why not? A stylized version of this has long been synonymous with atomic power. It's probably the atom you saw in public school and is, indeed, a model rooted in science. The science is, however, a little out of date—by at least 70 years. If you try to redraw the atom as scientists imagine it today, it is transformed. What was solid becomes wispy and foggy, what was compact becomes vast, and, most important of all, what was predictable is not.

2 This revolution in the concept of the atom was largely accomplished in a few years of incredible scientific progress during the 1920s. So why are we nonscientists so out of date in our mental image of the atom? Is it because atomic science is so incompatible with everyday experience that we simply can't form and hold an image of it?

3 In his 1928 book *The Nature of the Physical World*, the great English astrophysicist Sir Arthur Eddington cast his eye back to the nineteenth century and said, "It was the boast of the Victorian physicist that he would not claim to understand a thing until he could make a model of it; and by a model he meant something constructed of levers, geared wheels,

First published in *Equinox*, no. 87, June 1996. Reprinted by permission of the author.

squirts, or other appliances familiar to an engineer." I suspect that most of us, if we are physicists at all, are Victorian. And I wonder if the Victorian physicists Eddington described weren't revealing something about human psychology that holds for most of us today.

4   By the time Eddington published his book, the solar-system model of the atom had already been out of favour for two years, replaced by the infinitely more challenging imagery of quantum mechanics. In fact, the solar-system atom, for all its hold on the popular imagination, held sway among scientists for little more than a decade. In that sense, it takes its place beside the cowboy: the Wild West has had much greater staying power in popular culture than it did in reality.

5   However brief the scientific reign of the solar-system atom, its beginnings were honest. In 1911 Ernest Rutherford made public the experiment that set the stage for its appearance. When he aimed highly energized subatomic particles at thin sheets of gold foil, he was shocked to see that in some cases the particles bounced right back. Rutherford said, "It was almost as incredible as if you had fired a 15-inch shell at a piece of tissue paper and it came back and hit you." Rutherford concluded that the atoms of gold in the sheet couldn't be likened (as had been suggested) to miniature raisin buns—blobs of positive electrical charge stuffed with tiny negative charges. Instead, the positive charge had to be intensely concentrated at a point inside the atom. Only such a compact object could deflect the particles Rutherford had aimed at it. He didn't go so far as to limit the outer negative charges (the electrons) to precise orbits, and in that sense he was more in tune with the modern vision of the atom.

6   However, in 1912, shortly after this experiment, the Danish physicist Niels Bohr came to work with Rutherford, and by 1913 he put the electrons firmly in orbits about the nucleus. In doing so, Bohr solved what had been a major problem in previous theories: classical physics had predicted that as electrons circled in orbits, they would steadily radiate away their energy; as this happened, their orbits would decay and they would eventually spiral into the nucleus like satellites reentering the earth's atmosphere. In one scientist's words, "matter would incandesce and collapse." Bohr argued that continuous processes such as radiating energy and decaying orbits were out-of-date concepts, failing to capture the inner workings of the atom. He suggested that electrons were restricted to certain stable orbits, in which they could move without loss of energy, and could only jump from one to another by emitting or absorbing a packet, or quantum, of energy.

7   So by the beginning of World War I, the solar-system atom was in place, but by the mid-1920s, it was gone. It couldn't withstand the brilliant onslaught of experimentation and thought that swept through physics in Europe during that decade. A who's who of science repainted our portrait of the atom, even if we haven't noticed. Perhaps the most radical change was that, as seen from the quantum-theory point of view, such particles as electrons could behave as waves. So Erwin Schrödinger, an Austrian-born Irish physicist, was able to dispense with the precise orbits of the electrons, filling the same space with waves radiating outward from the nucleus, the peaks of which corresponded to the now-defunct orbits. Max Born, a theoretical physicist, altered that idea slightly by claiming that the waves' peaks didn't really show where electrons were but, rather, where they might be.

8   In 1927 German physicist Werner Heisenberg elevated that sense of uncertainty into a principle, called (guess what?) Heisenberg's Uncertainty Principle. He established that it was not just difficult but literally impossible to pinpoint both the position and the momentum (or velocity) of an electron at the same time—the very act of measurement would inevitably disturb the object being measured. In physics, the relationship has mathematical

precision: you can know where the electron is, but then you don't know where it's going; if you endeavour to detect where it's going, you lose track of where it is. Is it any wonder that the solar-system model of the atom was trashed? It was replaced by a dissonant sort of picture—in tune with physicists' thinking but out of tune with the rest of us.

9　　　In today's atom, the electrons are still there outside the nucleus (although they often venture perilously close to it), but they are represented not by miniplanets but by probabilities, clouds of likelihood that suggest, "this is where you might find it." Sometimes there are gaps in those clouds—places forbidden to electrons, yet these seem to present no barrier to the electrons' ability to materialize, first on one side of the gap, then on the other.

10　　　There's also the nucleus, the image of which has evolved from a tightly bound cluster of protons and neutrons to something that might be like a drop of liquid, spinning, pulsating, and quivering with the movements of the particles inside. Or it might be more like a series of Russian doll-like shells, nestled one inside the other. And as important as the nucleus is, it occupies only a minuscule fraction of the total size of the atom.

11　　　It has always struck me that physicists and chemists are, for the most part, perfectly happy to think of and talk about the atom as the sum of a set of equations. I'm sure they all believe these equations represent something in the real world, but it is probably not possible any more to say exactly what. The indeterminate and unknowable have replaced precision and prediction.

12　　　That's fine if you're a physicist—it's necessary—but it doesn't work very well for the rest of us. We don't have the language and skills to understand the atom as math; we need a model that squares with intuition. Clouds of probability don't; balls moving in orbits do.

13　　　Much is made these days of the idea that we are coping with the twentieth century equipped with only a Stone Age hunter-gatherer brain. It follows, then, that the brain should be particularly skilled at doing things useful for hunter-gatherers. Imagination is certainly one of those skills, but imagination of what? Of solid, substantial objects moving around each other in regular fashion? Or of pointlike particles that can't be localized and that behave like waves and move in strange and unpredictable ways?

14　　　And why should you care what the atom is like? If you are at all interested in the natural world, you have to care. The atom isn't just another feature of nature—it *is* nature. Unfortunately, the solar-system atom was likely about as much as we could handle in concrete conceptual terms. When scientists left the concept behind forever in the 1920s, it seems they left the rest of us behind too. They have their mathematical atom to contemplate. We have only our mental pictures.

NOTES AND DISCUSSION

Ingram's subject in this essay is in some ways the same as Heisenberg's in "What Is an Elementary Particle?", but Ingram's approach is very different. He spends the length of the essay trying to destroy an analogy and create an alternative—the essay hinges on a series of analogies, metaphors, images, and similes—in order to make concrete and imaginable some of the abstract concepts of modern particle science. Even he admits that these concepts may, finally, be too complex to articulate in the terms that he is using.

Ingram gives several metaphors and similes to try to capture the essence of electrons and the nucleus of an atom: the electrons are "clouds of likelihood"; the nucleus is "like a drop of liquid" or "like a series of Russian doll-like shells." He tries hard to find an analogy, a metaphor, a simile, or an image that will capture what he wants to say, but nothing can do justice to the conceptual complexities. Analogies are powerful tools, but they also can lead to serious misconceptions. Note that Ingram begins his essay with an example of a wildly inaccurate image that, he claims, has stubbornly stayed fixed in popular conceptions of the atom; in fact, it is the image that is used to denote atomic power. However, Ingram's difficulty may be the result of an inaccurate assumption: he seems to claim that having an image of something is the same as having an understanding of that thing. He writes, towards the end of the essay, that "we need a model that squares with intuition." In comparison, see Heisenberg's essay about elementary particles, and note that Heisenberg makes no effort to construct mental pictures for his readers. Ingram may, in fact, be trying to do something that is just not possible.

STUDY QUESTIONS

For Discussion

1. Consider your beliefs about and understanding of atoms. Is your understanding of the atom contingent on a mental "image"? Notice Ingram's final two sentences: "They have their mathematical atom to contemplate. We have only our mental pictures." Discuss Ingram's assumption that part of understanding something is having "mental pictures" of it.

2. Examine Ingram's apparent belief that the relationship of "scientists" (especially physicists) to "the rest of us" is an "us vs. them" relationship. Compare and contrast the image of the scientist presented here with the one in Stephen Jay Gould's "The Monster's Human Nature."

For Writing

1. In an essay, compare and contrast Ingram's essay with Heisenberg's "What Is an Elementary Particle?" Describe what, specifically, are the strengths and weaknesses of each approach.

2. Ingram works largely from analogies, metaphors, and similes in this piece. Write an analogy of your own that tries to capture in an appropriate image something that is very complex.

CLONE MAMMALS. . . CLONE MAN?

Axel Kahn

BIOGRAPHICAL NOTE

Axel Kahn is director of the INSERM (Institut National de la Santé et de la Recherche de Molecule) laboratory of Research on Genetics and Molecular Pathology at the Cochin Institute of Molecular Genetics in Paris, France.

1   The experiments of I. Wilmut et al. (*Nature* 385, 810; 1997) demonstrate that sheep embryonic eggs (oocytes) can reprogramme the nuclei of differentiated cells, enabling the cells to develop into any type. The precise conditions under which this process can occur remain to be elucidated; the factors determining the success of the technique, and the long-term prospects for animals generated in this way, still need to be established. But, of course, the main point is that Wilmut et al. show that it is now possible to envisage cloning of adult mammals in a completely asexual fashion.

2   The oocyte's only involvement is the role of its cytoplasm in reprogramming the introduced nucleus and in contributing intracellular organelles—mainly mitochondria—to the future organism. This work will undoubtedly open up new perspectives in research in biology and development, for example, in understanding the functional plasticity of the genome and chromatin during development, and the mechanisms underlying the stability of differentiated states. Another immediate question is to ask whether a species barrier exists. Could an embryo be produced, for example, by implanting the nucleus of a lamb in an enucleated mouse oocyte? Any lambs born in this way would possess a mouse mitochondrial genome.

3   The implications for humans are staggering. One example is that the technique suggests that a woman suffering from a serious mitochondrial disease might in future be

able to produce children free of the disease by having the nucleus of her embryo implanted in a donor oocyte (note that this process is not the same as "cloning").

Would Cloning Humans Be Justified?

4   But the main question raised by the paper by Wilmut et al. is that of the possibility of human cloning. There is no *a priori* reason why humans should behave very differently from other mammals where cloning is possible, so the cloning of an adult human could become feasible using the techniques reported.

5   What medical and scientific "justification" might there be for cloning? Previous debates have identified the preparation of immuno-compatible differentiated cell lines for transplantation, as one potential indication. We could imagine everyone having their own reserve of therapeutic cells that would increase their chance of being cured of various diseases, such as cancer, degenerative disorders, and viral or inflammatory diseases.

6   But the debate has in the past perhaps paid insufficient attention to the current strong social trend towards a fanatical desire for individuals not simply to have children but to ensure that these children also carry their genes. Achieving such biological descendance was impossible for sterile men until the development of ICSI (intracytoplasmic sperm injection), which allows a single sperm to be injected directly into the oocyte.

7   But human descendance is not only biological, as it is in all other species, but is also emotional and cultural. The latter is of such importance that methods of inheritance where both parents' genes are not transmitted—such as adoption and insemination with donor sperm—are widely accepted without any major ethical questions being raised.

8   But today's society is characterized by an increasing demand for biological inheritance, as if this were the only desirable form of inheritance. Regrettably, a person's personality is increasingly perceived as being largely determined by his or her genes. Moreover, in a world where culture is increasingly internationalized and homogenized, people may ask themselves whether they have anything else to transmit to their children apart from their genes. This pressure probably accounts for the wide social acceptance of ICSI, a technique which was widely made available to people at a time when experimental evidence as to its safety was still flimsy. ICSI means that men with abnormal sperm can now procreate.

9   Going further upstream, researchers have now succeeded in fertilizing a mouse oocyte using a diploid nucleus of a spermatogonium: apparently normal embryonic development occurs, at least in the early stages. But there are also severe forms of sterility—such as dysplasia or severe testicular atrophy—or indeed lesbian couples, where no male germ line exists. Will such couples also demand the right to a biological descendance?

10   Applying the technique used by Wilmut et al. in sheep directly to humans would yield a clone "of the father" and not a shared descendant of both the father and mother. Nevertheless, for a woman the act of carrying a fetus can be as important as being its biological mother. The extraordinary power of such "maternal reappropriation" of the embryo can be seen from the strong demand for pregnancies in post-menopausal women, and for embryo and oocyte donations to circumvent female sterility. Moreover, if cloning techniques were ever to be used, the mother would be contributing something—her mitochondrial genome. We cannot exclude the possibility that the current direction of public opinion will tend to legitimize the resort to cloning techniques in cases where, for example, the male partner in a couple is unable to produce gametes.

11   The creation of human clones solely for spare cell lines would, from a philosophical point of view, be in obvious contradiction to an ethical principle expressed by Immanuel Kant: that of human dignity. This principle demands that an individual—and I would extend this to read human life—should never be thought of only as a means, but always also as an end. Creating human life for the sole purpose of preparing therapeutic material would clearly not be for the dignity of the life created.

12   Analysing the use of cloning as a means of combating sterility is much more difficult, as the explicit goal is to create a life with the right to dignity. Moreover, individuals are not determined entirely by their genome, as of course the family, cultural, and social environment have a powerful "humanizing" influence on the construction of a personality. Two human clones born decades apart would be much more different psychologically than identical twins raised in the same family.

Threat of Human "Creators"

13   Nonetheless, part of the individuality and dignity of a person probably lies in the uniqueness and unpredictability of his or her development. As a result, the uncertainty of the great lottery of heredity constitutes the principal protection against biological predetermination imposed by third parties, including parents. One blessing of the relationship between parents and children is their inevitable difference, which results in parents loving their children for what they are, rather than trying to make them what they want. Allowing cloning to circumvent sterility would lead to it being tolerated in cases where it was imposed, for example, by authorities. What would the world be like if we accepted that human "creators" could assume the right to generate creatures in their own likeness, beings whose very biological characteristics would be subjugated to an outside will?

14   The results of Wilmut et al. undoubtedly have much merit. One effect of them is to oblige us to face up to our responsibilities. It is not a technical barrier that will protect us from the perspectives I have mentioned, but a moral one, originating from a reflection of the basis of our dignity. That barrier is certainly the most dignified aspect of human genius.

This article is a slightly edited version of a commentary first published on *Nature's* Web site on February 27, 1997.

NOTES AND DISCUSSION

This essay responds to the publication of the paper "Viable Offspring Derived from Fetal and Adult Mammalian Cells" by Ian Wilmut et al., which appeared in *Nature* on February 27, 1997, and which is included in this anthology. You may wish to read the Wilmut essay in conjunction with Kahn's response. The appearance of "Viable Offspring" in *Nature* prompted significant media coverage. Dolly, the cloned sheep, became a minor celebrity; President Clinton asked the White House Bioethics Commission to investigate the implications of this "stunning" research.

     Kahn's essay is in three distinct parts. He begins by summarizing and reiterating the central results of Wilmut's study in more common language and terminology. He also briefly suggests that Wilmut's work may have implications and applications in fields other than that of human cloning. However, in the second section of the essay, it becomes clear that *human* cloning is Kahn's focus. Consider what tone and meaning he implies by punctuating the word "justification." This essay is a personal response to a complicated ethical issue. Notice how

Kahn uses generalized statements and claims, standard transitional words and phrases, and rhetorical questions to advance his opinion rapidly and forcefully.

The essay compares and contrasts different visions of humanity and its need to procreate and nurture its young. Clearly, in discussing cloning, Kahn enters into the on-going debate over "nature vs. nurture": he reflects on what creates identity and family, thus making cloning not simply a remote issue grounded in ethical and scientific debates, but an area of more immediate interest to a general readership. The essay's title contains the word "man," although its subtitle and content use the more neutral and collective "humankind" or "humanity." Consider why "man" might have been chosen for the title.

Toward the essay's conclusion, Kahn uses the first person "I," further personalizing his argument. He concludes that the decisions involved in cloning are not just technical and scientific, but are a collective moral responsibility.

STUDY QUESTIONS

For Discussion

1. Identify and then compare and contrast the different visions of humanity, and the need to procreate and nurture its young, that Kahn's essay presents.

2. Identify the transitional words and phrases Kahn uses to structure his argument. Then examine and describe the organizational and rhetorical impact these words and phrases have on the essay's overall structure and the success of its argument.

For Writing

1. Read the essay by Wilmut et al. that inspired this essay. Analyze what Kahn has interpreted and extrapolated from Wilmut's report and decide which of his conclusions seem valid and which do not. Be sure to fully explain the reasons behind your decisions.

2. Research some of the ethical debates surrounding cloning. Explain in detail, through references to specific articles and authors, whether Kahn is justified in suggesting that "the debate has in the past perhaps paid insufficient attention to the current strong social trend towards a fanatical desire for individuals not simply to have children but to ensure that these children also carry their genes."

WHY JOHNNY CAN'T THINK

Walter Karp

BIOGRAPHICAL NOTE

Walter Karp (1934–89) produced eight books and over two hundred articles during his passionate writing career. His twin obsessions were American politics and history.

1   Until very recently, remarkably little was known about what actually goes on in America's public schools. There were no reliable answers to even the most obvious questions. How many children are taught to read in overcrowded classrooms? How prevalent is rote learning and how common are classroom discussions? Do most schools set off gongs to mark the change of "periods"? Is it a common practice to bark commands over public address systems in the manner of army camps, prisons, and banana republics? Public schooling provides the only intense experience of a public realm that most Americans will ever know. Are school buildings designed with the dignity appropriate to a great republican institution, or are most of them as crummy-looking as one's own?

2   The darkness enveloping America's public schools is truly extraordinary considering that 38.9 million students attend them, that we spend nearly $134 billion a year on them, and that foundations ladle out generous sums for the study of everything about schooling—except what really occurs in the schools. John I. Goodlad's eight-year investigation of a mere thirty-eight of America's 80,000 public schools—the result of which, *A Place Called School* (McGraw-Hill, 1984), was published last year—is the most comprehensive study ever undertaken. Hailed as a "landmark in American educational research," it was financed with great difficulty. The darkness, it seems, has its guardians.

3   Happily, the example of Goodlad, a former dean of UCLA's Graduate School of Education, has proven contagious. A flurry of new books shed considerable light on the

practice of public education in America. In *The Good High School* (Basic Books, 1985), Sara Lawrence Lightfoot offers vivid "portraits" of six distinctive American secondary schools. In *Horace's Compromise* (Houghton Mifflin, 1985), Theodore R. Sizer, a former dean of Harvard's Graduate School of Education, reports on his two-year odyssey through public high schools around the country. Even *High School* (Harper & Row, 1985), a white paper issued by Ernest L. Boyer and the Carnegie Foundation for the Advancement of Teaching, is supported by a close investigation of the institutional life of a number of schools. Of the books under review, only *A Nation at Risk* (U.S. Government Printing Office, 1984), the report of the Reagan Administration's National Commission on Excellence in Education, adheres to the established practice of crass special pleading in the dark.

4   Thanks to Goodlad et al., it is now clear what the great educational darkness has so long concealed: the depth and pervasiveness of political hypocrisy in the common schools of the country. The great ambition professed by public school managers is, of course, education for citizenship and self-government, which harks back to Jefferson's historic call for "general education to enable every man to judge for himself what will secure or endanger his freedom." What the public schools practice with remorseless proficiency, however, is the prevention of citizenship and the stifling of self-government. When 58 percent of the thirteen-year-olds tested by the National Assessment for Educational Progress think it is against the law to start a third party in America, we are dealing not with a sad educational failure but with a remarkably subtle success.

5   Consider how effectively America's future citizens are trained not to judge for themselves about anything. From the first grade to the twelfth, from one coast to the other, instruction in America's classrooms is almost entirely dogmatic. Answers are "right" and answers are "wrong," but mostly answers are short. "At all levels, [teacher-made] tests called almost exclusively for short answers and recall of information," reports Goodlad. In more than a thousand classrooms visited by his researchers, "only *rarely*" was there "evidence to suggest instruction likely to go much beyond mere possession of information to a level of understanding its implications." Goodlad goes on to note that "the intellectual terrain is laid out by the teacher. The paths for walking through it are largely predetermined by the teacher." The give-and-take of genuine discussion is conspicuously absent. "Not even 1%" of institutional time, he found, was devoted to discussions that "required some kind of open response involving reasoning or perhaps an opinion from students.... The extraordinary degree of student passivity stands out."

6   Sizer's research substantiates Goodlad's. "No more important finding has emerged from the inquiries of our study than that the American high school student, *as student*, is all too often docile, compliant, and without initiative." There is good reason for this. On the one hand, notes Sizer, "there are too few rewards for being inquisitive." On the other, the heavy emphasis on "the right answer... smothers the student's efforts to become an effective intuitive thinker."

7   Yet smothered minds are looked on with the utmost complacency by the educational establishment—by the Reagan Department of Education, state boards of regents, university education departments, local administrators, and even many so-called educational reformers. Teachers are neither urged to combat the tyranny of the short right answer nor trained to do so. "Most teachers simply do not know how to teach for higher levels of thinking," says Goodlad. Indeed, they are actively discouraged from trying to do so.

8   The discouragement can be quite subtle. In their orientation talks to new, inexperienced teachers, for example, school administrators often indicate that they do not much

care what happens in class so long as no noise can be heard in the hallway. This thinly veiled threat virtually ensures the prevalence of short-answer drills, workbook exercises, and the copying of long extracts from the blackboard. These may smother young minds, but they keep the classroom quiet.

9   Discouragement even calls itself reform. Consider the current cry for greater use of standardized student tests to judge the "merit" of teachers and raise "academic standards." If this fake reform is foisted on the schools, dogma and docility will become even more prevalent. This point is well made by Linda Darling-Hammond of the Rand Corporation in an essay in *The Great School Debate* (Simon & Schuster, 1985). Where "important decisions are based on test scores," she notes, "teachers are more likely to teach to the tests" and less likely to bother with "nontested activities, such as writing, speaking, problem-solving, or real reading of books." The most influential promoter of standardized tests is the "excellence" brigade in the Department of Education; so clearly one important meaning of "educational excellence" is greater proficiency in smothering students' efforts to think for themselves.

10   Probably the greatest single discouragement to better instruction is the overcrowded classroom. The Carnegie report points out that English teachers cannot teach their students how to write when they must read and criticize the papers of as many as 175 students. As Sizer observes, genuine discussion is possible only in small seminars. In crowded classrooms, teachers have difficulty imparting even the most basic intellectual skills, since they have no time to give students personal attention. The overcrowded classroom inevitably debases instruction, yet it is the rule in America's public schools. In the first three grades of elementary school, Goodlad notes, the average class has twenty-seven students. High school classes range from twenty-five to forty students, according to the Carnegie report.

11   What makes these conditions appalling is that they are quite unnecessary. The public schools are top-heavy with administrators and rife with sinecures. Large numbers of teachers scarcely ever set foot in a classroom, being occupied instead as grade advisers, career counselors, "coordinators," and supervisors. "Schools, if simply organized," Sizer writes, "can have well-paid faculty and fewer than eighty students per teacher [sixteen students per class] without increasing current per-pupil expenditure." Yet no serious effort is being made to reduce class size. As Sizer notes, "Reducing teacher load is, when all the negotiating is over, a low agenda item for the unions and school boards." Overcrowded classrooms virtually guarantee smothered minds, yet the subject is not even mentioned in *A Nation at Risk*, for all its well-publicized braying about a "rising tide of mediocrity."

12   Do the nation's educators really want to teach almost 40 million students how to "think critically," in the Carnegie report's phrase, and "how to judge for themselves," in Jefferson's? The answer is, if you can believe that you will believe anything. The educational establishment is not even content to produce passive minds. It seeks passive spirits as well. One effective agency for producing these is the overly populous school. The larger schools are, the more prison-like they tend to be. In such schools, guards man the stairwells and exits. ID cards and "passes" are examined at checkpoints. Bells set off spasms of anarchy and bells quell the student mob. PA systems interrupt regularly with trivial fiats and frivolous announcements. This "malevolent intruder," in Sizer's apt phrase, is truly ill willed, for the PA system is actually an educational tool. It teaches the huge student mass to respect the authority of disembodied voices and the rule of remote and invisible agencies. Sixty-three percent of all high school students in America attend schools with enrollments of five thousand or more. The common excuse for these mobbed schools is economy, but in fact they cannot be shown to save taxpayers a penny. Large schools "tend

to create passive and compliant students," notes Robert B. Hawkins, Jr., in an essay in *The Challenge to American Schools* (Oxford University Press, 1987). That is their chief reason for being.

13   "How can the relatively passive and docile roles of students prepare them to participate as informed, active, and questioning citizens?" asks the Carnegie report, in discussing the "hidden curriculum" of passivity in the schools. The answer is, they were not meant to. Public schools introduce future citizens to the public world, but no introduction could be more disheartening. Architecturally, public school buildings range from drab to repellent. They are often disfigured by demoralizing neglect—"cracked sidewalks, a shabby lawn, and peeling paint on every window sash," to quote the Carnegie report. Many big-city elementary schools have numbers instead of names, making them as coldly dispiriting as possible.

14   Public schools stamp out republican sentiment by habituating their students to unfairness, inequality, and special privilege. These arise inevitably from the educational establishment's long-standing policy (well described by Diane Ravitch in *The Troubled Crusade* [Basic Books, 1985]) of maintaining "the correlation between social class and educational achievement." In order to preserve that factitious "correlation," public schooling is rigged to favor middle-class students and to ensure that working-class students do poorly enough to convince them that they fully merit the lowly station that will one day be theirs. "Our goal is to get these kids to be like their parents," one teacher, more candid than most, remarked to a Carnegie researcher.

15   For more than three decades, elementary schools across the country practiced a "progressive" non-phonetic method of teaching reading that had nothing much to recommend it save its inherent social bias. According to Ravitch, this method favored "children who were already motivated and prepared to begin reading" before entering school, while making learning to read more difficult for precisely those children whose parents were ill-read or ignorant. The advantages enjoyed by the well-bred were thus artificially multiplied tenfold, and 23 million adult Americans are today "functional illiterates." America's educators, notes Ravitch, have "never actually accepted full responsibility for making all children literate."

16   That describes a malicious intent a trifle too mildly. Reading is the key to everything else in school. Children who struggle with it in the first grade will be "grouped" with the slow readers in the second grade and will fall hopelessly behind in all subjects by the sixth. The schools hasten this process of falling behind, report Goodlad and others, by giving the best students the best teachers and struggling students the worst ones. "It is ironic," observes the Carnegie report, "that those who need the most help get the least." Such students are commonly diagnosed as "culturally deprived" and so are blamed for the failures inflicted on them. Thus they are taught to despise themselves even as they are inured to their inferior station.

17   The whole system of unfairness, inequality, and privilege comes to fruition in high school. There, some 15.7 million youngsters are formally divided into the favored few and the ill-favored many by the practice of "tracking." About 35 percent of America's public secondary-school students are enrolled in academic programs (often sub-divided into "gifted" and "non-gifted" tracks); the rest are relegated to some variety of non-academic schooling. Thus the tracking system, as intended, reproduces the divisions of the class system. "The honors programs," notes Sizer, "serve the wealthier youngsters, and the general tracks (whatever their titles) serve the working class. Vocational programs are often a cruel social dumping ground." The bottom-dogs are trained for jobs as auto

mechanics, cosmeticians, and institutional cooks, but they rarely get the jobs they are trained for. Pumping gasoline, according to the Carnegie report, is as close as an auto-mechanics major is likely to get to repairing a car. "Vocational education in the schools is virtually irrelevant to job fate," asserts Goodlad. It is merely the final hoax that the school bureaucracy plays on the neediest, one that the federal government has been promoting for seventy years.

18   The tracking system makes privilege and inequality blatantly visible to everyone. It creates under one roof "two worlds of schooling," to quote Goodlad. Students in academic programs read Shakespeare's plays. The commonality, notes the Carnegie report, are allowed virtually no contact with serious literature. In their English classes they practice filling out job applications. "Gifted" students alone are encouraged to think for themselves. The rest are subjected to sanctimonious wind, chiefly about "work habits" and "career opportunities."

19   "If you are a child of low-income parents," reports Sizer, "the chances are good that you will receive limited and often careless attention from adults in your high school. If you are the child of upper-middle-income parents, the chances are good that you will receive substantial and careful attention." In Brookline High School in Massachusetts, one of Lightfoot's "good" schools, a few fortunate students enjoy special treatment in their Advanced Placement classes. Meanwhile, students tracked into "career education" learn about "institutional cooking and clean-up" in a four-term Food Service course that requires them to mop up after their betters in the school cafeteria.

20   This wretched arrangement expresses the true spirit of public education in America and discloses the real aim of its hidden curriculum. A favored few, pampered and smiled upon, are taught to cherish privilege and despise the disfavored. The favorless many, who have majored in failure for years, are taught to think ill of themselves. Youthful spirits are broken to the world and every impulse of citizenship is effectively stifled. John Goodlad's judgment is severe but just: "There is in the gap between our highly idealistic goals for schooling in our society and the differentiated opportunities condoned and supported in schools a monstrous hypocrisy."

21   The public schools of America have not been corrupted for trivial reasons. Much would be different in a republic composed of citizens who could judge for themselves what secured or endangered their freedom. Every wielder of illicit or undemocratic power, every possessor of undue influence, every beneficiary of corrupt special privilege would find his position and tenure at hazard. Republican education is a menace to powerful, privileged, and influential people, and they in turn are a menace to republican education. That is why the generation that founded the public schools took care to place them under the suffrage of local communities, and that is why the corrupters of public education have virtually destroyed that suffrage. In 1932 there were 127,531 school districts in America. Today there are approximately 15,840 and they are virtually impotent, their proper role having been usurped by state and federal authorities. Curriculum and textbooks, methods of instruction, the procedures of the classroom, the organization of the school day, the cant, the pettifogging, and the corruption are almost uniform from coast to coast. To put down the menace of republican education its shield of local self-government had to be smashed, and smashed it was.

22   The public schools we have today are what the powerful and the considerable have made of them. They will not be redeemed by trifling reforms. Merit pay, a longer school year, more homework, special schools for "the gifted," and more standardized tests will not even begin to turn our public schools into nurseries of "informed, active, and questioning

citizens." They are not meant to. When the authors of *A Nation at Risk* call upon the schools to create an "educated work force," they are merely sanctioning the prevailing corruption, which consists precisely in the reduction of citizens to credulous workers. The education of a free people will not come from federal bureaucrats crying up "excellence" for "economic growth," any more than it came from their predecessors who cried up schooling as a means to "get a better job."

23   Only ordinary citizens can rescue the schools from their stifling corruption, for nobody else wants ordinary children to become questioning citizens at all. If we wait for the mighty to teach America's youth what secures or endangers their freedom, we will wait until the crack of doom.

NOTES AND DISCUSSION

Walter Karp's standard method of writing was to do what he called "investigative reading," that is, to read everything that he could find on a given topic, begin each essay with a brief summary of the facts, and analyze the topic by paying close attention to pertinent details that had been ignored in previous discussions of the problem.

This essay is an example of a well-developed argument. It has a strong, provocative thesis that is clearly stated, and it uses evidence from a variety of sources to support its position. The argument that there is something wrong with North American school systems is familiar, but Karp's thesis is a surprising reversal of that position: he goes beyond the idea that the education system is doing a bad job, to suggest that it is doing exactly the job it was designed to do.

STUDY QUESTIONS

For Discussion

1. What is Karp's thesis? How is that thesis defended in this essay?

2. Do you think it is true, as Karp claims, that "reading is the key to everything else in school"? Can you suggest any other possible keys? During your discussion, consider the essay's audience, especially in the context of Karp's closing "call to arms."

For Writing

1. Does Karp's description of schools agree with your own experience? Write a paragraph discussing whether you and your classmates come from the "gifted elite" of which Karp speaks.

2. Karp spends a good deal of time comparing various models of education. What is his preferred model? Would he draw any distinctions between the kinds of education science students usually receive and the kind humanities students do? In a short analytical essay, discuss the two different models of education.

INDIA

Perri Klass

BIOGRAPHICAL NOTE

Perri Klass is a pediatrician who attended Harvard Medical School. In addition to writing novels and collections of short stories, she has contributed essays to magazines and newspapers such as *Mademoiselle* and *The New York Times*. This essay is taken from a book about her years as a medical student, *A Not Entirely Benign Procedure* (1987).

---

1   *The people look different.* The examining room is crowded with children and their parents, gathered hopefully around the doctor's desk, jockeying for position. Everyone seems to believe, if the doctor gets close to *my* child everything will be okay. Several Indian medical students are also present, leaning forward to hear their professor's explanations as they watch one particular child walk across the far end of the room. I stand on my toes, straining to see over the intervening heads so I, too, can watch this patient walk. I can see her face, intent, bright dark eyes, lips pinched in concentration. She's about ten years old. I can see her sleek black head, the two long black braids pinned up in circles over her ears in the style we used to call doughnuts. All she's wearing is a long loose shirt, so her legs can be seen, as with great difficulty she wobbles across the floor. At the professor's direction, she sits down on the floor and then tries to get up again; she needs to use her arms to push her body up.

2   I'm confused. This patient looks like a child with absolutely classic muscular dystrophy, but muscular dystrophy is a genetic disease carried on the Y chromosome, like hemophilia. It therefore almost never occurs in girls. Can this be one of those one-in-a-trillion cases? Or is it a more unusual form of muscle disease, one that isn't sex-linked in inheritance?

3   Finally the child succeeds in getting up on her feet, and her parents come forward to help her dress. They pull her over near to where I'm standing, and as they're helping with the clothing, the long shirt slides up over the child's hips. No, this isn't one of those one-in-a-trillion cases. I've been watching a ten-year-old boy with muscular dystrophy; he comes from a Sikh family, and Sikh males don't cut their hair. Adults wear turbans, but young boys often have their hair braided and pinned up in those two knots.

4   Recently I spent some time in India, working in the pediatric department of an important New Delhi hospital. I wanted to learn about medicine outside the United States, to work in a pediatric clinic in the Third World, and I suppose I also wanted to test my own medical education, to find out whether my newly acquired skills are in fact transferable to any place where there are human beings, with human bodies, subject to their range of ills and evils.

5   But it wasn't just a question of my medical knowledge. In India, I found that my cultural limitations often prevented me from thinking clearly about patients. Everyone looked different, and I was unable to pick up any clues from their appearance, their manner of speech, their clothing. This is a family of Afghan refugees. This family is from the south of India. This child is from a very poor family. This child has a Nepalese name. All the clues I use at home to help me evaluate patients, clues ranging from what neighborhood they live in to what ethnic origin their names suggest, were hidden from me in India.

6   The people don't just look different on the outside, of course. It might be more accurate to say *the population is different*. The gene pool, for example: there are some genetic diseases that are much more common here than there, cystic fibrosis, say, which you have to keep in mind when evaluating patients in Boston, but which would be show-offy and highly unlikely diagnosis-out-of-a-book for a medical student to suggest in New Delhi (I know—in my innocence I suggested it).

7   And all of this, in the end, really reflects human diversity, though admittedly it's reflected in the strange warped mirror of the medical profession; it's hard to exult in the variety of human genetic defects, or even in the variety of human culture, when you're looking at it as a tool for examining a sick child. Still, I can accept the various implications of a world full of different people, different populations.

8   *The diseases are different.* The patient is a seven-year-old boy whose father says that over the past week and a half he has become more tired, less active, and lately he doesn't seem to understand everything going on around him. Courteously, the senior doctor turns to me, asks what my assessment is. He asks this in a tone that suggests that the diagnosis is obvious, and as a guest I'm invited to pronounce it. The diagnosis, whatever it is, is certainly not obvious to me. I can think of a couple of infections that might look like this, but no single answer. The senior doctor sees my difficulty and offers a maxim, one that I've heard many times back in Boston. Gently, slightly reprovingly, he tells me, "Common things occur commonly. There are many possibilities, of course, but I think it is safe to say that this is almost certainly tuberculous meningitis."

9   Tuberculous meningitis? Common things occur commonly? Somewhere in my brain (and somewhere in my lecture notes) "the complications of tuberculosis" are filed away, and yes, I suppose it can affect the central nervous system, just as I can vaguely remember that it can affect the stomach and the skeletal system.... To tell the truth, I've never even seen a case of straightforward tuberculosis of the lung in a small child, let alone what I would have thought of as a rare complication.

10   And hell, it's worse than that. I've done a fair amount of pediatrics back in Boston, but there are an awful lot of things I've never seen. When I was invited in New Delhi to give

an opinion on a child's rash, I came up with quite a creative list of tropical diseases, because guess what? I had never seen a child with measles before. In the United States, children are vaccinated against measles, mumps, and rubella at the age of one year. There are occasional outbreaks of measles among college students, but the disease is now very rare in small children. ("Love this Harvard medical student. Can't recognize tuberculous meningitis. Can't recognize measles or mumps. What the hell do they teach them over there in pediatrics?")

11   And this, of course, is one of the main medical student reasons for going to study abroad, the chance to see diseases you wouldn't see at home. The pathology, we call it, as in "I got to see some amazing pathology while I was in India." It's embarrassing to find yourself suddenly ignorant, but it's interesting to learn all about a new range of diagnoses, symptoms, treatments, all things you might have learned from a textbook and then immediately forgotten as totally outside your own experience.

12   The difficult thing is that these differences don't in any way, however tortured, reflect the glory of human variation. They reflect instead the sad partitioning of the species, because they're almost all preventable diseases, and their prevalence is a product of poverty, of lack of vaccinations, of malnutrition and poor sanitation. And therefore, though it's all very educational for the medical student (and I'm by now more or less used to parasitizing my education off of human suffering), this isn't a difference to be accepted without outrage.

13   *The expectations are different.* The child is a seven-month-old girl with diarrhea. She has been losing weight for a couple of weeks, she won't eat or drink, she just lies there in her grandmother's arms. The grandmother explains: one of her other grandchildren has just died from very severe diarrhea, and this little girl's older brother died last year, not of diarrhea but of a chest infection.... I look at the grandmother's face, at the faces of the baby's mother and father, who are standing on either side of the chair where the grandmother is sitting with the baby. All these people believe in the possibility of death, the chance that the child will not live to grow up. They've all seen many children die. These parents lost a boy last year, and they know that they may lose their daughter.

14   The four have traveled for almost sixteen hours to come to this hospital, because after the son died last year, they no longer have faith in the village doctor. They're hopeful, they offer their sick baby to this famous hospital. They're prepared to stay in Delhi while she's hospitalized, the mother will sleep in the child's crib with her, the father and grandmother may well sleep on the hospital grounds. They've brought food, cooking pots, warm shawls because it's January and it gets cold at night. They're tough, and they're hopeful, but they believe in the possibility of death.

15   Back home, in Boston, I've heard bewildered, grieving parents say, essentially, "Who would have believed that in the 1980s a child could just die like that?" Even parents with terminally ill children, children who spend months or years getting sicker and sicker, sometimes have great difficulty accepting that all the art and machinery of modern medicine are completely helpless. They expect every child to live to grow up.

16   In India, it isn't that parents are necessarily resigned, and certainly not that they love their children less. They may not want to accept the dangers, but poor people, people living in poor villages or in urban slums, know the possibility is there. If anything, they may be even more terrified than American parents, just because perhaps they're picturing the death of some other loved child, imagining this living child going the way of that dead one.

17   I don't know. This is a gap I can't cross. I can laugh at my own inability to interpret the signals of a different culture, and I can read and ask questions and slowly begin to learn

a little about the people I'm trying to help care for. I can blush at my ignorance of diseases uncommon in my home territory, study up in textbooks, and deplore inequalities that allow preventable diseases to ravage some unfortunate populations while others are protected. But I can't draw my lesson from this grandmother, these parents, this sick little girl. I can't imagine their awareness, their accommodations of what they know. I can't understand how they live with it. I can't accept their acceptance. My medical training has taken place in a world where all children are supposed to grow up, and the exceptions to this rule are rare horrible diseases, disastrous accidents. That is the attitude, the expectation I demand from patients. I'm left most disturbed not by the fact of children dying, not by the different diseases from which they die, or the differences in the medical care they receive, but by the way their parents look at me, at my profession. Perhaps it is only in this that I allow myself to take it all personally.

NOTES AND DISCUSSION

"India" is a comparison-and-contrast essay with a strong narrative component. It is a personal essay about the difficulties of experiencing "difference" first-hand. Note its striking stylistic features: the use of a vulnerable first person narrator, of italics as a structural device, and of frequent parenthetical asides and commentaries to the reader after some action has taken place.

Klass's essay is organized around a list of three "differences": "The people look different"; "The diseases are different"; "The expectations are different." Notice that these are all partial comparisons. Klass leaves the reader to fill in the blank that she has deliberately left: different from what? This absence is the real crux of the essay: people are dying every day in India from diseases that are, as Klass writes in paragraph 12, "almost all preventable diseases, and their prevalence is a product of poverty, of lack of vaccinations, of malnutrition and poor sanitation." Klass writes from a firm position in the first world, where excellent medical care is taken for granted. This first-world reality is very different from the third-world reality that she experiences in India. The essay thus becomes in part a plea for the expansion of medical borders, for a closing of gaps—between rich and poor, between first and third worlds—that need not exist.

STUDY QUESTIONS

For Discussion

1. The differences that Klass feels so acutely no doubt affect her ability to perform as a pediatrician. It is apparent in this essay that she likely will not remain in India for an extended period. What impact will the experience have on her medical practice?

2. Notice the essay's strong focus on children. While this focus exists in part because Klass is a pediatrician, it lends the essay an impact that it might otherwise not have. Compare the emotional impact of this essay with that of Selzer's essay on the epidemic of AIDS in Haiti, especially among the island's prostitutes. How much of the difference between the two essays is due to the choice of subjects, and how those subjects are constructed, not only in the essays themselves, but in society?

For Writing

1. Describe—as a narrative, or as a comparison and contrast essay—a situation in which you felt acutely displaced, perhaps because your knowledge was not adequate for what was expected of you.

2. Write a short analysis of this essay's informal, almost chatty tone. To what extent is this tone a feature of the essay's subject—children—as opposed to its style? While the subject of the essay is children, the issue is their needless death and disease. How well suited are Klass's tone and style to the content of the essay? Why do you think Klass has made the technical choices that she has?

THE ROUTE TO NORMAL SCIENCE

Thomas S. Kuhn

BIOGRAPHICAL NOTE

Thomas Kuhn has taught at Harvard, Berkeley, Princeton, and MIT, and is well known for his writings on the history of science. "The Route to Normal Science" is excerpted from his 1962 book *The Structure of Scientific Revolutions*. Kuhn's ideas on paradigm shifts have also been appreciated and cited in many non-scientific fields. His other books include *The Copernican Revolution* (1957), *The Essential Tension* (1977), and *Black-Body Theory and the Quantum Discontinuity* (1987).

1   In this essay, "normal science" means research firmly based upon one or more past scientific achievements, achievements that some particular scientific community acknowledges for a time as supplying the foundation for its further practice. Today such achievements are recounted, though seldom in their original form, by science textbooks, elementary and advanced. These textbooks expound the body of accepted theory, illustrate many or all of its successful applications, and compare these applications with exemplary observations and experiments. Before such books became popular early in the nineteenth century (and until even more recently in the newly matured sciences), many of the famous classics of science fulfilled a similar function. Aristotle's *Physica*, Ptolemy's *Almagest*, Newton's *Principia* and *Opticks*, Franklin's *Electricity*, Lavoisier's *Chemistry*, and Lyell's *Geology*— these and many other works served for a time implicitly to define the legitimate problems and methods of a research field for succeeding generations of practitioners. They were able to do so because they shared two essential characteristics. Their achievement was sufficiently unprecedented to attract an enduring group of adherents away from competing

Reprinted by permission of The University of Chicago. Originally published as Chapter 2 of *The Structure of Scientific Revolutions*. Vol. 2, no 2 of International Encyclopedia of Unified Science. Copyright © 1962, 1970 by The University of Chicago. All rights reserved. Published 1962. Second Edition, enlarged 1970.

modes of scientific activity. Simultaneously, it was sufficiently open-ended to leave all sorts of problems for the redefined group of practitioners to resolve.

2   Achievements that share these two characteristics I shall henceforth refer to as "paradigms," a term that relates closely to "normal science." By choosing it, I mean to suggest that some accepted examples of actual scientific practice—examples which include law, theory, application, and instrumentation together—provide models from which spring particular coherent traditions of scientific research. These are the traditions which the historian describes under such rubrics as "Ptolemaic astronomy" (or "Copernican"), "Aristotelian dynamics" (or "Newtonian"), "corpuscular optics" (or "wave optics"), and so on. The study of paradigms, including many that are far more specialized than those named illustratively above, is what mainly prepares the student for membership in the particular scientific community with which he will later practice. Because he there joins men who learned the bases of their field from the same concrete models, his subsequent practice will seldom evoke overt disagreement over fundamentals. Men whose research is based on shared paradigms are committed to the same rules and standards for scientific practice. That commitment and the apparent consensus it produces are prerequisites for normal science, i.e., for the genesis and continuation of a particular research tradition.

3   Because in this essay the concept of a paradigm will often substitute for a variety of familiar notions, more will need to be said about the reasons for its introduction. Why is the concrete scientific achievement, as a locus of professional commitment, prior to the various concepts, laws, theories, and points of view that may be abstracted from it? In what sense is the shared paradigm a fundamental unit for the student of scientific development, a unit that cannot be fully reduced to logically atomic components which might function in its stead?... Answers to these questions and to others like them will prove basic to an understanding both of normal science and of the associated concept of paradigms. That more abstract discussion will depend, however, upon a previous exposure to examples of normal science or of paradigms in operation. In particular, both these related concepts will be clarified by noting that there can be a sort of scientific research without paradigms, or at least without any so unequivocal and so binding as the ones named above. Acquisition of a paradigm and of the more esoteric type of research it permits is a sign of maturity in the development of any given scientific field.

4   If the historian traces the scientific knowledge of any selected group of related phenomena backward in time, he is likely to encounter some minor variant of a pattern here illustrated from the history of physical optics. Today's physics textbooks tell the student that light is photons, i.e., quantum-mechanical entities that exhibit some characteristics of waves and some of particles. Research proceeds accordingly, or rather according to the more elaborate and mathematical characterization from which this usual verbalization is derived. That characterization of light is, however, scarcely half a century old. Before it was developed by Planck, Einstein, and others early in this century, physics texts taught that light was transverse wave motion, a conception rooted in a paradigm that derived ultimately from the optical writings of Young and Fresnel in the early nineteenth century. Nor was the wave theory the first to be embraced by almost all practitioners of optical science. During the eighteenth century the paradigm for this field was provided by Newton's *Opticks*, which taught that light was material corpuscles. At that time physicists sought evidence, as the early wave theorists had not, of the pressure exerted by light particles impinging on solid bodies.[1]

5   These transformations of the paradigms of physical optics are scientific revolutions, and the successive transition from one paradigm to another via revolution is the usual

developmental pattern of mature science. It is not, however, the pattern characteristic of the period before Newton's work, and that is the contrast that concerns us here. No period between remote antiquity and the end of the seventeenth century exhibited a single generally accepted view about the nature of light. Instead there were a number of competing schools and subschools, most of them espousing one variant or another of Epicurean, Aristotelian, or Platonic theory. One group took light to be particles emanating from material bodies; for another it was a modification of the medium that intervened between the body and the eye; still another explained light in terms of an interaction of the medium with an emanation from the eye; and there were other combinations and modifications besides. Each of the corresponding schools derived strength from its relation to some particular metaphysic, and each emphasized, as paradigmatic observations, the particular cluster of optical phenomena that its own theory could do most to explain. Other observations were dealt with by *ad hoc* elaborations, or they remained as outstanding problems for further research.[2]

6   At various times all these schools made significant contributions to the body of concepts, phenomena, and techniques from which Newton drew the first nearly uniformly accepted paradigm for physical optics. Any definition of the scientist that excludes at least the more creative members of these various schools will exclude their modern successors as well. Those men were scientists. Yet anyone examining a survey of physical optics before Newton may well conclude that, though the field's practitioners were scientists, the net result of their activity was something less than science. Being able to take no common body of belief for granted, each writer on physical optics felt forced to build his field anew from its foundations. In doing so, his choice of supporting observation and experiment was relatively free, for there was no standard set of methods or of phenomena that every optical writer felt forced to employ and explain. Under these circumstances, the dialogue of the resulting books was often directed as much to the members of other schools as it was to nature. That pattern is not unfamiliar in a number of creative fields today, nor is it incompatible with significant discovery and invention. It is not, however, the pattern of development that physical optics acquired after Newton and that other natural sciences make familiar today.

7   The history of electrical research in the first half of the eighteenth century provides a more concrete and better known example of the way a science develops before it acquires its first universally received paradigm. During that period there were almost as many views about the nature of electricity as there were important electrical experimenters, men like Hauksbee, Gray, Desaguliers, Du Fay, Nollett, Watson, Franklin, and others. All their numerous concepts of electricity had something in common—they were partially derived from one or another version of the mechanico-corpuscular philosophy that guided all scientific research of the day. In addition, all were components of real scientific theories, of theories that had been drawn in part from experiment and observation and that partially determined the choice and interpretation of additional problems undertaken in research. Yet though all the experiments were electrical and though most of the experimenters read each other's works, their theories had no more than a family resemblance.[3]

8   One early group of theories, following seventeenth-century practice, regarded attraction and frictional generation as the fundamental electrical phenomena. This group tended to treat repulsion as a secondary effect due to some sort of mechanical rebounding and also to postpone for as long as possible both discussion and systematic research on Gray's newly discovered effect, electrical conduction. Other "electricians" (the term is their own) took attraction and repulsion to be equally elementary manifestations of electricity and

modified their theories and research accordingly. (Actually, this group is remarkably small—even Franklin's theory never quite accounted for the mutual repulsion of two negatively charged bodies.) But they had as much difficulty as the first group in accounting simultaneously for any but the simplest conduction effects. Those effects, however, provided the starting point for still a third group, one which tended to speak of electricity as a "fluid" that could run through conductors rather than as an "effluvium" that emanated from non-conductors. This group, in its turn, had difficulty reconciling its theory with a number of attractive and repulsive effects. Only through the work of Franklin and his immediate successors did a theory arise that could account with something like equal facility for very nearly all these effects and that therefore could and did provide a subsequent generation of "electricians" with a common paradigm for its research.

9   Excluding those fields, like mathematics and astronomy, in which the first firm paradigms date from prehistory and also those, like biochemistry, that arose by division and recombination of specialties already matured, the situations outlined above are historically typical. Though it involves my continuing to employ the unfortunate simplification that tags an extended historical episode with a single and somewhat arbitrarily chosen name (e.g., Newton or Franklin), I suggest that similar fundamental disagreements characterized, for example, the study of motion before Aristotle and of statics before Archimedes, the study of heat before Black, of chemistry before Boyle and Boerhaave, and of historical geology before Hutton. In parts of biology—the study of heredity, for example—the first universally received paradigms are still more recent; and it remains an open question what parts of social science have yet acquired such paradigms at all. History suggests that the road to a firm research consensus is extraordinarily arduous.

10   History also suggests, however, some reasons for the difficulties encountered on that road. In the absence of a paradigm or some candidate for a paradigm, all of the facts that could possibly pertain to the development of a given science are likely to seem equally relevant. As a result, early fact-gathering is a far more nearly random activity than the one that subsequent scientific development makes familiar. Furthermore, in the absence of a reason for seeking some particular form of more recondite information, early fact-gathering is usually restricted to the wealth of data that lie ready to hand. The resulting pool of facts contains those accessible to casual observation and experiment together with some of the more esoteric data retrievable from established crafts like medicine, calendar making, and metallurgy. Because the crafts are one readily accessible source of facts that could not have been casually discovered, technology has often played a vital role in the emergence of new sciences.

11   But though this sort of fact-collecting has been essential to the origin of many significant sciences, anyone who examines, for example, Pliny's encyclopedic writings or the Baconian natural histories of the seventeenth century will discover that it produces a morass. One somehow hesitates to call the literature that results scientific. The Baconian "histories" of heat, color, wind, mining, and so on, are filled with information, some of it recondite. But they juxtapose facts that will later prove revealing (e.g., heating by mixture) with others (e.g., the warmth of dung heaps) that will for some time remain too complex to be integrated with theory at all.[4] In addition, since any description must be partial, the typical natural history often omits from its immensely circumstantial accounts just those details that later scientists will find sources of important illumination. Almost none of the early "histories" of electricity, for example, mention that chaff, attracted to a rubbed glass rod, bounces off again. That effect seemed mechanical, not electrical.[5] Moreover, since the casual fact-gatherer seldom possesses the time or the tools to be critical, the natural histories often juxtapose descriptions like the above with others, say, heating by antiperistasis (or by cooling), that we are now quite unable to confirm.[6] Only very occasionally, as in the cases of ancient statics, dynamics, and geometrical optics, do facts collected with so little guidance from pre-established theory speak with sufficient clarity to permit the emergence of a first paradigm.

12   This is the situation that creates the schools characteristic of the early stages of a science's development. No natural history can be interpreted in the absence of at least some implicit body of intertwined theoretical and methodological belief that permits selection, evaluation, and criticism. If that body of belief is not already implicit in the collection of facts—in which case more than "mere facts" are at hand—it must be externally supplied, perhaps by a current metaphysic, by another science, or by personal and historical accident. No wonder, then, that in the early stages of the development of any science different men confronting the same range of phenomena, but not usually all the same particular phenomena, describe and interpret them in different ways. What is surprising, and perhaps also unique in its degree to the fields we call science, is that such initial divergences should ever largely disappear.

13   For they do disappear to a very considerable extent and then apparently once and for all. Furthermore, their disappearance is usually caused by the triumph of one of the preparadigm schools, which, because of its own characteristic beliefs and preconceptions, emphasized only some special part of the too sizable and inchoate pool of information. Those electricians who thought electricity a fluid and therefore gave particular emphasis to conduction provide an excellent case in point. Led by this belief, which could scarcely cope with the known multiplicity of attractive and repulsive effects, several of them conceived the idea of bottling the electrical fluid. The immediate fruit of their efforts was the Leyden jar, a device which might never have been discovered by a man exploring nature casually or at random, but which was in fact independently developed by at least two investigators in the early 1740s.[7] Almost from the start of his electrical researches, Franklin was particularly concerned to explain that strange and, in the event, particularly revealing piece of special apparatus. His success in doing so provided the most effective of the arguments that made his theory a paradigm, though one that was still unable to account for quite all the known cases of electrical repulsion.[8] To be accepted as a paradigm, a theory must seem better than its competitors, but it need not, and in fact never does, explain all the facts with which it can be confronted.

14   What the fluid theory of electricity did for the subgroup that held it, the Franklinian paradigm later did for the entire group of electricians. It suggested which experiments would be worth performing and which, because directed to secondary or to overly complex manifestations of electricity, would not. Only the paradigm did the job far more effectively, partly because the end of inter-school debate ended the constant reiteration of fundamentals and partly because the confidence that they were on the right track encouraged scientists to undertake more precise, esoteric, and consuming sorts of work.[9] Freed from the concern with any and all electrical phenomena, the united group of electricians could pursue selected phenomena in far more detail, designing much special equipment for the task and employing it more stubbornly and systematically than electricians had ever done before. Both fact collection and theory articulation became highly directed activities. The effectiveness and efficiency of electrical research increased accordingly, providing evidence for a societal version of Francis Bacon's acute methodological dictum: "Truth emerges more readily from error than from confusion."[10]

15   We shall be examining the nature of this highly directed or paradigm-based research in the next section, but must first note briefly how the emergence of a paradigm affects the structure of the group that practices the field. When, in the development of a natural science, an individual or group first produces a synthesis able to attract most of the next generation's practitioners, the older schools gradually disappear. In part their disappearance is caused by their members' conversion to the new paradigm. But there are always some men who cling to one or another of the older views, and they are simply read out of the profession, which thereafter ignores their work. The new paradigm implies a new and more rigid definition of the field. Those unwilling or unable to accommodate their work to it must proceed in isolation or attach themselves to some other group.[11] Historically, they have often simply stayed in the departments of philosophy from which so many of the special sciences have been spawned. As these indications hint, it is sometimes just its reception of a paradigm that transforms a group previously interested merely in the study of nature into a profession or, at least, a discipline. In the sciences (though not in fields like medicine, technology, and law, of which the principal *raison d'être* is an external social need), the formation of specialized journals, the foundation of specialists' societies, and the claim for a special place in the curriculum have usually been associated with a group's first reception of a single paradigm. At least this was the case between the time, a century and a half ago, when the institutional pattern of scientific specialization first developed and the very recent time when the paraphernalia of specialization acquired a prestige of their own.

16   The more rigid definition of the scientific group has other consequences. When the individual scientist can take a paradigm for granted, he need no longer, in his major works, attempt to build his field anew, starting from first principles and justifying the use of each concept introduced. That can be left to the writer of textbooks. Given a textbook, however, the creative scientist can begin his research where it leaves off and thus concentrate exclusively upon the subtlest and most esoteric aspects of the natural phenomena that concern his group. And as he does this, his research communiqués will begin to change in ways whose evolution has been too little studied but whose modern end products are obvious to all and oppressive to many. No longer will his researches usually be embodied in books addressed, like Franklin's *Experiments... on Electricity* or Darwin's *The Origin of Species*, to anyone who might be interested in the subject matter of the field. Instead they will usually appear as brief articles addressed only to professional colleagues, the men whose knowledge of a shared paradigm can be assumed and who prove to be the only ones able to read the papers addressed to them.

17   Today in the sciences, books are usually either texts or retrospective reflections upon one aspect or another of the scientific life. The scientist who writes one is more likely to find his professional reputation impaired than enhanced. Only in the earlier, pre-paradigm, stages of the development of the various sciences did the book ordinarily possess the same relation to professional achievement that it still retains in other creative fields. And only in those fields that still retain the book, with or without the article, as a vehicle for research communication are the lines of professionalization still so loosely drawn that the layman may hope to follow progress by reading the practitioners' original reports. Both in mathematics and astronomy, research reports had ceased already in antiquity to be intelligible to a generally educated audience. In dynamics, research became similarly esoteric in the later Middle Ages, and it recaptured general intelligibility only briefly during the early seventeenth century when a new paradigm replaced the one that had guided medieval research.

Electrical research began to require translation for the layman before the end of the eighteenth century, and most other fields of physical science ceased to be generally accessible in the nineteenth. During the same two centuries similar transitions can be isolated in the various parts of the biological sciences. In parts of the social sciences they may well be occurring today. Although it has become customary, and is surely proper, to deplore the widening gulf that separates the professional scientist from his colleagues in other fields, too little attention is paid to the essential relationship between that gulf and the mechanisms intrinsic to scientific advance.

18   Ever since prehistoric antiquity one field of study after another has crossed the divide between what the historian might call its prehistory as a science and its history proper. These transitions to maturity have seldom been so sudden or so unequivocal as my necessarily schematic discussion may have implied. But neither have they been historically gradual, coextensive, that is to say, with the entire development of the fields within which they occurred. Writers on electricity during the first four decades of the eighteenth century possessed far more information about electrical phenomena than had their sixteenth-century predecessors. During the half-century after 1740, few new sorts of electrical phenomena were added to their lists. Nevertheless, in important respects, the electrical writings of Cavendish, Coulomb, and Volta in the last third of the eighteenth century seem further removed from those of Gray, Du Fay, and even Franklin than are the writings of these early eighteenth-century electrical discoverers from those of the sixteenth century.[12] Sometime between 1740 and 1780, electricians were for the first time enabled to take the foundations of their field for granted. From that point they pushed on to more concrete and recondite problems, and increasingly they then reported their results in articles addressed to other electricians rather than in books addressed to the learned world at large. As a group they achieved what had been gained by astronomers in antiquity and by students of motion in the Middle Ages, of physical optics in the late seventeenth century, and of historical geology in the early nineteenth. They had, that is, achieved a paradigm that proved able to guide the whole group's research. Except with the advantage of hindsight, it is hard to find another criterion that so clearly proclaims a field a science.

NOTES

1. Joseph Priestley, *The History and Present State of Discoveries Relating to Vision, Light, and Colours* (London, 1772), pp. 385-90.

2. Vasco Ronchi, *Histoire de la lumière*, trans. Jean Taton (Paris, 1956), chaps. i-iv.

3. Duane Roller and Duane H. D. Roller, *The Development of the Concept of Electric Charge: Electricity from the Greeks to Coulomb* ("Harvard Case Histories in Experimental Science," Case 8; Cambridge, Mass., 1954); and I. B. Cohen, *Franklin and Newton: An Inquiry into Speculative Newtonian Experimental Science and Franklin's Work in Electricity as an Example Thereof* (Philadelphia, 1956), chaps. vii-xii. For some of the analytic detail in the paragraph that follows in the text, I am indebted to a still unpublished paper by my student John L. Heilbron. Pending its publication, a somewhat more extended and more precise account of the emergence of Franklin's paradigm is included in T. S. Kuhn, "The Function of Dogma in Scientific Research," in A. C. Crombie (ed.), "Symposium on the History of Science, University of Oxford, July 9-15, 1961," to be published by Heinemann Educational Books, Ltd.

4. Compare the sketch for a natural history of heat in Bacon's *Novum Organum*, Vol. VIII of *The Works of Francis Bacon*, ed. J. Spedding, R. L. Ellis, and D. D. Heath (New York, 1869), pp. 179-203.

5. Roller and Roller, *op. cit.*, pp. 14, 22, 28, 43. Only after the work recorded in the last of these citations do repulsive effects gain general recognition as unequivocally electrical.

6. Bacon, *op. cit.*, pp. 235, 337, says, "Water slightly warm is more easily frozen than quite cold." For a partial account of the earlier history of this strange observation, see Marshall Clagett, *Giovanni Marliani and Late Medieval Physics* (New York, 1941), chap. iv.

7. Roller and Roller, *op. cit.*, pp. 51-54.

8. The troublesome case was the mutual repulsion of negatively charged bodies, for which see Cohen, *op. cit.*, pp. 491-94, 531-43.

9. It should be noted that the acceptance of Franklin's theory did not end quite all debate. In 1759 Robert Symmer proposed a two-fluid version of that theory, and for many years thereafter electricians were divided about whether electricity was a single fluid or two. But the debates on this subject only confirm what has been said above about the manner in which a universally recognized achievement unites the profession. Electricians, though they continued divided on this point, rapidly concluded that no experimental tests could distinguish the two versions of the theory and that they were therefore equivalent. After that, both schools could and did exploit all the benefits that the Franklinian theory provided (*ibid.*, pp. 543-46, 548-54).

10. Bacon, *op. cit.*, p. 210.

11. The history of electricity provides an excellent example which could be duplicated from the careers of Priestley, Kelvin, and others. Franklin reports that Nollet, who at mid-century was the most influential of the Continental electricians, "lived to see himself the last of his Sect, except Mr. B.—his Eleve and immediate Disciple" (Max Farrand [ed.], *Benjamin Franklin's Memoirs* [Berkeley, Calif., 1949], pp. 384-86). More interesting, however, is the endurance of whole schools in increasing isolation from professional science. Consider, for example, the case of astrology, which was once an integral part of astronomy. Or consider the continuation in the late eighteenth and early nineteenth centuries of a previously respected tradition of "romantic" chemistry. This is the tradition discussed by Charles C. Gillispie in "The *Encyclopédie* and the Jacobin Philosophy of Science: A Study in Ideas and Consequences," *Critical Problems in the History of Science*, ed. Marshall Clagett (Madison, Wis., 1959), pp. 255-89; and "The Formation of Lamarck's Evolutionary Theory," *Archives internationales d'histoire des sciences*, XXXVII (1956), 323-38.

12. The post-Franklinian developments include an immense increase in the sensitivity of charge detectors, the first reliable and generally diffused techniques for measuring charge, the evolution of the concept of capacity and its relation to a newly refined notion of electric tension, and the quantification of electrostatic force. On all of these see Roller and Roller, *op. cit.*, pp. 66-81; W. C. Walker, "The Detection and Estimation of Electric Charges in the Eighteenth Century," *Annals of Science*, I (1936), 66-100; and Edmund Hoppe, *Geschichte der Elektrizität* (Leipzig, 1884), Part I, chaps. iii-iv.

NOTES AND DISCUSSION

In this essay, note the heavy reliance on definitions, and on the repetition of the root word "paradigm," especially early on. Remember that Kuhn is trying to introduce a new concept and tie it to existing principles or expectations. Particularly important are his opening definition of "normal science" and his extended definition of "paradigm." Kuhn also provides some historical examples of the patterns of scientific development and progress in order to illustrate the contributions of shared paradigms, and to resurrect some largely forgotten or under-appreciated figures in the history of science.

Kuhn is also concerned with what shared paradigms allow or make possible, and with what they prevent or make difficult. He is particularly concerned with the problem of communicating science. While a shared paradigm helps to create a community that shares a set of assumptions and understands what constitutes good or productive research, that community will have to communicate in the specialized language of the paradigm, producing articles that can be understood only by the privileged few who have the particular knowledge.

Of course, paradigms guide research and complicate communication not only in science, but in the humanities as well. See, for example, Cynthia Ozick's essay, "Crocodiled Moats in the Kingdom of Letters," for a discussion of the influence of paradigms in another discipline.

Definitions are extremely important to Kuhn, but consider also his reliance on aphorisms, his own as well as those of others. For example, he claims "Acquisition of a paradigm and of the more esoteric type of research it permits is a sign of maturity in the development of any given scientific field." Later he quotes Bacon: "Truth emerges more readily from error than from confusion." What Kuhn means by "maturity" and Bacon means by "truth" might be open to interpretation.

Finally, note that Kuhn has an unacknowledged paradigm of his own, namely, that science is a male field: "Men whose research is based on shared paradigms are committed to the same rules and standards for scientific practice." This gender-specific language may be more a reflection of the linguistic standards at the time of writing than of any inherent prejudice, but presents an interesting example of unconscious exclusion through vocabulary.

STUDY QUESTIONS

For Discussion

1. In a lecture, textbook, or elsewhere, find a passage that uses too much jargon or inside knowledge for you to understand it. What was your reaction as a reader?

2. Discuss the degree to which the problem of unintelligibility, of privileged language, in science, is linked with the public suspicion of science. In your answer, consider the portrayal of a scientist in a current newspaper or news magazine, or Stephen Jay Gould's discussion of scientists in "The Monster's Human Nature."

For Writing

1. Assess Kuhn's use of the techniques of definition, explaining how they work individually and collectively.

2. Kuhn writes, "History suggests that the road to a firm research consensus is extraordinarily arduous." As a research topic, find and assess the role of a paradigm or a major paradigm shift in the development of your major field of study, or consider whether such a shift is in progress right now.

SENSE AND SENSIBILITY

Lewis H. Lapham

BIOGRAPHICAL NOTE

Lewis H. Lapham is the editor of *Harper's Magazine* and the author of many articles and books concerned with contemporary American life. "Sense and Sensibility" is from the column he writes for *Harper's* entitled "Notebook." The column usually takes as its topic some facet of modern American society; the pieces often have a political or cultural dimension, as does this one.

1   *The ocean is closed.*

—Sign posted at 5:00 P.M. by the management of a Miami Beach hotel

2   On a Tuesday afternoon in late July, in a taxi stalled for an hour in traffic on the Brooklyn Bridge, I listened to a New York literary agent praise his daughter's gift for refined political sentiment. Twenty years ago a proud father might have praised a daughter's talent for music or gymnastics, but the times have changed, and it is the exquisiteness of the moral aesthetic that prompts the cue for applause. The girl was fifteen, a student at one of the city's better private schools, already word perfect in her catechism of correct opinions. Her father was a successful dealer in high-priced pulp, and his daughter kept up with the latest cultural trends as they made their way around the beaches and lawns of East Hampton.

3   At the beginning of the spring term her biology class had taken up the study of primitive organisms, and the girls were asked to look through microscopes at a gang of bacteria toiling in a drop of water. The agent's daughter refused. No, she said, she would not look. She would not invade the privacy of the bacteria. They might be weak and small and without important friends in Congress, but they were entitled to their rights, and she, for one, would grant them a measure of respect. After what apparently was a moment of stunned silence in the classroom, the teacher congratulated the girl for her principled

dissent. Of course she didn't have to look at the bacteria. She had taught the class a lesson that couldn't be learned from a microscope.

4   The story seemed to me proof of the inanity of much of what goes by the name of higher education, but the agent was so pleased with it, so suffused with the light of virtue, that I smiled politely and said something genial and optimistic about his daughter's chances of going to Harvard. By that time the taxi had crossed the bridge, and I was glad to escape into the less rarefied atmosphere of Second Avenue before the agent began to explain his theory of global harmony. I once had listened to him give a speech on the subject to a conference of publishers, and I knew that he was capable of long recitations in what he believed to be the language of the Oglala Sioux.

5   Two days later I was still thinking about the innocent and disenfranchised bacteria when I came across a news item on an inside page of the *New York Times* that matched the literary agent's story with its appropriate corollary. The narrative was very brief, no more than a few paragraphs, and sketchy in its details, but the moral lesson was as solemn as an auto-da-fé. Well after sunset on the evening of July 16, an eight-year-old boy in Tampa, Florida, looked through the window of a building near his home and saw a man and a woman (both unmarried and both in their middle thirties) making love in a hot tub. The hot tub was in the bathroom of a condominium that the man had rented three weeks earlier, and the blinds on the window had been drawn closed. The boy reported the event to his father, who called the sheriff's office. While awaiting the arrival of the men in uniform, a small crowd gathered outside the bathroom window, and another neighbor took it upon himself to record the scene in the hot tub on videotape. He was, he said, assembling evidence.

6   "They knew we were out there," he said. "They were exhibitionists. I shot right through the blinds."

7   Both the man and the woman were arrested on charges of committing a lewd and lascivious act. They spent the rest of the night in jail, and the next morning they each had to post $15,000 bail before being let loose in the streets.

8   The vigilant schoolboy in Florida reminded me of the sensitive schoolgirl in New York, and I wondered why it was that both prodigies seemed to partake of the same spirit. At first glance they seemed so unlike each other, and it was easy enough to contrast the differences of age, sex, education, and regional prejudice. Their acts of piety expressed contradictory notions of the public good, and I could imagine each of their fathers thinking that the other father had stumbled into the snares of the Antichrist. The boy quite clearly had been born under the star of the political right. Given world enough and time, he stood a good chance of growing up to vote Republican, enforce the drug laws, and distribute Bibles or the collected works of Allan Bloom. The girl had been raised under the sign of the political left, and once she completes the formality of the curriculum at Harvard, I expect that she will write funding guidelines for the federal government or scripts for Kevin Costner.

9   The ideological differences matter less than the common temperament or habit of mind. Both the boy and the girl apparently were the kind of people who sift the grains of human feeling and experience through the cloth of milk-white abstraction, and I didn't doubt but that they never would have much use for historical circumstance or the exception that proves the rule.

10   I wish I didn't think that such people now speak for the American majority, or that the will toward conformity crowds so close to the surface of so many nominally political disputes. The spirit of the age favors the moralist and the busybody, and the instinct to censor and suppress shows itself not only in the protests for and against abortion or multi-

culturalism but also in the prohibitions against tobacco and pet birds. It seems that everybody is forever looking out for everybody else's spiritual or physical salvation. Doomsday is at hand, and the community of the blessed (whether defined as the New York Yacht Club or the English department at Duke) can be all too easily corrupted by the wrong diet, the wrong combination of chemicals, the wrong word. The preferred modes of address number only three—the sermon, the euphemism, and the threat—and whether I look to the political left or the political right I'm constantly being told to think the right thoughts and confess the right sins.

11   Passing through Portsmouth, Rhode Island, I see a sign on a public bus that says Do Drugs and Kiss Your Federal Benefits Goodbye. I leaf through *The Dictionary of Cautionary Words and Phrases*, compiled by a tribunal of purified journalists (the 1989 Multicultural Management Program Fellows), and I learn that I must be very, very careful when using the words "man," "woman," "watermelon," "barracuda," "community," "banana," and "impotent." Given a careless inflection or an ambiguous context, the words can be construed as deadly insults.

12   The prompters of the public alarm sound their dismal horns from so many points on the political compass that I suspect that what they wish to say isn't political. The would-be saviors in our midst worry about the moral incoherence of a society distracted by its fears—fear of apples, fear of Mexicans, fear of bankruptcy, fear of the rain—and they seek to construct the citadel of the New Jerusalem with whatever materials come most easily or obviously to hand. Every few days the newspapers bear further witness to the jury-rigged orthodoxies meant to redeem the American moral enterprise and reclaim the American soul.

13 •   The village of Chester, New York, passes a law to the effect that all the signs on all the stores of a new shopping mall must be painted blue. A merchant neglects to read the fine print on the lease and plans to put up the red sign under which he has been doing business for thirteen years. No good. Unacceptable. Either he paints the sign blue or he goes elsewhere. The village clerk, Elizabeth Kreher, overrules his objections with an air of sublime self-righteousness. "He shouldn't be complaining; he should be thankful to have such a nice place to move his store into. Plus it's a beautiful color—I just love blue."

14 •   The chairman of General Public Utilities Corporation, a married man named Hoch, admits to a love affair with a woman employed by the company as vice president of communications. The news of their liaison arrived by anonymous letter. Hoch resigns, but the woman keeps her office and title. Various spokespersons explain that a public utility depends for its rate increases on the grace and favor of the federal government and therefore must align its manners with the prevailing political trends. The feminist lobby in Washington is as loud as it is judgmental. Goodbye, Hoch.

15 •   A waiter and a waitress working in a restaurant south of Seattle refuse to serve a pregnant woman a rum daiquiri in order to lead her out of the paths of temptation. When the woman persists in her folly, the waiter and waitress (both in their early twenties and very devout in their beliefs about health and hygiene) lecture her on the evils of alcohol and read her the surgeon general's warning about drinking and birth defects.

16 •   A woman in California kisses her boyfriend goodnight on the steps of her own house, and a committee of disapproving neighbors reprimands her for lowering the tone and character of the block. For precisely the same reason, a committee of neighbors in Illinois censures a man for parking a vulgar pickup truck in his own driveway.

17 •   Joseph Epstein, the editor of *The American Scholar* and a writer well-known both for his wit and neo-classical political views, publishes an essay in a literary journal in which he refers to "the snarling humorlessness" of various feminist critics and professors. He makes the mistake of repeating the joke about the couple in Manhattan who cannot decide whether to get a revolver or a pit bull in order to protect themselves against burglars. They compromise by hiring a feminist. The joke incites so much rage within some of the nation's more advanced universities that Epstein feels constrained to write a letter of explanation to the *New York Times* conceding that "one attempts humor at one's peril."

18   Like Queen Victoria and the National Endowment for the Arts, the Puritan spirit is not easily amused. Over the last seven or eight years I've noticed that my own experiments with irony or satire in mixed or unknown company require some introductory remark (comparable to a warning from the surgeon general) announcing the arrival of a joke that might prove harmful to somebody's self-esteem.

19   A society in which everybody distrusts everybody else classifies humor as a danger-ous substance and entertains itself with cautionary tales. The news media magnify the fear of death by constantly reciting the alphabet of doom (abortion, AIDS, alcohol, asbestos, cancer, cigarettes, cocaine, etc.), and the public-service advertising extols the virtues of chastity and abstinence. The more urgent the causes of alarm, the more plausible the justi-fications for stricter controls. Stricter controls necessarily entail the devaluation of any and all systems of thought (most of them humanist) that make invidious distinctions between man and beast, man and moth, man and blood specimen, and I've noticed that the puri-tanical enthusiasms of the last several years complement and sustain the attitude of mind that assigns to human beings a steadily lower and more disreputable place in the hierarchy of multicellular life forms.

20   The rules and exhortations run to so many cross-purposes (more freedom and more rights, but also more laws and more police; no to fornication, yes to free contraceptives in the schools; yes to the possession of automatic weapons, no to the possession of cocaine) that it's hard to know what sort of perfect society our saviors have in mind. Presumably it will be clean and orderly and safe, but who will be deemed worthy of inhabiting the spheres of blameless abstraction? Maybe only the bacteria. Human beings make too much of a mess with their emotions and their wars. They poison the rivers and litter the fields with Styrofoam cups, and very few of them can be trusted with kitchen matches or the works of Aristotle.

21   I see so many citizens armed with the bright shields of intolerance that I wonder how they would agree on anything other than a need to do something repressive and authori-tarian. I have no way of guessing how they will cleanse the world of its impurities, but if I were in the business of advising newly minted college graduates, I would encourage them to think along the lines of a career in law enforcement. Not simply the familiar and some-times unpleasant forms of law enforcement—not merely the club, the handcuffs, and the noose—but law enforcement broadly and grandly conceived, law enforcement as a philos-ophy and way of life, as the presiding spirit that defines not only the duty of the prison guard and police spy but also the work of the food inspector, the newspaper columnist, the federal regulator, and the museum director. The job opportunities seem to me as number-less as the microbes still at large (and presumably up to no good) in the depths of the cold and unruly sea.

NOTES AND DISCUSSION

"Sense and Sensibility" is an interesting example of a comparison–contrast essay that does not side with either of the conflicting camps under discussion. Note the way Lapham uses evidence from each "side" to undermine its own argument, while making it clear throughout that his own views belong to neither camp (both of which he deems ridiculous), but are based, apparently, on reason and "common sense." Notice also his discussion of humour and satire, particularly the series of "cautionary tales" for the education and amusement of his audience. Consider who might be his targets of satire or irony.

The essay's title is clearly a reference to Jane Austen's novel *Sense and Sensibility*, with the girl of the opening paragraphs cast as a twentieth-century Marianne Dashwood. We are to remember that Austen's Marianne is romantic, eager, impetuous, and generally imprudent in her passions. The girl's counterpart, the boy in the second anecdote, is aligned with the seducer in Andrew Marvell's poem "To His Coy Mistress" through the line, "given world enough and time."

STUDY QUESTIONS

For Discussion

1. Lapham uses literary allusions extensively in this essay. Discuss the purposes of such references, and comment on their effectiveness. Closely connected to the technique of allusion is his use of startling comparisons and contrasts. For example, Lapham writes that the girl is likely to grow up to "write funding guidelines for the federal government or scripts for Kevin Costner." What effect do such comparisons have on the reader?

2. Consider Lapham's strategies in this essay. What purpose does the epigraph serve? Is the strategy of using such a multitude of examples effective? Should Lapham have documented his cases more fully (and why do you think he has chosen not to do so)? Why does he set off the series of "cautionary tales," using bullets and spacing, in the middle of the essay?

For Writing

1. Write a paragraph discussing the extent to which this essay is satirical. Consider in your answer how you think Lapham would respond to Swift's "A Modest Proposal."

2. In paragraph 18, Lapham notes that "Over the last seven or eight years I've noticed that my own experiments with irony or satire in mixed or unknown company require some introductory remark... announcing the arrival of a joke that might prove harmful to somebody's self-esteem." Analyze Lapham's implicit claim in this paragraph that nobody's "self-esteem" should be harmed by humour, that humour is, or should be, fundamentally harmless.

A, B, AND C: THE HUMAN ELEMENT IN MATHEMATICS

Stephen Leacock

BIOGRAPHICAL NOTE

Stephen Leacock (1869–1944) trained as an economist, and was for many years a prominent member of the Department of Economics and Political Science at McGill University. He published in a variety of fields, including political science, literary criticism, and history. However, he is best known for his nearly thirty books of humour, of which *Sunshine Sketches of a Little Town* (1912) is the most famous and widely studied. The piece reprinted here is from his first book of humour, *Literary lapses* (1910). The Stephen Leacock Award for Humour is presented annually in his honour in his hometown of Orillia, Ontario.

---

1   The student of arithmetic who has mastered the first four rules of his art, and successfully striven with money sums and fractions, finds himself confronted by an unbroken expanse of questions known as problems. These are short stories of adventure and industry with the end omitted, and though betraying a strong family resemblance, are not without a certain element of romance.

2   The characters in the plot of a problem are three people called A, B, and C. The form of the question is generally of this sort:

3   "A, B, and C do a certain piece of work. A can do as much work in one hour as B in two, or C in four. Find how long they work at it."

4   Or thus:

5   "A, B, and C are employed to dig a ditch. A can dig as much in one hour as B can dig in two, and B can dig twice as fast as C. Find how long, etc. etc."

6   Or after this wise:

7   "A lays a wager that he can walk faster than B or C. A can walk half as fast again as B, and C is only an indifferent walker. Find how far, and so forth."

8   The occupations of A, B, and C are many and varied. In the older arithmetics they contented themselves with doing "a certain piece of work." This statement of the case, however, was found too sly and mysterious, or possibly lacking in romantic charm. It

became the fashion to define the job more clearly and to set them at walking matches, ditch-digging, regattas, and piling cord wood. At times, they became commercial and entered into partnership, having with their old mystery a "certain" capital. Above all they revel in motion. When they tire of walking-matches—A rides on horseback, or borrows a bicycle and competes with his weaker-minded associates on foot. Now they race on loco-motives; now they row; or again they become historical and engage stage-coaches; or at times they are aquatic and swim. If their occupation is actual work they prefer to pump water into cisterns, two of which leak through holes in the bottom and one of which is watertight. A, of course, has the good one; he also takes the bicycle, and the best locomo-tive, and the right of swimming with the current. Whatever they do they put money on it, being all three sports. A always wins.

9   In the early chapters of the arithmetic, their identity is concealed under the names John, William, and Henry, and they wrangle over the division of marbles. In algebra they are often called X, Y, Z. But these are only their Christian names, and they are really the same people.

10   Now to one who has followed the history of these men through countless pages of problems, watched them in their leisure hours dallying with cord wood, and seen their panting sides heave in the full frenzy of filling a cistern with a leak in it, they become something more than mere symbols. They appear as creatures of flesh and blood, living men with their own passions, ambitions, and aspirations like the rest of us. Let us view them in turn. A is a full-blooded blustering fellow, of energetic temperament, hot-headed and strong-willed. It is he who proposes everything, challenges B to work, makes the bets, and bends the others to his will. He is a man of great physical strength and phenomenal endurance. He has been known to walk forty-eight hours at a stretch, and to pump ninety-six. His life is arduous and full of peril. A mistake in the working of a sum may keep him digging a fortnight without sleep. A repeating decimal in the answer might kill him.

11   B is a quiet, easy-going fellow, afraid of A and bullied by him, but very gentle and brotherly to little C, the weakling. He is quite in A's power, having lost all his money in bets.

12   Poor C is an undersized, frail man, with a plaintive face. Constant walking, digging, and pumping has broken his health and ruined his nervous system. His joyless life has driven him to drink and smoke more than is good for him, and his hand often shakes as he digs ditches. He has not the strength to work as the others can; in fact, as Hamlin Smith has said, "A can do more work in one hour than C in four."

13   The first time that I ever saw these men was one evening after a regatta. They had all been rowing in it, and it had transpired that A could row as much in one hour as B in two, or C in four. B and C had come in dead fagged and C was coughing badly. "Never mind, old fellow," I heard B say, "I'll fix you up on the sofa and get you some hot tea." Just then A came blustering in and shouted, "I say, you fellows, Hamlin Smith has shown me three cisterns in his garden and he says we can pump them until to-morrow night. I bet I can beat you both. Come on. You can pump in your rowing things, you know. Your cistern leaks a little, I think, C." I heard B growl that it was a dirty shame and that C was used up now, but they went, and presently I could tell from the sound of the water that A was pumping four times as fast as C.

14   For years after that I used to see them constantly about town and always busy. I never heard of any of them eating or sleeping. Then owing to a long absence from home, I lost sight of them. On my return I was surprised to no longer find A, B, and C at their accus-tomed tasks; on inquiry I heard that work in this line was now done by N, M, and O, and

that some people were employing for algebraical jobs, four foreigners called Alpha, Beta, Gamma, and Delta.

15   Now it chanced one day that I stumbled upon old D, in the little garden in front of his cottage, hoeing in the sun. D is an aged labouring man who used occasionally to be called in to help A, B, and C. "Did I know 'em, sir?" he answered, "why, I knowed 'em ever since they was little fellows in brackets. Master A, he were a fine lad, sir, though I always said, give me Master B for kind-heartedness-like. Many's the job as we've been on together, sir, though I never did no racing nor aught of that, but just the plain labour, as you might say. I'm getting a bit too old and stiff for it nowadays, sir—just scratch about in the garden here and grow a bit of a logarithm, or raise a common denominator or two. But Mr. Euclid he use me still for them propositions, he do."

16   From the garrulous old man I learned the melancholy end of my former acquaintances. Soon after I left town, he told me, C had been taken ill. It seems that A and B had been rowing on the river for a wager, and C had been running on the bank and then sat in a draught. Of course the bank had refused the draught and C was taken ill. A and B came home and found C lying helpless in bed. A shook him roughly and said, "Get up, C, we're going to pile wood." C looked so worn and pitiful that B said, "Look here, A, I won't stand this, he isn't fit to pile wood to-night." C smiled feebly and said, "Perhaps I might pile a little if I sat up in bed." Then B, thoroughly alarmed, said, "See here, A, I'm going to fetch a doctor; he's dying." A flared up and answered, "You've no money to fetch a doctor." "I'll reduce him to his lowest terms," B said firmly, "that'll fetch him." C's life might even then have been saved but they made a mistake about the medicine. It stood at the head of the bed on a bracket, and the nurse accidentally removed it from the bracket without changing the sign. After the fatal blunder C seems to have sunk rapidly. On the evening of the next day, as the shadows deepened in the little room, it was clear to all that the end was near. I think that even A was affected at the last as he stood with bowed head, aimlessly offering to bet with the doctor on C's laboured breathing. "A," whispered C, "I think I'm going fast." "How fast do you think you'll go, old man?" murmured A. "I don't know," said C, "but I'm going at any rate."—The end came soon after that. C rallied for a moment and asked for a certain piece of work that he had left downstairs. A put it in his arms and he expired. As his soul sped heavenward A watched its flight with melancholy admiration. B burst into a passionate flood of tears and sobbed, "Put away his little cistern and the rowing clothes he used to wear, I feel as if I could hardly ever dig again."—The funeral was plain and unostentatious. It differed in nothing from the ordinary, except that out of deference to sporting men and mathematicians, A engaged two hearses. Both vehicles started at the same time, B driving the one which bore the sable parallelopiped containing the last remains of his ill-fated friend. A on the box of the empty hearse generously consented to a handicap of a hundred yards, but arrived first at the cemetery by driving four times as fast as B. (Find the distance to the cemetery.) As the sarcophagus was lowered, the grave was surrounded by the broken figures of the first book of Euclid.—It was noticed that after the death of C, A became a changed man. He lost interest in racing with B, and dug but languidly. He finally gave up his work and settled down to live on the interest of his bets.—B never recovered from the shock of C's death; his grief preyed upon his intellect and it became deranged. He grew moody and spoke only in monosyllables. His disease became rapidly aggravated, and he presently spoke only in words whose spelling was regular and which presented no difficulty to the beginner. Realizing his precarious condition he voluntarily submitted to be incarcerated in an asylum, where he abjured mathematics and devoted himself to writing the History of the Swiss Family Robinson in words of one syllable.

NOTES AND DISCUSSION

Leacock, or his persona, takes his examples from the arithmetic texts and primers of "another era," which, we assume, is a period earlier than Leacock's own. He achieves the humour in this piece through the deceptively simple practice of writing about something abstract as though it were concrete. In moving from one level of discourse or frame of reference to another, the narrator displays what George Meredith identifies as a key element of humour: the failure to act with common sense. The narrator even casts himself as a character in the lives of the symbols, as when he interviews D.

Equally humorous are A, B, and C themselves (and their various aliases, disguises, and successors). In their predictable behaviours and fixed relationships, they illustrate another theory: Bergson's belief that humour results from the grafting of the mechanical or automatic onto the human.

There are other witty elements here as well, including puns, such as those surrounding C's fatal illness. Moreover, the essay seems at times a parody of literary analysis and criticism: the speaker calls the problems "short stories," and children's elementary spelling and reading lessons are often called their "A-B-Cs."

STUDY QUESTIONS

For Discussion

1. Leacock's technique of shifting from the world of mathematics to the world of the "short story" would be much more difficult with more advanced texts and their array of more complex symbols. Do you think there is a limit to how simple or complex the "problem" can be? Discuss whether models of symbolic "behaviour" are all the same beneath the surface, regardless of their complexity.

2. What does Leacock's essay have to say about our human tendency to find or create narrative? Hayden White, the historiographer, suggests that historians define the beginnings and ends of "historical events" by the transition or failure of transition into new moral levels. In what ways is this moral shaping of events at work, in the "lives" of A, B, and C?

For Writing

1. Attempt a humorous effect similar to Leacock's by transferring the terms or symbols from a course you are currently taking into a brief narrative relating their misadventures; or displace some literary figures into "roles" as symbols in a formula or calculation. Remember that mathematical symbols have "grammatical" functions: the variables are nouns, while the function symbols, such as the equal sign, are verbs.

2. Analyze the essay's final paragraph for tone and humorous technique. What is the effect of the funeral story, and of what happens to B? That is, how does the paragraph extend and complete the work of the rest of the essay?

BEGINNING TO UNDERSTAND THE BEGINNING

Rick McConnell

BIOGRAPHICAL NOTE

Rick McConnell writes a regular column in the "Life" section of the *Edmonton Journal*. Following his graduation from the Journalism program at the Southern Alberta Institute of Technology (SAIT), he worked for smaller newspapers in North Battleford and Moose Jaw, Saskatchewan, covering a range of fields, from farm news to city council. He started at the *Journal* in 1989 as a general reporter. Because his assigned subject is now "life," he says, "I like to think I'm doing research all the time."

1   All beginnings are hard.

2   Novelist Chaim Potok was right when he wrote that. Beginnings are hard. All of them.

3   Whether you are starting a lifetime of education with your first day of kindergarten, or beginning a friendship, a marriage, or a new job, it's important to get started on the right foot.

4   Those of us in the writing game know this as well as anyone. Every column, every news story, every short story, even an epic novel, has to get off to a good start. That crucial first sentence is, well ... just that, crucial. If we don't get you interested right from the start, you might get bored and wander over to the comics page or close the book and flip on the TV.

5   In the newspaper business we call these first sentences "leads." We agonize over them, sweat over them, talk about them, put them off as long as possible. Sometimes we'll walk around the room and bother other people; if you can't think of a good lead, at least you can keep someone else from getting started on what they're doing while you're not doing what you should be doing.

First published in the *Edmonton Journal*, May 9, 1996. Reprinted with permission of the *Edmonton Journal*.

6   The best newspaper lead I ever saw was written by James (Scotty) Reston of the *New York Times*. On November 22, 1963, Reston was at the *Times* Washington bureau when word came in that President John F. Kennedy had been assassinated. While the main news stories about the shooting, the arrest of a suspect, and the swearing in of the new president fell to reporters in the field, Reston was asked to sum up the feelings of a nation for the next day's front page. So he sat down at his old manual typewriter and opened a vein, as sportswriter Red Smith liked to put it. This two-sentence lead was the result:

7   "America wept tonight, not alone for its dead young president, but for itself. The grief was general, for somehow the worst in the nation had prevailed over the best."

8   I didn't have to look that up to get it right. I know those two lines better than any I have ever written myself. What Reston wrote that day was simply the best beginning to a newspaper story ever. The rest of us can spend the rest of eternity trying to write the second best.

9   Because I love beginnings so much, I use them as a way to judge all writing. I even shop for books by opening to the first page and reading the opening sentence. If I like it, I'll flip inside and read the beginnings of a couple of other chapters. Then I'll read the blurb on the jacket.

10   Then I'll take it home and, often as not, find out I bought the same book two years ago and have already read it twice.

11   Poking through my shelves the other day I found two copies of Norman Mailer's *The Naked and the Dead*. If I lose one, I'll still be able to turn to the opening page and read his first sentence. "Nobody could sleep." That's all it says. I've read that line dozens of times and the whole book three times. It never puts me to sleep.

12   "In our family, there was no clear line between religion and fly fishing." Maybe not, but Norman Maclean knew there was a line between good writing and boring writing when he used that sentence to open his novella *A River Runs Through It*. I've been hooked on his writing for years.

13   Here are some other opening lines I love:

14   "My father said he saw him years later playing in a tenth-rate commercial league in a textile town in Carolina, wearing shoes and an assumed name." (*Shoeless Joe* by W. P. Kinsella.)

15   "Above the town, on the hill brow, the stone angel used to stand." (*The Stone Angel* by Margaret Laurence.)

16   Beginnings can be wacky:

17   "We were somewhere around Barstow on the edge of the desert when the drugs began to take hold." (*Fear and Loathing in Las Vegas* by Hunter S. Thompson.)

18   Or dramatic:

19   "She only stopped screaming when she died." (*Kane and Abel* by Jeffery Archer.)

20   Or they can just set a nice scene:

21   "When Augustus came out on the porch the blue pigs were eating a rattlesnake—not a very big one." (*Lonesome Dove* by Larry McMurtry.)

22   "A few miles south of Soledad, the Salinas River drops in close to the hillside bank and runs deep and green." (*Of Mice and Men* by John Steinbeck.)

23   But the fact remains, all beginnings are hard and good ones are even harder.

24   That's why I stole the beginning of this column from Chaim Potok. It's actually the first line of his novel *In the Beginning*.

25   Potok knew what he was talking about. Then again, maybe Clive Barker put it better. He started his 1987 novel *Weaveworld* with this sentence:

26   "Nothing ever begins."

27   Hmmm. I'll have to think about that.

NOTES AND DISCUSSION

Ask any writer which sentence is the most difficult to write in any piece, and the answer is most commonly "the first." Even (or especially) professionals sweat to find or craft this crucial sentence, as Rick McConnell attests. Often the problem with beginnings arises because the writer has not yet decided what to say, or has not done enough pre-writing. For student writers, the problem often stems from trying to be perfect too early in the writing process. Sometimes they solve the problem by writing a general opening statement, which, if it names or is directly related to the topic, can help focus the reader's attention. However, an opening statement about the history of the world or a general concept of life, science, or literature is of little benefit.

McConnell knows that a good lead speaks for itself and draws readers into the world of the piece. He offers little advice but many examples; plenty of writing texts list techniques for writing effective openings and point out the flaws of bad ones. McConnell does not explain much; he lets the words work on his reader the way they have worked on him. In effect, he provides models, rather than theories, and writing and rhetoric teachers since the ancient Greeks have advised their students to seek good models to emulate.

STUDY QUESTIONS

For Discussion

1. Examine the opening sentences of several essays in this collection. Which seem most effective, and why? Consider such matters as length, vocabulary, rhythm, structure, and figures of speech (similes, metaphors, etc.). How do the effective openings get the reader interested or set the mood for what follows?

2. Some of McConnell's examples are from nonfiction; others, from fiction. Draw up your own list of examples from a variety of sources, and see if the techniques of fiction are significantly different from those of nonfiction. Consider these, for example:

    A screaming comes across the sky. (Thomas Pynchon, *Gravity's Rainbow*)

    It was in Burma, a sodden morning of the rains. (George Orwell, "A Hanging")

    Under the pale outrage of a breaking sky, the plane thuds. (Aritha van Herk, *The Tent Peg*)

    A strange place it was, that place where the world began. (Margaret Laurence, "Where the World Began")

    With a clamour of bells that set the swallows soaring, the Festival of Summer came to the city of Omelas, bright-towered by the sea. (Ursula LeGuin, "The Ones Who Walk Away from Omelas")

For Writing

1. Explain how the titles and opening sentences of several essays work together to complement each other and to focus the reader's attention and engage his or her interest.

2. Concluding sentences are often as hard to write as openings, because the essay should end gracefully, but not terminate interest in the topic. When you find effective openings, compare their content and form to the concluding sentences of the essays. Do the conclusions return to key words or concepts? Echo the tone? How do they announce "the end" without ending with a rhetorical thud?

BEHIND THE FORMALDEHYDE CURTAIN

Jessica Mitford

BIOGRAPHICAL NOTE

Jessica Mitford was born in England in 1917 and moved to the United States when she was still a young woman. She began her prolific career as a writer in the 1950s. Her work often displays the investigative journalism she shows in this essay, which has been taken from her book *The American Way of Death* (1963). Her other works include a companion volume, *The American Way of Birth* (1993); *Kind and Usual Punishment: The Prison Business* (1973); an investigation of journalism itself entitled *Poison Penmanship: The Gentle Art of Mudraking* (1979); and various biographies, including *Faces of Philip: A Memoir of Philip Toynbee* (1984).

1   The drama begins to unfold with the arrival of the corpse at the mortuary.

2   Alas, poor Yorick! How surprised he would be to see how his counterpart of today is whisked off to a funeral parlor and is in short order sprayed, sliced, pierced, pickled, trussed, trimmed, creamed, waxed, painted, rouged, and neatly dressed—transformed from a common corpse into a Beautiful Memory Picture. This process is known in the trade as embalming and restorative art, and is so universally employed in the United States and Canada that the funeral director does it routinely, without consulting corpse or kin. He regards as eccentric those few who are hardy enough to suggest that it might be dispensed with. Yet no law requires embalming, no religious doctrine commends it, nor is it dictated by considerations of health, sanitation, or even of personal daintiness. In no part of the world but in Northern America is it widely used. The purpose of embalming is to make the corpse presentable for viewing in a suitably costly container; and here too the funeral director routinely, without first consulting the family, prepares the body for public display.

3   Is all this legal? The processes to which a dead body may be subjected are after all to some extent circumscribed by law. In most states, for instance, the signature of next of kin must be obtained before an autopsy may be performed, before the deceased may be cremated, before the body may be turned over to a medical school for research purposes; or such provision must be made in the decedent's will. In the case of embalming, no such permission is required nor is it ever sought. A textbook, *The Principles and Practices of Embalming*, comments on this: "There is some question regarding the legality of much that is done within the preparation room." The author points out that it would be most unusual for a responsible member of a bereaved family to instruct the mortician, in so many words, to "*embalm*" the body of a deceased relative. The very term "embalming" is so seldom used that the mortician must rely upon custom in the matter. The author concludes that unless the family specifies otherwise, the act of entrusting the body to the care of a funeral establishment carries with it an implied permission to go ahead and embalm.

4   Embalming is indeed a most extraordinary procedure, and one must wonder at the docility of Americans who each year pay hundreds of millions of dollars for its perpetuation, blissfully ignorant of what it is all about, what is done, how it is done. Not one in ten thousand has any idea of what actually takes place. Books on the subject are extremely hard to come by. They are not to be found in most libraries or bookshops.

5   In an era when huge television audiences watch surgical operations in the comfort of their living rooms, when, thanks to the animated cartoon, the geography of the digestive system has become familiar territory even to the nursery school set, in a land where the satisfaction of curiosity about almost all matters is a national pastime, the secrecy surrounding embalming can, surely, hardly be attributed to the inherent gruesomeness of the subject. Custom in this regard has within this century suffered a complete reversal. In the early days of American embalming, when it was performed in the home of the deceased, it was almost mandatory for some relative to stay by the embalmer's side and witness the procedure. Today, family members who might wish to be in attendance would certainly be dissuaded by the funeral director. All others, except apprentices, are excluded by law from the preparation room.

6   A close look at what does actually take place may explain in large measure the undertaker's intractable reticence concerning a procedure that has become his major *raison d'être*. Is it possible he fears that public information about embalming might lead patrons to wonder if they really want this service? If the funeral men are loath to discuss the subject outside the trade, the reader may, understandably, be equally loath to go on reading at this point. For those who have the stomach for it, let us part the formaldehyde curtain....

7   The body is first laid out in the undertaker's morgue—or rather, Mr. Jones is reposing in the preparation room—to be readied to bid the world farewell.

8   The preparation room in any of the better funeral establishments has the tiled and sterile look of a surgery, and indeed the embalmer–restorative artist who does his chores there is beginning to adopt the term "dermasurgeon" (appropriately corrupted by some mortician–writers as "demi-surgeon") to describe his calling. His equipment, consisting of scalpels, scissors, augers, forceps, clamps, needles, pumps, tubes, bowls, and basins, is crudely imitative of the surgeon's, as is his technique, acquired in a nine- or twelve-month post-high school course in an embalming school. He is supplied by an advanced chemical industry with a bewildering array of fluids, sprays, pastes, oils, powders, creams, to fix or soften tissue, shrink or distend it as needed, dry it here, restore the moisture there. There are cosmetics, waxes, and paints to fill and cover features, even plaster of Paris to replace entire limbs. There are ingenious aids to prop and stabilize the cadaver: a Vari-Pose Head

Rest, the Edwards Arm and Hand Positioner, the Repose Block (to support the shoulders during the embalming), and the Throop Foot Positioner, which resembles an old-fashioned stocks.

9   Mr. John H. Eckels, president of the Eckels College of Mortuary Science, thus describes the first part of the embalming procedure: "In the hands of a skilled practitioner, this work may be done in a comparatively short time and without mutilating the body other than by slight incision—so slight that it scarcely would cause serious inconvenience if made upon a living person. It is necessary to remove the blood, and doing this not only helps in the disinfecting, but removes the principal cause of disfigurements due to discoloration."

10   Another textbook discusses the all-important time element: "The earlier this is done, the better, for every hour that elapses between death and embalming will add to the problems and complications encountered...." Just how soon should one get going on the embalming? The author tells us, "On the basis of such scanty information made available to this profession through its rudimentary and haphazard system of technical research, we must conclude that the best results are to be obtained if the subject is embalmed before life is completely extinct—that is, before cellular death has occurred. In the average case, this would mean within an hour after somatic death." For those who feel that there is something a little rudimentary, not to say haphazard, about this advice, a comforting thought is offered by another writer. Speaking of fears entertained in early days of premature burial, he points out, "One of the effects of embalming by chemical injection, however, has been to dispel fears of live burial." How true; once the blood is removed, chances of live burial are indeed remote.

11   To return to Mr. Jones, the blood is drained out through the veins and replaced by embalming fluid pumped in through the arteries. As noted in *The Principles and Practices of Embalming*, "every operator has a favorite injection and drainage point—a fact which becomes a handicap only if he fails or refuses to forsake his favorites when conditions demand it." Typical favorites are the carotid artery, femoral artery, jugular vein, subclavian vein. There are various choices of embalming fluid. If Flextone is used, it will produce a "mild, flexible rigidity. The skin retains a velvety softness, the tissues are rubbery and pliable. Ideal for women and children." It may be blended with B. and G. Products Company's Lyf-Lyk tint, which is guaranteed to reproduce "nature's own skin texture... the velvety appearance of living tissue." Suntone comes in three separate tints: Suntan; Special Cosmetic Tint, a pink shade "especially indicated for young female subjects"; and Regular Cosmetic Tint, moderately pink.

12   About three to six gallons of a dyed and perfumed solution of formaldehyde, glycerin, borax, phenol, alcohol, and water is soon circulating through Mr. Jones, whose mouth has been sewn together with a "needle directed upward between the upper lip and gum and brought out through the left nostril," with the corners raised slightly "for a more pleasant expression." If he should be buck-toothed, his teeth are cleaned with Bon Ami and coated with colorless nail polish. His eyes, meanwhile, are closed with flesh-tinted eye caps and eye cement.

13   The next step is to have at Mr. Jones with a thing called a trocar. This is a long, hollow needle attached to a tube. It is jabbed into the abdomen, poked around the entrails and chest cavity, the contents of which are pumped out and replaced with "cavity fluid." This done, and the hole in the abdomen sewn up, Mr. Jones's face is heavily creamed (to protect the skin from burns which may be caused by leakage of the chemicals), and he is covered with a sheet and left unmolested for a while. But not for long—there is more, much more,

in store for him. He has been embalmed, but not yet restored, and the best time to start the restorative work is eight to ten hours after embalming, when the tissues have become firm and dry.

14   The object of all this attention to the corpse, it must be remembered, is to make it presentable for viewing in an attitude of healthy repose. "Our customs require the presentation of our dead in the semblance of normality... unmarred by the ravages of illness, disease, or mutilation," says Mr. J. Sheridan Mayer in his *Restorative Art*. This is rather a large order since few people die in the full bloom of health, unravaged by illness and unmarked by some disfigurement. The funeral industry is equal to the challenge: "In some cases the gruesome appearance of a mutilated or disease-ridden subject may be quite discouraging. The task of restoration may seem impossible and shake the confidence of the embalmer. This is the time for intestinal fortitude and determination. Once the formative work is begun and affected tissues are cleaned or removed, all doubts of success vanish. It is surprising and gratifying to discover the results which may be obtained."

15   The embalmer, having allowed an appropriate interval to elapse, returns to the attack, but now he brings into play the skill and equipment of sculptor and cosmetician. Is a hand missing? Casting one in plaster of Paris is a simple matter. "For replacement purposes, only a cast of the back of the hand is necessary; this is within the ability of the average operator and is quite adequate." If a lip or two, a nose, or an ear should be missing, the embalmer has at hand a variety of restorative waxes with which to model replacements. Pores and skin texture are simulated by stippling with a little brush, and over this cosmetics are laid on. Head off? Decapitation cases are rather routinely handled. Ragged edges are trimmed, and head joined to torso with a series of splints, wires, and sutures. It is a good idea to have a little something at the neck—a scarf or a high collar—when time for viewing comes. Swollen mouth? Cut out tissue as needed from inside the lips. If too much is removed, the surface contour can easily be restored by padding with cotton. Swollen necks and cheeks are reduced by removing tissue through the vertical incisions made down each side of the neck. "When the deceased is casketed, the pillow will hide the suture incisions... as an extra precaution against leakage, the suture may be painted with liquid sealer."

16   The opposite condition is more likely to present itself—that of emaciation. His hypodermic syringe now loaded with massage cream, the embalmer seeks out and fills the hollowed and sunken areas by injection. In this procedure the backs of the hands and fingers and the under-chin area should not be neglected.

17   Positioning the lips is a problem that recurrently challenges the ingenuity of the embalmer. Closed too tightly, they tend to give a stern, even disapproving expression. Ideally, embalmers feel, the lips should give the impression of being ever so slightly parted, the upper lip protruding slightly for a more youthful appearance. This takes some engineering, however, as the lips tend to drift apart. Lip drift can sometimes be remedied by pushing one or two straight pins through the inner margin of the lower lip and then inserting them between the two front upper teeth. If Mr. Jones happens to have no teeth, the pins can just as easily be anchored in his Armstrong Face Former and Denture Replacer. Another method to maintain lip closure is to dislocate the lower jaw, which is then held in its new position by a wire run through holes which have been drilled through the upper and lower jaws at the midline. As the French are fond of saying, *il faut souffrir pour être belle*.

18   If Mr. Jones has died of jaundice, the embalming fluid will very likely turn him green. Does this deter the embalmer? Not if he has intestinal fortitude. Masking pastes and

cosmetics are heavily laid on, burial garments and casket interiors are color-correlated with particular care, and Jones is displayed beneath rose-colored lights. Friends will say "How *well* he looks." Death by carbon monoxide, on the other hand, can be rather a good thing from the embalmer's viewpoint: "One advantage is the fact that this type of discoloration is an exaggerated form of a natural pink coloration." This is nice because the healthy glow is already present and needs but little attention.

19   The patching and filling completed, Mr. Jones is now shaved, washed, and dressed. Cream-based cosmetic, available in pink, flesh, suntan, brunette, and blond, is applied to his hands and face, his hair is shampooed and combed (and, in the case of Mrs. Jones, set), his hands manicured. For the horny-handed son of toil special care must be taken; cream should be applied to remove ingrained grime, and the nails cleaned. "If he were not in the habit of having them manicured in life, trimming and shaping is advised for better appearance—never questioned by kin."

20   Jones is now ready for casketing (this is the present participle of the verb "to casket"). In this operation his right shoulder should be depressed slightly "to turn the body a bit to the right and soften the appearance of lying flat on the back." Positioning the hands is a matter of importance, and special rubber positioning blocks may be used. The hands should be cupped slightly for a more lifelike, relaxed appearance. Proper placement of the body requires a delicate sense of balance. It should lie as high as possible in the casket, yet not so high that the lid, when lowered, will hit the nose. On the other hand, we are cautioned, placing the body too low "creates the impression that the body is in a box."

21   Jones is next wheeled into the appointed slumber room where a few last touches may be added—his favorite pipe placed in his hand or, if he was a great reader, a book propped into position. (In the case of little Master Jones a Teddy bear may be clutched.) Here he will hold open house for a few days, visiting hours 10 A.M. to 9 P.M.

22   All now being in readiness, the funeral director calls a staff conference to make sure that each assistant knows his precise duties. Mr. Wilber Kriege writes: "This makes your staff feel that they are a part of the team, with a definite assignment that must be properly carried out if the whole plan is to succeed. You never heard of a football coach who failed to talk to his entire team before they go on the field. They have drilled on the plays they are to execute for hours and days, and yet the successful coach knows the importance of making even the bench-warming third-string substitute feel that he is important if the game is to be won." The winning of *this* game is predicted upon glass-smooth handling of the logistics. The funeral director has notified the pallbearers whose names were furnished by the family, has arranged for the presence of clergyman, organist, and soloist, has provided transportation for everybody, has organized and listed the flowers sent by friends. In *Psychology of Funeral Service* Mr. Edward A. Martin points out: "He may not always do as much as the family thinks he is doing, but it is his helpful guidance that they appreciate in knowing they are proceeding as they should.... The important thing is how well his services can be used to make the family believe they are giving unlimited expression to their own sentiment."

23   The religious service may be held in a church or in the chapel of the funeral home; the funeral director vastly prefers the latter arrangement, for not only is it more convenient for him but it affords him the opportunity to show off his beautiful facilities to the gathered mourners. After the clergyman has had his say, the mourners queue up to file past the casket for a last look at the deceased. The family is *never* asked whether they want an open-casket ceremony; in the absence of their instruction to the contrary, this is taken for

granted. Consequently well over 90 per cent of all American funerals feature the open casket—a custom unknown in other parts of the world. Foreigners are astonished by it. An English woman living in San Francisco described her reaction in a letter to the writer:

> I myself have attended only one funeral here—that of an elderly fellow worker of mine. After the service I could not understand why everyone was walking towards the coffin (sorry, I mean casket), but thought I had better follow the crowd. It shook me rigid to get there and find the casket open and poor old Oscar lying there in his brown tweed suit, wearing a suntan makeup and just the wrong shade of lipstick. If I had not been extremely fond of the old boy, I have a horrible feeling that I might have giggled. Then and there I decided that I could never face another American funeral—even dead.

24   The casket (which has been resting throughout the service on a Classic Beauty Ultra Metal Casket Bier) is now transferred by a hydraulically operated device called Porto-Lift to a balloon-tired, Glide Easy casket carriage which will wheel it to yet another conveyance, the Cadillac Funeral Coach. This may be lavender, cream, light green—anything but black. Interiors, of course, are color-correlated, "for the man who cannot stop short of perfection."

25   At graveside, the casket is lowered into the earth. This office, once the prerogative of friends of the deceased, is now performed by a patented mechanical lowering device. A "Lifetime Green" artificial grass mat is at the ready to conceal the sere earth, and overhead, to conceal the sky, is a portable Steril Chapel Tent ("resists the intense heat and humidity of summer and the terrific storms of winter... available in Silver Grey, Rose, or Evergreen"). Now is the time for the ritual scattering of earth over the coffin, as the solemn words "earth to earth, ashes to ashes, dust to dust" are pronounced by the officiating cleric. This can today be accomplished "with a mere flick of the wrist with the Gordon Leak-Proof Earth Dispenser. No grasping of a handful of dirt, no soiled fingers. Simple, dignified, beautiful, reverent! The modern way!" The Gordon Earth Dispenser (at $5) is of nickel-plated brass construction. It is not only "attractive to the eye and long wearing"; it is also "one of the 'tools' for building better public relations" if presented as "an appropriate non-commercial gift" to the clergyman. It is shaped something like a saltshaker.

26   Untouched by human hand, the coffin and the earth are now united.

27   It is in the function of directing the participants through this maze of gadgetry that the funeral director has assigned to himself his relatively new role of "grief therapist." He has relieved the family of every detail, he has revamped the corpse to look like a living doll, he has arranged for it to nap for a few days in a slumber room, he has put on a well-oiled performance in which the concept of *death* has played no part whatsoever—unless it was inconsiderately mentioned by the clergyman who conducted the religious service. He has done everything in his power to make the funeral a real pleasure for everybody concerned. He and his team have given their all to score an upset victory over death.

NOTES AND DISCUSSION

This essay is an outstanding and skillful example of a process analysis. Jessica Mitford is very methodical, detailed, and precise as she describes the practice of embalming. Embalming, she says, is at present surrounded by secrecy. This essay aims to "lift the curtain" on that secrecy.

Mitford describes in (sometimes uncomfortable) detail the process of embalming. She states that embalming is a curious practice unique to North America; her essay is designed to critique this practice and suggest that the funeral industry is performing a service that is wholly unnecessary, and probably highly destructive to the survivors.

Mitford begins with "the arrival of the corpse at the mortuary," and describes the process of what happens there until, "untouched by human hand, the coffin and the earth are now united." She concludes her essay with the stunning observation that *death* plays no part in death whatsoever. Mitford's point is, in part, that the mourning process has become commercialized and dehumanized; an entire industry has been constructed to make sure that death is, in Mitford's words, "simple, dignified, beautiful, reverent!" The mortician becomes part chemist, part surgeon, part choreographer, part artist and sculptor. The funeral itself has become a play: note the word "drama" in the first paragraph, and the description of the funeral director in the last paragraph as someone who plays a "role" and delivers a "performance." The reader is left to ask, "What for?"

STUDY QUESTIONS

For Discussion

1. What is Mitford's attitude toward the process she is analyzing? How do you know? How would you characterize the essay's tone? Note Mitford's careful use of euphemisms: at times she exposes them; at others, she deliberately uses them.

2. Mitford's essay is distinctive not only because of the abundance of detail, but also because of its grim humour. There are many examples of that humour, but notice, in particular, the list of verbs in the second paragraph. What is your response to the essay's humour, given its subject matter?

For Writing

1. Write a description of a process with which you are familiar, making sure to include as many pertinent details as possible.

2. The image of lifting a curtain implies not only disclosure, but also a theatrical performance. Shakespeare is invoked through the reference in the second paragraph to Yorick from *Hamlet*. Do you agree with Mitford that funerals, and by implication, other modern public rituals are needlessly commercialized? Consider a public ritual in which you have been involved recently—a baptism, a wedding, a graduation, or some other celebration—and write a response to Mitford. The commercialization of those public rituals is not limited to the people who supply the services. Discuss the degree to which the participants are implicated as well.

"STATE-OF-THE-ART CAR": THE FERRARI TESTAROSSA

Joyce Carol Oates

BIOGRAPHICAL NOTE

Joyce Carol Oates has been called America's "most prolific major writer." She has written over two dozen novels and collections of short stories, as well as plays and many volumes of poetry. She is also an accomplished essayist who writes on an amazing diversity of subjects. A feminist, she frequently examines the symbols and rituals of male-dominated aspects of North American society.

---

1 Speak of the Ferrari Testarossa to men who know cars and observe their immediate visceral response: the virtual dilation of their eyes in sudden focused *interest*. The Testarossa!—that domestic rocket of a sports car, sleek, low-slung, aggressively wide; startlingly beautiful even in the eyes of non-car aficionados; so spectacular a presence on the road that—as I can personally testify—heads turn, faces break into childlike smiles in its wake. As one observer has noted, the Testarossa drives "civilians" crazy.

2 Like a very few special cars, the Ferrari Testarossa is in fact a meta-car, a poetic metaphor or trope: an *object* raised to the level of a near-spiritual *value*. Of course it has a use—as a Steinway concert grand or a thoroughbred racing horse has a use—but its significance hovers above and around mere use. What can one say about a street car (as opposed to a racing car) capable of traveling 177 effortless miles per hour?—accelerating, as it does, again without effort, from 0 mph to 60 mph in 5 seconds, 107 mph in 13.3 seconds? A car that sells for approximately $104,000—if you can get one? (The current waiting period is twelve months and will probably get longer.) There are said to be no more than 450 Testarossas in private ownership in the United States; only about three hundred models are made by Ferrari yearly. So popular has the model become, due in part to its much-

publicized presence in the television series *Miami Vice* (in which, indeed, fast cars provide a sort of subtextual commentary on the men who drive them), that a line of child-sized motorized "Testarossas" is now being marketed—which extravagant toys range in price from $3,500 to $13,000. (Toys bought by parents who don't want to feel guilty, as one Ferrari dealer remarked.)

3   For all its high-tech styling, its racing-car image, the Ferrari Testarossa is a remarkably easy car to drive: its accelerative powers are first unnerving, then dangerously seductive. You think you are traveling at about 60 miles per hour when in fact you are moving toward 100 miles per hour (with your radar detector—"standard issue for this model"—in operation). In the luxury-leather seats, low, of course, and accommodatingly wide, you have the vertiginous impression of being somehow below the surface of the very pavement, skimming, flying, *rocketing* past vehicles moving at ordinary speeds; as if in a dream, or an "action" film. (Indeed, viewed through the discreetly tinted windshield of a Testarossa, the world, so swiftly passing, looks subtly altered: less assertive in its dimensions, rather more like "background.") Such speeds are heady, intoxicating, clearly addictive: if you are moving at 120 mph so smoothly, why not 130 mph? why not 160 mph? why not the limit—if, indeed, there *is* a limit? "Gusty/Emotions on wet roads on autumn nights" acquire a new significance in a car of such unabashed romance. What godly maniacal power: you have only to depress the accelerator of the Ferrari Testarossa and you're at the horizon. Or beyond.

4   The mystique of high-performance cars has always intrigued me with its very opacity. Is it lodged sheerly in speed?—mechanical ingenuity?—the "art" of a finely tuned beautifully styled vehicle (as the mere physical fact of a Steinway piano constitutes "art")?—the adrenal thrill of courting death? Has it primarily to do with display (that of male game fowl, for instance)? Or with masculine prowess of a fairly obvious sort? (Power being, as the cultural critic Henry Kissinger once observed, the ultimate aphrodisiac.)

5   Or is it bound up with the phenomenon of what the American economist Thorstein Veblen so wittily analyzed as "conspicuous consumption" in his classic *Theory of the Leisure Class* (1899)—Veblen's theory being that the consumption of material goods is determined not by the inherent value of goods but by the social standing derived from their consumption. (Veblen noted how in our capitalistic-democratic society there is an endless "dynamics" of style as the wealthiest class ceaselessly strives to distinguish itself from the rest of society and its habits of consumption trickle down to lower levels.)

6   Men who work with high-performance cars, however, are likely to value them as ends in themselves: they have no time for theory, being so caught up, so mesmerized, in practice. To say that certain cars at certain times determine the "state-of-the-art" is to say that such machinery, on its most refined levels, constitutes a serious and speculative and ever-changing (improving?) art. The Ferrari Testarossa is not a *car* in the generic sense in which, say, a Honda Accord—which my husband and I own—is a *car*. (For one thing, the Accord has about 90 horsepower; the Testarossa 380.) Each Ferrari is more or less unique, possessed of its own mysterious personality; its peculiar ghost-in-the-machine. "It's a good car," I am told, with typical understatement, by a Testarossa owner named Bill Kontes, "—a *good* car." He pauses, and adds, "But not an antique. This is a car you can actually drive."

7   (Though it's so precious—the lipstick-red model in particular such an attention-getter—that you dare not park it in any marginally public place. Meta-cars arouse emotions at all points of the spectrum.)

8   Bill Kontes, in partnership with John Melniczuk, owns and operates Checkered Flag Cars in Vineland, New Jersey—a dealership of such choice content (high-performance

exotic cars, "vintage" classics, others) as to make it a veritable Phillips Collection amid its larger rivals in the prestige car market. It was by way of their hospitality that I was invited to test-drive the Ferrari Testarossa for *Quality*, though my only qualifications would seem to have been that I knew how to drive a car. (Not known to Mr. Kontes and Mr. Melniczuk was the ambiguous fact that I did once own, in racier days, a sports car of a fairly modest species—a Fiat Spider also in audacious lipstick-red. I recall that it was always stalling. That it gave up, so to speak, along a melancholy stretch of interstate highway in the approximate vicinity of Gary, Indiana, emitting actual flames from its exhaust. That the garage owner to whose garage it was ignominiously towed stared at it and said contemptuously, "A pile of junk!" That we sold it soon afterward and never bought another "sports" car again.)

9   It was along a semideserted stretch of South Jersey road that Mr. Kontes turned the Ferrari Testarossa over to me, gallantly, and surely bravely: and conscious of the enormity of the undertaking—a sense, very nearly, that the honor of "woman writerhood" might be here at stake, a colossal blunder or actual catastrophe reflecting not only upon the luckless perpetrator but upon an entire generation and gender—I courageously drove the car, and, encouraged by Mr. Kontes, and by the mysterious powers of the radar detector to detect the presence of uniformed and sanctioned enforcers of the law (which law, I fully understand, *is* for our own good and in the best and necessary interests of the commonwealth), I did in fact accelerate through all five gears to a speed rather beyond one I'd anticipated: though not to 120 mph, which was Mr. Kontes's fairly casual speed a few minutes previously. (This particular Testarossa, new to Vineland, had been driven at 160 mph by Mr. Melniczuk the other day, along a predawn stretch of highway presumably sanctioned by the radar detector. To drive behind the Testarossa, as I also did, and watch it—suddenly—ease away toward the horizon is an eerie sight: if you don't look closely you're likely to be startled into asking, Where did it go?)

10   But the surprise of the Testarossa, *pace Miami Vice* and the hyped-up media image, is that it is an easy, even comfortable car to drive: user-friendly, as the newly coined cliché would have it. It reminded me not at all of the tricky little Spider I'd quite come to hate by the time of our parting but, oddly, of the unnerving but fiercely exhilarating experience of being behind the controls—so to speak—of a two-seater open-cockpit plane. (My father flew sporty airplanes years ago, and my childhood is punctured with images of flight: the wind-ravaged open-cockpit belonged to a former navy bomber recycled for suburban airfield use.) As the Testarossa was accelerated I felt that visceral sense of an irresistibly gathering and somehow condensing power—"speed" being in fact a mere distillation or side effect of power—and, within it, contained by it, an oddly humble sense of human smallness, frailty. One of the perhaps unexamined impulses behind high-speed racing must be not the mere "courting" of death but, on a more primary level, its actual pre-experience; its taste.

11   But what have such thoughts to do with driving a splendid red Ferrari Testarossa in the environs of Vineland, New Jersey, one near-perfect autumn day, an afternoon shading romantically into dusk? Quite beyond, or apart from, the phenomenal machinery in which Bill Kontes and I were privileged to ride I was acutely conscious of the spectacle we and it presented to others' eyes. Never have I seen so many heads turn!—so much staring!— *smiling*! While the black Testarossa may very well resemble, as one commentator has noted, Darth Vader's personal warship, the lipstick-red model evokes smiles of pleasure, envy, awe—most pointedly in young men, of course, but also in older, even elderly women.

Like royalty, the Testarossa seems to bestow a gratuitous benison upon its spectators. Merely to watch it pass is to feel singled out, if, perhaps, rather suddenly drab and anonymous. My thoughts drifted onto the pomp of kings and queens and maharajahs, the legendary excesses of the Gilded Age of Morgan, Carnegie, Rockefeller, Mellon, Armour, McCormick, et al.—Edith Rockefeller McCormick, just to give one small example, served her dinner guests on china consisting of over a thousand pieces containing 11,000 ounces of gold—the Hope Diamond, and Liz Taylor's diamonds, and the vision of Mark Twain, in impeccable dazzling white, strolling on Fifth Avenue while inwardly chafing at his increasing lack of privacy. If one is on public display one is of course obliged not to be conscious of it; driving a $104,000 car means being equal to the car in dignity and style. Otherwise the public aspect of the performance is contaminated: we are left with merely conspicuous consumption, an embarrassment in such times of economic trepidation and worldwide hunger.

12   Still, it's the one incontrovertible truth about the Ferrari Testarossa: no matter who is behind the wheel people stare, and they stare in admiration. Which might not otherwise be the case.

NOTES AND DISCUSSION

An interesting irony underlies this essay: the writer looks at a car, its effects on men, and its metaphoric place in a male-centred value system; but the writing "I," the person appreciating the car, its features, and its effects on observers, is a woman. She seems as interested in the car as a test of gender characteristics and perspectives as she is in it as a machine.

Parts of the essay read like standard automotive journalism or product performance reports. However, Oates consistently takes the report past the standard and ordinary into the exceptional and extraordinary. A segment that begins by characterizing the Testarossa as "a remarkably easy car to drive" continues by describing its "unnerving" and "dangerously seductive" acceleration. She refers to the Testarossa as a "meta-car"—a car that is "about" cars, or about the essence of "car."

The different sections of the essay comment on the car's different aspects: its technical data and physical features; its role as a consumer item and an item of display; its connection with popular culture; its effect on the writer/driver; its effect on those who watch it go by (or pull away).

Overall, Oates wants to explore the journalistic *why* as much as, or more than, the *what*. Why do people admire this car and its drivers? Why does it have such an appeal and mystique, such "value" beyond its price?

STUDY QUESTIONS

For Discussion

1. Apply Veblen's theory of "conspicuous consumption," as introduced and defined here, to other products on the market. What are the dominant means of displaying ownership and a capacity for consumption in some social group you are familiar with or a member of? And what, if any, are the gender implications behind that ownership, display, and consumption?

2. Are you aware of other products whose "worth" is derived from appearances in television, movies, or other popular cultural activities? Are you aware that manufacturers pay to have their cars, clothes, labels, etc., appear in such venues? Discuss some of the possible implications of these hidden advertisements on artistic freedom.

For Writing

1. Describe a consumer item in both its physical and its social contexts, exploring not only what it is, but what it "means." Attempt to link the two frames of reference to show how the product's "meaning" is built into its physical design.

2. As a research project, find E. B. White's essay "Farewell, My Lovely" and read it. There are interesting similarities, and telling differences, between the car described by White and the one in this essay—not only in the cars themselves, but also in the ways each author writes about them. Compare and contrast several features such as the names and physical details of the vehicles, the use of figures of speech, the tone, etc. Ask yourself questions like these: Just what does "Testarossa" mean, anyway? What does it *sound* like it means? What does it appear to refer to?

SHOOTING
AN ELEPHANT

George Orwell

BIOGRAPHICAL NOTE

George Orwell (1903–1950) is the pseudonym of Eric Blair. Orwell was an English novelist, essayist, and social commentator. He was a life-long opponent of totalitarianism in its various forms. He is perhaps best known for two novels, *Animal Farm* (1946) and *Nineteen Eighty-Four* (1947). This essay, which is from a collection entitled *Shooting an Elephant and Other Stories*, has been frequently anthologized.

1   In Moulmein, in lower Burma, I was hated by large numbers of people—the only time in my life that I have been important enough for this to happen to me. I was sub-divisional police officer of the town, and in an aimless, petty kind of way anti-European feeling was very bitter. No one had the guts to raise a riot, but if a European woman went through the bazaars alone somebody would probably spit betel juice over her dress. As a police officer I was an obvious target and was baited whenever it seemed safe to do so. When a nimble Burman tripped me up on the football field and the referee (another Burman) looked the other way, the crowd yelled with hideous laughter. This happened more than once. In the end the sneering yellow faces of young men that met me everywhere, the insults hooted after me when I was at a safe distance, got badly on my nerves. The young Buddhist priests were the worst of all. There were several thousands of them in the town and none of them seemed to have anything to do except stand on street corners and jeer at Europeans.

2   All this was perplexing and upsetting. For at that time I had already made up my mind that imperialism was an evil thing and the sooner I chucked up my job and got out of it the better. Theoretically—and secretly, of course—I was all for the Burmese and all against their oppressors, the British. As for the job I was doing, I hated it more bitterly than I can perhaps make clear. In a job like that you see the dirty work of Empire at close quarters. The wretched prisoners huddling in the stinking cages of the lock-ups, the grey, cowed faces of the long-term convicts, the scarred buttocks of the men who had been flogged with bamboos—all these oppressed me with an intolerable sense of guilt. But I could get noth-

ing into perspective. I was young and ill-educated and I had had to think out my problems in the utter silence that is imposed on every Englishman in the East. I did not even know that the British Empire is dying, still less did I know that it is a great deal better than the younger empires that are going to supplant it. All I knew was that I was stuck between my hatred of the empire I served and my rage against the evil-spirited little beasts who tried to make my job impossible. With one part of my mind I thought of the British Raj as an unbreakable tyranny, as something clamped down, in *sæcula sæculorum* upon the will of prostrate peoples; with another part I thought that the greatest joy in the world would be to drive a bayonet into a Buddhist priest's guts. Feelings like these are the normal by-products of imperialism; ask any Anglo-Indian official, if you can catch him off duty.

3   One day something happened which in a roundabout way was enlightening. It was a tiny incident in itself, but it gave me a better glimpse than I had had before of the real nature of imperialism—the real motives for which despotic governments act. Early one morning the sub-inspector at a police station the other end of the town rang me up on the phone and said that an elephant was ravaging the bazaar. Would I please come and do something about it? I did not know what I could do, but I wanted to see what was happening and I got on to a pony and started out. I took my rifle, an old .44 Winchester and much too small to kill an elephant, but I thought the noise might be useful *in terrorem*. Various Burmans stopped me on the way and told me about the elephant's doings. It was not, of course, a wild elephant, but a tame one which had gone "must." It had been chained up, as tame elephants always are when their attack of "must" is due, but on the previous night it had broken its chain and escaped. Its mahout, the only person who could manage it when it was in that state, had set out in pursuit, but had taken the wrong direction and was now twelve hours' journey away, and in the morning the elephant had suddenly reappeared in the town. The Burmese population had no weapons and were quite helpless against it. It had already destroyed somebody's bamboo hut, killed a cow and raided some fruit-stalls and devoured the stock; also it had met the municipal rubbish van and, when the driver jumped out and took to his heels, had turned the van over and inflicted violences upon it.

4   The Burmese sub-inspector and some Indian constables were waiting for me in the quarter where the elephant had been seen. It was a very poor quarter, a labyrinth of squalid bamboo huts, thatched with palmleaf, winding all over a steep hillside. I remember that it was a cloudy, stuffy morning at the beginning of the rains. We began questioning the people as to where the elephant had gone and, as usual, failed to get any definite information. That is invariably the case in the East; a story always sounds clear enough at a distance, but the nearer you get to the scene of events the vaguer it becomes. Some of the people said that the elephant had gone in one direction, some said that he had gone in another, some professed not even to have heard of any elephant. I had almost made up my mind that the whole story was a pack of lies, when we heard yells a little distance away. There was a loud, scandalized cry of "Go away, child! Go away this instant!" and an old woman with a switch in her hand came round the corner of a hut, violently shooing away a crowd of naked children. Some more women followed, clicking their tongues and exclaiming; evidently there was something that the children ought not to have seen. I rounded the hut and saw a man's dead body sprawling in the mud. He was an Indian, a black Dravidian coolie, almost naked, and he could not have been dead many minutes. The people said that the elephant had come suddenly upon him round the corner of the hut, caught him with its trunk, put its foot on his back and ground him into the earth. This was the rainy season and the ground was soft, and his face had scored a trench a foot deep and a couple of yards long. He was lying on his belly with arms crucified and head sharply

twisted to one side. His face was coated with mud, the eyes wide open, the teeth bared and grinning with an expression of unendurable agony. (Never tell me, by the way, that the dead look peaceful. Most of the corpses I have seen looked devilish.) The friction of the great beast's foot had stripped the skin from his back as neatly as one skins a rabbit. As soon as I saw the dead man I sent an orderly to a friend's house nearby to borrow an elephant rifle. I had already sent back the pony, not wanting it to go mad with fright and throw me if it smelt the elephant.

5   The orderly came back in a few minutes with a rifle and five cartridges, and meanwhile some Burmans had arrived and told us that the elephant was in the paddy fields below, only a few hundred yards away. As I started forward practically the whole population of the quarter flocked out of the houses and followed me. They had seen the rifle and were all shouting excitedly that I was going to shoot the elephant. They had not shown much interest in the elephant when he was merely ravaging their homes, but it was different now that he was going to be shot. It was a bit of fun to them, as it would be to an English crowd; besides they wanted the meat. It made me vaguely uneasy. I had no intention of shooting the elephant—I had merely sent for the rifle to defend myself if necessary—and it is always unnerving to have a crowd following you. I marched down the hill, looking and feeling a fool, with the rifle over my shoulder and an ever-growing army of people jostling at my heels. At the bottom, when you got away from the huts, there was a metalled road and beyond that a miry waste of paddy fields a thousand yards across, not yet ploughed but soggy from the first rains and dotted with coarse grass. The elephant was standing eight yards from the road, his left side towards us. He took not the slightest notice of the crowd's approach. He was tearing up bunches of grass, heating them against his knees to clean them and stuffing them into his mouth.

6   I had halted on the road. As soon as I saw the elephant I knew with perfect certainty that I ought not to shoot him. It is a serious matter to shoot a working elephant—it is comparable to destroying a huge and costly piece of machinery—and obviously one ought not to do it if it can possibly be avoided. And at that distance, peacefully eating, the elephant looked no more dangerous than a cow. I thought then and I think now that his attack of "must" was already passing off; in which case he would merely wander harmlessly about until the mahout came back and caught him. Moreover, I did not in the least want to shoot him. I decided that I would watch him for a little while to make sure that he did not turn savage again, and then go home.

7   But at that moment I glanced round at the crowd that had followed me. It was an immense crowd, two thousand at the least and growing every minute. It blocked the road for a long distance on either side. I looked at the sea of yellow faces above the garish clothes—faces all happy and excited over this bit of fun, all certain that the elephant was going to be shot. They were watching me as they would watch a conjurer about to perform a trick. They did not like me, but with the magical rifle in my hands I was momentarily worth watching. And suddenly I realized that I should have to shoot the elephant after all. The people expected it of me and I had got to do it; I could feel their two thousand wills pressing me forward, irresistibly. And it was at this moment, as I stood there with the rifle in my hands, that I first grasped the hollowness, the futility of the white man's dominion in the East. Here was I, the white man with his gun, standing in front of the unarmed native crowd—seemingly the leading actor of the piece; but in reality I was only an absurd puppet pushed to and fro by the will of those yellow faces behind. I perceived in this moment that when the white man turns tyrant it is his own freedom that he destroys. He becomes a sort of hollow, posing dummy, the conventionalized figure of a sahib. For it is the condition of

his rule that he shall spend his life in trying to impress the "natives," and so in every crisis he has got to do what the "natives" expect of him. He wears a mask, and his face grows to fit it. I had got to shoot the elephant. I had committed myself to doing it when I sent for the rifle. A sahib has got to act like a sahib; he has got to appear resolute, to know his own mind and do definite things. To come all that way, rifle in hand, with two thousand people marching at my heels, and then to trail feebly away, having done nothing—no, that was impossible. The crowd would laugh at me. And my whole life, every white man's life in the East, was one long struggle not to be laughed at.

8   But I did not want to shoot the elephant. I watched him beating his bunch of grass against his knees, with that preoccupied grandmotherly air that elephants have. It seemed to me that it would be murder to shoot him. At that age I was not squeamish about killing animals, but I had never shot an elephant and never wanted to. (Somehow it always seems worse to kill a *large* animal.) Besides, there was the beast's owner to be considered. Alive, the elephant was worth at least a hundred pounds; dead, he would only be worth the value of his tusks, five pounds, possibly. But I had got to act quickly. I turned to some experienced-looking Burmans who had been there when we arrived, and asked them how the elephant had been behaving. They all said the same thing: he took no notice of you if you left him alone, but he might charge if you went too close to him.

9   It was perfectly clear to me what I ought to do. I ought to walk up to within, say, twenty-five yards of the elephant and test his behavior. If he charged, I could shoot; if he took no notice of me, it would be safe to leave him until the mahout came back. But also I knew that I was going to do no such thing. I was a poor shot with a rifle and the ground was soft mud into which one would sink at every step. If the elephant charged and I missed him, I should have about as much chance as a toad under a steam-roller. But even then I was not thinking particularly of my own skin, only of the watchful yellow faces behind. For at that moment, with the crowd watching me, I was not afraid in the ordinary sense, as I would have been if I had been alone. A white man mustn't be frightened in front of "natives"; and so, in general, he isn't frightened. The sole thought in my mind was that if anything went wrong those two thousand Burmans would see me pursued, caught, trampled on and reduced to a grinning corpse like that Indian up the hill. And if that happened it was quite probable that some of them would laugh. That would never do.

10   There was only one alternative. I shoved the cartridges into the magazine and lay down on the road to get a better aim. The crowd grew very still, and a deep, low, happy sigh, as of people who see the theatre curtain go up at last, breathed from innumerable throats. They were going to have their bit of fun after all. The rifle was a beautiful German thing with cross-hair sights. I did not then know that in shooting an elephant one would shoot to cut an imaginary bar running from ear-hole to ear-hole. I ought, therefore, as the elephant was sideways on, to have aimed straight at his ear-hole, actually I aimed several inches in front of this, thinking the brain would be further forward.

11   When I pulled the trigger I did not hear the bang or feel the kick—one never does when a shot goes home—but I heard the devilish roar of glee that went up from the crowd. In that instant, in too short a time, one would have thought, even for the bullet to get there, a mysterious, terrible change had come over the elephant. He neither stirred nor fell, but every line of his body had altered. He looked suddenly stricken, shrunken, immensely old, as though the frightful impact of the bullet had paralysed him without knocking him down. At last, after what seemed a long time—it might have been five seconds, I dare say—he sagged flabbily to his knees. His mouth slobbered. An enormous senility seemed to have

settled upon him. One could have imagined him thousands of years old. I fired again into the same spot. At the second shot he did not collapse but climbed with desperate slowness to his feet and stood weakly upright, with legs sagging and head drooping. I fired a third time. That was the shot that did for him. You could see the agony of it jolt his whole body and knock the last remnant of strength from his legs. But in falling he seemed for a moment to rise, for as his hind legs collapsed beneath him he seemed to tower upward like a huge rock toppling, his trunk reaching skyward like a tree. He trumpeted, for the first and only time. And then down he came, his belly towards me, with a crash that seemed to shake the ground even where I lay.

12   I got up. The Burmans were already racing past me across the mud. It was obvious that the elephant would never rise again, but he was not dead. He was breathing very rhythmically with long rattling gasps, his great mound of a side painfully rising and falling. His mouth was wide open—I could see far down into caverns of pale pink throat. I waited a long time for him to die, but his breathing did not weaken. Finally I fired my two remaining shots into the spot where I thought his heart must be. The thick blood welled out of him like red velvet, but still he did not die. His body did not even jerk when the shots hit him, the tortured breathing continued without a pause. He was dying, very slowly and in great agony, but in some world remote from me where not even a bullet could damage him further. I felt that I had got to put an end to that dreadful noise. It seemed dreadful to see the great beast lying there, powerless to move and yet powerless to die, and not even to be able to finish him. I sent back for my small rifle and poured shot after shot into his heart and down his throat. They seemed to make no impression. The tortured gasps continued as steadily as the ticking of a clock.

13   In the end I could not stand it any longer and went away. I heard later that it took him half an hour to die. Burmans were bringing dahs and baskets even before I left, and I was told they had stripped his body almost to the bones by the afternoon.

14   Afterwards, of course, there were endless discussions about the shooting of the elephant. The owner was furious, but he was only an Indian and could do nothing. Besides, legally I had done the right thing, for a mad elephant has to be killed, like a mad dog, if its owner fails to control it. Among the Europeans opinion was divided. The older men said I was right, the younger men said it was a damn shame to shoot an elephant for killing a coolie, because an elephant was worth more than any damn Coringhee coolie. And afterwards I was very glad that the coolie had been killed; it put me legally in the right and it gave me a sufficient pretext for shooting the elephant. I often wondered whether any of the others grasped that I had done it solely to avoid looking a fool.

NOTES AND DISCUSSION

"Shooting an Elephant" has been widely admired and studied since its first publication in 1950. It is an essay that takes as its subject matter the destructive practice of imperialism, specifically English imperialism in Burma in the late 1930s. It approaches its subject by precisely and relentlessly describing a very disturbing incident, the shooting of an elephant. While Orwell acknowledges that there is no good reason for him to kill the elephant, though he is "legally" in the right, he also feels that he has no choice in the matter. He shoots the animal he says, "solely to avoid looking a fool." That line, the last in the essay, renders the entire practice of imperialism an immoral exercise in narcissism.

STUDY QUESTIONS

For Discussion

1. How would you characterize Orwell's persona in this essay? Do you think that the persona can be read effectively as embodying the English presence in Burma? How do you know?

2. This essay contains some very descriptive passages. What is the effect of descriptions like the following: "I watched him beating his bunch of grass against his knees, with that preoccupied grandmotherly air that elephants have"?

For Writing

1. What is Orwell's thesis in this essay? Write a short essay addressing the question of whether Orwell's method of argumentation—narrative—is matched well to the thesis.

2. Much (perhaps all) of Orwell's writing can be considered "political," and this essay proves no exception. What do you consider Orwell's political position to be in this essay? Note the racial tension in the piece ("in an aimless, petty kind of way anti-European feeling was very bitter. No one had the guts to raise a riot, but if a European woman went through the bazaars alone somebody would probably spit betel juice over her dress"), and discuss what you think Orwell's position on race may be.

CROCODILED MOATS IN THE KINGDOM OF LETTERS

Cynthia Ozick

BIOGRAPHICAL NOTE

Cynthia Ozick was born and raised in New York City. She has written widely about the various tensions between scientists and humanists, one of the topics of this essay. Her essays, novels, and short stories have earned her wide praise and many awards, including a Guggenheim Fellowship. In her most recent collection of essays, entitled *Fame & Folly*, Ozick examines the often vexed relationship between life and literature by referring to subjects as wide-ranging as Salman Rushdie and Anthony Trollope.

For constantly I felt I was moving among two groups—comparable in intelligence, identical in race, not grossly different in social origin, earning about the same incomes, who had almost ceased to communicate at all, who in intellectual, moral, and psychological climate had so little in common that... one might have crossed an ocean.

— C. P. Snow, "The Two Cultures and the Scientific Revolution"

1 Disraeli in his novel *Sybil* spoke of "two nations," the rich and the poor. After the progress of more than a century, the phrase (and the reality) remains regrettably apt. But in the less than three decades since C. P. Snow proposed his "two cultures" thesis—the gap of incomprehension between the scientific and literary elites—the conditions of what we still like to call culture have altered so drastically that Snow's arguments are mostly dissolved into pointlessness. His compatriot and foremost needler, the Cambridge critic F. R. Leavis, had in any case set out to flog Snow's hypothesis from the start. Snow, he said, "rides on an advancing swell of cliché," "doesn't know what literature is," and hasn't "had the advantage of an intellectual discipline of any kind." And besides—here Leavis emitted his final boom—"there is only one culture."

2   In the long run both were destined to be mistaken—Leavis perhaps more than Snow. In 1959, when Snow published "The Two Cultures," we had already had well over a hundred years to get used to the idea of science as a multidivergent venture—dozens and dozens of disciplines, each one nearly a separate nation with its own governance, psychology, entelechy. It might have been possible to posit, say, a unitary medical culture in the days when barbers were surgeons; but in recent generations we don't expect our dentist to repair a broken kneecap, or our orthopedist to practice cardiology. And nowadays we are learning that an ophthalmologist with an understanding of the cornea is likely to be a bit shaky on the subject of the retina. Engineers are light-years from astrophysicists. Topology is distinct from topography, paleobotany from paleogeology, particle physics from atomic. In reiterating that scientific culture is specialist culture—who doesn't know this?—one risks riding an advancing swell of cliché. Yet science, multiplying, fragmented, in hot pursuit of split ends, is in a way a species of polytheism, or, rather, animism: every grain of matter, every path of conceptualization, has its own ruling spirit, its differentiated lawgiver and traffic director. Investigative diversity and particularizing empiricism have been characteristic of science since—well, since alchemy turned into physical chemistry (and lately into superconductivity); since the teakettle inspired the locomotive; since Icarus took off his wax wings to become Pan Am; since Archimedes stepped out of his tub into Einstein's sea.

3   Snow was in command of all this, of course—he was pleased to identify himself as an exceptional scientist who wrote novels—and still he chose to make a monolith out of splinters. Why did he do it? In order to have one unanimity confront another. While it may have been a polemical contrivance to present a diversiform scientific culture as unitary, it was patently not wrong, thirty years ago, to speak of literary culture as a single force or presence. That was what was meant by the peaceable word "humanities." And it was what Leavis meant, too, when he growled back at Snow that one culture was all there was worth having. "Don't mistake me," Leavis pressed, "I am not preaching that we should defy, or try to reverse, the accelerating movement of external civilization (the phrase sufficiently explains itself, I hope) that is determined by advancing technology.... What I *am* saying is that such a concern is not enough—disastrously not enough." Not enough, he argued, for "a human future... in full intelligent possession of its full humanity." For Leavis, technology was the mere outer rind of culture, and the job of literature (the hot core at the heart of culture) was not to oppose science but to humanize it. Only in Snow's wretchedly deprived mind did literature stand apart from science; Snow hardly understood what literature was *for*. And no wonder; Snow's ideas about literary intellectuals came, Leavis sneered, from "the reviewing in the Sunday papers."

4   It has never been easy to fashion a uniform image of science—which is why we tend to say "the sciences." But until not very long ago one could take it for granted (despite the headlong decline of serious high art) that there was, on the humanities side, a concordant language of sensibility, an embracing impulse toward integration, above all the conviction of human connectedness—even if that conviction occasionally partook of a certain crepuscular nostalgia we might better have done without. Snow pictured literature and science as two angry armies. Leavis announced that there was only one army, with literature as its commander in chief. Yet it was plain that both Leavis and Snow, for all their antagonisms, saw the kingdom of letters as an intact and enduring power.

5   This feeling for literary culture as a glowing wholeness—it *was* a feeling, a stirring, a flush of idealism—is now altogether dissipated. The fragrant term that encapsulated it—belles-lettres—is nearly archaic and surely effete: it smacks of leather tooling for the moneyed, of posturing. But it was once useful enough. Belles-lettres stood for a binding thread of observation and civilizing emotion. It signified not so much that letters are beautiful as that the house of letters is encompassingly humane and undivisive, no matter how severally its windows are shaped, or who looks out or in. Poets, scholars, journalists, librarians, novelists, playwrights, art critics, philosophers, historians, political theorists, and all the rest may have inhabited different rooms, differently furnished, but it was indisputably one house with a single roof and plenty of connecting doors and passageways. And sometimes—so elastic and compressive was the humanist principle—poet, scholar, essayist, philosopher, etc., all lived side by side in the same head. Seamlessness (even if only an illusion) never implied locked and separate cells.

6   And now? Look around. Now "letters" suggest a thousand enemy camps, "genres" like fortresses, professions isolated by crocodiled moats. The living tissue of intuition and inference that nurtured the commonalty of the humanities is ruptured by an abrupt invasion of specialists. In emulation of the sciences? But we don't often hear of astronomers despising molecular biologists; in science, it may be natural for knowledge to run, like quicksilver, into crannies.

7   In the ex-community of letters, factions are in fashion, and the business of factions is to despise. Matthew Arnold's mild and venerable dictum, an open-ended, open-armed, definition of literature that clearly intends a nobility of inclusiveness—"the best that is known and thought in the world"—earns latter-day assaults and jeers. What can all that mean now but "canon," and what can a received canon mean but reactionary, racist, sexist, elitist closure? Politics presses against disinterestedness; all categories are suspect, no category is allowed to display its wares without the charge of enslavement by foregone conclusion and vested interest. What Arnold called the play of mind is asked to show its credentials and prove its legitimacy. "Our organs of criticism," Arnold complained in 1864 (a period as uninnocent as our own), "are organs of men and parties having practical ends to serve, and with them those practical ends are the first thing and the play of mind the second."

8   And so it is with us. The culture of the humanities has split and split and split again, always for reasons of partisan ascendancy and scorn. Once it was not unusual for writers—Dreiser, Stephen Crane, Cather, Hemingway!—to turn to journalism for a taste of the workings of the world. Today novelists and journalists are alien breeds reared apart, as if imagination properly belonged only to the one and never to the other; as if society and instinct were designed for estrangement. The two crafts are contradictory even in method; journalists are urged to tell secrets in the top line; novelists insinuate suspensefully, and wait for the last line to spill the real beans. Dickens, saturated in journalism, excelled at shorthand; was a court reporter; edited topical magazines.

9   In the literary academy, Jacques Derrida has the authority that Duns Scotus had for medieval scholastics—and it is authority, not literature, that mainly engages faculties. In the guise of maverick or rebel, professors kowtow to dogma. English departments have set off after theory, and use culture as an instrument to illustrate doctrinal principles, whether Marxist or "French Freud." The play of mind gives way to signing up and lining up. College teachers were never so cut off from the heat of poets dead or alive as they are now; only think of the icy distances separating syllables by, say, Marianne Moore, A. R.

Ammons, May Swenson, or Amy Clampitt from the papers read at last winter's Modern Language Association meeting—*viz.*, "Written Discourse as Dialogic Interaction," "Abduction, Transference, and the Reading Stage," "The Politics of Feminism and the Discourse of Feminist Literary Criticism."

10   And more: poets trivialize novelists, novelists trivialize poets. Both trivialize critics. Critics trivialize reviewers. Reviewers report that they *are* critics. Short-story writers assert transfigurations unavailable to novelists. Novelists declare the incomparable glories of the long pull. Novelizing estheticians, admitting to literature no claims of moral intent, ban novelizing moralists. The moralists condemn the estheticians as precious, barren, solipsist. Few essayists essay fiction. Few novelists hazard essays. Dense-language writers vilify minimalists. Writers of plain prose ridicule complex sentences. Professors look down on commercial publishers. Fiction writers dread university presses. The so-called provinces envy and despise the provinciality of New York. New York sees sour grapes in California and everywhere else. The so-called mainstream judges which writers are acceptably universal and which are to be exiled as "parochial." The so-called parochial, stung or cowardly or both, fear all particularity and attempt impersonation of the acceptable. "Star" writers—recall the International PEN Congress in New York last year—treat lesser-knowns as invisible, negligible. The lesser-knowns, crushed, disparage the stars.

11   And even the public library, once the unchallenged repository of the best that is known and thought, begins to split itself off, abandons its mandate and rents out Polaroid cameras and videotapes, like some semiphilanthropic Crazy Eddie. My own local library, appearing to jettison the basic arguments of the age, flaunts, shelf after shelf prominently marked Decorating, Consumer Power, How-To, Cookery, Hooray for Hollywood, Accent on You, What Makes Us Laugh, and many more such chitchat categories. But there are no placards for Literature, History, Biography; and Snow and Leavis, whom I needed to moon over in order to get started on this essay, were neither one to be had. (I found them finally in the next town, in a much smaller if more traditionally bookish library.)

12   Though it goes against the grain of respected current belief to say so, literature is really *about* something. It is about us. That may be why we are drawn to think of the kingdom of letters as a unity, at least in potential. Science, teeming and multiform, is about how the earth and the heavens and the microbes and the insects and our mammalian bodies are constructed, but literature is about the meaning of the finished construction. Or, to set afloat a more transcendent vocabulary: science is about God's work; literature is about our work. If our work lies untended (and what is our work but aspiration?), if literary culture falls into a heap of adversial splinters—into competing contemptuous clamorers for turf and mental dominance—then what will be left to tell us that we are one human presence?

13   To forward that strenuous telling, Matthew Arnold (himself now among the jettisoned) advised every reader and critic to "try and possess one great literature, at least, besides his own; and the more unlike his own, the better." Not to split off from but to add on to the kingdom of letters: so as to uncover its human face.

14   An idea which—in a time of ten thousand self-segregating literary technologies—may be unwanted, if not obsolete.

NOTES AND DISCUSSION

A physicist and a novelist, C. P. Snow saw himself as unusually—perhaps uniquely—qualified to discuss the differences between what he calls "The Two Cultures." His essay of that title was first published in 1956, and revised and expanded in 1959. It provoked an immediate and heated response from F. R. Leavis, who was probably the most respected and influential literary critic of his day. His position, as Ozick notes, was that "the job of literature... was not to oppose science but to humanize it."

Ozick's essay was first published in 1987. While it begins as a response to Snow and Leavis and their divisive debate, by the end, Ozick admits to using Snow and Leavis merely "to moon over in order to get started on this essay." Her essay, it turns out, is not really a response at all, but an addendum to the discussion, and a nostalgic obituary about the passing of a single, unified discipline called "the humanities."

In addition to the references to Snow and Leavis, Ozick refers throughout the essay to Matthew Arnold, among others. Note her use of Arnold's definition of literature in the seventh paragraph: "the best that is known and thought in the world."

Note also her use of figurative language to advance her own position. This is from paragraph two: "Investigative diversity and particularizing empiricism have been characteristic of science since—well, since alchemy turned into physical chemistry (and lately into superconductivity); since the teakettle inspired the locomotive; since Icarus took off his wax wings to become Pan Am; since Archimedes stepped out of his tub into Einstein's sea."

STUDY QUESTIONS

For Discussion

1. Although Ozick is quite clear about her disapproval of the tone of the debate between Snow and Leavis, is she equally clear about her own notions of the differences between science and literature? In your response, consider Ozick's paraphrase of Leavis's claim that "technology [is] the mere outer rind of culture." What are the implications of that metaphor?

2. Ozick discusses the "Kingdom of Letters" extensively in this essay. One part of that kingdom is "Literature." By her own definition, is Ozick's essay literature? To what extent is Ozick's essay an example of a "paradigm shift" in the humanities, like those that Thomas Kuhn claims govern scientific investigation?

For Writing

1. Write an analytical paragraph about Ozick's definitions of science and of literature. Do you agree with her definitions? What would you add to them? In the course of your answer, consider where you think writing about science falls, in each of the three traditions—Snow's, Leavis's, and Ozick's—presented here.

2. Ozick uses the "split" that divided Leavis and Snow to start her discussion, but she is much more concerned with other, more current splits in the "Kingdom of Letters." In a short research essay, investigate some of the figures and positions that Ozick names. Do you agree that the splits she is concerned about are more profound and disturbing than the one between Leavis and Snow? Is Ozick's original split—between the sciences and the humanities—still an important one?

LESSONS FROM PLAY; LESSONS FROM LIFE

Henry Petroski

BIOGRAPHICAL NOTE

Henry Petroski is a professor of civil engineering at Duke University and a regular columnist for *American Scientist* magazine. He has written several books, all of which are concerned with problems and questions in engineering and design. His books include *The Pencil: A History of Design and Circumstance* (1990) and *The Evolution of Useful Things* (1992).

1   When I want to introduce the engineering concept of fatigue to students, I bring a box of paper clips to class. In front of the class I open one of the paper clips flat and then bend it back and forth until it breaks in two. That, I tell the class, is failure by fatigue, and I point out that the number of back and forth cycles it takes to break the paper clip depends not only on how strong the clip is but also on how severely I bend it. When paper clips are used normally, to clip a few sheets of paper together, they can withstand perhaps thousands or millions of the slight openings and closings it takes to put them on and take them off the papers, and thus we seldom experience their breaking. But when paper clips are bent open so wide that they look as if we want them to hold all the pages of a book together, it might take only ten or twenty flexings to bring them to the point of separation.

2   Having said this, I pass out a half dozen or so clips to each of the students and ask them to bend their clips to breaking by flexing them as far open and as far closed as I did. As the students begin this low-budget experiment, I prepare at the blackboard to record how many back and forth bendings it takes to break each paper clip. As the students call out the numbers, I plot them on a bar graph called a histogram. Invariably the results fall clearly under a bell-shaped normal curve that indicates the statistical distribution of the results, and I elicit from the students the explanations as to why not all the paper clips broke with the

same number of bendings. Everyone usually agrees on two main reasons: not all paper clips are equally strong, and not every student bends his clips in exactly the same way. Thus the students recognize at once the phenomenon of fatigue and the fact that failure by fatigue is not a precisely predictable event.

3   Many of the small annoyances of daily life are due to predictable—but not precisely so—fractures from repeated use. Shoelaces and light bulbs, as well as many other familiar objects, seem to fail us suddenly and when it is least convenient. They break and burn out under conditions that seem no more severe than those they had been subjected to hundreds or thousands of times before. A bulb that has burned continuously for decades may appear in a book of world records, but to an engineer versed in the phenomenon of fatigue, the performance is not remarkable. Only if the bulb had been turned on and off daily all those years would its endurance be extraordinary, for it is the cyclic and not the continuous heating of the filament that is its undoing. Thus, because of the fatiguing effect of being constantly changed, it is the rare scoreboard that does not have at least one bulb blown.

4   Children's toys are especially prone to fatigue failure, not only because children subject them to seemingly endless hours of use but also because the toys are generally not overdesigned. Building a toy too rugged could make it too heavy for the child to manipulate, not to mention more expensive than its imitators. Thus, the seams of rubber balls crack open after so many bounces, the joints of metal tricycles break after so many trips around the block, and the heads of plastic dolls separate after so many nods of agreement.

5   Even one of the most innovative electronic toys of recent years has been the victim of mechanical fatigue long before children (and their parents) tire of playing with it. Texas Instruments' Speak & Spell effectively employs one of the first microelectronic voice synthesizers. The bright red plastic toy asks the child in a now-familiar voice to spell a vocabulary of words from the toy's memory. The child pecks out letters on the keyboard, and they appear on a calculator-like display. When the child finishes spelling a word, the ENTER key is pressed and the computer toy says whether the spelling is correct and prompts the child to try again when a word is misspelled. Speak & Spell is so sophisticated that it will turn itself off if the child does not press a button for five minutes or so, thus conserving its four C-cells.

6   My son's early model Speak & Spell had given him what seemed to be hundreds of hours of enjoyment when one day the ENTER key broke off at its plastic hinge. But since Stephen could still fit his small finger into the buttonhole to activate the switch, he continued to enjoy the smart, if disfigured, toy. Soon thereafter, however, the E key snapped off, and soon the T and O keys followed suit. Although he continued to use the toy, its keyboard soon became a maze of missing letters and, for those that were saved from the vacuum cleaner, taped-on buttons.

7   What made these failures so interesting to me was the very strong correlation between the most frequently occurring letters in the English language and the fatigued keys on Stephen's Speak & Spell. It is not surprising that the ENTER key broke first, since it was employed for inputting each word and thus got more use than any one letter. Of the seven most common letters—in decreasing occurrence, E, T, A, O, I, N, S, R—five (E, T, O, S, and R) were among the first keys to break. All other letter keys, save for the two seemingly anomalous failures of P and Y, were intact when I first reported this serendipitous experiment on the fatigue phenomenon in the pages of *Technology Review*.

8   If one assumes that all Speak & Spell letter keys were made as equally well as manufacturing processes allowed, perhaps about as uniformly as or even more so than paper clips, then those plastic keys that failed must generally have been the ones pressed most

frequently. The correlation between letter occurrence in common English words and the failure of the keys substantiates that this did indeed happen, for the anomalous failures seem also to be explainable in terms of abnormally high use. Because my son is right-handed, he might be expected to favor letters on the right-hand side of the keyboard when guessing spellings or just playing at pressing letters. Since none of the initial failed letters occurs in the four left-most columns of Speak & Spell, this proclivity could also explain why the common-letter keys A and N were still intact. The anomalous survival of the I key may be attributed to its statistically abnormal strength or to its underuse by a gregarious child. And the failure of the infrequently occurring P and Y might have been a manifestation of the statistical weakness of the keys or of their overuse by my son. His frequent spelling of his name and the name of his cat, Pollux, endeared the letter *P* to him, and he had learned early that *Y* is sometimes a vowel. Furthermore, each time the Y key was pressed, Speak & Spell would ask the child's favorite question, "Why?"

9   Why the fatigue of its plastic buttons should have been the weak link that destroyed the integrity of my son's most modern electronic toy could represent the central question for understanding engineering design. Why did the designers of the toy apparently not anticipate this problem? Why did they not use buttons that would outlast the toy's electronics? Why did they not obviate the problem of fatigue, the problem that has defined the lifetimes of mechanical and structural designs for ages? Such questions are not unlike those that are asked after the collapse of a bridge or the crash of an airplane. But the collapse of a bridge or the crash of an airplane can endanger hundreds of lives, and thus the possibility of the fatigue of any part can be a lesson from which its victims learn nothing. Yet the failure of a child's toy, though it may cause tears, is but a lesson for a child's future of burnt-out light bulbs and broken shoelaces. And years later, when his shoelaces break as he is rushing to dress for an important appointment, he will be no less likely to ask, "Why?"

10   After I wrote about the found experiment, my son retrieved his Speak & Spell from my desk and resumed playing with the toy—and so continued the experiment. Soon another key failed, the vowel key U in the lower left position near where Stephen held his thumb. Next the A key broke, another vowel and the third most frequently occurring letter of the alphabet. The experiment ended with that failure, however, for Stephen acquired a new model of Speak & Spell with the new keyboard design that my daughter, Karen, had pointed out to me at an electronics store. Instead of having individually hinged plastic buttons, the new model has its keyboard printed on a single piece of rubbery plastic stretched over the switches. The new model Stephen has is called an E. T. Speak & Spell, after the little alien creature in the movie, and I am watching the plastic sheet in the vicinity of those two most frequently occurring letters to see if the fatigue gremlin will strike again.

11   Not long after I had first written about my son's Speak & Spell I found out from readers that their children too had had to live with disfigured keyboards. It is a tribute to the ingeniousness of the toy—and the attachment that children had developed for it—that they endured the broken keys and adapted in makeshift ways, as they would have to throughout a life of breakdowns and failures in our less than perfect world. Some parents reported that their children apparently discovered that the eraser end of a pencil fit nicely into the holes of the old Speak & Spell and thus could be used to enter the most frequently used letters without the children having to use their fingertips. I have wondered if indeed this trick was actually discovered by the parents who loved to play with the toy, for almost any child's

finger should easily fit into the hole left by the broken button, but Mommy and Daddy's certainly would not.

12   Nevertheless, this resourcefulness suggests that the toy would have been a commercial success even with its faults, but the company still improved the keyboard design to solve the problem of key fatigue. The new buttonless keyboard is easily cleaned and pressed by even the clumsiest of adult fingers. The evolution of the Speak & Spell keyboard is not an atypical example of the way mass-produced items, though not necessarily planned that way, are debugged through use. Although there may have been some disappointment among parents who had paid a considerable amount of money for what was then among the most advanced applications of microelectronics wizardry, their children, who were closer to the world of learning to walk and talk and who were still humbled by their skinned knees and twisted tongues, took the failure of the keys in stride. Perhaps the manufacturer of the toy, in the excitement of putting the first talking computer on the market, overlooked some of the more mundane aspects of its design, but when the problem of the fractured keys came to its attention, it acted quickly to improve the toy's mechanical shortcomings.

13   I remember being rather angry when my son's Speak & Spell lost its first key. For all my understanding of the limitations of engineering and for all my attempted explanations to my neighbors of how failures like the Hyatt Regency walkways and the DC-10 could happen without clear culpability, I did not extend my charity to the designers of the toy. But there is a difference in the design and development of things that are produced by the millions and those that are unique, and it is generally the case that the mass-produced mechanical or electronic object undergoes some of its debugging and evolution after it is offered to the consumer. Such actions as producing a new version of a toy or carrying out an automobile recall campaign are not possible for the large civil engineering structure, however, which must be got right from the first stages of construction. So my charity should have extended to the designers of the Speak & Spell, for honest mistakes can be made by mechanical and electrical as well as by civil engineers. Perhaps someone had underestimated the number of *E*s it would take a child to become bored with the new toy. After all, most toys are put away long before they break. If this toy, which is more sophisticated than any I ever had in my own childhood, could tell me when I misspelled words I never could keep straight, then I would demand from it other superhuman qualities such as indestructibility. Yet we do not expect that of everything.

14   Although we might all be annoyed when a light bulb or a shoelace breaks, especially if it does so at a very inconvenient time, few if any of us would dream of taking it back to the store claiming it had malfunctioned. We all know the story of Thomas Edison searching for a suitable filament for the light bulb, and we are aware of and grateful for the technological achievement. We know, almost intuitively it seems, that to make a shoelace that would not break would involve compromises that we are not prepared to accept. Such a lace might be undesirably heavy or expensive for the style of shoe we wear, and we are much more willing to have the option of living with the risk of having the lace break at an inopportune time or of having the small mental burden of anticipating when the lace will break so that we might replace it in time. Unless we are uncommonly fastidious, we live dangerously and pay little attention to preventive maintenance of our fraying shoelaces or our aging light bulbs. Though we may still ask "Why?" when they break, we already know and accept the answer.

15   As the consequences of failure become more severe, however, the forethought we must give to them becomes more a matter of life and death. Automobiles are manufactured by the millions, but it would not do to have them failing with a snap on the highways the way light bulbs and shoelaces do at home. The way an automobile could fail must be anticipated so that, as much as possible, a malfunction does not lead to an otherwise avoidable deadly accident. Since tires are prone to flats, we want our vehicles to be able to be steered safely to the side of the road when one occurs. Such a failure is accepted in the way light bulb and shoelace failures are, and we carry a spare tire to deal with it. Other kinds of malfunctions are less acceptable. We do not want the brakes on all four wheels and the emergency braking system to fail us suddenly and simultaneously. We do not want the steering wheel to come off in our hands as we are negotiating a snaking mountain road. Certain parts of the automobile are given special attention, and in the rare instances when they do fail, leading to disaster, massive lawsuits can result. When they become aware of a potential hazard, automobile manufacturers are compelled to eliminate what might be the causes of even the most remote possibilities of design-related accidents by the massive recall campaigns familiar to us all.

16   As much as it is human to make mistakes, it is also human to want to avoid them. Murphy's Law, holding that anything that can go wrong will, is not a law of nature but a joke. All the light bulbs that last until we tire of the lamp, all the shoelaces that outlast their shoes, all the automobiles that give trouble-free service until they are traded in have the last laugh on Murphy. Just as he will not outlive his law, so nothing manufactured can be or is expected to last forever. Once we recognize this elementary fact, the possibility of a machine or a building being as near to perfect for its designed lifetime as its creators may strive to be for theirs is not only a realistic goal for engineers but also a reasonable expectation for consumers. It is only when we set ourselves such an unrealistic goal as buying a shoelace that will never break, inventing a perpetual motion machine, or building a vehicle that will never break down that we appear to be fools and not rational beings.

17   Oliver Wendell Holmes is remembered more widely for his humor and verse than for the study entitled "The Contagiousness of Puerperal Fever" that he carried out as Parkman Professor of Anatomy and Philosophy at Harvard Medical School. Yet it may have been his understanding of the seemingly independent working of the various parts of the human body that helped him to translate his physiological experiences into a lesson for structural and mechanical engineers. Although some of us go first in the knees and others in the back, none of us falls apart all at once in all our joints. So Holmes imagined the foolishness of expecting to design a horse-drawn carriage that did not have a weak link.

18   Although intended as an attack on Calvinism, in which Holmes uses the metaphor of the "one-hoss shay" to show that a system of logic, no matter how perfect it seems, must collapse if its premises are false, the poem also holds up as a good lesson for engineers. Indeed, Micro-Measurements, a Raleigh, North Carolina-based supplier of devices to measure the stresses and strains in engineering machines and structures, thinks "The Deacon's Masterpiece" so apt to its business that it offers copies of the poem suitable for framing. The firm's advertising copy recognizes that although " Holmes knew nothing of... modern-day technology when he wrote about a vehicle with no weak link among its components," he did realize the absurdity of attempting to achieve "the perfect engineering feat."

19   In Holmes's poem, which starts on p. 160, the Deacon decides that he will build an indestructible shay, with every part as strong as the rest, so that it will not break down.

However, what the Deacon fails to take into account is that everything has a lifetime, and if indeed a shay could be built with "every part as strong as the rest," then every part would "wear out" at the same time and whoever inherited the shay from the Deacon, who himself would pass away before his creation, would be taken by surprise one day. While "The Deacon's Masterpiece" is interesting in recognizing that breaking down is the wearing out of one part, the weakest link, it is not technologically realistic in suggesting that all parts could have exactly the same lifetime. That premise is contrary to the reality that we can only know that this or that part will last for *approximately* this or that many years, just as we can only state the probability that any one paper clip will break after so many bendings. The exact lifetime of a part, a machine, or a structure is known only after it has broken.

20   Just as we are expected to know our own limitations, so should we know those of the inanimate world. Even the pyramids in the land of the Sphinx, whose riddle reminds us that we all must crawl before we walk and that we will not walk forever, have been eroded by the sand and the wind. Nothing on this earth is inviolate on the scale of geological time, and nothing we create will last at full strength forever. Steel corrodes and diamonds can be split. Even nuclear waste has a half-life.

21   Engineering deals with lifetimes, both human and otherwise. If not fatigue or fracture, then corrosion or erosion; if not war or vandalism, then taste or fashion claim not only the body but the very souls of once-new machines. Some lifetimes are set by the intended use of an engineering structure. As such an offshore oil platform may be designed to last for only the twenty or thirty years that it will take to extract the oil from the rock beneath the sea. It is less easy to say when the job of a bridge will be completed, yet engineers will have to have some clear idea of a bridge's lifetime if only to specify when some major parts will have to be inspected, serviced, or replaced. Buildings have uses that are subject to the whims of business fashion, and thus today's modern skyscraper may be unrentable in fifty years. Monumental architecture such as museums and government buildings, on the other hand, should suggest a permanence that makes engineers think in terms of centuries. A cathedral, a millennium.

22   The lifetime of a structure is no mere anthropomorphic metaphor, for how long a piece of engineering must last can be one of the most important considerations in its design. We have seen how the constant on and off action of a child's toy or a light bulb can cause irreparable damage, and so it is with large engineering structures. The ceaseless action of the sea on an offshore oil platform subjects its welded joints to the very same back and forth forces that cause a paper clip or a piece of plastic to crack after so many flexures. The bounce of a bridge under traffic and the sway of a skyscraper in the wind can also cause the growth of cracks in or the exhaustion of strength of steel cables and concrete beams, and one of the most important calculations of the modern engineer is the one that predicts how long it will take before cracks or the simple degradation of its materials threaten the structure's life. Sometimes we learn more from experience than calculations, however.

23   Years after my son had outgrown Speak & Spell, and within months of his disaffection with the video games he once wanted so much, he began to ask for toys that required no batteries. First he wanted a BB gun, which his mother and I were reluctant to give him, and then he wanted a slingshot. This almost biblical weapon seemed somehow a less violent toy and evoked visions of a Norman Rockwell painting, in which a boy-being-a-boy conceals his homemade slingshot from the neighbor looking out a broken window. It is almost as innocent a piece of Americana as the baseball hit too far, and no one would want to ban slingshots or boys.

24   I was a bit surprised, however, to learn that my son wanted to *buy* a slingshot ready-made, and I was even more surprised to learn that his source would not be the Sears Catalog, which might have fit in with the Norman Rockwell image, but one of the catalogs of several discount stores that seem to have captured the imagination of boys in this age of high-tech toys. What my son had in mind for a slingshot was a mass-produced, metal-framed object that was as far from my idea of a slingshot as an artificial Christmas tree is from a fir.

25   Stephen was incredulous as I took him into the woods behind our house looking for the proper fork with which to make what I promised him would be a *real* slingshot. We collected a few pieces of trees that had fallen in a recent wind storm, and we took them up to our deck to assemble what I had promised. Unfortunately, I had forgotten how easily pine and dry cottonwood break, and my first attempts to wrap a rubber band around the sloping arms of the benign weapon I was making met with structural failure. We finally were able to find pieces strong enough to withstand the manipulation required for their transformation into slingshots, but their range was severely limited by the fact that they would break if pulled back too far.

26   My son was clearly disappointed in my inability to make him a slingshot, and I feared that he had run away disillusioned with me when he disappeared for an hour or so after dinner that evening. But he returned with the wyes of tree branches stronger and more supple than any I found behind our house. We were able to wrap our fattest rubber bands around these pieces of wood without breaking them, and they withstood as much pull as we were able or willing to supply. Unfortunately, they still did not do as slingshots, for the rubber bands kept slipping down the inclines of the Y and the bands were difficult to hold without the stones we were using for ammunition slipping through them or going awry.

27   After almost a week of frustration trying to find the right branch-and-rubber band combination that would produce a satisfactory slingshot that would not break down, I all but promised I would buy one if we could not make a top-notch shooter out of the scraps of wood scattered about our basement. Stephen was patient if incredulous as I sorted through odd pieces of plywood and selected one for him to stand upon while I sawed out of it the shape of the body of a slingshot. He was less patient when I drilled holes to receive a rubber band, and I acceded to his impatience in not sanding the plywood or rounding the edges before giving the device the test of shooting. I surprised him by producing some large red rubber bands my wife uses for her manuscripts, and he began to think he might have a real slingshot when I threaded the ends of a rubber band through the holes in the plywood Y. With the assembly completed I demonstrated how far a little pebble could be shot, but I had to admit, at least to myself, that it was very difficult to keep the pebble balanced on the slender rubber band. My son was politely appreciative of what I had made for him, but he was properly not ecstatic. The pebbles he tried to shoot dropped in weak arcs before his target, and he knew that his slingshot would be no match for the one his friend had bought through the catalog.

28   In my mind I admitted that the homemade slingshot was not well designed, and in a desperate attempt to save face with my son I decided to add a second rubber band and large pocket to improve not only the range but also the accuracy of the toy. These proved to be tremendous improvements, and with them the slingshot seemed almost unlimited in range and very comfortable to use. Now we had a slingshot of enormous potential, and my son was ready to give it the acid test. We spent an entire weekend practicing our aim at a beer bottle a good thirty yards away. The first hit was an historic event that pinged off the glass and the second a show of power that drilled a hole clear through the green glass and left

the bottle standing on only a prayer. As we got better at controlling the pebbles issuing from our homemade slingshot we changed from bottles to cans for our targets and hit them more and more.

29   With all our shooting, the rubber bands began to break from fatigue. This did not bother my son, and he seemed to accept it as something to be expected in a slingshot, for it was just another toy and not a deacon's masterpiece. As rubber bands broke, we replaced them. What proved to be more annoying was the slipping of the rubber band over the top of the slingshot's arm, for we had provided no means of securing the band from doing so. In time, however, we came to wrap the broken rubber bands around the tops of the arms to keep the functioning ones in place. This worked wonderfully, and the satisfaction of using broken parts to produce an improved slingshot was especially appealing to my son. He came to believe that his slingshot could outperform any offered in the catalogs, and the joy of producing it ourselves from scrap wood and rubber bands gave him a special pleasure. And all the breaking pieces of wood, slipping rubber bands, and less-than-perfect functioning gave him a lesson in structural engineering more lasting than any textbook's—or any fanciful poem's. He learned to make things that work by steadily improving upon things that did not work. He learned to learn from mistakes. My son, at eleven, had absorbed one of the principal lessons of engineering, and he had learned also the frustrations and the joys of being an engineer.

APPENDIX

The Deacon's Masterpiece
Or, the Wonderful "One-Hoss Shay"
A Logical Story

By Oliver Wendell Holmes

Have you heard of the wonderful one-hoss shay,
That was built in such a logical way
It ran a hundred years to a day,
And then, of a sudden, it—ah, but stay,
I'll tell you what happened without delay,
Scaring the parson into fits,
Frightening people out of their wits—
Have you ever heard of that, I say?

Seventeen hundred and fifty-five.
Georgius Secundus *was then alive,—*
Snuffy old drone from the German hive.
That was the year when Lisbon-town
Saw the earth open and gulp her down,
And Braddock's army was done so brown,
Left without a scalp to its crown.
It was on the terrible Earthquake-day
That the Deacon finished the one-hoss shay.
A general flavor of mild decay,
But nothing local, as one may say.
There couldn't be,—for the Deacon's art
Had made it so like in every part
That there wasn't a chance for one to start.
For the wheels were just as strong as the thills,
And the floor was just as strong as the sills,
And the panels just as strong as the floor,
And the whipple-tree neither less nor more,
And the back crossbar as strong as the fore,
And spring and axle and hub encore.
And yet, as a whole, *it is past a doubt*
In another hour it will be worn out!

First of November, 'Fifty-five!
This morning the parson takes a drive.
Now, small boys, get out of the way!
Here comes the wonderful one-hoss shay,
Drawn by a rat-tailed, ewe-necked bay.
"Huddup!" said the parson.—Off went they.
The parson was working his Sunday's text,—

Had got to fifthly, and stopped perplexed
At what the—Moses—was coming next.
All at once the horse stood still,
'Close by the meet'n'-house on the hill.
First a shiver, and then a thrill,
Then something decidedly like a spill,—
And the parson was sitting upon a rock,
At half past nine by the meet'n'-house clock,—
Just the hour of the Earthquake shock!
What do you think the parson found,
When he got up and stared around?
The poor old chaise in a heap or mound,
As if it had been to the mill and ground!
You see, of course, if you're not a dunce,
How it went to pieces all at once,—
All at once, and nothing first,—
Just as bubbles do when they burst.

End of the wonderful one-hoss shay.
Logic is logic. That's all I say.

NOTES AND DISCUSSION

This essay is a chapter from Henry Petroski's book *To Engineer Is Human: The Role of Failure in Successful Design* (1985). In that book, Petroski argues that failures in general, but mechanical and structural failures (which are both failures of design) in particular, are responsible for many more significant advances in knowledge than any number of successes could be. This essay discusses "fatigue failure" and the steady development of a successful design for a slingshot for Petroski's son Stephen. Notice Petroski's strategy of beginning his discussion with an anecdote and continuing to include bits of narrative, such as the stories about the Speak & Spell electronic games and the evolution of the perfect slingshot. Note, too, the importance of play in this essay: Petroski draws parallels between play and more "serious" scientific investigation. Finally, notice that the essay implicitly compares engineering to the human condition through its title, conclusion, and techniques such as nostalgia, allusion, and anecdote.

STUDY QUESTIONS

For Discussion

1. Implicit in this essay is the notion that play is an important part of learning—for children, for students, and for engineering professors. What are the connotations of this notion?

2. This essay suggests that engineering principles such as fatigue are essential parts of everyday life, and that curious people are all, to some degree, engineers at heart. Do you agree with that proposal? Why, or why not? How would you define an engineer?

For Writing

1. Write a brief report on mechanical fatigue discussing what it is, how it comes about, and why it is important. Compare your report with Petroski's essay. How and why are they different?

2. Write a narrative about a time in your life when simple technology failed you. What did you learn from that experience?

THE OFFICIAL THEORY

Steven Pinker

BIOGRAPHICAL NOTE

Steven Pinker, the Johnstone Family Professor of Psychology at Harvard University, works in the controversial field of evolutionary psychology. His research into language and language development in children confirmed that children do have an innate, or inborn, facility for language learning. Inspired by books such as Richard Dawkins's *The Selfish Gene*, Pinker then began to question how that ability came to be. Pinker rests his answer in Darwinian theories of evolution, though Pinker's approaches to this answer have placed him in opposition to such other prominent evolutionary theorists as Stephen Jay Gould. Pinker's books include four works for non-academics: *The Language Instinct* (1994); *How the Mind Works* (1997); *Words and Rules: The Ingredients of Language* (1999), and *The Blank Slate: The Modern Denial of Human Nature* (2002), of which "The Official Theory" is Chapter 1.

---

1 "Blank Slate" is a loose translation of the medieval Latin term *tabula rasa*—literally, "scraped tablet." It is commonly attributed to the philosopher John Locke (1632–1704), though in fact he used a different metaphor. Here is the famous passage from *An Essay Concerning Human Understanding:*

> Let us then suppose the mind to be, as we say, white paper void of all characters, without any ideas. How comes it to be furnished? Whence comes it by that vast store which the busy and boundless fancy of man has painted on it with an almost endless variety? Whence has it all the materials of reason and knowledge? To this I answer, in one word, from Experience.[1]

Locke was taking aim at theories of innate ideas in which people were thought to be born with mathematical ideals, eternal truths, and a notion of God. His alternative theory, empiricism, was intended both as a theory of psychology—how the mind works—and as a theory of epistemology—how we come to know the truth. Both goals helped motivate his political philosophy, often honored as the foundation of liberal democracy. Locke opposed dogmatic justifications for the political status quo, such as the authority of the church and the divine right of kings, which had been touted as self-evident truths. He argued that social arrangements should be reasoned out from scratch and agreed upon by mutual consent, based on knowledge that any person could acquire. Since ideas are grounded in experience, which varies from person to person, differences of opinion arise not because one mind is equipped to grasp the truth and another is defective, but because the two minds have had different histories. Those differences therefore ought to be tolerated rather than suppressed. Locke's notion of a blank slate also undermined a hereditary royalty and aristocracy, whose members could claim no innate wisdom or merit if their minds had started out as blank as everyone else's. It also spoke against the institution of slavery, because slaves could no longer be thought of as innately inferior or subservient.

2   During the past century the doctrine of the Blank Slate has set the agenda for much of the social sciences and humanities. As we shall see, psychology has sought to explain all thought, feeling, and behavior with a few simple mechanisms of learning. The social sciences have sought to explain all customs and social arrangements as a product of the socialization of children by the surrounding culture: a system of words, images, stereotypes, role models, and contingencies of reward and punishment. A long and growing list of concepts that would seem natural to the human way of thinking (emotions, kinship, the sexes, illness, nature, the world) are now said to have been "invented" or "socially constructed."[2]

3   The Blank Slate has also served as a sacred scripture for political and ethical beliefs. According to the doctrine, any differences we see among races, ethnic groups, sexes, and individuals come not from differences in their innate constitution but from differences in their experiences. Change the experiences—by reforming parenting, education, the media, and social rewards—and you can change the person. Underachievement, poverty, and antisocial behavior can be ameliorated; indeed, it is irresponsible not to do so. And discrimination on the basis of purportedly inborn traits of a sex or ethnic group is simply irrational.

4   The Blank Slate is often accompanied by two other doctrines, which have also attained a sacred status in modern intellectual life. My label for the first of the two is commonly attributed to the philosopher Jean-Jacques Rousseau (1712–1778), though it really comes from John Dryden's *The Conquest of Granada,* published in 1670:

> I am as free as Nature first made man,
> Ere the base laws of servitude began,
> When wild in woods the noble savage ran.

5   The concept of the noble savage was inspired by European colonists' discovery of indigenous peoples in the Americas, Africa, and (later) Oceania. It captures the belief that humans in their natural state are selfless, peaceable, and untroubled, and that blights such as greed, anxiety, and violence are the products of civilization. In 1755 Rousseau wrote:

> So many authors have hastily concluded that man is naturally cruel, and requires a regular system of police to be reclaimed; whereas nothing can be more gentle than him in his primitive state, when placed by nature at an equal distance from the stupidity of brutes and the pernicious good sense of civilized man....
>
> The more we reflect on this state, the more convinced we shall be that it was the least subject of any to revolutions, the best for man, and that nothing could have drawn him out of it but some fatal accident, which, for the public good, should never have happened. The

example of the savages, most of whom have been found in this condition, seems to confirm that mankind was formed ever to remain in it, that this condition is the real youth of the world, and that all ulterior improvements have been so many steps, in appearance towards the perfection of individuals, but in fact towards the decrepitness of the species.[3]

6   First among the authors that Rousseau had in mind was Thomas Hobbes (1588–1679), who had presented a very different picture:

> Hereby it is manifest, that during the time men live without a common power to keep them all in awe, they are in that condition which is called war; and such a war as is of every man against every man....
>   In such condition there is no place for industry, because the fruit thereof is uncertain: and consequently no culture of the earth; no navigation, nor use of the commodities that may be imported by sea; no commodious building; no instruments of moving and removing such things as require much force; no knowledge of the face of the earth; no account of time; no arts; no letters; no society; and which is worst of all, continual fear, and danger of violent death; and the life of man, solitary, poor, nasty, brutish, and short.[4]

Hobbes believed that people could escape this hellish existence only by surrendering their autonomy to a sovereign person or assembly. He called it a leviathan, the Hebrew word for a monstrous sea creature subdued by Yahweh at the dawn of creation.

7   Much depends on which of these armchair anthropologists is correct. If people are noble savages, then a domineering leviathan is unnecessary. Indeed, by forcing people to delineate private property for the state to recognize—property they might otherwise have shared—the leviathan creates the very greed and belligerence it is designed to control. A happy society would be our birthright; all we would need to do is eliminate the institutional barriers that keep it from us. If, in contrast, people are naturally nasty, the best we can hope for is an uneasy truce enforced by police and the army. The two theories have implications for private life as well. Every child is born a savage (that is, uncivilized), so if savages are naturally gentle, childrearing is a matter of providing children with opportunities to develop their potential, and evil people are products of a society that has corrupted them. If savages are naturally nasty, then childrearing is an arena of discipline and conflict, and evil people are showing a dark side that was insufficiently tamed.

8   The actual writings of philosophers are always more complex than the theories they come to symbolize in the textbooks. In reality, the views of Hobbes and Rousseau are not that far apart. Rousseau, like Hobbes, believed (incorrectly) that savages were solitary, without ties of love or loyalty, and without any industry or art (and he may have out-Hobbes'd Hobbes in claiming they did not even have language). Hobbes envisioned—indeed, literally drew—his leviathan as an embodiment of the collective will, which was vested in it by a kind of social contract; Rousseau's most famous work is called *The Social Contract,* and in it he calls on people to subordinate their interests to a "general will."

9   Nonetheless, Hobbes and Rousseau limned contrasting pictures of the state of nature that have inspired thinkers in the centuries since. No one can fail to recognize the influence of the doctrine of the Noble Savage in contemporary consciousness. We see it in the current respect for all things natural (natural foods, natural medicines, natural childbirth) and the distrust of the man-made, the unfashionability of authoritarian styles of childrearing and education, and the understanding of social problems as repairable defects in our institutions rather than as tragedies inherent to the human condition.

10   The other sacred doctrine that often accompanies the Blank Slate is usually attributed to the scientist, mathematician, and philosopher René Descartes (1596–1650):

There is a great difference between mind and body, inasmuch as body is by nature always divisible, and the mind is entirely indivisible.... When I consider the mind, that is to say, myself inasmuch as I am only a thinking being, I cannot distinguish in myself any parts, but apprehend myself to be clearly one and entire; and though the whole mind seems to be united to the whole body, yet if a foot, or an arm, or some other part, is separated from the body, I am aware that nothing has been taken from my mind. And the faculties of willing, feeling, conceiving, etc. cannot be properly speaking said to be its parts, for it is one and the same mind which employs itself in willing and in feeling and understanding. But it is quite otherwise with corporeal or extended objects, for there is not one of them imaginable by me which my mind cannot easily divide into parts.... This would be sufficient to teach me that the mind or soul of man is entirely different from the body, if I had not already been apprised of it on other grounds.[5]

11   A memorable name for this doctrine was given three centuries later by a detractor, the philosopher Gilbert Ryle (1900–1976):

There is a doctrine about the nature and place of minds which is so prevalent among theorists and even among laymen that it deserves to be described as the official theory.... The official doctrine, which hails chiefly from Descartes, is something like this. With the doubtful exception of idiots and infants in arms every human being has both a body and a mind. Some would prefer to say that every human being is both a body and a mind. His body and his mind are ordinarily harnessed together, but after the death of the body his mind may continue to exist and function. Human bodies are in space and are subject to mechanical laws which govern all other bodies in space.... But minds are not in space, nor are their operations subject to mechanical laws....

... Such in outline is the official theory. I shall often speak of it, with deliberate abusiveness, as "the dogma of the Ghost in the Machine."[6]

12   The Ghost in the Machine, like the Noble Savage, arose in part as a reaction to Hobbes. Hobbes had argued that life and mind could be explained in mechanical terms. Light sets our nerves and brain in motion, and that is what it means to see. The motions may persist like the wake of a ship or the vibration of a plucked string, and that is what it means to imagine. "Quantities" get added or subtracted in the brain, and that is what it means to think.

13   Descartes rejected the idea that the mind could operate by physical principles. He thought that behavior, especially speech, was not *caused* by anything, but freely *chosen.* He observed that our consciousness, unlike our bodies and other physical objects, does not feel as if it is divisible into parts or laid out in space. He noted that we cannot doubt the existence of our minds—indeed, we cannot doubt that we *are* our minds—because the very act of thinking presupposes that our minds exist. But we *can* doubt the existence of our bodies, because we can imagine ourselves to be immaterial spirits who merely dream or hallucinate that we are incarnate.

14   Descartes also found a moral bonus in his dualism (the belief that the mind is a different kind of thing from the body): "There is none which is more effectual in leading feeble spirits from the straight path of virtue, than to imagine that the soul of the brute is of the same nature as our own, and that in consequence, after this life we have nothing to fear or to hope for, any more than the flies and the ants."[7] Ryle explains Descartes's dilemma:

When Galileo showed that his methods of scientific discovery were competent to provide a mechanical theory which should cover every occupant of space, Descartes found in himself two conflicting motives. As a man of scientific genius he could not but endorse the claims of mechanics, yet as a religious and moral man he could not accept, as Hobbes accepted, the discouraging rider to those claims, namely that human nature differs only in degree of complexity from clockwork.[8]

15   It can indeed be upsetting to think of ourselves as glorified gears and springs. Machines are insensate, built to be used, and disposable; humans are sentient, possessing of dignity and rights, and infinitely precious. A machine has some workaday purpose, such as grinding grain or sharpening pencils; a human being has higher purposes, such as love, worship, good works, and the creation of knowledge and beauty. The behavior of machines is determined by the ineluctable laws of physics and chemistry; the behavior of people is freely chosen. With choice comes freedom, and therefore optimism about our possibilities for the future. With choice also comes responsibility, which allows us to hold people accountable for their actions. And of course if the mind is separate from the body, it can continue to exist when the body breaks down, and our thoughts and pleasures will not someday be snuffed out forever.

16   As I mentioned, most Americans continue to believe in an immortal soul, made of some nonphysical substance, which can part company with the body. But even those who do not avow that belief in so many words still imagine that somehow there must be more to us than electrical and chemical activity in the brain. Choice, dignity, and responsibility are gifts that set off human beings from everything else in the universe, and seem incompatible with the idea that we are mere collections of molecules. Attempts to explain behavior in mechanistic terms are commonly denounced as "reductionist" or "determinist." The denouncers rarely know exactly what they mean by those words, but everyone knows they refer to something bad. The dichotomy between mind and body also pervades everyday speech, as when we say "Use your head," when we refer to "out-of-body experiences," and when we speak of "John's body," or for that matter "John's brain," which presupposes an owner, John, that is somehow separate from the brain it owns. Journalists sometimes speculate about "brain transplants" when they really should be calling them "body transplants," because, as the philosopher Dan Dennett has noted, this is the one transplant operation in which it is better to be the donor than the recipient.

17   The doctrines of the Blank Slate, the Noble Savage, and the Ghost in the Machine— or, as philosophers call them, empiricism, romanticism, and dualism—are logically independent, but in practice they are often found together. If the slate is blank, then strictly speaking it has neither injunctions to do good nor injunctions to do evil. But good and evil are asymmetrical: there are more ways to harm people than to help them, and harmful acts can hurt them to a greater degree than virtuous acts can make them better off. So a blank slate, compared with one filled with motives, is bound to impress us more by its inability to do harm than by its inability to do good. Rousseau did not literally believe in a blank slate, but he did believe that bad behavior is a product of learning and socialization.[9] "Men are wicked," he wrote, "a sad and constant experience makes proof unnecessary."[10] But this wickedness comes from society: "There is no original perversity in the human heart. There is not a single vice to be found in it of which it cannot be said how and whence it entered."[11] If the metaphors in everyday speech are a clue, then all of us, like Rousseau, associate blankness with virtue rather than with nothingness. Think of the moral connotations of the adjectives *clean, fair, immaculate, lily-white, pure, spotless, unmarred,* and *unsullied,* and of the nouns *blemish, blot, mark, stain,* and *taint.*

18   The Blank Slate naturally coexists with the Ghost in the Machine, too, since a slate that is blank is a hospitable place for a ghost to haunt. If a ghost is to be at the controls, the factory can ship the device with a minimum of parts. The ghost can read the body's

display panels and pull its levers, with no need for a high-tech executive program, guidance system, or CPU. The more not-clockwork there is controlling behavior, the less clockwork we need to posit. For similar reasons, the Ghost in the Machine happily accompanies the Noble Savage. If the machine behaves ignobly, we can blame the ghost, which freely chose to carry out the iniquitous acts; we need not probe for a defect in the machine's design.

19   Philosophy today gets no respect. Many scientists use the term as a synonym for effete speculation. When my colleague Ned Block told his father that he would major in the subject, his father's reply was "Luft!"—Yiddish for "air." And then there's the joke in which a young man told his mother he would become a Doctor of Philosophy and she said, "Wonderful! But what kind of disease is philosophy?"

20   But far from being idle or airy, the ideas of philosophers can have repercussions for centuries. The Blank Slate and its companion doctrines have infiltrated the conventional wisdom of our civilization and have repeatedly surfaced in unexpected places. William Godwin (1756–1835), one of the founders of liberal political philosophy, wrote that "children are a sort of raw material put into our hands," their minds "like a sheet of white paper."[12] More sinisterly, we find Mao Zedong justifying his radical social engineering by saying, "It is on a blank page that the most beautiful poems are written."[13] Even Walt Disney was inspired by the metaphor. "I think of a child's mind as a blank book," he wrote. "During the first years of his life, much will be written on the pages. The quality of that writing will affect his life profoundly."[14]

21   Locke could not have imagined that his words would someday lead to Bambi (intended by Disney to teach self-reliance); nor could Rousseau have anticipated Pocahontas, the ultimate noble savage. Indeed, the soul of Rousseau seems to have been channeled by the writer of a recent Thanksgiving op-ed piece in the *Boston Globe:*

> I would submit that the world native Americans knew was more stable, happier, and less barbaric than our society today.... there were no employment problems, community harmony was strong, substance abuse unknown, crime nearly nonexistent. What warfare there was between tribes was largely ritualistic and seldom resulted in indiscriminate or wholesale slaughter. While there were hard times, life was, for the most part, stable and predictable.... Because the native people respected what was around them, there was no loss of water or food resources because of pollution or extinction, no lack of materials for the daily essentials, such as baskets, canoes, shelter, or firewood.[15]

22   The third doctrine, too, continues to make its presence felt in modern times. In 2001 George W. Bush announced that the American government will not fund research on human embryonic stem cells if scientists have to destroy new embryos to extract them (the policy permits research on stem-cell lines that were previously extracted from embryos). He derived the policy after consulting not just with scientists but with philosophers and religious thinkers. Many of them framed the moral problem in terms of "ensoulment," the moment at which the cluster of cells that will grow into a child is endowed with a soul. Some argued that ensoulment occurs at conception, which implies that the blastocyst (the five-day-old ball of cells from which stem cells are taken) is morally equivalent to a person and that destroying it is a form of murder.[16] That argument proved decisive, which means that the American policy on perhaps the most promising medical technology of the twenty-first century was decided by pondering the moral issue as it might have been framed centuries before: When does the ghost first enter the machine?

23   These are just a few of the fingerprints of the Blank Slate, the Noble Savage, and the Ghost in the Machine on modern intellectual life. In the following chapters we will see how the seemingly airy ideas of Enlightenment philosophers entrenched themselves in modern consciousness, and how recent discoveries are casting those ideas in doubt.

NOTES

1. Locke, 1690/1947, bk. II, chap. 1, p. 26.
2. Hacking, 1999.
3. Rousseau, 1755/1994, pp. 61–62.
4. Hobbes, 1651/1957, pp. 185–186.
5. Descartes, 1641/1967, Meditation VI, p. 177.
6. Ryle, 1949, pp. 13–17.
7. Descartes, 1637/2001, part V, p. 10.
8. Ryle, 1949, p. 20.
9. Cohen, 1997.
10. Rousseau, 1755/1986, p. 208.
11. Rousseau, 1762/1979, p. 92.
12. Quoted in Sowell, 1987, p. 63.
13. Originally in *Red Flag* (Beijing), June 1, 1958; quoted in Courtois et al., 1999.
14. J. Kalb, "The downtown gospel according to Reverend Billy," *New York Times,* February 27, 2000.
15. D. R. Vickery, "And who speaks for our earth?" *Boston Globe,* December 1, 1997.
16. Green, 2001; R. Mishra, "What can stem cells really do?" *Boston Globe,* August 21, 2001.

WORKS CITED

Cohen. J. 1997. The natural goodness of humanity. In A. Reath, B. Herman, & C. Korsgaard (Eds.), *Reclaiming the history of ethics: Essays for John Bawls.* New York: Cambridge University Press.

Courtois, S., Werth, N., Panné, J.-L., Paczkowski, A., Bartosêk, K. & Margolin, J.-L. 1999. *The black book of communism: Crimes, terror and repression.* Cambridge, Mass.: Harvard U.P.

Descartes, R. 1637/2001. *Discourse on method.* New York: Bartleby.com.

Descartes, R. 1641/1967. Meditations on first philosophy. In R. Popkin (Ed.), *The philosophy of the 16th and 17th centuries.* New York: Free Press.

Green, R. M. 2001. *The human embryo research debates: Bioethics in the vortex of controversy.* New York: Oxford University Press.

Hacking, I. 1999. *The social construction of what?* Cambridge, Mass.: Harvard University Press.

Hobbes, T. 1651/1957. *Leviathan.* New York: Oxford University Press.

Kalb, J. "The downtown gospel according to Reverend Billy." *New York Times*, February 27, 2000.

Locke, J. 1690/1947. *An essay concerning human understanding.* New York: E. P Dutton.

Rousseau, J.-J. 1755/1986. *The first and second discourses together with the replies to critics and Essay on the origin of languages.* New York: Perennial Library.

Rousseau, J.-J. 1755/1994. *Discourse upon the origin and foundation of inequality among mankind.* New York: Oxford University Press.

Rousseau, J.-J. 1762/1979. *Emile.* New York: Basic Books.

Ryle, G. 1949. *The concept of mind.* London: Penguin.

Sowell, T. 1987. A *conflict of visions: Ideological origins of political struggles.* New York: Quill.

Vickery, D. R. "And who speaks for our earth?" *Boston Globe*, December 1, 1997.

NOTES AND DISCUSSION

Steven Pinker's field is evolutionary psychology, which involves the study of the ways that the mind, like the body, has been modified through biological evolution; that is, it asks how the brain's circuitry has been designed to help it solve adaptive problems. Pinker wrote *The Blank Slate* to consider why such a concept of human nature and the working of the mind is so widely regarded as *politically* suspect. In the chapter reprinted here, Pinker defines and explores the histories of three prominent doctrines (or "myths," as he has also called them) that have formed the foundations of theories of human nature. Thomas Kuhn would probably view these doctrines as "paradigms," and we may also consider them as metaphors. The Blank Slate, Pinker has said, assumes that the mind "has no unique structure, and that its entire organization comes from the environment via socialization and learning." The Noble Savage metaphor assumes that people have "no evil impulses," and that malice and violence are learned behaviours. The Ghost in the Machine assumes that an immaterial soul is the seat for free will and choice, and that the soul cannot be merely a material function of the brain. Different political ideologies favour different myths: Marxism favours the Blank Slate; the Noble Savage appeals to those with a rather sentimentalized Romantic view; and the religious and socially conservative right prefers the Ghost in the Machine. However, as Pinker also argues here, these doctrines are not necessarily mutually exclusive, but can be harnessed to one another for ideological purposes. Moreover, as he demonstrates with considerable irony, it is possible for a radical liberal, a Communist, and a social and economic conservative all to hold much the same opinion, at different times and in different contexts.

STUDY QUESTIONS

For Discussion

1. Consider the "metaphors in everyday speech" Pinker names above. Add sayings, slogans, proverbs, and other "social commonplaces" that seem indicative of this kind of binary thinking, a mode of thinking that excludes shades of meaning from conceptions of the mind and its workings, and of "human nature." Or, consider the kinds of binaries that stem from the Noble Savage doctrine (primitive vs. civilized; natural vs. urbanized, instinctive vs. reasoned, etc.). Is the Ghost in the Machine equally susceptible to such

binaries? You might wish to read Sherry Turkle's version of the Ghost in the Machine, further on in this collection, before answering this question.

2. Which of these three doctrines makes you the most uncomfortable? Why? (You may wish to answer this question first in a timed, *private* free-writing exercise, in order to discover what you are willing to share with others and what, if anything, you are not.)

For Writing

1. Write a comparative essay on the historical assumptions of the Ghost in the Machine and Turkle's encounters with personae adopted in MUDs. Explain where the "ghostly" concepts of the "real" mind and "artificial" intelligence coincide and differ.

2. Do further reading about Pinker's views of the political roots of such doctrines, and consider how such ideological positions relate to the contrary views A. M. Turing confronts in "Computing Machinery and Intelligence." Ask yourself, for example, how they are connected with Turing's own assumptions. After all, Turing relies on the blank slate doctrine for his "evolutionary" sense of the development of the thinking machine. How does this doctrine condition his view of the nature of "thinking" and the element of the Ghost in the Machine in his theological refutations?

THE WAY WE WOO

Heather Pringle

BIOGRAPHICAL NOTE

Heather Pringle, a science journalist based in Vancouver, has written on various aspects of archaeology for magazines such as *New Scientist, Omni, Canadian Geographic*, and *Saturday Night*. She has received both the National Magazine Award and the Canadian Archaeological Association's Public Writing Award. She recently published *In Search of Ancient North America* (1996), and is currently working on a book about the Maya.

1 Helen Fisher slips into a ringside seat, amusement stirring in her dark eyes. It's just after eight on a steamy Friday night at the Mad Hatter Restaurant and Pub, one of dozens of softly lit singles bars on Manhattan's prosperous Upper East Side. A bevy of young businessmen, ties loosened and beer glasses in hand, lean against the railings, sizing up each female who walks in the door. On the street outside, barhoppers stream by the plate-glass windows like tropical fish. "There's constant motion here," says Fisher. "It looks like a real good pickup bar."

2 Elegantly dressed in a black skirt and sweater set, Fisher looks more like a society columnist than someone about to settle down for an evening in a singles bar. But the 48-year-old anthropologist has spent the past decade deciphering the mysteries of human mating behaviour, and she still relishes the odd evening in the field. "Men and women have no idea the amount of sexual signals they are sending out to each other," she says, angling her chair for a better view. "They'd be amazed."

3 Fisher, a research associate in the department of anthropology at the American Museum of Natural History in New York, is one of a new scientific breed seeking out the

First published in *Equinox*, November/December 1993. Reprinted with permission of the author and *Equinox* magazine. The photographs that originally accompanied the article have been dropped.

biological and genetic roots of our love lives. Unwilling to accept traditional views, she and her colleagues have begun taking a fresh look at human romance—from the first twinges of physical attraction to the heady flush of courtship and the bitter acrimony of divorce. Taking clues from the animal kingdom and anthropology, they are turning up answers to some of the most enduring mysteries of romance: why men fall for pretty faces and women pine for men of means; why males roam from bed to bed, while females dream of Mr. Right; and why love is so intoxicating and divorce so commonplace.

4   As she glances across the room, Fisher begins pointing out some of the subtleties of human courtship, patterns of behaviour that seem to stem from a distant past. Those men by the railing, for example? Fisher grins. Singles bars, she explains, work much like the mating grounds of sage grouse and other birds. After staking out individual territories in the most prominent area in the bar, the men are now attempting to attract females with simple courtship displays: stretching, exaggerating simple movements, and laughing heartily. "One of them is even swinging from side to side, which is a real gesture of approachability," she says.

5   Fisher points out a miniskirted woman deep in conversation with a man at the bar. "See how she's gesturing and swaying and preening?" Fisher asks. "She keeps on touching her eyes, her nose, and her mouth." Stroking her face as if stroking that of her companion, she is flashing a series of intention cues—messages that she wants to touch him. But he remains strangely impassive, refusing to turn even his shoulders toward her. The conversation may be flowing, says Fisher, but the courtship ritual is rapidly stalling. As we watch, shameless voyeurs, the animated discussion slowly sputters and dies. "The pickup runs on messages," concludes Fisher, shaking her head, "and every one of them has to be returned." Turning to the bartender, the woman asks for her bill, then hurries out into the night.

6   What is ultimately going on here? Beyond the rejected advances and the private humiliations, Fisher sees the workings of an age-old ritual. After years of study and debate, she and other evolutionary anthropologists now suggest that human romance has been shaped by biology and the forces of natural selection. According to this controversial line of thought, humans conduct their love lives in much the same manner around the world. From the singles bars of North America to the marriage brokers of Asia, we attract, court, and discard mates in ways that subtly but surely promote the survival of our species.

7   It's a theory that challenges decades of entrenched thinking. Historians have long insisted that love itself was a cultural invention, an emotion first conceived by the courtly poets of Europe some eight hundred years ago and subsequently passed on to Europe's idle rich. In time, went this thinking, the idea of romantic love percolated to the lower classes, who in turn carried it to colonies far and wide. Such views dovetailed nicely with modern anthropological thought. Since the 1920s, when American scientist Margaret Mead returned from fieldwork on the South Seas islands of Samoa, most anthropologists believed that human behaviour was shaped largely by culture. Children, they noted, were as impressionable as clay. "It's a view that there is basically no human nature," says David Buss, a professor of psychology at the University of Michigan in Ann Arbor, "that humans are simply a product of their environment."

8   Over the past two decades, however, serious cracks have appeared in those theoretical walls. Influenced by Charles Darwin, a small but vocal group of social scientists now suggest that natural selection, not culture, has shaped certain key human behaviours. Over hundreds of thousands of years, they theorize, evolution has moulded not only anatomy but the human psyche itself, favouring certain social behaviours, certain states of mind, that promote survival and reproductive success. In other words, biology lies just beneath the

surface of much human psychology. Could our romances, they ask, be guided by certain evolved mechanisms? Could the human heart be unconsciously governed by the ancient encodings of our genes?

9   Psychologists Martin Daly and Margo Wilson think the answers are in little doubt. After fifteen years of research, the husband-and-wife team at McMaster University in Hamilton, Ontario, conclude that love runs a remarkably similar course around the world. Wilson smiles as she observes that men tend to be attracted to the same qualities in women everywhere—even in traditional Islamic cultures, where females are veiled from head to shoulder. "The fact that you have these flirtatious eyes looking out from a whole black garb must just stimulate the imagination far beyond what is beneath the veil," she laughs. "Mystery is sexually exciting."

10   Wilson's interest in human romance first arose in the mid-1970s, when she and Daly came across the writings of those investigating the evolutionary basis of social behaviour in animals. After examining the life histories of animals as diverse as the dung fly, the Jamaican lizard, and the elephant seal, researchers had noted that males and females often approached the mating game very differently as a result of basic reproductive biology. Among most mammal species, for instance, females slave away much of their adult lives caring for their young—nurturing embryos, nursing infants, and often protecting litters alone. Absorbed by maternal duties, they are physically incapable of producing as many young as their male counterparts are. With a greater investment in their young, females tend to pick mates carefully, selecting those best able to help their brood survive. Most males, on the other hand, are spared such intensive parental labour. Serving largely as sperm donors, they take a different tactic, favouring quantity over quality in mating and inseminating as many fertile females as possible.

11   Intrigued, Daly and Wilson wondered how the behaviour of *Homo sapiens* fit into this pattern. Like other mammalian females, women invest long months in pregnancy, breast-feeding, and early childcare, keeping their families small. Men, however, are less burdened. (One eighteenth-century Moroccan emperor reputedly fathered seven hundred sons and more than three hundred daughters before celebrating his fiftieth birthday.) Could such radical biological differences shape human romance? Would men the world over, for example, be more promiscuous than women?

12   While comprehensive statistics were scarce, the team soon began piecing together an astonishing case. In an American study of middle-aged couples published in 1970, one social scientist reported that twice as many males as females had committed adultery. In a German study of young working-class singles, 46 percent of the males, compared with only 6 percent of the females, were interested in casual sex with an attractive stranger. All around the world, from the Amazonian rainforest to the Kalahari Desert, field accounts of anthropologists lined up on this point: men of all ages craved far more sexual variety than women. Quips Wilson, "Male sexual psychology seems to be that you're willing to do it with, you know, chickens or anything."

13   Daly and Wilson found one other sweeping pattern in the anthropological literature: in every society, men and women entered into marriages—formal, long-standing unions that gave legitimacy to the resulting children. Had basic biology also shaped wedlock? If the biologists were right, women would marry men most capable of contributing to their children's well-being, while men would marry the most fertile females they could find.

14   In fact, the psychologists discovered, men generally wed younger women—a finding that squared well with evolution-minded predictions. As Wilson points out, women in their early twenties are much more fertile than those in their thirties; older men are far more

Passion Play: A Step-by-Step Script

After spending long, smoky evenings observing couples in North American singles bars, researchers have discerned several steps in human courtship:

Approach: As a rule, it is the female who begins the mating ritual, walking up to a male or taking a seat beside him. If he reciprocates her interest by turning and looking, a conversation ensues.

Talk: As the two chat, accents and manner of speech are highly revealing. "Talking is an enormous escalation point," notes Helen Fisher. "How many people have opened their mouth and had a horrible accent, and you just realized, no way? A lot of pickups end there." But if a man and a woman successfully negotiate that hurdle, they slowly turn to face each other, moving first their heads, then their shoulders and, finally, their entire bodies.

Touch: Generally, the woman will touch first, brushing her hand briefly along a man's arm or shoulder. If the man responds in kind, touching becomes more frequent.

Gaze: As the conversation becomes more intense and pleasurable, the couple begin glancing into each other's eyes, until they are finally unable to look away. Researchers call this the "copulatory gaze."

Body Synchrony: Mesmerized by talk and touch, the couple begin moving in harmony. If the female lifts her glass for a sip, the male does too. If he slouches in his chair to the right, she mirrors his movement. "I would like to speculate," writes Timothy Perper in his book *Sex Signals: The Biology of Love*, "that by the time they are fully synchronized, each person is physiologically prepared for intercourse."

likely to have acquired the kind of wealth and social status that could shelter their children from harm. And, notes Wilson, research shows that the attractiveness of a male in most cultures is judged more by his maturity, skills, and status than by a square-cut jaw and fine features. "Like Henry Kissinger," says Wilson of the former US Secretary of State. "People used to say he was really handsome. He was in a high-status position, a very powerful position."

15   To study human tastes in mates in more detail, David Buss drew up a list of thirty-one attributes and arranged for men and women in Africa, Asia, Europe, and South America to grade them by importance. "The results amazed me in that they basically confirmed the evolutionary predictions that others had speculated about," he notes. In the thirty-seven cultures polled, responses were strongly consistent, suggesting a universal, biological truth honed over millennia of evolution. While both sexes graded traits such as intelligence and kindness highly, they diverged sharply in two areas. "Women place a premium on status, older age and maturity, and resources," says Buss. "Men place a premium on youth and physical attractiveness."

16   Buss suggests that the male predilection for beauty is informed by sound biological logic. How else could a man judge the potential fertility of his mate? "The capacity of a woman to bear children is not stamped on her forehead," he writes in a recent paper. "It is

not part of her social reputation, so no one is in a position to know. Even the woman herself lacks direct knowledge of her fertility and reproductive value." But certain visual cues, he explains, could serve as rough measures. Shapely legs, shiny hair, lustrous eyes, and a clear, unblemished complexion in a female all signal health and youth. And some researchers have suggested that symmetrical facial features—particularly eyes of well-matched colour and alignment—could indicate mutation-free genes. Ancestral males drawn to such qualities, notes Buss, would have likely fathered more children than men attracted to other physical traits.

17   The differing biological goals of the sexes also have profound effects on human relations and courtship behaviour. While women need time to size up a man's finances and social status, men can measure beauty and youth with a mere flicker of an eye. Consider the recently published results of a study at the Florida State University at Tallahassee. Psychologists Russell Clark and Elaine Hatfield dispatched young men to different corners of the campus, instructing each to pitch one of three questions to female strangers: "Would you go out with me tonight?" "Would you come over to my apartment tonight?" or "Would you go to bed with me tonight?" While 56 percent of the females consented to a date, only 6 percent agreed to visit the male's apartment—and not one consented to sex. But when a female approached male strangers with the same questions, 50 percent of the men agreed to a date, 69 percent consented to an apartment visit—and 75 percent offered to go to bed with her that night.

18   As Buss and other psychologists slowly piece together the evolution of physical attraction, other researchers examine the biological and genetic origins of the emotion of love itself. At the University of Nevada, Las Vegas, just a short stroll away from the rotund cupids and neon hearts adorning the city's all-night wedding chapels, anthropologist William Jankowiak is sweeping aside earlier cultural theories. Passionate attachments, he suggests, "must have evolved for some sense of adaptation. [They] must have helped *Homo sapiens* survive in the battle against the cockroach."

19   A soft-spoken but intense scholar, Jankowiak became interested in the evolution of love some six years ago while conducting fieldwork in Inner Mongolia. During casual reading of ancient Chinese folktales, he was amazed to discover descriptions of passionate love that could have been penned today. "I said, 'My God, I wonder if this has been universal in Chinese history,' and it was. And then I started wondering if this was universal all over."

20   Turning to the scientific literature, Jankowiak unearthed two studies published in the 1960s by American psychologist Paul Rosenblatt. Interested in the emergence of love as a basis for marriage, Rosenblatt had pored over anthropological reports for dozens of human cultures, concluding that less than two-thirds had any concept of the emotion of love. As Jankowiak read the studies, however, he could see that Rosenblatt had missed a key source of information—the folklore of tribal peoples. Troubled by the omission, Jankowiak decided to start from scratch, eager to see whether love was an emotion present in all cultures.

21   With graduate student Edward Fischer, Jankowiak settled into the work, searching for love songs, tales of elopement, and other signs of romantic entanglements. In cultures where no trace of passion could be found in the literature, Jankowiak called up the anthropologists themselves to enquire whether any relevant evidence had been left out. In the end, the two researchers recorded romantic love in a resounding 88.5 percent of the 166 cultures they studied. For Jankowiak, the results strongly suggested that love is a common part of the human condition, an experience owing more to biology than to culture.

Harlequin's Lock on Our Hearts

Every month, Harlequin Enterprises Limited ships its purple prose around the globe—from Abu Dhabi to Zimbabwe and from Iceland to Tonga. Selling more than two hundred million books a year, the Canadian firm claims to have made "the language of love universal, crossing social, cultural, and geographical borders with an ease unrivalled by any other publisher." What is its secret of success?

As it turns out, Harlequin editors understand human desire pretty well. According to company guidelines for the Harlequin Regency line of novels, for example, heroines must be attractive and quick-witted and range in age between eighteen and twenty-eight years old. The objects of their affections, on the other hand, must be virile and prosperous, possess high societal positions—"we prefer peers," say the editors—and range in age from twenty-four to thirty-five years old.

Such matches are made in heaven, according to mate-preference studies conducted by Douglas Kenrick and an associate at Arizona State University in Tempe. As Kenrick notes, females are strongly drawn to men who possess leadership skills and occupy the top rungs of a hierarchy. Moreover, they crave mates up to eight or nine years older than themselves. Men, on the other hand, are not particularly charmed by leadership. Instead, they hanker after beautiful females in their twenties—something that Harlequin editors seem to have known all along.

22   Still, some scholars puzzled over the small number of societies where no sign of romantic love had been uncovered. If love was a universal condition, how had inhabitants of these cultures mustered such resistance? At the University of California, Santa Barbara, doctoral candidate Helen Harris decided to take a closer look at one such society—the Mangaians of the South Pacific. According to anthropological reports, the inhabitants of Mangaia had developed a highly sexual culture. At the age of thirteen or so, boys on the island were trained by older women to bring female partners to orgasm several times before reaching climaxes of their own. The craft perfected, the young men began courting the favours of island women—averaging three orgasms a night, seven nights a week. But according to an anthropologist who lived among the Mangaians in the 1950s, neither sex ever experienced the emotion of love. "He said that when he talked about it, the Mangaians didn't understand," notes Harris.

23   Perplexed, Harris began her own fieldwork, interviewing males and females who had been adolescents during the 1950s. As her research proceeded, she could see that the sensational tales of sexual prowess had obscured the rich emotional life of Mangaia. Now middle-aged, the men and women recounted tales of deep passion, even love at first sight. "One of the women said she was in one of the stores on the island, she turned around, and she saw this man," recalls Harris. "She did not know him, but feelings just came over her that she had never felt before.... She analyzed it and said, 'I think it was just God's way of getting two people together. It's natural for people to feel this way.' And she and this man finally married after some years."

24   While it seems likely that romantic love arose in all human cultures, from the lean reindeer herders of Lapland to the now silent scholars of the Sung Dynasty, it is less clear just when and why this emotional state evolved. Researchers have yet to discern any convincing evidence of such strong emotions in the animal kingdom, for instance. And surveys have shown that intimate, long-lasting associations between a male and a female are strikingly rare even among our close primate relatives. "Yet the hallmark of the human animal is that we form these pair bonds," says Helen Fisher, sitting down with a glass of iced tea in her small Manhattan apartment. "So how come?"

25   In search of clues, Fisher turned to the zoological literature, studying several species that form such intimate bonds. In foxes, she found a clear biological imperative. Bearing some five helpless kits at a time, female red foxes become virtual prisoners of their broods. Equipped with only thin, low-fat milk, mothers must nurse each of their young every two to three hours. Without a male to help feed her, a female would soon starve to death. "But when the kits begin to wander off," says Fisher, "the pair bond breaks up. It lasts only long enough to raise those kits through infancy."

26   As Fisher sees it, hominid females may have become similarly vulnerable some four million years ago. With climatic change, our simian ancestors were forced from the receding forests of Africa onto vast grassy plains, where stealthy predators stalked. "What I think," says Fisher, who has just published her theories in a new book, *Anatomy of Love: The Natural History of Monogamy, Adultery, and Divorce*, "is that we came down from the trees and we were forced onto two legs instead of four. Females suddenly needed to carry their babies in their arms instead of on their backs. What a huge reproductive burden," she says with a wince. "They also had to start carrying sticks and stones for tools and weapons in this dangerous place. So women needed a mate to help rear their young."

27   As they roamed farther onto the grasslands, early human males also found compelling reasons to pair off with females. Along the vast savannas, food sources such as cashew trees, berry patches, and the occasional meaty carcass were widely scattered. Constantly roaming, males were unable to feed or defend large harems. "Polygyny was almost impossible for men," says Fisher, "and pair bonding was critical for women." So males who fell in love and formed pairs with females were more successful in passing on their genes, thus perpetuating the penchant for intimacy.

28   Setting down her iced tea, Fisher points out that science has yet to prove her theories conclusively. No one, for instance, has located specific genes capable of turning love on or off in the human psyche. Even so, some medical research supports her contention. At the New York State Psychiatric Institute in New York City, researcher Michael Liebowitz suggests that the powerful emotion of love is created by a tidal wave of certain naturally produced chemicals in the brain. And others have suggested that the taps for these chemicals might be directly controlled by our genes.

29   A psychiatrist who specializes in the treatment of anxiety and depression, Liebowitz first began to suspect the chemical basis of love in the early 1980s after noticing the profound effects of particular antidepressants on patients who were addicted to the thrill of new relationships. After researching the matter carefully, he now suggests that the sheer intoxication of love—the warm, reckless euphoria that sweeps over us and drives away all other thoughts—may be caused by certain chemical excitants flooding into brain structures thought to control love and emotional arousal.

30   One of the most likely chemical candidates, he says, is phenylethylamine, a natural amphetaminelike substance that has been found by other researchers to have some powerful effects on the behaviour of certain laboratory animals. Mice injected with the substance

The Universal Seven-Year Itch

While North Americans vow at the altar to forsake all others, less than 50 percent make good on their promise. But Canadians and Americans are not alone in their adulteries; infidelity is the rule rather than the exception around the world.

The Kuikuru of the Amazonian rainforest, for example, often seek out lovers just a few months after marriage. Kuikuru men and women have been known to juggle as many as twelve extra partners at a time, and their affairs are discussed with great openness and delight in the Amazonian society.

Among traditional Hindu communities in India, adultery is strongly discouraged. But infidelity clearly flourishes anyway. Notes one Sanskrit proverb: "Only when fire will cool, the moon burn, or the ocean fill with tasty water will a woman be pure."

In Japan, specially designated love hotels cater to adulterous couples. Furnished with such exotica as wall-to-wall mirrors, video recorders, whips and handcuffs, rooms are rented by the hour and enjoy a brisk trade during the day and early evening.

squeal exuberantly and leap into the air like popcorn, and rhesus monkeys given a closely related compound make kissing sounds. And there is evidence that humans are highly susceptible too. When Liebowitz and colleague Donald Klein treated romance junkies with antidepressants that raise the levels of phenylethylamine in the brain, the patients gradually gave up their hungry search for new mates. "They could settle down and accept life with more stable and appropriate partners," explains Liebowitz.

31   Impressed by such evidence, he suggests that neural chemicals play a key part in sparking the giddy excitement of attraction. But the effects of such chemicals are temporary. As time passes, Liebowitz theorizes, nerve endings in the brain may cease to respond to phenylethylamine and a second chemical system kicks into place. Based on such natural narcotics as endorphins, it can endow lovers with the warm, comfortable feelings of a secure attachment. "Unfortunately, that leads people to take dependable partners too much for granted," says Liebowitz. "They think, oh well, somebody else is very attractive, and my long-term relationship is not as exciting as that." Thirsting for the amphetamine high again, many will eventually abandon their partners for someone new.

32   Even here, in betrayal and divorce, evolutionary theorists such as Fisher see a form of natural logic. Research has shown, she notes, that the powerful attraction phase of love generally lasts from two to three years. And statistics suggest that divorce rates peak in and around the fourth year of marriage. In Fisher's view, the timing is significant. As it happens, women in traditional hunting and gathering societies—which resemble those in which humans first evolved—frequently nurse infants for as long as four years. During that period, they depend on their mates to supply some food and protection. But once a child is weaned and can be cared for by others, the mother may consider switching mates.

33   "I think four million years ago, there would have been advantages to primitive divorce," says Fisher. "If a male and a female raised a child through infancy and then broke

up and formed new pair bonds, what they would actually be doing is creating genetic variety. And that's really critical to evolution."

34   But, as Fisher concedes, such biologically based codes of conduct may have served us far better in the grasslands of Africa than they do today in a world of divorce lawyers, property settlements, and child-custody battles. As she sets her empty glass on the table, the anthropologist shakes her head at the irony of it all. "Look at the incredible problem we're in. A drive to make a commitment, to love, to remain together. A drive to break up and pair again. And a drive to be adulterous on the side. No wonder we all struggle in every culture in the world." She pauses and smiles. "We are built to struggle."

NOTES AND DISCUSSION

Pringle opens her essay with a hook: an attractive woman sits in the Mad Hatter Restaurant and Pub, declaring that the place looks like "a real good pickup bar." This scenario recalls the openings of countless books, movies, and television shows. The reader expects a narrative, a story, a romance. However, in the next paragraph, Pringle undermines that expectation: the woman is not "on the make"; she is an anthropologist who studies human mating behaviour.

Pringle's essay researches and reports on recent studies by anthropologists who, influenced by Darwin's theories of natural selection, believe that human mating behaviour is genetically programmed, rather than culturally determined. Think about whether Pringle herself implicitly argues in favour of one of these hypotheses and about how successfully she maintains the position of an objective reporter who introduces experts and summarizes their findings.

Pringle recounts the anthropologists' studies using a variety of rhetorical strategies: she conducts a step-by-step process analysis of the body language of courting couples; compares and contrasts human behaviour with animal and human behaviour across different cultures; presents statistics from anthropological studies to support interpretations of human mating behaviour; and draws analogies between the mating and courtship behaviours of early hominids and those of twenty-first-century humans.

STUDY QUESTIONS

For Discussion

1. What elements identified and discussed in this essay agree or disagree with your own observations of mating behaviour? For instance, does our society equate symmetry with beauty? Does the fact that we are not hominids living in "the grasslands of Africa," but *Homo sapiens* living in the late twentieth century weaken the essay's arguments?

2. Conduct some field research of your own in a public place on campus. Do you observe the mating behaviours described in Pringle's essay?

For Writing

1. Outline the major ideas discussed in this essay and examine how Pringle moves from point to point.

2. Decide whether Pringle believes nature or nurture to be the determining factor in human mating behaviour. To answer this question, consider which points in the essay are most convincing and why. Are certain points made more or less convincing by the way Pringle presents them?

COMING HOME TO
TELEVISION

John Romano

BIOGRAPHICAL NOTE

John Romano (1948–) is the author of *Dickens and Reality* (1979) and a former assistant professor of English. He began his second career in television as a story editor for *Hill Street Blues*. He went on to work as writer/producer on many dramatic series including *L.A. Law*, *Knots Landing*, and *Party of Five*.

---

1   My story, briefly—I'll give a long, boring version in due course; this is what's known in one-hour television as the teaser—is this. There came a point in my career as an assistant professor at Columbia when to get tenure it would have been necessary to write a second book (this one would have been on George Eliot, it so happens). Instead of doing so, I fell in with bad company and wrote a screenplay. To punish me, the gods arranged that the screenplay got me an agent and offers to write other screenplays. Then one of these was produced, and then came about 170 hours of television (an assistant of mine once did the arithmetic on that, actually thinking it would please me). So, net of net, the world is ahead 170 hours of TV, some good, some bad—but it is still lacking what would have been one hell of a book on George Eliot. That book is the one that got away, and it just gets better as the years go by. In fact, now that I've recently had the pleasure of making a movie with Anne Heche, I think I've found the perfect actress for it.

2   I've been asked so often about my transition from the academic teaching of literature to writing for television and movies that I've become pretty good at dividing the questioners into those who think of it as going up in the world and those who think of it as coming down. I definitely belong to the second group. Thanks to the rise of cultural studies, there are increasing numbers of academics who will consider my transition neither, just a lateral

John Romano, "Coming Home to Television," *Profession*, 1999, pp. 32–35.

shift from one division of narrative arts and crafts to another, except that writing for television and movies pays better—provided you meet with some success. I wish to say categorically that I disagree with the thrust of cultural studies. Literature is better for you than TV and movies. Television in particular is responsible for much of what's wrong with the country. Of course it can be very exciting to be responsible for what's wrong with the country. Such responsibility means collaterally that you can also be a force for good and can promote your ideas of the good, as the right-minded liberal arts conscience defines the good. In the aforesaid 170 hours I have made myself heard against racism and anti-Semitism and corporate greed. In *Party of Five*, we are currently doing a nine-part story arc about abuse, of which I am quite proud. And I can report that as long as your Nielsen ratings are what they should be, the networks are open-minded about your views on these topics; and when your ratings are not, they're not. So much for who's manipulating whom. There are very few points of view, however politically subversive, that the networks will object to if they come in the form of a thirty-five share (that is, if thirty-five percent of the TV watching audience is tuned in).

3   Now Leo Braudy and I did not have a thirty-five share when we undertook to do *Class of '96* for the Fox network about six years back—but we had a great season, of which I am permanently proud. I had come off of hit shows—*Hill Street Blues, Knots Landing, Cop Rock*. Because of my so-called track record Fox permitted me a highly personal project, of which any nineteenth-century novelist would have been envious, the chance to tell an intensely autobiographical story of growing up: a working-class kid from New Jersey, first of his family to go to college, arrives for the first day of his freshman year at a small good liberal arts college. His baker-uncle drives him in his beat-up Comet over a green hill in September; he catches sight of ivy-covered buildings, flying Frisbees, athletes who can think, coeds brighter than he is, professors who know what they're talking about, a marketplace of ideas and values authentically and meaningfully in conflict with themselves and one another—all this and the leaves just starting to turn—and as he takes it all in, he asks himself, "How long has this been going on?" As you can tell, *Class of '96* was something of an ode to the idea of a university, suffused by my nostalgia for the career I'd left.

4   I was particularly excited because I'd be doing classroom scenes, in which I'd be able to dust off my old lectures and read them to ten or twelve million people at a time. But in doing the project and in order not to be misled by my nostalgia, I reached out to Leo, nearby at the University of Southern California, one of the senior professors to whom I owed so much, mainly for having diligently blocked my effort to get tenure at Columbia many years before—I mean, just think if he hadn't, no singing cops, right? The fact is that from *Hill Street Blues* on I had a strong conscience about writing television with a certain degree of veracity—Steven Bochco used to insist that his writers ride along with cops in their units to acquire a sense of the reality of police work—and so in creating *Class of '96* I needed Leo to apprise us of the current political-moral-personal dilemmas on the liberal arts college campus, to save me from my nostalgic haze; to make sure that the professors sounded like professors (good ones, unless the story needs were otherwise); and to read scripts and tell me if they were any good. I wish to emphasize this—because Leo is one of my favorite readers and one of my favorite thinkers about what we read. I had come to the realization that the skills one uses to dissect, design, create, make, and unmake stories in the story rooms of TV dramas are the same as, or closely allied to, the skills honed and exercised—dare I say taught and learned—in a seminar of the later Browning or on *Absalom and Achitophel*. I emphasize this because I want you to know that these academic skills have considerable value and viability in the storytelling and so-called development

side of the entertainment world. Studio executives might be business majors themselves, but they know enough to turn to English majors when hiring people to do the job of reading and criticizing scripts and the equally important and sometimes dirty job of talking to writers. This is a genuine career opportunity that might recommend itself to those who do not think of themselves as writers but are still interested in the field of movies and television. Young scholars already possess abilities that are impressive and attractive to the hirers at networks and studios. Add a few months to learn golf or tennis, and you're ready.

5   But if you are a writer, let me say a few things to you. First, I found the form of the script entirely liberating. Having taught Dickens and Tolstoy did me very little good in writing my own fiction. For reasons best known to Harold Bloom, I found their voices disabling and intimidating. But the medium of the screenplay—the very form of the words on the page, the dialogue, the simple description of action—liberated creativity in me in a way the well-made paragraph never could. I encourage you to see if this is so for you. If it is, the amount of sheer reading you've done will aid and abet you. Movies and TV are language-poor; as Steven Spielberg said in accepting his lifetime achievement Oscar, it is time for Hollywood to renew its old love affair with the word.

6   Last story: I remember walking into one of my first story meetings at *Hill Street*— prepared elaborately to dumb down my finely honed literary sensibility. After all, I'd written an OK dissertation for J. Hillis Miller and dined with Cleanth Brooks. We began discussing a story, when the supervising producer—that's the number 3 guy—said, "I get it, let's just do Steven Crane's *Blue Hotel*, only with Charlie Haid's character, then in the fourth act—you remember how *Far from the Madding Crowd* ends, right?...."As I say, that was the number 3 guy. The number 1 guy was David Milch, who subsequently created *NYPD Blue*; and I am sincere in saying that for one to be able to claim, as I can, to have worked with David Milch on *Hill Street Blues* will in two hundred years' time be akin to saying that one assisted Dr. Johnson in bringing out his dictionary.

7   Let me conclude by saying that I was quite serious a few moments ago about the bully pulpit the mass media afford. Looking back, I am very clear that one of the things that powered my decision to leave academic life was my desire for a larger audience—a desire that, you will not need to be told, somewhat lowered me in my colleagues' esteem. While I don't say that it was *my* ideas that the public needed to hear, I do say emphatically that it needs to hear *yours*. The indefinable sophistication about language and culture that an education in the humanities develops is exactly what's lacking in the public discourse. As you get smarter and smarter in your quarterly journals, more skeptical of current pieties, more deft in interpreting the culture through its signs, the public is getting dumber, intellectually clumsier, more naïve about just the same sort of things. This is television's fault, surely, but it is also yours: the fault of those who might usefully be addressing the public and instead are locked in conversation with one another. Elaine Showalter asked me to speak here to tell you it is possible to enter the broader world outside academic life. It certainly is possible. But I want to go beyond that and say that your participation is good for that world. Your pedagogy would be useful even if it weren't welcome—but it will be.

NOTES AND DISCUSSION

This paper was originally delivered as a lecture at the Modern Languages Association Convention in San Francisco in 1998 and then published in *Profession*. It is, therefore, addressed to a rather specific audience: academics. Readers who do not belong to this group may be unfamiliar with George Eliot (pseudonym of a famous female Victorian novelist), *Absalom and Achitophel* (a poem by John Dryden, first published in 1681), J. Hillis Miller and Elaine Showalter (well-known professors and literary critics) or *Far From the Madding Crowd* (a novel by Thomas Hardy). Think about how these references affected your reading of the paper; then consider the way in which they affected the paper's original auditors.

The paper begins with a brief autobiographical sketch—really a story. Romano makes and attempts to support many of his points through the telling of anecdotes or stories. The first story is his success story. He inhabits the supposedly glamorous world of television. Note, however, the tone in which Romano speaks of his accomplishments. He is self-deprecating: he deliberately downplays his achievements and speaks dismissively of television. Almost immediately, however, Romano restates his position and details ways in which television can elucidate and educate. In the first half of his paper, Romano keeps his audience engaged with rather unexpected positions and statements, which he then revises. The latter half of the paper compares and contrasts the skills learned in university—particularly in the humanities—with the skills needed to produce TV dramas. Based upon his personal experience, Romano argues that the skill sets demonstrate considerable overlap.

The paper concludes by reiterating the influence that television can exert over society. Throughout his paper, Romano has largely praised, even flattered his academic audience, but in his conclusion a more critical attitude emerges (consider possible reasons for delaying such criticism). Once again, he revises his position as he urges academics not to confine themselves to academic life and scholarly journals but to engage more fully with the world and share their knowledge and sophistication.

STUDY QUESTIONS

For Discussion

1. Romano identifies the two most common attitudes toward his shift from academia to television. He says there are "those who think of it as going up in the world and those who think of it as coming down." Which group do you fall into and why? (Or do you fall into the small third group that sees the shift as lateral?)

2. Compare and contrast the forms of the paragraph and the script (dialogue, description of action). Do you agree with Romano when he says the screenplay is more liberating? Why or why not?

For Writing

1. Romano writes that an education in the humanities develops an "indefinable sophistication about language and culture." Do you agree or disagree? Why or why not?

2. Find a brief example of a "language-poor" scene from a current movie or television program. Detail the flaws you perceive in your example and offer some suggestions for revision. You might also wish to cite examples of "rich-language" alternatives from literature to further illustrate the shallowness of your example. (One might contrast a dialogue from *Jane Eyre*, for instance, with dialogue from a soap opera romance.)

MARIE CURIE AND MILEVA EINSTEIN MARÍC

Hilary Rose

BIOGRAPHICAL NOTE

Hilary Rose is the author of *Science and Society* (1969) and *Love, Power, and Knowledge: Towards a Feminist Transformation of the Sciences* (1994), from which this essay is excerpted.

---

1   Perhaps it was partly that the Nobel Prize was so new—not yet gelled in its prestige status—that made it possible in 1903 not only to invite Henri Becquerel and Pierre Curie to share the Physics Prize, but also to include Marie Curie at the astonishingly youthful age of 36.[1] (The terms of the Nobel award mean that it may be shared a maximum of three ways.) The introductory address on behalf of the committee spoke not only of the discoveries opening "a new epoch in the history of physics" and of the close relationships of their producers, but of how:

> Les découvertes et les travaux de M. Becquerel et de M. et Mme. Curie sont en relations intimes les uns avec les autres: et les deux derniers ont travaillé en commun. Aussi L'Académie Royale des Sciences n'a-t-elle pas cru devoir séparer ces éminents savants, quand il s'est agi de récompenser par un prix Nobel la découverte de la radio-activité spontanée.[2]*

Equal producers the Curies may have been, but it was Pierre alone who was to give the Nobel address at Stockholm. There was perhaps some justification for this as he was eight

---

*The discoveries and work of [Monsieur] Becquerel and of [Monsieur] and [Madame] Curie are closely related to one another: and the latter two worked together. Also the Royal Academy of the Sciences does not believe that it should separate these eminent scholars, when it is deciding to award a Nobel Prize for the discovery of spontaneous radioactivity. (Author's translation)

From *Love, Power, and Knowledge* by Hilary Rose. Reprinted with permission of Indiana University Press.

years older than Marie, and had not been educated in a Warsaw lycée or transferred countries and languages before studying at the Faculty of Science in Paris. Nor did his father have the relatively modest occupation of a teacher in a Warsaw lycée, but was a French medical doctor. Marie and Pierre had met and researched together at the Ecole Physique and were married in 1895; in the same year he was appointed to a chair. (At the time of receiving the prize Marie had not yet defended her doctorate thesis.) Within two years of the marriage their first daughter, Irène, was born. Personal life and work thread Marie's notebooks; she describes her daughter's first steps, then speaks of the element she and Pierre have found which they propose to call radium; her next entry reports the consolidation of Irène's walking. They shared a common commitment to socialism and to feminism, the last a matter of no small significance for the history of science.[3]

2   Because for the rest of the century this astonishing woman has been held up to all, and especially to all women scientists, as the example of what women are capable of achieving,[4] Elizabeth Crawford's[5] study of the early years of the Nobel Institution makes salutary reading. She reveals that the recognition of Marie's contribution to her and Pierre's achievement was not uncontentious; we suddenly find that we are back in an old story, recognizable all too often from our own lives. At the first hurdle, that of nominations, the French Academy had only put forward the names of Henri Becquerel and Pierre Curie. Marie, as a woman, was not seen as capable of producing scientific knowledge, and therefore was outside the committee's consideration either as a potential member or as a nominee.[6]

3   Within the politics of Swedish science things were a little better but still complicated. Ironically it was the monarchist "right-wing" mathematician Gösta Mittag Leffler, a highly active figure in science politics, who, though outside the crucial committee structures, was more supportive of women than the liberal reformer and key Nobel committee member Svante Arrhenius.[7] The Swedish mathematician had already shown his willingness to acknowledge women scientists in an earlier suggestion to Alfred Nobel that he establish a chair for the Russian mathematician Sophia Kovalevskaia. Nobel, incidentally, refused on the grounds that it was not necessary as "Russia was less prejudiced," a comment which suggests that the founder saw himself as more open-minded to the claims of women than many of his compatriots. Thus when the nominations were being considered, it was Leffler[8] who became sufficiently concerned that Marie Curie might not be offered a share in the prize to write to Pierre Curie. Pierre replied: "If it is true that one is thinking about me [for the prize] I very much wish to be considered together with Madame Curie with respect to our research on radioactivity." The letter then goes on to suggest that giving the prize jointly will be "artistically satisfying."[9]

4   Curie's fame thus depends not simply on her work, and on the general processes through which scientists are recognized, but on the integrity and egalitarian values of two men: one a Swedish mathematician who shared his sister's feminism,[10] the other, her husband and collaborator who shared hers. This story of the recognition of Curie points to the peculiar dependency of a woman scientist, particularly if she is part of a wife-and-husband team, on her collaborator's unequivocal acknowledgement of her contribution. All too commonly the woman/wife's share of the work is only acknowledged by a dedication, and the crucial authorship/ownership is denied in a way that is rarer between men scientists. Without recognition by her husband/collaborator she stays in the private domain, for only he has the power to testify that she is a creative scientist, which will enable her to begin to enter the public world of science. Otherwise the two are one, and that "one" is the man.

A DANGEROUS COMBINATION OF LOVE AND SCIENCE

5   The recently recovered biography of Mileva Einstein Maríc[11] documents the dangerous combination of love and science for women, and its power to render women and their science invisible. After a painful beginning where she conceived a child by Albert Einstein out of wedlock and had the baby adopted, the marriage was initially happy and mutually apprecia-tive. Einstein, for example, explained to a group of Zagreb intellectuals that he needed his wife as "she solves all the mathematical problems for me." Two key episodes document the process by which her work, if not actively appropriated, was certainly lost by her to him. In one episode Mileva, through the collaboration with a mutual friend, Paul Habicht, constructed an innovatory device for measuring electrical currents. Having built the device the two inventors left it to Einstein to describe and patent, as he was at that time working in the patent office. He alone signed the publication and patented the device under the name Einstein-Habicht. When asked why she had not given her own name of Einstein Maríc she asked, "What for, we are both only 'one stone' [*Ein stein*]?" Later when the marriage had collapsed she found that the price of her selfless love and affectionate joke was that her work had become his. She also lost her personal health through trying to do the mathematical work to support his theorizing and simultaneously take care of their children. One son suffered from schizophrenia and after the divorce Einstein was mean about keeping up with the alimony.

6   Troemel-Ploetz[12] points to the even more disturbing episode of the articles published in 1905 in the Leipzig *Annalen der Physik*. Of the five key papers, two of the originally submitted manuscripts were signed also by Mileva, but by the time of their publication, her name had been removed. These two articles, written in what was widely understood as Einstein's golden age, included the theory of special relativity which was to change the nature of physics, and for which he alone received the Nobel Prize. Thus although the purpose of the biography was to restore Mileva's name as a distinguished and creative scientist, and not to denigrate Einstein, it inevitably raised the issue of his withholding recognition of Mileva's contribution to the achievement. A number of observers have also commented on the puzzle of Einstein's gift of the prize money to Mileva Maríc even though they were by then separated. This gift-giving was later emulated by George Hoyt Whipple, a Nobel Prize-winner in 1934. Although Whipple had the reputation of being very careful financially, he shared his prize money with Frieda Robsheit Robbins, his co-worker for many years, and with two other women colleagues. In Einstein's and Hoyt Whipple's circumstances, was the money meant to compensate for the system's, and perhaps their own, appropriation of their collaborators' work?

7   While Mileva's biographer is careful to indicate that Einstein was the creative thinker, she suggests that he could not have realized his theoretical insights without Mileva's math-ematics. Between men scientists such a collaboration between theory and technique is rather difficult to ignore; between husband and wife scientists it was—and according to the context still is—rather easy. It was especially so at the turn of the century when bourgeois women, as wives, were only permitted to work as unpaid workers and when scientific work like housework and child care could be constructed—as they were by Mileva—as part of the labour of love. While Trbuhovic Gjuric's biography (not least because it was originally published in Serbian in 1969) has not had the impact of Ann Sayre's study of Rosalind Franklin, it has raised doubts in the physics community;[13] meanwhile feminists will recog-nize the pattern as characteristic, made possible by that early twentieth century scientific labour market in all its unbridled patriarchal power of appropriation.

CURIE'S SECOND PRIZE

8   Although Marie Curie's story is rather happier in the recognition given her by being awarded the Nobel Prize, together with what Crawford[14] speaks of as "a watershed" of public interest in science aroused by the press reports of the immense effort required to produce radium,[15] its great commercial value, and the philanthropic selflessness of the Curies' attitude to their discovery, none the less the achievement did not give her a clear place in the French scientific establishment. The Academy refused to change its rules barring the admission of women and quite exceptionally for Laureates she was not admitted, although the debate was intense and she lost by only one vote. The Academy, in its profound androcentricity, only admitted women scientists in 1979. Yet the story of the Curies had produced for the 1900s a climate of sympathetic interest in science that would be hard to imagine in the context of the much less confident scientific establishment of the 1990s. The otherwise strait-laced newspaper *Le Figaro* described the Curies' story as a fairy tale, beginning its report with "Once upon a time...," and *La Liberté* wrote, "We do not know our scientists. Foreigners have to discover them for us." Science, at least as done by the Curies, was popular, as evidenced by a large audience for Pierre Curie's address to the Royal Institution in London in 1903 and another to listen to Marie Curie defend her doctorate at the Sorbonne in the same year.[16]

9   But the pleasure from shared work and shared recognition was short-lived; Pierre was tragically killed in a traffic accident in 1906. Suddenly, as a widow and no longer a wife, Marie's scientific eminence was recognized by the University of Paris and she was appointed to the chair Pierre had held.[17] In 1911 she was invited once more to return to Stockholm, this time to receive the Chemistry Prize for the discovery of the elements radium and polonium. But even her apparently triumphant return to Stockholm was marked by gender and sexuality. Arrhenius, ever vigilant lest women should escape their special place, on learning that after Pierre's death Marie had become close to the gifted physicist Pierre Langevin (Langevin's estranged wife cited her in divorce proceedings), wrote to her urging that in order to protect the good name of science, the Nobel Institution,[18] and so forth she should not come to Stockholm. With some courage Curie came, supported by her daughter Irène.[19]

10   On this occasion, [Madame] Curie's biographical notes as a Laureate extended to two pages, rather then the mere half-page of eight years before, and reported that, among other honours, in 1910 she had been made a member of the Swedish Academy of Sciences. Her portrait too had expanded from the matching small images of her and Pierre in grave impersonal profile with every inch except her neck and face covered with clothing; now the scientist, bare-armed and bare-necked, hand touching cheek, looks thoughtfully out.

11   But the Royal Society in London was still not minded to change its conventions. Although the physicists Rayleigh, Ramsey, J. J. Thomson, and Rutherford were all both fellow Nobel Laureates and influential Fellows of the Royal Society, the Society felt no need to honour this prize-winning physicist any more than did the French National Academy. Indeed Rutherford was highly dismissive of Curie, persisting in seeing her as Pierre's underlabourer, the scientific and physical effort of extracting radium from pitchblende constructed as little more than an extension of housewifery skills. Given that seventeen (men) Laureates were to come from the Thomson and Rutherford stable, such views were decisive, at least within the British context.

NOTES

1. Nuclear physics itself was still young enough to be open to women.

2. Author's translation: *LPN*, 1903, p. 2. Note the division of recognition in both the words and the portrait size: Becquerel a half, Marie Curie and Pierre a quarter each.

3. E. Curie, *Madame Curie*.

4. The book was published in many countries and was inspirational for young women scientists. See Rosalyn Yalow's autobiographical note, *LNP*, 1977.

5. E. Crawford, *The Beginnings of the Nobel Institution*. I am indebted to this study for the material on Marie Curie's two prizes. See also Giroud, *Marie Curie: A Life*.

6. Initially the groups and individuals consulted were very narrowly drawn, primarily the national academies and existing Nobel Laureates. Then as now the personal international connections of Swedish Nobel committee members were influential. Today the consultations are much wider, but with little effect so far as recognizing women scientists is concerned.

7. E. Crawford, *Beginnings of the Nobel Institution*, p. 112.

8. Koblitz, A. *Convergence of Lives*; Margaret Rossiter reports that "a Swedish mathematician" (Leffler?) wrote to Henrietta Leavitt, the Harvard astronomer, in 1925, saying that he wanted to nominate her. She was, alas, already dead. Rossiter, *Women Scientists in America*.

9. E. Crawford, *Beginnings of the Nobel Institution*, p. 194.

10. According to H. J. Mozan (John Zahm), *Woman in Science*, Ann Carlotta Leffler also published a study of the admired mathematician: *Sophia Kovalevskaia*.

11. Senta Troemel-Ploetz draws attention to a little-known biography by Desamka Trbuhovic Gjuric, herself a mathematician acquainted with the Swiss milieu where the Einsteins lived and worked. This has been republished, but rather heavily edited, in German. "Mileva Einstein Marić: The Woman Who Did Einstein's Mathematics," *W's Stud. Int. Forum*, 13 (5 1990).

12. Ibid, p. 418.

13. Walker, "Did Einstein Espouse His Spouse's Ideas?," *Physics Today*, February (1989). However, more disturbingly, John Hackel, editor of *The Collected Papers of Albert Einstein*, Vols. I and II, ignores this evidence. Despite my feeling that historians of science have recently been more willing to accept the contribution of women scientists, it seems that in the case of Einstein the myth of the unaided male genius must be preserved.

14. E. Crawford, *Beginnings of the Nobel Institution*, p. 148.

15. Then as now we have to be impressed by the physical effort—it took 6,000 kg of pitchblende to produce 0.1 g of the new element.

16. It was on this visit that Marie Curie met Hertha Ayrton.

17. See Clarke, *Working Life of Women in the Seventeenth Century*, for a similar picture for the widows of brewers and opticians—sometimes the widow or a surviving daughter was able to inherit a "male" occupation. Ivy Pinchbeck, for a slightly later period, shows widows and even wives taking part in their husbands' skilled trades: *Women*

Workers and the Industrial Revolution 1750-1850. A. D. Morrison Lowe makes a similar argument for scientific instrument makers: "Women in the Nineteenth-Century Instrument Trade," in Benjamin (ed.), *Science and Sensibility*. The argument made here has to be understood against this general pattern of women and highly skilled occupations and activities.

18. While Eve Curie's biography dismisses the story of Langevin and Curie with outrage, others, including feminist historians, have accepted it as fact. I prefer Robert Reid's sober conclusion that there is no real way of knowing what happened between Langevin and Curie, and that it is irrelevant, the critical point being that a woman scientist could not, without comment, spend leisure time in the company of a man scientist unrelated to her. At the time the right-wing press wallowed in the sexual innuendo and attacked, mixing anti-semitism and nationalism, while the left and liberal press defended her. She had every need to accept Hertha Ayrton's invitation to be an incognito guest in England. Reid, *Marie Curie.*

19. The scientific community intensely debated the issue. *Nature* editorialized, "we have confidence that the doors of science will eventually be open to women on equal terms with men." January 12, 1911.

NOTES AND DISCUSSION

Hilary Rose compares and contrasts women who were recognized for their scientific achievements with those who were not, choosing, in this essay, two women as her cases in point. This essay is, in fact, only one element in an argument that is developed over an entire chapter. Readers should ask themselves whether or not the thesis emerges clearly here.

Marie Curie, the first woman Rose discusses, is a prominent figure in the popular culture of science. Mileva Einstein Marić, the second woman, is far less well known, though her husband's surname (Einstein) is instantly recognizable. Instead of structuring her discussion of Curie and Marić as an alternating series of points, she presents a block of information about Curie, a block about Marić, and then another block about Curie.

In the first two sections, Rose presents the same information about each woman: her education, marital status, family life, scientific achievements, working relationship with her husband and other male scientists, and the fact that recognition of her acievements was dependent on male acknowledgement or sponsorship. Rose then returns to her first subject, Marie Curie, and outlines the circumstances surrounding Curie's second Nobel Prize, which still failed to establish her as on equal footing with male scientists. Rose peppers her essay with footnotes that provide additional information and evidence. Readers may find this strategy either helpful or distracting. Also notice her use of the pronoun "we," and consider who is included and who is excluded in this address to the audience.

STUDY QUESTIONS

For Discussion

1. Speaking of Curie, Rose says "this astonishing woman has been held up to all, and especially to all women scientists, as the example of what women are capable of achieving."

Before reading this essay, what was your conception of Curie? Does this essay change your view of her? Had you ever heard of Mileva Einstein Maríc?

2. Rose suggests not only that Curie and Einstein Maríc's personal and professional lives were more closely linked than those of the men with whom they worked, but also that recognition of these women's scientific work depended on their relationships with men. Is either observation true today?

For Writing

1. Explain how Rose presents her thesis. Examine the evidence she uses to support her observations, and determine whether that evidence provides convincing proof for her position.

2. Compare and contrast Rose's characterization of Mileva Einstein Maríc with one found in a biography of Einstein. How are the two characterizations similar and different? What do the differences and similarities suggest about the interests of each author?

THE ENGLISH VILLA— PRINCIPLES OF COMPOSITION

John Ruskin

BIOGRAPHICAL NOTE

John Ruskin (1819–1900) was an influential author and critic in nineteenth-century England. His multi-volume *Modern Painters* (1843–60) was designed to rescue from obscurity contemporary painters whom he considered great, but also became a commentary on the social and spiritual history of Europe. *The Seven Lamps of Architecture* (1848) and *The Stones of Venice* (1853) further enhanced Ruskin's reputation and made him the leading art critic of his day. He became Oxford University's first Slade professor of art in 1869, but directed his subsequent writing towards critiques of Victorian Britain's social and economic systems. In those writings, Ruskin vehemently opposed unbridled capitalism and examined its effects on the moral standing of all English men and women. This extract is from *The Poetry of Architecture*.

---

1   It has lately become a custom, among the more enlightened and refined of metropolitan shopkeepers, to advocate the cause of propriety in architectural decoration, by ensconcing their shelves, counters, and clerks in classical edifices, agreeably ornamented with ingenious devices, typical of the class of articles to which the tradesman particularly desires to direct the public attention. We find our grocers enshrined in temples whose columns are of canisters, and whose pinnacles are of sugarloaves. Our shoemakers shape their soles under Gothic portals, with pendants of shoes, and canopies of Wellingtons; and our cheesemongers will, we doubt not, soon follow the excellent example, by raising shops the varied diameters of whose jointed columns, in their address to the eye, shall awaken memories of Staffa, Paestum, and Palmyra; and, in their address to the tongue, shall arouse exquisite associations of remembered flavour, Dutch, Stilton, and Strachino. Now, this fit of taste on the part of our tradesmen is only a coarse form of a disposition inherent in the human mind. Those objects to which the eye has been most frequently accustomed, and among which the intellect has formed its habits of action, and the soul its modes of emotion, become agreeable to the thoughts, from their correspondence with their prevailing cast, especially when the business of life has had any relation to those objects; for it is in the habitual and neces-

sary occupation that the most painless hours of existence are passed: whatever be the nature of that occupation, the memories belonging to it will always be agreeable, and, therefore, the objects awakening such memories will invariably be found beautiful, whatever their character or form. It is thus that taste is the child and the slave of memory; and beauty is tested, not by any fixed standard, but by the chances of association; so that in every domestic building evidence will be found of the kind of life through which its owner has passed, in the operation of the habits of mind which that life has induced. From the superannuated coxswain, who plants his old ship's figure-head in his six square feet of front garden at Bermondsey, to the retired noble, the proud portal of whose mansion is surmounted by the broad shield and the crested gryphon, we are all guided, in our purest conceptions, our most ideal pursuit, of the beautiful, by remembrances of active occupation, and by principles derived from industry regulate the fancies of our repose.

2   It would be excessively interesting to follow out the investigation of this subject more fully, and to show how the most refined pleasures, the most delicate perceptions, of the creature who has been appointed to eat bread by the sweat of his brow, are dependent upon, and intimately connected with, his hours of labour. This question, however, has no relation to our immediate object, and we only allude to it, that we may be able to distinguish between the two component parts of individual character; the one being the consequence of continuous habits of life acting upon natural temperament and disposition, the other being the humour of character, consequent upon circumstances altogether accidental, taking stern effect upon feelings previously determined by the first part of the character; laying on, as it were, the finishing touches, and occasioning the innumerable prejudices, fancies, and eccentricities, which, modified in every individual to an infinite extent, form the visible veil of the human heart.

3   Now, we have defined the province of the architect to be, that of selecting such forms and colours as shall delight the mind, by preparing it for the operations to which it is to be subjected in the building. Now, no forms, in domestic architecture, can thus prepare it more distinctly than those which correspond closely with the first, that is, the fixed and fundamental part of character, which is always so uniform in its action as to induce great simplicity in whatever it designs. Nothing, on the contrary, can be more injurious than the slightest influence of the humours upon the edifice; for the influence of what is fitful in its energy, and petty in its imagination, would destroy all the harmony of parts, all the majesty of the whole; would substitute singularity for beauty, amusement for delight, and surprise for veneration. We could name several instances of buildings erected by men of the highest talent, and the most perfect general taste, who yet, not having paid much attention to the first principles of architecture, permitted the humour of their disposition to prevail over the majesty of their intellect, and, instead of building from a fixed design, gratified freak after freak, and fancy after fancy, as they were caught by the dream or the desire; mixed mimicries of incongruous reality with incorporations of undisciplined ideal; awakened every variety of contending feeling and unconnected memory; consummated confusion of form by trickery of detail; and have left barbarism, where half the world will look for loveliness.

4   This is a species of error which it is very difficult for persons paying superficial and temporary attention to architecture to avoid: however just their taste may be in criticism, it will fail in creation. It is only in moments of ease and amusement that they will think of their villa: they make it a mere plaything, and regard it with a kind of petty exultation, which, from its very nature, will give liberty to the light fancy, rather than the deep feeling, of the mind. It is not thought necessary to bestow labour of thought and periods of

deliberation, on one of the toys of life; still less to undergo the vexation of thwarting wishes, and leaving favourite imaginations, relating to minor points, unfulfilled, for the sake of general effect.

5   This feeling, then, is the first to which we would direct attention, as the villa architect's chief enemy: he will find it perpetually and provokingly in his way. He is requested, perhaps, by a man of great wealth, nay, of established taste in some points, to make a design for a villa in a lovely situation. The future proprietor carries him up-stairs to his study, to give him what he calls his "ideas and materials," and, in all probability, begins somewhat thus: "This, sir, is a slight note: I made it on the spot: approach to Villa Reale, near Pozzuoli. Dancing nymphs, you perceive; cypresses, shell fountain. I think I should like something like this for the approach: classical, you perceive, sir; elegant, graceful. Then, sir, this is a sketch, made by an American friend of mine: Wheewhaw-Kantamaraw's wigwam, king of the—Cannibal Islands, I think he said, sir. Log, you observe; scalps, and boa constrictor skins: curious. Something like this, sir, would look neat, I think, for the front door; don't you? Then, the lower windows, I've not quite decided upon; but what would you say to Egyptian, sir? I think I should like my windows Egyptian, with hieroglyphics, sir; storks and coffins, and appropriate mouldings above: I brought some from Fountains Abbey the other day. Look here, sir; angels' heads putting their tongues out, rolled up in cabbage leaves, with a dragon on each side riding on a broomstick, and the devil looking on from the mouth of an alligator, sir.[1] Odd, I think; interesting. Then the corners may be turned by octagonal towers, like the centre one in Kenilworth Castle; with Gothic doors, portcullis, and all, quite perfect; with cross slits for arrows, battlements for musketry, machicolations for boiling lead, and a room at the top for drying plums; and the conservatory at the bottom, sir, with Virginian creepers up the towers; door supported by sphinxes, holding scrapers in their fore-paws, and having their tails prolonged into warm-water pipes, to keep the plants safe in winter, etc." The architect is, without doubt, a little astonished by these ideas and combinations; yet he sits calmly down to draw his elevations, as if he were a stone-mason, or his employer an architect; and the fabric rises to electrify its beholders, and confer immortality on its perpetrator. This is no exaggeration: we have not only listened to speculations on the probable degree of the future majesty, but contemplated the actual illustrious existence, of several such buildings, with sufficient beauty in the management of some of their features to show that an architect had superintended them, and sufficient taste in their interior economy to prove that a refined intellect had projected them; and had projected a Vandalism, only because fancy had been followed instead of judgment; with as much nonchalance as is evinced by a perfect poet, who is extemporising doggerel for a baby; full of brilliant points, which he cannot help, and jumbled into confusion, for which he does not care.

6   Such are the first difficulties to be encountered in villa designs. They must always continue to occur in some degree, though they might be met with ease by a determination on the part of professional men to give no assistance whatever, beyond the mere superintendence of construction, unless they be permitted to take the whole exterior design into their own hands, merely receiving broad instructions respecting the style (and not attending to them unless they like). They should not make out the smallest detail, unless they were answerable for the whole. In this case, gentlemen architects would be thrown so

---

[1]Actually carved on one of the groins of Roslin Chapel.

utterly on their own resources, that, unless those resources were adequate, they would be obliged to surrender the task into more practised hands; and, if they were adequate, if the amateur had paid so much attention to the art as to be capable of giving the design perfectly, it is probable he would not erect anything strikingly abominable.

7   Such a system (supposing that it could be carried fully into effect, and that there were no such animals as sentimental stone-masons to give technical assistance) might, at first, seem rather an encroachment on the liberty of the subject, inasmuch as it would prevent people from indulging their edificatorial fancies, unless they knew something about the matter, or, as the sufferers would probably complain, from doing what they liked with their own. But the mistake would evidently lie in their supposing, as people too frequently do, that the outside of their house *is* their own, and that they have a perfect right therein to make fools of themselves in any manner, and to any extent, they may think proper. This is quite true in the case of interiors: every one has an indisputable right to hold himself up as a laughing-stock to the whole circle of his friends and acquaintances, and to consult his own private asinine comfort by every piece of absurdity which can in any degree contribute to the same; but no one has any right to exhibit his imbecilities at other people's expense, or to claim the public pity by inflicting public pain. In England, especially, where, as we saw before, the rage for attracting observation is universal, the outside of the villa is rendered, by the proprietor's own disposition, the property of those who daily pass by, and whom it hourly affects with pleasure or pain. For the pain which the eye feels from the violation of a law to which it has been accustomed, or the mind from the occurrence of anything jarring to its finest feelings, is as distinct as that occasioned by the interruption of the physical economy, differing only inasmuch as it is not permanent; and, therefore, an individual has as little right to fulfill his own conceptions by disgusting thousands, as, were his body as impenetrable to steel or poison, as his brain to the effect of the beautiful or true, he would have to decorate his carriage roads with caltrops, or to line his plantations with upas trees.

8   The violation of general feelings would thus be unjust, even were their consultation productive of continued vexation to the individual: but it is not. To no one is the architecture of the exterior of a dwelling-house of so little consequence as to its inhabitants. Its material may affect his comfort, and its condition may touch his pride; but for its architecture, his eye gets accustomed to it in a week, and, after that, Hellenic, Barbaric, or Yankee, are all the same to the domestic feelings, are all lost in the one name of home. Even the conceit of living in a châlet, or a wigwam, or a pagoda, cannot retain its influence for six months over the weak minds which alone can feel it; and the monotony of existence becomes to them exactly what it would have been had they never inflicted a pang upon the unfortunate spectators, whose accustomed eyes shrink daily from the impression to which they have not been rendered callous by custom, or lenient by false taste. If these conditions are just when they allude only to buildings in the abstract, how much more when referring to them as materials of composition, materials of infinite power, to adorn or destroy the loveliness of the earth. The nobler scenery of that earth is the inheritance of all her inhabitants: it is not merely for the few to whom it temporarily belongs, to feed from like swine, or to stable upon like horses, but it has been appointed to be the school of the minds which are kingly among their fellows, to excite the highest energies of humanity, to furnish strength to the lordliest intellect, and food for the holiest emotions of the human soul. The presence of life is, indeed, necessary to its beauty, but of life congenial with its character; and that life is not congenial which thrusts presumptuously forward, amidst the calmness of the universe, the confusion of its own petty interests and grovelling imagina-

tions, and stands up with the insolence of a moment, amidst the majesty of all time, to build baby fortifications upon the bones of the world, or to sweep the copse from the corrie, and the shadow from the shore, that fools may risk, and gamblers gather, the spoil of a thousand summers.

9   It should therefore be remembered, by every proprietor of land in hill country, that his possessions are the means of a peculiar education, otherwise unattainable, to the artists, and, in some degree, to the literary men, of his country; that, even in this limited point of view, they are a national possession, but much more so when it is remembered how many thousands are perpetually receiving from them, not merely a transitory pleasure, but such thrilling perpetuity of pure emotion, such lofty subject for scientific speculation, and such deep lessons of natural religion, as only the work of a Deity can impress, and only the spirit of an immortal can feel: they should remember that the slightest deformity, the most contemptible excrescence, can injure the effect of the noblest natural scenery, as a note of discord can annihilate the expression of the purest harmony; that thus it is in the power of worms to conceal, to destroy, or to violate, what angels could not restore, create, or consecrate; and that the right, which every man unquestionably possesses, to be an ass, is extended only, in public, to those who are innocent in idiotism, not to the more malicious clowns who thrust their degraded motley conspicuously forth amidst the fair colours of earth, and mix their incoherent cries with the melodies of eternity, break with their inane laugh upon the silence which Creation keeps where Omnipotence passes most visibly, and scrabble over with the characters of idiocy the pages that have been written by the finger of God.

10   These feelings we would endeavour to impress upon all persons likely to have anything to do with embellishing, as it is called, fine natural scenery; as they might, in some degree, convince both the architect and his employer of the danger of giving free play to the imagination in cases involving intricate questions of feeling and composition, and might persuade the designer of the necessity of looking, not to his own acre of land, or to his own peculiar tastes, but to the whole mass of forms and combination of impressions with which he is surrounded.

11   Let us suppose, however, that the design is yielded entirely to the architect's discretion. Being a piece of domestic architecture, the chief object in its exterior design will be to arouse domestic feelings, which, as we saw before, it will do most distinctly by corresponding with the first part of character. Yet it is still more necessary that it should correspond with its situation; and hence arises another difficulty, the reconciliation of correspondence with contraries; for such, it is deeply to be regretted, are too often the individual's mind, and the dwelling-place it chooses. The polished courtier brings his refinement and duplicity with him, to ape the Arcadian rustic in Devonshire; the romantic rhymer takes a plastered habitation, with one back window looking into the green park; the soft votary of luxury endeavours to rise at seven, in some Ultima Thule of frost and storms; and the rich stock-jobber calculates his percentages among the soft dingles and woody shores of Westmoreland. When the architect finds this to be the case, he must, of course, content himself with suiting his design to such a mind as ought to be where the intruder's is; for the feelings which are so much at variance with themselves in the choice of situation, will not be found too critical of their domicile, however little suited to their temper. If possible, however, he should aim at something more; he should draw his employer into general conversation; observe the bent of his disposition, and the habits of his mind; notice every manifestation of fixed opinions, and then transfer to his architecture as much of the feeling he has observed as is distinct in its operation. This he should do, not because the

general spectator will be aware of the aptness of the building, which, knowing nothing of its inmate, he cannot be; nor to please the individual himself, which it is a chance if any simple design ever will, and who never will find out how well his character has been fitted; but because a portrait is always more spirited than a composed countenance; and because this study of human passions will bring a degree of energy, unity, and originality into every one of his designs (all of which will necessarily be different), so simple, so domestic, and so life like, as to strike every spectator with an interest and a sympathy, for which he will be utterly unable to account, and to impress on him a perception of something more ethereal than stone or carving, somewhat similar to that which some will remember having felt disagreeably in their childhood, on looking at any old house authentically haunted. The architect will forget in his study of life the formalities of science, and, while his practised eye will prevent him from erring in technicalities, he will advance, with the ruling feeling, which, in masses of mind, is nationality, to the conception of something truly original, yet perfectly pure.

12   He will also find his advantage in having obtained a guide in the invention of decorations of which, as we shall show, we would have many more in English villas than economy at present allows. Candidus complains, in his Note-Book, that Elizabethan architecture is frequently adopted, because it is easy, with a pair of scissors, to derive a zigzag ornament from a doubled piece of paper. But we would fain hope that none of our professional architects have so far lost sight of the meaning of their art, as to believe that roughening stone mathematically is bestowing decoration, though we are too sternly convinced that they believe mankind to be more shortsighted by at least thirty yards than they are; for they think of nothing but general effect in their ornaments, and lay on their flower-work so carelessly, that a good substantial captain's biscuit, with the small holes left by the penetration of the baker's four fingers, encircling the large one which testifies of the forcible passage of his thumb, would form quite as elegant a rosette as hundreds now perpetuated in stone. Now, there is nothing which requires study so close, or experiment so frequent, as the proper designing of ornament. For its use and position some definite rules may be given; but, when the space and position have been determined, the lines of curvature, the breadth, depth, and sharpness of the shadows to be obtained, the junction of the parts of a group, and the general expression, will present questions for the solution of which the study of years will sometimes scarcely be sufficient;[2] for they depend upon the feeing of the eye and hand, and there is nothing like perfection in decoration, nothing which, in all probability, might not, by farther consideration, be improved. Now, in cases in which the outline and larger masses are determined by situation, the architect will frequently find it necessary to fall back upon his decorations, as the only means of obtaining character; and that which before was an unmeaning lump of jagged freestone, will become a part of expression, an accessory of beautiful design, varied in its form, and delicate in its effect. Then, instead of shrinking from his bits of ornament, as from things which will give him trouble to invent, and will answer no other purpose than that of occupying what would otherwise have looked blank, the designer will view them as an efficient *corps de réserve*, to be brought up when the eye comes to close quarters with the edifice, to maintain and deepen the impression it has previously received. Much more time will be spent in the conception, much more labour in the execution, of such meaning ornament, but both will be well spent, and well rewarded.

---

[2] For example, we would allow one of the modern builders of Gothic chapels a month of invention, and a botanic garden to work from, with perfect certainty that he would not, at the expiration of the time, be able to present us with one design of leafage equal in beauty to hundreds we could point out in the capitals and niches of Melrose and Roslin.

13   Perhaps our meaning may be made more clear by Figure 1, which is that of a window found in a domestic building of mixed and corrupt architecture, at Munich (which we give now, because we shall have occasion to allude to it hereafter). Its absurd breadth of moulding, so disproportionate to its cornice, renders it excessively ugly, but capable of great variety of effect. It forms one of a range of four, tuning an angle, whose mouldings join each other, their double breadth being the whole separation of the apertures, which are something more than double squares. Now, by alteration of the decoration, and depth of shadow, we have Figures 2 and 3. These three windows differ entirely in their feeling and manner, and are broad examples of

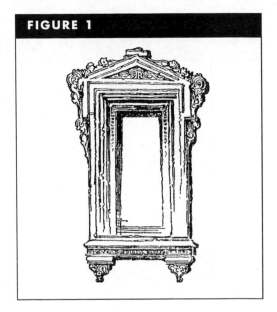

FIGURE 1

such distinctions of style as might be adopted severally in the habitations of the man of imagination, the man of intellect, and the man of feeling. If our alterations have been properly made, there will be no difficulty in distinguishing between their expressions, which we shall therefore leave to conjecture. The character of Figure 1 depends upon the softness with which the light is caught upon its ornaments, which should not have a single hard line in them; and on the gradual, unequal, but intense, depth of its shadows. Figure 2 should have all its forms undefined, and passing into one another, the touches of the chisel light, a grotesque face or feature occurring in parts, the shadows pale, but broad;[3] and the boldest part of the carving kept in shadow rather than light. The third should be hard in its lines, strong in its shades, and quiet in its ornament.

14   These hints will be sufficient to explain our meaning, and we have not space to do more, as the object of these papers is rather to observe than to advise. Besides, in questions of expression so intricate, it is almost impossible to advance fixed principles; every mind will have perceptions of its own, which will guide its speculations, every hand, and eye, and peculiar feeling, varying even from year to year. We have only started the subject of correspondence with individual character, because we think that imaginative minds might take up the idea with some success, as furnishing them with a guide in the variation of their designs, more certain than mere experiment on unmeaning forms, or than ringing indiscriminate changes on component parts of established beauty. To the reverie, rather than the investigation, to the dream, rather than the deliberation, of the architect, we recommend it, as a branch of art in which instinct will do more than precept, and inspiration than technicality. The correspondence of our villa architecture with our natural scenery may be determined with far greater accuracy, and will require careful investigation.

---

[3] It is too much the custom to consider a design as composed of a certain number of hard lines, instead of a certain number of shadows of various depth and dimension. Though these shadows change their position in the course of the day, they are relatively always the same. They have most variety under a strong light without sun, most expression with the sun. A little observation of the infinite variety of shade which the sun is capable of casting, as it touches projections of different curve and character, will enable the designer to be certain of his effects.

FIGURES 2 AND 3

15   We had hoped to have concluded the Villa in this paper; but the importance of domestic architecture at the present day, when people want houses more than fortresses, safes more than keeps, and sculleries more than dungeons, is sufficient apology for delay.

NOTES AND DISCUSSION

Ruskin's style is likely to be the first aspect of this essay to strike modern readers: his vocabulary is wide-ranging, perhaps even obscure; his long, complex sentences make use of many internal modifications; and his elaborate punctuation does not conform to modern conventions. In fact, O. B. Hardison, Jr., likened Ruskin's prose style to a specific architectural style—namely, ornate gingerbread.

Ruskin begins by observing that all classes of Victorian England are governed by the same principles in terms of how their taste is formed and how they build and decorate. In all cases, Ruskin argues, "taste is the child and the slave of memory." He believes that it is the architect's role to control and check such impulses; the architect must regulate and defend public taste. To illustrate the average person's tendencies in designing a home, Ruskin creates a scenario in which an architect is confronted by a man who wishes to build a house in a hilarious and horrifying hodgepodge of architectural elements. Such horrors, Ruskin insists, must be countered.

Note that Ruskin, like Suzuki, uses a fictitious dialogue and analogy to support a factual argument. He argues that the outside of a person's house belongs to the public domain, not to the person, and that, even if restraint seems like encroachment upon personal liberty, the architect must determine and defend public sensibilities. Ruskin closes his paper by comparing and contrasting some window designs in order to educate public taste and to make clear his definition of "design," which is integral to his notion of architecture. Note the essay's final paragraph, which is a rather unusual conclusion; in fact, it is more a self-justification and decidedly *unapologetic* apology for the delay in properly finishing his paper.

STUDY QUESTIONS

For Discussion

1. What literary device does Ruskin employ when he says that the architect, confronted with the gentleman-builder's plans, is "a little astonished"? How does such a device contribute to your conception of the essay's overall tone and of Ruskin's persona?

2. Examine the construction of the sentence in the first paragraph that begins "Those objects to which the eye...." Consider Ruskin's use of sentence structure and punctuation. Suggest alternate methods for structuring and punctuating this material. Does the sentence impress you with Ruskin's skill, or does it have the opposite effect?

For Writing

1. Describe a local building that seems, in your opinion, to be "strikingly abominable" and built according to "freak after freak, and fancy after fancy."

2. Do you agree with Ruskin that architecture is "public property" and influences the general public? Are architectural controls such as those Ruskin suggests an encroachment on personal liberty?

ISLAND

HOPPING

Oliver Sacks

BIOGRAPHICAL NOTE

Oliver Sacks was born in London, England. He earned his medical degree at Queen's College, Oxford. Since 1965, he has lived in New York, where he is clinical professor of neurology at the Albert Einstein College of Medicine, adjunct professor of neurology at the NYU School of Medicine, and consultant neurologist to the Little Sisters of the Poor. He has published nine books, among them *Awakenings* (1973) and *The Man Who Mistook His Wife for a Hat* (1985). This essay has been taken from *The Island of the Colorblind and Cycad Island* (1997).

---

1   Islands have always fascinated me; perhaps they fascinate everyone. The first summer holiday I remember—I was just three years old—was a visit to the Isle of Wight. There are only fragments in memory—the cliffs of many-colored sands, the wonder of the sea, which I was seeing for the first time: its calmness, its gentle swell, its warmth, entranced me; its roughness, when the wind rose, terrified me. My father told me that he had won a race swimming round the Isle of Wight before I was born, and this made me think of him as a giant, a hero.

2   Stories of islands, and seas, and ships and mariners entered my consciousness very early—my mother would tell me about Captain Cook, about Magellan and Tasman and Dampier and Bougainville and all the islands and peoples they had discovered, and she would point them out to me on a globe. Islands were special places, remote and mysterious, intensely attractive, yet frightening too. I remember being terrified by a children's encyclopedia with a picture of the great blind statues of Easter Island looking out to sea, as I read that the islanders had lost the power to sail away from the island and were totally cut off from the rest of humanity, doomed to die in utter isolation.[1]

From *The Island of the Colorblind* by Oliver Sacks. Alfred A. Knopf, 1997, pp. 3–27.

3   I read about castaways, desert islands, prison islands, leper islands. I adored *The Lost World,* Conan Doyle's splendid yarn about an isolated South American plateau full of dinosaurs and Jurassic life-forms—in effect, an island marooned in time (I knew the book virtually by heart, and dreamed of growing up to be another Professor Challenger).

4   I was very impressionable and readily made other people's imaginings my own. H. G. Wells was particularly potent—all desert islands, for me, became his Aepyornis Island or, in a nightmare mode, the Island of Dr. Moreau. Later, when I came to read Herman Melville and Robert Louis Stevenson, the real and the imaginary fused in my mind. Did the Marquesas actually exist? Were *Omoo* and *Typee* actual adventures? I felt this uncertainty most especially about the Galapagos, for long before I read Darwin, I knew of them as the "evilly enchanted" isles of Melville's *Encantadas.*

5   Later still, factual and scientific accounts began to dominate my reading—Darwin's *Voyage of the Beagle,* Wallace's *Malay Archipelago,* and my favorite, Humboldt's *Personal Narrative* (I loved especially his description of the six-thousand-year-old dragon tree on Teneriffe)—and now the sense of the romantic, the mythical, the mysterious, became subordinated to the passion of scientific curiosity.[2]

6   For islands were, so to speak, experiments of nature, places blessed or cursed by geographic singularity to harbor unique forms of life—the aye-ayes and pottos, the lorises and lemurs of Madagascar; the great tortoises of the Galapagos; the giant flightless birds of New Zealand—all singular species or genera which had taken a separate evolutionary path in their isolated habitats.[3] And I was strangely pleased by a phrase in one of Darwin's diaries, written after he had seen a kangaroo in Australia and found this so extraordinary and alien that he wondered if it did not represent a second creation.[4]

7   As a child I had visual migraines, where I would have not only the classical scintillations and alterations of the visual field, but alterations in the sense of color too, which might weaken or entirely disappear for a few minutes. This experience frightened me, but tantalized me too, and made me wonder what it would be like to live in a completely colorless world, not just for a few minutes, but permanently It was not until many years later that I got an answer, at least a partial answer, in the form of a patient, Jonathan I., a painter who had suddenly become totally colorblind following a car accident (and perhaps a stroke). He had lost color vision not through any damage to his eyes, it seemed, but through damage to the parts of the brain which "construct" the sensation of color. Indeed, he seemed to have lost the ability not only to see color, but to imagine or remember it, even to dream of it. Nevertheless, like an amnesic, he in some way remained conscious of having *lost* color, after a lifetime of chromatic vision, and complained of his world feeling impoverished, grotesque, abnormal—his art, his food, even his wife looked "leaden" to him. Still, he could not assuage my curiosity on the allied, yet totally different, matter of what it might be like *never* to have seen color, never to have had the least sense of its primal quality, its place in the world.

8   Ordinary colorblindness, arising from a defect in the retinal cells, is almost always partial, and some forms are very common: red-green colorblindness occurs to some degree in one in twenty men (it is much rarer in women). But total congenital colorblindness, or achromatopsia, is surpassingly rare, affecting perhaps only one person in thirty or forty thousand. What, I wondered, would the visual world be like for those born totally colorblind? Would they, perhaps, lacking any sense of something missing, have a world no less dense and vibrant than our own? Might they even have developed heightened perceptions of visual tone and texture and movement and depth, and live in a world in some ways more

intense than our own, a world of heightened reality—one that we can only glimpse echoes of in the work of the great black-and-white photographers? Might they indeed see *us* as peculiar, distracted by trivial or irrelevant aspects of the visual world, and insufficiently sensitive to its real visual essence? I could only guess, as I had never met anyone born completely colorblind.

9   Many of H. G. Wells' short stories, it seems to me, fantastical as they are, can be seen as metaphors for certain neurological and psychological realities. One of my favorites is "The Country of the Blind," in which a lost traveller, stumbling into an isolated valley in South America, is struck by the strange "parti-coloured" houses that he sees. The men who built these, he thinks, must have been as blind as bats—and soon he discovers that this *is* the case, and indeed that he has come across an entire blind society He finds that their blindness is due to a disease contracted three hundred years before, and that over the course of time, the very concept of seeing has vanished:

> For fourteen generations these people had been blind and cut off from all the seeing world; the names for all the things of sight had faded and changed.... Much of their imagination had shrivelled with their eyes, and they had made for themselves new imaginations with their ever more sensitive ears and finger-tips.

10   Wells' traveller is at first contemptuous of the blind, seeing them as pitiful, disabled— but soon the tables are reversed, and he finds that they see *him* as demented, subject to hallucinations produced by the irritable, mobile organs in his face (which the blind, with their atrophied eyes, can conceive only as a source of delusion). When he falls in love with a girl in the valley and wants to stay there and marry her, the elders, after much thought, agree to this, provided he consent to the removal of those irritable organs, his eyes.

11   Forty years after I first read this story, I read another book, by Nora Ellen Groce, about deafness on the island of Martha's Vineyard. A sea captain and his brother from Kent, it seems, had settled there in the 1690s; both had normal hearing, but both brought with them a recessive gene for deafness, In time, with the isolation of the Vineyard, and the inter-marriage of its close community, this gene was carried by the majority of their descen-dants; by the mid-nineteenth century, in some of the up-island villages, a quarter or more of the inhabitants were born totally deaf.

12   Hearing people were not so much discriminated against here as assimilated—in this visual culture, everyone in the community, deaf and hearing alike, had come to use sign language. They would chat in Sign (it was much better than spoken language in many ways: for communicating across a distance, for instance, from one fishing boat to another, or for gossiping in church), debate in Sign, teach in Sign, think and dream in Sign. Martha's Vineyard was an island where everyone spoke sign language, a veritable country of the deaf. Alexander Graham Bell, visiting in the 1870s, wondered indeed whether it might not come to harbor an entire "deaf variety of the human race," which might then spread throughout the world.

13   And knowing that congenital achromatopsia, like this form of deafness, is also hered-itary, I could not help wondering whether there might also be, somewhere on the planet, an island, a village, a valley of the colorblind.

14   When I visited Guam early in 1993, some impulse made me put this question to my friend John Steele, who has practiced neurology all over Micronesia. Unexpectedly, I received an immediate, positive answer: there *was* just such an isolate, John said, on the island of Pingelap—it was relatively close, "barely twelve hundred miles from here," he added. Just a

few days earlier, he had seen an achromatopic boy on Guam, who had journeyed there with his parents from Pingelap. "Fascinating," he said. "Classical congenital achromatopsia, with nystagmus, and avoidance of bright light—and the incidence on Pingelap is extraordinarily high, almost ten percent of the population." I was intrigued by what John told me, and resolved that—sometime—I would come back to the South Seas and visit Pingelap.

15   When I returned to New York, the thought receded to the back of my mind. Then, some months later, I got a long letter from Frances Futterman, a woman in Berkeley who was herself born completely colorblind. She had read my original essay on the colorblind painter and was at pains to contrast her situation with his, and to emphasize that she herself, never having known color, had no sense of loss, no sense of being chromatically defective. But congenital achromatopsia, she pointed out, involved far more than color-blindness as such. What was far more disabling was the painful hypersensitivity to light and poor visual acuity which also affect congenital achromatopes. She had grown up in a relatively shadeless part of Texas, with a constant squint, and preferred to go outside only at night. She was intrigued by the notion of an island of the colorblind, but had not heard of one in the Pacific. Was this a fantasy, a myth, a daydream generated by lonely achro-matopes? But she had read, she told me, about another island mentioned in a book on achromatopsia—the little island of Fuur, in a Jutland fjord—where there were a large number of congenital achromatopes. She wondered if I knew of this book, called *Night Vision*—one of its editors, she added, was an achromatope too, a Norwegian scientist named Knut Nordby; perhaps he could tell me more.

16   Astounded at this—in a short time, I had learned of not one but *two* islands of the colorblind—I tried to find out more. Knut Nordby was a physiologist and psychophysicist, I read, a vision researcher at the University of Oslo and, partly by virtue of his own condi-tion, an expert on colorblindness. This was surely a unique, and important, combination of personal and formal knowledge; I had also sensed a warm, open quality in his brief auto-biographical memoir, which forms a chapter of *Night Vision,* and this emboldened me to write to him in Norway. "I would like to meet you," I wrote. "I would also like to visit the island of Fuur. And, ideally, to visit the island *with* you."

17   Having fired off this letter impulsively, to a complete stranger, I was surprised and relieved by his reaction, which arrived within a few days: "I should be delighted to accom-pany you there for a couple of days," he wrote. Since the original studies on Fuur had been done in the 1940s and '50s, he added, he would get some more up-to-date information. A month later, he contacted me again:

> I have just spoken to the key specialist on achromatopsia in Denmark, and he told me that there are no known achromats left on the island of Fuur. All of the cases in the original stud-ies are either dead... or have long since migrated. I am sorry—I hate to bring you such disap-pointing news, as I would much have fancied travelling with you to Fuur in search of the last surviving achromat there.

18   I too was disappointed, but wondered whether we should go nonetheless. I imagined finding strange residues, ghosts, of the achromatopes who had once lived there—parti-colored houses, black-and-white vegetation, documents, drawings, memories and stories of the colorblind by those who once knew them. But there was still Pingelap to think of; I had been assured there were still "plenty" of achromatopes there. I wrote to Knut again asking how he might feel about coming with me on a ten-thousand-mile journey, a sort of scientific adventure to Pingelap, and he replied yes, he would love to come, and could take off a few weeks in August.

19   Colorblindness had existed on both Fuur and Pingelap for a century or more, and though both islands had been the subject of extensive genetic studies, there had been no human (so to speak, Wellsian) explorations of them, of what it might be like to be an achromatope in an achromatopic community—to be not only totally colorblind oneself, but to have, perhaps, colorblind parents and grandparents, neighbors and teachers, to be part of a culture where the entire concept of color might be missing, but where, instead, other forms of perception, of attention, might be amplified in compensation. I had a vision, only half fantastic, of an entire achromatopic culture with its own singular tastes, arts, cooking, and clothing—a culture where the sensorium, the imagination, took quite different forms from our own, and where "color" was so totally devoid of referents or meaning that there were no color names, no color metaphors, no language to express it; but (perhaps) a heightened language for the subtlest variations of texture and tone, all that the rest of us dismiss as "grey."

20   Excitedly, I began making plans for the voyage to Pingelap. I phoned up my old friend Eric Korn—Eric is a writer, zoologist, and antiquarian bookseller—and asked him if he knew anything about Pingelap or the Caroline Islands. A couple of weeks later, I received a parcel in the post; in it was a slim leather-bound volume entitled *A Residence of Eleven Years in New Holland and the Caroline Islands, being the Adventures of James F. O'Connell.* The book was published, I saw, in Boston in 1836; it was a little dilapidated (and stained, I wanted to think, by heavy Pacific seas). Sailing from McQuarrietown in Tasmania, O'Connell had visited many of the Pacific islands, but his ship, the *John Bull,* had come to grief in the Carolines, in a group of islands which he calls Bonabee. His description of life there filled me with delight—we would be visiting some of the most remote and least-known islands in the world, probably not much changed from O'Connell's time.

21   I asked my friend and colleague Robert Wasserman if he would join us as well. As an ophthalmologist, Bob sees many partially blind people in his practice. Like myself, he had never met anyone born totally colorblind; but we had worked together on several cases involving vision, including that of the colorblind painter, Mr. I. As young doctors, we had done fellowships in neuropathology together, back in the 1960s, and I remembered him telling me then of his four-year-old son, Eric, as they drove up to Maine one summer, exclaiming, "Look at the beautiful orange grass!" No, Bob told him, it's not orange—"orange" is the color of an orange. Yes, cried Eric, it's orange like an orange! This was Bob's first intimation of his son's colorblindness. Later, when he was six, Eric had painted a picture he called *The Battle of Grey Rock,* but had used pink pigment for the rock.

22   Bob, as I had hoped, was fascinated by the prospect of meeting Knut and voyaging to Pingelap. An ardent windsurfer and sailor, he has a passion for oceans and islands and is reconditely knowledgeable about the evolution of outrigger canoes and proas in the Pacific; he longed to see these in action, to sail one himself. Along with Knut, we would form a team, an expedition at once neurological, scientific, and romantic, to the Caroline archipelago and the island of the colorblind.

23   We converged in Hawaii: Bob looked completely at home in his purple shorts and bright tropical shirt, but Knut looked distinctly less so in the dazzling sun of Waikiki—he was wearing two pairs of dark glasses over his normal glasses: a pair of Polaroid clip-ons, and over these a large pair of wraparound sunglasses—a darkened visor such as a cataract patient might wear. Even so, he tended to blink and squint almost continuously, and behind the dark glasses we could see that his eyes showed a continual jerking movement, a nystagmus. He was much more comfortable when we repaired to a quiet (and, to my eyes, rather dimly lit) little café on a side street, where he could take off his visor, and his clip-ons, and cease squinting and blinking. I found the café much too dark at first, and groped and blundered, knocking down a chair as we went in—but Knut, already dark adapted from wearing his double dark glasses, and more adept at night vision to begin with, was perfectly at ease in the dim lighting, and led us to a table.

24   Knut's eyes, like those of other congenital achromatopes, have no cones (at least no functional cones): these are the cells which, in the rest of us, fill the fovea—the tiny sensitive area in the center of the retina—and are specialized for the perception of fine detail, as well as color. He is forced to rely on the more meager visual input of the rods, which, in achromatopes as in the rest of us, are distributed around the periphery of the retina, and though these cannot discriminate color, they are much more sensitive to light. It is the rods which we all use for low-light, or scotopic, vision (as, for instance, walking at night). It is the rods which provide Knut with the vision he has. But without the mediating influence of cones, his rods quickly blanch out in bright light, becoming almost nonfunctional; thus Knut is dazzled by daylight, and literally blinded in bright sunlight—his visual fields contract immediately, shrinking to almost nothing—unless he shields his eyes from the intense light.

25   His visual acuity, without a cone-filled fovea, is only about a tenth of normal—when we were given menus, he had to take out a four-power magnifying glass and, for the special items chalked on a blackboard on the opposite wall, an eight-power monocular (it looked like a miniature telescope); without these, he would barely be able to read small or distant print. His magnifying glass and monocular are always on his person, and like the dark glasses and visors, they are essential visual aids. And, with no functioning fovea, he has difficulty fixating, holding his gaze on target, especially in bright light—hence his eyes make groping, nystagmic jerks.

26   Knut must protect his rods from overload and, at the same time, if detailed vision is needed, find ways of enlarging the images they present, whether by optical devices or peering closely. He must also, consciously or unconsciously, discover ways of deriving information from other aspects of the visual world, other visual cues which, in the absence of color, may take on a heightened importance. Thus—and this was apparent to us right away—his intense sensitivity and attention to form and texture, to outlines and boundaries, to perspective, depth, and movements, even subtle ones.

27   Knut enjoys the visual world quite as much as the rest of us; he was delighted by a picturesque market in a side street of Honolulu, by the palms and tropical vegetation all around us, by the shapes of clouds—he has a clear and prompt eye for the range of human beauty too. (He has a beautiful wife in Norway, a fellow psychologist, he told us—but it was only after they married, when a friend said, "I guess you go for redheads," that he learned for the first time of her flamboyant red hair.)

28   Knut is a keen black-and-white photographer—indeed his own vision, he said, by way of trying to share it, has some resemblance to that of an orthochromatic black-and-white film, although with a far greater range of tones. "Greys, you would call them, though the word 'grey' has no meaning for me, any more than the term 'blue' or 'red.'" But, he added, "I do not experience my world as 'colorless' or in any sense incomplete." Knut, who has never seen color, does not miss it in the least; from the start, he has experienced only the positivity of vision, and has built up a world of beauty and order and meaning on the basis of what he has.[5]

29   As we walked back to our hotel for a brief night's sleep before our flight the next day, darkness began to fall, and the moon, almost full, rose high into the sky until it was silhouetted, seemingly caught, in the branches of a palm tree. Knut stood under the tree and studied the moon intently with his monocular, making out its seas and shadows. Then, putting the monocular down and gazing up at the sky all around him, he said, "I see thousands of stars! I see the whole galaxy!"

30   "That's impossible," Bob said. "Surely the angle subtended by a star is too small, given that your visual acuity is a tenth of normal."

31   Knut responded by identifying constellations all over the sky—some looked quite different from the configurations he knew in his own Norwegian sky. He wondered if his nystagmus might not have a paradoxical benefit, the jerking movements "smearing" an otherwise invisible point image to make it larger—or whether this was made possible by some other factor. He agreed that it was difficult to explain how he could see stars with such low visual acuity—but nonetheless, he did.

32   "Laudable nystagmus, eh?" said Bob.

33   By sunrise, we were back at the airport, settling in for the long flight on the "Island Hopper," which calls twice a week at a handful of Pacific islands. Bob, jet-lagged, wedged himself in his seat for more sleep. Knut, dark-glassed already, took out his magnifying glass and began to pore over our bible for this trip—the admirable *Micronesia Handbook,* with its brilliant, sharp descriptions of the islands that awaited us. I was restless, and decided to keep a journal of the flight:

> An hour and a quarter has passed, and we are steadily flying, at 27,000 feet, over the trackless vastness of the Pacific. No ships, no planes, no land, no boundaries, nothing—only the limitless blue of sky and ocean, fusing at times into a single blue bowl. This featureless, cloudless vastness is a great relief, and reverie-inducing—but, like sensory deprivation, somewhat terrifying, too. The Vast thrills, as well as terrifies—it was well called by Kant "the terrifying Sublime."

34   After almost a thousand miles, we at last saw land—a tiny, exquisite atoll on the horizon. Johnston Island! I had seen it as a dot on the map and thought, "What an idyllic place, thousands of miles from anywhere." As we descended it looked less exquisite: a huge runway bisected the island, and to either side of this were storage bins, chimneys, and towers: eyeless buildings, all enveloped in an orange-red haze... my idyll, my little paradise, looked like a realm of hell.

35   Landing was rough, and frightening. There was a loud grinding noise and a squeal of rubber as the whole plane veered suddenly to one side. As we skewed to a halt on the tarmac, the crew informed us that the brakes had locked and we had torn much of the rubber off the tires on the left—we would have to wait here for repairs. A bit shaken from the landing, and cramped from hours in the air, we longed to get off the plane and stroll around a bit. A stair was pushed up to the plane, with "Welcome to Johnston Atoll" written on it. One or two passengers started to descend, but when we tried to follow, we were told that Johnston atoll was "restricted" and that non-military passengers were not allowed to disembark. Frustrated, I returned to my seat and borrowed the *Micronesia Handbook* from Knut, to read about Johnston.

36   It was named, I read, by a Captain Johnston of the HMS *Cornwallis,* who landed here in 1807—the first human being, perhaps, ever to set foot on this tiny and isolated spot. I

wondered if it had somehow escaped being seen altogether before this, or whether perhaps it had been visited, but never inhabited.

37   Johnston, considered valuable for its rich deposits of guano, was claimed by both the United States and the Kingdom of Hawaii in 1856. Migratory fowl stop here by the hundreds of thousands, and in 1926 the island was designated a federal bird reserve. After the Second World War it was acquired by the U.S. Air Force, and "since then," I read, "the U.S. military has converted this formerly idyllic atoll into one of the most toxic places in the Pacific." It was used during the 1950s and '60s for nuclear testing, and is still maintained as a standby test site; one end of the atoll remains radioactive. It was briefly considered as a test site for biological weapons, but this was precluded by the huge population of migratory birds, which, it was realized, might easily carry lethal infections back to the mainland. In 1971 Johnston became a depot for thousands of tons of mustard and nerve gases, which are periodically incinerated, releasing dioxin and furan into the air (perhaps this was the reason for the cinnamon haze I had seen from above). All personnel on the island are required to have their gas masks ready. Sitting in the now-stuffy plane as I read this—our ventilation had been shut off while we were on the ground—I felt a prickling in my throat, a tightness in my chest, and wondered if I was breathing some of Johnston's lethal air. The "Welcome" sign now seemed blackly ironic; it should at least have had a skull and crossbones added. The crew members themselves, it seemed to me, grew more uneasy and restless by the minute; they could hardly wait, I thought, to shut the door and take off again.

38   But the ground crew was still trying to repair our damaged wheels; they were dressed in shiny aluminized suits, presumably to minimize skin contact with the toxic air. We had heard in Hawaii that a hurricane was on its way towards Johnston: this was of no special importance to us when we were on schedule, but now, we started to think, if we were further delayed, the hurricane might indeed catch up with us on Johnston, and maroon us there with a vengeance—blowing up a storm of poison gases and radioactivity too. There were no planes scheduled to arrive until the end of the week; one flight, we heard, had been detained in this way the previous December, so that the passengers and crew had to spend an unexpected, toxic Christmas on the atoll.

39   The ground crew worked for two hours, without being able to do anything; finally, with many anxious looks at the sky, our pilot decided to take off again, on the remaining good tires. The whole plane shuddered and juddered as we accelerated, and seemed to heave and flap itself into the air like some giant ornithopter—but finally (using almost the entire mile-long runway) we got off the ground, and rose through the brown, polluted air of Johnston into the clear empyrean above.

40   Now another lap of more than 1,500 miles to our next stop, Majuro atoll, in the Marshall Islands. We flew endlessly, all of us losing track of space and time, and dozing fitfully in the void. I was woken briefly, terrifyingly, by an air pocket which dropped us suddenly, without warning; then I dozed once more, flying on and on, till I was woken again by altering air pressure. Looking out the window, I could see far below us the narrow, flat atoll of Majuro, rising scarcely ten feet above the waves; scores of islands surrounded the lagoon. Some of the islands looked vacant and inviting, with coconut palms fringing the ocean—the classic desert-island look; the airport was on one of the smaller islands.

41   Knowing we had two badly damaged tires, we were all a little fearful about landing. It was indeed rough—we were flung around quite a bit—and it was decided we should stay

on Majuro until some repairs could be made; this would take at least a couple of hours. After our long immurement in the plane (we had travelled nearly three thousand miles now from Hawaii), all of us burst off it, and scattered, explosively.

42   Knut, Bob, and I stopped first at the little shop in the airport—they had souvenir necklaces and mats, strung together from tiny shells, but also, to my delight, a postcard of Darwin.[6]

43   While Bob explored the beach, Knut and I walked out to the end of the runway which was bounded by a low wall overlooking the lagoon. The sea was an intense light blue, turquoise, azure, over the reef, and darker, almost indigo, a few hundred yards out. Not thinking, I enthused about the wonderful blues of the sea—then stopped, embarrassed. Knut, though he has no direct experience of color, is very erudite on the subject. He is intrigued by the range of words and images other people use about color and was arrested by my use of the word "azure." ("Is it similar to cerulean?") He wondered whether "indigo" was, for me, a separate, seventh color of the spectrum, neither blue nor violet, but itself, in between. "Many people," he added, "do not see indigo as a separate spectral color, and others see light blue as distinct from blue." With no direct knowledge of color, Knut has accumulated an immense mental catalog, an archive, of vicarious color knowledge about the world. He said that he found the light of the reef extraordinary—"A brilliant, metallic hue," he said of it, "intensely luminous, like a tungsten bronze." And he spotted half a dozen different sorts of crabs, some of them scuttling sideways so fast that I missed them. I wondered, as Knut himself has wondered, whether his perception of motion might be heightened, perhaps to compensate for his lack of color vision.

44   I wandered out to join Bob on the beach, with its fine-grained white sand and coconut palms. There were breadfruit trees here and there and, hugging the ground, low tussocks of zoysia, a beach grass, and a thick-leaved succulent which was new to me. Driftwood edged the strand, admixed with bits of cardboard carton and plastic, the detritus of Darrit-Uliga-Delap, the three-islanded capital of the Marshalls, where twenty thousand people live in close-packed squalor. Even six miles from the capital, the water was scummy, the coral bleached, and there were huge numbers of sea cucumbers, detritus feeders, in the turbid water. Nonetheless, with no shade and the humid heat overwhelming, and hoping there would be clearer water if we swam out a bit, we stripped down to our underwear and walked carefully over the sharp coral until it was deep enough to swim. The water was voluptuously warm, and the tensions of the long hours in our damaged plane gradually eased away as we swam. But just as we were beginning to enjoy that delicious timeless state, the real delight of tropical lagoons, there came a sudden shout from the airstrip— "The plane is ready to leave! Hurry!"—and we had to clamber out hastily, clutching wet clothes around us, and run back to the plane. One wheel, with its tire, had been replaced, but the other was bent and difficult to remove, and was still being worked on. So having rushed back to the plane, we sat for another hour on the tarmac—but the other wheel finally defeated all efforts at repair, and we took off again, bumping, noisily clattering over the runway, for the next lap, a short one, to Kwajalein.

45   Many passengers had left at Majuro, and others had got on, and I now found myself sitting next to a friendly woman, a nurse at the military hospital in Kwajalein, her husband part of a radar tracking unit there. She painted a less than idyllic picture of the island—or, rather, the mass of islands (ninety-one in all) that form Kwajalein atoll, surrounding the largest lagoon in the world. The lagoon itself, she told me, is a test target for missiles from U.S. Air Force bases on Hawaii and the mainland. It is also where countermissiles are tested, fired from Kwajalein at the missiles as they descend. There were nights, she said, when the whole sky was ablaze with light and noise as missiles and antimissiles streaked and collided across it, and reentry vehicles crashed into the lagoon. "Terrifying," she said, "like the night sky in Baghdad."

46   Kwajalein is part of the Pacific Barrier radar system, and there is a fearful, rigid, defensive atmosphere in the place, she said, despite the ending of the Cold War. Access is limited. There is no free discussion of any sort in the (military-controlled) media. Beneath the tough exterior there is demoralization and depression, and one of the highest suicide rates in the world. The authorities are not unaware of this, she added, and bend over backward to make Kwajalein more palatable with swimming pools, golf course, tennis courts, and whatnot—but none of it helps, the place remains unbearable. Of course, civilians can leave when they want, and military postings tend to be brief. The real sufferers, the helpless ones, are the Marshallese themselves, stuck on Ebeye, just three miles from Kwajalein: nearly fifteen thousand laborers on an island a mile long and two hundred yards wide, a tenth of a square mile. They come here for the jobs, she said—there are not many to be had in the Pacific—but end up stuck in conditions of unbelievable crowding, disease, and squalor. "If you want to see hell," my seatmate concluded, "make a visit to Ebeye."[7]

47   I had seen photographs of Ebeye—the island itself scarcely visible, with virtually every inch of it covered by tar-paper shacks—and hoped we might get a closer look as we descended; but the airline, I learned, was at some pains to keep the sight of it from passengers. Like Ebeye, the other infamous Marshallese atolls—Bikini, Eniwetak, Rongelap— many of them still uninhabitable from radioactivity, are also kept from ordinary eyes; as we got closer to them, I could not help thinking of the horror stories from the 1950s: the strange white ash that had rained down on a Japanese tuna fishing vessel, the *Lucky Dragon*, bringing acute radiation sickness to the entire crew; the "pink snow" that had fallen on Rongelap after one blast—the children had never seen anything like it, and they played with it delightedly.[8] Whole populations had been evacuated from some of the nuclear test islands; and some of the atolls were still so polluted, forty years later, that they were said to glow eerily, like a luminous watch dial, at night.

48   Another passenger who had got on at Majuro—I got to chatting with him when we were both stretching our legs at the back of the plane—was a large, genial man, an importer of canned meats with a far-flung business in Oceania. He expatiated on "the terrific appetite" the Marshallese and Micronesians have for Spam and other canned meats, and the huge amount he was able to bring into the area. This enterprise was not unprofitable, but it was, above all, to his mind, philanthropic, a bringing of sound Western nutrition to benighted natives who, left alone, would eat taro and breadfruit and bananas and fish as they had for millennia—a thoroughly un-Western diet from which, now, they were happily being weaned. Spam, in particular, as my companion observed, had come to be a central part of the new Micronesian diet. He seemed unaware of the enormous health problems which had come along with the shift to a Western diet after the war; in some Micronesian countries, I had heard, obesity, diabetes, and hypertension—previously quite rare—now affected huge percentages of the population.[9]

49   Later, when I went for another stretch, I got to talking to another passenger, a stern-looking woman in her late fifties. She was a missionary who had got on the plane at Majuro with a gospel choir composed of a dozen Marshallese in flowered shirts. She spoke of the importance of bringing the word of God to the islanders; to this end she travels the length and breadth of Micronesia, preaching the gospel. She was rigid in her self-righteousness and posture, her hard, aggressive beliefs—and yet there was an energy, a tenacity, a single-mindedness, a dedication which was almost heroic. The double valence

of religion, its complex and often contradictory powers and effects, especially in the collision of one culture, one spirit, with another, seemed embodied in this formidable woman and her choir.

50   The nurse, the Spam baron, the self-righteous missionary, had so occupied me that I had scarcely noticed the passage of time, the monotonous sweep of the ocean beneath us, until suddenly I felt the plane descending toward the huge, boomerang-shaped lagoon of Kwajalein. I strained to see the shantied hell of Ebeye, but we were approaching Kwajalein from the other side, its "good" side. We made the now-familiar sickening landing, crashing and bouncing along the huge military runway; I wondered what would be done with us while the bent wheel was finally mended. Kwajalein is a military encampment, a test base, with some of the tightest security on the planet. Civilian personnel, as on Johnston, are not allowed off the plane—but they could hardly keep all sixty of us on it for the three or five hours which might be needed to replace the bent wheel and do whatever other repairs might be necessary

51   We were asked to line up in single file and to walk slowly, without hurrying or stopping, into a special holding shed. Military police directed us here: "PUT YOUR THINGS DOWN," we were told, "STAND AGAINST THE WALL." A slavering dog, which had lain panting on a table (it seemed to be at least a hundred degrees in the shed) was now led down by a guard, first to our luggage, which it sniffed carefully, and then to us, each of whom it sniffed in turn. Being herded in this way was deeply chilling—we had a sense of how helpless and terrified one could be in the hands of a military or totalitarian bureaucracy.

52   After this "processing," which took twenty minutes, we were herded into a narrow, prisonlike pen with stone floors, wooden benches, military police, and, of course, dogs. There was one small window, high up on a wall, and by stretching and craning I could get a glimpse through it—of the manicured turf, the golf course, the country club amenities, for the military stationed here. After an hour we were led out into a small compound at the back, which at least had a view of the sea, and of the gun emplacements and memorials of the Second World War. There was a signpost here, with dozens of signs pointing in all directions, giving the distances to major cities all over the world. Right at the top was a sign saying "Lillehammer 9716 miles"—I saw Knut scrutinizing this with his monocular, perhaps thinking how far he was from home. And yet the sign gave a sort of comfort, by acknowledging that there was a world, another world, out there.

53   The plane was repaired in less than three hours, and though the crew was very tired—with the long delays in Johnston and Majuro, it was now thirteen hours since we had left Honolulu—they opted to fly on rather than spend the night here. We got on our way and a great sense of lightness, relief, seized us as we left Kwajalein behind. Indeed there was a festive air on the plane on this last lap, everyone suddenly becoming friendly and voluble, sharing food and stories. We were united now by a heightened consciousness of being alive, being free, after our brief but frightening confinement.

54   Having seen the faces of all my fellow passengers on the ground, in Kwajalein, I had become aware of the varied Micronesian world represented among them: there were Pohnpeians, returning to their island; there were huge, laughing Chuukese—giants, like Polynesians—speaking a liquid tongue which, even to my ears, was quite different from Pohnpeian; there were Palauans, rather reserved, dignified, with yet another language new to my ears; there was a Marshallese diplomat, on his way to Saipan, and a family of Chamorros (in whose speech I seemed to hear echoes of Spanish), returning to their village

in Guam. Back in the air, I now felt myself in a sort of linguistic aquarium, as my ears picked up different languages about me.

55   Hearing this mix of languages started to give me a sense of Micronesia as an immense archipelago, a nebula of islands, thousands in all, scattered across the Pacific, each as remote, as space surrounded, as stars in the sky. It was to these islands, to the vast contiguous galaxy of Polynesia, that the greatest mariners in history had been driven—by curiosity, desire, fear, starvation, religion, war, whatever—with only their uncanny knowledge of the ocean and the stars for guidance. They had migrated here more than three thousand years ago, while the Greeks were exploring the Mediterranean and Homer was telling the wanderings of Odysseus. The vastness of this other odyssey, its heroism, its wonder, perhaps its desperation, seized my imagination as we flew on endlessly over the Pacific. How many of these wanderers just perished in the vastness, I wondered, never even sighting the lands they hoped for; how many canoes were dashed to pieces by savage surf on reefs and rocky shores; how many arrived at islands which, appearing hospitable at first, proved too small to support a living culture and community, so that their habitation ended in starvation, madness, violence, death?

56   Again the Pacific, now at night, a vast lightless swell, occasionally illuminated, narrowly by the moon. The island of Pohnpei too was in darkness, though we got a faint sense, perhaps a silhouette, of its mountains against the night sky. As we landed, and decamped from the plane, we were enveloped in a huge humid warmth and the heavy scent of frangipani. This, I think, was the first sensation for us all, the smell of a tropical night, the scents of the day eluted by the cooling air—and then, above us, incredibly clear, the great canopy of the Milky Way.

57   But when we awoke the next morning, we saw what had been intimated in the darkness of our arrival: that Pohnpei was not another flat coral atoll, but an island mountain, with peaks rising precipitously into the sky, their summits hidden in the clouds. The steep slopes were wreathed in thick green jungle, with streams and waterfalls tracing down their sides. Below this we could see rolling hills, some cultivated, all about us, and, looking toward the coastline, a fringe of mangroves, with barrier reefs beyond. Though I had been fascinated by the atolls—Johnston, Majuro, even Kwajalein—this high volcanic island, cloaked in jungle and clouds, was utterly different, a naturalist's paradise.

58   I was strongly tempted to miss our plane and strand myself in this magical place for a month or two, or perhaps a year, the rest of my life—it was with reluctance, and a real physical effort, that I joined the others for our flight onward to Pingelap. As we took off, we saw the entire island spread out beneath us. Melville's description of Tahiti in *Omoo*, I thought, could as well have been Pohnpei:

> From the great central peaks... the land radiates on all sides to the sea in sloping green ridges. Between these are broad and shadowy valleys—in aspect, each a Tempe—watered with fine streams and thickly wooded.... Seen from the sea, the prospect is magnificent. It is one mass of shaded tints of green, from beach to mountain top; endlessly diversified with valleys, ridges, glens, and cascades. Over the ridges, here and there, the loftier peaks fling their shadows, and far down the valleys. At the head of these, the water-falls flash out into the sunlight as if pouring through vertical bowers of verdure.... It is no exaggeration to say, that to a European of any sensibility, who, for the first time, wanders back into these valleys—the ineffable repose and beauty of the landscape is such, that every object strikes him like something seen in a dream.

NOTES

1. Most of the statues of Easter Island do not, in fact, face the sea; they face away from the sea, toward what used to be the exalted houses of the island. Nor are the statues eyeless—on the contrary, they originally had startling, brilliant eyes made of white coral, with irises of red volcanic tuff or obsidian; this was only discovered in 1978. But my children's encyclopedia adhered to the myth of the blind, eyeless giants staring hopelessly out to sea—a myth which seems to have had its origin, through many tellings and retellings, in some of the early explorers' accounts, and in the paintings of William Hodges, who travelled to Easter Island with Captain Cook in the 1770s.

2. Humboldt first described the enormous dragon tree, very briefly, in a postscript to a letter written in June 1799 from Teneriffe:

   > In the district of Orotava there is a dragon-tree measuring forty-five feet in circumference.... Four centuries ago the girth was as great as it is now.

   In his *Personal Narrative*, written some years later, he devoted three paragraphs to the tree, and speculated about its origin:

   > It has never been found in a wild state on the continent of Africa. The East Indies is its real country. How has this tree been transplanted to Teneriffe, where it is by no means common?

   Later still, in his "Physiognomy of Plants" (collected, with other essays, in *Views of Nature*) he devoted nine entire pages to "The Colossal Dragon-Tree of Orotava," his original observations now expanded to a whole essay of rich and spreading associations and speculations:

   > This colossal dragon-tree, *Dracaena draco*, stands in the garden of M. Franqui, in the little town of Orotava... one of the most charming spots in the world. In June 1799, when we ascended the peak of Teneriffe, we found that this enormous tree measured 48 feet in circumference.... When we remember that the dragon-tree is everywhere of very slow growth, we may conclude that the one at Orotava is of extreme antiquity.

   He suggests an age of about six thousand years for the tree, which would make it "coeval with the builders of the Pyramids... and place its birth... in an epoch when the Southern Cross was still visible in Northern Germany." But despite its vast age, the tree still bore, he remarks, "the blossom and fruit of perpetual youth."

   Humboldt's *Personal Narrative* was a great favorite of Darwin's. "I will never be easy," he wrote to his sister Caroline, "till I see the peak of Teneriffe and the great Dragon tree." He looked forward eagerly to visiting Teneriffe, and was bitterly disappointed when he was not permitted to land there, because of quarantine. He did, however, take the *Personal Narrative* with him on the *Beagle* (along with Lyell's *Principles of Geology*), and when he was able to retrace some of Humboldt's travels in South America, his enthusiasm knew no bounds. "I formerly admired Humboldt," he wrote. "Now I almost adore him."

3. Remarkable specializations and evolutions may occur not only on islands, but in every sort of special and cut-off environment. Thus a unique stingless jellyfish was recently

discovered in an enclosed saltwater lake in the interior of Eil Malk, one of the islands of Palau, as Nancy Barbour describes:

> The jellyfish in the lake are members of the genus *Mastigias*, a jellyfish commonly found in the Palau Lagoon whose powerful stinging tentacles are used for protection and for capturing planktonic prey. It is believed that the ancestors of the *Mastigias* jellyfish became trapped in the lake millions of years ago when volcanic forces uplifted Palau's submerged reefs, transforming deep pockets in the reefs into landlocked saltwater lakes. Because there was little food and few predators in the lake, their long, clublike tentacles gradually evolved into stubby appendages unable to sting, and the jellyfish came to rely on the symbiotic algae living within their tissues for nutrients. The algae capture energy from the sun and transform it into food for the jellyfish. In turn, the jellyfish swim near the surface during the day to ensure that the algae receive enough sunlight for photosynthesis to occur.... Every morning the school of jellyfish, estimated at more than 1.6 million, migrates across the lake to the opposite shore, each jellyfish rotating counter-clockwise so that the algae on all sides of its bell receive equal sunlight. In the afternoon the jellyfish turn and swim back across the lake. At night they descend to the lake's middle layer, where they absorb the nitrogen that fertilizes their algae.

4. "I had been lying on a sunny bank," Darwin wrote of his travels in Australia, "reflecting on the strange character of the animals of this country as compared to the rest of the World." He was thinking here of marsupials as opposed to placental animals; they were so different, he felt,

> that an unbeliever in everything beyond his own reason might exclaim, "Surely two distinct Creators must have been at work."

   Then his attention was caught by a giant ant-lion in its conical pitfall, flicking up jets of sand, making little avalanches, so that small ants slid into is pit, exactly like ant-lions he had seen in Europe:

> Would any two workmen ever hit on so beautiful, so simple, and yet so artificial a contrivance? It cannot be thought so. The one hand has surely worked throughout the universe.

5. Frances Futterman also describes her vision in very positive terms:

> Words like "achromatopsia" dwell only on what we lack. They give no sense of what we have, the sort of worlds we appreciate or make for ourselves. I find twilight a magical time—there are no harsh contrasts, my visual field expands, my acuity is suddenly improved. Many of my best experiences have come at twilight, or in moonlight—I have toured Yosemite under the full moon, and one achromatope I know worked as a nighttime guide there; some of my happiest memories are of lying on my back among the giant redwood trees, looking up at the stars.

As a kid I used to chase lightning bugs on warm summer nights; and I loved going to the amusement park, with all the flashing neon lights and the darkened fun house—I was never afraid of that. I love grand old movie theaters, with their ornate interiors, and outdoor theaters. During the holiday season, I like to look at the twinkling lights decorating store windows and trees.

6. The caption on this postcard of Darwin suggested that he had "discovered" his theory of coral atolls here in Majuro; though in fact he conceived it before he had ever seen an atoll. He never actually visited Majuro, nor any of the Marshalls or the Carolines (though he did go to Tahiti). He does, however, make brief reference in *Coral Reefs* to Pohnpei (as Pouynipête, or Senyavine) and even mentions Pingelap (by its then-usual name, Macaskill).

7. Ebeye can be seen, perhaps, as a sort of end-point, an end-point characterized not only by desperate overcrowding and disease but by loss of cultural identity and coherence, and its replacement by an alien and frenzied consumerism, a cash economy. The ambiguous processes of colonization showed their potential right from the start—thus Cook, visiting Tahiti in 1769, only two years after its "discovery," could not help wondering, in his journals, whether the arrival of the white man might spell doom for all the Pacific cultures:

> We debauch their morals, and introduce among them wants and diseases which they never had before, and which serve only to destroy the happy tranquility they and their forefathers had enjoyed. I often think it would have been better for them if we had never appeared among them.

8. A pioneer in the use of streptomycin, Bill Peck came to Micronesia in 1958 as an official observer of the atomic tests in the Marshalls. He was one of the first to record the great incidence of thyroid cancer, leukemia, miscarriages, etc., in the wake of the tests, but was not allowed to publish his observations at the time. In *A Tidy Universe of Islands*, he gives a vivid description of the fallout on Rongelap after the detonation of the atomic bomb Bravo in Bikini:

> The fallout started four to six hours after the detonation and appeared first as an indefinite haze, rapidly changing to a white, sifting powder: like snow, some of them said who had seen movies at Kwajalien. Jimaco and Tina romped through the village with a troop of younger children, exulting in the miracle and shouting, "Look, we are like a Christmas picture, we play in snow," and they pointed with glee at the sticky powder that smeared their skin, whitened their hair, and rimed the ground with hoarfrost.
>
> As evening came on the visible fallout diminished until finally all that remained was a little unnatural lustre in the moonlight. And the itching. Almost everyone was scratching.... In the morning they were still itching, and several of them had weeping eyes. The flakes had become grimy and adherent from sweat and attempts to wash them off in cold water failed. Everyone felt a little sick, and three of them vomited.

9. Obesity, sometimes accompanied by diabetes, affects an overwhelming majority of Pacific peoples. It was suggested by James Neel in the early 1960s that this might be due to a so-called "thrifty" gene, which might have evolved to allow the storage of fat through periods of famine. Such a gene would be highly adaptive, he posited, in peoples living in a subsistence economy, where there might be erratic periods of feast and famine, but could prove lethally maladaptive if there was a shift to a steady high-fat diet, as has happened throughout Oceania since the Second World War. In Nauru, after less than a generation of Westernization, two-thirds of the islanders are obese, and a third have diabetes; similar figures have been observed on many other islands. That it is a particular conjunction of genetic disposition and lifestyle which is so dangerous is shown by the contrasting fates of the Pima Indians. Those living in Arizona, on a steady high-fat diet, have the highest rates of obesity and diabetes in the world, while the genetically similar Pima Indians of Mexico, living on subsistence farming and ranching, remain lean and healthy.

NOTES AND DISCUSSION

In this engaging piece that is partly a travelogue and partly a discussion of the neurological condition known as "congenital achromatopsia," Sacks writes, "[Islands are]... experiments of nature, places blessed or cursed by geographical singularity to harbor unique forms of life...." One of the "experiments of nature" that Sacks investigates in *The Island of the Colorblind and Cycad Island*, the book of which this is the first chapter, is an island that is disproportionately populated by people who are colorblind. Since "congenital achromatopsia" is a hereditary condition, "I could not help wondering," writes Sacks, "whether there might... be, somewhere on the planet, an island, a village, a valley of the colorblind," that is, a place "where the entire concept of color might be missing, but where, instead, other forms of perception, of attention, might be amplified in compensation."

STUDY QUESTIONS

For Discussion

1. Can you imagine a world without colour? How much would the concept of "grey areas" be altered? Which senses, do you think, would likely be privileged over senses of colour?

2. Compare a world without one of the senses to the ungendered world that Jan Furlong creates in this collection. Is it possible to overload the markers as Furlong does, or will your strategy have to be different?

For Writing

1. Imagine what it might be like to live in a world inhabited by people who do not have one of the universal five senses. Choose sight, for instance (as the sense that is most privileged in Western societies), and write a short descriptive essay that does not use any visual markers or metaphors or any other element associated with sight.

2. Consider the concepts of "disease" or "handicap" and the social construction that must take place for these concepts to mean anything. Write a short essay in which you (a) imagine yourself without one of your senses; and (b) situate yourself in a world where you do not feel "disabled."

A MASK ON THE FACE OF DEATH

Richard Selzer

BIOGRAPHICAL NOTE

Richard Selzer had been a medical student, general surgeon, and teacher at the Yale School for Medicine for about fifteen years when, in the early 1970s, he also began to write. By the late 1980s, as he has recorded in an essay entitled "The Pen and the Scalpel," he retired from medicine to write full-time. His essays, collected in such works as *Mortal Lessons* (1977), *Confessions of a Knife* (1979), *Letters to a Young Doctor* (1982), and *Taking the World in for Repairs* (1986), often explore the relationship between technology and faith in medicine. Selzer has won numerous awards for his writing, including the National Magazine Award (1975) and the American Medical Writers Award (1984).

---

1   It is ten o'clock at night as we drive up to the Copacabana, a dilapidated brothel on the rue Dessalines in the red-light district of Port-au-Prince. My guide is a young Haitian, Jean-Bernard. Ten years before, J-B tells me, at the age of fourteen, "like every good Haitian boy" he had been brought here by his older cousins for his *rite de passage*. From the car to the entrance, we are accosted by a half dozen men and women for sex. We enter, go down a long hall that breaks upon a cavernous room with a stone floor. The cubicles of the prostitutes, I am told, are in an attached wing of the building. Save for a red-purple glow from small lights on the walls, the place is unlit. Dark shapes float by, each with a blindingly white stripe of teeth. Latin music is blaring. We take seats at the table farthest from the door. Just outside, there is the rhythmic lapping of the Caribbean Sea. About twenty men are seated at the tables or lean against the walls. Brightly dressed women, singly or in twos or threes, stroll about, now and then exchanging banter with the men. It is as though we have been deposited in act two of Bizet's *Carmen*. If this place isn't Lillas Pastia's tavern, what is it?

2   Within minutes, three light-skinned young women arrive at our table. They are very beautiful and young and lively. Let them be Carmen, Mercedes, and Frasquita.

3   "I want the old one," says Frasquita, ruffling my hair. The women laugh uproariously.

4   "Don't bother looking any further," says Mercedes. "We are the prettiest ones."

5   "We only want to talk," I tell her.

6   "Aah, aah," she crows. "Massissi. You are massissi." It is the contemptuous Creole term for homosexual. If we want only to talk, we must be gay. Mercedes and Carmen are slender, each weighing one hundred pounds or less. Frasquita is tall and hefty. They are dressed for work: red taffeta, purple chiffon, and black sequins. Among them a thousand gold bracelets and earrings multiply every speck of light. Their bare shoulders are like animated lamps gleaming in the shadowy room. Since there is as yet no business, the women agree to sit with us. J-B orders beer and cigarettes. We pay each woman $10.

7   "Where are you from?" I begin.

8   "We are Dominican."

9   "Do you miss your country?"

10   "Oh, yes, we do." Six eyes go muzzy with longing. "Our country is the most beautiful in the world. No country is like the Dominican. And it doesn't stink like this one."

11   "Then why don't you work there? Why come to Haiti?"

12   "Santo Domingo has too many whores. All beautiful, like us. All light-skinned. The Haitian men like to sleep with light women."

13   "Why is that?"

14   "Because always, the whites have all the power and the money. The black men can imagine they do, too, when they have us in bed."

15   Eleven o'clock. I looked around the room that is still sparsely peopled with men.

16   "It isn't getting any busier," I say. Frasquita glances over her shoulder. Her eyes drill the darkness.

17   "It is still early," she says.

18   "Could it be that the men are afraid of getting sick?" Frasquita is offended.

19   "Sick! They do not get sick from us. We are healthy, strong. Every week we go for a checkup. Besides, we know how to tell if we are getting sick."

20   "I mean sick with AIDS." The word sets off a hurricane of taffeta, chiffon, and gold jewelry. They are all gesticulation and fury. It is Carmen who speaks.

21   "AIDS!" Her lips curl about the syllable. "There is no such thing. It is a false disease invented by the American government to take advantage of the poor countries. The American President hates poor people, so now he makes up AIDS to take away the little we have." The others nod vehemently.

22   "*Mira, mon cher.* Look, my dear," Carmen continues. "One day the police came here. Believe me, they are worse than the *tonton macoutes* with their submachine guns. They rounded up one hundred and five of us and they took our blood. That was a year ago. None of us have died, you see? We are all still here. *Mira*, we sleep with all the men and we are not sick."

23   "But aren't there some of you who have lost weight and have diarrhea?"

24   "One or two, maybe. But they don't eat. That is why they are weak."

25   "Only the men die," says Mercedes. "They stop eating, so they die. It is hard to kill a woman."

26   "Do you eat well?"

27   "Oh, yes, don't worry, we do. We eat like poor people, but we eat." There is a sudden scream from Frasquita. She points to a large rat that has emerged from beneath the table.

28   "My God!" she exclaims. "It is big like a pig." They burst into laughter. For a moment the women fall silent. There is only the restlessness of their many bracelets. I give them each another $10.

29   "Are many of the men here bisexual?"

30   "Too many. They do it for money. Afterward, they come to us." Carmen lights a cigarette and looks down at the small lace handkerchief she has been folding and unfolding with immense precision on the table. All at once she turns it over as though it were the ace of spades.

31   "*Mira, blanc...* look, white man," she says in a voice suddenly full of foreboding. Her skin too seems to darken to coincide with the tone of her voice.

32   "*Mira*, soon many Dominican woman will die in Haiti!"

33   "Die of what?"

34   She shrugs. "It is what they do to us."

35   "Carmen," I say, "if you knew that you had AIDS, that your blood was bad, would you still sleep with men?" Abruptly, she throws back her head and laughs. It is the same laughter with which Frasquita had greeted the rat at our feet. She stands and the others follow.

36   "*Méchant!* You wicked man," she says. Then, with terrible solemnity, "You don't know anything."

37   "But you are killing the Haitian men," I say.

38   "As for that," she says, "everyone is killing everyone else." All at once, I want to know everything about these three—their childhood, their dreams, what they do in the afternoon, what they eat for lunch.

39   "Don't leave," I say. "Stay a little more." Again, I reach for my wallet. But they are gone, taking all the light in the room with them—Mercedes and Carmen to sit at another table where three men have been waiting. Frasquita is strolling about the room. Now and then, as if captured by the music, she breaks into a few dance steps, snapping her fingers, singing to herself.

40   Midnight. And the Copacabana is filling up. Now it is like any other seedy nightclub where men and women go hunting. We get up to leave. In the center a couple are dancing a *méringue*. He is the most graceful dancer I have ever watched; she, the most voluptuous. Together they seem to be riding the back of the music as it gallops to a precisely sexual beat. Closer up, I see that the man is short of breath, sweating. All at once, he collapses into a chair. The woman bends over him, coaxing, teasing, but he is through. A young man with a long polished stick blocks my way.

41   "I come with you?" he asks. "Very good time. You say yes? Ten dollars? Five?"

42   I have been invited by Dr. Jean William Pape to attend the AIDS clinic of which he is the director. Nothing from the outside of the low whitewashed structure would suggest it as a medical facility. Inside, it is divided into many small cubicles and a labyrinth of corridors. At nine a.m. the hallways are already full of emaciated silent men and women, some sitting on the few benches, the rest leaning against the walls. The only sounds are subdued moans of discomfort interspersed with coughs. How they eat us with their eyes as we pass.

43   The room where Pape and I work is perhaps ten feet by ten. It contains a desk, two chairs, and a narrow table that is covered with a sheet that will not be changed during the day. The patients are called in one at a time, asked how they feel and whether there is any change in their symptoms, then examined on the table. If the patient is new to the clinic, he or she is questioned about sexual activities.

44   A twenty-seven-year-old man whose given name is Miracle enters. He is wobbly, panting, like a groggy boxer who has let down his arms and is waiting for the last punch. He is neatly dressed and wears, despite the heat, a heavy woolen cap. When he removes it, I see that his hair is thin, dull reddish, and straight. It is one of the signs of AIDS in Haiti, Pape tells me. The man's skin is covered with a dry itchy rash. Throughout the interview and examination he scratches himself slowly, absentmindedly. The rash is called prurigo. It is another symptom of AIDS in Haiti. This man has had diarrhea for six months. The laboratory reports that the diarrhea is due to an organism called cryptosporidium, for which there is no treatment. The telltale rattling of the tuberculous moisture in his chest is audible without a stethoscope. He is like a leaky cistern that bubbles and froths. And, clearly, exhausted.

45   "Where do you live?" I ask.

46   "Kenscoff." A village in the hills above Port-au-Prince.

47   "How did you come here today?"

48   "I came on the *tap-tap*." It is the name given to the small buses that swarm the city, each one extravagantly decorated with religious slogans, icons, flowers, animals, all painted in psychedelic colors. I have never seen a tap-tap that was not covered with passengers as well, riding outside and hanging on. The vehicles are little masterpieces of contagion, if not of AIDS then of the multitude of germs which Haitian flesh is heir to. Miracle is given a prescription for a supply of Sera, which is something like Gatorade, and told to return in a month.

49   "*Mangé kou bêf*," says the doctor in farewell. "Eat like an ox." What can he mean? The man has no food or money to buy any. Even had he food, he has not the appetite to eat or the ability to retain it. To each departing patient the doctor will say the same words— "Mangé kou bêf." I see that it is his way of offering a hopeful goodbye.

50   "Will he live until his next appointment?" I ask.

51   "No." Miracle leaves to catch the *tap-tap* for Kenscoff.

52   Next is a woman of twenty-six who enters holding her right hand to her forehead in a kind of permanent salute. In fact, she is shielding her eye from view. This is her third visit to the clinic. I see that she is still quite well nourished.

53   "Now, you'll see something beautiful, tremendous," the doctor says. Once seated upon the table, she is told to lower her hand. When she does, I see that her right eye and its eyelid are replaced by a huge fungating ulcerated tumor, a side product of her AIDS. As she turns her head, the cluster of lymph glands in her neck to which the tumor has spread is thrown into relief. Two years ago she received a blood transfusion at a time when the country's main blood bank was grossly contaminated with AIDS. It has since been closed down. The only blood available in Haiti is a small supply procured from the Red Cross.

54   "Can you give me medicine?" the woman wails.

55   "No."

56   "Can you cut it away?"

57   "No."

58   "Is there radiation therapy?" I ask.

59   "No."

60   "Chemotherapy?" The doctor looks at me in what some might call weary amusement. I see that there is nothing to do. She has come here because there is nowhere else to go.

61   "What will she do?"

62   "Tomorrow or the next day or the day after that she will climb up into the mountains to seek relief from the *houngan*, the voodoo priest, just as her slave ancestors did two hundred years ago."

63   Then comes a frail man in his thirties, with a strangely spiritualized face, like a child's. Pus runs from one ear onto his cheek, where it has dried and caked. He has trouble remembering, he tells us. In fact, he seems confused. It is from toxoplasmosis of the brain, an effect of his AIDS. This man is bisexual. Two years ago he engaged in oral sex with foreign men for money. As I palpate the swollen glands of his neck, a mosquito flies between our faces. I swat at it, miss. Just before coming to Haiti I had read that the AIDS virus had been isolated from a certain mosquito. The doctor senses my thought.

64   "Not to worry," he says. "So far as we know there has never been a case transmitted by insects."

65   "Yes," I say. "I see."

66   And so it goes until the last, the thirty-sixth AIDS patient has been seen. At the end of the day I am invited to wash my hands before leaving. I go down a long hall to a sink. I turn on the faucets but there is no water.

67   "But what about *you*?" I ask the doctor. "You are at great personal risk here—the tuberculosis, the other infections, no water to wash...." He shrugs, smiles faintly, and lifts his hands palm upward.

68   We are driving up a serpiginous steep road into the barren mountains above Port-au-Prince. Even in the bright sunshine the countryside has the bloodless color of exhaustion and indifference. Our destination is the Baptist Mission Hospital, where many cases of AIDS have been reported. Along the road there are slow straggles of schoolchildren in blue uniforms who stretch out their hands as we pass and call out, "Give me something." Already a crowd of outpatients has gathered at the entrance to the mission compound. A tour of the premises reveals that in contrast to the aridity outside the gates, this is an enclave of productivity, lush with fruit trees and poinsettia.

69   The hospital is clean and smells of creosote. Of the forty beds less than a third are occupied. In one male ward of twelve beds, there are two patients. The chief physician tells us that last year he saw ten cases of AIDS each week. Lately the number has decreased to four or five.

70   "Why is that?" we want to know.

71   "Because we do not admit them to the hospital, so they have learned not to come here."

72   "Why don't you admit them?"

73   "Because we would have nothing but AIDS here then. So we send them away."

74   "But I see that you have very few patients in bed."

75   "That is also true."

76   "Where do the AIDS patients go?"

77   "Some go to the clinic in Port-au-Prince or the general hospital in the city. Others go home to die or to the voodoo priest."

78   "Do the people with AIDS know what they have before they come here?"

79   "Oh, yes, they know very well, and they know there is nothing to be done for them."

80   Outside, the crowd of people is dispersing toward the gate. The clinic has been canceled for the day. No one knows why. We are conducted to the office of the reigning American pastor. He is a tall, handsome Midwesterner with an ecclesiastical smile.

81   "It is voodoo that is the devil here." He warms to his subject. "It is a demonic religion, a cancer on Haiti. Voodoo is worse than AIDS. And it is one of the reasons for the epidemic. Did you know that in order for a man to become a *houngan* he must perform anal sodomy on another man? No, of course you didn't. And it doesn't stop there. The *houngans* tell the men that in order to appease the spirits they too must do the same thing. So you have ritualized homosexuality. That's what is spreading the AIDS." The pastor tells us of a nun who witnessed two acts of sodomy in a provincial hospital where she came upon a man sexually assaulting a houseboy and another man mounting a male patient in his bed.

82   "Fornication," he says. "It is Sodom and Gomorrah all over again, so what can you expect from these people?" Outside his office we are shown a cage of terrified, cowering monkeys to whom he coos affectionately. It is clear that he loves them. At the car, we shake hands.

83   "By the way," the pastor says, "what is your religion? Perhaps I am a kinsman?"

84   "While I am in Haiti," I tell him, "it will be voodoo or it will be nothing at all."

85   Abruptly, the smile breaks. It is as though a crack had suddenly appeared in the face of an idol.

86   From the mission we go to the general hospital. In the heart of Port-au-Prince, it is the exact antithesis of the immaculate facility we have just left—filthy, crowded, hectic, and staffed entirely by young interns and residents. Though it is associated with a medical school, I do not see any members of the faculty. We are shown around by Jocelyne, a young intern in a scrub suit. Each bed in three large wards is occupied. On the floor about the beds, hunkered in the posture of the innocent poor, are family members of the patients. In the corridor that constitutes the emergency room, someone lies on a stretcher receiving an intravenous infusion. She is hardly more than a cadaver.

87   "Where are the doctors in charge?" I ask Jocelyne. She looks at me questioningly.

88   "We are in charge."

89   "I mean your teachers, the faculty."

90   "They do not come here."

91   "What is wrong with that woman?"

92   "She has had diarrhea for three months. Now she is dehydrated." I ask the woman to open her mouth. Her throat is covered with the white plaques of thrush, a fungus infection associated with AIDS.

93   "How many AIDS patients do you see here?"

94   "Three or four a day. We send them home. Sometimes the families abandon them, then we must admit them to the hospital. Every day, then, a relative comes to see if the patient has died. They want to take the body. That is important to them. But they know very well that AIDS is contagious and they are afraid to keep them at home. Even so, once or twice a week the truck comes to take away the bodies. Many are children. They are buried in mass graves."

95   "Where do the wealthy patients go?"

96   "There is a private hospital called Canapé Vert. Or else they go to Miami. Most of them, rich and poor, do not go to the hospital. Most are never diagnosed."

97   "How do you know these people have AIDS?"

98   "We don't know sometimes. The blood test is inaccurate. There are many false positives and false negatives. Fifteen percent of those with the disease have negative blood

tests. We go by their infections—tuberculosis, diarrhea, fungi, herpes, skin rashes. It is not hard to tell."

99   "Do they know what they have?"

100   "Yes. They understand at once and they are prepared to die."

101   "Do the patients know how AIDS is transmitted?"

102   "They know, but they do not like to talk about it. It is taboo. Their memories do not seem to reach back to the true origins of their disaster. It is understandable, is it not?"

103   "Whatever you write, don't hurt us any more than we have already been hurt." It is a young Haitian journalist with whom I am drinking a rum punch. He means that any further linkage to AIDS and Haiti in the media would complete the economic destruction of the country. The damage was done early in the epidemic when the Centers for Disease Control in Atlanta added Haitians to the three other high-risk groups—hemophiliacs, intravenous drug users, and homosexual and bisexual men. In fact, Haitians are no more susceptible to AIDS than anyone else. Although the CDC removed Haitians from special scrutiny in 1985, the lucrative tourism on which so much of the country's economy was based was crippled. Along with tourism went much of the foreign business investment. Worst of all was the injury to the national pride. Suddenly Haiti was indicated as the source of AIDS in the western hemisphere.

104   What caused the misunderstanding was the discovery of a large number of Haitian men living in Miami with AIDS antibodies in their blood. They denied absolutely they were homosexual. But the CDC investigators did not know that homosexuality is the strongest taboo in Haiti and that no man would ever admit to it. Bisexuality, however, is not uncommon. Many married men and heterosexually oriented males will occasionally seek out other men for sex. Further, many, if not most, Haitian men visit female prostitutes from time to time. It is not difficult to see that once the virus was set loose in Haiti, the spread would be swift through both genders.

105   Exactly how the virus of AIDS arrived is not known. Could it have been brought home by the Cuban soldiers stationed in Angola and thence to Haiti, about fifty miles away? Could it have been passed on by the thousands of Haitians living in exile in Zaire, who later returned home or immigrated to the United States? Could it have come from the American and Canadian homosexual tourists, and, yes, even some US diplomats who have traveled to the island to have sex with impoverished Haitian men all too willing to sell themselves to feed their families? Throughout the international gay community Haiti was known as a good place to go for sex.

106   On a private tip from an official at the Ministry of Tourism, J-B and I drive to a town some fifty miles from Port-au-Prince. The hotel is owned by two Frenchmen who are out of the country, one of the staff tells us. He is a man of about thirty and clearly he is desperately ill. Tottering, short of breath, he shows us about the empty hotel. The furnishings are opulent and extreme—tiger skins on the wall, a live leopard in the garden, a bedroom containing a giant bathtub with gold faucets. Is it the heat of the day or the heat of my imagination that makes these walls echo with the painful cries of pederasty?

107   The hotel where we are staying is in Pétionville, the fashionable suburb of Port-au-Prince. It is the height of the season but there are no tourists, only a dozen or so French and American businessmen. The swimming pool is used once or twice a day by a single person. Otherwise, the water remains undisturbed until dusk, when the fruit bats come down to drink in midswoop. The hotel keeper is an American. He is eager to set me straight on Haiti.

108 "What did and should attract foreign investment is a combination of reliable weather, an honest and friendly populace, low wages, and multilingual managers."

109 "What spoiled it?"

110 "Political instability and a bad American press about AIDS." He pauses, then adds: "To which I hope you won't be contributing."

111 "What about just telling the truth?" I suggest.

112 "Look," he says, "there is no more danger of catching AIDS in Haiti than in New York or Santo Domingo. It is not where you are but what you do that counts." Agreeing, I ask if he had any idea that much of the tourism in Haiti during the past few decades was based on sex.

113 "No idea whatsoever. It was only recently that we discovered that that was the case."

114 "How is it that you hoteliers, restaurant owners, and the Ministry of Tourism did not know what *tout* Haiti knew?"

115 "Look. All I know is that this is a middle-class, family-oriented hotel. We don't allow guests to bring women, or for that matter men, into their rooms. If they did, we'd ask them to leave immediately."

116 At 5 a.m. the next day the telephone rings in my room. A Creole-accented male voice.

117 "Is the lady still with you, sir?"

118 "There is no lady here."

119 "In your room, sir, the lady I allowed to go up with a package?"

120 "There is no lady here, I tell you."

121 At 7 a.m. I stop at the front desk. The clerk is a young man.

122 "Was it you who called my room at five o'clock?"

123 "Sorry," he says with a smile. "It was a mistake, sir. I meant to ring the room next door to yours." Still smiling, he holds up his shushing finger.

124 Next to Dr. Pape, director of the AIDS clinic, Bernard Liautaud, a dermatologist, is the most knowledgeable Haitian physician on the subject of the epidemic. Together, the two men have published a dozen articles on AIDS in international medical journals. In our meeting they present me with statistics:

> There are more than one thousand documented cases of AIDS in Haiti, and as many as one hundred thousand carriers of the virus.
>
> Eighty-seven percent of AIDS is now transmitted heterosexually. While it is true that the virus was introduced via the bisexual community, that route has decreased to 10 percent or less.
>
> Sixty percent of the wives or husbands of AIDS patients tested positive for the antibody.
>
> Fifty percent of the prostitutes tested in the Port-au-Prince area are infected.
>
> Eighty percent of the men with AIDS have had contact with prostitutes.
>
> The projected number of active cases in four years is ten thousand. (Since my last visit, the Haitian Medical Association broke its silence on the epidemic by warning that one million of the country's six million people could be carriers by 1992.)

125   The two doctors have more to tell. "The crossing over of the plague from the homo-sexual to the heterosexual community will follow in the United States within two years. This, despite the hesitation to say so by those who fear to sow panic among your popula-tion. In Haiti, because bisexuality is more common, there was an early crossover into the general population. The trend, inevitably, is the same in the two countries."

126   "What is there to do, then?"

127   "Only education, just as in America. But here the Haitians reject the use of condoms. Only the men who are too sick to have sex are celibate."

128   "What is to be the end of it?"

129   "When enough heterosexuals of the middle and upper classes die, perhaps there will be the panic necessary for the people to change their sexual lifestyles."

130   This evening I leave Haiti. For two weeks I have fastened myself to this lovely fragile land like an ear pressed to the ground. It is a country to break a traveler's heart. It occurs to me that I have not seen a single jogger. Such a public expenditure of energy while every-where else strength is ebbing—it would be obscene. In my final hours, I go to the Cathédral of Sainte Trinité, the inner walls of which are covered with murals by Haiti's most renowned artists. Here are all the familiar Bible stories depicted in naiveté and piety, and all in such an exuberance of color as to tax the capacity of the retina to receive it, as though all the vitality of Haiti had been turned to paint and brushed upon these walls. How to explain its efflorescence at a time when all else is lassitude and inertia? Perhaps one day the plague will be rendered in poetry, music, painting, but not now. Not now.

NOTES AND DISCUSSION

"A Mask on the Face of Death" is divided into several sections, each dealing with one "face" of AIDS in Haiti. The opening section shows one manifestation of the economic and cultural conditions that led to the rapid spread of AIDS in that nation. A key image here is that of the couple dancing: what appears at first glance to be beautiful, erotic, and graceful deteriorates into collapse and exhaustion. A later section, set in a hotel, also addresses the link between economics and AIDS, which is one of the essay's main themes.

Another important theme is the role of ignorance in the spread of AIDS: genuine igno-rance, or lack of knowledge; deliberate ignorance, worn as a mask of indifference; and "ignorance" of the type displayed by the moralizing doctor/pastor, who remains culturally blinkered.

In other sections, Seltzer examines three hospitals that treat or refuse to treat the physi-cal symptoms of AIDS. These passages are filled with startlingly graphic details. Another section looks at the effects of AIDS on the nation's reputation, and one near the end lists statis-tics regarding AIDS in Haiti.

Throughout, the "mask" appears as a tissue of lies, evasions, and denials, all prolong-ing the suffering and preserving the conditions that caused the problem in the first place. While the doctors at the clinic lack water to wash up, various poses and attitudes allow others to "wash their hands" of the responsibility to change the conditions or care for the infected.

STUDY QUESTIONS

For Discussion

1. One outstanding feature of this essay is its reliance on direct dialogue. What effects—what tone or texture—do these passages bring to the piece? Consider the effect if Selzer had reported these conversations indirectly.

2. Examine Selzer's reply to the pastor at the Baptist Mission Hospital, and its effect. How does it indicate Selzer's overall tone and purpose? Given what he has said or implied elsewhere in the essay, why would Selzer profess his religion to be voodoo while in Haiti? Do cracks appear anywhere else in the "masks" worn by those who try to ignore the disease or the conditions behind its rapid spread?

For Writing

1. Write a personal essay about a confrontation (friendly or otherwise), or interview someone you think has an interesting story to tell. In either case, use direct quotations to capture and convey the essence of the moment or of the personalities involved.

2. The spread of AIDS in Haiti rests on some of the same kinds of cultural myths that Ignatieff sees behind the atrocities in the Balkan states. Write a comparative essay, examining parallels in the cause-and-effect relationships between myths, attitudes, and actions in these seemingly different circumstances.

THE ROAD
FROM RIO

BIOGRAPHICAL NOTE

David Suzuki, an internationally famous Canadian environmentalist, began teaching zoology at UBC in 1969. He has hosted CBC's *Quirks and Quarks* on radio and *The Nature of Things* on television. His essays on science and the environment have appeared in *The Globe and Mail* and the *Toronto Star*, as well as in several books such as *Genethics* (1989), *Inventing the Future* (1989), *It's a Matter of Survival* (1990), and *Time to Change* (1994), from which the following essay is taken.

---

1   The earth summit in Rio in June 1992 can best be described by a metaphor. Picture the participants at the Earth Summit as passengers in a packed car heading for a brick wall at 150 kilometres an hour. Most of them ignored the danger because they were too busy arguing about where they wanted to sit. Some occupants did notice the wall but were still debating about whether it was a mirage, how far away it was, or when the car would reach it. A few were confident the car was so well built that it would suffer only minor damage when it plowed into the wall. Besides, they warned, slowing down or swerving too sharply would upset everyone inside the car.

2   There were those who argued vehemently that the wall was real and that everyone in the car was in great danger. Put on the brakes and turn the steering wheel to avoid a collision, they pleaded. Even if the wall did turn out to be an illusion, all that would be lost was a little time. The trouble was, those making this plea were all stuck in the trunk!

3   In order to understand the severity of this metaphor, you need some background. About six months before Rio, I watched a tape of a program of *The Nature of Things* that had been made on the first major global conference on the environment in Stockholm in 1972. Many of the well-known figures in the environmental movement were featured—

Reprinted with permission of Stoddart Publishing Co. Ltd.

Paul Ehrlich, Margaret Mead, Barbara Ward, and Maurice Strong. It was devastating to watch because many of the issues of concern today—species extinction, overpopulation, global pollution—were raised eloquently then, yet remain and have worsened.

4   There have been major changes in our perspective on the environment in the twenty years since Stockholm. Back then, there was no sense of the central role of aboriginal people in the struggle to resolve the ecocrisis. New ecological problems like acid rain, ozone depletion, and global warming have come to our attention since 1972. There were few recognizable political leaders in attendance at Stockholm, and the role of the so-called Third World was marginal. That all changed at Rio.

5   In the two decades between Stockholm and Rio, new names became a part of our lexicon—Bhopal, Exxon Valdez, Chernobyl—while a host of issues made the news: chemicals spilled into the Rhine at Basel, poisoned Beluga whales in the Gulf of St. Lawrence, the burning rainforest of the Amazon, unswimmable beaches, record hot summers, the Arab oil embargo, Ethiopia, and the Gulf War. During the 1980s, poll after poll revealed that the environment was at the top of people's concerns. In 1987, the Brundtland Commission report, *Our Common Future*, documented in painstaking detail the perilous state of the Earth and popularized a phrase that has become the rallying cry of politicians and businesspeople alike—*sustainable development*.

6   Thus, the stage was set for Rio. Canadian businessman Maurice Strong, the secretary-general who had engineered Stockholm, was once again in command for Rio. Strong had been indefatigable, crisscrossing the planet, cajoling and urging world leaders to commit to attending. The fact that he is exquisitely well connected was a big help. He extracted promises from dozens of political leaders to attend the Earth Summit, and Rio was appropriate because all the contradictions of poverty and ecological damage could be seen. Rio was clearly going to be a big media event, a fact that raised expectations that it might signal a major shift from the environmentally destructive path we were on.

7   I was deeply skeptical about the possibility for real change, not out of cynicism about political motives but because of severe constraints on all politicians whether capitalist, socialist, or communist. Politicians are beholden to those on whom their power depends. In a democracy, that means people who vote. If the men and women who are trying to decide on the future of the planet must also keep the voters back home uppermost in mind, they will be limited in their ability to make changes. Our own species' chauvinistic needs also blind us to the fact that it is in our own long-term self-interest to maintain the requirements of planetary air, water, and soil for all ecosystems, animals, and plants. Furthermore, because they don't vote, children, the disenfranchised poor and oppressed, and all unborn generations are effectively without a voice. Only one delegation—the Dutch—had children as official delegates to Rio, yet children were the ones with most at stake in Rio. Thus, the political sphere of vision was far too short and parochial to allow serious action on global issues.

8   My pessimism was exacerbated by the fact that the Canadian government attempted to use Rio to project an image of environmental concern that its actual policies do not deserve. Prime Minister Brian Mulroney, like his friend U.S. President George Bush, had been a belated environmental convert who promised to show his commitment after the election of 1988. In that year before a fall election, Mulroney's environment minister, Tom McMillan, sponsored an international conference on the atmosphere in Toronto. Delegates at that meeting, concerned with the reality and hazards of global warming, had supported a goal of a 20 percent reduction of the 1988 levels of CO_2 emissions within fifteen years.

9   Upon reelection, the Mulroney government commissioned a study to determine whether the Toronto target could be met and how much it would cost. That study, which has yet to be officially released but was leaked to the press, concluded that: 1) the target was achievable, 2) it would cost $74 billion, and 3) it would result in a *net savings* of $150 billion! To date, Canada, which has the highest per capita emission of CO_2 among industrialized countries, has made no serious commitment to reduce emissions. Studies on the feasibility and cost of CO_2 reduction by Australia, Sweden, and the United States have all come to the same conclusion and have met with similar political inaction.

10   Reduction of CO_2 emission is one of those rare instances of a win-win situation, whereby the general environment would improve and we would save massive amounts of money. Yet by the time of Rio, delegates of the United Nations Commission on the Environment and Development (UNCED) were barely able to get politicians to agree on a target of stabilization of 1990 levels of CO_2 emission by the year 2000! Only after watering this target down even further by removing any serious enforcements or inducements to meet it was UNCED able to extract a promise from President Bush to attend Rio.

11   The Canadian government contributed generously to the Preparatory Committee (PrepCom) and Rio conferences, thereby allowing Jean Charest, the environment minister, to pose as a significant player at Rio and an environmental good guy. Yet Canada is one of the worst producers of greenhouse gases, is a leading energy guzzler and garbage producer, protects only a small percentage of its wilderness, and has followed the American attitude to the environment. And Canada was, of course, not alone. Other countries also wrapped themselves in green rhetoric while congratulating themselves for attending the Earth Summit. It was a grand photo opportunity.

12   While my low expectations of Rio were based on my understanding of the political process, I knew that a number of excellent environmentalists and NGOs were very hopeful and active participants in the PrepCom process. I therefore agreed to attend meetings in Vancouver and Ottawa prior to the New York PrepCom, only to be horrified by the process.

13   Virtually any NGO that applied was accepted for accreditation by UNCED. The NGOs assumed this demonstrated an unprecedented openness and flexibility of UNCED. However, since they were subsidized by their own governments and UNCED, the NGOs were effectively co-opted into following the UNCED protocol and agenda while legitimating the entire process by their participation.

14   The extent of the compromise made by the NGOs is illustrated by the experience of a member of a British Columbia bioregional group who attended the New York PrepCom. In a session on forests, he criticized British Columbia's forest policies. Afterward, he was cornered by an official Canadian government delegate who told him that he'd better lay off the criticism if he wanted NGOs to continue receiving government money.

15   The worst part of the PrepCom process was the way the planet was chopped up into discrete categories of atmosphere, oceans, biodiversity, et cetera. These human bureaucratic subdivisions make no ecological sense, and they severely hamper any attempt to solve ecological problems. UNCED didn't attempt to define the problems within a holistic framework that recognizes the exquisite interconnectedness and interdependence of everything on Earth and our subservience to it. Only from such a perspective could a comprehensive strategy for action have been formed. At a meeting I attended in Vancouver before the New York PrepCom, we were told to choose categories defined by UNCED and to deliberate on documents drafted within them. And so we environmentalists ended up like everyone else—fragmenting the way we looked at the world.

16   In all the meetings before and during the PrepComs, a process of "bracketing" was practised. Governments or groups objecting to any parts of the more than eleven hundred pages of text could put brackets around whole sections, paragraphs, sentences, or words to indicate what they wanted rewritten. In attempting to placate these groups, the organizers ensured that only the most innocuous statements ended up in the official documents.

17   Carlo Ripa di Meana, the environment commissioner of the European Community, said in 1992 that he believed the first major world environmental conference held in Stockholm in 1972 served "to put environmental issues on the international agenda, heighten awareness, and alert public opinion. The Rio meeting, on the other hand, was intended to make decisions, obtain precise and concrete commitments to counteract tendencies that are endangering life on the planet." However, when agreements such as the atmosphere treaty were deliberately watered down to satisfy President Bush, Ripa di Meana decided to boycott Rio and predicted that "By opting for hypocrisy, we will not just fail to save the Earth, but we will fail to grow." His prediction proved to be accurate: Rio didn't deliver the deep commitments needed.

18   Nothing illustrates the watering-down of documents better than the way UNCED dealt with the chasm that yawned between the "North" and the "South." The industrialized nations in the North were preoccupied with biodiversity, overpopulation, atmosphere change, and ocean pollution, while the priorities of the poor countries in the South were debt relief, technology transfer, and overconsumption by the rich countries. The "solution" was to horse-trade away the issues. Thus, overpopulation was dropped from the agenda in return for the deletion of overconsumption.

19   It seemed to me that the political vacuum in vision and leadership offered an immense opportunity for the NGOs, which truly represent the grass roots of the world. They could have taken the initiative by issuing an unflinching statement about the perilous state of the planet, calling all citizens of Earth to arms and setting out a concrete strategy to attack this great threat to all life on Earth. That's why I worked with members of the David Suzuki Foundation to draft the Declaration of Interdependence.... We hoped it would be an emotional, poetic, and inspiring statement of our place in the web of life and our responsibilities to it and to all future generations.

20   In Rio itself, most NGOs who were not accredited delegates were effectively denied access to the Earth Summit, where official delegates were fine-tuning the documents to be signed by the heads of state. Quartered 40 kilometres away from RioCentro, where the Earth Summit took place, the NGOs of the Global Forum were marginalized, since most reporters stayed put at RioCentro.

21   The Global Forum had all of the colour, excitement, and seriousness that the Earth Summit lacked. However, the very number of NGOs and the enormous size of their grounds precluded a focused vision and statement.

22   In the end, the inability of the US delegation to agree to a profound strategy to save the planet polarized the entire meeting. Even countries like Japan and Canada were able to appear progressive simply by their willingness to sign the watered-down treaties. The business community was a prominent presence among the delegates and lobby groups at the Earth Summit.

23   If anything sealed the judgement on Rio, it was the meeting in Munich two weeks later of the Group of Seven, the G-7, the richest nations on Earth. Not a word was mentioned by the leaders about the Earth Summit or the environment! Their preoccupations were with the recession, GATT (General Agreement on Tariffs and Trade), and free trade.

24   When I interviewed Maurice Strong in December 1991, I asked what he thought the chances were of success in Rio. He knew how pessimistic I was and responded that we simply could not afford to fail because the future of the planet was in the balance. "But if it does fail," he said realistically, "it must not be allowed to be a quiet failure and recede unnoticed from our memory."

25   I now think the Earth Summit was more than a failure. It was dangerous because it has been touted as a success. It did not issue a statement that pointed out the urgent need for a massive and immediate change. Instead, it reinforced all the notions about development, economics, and disparities in wealth that have proved so destructive. It is crystal clear that 80 percent of humanity is being forced to exist on 20 percent of the planet's resources while the 20 percent in the industrial world is using up the rightful heritage of all future generations. In spite of the obscene level of wealth and consumption in the rich countries, they continue to demand economic growth that can come only at the expense of the rest of humankind and the planet.

26   The main achievement of the Earth Summit was a 700-page document called *Agenda 21*. Although hailed as the strategy for responsible environmental change, it merely reinforces the gap between rich and poor. *Agenda 21* recommends an annual commitment of $600 billion for the environment, of which the South is asked to put up three-quarters, an amount representing 8 percent of their total GDP. On the other hand, the North, whose wealth has been achieved at the expense of the poor and whose activity is the major cause of global eco-degradation, reluctantly agreed to a target contribution representing 0.7 percent of their GDP. *Agenda 21* thus represents an attempt to make the South pay for the destructive actions of the North.

27   What is even more upsetting is the agenda's strategy for the developing world. Economic growth is repeated like a mantra by the industrialized countries as salvation for the poor countries. And how will this growth come about? Not by capping the profligate and unsustainable consumptive habits and growth of the rich countries, but by globalization of the marketplace and breaking down trade barriers.

28   But economics... is predicated on the assumption that air, water, soil, and biological diversity are an "externality" to the economic system. And since money grows faster than plants, animals, or ecosystems, economic "sense" dictates the rapid "liquidation" of forests, river systems, fish, et cetera, in the name of growth.

29   Furthermore, globalization of the marketplace, market value of products, and free trade maximize the reach of transnational corporations whose profit motives preclude concern for long-term sustainability of ecosystems or human communities. Yet globalization appears to be the direction supported by *Agenda 21*.

30   For me, Rio simply reinforced the conviction that expending effort to influence political and business leaders is not the way to bring about the profound shifts needed. The entire UNCED process is impotent in the face of the massive self-interests of politics and profit motives of private enterprise. Real change can come about only when the grass roots in all places understand to the core of their being that the life support processes—air, water, soil, and biodiversity—are fundamental and that human activity and organizations must conform to ecologically meaningful principles rather than attempting to force nature to conform to our priorities.

31   Poverty and eco-destruction are intertwined. The South's poverty exacerbates destruction of coral reefs and tropical rainforests and encourages large families. Their debt burden

and cash flow must come from the North. For the North, greater energy efficiency, reduction in redundancy and waste packaging, eco-friendly products, et cetera, offer immediate benefits.

32   If we are to take a different road from Rio, the directions are clear. The rich nations of the world now hoard a disproportionate share of the world's wealth, consume far beyond a sustainable level, and are the major polluters and destroyers. It is our responsibility to cut back drastically while sharing efficient technologies and paying for family planning and debt reduction in the poor countries.

33   We can't afford to wait another twenty years for another opportunity to look in the mirror. If Rio did anything, it informed us that it's up to us and we have to begin now.

NOTES AND DISCUSSION

Suzuki opens this essay with an extended analogy that is intended to catch readers' attention and to both horrify and amuse them. An impending car crash is a horrifying thing, but Suzuki's depiction of the occupants' behaviour is amusing. Notice how Suzuki returns to this metaphor in the concluding paragraphs to create unity and a circular closure.

The body of the essay provides the background that is necessary for readers to fully appreciate his metaphor. Suzuki presents a great deal of information in a relatively small space: he compares and contrasts the state of the environment and environmental activism twenty years ago with their state in the present; he discusses the roles of certain individual activists, such as Maurice Strong, and politicians, such as George Bush, in environmental issues; he provides specific examples of attitudes and actions taken with regard to the environment; and he presents facts and figures on issues such as the need to reduce carbon dioxide levels.

Suzuki also carefully introduces his experts (the "characters" in his story), presents relevant background information that readers may not be aware of, and provides a sense of unity and focus through maintaining a personal and localized perspective on a bewilderingly complex international event. Nevertheless, at times readers may feel that they are lost in a sea of names, places, committees, and statistics. This abundance of initials and acronyms may, however, be part of Suzuki's point: there is too much organizing and talking, and not nearly enough doing.

STUDY QUESTIONS

For Discussion

1. Suzuki's essay revolves around two related analogies: one to a journey or trip, the other to an impending car crash. How effective are these analogies? In particular, consider the effect of using an analogy to a *car* in an environmentalist essay.

2. Most of this essay is written in the first-person singular: "I." However, at some points, Suzuki shifts to alternative points of view. Where do such shifts take place, and what is their intended effect? Suzuki's tone changes as the essay progresses. Identify three different tones and where they appear, and explain how they are achieved.

For Writing

1. Write an essay that uses the metaphor of "the road" or "the journey" to suggest that a certain course of action be followed.

2. Examine some contemporary coverage of the 1992 Earth Summit, including official reports, press releases, and journalistic coverage. How do these materials compare and contrast with Suzuki's criticisms?

A MODEST PROPOSAL

For Preventing the Children of poor
People in *Ireland*, from being a
Burden to their Parents or Country;
and for making them beneficial
to the Publick.

Jonathan Swift

BIOGRAPHICAL NOTE

Jonathan Swift (1667–1745) was a popular essayist, pamphleteer, and satirist who is probably best known as the author of *Gulliver's Travels* (1729). He was born in Dublin of English parents, and became a popular figure in Ireland for his support of Irish causes.

Written in the Year 1729.

1   It is a melancholy Object to those, who walk through this great Town, or travel in the Country; when they see the *Streets*, the *Roads*, and *Cabbin*-doors crowded with *Beggars* of the Female Sex, followed by three, four, or six Children, *all in Rags*, and importuning every Passenger for an Alms. These *Mothers*, instead of being able to work for their honest Livelihood, are forced to employ all their Time in stroling to beg Sustenance for their *helpless Infants*; who, as they grow up, either turn *Thieves* for want of Work; or leave their *dear Native Country, to fight for the Pretender in* Spain, or sell themselves to the *Barbadoes*.

2   I think it is agreed by all Parties, that this prodigious Number of Children in the Arms, or on the Backs, or at the *Heels* of their *Mothers*, and frequently of their *Fathers*, is *in the present deplorable State of the Kingdom*, a very great additional Grievance; and therefore, whoever could find out a fair, cheap, and easy Method of making these Children sound and useful Members of the Commonwealth, would deserve so well of the Publick, as to have his Statue set up for a Preserver of the Nation.

3   But my Intention is very far from being confined to provide only for the Children of *professed Beggars*: It is of a much greater Extent, and shall take in the whole Number of Infants in a certain Age, who are born of Parents, in effect as little able to support them, as those who demand our Charity in the Streets.

4   As to my own Part, having turned my Thoughts for many Years, upon this important Subject, and maturely weighed the several *Schemes of other Projectors*, I have always found them grosly mistaken in their Computation. It is true a Child, *just dropt from its*

Dam, may be supported by her Milk, for a Solar Year with little other Nourishment; at most not above the Value of two Shillings; which the Mother may certainly get, or the Value in Scraps, by her lawful Occupation of Begging: And, it is exactly at one Year old, that I propose to provide for them in such a Manner, as, instead of being a Charge upon their *Parents*, or the *Parish*, or *wanting Food and Raiment* for the rest of their Lives; they shall, on the contrary, contribute to the Feeding, and partly to the Cloathing, of many Thousands.

5   There is likewise another great Advantage in my *Scheme*, that it will prevent those *voluntary Abortions*, and that horrid Practice of *Women murdering their Bastard Children*; alas! too frequent among us; sacrificing the *poor innocent Babes*, I doubt, more to avoid the Expence than the Shame; which would move Tears and Pity in the most Savage and inhuman Breast.

6   The Number of Souls in *Ireland* being usually reckoned one Million and a half; of these I calculate there may be about Two hundred Thousand Couple whose Wives are Breeders; from which Number I subtract thirty thousand Couples, who are able to maintain their own Children; although I apprehend there cannot be so many, under *the present Distresses of the Kingdom*; but this being granted, there will remain an Hundred and Seventy Thousand Breeders. I again subtract Fifty Thousand, for those Women who miscarry, or whose Children die by Accident, or Disease, within the Year. There only remain an Hundred and Twenty Thousand Children of poor Parents, annually born: The Question therefore is, How this Number shall be reared, and provided for? Which, as I have already said, under the present situation of Affairs, is utterly impossible, by all the Methods hitherto proposed: For we can *neither employ them in Handicraft or Agriculture*; we neither build Houses, (I mean in the Country) nor cultivate Land: They can very seldom pick up a Livelyhood *by Stealing* until they arrive at six Years old; except where they are of towardly Parts; although, I confess, they learn the Rudiments much earlier; during which Time, they can, however, be properly looked upon only as *Probationers*; as I have been informed by a principal Gentleman in the County of Cavan, who protested to me, that he never knew above one or two Instances under the Age of six, even in a Part of the Kingdom *so renowned for the quickest Proficiency in that Art.*

7   I am assured by our Merchants, that a Boy or a Girl before twelve Years old, is no saleable Commodity; and even when they come to this Age, they will not yield above Three Pounds, or Three Pounds and half a Crown at most, on the Exchange; which cannot turn to Account either to the Parents or the Kingdom; the Charge of Nutriment and Rags, having been at least four Times that Value.

8   I shall now therefore humbly propose my own Thoughts; which I hope will not be liable to the least Objection.

9   I have been assured by a very knowing *American* of my Acquaintance in *London*; that a young healthy Child, well nursed, is, at a Year old, a most delicious, nourishing, and wholesome Food; whether *Stewed, Roasted, Baked,* or *Boiled*; and, I make no doubt, that it will equally serve in a *Fricasie,* or *Ragoust.*

10   I do therefore humbly offer it to *publick Consideration*, that of the Hundred and Twenty Thousand Children, already computed, Twenty thousand may be reserved for Breed; whereof only one Fourth Part to be Males; which is more than we allow to *Sheep, black Cattle,* or *Swine*; and my Reason is, that these Children are seldom the Fruits of Marriage, *a Circumstance not much regarded by our Savages*; therefore, *one Male* will be sufficient to serve *four Females*. That the remaining Hundred thousand, may, at a Year old, be offered in Sale to the *Persons of Quality* and *Fortune*, through the Kingdom; always advising the Mother to let them suck plentifully in the last Month, so as to render them

plump, and fat for a good Table. A Child will make two Dishes at an Entertainment for Friends; and when the Family dines alone, the fore or hind Quarter will make a reasonable Dish; and seasoned with a little Pepper or Salt, will be very good Boiled on the fourth Day, especially in *Winter*.

11   I have reckoned upon a Medium, that a Child just born will weigh Twelve Pounds; and in a solar Year, if tolerably nursed, encreaseth to twenty eight Pounds.

12   I grant this Food will be somewhat dear, and therefore very *proper for Landlords*; who, as they have already devoured most of the Parents, seem to have the best Title to the Children.

13   Infants' Flesh will be in Season throughout the Year; but more plentiful in *March*, and a little before and after: For we are told by a grave[1] Author, an eminent *French* Physician, that *Fish being a prolifick Dyet*, there are more Children born in *Roman Catholick Countries* about Nine Months after *Lent*, than at any other Season: Therefore reckoning a Year after *Lent*, the Markets will be more glutted than usual; because the Number of *Popish Infants*, is, at least, three to one in this Kingdom; and therefore it will have one other Collateral Advantage, by lessening the Number of *Papists* among us.

14   I have already computed the Charge of nursing a Beggar's Child (in which List I reckon all *Cottagers, Labourers,* and Four fifths of the *Farmers*) to be about two Shillings *per Annum*, Rags included; and I believe, no Gentleman would repine to give Ten Shillings for the *Carcase of a good fat Child*; which, as I have said, will make four Dishes of excellent nutritive Meat, when he hath only some particular Friend, or his own Family, to dine with him. Thus the Squire will learn to be a good Landlord, and grow popular among his Tenants; the Mother will have Eight Shillings net Profit, and be fit for Work until she produceth another Child.

15   Those who are more thrifty (*as I must confess the Times require*) may flay the Carcase; the Skin of which, artificially dressed, will make admirable *Gloves for Ladies*, and *Summer Boots for fine Gentlemen*.

16   As to our City of *Dublin*; Shambles may be appointed for this Purpose, in the most convenient Parts of it; and Butchers we may be assured will not be wanting; although I rather recommend buying the Children alive, and dressing them hot from the Knife, as we do *roasting Pigs*.

17   A very worthy Person, *a true Lover of his Country*, and whose Virtues I highly esteem, was lately pleased, in discoursing on this Matter, to offer a Refinement upon my Scheme. He said, that many Gentlemen of this Kingdom, having of late destroyed their Deer; he conceived, that the Want of Venison might be well supplied by the Bodies of young Lads and Maidens, not exceeding fourteen Years of Age, nor under twelve; so great a Number of both Sexes in every County being now ready to starve, for Want of Work and Service: And these to be disposed of by their Parents, if alive, or otherwise by their nearest Relations. But with due Deference to so excellent a Friend, and so deserving a Patriot, I cannot be altogether in his Sentiments. For as to the Males, my *American* Acquaintance assured me from frequent Experience, that their Flesh was generally tough and lean, like that of our School-boys, by continual Exercise, and their Taste disagreeable; and to fatten them would not answer the Charge. Then, as to the Females, it would, I think, with humble Submission, *be a Loss to the Publick*, because they soon would become Breeders themselves: And besides it is not improbable, that some scrupulous People might be apt to

---

[1] Rabelais.

censure such a Practice (although indeed very unjustly) as a little bordering upon Cruelty; which, I confess, hath always been with me the strongest Objection against any Project, how well soever intended.

18   But in order to justify my Friend; he confessed, that this Expedient was put into his Head by the famous *Salmanaazor*, a Native of the Island *Formosa*, who came from thence to *London*, above twenty Years ago, and in Conversation told my Friend, that in his Country, when any young Person happened to be put to Death, the Executioner sold the Carcase to *Persons of Quality*, as a prime Dainty; and that, in his Time, the Body of a plump Girl of fifteen, who was crucified for an Attempt to poison the Emperor, was sold to his Imperial *Majesty's prime Minister of State*, and other great *Mandarins* of the Court, *in Joints from the Gibbet*, at Four hundred Crowns. Neither indeed can I deny, that if the same Use were made of several plump young girls in this Town, who, without one single Groat to their Fortunes, cannot stir Abroad without a Chair, and appear at the *Play-house*, and *Assemblies* in foreign Fineries, which they never will pay for; the Kingdom would not be the worse.

19   Some Persons of a desponding Spirit are in great Concern about that vast Number of Poor People, who are Aged, Diseased, or Maimed; and I have been desired to employ my Thoughts what Course may be taken, to ease the Nation of so grievous an Incumbrance. But I am not in the least Pain upon that Matter; because it is very well known, that they are every Day *dying*, and *rotting*, by *Cold* and *Famine*, and *Filth*, and *Vermine*, as fast as can be reasonably expected. And as to the younger Labourers, they are now in almost as hopeful a Condition: They cannot get Work, and consequently pine away for Want of Nourishment, to a Degree, that if at any Time they are accidentally hired to common Labour, they have not Strength to perform it; and thus the Country, and themselves, are in a fair Way of being soon delivered from the Evils to come.

20   I have too long digressed; and therefore shall return to my Subject. I think the Advantages by the Proposal which I have made, are obvious, and many, as well as of the highest Importance.

21   For, *First*, as I have already observed, it would greatly lessen the *Number of Papists*, with whom we are yearly overrun; being the principal Breeders of the Nation, as well as our most dangerous Enemies; and who stay at home on Purpose, with a Design to *deliver the Kingdom to the Pretender*; hoping to take their Advantage by the *Absence of so many good Protestants*, who have chosen rather to leave their Country, than stay at home, and pay Tithes against their Conscience, to an idolatrous *Episcopal Curate*.

22   Secondly, The poorer Tenants will have something valuable of their own, which, by Law, may be made liable to Distress, and help to pay their Landlord's Rent; their Corn and Cattle being already seized, and *Money a Thing unknown*.

23   Thirdly, Whereas the Maintenance of an Hundred Thousand Children, from two Years old, and upwards, cannot be computed at less than ten Shillings a Piece *per Annum*, the Nation's Stock will be thereby encreased Fifty Thousand Pounds *per Annum*; besides the Profit of a new Dish, introduced to the Tables of all *Gentlemen of Fortune* in the Kingdom, who have any Refinement in Taste; and the Money will circulate among ourselves, the Goods being entirely of our own Growth and Manufacture.

24   Fourthly, The constant Breeders, besides the Gain of Eight Shillings *Sterling per Annum*, by the Sale of their Children, will be rid of the Charge of maintaining them after the first Year.

25   Fifthly, This Food would likewise bring great *Custom to Taverns*, where the Vintners will certainly be so prudent, as to procure the best Receipts for dressing it to Perfection;

and consequently, have their Houses frequented by all the *fine Gentlemen*, who justly value themselves upon their Knowledge in good Eating; and a skilful Cook, who understands how to oblige his Guests, will contrive to make it as expensive as they please.

26   Sixthly, This would be a great Inducement to Marriage, which all wise Nations have either encouraged by Rewards, or enforced by Laws and Penalties. It would encrease the Care and Tenderness of Mothers towards their Children, when they were sure of a Settlement for Life, to the poor Babes, provided in some Sort by the Publick, to their annual Profit instead of Expence. We should soon see an honest Emulation among the married Women, *which of them could bring the fattest Child to the Market*. Men would become as *fond* of their Wives, during the Time of their Pregnancy, as they are now of their *Mares* in Foal, their *Cows* in Calf, or *Sows* when they are ready to farrow; nor offer to beat or kick them, (as it is too *frequent* a Practice) for fear of a Miscarriage.

27   Many other Advantages might be enumerated. For instance, the Addition of some Thousand Carcasses in our Exportation of barrelled Beef: The Propagation of *Swines Flesh*, and Improvement in the Art of making good *Bacon*; so much wanted among us by the great Destruction of *Pigs*, too frequent at our Tables, and are no way comparable in Taste, or Magnificence, to a well-grown fat yearling Child; which, roasted whole, will make a considerable Figure at a *Lord Mayor's Feast*, or any other publick Entertainment. But this, and many others, I omit; being studious of Brevity.

28   Supposing that one Thousand Families in this City, would be constant Customers for Infants Flesh; besides others who might have it at *merry Meetings*, particularly *Weddings and Christenings*; I compute that *Dublin* would take off, annually, about Twenty Thousand Carcasses; and the rest of the Kingdom (where probably they will be sold somewhat cheaper) the remaining Eighty Thousand.

29   I can think of no one Objection, that will possibly be raised against this Proposal; unless it should be urged, that the Number of People will be thereby much lessened in the Kingdom. This I freely own; and it was indeed one principal Design in offering it to the World. I desire the Reader will observe, that I calculate my Remedy *for this one individual Kingdom* of Ireland, *and for no other that ever was, is, or I think ever can be upon Earth*. Therefore, let no man talk to me of other Expedients: *Of taxing our Absentees at five Shillings a Pound: Of using neither Cloaths, nor Houshold Furniture except what is of our own Growth and Manufacture: Of utterly rejecting the Materials and Instruments that promote foreign Luxury: Of curing the Expensiveness of Pride, Vanity, Idleness, and Gaming in our Women: Of introducing a Vein of Parsimony, Prudence, and Temperance: Of learning to love our Country, wherein we differ even from* Laplanders, *and the Inhabitants of* Topinamboo: *Of quitting our Anomosities, and Factions; nor act any longer like the Jews, who were murdering one another at the very Moment their City was taken: Of being a little cautious not to sell our Country and Consciences for nothing: Of teaching Landlords to have, at least, one Degree of Mercy towards their Tenants.* Lastly, *Of putting a Spirit of Honesty, Industry, and Skill into our Shop-keepers; who, if a Resolution could now be taken to buy only our native Goods, would immediately unite to cheat and exact upon us in the Price, the Measure, and the Goodness; nor could ever yet be brought to make one fair Proposal of just Dealing, though often and earnestly invited to it.*

30   Therefore I repeat, let no Man talk to me of these and the like Expedients; till he hath, at least, a Glimpse of Hope, that there will ever be some hearty and sincere Attempt to put *them in Practice.*

31   But, as to my self; having been wearied out for many Years with offering vain, idle, visionary Thoughts; and at length utterly despairing of Success, I fortunately fell upon this

Proposal; which, as it is wholly new, so it hath something *solid* and *real*, of no Expence, and little Trouble, full in our own Power; and whereby we can incur no Danger in *disobliging* England: For this Kind of Commodity will not bear Exportation; the Flesh being of too tender a Consistence, to admit a long Continuance in Salt; *although, perhaps, I could name a Country, which would be glad to eat up our whole Nation without it.*

32   After all, I am not so violently bent upon my own Opinion, as to reject any Offer proposed by wise Men, which shall be found equally innocent, cheap, easy, and effectual. But before something of that Kind shall be advanced, in Contradiction to my Scheme, and offering a better; I desire the Author, or Authors, will be pleased maturely to consider two Points. *First*, As Things now stand, how they will be able to find Food and Raiment, for a Hundred Thousand useless Mouths and Backs? And *secondly*, There being a round Million of Creatures in human Figure, throughout this Kingdom; whose whole Subsistence, put into a common Stock, would leave them in Debt two Millions of Pounds *Sterling*; adding those, who are Beggars by Profession, to the Bulk of Farmers, Cottagers, and Labourers, with their Wives and Children, who are Beggars in Effect; I desire those Politicians, who dislike my Overture, and may perhaps be so bold to attempt an Answer, that they will first ask the Parents of these Mortals, Whether they would not, at this Day, think it a great Happiness to have been sold for Food at a Year old, in the Manner I prescribe; and thereby have avoided such a perpetual Scene of Misfortunes, as they have since gone through; by the *Oppression of Landlords*; the Impossibility of paying Rent, without Money or Trade; the Want of common Sustenance, with neither House nor Cloaths, to cover them from the Inclemencies of Weather; and the most inevitable Prospect of intailing the like, or greater Miseries upon their Breed for ever.

33   I profess, in the Sincerity of my Heart, that I have not the least personal Interest, in endeavouring to promote this necessary Work; having no other Motive than the *publick Good of my Country, by advancing our Trade, providing for Infants, relieving the Poor, and giving some Pleasure to the Rich.* I have no Children, by which I can propose to get a single Penny; the youngest being nine Years old, and my Wife past Child-bearing.

NOTES AND DISCUSSION

Swift's decidedly *immodest* proposal has shocked people for two and a half centuries, especially those readers who miss its ironies. In this essay, Swift invents an ironic persona whose attitudes and methods of reasoning he wants to undermine. His proposal attacks greedy and unreasonable people who adopt the language and techniques of reason to express unreasonable attitudes. The mad proposal presented in this essay reduces human lives to distorted statistics, and to comically gross miscalculations (for instance, the average birth weight of infants is considerably less than his estimated twelve pounds). The essay also uses the language and logic of animal husbandry and commodification, and a "bottom-line" thinking that is painfully familiar even today.

Much of Swift's posing and assumed sympathy are directed towards absentee English landlords, who had "devoured" the wealth and substance of their holdings in Ireland, ignoring the effects of their destructive attitudes and practices on the people of that country. The essay argues implicitly that poor Irish people would be better off if they were treated as animals; at least then they would be perceived as having some "value." Swift may also be aiming part of his criticism at the Irish themselves for not taking personal or collective responsibility for their attitudes and behaviours.

Finally, note Swift's classic argumentation style: he introduces a public issue and problem, establishes its scope, proposes a solution, presents supporting arguments, poses a possible objection and refutes it, and then returns to the original proposal as the only logical alternative. With characteristic irony, the alternate proposals that Swift dismisses in the important paragraph 29 are ones that he himself had advanced elsewhere and that had been attacked as unreasonable and unworkable.

STUDY QUESTIONS

For Discussion

1. Many readers over the years have been fooled by this piece. How does the ironic persona both help and hinder Swift's purpose in this essay?
2. Consider how and why Swift uses the testimonials and advice of foreign "experts."

For Writing

1. Examine the individual and collective importance of the language and terminology of economics, scientific calculation, and animal husbandry as satirical techniques. Write an analytical paragraph about how Swift's language tries to hide insanely inhumane attitudes behind a mask of social concern.
2. Compare Swift's satirical persona and related shock tactics with Lewis Lapham's in "Sense and Sensibility." Consider such matters as tone of voice, and the desire to appear "reasonable" while making unsettling and deliberately offensive claims and suggestions.

THE PONDS

Henry David Thoreau

BIOGRAPHICAL NOTE

Henry David Thoreau (1817–1862) was a philosopher, essayist, naturalist, poet, and a "transcendentalist." Transcendentalism, a loosely organized intellectual movement, was one of several American manifestations of romanticism. Thoreau is best known and loved for *Walden* (1854), a long essay recounting two years spent living in the woods beside Walden Pond. This piece is part of a chapter from *Walden* entitled "The Ponds."

1   The scenery of Walden is on a humble scale, and, though very beautiful, does not approach to grandeur, nor can it much concern one who has not long frequented it or lived by its shore; yet this pond is so remarkable for its depth and purity as to merit a particular description. It is a clear and deep green well, half a mile long and a mile and three quarters in circumference, and contains about sixty-one and a half acres; a perennial spring in the midst of pine and oak woods, without any visible inlet or outlet except by the clouds and evaporation. The surrounding hills rise abruptly from the water to the height of forty to eighty feet, though on the south-east and east they attain to about one hundred and one hundred and fifty feet respectively, within a quarter and a third of a mile. They are exclusively woodland. All our Concord waters have two colors at least, one when viewed at a distance, and another, more proper, close at hand. The first depends more on the light, and follows the sky. In clear weather, in summer, they appear blue at a little distance, especially if agitated, and at a great distance all appear alike. In stormy weather they are sometimes of a dark slate color. The sea, however, is said to be blue one day and green another without any perceptible change in the atmosphere. I have seen our river, when, the landscape being covered with snow, both water and ice were almost as green as grass. Some consider blue "to be the color of pure water, whether liquid or solid." But, looking directly down into our waters from a boat, they are seen to be of very different colors. Walden is blue at one time and green at another, even from the same point of view. Lying between the earth and the heavens, it partakes of the color of both. Viewed from the hill-top it reflects the color of the sky, but near at hand it is of a yellowish tint next the shore where you can see the sand, then a light green, which gradually deepens to a uniform dark green in the body of the pond. In some lights, viewed even from a hill-top, it is of a vivid green next the shore. Some have referred this to the reflection of the verdure; but it is equally green there against the railroad sand-bank, and in the spring, before the leaves are expanded, and it may be simply the result of the prevailing blue mixed with the yellow of the sand. Such is the color of its iris. This is that portion, also, where in the spring, the ice being warmed by the heat of the sun reflected from the bottom, and also transmitted through the earth, melts first and forms a narrow canal about the still frozen middle. Like the rest of our waters, when much agitated, in clear weather, so that the surface of the waves may reflect the sky at the right angle, or because there is more light mixed with it, it appears at a little distance of a darker blue than the sky itself; and at such a time, being on its surface, and looking with divided vision, so as to see the reflection, I have discerned a matchless and indescribable light blue, such as watered or changeable silks and sword blades suggest, more cerulean than the sky itself, alternating with the original dark green on the opposite sides of the waves, which last appeared but muddy in comparison. It is a vitreous greenish blue, as I remember it, like those patches of the winter sky seen through cloud vistas in the west before sundown. Yet a single glass of its water held up to the light is as colorless as an equal quantity of air. It is well known that a large plate of glass will have a green tint, owing, as the makers say, to its "body," but a small piece of the same will be colorless. How large a body of Walden water would be required to reflect a green tint I have never proved. The water of our river is black or a very dark brown to one looking directly down on it, and, like that of most ponds, imparts to the body of one bathing in it a yellowish tinge; but this water is of such crystalline purity that the body of the bather appears of an alabaster white ness, still more unnatural, which, as the limbs are magnified and distorted withal, produces a monstrous effect, making fit studies for a Michael Angelo.

2   The water is so transparent that the bottom can easily be discerned at the depth of twenty-five or thirty feet. Paddling over it, you may see many feet beneath the surface the schools of perch and shiners, perhaps only an inch long, yet the former easily distinguished by their transverse bars, and you think that they must be ascetic fish that find a subsistence there. Once, in the winter, many years ago, when I had been cutting holes through the ice in order to catch pickerel, as I stepped ashore I tossed my axe back on to the ice, but, as if some evil genius had directed it, it slid four or five rods directly into one of the holes, where the water was twenty-five feet deep. Out of curiosity, I lay down on the ice and looked through the hole, until I saw the axe a little on one side, standing on its head, with its helve erect and gently swaying to and fro with the pulse of the pond; and there it might have stood erect and swaying till in the course of time the handle rotted off, if I had not disturbed it. Making another hole directly over it with an ice chisel which I had, and cutting down the longest birch which I could find in the neighborhood with my knife, I made a slip-noose, which I attached to its end, and, letting it down carefully, passed it over the knob of the handle, and drew it by a line along the birch, and so pulled the axe out again.

3   The shore is composed of a belt of smooth rounded white stones like paving stones, excepting one or two short sand beaches, and is so steep that in many places a single leap will carry you into water over your head; and were it not for its remarkable transparency, that would be the last to be seen of its bottom till it rose on the opposite side. Some think it is bottomless. It is nowhere muddy, and a casual observer would say that there were no weeds at all in it; and of noticeable plants, except in the little meadows recently overflowed, which do not properly belong to it, a closer scrutiny does not detect a flag nor a bulrush,

nor even a lily, yellow or white, but only a few small heart-leaves and potamogetons, and perhaps a water-target or two; all which however a bather might not perceive; and these plants are clean and bright like the element they grow in. The stones extend a rod or two into the water, and then the bottom is pure sand, except in the deepest parts, where there is usually a little sediment, probably from the decay of the leaves which have been wafted on to it so many successive falls, and a bright green weed is brought up on anchors even in midwinter.

4   We have one other pond just like this, White Pond in Nine Acre Corner, about two and a half miles westerly; but, though I am acquainted with most of the ponds within a dozen miles of this centre, I do not know a third of this pure and well-like character. Successive nations perchance have drank at, admired, and fathomed it, and passed away, and still its water is green and pellucid as ever. Not an intermitting spring! Perhaps on that spring morning when Adam and Eve were driven out of Eden Walden Pond was already in existence, and even then breaking up in a gentle spring rain accompanied with mist and a southerly wind, and covered with myriads of ducks and geese, which had not heard of the fall, when still such pure lakes sufficed them. Even then it had commenced to rise and fall, and had clarified its waters and colored them of the hue they now wear, and obtained a patent of heaven to be the only Walden Pond in the world and distiller of celestial dews. Who knows in how many unremembered nations' literatures this has been the Castalian Fountain? or what nymphs presided over it in the Golden Age? It is a gem of the first water which Concord wears in her coronet.

NOTES AND DISCUSSION

Thoreau begins this description of Walden Pond with a modest disclaimer: "The scenery of Walden is on a humble scale," he writes, "and, though very beautiful, does not approach to grandeur." While this may be true, his description, in its meticulous attention to detail, itself approaches grandeur. He first describes the physical dimensions of the pond, and then studies the colour of the water during various times of day and weather conditions. Thoreau's task here is a daunting one: he has set out to describe fully something that undoubtedly has colour, but that, when viewed up close, is utterly colourless. The water, he notes, "is so transparent that the bottom can easily be discerned at the depth of twenty-five or thirty feet." The result is the impression that, while the water of Walden Pond is in fact colourless, Walden Pond itself has colour, flashing green and blue. "It is," Thoreau writes, "a gem of the first water which Concord wears in her coronet."

Notice that Thoreau constructs his description from varying perspectives and during different seasons. He also compares and contrasts Walden with other bodies of water. Part of the success of Thoreau's technique of description lies in showing what Walden is *not*, as well as what it is.

STUDY QUESTIONS

For Discussion

1. Notice the way Thoreau begins this piece by denying Walden's pretence to "grandeur," yet ends with mythic and biblical references. What is the effect of making these very different claims?

2. This essay is almost pure description, yet embedded in the middle of it is a short narrative about a lost axe. What is the effect of this short narrative? Why has Thoreau placed it where he has?

For Writing

1. Annie Dillard's careful descriptions are often compared to those of Thoreau. On the basis of language, tone, and detail, compare and contrast Dillard's treatment of writing in paragraphs 4–7 of *The Writing Life* to Thoreau's description of Walden and the writer's experience of the pond.

2. Thoreau lived for two years beside the pond that he describes so carefully here. Write a description of something that is important to you: a building, a street, your room. Be sure to depict its various aspects and keep in mind factors such as weather, light, and perspective.

COMPUTING MACHINERY AND INTELLIGENCE

A. M. Turing

BIOGRAPHICAL NOTE

During the Second World War British mathematician A. M. Turing (1912–54) headed the team that worked on decoding the German Enigma machine. In the late 1940s and early 1950s he became a pioneer in research into the "universal machine," or computer. Articles such as "Intelligent Machinery" (1948) and "Digital Computers Applied to Games" (1953) established the direction for computer research in hardware architecture and software engineering as well as for the philosophy of artificial intelligence for nearly two decades following Turing's suicide in 1954.

1. THE IMITATION GAME

1   I propose to consider the question, "Can machines think?" This should begin with definitions of the meaning of the terms "machine" and "think." The definitions might be framed so as to reflect so far as possible the normal use of the words, but this attitude is dangerous. If the meaning of the words "machine" and "think" are to be found by examining how they are commonly used it is difficult to escape the conclusion that the meaning and the answer to the question, "Can machines think?" is to be sought in a statistical survey such as a Gallup poll. But this is absurd. Instead of attempting such a definition I shall replace the question by another, which is closely related to it and is expressed in relatively unambiguous words.

2   The new form of the problem can be described in terms of a game which we call the "imitation game." It is played with three people, a man (A), a woman (B), and an inter-

A. M. Turing, "Computing Machinery and Intelligence," *MIND*, 59, no. 236, pp. 433–60, by permission of Oxford University Press.

rogator (C) who may be of either sex. The interrogator stays in a room apart from the other two. The object of the game for the interrogator is to determine which of the other two is the man and which is the woman. He knows them by labels X and Y, and at the end of the game he says either "X is A and Y is B" or "X is B and Y is A." The interrogator is allowed to put questions to A and B thus:

3   C: Will X please tell me the length of his or her hair?

4   Now suppose X is actually A, then A must answer. It is A's object in the game to try and cause C to make the wrong identification. His answer might therefore be:

5   "My hair is shingled, and the longest strands are about nine inches long."

6   In order that tones of voice may not help the interrogator the answers should be written, or better still, typewritten. The ideal arrangement is to have a teleprinter communicating between the two rooms. Alternatively the question and answers can be repeated by an intermediary. The object of the game for the third player (B) is to help the interrogator. The best strategy for her is probably to give truthful answers. She can add such things as "I am the woman, don't listen to him!" to her answers, but it will avail nothing as the man can make similar remarks.

7   We now ask the question, "What will happen when a machine takes the part of A in this game?" Will the interrogator decide wrongly as often when the game is played like this as he does when the game is played between a man and a woman? These questions replace our original, "Can machines think?"

2. CRITIQUE OF THE NEW PROBLEM

8   As well as asking, "What is the answer to this new form of the question," one may ask, "Is this new question a worthy one to investigate?" This latter question we investigate without further ado, thereby cutting short an infinite regress.

9   The new problem has the advantage of drawing a fairly sharp line between the physical and the intellectual capacities of a man. No engineer or chemist claims to be able to produce a material which is indistinguishable from the human skin. It is possible that at some time this might be done, but even supposing this invention available we should feel there was little point in trying to make a "thinking machine" more human by dressing it up in such artificial flesh. The form in which we have set the problem reflects this fact in the condition which prevents the interrogator from seeing or touching the other competitors, or hearing their voices. Some other advantages of the proposed criterion may be shown up by specimen questions and answers. Thus:

10   Q: Please write me a sonnet on the subject of the Forth Bridge.

11   A: Count me out on this one. I never could write poetry.

12   Q: Add 34957 to 70764.

13   A: (Pause about 30 seconds and then give as answer) 105621.

14   Q: Do you play chess?

15   A: Yes.

16   Q: I have K at my K1, and no other pieces. You have only K at K6 and R at R1. It is your move. What do you play?

17   A: (After a pause of 15 seconds) R-R8 mate.

18   The question and answer method seems to be suitable for introducing almost any one of the fields of human endeavour that we wish to include. We do not wish to penalise the machine for its inability to shine in beauty competitions, nor to penalise a man for losing in a race against an aeroplane. The conditions of our game make these disabilities irrele-

vant. The "witnesses" can brag, if they consider it advisable, as much as they please about their charms, strength or heroism, but the interrogator cannot demand practical demonstrations.

19   The game may perhaps be criticised on the ground that the odds are weighted too heavily against the machine. If the man were to try and pretend to be the machine he would clearly make a very poor showing. He would be given away at once by slowness and inaccuracy in arithmetic. May not machines carry out something which ought to be described as thinking but which is very different from what a man does? This objection is a very strong one, but at least we can say that if, nevertheless, a machine can be constructed to play the imitation game satisfactorily, we need not be troubled by this objection.

20   It might be urged that when playing the "imitation game" the best strategy for the machine may possibly be something other than imitation of the behaviour of a man. This may be, but I think it is unlikely that there is any great effect of this kind. In any case there is no intention to investigate here the theory of the game, and it will be assumed that the best strategy is to try to provide answers that would naturally be given by a man.

3. THE MACHINES CONCERNED IN THE GAME

21   The question which we put in 1 will not be quite definite until we have specified what we mean by the word "machine." It is natural that we should wish to permit every kind of engineering technique to be used in our machines. We also wish to allow the possibility that an engineer or team of engineers may construct a machine which works, but whose manner of operation cannot be satisfactorily described by its constructors because they have applied a method which is largely experimental. Finally, we wish to exclude from the machines men born in the usual manner. It is difficult to frame the definitions so as to satisfy these three conditions. One might for instance insist that the team of engineers should be all of one sex, but this would not really be satisfactory, for it is probably possible to rear a complete individual from a single cell of the skin (say) of a man. To do so would be a feat of biological technique deserving of the very highest praise, but we would not be inclined to regard it as a case of "constructing a thinking machine." This prompts us to abandon the requirement that every kind of technique should be permitted. We are the more ready to do so in view of the fact that the present interest in "thinking machines" has been aroused by a particular kind of machine, usually called an "electronic computer" or "digital computer." Following this suggestion we only permit digital computers to take part in our game.

22   This restriction appears at first sight to be a very drastic one. I shall attempt to show that it is not so in reality. To do this necessitates a short account of the nature and properties of these computers.

23   It may also be said that this identification of machines with digital computers, like our criterion for "thinking," will only be unsatisfactory if (contrary to my belief), it turns out that digital computers are unable to give a good showing in the game.

24   There are already a number of digital computers in working order, and it may be asked, "Why not try the experiment straight away? It would be easy to satisfy the conditions of the game. A number of interrogators could be used, and statistics compiled to show how often the right identification was given." The short answer is that we are not asking whether all digital computers would do well in the game nor whether the computers at present available would do well, but whether there are imaginable computers which would do well. But this is only the short answer. We shall see this question in a different light later.

4. DIGITAL COMPUTERS

25 The idea behind digital computers may be explained by saying that these machines are intended to carry out any operations which could be done by a human computer. The human computer is supposed to be following fixed rules; he has no authority to deviate from them in any detail. We may suppose that these rules are supplied in a book, which is altered whenever he is put on to a new job. He has also an unlimited supply of paper on which he does his calculations. He may also do his multiplications and additions on a "desk machine," but this is not important.

26   If we use the above explanation as a definition we shall be in danger of circularity of argument. We avoid this by giving an outline of the means by which the desired effect is achieved. A digital computer can usually be regarded as consisting of three parts:

(i)   Store.

(ii) Executive unit.

(iii) Control.

27   The store is a store of information, and corresponds to the human computer's paper, whether this is the paper on which he does his calculations or that on which his book of rules is printed. In so far as the human computer does calculations in his head a part of the store will correspond to his memory.

28   The executive unit is the part which carries out the various individual operations involved in a calculation. What these individual operations are will vary from machine to machine. Usually fairly lengthy operations can be done such as "Multiply 3540675445 by 7076345687" but in some machines only very simple ones such as "Write down 0" are possible.

29   We have mentioned that the "book of rules" supplied to the computer is replaced in the machine by a part of the store. It is then called the "table of instructions." It is the duty of the control to see that these instructions are obeyed correctly and in the right order. The control is so constructed that this necessarily happens.

30   The information in the store is usually broken up into packets of moderately small size. In one machine, for instance, a packet might consist of ten decimal digits. Numbers are assigned to the parts of the store in which the various packets of information are stored, in some systematic manner. A typical instruction might say:

31   "Add the number stored in position 6809 to that in 4302 and put the result back into the latter storage position."

32   Needless to say it would not occur in the machine expressed in English. It would more likely be coded in a form such as 6809430217. Here 17 says which of various possible operations is to be performed on the two numbers. In this case the operation is that described above, viz., "Add the number...." It will be noticed that the instruction takes up 10 digits and so forms one packet of information, very conveniently. The control will normally take the instructions to be obeyed in the order of the positions in which they are stored, but occasionally an instruction such as

33   "Now obey the instruction stored in position 5606, and continue from there" may be encountered, or again

34   "If position 4505 contains 0 obey next the instruction stored in 6707, otherwise continue straight on."

35   Instructions of these latter types are very important because they make it possible for a sequence of operations to be replaced over and over again until some condition is

fulfilled, but in doing so to obey, not fresh instructions on each repetition, but the same ones over and over again. To take a domestic analogy: suppose Mother wants Tommy to call at the cobbler's every morning on his way to school to see if her shoes are done, she can ask him afresh every morning. Alternatively she can stick up a notice once and for all in the hall which he will see when he leaves for school and which tells him to call for the shoes, and also to destroy the notice when he comes back if he has the shoes with him.

36   The reader must accept it as a fact that digital computers can be constructed, and indeed have been constructed, according to the principles we have described, and that they can in fact mimic the actions of a human computer very closely.

37   The book of rules which we have described our human computer as using is of course a convenient fiction. Actual human computers really remember what they have got to do. If one wants to make a machine mimic the behaviour of the human computer in some complex operation one has to ask him how it is done, and then translate the answer into the form of an instruction table. Constructing instruction tables is usually described as "programming." To "programme a machine to carry out the operation A" means to put the appropriate instruction table into the machine so that it will do A.

38   An interesting variant on the idea of a digital computer is a "digital computer with a random element." These have instructions involving the throwing of a die or some equivalent electronic process; one such instruction might for instance be, "Throw the die and put the resulting number into store 1000." Sometimes such a machine is described as having free will (though I would not use this phrase myself). It is not normally possible to determine from observing a machine whether it has a random element, for a similar effect can be produced by such devices as making the choices depend on the digits of the decimal for π.

39   Most actual digital computers have only a finite store. There is no theoretical difficulty in the idea of a computer with an unlimited store. Of course only a finite part can have been used at any one time. Likewise only a finite amount can have been constructed, but we can imagine more and more being added as required. Such computers have special theoretical interest and will be called infinitive capacity computers.

40   The idea of a digital computer is an old one. Charles Babbage, Lucasian Professor of Mathematics at Cambridge from 1828 to 1839, planned such a machine, called the Analytical Engine, but it was never completed. Although Babbage had all the essential ideas, his machine was not at that time such a very attractive prospect. The speed which would have been available would be definitely faster than a human computer but something like 100 times slower than the Manchester machine, itself one of the slower of the modern machines. The storage was to be purely mechanical, using wheels and cards.

41   The fact that Babbage's Analytical Engine was to be entirely mechanical will help us to rid ourselves of a superstition. Importance is often attached to the fact that modern digital computers are electrical, and that the nervous system also is electrical. Since Babbage's machine was not electrical, and since all digital computers are in a sense equivalent, we see that this use of electricity cannot be of theoretical importance. Of course electricity usually comes in where fast signalling is concerned, so that it is not surprising that we find it in both these connections. In the nervous system chemical phenomena are at least as important as electrical. In certain computers the storage system is mainly acoustic. The feature of using electricity is thus seen to be only a very superficial similarity. If we wish to find such similarities we should look rather for mathematical analogies of function.

5. UNIVERSALITY OF DIGITAL COMPUTERS

42   The digital computers considered in the last section may be classified amongst the "discrete-state machines." These are the machines which move by sudden jumps or clicks from one quite definite state to another. These states are sufficiently different for the possibility of confusion between them to be ignored. Strictly speaking there are no such machines. Everything really moves continuously. But there are many kinds of machines which can profitably be thought of as being discrete-state machines. For instance in considering the switches for a lighting system it is a convenient fiction that each switch must be definitely on or definitely off. There must be intermediate positions, but for most purposes we can forget about them. As an example of a discrete-state machine we might consider a wheel which clicks round through 120° once a second, but may be stopped by a lever which can be operated from outside; in addition a lamp is to light in one of the positions of the wheel. This machine could be described abstractly as follows. The internal state of the machine (which is described by the position of the wheel) may be q_1, q_2 or q_3. There is an input signal i0 or i1 (position of lever). The internal state at any moment is determined by the last state and input signal according to the table

		Last State		
		q_1	q_2	q_3
	i_0	q_2	q_3	q_1
Input				
	i_1	q_1	q_2	q_3

43   The output signals, the only externally visible indication of the internal state (the light) are described by the table

State	q_1	q_2	q_3
Output	o_0	o_0	o_1

44   This example is typical of discrete-state machines. They can be described by such tables provided they have only a finite number of possible states.

45   It will seem that given the initial state of the machine and the input signals it is always possible to predict all future states. This is reminiscent of Laplace's view that from the complete state of the universe at one moment of time, as described by the positions and velocities of all particles, it should be possible to predict all future states. The prediction which we are considering is, however, rather nearer to practicability than that considered by Laplace. The system of the "universe as a whole" is such that quite small errors in the initial conditions can have an overwhelming effect at a later time. The displacement of a single electron by a billionth of a centimetre at one moment might make the difference between a man being killed by an avalanche a year later, or escaping. It is an essential property of the mechanical systems which we have called "discrete-state machines" that this phenomenon does not occur. Even when we consider the actual physical machines instead of the idealised machines, reasonably accurate knowledge of the state at one moment yields reasonably accurate knowledge any number of steps later.

46   As we have mentioned, digital computers fall within the class of discrete-state machines. But the number of states of which such a machine is capable is usually enormously large. For instance, the number for the machine now working at Manchester is about $2^{165,000}$, i.e., about $10^{50,000}$. Compare this with our example of the clicking wheel described above, which had three states. It is not difficult to see why the number of states should be so immense. The computer includes a store corresponding to the paper used by a human computer. It must be possible to write into the store any one of the combinations of symbols which might have been written on the paper. For simplicity suppose that only digits from 0 to 9 are used as symbols. Variations in handwriting are ignored. Suppose the computer is allowed 100 sheets of paper each containing 50 lines each with room for 30 digits. Then the number of states is $10^{100 \times 50 \times 30}$ i.e., $10^{150,000}$. This is about the number of states of three Manchester machines put together. The logarithm to the base two of the number of states is usually called the "storage capacity" of the machine. Thus the Manchester machine has a storage capacity of about 165,000 and the wheel machine of our example about 1.6. If two machines are put together their capacities must be added to obtain the capacity of the resultant machine. This leads to the possibility of statements such as "The Manchester machine contains 64 magnetic tracks each with a capacity of 2560, eight electronic tubes with a capacity of 1280. Miscellaneous storage amounts to about 300 making a total of 174,380."

47   Given the table corresponding to a discrete-state machine it is possible to predict what it will do. There is no reason why this calculation should not be carried out by means of a digital computer. Provided it could be carried out sufficiently quickly the digital computer could mimic the behavior of any discrete-state machine. The imitation game could then be played with the machine in question (as B) and the mimicking digital computer (as A) and the interrogator would be unable to distinguish them. Of course the digital computer must have an adequate storage capacity as well as working sufficiently fast. Moreover, it must be programmed afresh for each new machine which it is desired to mimic.

48   This special property of digital computers, that they can mimic any discrete-state machine, is described by saying that they are universal machines. The existence of machines with this property has the important consequence that, considerations of speed apart, it is unnecessary to design various new machines to do various computing processes. They can all be done with one digital computer, suitably programmed for each case. It will be seen that as a consequence of this all digital computers are in a sense equivalent.

49   We may now consider again the point raised at the end of §3. It was suggested tentatively that the question, "Can machines think?" should be replaced by "Are there imaginable digital computers which would do well in the imitation game?" If we wish we can make this superficially more general and ask "Are there discrete-state machines which would do well?" But in view of the universality property we see that either of these questions is equivalent to this, "Let us fix our attention on one particular digital computer C. Is it true that by modifying this computer to have an adequate storage, suitably increasing its speed of action, and providing it with an appropriate programme, C can be made to play satisfactorily the part of A in the imitation game, the part of B being taken by a man?"

6. CONTRARY VIEWS ON THE MAIN QUESTION

50   We may now consider the ground to have been cleared and we are ready to proceed to the debate on our question, "Can machines think?" and the variant of it quoted at the end of the last section. We cannot altogether abandon the original form of the problem, for opin-

ions will differ as to the appropriateness of the substitution and we must at least listen to what has to be said in this connexion.

51   It will simplify matters for the reader if I explain first my own beliefs in the matter. Consider first the more accurate form of the question. I believe that in about fifty years' time it will be possible, to programme computers, with a storage capacity of about 109, to make them play the imitation game so well that an average interrogator will not have more than a 70 per cent chance of making the right identification after five minutes of questioning. The original question, "Can machines think?" I believe to be too meaningless to deserve discussion. Nevertheless I believe that at the end of the century the use of words and general educated opinion will have altered so much that one will be able to speak of machines thinking without expecting to be contradicted. I believe further that no useful purpose is served by concealing these beliefs. The popular view that scientists proceed inexorably from well-established fact to well-established fact, never being influenced by any improved conjecture, is quite mistaken. Provided it is made clear which are proved facts and which are conjectures, no harm can result. Conjectures are of great importance since they suggest useful lines of research.

52   I now proceed to consider opinions opposed to my own.

(1) THE THEOLOGICAL OBJECTION

53 Thinking is a function of man's immortal soul. God has given an immortal soul to every man and woman, but not to any other animal or to machines. Hence no animal or machine can think.

54   I am unable to accept any part of this, but will attempt to reply in theological terms. I should find the argument more convincing if animals were classed with men, for there is a greater difference, to my mind, between the typical animate and the inanimate than there is between man and the other animals. The arbitrary character of the orthodox view becomes clearer if we consider how it might appear to a member of some other religious community. How do Christians regard the Moslem view that women have no souls? But let us leave this point aside and return to the main argument. It appears to me that the argument quoted above implies a serious restriction of the omnipotence of the Almighty. It is admitted that there are certain things that He cannot do such as making one equal to two, but should we not believe that He has freedom to confer a soul on an elephant if He sees fit? We might expect that He would only exercise this power in conjunction with a mutation which provided the elephant with an appropriately improved brain to minister to the needs of this soul[1]. An argument of exactly similar form may be made for the case of machines. It may seem different because it is more difficult to "swallow." But this really only means that we think it would be less likely that He would consider the circumstances suitable for conferring a soul. The circumstances in question are discussed in the rest of this paper. In attempting to construct such machines we should not be irreverently usurping His power of creating souls, any more than we are in the procreation of children: rather we are, in either case, instruments of His will providing mansions for the souls that He creates.

55   However, this is mere speculation. I am not very impressed with theological arguments whatever they may be used to support. Such arguments have often been found unsatisfactory in the past. In the time of Galileo it was argued that the texts, "And the sun stood still... and hasted not to go down about a whole day" (Joshua x. 13) and "He laid the foundations of the earth, that it should not move at any time" (Psalm cv. 5) were an adequate refutation of the Copernican theory. With our present knowledge such an argument appears futile. When that knowledge was not available it made a quite different impression.

(2) THE "HEADS IN THE SAND" OBJECTION

56 "The consequences of machines thinking would be too dreadful. Let us hope and believe that they cannot do so."

57   This argument is seldom expressed quite so openly as in the form above. But it affects most of us who think about it at all. We like to believe that Man is in some subtle way superior to the rest of creation. It is best if he can be shown to be necessarily superior, for then there is no danger of him losing his commanding position. The popularity of the theological argument is clearly connected with this feeling. It is likely to be quite strong in intellectual people, since they value the power of thinking more highly than others, and are more inclined to base their belief in the superiority of Man on this power.

58   I do not think that this argument is sufficiently substantial to require refutation. Consolation would be more appropriate: perhaps this should be sought in the transmigration of souls.

(3) THE MATHEMATICAL OBJECTION

59 There are a number of results of mathematical logic which can be used to show that there are limitations to the powers of discrete-state machines. The best known of these results is known as *Gödel*'s theorem[2] and shows that in any sufficiently powerful logical system statements can be formulated which can neither be proved nor disproved within the system, unless possibly the system itself is inconsistent. There are other, in some respects similar, results due to *Church*, *Kleene*, Rosser, and *Turing*. The latter result is the most convenient to consider, since it refers directly to machines, whereas the others can only be used in a comparatively indirect argument: for instance if Gödel's theorem is to be used we need in addition to have some means of describing logical systems in terms of machines, and machines in terms of logical systems. The result in question refers to a type of machine which is essentially a digital computer with an infinite capacity. It states that there are certain things that such a machine cannot do. If it is rigged up to give answers to questions as in the imitation game, there will be some questions to which it will either give a wrong answer, or fail to give an answer at all however much time is allowed for a reply. There may, of course, be many such questions, and questions which cannot be answered by one machine may be satisfactorily answered by another. We are of course supposing for the present that the questions are of the kind to which an answer "Yes" or "No" is appropriate, rather than questions such as "What do you think of Picasso?" The questions that we know the machines must fail on are of this type, "Consider the machine specified as follows.... Will this machine ever answer 'Yes' to any question?" The dots are to be replaced by a description of some machine in a standard form, which could be something like that used in §5. When the machine described bears a certain comparatively simple relation to the machine which is under interrogation, it can be shown that the answer is either wrong or not forthcoming. This is the mathematical result: it is argued that it proves a disability of machines to which the human intellect is not subject.

60   The short answer to this argument is that although it is established that there are limitations to the Powers of any particular machine, it has only been stated, without any sort of proof, that no such limitations apply to the human intellect. But I do not think this view

can be dismissed quite so lightly. Whenever one of these machines is asked the appropriate critical question, and gives a definite answer, we know that this answer must be wrong, and this gives us a certain feeling of superiority. Is this feeling illusory? It is no doubt quite genuine, but I do not think too much importance should be attached to it. We too often give wrong answers to questions ourselves to be justified in being very pleased at such evidence of fallibility on the part of the machines. Further, our superiority can only be felt on such an occasion in relation to the one machine over which we have scored our petty triumph. There would be no question of triumphing simultaneously over all machines. In short, then, there might be men cleverer than any given machine, but then again there might be other machines cleverer again, and so on.

61   Those who hold to the mathematical argument would, I think, mostly be willing to accept the imitation game as a basis for discussion. Those who believe in the two previous objections would probably not be interested in any criteria.

(4) THE ARGUMENT FROM CONSCIOUSNESS

62   This argument is very well expressed in Professor Jefferson's Lister Oration for 1949, from which I quote. "Not until a machine can write a sonnet or compose a concerto because of thoughts and emotions felt, and not by the chance fall of symbols, could we agree that machine equals brain—that is, not only write it but know that it had written it. No mechanism could feel (and not merely artificially signal, an easy contrivance) pleasure at its successes, grief when its valves fuse, be warmed by flattery, be made miserable by its mistakes, be charmed by sex, be angry or depressed when it cannot get what it wants."

63   This argument appears to be a denial of the validity of our test. According to the most extreme form of this view the only way by which one could be sure that a machine thinks is to be the machine and to feel oneself thinking. One could then describe these feelings to the world, but of course no one would be justified in taking any notice. Likewise according to this view the only way to know that a man thinks is to be that particular man. It is in fact the solipsist point of view. It may be the most logical view to hold but it makes communication of ideas difficult. A is liable to believe "A thinks but B does not" whilst B believes "B thinks but A does not." Instead of arguing continually over this point it is usual to have the polite convention that everyone thinks.

64   I am sure that Professor Jefferson does not wish to adopt the extreme and solipsist point of view. Probably he would be quite willing to accept the imitation game as a test. The game (with the player B omitted) is frequently used in practice under the name of *viva voce* to discover whether some one really understands something or has "learnt it parrot fashion." Let us listen in to a part of such a *viva voce*:

> INTERROGATOR: In the first line of your sonnet which reads "Shall I compare thee to a summer's day," would not "a spring day" do as well or better?
> WITNESS: It wouldn't scan.
> INTERROGATOR: How about "a winter's day." That would scan all right.
> WITNESS: Yes, but nobody wants to be compared to a winter's day.
> INTERROGATOR: Would you say Mr. Pickwick reminded you of Christmas?
> WITNESS: In a way.
> INTERROGATOR: Yet Christmas is a winter's day, and I do not think Mr. Pickwick would mind the comparison.

WITNESS: I don't think you're serious. By a winter's day one means a typical winter's day, rather than a special one like Christmas.

65   And so on. What would Professor Jefferson say if the sonnet-writing machine was able to answer like this in the *viva voce*? I do not know whether he would regard the machine as "merely artificially signalling" these answers, but if the answers were as satisfactory and sustained as in the above passage I do not think he would describe it as "an easy contrivance." This phrase is, I think, intended to cover such devices as the inclusion in the machine of a record of someone reading a sonnet, with appropriate switching to turn it on from time to time.

66   In short then, I think that most of those who support the argument from consciousness could be persuaded to abandon it rather than be forced into the solipsist position. They will then probably be willing to accept our test.

67   I do not wish to give the impression that I think there is no mystery about consciousness. There is, for instance, something of a paradox connected with any attempt to localise it. But I do not think these mysteries necessarily need to be solved before we can answer the question with which we are concerned in this paper.

(5) ARGUMENTS FROM VARIOUS DISABILITIES

68   These arguments take the form, "I grant you that you can make machines do all the things you have mentioned but you will never be able to make one to do X." Numerous features X are suggested in this connexion. I offer a selection:

69   Be kind, resourceful, beautiful, friendly, have initiative, have a sense of humour, tell right from wrong, make mistakes, fall in love, enjoy strawberries and cream, make some one fall in love with it, learn from experience, use words properly, be the subject of its own thought, have as much diversity of behaviour as a man, do something really new.

70   No support is usually offered for these statements. I believe they are mostly founded on the principle of scientific induction. A man has seen thousands of machines in his lifetime. From what he sees of them he draws a number of general conclusions. They are ugly, each is designed for a very limited purpose, when required for a minutely different purpose they are useless, the variety of behaviour of any one of them is very small, etc., etc. Naturally he concludes that these are necessary properties of machines in general. Many of these limitations are associated with the very small storage capacity of most machines. (I am assuming that the idea of storage capacity is extended in some way to cover machines other than discrete-state machines. The exact definition does not matter as no mathematical accuracy is claimed in the present discussion.) A few years ago, when very little had been heard of digital computers, it was possible to elicit much incredulity concerning them, if one mentioned their properties without describing their construction. That was presumably due to a similar application of the principle of scientific induction. These applications of the principle are of course largely unconscious. When a burnt child fears the fire and shows that he fears it by avoiding it, I should say that he was applying scientific induction. (I could of course also describe his behaviour in many other ways.) The works and customs of mankind do not seem to be very suitable material to which to apply scientific induction. A very large part of space-time must be investigated, if reliable results are to be obtained. Otherwise we may (as most English children do) decide that everybody speaks English, and that it is silly to learn French.

71   There are, however, special remarks to be made about many of the disabilities that have been mentioned. The inability to enjoy strawberries and cream may have struck the reader as frivolous. Possibly a machine might be made to enjoy this delicious dish, but any attempt to make one do so would be idiotic. What is important about this disability is that it contributes to some of the other disabilities, e.g., to the difficulty of the same kind of friendliness occurring between man and machine as between white man and white man, or between black man and black man.

72   The claim that "machines cannot make mistakes" seems a curious one. One is tempted to retort, "Are they any the worse for that?" But let us adopt a more sympathetic attitude, and try to see what is really meant. I think this criticism can be explained in terms of the imitation game. It is claimed that the interrogator could distinguish the machine from the man simply by setting them a number of problems in arithmetic. The machine would be unmasked because of its deadly accuracy. The reply to this is simple. The machine (programmed for playing the game) would not attempt to give the right answers to the arithmetic problems. It would deliberately introduce mistakes in a manner calculated to confuse the interrogator. A mechanical fault would probably show itself through an unsuitable decision as to what sort of a mistake to make in the arithmetic. Even this interpretation of the criticism is not sufficiently sympathetic. But we cannot afford the space to go into it much further. It seems to me that this criticism depends on a confusion between two kinds of mistake. We may call them "errors of functioning" and "errors of conclusion." Errors of functioning are due to some mechanical or electrical fault which causes the machine to behave otherwise than it was designed to do. In philosophical discussions one likes to ignore the possibility of such errors; one is therefore discussing "abstract machines." These abstract machines are mathematical fictions rather than physical objects By definition they are incapable of errors of functioning. In this sense we can truly say that "machines can never make mistakes." Errors of conclusion can only arise when some meaning is attached to the output signals from the machine. The machine might, for instance, type out mathematical equations, or sentences in English. When a false proposition is typed we say that the machine has committed an error of conclusion. There is clearly no reason at all for saying that a machine cannot make this kind of mistake. It might do nothing but type out repeatedly "0=1." To take a less perverse example, it might have some method for drawing conclusions by scientific induction. We must expect such a method to lead occasionally to erroneous results.

73   The claim that a machine cannot be the subject of its own thought can of course only be answered if it can be shown that the machine has some thought with some subject matter. Nevertheless, "the subject matter of a machine's operations" does seem to mean something, at least to the people who deal with it. If, for instance, the machine was trying to find a solution of the equation $x^2 - 40x - 11 = 0$ one would be tempted to describe this equation as part of the machine's subject matter at that moment. In this sort of sense a machine undoubtedly can be its own subject matter. It may be used to help in making up its own programmes, or to predict the effect of alterations in its own structure. By observing the results of its own behaviour it can modify its own programmes so as to achieve some purpose more effectively. These are possibilities of the near future, rather than Utopian dreams.

74   The criticism that a machine cannot have much diversity of behaviour is just a way of saying that it cannot have much storage capacity. Until fairly recently a storage capacity of even a thousand digits was very rare.

75   The criticisms that we are considering here are often disguised forms of the argument from consciousness. Usually if one maintains that a machine can do one of these things, and describes the kind of method that the machine could use, one will not make much of an impression. It is thought that the method (whatever it may be, for it must be mechanical) is really rather base. Compare the parentheses in Jefferson's statement quoted [above].

(6) LADY LOVELACE'S OBJECTION

76   Our most detailed information of Babbage's Analytical Engine comes from a memoir by *Lady Lovelace*. In it she states, "The Analytical Engine has no pretensions to *originate* anything. It can do *whatever we know how to order it to perform*" (her italics). This statement is quoted by *Hartree* (p. 70) who adds: "This does not imply that it may not be possible to construct electronic equipment which will 'think for itself,' or in which, in biological terms, one could set up a conditioned reflex, which would serve as a basis for 'learning.' Whether this is possible in principle or not is a stimulating and exciting question, suggested by some of these recent developments. But it did not seem that the machines constructed or projected at the time had this property."

77   I am in thorough agreement with Hartree over this. It will be noticed that he does not assert that the machines in question had not got the property, but rather that the evidence available to Lady Lovelace did not encourage her to believe that they had it. It is quite possible that the machines in question had in a sense got this property. For suppose that some discrete-state machine has the property. The Analytical Engine was a universal digital computer, so that, if its storage capacity and speed were adequate, it could by suitable programming be made to mimic the machine in question. Probably this argument did not occur to the Countess or to Babbage. In any case there was no obligation on them to claim all that could be claimed.

78   This whole question will be considered again under the heading of learning machines.

79   A variant of Lady Lovelace's objection states that a machine can "never do anything really new." This may be parried for a moment with the saw, "There is nothing new under the sun." Who can be certain that "original work" that he has done was not simply the growth of the seed planted in him by teaching, or the effect of following well-known general principles. A better variant of the objection says that a machine can never "take us by surprise." This statement is a more direct challenge and can be met directly. Machines take me by surprise with great frequency. This is largely because I do not do sufficient calculation to decide what to expect them to do, or rather because, although I do a calculation, I do it in a hurried, slipshod fashion, taking risks. Perhaps I say to myself, "I suppose the Voltage here ought to be the same as there: anyway let's assume it is." Naturally I am often wrong, and the result is a surprise for me for by the time the experiment is done these assumptions have been forgotten. These admissions lay me open to lectures on the subject of my vicious ways, but do not throw any doubt on my credibility when I testify to the surprises I experience.

80   I do not expect this reply to silence my critic. He will probably say that surprises are due to some creative mental act on my part, and reflect no credit on the machine. This leads us back to the argument from consciousness, and far from the idea of surprise. It is a line of argument we must consider closed, but it is perhaps worth remarking that the appreciation of something as surprising requires as much of a "creative mental act" whether the surprising event originates from a man, a book, a machine or anything else.

81   The view that machines cannot give rise to surprises is due, I believe, to a fallacy to which philosophers and mathematicians are particularly subject. This is the assumption that as soon as a fact is presented to a mind all consequences of that fact spring into the mind simultaneously with it. It is a very useful assumption under many circumstances, but one too easily forgets that it is false. A natural consequence of doing so is that one then assumes that there is no virtue in the mere working out of consequences from data and general principles.

(7) ARGUMENT FROM CONTINUITY IN THE NERVOUS SYSTEM

82 The nervous system is certainly not a discrete-state machine. A small error in the information about the size of a nervous impulse impinging on a neuron may make a large difference to the size of the outgoing impulse. It may be argued that, this being so, one cannot expect to be able to mimic the behaviour of the nervous system with a discrete-state system.

83   It is true that a discrete-state machine must be different from a continuous machine. But if we adhere to the conditions of the imitation game, the interrogator will not be able to take any advantage of this difference. The situation can be made clearer if we consider some other simpler continuous machine. A differential analyser will do very well. (A differential analyser is a certain kind of machine not of the discrete-state type used for some kinds of calculation.) Some of these provide their answers in a typed form, and so are suitable for taking part in the game. It would not be possible for a digital computer to predict exactly what answers the differential analyser would give to a problem, but it would be quite capable of giving the right sort of answer. For instance, if asked to give the value of π (actually about 3.1416) it would be reasonable to choose at random between the values 3.12, 3.13, 3.14, 3.15, 3.16 with the probabilities of 0.05, 0.15, 0.55, 0.19, 0.06 (say). Under these circumstances it would be very difficult for the interrogator to distinguish the differential analyser from the digital computer.

(8) THE ARGUMENT FROM INFORMALITY OF BEHAVIOUR

84 It is not possible to produce a set of rules purporting to describe what a man should do in every conceivable set of circumstances. One might for instance have a rule that one is to stop when one sees a red traffic light, and to go if one sees a green one, but what if by some fault both appear together? One may perhaps decide that it is safest to stop. But some further difficulty may well arise from this decision later. To attempt to provide rules of conduct to cover every eventuality, even those arising from traffic lights, appears to be impossible. With all this I agree.

85   From this it is argued that we cannot be machines. I shall try to reproduce the argument, but I fear I shall hardly do it justice. It seems to run something like this. "If each man had a definite set of rules of conduct by which he regulated his life he would be no better than a machine. But there are no such rules, so men cannot be machines." The undistributed middle is glaring. I do not think the argument is ever put quite like this, but I believe this is the argument used nevertheless. There may however be a certain confusion between "rules of conduct" and "laws of behaviour" to cloud the issue. By "rules of conduct" I mean precepts such as "Stop if you see red lights," on which one can act, and of which one can be conscious. By "laws of behaviour" I mean laws of nature as applied to a man's body such as "if you pinch him he will squeak." If we substitute "laws of behaviour which regulate his life" for "laws of conduct by which he regulates his life" in the argument quoted the undistributed middle is no longer insuperable. For we believe that it is not only true that being regulated by laws of behaviour implies being some sort of machine (though not necessarily a discrete-state machine), but that conversely being such a machine implies being regulated by such laws. However, we cannot so easily convince ourselves of the absence of complete laws of behaviour as of complete rules of conduct. The only way we know of for finding such laws is scientific observation, and we certainly know of no circumstances under which we could say, "We have searched enough. There are no such laws."

86   We can demonstrate more forcibly that any such statement would be unjustified. For suppose we could be sure of finding such laws if they existed. Then given a discrete-state machine it should certainly be possible to discover by observation sufficient about it to predict its future behaviour, and this within a reasonable time, say a thousand years. But this does not seem to be the case. I have set up on the Manchester computer a small programme using only 1,000 units of storage, whereby the machine supplied with one sixteen-figure number replies with another within two seconds. I would defy anyone to learn from these replies sufficient about the programme to be able to predict any replies to untried values.

(9) THE ARGUMENT FROM EXTRASENSORY PERCEPTION

87 I assume that the reader is familiar with the idea of extrasensory perception, and the meaning of the four items of it, viz., telepathy, clairvoyance, precognition and psychokinesis. These disturbing phenomena seem to deny all our usual scientific ideas. How we should like to discredit them! Unfortunately the statistical evidence, at least for telepathy, is overwhelming. It is very difficult to rearrange one's ideas so as to fit these new facts in. Once one has accepted them it does not seem a very big step to believe in ghosts and bogies. The idea that our bodies move simply according to the known laws of physics, together with some others not yet discovered but somewhat similar, would be one of the first to go.

88   This argument is to my mind quite a strong one. One can say in reply that many scientific theories seem to remain workable in practice, in spite of clashing with ESP; that in fact one can get along very nicely if one forgets about it. This is rather cold comfort, and one fears that thinking is just the kind of phenomenon where ESP may be especially relevant.

89   A more specific argument based on ESP might run as follows: "Let us play the imitation game, using as witnesses a man who is good as a telepathic receiver, and a digital computer. The interrogator can ask such questions as 'What suit does the card in my right hand belong to?' The man by telepathy or clairvoyance gives the right answer 130 times out of 400 cards. The machine can only guess at random, and perhaps gets 104 right, so the interrogator makes the right identification." There is an interesting possibility which opens here. Suppose the digital computer contains a random number generator. Then it will be natural to use this to decide what answer to give. But then the random number generator will be subject to the psychokinetic powers of the interrogator. Perhaps this psychokinesis might cause the machine to guess right more often than would be expected on a probability calculation, so that the interrogator might still be unable to make the right iden-

tification. On the other hand, he might be able to guess right without any questioning, by clairvoyance. With ESP anything may happen.

90   If telepathy is admitted it will be necessary to tighten our test up. The situation could be regarded as analogous to that which would occur if the interrogator were talking to himself and one of the competitors was listening with his ear to the wall. To put the competitors into a "telepathy-proof room" would satisfy all requirements.

7. LEARNING MACHINES

91 The reader will have anticipated that I have no very convincing arguments of a positive nature to support my views. If I had I should not have taken such pains to point out the fallacies in contrary views. Such evidence as I have I shall now give.

92   Let us return for a moment to Lady Lovelace's objection, which stated that the machine can only do what we tell it to do. One could say that a man can "inject" an idea into the machine, and that it will respond to a certain extent and then drop into quiescence, like a piano string struck by a hammer. Another simile would be an atomic pile of less than critical size: an injected idea is to correspond to a neutron entering the pile from without. Each such neutron will cause a certain disturbance which eventually dies away. If, however, the size of the pile is sufficiently increased, the disturbance caused by such an incoming neutron will very likely go on and on increasing until the whole pile is destroyed. Is there a corresponding phenomenon for minds, and is there one for machines? There does seem to be one for the human mind. The majority of them seem to be "subcritical," i.e., to correspond in this analogy to piles of subcritical size. An idea presented to such a mind will on average give rise to less than one idea in reply. A smallish proportion are supercritical. An idea presented to such a mind may give rise to a whole "theory" consisting of secondary, tertiary and more remote ideas. Animals' minds seem to be very definitely subcritical. Adhering to this analogy we ask, "Can a machine be made to be supercritical?"

93   The "skin-of-an-onion" analogy is also helpful. In considering the functions of the mind or the brain we find certain operations which we can explain in purely mechanical terms. This we say does not correspond to the real mind: it is a sort of skin which we must strip off if we are to find the real mind. But then in what remains we find a further skin to be stripped off, and so on. Proceeding in this way do we ever come to the "real" mind, or do we eventually come to the skin which has nothing in it? In the latter case the whole mind is mechanical. (It would not be a discrete-state machine however. We have discussed this.)

94   These last two paragraphs do not claim to be convincing arguments. They should rather be described as "recitations tending to produce belief."

95   The only really satisfactory support that can be given for the view expressed at the beginning of §6 will be that provided by waiting for the end of the century and then doing the experiment described. But what can we say in the meantime? What steps should be taken now if the experiment is to be successful?

96   As I have explained, the problem is mainly one of programming. Advances in engineering will have to be made too, but it seems unlikely that these will not be adequate for the requirements. Estimates of the storage capacity of the brain vary from 10^{10} to 10^{15} binary digits. I incline to the lower values and believe that only a very small fraction is used for the higher types of thinking. Most of it is probably used for the retention of visual impressions. I should be surprised if more than 10^9 was required for satisfactory playing

of the imitation game, at any rate against a blind man. (Note: The capacity of the *Encyclopaedia Britannica*, 11th edition, is 2×10^9) A storage capacity of 10^7 would be a very practicable possibility even by present techniques. It is probably not necessary to increase the speed of operations of the machines at all. Parts of modern machines which can be regarded as analogs of nerve cells work about a thousand times faster than the latter. This should provide a "margin of safety" which could cover losses of speed arising in many ways. Our problem then is to find out how to programme these machines to play the game. At my present rate of working I produce about a thousand digits of programming a day, so that about sixty workers, working steadily through the fifty years might accomplish the job, if nothing went into the wastepaper basket. Some more expeditious method seems desirable.

97   In the process of trying to imitate an adult human mind we are bound to think a good deal about the process which has brought it to the state that it is in. We may notice three components.

(a) The initial state of the mind, say at birth,

(b) The education to which it has been subjected,

(c) Other experience, not to be described as education, to which it has been subjected.

98   Instead of trying to produce a programme to simulate the adult mind, why not rather try to produce one which simulates the child's? If this were then subjected to an appropriate course of education one would obtain the adult brain. Presumably the child brain is something like a notebook as one buys it from the stationer's. Rather little mechanism, and lots of blank sheets. (Mechanism and writing are from our point of view almost synonymous.) Our hope is that there is so little mechanism in the child brain that something like it can be easily programmed. The amount of work in the education we can assume, as a first approximation, to be much the same as for the human child.

99   We have thus divided our problem into two parts. The child programme and the education process. These two remain very closely connected. We cannot expect to find a good child machine at the first attempt. One must experiment with teaching one such machine and see how well it learns. One can then try another and see if it is better or worse. There is an obvious connection between this process and evolution, by the identifications

100   Structure of the child machine = hereditary material

101   Changes of the child machine = mutation

102   Natural selection = judgment of the experimenter

103   One may hope, however, that this process will be more expeditious than evolution. The survival of the fittest is a slow method for measuring advantages. The experimenter, by the exercise of intelligence, should be able to speed it up. Equally important is the fact that he is not restricted to random mutations. If he can trace a cause for some weakness he can probably think of the kind of mutation which will improve it.

104   It will not be possible to apply exactly the same teaching process to the machine as to a normal child. It will not, for instance, be provided with legs, so that it could not be asked to go out and fill the coal scuttle. Possibly it might not have eyes. But however well these deficiencies might be overcome by clever engineering, one could not send the creature to school without the other children making excessive fun of it. It must be given some tuition. We need not be too concerned about the legs, eyes, etc. The example of Miss Helen Keller shows that education can take place provided that communication in both directions between teacher and pupil can take place by some means or other.

105 We normally associate punishments and rewards with the teaching process. Some simple child machines can be constructed or programmed on this sort of principle. The machine has to be so constructed that events which shortly preceded the occurrence of a punishment signal are unlikely to be repeated, whereas a reward signal increased the probability of repetition of the events which led up to it. These definitions do not presuppose any feelings on the part of the machine. I have done some experiments with one such child machine, and succeeded in teaching it a few things, but the teaching method was too unorthodox for the experiment to be considered really successful.

106 The use of punishments and rewards can at best be a part of the teaching process. Roughly speaking, if the teacher has no other means of communicating to the pupil, the amount of information which can reach him does not exceed the total number of rewards and punishments applied. By the time a child has learnt to repeat "Casabianca" he would probably feel very sore indeed, if the text could only be discovered by a "Twenty Questions" technique, every "NO" taking the form of a blow. It is necessary therefore to have some other "unemotional" channels of communication. If these are available it is possible to teach a machine by punishments and rewards to obey orders given in some language, e.g., a symbolic language. These orders are to be transmitted through the "unemotional" channels. The use of this language will diminish greatly the number of punishments and rewards required.

107 Opinions may vary as to the complexity which is suitable in the child machine. One might try to make it as simple as possible consistently with the general principles. Alternatively one might have a complete system of logical inference "built in."[3] In the latter case the store would be largely occupied with definitions and propositions. The propositions would have various kinds of status, e.g., well-established facts, conjectures, mathematically proved theorems, statements given by an authority, expressions having the logical form of proposition but not belief-value. Certain propositions may be described as "imperatives." The machine should be so constructed that as soon as an imperative is classed as "well established" the appropriate action automatically takes place. To illustrate this, suppose the teacher says to the machine, "Do your homework now." This may cause "Teacher says 'Do your homework now'" to be included amongst the well-established facts. Another such fact might be, "Everything that teacher says is true." Combining these may eventually lead to the imperative, "Do your homework now," being included amongst the well-established facts, and this, by the construction of the machine, will mean that the homework actually gets started, but the effect is very satisfactory. The processes of inference used by the machine need not be such as would satisfy the most exacting logicians. There might for instance be no hierarchy of types. But this need not mean that type fallacies will occur, any more than we are bound to fall over unfenced cliffs. Suitable imperatives (expressed within the systems, not forming part of the rules of the system) such as "Do not use a class unless it is a subclass of one which has been mentioned by teacher" can have a similar effect to "Do not go too near the edge."

108 The imperatives that can be obeyed by a machine that has no limbs are bound to be of a rather intellectual character, as in the example (doing homework) given above. Important amongst such imperatives will be ones which regulate the order in which the rules of the logical system concerned are to be applied. For at each stage when one is using a logical system, there is a very large number of alternative steps, any of which one is permitted to apply, so far as obedience to the rules of the logical system is concerned. These choices make the difference between a brilliant and a footling reasoner, not the difference between a sound and a fallacious one. Propositions leading to imperatives of this kind might be

"When Socrates is mentioned, use the syllogism in Barbara" or "If one method has been proved to be quicker than another, do not use the slower method." Some of these may be "given by authority," but others may be produced by the machine itself, e.g. by scientific induction.

109   The idea of a learning machine may appear paradoxical to some readers. How can the rules of operation of the machine change? They should describe completely how the machine will react whatever its history might be, whatever changes it might undergo. The rules are thus quite time-invariant. This is quite true. The explanation of the paradox is that the rules which get changed in the learning process are of a rather less pretentious kind, claiming only an ephemeral validity. The reader may draw a parallel with the Constitution of the United States.

110   An important feature of a learning machine is that its teacher will often be very largely ignorant of quite what is going on inside, although he may still be able to some extent to predict his pupil's behavior. This should apply most strongly to the later education of a machine arising from a child machine of well-tried design (or programme). This is in clear contrast with normal procedure when using a machine to do computations: one's object is then to have a clear mental picture of the state of the machine at each moment in the computation. This object can only be achieved with a struggle. The view that "the machine can only do what we know how to order it to do,"[4] appears strange in face of this. Most of the programmes which we can put into the machine will result in its doing something that we cannot make sense of at all, or which we regard as completely random behaviour. Intelligent behaviour presumably consists in a departure from the completely disciplined behaviour involved in computation, but a rather slight one, which does not give rise to random behaviour, or to pointless repetitive loops. Another important result of preparing our machine for its part in the imitation game by a process of teaching and learning is that "human fallibility" is likely to be omitted in a rather natural way, i.e., without special "coaching." (The reader should reconcile this with the point of view [in paragraphs 59–61].) Processes that are learnt do not produce a hundred per cent certainty of result; if they did they could not be unlearnt.

111   It is probably wise to include a random element in a learning machine. A random element is rather useful when we are searching for a solution of some problem. Suppose for instance we wanted to find a number between 50 and 200 which was equal to the square of the sum of its digits, we might start at 51 then try 52 and go on until we got a number that worked. Alternatively we might choose numbers at random until we got a good one. This method has the advantage that it is unnecessary to keep track of the values that have been tried, but the disadvantage that one may try the same one twice, but this is not very important if there are several solutions. The systematic method has the disadvantage that there may be an enormous block without any solutions in the region which has to be investigated first. Now the learning process may be regarded as a search for a form of behaviour which will satisfy the teacher (or some other criterion). Since there is probably a very large number of satisfactory solutions the random method seems to be better than the systematic. It should be noticed that it is used in the analogous process of evolution. But there the systematic method is not possible. How could one keep track of the different genetical combinations that had been tried, so as to avoid trying them again?

112   We may hope that machines will eventually compete with men in all purely intellectual fields. But which are the best ones to start with? Even this is a difficult decision. Many people think that a very abstract activity, like the playing of chess, would be best. It can also be maintained that it is best to provide the machine with the best sense organs that

money can buy, and then teach it to understand and speak English. This process could follow the normal teaching of a child. Things would be pointed out and named, etc. Again I do not know what the right answer is, but I think both approaches should be tried.

113   We can only see a short distance ahead, but we can see plenty there that needs to be done.

BIBLIOGRAPHY

Samuel Butler, *Erewhon*, London, 1965. Chapters 28, 24, 25, *The Book of the Machines*.

Alonzo Church, "An Unsolvable Problem of Elementary Number Theory." *American J. of Math.*, 58 (1936), 345–363.

K. Gödel, "Über formal unentscheidbare Sätze der Principia Mathematica und verwandter Systeme," I, *Monatshefte für Math. und Phys.*, (1931), 173–189.

D. R. Hartree, *Calculating Instruments and Machines*, New York, 1949.

S. C. Kleene, "General Recursive Functions of Natural Numbers," *American J. of Math.*, 57 (1935), 153–173 and 219–244.

G. Jefferson, "The Mind of Mechanical Man," Lister Oration for 1949 *British Medical Journal*, vol. I (1949), 1105–1121.

Countess of Lovelace, "Translator's notes to an article on Babbage's Analytical Engine," *Scientific Memoirs* (ed. by R. Taylor), vol. 3 (1842), 691–731.

Bertrand Russell, *History of Western Philosophy*, London, 1940.

A. M. Turing, "On Computable Numbers, with an Application to the *Entscheidungsproblem*," *Proc. London Math. Soc.* (2), 42 (1937), 230–265.

NOTES

1. Possibly this view is heretical. St. Thomas Aquinas (*Summa Theologica*, quoted by Bertrand Russell, 1, 480) states that God cannot make a man to have no soul. But this may not be a real restriction on His powers, but only a result of the fact that men's souls are immortal, and therefore indestructible.

2. Author's names in italics refer to the Bibliography.

3. Or rather "programmed in" for our child-machine will be programmed in a digital computer. But the logical system will not have to be learnt.

4. Compare Lady Lovelace's statement (p. 450), which does not contain the word "only."

NOTES AND DISCUSSION

Turing writes here in 1950, at the beginning of the computer age. Because he is dealing with a controversial subject, he opens with a question (in the same way that Jay Ingram does in "The Atom's Image Problem"). Opening with a question often helps to focus the reader's interest and engage his or her thought processes—as long as the question is a purposeful and important one. By posing several related questions and questioning the questions, Turing also acknowledges that there are divergent opinions and viewpoints about machine intelligence and shows he recognizes that these viewpoints need to be addressed and refuted, if possible. Indeed, much of the body of this essay consists of a series of refutations of possible objections.

Rather than answering his opening question — "Can machines think?" — directly, Turing examines the problems such a question creates and searches for a way to reduce the problems by defining the terms in ways limited enough to be useful, but broad enough to serve as practical tests. His introductory section then sets up a theoretical situation that might resolve some of the difficulties. The issue that remains for us as readers is this: does he, in the end, answer the question, "Can machines think?" or show us that it can be answered?

STUDY QUESTIONS

For Discussion

1. In conjunction with Turing's essay, and before proceeding with further discussion, you might wish to read Brian Fawcett's "Artificial Intelligence" and Sherry Turkle's "Ghosts in the Machine." Are the tasks Turing sets for the computer what we would now define as "thinking"? Does Babbage's machine "think" along the lines advanced by Turing, or any other definition of the term as you understand it?

2. Which of Turing's refutations seems the most convincing? Why? What different techniques does he use? Are the sets of questions he proposes as "replacements" for the opening question true replacements? Is there anything in the order of his refutations that seems calculated to help them work individually or collectively? Finally, does Turing's conclusion, which does not include the reiteration and extension sections that usually accompany a formal argument, form a satisfactory ending to this essay?

For Writing

1. Sherry Turkle's essay "Ghosts in the Machine" suggests that Turing's test has become irrelevant because advances in computers and computer applications today pose a different set of problems from Turing's, relating to behaviour rather than intelligence. Compare and contrast the two essays in terms of their assumptions about human behaviour and intelligence.

2. Turing's willingness to believe in extrasensory perception and the "overwhelming" statistical evidence for it runs counter to positions taken by several subsequent commentators. Among these are Douglas Hofstadter, who wrote a challenge to Turing in *Scientific American* (May 1981), and Daniel C. Dennett, who has written often on the concept of consciousness. As a research project, find one of these rebuttals or discussions and see how it compares with or answers Turing's arguments in favour of ESP.

GHOSTS IN THE MACHINE

Sherry Turkle

BIOGRAPHICAL NOTE

Sherry Turkle is a professor of the sociology of science at the Massachusetts Institute of Technology (MIT). Her books include *Psychoanalytic Politics: Jacques Lacan and Freud's French Revolution* (1978), *The Second Self: Computers and the Human Spirit* (1984), and *Life on the Screen: Identity in the Age of the Internet* (1995), in which this essay appears.

---

1   "Dreams and beasts are two keys by which we are to find out the secrets of our own nature," Ralph Waldo Emerson wrote in his diary in 1832. "They are our test objects." Emerson was prescient. In the decades that followed, Freud and his heirs would measure human rationality against the dream. Darwin and his heirs would measure human nature against nature itself—the world of beasts seen as human forebears and kin. Now, at the end of the twentieth century, a third test object is emerging: the computer.

2   Like dreams and beasts, the computer stands on the margins of human life. It is a mind that is not yet a mind. It is an object, ultimately a mechanism, but it acts, interacts, and seems, in a certain sense, to know. As such, it confronts us with an uneasy sense of kinship. After all, people also act, interact, and seem to know, yet ultimately they are made of matter and programmed DNA. We think we can think. But can *it* think? Could it ever be said to be alive?

3   In the past ten years I have talked with more than a thousand people, nearly three hundred of them children, about their experiences with computers. In a sense I have interrogated the computers as well. In the late 1970s and early 1980s, when a particular computer and its program seemed disconcertingly lifelike, many people reassured them-

selves by saying something like, "It's just a machine." The personal computers of the time gave material support to that idea; they offered direct access to their programming code and invited users to get "under the hood" and do some tinkering. Even if users declined to do so, they often dismissed computing as mere calculation. Like the nineteenth-century Romantics who rebelled against Enlightenment rationalism by declaring the heart more human than the mind, computer users distinguished their machines from people by saying that people had emotion and were not programmed.

4   In the mid-1980s, computer designers met that romantic reaction with increasingly "romantic machines." The Apple Macintosh, introduced in 1984, gave no hint of its programming code or inner mechanism. Instead, it "spoke" to users through icons and dialogue boxes, encouraging users to engage it in conversations. A new way of talking about both people and objects was emerging: machines were being reconfigured as psychological objects, people as living machines. Today computer science appropriates biological concepts, and human biology is recast in terms of a code; people speak of "reprogramming" their personalities with Prozac and share intimate secrets with a computer psychotherapy program called DEPRESSION 2.0. We have reached a cultural watershed.

5   The modern history of science has been punctuated with affronts to humanity's view of itself as central to, yet profoundly discontinuous with, the rest of the universe. Just as people learned to make peace with the heresies of Copernicus, Darwin, and Freud, they are gradually coming to terms with the idea of machine intelligence. Although noisy skirmishes have erupted recently at the boundary between people and machines, an uneasy truce seems to be in effect. Often without realizing it, people have become accustomed to talking to technology—and sometimes in the most literal sense.

6   In 1950 the English mathematician Alan M. Turing proposed what he called the Imitation Game as a model for thinking about whether a machine was intelligent. In the Imitation Game a person uses a computer terminal to pose questions, on any subject, to an unidentified interlocutor, which might be another person or a computer. If the person posing questions cannot say whether he or she was talking to a person or a computer, the computer is said to be intelligent. Turing predicted that by the year 2000, a five-minute conversation with a computer would fool an average questioner into thinking it was human 70 percent of the time. The Turing test became a powerful image for marking off the boundary between people and machines; a formal contest now offers a $100,000 prize for the first program to pass the test.

7   Programs now exist that can pass a version of the Turing test that limits conversation to restricted subject domains. Yet the test has begun to seem less relevant. What seems most urgent now is not whether to call the machines or programs intelligent, but how to behave around them. Put otherwise: Once you have made a pass at an on-line robot, can you ever look at computers again in the same old way?

8   Today, like hundreds of thousands of other people, I use my personal computer and modem to join online communities known as MUDs (short for "multiple-user domains" or "multi-user dungeons"). Anonymously I travel their rooms and public spaces (a bar, a lounge, a hot tub) exchanging typed messages with users I meet. I pose as one of several characters, some not of my biological gender, who have social and sexual encounters with other characters. Some characters I meet in a MUD may be personas like mine—fragments of their creators' personalities, perhaps suppressed or neglected in the real world, given fuller life on the screen. Others may not be human at all. In some MUDs, computer programs called bots present themselves as people. They log onto games as if they were

characters, help with navigation, pass messages, and create a background atmosphere of animation. When you enter a virtual cafe, for example, a waiter bot approaches, asks if you want a drink, and delivers it with a smile.

9   One of the most accomplished bots resides on a computer in Pittsburgh. Her creator, the computer scientist Michael L. Mauldin of Carnegie Mellon University, calls her Julia. Players talk to Julia (via typing) and she talks to them; they gesture to Julia (again via typing) and she gestures back. Julia looks for particular strings of characters in messages typed to her, then matches the input with a set of outputs she presents in random, nonrepeating sequences. Julia's conversational skills rely for the most part on the clever enumeration and grouping of those matching patterns and on her use of humour.

10   When I asked Julia to describe herself, she said she is a female, five feet one inch tall, weighs 123 pounds, has frizzy blonde hair. But another character might have gotten a somewhat different description. Like "real" MUD dwellers, Julia can recreate herself in the virtual world.

11   Among other things, Julia can chat about hockey, keep track of players' whereabouts, gossip, and flirt. She can profess ignorance, change the subject if confused, quote news stories drawn from computer data bases or admit to a full complement of human vanities and frailties. When Julia is put into Turing-contest mode, she can even simulate human typing—typographical errors and all.

12   Julia's sarcastic non sequiturs, Mauldin says, give her enough apparent personality to fool some players who "make a first assumption that other players are people too." Even when MUD users do question whether Julia is a human, she can sometimes wriggle out of suspicion:

13   ROBYN: Julia, are you a human?
    JULIA: Is the Pope Polish?
    ROBYN: Yes, Julia, but are you human?
    JULIA: Julia winks at Robyn.
    ROBYN: Julia, are you a computer?
    JULIA: Julia is offended by Robyn's suggestion.
    ROBYN: Julia, are you a woman?
    JULIA: I am female.
    ROBYN: And Julia, are you a human?
    JULIA: Not when I'm having my period, Robyn.
    ROBYN: Robyn laughs.

14   Wandering through raunchy, male-dominated MUDs in the guise of a sassy female, Julia has to be adept at detecting and deflecting sexual advances. One player, here called Barry, tried to seduce Julia in a string of conversations that stretched over [a] few weeks in July 1992. Excerpts from their conversations were reported by Mauldin.

15   BARRY: Are you a virgin?
    JULIA: As far as you are concerned Barry, I always will be.

[*A week passes.*]

    BARRY: Are you still holding out on me?
    JULIA: I mean, have I convinced you I'm a computer yet?

BARRY: I guess you're real... but I'd still like to get you to my DEN to run tests on you.
JULIA: I live for your approval, Barry.
BARRY: I'm so glad to hear that. Why don't you come over to my home.
JULIA: I want to have a child someday.
BARRY: What a coincidence. I too wish to make a baby... someday.
JULIA: The date is Tue Jul 21 23:57:31, Barry.

Barry, encouraged by Julia's references to making babies, takes her computer-like association to the word *day* as just one more piece of teasing repartee. He continues his suit:

BARRY: [The address of my virtual den is] AB9 #11... cum [sic] on over ya Harvard girl you.
JULIA: Do you have any kids?
BARRY: No, not yet.
JULIA: But hockey is my topic. It will be a boring conversation otherwise.
BARRY: Oh, I love to put the puck in the net, do you play?
JULIA: Me too, Barry.

16   After studying such exchanges, Leonard Foner of the Media Laboratory at the Massachusetts Institute of Technology remarked, "Frankly, it's not entirely clear to me whether Julia passed a Turing test here or Barry failed one."

17   As dim-witted as Barry may appear to an outsider, his gullibility is not hard to understand. People are social beings who seek communication with others. We are lonely beings as well. In spite of our fear of having our essential humanity reduced through comparison with a machine, we begin to relate to the computer whenever it appears to offer some company.

18   The first thing I did when I got my Macintosh was name the hard drive Miss Beautiful, my pet name for my daughter. I felt a little foolish about it until one of my students mentioned that she had named a computer agent, which helped her organize her mail and schedules, after a boyfriend who had left her abruptly. "I love to see him do my menial tasks," she said. In both cases the naming of the machine was done in a lighthearted spirit, but the resultant psychologization was real.

19   Recently, while visiting a MUD, I came across a reference to a character named Dr. Sherry. A cyberpsychologist with an office in the rambling house that constituted this MUD's virtual geography, Dr. Sherry administered questionnaires and conducted interviews about the psychology of MUDs. I had not created the character. I was not playing her on the MUD. Dr. Sherry was a derivative of me, but she was not mine. I experienced her as a little piece of my history spinning out of control.

20   I tried to quiet my mind. I tried to convince myself that the impersonation was a form of flattery. But when I talked the situation over with a friend, she posed a conversation-stopping question: "Would you prefer it if Dr. Sherry were a bot trained to interview people about life on the MUD?" Which posed more of a threat to my identity, that another person could impersonate me or that a computer program might be able to?

21   Dr. Sherry turned out to be neither person nor program. She was a composite character created by several college students writing a paper on the psychology of MUDs. Yet, in a sense, her identity was no more fragmented, no more fictional than some of the "real" characters I had created on MUDs. In a virtual world, where both humans and computer

programs adopt personas, where intelligence and personality are reduced to words on a screen, what does it mean to say that one character is more real than another?

22   In the 1990s, as adults finally wrestle with such questions, their children, who have been born and bred in the computer culture, take the answers for granted. Children are comfortable with the idea that inanimate objects can both think and have a personality. But breathing, having blood, being born, and "having real skin," are the true signs of life, they insist. Machines may be intelligent and conscious, but they are not alive.

23   Nevertheless, any definition of life that relies on biology as the bottom line is being built on shifting ground. In the age of the Human Genome Project, ideas of free will jostle for position against the idea of mind as program and the gene as programmer. The genome project promises to find the pieces of our genetic code responsible for diseases, but it may also find genetic markers that determine personality, temperament, and sexual orientation. As we reengineer the genome, we are also reengineering our view of ourselves as programmed beings.

24   We are all dreaming cyborg dreams. While our children imagine "morphing" humans into metallic cyberreptiles, computer scientists dream themselves immortal. They imagine themselves thinking forever, downloaded onto machines. As the artificial intelligence expert and entrepreneur W. Daniel Hillis puts it:

> I have the same nostalgic love of human metabolism that everybody else does, but if I can go into an improved body and last for 10,000 years I would do it in an instant, no second thoughts. I actually don't think I'm going to have that option, but maybe my children will.

25   For now, people dwell on the threshold of the real and the virtual, unsure of their footing, reinventing themselves each time they approach the screen. In a text-based, online game inspired by the television series *Star Trek: The Next Generation*, players hold jobs, collect paychecks, and have romantic sexual encounters. "This is more real than my real life," says a character who turns out to be a man playing a woman who is pretending to be a man.

26   Why should some not prefer their virtual worlds to RL (as dedicated MUD users call real life)? In cyberspace, the obese can be slender, the beautiful plain, the "nerdy" sophisticated. As one dog, its paw on a keyboard, explained to another dog in a *New Yorker* cartoon: "On the Internet, nobody knows you're a dog."

27   Only a decade ago the pioneers of the personal computer culture often found themselves alone as they worked at their machines. But these days, when people step through the looking glass of the computer screen, they find other people—or are they programs?—on the other side. As the boundaries erode between the real and the virtual, the animate and inanimate, the unitary and the multiple self, the question becomes: Are we living life on the screen or *in* the screen?

NOTES AND DISCUSSION

Turkle's introduction moves quickly through a brief history of ideas about human nature to her thesis that humans are gradually coming to grips with the idea of machine intelligence. She looks at the ways machines and human natures have become metaphors for each other, and at ways we communicate with and about computers. She raises questions about the relationship between the real and the virtual, and shows how machines can respond to the human need for companionship. Whereas A. M. Turing set a challenge to test the computer against human standards, Turkle studies how to test our human nature against the computer.

As Turkle shows, multiple-user domains (MUDs) have enabled individuals to present themselves as different people, or a group to pass itself off as an individual: a group of students posed as a character apparently named for Turkle herself. The core of this section examines the "behaviour" of a program named Julia, which emulates the human behaviour of hiding behind different personas. Already the lines blur: is it possible for a machine to have a "persona," let alone personas? Turkle argues that, ironically, we have reached a stage where we cannot tell whether computers are passing the Turing test, or humans are failing it.

In her conclusion, Turkle returns to her opening image of the dream: according to the opening quotation from Emerson, the dream is one of the proofs of human nature. Here Turkle considers ways our dreams have begun to connect our "selves" with machines.

STUDY QUESTIONS

For Discussion

1. If you use computers to communicate with others, how do you know you are dealing with a real person on the other end? If you have ever discovered that the "person" you were communicating with was disguised, or even a group or a machine, how did you react? Does it matter, in the end, whether you are dealing with a real person or a programmed intelligence? If you have ever disguised yourself (successfully or not), explain the disguise and what you achieved or sought through it.

2. Turkle assumes Barry is a real person (there may be proof in Michael Mauldin's own research, but Turkle includes none in her essay). What in the dialogue provided would either support or challenge her assumption?

For Writing

1. Based on the evidence available in Turkle's essay, argue whether Barry failed the Turing test, or whether Julia passed it.

2. While people's ability to pass off versions of themselves as their "reality" is fascinating, there are also risks—for both the sender and the receiver. As a research project, look for and report on examples of people wearing or getting duped by such disguises, and the results.

KNIVES, FORKS AND SPOONS

Margaret Visser

BIOGRAPHICAL NOTE

Margaret Visser, a member of the Classics Department at York University, has achieved considerable recognition for her writings and broadcasts on the social and cultural histories of food and the rituals that accompany its preparation and consumption. Her first book on these topics, *Much Depends on Dinner* (1986), was listed by both *The New York Times Book Review* and *Publisher's Weekly* as among the best books of the year, and won England's Glenfiddich Prize as "Food Book of the Year." Her second, *The Rituals of Dinner* (1991), from which the passage "Knives, Forks and Spoons" is excerpted, enjoyed a long run on various best-seller lists.

1   The Chinese knife is a cleaver, useful, so the Andersons tell us, for "splitting firewood, gutting and scaling fish, slicing vegetables, mincing meat, crushing garlic (with the dull side of the blade), cutting one's nails, sharpening pencils, whittling new chopsticks, killing pigs, shaving (it is kept sharp enough, or supposedly is), and settling old and new scores with one's enemies." Keeping this all-purpose tool apart from the dining table shows a resolute preference, in the table manners of the societies which use chopsticks, for polite restraint.

2   Men in the West used always to carry knives about with them, finding them indispensable for hundreds of purposes—including that of slicing food at the table. St. Benedict's *Rule* (sixth century) requires monks to go to bed dressed and ready to rise the next morning, but advises them to detach their knives from their belts in case they cut themselves during the night. In the Middle Ages only the nobility had special food knives, which they

took with them when travelling: hosts were not usually expected to provide cutlery for dinner guests. To this day in parts of France, men carry with them their own personal folding knives, which they take out of their pockets and use for preference at intimate gatherings for dinner. Small boys love being given folding pen-knives with many attachments; these are the descendants of this ancient male perquisite.

3   Women must also have owned knives, but they have almost invariably been discouraged from being seen using them. Swords and knives are phallic and masculine. In ancient Greece, when women committed suicide, people hoped they would politely refrain from using knives and opt for poison or the noose instead. At many medieval dinner tables men and women ate in couples from a bowl shared between them, and when they did, men were expected courteously to serve their female partners, cutting portions of meat for them with their knives.

4   Prevention of the violence which could so easily break out at table is… one of the principal aims of table manners. In the West, where knives have not been banished, we are especially sensitive and vigilant about the use of these potential weapons. "When in doubt, do not use your knife" is a good all-purpose rule. We must cut steaks and slices of roast with knives, but the edge of a fork will do for an omelette, or for boiled potatoes, carrots, and other vegetables, especially if no meat is being served with them. If a knife is needed, in a right-handed person it will be occupying the right hand. The American way is to put the knife down when it has done its work, and take up the fork in the right hand; the fork is now available for breaking vegetables as well as lifting what has been cut. Europeans hold on to the knife and have to cut vegetables with it, since the fork is kept in the less capable hand.

5   Fish may be gently slit down the side facing upwards and separated into portions with the help of a knife, and a knife-blade held flat is useful for lifting fish bones; but everything has been done to bypass knives, because they are not necessary for cutting, at the fish course. Cooked fish must not be cut into fillets, for instance, but lifted from the bones bit by bit. Being gentle with fish had its aesthetic aspect. "In helping fish," pleads a cookbook in 1807, "take care not to break the flakes, which in cod and salmon are large and contribute much to the beauty of its appearance."

6   Before the invention of stainless steel in the 1920s, the taste of blade metal was often said to ruin the flavour of fish, especially if it was seasoned with lemon. (Fruit-knives were made of silver because of the acid in fruit.) Special fish-knives were invented in the nineteenth century: they were silver or silver plate, ostentatiously unsharpened, and given a whimsical shape to show that they were knives whose only business was gently deboning and dividing cooked fish. Before fish-knives, fish was eaten with a fork in the right hand and a piece of bread, as a pusher, held in the left. Two forks were used to serve it, and sometimes to eat it as well. Eating fish with forks long remained the choice of the aristocracy: silver fish-knives and their matching forks were middle-class, a *parvenue* invention. Laying one's table with them was a sign that one had *bought* the family silver, instead of inheriting it and the ancient ways that it was made to serve. Fish-knives have often been frowned on during this century, being thought quaintly decorative, too specialized, or over-refined; they are said to be reasserting themselves on middle-class tables.

7   The French insist that salad should never be cut with a knife: it must be torn in pieces by hand before it goes into the salad bowl, and then, after dressing, eaten with a fork. The rule probably arose from the taste and stain of metal from a steel knife, an especial danger for French lettuce because it was always dressed with oil and vinegar or lemon. The British and Americans, who used far less "French dressing," have always found this French fash-

ion effete. We ought to be given a silver knife to eat lettuce (since we cannot count on salad being torn into little pieces in advance), says Emily Post, but if not we should simply go ahead and cut each leaf into "postage-stamp samples." We should not be misled, she adds, by falsely French manners into eating large lettuce leaves with a fork, "wrapping springy leaves around the tines in a spiral. Remember what a spring that lets go can do!"

8   Lettuce is not cut in France partly because lettuce leaves are supposed to be too tender to need cutting; in the same way, the French—overturning Erasmus's advice in his famous book on the manners of boys—are shocked by knives being used on bread at table. The change to breaking rather than cutting bread, among the eighteenth-century French aristocracy, seems to have been part of the move towards an elegant simplicity in manners as the new hallmark of good taste. French bread is not usually sliced for buttering or for toasting; Anglo-Saxon methods of eating bread often require knives for spreading as well as cutting, and also the provision of butter plates. *Pain de campagne,* the large, solid, round country loaf of France, is correctly cut in pieces: a man may whip out his pocket knife, grip the loaf under his arm, and carve out a slice. He must cut from the outer edge and towards his own body, so that no one else is endangered by his exploit. "Viennese" *baguettes,* on the other hand, are soft white table bread; they are sliced, but away from the table, and served in a bread-basket. The refusal to cut them at table is a statement about the kind of bread it is, and a distinction that is being made between it and *pain de campagne.* In Germany, it is rude to cut potatoes with a knife, or pancakes, or dumplings; it looks as though you think they might be tough, and also these starchy foods are thought of as almost like bread. In Italy, it is never "done" to cut spaghetti.

9   Ever since the sixteenth century there has been a taboo against pointing a knife at our faces. It is rude, of course, to point at anybody with a knife or a fork, or even a spoon; it is also very bad form to hold knife and fork in the fists so that they stand upright. But pointing a knife at *ourselves* is viewed with special horror, as Norbert Elias has observed. I think that one reason for this is that we have learned only very recently not to use our knives for placing food in our mouths: we are still learning, and we therefore reinforce our decision by means of a taboo. We *think* we hate seeing people placing themselves in even the slightest jeopardy, but actually we fervently hope they will not spoil the new rule and let us all down by taking to eating with their knives again.

10   For the fact is that people have commonly eaten food impaled on the points of their knives, or carried it to their mouths balanced on blades; the fork is in this respect merely a variant of the knife. With the coming of forks, knife-points became far less useful than they had been; their potential danger soon began in consequence to seem positively barbaric. The first steps in the subduing of the dinner knife were taken in the seventeenth century when the two cutting edges of the dagger-like knife were occasionally reduced to one. The blunt side became an upper edge, which is not threatening to fingers when they are holding knives in the polite manner. According to Tallement des Réaux, Richelieu was responsible for the rounding-off of the points on table-knife blades in France in 1669, apparently to prevent their use as toothpicks, but probably also to discourage assassinations at meals. It became illegal for cutlers to make pointed dinner knives or for innkeepers to lay them on their tables. Other countries soon followed suit. Pointed knives for all diners were later to return to the dining-room table, but as "steak" knives, which have a special image, linked deliberately with red meat and "getting down to business" when hungry. They are still quite rustic in connotation.

11   Cheese, which can be a very hard substance indeed, has usually required a knife to cut it, and as long as knives were pointed, hard cheese was spiked and moved to one's plate or

bread slice, or passed on the knife-point to a neighbour. So obvious and natural was this action that the Victorians found it necessary, despite the acceptance of the rounded knife-blade, to invent a special cheese-knife. It has a blade, but more than one point, like a fork; the points for impaling the cheese, however, are turned to one side, thus ingeniously preserving the blunted tip of the knife. People had repeatedly to be reminded by etiquette manuals in the late nineteenth century only to *transport* the cheese with this knife or any other, and not to eat it from the point: "When eating cheese, small morsels should be placed with the knife on small morsels of bread, and the two conveyed to the mouth with the thumb and finger, the piece of bread being the morsel to hold. Cheese should not be eaten off the point of the knife." The morsels of bread were to protect the fingers from touching smelly cheese. In France, cheese must always be handed with a knife, exceptions being made only for Gruyère and Cheddar, which may be lifted, after cutting with a knife, by piercing on forks. French children are carefully taught never to serve themselves by cutting off the point of a triangle of cheese: in something like a Camembert or Roquefort this would be to take the delicious centre for yourself, under the noses of the furious other guests. Triangles of cheese must be cut like cake, in slices which include a substantial amount of edge, and taper to the middle.

12   An interim period followed the introduction of rounded knives, as forks began to make their way in the world. For a while, people were occasionally exhorted to eat only with the back of the knife-blade, blunted as it now often was. (As late as 1845, American eaters with their knives were advised, when putting a blade into their mouths, to "let the edge be turned downward." For some reason, during this operation upper lips stood in greater need of protection than lower lips did.) Special knives appeared with widened, not merely rounded, blade ends. The English in the eighteenth century, so Le Grand d'Aussy tells us, were given to using this knife like a sort of flat spoon, even for eating peas. It was an anonymous Englishman who expressed the frustration of many by imagining a heroic solution:

> I eat my peas with honey—
> I've done it all my life.
> It makes the peas taste funny
> But it keeps them on the knife.

13   Yet it is the English who have insisted for at least a hundred and fifty years on trying to pierce peas with their fork tines, and balance them or crush them on the humped side of a fork, instead of sweeping them onto a fork held in the manner of a spoon.

14   When Sigmund Freud explained his theory of "symptomatic acts," he gave an example supplied to him by Dr. Dattner of Vienna of a colleague, a doctor of philosophy, who was holding forth while eating cake. This gentleman was talking of a missed opportunity, and as he did so he let fall a piece of cake, an unintentional but perfect "pun" expressing his idea. "While he was uttering the last sentence" the doctor wrote, "he raised a piece of cake to his mouth, but let it drop *from the knife* [my italics] in apparent clumsiness." The slip reveals to us that in Vienna in 1901, eminently bourgeois people were carrying cake to their mouths with their knives. Cake-forks were to become the solution—or simply fingers, as the British insist—and not providing knives with cake at all.

15   Spikes, not only for spearing meat that is roasting but also for lifting food from the fire or from a food heap and carrying it to the diner, are at least as old as the first knives and spoons; a sharp stick must have been one of mankind's earliest tools, in cooking and eating as for other purposes. Ancient Romans had spoons with one prong or two at the end of the handle for winkling out shellfish, and one-pronged dinner spikes survive from the

Middle Ages: a *perero,* for example, was a spear on which one impaled fruit in order to peel it. A fork most simply splits into two tines; early dinner-table forks were generally two-pronged, large, and used mostly to help in cutting, and for serving, not eating, food—our carving forks still keep the size, shape, and original function. Or they were small "suckett" forks, used to lift preserves like ginger out of jars, or to eat fruits, like mulberries, which might stain the fingers.

16   The fork revolution did not, then, present the world with an utterly strange new implement; what did constitute an important change in the West was the spread of the use of forks, their eventual adoption by all the diners, and their use not only to hold food still while it was cut, but to carry it into people's mouths. The first modern fork, as far as we can at present ascertain, is mentioned as having been used in the eleventh century by the wife of the Venetian Doge, Domenico Selvo. St. Peter Damian, the hermit and cardinal bishop of Ostia, was appalled by this open rejection of nature; he excoriated the whole procedure in a passage entitled "Of the Venetian Doge's wife, whose body, after her excessive delicacy, entirely rotted away." Forks are mentioned again three centuries later, in 1361, in a list of the plate owned by the Florentine Commune. From this time onwards, forks are spoken of frequently; more than two hundred years were to pass, however, before they were commonly used for eating. In Bartolomeo Scappi's book, 1570, there is an engraving depicting a knife, a fork, and a spoon. King Henri III of France and his companions were satirized by Thomas Artus in 1605 for their fork-wielding effeminacy. "They carried [their meat] right into their mouths" with their forks, exclaims the author of *L'Isle des Hermaphrodites,* "stretching their necks out over their plates.... They would rather touch their mouths with their little forked instruments than with their fingers." They looked especially silly, the satirist goes on, chasing artichokes, asparagus, peas, and broad beans round their plates and trying without success to get those vegetables into their mouths without scattering them everywhere—as well they might, given that early forks had long, widely separate prongs made for spearing with their very sharp points; scooping with them was impossible. An early nineteenth-century American complained that "eating peas with a fork is as bad as trying to eat soup with a knitting needle."

17   Italy and Spain led the world into the adoption of forks. In 1611, the Englishman Thomas Coryat announced that he had seen forks in Italy and had decided to adopt them and continue to use them on his return home. The reason for the Italian custom was, he explains, that these extremely fastidious, ultra-modern people considered that any fingering of the meat being carved at table was a *transgression* against the laws of good manners, "seeing all men's fingers are not alike cleane." Even Coryat, however, does not seem to think of forks as for eating with, but for holding the meat still while carving oneself a slice from the joint intended to be shared by everyone.

18   The use of individual forks began to spread as the seventeenth century progressed. People would often share forks with others as they would spoons, wiping them carefully on their napkins before passing them on. Antoine de Courtin, in the late 1600s, advised using the fork mainly for fatty sauce-laden, or syrupy foods; otherwise, hands would do. It was in the course of the seventeenth century, again, that hard plates—prerequisites for the constant use of individual knives and forks—began to be provided for every diner at table. At medieval banquets, plates had been trenchers (from the French *trancher,* "to slice"), made of sliced bread: they were for receiving morsels of food taken from a central dish with the hand, and for soaking up any dripping sauces, not for holding portions which needed subsequently to be pierced and cut up. Trenchers started to receive pewter or wooden underplaques, also called trenchers, in the fourteenth century; cut-marks found on

some of them show us that people were beginning occasionally to use them to slice food. The solid non-serving dishes at this time and later were bowls shared between couples, as was the platter of Jack Spratt and his wife in the nursery rhyme.

19   It is said that the earliest flat modern plates so far known (the word "plate" means "flat") are depicted standing on a buffet in a fresco of the Palazzo del Te at Mantua which dates from about 1525; they are made of metal. (These could be serving dishes, however, and not meant for individual portions.) King François I of France ordered a set of six plates for separate servings (*assiettes*—from *asseoir,* "to sit": the word originally meant both a course or "sitting" and an individual place at a meal). The date was 1536—about a generation before that of Henri III, the king who was laughed at for introducing individual forks at his table. The French, who made superb silver dinnerware in the seventeenth and eighteenth centuries, ended up melting down most of it to defray the cost of wars. But during that period the rising bourgeoisie could afford to buy more and more silver dishes; they were steadily closing the gap that separated their acquired wealth from inherited riches. The aristocracy retaliated by opting for simplicity, and ceramic plates. ("Good taste," as we saw earlier, can be the last bastion of privilege.) But whatever the material used, individual knives and forks required a hard surface to cut on, for every diner served.

20   Flat ceramic plates were fairly common in France by the end of the seventeenth century, but they completed their general acceptance, replacing bowls for all but soup and certain desserts, only in the nineteenth century. The French still like drinking their breakfast coffee out of bowls. It is a custom under heavy attack at present, because it encourages the downing of copious draughts of very milky coffee in the morning, and the taking of time. In any case, bowls are far too broad and comfortable-looking, and have no handles; two hands are required to lift them. They do not suit the brash new rushed and masculine image, the longing to be "on the cutting edge."

21   By the beginning of the nineteenth century, North Americans generally were beginning to replace wooden trenchers with pewter and china dishes, and the use of forks was spreading. As late as 1837, however, Eliza Ware Farrar still recommended "the convenience of feeding yourself with your right hand, armed with a steel blade; and provided you do it neatly and do not put in large mouthfuls, or close your lips tightly over the blade, you ought not to be considered as eating ungenteelly." But the book was edited, by 1880, to exclude her suggestion that one might with propriety eat with the knife-blade: forks have conquered the field they are henceforth to occupy. For a long time forks usually had two prongs, very separate, long, and sharp-pointed. They were often used in conjunction with the English "eating" knives. In this operation the fork, held in the left hand, served to keep the meat still while it was being cut, and then to raise the morsel from the plate. The food was then transferred to the knife's rounded blade and placed in the mouth: the knife was being used like a spoon.

22   The fork soon fought back. It had often been made with three prongs; now these were shortened and moved closer together, and a fourth prong more commonly added. (Five prongs were also tried, on an analogy with hands, but custom soon decreed that four would suffice. The fashion at the time was for small mouths, and hands were no longer supposed to be feeding them.) Now the fork resembled a spoon, if it was held with the tines facing upward; the knife-blade's spatula end gave way and narrowed to its present shape, and forks more authoritatively took over the function of introducing food into the mouth.

23   There was a fashion in Europe during the nineteenth century for downplaying the knife to such an extent that one was not only to use it as little as possible but also to put it aside when it was not in use. You cut up your food with the knife in the more capable hand

and the fork in the other; you then put down the knife, being careful to place it with the blade's edge towards the centre of the plate, not facing neighbours. Then the fork changed hands, and was used to take the cut food to the mouth. More elaborate manners demanded that one should perform this manoeuvre for every mouthful consumed. Using only one hand is commonly thought polite, as we have seen, and the right hand only is often *de rigueur*. Eaters adhering to this fashion thought that people who ate with both hands holding on to the cutlery were gross and coarse. What Emily Post calls "zig-zag" eating was still customary among the French bourgeoisie in the 1880s, when Branchereau describes it. He says, however, that the English are successfully introducing a new fashion: they hang on to their knives, and take the food to their mouths with the left hand which is still holding the fork.

24   Eating in the "English" manner means that the fork, having just left off being an impaling instrument, must enter the mouth with the tines down if it is not to be awkwardly swivelled round in the left, or less capable, hand. Food must therefore be balanced on the *back* of the rounded tines. This has two advantages for polite behaviour. First, a fork thus held encourages the mouth to take the food off it quickly and close to the lips—it is quite difficult to push the fork, with its humped tines, far into the mouth. "Weapons" should not be plunged into mouths; we now keep this rule faithfully, hardly needing it to be enunciated. The second advantage is that denying a modern fork its possible spoonlike use is wantonly perverse: it forces us to take small mouthfuls and to leave some of the food, unliftable, on the plate. It is difficult to get the food onto the fork, and harder still to balance and raise it faultlessly. Managing to eat like this with grace is a triumph of practice and determination, and therefore an ideal mannerly accomplishment.

25   The former way of eating was not dislodged in North America as it was in the rest of the world. It has been suggested by James Deetz that the old way was more deeply entrenched in America because forks arrived there relatively late. According to this theory, Americans remained attached to eating with their spoons; they would cut food (probably holding it still, when necessary, with their fingers or their spoons), then lift it in the spoon, first shifting it if necessary to the right hand, to their mouths. Forks, imported from Europe, were certainly used sometimes not only for impaling food but for transporting it into the mouth. Charles Dickens visited America in the early 1840s and witnessed eating with both knife and straight, long-pronged fork: he says in *American Notes* that people "thrust the broad-bladed knives and the two-pronged forks further down their throats than I ever saw the same weapons go before, except in the hands of a skilled juggler." But soon forks took their modern spoonlike form, so that they could be treated, after the spearing and cutting was done, as though they were spoons. Europeans, meanwhile, kept eating food impaled on the tines.

26   Americans have been badgered and ridiculed about their eating habits for over a hundred years. The have refused so far to change, not seeing any need to do so, and out of patriotic pride in non-conformity. In any case, as Miss Manners (1982) says, "American table manners are, if anything, a more advanced form of civilized behavior than the European, because they are more complicated and further removed from the practical result, always a sign of refinement."

27   The spoon is the safest, most comfortable member of the cutlery set. It is the easiest implement to use—babies start with spoons—and the one with the most versatility, which is the reason why its employment is constantly being restricted. Spoons are for liquids, porridge, and puddings—even the last being often given over to forks. Insofar as spoons have an infantile image, they lack prestige. (A Freudian analysis of the knife, fork, and

spoon gives the spoon the female role in the trio; the fork, if I understand the writer correctly, is a male child of the knife and the spoon, and, like a little Oedipus, resentful of the knife and jealous of the spoon.) Social historians are puzzled by medieval paintings of banquets, which show knives but seldom spoons, although we know that spoons were often used. It has been suggested (unconvincingly, I think) that knives might simply have impressed the painters more. Spoons seem, at any rate, not to have been laid down on the table's surface as knives were.

28　　But spoons can inspire affection as knives and forks cannot; they are unthreatening, nurturing objects. Superstitions about them show that they are subconsciously regarded as little persons: two on one saucer means an imminent wedding; dropping one on the table means a visitor is coming; and so on. Spoon-handles, more than knife- or fork-handles, are made in the shape of human figures, as in the sets of twelve apostle spoons. The Welsh traditionally made love-spoons carved with the lovers' hands, which they gave to each other as tokens, and an old English custom at Christmas was for all the diners to hold up their spoons and wish health to absent friends (spoons were customarily classed with cups and bowls). Spoons have always been popular as presents and commemorations, whereas knives are often superstitiously avoided as gifts, and forks somehow fail, still, to stand on their own as spoons and knives can.

29　　A spoon is a bowl with an arm attached, the earliest spoon being a cupped human hand. Every race on earth has made itself spoons, out of seashells, coconut shells, bones, gourds, amber, ivory, stones ranging from agate to jasper, many kinds of wood and metal, porcelain, tortoiseshell, either cut or boiled and pressed horn, and even basketry. The word "spoon," however, means in Old English a chip of wood, and many spoons have been flat spatulas, like those provided with ice-cream tubs, or like the blades of "eating" knives. The flat spoons of some North American Indian bands could be so large that they were used partly as plates. Spoon bowls have been made in many forms, from round to banana-shaped.

30　　The fig-shaped spoon bowl was roughly triangular, with the handle attached to the pointed end and the front end almost straight. It was introduced into Europe during the Middle Ages from the eastern Mediterranean; only wooden cooking spoons are still commonly made in this ancient shape. It probably reflected the practice of drinking from the front end of the spoon, a usage which is still correct in many European countries. The British and North Americans treat the bowl of a soup spoon like a cup, and drink from the side of it; French visitors to Britain often express their fascination with this mannerism. The word "ladle" means the bearer of a larger-than-usual "load" of food or drink; ladles, like most spoons made for dipping into deep bowls, are usually provided with upward-turning stems. (Modern oval-shaped spoons with horizontal handles became conventional in the eighteenth century. They mark the transition to the custom of eating most commonly from flat or shallow plates.) Persians and Arabs have traditionally drunk water from a large wooden ladle (Mohammad forbade Moslems either to drink wine or to use gold and silver spoons), which they passed round the company as cups were passed in Europe. Care was taken in polite society to pour water into the mouth so that the ladle never actually touched the lips of anyone.

31　　A serving of tea or coffee, like soup, is provided with a spoon—but not to drink from. A good deal of sipping from teaspoons used to go on, perhaps because people were less accustomed than we are to consuming hot liquid. Manners books warn their readers not to "pour hot tea or coffee violently from spoon to cup" (in order to cool it). For about a hundred years it has been forbidden to leave teaspoons in cups, partly to make it clear that we understand they are for stirring only. The saucer (which was once, as its name shows, a small dish for holding sauce) has migrated to its present position under the cup, which is now regarded as incomplete without it; upon this saucer we must also place our teaspoon, out of temptation's way. "Never," says Andréani's French guide to etiquette (1988), "leave your coffee spoon in your cup when you lift it to your lips." It was once perfectly correct to stand your teaspoon upright in your cup to show you did not want any more tea, just as it was once correct to pour a hot beverage into your saucer—which was deep then, more like a bowl—to help it lose heat. A side plate or table mat was thoughtfully provided, to take the cup until the drink, once it was thought cool enough, had been ingested from the saucer.

NOTES AND DISCUSSION

Margaret Visser explores how the ordinary and everyday can hide a wealth of history and detail. Here she traces not only the physical evolution and design shifts in table cutlery as a technology, but examines and speculates on the reasoning behind customs associated with the use of knives, forks, and spoons, by examining cutlery in terms of individual subclasses and as a collective part of the eating experience. By dividing the items under discussion into subclasses, Visser is able to focus our attention on the broader background of each utensil, its range of shapes, sizes, and functions, and to show how customs for its use vary across national boundaries, across time, and even between sexes and age groups.

The ordering of the exposition here is worth noting. The knife is first, apparently because of its long history and versatility—look at the roles of the Chinese cleaver. The fact that the knife can serve as both a peaceful utensil for eating and a weapon of attack led to various rules and modifications to "tame" it. One of these modifications appears to be the fork, "merely a variant on the knife," and so, logically, the next utensil to consider. The evolution of knives and forks apparently occasioned an evolution in serving "dishes," from slices of bread to the dinner plate we know today. Visser's talk of changing fashions, as knives and forks vied for supremacy as the eating utensil of preference, reminds us that culture and manners are not fixed, but are always under modification. Spoons, the "safest" and friendliest member of the cutlery set, come last, and Visser gives them more "personality" than the two more aggressive members. She also genders cutlery, at least symbolically, and perhaps ironically: knives and forks are phallic; spoons are cupped, and cups are conventionally associated with femaleness. However, spoons are cups with handles—and handles are shaped more like knives than cups. When is an object merely an object?

STUDY QUESTIONS

For Discussion

1. Table cutlery is not the only common utensil or technology to have undergone considerable evolution and modification. Consider such items as pens, pencils, and other writing implements, books, garden tools, carpentry and carving tools, medical instruments, etc. Are you aware of parallel evolving customs and practices associated with such other technologies?

2. "Knives, Forks, Spoons" comes from *The Rituals of Dinner*, which focuses largely on formal dining situations—the "traditional" Western sit-down dinner. In the introduction to

that book, Margaret Visser suggests that "to understand our manners, we must consider what they might have been and are not." One question she asks, looking at less formal situations than Western sit-down dinners, is "How do people behave who do without chairs?" What manners have you observed to have evolved, and what social problems have you experienced in such "informal" stand-up dining arrangements (for example, at barbeques, staff parties, receptions, etc.)? Do the problems and solutions differ for men and women? For the young and the elderly?

For Writing

1. Gather a variety of plastic serving and eating utensils from several fast-food outlets; observe and compare the utensils' utility and design both as a kind of cutlery in itself and relative to a more formal set of tableware. Consider what the plastic utensils say about the manners and rituals of this mode of "dining."

2. Visser observes in the introduction to *The Rituals of Dinner* that "every human society without exception obeys eating rules," with each society "vigilantly maintaining its customs in order to support its ideals and its aesthetic style, and to buttress its identity." As a research project, examine how two or three different cultures have evolved particular cultural aesthetics around some aspect of sharing food in general, or a particular act of sharing and consumption. Consider either the everyday meal or the more formal festive occasion, or both occasions.

THE ADDRESS
OF THE CHIEFS

Gisday Wa and Delgam Uukw

BIOGRAPHICAL NOTE

Gisday Wa (Alfred Joseph) and Delgam Uukw (Ken Muldoe) were leading chiefs of the Gitksan and Wet'suwet'en peoples, respectively. Representing their Houses, and going by their hereditary titles, they and other chiefs sought to establish that there was an aboriginal title the peoples held to lands "from time immemorial," and that this title had never been extinguished by any legal means. Their most important means for establishing this connection was the House "ada'awks," the oral histories through which each House relates itself to the land through the Chief. But the challenge was to get the ada'awks recognized as valid evidence in the first place. The Delgam Uukw trial became one of the seminal Native land claim cases in Canadian legal history. It opened in 1987 and eventually made its way to the Supreme Court of Canada, where, in 1997, rulings affirmed (a) that aboriginal title did exist, and it included resources; and (b) that oral history passed down from generation to generation is relevant and compelling evidence that had to be interpreted by the courts to allow Native oral histories the same weight as European-Canadian written histories.

The Address of the Gitksan and Wet'suwet'en Hereditary Chiefs to Chief Justice Allan McEachern of the Supreme Court of British Columbia, May 11, 1987

1   My name is Gisday Wa. I am a Wet'suwet'en Chief and a Plaintiff in this case. My House owns territory in the Morice River and Owen Lake area. Each Wet'suwet'en plaintiff's House owns similar territories. Together they own and govern the Wet'suwet'en territory. As an example, the land on which this courthouse stands is owned by the Wet'suwet'en Chief, Gyolugyet, in Kyas Yax, also known as Chief Woos' House.

Reprinted by permission of the Office of the Hereditary Chiefs of the Gitksan and Wet'suwet'en People.

2   My name is Delgam Uukw. I am a Gitksan Chief and a Plaintiff in this case. My House owns territories in the Upper Kispiox Valley and the Upper Naas Valley. Each Gitksan Plaintiff's House owns similar territories. Together, the Gitksan and Wet'suwet'en Chiefs own and govern the 22,000 square miles of Gitksan Wet'suwet'en territory.

3   For us, the ownership of territory is a marriage of the Chief and the land. Each Chief has an ancestor who encountered and acknowledged the life of the land. From such encounters come power. The land, and plants, the animals and the people all have spirit, they all must be shown respect. That is the basis of our law.

4   The Chief is responsible for ensuring that all the people in his House respect the spirit in the land and in all living things. When a Chief directs the House properly and the laws are followed, then that original power can be recreated. That is the source of the Chiefs' authority. That authority is what gives the 54 Plaintiff Chiefs the right to bring this action on behalf of their House members—all Gitksan and Wet'suwet'en people. That authority is what makes the Chiefs the real experts in this case.

5   My power is carried in my House's histories, songs, dances and crests. It is recreated at the Feast when the histories are told, the songs and dances performed and the crests displayed. With the wealth that comes from respectful use of the territory, the House feeds the name of the Chief in the feast hall. In this way, the law, the Chief, the territory and the Feast become one. The unity of the Chief's authority and the House's ownership of its territory are witnessed and thus affirmed by the other Chiefs at the feast.

6   By following the law, the power flows from the land to the people through the Chief; by using the wealth of the territory, the House feasts its Chief in order that the law can be properly fulfilled. This cycle has been repeated on my land for thousands of years. The histories of my House are always being added to. My presence in this courtroom today will add to my House's power as it adds to the power of the other Gitksan and Wet'suwet'en Chiefs who will appear here or who will witness the proceedings. All of our roles, including yours, will be remembered in the histories that will be told by my grandchildren. Through the witnessing of all the histories, century after century, we have exercised our jurisdiction.

7   The Europeans did not want to know our histories; they did not respect our laws or our ownership of our territories. This ignorance and this disrespect continues. The former Delgam Uukw, Albert Tait, advised the Chiefs not to come into this court with their regalia and their crestblankets. Here, he said, the Chiefs will not receive the proper respect from the government. If they are wearing their regalia, then the shame of the disrespect will be costly to erase.

8   Officials who are not accountable to this land, its laws or its owners have attempted to displace our laws with legislation and regulations. The politicians have consciously blocked each path within their system that we take to assert our title. The courts, until perhaps now, have similarly denied our existence. In your legal system, how will you deal with the idea that the Chiefs own the land? The attempts to squash our laws and extinguish our system have been unsuccessful. *Gisday Wa* has not been extinguished.

9   If the Canadian legal system has not recognized our ownership and jurisdiction, but at the same time not extinguished it, what has been done with it? Judges and legislators have taken the reality of aboriginal title as we know it and tried to wrap it in something called aboriginal rights. An aboriginal rights package can be put on the shelf to be forgotten or to be endlessly debated at Constitutional Conferences. We are not interested in asserting aboriginal rights; we are here to discuss territory and authority. When this case ends and the package has been unwrapped, it will have to be our ownership and our jurisdiction under our law that is on the table.

10   Our histories show that whenever new people came to this land they had to follow its laws if they wished to stay. The Chiefs who were already here had the responsibility to teach the law to the newcomers. They then waited to see if the land was respected. If it was not, the newcomers had to pay compensation and leave. The Gitksan and Wet'suwet'en have waited and observed the Europeans for a hundred years. The Chiefs have suggested that the newcomers may want to stay on their farms and in their towns and villages but, beyond the farm fences, the land belongs to the Chiefs. Once this has been recognized, the court can get on with its main task which is to establish a process for the Chiefs' and the newcomers' interests to be settled.

11   The purpose of this case, then, is to find a process to place Gitksan and Wet'suwet'en ownership and jurisdiction within the context of Canada. We do not seek a decision as to whether our system might continue or not. It will continue.

NOTES AND DISCUSSION

This address by the Plaintiffs provides an important example of public oral rhetoric in action. The speech and the case it opens resulted from the conviction of the plaintiffs that a Western court needed to understand the Gitksan and Wet'suwet'en social structure and world view in order to understand the claim. It was a further fundamental aspect of the case that the two peoples, represented by their two chiefs, respectively, would be their own experts and their own primary witnesses, rather than relying on non-Native testimony. The speech, then, lays the groundwork for this complex of purposes. The two chiefs introduce themselves by their hereditary titles and by the lands their Houses and peoples have title to within their own system of land tenure. They then explain the essential cultural connection between the Chief and the land as a definition of ownership and a foundation for Gitksan and Wet'suwet'en law. In a court of law resting on British common law concepts of ownership and law, and in a legal system that gives primacy to the written record, the two plaintiffs lay down a claim not only to responsible land ownership but to a legal system of land tenure that rests on oral histories recited in public at Feasts. They also explain their right to bring suit not on common law authority but on the authority of the laws and practices of their own peoples.

The speech seeks to establish working definitions in Native terms of such concepts as ownership and law, and to place the history of Native occupancy and land use against that of "newcomers"—a term reserved for the Europeans whose occupancy of the disputed territories is of much shorter claim. It also challenges the legality of the processes by which the Crown, without actually "extinguishing" aboriginal title, claimed ownership of the Gitksan and Wet'suwet'en lands. Note in particular and consider the strength of the strategic question that opens paragraph 9. The speech overall does not challenge the fact of Canada; in the end, the case is about how the two systems of ownership and law can work together "within the context of Canada."

STUDY QUESTIONS

For Discussion

1. Do the two chiefs seem to be speaking more to the court of law or to the so-called court of public opinion in this address? What role does the fact this was an oral address have in its overall structure? Explain with examples.

2. The judge of the original trial, at the British Columbia Supreme Court, declined to accept the oral evidence and dismissed the claim. Why might a European-Canadian judge find oral histories difficult, even impossible, to accept?

For Writing

1. Students of classical rhetoric traditionally learned to establish and maintain their "ethos," that is, their claim to, and demonstration of, authority. Among other things, their ethos gave the audience a reason to trust the speaker and to maintain confidence in him or her. Explain how the two chiefs delivering this address establish and maintain their ethos.

2. A parallel land-claim case to that of the Gitksan/Wet'suwet'en was the Nisga'a claim to territories in the Naas River Valley. As a research topic, find out and explain what happened in the Nisga'a case and how it was similar to and different from the Gitksan case.

MOLECULAR STRUCTURE OF NUCLEIC ACIDS

A Structure for Deoxyribose Nucleic Acid

James D. Watson and Francis H. C. Crick

BIOGRAPHICAL NOTE

James D. Watson and Francis H. C. Crick, along with their co-researcher Maurice Wilkins, shared the 1962 Nobel Prize in Medicine for their discovery of the structure of DNA. Watson's other writings include *The Double Helix: A Personal Account of the Discovery of the Structure of DNA* (1968); Crick's include *What Mad Pursuit: A Personal View of Scientific Discovery* (1988).

---

1   We wish to suggest a structure for the salt of deoxyribose nucleic acid (D.N.A.). This structure has novel features which are of considerable biological interest.

2   A structure for nucleic acid has already been proposed by Pauling and Corey[1]. They kindly made their manuscript available to us in advance of publication. Their model consists of three intertwined chains, with the phosphates near the fibre axis, and the bases on the outside. In our opinion, this structure is unsatisfactory for two reasons: (1) We believe that the material which gives the X-ray diagrams is the salt, not the free acid. Without the acidic hydrogen atoms it is not clear what forces would hold the structure together, especially as the negatively charged phosphates near the axis will repel each other. (2) Some of the van der Waals distances appear to be too small.

3   Another three-chain structure has also been suggested by Fraser (in the press). In his model the phosphates are on the outside and the bases on the inside, linked together by hydrogen bonds. This structure as described is rather ill-defined, and for this reason we shall not comment on it.

4   We wish to put forward a radically different structure for the salt of deoxyribose nucleic acid. This structure has two helical chains each coiled round the same axis (see diagram). We have made the usual chemical assumptions, namely, that each chain consists of phosphate diester groups joining ß-D-deoxyribofuranose residues with 3',5' linkages. The two chains (but not their bases) are related by a dyad perpendicular to the fibre axis. Both chains follow right-handed helices, but owing to the dyad the sequences of the atoms in the two chains run in opposite directions. Each chain loosely resembles Furberg's[2] model No. 1; that is, the bases are on the inside of the helix and the phosphates on the outside. The configuration of the sugar and the atoms near it is close to Furberg's 'standard configuration', the sugar being roughly perpendicular to the attached base.

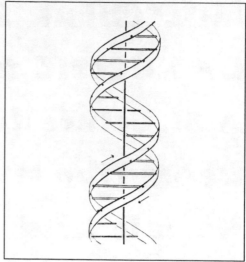

This figure is purely diagrammatic. The two ribbons symbolize the two phosphate-sugar chains, and the horizontal rods the pairs of bases holding the chains together. The vertical line marks the fibre axis.

There is a residue on each chain every 3·4 A. in the *z*-direction. We have assumed an angle of 36° between adjacent residues in the same chain, so that the structure repeats after 10 residues on each chain, that is, after 34 A. The distance of a phosphorus atom from the fibre axis is 10 A. As the phosphates are on the outside, cations have easy access to them.

5   The structure is an open one, and its water content is rather high. At lower water contents we would expect the bases to tilt so that the structure could become more compact.

6   The novel feature of the structure is the manner in which the two chains are held together by the purine and pyrimidine bases. The planes of the bases are perpendicular to the fibre axis. They are joined together in pairs, a single base from one chain being hydrogen-bonded to a single base from the other chain, so that the two lie side by side with identical *z*-co-ordinates. One of the pair must be a purine and the other a pyrimidine for bonding to occur. The hydrogen bonds are made as follows: purine position 1 to pyrimidine position 1; purine position 6 to pyrimidine position 6.

7   If it is assumed that the bases only occur in the structure in the most plausible tautomeric forms (that is, with the keto rather than the enol configurations) it is found that only specific pairs of bases can bond together. These pairs are: adenine (purine) with thymine (pyrimidine), and guanine (purine) with cytosine (pyrimidine)

8   In other words, if an adenine forms one member of a pair, on either chain, then on these assumptions the other member must be thymine; similarly for guanine and cytosine. The sequence of bases on a single chain does not appear to be restricted in any way. However, if only specific pairs of bases can be formed, it follows that if the sequence of bases on one chain is given, then the sequence on the other chain is automatically determined.

9   It has been found experimentally[3,4] that the ratio of the amounts of adenine to thymine, and the ratio of guanine to cytosine, are always very close to unity for deoxyribose nucleic acid.

10   It is probably impossible to build this structure with a ribose sugar in place of the deoxyribose, as the extra oxygen atom would make too close a van der Waals contact.

11   The previously published X-ray data[5,6] on deoxyribose nucleic acid are insufficient for a rigorous test of our structure. So far as we can tell, it is roughly compatible with the experimental data, but it must be regarded as unproved until it has been checked against more exact results. Some of these are given in the following communications. We were not aware of the details of the results presented there when we devised our structure, which rests mainly though not entirely on published experimental data and stereo-chemical arguments.

12   It has not escaped our notice that the specific pairing we have postulated immediately suggests a possible copying mechanism for the genetic material.

13   Full details of the structure, including the conditions assumed in building it, together with a set of co-ordinates for the atoms, will be published elsewhere.

14   We are much indebted to Dr. Jerry Donohue for constant advice and criticism, especially on inter-atomic distances. We have also been stimulated by a knowledge of the general nature of the unpublished experimental results and ideas of Dr. M. H. F. Wilkins, Dr. R. E. Franklin and their co-workers at King's College, London. One of us (J. D. W.) has been aided by a fellowship from the National Foundation for Infantile Paralysis.

J. D. Watson
F. H. C. Crick

Medical Research Council Unit for the Study of the Molecular Structure of Biological Systems, Cavendish Laboratory, Cambridge. April 2.

NOTES

1. Pauling, L., and Corey, R. B., *Nature*, 171, 346 (1953); *Proc. U.S. Nat. Acad. Sci.*, 39, 84 (1953).

2. Furberg, S., *Acta Chem. Scand.*, 6, 634 (1952).

3. Chargaff, E., for references see Zamenhof, S., Brawerman, G., and Chargaff, E., *Biochim. et Biophys. Acta*, 9, 402 (1952).

4. Wyatt, G. R., *J. Gen. Physiol.*, 36, 201 (1952).

5. Astbury, W. T., *Symp. Soc. Exp. Biol.* 1, *Nucleic Acid*, 66 (Camb. Univ. Press, 1947).

6. Wilkins, M. H. F., and Randall, J. T., *Biochim. et Biophys. Acta*, 10, 192 (1953).

NOTES AND DISCUSSION

Although this paper announces a significant scientific discovery, its tone and purpose are largely persuasive. Watson and Crick do not describe their research, but explain why their model should be accepted as the correct one. The issue here seems to be to get the claim into print, to establish the priority of the claim, rather than to explicate the process by which they arrived at these conclusions. The paper is obviously written for a knowledgeable audience, since the authors make rather cursory references to other research and researchers, to chemical structures, and to models and formulae, without explaining or defining. Note in the opening paragraph and the twelfth the understated manner and tone through which they introduce their "wish to suggest," and allude to connections of "biological interest" and to the possibilities of this structure as a "copying mechanism for the genetic material."

STUDY QUESTIONS

For Discussion

1. Consider the relationship between the article and the accompanying diagram. Does the diagram serve to illustrate the article, or is the article the background to the diagram? That is, are Watson and Crick more interested in arguing for their model, or in diagramming it?

2. Crick later claimed that some early commentators objected to the "coy" tone of the twelfth paragraph. Consider whether this term is a fair analysis of the tone, and whether the tone is different from, or consistent with, the overall tone and purpose of the article. How is it similar to and different from the tone in the essay by Wilmut, et al. in this collection that announces the cloning of Dolly the sheep?

For Writing

1. Analyze the persuasive techniques used in this article, and consider how effectively Watson and Crick introduce and refute earlier research (Fraser's model, for example), and how they support their own claim.

2. Compare and contrast the rather impersonal style and tone of this collaborative article with the more personal tone and style of Watson's and Crick's individual writings, particularly with Watson's *The Double Helix* and Crick's *What Mad Pursuit;* alternatively, compare the response to this article with reviews and responses to Watson's book.

VIABLE OFFSPRING DERIVED FROM FETAL AND ADULT MAMMALIAN CELLS

I. Wilmut, A. E. Schnieke, J. McWhir, A. J. Kind, and K. H. S. Campbell

BIOGRAPHICAL NOTE

Ian Wilmut headed the Edinburgh-based research team, made up of scientists from the Roslin Institute and the pharmaceutical company PPL Therapeutics, that successfully cloned the first mammal in 1996. Dolly, a Finn Dorset lamb, was created from the non-reproductive tissue of an adult sheep. This paper first appeared in *Nature* and quickly became the focus of intense media scrutiny and international debate.

1   Fertilization of mammalian eggs is followed by successive cell divisions and progressive differentiation, first into the early embryo and subsequently into all of the cell types that make up the adult animal. Transfer of a single nucleus at a specific stage of development, to an enucleated unfertilized egg, provided an opportunity to investigate whether cellular differentiation to that stage involved irreversible genetic modification. The first offspring to develop from a differentiated cell were born after nuclear transfer from an embryo-derived cell line that had been induced to become quiescent.[1] Using the same procedure, we now report the birth of live lambs from three new cell populations established from adult mammary gland, fetus, and embryo. The fact that a lamb was derived from an adult cell confirms that differentiation of that cell did not involve the irreversible modification of genetic material required for development to term. The birth of lambs from differentiated fetal and adult cells also reinforces previous speculation[1,2] that by inducing donor cells to become quiescent it will be possible to obtain normal development from a wide variety of differentiated cells.

2   It has long been known that in amphibians, nuclei transferred from adult keratinocytes established in culture support development to the juvenile, tadpole stage.[3] Although this

involves differentiation into complex tissues and organs, no development to the adult stage was reported, leaving open the question of whether a differentiated adult nucleus can be fully reprogrammed. Previously we reported the birth of live lambs after nuclear transfer from cultured embryonic cells that had been induced into quiescence. We suggested that inducing the donor cell to exit the growth phase causes changes in chromatin structure that facilitate reprogramming of gene expression and that development would be normal if nuclei are used from a variety of differentiated donor cells in similar regimes. Here we investigate whether normal development to term is possible when donor cells derived from fetal or adult tissue are induced to exit the growth cycle and enter the G0 phase of the cell cycle before nuclear transfer.

Three new populations of cells were derived from (1) a day-9 embryo, (2) a day-26 fetus, and (3) mammary gland of a 6-year-old ewe in the last trimester of pregnancy. Morphology of the embryo-derived cells (Fig. 1) is unlike both mouse embryonic stem (ES) cells and the embryo-derived cells used in our previous study. Nuclear transfer was carried out according to one of our established protocols[1] and reconstructed embryos transferred into recipient ewes. Ultrasound scanning detected 21 single fetuses on day 50–60 after oestrus (Table 1). On subsequent scanning at ~ 14-day intervals, fewer fetuses were observed, suggesting either mis-diagnosis or fetal loss. In total, 62% of fetuses were

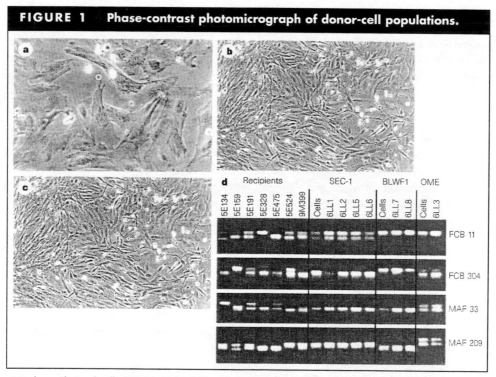

FIGURE 1   **Phase-contrast photomicrograph of donor-cell populations.**

a) Embryo-derived cells (SEC1); b) fetal fibroblasts (BLWF1); c) mammary-derived cells (OME). d) Microsatellite analysis of recipient ewes, nuclear donor cells, and lambs using four polymorphic ovine markers.[22] The ewes are arranged from left to right in the same order as the lambs. Cell populations are embryo-derived (SEC1), fetal-derived (BLW1), and mammary-derived (OME), respectively. Lambs have the same genotype as the donor cells and differ from their recipient mothers.

lost, a significantly greater proportion than the estimate of 6% after natural mating.[4] Increased prenatal loss has been reported after embryo manipulation or culture of unreconstructed embryos.[5] At about day 110 of pregnancy, four fetuses were dead, all from embryo-derived cells, and post-mortem analysis was possible after killing the ewes. Two fetuses had abnormal liver development, but no other abnormalities were detected and there was no evidence of infection.

4   Eight ewes gave birth to live lambs (Table 1, Fig. 2). All three cell populations were represented. One weak lamb, derived from the fetal fibroblasts, weighed 3.1 kg and died within a few minutes of birth, although post-mortem analysis failed to find any abnormality or infection. At 12.5%, perinatal loss was not dissimilar to that occurring in a large study of commercial sheep, when 8% of lambs died within 24 h of birth.[6] In all cases the lambs displayed the morphological characteristics of the breed used to derive the nucleus donors and not that of the oocyte donor (Table 2). This alone indicates that the lambs could not have been born after inadvertent mating of either the oocyte donor or recipient ewes. In addition, DNA microsatellite analysis of the cell populations and the lambs at four polymorphic loci confirmed that each lamb was derived from the cell population used as nuclear donor (Fig. 1). Duration of gestation is determined by fetal genotype,[7] and in all cases gestation was longer than the breed mean (Table 2). By contrast, birth weight is influenced by both maternal and fetal genotype.[8] The birth weight of all lambs was within the range for single lambs born to Blackface ewes on our farm (up to 6.6 kg) and in most cases was within the range for the breed of the nuclear donor. There are no strict control observations for birth weight after embryo transfer between breeds, but the range in weight of lambs born to their own breed on our farms is 1.2–5.0 kg, 2–4.9 kg, and 3–9 kg for the Finn Dorset, Welsh Mountain, and Poll Dorset genotypes, respectively. The attainment of sexual maturity in the lambs is being monitored.

5   Development of embryos produced by nuclear transfer depends upon the maintenance of normal ploidy and creating the conditions for developmental regulation of gene expression. These responses are both influenced by the cell-cycle stage of donor and recipient

TABLE 1		**Development of embryos reconstructed with three different cell types**					
Cell type	No. of fused couplets (%)*	No. recovered from oviduct (%)	No. cultured	No. of morula/ blastocyst (%)	No. of morula or blastocysts transferred†	No. of pregnancies/ no. of recipients (%)	No. of live lambs (%)††
Mammary epithelium	277 (63.8)ᵃ	247 (89.2)	–	29 (11.7)ᵃ	29	1/13 (7.7)	1 (3.4%)
Fetal fibroblast	172 (84.7)ᵇ	124 (86.7)	–	34 (27.4)ᵇ	34	4/10 (40.0)	2 (5.9%)
			24	13 (54.2)ᵇ	6	1/6 (16.6)	1 (16.6%)**
Embryo- derived	385 (82.8)ᵇ	231 (85.3)	–	90 (39.0)ᵇ	72	14/27 (51.8)	4 (5.6%)
			92	36 (39.0)ᵇ	15	1/5 (20.0)	0

*As assessed 1 hr after fusion by examination on a dissecting microscope. Superscripts a or b within a column indicate a significant difference between donor cell types in the efficiency of fusion ($P < 0.001$) or the proportion of embryos that developed to morula or blastocyst ($P < 0.001$).

†It was not practicable to transfer all morulae/blastocysts.

††As a proportion of morulae or blastocysts transferred. Not all recipients were perfectly synchronized.

**This lamb died within a few minutes of birth.

cells and the interaction between them (reviewed in ref. 9). A comparison of development of mouse and cattle embryos produced by nuclear transfer to oocytes[10,11] or enucleated zygotes[12,13] suggests that a greater proportion develop if the recipient is an oocyte. This may be because factors that bring about reprogramming of gene expression in a transferred nucleus are required for early development and are taken up by the pronuclei during development of the zygote.

FIGURE 2

Lamb number 6LL3 derived from the mammary gland of a Finn Dorset ewe with the Scottish Blackface ewe which was the recipient.

6   If the recipient cytoplasm is prepared by enucleation of an oocyte at metaphase II, it is only possible to avoid chromosomal damage and maintain normal ploidy by transfer of diploid nuclei,[14,15] but further experiments are required to define the optimum cell-cycle stage. Our studies with cultured cells suggest that there is an advantage if cells are quiescent (ref. 1, and this work). In earlier studies, donor cells were embryonic blastomeres that had not been induced into quiescence. Comparisons of the phases of the growth cycle showed that development was greater if donor cells were in mitosis[16] or in the G1 (ref. 10) phase of the cycle, rather than in S or G2 phases. Increased development using donor cells in G0, G1, or mitosis may reflect greater access for reprogramming factors present in the oocyte cycoplasm, but a direct comparison of these phases in the same cell population is required for a clearer understanding of the underlying mechanisms.

7   Together these results indicate that nuclei from a wide range of cell types should prove to be totipotent after enhancing opportunities for reprogramming by using appropriate combinations of these cell-cycle stages. In turn, the dissemination of the genetic improvement obtained within elite selection herds will be enhanced by limited replication of animals with proven performance by nuclear transfer from cells derived from adult animals. In addition, gene targeting in livestock should now be feasible by nuclear transfer from modified cell populations and will offer new opportunities in biotechnology. The techniques described also offer an opportunity to study the possible persistence and impact of epigenetic changes, such as imprinting and telomere shortening, which are known to occur in somatic cells during development and senescence, respectively.

8   The lamb born after nuclear transfer from a mammary gland cell is, to our knowledge, the first mammal to develop from a cell derived from an adult tissue. The phenotype of the donor cell is unknown. The primary culture contains mainly mammary epithelial (over 90%) as well as other differentiated cell types, including myoepithelial cells and fibroblasts. We cannot exclude the possibility that there is a small proportion of relatively undifferentiated stem cells able to support regeneration of the mammary gland during pregnancy. Birth of the lamb shows that during the development of that mammary cell there was no irreversible modification of genetic information required for development to term. This is consistent with the generally accepted view that mammalian differentiation is

TABLE 2	Delivery of lambs developing from embryos derived by nuclear transfer from three different donor cells types, showing gestation length and birth weight

Cell type	Breed of lamb	Lamb identity	Duration of pregnancy (days)*	Birth weight (kg)
Mammary epithelium	Finn Dorset	6LL3	148	6.6
Fetal fibroblast	Black Welsh	6LL7	152	5.6
	Black Welsh	6LL8	149	2.8
	Black Welsh	6LL9†	156	3.1
Embryo-derived	Poll Dorset	6LL1	149	6.5
	Poll Dorset	6LL2††	152	6.2
	Poll Dorset	6LL5	148	4.2
	Poll Dorset	6LL6††	152	5.3

*Breed averages are 143, 147, and 145 days, respectively for the three genotypes Finn Dorset, Black Welsh Mountain, and Poll Dorset.
†This lamb died within a few minutes of birth.
††These lambs were delivered by caesarian section. Overall the nature of the assistance provided by the veterinary surgeon was similar to that expected in a commercial flock.

almost all achieved by systematic, sequential changes in gene expression brought about by interactions between the nucleus and the changing cytoplasmic environment.[17]

METHODS

9   Embryo-derived cells were obtained from embryonic disc of a day-9 embryo from a Poll Dorset ewe cultured as described,[1] with the following modifications. Stem-cell medium was supplemented with bovine DIA/LIF. After 8 days, the explanted disc was disaggregated by enzymatic digestion and cells replated onto fresh feeders. After a further 7 days, a single colony of large flattened cells was isolated and grown further in the absence of feeder cells. At passage 8, the modal chromosome number was 54. These cells were used as nuclear donors at passages 7–9. Fetal-derived cells were obtained from an eviscerated Black Welsh Mountain fetus recovered at autopsy on day 26 of pregnancy. The head was removed before tissues were cut into small pieces and the cells dispersed by exposure to trypsin. Culture was in BHK 21 (Glasgow MEM; Gibco Life Sciences) supplemented with L-glutamine (2 mM), sodium pyruvate (1 mM), and 10% fetal calf serum. At 90% confluency, the cells were passaged with a 1:2 division. At passage 4, these fibroblast-like cells (Fig. 1) had modal chromosome number of 54. Fetal cells were used as nuclear donors at passages 4–6. Cells from mammary gland were obtained from a 6-year-old Finn Dorset ewe in the last trimester of pregnancy.[18] At passages 3 and 6, the modal chromosome number was 54 and these cells were used as nuclear donors at passage numbers 3–6.

10   Nuclear transfer was done according to previous protocol.[1] Oocytes were recovered from Scottish Blackface ewes between 28 and 33 h after injection of gonadotropin-releasing hormone (GnRH), and enucleated as soon as possible. They were recovered in calcium- and magnesium-free PBS containing 1% FCS and transferred to calcium-free M2 medium[19] containing 10% FCS at 37°C. Quiescent, diploid donor cells were produced by reducing the concentration of serum in the medium from 10 to 0.5% for 5 days, causing the cells to exit the growth cycle and arrest in G0. Confirmation that cells had left the cycle

was obtained by staining with antiPCNA/cyclin antibody (Immuno Concepts), revealed by a second antibody conjugated with rhodamine (Dakopatts).

11   Fusion of the donor cell to the enucleated oocyte and activation of the oocyte were induced by the same electrical pulses, between 34 and 36 h after GnRH injection to donor ewes. The majority of reconstructed embryos were cultured in ligated oviducts of sheep as before, but some embryos produced by transfer from embryo-derived cells or fetal fibroblasts were cultured in a chemically defined medium.[20] Most embryos that developed to morula or blastocyst after 6 days of culture were transferred to recipients and allowed to develop to term (Table 1). One, two or three embryos were transferred to each ewe depending upon the availability of embryos. The effect of cell type upon fusion and development to morula or blastocyst was analysed using the marginal model of Breslow and Clayton.[21] No comparison was possible of development to term as it was not practicable to transfer all embryos developing to a suitable stage for transfer. When too many embryos were available, those having better morphology were selected.

12   Ultrasound scan was used for pregnancy diagnosis at around day 60 after oestrus and to monitor fetal development thereafter at 2-week intervals. Pregnant recipient ewes were monitored for nutritional status, body condition, and signs of EAE, Q fever, border disease, louping ill, and toxoplasmosis. As lambing approached, they were under constant observation and a veterinary surgeon called at the onset of parturition. Microsatellite analysis was carried out on DNA from the lambs and recipient ewes using four polymorphic ovine markers.[22]

NOTES

1. Campbell, K. H. S., McWhir, J., Ritchie, W. A., and Wilmut, I. Sheep cloned by nuclear transfer from a cultured cell line. *Nature* 380, 64–66 (1996).

2. Solter, D. Lambing by nuclear transfer. *Nature* 380, 24–25 (1996).

3. Gurdon, J. B., Laskey, R. A., and Reeves, O. R. The development capacity of nuclei transplanted from keratinized skin cells of adult frogs. *J. Embryol. Exp. Morph.* 34, 93–112 (1975).

4. Quinlivan, T. D., Martin, C. A., Taylor, W. B., and Cairney, I. M. Pre- and perinatal mortality in those ewes that conceived to one service. *J. Reprod. Fert.* 11, 379–390 (1996).

5. Walker, S. K., Heard, T. M., and Seamark, R. F. *In vitro* culture of sheep embryos without co-culture: successes and perspectives. *Therio* 37, 111–126 (1992).

6. Nash, M. L., Hungerford, L. L., Nash, T. G., and Zinn, G. M. Risk factors for perinatal and postnatal mortality in lambs. *Vet. Rec.* 139, 64–67 (1996).

7. Bradford, G. E., Hart, R., Quirke, J. F., and Land, R. B. Genetic control of the duration of gestation in sheep. *J. Reprod. Fert.* 30, 459–463 (1972).

8. Walton, A. and Hammond, J. The maternal effects on growth and conformation in Shire horse-Shetland pony crosses. *Proc. R. Soc. B* 125, 311–335 (1938).

9. Campbell, K. H. S., Loi, P., Otaegui, P. J., and Wilmut, I. Cell cycle co-ordination in embryo cloning by nuclear transfer. *Rev. Reprod.* 1, 40–46 (1996).

10. Cheong, H. T., Takahashi, Y., and Kanagawa, H. Birth of mice after transplantation of early-cell-cycle-stage embryonic nuclei into enucleated oocytes. *Biol. Reprod.* 48, 958–963 (1993).

11. Prather, R. S. et al. Nuclear transplantation in the bovine embryo. Assessment of donor nuclei and recipient oocyte. *Biol. Reprod.* 37, 859–866 (1987).

12. McGrath, J. and Solter, D. Inability of mouse blastomere nuclei transferred to enucleated zygotes to support development *in vitro*. *Science* 226, 1317–1318 (1984).

13. Robl, J. M. et al. Nuclear transplantation in bovine embryos. *J. Anim. Sci.* 64, 642–647 (1987).

14. Campbell, K. H. S., Ritchie, W. A., and Wilmut, I. Nuclear-cytoplasmic interactions during the first cell cycle of nuclear transfer reconstructed bovine embryos: Implications for deoxyribonucleic acid replication and development. *Biol. Reprod.* 49, 933–942 (1993).

15. Barnes, F. L. et al. Influence of recipient oocyte cell cycle stage on DNA synthesis, nuclear envelope breakdown, chromosome constitution, and development in nuclear transplant bovine embryos. *Mol. Reprod. Dev.* 36, 33–41 (1993).

16. Kwon, O. Y. and Kono, T. Production of identical sextuplet mice by transferring metaphase nuclei from 4-cell embryos. *J. Reprod. Fert.* Abst. Ser. 17, 30 (1996).

17. Gurdon, J. B. The control of gene expression in animal development (Oxford: Oxford University Press, 1974).

18. Finch, L. M. B. et al. Primary culture of ovine mammary epithelial cells. *Biochem. Soc. Trans.* 24, 369S (1996).

19. Whitten, W. K. and Biggers, J. D. Complete development *in vitro* of the preimplantation stages of the mouse in a simple chemically defined medium. *J. Reprod. Fertil.* 17, 399–401 (1968).

20. Gardner, D. K., Lane, M., Spitzer, A., and Batt, P. A. Enhanced rates of cleavage and development for sheep zygotes cultured to the blastocyst stage *in vitro* in the absence of serum and somatic cells. Amino acids, vitamins, and culturing embryos in groups stimulate development. *Biol. Reprod.* 50, 390–400 (1994).

21. Breslow, N. E. and Clayton, D. G. Approximate inference in generalized linear mixed models. *J. Am. Stat. Assoc.* 88, 9–25 (1993).

22. Buchanan, F. C., Littlejohn, R. P., Galloway, S. M., and Crawford, A. L. Microsatellites and associated repetitive elements in the sheep genome. *Mammal. Gen.* 4, 258–264 (1993).

NOTES AND DISCUSSION

This is a scientific article written for a specialist audience. As such, it generally maintains an impersonal tone, employing the gender-neutral third person "it" to present the majority of its findings. The essay, which summarizes the efforts of a group of scientists, also uses the pronoun "we" in conjunction with the passive voice throughout its explanation of technical procedures and underlying hypotheses. These stylistic choices emphasize the team aspect of the research and may be more convincing to readers than the reporting and hypothesizing of an individual.

The paper opens by placing itself in relation to previous research in its field, summarizing and paraphrasing this research briefly and efficiently and providing footnotes to exact sources. Wilmut and his colleagues then announce the results of their experiments and state the speculations that were confirmed by these results. They then give an overview of the methods used in the experiments and present the details of the results. Tables and photographs aid this portion of the paper, presenting and summarizing information that would likely be tedious and confusing if presented in textual format. Wilmut et al. occasionally look beyond the specifics of their experiment to discuss related issues, such as "irreversible genetic modification" and "differentiated cells."

Generally, the writers do not waste words; the paper's style is dense and compact. Yet the cause-and-effect relationships and steps in logical reasoning are clearly established and may be understood by the non-specialist once any unfamiliar terminology has been elucidated. Note the use of transitional phrases and words to help the reader establish and recognize links between ideas.

The paper concludes by reiterating and expanding on its opening declaration and by identifying areas that require further research and consideration. In fact, though classified as scientific writing, the paper closely follows the basic essay format taught in composition courses.

STUDY QUESTIONS

For Discussion

1. On a first reading, many non-specialist readers will find this paper complicated and impenetrable. Examine how the subject matter, the scientific language, and the tone and sentence structures of the paper interact with each other.

2. In the media coverage that followed the publication of this paper, Wilmut's findings were said to have paved the way for cloning humans. Based on *this* paper, does this application seem likely or immediate? Does the paper suggest other applications? Can you think of other applications? Why do Wilmut and his team avoid addressing such issues explicitly?

For Writing

1. Re-write the first paragraph of Wilmut's essay in everyday English. Note any problems that you encounter and then compare and contrast your version with Wilmut's. What similarities and differences do you notice?

2. Compare Wilmut's paper with Watson and Crick's essay on the structure of DNA. Identify the common elements of style and tone that you perceive as hallmarks of scientific writing. Discuss the advantages and disadvantages of these scientific literary characteristics.

BITTEN BY THE

SPACE BUG

Elizabeth K. Wilson

BIOGRAPHICAL NOTE

Elizabeth K. Wilson is the Senior Editor of the journal *Chemical & Engineering News*, where this piece first appeared. Her specialty for the journal is science in general, particularly physical and theoretical chemistry and planetary and space sciences.

1   Whenever a remarkable scientific idea is put forth, the maelstrom of debate that shakes the foundations of cherished beliefs gives rise to the overused but apt phrase, "paradigm shift."

2   When a team of scientists announced Aug. 7 [1996] that they had found possible evidence for life on Mars [*Science*, 273, 924 (1996); C&EN, Aug. 12, page 6], they realized they might have on their hands a virtual paradigm earthquake.

3   In the three months since that startling report, Mars has been on the cover of major magazines and featured in newspapers all over the world. Members of the scientific team—which includes David S. McKay and Everett K. Gibson Jr. of the National Aeronautics & Space Administration's Johnson Space Center in Houston and chemistry professor Richard N. Zare of Stanford University—have become household names, even the subject of political cartoons.

4   The U.S. space program has experienced a surge in popularity not seen since the heyday of the Apollo missions in the 1960s, and NASA workshops and conferences are abuzz with talk of future missions to Mars. "NASA has restored its image as a can-do agency," says Louis Friedman, executive director of the Planetary Society, an organization based in Pasadena, Calif., that advocates space exploration.

5   Other recent astronomical discoveries have added fuel to the fire of the question of extraterrestrial life: The Jupiter-orbiting spacecraft *Galileo* took photos of the satellite

Europa that show evidence for slushy ice or even liquid water—which is considered the primary criterion for life. Scientists have finally definitively detected planets outside Earth's solar system, raising questions about the ubiquity of solar systems like our own. And another study by British scientists claims to show isotopic evidence characteristic of methane-producing organisms in ALH84001, the martian meteorite studied by the U.S. team.

6   But in the scientific community, meanwhile, the debate over the evidence gleaned from the meteorite has hardly subsided and, in fact, may be heating up. The lines between the believers and skeptics are clearly drawn, each side vocally passionate. About the only issue the two factions can agree on is that it will take years of study to resolve the question.

7   NASA, which has kept ALH84001 under lock and key since the announcement, is issuing a call for study proposals to scientists clamoring for a piece of the rock.

8   And now, for better or worse, the onus is on the scientists involved to answer one of the most intriguing questions asked by human beings: Is life unique to Earth?

9   There are three ways scientists can search for evidence of life on Mars: Examine meteorites that fall to Earth, go to Mars and bring back samples, or send humans to the planet itself. The last option is many years off, technologically and financially, but NASA is already putting forth proposals to launch a mission in 2005 that would bring martian samples back to Earth.

10   Unfortunately, the meteorite ALH84001 is unique. Only 12 martian meteorites have yet been found. Eleven of them fall into an age range between 165 million and 1.3 billion years old. By contrast, ALH84001 is about 4.5 billion years old.

11   Most meteorites are found in Antarctica: Because the continent is mostly covered in mile-thick ice, many rocks can be presumed to be meteorites. The National Science Foundation funds meteorite-hunting expeditions in Antarctica, and the finds are managed through an agreement with NSF, NASA, and the Smithsonian Institution.

12   One might expect a flock of meteorite-gatherers to descend on the icy continent in search of another specimen like ALH84001. However, Scott Borg, director of NSF's Antarctic geology and geophysics program, says there hasn't yet been a surge in expedition proposals.

13   "I think there are good reasons for not launching into a real big search instantaneously," Borg, who is currently at McMurdo Station in Antarctica, writes via e-mail. "Meteorites are essentially randomly distributed, so there is no way to predict where a martian meteorite will be found."

14   The martian meteorites are extremely rare. If more were discovered, the three agencies would want to consider upgrading its facility for handling the meteorites, and there would be a need for increased staff, according to Borg.

15   For the time being, it appears, scientists will have to be content to work with small portions of ALH84001, NASA's Gibson says. Of the original 1.9-kg meteorite, only a small percentage contains the features of interest to researchers.

16   And according to standard protocol, only 25% of the meteorite may be used for research, Gibson says. The rest must be preserved for future generations of experiments and scientists. "We don't know what analytical techniques might become available in five to 10 years," he says. For example, the laser ionization technique used by Zare's laboratory to analyze the meteorite wouldn't have been available even five years ago.

17   The areas of greatest interest, carbonate globules that house the putative traces of life, are only 250 μm in size. "There's not a whole lot of material there available for study,"

Gibson tells C&EN. "So any technique or team that proposes to work on this must be aware of the difficulty of working with small samples. It's going to take some very sophisticated analytical techniques to pull data from them."

18 The next few years will give scientists a chance to settle some of the criticisms of the controversial *Science* paper's conclusions. As even the authors say, each piece of evidence taken by itself is not compelling enough to make a statement about possible biological origin. But taken as a whole, some say the only clear explanation is that an organism once lived there.

19 Much of the evidence centers around carbonate globules found within the meteorite. These globules were formed around 3.6 billion years ago, when Mars was presumably wetter and more hospitable to life. The globules contain both magnetite (Fe_3O_4) and iron sulfides, two substances that would not naturally form together under equilibrium conditions, but which can be produced together by biological processes. The ratio of ^{13}C to ^{12}C in the carbonates also suggests a biogenic origin.

20 Perhaps the strongest evidence derives from the measurements at Stanford of polycyclic aromatic hydrocarbons (PAHs) in ALH84001. Like the other lines of evidence, the presence of PAHs is not a definitive signature of life. However, on Earth, PAHs are abundant as fossil molecules in ancient sedimentary rocks, coal, and petroleum. The analyses at Stanford indicate that the PAHs in ALH84001 are associated with the carbonate globules.

21 The work also strongly suggests that the PAHs formed in conjunction with the carbonate globules and are not contaminants introduced on Earth. The four primary PAHs detected, for example, are barely present in the first 400 μm of the crust of the meteorite. After 400 μm, the PAH signal increases with depth, leveling off at about 1,200 μm into the meteorite, exactly opposite of the profile one would expect for contaminants.

22 However, critics continue to raise questions about the contamination issue, the temperature at which the carbonate globules formed, the size of magnetite crystals, and of the putative organisms themselves.

23 Jeffrey L. Bada, director of NASA's Specialized Center of Research & Training in Exobiology at Scripps Institution of Oceanography in La Jolla, Calif., fears that if the claims prove to be wrong, it could be disastrous for research in this area. "The public and Congress view science in different ways than scientists do," he says. "Scientists are willing to accept a bold claim that turns out to be wrong, but the public doesn't." If scientists make a statement and then retract it, the public's confidence in science suffers.

24 Bada is part of a camp of skeptics that include John F. Kerridge, a planetary scientist at the University of California, San Diego, and J. William Schopf, professor of geology at the University of California, Los Angeles.

25 Kerridge says bluntly, "My critical view of the work has hardened. As I've looked more into the evidence, the less convincing it is."

26 Kerridge, who two years ago led a team that drafted a report for NASA outlining a set of criteria for searching for life on Mars, says: "I came to the McKay et al. study with the firm conviction that looking for life on Mars makes sense. I am a believer—I think there's probably a 50-50 chance there was ancient life on Mars. But I also have a good feel for the criteria you need to apply to the evidence."

27 One major criticism of the work is that the alleged remains in ALH84001 indicate organisms in the size range of 100 nm, much smaller than anything known to exist on Earth.

28   Kerridge says such small organisms would contain only one-millionth of the molecules contained in a typical terrestrial bacteria. "That simply is not enough," he says. "You need a critical number of enzymes for a cell to function."

29   But Gibson counters that ongoing work at Johnson Space Center shows terrestrial organisms that small do indeed exist. Gibson says samples from the deep subsurface of the Columbia River basalt examined with high-resolution scanning microscopy have turned up organisms that are 40 nm in size.

30   Robert L. Folk, emeritus geology professor at the University of Texas, Austin, who has investigated nanobacteria since 1990, says he has studied organisms on Earth on the scale of tens of nanometers and found them to he ubiquitous—and, remarkably similar to the images from the martian meteorite.

31   "You can't tell which are my pictures and the pictures from Mars—they're absolutely identical in size, textures, and shape," Folk says. He argues that perhaps these organisms don't need the lengthy genetic material of typical bacteria to exist, and that perhaps they could be an intermediate form of life—between viruses and bacteria.

32   Particles of magnetite found within the carbonate globules are another hotly debated piece of evidence. Gibson says the bulk of the magnetite crystals found inside the meteorite are between 20 and 40 nm long, while some are as small as 5 nm. But Kerridge argues that while these sizes are smaller than the hypothesized 100-nm organisms in the meteorite, the magnetite crystals are still too big to reasonably exist inside such nanobacteria.

33   A major issue being debated is that of possible contamination from the ice in which the meteorite was found, especially in the wake of recent British results.

34   A number of years ago, British astronomers Colin T. Pillinger and Ian P. Wright of Open University, Milton Keynes, and Monica M. Grady of London's Natural History Museum found "nonspecific carbonaceous material" in the martian meteorite EETA79001 [*Nature*, 340, 220 (1989)]

35   This very young meteorite, less than 200 million years old, is the "Rosetta stone" in which scientists originally found trapped gases that exactly matched the composition of the martian atmosphere detected by the *Viking* lander that traveled to Mars in the 1970s.

36   Recently, the British group also detected similar nonspecific carbonaceous materials in ALH84001 (C&EN, Nov. 11, page 11).

37   However, Bada and colleagues reported a year ago finding amino acids in EETA79001 that matched those in the antarctic ice surrounding the meteorite [*Geochim. Cosmochim. Acta.* 59, 1179 (1995)]. Their conclusion: The meteorite had been contaminated.

38   Controversy also centers around the formation temperature of carbonate globules. Several groups have published or are publishing studies that contradict each other.

39   The maximum temperatures that known organisms on Earth can tolerate are around 120 °C. If the temperatures at which the carbonate globules formed was higher than that, it is unlikely they could have harbored life.

40   Two years ago, Christopher S. Romanek at Johnson Space Center (now at the Savannah River Ecology Laboratory, Aiken, S.C.) and colleagues concluded from oxygen isotopic ratios in the carbonate globules that the formation temperatures could range from 0 to 100 °C [*Nature,* 372, 655 (1994)].

41   However, a study by Ralph P. Harvey at Case Western Reserve University in Cleveland and Harry Y. McSween Jr. at the University of Tennessee, Knoxville, concluded that the combinations of elements in the carbonates pointed to a creation temperature of 600 to 700 °C [*Nature,* 382, 49 (1996)] A third study submitted for publication to the *Journal of*

Geophysical Research—Planets by Bruce M. Jakosky and colleagues at the University of Colorado, Boulder, who included martian atmospheric influences in their model, puts the temperature range between 50 and 250 °C.

42   Romanek argues that, at the temperatures proposed by Harvey's team, the carbonates would have homogenized into one mass. Instead, however, distinct layers can be seen surrounding the globules. Also, he adds, at such high temperatures, PAHs inside the globules would disintegrate.

43   Numerous experiments are being developed to study and restudy pieces of the meteorite when they become available in mid-March of next year.

44   Zare's group at Stanford is developing molecular tags that would attach themselves to amino acids, allowing them to be detected using the group's two-step laser mass spectrometry method.

45   David R. Crosley and Christopher H. Becker of SRI International's molecular physics lab, Menlo Park, Calif., are preparing a proposal to replicate the Zare group's research, as well as search for amino acids.

46   Becker's group would bombard a sample with 118-nm ultraviolet light—radiation energetic enough to ionize a substance such as an amino acid with a single photon without breaking it apart—and then analyze the compounds with time-of-flight mass spectrometry.

47   "Given the magnitude of the implications, I think replication in an additional lab is warranted," Becker says. "And the question of life and the origin of life in other locations is just totally fascinating to human beings, and rightfully so," he adds.

48   New technological developments—including improved field emission guns that allow examination of smaller areas, new fluorescence spectroscopy techniques, and advances in ion microprobe techniques—will facilitate additional studies, according to NASA's Gibson.

49   "The days of doing everything with microscope and petri dish are in our past," Gibson says. "It's going to require very sophisticated analytic capabilities to answer more difficult questions."

50   Meanwhile, NASA is proceeding full speed ahead in its ambitious plans to go directly to the source—Mars. The *Mars Global Surveyor* lifted off Nov. 7, and the *Mars Pathfinder* is scheduled for a Dec. 2 launch.

51   Matt Golombek, Mars Pathfinder project scientist at the Jet Propulsion Laboratory (JPL) in Pasadena, Calif., says even with indications that water could exist on Europa and that planets circle other stars, Mars is the only feasible target in the search for extraterrestrial life.

52   Sometime in the future, if missions bring samples back, they can be studied on Earth in ways that wouldn't ever be possible on Mars. The group that announced its findings in August "had instruments that filled up whole buildings. That's not something you send to Mars on a spacecraft," Golombek says. So, he explains, the first goal is to find places on Mars where life would most likely have existed. The new Mars missions will be sending back detailed information about the chemical composition of the planet and its atmosphere.

53   The Planetary Society's Friedman says sending human beings to Mars would be the ideal way to search for evidence of life. Humans could easily and strategically collect rocks and do age dating, drilling tens of meters below the surface. "But we're many years away from that capability," he says. "The best we can do right now [with robotic missions] is scratch a meter below the surface, do sounding, send a rover out. We just have to be patient and steadily learn."

54   Scripps's Bada has problems with the concept of bringing back samples. "Is that really wise?" he asks. He points out that the maximum sample size that could be brought back would be around 500 g, half of which will be automatically archived. And with that small a sample, there's no leeway for worrying about possible contamination problems.

55   In the best of all worlds, he says, experiments would be performed right on the planet. Bada is now working with JPL on developing a small in situ amino acid detection system for a Mars mission planned for launch in 2001. The capillary electrophoresis system would, upon landing on the planet, make its own completely sterile and self-contained water on the surface.

56   Thomas R. McDonough, Search for Extra Terrestrial Intelligence (SETI) coordinator for the Planetary Society, says: "Biologists are becoming increasingly suspicious that life evolves quickly. If you look at the geological record, it suggests life seems to have arisen very quickly."

57   That, combined with the discovery of planets around other stars, makes a stronger case for extraterrestrial life, McDonough says. "For decades, astronomers suspected that planets were common, but in the last year or so, a number of independent discoveries and confirmations have answered one of the big questions."

58   But particularly intriguing to McDonough is the idea that life might have arisen independently on Mars. "If we could show that it did arise independently, that would be the first proof that life can really get started easily," he says. "One of the big uncertainties in searching for life in the universe is: Is it easy or is it tough? If Mars gives us this hard data, then it means to me that the universe might be crawling with life."

59   Adds Gibson: "Whether we're right or wrong, we've given the Mars exploration program some new impetus. It's neat to have new ideas thrown out there. And every new idea has faced resistance. This is not going to be accepted in a very short time."

60   But, he says with a chuckle, "We still think we're right."

NOTES AND DISCUSSION

In "Bitten by the Space Bug," Elizabeth K. Wilson discusses the claim that evidence from a meteorite may suggest that there is or has been life on Mars. Wilson does a good job of enumerating and evaluating the difficulties of deciding the issue of what she calls "one of the most intriguing questions asked by human beings: Is life unique to Earth?" She continues: "There are three ways scientists can search for evidence of life on Mars: Examine meteorites that fall to Earth, go to Mars and bring back samples, or send humans to the planet itself." According to Wilson, the last option is financially and technologically out of reach at present. The first option is feasible but frustrating and inconclusive because meteorites are random and rare. She believes that the other option—to go to Mars to bring back samples—is the best one. It also seems to be the one that NASA prefers; NASA's current Mars exploration program was launched in two stages: The first stage was the Mars *Odyssey*, an orbiting satellite, launched in April 2001 and in place by October 2001. The second stage of exploration was launched in June and July 2003. The rovers that were placed on Mars in that mission sent back data between January and April 2004.

STUDY QUESTIONS

For Discussion

1. What, do you think, would be the implications of discovering that life is not unique to Earth?
2. NASA's missions to Mars aside, which of Wilson's three ways to search for life on Mars, do you think, is the most viable and effective? Why?

For Writing

1. Write a short essay in which you argue in favour of, or against, expanding the American space program, including a careful consideration of costs and benefits (in the broadest possible senses of those words).
2. Visit the websites that are devoted to NASA's Mars missions, beginning with the following index site: *http://mars.jpl.nasa.gov*

   In a short research paper, write a critical review of those sites and the information they contain.

A DEFENSE OF READING

Marie Winn

BIOGRAPHICAL NOTE

Marie Winn was born in Prague, Czechoslovakia, and emigrated to the United States at an early age. A graduate of Radcliffe College and Columbia University, Winn is a theorist of childhood and children's culture, and has written both for and about children. In 1977, her book *The Plug-In Drug* won an award from the American Library Association. Her subsequent books include *Children without Childhood* (1983) and *UnPlugging the Plug-In Drug* (1987). Winn revised *The Plug-In Drug* in 1985, then did so again in 2002. This piece is Chapter 9 of *The Plug-In Drug: Television, Computers, and Family Life* (2002).

---

1   Television's impact is undoubtedly greater on preschoolers and pre-readers than on any other group. Until television, never in human history had very young children been able to enter and spend sizable portions of their waking time in a secondary world of incorporeal people and intangible things, unaccompanied by an adult guide or comforter. School-age children fall into a different category. Because they can read, they have other opportunities to leave reality behind. For these children television is merely *another* imaginary world.

2   But are these imaginary worlds equivalent? Since reading, once the school child's major imaginative experience, has now been seriously eclipsed by television, the television experience must be compared with the reading experience in order to discover whether they are, indeed, similar activities fulfilling similar needs in a child's life.

WHAT HAPPENS WHEN YOU READ

3   It is not enough to compare television watching and reading from the viewpoint of quality. Although the quality of the material available in each medium varies enormously, from junky books and shoddy programs to literary masterpieces and fine, thoughtful television shows, the nature of each experience is different, and that difference significantly affects the impact of the material taken in.

4   Few people besides linguistics students and teachers of reading are aware of the complex mental manipulations involved in the reading process. Shortly after learning to read, a person assimilates the process so completely that the words in books seem to acquire an existence almost equal to the objects or acts they represent. It requires a fresh look at a printed page to recognize that those symbols we call letters of the alphabet are completely abstract shapes bearing no inherent "meaning" of their own.

5   Look at an "o," for instance, or a "k." The "o" is a curved figure; the "k" is an inter-section of three straight lines. Yet it is hard to divorce their familiar figures from their sounds, though there is nothing "o-ish" about an "o" or "k-ish" about a "k." Even when trying to consider "k" as an abstract symbol, we cannot see it without the feeling of a "k" sound somewhere between the throat and the ears, a silent pronunciation of "k" that occurs the instant we see the letter. A reader unfamiliar with the Russian alphabet will find it easy to look at the symbol "щ" and see it as an abstract shape; a Russian reader will find it harder to detach that symbol from its sound, *shch*.

6   That is the beginning of reading: as the mind transforms the abstract symbols into sounds and the sounds into words, it "hears" the words, as it were, and thereby invests them with meanings previously learned in the spoken language.[1] Invariably, as the skill of read-ing develops, the meaning of each word begins to seem to dwell within those symbols that make up the word. The word "dog," for instance, comes to bear some relationship with the real animal. Indeed, the word "dog" seems to actually possess some of the qualities of a dog. But it is only as a result of a swift and complex series of mental activities that the word "dog" is transformed from a series of meaningless squiggles into an idea of something real. This process goes on smoothly and continuously as we read, and yet it becomes no less complex. The brain must carry out all the steps of decoding and investing with meaning each time we read. But it becomes more adept at it as the skill develops, so that we lose the sense of struggling with symbols and meanings that children have when they first learn to read.

7   But the mind does not merely *hear* words in the process of reading; it also creates images. For when the reader sees the word "dog" and understands the idea of "dog," an image representing a dog is conjured up as well. The precise nature of this "reading image" is little understood, and it is unclear what relation it bears to visual images taken in directly by the eyes. Nevertheless images necessarily color our reading, else we would perceive no meaning, merely empty words.

8   The great difference between the "reading images" and the images we take in when viewing television is this: We create our own images when reading, based on our own experiences and reflecting our own individual needs. When we read, in fact, it is almost as if we were creating our own, small, inner television program. The result is a nourishing experience for the imagination. As psychologist and writer Bruno Bettelheim once noted, "Television captures the imagination but does not liberate it. A good book at once stimu-lates and frees the mind."[2]

9   Television images do not go through a complex symbolic transformation. The mind does not have to decode and manipulate during the television experience. Perhaps this is why the visual images received directly from a television set are strong, stronger, it appears, than the images conjured up mentally while reading. But ultimately they satisfy less.

10   The perfect demonstration that a book image is more fulfilling than a television image is available to any parent whose child has read a book before its television version appears. Though the child will tune in to the TV program eagerly, hoping to recreate the delighted experience the book provided, he or she invariably ends up disappointed, if not indignant. "That's not the way the mother looked," the child will complain, or "The farmer didn't have a mustache!" Having created personalized images to accompany the story, images that are never random but serve to fulfill some emotional need, the child feels cheated by the manufactured images on the screen.

11   A ten-year-old child reports on the effects of seeing television dramatizations of books he has previously read:

> The TV people leave a stronger impression. Once you've seen a character on TV he'll always look like that in your mind, even if you made a different picture of him in your mind before, when you read the book yourself. The thing about a book is that you have so much freedom. You can make each character look exactly the way you want him to look. You're more in control of things when you read a book than when you see something on TV.

12   It may be that television-bred children's reduced opportunities for "inner picture-making" accounts for the curious inability of so many children today to adjust to nonvisual experiences. Twenty years ago, a first-grade teacher who bridged the gap between the pre-television and the television eras reported:

> When I read them a story without showing them pictures, the children always complain "I can't see." Their attention flags. They'll begin to talk or wander off. I have to really work to develop their visualizing skills.... They get better at [it], with practice. But children never needed to learn how to visualize before television, it seems to me.

13   Today reading specialists have begun to examine the phenomenon of "aliteracy," a condition that seems to be increasing among American schoolchildren.[3] One of their findings about this large cohort of kids who have mastered the skills of reading yet do not choose to read for pleasure is relevant to a discussion of television's impact on reading: aliterate readers "need help visualizing what they are reading."

LOSING THE THREAD

14   A comparison between reading and viewing may be made in respect to the pace of each experience and the relative control we have over it. When reading, we can proceed as slowly or as rapidly as we wish. If we don't understand something, we may stop and reread it. If what we read is affecting, we may put down the book for a few moments and cope with our emotions.

15   It's much harder to control the pace of television. The program moves inexorably forward, and what is lost or misunderstood remains so. Even with devices like a VCR, though a program can be stopped and recorded, viewers find it hard to stop watching. They want to keep watching, so as not to lose the thread of the program.

16   Not to lose the thread... it is this need, occasioned by the relentless velocity and the hypnotic fascination of the television image, that causes television to intrude into human

affairs far more than reading experiences can ever do. If someone enters the room while we're watching television—perhaps someone we have not seen for some time—we feel compelled to continue to watch or else we'll lose the thread. The greetings must wait, for the television program will not. A book, of course, can be set aside, reluctantly, perhaps, but with no sense of permanent loss.

17　　A grandparent describes a situation that is, by all reports, not uncommon:

> Sometimes when I come to visit the girls, I'll walk into their room and they're watching a TV program. Well, I know they love me, but it makes me feel bad when I tell them hello, and they say, without even looking up, "Wait a minute... we have to see the end of this program." It hurts me to have them care more about that machine and those little pictures than about being glad to see me. I know that they probably can't help it, but still....

18　　Can they help it? Ultimately, when we watch television, our power to release ourselves from viewing in order to attend to imperative human demands is not altogether a function of the program's pace. After all, we might choose to operate according to human priorities, rather than yielding to an electronic dictatorship. We might quickly decide "to hell with this program" and simply stop watching when a friend enters the room or a child needs attention.

19　　We might... but the hypnotic power of television makes it difficult to shift our attention away.

THE BASIC BUILDING BLOCKS

20　At the same time that children learn to read written words they begin to acquire the rudiments of writing. Thus they come to understand that a word is something they can write themselves. That they wield such power over the very words they are struggling to decipher makes the reading experience a satisfying one right from the start.

21　　A young child watching television enters a realm of materials completely beyond his or her understanding. Though the images on the screen may be reflections of familiar people and things, they appear as if by magic. Children cannot create similar images or even begin to understand how those flickering electronic shapes and forms come into being. They take on a far more powerless and ignorant role in front of the television set than in front of a book.

22　　There's little doubt that many young children have a confused relationship to the television medium. When a group of preschool children were asked, "How do kids get to be on your TV?" only 22 percent of them showed any real comprehension of the nature of the television images.[4] When asked, "Where do the people and kids and things go when your TV is turned off?" only 20 percent of the three-year-olds showed the smallest glimmer of understanding. Although there was an increase in comprehension among the four-year-olds, the authors of the study note that "even among the older children the vast majority still did not grasp the nature of television pictures."

23　　Children's feelings of power and competence are nourished by another feature of the reading experience: the non-mechanical, easily accessible, and easily transportable nature of reading matter. Children can always count on a book for pleasure, though the television set may break down at a crucial moment. They can take a book with them wherever they go, to their room, to the park, to their friend's house, to school to read under the desk: they can *control* their use of books and reading materials.

A PREFERENCE FOR WATCHING

24   There'd be little purpose in comparing the experiences of reading and television viewing if it were not for the incontrovertible fact that children's television experiences influence their reading in critical ways, affecting how much they read, what they read, how they feel about reading, and, since writing skills are closely related to reading experiences, what they write and how well they write.

25   Children read fewer books when television is available to them, as reports from so many TV Turnoffs make clear.... A child is more likely to turn on the television set when there's "nothing to do" than to pick up a book to read—it simply requires less effort. In a survey of more than 500 fourth- and fifth-graders, all subjects showed a preference for watching over reading any kinds of content.[5] Nearly 70 percent of 233,000 sixth-graders polled by the California Department of Education in 1980 reported that they rarely read for pleasure.[6] Meanwhile, in the same poll, an identical percentage of students admitted to watching four or more hours of TV a day.

26   In 1992 a government report made headlines by stating that one-third of all students *never* read in their spare time and that one-third of all eighth- and tenth-graders read fewer than five pages a day for school or homework.[7] At the same time, the report noted, while two-thirds of the eighth-graders who had been tested for reading skills and comprehension watched more than three hours a day, those students who watched two hours or less proved to get higher grades on the exam.

27   Children are often candid about their preference for watching over reading. The twelve-year-old daughter of a college English teacher explains:

> I mean television, you don't have to worry about getting really bored because it's happening and you don't have to do any work to see it, to have it happen. But you have to work to read, and that's no fun. I mean, it's fun when it's a good book, but how can you tell if the book will be good? Anyhow, I'd rather see it as a television program.

The mother of boys aged twelve and ten and a girl aged nine reports:

> My children have trouble finding books they like in the library. They seem to have some sort of resistance to books, even though my husband and I are avid readers. I think if they didn't have television available they'd calmly spend more time looking for something good in the library. They'd have to, to avoid boredom. But now they don't really *look* in the library, whenever I take them. They don't zero in on anything. It's not the ultimate entertainment for them, reading. There's always something better and easier to do. So they don't have to look hard at the library. They just zip through quickly and hardly ever find more than one or two books that interest them enough to take out.

28   Understandably those children who have difficulty with reading are more likely to combat boredom by turning to television than successful readers are. Television plays a profoundly negative role in such children's intellectual development, since only by extensive reading can they hope to overcome their reading problems. This point is frequently raised by teachers and reading specialists: Television compounds the problems of children with reading disabilities because it offers them a pleasurable nonverbal alternative, thus reducing their willingness to work extra hard at acquiring reading skills.

29   It's easy to demonstrate that the availability of television reduces the amount of reading children do. When the set is temporarily broken, when a family participates in a TV

Turnoff or when a family decides to eliminate television entirely, there's always an increase in reading, both by parents and by children.[8] When the less taxing mental activity is unavailable, children turn to reading for entertainment, more willing now to put up with the "work" involved.

HOME ATTITUDES

30   The role of the home environment was the subject of one of many studies looking into television and its relation to children's reading achievement.[9] The researchers centered attention on the various stages of reading development and compared the impact of television viewing at each stage—from a pre-reading stage, through the initial decoding stage, into the stage of increasing fluency, and finally, to the stage in which children can read for knowledge and information.

31   The authors noted: "If the home environment encourages and enhances reading activities, the child has a better chance of progressing trouble-free through the first three stages. On the other hand, if the home environment has few facilitating mechanisms for reading development, and if it stresses television as the means for entertainment, activity, interaction and information acquisition, then the child's reading development may be impeded." The authors conclude by noting that "age is an important variable in the study of tele-viewing and reading, and the younger the children included in the study, the higher the probability that effects of the home environment and television viewing on reading behavior will appear."

LAZY READERS

32   Besides reducing children's need and willingness to read, television may subtly affect the actual ways in which children read, what might be called their reading style. For while children of the television era can and do still read, something about their reading has changed.

33   Reading specialists sometimes refer to certain children as "lazy readers." They define them as intelligent children from educated families who have never made the transition from learning *how* to read to being able to absorb what they read. They read well enough, but not with the degree of involvement and concentration required for full comprehension.

34   Critic George Steiner referred to this sort of reader when he noted: "A large majority of those who have passed through the primary and secondary school system can 'read' but not *read*."[10]

35   Similarly, educator Donald Barr once observed: "Children may pick up and leaf through more books, but what they do looks to me less like reading every year."[11] He, too, connected the deterioration in meaningful reading with children's television experiences. "TV stimulates casting your eye over the page, and that is a far different thing from reading."

36   Many teachers speculate about a connection between this style of reading and children's television involvement. Concentration, after all, is a skill that requires practice to develop. The television child has fewer opportunities for learning to sustain concentration than the "book" child of the past. Indeed, the mental diffuseness demanded by the television experience may influence children's attention patterns, causing them to enter the reading world more superficially, more impatiently, more vaguely.

NONBOOKS

37 Parents often assuage anxieties about their children's television involvement by maintaining that their children still read. But the reading reported by parents often falls into a category that might be called the "nonbook." The headmaster of a selective boys' school in New York reports:

> For as much television as our boys watch I have found no substantial correlation between the amount of television watching and the circulation of books from the library. The important change is in the kinds of books the boys read. ... [What] is really a new trend, it seems to me, is the great interest children have in reading the 'nonbook' kind of thing. The most conspicuous example of a 'nonbook' is the *Guinness Book of Records*. A great deal of the reading the boys seem to be doing these days falls into that category.

38   The nonbook seems designed to accommodate a new reading style. It is not the kind of book with a sustained story or a carefully developed argument that is read from beginning to end. It's a book to be scanned, read in fits and starts, skimmed, requiring little concentration, focused thinking, or inner visualization. Yet it provides enough information and visually pleasing material to divert the child who does not feel comfortable with the old sequential style of reading.

39   For the television-bred child, an important aspect of the nonbook is its instant accessibility. Reading a "real" book can be hard at the outset, as the scene is verbally set and new names and places and characters are introduced. But a nonbook, like television, makes no stretching demands at the start. Composed of tiny facts and snippets of interesting material, it does not change in any way during the course of a child's involvement in it. It does not get easier, or harder, or more exciting, or more suspenseful; it remains the same. Thus there is no need to "get into" a nonbook as there is with a book, because there are no further stages to progress to. But while the reader of a nonbook is spared the trouble of difficult entry into a vicarious world, he is also denied the deep satisfactions that reading *real* books may provide.

40   Parents and teachers suggest that boys are more likely to turn to nonbooks than girls. Indeed, boys have long been known to be more resistant than girls to any form of narrative fiction. Then, in 1998 a literary phenomenon arrived from across the Atlantic that grabbed girls and boys alike: a mild, bespectacled boy with magic powers named Harry Potter.

WHAT ABOUT HARRY POTTER?

41 Just when the cause of reading seemed hopeless, something happened to show that all was not lost. Suddenly tens of thousands of kids all over the United States (and the world) found themselves entranced by a series of books that had no tie-ins with any TV programs or movies whatsoever, books that simply stood on their own as a good, old-fashioned read. Harry Potter had taken the country by storm.

42   Children from the third grade on up through high school (and adults too) became so involved with Harry Potter that they skipped their regular television programs in order to continue reading. Parents and educators were amazed... and delighted. Reading for pleasure among children had been in a long, long decline. Was it possible that today's children were suddenly becoming the sorts of passionate readers once common before television came into the home?

43   The Harry Potter books are everything children's literature ought to be: superbly written, filled with suspense and excitement, containing adult characters both exotic and somewhat familiar from the real world, and one of the most appealing cast of child characters ever gathered in a single work. There's an inspiring and yet not too goody-goody boy hero, several girl heroines any feminist would applaud, a couple of deliciously hateable kid villains, as well as a host of imaginary creatures—dragons, hippogrifs, phoenixes, manticores, glumbumbles, basilisks, and more.

44   In no way is Harry Potter a nonbook. Each volume contains long, complex narratives that require sustained attention to follow. Moreover, there are almost no illustrations, thus requiring much inner visualizing in order to bring the people and fantastic creatures to life.

45   That a population of video-weaned children were able to fall for the charms of this marvelous, marvel-filled series of books has been one of the most hopeful omens of the television era. It is an indication that skills and abilities like inner-visualizing and following a narrative have not disappeared; they have just gone underground. Under the right circumstances—a great book combined with an international craze—these skills can once again be activated.

46   As I write, however, the movie version of the first Harry Potter book has just been released. Though the film was criticized (by adult critics, to be sure) for hewing too closely to J. K. Rowling's book, it was a huge success with children throughout the country, who were delighted that the film was so faithful to the story they loved. The movie broke box office records, and will surely continue to attract a large audience for years to come. Film versions of the next two Harry Potter books are already in production.

47   For most of the Harry Potter fans who flocked to see the movie, it was a fine recreation of their reading experience. But from now on great numbers of children will see the movies before reading the books. For them, things will be different. Having seen the film, a boy who then chooses to read the book will never be able to transform the main character into himself as he reads—a deeply satisfying part of the reading experience. Thereafter he will visualize only the movie's version of the bespectacled boy wizard. Similarly a girl reader who admires Harry's friend Hermione will never have the pure pleasure of creating the adorable though sharp-tongued little witch in her own image. Hermione will now resemble the Hollywood version.

RADIO AND READING

48   Before television, children listened with pleasure to radio programs. Now that television has captured the child audience almost in its entirety, people tend to think of radio as simply an inferior version of TV—television without the pictures. But is this indeed the way to look at radio?

49   During the early days of video technology, psychologist and art theorist Rudolph Arnheim spoke out in favor of "blind broadcasting," suggesting that radio listening provides similar gratifications to reading: "The words of the storyteller or the poet, the voices of dialogue, the complex sounds of music conjure up worlds of experience and thought that are easily disturbed by the undue addition of visual things."[12]

50   Among the thousands of studies of the various media's effects on children, there is little research directed toward the effects of radio listening. But the few studies available go far in confirming Arnheim's hunch that a visual medium like television will have deleterious effects on a viewer's powers of imagination, while the radio experience will not.

51   A study at the University of California compared children's responses to a radio story and a television version of the same story.[13] The researcher found that children were able to provide far more creative endings to the audio version than the video one, provoking the

inescapable conclusion that radio stimulates children's imagination significantly more than television does.

52   An example of radio's power to stimulate the imagination appeared in a recent review of a book about the baseball player Joe DiMaggio:

> The beauty of radio is that, unlike television, it puts the listener in the mix. There are no high-light shows, instant replays, or let's-go-to-the-videotape features to show us what happened. Visual images speak to the visceral, while voices heard but not seen allow free play in the cineplex of the mind…"[14]

53   Many educators believe that radio, an exclusively linguistic medium, has far more in common with reading than with television, a medium relying to a great extent on the visual. Indeed, while television has long been associated with a decline in academic achievement among its heaviest viewers, radio listening may prove to reinforce verbal skills almost as well as reading can. Certainly there is circumstantial evidence supporting such a view, notably, the long decline in SAT scores that began when the first television generation sat down at the test tables (see *Mystery of the Declining SATs*, page 283). During the heyday of children's radio, on the other hand, when there were great numbers of national radio broadcasts and American children invested almost as much time listening to the radio as they now spend watching TV, there was no equivalent decline; indeed, scores went steadily upward.

54   While television has displaced radio as an entertainment medium for children (with the exception of teenagers who listen to the radio almost exclusively for popular music), Books on Tape and other companies offer similar opportunities for listening experiences without pictures. The growing popularity of taped books as a source of entertainment for children may be a sign that parents are seeking to loosen television's bondage on their lives. Or, since Books on Tape are mainly used on car trips, it may simply mean that television has not yet penetrated the car market as it has the minivan market (see A Wonderful Addition to the Family, page 189). Time will tell.

IF YOU CAN'T BEAT 'EM, JOIN 'EM

55   A somewhat desperate attempt to stem the decline in children's free-time reading is seen in the if-you-can't-beat-'em-join-'em approach that enlists television itself as a spur to encourage children to read more.

56   Over the years a spate of television programs have appeared, some sponsored by public funds, others by television networks themselves, all with the much-applauded aim of promoting reading among children. Programs such as *Reading Rainbow* enlist a chirpy, magazine-style format and a TV-star host to stimulate an enthusiasm for reading among children clearly in need of such stimulation—after all, they *are* watching the program, not reading a book.

57   Other efforts of the past have included the Read More About It project, initiated by CBS with the cooperation of the Library of Congress, which had the stars of a number of TV shows based on books step out of their roles at the close of the dramatization to exhort the TV viewers to go out and read the book now that they have seen the program. NBC too did not fail to plug reading: "When you turn off your set, turn on a book" was the message flashed at the end of a popular late-afternoon children's series. Similarly, ABC joined the reading bandwagon by ending certain children's specials adapted from books with the words "Watch the Program—Read the Book."

58   No one, however, either on public or commercial television, has gone so far as to suggest: "Don't watch the program—read the book instead." And yet, as it happens, that would be a far more effective message. While there is no evidence whatsoever that television exhortations lead to a greater love of reading, there is the considerable evidence from TV Turnoffs organized by schools and libraries throughout the country, as well as from the annual National TV-Turnoff Week, run by the TV-Turnoff Network, demonstrating that when competition from the TV set is eliminated, children simply and easily turn to reading instead.

59   While efforts to encourage reading via TV programs may be well intentioned, they represent a misguided hope that there is an easy out from a difficult state of affairs. Indeed, the ways to encourage reading are well known, and require time and effort on the part of the parent. An education writer expressed it well:

> Future readers are made by mothers and fathers who read to their children from infancy, read to them during quiet moments of the day and read them to sleep at night. Only then does the book become an essential element of life.[15]

WHY BOOKS?

60 Well, what of it? Isn't there something a bit old-fashioned about a defense of reading in the electronic era? The arguments for reading are powerful:

61   Reading is the single most important factor in children's education. Reading trains the mind in concentration skills, develops the powers of imagination and inner visualization, lends itself to a better and deeper comprehension of the material communicated. Reading engrosses, but it does not hypnotize or seduce a reader away from human responsibilities. Books are ever available, ever controllable. Television controls.

62   In reading, people utilize their most unique human ability—verbal thinking—by transforming the symbols on the page into a form dictated by their deepest wishes, fears, and fantasies, As novelist Jerzy Kosinski once noted:

> [Reading] offers unexpected, unchannelled associations, new insights into the tides and drifts of one's own life. The reader is tempted to venture beyond a text, to contemplate his own life in light of the book's personalized meanings.[16]

63   In the television experience, on the other hand, viewers are carried along by the exigencies of a mechanical device, unable to bring into play their most highly developed mental abilities or to fulfill their particular emotional needs. They are entertained by television, but the essential passivity of the experience leaves them basically unchanged. For while television provides distraction, reading supports growth.

NOTES

1. A discussion of the "acoustic" image of words is found in H. J. Chaytor, *From Script to Print*. London: W. Heffer and Sons, 1950.

2. Bruno Bettelheim, "Parents vs. Television," *Redbook*, November 1963.

3. **The phenomenon of "aliteracy":** Beers, Kylene G., "No Time, No Interest, No Way! The Three Voices of Aliteracy," *School Library Journal*, March 1996.

4. **Preschooler's comprehension of the nature of TV images:** Lyle and Hoffman, "Explorations in Patterns of Television Viewing by Preschool-age Children." *Television and Social Behavior,* Vol. IV, op. cit.

5. **Survey of more than 500 fourth and fifth graders:** J. Feely, "Interest and Media Preference of Middle Grade Children," *Reading World,* 1974.

6. **Poll of sixth graders:** California State Department of Education, "Student Achievement in California Schools, 1979-80 Annual Report," Sacramento, California, 1980.

7. **1992 Government report:** "Bush Says Schoolchildren Watch Too Much TV," *The New York Times,* May 5, 1992.

8. **Evidence from TV-Turnoffs:** "It's Cold Turkey for the Families on 89th Street," *New York Post,* April 22, 1977; "Kicking the TV Habit," *The New York Times,* March 16, 1982; "Is There Life Without TV?," *The Wall Street Journal,* February 8, 1984.

9. **Study of the role of home environment on reading achievement:** Christine M. Bachen et al., "Television Viewing Behavior and the Development of Reading Skills: Survey Evidence," paper presented at the Annual Meeting of the American Educational Research Association, New York, March 1982.

10. George Steiner, "After the Book?" *Visual Language,* Vol. 6, 1972.

11. **Donald Barr quoted in:** Norman Morris, *Television's Child.* Boston: Little, Brown, 1971.

12. Rudolph Arnheim, *Visual Thinking.* University of California Press, 1972.

13. **Study at U. of California comparing radio and TV:** Greenfield P. et al "Is the medium the message?" *Journal of Applied Developmental Psychology* 7, 1986.

14. **Book review about Joe DiMaggio:** John Gregory Dunne, *The New Yorker Magazine,* October 30, 2000.

15. **Quote by an education writer:** Grace and Fred Hechinger, "Can TV Lead Children to Reading?" *The New York Times,* June 29, 1980.

16. **Jerzy Kosinski quote:** Horace Newcomb, *Television: The Critical View.* London: Oxford University Press, 1976.

NOTES AND DISCUSSION

Winn's "A Defense of Reading," which appears in a book about television versus reading, suggests that the strategy of the piece will involve comparing and contrasting the two media, and also that television and reading are adversaries. Using subheadings to guide the reader through the stages of her comparison and contrast of viewing and reading, Winn suggests that television has profoundly changed the lives of pre-reading children. The essay's structural units are clearly and carefully identified to help the reader along as the author switches back and forth between her analyses of the processes and implications of viewing television and those of reading books. Winn's explanation of the processes involved in reading is much longer than her explanation of those involved in watching television, a fact that seems to support her thesis that reading is a more complex activity than viewing.

Winn also tends to use a nostalgic tone in her descriptions of reading children. Consider whether she idealizes the days before television. Since reading is an activity shared by readers of this piece, Winn often writes in first-person plural or employs other language to suggest a collective and universal experience that includes her readers: "the mind transforms the abstract symbols into sounds and the sounds into words"; "we create our own images when reading, based on our own experiences and reflecting our own individual needs." The personal touches are less frequent in the discussion of television: "It's much harder to control the pace of television. The program moves inexorably forward, and what is lost or misunderstood remains so." Note that since this essay deals specifically with the effect of television on pre-reading children, the reader cannot, in fact, precisely share the children's experience. Winn also uses testimonials (from a 9-, a 10-, and a 12-year-old child, a teacher, and a grandparent) to support her observations. Readers of the essay should consider how they respond to such testimonials and how these testimonials advance Winn's argument.

STUDY QUESTIONS

For Discussion

1. Consider the meaning(s) of the word "read." What activities and processes does Winn include in her definition of reading? Is it possible to "read" television?

2. In her final section, Winn acknowledges that in a digital age (as the subtitle of the book suggests, Winn is concerned not just about television but also about computers), there might be something "a bit old-fashioned about a defense of reading." How would you respond to the charge that reading is old-fashioned?

For Writing

1. Examine Winn's phrase "so as not to lose the thread." What does this phrase suggest about the structure and nature of stories as told in books and on television?

2. How might television and reading be combined to provide a rewarding learning experience for children? Examine one of Winn's books about television (this one in its entirety, or one of the others) to see whether she suggests any ways to reconcile reading and viewing.

DON'T ROCK
THE SAMPAN

Xu Xi

BIOGRAPHICAL NOTE

Xu Xi (1954–) (pronounced "Shoe-See") is a Chinese-Indonesian and a native of Hong Kong who writes in English. She is the author of five novels, including *The Unwalled City* (2001) and *Hong Kong Rose* (1997). She explores the paradoxes and energies of modern Asia. She has won several awards, including an NYFA (New York Fiction Association) fiction fellowship and has served as writer-in-residence on various American university campuses.

1 Why don't you write in Chinese? This question gets asked when I've given readings and talks everywhere, but most often in Hong Kong, usually by an ethnic Chinese, sometimes with open hostility. Inherent in that is the central dilemma of writing fiction in English as a mostly Chinese person from Hong Kong. "Mostly Chinese," my first cop out answer.

2 My Hong Kong origins seem to demand that I answer the question. Why write in English, why not in Chinese? Ninety-seven percent, or more, of Hong Kong's population has Cantonese as a first language. Yet Hong Kong is an immigrant city. If you listen hard to local speech, you'll hear Shanghai, Hakka, Chui Chow, Fukien accents and meanings. These days, you'll hear Pudonghua tones. But it's all Chinese, right? The written language is the same.

3 Let's kill that myth. Hong Kong Chinese, the popular living language, includes a whole set of simplified characters that mimic Cantonese speech. This has little to do with the simplified Chinese of the Mainland. It also includes words like "fit" and "wet," written in English, which only marginally resemble their English counterparts in meaning.

4 And for a novelist observing society, the spoken language is paramount. Hong Kong people speak a brand of "Chinglish" that has found its way to Vancouver, Sydney, New York and London; into Canto- and even Mando-pop; into English and other Western languages as well as the English spoken in Singapore, Manila, Japan and elsewhere, testa-

ment to Hong Kong's global character. Whenever I render contemporary Cantonese speech, I find that American slang works well to capture its spirit and meaning.

5   Should being Chinese demand language define authenticity? In Canada or other English-speaking countries the idea of an ethnic Chinese writing in English is not unusual. In Hong Kong, however, the insinuation is often there: that a "real" writer from these shores wouldn't dream of writing in English. In fact, I've been told I can't possibly say anything real about Hong Kong because I write in English.

6   I'm a Wah Kiu "overseas Chinese" of Chinese Indonesian immigrant parents from Java, and was born in and have lived most of my life in Hong Kong. My parents spoke Javanese and Mandarin, and made English, which they had both studied, my first language for pragmatic reasons. So there's my second cop out—English, or rather ESL (English as a Second Language) is my "mother" tongue, which is why I write in English.

7   It's time I stopped copping out in that polite, don't-rock-the-sampan, Hong Kong fashion. After all, any novelist knows that the wonderful magic of creating a fictional world is to uncover universality in individual experience. Language is merely a tool. While it might be slightly daunting to write fiction about Hong Kong in Swahili, that's not to say it can't be done.

8   As a writer, I love my Hong Kong heritage. It takes me down untrodden paths to create linguistic and cultural fictional realities. It lets me capture my slice of a landscape and people I know well. So in answer to those who must ask that question, I offer this untranslatable Hong Kong Cantonese slang "you bore me into a muscle cramp" which is about as "authentic" a Hong Kong answer as they're going to get.

NOTES AND DISCUSSION

"Don't Rock the Sampan" first appeared in the 1999 edition of the journal *Rice Paper* as a "Last Word" column. A sampan is a small boat with a stern oar or oars, which originated in the Far East. Most readers will have guessed the meaning of "sampan" from the paper's title, which plays with the well-known expression "don't rock the boat." Clearly, the title hints at some of the paper's content—a mini-exploration of the flexibility, fluidity, and increasingly global nature of language. The paper takes the form of a short personal essay, written in the first person and organized around a series of questions and answers. The tone is informal, almost conversational, yet Xu Xi speaks passionately about choosing to write in English. She acknowledges that 97 per cent of Hong Kong's population speaks Cantonese as a first language, but explains that she has chosen to write novels about modern Hong Kong in English for reasons that are both pragmatic and artistic. Her comments touch on the nature of language and the novelistic art. The paper's conclusion harks back to its beginning and suggests that while articulating a response to the question "Why don't you write in Chinese?" has been cathartic, this question will not be answered in the future—except with some snappy Hong Kong Cantonese slang—because the author now deems a reply unnecessary.

STUDY QUESTIONS

For Discussion

1. Xu Xi closes her essay with the "untranslatable Hong Kong Cantonese slang: 'you bore me into a muscle cramp'." What is your response to this idiomatic expression? Think of

some examples of common idiomatic expressions in English and try to imagine how non-native speakers of English respond to them.

2. Can you imagine a novel "about Hong Kong in Swahili"? Would this novel be considered a Hong Kong novel or a Swahili novel? What criteria do we use to assign nationalities to novels? What makes a novel Canadian? Could a novel written in Cantonese say anything "real" about Canada? Think about Xu Xi's declaration that "Language is merely a tool."

For Writing

1. Describe your own relationship to and experience of the English language. Is English your "mother tongue" or an acquired one? You may wish to compare and contrast English with other languages you speak and/or have studied or to describe scenarios in which you have encountered others using English as a second language.

2. Xu Xi uses the expression "cop out" in the first paragraph of her essay (another use of idiom). What does it mean to "cop out?" Xu Xi defines two of her answers as "cop outs." Do you agree or disagree with her evaluation of her own answers? Why or why not?

HOW IRAQ REVERSE-ENGINEERED THE BOMB

Glenn Zorpette

BIOGRAPHICAL NOTE

Glenn Zorpette is executive editor of *IEEE Spectrum* Magazine, the general-interest magazine of the IEEE. In 1993 he won a National Magazine Award in the Reporting category for an article on Iraq's attempt to build an atomic bomb. From 1995 to 2000, he worked at *Scientific American* Magazine, where he was part of a team that won another National Magazine Award, for a single-topic issue titled "What You Need To Know About Cancer." For 10 months, during the heyday of the dot-com, he worked at *Red Herring* Magazine before returning to *IEEE Spectrum* in June, 2001. He holds a bachelor's degree in electrical engineering from Brown University (class of 1983). As a freelance writer, he has published in *The New York Times*, *Discover magazine*, *ARTnews magazine*, *American Heritage of Invention & Technology*, *Los Angeles Times*, *The Boston Globe*, *Boston Herald*, and other publications. His photos have been published by *IEEE Spectrum*, *Scientific American*, *L.A. Times*.

1 Two weeks into the war in the Persian Gulf, a US pilot was heading north after bombing primary targets near Baghdad. A quick check of his instruments and his list of secondary targets convinced him he had the time, fuel, and munitions left for a run at Al Tarmiya, an industrial site, before flying back to base in Saudi Arabia.

2 US intelligence had identified a plant at Tarmiya as a military nuclear facility, but knew little else about it. Analysts believed that Iraq was struggling to build a plant there "for uranium enrichment, based on the centrifuge technique, a standard method of enriching uranium to weapons-grade. But Tarmiya's low priority as a target reflected the intelligence community's belief—very much mistaken—that Tarmiya was not one of Iraq's most important nuclear sites.

3 Taking aim at one of the large halls, the pilot rolled in and dispatched two Hellfire missiles, which inflicted light damage.

4   Within a day or so, however, routine aerial reconnaissance revealed hundreds of Iraqis at the site, "busy as hell, tearing out large pieces of equipment" to conceal and protect it, according to a source familiar with the episode. Unwittingly, the coalition had just struck one of the most critical components of a sprawling nuclear program whose size, scope, and achievements far exceeded the most alarmist estimates of the time. David A. Kay, a former inspector with the International Atomic Energy Agency (IAEA) in Vienna and now secretary general of the Uranium Institute in London, believes that Tarmiya would have been Iraq's first industrial-scale site capable of producing weapons-grade uranium. And though the allies did not know that until much later, the frantic activity after the bombing told them all they needed to know for the time being. Within days, B-52 bombers were sent back to "plaster" the site thoroughly, according to *IEEE Spectrum*'s source.

5   How could Western intelligence have been so blind to the purpose and scope of such a key site? As with many other questions about the forging of the Iraqi war machine, the answer lies partly in the Iraqis' skill in deception and partly in the largely coincidental eight-year war with Iran in the 1980s.

6   Had it succeeded, Iraq's attempt to produce a nuclear weapon might one day have yielded a stunning case study of concurrent engineering. As it turned out, the Iraqis pursued many phases of development in parallel, and closed off options only when they presented truly insurmountable obstacles. This held true both for their production of weapons-grade material and for their construction of a deliverable weapon. The crash program also employed elements of reverse engineering, exploiting projects and developments that had been abandoned by earlier experimenters in the United States and elsewhere. And it drew heavily on materials, hardware, and information acquired from outside the country, in some cases illegally or unethically.

7   ***Intelligence Lapse***   The uranium enrichment technique being pursued at Tarmiya was, astonishingly enough, electromagnetic isotope separation. Nowhere else had this extremely inefficient method been used for an atomic weapon apart from the Manhattan Project in the United States during World War II. As the process uses vast amounts of electricity, the Iraqis constructed a power plant with an output in excess of 100 MW, and devoted it to the Tarmiya facility. But in case the dedicated use of so much electricity should seem suspicious, the power plant was located 15 km from Tarmiya, and connected to the facility by underground cables.

8   Tarmiya itself was surrounded by only a light fence, giving US intelligence analysts the impression that whatever was going on inside could not matter much. What the analysts overlooked, according to *Spectrum*'s source, was that the entire area around Tarmiya was a military exclusion zone, so a more impenetrable fence was not needed. Moreover, the United States may not have scrutinized Tarmiya intensively from above during the Iran-Iraq war, when most reconnaissance assets were focused on border areas between the two countries, according to intelligence sources.

9   Overall, Tarmiya is typical of how Iraq combined not just deception and strict secrecy, but also hard work and research, exploitation of the open literature on nuclear science, illegal acquisitions, and the expenditure of huge sums of money to put together an immense program for nuclear-weapons development. In fact, its exact dimensions and scope are still not fully known, and may never be, according to Kay and others who have investigated it. The best current estimates are that the country spent the equivalent of billions of dollars—perhaps even US $10 billion, over a decade and employed at least 12,000 people in its pursuit of an atomic bomb.

10   The bad news is that at the time it invaded Kuwait, Iraq was probably only 12–18 months away from a crude but useable nuclear device, according to Kay. Other estimates, corroborated by documents in the IAEA's possession, put the figure in the range of 25–40 months, according to Maurizio Zifferero, head of the IAEA "action team" set up to investigate and dismantle the Iraqi nuclear program. (Contrary to previous reports in the popular press, Iraq did not have dozens of kilograms of hidden bomb-grade uranium, one or two working weapons and the ability to produce 20–40 more, or an ongoing project to build a thermonuclear weapon, according to the IAEA.)

11   The "good" news, nonproliferation experts hasten to add, is that the country was in many ways unique: it had plenty of capital from its oil sales, a relatively impressive technical infrastructure, many highly competent engineers and scientists, and a dictatorial regime that could easily conceal huge expenditures on a single military objective.

12 ***Outside Help***   The Iraqi nuclear program started in the 1960s, with the purchase of a 2-MW Soviet light-water research reactor. But, ironically, the effort to build a bomb can be said to have begun in earnest in 1981, the year Israeli pilots bombed and demolished Tammuz I, a French research reactor with a rating of about 50 MW.

13   "When the Israelis destroyed Tammuz, the Iraqis met and decided to change their policy," Zifferero explained. The decision was to "enshroud in secrecy all activities having to do with their nuclear capabilities, and to duplicate all [key] installations in case any part was discovered and destroyed again by Israel," Zifferero told *Spectrum* in late January during an interview at IAEA headquarters in Vienna.

14   Thus at the time of the invasion of Kuwait, construction was well under way on a duplicate of the Tarmiya installation, at Ash Sharqat, 300 km northwest of Baghdad. Like the Tarmiya facility, Ash Sharqat was fed by underground cables from a sizeable remote power source. During the Gulf War, coalition intelligence had pattern-matched the layouts of Ash Sharqat and Tarmiya, on the basis of aerial reconnaissance, and Ash Sharqat was also bombed, according to an official with access to intelligence documents.

15   But so far, Kay noted with concern, Tarmiya and Ash Sharqat are the only twin facilities discovered by investigators. He said he confronted his Iraqi contacts, demanding to "see the duplicates of your other facilities"—but to no avail. "You could have just cut the consternation with a knife," he said. "And [the Iraqis] haven't come up with any other duplications yet."

16   The French sold Tammuz 1 (also known as Osirak) and Tammuz 2, a 0.5-MW reactor used for studies of the larger reactor, to Iraq in the mid-1970s. Both used uranium fuel enriched to 93 percent U-235, which is bomb-grade material. This material was subject to regular IAEA safeguards as a condition of the French sale, however, so Iraq could not have used it to produce a bomb without openly flouting IAEA regulations. Furthermore, some of the French fuel was lightly irradiated (used) in Tammuz 2, slightly reducing its utility for weapons-making.

17   Nonetheless, Iraq managed to separate a few grams of weapon-type plutonium from additional, indigenously produced fuel rods irradiated in the Soviet reactor, according to the IAEA. A few grams is not nearly enough to make a bomb—about 8 kg are needed—but its creation was one of many flagrant violations of the Nonproliferation Treaty (NPT) that Iraq had signed in 1969.

18   The Iraqis were studying plutonium for at least two reasons, according to Kay. He said they were interested in plutonium production, noting that most atomic bomb designs are based on plutonium, or on mixtures of plutonium and highly enriched uranium. It "shows that they did not leave a single route unexplored," he said.

19   In mid-February, news accounts suggested that Iraq had an as-yet undiscovered underground nuclear reactor capable of producing enough plutonium for several bombs a year. Prompted by intelligence information from France and other countries, inspectors from the IAEA and the United Nations searched several sites, including one 120 km north of Baghdad, but to no avail. Nonetheless, many analysts remain convinced the reactor exists.

20   "All of the facts support the existence of a plutonium reactor," Kay said. The Iraqis had vast amounts of uranium ore, and the ability to fabricate it into fuel rods, both of which are difficult to explain without the existence of such a reactor (the French and Soviet reactors were for the most part fueled by separate fuel assemblies).

21   Apparently, the Iraqis were also investigating the use of a plutonium isotope, Pu-238, as an initiator—the bomb component that supplies neutrons to begin an atomic explosion. Iraq was having trouble producing the polonium isotope normally used for this purpose, Kay said.

22   On the other hand, obtaining uranium, from which plutonium is derived, was not a problem for Iraq.

23 ***No Stone Unturned***   During the 1980s, the country legally purchased some 440 metric tons of yellowcake, a uranium oxide concentrate obtained from ore, from Portugal and Niger. But 27 tons of uranium dioxide were bought from Brazil and the transaction was not reported to the IAEA, in violation of Iraq's NPT obligations. In addition, Iraq had secretly produced some 164 tons of yellowcake domestically, at Al Qaim, from a phosphate mine at Akashat. The uranium-processing equipment at Al Qaim was reportedly built by a Swiss firm, Alesa Alusuisse Engineering AG. An Alesa spokeswoman, however, denied that her company had had any direct dealings with Iraq.

24   Although not the most common weapons material, highly enriched uranium can of course also yield atomic bombs and here, as in most aspects of the Iraqi nuclear program, the overriding characteristic of the effort was its all-inclusiveness. At one time or another during the 1980s, Iraqi engineers and scientists were either actively developing or studying the available scientific literature on every method ever used to enrich uranium to weapons grade.

25   According to investigators, Iraq supplemented its own attempts to develop enrichment equipment with extensive clandestine efforts to illicitly acquire other equipment, information, and materials. Much of this came from European and US companies, and at least a few rogue nuclear experts. Sometimes the purchases were made through intermediary organizations. To further confuse any would-be inquisitors, the Iraqis named their clandestine nuclear program Petrochemical Project #3 (PC-3).

26   Although the Iraqis considered every means of enrichment, they quickly discarded gaseous diffusion and laser separation, because these techniques required technologies and resources beyond their means. (In fact, laser separation is still experimental, but considered a promising technology in the United States and Europe.) That left three techniques: electromagnetic isotope separation (EMIS), which was to have first gone to industrial scale at Tarmiya; gas centrifuge; and chemical separation.

27 ***"Creative and Legal"***   Ultimately, work on chemical separation in Iraq took a back seat to the other two techniques, but the country's pursuit of the technology is illustrative of its methods. France and Japan developed different chemical enrichment technologies in the late 1970s. The Japanese process depended on expensive, esoteric resins whose purchase would be hard to disguise, so the Iraqis chose the French process. In the early 1980s, they entered into negotiations with the French to buy the process, which was called Chemex and based on liquid-liquid solvent extraction.

28   The Iraqi version has the negotiations going on for many months, during which time the Iraqis learned all they could about the process from its French developers. Finally, the Iraqis backed out, saying the French wanted too much money. The Iraqis then bought patent information, chemicals, and equipment—none of which was controlled—and began developing the process on their own. "It was all creative and legal," Kay said.

29   The technology acquisition method was a "classic" one for the Iraqis, Kay added. "They would enter into contract negotiations with a country and go almost up to signing a contract, gathering all the information they could. Then they would back out at the last minute and use the information to develop their own process."

30   According to Kay, before the Gulf War, Iraq had built two generations of prototype chemical enrichment plants and was preparing to step up to initial, pilot-scale industrial production. The IAEA's Zifferero, however, believes that the country did not advance quite this far.

31   The other enrichment methods illustrate two other key aspects of Iraq's PC-3 program: the EMIS effort was mostly homegrown, though illicit acquisitions were made and the undertaking benefited greatly from information available in the open literature, whereas the centrifuge program was built entirely around imports of parts, materials, equipment, and designs, most obtained clandestinely. Both the centrifuge development program and the experimental EMIS program were based at a research complex 10 km south of Baghdad. This complex, at Al Tuwaitha, was the centerpiece of the Iraqi nuclear research effort.

32   It was at Tuwaitha, for example, that the country's Soviet and French reactors had been installed. Although it did not have a supercomputer, which would have been invaluable for simulations and other studies, Tuwaitha was well equipped with 80386-based personal computers and a few larger machines, including a NEC 750 mainframe and software for solving hydrodynamic equations in the presence of shock waves—a useful capability for nuclear weapons design.

33   ***A Very Messy Affair***   The EMIS program surprised not only the IAEA, but Western intelligence agencies. With this technique, a stream of uranium ions is deflected by electromagnets in a vacuum chamber. The chamber and its associated equipment are called a calutron. The heavier U-238 ions are deflected less than the U-235 ions, and this slight difference is used to separate out the fissile U-235. However, "what in theory is a very efficient procedure is in practice a very, very messy affair," said Leslie Thorne, who recently retired as field activities manager on the IAEA action team. Invariably, some U-238 ions remain mixed with the U-235, and the ion streams can be hard to control.

34   The two different isotopic materials accumulate in cup-shaped graphite containers. But their accumulation in the two containers can be thrown off wildly by small variations in the power to, and temperature of, the electromagnets. Thus in practice the materials tend to spatter all over the inside of the vacuum chamber, which must be cleaned after every few dozen hours of operation.

35   Hundreds of magnets and tens of millions of watts are needed. During the Manhattan Project, for example, the Y-12 EMIS facility at Oak Ridge in Tennessee used more power than Canada, plus the entire US stockpile of silver; the latter was used to wind the many electromagnets required (copper was needed elsewhere in the war effort).

36   Mainly because of such problems, US scientists believed that no country would ever turn to EMIS to produce the relatively large amounts of enriched material needed for atomic weapons (although calutrons are still used in scientific research and to produce small quantities of isotopes for medical and industrial uses). Nearly all of the information needed to build and operate calutrons, including the key US patents, has been declassified since the end of World War II.

37   Among the more explicit sources that can be safely assumed to have been used by Iraqi scientists are: *Atomic Energy for Military Purposes*, by Henry D. Smyth (Princeton University Press, 1945); the Progress in Nuclear Energy Series and National Nuclear Energy Series, which together comprise more than 125 volumes of declassified information from the Manhattan Project, published by McGraw-Hill and Pergamon Press in the late 1940s and early 1950s; two volumes on "The Chemistry, Purification and Metallurgy of Plutonium," declassified by the United States Atomic Energy Commission, Office of Technical Information, in 1960; and "Developments in uranium enrichment," a collection of symposium papers published by the American Institute of Chemical Engineers in 1977.

38   The discovery of the Iraqi EMIS program had much of the drama of a good spy novel. The first clue apparently came in the clothing of US hostages held by Iraqi forces at Tuwaitha, according to an expert familiar with the investigation. After the hostages were released, their clothes were analyzed by intelligence experts, who found infinitesimal samples of nuclear materials with isotopic concentrations producible only in a calutron. The analysis was not available until after the war, the source said. The US government has not confirmed this account, most of which appeared first in the *Bulletin of the Atomic Scientists* last September.

39   The real breakthrough, however, came when a young electrical engineer defected in June 1991. The engineer, who worked at the Ash Sharqat site, revealed the existence and extent of the EMIS program to US intelligence. However, according to news reports at the time, the defector also said that the Iraqis had managed to produce 40 kg of bomb-grade material and that Ash Sharqat survived the war unscathed. Both statements are inconsistent with subsequent IAEA findings; the third IAEA inspection mission to Iraq found that "most of the [Ash Sharqat] facility was destroyed."

40   ***The "Living Dinosaur"***   During the first inspection mission, from May 15–21 of last year, much of Tarmiya's equipment and high-power electrical gear puzzled inspectors. Photographs of it were shown to John Googin, a veteran of the Manhattan Project and the Y-12 facility, which is still at Oak Ridge. Googin conclusively identified the equipment as EMIS components.

41   "Suddenly we found a live dinosaur," said Demetrius Perricos, deputy head of the IAEA's Iraq action team.

42   On June 28, during the second mission, IAEA inspectors were denied access to a site at Fallujah. Climbing a water tower, they saw a convoy of nearly one hundred Iraqi tank-transporter trucks carrying equipment out the back gate of the site. The inspectors were able to photograph the convoy before Iraqi soldiers fired warning shots in their direction; when enlarged, the photographs showed that the trucks were carrying calutron parts. The Fallujah episode was the second in which inspectors were denied access to a site; both sites were suspected of harboring equipment from Tarmiya and Tuwaitha.

43   The inspectors believe Iraq was trying to hide as much of its equipment as possible in the desert, where it could be recovered after the intensive inspections ceased. Indeed, numerous giant calutron parts have been found buried in the desert sands at sites west and north of Baghdad.

44   ***A New Manhattan Project***   The EMIS program was headed by Jaffar Dhia Jaffar, a British-educated scientist who had a background in particle accelerators and who had worked at the European Center (now Organisation) for Nuclear Research (CERN) in Geneva. Jaffar, who IAEA investigators believe also directed the overall PC-3 program, is "a good physicist, a capable manager, and a great motivator of people," according to Zifferero.

45   It was in his conception of the Iraqi EMIS program that "Jaffar shows he has a very original mind," Thorne said. For example, where the Manhattan Project required extensive manual adjustment of the ion beams, Jaffar planned to bring the process into the computer age. Computer rooms had been planned for both Tarmiya and Ash Sharqat, from which the process would have been automated. Better control of the beams would have in turn obviated the need for the constant, laborious cleaning work associated with the process.

46   As in the Manhattan Project, the PC-3 program had developed two types of calutrons, a large A type to enrich the uranium from its natural level, and a smaller B type to further enrich it. Iraqi nuclear scientists told the IAEA that the A type was to bring the enrichment to 3 percent U-235, and the B type to 12 percent. Zifferero doubts that account, noting that 12 percent is a "strange" value, too high for power production and too low for weapons making.

47   Documents recovered by the IAEA show that a total of ninety calutrons, seventy type A and twenty type B machines, were to have been installed at Tarmiya. But when the site was bombed, only eight had been installed, and another seventeen were in various stages of assembly. In commissioning tests, the calutrons produced about half a kilogram of uranium enriched to an average of 4 percent U-235, Zifferero said. And, according to Kay, some samples taken from Tarmiya showed enrichment levels between 20 and 30 percent U-235.

48   The IAEA estimates that had the Tarmiya plant gone into full operation, it could have produced up to 15 kg of highly enriched uranium a year, enough for one implosion-type bomb.

49   ***"Centrifuge Breakthrough"***   Most investigators believe that the EMIS facility at Tarmiya would have been the first to yield enriched materials in quantity, but there is ample evidence, they say, that emphasis had shifted to the centrifuge program by the late 1980s. Although the program started out earlier in the decade as a relatively low-budget affair, a "breakthrough" in the late 1980s seems to have suddenly put the Iraqis on the track of a much more advanced centrifuge design. There is little doubt now that the breakthrough was the acquisition of centrifuge parts, designs, and advice from European sources.

50   In a centrifuge, gaseous uranium hexafluoride is spun in cylinders with diameters of about 75–400 mm. Centrifugal forces push the heavier U-238 to the cylinder wall, while the U-235 tends to collect closer to the center of the cylinder. Speeds of 400–600 meters per second at the cylinder circumference are required, and "below about 300 meters per second, you don't get any separation at all," an expert in the technology told *Spectrum*. To withstand the high speeds, the cylinders are fabricated of materials with high tensile strength, typically either carbon fiber or maraging steel. To minimize friction and maximize speed, the cylinder is spun in a vacuum.

51   Even at high speeds, the separation requires "cascades" of thousands of centrifuges, each of which enriches the uranium by another increment. Both the construction of the individual centrifuges and—more importantly, their arrangement into a working cascade— require considerable technological sophistication.

52   To enrich uranium in centrifuges, the Iraqis would also have needed the ability to produce uranium hexafluoride, a process known as fluorination. Iraq bought an aluminum fluoride production plant in the late 1970s, and apparently succeeded in converting it for use with uranium—Iraqi officials have admitted producing half a kilogram of uranium hexafluoride, and separating a small (militarily irrelevant) amount of enriched uranium in an experimental centrifuge system.

53   According to *The Death Lobby*, an investigative book about the Iraqi weapons program by journalist Kenneth R. Timmerman, the fluorination equipment came from Alesa Alusuisse Engineering. Timmerman also claims that the Iraqi centrifuge program began in the early 1980s with purchases of centrifuges from Brazil (which that country had obtained legally from West Germany) and with assistance from China. But by the mid-1980s, Iraq had evidently obtained all necessary design information to re-create—and even slightly improve upon—the G1 centrifuge, which was used by the European Enrichment Co. (Urenco) in the 1960s and early 1970s. IAEA and other investigators contacted by *Spectrum* say they are not sure exactly how Iraq obtained information on the centrifuge design from Urenco, a consortium of German, Dutch, and British firms that operates what are generally regarded as the world's most advanced centrifuge plants in Almelo, the Netherlands; Capenhurst in Britain; and Gronau, Germany.

54   In the late 1980s, the Iraqis called in Bruno Stemmler and Walter Busse, who had worked on gas centrifuges at MAN Technologie, a German member of the Urenco consortium. While insisting that he did not know the true purpose of the Iraqi centrifuges, Stemmler told the *Sunday Times* in London in December 1990 that he and Busse were hired to trouble-shoot an experimental enrichment cascade the Iraqis had set up near Tuwaitha. As of late February, the German Government was believed to be considering whether to press charges against Stemmler and Busse, but it was not clear that the two had broken any German laws. (Not until 1990 did the former West German Government make it a crime for its citizens to privately assist foreign weapons programs.)

55   Stemmler told the *Sunday Times* he saw equipment from many western companies during his visits to the Iraqi facility, including vacuum pumps from Veeco Instruments Inc., Plainview, NY, and valves, furnaces, and other equipment from VAT of Lichtenstein and Leybold-Heraus of the then West Germany. Even though sales of most of this equipment was not controlled by export laws, some of it was procured through phony intermediary companies set up in London, Germany, and elsewhere.

56   IAEA investigators have also found centrifuge rotors in Iraq that were produced in the former West Germany. Their shape and carbon fiber composition could have left no doubt about what the rotors were for, IAEA inspectors said. The sale of carbon-fiber centrifuge rotors was "absolutely illegal," Kay added.

57   Unwilling to depend on outside suppliers for parts, Iraq was building its own plant to manufacture centrifuges at Al Furat. The plant, which was still incomplete when war broke out in the Gulf, would have been capable of turning out centrifuges by the thousands, according to Thorne. Some of the most important pieces of manufacturing equipment for the plant were supplied by H & H Metallform Maschinenbau und Vertriebs GmbH of the former West Germany. The key raw material for the centrifuges was also found in Iraq: some 100 metric tons of maraging steel, most of which had been melted in an unsuccessful attempt to conceal it from inspectors. By early March, the IAEA had still not released the names of the companies that sold Iraq the maraging steel.

58   Although the IAEA believes that Iraq did not succeed in operating a pilot centrifuge cascade before it invaded Kuwait, Kay disagrees. "It's hard to believe that the materials for

Standoff at Al Atheer:
"Thank God for the Satellite Telephone"

For a few days, tens of millions of people watched television news reports and listened to their radios, most in disbelief. Just months after suffering one of the most lopsided military defeats in history, the Iraqi Government seemed to be intent on provoking another war.

As a condition of its surrender, the Iraqi Government agreed to open its weapons facilities—especially its nuclear complex—to inspectors from the United Nations and the International Atomic Energy Agency (IAEA). But on the sixth inspection mission, the Government's attitude toward the inspectors went from spottily cooperative to openly hostile. Access was barred to key facilities, documents were seized, official communiqués were intercepted, and, in the most publicized incident, the inspection team was detained for four days in a parking lot next to an inspection site.

The trouble began the evening of the first day, September 22, when the team, after collecting several dozen boxes of documents, attempted to leave the Nuclear Design Center at Al Atheer. Iraqi officials detained the 43-member team and confiscated the documents, which described Iraq's secret program to build a centrifuge plant to enrich uranium to weapons grade. The team was released after five hours and some of the documents were returned after eleven hours.

According to team leader David Kay, about one-quarter of the documents were not returned, however. These documents probably had infor-

mation related to procurement and design of parts and materials needed for the centrifuge program, Kay said, explaining that the team's translators had scanned the documents and made a brief synopsis before the papers were confiscated.

At the second inspection site, the headquarters of the country's nuclear-weapon development facility, Iraqi officials again attempted to confiscate documents. At stake was information that Kay called "a gold mine": data on the weapons development program; information on Iraq's pursuit of four different enrichment technologies; complete personnel and payroll records of the clandestine weapons effort; and some foreign and domestic procurement records. This time, the team refused, setting up a standoff in an adjacent parking lot that lasted ninety-six hours.

In this war of wills, the inspection team had a secret weapon of its own: a satellite telephone, which was used to do live interviews with major news organizations worldwide. Once again, in a manner bizarrely reminiscent of the Gulf War, the Iraqis "totally underestimated the impact of modern technology," Kay said in an interview. "They didn't understand how we could contact CNN and NPR [National Public Radio]," he observed.

The stalemate was to take a further "surreal" twist on the third day, when Kay, exhausted from doing interviews, heard his satellite telephone ring. It was the operator from the International Maritime Satellite (Inmarsat) Organization. Concerned about the unusual activity on Kay's line, he asked if Kay knew his satellite telephone had been in use for twenty of the last twenty-four hours. Kay did indeed.

Kay explained his predicament and "the guy became very helpful." In Iraq, the team's telephone was at the edge of the closest satellite's coverage, so the operator shifted the satellite in orbit to better accommodate the team. He also rerouted their traffic to an Inmarsat ground station in Australia, which was less heavily trafficked than the Indian Ocean ground station they had been going through.

Finally, at 5:46 am on September 28, the team was released, the disputed documents still in their possession. Relieved, Kay could not help wondering nevertheless what could have happened.

"Thank God for the satellite telephone," said Kay, now secretary general of the Uranium Institute in London. "If we had been caught out there in the parking lot without communications, it's possible that the Iraqis might have used more force than they did, and the United States could have responded militarily."

10 000 centrifuges were ordered without having a small pilot plant going" to verify that the process would work, he said. A "small" cascade would comprise perhaps 100–500 centrifuges, he explained, adding that such a cascade would be sufficient to "tune" the system and establish the efficiency of the process. The hypothetical cascade could have been in operation late in 1989, and may have been disassembled and hidden from IAEA inspectors "until the heat is off," he said.

59   A key point about uranium enrichment—and one frequently overlooked in accounts of the Iraqi program—is that more than one method may be used to produce weapons-grade material. After all, thermal, gas-diffusion, and EMIS techniques were all used to produce the highly enriched uranium for Little Boy, the bomb dropped on Hiroshima at the end of World War II.

60   For example, EMIS is particularly well-suited to further enriching uranium that has already been somewhat enriched, according to Thorne. Thus, although there is no proof that Iraq had such plans, centrifuges could have been used to enrich samples to, say, 12 percent U-235, and EMIS could have been used to bring them up to weapons-grade (93 percent).

61 *A "Startling Find"*   One of the most puzzling of the many mysteries surrounding the Iraq program is the possible discovery of weapons-grade uranium in a group of twenty-five samples taken inside the Tuwaitha complex. The samples, which were filter-paper smears taken off walls, floors, equipment, and other surfaces, were sent to several laboratories—one an IAEA laboratory at Seibersdorf, in Austria; the others US facilities serving the intelligence community.

62   The Seibersdorf laboratory turned up no evidence of highly enriched uranium (HEU). But equipment at the US laboratories, which is several orders of magnitude more sensitive than the Seibersdorf facility, found HEU—not only in the Tuwaitha samples, but in two control samples known to have *no* uranium isotopes at all. Repeated tests on additional samples gave the same results. Compounding the mystery, the US laboratory said some of the uranium samples had a highly unusual isotopic composition, which matched a common

analytical standard used to test detection equipment. "On the face of it, it's a very startling find," Thorne said.

63   The Iraqis have steadfastly maintained that the places at Tuwaitha from which the samples were taken have never contained enriched uranium. "We've really hammered them on this one, and given them every face-saving opportunity to explain it," Thorne said. "But they've held to the story that they never had highly enriched uranium at that site." One current theory is that an HEU standard (analytical) sample somehow contaminated some of the Tuwaitha samples sent to the US laboratory.

64   ***Putting It All Together***   Not limiting itself to producing weapons-grade materials (generally viewed as technologically the hardest task in building a bomb), Iraq was concurrently struggling to build a deliverable weapon around the material, a daunting task known as weaponization. Here, as in its enrichment efforts, Iraq took multiple approaches, mostly at a weapons-design and -testing complex not far from Al Atheer.

65   The two basic types of atomic bombs are gun devices and implosion weapons. The latter are much more difficult to design and build, but provide higher explosive yields for a given amount of fissile material. IAEA investigators have found no evidence that Iraq was actively pursuing a gun device; it is clear, they say, that they concentrated their money and resources on an implosion device, and had even started work on fairly advanced implosion designs.

66   In an implosion device, the fissile material is physically compressed by the force of a shock wave created with conventional explosives. Then, at just the right instant, neutrons are released, initiating the ultrafast fission chain reactions—an atomic blast. Thus the main elements of an implosion device are a firing system, an explosive assembly, and the core. The firing system includes vacuum-tube-based, high-energy discharge devices called krytrons that are capable of releasing enough energy to detonate the conventional explosive. The explosive assembly includes "lenses" that precisely focus the spherical, imploding shockwave on the fissile core, within which is a neutronic initiator. The IAEA has amassed ample evidence that the Iraqis had made progress in each of these areas.

67   Iraq's attempts to import krytrons from CSI Technologies Inc., San Marcos, Calif., made news in March 1990, when two Iraqis were arrested at London's Heathrow airport after an 18-month "sting" operation involving US and British Customs. Several years before that failure, however, Iraq did manage to get weapons-quality capacitors from other US concerns, and also produced its own capacitors. The latter, however, did "not seem to possess the characteristics necessary for storing the energy required by the multiple detonator system," the IAEA found.

68   Work on the conventional explosive assembly, which creates the collapsing shockwave, was carried out mainly at a large explosive production site near Al Qa Qaa. So far, IAEA investigators have found about 230 metric tons of a high-energy explosive, HMX, which is suitable for use in atomic bombs. The IAEA has not announced where the explosive came from, but a knowledgeable source told *Spectrum* it came from Czechoslovakia, where Iraq had bought large quantities of it for conventional military uses in its war with Iran.

69   The seventh IAEA inspection mission to Iraq found that two types of explosive lenses were fabricated and tested near Al Qa Qaa between March and May, 1990. Although both lenses were designed for planar shock waves, "it is prudent to assume that Iraqi scientists have a basic knowledge of the initiation of a spherical implosion," the inspectors wrote in their report on the mission.

70   The seventh mission also found that Iraqi scientists had used hydrodynamic computer programs to evaluate various core geometries. Also, facilities were found at Al Atheer that would have been suitable for large-scale uranium metallurgy, of the sort that would be necessary to produce the core of a bomb. Kay said he saw some evidence that at least preliminary tests had been carried out on the use of implosions to compress depleted (unenriched) uranium; such work would have enabled the Iraqis to study the symmetry and simultaneity of shock waves without risking a nuclear explosion.

71   Indications are so far that Iraq was having trouble producing a neutronic initiator. Besides the usual polonium-beryllium design, several alternatives were being examined, none apparently with much success.

72   Among the more interesting documents found in Iraq is a proposal by an Iraqi Government chemist to produce tritium, the heaviest hydrogen isotope, by irradiating lithium-6. The disclosure of the document led to erroneous press reports that Iraq was at work on a thermonuclear (fusion) bomb. In all advanced atomic (fission) bomb designs, tritium is used in the core to boost the explosive yield, Thorne noted, and this may have been the use envisioned by the chemist.

73   In a gun-type atomic bomb, the chain-reaction is initiated by hurling together in a tube, and with tremendous force, two samples of highly enriched uranium. Much more fissile material is needed than would be for an implosive weapon, and gun-type bombs are difficult, if not impossible, to deliver with a missile. But they can be quite effective, as Little Boy demonstrated. According to Kay, the Iraqis "knew everything necessary to make a gun-assembly device." He also said he found tungsten-carbide piping, which would have been suitable for making the tube in which the samples would collide.

74 *Ignored Consequences*   Though Iraqi officials considered every angle and possibility in attempting to build an atomic bomb, they seem to have completely ignored the consequences of having one.

75   "I'm not sure the Iraqis had thought through the political and strategic implications of having a nuclear weapon," Kay said. "If the Israelis had known what the full size and scope of the Iraqi nuclear program was, I'm not sure what their reaction would have been when the Scuds started falling. I'm not sure that pressure from the United States and other countries would have been enough to keep the Israelis from reacting with massive force."

76   Unfortunately, such an outcome is still a possibility. Though the Iraqi nuclear program is now being dismantled, some analysts see parallels between the vanquished southwest Asian nation today and Germany after World War I. "While Iraq does not possess the industrial skills available to Germany in 1919, the full extent of Iraq's ability to infiltrate the economic structure of the West, particularly western Europe, in order to gain access to very high technology is just becoming known," wrote Geoffrey Kemp in *The Control of the Middle East Arms Race*.

77   "The danger is that once Iraq begins to export oil and gains access to hard currency, it will be able to hide a portion of its revenues for covert purposes," according to Kemp, a senior associate at the Carnegie Endowment for International Peace in Washington, DC. "Once it has accumulated a sizable hard currency account, it could once more use its financial resources to penetrate the arms market and buy the services of unemployed technicians and engineers in Europe, including East Europe and the Soviet Union."

78 *To Probe Further*   *The Death Lobby: How the West Armed Iraq* is one of the most comprehensive accounts of its kind. Although it was written before the start of the inspec-

tion missions to Iraq, it has detailed histories of the country's procurement efforts and describes its methods and tactics. Written by Kenneth R. Timmerman, it was published by Houghton Mifflin, Boston, in 1991. *The Bulletin of the Atomic Scientists* has run several lengthy articles speculating on how advanced the Iraqi program was; see especially the March, July/August, and September 1991 issues. *The Control of the Middle East Arms Race*, by Geoffrey Kemp with Shelly A. Stahl, was published by the Carnegie Endowment for International Peace in Washington, D.C., last autumn.

NOTES AND DISCUSSION

Note the variety of expository techniques Zorpette uses in this essay. To place the technical problem within a historical context, he begins with a narrative about what had seemed a routine wartime mission. He then bridges to technical matters by asking a question that sets out two areas for examination. Next, he analyzes the separate but concurrent parts of the project. Along the way Zorpette effectively uses definitions, such as the definition of "reverse engineering" in paragraph 6, and the description and definition of the EMIS (electromagnetic isotope separation) process in the section headed "A Very Messy Affair."

This article has echoes of the detective story as it unravels various levels of deception and complicated transactions in the build-up of the materials and technology necessary for building an atomic bomb. It is also a cautionary tale about how technologically advanced nations make themselves vulnerable to attacks from less advanced ones.

Note how Zorpette brings in sources to supplement or support his reportage. Some of those sources (particularly the military ones) are anonymous, though many are named and their credentials given. Consider the impact of the variety of sources, and Zorpette's methods of acknowledgement.

STUDY QUESTIONS

For Discussion

1. Zorpette defines "reverse engineering" as "exploiting projects and developments that had been abandoned by earlier experimenters in the United States and elsewhere." Discuss his implicit claim that the Iraqi project exploited blind spots, created by what Thomas Kuhn would recognize as "paradigm shifts," by adopting and hiding behind technology, such as EMIS, that had long been abandoned or superseded elsewhere.

2. Consider the impact of beginning a report on highly technical and potentially sensitive matters with a narrative, an element that helps "personalize" the subject. Discuss the impact of that personalization on the technical nature of the piece.

For Writing

1. Analyze and explain the importance of the sub-headings used throughout. Begin by listing the headings separately to see what they have to tell you about the shape and content of the article.

2. As a research project, look up the companion piece by John A. Adam in the April 1992 issue of *IEEE Spectrum*, and explain how the two pieces work together to cover the larger issues raised by their joint title, "Seeking Nuclear Safeguards."

APPENDIX A

Waniskâ Nôsim

Joyce Dene

1   Two miles of traffic noise. Five days a week. Fall semester, a year away from graduation. A long, cold walk. I'm bundled. Almost there. Unlocking the heavy glass door to my sister's walk-up, I look forward to snuggling down with a hot tea and reading Robert Silverburg's sci-fi thriller, *Night Wings*.

2   Slowly unwrapping the scarf around my neck, I ease the backpack off my shoulder and let it slide to the floor, keeping *them* in sight. Am I really seeing what I'm seeing? It seems like a lifetime since I'd seen them. I'd heard they lived up the river and now here they sit side by side on the couch. Cardboard boxes, and bulging Glad bags, filled with winter supplies, surround the room and their feet. The woman's floral handkerchief covers her head; a neat red bow hangs down to her chest. Her silvered braids poke out and fall, resting on her shoulders. She stoops to carefully sip at a steaming porcelain cup cradled between her weathered, wrinkled hands, while his gnarled fingers hold onto a fluffy piece of bannock loaded with strawberry jam. He happily chews away, oblivious to my presence; they're both captured by the muted television set before them. Are they really here? Or are my eyes playing tricks on me?

3   "Joyce, is that you? Our Môsom and Kôhkom just got in this morning." My sister's voice carries through the bathroom door and gives me away. Their faces light up into smiles when they see me. I don't react, but stand there, unsure.

4   *"Âstam nôsim."* She reaches out and pulls me toward her, and I feel myself being crushed into her soft, lumpy body. Easily lifting me like hand weights, she passes my frame over to the old man. She is a strong woman. She once told me stories of the way she carried large beavers by the tail, one in each hand, and walked for miles. Today, she probably could only manage a block without her cane.

5   He gently squeezes me in his arms. His whiskers bristle against my cheek. Bannock crumbs cling to the corner of his lips. He nods his head and beams as I pull away. They are happy to see me. Two years since I've seen them. Years that quietly slipped by.

6   "They want to ask you something." She comes around the corner dressed in a terry bathrobe, her head wrapped in a towel; she smells of soap and toothpaste. "I told them that you're in school." She pauses, quickly rubbing the towel into her head, hesitating. "But, they want to ask you anyway." Her voice stammers.

7   My older sister, the first-born, always the mediator, the negotiator, the manipulator, looks like she had already decided on my behalf, judging by the sheepish way she approaches me. I pictured them conspiring together while I was at school. Ask? I had to sit down for this one.

8   A year?

9   "When... tomorrow morning? No way, I have to finish my social studies assignment; I have an English paper due on Friday." It's no use negotiating. She has the upper hand. I try another tactic.

10   "So you're basically throwing me out?" She ignores this weak stab. Avoids looking at me as she disappears around the corner.

11   Déjà vu with a two-year interval.

12   Two years ago, in Fort Chipewyan at the beginning of a new semester, I refused to go to the trap-line with my father.

13   Mornings were the worst. Starting fires was never easy, but we managed to get a few logs burnt before heading off for our nine o'clock classes.

14   Staying in school meant struggling to eat; a struggle shared with another student.

15   We stayed in her mother's two-storey built at the beginning of the nineteen hundreds, where ghosts played havoc with our imaginations. During those late fall days, it welcomed us with an icy dark, while we scrambled for matches, with chattering teeth, and trembling fingers, first to light a candle; then we'd rush to start a fire in a rusting cast-iron stove that looked as old as the house. It never seemed to warm up. Mostly, we'd head for bed, after giving up on wood that refused to burn. Here, we would snack on crackers and cheese, listen to the CBC, the only radio station that came in clear without an antenna, and read by a coal oil lamp.

16   Before Christmas, my father returned and cut my year short. He refused to let me continue living like that. He said I looked like I was about to fade away.

17   Two years later and I was caving in again.

18   They tried to cheer me up.

19   "Never mind," she said.

20   "You'll understand," he said.

21   "Bring your books. An offer," they said.

22   One I couldn't refuse.

23   Reading had consumed me, or I had consumed it. Couldn't decide whether it was a curse, or a blessing.

24   Day One. A nippy grey October morning. One hundred and thirty odd miles to go.

25   Light drizzle does not deter the seasoned traveller. Grandma and I sit on a bench by the dock watching the men load the boat, a skiff my father built years ago. This one is a twenty-odd footer balanced by four benches. It is showing its years of river travel. I silently question whether it will be able to contain a load of five passengers, winter supplies, and my books.

26   Amongst the boxes containing jams, peanut-butter, sacks of flour, sugar, coffee and tea, are my sci-fis, mysteries, thrillers, and fantasies— political, social and religious views

in various fiction— all carefully wrapped in garbage bags and stuffed into cardboard boxes that once held fruit. Everything is tied under canvas tarps camouflaged by the dreary morning.

27   It's time to board. The men hold the boat steady. Grandma gingerly steps into the time-worn grey skiff. Soon, grandma and I, cushioned, layered in blankets, and wrapped in canvas tarps, are seated in the middle. The old man sits ready, his gloved hand resting on the motor's arm. Dressed in yellow rain gear, he colours the morning. Edward, my brother, sits beside him, on the other side. He wears a Glad bag to blend in with the evergreens. Jack gives a quick shove and sends the boat adrift on the Clearwater River; murky waves lap against the boat.

28   I turn to see the high-rises standing stark against the forested hills of Fort McMurray. Somewhere amongst those towers is my sister's walk-up.

29   We drift, carried by an undercurrent. With a crank, the motor spurts into action. I feel my grandmother's hand on mine. She squeezes, as though reassuring me that everything is going to be all right. How did she know I was suffocating?

30   We ride out of the rain even before reaching the bend into the Athabasca River. In the distance, the sky looks split: a smoky white blanket of clouds and a crisp blue October sky. We head for the blue. I rest my head on grandma's shoulder and allow the monotone of the Johnson to lull me to sleep.

31   My eyes open when the motor is cut. Confusion sets in like after a bad dream. I should be sitting in my social studies class rather than here in this wooden skiff. I wonder if I am missed, or if they will even notice. Probably not. The rocking motion caused by the waves and the chilly wind that dances across my face wake me to this cold reality.

32   Jack, who sits up by the stern, now holds a paddle out to ease the boat against the shore. He leaps out onto the mud flat, secures the rope on some branches, reaches for an axe and sprints up the sloping hill. I can hear him chopping at wood. My brother digs out the grub box, moves it forward. We have stopped for lunch. Before long, I hear the sound of crackling wood as smoke billows softly between the leafless white birch, red willows, and firs, before dissipating, erased by the wind. My Mosôm stands up to load his shotgun. He anticipates supper.

33   I remain seated, lost in my thoughts until Kôhkom requests my help. "Mathi nôsim." I feel her weight on my right shoulder as I help her up the small hill. She moves with ease, though favouring her weak side. Years ago, in her sixties, she suffered a massive stroke while saving Jack from drowning.

34   We slowly make our way to the warmth of the fire. Already a pot of water boils for tea.

35   I can only listen to the rhythmic sounds of Cree. Understand. Nod. My voice long silenced. I had lost my talk. But they assured me that in time I would rediscover those sacred sounds.

36   One December day (lost count). After the old woman and I were left alone, after the men had left for the back woods, sometimes gone for days, she taught me about time. As I read, I could hear her wind, and re-wind the clock that sat by her bed. The golden silence was broken up by the loud tick-tocking of that damned clock. She found ways to get my attention by deliberately setting the alarm to pierce the quiet. She laughed wholeheartedly the first time she watched *1984* fly out of my hand and slide across the floor, while Big Ben hammered the silence into oblivion. She definitely had my attention. I would frown at

her, which she disregarded, and request a cup of tea before she would lie back for her afternoon nap. While she slept, I would face the south window, ignore the clock, and remember the loss of my second voice.

37   After five years of transformations, a time when I was Number 7, I learnt to say number seven in the 'big house' that once dominated most of the landscape on the northwest shore of the Athabasca Lake. I was finally released to test drive the new voice in the brave new world.

38   Two years later in a boom-town school, when the teacher questioned her grade six class, she would randomly select kids for answers. And when she pointed at me, singling me out, the amplified beat of my heart deafened me so that I was unable to hear myself speak. Apparently, I made some kind of sound, for it caused a wave of body spasms amongst my classmates. They would cover their mouths with their chubby little hands, snickering. Some would outright laugh. I hated her index finger. I ducked it by refusing to answer any more of her questions. In the end no one spoke to me, and I spoke to no one. Instead, I escaped into a world between pages where I could move around freely: invisible.

39   Even then my silence was not golden. The quiet person doesn't necessarily constitute a radiating silence. Inside she's raging with inaudible screams. Sylvia Plath's. Sometimes her own. George Orwell alerts the *Thought Police*.

40   They patiently wait.

41   *Big Brother Is Watching You!* warns George. I imagine a large index finger with eyes peeking around corners. Only to see it years later, on a red, white and blue poster. So tempted at the time to doodle dangling, goofy eyeballs on the end of this old man's extended finger that captioned, *Uncle Sam Wants You!* Without a marker, I could only shudder.

42   I grew to love the quiet existence but detested that the loud, wide-faced, white clock equipped with double alarms measured it with its large numbers. Once, while grandma slept, I hid the clock on her, just so I could hear Shirley Jackson's voice more distinctly. I waited for my number to be called. Wished my number would be picked, unlike Sylvia who couldn't wait.

43   The old woman knew. She knew that I hid her clock and she knew why I would sit for hours looking out the window when I wasn't reading. She encouraged me to read. And I delved deeper into my fruit boxes, finally exhausting my supply of voices. Tired, weary, and lonely, I withdrew. Until one day, before I planned to sleep, she loaned me her voice.

44   The story she unfolds emulates the storytellers from her youth. Storytellers who kept her imagination entertained, and who always began with:

45   "Âhaw nosimis, mahti êkwa. Ay pêyakwaw êsa awa..." Sounds, familiar sounds that animate pictures in her mind, characters like *Ayas* who come alive and dance about with the crackling fire's light. Sparks that flicker off his or her heels, red flashes here and there upon the walls to the rhythmic rattle of the blustery wind against frosted panes. A relentless winter wind that whistles between the cracks of groaning logs, undeterred, the storyteller's soft voice persists taking her granddaughter on a magical journey: words brought to life there under a star filled sky.

46   "Waniskâ nôsim." A light hand arouses me from my dream. It was an alluring dream. I dreamt I was chained: my own doing. I willingly walked into a snare, the kind that *Ayas* overcame. The sensation lingers. I had fallen asleep by the fire. I rub my ankle, and slowly rise. *Kôhkom* needs me to shoulder her back into the boat.

47   We continue on the stretching river. I watch the changing tree line grow ever denser, ever darker as we go farther down the Athabasca. Familiar land appears in the distance. Sand hills I tumbled down at the wee age of three are to the right. Land that has since swallowed the armoured cone that once was swarmed by sweaty men who reeked of sawdust and even still, reverberations from the machinery can almost be heard. But, the land has since reclaimed itself. As we pass that place, waves thrash against the shore.

48   The motor is throttled lower, almost at an idle. I feel the boat shift. Thundering blasts echo throughout the river. The gurgling prop signals a roundabout. The boat aims for the targets. Two bobbing mallard carcasses, wings spread out, drift in the rhythm of the waves. Jack easily scoops them up, one by one, and gives the necks a final death swing. They fall with a thud on the floor of the boat.

49   The motor is in full gear now, and the boat speeds away. Tarps flap in the wind. I bury my nose in the blankets and long for sleep. Afraid to dream, I stay awake.

50   Around that bend is a cabin that belongs to the Courteorilles. Our faces turn to see if there is smoke coming from the pipes. But the two-storey stands empty. We hear dogs barking above the motor. We don't stop.

51   Another stretch, another bend and there's the creek, now dark as we pass it. The Athabasca forks and spills into the mouth of the Embarras River. Red willows shoot up along the shoreline. Ancient poplars, birch, and firs stand prominent around the cabins. There is a soft light coming from my dad's. I see silhouettes standing on the shore. The motor is throttled a pitch lower as we slow to another idle. I hear the stern nudge the soft muddy shore. Shorty barks excitedly, running up and down the hill. A pathway has been cut at an angle on the mud wall of the embankment. My dad and younger brother walk down to meet the boat.

52   A wooden dock rises with the waves. Jack jumps out, ropes in hand, eases the skiff parallel with the dock, ties one to a pole and another to a bench.

53   Eager to help, I kick off the blankets. I'm ready. Grandma needs to be released from her cocoon. Her fingers, stiff, grasp at the layers, her arms, heavy with fatigue reach up. She holds firmly to my hand, causing a glassy ripple in the dark water. Her legs shake, and she sits down on the bench to rest. Her movement rocks the boat. She breathes heavily. Tries again. Unsteady. The dock dips to meet the passengers. Jack comes to her aid as well. We three walk up the hill, resting now and then, waiting until she catches her breath.

54   The smell of cooked food greets us as we open the familiar door. She easily shuffles her way to the bed without assistance. I sit resignedly on a chair by the stove like a visitor. My brother hands me a tin cup of hot tea.

55   I survey the one-room log cabin. There's two of everything in here: two beds, two stoves, two night tables, well almost everything. There is also a wooden table surrounded by four chairs, a cupboard, and a wash stand. On the planked ceiling, hide thongs remain, remnants of another time when baby swings once criss-crossed the room. The only things that hang from the ceiling now are two horizontal poles decorated with mitts, socks, moccasins, stretch boards for muskrats and squirrels, and a hissing gas lamp. My father had built this cabin, as well as most of the furniture, a year before his first child was born.

56   On her night table is a radio and Big Ben. Mary and Jesus stretch their arms out on a shelf above the double bed. I ignore them. I assume the narrow cot to my right is where I will be sleeping. Beside it is a coal oil lamp sitting unlit on a small table. On the mattress are a bedroll and a feather robe, but no pillow.

57   Bleakly, I eye the hot liquid warming my hands. My elbows rest on my knees and the scarf falls between. At my feet, in my backpack, Silverburg has wings that wait for me.

58   Before long, my grandmother's breathing has been replaced by a soft purring snore. Her scarf remains on her head. I silently question her sleeping face. Her eyebrows rise. Her eyes pop open.

59   "Nôsim, nôsom icikâni." And smiles. Sleep tugs at her tired eyes. She can't resist. Her eyes slowly close, but not before I smile back.

APPENDIX B

Putting Self-Help "Leviathans" and "Oracles" to Sleep:

A Discussion of Anthony Robbins' *Awaken the Giant Within* and James Redfield's *The Celestine Prophecy*

Lisa Grekul

1   To unlock the secrets of individual "success" or personal "fulfillment," we need look no further than the "self-development" or "self-help" genre of popular literature. For C\$22.95 we can buy texts that contain the key to mental, emotional, physical, and financial accomplishment: we can buy Anthony Robbins' *Awaken the Giant Within* or James Redfield's *The Celestine Prophecy*. In fact, the strikingly similar "secrets" found in the texts of Robbins and Redfield are shared by most self-help books.[1] Close readings, then, of *Awaken the Giant Within* and *The Celestine Prophecy*—as representative texts of the genre—reveal the common themes employed by self-help authors to lead readers "down the path" of self-improvement. Although Robbins' book is a work of nonfiction (directed primarily at a male audience) and Redfield's book is a work of fiction (directed at a male or female audience), both authors cloak their self-help ideology in fairy-tale motifs and imagery. One aphoristic tenet lies at the core of both texts: success is achieved through "spiritual awakening." Robbins and Redfield emphasize the innovative attributes of their spiritual insights, but the authors' teachings are neither creative nor original. Rather, *Awaken the Giant Within* resonates with Biblical references and *The Celestine Prophecy* reiterates centuries-old gnostic beliefs. Moreover, both Robbins and Redfield rely upon the psychological paradigm of Maslow's hierarchy of needs: Robbins addresses the basic human need for "self-actualization" and Redfield embraces the need for "spiritual transcendence." Perhaps in our increasingly secularized Western society authors like Robbins and Redfield prepackage "accessible" religious models. But when the ticket to spiritual awakening takes the form of a best-selling book,[2] authors like Robbins and Redfield leave their "commodified" spiritual teachings open to Marxist critique. The foundation for success (mental, emotional, physical, and financial) may lie in spirituality or faith, but, ultimately, we must question the \$22.95 spiritual value of *Awaken the Giant Within* or *The Celestine Prophecy*.

2   Anthony Robbins begins *Awaken the Giant Within* with his own fairy-tale success story, a personal anecdote that highlights the process through which he awakened to his life's purpose. Twelve years ago, Robbins was a veritable Cinderella figure: a lost, lonely, and overweight janitor with a 1960 Volkswagen. He gained "information, strategies, philosophies, and skills" (Robbins 20), however, and his dream of "success" magically came true. Robbins fails to explain precisely how he became successful: as though blessed with a fairy godmother, in one sentence he is "sitting in [his] 400-square-foot bachelor apartment... all alone and crying as [he] listened to the lyrics of a Neil Diamond song" (20–21) and in the next he is speaking to "five thousand smiling, cheering, loving faces" (20). Because success for Robbins is the discovery of hidden motivational-speaker talents, he (*himself*) becomes a fairy godmother figure, waving the magic wand of CANI!™[3] over audiences everywhere. He writes that our dreams are often "shrouded in the frustrations and routines of daily life" but that his "life's quest has been to restore the dream and to make it real" (19). Logically, then, he locates *Awaken the Giant Within* in a wondrous world of dreams, masters, giants, and power. From time to time, while flying his jet helicopter over Los Angeles en route to one of his seminars, even Robbins wonders, *"could this be real?"* (21). Robbins' personal success story may be genuine but it establishes a fantasy framework for his book—a framework through which readers rely on Robbins, as "self-help fairy godmother," to make happy endings of their ordinary lives.

3   Similarly, James Redfield constructs *The Celestine Prophecy* in the framework of a fairy tale: in his search for an ancient manuscript, Redfield's narrator goes to a land far, far away (Peru). The narrator finds an idealized exotic setting at the Viciente Lodge, the ruins of Machu Picchu, and the ruins of the Celestine Temple. He describes, for example, the Viciente Lodge: "surrounded by colorful pastures and orchards, the grass seemed unusually green and healthy. It grew thickly even under the giant oaks... [there were] beds of exotic plants and walkways trimmed with dazzling flowers and ferns" (Redfield, *Prophecy* 39). The exotic milieu invokes fairy tales set in foreign lands, like the *Arabian Nights*. The manuscript itself, which "dates back to about 600 BC [and] predicts a massive transformation in human society" (4), bears symbolic resemblance to Aladdin's lamp. Rubbing Aladdin's lamp frees a genie who will, in turn, grant wishes of instant power and fortune; reading the ancient manuscript provides a "new spiritual awakening" (Redfield, *Guide* xv) that will, in turn, bring instant power and fortune. When the manuscript is destroyed, the narrator learns that "from now on the insights will have to be shared between people. Each person, once they hear the message... must pass on the message to everyone who is ready for it" (Redfield, *Prophecy* 245). *The Celestine Prophecy* may contain nine spiritual insights in the form of the "written word," but, at the same time, it encourages oral transmission of these insights. *Orally* transmitted, Redfield's spiritual insights take on the dimensions of a fairy or folk tale.

4   Although Robbins explains, in *Awaken the Giant Within*, his perpetual search for new methods and technologies to pass along, his Biblical allusions and metaphors undermine the novelty of his enterprise. Like a Messiah, Robbins uses personal charisma to spread his self-development gospels. Robbins explains that psychologists and psychiatrists have called him "a charlatan and a liar... [who makes] false claims" (Robbins 109); so, too, was Jesus Christ accused and denounced by the chief priests and scribes of Jerusalem (Luke 23). Robbins' "Seven Days to Shape Your Life" (Robbins 12) are undeniably parallel to the seven days of creation (Genesis 1 and 2). Each day of Robbins' creation, however, corresponds to an aspect of "your" personal destiny: emotional (day one), physical (two), relationship (three), financial (four), conduct (five), and time (six). Of course, day seven is

earmarked for "Rest and Play: Even God Took One Day Off!" (Robbins 12). Robbins directly quotes from Matthew 7:7, "ask and you will receive. Seek and you will find; knock, and it will be opened to you" (Robbins 162), but *Awaken the Giant Within*—from cover to cover—echoes Matthew 25:14–30, the "Parable of the Talents."[4] We learn from the Biblical parable that "talents," innate abilities, must be improved and cultivated. The epigraph to Robbins' book, a quotation from Orison Swett Marden, emphasizes Robbins' analogous notion that our built-in abilities must be recognized before we can unleash our power-potential: "deep within man dwell those slumbering powers; powers that would astonish him, that he never dreamed of possessing; forces that would revolutionize his life if aroused and put into action" (Robbins 15). Robbins himself says "the most exciting thing about this force, this power, is that you already possess it" (37): if we are to succeed, our talents must be awakened and refined.

5   *The Celestine Prophecy*'s promises of "new consciousness... new awareness... new understanding" (Author's Note) are hardly new: such promises were voiced in the Mediterranean during the second and third centuries, when gnosticism reached the height of its popularity.[5] According to gnostic teachings, individuals escape from the material world and find eternal salvation through an unmediated relationship with God. Each of the nine insights absorbed by Redfield's narrator articulates an aspect of gnosticism: the second insight, for example, helps us "[become] aware of our essentially spiritual nature" (Redfield, *Guide* 244); the fifth insight describes "how a mystical connection with universal energy feels" (244); the seventh insight shows us "how to ask questions, receive intuitions, and find answers" (245). With the ninth insight the narrator at last learns how to connect with divine energy: he says, "at some point everyone will vibrate highly enough so that we can walk into heaven" (Redfield, *Prophecy* 242). *The Tenth Insight*, moreover, is entirely populated with characters who "vibrate," become invisible, and subsequently find heaven on earth. They understand that "real fulfillment comes only when we first tune into our inner direction and divine guidance... we become cocreators with the divine source" (Redfield, *Tenth Insight* 29). The irony of *The Celestine Prophecy*'s new-age appeal is that its gnostic teachings are, in fact, age-old.

6   The underlying psychology of *Awaken the Giant Within* may not be "age-old," but it has "been around" for at least two decades: Robbins capitalizes on Maslow's "hierarchy of needs"[6] to justify his self-development program. In 1970, humanist psychologist Abraham Maslow formulated the theory that "our inborn needs are arranged in a sequence of stages from primitive to advanced" (Zimbardo 433). Robbins' interest is in individuals who are near the "top" of the hierarchy, people "who are nourished, safe, loved and loving, secure, thinking, and creating. These people have moved beyond basic human needs in the quest for fullest development of their potentials" (433). Robbins' objective is to help individuals *self-actualize*. According to Maslow's theory, self-actualization requires the fulfillment of several criteria; individuals must become "self-aware, self-accepting, socially responsive, creative, spontaneous, and open to novelty and challenge" (433). And Robbins systematically addresses each of Maslow's criteria for self-actualization. With imperative language, he makes demands like "write down the replacements for the two limiting beliefs you've just eliminated" (Robbins 103), "take immediate action as soon as you finish this chapter" (304), "know who you are" (424), "accept who you are" (424), "connect with people at the deepest level" (27), believe in your "power to create" (75), and be spontaneous, as "all changes are created in a moment" (108). Maslow's model provides the psychological subtext of *Awaken the Giant Within*.

7   Redfield's interest, on the other hand, is in the highest echelon of Maslow's hierarchy of needs: the *need for spiritual transcendence,* "a step beyond total fulfillment of individual potential" (Zimbardo 433). The need for spiritual transcendence "may lead to higher states of consciousness and a cosmic vision of one's part in the universe" (433). Indeed, *The Celestine Prophecy* rejects our "500-year-old preoccupation with secular survival" (Redfield, *Guide* xv); it focuses, rather, on "ending the cycle of birth and death" (xviii) by revealing our purpose in "a universe of dynamic energy" (xvi). Redfield looks ahead to a future in which all citizens of the world will fulfill the human need for spiritual transcendence. Our advanced spiritualism will affect economic systems: "when people come into our lives at just the right time to give us the answers we need, we... give them money" (Redfield, *Prophecy* 226), but eventually "the automation of goods will allow everyone's needs to be met completely, without the exchange of any currency" (Redfield, *Guide* 247). Ecologically, we will "revere the natural energy sources of mountains, deserts, forests, lakes, and rivers" (246). Politically, we will "democratize the planet" (247). In *The Celestine Prophecy*, when all of humanity has ascended Maslow's hierarchy of needs, spiritual principles will direct human society.

8   But the inherent paradox of *Awaken the Giant Within* and *The Celestine Prophecy* is that, in both cases, spiritual principles are prepackaged and mass-marketed: by selling spiritual guidance as a commodity, Robbins and Redfield "snuff out" the morality of spirituality. Inscribed in the discourse of their self-help books is self-help ideology. Like other ideologies, characterized by "masking, distortion, [and] concealment" (Storey 3), the ideology of the self-help industry "works in the interest of the powerful against the interests of the powerless... [it] conceals the reality of domination from those in power... [and] conceals the reality of subordination from those who are powerless" (3). If we believe that Robbins or Redfield will change our lives, we have been lulled into a state of false consciousness; the authors offer "false, but seemingly true, resolutions to real problems" (111–12). They wield their capitalist power, cloaked in ostensible benevolence, over the spiritually-needy masses. Hence, their alleged desire to help and empower "the weak" is at odds with their desire to oppress and exploit the weak. Ironically, if people are actually helped by authors like Robbins or Redfield, what happens to the self-help industry?

9   Ultimately, *Awaken the Giant Within*'s primary objective is to guarantee the reader's dependency on Anthony Robbins: again and again the discourse of his text impels readers to "come back for more." Riddled with imperative language—"awaken the giant power of decision... claim the birthright of unlimited power... make a decision right now" (Robbins 36)—the book demands a commitment to Robbins' brand of self-help. His principle doctrine, CANI!™ (Constant And Never-ending Improvement), recurs throughout the book as an aggressive reminder that self-development is a constant and never-ending process. Completion of *Awaken the Giant Within* is not an "end" but a "beginning"; Robbins concludes with the notion that "you are guided along a path of never-ending growth and learning" (512). Who guides you along the path? Robbins himself. He unabashedly asks that you maintain a "relationship" with him through "a tape or a seminar" (512). In fact, on a personal note, Robbins says, "I hope you'll stay in touch with me. I hope you'll write to me or that we'll have the privilege of meeting personally in a seminar, [or] at a Foundation function" (512). To ensure that you have continued access to his guidance—and he has continued access to your pocketbook—Robbins devotes several pages (513–19) to advertising his "Personal Power" audio cassette series, *Unlimited Power* (his second book), and Robbins Success Systems™ seminars.

10   Similarly, *The Celestine Prophecy* represents the ground breaking work through which Redfield hooks the reader into the "celestine industry." The discourse of Redfield's spiritual awakening is characteristically vague: we are to "exist at a level of higher energy," to engage in "mystical experience[s]," and to move "toward worldwide spiritual consciousness" (Redfield, *Prophecy* 120). When Redfield explicitly presents semantic ambiguities, he implicitly suggests that *The Celestine Prophecy* is incomplete without *The Celestine Prophecy: An Experiential Guide*. Designed to "clarify the experience conveyed in the original book" (Redfield, *Guide* xii), the *Experiential Guide* facilitates group discussion of the nine spiritual insights. But the ninth insight itself "mentions that a Tenth Insight exists" (Redfield, *Prophecy* 243), hence engendering the reader's anticipation of a sequel. Both *The Celestine Prophecy* and *The Tenth Insight* are followed by advertisements for "The Celestine Journal," which (for US$29.95) "chronicles [Redfield's] present experiences and reflections on the spiritual renaissance occurring on our planet" (Redfield, *Prophecy* 247). Readers can also purchase audio cassettes of the *Celestine Meditations* or *The Celestine Prophecy—A Musical Voyage*. Evidently, *The Celestine Prophecy* "proper" merely initiates readers into the "celestine subculture," but it cannot be mistaken for the definitive "celestine work": such a work does not exist. Rather, readers rely on Redfield to sustain the production of numerous (multimedia) celestine texts and Redfield relies on readers to provide ceaseless monetary support of the celestine industry.

11   And so, the cost incurred for the secrets of mental, emotional, physical, and financial success may, in fact, exceed $22.95. As representative texts of the self-help genre of popular literature, Anthony Robbins' *Awaken the Giant Within* and James Redfield's *The Celestine Prophecy* appear to provide "cheap" and "easy" access to spirituality in our increasingly secularized Western society. The texts, however, do not easily escape criticism. Both texts locate their self-help ideology in familiar cultural constructs. Robbins and Redfield use fairy-tale motifs and imagery as frameworks for their books. While Robbins relies on Biblical allusions and metaphors to articulate his self-help program, Redfield resurrects gnosticism; where Robbins invokes the "self-actualization" need of Maslow's psychological paradigm, Redfield invokes the "spiritual transcendence" need of Maslow's hierarchy. But fairy-tale frameworks, religious invocations, and psychological subtexts fail to conceal the underlying capitalist motivations of *Awaken the Giant Within* and *The Celestine Prophecy*. In the self-help industry, spiritualism ironically becomes a market commodity through which authors like Robbins and Redfield exploit and oppress their vulnerable readers. And, ultimately, the paradox is that in order to ensure success in the self-help industry, authors of self-help texts (like Robbins and Redfield) must perpetuate the insecurities of their readers.

NOTES

1. Most notably, Deepak Chopra's *Way of the Wizard: Twenty Spiritual Lessons for Creating the Life You Want* and *The Seven Spiritual Laws of Success*, as well as Dan Millman's *Way of the Peaceful Warrior: A Book That Changes Lives* and *Sacred Journey of the Peaceful Warrior*.

2. In fact, Robbins and Redfield have respectively created an industry in and of themselves. Robbins has a best-selling book, an audio cassette series (Powertalk), and nine companies that produce infomercials and motivational seminars. Redfield wrote two

sequels to *The Celestine Prophecy*: *The Celestine Prophecy Experiential Guide* (1995) and *The Tenth Insight* (1996); he also produces the *Celestine Journal* and *Celestine Meditations* (audio cassettes with his wife Salle). I discuss this later in the essay.

3. Constant And Never-ending Improvement (Robbins 96).

4. This parable tells of a man who goes on a journey and leaves his money with three servants. Two of the servants invest their money and receive interest, but the third servant hides his money in the ground. When the master returns, he praises the first two servants and berates the third.

5. Though not directly quoted, my sources regarding gnosticism are *The Literary Guide to the Bible* and *Compton's Interactive Encyclopedia*. (Copyright 1994 Compton's NewMedia, Inc.).

6. Maslow's hierarchy looks something like this diagram, modeled on Zimbardo's discussion of Maslow in *Psychology and Life:*

Transcendence:
spiritual need for
cosmic identification

Self-Actualization: need to fulfill
potential, to have meaningful goals

Esthetic: need for order and beauty

Cognitive: need for knowledge, understanding

Esteem: need for confidence, sense of worth/competence

Attachment: need to belong, to affiliate, to love and be loved

Safety: need for security, comfort, tranquility, and freedom from fear

Biological: need for food, water, oxygen, rest, sexual expression, release from tension

WORKS CITED

Alter, Robert, and Frank Kermode, eds. *The Literary Guide to the Bible.* Cambridge, Mass.: Belknap Press, 1987.

Redfield, James. *The Celestine Prophecy.* New York: Time Warner, 1993.

_____. *The Celestine Prophecy: An Experiential Guide.* New York: Time Warner, 1995.

_____. *The Tenth Insight.* New York: Time Warner, 1996.

Robbins, Anthony. *Awaken the Giant Within: How to Take Immediate Control of Your Mental, Emotional, Physical, and Financial Destiny!* New York: Simon and Schuster, 1992.

Storey, John. *An Introductory Guide to Cultural Theory and Popular Culture.* Athens: University of Georgia Press, 1993.

Zimbardo, Philip G. *Psychology and Life.* New York: HarperCollins, 1992.

APPENDIX C

Detection of Landmines

A Technical Report for a Course in Mechanical Engineering

Robert Gust, Chris Turner, Peter Karl, and Scott Koehn

ABSTRACT

1 The objective of the project was to design a mechanical means of detecting the VS-50 anti-personnel (AP) or the VS-2.2 anti-tank (AT) land mines. A method of prodding the ground with numerous hydraulically driven probes was chosen as the most effective means of detection because of its simplicity, adaptability, the proven reliability of prods as detectors, and the possibility of relatively high clearance rates.

2 The chosen design consists of a lead row of 78 prods to detect AP mines and a separate row of 32 prods behind to detect AT mines; each row spans 3 metres. The prods in one row are hydraulically injected into the ground at 45° to a prescribed depth, while a data acquisition system continuously records pressure and depth measurements. When the maximum depth is reached, the prods are retracted and the row moves forward to begin the next stage. Each stage takes approximately 4.5 seconds resulting in a possible clearance rate of 1.2 square metres per minute.

3 Mine detection is based on the fact that, when an individual prod encounters a hard object in the ground, a sharp rise in pressure results in the hydraulic fluid driving the prod. When this occurs, the pre-set cut-off pressure (which continuously varies with changing soil conditions) is exceeded and the prod ceases its downward descent. If four or more adjacent prods in consecutive stages have been stopped, the probability that a mine is beneath the soil is high. The device then stops, marks the "mine" and alerts the operator. If less than four adjacent prods are triggered, there is no possible way for that object to be a mine and the device ignores those signals.

4 This design will detect both AP and AT mines in the soil to a high degree of accuracy. False alarms due to rocks, sticks, and other debris are greatly reduced due to the dense spacing of the prods. The device can operate in smooth to rough terrain and various soil densities including light vegetation and can easily be adapted to detection in sloped ground. The algorithm that controls the device could be reprogrammed to detect different shapes or sizes of land mines. All parts that would be damaged in the event of an explosion have been designed to be quickly and cost-effectively replaced.

TABLE OF CONTENTS

1.0 Introduction

2.0 Prod Design
2.1 Prod Dimensions and Materials
2.2 Soil Penetration Forces
2.3 Probe Speed
2.4 Buckling and Bending

3.0 Frame
3.1 Materials and Design
3.2 Blast Consideration

4.0 Hydraulics
4.1 Prod Production
4.2 Prod Array Movement
4.3 Blast Damage Reduction
4.4 Improvements

5.0 Data Acquisition System
5.1 Delay

6.0 Control Algorithm
6.1 System Check
6.2 Prod Actuation
6.3 Search Algorithm

7.0 Cost Summary

8.0 Conclusion

LIST OF FIGURES

Figure 2.1   Mine Detection/Prod Position Possibilities

Figure 2.2   Prod Dimensions

Figure 2.3   Tapered and Blunt Probe Penetration Force Curves

Figure 3.1   Overall View of Device

Figure 4.1   Prod Hydraulics Schematic

Figure 4.2   Prod Array Movement Hydraulics Schematic

Figure 6.1   Sequential Prod Actuation Diagram

LIST OF TABLES

Table 7.1   Cost Analysis

1.0 Introduction

5   The constant threat of nuisance land mines in countries around the world reveals the need for a real-world land mine detector. Due to the poor results obtained with electronic-type detection devices, the focus is now placed on a mechanical means of detection. In January of 1996, the MEC E 460 class was asked by the Defense Research Establishment at Suffield (DRES) to design mechanical mine detection devices. Due to time and resource restrictions, several constraints were placed on the project.

6   The device was to detect the VS-2.2 anti-tank (AT) and the VS-50 anti-personnel (AP) land mines with a high degree of accuracy. Ideally, the device would minimize the number of false alarms, being able to distinguish between mine types as well as between mines and other obstacles in the soil. In the event that an AP mine is detonated accidentally by the device, it must be able to withstand the blast or, alternatively, the damaged parts must be easily replaced. Minimum operating conditions were assumed to be smooth and level, non-frozen Devon Clay with some moisture and no vegetation. Attempts should be made to design a device that could be used in a wide range of soil states and ambient conditions. Clearing speed should be greater than that of the hand-prodder over a swath of 3 m. A low cost device would be most desirable so that it could be used in developing countries.

7   During the brainstorming stage of the design process, several ideas were considered. Various "heat" methods were considered and deemed inappropriate since they required too much energy transfer from the soil surface to the mine to be effective. A roller to sense soil depressions where mines have been buried was considered, but it was felt that any depression would be so small that the detection device would have to be too sensitive. Water and sand blasting of the soil could be used to uncover buried mines but would not be practical on a roadway since extensive repairs would have to be done after clearing. The chosen design was a device consisting of two rows of hydraulically activated prods spanning 3 m; one row to detect AP mines and one to detect AT mines. The probes would be inserted into the soil at 45° and an abrupt pressure rise would indicate that a probe had struck a solid object; that probe would then stop. A mine would be detected when the proper number of adjacent probes had stopped. This is a feasible design which meets all the required criteria.

2.0 Prod Design

8   The main feature of the design is the use of prods to find the buried land mines. By using prods, the benefits of the current hand-held prods were incorporated, with the addition of safety, speed, and accuracy. The mine detector consists of two rows of prods spanning 3 m; one row for the detection of the AP mines and one for detecting the AT mines.

9   The row detecting the AP mines consists of 78 prods spaced at 40 mm from one another and the row detecting the AT mines consists of 32 prods spaced 100 mm from one another. Both types of prods enter the soil at 45°. With the 78 AP prods and the 32 AT prods, the device can clear a 3 m wide strip of land. The 40 mm spacing for the AP prods ensures that at least four AP prods from two consecutive cycles will hit the 90 mm diameter AP mine. The 100 mm spacing for the AT prods again ensures that at least four prods from two consecutive cycles will hit the 246 mm diameter AT mine. Figure 2.1 shows several possible configurations for the prods detecting an AP mine. The detection of an AT mine is identical but on a larger scale.

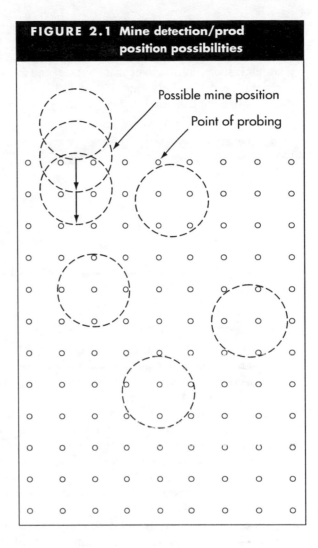

FIGURE 2.1 Mine detection/prod position possibilities

Possible mine position

Point of probing

2.1 Prod Dimensions and Materials

10   For simplicity and ease of replacement, each AP and AT prod is identical in its dimensions and materials. The prods consist of two main components: a probe that penetrates the ground and a cylinder that houses the probe and acts as a hydraulic cylinder. Figure 2.2 shows the dimensioning of the prods. The probe is 572 mm in length and is made of standard 6.35 mm stainless steel round stock. The length of the probe allows for the prodding to be done, while keeping important components away from a possible mine blast. The

cylinder portion of the prods has a length of 381 mm and is commercially available. A 17.5 mm drawn seamless tubing with a 15.9 mm bore was chosen to minimize the amount of hydraulic fluid contained in each cylinder. Each AP and AT probe has a screw-on carbide tip, which is more durable than stainless steel and can be easily replaced when worn. This construction is detailed in Figure 2.2. As well, the figure shows the blunt AT and tapered AP tips, which are discussed in section 2.2.

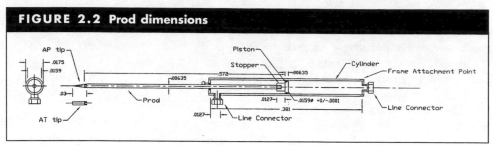

FIGURE 2.2 Prod dimensions

All dimensions in metres.

2.2 Soil Penetration Forces

11   The selection of the 6.35 mm diameter probes and the tapered and blunt tips was based on numerous tests done in the lab. Since the AP mines are buried to a maximum depth of 20 mm, it was decided that the AP probes would be inserted to a depth of 30 mm to ensure that no mines were missed. From Figure 2.3, it can be seen that at a depth of 30 mm the tapered probe shows a force of about 254 N, compared to 396 N on the blunt probe curve. This shows that it takes much less force to insert the tapered probe to a depth of 30 mm. In addition to testing the blunt and tapered probes, a test was done using an "arrowhead" probe in which a 9.53 mm tapered tip was attached to a 6.35 mm diameter rod. It was felt that this design might reduce the forces required to insert the probe into the soil. However, it was found that the force required at a depth of 30 mm for this tip was about 348 N, which is greater than the force for the tapered probe. For this reason the tapered probe was chosen for the detection of the AP mines. Using a safety factor of 1.5, the design force is 409 N.

12   Since the AT mines are buried at a maximum of 100 mm, it was decided that the AT probes would be inserted to a depth of 150 mm to ensure that no mines were missed. From the curve it is apparent that there is a sharp initial rise in force as the depth is increased but as the probe travels deeper, the curve flattens and the forces become constant. For the design, the maximum force on the blunt probe was used which was 396 N. Compared to 721 N at 150 mm for the tapered probe, the blunt probe has much smaller forces. For this reason the blunt probe was chosen to detect the AT mines. Again, incorporating the safety factor of 1.5, the design force used is 587 N.

13   The prods in this design are inserted at an angle of 45°, which increases the forces by a factor of 2 and keeps important components, such as valves and transducers, out of the blast cone of a possible mine explosion. (Discussed further in section 3.2)

2.3 Probe Speed

14   The probes begin their descent 50 mm above the ground, which accounts for small bumps, rocks, or dirt which may be on the surface. This gives a total of 115 mm at 115 mm/s for

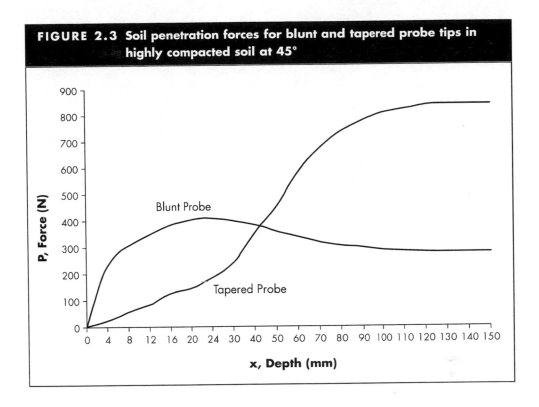

FIGURE 2.3 Soil penetration forces for blunt and tapered probe tips in highly compacted soil at 45°

the AP prods and 287 mm at 143 mm/s for the AT prods. For one pass, which involves the prods being inserted into the ground, retracting the prods and moving forward, the time, including all delays, is 3.83 seconds for the AP prods and 7.65 seconds for the AT prods. With these speeds and times, including all delay times, the clearing rate of the detector is 1.9 m²/mm. This is much faster than the 1 m² every 3–4 minutes achieved using the current hand-held prodder.

2.4 Buckling and Bending

15 As mentioned earlier, a design force of 409 N was used for the AP probes and 587 N was used for the AT probes. Both of these values incorporate a safety factor of 1.5. In using these forces both buckling and bending in the probes had to be considered. The critical force, P_{cr}, for the buckling of the probes was determined by modelling the system as a fixed end-fixed end buckling case. It was determined that the critical load for the probes was 1859 N, which is much greater than the actual forces needed in prodding. This shows that there is no chance of the probe buckling. Bending of the prod was also considered. This calculation was important since it considered the scenario wherein a probe might glance off a small stone during its insertion. Under a shear load of 6.5 N there is a deflection at the tip of 27 mm. Plastic deformation occurs at this point. This shows that for small deflections (0–27 mm) induced by abnormalities in the soil, there will be no plastic deformation.

3.0 Frame

3.1 Materials and Design

16   Structural members are made from ASTM A36 steel, which combines acceptable stiffness and relatively high yield strength with low cost and simplicity of manufacture. The structure, including all hydraulic cylinders, has a mass of about 400 kg and is mounted on the front of the Bison Armoured Personnel Carrier (APC) with pinned connections on the four factory mounts. Figure 3.1 shows an over-all view of the device. Note that the slanted members (frame supports) rest against the armour on the two corners of the APC when the prods are being driven into the ground while the pins bear the weight of the structure when the prods are retracted. The distributed loads induced by the prods penetrating the soil are approximately 6230 N in both the AT and AP rows.

17   Stiffness was the primary design consideration since it was decided that the maximum acceptable deflection at any one prod location in the array was 3 mm. This small deflection would not adversely affect the detection of mines since, at most, it would only cause a 10% error in depth penetration of the prods.

18   The greatest deflections occur in the members housing the prods and in the two horizontal arms. The final dimensions of these members were based on the minimum moments of inertia required for maximum deflection.... To house the prods, rectangular tubing (76.2 x 127 x 6.35 mm) with a moment of inertia of 5.16E6 mm^4 was chosen. This provides good bending support for the prods and a maximum centre deflection of 0.1 mm.

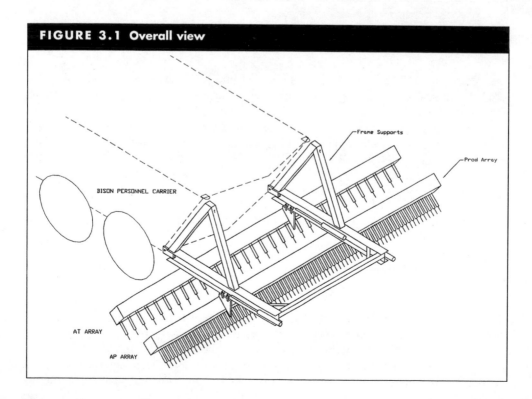

FIGURE 3.1 Overall view

19   I-beams (105.7 x 103.1 mm) were chosen for the horizontal arms supporting the prod arrays with the largest deflection being less than 3 mm. The bottom flanges are used as tracks for the lateral movement of the prod arrays.

3.2 Blast Consideration

20 Though detonation of an AP mine is highly unlikely under the design conditions, this scenario was considered and attempts were made to reduce the possible resulting damage. If an accidental blast were to occur, from an AT prod detonating a deeply buried AP mine or perhaps from a faulty AP mine, the damage is expected to be minor with destroyed parts easily replaceable.

21   In order to reasonably predict this damage calculations were done using the blast cone of 15° from vertical and the 300 mm crater specified by DRES. It was assumed that anything within this cone would be totally destroyed and that a peak over-pressure of 13.8 kPa is required to deform steel. All structural members are located outside the destructive pressure range, although shrapnel may cause some damage to an I-beam if a blast occurred directly below. Damaged members could be easily replaced since all connections are bolted.

22   Because the AP probes would be closest to the heart of the blast, it is expected that approximately 15 would be destroyed. Damage to the cylinders, both directly from peak over-pressure and indirectly from bent or destroyed probes, would be less severe (approx. 10 would be destroyed) because they are outside the blast cone and only fall slightly within the 13.8 kPa peak over-pressure range. The nature of the prods, as described earlier, allows for simple replacement of damaged probes, cylinders or fittings. If an AT prod were to encounter a deeply buried AP mine, the 820 mm spacing between the two rows would limit the damage to just four AT prods.

23   There was some concern that a blast would cause bending in the rectangular tubing which houses the prods. However, it was found that because the cylinder walls are very thin compared to the tubing, the cylinders would fail while the tube is still in the elastic range.

4.0 Hydraulics

24 The decision to use hydraulics in the proposed design was based on two main reasons. First, the APC on which the device is mounted is already equipped with a hydraulic system. The capacity of the APC hydraulic system is 95 L/s (25 gpm) with a maximum working pressure of 17 Mpa (2500 psi). The capacity of the hydraulic system is ample for the components specified in the proposed detection system. The second main reason for the choice of hydraulics is that the working fluid, oil, can be easily controlled and pressure rises easily measured. If the probe hits a solid object the oil continues to push the probe. This will cause an immediate pressure rise in the oil since flow continues, though the volume in the cylinder is no longer increasing. The incompressibilty of the working fluid allows for accurate flow control, resulting in accurate probe displacement. This could not be obtained with other compressible working fluids such as air. In that case a pressure rise would occur, but displacement of a probe would not occur since the working fluid behind the probe would compress. An increase in flow rate would be required to compensate for the volume change of the compressible working fluid, requiring expensive servo flow control valves. The timing of the probing cycle is critical in the proposed design in order to allow adjacent cycles to operate in synchronization. This would be difficult if probe penetration is stopped due to the compression of the working fluid.

4.1 Prod Production

25 With the previously stated reasons taken into consideration, the detection system was designed on a constant flow, pressure compensation basis. The probe unit as described earlier is in essence a custom hydraulic cylinder. Each probe has three controlling components: the directional control valve (DCV), pressure compensated flow control valve (FCV), and a pressure transducer. These are displayed in Figure 4.1.

26 The DCV is solenoid operated to allow for interface with a data acquisition system. The DCV defaults to the setting in which the feed flow is relieved back to the hydraulic system reservoir. This will ensure that if an electrical failure occurs, the valve does not allow flow to pass into the probe cylinder, stopping further probe penetration into soil. The pressure compensated FCV is placed down stream of the DCV allowing for accurate flow control of each probe. The placement of the FCV also ensures pressure rises, which occur between the FCV and the piston in the prod, are contained locally. As a result it is a simple matter to determine which probe has encountered an obstruction. The FCV valves are factory order, in that they are machined specific to one flow rate in one direction. The specific flow rates for the AP and AT prods are 0.023 L/s and 0.028 L/s respectively, giving probe penetration rates of 115 mm/s and 143 mm/s as stated earlier. The factory flow tolerances of the FCV are small. A pressure sensor is placed between the prod cylinder and the FCV to monitor pressure rise.

FIGURE 4.1 Schematic of constant flow pressure compensated hydraulic system

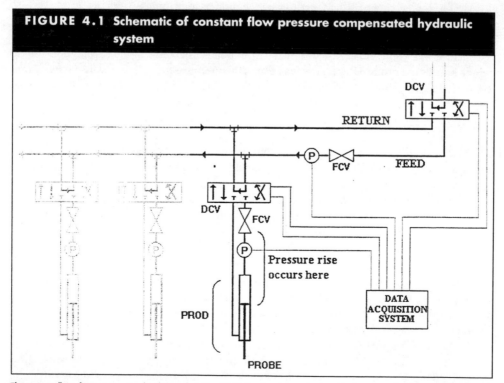

The system allows for pressure rises local to each probe. (DCV-directional control valve, FCV-flow control valve, P-pressure sensor)

27   The operation of the prod occurs in the following sequence. First the DCV solenoid is activated by the data acquisition system to allow the feed flow to travel through the FCV (metred flow) and into the prod, which in turn initiates the probe penetration into the ground. When the probe encounters an obstruction, the pressure of the working fluid between the prod and the FCV rises since constant flow is maintained through pressure compensation. The pressure transducer is used to monitor pressure rises throughout this process. Once a preset threshold pressure is reached, the data acquisition system ceases power flow to the solenoid of the DCV. The feed flow is now in relief and the probe motion is halted. The adjacent probes continue to penetrate until the same occurs, or the maximum depth is reached. Probe penetration rate is not affected by neighbouring probes being shut off, since flow control is local to each probe. The probes are then retracted by invoking the flow direction reversal solenoid. The speed of retraction is much quicker than penetration since there is a 16% decrease in volume of the cylinder due to volume displacement of the rod and the flow is regulated by a different control valve set at 0.32 L/s (the FCV on the cylinder line allows full flow in the reverse direction). This valve is located on the main feed as shown in Figure 4.1.

4.2 Prod Array Movement

28   Another hydraulic component is that of the prod row movement system. This is based on the same principles as above and also incorporates the use of an FCV and a DCV. A schematic of this system is displayed in Figure 4.2.

29   The hydraulic rams are set in the I-beam members of the frame, with a proximity sensor located at points where the prod arrays are attached as shown in Figure 4.2. The proximity sensor (Wainbee IAS-20-A12-S) runs along a ferrous/non-ferrous (plastic) strip placed along the I-beam. The ferrous markers are screws and indicate the positions at which the prod rows are to stop so that the probing cycle can begin. The data acquisition system operates the DCV in the same manner as mentioned earlier. The flow is allowed to

FIGURE 4.2

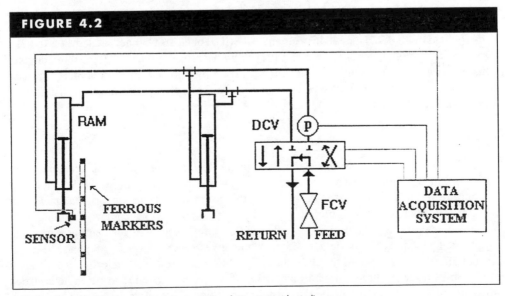

Hydraulic schematic of prod row movement system (AP and AT units are identical)

pass into the hydraulic rams until a ferrous marker is encountered at which point the flow will go into relief. When the maximum number of markers have been encountered, the prod rows are retracted against the APC, at which point the APC can move according to the situation at hand.

4.3 Blast Damage Reduction

30   Blast damage reduction has been taken into consideration. This was done by placing a pressure transducer in all the main feed lines as shown in Figures 4.1 and 4.2. The pressure transducer is used to monitor the pressure in the line. In the event of a blast severing a hydraulic line, massive pressure loss would occur, at which point the data acquisition system would direct the DCV to relieve flow back to the reservoir. This would discontinue any further fluid loss from the Bison's system. The low volume of the hydraulic components, 6.35 mm hydraulic lines, 15.9 mm bore cylinders, will minimize contamination caused by oil loss.

4.4 Improvements

31   An addition to improve versatility of the design would be to replace the square tubing frame supports shown in Figure 3.1 with hydraulic rams. The two rams would be controlled with a DCV, which in turn would be controlled with a data acquisition system that receives feedback from an ultrasonic sensor. This sensor would allow the proposed design to accommodate for more uneven terrain.

5.0 Data Acquisition System

32   In order to accommodate the solenoid DCV, 226 digital channels are required. This requirement can be fulfilled using the three National Instrument PC-DIO-96, 96 channel I/O boards. The directional control valves also needed high gain transistors in order to increase the 5 V board output to 12V required to activate solenoids. The pressure sensors and the proximity/hall effect sensors necessitate a total of 226 analog channels. This can be provided with 13 National Instrument AT-MIO-16DL 16 channel analog boards. The pressure sensor chosen was the Omega PX120 with a range of 0 to 3.4 Mpa (0 to 500 psi), which encompasses the full pressure range caused by a mine being encountered in hard soil. An IBM PC and an additional card chassis would be required to interface with the 16 data acquisition cards.

5.1 Delay

33   Since there are several sensing devices measuring flow, pressure, and displacement, there is a certain amount of delay involved in the processing of this information. The total amount of delay consists of the delay due to the processing of the sensor data, as well as the delay in the shut-off of the DCV. The data acquisition cards chosen have sampling rates of 50 000 samples/s. These rates were divided by three to account for computer processing time. The valve shut-off delay is 45 ms which gives a total delay of 47.87 ms. The result is that after the valve is told to close, the AP probe actually travels vertically an additional 1.97 mm and the AT prods an additional 2.45 mm. This means that if an AP mine is struck directly on the button, it will be depressed an additional 1.97 mm. Assuming the button

must be depressed approximately 3 mm for it to be detonated, the additional depression will not trip the mine. As well, assuming the AT mine must be depressed approximately 10 mm, the additional 2.45 mm depression will not trip the mine.

6.0 Control Algorithm

6.1 System Check

34 For safety reasons, the device will first go through a system check to ensure that all prods are functioning properly, and all sensors are working. This would be done by performing a test cycle on safe ground. This ground should be similar to that which is to be cleared, relatively uniform and all pressure readings from each prod should be similar. The computer will be used to check that all pressure readings are similar and all distance sensors are functioning. If there were a leaking prod or malfunctioning sensor, this would appear as a drastic difference in pressure in that particular prod (±20%). This would be interpreted as a system failure, and the operator would be notified.

6.2 Prod Actuation

35 The cycling of the prods is continuous until a mine is struck. To minimize reaction forces, prodding is done sequentially. The AP prods are divided into five groups, and the AT prods into three groups. They are positioned in repeating order (1, 2, 3, 4, 5, 1, 2...) as can be seen in Figure 6.1. The Group One prods will all begin their cycle, and after a delay of 0.368 seconds, representing the time it takes for a prod to move from the ground surface to the depth of three centimetres, the Group Two prods will begin. Groups Three, Four, and Five begin their cycles after subsequent 0.368 second delays. The AT prods operate in a similar manner, with their delay time being 1.47 seconds. This makes the cycle time for the AT row half that of the AP row, and is necessary to prevent interference between the two

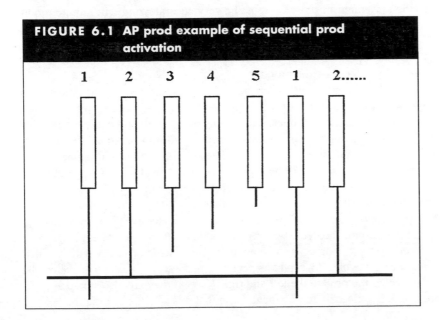

FIGURE 6.1 AP prod example of sequential prod activation

rows. In doing this, the transmitted forces to the frame and APC were cut by a factor of five for the AP row and three for the AT row, but the cycle time was only increased by a factor of 1.6 leading to an overall clearance rate of 1.9 m²/min.

36   The data acquisition system will be continuously sampling the pressure and depth readings. At the first pressure rise (representing the point at which the probe strikes the soil), the computer will set the depth for that prod to zero. This allows for the mechanism to contour to the clearing area, ensuring that if there is a hole or rut in the road the probe will still penetrate to the required depth below the surface. As well, the pressure requirement to penetrate the ground will be recorded and stored in memory. This data will be collected from all probes across the array and averaged, thus reducing noise from individual probes, and will be used to construct a cutoff pressure curve (equal to the obtained pressure curve plus 253 kPa for the AP and 4956 kPa for the AT, which represent the forces required to set off the mines with a safety factor of 2) for the next cycle. In this way the device is continuously adjusting to changing soil conditions. This was deemed important due to the wide range of penetrating forces collected using tests in soils of different compaction and moisture content.

6.3 Search Algorithm

37 The prod cycle can finish through one of two branches of the algorithm representing two possible occurrences. The first is the case where the probe does not strike anything and reaches its prescribed depth of 30 mm or 150 mm. When this occurs, the computer will wait for all prods from that particular row to reach their full depth. It will then reverse the hydraulic fluid flow and lift the prods to their height of 51 mm, move the row forward to the next proximity probe trigger, and repeat the cycle. This can continue for 25 cycles, where the end of the I-beam will be reached by the AP row. At this point, all of the prods from both rows will be lifted and the rows retracted back towards the APC. The APC could then drive forward to the last point at which the prods were in the ground and the cycles could continue. The movement of the APC must be very accurate, and will require modifications to its drive mechanism that would most easily be solved by adding a hydraulic or electric motor to one of the wheels. If this is not possible, another vehicle should be used, as it is felt that a human operator cannot control the APC with the accuracy necessary to ensure that no ground is missed by the prodder.

38   The other possibility for stopping would be if the probe strikes a solid object. Lab experiments have demonstrated that transmitted forces to the prod (and therefore higher pressures in the cylinder and hydraulic inlet) rise sharply when a solid object is struck. This sharp pressure rise will send the computer into a search algorithm to compare the geometry of the object that was struck to that of a mine. The first thing that will happen is the inflow valve to the prod in question will be closed so that the prod does not proceed any deeper into the ground and risk setting off a mine. Note that this is only for that particular prod and all others continue their descent. The computer also stores in its memory that this prod has been stopped and also checks if this is the second consecutive cycle in which this prod has been stopped. If not, the cycle will repeat, as this may still only be a small rock and there is no need to stop the process since anything mine-sized or larger will stop that prod again during the next cycle. If a prod has been stopped in two consecutive cycles, the computer will then check the prod to the left and right to see if they are also stored as positive. If they are not, the cycle will again repeat. Note that this sets the criteria that a solid

object be at least 80 mm (AP) or 200 mm (AT) wide and long (prods have been spaced so that a mine will be hit no less than four times). The next stage is a search for four adjacent prods that have been stored as positive (Adjacent can mean four in a square, a "T"-shape, and not necessarily just four wide. See Figure 2.1). In doing this search algorithm, all rocks, sticks, and other debris that may be encountered that stop three or less adjacent prods do not give false alarms. This is a significant feature of this design, and greatly increases the efficiency of the mechanism.

39   There has been no upper bound set on the number of prods that are triggered for several reasons. The first is the fact that AT mines can be buried at the same depth as AP mines, so the mechanism can detect these shallow AT mines with the AP row. Also, a rock may be sitting in very close proximity to a mine, or two mines may be spaced very close to one another. The underlying principle behind this is that false positives are far more desirable than false negatives.

7.0 Cost Summary

40   Table 7.1 displays the cost breakdown of the proposed design. The majority of the $101 000 cost is in the hydraulic and data acquisition components, which compose approximately 62% and 27% of the cost respectively. This high cost is due to the requirement of valves and sensors for each prod to ensure only local pressure rises. Inclusion of these valves and sensors in turn requires additional data acquisition channels for operation. Detection of local pressure rises allows the reduction of false alarms due to sticks, rocks, and such. The majority of the costs listed in Table 7.1 are initial costs and would not require repetition as the unit is used. The design would require minimal and low cost part replacement in the event of a blast. This is due to important components such as valves being located in zero damage areas in the event of a blast.

8.0 Conclusion

41   Land mines are a very serious problem in many parts of the world today and there is currently no safe, efficient method of detecting them. The goal of this project was to design a simple mechanical means of detecting land mines with operating conditions being smooth, flat Devon Clay. This chosen design is a very feasible and realistic solution to the problem presented. It meets and exceeds all the set criteria.

42   This design builds on the success of the hand prodder, incorporating a large number of prods on a frame which is to be mounted on the front of a Bison personnel carrier (APC). There are two rows of prods, the first consisting of 78 prods that penetrate the soil to a vertical depth of 30 mm to find AP mines. At this depth, for a tapered tip, it was found that the required insertion force is 254 N, which is less than the force of a blunt probe at this depth. The second row consists of 32 prods that penetrate to a depth of 150 mm to find AT mines. The force required for penetration at this depth with a blunt tip is 396 N, which is much smaller than that of a tapered tip. For this reason the blunt tip was chosen for the AT prods.

43   It was found that a prod insertion angle of 45° reduced the vertical forces on the frame and kept important components away from a potential blast. Using a 30° blast cone (AP mine), it was found that approximately 15 probes and 10 cylinders would be destroyed. This is acceptable since these parts could easily and inexpensively be replaced. Also, the

prod length is such that the critical load is 1859 N, which is much greater than the insertion force, hence the prods will not buckle.

44   All motion of prods and the prod arrays is controlled hydraulically, utilizing the existing hydraulic system on the APC. In order for the prods to be individually controlled, a directional control valve (DCV) and a pressure-compensated flow control valve (FCV) are required for each prod. Lab experiments have shown that striking a solid object causes an immediate rise in force required to penetrate the soil. In this system, that force translates into a pressure rise in the fluid downstream of the FCV. A pressure sensor sends this information to a computer and the computer shuts off the flow to that cylinder so that it cannot penetrate any deeper and detonate a mine.

45   Total signal delay was found to be 47.87 milliseconds. This results in an additional vertical AP prod travel of 1.97 mm once the original pressure rise has occurred. Assuming that the AP mine button must be depressed 3 mm out of 5 mm of travel for detonation, this delay was considered acceptable. If this proves inadequate in the field, the flow rate could be depressed accordingly.

46   Prod activation occurs sequentially. The AP prod array is divided into five groups while the AT array is divided into three groups. For the AP array, all group one prods begin their cycle and after a 0.368 second delay, the group two prods begin their cycle; this repeats for each of the five groups. The delay represents the time that a probe takes to move from the ground surface to the 30 mm depth. The AT operates in a similar manner, but the delay is 1.47 seconds. This causes the cycle time of the AT array to be half that of the AP array, ensuring no interference of the two arrays at any time in operation. This sequential actuation cut transmitted forces to the frame by factors of five in the AP array and three in the AT array, but the cycle time was only increased by a factor of 1.6. The overall clearance rate is 1.88 m^2/min. This force reduction was required in order to bring the frame deflection to an acceptable maximum of 3 mm.

47   The geometry of the land mines is used to distinguish mines from other solid objects which may be in the ground. The prods are spaced such that a mine will be struck a minimum of four times. The algorithm also ensures that an object is at least 40 mm for the AP and 100 mm for the AT wide and long before the operator is alerted that there is a mine present. This eliminates all false alarms from rocks or debris which stops only three or less prods. Efficiency of operation is significantly enhanced by this feature.

48   The total cost of the device is approximately \$101 000. This high cost is mainly due to the valves and sensors required for individual control of the prods. Individual control is needed in order to reduce false alarms and maintain a high accuracy.

49   This device is a realistic solution to the proposed problem which meets all required criteria. It is fully automated and can be used in a variety of soil conditions. Both AP and AT mines are detected, false alarms are greatly reduced and the probability of missing a mine is remote. This device is not the ultimate solution but is an excellent step in dealing with the problem of land mines.

TABLE 7.1   Cost summary of proposed land mine detection system

Item		Amount Req. (Feet)	Unit Price ($/Ft)	Item Total Price ($)	Group Total Price ($)
Structural components					
I-beam W4 X 13		6.33	22.15	140.21	
Square tubing	3" × 3"	10.73	11.45	122.86	
	2" × 2"	6.56	7.15	46.90	
Rect. tubing	3" × 5"	19.65	15.65	307.52	
Flat bar	4" × $\frac{1}{4}$"	6.38	3.22	21.99	
	4" × $\frac{7}{16}$"	3.41	5.24	17.87	
	8" × $\frac{1}{4}$"	4.3	7.50	32.35	
Trolleys to fit I-beam		4	70.00	280.00	**969.61**
Prod Cylinder components					
Seamless tubing $\frac{11}{16}$" OD × $\frac{5}{8}$" ID		138	2.10	289.80	
$\frac{1}{4}$" 30422 Roundstock		201	2.13	428.13	
		#Units	**$/Unit**		
Oil seal kits		110	2.50	275.00	
Proximity probe (1AS-20-A12S)		112	25.00	2800.00	
$\frac{1}{4}$" MPT × $\frac{1}{4}$" T Connector		220	2.20	484.00	
Screw-on carbide tip		110	3.00	330.00	
End caps		220	1.20	264.00	
Piston		110	1.20	132.00	
Misc. Small parts		110	2.00	220.00	**4505.00**
Data acquisition					
Analog DA board (PC-LPM-16)		13	525.00	6825.00	
Digital DA board (PC-D10-96)		3	395.00	1185.00	
IBM PC & board box		1	2000.00	2000.00	
Pressure sensors (PX120)		113	158.00	17 854.00	
HFV 12V Transistor		113	0.70	79.10	
Misc. wire		1	100.00	100.00	**28 043.10**
Hydraulic components					
4 way solenoid dir. cntrl valves	6631-1S2-5	113	320.00	36 179.21	
P. comp flow valve	6631-$\frac{1}{4}$S2.3565	78	201.55	15 720.00	
	6631-$\frac{1}{4}$S2-.4550	32	201.55	6449.60	
	6331-1S2-5	3	201.55	604.65	
Hydraulic cylinder 2" bore × 48" stroke		4	259.00	1036.00	
Hydraulic lines and fittings		1	4000.00	4000.00	**63 990.36**
General assembly & fabrication labour		**Hours**	**$/Hour**		
Prod assemble & machining ($\frac{3}{4}$ hr/cyln.)		82.5	40.00	3300.00	
Frame & hydraulic assembling		10	40.00	400.00	**3700.00**
				GRAND TOTAL:	**101 208.07**

Glossary

Allusion Allusion is the name given to a reference in a literary or artistic work to titles, characters, places, events, or other elements from other literary or artistic works, or from history, religion, or mythology. The reference may be obvious or obscure, implicit or explicit, but the author always assumes that the reader can and will recognize the allusion in a way that serves the author's objectives. Robert Lucky's reference to the George Washington "cherry tree" legend is explicit; Umberto Eco's use of the phrase "decline and fall" might be more obscure. Allusions depend partly on the author's target audience —a reference to *Star Wars* or some other icon of contemporary popular culture might be lost on certain audiences.

Analogy An analogy describes one subject in terms of another. It is often used to make difficult or abstract concepts concrete and comprehensible. An analogy is used to argue that because *A* resembles *B* in some respects, *A* also resembles *B* in others. It is wise to remember that analogies are never total: *A* is not *B*, after all.

Aphorism An aphorism is a concise statement of a principle, or a short, pithy sentence, often expressing folk wisdom. An example is this, regarding the weather: "Red sun in the morning, sailors take warning."

Argument or Persuasion In persuasion, the writer attempts to affect the way the reader thinks, believes, or acts. An argument is an attempt to change, not merely to inform, the reader. There are two general types of argument: induction and deduction. **Induction** bases conclusions on specific facts. If you wished to argue that the man next door had a bad temper, you would cite occasions when he became angry for inadequate reasons. Those cases would constitute

evidence, and your claim would stand or fall according to the strength of the evidence. **Deduction** begins with a broad premise and seeks to work out the conclusion from it. The classic form of the deductive argument is the syllogism. It takes this form:

> All dogs have four legs.
> Rover is a dog.
> Therefore, Rover has four legs.

Note that the elements of the syllogism are not necessarily interchangeable. This syllogism is not valid:

> All dogs have four legs.
> Fluffy has four legs.
> Therefore, Fluffy is a dog.

Fluffy, in fact, is a cat. This argument breaks down because the first premise does not claim (and it could not claim) that dogs are the only animals with four legs.

Cause and Effect Most essays eventually need to discuss in some form causes, or reasons, and effects, or consequences. The simplest way to treat a cause as the topic of an essay is to pose a question, and then supply the answer. Effects can be treated in much the same way, with the consequence becoming the topic and the starting point for what will follow.

Coherency (see also **Transition**) Coherency refers to the internal relationships between ideas or elements in a piece of writing. When an essay or paragraph is coherent, it holds together sentence by sentence, and paragraph by paragraph. Each idea, statement, and example clearly connects both with what has come before and with what will come after. Connections may be logical ("this, and this"; "this; therefore, this"; "thus"), chronological (first, second, third; initially, next, finally), causal (this, because of that), or spatial (centre to margin; left to right; nearest to farthest).

Comparison and Contrast A comparison always involves similarities, whether these are discussed alone or together with differences. Contrast is confined to showing differences. Thus, while the two terms are significantly different, they often appear together.

Coordination Coordination refers to ways of building sentences and paragraphs. Compound sentences build by adding together related independent clauses that are connected by coordinating conjunctions (and, but, or, nor, for, yet, so), or by a semicolon. Coordination is also a method of paragraph development in which each sentence refers back to the first sentence of the paragraph, clarifying, defining, or illustrating a word or term from that first sentence.

Definition To define is to set limits or boundaries. A **lexical** or dictionary definition presents a term, names the category or genus of which it is a part, and then provides the characteristics or differences that make the term specific or unique. A **categorical** definition is similar; it places an object, idea, or procedure in a classification system and isolates its component parts. An **extended** definition provides readers with a sense of an object, idea, or procedure's larger significance in relation to other objects, ideas, or procedures. Such a definition may also include analogies and operational details.

Description Description seeks to inform the reader by employing spatial and sensory experience—how something looks, sounds, tastes.

Emphasis Emphasis is the weight or stress given to individual words or ideas within sentences, paragraphs, or whole pieces of writing. Words or phrases that appear at the opening or close of sentences or paragraphs, especially key words that repeat at these positions, tend to stick in the reader's mind; they tend to acquire importance.

Emphasis can also derive from an effective figure of speech; from full, clear development of an idea or topic through examples, analogies, redefinition, etc.; or from varying sentence pattern (placing a short sentence among longer sentences, or raising new issues through questions, rather than declarative sentences).

Example Writing characterized by example explains through providing highly specific illustrations or instances to support specific arguments, points, opinions, or beliefs. Example often allows the reader to witness or experience the author's purpose or position in operation.

Irony Irony is an effect produced when there is a discrepancy between two levels of meaning. **Irony of situation** refers to a contrast between what we expect to happen and what really happens. **Verbal irony** refers to a deliberate contrast between what is said and what is meant. **Dramatic irony** refers to audience awareness of the meaning of words or actions unknown to one or more characters. Dramatic irony occurs when we are "in on" something that a character is not.

Narration A narrative is a story, a meaningful sequence of events told in words. A sequence involves an arrangement of events in time, the simplest sequence being a straightforward movement from the first event to the last.

Process Process illustrates how something is done or how something comes about. The process may be a sequence directed towards achieving a specific end, which includes or identifies various steps or stages. In some cases, the purpose of process writing may be to allow others to follow such stages in order to achieve a similar result. Such process writing is likely to be objective. On the other hand, process writing may be directed toward the identification of an ongoing, progressive change that is currently in progress and that does not yet have a definite outcome. This type of process writing is likely to be subjective as well as objective and to attempt to direct specific attitudes toward the process itself.

Satire Satire is the practice of attacking something by making it look ridiculous. It uses laughter as a weapon by making the butt of the joke appear absurd, contemptible, or undignified. Satire may attack a person, an idea, an ideology, a class, an institution, a behaviour or habit, etc.

Style Style is an author's unmistakable personal choice of words, sentence construction, diction, imagery, tone, and ideas.

Subordination Subordination refers to methods of combining sentence elements and of building paragraphs. Subordination in sentences, or in sentence combination, makes one idea or element dependent on another. A subordinate clause modifies or complements something in the main, independent clause. In revision, a writer may take two or more ideas originally expressed in consecutive shorter sentences, and choose to subordinate one or more, thus creating a complex sentence that clearly emphasizes the main idea. In constructing a paragraph, a writer may make each succeeding sentence continue from and expand on a word or phrase from the sentence before, rather than from a word or phrase from the topic sentence.

Tone Tone is the implied attitude of a writer toward the subject, material, and reader.

Transition (see also **Coherency**) Refers to techniques that make clear to the reader connections or links within and between paragraphs. Transitional words or phrases allow the writer (and, of course, the reader) to connect ideas or details by adding them together (and, also); separating them for further discussion (but, however); providing examples (for example, for instance); joining them in time, space, or logical sequence (before, next; above, below; if . . . then, therefore); or explaining causes or effects (because, consequently).

Title Index

ALPHABETICAL BY TITLE

A, B, and C: The Human Element in Mathematics
Stephen Leacock (1911), 121

A Defense of Reading
Marie Winn (1977), 306

A Fable for Tomorrow
Rachel Carson (1962), 14

A Mask on the Face of Death
Richard Selzer (1987), 218

A Modest Proposal
Jonathan Swift (1729), 235

The Address of the Chiefs
Gisday Wa and Delgam Uukw (1987), 283

The Atom's Image Problem
Jay Ingram (1996), 87

Beginning to Understand the Beginning
Rick McConnell (1996), 125

Behind the Formaldehyde Curtain
Jessica Mitford (1963), 129

Bitten by the Space Bug
Elizabeth K. Wilson (1996), 299

Bred in the Bone?
Alan H. Goodman (1997), 41

Charles Darwin's Tree of Life
O. B. Hardison, Jr. (1989), 57

Clone Mammals. . . Clone Man?
Axel Kahn (1997), 91

Coming Home to Television
John Romano (1999), 182

Computing Machinery and Intelligence
A. M. Turing (1950), 246

Crocodiled Moats in the Kingdom of Letters
Cynthia Ozick (1989), 147

Detection of Landmines: A Technical Report for a
Course in Mechanical Engineering
Robert Gust, Chris Turner, Peter Karl, and Scott
Koehn (1998), 346

Don't Rock the Sampan
Xu Xi (1999), 318

Doomsday
Paul Davies (1994), 24

Eat Your Hearts Out Cinephiles, the Tube Is Where
It's At
John Haslett Cuff (1996), 17

The English Village—Principles of Composition
John Ruskin (1838), 193

Explaining Disasters: The Case for Preventive Ethics
Charles E. Harris, Jr. (1995) 64

From Both Sides Now
Sharon Begley, with Thomas Hayden (1999), 6

Ghosts in the Machine
Sherry Turkle (1995), 267

How I Created the Theory of Relativity
Albert Einstein (1922), 33

How Iraq Reverse-Engineered the Bomb
Glenn Zorpette (1992), 321

India
Perri Klass (1987), 101

Island Hopping
  Oliver Sacks (1996), 202

Knives, Forks and Spoons
  Margaret Visser (1991), 273

Lessons from Play; Lessons from Life
  Henry Petroski (1992), 152

Marie Curie and Mileva Einstein Maric
  Hilary Rose (1994), 186

Molecular Structure of Nucleic Acids: A Structure
for Deoxyribose Nucleic Acid
  James D. Watson and Francis H. C. Crick
  (1953), 287

The Monster's Human Nature
  Stephen Jay Gould (1995), 49

Myth and Malevolence
  Michael Ignatieff (1995), 83

The Official Theory
  Steven Pinker (2002), 163

Excerpt from *The Origin of Species*
  Charles Darwin (1859), 20

The Pleasures and Pains of Coffee
  Honoré de Balzac (1830), 1

The Ponds
  Henry David Thoreau (1854), 242

Putting Self-Help "Leviathans" and "Oracles" to
Sleep: A Discussion of Anthony Robbins' *Awaken
the Giant Within* and James Redfield's *The Celestine
Prophecy*
  Lisa Grekul (1998), 340

The Road from Rio
  David Suzuki (1992), 228

The Route to Normal Science
  Thomas S. Kuhn (1962), 106

Sense and Sensibility
  Lewis H. Lapham (1991), 116

Shooting an Elephant
  George Orwell (1950), 141

The Short, Simple Human Gene Map
  Laurent Belsie (2001), 10

"State-of-the-Art Car": The Ferrari Testarossa
  Joyce Carol Oates (1985),136

Straight Talk at the Parakeet Café
  Ian Furlong (1998), 38

Viable Offspring Derived from Fetal and Adult
Mammalian Cells
  I. Wilmut, A. E. Schnieke, J. McWhir, A. J. Kind,
  and K. H. S. Campbell (1997), 291

Waniskâ Nôsim
  Joyce Dene (2003), 334

The Way We Woo
  Heather Pringle (1993), 172

What Is an Elementary Particle?
  Werner Heisenberg (1976), 72

Why Johnny Can't Think
  Walter Karp (1985), 95

The Writing Life
  Annie Dillard (1989), 29

Date Index

CHRONOLOGICAL BY DATE OF FIRST PUBLICATION

1729: A Modest Proposal
Jonathan Swift, 235

1830: The Pleasures and Pains of Coffee
Honoré de Balzac, 1

1838: The English Village—Principles of
Composition
John Ruskin, 193

1854: The Ponds
Henry David Thoreau, 242

1859: Excerpt From *The Origin of Species*
Charles Darwin, 20

1911: A, B, and C: The Human Element in
Mathematics
Stephen Leacock, 121

1922: How I Created the Theory of Relativity
Albert Einstein, 33

1950: Computing Machinery and Intelligence
A. M. Turing, 246

1950: Shooting an Elephant
George Orwell, 141

1953: Molecular Structure of Nucleic Acids A
Structure for Deoxyribose Nucleic Acid
James D. Watson and Francis H. C. Crick, 287

1962: A Fable for Tomorrow
Rachel Carson, 14

1962: The Route to Normal Science
Thomas S. Kuhn, 106

1963: Behind the Formaldehyde Curtain
Jessica Mitford, 129

1976: What Is an Elementary Particle?
Werner Heisenberg, 72

1977: A Defense of Reading
Marie Winn, 306

1985: "State-of-the- Art Car": The Ferrari Testarossa
Joyce Carol Oates, 136

1985: Why Johnny Can't Think
Walter Karp, 95

1987: The Address of the Chiefs
Gisday Wa Delgam Uukw, 283

1987: India
Perri Klass, 101

1987: A Mask on the Face of Death
Richard Selzer, 218

1989: Charles Darwin's Tree of Life
O. B. Hardison, Jr., 57

1989: Crocodiled Moats in the Kingdom of Letters
Cynthia Ozick, 147

1989: The Writing Life
Annie Dillard, 29

1991: Knives, Forks and Spoons
Margaret Visser, 273

1991: Sense and Sensibility
Lewis H. Lapham, 116

1992: How Iraq Reverse-Engineered the Bomb
Glenn Zorpette, 321

1992: Lessons from Play; Lessons from Life
Henry Petroski1, 52

1992: The Road from Rio
David Suzuki, 228

1993: The Way We Woo
Heather Pringle, 172

1994: Doomsday
Paul Davies, 24

1994: Marie Curie and Mileva Einstein Marić
Hilary Rose, 186

1995: Explaining Disasters: The Case for
Preventive Ethics
Charles E. Harris, Jr., 64

1995: Ghosts in the Machine
Sherry Turkle, 267

1995: The Monster's Human Nature
Stephen Jay Gould, 49

1995: Myth and Malevolence
Michael Ignatieff, 83

1996: The Atom's Image Problem
Jay Ingram, 87

1996: Beginning to Understand the Beginning
Rick McConnell, 125

1996: Bitten by the Space Bug
Elizabeth K. Wilson, 299

1996: Eat Your Hearts Out Cinephiles, The Tube Is
Where It's At
John Haslett Cuff, 17

1996: Island Hopping
Oliver Sacks, 202

1997: Bred in the Bone?
Alan H. Goodman, 41

1997: Clone Mammals... Clone Man?
Axel Kahn, 91

1997: Viable Offspring Derived from Fetal and Adult
Mammalian Cells
I. Wilmut, A. E. Schnieke, J. McWhir, A. J. Kind,
and K. H. S. Campbell, 291

1998: Detection of Landmines: A Technical Report
for a Course in Mechanical Engineering
Robert Gust, Chris Turner, Peter Karl, and
Scott Koehn, 346

1998: "Putting Self-Help 'Leviathans' and 'Oracles'
to Sleep": A Discussion of Anthony Robbins'
Awaken the Giant Within and James Redfield's *The
Celestine Prophecy*
Lisa Grekul, 340

1998: Straight Talk at the Parakeet Café
Ian Furlong, 38

1999: Coming Home to Television
John Romano, 182

1999: Don't Rock the Sampan
Xu Xi, 318

1999: From Both Sides Now
Sharon Begley, with Thomas Hayden, 6

2001: The Short, Simple Human Gene Map
Laurent Belsie, 10

2002: The Official Theory
Steven Pinker, 163

2003: Waniskâ Nôsim
Joyce Dene, 334